THE
EBBING TIDE

The National Library of Poetry

Richard Schaub, Editor

The Ebbing Tide

Library of Congress
Cataloging in Publication Data

ISBN 1-57553-068-6

Proudly manufactured in The United States of America by
Watermark Press
One Poetry Plaza
11419 Cronridge Dr., Suite 10
Owings Mills, MD 21117

Editor's Note

Artistry can at times be mistakenly labeled an "artist's interpretation of the mechanics of nature." The many cycles of nature have fascinated artists for centuries. Consider the countless literary allusions to the waxing and waning shapes of the moon, the changing seasons, and the ebb and flow of the ocean tides. All of these things have perpetuated a deep-rooted desire for humanity to understand its natural environment. Unfortunately, however, some critics wish to limit the scope of art to only these specific categories, opting to ignore the many arenas outside the realm of nature. Thus, political poetry, poetry of human relationships, and even metaphysical poetry would not be considered art. While the world of nature is rich in possibilities and there is great potential for fresh interpretation, it is not the only subject worthy of investigation.

The Ebbing Tide represents the accumulation of thousands of ideas carefully formulated and meticulously crafted into works of art. The poets in this anthology remind us that the beauty of art is not restricted to any one particular subject. Represented in this anthology is a vast expanse of creativity rendered by many different people from many different backgrounds. Poets often vary their interests and concerns for new subject matter to expand the possibilities for their work. One such poet is Second Place Prize winner Peter Kerns who tackles a difficult political subject in a very interesting fashion. Kerns's poem "The Parade" re-creates the situation surrounding the assassination of President John F. Kennedy. The difficulty in attempting a poem of this kind is in portraying a work that is true to history and yet still imaginative. Kerns meets this challenge very eloquently by playing off the media's news and film footage and yet using fresh images to describe the sequence of events.

> *Camera ready.*
> *Slowly sweeping. Fading in.*
> *Lens guzzling sun.*
> *Succulent brightness leaving the haunting to stay.*

These first four lines of "The Parade" set a mood and scene for this work that places the subject in a framework that can be easily understood: television. More than three decades after that fateful day when Kennedy was murdered, one is dependent on the media coverage of that time to help us understand the experience. Kearns's awareness of our media dependence enables him to place the occurrence in a frame of reference to which most of the world can relate. However, it is important to recognize that the poet does much more than this by adding color and sensation to the poem. The phrase "lens guzzling sun" helps to take this image into techni-color by giving it poetic sound and shape.

As the poem moves forward, Kerns continues to brandish his skills by making even more references to the media and popular-culture, while maintaining a vivid re-imagining of the event. It is the poet's eloquent choice of images that makes this work so unforgettable and disturbing.

> *Movie dust, movie smoke*
> *Misted extras in polaroid diagonal silhouette*
> *Shots cut across all heads,*
> *Save one: They cut. (Cut into explosion.)*

While the poet skirts around the primary significance of the "drive down Elm in cowboy town," the last stanza brutally crystallizes its significance and firmly identifies this "parade" as the Kennedy assassination. Once again by playing off the media interpretations of this event, Kerns is able to reveal the full relevance of his subject. We see in this last stanza the conspiracy theory, as well as the very disturbing image of Kennedy's head being hit by the assassin's bullet.

> *Plain murder. Blood. Blow back gore.*
> *Classified. Eyes only. Liquid affairs.*
> *Under the blood-halo of a butchered head.*

By using sharp images and linking them with the significance of a very important political and historical moment, Kerns creates a very imaginative piece of poetry that enhances our understanding of the Kennedy assassination.

Political poems, much like poems about nature, operate on a sensual level. In order to experience a poem -- whatever the subject -- we must feel the poet's ideas. In this sense, all poetry has a common bond by which we interpret the information being related. Our minds process information deeply when it appeals to each of our senses. And when this is coupled with the music of language, it is poetry, regardless of subject.

The twentieth century has changed the landscape of poetry. Many subjects never before considered worthy of poetry have now become welcomed by poets the world over who wish to expand the poetic possibilities in our strange and unnatural world. One such subject is examined in R. E. Shenberger's poem "Steelmill." The title alone suggests the kind of path down which Shenberger will lead in this excellent work. The poem describes the physical appearance of a woman through the metaphor of a steelmill. Shenberger masterfully shapes "Margret," the subject of the piece, with amazing clarity and skill by using terms more often associated with the cold world of a steelmill.

> *i remember margret*
> *...her straight uniform needle tipped hair jagged*
> *molded square at the shoulders forehead protecting*
> *helmet guarding approach touch*

By using no punctuation and rather abrupt language, Shenberger reveals the kind of person Margret is: "absorbing concealing revealing." The cold and distant speaker seems to speak slowly and deliberately as if he or she, while attempting to describe Margret, could also be revealing even more about him or herself.

> *her cutting blue eyes chiseled sculpted slits*
> *warning penetrating slicing the intruder*
> *her uninviting closed narrow lips bound shut*

The clearest descriptions of Margret's "Steelmill" characteristics are revealed near the end of the poem. The poet breaks down the character into the barest rudiments of iron and steel and reveals the sadness in a character like Margret, who seems trapped in her armor, unable to escape the fate of her own existence.

> *never witness to her creator manufacturer*
> *never testimony to her assembly process abuse*
> *her welded tight silence shame guilt knowledge*
> *of who forged her steel pounded her shield's shape*

The persona's description reveals some form of childhood abuse which forced Margret into the steel shell she currently inhabits. Perhaps, never knowing her "creator" she is unable to give testimony to her "assembly process," and thereby unable to escape the prison that perhaps at one time protected her from the pain of abuse, but now only hides her from the outside world. Margret is trapped because she does not see herself as the creator of her "fortress."

> *of who forged her steel...*
> *erected her impenetrable fortress secreting from the world*
> *a beautiful ten year old girl adorned with a party dress*

Traditional forms of structured poetry allow a formula or outline through which a poet can build interesting ideas within the structured confines of the form. More often than not, however, these structures become a hindrance to a developing poet rather than serving as a guideline for creativity. It is with careful skill and deliberation that a practiced poet uses a traditional form to its fullest potential. The fourteen-line sonnet offers a particular challenge because of its demanding meter and rhyme scheme. Occasionally, however, a poet is able to use a traditional structure with such grace and skill that he or she elevates their subject far above the limitations of the form. It is for her ability to do this that CherylAnn Whelchel's "Sonnet One" was given the Grand Prize in the North American Open Poetry Contest.

"Sonnet One" is not only a well written poem that subtly uses structure to its fullest potential, but it also reveals a careful balance between the nature of relationships. Whelchel's poem shows the co-dependence of complementary elements and reveals the breakdown of distinguishing separate characteristics. In the issue of nature poetry and poetry outside the realm of nature, it can be said that both forms of poetry share so many commonalties that it is sometimes difficult to distinguish a noticeable difference. Whelchel's poem deals with this same issue in terms of personal relationships.

The poem begins by analyzing how and to whom one gives credit for the creation of something as complex as a jet. After analysis, it becomes apparent that the invention of the jet was the culmination of years and years of work, and is impossible to attribute it to a single person. By even attempting to find out that information, Whelchel suggests we "kindle needs we never satisfy."

> *A point of silver light, a jet, shot by*
> *framed half by hope, half by a maple tree;*
> *and made me wonder who might ever be*
> *paid honor to, whatever arcs we fly,*

Whelchel also says that a personal relationship is equally elusive in its structural makeup. There are no dividing lines in a relationship revealing the individual's role in the structures that make-up a relationship, i.e. financial responsibility or, more importantly, who loves whom and how much.

> *we kindle needs we never satisfy;*
> *along whatever blue periphery*
> *(my love for you and yours for me;*
> *the line that marks off land from sky).*

The structures of the world, the poet goes on to suggest, are named in order to be understood. What we call a jet, others less informed might call "a point of silver light." Though these names help us to understand life, they do not reveal all of the inherent structure; instead they label that structure as an object. This naming forces us, as observers, to grow accustomed to these names and forget the deeper significance.

> *Whatever we've called up we've called by name*
> *to take life fully, to participate*
> *in cosmos, fuse in flesh and bone;*
> *object and observer both grown tame,*

Whelchel concludes in the ending couplet that humanity, in its understanding of the universe, is only able to scratch the surface of its pursuits, and it is also unable to see anything beyond what we are capable of perceiving.

> *committed to dynamics inchoate*
> *in darkness, ineluctable as stone.*

The poets appearing in **The Ebbing Tide** have created a wealth of literature worthy of long perusal. Examine these poems thoroughly and I am sure you will find it a rewarding experience. In particular I would like to call your attention to the following excellent award winning poems: Daniel Wilkens's poem "Big Red Box," Matthew Nierenberg's poem "Uncle (And Angelic Overtures), Lisa Howard's poem "Reverie Of Sumer Past," and Eva Acqui's poem "Memories."

The Ebbing Tide is the culmination of many hard working NLP employees. I wish to offer a very sincere thank you to all of the editors, assistant editor's, customer service representatives, data entry workers, and everyone else who had a hand in making this excellent volume possible.

May the tides that guide your imagination flow into deep and shimmering waters that reveal profound and meaningful insights.

Richard Schaub,
Editor

Cover Art: Tracy Hetzel

Winners of the North American Open Poetry Contest

Grand Prize Winner

CherylAnn Whelchel / Forest Park, GA

Second Prize Winners

Eva Acqui / Baia Sprie, Romania
Richard Chapman / Pinehurst, NC
Ed Devany / Chapel Hill, NC
Rebecah Hall / Albuquerque, NM
Lisa Howard / North York, ON Canada

Miriam Kapner / Boston, MA
Peter Kerns / New York, NY
Matthew Nierenburg / La Jolla, CA
Poet Shenberger / Clinton, NY
Daniel Wilkens / Tillsonburg, ON Canada

Third Prize Winners

J. Chang Alloy / Etobicke ON Canada
Amy Anderson / Athens, GA
Laura Baldino / Philadelphia, PA
Staci Barker / Marlow, OK
Harold Beckles / Durham, NC
Kerri Brannan / Westland, MI
April Britton / BC, Canada
Nikolay Brovcenko / Kilkenny, Australia
E. Simone Buttry / Lake View Terrace CA
Helen Carl / Neuilly Sur Marne, France
Herbert Channick / Rockford, IL
D. Alex Chunag / Castle Rock, CO
Deborah Collins / BC, Canada
Andrew Conant / Ann Arbor, MI
Ann Creer / Coleman, AB Canada
Kim Dawn / NS, Canada
Henry Deas III / Los Angeles, CA
Patrys Destin / Chicago, IL
Dante Golio / Pembroke Pines, FL
Stacey Graham / Douglasville, GA
Kristen Grubert. / Dear Park, NY
Lauren Jane Heimberg / Manhattan Beach, CA
David Hughes / Saint George, UT
Zoran Jungic / BC, Canada
Donna Kavin / ON, Canada
Jon Kirkwood / Monaca, PA
Earl Knight / ON, Canada
Mattthew Lancaster / Denver, CO
Haye Lewis / Jamaica Estates, NY
Sarah Martin / Aiea, HI

Chris Mastrogiovanni / Vail, CO
Tony Mazzara / Boca Raton, FL
Richard C. Miller / Davenport, IA
Denise Moline / Calgary, AB, Canada
Douglas Mortimer / Des Moines, IA
Carlos Murrell / Raleigh, NC
Gretchen Oswald / Denver, CO
Rebecca Pearson / Hamilton Square, NJ
Scott Potter / Grand Rapids, MI
Mahendra Persaud / North Bay Village, FL
Russell Phillips / Humboldt, TN
Joseph Posner / Massapequa, NY
Karoline Ross / Evansville, WI
Dominick Scarchello / Yardley, PA
M. Lee Sherburne / Humboldt, NE
M. L. Smith / Bartsville, OK
Margo Sosa / Ithaca, NY
Louise Thomas / Shawnee, OK
Fernando Tiberini / Baden, Switzerland
Toni Tuminella / Pittsburgh, PA
Lonnie Upshur / Trenton, NJ
Michelle Van Rhyn / Spray Village, CA
Phillip Waugh / St. Croix, MN
Alan Webb / Townsville, Australia
Andy Whyte / PQ, Canada
Philo Wilson / Orleans, MA
Donald Whitee / West Springfield, MA
Mandy Wood / Victoria, BC, Canada
Ramsay Wood / London, UK

Congratulations also to all semi-finalists.

The National Library of Poetry · 11419-10 Cronridge Drive · PO Box 704 · Owings Mills, MD 21117

Grand Prize Winner

Sonnet One

A point of silver light, a jet, shot by
framed half by hope, half by a maple tree;
and made me wonder who might ever be
paid honor to, whatever arcs we fly,
we kindle needs we never satisfy;
along whatever blue periphery
(my love for you and yours for me;
the line that marks off land from sky).

Whatever we've called up we've called by name
to take life fully, to participate
in cosmos, fuse in flesh and bone;
object and observer both grown tame,
committed to dynamics inchoate
in darkness, ineluctable as stone.

CherylAnn Whelchel

The Hidden Gift Of Snow

The winter snow that I love so much......
So delicate, so pure and white.....
Has said: "Good-Bye"....and slipped out of sight.....
For it heard the earth cry..."In thirst".....

It gave of itself till it could give no more....
The last I saw of the glistening snow.....
It was shedding tears to the earth below..
I watch the droplets of the beautiful snow.....
As it trickled into the earth.....

For the snow had served a great purpose.....
And in spring....I will rejoice....
For I will see the sacrifice made in new birth....
From mother earth....

And I will remember the beautiful snow....
For it is a gift of life.....
That is hidden under a blanket of white....

Florence Mick

Lost In Tears

It rained on me today,
Alone, inside, in bed;
Thru the blinds a single ray,
Found a tear upon my head;
Slowly weeping down, it fell onto my cover,
Reality soaking in: I lost my only lover.

James M. Henley Jr.

The Rose Will Bloom Again

The rose will bloom again, just you wait and see.
When my Jesus, he will come, will come after me.
The trails that I'm in they won't fade away,
Lord I'm longing and I'm waiting
for that great judgement day.
Let the rose bloom again, let the rose bloom again.
Let the rose of Sharon give me peace within.
He's my shield and my armor, the bright
and morning star, Lord I know who
you are; let the rose bloom again.
I'd stopped one day and felt him in my heart.
He'd given me a peace of mind and a new life to start.
I'm opening the door once more to
let you in; I know without doubt,
that the rose will bloom again.

Debbie J. Cates

Orient Express

As I stepped aboard, I moved cautiously;
as though something or someone was about.

Great notables had once preceded me,
of their presence there was no doubt.

I knew not fear... mere curiosity
and did poke and explore where I could.

Somehow, I felt not an intruder;
no matter that I didn't... nor I should.

Dastardly deeds were done in this place;
mysteries forgotten, hidden away!

I resolved, somehow, to unravel them all;
Though would take much more than one day.

As the great horse lumbered along,
I felt almost a warm caress...

And kinship with "Aggie" and "Poirot"...
As I traveled on the Orient Express.

Lana Robinson

Stigma On Humen Faces

My heart filled with desires, limit is sky;
My head tilted with dire consequences to fly.

My pen filled with ink, obsolete to repeal;
My decree charged with authority, stigma to peal.

My people willed with oriflamme, to do or die;
My people, Ah! Himalayans, commandments to defy.

My world, Ah! yet patronizes the mafia and apartheid
My U.N., Ah! yet "justice delayed, justice denied."

My world, yet patronizes the ignobles and heinous:
My world, yet patronizes the irresponsible and insidious.

My brothers and sisters in seige before Serbians and Somalians:
And mass massacred before the Bolsheviks, Nazis and Rwandans!!!

My world is Beirut, Gaza and South of Africa;
My world is Afghanistan, Kurdistan and Horn of Africa.

My orgy is loot, arson and riots in Kashmir-desh:
My Biharis' camps' ordeal and episodes in Bangladesh.

I'm, a bitter fact, not supposed to be, sinking in shame!!!
I'm, in fact, supposed to be, Deputy to God, ranking in fame!!!

Shah Ahmed

"My Special Angel"

Thinking back of all the pain and suffering you had to endure,
You kept of face and faith; for we knew there was no cure.
Lucky we were to have had these years,
Yes, together we've shared many laughs and tears.
We had discussed what was to take place,
Yet, we were never prepared in any case.
We began ours days with traditions we'd formed,
This day was no different; just the norm.
One minute you were here and in a second you were gone.
Life ceased to exist, now I am all alone.
Gallantly you braved your final days,
No fears to be shown; that was your way.
To have prospered in love was our greatest accomplishment.
Though doubted by most, we excelled in life with amazement
and wonderment.
Rich with memories we have shared;
you'll live on through me, for our
love is mine to keep.
With our motto of "Together as one we will succeed."
We've crossed all barriers; a proven fact indeed.
Our love stood strong for always and forever.
Now more than ever, please my love, help me to bear the rest of my
life's unexpected endeavors.
All my love until we meet,
Give me your strength and guidance, I beseech.

Glenda Richard Leleux

Child's Play

The silence of the country side
forebodes the scene.
The elements conspire from distant thrones.

Our mundane members yield
to winds and weepings
not our own,

to dreams and visions
sewn
by children playing God.

James Hartsell

Old Home

The old farm house by the side of the road,
Was where many travelers dropped their load.
To rest and cool in the welcome shade,
Of the old oak trees and the wild grass glade.
The house itself was not fine or bold,
But the folk it housed were good I'm told.

This house befriended all mankind;
The rich, the poor, or any who'd find,
The old panelled gate that swung open wide,
To any who wished to come inside.
When once they entered they were sure to see,
The love in this home and hospitality.

The peddler, the lumberman, the beggar, or preacher,
Poor wanting help, or children, a teacher;
Each one of his kind found peace, love, and rest,
And went on his way feeling that he had been blessed.
By entering the gate to a welcome land,
Where charity and kindness were always at hand.

Naomi Dale

Gift Of Love

God hath made so many things
For all the world to see.
But none can be so beautiful
As the gift of love made for me and thee.

The Lord was on this earth, so dear,
For such a short, short time.
The miracles of love performed
Were as a stitch in time.

The Gift of love was given me
For all the world to see.
But the greatest gift God hath given me
He's also given to thee.

God's greatest gift was of himself
For all the world to see.
When Jesus came and died for thee,
He also died for me.

Barbara Switzer

"I'll Be Happy"

When all war is gone from the earth
When more babies are allowed the joys of birth
When the drugs are no longer on our streets
When togetherness is what everyone sees
When I find someone all my own
When the homeless people have a home
When a black man and a white can be friends
When a new year begins as an old one ends
When the cure to it has been found
When laughter becomes the most familiar sound
When the hungry have plenty to eat
When the air we breathe is finally cleaned
When everyone knows the meaning of peace
When I have all these.... I'll Be Happy!

James M. Sager

The Heavenly Chair

There was this little lady in a nursing home.
I adopted her for my very own.
I would sit beside her in a chair
As the weekly worship service we would share.
We would often talk of Heaven as our thoughts we would bare.
She said when she got to Heaven she would save me a chair.
Now I can almost hear her there,
"I am here and I am saving you a chair."

Virginia Skinner

I Am

I am a good person who has but one dream
I wonder what the future holds for me
I hear the splashing of waves against the shore
I see the sunset rise at the crack of dawn
I want to live my dreams so that I am happier than ever before
I am a good person who has but one dream

I pretend that I don't feel remorse for those I've lost
I feel the pressure of life
I touch the sunset, the sky, the clouds
I worry about where I'll go when I'm gone
I cry for all the starving people and abused children of the world
I am a good person who has but one dream

I understand that in order to get what you
Want you have to do your best to get it
I say I can handle all problems thrown my way
I dream of being a famous actress
I try to be all I can be and do all I can do
For this dream to come true
I hope I reach all my goals of life
I am a good person who has but one dream

Misty Pruitt

Untitled

Tear down the walls so you can hear silence
and listen to the air taste the sun.
Walk into the night and you will feel green leaves;
Follow your shadow so you can be free.
Set your own boundaries
To chase after a dream
But stop
To watch rainbows shine brightly
Through dissipated rain,
And realize the beauty though seldomly seen.
Know there's a difference from what was once known
Dark skies are white when all stars appear...
Go tap tap tapping your sticks on my fence
But go placidly thinking
If I'd never known a tree
Could I have this stick in sight of me?
And if I'd never known a thing
What would I know
Experience
To be?

Kiri A. Roberts

Peace

Peace is letting life's cares
Roll over your head while
Stamping on them with both feet.
It is daily maintaining control
Of the body, mind and soul.
Peace is steering away from snares
And not taking on life's gloomy cares.
It is being like falling snowflakes
Wonderfully resting serenely as you
Lie on your bed when sick or well.

Peace is letting God have complete control
Of troubles, misery and gloom.
Peace never entertains sorrow
But firmly grips hope for each tomorrow.
Sometimes, peace says speak.
Frequently, peace says be silent.
Peace dwells deep within you and me
Where no mortal being can reach.
Peace cries, "Never let me go
For I am yours to forever keep."

Florence M. Jones

Grandma's Never Been To Paris

Grandma's never been to Paris or sailed the ocean blue.
Grandma's always been a lady, right here for me and you.
In good times and in bad times, Grandma's been right there
when no one else can understand, Grandma, she will care.

She was there for all the falls we took, when we all learned to bike.
And taught us to find beauty where ever we would hike.
She's there for the milestone each of us will reach.
And if we should hit bottom, she will never preach.

But Grandma's never been to Paris or sailed the ocean blue.
Grandma's spent her whole life caring and loving me and you.
Remember all the good times and remember too, we care.
We'll always be a family, as long as love we share.
Susan Bloczynski

A Story

Today I wrote a story small
   Told the truth to one and all.
Some heaped praise upon my head
   Others were shocked by what I said.

It's never easy to write or say
   The truth about the world today.
So much beauty; so much hate
   So little kindness, what is our fate?

No one willing to take the blame
   For things so wrong, they bring us shame.
Who holds your hand, stands by your side;
   Teaches the children of hope and pride?

Lost to us are many things
   Just a little caring brings...
We've forgotten how to smile
   Or give a hug once in awhile.

Show some kindness, be a friend
   Give of love that never ends.
Open your heart, to the young and old
   Change my story, as it's been told
Virginia Brooks

All These Things

A cheer to brighten the day,
A bird chirping along its way.

A snowflake sparkling in the sun,
Two great friends having fun.

A beautiful sunrise, the beginning of light,
The sun setting, slipping out of sight.

The ocean waves splashing on the shore,
A heart full of love with room for more.

A rainbow colored so very bright,
A walk on a star filled night.

A full moon shining in the dark,
A picnic for two in the park.

To feel your love or to taste your kiss,
Is far better than any of this.

All of these things can make me smile,
But I would give them all for your love awhile.
Melinda Wells

Emotion

I feel deep, deep rumbling emotion
Way down in the depth of my soul;
Thrashing around like the stormy waters
Fierce, dashing, fearless and bold.

Rolling, tumbling, it has no bounds
Rising, reaching up, up to the ship
Easing down ever so slowly
Like the out going tides.

Then they are still, like a warm spring day
When the breeze is calm and almost still
Looking out over the grass so green;
Then a cool, easy breeze, and the air is chilled.

So much is happening deep inside
The emotions rise up with leaps and bounds
Just as quickly they suddenly go away
Yet I sit still, not making a sound.
Valeria F. Seay Shepard

Daily Living

Have you ever stood by a window
And gazed at the setting sun
And wondered what God in his heaven
Has thoughts of the day just done
Is God pleased with the progress your making
As daily you wander the earth
Are you wise in the way you are living
With no thoughts for the friends cross the way
With no heed to the help or the comfort
You could give to some needy today
Could you answer if God were to ask you
How you handled the gifts he bestowed
There's still time to lighten the burden
Of someone on lifes weary road
There's still time to work in God's kingdom
If only you'll take up the load
So remember, the sun will soon vanish
And darkness will shut out the light
And you'll answer to God for your actions
And he will know if the answer is right.
Hazel J. Berg

Cancer

For ten years she fought against the odds and she lost...
Time eases the pain, but the memory of her stays the same.

They told me not to cry, be strong
   talk to her as she lay as though nothing was wrong.
Heavy her labored breath, with her ever staring eyes.
Could she hear, see, since us?
Know we were there to say our good-byes?

Never to forget the over whelming fear,
praying for that miracle cure.
As they all talked around her, that last day as she lay
finally along I begged
"Don't go, you can't leave me!" don't let it be today.
Her head moved, once, slowly back-n-fourth,
   realizing she had heard me, my tears flowed.
As I bowed my head, while holding her hand,
   I knew God had answered, he's taking her to his heavenly fatherland

She now lies in his hands protected from all evil
   and the disease called cancer that helped gain her halo.
Ashes in the crater of Mt. Rainier,
her cherry tree blossoming every year.
Time eases the pain, but the memory of her will always stay the same.
Renee L. Salnave

Our Love

Our love is like...
The hypnotizing stars in the night skies.
Like a calm misty morning sunrise.
Like crystals in the icy snow.
Like water rushing over mossy stones.
Our love is like...
The beauty of birds in circled flight,
In the tranquility of the night.
Like beautiful frothy ocean waves,
On the cool wet sands.
Like watching all the animals,
Playing on the lands.
Our love is like...
All of this plus much, much more.
Our love is forever more.

Tina Russell

Breakfast For Dad

In my memory his face appears,
Like bright sun glancing off a mirror,
He's standing alone, dust in his hair,
In the mist of early morning air,
I drive up, holler, "Daddy I'm here",
The old car jerks suddenly in parking gear,
I hear mama say "don't let these get cold,"
The air smells like ham biscuits and cinnamon rolls,
He's behind the fence as I walk up,
Seems like he's drinking something from a cup,
I leave saying "enjoy your meal",
In the background I still hear....The Mill.

Linda T. Sanders

Body, Heart And Soul

Take my body, heart and soul,
Only you posses my being whole.
Will you my dearest object be?
Then ever let me cling to thee.

Come, let me have your better part,
And I will give thee all my heart.
Whom else have I on earth below?
There's only you to love and know.

All my treasure is yours, my love,
My best value is yours to prove.
Satisfied by what your love provides,
Withdrawing from all this world decides.

There is nothing more my life requires,
Just let my love, you alone desire.

Sybil Myers

Three Senses

I've never seen the mighty ocean blue
I've never seen an acre of roses covered in dew
But the sweetest thing I ever hope to see
is the love in your eyes when you look at me

I've never heard a newborn babies first cry
I've never heard a loved one say a final goodbye
But the sweetest thing I ever hope to hear
Is the sound of your voice when you say I love you dear

I've never touched a rainbow after the rain
I've never touched a burning flame
But the sweetest thing I ever hope to feel
is the touch of your hand when my heart you steal

Martha Welfel

A Question Of Love

I have nothing to offer to you, but my heart
Of course, you knew that right from the start.
I look in your eyes and I see forever
I want to face life with you... together.
Good times will come, hard times will too
But nothing can change how much I love you.
Where do we go from here? You may ask
I say choose love, it's not a tough task.
Open the door and let me walk through it
Open your heart and just simply do it.
I say choose me and let go of the past
I couldn't be first, but I can be the last.
Let me take your hand, your heart, and your love
Take mine in return and be blessed from above.
Say yes to a love...
    That can set your heart free
Say yes to the question....
    Will you marry me?

Rhonda K. McCulley

Strange Is The Means Of Placidity

Transcendence into the tranquil twilight,
Dreams and ambitions take her to flight
As she travails through dawns predecessor, the night.
Where shimmering stars dance in the sky
Looking upon the world; sparkling eyes
These with the pale moon now hidden by waves
By tides of cascading hair reaching her nave.

Here through which sails an ocean of tears
Washing away sunshine of the years
Boundaries beset, never truly free
With impetuous passion she circles the sea.

Drifting in thought into the seeping deep
Herself with incredulous emotions steeped
A ripple of experience for a lifetime of sleep.

Cory Desrosiers

Fall

I love the trees;
in their foliage, of multi-colored leaves;

Of red and orange and yellows galore;
waiting patiently, to cover, the earth's floor;

As one by one, they quietly, fall to the ground;
whirling and swirling, round and round;

Without making a sound;
as they blanket the ground;

Looking like, a patchwork quilt;
slowly changing, as they wilt.

There is no valor; they have no choice;
sometimes dry and sometimes moist;

Wherever they lye;
they wither and curl, and roll up and die;

Changing, from a brown to a rust;
as they gradually, change into dust;

Leaving the trees, looking mighty bare;
with no leaves on, to stop, the cold air;

While hoping, winter, won't last long;
when it's time, to put, a new coat on!

Robert E. Filip

After The Rain

Cactus greens became more brilliant when the dusting of sand was cleansed from their every crevice. The dull grays took on a different hue, as though touched ever so lightly with silver threads. Nondescript browns had turned to a fawn color. What once appeared as a bleak, barren desert mountain, suddenly became alive; after the rain. The barrel cactuses, scattered amongst the glistening rocks, had rooster red tips unfurling. The outstretched arms of the Joshua trees held bouquets of white blossoms, announcing the birth of spring.

Tiny rivulets had crept through hardened soil creating a jig-saw puzzle pattern. Puddles had formed in the shallows, miniature ponds had dotted the desert floor, offering a place to quench the thirst of the tiniest desert creatures.

Misty clouds had risen from their resting places along the ledges of the desert mountains. They had performed their last ballet dance as they moved with graceful splendor to a loftier plain. The steel gray sky had floated away to the North. Patches of robin's egg blue had brightened the sky, after the rain.

This had been the desert's gift to us all when the season changed from winter to spring, after the rain.

Lynn Lehman

An Affirmation For Strength Of Endurance

I am a child of God! Wherever I am, God is!
Giving me strength to endure, physical and spiritual healing
To mind body and soul.
And the ability to have faith, hope, and charity
With love, respect, understanding and forgiveness
Of others as well as myself.
For all these things, I give thanks to the trinity...
"God" Our Father "Jesus Christ", his son and the "Holy Spirit",
"Mother, Father light in action" which is in us all.
Thank you,
Amen...

Maxine Witte Aballi

Dear Sis

I thought about your birthday, but forgot to send the card.
I think about a lot of things, but find it very hard
To find the time to do things when I think of them, and then
When I have the time to do them, I've forgotten them again!

It wouldn't matter anyway if I braved snow and hail
And had it written early, it still wouldn't make the mail.
The members of my family are all masculine, you know,
And they mail all my letters and that's why I'm so slow.

I find my correspondence in coat pockets and the car,
And some I never find at all, tho I look near and far.
So if you get this message, I shall be very glad.
I hope twas the happiest birthday that you have ever!

Zetta Cook

Pride

At a time like this we need our pride.
For blue and white are on our side.

Stand up straight,
Hold your head high,
While we lower our flag for those who died.

Keep our town hand and hand
Explain to those who don't understand.
Our town needs power, strength, and pride.

Please don't forget those who died.
*(Christina's Sister was tragically killed
    by a speeding Metro Train)*

Christina Fulham

Mending Shattered Dreams

When the ground beneath you crumbles
and your heart's in sinking sand,
There is only one place you can go to for a helping hand.
He is your sure foundation and the anchor of your soul,
He is the One who can make your shattered life be whole.

Your dreams lie in ashes all around your feet,
And the life you now are living seems to spell defeat.
There is no hope in natural man to mend your shattered life,
And the broken pieces reveal your constant strife.

But there is a wondrous way that you can be made whole,
Despair can turn to peace and joy and mend the hurting soul.
Call upon the One true friend who really cares for you,
He'll fill your heart with love and hope and give you strength anew.

There is no problem that's too great or a life too torn to mend,
For when Jesus comes into your heart, the battle you will win.
He will heal your aching soul with His gentle caring ways,
And turn your shattered dreams into a vision for all your days.

Sandra Poynor

Whistling In The Wind

I love it when the wind whistles through,
Whatever it is the wind whistles through,
Those times when the house leans away,
When the windows shake and rattle,
And puffs of dust arise with each new draft,
With a fire in the old wood stove,
My union suit upon my back the flap buttoned tight,
The dogs at my feet breathing slow and regular,
As the security light flashes on and off,
Catching the wind blown trees,
And stopping them in their tracks,
I could watch for hours as the clouds flow by the moon,
First darkness then the ringed fullness of the light,
The sparkling of the newly fallen snow,
That lies in waves across the open field,
Nothing alive will move tonight,
And in their warmth and hunger hope,
That tomorrow will not move so fast or so cold

Steven C. Heaton

A Cry In The Crowd

Listen!
    Can't you hear my silent cries for help? Please listen to me, please.
    I am losing ground and drowning in these cold, unfriendly seas.
     I have struggled for so long
      And the current is so strong
    And I've lost the will to fight, so won't you listen to my pleas?

Look!
    Can't you see my spirit's broken and I've lost the will to live?
    A friendly word, a kindly glance, not much for you to give.
     Help! The waves are getting higher
      And my spirit starts to tire.
    Can't you see me? Don't you care or don't want to see me live?

Help!
    Please save me! I'm not asking much, just for help to reach the shore.
    Won't you reach out a friendly hand, I can't struggle any more.
     Please don't turn your back on me.
     Take a look and you will see
    I am every human being who has drifted from the shore.

Eva R. Beatty

A Budding Romance

I thank God each day for the blessing of love
That has come our way from the Lord above
A budding romance is near full bloom
The flowering of love needs plenty of room
To climb the trellis of life as it grows
The excitement sends shivers from my head to my toes
My dreams of a friend and a lover are coming true
I pledge my love and faithfulness, Bud, to you
You will always be uppermost in my heart
I'm glad you think I'm special right from the start?
Whatever the future holds in store for us
I'll be by your side with nary a fuss
Your smile and your teasing, kindness and wit
Keep my heart filled with laughter and joy as I sit
Pondering the happiness that we've recently felt
It's certain to grow, and our hearts will melt
Into one glorious union meant to forever last
Our memories are blended with events from the past
I truly love you and hope that our lives will be
Always a sharing of our love between you and me

Lucretia A. Gorham

"This Christmas"

Christmas a time to love and remember
To cherish the memories we've gathered all year
To stay cozy at home as the snow falls in december
As little Jesus's birthday draws near

Bake cookies and share them with a lonely neighbor
Leave a card for the mailman in your box
The butcher the grocer who may have done you a small favor
Leave some candy or ginger bread men or the durable pair of socks

Remember the sanitation crew who pick up everything you throw out
Or when they helped you pull your car off the ice
It's all a part of what christmas is about
Taking the time to be a little extra nice

Remember your loved ones buried in the snow
Light a candle to guide their way
Settle down for the new year and watch your children grow
Loving them always as you do this christmas day.....

Catherine Olivera

The Littlest Escape

Cusie was only four when he escaped the Nazis
too young to walk in pace with the rest,
his mother and his sisters and his brother
when they were taking their walk towards death.
He found out they could not longer see him
as they turned around on the mountain side
he made turn along the mountain path and run for life
His father viewed him from across the mountain
"An object small," he said "that moves in the terrain
He took a second look and then he cried
"One of my children alive has remained."

Sophia Demas

Soul Depth

I went deep through your breath
And discovered your soul and depth,
I saw in you worlds of faces,
And love in you as in the infinite graces.
You my heart does prefer,
All my delight is in you, you are her
That brings out my love like a waterfall,
That brings out rivers of love; just about feelings all.

Anatole Kantor

Competition!

Competition is a fitness trial, a testing of your skill,
Not just a case of win or lose, a stimulating thrill.
You enter in the contest, with a lot of motivation,
And you see yourself a winner, in your own imagination.
With total effort to excel, from all who enter in,
The aim in competition, is to be the one to win.
Some forms of competition, use the muscles full of zest,
With others; as in writing; it is more a mental test.
In all of them, if effort made, has failed to win the prize,
Remember! There's another trial, another exercise.
The benefits that you receive, each time you enter in,
Are making you a winner, that's the way they all begin.

Richard Baird

Why Do We?

Why do we call Jesus mighty for?
    He is the wondrous savior!
Jesus saves souls from sin,
    What a marvelous friend.
Who else in this world would give such a gift!
    He places his hands underneath us and lifts
Us out of miseries.
    Where we feel under our feet the breezes
Of turmoil, that we would have known;
    If we had stood like a stone
Upon our pride -
    But we did not reside
Inside the burdened-heart we normally desired,
    But we acquired
The Holy presence of the Lord,
    As we listened to His sweet word
Deep down in our heart.

Luthia Shaw

A Bald-Headed Woman

It is like a bald-headed woman,
what an amazing sight to behold!
Her enemy woefully shaved off her covering and beauty,
That true natural covering of peace, tranquility and guidance!
Nature is still wondering and sympathizing;

Now, listen to me,
Give heart to my lamentation!
Indeed, my tongue is full of today's question,
A bald-headed woman? Only this AGE have a product!
For she, the real image of today's world,

Oh total annihilation has uncovered itself!
Craziness, the degree achievement of modern era,
Like a bald-headed woman,
Darkness has been revealed
To show it deepness of woe!

Yes, she has been found wanting,
Weighed with the scale of ignorance,
Blind, naked and yet not aware!
Introducing her Hell of tomorrow's doom,
There she belongs!

Robert VanEarl Danso

A Wistful Sigh

Who's that dancing with my shadow, when I
walk alone, prairie dust and cactus tears,
are in my thoughts throughout the years,
love's sweet touch, with memory's songs,
without life's fears, my thoughts are
precious, to lofty heights of grandeur stay.
To you my love, 'What will you say.'

T. R. Woodward

Sweet Compensation

Instruments marry to create a fine tune.
What a charming and provocative thought!
envision the joining - that, makes sweet harmony.
  In quiet reverie - the melody haunts, repeats
and repeats - never ending.
  The instruments blend, as, if one, and play
with a singular joy.
  That, tightest blending, has just given
birth, the notes rise and fall, filling
the air, creating, beautiful sound everywhere.
  Thoroughly caught and enraptured - flow
into the sound and its beauty.
  That musical beauty so, sweet and low.
The marriage, that music can bring, into
your heart mind, and soul.
  Instruments marry, and wedded
make music.
  The most perfect compensation, for
most, of man's woes.

  Sharon Grove Mack

The Return

He walked along the back roads, on tired, aching feet,
The late summer sun low in the sky, and pale;
Close to the hedgerows in fear of those he'd meet,
Who may wish him harm, or throw him in jail.

Sinking behind the crest, its warmth gone with the light
The sun's exodus paints the clouds purple and blood red.
A chill runs through him, facing another long night
With the same dreaded question, will he find a bed.

The wandering lane makes way for a town. What a welcome sight!
But the people stare and point and shout "Get out, get out o'here!"
Compassion is forgotten, for they are full of fear and fright
At this shuffling old man, his eyes filled with briny tears.

Head bowed low, he leaves in disgrace. What has he done?
He couldn't fathom this place! "Worse than a stray dog I'm treated"
He sighed, "in the town of my youth, once home, sweet, sweet home!"
But no-one remembers, and nobody cares. He leaves, again defeated!

"Don't go!" called the voice, as he stumbled down the lane.
"Here's a room, with warm blankets, a shower and hot food!"
He turned.....They found him next day, laying out in the rain,
A look of serenity that none could explain, but dead, just the same!

  Kathleen M. Hall

Wappapello

  You were named after a proud Indian Chief.
beautiful lake Wappapello, glistening in the
silver moon-light, you truly live up to your name.
  Dear Wappapello, you hold my heart, a feeling
I can't shake. Memories of you bring me peace in
this world of turmoil, I hear you call to me,
some day I shall return.
  Oh my cherokee ancestors, look down on me,
send down your gentle breezes and cool my aging brow.
  This lake Wappapello, named after one of your own,
when I stand by you, holding my face up toward the
heavens, I seem to sense others long gone.
  Wappapello, in the state of Missouri where the
sun shines warm and sweet, and the wind is soft and clean.
  It's where my mom and dad lie sleeping,
hold them close with sweet love for-ever.

  Willie-Dean Bartlett

Untitled

The deadly venom of a rattlesnake,
  comes in many forms.
It comes thru words —
  that linger in our minds;
  poisoning each though, that becomes a memory.
It comes thru actions —
  biting us with fangs;
  that seep in thru our bloodstream;
  making us faint and numb all over.
It comes thru treatment —
  playing the games of the heart;
  that taunts us from the beginning of the attack.
Such an ugly reptile,
  this venomous snake is.
No wonder, Mary of God,
  has her foot upon his head!

  Naomi Carius

Every Now And Then

Every now and then, doubts disarm my confidence,
Uprooting my defences, challenging my resilience;
Haunting memories of old, return to threaten me,
I'm running on a dream, but they won't let me be;
I trudge along the new road I have chosen to pave,
While my restless past rolls around in a shallow grave.

My head is spinning between the winning and the losing,
The going up and the coming down make life so confusing!
A wayward tear finds me trying to shift with the tide,
As I stand alone and afraid, with no place to hide;
So every now and then, I run miles in the pouring rain,
Searching for a little hope, to make me believe again...

I wait on The Lord, knowing His promises to be true,
He'll invade the darkness and I'll find my way through;
Not long ago, I vowed to serve Him with a burning desire,
I bet my soul on Him, as He filled me with new fire;
I guess I know what went wrong - I didn't fan the flame,
For, every now and then, I forget to call upon His name.

  Margaret S. Wilson

Grandfather Clock

The old Grandfather clock stands straight and tall,
  giving its chimes for one and all.

I wonder how many besides my self,
  has problems at times as I do.

When one waits for medication to work
  and breathing is hard to achieve.

But one is never alone as I say a prayer
  and know Angel's are there while all asleep.

One waits for the chimes and ever hour the tolls,
  as one waits in the dark for hours to pass.

One thinks of time's all in the past of places one has been
  and places one has seen and places one would love to go.

What wonderful company is old Grandfather Clock
  as it stands so tall and gives out the time.

As one waits for the hours to pass and morning light to appear.

  Nellie M. Brand

Why Are There So Many?

Why are there so many horses asses, and very few horses around?
It seems to me a horses ass, is so easy to be found.
They pop-up here, and they pop-up there-no one likes to see them.
Why don't they stay in the horse's rear, instead they must
precede them.

Why do they show themselves to us? Do they need to cause a stink?
Don't they know that they're not liked?
Why don't they stop and think?
Do they just want to let us know, such things as they exist?
Is that why everyday it seems, another makes the list?

They appear to be in great supply, they sure do get around.
You might see one on the interstate as it passes through your town.
You could meet one at the supermarket, the theatre, or a bar.
And they love to spring and pounce on you, as you're driving
in your car.

They'll cut in front, and run red lights, and blow their horns SO LOUD
And there's always a big ol' horses ass wherever there's a crowd.
So keep looking 'til you spot, and you'll marvel just like me —
A horses ass - without the horse! You'll wonder — how can it be?!

Ernest L. Akers

Hidden Veils

Fading shadows silently seen
On winding roads where travelers dream
Journeys down each path unveil
An easily marked and well-trodden trail

Tarnished droplets of wind-blown mist
Cling to seekers like a stolen kiss
As a haunting eloquence echoes the scene
Like silver dewdrops of a mirrored stream

Journeyman find a beauty so rare
And tender secrets so worn and bare
For this is the prize no man can measure
Mother Earth's quietly laid treasure!

Gene Larrimore

Silent Snow

I watched the snow from my picture window.
It falls silently, slowly,
In a graceful dance of flakes
That meander this way and that,
In contrapuntal style.

Each snowflake does not seem
To be important, and yet
Each one adds its crystals
To the white blanket that is gradually
Covering the earth, quietly
Spreading its softness over dirt
And dead leaves and trash.

A feeling of peace settles gently
Within my spirit, whiting out
My busy-ness, my cares and frustrations,
As I watch the silent snow.

Barbara D. Schriever

Untitled

When I met you I knew not of love,
It was something in song and stories alone.
Since I met you I have learned of love,
It is real indeed. It's not something you see or do,
It's something from the heart that emanates within.
You are so full of love it rubbed off on me,
Now I know for sure what love is so I'm writing this to say
to you, I love you.

Richard Deily

Climbing Roses

She strolls graciously thru the arbor covered with climbing
roses of every color.
Garden gloves, hat and pruning tools, she approaches a small
concrete, white bench at the end of her sanctuary.
Her soul, and spirit is shaped. Two generations of caring
and wisdom have passed in this garden.
Suddenly, a skip, skip of little feet approaches.
Mamaw, Mamaw, she cries. Can I pick a rose?
Without waiting for a reply, the little hands reach up to
pluck a delicate rose.
Watch out! Watch out! Watch out for the thorns the older and
wiser one replies.
A split second is gone.
Her place, time and purpose is now.
Upon these the loving task is passed and continues.

Sandra F. Mitchell

"Mother/Daughter Miracle"

Daughter you have grown so fast,
    A mother you soon will be.
It didn't seem that long ago,
    I was holding your tiny body close to me.
Treasure this miracle that we now share,
    And give thanks to God daily in a prayer.
Treasure the child in a thousand ways,
    Love it, guide it in future days.
And as this child grows, a parent it too will be,
    We'll have another miracle to share...
        your child,
        You
        and Me.

Jan Paquette

Brotherly Love

Just thinking of you, this very day;
Wondering perhaps, if you would say:
'Neath all the stars that shine above,
There's nothing greater than Brotherly Love.

We all have differences, needless to say,
And make mistakes 'most every day.
No one is perfect, to stand so tall,
On the highest pedestal, only to fall.

So friend, let bygones be in the past,
And give thy Brotherly Love to last.
Do this today, and please don't wait;
One day at a time, may be a day late!

Nelson D. Bartlett

Love Bird

A home with love is empty if never a bird one sees,
passing its sweet love lyrics, winging from tree to tree.

The flutter of wings so gently sings its daily rhapsody,
Of morning light, of distant night, of all that's in between.

Love can fill a house with hopes, with dreams and wishes true,
But only the wings of a bird in flight can bring them all to you.

This little bird I tell of holds the key to your hearts desires,
Its little heart to beat with yours, to sing with through the hours.

This little bird you might have heard does not a feather have,
But little hands to hold you close and songs to make you laugh.

In all the days of love you share and many may they be,
I wish for you a little bird, to sing with most joyously.

Charmaine Rochon

To Santa

Santa do you care how much I miss my teddy bear.
  He's strong and cuddly
   Warm and Safe
  This special Teddy Bear
I'm writing just in case you've seen my
   Teddy Bear.
I thought I'd never lose this special Teddy Bear.
  It's Christmas time and this request
   Santa needs to hear.
Make sure you send the same special one,
  I've had with me before.
We've walked together arm in arm along
   The Rocky Shore.
He's warm to hold and peace surrounds
   When I'm with
    Teddy Bear.
It's times we've shared I miss the most
   with
   "Special Teddy Bear."
Donna Foy Jones

On Value

When loved one has left our boundary,
immediate thoughts of the past returns.
Life's accomplishments loses meaning as
reality of the time is heard.
The joys and hardships of living, fades
like worn strands of woven cloth.
Life experiences and deeds well done,
emerges to the fore of thought.
We hope to quietly leave, with thoughtful
memories and deeds, as our time has run its
course and now tis time to leave.
With hopeful epitaph, to friendships and
loving life complete. Inscribed for us forthwith,
then nothing more, nothing more.

  Jack Wakamatsu

The Climber

Morning air, crisp and clean
Much lay ahead to test his noble mien

Enthusiastically he climbed, summoning
Energy from source sanguine

At midday the climber
Reached median, strong purpose determining

The day wore, the goal sharply deemed,
Exerting reserve energy supreme

With dusk, he continued
The climb, undaunted by weariness and time

By dark, the finish
Was his victory sublime.

That night he rested long and well
Glad for the darkness that reliably fell

Rest and peace were earned in sum,
All hoped for dreams had finally come.

Next day, he rose little past
His usual hour, dressed and ate with savor unbounden...

Hours later, lifting his heavy pack
He started toward another more rugged distant mountain.

  Carmine T. Vigorito

The Sky Sox Win!

It is the bottom of the ninth. The score is tied.
Two outs, full count, Jimmy Tatum is up to bat.
Here's the pitch,
There's the swing, it's popped up.
Ced Landrum comes in to score.
The Sox Won!
The Sky Sox have won the PCL Championship!
The players are cryin', they're thrown' balls and hats into the stands,
The crowd is screamin',
Craig Counsell, Harvey Pulliam, Quinton McCracken,
and Mark Thompson
Are called up to the Rockies.
Jorge Brito, Alan Cockrell, Ty vanBurkleo, Ryan Hawblitzel,
Jim Czajkowski, Webster Garrison,
and Pedro Castellano are awaiting their turn.
"Oi" is played over the loudspeakers.
The crying announcer calls "Jayhawk Owens and Trenidad Hubbard,"
Are they here? No, they've been up at the Rockies since August.
But they're the ones who helped get us here.
They got their moment of glory even if it was sixty miles away.

  Cristi Gower

Peace

The silence of war machines
Killings stopped
Solutions discussed at a table,
With heads of nations willing and able
To bring harmony to all lands.

Let everyone share in the progress
Work and earn their place
In lives that are fruitful
With kindness, happiness and grace.

A freedom to wander over all the land,
To greet our neighbors and shake their hands
To nurture our families and our faith
To make our world snug and safe.

When this harmony is attained
And we are led down peaceful lanes,
Then we can bow our heads
And reap our heavenly rest.

  Mary M. Calderone

A Tribute

Everyone experiences revelations—
a few moments of crystal clarity.
Leafing through a famous painter's autobiography
I came to his portraits of nude women.
The sheer magnificence of the female form
left me almost breathless.
I suddenly realized why mankind will endure.
Remembering my mother's unflinching courage,
her optimism, undaunted by horrendous poverty,
I gazed in awe and felt the power
and determination of this wonderful creation.

  Harry W. Gordon

Sanctuary

I will find my place in the sun.
A place that is meant for me alone
Where contemplation comes about undisturbed
Regardless of the world around.

  Jacqueline L. Childs

Life Today

Scared to leave your home, cautious be
Snipers, killers, robbers, be on guard
They can be anywhere you are
More so now than ever before
Will you become a victim
No safe haven in this world
Tempers flare easily
Today and tomorrow so uncertain
No security, no guarantees
Health Care, unemployment, every day life
Disasters, tragedy, terrorism all around
Weighing heavy on your mind
You try to hold fast to how
Life was so long ago, way back when
But gone are those carefree days
A thing of the past, laid to rest
We must go on, hoping the best to see
Praying for a safe day, a long life
Thankful when each day has ended well
This to will pass-peace and happiness forever...

Anita Rogers

Poetic Seduction

She silently welcomes the music's soft melodious tone,
with closed eyes she imagines, she and lover alone.

Ever so sweetly to her heart he plays,
his declaration of feelings, her heart to steal away.

She feels herself on the verge of surrender,
her captured heart, to him she will render.

He tempts her thoughts with impassioning sound,
to the inflaming concerto, she finds herself bound.

She has fallen under his rapturous spell,
his rhapsodical flirtation, she can not quell.

At reaching his crescendo he now does leave,
his sensuous movement, to be perceived.

She reflects upon her feelings, in a poetic way,
of musical encounter, with her lover that day.

Unknown unto her what was to befall,
of music's seduction, as she sat in Symphony Hall.

Crystal Black

A Soldier's Farewell

Good-by my love
You are the light of my life
Were the words of a soldier
As he embraced his young wife...
But, I must be going
Don't cry for me my love, or show no sorrow
For I shall return tomorrow...
I can see now the dawning of anew morn
Yonder, by the camp, the soldiers start to form
And if you listen, a bugle is playing reveille..
It was one evening after a savage battle
Many lie wounded and moaning
Some won't utter a sound.. A dark cloud looms
Over the battleground
Now, softly she speaks, last night I had a dream
Oh! So real it seems, I saw an Angel
Standing there by Michael
And he whispers softly to me
Please don't cry for me my love or show no sorrow
For I shall return tomorrow...

Joel Camacho

You Forgot Something

Memories - I have found are funny things.
They seem to show up in all your dreams.

I remember wishing upon a star - and "you" came true.
Now that you're gone - I'm not sure what to do.

Because when you said good-bye - you left some things behind.
Some of them are tangible, but others are nestled in my mind.

The first thing I noticed was your toothbrush in the holder,
A pair of socks, a video, and a couple of work folders.

But, you also left your scent, which lingers in the covers.
The ones we used to snuggle in, back when we were lovers.

And in my bed - where you always - made everything - seem so right.
There now is an empty spot that I keep reaching for each night.

All of the material items, I can wash, forget, or throw away.
But the memories just don't seem to want to stray.

I'm trying to forget it all - and make a brand new start.
If only I could fill this vacant spot in my heart.

You see I really miss your smile and hunger for your touch.
Why did I allow myself to want you so much?

Getting over your would have been faster and a lot less of my time spent.
If you had simply taken your memories - with you - when you went.

Lisa A. Hanebrink

Tika

No one and nothing compares to you,
    not oceans, nor mountains, nor skies of blue.
Not stars in the sky, not the moon up above,
    Not the riches of man, not the wings of a dove.

Of the songs of the world of love have been sung,
    not one is compared with my heart's own tongue.
For of you it sings timeless with not words of the world,
    but with those of great passion, with those of the soul.

Three years gone past is the time since we married,
    To you I grow closer, by my heart I am carried.
My world you give meaning, direction, and light,
    Without you I'd wither, absent passion to fight.

Fear not I am yours, til the day we take flight,
    and are carried away to the wondrous light.
My love is a fire, burning each day a new,
    for no one and nothing compares to you.

Darren Ball

Let God Show Me The Way

I walk my path of life alone, my wife has left my side.
I never knew the pain divorce could cause a man inside.

The sparkle's missing from my eyes, my face is cloaked in pain,
I search to find some logic in a world that's gone insane.

I feel I'm but a hollow shell, my dreams die in a heart
Devoid of strength to carry on for it lies torn apart.

I find no pride in doing well. I've learned unless you share,
Accomplishments mean nothing when there's no one close to care.

Perhaps some day the pain will ebb— the daily tears will end—
Perhaps some day new dreams will form as my heart starts to mend.

I'll rediscover peace and joy and love perhaps some day—
With patience I must keep faith and let God show me the way.

Richard Day

New Beginnings

Today begins a brand new year,
with room for new memories to make;
A fresh new time to give some thought,
to the steps that we will take.

Out with the old and in with the new,
bad habits soon should depart;
Wiping the slate totally clean,
to help make for a clear fresh start.

Change of ways and resolutions,
a whole new year to grow;
Hope that at the end of this year,
you have wonderful things to show.

Set your goals and work for more,
put yourself to the test;
And all the days of this bright new year,
focus on being your best.

Deanna L. Martinez

Family Name

Of my brother I was so proud
　he stood up for me, he was quite loud.
But speaking up for me didn't last long,
　because he wasn't taught to be strong.
One day I thought he would get on the right trail,
　but he won't, he's jut a male.
I say a male and not a man,
　there is a difference I now understand.
A male child brings much adoration,
　but a man can keep his family from separation.
No one in this family ever held up the other,
　not the father, the mother or the brother.
I figured when you were younger you were afraid,
　that you'd outgrow it, it was only a stage.
My pride in you is gone without a trace,
　you are now talking from both sides of your face.
I hope you're happy in your new selection,
　you're acquiring quite the collection.
Yes, there's no greater blessing to proclaim,
　than the honor of a good family name!

Danene Whitney

One Night Stand

　My dream is running around.
He has been with most of the girls in town.
My body he needs. I'll continue my deed.
For the hope that someday love will follow.
Never before did love making come before love,
did I allow. Except for now.
　The more I know the more I want.
My eyes no longer want to hurt.
I now do things I thought I'd never do.
But now my heart is telling me go.
My hunger grows as everyday goes by.
I thought I could never be satisfied,
without someone by my side.
　But now everything is seeming to workout
just right. I love the way he smiles
it is the sight I wait to see. Even though
there is a chance that our love could be.
But if not then I'll understand as long as
he stays my one night stand.

Michell Manuel

Aloha, Mahalo

Aloha, Mahalo, Aloha Lei
Enchanting are the songs from far away.
Aloha, Mahalo, Aloha Lei
Hawaii sends a flower lei.

　Leave the worries of this world behind
　 happiness abounds here for you.
　Hawaii offers peace of mind
　and lets your dreams come true.
　Aloha, Mahalo...

　Palm trees swaying gently in the breeze
　beckon you ashore to enjoy
　and island people call to please
　with luaus, leis and poi.
　Aloha, Mahalo...

　Magic casts a spell on plants and trees
　beautiful and bright in the sun
　and in the moonlight mysteries
　another day is born.
　Aloha, Mahalo...

　Ute M. Lorenz

If Only I Could Understand

If only I could understand.
Why people die in the wrong accordance of nature?
Why other people think they have a right to take another's life?
Not wondering who is left to try and survive.

Who has the right?
The 25 year old man who took my son's life.
My son who had a life that was troubled and in misery.
He tried as a youngster to understand.
What was wrong between Mom and Dad?
Never quite figuring it out. He went on.
With little self-esteem and never understanding.

I, as Mom should never have left him at ten.
Left him with the man, who harmed him for eternity.
But, I did as I tried to repair it at 15.
It was too late.

Now, he is gone, and I miss him immensely.
I guess I will never understand. Why God took him first?
It should have been me first. Him last.
I miss him so very much.
If I could only understand.

Dawn Anne Remick

Flight Of The Giants

Oh clapping giants skyward bound
Ushering breezes my way and crowned
With noble beauty alive before me
Destined for true glory.
In a moment captured breath doth flee,
Surrendered by your majesty.
You reach for Heaven; I'm so rendered
Awestruck by such towering splendor.
Whisper tales of time dearly spent
Of years, and youth and sentiment.
Reflecting ages of reason and rhyme,
Forever soar higher; oh, peaceful sublime.

Kristy A. Roberson

Perhaps Tomorrow

The work is there it must be done
But I want to spend time in your warmth my sun.
I want to sit and look at you blue sky.
But no time to watch your clouds roll by.
  Perhaps Tomorrow.

There's no time to watch you rippling brook
As you search toward the seas.
No time to enjoy your softness now,
My warm and gentle breeze.
  Perhaps Tomorrow.

God has given us his treasures,
To enjoy, to seek to find.
And the day he beckons us to him
We'll leave all these gifts behind.
  Perhaps Tomorrow.

  Aline L. Williams

Us

Five loving sisters are we
Josie, Johanna, Dolores and Marie
  spelled with an A
  like in F-R-I-E-D-A
Josie born second after first Josie died
Named Josie for Grandma, because Papa cried
"Mama loved Papa too much," did you say?
Oh! No! She named Maria with an A
For her mama to even the score
She named all the others, total: four.
Mama said, "Papa will name all the
  boys, when there's more,"
Sons never came. The girls had no brother
But Papa was happy - one girl named for Mother
The names are just letters, it's people who care
Who love like a family, it's burdens to share.
We're five happy women with blessings galore
Growing older and wiser, many memories to store.

  Frieda Pantuso Farinelli

"Extinction"

The point-
sight's blackest mind's edge ends.
The fading-cascading-
earth's blood of life-
nimbly jumps-
to the rivers winding way
and falls short of life's steady flow.

Limping desperately
Earth's blood of life
found no footing
on a world breastless, and with no ground,
as cracks that long ago appeared
sliced darker-and split the world in pieces.

The point-
a single shard of sand
flung outward on ribbons of red
looses the cry
that arrived to late-
in his world to stop
the last point of sand from dying.

  David Hughes

A Window To My Past

When I was a little girl
My mom said I was nice.
Now that I'm a young girl,
She says I'm full of spice.
I guess you change as time goes by,
From sun up till mornings nigh.
When I think back years ago,
Memory after memories flow.
I've loved my life from the very beginning
I can't imagine my life ever ending.
When I think of the memories years ago, I have such a blast.
Because I think of the window to my past.

  Tina Thrash

A Kid Best Friend

Santa Claus is a kid's best friend.
From the first of December, clear to the end.
The kids try to please him, to love and obey
their Moms and Dads with each passing day.

They know Santa's watching, they don't even try
to kick, pinch, tattle or make someone cry.
They visit him often when he comes to town,
with a list miles long of things written down
that they would like their best friend to bring,
on the night when all children's glad hearts sing.

Now I've been thinking this to myself,
In fact I've discussed it with Santa's chief elf.
If I love Santa so much in December
He's been good to me, I'll always remember.

And because he's my dearest friend.
I'll try to be dear.
Not for just one month.
But for the whole year!

  Betty Romero

My Family

My husband and my sons have brought
The kind of love that I have sought.
Today I am so glad to see
The joys of you, my family.

Whene'er I feel the least bit blue,
I only have to think of you,
To know that life is still worth all
The ups and downs with its pitfalls.

You've given me the kind of home
So that I'll never have to roam.
My hopes and dreams securely set;
I'm settled in with no regrets.

For you, my loves, I live and breathe;
I find my utmost is achieved.
When working or playing for you I strive
To give you back the joys I've derived.

My husband, my sons, I see as One,
One complete and total sum,
For whom I want to always show
My life is lived your love to know.

  Brenda Fullerton

Frustration

"This is the day the Lord has made-let us rejoice and be glad in it"
I rose to comply, opened the coffee can -
but there was nothing in it.
So I went to do some cleaning -
the bottle said "To open press down and turn."
Which I simply can not do, for easy lids I yearn.

Next I tried to make a call some business to complete.
By the time I heard "Press 7", I had to admit defeat.

The weather did not cooperate, the day was dull and gray.
"Aha", I thought. "Some soup will go well today."
I put the soup bones on the gas up high I turned
To get it started quickly. But I forgot and so it burned.

I left the house discouraged, went to the station to fill my tank.
Some one was using my pump and (so to be frank)
In my frustration I ran into a post newly painted white
Which left a big white blotch and broke my parking light.
Although I got the light fixed the blotch caused my down fall
For I had to tell my husband about it all.

When I sank at last, into my chair recounting how I'd been abused,
Someone seemed to speak to me as if He was amused.
Then as I listened I heard a still small voice
That said "Just laugh, my dear, and in this day rejoice.

Mary Jane Harns

Love Within

Good morning Dear Lord, it's a beautiful day,
I must talk with you Lord, then be on my way,
Got a busy schedule looking at me,
Lord help me to take help those in need,
not selfishly desiring my own gain,
Help me show love to others so they may see,
Your light Dear Lord Jesus glowing in me,
So many are lost and in so much strife,
They haven't heard Lord, your the way, truth and life,
I want to tell them so desperately,
as your merciful love sent someone to me,
I pray that my words and my actions will say,
Dear Jesus your living within me this day.

Carol Kubat

Silent Tears

The tears that are shed in silence,
will also not be seen or felt.
Except for those who shed them,
but who cannot cry out for help.

They are shed by young and old alike.
They are shed by the wealthy and poor.
They are shed in every time and place,
in a silent, eternal war.

They are shed for loves that were won and lost,
or for loves that could have been.
They are shed for crimes as yet unpunished,
or for scars that will never mend.

To look at their faces, you would never guess,
the silent tears they must endure.
But the face is a mask the tears betray,
and for that, there is no cure.

Aaron Madison

Sweet Mother

This is a poem to my mother, who is a sweet mother,
Whose love for me, remains a source of inspiration.
Oh!, my sweet mother,
When I was hungry, you gave me something to eat.
When I was sick, you prayed that I got well quick,
You spent sleepless nights, taking care of me,
You will not sleep, untill you've lured me to sleep.
All that you did for me, will run pages.
Ebony black, mother you are beautiful,
You are sweet, sweet mother.
I cannot forget that early January morning.
When the cold hand of death, snatchedyou away from me,
You died,
When I needed you most,
Unwilling, you went to the world beyond.
So, I write this poem for love, for life, in memory,
As a tribute to you my dear sweet mother,
Who died nine years ago,
Struggling to educate me.
Sweet mother, the struggle continues.

Michael Nnaemeka Okonkwo

It Has Finally Come!!

We have waited so long,
Now, there's a smile on my face
And I'm singing a new song.
My people struggled!
My people died!
While waiting for this day!
Yes, I SMILE!
Our head's up high!
And we're chanting with pride!
So, look up young brother,
There's nothing to hide.
Grab the new flag and run to the mountain top,
And keep on running, for we must not stop!
We have waited so, very long!
To sing and dance the FREEDOM SONG!!!!

Ozzie Morrow

Nature's Pain

As I dreamt I walked with nature.
I could hardly see my hand before
me, the air was full of smoke. I walked
in a fog for what seemed like forever.
As I dreamt I walked with nature.
I took a sharp turn and suddenly
all bout me was green. Forest green.
The air was still as the night sky.
I moved slowly forward. My foot crushed
leaves and dead twigs. The sound was
blood curdling and with every step I
felt nature's pain.

Eileen Hughes

What If...??

What if the sun were blue?
What would you say? What would you do?
And what if ocean waves were pink?
How would you feel? What would you think?

Now picture clouds of fluffy green
And bouncing rabbits of tangerine.
Silver bees, a yellow sky
And a polka-dotted you and I.

Valerie Ann King

Sonnet To Sergei

They could not hide the love in their eyes
Melting the sheen that they danced upon
They could not hide from their fate
As the light of their future grew dim then gone
She once had gold glimmering around her neck and in her arms
A strength absorbed through her skin from his
Trusting to keep her from all harms
So full of promise, so full of life
Hand in hand as children, and as husband and wife
Without a warning, his strong hand slipped away
Leaving her tiny hand reaching for forever from this day
Frozen tears cut paths down cheeks of those left behind
As Moscow's angels weep flurries upon those trying to find
The strength to go on and to remember
The Russian bear that was as gentle as strong
The elegance and passion he lived through every breath and song
The memories will never fade, just as his smile always strong
Through masterpieces of motion he will forever live on
The sullen face lifts skyward as she manages to smile
Perhaps knowing in her heart, she will have him all the while.

Pamela S. Owens

Untitled

Gentle breezes blowing through my window
brushing away stale memories that have
settled in an inch of summer-dust
unwanted upon the furniture.

In having a sense of moving on do I
drop the past like out-moded ways,
like stone-aged thinking.

New chances taken, more life to be lived.
Tomorrow still evades me,
for upon grasping it, I find it's only today.

So I take it and fill it with more memories
to be preserved from a stale existence.
Memories that are jazz colored and taste of pungent espresso
and a good read.

Ears filled with possible poetry and breaking hearts
smiles and tears, boredom and busy-ness.

Thus is the spice in my taste-budded hours
that bring curled noses of the rankness or
desired devouring of a glutton.

It is everything set altogether in Pandora's box.

Amber-Dawn Germany

Distant Wave

Will time run out and leave me here
Without a memory of you to share?
Will moments spent with you in thought
Drift faraway as if you were not?

Oh wave of memory from distant shores,
Bring back to me all time mine and yours.
I wait in hope for you to be
My special thought in memory.

The time does change, but you remain
The force in my heart, a treasure unchanged.
I wait to share our time once more;
A wave of laughter upon our shore.

Patti Weber

If We Could See

If we could see what a small boy imagines,
    What do you think we would see,
Puppies, ponies and dragons,
    Or pirates that sail on the sea?

Rockets that fire to the planets,
    Cowboys that ride on the plains,
Airplanes that roar through the heavens,
    Hitch a ride on a big circus train?

If we could see what a small girl imagines,
    What do you think we would see,
Lace and small satin slippers,
    Fairies dancing with magical glee?

A princess with gowns all a-flowing,
    A crown that glows from her head,
Prince Charming on a white stallion,
    Or a kitten that sleeps on her bed?

If we could look with such innocent wonder,
    Feel love that's as pure as can be,
Let our spirits soar with no shadows,
    Their dreams are what we would see!

Claudette T. Allen

Untitled

I want to tell you about
a very special place that everyone has.
A place that makes your dream come true.
Where you can make yourself a pirate or
even a kings knight.
You and your friends can be stranded
on an island.
Even you in an animal's point of view.
If you would like to eat dog food
you are welcomed to.
Would you like to know why?
Well, because silly you can eat anything
you please.
You could dress in fish scales or even
amphibian skin.
It's all up to you, because it's your
imagination.
Won't you come and imagine?

Nicole Ball

Present Moment

With my new found knowledge
I can clearly see your thoughts
are not your friend
They bring you only confusion
of what was and what could be
Our inner mind the beast within
cannot solve, either
From day one of our birth
divine providence keeps trying to come through
The beast within sensing lost of
control continue to block its birth
Yet when those few who seek truth
and freedom discover the ever sending voice
New found peace and direction are theirs
Our thoughts from the heart the key
focus to the most important being present moment
When we realize what was or what could be
is not decided by our minds
A new freedom is born within us, ever lasting

Terry Lee Greger

"Certainties"

Under the tearful clouds the day prevailed
a little longer — a little lighter
    spring will come again

Like phantoms of a dream
    life's warm sun
brings back those sunny hours
    bright days — gentle nights

Thoughts of winter gloom — winter wind
    disappear with the year
should snow fall on new years day
    I will see springs flowers

Perhaps I shall sit by a pond and
    watch it flow
to the ocean of eternity — my imagination
    has achieved timelessness

To think about the affirmation of my life
    is to realize
happiness, growth, freedom, love and
    the new year with you

Robert J. Cece

Ashes To Ashes

He really hadn't meant to cause her pain.
Somehow he never made it home last night
and morning finds him walking in the rain
turning over ways to set things right.
He turns his collar up against the cold,
fearing she's already taken fight.
Last night he left so smug, today, just old.

His fear, despair and sorrow make him bold
enough to try, somehow, to make amends,
to save this love, his life that she now holds;
his grace, tomorrow, future he suspends.
If only she will listen, hear his pain.
He falters...turns away into the rain.

Treva Myatt

The Changing World

It seems the world is changing, and if this fact you doubt.
Look twice at all the problems, we fear and talk about,
The wars in other countries, near-war on city streets,
The viruses that sicken, E-Coli in our meats.

The greed in high-up places, is not the only sin,
The scorn we show a black man, whose lily-white within,
Addictions, sex, and violence, from which some won't return,
We scoff at Christian values, from which we used to learn,

Beware we say of neighbors, keep all doors shut and locked,
We hate to use a street where, a friend is being stalked,
No love for one another, some kids have fathers "five",
Not raised, just simply growing, quite empty, they survive.

And what about the earthquakes, so frequent anymore,
Tornadic winds and flooding, with lost lives by the score,
Abortion is our choosing, to kill the child we make,
And now we tell our "Old Folks", their own lives they can take!

Perhap's we need God's blessing, with prayers he's listening for,
Let's hope he isn't angry, we kicked him out the door!
It's true, the world is changing, to what? Some say it's clear,
The Bible gives fair warning; the "End Times" may be near!

Hazel Burnworth

Of Ahdenoff's Terrible Deed

As the Ent walked out of sight, singing aloud
Of many an adventure, the residents waved
Good-bye, silently, dreadfully, behind the cloud
Of fear that he would not return unscathed.

And once out of sight, he cried a single tear
For the fear that was in his heart, slowly building
Into the most dreaming emotions called fear,
But did not dwell on the subject long. Buying

His time by using magic, with the purest of heart
At the crossroads he met — met a strange face
And asked for directions to his home and went
Along his way. But evil was he, and in haste

The Ent did not notice thus until he,
Was gone. And trapped on the beaches of the sea.

Tommy Carlson

How May I Help

Stark and lonely creatures enveloped in greed.
Sterile selfish people aiming only to succeed.
Cumulating riches far beyond measure,
ignoring any loving sharing pleasure.

Escaping the race, seeking spiritual thought.
The highway deadends, tourists come naught.
It's barren of inns, no room to tarry.
Come to oneself, unnerving and scary.

Sensing gentle cleansing from every wave,
finding understanding, striving to be brave.
The ocean's rhythmic pulsing washing evil from my mind,
leaving me the challenge of responding in kind.

The agony of changing from my former greedy pace,
to a thoughtful caring person etched deeply on my face.
Uneasily submitting to my new evolving self,
what's in it for me becoming "how may I help".

Cleve Anderson

A Child

A child wonders from the path it knows so well,
oh, what the hell.
The way seems fun and full of light,
follow the sun just out of sight.

Time passes where I don't know,
the light dims to an eerie glow,
Calls to return it will not heed,
This path is fine there is no need,

The good is gone the shadows darken,
The voices are those she will not harken,
The voices say return to the way,
The Lord is here for you each day.

Tears are wept by those who care,
Their sorrow, their grief are hard to bear,
Days of trouble build to a load of care,
The voices return saying the Lord is there.

Donald E. Barron

Beauty

When your thoughts are weary and your body is tired
Lift up your eyes and look at the sky,
The splendor and beauty will set you on fire
And your soul is rested and shall never die.

Whenever darkness approaches
Forever react the same way
For your mind and body will be refreshed
With the dawn of each new day.

Carrie Bachrach

The Trap

Leaf for a roof-hiding place webs strung on twig's and stick's
high in a young orange tree like crochet magnified
a hundred times or more, Perfect art in the twilight of dawn.
Small world-independent home.

Drop-lets of dew small prisms of red and blue
when sun shines through
Out of sight waiting for prey as fly circles looking to lit.
Webs of glue no fly should venture into.
Struggles wont let go, no escape.

Like on a trapeze-balancing act spider attacks,
Quick as a flash shot fly in the head retreats to wait for death.

Cocoon of silk fly at rest spiders wait the next victim to attempt the test.

William J. Cedar

To Be

To be submerged in serenity.
To be embraced by time.
To be in the waves of water.
To have peace in mind.
To be completely and totally free, for what
I am, I am proud to be.
Contemplating the moments in life
achieving the goals that I strive.
I am but one of many whose eyes can see
of what i s really meant to be.
To feel me for I am the wind.
To hear me for I am the waves.
To smell me for I am the air.
To touch me for where ever you are,
I will also be there.
Walk with me and hold my hand,
letting our feet become subdued in the sands.
Life and love will sometimes come together,
just as eternity was meant to last forever.
What is it that you see, for it is me that I am to be.

F.M. Cooper

Picture Window

Inside this picture window is my fantasy come true
It gives to me the power of love that keeps me close to you

I think of you and suddenly the real world disappears
A fantasy so real, and yet, I know the end is near

I find myself a secret place somewhere behind the times
To have a love affair extinct, a rendezvous of minds

And when I've lost myself in love with no trail leading back
The real world seems to pave the way...the picture windows cracks.

Belvha LeValle-Harris

Today Be Thankful

Today you praise God for today
You thank Him for yesterday
And you ask Him for tomorrow
Today be thankful that you met no sorrow

You thank Him for each night
The moon and stars shine so bright
For each new morning
You rise and face a brand new dawning
Today you just be thankful

And last but far from least
You thank Him for His Son
For He's the only one
Who can give us today, yesterday
And all our tomorrow, so let us
Today be thankful

Betty J. Davis

"The Autumn Must Be His"

'Twas in the Autumn of our life, God blessed us with a child
A sweet and precious daughter to love and cherish for awhile
A once in a lifetime angel with heart of purest gold
One who was so full of life, a beauty to behold.

She always loved the Autumn, with cool gentle breezes,
golden leaves falling.
We'd laugh and talk and walk along down each lane of red and gold,
Then she's hurry back to see her friends,
and down the road they'd go.

Years went by and seasons passed and dark clouds gathered in
Losing what our hearts beat for, our grief, too much to comprehend
I guess it was by faith alone that we survived the days,
Of deep despair and broken dreams, she'd suffered so many ways.

Throughout those crimson Autumn days, we felt him near in many ways
Her life touched so many hearts and many friends so dear
And sharing all the laughter, memories, pain and tears,
We had to cram a lifetime into a few short years.

In the lovely season that he sent her, he came back to take her home
She is now gone back to him, around God's golden throne
We trembled, when Autumn called her name,
our angel, we'll surely miss
Loving and knowing her for what she is,
we know the Autumn must be his

Bulah McCall

Change of Heart

After awhile you learn the subtle difference...
Between holding a hand and imprisoning a soul.

And you learn that love doesn't mean security,
While you begin to understand that kisses aren't binding contracts.

Words or gifts aren't promises of forever
You accept defeats in reality.

With your head held high and your eyes open wide,
Take it as the grace of a woman, not the grief of a child.

Then you learn to build all your roads on today,
Because tomorrow's ground is too uncertain

futures have a way of failing in full flight,
After awhile you learn that sunshine burns when you get too much.

So you plant your own garden and decorate your soul,
Instead of waiting for someone else to bring you flowers that
will whither in the wind.

It's then that you learn to endure... and endure...
Endure even more
You discover that you really are strong, a survivor.
And you learn that you really are worthwhile...
You learn and learn... that's life!
Jay Warren Downs

Jay Downs

Our Private World

In the morning next to me is sunshine
Even if the rain clouds gather at my window
A gentle wind blows across my heart,
and strikes the chords of love that dwell there in.
His tender smile caresses me, and for
precious moments the world is held at bay
Til smaller voices of love come
stealing in, and quickly melt our
private world away

Linda Pittman

To Craig, Dying Of AIDS

Yet stay awhile sweet youth in my embrace
Nor care that sad intangibles await;
Now lies a loveliness upon earth's face
And quietude has claimed us for its state.

The rhetoric of rain shall be our prayers
And eloquence of winds a David's psalm
To soothe this troubled Saul beset with cares
While thoughts like cowled monks walk by in calm.

Each day my eyes weighed down with unwept tears
Must scale the craggy contours of your head
To read thereon the same unspoken fears
Of what laid you low at last upon your bed.

Ah, look up love and tell me if despair
Can last so long our dust shall find it there.

Robert Clermont

With You Eternally

I am in the air you breath,
I am in the rain softly falling on a summer's day
I am the streams ever running on their way,
I am the flowers blooming throughout the universe.

I am the grass a green carpet so lush,
I am the trees so stately and tall,
I am the birds singing ever so sweetly,
I am the winds that gently blow.

I am the snow so glistening white,
I am the children's voices gleefully singing,
I am the earth from which we begin.

I am no longer here, but yet I am everywhere,
For I have passed into the unknown,
But still I am here with you every step you take,
Till we can be as one again some day.

So weep not and feel no grief,
For I've not died you see,
I've stepped into a void of which you cannot be
But yet, I will be with you for all eternity.

Philomena Rossi

"Courage"

Courage in peace, courage in war,
Courage at home, courage abroad.
Reach for the stars, walk on the moon.
Scan the ocean, scan the skies.

Take heart, be not despised,
Courage in marriage, courage in life.
Forget the fear of being afraid,
Be not dismayed.

When climbing a mountain, climb with your might
For a heavy heart has no place in upward flight
Courage is not a paper tool, nor is it iron or steel
It's the heart's deep need.

Be courageous now and make up your mind.
Those worthy of honour are those who have led.
Victorious battles and never said die,
But rather they shouted, get up and try.

Do not think of your enemies faces at all.
See David seemed short and Goliath tall.
But the courageous one outweighed them all,
Be strong! Be strong!

Victoria A. Huntley

Young Girls

Young girls, footloose and fancy free
But are they really?
They are full of fun and mischievous acts
At an age where they are trying to discover so much
They have to do what they have to do to make those discoveries,
no matter what
They are not only trying to discover themselves,
but also the world around them, including boys, and how they
fit into the world
Not still a child, not yet a woman
Bodies change, minds confused
Calling Red Rover, Red Rover-come on over
Come from childhood, enter into womanhood
Shootin' baskets, playin' ball
Hittin' boys, then thoughts turn to kissin' boys
Growin' up and not sure that they want to, or are ready to
Wanting to still be a little girl, yet seeing the world in a different light
Skating rinks and dances
Swimming holes and play houses boys and first kisses

Sheila Holwell

Nature Cries

Aura of honeysuckle, wisp of the wind
Dandelions in full bloom, roses on the stem
Wind lingers in the shadows of the huge oak trees
Mother nature reaches forward to quench her needs
Anchored mountains clasp their rigid arms together
But set no limit
Water races onward without an ending.

Appearing before all this monetary treasures evolved man
Earth's counter-partner with no will to understand
Rapacious destruction expands thru the years
Devastation and starvation rapidly appear
The huge oak trees cry out as their branches tumble down
Anchored mountains no longer echo their bellowing sound.

Whispering winds pine for the chance to touch
The roses on the stem there was so much of
Caution thrown to the wind, give us the caring hand,
God grant us the wisdom to understand.

Judy Lackey

Happy Mother's Day

Happy Mother's Day to a mom whose super-great,
A mom who got me ready for school, without being late,
A mom who taught me how to treat a lady on a date,
A mom who enforced table manners as I ate.

Thanks for baking me chocolate chip cookies and cherry pie,
And when I was sad, wiping the tears from my eye.
Thanks for weighing my food when I was sick,
And visiting me in the hospital, till the candle was just a wick.

Your special to me in so many ways,
You tolerated me through every kid-crazed phase,
You disciplined me when I was bad,
When I was successful, you gave me praise,
Shared my joys when I was glad,
And took me to Pueblo during my orthodontist days.

My Mom: who raised me and 4 sisters, but didn't complain,
My Mom: who washed my clothes when I got a stain,
My Mom: who when I get hurt, shared my pain,
My Mom: who dried me off when I came in from the rain,
My Mom: pretty, kind, loving, gentle and somehow still sane.

Pat Kastler

Spiritual Life

Living a "spiritual centered life" makes my life complete and true
The armies of heaven are on our side in all we seek to do
To stay with him in daily prayer
To always speak and know he is there
He always knows the out come of all we seek to do
Divine grace "Assures Me"
He will always "see us through"
He guides you to the answer
To all who "seek to know"
God only wants what's "best for us"
Where ever you may go.
He'll stay with you and pray for you
He always wants to share
Through "Grace we can begin again"
'He's with us everywhere.

Alice B. Kell

Cool Blue Nights

On cool blue nights
When nothing matters more
Than soulful sounds,

Horns pressed tightly, slightly turned
Like some kaleidoscopic floral design
Bound for freedom,

Mallets poised, noiselessly obscured
Like sunlight beating down passageways
To heart's golden door,

Just one thought of you
Moves me beyond worldly compare
Through runnels, waves and planes, forevermore

Soaring like jazzy men and women
Dazzling on spiced jasmine,
Preying on passioned delight,

Now a vessel, warmed
When nothing matters more
On cool blue nights.

Susan M. Marchese

Think Of Jesus

When you think about the hard times you are going through
Think of those things Jesus did for you

Jesus wasn't given roses - instead he was given thorns
He never got a pat on the back - he got his back torn with a
Roman scourge
He didn't get to walk a smooth highway
He had to walk up a rocky hill that day

He didn't worry about things lost
He allowed them to nail him to a cruel cross

He never had a fancy room
Instead he was laid in a cold, dark tomb

His enemies thought he was put in that tomb to stay
But he rose again on the third day

So friend, before you complain about troubles this world hands you
Remember the saviour and the troubles he went through

Then, and only then, can you truthfully say
I have the victory over Satan today!

Terry L. Coons

Kid Sisters

Sisters close as peas sometimes, like twins
    neatly enclosed and wrapped like a gift.
Oldest, youngest, which one is she in the
    middle of that black and white photograph
holding a puppy, and our braces yet to come.
    Swimming in a lily pond. Summers remembered
like Mom and Dad.
    Little spats. She wore a frown because the
gown borrowed didn't fit and she had one when
    the seams of life split.
Away from dolls or sibling dreams, off to
    boarding a train and schools, to marriage
in another town.
    The letter came when nothing came between
them, except that distance and death.
    I miss you dearly Sister of my heart.

Ruth Allen Raymond

Paternalism

My failings, frailties and being
their seeing, thinking and shaping

My teaching, philosophizing and requiring
their analysis, emphasis and effectiveness

My channeling, instilling and pricing
their assertion, resolution and comprehension

My providing, allowing and showing
their protection, affection and compassion

My avoiding, balancing and saving
their ethics, conflicts and values

My caring, demonstrating and establishing
their mentality, roles and soul

My paternalism
their self determination

Carl Casteel

One Night

Dear..........
I thought I should write you......
After all it is only fifteen years since we met......

It was in March.....on a windy day......
You standing handsome and tall in your suit....
I young, sweet, and petite in my red sweater.....

You crushed me with your love......
I was enveloped by your charm.....
You knew the answers.....you could protect me....

Over the years we have loved and laughed and fought back the
disappointments together....
We have been there for each other on other cold....windy days...

Today is another day in fifteen years....
but you are not with me...
I sleep alone tonight...wanting you near...

Please come to me tonight and shield me....
I am afraid of spending another fifteen years without you...
Please stay one more night....

Leslie K.

Illegal Granny

They load Granny off to jail
There was no one to go her bail
She said sorry, look after my mail
Granny was in a daze
Her son was outrage
She was no stranger to the law
She serving ten to twenty days
Granny needs to change her ways
Granny was caught bootlegging
Granny says it beat begging
People come from miles around
All across town, to Granny Shaer
On Shanny RD to chat, listen to the blues
Low down dirty
Blues, so deep
On the juke box
Make one weep
To play pool, and dominoes, drink
You see granny cross the line of the law
She has been fined, will serve time

Maxcine Fuller

All Of You

The warm air takes my breath
as the tropical mist falls like dew.
The palms sway, the birds sing
ever so softly, but...
I hear them, I hear them all.
The night stars flicker and spark
cascading to the shores.
Iridescent sand glistening in the moonlight,
I stand in it alone, but...
I see it, I see it all.
His hand falls over my eyes.
Water drips onto my fingers, pale and somber.
His eyes dark and shadowy
hair falling to one side, but...
I touch it, I touch it all.
I drink his smile and taste his laughter.
I breath his peace and hold his love.
I hear his heart and listen ever so softly
to the fears, but...
I love him, I love him all.

Holly Fazio

I Remember

I remember the games we played-
and the nights, at your house I stayed-

I remember being together doing dishes-
you had brothers, one of my wishes-

I remember the dances, the picnics and chances - we took,
I remember the strawberries, we ate on the sly -
Gee, they tasted good, my oh my!

I remember us growing older
and how we became bolder -

I remember your marriage and mine -

I remember our laughter, joys and tears -
the sorrow and fun times, over the years.

I remember our families have grown, and gone their own way
But we have our friendship, it's here to stay.

Beverly J. Williams

Appreciation

Hospitable
How
You made me feel —
So comfortable
Like a (bugles) meadow walk
on a just-right summer's day.

The worries pause
And realize
They're not so important
And they stop clambering for my attention.

The made pace
Stops for a moment
And while there remembers
What the goal was
in the first place.

And all because
You are so
Hospitable
And you make me feel so welcome here.

And thank you for this space to simply be.

Wrennie N. Warren

Journey Into Light

We died, the ghosts of soldiers dance
upon the graves, at close of day.
We love to dance the night away
at full of moon. We try to say
we gave our bodies
listen to our spirits now
and let us try to tell you how
to reach the moon, and reach the stars
and even to the planet mars.

Clasp hands with friends
and every man and woman
dance in circles now
and look into their eyes
you'll see the life and spirit there within, the joy of living,
then you'll win a place in heaven
here on earth. Rejoice at every saviors birth,
for God is love, and love is God, and every
child born to man and woman, is a savior.
Clap hands and laugh at every death, and when the
breath of life expires - give thanks to God.

Amy Taylor

A Raging Storm

The waves were crashing on the western shore.
The wind screamed through the busted door.
The old frame house creaked and moaned.
The axe was sharp and the sythe had been honed.

The people had fled to higher ground.
The water was rising all around.
When far to the east there was a haunting cry.
Of a child that was lost, and was sure to die.

But the people heard and would not let it be so.
The men formed a chain and would not let go.
They reached the child as the water reached her chin.
The men made sure the storm would never win.

Ken Flanders

In Orbit With God And Man

When we become Christians, it is a small step for God
A giant step for man
As each of us climbs the path of life for a closer walk with God
We are each in a different orbit; a different learning pattern
As with our grades in school
With our growing and learning process, each step, each orbit
Each increase in knowledge and love, becomes more difficult
We must take each step as a little child, turning to the teacher, the Father
When the road gets rough in one orbit, temptations to go
against God may be less
Temptations to go against man (or be less understanding of the
Man on the outer rim) may be greater
When one of us falters, we need man as well as God to run and
Comfort us; to say "We understand, we will help you, we know
the pressures, forgive yourself and go on!"
As with the shepherds, when they saw "The glory of the Lord" and
"Were sore afraid", man should remember that he is not able to
See the full glory of God
For he would be blinded by His magnificence, 'till he reaches
The other side

   Dorothy Melton

The Danish Dresser

"I want this," she said, touching it tenderly..meaning
after I'm gone and won't need earthbound treasures.
What she wants is my sturdy, Danish, dresser.
Ah, yes, in her solitary childhood, this was not
just a dresser. It was her Fantasy Land:
brand-new then, with a four-foot mirror on the right;
slender but functional with nine drawers, spaced
three in a row; colored like papershell pecans
and a three-inch ledge near the bottom
where she stood, moving "Windsong," "Chantilly,"
and miniature perfume bottles all around.
She called them people.
What do Bottle People do?
Eat lunch on a round table, dusting powder box,
recline beneath a pink shade, tree lamp,
or ice skate on white, dresser-scarf lake?
She shall have their dresser.
Her scuff marks on the ledge prove squatter's rights.
Some special day, she'll look at it and remember
the little girl, who stood on the edge of Fantasy Land.

   Adeline Erwin

To Kathy

   It was a day much the same as any other.
Late autumn sun, hazy sky, lingering flowers,
and a hush of expectancy in the air.
Nothing out of the ordinary, to separate it from
a chain of just such days that tie fall's ending and
winter's beginning. To a weary young woman,
it seemed not only the ending of a season but the bridge
to an awesome new world. This day was long awaited and
sometimes feared by a girl barely turned from child to woman.
No amount of dreaming or speculation through childhood,
growing up, love or marriage could prepare her for this day
of pain, of fear, of wonder and completeness. It was a
day much as any other in the chain of late autumn days,
but it marked the beginning of my reason for living -
that rare and wonderful day my baby girl was born.

   Harvene McAuley

Nature's Fatal Overture

The dangling branch weighs down heavy, lifeless,
   burdened by dripping blankets of white, wintry slush.

A January storm always packs a wallop, but this
   furious, unnumbered movement was being composed
   during the first few bars of November.
      For music has no era.

Though unusually surprising, unmercifully relentless...
   A few brown, brittle leaves cling to life,
   soon to snap- and fall; returning feebly to
   fertilize the earth's quite, niveous terrain.

Etched into memory of the weakening branch, a young
   sapling, happier times.. when newborn leaves,
   rubber like, vibrant, sang through the branch in
   octaval unison; waving hello! to the world,
   orchestrating a joyful overture in C major.

Succumbing to many years of weathering countless
   beatings, the once mighty, now aged limb
   snapped - and fell. Amidst a free fall, the
   lifeless branch heard the final chord
   ring out - in F minor.

   Ronald A. Busse

The Storm

Thundering in its delirium, Lord over all,
The fates are set against us.
Frightening yet splendid in it's passion.
Rain seems to penetrate our very consciousness.
Sifting waves beat the shore with frenzied fists
Like a raging battle as yet unwon.
Compelling in it's fury, yet not stopped,
For man has no power now,
Proof that nature's forces are stronger still.
Meaningless, insurgent, are our laws to You.
Winds cease now, their mournful cries no longer heard.
Trees bow no longer at the Masters feet
For you are free again.
Washed of imperfections, cleansed and shining,
The storm is past.

   Betty G. Bruce

Smile Santa Is Coming

'Tis the night before the old fellow
Dressed in red comes down the chimney

A jolly old fellow he is
Never mind if a chimney you do not have
Never mind if you do not live in a house
He will come

Believe in magic
He will come
Believe in dreams
He will come

He will come
If you believe good things can happen

He will come
If you believe in his flying reindeer
Or the twinkle in his eye

You see
If you believe in the goodness of mankind
Christmas will happen for you
Because Christmas is that jolly old fellow in red
Always near by ready to dry your tears away
With his radiating smile

   Harold Colon

"Women Are Farmers Too"

Imagine if you will a herd of Jersey cattle grazing on the hillside,
All at once at the sound of a womans voice they run full force being
  careful not to slide.
To see someone clap their hands and say, come to momma, is a unique
  sight,
It's as if the animals and the farmer have a bond which is different,
  but not a fright.
She doesn't have three arms, four legs, or purple skin,
She's just a woman farmer, which makers her different for most men.
There are 90 animals she is mistress of,
And the trust and understanding between them is as if sent from up
  above.
Some tell her she's crazy and should be locked up in a zoo,
But, she is taught the old way that "women are farmers to."
She cleans her barn by hand cause the barn cleaners broke,
And can't afford a new one, which makes her most people joke.
There are many jobs she could do but wouldn't enjoy,
Since with animals there is no time clock and she is her own employ.
Some tell her she must be hard to the core and tough as nails,
But they don't see her in the barn, when the tears can fill milk
  pails.
She has told people the animals accept you for who you are,
Not if you are rich, poor, or some great movie star.
For she is one of the few proud to say while looking up at you,
I am a woman, and "Women are farmers too."

Patty Nichols

Stories Untold

At twilight in the garden
When the bells began to chime,
I chanced to stroll along the path
That leads to the gnarled pine.

As I looked at it's majestic height
I wondered as of old,
If this great tree, had a story for me
A story never told.

A story of nights when the wind is cold
When the wolves and the coyotes howl.
Or a night when the eagle soared its height,
And is heard the hoot of the owl.

A story of days when the Indians camped
Beneath its lofty boughs,
And around the campfire sat the tribe
And puffed smoke into clouds.

No doubt many stories could be told
About this splendor tree
But only God knows it's secrets
And He'll not tell...even Me!

Deane Query

The Calm Of The Sea

As I stand by the sea and the water is calm
The birds above singing their own sweet song
Little creatures crawling on the sand to and fro
The blue sky above and the warm sun heating my body all over
I feel this inner sense of peace.

But soon the sea becomes turbulent and the sky grows gray
The waves sound their own angry roar
The winds become stronger.
As I sense the storm is here
As I watch the storm
I know that soon there will be a return of the calm of the sea.

So when trials in life appear,
I try to remember the calm of the sea.

Rosette Mines

New Sight

I've wondered of diamond rings,
Of gold and gems and precious things,
Owning a mansion on a wooded hill,
But I never heard the Whippoorwill.

I've wondered of a plane so fine,
Wealth enough to call it mine,
Then I could soar to places high,
But I never saw the endless sky.

I've wondered of plantations vast,
And I would own at long last,
The harvests serving all my needs,
But I never thought of its gifted seeds.

I've wondered of riches and things of power,
But I never thought of nature's bower,
I saw the mansion but not the hill,
And I never heard the Whippoorwill.

Now I wonder at things I should have seen,
Blue sky, flowers, grass so green,
Spring, summer, fall, and winter's frost,
And I realize what I almost lost.

George J. Luther

Through The Eyes Of A Child

To see their wonderful smile,
So full, yet free from guile,
So innocent, so undefiled,
To see - through the eyes of a child.

To see there time of play,
Never thinking of the pain of yesterday,
With a heart so happy and mild,
To see - through the eyes of a mild a child.

To see how quick they are to forgive,
To love, to cherish, and to live.
No poet can tell it - not even Oscar Wilde.
To see - through the eyes of a child.

To see there peace of heart,
How quickly their troubles depart!
In a world so crazy, so wild,
To see - through the eyes of a child.

In our Heavenly Father, we ought to rest,
As a child doth so blest.
Free from care in a world so defiled,
To see - through the eyes of a child!

Gene Griffin

The Whirlwind

Listen to the howling wind
as it tears through the tree branches...

As it screams in fear
yet we wonder what
it has to be afraid of...

Perhaps fear itself,
Perhaps terror of its own power...

Its lack of discipline
could either soothe or destroy.

Its significance could cut both ways.
Perhaps we sometimes feel it...

We find ourselves lost
in its rage...

In this whirlwind
that most of us call "life."

Jordan Slutsky

Freedom

To awake on a morn so fresh and new.
To walk through the garden covered with dew.

To find new meaning in a life so confused.
To feel loved and wanted, and not just used.

To see life as God meant it to be.
To really be happy with just being me.

To know that I'm wanted and highly prized.
To be somebody special in somebody's eyes.

These are the things we all long to see.
For these are the things that set souls free.

Daniel James Gerkin

Grandpa

Holding Grandpa's hand, one last time,
The warmth and strength, still there,
His eyes were closed, his breathing light
Yet, he squeezed our hands, to show his care.

Tears filled the eyes of the family in the room,
We watched as his life peacefully faded away;
Goodbyes and I love you's filled the silent air,
To see him at peace, no one begged him to stay.

Years of memories passed through each mind,
Bits of laughter, mixed with tears.
The love and pride for his family was known,
An honorable man, to so many, through his years.

Quietly he left us, his hands will gripping ours,
But somehow when his heart was gone,
A warmth filled the room, drying my tears.
Death to grandpa came quickly, as he wanted all along.

Sure, I'll miss my Grandpa's head, very much;
He's been a big part of my life —
He left the struggles and pains that came with age
Yet, he left his wonderful wife.

Brenda Head Lasch

The Nomad Man

The ride never stops for the Nomad Man.
Looking for a home,
He has traveled from the hills of Indiana to the windy city,
From the country's capital to the Green Mountain State,
From the sunny shores of Florida to the harshness of a Buffalo winter.
From the west to the east moving north and south.
Running from town to town,
His head spinning round and round
The ride never stops for the Nomad Man.

He's stood on the mountain tops, seen the biggest lakes,
the largest rivers.
Yet Nomad Man is always searching for the home that disappeared.
He hears Long Island calling him back,
Knowing this move will get him back on track,
Where it all began so many years ago.

Sick of feeling like a misfit clown.
Going from town to town
Hoping to make all the wrongs right,
Finally seeing the light,
Nomad man is nearing the end of his journey,
The journey home!

Thomas Berntsen

I Went To The Zoo

I went to the zoo,
I saw "Lions and Giraffes.
Their necks were so Long,
It made me laugh.
I saw a Zebra, he was a sight.
He had stripes of "Black and White".
IT looked like an artist, had painted with a Brush.
The stripes so even, it made me Hush!
My favorite was the monkeys, up in a tree,
THEY kept looking-strait at me!
Then they jump up and down and turn around!
They were chirping with glee, as to entertain me!
I saw the peacocks, with "Rainbow-Feathers,"
They pranced all around, but keeping together.
An "Elephant" pick a little-girl up, with its trunk,
She was as "Happy", as a "chipmunk!"

Winifred Bullard

Reflections

Greet the morning with a smile,
for we only have it a little while.
Soon this day will surely pass; and,
we must earn our merits towards repast.

Enjoy this time; for tomorrow
we know not, whether
that brings joy or sorrow!
Look for the positive aspects of life,
and savor the present; delete the strife.

The more negative a situation can be;
stop, reflect deeply and you will see,
there is a good measure of tender care
in just knowing you've done your share.

Dwell not upon disappointments and strife;
just chalk it up to - "well that's life!"
Pray to the Lord who sees all things,
and in his "own time" will bring,
fulfillment of all your dreams.

Elva D'Antoni

An Animal Anthology

An aardvark addressed an anteater,
"By battle boasts best bug beater."
Capturing, catching,
Digging, dispatching,
Each endeavored, earning "Eminent Eater."

An ant army attacks an apiary:
Bees battle boldy before beehives bury.
Contesting, contending,
Divesting, defending,
Each enemy evinces effort extraordinary.

A slug slithering slimily slow
Met a moth moving merrily mid "moon glow"
A journeying jaunter;
A fluttering flaunter;
But both bestowing brash bravado.

Henry M. Ditman

Wake Me Up Before It's Too Late

We play games with each other
And make pretend we're lovers
Everyday and in every way
We want to leave and we want to stay
In silence we pretend that we know how
   to play our game
But in the end, everything always ends up the same
We both get mad at ourselves after a short while
Then we see we begin to lose our patients and don't
   go the extra mile
Then we start to give in to one another after we've
   earned the time
And start to realize that what we have isn't really
   yours or mine
Just like when we were both innocent
Before a love we ever met
Life can be sunny and then in an instant
   make us all wet
It's really not ours to hold or keep
Just to have for a while, then fall fast asleep

    Robert Lee Elliott II

Danny's Version Of Santa Claus
(Santa Through The Eyes Of A Five Year Old)

Santa is so very old
Lives way up in the cold
Santa is nearly twenty-nine
And his health is still quite fine
Mrs. Claus throws white powder all over him
That's supposed to try to keep him slim
The powder keeps him healthy too
Yes, Mrs. Claus knows just what to do
Mrs. Claus is ancient too
She is nearly twenty-two
They are both as old as can be
But will keep all kids happy eternally

    Winniferd Gilchrest

Snow

Snow - all the boundaries you create
Your coldness enters my heart
And there is a bleakness
Without and within
I feel an icy chill creeping
throughout my body as all
the turbulent emotions
start to take over
Suddenly I am thrust into a pool of ice...
Fighting to regain that
tranquility and joy that
has kept my head above the water
But this will pass and
I will see the loveliness
in your icy patterns

    Shirley Campbell Horton

Peace

Peace is a solitude place within us.
Its characteristics favor a place we have been.
A place where our spirit can sore freely, and our soul can rest.
A place where, we are not searching for anything, for our mind is at
ease and our thoughts are adventurous.
A place where time stands still and the world revolves around our being.
We do not look to seek, but see without looking.
For in this place we feel the beauty and take in its wisdom and
allow solitude to capture our presence.

"Think of a beautiful place and peace will follow."

    Gina Whitacre

Purer Than Snow

The year is now dying. These trees, bent with care,
Are growing old gracefully—gracefully fair.
Robed in white splendor, their heads bowing low,
They are whiter and purer than even the snow.

God's love has adorned them, these saints of the earth,
And showered their lives with rich blessings since birth:
They are free from all sin; they age without worry,
Growing old wealthily, rich in His glory.

Man differs greatly. Can he really be blamed,
Plodding on sinfully—sinfully shamed?
Age creeps upon him, he thinks of his youth,
Budded in innocence, blossomed in truth.
His prayer becomes this, as his time draws nigh:
Let me live beautifully—beautifully die.

    Owen E. Humphrey

A Fine Lady

"Ma" she was called, a very common name.
Although old women may seem the same
With snow white hair and wrinkled face
Nothing was common about her.

"Ma" had a heart as big as the world.
Barren of children though she was
Her home welcomed children of the world.
Black or white - foster children found love.

Twenty three at one time was not too much
For "Ma" to cook and clean. She still found time
To love and nurse, a time to advise or restrain
A time to kiss away all hurts.

In later years the children grown, would write and send money.
Blessed the only mother they ever knew.
At eighty-two she went to her reward.
Heaven must have welcomed her with open arms!
A fine lady full of love!

    Dorothy Jefferson

"The Beast Within"

My dream is to be a poet. My words for all to read.
To educate and illuminate. God plants the poet's seed.

I'll write about our universe. Equality and Peace.
I'll try to soften, the hearts of stone. Destroying "The Evil Beast"

If I succeed in doing that, through the words I write.
The Beast will have nowhere to go, for I have won the fight.

So, Evil Beast, don't show your face, your emotion being hate.
With God's help, I'll soften the hearts. Soon you'll meet your fate.

I'll free the hearts, that you possess, through the words I write.
They'll be free, from you evil emotion. May they see the light.

Listen, evil beast within. You don't have a chance.
I've beaten you many times before. Again, I take a stance!

Do what you will do in life, as I write my mighty words.
Souls will turn away from you. For my message, will be heard.

    Susan L. Kline

My Mask

Oh mask that rest upon my face, wished I
  dared lift you from your place

For you do hide from them I meet, the man and
  soul I think they seek

But then again what do I know, for who am I
  and where's my soul

How often I pretend to be, the kind of man
  I hope they see

But who is fooled by this game I play, is it
  me or them, I couldn't say

David G. Turner

Smoldering

The same eyes beheld you but for the first time
Red hot liquid scorches my innards
My fingers itch to run through your thick hair
And spread ripples of fire

I have just discovered who you are
But I cannot forget who I am

I look away
Don't even smile

Beneath my mask
Embers glow and catch fire
Frustrated desire undulates
Like sun warmed currents trapped against the hot white sand

Zilla Martin

The New Baby

A precious little angel,
A new baby girl;
As cute as a button,
As beautiful as a pearl.

She's the apple of Daddy's eye,
and Mommy's little sweetheart;
Her 2 big brothers will spoil her,
With Grandma and Grandpa playing their part!

Just give her all your love,
With special attention too;
And she'll turn out just
As wonderful as all of you!

Carolyn McFarland

Dad - Six Sons

It's been many years since Jesus called,
But, Dad, you're still a part
Of structuring our lives for God,
Because you left your heart.

God placed your heart in each of us,
A giving, caring one,
To carry out a plan of love,
The work YOU would have done.

You never seemed to see a need
That you refused to meet,
And satan thought to take your life
Would leave us in defeat.

But Jesus intervened again,
And now the devil's mad,
Six times the heart is beating now
That beat inside our Dad.

Ann A. Reynolds

Night Dance Of The Magic Hula

Dark Hawaiian beauty
Dance by the phallic stone;
Erotic sway and movement
Make the rock your own.

On mountain top young flower high
Above Kalaupapa Moloka'i;
Only fertile moment stop the
Night dance of the magic hula.

Dance in the moonlit black forest sea,
See through eyes that slit the dark;
Hungry preying owls in a tree
Scratch at the itching bark.

Tease a strand of black coarse hair,
Drop your skirt and hot, soft bare;
Ebbing arms beckon, ebon eyes invite,
Come phallus flood—spirit, arise tonight.

A manly spectre screws, then heaves with rude attire
Deep in carnal feast doth quench the objects of desire;
At last the life lance leaves, when first the light of day
Shines on a woman and mother to be, flushed about her way.

Keoni Aloha

"A Piece About Peace"

"Many words do sound the same,
Like peace and piece it's true-
These words have different meanings,
Their spelling differs too."

"Bosnia seeks a lasting peace,
To rebuild its country wide-
Everywhere is devastation,
Its citizens have no place to hide."

"The Serbs desire a greater piece,
Of Bosnia, far and wide-
Their aggression has taken a very large toll,
Not satisfied with peace and won't abide."

"Our U.S. troops are there to aid.
To make sure that peace will stay-
The U.N. and other countries will help,
To make sure the fighting stops someday."

"World Peace would be a wonderful thing,
I believe it would be best for all-
People should live their lives as they choose,
And not have to answer the War's call."

Marty Rollin

The White-Hat Clan

Chest swells when think about our clan,
Universal White-hats, to date God's plan.
There the universality ends,
Numbers range, occupations at alphabet's both ends.
As each new one takes a bow,
New total number, wow.
Two senior families each with five,
Like the one with twelve, all thrive,
Executive, lawyer, fireman-chief,
Proprietor, policeman, but no horse-thief,
These and others with talents more,
Make it difficult to keep score.
Around the saloon corner do not peek,
There may lurk the Black-hat we do not seek.

Joseph Rutkowski

Grandpa With His Hat Backwards

He found hill made of dirt,
That was Real high and Real low,
He reved up his old jalopy,
And turned his ball cap backwards.

Us kids would always laugh and scream,
As we went straight up,
And then he put the car in neutral,
And Flew down the gravel road.

Mom screamed "we'll die! Stop, stop! No more!
But Grandpa had the thrill, of scaring here to death
and us? All we shouted was "more!"

Joyce Santos

Adolescence

Unsteady—gently groping the darkness—
yet surging ever forward—boldly!
filled with wonder, fear-eager expectation...
Knowing nothing of boundaries, time, evolution—
nor its part of these;
it is still wild, free-a single swirling atom
romping across fields of the Universe—
living for love, loving for life;
racing headlong to its ultimate reckoning
with the new dawn: The exaltation of its
inexorable self.

From hence, freedom and night fade;
the mighty Warrior—though strong—
yet still blossoming with iron youth—
must surrender this unbridled freedom
upon the Altar of the Equinox and there,
in the ascending day, await Aurora's
New Birth—Aurora's New Song.

Mel Scott

"Sisters"

Conceived out of love, yet a tragic ending;
it's only many years later, there's a new beginning.

No one knew what they were missing out on;
until happiness arrived with the ring of the phone.

We communicate through letters and thoughts of love;
the beauty of our finding came from God above.

Although we missed making mud pies and playing in the rain;
we'll see each other soon and bypass all that pain.

We'll laugh and sing and do the things that sisters do;
many may resent it, but before we're done, they'll be singing too.

We can share the present, the future, and even our past;
and we can rest assured that a sisters love will always last!

Kathy Seibert

Numen

There is a quality in music that
cannot be named by man, eluding to
Immortal planes where melody and thought
are one, where every biding strain construes
concept more exact than simple sound.
What is it that in music causes kings
to weep and babes to let scorned sleep surround
their hearts and minds? And why, when robins sing
does Spring return with eager haste to brush
a shaded winter scene with songs of brighter
hue? And why did Heaven cease its hush
when Christ was born, all darkness to deter?
There is a power lies in music that
no dark, no light, no mortal can combat.

Rebecca McGovern

Violence Of Wind

Gust of winds we hear with our ear,
Our body can feel it when it is near.
Windows quiver, shake and rattle
    as the winds dance against the glass,
Violent strong wind, cold bustling wind,
    so noisy as they pass.
Beautiful tall trees with giant arms
    torn apart as they fall to the ground
Our eyes are shocked as we look around.
Often we see strong buildings torn in shreds,
Many times people thrown right out of bed.
"Well! Mr. Wind - Why are you so violent?"
After your visit we look around in wonderment.
Our hats fly high in the sky,
    riding on the giant wind gusts passing by.
Frighten we are as swirling wind push us around
Our bodies landing on the ground.
All the beauty on this earth — can be demolished in seconds of time
Grateful we are when volunteers arrive,
Restoring everything to a bright shine getting rid of the grime.

Ethel M. Shannon

Glory to the Babe

Glory to the babe who is exceedingly blessed.
Laying in a manger to get a little rest.
The heavenly angels announced it bold.
When this story was foretold.
Glory to the lamb! Glory to the lamb!
The heavenly host proclaim the name
Now the world will never be the same
Praise to God on high.
The Messiah has come to die
For the sins of all mankind
His coming was right on time
For Jesus came to reconcile man back to God
His coming was not a facade
Glory! Glory! Glory!
Praise His Holy Name, Glory! to the new born King.

Harriet A. Sims

Passing Youth

In the bloom of youth, I was quite bold,
Exciting and adventuresome, or so I was told;
Nothing was too daring, nothing out of bound,
Wherever gaiety was, there was I to be found.

But boldness fades in the passing of years,
Adventure passes with the coming of fears;
Excitement has gone in advancement of time;
And gaiety no longer is a concern of mine.

In the mirror, youth no longer do I see;
How, and why could this happen to me?
But age and wrinkles now line my face,
The person I used to be has left no trace.

Shelby J. Smith

"Eyes"

There are black ones, blue ones and brown ones,
There are Hazel ones, green ones and grey ones,
Some see far.
Some see near,
Some see not at all,

Some see not as clearly as they should.
Some see too well,
Some see only what they recall,

Eyes are connected to the mind,
That is why, so many are blind.

Mattie M. Stewart

Battles

Surreal mist covers the plain
Upon which the battle is fought.
Existing not in a physical realm,
Yet trapped in the dimension of thought.
The knight inspects his tack,
Casting his gaze across the field
Upon the enemy's superior number,
Refusing the compulsion to yield.
A seething wave of dark despair
Threatens to devour, by advancing, the light.
Wearily the battle stance is adopted
As he prepares to stop the blight.
Thrust and parry, block and slash
Gallantly the knight defends.
Drawing strength deep within
From the light of family and friends.
For it is his own dark thoughts
Which threaten his soul to consume.
He must never retreat nor surrender
Lest he become sealed in Death's dark tomb.

Darrell W. Sutton Jr.

Always Together

My Faith rests on God's promises, they're faithful and true,
The Lord goes with me everywhere, and in all that I do.

I felt of God's Presence as the sun kissed my face,
Knew in my weakness, I had His Strength and His Grace.

Entering my secret place to be alone with the Lord,
Prayed, paused, then listened, heard Him speak by His Word.

Went to the doctor, lo and behold, God was there,
Sharing our faith, 'Jesus' sweet Spirit soon filled the air.

Knowing God's children in whom Christ lives His life through,
And out of their well of love, freely from it I drew.

In the Valley of Weeping God comforted me in my sadness,
Then poured me out a blessing, He delighted in my gladness.

God laid on me this burden to plant His precious Seeds,
That others know the Savior and live with Him indeed.

I know my sins are forgiven for Jesus paid them all,
Therefore, we're always together in great things or in small.

I've been through many changes, some losses and some gains,
But the Lord never changes, His Kingdom shall remain.

Yes, my Redeemer lives for He lives His life in me,
The best is yet to come, then my Savior's face I'll see!

Berthe N. Welch

I Call That Love

You look pretty and happy. You look great with those cute jeans and dresses. Wow! Your inside track carries my dreams of love... My heart is filled with glorious rejoicing. Yes honey! You are the greatest...Honey, I found, genuine happiness in your embracing love. You conquered my heart. Inside your body swim those hot genes. They yearn to fulfill glory. I'm your thankful mate... Glorious you! You drip with honey. Your soul is laced with happy invitations. Wow! Your loving kindness, lives deep inside my motives. It's those good genes that sing - "Give me dresses, jeans and shoes that dance." Love's glory told me to unite. Honey, you adorn me with happiness. You fill my heart with love. Such truth! You reside, inside my heart...You reside, inside my soul...Our wonderful genes make future life. Our happiness thrives on milk and honey. We yearn for heaven's glory. You honored my seeds of love. You did it! Our needs of love are fulfilled. "Presto!" Inside your body, our thankful genes united. It's God's glory. Now that's fulfillment. Honey, what a thrill. We are happy. Our happiness swims inside your jeans...and consumes glorious honey... "I Call That Love."...

Willard R. Fox

Purple Horse

A purple horse -
Is there such a thing?
A h
yes, there is.
Black as coal
and glistening
as the purple in the sunset of the sky,

For in the distance
on a knoll
He is romping;
with his maine catching the wind
as his fleeting hoofs dash across the green,

There He stands
Majestic as a King.
Nodding to all who will follow
Come and dance with me
In the Rays of the beaming Son.

Pauline Hilton

My Teddy Bear

You've been there through the hard times,
You've been there for the fun.
You've always been there listening
And smiling whenever I got done.
I never went a single night
Without you by my side,
I think you are my one true friend
Because to me you're never lied.
I never had to explain to you
The reasons I was mad,
You never even bothered to question me
Whenever I was bad.
You were always there for me to hold
Whenever I wanted to cry.
You'd always reach up your hand to me
To wipe the tears away from my eyes.
Some people think there comes a time
When they're to old for a bear.
But how could they let go of the one thing
You know will always be there!

Alicia Driskill

Untitled

You never find what you want
if you try to create it.
It must happen without
expectations or demands.
Looking too hard,
wanting too much
the intimacy of love,
constant disappointment
and heartbreak,
a roller coaster ride
in your travels through life.
Running when we should have walked,
looking but yet never really seeing,
imagining but not realizing
differences between real and unreal.
Sometimes what we seek most
was never beyond the reach
of our outstretched arms,
too distant our focus,
too great were our expectations and demands.

Richard L. Walton

Arrival...

As I sit here and wonder, when our 2 will become 3,
  I look back into the past, when I though it would be only you and me.

As we've waited patiently these last 9 months, wondering what kind of
  parents we will be,
  It also made me wonder, will it be a he or she.

It really doesn't matter, whether it will be a girl or boy,
  All that's important to remember, is that we made this bundle of joy.

It's not long now, before the big day, if it doesn't happen tonight
  or tomorrow,
  it will arrive on the 20th of May.

I'm getting a little scared, of becoming a new mom,
  Will I do all the right things, to fulfill this job.

The baby didn't arrive over the weekend, even after dancing all
  night at the prom,
  So I'm to be at the hospital in the morning to induce and have
  this little one.

I've returned from the hospital, I had a little boy,
  We gave him the name "Tyler Lane," and he is a "bundle of joy."
  Valerie Crafton

"What Are We Doing To The Children Of The World"

What are we doing to the children of the world?
What are we saying to them?
 Why can't we show them the love that they so justly deserve?
They should not be the answer to adult problems.
They should not have to suffer the consequences when something goes wrong.
Why don't we let them know how much they are loved, needed, and wanted!

The children of the world are our future.

What are we doing to help these children grow up to be adults who care;
who want to help others; who want to love someone; and who want to be loved?
Children need love; not pain or hurt. They need to have people who will go the
"extra mile" for them. Children of the world should not have to
turn to gangs, to drugs, to alcohol, or to the streets to achieve these goals.
Their lives should not be cut short because no one was there for them.

We need to change our ways of treating our children.
We need to do more listening and less hurting.
We need to show them they are loved and are very special to us.
We need to protect our future. They will be the leaders one day,
and they need to know there are good people in the world.
We need to tell them we're sorry! We need to say we LOVE them!
A HUG can last a lifetime! Children of the world need to know
they have a place they can call HOME!
  Rachel Wallace

Love Letter

Love games are for the nymphs and fairies that live in dreams.
Only through truth and honesty does love flourish.
Our time-weathered love creates blessed eternal bonds.
Ceaseless are the winds of adversity but love guides us
through this journey we call life.
For our time together is surely meant to be, as the heavens
above have always known.
So lucky am I to know true love.
Let us share our love with all of God's creatures.
May peace on earth flourish in abundance.
Let us live consciously, live honestly, and love with all
our hearts.
  Ann Garrett Grogan

Today

Along a dark and dreary path,
A man doth linger to consume his wrath,
And does he pray for that blessed key,
That holds the secret of his destiny;

A man is born into this forsaken world,
To meet the labors of his endless toils,
And when he lay thee down to sleep,
Even then, he dammed his soul to keep;

The mist has risen, the dawn has reared,
There is only one that must be feared,
And on upon this summer's day,
Think not the thoughts of yesterday,
A new day is born for all to see,
Breath deeply my friend, it's all for free;

For tomorrow shows its ugly shadow,
Be a man whose not so callow,
For those who dream, and dream, and dream,
Never know just what it all does mean.
  Donald Braverman

Fleeting Love

He took my hands and drew me close,
And whispered, "I love you."
There in his eyes I could see the gross
Of his love in their brilliant blue.

I smiled and whispered, "I love you, too,"
For I truly loved him so.
But his eyes turned cold and said, "It's true,
"Away forever I must go."

I felt this ice pierce to my soul,
And to my broken heart.
My life had once been safe and whole,
But right then fell apart.

He kissed me once and walked away
And I saw my love, my dear
Walk through the trees on a summer's day,
And finally disappear.

So I pulled myself into my womb,
Completely safe from sorrow.
My mind was filled with thoughts of gloom,
And the hell that was tomorrow.
  Jamie Woolsey

The First Thanksgiving

The purple twilight revealed his face,
As the Pilgrims said their grace;
The breeze ruffled his feathers, but made no sound
As he tried to understand this new band
Of men who walked the same as he
Strangely dressed, who could not see
That the muskets their men wield
Could not take his country's yield.
It was by accident, for he was still,
That a Pilgrim spied his quill.
And faced his squarely, and kindly said,
"Tomorrow, when we break bread,
Will the natives of this land
Join us and be on hand
For a great feast and thanks to God
Who blesses us with staff and rod.
Help us to express our love,
As He looks down from above.
You shall live as you did before.
And we'll be friends forevermore.
  Barbara W. James

"Fame And Wealth"

We stood back and took a look
at the way some live today,
in a demanding world and fast paced lives . . .
in need of time and play.

While striving to achieve their goals,
comprised of "FAME AND WEALTH";
they overlooked the benefit of . . .
time for love, good friends and health.

Success in life and its relationships,
depends on how and where we place;
priorities within our lives . . .
to bring smiles to many a face.

You bring out the best in me,
you say "I the best in you"!
So glad we chose not "FAME AND WEALTH",
what we have holds more value!

We wouldn't trade what we have now
for "FAME AND WEALTH" achieved.
They have no one to share it with.
It wasn't worth it . . . if they grieved!

Patricia A. Wessel

Untitled

Again, last night, the angels appeared to me.
with an omni-presence that only I could see.
I was not afraid of what they had to say
For the love that radiated would carry me another day.
Such a feeling of so much warmth and peace
I wanted to keep that feeling; never to let it cease
They told me the time was soon to be near
But of what it is, I have no fear.
If it is my time to cross over
I know I'll be happy, running barefoot through clover.
I have become so very tired and weary
A lot of times, my eyes became teary.
Over wrought with so very much pain
Even the very strongest would go insane
And when I begin my journey to the other side
Others will be along the way to be my guide.
Thus, when I arrive at heaven's pearly gates
I know the ones who for me patiently wait.
The angels I know will come again
Take me forever from this cruel world of sin.

Cathy Wilder

A Vessel Of Honor

Make me a vessel of honor Lord,
    Never to bring reproach upon Your name;
Pour me out, Oh God,
    That when you are finished I'll not be the same.

Already You've brought me from a life
    of terrible sin and shame;
Set my feet upon the rock
    of my blessed Jesus' name.

Give me Holy boldness Lord,
    To tell all I meet of You;
Of the wonderful changes You've brought into my life
    and how, for them, You'll do it too.

Allow the glory of Your love
    to show upon my face;
That when I speak of You -
    It shall not be common-place.

Margaret Campbell Riddlebaugh

Metamorphose At Eckley — for Dave

Just before dawn the old company house is desolate, no paint,
side porch collapsing from the weight of a hard Pennsylvania winter,
supported only by two 4 x 4's leaning toward it.
The sun begins to rise, the reflection of light off the windows
revealing the tulips just breaking through the ground. As the light
intensifies, the new grass shows itself, a grasshopper hopping about.
The form of an apple tree appears, just sprouting its buds, soon
to be white with flowers. If I close my eyes I can picture the red
round fruit and then imagine the smell of cinnamon and apple in
a newly baked pie.
As I glance toward the broken porch, I see a little nose poke out,
then another and another. A litter of kittens makes its way out
into the day. They roll about with each other until Mom comes
and swats one's nose. They then follow their mother to a
morning feast.
Now the sun is fully risen, I look up into the cloudless sky with
its shades of azure and sapphire unmarred by man, made
glorious by nature.
I look again toward the house to see that the door is painted a
bright green, the color of hope. The house looks no longer
desolate, it is such a beautiful, wonderful house.

Lynda Woolf

My Love

Like a flower blushing unseen
She hides her looks in her white sheen
O What a blush! I had never seen
So tickling a moment there had never been.

As I draw near, she unveils her face
So beautifully chiselled in all its grace
As if inviting a soothing kiss
A moment in my life never to miss.

First a kiss on her lips so tender
Then on her cheeks, which emotions can render
A silent embrace to clasp her heart
A soft corner in the secrecy of my heart.

ROMANCE, LOVE, POETRY - miles of these
Lie lined across to bear her with ease
MY LOVE, so lovely by far
To steal my heart, a lovely star.

Bulusu Lakshman

Oneness

It's all right here before your eyes
Do not be fooled by illusions that lie.
See the light, have faith, feel the joy
Forgive the anger and hate.

For you each there is peace
Let it happen
Recognize fears that are unreal
Allow your mind to reveal
    The thoughts that have no form
    Where there are no struggles and there is no storm.

Let the clouds pass you by.
Keep love by your side.
Giving and receiving are one
Find out yourself that giving is fun.

Open your heart and let love flow
Open your mind and let the pain go
Open your arms and accept happiness
Feel the love and tenderness.

Yvonne A. Fischer

"A Secret"

I had no one with whom to share a secret,
not until the day you took my hand.
Then it was so easy to reveal it,
that's because I knew you'd understand.
When your eyes were looking into mine, dear,
I knew exactly what I had to do...
That is when I tenderly embraced you,
and said my secret was "How I love you."

Merle W. Kinne

Can It Be I?

He thought that things could not be worse,
The maker of the universe.
He sadly looked from up above
For some faint spark of his great love.
Then all at once there was a sigh,
A radiant smile lit up the sky,
For there it was! Now he could rest;
Mankind at last had passed the test.
The loving creature down below,
Somehow did know where from the glow,
In wonder looked up at the sky
And asked, "Dear Lord, can it be I?"

Anthony Gutowski

Forgiving And Forgetting

In order to forgive, you must also forget -
for until you do, forgiveness is not valid yet!
Someday, somehow, the memory will accost you when you're
unaware, and the hurt you thought you had forgotten,
  you'll find lurking there,
All the anger and grief that resulted from the transgression
has not really gone away - it's still in your possession!
You'd only pushed it from your mind - buried it quite deep -
Someday it will rise again - perhaps in a dream while you're asleep.
Remember the lesson you learned - but the hurt itself forget;
As long as it can call forth hurt and wrath, it's not forgiven yet!
Oh what trouble I would know if God remembered every err!
I pray I can forgive another's "sin" against me -
place it in God's hands, and leave it there!
Everyone has made mistakes - others do it - I do too!!
Lord, I ask Your help to forgive and forget -
showing love and understanding
such as I receive from You!!

Betty D. Mason

The Red Convertible Car

In days of old, when knights were bold,
I had my first beau at thirteen years old
He had beep blue eyes, curly black hair,
A beautiful smile — was quite debonair —
But surpassing all this, by far:
"He owned a red convertible car."

However, our beautiful association
Was of very short duration,
For neighborhood boys, ready for war,
Appeared one evening, wielding baseball bats
And chased Sam and his red convertible car
Back to his own habitat.

I wouldn't know Sam after sixty-six years
But I'll always remember my bitter tears
That were shed that summer night
As my shining, handsome, errant knight
Accelerated that motor
And sped out of sight.

Loretta M. Hanneman

Top of God's World

I see you Lord in the grass so green
In the trees - that blow in the breezes,
In the beautiful birds that sing
I see you Lord in everything!

Sometimes the clouds cover the sun
But above it all it still shines,
I am so thankful to know the ONE
Who makes peace and contentment mine.

You ask how I can be full of glee
When troubles are all around,
Because His love consumes me
And I know I'm heaven bound.

I'm on top of Gods world today
Troubles come but they don't stay,
Time soon washes them all away
When you're on top of Gods world!

Mary Allene Brogdon

Do You Ever Look At The Sky?

Do you ever look at the sky? What do you see?

Do you see the sun rising at the far horizon
Filling the sky with intense light and color?
Do you feel its warmth, its life giving energy?

Do you see the dense clouds covering the blue?
Do you see the gray sky and the wet falling rain?
Do you see the gloom or its life giving power?

Do you see a rainbow in its enchanting colors
Encircling the earth in a real aura of glory?
Tying us all together in a ring of true love?

Do you see the darkness, the blackness of the night?
Or the myriads of bright, twinkling little stars?
Do you see the infinite immensity of the universe?

Do you see your spirit deep, very deep within
Filled with energy, power, and infinite love?
Do you see in your spirit the meaning of it all?

Do you ever look at the sky? What do you see?
Do you have a glimpse, just a glimpse of eternity?

Silvino R. Foglia

Untitled

Running around on a bike is great
Specially with you as my running mate
Through the mountain rain and the desert heat
It's really great fun and hard to beat

you balance the bike and hold me tight
We just ride along with no care in sight
You rub my back and put me at ease
But I really get high with a quick chilly breeze

I like it a bunch when you snuggle in close
You hold me and warm me, you're really the most
We fly along Dunlap at least 85
And being with you, is being alive

We stop for a beer or to look at the sun
I really didn't know that love was such fun
This little boy's safe all wrapped in your arms
And very aware of your mystical charms

Richard G. Williams

"Two Dogs"

Two dogs
One young, one old
One black, one yellow
One short-haired, one long-haired
One with sharp ivory-white teeth, one with worn, but effective
teeth
One skinny, one fat, one male, one female
One uncut, one cut
One stubby tail, one long tail
One Doberman, one lab
One hyperactive, one laid-back
One annoying, one sweet, one jumps at you, one wags her tail
One fast, one, what's the hurry
One risks death, one gets out of the way
One heat absorber, one shade dog
One shiverer, one, the weather's fine
One red, tattered collar that belonged to the other,
   one, naked neck
One pup, one dog
One Davidson, one Biscuit (formally Brisket)

Donald James Pitts

Untitled

Crispness of starch are these early autumn morns,
even the wind has a different voice.
Lazy spider webs ebb down,
only seen when sunlight filters down through the bog,
moss encompasses all.
Pine cones one by one roll to the ground,
and are heard by none.
As apples drop, bees seize their prey aware of this
last feast.
Geese show their splendor, as they fly in array,
bidding farewell to the place they call home.
clouds once soft and billowy, are now straight forth
and challenging.
Animals playful, labor now in preparation of coming
months.
Leisurely walks turn to brisk strides.
Tank tops to cardigans, autumn is here.!

Robin Lynne Coughlin

My Journey

Walking down the road of plenty
shoulder and shoulder with the many
lonely and in search of if any
I'll plan if I can
and can if I plan
to instill the will to climb that hill
a tear is near
it's abundantly clear
my road is long and winding
my determination grinding
out the thrill of my will to climb that hill
in search of if any
and what if I find as I fall behind
no thrill of my will to climb that hill
tales and wails of a traveler

Robert L. Whitsitt

Who Am I?

I am a square peg trying to fit into a
   round hole.
I know this is impossible as my life
   unfolds.
I have learned to appreciate my uniqueness
   while I explore life's unbounded
   completeness.

Eleanor Lynar-Cohen

Music And Poetry

Poetry when put to music is beautiful to hear
it makes you stop and listen if the words are very clear
yes it can be a lesson for all to learn from to
a lesson as to what everyone should and should not do
so put a poem and music together and you soon will see
that your message is understood just what it should be
it may be about two lovers who have parted now and then
then they both decide to try togetherness again
or it may be about a child's quarrel with their Mom and Dad
about all the things they want that they never had
but the best words and music is all a point of view
so if someone writes the music I will write a poem for you
yes it often takes two people to write a song, you see
so if you write the music you can use this poem from me.

Bernice M. Spych

Chicken Soup

There's so much more to chicken soup,
Made from the chickens that flew the coop.
It warms your body,
It heals your soul,
And smells so good
In the bowl,
You'll feel better soon,
And start to mend,
Not a soul will you offend.

Susanna G. Taubenberger

Dream Lightly

Dream lightly, young lover.
For in your dreams lay truth.
Of who you were, who you are,
And all the "whos" you'll be.

So dream lightly, young lover.
And mark your dreams
As they are your gateway through tomorrow.
And through them will reality unfold.

Dream deeply, young lover.
And if, perchance, she calls to you,
Answer her strong
And go to her.

Now wake gently, young dreamer,
And pull your dreams through with you.
Spread them wide before you
And tread surely through tomorrow.

Robb Flynn

Frivolous Satin

Glimmering, shimmering, elegant satin -
Yearning for it in Cleveland, Chicago, or Manhattan,
Rag-a-muffin, prim and proper, or in-between,
Altering the scenario from what has been.
Destitute who accept cotton or polyester,
Haughty who neglect and let fester
Attitudes of hurt and frustration.
Idealists who skim above the surface
To rebuild, renew and refurbish,
Society crying for attention -
Causes too numerous to mention;
Multitudes agonizing in tatters
Relinquishing values that matter.
Caucasian, Black, Asian, or Latin,
Searching for elusive, but attainable, satin.
Be wary about what you're longing for
Lest with fulfillment you slide to the floor -
Slippery, frivolous, impractical satin.

Floriana Hall

Ode To Jesus And Mary

In what distant land do you this joyful day
appear? Your humble visit, though seen
by few, consecrates all forever, and your
glowing starry crown and Immaculate Pious
Heart fill our souls with peace, warmth and love.

What joy was felt by all Bethlehem when you
bore your son! What a special day—
for our Redeemer came as flesh and blood to
save us all — a child King who could never sin
but wholly love as only he could do!

You are blessed by the generations of
all of humankind. Born free of sin,
so worthy of God, chaste and pure of heart—
ever virgin daughter of Anne you magnify
the Lord! You are Mary, our friend and guide!

True Son of God, born in the manger, the
Word in flesh, King of Truth and Love—
you came a child to save us all from sin.
O Jesus can mere words demonstrate our love for
you? Christ Jesus you are the Savior of the world!

William Sutherland

Grief's Acceptance Short And Sad Bad And Deep!!!

Wolfing the benefits; .... savor not, the excuse.
  Greener than many; not yet, his
Last training composite, repertoire!!
  The bow, of adieu.... a, brief
Respite of trainings long.... end's
  Approach, with more practical thoroughness,
Than, most;
  The newness of the sixties plight
Seemed... only a... faint, faint,
  Ringing.... on, as deja vu of
Old. Eight months of intenseness ... on,
  And off the record... wait.
A bold feeling of being
  Ever — eried, and S. Diego - bold;
And warily deft... at official's
  Ire... presence to carry on; as,
Thy... needs! Sky!

Richard C. Miller

Ride The Wolf

I rode the frantic, raging wolf today.
It was just like grandpa and Pa had done.
The world roared and tore in feral display.
Senses reeled until the very sun spun.

Peel outs and side surfs become eddy turns.
Wisconsin's Wolf River speeds high and riled.
The boulder strewn whitewater snarls and churns.
The miles long maelstrom scuds amok and wild.

Melting snow and spring rains fuel its quick rage.
Self-rescue swimming is indeed a must.
Your nerve and skill form a life saving gauge.
A body-ferry is something you trust.

When young you learn balance and the oar stroke.
The canoe and life-jacket are your tools.
The day will come when you must go for broke.
You must remember the life saving rules.

People raft mountain rivers of the West.
I've shot the Colorado and the Snake.
The Wolf River still is rated the best.
This is where stark thrills and verve do awake.

Frank Ducat

Added Touch

Sound and light travel through the air.
Solid walls no barrier.
Pictures bounce upon the screen.
I see people, but they don't see me.
They turn away when I try to grab them.
Why that happens, I can't fathom.
Light must travel light, I know,
but can't it carry more cargo?
Near the year 2025,
TV screens will come alive.
Simulation never was enough.
There'll be two way talk, taste, smell and touch

Genevieve Griffin

Fifty Anniversary Ode

Fifty years ago today, you began an exciting sojourn.
Lead by dreams, unaware of what you would soon learn.
Enticed by love, you stepped forth, on the pathway of married life.
Together you have shared, sunny days of joy, cloudy days of strive.
That road has taken you, through great joy and much sorrow,
Sometimes with very little hope, for a bright tomorrow.
You have experienced trials and trouble, worry and woe,
Especially while feeding and keeping six children in tow.
You have shown love for each other and all six of us,
Faithfully giving each day, strength, loyalty and trust.
Today our prayer is that, you grow closer as you travel on.
Because together is right where you two, will always belong.
As we express our love and devotion, with happy tears,
We lift our glasses, "Here is to another fifty years."

Patricia Stone Guynn

Sand Creek Witnessed My Grandparents'
Homestead Appearance

In 1887, my grandparents arrived near Sioux Falls, South Dakota
Hoping, in all earnestness, to locate a homestead.
Not until 1906 did their misfortune turn about
When a disappointed homestead owner's overtures became intent.

My grandparents headed north to a place eventually near
Temvik, North Dakota, about sixty miles south of Bismarck.
There, Sand Creek welcomed my grandparents with tears
To his land of opportunity without a single remark.

My grandparents and ten children succeeded in their first major goal
Drilling a well hole into which a manual water pump was installed
A quarter mile north of Sand Creek near home and fold,
Safely distanced from seasonal Sand Creek flooding sprawl.

Slowly, things progressed and food shortages ceased to be a problem,
Because this large family planned well for preservation.
The General Welfare was attained by an honest work emblem
Which these grandparents promoted without reservation.

At last, aging, my grandparents moved into Temvik,
Owning three homes, a horse livery stable, and a cream station.
This property was always, temporarily, available for serving
Any family member in the event of their personal privations.

Theodore R. Reich

Rain

Rain, rain, all the day long
Birds huddled in trees, devoid of song.
Tears of water, down the windows stream,
As stormy skies keep out the sunbeams.
Puddles accumulating on the ground
Raised umbrellas seen, all around.
Green grass glistening with rain.
Flowers hanging their heads as if in shame.
From a light sprinkle to a heavy downpour,
For a little while, then the sun will shine once more.

Patricia Burney

Old John

He was feeble and frail, rather small for today
As he made his way from his home by the bay.

Towards the shore he shuffled along,
Thinking of surroundings where he used to belong.

The children made fun of his wobbly gait,
Threw stones at the man with the silvery pate.

They teased him and badgered him as he walked,
They called him names, and made nasty talk.

The old man's mind was not on this scene,
'Twas far away on the bounding main.

His vessel at sea, whose captain he was,
Was sounding the "Horn", in wintery blast.

And this is the man they're laughing at now,
As he totters along, his head in bow.

Oh, how different are his days today,
Away from his ship and the oceans spray.

But the day is not long, not too far away,
When old, John, the sailor will go away,

Gone to be a land where respect is returned,
Where man is rewarded for what he has earned.

Clifford Ward Handy

A Secret

There is a secret that I hold
something I have never told.
It's just for me, and me alone to know
but someday I will let it go.
I don't know how, or when it will be
but I do know in time everyone will see.
The secret then will be no longer
and in return, in a sense,
I will have become stronger.
There is a secret that I hold
something I have never told.

Kimberlee Jenca

A Fading Bounty

Our mother is the Earth, our father is the sun
We have our creator who gave life, we think of the three as one
Our mother sings a song of sorrow as its injuries bleed from man
Her tears cover the tired soil trying to nourish our sore land
Trees, rocks, skies and man all possess harmony and peace
But when will man awaken, when will the damage cease
Our hands are the devices of our essence, the warriors of our wrath
But we have the power of mind we can stop this hell-bent path
Think of the many pleasures given from above that are ours to treasure
When the sky if fast asleep and daylight shuts her eyes
Under the spotlight of stars, for us the moon will rise
Listen to the music of the passing breeze
Or the tune of the songbirds lazing happily in the trees
Have you ever found yourself companion to the lonely moon
And then seem so fulfilled that the night ends to soon
There is no bridge to yesterday, no path that we may return
Left with regrets and excuses we must live and learn
Given precious gift's from Heaven we have no right to abuse
Where and who will we turn to when we realize we're the ones to lose

Debi Travers

Spiritual Wedding Vows

Into your hands, I laid my trust.
Until death due us part, I gave my love.
"True Companion" is the name I gave thee,
Sharing my life with you is how I dreamed it would be.

Now I submit to a greater power up above,
Just like a father who gives his daughter in love.
How my joy overflowed when I found,
A woman who's love for the Lord abounds.

Submerged in water to wash earthly cares away,
Rising on high in hope of living eternal days.
The stage is set, the invitation has been accepted.
Heavenly beings sing praises on high!

The servant of the Lord asks the question,
"Will you take Jesus to be your Savior?"
The spirit within responds with praise,
"I accept Him with total love this day!"

Let us build our life on the Rock of Christ;
"Keep God first" is our only advice.
We will love and cherish Him until death due us part,
Until Christ comes again and takes us eternally into His heart.

James Robert Webb

It's Me!

I am a bright star in the sky at night...
I am the soft breeze of a bird in flight...
Do not feel like my life is gone.
Look up - that's where I live...
it's me!

I am the sweet song of the mourning dove...
I am the tenderness of a new baby's love.
Do not stand at my grave and cry.
I am not there - I did not die...
Look up and feel the love...
it's me!

I am the dream that finally came true....
I will love and laugh forever through you....
Do not bow your head and cry.
Look up that's where I live...
feel the love, oh, feel the love...
it's me!

Jo Tucker

The Lady

Gabrielle was a lady, a cat.
Who came to live at Chris Bell's house
One night she brought in a present
a nice fat juicy dead mouse!

Her main goal in life was plotting how
That when the front door was opened.
She'd make a dash for it
and think "I must get in now!"

For food Gabrielle would not you see
lower herself to beg or to rub around on a persons legs.
it was beneath her dignity!

But you know...it was neat
when she wanted what you were trying to eat
even though she would not whine or cry
You could tell what she wanted, by the look in her eye.

Then one day Gabrielle just up and went away.
Never a back ward glance
She didn't even give me a chance...
to tell her what a joy she'd been
This cat who had become my friend!

Christine Marie Bell

Lost Child

Lost child how far away are you?
Can you ever find your way back home
You been traveling so far and for so long
Lost in the wilderness, and lost in the storm
How far away are you?
Can you ever find your way back home
Reach out to me and I'll be there
Lost child how far away are you?
Lost in the dessert hungry and in pain
Won't you ever come home again?
Lost child you made a wrong turn
Call out in the wind, and my voice you will hear
Lost child alone and confuse
Don't you know your way back home?
Alone with no where to go lost in your own world
How far away are you?
    Lost

Ana Pabon

"A Rhymn In Signs"

Sitting at the bar in the Eagles' Club,
    With thoughts wandering out into space.
One's mind starts to roam, and up comes a poem,
    About the signs in this place!

If that barmaid would just stand still,
    You could see by the sign near the till,
"No Profanity allowed" that's cussing out loud.
    But somehow, someone always will!

Wearing hats indoor, seems rather queer.
    By the bald heads, it would appear.
To the signs they adhere, which says very clear:
    "Wear a hat in here - you'll buy the folks a round of cheer!"

And if you go downstairs to eat,
    Posted there is a sign hard to beat.
It couldn't be said better - it fits to the letter.
    "Up your bucket, colonel - our chicken's better!"

But there's always one single sign,
    That's really so hard to find.
You know that it's there - but heavens knows where.
    Locating "rest rooms" can blow your old mind!"

Richard E. Nickel

Who Are You!

To whom do you pray
What color is it
Where can it be found
No one knows
But your faith will take you to the same thing
    and you will seek it over and over again
    in the same place
Your creator is not visible nor is he physical
He has no color and no human wealth
Yet he is considered greater and mightier than any
    living thing
You salute and honor him with ultimate reverence
Why then do you a follower and believer
Make such a fuss about your brother's color, or the
    riches you pursue, or your social stature or your race
Are these really important to your creator
If so, he would have chosen a human form, race, color,
    and a place to hoard his wealth
Instead he remains anonymous - why!
Then who are you!

John Rodriguez

Boyhood

There's a tree in the meadow, one of many
in a sycamore stand, where I carved my
initials as a boy to lay claim to my piece of land,

A gentle stream close by, where you can
hear the ripple of the water, flowing
over a beaver dam and watch the antics
of an otter,

I loved to go fishing there, up with the
morning light, with a slight drizzle of
rain the fish were sure to bite,

As I look towards the Summer sky for
perhaps a change in weather, I can see
the grass blowing to and fro like that of
Irish Heather,

The trill of the mocking bird, the cooing
of a dove, the smell of a clover field are
among the things I love,

As we live our lives full circle from the
beginning to the end, it's the trying to
piece together the many places we have been.....

Leamon C. Ryan

"The Shadow Of The Soul"

How dismal, life without light, the gloom engulfs me.
Groping, yet not finding the way out, the sounds, like stabbing pains.
To go on is to fall in the depths, calling silent cries unrecognized.
Abandoned, un-nurtured, unwanted, giving all,
    becoming a wasted one.
The barrier looms, casting a shadow. Cold exists in that shadow.
Storms cause shadows to disappear, but the storm within my
    being back lashes to my undoing.
Dreadful is the night when sleep eludes me, sleep that only over
    takes me in living death, breathing, but dead.
What have I lost, possibly never had?
Has the shadow stolen who I am?
Causing me to grope in darkness, will I ever awaken to my light?
What keeps me struggling, why do I not give in?
From where does my strength grow, why torment myself so?
I sit, dismal and despondent, why?
Am I waiting for the shadow to disappear?"
When it has dissolved, will I survive?
Am I so lost without it, shall I die?

Geraldine J. Arvanites

"Star Of Night"

Star, star in heaven, you are so bright
The North stars in the biggest yes, that's right.

Star of wonder, Milkyway in the sky,
as I watch it passes right by.

My breathes I take, keep going on,
the power of God is on his throne?

King forever, ceasing never the heavenly star on high
still proceeding, guide us to the light,
Westwood heading all through the night.

No sighing, no dying, no crying stay in the sky,
still will guide us to the perfect bright star,
star of the night

Rhunette Liles

The New Year

Come January first, you shall begin again
The word of authority was spoken unto me
The living word I heard (audibly)
The voice of the Lord
I was not surprised to hear
The truth say unto me, (so clear)
Come January first, you shall begin again

Straightway, as a mighty rushing wind
The truth came in, I am delivered from sin
By the power of the blood of Jesus the Christ
Through his death, burial and resurrection
I believe and offer my repentance, my confession
Satan, you are powerless! No more connection!

Come January first, I shall begin again
For I am born again
A child of the living God with eternal life
Reconciled and sanctified unto him
Redeemed through jesus the Christ
The way, the truth and the life
The holy one of God, the heavenly sacrifice
Martus

Boot Camp Bound

The girl I left behind...
Was sweet kind and divine...
For it was I...
That was given the chance to find...
The beauty of the girl left behind...

As I sit and reminisce of the girl I miss.
And the times when we laughed and cried...
Her purity and grace I will always embrace...
The beauty of the girl I left behind...

Thoughts and memories I will never forget...
Like the singing of Auld Lang Syne...
She will lay still in my mind...
For the rest of my time...
The beauty of the girl I left behind...
Raymond McEvoy

Looking Glass

The problem with people
Is that I am a person
And what bothers me most about you
Is what's dysfunctional about myself.

The trouble with society
Stems from my own anxiety
And what disturbs me about the world
Are those many faults we have in common.

Through our own subjective vision
We see ourselves in everyone else
And if we find we love no other
'Tis largely 'cause we do not like ourself.
Jerry Olney

Honesty

All I ask from you is honesty
Through time and events this will
help our love grow
Honesty brings forth the special glow
With honesty you have everything we need
Honesty is like planting a seed
And when it begins to grow
My love for you will also
Barbery M. Evans

The Reign

Today to be crowned the KING OF EXTREMES.
The lack of the grey
Speaks more than it seems.
Pain crystallizes,
Forms pointed shards
That blind mine eye to the fortunate cards.

Accomplishments many,
Goodness exists.
Concentration on what's lacking,
How it binds and it twists.
Regrets may seem few,
But they taint the whole glory.
I endeavor to not.....
Blow a hole in my story.
Keith Robert Gebbia

The Flight Of Anonymity

Bearing the gifts away without a thought,
the Santa Claus syndrome hangs from the tree,
just over the red curtain-draped cloth
strewn freely around the stand.
Down the chimney comes the gift,
the child still remaining in each one of us,
all waiting for more than the red suit and
presents released from his hand,
those unimportant gifts from the imaginary man.
There will be no names dripping,
no fame slipping from one tongue to the other,
only reverence in the grace of day,
only our desire to continue to play.
Henry Deas III

Innocence Lost

What is happening to our children?
Why have we taken the joy out of childhood?
Innocence lost in the hatred of the parents.
Blank eyes staring out of empty sockets.
Faces branded by the trauma in the trenches.
Human pincushions, human ashtrays,
Hands severed at the wrists,
Putrid remains of yesterday's love.
Voices silenced forever by
Parental firing squads.
Julio Bernal

Faces

As I walk down the street, I look at all the faces.
Each one is a book, sometimes asking to be read, sometimes not.
Some are paperback novels, read once or twice, their covers
    bent and dog-eared, then discarded, or shoved on a back
    shelf, never or rarely to be seen again.
Others are hardcover masterpieces, Shakespeare, Melville, Shelley.
    These are pristine, barely touched at all; to
    even deign to look at them is sacrilegious.
There are some that lie there, gold-gilded, shining, begging
    to be looked upon, but once the pages are opened, there
    is nothing worth looking at.
And their foils, those that look like they have no place on
    any bookshelf, so "ugly" they look worthless.
    But within, the words have a life unlike any others.
Then the greatest of them all. The story that is never
    cold, for the reader's hands barely leave it.
    It may be tattered or worn, but that is no matter, for it is
    the story that counts, that gives it life.
The faces. All of them a tale; waiting, waiting to be read.
Gregory Miska

Optimism

We tend to hide sometimes, inside an empty glass . . .
Unreachable to relations, Why?

Obstacles in life . . .
We overlook . . . we are not the only.
We neglect . . . what we have.
We recognize . . . what we do not.

Very guilty . . . am I, for many things have not gone as planned . . .
So, I have broken that glass, that prison . . .
To which I conform . . . for such a very long time.

With laughter and a joke, I learn to cope.
As amusing as it may not be . . .
To make light of, keeps my empty glass broke . . .

REMEMBER . . . EXISTENCE . . .
Not, "Perpetually" A day at the beach . . .
Yet, with all our relations, we can turn a grimace into a grin.
If only for one moment.

A Tender Smile, A Joyous start . . .

Heidi Hoffman

The Web

Glimmering strands are revealed only to tearful eyes,
Silvery lace has been woven and is now threatened.
Gossamer threads bind together dancers.

It was never visible before a dancer slipped,
The thread was woven through the other dancers,
Now the web must be repaired and the dance is harder
    because the dancers know they may fall.
All that felt the threads pull as he fell know it is not
    dew that glistens on the web...it is tears.

Now that it has been seem it is easier to destroy.
The dancers hold the elusive gossamer tightly,
The dance grows more difficult as the web grows more
    intricate with every move.

Carinn J. Sprecher

The Night

The night is my protector
I can hide behind the darkness
If I want to shine
The moon will be my spotlight
There is mystery in the night
And the shadows play games
With my still adjusting eyes
Death feels near yet I am so alive
I can dance on the calm black water
Or play among the stars that shine
Like diamonds on the beautiful necklace of
The night

Nikole Meier

Nature

The birds and the bees are
a pretty sight to see. When
I walk outside in the great
outdoors I look at the pretty
sight, I might pick a flower
or two, but still I respect
Mother Nature's nature. But in my heart,
I know there lies a spirt in every
living thing.

Clarissa Milton

Danse A La Ville (After The Painting By Renoir)

Her hand
Quivers like a palm leaf
Perfect nonchalance
Floating gently through the music
Blue shadows gather in starched lace
They both wear gloves

He dips forward into the waltz
(the tempo, after all, must be kept)
His nose brushes upswept hair
Her rose adornment slips closer to her cheeks
As lips do not blend past his harsh tuxedo jacket
None of the tea room ladies fluster

It makes a shadow-lover consider
Whether she can feel his subtle breath
In such a proper ballroom

Katherine Plante

Saying Goodbye

I say my prayers and go to bed, sometimes angry, sometimes sad,
But I know now what I must do and say goodbye for the final time
to this wonderful man, so unique in his ways,
touching everyone he meets in some special way.
A warrior dying the way he dreamed,
taking with him his legend of gold.
So devoted to our God, so well blessed in his jobs,
so awesomely patient with his lost sheep and compassionate
beyond belief.
A man to admire, so deeply loved. It is true we will miss him much.
But I can hear my Lord saying now,
"Come with me my good and faithful servant,
you have earned my riches". I can see him in heaven,
at His feet, praising Him, singing and dancing with glee.
And though I know he has no more sorrow,
It does not make it any easier to say and do what I must.
So, dear Grandpa, look down and hear me now,
As I say my goodbyes one not so final time.
You have gone away to an awesome place, a trip from which you
will not return.
But I know a day will come when it will be my time to journey on.
And when I do, you and I will be together.
So, till then, goodbye dear father. And now the waiting begins.

Michelle Ellington

Ode To Momma

Elaine, Elaine. O Momma! I never met thee.
I never had the chance to wipe your brow and kiss your cheek.
I never got to hold your hand or wash your feet.
I never wrote a letter for you or read to you.
I never got to fluff your pillows or tuck you under the covers.
My hands never got to brush your hair nor rub your back.
You never got to hear my lullabies.
We didn't get to share those women stories —
    of first loves and husbands and first babies.
We never got to share recipes. I didn't get to learn from you
to hear your wisdom or question the pain of womanhood - of
being wife and mother, of sacrifices for husband and children.
I never got to love you up close to empty my heart on your breast.
O Momma! I was not there for you! And Momma, I didn't get to
thank you for what you gave me to me - we had so much in common —
    your first born - my last love. I never got to tell you
how much he means to me. O the joy to have cared for you!
We didn't get to share Jesus - we didn't get to say goodbye.
Aloha Momma. I pray we'll meet in His time. I love you so!

Dorothy L. Toulson

In Memory of Mom-mom

You were the dawn of a bright sunny day
You were the calm in the middle of the storm
My pot of gold of the end of a rainbow
And like a thief in the night
You were here one minute and gone the next!

You were my Mom-Mom, my Grandmother
You loved, cared for, raised and taught me
You were my mother, my father, my friend
And believe it or not, I did listen
Many times when you thought that I hadn't.

But on the day that you departed from this life
The pain that I felt when you were gone
Was no greater that the guilt that I felt
For you were gone before I said that
"I love you very much!"

Cheryl D. Brown White

Friends Of Color

I had a good friend
who lived just around the bend.

We played stick ball
and sometimes cruised the mall.

We went to the movies every week
and ate candy until our glucose peaked.

I took him to church with us
and discovered that this was a bust.

For some reason people weren't receptive
and I soon learned the reason was deceptive.

Unfortunately, some could not
see beyond the skin,
but he had many
qualities that were within.

Vic Tomlinson

We Were Friends, We Are Friends

We were friends, we are friends, we may still be friends
In the future, the far off future.
We were friends, we are friends, we may not stay friends
In the future, the far off future.
On a cold winter day we may start up a fight
Or maybe we'll stay as we are.
For me the breakup can't last up until night
But what about for her?
And then I'd come home and burst in to tears
And wish for it all to be over.
And when we make up I'll be happy until
It'll quickly begin all over.
We were friends, we are friends, why can't we stay friends
In the near, far off future?

Olga Kamensky

Trust And Deception

Trust and deception.
Do they go hand in hand?
Do we trust someone only to be deceived?
Or do we deceive only to be trusted?
Do we love those we trust and
despise those who deceive?
Or are we loving those we deceive and
despising those who we love?

Jacquelyn J. Moore

Why Did You Come?

Beasts of the night why did you come and take my precious little one?
You killed with treacherous might, hate, spite
    and only leave fright!
The pain of loss hurts and cuts me deep... I scream; I cry; I weep.
No peace I find... only anger and bad dreams
    while you still run free.
Probably killing others, including me.
And now I am totally alone... nothing to share my home.
No one to know when I leave, come and go.
I miss her... my friend... I love her still...
And it is now you I want to kill
I hope and pray for some kind of peace
But for now, I can find no release.

Kim D. Lawson

True Love

We both have had bad loves in our past.
But God brought us together and I know that it will last.

The wind is blowing up against my window pane.
I look out and see, the falling rain.

Sitting here remembering how we walked in the rain
You looked at me, and I looked at you and we kissed so tenderly.

We both knew our love will never be the same.
For we found true love walking in the rain.

Remembering how the moon was shinning up above just right
How I saw the twinkling of the stars by the shiny moonlight.

It is so nice to be with the one you love
For you think about them day and night
And you pray constantly to God almighty
That they will treat you right,

And in your prayers you pray they will love you.
For the rest of your life God brought us together.
And we knew our love was meant to last true love.

LaFair Pardon

Pieces

Eyes like dying stars peer into the void
Finding faded memories and broken dreams.
Things better left forgotten...
Things better left for dead.

The hall of shattered mirrors
On the sea of ebon black
Follows the whisper in the dark.

Silence is the deadliest weapon of all
As we play hide-and-seek with blind eyes.
Drifting in our confusion...
To the tattered, up-rooted remains of Eden
Where the only religions are worshipped by fools,
And false prophets are half mad with greed.

Tom Herchenrader

Happy Anniversary

You have traveled
Many years on the road of life
As a happy husband and wife.

We wish you good luck and happiness too.
So keep traveling that road
For you have reached the silver,
And now go for the gold.

Earl Denniston

How Men Talk

While I waited at WESTERN AUTO
I listened to how men talk.
Would you believe they also worry
About how they look and how they walk?

Oh yes, they do, and that's all ages
From 40 on they re-counted pages
Of what life is about and a lot about cars
They hardly talked about the wars.

Oh yes, they remembered about the bars
The "Cozy," the "Zanzibar" and the "Star."
No matter what it was about
They always got back to talk about cars!

Mercedes Conner

We Are The Youth

We are the youth!
Rising from a war-torn world,
Witnessing an era of ruthless bloodshed —
Living remains of disease and starvation,
Survivors of death, torture and depression.

Yes, we are the youth!
Envisaged by a world gone mad,
Beckoned by the future, obscure and darkened
By woes and trials of government,
Economic strife and peace pacts unsettled.

But while all adversities blast,
Hopeful still, naught will dismay
Our youthful dreams, nor turn aghast
Our ardent hearts, Therefore, O, St. Williams,
We've come to stay 'neath your paternal guidance.

In part to us true wisdom and knowledge,
But not the wisdom of the atomic sage.
Grant to us the wisdom of the heavenly saints,
That while we live, we may still be the hope of the
Fatherland!
The unshakable pillars of the Mother Church.

Remedios V. Miguel

Say It's Not So

She's sweet and innocent at the age of 10.
Her mother meets a man and marries again.
It seems that she can never win.
Her new dad takes her into the den,
and performs the ultimate sin.

Say it's not so.

Ten years from that place
same incident, different face.
He ties her wrists and ankles with tape.
She starts to cry as she's being raped.

Say it's not so.

Ten more years; she's married to a business man.
He lays down the law with the back of his hand.
She believes it's her fault,
so she locks it in her memory — her vault.

Say it's not so.

At the age of 40, she thinks things cannot get worse.
She pulls a gun out of her purse,
and puts it up to her head.
Her world of broken dreams is now covered with red.

Ty Glander

Tears On My Pillow

I wished upon a falling star,
I turned around and there you are.
You were sent here for reason, not by fate,
You were sent here to change my life, not to late...

I grew to adore you, I needed your touch,
Your smile made my heart melt, your eyes said so much.
I tried to ignore it, I tried not to see,
The power of love, that had captured me...

Your love made me happy, your love gave to me,
Contentment, fulfillment, your all that I need
You promised you'd be here and not go away,
To stay right beside me and help lead the way...

Then one day you left me, you went far away,
I cried and I cried for you, day after day.
I waited and waited, I needed you so,
Each day seemed a challenge, I wanted to know...

Why don't you call me, why don't you write,
To tell me you love me, and miss me each night.
My heart has been broken, my eyes fill with tears,
What we had once is over, and now the end nears...

Trika Rauls

Divine Mortality

Passing through time,
Absorbing its rhythm - life's journey on a treadmill,
Its cadence counting events that sweep me along,
Momentum accelerating, empty striving, actualizing self,
Passing through life's ages on a continuous circle;
Beginning and ending together, I, the dust of the earth.

Breaking the cadence, slowing its consuming pace
To the beat of my heart and the dulcet tones of the verdant earth;
My outstretched hands reach to touch the horizon where earth
and eternity meet,
A cry of anguish pierces the black night;
Light and peace comes, finally,
I am cognizant of eternal secrets I once knew.

I am a being of spirit, life is more than a concourse of events
Carrying me along to a hollow grave;
I will gather earth's wild flowers to me
And breathe in the sweet fragrance,
I will sow their seed as I go and create meadows in my passing;
Those who follow this path will remember the secrets and live
forever.

Rita L. Foster

A Perfect World

I wish there was a perfect world. Where there was
No black, no white no wrong just right.

I wish there was a perfect world where all the
problems were solved and all the Bad people
were captured by law.

I wish there was a perfect world where all people
were friends and poverty would end.

I wish there was a perfect world where hearts weren't
broken and there was no drugs or smoking.

I wish there was perfect world where life always
had a surprise and no people had to cry.

I wish there was perfect world where animals
could play and there was no rain just sunny days.

I hope that life will soon uncurl and we can all have a
perfect world.

David M. Fanning

Goodbye To A Friend

When I think of you my dear friend, I feel so sad,
you were the best friend that I have ever had.
We have known each other for many wonderful years,
now my friend, you're gone, I cry for you bitter tears.

My friend, you will always have a special place in my heart,
I remember when we met and how our friendship got its start.
Days have gone by, there are times your smile I can plainly see,
the places we use to go, I now go alone, there I wished you'd
be.

I miss talking to you and hearing the things you use to say,
my friend, so many times, I've asked, why did you go away.
Your going away my friend has left an emptiness in my life,
it filled my life with sorrow when you left on April 19, 1995.

So many times I imagine seeing you standing there in the crowd,
then I remember you're gone as I start to call your name out loud.
I'll cherish our friendship, tho your leaving has left an empty space
time will mend the heart but no other friend will take your place.

The pain of loneliness and emptiness for a friend who was always near
never again to see the face or hear the voice of a friend who was so
   dear.
I am glad we met and that I had you for a friend for just a short time
with a heavy heart, I say goodbye to a very dear friend of mine.

   Lillie M. Perry

A Wife In Waiting

It's been seventeen long years since
our hearts have met.

I remember it so well the night you
drove up in your pearl white corvette;
You treasured that car and soon
I became a part of that treasure.

You showed me a love I've never
experienced. You let me into you
world, a place where no one ventured.

You seduced my heart, mind, soul,
and body into accepting and trusting
you, then you released the secrets
from your subconscious that you
vowed never to reveal.

You told of a child that meant so much,
of a love made in heaven, you paralyzed my
emotions and second handly gave me your last name
which I graciously accepted.
But now the long years of awaiting doesn't matter, because
they have made me a wife of love, warmth, and wisdom.

   Vicky P. Pollens

Whispers

Janice....I heard a whisper in the middle of the night,
I could not tell where it was coming from as I sat up with a fright
Was it from my pillow, or somewhere in the dark of night
Then I realize it was my own voice whispering your name in the night

I'm not sure what the dream was about,
We may have just been standing close together,
Or holding hands as we walked for awhile.
Or maybe I was just looking in amazement at your beautiful smile.
I guess I'll never know just what my dream held in store;
But as I layed back down to sleep,
I said a little prayer;
"God please let me dream just a little more"

   R. Dwayne Hall

A Greek Fable Of Old

Aesop told us the story
Of a young mouse that was nearly
swallowed up by a lion hungry.

She pleaded with him,
Calling him "Big Jim,"
Please don't eat me,
Of any further service to you I couldn't be!"

"How could you,
You're so small and so insignificant..."

"Oh then you think I can't
be of any use to you,
One day I might surprise you."

That day happened. The lion mighty
was caught up in a snare
On the prairie in the open air,
In his net a dumbfounded prisoner.

Was he ever pleased to see her!
She did a very good job of gnawing away
The meshes of the net, and set him free,
That's what can do for you a friend, even very wee.

   Claudette Aubert

Tenderness Of Life

Like a star shining in the sky,
was that first day I looked in your eyes.

The softness of your body.
That first touch that makes emotions rise.

My mother always told me, and now I know
how wonderful the mistress of life.

If there is something I want more,
is to always protect you.

Life is tough, life is cruel,
but don't worry my baby;
I will always be with you.

   Luz E. Festoff

For Jennifer

If only I could find a word,
Or know a song to sing,
Of the pale and graceful bird,
With frail and fragile wing,

Who flies above the land, so high,
Who soars above a fretful sea,
In an azure blue, sun-drenched sky,
On feathered wings so coveted by me.

Who in her high and airey loft,
So far above and well beyond us all,
Builds her nest with plumes so soft,
And taunts me with her dreamlike call.

My feathered friend, I long to be as you.
Could it be, somehow, that you envy me, too?

   Rod Grille

The Frost

As the frigid February winds surge outside with such ferocity
One can only wonder in amazement
How when they mysteriously combine with equal parts
of gelid temperature and slight drops of moisture
Something so brutal can create such delicate
beauty on every window pane.

It must be divine fingertips creating such
intricate and fragile works of art.

Lucinda M. Wetzel

My Mentor

There are many diverse people in this world today,
My focus is one individual that came into my life in a special,
    unique way.
His kindness and generosity would melt your heart,
He did his research faithfully for he was very smart,
Everything in the world to him seemed to be a piece of cake,
For he preached that it is better to give than to take.
He taught me almost everything that I needed to know,
for his character could certainly put on a worthwhile show!
Every time I look through the obituary page,
I cannot forget that GOD took him at a young age!
As I stand by his grave,
I know that in my heart he would want me to be brave.
HE was a LEADER, not a follower,
YES, indeed that was my FATHER!

Carla Capone

And The Lord Spoke Unto Them

The time of penance is at hand
For those who denounced my name in thoughtless ridicule of non-belief
One by one to the second power
For their wounding words by killing sword shall lift high
High above their pitiful world
To gain strength from every bloodied soul it has elected to receive
    the truth
You, as well as I, know who you are
Accomplice and procreator alike
Guilt shall engulf you as the darkness greatens within your heart
Forgiveness doth not come in prayer nor sorrow
Amendments are made only in realization
Realization is the enlightenment of fraudulent words
Enhanced by ones vocal cords
To accommodate the eager consumption of non-merited worth
By naive ears

Derek Hosselkus

My Beloved Father

I feel peace as the wind blows through my hair.
It's been a long time since I felt this way.
How I've longed to be able to see you again.
God sent you here to help guide my way.

I don't know why you were taken away so fast.
The nights and days have gone on so long.
The sweet words you whisper in my heart.
They come to me with the spirit of song.

I hope to see you again someday.
While your light shines through my soul.
And when I die we will be in paradise.
With that memory, it will be my only goal.

Your shadow has enlightened my being.
I shall never forget you.
And as long as we can be together again.
Your essence will always remain soft and true.

Randi M. Grossman

"God's Night"

Without a mortal around came this
thing from the ground it grew not too tall
But big around brought food shelter
And sound. This thing from the ground...
Can you see me I'm a tree... God's
Gift to you and me.

Richard Yoeman

If The World Should End Tonight

If the world should end tonight; let the angels find me
in your arms tomorrow
If heaven is a myth and darkness is our final peace; then
let my last sensations of life be mixed with yours
If in this life I have said anything of meaning and true
value; then let me say "I love you" before I close my eyes
Let your touch be my final memory, your kiss my final
indulgence, your smile my final happiness
If the curtain should fall tonight; let our love be our
last ecstasy, let our last ecstasy be our greatest sin;
let your name be my last breath

Michael M. Jones

Covered Spirits

Your looks confuse me, my friend.
Yes, I am your friend. I do love you.
Yet, I am unable to comprehend what my eyes see before me.

I sense your womanhood
your core essence moves me.
I am at home in your presence
thought your physical appearance baffles me.

How is it that someone so lovely and stately
adorns and covers herself with garbs of harsh lines and angles?

I seek a goddess at your temple
whence I'm summoned
only to arrive
I find you sitting in remnants of
nails and bolts — your father's clothing.

I understand you like neither
your mother's frocks nor frills
they once were worn with disdain
But I ask you — my sister
    where are your clothes???

E. Simone "Tina" Buttry

And The World Watched In Silence

From Warsaw to Paris, Jews were taken—then exterminated,
From the Ghetto to the country, Jews were taken—then exterminated,
Jews were branded like cattle-then exterminated,
Jews were made to labor until exhaustion—then exterminated,
Jews were fed rotten food, if fed at all—then exterminated,
Jews were made emaciated and weak—then exterminated,
Jews were robbed of all dignity—then exterminated,
Jews were made to dig mass graves—then exterminated,
Jews were used as lab rats—then exterminated,
Jewish women were raped—then exterminated,
Jewish men were castrated—then exterminated,
Jews were lashed—then exterminated,
An entire race was vanishing,
America, where the Hell were you!
Justice, where the Hell were you!
They were just Jews,
So nobody cared,
And the world watched in silence!

Jonathan Kanze

Through The Eyes Of Depression

Weak, tired and in distress.
Tears flowing down my cheeks
I lay covered completely in my bed.
For, this is the only security and comfort that I need.
Don't bother to touch or speak a word to me.
For, at this moment, I'm definitely out of reach.
The mind is traveling at a rapid speed.
If it would just come to a red light, oh, what an ease.
My heart is beating like drums in the villages of Africa.
Loud, at its own steady and musical beat.
I must find a path to get back in control.
If not, I'll lose it all together, Lord only knows!
A word to myself, stay focus, let positive thoughts creep up into
  my mind.
Let the bells of peace began to chime.
I'm feeling stronger, my tears are almost dry.
Touch me, let me feel your warmth
My mind has reached that red light and my heart is back on beat.
I'll lay here a little longer, get some peaceful sleep.
Praise God, Praise God, I'm no longer at this time depressed.

Christine Young-Robinson

Untitled

To look upon the heavens, as if to see your sweet smile.
Like venus upon the night sky, you eclipse all that surround you.
Like venus you shine for everyone to see, and then you're gone.
The sky, no longer quite the same.
As if you're in another world.
If only I could cross over to you.
Maybe to reach out to caress your face,
As if it will take me there.
As if I've known you all my life, as if you were a part of me.
If only you were a dream to never wake, always
would I stay with you.
Forever would I reach out, if only to touch your heart.
If only to see your smile

Rick Huffman

The Paths Of Life

Through the years we change and grow
We come to find what we need to know
The seasons change and time goes by
We realize someday we all will die
As time passes on we learn about life
And love and how we must help others
Before they are gone.

We see that peace is the key
To the way our happiness must be
We find that life is not a game, but
A path of many ways, we must reach
In our hearts and find that our paths
Are not the same, we all have to part
At least for a while, it'll break
My heart, but I know you'll be
At the end with a smile, we must
Search for what God put us here
To do, when we see it we'll know all along
That we knew.

Melissa Ann Martinez

Friends

Friends are there when you need them.
You count on them to be there.
They become apart of you and only you.
  The laughter becomes memories of the magical wind.
Your childhood always remains with you just like your friends.

Maria McLaughlin

Simple Pleasures That Relate

The mountains roared back at the mighty winds;
It was a long walk I would walk to the end.
I fought and fought to make my way to shelter.
Various feelings of heartache
Attacked me.
The sounds became softer with the ease to my ears,
I was waiting for the God of the morning to appear.
Winding wind
Through the shattered soul,
Would only hurt if left untold.
Snowballs flew into the trees
Only to fall and plead;
That the hardness would turn soft
And gently slow them down.
The birds screamed at the big bears but they should of kept on
singing.
I stood on the highest mountain and cried,
No longer felt cold
No longer felt weak
And the snow blew off the top.

Nicole Bafford

Change

As the Autumn leaves birth new color,
The northern winds usher out the summer.
The birds fly south in search of the sun,
All is accomplished yet Winter is done.

Season to season, new beginnings are formed,
Change is nature, seasons forewarned.
Our Father prepares the earth to revolve,
To accept each season and all it involves.

So too our lives parallel with the seasons,
Change always occurs for various reasons.
Our Father prepares us for the path we must go,
With His trust and endurance, the winds of change
    start to blow.

Robert Lee Rose III

Grand Mother

The wind whips through my soul as a run-away train might
yet, where do I stand.
The question is an irrelevancy, life is lost, I hate all!
When I was a young boy you where my support,
my confidant, my savior.
Yet, here again I sit pondering on the remembrance of thee.
I miss you with all my heart, tears have dried,
you've become a lost dream.
Everything has become a new awakening.
Life is still an unexplored frontier to me, that is with out you.
The complications are something of a lost trend.
You where truly my lost soul mate, yet, again lost too the age's.
Why? I ponder the ideals lost and the truth is something of
an extremity too me.
Hazel is the name of witches, you where of another,
an icon comes too mind.
I still have yet to see your grave, and why,
because that's the reality of death.
All I can promise too you is this, I will make you immortal!
Life is a lost personality and you in death are more of an
influence then you were, even in life.
May God have mercy on my tormented soul!

Christian A. Miller

Of His Heart

Your words are like the wind
  you speak and the world is talking.
You rest your wings in a nest of stillness,
  to hatch your fears, your happiness, and your dreams.
I do not always hear the words you say,
  instead I hear the love and the caring.

Your words reflect the armor you wear,
  when loving, when sharing, to keep the aching out.

It is the wisdom of your words,
  that have answers to everything.
  It wears your self-importance and sits in the back seat
  and directs all your travels.

Your words reflects the loneliness in you
  and the need to be understood.
  And though you mask yourself with moods and silences,
  your needs leap out from all you do
  and speak to those alike.

But what are the words of this man?
  It is the silent singing within his heart,
  that only another heart can hear!

   Edna Overton

Things To Do

Make regular contact with reality,
stop visiting my past lives and try living this one,
Categorize my 2,176 books, read them.
Defrost my refrigerator and find out what's underneath all that snow,
Throw out everything covered with blue mold, keep the stuff
with green mold, it's pretty.
Take a head count of all the cats that are currently living in my
apartment, ask some to leave or at least to stop bringing their
friends home for dinner,
Go through my closet and get rid of the clothes
belonging to the people whose lives I no longer live,
Smile, look pretty, be here now, be centered, find myself, find my
shoes, become organized, pray for miracles, reach enlightenment,
make more novenas, stop putting my crystal ball in the dish water,
eat my vegetables, take my vitamins, drink my Lourdes water
and hope for the best, save the whales, free the dolphins, and
bring back the leprechauns, visualize world peace.
Disarm the warheads that stand inside me.

   Serena Fletcher

To Sea!

There's a small craft advisory today
Along the coast and on the bay
Keep your boat in port the old salts say
But I'm yearning to sail and go anyway

Alone I leave to face the sea
To test my vessel and challenge me
The ocean in March is a frigid degree
But my spirit is hot and my soul is free

To starboard the Cape Henry light I spy
With a background of gray and pale blue sky
The white caps and olive green sea slip by
Praise Neptune, Mother Nature and God on High

An in bound freighter to port goes past
I await her wake, it's moving fast
I pray my sail and mast will last
What the hell
  To sea!
    My fate is cast

   Brian James Huddy

Climacteric

Be advised: It is too late in the season
To plant in my garden;
The seeds you carry in your sack
Will not grow here.
But the morning sun
Is deceptively warm
And a heavy dew has rendered
A promising appearance
To the tired clay;
So, for this moment,
We may pretend at the ritual;
Ready your plow,
And I will yield;
Cast a prayer upon my soil,
And perhaps I shall surprise us both
With a tender green memory.

   Lynn Tucker

Death

Life was the one thing I feared most,
even more than Death herself.
I would accept death wherever I could meet it.
I searched, but no one would accept the offer.
I tried suicide.
My attempt failed; not once, but several times.
However, I did not give up.
Day after day, night after night, I was persistent.
Finally I gave up; I became sleepy.
But, it was no sooner than the moment that I closed my eyes,
that I met death.

Darkness surrounded me; that was until Death had opened the door.
Rays of light struck my eyes, like lightning striking a beam of metal.
Death had entered the room.
I sensed her presence.
I had an image of her: young and beautiful.
Questions filled my thoughts.
I searched for answers; none.
She called my name. I reached out.
She led me into the light.
Now I knew I would never be seen again.

   Sumit Sahdev

When Will You Know I'm The One

Do you faithfully believe in Me - Or just what seems to be.
When will you know - I am the one.
The last days see us having too much fun.

Too much lust; too much pain. Men, you want to call out my name.
I accept you when you claim me as your Lord
My Son Jesus, to you I give.

I gave so that, through him, you would learn my way
And love each other - as I my son

When will you know - I am the one?

Will it be when you rebuke Satan out of your life?
Will it be when you deny cheating on your wife?
Will it be after you have been convicted of crime?
Will it be after I have given you all the signs?
Will it be when you hit the lottery and money overflows?
Will it be it be today? Tomorrow? Do you really know?
Will it be when you put others on a pedestal - a throne?
Will it be when the birds stop singing - Or the sun doesn't rise?

NOW is the time - for the Lord's Way to redirect our lives!

   Michelle Christine Johnson

One Day

One day the earth was born
in the consciousness of time
That day the earth gave life to man
and made its secrets ours to find
One day mankind made love to hate
and begot military might
The seams of war were stitched in fear
a cloth to conceal our fright
One day our species discovered strength with
sharpened lead and steel
Thus the rise of kings with crowns
to harvest killing fields
One day they stayed the enemy
with a billion clubs they crushed
One day we took a closer look
and found the fallen foe was us

M. Andrew Dean

Memories

Memories are what make the world go round.
If memories were no longer in existence where would we
be? Lovers of the past, quiet special places where you
could relax, all would be forgotten.

If this were true and memories weren't
Manufactured, how could we teach our children to
behave. You wouldn't be able to remember how you acted
and how to avoid the same mistakes you made. All the
wonderful books, songs, and voices would all be lost forever.

Meeting that special someone. The fond
memories of grandparents. And those of your
grandchildren playing ring-around-the-rosy.

If these memories didn't exist, the world and
all of its memories would go down in ruins. Nothing would
be left, to REMEMBER!

Denise Alexander

Dreams

Dreams are always a most precious thing
    They can make us happy in times of bad
Allowing us to forget our many ills
    And bring us much hope without being sad.

Dreams will put us into a state of mind
    Of joy and happiness and positive thought
They take us on journeys both near and far
    Giving us the more complete life which is sought.

Each of us dreams about many a thing
    Whether we be asleep or in a conscious state
Dreams take away our pressures and tensions and fears
    Letting us live a more complete life with our mate.

Yes! Dreams are always a most precious thing
    We can keep them throughout our work and play
Dreams make our hopes really begin to grow
    By concentrating on the good and letting the bad go astray.

Emil H. Hoch

Sunrise

The rooster crows at the crack of dawn,
Welcoming the sun to break the night.

The sun pushes the moon out of the way,
Leaving no room to linger behind.

The sun stays up all through the day,
Til the moon comes back to take revenge.

Jessica Washburn

The New Year

The time for making a brand new friend
To let old wounds to begin to mend,
Forgetting old memories your enemy as done
Looking to the Lord for forgiveness through his son.
It's the time to forget the old self and start anew
Living for the savior who is faithful and true,
What a great time to help a person in need
To do God's will and plant his seed.
This also is a good time to show love to your spouse
And give thanks to God for your spiritual house,
No greater moment can come but right now
For a person to be like Christ who will show you how.
A new year is a time that the calendar is new
This is the best of times God has now given to you,
Now is the time to accept his salvation
To put an end to a life of lamentation.
The new year can become as a Genesis
A time to begin, acquainted with the Lord Jesus.
Today everyone can find him for he is near
What a beautiful way to start your new year.

Phillip A. Headley

You're Not There

I can go into a place where no one else can be
Hide away from everyday and live there rent free
See myself in every way that I have known
I could move around with every thought and know they're all my own
I could place myself amongst the best never bothering with the rest
I could lay back on a memory sun bathe through my eyes
When I get hungry I will go over to my past
And pick a certain somewhere where my taste bud had a blast
I could set a certain time to visit any friend
I've ever had from the beginning to the end
I could go to work, if I got bored and pick one I like best
Clock out anytime and go somewhere and rest
I can be alone with every word and no one disagree
I can dance and shout and spin about with no one to hear me
But, if I wanted a love for a night or two there would be no one there
BECAUSE...I'VE NEVER MET YOU

Ali Vance

Winter

Yesterday the west winds wrestled,
Tossing snow in curtained whirls.
Fence posts deep in snowdrifts nestled.
Roadways grayed mid snowy twirls.

Winter cloaked in icy bleakness.
Timbers quaking in the winds.
Sun rays disappeared in meekness
Daunted by dark cloudy fiends.

Then today the morning sunbeams
Filtered through the waning greys
Glistening the children's snow dreams,
Sleds and snowmen, horse drawn sleighs.

Yes, there is charisma, wonder
In this soft white renaissance.
Clear crisp silence lets me ponder
Winter's sounds—sweet resonance.

Oh! That we might keep our hearts warmed,
Sensitized by life and love
To this milieu flawless formed
By a Loving Hand above.

Jane M. Johannsen

"Hearts On Fire"

Sometimes when I'm tossing and turning,
I know my heart is burning.
It start out with a flame,
Then it turns into pain.
I then know that something's wrong,
When I try to find it, it's gone.
My heart beats very fast.
I think this burning has past.
I hear a voice, "Put the fire out,"
I start to scream and shout.
I thought death has come to take me away,
I get on my knees and start to pray,
And then the fire has gone away.

Yvette Carter

Muffin

Muffin is my dog you see;

   she really likes to play and pee.
She eats and eats and eats all day
   and then she goes and lays to stay.
Her favorite toy is any ball
   but when you call she always stalls.
She licks my bear till it has no hair.
She chews my socks and underwear.
She's quite a clown
   this big fluff of brown.
She's just a dog you see,
   but a best friend to me.

Jennifer Leaman

This Little Town

The people in this little town, meeting at the post office,
seek to hide their pain in smiles and chat,
but this little town conjectures about it on the phone,
at the coffee shop, in the real estate office.

People here
are not always vigilant.
They leak their pain in a look,
then hurriedly conceal it in a quip.

There are those
who long to share their pain,
to ease their hearts,
but fear the undefined penalty.

So, the people in this little town
hide their pain,
increase their pain,
withhold their pain from their neighbor.

But then she knows all about this little town's pain,
she hides her own.

H. Patricia Oates

Untitled

As I look out through the window I see my life go past
I think of all the things I did and want to take it back
I wish that I could start again using my own script
Make up for all the mistakes I've made using a brand new pen
When I look upon the canvas that shows the story of my life
I wish that I could paint it over using a new brush
All of that is gone by now, left behind in the dust
The little girl that I was calls out for me
I wish I could help her up

Elizabeth Ann Hensley

Loosing A Loved One

We live on earth for only a short time,
Trying to live our lives to the prime.
No matter how young or old we maybe,
We all hold in our mind sweet memories.
As we stand grieving by the grave,
We remember the love which you gave.
As tears fall down like rain,
Only time will heal the pain.
The heartache of having to say good-bye,
You're now an angel with wings to fly.
We'll be with you in heaven someday,
Together again we will always stay.

Linda M. Deibler

The Mightiest Dilema

A sepulcher shrouded by flowers
Above the plot, this grave towers
A great person was laid here to rest
Now worms feed upon his breast
The kingdom of living is by far the best
The worms feed on all the rest
of the man that once held greatness.
Death might just set you free,
of the problems that others see.
The answer lies deep within
as this process repeats itself
again and again...
Problems just seem to never end.

Derrick Terrell

In Nostalgia For Him

She sentimentally called him the blue-eyed prince
A rather warm and majestical description
But there have been many princes and princesses since
His hard reign of counterculture and impending change
Joni, Judy, Jackson and she also tried changing society
Courageous and vociferous, yes; inspirational absolutely, but tame
Compared to the "unwashed phenomenon,"
   very unique, who wanted the same
Was it because he was Jewish—Zimmerman—
   that he was a compassionate man
Or was it because he was just aiming for the promised land
But you've got to admit that his literature
Sure changed the conscience landscape
Erza Pound and T.S. Eliot can't compare in which they can't escape
Her admiration and awe for this slick man cannot be stressed enough
Even when nostalgia strikes and the times get rough
Some people called his writing and singing lousy and very odd
Miraculously, it fit just right with the invasion and the mod
He will be one of the greatest composers of his time with his
   rhythms and rhymes
Such a talented individual whom she will always hold in high-esteem
Joan and Bob would have made a great team

Scott Darryl Imamura

"Not Now"

I think I'll plant some strawberries, on second thought not now.
I've planted things on my own time and now they wear the smiles.
Strawberries, like little children, they grow and grow forevermore and
then they multiply; but the fruit of little children will never, never die.

Carol Ann Zuber

Lost Soul

Throughout his life, Jim received minimal love.
His father, set on his Asian masculinity never showed his affection.
From the attitude given by his father, he became a lonely child.
Jim feared going to school because he didn't think he
Could make it through the day knowing he had no true friends.
At the age of seven, he would bribe the children
At school with candy and toys so they would play with him.
As the years passed, conditions at home did not improve.
His father became more bitter and abusive.
Jim grew and became the boy no one thought he would be.
He fought in school, did no homework, stole, and lied frequently.
Only at twelve, and he was already out of control.
He conquered the mediocre activities from amateur to professional.
Now like a criminal in the mist of the night, he roams the streets.
In people's properties no one sees until they find their goods
   missing.
He made a life for himself out in the streets.
He always wanted to fly, fly like a free bird in the wind.
He proved it at home but ironically, he caged his life in his future.
He is forever lost until he picks up the broken pieces of his life.
I hope I haven't lost him yet, have I?

   Julia Hanh Le

Destiny

Ripples.
Concentric circles
Spreading ever outward.
Touching lives, altering perspectives.
Light, darkness, growth, decline, salvation,
Or oblivion await humanity.
Are we prisoners
Upon relentless
Ripples?

Ripples.
Strong character
Overcomes human frailties.
Nuclear winter? Global warming?
Transcend ignorance! Vanquish apathy! Mankind
Alone throws pebbles into
His earthly pond,
Making eternal
Ripples.

   David C. Grier

Words

Teach me words of wisdom Lord -
words to comfort my weary soul.

Words to help me feel secure -
while this painful life I endure.

Knowledgeable words that come from you -
words of meaning, that I know are true.

Courageous words to make me strong -
forgiving words when I do wrong.

Words of love to give me faith -
patient words so I may learn to wait.

Words of kindness for my brothers -
so I may see the good in others.

Words of comfort, for life often is absurd -
please, oh Lord, teach me the right words.

   Connie J. Johnson

Today, Tomorrow And The Day After That

Today, tomorrow and the day after that,
I'll have to clean up after that pesky cat.
He runs all day, he runs all night,
And when ever I try to stop him, we get into a fight.
His naptime is 2:00 in the afternoon,
And to get him asleep I have to play a tune,
His favorite singers are Sunny and Cher,
And he sleeps with his little teddy bear.
There is something weird about my little old cat, Jack,
He will always sleep on his little old fat back.

   Jennifer A. Moore

When She's Gone

I will, in the future many times
Smile at the thought of her
A tear or two might appear
As I play what was and might have been.

I won't, anger and rage cannot rule
Forever there will be no blame
As I play what was and might have been.

I can, let go, set free
Secure in the knowledge of her and me
As I play what was and might have been.

I have, found joy and sadness
Within her arms sweet pleasure, great pain
As I play what was and might have been.

I should, no resentments I will hold
Nor blame upon her shoulders.
Look inward toward all causes
As I play what was and might have been.

I will, love forever - heart and soul
Let go, set free
As I play what was, and will forever be.

   James Munyon

A Time for Recycling

I have yet to find
a way to recycle
the litter of my life
the unfocused dashings
to and fro
that fill so much my time.

If I could bundle
these distractions
and throw them in some
green bin for litter-acy,
I'd be truly free
to languish literately
on the blank page
or the blank screen
with free verse that
would freely flow
after this undertow
of litter is discharged.

The small urgency of literacy cannot
compete with the largesse of litter in my life.

   Martha Wessells Steger

Broken Dreams....

Do you know how it feels lying here without you.
You could never understand what's happening to me.
So alone nothing's real.
I just dream about you and forever wonder why you had to break free.
I would give my hear to have you here just to hold you once again.
It's so hard to believe I don't have right beside me as long as to
touch you but you're out of my reach and my heart doesn't feel.
It's so very cold inside.
I'm just a shadow of someone I use to be.
You were the only I allowed inside my heart.
Now I'm just holding or to something so far gone.
Where did I go wrong?

Samantha Graber

Untitled

Feeling so very alone.
The past has found it's way to the present,
bringing back memories best forgotten.
But yet, how can they ever forget?
Life does go on, but the black clouds hang ready to strike again.
Will true happiness ever be found to chase them away?
One thinks it will at times.
But then the future only brings more and more sadness.
What was ever done to deserve this? Feeling so very, very, alone.
There's no one to turn to when times are tough.
But then again, how can one handle it on their own?
Wishing there was someone. Someone to hold, to talk to.
Anyone. Anyone at all.
Asking people of themselves is an impossible thing.
No one is ever completely on your side.
What about the people who need that?
What do they do? They keep hoping for tomorrow.
Hoping and wishing someone will come along.
But there will come a time when no hope is left.
What does one do then?
They leave the world alone, like they entered it.

Kelly J. Miller

Peace

I think of peace as tranquility or quiet
Not a fight or a riot,
A dove sitting on a perch
Or waking up Sunday and going to church.
I think of peace watching the moon glow
Or making angels in new fallen snow.
I think of peace when I'm alone.
Not watching T.V. or on the phone.
It is peace watching the stars in the sky
Or giving food to a homeless guy.
I think of white - it is pure.
When you're having a bad day,
Peace is the cure.

Z. F. Spaulding

Acceptance

I'm beginning to find the affections
  of the heart an inevitable trap
Perilous and unquenchably sought of after;
A chasm of confusion and bitter agony
  which reeks havoc upon one's mental landscape

This crime unknowingly besought by those
  who seek the simple company of another
Grows more wise over time's wings
  and learns to fly deceitfully into one's heart

And slaughter the peaceful thoughts that were
  once an everlasting bounty!?

Jorge Torres

I Am

I am caring and sensitive
I wonder how many children die each breath I take
I hear the fading heartbeats of children slowly dying in pain
I see crying children that are starving
I am caring and sensitive

I pretend that I can feed all of the starving children but I know
  I can't
I feel of the starving children's pain
I touch their hearts with a prayer
I worry about all of the starving children
I cry when I think that they starved to death
I am caring and sensitive

I understand that they don't have any money to buy food
I say "But there has to be a way."
I dream of those children eating and becoming healthy again
I try to help them by giving them the money I earn
I hope they find a way
I am caring and sensitive

Stephanie Mumma

The Coming Of Dawn

A title of: Entering the poetry contest
Any subject, any style, but limited: No more than 20 lines
Any one may enter the competition
But you'll end asking for petition
If you write from the heart, it is such an art.
If you write for the price, you're still titled under art.
Both ways the words caused by hurt.
The dead line for entry is marked
My case of cancer also is marked.
I prayed till I'm healed
My body is the poetry contest
Each publication will enter with different title of impact
They have a ten year history of awarding prizes
I've ten coming years to be a history
Proving the healing power against cancer
We need to challenge, to change and no more chains
of 20 lines limited
The new poetic talent of next feature to be titled:
The Power of Healing
It is full of natural talent!

Najat Sukhun

Breathless

As time goes by you stay waiting,
Wondering of the next moments, to show
Your emotions is like conquering your greatest fear,
The power of a kiss that was so long awaited,
lie breathless - breathless you lie,

To be created for one who was not created for you,
Uncertain where pain is quoted
  in the definition of love,
Sitting under the stars - curious
  about who really composes them,
lie breathless - breathless you lie,

The destiny of your true love is silent
  'Till your heart ceases,
lie breathless - breathless you lie...

Amy Johnson

Seasons

Winter
The days seem, at first, dark and dreary;
But the snow, falling softly to the ground
Makes someone feel lighthearted.
A beautiful sight, with no sound.
    Spring. Flowers, lifting heads to the sunshine,
Patches of snow here and there.
I feel like singing and shouting:
"Spring is awake everywhere!"
    Summer. The dew glistens on fresh summer grass
As the sun shines its morning rays down.
The king-like clouds in the sky.
Are wearing the sun as a crown.
    Autumn. A rainbow of colors is autumn.
The leaves dressing up in their best.
The trees dropping off all their clothing,
Getting ready for their winter rest.
Thank you
I love every one of the seasons:
Winter, spring, summer, and fall.
And, although I have my favorites,
Thank you, God, for them all!

Holly Susan Dempsen

Answers

My mind goes blank and I begin to quiver with fear,
    Fear of my love...
Fear of a way to explain myself to you.
So loved...so loved in a way you do not know.
My mind is an empty pot of nothing
But at the bottom of that nothingness,
    There is a light.
A light that shines, shines with your name
    Your name is love...in love?
    In love you ask? How to be in love,
    How so fast, how so sudden...
How afraid am I to propose my love
And my emptiness fills with hopes of you
    You proposing yours to me.
Proposing a love so strong that nothing,
    Even ourselves could break.
The bind of love that we have for each other...
    For each other
    I love you.

Michael P. Trioli

Reflections Your Mother And Me

Reflect with me to childhood days
I was care-free then you see.
Days filled with childish things
As I imagined Life would be.

As I grew older, on my own
I searched for answers, all alone.
I thought, is there a hidden plan
That one must find, to become a man?

Soon I found someone who loved me, and only me.
Who was very proud of me, you see.
Immediately I loved her, as no other
And this young lover, became your mother.
No finer person, you will agree
Your mother is - and ever will be.
There is none like her - none to compare
Willing to give - eager to share.

From that first day, at the altar
Always there - never to falter.
Finding her was my lucky day
Yours too, wouldn't you say?

Walter A. Alexander

Inner Heat

All my life, I wanted a touch.
A touch that was so hot,
it would burn your soul.
A touch that was so hot,
it would leave a mark.
Not as a scar on your body,
but an impression on your heart.
It's a feeling so strong.
And electricity you only feel-
when you're in love with the one who is real.
You can love many, but you'll only find one.
who will have that touch
The touch that burns body, soul and mind.
and you begin to melt.
The heat is so strong, the love so intense.
Please touch me again and hold my hand.
I want to feel that burn only you alone can give.

Laura Wilkison

Untitled

Fatalistic, Phallic Fantasies
Chaste not by choice
Probing mindless thoughtless things
Watching, Waiting. Wanting to be, not me,
Someone else. No choice.
Yelling silent Subliminal screams
Can't be heard, Can't be seen,
    No Voice.
Falling, Failing Fallacies
Nailed to voyeuristic tendencies
Surrounded by white noise
Tearing. Sharing. Staring out
Locked inside a vacancy
Brow creased in useless pondering
Lips pursed and dry,
    Not moist.
Singing, Ringing Stinging Slap
of feelings left unvoiced.

Marcell Cleinow

Life's Challenge

We came from the heavens to the earth
The life we are given is so unsure
We're put to the test from up above
Who really understands this part of life
There's always a challenge from the skies
That we know we must survive
Us being together there's a reason why
Its give us the challenge of life
There's no explaining this crazy thing
It's just happened to you and me
And from my side there's no arguing
It came from the heavens unto our live
We share this together you and I

Cory P. Marazita

True

The sun and its shining light
The dog and its killing bite
A child with his bright smile
A road and its winding mile
A mirror and its true reflection
A wound with its spreading infection
A woman without a choice
A man with no power to rejoice
These facts all true, no statement false
As true as dead, is without a pulse

Heather Harrington

What Is Blue

Blue is the color of the midnight sky
Blue is the color of an officers tie
Blue is the feeling of a sadness inside
Blue is a babies lonesome cry
Blue is a ribbon you can tie in your hair
Blue is lonesome or sometimes a dare
Blue is a piece of bubble gum
Blue is a flax picked by your thumb
Blue is a snowflake fall on your nose
Blue is a color of painted toes
Blue is evening sunset or shoe
Blue is the ocean, sky or bloom
Blue is baby blue eyes
Blue is the smell of a blueberry pie
Blue is the color of bread after time
Blue is a friend or valentine
Blue is a crayon you dropped on your shoe
Blue is a whale crying to you
Blue is a book of romantic scenes
Blue is the smell of morning or dream ..... Blue

Stephanie Stewart

Lingering Memories

Easter was over, egg hunts were in the past
Parents and children had gone home to rest at last
Soon it was back to work, and on the way.
Children were left in the nursery to play
No one dreamed that danger would come to them that day
Driving a ryder truck a man with a heart of stone
Took many precious lives away from friends at home
The big boom was so loud, smoke rolled up like a huge black cloud

As floors fell through
People did what they had to do
Emergency cars how they did drive
Men dug in the rubble hoping to find someone alive
Folks say McVey was the man
They brought him back to justice his final trial to stand

Leota S. Ward

Untitled

Crust on a dampened lash,
My arm lying on the down,
the Room shall never hear...
the hammer of the breast.
No humm in the cell.
Weary of Their numb words,
and my mythical roles.
Broke all my utensils-
Destroyed all my books;
shattering their identities...
There'll always be silence and dampness.
No poetry to compose,
No Poem to breath long.
No arms for any poet to encounter...
or ever clutch on to mire passion with.
    Will fate ever bid mercy on a poet's pious soul?

Kathy Valos

A True Friend

A friend is an individual that
understands who you are. No matter
what you achieve great or small.
When you fall down in life, they'll be
there to pick you up and help you
stand tall. Through shortcomings and
fortune, good times and bad, a good friend
will try to make you happy, and keep you
from being sad. A kind word or a cheerful
smile, when you don't think you can go
the distance, will carry you that extra
mile. Sometimes the silence and unspoken
words from a true friend who knows you,
makes you feel understood.

Cynthia Susan Ostrunic

Green River

I wanted the moon to be more
    than just a beautiful object in the sky —
I wanted to become part of it,
    a longing inside to be fulfilled.

What would I have him say
    if he had sat to watch the moon beside me?
Or would I say to him?

That this is a unique occurrence in our lives
    to be here at this time —
Watching the full orange moon rise over the desert horizon
    and it makes me happy to share it with someone I love.

He says he should try harder
She says she shouldn't expect so much

Like the Continental Divide of their marriage
    He flows one way
    She flows another.

Marjorie Schallau

Don't Give Up Hope

I gave up a baby many years ago...
Where she'd end up, I'd NEVER know.
26 years later, a phone call came...
She was looking for me, wants to know my name.
With my consent, she called me on the phone...
her adoptive parents died, leaving her alone
We hugged when we met, so Sweet and Dear...
I'm a Mother-in-Law and Grandma, I shed a Tear.
I feel so Strange and my family has GROWN!!!
A feeling of which, I have NEVER known!!!

She needed to know about who gave her birth...
and if this lady was still living on this earth.
Curious of her looks, personality and health,
to find her Birth Mother, would help find HERSELF!!!
It's been 2 months, it's all so new...
If you've given up a child, this could be you!!!
I NEVER FORGOT HER, ESPECIALLY WHEN I'D PRAY...
DON'T GIVE UP HOPE, today may be YOUR day!!!
I feel so complete, my mind is at rest...
To MAKE-UP for lost time, will be my QUEST!!!

Sheila Grue

Failure

In the petite death of early morning sleep, I smell success around me like blue water, breaking and crashing against my hull as I cut through the vast ocean of life.
I have become king where fear and hatred have been exiled like abused and estranged brothers brought to justice for their vulgar displays of evil.
I have been gently plucked from personal purgatory and scattered across years of journey to rest with the clouds above and smile downward.
But an underlying dread like back-to-work monday is that body back home in bed, stirring enough to open one eye and remember - awakened.

The first light meets my brow like a groping yellow sensor and reads aloud to me what's inside - my sunrise confessions: Lies I told the night before, money I drank in crumpled remains in urine-soaked heavy denims, have me heaving and wrestling myself naked as I vomit tears, lower my head, beaten and sob. Depressed and sorry for myself, naturally. Still a spoiled boy faking sickness for attention. Sickness the reason to stay home, safe from failure.

Douglas Neal McLaughlin

Untitled

Like the logic of life, you leave me without having come
You walk away as if in a mission,
staying with me just the necessary time to distort the poles of my world, living me adrift
Like a storm, you run through the pores of my skin
covering me, covering you
then you go away and my universe is in ruins,
like a catastrophe of chaotic proportions
which cannot sink into oblivion, and which will remain
in my darkest and most fearful memories,
those that shall make me awake in the middle of the night crying your name,
just to realize in the end that it all was a sweet nightmare

You leave and there's emptiness behind you,
After all you were inside me like a curse
that cannot be revoked,
until the time comes that the winds of a newly found love knocks on my door
then your time will be in the past
and everything will be blown into place like before

Michel Gonzalez

Untitled

Where are you, my one true love,
  Everyone has one I'm told.
I can't find mine, but I keep
  Looking, it's my goal.
I know he's out there somewhere,
  So I will keep searching for him.
Day by day, I keep longing,
  Watching and wondering when -
Is he close by - or maybe far away,
Blond? Black hair, thin or fat?
Maybe I'm looking too hard,
I hadn't thought about that!
Think I'll relax and just see what happens.
I'm sure he will find me at
the least expected time,
Until then I'll be patient,
for in the end, true love will be mind.

Nina L. Williams

Untitled

Standing in the dark waiting it out
Not knowing why we're always apart
So many things we should be sharing
Why does it seem one is less caring
How can u love as much as u do
And I still not know if this is true
All I want is our hopes and dreams
to become one in the same
All of these thoughts going through my mind
Why does it seem I'm always so blind
Who would have thought a man could love
A women so much he'd sacrifice his own life
Why is loving you so hard to do
Not knowing the outcome within my mind
Not knowing from day to day where it is I stand
Loving and hurting one in the same

Michael A. Casto

My Love

I know you used to care for me
but now I clearly see
that your heart has drifted away
and was never here to stay
I should be getting over you
like a I know I can do
but each time I try
I just see you in my eyes.
Each time I see your face
in place after place
I just fall more and more in love.
Someday I will tell you how I feel
then maybe our love will be real
but until that day my heart will find a way
to fall more in love with you each day.

Ashlee McMicken

If I Could Fly

If I could fly, with no worry in sight,
Up where the sky is clear.
I'd pick you up, and hold you tight,
Just to have you near.

You've touched me in a special place,
That place, it is my heart.
I love you more each passing day,
If you're here, or we're apart.

If we could fly, we'd sail on together,
In love, forever true.
We'd never land, but sore higher and higher,
In skies, forever blue.

Tina G. Span

Thy Love

Your image doth giveth life
Your vision doth taketh breath
You giveth thou reining dream
And yet nothin's lef'

You leadeth thou to the mountain stream
Doth dance upon thy bellows
Silent smiles entangle thee
I'm lost within thou meadows

Thy violet valley trickles light
When in doth heart thou mine
Drinketh together sweetened wine

Be with me all time
Michael Q. Williamson

The Burch's

For Monica and Jim Burch
The angels, they will perch
Outside, your window.....
Til all this sadness
Turns to gladness

The path, must have been dark and dreary
Fearful and far from clear
Well, now he's home!
No more will he have to roam

One night in a dream, he will come and whisper
Only something you can hear
I'm fine, it's beautiful here
In this place I have no fear
So sleep my Father and my Mother
And cling to one another....
The gates of heaven, will open, I know not when
But, come and see me when you can

Nancy Dallmann

Abused

She stands back in the shadows
Afraid to show her face
She hides behind a mask
A front for her disgrace
She tries to stay awake
Because the dreams she knows are there
The pain inside won't disappear
It takes someone to care
He'll come again, she knows for sure
A threat he's made before
Still no one hears the cry of her
It echoes forevermore
The handle turns, the door swings wide, she cowers back in fright
Her heart beats fast, but still she has nowhere to go
The echo lasts a lifetime as she screams out, "DADDY NO!"

Jeffrey Matthew Burr

Voiceless Conversations

I have accepted the hint of the rising sun,
Ending a dream created by
Voiceless conversations that have mislead
My heart while it seeks a new place.

I have thoughts that feelings,
Unknown to existence, can be disguised,
Yet recognized by one equal within
The same force of imagination....
And they were,

And now, I have been discovered.
No longer the explorer, and I find
The dream has already been exposed
As a futile and foolish opportunity
That will never come.

But, the sounds not heard
In the voiceless conversations,
Still lead me To a ship of fools,
Burdened with intoxications kegs of dreams.

M. L. Smith

Barren Is...

A lackadaisical landscape
clasping onto murky memories of a flourishing flora and fauna
A lilting lady singing lullabies to a wilted womb
A blustery broker
bequeathing his life to an insatiable image of success
A sullen society
inhibiting the innocence of a chameleon child
A pontifical professor
hiding behind the crumpled clippings of published prose
A sun-strewn day
failing to warm the callous countenances of its hominid habitants
A haughty heart
unwilling to enunciate emotional cravings for fear of not being fed

Barren is a multitude of meanings and a variety of visages,
yet its essential emptiness leaves a rather apathetic afterstate
upon my tongue

Denise E. Meeks

One Chance

With their hands jammed down their pockets
They don't notice
What's passing by at incredible speeds.
Not grabbing on but holding tight
To what they know best
Which could be the wrong thing to do.
Letting big chances and high futures
Fall through their fingers
Like grains of sand.
Waiting for money, lovers, pleasures,
And friends, brought to them.
They wonder why they missed the fun times
The best four years of their life
Friends, lovers, and childhood pranks,
And most importantly 'magic and
Laughter of their youth.
Yet they finally notice...
When it's too late...too late for life.

Aaron R. Sanchez

Danny's Colors

Orange like the sunset he'd watch when he wanted
    his problems to go away.
Green like the grass he'd lay on, hoping no one would find him,
    wishing the earth would just swallow him up.
Blue like the sky he'd gaze upon,
praying that he'd fly away someday.
Pink like the knuckles on his hands,
begging someone to reach out and
    hold them, telling him everything's alright..
Gray like his world, where no one knew and no one cared.
Red like the anger he felt everyday for no reason at all.
Purple like the sadness he was living with.
Black like the gun he used 'cause he thought it was the only way out
Yellow like the sun that was blazing bright as we all stood around
    his coffin to say goodbye for the last time.

Cyra Sherburn

Forest

As I walk through the forest on a lovely fall day,
I hear the wonderful birds.
I shut my eyes and just listen.
Just for one second,
I thought the whole world understood the meaning of peace.
It was great!
After that day I looked at everything differently.
I lived my life as if everyday was the last.
Meaning what?
Know that's your choice to make.

Ann French

Miss Sarah Chadwick Remembers...

She sat in a white wicker chair
The wind blows warm against her cheek
She smiles... remembering summers past
The wind turns cold with the smell of lilac and roses
Tears start to fall from her eyes
Is it the smell of lilac and roses that made her cry

The wind again turns warm.... a stranger appears
Is this the man she dreams of?
His eyes glimmered like rays of blue light
Miss Sarah Chadwick raises from her chair
She drifts to where he stands
Holding a bouquet of lilac and roses
Their hands meet on the bouquet
As the wind blows... she spins in a circle
She looks out to where he stood.....
There are only the waves crashing upon the shoreline
She looks down to her hands.... the bouquet is gone
With the smell of lilac and roses
Miss Sarah Chadwick remembers....that day.

Jessica Constantine

A Poem Of Enlightenment

You will change my life.
Your love will find its way
to the deepest bring out of the darkness
You will bring out of the darkness
the me who has been crying alone.

Did I ever know anyone could get there?
Did I ever think anyone would try?
Care to try?
Care enough to try and try some more?
That's what love does.

I have never really known the awesome power of love
Only read about it, only believed it was.
My heart is touched so deeply by this man's love,
that my weeping for joy suddenly turns to leaping
and shouting for joy.

Just to know that when I am fully healed
I will need nothing but to sit at his feet
my head resting in his lap.
I will be serene.

Jan Nimchuk

Wrath Of The Wind

On cold winter nights when the wind is so mean
You can hear it schrill its piercing scream
How that wind makes the snowflakes crystallize
And spins them wickedly from the wintery skies
You watch it rush across lawns and streets
You see it turn water into icy sheets
Yet you dare face that wicked wind
You feel its frosty breath slapping your skin
The feeling so bitter like it wants you to bleed
Making you vulnerable you beg, you plead
You rush to get away from this wicked feeling
Long to take shelter so your skin can start healing
Knowing you suffer when the wind has the furor to freeze
Yearning for the day it will again be a breeze

Mary Elizabeth Sievert

Suffer-Blue

My far-flung obscenities smear your mirage,
but cannot hope to stay
your resurrection.
(Blinded desecrations hold no sway)
Like skins, shed sins decay with time.

My net of close-knit cruelty snared you,
and barbed words bled you,
for your own good.
Compassion's masochism kept you close,
but offered no protection from my abuse.

I killed you, finally, on a plain;
you died when your eyes could no longer reach mine.
The blade used slit the wrists
Of your hopes;
they were not as fertile as my despair.

My color now stains the tears you cry,
breaching faith's walls to knock you down.
I flaunt your fault-line to your peers;
with torments veiled as need, I burden you.
I win.

Malcolm Carstafhnur

A Long Way From Home

Time and Circumstance are basic keys
    around which all life infinitely concedes,
      and in one thought the mind may roam
        — taking you long distances away from home.

Though you may travel far and wide
    in the futile search, as you hide
      your motives and your greatest of fears
        causing the search to extend thru the years . . .

        but, in the end you find as others do

Time and Circumstance brought some ultimate truths;
    invading the sleep, transcending all that is known . . .
      returning you from your journey —
        though, not alone . . .
          the journey that took you . . .
            . . . a long way from home.

Mary L. Adefala

"The Quiet Place"

In my mind there is a place,
with peace and quiet and plenty of space.

Country roads and grassy hills
herds of cows and corn in fields.

Bales of hay all nicely rolled,
small towns and fishing holes.

Horses, pigs and sometime sheep,
skyride tours of the rivers deep.

Scenic routes with so much to see,
blue skies and eagles free.

A place for us that's far from home,
filled with space where we can roam.

Swimming pools and pony rides,
miniature golf and game room inside.

Sandy playgrounds where we can swing,
ooh there's so many things.

But with all the problems that we may face,
it's good to have our quiet place.

Nadine A. Williams

Untitled

Jeez I miss his dance I miss his song
I wonder where ol' Irish has gone

That he was from Ireland the wonderful warbling
Inflection of his voice left no doubt

The Catskills were his home is summer
The canyons of Big Apple in winter

We quaffed pints of pallid stout at Sylvan Lake
Later on at Grossingers' Liberty where he patronized
An ol' temperance warrior who of necessity kept a tavern
A fact that left rough edges on his disposition in the mornings

I ask him once had he ever been married he gave no reply
I ask him once had he ever been in love
He peered into my marrow through a cocked and furrowed eye
   ...Mon eyre mon as ben en luv

We parted one fall at the Beacon Ferry
He aboard Short Line for Bowery dugouts and Sterno fired coffee

Me in a bathtub Rambler into the darkness
of the Berkshires . . . marriage . . . purgatory

I wonder where ol' Irish has gone
Jeez I miss his dance I miss his song
   Garry O. Knicely

Lightness

Spires compete for stellar dreamscapes and confiscate your "id"
A subliminal subconscious reality of dream spaces void in their own
   right
Until the angels with a voice send a message
Listen, hear, feel and respect the darkness,
silence
until lightness
floating
sunshine
birds singing
uplifting you into a rebirth of
your soul and spirit
Rejuvenation not resignation
Hope not prayer.
   Lauren Jane Heimberg

Dream

Upon the waves of the silver moon,
I see my sweetheart there marooned.
She glances my way and what do I see?
A face filled with wonder looking at me.
I reach out to her, she takes my hand.
I marry her in the silver sands.
Her hair blows softly against my cheek,
I love her for she is meek.
And then I turn and hear the scream,
Of my sweetheart, in my ears it rings!
I catch her and kiss her sweet,
But that is the end and I retreat.
Loneliness comes into my heart,
But never again will I start,
To fall in love and hear the scream,
Of another sweetheart in my dreams.
   Stephanie Bahr

When Love Flew

Shrouded words
wispy webs of shredded past clinging-love
flew from our hands in a fancy
resort surrounded by honey mooners
and couples rekindling gray ashes into
flame flickering lights in their eyes
trembling with the stars of night. At two a.m.
we wrapped white soft towels
around our hips and slipped into the warm
dark morning smelling of oleanders
starfilled moonfilled beside the hushed motel pool. We
sliced through blue lighted water
sleek dark shadows dancing. We rose
dripping laughing eager to flip
over and over making circles
of pale moon-stuck until
we were thrilled and exhausted
like love.
   Karen Herrera

The Village In The Woods

Whose woods these are I think that I know.
Her house is in the lonely village though;
She will not see me stopping here
To look at her woods fill up with snow.

My little horse must think it queer
To stop without a farmhouse near
The dusk of the year.

She gives the harness bells a shake
To ask if there might be a slight mistake.
The only other sound's the sweep
of easy wind and downy flake.

The woods are lovely, gloomy and so deep,
But I have so many promises to keep,
And so many miles ahead before I can sleep,
And so many miles ahead before I can sleep.
   Carrie Jones

Charisma

Could he be a Saint?
One for the devil...
He ain't
He sits on some level

Is he an advisor, messenger or defender?
Maybe a prophet
For sure he's a healer
Not for profit

Will he spiral up?
He'll never go down
He's just a pup
He's known in this town

Unusual he is
Integrity, morals and ethics her retains
He is a wiz
He seeks no gains

All he wants to do is suggest
Some think he's a pest
But those who are important...
Treat him as an invited guest
   Adam Meredith Dash Sd.

The New Englanders

As surely as a New England Winter
Follows summer at the Cape,
Changes come into our lives
Whether we're prepared for them or not.

New Englanders are a hearty breed.
The first Nor'easter of the fall
Finds them battening down the hatches,
Securing all on deck in a calm,
Yet determined way,
As the oncoming storm approaches.

Many of us are like the New Englanders,
If we give ourselves a chance.
We are not weak or incapable.
We can deal with the cards as they fall to us,
Kings and threes alike.
We know we can't control the deal,
But, ultimately, we shall be judged on how
We handle our fate
And not on the damage
That the storm leaves behind.

Jeff Murdock

The Heart Of A Stranger

They sat
The happy couple.
They sat and shared words with each other
Over coffee and cake.
I was silent,
Watching them lose themselves in an invisible sea of contentedness:
Their smiles almost in sync with the subtle rising of their chests;
The atmosphere of their conversation as intimate as sex
On a hot summer afternoon, in the heart of a restless city.
And I, a stranger on the outside looking in,
Felt more alienated there than I had ever felt in my life.
On the outside of the warmth they created
I sat still, until it warmed my cold heart and comforted my soul.
And when they left,
The two of them,
I continued to sit
One lone guest at a table for two
Sitting until I had finished my coffee
And was prepared to bear the beatings of the cold wind
Against my chest.

Richard Haynes

Rusting Chains Of Time

Wrapped in silence about the redwood pole
the old rusting chain speaks with tears.
Memories shroud my heart of yesteryears
of my lamb-white shepherd friend once near.

I touch a remnant of our time
Entwine the rusting chains of time
within my yearning hands.
Aching fingers faint within their plans
to touch that captured moment of our time.

Now, I know, I cannot capture time.
For now, my heart must ache, Oh Pilgrim mine,
Until the rusting chains of yesteryears
Lie broken by God's time when you appear.

Glenda Dunn

My Miracle

I counted five fingers on each tiny hand
He grabbed at my finger with urgent demand
My hand was his partner, never tired,
Always true.
But as he grew older it seemed to
Slip through
Now as I hold my hands in his warm
Strong tight grasp
I know that my son is a man now
At last
So treasure each moment as
If they are gold, for I have
just watched a miracle unfold

Marylin J. Clark

Chasing A Dream

Dreams come and dreams go, but there is
always one that continues to grow.
It enters your mind and takes over your heart.
A little voice tells you it's a start.
Chase this dream wherever it goes;
through mountains, through woods, through
sleet and snow.
If you chase this dream faithfully and with
constant desire, you will see that your
heart is not a liar.
As time passes by look yourself deep in the
eye, and you'll see that your dream will never die.
Continue to believe, and soon you will find,
the dream that has been engraved in your mind.

Gina Bartolo

The Corner Store

I looked to see the face of a stranger,
instead I saw my past.
What use to be my everything,
that ended with less of a goodbye.
And was it no long ago
that we were speaking of our hopes and dreams.
Just to meet again and realize we're so far off.
Must I play the invalid?
Do I fit the suit?
Now I know of nothing,
to me I see a stranger.

Jennifer M. Douglas

No One Can Know

No one can know the true feelings and thoughts of another person;
   Therefore trust is out of the question.

No one can know whether someone will be hurt or not;
   Therefore it is best never to mention.

No one can know when somebody will reach the breaking point;
   Therefore we must ease the tension.

No one can know if their future is made;
   Therefore we must conceive the invention.

No one can know what is real and what is not;
   Therefore we must continue to exist in this cruel dimension.

James A. Turner

To Daddy

I used to come and talk too you alot
I always think of you and never forgot
Sometimes the load gets so heavy
I'd like to load up and run away in your old Chevy
How can we know if we do right
Seems we never get a ray of hope in sight
So many say good wishes about all
But some day I feel like I'm gonna fall
Seems there are many memories to wonder
What more could be added to the plunder
Just must keep doing as you said
Live your life as can be read

Crystal Hanna

Dreams Of Destiny

Destiny...it is something that I have
    always thought was not possible for me....

Destiny...it is something that you have
    to believe in with your mind, your heart and soul...

Destiny...it is something that I have
    dreamed of and longed for and wished for...

Destiny... it appear's right in front of your
    eyes when you least expect it.
    When it does, you need to reach for it and never let go of it...

Destiny...it is something that I never thought
    I would grab on to until it appeared before my eyes...

Destiny...it was then that I realized that
    all of my hopes and dreams of finding destiny
    came true, my search was over...

For it was destiny that led me to you!

Kenya Beth Brown

The Whisper Of Pines

The Whispering of Pine trees along the misty river,
When You watch in early morn it gives a twisted shiver.

The icy water swirl and twist,
To put one hand you'd in freeze your fist.

Morning comes and morning goes,
But along the river the pines stand in rows.

In Noon's hot beams of golden light,
The beautiful river is such a sight.

The silver sparkles dance in the water,
As the day gets hotter and hotter.

In the jade-green waters,in the current lurks fun,
Near the dark pines, that's bows hide the sun.

Evening comes swift and true,
The sky quickly changes from pale to dark blue.

When the blazes dim when the blazes die,
The chill returns when asleep you lie.

Icy fingers seem to brush on your face,
If you are here, at this time, at this place

In just one minute the river will awake,
And the whispering of pines the river will take.

Merrielle T. Spain

Yesterday's Journey Is Today's Memories

We may have walked
on roads made of
gravel, dirt, or stone.

During the walk,
we may have felt
like we were all alone.

We fought to travel
up the road;
but looking back now,
the streets appear
to be paved with gold.

We see now
that there were
family and friends
who helped along the way,
who guided us
through the treacherous pathway.

Yesterday's journey,
no matter how sad or sweet,
are today's memories that seem to be a treat.

Alisa Alexander

Waiting

We are a tight group, waiting for our loved ones
    Who are "under the knife" so to speak.
Young, old, in between, waiting for surgery to be done.
    Talking, consoling, comparing, with fear at its peak.

Time goes slowly—was it only five minutes ago we asked?
    How do we each treat this agonizing waiting?
Some laugh, play cards, drink coffee; others pray for the task
    That skilled hands are being guided as we are aching.

Aching for the surgeon's return, stating all is well
    With the task just performed on our special person.
As each family's time of waiting ends, the rest can tell
    If the news is good or bad by sounds behind the curtains.

Moments of sadness seldom shared, privacy overshadows tightness.
    Silently, the unfortunate slip away with nary a glance.
Happiness is momentarily shared with hugs and lightness.
    Even they break away, relishing their good chances.

Those left, after long periods of time, pull away from the group too,
    Fearing that hopes are lessened with each passing hour.
Each pulls away into lonely, waiting families in separate pews;
    No longer interested in others, engrossed in prayer power.

Rose M. Kuter

When Curtains Fall

"The world's a stage and we're but players,"
The chief of playrights said.
The cast complete, the scripts are learned,
Each to his place is led.

"The play's the thing," we do assert,
But question not our part
That's given us once to perform.
We act with all our heart.

Approval from our audience!
(The aim is plain to see.)
We grovel for a loud applause,
The hero seek to be.

But 'ere this play of life is o'er,
Soliloquize we must:
"When curtains fall, ovations done,
'Return, O man, to dust.'"

Orvind White

Love Fulfilled

I saw a man riding in a horse,
Why the hurry, he came from the north,
I received his letter before yesterday
"Tomorrow my darling" I'll be back to school.

Yes, indeed, he will come to say goodbye,
In his bag he has a present for me, and a pie,
The long school days are hard to wait,
To shake hands again and have a kiss.

We are waiting for the days to come,
The promise we vowed-do you understand?

Two little creatures happily in love!
Writing love letters will not be enough
To console themselves when they're far apart.

Each one say, "it's so silly,"
Why I should be so unhappy,
Keep on waiting till the day
The promise, hope, will stay.

Day dreaming as the days passed by,
Our sincere love-now you understand?
For she and he, are now wife and husband.

Francisca F. Cacdac

Renewal

The sun, red as fire, slowly melted away resistance
against the cold world.
Crisp cool air, whipped about by lashing winds, scarred
the hill that was once brazen with wild flowers.
The soul of the earth was touched by sorrow.
Broken and battered, yet not quite smothered completely.
A droplet, strewn by the tears of an Angel, fell upon the ruin.
Tiny, yet ever so powerful, it grew, spawning rivers and oceans.
Mountains, once again were green with life
Birds returned to singing and natures balance was almost again.
Peace overcame the harsh world that was.
I sighed inside for I knew I had been touched
in heart to dream such a dream!
Renewal

Dianne M. Lee

Thistles

Once I walked on Holy Ground.
Consecrated by the blood in it.
And the blood cried out to me.
In unknown tongues.
Hukoida gonbwe, plus jamais, nie wieder.
A king walked with me that day.
Crowned with a yarmulke.
Adorned with a tattoo.
A king of another sort decreed.
"Let us pull up the thistles.
That we may walk in safety.
To see the shrubs,
And to smell the flowers."
But the shrubs were hemlock,
from which they were made to drink.
And the flowers were night shade,
from which they were made to breathe.
And the blood cried out to me.
In a tongue I know.
Never again.

Douglas A. Cook

In The Garden

I go to the garden alone.
I go to find my lover there.
He says stay with me.
My beloved is mine and I am his.
I held him, I would not let him go.

I have gone into my garden to stay.
My lover has given it to me, to keep.
I can go and come as I please.
He has given me the key.

He satisfies my soul with his love.
My lover feeds me from his hands,
As I sit under the shady tree.
My lover has other companions, lovers like me,
that seek his love throughout all eternity.

The lover of my soul will knock on your door,
calling on you.
Mine is not a selfish love, I'll share with you.
""Listen", there he is in the garden.
The God that has created you and me.

Norma Jean Griffin

Placement

I feel small enough to walk between the blades of grass,
and never really see the sun. I've felt its warmth, know
the darkness follows the light, feel the coldness coming
when the green begins to fade, but I have not seen the sun.
I only know it must be so.

I feel scared enough to drift forever amongst the same dirt,
and never really know another soil. I know there are those
with different colored earth beneath their feet, and some seem
to walk best when the turf is soft, and some when it is hard.
But, I have not seen another place. I only know it must be so.

I am weak enough to stay near familiar green when the storms
come, so as not to lose my way. If I am blown by a gust of wind,
or cold wave of water, I will find myself alone and frightful of
tomorrow. I am not proud, or arrogant, there is no peace in fear.
Others will only visit here. I only know it must be so.

Oh, to dream enough to rise above the ground, and feel strength
in the colors of flowers, and power near the tops of trees.
I envision the earth to be generous with forms of life like me.
Now I climb to the mountain, and fling my arms amid
A blue and naked sky. This I know. I dream it so.

Diane Stofko

Now, I See

To see beyond the skin's hue,
to the richness of each other's view.
To find the point at which we meet,
to find a common ground or street.
To meet the need within each heart,
seems to me to be a start.
To see the work of each man's hands,
reflections of his goals and plans.
We've reached beyond each separate dream,
integrity, dignity - love it seems.

To be accepted, to be loved—
A need defined, a common goal,
reflected now, I see, within each soul.
No matter what each skin's hue,
we share a common bond, a view.
To love, to live, to share ourselves—

To have value, to have worth,
to have dignity upon this earth.
Our hopes, our dreams, the same you see
The same for you as for me.

Sharon Wood

Metropolis, Vivacious Necropolis

Domineering atop the deceased below,
Stand guard the head stones praised and built
by all the corpses represented, though
these tombs show not their remorseless guilt.
Bright lighting streaking red and blue,
illuminating the scenes where peace collapsed
and, because of clouds one can't see through,
unknown thunder clapped as time elapsed.
Glowing eyes roam the neon rows,
the mourning groups help acid tears
fall vengefully down, the reaper bestows
death upon he who the faction endears.
This dying life needs itself reprimand
itself for its ever-living will to expand.
        Dillon Wallace

Far Off Playmate

Remember Me,
Dancing in the wet streets of our hometown
infinitely youthful, heads bursting with dreams
Now it seems,
as though we've both misted into separate clouds
free on the winds breath, gliding aimlessly toward a goal
will we ever reign together?
empty into pools of thick puddles, enjoying earth's stability
one more time
I miss swimming in the same waters as you miss you
perhaps one day, we'll both come to rest in the ocean together
far from the airy clouds that seem to drift endlessly apart.
        Shay Voss

Where Are You My Son...

The sky is blue...
The clouds are white...
But what will I do without you.

You were my dream,
You were my life,
Where are you my son,
Without your life.

Deep as the sea is my love for thee...
Shall I go in sorrow,
Without you my son there is no tomorrow for me,
You were my dream it seems.
        Marie Six

Two Love Birds

Two love birds
Just had to fly north
To express great affection
Destined to come forth

For spring has blossomed unique and colorful flowers
And this tender new born affinity,
For spring has nourished this amour of ours
And filled it with unfamiliar serenity

Gazing into space,
The birds received a notion
That fate and existence
Was the only love potion

Two love birds
Must never stop flying
For that is the only way
To prevent their love from dying
        F. Roberts Yates Jr.

What I See High In The Sky

When I see the sun high in the sky,
The sun looks like a great big bold circle of golden fire
High in the sky.

When I see the moon high in the dark blue sky,
The moon looks like the center of a flower high in the sky.

When I see the stars high in the dark blue sky,
The stars in the sky resemble the petals of a flower
High in the sky.

The petals of the flower are blue and gold, standing as the
Flower of the night shinning high in the sky.

When I see the thunder of night and day high in the sky,
The thunder of night and day looks like a mad strike of anger
That is loud and crying full of rain, obsessed with rage and envy
High in the sky.

When I see the rainbow high in the sky,
The rainbow brings color of all human races on earth, good luck,
Happiness and joy.

This is what I see high in the sky.
        India Ivory

But A Fool

Looking into the mirror and what do I see?....
    But a Fool looking at me...

Hoping your call would come my way....
    For it would be a brighter day.

I'm missing you as you can see...
    Even though you're not thinking of me.

I'm always here to be a friend...
I'm always here to lend a hand...
But I guess, you have other plans that don't include me.
Played for a Fool once again I see...
I guess learning to play the game is not for me...
You have fallen out of sight... only to have been suddenly dropped,
Although everything I've said and did...I've meant it with my heart.
Being sincere, you always pay a price...
Though at the time you don't think twice.

Yes...one look in the mirror and what do I see?,...
    But a Fool looking at me!
        Mary Sue Tumminello

Lion

With a ferocious tenacity he eyes his prey,
She lay there defenseless
What can she do to stop him,
What can she say?
Absolutely nothing.
What he want's, he takes.
Her dignity, her feelings, her trust
She hates to love him.
Yet she can not bring herself to hate him.
She runs for awhile,
Her endurance is lacking when compared to his.
The king of his concrete jungle, he devours her,
Slowly, with a lustful pleasure.
Already Master of his own domain.
He becomes Master of her's.
        Grant J. Combs

Chewing Gum

The war begins.
Troops meet the enemy,
attacking it and pulling it
further into the heat of battle.
Infantrymen appear
gleaming white, proud
and pummel the enemy with their
devastating assaults.
The fusillade continues until the
cavalry arrives for one last blow.
Pressure mounts, attacks increase, finally
a tremendous explosion rings out!
Tired and defeated, the enemy retires
to a life of world travel at the bottom
of a shoe.

Travis Hoffman

Haunt Me

"i will always love you" were her last words that night
cold words for a cool summer night, he listened, quiet
ed by hurt and not knowing how to respond. she
hung up without a goodbye. all that could be heard
was the slow hum of the dial tone flatlining what
was once love. he found solace in darkness arms.
he lay in his bed and softly wept as her beau
tiful smile and whispered words haunted and made love
to him until the screams lost their passion and sleep was but
a dream away. he welcomed it. he wanted it. maybe to forget.
but her smile. her voice. the memories. they tossed and turned him
until exhaustion betrayed him into sleep's patiently waiting arms.
each night thereafter was the same until time dried the tears and
the pain gave way to numbness. yet, he had not forgotten her, or her
whispered words. six months later and her words still echo
in his broken heart reminding him of a love
no more.
        "i will always love you"
                no goodbye...just
   a dial tone flatlining what once was...

Richard Gipson Jr.

Desert Sand Storm

Loneliness is like a desert sand storm.
Seconds become like grains of sand . . .
They blow through your life, like the wind across a dune.
If allowed to . . . they carve into your soul like chisels in stone.
The wind can swirl dust into circles,
As loneliness can become tornadoes of self pity.
The heat of the desert . . .
The burning of a broken heart . . .
The choices of life's direction are as vast
As the wide expanse of the desert.
Beauty can be found both in life, and in the desert . . .
If one takes the time and effort to observe.
Loneliness can be used to soul-search and renew . . .
As grains of sand can blow softly to sculpt a dune,
Or blow hard to polish a stone to a shining perfection.
Both are essential and mere moments in time . . .
For the rains bring refreshing new life, to a once barren land . . .
As a new love can heal pain and confusion,
With the wave of God's hand.

Betty Mueller

What Became Of Gentle Rain?

What became of gentle rain,
Of patters on the window pain?
Rain which coaxes one to sleep.
Not any need for counting sheep!

Rain that soaks into the ground,
Doesn't swish the soil around.
Makes air we breathe all fresh and clean;
Makes leaves and grass look brightly green.

Last nights rain was a down pour.
Lightening struck too near my door.
Thunder raged and rumbled loud.
Above our town was a black cloud.

Hail pounded on the window casement.
Sirens sent us to the basement.
Winds blew sixty miles an hour.
Electricity lost power.

Is a cloud burst now the norm?
Every rain a thunder storm?

Mary Louise Rodenberger

Eng. Comp. '95—Villanelle

How have my classes changed in fifteen years?
Melissa's sonagram suggests a son.
Her felt-tipped sentences are smeared with tears.

Guidance counselors fault the stress from peers.
Tuition, tutors, tests. Cheating? Everyone.
How have my classes changed in fifteen years?

Backfield's booked on DUI; caught with beers.
Student athletes lost, but the game was won.
Their felt-tipped sentences are smeared with tears.

Michael's mom tracks two jobs; Dad's in arrears.
Younger latchkey sisters can't see the sun.
How have my classes changed in fifteen years?

Good girls, nice boys. They've hidden frail their fears.
Metal detectors: "Gobble up that gun!"
Their felt-tipped sentences are smeared with tears.

Composition's cruel as adulthood nears.
I feel their pain! Is Brave New World a pun?
How have my classes changed in fifteen years?
Their felt-tipped sentences are smeared with tears.

Toni Tuminella

An Item Of Beauty

You are a blossoming rose that will last an eternity
and with your thorns you cannot hide
that beauty resting so deep inside.

You are so young and special
and the sweetness of sugar can not compare
to a lifetime of your tender love and care.

Your mind is so wondrous
that I cannot help but seek
all the words of wisdom that you speak.

We are separated by generations,
oh, but we cannot detour,
for from us, life will endure.

David Lawrence Bruman

The Meaning Of Forgiveness

The hardest part of a relationship
Is being able to grow along with each other,
Knowing when changes need to be made,
and not being afraid to help each other.
    To begin a new life together
Does not include forgetting the past,
But it means remembering the differences
So that the love can last.
    Never let the love grow so weary
That the time is not taken to be alone,
Do not grow so impatient with each other
That you decide to change only after the love is gone.
    No one is perfect, humans are subject to err;
Do not let the bond be weakened by the rough times;
Rather let it grow more stronger and loving,
Do not turn caring for each other into a crime.
    Do not let past hurts and angry words
Build walls between your hearts,
Learn the meaning of forgiveness
And nothing will be able to tear you apart.

Gwendolyn M. Clark

Heart And Soul

Throughout the years since time began, the children of our nation
Have grown up knowing they might fight for freedom and salvation;

With courage, pride and, yes, some fear, to battles they would go;
Some returned, some never did, but all the world would know

That these were true Americans, the protectors of our land;
They gave so much - sometimes their lives - to keep our country grand.

From coast to coast, we'd welcome them as they returned back home;
We'd let them know how proud we were of the courage they had shown.

Then, some time along the way, through politics intense
The wars that they were asked to fight no longer made much sense.

With all the problems here at home, why put them in harm's way
And make them fight for goals unknown, with such a price to pay?

But, still, our men and women go, to "keep the peace", they're told;
And, like the patriots that they are, they fight with heart and soul.

Let's never cease to honor them, despite how we might feel,
Because each loss is still so great, and each sacrifice so real!

Judy A. Murphy

In The Forest

When living becomes a depression,
I leave for the forest.

My heart goes first
laying on the plains of wild white flowers.
Mother's milky fragrance
rises by my side.

In the forest
the green absorbs the whole of me.
Only the shell of my existence remains.

Oh! It is
the unseen source of my power.

Every night, without moan,
busting new leaves,
nestles
the innocent creatures.

When living becomes a depression,
to the forest, I want to move.
I long to lose myself in the forest.

Haeng Ja Kim

In Memory Of Mary

The day that mourned her
    passing...
Craggy hill climbed upwards,
    past the shrouding clouds
In her beloved Scotland;
The filmy mist cloaked the trees,
    smothering their brilliant green.

The sun was slow to rise,
    the moon had bedded early;
The twinkling stars had lost their shine,
    and stared in grim despair;
The thunder grumbled in irate frustration;
The clouds wept with deep sorrow
    to inundate the dark land.

The red-breasted Robin kept quiet
    his song;
The sheep wandered listlessly,
    heads low with empty eyes;
An old Border Collie, poor lassie,
    laid at the feet of her grieving masters.

Heather Black

A Love Of A Lifetime

Blazing passions of fiery desire surge through the rapid beating heart
Spreading out like wild fire . . . Free and Uncaring.
Hot, dangerous unyielding rapture of love so profound and vast,
Feelings of Unbridled joy . . . to Cherish without restrain,
Breathless affections.

Broken away from the "polite" society,
Uncaring of rules liberated from the human cares and regretful
    consequences.

Glorifying in the scorching tempest, which
only two people of one heart can make when the flame of love is
    burning brightly.
Feelings beyond description and understanding.
Stirring deep within the dark, sable chambers.
A breaking of light through the heavy shroud.

The flame is burning feverishly - out of control.
White explosion of one soul
Floating without care - without movement.
Sensual bliss — pure Heaven . . . Eternal Eden

U'ilani

The Clouds

That God should grant me the privilege to see,
The clouds as they float in the sky,
That God should grant me the privilege to hear,
The rain as it falls from on high.

Soft flakes in the air, they twist round & round,
And sometimes gently, light on the ground,
I look to the sky, then I say,
What will it be with those clouds today?

Now everythings balanced, I should surely know,
I made "three score and ten along time ago."
Dark and foreboding, clouds meet in the sky,
And wait for instructions, how or why,

Earthquake or fire, they rip up the air,
No one can stop, and no one can care,
And then to my great amazement, I see,
Everything turned in, as it used to be.

Rezoned and recycled, they float against blue,
Fluffy and white, too-good to be true,
and if they could talk, I know they would say,
Our time is forever, yours may be today.

Helen E. Robinson

"A Baby That Won't Be Born"

Oh, little baby not yet been born
From your mother and father your were torn

We were all surprised by your coming birth
God decided not good enough was this earth

A little broken hearted we became to be
When we found out there won't be a baby

But God made a decision we understand
About the baby we will never hold in our hand

So life goes on and in some future day
We know a baby will come to stay

Carol M. Crystian

I Hear God Speaking

I hear God speaking in the rustling leaves.
I hear God speaking in the morning breeze.

I hear God speaking in the golden setting of the sun.
I hear God speaking in the laughter of a child's voice when he's
  having fun.

I hear God speaking when all seems to have failed.
I hear God speaking as I stand holding onto life's rough, jagged rail.

I hear God speaking and His voice is so sweet,
It says, "My child I've never suffered defeat".

I hear God speaking saying to
"hold on for your day is coming and it won't be long".

Sh-h-h-h...
I hear God speaking.

Mable Carter Robinson

A Mother's Love

My girl, my boy. Oh what a joy!
As he stands by the plate and swings the bat.
As the ball sails by, he shouts.
Did you see that!
Just a typical little boy. Ah, but never,
never, to me. He is so special can't
everyone see?
   She with her long dark hair and flashing
smile. Just a little girl for such a short
while. Rapidly approaching womanhood.
Would I stop time if I could?
All these things that I feel. Oh how
can I say. Please God make me a
wise mother I dearly pray.

Mary Ingallinera

Fall: Westerville 1973

Saturday afternoons
Turtleneck sweaters, hot coffee
The sun shining clear and brilliant
The cool crisp fall air drifting through
The open window

Old rocking chairs
Children playing, fresh cigarettes
The music filtering gently throughout the rooms
Filling us with the peace and tranquility
Of living

Straw flowers
Worn out shoes, school books and papers
This room has seen and heard so much
Yet, here is where we stay learning
Of love

Hollis Lee Donisi

Foregoing Eden

Perhaps today will go according to plan.

Following every turn and curve with the ease
  of someone who has lived on mountain roads
  all their life and knows nothing other than
  treacherous switchbacks buffeted by rough
  winds and slicked by winter ices.

The gray sky and incessant rain could mean
  nothing.

They don't have to be a forewarning to hard
  lessons learned unwillingly or the mood of
  rather unpleasant characters mourning the
  loss of a locally respected nobody who leaves
  the stench of depravity and poverty in their
  nostrils.

No, today is filled with the possibility of
  excellence.

Hope Kalbach

"Sadness"

Being trapped within one's own soul
Clawing, scrapping, fighting to be set free
Of the sadness that subdues
One from inside themselves

THEN COME THE TEARS

Falling, flowing, streaming down the cheek
One after another, the endless reserve
Does not stop, until

The mind, the emotional valve,
turns the river off.

Then, no more tears
Only tiresome tremors of sadness.

But then comes the sweet soft sadness,
An emotional cover that hides
the true sadness to the rest of the society

Joseph T. Meier

Alone

Out there in the world,
It's just me, facing every thing.
Day by day, my mind tells me
something different, but I know
it's me all alone. Time comes around
like the hand on an Old Grandfather's
clock, saying it's that time again for
love, hate, joy, or death. To me it's
just something out there for me that
I don't know. At the end I found
love, something that is happy, enjoying
But love is a chance that we all
learn from for the good, bad, beautiful,
Ugly or worst but I know that it's
me out there saying the same old words.
It's me all alone in this world
Whether I'm going up or down or in or out.
It's me, only me to face it all, troubles,
love, sex, or anything else it's me yes, me.
All alone

Sarah Grant Smith

A Reflection

I feel time lost, a sting, erosion
Children laugh in snow kingdoms, mothers look warm
Sweetest hours ever known, unfelt
Glowing television holding hands, embarrassed
A kiss, a vacant dream
Feel this absence

Another way up from the carpet, thorny and cold
Unlike models, ideals to romanticize
Taste hours alone in bed, angry brine tears and wrist-blood
Neverending screams of progenitors, downstairs, drawn in
Silent telephone, junk mail, advice uncomprehended
Dead friends and embers of friendships
Hatred from the outside in, then out again
In words, in music, in looks, a distance farther away

Want to leave, move beyond deaths and addresses
Another world, another sky, clean grass and love
Touching the ink of night, peppered with stars
Yet sad, cry, the impossible heaven
The light of a brighter sun, unknown to my eyes

Jay A. Sorrels

Proud Patriotism

Shinng! Crackle! Bang! A rainbow of color lights up the sky,
Watched by millions of dazzled eyes,
A celebration on the fourth of July.
Reminding me of why I am proud,
Of America's freedom shouting out loud.
Learning from my elders about the past,
Of America's wars and the scars they cast.
Our flag waving proud and free,
America, America how I love thee.
50 stars and 13 stripes,
Teaches us of our country's life.
The thousands of people whose lives they paid,
Proudly remembered on Veteran's Day.
All reasons patriotism should be respected,
By students of America who seem to reject it.
The warmth of my country hovers over me,
America, America how I love thee,
Yes America, America I really love thee.

Sara A. Clements

An Opportunity Missed

An opportunity came knocking at my door today
But I was busy dreaming, so it went away,
When from my bed I finally did rise
I looked for it, but never opened my eyes...

I searched for opportunity all over the place,
I looked in its eyes, not knowing its face.
It only knocks one time, somebody said—
You should have been watching, instead of in bed.

They don't know me, or the shape I'm in—
If opportunity is for real, won't it knock again?
Besides, I'm tired of looking, I've got to lay down,
But I'll listen real hard, in case it comes back around.

An opportunity came knocking at my door today,
But I was busy dreaming...so it went away.

Steven J. Nelson Sr.

Grandaddy

Grandaddy led a very special life.
And he also shared it with a special wife.
They lived thru hard times in this world.
But always made it with the help of the Lord.
When times were hard and not lots to eat.
They worked together to make ends meet.
They loved their family with all their might.
And prayed for the Lord to protect them each night.
They gave their family all that they had.
And was there to help them when times were bad.
They touched everyone in a special way.
Whenever you saw them it would brighten your day.
They often spoke of the good ole days.
As they always smiled with a glorious praise.
They loved the Lord with a special grace.
As you always could tell by the smile on their face.
Their love was stronger than the biggest chain.
And when he died Granny bared the pain,
She knew that he'd gone to heavens land.
And would be waiting there with a loving hand.

Chester Jones

A Child Of Mine

The day that you came into my life
was one of the happiest.
The day that you left my life
was the saddest of all.
All of your cry's and cuddles remain
a memory each and every day.
All of those booties of yours that remain
unworn are kept and treasured.
All of the pictures and memories of
you will always remain hanging.
There is never a day that goes by
that I don't think about you.
I think about how you would've grown
up and what you would've done;
However those thoughts will never become
true because I will never know.
I can't take you back, but I can carry
you in my heart forever.
Once a Child Of Mine, but now
a Child Of Heaven above.

Denise Marie Trieglaff

My Garden

Weeds flourish in my garden
Sturdy and florid,
Towering o'er all, and then —
Boldly, their descendents spread.
But - some flowers beautiful and budding
With blossoms stay.
Taking the sight and sting
Of many weeds away.

Others become stunted and sparkless.
Starving for a gentle glance,
Or a kind word, a little caress
To nourish their existence.
They droop their heads,
And turn back their foliage.
To hide within their beds.
Only to turn pale, and loose parentage.

Pray, that someday, these flower
Thou lacking the essential nutrients,
Thru their struggling, shall stir
In others, courage, peace and contentment.

Vinan Archie Mathews

Discovering

He discovered new things
with the one he loved most.

He felt and touched new things
and feelings held within him.

She opened a new world
for her and her lover.

They discovered, felt, touched, and
expressed feelings held within themselves.

The agressiveness came from the hot desireable feelings
they had for each other.

They hunger for clean pure flesh
Which was only found within each other.

A love discovered at young age.

Two mature young lovers
joined together to fill
their empty souls, hearts
and lives.

　Lets discover the unknown my love...
　　Idania Moncada

Murder Mouth

The words spew from his mouth like weapons of death,
cutting into the sacred flesh of my soul,
he leaves a weeping hole.
He's murder mouth.

Like a knife sharpened to the ultimate degree,
he sends his hateful message to me,
leaving scars and wounds from which I can't escape.
Is this my fate?
He's murder mouth.

He makes cuts to the psyche that cannot be seen,
they never can heal, they're etched in my being.
His hate reveals evil that's almost unreal,
his hatred of women he tries to conceal.
He's murder mouth.

He disarms you with charms that are carefully cultivated,
clutching you back into the web that he has created,
he cannot love you or even see you,
the problem is, he wants to be you,
so he tries to kill you with his words.
He's murder mouth.

　　Marsha Zebin

Something + Rain

I have given my time to the rain
In night streets walking while its skin tightening wet
lashed speckled harshness
whistled cold into my pores
igniting images of home so bright
its imaginary luminescent light lit the way
and home again beneath the covers, head set free, skull-less
to sweet sensation of drifting, drifting, into starry space
above the sheeting clouds and feet free of weighty shoes
released at last to cold sheet corners and partnered toes
while the rain
its wetness now a distant glow danced like a tribe
of African elves upon the roofs flow. While I
enfolding into slumber
unfolding into dreams breathed forward to future dates
and giving time to the rain.

　　Peter J. Warren

Emotional Scraps

Hope is the spark my heart leaps at,
Though it may defy all rationality.
It is the spark that still exists
After my mind admonishes me,
"It cannot be so."

Love is the hope of my heart.
That spark rebelling against rationality,
It glows with promises yet to come.
Yet all the while my mind cautions,
"It cannot be so."

Devotion is the love and hope of my heart,
The belief in the rationality of the irrational.
It is the spark that forces my mind to follow.
The now-humbled leader accedes,
"It cannot be so, but it is."

I rejoice in you, my emotional scraps.
Leftovers from the meal my mind picks through.
Through all your collective sparks
Does a fire blaze in my heart and soul,
My one true link to humanity and God.
　　Vaishali N. Mane

The Tree

I think that I would like to be
a great big Oak, or at least a tree

A tree that stands so straight and tall
its branches hung from wall to wall

Its head pushed high into the sky
to touch each cloud that passes by

To touch each cloud that might come near
just to say, "I'm standing here"

A tree with branches e'er so thin
hanging there with life within

The life within each hanging branch
waits in abeyance to advance

It waits for Spring to come each night
so it can bring the tree to life

The tree of life, Oh can it be
the driving force inside of me?

The driving force inside of me
that makes me want to be a tree
　　Daniel J. Snook

Damn The Gunpowder, Full Peace Ahead

The stench of saltpeter, nostrils laden,
　unnoticed neath the agony of missing limbs
by a ten year old squirming on a bed of rags,
　improvised comfort while the bearers of peace
in roaring tanks, whooshing planes, and afoot,
　surround him with promises for the future.

An olive branch, too weighty for the raving mouths
　of pretentious politicians preaching peace
throughout a world of confused, wonderful people.
　Another "save" for an elite level of grasping souls
in a world of their own making, leaders unto leaders,
　uncaring of a populace suffering 'neath their rule.

Peoples who would be basking in the warmth of
　amicable coexistence, were such a condition not
threatening to certain selfish plans and personal aims.
　Gunpowder for talc, land mines for security,
violence for control, and peace,
　a world peace, but a gunshot away?
　　Donald F. Withee

"A Friendly Demise"

Revenge is branded with steel in thy heart,
and blood from my own vein.
All that is strange may sooneth depart,
will only fill thee with pain.
This beauty distilled with changing eyes,
on a face that hath no sleep.
In midnight hours that reek with lies,
and from this I do weep!
I touch the hair of an angel at night,
and by morning my heart hath changed.
And days do pass with all loss of sight,
it seems more was gone than I had ranged.
And all those faces and words
are done and can't be pushed away.
Not a tear in your eye, this stab in my back,
will always sit and stay.
I see you are foolish, now time to be learned,
must wither away and be carried by dove.
Nay ever disrupt your hand that I've earned,
nor curse our beautiful love.

Austin Mahlon Reece

Death's Revenge
(An Answer To John Donne's Holy Sonnet 6)

O man who mocks me,
Thou art a brave fool.
My powers are beyond your understanding.
Do you think I am tortured so by making my home with poison,
     war, and sickness.
To witness suffering is what I do enjoy most.
'Tis not a world of torture to me but more of a Utopia.
And, 'tis true I must take all,
But, what thou dost not comprehend is that I do have choice as
     to when.
So young brave fool, thou suffering shall be long.
You shall be so stricken with illness and pain that you will call
     upon me,
Hoping I might ease your woes.
This is where my revenge shall come.
I will tease you with sleep and graze you with my sickle,
And just when you think you will close your eyes forever,
You shall awaken to another day of pain.
Maybe 'tis true that I, Death, will die to you when you have
     passed into the hereafter,
But my revenge will be sweet when you must live on eternally
     with the memories
Of pain and torture.
Remember fool, that I shall always live on to others.
Death shall never wholly die.

Michele Pollio

Introit

Arch the stars high, indigo-black cool forever.
Lean gently, breathe softly
On downs rolling seaward in velvet gray starlight.
   Secret hollows fold tree blackness.
Look down, look down. Forest gathers a village.
A village far back in memory yet an intimate of my soul.
Oh, there. Smudge of orange glow, a lamp waits in the center of
the window, the village, the forest, the downs, the universe.
The traveler has come home.

Evelyn Swift

Why???

Yitzak Rabin was assassinated yesterday.
One of his own gunned him down.
This was a Great man Peace for the world;
Not only passing Peace through his town.
He met with National Leaders throughout the globe.
His light shined bright.
It was a twenty eight year old man
who decided that the light was not quite right.
What is it that possesses such plain and unspiritual that show
that some choose to live their lives planning to other's lives slow?
The smallest aggravation is able to pull these demons out amongst us all.
What about the major issues, like Peace, makes the lighted candle
surely fall and break into millions of pieces
and is able to cause a Worldy brawl.
Are we so blind that we can not see the effects
that this has on this Earth?
Each and every single day many more brought here by birth.
There must be a solution but yet it seems to hide.
Or else we haven't even begun the search that, indeed, is Worldwide.

Lisa M. Lindstrom

The Ballad Of Her Falling Asleep

Your hands between two trees
Where is the difficulty to reach a flame
And remain innocent?
Between the fires was a disharmony
Requiring pieces of reminiscence
At the dreamy birthday
The day when was born the doll
At the branch
When she learned to cry
At the sheer rock
And the friends depart.

(Over the empty sky
Cry the hawkers....)

To lie on a shore of rocks,
To whisper by the pebbles of moonlight;
You forebode fists which appear out of water,
Bloody fists appear out of water

Over the empty sky cry the hawkers.

Denis Fetahagic

The Key Master

Eyes open wide ... Prejudice to one's own self.
Harshly judged ... Finding endless faults.
Locked doors to your inner self.
Close your eyes ... Clear your mind.
Naked and free ... You stand before me and the mirror.
The mirror is your enemy ... Viewing only what is skin deep.

Eyes open - faults, wrong choices cloud your mind.
Close your eyes and be with me!
I'm the Soul Searcher ... The Key Master.
I know what is hidden.
I hold the keys to unlock the depths of your soul and mind.

Naked and free standing before me ... Uninhibited!
The warmth of your smile hidden behind unspoken soft lips.
The security of your arms crossed against your chest.
The mystery lost with in your eyes unfocused on the future,
haunted by the past.

These locks I can open... My key ... My touch ...
Let them set you free.
Soul Searcher standing next to you.
Naked and free ... Eyes Closed ... Speak to me.
Let me into that hidden world ... Behind closed lock doors ...
So much to see.
The YOU, no one else can see, but ME!

Ellen M. McConnell

"Beautiful"

Beautiful, I've often heard this word, but I never knew quite what it meant; until you came into my life!

Now it's as clear to me as light from darkness. Your quality of beauty cannot be measured, for it is unfathomable in every respect.

And I have become so amorous with your beauty, so fervent, so over powered, that there is no turning back for me now.

I must openly declare to you the awe and respect my own being has grown to have of you.

As the midnight hour approaches upon me like a dark cloud pouring loneliness over my entire body, the only hope for me now, to make it through the darkness of life, is your beauty.

Your delicate touch is like an ocean full of precious jewels to me, coloring my very soul with shades of happiness and joy.

Your words are like a stream of rose petals dancing over my ears. The vibrations radiating from your heart has warmed my blood to boiling, granting me an unquenchable thirst for your specialness.

And you, well, there's just no one as beautiful as you, because you are you!

Burton Fariss

It's Much More Than A Toy

See her ride the new bicycle, given by her parents dear,
on the day of celebration of the passing of her second year.

She can ride that new bicycle, she can make the wheels spin.
Her feet barely reach the pedals, and she rides with a mischievous
  grin.

She's on the roads of Texas, pedaling Oh, so very far.
O'er the highways and the byways, through the gravel, dirt and tar

She can ride with speed of lightening as she passes cross the sky.
Through the clouds of cotton candy, to the North Pole she will fly.
She has pedaled many a mile, and the trip was long, but fun.
But now the day is over as we watch the setting sun.

The adventures have been many, and she'll keep them in her head.
But, for now the day is over, and it's time to go to bed.

She has traveled o'er the country without leaving her own home.
Oh!, the wonders of a child's mind caught briefly in a poem.

The lessons we can learn from her, if only we'd take heed,
to all the fun that children have, we wish them all God's speed,
in all their trips of fantasy, in all their fun and joy
aboard their magic bicycles...it's more than just a toy.

William H. Garton

Untitled

My little Sarah, you've given my life so much joy.
Your smile can chase the storm clouds away.
The light from your eyes have been like beacons in the night
guiding this ship home to the harbor of your heart.

I have been so proud to watch you grow from infancy
to this innocent young lady whose radiance demands the favor of kings
  and princesses.
You have filled my life with meaning and kept hope alive my soul.
Your intuition and tenderness of heart still amaze me and
I struggle to remind myself that you've only been with us 9 years.

Holding my hand at the zoo when you knew my heart was broken,
Piercing my darkness with the light of your love.

You are my legacy to pass on to this world
To take the goodness that was in me and pass it on
To refresh us all with your love and compassion
A godly woman will always be in fashion.

The grace and beauty, the innocence of a dove
I will be so proud to watch from above.

Michael Keeterle

Sunset

Far off in the distance
The sun begins to set
And where the sky and earth meet
The sun there too is met
A torch of reddish luster
Is stretched across the line
Where sky and earth and sun
Together than combine
But only for a short time
Does all this beauty last
Extending out its brilliance
With a glow that's unsurpassed
Crossing the great horizon
Descending there between
An illuminating sunset
Cast its farewell sheen
For soon the dark will blacken
The line that flames so bright
Where sun and sky and earth meet
In the twilight of the night

Robert J. Pool

Stranger In The Night

Death called ...
And youth walked alone
She was like a stranger
In the night,
But he welcomed her
His arms reached out,
And she enfolded him.
Sweet, sweet youth of a battlefield,
You are beyond human evaluation!

Muriel D. Glaister

Mother's Yesterdays

One cold and cloudy day, death knocked
At our door, but did not stay.
Leaving nothing but a shell, then went
His way to cast another spell.
Now those eyes are shallow tombs,
Of past days and tomorrow's gloom.
That body bent so gray and frail,
Now lives in a dimension of time,
I cannot tell.
Laughter like a child at play,
Tears that flow day by day.
Far away look, the mind has strayed,
I wonder where she is today?
I cannot break this evil spell,
Only God in his wisdom could ever tell.
Please bring her peace, oh Lord I pray
Or is it for me that I plea?

Kathy Scarbro

Trust

I am a splinter floating,
In the universal dust,
I am a splinter drifting,
To a universal must,
A speck of cosmic matter,
Swimming in a sea,
A small splinter searching,
For my destiny,
I am a splinter hoping,
For a world that's just,
I am a splinter floating,
A splinter of trust.

William R. Davis

To My Best Friend - The Rose

I went walking through a garden one sunny day, picking and choosing
flowers along the way. As I walked down the straight, lonely path,
I noticed on the side sat a thorny bush, the thorniest by far. And
in the middle of that bush stood an unopened rose. I couldn't bring
myself to let its natural beauty be hidden by the thorns, so I picked
it, put it into my bundle of flowers and continued on.

As the days moved by, the flowers that I had picked from that garden
bloomed, wilted and died...all except for that simple rosebud. Later
I picked more flowers but they too died and the surviving rose stood
alone, unopened.

I tended to that single rose, each day clipping thorns off its side.
Until one day, that simple rose bud that I had picked from the
thorniest of bushes, blossomed. On that very day tears flowed from
my heart, not in sadness, but in overwhelming joy, for before me
stood the most beautiful sight the world had ever beheld.

That rose has meant more to me today than words would ever express.
For beyond its pink, soft petals, fragrant scent, and green stem,
laid a hidden beauty that only I could see. On that one day, that rose
showed me strength, happiness, courage, friendship, bravery, and love.
I will never be able to repay that rose because it changed my life, forever.

So I saved that rose, and put it into a separate chapter in the book of my life.
A chapter that shall live forever and never be forgotten.
For that rose belongs here and nowhere else...in the chapter of my heart.

Jason DuBose 9/15/95

The True Meaning Of Christmas

Christmas is home with family, trimming trees and present giving,
decking hall's with boughs of holly, laughing merrily as memories
passe' are recalled of fun and folly.
Delicious smells emit from kitchens teasing the senses delight,
turkey with fixings of all kinds,
plum pudding and assorted pies to tempt the appetite.

Traditional decorating of homes with lights
send out multi-colored glows in the darkened night.

The chill of the air with sometimes snow delights the young and old alike.
If ice on the pond there's skating,
snow on the hill slopes sledding or toboggan racing.
While other's just enjoy from sleigh's the sights while gliding o'er
the snow and ice.

Although a fun filled holiday,
we must never forget the true meaning of Christmas, Christ.
Rejoicing in this blessed birth by celebrating
God's greatest gift to man on earth.
A gift bestowed with love, giving his only son Jesus Christ
who shed his blood for us, the sacrificial lamb of God.

Before I lay me down to rest my head upon my bed,
I bend my knees to God in prayer,
Thanking him for his wondrous gift of our Lord Jesus Christ,
Who came to save us our sins and give eternal life.

Marolyn E. Baker

A Mother's Precious Memories

I watched you in that big yellow bus as it drove on down the lane,
you looked so tiny in that big seat you barely knew your name

You seemed just like a baby when you first went to school, but
you were very eager to learn the golden rule

You brought me flowers everyday you picked down by the old horse stall,
you made me pretty pictures that you hung on the kitchen wall

First grade went so very fast now second grade's so brand new,
you'll learn so many things this year and I'm so very proud of you

You've come a long way buddy, from that little boy on the bus,
respect your parents and yourself, and God will bring you
"Safely home to us."

Elaine Kearney

Lapping Liquid

The gentle rippling
waves of the majestic lake
smoothly flow inward.

Virginia Hovdestad

My Angel And I

Today my angel is here
Invisible as always,
But clearly audible
As it sits on my shoulders
To whisper a command
That makes me quickly forget
Any regrets I may have
From the present or the past,
For then I become its scribe
Threading words reassuring me
That there is nothing more dear
Than a life lived without fear,
In all its fullness and hopes,
Wishing my day in the sun
Sooner or later will come.
And if it doesn't, at least,
I can console myself with the fact
That I tried to make the best
Of whatever speck of creativity
Within me remained alive.

Horatio Costa

Little Yellow Butterfly

Little yellow butterfly,
you seem the last to leave.
Alone, you dance and dip
into late Autumn blossoms,
unaware of cloudless skies.

Little yellow butterfly,
this very night moon and stars
will settle, cold and still,
on frozen flower cups
of nectar.

Sandy Fink

My God And I

God's not finished with me
He watched me climb the tree
The limb broke down and I went around
Saying he is not finished with me.

He's still making me now
Some days He has me plow,
Up a flower bed, to plant flowers red -
Cause God's not finished with me.

Give God plenty of room-
Give Him a finishing spoon
The need is great, make no mistake
His making me over right now.

But, then "He, didn't ask me."
But beckoned me down from a trees
He molded the clay on a sun shiny day.
"Thank God, it's Heaven for me"

Argatha Hamilton Merchant

My Fantasy Lover

Outside the wind is blowing the branches of my tree,
  the moon is almost full,
the sweet smell of night blooming jasmine is in the air.

Inside I lie alone, wondering what is in store for me,
knowing that something has been awakened that is familiar,
but thought long gone,
never to waken again.

I wonder what you are doing long into the night. I felt like I was
beside you, feeling you next to me, imagining what making love to you
would feel like, how your hands feel, how you breathe,
where you wanted me to touch you.

I stirred several times during the night, you were like a spirit
haunting my dreams and my physical being.
Who are you, what are you, will you be good to me?

You've pushed into my thirsty spirit, causing such a stir in my soul,
  into my very being.
It's good to feel again, but it scares me, my fantasy lover.

I love the sound of your voice, I feel the caress of your hands,
I sense your kindness, your humor, your earthiness,
I feel our spirits merging. We seem alike, yet different, you and I.

Will we meet, will the galaxy explode like fireworks when we make love?
Or will we let each other go and never know what the answer is.

I'm frightened, yet adventurous, cautious, yet curious.
Don't hurt me,
I'm still too fragile, my spirit has been broken into shards of glass,
only slowing rising and daring to put myself together again.

I'm yearning to meet you in the moonlight, let the wind kiss our skin
  and lift us to the stars.
We will look down on this place we call earth, and say,
  "we rose above that."
 What is so special, why were we destined to be?

    Janice Lee Reilly

The Racial Divide

Why do you sit there acting so surprised, could it be your mind has
been hypnotized. Come on now tell me the truth; WHAT IS THE RACIAL
DIVIDE? Sounds worse than, a stinking rotten tooth.
Is it a great big ocean full of hate and discontent? Or, is it a
code phrase created by the government? Is it black and white or is
it yellow and red? Maybe, it's just an ill feeling planted in
our heads. Let us not deny that racism does exist. However,
coining catchy phrases will not help us deal with it. From this
day forth let us be courageous, and admit when we are wrong about race,
it might just become contagious.

Racism is a disease that eats away at our psyche.
You'll find it in boardrooms all across America, from Toyota to McDonalds to Nike.
Rise! Up America let's move to a place, where affirmative action
will never again be needed, to define a particular race. Let's
take our case a to place where judgement is fair, somewhere we can
compromise without any despair. The racial divide can be whatever
you and I wish it to be, let's learn to celebrate our difference,
only then can we truly be free. The racial divide will create
a genocide, if we continue to shuffle our feet. Let's try to
respect and understand, each and every man, every time we meet.

I'll never give in to hatred, Racism will not devour me.
I'll extend kindness to everyone, until this war is won, and then
I'll pass the legacy on to my growing son. The racial divide,
the racial divide is whatever we will it to be. I'm making that
divide a little less wide, with compassion plus understanding using
God as my guide.

    Kevin T. Prince Sr.

By Accident

She doesn't seem
To remember
That just a week ago she was sitting
(Straddling me)
Giving me kisses that almost left me
Breathless

She apparently doesn't
Know
How I was kissing
And touching
Her body
All over
And how my pulling her hair
Made her moan

She painfully
Recalls
How she let me
Gather her ecstasy in my arms
And now she
Regrets the act

    John C. Bystra III

What Might Have Been

There was a time when the sun set,
without structures or wires.
When the night's glow came from Heaven,
not street light fires.

Was a time when rainbows,
were luminous and clear.
A time when a star fell,
not far from here.

It seems so long ago,
in a distant sunrise.
I saw the golden morning,
with wondering eyes.

How the years have passed,
in the whispering wind.
I find myself waiting,
for a message it sends.

Dreaming in the moon glow,
the night begins.
Wishing on a starfall,
and this heart to mend.

    Robert A. Sabatini

Blue Skies

Where has all the blue gone
Now all is gray and black
Will the blue return?
I hope it's coming back.

Where has all the blue gone
All we see are clouds and mist
Will the blue return?
Or is it all a myth?

Where has all the blue gone
The sky is dark or pale
Will the blue return?
Enough of winds and gale.

Where has all the blue gone
The sun is shining through
Soon the blue will return
Triumphant and renewed.

    Gordon C. Pierce

The Return Of One

Dear dejected soul,
   I called on your will the other day to aid my escape. I had to
run, run so far, to save all I was, all I had left, to save my place.
Smooth sorrows told of timely tales left in the hands of widowed
mountains, severed from the preserve of sky. Hoping, looking, to Heaven.
   Smooth sorrows calling my name. Calling me back again to
play the final chorus of goodbye, but my needs would not falter.

My commands lived to tell the story of my escape.
Reach fast my feet to leave.
Carry, carry soon if not quicker the name of this victor to a home on high.
Calm passion these notes of courage ringing true over harmonies of
Love and resurrection.
At last deserted days pass away to open the chest of laughs.
Swallow me whole joy.
   Temptation played her game with poison dripping sweet eyes,
calling me to touch. Allow me sleep that I may awake only to hear.
Feast me knowledge that all may come to right my wrongs and cheer all doubts.
Create a harp to accompany this choice.
Leave me a trumpet to bring forth my Father.
 Sound all souls to receive sweet sight for my coming is now.
                    Receive again this ONE.
   William M. Collins III

Dawn at the Edge of the Forest and Meadow

Dawn at the edge of the forest and meadow.
The beginning of a new day.
Bright in the eyes of a man a woman absorbed in the joys of each other
Their bodies intertwined, their souls mix.

The rays of light filter down through the leaves like ribbons of
silver, and envelope the two lovers.
Their Aura is electric as their energy merges with the energy of nature.
There is power in this moment.
Power so pure it cannot be harnessed!
Power that brings them closer together allowing them to unite and
reach a spiritual plain experienced only by a few.

The power ebbs, but the two linger at this higher level holding
   each other close.
Being so close they cherish the time together envisioning an Eden
   created in the mind's eye.
The power fades to a calm appreciation of each other.
Their bodies unwind becoming separate again, but closer.
They peer into each other's eyes with a new awareness of the other,
And in each others arms they relax knowing that they are alive
   together, FOREVER.
   Robert Owen Ramsey

Angel (Ode To An Old Friend)

Angel in the light,
   sending a ray in my darkness.

Out there she shines somewhere.
   I will never see daylight again,
   I hope she never sees the night.
For she should be among the stars,
   blinding out the sun.

Sometimes I look at the moon,
   and picture it's her.

She is my Idol,
   my angel,
      my goddess of light

I wait patiently for the next sunrise;

      hoping to see her again.
   Kevin Doherty

"The Fairest Of Them All"

Pretty girl...
oh, pretty girl...
Why are you so beautiful?

Is it your upturned nose?
Your paper-thin lips?
Your well-trained hair?

When you open your mouth,
people stare.
When you strut into a room,
men swoon
at the sight of your regal profile,
carved by a loving hand.

Tell me, what secrets do you hide
within your piercing eyes
and addictive smile?

Why,
out of all of His children,
did God choose you,
and forget about the rest of us?
   Rashida Bowman

Words

In the beginning was the world
Words can be spoken
Words can be mumbled
Words can heal
Words can hurt
Words can tell truth
Words can lie
Words are important
Words can be unimportant
Words can teach hate
Words can teach love
Words can explain
Words can confuse
In the end one world will stand. GOD!
   Darlene Durham

Cascade of Memories

Silver Streams, Silver Dreams
Memories of an aspiring queen

Carried with lucid recollections
of her golden hair dancing,
glistening so freely
in the warmth of the breeze

Suddenly my countenance was lost
amidst it's wondrous frolicking
such a meritoriuos cost
for the pleasure that would bring

Often I'd pretend upon those hairs
becoming locking arms
around my palpable physique

and then she would turn with
an ever so graceful gesture

and enrapture my soul to the heavens
as her crimson lips and pearls so play
would send an enthralling smile my way
   Ron Bigalke Jr

Feathered Shadows

Poet! Oh poet! Pen the word.
The sweetest voice ever heard.
  Spirit! Spirit!
I hear your call.
Feathered shadows on my wall;
Musical voices call to me.
  Angel! Angel!
Your wings I see.
Heralded words from heaven's door
reflecting on my bedroom floor.
  Wake up! Wake up!
My soul rejoices. Answer! Oh answer
the heavenly voices.
Verses float across the early morn.
Beautiful words, a song is born:
Feathered shadows on my wall.
  Answered! Oh answered,
the composer's call!

Doris Hartsell Brewer

Lucky In Love

As we held each other close
My heart started to pound
At long last my true love I found
Tall dark and handsome
He's all mine
The most compassionate soul
So hard to find
Always thinking of me
Never letting me down
No longer do I wear a frown
I'm the luckiest woman alive
Then I smiled to myself
Thank God for imagination
Since this is how my love appears
I close my eyes as I cuddle my bear
Knowing soon my love will reappear

Jennifer Tatem

Straddling

When politicians straddle,
  Their credentials become weak:
They're branded pussy-footers,
  Then their future becomes bleak.

Their effectiveness dwindles
  When they cannot yet decide;
They are pictured as straddling,
  With one foot on either side.

But perhaps one needs more facts
  To make up a searching mind;
Too bad one seems expected
  To fake or to fall behind.

Many problems are complex
  And drive honest persons mad;
Let's ask some hard-nosed critics,
  Is straddling quite all that bad?

Do we want a congressman
  Who hip-shoots at noon high,
Or one who takes careful aim
  And hits the bull in the eye?

William A. Paff

"Railroad"

Many years ago walking one day down
the railroad tracks a little girl came
up to me & started talking. I'll never
forget the words she said to me that
day. Do you know how to stop blood?
She said I will tell you, this is what
you say. As I passed by the & saw
the in thine own blood. Ya tho
I say unto the live. Far on down
the line of tracks I saw a vision
of someone. I would see down
the line that maybe someday would
be mine.

Ramona Hamric

A Happy Time

Winter is a joyful season
Where you can run and play
On snow covered grass
Every hour of the day,

There's always a gentle breeze
Which makes the air fresh and cool
And we're just as happy as can be
Skating on the ice covered pool.

Our hearts are all a glow
With sheer happiness and fun
We can hear laughter and joy everywhere
As our love appears to flow

While we watch the setting sun
Just knowing it's a happy time
And now the day is all done
The time is a passing memory,

So now we sit by the fireplace
As we give thanks and praise
To our Father, who's full of grace
For all He allows us to see.

Robert E. Dafft

Home Sweet Home

I once lived in the country,
But I just did not belong,
Even though the flowers were pretty
And the birds burst into song.

There's another place I know of
With its flowers and birds so merry
It's that lovely formal garden
That they call a cemetery.

So I moved back to the city;
Twas the only real solution;
I don't want to die of boredom;
Let me die of air pollution.

Marion Ahlborn

"World Of Skin Color Issues?"

If...red men were to..constantly...
Hate white men...due to...history...
If black men were to ..contemplate...
Revenging back for...slavery...
If yellow men would follow..suit...
People!...
In techni-skin-colors..monster-hue
God's green earth...would be painted..
Tragically.......blue!

Nefertiti Louiza Flama Meyer Jr.

The Beast Within

Deep within the cave he lies;
An angry beast with raging eyes.
Smoke pours from his ugly snout.
The air is thick with fear and doubt.

Around his leg he wears a chain.
Against it, he does pull and strain,
But cannot be free from his dark bonds;
Cannot escape to worlds beyond.

He belches forth steam and fire;
His eyes glow red with raging ire,
And the scales from his body fall
As he struggles in the slimy thrall.

Then, exhausted, he must rest.
But the beast remains distressed;
This beast who dwells in the dark hole;
In the cavern of my soul.

Kathy A. Carder

Silent Night, Peaceful Night

In a forgotten war long ago,
Peacemakers were talking.
Guns were firing,
Men were fighting.
The peacemakers kept talking.
The guns kept firing.
Men kept dying.
The peacemakers reached accord,
Only twelve more hours of war.
The guns kept firing.
Men kept dying.
Light faded, darkness fell,
The time grew near.
The guns kept firing.
The men caught hell.
An eternity passed.
The hour was here.
The guns fired their last.
Silent night, peaceful night.

Walter Randolph Johnson

The One For Me

The guy I love, the one for me,
Something I dream so perfectly.
The misting rain, stars shining bright,
I feel your arms holding me tight.
Your gentle lips and silky skin,
What is this heaven I am in?
Can this moment last forever,
You and me, alone together?
A passionate kiss and long embrace,
That sacred look upon your face.
And then it's dark and I can't see,
Was he ever a reality?
Morning has come, I wake again,
And things are as they've always been.
No perfect night, no perfect guy,
Alone again, I start to cry.
I wish upon each star above,
That someday soon I'll find this love.
When my dreams become reality,
With the guy I love, the one for me.

Jaime Mallett

Look To The Future

Teach the little children
Teach them right from wrong
Teach the little children
Teach them to be strong.

Fill their hearts with wonder
See the happiness in their smile
Fill their eager minds with knowledge
See the wisdom in their eyes.

Teach the little children
All so innocent and bright
They are the future generation
And deserve the best in life.
Linda Gavana

Lacy Snowflakes

Whirling in
the dark
night,
Lacy snowflakes of
silver and white
softly fall
dancing all
around,
blown into a hazy
mist,
creating a blanket
of twisting
snowflakes,
the moonlite
shines brightly
across the snow.
Meghan Farrell

A Question (?) Of Why

Just the other day she asked me?
Why I linger

She said tell me just the reason Why.

And Why do you pursue me?
Why am I your desire

And I say

You see, I am like a flower
that blooms Everyday

And your Essence is like the Sun
And I drink your every Ray.
Christopher Trigg

The Journey

O life you are as a river,
    ever moving on and one.

Sometimes a rage of rapids,
    sometimes very calm.

Sometimes plunging over falls,
    sometimes over rocks - I see.

A cork upon the ocean,
    a ship upon the sea.

Nothing for an anchor,
    or security.

But when I meet the ocean,
    the droos shall break away.

And I shall rest in my
    Father's arms that day.
Jessie M. Combs

How Do I Know

I can cry with her
Or I used to be able to
Because she's large
And unambitious

She says she was ambitious
But two breakdowns stopped her
She can function well
But is afraid to push

When I saw we're incompatible
She calls me a judgmental
Psychiatrist - to - be
Upwardly mobile
P.I.
Uptight
New Yorker

Since she's right
How do I know
If to leave
Laura L. Post

November Snow

OCTOBER left NOVEMBER
her leaves still golden green.
Not waiting for DECEMBER, SNOW
slipped in upon the scene.

Snowflakes now lightly falling -
each one, its own design -
on balsam wreath and evergreens,
on every lacey vine.

Softly fell the snowflakes
on everything in sight.
Soon Maple leaves were wearing
capes of snowy white.

Snow blossoms in the ivy,
a carpet on the lawn,
a snowcap on the wren house,
came morning, she had gone.
Velma Ilsley

Love

Love is like a burning candle.
It always burns strong,
And lasts all night long.
But sometimes when the flame
Burns down,
The relationship ends.

But sometimes,
Love is like the ocean waves,
They always come crashing
Against the soft, wet sand.
But one day,
When the waves stop
Coming, and the sand
Stays hard and dry,
You know the love is
Gone.
Cherilyn Swenson

Aspens

Winds blow Aspen trees
Turning their leaves upside down
Yellow until spring
Jeanine Cappuccino

Another World

Sitting on my bed
Our legs braided
Warming my feet with
His loving touch

Probing my eyes
For a clue of
Where I had gone

I was dreaming of
Another world
Another time
Another place
Where my roots are woven

But my leaves touch
The wind
Blowing my soul to
Another world
Where I might find
The love
I so desperately need
Debra A. Ruby

Banjo Ode

What cool shadow of some
Bright light kisses my eye
Leaving that emerald green
Wreath around my heart
And swells my thirsty lungs
With such passionate heat
That I stretch into every
Tomorrow, breathing eternity's
Sweet everlasting breath
And view my laughing self
On the high-cumulus mirrors
Of ever-present intellect?
Michael Scott

If You Call That A Relationship
I Must Be Crazy To Want You Back

You left me behind without a word.
To stick around I would've preferred.
No hide, no hair, no trace to be found.
I scream at the sky, a rock I pound.

Our lust
My trust
Turned into rust.

Your last gift to me was only pain.
Standing here by myself in the rain.
Pins in my eyes, a knife in my heart.
To let you go is the hardest part.

You gave
My grave
Cannot be saved.

Your soft caress, your tender kisses.
No one listening to my wishes.
Asleep in my bed without a care.
I thought we made a wonderful pair.
Mark Brannan

Flowering

I am like a flower
Waiting to blossom
Give me a little care
And I shall open my petals
And grow beautiful with you.
Marjorie T. Sommerville

Chasing Dreams

Don't go chasing butterflies
Why run after the wind
Dreams show through your eyes
And love shows from within

Why do you search for a clover
Why are you wishing on a star
Why stand till the anthem's over
You can dream right where you are

Looking for a pot of gold
At every rainbow's end
Will only make you gray and old
I want to be your friend

Plant your feet on the ground
Here's where you need to be
Two hearts make a lovely sound
Why don't you dream of me

Why trust your wishes on a star
When I'll make them all come true
Don't toss your dreams out so far
I'm down here waiting for you

Ginger Adkins

Public Conscience

I see Him in the beam of sun
Dancing on the bars.
I know He is the Only One
As I look up at the stars.

My Master's shoes I'll never fit
As hard as I try to be humble.
How did I get into this pit?
Night sweats hear me mumble.

My innocent cry is ignored
The court was cruel to me.
But in my cell I'm never bored
God brings me to my knee.

Bankrupted is our freedom fund
God needs to clearly call.
When one boy is unjustly prisoned
Man has imprisoned all.

When the system seems to fail you
Think a little bit about me.
Speak out with your conscience true
That's the only way I'll ever be free.

Charlotte Vogel

Untitled

Of all the things twixt mice and men
nothing equals my old white hen
While I am at play
she for me an egg doth lay
If I can keep this biddie on my knee
I could go on to eternity
With BOOTS beside me on the floor
I could go on for evermore
and when we meet St. Peter at the gate
we will never, never have to wait

Jerry Crozier

Friends

Keep this picture on your wall,
In hope your spirits never fall.
Remember me, but please don't cry,
I know our friendship will never die.

Julie Hunter

"My People"

Come to our home and sit awhile.
We can reflect and wear a smile.
We'll talk about our daily due,
To all of our pals, just like you,
And just remember this my "friend,"
That's what you are until the end!

N. A. Thompson

In Here

If you can see
from where you are
the very cold
and grey of day
then you're with me
inside somewhere.
The fire's warm.
Oh, about life,
we do not care.
So hide away
inside that place
and you will find
it's not so bad.
It's better than
the war out there.

Greg J. Gunsch

Seagulls

If the years pass without posin'
they would be white clouds
of strange seagulls...
But if passing
the years are posed,
just laugh of its disillusions...

Guido Féliz

Winters Near

The wind is blowing
Crisp and clear. The air on
My face smells of winter
Near. The leaves on the trees
Are turning brown, and in a
While there will be snow on
The ground.

Children will slide
Out on the ice and play in
The snow until time to
Go in the house. They will drink
Hot chocolate and warm their
Hands, then be ready to go
Out again.

When evening comes and they
Are all in the house. They will
Snuggle by the fire as quiet
As a mouse. The wind outside
Is cold and clear. That is
When we know that winter is
Near.

Maxine Talley

Bedding

A rack of hay.
A stall of straw.
Not for
The thoroughbred racer;
But a place for me.
Homeless!

Donald W. Lawrence

Night

I am the sun smart and silent
my friend the sky light and dark
plays with magic stars
I cry to the moon my love
who whispers dreamy music to me
inside the song is night
that slowly twirls out upon all.

Nicole Kathryn Ramsey

The Voyage

The wind is in the sails
and the ship is out to sea
What has this to do
with such as you and me?

Now, sweeping by an iceberg,
given birth by frigid air
we're coming into danger,
most would never dare.

A whirlpool's foamy edge
compels us closer yet;
Though we manage to escape
the worst has not been met.

Upon a sandy bar we're washed,
a most forsaken place;
At last, a blustery gale
draws us into forward pace.

Forboding clouds reveal
our meager plans are still
Inept to meet the challenge.
it's time to seek God's will.

Florence P. Bullis

Survival

What can a soul do to retain
its essence, lacking due to pain
inflicted and which now remains
within it so engrained.

Surrounded by great loneliness
it cannot help but to regress
in silence, to feel its distress
and its healing to address.

Once healed, this soul will survive
and in it will there be imbibed
the formula which was prescribed
for it to be revived!

Judith Acevedo

Forgiving

Sometimes it really hurts,
Admitting we are wrong.
People write it in a poem,
Others say it with a song.

Just to say "I'm sorry,"
Today, does not hold true.
Sincere apologies aren't said by words,
Rather, by actions that we do.

So, leave the past behind,
And judge not wrong or right.
For time will heal old wounds;
The future can be bright.

N. Loy Higgins

Earth

Earth
  loaned, but only for awhile
  taken for granted
  our future in jeopardy
Animals
  sleek, beautiful, free
  slaughtered, endangered, extinct
  only for money, for enjoyment
Rivers
  once flowing wide, clean, deep
  now empty, polluted
  what do we drink tomorrow?
Trees
  so tall, touching the heavens
  cut down, dead
  giving us life nor shade anymore
Humans
  at fault, killing our own
  changing, giving new life, new hope
  its never to late to change

    Jenny Lynn Durst

Money Woes

As a child I was told-
Don't spend every cent
Or one day when you are old
You'll wonder where it went.
That is Money Woes!

You work all day long
For food and rent
You wonder what went wrong
And ask where it was spent.
That's Money Woes!

Very little went for enjoyment-
Necessities for you-kids and wife.
Hanging on by God's providence
Just barely enough to sustain life.
That's Money Woes!

You can't take it with you I'm told
Your worldly goods you must leave,
Shucks, I didn't have enough to hold
Just debts with which to grieve.
Now that's Money Woes!

    Odessa Roberts

Texas Snow

Drifting silently
Caught up on the wind,
It swirls through the air.
Frozen water confetti
Falls to the earth.
From the sky to the ground,
It melts into the dirt.
Nothing really more than
Dressed-up rain.

    Heather Loyd

To My Son Pete

Oh! Where oh where is my sailor
I wonder where he can be?
Is he wandering over the land?
Or is he sailing the seas?
You know I love my sailer boy,
I miss him constantly.
And every night I pray for the day,
When he'll be returning to me.

    Grace Washburn

Nostalgia

How could I know in childish dark
That the whistle of a field lark
Would at some future date
Bring to mind a nostalgic state

And how could I know
As onward I'd go
That wind whistling through trees
Would recall past memories

When as a child on a farm
Though no cause for alarm
Sometimes I'd be afraid
As I sat in the trees shade

How could I know these would be
Things I'd have with me
For a lifetime through
To share and enjoy here with you

    Cleo Mills-Coffin

Early Christmas Morning

I saw a ship come sailing in
To placid Biscayne Bay.
The air was cool and crystal clear,
'Twas early-a blessed day.
From the ship resounding notes
Buoyed 'cross a sandy bar.
A joyous sound of happiness,
For souls both hear and far.
I ask a friend to name the strain,
The music was so pure.
Every eye within its range,
Had tears like mine I'm sure.
Notes so clear, like silver bells,
Caused my frame to sway.
'Twas a joyful tune a bugler blew-
For it was Christmas Day.

    A. R. Jack Banks

The Feel Of Being Here

I like the feeling of being here
A part of the wind and sea.
I even think the great big moon
Is some sort kin to me.

Oh, I like the feel of being here,
A part of the happy crowd.
In a parade I love to march,
Because you just so proud.

On frosty days I feel the sun
As warm as a kiss of love.
I climb the highest hill
And feel protected from above.

On summer days I find a big old tree
Full of singing birds,
And read a stirring book
Or make up songs to my own words.

Just any old thing to know I'm here,
And that's why I feel so proud.
Along with heaven, earth and you!
I was allowed.

    Alice Spohn Newton

Keeping Marriage Alive

Marriage is a leap of faith
Into the future taken
This is a holy union
Sometimes forgotten by humans

Be a kind and faithful mate
Making marriage happy estate
Humble yourself and be meek
Enjoying bliss so unique.

Mutual interest do invoke
Days for pleasure you devote
Take time for daily prayer
Respect and understanding share.

Like a record marriage is
Receiving both sides sometimes a quiz
To their husband wives submit
Trusting your knowledge to commit.

Compare not your lot with others
Thanking God for being together
When you are aged and gray
Keep loving in the same way

    Shirley Brigham

Nostalgia

Romance used to beckon me
To follow her each place,
Through Art, and Love, and Science,
She led a merry chase.

She startled me, surprised me,
By her beguiling airs,
And though I thought I knew her well,
She always caught me unawares.

She showed me untold beauty,
And laid her treasures bare,
So I might catch a glimpse of love
And find enchantment everywhere.

But then, one day, I lost her
Through human frailty,
And now, I cannot reach her,
She wants no part of me.

Sometimes, I chance to meet her,
And she will talk with me,
Emotionless, passionless,
Of days that used to be.

    Virginia W. Loehlein

Autumn Muse

Autumn's here, and I do fear
that winter's coming soon;
until then, with leaves again
ablaze in varied hues,
trees are crowned with "hats" renowned
that they so soon will lose.

Easter's parade with hats arrayed
can never match this scene;
golden, reds, russet heads
amid the shades of green.
Color abounds and rustling sounds
do fill the senses keen.

Soon I know, cold winds will blow,
the leaves will flutter down;
barren trees respond to freeze,
the "hats" will turn to brown.
So will end as leaves descend,
the time of harvest moon.

    Edith S. Anderson

Contests

Another contest?
Now what can I write?
What new theme or text?
Something rather light
Something bright, airy
Doesn't seem to rhyme
Must be smooth, merry
And must be all mine
But when your old mind
Goes completely blank
Wouldn't it be kind
For one to be frank
And to just admit
Though you'd like to be
You're really no wit
As anyone can see.

Florence H. Walker

Caress The Faith

So confident, strong, big and brave.
  Warm as a flickering flame.
It stands behind the door and wait
  As some grave heart is tamed.

The focus is on many dreams
  That often drift away.
There is so many doubts inside
  Faith has no place to stay.

Why do we let it go so quick,
  To grab the deeds of doubt?
When all the keys of doubt won't fit
  The door that is so stout.

Just turn the key to that stout door
  And dream your dreams of life
Caress the faith that lies behind
  To void the coming strife

Brenda Gibson

The New King

Let us worship the new king,
Let us follow the star
Shining over a stable,
Guiding us from afar.

Angels came to the shepherds
In the early morn
Heralding the tidings,
The holy child is born.

In a manger Jesus lay,
He has come to us this day;
If we serve Him and adore
We shall live forevermore.

Let us find the manger,
Let us tribute bring;
God our Father sent us
His most precious thing.

What shall we give to Jesus
Sent from Heaven above?
He who came to save us
Let us give Him our love.

Margaret Evans Wright

'The Kid In The Hall'

Was he real or wasn't he
She really had to know
So she decided to stay up late
She wouldn't let Santa go.
She quietly got out of bed
And slipped into the hall
There she sat an hour or two
Watching the tree so tall.
Would Santa come our wouldn't he
With his reindeer and his sled?
She watched and waited patiently
Though she should have been in bed.
Then Mom came into the room
Carrying presents in her arms
A dollhouse, big and beautiful
With elegant style and charm.
Now the secret was no more
As Mom bent beneath the tree
Her eyes fell on the little girl
And that little girl was me.

Esther M. Thomas

A Bright Light

A bright light came
Shinning forth on a cold
Dark night so long ago
It shone upon a crude
Manger, where a new born
Child did lay

From miles and miles the
Travelers came to worship
An adore
Who would think that
Thousands of years later
That same baby's birth
Would be celebrated with
Songs, Christmas trees
And mistletoe

Yes, today that bright
Light still shines
Fourth and gives the
Gift of hope, peace
And law

Cloamae Suiters

Dreaming Of Winter

The time goes
The wind blows
The seasons come and go
First it's spring
Then it's fall
Then it starts to snow
Some love the sun
When there's time for fun
On the beach and in the water
But in the fall
I hear the call
Of the forest and the otter
The owl hoots
The deer runs
The fox is in his den
The snow falls
The wolf calls
Winter's come again

Mary Ellen Steinhagen

Beacon

A candle in the window, a light,
to show the way. The lost and,
lonely soul, struggling to find its
place, confused, empty, a heart
so full of pain, The burning brightly,
candle, dripping wax forever, if need
be. Should the lonely soul pass by,
sees the candle in the window. The
heart will heal itself, the soul free
of loneliness, to know at last, a place
with love, and warmth, a place, called
  home. The candle put to rest!

Wendy Casey

"Birthday Wishes"

You know your getting old
When your skin starts to
look like an old lace curtain.
And your feet are always cold
You not at all certain
what color your hair used to be
You need glasses to see
Dentures are a must
and you have to look
in the dictionary for the
meaning of lust!
But getting old isn't so bad.
So cheer up don't be sad
after all it's just another day
and he glad your still alive!
Happy Birthday!

Hilda Horton

The Way That Beauty Goes

Beauty rises in the spring
Though not an everlasting thing
Just as the melting winter snows
Such is the way that beauty goes.

Once the flowers met by frost
One can see the beauty lost
Much like the wilting of a rose
Such is the way that beauty goes.

Dare I pose the question why
Does the beauty have to die
For as everybody knows
Such is the way that beauty goes.

Mitchell Coleman

Singles Bar

I mingled with the crowd
A single plot exposed to hope
A lot for me
Then filling a vacancy
For two
Motioned up myself a brew
I drank the rhythms
While the drink went flat
Nursed thinking this is where it's at
But when the future
Would... Not... Come
I ordered up two coffees
Black for one
And two to go

Mila Vonderheid

Tears Quietly Shed

With a lock of hair
and a cross of silver
you will be burned.

Tears of children are
quietly shed as they
are forced to learn.

The church bells won't be
ringing and the earth will
remain unturned.

Mournful crowds are numb
with grief, as they attempt
to fray the hurt.

Longing for days gone
by, but knowing we must
continue on.

Your love will always
be felt, remembered and
vital to us.

Jennifer Moskal

Clouds

Did you ever take time
To look up in the sky?
To watch the white clouds
As they go floating by?

They take forms and shapes.
Sometimes thin out or thicken.
There's one looks like a parasol
And that one a fluffy kitten.

That one looks like
A long string of pearls
And that one looks like
Two curly haired girls.

There's a little dog
And there's a horse
And he's pulling something,
It's a wagon, of course.

Just use your imagination
And you will see,
All the fun you can have,
And it's absolutely free.

Fanny Lee Baker Shaw

Untitled

   Angels filled the hand of God
while darkness covered all —
   He let them loose to beautify
a world that soon would fall —
   Now, Lights of Night, the angels
shine and brighten the night sky —
   Like stars, the angels, they
do shine like the twinkle of
God's eye —
   I thank you, LORD, for your
creation; the beauty of the
night —
   I thank you, LORD, my true
friend, for your angels, our
starlight —

Brian Stuchell

The End Of The Road

The end of the road, I cannot see.
Its path gives me no clue.
At each new fork, I pause a while
to determine what to do.
A time of peace to clear my thoughts —
explore some new insight.
Each dendrite path implores me
to choose its path outright.
Each path stems from common seed
planted deep inside of me.
The end can only yield the fruit
of my thought's pedigree.
Greeting me at the end of the road,
whether good or catastrophe,
is consequence of one root cause
—desire's heredity
Go here. Go there or go no where,
are choices I can make.
What meets me at the end of the road
is never a mistake.

Hazel Goodwin

"My Grandfather"

Grandfather, I lost you one day
I still wonder why

There never was a day go by
that I wasn't sad

I guess it's the way
God intended it to be

I felt like my heart was gone
I didn't want to live on

I wanted to go with you
but maybe it wasn't meant to be

I wanted to say goodbye
But everything I tried
inside I'd just die

I know your still a part of me
that's the way you will remain

Everyday in my heart
forever you will be

Kimberly A. Gill

Unrequited Interlude

I remember a late summer day,
And the journey of your hands
Against the smoothness of my skin.
Traveling my body
As though they'd been there before.
I remember the fullness of your mouth
Pressed softly against mine.
The tenderness of your lips
As you inspired me to greater passion.
The breathlessness of our bodies
Intertwined in desire.
I remember the warmth,
The smell,
The taste of you.
I don't understand,
When you say,
That what you felt
Was empty.

Geri Swift

Seeking Stability

Inner madness,
That crazy part
   which defies
   life's realities;
And nurtures
Its own self.

Inner madness,
That chaos
   which is unto itself
   and impregnates
The given reality
Of everyday life.

Lawrence Michael Dickson

A Picture Of You

I'll paint a picture of you
A lovely moon beam
A star or two
But where will I put little me?

I'll smear a cloud across the sky
Like fresh dipped ice cream
And then I'll close my eyes to look
And dream and dream and dream.

I'll paint a picture of you
A lovely moon beam
A star or two
But where will I put little me?

John M. Altman Sr

The Beltway Scene

On long stretches of concrete lanes
Move life's must do weekly game
Bumper to bumper of metal lines
Snail's pace getting to work on time.
Fingers tap on steering wheels
As if the rhythm could heal
Frustration that seethe within
It's Friday and grid-lock again.
Radios blast rattling brains
With rap music and talk show complaints
Thoughts of the day come through
To be or not your contract renew.
An optimist honks from behind
An angry retort comes into mind
You grit your teeth taut your neck
Better to keep your temper in check.
A boom of thunder deluge of rain
Summer's heat can drive one insane
The car in front picks up speed
Life moves on in the beltway scene.

Eleanor F. Basinger

Sharin' The Sporran

Gordon sired two bonny bairns —
Shy Martin and bold Harry.
Both eschewed lowlander's kilt
Till day lads chose to marry
Highland lassies top of brae
Where they by choice would tarry —
Mild Martin clad in tartan,
Wild Harry in Glengarry.

Judith Pike Boos

Rivers Edge

At
rivers edge,
a sparkling day
of rest,
a soft caress
shimmering
in light of
shadows and shade
whispering
haunting melodies
on oceans of wind
abundantly inviting
a rambling stroll
wandering aimlessly
upon smiles
and frowns
setting wonders free
where mountains rise
to meet the sky
and rainbows passing by.

Marvin Blevins

Don't Stand At My Grave

Do not stand at my grave and weep
I am not there, I do not sleep
I'm all you feel, both love and pain
The soft and gentle autumn rain
I am a thousand winds that blow
And diamond glints upon the snow
I leave you, with a smile of mine
I'm still with you, all the time
So, don't stand at my grave and cry
I am not there, I did not die-

Dori Dennis-Vasquez

No Telling

I was going to tell everyone about him
But there wasn't much to tell
A week's flirtation, a few sweet notes
A beautiful book
Now nothing.
If I had bragged
I'd have to make excuses
While everyone asked
Where'd he go?
I did tell a few friends
Who now hear me sob
If he ever writes again
I won't even tell myself.

Barbara R. DuBois

The Simple Things

The simple things
That mean so much
Seem always to be
Just beyond touch

A life to share
A love to hold
Someone to care for
As I grow old

Sweet memories to carry
To our golden years
Not sitting alone
Blinded by my tears—

Jim Brogan

Withering Away

As your lying there
and withering away
I ask the Lord
Just to take you away
To spare you of all
the pain that you have
Taking you home and
freeing you at last

But if it's God's will to keep you here
With all your pain and suffering
I pray that soon, this is the day
He will come down to pardon you
Yet we know as God's children
A cross we do carry
And when it's done
And the race is won
Our Eternal home we can cherish

Iva L. Foor

Pen As Piton As Pen

He is ever aware of plummeting
to his death
whenever he meets the challenge
in the clouds.

The poet like the mountain climber
scaling to
reach the pinnacle of his dream,
also wary.

Both seek limits far beyond
endurance.
One uses pitons, ropes
and courage.

The other, ideas, words and sheer
audacity.
The climber's poem is massive;
Everest is!

But a mountain is no loftier
than a poet's
impassionate
bid for truth.

Dorothy Hom

Untitled

And someone reached
the center
and found it sharp
and hard

God know's it's solid
That's what makes us tick

And someone found it weighty,
like lead,
only harder, more severe

It's always so rigid here —
at our core

There's no place to lay your head
We just carry on
and place our bets

We gamble on ourselves again
and expect to come up Aces

Yet, here we are strip mining —
holding spades

P. J. Neary

Narrow Is The Way

Nettled-narrow is the win-ward way,
Man-mined and mettle-measuring for
Miles and miles, more miles of
Blinders on, atop buffoonery's back,
On cramped-course carousel
Near jaded jungle jammed with
Jeering jealous and with
Myriad monsters of the mix,
Through elongated ebony
Till mercy-morning when
Closed channel widens into field of
Reckoned wreaths and laurel leaves—
Where lingering Love laughs last.

John Lenox

"It's Mine"

"Don't touch it," it's brittle,
and it's mine.
Just let what's inside,
Be given to one who,
Is now deserving.
I guess I must
be now conserving,
With what I have left
Of that brittle pierce.
I can confide, in time,
That inside, there's a love so divine
Not just anyone is worthy,
Of this would be cherished port.
I must not intrust it.
In the wrong hands again.
For it's brittle, and it's mine,
Everything has the proper place.
It may be brittle, but it's mine.
I must not intrust it,
In the wrong hands again.

Mary Christine Lucas

A Gift Sent From Heaven

I'm so excited
to finally hear,

I'm sure you're lit up
and filled with cheer.

His little hands
reaching up to say,

How special it is
this glorious day.

How precious he is
so fragile and small

But watch him closely
and remember it all.

You see his eyes
and head of hair,

And you thank the Lord
from Heaven up there.

Now he's here
and you're filled with joy,

Congratulations
on your new baby boy.

Janice Pierson

The Wife

I sit at home
and wait and wait
to give applause
and fill his plate
and wash the floor
and walk the dog
and again, in bed, applaud.

And later
when I'm all alone
I bake the bread
and dust his throne
and wait to cheer
him so some more
and forget, again, what for.

A dreamy, lazy kind of life
with no demands;
I play the wife
and clap my hands.

Susanna Ralli

Miniature Music Boxes

Children's minds are
Intricately tuned
Delicate music boxes;
Small carved containers
Engraved with colors
Hold their inner sounds.

When sensitive hands
Gently touch them
And open the lids,
Lovely little melodies
Come pouring forth,
And beauty unfolds.

Mary Sullivan

Dreams

When young and carefree
Dreams of great deeds,
Of accomplishing the impossible,
Are ours to possess.

If a dream is shattered
We simply replace with another;
Put together from the pieces
And set a new course.

One key to staying young,
Is having the ability
To keep dreams alive,
When faced with the impossible.

Dreams are the fuel,
Keeping hopes alive;
Keeping us looking to the future;
Giving us a vision
"That tomorrow will be a better day."

Kenneth A. Tucker

Untitled

I like shopping, basketball
Baseball, soccer, and a swoop
In the goal!

I like school, classmates,
Books, and to be cool!
Boyfriends, girlfriends, and
My teacher too!

Katie Gann

A Mothers Prayer

Heavenly Father
So full of love and grace
Bless my son's cute little face
Bless his hair and that little curl
He's the cutest in the world
Bless his hands that are so small
Bless the way that he plays ball
Bless his feet that like to run
And bless the way the he has fun
Bless his kisses that are so sweet
Just bless my son from his head
to his feet.

Donna Langley

The Greatest Peace

Just to sit and stare,
sometimes, is the greatest peace.
Just to watch the wind through
the trees, or the water glisten
with a certain ease.
Leaves my soul rested.
To be able to sit silently, with
thoughts about everything
running through my head...
is the most wonderful quiet.
A bird here and there
could never interrupt, the joy
of my heart,
When I peacefully, quietly
stare from the deck, content, with
myself, and the world.

Katherine M. Watters

Remember The Raincrow

One time I heard its haunting call
When I was young and very small,
"What is that bird?" I asked beguiled,
My wise and gentle father smiled,
"It is the raincrow, and its trill
Is heard by those who think no ill.
My golden child, your soul is new
And that is why it called to you,
You think no ill, but as you grow
You must remember the raincrow."
I trained my ears to know the note
That came from its elusive throat,
I sought it on the highest hill
And listened for its call until
My ears became undisciplined,
The sounds I heard were just the wind.
I thought the forest might reveal
Or that the wilderness would yield
The mystic bird I longed to see,
But never more it called to me...

Rosemary Muntz Yasparro

When Is It Spring?

When rain is falling everywhere
When magic is in the air
When grass gets greener everyday
When kids are out to play
When bicycles call to our feet
We know we can't stay on one street
When we hear baby birds sing
We're definitely sure it's spring!

Shannee S. Koenig

"Shipwrecked"

She's going down
After 20 years of "sailing" together.
She's going down.
I'll be swimming
alone,
In the endless sea.

She's going down,
After we have "sailed"
late, in our years.
The "voyage" has been
a "happy voyage"

but
Her mind is going
slowy.

Our adventure
is ending with
happy memories.
Sadly,
She's going down!

Allan L. Gauntlett

Rising Above The Circumstance

Father, take me above the clouds
To skies clear and blue
High above the circumstance
That lingers here like dew.

I want to look to you on high
And find peace within your face
Rising above pain and strife
Once more receiving your grace.

You are all sufficient
To meet my every need
You call me far beyond
Life's care if I will heed.

By faith you renew my strength
I'll soar on eagle's wings
Singing praises to you
Will remove me from earthly things.

Thank you Lord, for your provisions
That enable me to flee
Once more to your throne of grace
Your faithfulness to see.

Peg Antle

Aftermath

When candles burn with black flames,
the guilt of one,
who no one blames,
the last setting of the sun,
as endless night descends,
I treasure what I see one last time,
the way a day ends,
even if it is only filth and grime,
today I bid farewell,
to the master of the lofty heights,
the ringing of the bell,
for on and on only nights,
the unvoiced question why,
echoes softly as I cry.

Caitlin Reynolds

Memories

Memories dance through my mind
  on winged feet.
Thoughts of days and nights past
  linger long behind the windows
  of my eyes, chasing sleep, twisting
  and turning toward the dawn of
  another page of my life.

Shall I turn the memories loose,
  let them float away? Or shall
  I hold them close, remembering
  all that has gone before?
Shall I throw away the good memories
  and keep the bad?
  Letting the good ones slide under
  the curtain of time, to bring
  happiness to other minds,
  keeping the bad ones confined,
  so they can neither corrupt
  nor blind?

  Phyllis Peter

Writing

When the pen writes
  blotches become words
  a stroke of genius

When the pen writes
  words from meaning
  progress awaits

When the pen writes
  imagination takes shape
  sentences bring life

This is communicating
  imparting one's own self

  Julianne Blommer

"When You Do That You Do"

When you do that you do
Let it be that and done
Do the best that you can
Let it all be in fun
Practice hard, work it good
Give it all that you've got
Finish entirely, prize it helpful
While it's still running hot
Tag it priceless, honor it double
Reveal to show the world your best
Display the joy you've found creating
"Tis done" a worthwhile treasure chest

  Rhonda K. Vaughn-Flowers

Let Me Lean On You

Keep your eyes upon me,
Keep me in your sight,
Help me down the crooked road,
Lead me to the light.
The road I'm on is dark,
I'm not sure I know the way,
Yet with you right beside me,
I'm certain I won't stray.
Protect me from the world,
I know we'll make it through,
Give me all the strength I need,
Let me lean on you.

  Rachel Sonnett

And That Ain't Far

The snow on the ground —
Makes the year all new,
And when I close my eyes,
I can envision you.

Sitting by the fire —
Smiling and warm,
Knowing that I,
Will keep you from harm.

The memories you gave me —
Before you left,
Will settle my —
"I miss you" debt.

Just remember this —
Wherever you are —
You are in my mind,
And that ain't far.

  Wendy Lacy

"The House We Built"

We built a house before
the storms could rage
the howling wind gave
the roof a jar.
We felt our work was
a stumbling failure
Then the winds
and sun with
blooms came.
Our home has creaks
and troubles to
But comfort we feel
And safe and secure.
Our house of love
Is now a home.

  Barbara Grass

Don't Hurt God's Little Children

Somewhere a child is suffering
  At the hands of someone cruel.
Beaten and neglected
  Not able to go to school.

A little heart is so sad
  And doesn't understand
Why he keeps hitting her,
  This big grown man.

Don't hurt God's little children.
  Be gentle and kind to them.
He tells us to take care
  For they belong to Him.

God only loaned them to us
  From Heaven up above.
He gave them to us a short time
  To cuddle, teach and love.

  Alma Smith

Girl

I notice men
  looking at me
from a distance

They used to
  look away
as they got close

But now
  they keep looking

  Kenneth Nohe

Untitled

To hold your hand
Look into your eyes
kiss your lips
these actions tell no lies

To whisper softly
or to deeply converse
we get along so well
and without rehearse

To laugh comes natural
to smile with ease
my expressions will tell you
it's my heart that you please

So I'll tell you again
and not just times two
this is forever baby
I LOVE YOU!

  Wileen Gausman

Life

  Life itself does not bring
us happiness; it is the people
we share our lives with that
make us smile.

  Life itself does not bring
us sorrow; it is the things
that happen to the one's we
love that make us frown.

  Life without someone to love;
is as bad as life without
being loved.

  If a life of love you need
to live; than a life of love
you need to give.

  Robert J. Boucher

Timeless Message

Don't wait to say "I Love You"
To someone you hold dear
Don't wait for perfect timing,
But tell them while they're here.

It's such a small, small gesture
That means so very much
It fills the heart with gladness,
Like a mighty magic touch.

Much sorrow would be fleeting,
If we only learned to say
With feeling and with meaning,
"I Love You More Each Day".

Don't wait to say "I Love You"
You may not have the time,
But let God's love within you
Reflect your love sublime.

  Ruth Sievers

As Feelings Change

As the sun sets slowly,
the beautiful colors fade.
The red, yellow, and orange
start to become gray.
Loneliness sets in,
when gray turns to black,
and all I have are memories,
while wishing for you to come back.

  Brian Marain

The Holiday Season, The ACLU And A Nightmare Of Ignorance

The nightmare prevails:
the town lays dark and quiet:
burlap shrouds drape mosque,
synagogue and cathedral spire:
bells silenced
menorahs unlit
lest these symbols of faith
unite in celebration and,
somehow, cross-pollinate.

Mind in turmoil
struggles thru' silent scenes
of nothingness: wavering
until a searching eye gleans
un-shrouded skies
where the universe
glitters with brilliance
that illuminates beyond
control of human ignorance.

The defining touch of "GOD"?

Sara Hewitt Riola

Truth

The spark was ebbing
its brief and bleak flickering
pulsed ever slowly
until, in the dying embers, where
only the fading core could be
perceived,
came a flash
nurtured and strengthened by
the voice of the wind
and it flickered, out of impulse
at first, then with confidence
spread into flame and raged
until its anger mellowed
into the warm light of truth
and
burned
brightly.

Chris Mastrogiovanni

Untitled

Babies cry,
the sound is lost
in the wind,
children cry,
the sound is scattered about,
the dead cry out,
the sound echoes in our minds,
who is living? Who is dead?
Who is crying? Who is silent?

Listen to the winds,
they hold the knowledge you've known,
listen to the echoes,
they hold the secrets you never knew,
listen to the children,
they hold the purity you've lost,
listen to the world,
and open your mind and soul,
so when YOU die,
YOU'LL have lived.

Aviva Shinnar

A Talk In The Night

I lift up my prayers
Like incense.
They rise from me like hiccups.

My petitions hang
Like wind-tossed webs
In leafless trees.

I stare into the numbness
Of the night —
Like into oppression;
Unable to behold your face.

My desire for your closeness
Squeezes my heart
Like a heart attack.

Can't hear your voice;
Through my cries.
Only a wail of a lonely cat,
And crickets praising you.

My needs suffocate my praises.
My heart beats like snare drums
Against the black, lacy night.

Leila Lisebet Tuori Kallio

The Other World

The world is so small tonight;
The way is dark without the light
That shines upon that other plane;
Gladly would I return again.

My soul was stripped of all desire
For human things; a holy fire
Consumes me; I know harmony
And love - and sacred unity.

I am merged within the Ocean,
Swept along by rhythmic motion
To the shore of that strange land
That lies within the Father's hand!

Amelia Nyers

The Surrounding Spell

It is here, love so dear
When one's heart feels mighty
Hear the bell, it's a spell
That of Aphrodite.

It is there, love so fair
Blindly dance the cosmos
Fare thee well, it's a spell
Cast by fledgling Eros.

It's around, love so bound
To be up on cloud nine
Sound the shell, it's a spell
That of St. Valentine.

It is near, fearless fear
It is everywhere
Sear the heart, ne'er apart
Dare thee to tell, to dare.

Michael Brandon Puskar

The One

He's gone.
He'll always be gone,
I may never see him again.
I'll close myself up,
I'll let no one in.
And when that one comes,
If he comes,
He'll feel the pain I did.

Kelly Maddux

A Stupid Poem

Sometimes, somewhere,
If you search
The misty air,
You - yes, you-are sure to find
Something that you'll surely mind.
When your alone,
It knows your secrets,
When your thinking,
It knows your thoughts.
That's whats so scary about it.
Do you know
What I'm saying?
Do you realize
What I mean?
You don't? Too bad,
Because neither do I.
Alone I am alone,
I am alone, I am alone,
My heart aches for laughter.

Jennifer Kipp

A Mothers Love

A mothers love
Is God's blessing sent from above.
Present and never ending
Always endless

A mother love
Who we are guiding us showing the
way, going on through others.
The greatest gift one could receive
from that love.. life

Nothing is as good or as pure
as a mothers love.

True from the heart
bonding forever.
A Mother's love.

Linda Forbes

I Love You Already

Come!
Tell me about
Yourself....

Hurry!
For I get older
By the second..

Also!
Wiser...
So!
Be truthful...

For!
I love you
Already....

Robert Gene Davis

Glimpse

Today I saw
A man with a cane
And a limp of pain
Walking the wet beach sand;
And a very small boy
With face full of joy
Attached to his other hand.

Today I saw
Pure love from the wise,
And the upturned eyes,
Under a baseball cap.
They didn't see me
They were too busy
Closing the generation gap.

Lucille M. Hansen

Power Of Evil

Marching to a stiffened gait.
In uniforms of Blackened slate.
Above their shoulders beyond the eye
A grisly creature with bloodied scythe.

To claim their victory laurels reap.
A rape of peace, their fortunes keep.
Needless lives will soar away.
Bodies draped in horrid display.

In bloody birth chaos reign.
And in broken body maim.
Somewhere the white dove slain.
For power and gold to gain.

Only through sacrifices plain.
Can freedom ever hope regain.
Respiration of peace from the scythe.
For this men, willing to die.

A return of sober sanity.
From death, greed, and vanity.
Ever watchful at the gate.
Catch evil early instead of late.

Thomas Thompson

To Nan

I see myself in you,
A mirror'd reflection
Of gone and coming time.

I hear myself in you,
A need, a longing,
A cry for love.

I feel myself in you,
The impassioned pain
Of inward seeking.

I touch myself in you.
My soul shivers
Against our anguish.

I am myself in you,
In love and sorrow
Complete at last.

Bruce R. Parker

Searching Is Over

You're in my heart,
you're in my soul,
you're in my dreams,
and soon in my life.
I can't imagine a day without you,
in my arms,
or by my side.
Such emptiness fills my world,
When I think of you gone for good,
such inadequacy,
such sadness,
such pain.
You're a wonderful person to me,
no matter what your downfalls,
both past and present,
for if I wanted perfection,
I would spend eternity searching
for something not possible,
and pass something so right,
and so good, you.

Raymond R. Harrold

"Summer Time"

Summer time is just for fun;
go and play out in the sun.
Maybe swimming, maybe talking,
maybe go and do some walking.
Maybe go to other states,
maybe stop and take a break.
Maybe coming home from college,
maybe using new found knowledge.
Throughout the summer having fun,
Before too long it will be gone!

Heather Monteith Warren

Journey Of Life

"In this life
We all endeavor,
To find that peace
And joy forever,
So as we struggle
With all our might,
And always seek
To do what's right,
So that when we cross
To that mystic realm,
We will surely know
Who man's the helm."

Hughie Dale

Untitled

There was a young lady named Rhonda
Whose name inspired quite a quota.
She rode a bike.
She rowed a boat.
She wrote a book
Which wise men quote.
She married Jack Tiller,
A man of great charm.
She's now Rhonda Tiller
And lives on a farm.

Elizabeth M. Worthington

Life's Evanescent Dream

Alas, too soon my spirit tired.
Now my mournful heart, once inspired,
Has become a wound within my breast
Leading me to eternal rest.
The fleeting years have taken toll
On the youthful musing of my soul.
And all my happy childhood dreams,
That danced amongst the soft moonbeams,
Are buried inside a dreary cloud,
Entombed within its ashen shroud.

Yet, somewhere in dusk's gloomy spell
There is a land where dreamers dwell.
A mystic land where all may see
The truth of love's reality.
So as I lose my mortal breath,
And lapse into the sleep named death,
I shall seek that land beyond the sun
Where all people live as one.
Where hope presides and spirits soar.
Then perhaps I can dream once more.

David R. Hoffman

Blackened

Mothers roses are dying
They're fed by tainted hands
the soil has been neglected
the thorns are all that stand

The tender petals fall away
Darkened by lack of light
they crumble into nothingness
becoming black as night

Fathers hands are scarred
they bleed of ignorance and fear
the nails are buried deep
his ears, they do not hear

Summoned rain is screaming
the voices plead to be heard
to laugh becomes a dream
the violence within has stirred

The streets become a shelter
a place to vent their rage
their hands become as weapons
here starts the blackened stage

Leeann Hansen

Things Must Change

The sun shines through the clouds
Raindrops fall from the sky
Mocking birds do sing
In early spring
Seasons do change
Winter, summer, fall and spring
People do grow old
Mistries do unfold
These are some of the things
that we can be sure about
This is the time to have the
joy of your life
Things must change
Plano make beautiful sounds,
that can be heard all over town
Butterflies do fly
Soar like an eagle in the sky and
when they come down
Light on a flower on the ground
Things must change

Willie McKinney Jr.

Love's Song

Beautiful,
 they sit together
Hand softly caressing neck
His fingers
 gliding across her body
Together,
 beautiful music is made
Each possessing the gift,
 but only together
 can create it

His soul,
 pouring out
 through his fingertips
Her heart,
 singing out with joy

Each alone,
 beauty.
Together,
Beautiful.

Jennifer Taylor

Thoughts

Thoughts are like clouds
 Light, floating in space
 Rolling, gathering momentum
 Darkening, threatening
Embracing a universe
 Unseen.

Thoughts are mysterious
 Invisible, powerful,
 Driving, restraining,
 Revealing deep recesses
 Of the mind.

Thoughts are like rain
 Reaching seed
 Within the barren earth
 Reviving buried emotions
 To bring forth
 A harvest of love.

Muriel J. Battiste

Quiet Of Winter

In the distant quiet of winter
When all sit warm by the hearth
I ponder the deepest questions
Of love and its worth

In the shadow of midnight
While all are safe asleep
I dwell on all the memories
That my mind tries to keep

By the break of day
When the sleepers begin to stir
I'm still sitting by the fire
Whispering forgotten words

When the sun rises to the sky
And falls again into the sea
You can still find me here
Thinking of love and what it means

The black of night surrounds me
Thus this day I must depart
Learning at the end of life
Love was always in my heart

Caleb Holt

Boot Camp

Sarafina or Serena
no one should really care
for names are unimportant when
a girl is young and fair

Her hair is black as Plato's cave
her raven eyes are bright
her smile so warm unneeded are
the campfires of my night

In rage I hear the breathing on
this smoke-filled barroom air
from soldiers who would like to get
my jewel out of there

She sees me as the only man
among this bunch of sots
whose mind reflects Platonic thoughts
that's why I grin a lot.

Joseph C. Scanlon

Meeting You At The Alter

As I come down the isle,
tears take over my eyes.
I look around and see all
our friends and family who
have joined together to
celebrate this day with us.

The church is beautifully
decorated with flowers and
candles. As I take your
hand, I can't help but
think how handsome you look.

I can't help but notice
the sparkle in your eye.
It's the same sparkle
I saw on our first date.
Tears also take over your eyes.

This is the day we've been
waiting for, the day we
come together as one.

Tannya Yohn

Angels Unaware

For MCA
She sleeps
How the angels sleep
I can forgive you everything
Because of your cheeks
I'll forgive anything
Because of her cheeks
The Savior kissed
Does she see this earth
When she smiles at me
Are we in heaven
When she dreams
Am I
When she awakens
Why does she return
And make her morning mine
She sleeps
In my hand
She sleeps
And my hand is so small
And she, she is everything

Michael Adamovich

Winter Snow

It painted....A picture
 That pure white snow...
And colored the land...
 Where the flowers grow...

It draped...the trees...
 And the river banks...
It is....to Mother nature...
 That we owe our thanks...

When nighttime falls...
 All...the colored lights glow...
to form...various patterns....
 On the pure White Snow...

The winter scenery...
 Is a sight to behold...
No matter how young...
 No matter how old....

But not matter what...
 Or, for whatever reasons...
To most...it's more popular...
 Of all the four seasons...

Howard Reds Lafty

Funereal

I want the ominous death toll rung;
I want the Dies Irae sung
 At my funeral.

Announce as heretofore
By bell and sacred hymn:
 My fate is sealed.

Let those who morn, with time unspent,
Heed their degree of love
 Of loving fellowmen.

Too late for solace for my sins —
My time is spent; eternity now begins.

I know I must be ready
Before His realm to stand
 And face God's judgment.

His wrath is due, for me.
I've seen His mercy humanly;
 I know He sees me inwardly.

I know You will measure now
Only Thyself wrought out in me.
 Be merciful, I plea.

Anne Marie Behen

Untitled

 Eleven years ago I thought
my life had fell apart;
 But I found out all I
had was a broken heart.
 For my Mom had
passed away;
 And left me on this
earth to stay.
 God must of had a
reason to let her go;
 But till this day the
reason I still don't know.
 I know she loved me;
 Her baby I will always be.
 Until we meet again
 May God love and bless
her - till the end.

Deborah L. Perro

Tears At Midnight

Oh tears
Leave me tonight
I now lie in bed
Too weak to fight
Don't hold me bound
To so much crying
For tomorrow
Is fast approaching.

Tonight I must sleep
Clear my mind
And forget my grief
For I know
When daylight comes
I'll be driven
To weep again
Remembering yesterday's pain.

Florence Pabros Ragudo

'As One'

The gentle breeze
Wraps upon my tiny frame.
A coat almost mother like,
the shadows of past spirits
have coiled together
Mother Earth has spoken
listen to her, in her morning songs
that fill the trees or the
nightly air that fills
an unawakened dawn
Enjoy her womb,it is
our heaven
Mother Earth has spoken.

Brendan Crowley

The Willow Tree

Are we like the willow tree?
Or should we try to be like thee?

Strong yet we can feel the pain
inside.
Yet weeping for some love
outside.

Our branches slanting low
to the ground.
Trying to reach for some
help around.

We are scared, but we try
to hide.
We are strong, but we hurt
deep inside.

So I ask myself...

Are we like the willow tree?
Or should we try to be like thee?

Christina Montano

As I

As I walk through the streets
So empty, and, oh, so all alone,
I wonder about the heartbeats
That now no longer drone.

He walks before me in peace.
The home of God he's found,
His soul no sin shall ever crease
Because to Heaven he's bound.

Joan Wilganowski

My Korean Clock

Its appearance is old and worn,
and its chimes are all chipped.
Yet its spirit is not torn,
and its still well equipped.
Its weathered hands still tick,
and its gears still turn.
Its insides do stick,
but it still can learn.

My Korean clock will never die.
Why it lives on inside of me.
She could never tell a lie,
for good and glad is she.
We all have an old clock,
perhaps known or forgot.
Just always keep her in stock,
and love her a lot.

Elizabeth Lee

Untitled

The rising sun had
no mercy to spare
for I saw death
in your face.
Skin sucked into bone
bulb hollowed sockets
once flesh rested there.
Weary the tendons
that tied muscle and tissue
and bound the body as one.
Sharp and round
protrusions abound
where once there had been none.
Gone all adornment
of human pretension
no hope now for restoration.
Empty the chambers
of my heart
for your soul has already fled.

Susan H. Miller

Regret

Every night the same man
dressed in black, walks
down a dark path
next to the same, old
graveyard, wishing he
had not done what he
had done, his heart
a nonstop drum. People
watch him pass on by,
clutching a drenched handkerchief,
trying to forget everything
that ever happened.

Sabrina Magid

Winter

Winter, it's the best time,
Winter, it's the best time of the year,
Don't you love when it comes here,
We have a snowball fight,
It looks real pretty in the night,
Winter, I love it like a friend,
I like it till the end.

Jordan Coleman

Autumn Princess

The leaf fell like
A princess for a day,
All dressed up in her
New scarlet gown,
Folded and creased
Like party crepe paper.
She waited all summer
To be old enough to go.
Now her mother releases her hand
And she glides elegantly,
Like a kiss blown through the air.
She dances across the earth,
Twirling and skipping,
Like a marionette on a string.

Lisa K. Manwill

Outside

I look outside, and all I see,
Are the birds, hiding in the tree.
Over yonder,
Over there!
Where? They say, where?
How will they see, my little tree,
and all the birds,
and all the bees?
My little tree,
over yonder,
over there.

Lori Yoder

A Grim Fairy Tale

You see, he was my lover;
A noble man was he,
With laughing eyes and tender ways
And standing six foot three.

We'd walk along the river bank
And sing our special song;
I could hardly wait until the day
Our wedding would come along.

We made so many happy plans,
About children, two or three;
We couldn't have been happier,
Such a noble man was he!

I didn't mind his using drugs
Or having another lover;
"Everybody does," he said;
It's fun, as you'll discover."

Well, now my dream is dead and gone
And, sadly, so is he;
You see, as I lie here dying,
I caught his H.I.V.

Bonnie Marriott

Love Has Life To Sell

Eyes that love you...
Spirits that delight,
Holy thoughts that shine
in the night.
Arms that hold
Music rich as gold,
Love has life to see...
Spend all you have on life,
no matter what the cost.
For ever breath of ecstasy...
There as to be a little more.
Love has life to sell.

Helen Studley

Thinking Back

Rainbow colored lights on the water
On a bench sitting close, you and I
Your strong arms wrapped around me
We watched the people pass by

Your lips were sweet like licorice
Your tongue was soft and warm
Your brown eyes bright and sparkling
Your smile so full of charm

We laughed and talked together
We shared our points of view
It was then I knew I loved you
I think you knew it too

Sometimes I still go back there
I sit on that bench all alone
the lights still color the water
they seem to flicker just one-by-one

I think of that night and its colors
though I know it is now in the past
Of the memories we've woven together
In my heart it's the one that will last

Tracy Kelly

Take A Chance

You get a clear view,
as clear as crystals.
Your view is a hollow
hole.
It holds darkness
and anger.

Up ahead is a door.
Behind the door is
happiness and love.
It calls to you.
It's your chance.
Take it.

Amber Gibson

The Game

Evil is an ancient game,
Before that of man or time,
Its control reaches everything,
And all shall play its rules.

Suffer all ye children,
For it comes from within,
None escape from the board,
And all shall feel its wrath.

Who can fight its will,
Look inside its heart,
All will be seen by the brave,
And it shall feast upon the weak.

What is to be learned,
Deep where few dare to go,
Horror awaits the trespasser,
And yet all must try.

Kenneth A. Cook

Crescent Star

If the moon is full
Then something's empty
Maybe my pockets
But not my thoughts
They are full of
Endless rainbow visions
They cast light over
A shadowy day
They make worth of
This my life
I could not trade them
For anything else
But if you wish
I'll share them with
With you until
The moon is full
I would empty my pockets
For you
Hold my thoughts
But not too tight.

Kameron F. Kalb

"The Violet Haze"

Darkness filled
The moon's light.
Clouds covered
The star's blight.
An angel has fallen
To dust this night . . .
Babes mourn
And the children cry.
Why did our hero
Have to die . . .
As the clothes of purple.
Gathered in circle.
Reflections of
The dark light . . .
The green and the red
Turned to each other.
Why, o'why
Did we kill our brother . . .

Ridge Reinhart

Selfishness

You can sit in the dark,
But will it wash away the pain?
You can eternally be alone,
But will it keep away the shame?
They say that you can run-
But you can never, ever hide
So if you run from the truth,
Will you be caught in the tide?
You are only hiding from yourself
Down in that empty shell
You can call it your heart,
But it won't break the spell
For love can be crushed,
And souls can depart,
But no one can fix
A broken heart

Megan Moerke

Life Goes On

When you think
you have that right
    Someone you Love
him to Death
    Then he breaks
up with your for no
reason you want to
die, you don't want
to live because you
don't have that special
someone in your life.
    So what do you
do, I guess you wait
and see if your life
goes on.

Katie Burks

The Golden Arrow

You are the golden arrow that
    runs straight through my heart,
It is very thin and narrow,
    but without it I'd be torn apart.
You may not think you mean
    that much to me,
But are you so blind
    that you cannot see?
I love you, I need you.
I really do.
For if you break that arrow,
    you will break my heart,
Then I will never be the same,
    for I'd be torn apart.

Danielle Sparacio

The Spider Of Spin

Vacant walls
A universe within
The nipple of the earth
A spider of spin
Perverted webs
Ambiguous thoughts
A trap for the prey
For which he is caught
No hope for tomorrow
No knowledge of sin
Suppressed
By the spider of spin

Alison Brita

Friends Forever

Friends are there when you
need them the most.
Friends can be far, yet close
There's one thing about a friend
that doesn't have to be
Here, everyday, for you to see,
When you think about a friend
A smile comes across your face
For no matter what the problems
With friends you feel safe
Friends cannot be measured in money,
Nor any other treasure
Friends are, such a pleasure
Though we're not together.
We will always be
Friends, forever, you and me.

Clarita Tucker Cook

Till Death

Darkness falls
Makes me shiver
Breath lost
Body aches
Time moves slowly
Feel your presence
Silent life
You whisper softly
Words mingle with moans
I can't understand
Hand on my face
So cold and lifeless
Closer now
I smell your breath
Strangely sweet
Of earth and beyond
You whisper again
This time I hear
The words chill me
"Love is forever"

Tracy Dozois

Simon Says

Simon says go
Simon says stop.
One is in love
the other one not.

Simon says one
Simon says other.
One is a flower
the other one none.

Simon says quit
Simon says stay.
One doesn't have
One little say.

None gets other
flower gets hurt.
Now flower has
not one lover.

Simon says bye
Simon says cry.
Flower is done
He has died.

Marelena Gonzales

The Game

She plays her game slow
  In silent deliberation,
Her eyes open wide
  breathing awareness,
Holding on to Faith, hoping
Waiting for chance, calculating
Risk, and she smiles serenely,
'Go slow' she says,
'The world is my field of green,
I will play as I wish,'
  (as I believe)
Slowly she makes her decision
Graceful, an artist, she moves.
Understanding the rules,
  Unaccommodating.
'You must take time,' she says,
Looking at the bewilderment around her.
And she leaves behind
all that is ineffective,
Carrying herself erect, the winner.

Lisa Mathews

My Cloak

Darkness settles about me.
This cloak I've donned
to match the mask
that hides my face
so as not to allow
my eyes to be seen.

I wear the cloak
so no one gets close
close enough to see
to see beyond the mask
that hides my face
to see into my eyes

For that is where the story lies.
The story of loss, defeat,
of pain, of grief,
hopelessness, violation,
and grim despair
too much, too fast,
too soon, without relent

Brian T. Hudgens

Sarah's Dreams

With moonbeams at her fingertips
With caring words upon her lips
Dear Sarah speaks of times to come
Within her heart, the rising sun

The beauty of a young girls laughter
Falling stars and peace thereafter
Sarah's dreams will help her grow
Help her learn what seeds to sow

In her future lies the truth
Found in dreams of Sarah's youth
Sarah sees a world that's kind
In the ripples of her mind

Ponytail, glasses, turned up nose
Dreams that only Sarah knows
Sarah dreams of times to come
Within her, heart and soul are one

Carol A. Rogers

The Vigil

There is a place at journey's end.
Where time begun begins again.
Faint and shy its shadows creep.
Round every corner at verge of sleep.

Beyond the raging world of time,
In quietude rests life sublime.
Sought by many far and wide,
As Shangrila and Paradise.

Where falling back is moving on.
And darkness is the break of dawn.
So softly now with patience deep.
My vigil I will stalwart keep.

Edward A. Wiltsie

Distant Violets

The distant violets caress the wind,
a lover's name upon my lips.

The forgone days of sensual bliss,
a lover vanished through the mist.

The yearnings spurn the endless night,
a lover missing from my side.

The haunting presence fills my soul,
a lover's breath forever cold.

The gripping pain of despair,
the violets and I caress thin air.

Olga V. Romeos

Shadows

The sun goes down, the moon rises
and day gives into night
yet not all sleeps peacefully
for one lies awake in fright

Afraid of closing his eyes
and recalling that painful night
A night of great disaster
of a group's final farewell flight

Scared of being left alone
having never said any good-byes
He lives each day with the pain
of the lose of four great guys

With each new day he grows weaker
He tries to give up on life
but he just can't pull the trigger
or through the heart push the knife

And with each new sun rise
he glances at that knife
and prays again and again
for God to take his life.

Bill Johnson

A Cry for Help

Walking through the dungeons of time
I seek revenge to get what's mine
Slowly drifting in the wind
Visions haughty me of long lost sins

Spirits rising of long lost loves
Reveal an evil fate
Piercing my soul, it steals my breath
I now no I can't escape

Help me please I'm drowning here
In my sorrows and greatest fears
I'm lying here in bed alone
On a destine journey to a danger zone.

Alexis J. Ryan

A Prayer

We thank you for this moment
A time to pause in prayer

To thank you for the many things
You give to us to share

Like love and hope and happiness
and light to guide our way

Is it any wonder
that we come to you and pray

Phyllis Thompson

Gambling Daze

Black salted silk
Immortal wager
Ivory dare
And a sleeve of spades
Pascal dealt
This four card haze

All face down
The hiding clowns
Are bowing West
Under Crass-like laughs
At the right hand bets

And on the dealer sails
From age to age
Dancing with the lily
Of our soul
Through fading grace

Ante up
And douse the Blaze
Pick a square
Amazing haste
Kevin Nix

Untitled

Tension expanding
anger rising

Words exchanged
words not intended

Feelings hurt
a storm brewing

Alone and lost
floating in a daze

Realization hit
tears flow

Misery invades
sorrow follows

Suicidal thoughts
utter dejection

A desolate figure
waiting for your return.
Cassie Sweet

Letting Go

My life is not the same
  since you walked out the door
It's hard for me to accept
  that you don't love me anymore
Every day that goes by
  I think of you
And remember the days
  that our love was so true
The love in your eyes
  all those warm feelings inside
The things we did together
  and those yet left to do
The memories we created
  I'll carry my whole life through
One thing I know for sure
  I will always love you
Melinda Leonard

Lonely Love

You may not see the emptiness
of a lonely heart
where tender love is mounting always
You may not experience-
the fabulous warmth of caresses

I've so long been possessing
the passion of love
for someone like you
who is as special to me
as no one would ever be

Let's cull and explore
love's hidden beauty.
Let's step through the passage
and turning sorrow to rejoice
by shattering the stone wall of silence
Mohammad Kamal

The Learning Fields

Where are the boundaries
which have no force...could
there be such a place
where images cannot be contained,
where the rush of stability
does not stalk us?

Without force there is no form,
only fields of energy vibrating
with each new thought...
there, far-from-equilibrium,
my ideas go roving into space,
and carry me along.

The business of matter, form, or place
seems less pressing now,
although not entirely forgotten...
like some ancient ritual, perhaps,
my mind remembers, but
lingers not.
Pamela S. Mayer

A Fallen Paradise

Why is there so much death
and hate in our future to come.

When will people learn to love,
work together and never act numb.
Toward's feeling's and idea's about
others outside their race.

Jesus has made me dream the
future's end with despair.

Singing from all of his children
he bow's his head in disgrace.

Why the future is so clear to
me it hurt's to care.

I love every living thing on this
earth with all my heart.

And I hope all will listen
to this poem.

My love isn't strong enough
to make a start.

But believe me when I say
the Lord is coming home.
Kyals Howard

Awakening

I did not know
Until I became
And grew

I did not feel
Until I shared
My heart

I did not see
Until I opened
My mind

I did not hear
Until I listened
Inside

I did not taste
Until I took
The time

I did not touch
Until someone
Touched me
Christy R. Owens

"Loneliness"

Loneliness is a time of confusion,
unaware of society's reasons
for allowing them to find and scold us
for our weaknesses

Loneliness is a time of thought
letting the mind wander,
to ponder the "what ifs..."
and create your own world

Loneliness is a time for control,
release the hidden feelings,
discipline the negativity and hate,
treasure memories and love,

Loneliness is what you make of it
good or bad, ashamed or proud
you may get used to it
and still not like it
but chances are - it likes you.
Kevin Weishan

How Much I Love You!

I once had a heart and it was true
But know it's gone from me to you
Keep it as I have done
Cause you have two and I have none
I do believe God above
Created you for me to love
He picked you from all the rest
Cause he knew I would love you the best
If I go to heaven and you're not there
I'll wait by are special star
If you're not there by judgement day
I'll know you went the other way.
To prove my love for you
I'll give up my angel's wings
Golden harp, and pretty things
To go to hell and be with you
That's how much I love you!
Melissa Stiefel

Serenity

That mighty mall awaits us all.
Above, around, within
so near and dear.
Thank you Lord who is
knowing. You're extreme
supreme in showing.
For us in sleep. I pray our
souls not weep.
Please forgive my short.
Comings and woes. Ones
who do not and those that
knows our blessings be
that comes from thee.

Bette B. Parks

Light Of Eternal Love

The beating of my heart
I could not hear,
But, I remember feeling things
From here and there.
The light drew me down a path
Of serenity and love.
The past, present, and the future
Became as one.
Reality was simple
Yet complicated too.
Love is an eternal gift
Given for us to use.
Brought back into myself
I remember wondering why,
I had to leave such peacefulness
To live with pain and pride.
Did it really happen,
Or was it just a dream?
Echoes I hear in my head
Narrate what it seems.

Sue Charles

Memories

Memories are made of homemade things
The care that you gave me
The love you would bring
The laughter in times when
Sorrow was near
To take away hurts and wipe away tears
I love you my sister, my teacher,
My friend
This love that I have
Will never...ever...end

Jodie Stevens

The World Without Music

The world without music
would be like an ocean without
water - Empty.

The world without music
would be like a flag without
stars or strips - Blank.

The world without music
would be like a person without
a family - Lonely.

The world without music
would be like a friend without
a heart - Bitter.

My world would be empty -
without Music.

Shaun Swigart

Marriage

Marriage is the most precious
Years of life with work,
Trust and patience as a loving
Man and wife working and
Planning things together,
Watching your dreams come true,
All those precious little
Secrets known only by you two.

Understanding all those sad
And happy tears, that's why
They are known as the priceless,
Precious golden years.

When the way seems rough and
Darkest to you, turn to the Lord,
He'll carry you through
He will lighten your load and
Brighten the way,
If you will only trust in him
Day by day.

Sarah G. Bradshaw

"No"

I feel your knife enter me,
the pain is sharp and hot.
This weight is so unbearable
I'm afraid my heart has stopped.

You took with you my flesh and blood
and left me only with pain.
I can't even stop to imagine
what it is you hoped to gain.

I tried to push the knife away,
but your will was just too strong.
I'll just close my eyes and hope
this won't take too long.

Do you want me to forgive?
Do you expect me to forget?
Do you believe this is what I deserve?

No.
I said no.

Rachel Rhatigan

Stories Yet To Be Told

Things you don't use
could atrophy.
Is that true of the mind?

things put in the back
of the frig. That turn green
that you might never find.

Papers in boxes in the garage
that are yellow with age
could rip and shred.

Places you think about
but never go to
like a Club Med.

The wonders of life.
Things unused, lost, grown old.
Places out there you'll never see
but lots of stories yet to be told.

Denny Sternberg

Perennial

Winter's the sleep that
  follows the wine

Of Autumn, lovely concubine,
  who, stealing Time,
  Summer's lover,

Sleeps, lost Mother Earth
  discover the fraud.

Winter's sleep that
  rests Earth's whole
  exhausted, worn,
  maternal soul;

From which she wakes midst
  joy of birth

To Spring, conceived of
  very mirth of God.

Eileen Hayes Lupoli

Memory

The Angels in Heaven Rejoice and
Praise my Lord, His love and goodness
Is their reward.
Although I sit all alone
My memory serves
My lonely soul.
I praise the memory
Of one so dear
I feel their presence
Although not here
The apple of my eye
The essence of my soul
Thank you Lord above
Our memory's
Can not be parted

William R. Sturdivant

To Me She Is...

A radiant rose,
and a honeyed tune.
A graceful prose,
and a summer's June.

A peaceful lake,
A golden flower,
A memory's take,
and an emerald shower.

A laugh not heard,
and a smile not seen.
An ocean of pearls,
and a touch as keen.

To me she is,
everything held,
the reason I live,
for nothing else.

Chris Tillery

The Deer

As you walk through the
field and you look up and
there he is. Standing as
gracefully as ever. You look
into his big brown eyes and
there you read his story.
You reach out to touch him and
in a heartbeat he's gone.

Stephanie Crocker

"Don't Give Up"

Never let it go, don't let it loose,
once you start on your dream,
keep it up, soon you'll have your
Ice cream, "Don't give up"
Once your mind is set on your goal,
put your best foot forward,
You'll start making it on your way
to the top, never thinking once,
should I stop, "Hell no"
I'm going to be all I can be,
my friends, strangers, even family,
will see that once I start,
my goal, my fantasy, I don't give up,
I'll stand tall, always keeping
my head up, rough roads may come,
but in between I'll remember
my dream, my goal, "Don't give up,"

Peace.

Vanessa C. Tramble

Untitled

Should - things make me feel Good:
events make me feel Warm:

if only Should would be a Could.
Life will be much easier
compliments of "LOVE"
breakfast-in-a-basket
Honor with Dignity and the last word.

should - our "gratefulness"
as Elements of Triumph
anything is possible...
If one can just Believe it.

Should -
be Life's greatest pleasures.
Hearing GOOD for decisions/
Accomplishments made.
Elements of Triumph
makes me feel Good!

Vicki Ann Berry

Jingle

Poem - readers like them simple -
No rule nor form need be;
A laugh - arresting jingle
Will activate their glee.

There's one about the pimple
Upon Old Santa's face
In the middle of the __?__
A very likely place.

It caused his eyes to twinkle
This rosy little pimple
In the middle of his __?__
While the sleigh - bells did jingle!

(? rhymes with "pimple")

Vera M. Snyder

Love

　The river goes on,
It twists and bends,
It leads to a waterfall,
It leads to the end,
　But when love comes,
And knocks at your door,
　You don't have to be,
A victim of this game anymore,

Jillian Lea Kirkland

Anne

The heavens wept the day we kept,
　Your form away from God,
And in their weeping, they
　gently softened,
The bed where you are sleeping,
　And thrice-blest was the sod.

Though we gave you back,
　Regretting, and with much sorrow,
Surely He will forgive us,
　For keeping you, til the
　　End of each tomorrow.

Syd Caplan

Horse Freedom

As I run through the icy
water, the air flows through
my dark black hair. I
do not care what happens
to me. It does not matter
because I'm free.

I jump the waves and prance
in the sand leaving my tracks
behind me.

I am safe from harm with my
special charm. The yellow thing
on the horizon keeps me warm.
The ghostly dot in the sky when
the land is dark, guides me.

All that matters is that I am
Free!

Wendy Elliott

A Tree In Winter

I love a tree in winter
So sturdy, strong, and free.
Each tiny twig becomes a part,
United there by Nature's Art,
Combined to make the tree.
Not hid by leaves, its grace and form
Are there for all to see.
A tree in winter speaks to me
Of souls as seen by God.
He sees what we are like inside
And not what people see.
We cover up each fault and sin
With words that aren't sincere,
But God who made the winter tree
Knows what we're like within.

Laura Shelton Thurmond

Untitled

Complete is how I feel
When I'm with you
Feeling whole and loved
Is something new
I have no doubts
When you say how you feel
I know your love is,
and always will be real
I'm happy
like I always wanted to be
and what makes me happy
is you loving me

Rebekah Bell

"Come With Me"

My hand is open, palm outstretched:
"Please come," I beg.
"Yes, come," I cry.
The clouds above float softly on
While whispering, "Not I."

My eyes are open, seeing sights:
"You'll come?" I ask.
"Do come!" I say.
The fields of flowers softly nod
And murmur, "Not today."

My heart is open, craving joy:
"Please come!" I plead.
"You'll see!" I vow.
The river hurries on its way
And sweetly sings, "Not now."

My spirits sink, my gladness fades;
"None care," I sigh,
"To seek and know."
Then suddenly, behind my back,
My shadow calls, "I'll go!"

Nicole Anderson

Untitled

Many many years ago
When I was in my teens
I met a boy who I never told
Was always in my dreams
We parted and went our ways
He was always on my mind
I hoped we would meet someday
And talked about old times
After 40 years of wondering
We met again one day
He came upon my door step
I hoped he came to stay
We talked about years ago
When we were very young
He suppose to be me best friend
But this is what he's done
We started writing letters
I enjoyed it very much
I sure would love to hear from him
But he has given up.

Virginia N. Crandall

Summer Begins

And so another summer is upon us,
as I watch they day break void
of the harshness of winter.
Birth of another seasons cycle
not like childbirth at all, but a very
gentle beginning, as the morning dew
sprays a light mist followed by a
soft warm breeze; just enough to
ruffle a leaf or two.
Once again I am part of universal law,
everything on cue. I have wondered
how many of God's rehearsals it
took to get it right. The ever
changing cycle of the seasons.
Summer, Winter, then summer again.

Paul Price

My Journey Home

Relentless time leads me on,
Etches furrows in my brow,
Dampens passion's blazing fire,
Draws the shades o'er tired eyes.
Drums are muffled, the tempo slows.
A short trip,
An apprenticeship.
Now's the hour for summing up.

I see the beauty of the hyacinth,
The azure sky, a grandson's smile.
Forgive the failings of my friends,
Harder yet, forgive my own.
Know love that passed the test of time
Find my place and Peace of Mind.

From mother's womb to humble grave,
So soon over! Earth stakes her claim.
My Father's house has many mansions;
there's a place prepared for me.
Soon, enfolded in His arms,
I will make my journey Home.

John D. Coggins Jr.

Paper

Falls
Among the musky smell
of boys sleeping;
and the pond
grows
still
Rippling only under
the spidery water bug.
Mother
begins
to cry
24 and then
25,
sad
men die;
You become again
the cowboy in your
washed-out
dreams
of loneliness.

Staci Barker

Dark

Dark and dreary
rain drenched with tears
beyond understanding
nightmares, fears
the moon's illumination
in nightly skies
darkest before the dawn
howling cries
see beyond the rainbow
can't see the forest for the trees
bending down in loneliness
to fall upon my knees, and pray
because I'm afraid

Allen Davenport

I Love It When It Sweeps
The Ground

I love it when it sweeps the ground,
And whistles while it works.
A train that always is northbound-
It groans and moans and jerks.

It tosses balls and big balloons
Way up into the air,
It chases them through hill and dale,
It plays without a care.

When ushering in a stormy day,
It screams the whole day long.
It hoots and hollers all the way,
While whistling an old song.

It loves to waltz with flowers gay,
It tangos with the trees,
And when it serenades the Earth,
I am so very pleased.

Terry Outlaw

Untitled

Their love.
Flows in each others body,
like the blood in
their veins.
Frustrated, because
the words they want
to say,
they cannot say.
Their emotions.
Are hard to share,
because they never
felt this way.
Actions are loud,
but its those three words
that are louder,
and easier to
understand.
Their love.

Lemuel Kwame Johnson

The Plea Of An Orange

I'd gladly lose my skin for you
I'm anxious as can be,
I wish that you would turn your head
And kindly notice me.

My lovers come from everywhere
Why do you resist me,
And I am so delightful that
The sun has even kissed me.

Your attitude is strange and it
Has left me up a tree,
I cannot understand why you
Don't listen to my plea.

You're welcome to come squeeze me and
You're foolish not to try
But if you want to leave me now,
I can wave goodbye.

So why not take me home with you
It really isn't wrong,
I have a juicy feeling that
I won't be 'round for long.

Rosalie Crisfulla

For My Mother

If I were to be stuck on an island,
That was filled with white sand,
And could only take one thing,
It would definitely not be a king.

This person would have to be great,
So it couldn't be a mate.
The person would be my mother,
Like her, there is no other.

She will always love me,
No matter what I do wrong.
Her kindness is easy to see,
For her voice is as sweet as a song.

She makes or bakes my food,
So that I am never hungry,
And is always in a good mood,
While she doesn't often get angry.

My mother is priceless,
I will follow her faithfully,
Even into a cave of darkness,
For I love her very dearly.

Imelda Tamayo

The Weed...

I sat once with someone
and gazed at many trees
those trees are cut to perfection
but what a shame indeed
"yes" they're cut to perfection
and all to be the same
but if one grows new branches
and others grow new leaves
then they're not in perfection
but do they shame the other trees?
It's a shame that perfection
is looked upon that way
for perfection is to be
yourself and not to be the same

Steven M. Kerper

Falling Star

Your eyes are like the stars
in the sky,
Shining brightly on a
moonlit night.
Your touch is like the warmth
of day
Warming me in every way.
Your laughter like the breeze,
Enveloping my sensitive skin.
It seems you're the only
one in this world for me,
And someday you'll be all mine.
I'll catch you like a falling star,
To keep for the rest of my life.

Amelia Regalado

My Son

You are my first born son,
I'll never forget you. I will
miss you, but you'll always
be remembered. Your father
and I will see you in heaven.
Look down on us and smile. I'll
look up and smile back. May
God keep you close to his heart
as you are to mine. Goodbye.

Kamillah Smith

Anything!

You can be anything you
want they say!

You can have anything you
want they say!

You have the world at your
disposal they say!

How easy for them, to say
these things!

I say, I need to want to live first.
Rose M. Audet

Psaw Him 1:36

Where is God?
  Gone
    Among the
    Dead?

I do not know.

I can not say that He
  ignores all prayers
But I do not feel Him.
  my heart cries OUT!
Please be reality and not some
  silly invention.
All is lost without you.
Amen
Losing
Life

all men
Sarah Croy Avan Rooley

"My Anger is a Fountain"

My anger is a fountain
it bubbles from within

It's darkness is a state of mind
with which I cannot win

The rumble of a mighty thunder
rolls inside my soul

This kinesthetic plague intact
creates an empty hole

And in that hole I'll fall to death
where evil satan lay

For anger is a wanton friend
my being it betrays
Stacia Jo Mullen

Autumn . . . What A Change!

Autumn's the time when summer's
air goes away and frost
begins to bloom

Autumn's the time when leaves
loose their pigment and
turn scenic colors

Autumn's the time of changing
from sunny to chilly
without notice

Oh . . .
  Autumn . . .
    What a change!
Laura Oberne

Christ, Our Strength

Many times we feel down-hearted,
Not knowing which way to go;
But if we look to Jesus
He'll guide is here below.

Our family and friends may fail us,
When at times we need them most;
But, with Jesus as our pilot
We can fight the world's host.

"God's to blame," we often say
For things that happen from day to day.
But why blame God for our mistakes
And the foolish steps we often take?

Why not let him help you
As you live from day to day?
He will always lead and guide you,
As you live for him and pray.

Merely take him at his word;
His promise believe;
And you'll be simply startled
With the blessings you'll receive.
Mary Rosenberry

My Inner Soul

God as I am in your house
And everything is quiet as a mouse

My thoughts and prayers
To heaven soar
I hope they do get
Through your door

An answer to them
Yea or nor
I still do thee adore

Inside me deeply is thy presence
You are my very essence

On days when I can hardly cope
I turn to you and it gives me hope

For life is but
The time to pass
For final life
With thee at last
Judith F. Schultz

Can Someone Tell Me

Can someone tell me
How can love be so blind
Between him and I
Can someone tell me
What his mind
Was telling him
What his heart felt
To come back to me
Can someone tell me
How two people
Care for one another
Can hurt one another
Can someone tell me
How two people
Can't stand one another
But yet can't be without
Can someone tell me
What makes me stay
Can someone tell me
Is this what they call love
Bethan Ovellette

The World As A Family

The world is our home
We share with all race

It was God's intentions
To share with lightning pace

Is the color of our skin
A reason for us to hate
Beauty is with in
For goodness sake

God created all man equal
All of us on borrowed time
Life is what we all share
Is this such a crime

Life is very short
Take care of each other
Nobody really wins this game
Treat all man like a brother

The proof is in our blood
To show your family and mine
We all bleed the same color
Let's stop wasting time.
John Fernandez

Mr. Man

Hey! Mr. Man
Where's ya worn coat today?
It's cold outside and the sky is gray.
Oh, God! How did you end up this way?

What did society do to you?
You're fighting to stay warm,
With your little brown bag,
Under your arm!
Oh, Mr. Man! I feel for you!

Where's your family?
Don't they know, you are in need?
Why does this have to be?
I hope this wasn't your choice.
Mr. Man, it takes a voice,
To make people understand,
What it's like for you!
Oh, Mr. Man! I feel for you!

What a price you have to pay,
Living this way!
Oh, Mr. Man! I feel for you!
Ninna Milliken

Untitled

It hurts being here
when the only place I want to be
Is in your arms.
It hurts seeing him
Knowing I only love you.
It hurts looking at the night sky
Because in the blackness
I only see your eyes.
It hurts knowing
That you'll probably find someone else
To replace me
Before I can escape this hellhole
To come to you.
I hurt
Because I know
I don't mean half as much to you
As you do to me.
Nicole K. Storing

Singing Sands

Shuffling along
The sand signs
Underneath my feet
The grains rubbing together
Between my toes.

Waves hiss
Pushing higher on the shore
Attacking more of my playground.

On the dune
Tall grass whistle
A care-free tune
While the breeze
Always in hurry
Rushed by.

Jennifer Gresley

Dreams Are Like An Ocean

For some, dreams are like an ocean,
And we are but the wave,
They carry us, we toss and turn,
Slowly, day by day.

For others, they are shown
Through work and security,
They pull us through, they help us,
They tell us what we'll be.

Or dreams may be your rainbow,
Forever out of reach,
You always try, you never make it,
However you jump and leap.

As for me, well,
Dreams are in my heart,
And in my joys, my pains, my words
I know where I can start.

Kimberly Ferrero

Torn

You'll never know what
  crosses my mind
Maybe it's best
  that you leave me behind.

I sense in you something
  I can't express
A pain? Or a sorrow
  that should be addressed?

I'd never hurt you
  by probing too deep
This one is yours
  for you only to keep.

If perhaps in some faraway when
  you decide your burden to share
I'll be there to listen
  I can't help but care.

Patricia A. Mullen

Flight 143

Our love is terminal.
The mesh of our life
together unravels
like a knitted airplane
whose loose ends
are being held
by the air traffic controller,
who can't find it in her heart
to let us take off.

Andrew Spackman

Shadows

Like black casts
Upon the night
Like gray ghosts
Without a fright

Light is the force
That allows them to play
Hovering and following
You along the way

They're sometimes gray
And sometimes black
And not even a care
Upon their back

They're out at night
And in sun's light
And free as a bird in its flight

They chance their shape
And reposition and creep as if
They're under suspicion

As a friend so loyal and true
Does your shadow follow you?

Lincoln Wade Rogers

Peace

Peace is happiness
peace is love.
Peace doesn't mean carry
guns and playing dead.
Peace is something that
you should remember.
Peace is something
forever and ever.
Peace can be different
in lots of ways it could
mean night it could mean day.
People with violence don't
know what peace means at all.
But they should look back
and remember it all.
Peace means no fights,
no guns, no drinking, no violence.
So when I say these words
you should remember.
Keep in your mind forever and ever.

Vlada Gutman

"Silence No More"

In the fields,
There is silence,
There heals a wounded one,
there is no silence,
The sounds fill up the air,
With whimpering,
Cries of pain,
Footsteps of humans running,
The cries of a puppy,
The shot of a gun,
There lays a wounded one,
There is silence no more,
He lays still,
He went somewhere special,
With happiness,
And joy.

Jennifer Buechner

Time

In all of my given years.
What they say,
Is not what appears.

Even my size, oh how long.
And I'm still growing strong.

I have seen many kings,
Rise in my strength.
But for a moment,
Without atonement.
Death was my length.

As I watch for the eclipse
What? Is there no one left?

At my best, I was my stay.
Even the wind faded away.

Father Time Father Time
Leaving worlds behind.
Father Time Father Time
Outlasting all of earth's kind.

Rudolph V. Speight

I Wonder

Does she love me most completely
Am I the subject of a fetch
Does she speak to me sincerely
Or do I simply fill a niche
I wonder

Of the words she never uses
Can it be they hide a canter
Does she speak the more with substance
With her eyes and in her laughter
I wonder

Should I believe her when she tells
Of the essence we shall share
Does her heart within her swell
Will she her feelings true declare
I wonder

John L. Herold

Time Rolls On

I close my eyes and dream
I see the things I never seem
  to be able to say to you.

I hear pictures in my mind
Reminding me all the time
of what we once meant to each other.

But, Time rolls on
We can't stop Time
Or turn back the clock
to redo all the mistakes we made
I'm not sure I'd like to, anyway.

Gazing off into space,
  daylight fades fast.
Standing here in my loneliness,
  it's hard not to think of the past
    and it hurts.

Laura Hafdelin

This Thing Called Love

Pull me through a sunset
And don't protect my eyes
Prepare for me the growing love
That somewhere under lies.

Send me like a butterfly
And fill me with rebirth
Spread your mind like
Trees upon this selfish dying earth.

Turn to me for reassurance
You won't believe my worth
I finally found a way for you
To cease your endless search.

Now you feel this thing called love
I spoke of once before
More beautiful than rainbows
And lasting evermore.

Without your fears and salty tears
I think that you will find
To captivate our steadfast love
Will surely ease your mind.

Michelle Hoke

My Life

My life is but a passing thing,
A feather in the wind.
It lasts but oh, so briefly
And then comes to an end.

Oh, may I be a blessing
As I pass along this way,
And may my life touch someone's heart
Each and every day.

If by some friendly gesture
Or just a simple smile,
I can lift the spirit
Of even one small child;

Or if with but a kind word
I can brighten someone's day,
If I can touch a heavy heart
And chase a care away,

Then my life will find meaning,
And my heart will be content
To know I was a blessing
Each day my life was spent.

Gale Eggerton Monk

Life Of 3 Seasons

I am green.
My color glistens.
Minuscule at birth.
I die a giant.
I live off my mother.
My entire life.

Comes summer.
Joy and prosperity.
Bold and true.
I face the world.

Comes the age of autumn.
My age grows.
Wrinkles and shrivels,
The world has turned grey.
My way is filled,
My destiny is preplanned.
I leave my mother.

Leaf.

Jason Hsien

In Dream I Can See You

My heart cries out, although
I receive no answer.
My tears long for your touch,
although I feel nothing.
My eyes search for you,
although I'm alone.
But I can always hope and
close my eyes, in dream I can see you.

In dream my mind takes over
my heart cries out no more
for in dream I have found you.

Jill Pasqualetto

Angels

My Guardian Angel has
wings of pearl.
A smile of sunbeams and
a halo of gold.
She surrounds me with white
light, gives me her hand to hold.
My Guardian Angel is a
connection to comfort me in the
dark of night.

LuJuan Bartlett

Life

Why does life have
To be this way?
It gets more
Confusing everyday.

Not a single day
Goes by,
That I just
Don't wonder why.

I do what they want,
I do what I'm told,
It's like this everyday,
And is getting old.

As I try to understand
Everyone's pain,
I go through life,
With some of my own strain.

Candace Smith

"Parents"

Parents can be mean
They can be a team

But mostly aren't
And come apart

So they break-up
And never make-up

They hurt the family
That's very sadly

The kids feel bad
Because they lost their Dad

Now the Mom's all alone
Can't stay home

Move in with Mom
And kids come along

Now Mom and Dad are friends

That's a good start
So they won't be apart

Monica Precie

Untitled

One night I dreamed
I was a fish
in the deep blue
Caribbean Sea

And divers from
all the Islands
dove in just to get
a glimpse of me.

I was quite a beauty
my colors were
silver, torquoise and red

And its no wonder why
I dreamed I was a fish,
I went to sleep
on a water bed!!!

Marie E. Komar

Mother

When I was just a little girl
I sat on Mother knee.
She hugged me tightly to her breast
and told how she loved me.
I never realized how good she was
until God took her home.
The house is oh so quiet now that
she is gone.
Her Rocking Chair is empty, and I
am all alone.
I pray that God will comfort me.
Until he takes me home.
I know that she will be waiting
To hold me on her knee
I love her oh so dearly.
What a pleasure it will be.

Lida Schmidtke

Life

Life is short
or so it seems
When we try to fulfill
our hopes and dreams.

We struggle along
day by day
To reach success
along the way.

To leave a legacy
for our youth
Who don't always listen
to the truth.

We want to demonstrate
right from wrong
And make others feel
like they belong.

At times we're discouraged
at times we've cried
The best we can do
is say that we tried.

Maryjo A. Price

Untitled

I shot my arrow to the sky
It the old mockingbird
that flew up high
She withered up and
then she died

Rachel Ghansah

Memories

I remember being young,
Making play houses in the tall grass,
Lying on my back watching white clouds
Float across the bright blue sky,
Making mud pies. And muddy tea.
Or coffee as I preferred,
Playing marbles with my cousin,
And riding stick horses,
Learning my a db cps,
And counting on my fingers
From one to ten,
This might be simple and humble
For some, but for me it was fun.

Lois Watson

Angel Of Love

How can one speak to an angel,
When she does not know
Of the feelings so hard to tell,
Of the way one's heart flows?

How can I say to this creature,
Without stumbling over my own path;
Without losing her kind feature
To a cold and hard wrath;

That my adoration for her soul
Is more than I can bear
To keep and to hold
Away from her fair ear?

Alas! Though she with another
Has made her pact
I shall never my love
From this angel take.

Matthew Davis

"A Family"

A family
is like a hand.

The forefinger can oppose
the thumb,

or all five can clench
together, forming a fist.

No finger can deny
its relation to any other,

Since they are connected
by flesh.

Patricia Luedke

Happy Birthday Bob

I thought of you with love today,
but that was nothing new
I thought about you yesterday
and days before that too
I think of you in silence
I often speak your name
All I have are memories
and your pictures in their frames
Your memory is my keepsake
with which I'll never part
God has you in His keeping
But I have you in my heart
I love you forever, and miss
you oh so very much!

Roni Lane Skaggs

"The Gift Of Children"

I rummage through the photographs
With thoughts rushing through my mind
Of birthday parties, baby dolls
And homemade cards of the dearest kind

I think of all the fun we've had
Cooking cakes, playing games, the beach
The stormy, rainy, summer days
And to each other we would reach

Mending "boo boos" took just my kiss
To brighten teary eyes
And my soothing mother's touch
To comfort all their cries

Sometimes parents take for granted
In the fast pace we all go
The precious gift of children
Is one we should take slow

Babies today, grown tomorrow
How fast time does go by
But all the love and memories
I'll always have inside.

Connie L. Halford

No Mercy

No place is safe.
Wherever you look.
The presence of gangs
just can't be shook.
They cross paths with each other
and not thinking twice,
pull out their guns
to take someone's life.
An innocent child,
his life now ending.
A stray bullet has found him,
the damage unmending.
This boy's chance is gone,
there will be no tomorrow.
His future, his dreams,
his life ends in sorrow.
They destroy with no conscience.
Allowed to run wild.
We must take action swiftly,
their next victim - your child?

Teresa Fernandez

Beloved

You my beloved
are true inspiration

My heart sings
My soul rejoices

For you my beloved
these words pour forth
like springs of living water
like an oasis in a dry desert
like dew drops on a delicate rose.

Sandra Mahula

Friends Going Through Time

As our lives move far apart,
You will make new friends who
are dear to your heart.

But when friends come to mind,
None will love you more
Than those you left behind!

Cora McKenna

Gentle Soul

The gentleness of the soul
and the warmth of the heart
far outweigh the severe
injustices we bestow
willingly upon ourselves

It is not always what the
eye behold that catches
the attention of some
but, ofttimes it is the soul
inside that captures the heart.

Beverly George

Christmas Time

Christmas is a time of joy
When children get their toys
families come from different places
you're excited to see their faces
girls walk and play with their dolls
boys run and bounce their balls
girls try on their skates
while mothers fix their plates
everyone sits by the fire
dressed in their best attire
kids put on a show
while parents sit in rows
Christmas is a time of joy
when family's reunite

Jasmine Taylor Stells

Normal

I want to hear your hand
like your elbow
tickle your bellybutton
touch your ear
listen to your back
giggle with your leg
talk to your knee
whistle in your instep
smile on your chest
and be really crazy with your shoulder

I could
kiss your mouth
hold your hand
listen to your heart
rub your back
blow in your ear
sit on your lap
play with your toes
but I only like being normal
on Sundays.

Starr Russell-Harris

Childhood

Childhood is taking your first steps,
and falling flat on your face.
Childhood is refusing to swim
in your pool,
because you are convinced
"Jaws" lives there
Childhood is sucking on a lemon
for an hour,
and never noticing
how sour it is.
Childhood is saving your puppy
from drowning,
and gaining a best friend, for life.

Jaclyn Sabol

Untitled

Writing thoughts forbidden
To speak
Phrasing words as if pulled
From the heart
Emotions are felt but cannot
Be shown
Anger and love act together to
Form sentences never told
Terms of sadness and happiness
Are unknown to all
But as darkness grows closer
Minds and hearts weaken
They cannot confide in the
Closeness of there eyes
Complete dark is know and no
More is felt

Paul A. Stengel

Paper Snowflakes

What I've found is so innocent
   I've drowned
      been the first to go under
         hoping she'd stay

impoverished impulses
   in the magnitude of one

      snippets of regret
         from paper snowflakes

What I've found is so innocent
   I've drowned
      been the first to blunder
         hoping she'd stay

impertinent impulses
   in the magnitude of one

      snippets of her picture
         fall like paper snowflakes

What I've found is so innocent
   I've drowned
      been the first to thunder
         when she went away

James Andrew Bowers

Hope

Little ones so dear and true,
are the babies born to you.
They grow up so big and strong,
but it isn't very long,
comes a war and soon they're gone.
Mothers wonder for how long.
Sometimes they return unharmed,
to their mothers waiting arms,
but for those who n'er return,
grief and sadness knows no home.
Is there any answer God,
to remove this awful plot,
to end a life so pure from God?

Anna L. Stift

Books

Fantasies spinning through my head,
coming from all the books I've read.

Adventures I have never known,
companions for my times alone.

Jerine Loy

Untitled

There is someone
standing across the room,
   Their eyes shine as
bright as the moon.
   What they see or what
they hear,
   Does not compare to
my fear.
   I am sitting alone by
a clock
   Without a key of a lock.
   There are people, places,
and things
   Who think they are better
think they are kings.
   The light is getting
darker, I can't see very clear.
   I am like a ship who
can't find its pier.

Lindsey Siegel

America

Our flag means freedom,
So that means we're free.
Don't come in my country
   Shooting at me.
   Racism is bad!
There's no time to get mad!
We're all in this together.
Don't give up, not ever!
The government needs to do more
To help the poor!

Mario Concepcion Jackson

Fertile Time

Our time on Earth is measured in hours
Wasted time a huge banked cloud
Blighted thoughts our pride devours
Stunting growth of which we're proud

Life can resemble the original garden
If sowed with only fertile seed
Be reaped without our begging pardon
For biting apples in our greed

If life is full as hair turns grey
And we've smiled more than we've cried
And shared the best of every day
Reflections are our tithe of pride

Misspent youth and fruitless years
Sown without a backward glance
Can't be regained with belated tears
Your seasons over, no second chance

What would our futures hold in store
if we only took, and rarely gave?
Live to love, and give much more
"Should Haves" mark a lonely grave

Sonia D. McSwain

"Life"

Simply
If we hang our heads together,
laugh like we're fit to die,
cry in our joy and sigh,
we'll make it.

William R. Toczylowski

Portrait Of My Granddaughter

Sunny little girl,
does that smile light your eyes
especially for me?
Does it try to tell me
that in your first imprinting
there is an image of me?
And you still remember
that in those first moments
when your cries called someone,
I was one who answered.

Charlene F. Schatz

Parents Of This Girl

This girl wishes to state
   for all the world to hear.
That her parents are loving and kind.
   That they are very dear.

Sometimes I forget to tell them
   as the days go drifting by.
How very much I love them
   and I am glad that they are mine.

My mother is more like a friend to me
   and a big sister too.
My father is there to answer questions
   and teach me a thing or two.

Like true friends who know that
   one hand washes the other,
a nicer father and mother
   I can find in no other.

So I cherish the days we have together
   like a rare and precious pearl.
For I love them dearly.
   Those parents of this girl.

Nancy Walter

Careless Lessons

I don't know;
I've said it once, I'll say it twice.
Burn your mind on comfort found,
pretend you're nice.

But are you true to being you?
Or do you hide in chains of now
that answer how?

Faith is just a nothing trust.
Can't you feel that what is real
is what you choose to steal;
to heal.

Condemn your friends,
predict their end,
While you save face in written grace
Of past unknown.
Reap what you've sewn.

Is it hate that makes you great,
and love you preach is out of reach?
Watch what you teach.

Jason Michael Lupei

Lost

Desolate and lonely,
Afraid and unaware,
Of all that is around you,
Lost,
And no one cares.

W. N. Warren

Concerning A Girl

Asymmetrical
curves
molded and
flat and
so smooth and
you can't help but
imagine

Forever
is sitting next to you
silent
when I have a million things to say

Where did you come from
I'm so plain
you shine like a
midnight moon
as I look up at the stars
my feet planted firmly
on the ground

Luke Schoenbaum

"Stood It To The Last"

We knew it would someday happen
Cause these things must certainly past.
They said that God was gathering roses,
That had stood it to the last.

We also knew that time would age,
The flowers that God had made.
It's very hard to watch sometimes
When they begin to fade.

But while you bloomed, we always knew,
You were the very best.
Cause in happy times or trying times,
You always pass the test.

When life got hard and others quit,
And didn't know what to do,
You always had your special way,
To pull your family through.

As we live on, we may forget,
Some things about our past.
But we never will forget the one
"That stood it to the last"

Ralph Jones

Siting On That Same Old Lap

Looking at him across the way
wondering what he'll say if
I give him a note so, strong and clear
I'd give anything to hold him near
even if his hate hits me like a bat
or he loves me like a cat
I'd still want to sit on
that same old lap even if his
mom gives me his lap. I'd do
even if he's half black still my heart
goes click and clack I hope he
cuts me some slack he the
one I love is slick gee I hope
it's clicked the time has
ticked it's tick for hundreds of
years it seems all this time
I've waited for the right guy
and even if he is half black
I'd still want to sit on that
same old lap.

Kami Wood

Black Dancer

She dances naked in the rain
she talks to plants and trees
she sleeps inside the lion's den
she'll do what ever she please

i'm the firelord, my princess
i came for Middle-earth
i'm the ring of death, my princess
i'm Volcan, and I'm Pearth

She dances circles around my dead
she laughs at all the pain
she eats small children while i sleep
she gives me all the blame

i am death alive
the dead who walks
  i truly don't exist
she feeds on me
she drinks my soul
  i'm sure i won't be missed.

Levi Rawlins

Untitled

The children are crying
can you hear them?
If you can't
listen closer
for I hear them
I hear them every day
I hear them in my sleep
And I feel the
tear drops
falling from their
eyes
as they land
directly on my
heart I can feel
their pain
we all must begin to
feel their pain but it
is not until we can hear them
cry can we feel their pain
our children are the future

Joel D. Harper

"As I Look Out My Window"

As I look out my window
I hear the sweet sound
Of a cardinal tweet.

As I look out my window
I feel a cool crisp fall breeze
Blow in my face,
Relieving me of all worries.

As I look out my window
The sun gleams onto the
Glistening morning dew
Almost lighting the ground up.

As I look out my window
Body and soul are released
Into thoughts of peace and love
As I look out my window.

Andrew Grenell

I Am

I am original
the life that has not been lived
a flower that has not been planted
a bird that has not flown a flight
I am born
and reborn again
taste will taste better
smell shall smell fresher
sight shall be clear forever more
I am here
arrived into life
discoveries to notice
technology is complete
life its self is complete
I am complete
I am me

Annie Laurie Walker

Why Worry?

Why worry about yesterday
When it's already gone
Why worry about today
When it wili be gone in the morn

Why worry about tomorrow
For it may never be
Live life to the fullest
Be happy and worry free

Triccilla Brown

Untitled

Holding a young rose in my hand,
Feeling the love from it in my heart.
Grasping this tiny captured soul,
Knowing this moment will soon part.

So close to love, yet distant,
Onto the rose tears of grief fall.
What's a lonely heart to do,
When father time begins to call?

I can't stop this rose from dying,
Don't want to leave it to subside.
It's not fair life can't just cease,
Can't I keep it all inside?

Wish I could hold it forever,
This rose, this living work of art.
All this love in it flowing out,
From this dying captive heart.

Esther Lin

Signs Of Love

The tongue speaks madness
the smile reeks gladness
the kiss lasts longer
the heart beats stronger.

Love tastes sweet as candy
it knocks you out like brandy
it heightens your sounds
your entire being pounds.

The eyes become blind,
and reason flees the mind
passion reaches deep
emotions make you weep.

You'll always be together
fleeing will be never
life within you starts
and only gloom departs!

Winston W. Wilson

"The Diamonds Of Your Eyes"

The value of a diamond
Is great, or so I'm told,
But as for me— I'll take
The roses that unfold.

I'll take a song, a smile or two
A little fun and laughter,
For to my mind those are the things
That lingers ever after.

I'll take the TREES, a soft blue sky
The rumbling of a stream,
The whisper of a summer's breeze
That makes me drift and dream.

I'll take the snows of winter
The tears a baby cries,
And still before most of all,
The LOVE-LIGHT of your EYES.

For your eyes LIGHT the way for me
Without them,— I'd be lost,
They outshine the brightest DIAMOND
That help me to pay the cost.

Rajandra K. Bubhan

Mourning

Do not mourn my passing
Even though my stay
On earth was short
Rejoice in my new life
For I am at peace
I now live in
The House of God
Remember my deep love
For family and friends
Smile and give each
A strong embrace
Also remind them
When there day comes
I shall meet each one
With open arms
And a heart full of love.

James P. Bankston

Ocean Child

I'm yearning for the ocean,
I long to see the beach,

It is in my dreams at night,
but, it I cannot reach.

I long to hear the crash of waves,
I want to feel the sand,

I would walk out in it
And right there I would stand.

It is my fascination,
Its in my heart and soul,

And even when it's distant,
My mind can feel it's roll.

If I were a bird,
and I could fly away,

I'd fly down by the ocean,
and right there I would stay.

Kendra G. Hatcher

Reliving The Past

We're still fighting, still at war.
Are we reliving the sixties once more?
Sixties fashions are back around;
A second Woodstock with muddy
ground.

The blacks are back to rioting.
But now they call it gang banging.
They're busy killing off each other.
Whatever happen to peace my brother?

The whites are as worse as ever.
The KKK is still considered clever.
And the children being raised in this,
As in the sixties, they will resist.

So we're back to praying for peace.
Love and caring; hate must cease.
It won't be easy but can be done.
For in the sixties we united as one.

We must learn to live together,
Through the smooth or stormy weather.
For if we stand hand-in-hand within,
The circle of life is complete—we win.

Barbara Smith

Weatherman's Forecast Of Rain

Last night we bought equipment
for tomorrow's forecast of rain.

Something to stand under while
we wait for the 8:22 bus
that never comes on time.

That morning

Peered through the blinds
expecting the drip-drop sounds
and the matching visuals on the pool
of a generous precipitation.

But there is none

except for the mist
that could hardly be considered rain.

So we cross the street defenseless
to the red-marked sidewalk stop.

Nothing to stand under while
wc wait for the 8:22 bus
that never comes on time.

Danilo Tizon

Father Time

Thunder roars
as the trigger is pulled.
The gray long eared rabbit lays limp
like dinner on the table.

Grandpa settles in front of the TV.
His feet elevate as the smoke lingers.
Tales escape from his breath
like powder from a pistil.

Dust is collected
as spiders occupy the barrel.
Silence overcomes the room.
The thunder roars no more.

The shovel throws dirt,
as the sun hides behind the clouds.
Moisture falls like tears,
time stops.

Nathan Schmidt

The Miracle Of Day

Look to the east for the light
Where a day is born,
And the darkness with the night
Fades at break of dawn.

Look to the east for the sun
to give its hint of day.
Its rise to heaven just begun,
and rays in color play.

Look to the east for its birth
which clearly you will see.
The miracle of day on earth.
a gift for you and me.

John R. Leone

The Awakening

Oh! Sleeping prince —
How soundly you retire;
The realm of comfort
Should you desire:
Thoughts of wonder
Or murmurs of sweet;
When lest the hour,
The moment We meet —
To once again exalt the mood;
So precious or vain
As memories lost in time
Like tears in rain
The way of all life
As angels do call;
A spirit alighted dawn to dawn:
White streams crossing oceans
Of time unknown
The infinite Journey —
Alas Soul meets Soul...

Roanne Traficenti

Quiet Revelation

No burning bush
Beckons
No almighty voice
Quakes or thunders above;
But like the evening mist
That steals upon the valley
The almost imperceptible shift
Of air
That ripples through the trees
Meshing wisp with wisp
Weaving a snare
Of quiet revelation
More profound than
Dawn's explosion
More poignant than sunset's passing
You did not speak
You did not move
You did nothing
And in that stillness
The world was forever changed.

C. L. Vargo

My Wife

You gave me your heart
I filled it with love
And connected it with mine
Never to depart...

Marc Wuttke

I Am Fish

See you staring
a seed to grow,
You laugh the tears
I cry to know.

A fish you are
to look at me,
A stepping stone
for all to see.

Vacant thoughts
you long to hear,
You should be afraid
of all my fear.

Kiss my face and it's on it's way,
You said I died that very day.

Feed my mouth
with green salt water, there I lay
upon the alter.

Fish you are
to breathe my air
Dead I am and you don't care.
Tami Hankins

The Window

As I sit here looking out,
I'm reminded of what life is about.

So much joy, yet so much pain,
When will I be in love's domain?

Everyday I watch him walk by,
How can I catch love's eye?

I don't see, nor do I know,
So I'll keep watching through my window.
Kristy Riker

Holiday Preserves

Some folks harvest crops
for less plentiful time of year
If only we could do the same
with this season of good cheer
If we could save and cherish
some of the warmth and love
And capture in our hearts
the gentleness of doves
If we could step in tune
with the softest morning flurry
And not always be
in such a blasted hurry
If only we could preserve
this joyous time of myrth
We might just find a way
to harvest PEACE ON EARTH
Susan M. Smith

Speak Not

Today is a day of celebration,
Speak not of things past.
Today is a day of happiness,
Speak not of things sad.

Why do you speak not to me?
For I am here with you.
Why do you speak not of me?
For I am the one you love.

Speak to me once more...
Hsiao-Lung Chang

Piano, Pianissimo

How bends the listening heart
    To hear the bright sounds soar
When wild crescendos part
    And fall with crashing roar!

How thrills the yearning soul
    To hear the clean, clear line
Run to be merged, made whole,
    The symphony define!

How slow we are to learn:
    The hardest notes to play
Are those so soft they burn
    Into our minds to stay!

We trace that crystal tone,
    So soft it seems a sigh
Whose song goes on and on,
    So pure it cannot die!

And so with God's Own Word;
    It is His sovereign choice
To have His speaking heard
    In this: The still, small voice.
Ruth Joan Geiger

Longings

Oh, the surge of the sea
a love song for me,
In the still of the night
when all is quiet,
Even though I'm alone
my thoughts tend to roam,
Yet I know deep within
He has pardoned all my sin,
And these longings of my soul
will continue as the waves roll,
No matter how large or small
He still cares for them all.
Kathy Windham

Enigma

In the dry corridors of my soul
wind sorrows around me, stretching
shame into zip-locked silences
where words crumble and vaginal cords
have forgotten how to sing.
But when I wanted to become liquid,
I reached with a furious burning
for a pure touch. God, maybe. Or
a man in His likeness. And he
became me. I became him.
And we are one for a time
ignoring distance or circumstance
holding onto nothing except
a squeezed heart
that refills with hesitation
a silver pearl
that cups the breath and textures
of his inaccessible skin.
Joyce Elaine Ross

Justice

JUSTICE...
    Her blindfold
      In tatters,
        Winks

And weighs her thumb
To tip the scales.
Jeanette Weld Otter

Cold Winter Days

The cold is here and I hope not
to stay. But the cold sure
matches these old cold gray
days. Wouldn't be so bad if
the snow would come down.
And cover the old cold ground.
Where we could go out and
slide around.
April Inman

The Star

Out of darkness came a light,
A shining sign on Christmas night.
The Son has come, salvation's here,
The light of God, in Christ, is near.

Those who seek with hopeful heart,
    Will see a beacon in the dark.
In Jesus' life, God's light has shone,
And leads us to the Father's throne.

Oh light of God, please shine in me.
Transform the darkness that you see.
    May my life be ever bright,
A beaming lighthouse in the night.
Dawn M. Angus

The Child

It is quite convenient
in the shadows of the night
to abandon a soul so lost and troubled
failure of the first providers
the secret cause.

False saviors fearing spirituality
allow their dogma
to become a weakened god
tying to define for all the world
some right and wrong.

Who will teach acceptance
the shades of gray lying in-between
to help this child begin to know
the courage born of wisdom
to find her sacred path?
Susan G. Spoelma

Mirage?

The sun has torched the desert sky
The clouds have run away
He wipes his brow and squints his eyes
In search of precious shade
His lips are parched, his skin is red
There's pain and much despair
The time is nigh for him to die
As vultures fill the air

Yonder hills turn round and blue
Like waves upon the sea
Palm trees sway where cactus grew
Gentle is the breeze
The sand is cooled by the island's surf
The vines grow tall and green
He tells himself this can't be true
Is it a mirage or capricious dream?
A. Younger

Birthday Songs

Powdered face, tear drops
dowager stares
life gawking back
mimicking in mockery

Dirty dirty business, pithy tricks
marble faces
hiding behind the bar
people want and people get

Counting candles, posting invitations
phantom guests
fistful of greenback
away a young life

Overdue sorrows, regrets
upturn party hats
empty room
echoing a happy birthday song

D. Alex Chuang

Christmas

It starts with
  Joseph and Mary

To Bethlehem a mule
  did carry

A stable and a
  manger

Kept the newborn
  King from danger

Kings, shepherds, wise
  men traveled far

Only guided by a
  star

Gold, myrrh, frankincense
  were brought

To the King whom
  all sought

This is Christmas
  we mustn't forget

He who though we
  never met

Erica Fies

The Winter River

Snow, mist, icelets
forming along the edges
of the quiet, still pools.
Far out, the water rushes
hurling itself along the rocks
and against the banks in
a never-ending race to escape
the freeze, although it can't be done.
The freeze is inevitable - it will come
as always, and snow and ice
will take over the Winter River!

John H. Horner

"Rain"

Rain falls
hitting the window pain
and the pain in my heart
the pitter patter of the rain
reminds me of the days
I spent with her
sitting, listening, waiting
for the moment when
the rain stops and all we hear
is nothing.

Dustin Montgomery

Dreams

In my dreams I dance
You would do it so well
A thought you let slip
A wish from your lips

In my dreams I dance
I know you can tell
Your music moves my life
I would make you my wife

In our dreams we dance
We could do it so well
We two move as one
Oh let it be done

In our dreams we dance
I love you I must now tell
To move to soar to leap
Together we must sleep

B. W. Leversee

Unrecorded Thought

The shifting sands of Time
Record our footsteps where we tread.
But what preserves the journey line
Of thoughts within our head?

Reversals in the sand press printouts
Clear to recognize,
But mental twists and turns
'Oer which we fret and agonize
Leave naught to measure progress
Nor even cue to sympathize.

So with our feet we lurch and leap,
And strive to hurdle high,
All the while our heads churn on,
Blank sentinels to Time gone by!

Jane Hays

Apron Strings

How precious to remember
  the joy of yesteryear,
The tugging of the apron strings
  that only a mother holds dear.

First used by your brother
  and then your sister to,
The apron strings were strong enough
  to meet all needs for you.

Tonight I cut these apron strings
  to the happiness I've known,
And loose myself in memories
  for the years have quickly flown.

Minnie Jackson

This Man Of Dust And Gold

Angels sigh
And women cry,
While souls are bought and sold;
Endless sands
Fall through his hands,
This man of dust and gold.

Through his eyes
I realize,
The secrets to be told;
In my sleep
I'll never weep,
For this man of dust and gold.

Goodnight all
It's time to fall,
Asleep amidst the cold;
Sorrow fills
These ancient hills,
This man of dust and gold.

John Hahn

The Last Covered Bridge
(Sergentville, New Jersey)

The last covered bridge
Near the swollen creek,
Stands now alone
Unable to speak.

Though the bridge can't talk
It remembers those days,
The heavy boots of Farmer Brown
The tiny feet of Sally Hayes.

There were stormy times
When the rain beat on down,
There were bitter cold days
With snow covered ground.

But the last covered bridge
Will shed no tears,
There's been wonderful days
Down through the years.

Peter Coyle

Lady, Like A Rose

Your legs are the stem
That holds the blooms.

Your arms are the petals
That reach out to others,

Your smile is the fragrance
For it is so sweet.

Your eyes are the colors
For they are so bright.

Your heart is the bud
That blooms out to everyone,

But must of all, you are the rose
That blooms all year long.

Estelle Hahn

Arthur

Arthur Laurence Fuller is he
that silly cat of mine.
Popcorn, jello,
a marsmallow,
These foods he says; "Are mine!"

Katherine Helen Fuller

H?RO

Amidst the blaze of battles gone
he stands amazed and wanders on
the bell does toll... his soul set free
the worlds unfold... we cease to be
and though his name it echoes round
he stays the same beneath the ground
yet to his face there comes a smile
I cannot place nor reconcile
and though his name I soon forgot
he stays the same herO or not

Kevin Sexton

Death

For some, death is one with life
Knowing from the heart and soul
It is something very rife.

To be there with-in the ring
And rest at the author's feet
To be with-out suffering
For this is very complete

Knowing that I, and divers
Will soon be gone from this sin
Knowing a new universe
And ingressing there from then

Being set free from evil
Knowing Christ was, and is still
The only way to have life
Beyond celestial bliss.

Charles Cejka

Untitled

last night i cried
   words of wisdom
      underneath the
      pear tree
no one heard the words
   i cried nor
      the pain from
         which they came
nor did anyone hear
   the tear drops
      fall upon the cool
         autumn earth
no one heard the thunder
   send lightning
      to strike the tree
      dead
no one saw the pears fall

someone was there today
   someone chasing
      those tears away
dangerous are the
   tears of knowledge and
      tear-soaked pears
         never to be eaten
as for the tree
   it still stands
      leaning to one side
      with poison in its hands

Alena Schaim

Winter

Winter comes like a thief in a night,
It roams about like a roaring lion,
No mercy except for little children,
Tomorrow shall hold what?
Enter the wonders of winter,
Ready or not here it comes!

Jesse Arza

The True Meaning Of Christmas

We spend until we're placed in debt
and our spirits are running low
We haven't found the meaning yet
so what we all should know
On this day a child was born
and he gave to make things right
We are taught we should obey and adorn
and follow in his light
But somewhere down this path in time
we seem to have lost our way
So giving for this child form the heart
is the true meaning of Christmas Day.

David K. Ebersole II

Untitled

Spanish English
LUNA Moon
TRISTE LUNA Sad moon
LUZ INERTE Inert light
CARA DE LA MUERTE Face of death
LUNA AZUL Blue light
NULA LUZ Null light
MITAD DE DIA Half of Day
IDA TIMIDA Timid sally
LUNA Moon

Salvador Lugo

Untitled

I see my mother's hands
whenever I look

Carefully down into
the creases that map their way

Across my own.
Her knuckles are now my knuckles,

Both wrinkled and tired.
Each one sits cradled by

Out-stretched fingers
that peek shyly from beneath

The veneer
of what was once thought

To be a precocious childhood.

Maria Daversa

No Comfort In Distance

There must be no comfort in my distance
   from violence
   a slap of your face must sting mine
   as much
   when you bleed, I too must become
   weakened
   if you fear for your life, no less
   must I.

Bob Bartlett

Untitled

Thank you, Father,
   for this day —
Another day
   to serve—to pray.
To pray for those
   who need thy touch.
Thy touch of healing
   Thy touch of love..

Esther Dearborn

Winter Park

Still and silent
Trees snow-rooted

Stretch high into
The morning wonder.

I thank them for
Being brothers here,
My tall steadfast
Stalwart companions.

They clean my breathing
Heal my soul
So sullied so wounded

Outside the wood.

Their virgin reach
Makes me twist
My neck to see their
Brain-topped branches.

As I commune my thanks
Gentle air moves stately limbs
In gracious acknowledgment
Of my solemn prayer.

Audrey St. Mark

Untitled

On quiet nights
I lay awake
and remember my comrades.

I hear, at times, their laughter
and relive their joy.
I feel, sometimes, their losses
and recall their pain.

But always I remember
the power of our gathering;

A sense of being which
no union,
no lover,
no triumph
has ever reflected.

In eternity
our paths again merge;
we will regroup

And our souls
will sing
as one.

Dondi Koenig

What Is Christmas's Greatest Joy

To have a friend
A family tried and true.
To know they are always there
When they need you
It isn't so much what they
    ask, as what they do.

The tree is lit with lights so bright
A halo soft, shines around each light
A song is sung by children who dream
What toys will Santa bring?

A fire aglow, for each we know
to bring cheer within and warmth
    bestow
We see bright cards, merry cards,
    tinsel and mistletoe
Life's memories of moments are
    stored for review
A Merry Christmas for friend
    and family too.

Frances L. Van Middle

Life In Blackface

So white — these hands of mine —
Outstretched,
To you, black sister.

I wish I didn't see colors,
Or that I did, but seeing them didn't
Carry so much weight,
Like a stone
Tied 'round the neck
Of a man struggling to swim.

The world is black and white
And I don't know why
We think
That makes it clearer.

Here, now, I am aware of my color,
Or lack thereof.
And just for a little while,
In the smallest way,
Begin to imagine being aware
So conscious and continually reminded
All day, everyday.

Jennifer Chassman

"The Two Of Us"

If there were just the two of us,
to fly away on distant wing.
I'd never, ever find a word,
that expresses the joy you bring.

To soar above the clouds so high,
with you so close to me,
Is all I would ever wish for
'cause with you alone I'd be.

Just to soar above the mountains,
or across the oceans green.
To gaze upon the earth below,
with the air beneath our wings.

But our lives have us here below,
with our feet upon the ground.
How nice it is, that I can hold you,
with my arms around.

C. W. Coster II

Life's Glow

On the open range,
The prairie grass ablaze.
The animals flee,
This dreaded misery.
You can hear their sorrowful pleas!
Oh, peace let there be,
In the middle of this catastrophe.

Here and there the fire dies,
Now and then a bird flies,
Oh, how they soar so high,
Into that beloved sky!

A green bud sprouts
Out of that charred soil.
A beautiful bloom unfolds
To show its pedals, so royal.
It turns towards the heavens
To praise our God,
For the wonders of nature
And for what HE has done.

Kristy Holubar-Walsh

River Of Love

Love is like a river,
that has no real end
Its long, beautiful and looks happy,
like the way you feel within.
When someone says "I love you",
it makes you feel warm inside.
Like the way the sun does to the river,
When its high up in the sky.
Love is not a game,
it's not something you pretend.
Like the way the river does,
When it makes a sudden bend.
So when you're in love,
keep your hopes up high.
As the water in the river,
go rushing by.
And make your partner,
a life long friend.
For the river for you,
has no end.

Brandi Lawson

My Church

My church, a forest of trees
churned with leaves
fertile ground rapture of growth
the odors flow through
Exhaling, I have been quenched.

My church, the break of the ocean
winged beings swooping down
claiming food.
Beauty stirred filling emptiness
a cry, is it mine?
Soaring flight a pattern of freedom
Refreshed, I am cleansed.

My church, an endless mountain
Animals peek in silence
we look
Never seeing the same view.
Understanding, my heart sees.

My church, structured
by God's hand, where no one speaks
yet we hear.

Jeanette Klimszewski

The Herd

Plagued with intelligence,
I've thought feverishly of it all,
Going to the market a journey,
Seemingly hours down a hall.

Thinking what if, if when,
And if ever, how,
With disgust, with hatred,
I join the other cows.

I join momentarily
For the necessities of life.
I eat and I drink
As if under a knife.

No time to frolic,
No time for games,
I simply tread along,
Not paying attention to names.

Although madness is setting,
I know soon I shall be,
Resting comfortably under
My own little shade-tree.

Robert B. Jarrell

Come Dream With Me

Come dream with me
    In a far away land
Come dream with me
    And play in the sand

Can you build a castle
    As big as mine
Can you build a castle
    From the sands of time

With turrets and windows
    That reach to the sky
Right here in the sand
    With the ocean near by

Better hurry and build
    Here comes the tide
Better hurry and build
    Before they collide

Come dream with me
    In a far away land
Come dream with me
    And play in the sand

Robert D. Yates

To Hana

Hana I go,
Winding to and fro
Green forest blankets valley
    everywhere
Mirrored falls and brooks
    murmur along the way
Morning sun glitters thousand
    diamonds out to sea
Tradewind whispers lullaby
    to my wife and me
Wished that progress never
    comes this way,
Truly an Eden to see.

Eduardo L. Ricote

Voyage Within

I see your breaking smile in the sun
  when it rises in the morning,
And the sparkle in your eye
  in the dew on the grass.
I hear your voice in the gurgling water
  coming down the creek.
The wind on my cheek feels
  like the soft touch of your hands.
But it is your love for me
  that is everywhere.
I see it, I hear it, I feel it
  the flow of it, the energy
And as it passes through my heart,
  it turns into my love for you
    to make the flow eternal.

Dorito Marringa

Dreams Of Love

One day he will come,
come to you and steal your heart
You follow blindly into the darkness.

Relying only on the artificial
love which surrounds you.

Without notice you hear a
voice scream.
What is that? You ask.
What can make such a noise?

Nothing, he says, as blood streams
down his chin.

It's only your heart, which you
gave freely to me.
He turns,
only to leave you alone in the darkness.

Rande Moreno

Early Morning East Of Here

You can't just look out
over the pacific ocean
and see red orange blooming
maroon into dusk and darkness
without having it in your mind
what it looks like early morning
east of here.

You can't just see the glare
without seeing the brightness
nor taste the mud of a river
without tasting its sweetness
nor hate
without first loving
nor deprecate
without appreciating
nor die
before you have lived.

Storm Lawrence

Untitled

I am a bulb
in the Spring
I am a flower
waiting.

I am nature
come often
for tea.

Emily Elizabeth Sogg

Beauty

When beauty comes turn it away not.
Stare and adore,
and beauty preserve.
Picture beauty in your heart,
bask in beauty's eyes you may.
Do all above but turn it away not.

When beauty sings, savor.
When away she ambles, bow and cry,
but beauty's picture always preserve.
For beauty again may strike.

Fabio Malagisi

"Mr. Odd"

Once there was a little boy
He was skinny as a rod.
His parents undecided what to call him
So they called him "Mr. Odd."
All the children would tease him
They laughed about his name
And as he grew much older
The people did the same
He never mingled with anyone
And always stayed at home
No one would ever visit him
He wanted to live alone
As he guest older they still teased him
And they called an old crank
So he decided when he lies
His frame stone will he bland
So when people come to see his grove
They would whisper and just nod
And the only words they would say
  "There lies Mr. Nod"

W. M. Chescrow

Inside Heaven

Inside of heaven is a
beautiful castle, the color is
like snow. A unicorn as white
as flour soars by. The white
clouds are as fluffy as a pillow.
I see a rose as pink as my lips.
I feel happy while I watch
all the unicorns soar by, playing
and enjoying themselves. As they
soar higher, one puts
me on its back. As I ride higher
and higher, I smile at the unicorns
by me. I see a white swan, swimming
and playing with its baby. On the
left side is a white baby buffalo.
I am as happy as a winner. I feel
like a lucky person.

Tiffany Jenna Stells

Untitled

I still hear her hurried breath
I still taste her sweet lips
I still feel her soft caress
A mere half day has passed
Yet it seems an eternity
Might this be love I sense
Or merely a pleasant dream

Kevin Dru Boen

Corky The Dog With The Human Soul

Corky
Happy to be near his mistress
  Not needing much more
Ready to defend and always adore
  The one that saved his life
Eyes more human than animal because
  Of the emotions so easily seen
Fourteen years of life
  Long but so short with a dog
  Like Corky
Oh if we poor human beings could so
  Emulate his love
What a better world this would be!

Carmel Rossini

Endless

Once again I walk away
And feel as though
A part of me is gone
Like pieces of marble
Cast aside by an artist's hand
To wait for wind and rain
And time - endless time
To smooth and heal
That which only time can

Eunice Kopp

I'm O.K.

I didn't want to leave you Mommy.
But God said I must.

I will be taken care of.
In God we have to trust.

Don't be afraid Mommy,
just think of the happy
times together.

I'm still in your heart
and I'll be there forever.

I look just like you
of this I'm very proud.
We are so beautiful
just like a big white cloud.

I didn't want to
leave you Mommy, but
God said it's o.k.

I loved you yesterday,
but even more today.
I love you, Mommy.

Marc Johnson

Lawrences'

Lawrences' are loving,
Loving as can be,
Loving wide as a river,
Loving deep as a sea,
Loving like an eagle,
Soaring in the sky,
Loving like a snail,
While it slowly passes by,
Lawrences' are loving
Loving as can be,
I'm glad I'm a Lawrence,
Because a Lawrence is me.

Nichole Lawrence

Autumn Requiem

I yearn for Autumn's time gone by
When evening black ducks filled the sky
On wings compelling them to seek
The nighttime solace of the creek.

Silent, ghostlike o'er the hill,
Their images that haunt me still
Seem real and yet, as dusk descends,
I see them not, harsh truth transcends.

That time is gone, the era's past
And evening flocks no longer fast
Approach and cross the woods in light
That softly silhouettes their flight.

That time is gone but now, as then,
My memories make them fly again.

Robert E. Weet

The Band

Upward soaring toward the stars
Joyful band launched a thousand notes,
Slashing, dashing scimitars
And eerie incandescent ghosts,
Ricocheting from moon to Mars.

On they flew through icy space,
From Jupiter to Mercury to Neptune,
Bouncing off Uranus' face,
Barren rock and sandy dune,
Asteroids and comets chase.

String and brass, drum and wood,
Symphonic poems above the war
Of little men who never could
See above grim, earthbound chore,
The triumph of one tapping foot.

Still, they form and recreate,
Men and women playing together,
And through the joy they emanate,
Lift weary minds from the nether,
And heavenly musings contemplate.

Robert J. Carroll

Carnivalized

I am the jester in your eyes.
Cavorting clowns in a row
Stretched tissue thin.
I am Vegas.
White smiles catch your star
In the funhouse
And I try to reel you in
On lipstick red alone.
But alas, love is the foodstuff
Of the gods,
And I am earthly bound by pride;
Too cool to tarry in your warmth.
Fluid colors move steely thoughts
Tainted by damp heat,
Your hand between my legs,
Only to discover amputation
And its wicked tauntings.

Wendy Skillin

A Time Bomb

Tick tock goes the clock of strife
Ending my breathing,
Ending my life.
Eyes closing slowly,
Heart stopping fast
I'll be gone - but alas...
There'll be nothing good
All bad.
No one happy
Many sad.
Many loses
Fewer gains
All this madness
Drives me insane
Give me flowers now
Not after
Show me the love
Let me taste the laughter,
Tick tock goes the clock of strife
Tick tock the rest of my life.

Tabatha Bernice Berry

Alone

She walked along the path
To be alone with it
To see the deal she made
She looked around the place

She thought about the deal
She made to save the one
She thought she could live with
But now she could be wrong

Her heart torn out, now crushed
She cries alone, out loud
No one to hear, to care
To hold, to help,
  ALONE.

Michael D. Smigelski

Untitled

Stop and take some time
To look at all you see
The beauty of the world
Is shown through poetry.

The sky so high above
The sun it shines so bright
The stars that fill the sky
In the darkness of the night.

The earth so colorful
With browns and blues and greens
The life it gives to us
Can you see just what it means?

So stop and smell the flowers
And see that mighty tree
'Cause in and all around us
Is natural poetry.

Linda R. McGinnis

An Illusion

In order for us to be together
I must forfeit my own happiness
Peace of mind goals and desires
I must conform to the mold
He has created
In order for us to be together
I can not be true to myself

Beverly Lowman

If

If you were my one and only true love,
why did you have to leave?
If I ever wanted anyone more,
you know it would be thee.
If I could have you by my side
to touch, see, and hear,
I would do whatever the request
just so we wouldn't cry the fear.
If I could tell you my feelings now
to help my heartache,
then you'd know I'll never forget you
and still our love I wish they wouldn't
have had to take.

Beth Ann Clark

What Is?

The casket and the vault
But that awesome thought
That keeps us from
Our destined rot

We, oh, so little
As we push, pull and whittle
At each, our lonely selves
Really, aren't we peas in the kettle

To the willows weeping
Of internal striving
Revolving 'round this earthen sphere
Is, but our selfish trifling

Life? Is but a way
Transformation, let us say
For Universal Energy
To view it's Grand Array

Frank Thornton

My Love

I want to love you,
  but I can't find you.
It always seems like I'm one step
  behind you.
I need you, whoever you are

There's no place to big,
  no distance too far.
I will be yours - you'll be mine
  Our love will grow - through all
    space and time
Just want to hold and squeez you tight
You and I together would be so right.
I pray we will meet some day soon,
  for my life without you is
    nothing but doom.

Marcellus James Batchelor

Open Up

When you open your heart
  and it's filled with pain.
Nothing will help cause
  you have so much shame.

When you open your mind,
  to the world outside.
Love comes in
  so you have nothing to hide.

When you open your eyes
  and look to see.
You see a world where
  most everyone is free.

Katrina R. Edwards

Humanity

Early, virgin light,
crawling fusion,
under a solar blanket,
all are equal.

Drop upon deluge,
myriad, molecular fall,
sizzle, whisper, vapor,
under a sudden crash,
all are equal.

Crystal, silent, drifts,
ivory, tender, lace,
under a gentle softness,
all are equal.

Cycle, brought to rest,
years, to decades turn,
quiet, stillness, eternity,
under an earthen blanket,
all are equal.

Kristen Grubert

Untitled

Softly on the wings of night
a whisper comes to me.

It calls me on to deeper dreams,
of my love, her love and we.

Hiding within the shadows, just
out of awakenings reach,
The taunting breath of wonder
slips in-between the sheets.

Veltorina Lauterio

Did You Ever Wonder

Did you ever wonder
  What it's like
    Not to be a jock?
      Or a bubble brain?
        Or a teenage revolutionary?

What it's like
  Not to be black?
    Or white?
      Or yellow?
        Or red?

Did you ever wonder
  What it's like
    To be free of
      Judgement?
        Hate?
          Ignorance?
Did you ever wonder?

Jennifer L. Nielsen

"Valentine"

Hopes are my cargo
Love is my crew
As I go sailing
Directly to you.

May you always be
Happy and fine
My one and only
My Valentine.

Brevard Keyser Titter

Prison of Doubt

Enclosed behind a wall
You or me that's behind it?
So much is beyond that scope,
unbound and unconcerned with
reasons for barriers.

But you and I exist
on opposite sides of that chain link,
Grasping the cold metal diamonds
sometimes brushing each others' hands.
Looking, watching, waiting...
maybe hoping,
maybe predicting the worst;
witnessing Hell.

But still there,
looking to the blue sky
biding our time
calculating the risk.
I wait with you
for the day we can
travel beyond.

Lisa Van Breedam

Does It Matter

A poet without feelings,
A human without sound
Eyes in the darkness
Being consumed by the heart
Born under dark clouds
A poet without words

Does it matter
That my life isn't complete
How can love be blissful
When my life can't understand
What's better for me
Does it matter
That a poet slowly dies in me

Once the romantic
Letting seasons change
Before my eyes
I let years go by
I watch the world burn in flames
People worry over small things
The poet in me just slowly drains away.

Delia Santos

Triviality

They have mastered
The Art of the
Inconsequential.
What to wear
For what occasion.
What to serve,
And how to serve it.
Who went here,
And who went there-
As if this mattered
Anywhere.
All this talk
Of trivial things,
Means they never
Ever
Speak of what's
Important.

Joyce A. Vernooy

The Man

I miss the man
I knew long ago.
The man who...
Gave me my first fishing pole.

I miss the man
I knew yesterday
For you see...
He passed away.

I miss the man
Who taught me right from wrong
For who will do...
The things that man could do.

I miss the man
That I called Papa
For to me...
He was my dad, too.

I miss him dearly
I miss him so...
I miss my Papa,
My dad, My friend.

Vickie A. Templeton

A Rose Is Love

Love is like a rose
  in so many ways...

The bud is the formation
  of love, the joy and ecstasy
  of its completeness.

The color is the beauty
  that surrounds love.

The petals represent the
  tenderness that is...love.

The leaves are the arms
  that reach out and touch
  the one in need of love.

And the thorns...they are
  the obstacles that sometimes
  come with love;

But there aren't many,
  for the stem is the strength
  which holds the rose
  together as one...

  And that is love.

Mary Eunice Erb

Untitled

He washed my body
With hands like fine wine
Nipping at my tongue

Round and round each
Smooth breast
His soap softly glistened

I struggled to rest
My vulnerable mind
Toes curled, belly panted
Heart floated open

Love bubbling deep from
My soul's thousand paths

  Surrendered me.

Sherlin Hendrick

Bed Time

Day is done,
time to sleep
and dream,
for tomorrow
is nearer more.

Dream happy dreams
my little angel.
Popcicle forests to wear
out your tongue,
and of soda-lakes
with ice-cream fish to catch.

Sleep well my little one,
for when you awake,
your life once more
will be renewed.

Rest my little angel,
and know you are loved.
You are,
I do.

Odie F. House Jr.

Your Day Will Come

Not only did you break my heart
You broke my soul as well
You carried me on wings to heaven
Then dropped me into hell.

But I will say with confidence
I'll overcome the pain
And all the hurt I'm feeling now
Will not have been in vain.

My inner strength will see me through
And I will rise once more
I will emerge like tempered steel
And stronger than before.

So go your own way if you must
It's not important why
But be assured the day will come
When it's your turn to cry.

Melanie Pedersen

A Child's Creed

I'm deeply touched by what I see
When you cast your eyes on me
You never cease to understand
That inside of me lives heartaches
and pains!
I'm eager to learn
I want to know
Give me guidance so that I may grow
Hold my hands and guide my feet
Make me an example for the world
to greet!
Challenge my mind
And you will see
I can become
Whatever I want to be
I'll make a difference
I want stop
I'll keep searching
Until I reach the top!

Julia F. Kearns

Love Is....

Love is a wishing stone from
a far away country.
Love is a red rose.
Love is a play.
Love is a kiss and hug.
Love is a baby.
Love is a flower bright as can be.
Love is a country side.
Love is a cat and dog together.
Love is Valentines day.
Love is America.
Love is Christmas.
Love is Easter.
Love is a card.
Love is a church.
Love is a friend.
Love is parents.
Love is God.

Jenica Jones

Love Must Be Evident

Love presets no limit
Love respects no bound
Love knows its origin
For in Christ, it's found

Love seeks no chartered course
It just craves fulfillment
Relying on its source
Pledges deep commitment

Love thrives on expression
Its light is clearly seen
Each act - a reflection
Of love's radiating beam

Love reciprocates love
Enriching hearts and lives
When joined with Christ above
Love forever resides

Dawn S. Spence Applewhite

Poetry - Haiku

Earths history viewed
In metamorphic array
Mammoth Cave's display.

Wind, water and time
With God as the architect
Formed the Grand Canyon.

Majestic water
Falling foaming constantly
Niagara Falls show

Mary K. Lacy

Sepulchral Flight

A spineless thing she is
a snail or so she says.
With her eyes innocence
she is the beautiful cowardess
clothed in robes of pure.
Yet her pains still endure
so she has clipped her very own wings
epitome of spineless things.

Lindsey Dresser

"Come To Ohio"

Come to Ohio;
Come take a ride
O'er the rolling hills
And green countryside;

O'er rivers and lakes
And streams winding through
The bountiful farms
And historical views;

O'er rail ways and mines
And caverns and mounds,
Factories and suburbs
And cities and towns.

"Mother of Presidents,"
"Mother of states,"
Everchanging seasons,
And people of all traits;

"Beautiful Ohio;"
Heed her call;
Come to Ohio;
"The Heart of It All."

Leah Findlay

Have You Heard?

Where are the lovely song birds
Where, did they go
Pretty little creatures
With greetings in the morn
Look up and through the trees
Where have they gone

How I long to hear their voices
Lifting my spirit from dawn to dusk
This imbalance of nature
Now I wonder
What will happen to us

Their music gives healing and solace
To those they trust
Look up and through the trees
Where are the lovely song birds
Where have they gone

Joan Knoblauch Washburn

"Imagine Me"

Imagine me -
How happy and free
I could be.
If I took me
A little less seriously.

If I laughed at my faults
Every once and awhile.
Accepting my mistakes
Sometimes with a smile.

If I took little setbacks
And failures in stride.
While remembering that crying
Is only a part of pride.

Imagine me-
How happy and free
I could be.
If I could just enjoy
Being me.

Michael D. Williams

The Beginning

Our world is marvelous
For all who can see,
The beautiful things
God created for thee.

So perfectly brilliant
Created he light,
He called the light day
And the darkness called night.

Then formed he dry land
And waters called Sea,
God saw it was good
For it answered his plea.

He brought forth green grass
Flowers and trees fit his plan,
Then brought forth living creatures
Greatest of all being man.

God saw all was good
And rested the seventh day,
For heaven and earth
Were now on display.

Shirley M. Kohls

When Darkness Falls

When darkness falls,
You cannot see,
The lark of depression,
The lark of nothing.

The only character,
Is darkness,
For the bells ring clear,
Only clear to the ear.

You only see
What you hear,
What you touch,
What you feel.

The life of all,
Is lifeless to you,
For you cannot grab hold of it,
For you are not part of it.

When darkness falls,
You are nothing,
And we are all,
For you cannot see in darkness.

Anjuli Sinha

St. Peter's Birds

How solitary the long view
of the water was—
only the waves caressing
each other's foamy curves
with the ephemeral rhythm
of the cold, wintry sea.

Two stormy petrels on the wing
circled the ever-changing sand dunes
of the brown, rocky beach.
Time seemed to repeat the same hour,
and the perplexed sun
chose to stand still.

How lonely my soul was—
and yet how peacefully quiet.

Mercedes Paz Carty

Tender Tabby

Can you love a cat?
Yes, you can and that's a fact!
She's charming and discreet
Certainly a rare treat.
A joy to have around
between purring and mewing
It's the ultimate sound.
Curled up like a furry ball
Is a favorite position of sleep,
I kiss her gently and
Out of pure love almost weep.
This little creature
With perfect features
Has won my heart
Right from the start.

Pearl Zwerdling

Between You And I

What do you get
When you're feeling down
Feeling rather sad
And there's trouble all around

I know what you get
You get feelings of uncertainty
Looking for someone to talk to
Friend, come and talk to me.

People get sick or suffer with pain
And some even die
I wish I knew, I wish you knew,
I wish we knew why.

All I do when I don't know why
I absorb everyone's feelings,
Smile, and look to the sky.

I have but one wish
When we don't know why
I hope we keep this special bond,
Between you and I.

Donna L. Yanez

All Around Me

Oh, I wish that everyone could live
as happily as me
and see what I see
all around me.

Graceful trees reaching toward the sky
green and grassy fields
blowing on by
all around me.

Painted butterflies in flight
busy little bumblebee
birds singing joyfully
all around me.

Flowers blooming in the sun
growing along the bank
where the sparkling river runs
all around me.

Oh, I wish that everyone could see
what God has given me
for this is what I see
all around me.

Nina Marie Lawson

The Truth

We each receive our share of days
And life sometimes can seem a maze
We cannot know what comes with years
Sometimes happiness, sometimes tears

On stormy seas we may be tossed
Until we fear all hope is lost
And yet somehow we find a way
To make it through another day

On sunny days our spirits rise
We win the game and gain the prize
And feel there's nothing we can't do
Our inner self is born anew

Within the years the seasons fly
Like drifting clouds across the sky
Till in my daughters eyes I see
The vision of all I'd hoped she'd be

If there's one truth I could impart
It be to listen to your heart
Dare to try and take the chance
And in your heart your soul will dance

Susan Sponseller

Upon The Waves

They dance upon the waves,
Like angels,
Laughing happily,
With their shimmering laughter,
Rolling away like the wind.

The sun glistens on their hair,
While they dance like gypsies,
Of danger and fear unaware,
Only of the love they share.

But soon it may die,
And tear them apart,
So they enjoy it now,
Upon the waves.

Kavita Murthy

The Sands Of Time

Glistening, golden granules gliding
Silently along the curves of glass,
Each tiny crystal reflecting moments
Of the future, present, and past.

The sands of time yet to come,
Still softly sifting above the rest,
Gently tumble and envelop
The future in a golden nest.

Slowly slipping into any abyss
Of swirling, spiraling sands,
Future mixes with the present
And falls into past's frozen hands.

In the still, quiet depths
Of the frigid past,
Lies yesterday and yesteryear
And all of history passed.

The sands are forever flowing
Throughout eternity,
Tiny prisms refracting time
Into lives, for infinity.

Leah Campbell

The Great And Small Of Christmas

The flurry of snow
So it's the season

The dancing of light's
Brought about reflection

The goodwill of Man
Our selfless and loving friendships

Goodwill of Man to Man
A universal commitment

Love of Creatures
Our animal friends

We sing in merriment
About hopes, contentment, expectations

Many call it Christmas
And renew their faith in all
Jane M. DeWitt

Gethsemane

I want to weep, my eyes are dry.
No welcome tear will wet my eye.
My heart is heavy like a stone.
I am alone. I am alone.

My voice does echo in my ears,
And in my mind, I part the years.
And in my eyes, — Gethsemane!
My precious God! You are with me!

Olga M. Drahozal

Rainbow

My name is Rainbow,
So, pretty in the sky

My name is rainbow,
You wonder why

A name that was given just to me,
It reflects on my family tree

I am colors of the rainbow,
Purple, blue and white
(Filipino) (Hawaiian) (Haole)

I am colors of the rainbow
7, tall and bright

My name is rainbow...
Of the colors up above

My name is rainbow...
From a grandfather's love
Lovelyn M. Kekino

We

We are so alike,
In oh so many ways.
We are the sunshine,
Giving joy to all the days.
We are the songs,
And we are the singing.
We are happy bells,
Laughing and ringing.
We are the days,
and we are years.
We are the laughter,
And we are tears.
we are the earth,
And the heavens above.
But most of all,
We.....are love.

Richard C. Mays

Lost Soldier's Song

Saint Peter, don't you know.
It weren't my fault.
I gave my body,
they stole my soul.

Hell no, we won't go,
scratched on my gun.
They gave no choice,
they wouldn't take no.

I push up daisy's,
which offers no seed.
If it wasn't me; Peter,
who else would you see.

But it is true,
it was me.
Duty bound,
with my weapon,
i soiled the ground.

My body so cold.
I just wanted to grow old.
Kenn E. McDaniel

"My Daddy Left A Year Ago"

My Daddy left a year ago
he had better things to do.
God needed him in heaven
to start his life anew.

It's peaceful there where he's at
Not a problem can be found.
No wars no aids, no drugs, no crime
Just pretty flowers all around.

I think he has a job there
moving furniture around.
And every time it thunders
I enjoy its every sound.

I know that he is happy
I see a smile on his face.
I'll remember when I think of him
That he's in a better place.

So I close my eyes and say my prayers
Just thanking God above
That he was kind enough to give to me
My Daddy that I loved.
Betty Ann Stoneburgh

Today I Celebrate Me

Treading upon the words
of
Duplicity
and
Your broken promises
I
Chose to
eliminate the
Lies and
Enabling
Behaviors as
Reality and realization
Avenged
the
evil
Manifestation
Encountered.

Diane Adele Pomeroy

Thoughts Of You

Old Shelley, he may like
To a West Wind write at night,
Or in the bright of day
To a Skylark honor pay.
My time is better spent,
Telling you how much you meant.

Keats on the other hand,
A Grecian Urn, he thinks is grand,
What else I can not say
I shan't give him time of day.
What I write is for you,
To me you are a "who's who."

Byron's England Farewell,
Many lads have learned to tell,
On Ocean's what he wrought,
Teachers they have always taught.
But what I want to state,
you brighten our every date.
Guy E. Tuttle

Friend

There are many treasures
in this world.
Like rubies, diamonds,
emeralds and pearls.

All these things
cannot replace,
the happy smile,
on your familiar face.

Nor can they give,
the love and devotion
that a friend gives
with deep emotion.

There is no treasure
more valuable and known
than that of a friendship
that's full grown.
Dorothy J. Steele

Journey Through

On the face of time
We are simple teardrops
given only moments to shine
Then we fade away
Down the cheek of life
falling, falling
Each second moving faster

We have so little control

hit the ground
our final resting place
lay still
awaiting the moment
we are gone
H. L. Charleston

Love

Love changes the look
Love shortens the mind
Love makes it hard
to except little time
Love brightens the day
and enhances the night
It makes it look like
it's worth the fight
Bonnie J. Clauser

Unleashed Sight

I see the wind...
I allow my eyes to wander,
watching the clouds.
Passions emerge and find
the way to words, but it is
I, the hesitant, who disowns them.
So with my head,
laying on the pillow of grass,
I look up into the blueness.
My mind and the Earth are one;
I soak it like a plant,
filling my roots,
until, at last I am in peace.
Quiet, serene, a thousand images
are breathed into vision,
for I can see the wind.

Andrew Neal

On Coming Of Fever

Yellow road. Road is yellow.
Yellow is road. Quite yellow.
Yellow. Road.
Yellow and road.
Road and yellow.
Road is yellow.
And yellow, yellow, and yellow.
Yellow and yellow.
Yellow road. Quite yellow.
The road is yellow.
Road? Yellow!
Yellow is road.
Silence, please.
Perhaps, I am blind.

Milos Vujasinovic

On Bended Knee!

Home of the brave
Land of the free..
That's what America
Used to be!

But now we sit
Behind locked doors.
When our children are at school,
In fear; we pace the floors!

Will they return home
Safe and drug free?
Or will I be called to the morgue,
Or hospital emergency!

God bless America,
God bless me.
With your loving hands,
Bring my child home to me.

Janet L. Buchanan

Falling Stars

We were young.
We were lost.
We were old.
We paid the cost.
We were real.
We had fought.
We had dreams,
We had sought.
Until it seemed,
We were all just falling stars.
Falling stars...

Claire Porter

The Gift

You gave me a gift,
But before I realized it,
    I threw it away.

This gift took a long time to make.
As time went by,
    I watched you work,
Intensely...
    Carefully...
Until it was completed.

You set it in my hand,
I tore it while your tears fell.
    Only now,
Did I realize that the gift you gave,
    was the gift of love.

Margaret Smith

Equality At The Center

Earnest seeker comes home
Quest for truth fulfilled
Universe embraces itself
All pain included in the love
Love knows no bounds
Illumined mind at peace
Thrilling waves of liquid fire
Yield to bliss

All-Mighty God is self
There is none else

Thou art that
Here, now
Equality births compassion

Certainty at last
Energy a fountain of life
No restriction whatsoever
Truth and beauty, love and joy
Everlasting praise and thanks
Revelation in the heart of being

Arisa Victor

Twinkle, Twinkle

Twinkle, Twinkle
the cold, crisp snow
lingered down
ever so slow.
Twinkle, Twinkle
gazed my eyes
at the magical moment
in the skies.
Twinkle, Twinkle
the fire glowed
as it warmed my
longing fingers and toes.
Twinkle, Twinkle
the night wept
like a baby
who never slept.
Twinkle, Twinkle
the cold, crisp snow
lingered down
ever so slow.

Ellen Wilshusen

Sandpiper

Chasing the surf
little twig-legged
creature
of the sea and sand.
Pulling a wave in
with your zipper track.
Turning to see it
laugh merrily as it runs
back to sea
erasing your zipper
as it goes.

Your turn now.
You take to wing
shrilly chattering
swooping down
"Tag! You're it!"
You touch the sand
zipping the sea to shore
only to have it
ripped away once more.

Jimmie S. Faris

Emotional Waves Of Blue

Soothing waves of blue
as the ocean rhythmically
pounds against the beach
give a calm feeling.

Depressing waves of blue
as life seems unbearable
working through the pain
brings you down.

Aspiring waves of blue
as the eagle flies across
the sky soaring away
lift your spirits.

Twisting waves of blue
as you write about life's
cruel bumps and turns
spins you around.

Rippling waves of blue
as the wind brushes
the smooth pool of water
stir the emotions.

Evelyn Proctor

My Parents

To hear some one say it,
how lived long ago,
We know nothings of troubles
and nothing of woes.
The troubles were harder back
then in those days, we carried
our water and held our own hay.
We thought of our neighbor as
they were our selfs.
We look after our brother for
not one bit of wealth.
We taught of our children not
to make our mistakes.
Mean while praying to God
he'd lead the way.
We know were not perfect because
of the date.
Were just saying we love you
don't make our mistakes.

Margaret Anne Massey

Nurses

Angels of mercy
Dressed all in white;
Watching and waiting
Through the long night.

Like a guardian angel
Hovering near;
Easing the pain
Dispelling each fear.

Silent as shadows
Watching with care;
No matter the hour
An angel is there.

Bernice Roder

"My Vision"

My mother came to say good-bye
She was the highest in the sky
Upon the wings of a bird she took
Coming by for one last look
I knew she wouldn't go away
Without seeing me one more day
She told me that she loved me so
But she would shortly have to go
She said hey look don't worry much
You know I'll always keep in touch
Just remember what I say
I love you now and every day
A part of me lives on in you
Remember this and don't feel blue
That is the last I've seen of her
It's helped me some I know for sure
Yet she has gone and I remain
My world will never be the same

Jane Hinz

Star Led

In such a rush we go
From shop to shop in town
Up the streets and down
Everything is bright and shinny
To celebrate the birth
of the Christ child
We welcome him a
new each year
with all the traditions
we hold so dear.
This year let us be
star led and wonder bound
Till in all of the world
joy and peace is found.

Nancy Alford

Dreams

I can be a pirate
on a pirate ship,
I can see a Martian
from another world
or be a whale in the
sea, or possibly go back in
time to meet a dinosaur
oh so many things I can
be or see, where you ask
In my dreams, that's where
I can be or see anything
I want be.

Liz Wiemken

Shatter

Woman bound in linen tightly,
sarcophagus wombed,
see your life
reflections upon
rippled silver
outside in.

The cloth ravels, yet you take
no step away from
warped beveled
edges, or the
struggle shattered glass
at your feet,
as though you have no choice
beyond your winter
mantled mind.

Rebecah Hall

Who?

When you are
    what you are,
        you'll be liked
            for what you are.

When you are
    what you aren't,
        you'll be liked
            for what you're not.

Then when you are
    what you aren't,
        you won't be liked
            for what you are.

Elizabeth Ann Yowell

Perspective Of The Moment

Summer sun
Hot on your face
Forget the winter darkness

Coral beach
Your joyful floor
Distant from the icy pavement

Ocean waves
Your private bath
Untouched by the day's debris

This moment in time
A mist of melancholy
A plaintive pause before blue skies

Lawrence S. Fowler

Half A Circle

Half a Circle, what have I done.
I've made a have, half a circle
Where someone can or can not complete
    Half a Circle, what have I done

A child will laugh, play or run
Shall be complete
For I have made a half a circle
With love this day.

Josephine Frances Deneen

The Heart's Desert Rose

Ragged edges
Lifeless ledges
Gall midges on sedges
Warring wedges, broken pledges.

Brambles and thorns
Border bleak morns
Trudging on corns
Wanderer forlorn, mourns.

Trust lost
New world the cost
The fleeced tossed
The dispossessed bossed.

Within wasteland's desolation
Wrought by Rebel's defoliation
A dark red rose the emancipation
Pilgrim's supernal consolation.

Though by faithless hated
Leading Lodestar never fated
Cross and crown now mated
The heart's deepest longing sated.

Robert J. Palma

Bowler's Lament

A perfect score I don't expect
Of course, I'd gladly take it;
But until then, I'll struggle on,
With miracles... I'd make it!

The game is fun, we all admit
With challenge ever there;
If skill does not afford a strike,
Then luck might lend a spare.

The gutter balls, the splits and blows
Are not considered "nice,"
But then, I get my money's worth
I roll that ball down twice!

Phyllis F. Smith

A Child's View

(The Cave)

Going back to my roots?
What roots?
Are they in the
    rounded leaves
Of sea grapes
Or the rocky climb
Between the Bishop's Pond
And the frantic,
    rushing sea
In its mysterious
Hypnotic path
(My heart-beat suspended
With fear and fascination,
And my father's hand
Intertwined firmly
With mine)
As the sea enters
The cave
Underneath
The lighthouse.

Febe Gonzalez

Say Hello

You only have to say hello
And instantly I find
My heart is filled with smiles of joy
My cares are far behind

You only have to say hello
And suddenly I feel
A special glow inside of me
So very warm and real

And when I need the morning sun
To start my day off right
You only have to say hello
And life is sweet and bright.

Kimberly Graves

Untitled

I shall stand taller than
    a palm tree
I shall set my spirit free
It shall soar higher
    than an eagle
Now that I am off my knees,

For I no longer have a
    need for you,
I bore my children,
    I shared them too!

I have kept my pride and
    dignity
Through the years I've
    guarded my identity
You no longer can be little me,
I am free.

Eloina M. Giron

Outside My Window Frame

Outside my window frame,
there is a cycle like a game.

In front of my window not far away,
there is a forest of trees,
it is beautiful and buzzing
with the sound of bees.

Behind of there,
there is a mountain setting there,
wise and witty.
In the winters,
him I pity.

Beyond there,
I have not a clue.
But for all I know,
there is blue.

Heather Henderson

Snow

Snow is so beautiful,
Falling through the air.
Snowflakes running, dancing,
Maybe even prancing.
Snowflakes so fragile, and gentle,
Falling to the ground.
There's a white blanket,
Lying all around.
Snow is like a fluffy pillow,
As though it were a cloud.
Kids hoping for no school,
As the snow falls so proud!

Ashley K. Luhrs

Untitled

If I had an Island
Way out in the sea,
then you would be the only one
Way out there with me

And if I had an Island
all to my very own
then you would be the only one
that I had ever shown

And if I had on Island
no matter what the size
then you would be the only one
right there before my eyes

So if I get an Island
Please come along with me
for you would be the only one
I'd ever want to see

Ken Bika

The Birth Of A Garden

I awoke one morning, my heart,
my mind, and my soul in a craze.
I had dreamed of a garden, a
beautiful garden, and I was in a daze.
I dreamed of tomatoes, carrots,
beans and of tall sweet corn.
This very day, this very dream,
this very garden was born.
I turned the soil, I set the
rows and I sowed the seeds.
I realized someone had
given my garden just what it needs.
Now I gaze across my garden
with very satisfying pride.
I knew I had help because
God was on my side.
He gave it the sun, the moon,
the rain and the Earth.
I thank God for giving
you, me, and my garden its birth.

Ronald Cloud

One Day (Veteran's Day)

There's one day of sorrow,
One day to cry,
One day of honor,
And all know why.
We go to the Wall,
See the men who fought.
So hang your head low,
For this very sad thought.

Preston Kwok-Wai Chan

Avoiding Reflection

Avoiding reflection
Seeing into the
Windows
Black in all directions
Weeping as the
Willow
Until on second
Glance
Seeing into the blue
Given another chance
To begin anew

Tiffany Adams

Desperate For You To Know

Hear me out,
My feelings are noticeable.
Hear me shout,
I have no bound.
See my fear in front of my eyes,
See me cry,
I feel like..
Dying.

So little of words said,
So huge of meaning.
Hear me out!
Hear me shout!
Save me,
Oh,
Please, save me!

Cecilia Awayan

Rhythms

I ride the swells
that shift and beat the ship
I shift in those rhythms
that lift and swing and drop
lift and swing and drop
and I am an infant
in a mother's womb
swaying
swaying with her breathing
feeling
the beating drum
that pounds the chest
and beats this fragile hull
creaking
wailing louder
in the relentless rhythms
of the sea

Harland J. Hand

Essence Of Existence

I have concluded...
In essence;
    That on this...
"Plane of Existence"...
    It is not "PEOPLE";
"WE"...as individuals,
    Who are of utmost
Importance!
    Rather...
It is our "BEST"...
    "THOUGHTS" and "ACTIONS"
That are of "TRUE"
    Significance!
For, these, indeed ARE...
    Crystalline "GEMS"
Emanating from...
    The "SOUL"... of "GOD"

David L. Johnson Sr.

Thoughts On Spring

Floating above and all around
    Puffy white clouds abound
A clear and lovely spring day
If I could... this feeling delay
    A soft and gentle breeze
    My mind is so at ease
The sky is a bright deep blue
    To myself I must be true.

Janet H. Lassen

Nothing Is Really Wasted

Oh, the times
We've wondered why
a long - awaited dream
is gathered up in tears and sighs,
and life's joy is gone, so it seems.
But, nothing is really wasted,
not even tears;
They clear the heart's mind
making a path for new joys to find.
Oh, the times
we walk a lonely way
and no one seems to care.
There's not much we can do or say,
our thoughts tumble everywhere.
But, nothing is really wasted,
not even loneliness;
Because somewhere along the way
a friend helps to ease the stress
with just the right words to say!

Frances F. Reed

One Nation Under God

This is a nation under God
Walk nobly on this holy Sod;
Let us declare - each one of us
"In God alone we fully trust!"
No nation without God can rise,
Nor long hold on to freedom's prize;
For freedom God has set us free
Stand firm and live in liberty!

This is a nation strong and great,
But one thing's sure to seal our fate:
We cannot long on earth endure
With our foundation unsecure.
Now let us with one voice proclaim:
"Our God has given us our fame!
With Him as all our strength and power
We will yet see our greatest hour!"

Harry Hodges Cunningham

"A Precious, Special Angel"

The moment that I saw her,
in my heart I knew
She was a precious, special angel,
a dream of mine come true
For years I hoped and prayed,
of wanting to someday
To know that when I saw her,
I could not look away
It all worked out so beautifully,
just like a fairy tale
About a man believing,
who set his dreams assail
Seeing is believing,
and feeling is to know
That even without a spoken word,
It's in her eyes that show
So after years of hopes and prayers,
I finally know I'm loved
By an angel sent to me,
down from above.

Gail P. Sudul

Same Heart

The day moves smoothly
knowing as I do
that it will end beyond the sunset
and I will be with you

We may not be together
and perhaps we won't even speak
but when I rest my head on my pillow
I need not want nor seek

Because you are always here
inside my heart so warm
and although I may miss you next to me
my thoughts of you take form

We never have to worry
when we are apart
because feeling the way we do
we are one in the same heart

Helen-Louise C. Xiques

Untitled

If I could have one wish
Of what I'd like to be,
I'd want to be a mountain
So I could make you happy!

You'd rest your head upon my grass,
And tread upon my dirt,
Take your nourishment from my streams,
I promise it won't hurt.

And if one wish you could have,
I know what it would be,
To be a "Mountain Man," my love
So you could be close to me!

Christine J. Karl

"Let's Get Married"

Congratulations!
This is real
Not fake so let's kneel.
Praise the Lord for how we feel
cause today is the day we make a deal.
Life goes on after this
so let's get married
like we wished
Love is all that really counts
and that's what I'm going to announce.
Let's go on a honeymoon
far, far away.
But not too soon
for this is the day
we made a deal
and let's both feel
that this is real.

Kathy Kalich

Giraffe

Seeing to eternity
Tallest of the tall
Pattern of complexity
Puzzling over all.

Head held high with tongue-in-cheek
Listening to my voice
Valentine of lofty heights
Gentleness your choice.

Ann Daigle

Maybe Love

Maybe love is like a resting place
a shelter from the storm
it exists to give you comfort
it is there to keep you warm
and in those times of trouble
when you feel most alone
the memory of love will bring you home.

Maybe love is like an ocean
full of conflict, full of change
like a fire when its cold outside
or thunder when it rains.

Maybe love is like a window
maybe an open door
it invites you to come closer
it wants to show you more
and even if you lose yourself
and don't know what to do
The memory of love will always
see through.

Lora Brownlee

Not Random

When our smiles overlapped
And we joked about
Vanilla latte promises
Toilet paper ideas
Watching a TV that wasn't really there
Our backs were to the door...
What time was it
When you killed the cockroach,
The kitchen critter?
I couldn't understand HOW.
I didn't think you had it in you.
What time was it
When the lava lamp exploded
And your screams locked the door?
My votives flared with rage...
What time was it
When you shaved off your milk mustache
And painted on a shadow?
Your alarm clock woke me...
I still don't know how to turn it off.

Miriam Kapner

Feelings From Far Away

So far
from you
I ache a lake of
lonely.

Only
not a burly giant lake
slamming shores
with waves of
anguish.

And not a turgid
flatland pond,
opaque with silt and
restless.

I ache a mountain lake:
remote,
crystal,
cold,
deep,
and lonely.

Ted L. Gibbons

Joy

Born again
　Thank the Lord!

Pay attention,
　Here comes the baby,
Pray again,
　Thank the Lord!
Amen! Amen!

Stay again,
　There's loves laughter
Safe again
　Thank the Lord!

Leave again,
　Die again.
To be born again,
　Thank the Lord!
Amen! Amen!

　　Adrienne B. Fried

Autumn Passage

The stillness
　of September,
The warmth of
　the sun.
The life cycle has ended,
　the retreat has begun.
The birds have gathered
As from an unseen hand.
That will gently direct them,
　from the cold, icy land.

If human's could only believe
　what they see
To trust in the seasons of life
　and be free.
To trust in the retreat
To give into the Hand
That gives direction to birds,
That gives meaning to Man.

　　H. L. Junkin Jr.

Tranquility

The water laughed at our feet,
Delighted at our surprise!
It danced in gay abandon,
Jade aprons with white bow ties.

The sand castles of the children
Vanished quickly away!
And we hastily ran shoreward,
Lest we go the same as they!

The clouds put the mountains to sleep
In blankets of snowy white;
And the stars lay down like sheep
And were folded in by the night.

　　Florence M. Brown

Gopher Tortoise

Wise
ancient
dirt encrusted.
The embodiment of mother earth
dwells deep within her
filled with her secrets,
her wisdom
to share with us
newcomers to the planet.

　　Cheryl Lincoln

Now

I put on my pink skirt
And little pearl shoes
I let my hair down
Touch my face with rouge
I am beautiful tonight

Scrape up some rainbow
To paint on a smile
Forget the rage
Escape for a while
Night's cool kiss awakens desire
I vibrate with hope
To feel life's fire

Expect the unexpected
My mind clear and sound
My spirit soars on a starlit sky
Observe myself a moment
Long enough
It's okay
Just right
I am beautiful tonight

　　Katarzyna Galazka

Tempest

A Dragon
You slithered upon me
A mist
You hypnotized me
Oh such clever words
Fingers so precise
Your prey
To tempt and to entire
Seduced
Your windily empire
Bewitched
A captive of desire
How I craved for more
Loving you with greed
My soul devoured
Left to bleed
Every corner turned or whisper heard
I look for you
Every night in solitaire
I reach, I feel for you

　　Anna Marie Rocca

Marathon

When you're all soaked in sweat
And you just can't forget
'Bout the pain in your feet
From hitting concrete,
You've just begun.

When your lungs beg for air
And you find it's not there
'Cause the whole world's a blur
And your head's in a whir,
Keep it up.

When you've done all you dare
And you find you can't bear
To take one more step,
For you've lost all your pep;
Strive for more.

When you're nearing the end
For it's just 'round the bend
You'll be glad you stayed in:
You can win!
You can win!

　　Emily E. Bright

Life's Greatest Rewards

The greatest of life's rewards
lies sleep on the children's ward
a baby bold and pretty
wondering if it's witty.

Each time we see the newborn
life again is at it's dawn
as he kicks and hollers his way
he's telling us it's his day.

As he grows and learns his name
life will never be the same
If he doesn't leave too soon
He'll descend on many moons.

Time will surely come
no matter where he's from
when all will gather to
Bless the things he do.

　　James H. O. Chisley

Time

Let go
And let time
Perform
The sublime.

My concept of God
Is defined by time
The devout might say
An irreverent crime.

If you suffer enough
Death becomes a friend
The hopeless can embrace
Hoping hurt may end.

When I see
Suffering everywhere
Comfort comes
Knowing time is there.

　　Grant T. Smith

Untitled

I saw,
　A fairy in the forest
　Early in the morning
　　When the grass is still wet
I saw,
　A fairy from yesterday's
　A spirit of the forest
　　Dancing, quietly
　In a sleepy silence
When the air is still
　Red and yellow
And clouds of peace
　Came over me
When I saw a fairy
　A dream
　From another world
　　Untouchable? Impossible?
Shh!! Don't break the magic
It's all within you

　　Eija DeLa Garza

M e

Solitude brings Phantoms
From another place and time
They carry on with Their Parade
Atop this Masquerade of mine

Solitude brings Shadows
From behind the scenes I play
They dance of truths that I deny
To all who glance my way

Solitude brings Voices
Echoes buried deep within
They speak to me of times long gone
They run the Circus of my mind

Solitude removes My Veil
Where lay concealed a dagger
It takes away my Painted Smile
Of normalcy and laughter

Solitude removes The Stage
Where I perform you see
A Clown until the curtain falls
And there is only... Me

Beatriz M. Pena/mina

Dreams

We all have dreams
Some dreams seem to
take forever
Few dreams my
Come true
We work hard
still we keep believing
Dreams can be shattered
at once
Still we have the
determination
When a dream comes true
we feel anything is
possible
When dreams fail the
disappoint overwhelms us
However tomorrow is
another day and our
other dreams are waiting to
prevail

Sue Gillespie

That's My Mother

Sweet and gentle
loving, too
That's my mother
all year thru.

Thoughtful - kind
That's her charm
She's a dear
that mother mine.

Do I love her?
Treasure her, too?
You're dog gone right
You bet I do!

Brycie Click

Snowflakes

Small white stars
Floating down
Crystal raindrops
On the ground

Slowly they float
Down from the sky
From cotton clouds
That sits on high

Flakes of snow
So beautifully white
They glow on their own
With an inner light

No two are alike
This I know
These graceful crystals
Made of snow

Heather Cameron

The Sea

The sea comes in like
a blue brocaded gown.

Tossing and turning all
around

Suddenly it burst upon
the shore

Then everything is calm
once more

Judith Lyle Jones

A Heartbeat

I lie my hand upon your chest
and feel your heart beat through
the longer I lay by your side
the faster mine beats too
A rhythm pounding through
the air out from you to me
We've done what we dare and
we are what we dare to be
A sound only ears of love
can hear
older things were not as they
appeared
That rhythm beats within
my reach
imagine the beautiful words
we'd hear if a heartbeat
speaks

Tina Lynn Porth

The Bird

I am a bird
I fly around
I soar above
The tiny town
With wings of fluff
And a beak of gold
I see the people
Young and old
And when I fly
Above their heads
You'd never guess
The things they've said
After I went....
SPLAT!

Katie Bauer

Advent - Exodus

You came -
And at once
My every room
Filled with beauty.
All nooks and crannies
In my home
Echoed your
Jocund liveliness.

You left -
And at once
My every room
Spilt its joy.
All nooks and crannies
In my home
Echoed my
Deep loneliness.

Rose Anglin

Children Without Faces

Great-Grandma used to see children.
Children without names, without faces.
Children wearing old-fashioned clothes.
Children ever quiet
With her 'til she died.
Grandpa too has seen those children.
Still nameless, still faceless.
Still wearing the same clothes.
Still ever so quiet.
Grandpa too has died.
These children without faces.
Who are they? Where are they from?
What do they want?
They seem to look right thru you,
ever knowing, ever watchful.
What are they trying to say?
You see I too have seen them.
In a dream.
What will became of me?

Susan K. Branch

Spiral Of Life

Though the night has fallen
On a friendly face
A new star shines brightly
To take their place
A heavenly reminder that they
Are never really gone
And an earthly reminder
That we must carry on
Do not feel sorrow but
Rather look above
His glory will shower you
With unseen love

Shann E. Butler

Linked Souls

Shiny bright O' Wondrous Star
I am so thankful, for who you are.
Soft Kittens and Rainbows' End.
You are who, I call my friend.
Full of life and love and whim.
One who listens again and again.
God bless you all ways and always.
For you bring me close to Him.
Shiny bright o' Wondrous Star
Your powerful light shall never dim.

Sandra Kay Kidder

Little Weed

May the rose bring hope and grace.
As such a splendid creation;
is a light of life.

Let me be the rose for once,
I want to bud gloriously.
Let me in grow in the earth;
And have my moment of bloom.

To be wanted among all.
To be beautiful inside and out;
and be the hearth of love.

No, not me.
I just wait on the side;
Trampled and without life.

Just little old me;
A little weed.

Leida Deanne LePage

Truth Seeker

As I walk life's curious
pathways,
I seek out curious places
curious
things.
Seeking the connecting
tendons
That make sense out of the
muscle of life.
Sketchy timelines stretch
through my mind.
A spiritual pencil makes note
of all I discover.
Thoughts race
about my head
Seeking their proper places in
my mental rainbow.
From creation to destruction
I seek truth in all I see.

Kimberly Kozee

At Days End...

Just to look into your eyes,
Reveals the truth and tells no lies,
Gaze further deep into your soul,
I feel the warmth inside its hold.

Embrace its love, possess its lust,
Until the day returns to dust,
But still I'm here, we're not apart,
Safe in your arms when all is dark.

When all is gone, when all is black,
You tell me things to ease me back,
Your gentle voice delivers words,
And one by one they're softly heard.

Inside my head you fill my dreams,
You stop the pain, you silence screams,
To ease my mind is all I ask,
To resurrect me from my past.

To lead me on into the night,
To let me know that all is right,
And when you do you're at your best,
Until I close my eyes to rest....

C. William Brenize

Love In Bloom

Love is like a rose
Vivid and bright
Wilted at the edges
Yet still a beautiful sight

Each beautiful pedal
Formed from the start
Allowed to grow
With warmth and heart

Each little thorn
Sometimes pricks
The painful feeling
Seldom sticks

Allowed to grow freely
Year after year
Knowing it will blossom
without fear

Love is like a rose
Given patience and care
The beauty that comes from it
was meant to share

Charlotte J. Jennings

Growing Up Or He Is Becoming

There he is
At the distant edge
Of his own mind.

Teetering
On the brink
Of maturity,
He rushes headlong,
Unknowing and fearful,
Into a future
Waiting to be discovered.

Uncertain of each step,
He blindly reaches out and
Finds a hand
To stabilize him
On his journey.

The boy becomes a man.

Troy R. Hailparn

Oh Mother, Mine

Oh Mother, mine,
Beside your grave I reminisce and pine
For happy days that I once knew
Until the day you passed away.

Full of patience and so good,
You were the example of motherhood;
Endowed with God's gift of love,
You imparted it to all of us.

Also the sweetest, dearest Mother
To my sisters and my brother,
You brought laughter to our hearts
And sunshine into our home.

Oh Mother, mine,
Upon my knees
I join my hands and pray
That you may rest in peace.

Irene T. Xavier

You And I

I look at you and I know
You are everything I ever wanted for me
I will never have you
You will never have me.

You will be married
I will be single
You will be free
I will be me.

You will have love
I will have hate
You will have a significant other
I will have significant others.

You will make children
I will make none, you will make a home
I will make a room.

You will grow old together
I will grow old alone
We could have had each other
We could have been together
You chose for us to have another.

Shannon Kaupp

Because

She has a small round face
And she's cute as a button
If I knew she was mine
I'd sure be a strutting

She has a smile to die for
And a body to match
For millions of men
She would be quite a catch

She's wonderful, she's smart
She's sweet and she's witty
She has skin so soft
And a smile so pretty

To me she's the wild one
No way to control
But my desire for her is endless
It goes clear through my soul

Do I have her on a pedestal
Why should I care
Because...I LOVE HER
I said it so there.

Michael W. Cave

"Bouncing The Budget"

How easily you reach your hand
into the poor man's pocket.
How quickly you do close
compassion's open door, and lock it.

While to the money-hungry ones
you listen very well
and would ease the burden of their tax
while their huge profits swell.

However to the elderly
and handicapped you say
"Your life of luxury must cease
we must take it away!"

And welfare also cannot be
for even those in need.
but when you wish to raise your pay
you are certain to succeed.

Oliver J. Larlham

My Loss

Your shoulder was always there,
For me to lean upon.
During my despair and toils,
You listened and cared for me.

You were always there for me,
To cheer and encourage me
During my victories, you
Congratulated and celebrated with me.

Now, your shoulder is not there
For me to lean upon.
Your encouraging words and
Congratulating expressions are gone.

You were my best friend,
Always so willing to care
You always seemed to keep
The secret that I've shared.

But now oh friend,
What have I done?
I've lost my best friend
Who was always there.

Michelle Mah

Silently Sirocco Speaks

A gentle breeze is whispering
of tendrils loose and nursery rhymes.
The day wisely halts awhile,
youthful exuberance devoid of time.

A gust blows up tumultuous
blowing fierce and wild.
So sudden in duration
borne so meek and mild.

The wind blows, firm, it whistles
is heard a pretentious tune.
With sturdy stalks the wildflowers
raise heads in mighty bloom.

The lengthened day is quiet
aft cross winds tempest peaks.
The morning glorious lay their heads
as silently sirocco speaks.

Tari Meyers

Age Before Beauty

With hesitation
deeply rooted in fear
he keeps her at arms length
yet desires her near

So the looking glass reflects
the years surely gaining
there's much left to do
with the time remaining

Still the autumn of his wisdom
courts the summer of her being
and frozen winter melts
into the springtime of believing

For the fancies of the heart
know little rhyme or reason
and there is much beauty to behold
in the union of the seasons

Annette R. Aben

Watching

As I listen to the river's laughter,
I hope that it will stay thereafter,
Content and happy to run downstream.

As I watch the beauty of the dawn,
I hope the colors will stay on,
The crimson red, as night becomes day.

And I watch the full moon rise,
I revel at it making small cried,
To welcome the night to me.

As I watch the world go around,
I keep my feet upon the ground,
And I let my head fly through the sky.

As I watch the stars twinkle up above,
I wish that there will always be love,
That I can always feel.

Sarah Allsop-Fine

Slaves Of Time

Celestial field of
spirits and minds.
Love for energy;
slaves of time.

Film melts to memories,
images in our mind.
Eyes of the world;
uniting all as mankind.

Dreams of chaos,
in time and space.
Cycles of energy
universal race.

A brink of reality
I breathe and see.
Balanced for eternity;
Alive-we'll never be.

Devin Spencer

A Simple Gesture

My baby thinks in metaphors,
    gathering full stride
With a display of splendid plumage,
    the eyes of Hera's lover,
His rainbow fan of pride
    the green peafowl of Assam.

My baby speaks with pictures
    and like a child
I'm caught in his web of fascination,
    the images are swift and sure,
My head spinning wild
    I'm amazed with each revelation.

My baby has his own culture
    the myths and legends
A message drawn on a single feather:

My baby thinks in metaphors,
    My baby speaks with pictures,
Gathering full stride and like a child
    The myths and legends
Unfold with a simple gesture.

Sally VanHorn

The Remnant

Remnants of passion, remnants of love,
Remnants of living are all that remain.
Crumbs from the table once resplendent
With delectable, succulent feast
From which senses were titillated,
Appetites assuaged.
The cup was drained and filled,
And drained again.
Age that once was longed for
Just to be "old enough"
To live, to love,
Has stalked, overtaken and assaulted,
Viciously leaving in its wake
A shell, a once-was,
A remnant.

Dottie Jones

Waiting

Leaves rustling in the trees
Turn from green, to red, to brown
Turn from swaying to on the ground
Turn to crunching under my feet
I can hear the sound in my ear
Autumn is here

No leaves are on the trees
The air is cold and still
Everything is crystallized
From the falling snow
Frost and ice have come,
The sun and warmth have gone
Winter is here

Buds are growing on the trees
In the air there is a breeze
It is getting warmer out
Children play, I hear them shout
March has come, February gone
Spring is here

But I'm still waiting for Summer

Jessica Hallett

30th St Station Philadelphia

Eyes: Yellow radials —
a destination moved
into (temporal) stillness
temporal — no longer
yours.

Viscouswollen under
indoor table umbrellas
unmoved smoke
becomes self reflexive
aether: Eyes between
the I
will walk fingers of synthetic
spokes —

What is torn from
you becoming tangible
  as I move into
what congeals beneath the moving
eye.

A. Hunter Bivens

Honor Guard

I watch the Canadian geese
wheel low over the dead city.
No water here, but I know
why they land to step web-footed,
solemn, stately soldiers
among the gray stones.
Four scouts come first,
reconnoiter the quiet slopes.
Winged trumpets from the sky
announce the rest
of the graceful-necked platoon.
They search for one of their own
whose soul is cycling
from man to bird once more.
The lodestone of his soul beams
out their course, asks to be taken
where his gentleness
will not be misunderstood.

S. R. Tomanek

Alone

They walk hand in hand,
They speak in hushed tones,
They laugh with their eyes,
And she watches - alone.

She looks in the mirror,
Surprised at such sadness.
Her soul is moaning
With increasing madness.

She can't sleep at night
with thoughts of love they share.
Love she may never know
Her terrifying nightmare.

People may never know
The pain she doesn't show.
It hurts to see them everyday
Yet she cannot seem to look away.

They walk hand in hand,
They speak with hushed tones,
They laugh with their eyes,
And she watches - alone.

Antonietta Suppa

The Duel

I have two
faces in the light of day;
the face revealed
is what
you need
me
to be.
Nothing
more.
And the other
lies
in shadows
chasing
me
to be.
Something
more
than the other.

Mona Jordan

"Come, Come!"

Why did they believe what you said that you wouldn't die and stay dead
When they saw you rise again?
How could they have said it couldn't have been?
The only son of God!

Still today I wonder why They don't believe you're still alive?
And fools still mock your name,
But they'll find out without a doubt the time you come again.

Swift and silent like the night, leaving them in an awful fright.
Because they thought you just to be a fable But when the end time
comes, they'll be the ones who will have it worse than being born in
a stable. Yet it seems like I can see and hear you crying:

"COME, COME! look what I have done! I've come to this earth to save
the earth and all that is lost among, COME, COME!
I came here for YOU! I died for YOU! the lost and wretched ones!
COME, COME! before the time is done!"

Yet many may come your way, There are millions that still won't come.
The trumpets are getting ready, The sound's about to come.
Still I hear your soft loving voice saying:

"COME, COME! before the trumpet's sound!
The angels are ready for the battle call, but the battle won't take long at all.
"COME, COME! before time will come!

Michael Curtis Johnson

The Rage Within

So you say you want a companion?, but didn't anyone tell you that's
not good enough? If you wait on the Lord, he will renew your
strength; yea, sure, but will he send you your mate?
Of course he will.
He's the beginning and the end, the marriage and the death, in
Him we have everything! So you say you want a friend?,
but didn't anyone tell you that's not good enough?
A true friend is hard to come by,
and when one is found, the journey
to trust and friendship is narrow with a lot of caution signs.
Don't want to be no caution sight!
Don't let it be said that I stopped progress.
Oh, the many days of loneliness now left behind,
but were they ever truly lonely days at all?
Is it possible that lonely is just a state
of mind or maybe a state of shock and panic!
Don't take your eyes off the Master!
He holds the answers in the palm of His Hand!
Lean not to thine own understanding, for in the long run,
you'll see that you truly didn't understand at all.
Pray for the wolves, for they surround you with smiles while making
the pot hot for your feasting. Oh, the many wolves!, smiling with
sharp teeth intended to shred your very soul.
But even the sharpest teeth, polished with greed,
envy and jealousy can't penetrate a peaceful, believing heart!
Woe unto you, you ravenous wolves!,
for the hearts you seek to feast on will soon be your own!
Be mindful of the pot you heat for someone else-
for you will soon not understand why it is your head being
revealed at the dinner table.
Peace unto you, you meek and humble servants!
for the rewards of your labor will be many!
And once again, when God uses your light to show
the wolves that He alone is supreme, you'll be able to shout the
victory and pray the rage within the wolves will calm and quite down
so that they too may experience true peace.

Jozette Maxwell

The Old Log House

Fifty years the log house stands
It was built by my father's hands.
The logs have become weathered and worn,
For the good old days I do not mourn.

Most of my childhood was spent here.
Those childhood dreams are still so clear.
The hours spent on the stairway each day
Have taught me patience will usually pay.

Those memories of the old out house
With spiders, flies, bugs and sometimes a mouse
Have been dimmed by modern inventions.
And no more out-houses are my intentions.

So large to us this log house seemed
By standards of yesteryear-so we gleaned.
Now small and sedate it stands
This house built by my father's hands.

Jessie Sparks Thomas

I Love My Country

I am a Vietnamese who loves his country,
that has more than four thousand years of history,
and where my ancestors are sleeping eternally.
For me, it is the best place in the world to be.

I want my country to become wealthy,
my people to live happily in freedom.
I had to sacrifice almost my whole life
to fight against the invasion of the Communism.

My dream did not turn to reality.
This cost me five years in prisons,
six years after in mental harassment,
and my family seventeen years in discrimination.

My people's aspiration did not come true.
This made the entire nation turn into a huge prison,
more than one million people leave it for freedom,
and hundreds of thousands of them drown in the ocean.

I lost my country, then became an exile in America.
People here welcome and treat me very enthusiastically.
I am living under the protection of the Goddess of Liberty.
Many thanks to American, but I can't forget my country.

Tham Huy Vu

The Smiling Face

The sun is shining, the sky is awake
The wind is cool and free
I sit in a field of blossoming life
There is no one there but me

I hear soft laughter, I turn and see
A smiling face welcoming me

It's been a long time — nice to see you again
The years of pain erased
We talked with ease, with joy and love
Remembering the dreams we chased

I've missed your smile, your warmth, your glow
Nice to have you back — I've missed you so

As if time stood still, never a moment of sorrow
We laughed and played looking forward to tomorrow

Now the sun has gone down, the sky is asleep
The wind is still cool and free
I sit alone in the field of blossoming life
And realize...the smiling face was me.

Connie Winter

Kisses On Winter

I forgot for a while the kisses of winter
Or, my red, always wet, woolen gloves
Which after the playing, will jump
Somewhere, each in a different corner of my room
I forgot for a while his eyes and beautiful long fingered hands,
His coat where I'd look every time for some candy
I didn't like him then,
When each winter afternoon
he came to take me home each day from school
So that none of the boys will throw snowballs at me.
While thousands of little pieces of paper, would fall upon us
We'd walk hand in hand, quiet and sober;
And than, it happened over night;
he needed than my hand and we forgot
together when kisses came from winter.

Andreea Petric

Orient Express

As I stepped aboard, I moved cautiously;
as though something or someone was about.

Great notables had once preceded me,
of their presence there was no doubt.

I knew not fear....mere curiosity
and did poke and explore where I could.

Somehow, I felt not an intruder;
no matter that I didn't...nor I should.

Dastardly deeds were done in this place;
mysteries forgotten, hidden away!

I resolved, somehow, to unravel them all;
Though would take much more than one day.

As the great horse lumbered along,
I felt almost a warm caress...

And kinship with "Aggie" and "Poirot"...
As I traveled on the Orient Express.

Lana Robinson

Angel Of Life

God sees as we grow grandly in a worldly universe of panacea, but remembering the dearest love - knowledge in innate energies conceal the facts of the living dead and inhabits terminals in a badland.

We can recondition the embodiment of virtue, but fanatically carnivorous consumption leads to our suffering. Gifted persons of today surely know purification, diet and rejuvenescence are related - "modulated" the measures of God can live forevermore.

"Yes" unless the tables turn, the seeds of life and love shall not bear the truth in amazing grace... A life and love dying must be recognized as lush ridden from the future, as doom ceases from the womb, and meat is spared from the lustiness of our mouths.

Being part of Gods family tree's we are with branches of supreme ability - the dreams of leaves blooming unto angelic trust, fruits of an almighty eminency remembering and seeing the conations of power in a worldly universe of "Dear Love."

- The Institute Of Loves Enterprise -

Rasool James Carey

Answers

I once asked a man if I was beautiful.
He smiled and touched my leg.
I once asked a woman if I was beautiful.
She smiled and stroked my hair.
I once asked a child if I was beautiful.
No, the child replied.

Tai Garcia

Songs

The wind, warm and gentle on my face,
combines with crystal clear
sunshine to bring serenity to my mind.

With eyes closed,
I embrace the moment graciously as birds bring
forth their songs.

Songs of flight uninhibited
by the constraints of landbound perimeters.
Songs of mothers scolding
their children for straying too far from protection.

Songs of loneliness,
the calling for a mate to share this freedom with.
Songs of territory, songs of joy.

Each different yet the same.
In perfect tune with the season.
So it is with all living things.
Unavoidably fulfilling the wishes of nature,
and nature fulfilling the wishes of GOD,
and me in the middle of it all filled
with awe and wonder can only say . . .
Thank You!

Darrell Jackson

Seasons

Winter days are here at last. The beauty of autumns leaves
Has come and passed.

Leafless trees so tall and bare, sways in the breeze without
A care.
Winter has passed and spring is here. Budding of trees,
Green grass and flowers, has no fear.

Warm sprinkles of April showers tells us truly there will
Be may flowers.

In the mid-of-summer heat, an ice cold lemonade will surely
Be a treat.

Coloring of leaves are now in sight. All around us will
Soon be a golden bright.
Mother nature knows when there is a reason. She puts on a
Show for every season.

W. G. Daughtry

Angelica

She came out of my darkness days-
When voices from others rained goodbyes
Only to be lost of a depth I lay-
To be saved and a different truth sanctified.

Softly glowing her warmth of another-
Shades of feathers trail a psalm to nature
Where crossroads touched to give me life-
While holding my hand she smiles, lesson.

Soaring above while the thunder rolls,
And looking in the mirror of my soul-
She may seem a wonders dream back
Giving me life from inside salvation destined.

There can be only one on my shoulder-
With infinite wisdom to a miracle
Awakened by her touch I couldn't feel-
Her eyes of truth are always watching me.
A SILENT HEART ECHOES

Michael W. Tavares

The Wind, My Peace

I soar with the birds when I am free
I ride with the wind wherever it takes me
The air is so pure and the sky is so blue
When I'm this high, I study its perfect hue
I am as light as a feather on a bird's back
When I know that sadness is the only thing I lack
My feet are light and my body carries me
Wherever the wind decides to take me
My worries are carried away by the wind
And I feel freedom in the tingle of my skin
So come soar with me and see
How peaceful this freedom can be
Let the quiet air take you away
To meet the sunshine's beautiful rays
Let the wind move through you way up above
And then you'll understand the symbol of the dove.

Marie-Catheline Jean-Francois

Rain Dancer

It took a lifetime to find where you are
searching forever from every star
trying to dance to the music you know
I can't seem to hold you, I can't let you go
I see you now in a field not far
dancing, singing, stealing my heart

Rain dancer, Rain dancer won't you dance for me
sing me a story, let me see what you see
rain dancer, rain dancer let me look in your eyes
there's a storm brewing to fill my lonely nights

I hear a tune that lovers have played
around the night in the warmth of their beds
dancing, swaying never missing a beat
you're always around when I fall asleep
come, dance faster spinning 'round in the rain
now in my dreams, your future begins

Keep dancing lovely lady for you're safe in the night
and soon the sun will take you from the glow of the firelight
and those dancing flames reaching through the night
as I feel myself, once again becoming one with you tonight

Carolyn Custer

The Lake

By a lake calm and serene
 O'er the surface floats a fog,
From the depths rises of fish as big as a log.
 It's as if it's all from a dream,
I ponder upon the whole scene.
 A lake comes from the flow of a stream,
Below where eyes have seen.
 It takes its rest in the earth's crust.
Where it will be in our trust,
 To be kept pristine and clean.

Scott J. Blanchard

Happy Anniversary To My Husband

Thanks for the sorrow, thanks for the joy.
Thanks for the little girl and thanks for the big boy.
He's handsome, dashing and a good father to three.
She's beautiful, career-minded and will be on TV.
They're a little like you and a little like me.
His wife is a comfort and suits him to a tee.
There are three Grands: a boy, a girl and a soon-to-be.
They're all a little like you and a little like me.
God blessed our thirty-one year old family
with two new generations for all to see
a little of you and a little of me.

Jenny Eaves

The Thespian Death Of The Day

My eyes explode as the sinking sun ignites the clouds and sets
my mind ablaze by inferno of thought arisen by the descent.

The torch strikes the heavens, the sea consumes the blaze,
And the sky bursts aflame into a raging gale of nature's fury.

This fiery apocalypse, bursting God's canvas, pushes ripples
never ceasing in the sea of weightless tides, and laps the clouds
upon each other without smoldering, as the horizon sears
without ashes, and the firmament scalds in a wash of hue.

Coursing through my throbbing veins, my boiling blood surges.
The pulsating chambers of my melting core forebode to burst
asunder, saturating my soul with the bittersweet brine of fear and awe.

I clutch my faces as to avert my burning gaze from the hypnotic
marvel that overwhelms my simple mind and glorifies my aged soul.

Shall I be vanquished by the vim of God's magnum opus
My being enslaved, flung to my knees and drowned by my
deluge of soul sanctifying tears.

This catharsis evoked within, purges the depths of my heart,
and awakens my dormant ears with the power of silent screams
as the colors collide with each other. My lips begin to quiver,
as my mortal mold trembles, for the Thespian death of the day
has dissolved........me.

Christen Parker

Sequences Of Time

That feeling of freedom, pure essence of life
That fire in your eyes will always burn bright
A spirit of an angel including heart and soul
Hold still my world, as life unfolds.

Such a word of life is time
A journey all unknown
Not a rule to be had
Just a conscience to go on.

Entered in by two
Creating love and lust for life
A gift of human nature
We take pleasure with much delight.

Our side or the flip side
The downward spin we go
The end of the long journey
Now the knowledge we behold.

Time is never ending
With its promise that it holds
That change will never cease
Only sequences of time between young and old.

Diane Harclerode

"A Father Is:"

A father is someone who is there.
A father is a someone who cares.
A father is willing to share good times
And bad, happy and sad.
A father is there when you are sad to give a hug.
A father is able when needed, to give a tug.
A father is someone who believes when you can not.
He can turn a frown upside down.
With his smile he can make you want to walk a mile.
MY father is all these things and much, much more.
For that I am sure, sure, sure!
I love you, Dad.

Sharon Tauber

The Space In Front Of Us

She moves through her days wishing for return.
For wet grass she can fall into laughing.
The park spins silver as it makes her turn

The wild mushrooms, delicate, dissolving.
Words are an intricate dance which evokes
Wet grass she can fall into laughing.

Her desire, sweet and sour for the spokes
Of a wheel, the slope of a hand inflames.
Words are an intricate dance which evokes

Lemon popsicles, tree bark, rain.
The names burn through her like electric volts.
The hub of a wheel, the slope of a hand inflames.

She cannot breathe freely in the park.
Sub text is dizzy, and is in everything.
Burning her with electric volts, the hub

Of her heart, possession of her longing.
She moves through her days wishing for return.
Her treasure narrows and is dissolving.
She spins silver in the park. The trees turn.

Susan Rogers

He Visited Me

I called on the LORD and He visited me.
I sat at His feet with my head on His knee.

My hand in His hand as plain as could be,
When I called on the Lord and He visited me.

My faults I confessed, all that troubled me.
He knew all my needs and He comforted me.

I could feel the peace flow as the Light I did see.
When I called on the Lord and He visited me.

Like the water He calmed in that storm raging sea,
He called out the Demons that were raging in me.

The void filled with song, a heart filled with glee,
When I called upon GOD and He visited me.

Orr B. Morris

Unitarian Truths?

Ku Klux Klan burning crosses
World's religion's count their losses

Nazi Skinheads killing Jews
Preachers sermons to empty pews;

Black Panthers segregate from Whites
Religions bicker over which one is right;

People starving-die in vain
Evangelist's yelling won't help their pain.

Why do we wonder which religion is for real?
They all teach good virtues-not to lie, cheat or kill.

People who are Buddhists, Moslems and Hindus
Are they really that different from Christians, Catholics and Jews?

Why do we criticize what we don't understand?
Is the final decision going to be up to man?

Maybe combining the beliefs of all faiths
Would put us that much closer to Heavens Golden Gates.

What about people who have never heard God's Word?
Are they completely clueless or just misunderstood?

Why do we need only one religion to be true?
Why would God limit Himself to so few?

Jason T. Gatts

The Keeper Of Emotion

He's let them out again
Misery seeps down the walls
Disgust hangs from the ceiling

Pity has sprawled itself upon my bed
And fear is walking hand in hand with dread

Sadness casts its shadow from this pen
While ridicule laughs out loud inside

Anger has no place at all
Frustration makes the curtain call

Confusion makes my temples ache
Guilt says it was my mistakes

Pain convinces confusion
That love is once more to blame
And someday He'll forget my name
But not "The keeper of emotions"

Lizette D. Nielsen

Mother To Son

A new mother gazes at her baby with wonder
She wants him to grow with fire and thunder

A soul so great Gods perfect creation
His eyes show courage, trust and salvation

Will he grow to be true, courageous and right
A leader of people with wisdom and might

Or will he stray from Gods chosen path
To fill the world with abandon and wrath

In his life I know it won't be true
Because something so bad could never be you

Your eyes reflect a light like mirrors of wisdom
To show your soul the path to Gods kingdom

Raymond Allen Freitas

Untitled

As I lie awake in bed at night
I envision the Christmas snow so white
Seeing the smiles on my children's faces
from the gifts they were blessed from different places
To be so grateful for my wonderful life
this could not be lived without my wife
She has given me so much love to endure
and two beautiful children to be thankful for.
Christmas is the time to share and to love
to this wonderful year, I thank my lucky stars above

Richard Courtright Jr.

Brotherly Love

I hear the patter of raindrops
    Against my window pane,
But can I feel secure as I lay in bed
    In this world of peace, so they claim?

What of the boys still over there
    Manning our bastions afar?
Do they know there's peace in the wartorn world
    When they see the door of peace ajar?

There can't be peace until freedom reigns
    On land, sea and sky above
And only then when people learn
    The meaning of brotherly love.

Thomas Howard

My Friend

I remember you . . .
I remember the times we had together, you are a poet.
You are a part of something that I have always wanted to be.
The way you write inspires and I long to read your words.
I long to remember everything I learned from you.
But it isn't as deep now . . .
When I think about it I remember,
when I remember the feelings come back.
The desire to live life to the fullest!
The desire . . . desire!
The joy . . . the deep joy!
How can I remember . . .
How can I remember?
Please help me remember!
There was a sunset I wanted to share with you tonight,
you would have loved it.
Love.
You taught me a lot about that.
Oh, how blessed we are, there is beauty all around us.
Thank you . . . I'll never forget.

Susan Jorgensen

Oh Cowboy!

I came to Oklahoma from a Mississippi town
Just a naive southern girl who had never been around
The first time I saw a cowboy my head was in a whirl
Nothing has been the same since for this small town girl

Oh cowboy! do you know what you do to me?
My heart will never be free
Say you love me too
I will always be true to you

I used to think no other man could compare
To the southern gentleman with his fancy air
But Oh cowboy that was before I knew
Somewhere in this world there was a man like you

I married my cowboy, we live in perfect bliss
We still see fireworks everytime we kiss
We two-step around our world hand in hand
Oh cowboy! life with you is grand

Margaret Thomas Becknel

My Rose In Heaven

Looking back when mama and me
proudly worked this land. And
walked together hand in hand.

Proudly she planted this rose she
called, my rose my love. I lost my dear
one that winter. Now I have a rose in
heaven above.

The days seem long, the nights
are lonely. Wishing she could be here
beside me. I know that can not be.
She is up there waiting for me.

My memory my thoughts they are
memory. They take me back the things we
did. Places we went together through
out this land.

I know she waiting with open arms,
a smile on her face. Sparked in her eyes.
Then again. We'll walk together hand
in hand.

Eddie Skvarla

The Road Of Friendship

Friendship can be like a long and windy road;
With many turns, forks, and intersections.
And even though we may each choose a different
Path along this road,
I know you will always be with me,
Even if only in my heart, for now.
No matter how far apart our different paths may take us,
I want you to know,
I will always be here for you.
And someday, I'm sure, our paths will cross again.
Whether it be here on Earth,
Or up in Heaven with our dear Lord,
I know we will see each other again.
And until that wonderful day comes,
My memories of you will keep my love strong.

Beth Davis

Hug Me

Just a hug now and then
To say you love me still,
Give me hope, perhaps I'll live
A little while longer, if God will.

Don't just stand there and stare
Give me hug, and pull up a chair.

You hugged me when I was born,
You hugged me as a child
When I would cry,
So, hug me now before I die.

Show me some warmth and affection
For in your arms I'll feel protection.

Don't make me feel helpless, worthless and alone,
Hug me, Mother, and make me feel that I still belong.

Don't darken the room, give me light!
Give me a hug to help me fight.
Other battles have been fought and won,
So, hug me Mother, I'm still your son.

Ruby J. Jackson

The Dead Of The Night

In the dead of the night
The dead hour strikes
Bringing a frightening thump in the heart.
The men of mischief
And the ghouls of fright
Come out to play in the dead of the night.
A screech of horror
A drop of blood
Are the sounds in the dead of the night.
Hell comes alive
And heaven grows tired
In the dead of the night.
To dance is to die
And to laugh is to cry
In the dead of the night.
No more, no less
Then thy pain
To caress
In the dead of the night.

Chris Kolodziej

Safe Haven

My whole world is upside down
I don't feel there's a safe
haven in sight

I've never felt so unsure of my path

Do I fly away from what I have called home?

The beautiful watercolors
of my visions, have now turned
to muddled dark oils

My senses have been stirred,
the blue waters now murky

I feel my love of life has lead my astray

Sometimes trying to breath immobilizes me

I feel a need to purge my soul
and the need for vitality to
infuse my body

Would a new surrounding
recaptivate my enthusiasm for living?

I ponder, if a new haven would
ease my weary soul, to let
memories and bygones be just that.

Judy Wong

Dr. Jekyll And Mr. Hyde

The monster longs inside us
We know not where
We know not why
He lives here forever
He shall never die

"I shall kill this monster"
A foolish doctor said
Then the next month
They would find him dead
For he did not know the power of what he said

No man nor child would be
The rat
So the foolish doctor said
"Then I shall be just that"
He sounded full of joy until the next day when he was "Ed"

Brett Cole

Wounded Helpless Hearts

The anguish not to be endured as
seen through the eyes of the wounded child.

The melancholy tears for a soul lost forever
to a Heavenly home.

Wounded children emotionally limp.
So much despair.

Powerless to control the sorrow, fear, and
loss of desire. Wondering why

To take it away, the pain, fear heartbreak
and sorrowful tears we are powerless.

You hold on tight and listen to thoughts
and pray for Angels to guard and heal those
wounded helpless hearts.

Sandy Taylor

Sucker

It was tattooed colorfully
on my forehead.

Bright, bold, capital letters.
It's gone now.

Although I feel quite liberated.

A guy I fell madly in love with
unknowingly helped me etch it
off little by little with a very
dull razor, chisel and ice pick.

Of course the blood always ran
down my painted face.

The rush of blood was diluted by
my tears and always fell to the
ground beneath my feet, like a
reddish waterfall.

Unvaryingly staining the shade
of my days to follow.

What remains are some very deep scars.
Make-up and a smile has helped me cover them.

But it's not there anymore. No more SUCKER.

J. Wong

Wicked Charms

When you wrap your arms around me so tight,
It sends chills down my spine, like a breeze of the night.
And even on a chilly morn,
Your tender kiss keeps me warm.

I want to melt in your arms,
I always fall prey to you're wicked charms.
And every time you make me smile,
I feel this is just so worthwhile.

Every time you look at me,
I feel you are so true to me, and it be.
That I can hold you in my arms,
And you will never lose those wicked charms.

Is this all what it seems,
Or is it all just a dream...?

Mildred Planas

Life Corridor

Feels like walking down an endless corridor of
dreams unthought and thoughts undead

Life...cold air
The warm breezes of childhood lead to this door
big door covered with ivy
Opens my senses to the dank deeps and dark love
of books
of mind
of frustration
of accomplishment
of friendship
of woman of man
of bottles breaking
of diversity and racism
Yet a bright light pierces
Large dark arms reach out smelling of sweat and tears
Unity Love Strength
The gates swing open to a new dawn
dreams unthought
thoughts undead I am

Nancy Vanessa Brown-Holt

Unaccompanied

I sit alone with my thoughts the manner of them is unimportant.
However, in this respect I am not alone.
The thoughts that I have are my companions.
They befriend me when all else fails,
And they are with me always.
But these thoughts that form my being,
Can likewise destroy this being
If I in my infinite imperfections
Let them rule me and become my only friends.
For in this way - my life would be myself.
And my loneliness my happiness - thus, I pass without notice,
And as I fade, as do my thoughts, and therefore my life,
Hopelessness would overtake me - and thus my thoughts
And I would be thrust into an unending hopeless parallel to
   reality.
In this way I sit alone,
Not surrounded by hopelessness - but happiness.
For it is not myself for whom I live,
And clearly not myself whom I befriend.
Thinking is not living - therefore I am alone.

Andra Teten

"Click"

A bit beyond the horizon and
a dreamer's stretch past left or right of center,
one may
with an averted eye
detect a sense of its shadow
or hear the echoes of its clatter . . .
but it is in the charred charity of blackness,
punctuated only by a whoop of suddenness
that it may be most nearly recognized
and then,
with all breath sucked away,
there are no words
with which to tell of it.
You know
what I mean.

Esse Vaughn Rhodes

Eclipse

Tonight burns my eyes.
Tonight of torches moving coming slowly coming.

In red light, my eyes melt red and night a torch dance through the
   foggy valley.

Moon,
burning through the silent, foggy valley,
I torch dance through thick hills mist,
cold and blind as the moon
silent laughter.

I am the blindfolded torchbearer of a new year
searching my mind for the moving moon.
Out here, a flickering world's black dance to night
night's dance to silence
still coming to come to offer my hands
   full of burnt, blue stones.

Now!
Dance of sucking tides and flames,
hour of dim laughter, chain
of hours, through wet-smoked hills and valleys
to resonating stars
moon gone
blind.

Laura Alderdice

Lost In The Black Sea

autumn has come, like a brush
painting the rich scenery dull and black, and
realizing all life will soon be gone
i cry - shedding empty tears upon the
lifeless leaves of concrete below my feet. And I
wonder when will this pass, this
emptiness I feel as I try to
elude reality and continue living in a
kingdom made of dreams.
someday, maybe, all the hardships will pass
    and spring will come again into my life.

Jose Aliaga-Caro

One Mother To Another

Ode' to the other mother,
written with love from another.
All they really see is the back of me,
as I look upon the stars there is little respect you see.

"Oh Mom" as I hear quite often you see,
all that they see may really not be me!
All I am is one mother to another
I am who I am for the world to see.

One mother to another I am like no other,
you will always be my baby
As your own shall always be.
One mother to another, we have the love for each other.

Now that you have grown older and wiser,
you will see how it will feel to be a mother,
from one to another, the years will go by
and you will be where I am today
as one mother to another.

From one mother to another,
with love and respect,
Friends to the end, there is no other!

Nadine Anzures Brodd

Friends...

And, where on Earth, would you say,
one might find such loving friends?....
Around the corner?...Nay!!!
'Tis God!!!...
who brings their comet's sails
from a long time away....
To stir alive old mem'ries 'n tales
of a by-gone youth and faster days.....

So sit back, my love...
Enjoy!!!!.....
It's a present from Above...

For in the End....
Beauty.... is all that 'er remains,
reinforced with Purpose, and rooted in Love....
And the sharing of Old Friends....

Jose A. Buil

My Poem

    The sky is blue, the stars
are bright, I say my prayers every
night and I sleep all through the night.
The wind is blowing and people are cold.
A piece of love will warm their souls.
People are happy, people are sad;
give them happiness and they will feel glad.
I'm going to sleep for the night.
May the stars shine brightly
on everyone's sight.
    Good night!

Heather Heidenthal

Untitled

The anger welled up inside of me is like a wave
in the ocean that is just about to break
and come crashing down onto the sand only
to be swept back into the mass of endless sea.

Tamara Erdley

Life Is Castor Oil?

If life to you is castor oil,
Whatever dreams you have will spoil,
If you believe you can recoil,
From disappointment, and succeed.

To run and hide yourself away,
Is to deny the fullness of today,
Is to defeat life's hard lessons learned
And leave your essence scorched and burned.

In such a bountiful world as this,
Please tell me, from whence comes the greed
To change what is into a "something,"
We all know we really don't need.

To face defeat and pass on through,
To the next event with much to do,
Is to keep pace with curved space and time,
And not waste your moment, or your rhyme!

Nancy V. Logan

Within A Seed

In the morning tide of rays
a tiny bud is born from within
the rich soil, soon it will unfold
its curious little petals, and reach
for the sky.

Dew drops glisten on each ever
growing leaf. What once existed
as a petite blossom, is now an
extraordinary beautiful rose.

The sun falls into a deep blackness
as a bleak wind blows the voice of
Gods speaking softly in an eternal mood.
Slowly the flower begins to wilt and
wither, the silver waters shimmer
as the last petal Returns to the
Earth from which it came.

Kerry L. O'Brien

"Christmas Wish"

Snowmen, ice castles and dreams come true
my wish for christmas is for you

To cast away all your troubles, doubts and fears
through out this and the coming years

To lay to rest what has past
to believe in relationships that really do last

To be happy and a smile on your face
to tenderly caress me with your embrace

For these are my wishes certain and clear
Merry Christmas and Happy New Years

Stephen Wayne Mullins

A Rose In My Garden

You were like a beautiful rose growing in my garden,
your petals so soft my hand caressed, but the rose
without me knowing soon withered, and in my soul is
the memory and the essence of the rose.

Why did you leave me, why did you leave me like this,
that is what I cannot understand, I see your face
wherever I go, I see the emptiness and I think
of the lost dreams which are never to return.

Why did you leave me my love, the pain is too intense,
and wherever you are, I want you to feel my love,
and with every teardrop I cry, I water the rose, but your
petals will never shine again.

E. Diaz Ocampo

Inheritance

As children
They walked the same, they talked the same —
These sons of ours.

As men,
They walk the same, they talk the same —
These different ones or ours.

How different, but how much the same!
They care, they serve, they give, they love
But each by his own means.

And oh — the very richness of their selves!
The unity and diversity
Of the genes!

Patricia L. Roberts

I Need Only To Remember

Whenever I am weary with life's trials along the way
And I need a place to go for all those trials to fade away
When my nerves are shot, I'm frazzled and about to come unglued
I need only to remember what it's like to be with you

If I'm worried and befuddled with a frown upon my face
And my world runs 'round in circles at a harried, frenzied pace
When I'm lost for words and can't express things as I'd like to do
I need only to remember what it's like to be with you

You make my whole world different, it sounds crazy, but it's true
And the memory of the love you give makes every day brand new
The reason it's so special, and I feel the way I do
Is because I need only to remember what it's like to be with you

You can't take away a memory that's imbedded in my heart
And the love we share will always be the most important part
And I treasure life since loving you is all I want to do
And I need only to remember what it's like to be with you.

Marcia Peatross

Crack Mother

Hey crack mother:
   Where is your head?
Your shady, your filthy, just about dead
Take a look at yourself one long time,
What you have turned into is a senseless crime...
Hey crack mother:
   Where is your heart?
What makes you think you don't have to do your part
Your babies are hungry, crying and wet,
Yet you would sell them to cover a drug debt...
Hey crack mother:
   Snap out of it fast,
Before you become a thing of the past,
If a mother you are, then damn it, a mother you be
Hey mother; don't you know your part of the giving tree!

Roslyn. B. Kraus

Together With Age

When we were kids and full of play
We used to laugh and always say
Hugging and kissing what yucky stuff
Now we're adults we love and lust.

With emotions full of energy
In a world that's full of life
I know one thing to be true,
The longer we stay with each other
The more that I will love you.

In this time of age we grow up fast
Together we'll decide if things will last.
Growing as one we'll coincide
Lasting forever longing for life.

For today, tomorrow, for the rest of our lives
We'll walk hand in hand, together, side by side
Together forever, just you and I, led by our emotions.
But when I'm not there to give a hug
Just think and remember,
I always have, and always will, Love You.

Derek Nelson

Let Us Spend Time

Let us spend time, to understand each other, and to "laugh" and "cry"
   together.
Let us spend time, to know what makes each other "happy."
And to have
   a desire to bring "happiness" and "joy" to each other.
Let us spend time, to be "sensitive" to each others' "needs."
Let us spend time, to "enrich" and "touch" each other's lives
and to give to each other "Wisdom."
Let us spend time, to be "patient" and "tolerant" with each other.
Let us spend time, to "be there" for each other to "lean on" and to
   "console" one another.
Let us spend time, to give our "love" a chance to "grow".
Let us spend time, to look past "age" or "looks" and "short comings"
   we might find in each other.
Let us spend time, to make "sweet memories" and to give to each other
   "much love."
And when one has "gone," let us spend time to "remember" each other.
But! Before that time of "departure", let us spend time to "hold,"
   "hug", "kiss" and tell each other how much we "love them!"

Charles R. Flowers

Everything The Lord Does Is Good

When the day seems long and demanding,
Remember to let the Lord do the commanding.
He will guide and comfort you as He forgives your sin,
You will be free to begin again.
Be glad and rejoice in each day,
Do not let the evil one lead you astray.
You may ask for grace and love,
He will send it to you from above.

Keep your faith in the Lord and believe,
That everything the Lord does is good.

Pray each day and ask for His grace,
The strength you will gain will help win the race.
His comforting arms will hold you each day,
Be thankful for this and remember to pray.
Search for the Lord with all your heart,
Don't let the world keep you apart.
The Lord wants you with Him your whole life,
Your faith in Him will ease the strife.

Keep your faith in the Lord and believe,
That everything the Lord does is good.

Janis Dixon

Memories We'll Never Erase

This is a time of pain and grief
A time the family's in disbelief
A time of pain, a time of sorrow
Just one more day we wish we could borrow
To let her know how much she was loved
With the Lord she lives, up above
But it's also a time to be strong
even though what's happened is so wrong
There's a beautiful little girl
that needs to be raised
Her mother's dear life was taken away
For in Rebecca we'll be able to see
a bit of Theresa everyday
Her eyes, her hair, her beautiful face,
memories of Theresa we'll never erase.

Constance L. Cornett

Dear Mr. Stick

It's no use no more
'Cause I won't go and fight in your little war
People are dropping all over the land
We need to give them a helping hand
If they won't go, just leave them there
And look into their motionless stare
I know it is useless to sit here and fight
Against a system which thinks it is right
But as I sit here and think of my friend
Most of their lives have come to dead ends
Right beside me there is a pail
It's all filled up with half written tales
Of people like me and their friends
Whose lives have all come to dead ends
And I guess I might finish them just for you
Or I just might sell them for a buck or two
But now I must go for it is getting late
And I must get ready for my big date
For you see I still have one friend
Her name is Kari and we'll be together until the end.

Joshua Farkas

A Fall Afternoon Somewhere

Junco's chirp to find companionship.
Red tail hawks ride the warm updrafts.
An unmistakable hum from a nearby highway,
sets the soft tone for the
    background.
Leaves, brown and lifeless fall off trees with the smallest of gusts.
The loud crunching sound of dead foliage overrides the perpetual hum
    and gets closer.
A single small yearling meanders by.
More similar clamor comes from behind the malnourished animal.
Two blaze orange mammals duck behind leafless oaks and low lying
    bushes
They successfully elude the object in their cross hairs, and persist
    in the one-sided chase.
Chipmunks rummage around the ground, filling their cheeks,
A gray horned owl sits quietly, powerfully on top of an old red oak,
waiting for the cover of night to do his preparation and survival.
A shot rings out, followed closely by another.
Hawks abruptly leave their sky dance, chipmunks bury themselves
under fallen leaves, the owl spreads his great wings and flies away,
    shaking the old oak to its roots.
Silence . . .
A brave Junco breaks this seemingly uncomfortable situation with three
    quick calls.
Motion resumes, life continues.

Justin Machus

No Questions

How can you thank the night for its darkness?
How do you thank the Summer for breeze?
Has anyone heard the sun tell her story?
Have I ever thanked you for caring for me?

How do you tell the wind of its purpose?
Why do the waves return to the sea?
Does the bright moon know of its beauty?
Do you know what you mean to me?

How do you tell a star when to fall?
How do you ask the morning for dew?
How does the world know to keep turning?
How can I show you my feelings are true?

Some questions can never be answered.
Some answers hide in the dark.
But look in my eyes; my love can not hide;
The answer lies in my heart.

Stephanie Cowan

A Gangster's Prayer

Heavenly Father, please hear me tonight,
I need so much guidance; to live my life right.
I often wonder if anyone cares,
How can I wake up and face a new day,
Knowing I have to live my life this crazy way.

Heavenly Father, forgive all my sins,
I want to change, but where do I begin?
Give me the strength to resist the wild life I desire.
Help me get away from the nightly gunfire.

Please God, bless my mother; who cries every night
worrying I'll be killed in yet another gang fight.
Heavenly Father, what's it all for?
To prove to my homies, 'Yea, I'm down... I'm a hard core.'
How will I die? By a bullet wound... or a knife in my side.

Heavenly Father, please hear me Lord,
give me the courage and strength to live my life right.
Please show me the way; Lord show me the light.
Thank You for still being there, Lord
And most of all, Thank you for listening, to this sinner's prayer,
Amen.

Melissa Cryer

The Children Are Away

In the quiet of the evening when it's time to kneel and pray
When the cares of day have ended, folded up and put away
Then in fancy I can hear the voices of the children as they play
But those days are gone forever for the children are away

It seems like only yesterday, they romped the house in play
And listened to the stories at the even'n of the day
Oh my heart is sometimes lonely when it's time to kneel and pray
Home will never be the same again for the children are away

Some folk never seem to care what happens to their lambs
They early send them into life to go where they can
But my heart it never will give in to just let them go their way
I can't help but be so lonely for the children are away

I'm glad that they are trying hard to make this hard life pay
Daily I pray to the God of heaven that He in their hearts may stay
And I gather them into my heart as tonight I kneel to pray
To the very God of heaven for the children are away

Robert J. Jones

Loneliness Is —

WAITING —

A silent phone,
A bird unheard,
Lonely laughter.

WAITING —

A secret with no one to share it with,
No one to show — I care.
An intimacy tho't but yours;
But, shared by all.

WAITING —

Alone in the crowd, looking — searching.
Early dew on a bloom, unseen.
Shells of empty words, washed up
on the beach of your dreams.

STILL WAITING.

Robert R. Scruggs

Southeast Of Eden

Los Angeles, city of Angels, and tiny demons nipping at their heels,
schizoid mentality, split-brain, West LA, East LA...
a venomous water snake, and a long boring bridge,
two souls, two skins, and a wall in between
an invisible wall, subtle, infallible,
untouchable, easily traversed, yet an infinite divide.
This is not Wall Street, this is a wall in the streets
This is not Hall of Fame, this is a Wall of Shame
The Berlin Wall crumbled but you, invisible wall, when...? when...?
Angels, close your wings in disgrace you don't deserve flying
infantile tears chill my bones when I hear your misery
a febrile shiver inundates my brain as I notice your matter decaying
tortilla flats, flats full of tortillas, y mujeres de rodillas.
Rembetes on the street, beggars on the beat, squalid kids on Skid Row.
Popcorn, smiles and a desire of permanence on one side,
Yuppies driving in the fast lane, valets waiting in luxurious parking lots.
Famine, sorrows, cries of freedom and revolt on the other side,
a bullet in the head cut one life short in a drive-by shooting.
No one can stop the war, the wall is growing tall, it may never fall
Oh! wall, I beg you, let them free, let them be, they were here before

Carlos Cepeda

Me, A Cynic? Never!

Upon a lush green hill, I stand alone.
(WHERE IS EVERY ONE?)
The perfume of life circles amid the clouds.
(WHAT SMELL?)
An aria of music from lover's songs gilds the sun.
(WHERE IS DAWN?)
The sweet intoxication of the essence of life fills the cup.
(MINE HAS A LEAK!)

Rosalie S. Paczkowski

On A Friend's Suicide

Beneath the rough, rigid limbs
of an oak
hang the words we might have spoken.

Never touching one another,
the leaves grow ragged among the empty nests.
in the bruised purple sky,
gaunt birds scream and swoop and whirl about,
clawing at the swollen bellies of gray clouds
which will never give birth to rain.

Stephen J. Chonoles

My Dearest Friends

Though many miles have passed
And our road's courses have changed, so fast;
The friendships we've nurtured from close and clinging
To the memories and remembrances in our hearts singing,
Forever have bound us through fate, love, and hope.
Our spirits rekindled by each word or note.
The joys in which my heart is filled
Are savored, reveled, and solidly sealed.
Forever my friend,
Forever my friend,
I will take you to the end
Forever my dearest Friends.

Jeanne Kilroy

I Am

I am the weak.
Yet my body never breaks, it only bends
Beneath this weight of the world that I carry.

I am the silent.
Yet not a day goes by that my words
Don't ring in someone's ear.

I am the lover.
Yet my broken heart can never mend.
'Tis just broken again and again.

I am the dreamer.
Yet my dreams are not fulfilled
For my life has no room for such luxury.

I am the weaver.
Each thread upon my loom
Creates illusion or reality, beauty or pain.

I am the newborn and the withered.
I am everything and nothing at all.
I am the wielder of the Magic of Words.

Therefore, I am the Poet.

Brandi Gates

Roses And Thorns

I used to be the rose with no petals
All others had nothing but thorns.

Then I became the rose with closed petals
Still all others had nothing but thorns.

Now I am the rosebud about to bloom
The others are loosing there thorns.

But with Gods help I hope soon to be
A blooming rose for all to see.

Hermine Maria Fisch

"Freedom Train"

Freedom train a'coming my way,
For I's gon' be free one blessed day.
Ain't gon' work in nobody's field,
Ain't gon' hide behind nobody's shield.
Ain't no white man gon' tell me what to do,
For I's gon' be free, maybe you will too.
Done got tired of hoeing 'dem corn,
Done got tired of wearing clothes 'dat torn.
Done got tired of climbing life's hills.
But I ain't gon' work no more one day,
Cause the freedom train a'coming way.

Juanita Simmons

"Dear To My Heart"

To my adopted birth daughter,
born some many years ago;
who ever wherever you are,
I hope someday I will know.

Have often wondered off in thought,
where you live and how you are;
I imagine you must be unique and beautiful,
and as bright as the shiniest star.

Your mother was kind and precious,
with deep dark brown eyes;
The resemblance of her and I,
you cannot disguise.

I being your birth father,
have hazel and green eyes and hair that is dark;
this January 1st 1996 this poem I dedicate to you,
this day I mark.

The ranch I own in this small town,
is a home for wild life and somewhat new;
if I ever know who you are,
this ranch I leave to you.

Arjay A. Alkire "Wahoo"

Salute To My Comrades

Cry for the wounded
Cry for the maimed
Cry for those that didn't make it
But, cry all the same.

We, the living who are so few
We foresaw the future, call it precognition
But, somehow, we knew.

Some prayed that they would make it home
This was their only goal
For some, their prayers were answered
Now, we lay blessing on their soul.

We didn't know all the answers
I guess we never will
Please God, deliver us from this place
So no more American blood will spill!

Kenneth J. Boyer

Searching

I'm searching inside for the person
that's "me." Not the one that's visible for
others to see. There's so much I find that's
hard to face. I'm tempted to leave everything
in it's place. But then, I know I must
bring to light each deep hidden sin. There's
so much to right. I speak so glibly. Am
I always sincere? Compassion I have, but
not enough I fear. As for helping others,
do I do all I can? Or, do I selfishly
continue on with my plan. Yet, Jesus
knows the "inner me." It's like a diagram
for him to see. As each sin rears it's
ugly head. Jesus takes it in my stead.
He is my savior and on "that day," he'll
go before me to lead the way.

Marjorie Peebles

Just One More Time

If I could have just one more time
To say the things I should,
I'd tell you how much I love you
While yet I could.
If I could have one more chance
To change the way I live,
I'd devote my time to things of worth
To help my fellow man live.
I would give of myself
In any way I could
To improve the conditions of mankind.
I surely would; I surely would!
So often we don't have the chance
To make a difference in this life,
Perhaps because we don't measure
Our gifts and talents and all our might.
If I could have one more time to build bridges new,
I'd try to correct the wrongs I've done
And live my life for you.
Just you, dear God, just you!

Alice P. Jowers

Poison

Your burning anger lashes out at me
My body screams out in mortal pain
With a thousand of your barbed words
All sticking in my soul
Your smile of sadistic cruelty
Haunts my broken mind
And rips my soul into shreds
My eyes are clouded with red agony
Anguish chokes my blood
Your death is acted out in one hundred ways
All in my twisted head
Your disease poisons my heart
And pushes me away from your coldness
I cry out with a primal rage
And claw for a choking freedom
Which will only end up
Beating me into blinding oblivion
Fly away to your own little world
Of ignorance and stupidity
But I will not follow.

Camille Robinson

My Prayer For Peace

Lord, they are so far away
When we have night, they have the day.
The message they send is "Saddam go home"
But in Kuwait he still does roam.

We fight for peace, we know its right,
Please help us in this desperate fight.
There will be death, we know it now
The tears are showing, there's sweat on our brow.

There are fathers, husbands, sons, and daughters
Friends and neighbors, and countless others.
Their courage is strong, in their heart they know
To fight for freedom, it's a must they go.

Lord it is your shadow that we need
To follow our loved ones..this is our plea.
Bring them home safely, let the war cease...
May we finally have harmony and peace.

April S. Howser

The Man With The Hand

When you are only eight years old,
And you've lost your home in a flood,
The whole world seems a frightening place
Of muck, and sticks, and rocks, and mud...
And...you look for a hand to hold
Because you're full of fright and fear...
You reach, you hunt, and you're surprised
When your hand touches one so near...
To be sure that big hand is real,
You cling to it with all your might.
And then that hand closes over yours
To hold it, oh, so very tight.

It makes you feel so warm inside
When you find a man with a hand
That holds yours when you're cold and scared,
And the flood covers the whole land...
It makes the scare go far away
And warms your body through and through....
When you're just eight, it makes you feel
The man with the hand cares for you.

Macel D. Sarm

Finally

On a beautiful day her horses roam free.
She looks up and prays it was meant to be.
Her heart is heavy and her chores multiply.
While she hopes and prays her will won't die.
God above sent her the one thing she needed.
After she had argued and cried and begged and pleaded.
She dreamed one night on a plane ride home,
That one day, behind her house a horse would roam.
She waited ten long years for that day to arrive.
Now she has two beautiful horses that are well and alive.
They may not know much for what people may say.
But when they are older those people will pay.
Those people who told her what does and doesn't go.
Will look in surprise as they win their first show.
But now she watches the prettiest thing that could ever be,
She got what she wanted, finally.

Amanda Tuttrup

Shame Master

I am a master of my game
What masters me is my shame

From dawn to dusk
To hide from it I do what I must

I fill my mind irrelevant things
Then maybe I can forget it, fly away, take wings

Even though the clutter of the empty chatter
It stalks me, hunts me down.
Then it utters what really matters:

To master me you must stop fighting your destiny
It becomes you, it's at the door, it's calling
Until you follow me you will continue falling

You're destined to make it, there's nothing you can do
When you end your torment is strictly up to you

Release your denial and belligerence and I will follow
Until that time you will remain hollow

I've unlocked the mystery, given to you the only key.
Use it or you will never be rid of me

I will follow you without sympathy, relentlessly
Until your destiny is fulfilled, which means you've mastered me.

Cassandra Jenkins

The Ultimate Night Illusions

Use your illusions said the Lords of the illusion,
Flying through the air with the salem witches,
Running for your life from the wicked warlocks,
Skeletons slashing steal swords in your directions,
Shadows dancing under the sliverly moon,
Diving from the fired flame being throw by the giant
Demented winged dragons.
Can you escape the deadly dreams of the wizards.

Jennifer Minnick

Time And Eternity

The tide of time is ever moving toward the heavenly shore,
Where we will meet our Jesus and time will be no more.

The loved ones gone before us sing praises to our King.
We too will join the chorus and let our praises ring.

Never fret about the journey the price is already paid...
HIS life for ours...HIS choice so joyfully made.

As we the sheep of His pasture accept freedom in His love,
Freedom from sin and sickness, we will meet again above.

Martha E. Fessler

At Night

At night, beyond the quotidian, Life's estuary,
Where sleep stands to harbor, unload
Wares, stevedored, let fall to tower,
Arbitrary collections from the black hold,
Illuminated in the eerie moonlit gloom,
Cast readings, faintly legible, on the dark drenched eye.

And who to purchase in the macabre market?
The tenuous plank recedes.
These articles, which rose like flotsam on Memory's sea,
Were neither bought nor sold.
The commerce of day has no kinship,
With the province of night.

And yet who to we arrest, discurrent, this perpetual discourse,
With ourselves or some untimely shade?

James Donnellan

A World Without Plants

Can you imagine a world with no plants?
That would mean no harvester ants
No cows or elephants or beetles or deer
And absolutely no other animals to fear

But you need not worry about the human race
For with the earth we can keep pace.
You see we only need live in a bubble
For no more air will cause you much trouble

And humans won't have mouths running like trucks
For without use they have become stuck
Why? The keyboard is our communication
And our food is only our education

And how will we sleep without trees to shade?
Curled up in our bubble is how we have laid
We don't walk for our bubble will float
So our legs have grown weak in our bubble boat

There is no scenery on which to look
And no more beaches for the sun to soak
Can you imagine a world without trees?
It could have only a bleak outlook indeed

Jenny Stewart

Junior

My old dog
Sitting beneath the mimosa tree
wagging his tail and looking at me

My old dog
   Lying in the sun
just lying and waiting
for the work to get done

My old dog
   Just sitting and waiting
for Travis to come out and play
Oh how he loves for Travis to pet him at the end of the day.

My old dog
   He just watches and waits,
while the squirrels play,
and the birds flit about,

My old dog
   Was all heart and faithful to the end.

   Euna Armstrong

Painted Sunset

The sky ablaze with colors from the setting of
   the sun
A road stretched forth shadows the journey as
   time continues on

The moon full and bright surrounded by glittering
   stars
Dreams, hopes, desires, and wishes lift to
   heaven afar

Out on the crest of the freshly falling snow
Purity and rebirth sets the new years morning
   aglow

   Lisa Ann Server

Paw Prints

As the snow is falling from the sky
and covers up the ground,
all the animals run and hide
and some don't make a sound.

While some animals hibernate,
and others just fly south,
the squirrels gather all the nuts
and stick them in their mouths.

The wild cats run across the field
playing in the snow,
leaving behind them pretty little paw prints
and no one even knows.

   Lindsey Clark

A Walk In The Woods

Passing through tunnels of greens and golds
A wood's secret beauty quickly unfolds.
Nature's gifts are all around
In various shapes and sizes they abound.
The petals of flowers yet to bloom
The leaves of trees and a sparrow's plume.
As I picked up a piece of ancient wood,
I smiled in silence and understood.

   Ana R. Driggs

Her Gift

We had stood, she and I
graveside
on a leaden frigid February morn
watching our world slip into the soil
Ice crunched beneath our feet as I left a father
she a husband
She reached to comfort me

Alone I stood
graveside
on a fine morn in May
fighting the golden sunshine and soft breeze
wanting winter for my grief

Instead
wild violets nestled in the grass
as I walked the awful path again
I left behind a mother
but still she reached to me from the soil
comforting
making the Earth hers, mine

   Kathryn Finegan-Clark

Love Refused

My heart, my mind, my eyes and hands,
All instruments of love —
Yet denied the very power thereof,
Because you refused love or did not know.

My heart desires to feel for you,
My mind, to learn and know.
My eyes desire to look into your soul,
My hands to touch, and to hold.

But these instruments of love
Can not feel, or learn, or see or touch,
Your walls are thick and wide.
All because you refused my love, or
Because you just did not know.

   Linda Haynes

Graceful Faith

Blinded within myself by troubles. So confused and
lost that my body is numb.
Wondering why do I keep struggling and fighting to
go on? Is there a better way?
Feeling so alone and helpless.
I close my eyes and pray.
It is then I realize, I hold the key within me.
It is my faith that will carry me thru anything.
By the grace of my faith.
I open my heart, mind, and soul.
Our father had answered my prey!
My journey in this life maybe long and hard.
And I may not always know right from wrong.
But I know I will always have my faith to carry me
thru what ever may come my way.

   Lori Ann Schaefer

Walk With Me

Come, my love, walk with me along the shores of time.
Take my hand and walk with me—I'm yours—you are mine.
Together, forever, to walk this life in good times and in bad.
Laugh together, cry together, sometimes happy—sometimes sad.
All alone I walked—just walked with me—upon this sea of time.
Never finding love—finding love complete till your hand
   slipped into mine.
So come, my love, my life, walk with me throughout eternity.
Forever we will live and love; then my heart can fully see.
How much I could and would have lost—how all alone I'd be.
If never you had walked with me—along life's endless sea.

   C. Elaine Sorrow

Untitled

Love and life they are to cherish
As our loved ones perish;
We remain the same,
To conquer our dreams,
To play our scenes,
But all the while - we hurt,
We love, we care, and share;
Memories that are forever in our minds.
Erase; no such thing.
They are forever just as you and I.
Forever in love, forever in friendship,
Trust, pain, sorrows, forever.
I'm in love with you my one and only true,
Faithful, loving, beautiful man,
I love you forever, our
Dreams will some day come true,
And we will have a wonderful
Life together forever.

Michelle Carpenter

The Gift Of Life

Once upon a time in a land far away,
a star shone bright for three kings to lead the way.
When they saw Him, oh what praises to sing,
for they came to worship the newborn King!
Laying in a manger with a crowd gathered 'round,
worshipping and praising, gifts of love abound.
The King of kings, the Lamb, the Son of God
who would, one day to come, carry the cross.
He carried that cross to Mount Calvary
and there He died for you and for me.
To free us from our sins, His love was so much
that the gift of life was given to us.
A place in heaven is for those who believe,
to live eternally with the King of kings.
So praise Him with all your heart, soul and mind.
In the Lord Jesus, peace and joy you shall find.
Think it over this day and give Him your life
so that when He comes again, you won't be left behind.

Darylene Iacovetto

Untitled

Your emptiness built my pedestal
and in my emptiness I sat atop it wobbling.

You choke, you hate me
Words from your mouth come stunted, prickly, and
carefully, carefully measured. You hate me now.

What is it I did to you I lied to you I betrayed your love
I refused your love I tasted your love then made a polite face
and pushed the plate away
Left you weeping and shaking at your front door

You hate me now.

My new love mocks you and you think
I am pathetic and sick and without integrity
I had black and white dreams of you women singing
and forgetting the lyrics abandoned buildings on fire
It was me and you in a tower.
In a black, queasy, light-headed tower
Me and you and a rope and a stool; a sick grin on your face.

"Watch me, I'll do it I'll make you watch me."
I watched you I fled you hate me

I left you standing on the pedestal you constructed in my honor
And where are you standing now?

Shelley Lane Kommers

Rise Up, Nation!

Wake up people, the time is now!
Listen to me, the question is how?
How to come together as one race...
How to look each other in the face...
With a nod and a gentle smile...
How to walk together that extra mile.
The time is now to stop the hate,
The time is now before it's too late.
Yellow, red, brown, black and white,
The time is now for us to see the light.
Why can't we walk together hand in hand
Across this beautiful spacious land?
Why can't we look past the colors we see
And realize for all the differences, you're just like me.
Believe me when I say, this is the key!

Debra L. Johnson

I Know I Shouldn't

I know I shouldn't think of you all of the
time, because I have to get over you, or
at least I'll try.
You have to move away to a whole different town,
I'll never be happy cause I'll always be down.
We were just like best friends in sixth and seventh
grade, then we stopped talking when we got into
eighth.
I liked you a lot and you didn't even know, I
wish with all my heart, you didn't have to go.
I could always tell you anything and that's just
what I did, except for the secret, the one thing I hid.
I like you to much to watch you go away, so I'll
only ask you once, will you please stay?
I know you can't stay here so when I see
you around, I know I'll cry and so I'll look at
the ground.

Heather Owens

A Spring Debut

I looked out my window to a glorious burst of yellow.
  The forsythia is in bloom. How lovely it is.
Little sparrows darting in and out, pecking at this and that,
  Looking for whatever...
Their little dark bodies, like polka dots against the blaze of
  golden petals, enhance the bush's beauty.

Spring in all its wonder of God's creations has arrived
  once again. Thankful am I.
Winter has its place in our 4 seasons year, with its
  glistening snow and cold with pointed icicles but,
Spring is the promise of new life, new hope, that our hearts
  are in need of...to rejoice once more.

So, welcome sweet Springtime, I love you. Your colors, your
  sights, your smells endear you to me.
And thankful am I, that I am here once again to witness
  your entrance and enjoy your miraculous beauty.

Lena C. Krauss

A Dream Come True

When we fell in love it was a dream come true.
Because when I saw you, you reminded me of a
yellow rose that I have once seen before.
And with your eyes that reminded me of the
twinkling stars in the sky.
And when you smile, your lips form a perfect heart shape.
And when I run my fingers through your hair,
so self and wavy, I know then, that it is a dream come true.

Tabitha Hanlan

Doors

Open the doors of your mind,
Search into the far valleys below,
It is very hard to find,
The things that you just don't want to know.
The things that were in the past,
Something that may be happening now.
If it seems to go too fast,
And you don't know what or why, or how,
Open the door to your mind,
Search into the far valleys below,
If love is what you still find,
You'll find happiness, I have, I know.

Steve A. Gorlinski

Untitled

If I were a work of art, I'd be either a Rousseau or a Haitian
    painting:
    -a little naive
    -no great depth of perspective
    -sun-warmed and happy at the core
    -with an outer touch of exotica
I think of you as a Klee or a Gris:
    -abstract and elusive
    -difficult to define
    -happy, creative spirits that can't be tied down
    -with an unclear sense of time, ground, or gravity
The world we share takes me through Caligari expressionism,
Creates moments Monet soft and comfortable,
Gauguin warm and relaxed,
Nolde intense.
Schiele passionate,
Picasso hungover.

Wendy Temple

Winter's Night

I stand alone in this cold winter's night,
  awaiting the morning's first light.
Darkness surrounds me like a cloak,
  feeding off memories I try not to evoke.

My eyes fail to hide their heartsick look,
  yearning for the love that she forsook.
Night in its depths of darkness cannot hide,
  the hurt that will forever dwell inside.

'Twas love offered, and the promise to forever cherish,
  a lifetime of loving her was my fondest wish.
'Twas love rejected that was shoved into the cold dark,
  and my heart that will forever bear the mark.

It seems like this winter's night can never end,
  as I stand here feeling my heart twist and bend.
But the dark of the night knows not my plight,
  as I stand here waiting for morning's first light.

Timothy Lee Gamble

The Forest

There in the waterfall lies beauty unknown.
Each trickle sprays a tiny precious stone.
On a moon-lit night, phosphorescent glows.
The ripples shivering from the melting of the snows.
Shy deer come and drink the water, clean and crystal clear;
All the creatures of the forest do. For them, God placed it here.
From the flush forest the creatures secure their feed.
Each sharing without prejudice, but pious, without greed.
The nocturnal sky their roof, the neutral ground their beds.
They nestle down to sleep, the soft leaves rest their heads.
Yes, the beauty of the forest is far beyond compare.
Mother Nature created enough for all God's beings to share.

Shirley A. Davis

Fool

To live the life of a fool
Embracing both nice and cruel
Eager to learn what life can tell
Willing to jump into the unknown well
Travel all day from dawn to dusk
Only to find the night's wander lust
All who see this fool that pass
Will degrade, scowl, or only laugh
But this one truth I will say
No one loves life, the fool's special way
All life is adventure, with fear not feared
Not taken for granted, discarded, or sneared
For all who laugh, scowl, and degrade
I'd rather have joined, the fool's parade!

Tracy A. Bays

Best Friends Always, Love, Me

You're the very best friend I've ever had.
Always a shoulder to cry on, when I'm sad.
Not a moment goes by that I don't think of that day
When we met each other, and you asked me to play.
And from that point on, I knew right then
That we'd be friends forever, until the end,
Good times and bad times will always take part.
And there's a love we've grown within each other's heart.

Remember in kindergarten, when we first met each other?
And you started telling me about your big brother?
And I told you all about my mom and dad?
Thinking of that day, makes me sad.
I know it's been a great 12 years.
Thinking of the good times, bring back tears.
When you're old and gray, I hope a vision you see, is
    ...Best friends always, Love; Me

Kristian Renea Goodnight

Waves Of Love

Waves of love
Peaked with excitement
Calmed by repetition.

Waves of love
Rising with inception
Valleys of plateaus.

The strength of the current
Pulls us together in one direction
On each wave we learn to grow
Patiently we wait the swell. We are
Mesmerized by this incessant movement.

Only those who love the waves
know the waves will return.
Those who demand the waves
Grow impatient and lose sight
Of the beauty of that first wave ridden together.
Each successive wave loses importance.

And when the wind is still and the waves
Lap softly, pray tell we will recognize
Movement and not mistake our love's subtlety.

Christine M. Welsh

Holiday Cheer

The snow is falling fairly fast,
The people on the streets say hi to each other
A young child hugs its mother.
It's too bad the season cannot last,
Buying presents one after another,
Smiling faces everywhere
The season is filled with so much care.
Everyone acts as sister and brother,
Lovers holding hands walking past
People standing close to each other.
It's touching to see the love that is shared.

Robyn Smitt

What Is A Son?

A warm tiny hand she holds in her own,
These few precious moments, he's hers all alone.
Then diapers and feedings and colic an such,
She's alone and exhausted, it all seems so much.
Soon dirt in his pockets and gum in his hair,
He can't go to sleep without saying his prayers.
Now he's closing the door when taking a bath,
No more baby teeth smiles, braces show when he laughs.
His room is a mess, not a thing in it's place,
He's wearing an ponytail, growing hair on his face.
He stays out past midnight, spends a fortune on mousse,
He reads playboy. Just when did he quit Dr. Seuss?
She can't understand just where has time flown,
One minute he's helpless, next minute he's grown
His room is now empty, the posters are gone,
The house is so neat, things are were then belong.
Time has come for their lives to take a direction,
To go separate ways yet maintaining connection.
For a while, all they really had was each other.
And what is a son? Well, try asking a mother.

Patti Tripp

Fleeting Moments

Fleeting moments, the time we share,
The hours fly by, I know not where.
I long to share a sunset,
Or watch the waves pound the shore,
To brush our lips together,
And whisper forevermore.
I gaze into your eyes, a smile comes to your face
My soul comes to life, my heart starts to race.
Our times together have been joy mixed with fears,
When we are in each other's arms, gone are all the tear.
How I long to be alone with you,
A quiet place, just us two.
Soft music, candlelight, a glass of wine,
Sweet soft kisses, and you tell me you are mine.
This wonderful union has been delivered from above,
We are each but a half person,
Until united in our love.

Jeffrey M. Goldman

"My Tribute To A Special Man"

He was someone to share God's word with anytime of day.
Whenever you needed him he'd be on his way.
Forever faithful to the Lord in everything he'd done.
He was a true inspiration to each and everyone.
His kind and gentle ways had touched so many of us here.
Let's always keep those memories and hold them very dear.
Even though we all will miss him, God has reached out with his hand.
God has taken him to heaven and he has reached the promise land.

Donna Borger

Aliya

I hear the sound of her footsteps
They tell me that she's tumbled out of sleep
And tumbled out of bed
She runs as quickly as she can
Anxious to reaffirm her world
I am waiting for her
Ready to wrap her in her blanket
And in my arms
I want with all my heart
To make her a part of me again
But each day widens the scope of her world
And quickens her pace
I know the day will come, all too soon,
When she runs not towards me, but away
Off to conquer the world
No longer will I be able or allowed to wrap her in her blanket
And in my arms
But I know I'll want to
And if she wants me to...
I will

Deanna Frankel

Dancing The Universe

The dance in the street and the patterns of feet
call to a soul that's been dancing alone.

The sounds and the smells dance along the rails
as the tickets and seats make acquaintance.
Now...wheels upon rails, a rhythm prevails
and sunlight glances on metal.
Inside the glass, reflections dance and voices excitedly scurry.

Soon... there's a dance in the grass as the tall winds pass
and the birds dive their dance in the heavens.
To hear the wind blow is somehow to know
that the sky has a dance all its own.

And the waves on the beach seem forever to seek
their partners in the sand and the foam.
The leaves of the trees lend color to the breeze
as summer exits the stage in glory.

And the dance of the trout as they follow their route
in the sparkling dance of the stream
seems so like the dance of ribbons of chance
that swirl in a waking dream.

Ryan E. Fleming

"Memories"

Days may come and days may go,
but there is always a place in my heart for you.

Sometimes in the evening when I am lonely and blue,
I turn back the pages and search my memory for you.

I remember when we used to stroll down the trail by a
placid stream where the roses were in bloom and the
grass was always green, and the fragrance of spring
flowers filled the air.

Yes, days may come and days may go,
but my memories will live with me where ever I go,
and my thoughts will always be of you, because
my darling, I will always be in love with you.

Malvin L. Brown

What Is Love

That which we call love, many wonder what it is
Perhaps it is when we say "Forget it"
no matter whether fault be hers or his
Perhaps it is knowing there is always someone there for you
No matter whether your mood be happy or blue
Whenever your spirits are lowest it's what brings a smile
Love brings it every time not just once in a while
Love is being able to make the ultimate
sacrifice and give one's life for another
Even when the one is not your own brother
No matter what else is said, know that this is true
Love is the one who says "I am Always here for You."

Ben Grabber

Rainbow

All rainbows are beautiful in the far-distant skies,
We see them quite often, with wide-open eyes.
Now God has a SPECIAL one in his heaven so high,
Your loved ones are lost, not understanding why
You were taken so suddenly without any warning,
Leaving family and friends so deeply in mourning.

I knew you such a short, short while, but
I'll always remember your beautiful smile.
You even called me "Grandma" one warm, summer day
When you, Spring and Heather came over to play.

We'll miss you, sweet angel, with the beautiful smile,
And after each rain we'll look toward the skies
For OUR rainbow in heaven - relieved of all pain,
May God hold you close till we meet again.

Ruth Nagel

fountain square

all that eve in my dark corner i sat
gazed across the lively courtyard
dancing youths parading impeccable images
shrouds of identity displayed so proudly
woven so intricately with smiling faces and with lies
swapping lives and morals with every new wave
that would come crashing upon their angelic suburban existence
they revolt against authority and responsibility with apathy
oh, they are so misunderstood and so persecuted
that common thread which binds them all
with this they weave the banner for which they stand
but look, they don't stand, just sit
each follows the pattern of contrived idealism
they call it originality
ending as the same
their shroud becomes a muddled gray confusion
so like the blurred identity of each fiber

they seek each other because they cannot find themselves

Heather A. Wieczorek

The Rose

The long stemmed rose grows,
    isolated by her proud beauty.
Petals perfected by dew drops carefully placed
    by an oft ignored loving hand.

"Oh, ... me", is the murmur heard from her isolation.
"Me, me, me. I, I am ... , I Me. Glorious me."

A glass cage is less effective as a prison - it chafes.
The cage of Me is swept clean with the illusion of freedom.

A rose is to be picked, given away.
It's a vessel to hold the beauty of love for another.
Pride renders the vessel closed and hard
    unable to contain the rich perfume that is its perfection.

Clark Johnson

Life

All of our lives we search for things
that make our life a little more enjoyable.
Sometimes it takes time to understand
that life don't always play
fair and yea, it hurts like hell but
its "survival of the fittest" and those
of us who get stepped on, learn!

Yea, we learn, alright, everytime that
it happens we say, "enough of this
s**t," but inevitably, another comes along!
"You know who you are!"

So remember, if its going to make you
happy, get it! If your friends are true
they won't just stand by and watch
or ridicule you for your choices, because
even as friends or bro's we all must
put our feelings aside and choke
down a little pride to help those
we love and those who love us!

Justin William Herring

The Real Me

Sometimes I look at myself, thinking,
is this really me?
Or is there something more to me.
I'm not always happy with the way I look,
but I have to learn not to want the perfect, look,
I need to know that in this world,
I don't need to be the perfect girl,
I need to know there's more to me,
than just the face and looks that God gave me.
So when I look in the mirror at night,
I see a face that I can like,
maybe not what others want to see,
but just a face that makes me, me!!!
So now I know that I can be,
anything that I want to be!

Brandi Finch

Let Me

This life, forged from mentality and mortality, is a prison;
Cold, logical, nearly devoid of compassion and tender emotions.
Let me, the captive, be released from bondage for I am ready
To seize the heart of one who is open and desirous of affection.

I am a man of subdued passion, tempered by deep-seated morality;
Frustrated and longing to touch the soul of one I'm fond of.
Let me exceed the bounds of logic; the fetters that restrain,
To tender the life of one who longs for fidelity and respect.

If desire is the fuel for passion, let the conflagration rage;
A fire storm, unquenchable, that evaporated all resistance.
Let me say I love you to one who is ready to hear my entreaty,
Like one who is starving; yearning to join my banquet of devotion.

I can be a faithful friend; quick to listen; ready to advise;
Seeking to assist those in need of direction and confidence.
Let me be more than a friend; a lover who longs to hold you;
Bonding my soul with yours to form a union unable to be severed.

My emotions, tempered by rejection and exposed to disappointment;
Battered, yet survive to sustain my spirit and soul with sanity.
Let me emerge from this fortress of reason to fight all foes
That prevent the surrender and capture of your mind and heart.

Rick Badman

Stairway To Hell

I watch myself sitting on the bottom stair,
my body penetrated by a demon's stare.
He watches the blood flow through and out,
the gashes I put on my wrists about.
I cannot see the girl that drinks it all,
or paints hidden messages on my wall,
that I cannot see until it is too late,
because my soul is already filled with hate,
half of it real, the other half taught,
by the sight, to my blind eyes, life has brought.
I know the deeds that every man,
will go to if too much is laid in his hands,
all he can do is strive for more,
until everyone, but himself, is broken and poor,
and the bystanders, like myself, that did no right,
now have to to walk down a lonely flight, of stares.

Jeremy Lee Forhes

The Tiger

The tiger is like a mighty river,
Whose hand cuts through hard rocks.
The sight of her makes all animals quiver,
The wild oxen, the bear, she seems to mock.

The tiger is a volcano,
Erupting with speed and strength;
Her body like a torpedo,
She will kill her prey at any length.

The tiger smiles at herself after the kill,
Pleased with what she has done.
She will settle down and eat her fill,
Then lay with her tummy to the sun.

Nicolette L. Weaver

"What Lurks In The Shadows"

Life is carefree but full of hurt and pain,
Love lurks in the shadows, but it's not the same.

I've fallen in love and I won't call his name,
Love lurks in the shadows, but it's not the same.

We fell for one another, for we are the blame,
Love lurks in the shadows, but it's not the same.

He have ties and we're playing a dangerous game,
Love lurks in the shadows, but it's not the same.

Love doesn't come with fortunes or fames,
Love lurks in the shadows, but it's not the same.

My love for this man is love given in vain,
Love lurks in the shadows, but it's not the same.

Am I being modest or am I going insane,
Love lurks in the shadows, but it's not the same.

Opening the door and into my life he came,
Love lurks in the shadows, but it's not the same.

He has a wife and I'm just the dame,
Love lurks in the shadows, and it's not the same.

I have to let him go, for I can't stake any claims,
Love lurks in the shadows, I must never call his name!

Brenda Louise Smith

Epitaph Of A Planet

One sparrows falls, a velvet sound it makes,
Still, stagnant air surrounds its small remains,
Tall factories pour, with every puff of steam,
One surge of filth into the crystal stream,

High masted ships upon the melting brine,
Sight fountain spray on the horizon line,
One more harpoon brings one more whale down,
One less voice of mellifluous sound,

One sharpened are against the yielding bark,
White, empty fields, unforested and stark,
One lonely squirrel is left without its mate,
Yet one more beast to share the sparrow's fate,

Dark wooden box of ivory inlaid,
Chess pieces fine, of that same tusk were made,
Great dying bull lies on the grassy plains,
Where men disposed of elephant remains,

Two leaders pause, in disagreement stay,
Two angry hearts filled with an ancient hate,
Soft stifled cries, through gunfire unheard,
One little child to join that fallen bird.

Jhan Abercrombie

Cover-Up

A gauze of fog blurs outlines
slips its veil over abandoned lake of snow and ice
the sky, the lake, the shore
obscured in one inscrutable mass
of silver grey whiteness

A sheen of light behind it reflects from the snow
In the East, the tips of the quartzite bluffs
cast a shadow

Feel the silence

The still damp air hangs softly
waiting expectantly
to reveal what is behind the mist.

Sometimes
it is better not to know.

Kay Prosser

Powerful Darkness Sometimes Hurled

Earth's shadow crossed the moon's full face
last evening as midnight approached.
The sun, extinguished long before,
threw a powerful darkness directly
at the distant night orb, obscuring it.
We have named the occurrence, an eclipse.

Also with human experience,
powerful darkness is sometimes
hurled a vast distance at us and seems to
obscure otherwise bright events.

We must try to remember,
as I discovered this morning
when walking west at daybreak,
the temporary nature of such occurrences and
the return of events to normal conditions.
The large, orange orb of moon
broke free of clouds,
appeared whole once more
and descended into the western mountains.

Charles King

Anger

Thunder and rage about to explode.
Waves of emotion to be rode.
Taking our bodies to the end of life.
Cutting through our souls like a knife.

Dreams of joy leaving our skin.
Where hate and resentment begin.
Leaving others with the blame.
Holding on to all the shame.

Words of hate so easily said.
Letting our anger be fed.
Hurting others, when we know we are wrong,
Not even trying to get along,

Rage growing, hate flowing and all
The time anger showing.

Deborah Knight

Dunbar School Reunion Salute

To Deceased Alumni Tucson, Arizona

November 25, 1995
Across the vast sea of life,
Many elders have brought us to this nite.
They have supported and nurtured us to the pathways of life
we've quietly chosen.
Each in their own way, labored carefully and wisely to give us hope
for a better day and brighter future.

And when we cut the umbilical cord of support
and took flight into the world, they smiled and said "ALRIGHT."

Then in a fleeting moment, they vanished from our midst.
Who will lead us? Who will support us?
Who will build the foundation?
Our hearts screamed from the pain.
Then we looked around and smiled we did,
For we are the elders now.

Mattie Shepherd

"The Little Caboose"

God, sent for his best little angel and said to him,
You have to leave this place, my little guy,
Your mommy is waiting for you, that is why.
With a tear in his eyes he said,
When the bells are ringing, the gates will open up
Hurry outside, so again they can shut.
When you hear the last rings,
Leave your halo and wings,
With the big angel by the gate,
Go now, - you cannot wait!
The little angel climbed on a shooting star,
Who would take him down so very far.
God, watched the little guy depart,
As sadness settled in his heart.
Be always my good little angel
And you mommy's pride and joy,
You sweet little baby boy.

Barbara Korte Frame

Inside The Wall

From out in the open it looks safe.
  From a view it looks comforting.
From a glance it looks appealing.
  From here to there it looks like rain again.

Deep in the center is the storm, raging to find the way out to the
world. As the rage builds turning inside all that is left is one
burning soul locked in a prison of eternal madness, until the night
when all dark things come out to play the game of hide and seek.

K. M. Higgins

Grandma Dear

What did you think of Grandma Dear
When the time for the birth of your son was near
Did you sew his clothes with happy tears
Secure in the knowledge your husband was near

Did you ever look back to that dreadful day
When your father said "Be on your Way"
He understood not nor could he forgive
The words he knew were "Do as I say"

But you were in love with a loving man
He held your future in the palm of his hand
He promised you riches from a gold sprinkling can
On your finger he placed a bright wedding band

You made your son a little rag doll
Out of a sugar sack so they tell
You sewed into it your hopes and dreams
You would dream a while and then sew a spell

You didn't live to rear your son
Though I often think you would like to know
He grew up loving brave, and fine
Yes, Grandma, I thought you would like to know.

Dorothy L. Bussemer

Tell Me

When you cut me, is my blood blue
tell me how I am different from you
Does my hair grow green
that's something I haven't seen
your honey is made to eat
my honey is just as sweet

I like to party, dance, and have fun
Don't tell me that's something you're never done
So don't tell me one race is better than the other
The only true difference is our outside cover
once you peel that sheet back
it doesn't matter if you're yellow, white, or black

Shanique Chester

Let Me Be Free

Free. Free.
Please let me free.
So that I might fulfill my destiny.

You dominate my awakening hours,
Your presence is everywhere.
In the writer's song; little reminders emerge,
Your name electrifies the air.

Your gentle presence permeates every day,
Your name softly whispered in the breeze.
Just as flowers announce the coming of spring,
And a refreshing wind ripples through the trees.

Life's meaning is enriched because of you,
Inspiration overflows my soul,
I find uniqueness and meaning at the birth of each day,
Quiet strength to face challenges which unfold.

Free. Free.
Please let me be free.
If your love is a fruitless fantasy.
I'll take my aspirations, commitment, and dignity,
And continue to fulfill my destiny.

Iva J. Cooper

"A Bug's Eye View"

The figures below are all having fun
With their pointy beaks and flat pig noses
Poised upon those empty heads they fill with
A strange substance of boiling, clear liquid
Which makes them all act so joyous and gay,
And the hundreds of colors that float through
The air must have formed when that cloud did burst
At its seams, for surely it heard the odd
Noises those seashells make when the fancy
Penguins and posies do blow into them
After each sees some orb floating up to
The sky and huge roars blast from the picture
Box on the table and everyone grabs
Someone near, as finally they scream words of,
"Happy New Year!"

Adrienne B. Sherman

A Tribute To Maya Angelou

She waltzers in cool - as a late summer's breeze.
Wheeling women's heads. Dropping men to their knees.
It's more than her beauty, her dip and her sway,
though she's quite handsome
in an elegant way.
What's noticed the most is more feeling than fact.
She's a tempest contained with a modicum of tact.
Dancing to her own drum,
sounds only she hears.
Rhythms from a deep place -
seldom heard by her peers.
Alluring as an avatar, overwhelming to be near.
Swift as the current that draws us all here.
Raw power in harness, educated primal force.
Sureness mixed with secrecy, dedicated to course.
High priestess of poetry - she takes center stage.
Composition most magic - meted out by a sage.
Capturing the crowd - colors blend behind eyes.
Hearts lifting together, she enchants - -
"STILL I RISE"

Patricia A. Sim

The Kiss

I wanted to kiss you so bad
that when it did happen I wasn't prepared.
We sat on the couch you stared at me with your
big brown puppy eyes.
While I was staring at the TV you put your hand on mine.
I turned,
gently and slowly you moved forward.
I knew it was happening but wasn't sure how.
A million things running through my head.
Then the moment that I was longing for finally happened
our lips met.
I felt as if I was floating.
But then you pulled away
and asked if I wanted to go to the bedroom.
I got up and left.
I realized on my way home
that I was waiting for so long
for something so special to me.
But all you wanted was sex not me.

Nikki Ferraiolo

A Million Memories

I want to make a million memories with you by my side.
I want to walk in the rain holding hands;
or walk down a shady lane.

I want to make a million memories, one at a time,
taking the time to enjoy them all.
Feeling the warmth in my heart for only you.

Maybe a million and one;
that special one that comes in the morning watching you sleep.
Knowing that the love I feel will last a life time.

Or could it be a million and two;
remembering feeling your arms around me holding me tight,
when only your kiss could make the world all right.

No matter the number; no matter the times,
The best memory of all is just knowing
that you are mine.

Don Holley

Rainbow

Schizophrenic song,
Threading through my mind,
Confusing bits of laughter,
Rallying through time
Stronger, ever stronger
Changeling ribbon candy runs,
Dancing, spinning, colorfully disarrayed;
Incense bits with candle wax, burning bees
And leaving tracks, mud up to its knees;
Trampled flowers, mixed to plaster,
Caked screams, ice cream dripping blood.
Sharply panting, fluttering, gasp!
Ice and fire, unblended in a casque,
Death and Sex, Love and Violence,
The discarding of the mask
Which was never really a mask.

Jennifer Kho

Meaning

Do we have a purpose here on Earth,
or are we just supposed to survive?
Keep our heads above the water, keep ourselves alive?
Are we just wasting time here creating war and pollutants,
So eventually we'll live in bubbles
and give birth to ugly mutants?
There must be something more than merely just surviving,
It's answers to questions like this of which my mind is thriving.
Why does man do the devious things he does?
Are there reasons for his actions or is it just because?
If more time was spent uniting cultures of our race,
We would notice a change in the world,
it would be a better place.
Instead of competing for the good of one,
man should work together,
On finding a way to exist for not only now, but forever.
The frontier of our minds far exceeds what we know.
Think of the powers we posses and the places we can go.
Man must expand his quest to other dimensions of space,
And search for other beings that will help advance our race.

Robert R. Smith

Protest

Smile's gone. Once love, now forgotten.
I can't face another day,
But no one could guess.
Flimsy front, to protect from
Sympathy's glare.

Beth Edwards

Property Clerk

Energy quivers, singing deep inside the twisted metal
  of your bicycle
Relentless grey pauses to cradle the envelope that holds
  your broken eyeglasses
Your child scent is offered safe harbor within the cotton threads
  of your small t-shirt
Angry scuff marks injure the white leather
  of your tennis shoes
Howling energy shadows each penstroke
  as I write in thick black ink
Case inventoried/location:
Bin 7
Everything is in its place
Except,
A hungry chair sits forever at your family's table
And those that map the pathways of grief
And all who labored to save your precious heartbeat
  now struggle with new breath
And I, the guardian of lost memories
Will occasionally press my palm against the iron wall of Bin 7
Knowing
Everything is in its place
    Michele Hall

An Old Woman's Last Memory

The smell of the woods, the sounds of the birds
The heavenly sky so blue
The memory lingers on in the woman they now call old
She is spent and counts the number of her days
A city child taken from the grey steel and dark skys
To the wonderment of the woods
Discovering a wild rose among the shrub
Still comes back to the memory of the woods
She has lived through a life of happy moments
Sad moments and moments fulfilled
But yet her time is growing short
She wishes she could go back to those woods
God has given her life, but soon will see fit to take it
Again she comes to the memory
The beauty of the flower to the city child
Awake with the glorious song in her soul
the warm sun shining on her
Instead of the gray steel found in the city
Nature has bestowed a gift
God has seen fit to plant the memory
    Susan Laskin

I Give To You

I give to you all my strength.
To help you make it.
To make you strong.
I hope you take it.

I give to you all my love,
To help guide the way.
To help you through
Another day.

I give to you all my knowledge
To help you do what is right.
To help you teach others
And to help you through the night.

I give to you all my faith
To let you know I care.
To teach you to always listen
And to tell you I'll always be there.

I give you all these things
Because I love you best
But most of all, I give to you my encouragement
To top off all the rest.
    Jessie Allton

Eastertime

Happy easter to all girls and boys,
It's time to count our blessing and joys.
A time for family to get together,
Doesn't matter what kind of weather.

Your baskets are hid, but left you clues,
I know you'll find them cause you're no fools.
You'll have to help the little ones this year,
But soon they'll be racing with you, have no fear.

For the older ones, eggs I have hid,
Twelve eggs to find for each kid.
When they are all found, open with care,
Divide the goodies into an equal share.

Hope you have a fun time this year,
Be good till next time, you hear.
Off to the other homes I must go,
Happy easter to all, I love you, you know.

  Easter Bunny
    Barbara A. Green

Revelation: New Year's Eve, 1995

Tragedy moves punishing and relentless,
Thick and fast through ordered and successful lives.
Darkness and despair obscure the light,
Blinding choices and wisdom is in flight.

Divorce, 34 years shot to hell in one single act,
Business decisions gone awry in legal battles, truth and lies,
Fortune reversal and bankrupt dreams,
Emotions on edge, the ugly faces of distrust, anger and revenge.

A gradual demise from forces within, and beyond, control,
Years of infidelity come to a head.

Where is God in all this mess?
So silent, absent, after years of vineyard work,
In all the searching - a place to live, a job, an education,
Dating in the 90's, new life, new friends.

The best and worst, brought together in a single year of life.
And God is there, present in all the people and events,
The ups and downs, joys and sorrows that have brought,
The best and worst together in a single year of life.

PRAISE, HONOR, AND THANKSGIVING TO GOD,
WHOSE REVELATION OF SELF MADE THIS YEAR
  WORTH LIVING.
    Carolyn Aymond

My Good Friend

I have a good friend, who's been with me since birth,
and all my life he's been there, I never truly knew his worth,
the times of life he's shared with me, are my life's fondest memories
he has always been there, with his love and wise advice,
which always seemed a comfort, when my life was filled with strife,
Throughout my life my good friend, has always been close by,
But now our lives are changing, I said I would not cry,
There's things I need to tell him, things I need to say,
My good friend I care about, is moving far away,
I want to say I love him, for I do with all my heart,
I want to sat he'll always be my greatest friend,
despite the miles that keep us apart,
I hope this poem has done that job,
for it's so important that it has,
This man who is my good friend,
I still call him Dad!!
    Debbie S. Riddle

Tomorrow's Rainbow

The blue skies vanish as the clouds accumulate and darken;
The rain drenches everything in its path; then eases into a drizzle;
The sun breaks through to warm the earth...and life begins anew.

Losing hold of a loved one is one of
Life's most painful experiences.

Initially the tears come easy; then on and off
As memories flood back...disbelief, hopelessness,
Despair. A numbness sets in...a protective shield
From feeling for fear for being hurt again...the
Hardest part of love to accept is...the Pain. But,
Without the pain there is no love, no depth of feeling.

Yet, a different day will dawn for what's come and gone
Being, notably, of a higher quality for their special ways
Retained in our inner selves...since we have become
Enriched by their having touched our lives.

A new light will rise on the horizon and, somehow,
Everything that's passed will be put into prospective...as
Fortitude spawns tomorrow's rainbow.

Carolyn M. Aiello

Almost Home

Marines and sailors, mostly Marines,
Back home from war in peaces,
must never go back again.

A welcoming home 15 years too late, with a wall and a statue,
To be a healing Wall; it has helped, I hope,
The Wall, a statue of 3 soldiers,
and now of 3 nurses, all of bronze.

A tremendous emotional impact, bringing
back a rush of long lost feelings for me, a Nurse.
All those men on The Wall - dead.
All those thousands more with lives forever changed.

Welcome home, Soldiers!
Welcome home, Daughters of America!
At last!
NO! We are still not home.
The ghosts of war are still around.
MIA's, POW's - still unanswered questions.
Agent Orange, minds still at war, a government trying to forget...
We won't let them;
We're almost home.

Jean C. Skelton

Fear

Everyday, looking in the mirror
inspecting each purple-red mark on my legs and arms
because someplace I read about these things called lesions
maybe I'm paranoid
I thought we made love,
but how was I supposed to know?
I was, after all, only seventeen
And pure as those snow angels we made
That day I thought you loved me.
Tomorrow they will spear my arm, drawing out life's fluid
such a simplistic act
and I will await the results
feeling the noose tighten with each passing hour,
in front of gallows pole,
Praying that God will sever the rope
and exempt me from my mistake

Kimberly Elizabeth DeMaio

The Beautiful Bride

Dear Lord, the scriptures reflect your Bride
will be without spot or blemish-
a thing of beauty to see.
She will have purity of soul and, because
of your blood, dressed most righteously.

Lord, You know that Jessie is blind,
and Henry has singular vision.
Jim has an arm missing, and
sometimes Joe's brain is minus a mission.
Nevertheless, we await complete in You,
knowing that now our souls, and some
day our bodies, will be made anew.

William Henry Williams

Livin' In A Cage

Livin' in a cage of bars on every window,
and iron gates on every door
where crackerjack cops wheelin' shotguns,
roll down the streets
keepin' the fear alive,
keepin' us afraid of each other,
keepin' us inside the walls of oppression,
that they erected for us,
all those hundreds of years ago

Livin' in a cage that is covered with the blood
of our ancestors,
of our grandparents and,
oh my God, oh my God, they've gotten to our children too
where is our hope, where is our freedom

in a cage, that is not as strong as they'd like
because we are still alive,
still speakin' a language that they don't understand
still dancin' to rhythms that confuse their European feet
still alive with the life of our people

A cage, and only a cage, we'll blow away the dust when it
crumbles.

Leah Michelle Burton

Family And Friends

Sifting and drifting, down comes the snow
Covering footsteps where animals go
Gilding the branches of stark, leafless trees
Continually shifting with each aimless breeze.

Fogged in the sunshine, the stillness arises
Then quietly beckons to many surprises
And into the warmth of memories dear
A joyous new season comes crowding and near.

See all the children with sweet happy faces
Treasuring moments and loving embraces
Come closer, come closer and let us be one
Keeping the Yuletide as oft we have done.

Many the friends tucked deep in our hearts
Lovingly shared our time and our parts
Never forgotten you always will be
A part of our lives, thoughtful and free.

The wonders of Nature
That open our mind
Bring God to our hearths
And love to Mankind.

Joan M. Swanson

Alone

Do you know what it's like to be
deserted and left alone?
It's a cold feeling in the bottom of one's heart!
I've had this feeling since you left me.
It is also a feeling of emptiness.
My heart can never feel whole again.
In my heart is the hole that you used to fill up.
It will always belong to you forever.
I used to always be happy.
I used to have a warm heart and that feeling of wholeness,
But not anymore.
Not since you left me.
And never again until you come back home to me.
Maybe then my heart will be whole again.
But now I feel Alone.

Christina Canales

Our Maxi Our Taxi Of Love

Ad read "Yorkshire terror $10.00 not housebroken"
Left out was "Yorki 10,000 feelings of love and tenderness
When we met he wiggled and jumped high
With a tear in my eye, he sent my emotions to the sky
I patted, he licked my hand and
I experienced joy from another land
He weighs only seven from heaven, I see a ton of emotion
He seeks only a kind word and devotion
At home with my wife, we welcomed him to a better life
Once in awhile an accident will occur and
With sadness in his eye, he asks "please give me another try"
After a pat on the rear, our "Lil Lovebug" will respond with
A kiss on the cheek or a smooch in the ear.
Our lil "Maximillan, with a long name will
Pass any competition with fame.
Thank you "Man above, you have bestowed our belief in
Lasting love"

John P. Glynn

What America Means To Me

You asked me what America means to me?
The answer is plain and easy to see
I can work the land, plant what I please
Without the government trying to seize

I can go to church, I can go to school
I can practice each day the golden rule
We can live and learn just all we can
For it takes the best to run this land

I can play all day and daydream too
And know someday my dreams can come true
I can raise my voice loud and long
And help my government be brave and strong

And when I'm tired, I can sit and rest
Watch the TV programs I like best
And then to sleep the whole night through
Doesn't it seem just to good to be true?

Then I think of children across the sea
Who would be so proud and happy to be
A wonderful American, just like me

Doris M. Allen

Untitled

Afraid to love,
   Afraid to be hurt.
Wanting to get close and to care for someone.
   Afraid to lose the one who you do love.
   Afraid to love but afraid not to ever love.

Jennifer Lee Keeley

A New Day

I opened the door to a brand new day,
   what will be in store for me along the way?
Can I determine what kind of day this will be,
   or has fate already planned what I will see?
Does this day hold sunshine so I will feel okay,
   or be cloudy and a dull color of grey?
Will the day be eventful and make me proud,
   or a lonely one and I'll get lost in a crowd?
If the phone rings, will it be a friend,
   or a sales person to displease me to no end?
Does the mailman bring a letter to make me glad,
   or bills and advertisements that make me sad?
Could enjoyment be in store that brings fun,
   or will I be mad and take it out on someone?
Could this be the day I meet someone new,
   who brings happiness and washes away the blues?
Wouldn't it be wonderful for someone to share life,
   a good friend; it wouldn't have to be a wife.
A friend could wipe the pain away gathered along the way,
   that could start a new beginning on this new day.

Bob Rampani

T'is A Mystery

In Memory Of My Mother Ruth C. Damm

T'is a mystery to me
the things which were and are to be
Shadows passing by, leave their marks upon the wall
Painting the woes of life, E'er so great or small.

T'is a mystery to me,
the things which were and are to be
Would it were, like music sweet; the sorrows in life, we have to meet
All our wraths and woes, to reach the height of ecstasy
And then break forth in prose.

T'is a mystery to me
the things which were and are to be
Little "demons" whisper in my ear, the threads of life,
Are drawing near, and that which was it had to be
For Fate is e'er Destiny.

T'is a mystery to me
The things which were and are to be
But when judgement day doth come, life for me has just begun
No more earthly mysteries, Heaven's peace will better these,
and glorify the things on earth, we most defy

Leonor Clara Damm Hillock

Blinded By Colors

You definitely don't like me.
It's really not that hard to see.
Why do you hate me like you do?
I've never done anything to you.
These black and white games,
And all the pointless names
Just don't make sense.
Needless fear feeds our prejudice.
They're just like you and me.
Why do you refuse to see
That they're people too?
We should treat each other better than we do.
Blinded by colors,
Love one another.
Blinded by colors,
Brother vs. brother.
Blinded by colors
Certain to smother one another because we're
Blinded by colors.

Vanessa Minich

135

A Walk In Nature

When ever my spirits are low and I am in need of consolation,
I take a walk through nature and I admire all of God's creation.
While I take this walk through nature, I stop to admire the
birds and the bees, the flowers and the trees and not the diamond
rings or the fine automobiles.

From the dust in his own image God created man and gave him
total dominion over all the land. Since man is so dominant he
has taken many courses, but his concern is very limited when
it comes to our natural resources.

While I trod along I looked up in a tree, for I heard a bird
singing oh so sweetly. The song it was singing seems to say
from the dust is where it all came and in due time it will all
turn to dust again.

For man has the ability to build the automobiles that travels
the road and the big locomotives that carries the heavy load.
For man has built satellites that travels into outer-space,
but yet and still he says there just isn't enough food to feed
the entire human race.

So when things looks dull and mighty dim I love to take a walk
through nature and whisper a prayer every now and then.

Henry Williams Jr.

Silence Set Free

My silent pain, can someone know
To keep it quiet, or let it show
I want to scream, I want to share
The hurt I feel, but who should care
The trials are many, so hard to bare
But stop, look, and listen, it's Satan that's there
God does not give this spirit of fear
But power, love and sound mind, my dear
So put on the armor, pick up the sword
My place is in heaven and that's some reward
To focus on Jesus, and glorify Him
At times it seems tough, and looks kind of grim
But through trials we witness, and show God we trust
A test that He gives us, to pass it a must
I'll call on my God, to set this pain free
As I cherish, love and glorify Thee
It's His will, not mine, I need to ask for
To heal me, or use me, whatever's in store
I thank God He trusts me, to witness for Thee
Whatever it takes Lord, to set others free.

L. Jackie Ferguson

"To My Mother"

From the day I knew you were feeling blue
I covered my sadness with laughter and happiness
Nobody should ever see, nobody should ever know
How I feel about you; wish I could help you

Moments I blame myself maybe I neglected you
My conscience said no, "there's nothing much I can do
There are also when times tears fell from my weary eyes
I can't let you go because I love you so

My heart, my soul, my arms and my legs
We still be able to carry and take care of you
My son, my daughter, your husband and mine
Are all still here to help me through

So please! Mama don't go I still need you
Keep fighting for your life just like you always do
But, if God takes you because it is time for you to go
Take it to heaven all the love I have for you....

Estrella M. Chaco

My Berlin

A world of likeness
Separated by moral indifference, not by the persons,
(No, the persons are like me.),
But by human beings far away, not like us.

Pieces of stone, simple pieces of stone
Serve so much more.
Yet, no worthiness is this, this wall.

Just a step away, one step toward freedom.
My brother is there waiting for me.
I outstretch my arm, they slap it away.
I could reach him, my brother, if they would let me.

Envision it in my head, that is all I can do.
Those monsters - I would kill them if I could!

It stands there,
Blank without meaning anymore.
I hate it! I hate them!

Full of rage we violently tear it down!
Tear it apart, the wall between us.

Together we are now, forever in peace.
We stand where it stood - the Blockade.

Lensi Paige Goad

Poetry

Poetry that by many is understood
critics quickly say it is not so good

Poetry like classical music when rated very high
finds many asleep and others exit with a sigh

Poetry that is esoteric merely dampens the fire
poetry must be reconstructed to inspire

Poetry should rely on experience and intuition
no need to run to the dictionary for definition

Poetry critics are caught up in a fixation
poetry must free the spirit of all for reflection

J. Rajcic

The Lagoon

Running through the coral pool
  the sandpiper knows we are near
And hissing softly as embered smoke
  this gull circles the pattern of our communion.
Slow waves begin their sacred dance
  where the shoreline meets the water's edge
Beckoning this ocean's life to come closer to my shore.
Just the lure of the ocean's scent alone
  plays its force like gravity
  on wet, slow waves within close shores.

I would move to your shore
  with both the eagerness of the frenzied sandpiper
  and the patience of our gull's circling glide
But I can't come inside your mounting waves
And so this beauty at dusk
  makes my eyes sting with desire
Because your winding waves have not yet reached
  my coral shore.

Nan Hirleman Aalborg

A Little One's First Halloween

There are black cats - and spiders and witches all mean.
They hide in those shadows so as not to be seen.
The crawl all around you - But leave not a track
You fear that they've found you - You dare not look back.

So eerie and scary - It's just not much fun
To hear something whisper, "WATCH OUT LITTLE ONE!"
The wild winds are howling and it seems that you hear
THE SHRIEKING OF DEMONS RIGHT NEXT TO YOUR EAR

THEN WILD-EYED AND SCREAMING YOU CRY OUT, "OH NO!!"
You want to race home but which way to go?
Then DEEP FROM THE DARKNESS - A VOICE THUNDERS "BOO!"
Your feet begin running; your shoes follow too.

Your heart - is - a - pounding as you whiz through the trees,
And hope that the good Lord will hear all your pleas.
"OH PLEASE GOD - I PROMISE, I'LL NEVER MORE ROAM
IF YOU JUST GET ME SAFELY IN FRONT OF MY HOME."

Then right of nowhere your mom comes in sight.
You're real glad to see her this GHOST-GOBLIN NIGHT
SHE WRAPS HER ARMS 'ROUND YOU AS SHE WIPES OFF A TEAR
"WE'LL GO OUT TOGETHER - NEXT HALLOWEEN DEAR."

John Farrell

Untitled

Mysterious souls
Fluttering miraculously threw the journey of life:
self discovery
circumstance
challenge
Desperately seeking to father their intrinsic identity

Fear
doubt
veil of negativity is lifted
innate powers commence

Mysterious souls
search authentically for
truth
satisfaction
divine genius!

Nicole E. Ward

Alone

I hate being in a crowd of people
Yet feeling as if I'm a shadow upon the wall
What misery is this that grinds beneath the heels of society?
What toil, what trial,
Would cast out nature's child upon the whims of a blind worlds?
A world that is blind to the needs of its fellows
Hasn't an abandoned child in her midst
Who would see me? Who would love me?
No one hears the tears that fall from my eyes
No one sees the bitterness grow from years of abandonment
No one cares....

I shall break free from societies' chains
I shall capture the sun in my hand to hold forever more
And when the people turn and look
When they finally hear my cries
I will be soaring ever higher among the evergreens
Far away from my bitterness and sorrow
There will come a day when all others shall fall short
And with their gasping breaths to reach my status, they fall
And I stand alone once more....

Leilani Camacho

Escape

When storms of rage breach sanity,
The warm drill, piercing the clouds of doom, is a radiant beam
...And to the memory of you I escape

Overflowing reservoirs of desolated mentality are dammed
...When to your memory I escape

Great spirits, who encounter violent opposition, float under
The sustaining breath that pulsates from the heart of rare beauty
...And to the memory of you I escape

Each new portrait etched in an aging past, each new individual met,
Each smile replaced...cries incompleteness
The eternal circle can be drawn, perfectly round, splashed with bliss
...When to the memory of you I escape

Two lives remain separately parallel, a Utopia never built
Yet, imagination is powerful—the puzzle united is created
...When to the memory of you I escape

As each grain of sand crawls through the hourglass of time, a
Second soul yearns, lifts his eyes upward,
And thanks the angelic voices of heaven,
For winged deities sing perfect thoughts of you into an imperfect
   person

I beg God to once again raise the tides and wet me with
Rejuvenating waves
...And to the memory of you I escape

Michael S. Roope

Lost Love

I've a feeling of death that's in my heart,
Since the first day we were torn apart.
For I miss you dearly and wish you were near,
To live life without you is all that I fear.
Love and hate, they go hand in hand
I'm sorry what happened, please understand.
For loving you to much, is my only sin,
Surely your forgiveness, I shall never win.
All that has happened, can we not mend,
Because I still need you to call my friend
Or just to hold you in one last embrace,
I would travel through all, time and space,
But to part from you, without a good-bye,
Makes my heart empty, wither and die.

Dave Whitney

Untitled

I held up a candle at noon,
But wasn't much noticed at all.
Though all around me was gloom,
They still rushed and hurried to fall.

So I purchased a halogen light.
And kept pointing the way with my beam.
Their eyeballs were blurred with their sight.
Heard one say, "Things are not what they seem."

I held up my candle at night,
And though I spoke not a syllable of sound,
Darkness split at the glorious light,
And the searchers all gathered around.

Larry Koontz

Trees

The trees in our yard stand straight and upright.
A haven for birds at night.
The snow on the branches decorates them best.
Each bird thinks his nest is nicest.
Cardinals are red, wrens are brown.
No matter what color they, share the tree,
because a nest in the tree is better
than the cold ground.

Audrey Garcia

Unforgiven

Though I stand on my turning threshold
I can not remember my life.
For we are not what we remember of ourselves
But rather what people say we are.
I am who I am,
But who I am,
Who's to say who I am,
Or who I will become.
My unwritten future lies ahead.
I am chilled by my solitude.
I realize that time is only a frame in my mind.
I was never here to begin with,
I was always here,
Always will be.
It makes me sad to know
That my life was more than who I was.
And that I took the risk to remain closed in a badd,
Rather than taking the risk to blossom.

Becca Urciuolo

What's Inside

Don't know which way I'm going, unrest and fear is overflowing
Can't trust myself to pick myself up and start again
Unsure of things that I am trying
I feel the light inside me dying
I try to light the fire, once again the flame is dim
A road to search and one to deny
Either rain pours down or the well is dry
Both chances decrease my chances to survive the unavoided pain
The fork in the road cries indecision
Both shouting at me, blurring my vision
Between emptiness or thundering skies
I choose to wash out with the rain
I clear myself of the dirt in my eyes
Wash my soul with the truth, bearing no lies
Fight the pressure by letting what's inside control my retreat back to life
My thoughts of the days attacked by gray
Are darkened inside with a heartless cry
I drop my problems, only one thing to say
Life is too precious for me to deny.

Stephen M. Wellenc

A Perfect Fit

Her hair —
   A thousand silky tails
   Framing a delicate face of purest China.
Her eyes —
   Evanescent shards of God
   Radiating all that is love and kindness.
Her smile —
   A captivating purebred cheshire grin
   Exuding empathy while excluding all else.
Her height —
   Taller than my chin and lower than my hairline;
   When we hug we fit.

Jonathan Kuehnle

Untitled

Oh industry you beast
Who robs the children of their sleep
You strip families of dignity
And fill man's head with wanton needs
Upon the computer you feast
While our sons and daughters are riddled with disease

A PC with a virus
Call a repairman quick
For much money is being lost
With this poor thing sick

Cancer, AIDS, common colds that have no cures
But without a cool million you'll never know for sure
Father Time and Mother Earth
Will soon part over this mournful birth

Jesus hangs his head in shame
For it is His brother we all blame
And thus we have the perfect excuse
A dysfunctional Heaven is to blame for this abuse

Angie Clark

Untitled

I am the raven that watches from above.
I am the gone prey that it watches for.
I am the burning cold carried on the wind of autumn's end.
I am the small shifting that dances the leaves.
I am the intoxicating perfume of lavender moors.
I am the forgotten smell of ancient books and old memories.
I am the crimson stain splashed by the cup.
I am the dark spreading spilled by the sword.
I am the fragile peals of children's laughter.
I am the piercing cry of abandoned lovers.
I am the candles glittering at Samhain.
I am the smoke and flame of funeral piers.
I am the gossamer images of pleasant dreaming.
I am the crashing cold terror of nightmare.
I am violet sunsets and morning mist.
I am barren desert and moonless night.

I am.

Karen West

Youth

Hiding nakedness, but not that which is so barren,
the girl's black hair, knotted about
ripening eyes,
watches.

She presses dry hands, reveals broken nails, flat
against thighs, hardening,
terra cotta in the dry, gypsy sun.

Dust whorls, droplets roll along forearms and knuckles,
tracing callous-soot knees,
opening red earth
to swallow the tendrils,
the flashing, sepia stare,
and the weariness for someone too young.

Sarah E. W. Martin

Controversial Confusion

   They say if the sun faded away, we'd all die. "The sun is the threshold of all life." How? Without light, there is no color discrimination. No way to tell who looks better than who. No fingers pointed at anybody. In the dark, all is peaceful and quite. In the light there is war and hate. In the light, there is death. How can light be life? As the sun rises in the east, a new day has begun. It has charred the rest of the world and come back to us again. The sky gets lighter, the hate gets clearer. Time to start a new day.

Maliea Jordan

Moonlit Dreaming

It's night, it's dark, I'm outdoors,
I look, I see, the moon soars,
I stare, it's bright, it shines,
I listen, I hear, a coyote whines,
I think, I wonder, but how,
There's time, I think, and ponder now,
My thoughts, are lost, drifting around,
My peace, my heart, must be found,
The joy, the warmth, it brings,
Reminds me, life's reasons, such wonderful things,
I wish, I dream, I wait,
Something's happening, I know, and it's great,
I smile, I love, I fly,
Bad things, evil things, pass me by,
I give, send hope, send care,
My happiness, my joy, I will share,
It's time, it's come, everyone wakes,
I'm back, nothing's changed, my mind aches,
The moments, the few, escaping fears,
It's sunrise, it's morning the moon disappears.

Josh Sytsma

Visions

As I walked along the sandy beach
  I saw the most beautiful scene
It was too good for words
  Yet so far out of my reach
It was a full moon in the sky
  Shining brightly on the sea
It made me think of the future
  Hopefully what is meant to be
But also of my past, things left behind
  Some memories so vivid, I wish I could rewind
If I could go back, nothing would I change
  For I have learned that dreams are created
From the challenge of life's joy and pain
  I know the time will come
When I must face life on my own
  Meet the challenge of tomorrow
Things that are yet unknown

Monica Craig

"Innocence Lost"

In 1969 it exposed itself to me
A monster from the evilest of breeds.
Its actions you couldn't hear or see
It would commit the foulest of all deeds.

We were but children in that land time forgot.
We laughed and we joked — never giving it thought
Of what lay ahead, do we survive or do we not
With pain so great, sometimes death we sought.

This was the first sign of innocence lost.
Lost in a way, a way such as this.
I must live forever with the horror of it all.
In the air, the horrible, horrible taste of death.

Now I do not speak as do other men.
That monster again left his mark on me.
But in the end he did not win
For a beautiful spirit helped me to see.

Now I forget about monsters and memories;
They no longer control me at all.
I speak with more than any voice now
This beautiful spirit helped me tear down the wall.

Taylor Church

The Tree Of Life

I stand so lovely on the hill,
looking down at the old red mill,
I am a tree I stand so tall
I bring happiness and joy to all
The water of the Earth flows in my
roots, even though workmen stomp with their boots.
The light of man shines on my leaves,
which makes a safe home for all little bees.
Children have picnics under my
shade and think I'm the best thing
that God ever made.
Robins nest high in tops of me
and people say "What a beautiful tree!"
I love my job because I bring joy,
To each man, lady, girl, and boy.
The tree of life

Lauren Marie DiNardo

Enchantment

The countryside is wrapped this morning,
In a blanket soft, cold and white.
The snow that began in the twilight,
Continued on through the night.

Falling in muffled silence.
It tucked in the sleeping earth
Now peacefully all nature will slumber,
'Till gentle spring kindles her rebirth.

Tracks in the snow tell a story,
Rabbits scurried o'er the yard in great bounds,
A raccoon left hand prints by the creek bed,
Stray hounds have been nosing around.

Birds queue up by the feeder,
Like motions, an order exits,
The small and weak wait in subjection,
Knowing how futile it would be to resist.

Spring rains pattering on the roof tops,
Summer sun warming the earth with its glow,
Autumn colors transforming the land with their beauty
Are less enchanting then winters white, gentle snow.

Alice McMurry

Cracked Actor

Hey you! Looking so suave and debonair
With them razor-sharp sideburns and that greased-back hair
Feeling wild and hip-hop as you saunter on by
Dazzling little girls with a wicked, crazy smile

I hear life is just another Smash-and-Grab for you

Cracked Actor - Thought you were the real thing
Cracked Actor - Listen to you head sing

Watching and waiting - Watcha doin man?
Getting in over your head wasn't part of the plan
Playing games with your friends -
Who's going down with ya next?
What they don't know won't hurt them
(You guess)
Well, that's what I hear

Seen it all, lived it all - looking for your next buy
Smoked it all, done it all - Looking for your next high
(Thought you were smarter then that)

So, go ahead and kill yourself - do that nickel vial
But take no prisoners with ya sorry-ass self -
You're dead to me anyhow.

Sarah Laylah Evans-Cliff

Jerry

About 30 years before 1995,
Haight Ashbury was alive.
Kids' minds woke up, got out of bed
A little band started, the Grateful Dead.

Jerry got this band started, it was all his fault.
All the heads following looked like a strange cult.

More and more records came pouring out,
from Terrapin Station, to One From the Vault.

A jolly stout man, wild curly brown hair.
Looks don't matter when a heart's there.

Jerry kept playing, some band members gone.
His happy spirit kept trucking on.
From states and cities he brought much joy
to kids everywhere, every girl and boy.

Now in 1995 poor Jerry's dead,
but the music will thrive,
and take his place instead.
A heart attack killed him,
touring, heroin, cocaine,
but excuses won't take away the pain.

Tiffany A. Heitzer

Pastures Of Meadows

Molted rock, petrified layers of yearning for that special
moment laid wasted on a vast pasture of time.

Moments of hoping, built on towers piecing my sky.
Time of wanting balanced on leaded clocks now wound
too tight to click, tick, tock stop.

Yearnings so strong they seized my light - changing it into
tight fireballls - flung into dark ethers of space - lighting
my molted wasteland.

Walk on, fast - run - don't look back - nothing there but
past dreams, dreams not mature enough to take wings and
appear in sleep. Just dreams - no, not dreams - wishes -
wish to have, or be, or been there - once maybe.

Run, - pant - flee away where there's blades of grass, sky,
bounty of trees - pastures of meadows of hope, fulfilled
dreams, go where there's YOU.

Ardie Stuart Brown

"The Chalice"

The chalice is mine... I have only to drink of it.
Warm and sweet and strong, essence of the finest fruit.
It's intoxicating bouquet has left me weak and shaken
Light headed and light hearted... ready to soar.
    Perhaps falsely brave.
To drink for courage is surely fool hardy.
But to deny such spirits, to let it pass, is perhaps to perish alone..
Or is the passing of the cup the only way to live.

Poison or remedy... it is but a matter of tolerance
And that is not by choice but heritage,
so each must know their limit.
I have found where temptation overtakes reason
Where so hearty a drink would surely flow easier
Than the bitter stuff I know...
but which has nonetheless sustained me.

Blood of the vine, food for the heart.
A mask for reason or window for the soul...
Magic potion. Drink of life.   Drink of death.

It is cold and smooth and heavy in my hands.
My lips are whet, my breath is still...
Dark liquid glistens, reflecting anticipation.
The chalice is mine... I have only to drink of it.

Deborah Borci Ziegler

Young Love

I'd drink her beauty from afar,
As one who gazes on a star,
Yet fearful lest her eyes meet mine
In feasting on her shape, sublime.

Her smile would make my day seem bright,
And in my fancy I would fight,
A thousand martyrs for 'her grace'
And untold hardships I would face.

Gad, how I cursed my timid fate,
That caused my heart to palpitate,
And made my gulping throat run dry
Whenever she'd go strolling by.

Yes, this delightful little lass,
Was idol of our third grade class,
And 'tho her face gave me the slip
I'll bet she must have been a pip!

Jerrold Jack Rotwein

The Sculptor

The eye of the sculptor does contemplate
The essence of flesh that becomes a slave
To tenacity and courage to wait
For the future and the will to be brave
The hand of the sculptor departs in trust
To seek the beauty of strength in mind
And body where the verdict will be just
Although the long journey may be unkind
The promise of grace will begin to thrive
And realization of a dream does yield
Vitality in the artist alive
And the voice of destiny shall be sealed
The triumph of spirit sustains the course
The heart of the sculptor is at its source

Monique Karlen

Ride On The Trail

Ride on the Tamiami Trail for miles and miles.
Enjoying the sights will bring many a smile.
See Indian villages steeped in history,
And thousands of birds whose ways are a mystery.

If one could take an airboat ride,
Thru the Everglades they could look with pride.
Vast and beautiful and abounding with life,
But the struggle for survival must end with strife.

Oh, ride on the "Trail" and enjoy all the sights,
The canals, the fishing, the birds in flight,
See Ibis, Herons, Eggrets, and Cranes,
That swoop and dip like low flying planes.

Ride on the Trail for miles and miles.
See the swamplands, sawgrass, the Indian trails.
You'll never forget your trip through the "GLADES,"
On the TAMIAMI TRAIL'S passing parade

Ruth Mathas

Untitled

Snuggly warm and soft
a heart of pure love and
a friend that we'll never forget.

Our teddy bear shall always remain
in every part of our domain
We cuddle night after night
Our teddy bear removes all fright
what a wonderful sight our teddy bear

One who fills us with hope, dreams and cares
Something we all hold dear, but still we share
So others may feel the warmth
and love of our teddy bear that cares

Paul M. Ciraldo

The Christmas Tree

My Dad said only one Christmas tree.
My mom wanted two: A big and a little one.
Then there were three angel ornaments
that fell and busted.

Four Christmas lights were burnt out.
Five candy canes eaten by six people.
Seven presents already under the tree.
There were eight of same ornaments.
Nine people crying at its beauty.
Ten trains under the tree going in circles.
One Christmas star at the top.

Danielle Mancuso

Sandcastles

Sandcastles are temporary - like most things in life that are precious, you can't count on their beauty forever. The creation of something so unique to the eye. But fragile, when the tide - washed away what once was.

Just goes to show to enjoy what is there while you can, before it vanishes, like smoke in the air. People tend to destroy - What may not even be around for long, or what they don't understand to last. Instead of treating it with care - like a song gently sung, or a relationship that has begun, sandcastles are little hide-aways, that were man-made of love and creativity on a beautiful summer's day.

Sandcastles are little homes for dreams - that live and breathe in memory. Remaining vivid and clear in your mind, for however long you want. Way beyond the time they're gone.

Before the time the ocean rolled upon the shore - releasing the sandcastles' magic to the water, into the water's waves.
As particles disappeared their short-lived power now distantly far, Far away...

Carol Lynn Saccomandi

The Buzzard

The buzzard flew above the ground.
The black, attentive eyes looked down.
He saw some road kill by the road,
Ground like a hamburger, squashed like a toad.
A messy, gutty, bloody sight;
A yummy, gourmet buzzard's delight!

With a squawk and a squeak and a flap and a yell,
He rushed to the kill like a bat out of hell!
It tasted as good as green eggs and ham,
(The kill that he'd struck like a battering-ram.)
When he was done, he flew away,
Said, "Tomorrow is another day!"

Samantha Ann Kowalsky

Song Of The Aging Maid

It is dead!
(That fleshly part that craves —
though craving is a fly trapped in my grave)
But Freedom!
Like a spider's web I'm sent along a breeze
No longer wrenched between the clutching claws of Need
No — my mouth curls
Like saints in secret smile knowing
There's no earthly life for me yes
Knowing (and in knowing never waiting, wanting, hoping)
God is my lover; your child, my child, and love — I love you more
Divorced of greed (though still. The flesh dies slow:
my muscles twitch in one last lunge of terrifying Life,
a small voice cries but why I never asked
to go so high I only asked to be man's wife...)
Silly thing.
Lay back and let the earth absorb your pain
Your eyes roll quiet toward the sky and let
The knowing be your name

Heather Hutson

Hopeless Struggle

A life full of pain is all that I know
Years of struggle with nothing to show
Like an endless plunge to the bottom of the sea
The pressure builds and begins to crush me
As I gasp for air my body folds
Sinking deeper and deeper, another story untold
I can't break free from this force that holds tight
Which keeps me just inches from reaching the light
Exhausted from struggle, I try to hold on
But the fountain is dry and my faith long gone
I cry out in pain as I slip away
Slowly I die, lifeless I lay

Anthony T. LoPresti

If I Never Pass this Way Again

Please let it be told that I lent a helping hand.
There's a child that has no real life,
because of illness she must fight.
A young boy running the streets,
he has no home, no food, to eat.
An old lady sleeping on the bus stop,
she does not have a warm place to flop.
Children getting killed at school.
My God, Hijackers over there..
Hijackers over there!
None bother, nobody cares.
Why should it matter?
Is it you... Is it me?
No, so we throw our heads up high,
and close our eyes.
But, I tell you if I never pass this way again,
I will not..., I will not pretend,
Throw my head up, close my eyes,
because I feel their hunger,
their pain, their cry,
and so I lend them my hand. Why?
Because their just like you, and I, Human.

Sylvia Davis

Walk With Me

Will you walk with me? Here, take my hand;
as we tread through the remains of a desolate land.
Do not fear. Your eyes must remain sharp...
For we are approaching what some say is the most raven of parts.
Can you feel the chill, the dampness...there witness the rot?
View what's left of the trees of hope moldered in a helpless clot.

Look above you at the bleakish sky...
there are no birds of beauty, with wings flapping high.
Nor can be seen the rays of love and hope,
merely dusk and soot to itch thy throat.

Why do I take you on such a morbid trip?
Please, look closer with your questioning lips.
And what you'll see is more than just grave-ridden land...
but the sad yet veracious life of a decaying man.

What? Still, unable to see through?
Then take a moment from this decomposing view.
And allow your eyes to fall on yet another sight...
To your right, the mortal depiction of a sullen plight...

    Josephus Housey Jr.

Untitled

My life is a song, I perform each day.
I want my song to be simply divine, not just notes cluttering the
    page.
Lots of people don't like my song, but I find it rather nice myself.
They say it's too soft, too loud; too high or too low.
Sure, it has a flat note every now and then, but then again, don't
    they all?
They try to tell me how to rewrite my song;
Why, I just don't know.
Maybe it's meanness, bitterness or strife.
Or could it be jealousy; perhaps that's it.
But what they think, I really don't care, but there's one thing I do
    want to say;
In the words of Fanny Brice, "Don't rain on my parade".
My song is better than others think, you'll never understand.
You see, only I can sing my song;
Not Frank Sinatra, Judy Garland, or even Barbra Streisand.
However, my song lacks something, so let's make it a duet.
Our songs together blend so well, the love song I've longed to hear.
Our gentle notes, flamboyant chords, and the words that are our songs
Fit so well together to make ours a melody of romance, passion and
    ecstasy.
But since I'm singing solo, our duet flowing softly through the
    moonlit night,
I suppose will have to wait. That is, until I find you.

    Clint Morris

Forever

When you walked out you took
  my heart along with you
And left me here to sit and cry
  the whole night through
And there's no way that I can see
Another love will come to me,
It's over now, I'll stay this way forever,

They say that time heals everything
  but that's not true,
I think I've cried a million tears
  since I lost you.
The years have passed and
  I got by
And I don't know just how
  or why...
I only know I'll stay this way forever.

    Miriam Hoffman

"It's Over"

Now that she's gone and I alone
I call upon memory to bring her home

Most everything reminds me
Of sweet days long past
Of hopes and dreams that didn't last

All the promises that were never kept
Like leaves of the willow
All dried and wept

One couldn't find a love more true
Having searched earth's surface
And the heaven's too

They call this separation "Eternal Rest"
So final, unacceptable,
Heart breaking at best

People quick to add
We all go through it
At one time or another
Still difficult for me
Losing my heart's family
My wife, best friend, my lover

    George Nadeau

Two's A Crowd

Every day the one who shares my life slips,
in and out of my door. In the morning,
at lunch time, and in the evenings
he's always on my mind. He's known
We were meant to be together since he caught me
scribbling on the teachers' version
of the Ten Commandments.
Being more principled, he
argues with me over petty things
like why I'm not driving 55. I know
an argument is coming when he gets, what I
call affectionately, his holier than thou stance;
with his all knowing eyes and his determined sneer.
Often instead of accusing me he'll ask dumb questions
like "Do you really think you need that chocolate shake?"
I wonder why he doesn't just come out with the ugly, fat truth;
that's what he really means.
I've dumped him, but he's eager
for more. Uninvited, my conscience is back
at my door.

    Barbra White

Friendship's Worth

Your friendship is worth more to me
Than gold and silver could ever be
For it reaches way down you see
And sets this inner person free
Without your friendship I would die
Not outwardly, but, on the inside
On the inside, where it counts the most
I would be as a troubled ghost
I would have no reason to live
And tell me - what could I give?
Now I give joy and understanding you see
For that is just what you give to me
You give to me of yourself
And that gives me such great wealth
Now you see - your friendship is more to me
Than gold and silver could ever be!

    Dawn Darling Porche

Unknown Terror

Winds ablaze with scorching fire
Gusts blowing higher and higher
Crystal palace in all its might
Falls to earth with the fight
Clouds of dust begin to billow
Screams of terror crack overhead
Countless millions all are dead
Scorching bodies on the ground they lay
Awaiting new order in a darker day
Helpless victims plunged to their death
Screams heard afar with their dying breath
Fire spewing from the pits of hell
Burning flesh is the only smell
Wickedest of creatures is seen to laugh
With the burning of flesh in his path
Uncontrollable forces rage inside
Survivors all run and hide
White mare howls at the coming of dawn
Vanquishing the evil, the true hell spawn
Nevin Miller

I Am Poem

I am a bird
I wonder about life
I hear sweet harmony of the wild life
I see pretty flowers and calm leaves
I want to fly and see things no one else has seen
I am free

I pretend life is easy
I feel heart broken when I fail
I touch my heart and pray
I worry about whats going
   to happen the next day
I cry to afraid to show
   my worries and fears.
I am alone

I understand my friends in pain
I say to them I feel the same
I dream of what might
happen in the future I try to hold my
tears I hope someday I can live the life
I've always wanted to live I am my own person
Mandi Moreau

I Am Home

The big, blue, powerful waves crash against the rocky cliffs
like birds banging against the bars of their cage,
breaking free.

I look out against the blue stretch of water to the horizon
where I can see no further.
What is beyond that horizon?
What places?

Shall I go out there one day
and explore exotic places
unknown to the world?

I look out across the waters again,
and see wondrous things
the white sea foam, tropical fish and dolphins,
singing their sweet song.

I breathe the good sea air
and smell the harsh richness of sea salt.

And now I realize that I will not leave.
Because I could not be happier anywhere else
   because...
      I am home.
Alexis Alegria

Graduation Day

The time has come for me to let go
How hard it is you'll never know

It seems like only yesterday that you were small
Laughing and crying and playing ball

Now look at you, how much you've grown
It happened faster than I could have ever known

But the memories of your childhood I'll always
      keep safe in my heart
So that no matter where you are we'll never be far apart

So as you pack your suitcase, independence bound,
Remember that your mothers love will always be around

Wherever you go, it also goes with you
To help you and guide you and see you through

And if the time ever comes that life's too much to bear
May it bring you some comfort to know that I care

I wish you the best, including lots of success
A life full of joy and great happiness

Just remember to always stay on the right track
And be your own man instead of following the pack

So, good luck as your new life's begun
And thanks for being such a wonderful son.
Renee Huggins

Life's Dream

We search for the dark minded wonder -
will it appear before our end?
All day long we simply ponder,
as we strain to comprehend.

Daily, life presents its routine
while society tells us who we are.
Won't we let the true side be seen?
If we could only go that far.

Journey with me, down the path of life
as we search for any meaning.
The sights and sounds will replace our strife
as we see if there's more than dreaming.
Ryan Patrick

The Shadow Of A Memory

At the end of the day, in the darkened corners of the
room as various forms and shadows take shape, one tiny
shadow emerges from the rest.

He stood one foot tall, walked proud and bold upon four
tiny feet, yet tread so lightly as not to leave one
mark upon a satin sheet.

His aristocratic head was crowned with a fluff of jet
black fur fringed in silver white, richer than the
richest ermine; two deep brown, velvet pools for eyes;
a miniature heart that beat with the courage of a lion;
intelligence, compassion and understanding beyond
comprehension; love that demanded nothing in return.
His greatest joy to curl up at my feet, or snuggle next
to me in a chair, content my world to share.

These, and much more, are my memories of that tiny
shadow; but as I focus too hard in an attempt to bring
him more clearly into view I hear his tiny footsteps
echoing back through time as he gently fades away.
Again my heart must whisper, "farewell, La Pom",
remember I love you, even now, today.
Betty L. Nelms

A Walk In The Clouds

I spent my day looking at the big blue sky.
And others sit around and wonder why.

I love it for the joy it brings.
It filled with beauty and many things

It filled with birds and shapely clouds.
These are the things that make one proud.

It's filled with autumn beautiful leaves
It's filled with so much it's hard to believe.

It filled with the crisp fresh air.
All most to a point that we can't bare.

It's there clear and blue and bright.
And filled with the stars by night.

It's run's forever, as if one big stream.
So tranquil it all seem a dream.

For there you can travel at high rate of speed.
That's all the excitement that one needs.

The change can be hard that true.
But, the color so tranquil for me is blue.

Take one moment and look at the cloud.
What you see will make you proud.

K. Maholmes

Expecting

The feeling of anticipation, joy and sadness
wondering everyday, amidst all the madness
This could be the day. Again we try. Again
to our dismay.
The constant desire for new life
that enchanting delight shared
between husband and wife.
the results are in the doctor's confirm
The likes of parenthood
How long have we did yearn?
Our prayers have been answered
Oh the joy our hearts feel
Nine more months of countdown
It is finally real
No day could be harmed
Knowing our child is soon
To be in our arms.
The feeling of anticipation, joy and sadness
Soon to be a lifelong dream
Fulfilled
Amidst all the madness

Chrystine Ketcham

The Women In The Shade

A poet and
doesn't show it
a star in the sky
always flying high
shows no mercy on anyone
because she feels justice should be done
predictions are her best
but never tells the rest
"works too hard"
as said by Dianna Bard
weights about 94 and dresses to a "T"
which is how I want to be
She bombs everyone out
this is what my mom is about

Camille Brintzenhoff

Show Off Critter

Sammy Squirrel chatters and winks with glee
as if to say "Dude! Watch me up in this tree."
Then scampers and clutters to the very top
and shakes limber limb with a flippety flop.
Now a leap to the next tree to grab and to hold
with a haughty look meaning "Hey, ain't I bold."
Then one to another around a big ring
with each new branch like a see sawing spring.
At last the show's finished - he grins with disdain
then to the bird feeder to scratch out his claim.
Nose down - full stretch - he hangs by a toe nail
Avoid that blocking shield - alas to no avail.
Screeching birds chatter and swarm in - victorious
"So what!" THINKS Sammy, "My show's still meritorious."

Fred Charles Keill Sr

Ceilh! (Celebration)

I watch her now, sitting near her window, eyes downcast.

Sunlight has spun her long hair into pale gold;
the golden hair now a sudden flash
as she spins and leaves the window spot.

She moves with languid grace, like a dancer, unaware
of the beauty she has become...

No smile frames the narrow face, the lips almost
petulant; her eyes a deep blue, glacier and sad.

What hurts this child-woman, beauty, my Katie?

How can I reach inside and warm the heart?
I need her to know how special she is, so loved...
so lovely.

I will find a way...lift your eyes, Katie; raise
your arms, Katie...reach upward, unencumbered;

Free, like the eagle!

It is time to soar, strong and sure!
The World is at your feet...
That shy, hidden smile can light the sky!

Look up, Katie, look up. Fly...and
Celebrate! (Ceilh!)

Liz Tyre

Making The Bed

Every morning since we've been married,
My husband and I have made our bed together,
He on one side, I on the other,
And as we struggle
To get the sheets smooth and straight,
He'll say, "I need a little more sheet on this side,"
I'll counter with, "A little more blanket here,"
Together we end up with a bed smooth and comfortable
And inviting, ready for the night ahead.

I tend to think
As we celebrate our fiftieth anniversary
That making the bed is what marriage is all about,
Giving a little here,
Pulling a little there,
Working together side by side
To get the bumps out
Until everything is smooth and perfect.

Alma Hansen Langlois

Loveless

My soul is an empty void
where my blackened heart rests
while my mind roams a neon world
of love and lust
in a complete ecstasy
to cover up my pain
the pain that made my kind soul bitter
the world that made this red heart black
how long must I carry on
in this loveless world that I have found
one day love I'm sure to find
when I lay to rest the final time

Dave Cristen Lawrence

Untitled

I never meant to hurt
Or ever abuse
Something I searched a lifetime for
Someone who was to be forever more

I made terrible mistakes
I let it slip away
Never again to embrace
Your love for me erased

I need to let you know that my love for you remains
And I know for the rest of my life
That I could have called you my wife

I know we were different and problems arose
I should have known right from wrong

Your presence I feel everyday in a home we both made
I still call to you at night
And sense only silence and fright

I will still pray for the day a miracle may come my way
When a poem such as this will bring remembrance of a kiss

Peter Phillips

By The Gate

He's there
    waiting patiently, like always,
        though now his tear soaked neck lies cold
    his gentle understanding quiet beneath new
        snow that covers earth's wound.

He's not gone
    he lives in fabled fields that embrace warm breezes
        and cold starry nights
    he lives in a heart that shared dreams and joy and
        hope and love.

He waits
    at Glory's Gate
        where a gentle nicker and familiar toss of his head
            will greet me again
        for feedin' time and endless rides.

And the snowfall soothes a wounded heart.

B. J. Vardaman

Unseen Miracles

People held in earthly rings often fail to see
    The things that make life special - beyond their wildest dreams.

No time for reflection, caught in their daily routines,
    They soon lose sight of the ethereal schemes that each of our
lives bring.

Like the songs from the birds and scent from the trees,
    Sunsets and seashores - life's own melodies.

Look beneath the surface. A miracle there will be,
    underlying everything you hear, touch, taste and see.

Sense your very own miracle, the one that brings you here,
    that opens your heart and seeds your love for things that you
hold dear.

Keep this in mind and soon you'll see
    life's treasures need no special key
        for we already have one, hidden, inside of you and me.

Gary VanHoet

Athena Marie...

What does it mean? Poetry, beauty, sweet like honey
warm wet succulent skin, fresh flavorable flesh
screeching, silent, tender breathing
cold chilling embrace child like grace.
A pretty face that lightens, brightens
These dark doomly, gloomy filled days
who's love rains, pours down upon
around me in multiple, sensual, pleasurable rays
Innocence, lacking sin
entombed, encased, wrapped within a young girl
Purist form of ecstasy, sexually being
a Goddess of bliss, mistress of passion, pleasure, power
forever seeking a light to ignite, spark her,
Thee eternal flame, fire, the perfect flower,
oh another to say but a few of how
I love you

Joshua Bergeron

Racial Harmony (May 5, 1996)

Why must we fight amongst one another
    Do we really know each other as well as we feel we do;

Truth is shadowed through communication as false tones
what we vision behind falsehood with mortals souls within.
Fact and non-fact bonds the truth.

Product of the environment are what we strive as behind walls.
Break the chains and allow your essence to be free'd.

We allow chance to be our down fall
The worlds out look upon us is wrong, it is blind;
We all are equal in position, but not categorized the same.

Let emotion lead us and not ignorance, let us all follow
dictations lead by our own spirits.

David Wynter

"Mother To Mother"

Mother to mother, I can imagine your pains, to have to part
with your son is such a shame,
Mother to mother, you sent so many years, only to be left
now with so many tears,
Mother to mother, you're not to blame, for it is the system
in need of change.
Mother to mother, dry your weeping eyes, and pray O' Lord,
please hear my cry,
Mother to mother, there is not much time, for we must educate
our young to stop the dying...

Alton Wall

Ladder Of Life

One minute, one hour, one day,
Nobody knows how long we stay:

A mother in despair, who sat alone,
With a son who turned to stone:

Our childhood is a life of DREAMS,
For all that's how is seems.

One person alone, held in his hand,
Our families of a different land.

The secrets of many unknown,
Through the years grew very alone.

As wondered through the life of maze,
Oh, how we missed those lovely days:

The search of those was deeply sought,
Through GOD's Will and not forgot.

While we walk through the meadows of dew,
We gracefully think of those we knew.

For the ones who live and those whom gone,
We will share our memories from now on.

For the old who struggled with strife,
THE NEW ONES REIGN OUR LADDER OF LIFE:

Maxine Elaine Bridger

"Christmas Is A Busy Time; But Just How Busy Are You?"

Let us not be too busy, to share our joys with others,
or to remember the lonely, the sick and/or shut-ins or
someone's aged father or mother.

Let us not be too busy, to give our humble praise
for all the many bountiful blessings, for all our real perfect days!

Let us not be too busy, to help a little child...
To instill upon him or her the rights from the wrongs,
and help to make a positive attitude worthwhile.

Let us not be too buy, to use that human touch...
To reach out to help another, who may need it so very much!

Remember, just remember, as we are graced from day to day,
Can't we give the spirit of brotherhood,
patterned by the one who guides our way.

So at this busy christmas Season, take time to give a smile...
Spread the sunshine of happiness, to make all our lives worthwhile.

Merry, Merry Christmas and a Happy and Prosperous New Year!
Let us not be too busy... To share and to care,
with a stewardship of genuine love and cheer.

E. Vivian Williams

Concert

Win the tickets off the radio station,
Call a friend let them know the information.

You wait at home for a week,
Can't wait to get to the first row middle seat.

When it's finally time to depart,
Mom has to go to the kwick-e-mart.

Finally get to your seat after an hour,
People behind make you cower.

Then afterwards you go backstage with,
The best band there is AEROSMITH!

Richard Wooten

My Prayer

Dear God in your infinite wisdom,
  Be with me day to day.
Show me the path that I should trod
  And guide me on my way.

Your spirit within me makes the sun shine
  Even thought it be a cloudy day.
Your goodness and mercy lift me up
  And push the darkness away.

I look to the heavens and thank thee God
  For thy blessings from above.
For sustaining me here on earth
  And filling me with thy love.

Help me to find my place dear Lord,
  That I may help family, and all.
Give me strength to do my best for them
  That each of us may answer thy call.

Give me wisdom, oh Lord I pray
  To put good in all that I do.
To have complete faith by night and day
  Until my time on earth is through.

Shirley M. Knapp

"He Loves Me, He Loves Me Not"

When I see him,
My heart skips a beat.
And when he kisses me,
I'm swept right off my feet.
He loves me, he loves me not,
Is the game we use to play.
But now that simple game,
Has changed in every possible way.
The flower petals have turned to feelings,
Just thrown upon the ground.
And all my thoughts, and all my feelings,
Are being jumbled 'round.
When I'm not around him,
I miss him so much it hurts.
I have this craving for him,
It's like an undying thirst.
And when he looks into my eyes,
A chill runs down my spine.
I never, in my sweetest dreams,
Thought we'd have a love so divine.

Katherine E. Dallas

"My Only Act Of Violence Comes With A Pen And Paper"

I am a writer, an artist
It is my duty to tell about your conspiracies,
cover ups and white collar crimes.
You cannot hide from the pen and paper I hold
Yet I am considered an outcast, a menace to society,
by the wrong doer but....
"My only act of violence comes with a pen and paper"

My pen and paper are, instruments playing for all who care to hear
These instruments are food for the soul that hungers, a thought
for an empty mind, and a mending for a broken heart.
I ask you just to listen to my instruments play
They attempt to snatch my instruments away
Yet... "My only act of violence comes with a pen and paper"

Of all the things I do to make the world become better
I continue to have the odds against me
Still... "My only act of violence comes with a pen and paper"

Melissa Hudson

Don't Give Up

Lord, please help me make it through this night,
  And please give me the strength to fight.
Don't let me give up and say I'm through.
  Give me the wisdom to leave it up to you.
Cause what I'm going through with is in your plan,
  To strength someone else so they will be able to stand.
I'm not being punished for what I might have said or done,
  You are just preparing me for my journey home.
And when you get me exactly right,
  You will come and turn out the light.
And the pain I once went through will become a thing of the past.
  And I'll be able to go with you at last.
And the ones that helped me will be relieved,
  That they did all they could and won't be grieved.
Then I'll be able to lay down and take my rest,
  So please don't let me give up until I have done my best.

  Joseph Buckner

My Confusion

My mind is in one big block,
As I sit on this dock.
No where to go no where to be,
No one to run from in a desperate flee.

My confusion angers me,
Why does it have to be.
So much to know and learn,
It should all light up and burn.

I sit and watch the ships go by,
Wondering why people fight, cheat, and lie.
Like lightening.
My confusion is frightening.

  Ali Sharolli

Me To Me

And when my life has past, as I turn around to go,
I'll face the person I have been a thousand years ago,
Wiped clean of all deceit, no other place to hide,
I'll see the person I have been standing at my side,
And if I do not understand the things that I might see,
I'll turn and question who I was when I was shaping me.

There is but one to answer "how?"
With barren road before me now
There is but one who had the chance
To move in life or stare in trance.

For when last warmth has gone away
And the final movement stills the day,
You lie naked with your past;
When the closing moment comes at last,
There is but one person lying there
The one that mattered most and really cared.

  Judith Morgan

July 4th

This day amongst all others should be known why its sct aside,
It is a day for American's to show their national pride.
It is more than a day of fireworks and celebration,
It is a day for Americans to reminisce of our forefather's
  decisiveness and determination.
A day for Americans to set aside for remembrance,
Of this great nation's proclamation of independence.

It is dispiriting to think that any American does not know,
The great gift that our founding fathers sought to bestow,
On the future progeny that would inhabit the nation they would create.
Is this the future they envisioned? Is this the fate?
Are we a nation who can actually keep going forth,
If we do not know the significance of July fourth.

  Richard C. Fordham

Dipped In Silver - Wrapped In Silk

Dreamers dream dreams:
dreams of fulfillment, dreams of hope.
A dreamland is a lovely place
with streets of gold and fields of lace.
My dreamland is a place of refreshment
where the wind blows and whispers, the trees sway and willow
In the evening's brotherly breeze of love.

Dappled day, mercurial noctorious night
Cherubic appearances
Rich and poor all alike
Where freedom's friendliest followers find
Swirling pools of cirque to look at and not to touch
Dipped in silver wrapped in silks of saffron and mauve

Seek your dreams and you too will find
a glistening glimmer a sparkling surprise
the ways to success the route to freedom.
I perceive my dreams to be worthwhile
not a tantalizing wonder.

  Joy Dyer

The Lonely House

The old house stands silently waiting
Unaware that the owners will not return.
She was taken over a year ago
And for her he never ceased to yearn.

The walls of the house show the photographs
of happy family and joyous times.
Together as a couple for sixty years,
They endured many hard times.

The kitchen holds her prized possessions
Her cooking tools were her favorite things.
Her delight in life was to be busy
Preparing meals fit for a king.

His study appears as if he were interrupted
Amidst a busy task.
He has gone to be with her.
The house doesn't know he won't be back.

  Sandy Baker

Meg At Five

So now you are a five year old
You've been a blessing, I've been told
Your laughing heart and constant chatter
insanity reigns, that's whats the matter.

When you were small, wonder who you'd be
as Daddy bounced you on his knee
Now we know or maybe guess
a politician nothing less

No one talks as much as you
dinner time is just another coo
You lay the rules and enforce them hard
so your dictatorship is not marred

So now at five, I stop to write
at your expense I make light.
You are the bright spot in my days
as we run through life's long maze.

  Martin P. Bailey

Forever

Our souls have shared an eternity of sunsets together.
We've walked the paths of truth and freedom before.
Your words speak to my heart and mine to yours.
All thoughts now are reflections of memories past.
Bound to an earthly torture by flesh, we know of the same demons.
Greed and anger are the true disease of man.
Our time here is but a moment, a second in a thousand years.
There are but a few moments to remember, a smile, a word, a kind deed
Somehow they will seem familiar once again.
A compilation of past, present and future are fused.
Somewhere far, you are never more closer to my thoughts.
Whomever I meet I can find a quality paled by you.
Love and destiny are words of many meaning.
Love can be worn like a coat of desire;
But destiny to me can only mean that when we've gone from here
Somewhere, somehow, someplace the song that we alone know
will be sung again.

Gary J. Foster

Marriage Is And Is-Not

To my soul mate, My Emerald Mermaid Holly

Marriage is, a mutual union of endeavor,
    To be blessed 'n shared with a soul mate.
'Cause "God" created woman just for man,
    To be loved, cherished 'n to venerate.

Marriage is-not, words and ceremony,
    To be taken lightly or promiscuously.
But, with solemn genuine sincerity,
    Not frivolously or haphazardly.

Marriage is, an institution of love,
    For happiness 'n intimate togetherness.
Privileged according to "God's" plan,
    To fill the earth with sacredness.

Marriage is-not, a battle ground,
    For misfits or want-to-be lovers.
But, the best of best-friends,
    To make a lifetime of his 'n hers.

Marriage is, a lovingly covenant,
    Contracted forever with a huzza.
Established between a man 'n woman,
    Symbolized by a hebrew miz-pah.

Elmer A. Rasmusen

The Fire That Rages Within

Rejected by my sister, misunderstood by mother, ignored by father
and taunted by the neighborhood kids,
I was made aware that I was different from all the rest.
Second child of southern black parents and I liked to read.
For that sin I suffered and became aware of the hurt within.

My pleasure was in books, the back porch I always sat I escape to my
dream world the real world was too painful.
I didn't fit in with the crowd nor was I comfortable with my peers.
Rejected for my studious ways - called names by the uninterested,
Oh the pain of disappointment and the hurt that burned inside.

Slamming things around, answering abruptly and ignoring calls,
I was all too aware of the fire of the hurt raging inside.
The fire that burned through long sleepless nights and silent days.
What was the need to live or strive or fight - I was different.
Sad and frustrated, anger became the fire that raged inside.

I needed someone to recognize that it was not bad to be different.
Finding no sympathetic one - no silent partner, I wept.
Tired of criticism by the many, I looked inside for the answer.
The realization struck, the anger subsided, I realized, that only I
can put out the fire that raged inside.
I accepted me for who I am.

Mattie Smith Lucas

Cautiously Creeping

Cautiously creeping she runs with a rage
known only to the maddest of creatures
She drifts from my thoughts
Caressing me, consoling me
Drawing her claws like an ancient knight preparing for conflict
She illuminates an attraction that draws me closer
Igniting my curiosity
She show herself, she is a child lost from reality
As I watch her dance across the sands
She leads me to a waterfall
Reflecting a true meaning of what life is meant to be
Cautiously creeping I dive into the waterfall
Becoming one with my fears, hopes, and desires
She is my love, my inspiration
I will do anything to assure that all mankind knows and appreciates
Her existence
Cautiously creeping, I combat my desires,
stray from my curiosity
I am alone, I am a wanderer
I creep across the sky reaching for hope, seeking peace and conceive
That although she creeps away from my consciousness
Her scent will linger for eternity

Stephen B. Gerald

Steps Creaking

Steps creaking under little feet
Familiar white blood silently seats
The chipped warm knob reaching outward
Anxious tips stretch gently downward
and stop — to see such cold in heat.

Dead roses will not hear me creep
Such fruitful grain should not be reaped
Sharp blades and belts spin me coward
    Steps creaking.

The ring at the door damns my seat
Answering in tune without a peep
Ascending from the hallowed flowered
Tasting drops of rain now soured
Weak and thin with no snap, no shriek
    Steps Creaking.

Bridget Dowrick

Untitled

She sits there laughing away,
At all my silly jokes,
As she drinks her diet sprite,
And offers me some cokes.
I know that she is kind of old,
But to me she is still young,
She really is a kid at heart,
I mean...she likes to stick out her tongue!
She's been there for me forever,
We've talked about everything there is,
She's told me stories of long long ago,
And made me feel much older than a kid.
This woman is my grandmother,
I love her very much,
She's taught me about life and friends,
And blessed me with her sweet touch.

Kristen Anne Johnson

Letting Go

Hey, look! I let go!
Now what shall I do?
Dance with me feet, let's go, go, go!

Step here, step there with music only I know
Dancing and prancing to and fro.

CHOO CHOO! A train takes two . . .
here comes Mommy, her legs will do.
Across the room I follow behind,
Right foot, left foot, taking my time.

CHA CHA front, CHA CHA back.
Swing high and swing low,
Dancing like this makes my face glow.

Then I let go, wobbling away
Who will be my partner in the shimmy and sway?
Reaching out are big hands as I grab for his knee,
a waltz will be nice, just Daddy and ME!
Cheek to cheek, we're turning with ease.
Daddy is holding me close because I'm his big squeeze!

With a hug and a kiss I am on my own,
slow, slow . . . quick, quick
with each step I take I feel I have grown!

    Carol Sinoben-Jadali

Worn Strength

The pages are rippled
and the edges are torn.
Scripture verses are underlined
the cover is worn.
Tear stains fade the notes
several smudges here and there.
A few pages have fallen out
taped in place with loving care.
For our struggles and storms
inspiration fill its pages.
Hold on to its promises
a blessed message for all ages.
As we go through life's trials
stop and ponder this thought:

"The Bible that is gracefully falling apart,
is victoriously owned by someone who is not."

    Tina L. Fauble

Hooked

I'm hooked on a hug though I don't understand,
  How such a sweet, gentle touch turns all my high brick walls into
sand. How it touches my heart and then sets it free,
  Like the birds in the sky, the fish in the sea.

The hurt becomes less as old memories fade,
  And heart wrenching sorrow is sent far away.
Self-doubts become fewer as confidence grows,
  And making decisions gets easier as on time goes.

Guilt starts to fade when anger stops turning within,
  It can no longer haunt me, I won't let it win.
Fear ceases to threaten when one's courage grows strong,
  When one no longer lets himself be controlled all the day long.

Free from pain, doubt, guilt and fear,
  I'm free for as long as you hold me near.
I'm hooked on a hug but I don't understand,
  I'm hooked on a hug and oh! It feels grand!

    Elaine Ridley

The Swing

Like two kids, we head for the swings
Kicking our heals towards a clear blue sky
Just trying to go so high, trying to fly

Like two kids, we play in the park
We played until the sun went down and it was dark
Just trying to go so high, trying to fly

Like two kids, we play on the grass
Chasing each other around running skipping, going fast
Just trying to go so high, trying to fly

The child in me loves loving you
When all goes awry and my soul wants to cry
In my minds eye, I visit the swings

Free to do as we please
Acting like a couple of kites set free
In the winds above
Trying to find the one to take off with,
To soar through the sky
Just trying to fly

    Glen J. Rose

Enchantment

Upon walking in the forest today
I found the nymph and boar
Entwined in mirth and gaiety
Over delights and gifts galore.

From the heavens came some golden doves
Whirling the wind their wings
I was not sure who they came to see
The nymph, the boar or me.

There was a river encircling them
With the babblings of the wood
But the nymph and boar did not see
The doves, the brook, or me.

Enchantment is a slippery thing
Elusive as its glee
While the brook flows on forever
With its tales of everything

The brook has babbled our doings
And the doves have spun our tears
While the nymph and boar choose not to see
The dreams of things like me.

    Linda Curtis

My Love

My love that was here,
seems to have gone; this is
not my love, the one I love.

My love is drowning in a empty bottle.

My love that I grew to love;
my love that I can't see through
the liquid that fills my love,
fills my eyes.

My love I know was their is
temporarily no longer existing,
is my love that I do not love.

    Monica J. Carney

"Evanesce"

Sleeping buds all winter long awake in springtime, then they're gone
Sweet and fragrant, porcelain-pure, blossoms bloom one time each year
Petals gilded with golden sun drop to the ground but the tree lives on
Mixed with scents of death and birth, carrying life return to earth
Magnolia white, Magnolia gold, once you're young, then quickly old
Magnolia white, Magnolia gold, you are a wonder to behold
Through the grace of the magnolia tree, I give to you this legacy
To know my love will linger on as long as trees reach for the sun
To know that I will be with you as long as flowers gather dew,
And though my blossom fades away, with you my love will always stay
Magnolia white, Magnolia gold, once you're young, then quickly old
Magnolia white, Magnolia gold, time is the enigma we shed to unfold
So my children, remember me when you go by the Magnolia tree
Your springtime buds will quickly bloom, the gold dust gathered
     a bit too so
Then you will know within your heart, that of life's circle we're
     all a part
And in the spring this time next year, the love we share will still
     be here
Magnolia white, Magnolia gold, once you're young, then quickly old
Magnolia white, Magnolia gold, through your sweet life my story's told

Jamee Taylor Smith

Poem Of The Middle Ages

This is a story of long ago-happiness and joys that are now foretold.
This is now known as the Middle or Dark Ages.
We see the story as we turn the pages.

The tale of kings and queens, nobles, peasants,and serfs.
The days of old, The days of glory, The days of fury,
The days of knights-with their armor and chivalry,

Which brought them into long and bloodsome wars and fights.
The days of the Church and Pope,
when he was around the people did not mope.
For when they were around,
they gave people a sense of belonging and hope.

And now this story I have unfolded, a summary of glory come-glory past.
Although this all didn't last, that doesn't mean that this poem is undone.
There were many knights, lords, nobles, vassals and kings,

That did not mean that a king couldn't be a vassal.
Is that the warning bell that rings? Run, run, into the castle!
A war was ablaze, a great many people were in a daze,
who knew where to run or hide,

Unfortunately-these wars could last for hundreds of years,
I shall confide.
Now finally after the wars and plagues and famines,
The Middle Ages draws to a close,

I hope in the meantime you didn't doze,
Now there is a new style, new age, and new clothes-called the
Renaissance.

Lilian Moshinski

Wisdom

When I'm with my sweetheart, we exchange ideas and advice,
She asks me a question about a topic I know,
I give her advice, she smiles and thanks me for my patience,
Encouraging one another is so important from day to day.
We work as a team on projects.
Experience different things.
Yes, giving advice is so important.
It makes you feel good, especially when you follow
your own advice.

Malcolm Smith

The Survivor's Hymn

I
We shall get by.
We're still alive.
With love to guide,
We shall survive.

II
We're moving on,
Know right from wrong.
Through prayer and song,
We carry on.

Refrain
We know, the time is now.
To heal, our pain somehow.

III
We're not alone.
We'll make it known.
A loving home's
Where we belong.

IV
We shall recover.
New life discover.
What once was wrong,
Now makes us strong.

Refrain
We know, the time is now.
To heal, our pain somehow.

V
We shall get by.
We're still alive.
God's love will guide,
We shall survive.

Bruce A. Campbell

Finding My True Love

Why do you come to me, while I sleep?
Why do you come to me, while I think?
I had all I wanted, just me and Emily.
Now it's gone, I wish was my time.
For now I'm blue, from thoughts at not having you
If only you know.
If only you dreamed this too.
But this wish is nothing knew
It's only one of a show involving you
I've had them for quite awhile
I've walked with them for an unending mile,
For what starred as a small pile, is now a mountain
of deep feelings for only you, do you feel it too?
But still you come to me,
Even when I here nothing to see
You play with my old soft hour
That's loved you from the start
But then you go, where? I don't know.
And I feel a great loss that makes me fool
like I'm the one having alone from the great class.

Timothy Buchanan

Creation

Gazing out at God's creation,
Almost touching His eternal pulse —
G a p i n g, I.stood.
Through "bugged-out" eyes at once,
I projected the meaning of His Word —
"Behold, very good."
(Genesis:1:31)

Ronald G. Brown

Untitled

Grant me freedom and I will but hide in your cape
Loose the silken ties that bind and I will fly home
Give this captive heart the ample chance to roam
And I will taste no sweet success in the escape.
Rather, let me bide the time, watching the moon,
In his ceaseless chase of the sun. Her duty,
An endless rising. His will, led by her beauty,
Patient and content to follow, while I swoon.
Death will bring no Peace. My heart will beat
Your name and angels fair will sing
Your songs and echo the whispers of the strings
Of heaven's lute. And so, too, immortal rest will bring defeat.
For my Fate is etched for all Eternity
That I should spend my days in love with thee.

Melanie Evans

The Stallion

Among the swirls of fog and drisk,
Stood an imperious stallion of spirit and frisk.
   With his nostrils flared and his eyes ablaze,
He stared through the trees in an unearthly daze.
   He danced to the side, and then back he came,
Putting all commonplace horses to shame.
   He snorted, whinnied, and stomped at the ground,
Then stood mightily trembling not making a sound.
   He tossed up his head, testing his grace,
He then started off at a marvelous pace.
   His tail was up, his head was held high,
But stopped when he heard a lone coyote cry.
   Peace then broke through his untamed hide,
And he had a collected calmness inside.
   He disappeared over the mountainous chine,
That young, dark-eyed stallion, I wish he were mine.

Lori J. Critchfield

Words Of A Common Woman

I've always felt that written words were music to my ears
And whether fact or fiction, they stirred me thru the years.

To have the gift of written words was something I desired
But due to my fear of rejection, I have sat, solidly mired.

To set my thoughts to paper and to write what's in my heart
Has always been a problem of knowing where to start.

Some thoughts are very funny, others filled with tears
And some recall the memories of my childhood years.

Words can be used to harm, they can be used to heal
And sometimes what I write will hurt, because that's how I feel

I've never fought with my fists, I've always fought with words
And though I haven't always won, I have at least been heard.

What I right may entertain, may make you stop and pause
May bring a tear to your eye, may stir in you a cause

I do not mean to offend, nor cast dispersions on the lot
But the things that are the dearest, are the things we've hardest
fought.

Suzanne L. Hurley

Shades Of Green

Green is like a lovely sad dream.
Bright green is like a leaf, gently floating down.
Dark green reminds me of a doomy day.
Dark green also is like a day full of mystery.
Jungle green is like a soft and quiet place.
Green is like completing long, hard work.

Yossi Schulman

Diminished

Traumatic and terrible to learn
That those we crowned are not sublime,
Nor wonderful, nor even true.

Like waiting in an arctic room
To be in at the death of outgrown God's,
More bleak because in their demise
We recognize the grim portent
Of our descent to lesser realms
Where only pallid heroes reign.

Heather McPherson

The Beachcombers

We walk the beach, my dad and me,
Some driftwood in my hand.
It thumps and drags most rhythmically,
As I let it hit the sand.

The seagulls, stand a wary bunch,
As they wait by the edge of the sea.
They're waiting, waiting for their lunch,
As they let out squawks of glee.

The sea resounds with angry roars,
As it hits the land.
And I think of what was there
Before the sea took away the sand.

The foam at our feet,
We head for home.
I cannot wait until next week,
When again the beach we roam.

Kathleen Faith D'Angelo

Things That Glow

The sun glows on a sunny day,
as children's faces when it's time to play.
A mother's face glows when she sees her first born.
A ring which has a bright new stone.

The silver moon that shines up high,
reflects a lovers face when he looks into her eyes.
And the brightness of the lake by which they dance,
puts the two lovers in a trance.

Shiny eyes of the mother of the bride,
is a sure sign that there will be tears to dry.
And the stars which forever glow,
know things that you will never know.

Karla Su

My Love

When you entered the room I looked to the heavens
And saw the stars weeping
For the light that shone from your eyes
Paled their lackluster efforts.

And when I dared again violate the consummate
Perfection of your beauty with my gaze
The warmth of your smile melted the chains
That heretofore bound my imprisoned heart.

Freed, my heart took flight
And alighted upon a cloud suspended by your love.

From heavenly heights my heart regarded the infinite
And saw no wonder, marvel or miracle that equated your beauty.
The reaches of eternity appeared inconsequential,
Having glimpsed the depth of your soul.

David R. Samuel

Silly Toy

Fool, clown
Laugh turn upside down,
Dance and smile and sing.

Silly toy
Bright though foolish boy
Life is a painted butterfly wing.

Jester's mask
Silly questions you do ask
Clap your hands and catch the shiny ring.

Silly toy,
Bright though foolish boy
Fear not what life may bring.

Beneath your face
What disgrace
Into what pitfall will you fling?

Silly toy,
Bright though foolish boy
Prance and chatter on your master's string.

Rita G. Kroll

The Little Green Vase

In my mother's cupboard sits a little green vase
Etched with expressions on each child's face,
Etched with the sunshine of each passing day,
Filtering the joy and storing it away.

In my mother's cupboard sits a little green vase
Filled with the foliage of another time and place:
Filled with the flowers from a loved one's grasp,
Storing, still, the smiles of those special days past.

In my mother's cupboard sits a little green vase.
And, in my mother's sight should always be its place,
In my mother's sight to spark a thought or smile
As she recalls a memory from its treasured file.

In my mother's cupboard sits a little green vase,
For over fifty years, in all its style and grace.
If it were ever broken, it could never be replaced.
Yet, memories it holds will never be misplaced...

For in my mother's heart, is a little green vase.

Ruth Kain

Act Of Contrition

Wrapped to survive an ice age,
an old man makes angels in the snow
— spread open like an insect on display —
Arms, legs, and a
c a r e f u l   p e e l i n g
of his self from the indentations of the soul
left printed in the snow.
The man brushes the remaining traces of white from his back
    and moves forward.
Blinded by the reflecting light his one thousand Angels.

Anne Greenwood Brown

The Moment Passes

An elderly woman sits down with her family for dinner
The woman turns to ask her husband to pray
But someone else is sitting beside her
Someone else prays instead of her husband
The moment passes, and she begin to eat

The family begins to eat

Robert B. Wolcott

"I'm Only Away"

Please don't cry for my old broken body.
My sick diseased body, my weary soul.

I am not in this body.
I was ready, I'm away.

Remember me when I was young, happy, healthy and free,
when we laughed together.
When I hugged away your fears and say she's only away.

On Holidays when you see a pretty tree, say to yourself.
I live with my father. I'm only away.

When you see someone who was blind can now see.
Say there I am but I'm only away.

Remember the good times we all shared and know I still care.
Just say "she's only away."

Love each other and hold tight.
Remember I'm there with you day and night.
But "I'm only away."

Praise God who loved me so. I'm safe in his arms of love.
I don't fight for the breath I breathe,
I'm loved but, "I'm only away"

Prepare to meet me when your time comes,
and one day I will be there.
Then you can say, "she's come home, she's not away."

Gwen I. Conner

Back To See Daddy Again

Last night while I was sleeping, my mind went back in time
To a place that never changes, and boiled peanuts cost a dime.

The place is so dark and empty now, but I just had to see
If daddy was still in his old store; our Davis Pharmacy.

I pushed the old door open and I called my daddy's name
He answered from the back room and I hugged his neck again.

He said "you're still a sight for sore eyes and I hoped you'd come
again, 'cause I sure have missed you, honey, how long has it been?"

We talked all night of the good times—the fun we'd had in that old
store how we loved to watch the movies at the Pal Theater next door.

Through all those hot tobacco seasons we worked there side by side
My mother, sister and brother, we had laughed and we had cried.

Then we sang, "You Are My Sunshine," how daddy always loved that song
But it was time for me to go now, so I had to say, "so long."

Though I know daddy's been gone for all these years, to me he'll
always be, right back in Vidalia in that old store, just waiting
there for me.

So, I'll go back to Vidalia again and again; back to that old store again,
it's been such a long time but still in my mind

I go back to see daddy again.

Judy Davis Boyer

Special One

You've always been here
I've loved you always
You've been faceless and nameless
In my dreams you've danced with me
Walked with me, loved me
Your eyes have stared into my soul
I've longed so much to touch you
I know I would be hooked the moment I held you
You are a gift from heaven above
Just your presence is heaven on earth
Suddenly, you appear!!!
Just how I dreamed you'd be MY SPECIAL ONE

Shonda M. Brewer

Flame

Elegant warm and chilling
Dancing in the air
The effects are so thrilling
Killing and harming without a care
While gracefully destroying and putting in morn
A sacred soul is torn
Dancing until there's nothing in sight
It leaves the picture black and white

Nicole Drennan

A Friend Of Mine

Thought I've known you,
  only a very short time,

Consider yourself, a dear friend of mine.

We've shared each others sorrows,
  laughter and tears,

Emotional times to be remembered,
  down through the years.

You have a very special gift,
  that of touching lives,

Which many will never possess.

But, then not many have obtained,
  life's truest success.

The LOVE of GOD and commitment
  to do HIS WILL...

Dorothy Edwards

Untitled

Furies frustration the heart and mind blend
My sweet empty touch even that I not send
Strolling along numbered boxes crossed out
Dry now the river, produced not a pout
Deep in my chest cold the ice grow
Fairest of fairies positions don't know
Who art thou suffered bearing what cross?
Replete not my blood, more has been lost
Mine are the righteousness ways of the book
Still all I do is stand, cry, and look
Numb and futile the search has become
Is not my diligence worthy of some?
Take the forsaken the saints of that name
Somewhere, somehow, someone is the blame
The basic condition, the structure doth need
Building together the life of life seed
Locutions surplus now a dark spot
How is it possible this thing I have not?

John A. Lanzarone

Spring

Spring waketh the land
Zephyrus swayeth the petals in my hand

Spring beareth beauteous weather
Fieldeth the tulip, the crocus, and a myriad flower

Spring bringeth many a cool summer
And leaveth the heart truly much calmer

Spring showereth us with life and love
Giveth the flower its beauty, the lover his dove

Spring spreadeth sunshine everywhere
Stirreth my soul to music in the air

Goumya Neravetla

Window Of Regret

The cool morning wind tingles my face
As it flows through the window with angel's grace

It wavers at my bed, trembling with fear
And for multiple reasons, I shed a sad tear.
Emotion overcomes me as I'm struck with a thought
The reason I'm sad is depression I've caught

I feel old, gray, and withered, I've no longer to spare
I've been hollow and empty but finally, I care

I know that I've lost all control of my life,
but youth takes its place once again
As with a tear I picture myself
when I was so far from the end

If only I'd not been so cruel to all
instead kind to those back then,
I might not be so lonely right now,
but there's no time for making amends

If only I'd been a person who loved
I wouldn't be dependent on those up above

But now it's the reaper that I have met
Looking at me through my window of regret.

Erica Turcios

Vision

The rain fell feminine from the skies today.
And though leaf and branch blocked my look a little,
High in mid-airs above a glade brightly sunned,
Dark foliage further away for a backdrop,
I saw her from the shadows of tree shelters
Falling gently, lightly, blown by a babe's breath...
And not just falling gently, but so slowly
As if in secret descent for none to see.
How moving this maiden's mist of falling rain,
How sensuous this silken shawl from sunny
Shoulders falling was she that moisten'd meadow
So unaware of her hidden loveliness.
If women more worth to the eye secret seen
When they un'ware, slow un drape themselves to preen,
Does truth then ring clearest only glimpsed upon?
And the way: The nocturnal, horizontal
Thundercloud, unseen, unheard, not knowing it
There until looking directly at it the
Moment lightning illumes its immensity.

Jim Snyder

What I See?

When I look around me,
I see so much hostility.
I see crime on the streets,
And children that go days without something to eat.
I see black on black crime,
That people just don't pay any mind.
I see unemployment on the rise,
And I wonder why people despise.
I see people who don't help their fellow man,
And I just don't understand.
I see families that are being torn apart.
And some people just don't have the heart.
I see the world coming to an abrupt end,
And this is what I recommend.
Age, gender, color of your skin should not matter,
I think that ALL people should work together.
So let's join in and make this world a better place to live,
Remember: Don't destroy, let's build.

Belinda A. Myers

The Dark Water

The one to watch is the
face without features
the shifting perimeters
the dry ice
the numbed nerve ends.

Never to be kneeling in sewage
or lifted by the rich music of trees
leaves only the stark page.
Each night my brain heats up with electricity.
Still better these eyes opening everywhere
than no dreams.
I need the cage, the rusty nail
the open wound closing, the promise
the long wait.

The castle looks loveliest in the ashen twilight
when the town behind is burning with murderous fire;
and always beneath the drawbridge,
the dark water waiting.

Ron Cherry

The Sculptor

If we paint by numbers, or do it all alone,
If we mold in clay, or sculpt in stone,
Whether it's soft and supple, or brittle as bone,
What we have to work with, is all we own.

Happiness, sadness, love and hate,
Is what we use to create.
Our lives, our art, our imagination,
Will all affect our own creation.

The eyes of others, have criticized,
And priced our art, by weight and size.
They've tried to tell us of it's worth,
But all their words have only hurt.

Our art is our own, not bad or not good,
Made up of our will, and not of a should.
Made for ourselves, as time goes on,
Made for ourselves, "till time's all gone.

The art is my life, the sculptor is me.
The price I'm creating is priceless to me.
It's not just so perfect, as you will soon see.
But it's all I've got, my masterpiece is just me.

Rick Juel

The Driver

A driver on a long dust road
His mind filled with thoughts of his humble abode.
The road seems so different on this day
maybe he should have noticed, the bridge had fallen away.
Never did he stray from his thought of home
Never did he dream his wife and son, that night, would be alone.
He was headed for a journey much closer at hand
much further away if where bridge once stood there had been land.
A long journey from earth to heavenly paradise.
What was wrong with his home, he thought it was nice?
Why did he have to leave?
Leaving his son and wife to grieve.
Discontented to leave Earth for his heavenly place
as the car flew off the road he shot out the windshield and fell
on his face safely on the other side of the dark empty space.
God had saved that man that day.
But another day maybe not so soon
God again would call him away.

Maurice Potlongo

A Reckoning

You make me remember all the dreams I ever had
Of the perfect sphere of the moon
Broken into white knives by a shifting polished onyx sea
And of dust-belt cities whose people
Choke in a silence in memory
Of the voices they once had.
And now when I listen
I hear the flakes of snow crushing under
The weight of the flakes of snow
The winter bearing down upon centuries of advancing ice caps
Whose depth becomes earth's crust.
And I hear the iron wind
Hollowing amongst the locust and sycamore trees
Naked branches thrashing like spindly emaciated limbs
Tangled over a cape of new rocks on high shores.
In my mouth my tears taste stale
Oh the time spent waiting with questions
With ripe expressions of hope and penance.

Matthew N. Lancaster

"The Room Of Clowns"

The last rays of the winter sun
Gently touch a fallen toy,
Laying in the room of clowns,
Once loved by a small and gentle boy.

Bitter tears shed for broken family ties
Fall for days that might have been.
Sad faced clowns await his laughter,
Expecting it to fill the room again.

A house of sadness rules the day.
— A day of no return
To hopes and joys
And makes my heart within me burn.

Until forgiveness comes to heal,
I will feel this great despair,
Until that day comes to this room
The rays of winter sun will shine and die in there.

Marla J. Starry

Hugs

HUG, it's such a tiny little word,
but what a magnitude of feeling it can confer.

By definition, it means to embrace
and when you get one, it brings a smile to your face.

I know what I'm saying, because I'm a hugger
and I give them freely, for one reason or another.

There is nothing more touching than wen a person says to you,
do you think you could give me a hug or two?

You know right away, what your answer will be
and you give them that hug, maybe two or three.

And, afterward, doesn't it make you feel good,
knowing, in that embrace, you put all that you could.

In fact, when you're holding a person or friend,
you are giving a part of yourself, just to them.

This leaves you wide open, now, they know you care,
and your love and compassion, you are willing to share.

So, you see, what I've been trying to tell you about?
All the benefits of hugs, that make me want to shout.

Now, the next time you see someone, whose heart needs a tug,
Just put your arms around them and give them a HUG!

Ronda Kay Poppy

Go Fishin'

Humu humu nuku nuku apua'a. Humu humu nuku nuku apua'a.
Humu humu nuku nuku, humu humu nuku nuku...
Got your phone call. Here's the Eight Ball.

Humu humu nuku nuku apua'a. Humu humu nuku nuku apua'a.
Lost your day-o? Pass the mayo'.
Humu humu nuku nuku apua'a. Humu humu nuku nuku apua'a.

Humu humu nuku nuku
Humu humu nuku nuku
Take an aspirin. Eat a bufferin. No mo' sufferin'.

Humu humu nuku nuku apua'a.
Play the piano. Ahh!
Eat a banano. Yah!

Humu humu nuku nuku apua'a. Humu humu nuku nuku apua'a.
Humu humu nuku nuku
Humu humu nuku nuku

So! What's new, Daddy-O, under the sun?
Life is juicy!
So humdrum!

Doris A. Kaufman

"I Can See My God"

I can see my God in the leaves that fall,
I can see my God in the mountains tall.
I can see my God in the snow so cold,
I can hear his voice in the thunder bold.

Sometimes I can see him in the tall mountain pine.
I feel his nearness and a chill runs up my spine.
In the clouds by day and the star by night,
I can see my God's love and I can feel his might.
I hear him speak in a doves call
And I can see my God in a waterfall.
Because he created all of these and me,
In all of these things, my God I can see.

Ed Hicks

Rain

The rain beats upon my shoulders
My bones ache.
My ears still ring with shelling echoes;
I pick up the dead.

The rain washes the shattered bones clean
My soul screams.
My arms are limp from lifting the dead;
I move but don't feel.

The rain reveals a mass of olive-drab cloth
My heart breaks.
My eyes see the pieces of my buddy;
I cry but no tears come.

Thomas J. Evansew

Untitled

H elping poets who are undiscovered to express their ability
O ffering to them the kind of encouragement they can see
W isdom in matters of artistic talent is really evident
A lways making sure you get the writer's consent
R espected by your colleagues because you are a special man
D evising for them and yourself an interesting workable plan

E xceptional because you always endeavor to do the best you can
L istening with an attentive ear to what people have to say
Y ears from now you'll be remembered as the bright spot in their day

Hilda G. Woods

Mother

What a friend I have in Mother,
Oh, the beauty that I behold.
It's her inside - yes, God's transforming,
That makes her words - that's yet untold.

Oh, her hand that's rough from toiling.
Oh, her words both strict and warm.
Oh, her hug so strong yet gentle.
Such protection from Life's storm.

What a friend I have in Mother,
All my hurts she helps me bear.
What a comfort - she is courage,
And I know she's standing near.

Yes, she's a friend that is eternal.
She has love that will not go.
She is brave and so forgiving.
She's the sweetest that I know.

So it's okay to love her foremost.
It's okay to give praise to God.
For she's special - she's my Mother.
What a friend for me to love.

Mary Lou Jolly

A Song Of A Lie

As I look thru the window
    searching for the truth
I sink deeper and deeper within my lie.
    A lie that streams from my soul and
yet I face its song.

Close, Closer....I move to the music
    the notes of my song
A song of a lie which I dance
    In hopes of finding the truth.
This lie has become my world
    while honesty floats afar
I then look at my creation and the joy he brings
    Knowing this lie, my lie, my son, my BABY is the
NOTES of my song and the truth is buried in him.

Andrea Washington

The Song Of The Midnight Air

    I sang the song of the midnight air,
My voice crystal clear.
    It was the song only crickets and night creatures hear,
The song of the midnight air.

    My voice cried out,
A song that was forced deep from my soul,
    The song of the midnight air I sang,
The song that warms all that are cold.

    This song, oh mighty song,
Lifts the burdens off of my chest.
    This song of the midnight air,
Turns the worst of all to the best.

    My voice soared into the sky,
Warm, happy and free.
    This song of the midnight air
Can only be sung by me.

Joy Murphy

Remembering Brings Hope

When I'm weary in spirit I remember other times.
I remember times I felt so good; times of empowerment and confidence.
During these times I believed I could do anything I ever dreamed of.

I remember, I envision fragments of wonderful glorious moments in
life and I long to relive them over and over and over.

I remember experiencing seasons of such peace;
being filled with comfort and joy and yet feeling clean and empty.
Emptied of the worries and cares of this life.

I remember and I hear a sweet voice speak hope to my spirit.
My hope renewed, I remember, seasons change.

Faith L. Grieco

I Breathe In The Sky

I breathe in the sky, bleeding with life, tranquility
and the flow of a setting sun.
Crying out for time to seize the playful nightmare.
An angels falls, leaving her beauty on the land
gracing the trees with her wings.
Beneath a changing sky.
In the thunderous call, time haunts us all.
Black fades to green.
Drifting on empty seas, I breathe in this sky.
The sacred and the still.
The naked and the real.
Only a dream can pull me closer to reality.
I want to be as big as a mountain.
I want to fly as high as the sun.
If I were stronger
I could be a mountain range
If the night were longer
I could escape the day.
Feel with your soul.
You can see without eyes.

Charles Lloyd

Troubled Mind

I need each day to assess my life.
I need to plow through the cobwebs
Of my troubled mind
And find that hidden reason to survive.

Oh the price we pay for stubborn pride,
The loneliness we endure to avoid connection.
If only I could be free from the bondage on my fears,
Free to love and laugh and live.
Free to experience emotions repressed for a lifetime.

My soul is sad for days unlived.
My list of regrets is unending.
Dear God, I pray for the courage to change.
I pray for the eyes to see new beginnings...

Linda Gustafson

Spring Child

The child spring awakens from peaceful slumber.
She stretches, yawns, reaches for her coloring book.
Red, yellow, white, pink, green, oh so much green!
With crayon in clenched fist, she draws her thoughts...
Blossoms, blooms, beauteous and beautiful.
She imagines the smells and scents of her world,
The feel of its air. Just for good measure,
She blows through a whistle she finds nearby,
And a million birds answer in her mind.
She puts away her toys then she kneels, bows
Her head, whispering with eyes screwed shut
As the world awakens, the day made new.

Joel R. Blalock

Christmas Thoughts

Christmas morning never dawns,
Its evening never ends -
Without the thoughts of "good ole days"
And thoughts of good old friends.

It's the time of year, our hearts reach out,
To all those we hold so dear -
As we write to each - a CHRISTMAS CARD,
Which most of us do each year.

As each name comes up - in the address book,
It's nice to pause and think
Of the things we shared, in the years gone by,
Which made for a "special link".

Many of our ties have lasted years,
Adding happiness without end -
We for one feel favored indeed,
To have known you as a special friend!

For friends are special treasures,
Like gifts with ribbons tied -
Send each of them a little card
Sealed with your love inside.

Cora Lee Millenbach

Walls Of Time

My home is one of heartache, a place of steel and stone.
A barren cell, a home in Hell, and here I am alone.

For one brief crime I pay with time, where lights glare night and day.
And though I rage and pace my cage, I still must stay and pay.

Since every gate is one of hate, love has no place to hide.
For each lost fool who breaks a rule, the way to Hell is wide.

Shackled steel can never feel the things that I hold dear.
But chains of man are kinder than the men who keep me here.

It somehow seems that all my dreams must wait for each tomorrow.
My days and years are made of tears - misery and sorrow.

As convict knives take human lives, this jungle breeds more danger.
The years I stay both night and day, each man remains a stranger.

I breathe the sting - a bitter ring - of keys in metal locks,
And scrapes of feet upon concrete as guards patrol the blocks.

With these walls that never fall the damned all come to know
A row of cells - a special hell - called Solitary Row.

One cannot tell to those in hell the dreams I send above,
Nor how the shrill of whistles kills each passing thought of love.

To those who steal the things I feel and sow my heart with sorrow,
Each black farewell is bid in hell and lost inside tomorrow...

Dennis Ruiz

Native Americans Proudly They Stand

Native Americans proud of their home,
Free as the eagle,
The country did roam.
Hunting and fishing and gathering their food,
From the land so abundant to the sky so blue.

Until that day when the intruders came,
And took away their identity and brought them to shame,
To live now in places where they were told,
To live like the White Man to whom their lives had been sold.

The Native Americans so misunderstood,
Struggle each day to regain what was good,
To be a Native American,
To live proud again,
And regain a heritage free from pain.

Helene Meyerowitz

Real Blessing

The kids are small and the cupboard was almost bare,
Strangely enough everyone is happy and without a care;

A new ironing board for my birthday warmed my heart,
So many chores but all six did their part;

Why wasn't I told that they would grow up with no plans to stay,
Our endless days and nights together would quickly slip away;

The little ones are gone with babies of their own,
It happened suddenly as if I had not know;

Now I am over fifty and trying to write a verse,
To explain my role as wife, mother, friend and nurse;

These are my golden years so I have been told,
What happened to that young girl who was so bold;

New joys have replaced the old; grandchildren and some
days sleeping late,
If I had only had some warning that this was my fate;

I could have done more to make the carefree times last,
Perhaps turned back the clock and held onto the past;

With age comes the accepting of time without the fears,
The real blessing is not knowing the swiftness of the passing years.

Jean C. Moore

"Quarter Past Forever"

Words that you hoped to hide bring thoughts of old love letters.
Sometimes your feelings rhyme, some time for feeling better.
No matter what you find, your song will come together.
A gift of love takes time, a little more forever.

Hopes that you've kept alive rain tears confused for nectar.
Sometimes your first sunshine may feign the worst of weather.
Storm-clouds once wept inside, heart flowers do remember.
For now they grow beside the place long since surrendered.

Come forth by way of wine
and drown me in your splendor.
Control me.
You guide my fading light
where only dreams once entered.
You own me.

Her love became my life. The heart becomes the center.
Across the moon-lit night a wish I long to send her.
No promise etched in time, no perfect cruel love letter.

Just what was on my mind at quarter past forever.

Andreano

High Mountain Tonic

Over the eons mountains rising from the land
Hot red cools and sculptures to brown
A smattering or even a forest of trees fill the spaces
Moisture taking the forms of mist and fog
Traversing the mountains leaving something behind
Another era and the forest learned to think

The mountains have their own way of things
Its laws are different than from where you come
That's one thing that makes the mountains better
They're so quiet and yet important
The many phenomena awaiting within
Won't know until you actually go there

What the sky conceals in its upper levels
Clear truth and high precision dreams
Once you vacation here you'll never be the same
There's nothing like the mountain wind
Blowing like freedom through your hair
Soothing the spirit to its natural harmonious state

Jeffrey Sturm

Awaiting Love

In the chasm of loneliness and yet surrounded;
Praying that hope will, lift you from a life kept grounded;
Looking for the world's answers, but dying yourself, inside;
Ultimately knowing there is nowhere to run and hide...

Tired of hearing about one more death never to be avenged;
Wishing the insanity would disappear, hate not revenged;
Appalled at the murder of truth and the resurrection of lies
Wanting the change promised from beyond darkened skies...

In the moments of escape, wishing for reality;
Hearing of a love seemingly untrue, that can never be;
Likening the story of a Savior to a tale that sounds great;
Yet not sure if the story told now is a story told too late...

In the speed of a world moving too fast to care;
Looking for a solution when peace is very much rare;
Know the miracle you seek is not hidden at all;
There is an ear, just waiting to heed your call...

Jesus, the Savior that awaits...
Myama Boone

"BAT-istics"

What a marvel in all nature is the little nighttime bat,
A wondrous prodigy to this world and topflight aristocrat.

He's the only living mammal equipped to fly, you see.
Sans prop, jet or gimmick he soars by night so free.

Darting, dodging, dipping darling high above the ground.
Bat 'radar' predates man's eons 'fore it was "found."

Lest we forget, bats pioneered suspended animation.
After every "mission," upside down, they claim rejuvenation.

By the precedence of God the little bat is a lofty dignitary.
So, who are we to contest his right of primal priority?

Wayman W. (Whit) Whitley

Communion

Lifting eager eyes upward;
Scanning heaven's shining vault.
From what ancient mystery is derived this cosmic yearning?
What chemistry of the soul, what alchemy of the spirit
Prods our need for confirmation?

The answer....is it folded in rimpled vestments of clouds?
Or there in blinding afternoon sun across Lake Paolo,
Projecting diamond dancers, twirling and blinking on opaque glass,
Whilst plaid-coated pin-tails
Bob about like beaked corks?

Perhaps, there! Standing on russet bricks,
Overwhelmed by raucous, combustive bird songs:
Restive celebration of Spring's eternal promise.
And watching cardinals dive bombing-these small, red torpedoes
Assaulting tartan-clad holly trees-appetites sated with sweet berry wine.

Above this feathered bacchanal, cassocked crows,
Dark acolytes to priestly pines, send arcane messages
In occult communication; and westward, a spotted kite of shallows,
Wheels and darts down the fiery sky. It too searching for nourishment.
Part of the puzzle and the epiphany of Nature.

Richard D. Chapman

Hate

Hate is reality. Hate is love.
Hate is everything below and above.
Where does it live, where does it hide.
It hides in shadows, it hides in love.
I feeds off your heart, it feeds off love.
It multiplies and fills you with
hate until you kill and become hate itself.

Fred Russi

A Change For The Better

A great chaos filled the world,
problems of economic, political, social
woman wants change for the better, hermaphrodite winthrop.

Fifty trillion dollar deficit troubles nation,
solution: cut foreign aid, welfare, social security
   Nations annihilated and people starved.

Winthrop sees no liberty in communist regimes,
make it a democracy, free and pure like an eagle
   Dred Scott and Watergate.

Problems in racial name calling—redskins, niggers gooks,
improper: address as Native Americans, African Americans, Asian
Americans change in name and none in bias.

Women can't get good jobs in high places,
have Hilary president, Bill first gentlemen, women bosses in major
   Corporations men in low places and low wages.

Old timer walks up to hermaphrodite winthrop,
says "you've changed nothing"
shrug. Continue on revolutionary work...

A change for the better.

Brian Gum

"Glassy Glen"

Men bow their head as women shed their tears.
Children play as innocently as they can in the glassy glen.
Priest's read the word of God with their dignified fears.
As men carry his shell their only thoughts is, "When?"
When will the sadness of the passing depart into the night?
They walk through the glassy glen with his shell.
Concealing, hiding, not letting anyone see their terror, or fright.
The winds pick up the nauseating sweet smell.
The glassy glen cries not for the dead, but for the dying!
Thoughts of our death are more frightening than hell.
Don't let the children catch you crying...
The dead in the glassy glen...
They cry for the dying men.

Ezequiel J. Ramos

Middle Age

There are many stories written, and many stories told.
About the generation gap between the young and old.
Well I can still remember if you were thirty-five,
I thought your life was over, you were barely just alive.

Now that was several years ago, this I must admit,
Now thirty-five has passed me by, I've seen the last of it!
I remember too when I believed, that old I'd never be.
But then older people told me, "just you wait you'll see!!"
Well, I found but, they were right, the years have come and passed.
And I've aged just as others did, now the die is cast.
Still I'll always know, forget all else, that middle age for me.
Is just ten years more than what I am, whatever that may be!!!

Hazel R. Emmons

Constant

There is always one thing in my life that is constant.
When no one else would love me, there was constant.
When I was sick, there was constant.
When I felt my world was falling down all around me,
   there was constant.
When I needed someone to talk to, there was constant.
When I needed a boost of confidence, thee was constant.
Constant never lets me down.
Constant is unconditional.
Constant is MOM.

Miriam Appleton

The Living Dead

Her eyes were wide and empty,
   I could see in them too far.
   She did not have to talk.

Watching fast the street all day
   she did not see her mother's car
   nor hear her father's walk.

Though she has lived so short a time,
   her nose pressed hard against the pane,
   it seems she's watched for years.

She watches daylight fade to dark.
   One welcome sound would banish strain,
   one glimpse would dry her tears.

With courage feigned, she stared at me.
   Her face spoke fear and dread.
   My gaze moved away from her; my heart beat to survive.

No meaning could my answer have.
   "I wonder if they're gone," she said.
Though death can have a better claim - I whispered,

   They're alive."

Robert L. Taylor

Loss Of A Loved One

She didn't want to cry, but the tears
came anyway, she was in pain,
after all, she did lose a loved one.
The house felt cold, dark and empty,
the clothes she wore were dull and
colorless, but she didn't care after all,
she did just lose a loved one.
She spent the day preparing, phoning
and explaining the dismal situation
trying to hold herself together.
It hurt her, and she was tough but it hurt.
My Dad was there doing his job
of comforting, holding and ensuring
to my mother that things would be
alright, but the pain still came.
She tried hard to put on a front, but
I could see right through her,
she needed my Dad, and she needed me,
after all, she did just lose a loved one.
Her face looked as if it aged 30 years
in one day, but she didn't care, after
all, she did just lose a loved one.
Who was she going to get all dressed
up now, and share girl stuff with,
that little girl was gone now, and
with her, a piece of my mother!

Scott H. Johns Jr.

A River Sunset

As the sun sinks slowly behind the Brazos
Bursts of colors explode through the skies,
Constantly changing from minute to minute
A breathtaking sunset fills my eyes.

As colors drip from the Artist's paintbrush
Boldly streaking His canvas of blue,
Orange and purple mixed with yellow and red
Creating colors I never knew.

Mesmerized by this grandeur and beauty,
Nature's activities begin to cease,
Standing in awe and admiration
As the Artist finishes His masterpiece.

Oh how I long to thank this Artist
For each sunset He paints for me,
For ending a less than perfect day
With such peace and tranquility.

Jana Wiley English

Matrimony Math 101

BASIC
 One plus One equals two — me, you added ANEW
 One plus One becomes 3, 4, or more
 Two divided by Two equals One
 And carry the remainders

INTERMEDIATE
 The sum of triangles indie the perimeter
 of a rectangle divided by the radius of a square equals
 Living nowhere, minus true love and care
 Square root of children times two
 Sometimes with me, sometimes with you erase, redo
 Help our paper's ripping in two

APPLICATION
 Apply all learned logic to the parallel lines of life
 Minus, guilt, bitterness and strife
 Negative/positive experiences cancel each other out
 xy = give it another try
 End of Math course, your grade: A Divorce?

SOLUTION
 NO
 Do it over, remember rules, use all the tools X + Y equals XY
 Answer: XY =s Unconditional Love
 Great! You've solved the problem.
 Now continue working on the rest of them.

Dolores Degenhardt

Thoughts

In fire, hell upon this damned dream world
My love, how art thy thoughts thought — sister Cain
How art thy notions; such demonic pain
Sweeter art thou — sweeter art thou not so
In love, winds shall change hell's home — heavens known
In pain I live — why must thou kill — please go
Pathetic soul dream's cruel — love shall be shown
In love, art thou not joyous — find thy soul
In nonchalance thou lie — angel or ghoul
In thoughts thou love, in dreams we wed — my love
In Gothic sonnet I write — lost am I
In mirror's reflection haunts thy love — I cry
Bring peace o'heavenly bird — God's sweet dove
The beauty sets in — hells demise — love's world

Jack A. Dickson II

Untitled

Luminary orb, bright overhead uncover the murky shade from my bed.
I wake as the spun grasps my eyes blues, greens, and reds tantalize
The frost, the frost it glazes across the glade in my dreams I have
    once forgot.
The dew, the dew it seems to gleam as the sun shines though the top
    of the trees.
The wetness, the wetness it finally progresses through the top of my
    shoes in the place I snooze.
Lots and lots of grass blades caught as I freely walk and walk a lot.
Frying, frying the sun it's drying the grass which is almost dying.
That cage, there is a cage full of rage, so I stop for a minute to see
    what is in it.
What is in that cage? Why is he there? It looks like an ape in
    despair
When will he open his eyes? When will he wake? When the final signs
    of light break.
The shine, the shine is left behind, as an ape is prying its cage for
    it's trying you see.
The night, the night comes out of light hardly an irregularity as it
    comes into sight.
Nocturnal are finally escapes with the sun of sight it will make it
    alright.
Who will care? Who will see? I think to myself as it runs home to
    its family.
Across the lawn and through the dawn. I look at the animal and see
    it will not be gone from society long.

Mike Howerton

Welcome Home

Welcome to your inner sense,
Introductions long past due.
Where mind and spirit become one,
The journey fresh and new.

One hour of bliss, will tell you this,
How little we know of self.
For inward lies the truth my friend,
The truth of everlasting wealth.

Not fortune nor fame is found within,
But love from deep inside.
It's up to you to find the truth,
And surface those fears that hide.

Like you I'm scared, 'cause when I shared,
Rejection thrust deep in my heart.
It's hard to heal with fear inside,
And courage is just the start.

Have courage my friend, for in the end,
Your love will shine so bright.
One hour a day, you will find your way,
Back home in your own true light.

Kevin L. Householder

The Dance Of Sex

When I was fifteen it was like the swing, cool and crazy and a no-no.
When I was twenty it was baby making time, responsibility and all
    of that jazz.
When I was thirty, well no more kids, we ran that sex thing rag time
    ragged.
When I was forty it was my way now, when and where I wanted it.

Now I'm fifty and performances are over my man,
life's taken on a whole new meaning:
The dance of sex is now the waltz, but by and by when the moment's
    right,
I just might step a swing, a jazz or rag time — if the fancy strikes.

Yvonne M. Rice Sr.

Ray of Hope

The darkness that envelops me seems not to have an end
A single candle by my side its light my only friend
Time creeps along so slowly until you walk in the room
Your smile surrounds the darkness and eliminates the gloom
Our lives are now entangled my love is now complete
We shall never again know suffering or contemplate defeat
How can one have such effect upon another's fate
It almost seems impossible yet never shows the weight
Of the burden so impressive and the passion so intense
When our worlds come together we cannot help but sense
That the whole is somehow greater than the sum of our two parts
The equation comes together in the beating of our hearts
These moments are so precious when it's only just us two
I stop to take a look around and all I see is you
In a world that is so perfect so tranquil and ideal
I'm left in awe and wonder I cannot help but feel
That while we are together my heart shall never break
Yet this feeling that should always last
Ends when I awake.

Stuart Sands

Love Must Prevail

If we could arise in the morning,
With love in our hearts for mankind,
We would greet everyone as our brother,
In our hearts we would be color-blind.

Our friendships would not be limited,
To one race, color, or creed,
We would vow to stand by each friendship,
Through prosperity, illness, or need.

We are placed in this world for each other,
Let's pray that we'll all do our part,
And always be there for our brother,
With love and respect in our heart.

All this must begin with our children,
We must teach them good traits from the start,
To reach out in love to our neighbors,
And always with love in our hearts.

In order to teach love to children,
Our example should show them what's right,
By saying, "I love you" each morning - and not
"Where are my children tonight?"

Isleta Pelham Galloway

"Merry Go Round"

So Freely he Gallops up and down,
With his plastic face cutting
the wind and storms
That leave his glass eyes unteared.

So Large he appears to the little children
who ride upon his hollow back.
They clutch the reins,
as if they needed to.

So Beautifully the music Swells
inside my head.
Its ferocity Drowns out
the words I
Speak to You.

But I am not Fooled.
I am that horse.
My thoughts spin round and round,
until All is Blurred.

To you, I am a Plastic horse.
Just one part of the
carousel.

Lisa K. Mikula

Untitled

He stared into the wilderness
Lonely, forlorn and full of despair.
Gazing at the sky so blue
All he had was empty air.

The dark corners of the heart
Are haunting and perilous from the start.
Like the wail of a freight train
Which only increases heartfelt pain

Turning suddenly, he saw to his dismay
A beaver kissing a doe so dear
The sweet sight show him the way
He was no longer alone and had nothing to fear

Jane Olmstead

Careers

As a Professor, I'll stand up and tell all
As a Scientist, I'll explain the incredibly small.

As a Bee-keeper, I'll provide lots of honey
As a Broker, I'll wisely invest your money.

As a Policeman, I'll protect while you sleep
As a Counselor, I'll comfort when you weep.

As a Surgeon, I'll cut with a sturdy hand
As a General, I'll protect our greatland.

As a Guide, I'll navigate the river
As a Mother, I'll put out the painful sliver.

As a Waitress, I'll expect a good tip
As a Captain, I'll go down with my ship.

As a Carpenter, I'll pound a nail
As a Postman, I'll deliver your mail.

As a Florist, I'll brighten your day
As an Interpreter, I'll explain what they say.

As a Fireman, I'll save a life
As a Husband, I'll always love my wife.

So in the end, as if to start
Always remember, as a poet, I'll strive to change your heart!

Glen Alan Frost

Christ Child

If I had been there that Christmas Day
　　And gazed at the babe upon the hay,
If I had seen the wise men there
　　That brought gifts to the baby fair,
I know that I would have loved him too
　　Because he was sent for me and you.

If I had been on the hill that night,
　　Oh, wouldn't that have been a beautiful sight.
The angels sang carols to Jesus the babe,
　　While frightened shepherds soon did obey.
They found that the baby did not have a bed,
　　But was fast asleep where the animals fed.

Judith W. Ryan

Life

Wherever life leads we all must follow
even if it's somewhere we don't want to go.
Through its darkest paths and endless hollows
yet being not sure where they might go,
searching for what we can call are own
hoping someday that life will lead us home.

Steve J. McKeag

"Memory Lapses"

He forgot in the heat of our ravishing kisses
His careful; sure touch brought mutual blisses.
The force of life fever, how does it abate?
What banks such a burning? Just comfort or fate?
He slipped into comfort; a pleasant old shoe.
As wantonness left us without an adieu.
He forgot it's a passionate sensualist
Who's ironing his shirts and making store lists.
Thus the needy and greedy nymph that was me
Diminishably suffered; then just ceased to be.
Appropriate comments and timely attention
Quietly; simply; with never contention
Drove out the bright madness and magic of lusting.
Valium sameness. Energy rusting.
Departure to freedom and singleness give
Me the search for the heat it takes me to live.
Will he ever remember that which he forgot?
I'd like to feel hopeful, but I strongly think not.

Betty J. Merryman

Anticipation!

Anticipation of an usual, yet unusual event.
A huge ball glowing with warmth and light,
Hiding behind a bubbly mass of storm filled clouds.
Just a few more minutes and the victor will present itself.
The sky is becoming more colorful in the East,
While all around the edges of our valley
Mountains wear a heavy veil of rain or snow filled clouds;
Clouds that have to release some of their furry to light.
As gold edges trim the grey and white cotton fluff
Eyelids do not filter out the brilliance that holds more glow
    than gold.
I look away, knowing that the king of lights will be robed in
    beams of glory.
The sun!
Anticipation satisfied!

June Caplinger Richer

Nothing Too Small

Ponder the tiniest grains of sand,
Insignificant at best.
But savor the beauty of beaches formed
When each grain bonds with the rest.

Think of the brick's red rough-hewn form,
A mere baked chunk of clay.
But bonded with others in layers of walls
Will be strong cathedrals some day.

Look at the boulders scattered around,
Stumbling blocks where they lie.
But gathered together in organized piles
Make majestic mounts in the sky.

Consider a man in simplest state,
Just flesh and bone and blood.
But united with all men in faith and love
Are the very essence of God.

Dan F. Griffith

Solus

Left alone the sea will shape the stone,
Solus will shape the heart the same

John G. Henning

Distance And Time

Time can steal some moments from our lives,
And distance can try to keep us apart,
But there's nothing in this world that's known to man,
That could ever keep you away from my heart...

There's a hunger in my heart that's insatiable,
There's a fire burning brightly from within,
My feelings for you are so powerful
It's difficult to believe we've just began....

Well the heavens and the earth become as one,
Distance and time just fade away,
The birds begin to sing, the flowers start to bloom,
My love for you begins a brand new day...

So never question love based on latitude,
And never give up love 'cause of time,
For love has never known any boundaries,
And true love is so difficult to find...

S. Arthur Hampson

To Grandma

It's hard to hide the pain when a life you love runs out.
but the after life is promising and that's what death's all about.
My grandma always brought smiles to anyone she was near,
so we have to keep on smiling and not show our sorrow or fear.
The good times will be remembered they're too strong to ever fade,
from family gatherings to birthdays and all the memories we made.
She was always there with something new or even things you didn't need
She was always thinking of others first,
this in life was her pleasure indeed.
It's hard to understand the concept of life and death.
One minute she's with us, the next is her last breath
To ask yourself "Why" just makes things worse,
there was nothing anyone could do not a doctor or nurse.
I wish she were here to hear this
or see how much we all care,
but I know now it's forever and that I cannot bare.
I wrote this poem, as a symbol of my love,
So I hope she's listening from heaven above.
So one final thought, it's nothing new.
I want you to know, Grandma, I will always love you!!!

Kristy Ann Masseth

Untitled

Winter looms large around us
White and cold
Wind blows and winter shows it's the king
Snowing, blowing and bold
Snow and ice than slush and mush
Plans are changed and people are cold
Trees are bare and children take care to warm
Other things are put on hold
Streets glistens like glass
Right now this is the norm
Ice sickles sparkle like diamonds a far
Temperatures drop with a sudden foul weather storm
Weather not fit for man or beast
Skies and people feel forlorn
Dark butting clouds fill up the sky
But near the end we'll all be warned
of changes that are swift and sure
A time to die and then be born
So long to winter let's anew
Flowers bloom and then be warm.

Brian Donnelly Wolff

American Work Ethic

Many years ago—in another day
people worked long and hard for their pay.
They were amazingly productive, loyal and effective
for ensuring health, comfort and wealth was their objective.
Thankful to be employed and proud of their product
a can-do attitude was their standard of conduct.
A positive work ethic and high self-esteem
led to achieving the American dream.
Succeed we did and our country's stature rose
World class leaders — EVERYBODY KNOWS!!!

That was then — this is now
things have changed, but I don't know how.
Some changes were wrought by Theories X, Y and Z
others are evolving from the latest called TOTAL QUALITY.
Team building and stroking to encourage willing workers
may be resulting in protecting the shirkers.
YOU OWE ME — is more and more often the cry of the day.
Let me do what I want — but give me my pay.
If this attitude prevails and our economy slows
Will our world leadership continue — WHO KNOWS???

    Ted Schardt

A Rose

On the altar someone has placed a rose
Symbol that a new life today did begin
Lovely as can be, from this earth she arose
And she's crimson as the blood that runs in a vein.

It will take rhymes, not just any prose
To tell the world that our baby is born
But more than that it will take a rose
On our family tree this flower to adorn.

Tiny one is our book you're a beautiful rose
And you will take us all on the primrose path
But every so often we must stop and pose
To thank the Lord, before we reach the strath.

Every one's attention you will get very close
And already your agenda is well established
God has made plans as He long ago disclose
So we all have a chance to love and to cherish.

And now dear baby, our most promising rose
Knowing who you are but not what you will be
Grow forth and show the world the true purpose
Of your birth who's the symbol, a rose, it had to be.

    Yvette A. DiGangi

A Long Dry Spell

The bucket scrapes bottom mud and stone.
I am left with my scattered thoughts alone.
My mind a dried up well
after a long dry spell.
No water, no thoughts, no anything;
a shallow mountains spring.
It is not the illness as I grow old,
nor are my thoughts less bold,
nor are there less beautiful words or sounds,
nor are my thoughts less profound.
Too many trips leave a well run dry;
too many words and my mind questions "Why?"

    Walter A. Bryant

My Hearts Cry

My hearts cry is, that in the daily grind,
I'll stand on the Word and renew my mind.

My hearts cry is, when life gets demanding,
That I lean not on my own understanding.

My hearts cry is, when the going gets tough,
That I'll trust in Jesus and never give up.

My hearts cry is, when everything seems wrong,
I'll make a joyful noise to the Lord in song.

My hearts cry is, that in any situation,
I'll turn to the God of all creation.

My hearts cry is, that no matter the cost,
I'll humble myself and come to the cross.

My hearts cry is, also that you
Trust in Jesus and have victory too!

My hearts cry is, also that you
Trust in Jesus and have victory too!

My hearts cry is, above all, I pray,
I'm found faithful to do His will every day.

    Mary Alice Miller

When Did I Get Old?

Just when did I get old?
It seems like only yesterday
That I could run and play.
So, just when did I get old?

So many times we've lost one dear
As nature makes its choices.
We hold all close, those far and near
And long to hear their voices.

There's still one thing I'd like to know.
(Forgive me, Lord, I know I'm bold).
Please tell me now before I go -
Just when did I get old?

A postscript here I'd like to add:
There's joy in my life, full blown.
My heart is oh, so glad.
It's the best of times I've ever known.

My countenance portrays a lie.
So you see, I'm not REALLY old,
And my spirit's on a high.
Inside, I'm still as good as GOLD!!

    Evelyn Heise

Life

The sun and the moon all with a glow
Shining down on us from above
Is this life fast, or is it slow?
So many question we want to know

How did this world ever get started?
How did we come to feel nothing mattered?
What have our lives come to today?
Is life so bad we don't want to stay?

Let me tell you what I think about life
Its great its grand why can't you understand.
Its not what you have done, its what you can do.
Its giving yourself a medal for a job well done.

So let me tell you loud and clear
That there are people here that care
Give us a chance to show you too
That we can be a friend so true

    Judy Wensil

Standing On The Moon

Come with me and stand on the moon,
This sacred night; this night of June,

Gaze on Earth so crystal clear,
Let your heart stand still for He is near,

Enlightened one is standing on the moon,
Looking for us; to dance to His tune,

Let us speak of love and grace
    as we stand on the moon,
He speaks of you and you, so
    come very soon,

Come with me and stand on the moon,
Let your eyes and heart begin to commune,

How can I not speak thereof,
Of wonderful force, a force called love.

Dear one's, come with me,
    and stand on the moon.

Gary L. Durham

Friendship Garden

There is a garden in our lives
From which we pick our friends.
It's filled with colors bright and bold,
It's filled with whispered blends.

Some flowers in the garden spot
Are tall and catch our eye.
Some are hidden beneath the bold,
Sometimes we pass them by.

We sometimes pick a fresh bouquet
Of stems so strong and bright.
But soon we find them frail and weak,
And withering in our sight.

But if we look and search the mass
Of wonderment that's there,
Our needs will often come across
That flower that's so rare.

There, among the array of blooms,
One special rose will be,
Enclosed in crystal glass and locked
With friendship as its key.

Marty Yourman

Life

Is it that important?
Who will miss her when she's gone?
It's just the life of someone,
Who thinks she doesn't belong.
Her life to her is just misery,
All pain and nothing close to glory.
She is full of hurt inside
And having no place to hide,
She asks herself,
Is it that important?
No one cares and no one will remember her.
Her life is just another story that will live on forever.
She is afraid of the years to come,
So she takes her life but lives on in God's kingdom.

Rebecca Bromsted

Missing Peace

Life is nothing,
Without something.
What is that something,
That can make life nothing?
We have gangs, guns, war and fear.
What is that something that we hold dear?
Without that something the world may cease.
That something missing, is a thing called peace.

Stephanie Thomas

Final Journey

The light draws me near, calling me, wanting me.
My heart swells in the envelope of faith and love
that surrounds me. My body, left behind, is a mere
shell deteriorating and alone. For a moment I desire
to go back, but my future beckons me. As I race
toward the light parts of me succumb to the vacuum
of space. Love, hate, jealousy, greed and anger drift
toward the light and burn to ashes. They mean
nothing now. New emotions fill their place. Joy, but
not the joy I know. It's different, stronger, purer.
Love, no longer spelled lust, burns within me. The
light is closer now. I know things will never be the
same. I see new faces, old faces, one face, my face.
Colors, once invisible are now brilliant. Music
resonates within their hues. No longer bounded by
restrictions of space and time, I embrace the
freedom licensed to me. That old place is now just a
memory, fading. Yet that light, that glorious light
that drew me here will never fade.

Kathryn J. Long

Tragedy, And Love

  A happily married, pretty twenty year old girl,
With a loving husband, a baby boy, life starting to unfurl,
Not only pretty, but full of love, and endowed with strength,
Not aware that life would test her to the very utmost length.
With a far reaching epidemic, her young husband died,
I'm sure in her agony, she asked "why"? as she cried.
She was also very ill, and the little son ill too,
With her undaunted strength, and God's, they pulled through.
Then she was made aware, with utter shock one day,
She was carrying another baby, it was on the way.
How do you accept, one love lost, now another to gain?
Hard to untangle at the same time feelings of joy, and pain.
  The baby was born, a healthy little blue eyed Miss,
The Mother must have thought "what sort of a World is this?"
Now she had two children to take care of alone,
Determined she was, they would have a good home.
I respected, loved, and admired her, for you see,
That blue eyed little Miss, her daughter, is me.

Mary E. Horton

The Man

Sex, sex him till the sun comes up
passionately love him every night til he's mine forever
do you know this man..... well he is so sexy you might
want to rub your lips across his, your hands would
rush to embrace his dreaded locks of hair

His skin is so smooth you want to drip fine wine over it
drink it off him while the liquid shines luminating
moonlight through the room.... just to drink the wine
off his perfect body is passion it self, my body is
quivering just thinking about this man... I don't want
no other it's all for him to sex, sex me passionately
till the sun comes up, down and around.....

Kira Knight

Veterinarian

V is for the Veterinarian I would like to be.
E is for the Enormous animals I'll see.
T is for The many years of school I have to take.
E is for Every bit of money I'll make.
R is for the Rabies shots I'll have to give.
I is for how I'll help the animals to live.
N is for how I kNow exactly what to do.
A is for All the baby Animals so new.
R is for the Rabbits and Reptiles that come to me.
I is for the Important job this will be.
A is for All the work I'll do.
N is for hoping Nobody will sue.

Kaylie Brooke Dewitt

The Wall

He touches the black granite,
His hands, they move across.
He feels the emptiness inside,
He's numb with a hopeless sense of loss.
The images of war, he sees in his mind,
Is a Vet's cross, he can't leave behind.

He stands and stares and tries to recall,
The face of a man who's name is on "The Wall."
He was his comrade, he was his friend,
He fought in a senseless war that brought life to an end.
He sheds a tear he cannot hide,
He offers a prayer for those who died.

The dead are alive on that memorial of stone,
Some 58,000, they're never alone.
They're American heroes from a confrontation,
A raging battle that divided a Nation.
They died for their country, in that terrible war,
Now, they live in black granite, on "The Wall," evermore.

Mary Alice Sherer

Mother's Garden

How do we tend our gardens?
Do we carefully plant
ever-ripening corn in neat organized rows
Or do we let it go, over-grown and weary?
I question
her rough calloused hands that tend our gardens.
Are we really worth it?

I wonder why
the decrepit rotting apple falls
from a violent emerald tree
I'm curious of the wish-washy blue eyes
wrinkled with age and laughter
I wonder what they saw?
Or continue to see?
I wonder
What her hands feel picking up that mushy apple?
What did they feel
that I do not?
And what did those ever-wise eyes see
That I do not?

Samantha Mahon

My Affirming Friend

I look to you for affirmation,
You give me strength to do God's will.
You show me how I'm His creation.
I have a purpose to fulfill.

You are my spiritual friend,
You lift me up in prayer and praise.
You know what loving message to send
In my facing of the world's dark days.

No earthly friend has been so spiritual,
You are my manna where famine is found.
You turn my eyes toward life eternal
Your blessings ever flow and abound.

So when this world of put-downs and hurts
Start making me feel I have no worth,
I look to you and find that your words
Give me the value I've had since my birth.

So in return, as good friends should be
I'm lifting you up so you can see
How your praise has caused a victory
Of setting my spirit free.

Sue Ellen Lea

The Marks Of A Mother

She went through the tunnels of
death for a life of which she did not know

Unsure of what to do, what to say,
what to teach to her child that will grow

Not knowing what to expect, if
anything at all - but would only give her best

Which is what she did, from the
day her child was born with the
milk of her breast

A woman of remarkable standards,
courage and will, hoping she's done the right thing

For a child, her child with all
the joys he or she may bring

If you're a mother you could
understand, and a child who has
come of age will see

The marks of a mother, a
mark she made - she made for me!

Towanna L. Clegg

Untitled

Alone I sit on a deserted island,
with the wind blowing through my hair.
It whispers the past, present, and future,
reminding me of how I once cared.
It tells me lies, I never asked to hear.
It caresses my face, but does not take away fear.
It teases and plays with the clouds in the sky.
It tells me I should not give up,
I should never let hope die.
It blows in the rain, it sprinkles, it pours,
yet I stay still, sit quiet, on these empty shores.
I let it have its fun, untouched by its breeze.
Knowing it will calm, and put my hurt at ease.
Even if it blows in the worst,
while I am stranded here by the sea.
I know someday the wind will blow in my ship,
to come and rescue me.

Catherine Davidson

I Am Not Perfectly Square

I am not perfectly square.
What you see on the outside is not really me.
My actions, my words, all performed in deceit;
for that is the way they want me to be.
No one can touch, no one can see, what is really
  inside of me.
I am not perfectly square.
Each night I cry myself to sleep, and when I dream
I am free.
My heart is free to love whomever it pleases.
My soul is free to soar above the clouds.
My mouth is free to speak the truth, my mind has sought.
I do not try to please them in my dreams.
For my dreams are mine, and mine alone.
So when I sleep, you may touch, and you may see,
what is really inside of me.
When I sleep I am truly myself, and myself, I am alone.
I am not perfectly square, although that is the way they
make it seem.
And perfectly square, I never hope to be.

   Katrina E. Heintz

Good Night, My Son

Good-night, dear son so many miles away
Sweet dreams attend thee of a peaceful day
May God keep thee is his blessed care
And watch over thee while I am not there

Good-night, my son, this mother misses you so
More than you could ever even know
May God touch you with love and gentle hands
Keeping you safe until you return from foreign lands

Good-night, my son, that precious hour I await
When I shall hear your footsteps at the gate
May God grant this happiness and ecstatic joy to be
When I hear you Whisper "Good-night, Mom," to me

   Marian L. Houston

From The Inside Looking Out

The Ghetto- often described as a huge jail cell,
I'm Trapped- for eighteen years in this place I have dwelled.
An Inter-city Kid is what I am, with all odds against me,
A Struggle is ahead, including many obstacles before me.
My Future is said to be a wall, surrounded by a cage,
Because My Heart supposedly, has nothing in it but rage.
This Stereotype- has caused my race to suffer many years,
But mostly- the damage has been done by a portion of my black peers.

No Matter how hard we struggle or strive for the best,
It Seems as if my race will never be treated equally, like the rest.
But I'm Firm for my goal is to become a successful business man,
Living Life to the fullest, but never forgetting this wretched land.
Discrimination and segregation is what put me in the ghetto,
Admiration and determination is what's getting me out of the ghetto.
Nevertheless, a black man is what I am and a black man is what I
  will always be,
But, when will society begin to accept me for me?

   Damon G. Redding

The Vet

I know a man.
Who still walks with a limp.
Never bestowed a heroes welcome.
He still wrestles with a war,
fought years ago.
Over the airwaves of internal strife,
dispatched "orders",
that never seem to stop broadcasting.
Each day a new target to forget and forgive.
Through endless, sleepless nights,
"voices",
echo the cries of the past.
Waking in the crimson flash of a fire-fight,
tears stain his leathered face.
From distant rice paddies,
ghostly figures of guilt and anguish,
lurk and haunt,
gnawing the marrow of his very soul.

   Robert Hipkins

I Am Poetry

The thoughts are here, concealed within
the paper is in front of me and the pen is my friend.

I can become anything, or go anywhere with the movement of
my hand,
reality is not a factor and nowhere am I band.

I can destroy or create, I can love or hate
I can invent situations based on security or fear,
A crystal ball of my own,
that I alone make cloudy or clear.

I am master of my page, I am wizard of all
from sympathy to rage hear my words call.

A dimension that's unexplored
by the physical kind,
but if you close your eyes
and search you will find.
It's a beautiful sensation, to use the imagination.

And at the end of time
when everything is gone
one thing alone surely lives on
I am free I am poetry.

   Michael Marshall

Christmas

Christmas is a time for family
It is time for show
Christmas tree are a big part of it
Family giving gifts to me
It is time to deal with friends
and family
It is time to decorate the tree
Time to eat really good food
Then when the night is over you go to bed
I would try to see Santa.

   Marshall Eastridge

The Weeping Pool

A girl fell in love.
She feel in love with her teacher.
They had a secret meeting place.
That place was a lake hidden behind a hill.
They decided to have a picnic.
She brought the food, he brought the wine.
One day he didn't show up at the school.
And on that evening, he didn't come to the secret lake.
So she was so upset that she drowned herself in the pond.

Kimberly Lawson

Morning Supper Without You

Melon slices and juevos rancheros con leche
stirred into your coffee, just the way you like it.
I've had my second cup of kahlua,
sitting in my vinyl chair in nothing more than
the see through night gown you bought me last Christmas.
Mi cabeza spins como un whirl pool, feels like the time
you accidentally slammed me into the bathroom wall.
I counted ten thousand cracks on the ceiling, though
perhaps I lost count when the phone rang and it was only mama.
Mama and Papa in their sad accents asking when I'll be home
or if the baby is alright, "Esta bien la nina?"
I say you're in the shower but I think she heard past my pain.
I think tonight I'll brew mole and bathe in scalding hot water
as if it would make me forget.
La pero afuera barks like a screaming newborns and
I'm tempered to run out the back door and slam my foot on his tail
but I might miss your phone call then. "Ring Damn it!" I cry.
I think about dialing the operator to see if it's out of order but I
know it isn't ... it never is.

Aracelli Arellano

Thinking Of You

Memory's face cracks smiles elated,
The image in her eyes now faded.
Her broken heart spills life once liven',
All her love...a chance once given.

Her wasted breath remains unborrowed,
Surrounding all her silent sorrow.
Her tears by glance steal man's desire;
His aching to once more stand by her.

Behind closed eyes her face emerges,
The portrait's shadowed past resurges.
The message from her heart once broken,
Remembrance of love's word unspoken.

William James Weidner Jr.

Facets

The three of us played a game of chess. Evil on one
side, good on the other, I stood in the middle of the
board. Lust liked the white pieces so virtue played first
giving birth to the game. Sins move followed quickly.
The bishops tried to spread their word, and the rooks
built walls all over the land. The king and queen tried to
erect a monarchy, but the four horsemen struck their
wrath and all that stood was me and anarchy. I was a
pawn, eighteen percent grey. I played them all. They
were all a bore separately yet they were all wonderful
together. My whole life they fought for me, I suggested
checkers but none of them laughed. Neither team could
beat the other because I won't lose to myself. None
could have me alone so we all embraced each other, I
held them all, the devil's advocate.

Peter Talhame

Moonbeam Pathways

Moonbeams skip across the water,
Luminescent pathway across the lake;
Moving, shifting moon's reflection,
Always different, star-like

Summer's circle of cool white,
Dancing moonbeams prance along
Patterns of reflective light,
Engulfing the night.
Tranquil vista, serene, calms me,
Where words echo in my mind.

"Peace, be still" by another sea was said.
"Be still and know that I am God".
He is here now, unmistakable peace;
Enjoying His creation with me, and in me.

Strong and forcefully reaching hands
Stretched out to Peter, and the other learners.
He balanced on the lighted surface
Of the gentle swells, then, and invisibly today.

His powers to change creation,
Mirrors His power to change our life.

Beth Lynnette Kreiss

Foghorn Lullaby

Lull me to sleep with the foghorns
Let 'em croon the whole night long
For their low momentous moaning
Yields my favorite slumber song

Back in the days of my childhood
In a home above the bay
I learned to welcome the fog forms
Drifting in at close of day

At night the foghorns blew
To warn of perils of the bay
But for me 'twas assurance of safety on shore
To keep and dream securely

I've been away for a long time
Now I've come back home to stay
and I long to feel the fog freshness
Hear the distant foghorns play

I open windows wide tonight
Let fog wisps round me play
And I'll drift off to sleep
While foghorns repeat in San Francisco Bay

Rosa Pollard

Life

Racked inside your fear,
Engulfed in darkness,
Lonely, looking for the light.
A door opened and a path through the labyrinth found,
Love led the way.
Heaven sent or demon spawn?
Who cared?
Who knew?
Loneliness abated,
Pain assuaged,
Happiness sharp and tinged with bitterness.
The mixed blessings of life and death of love.
The fight to flee and to stay.
Love isn't a bright penny or a black cowl,
But a grey mantle worn for a time then cast away.

Katy M. Gilland

You And My Father

I was once afraid of boys like you
I rested my head in the softness
Of his flannel shirt and
Listened to his heart loving me

Until curiosity and stones
Tapped at my window
And your arms pulled me into night-dark
Away from him

A moment suspended between the wood sill
And the grass
Between childhood and
Whatever comes after that

Your car took me away
While my house slept on
He believing I was in my bed
While I kissed your evening-soft neck

I climbed back to where I came from
Under blankets, covering shame and wishing
It was enough to be a child in his arms

Safe from the world
            Bethann Tuzzio

Blind Faith

Glorious be this vision of mine
Behold such a sight
From the shadows of doubt emerged the light of tomorrow
Colors seem meaningless to the shade of pale
Blind faith
In the storm of bewilderment lies the realm of salvation
May I contemplate with such joy!
Forward motion encompasses my very soul
May this moment be rejoiced!
A sight behold a life risen
From the depth of sorrow leaps the essence of merriment
Faith without a vision
May you be so glorious to behold.
            Eddie Matt

"I Am"

I am a Catholic girl, who loves the Lord with all my heart.
I wonder what will become of me when I'm grown.
I hear a voice telling me to be a priest, others a doctor.
I see myself as a mother with children at my side.
I want to be like the Lord, loving, caring, and understanding.
I am a Catholic girl, who loves the Lord with all my heart.

I pretend that what is happening to the baby is fake, a dream.
I feel really bad that my mother had to go through all this.
I touch my heart when I think of all the pain in my family now.
I cry every night before I go to bed, about the baby.
I am a Catholic girl, who loves the Lord with all my heart.

I say that the Lord could do a miracle and let the baby live.
I dream about what life would be like if this baby lived.
I try to cheer everyone up at home during this sad time.
I am a Catholic girl, who loves the Lord with all my heart.

I understand why the Lord brought my John Paul to us.
I realize that the reason was to bring Love into my family.
I know it is in the Lord's hands, everything is.
I will never stop loving the Lord.
I am a Catholic girl, who loves the Lord with all my heart.
            Jana Du Charme

Trials And Trails Of Conflict

Those who dwell in logic and the sensible
Never daring to trespass else where
These are but petty paupers
When compared to the creative
Who don't submerge in the known
Just leap towards a bright star
Yet society has chosen logic over truth
Both close cousins in concept
Truth is felt where logic is seen
Brief are the moments when they agree
Still I'd rather upset my mind over my heart
Tending to travel on winding trails
I find it a much more scenic route
Other than straight and narrow paths
Which hold boredom surrounded by monotony
I know the road I wish to travel
care to journey with me?
            Jeffrey C. Holley

"3rd Millennium Kids"

They aren't in deep space age.
Those little people are in 1st grade.
Their playground called "TARHELL" land.
I ain't remember their eyecolour.

Bees' turn's come to end,
yellow butterflies'll fly away.
Fighttime's aged and ended.
Playground's got old and wise also.

Who's coming to play?
Millenniums came!
Millennium comes!

Newone isn't a bee.
That isn't belong to butterfly neither.
It isn't seeddgragon's guys.

Fruit's numbered, but not its; fruit of the womb
They won't be sparrow this time.
Think again oldman and C.O.!
Person isn't alone this time, but you were.
They're all together now.
They'll be free as a bird.
            Ehsan Zareian

Poetry Reading

How silly I was to think that only strange people engaged in
    poetry readings.
What a fool I've been—
    I've missed out on the sexuality,
        the sensuality,
            the serenity of our language.
Oh, and of course, the beautiful creature reciting his poem
A simple poem about soup
Yet so exciting, stimulating...
        captivating.
I don't know anything about him, yet when he reads his poem, it
    opens a window to his soul...revealing so much.
With his intense eyes piercing my soul as every word rolls off his
    full lips in a sensual way
While his deep voice penetrates my very being
His strong back hunched over his book
Like a lover with his mistress.
Caressing the pages so softly, so sweetly,
As I stare at him in awe...completely mesmerized,
Envious of the book in his hands.
            Kelly Krosnick

He's Home For Good

When you lose a child
No matter what his age.
It's hard to start your life a new
And turn to the next page.

He's been your life for all those years
and you have one regret
that he was taken much to soon
and you weren't finished yet.

The plans, the hopes, the dreams you shared
the things he could achieved
and now you lay him down to rest
it's so hard to believe.

It's through his love we celebrate
a brand new life for Kevin
as God has called him home for good
to live with Him in heaven.

Cheryl Moreno

"Silence"

Put my life on the public television channel
So no one watches.

I'll stay with my lover, silence, with his curls
And smooth chest I lean against.

We flirted and danced,
Now it's a thing, you know.

He lounges in my room in his nakedness,
I just watch him, like a wild animal, a cat.

He holds my breasts,
I hold my breasts for comfort.

I cry out and double over and
He takes me in, holds me in the break I make in him.

To me, he is everything,
And what he doesn't say far more important -

He knows how to pause, touch so I feel his love.
It's trite but he remakes me -

I feel strong and full, ruined for any
Other talky mortal.

The buzz of time is in his veins,
Flush of release and reprieve in his endless climax.

Elizabeth Degenhardt

Your Face, Your Love!

I went to sleep; I saw your face,
  It was enstroud in satin and lace.
The stars were in your eyes so bright,
  I knew, you were, mine tonight.
Your lips are full and taste of honey,
  Your smile is warm, and oh so sunny.
Your heart is beating ever so loudly.
  I know it's for me and I feel proudly.
Your arms are open and calling to me,
  I'm trying my damnest, but I can't get free.
The law is binding and I'm stuck in this place,
  and outside the fence, your beautiful face.
but do not worry, for our love is so,
  It'll always be pure as new fallen snow.
When I am free I'll make you mine,
  and we'll be together, till the end of time.

Paul H. Koermer

Circle Of Seasons

Mother's milk once fed
oceans blue, now poisoned
soured by neglect, disdain
for menacing wilds' promise.

Her breast bitten, scarred
by hatred, tribal wars unending
against all other, and then
souls battle selves, death-torn.

Technology's elixir oozes down crimson peaks,
cure and poison flow together as
truth obscured, simple beauty forgotten;
a tree ringed by millennia, sun-graced, emerald.

Suckling children weep salty regret
for us all, for a future
we know but cannot see
for desperate hope blinds wisdom.

As babes we search her eyes
with our own sanguine ones, humble
all pray to the source, at least once,
begging for her mercy, fogiveness, bliss...

Erin Sherman

Chase The Clouds Away

I thought my life was complete,
I thought I knew what happiness was.
But all I had was an inkling
Of the joys life had in store for me.
Now that I have known you,
If only for a short time.
I now know how to find
The simple joys of life.
The sun had always shone,
But never as bright as when you're around.
Your smile, your laugh,
Can brighten the darkest day,
And long after we have parted,
Your memory will still
Chase the clouds away.

Elizabeth Lembke

His Whispers

The dark and tumbling sea.
It's water rushing to the shore
with a salt-filled breeze
as it whips around once more.

White foam ripples toward me, then away
as if teasing me to come in and play.
I take a moment to ponder
as my mind is filled with wonder.

How awesome it is to see
all these forces working around me;
not knowing how they work at all.
No matter, these are His calls.

Such joy fills my heart
knowing I'm a special part
in the big plan of things.
It makes me want to sing.

To sing out with gladness and cheer
with a voice to be heard.
I'm alive! I'm here!
I'm free as a bird!

Deidre Robertson

"Loneliness"

Hanging from the bent branch of a desolate tree,
  A single, dried leaf sways in the wind.
A forgotten child, sobbing,
  Reaching out in a cold, dark room,
  Grasping nothing but silent emptiness.
The slow, mellow drone of church bells
  On a chilly, snow-filled day.
Like tired eyelids, once beautiful flowers droop
  In the musty air of a passed rain.
As cold as frosty snowflakes,
  Unshed tears puddle in the corners of searching eyes.
Searching for someone to hold onto,
  The eyes see only a vast, unwieldy desert.
A silent scream rolls through the air,
  Then slows to a murmuring whisper,
   Not ignored,
    But never recognized.

  Mary Neisen

Prompted By The Lord...

By fire I've tested to burn off your dark dross
Your flesh was in anguish and screamed quite a lot
But to your heart I was listening and it cried burn it out
for it's your image I'll be having or nothing at all

You flesh kept thrashing and throwing itself about.
But my image is quickly coming about
My path is now coming more clear to you.
So stay in my fire, till I bring you out.

Now you are looking in a glass darkly.
But soon you will see, so don't turn about.
My image you'll see reflected in you.
So stay in my fire, I AM is perfecting you

Unbelief is a vail that's being lifted from you

You stand in a doorway hanging between two worlds.
Which world will you walk in, they are calling to you.
Mine in the spirit of light and love or
that in the flesh of dead work
You stand in the threshold now what will you do?
Choose life, choose life. I AM is becking you.

  Carolyn Gillick

Our Beloved Daughter

As I look into their eyes so bright.
My thoughts go back as I reminisce tonight.

The day of their birth made us so proud.
Sweet and little and a cry so loud.

In my arms I rocked my precious girls
lots of hair and yes there were curls.

As they grew through the years.
We had laughter and some tears.

Sauntering through braces, schools and church
their way was made with some research.

In college they did well.
As a proud parent would tell.

Falling in love they chose to marry
Given our blessing they did not tarry.

Flowers, rings, while gowns with lace.
Two beautiful weddings did take place.

Thru children of their own
All special I can atone

I know the families will always find.
Their mothers so thoughtful and so kind.

  Lorraine Watson

Kindergarten

It's time to put my toys away
As I begin my life today
The year seemed long for it was new
To go to school the whole day thru
No longer could I sit and play
For I'm grownup and at school all day
I've grown a lot this year you see
As life begins from here, for me
I know to my parents, whom I love best of all
I still really look just a little bit small
But I can conquer the world, just wait and see
The beautiful part is .. it's all up to me!

  Barbara Patterson Boyd

Glorious Things Await Me

Babies born and unborn for me to love
  New friends to make and cherish
Songs of praise written for me to sing
Flowers to bloom to enjoy their fragrance
  Trees growing to shade me
   to hear luscious fruit to eat
Fields of grain to nourish my body
Delicious meals to enjoy
  some cooked by a friend
New exciting tastes to experience
  stir-fry in a wok.
Discoveries to be made
  to heal my schizophrenic daughter
  a cure for cancer that took my breast
  for strokes that took my Dad at 65
  and a coronary occlusion that took Mom
Happy times to recall through celebrations are scheduled
These and many other things arc scheduled
  Glorious things await me.

  Martha Downs

Fright

The ocean waves stricken waves
Trees shadow the blue water
it is scared and frightened.
The ocean wants to hide,
but has no where to go.
Boats race along its surface,
leaving scars along its wake.
It wants to be left alone,
but obstacles block the way.
The hard rain beats upon it
making it cry in pain.
As the sun sets it begins to relax.
Nothing can hurt it they have all gone away.
The ocean accepts the river
as if comforted by a mother's love.
It knows it has a friend by its side
someone who understands how it feels
to be scarred, shadowed, and beaten.
Together they look up at the stars as they rest,
hoping that tomorrow will never come.

  Angela Plank

Birds

Today, I woke up to the sound of birds whistling a lively tune.
Their vibrant colors are joy to my eyes.
Natures alarm clock.

They come to my window sill
Bringing joy to my soul.
Telling me to wake up, they are
Natures alarm clock.

  Tonya Vogt

For A Child Not Yet Twelve

Poised immaculate on the single instant,
soon comes the downward plunge of your nature;
now
you are innocent as a statue,
engraved and golden forever.

Time's flood I would freeze,
as in art I would stretch the pinpoint moment
to infinity.

But to you this time is
a chrysalis quick to be ripped
or a treasure hunt-trail
where, breathless, you follow the clues
to your future self.

Like water, you rush through my clutching fingers
and run laughing ahead to the fall.

Margaret H. Haskell

Empty Shell

Embrace the illness that stirs within me
If but merely a pound of flesh might sustain its hunger
grand would be the illusion...
For not, its fury consuming, rips the weight of emotion
from my bosom

Foe or comrade yet has to hear the cry
that stifled by corrupted sanctity.
Taste of despair interrupting an attempt to wretch,
that which is not within

Curtail thy heroics,
Lost is that which cannot be replaced.
Empty the existence, of the frigid,
desolate plain now traveled.

Scott A. Kunkel

Timebomb

Time tyrannical - out of sync -
Why must it always be - for me;
Stop watch living - insides quivering -
Pace car - race car smoking wheels - pit stop meals
Stomach full of acid rain - brain drain.

Hurry, hurry up and wait,
Motor revved, but standing still. . .
Horsepower straining at the gate.

Tick tock, wicked clock,
You have broken life in pieces -
seconds, minutes, hours, days;
Pleasure fleeting disappears like wisps of smoke,
Pain depleting plods and pokes.

Who has set these arbitrary rules
and fixed parameters on all of life.
I'm sick of time. . .
Metes and bounds - rigidity.
I envy wind and water and
Long for some unbroken flow, and time to grow -
Not older, only more serene.

Mean time - let me go.

Beverly Ann Starling

Zane

The powerful gift of life is a miracle to be had.
From the first moment I saw Zane,
I knew I'd never be the same.
His small wrinkled face and utterly unique presence
makes my heart glow with confidence.
When I look into his forever changing eyes,
they glimmer with a special vivacity.
One very simple facial gaze, and a soft sequencing babble
makes me smile with pleasure.
His delicate nature creates his entire image.
Each day he forms a spontaneous style,
of special character and witty smiles.
Changing so slightly everyday, I hadn't noticed enough to say
As the years pass and he's grown,
The world will be his to forever roam.
I love him more than words can say,
and my love grows stronger everyday.

Dawn Davison

Silhouettes Of Time

Looking through a window and who do we see?
A baby embracing every natural memory.
A child's curious eyes eager to conquer all that is new.
A teenager wondering if life is pure and true.
A pair of lovers embracing in the night.
A middle age couple full of fear and fright.
A loving partner dying -
    fighting for their life.
An elderly person dwelling in the past.
Silhouettes of time -
    memories that will forever last and last.

Irene H. Amann

"Happiness"

Happiness comes from deep within
From your soul, loose your win
If you're content all will know
From your heart your love will glow

Rain or shine, snow or sleet
Warm or cold, sunny or bleak
Windy or calm, skies of blue
When you're happy, all will know

Sad or joyful, tears anew
A frown on your face, will tell the gloom
Always smile, never let them know
The pain inside is how you feel

A smile always be
Your heart they will see
The sun will shine for all to beam
When the happiness comes from within

Cathy Peragallo

Victim Of A Mad Man

I see candid repercussions within my face.
Scars in my eyes.
Bruises on my lips.
Tears flow in my veins.
Semen and electrolytes drip from my teeth.
My hands burn.
My body aches.
My mind sleeps on the wine of eternal shame.

Tegan Rieske

What Is Inside Love?

Inside Love is something
That can never be sold.
It is not made of Silver,
Nor Diamonds, nor Gold.
What is inside Love
Can be gentle and caring,
But also at times,
Can be courageous and daring.
Inside Love is not riches and fame,
But is helping one another,
Whether they are different or the same.
Inside Love is family and friends,
That add color to our lives,
Like a beautiful rainbow that never ends.

Michael Disner

"The Old Farm Well"

The road which led to the old farm well
Is scarcely a trail today.
For those who fondly trod it then
Have long since passed away.

The massive wood curb leans slightly.
The pulley of iron wears a coat of rust.
A rope once strong and stealthy
Lies a rotted heap in the dust.

Upon the silence breaks a trickling,
A gurgle! A bubble! A splash!
The seeping drops are slapping
Each other, as swiftly they pass.

As fast as the drops the bottom reach -
They make a slight rebound.
Each contributes its little speech -
A faint mysterious sound.

Lois Lindsey Davis

Memory

Do I hear the drums a drumming?
Do I hear the trumpets call?
Can I see the flags a coming?
Can I hear the Sergeant's bawl?

Even so distant after battle
when the last saber long did rattle
and men slaughtered as if cattle,
do I feel it in my bones?

Yes, I must say is the answer
for war is like a cancer.
Its effects can be felt forever
because there is no like endeavor.

Though my eyes have grown the dimmer
and my hair has turned to gray,
I'll ne'er forget even one horror's glimmer
'til my last of living day.

James McArthur Dorton

Sad And Mad

Today is like tomorrow
and tomorrow is like today,
when yesterday I saw someone pray.
The praying person was very sad and at that
time I was feeling very mad. I was mad because
I do not like to see people sad.

So if you see someone sad,
you should be very mad.

Victoria Kawalewski

A Little Country Girl's Dream

The Summer that I turned thirteen,
My brother took me to New Orleans.
The things I saw made my head whirl
It was too much for this little country girl.

There were horse drawn carriages all around,
And I rode a street car to go down town
And my breath I could hardly draw.
I could not believe, what this country girl saw.

We went to the beach with some friends,
And I did not want the summer to end.
We went swimming and rode silly things,
It was a dream come true for a girl of thirteen.

Soon it was time for me to leave,
And I did not want to believe
That it was the end of her beautiful dream,
For the little country girl who was only thirteen.

My brother put me on a train
And this too was new and strange.
I was so scared and all alone
But this scared little country girl was going home.

I want to thank you for the fun we shared,
And I want you to know I love you and care.
The summer that I turned thirteen
You fulfilled a Country Girl's Dream.

Evelyn Smitherman

Untitled

A chance is what I asked you for,
    a chance, you said you'd give,
But I never even got started,
    to begin, my love to give.

You said you don't want a relationship,
    'cause you don't want for me any pain.
But I must love in order to chance being hurt,
    and Love is the name of the game.

You said you must sort out your feelings,
    and carry on with your life.
I want to be your friend and comfort,
    not another question in your life.

I'm not a very eloquent talker,
    but I think you understand.
I only want to care for you,
    with all the love I can.

You are a special lady to me,
    and I think you feel it too.
I just want to let you know,
    I have fallen in love with you.

Chuck D. Sperman

Marriage Of Love

I've been married 36 years,
Oh! there were plenty of tears,
There has to be a lot of respect,
Out of this everything falls into prospect;
We had six beautiful girl babies
I'd do it all over again without any maybe's!
Out of this Love
Given from above
Grandchildren flourished
Who will always be cherished.
Our lives are complete
With this wonderful feat
We will always have a great Valentie's Day
Because we are loved in a special way!

Jo-Ann Stocker

"To Remind Me Of You"

Beautiful flowers of colorful hues,
with sweet smelling fragrance, remind me of you.
Sunrise and rainbows, a beautiful view
songbirds and gardens, remind me of you...
Now there is one where once there were two,
Old pictures and perfume remind of you
with big hugs and kisses you used to say
"I love you my darling" this phrase rings loud
and true, for everytime I hear those words
they remind me of you.
Though you are gone my precious mother, still I love
you so much, I will always remember your
sweet smile, your loving touch.
Your memories will forever live on in my heart
just as today they do, for God has given
me all these beautiful things-to remind me of you.

Lisa N. Studensky

Ode To A Dream

We strive to be from the day we're born
The best, the first, the only one

To claim the prize that is ours alone
And carve our niche on a piece of stone

Pursuing the dream takes all we've got
We know one day we'll reach the top

How could we know how the fates perceived
A plan quite different from you and me

The dream moves on, the dreamer knows
The lessons learned teach us how to grow

How strange that the place we sought from the start
Was a place of peace buried in our heart!

Marie Winter

Eye To Eye

Opposing each other
They sat eye to eye,
With grossly graven eyes
The ashen, ugly and disfigured
Was first to speak
"My deeds are gaining with the
Blood stained shores of your young
Wedging distrust between all kind,
Turning husband against wife,
Brother against sister and
Disease and pestilence my
Trophy - of - Design..."
"These are all your accomplishments"
Said the purest of heart and
Clearest of eyes, "that is true.
Yet only one act from me
Wipes away your deeds
Spirit - for life
Has driven you away
You're no longer needed...Now go", said he.

James W. Keegan

Destiny

I want to remember how to laugh,
I want to remember how to live.
Dear God, please don't let the trials of my life,
    impede upon the hope I have for the future.

Let me see the sun peak through the clouds,
Let me climb the mountain to reach for the stars.
Help me to accept that your way is best,
Help me to accept that your way is mine.

Karen Hoino

Going Home

The time has come to say goodbye,
pictures and thoughts will still survive.
Before the end the pan is clear, focused
in grief making it real.
The mind racing, racing for stable ground.
While the gun is lifted that once was found.
Sweat flowing on a time high, injecting
power blown sky wide.
Emotions tumbling to an end, numbness, settling in.
Concentration at its peak, the reapers noose
conquering what it seeks.
Help me, help me, the words are said.
No one hears, for they are deaf and dead.
Silence stirs as the letters is signed,
with a blast and an echo farewell,
Farewell mankind.

Brian Steidle

Change

Every day a new dream, new story, new theme—
A new way of learning to solve the mystery.
A new cup of coffee, a new cup of tea,
A new little butterfly, a new bumblebee.
Each day, a new goal, a new direction,
A new way of loving and sign of affection.
Yesterday an adventure, tomorrow a dream,
A sky full of stars, with a silvery moonbeam.
Dawn brings the sun, dusk darkens the sky,
Night shines the stars, while the comets fly.
Tomorrow you may face decisions, struggles, strife
Tomorrow you could be truly living a new way of life.
We knew as the great day of new changing came,
That only change itself would remain the same.

Gina Moro

Watch The Children

With open hearts and trusting eyes; they look up to you.
And they believe that every word you speak; is nothing less than true.

And the life you live in front of them; is the right way to go.
But things aren't always what they seem; and they are just too young to know.

So willing and so eager to do anything to please.
But life has little twists and turns that will bring them to their knees.

And send them on a crooked path; when the way was planned straight.
Now you watch in horror; as life unfolds their fate.

As life got hard, as it sometimes does.
You weren't watching them; but someone else was.

So the next time your life is about to cave in;
WATCH THE CHILDREN; they're worth saving.

Pheyama L. Lincoln

The Lone Surfer

Cold wet power all around you,
Pruning your hands, cleansing your soul.
The mother of separating softens as you glide down the face
And drag a hand to say hello.
The beautiful soft pain ready to kill you if you offend it,
So offend it not, and take to flight.

Visit your mother.
All life comes from the sea; get back to the womb.
The mother being visited by the three finned children,
As they play in the front yard, occasionally scraping a knee.
Far away and yet so close.
Worries mumble on shore.
The life I dream of as I drink my coffee, watching the snow fall.

Max Kalchthaler

Love Of A Rose

A rose is like us humans, clinging to our
roots to grow.
A rose may fall or wither, but our stems will
hold us so.
A rose may be all for beauty or show, but
deep down in all it wants is tender love to grow.
Everyone wants to find that perfect rose,
but as they see they can't even come close.
Small, short, wide thin as every single rose is.
Until the day when that full perfect rose
appears, we turn away all others in tears.
Blind as we are, we don't see that all the
other roses needed was a little of our tender
love, to become the full blossom rose that
everyone wants and needs.

Lori Trudell

All Must Die

The sun is gone, all is gray
The rain descending is cold, thin, long, needlelike drops,
Causing small ripples in the dirty puddles
Has chased all of life from the streets.

Rivulets of raindrops running down the window panes
Bring a nostalgic sadness to my heart.
The occasional sound of a car
Breaks the incessant lonely sound of the pitter patter of raindrops
on the roof.

The room is warm but I am cold
For I see the bleakness of the world before me.
The trees are barren of the beauty they carried just a few short weeks ago.
They reach their empty arms to the sky like skeletons of Auschwitz
asking - why?

There are no answers, there are no reasons,
There is only the chilling wind whistling through their branches,
Causing the trees to bend in obedience and murmur
All must die.

Robert L. Ptaszek

Contentment

A chance first meeting, arranged by a friend
The beginning of a life, with many a bend.

She was cute and lively, though a bit naive
After pizza and bowling, could it be time to leave?

One week later, I knew I was had
To be so in love, could it be all that bad?

Each time she entered my thoughts or a room
My heart skipped a beat, then started with a boom!

After college and studies and a job so new
Marriage entered the picture with so much to do.

A new life together, just the two of us
Much growing and learning, with sometimes a fuss.

But after many a year, through children and debt
She's still cute and lively, though naive just a bit.

And each time she enters my thoughts or a room
My heart still skips a beat, then starts with a boom!

We've entered a life long journey as friends
And we'll survive though it winds and occasionally bends.

For the one I love is the rarest of gems
A companion, a wife, a lifelong friend.

Stephan E. Cheek

The Ring Master

Blue rabid dogs cluster in the halls
Drag queen winos, waiting for your call
Runaway children long for the night
Junkies sharing needles, tourniquets pulled tight
Carnival horses, faceless clowns
Doing what comes natural on this merry-go-round
Asphalt rivers down below
Hobo junction still in tow
In lieu of decree, cease to exist
Newspaper blankets comfort and bliss
Dark desolate streets, long shadows appear
Slipping a coin, swear it's sincere
Concrete circus, fantasy park
Step right up, it starts after dark.

Raymond J. Hughes

Serena

The tiniest little angel is four months old.
She lives in my house
And in my heart.

Her dainty, long fingers tug at my hair.
Her bright, toothless smile at my heart.

One moment she's still,
And I can see her thoughts;
Then suddenly her spirit cries out
Through vigorous movement.

She is love, she is beauty,
She is all that is good.

With a halo of gold
Like the hair on her head,
And soft, fluffy wings
Like the blanket beneath her,

She sleeps and she dreams
Like the angel she is.

Georgia Ann Mott

The Toughest Times As A Teenager

Now that you've been in the world 14 years
I do thank God you never had beer
But now temptations come far and near
Mom and Dad's help will always be here.
When you were young, Mommy defended you
But now you are grown, you must fight back too
As you go on in life, don't be a fool
Just remember you'll always be your family's jewel.
Please don't ever lose control
And let others drive your soul
God gave you a life to shape
In your own independent way.
Don't ever get caught in a drug bust
Through this you deserve your parents' trust
In all your decisions, be sure to be just
To have a successful life, it is a must.
You will meet many people in your days
Some of them may challenge your ways
Just continue with life and don't be afraid
Always strive for the best, and keep it maintained.

Steven Moore

Jesus (The Creator)

I said "I'm not worth it!"
He said "Would I have died for nothing?"
I said "But can't change myself!"
He said "I can".
I said "My sins are too ugly, too big".
He said "I love you, I see no sins".

He looked past the ugliness of my life,
to the little glimmer of light I had left.
He looked at what I could be instead
of what I was.
And then...He not only looked at what I
could be but he went on.
To show me what I could be.
And again he went on to create me.
(What I could..ME!)
And he still goes on

Thank you Jesus!!!

Shela J. Sidwell

Untitled

The frustrating sounds of life around us
The tormenting ego of man succumbed
Subjected to taunts from frustrated,
    chattering intellects.
The rebellious prognostications
    of malcontents.

The swirling, cycling whirlpool of living,
Freed only from the depths of the undertow,
And lifted to the current speed of life about us,
Only to be carried and swayed toward greater swirls.

The seeming endless swirls, each tattooing its mark,
Continues to haunt the lust, the greedy,
The rushing currents, the wide sweeping eddies,
    the quiet bay'ous,
All of these finding the last pool,
    the largest of them all,
The quiet and bigness of the ocean depths.

H. Nile Lamm

Stage Fright

The fabric that has unveiled many scenes
to amuse has now become my comfort.
In past
each thread
traced throughout its weave
of anxious
is now my blanket
of secure.
The polychrome fiber that has caught many
my stare
is now much less adorned
and what once seemed forbidden
is now within grasp.
Soon the curtain will part
exactly on center
and of each panel
pleats will swell in waltz
to its respective wing.
Now transformed to great columns of folds
the giant shroud stands magically awaiting to conceal.

Douglas E. Mortimer

Two Hearts

When two hearts are blending,
    Love will have no ending.
Across the miles, I see your smiles;
    your smiles of yesteryear.
Oh, how I loved you then.
    I even love you when
You're not near.
    You've been gone twenty and four,
But I couldn't love you any more,
    Than when you were at my side,
My sweet and beautiful bride.
    Ah, those years have gone so quickly by,
The time when we were young.
    But our's is not to cry.
I love you now, as much, as though it all...
    had just begun.

Eleanore J. Seidenburg

Understand "Love"

Love is something you must understand.
In woman it shows greater than man.
In child it grows without a hand.
In marriage it's love that's truly grand.

Though there is one thing I don't understand,
why divorce between woman, child, and man?
For if there's love that can command,
then love is worth a helping hand.

For this is what I understand,
because I love, love is grand,
between the woman, the child, and the man.

John Sipling

Untitled

When looking at your face,
I can feel the warmth of the sun.
The trust, love and knowledge
that I will protect your innocence,
flickers in the green pools of your eyes.
But yet, there is a doubt of exactly where
you fit into this world still so new to you.
My advice is to live life to the fullest.
Know that we, together, will learn the answers
and solve the problems with love and understanding;
true friends;
Father and son.

Roy L. McAtee

Dining In Saigon

Breakfast in the jungle
is not really breakfast at all,
amidst the leaves,
jungle trees,
enemy.
Food with the enemy,
a sound of fear,
the sound of the
birds.
A sound the same?
Breakfast in the jungle all sounds are the sound of fear.
Breakfast in the jungle.

George Ehrhorn

Through The Night

There above, the moon
Is shining so bright.
The stars will be twinkling soon
   At twilight.

The clouds of silvery, fleecy, white
Coming and going to and fro
Are sailing by in the quiet night
   At bedtime.

The wind is blowing soft and low.
Through the tops of the mighty trees
The trees are bending to and fro.
The birds are sleep in the tops of these
   At midnight.

The song of the wind is sweet and low.
The eastern sky is growing bright.
The dew is cool on the grass below.
the moon and the stars cease giving light
   At dawn!

    Mary Gwaltney Wynne

The Eighth Deadly Sin

There's a knife on the table,
warm silver slender point
a drug
The perfect drug to take me home.

I think of lines drawn on glass
paler grins on the pale flesh of my wrist
red light spurting,
drifting like memory,
falling into white.

The sunlight is cold
and the knife is
not enough.
I leave it on the table
and go
watch re-runs and static
on the old TV.

    Brad Greenberg

Ardent Blues

A velvet dream
can seem
to be an angel wing
used for the trip
when you unexpectedly say goodbye
to your partners
and you learn to swim with the shaman
when you are eagle, when you are bear
when you arc wolf with thick black hair
a time when lust is lost
and so is...
Gravity
to become flame in the fire of a spirit world
full of feathers and fur
Nothing like the place where you were
a time when your princess has come home...
alone
Farewell to a world that didn't understand you
the place where you never knew just where to go to find...
Home.

    Jay Zirkle

Retribution

I stabbed a man once long ago...
It was not the kind of a wound to show...
No spurt of blood to mark the place...
No flash of anguish on his face...
And only myself to know.

It was long ago when the world was new,
And I did not know what a word could do.
Yet the stab of a word when the world is young
can haunt the heart like a song unsung
And linger a whole life through.

Oh the wound has healed...there is scarcely a scar
To mark the place where the memories are;
And many a deeper hurt since then
Has been made on his heart by colder men
With crueler words by far.

Yet now I know...with no outward sign...
Though the wound was his, it was also mine.
For there is a scar upon my heart
At the place where the child and the woman part...
And the deeper wound was mine.

    Christena Bryson Kern

On Life's Voyage

The night is black;
The overhanging clouds have hid each star;
I hear the dashing of the restless waves;
The breakers roar.
There is no light to pierce the circling gloom,
And direful shadows round about me loom.
I cannot see his face or touch his hands,
But still I know
That there beside the wheel, my Pilot stands.

I hear his voice;
His messages to me are plain and clear.
He speaks, and bids my failing courage rise;
Dispels my fear.
Around me boisterous tempests fiercely blow,
But while my Pilot holds the wheel, I know
He'll guide me safely o'er the flashing foam,
And in the morn
We'll anchor safely in my Father's home.

    David Lehigh

Young Love

It was only a look a brief moment in time,
that made him feel special for no reason or rhyme.
He could swim any ocean, any mountain he could climb
just, because, of a look, a brief moment in time.

Then just a hug, one soft warm embrace,
that transported him back in time, dimension, and space.
A time when he was only a boy and he last saw her face.
When he knew a childlike love with one soft warm embrace.

It was just one simple kiss and nothing more,
that opened his heart to walk through loves door.
To experience emotions like he never knew before.
Where true love starts with a kiss and nothing more.

But, it was the three little words that "I Love You",
that made him remember why their love was so true.
A boy and a girl falling in love with memories for two,
with a look, a hug, a kiss and a special "I Love You."

    D. J. Reiber

Blue

Blue is the remembrance of days gone by.
Blue is the stars in the midnight sky.

Blue is the silent whisper of good-bye.
Blue is the warmth of a clear, azure sky.

Blue is the wind murmuring through the trees.
Blue is for the blue jays, the bluebells, and the bees.

Blue is a burning desire.
Blue is an intense, vivid, steel-blue fire.

Blue is as fresh as a summer breeze.
Blue is as cool as a winter on skis.

Blue is the sapphire waters cascading.
Blue is the veil of mist masquerading.

Janeen M. Carlson

Sonnet To Song

In the chant of the heart sings a rage of impart with a lust
For the art in the role to depart beyond earth to the realm
So divine that to man who is just tends the trust
And depends on who guideth in wisdom enchanted the helm.
Many ages to bring shall disperse with a fling of the voice
Entertaining the soul through the pulse of a note to regale.
Then the heavenly tune shall ring free with the theme of our choice
'Til with joy we implore all the host for the love to avail.
With a shout, with a jest, when in sport, when in quest do not flee
From the touch of the flesh that so warmly reveals to the sense
Of our burden the ease we achieve through the share of our glee.
Let us waft past his throne a crescendo replete so intense
That our fervor rejoice the angelic abode which shall lift
All mankind to ethereal peace and eternally save such a gift!!

Steve Spaugh

Memories Of Pain

Dedicated to all Holocaust Victims.
The blood curdling screams of panic break the sound,
Tears fall as fast as raindrops to the ground,
Cries for justice scream out into the night
for many victims do not want to die without a fair fight.
Rage rumbles through the roaring sky,
The brave dare to open their mortified eye.
A breath of hope blows through the air
asking for help, yet no one is there.
The line grows shorter and then the knees grow weak,
Silently pleading for a reprieval is what they seek.
Tired of the tricks, tired of the lies,
This is not a way for living souls to die.
The mind is paralyzed by conspirators hate,
while an abrupt end to their life is for what they wait.
And even though the innocent are tortured and punished before they die:
They shall be rewarded in heaven, giving a final sigh.

Laura Filbert

Untitled

As I see the sparkle in your eye
I hope you believe me when I say
I LOVE YOU, because it is not a lie
Knowing our love will not die

For you are always in my heart
I know our love was hard to start
I know now that I never want to part

For you my love is true
When we are not together, it makes me feel blue
For I will always LOVE YOU!
  BABE

Allan Adkison

Love

Love is like a shooting star
doesn't last too long, doesn't
go too far. It can make you
laugh, it can make you cry.
Sometimes it can make you die.
Love can make you go crazy
it can make you have babies
but it always ends up as a
simple little maybe. You love
your first until you burst and
say those three words unless
you know you mean it first. That
is love it's all the above I wish
it was like what I always thought of.
That is love it is strange in many ways.

Harry Nikolakis

Marriage Made In Heaven

"Inspired by God"
Entrance of elegance comes the bride,
  her gown with pearls of white
Beauty and holiness flowing,
  what an immaculate sight
The gown spread out draping,
  her train revealing God's saints
Christians who are the body of Christ,
  those who did not waver or faint
Each person linked to the bride,
  established their choice for Jesus
Walking down the isle of Heaven,
  entering gates of pearliness
Jesus, the Bridegroom waiting,
  as the bride walks toward her groom
The Glory of God's Majestic presence,
  choir of angels singing in radiant bloom
The Holy Spirit in Glorious endowment,
  as each bride makes their way
Having entered Heaven's open door,
  burst forth the illustrious eternal stay.

Jill Dugal

"The River Called Cheat"

The Cheat River hills are mean and wild.
Upon my first look I was only a child.
I loved her then and I love her now.
Upon every look brings back a smile.
When she's high and flowing fast, stay
off her back and out of her grasp.
When she's humble and down, hop on in at
Albright town.
Ride her down pass Hogback ridge.
Enjoy the scenery and stop at the Bull Run bridge.
When you look up you will see it's wearing thin.
It was built in 1912 by the Canton bridge builders men.
But don't stop there for goodness sake, from the
Bridge on down you can raft to Cheat Lake.
For those of you who know her not, take heed
upon this thought.
She's wide and steep, flowing and deep.
Don't take advantage of the Almighty Cheat.

Mark Thomas Calvert

Lost Muse

The canvas no longer beckons a stroke,
colors have lost their bright, rich call.
Lost brushes now are too heavy to lift,
carbons in broken pieces, lie on
scattered white pages.
Inks that once flowed pour forth no more;
the fountain has gone dry.

Uncorked heart that once spilled wild
now lies cold and empty.
Shades of gray are all the eyes now see,
mind is becalmed in rolling fog,
breath has become a conscious effort.
Windows are open to the day but dark
clings to the room,
no longer can I create within,
the studio has lost its light.

Rhys Solace

Heartache

Heartache is very hard to swallow
This pain lies in the pit of your stomach
Weighing down with every memory of him that passes through your head
After hanging onto his every word for so long,
It's hard not to hear the whisper of his voice in your ear
Your emotions take over and only crying helps,
But it will never be the same without him to wipe your tears away
You can't bear to see him with anybody but yourself
You hate him because if you don't, you'll never love again
You can't look at him, or even be near him
You go into a silent rage when you hear his name
But one day, he realizes he made a mistake
The question is - will you take him back?
Of course, you will because you love him
You'd rather be hurt a million times by someone you love
If it meant you could share one moment with that certain person
Even if that moment was a mere second,
You would give anything, even your heart
For that final good-bye.

Kelly Washart

Like A Child With A Candle

Like a child with a candle
His one ward against the night
A glimmer of love in a dark, cold world
You are my guiding light.

The hard times that would break up,
Instead bind us like a chain.
The rainbow memories guide us through
The hard times and the pain.

The river we float down may be rough,
Our patience may wear thin.
But the strength we need to pull us through
Will come from love within.

The pink rose of our friendship
Won't fade with passing years.
It will blossom and unfurl
Through our laughter and our tears.

Like a child with a candle
Whenever we're apart
I know that you are with me;
You are deep within my heart.

Jessica Elise Donaldson

I Need You Lord

Help me dear Lord as I strive today.
To be a better person in every way
meet me when I kneel to pray
and give me strength for another day.
It's only by your power
that I can survive another hour.
I am not striving for the world's towers.
I just want to be one of your flowers.
Then when traveling days are over
and no more can I look on fields of clovers.
Meet me on the other side
where I can rejoice with the
one who has been my guide
I will shout, and have no doubt
it's you my savior that brought me out.

Laura B. Brown

Life Of A Feather

In the air
Drifting through the clouds
Is a feather
Blowing freely through the wind
Flying

The feather
Is fluffy and white like the cotton clouds
Gliding gracefully through the air
Jostled and jerked by the fickle wind
Tumbling

Surrounded by the whiteness of the clouds
Is an agile feather
Ruffled by the wind
Dancing on air
Remembering

In the air
Drifting through the clouds
Is a feather
Blowing freely through the wind
Soaring out of view

Kim Crane

Knowing Your Leaving

How do I close my eyes at night
Without your arms, holding me tight,
How will I have a peaceful dream
Of you and I, walking by a stream,
How do I wake and face each day
Knowing your in heaven, so far away,
How will I stop my tears that easily fall
As I look at our pictures, on the wall,
How do I raise our daughter alone
Without you here, sharing our home,
How will I greet all the people we know
As my heart breaks, everywhere I go,
How do I possibly go on with my life
When I've only just, become your wife,
How will I face every month of May
On the anniversary, of our wedding day,
How do I keep the faith in my heart
Not understanding, why we must part.

Sue Ives

The Parade

Camera ready.
Slowly sweeping. Fading in.
Lens guzzling sun.
Succulent brightness leaving the haunting to stay.
Left-over lunch bones
Of spooks spotting spooks chasing spooks passing by.
Cut-outs dancing circles around
A drive down Elm in cowboy town.

Movie-dust, movie-smoke
Misted extras in polaroid diagonal silhouette.
Shots cut across all heads,
Save one: They cut. (Cut into explosion.)
Free-horror bounding around
A drive down Elm in cowboy town.

Murmur and happy trance fast dead with a bang.
Plain murder. Blood. Blow back gore.
Classified. Eyes only. Liquid affairs.
Under the blood-halo of a butchered head.
Following the panicked splattered parade covering the ground
On a drive down Elm in cowboy town.

Peter Kerns

Cobwebs

She lied awake gazing up at spider webs,
Spotting a grand daddy long-leg on the wall.
The plastic on the broken windows fluttered,
A mouse darted under the bed and down the hall.

She shivered from the cold and fear,
There was screaming in the room next door.
She heard broken glass and her mother's moans,
Her father yelling, "You're just a whore!"

After hours of yelling and hitting,
She closed her eyes to pray.
With scattered thoughts and muttered speech she stammered,
"Please God take me away."

That little girl got away,
From the run down shack in the woods.
She tried to survive and do her best,
She did all she would, could, and should.

She moved away to escape her pain,
But not much changed in fifteen years.
She clasped her hands and began to pray
But the words didn't pass through her tears.

Roxanna Rochele Graham

Untitled

After all was done,
   When everyone was repulsed but me
   (I didn't understand)
Those who were on my side were asking,
   "What happened?"
I lied to them, and I'll never forget that they don't know.
Why did I lie?
   "I love my daddy, and he loves me. There must
   be a mistake. This couldn't have happened to me."
Because I couldn't see you, I cried those nights by,
focusing on the lamp you made for me, back when we were all
together..
   "He hurt you."
   "When can I see him again?"
   (I didn't understand)
You never admitted it, but I remember.
Now, I can see it all.
   What I can not see
is how you could mock the innocence
every child deserves, needs.
   (I don't understand)

Evelyn Richardson

Hope For Spring

I look at the hills and see nothing but death.
Then I look again and hold my breath.
Was there a small tinge of color to see?
Is there a hope of spring to be?
It has been such a struggle this winter, you see.
Each time I look out my window, I only see
Dead trees, cliffs, and rocks, and brown leaves.
Surely this middle of March there would be
Some sign of life - a resurrection. But, oh me.
A closer look at the scene shows me no hope.
Bare branches are there, tree trunks, and the cliff.
But, yet, another glance and I swear I see
A tiny hope; a chance, of green. I must go see.
So, again I bundle: Don coat, boots and cap.
I open the door and face a winter chill.
I cross the road, and ditch, and climb the hill.
I stop to examine what I hope I had seen.
This tip of the branch of my favorite tree
Has a struggling bud, and a tinge of green.
Oh Hallelujah, praise God!
A few more days and life will begin again!

Marian May

Life's End

As I walk down the road of life
There is a river beside my path.
I see reflections off the water
Of the times I cried and laughed.
As my path grew slowly darker
I was struck with a feeling of dread.
My life long river was drying up
With so much left unsaid.
Just that moment I went to my knees
And prayed unto my Lord above.
I begged, "Dear God please don't take me
From all the ones I love!"
A feeling of peace rushed into my soul
As an angel did descend.
She said, "Take my hand, and fear not
My friend, for the river never ends."

Nick Nicolakis

"One Night"

A wood-smoke hint on evening's breeze
Helps set this perfect fall night scene,
As hand-in-hand we move along
These same safe streets we've always known.

The window glows from fires alight
In easy homes stood side-by-side,
Remind us of our alter dreams
Now snaking thin like chimney wisps.

And here an owl or young child's laugh
Will ripple through our silent stroll;
Though soon our footfall rhythms merge
Again with beats of scattered thoughts.

Then all at once this idyll's free
From 'neath our heavy, married steps,
To loose a length of crier's scroll
And whistle wind-borne wisdom true:

"One scene does not a fine film make,
One chord a timeless tune,
One tiny spark eternal light,
One night a mourning's bloom."

Alex Pearlstein

Sword And Nail

With furnace and heat the start of work,
The smith with patience and precision of skill,
Then molds the metal and gives it shape;
A hammer in hand, he pounds the anvil.

Now tempered with fire a tool is made,
A sword or nail both serve a purpose
Next dipped in water and left to cool,
Is work of weeks and days gone away.

Again thrust in flame to make it softer,
The metal an alloy, the metal made impure
Is done so purposely, to make it stronger;
After tasting the hammer, again immersed in water.

Every creation is unique, subtly each its own,
But all are made, are made by one;
With care and reason from the smith's hands,
The real test comes, true endurance yet shown.

When the tool is used, or left to be
Simply metal against metal or metal against wood,
The weight, the passing of time will reveal,
That all are useful and needed; with certainty.

Michael T. Warnock Jr.

Biscuits For Sale

As I dive into the flour
From above I get the power
To carry me along through the dough.

Now I cook by the book
Sure I check with a look
But I beckon to the call
Of the timer on the wall
Then fly back again through the dough.

It's soon to be time
For them to rise and shine
They look like pure gold
And are soon to be sold
Which makes it worth my trip through the dough.

First they're checked by sight
Then tested by the bite
And the race is on again through the dough.

Now the last mile is mine
And I'm home in the shower
Sure feels great to wash away the flour
For I have been through the dough.

Lettie C. Massey

I, blue

when I cry
the doves billow
the amber rose
begins to bloom
    Bop!

Tears—tears—tears
drip; drop; drip; drop
like the rain that beats against a window pane
    Hey!

Drums, unwantingly,
clammer at the edge of the sill..
The sun comes out to absorb them all
    Womp!

I cried because the doves had no more song.
Fa, fa, fa, fa, fa—
The rose willowed, but jazzmine lives on
    Be-Bop! Yeah!

Carlos Devonne Murrell

"My Blue-Eyed Rocker"

When she was just a tiny tot, and couldn't put on her shoe or sock,
She'd get up on the hands and knees and rock!
I said, "later rocking she'll outgrow."
And when a toddler she became, did she? Oh no! To and fro,
    still the same.
I coaxed and pleaded, go play with other children, outdoors among
    the flowers, but my little girl stayed indoors and rocked and
    rocked for hours.
During a ride in the car, I exclaimed, "an earthquake, it must be
    a whopper."
Then I discovered, no earthquake, 'twas just my blue-eyed rocker.
A new rocker I must buy, because the old one is all apart.
I don't mind, really, cause all these years she's been rocking in
    my heart.
Someday when married and grown, to drive her wild,
    I wish on her, her own.

Esta A. Sims

May Your Sock Drawers Never Rule Your Life

They live neatly in pairs
Two by two by two,
Lined up like soldiers on parade.
Argyles to the right, stripes to the left,
Black ones in the middle,
Their places never changing,
Sleeping rigidly year upon year,
Until at last worn out, they are discarded.

But the bold ones
They fling themselves out of the drawer,
Hanging precariously over the edge.
Green, pink, yellow, red-all colors and hues,
Matched and mismatched,
Popping in and out, ever changing,
Alive and laughing.
Until, one by one, they disappear,
Leaving a trail of sunshine.

Marjorie Wilson

Sweetness

You say you do not understand poetry. Want to know me?
Best friend, workmate, companion completely.
One in ten million? Is love so charming?
Sweetness is unaccountable, always disarming.

Truth when expressed, you should believe
the moment. You are not deceived!
You accuse me of cheating. Can love be so fleeting?
Is heart so deceiving, to cause such grieving?

Thoughts untrusting causes love's withdrawal,
Does love's loss manifest cheating?
Abandonment causes grief, helplessness
No end to emotional grieving.

Love explained is purity, fidelity, sounds.
Accept this love, or continue rounds.
Thoughts unjust challenge love's trust,
if I'm not me, do what you must.

Best friend, choose love's kin,
Intuition knows, feels, I did not sin.
There's no fault, let's begin again.
Sweetness is unaccountable, enamored within.

Tom Caudle

A Feel For Writing

Writing feels like happiness, like you're lost in your own world.
Writing feels like music flooding your body, washing out your
  worries and troubles.
Writing makes you want to fade into a dream and never come
  back toearth.
Writing gives you that special tingle of joy.
Writing is your survival when you're feeling low or depressed.
Writing is your shoulder to cry on when everyone has aban-
doned you.
Writing is the friend you never had.
Writing will always stand by you through bad times.
Writing is something you can put your emotions into,
  whether they are happy or sad.
Writing can be like sunshine on a pretty day or like big dark
  clouds on a rainy day.
Writing is the friend you always wanted.
Writing takes you into a whole new world,
  that you will never want to leave.

Heather Hynes

Kaleidoscope

Turn the kaleidoscope slowly
And colors come sifting down
Inspired with mood you laugh like a clown

Images wrapped in ribbons and bows
Turn it, moods vanish, happiness goes

A kaleidoscope world is just like a maze
With futures in abstract going opposite ways

Through a kaleidoscope all that you see
Is just how it is in reality

Rainbows of colors, kaleidoscopes change
Rainbows of colors re-arrange

Patterns and shapes clashing to blend
Is the scheme of today's world my friend

Turn the kaleidoscope slowly
To see colors sifting down
To inspire a mood, to laugh like a clown

B. J. Boden

Pain

Pain.
Pain seems red.
Like gushing blood.
I see a never-ending stream of violence.
I hear the horrified screams of a victim.
I smell a fear of death what
will soon come around.
I touch someone, for they need help.
I taste the salt of the
tears that cry.
Everyday, people are in trouble.
More children are getting shot.
There are more drugs being sold.
Pain.
Pain seems red.
Like gushing blood.

Stop the crime,
stop the hate!

Danielle Gardner

"The Job"

If ever there was a time I felt like an angel, it was when I met you.
And I asked the good Lord above "What is it you want me to do?"
This person like so many others, is confused in his head, for he has
seen all the wicked ways of the world, he said.
And I need someone like you to show him what it would be like,
to have someone love and care for him, and hold him tight.
 And I want you to listen when he needs someone to talk to,
cause I know you'll be understanding, and will know what to do.
Show him it's not the material things of the world, or the title of
ones name, nor is it how much money one has, or who's to
  "win" at life's little games.
For inside we've all done wrong in one way or another,
but you must help teach him again to have faith and to trust in
  one another.
For he has put a wall all around his heart, and
dares anyone to come near it and tear it apart. But my child I say
this to you, this is a very big job I'm asking you to do. For he
has turned so cold and cruel, and lives in a world of sin, and
your biggest challenge is to teach him to love again. And you
will know when your job is thru, with the touch of his hands and
the look in his eyes, and the whisper of his lips that can finally
say "I love you."

Janet Taylor Hadden

Reborn

I walked into her life, which was confused and
  shattered from broken love Affairs,

I used no heavy tricks or special charms to
  rebuild her still broken pieces,

I used my kind smile and a few bits of advice
  which I grew to learn myself in
  past experiences,

Time passed-and this girl became an over joyous
  bundle of laughter and happiness,

Now after many months which felt like years she
  is an ambitious and self-confident woman,
  fit to take the place of a gorgeous queen
  in her own world,

She now stands alone in her own glory, able to cope
  and conquer all that gets in her way,

Including... the drifting stranger who put her life
  together again!

Barbara Ceilura-Kleiber

Walk Of Life

Above my eyes, the moon cries,
The heavens hurt, an angel has died.
Most precious of life, Gods own wife.
Holy tears shall flood the Earthen Floor.

Angel of love between woman and man,
Never again will heaven withstand.
For the angel who died was mortal love,
Without her hand to guide, all love will slide.

No gossamer spirit to show the way,
Within ourselves our love will pay.
Tenderness of heart, sweetness of emotion;
Our soul's understanding-our love potion.

The walk of life, so lonely,
Please take my hand,
Be my one and true love only,
If I would die before we meet again,
Remember, I do so love you Jeannie Lynn.

Harvey McLemore

High Frontiers

With wind in my face I'll gleefully trace
  My trail through the limitless blue
To find in the sky an answer to why
  Men search for the strange and the new.

Like birds on the wing delighting to sing
  I'll laugh at the staid earth below
And seeking to pry the lid from the sky
  Surmount all the free winds that blow,

Barriers never really can sever,
  The searcher from what he may seek.
The losers but fail because they must quail
  From labors that stimy the weak.

The flush of the dawn is luring me on
  Far out to the frontiers of space
And all I would do is search for the new
  With wind of the stars in my face.

Earl Victor Shaffer

Autumn Tears

Muted, gloomy light
Soon day will turn to night
Rain pelting on the sill
Memories of day linger still
Cold, dreary, depressing day
Falls to night, darkens the gray
Makes you wonder if ever again
You'll feel the sweet, warm rays of spring
I sigh and glance out the window once more
Then make my way to the bed room door
I can hardly stand to be this depressed
It makes my heart feel so distressed

Elizabeth Thompson

Dance

Dance. More of an emotion than a movement. Those who teach it only drain the power out of it. You can not teach emotion it is just something contained deep inside you. Your mind moves your body without trying, legs twirling simultaneously with arms. You are unconscious to your surroundings as they slowly transform into blurs.
You are drawn into the serene world of dance. The emotion like love that takes you into its hands and spins you uncontrollably. And as your mind clouds over with thoughts of bewilderment and happiness, shivers run swiftly down your spine, tingling you all the way through with warmth.
You have been completely swallowed by dance.

Chelsea Sharon

"The Seashore"

The waves crashing against the sand,
a warm comforting walk hand in hand.
Everyone is making wishes,
while the wind, is blowing kisses.
Beautiful coral under the sea,
creatures lets count them 1,2,3.
There are shells many to see,
many people fill up with glee.
The clouds rolling and the sun peeking through,
if you go in the shops you can get something new.
When the stars come out it's the prettiest sight,
it's getting dark but the moon will shine bright.

Lynn Hamski

Creamy!

Mommy lifted Carolyn and
removed her from her cage
And introduced a brand new food
at very impressionable age
Just so you don't think that I'm
a baby jar food meany
Here to eat are yellow peaches
in a bowl
rich and sour creamy
Upon her tongue melted sour cream
sliding from her mouth so teeny
And Carolyn's first baby word
was consequently, creamy!
As years passed by into her teens
when all her friends said,
'Dreamy'
Cari slipped into her past and said, instead,
"It's creamy"

Adrienne Ferrol

Leopards

Drafted leopards whose search seems endless
In hopes of defeating its prey
Find mangled battered obstructions
Replacing reality with visual dismay.

Only at night do leopards play
Prancing swamps or manipulating sage
Following cues from well trained actors
Carefully stalking that well renowned stage.

Five in the mourn and years from dawn
For true daylight seldom appears
The leopards roam far from home
Praising courage while scorning fear.

The leopards gather one by one
Forming tight secluded wings
Roars belt out like lightning bolts
That form eternal rings.

Years roll past, dawn arrives
Yes the air smells quit upwinded
For cold, age, ill-minded leopards
The war is over thought never ended.

Jeff Southard

For The Living

What, for nothing lacking, is
  life without life,
  a bird without wings
  who longs for flight?
  In the throes of a strong wind's
  bluster he is tossed in strife.
  Nothing evil in the wind's intention
  that carries the fate of the bird's ill plight
What, for not living, is
  life without life?
  You and I have wings-of-thought.
  Soaring...
  We can be anywhere - do anything.
  Our bodies,
  like serpents to the ground;
  our spirits,
  like birds our-of-bounds.
Whom, with life's knowledge,
  lives life?
Those who dare to fly!

Darren Maurice Brady

Marina Bay

Swaying palms mark the spot
Where we make our turn, into
the cove we know as Marina Bay.

Surrounded by the tropical, lush
beauty of flowers, water, and trees.
We walk among the drifting boats
making music as they move against
the wooden docks.

So romantic, you can walk hand in hand
wondering about from boat to boat.
Making up stories of each one, ah the
fantasy you can create.

Come see our piece of paradise, our place
to share each other, come to our,
Marina Bay.

Loretta Knowlton

Senses

Vision, smell, taste, hearing, and touch,
Instruments for experimentation,
Interfaces between one and his environment.

Sight, a thin line between
A kaleidoscope of colors and an abyss of blackness.
Created by orbs of vision, destroyed by witnessing crimes.

Smell, an allusion to past experiences,
An encoding of lost but not forgotten experiences.
Summons old feelings upon thought,
And collects new ones simultaneously.

Taste, sample the flavors of the world,
Varying from person to person,
Sour to sweet, nation to nation.

Hearing, caves of music,
Free orifices with walls to bounce off of.
Sounds all so beautiful, poetry to music.

Hands of touch, boasting your deeds and actions,
Devices of labor, channeling your thoughts to another source.
The utensil that yields the result,
Of five senses working in unison.

Jonathan Sherman

Blind

Isn't it amazing, that the wisest man in the world
With a mind more vast than mountain ranges,
Who seems to know so much,
Could be so naive about two things.
Isn't it amazing, how the most gorgeous eyes in the world
That are as deep and blue as oceans,
Seem to be open and alert,
But instead are blind to two things.
The simplest to the most complex forms of love are displayed,
but he does not see them.
The tears well up in my eyes
And flow down ghost white cheeks
Plunging into pools at my feet.
My vision may be blurred,
But I can see well enough.
In silence I watch him stomp through these tear filled puddles
Without a notion of care.
He does not even notice that I am here.
Even though his eyes are open,
They are blind to love and me.

Amy Huddlestone

King Of The Desert

It's a bright, clear day.
I see you fly around the racetrack.

No one can stay on your back,
not even the best jockey in the country.

You're blacker than night, and name is lightning.
The name suits your speed, but to me you're "Shetan Malenka."

After ditching your jockey, you vault the fence.
Now I can believe it when people say you are the king.

Endurance and stamina show in your every move.
When you gallop, your legs are like pistons.

Glossy, muscular, never-ending movement,
Mane and tail streaming in the wind.

King of the Desert, you would be the pride of a sheik.
They would name you Shetan Malenka, just as I have.

Shetan Malenka, which means "Devil", truly describes you.
You are a raging wildcat.

I long to own you. The owner is willing to sell.

You're mine, but then maybe not,
You're a wild animal, not to be owned.

I'm going to return you to the desert.
Goodbye, Shetan Malenka. You're free. Run with the wind!

Angela Cheatham

A Child's Cry

I'm a child of love and hate.
Why didn't you just wait.
Now I'm the one to blame.
You say I've caused all the pain.
I have gone away, but I am near,
Just listen hard and you will hear.

You I must forgive.
For not letting me live.
I will keep on trying, even though inside I am dying.
You keep on lying, and I keep on crying.

I am not broken-hearted.
At least you finished what you started.
In case you haven't known.
I have a wonderful home.
I'm not what you wanted me to be .
Just listen hard and you can still hear me.

A child's cry, you can hear it in the night.
Please don't ignore it, it's an endless fight.
Try not to let it con you,
It goes on and on, A Child's Cry.

Tiffany Barge

Creation

What minds they were that conjured up the Taj
What hands to execute these grandest dreams,
Japan's Pagodas and the Angkor Wat,
The Lacy Palaces of Venetia's Doge.
With awe, past all imaginings it seems...
That unique man has easily wrought all that.
Till, out in space while sitting on the moon
He gazes back at earth, that pendant pearl,
And humbly sees that God's great granted boon
Gives him the most incomparable world
And in unmatched generosity
Let's man pretend to ape Him easily.
A joyful taste in genesis He gives
To sweeten hardship for man while he lives
Yet, lest his pride o'er run his puny place
Sets forth the sun in diadem of grace.

Rose C. Marchiano

October 11th

I live with you every day, so far from me.
Death is a comfort next to not knowing.
Don't be shocked by my feelings, it's just truth.
This is the hardest day of the whole year.

Dreams make me cry weeks before hand,
No one ever remembers your birthday.
But why should they really? You're not their pain.
Nine years later I'm still full of anger.

Your father is married with children now,
I wonder if he also lives with you.
Will I meet you someday? Will you hate me?
Can you understand what I can't explain?

Don't ask me. I don't remember just why.
All I know is I drank a lot after.
Blow out your candles, I'll kiss you good night.
This is the hardest day of the whole year.

AnneMarie Prodell

Buttons

Picking up a button from the ground
Starting thinking about what I'd found.

How we leave a trail of where we've traveled
Yet few pick up the pieces that come unraveled.

We lose our keys, our loves, our drive
They get replaced and we survive.

Who traveled before me on this trail?
What were they like? What was their tale?

Thinking of all the different times and places
Others lost their buttons, I saw their faces.

Keeping the lost button as a souvenir
A reminder to hold lives encountered dear.

For everyone I meet has a living soul
That may need mending, to be made whole.

Living needs to be like needle and thread
Sewing, mending, patching - instead,

Of ignoring the buttons that falls to the ground
Life cannot be repaired, if it is never found.

Kay L. Killian

Untitled

Sadness tapped me on the shoulder.
I turned to him; and yielded quickly.
For he reached in and tore
My innermost door.
He unveiled my only last secret.
So well I had hidden it.
Into such a little space;
My heart did not know it was even there.

But then; sadness tapped me on the shoulder.
I turned to him.
And now my mind is searching so;
For answers I cannot find.
And if all is true;
If he does not speak of lies,
Then there shall be pain at every turn.

Oh sadness;
Why must you do this to me?
Or do you wish?
Should I let it be?
And turn to you completely.

Juliana F. Herbst

Sing You

Recall from deepest soul depths
innermost
emotions.
Tap Virgin riches sleeping there
in unique, creative fashions.
Oh, record them: Fond memories, reflections...
All collective passions;
Creative life-song that sings you.
Echoing spirits
weaving eternal melodies;
forever
harmonizing
the universe.

Stella M. Trevino

Happy

Feeling like the only one, powerful.
Walk alone.
No one can see this, no one can be this.
It rises the soul to the clouds,
Walking on air, flying.
We haven't left.
We are around.
Surrounded by faces full of question,
Just as we feel, but ours is stronger.
Not on top, nor looking around.
But feeling like the only one.

Gustavo Dalphen

Fear

There is a fear
There is a fear within our souls
Allowing us to be conquered by ignorance
A dark shadow hovering over our hearts
A blindfold of envy and hatred covering our eyes
Creating a door between heaven and hell
There is a search for our inner-selves
A deadly obsession to find our destiny
The hunt for a purpose of our existence
There is a war
An unknown battle we constantly fight
A struggle never ceasing
Enormous pain of bombs exploding in the chest
Reluctant cries of loneliness contend for freedom
But pride keeps them imprisoned
There is fear
An enemy silently approaching
An adversary of life
Shall we allow ourselves to be conquered
Or shall we be conquerors?

Natasha L. Smith

Mother

A masterpiece - a work of art
I'm picturing, in my head, your heart
You love me now, you loved me then
When it comes to your love, I don't have to ask when.
I hope you know I feel the same
I love the sound of your sweet name
My feelings for you should overwhelm
This kind of love can't be captured on film
When your old and gray
And God beckons you to come his way;
I'll shed tears as everyone else
As God shall take you as his wealth,
I consider you a treasure, never to be met
Can I love you more ... No, I can't.

Mary Prater

"A Kiss Of Descending Fortune"

A kiss of descending fortune
Leads only to a game of malicious deception
The closer I get, the farther you pull away

She manifests a keen interest
I counter with the same
A kiss of descending fortune

The public event teeming with ecstasy,
Followed with a date full of passion
The closer I get, the farther you pull away

The evening concludes with the infamous kiss goodnight
You leave me to believe there is longing and aspiration
A kiss of descending fortune

I ask, again and again,
You respond with the perfect lie, if you respond at all
The closer I get, the farther you pull away

The day finally comes and your elegant, graceful beauty
Devours all, as you play me like a fiddle
A kiss of descending fortune
The closer I get, the farther you pull away

Joseph Posner

"Lord, Jesus"

If he should live before you die
You will have learned of his great try
To live and love with compassion great
For friends and fellow man of all slate
He is known through out the land
For bringing compassion to his fellow man
He is the seeker of man's soul
the shy, the great, the bold.
The believers and the non believers alike.
Will have found the Messiah, Jesus.
The most high.
He is Jehovah, Emmanuel, Hosanah, the Messiah, Jesus.
The prince of peace and love.
Who stands above us on the height.
Jesus will have lived before you die,
If you recognized any of the Most High!

James Edgehill

What Are You Doing Up Above?

I always knew that heaven,
Was beyond the sky above,
So filled with the tranquility,
The warmth of God's sweet love.
I never really thought about it,
Until you passed away,
Now I find myself looking toward the heaven
Each and everyday.
Sometimes I expect to see you on a cloud,
Waving down at me,
Or perched upon a star so bright,
For only my eyes to see.
I expect to see you walk about,
The amber moon so high,
Or see you ride a comet,
Zooming way across the sky.
Whatever you're doing in heaven,
I know you'll do it at your best,
With God in his beautiful kingdom,
You have finally found your rest.

Angie O. Dority

Valor Of The Heart

Among the many castles and rolling countrysides of green
I met a noble gentleman more precious than I had dreamed

He was not distinguished by wearing shining armor
But rather by averting cross swords to a lady's honor

Unpopular life decisions he decided to make
When faced with contrived events and yet others of fate

He acknowledge his share of the situation to this moment in time
Which was met with resistance from the lady so intertwined

Clad in great valor and resolve of steel
He responded to a drum within beating — this way up the hill

His gait is now slower but more determined is the stride
To keep marching forward as the pain of change subside

I see him climbing up life's hill with eyes of sadness still
Now cautiously choosing the steps to take toward dreams yet
   unfulfilled.

Barbara L. Bryant

When Windows Are Left Open

There are times, when windows are left open,
And the rugs, get dampened by the rain.
At these times, our secrets are worth keeping,
And our lies, become our closest friends.

And there are times, the willows bend to breaking,
But the spring, always brings them back again.
Sometimes time, can be the greatest healer,
But there are times, time can also break your heart.

And there are times, we try to write our feelings,
But end up, upon an empty page.
What should be, a simple, loving sonnet,
Turns out to be, unwritten books of praise.

Yes, there are times, when windows are left open,
And the winds, whistle music through the blinds.
At these times, mistakes seem meant to happen,
And our love, is one of these few times.

Mark Gruber

The Mystical Rose

White rose sounds like a young woman singing softly
Drifting off silently into her imagination
While the crow circles the white light, he is blinded
And collapses into the woman's imagination

The woman awakes with dark snow falling
While the white rose still shines bright
Now the woman becomes part of the never ending brightness
But now, the rose is black with pain and terror
As the snow whistles the warning of danger
And spreads his light over the terror

The black rose now collapses into the shivering blood of the snow
And becomes part of life itself
And the pain and agony over and over again

Nicholas S. Pizzino

Unforgotten Love

   I had never pondered all the injustices I had done to her,
and yet she always forgave. And now I find painful to put into
words all the memories that I have saved. She came to me as a lover,
and a friend. And still I left her over, and over again. To this
day she is the only one whom I could depend. I denied her love
for so long, I am sorry that I waited until now, it was wrong not
to speak of my love for her. But now is too late. She has passed on.
And all that remains of our unvowed love is memories, a child, our song,
and an unforgotten injustice to her which I see now was so wrong.

Rachel Henly

Charlene

The corn is high in the field as I pass;
day lilies bloom and we have cut the grass.

They say it's spring but summers heat is felt;
I prayed for a friends today when I knelt.

Her life has changed, made a very quick turn;
there's spaces to fill, so much to learn.

God gives us life and takes it away;
we said good-bye to a friend today.

We gazed for a moment at what could be;
at the grave side we shared in reality.

Does it have meaning I ask of thee;
pieces of a puzzle is what I see.

This is the beginning of what is now;
each day unfolds and show us how.

The corn will be picked and the grass will grow;
the world will round and round still go.

Janice L. Jewell

A Dog's A Dog

Oh, he's a dog all right.
   He may act human when he cocks his head
   To show he knows just what I've said.
The little imp can seem so bright!

Or when he keeps on nudging me
   To toss the ball he's placed nearby
   So he can run, and fetch, and try
To show how clever he can be.

 he yaps, "It's time to eat!"
   And when he's finished, he barks twice more
Which means, "Thank you" for his meat
   And then he heads right for the door.

His human traits are shed like that!
And dog-like he's off to chase the cat.

Elizabeth Yokley Terrell

Blackened Rose

I came from down under as nothing, yet still there was something
   deep within me wanting to erupt.
Then, a mist touched me deeply and I knew loneliness no more.
There was an uplifting light beaming through the seed of my being,
   and I was no longer in darkness.
Suddenly, I was uplifted with feelings I have never felt, sights I
   have never seen.
There were more like me, and yet more waiting to
   become like me — a tangible beauty, awaiting my beholder.
Now, time has passed and I have outlived my stay.
When I return from whence I came, I will know I have lifted
   another from loneliness, darkness, and the depths of despair to
   an experienced beauty to shine upon others and uplift those
   not knowing or believing there is more than existence.
As you mediate on my words, accept and allow that which uplifts,
   to higher dimensions.
After all, that is how: I was, I am, and I will always be.
So, please don't see me as a blackened rose, but as an experienced
   beauty.
Because I accepted not only the mist, but all which my
Creator created me to be.

Robin D. S. Torres

My World

Life is wonderful, life is great
Only if we could live without the hate
In my world, there would be no guns, murder or drugs
Instead may it be filled with kisses and hugs
I wouldn't have to worry about going out at night
Or wether the homeless are tucked in tight
Every one would have homes decorated nice
There would be enough food to go around twice
Chicken legs and vanilla cones would be a feast
Not to mention Ki-lime pie and that is not the least
I think about it all the time
To live in a world filled with love, instead of crime
What would it be like to live in a word so fine
A world that I could call mine
It would be great to elimate
All this un-needful hate

Lisa Zannelli

Silent Strength

A moment bursts and a new beginning is born;
with the anticipation of a child,
with the passion of a lover,
with the peace of a bird in flight.

The virgin moment is as damp clay in the potters hand.
Untouched by the complexity of routine yet to be performed,
or the distaste of thoughts and actions from selfish hearts.

We are the potters, the caretakers, the mothers of our moments in time.
We have the talent to mold our piece of art,
We have the ability to guard and protect from the influence of the enemy.
We have the strength and compassion to nurture to maturity.

When fatigued, we weep, yet rise again.
When victorious, we rejoice, yet remain humble.
When touched, we respond.
When rejected, we heal.
We are the Conducters who orchestrate our moments of time which
   produce the music of our lives.
Thanks to be God, we are the softness of life,
   we are the fragrance to the rose.

Julie L. Best-Speckel

Untitled

Have you ever heard the line from an old poem that starts
"How do I love thee let me count the ways"
There are so many ways to love
you said you will take me as your wife
I don't want to be your wife
I would rather be your friend, lover, confidant,
soul mate, partner, and companion
why should I be your wife?
A slave is a wife and a wife will be nothing more than your servant
believe that my love for you is beyond words
beyond heights of our imagination
I will be strong, true and faithful to you
encouragement is what I will give you
never discouragement because life gives you that already
I am your safe haven from the world because I am not your wife
but your friend, lover, confidant,
soul mate, partner, and companion
before me you thought you knew love
since knowing me you know only true love and glorious happiness.

Irish Denise Brown

Raindrops

Channels of moonlight beam on the canvas of night
sprinkled with raindrops reflecting off starlight.
Sounds of the night through darkness beckon me,
uncertain restless spirits longing to be free.
In the distance the sound of night birds in flight
soaring through peaceful stillness so close, yet out of sight.
The paths trodden with truth and with lies,
the night is afraid, reflecting the essence of their cries.
Following the raindrops through the night air
wondering what place in time they will fall and where.
As the winds of life toss them up and then down,
they search for a place to fall to the ground.
Not out of defeat or of tiresome quest
just simply looking for bitterness rest.
So when you see the raindrops falling all around
strive to look up, and never look down.

Phyllis J. Hensley

Alone Today

Rain in my day,
Tears in my mind,
Sun in my eyes,
But my eyes are blind.
Rain in my sky,
Tears in my soul,
Sun in my heart,
But my heart's torn apart.
Dreams in my day,
Dreams in my mind,
Sun in my grey,
And grey in my way;
Alone today.

Marshall C. Oldenburg

Forever Friend

I can't remember when we met, it seems so long ago.
Or maybe it was yesterday, sometimes I just don't know.
It really doesn't matter when our friendship came to be,
for in my heart I know you're a Forever Friend to me.

The friendship that we share will never falter, never end
for God himself ordained the day that you became my friend.
Enduring strong the test of time, our friendship, too will grow
through all the struggles, joys, and tears that we will come to know.

And should there come a day when both our paths may need to part,
remember that I'll always hold your friendship in my heart.
There is no distance, space, or time could cause this now to end
for you are now and always will be my Forever Friend.

Lisa L. Raimer

Death

It chokes me to confront the underworld,
It rapes me of my sins.
Normality can't face repentance,
Death only just begins.

A rivalry between vitality and mortality,
Only a thrust to disappear.
Why struggle in this world of vengeance,
Entanglement just grants us fear.

Swinging on the gates of heaven,
Magnetized towards hell.
Swimming on the waves of truth,
Drowning on this deceit I can't repel.

A rampage of a fight to lose-
Only in the end.
curiosity of the concealed darkness,
In hades it will suspend.

Kelly Sims

Last Word

Last time we met I forgot to say I love you,
I didn't know that you would stay only for a moment,
We shared a laugh or two and off you went,
I knew you would always be there, any given day,
I knew just where to find you.

When I needed a friend you were there,
when my life was so unclear and didn't
Know if it would clear, you gave me strength to go on,
you told me you would
Always be there, if I should fail, you made me so sure that
nothing could stand in my way.

And I went on taking life for granted,
knowing that you will always be there,
I found strength in you because you were my brother,
my world and my life,
I loved you more then I love myself, but yet,
you took my breath away.

I prayed each and ever day hoping
that you would stay until the day came,
When you went away, yes you went away, oh I knew you would go,
I just didn't know when, you left and so did I.

You took my life in the palm of your hands and held on tight,
Yea you held on to ever beat until it was time to say goodbye, oh
I knew you said it,
But I never heard the words, Oh I know you try,
but I was so far away,
And you cried, oh you cried
but the time was near when your heart said no more,
Your last word was goodbye.

Rose Rena Wagoner

I'm Bare

I'm bare,
and I don't care.
I would put clothes on,
but their on the lawn.
I'd go to the store,
but it gives me a great bore.
When I run down the street bare,
the people stare.
I look in the mirror at my head,
"I'm bald," I said.
I went to a lady,
her name is Katie.
She gave me a wig,
and it was too big.
So there, I'm bare,
and I don't have hair.

Joy Welch

She Is Always With Us

You speak of our mother as if she is not here
She passed in 1980, from house to house she went
When she is needed brothers and sisters, you've forgotten where to look
For years our mother has stood here, by my side
It is she that guide us every way with God his help, his pride
You've scattered far and wide you see
You've shouted and you've screamed
Forgotten how to pray the way our mother, on bended knee
Just, stop a while and stand right here
Then look from side to side
Then tell me brothers and sisters, the place our mother hides
I know the roads we often took were not narrow but wide
We stayed up late, we read the books and often wore no disguise
We talked a lot and washed the pots after cooking for all that came
My brothers and sisters I brought up the rear I know she is right here
In each of us, she looks at us from eyes across the room
She left the house to all of us, as she stands right here in this room

Roxanne D. Saunders

This Lost Child

I have this little voice. It's here inside of me. It cries all the
time and screams at me. Molested as a child there is no soul to be.
Where do I go where do I run. I talk to God but is he there. I do
not know how to pray. I get on my knees and I ask for God as I plea.
Take me from here I do not deserve to be. If I should die today will
he open his arms? Will he welcome me home to say come with me child
I willshow you the way? Will he tell me to return to earth for my
time has not come? For my job on earth is not yet done. He has touched me
with his golden hands. My soul he has returned to me from the promise
land. He holds my hand and he walks by my side. For this I know I
will survive. He says I have done no wrong. For the one that has
done this to me. He will be be judged by him for no one else to see.
He says when my time has come for me to return. He will be there with
his arms open wide with all my loved ones by his side. For he
is the Almighty God and I was just the lost little child. These words
come true from my heart and soul. These words I speak have brought
ease cause now I can let go and say I am free.

Laura Hodges

The Forty-Eighth Of My Life

Where did the time go? Now this is my forty-eighth year, still a
single as the old strong oak tree.

A single woman, a single woman.

I had a dream to be somebody special to someone - faithful, patience,
and confident, I had hoped for a long time.

I will be forty-nine in December.
My mother has never reached forty.
My mother died at thirty, a dear heart woman - suffering of cancer
departing her only deaf child at the stage of trust. My mother was
sweet, her eyes were soft brown and she was faithful, patient,
and a g - o - n - e - r. Who am I now?

A single woman, a single woman.

I have made good grades, good performance in school, and achieve to
become a good person for you, Moma more than once. I have inherited
your brown eyes, hair, and visages. A single woman mirroring Moma's
presence more than once. I am single woman now.

A single woman, a single woman.

If it is southwestern, if it is the last destination in my mind, I am
moving out into the new venture. Let me come to it whole-hearted
and challenge and courage out of my mother's pride - into my own
into my very own. There goes a single woman...

Patricia A. Geraghty

Untitled

Composure to the untamed soul, wildly expedient to capture this golden
prize, a silver box. Profound and confronted with decision, yes I hear,
the trees never sang. They were not mean to, yet now this box gleams
so wonderfully with brilliance that I aguishly, thwarted back by divinity,
quake. In fear, like a sinner under a hollowed hand.
In anxiety, like a paranoid. Both, yet separate. Both, yet the same.
I miss the hand to hold, and the arms to caress.

To you I sing this sonnet, a ballad in eruption, to usher forth what
I inquire, of you, to you, for you. All of this a shinny new silver
box I was afraid to open. I see your light, let it bathe me and heal
my decrepitness, an impairment of broken me; I am too joyous for my
words. This trance of light pacifies a tormented theory, not too
justified by actuality; I am to follow the piper.

An elated tear now fills my eye, with you to thank; I'm closer to myself.
The child quakes, please rest once more. You're safe with her,
your peace overflows, relax your grip, what's done has past your lives.

David Kasch

Open Our Hearts

I was watching a show on television today
Asking myself how can people live that way
People that live halfway around the world
Twenty-seven thousand deaths a day of young boys and girls
Dying because of sickness and also starving
When I heard the number of deaths it was alarming
We complain that we have things so bad
The little they have is so very sad
They don't have decent homes or education
Isn't it time we did a little meditation
God we must find a way to open our hearts
Give these people a chance at a new start
Twenty-seven dollars a month to sponsor a child
Is not much to ask and very worthwhile
Lets open our hearts and learn how to give
So the less fortunate in the world will be able to live.

Barb Wood

Getting Silver

When you are getting old and silver and full of sleep,
and nothing by the fire, take down your photo book,
and slowly read and dream of the soft look
your eyes had once and of their shadows deep.

How many loved your moments of glad grace,
and loved your beauty with love false on true,
but one man loved the pilgrim soul in you,
and loved the sorrows of your changing face

And bending down beside the glowing bars
murmur, a little sadly, how love fled
And paced upon the mountains overhead
And he'd his face amid a crowd of stars.

Joanna Van Bilsen

Between Lines

A world is right between lines
between the lines of the good an bad
between the love and hate
between Jesus Christ and lucifer.
A world full of small thinks and big moments
of different words and same hearts
of different religions and looking to find the same.
A world with small caress and hard hits
beautiful poems and great books
big decisions and awful wars
of fights between brothers and superior races.
Between the lines of the History great man born
big times and sad disillusions
Between the lines of the 1900 and the 2000,
we saw from the light and also we can touch the moon.
Every one of us have his own line
and nobody now if is gone be history or be write.
For that only can say that I am gonna be between lines
maybe the lines of one book or a poem
or maybe between the lines of one heart.

Claudia R. Villanueva

Hell's Reign

A sphere of light is plagued with fright
and the world tosses and turns;

Fires glow from the pits below and the lights
reign expires;

Shadows dance to and fro and people begin to
shutter

Because the devil came to reclaim the reigns
of the world we've come to know.

Mathieu James Horula

My Mother's Face

I can feel my ancestors in my veins, my double-veined passageway,
where two world's travel together
I can see my children smiling, but they won't know like I do, what
it was that caused their grace
I know the distance that I sometimes feel, is all a part of a longer
journey. I travel to fulfill my mother's race.
And in her face, I see my children and my past, in her color lies
the truth about our caste.

So it's my duty, to let my children feel - our ancestors - in their veins
No matter where we live, or how it comes to pass.

Here I am to connect the wild vine,
Leaking the sap of monarch's hearts
Though bridges parted us, here I am to show that all the bridges will decay
After millions have traveled back and forth
The blood that seeps through miles and miles of earth will dry,
Has dried, and nurtures growth.
The decayed bridges will fall into the water and will float
The debris will reach my kin and I.
My children will sail upon the wooden ruins
That much like stonehenge stand, with grace
And the beauty in its old and solemn structure
Will reign before their eyes, to bridge the gap,
between, within a race.

Fola Rae

Night Angel

Shall I compare thee to an evening breeze
the moon and the stars can not even compete
On my face soft feathery wind does tease
An angel of God whose job is complete.

Back to the Lord she flies up to the sky
a feeling of peace settles over me
She delivers my prayer to heaven high
Alone in the dark, only now I see.

The sweet night air comforts many lost souls
holding their hands and stroking their hair
Picking up pieces and making them whole
Whispering melodies of eternal care.

Back to the Lord the night angel will fly
delivering my prayer to God on high.

Sheridan P. Smith

"Chicken Butt Pleasures"

Here sitting am I all alone in this dark, demanding some reasons
as to why I embark. Contemplating my woes alone in my chair,
occupied is my mind in deepest despair.
Taking for granted all that life's been to me, wondering why life's
been so dame mean to me. Precious time has been wasted tis awfully
a shame, wallowing in self pities mundane.

When o'er by the couch is my middle son Ryan, standing there watching
me biding his time. With nary a smile he speaks onto me, "Know what
Dad"? Are the words the boy speaks. To speak to this boy I have
not an inkling, no words do I have to match his bright twinkling.
Again I'm enraged at this awful indignity, blind are my eyes to what
he has given me.

Pouting and steaming I answer back, "What"! These two words merely
I got, "Chicken Butt". Young Ryan lit up like a huge ball of fire,
he got his old Dad this was his desire. Tis funny somehow when the
All Mighty comes round, and shows us our ills without even his frown.
In the fast lanes of life depressions are plenty, don't dwell on them,
swell on them, there's pleasures too many.

Pleasures like that, of a young girl or boy,
wishing too make old Dad their new toy.

Michael F. Minger

A Mother-In-Law's Lament

You raise two sons that are as close as one
You're proud, you're pleased your work is done!
They each take wives to complete their lives
Your only daughters seem to want to throw knives
Not at you, but at each other
Should they be allowed to come between a brother?

The grandchildren come you're pleased as punch
They fill your day they come for lunch
You're not allowed to spoil them rotten
So they move away and you're soon forgotten
The saying goes a son is son until the takes a wife
A daughter is a daughter all of her life.

It's sad to say that you meant to be
The greatest mother-in-law that the world has seen
But is it because your boys have grown?
That you now sit alone with your thoughts to roam
to a place or places where you're not known
And give up everything including your home.

Jan Brown

Casus Belli

(Latin that which leads to or justifies a war)
The fragments of belief are being swept
and collected by those who work for
contradiction. This evening it has once
again invaded the land of strength; it
somehow knows the areas of weakness
and doubt in the newly recruited army.
Death By Hanging!!!
Yells contradiction to all of those barely surviving in the
land of strength. In single file the army is directed by
all the means nothing in the face of reality. As the last
noose is tightened around the weakest soldier's neck, a
voice is heard, screaming without words, something about
growing. The army is inspired by this voice which cannot be
identified. Despite the army's areas of weakness, which
contradiction will mostly likely manipulate again, its
soldiers unite in one last attempt to free themselves. The
entire army, including its weakest soldier, unties the noose
that so nearly ended their survival, and fights to preserve
their pride. With another minor victory, belief's shattered
frame is replenished with a more solid interior, and the
army in the land of strength march toward home, dragging
their hostage contradiction by the groin.

Anthony Cortese

Little Miss Baylee She Touched Our Hearts

A tragedy happened in America's heartland,
People came running to offer a hand.

A picture that touched everyone's heart
It must be Gods way, to keep you apart.

As she is gently cradled in a fireman's arms,
She is now in a place where she will never be harmed.

As we search for the words to try to explain.
We all feel the sorrow; we all feel the pain.

As prayers are being prayed more often than daily,
They're being prayed for you; and the one you called
"Little Miss Baylee".

As you lay her to rest in your own special way.
I hope that you know you'll be together some day

Although this city is left in a mess,
Time will bring healing, and to you,
God Bless
Oklahoma 1995

Randy Anderson

Four Gifts From God

In all the business of life, I cherish the quiet times. My mind is cleared, my peace fills up, my focus is made right. God beckons us to meet with him. He loves to hear our chatter. It's then that we can sit with Him and tell Him what's the matter.

But today...I am just grateful, blessed, and full of joy. I see so clearly now his gifts to me...and two of them are my boys.

Justin...so careful and practical. Questioning all the time. Learning about the world through books, travelling in his mind. His empathy towards others who don't quite measure up, is something precious given from God, and it's God who will continue to fill his cup.

Sweet Adam...so full of life and light; 5 dimples on his face. The places he feels most close to God is the woods or mossy place. His energy is unending, and his smile will melt your heart. Soon he's off and running and will quickly leave you at the start.

Jim...my life mate; Gentle, Kind, Loving me through it all. Your unconditional love for me is worth much more than gold. As we continue down life's road, it's yours and God's hand I want to hold.

The fourth gift comes from God himself: Salvation...sweet and simple. A veil was lifted, my life was shifted, now on the solid rock I'll stand. Grace and love, peace joy, all from my precious Father's hand.

These gifts were wrapped so plainly, no fancy colored bows. Be careful you don't miss your gifts...ones only you can know!

Sylvia M. Flint

Caroline

A blinding wash of headlights, then the collision. It happened so swiftly and flawlessly, as though it had been rehearsed Countless times before. Flawlessly, the hideous charcoal black tires Rolled over my friend, crushing her stunned body beneath their impact. So that she couldn't even open her mouth to scream in a voice choked With horror, as her distorted face indicated she yearned to do. And I stood, sneakers rooted to pavement, paralyzed with a terror. I'd never known, my palms clammy with perspiration, shivering and shaking like An autumn leaf whirling in a fierce gust of wind to earth, knowing all The while that Caroline's scream would be trapped within the confines Of her throat forever. So I screamed that scream for her. My shrill, Uncanny cries bounced off the trees that thronged the deserted Street, the piteous wail of the ambulance shattering the thick, Suffocating blanket of silence enveloping us in its entirety. It Was I, not Caroline, who suffered. She had lapsed away blissfully into The land of no return, leaving me to endure the agony that had ravaged her Body only a fraction of a second, cascading over me in icy waves, Drowning me in its intensity, So that my body was the agony and the agony was my body.

Laura Baldino

Closer

I climbed the tree unto its top, to get so close to the sky. I wanted so to have a talk, just you, the angels and I. I've missed you since you went away, never completely knowing why. At times when I want to talk with you, I fight so hard not to cry.

The world seems strange without you here, yet its hard saying these things. The thought of when we were friends, and the relief those memories bring. Maybe if I climbed a hill, or a glacier unto its peak. Maybe then I'd hear angels sing, or maybe I'd hear you speak.

If not a glacier or mountain, or a rocket that soars through space. Maybe I could dream or imagine, the heaven that's become your place. Keeping your laugh in my mind, seems to keep you close at my side. I know with the view you have, there's no place on earth I could hide.

The world seems busy as ever, and there is always something to do. Yet working and helping people, seems to always remind me of you. Until that time when we meet again, or I climb high enough we can speak. I'll continue your job of helping, the hurt, the hungry, and the meek.

Tim L. Bradley

Unconditional Love

Life is a maze filled with unexpected surprise But none can compare to your arrival, my sweet When you noisily made your grand entrance Emotions were mixed with tears and laughter With pounding heart, my eyes fastened on ones so blue That startling gaze which joined our souls Silently voiced, we will forever be one I shudder with thoughts of my life without you The pain seems so deep, there's a wrenching of my heart With God's grace, you'll go on and find love untold And leave this old one to reminisce on days passed Keep me close to your heart my special baby boy This is one promise I fervently make Gram will always be there to share your fears or joy For in body or spirit, it matters not Your guardian angel I have vowed to become I have but one goal in your regards To watch over you and yours to be A grandma's love is the tie that binds Forever my darling, you and I.

Diane Lapointe

The Wedding Vow

In time we learn that love is synonymous with pain But in that we loose we must remember what we gain. To love and to hold till death do us part Is spoken by many, but only few speak from the heart. On this day we are among family and friends And I am here to say that I shall love thee to the end. I shall honour and cherish the woman I love For her innocence and beauty is a gift from above. She has put a sparkle in my eye that can never be taken away For she has become my wife on this special and sacred day.

Gord Hysen

The Empty Eternity

The field lay lonely and desolate, Brightly colored flowers rose high from the ground. The engraving on the stones expressed so much love but the emptiness below shone through. The sobbing and weeping could still be heard although no-one stood near for miles. I spoke, but unheard were my words of respect and gratitude for the men of my country. Though they fought for their families and fought until death, I know I'm to blame while this field brightly blossoms. The world turns around me and war is not over, as these men lay to rest in their empty eternity.

Fay Turner

Winter Dreams

A soft fire's glow with flickering light Abounding around us, enticing the night. Windows all frosty forming patterns so real Of snowflakes, landscapes and images we feel. By sheer magic nature transpires her wonderland to white So pure and serene, a season of delight! Skiers enticed by the hills and countryside Nothing seems finer, not anywhere worldwide. Only nature can provide such glorious grandeur Awakening our dreams and luring to her splendor This winter wonderland of dreams come true.

Elizabeth Zurba

Untitled

Beautiful moments for you, pulsation in black light shine.
A million bloody sheets for you, night black hole am I.

Shocked in and out of this plane, swirling down and up mundane,
I walk....
Mocked up and out of this scene, fighting with my enemy green,
I stalk....

Too much for me today as I stumble across the all encompassing marsh,
sucking in my legs as I walk, sucking up my words as I talk.
Please mind my mind.

Pulsating black swirl of chaos pulls at me while I am changing.
Something has permeated my blood and is transforming me.

I see me here and I see me sound. I see I hear and I know the ground.

I have come to the point of summarization; I feel for the moist minds
of my fellow companions. Cluttered are we all, in a state of lover
toss up confusion.

What do I want to work with? What do I want to do? I am feeling
helpless next to you....sparkling mingled synonyms and translucent
aching fields, mindless numbing chanting, thoughtless to my appeal.
Forgiving thunderous backbone of the world I used to feel. Thinking
of the silence, screaming for my surreal eyes heavy, muscles weak -
drained and contained, I can bearly exclaim. My senses spiral toward
my window to the world. Must I go back to reality?

Rachel Harvey

Baby

No words to say
No song to sing;
Just a little prayer to think.
Think about your child unborn;
the way she'll feel within your arms.
So close, so tight, so soft, so small,
Baby forever - afterall.
So tiny, so helpless, so dependent upon you;
You'll be the one to give her a clue.
Tell her about the days back when -
things were great, when there was no end.
Now all grown up and gone away;
Baby forever will always stay.
She'll stay close to your heart and in your mind;
Even after the day when all has declined.

Mary LoPresti

In The Hallway

(Big black stencils)
5-3-6
Green door
holes
chips
cracks
rusty lock
Black knob level with me
Through the keyhole
purple light
All is night and the day's searching
for its 16 hour place
The light green floor leaks out of the room
like an ocean to where I sit

Jon M. Kirkwood

Winter Dreams

A soft fire's glow with flickering light
Abounding around us, enticing the night.
Windows all frosty forming patterns so real
Of snowflakes, landscapes and images we feel.
By sheer magic nature transpires her wonderland to white
So pure and serene, a season of delight!
Skiers enticed by the hills and countryside
Nothing seems finer, not anywhere worldwide.
Only nature can provide such glorious grandeur
Awakening our dreams and luring to her splendor
This winter wonderland of dreams come true.

Elizabeth Zurba

Call Her What You Like She's My Mamma!

Call her what you like, she's my Mamma!
Clad in her Sunday best, Baby Molly,
Your Mamma's in the street dallying:
Batting her eyes, flashing her flesh,
Smothering her lips, rosy red in sweet lust.
Offering her body and her virgin purity,
To covet lusty men in town for a quick run!
And a fast buck off the most fittest gun,
to satiate your father's lethal crazy dram,
And fetch you, hungry child your cup o milk.
Cos' your father's lethargic and ever jobless
Slithering around the pubs a begging a dram.
Ignoring your mother playing the sinner!
Omni-present God sees and mercifully pities her.
The world cruel certainly ridicules her;
Failing to understand her pathetic plight
"Woman! We happy! You aren't the vicious sinner!
Your Good Lord certainly knows you better."
To carve your Mamma's name indelibly in "Gold"

Ratna Perera

All Love Comes Together....

Again within my dreams, is the magic of the mind,
closely hidden from the heart, the soul so often finds.
Seen inside this vision, a loving force does mend,
only in silent sleeping hours, I begin to comprehend.

The mind is but a chamber, gathering all our thoughts,
fills it up one by one, with emotions they have brought.
With nowhere else to tarry, in dreams they come along,
times like this I'm reassured, the fact they do belong.

It discovers that the heart, is lulled by whispers deep,
and sees not very far away, the soul in perfect sleep.
Soft beating from the heart, I suddenly begin to hear,
quiet soul suggests to me, there's nothing else to fear.

The soul and heart in love, reaches to touch the mind,
again in whispers deep within, forever they will bind.
Dreams formed within the mind, are guided from above,
together with the heart and soul, floats on wings of love.

All inspiration is brought together, forever shines as one,
cuddled by a lofty evening star and visions from the sun.
The mind provides a spiritual food, nourished by the soul,
where all love comes together, to reach its ageless goal.

Harold A. Sutton

Celebrate Love

Our lives are often full of strife, we can't find time in the day,
To thank those who have touched our life, to speak the words we pray,
When we're alone within our thoughts, we say what's in our heart,
These words don't often reach our lips, the sounds don't often start,

Too many times we've said goodbye, to special loves we know,
With never having found the time, to say much more than hello,
We take for granted, they will always be there as our friend,
Then in a flash, they can be gone, your life with them can end,

You'll reminisce of olden days, comparing now with then,
Wondering why your love has gone, and just what might have been,
You look deep down, within your soul, to taste the fruits of love,
A taste so sweet, but gone with them, now somewhere up above,

I have a love, who shares my life, and lets my soul be free,
Who bestows a love so few can give, who aids my heart to see,
She gives me strength, to fight the winds that bend my tree of life,
And stands steadfast through fire storms, this treasure is my wife,

This diamond is a world of coal, outshines the brightest stones,
And brings such light and brilliance, to a heart once all alone,
She knows her worth within my soul, I speak the words I pray,
I celebrate the love we share, before time fades away.

Kelvin G. Semper

Morning Sings

Morning brings to my Heart's window
Tender messengers of Love
Flying here on wings of Joy . . .
    Birds are Angels from above.

Precious birds so bright in color
    Fluttering in Rays of Sun
Bathing in Life's living waters . . .
    Bringing beauty and sweet fun.

I am graced to have you near
    Close enough to feel your songs
Songs of Light that touch the shadows
    Healing wounds I thought were gone.

Thank you for your tenderness
Thank you for your soft caress
For the Freedom in your wings . . .

    The gift of Life that Morning Sings.

Maile Orme

Just A Phase?

Can you look at yourself in the mirror and truly say there is
    nothing that you regret?
Did you ever do something that you wish you hadn't and now you
    cannot forget?
Did you blow your problems out of proportion until you could
    think of nothing else?
Did you sit around all alone feeling sorry for yourself?

It's part of the process; an amalgamation of someone else's plan.
You continue on with problems to compare yourself to human.
You put your faith in someone else.
But could you count on a helping hand?
Predict your own future? Stay in command?

Can you envision yourself in a world of happiness?
Could you picture a time in life when you would have no shame or cares?
Do you think it's hard to smile?
Do you think it's a little too easy to cry?
You might as well come to terms, because someday you're going to die.

The father turns to his son and answers, "It's only a phase."
And as his son's eyes stare through his words, things remain unchanged.

Nick Province

And All Becomes Anyways (A History Of History)

One may sat that it projects itself forward
(beyond the accusation of personification there is an
underlying gradation: the existence of a
past/present/future which has intentionally strived
to become whole).
Could we have molded the unforeseen?

All confusion comes out of an empirical womb, thrust forth
into an existential nihilism. Truly there is an absence of
dogmatic persistence.
meanwhile/God's vision/has/Be/come/blanketed/by our creation

And one may say that it has no design, no purpose.
However, there is continuity.
A continuous
confusion that consistently seeks confirmation.
Does it matter from where the procedure stems?
And all becomes anyways.

Andy Whyte

The Child

In the fields of imagination, I am a child wandering
Far from home.
My complex mind is mistakable and mislead,
He who see's me understands not of where I come from
Understands not of who I am or my meaning to the
World,
I need love and honor, I am but a child.

I am a child, helpless and unheard, reality is far from
My reach,
I am an invisible face, not to be seen by anyone,
My creativity shows, yet no one see's it,
I am honored by those who love and care, not those
Beneath my understanding.
Understand me, I am a child.

Zuzana Stranska

"On Memories"

With feelings mixed I often do recall
Events which like the tides would rise and fall.
And times in which were felt anger and pain
And others which provided worthwhile gain
Tough times there were that brought with them distress.
And in their wake came loss and mental stress.

Rich memories there are of friendships true:
Familial love? Concern and caring too
That helped dissolve vicissitudes of life
Thereby succeeding to dispel its strife.

Precious were friendships made and kept those days
Marked with goodwill displayed in copious ways.
Happy delightful times I still recall
Times when it seemed life mostly was a ball.

Eustace H. Reis

Faith

Faith is the light parting the darkness through which we walk
Faith is the language of love allowing our hearts to talk
Faith is the friend that comes in the dark of the night
To say be still, be quiet, everything is alright
Faith is a mystery we cannot comprehend
A gift from God that gives us life without end
A gift so precious that we must never lose it
Honour it and love it and never abuse it
Faith has no boundaries, knows no time
Everyone has access to this joy sublime.

Joan Day

Checkmate

Surrounded by the strong,
Sacrificed is the pawn,
For the glory and the game,
Closer to the goal, few men remain.
The Master decides,
The others live or die.
When their role is at an end
Nothing is said for them.
So selfish, not even the woman is spared
When what seems necessary is declared.
The Master decides,
The others live or die.

Mireille Bilodeau

Our Choice

Clear skies of blue — grey, smoky haze,
Bright countryside — gloom over all,
Full range of hue — a blur of greys,
Green forests wide — trees, stunted, small,
Gay flowers nod — vines cease to climb,
Birds wheeling free — eggs, sterile, spoil,
Pure rivers broad — streams choked with slime,
Geese in a vee — ducks drenched with oil,
Glad children's cries — men without mirth
Full moon's splendour — starless heaven,
A paradise — a hell on earth,
Nature's wonder — man's pollution.

Dianne Leavens

Spring

The melting snow of the mountains
swells the rivers and streams.
The brown earth is waiting,
to do it's mantle of green.

The birds on the fly-way are noisy,
as they return to the nesting ground.
They herald the Spring in their coming,
Oh what a joyful sound!

The maple pours forth her sweetness
There are smells and sounds everywhere.
The sugar bush is buzzing and active,
with the song of spring in the air.

There is hope in the buds that are
bursting,
on flowers, bushes and trees.
The love of God's recreation,
is felt in the sun and the breeze.

A. E. Vermy

"Far Across The Sea"

You're a gentle saint to me,
Always in my heart and thoughts,
Far across the sea,
Like whispers on a breeze,
Your love spreads forth endlessly,
Within the warmth of your letters,
Each word cherished reverently,
Keeping us together in harmony,
Forging an everlasting unity,
Wherever we shall be.

Eamonn James McGrath

The Rainbow

It sneaks up on you after a storm.

After such terror and wetness,
a beautiful thing. How can it be?

Rows of colors. Red and orange.
An arch across the sky.

So beautiful. So peaceful.
With a promise of reward if
you find its end.

Untouched by man.
Controlled by nature.

If rain brings you sorrow,
Think of a rainbow.
Arching across the sky.
When the rain leaves,
And the sun arrives.

Amanda Barker

A Garden Full Of Flowers

Once there was
A garden full of flowers
And I adored it
For it's intoxicating smells.
And in it's heart
Lies a beautiful fountain
Inviting to visitors,
Calming my pain
Was it a dream?
Or
Was it reality?
Life is too short,
I don't want to think about it.

Yasmin Moavenian

The Vision

The Attic,
A lonely dark place,
Cold and misty.
A sheet of night surrounds the room.
There is a crack in the wall
A visiting fearless light
Makes its way through.

In the corner is a chair,
Smothered with cob webs.
The soft wooden floor beneath it,
Rotted from years of neglect.
A spine chilling breeze;
The chair starts to rock.
A blurred image appears;
An old woman with shriveled,
White skin.

Darrell Lewis

Is It Alright To Cry

Is it alright to cry when you're all alone
and there's no one to turn to?
Is it alright to cry when you're lost and
you can't find you're way back home?
Is it alright to cry when you're very
confused
and you think you're going crazy?
Is it alright to cry, just to cry...
Cause you can't hold it in forever?

Joanne Steenhuysen

You Are A Dream

I believe no one deserves
a long stem yellow rose,
unless it's sent to some one
from a loving heart that glows.

Your glowing radiating face
with glittering eyes full of gleam,
set my mind into wondering,
"You're a star within my dream."

I've sent you fragrant flowers
meant to tranquilize your heart,
overwhelmed by your beautiful eyes
has invigorated my heart never to part.

I know you deserve much more
than a fragrant long stem yellow rose,
your gleaming eyes are burnt with yes
to my electrifying ecstatic propose.

You are the dream of my heart,
invigorating it with warming ease,
your special methodical character
refreshes me more than a daily breeze.

Gino Fantillo

My Daring Young Brother

When I was a boy, I swore I would be,
A man of justice a man who was free.
But my young brother when small he swore
That he would grow up and fight in the war
And sure enough the war arrived
Yes he fought he didn't survive
I told my sister a strong fighter was he
But what had happened just had to be
He was beaten by others stronger than him
She asked me why "he had no sin"
I explained to her about his death
So she'd understand he tried his best
She kept on crying and asking me why
Some men fight to make others die
It was his choice I told her he swore
His one ambition was to fight in the war.
Because of him and others like he
Our country is now what it wants to be
So November Eleventh we put away
To think of these men it's remembrance day.

Angela R. Jackson

A Poem To Remember You By

If only God can make a tree,
A mountain, you, a bird or bee;
I seek your pardon, but please see
The helplessness which lies in me
To transcribe you in black and white
Yet well reflect the spectral light
Of all those features: 'Twould but blight
The vision should I try to cite
A radiant goddess so much blest
With favor; but then you may rest
Assured that minds will linger, lest,
In retreat from the manifest,
They lose the rapture which is there.
Now having seen, how could one dare
To desecrate, attempt to share
That artist's craft who made you fair?

Robert Hutchinson

October Ninety Five

The photograph was not crystal clear:
a shade visible was only after all
his head very small asleep in a deadly
evidence:
without any special consciousness
tiny face turned to the left in numbness
forever stranded in a shadow of lead
letters:
there was no end to the boy's deadened
apparition...

While nauseous during the time
of that total warkill
    of intestinal tearing apart
one desires only to be able to correct
    to be free and disappear
together with the appearance of exile
where the whole face of a boy becomes
cracked:
a splinter was left there
    at a dead place of divide:
entanglements of bitter battle rise
    killing death of the little innocent one
        graying nothingness of one's world
conception
marks the broken thread of silent collapse...

Zoran Jungic

The Toy

It sat on the dew damp lawn
    - a silent reminder
of a sweet life lost, gone

A worn toy, broken and bent
    - from the time
it was loved by a total innocent

Brown glass eyes and matted hair
    - an ugly beauty
this favorite playtime bear

A woman appeared, picked it up
    - with silent, sad face
stroked it as one would a pup

She carried it as far as the shed
    - to a tiny chair
beside books many times read

Left alone, the bear cried
    - for happier times
before the child died....

Barbara Oswald

What Is Art?

Art is a thing no one can explain
A world of paint that is insane
Splashes of colour everywhere
For you and for me so we can share
You can make - believe and dream
A time for everyone so hand to be seen.
You can't always say what the painter is saying
But you can imagine what the painter is playing
There is different kind of art
Like people, sculpture or even a chart
So when you see an art form and
your friend thinks something else of it —
    Don't be surprised.

Natalie Pastuszak

"Only In Passing"

Only in passing shall we see
A smile that use to be
By the wayside this child stands
Trapped inside a man

Look not this way
    For he is not here
The one you seek
    Has gone away

For where you stand
    He stands no more
And what you are
    He use to be

So only in passing
Give a smile
For yesterday is gone
And tomorrow - shall never be

George V. Lonsdale

Interconnectedness

The bright sun shining, my body warming,
A soft wind caressing my skin, blowing,
Sprinkles of water drops easing thirsty lawn,
This day will fall to rise again at dawn.

Your warm beautiful smile, my eyes shinning,
Your soft voice, warming sound caressing,
Thoughts of you sprinkles joy, memories
    quenching water,
When we say goodbye knowing later,
    never ever after.

The multitude colored flowers enhancing joyfully,
To give life in softness, harmoniously,
Trees create stability, a sense of security,
All will soon sleep to rise again in beauty.

Your laughter enhances how wonderful you are,
The softness of your words give life by far,
Your willingness give security and dependableness,
Thoughts of you, a sense of closeness,
Memories of you, a sense of
    nterconnectedness,
Although the miles separating, the next
    always lies in happiness.

Lise Tremblay

The Chimney's Child

Against a yawning, spreading blue carpet,
A strange spirit cunningly coils
Swirling and dancing beside its bright blanket,
It entices its background to move as a foil.

It narrows then stretches
It swells and it curves
It reaches and touches
The intention it serves.

The clever stream remains unbroken,
As it ever curls and puffs
In places fades, but leaves a token,
Of its endless misty touch.

On, it mysteriously ascends and sweeps
Gracing the very blanket that praised -
A smoky pillar that will not sleep
The chimney's child soars and plays.

Deborah Collins

Oddly Inspired

Red and white roses days after they die.
A thick dark hurricane with a pulsing red eye
Storm clouds just before they rain and pour
The slow high-pitched squeal of a
squeaky door
A soft fiddle melody that's played slow and shy
Sweet gentle tears from a child that cries.

Warm summer days, cool winter nights
Eating pizza, watching my neighbors fight
A wedding, a funeral, a rained out parade
sorting clothes in laundry day.

Racism, war, jobless, homeless,
Hatred, fear, death, prejudice.
Pollution, ozone, destruction, oil spill,
Endangered, extinct, development, landfill...

In a world where peace only comes from gun fire
it's no wonder I'm so oddly inspired.
To Ray

Rebecca Champion

Tomorrow

There she stands,
Abandoned,
Destitute,
Searching.

Please someone give me your hand,
Walk beside me, hold me.
Still there remains an empty shadow.

Your ignorance shatters my heart,
And my mind filled with wisdom and new
ideas.
A deep black hole threatens to consume
my destiny.
Unfounded worries,
Unsettled disputes,
All to be forgotten.
As the sun lowers it's entrancing head,
Deep below the earth's surface,
There is hope,
As tomorrow is the day for dreamers.

Hayley Blundell

Rwanda

Dark
Afraid
Alone
Lost forever
Cold
Hungry
No home
No parents
No reason
To live
No reason
To fight
Mad
Angry
Hurt
Scared
Momma
Daddy
Why?

Jennifer Klassen

Society Turmoil

All good is mine
All fame is mine
All glory is mine
All wealth is mine
All success is mine

All bad is yours
All defame is yours
All rags are yours
All losses are yours
All failures are yours

By lost in materialism
We lost ethicism
We lost humaneness
We lost glorious past
We lost our images

How hypocrite we became
We see us in global society
We can overcome vices
By turning impossible to possible
Justice equality is all that matters

Ikramul Haque

Angels

Angels come in
all shapes or forms
To help us through
our tragic storms.

They come to us.
at the time of birth.
They go with us
when we leave this earth.

They come to us
in our prayers.
to guide us from
our yester years.

They are our saviours
that we know.
For I will meet my angel
when it is my time to go.

They come from
heaven up above
to guide us through our lives
with happiness and love.

Deanna L. Valberg

Think Wise

Always think to be wise
And be wise through your life
Never think of being unwise
Or you will regret likewise

The world is full of deceit
To ponder you should not forget
Or beguiled you will be yonder
And its consequences you will have to suffer

A thinking being God made man
Superior of all His creation
Endowed to be wise and productive
through life
So always think wise and live wise.

Pamela Jane Guevarra

Remembrance Day

In Flanders Field the war men lay,
All their wives and families pray,
They lay down where the poppies grow,
All their grave stones row by row,
Everyone remembers them by fighting in war,
All their families sad and torn,
And that is why we always pray,
Because we now have Remembrance Day.

Kim Schmutz

A Dream

I think of us together
alone on a mountain
so far away
with soft candle light
romantic music
Holding and loving one another
in front of the fire

Take me away to this place
of love and beauty
Where we can forget the past
and forget our problems
where life can be happy
if only for a short time

Let me hold you and love you
Till you can stand no more
Lets walk and talk in the moonlight
and make plans for the future.
Lets be free
and happy at least for now
I am yours and you are mine
and together we'll just fine.

Laura Phillips

Jenny's Prayer

The pain is mine alone
   all the words have crossed my lips
in silent agony... split dimensions
Spirit, sweeten the shame that is not mine;
   tears to wash away my souls intrusions

Barriers of pride and confusion of emotion
   twist my reality
Share what!, I say in the misdirection of my life
Deserving and worthy I fight the chains
   that bound me from infinite love
Keep safe my heart, ...connect your strength
   and power with light

Make truth for this tormented child who
   shares with love
Gratefully, I receive what you offer —
   understanding and care
Guide my progression of bended will to taste
   the serenity you have created
Teach me the acceptance of life...
   which was given to me

J. J. Tremblay

Untitled

The sun does not see me
   away one's own light
The night does not see me
   away one's own darkness
How to conquer
   light and darkness
And become present.

Nada Bundalo

The Girl And The Woman

You are alone in the field,
Alone at harvest, alone in song.
Your only company is a chorus of crickets.
They grieve with you.

This summer, too, will pass, and many another,
And you will be alone.

Under your silk shirt you wish, you say,
To preserve your breast untouched.
Ample like ripening quinces,
Rising like the waters of spring.
In your voice the security of fire.
Probably from the colour of your face.

You lift a golden sheaf of wheat
And fall to the ground on well-rounded knees.
Knees anxious for yearning.
You do not care for anyone or anything.

Summers will follow summers and harvests will pass,
Harvests of wheat and youth.
Do you wish to be visited by flocks of fireflies?
Will you greet them and send them away
with a song?

Mustafa Jahic

Your Pain

There is a pain I cannot feel,
   Although to you it's very real.
To lay one's son down in the ground
   And no more hear his precious sound.

I've felt the pain of loved ones lost
   But there's really been no personal cost.
Grandparents, friends, and neighbors die,
   And pass on to their home in the sky.

I've felt the pain of friendships turned sour,
   The rejection that comes hour by hour.
Loneliness begs to be allowed in,
   And in my anger I strive not to sin.

I've felt the pain of unborn babies gone on,
   The sting of death had certainly won.
They're sitting secure on Jesus' knee,
   And someday He'll place them in my
arms to see.

I've not felt your pain of such great sorrow,
   Understanding it is as far as is tomorrow.
To have never know Derek; never got to say 'hi',
   Makes it even harder to share your
heart's cry.

Joanne F. Branscombe

'Thirsty Girl'

You've left me all thirsty
And I'm dehydrated with you,
I've got terrible pains in my chest
And my skins turned a permanent blue.
You've bitten all of my nails
And I've chewed the left side of my lip,
I've got to stop picturing you
Touching that place with your finger tip.
You've scarred all of my head
Where you beat my mind up till I cried,
I've got a permanent headache now
Because when you said all of that, you lied.
You've changed who I am
And I'm quite glad that you did that to me,
Yeah, you've left me all thirsty
But perhaps I always wanted to be.

Jacqueline Harrison

Our World

As much as there is hate
And anger and maybe even deep emptiness,
There is always a sense of forgiveness;
Thou very small and far below
It is never to be unnoble
To the understanding of the situation
Or the person or maybe even life's intentions.

As much as there is hurt
And pain and maybe even crumbling love,
There is always that tiny bit of caring;
Thou only a thing mist to the real waterfall
It can hold and cover the unintentional thoughts
Or the knowledge or maybe even
destiny's hurtful hand.

And as much as there is depression
And tears and maybe even new cancer-
ous marks upon the soul,
There is always that translucent particle of hope;
Thou lost in the swirling dust of pain
It can still fall upon the withering target
Or the society or maybe even tomorrow's
forgotten future.

Peter J. Ertl

Untitled

Today she takes a husband
   and he takes a wife
   Today is the day
   of a beginning new life

With family and friends
   all gathered around
To share this occasion
   and a new love found

When times get hard
   as they often do
We'll be thinking
   of all of you

Laughs and smiles
   will come to mind
We'll put our troubles
   far behind

Thank you all
   for sharing this day
Together, forever
   come what may.

Cecil S. Storring

Who Cares

There's a lot I wish, could change,
And lot's I'd like to rearrange.
People starving, children crying,
And before their time, people dying.

We see their faces on TV,
One Mother with her family.
Bet they're wondering if out there
How many people, really care!

It's always certain that their need.
Is down to someone else's greed.
And when we look into the past.
We never thought that it would last.

All this need, it should end.
Because on each other we all depend.
And who is different from the rest,
As we keep saying "We do our best!"

Jeff Hobson

"Salute To Robert Burns"

As long as Scottish hearts beat true,
And living voices sing,
No other Scotian name so true,
Is cherished like a king.

Burns taught us all to brothers be,
That everyman is great —
   (EVERYMAN)
That love - not money counts you see,
For God decides our fate.

His songs and poems taught of life,
A love of nature and of God —
A dream of peace and not of strife,
And freedom on each sod.

As long as Scottish bagpipes play,
And Earth does steadily turn;
We'll meet with "Auld Lang Syne" this day,
To honour Robert Burns!

Helen Penney

Stopping By The Wall

On A Snowy Evening

The spider looked to the abyss
And looked past it and looked at this:
A surface that looked liked a start
That yet seemed both strange and amiss.

The strand shot out as if a dart;
He felt success was close at heart.
The strand stuck tight against the wall
Then it just fell and fell apart.

The spider's failure cast a pall
He tried again, not sad at all.
He saw it cling and saw it hold
And saw the middle of it fall.

A closer surface seeming cold
Caught the last web, which from it lolled;
The spider inched with movements bold
Unto the breach, three times all told.

Richie Laskaris

Lonely Night

The sky is profoundly purple
And my heart is deeply blue
The spooky moon plays back the memories
To the day I first met you

My gracious eyes without its sight
And there you are appearing again tonight

Words that have meant to be
Long lost and forgotten
And now the shrieking wind carries back to me

My sorrow tears flooded heavenly
Fulfilled the emptiness of the vast hungry sea

I sit here all alone
And catch the cold in the air
Listening to the dark night cry
The voice that was once there

Jessica Trinh

MY GREATEST XMAS
FOR YOU, AND ME

My greatest Xmas wish, = for you and me
And people, = of every nation,
His for peace, and happiness,
No matter what their station

How nice to think, = the tools of war
Could = at last, be vanished
And that evil, word of "slaughter"
Abolished, instead, to lavish, all our love,
Upon = your "son or daughter"

Thus we would have paved the way
For the "rising generation"
It's now, = their turn, to show full
admiration
For tears, = blood and sweat,
Which paid that heavy price
So costly, and, so cruel.

Never let us have to fight
Again "that deadly duel"
So let us hope, and, "plan and dream"
"For that light" = at the end of the tunnel"
Will = "one day gleam"

James Grace

Grandma Remembers

She rubbed so gently the hard engraved name,
And quietly she cried out in pain.
The lonely tears softened her eye,
For she remembered the day Grandpa did die.

A young lad called to serve his fellowman,
He gave his life fighting to save his land.
The wall is a grim reminder of the price he had to pay,
So his family could enjoy the peace they have today.

"Please wear your poppy proudly," Grandma said,
"And pause to think of the blood that was shed."
She sadly walked away from the wall,
Remembering the soldiers who gave their all.

Joanna Boone

I Walk Alone

I walk alone
And see myself
As a pebble on a beach,
thrown into a sea where none can reach.

I walk alone
And feel myself
Being swept into a tide against my will,
While within my heart lies still.

I walk alone
And touch myself,
Finding a body stripped and bare,
And in the touching, finding nothing
there.

I walk alone
And taste myself,
The bitter, salty taste of tears,
That will wash away the sadness of the
years.

I walk alone
And hear myself
Talking to a God I know is there,
Showing me His Presence everywhere.

Cathryn Haywood

Anthea

In violet hues
and shimmering gold,
walks the goddess,
in peace.

Her footsteps
are light,
her garment
is the old forest.

Where she steps
grow flowers
dazzling in light,
myriad colours,
glowing with beauty.

Gary Trevor Barton

Speyside Splendour

The deer are in the pinewood
and the eagle soars above
the purple heather is blooming
all around this place I love

I Hear a piper playing
a lament on the pibroch
and I see the wild trout rising
on a lonely highland loch

I watch the evening sunset
as I stroll amongst the braes
I see the river sparkle
when caught by the suns rays

I look across the heather
and see the wild grouse shy and still
i look above the see the hawk
as I hear his cry so shrill

I see the snow capped mountain
so rugged rise above
I see the mist that shrouds these glens
of this dear land I love

Av Carlin

Justice

The Heavens were opened up
And the rain was pouring down,
The thunder was crashing
And lighting flashed all around.

The sky was all lit up
With a brilliance all its own,
The hanging tree casts its shadow
As the man hung there alone.

The jury were huddled together
Scared of what they had done,
Of how they had found him guilty
Trying to protect someone.

The jury were huddled together
As the thunder crashed all around,
And the rain continued to pour
As the lightning struck them down.

The jury had found him guilty
Of a crime he didn't commit,
The Lord had found them guilty
And sent them to the pit.

Dennis Ripley

Reflections

Too little time for dreams
    And to make them materialize;
    Not enough time for others;
Such happiness we could realize.

Too little time for friends;
    To see their countenance in gladness
    Wreathe with smiles galore;
Such thoughts bring only sadness.

Too little time for those we love
    And hurry home to greet;
    Somehow, we must ask why
All must ever hurry, with restless feet.

Take time to dream, to plan;
    Then bring these into view;
    Take time to build a sturdy house,
With foundations to keep it from becoming askew.

Take time for friends and family we love so much;
    These are the precious memories
    You will, time after time, recall,
And, change forever, the lives of those
you try to touch.

Elizabeth King

Our Village

Those meadows and heaths
    and velvet hills,
Enclosing that village, nestling deep.

Those timbered cottages 'round the green
Gables and mullions and latticed bays:
Ageless charms of Tudor days.

"The Bell and Dragon", that cozy pub,
With its old thatched roof
    and its swaying sign,
Beckoning locals to the brewers pint.

That tweedy gent with pipe in mouth
    and dog at heel,
Bending his way down the curving street
    to tea and scones and crony chat.

Bursts of a lazy, drowsy sun
    eclipsed by shadows of weeping clouds.

This our village:
Just a tiny spot on the English map.

Connie Laurent

Hope

The tides of peril
are on the rise
in this fatal chain
of consequences
my thoughts of you
have never ceased
they just threw me
into the trenches
of hardship
while the turbulence
of life goes on
standing alone
on the edge
at this midnight darkness
like the mourner I am
waiting for the sunlight
it seems forever

Fred Neubacher

Missing You

I look in my magic mirror,
and wonder where you are.
I miss you and your smiling face.
You'd bring me when I was down.
I'd never worry because you'd always be around.
But now your gone, the only one,
I ever really depended on.
So, I guess now it's time,
to depend on myself.
I go on every day with,
my new friends, but I never stop
thinking of you!
You were once there physically,
but your always there mentally.
Because I love you!
And love is never forgotten,
even till the day I die.
Your the true friend in my heart,
and I will love you,
Till death do us part.

Allison Fontaine

Love Unspoken

When I think of all the time that past
And your heart that may be broken,
I question why time past so fast
With words yet not spoken.

Was my love ever questioned
Within you tear-dropped eyes?
Was there a slight suggestion,
Before evergreen goodbyes?

Perhaps the truth lies within
A heart that's just a token,
Someday we may begin
To speak of Love Unspoken.

Daniel O'Brien

Passage For Nana

All life's events,
Are best with love.

A long life,
In it's turn.

A heart of courage,
A good life lived.

She who supported,
Our passages.

We support hers,
Held in our arms.

The circle of love,
A life complete.

Celebrate the life,
Cherish the memories.

Bill Aaroe

Memories

He meant the world to me!
But now he is gone.
To live in heaven
Where the skies are always blue
I miss him so very much I
And I know someday soon
We will be together again
Under the big shinny moon.

Loraine Crevier

"True Friends"

About my friend, I must tell you,
As for his appearance - not too lively I am afraid,
As for his temper - he doesn't have any,
Love - he abounds with it,
Freedom - I write what I please,
Listens - to everything I say
Affection - I have nothing more to ask for.
Name - well, you might call him a "diary."
I know him as my friend.

Prashanth Sabeshan

The Grass Is Greener?

Can you see them coming towards us
Are they coming to get us out
can you hear them calling
And can you hear them shout?

They want us to go in that lorry
There behind us pushing us on
We're frightened and huddle together
When the ramp shuts out the sun

The noise is loud and confusing
When we're pushed into a pen
At the market where people are shouting
And we're hit by big angry men

Somebody's bidding to buy us
But what do they want us for
Are we going back into a field
What's on the other side of that door?

Why did they send us to market
When we were happy where we were
Still, maybe this place will be better
Maybe the grass will be more

Carolyn Reed

Where Are They?

Where "are" the young men?
"Are" they on the blocks smoking drugs?
"Watching" the young ladies,
"take" the first step out.

Where "are" the young men?
"Are" they in jail?
"Hoping" that their mother,
Would "post" their bail.
Are they to "busy" sitting at home?
Are they "afraid" of "positive" responsibilities?

When would they "wake up" to reality...?
Where are the young men?
Tell me,
"Please,"
Where are they...?

Cowayne Comarcho

Untitled

Ambiguity sustains belief
Between these four walls,
The telephone's silence
Echoes stark rituals
Of intent
And I swallow my diet
Of desperation
And cold coffee comfort.

Robert Ellis

Superman/Batman

Whirling sounds
Around me
Flashing sounds
Astound me

I am falling down
Down to Emptiness

My head
Is spinning
My mind is turning

Around, around
To subliminal rest

My eyes are staring
My thoughts
Are sharing

Terror, terror
Beyond conquest

And as I reach before me
I feel, I see, with Glory
The end

Gord Fralick

The Old King

Long ago from a mere seedling he rose,
As a king rises above his subjects, he stood.
His limbs reaching for heaven itself
Staunchly, stubbornly, determined
To out shine all earthly features
The others were dwarfed by his obvious supremacy
But all kings grow old, his limbs
Droop like decaying flowers.
He no longer proudly challenges the clouds,
He has become hunched, an old man.
A new prince sprouts.
He dethrones,
The crown is lost to an arrogant youth.
He is grand just as old king was during
better times.

Cindy M. Ferguson

The Victim Of Rape

The weather was cold outside
As cold as her inside
She looked at herself in the mirror
Thinking back about her last horror
For that night she was kidnapped
And was brutally raped
She felt a slap across her face
And couldn't meet with anyone's gaze
Tears welled up in her eyes
Disgusted and humiliated she was
Outside the ground was soaked with rain
As she cut herself deep into the vein
What had she done to deserve this pain?
The hurt was left with her remains.

Isabella Gunawan

"Clouds"

Fleecy cream clouds like frolicking lambs
cover the landscape as far as eye scans
Chased by the wind over meadow and dell
Casting a happy, quite magical spell —

So much we perceive brings joy to the heart
Clouds, birds and trees all play their part
Wondrous and yet majestic the plan
"The fly in the ointment" most often is "man"...

Ralph E. Sullivan

The Knight's Quest

On a night as dark
as dark can be,
in a swamp that's
damp and cold,
A soldier rides
The morning mist,
His armor shining gold.
Three hundred years
He's rode the night.
Brave soldier of the past,
upon a steed of glistening black.
Long years ago a vow was made,
To a maiden young and fair,
that he'd return
from distant wars,
and they there love would share.
But lost upon a bog so dark,
where never the sun does shine,
He searches for a way to her,
so rides his love so blind.

John Shaw

What Will The Future Bring?

As we walk hand in hand,
As I gaze into his passionate eyes,
lurking his sorrow,
Will the feelings, I'm feeling,
last 'till tomorrow?
What will the future bring?
As he holds me tight,
And promises everything to be alright,
I think...
What will the future bring?
As we're on the floor, dancing to our song,
I wonder what will the future bring?
And as he whispers the words I love you,
My brain is scattered, is this a dream?
Or really true?
We continue walking hand in hand,
While I try to understand,
What will the future bring?

Jennifer Cuda

The Day The Wind Slept In

Nothing happened, all about was still.
As if motion had suddenly lost it's will
What peace, what tranquility,
what effortlessness and ease
As if all that man believe he'd lost.
Was mysteriously retrieved.

Could this be the final answer.
After many years for praying.
Or just a joke, the scientist were playing.
Could it be that all,
had travelled the required distance.
Or could it be that effort,
had surrendered to resistance.

Amidst a sea of external calm
Curiosity stirred within, greeted by
arousing thoughts,
Some how something was missing.
Compelled to action but no where to begin.
It was never noticed, that day,
the wind slept in.

Anderson Kellman

Raindrops Teardrops

I like to watch the rain
As it hits the ground
It makes me feel so good just
seeing it come down
But the raindrops in your eyes
I don't want to see
Because the more I see them
falling the more its hurting me
So dry your eyes lets go outside
and walk amidst the rain
Lets hold each other closely
while it washes away your pain
Now don't you feel much brighter
watching the rain hit the ground
You must admit its nicer than
seeing yours come down
Raindrops teardrops they both are
very small but those little drops
they hold so much I guess that's
why they fall

Ben McKay

Phantom Quest

I seek you, friend,
As seek I must,
On lonely moor,
By hedgerow dust.

The echoed call
By all was heard,
For you, my friend-
A phantom-word.

Within your self,
The wise have said,
"This whore-phantom
In death has bled.

The pregnant pain
Of stillborn quest,
Shall ever lie
Within your breast".

But now. "That Night -
No dream at dawn!"
Goodbye Phantom!
Unless reborn.

Daniel H. Pinner

Flowers Will Bloom In The Spring

Delivered from his sterile home
Beneath his mother's breast,
With lungs in rage and fury,
His child's birth pains could rest.
And the newborn infant cried.
Betwixt and between the child and the man
The youth in life's games rejoiced.
But as in all games, only one had triumphed,
The other, rejected, had lost.
And the heartbroken youth reclined.
The man was born from a woman's smile,
From her caress and adoration,
And with loving heart and tear-filled eyes,
He marvelled at his wondrous creation.
And the man stood erect with pride.
Perennial seeds were planted,
Some scattered by autumn wind,
They'll be nurtured beneath snow
covered valleys
And flowers will bloom in the spring.
And the old man weathered a sigh.

Anna M. Hefele

Dad

He looked down upon her small eyes,
and loved her
As she grew he would visit her at night,
and tell her bedtime stories.

Stories about Jesus and God's love
His voice was gentle and kind
His discipline was strict and fair
He knew how to say sorry,
and always showed his loved
For his little girl, he would give all he could
Many years passed, and the little girl grew up
As a teenager, she would go jogging with
Dad, and many talks they had.
As a young adult, she was now her Dad's friend
She became a nurse, as he had been her nurse
He taught her compassion, love and understanding
For her Dad, she will give all she can
She is his little girl forever...

Tammy Anderson

The Internecine And Belligerent Fascism Of ...

The Pine tree snappeth
As the Wind blows
The darkness loometh
As the Stream flows

Entropy shall lightly cometh
Lurking remaineth eternal Hate
For the claw o' Strife is offered
Wherefore not embrace this Fate

Laugh my dearest
The Bombast shan't last
Enjoy thy Purple
Ere the Final Blast

... One Quill here halteth

Adrian T. Mucalov

The Derelict

Have pity on yonder human desolate
Battered about like a bell bouy
on a rockbound coast
The soft, mourning eyes
The unkempt beard,
The slouched bearing of defeat
Make me want to cry out
To a fellow wayfarer
A rover like myself
But one who has run into far stormier seas

Is this an idealist end?
The fleeting refuge of a park bench,
A sailor's crib.
The greasy, raucous,
vulgar life of the poor?
Was this spectre
Once a youth with hope,
A full heart over flowing
Toward fellow man,
Laughing at life
in the pleasing complacency of youth?

Robert R. Flanagan

Last Cry Of Autumn

gone to yellow, leaves
flailing they shout against death
leave skeletons stand.

Carol Ritch

Memories

It's one thing to be together
Being apart is another.
At one time you are holding me in your arms
The next moment we are so far apart
we can't even hold hands

Our hearts break each time we say good-bye.
We long to be together.
Your heart belongs to me and
mine to you all.
Maybe someday we will be together.
Our hearts will mend.
Together we will be one again.

Loretta L. Rector

The Tree Is Me

The Woman in the tree

The air is cold and snow is falling
Blustery winds move the trees
Heavy laden with the might's accumulation
I gaze into the fuzzy distance
The movement is as if the trees are dancing
To the music of nature's winter song
One stands out from the rest
It resembles a woman
She does not hear the music though
Her movements are of stress
The weight she carries is heavy
Try as she might she can't stand straight
With each new gust she bends deeper
To the point of fear
My heart races as I watch the will to survive
The tree is me

Evelyn Gapp

Second Life

Seductive silence of sleep,
bodies engulf in satin sheets.
Eyes close, breath grows close,
as you surrender with solemn hope.
The perfect life lies beyond
the power to answer all that calls.
Glide the wind through the clouds,
sail the sea, control the ground.
Be the prince of distant lands,
to be the knife in a killers hand.
Feel the love of one so dear,
as you pull her near.
Gentle embrace, sound and sight:
Buzzing cuts like a knife;
a custom sound of the device
that wakes you from your second life.

David Pope

Reach Out

When a problem is hard to bear
Bring's sadness, despair,
Remember I care,
Reach out, I will be there.

When life is found to go awry,
Giving cause to cry,
Dry the tear from your eye,
Reach out, I will be close by.

When you feel alone,
From that moment on,
You won't be;
Reach out, you will find me.

James Innes

Fragile

The fiery halo up above
Brings a memory of that day
The forbidden love that began
With the single rose I gave to you

Our song ended too soon
It ended with a whippoorwill cry
But the music in me never died

I know you sleep peacefully
Our song lives on in my heart
I hope to see you again someday
When we may dance to an angel's chorus

Mike Darling

Changing Seasons

Spring time appears, birds singing,
  Buds forming,
    Love arrives...

Summer at last, flowers bloom,
  Water trickling,
    Promises made...

Warm moonlight evenings, long walks,
  Campfires crackling,
    Kisses under the stars...

Fall brings colour, mounds of leaves,
  Cool crisp air,
    Feelings begin to fade...

Winter winds chill, snowflakes fall,
  Beauty freezes,
    A heart soon forgotten...

But Spring will slowly break free,
  Thawing the soul,
    Warming the heart,
      Unveiling a brand new love...

Karen Halls

Unwise Eyes

Gazing up I notice
but a portion of the sky,
yet as vast as my stare may spread
across this azure heaven,
'tis hardly anything which my mind can see.

Looking down I cradle
innumerable grains of sand,
and I cannot count what bit of shore I hold,
neither can my eyes fathom
how many stone fragments span this
oceanside.

Gazing over I see
the remains of an eaten apple.
Thoughtfully staring at what was left behind
I see a lonely seed.
Tragically, my simple eyes cannot see a tree.

Looking at you I ponder
the countenance you possess.
I know the imperfections of your outer shell,
but my unwise eyes
can never see all that you are inside.

Lorretta Holmes

I Wish...

I wish that I could cry
but I have no more tears
I wish that I could laugh
but I hold too many fears
I wish that I could sing
But no one will listen to my voice
I wish that I could be happy
but I have nothing to rejoice
I wish that I could love
but you have gone away
I wish that you'd come back
but I'll never see that day
I wish that I could share
but I haven't got a friend
I wish that I could live
but I've finally reached my end

Rizalyn Reyes

Special Someone

I've known you for only a while
But it feels like its been years
The way your eyes sparkle
The way your smile lights up the room
It makes me realize how much you mean to me
Whenever I catch your glance
I'm overcome by emotions I don't
understand
I long for our time together
When we can share all our thoughts
A sweet stolen kiss
A light brush of hands
It all unleashes emotions
That are too strong too deny
I hope that as time passes
these feelings glow stronger
Feelings of happiness
That together we share

Michelle Edwards

The Humming Bird

A busy little humming bird,
Comes early every dawn,
Like a tiny helicopter,
In my garden and my lawn.

With her rapid moving wings,
Going swiftly up and down;
Waking every sleeping bud,
With music all around.

She kisses every flower,
Sipping all the honey dew;
As they bend to give her welcome,
And their friendship to renew.

Then she sits upon a twig,
And takes a little rest;
And picks her shining feathers,
And puffs her tiny chest.

Oh, she is so beautiful,
So joyous, cute, and gay;
She fills my heart with pure delight
Until she flies away!

L. P. Padarath

Our Loved One's Gone

Our loved one's gone
But we must go on
We still laugh and we still play
Seems like the same routine as yesterday
But there is an ache in our heart
And a tear in our eye
And we ask ourselves, why? Why?
Why?
Our loved one's gone
But we must go on

Pauline A. Lamb

Ambiguous We

In this wacky worldly race
can just ambition be the case?
For hubris people are breathless
Isn't all this madness?
Pinnacle induced over activity
why all this hindrance to creativity?
Careering through life with plenty of strain
Why is sanity going down the drain?
A world without cordial humanity
Isn't this real selves scarcity?
The diaphanous cicatrice of shame
Isn't it tattooed on every fame?
Money and success that's all as a goal
Certainly it's not the journey of the soul!
All are getting stuck in a quagmire
Who is the one who all this admires?
Even thought in it use do not believe
Why do we with it continue to live?

Meenakshi Sinha

My Land Of Darkness

Silent thunder
charges through the castles of light.
Endless torture is practiced in the flames of hell.
Your name is called as I am wounded.
The shadow of death awaits my arrival.
A cold dangerous voice enters my body
and says through me.
Let them come,
let them cry,
let them fear my crimson eyes,
let me be their midnight throne,
let them be my dark night slaves

Pupinder Mudan

Our Very Special Person

He is a very special person that
chosen son of ours,
  Our life was changed, our house
was changed, with noise and toys and diapers.
  But would we change it, not one bit,
he is our very "Special Person"

  Sometimes he is the perfect little lad,
then there are times when he seems so bad
  But when he says "I love you Mom,
I love you Dad"
We know he's our "Special Person".

Audrey Burns

Hom. Sap. Nunc Defunctus Est!

If some new fangled man made threat
Could patient Nature's plans abet
And at Creation's Big Bang pace
Blow all us humans into space,
It's sad and sorrowful to think
That as we shoot across the brink
Most animals will jubilate
At our ingenious man made fate.
Flowers would then have nought to fear
From our polluted atmosphere.
No clouds would pour down acid rain
On ancient forest or grassy plain.
Never with rapacious joy
Would we be able to destroy
The ozone in our habitat.
Upon that self destructive day
All other living things might say,
'It's really for the very best
THAT HOM. SAP. NUNC DEFUNCTUS EST.'

Allan Smit

Reverie Of Summer Past

A butter cup in sun-blushed hue
Craved my Lady's gown of dew.
She tickled in mirth and winked
At nymph maids perched in saffron blooms
    of water lilies' open plumes.

Water's abbess and current's weaving
Her bosom's children, tadpoles streaming
Through rifts of cattails leaning
With her tide.

Sun's honeyed ribbon sweeps down to iris nest
    in tranquil waters of the brook.
Her bright blue Bonnet trembles in its wake
    of owl call,
        from the forest's nook.

The scillas bow their dainty necks
    as tiny fragile sapphire specks
They take their repose at roots of trees
Where fern-dwelled realms they do not reach.

Lisa Howard

Early Riser

She struggles and falls,
Craving her needle.
Up her wiry legs,
her fish net stockings
are snugged with
shaking hands.
Red lips and blue liner,
billboard her trade.
Worn and weary,
her work, is behind her.
She plods towards home
like rain in a gutter.
A smile flickers across her face,
as she thinks about her
treasure at home.
As she mounts the stairs
the new dawn is breaking.
As bright and full of promise
as her two year old son,
awaiting his mom.

Mandy Wood

The Space Between

The amethystine forests
Crepuscular
Snake-eyed streams meander
Tongue tasting
The rock smooth chemistry
Moon streaked iridescence
Shagreened
Beneath fern deep skin

Flat bellied granite
Ripples to the touch
A frisson of pleasure-fear
Fingers the spinal fluid

Flood sculptured sinews
Flex gravity fed muscles
The earth's kiss whirlpools
Into black-holed coils
Sucked between subterranean ribs

The space where
Passion-feathered phoenix rise
A molten heart's beat

Alan Charles Webb

A Powerful Tool

Shells and bombs may blast and kill,
Cripple many a strong man's will
But never give you love and peace
put a troubled heart at ease.

Now, some may know a stronger means
To change the hearts of aged and teens.
On their knees in prayers plain
They enlist the high domain.

A prayer in faith will never harm,
Force its will with mighty arm.
Although it's pow'r can mountains stir,
In perfect love will this occur.

Josstein Rossby

Solitude

SILENCE, is all that I hear.
DARKNESS, is all I can see.
Does that make NOTHING,
all I can be?

AIR, is all that I smell.
WATER, is all I can taste.
These useless SENSES,
are such a waste.

SILENTLY and BLINDLY,
ODORLESS and TASTELESS,
Yet such a total and complete mess.
It's THOUGHTLESS.

SCREAMING sounds,
in a SILENT room.
Inside my head,
these sounds they BOOM.

FRIGHTENING pictures,
on a BLACKENED screen.
Make things so REAL,
things so unseen.

Leah Puckering

Tranquility

Arise to the misty waters set out for the
dawn of the day,
To be greeted by the sound of the loon
or the coyote with its mournful bay.

Here I drift with my thoughts in the
gentle breeze, at peace with myself.
So quiet, just the rustling of the leaves.

The moon is disappearing, the sun has arose.
Such warmth from her rays she poured,
To fill me with such peace that only it
could bring, this feeling of tranquility
that is coming from within.

Ina Relf

wandering

wandering in the woods
deep and lonely
wandering lost in shadows
shrouded in fog.
i am wandering alone
through this great forest
where trees live
and speak only to me.
wandering
sometimes aimlessly
sometimes with direction.
but in no hurry to join your world.
happy for the time to wander
in the deep dark forest
alone.
with natures arms
to surround and
comfort
me.

Linda Bowbyes

Two Worlds

A young body craves to be free.
Defying all rules to quench the need
Peace comes to you as the real world
Vanishes, in a smoky haze.
Again the veil is lifted, life emerges
As you join the real world, you wonder
Why you ever went away. Soon
Once more you stand on the threshold of
    temptation.
The majority quell your conscience.
You inhale the enemy, slowly, savoring
The sedentary sensation,
As you float away on a bubble
That all too soon will burst.
You awaken with sunshine
Flooding the room, as a voice
Inside of you tells, you, "you"
Can be strong that you are worthy of love,
Arts loved, needed and wanted
In the real world, with those
Who will protect you here.

Joyce B. Ferguson

The Parish Council

The council sat and sat,
Deliberating on policies apt.
There was some jesting and some anger,
At times it seemed a torture chamber.

An air of calm, a smile or two,
Some prayer, so the Holy Spirit knew,
That he'd come to a hallowed place,
Where differences achieved a state of grace.

'Tis a place where people meet,
To do God's work, and friendship greet,
It is the work of one and all,
To look for Jesus, instead of gall.

As we sit tonight in thought,
Lets to each other, love be brought,
We are all equal, special and unique,
And as God's children can achieve the feat.

Carol A. Millett

Now And Then

Where once wild, now civilization
Destroying nature, God's creation
Creatures retreat from their habitat
Man stands in awe, look at that!

In the distance a tower ever so tall
Below another shopping mall.
Nobody really gives a damn
As man savages and rapes the land.

As I so vividly in my youth recall,
Gardens forever, never a wall
Trees and bush, dust-swept roads
Creatures happy to share abodes.

Neil H. J. Groenewald

Baby Mine

Precious baby, smiling face,
Dimples almost every place.

Tousled hair, so soft and fine,
Sweet baby, sweet baby, mine.

Hands and feet up in the air,
Grabbing rainbows everywhere.

Little body, soft and sound,
Wiggling, squirming all around.

Special baby, dancing eyes,
Each day brings a new surprise.

Clinking spoons my baby heard,
Baby's mouth like baby bird.

Darling face with eyes that call,
Feed me, change me, or I'll bawl.

Cooing, cuddling, crying time,
Mommy loves sweet baby mine.

Oh, your so sweet my baby mine,
I could hug and kiss you all the time.

As my baby grows and grows.
My love will surely overflow.

Gwen Whissell

To Someone I Will Never Know

You touched my life today,
    Did You Know?

I hope, I in some small way touched yours,
    Though You Will Never Know.

I found you behind my garage today,
    A heap of old clothes and blurred senses.

When I asked if you were alright,
    You blearily peered at me from your own private place.

    Did You Know?

When I retreated to my safe world,
    I did not know how to choose.

You shook my world with a vision from
another place.

Who should I call? What was the right choice?
    Perhaps better to let you shuffle off to obscurity.

But, I called, they came, they were kind, yet firm,
    Soon you were gone.

Yet, still you linger in my thoughts.

I will think of you now and then,
    Perhaps say a prayer for you now and then.

    Did You Know?

Patricia Mae Peterson

When You Close Your Eyes

When you close your eyes at night
Do the fantasies ever come
and whisk you away
To a beautiful place
Where you and I are one?

When you close your eyes at night
Do you ever see
Slow songs and soft kisses...
Pure intimacy?

When you close your eyes tonight
Can you feel the warmth
Of my fantasy kisses upon your lips
As I hold you in my arms?

When you close your eyes at tonight
Leave some room in your dreams for me.
For one day soon I promise you
They will be reality.

Esan L. Ellis

Flight

The runway
down the trail
is the wind
no colour
just sound
I, on the plane
am the wings
looking around at everything
wanting to glide through the sky
patiently
then finally in a wonderful assent
I fly through the fresh and beautiful air
toward the neverending sun

Brooke Louise Martin

Lockmaster

Expecting masts on each horizon,
Dreaming sails, your eyes go white.

Here enigmas of arrival
Scale down to a barge or yacht,
Spoiling the best of ports.

Antwerp wharfs accommodate flat ships,
One by one they enter...

Noosed bollards numb up from the quays,
Cold change slipped in a pocket fades, and
Raising rooms of water the Lockmaster
    times when ropes lose their coils.

He spits remarkably
After the boatswain's whistle,

Addressing seas
Fills out again
Echoed from

One day's cargo funnel,
Asking for me.

With a finger
Vessels move like pews too close together;
Tires fall between.

Helen Carl

Druid Death

Stars spilled forth on the ancient path
Druids of knowing, spun of the light
Beings almighty, weaving the Godhead
Strange worlds of wonder in an empty void.

Void filled of light spinning the Godhead
Empty as being, filling as world
Being and knowing spinning the cosmos
Wonders and magic, created of stone.

Strange is this path woven of sorrow
Strange is the walking, wandering through time
Wonders of wisdom, taught in illusion
Waiting for death to open the shrine.

Mary Weber

Duel

I lie in my bed,
Dying and still alone,
I long to hold her precious hand,
To feel once again whole.

Denied from her,
My tortured life passed,
Knowing that upon me,
Her love would never be cast.

Apart were our lives spent,
Though I always tried to believe,
That by God's grace,
Somehow she would come back to me.

As I now look down from above,
Finally I watch her holding my hand.
I turn to God and strike him,
Make him beg the forgiveness of this
destroyed man.

Jishnu Mukerji

A Soulmate

We were like two lost and wounded birds
Each alone, frantically trying to flap our wings
Flying over the hills and down into the valleys
Desperately looking for the ONE other
spirit who could
Fulfill our lives with compassion and love.

It was there that our wings touched
Ever so lightly at first
Within moments of that first touch
It felt as if our lives had been HAND molded
Together for the lifetime
We were meant to share

It was this special love that was given to us
That gave us the courage to spread our wings
And fly again

Judy L. Riche

Agape

Three forms of love exist within
Each human's spiritual skin.
They who force, criticize and scorn,
Prevent hope's daylight entering souls unborn.

I've sailed into Darkness, faced the Eye of Storm,
Been cast alone into Man's Prisons of
abuse and scorn.
I've walked on Fire, Water and Air,
Faced Demons and Dragons fearing no evil,
God is there.

Eros, He raised His ugly head,
He stole from me the sanctity of a
marriage bed.
Brotherly affection, kindness to all,
Pride's sinful ways Prevented God's call.

Born a child of God, a Child of Light,
I've danced with Angels clapping in delight.
To err is human, to forgive Divine,
To die for another is Sublime.

Alone on the precipice of Life,
Trembling in fear, Soul shattered by strife,
God stands Mighty, Majestic and tall.
I've jumped into His arms, I am one with All.

Maggie Rosiak

The Skimmer

Staying again by the sea
Each tide pulls in and out
The memories of when
I was half a child

On my bicycle
Hurrying towards the pier
To meet the boys
Walk hand in hand
Its full length
Behind the rocks
To look for the skimmer
That would hop the farthest

But mine took me too far
And I wish I'd stayed
Two hops behind
In my own land

Dorothy Trus

Man Against Man

Man against man struggle for the top,
  Eats you away inside
From this burning hole in the heart;
  How long to be blinded?
  How long till we change?
  Power it rages like a fire,
  The fight for the top,
  It burns within us all.
Power it could be the end of all,
The reason for the appreciation
  for the wars,
That rages for the pleading,
Calls the desperation in all we fall,
But the need rages on how long,
How till the eyes see the light,
Or the fire that dies.

Cathy Ferchland

Emotions

Emotions are inside of you
Emotions play a big part too
A giggle, a laugh, a smile on your face
One emotion that has a special place

An emotion is as strong as can be
Emotions are what make us be
A sigh, a tear, a sad little place
One emotion that does not suit your face

Emotions will play games with that little
heart of yours
Emotions alert: They can last many hours
To share, to care, to give, to take
All of the above, emotions will make

A flame, a fire, a burning desire
An emotion to make one a live wire
Please let go to emotions you feel
It is what makes us people so real

Emotions are inside of you
Emotions play a big part too
A giggle, a sigh,
An emotion to let us feel real high

Deborah Guy

Autumn Symphony

Memories of summer, gathering wings
Ethereal flight; autumn sings.
Scintillating brilliance spattering stars
Sailing suspended from Saturn to Mars.
Slowly emerges from dawn's eastern sky
Orb of creation—millenniums cry.
Woodland awakens; fluttering leaves;
Advance call to harvest, gathering sheaves.
Last call of mother bird warning her young
Flowers have fled, 'tis time to go home.
Flurry of squirrels hiding their hoard
With reckless abandon for bounteous reward.
Sunshine or shadow, star-spark or moon,
A gala great festival has ended too soon.
While orchestra falters and symphony fails,
The grandeur and glory of Nature prevails.

Joan B. Grayer

Honesty

I feel today in my Heart —
Even the smallest Seed, needs a start.

Kindness and a gentle Smile —
Can win the Love, of most any Child.

Happiness! Can be found in most
everything —
All kinds of Nature, has a song to Sing.

Honesty and Trust, not Deceit
In Life, most Trials, they will Defeat.

A Home! can be built, most any place —
If; with God, we place all our Faith.

William J. Lambert

Weep Not Tears

I will go in a peaceful manner
Even though my spirit will roam
I will see Heaven's lights
or the Devil's glow
I don't know, but I know I'll go
When I go people won't know until
they find me in a soft, peaceful,
eternal sleep
Calm your fears
Don't shed tears
For that would hurt me even more
than what living did.

Laura Fedick

In Deed ...!

Life is so tough!!!
... Every one is busy!,
and no one is happy!!!.

Life is so tough!!!
There is no time! ... for laugh!!!

Indeed ...!!!
"LOVE"!!! is what we need!!!

Ahmad Al-Shammari

Gail

Le visage
  Eyes contain brilliance of spirit,
  eyebrows lend refinement.
  Forehead enshields mind.
  Nose gives character.
  Your lips - sensuality by invitation.
  Chin depicts strength of will.
  Cheekbones denote lineage.
  Ears gauge temperament.
  Hair evokes self-esteem.
  Skin radiates vitality
  Your smile-sweet heart's subtle animation

Le visage: apex stage of great art
  wholistic concept transfigured
  in crucible of exchange

Some are too exquisite
scarred by clever wit.
Let me show you perfection
found in a reflection,
  ton visage.

Rolland Levac

Return From .... "Out There"

Lips that smile ... "They man I know you."
Eyes that shine ... "It's good to see you."
Arms that beg ..... "Come let me hold you."
Hearts that beat ... "Our love is for you."
  Back again.....
    Black again....
      Home!

George A. Borden

It Was Meant To Be

I see your face every now and then,
Fate has brought me to you Jen.

Love overriding my every emotion,
For your sweet love, I would vow my
  everlasting devotion.

With passion pulsing through my soul,
With you in my life the puzzle seems whole.

So as we lay next to each other at night,
And embrace each other with all our might.

I thank the Lord in the heavens above,
For I know it was meant to be, I need your love.

William Meglic

Our Universe At Midnight

Through a harmony of air and light
filling the crisp clear ice-cold sky
heralding the rising star in the deep-blue night
before the moon shines high
and the heavens turn black
and the star-strew band of light,
so pretty, so fair, so intensely bright
protruding in places far and dear
shows us the depth of our universe
and how microscopically tiny we are here.

And then the mighty heavens bow down
and kiss us
with beautiful phrases of shadow and light
mystery and twinkle eyes
all over the huge dark twirling skies
out there in deep deep outer space
— a billion pin-point steady rays
of colour and light in a wispy maze
of giant kaleidoscopes, brilliant and bright,
spread across the vast starry extent
of our universe at midnight.

Paul C. Sandison

With Love

The time has come
For us to part.
The pain inside
Will never stop.

I wish you were here
With me today.
To make the pain
All go away.

I love you more
Than words can say.
I'd give my life
To have you with me today.

If I could have
Any wish at all.
I'd wish for you
To be here with us all.

Jackie Gibson

The Child

The child cried foul
for he could see.
The shame of the time
And place on thee.

Oh Magic Mountain
Far and wide -
Find a place
For this child to hide.

Onwards and upwards
The wind - it blew.
Up the mountain
The child - he flew.

Now the child
No longer fears.
For all the shame
Has been cleansed by tears.

Onwards and upwards,
Blows the wind.
UP to the child
Who once had been.

Colleen Duff

"Contentment"

Contentment in life is indeed good,
For healthy living it's the best food,
Always keeping you in a top mood,
Preventing situations to sit and brood,
Or ever becoming rough and rude,
And living in happiness which everyone could.

E. M. Best

"A New Beginning"

Today a new day's dawning
For yesterday has passed
While memories old are fading
Today some new ones made to last

Today is here for new found smiles
Not days filled with sorrow
for pain and suffering of days gone by
have no place in tomorrow

Todays for being happy
for learning how to laugh
for loving life and being free
for choosing the right path

For every day is a new today
and memories new are forming
and while sadness led to darkness
now the sun shines every morning

So live life for today
and build towards tomorrow
let yesterday be yesterday.......
.... for there's truly no more sorrow.

Lisa Norris

Passages Of Time

Minutes slipping into hours,
Hours turning into days,
Days fading into years
Merely markers of time.

Collections of experiences,
Expressions of love,
Impressions left behind
Just the passages of our time.

Maria Moccia

"Life"

When things in life aren't and as they
should be,
Frustration sets in with uncertainty,
And just when you think,
The road is rough,
And you can't get anywhere,
And you've had enough,
Remember in life it's up to fate,
"And all good things,
Come to those who wait."

Kelly Lynn Keddy

Untitled

Time's tick fades,
forgetting thought.
Lonely night shades,
lost dreams distraught.
  Eroding reality,
restless haze.
Distant sanity,
fantasy ablaze.
  Ending black night,
grey shadowy morn.
Blinding dream's sight,
tattered mind torn.
  Dawn's frozen frost,
disremembers dreams lost.

Ken Steigenberger

Cupid's Foolish Ways

A heart pierced
From an arrow's point.

Loss of rational thought,
A whirlwind of confusion.

As the one approaches,
Deeply falling.

Hands reaching,
As if to hug,

Suddenly wrenching
The arrow within.

Now loneliness begins.

Katherine Lee Horvat

One Universal Mind

We live our life
From day to day
What comes, what goes
Nobody but ONE knows

We live our life
From emptiness to fullness
If it wasn't for love
It would be loneliness
If it wasn't loneliness
It would be wantonness

We live our life
From start to finish
But in the end
Life is just beginning

Love and Strife
Hate and Life
Are all a state of
ONE UNIVERSAL MIND

Walter Schoen

A Lover's Kiss On A Night Of Bliss

A passion-filled kiss
From my lover's lips -
Kindling my nerves in rapturous bliss!

That passionate kiss
From my lovers lips -

Demanding, receiving,
Mutely questioning;
Silently reckoning

Painfully searing my virgin pride,
Teaching me, reaching me,
Challenging me to deny an eruption of
pure ecstasy!

A whirlwind ecstasy
Born of love - maybe
But awakened by a lover's kiss!

Dorna Blake

Only In My Mind

Your voice is calling to me,
From out of emptiness,
I feel your arms around me,
The wind is my caress,
You said I'd grow old lonely,
And this is loneliness,
But I still have you, if only in my mind

We walk through fields of heather,
The trees stand by me, we laugh and talk together,
Memories are my company,
You said I'd grow old lonely,
I'm lonesome as can be,
But I still have you, if only in my mind

You're hers to have and hold, now,
I still have my memories,
My future seems so cold now,
But I still have my fantasies,
You said I'd grow old lonely,
Yet, I feel you close by me,
For I still have you,
If only in my mind

Lorna Courtepatte

To Care

When two people have a lot to give
From the heart and much much more
You find that you really want to live
And open up and enter that brand new door
Then you find a wall close in on you

And you're alone wishing for a good true love
Now the sky has suddenly become brand new
A hand caresses me and I feel light above
And I feel dizzy with sweet delight

And a thousand bells sing in my head
And as you hold me all through the night
I know, the new lives, the old love is dead
Then I ponder is it all worthwhile?

The answer comes clear when I see you smile!!

C. M. Smoliak

Chiming Of The Bells

I heard small bells chiming,
from the house's form.
And I knew than
I was alone no more.
Shouting out
the words came
"If you are a holy spirit,
stay with me enlighten one."
"But if you are an old
and foul entity,
I expel you from this
humble domain.
A voice did not reply...
and all I heard
were the chiming of
the bells.

Isis Salé

Pleasure

Pleasure comes to those who seek it
From things within their grasp
Nature, music, love and friends
These contain it within a mask
Nature gives us birds and bees
Trees, insects and flowers
Music gives us lovely tones
Manifold symphonies to last us hours
Love, an innate trait of all
Is gentle and serene
As a mother hugs her child
Man and maiden in a woodland scene
Lastly, pleasure comes with friends
Who are her messengers bold
Friendship and pleasure can never part
If our friends we can but hold.

Frances Mary Milikic

With The Harmony...

With the harmony of our rhyming hearts
From which sunshine never departs
There's angels singing among the stars
Strumming their lyres and guitars...
...So here's to you with Love's compliment!...
Both our hearts dignified and content.
Isn't it 'just so?'. It now seems;
That our Love's harmony had begun,
From reveries and enchanted dreams,
That is gilded with a Rainbow which sprung;
From just a basic and 'Platonic Love'.
For now we watch our Love's bounty grow...
...Still being showered by Stardust,
For 'Chaste Love' to you and I is a MUST...

Eftalon Harman

Dinosaurs In The Sunlight

Dinosaurs in the sunlight,
gracefully swimming in a heart shape.
Dinosaurs in the moonlight
sipping tea under a maple tree
Dinosaurs run, Dinosaurs run
Sharp teeth are coming this way!
Volcanos are erupting
meteorites are falling
and the earth is shaking
how I wish I could help you.

Eleni Kelly

Autumn Reverie

Today I stood upon a hill
gazing down the valley.
Colours blazing everywhere
I could not help but dally.

I had to rush to beat the wind
I really had to hurry.
The leaves of brown and red and gold
were caught up in a scurry

When autumn dons her pretty coat
and sets the scene ablaze,
it makes me wonder why it is
the glory's gone in days.

To some Fall spells the end of things
For others a beginning
of winter snow and Christmas too,
a time for sports and winning.

The wind got up and swept away
the scene before my eyes.
The leaves are gone, the trees all bare
but still they hypnotize.

Pat Gateman

The Living Spirit

People, busy with their own lives,
Getting ready for school, going to work
and somewhere, a woman is going to labour
She's tired, in pain, and maybe even crying
Her anxiety and fear are replaced with joy
She is proud of her newborn child
And somewhere, a man is dying
He's tired, in pain, and maybe even crying
His anxiety and fear are replaced with peace
Although his life is over, the newborn
  babe's has just begun
His personality , his traits, his ideals
are memories in his loved ones' heart
The babe is searching for personality,
  traits and ideals
Through his loved one's hearts
All babies are born with spirits
Will this baby assumed the trait s of that
  dying man?
We know there is death after life
Is there life after death?
Through a newborn baby's eyes...

Julie A. Davieaux

Untitled

The motion beneath me was swaying,
giving, taking, wanting to be in control.
Slowly beating to the sound of my heart.
There was silence, comforting, I felt as one.
I was in control the master to the motion
beneath me.
The air was warm, sensual,
caressing every inch of my being.
The sky was aglow from a sun with no
beginning and no end.
I was well!
I was alive!
I was sailing!!

Linda Mellish

Dewdrops

Morning rain,
glistening dewdrops,
falling, whispering
"The morning rain has come".

The wind's gentle breeze
unearths the dew drops
from their hiding place.

Leaves with dewdrops
remind me of mother nature,
makes me wonder does
mother nature cry;
for the earth's destruction,
our unsettled world
has crumbled.

Gayle Lynn

Peace

Cherished by every good soul
good soul,
An opinion of a heart,
A courageous voice fighting against evil,
A symbol of hope,
An obstacle yet to conquer,
A dream dreamed by everyone,
A thought which could change your mind,
But also a word which means a
whole lot.
Peace.

Jasmine Swaich

Round Perception

Round perception is so skeptic
Greeks were saying: "don't you ever,
Keep regarding at the moon,
That so for, you will for ever
...lose your senses."

But, as a skeptic person,
Disregarding all of that,
I lost my sense forever,
As we've first met.

Your image was so pure,
Your body so discreet,
My senses were so deeper
Involved in our myth.

Nicolicescu Aurelian

Meditations On The First Philosophy

With half clouded vision, I walk around
half in, half out of reality
repeating over and over,
"I am, therefore I think"
images distorted, thoughts blurred
unable to make heads or tales of anything.
WHY? I ask, I scream, I beg!
yet there is no response
for you do not know the answer my friend
and I cannot give it to you
for the answer requires the ability of
one who is firmly rooted in reality.
Uncertainty.
 This is what makes me who I am.
Who I do not wish to be.

Kerri Kitchura

American Male

Fossils from an earnest reach,
Gush a nodding donkey's leash,
Sparking some prospectors glow,
In a modern gold-rush flow.

Oiling skins preserved as lead,
Casts removed by spanners heads,
Keeping safe an asset firm
And the folk with skills to learn.

Barrels brimming full of crude,
Swiftly shipped to waters new,
Piped to heat in forms redealt,
Expertise the first to smelt.

Troubleshoots' demands thru globe
Means and special quell of blow
One great handles sure to greet
catasrophic blanket's seat.

Red Adair a news hound's toast,
Does his work expelling roast
Of a repute not before,
First and foremost t'shooter's law.

David A. Bennett

Shiver

The full moon strikes,
Hard and heavy on the heart.
The chilling wind freezes the grass,
And trees shiver in the cold.

Apathetic resolutions blow through the mind
Willingness for nothing.
Integrity vanished, hope banished...
The calculating winter of love again arrived.

Deepest blueblack sky deepens
Into the soul-penetrating
The dark, cold spot that should be hidden,
And stars flourish in the midnight breeze.

Thawed tension and conjuring emotion
Feed the heat and rise the fire
To a roaring inferno, peltering
The pale, frozen core of a heart unshared.

Luke Spragg

Last Day Of Summer

The song of the crickets
has been quiet this year.
No thunderous roar
to echo the sultry days
and restless nights —
only a lull
  in the cool still night air.
A lone cricket
persists under the cloudy sky
devoid of the usual
shimmery summery stars.
No Jupiter for me tonight.
And no Southern Cross either.

Simone Simmons

Boomerang

If you love something, set it free
If it comes back, it's your's they say

Go on, then, and set me free
Throw me away, and we shall see

Stuck somewhere in a distant tree
Free at last, my soul will scream

Constance Demyris Helton

Time

The future, a mist,
Hazy and uncertain.
The past, clear,
But it can't help us now.
Time,
Stretches out,
In front of us.
Anything, could happen,
And anything will.
Things change,
Only memories remain.
So people hope, and pray,
For something,
New and good.
And eventually,
It comes.
But not soon,
Things take time.
And time...
Goes on forever.

Marie Jankowska

The Still Small Voice

The baby inside me was lonely...he left me,
He could feel, feel the emptiness through me

His heart told him not to stay...he is somewhere,
Somewhere else, where he can laugh
  and he can play

I feared I could not have given him
What he needs to be strong and true

He could feel these things about me
So he left me...he just knew

He could feel my pain and anger
He could feel my shame and fears

He could feel all this through me
And he left me with my tears

He touched my heart so softly
And whispered words so tender

I wish that he was here with me
To hold and cherish forever

I would caress away the fears
And assure him of my love

But he left me, as he flew one night,
Upon the wing of a gallant dove.

Deborah Mousseau

Discovery

In 1497 John Cabot set sail
He sailed from the Port of Bristol
in search of the new world.

The voyage was long and dreary
and hearts were filled with fear
as land failed to appear.

After many days of fear and gloom
what a wonderful surprise!
Land ahead, was the cry that rend the sky.

Oh happy sight!
A land full of potential
Where waters teamed with fish.

1997 will be 500 years
since John Cabot discovered
the Island of Newfoundland.

Daphne Rolls

Tears Of Pain

Five years ago, this November,
He had to leave this earth.
Although his life is over,
God has taken away his hurt.

Why couldn't he stay longer,
So I could say goodbye?
Now I know that forever,
I'll think of him and cry.

I try to think of the fun,
We had when he was here,
And I know through the rain and sun,
He watches every tear.

As I'm reminded of his smile,
I Know he rests in peace,
And as I walk that every mile,
I try to face the grief.

I know his time had come,
For him to say goodbye.
But at times it feels so wrong,
So young, I must know why.

Kimberley Bird

"Memories of a Friend"

I'd like to tell you about a friend of mine.
He isn't with us anymore,
Except in happy memories
Of days gone on before.

He was a kind and loving man
To family and friends;
And memories of that kind of person
Never, ever end.

He loved God, sunsets, fishing, trees and flowers,
Music, photography, and reading by the hour.

My friend enjoyed working with his hands,
Creating out of wood, houses, cupboards,
   beds, and shelves.
And many other things that we wished we
could do ourselves.

Sometimes I smile to think of things he
   used to do and say.
But then I cry and wish that he were here
   with me today.

I guess that happy memories shouldn't
   make me sad,
But God knows how much I miss this man—

My friend—
MY DAD

Brenda Cooper

My Mail Man

My mail man is a wonderful guy
he walks the streets
his head held high
the bag he carries
is full of mail
where ever he goes
he leaves a trail
a minute late
people begin to fear
Something has happened
to our mail man so dear.

Charlotte "Annie" Burgess

Untitled

Don't mention that rainy night to him,
He says it hurts too much.
The way he left, the way I cried,
The way he lied, looked me straight in the eye.

Try not to mention that night we met
For he may look back with sad regret.
He may recall the days we've shared,
He may get confused, believe he still cares.
He may want to call me up again
To give it a shot once more.
He may want my heart to try to forget
Just how hard he slammed that door.

But tomorrow morning reality will hit
The candle he blew out can't be relit.
He'll remember that it's gone, my time has passed.
And how his feeling for me just could not last.

So don't mention that 'morning after' to me,
Because dead feelings may arise - unintentionally.
Let's just talk about what tomorrow will bring
And leave "yesterday" lyrics for others to sing.

Robbyn Deroo

Misery

I saw a picture of a colored boy
he was bare and hungry
The world had betrayed him
and so, he no longer cared

I sang the song of a sparrow
struggling to free itself from man's trap
to fly away and live

I heard of a tiny baby
left by someone's door step
abandoned by those of supposed love
Why and when, God only knows

I saw an old woman crying
sitting in thin clothes on the side-walk
wanting another chance in life

I felt the hear-beat of one desperate girl
lying in a hospital bed
as she fought for dear life

I cry the tears of God
for only He sees us all at once
to discover so much pain

Hasti Kousha

The Hawk

The hawk she circled round and round
her watchful eyes scanning the ground
Soaring high and circling low
in search of food for her young at home
Her red tinged wings in the sunlight shone
as she dipped and dived around the emerald lawn
And then out of the day a sound so dread
and upon her breast her blood ran red
Slowly and awkwardly she dropped to the ground
and within a heartbeat was a lifeless mound
Off in the distance there came a sound
of her young in their nest calling her home
Calling her, calling her, calling her
home.......

Daryla Cuthbertson

Unearthed

The core of Humanity
held the crowbar that slowly
pried my identity free.
Five long stems gently
gripped the metal and would
not let go until my core
was released.
Finally my confined truths
became unshadowed, unearthed.
My wall has crumbled into
unuseful shambles of the identity
I forgot I possessed.
A flickering storm
of emotion has erupted
tonight as the crowbar
is layed to rest.
A white powdered dust now lays
to conceal my skeletons.
It will only take one blow of
his breath to create the harmonious
tornado.

Lindsay Blair

Our Spectacular Galaxy

It's like a large umbrella
Held high above our heads
A spray of diamonds glistening
Unsettled in their beds

Resembling a kaleidoscope
No two nights are the same
Northern lights will gather
To commence their dancing game

We've been invited to attend
This galaxy of mystery
Performing on this massive stage
For all the world to see

The moon will be the special guest
In a different size and shape
Man is searching to explore
It's majestic landscape

It's fascinated every child
He's seen it all since birth
Who would ever want to miss
This greatest show on earth.

H. Terri Swanson

Our Grandma

Her perceptive understanding,
Her stalwart but feeble frame,
Radiant rays of faith and love-
Gladys Shemilt is her name.

Her saucy, tittering manner,
Indispensably clever,
Had a frankness to embarrass
Flagrant minds forever.

Tea biscuits from nimble fingers,
Not as spry as in her youth,
Still amusingly presented,
Delightful, spirit of truth.

Her expressions grew laconic.
Infirmities settled in...
Yet her hums will be remembered
As radiant GEMs within.

Daniel B. Hanewich

Big Red Box

Uncertain striding
her head bowed in chaos
the seething young woman
with cloudy eyes
holds her tense frustration
like a handgun.

Like a hailstorm
wasting it's destruction
on unplanted cropland
she swears at circumstance
and her curses bounce harmlessly
on the pavement.

The pale ragged girl with rain matted hair
stalks the big red box.

Warily she glances
and with a movement
like stabbing a long time enemy
she pierces the mysterious chasm
with the envelope
and prays.

Daniel Wilkens

My Wonderful Friend

I have a wonderful friend,
He's gentle an he's kind.
His hair is soft and gold and white,
He has a stubborn type of mind.

He's loyal and he's happy,
And he really like to play,
He always likes to have his treats,
At any time of day.

If I'm feeling under the weather,
He will come over and sit by me,
And he looks up into my eyes,
And puts his paw upon my knee.

I imagine by now you've guessed it,
My friends a retriever dog,
He barks at birds and butterflies,
And sometimes little frogs.

I can't think of life without him,
He's really a very nice pet,
Just watching him's a pleasure.
It's the best fun you could get.

Jean Brohman

Untitled

If I could tell the story
How great our love has been
The sun moved shine forever
The stars in heaven beam
If I could tell the story.
Of all the lonely days
I spent in longing for you
Your touch, your loving ways
The clouds would draw their curtain
On life's eternal dream
And fill with tears of sorrow
For there was no tomorrow!
When God called you to heaven
Surrounding you with love
My heart was filled with thanks to him
And all the angels above
I knew you were at peace at last!
By sending me your blessings
And your eternal love.

Helga Szewczyk

Sam

Sam's not just another guy
He's kind, he's gentle, a little shy
If you need help, he's on the spot
He gives his all, and that's a lot

I'm sure there's times
When he feels pain
In Sam's own words
"No pain, no gain"

When we play golf
We laugh, we joke
Sam swings and misses
I count a stroke

Our game is over, we take a break
Sam orders decaf, I take mine straight
We check our scores, to see who won
It doesn't matter
We had great fun

Sam's kind, he's gentle, a little shy
Cause now, we all know
Sam's one heck of a guy.

Frank G. Thompson

Answered Delayed?

Cradle me in Your arms dear Lord,
Hold me close to Your side,
Envelop me with Your love, O Lord,
For in You alone peace abides.

You never send answers too early,
And You are never, ever too late
Your timing is always perfect, dear Lord,
For the child who will just trust and wait

When the answers I seek seem to be delayed,
Then this too is a part of Your plan.
For in your wisdom You are stretching my faith,
I must learn to rest rather than make demands

You are teaching me to keep my thoughts on You,
And not to be tossed to and fro like the sea.
You are Majestic God who is Holy and Just,
And nothing will hinder Your plans for me

So cradle me in Your arms, dear Lord,
Hold me close to Your side.
Shield me with Your wings, O Lord,
For in You alone my peace abides

Gloria Kelsey-Gilbert

Almost Death

As I walked toward the light,
I turned and looked behind,
I saw my family with tears in there eyes,
hoping they wouldn't have to say goodbye.
I didn't quite remember what had happened,
But I knew something was wrong,
What was the light in front of me,
And why were they crying,
How come they couldn't see me,
What were they all doing
I walked toward my family,
They all stopped crying
I heard their happy tears and wondered why?

Autumn R. J. Stephens

Home

My home's not new but 200 years old
Holding the memories of scenes untold
Mostly loving, I sense, in this beautiful setting-
A place to encourage forgiving, forgetting.

Rough stone walls defy gales and snow,
Have a future of many more years I know.
What matter if wild creatures live in the cracks
And under the eaves- a colony of bats!

Around us scenery breathtakingly pure,
Just as it was in days of yore.
Fresh sea breezes ensure our health,
Surrounded we are by nature's wealth.

But glad we are that our water is 'mains',
That a tanker comes to empty our drains;
A touch of a switch brings lighting and heat
And a car stands by ready to save our feet!

I think how they toiled- oh so long ago-
In this very place now with comfort aglow.
Could they have seen beauty, with so little leisure
In a world so harsh, with little pleasure?

Joan E. Clark

El Teatro

The patient is prepared in stages
Hypnotists do try pink-cloaked pirouettes
then prick to sleep with feathered darts
Once safe in trance

Acupuncturists plant new pain
the pin-flock lanced
rouged for incision

The body puts off pride and runs

The inept surgeon
slices an unscheduled vein

Irregular blood
jets from jaws
drains sunk feet

We too are mesmerized
dust-smocked
at the butcher's block

We did not do well
No-one was brave
Jeers and cushions pour into the open grave

Derek Wright

I Am

I am the eagle that soars up on high,
I am the ocean, the forests, the sky.
I am the flowers, the fields and the trees,
I am the storm and the whispering breeze,
I am the moon, the stars and the night,
I am the sun, the warmth and the light.
I am the future, today and tomorrow,
I am the joy, the happiness and the sorrow,
I am the mountain, the river, the stream,
I am the writer, the song and the dream.
I am beside you, whatever you do
For I become nothing, if there is no you.

Josephine Stock

I Can See The Fire

I can see the fire
I can feel the pain
But I do not understand
Why it is happening again
Why can't we be like women
Planting homes instead of bombs
In loving arms
Instead of nuclear arms
Let's stop these senseless killings
Let's have more feelings
Let's use our heads instead of our hearts
Let's ban these nuclear warheads
Let's not blow our world apart

Poh Kok Tan

Dear Daddy

When ever I feel sad,
I cry, I just can't think clear,
I just feel sorry for myself,
And I know that's no way to live,

I look around and who do I see,
But my daddy, I look up to him,
As if he is my whole world,
The only person who really understands me,

Who actually loves and cares for me,
I can feel it whenever I'm in pain,
When I cry there he is to cheer me up,
Then I don't have to cry, I'm not alone.

The times I think I have no friends,
There he is as my friend,
I just cannot dream a world,
Where a daddy or family doesn't exist.

Hasana G. Gulersonmez

Scorpio

Half past four
I did want more
But the lunar calender I could not consult
For fear of a Scorpio I would not insult

In Roma we will meet and in the fountain throw
A few pence, from a lamb's P.L.O.

Church fields and chapel lanes
Are nice numbers for water signs
Please spell Woodford for me
I'll buy us a suit at Cecil Gee
A dedicated follower of Kinks I'll never be

For domani is another day
In Paris night we will sway
Slumber is golden
But Sir William-peer
Will tell you about me when he appears

A sweet memory I will have on Arab palate
Of an Italian meal and
A statue that cannot but tell the whole
truth - Surgery
TKS 4 Alpha holy knight

Issa Kawar

Running To Reality

I once lived in grace and silver spoons.
My mother was a housewife, my father a tycoon.
My life was a dream I soon awakened from,
There was no evil, no fires, no bums.
That dream life wasn't for me.

That life was for a new tiny baby.
Well that baby came so I left.
My parents probably forgotten about me,
"A childish girl. What good was she?"
I now live in an alley.

Erin L. A. Calhoun

Fancy Seeing You

When first I saw you
I didn't know you for a little while
Now I remember, how you had pigtails
    when a little child
How you have grown up quite attractive
    with a lovely smile
Fancy seeing you here,
fancy seeing you here.

Back in our childhood days
We made a vow that we would never part
We graduated, and went our separate ways.
We broke our hearts, broke our hearts.

I'm glad I saw you
Strange it seems that we should meet again
This fated moment
I've always dreamed about since don't
    know when
Your eye's are saying
The many things that I've been saying too
Fancy seeing you here, fancy seeing you here.

S. Thomas

Untitled

As you held me tight,
I didn't want to let go.
I never felt so safe and loved,
In my entire life so.
Your touch was soft,
And your hands were strong.
You make me feel good inside,
Whenever I am feeling down.
You are the best thing that has ever
happened to me,
And I pray that you always stay in the
heart of me.
When you hold me again,
Please don't let go.

Melissa Mohammed

Warm Nights

Candles, lamps and lanterns that light
Having you here to warm the night.
Little windows of gold
glitter by the firelight.
Nowhere to go
-nothing to do.
Thank God for warm nights
and comforting thoughts of you.

Debbe Behnke

Mommy's Girl

Don't wear to much make-up;
I don't want to fight.
Please wear your jeans looser,
Your shirts not so tight!
I really don't care what the other
girls do; they may look flashy but
I don't want you to!!!
I do this for you;
I may sound like a witch, but
later you'll thank me,
And give your kids the pitch!!!
If we can be friends, I'm sure
we'll get along,
And someday you'll find that
its tough to be a mom.

Roberta Johnson

life, my friend

life, my friend
i don't want us to end
death is our enemy
both yours and mine
life, i welcome the time we've been given
to spend with my nieces
my family
my intimates
i truly delight in these blessings
i savor space to write
and the privilege to enjoy poetry
    and music
        and photography

and so life, my friend
i shan't complain
i've got you pretty good

i shall try to be strong in my hour of
reprieve
and brace up the hearts of my comrades
who grieve

Laurie Braithwaite

Rejection

You stay away so long
I fear for your return
The danger that envelops me
Ignites my loins to burn

You permeate my dreams
Where fantasy can live
But when I wake
My arms they ache
For love that you can't give

A passion unfulfilled
A deity unknown
A challenge unresolved
Searching for control

Fear of being abandoned
A fear that haunts my soul
Lingers there
Thickens the air
With a smell all of its own

Emma Ruth Thompson

A Recollection

I saw the ghost of love pass by.
I had not seen her in a year.
I thought I had been curéd of her,
But with the sighting came the fear

That never would I cured be
Of her sweet memory and grace -
The pain of recall, happy times,
The beauty of her smile, her face.

So let the throbbing pain return
With memories of what we shared:
I loved her then, I love her still,
I always will.

Brian J. McGrath

My House Sounds Like A Ship

As I lay in bed resting my youth,
I hear the walls crackling around,
  Escaped seconds are profound,
  Mark Twain saved me a minute;
  My room falls on the yard,
  Nearby the trees bruit growing,
  The hard wind beats by milliards,
  Mark Twain our houses are alike,
  Should a flood descend on land...
  ... I've been prepared for an ocean,
  My house shall be my ship.

Ray Blaze

Untitled

I saw that the mountain moved itself
I heard the cries of this people
later I thought about the pain of each person
but never did I forget my own
because my pain was so large
that I felt it was incomparable

I then mourned to be with life
I began to walk
and at each step a tear fell
as if my strength
each time was disappearing
leaving in me a mysterious loneliness
the loneliness of my people ruined
by the hunger and the injustice
my own loneliness of being alone
But suddenly there is born in me
an incredible force to save me from death
and to liberate so many confused minds
that make a people
be a people ruined.

Lucrecia Mendoza

The Meteor

A streak of light
Illuminates the sky.
A meteorite,
A streak of light,
A flashing brilliance in the night
Disappears as it goes by.
A streak of light
Illuminates the sky.

Kandice Ardiel

Respect

Statesmen,
I implore you.
Unite to face with courage
and understanding;
any menace of destruction,
of annihilation...
    without guns.

Replace all past mastery
over weaker things...
  with wisdom,
    superseded with love.

Cast aside the greed,
the blood-lust
of our decrepit characters...
  supplant it with sharing.

We have the good earth,
the miraculous beauty of all created
things...
They demand our respect!

Gladys Basaraba

Lost

I am lost in a web of fear
I know not who I am
I search and I search
Not knowing if I want
To find the answers I need

Am I afraid of the truth
That I so truly need
To set my mind at ease
For if I do find it
Will I want to accept it?

Do I deceive myself
That I may be
Something I'm really not
Will my hopes and dreams
Disappear in the face of truth?

Will I see the real me
That I've been searching for
Or will I see myself
Whom I've tried to hide
Inside the face of truth

Ellen Braun

To My Grandmother

I know your body is sore,
I know that you're in pain;
But I will always be with you,
snow sun or rain.

Grandma when the pain gets you down,
And you feel you want to frown;
I'll send kisses through the air,
To show you that I really care.
And when those kisses land on you,
You'll fear better through and through.

Laura MacRae

Untitled

Little by little, bit by bit
I learn to creep, walk and talk
Bringing forward joy
To Mom, Dad and
The rest of the family

Little by little, bit by bit
I played around with
The Alphabet from A to Z
Which grant me learning skills
To perfectly read, write and understand

Little by little, bit by bit
I seek help to clear
My views of disappointment
Making my fears disappear
And bring forward new pleasures

Narine Dat Sookram

Autumn

As I strolled into the woodlands
I lent against a tree.
It was one world of beauty as far as my
  eyes could see.
The leaves were amaze of colours it made
  me want to paint
A lovely autumn picture before it was too late
Oh, for the autumn beauty I shall never regret
The day I spent in the woodland,
I shall never forget.

Pamela Rose Hobson

Tragedy In The Night

While doing my homework last night,
  I listened with all my might,
For faint could I hear,
  The fire engine's siren, not near,
But far on the other end of town.

The fire was rapid,
  The men could not stop it,
With a sudden poof,
  It raged through the roof,
And burnt the whole house down.

There were ten people in that house,
  And like a poor mouse,
Eight perished in the fire,
  Because of the direr
Need for oxygen masks.

And one of those,
  As everyone knows,
Was the beauteous one around.
  Tomorrow she will go to the ground.
For her all flags fly half mast.

James A. Wells

The Circle

She looks back when he looks at her,
In some way designed by who knows who,
And he falls into her luscious self,
And she somehow signs she loves him true.

He's falling . . .
  . . . she's falling . . .
    . . . they fall,
Again, into a well so deep it ends
With just a touch or trace of smile,
Until he looks at her again.

Larry Aldrich

Today, Tonight, Tomorrow

I long to feel her touch
I long to see her smile
I long to hear the words,
It will be alright my child.

I remember her touch.
I remember her smile.
I remember her words,
It will be alright my child.

I cannot feel her touch.
I cannot see her smile.
I can never hear her say,
those words again,
It will be alright my child.

Rebecca English

Eternity

As I walk on the streets,
    I look to see you notice me;
But I'm not there.
    I'm transparent.
And if you do,
    it's just a sideways glance;
telling me there's no chance;
    For love.
It's a crazy wish, I know.
    I've seen too many movies.
A happy ending is all I want.
    One always desires what one cannot have.
Invisible people do not feel,
    I tell myself over and over again.
Feelings come from a living being,
    not one that lives to serve.
And I would gladly serve you for eternity
    for just one smile,
    a wink, a sign,
To show me that you see.

Karli Renee Smith

The Illusive Dream

Thru my journey on life's busy train,
I met a fairy , so complicated yet so plain.
Uncorrupted beauty, sat she there,
With soft music whispering through her hair.
A smile — darkness shattered by lightning,
Sent my pulse a leaping and my throat
    atightening.
Her life, her song, sweeter than the
    sweetest honey,
Made pauper a millionaire, regardless of
    his money.
The train slowed down, said she with a sigh,
"I'm getting off here, see you by and by!'
A tear here, a note there and off she went
My hopes, my dreams to earth she sent.
Oh! I want for us in haste to meet
To journey through life, thru bitter and sweet.
Without you this shredded life will not be
    the same,
Oh!!! Illusive dream,my rainbow in the rain.
They say, "It's life to meet and part,
Bid, part to meet the hope of every heart."
Though mountains and seas try to keep us apart,
I'll find you, fair maiden, you've stolen my heart.

Clarence Samuel

Fear

As I child I dreamed of acceptance
I needed to be like everyone else
Not fat. Ugly, stupid-and afraid

As a young man I strove for acceptance
I needed to love and be loved, successful
Especially with girls-and less afraid

As I got older I discovered women
Was accepted, successful-sometimes almost
Learned to control fear-appear unafraid

'Now-older-"I've made it"-"done it"
Accepted by women, success in my job
Good wife and kids, good relationships,
Achieved beyond my expectations

Now I know fear

John Vigrass

Willie (1938-1995)

I don't know why she had to leave
I only know how much I grieve,
And yet it's clear she still is near
And death is not a thing to fear
Her journey now has just begun
This life is not the only one
Don't think of her as gone away
We'll all be joined again someday
How innocent we both were then
The days before us care free
A child I was and she just ten
No thought of pain that could be
I cannot think she's gone away
Instead I feel she's resting
Some where in joy and warmth and sun
The peak of all her questing
I know she prays for no more tears
From all of those she touched
For nothing loved is ever lost.
And she was loved so much.

Catriona Braithwaite

The Dream Of The Black Child

Every time I close my eyes,
I see it.
There is in the distance,
It is perfect.
The dream of a black child,
A dream that only day,
Will become a reality.
My reality.
That will be the day...
The day when I can wear what I want to,
And still be respected.
When I can listen to any kind of music
I want to,
And still be accepted.
The day when I can walk pass a white woman,
And she'll smile and say "hi".
Instead of clutching her purse thinking I want it.
The day when things will get easier.
And the pain will subside even just a little.
And momma's tears will stop fallin' that's my dream.
The dream of a black child.

Kesha Christie

Dad

Even though he's not here
I sense him everywhere,
Even though he's not near
to hold me close
to still my fears
His silence hurts
never responding
hardly there
with care
but with you
you hold me close
still my fears
responding
always there
with care
luckily for me
you're my DAD

Lindsay Eillson

Today...

Today...
I shall not falter
And look behind me
Because today and only today
Remain in my focus

Today...
I shall not stumble
Or cry at yesterday's mistakes and
blunders
For its what goes on in the present
That matters the most

Today...
I will look and take each hour
One minute at a time
For yesterdays tears and yesterdays
mistake
Have long ago past

Today...
Is what remains most important
In my heart and in my mind.

Christine McFarlane

Sense Of Time (At Spynie Palace)

I see the Palace ruins bathed in sunshine,
I smell the new-mown grass and woodland pine.
I hear the children's chatter,
fledgling's birdsong.
And touch the golden sandstone,
Carved by masons, weathered by time.

I walk through arches into time forgotten,
Where Mary Stuart, Queen of Scots once stayed,
I sense the echo of a time that's long past,
No rhyme or reason now
To auld alliances once made.

The Watergate portcullis leads me no-where,
Though boats are gone,
the Spynie sea-loch drained,
I taste the bitter brine of Time relentless marching,
Unlike the land, our time once lost,
Can never be reclaimed.

Beryl McKenzie

Vet

It's quiet now, not much noise,
I soon will fall asleep.
To awake and find my best friend dead,
Lying at my feet.

The light it hurts my eyes,
As the sun, shines through the trees.
Is that the stench of death,
I smell within the breeze.

I yawn and stretch my arms,
To start another day.
The sound of war's not far behind,
So I am on my way.

Donald G. Rose

A Captain's Lament

O, how I wish that once again
I to the sea could go,
And sail my ship, the way I did
So many years ago.

No need to be a tall, tall ship
With masts standing high,
Just a schooner with two sails
And a compass to steer her by.

Standing on her wooden deck,
And leaning on her rail,
I would watch her push the waves aside,
As 'round the rugged cape we would sail.

Then with sails so full and firm,
I would put her out to sea.
The lighthouse on our starboard bow,
And leave ol' Harry on the lee.

But these are only dreams I dream,
As on my bed I lay,
For on her deck, no more I'll stand
And watch the riggins sway.

Harold White

Untitled

With sudden purposeless edges,
I transcend towards a roaring sky
The white hot flame inside me, flares up,
Engulfs the flesh, burns off this mortal ballast.
In purity brighter than the solace of suns,
Filling all the spaces that were laying
    empty-waiting,
I know the ecstasy of mediocrity dispersed.
Life's rugged waters start to part
To yield a glimpse of depths below;
The wind calls ringing to the quickening storm,
Rising faster than the floods of legend rivers,
To a place that living cannot go.
So fast, the event horizon blurs and at the
    edge of knowing,
I plummet like a wax-winged child.
Though once I felt it waiting,
At a point just past my fingertips,
Now not an echo of an echo's left for me.
And yet, a promise remembered leaves me
    waiting for the moment,
When the cacophony of sound will coalesce,
Into a single pure note.

Aimee Coueslan

Soaring To The Clouds

My heart has spread its wings and soared
    up to the clouds
I will love thee till my dying day, to this
    I have vowed
Take me, my love, again and again close
    to your heart
Your love, like a cocoon, envelopes me
    when we're together
    and when we're apart

Our spirits mingling together as one
So peaceful and warm, like lying in the sun

Whether we are together or if we are not
You're always with me and in my thoughts
So when I go to bed at night, my last
    thoughts are of you
When we will be together and will once
    again woo

Linda McCoy

Living Poor

As the sun sets, on the blue horizon
I wonder what life holds way beyond....
I hate to be poor, I say to myself
Born in poverty
Raised in poverty
Raising kids in poverty
In a poor neighborhood
You get no respect when you're poor
You're looked upon, worse than an
unpainted door
My body trembles with chills, cause I
have no skills
But, no matter the cost, I will have it all
So my kids won't drag no ragged cross
Against no ragged wall

Yvonne B. Forbes

That Old Backroad

Problems, questions, what's one to do?
If only I had an answer or two
Just like a poem, life doesn't always rhyme
I think I'll take one day at a time.

Sometimes life becomes a handful
And sometimes it seems to explode
Never know which way I'm headed
'Til I drive down THAT OLD
BACKROAD.

The country is fresh, so pure and clean
It's where I can breathe and wear bluejeans
If only life was that way everywhere
Pedal to metal, Backroad, I'm almost there.

Sometimes life becomes a handful
And sometimes it seems to explode
Never know which way I'm headed
'Til I drive down THAT OLD
BACKROAD.

Only a mile or two and I'm you no where
To my backroad in the midst of nowhere
So many memories, so much love
My destination is a gift from above!

Janie Lesiuk

No If's And's Or Butts!

With every day I exercise
I'll hopefully reduce my thighs
And every part that I despise.
I'll kiss my butt good-bye!

This morning much to my surprise
I lost the bags from 'neath my eyes
No need for make-up to disguise.
I'll kiss my butt good-bye!

A "Couch Potato" I won't be
I'm working out to my TV
Exercising vigorously.
I'll kiss my butt good-bye!

I bend, I twist, I stretch and turn
Until my muscles start to burn
My youthful shape, it will return.
I'll kiss my butt good-bye!

A figure trim, I'll work to find
With curves and muscles well defined
With nothing excess out behind.
I'll kiss my butt good-bye!

Roberta Whiskin

Untitled

A sight of hopeful becomings
In a sky of changing surroundings
Silence of a distant voice
Searching for its place of rejoice
A walk in a season of breathless skies
An ocean of beauty seen through her eyes
A flame of desire in a burning field
Radiance of the light makes his shield
Clouds of somber rain passing by
A white dove begins to die.

Jason K. Roy

Locked

Trapped
in an old dungeon
of hatred
everything I say
everything I do
they yell at me
"Shut up" they say
I can't go anywhere
I'm trapped
at home
at school
I'm locked in the dungeon
and I will never
be set free!

Holly Lynn Blair

"Wishes"

If wishes were reality, you'd be here
    in my arms,
If wishes were reality, you'd bless me
    with your charms.

But wishes are just wishes,
So I'll have to be content
To wish you health and happiness,
And love that's Heaven sent;

If you should ever realize
My wishes are yours too,
I'll spend each day together
Making your wishes come true!

Richard E. Pyefinch

The Subtropics Night After Rainy Season

The night curtain and down fully with the stars
In field singing the insets
To face blowing grass smelled wind

Dewdrop being left on grass leaf just saying
Yesterday's rain was very think very thick

This morning's mist was the farewell by rain
Tomorrow would be no longer worry
No longer muddy, no longer rainy
Standing water dispersed on ground
   twinkling like the stars
The clear sky the stars I could regard with curiosity

Liang Haisheng

The Orchid

The orchid blooms
In its exuberance.
Where is its beauty
And its charm
If there is none to behold?
The poetry and grandeur
The exquisite form
And tantalizing luster
Are as much in the beholder
As in the flower.
Alone one remains
An impersonal entity
With an unborn longing.
The difference creates the many.
The sense of separation
Brings the sensation
And flows in the joy
Of beauty and ecstasy
Of a reunion
Of what was always one.

Nirmal Chakravarty

Anticipation

I'm alone, so alone
In my cold dark room
With nought but my thoughts
And the encircling gloom.
As I sit in my chair
I dream of company
Coming out of the air.

The warmth of a body
Entwining with mine
Leaves me feeling lightheaded
Though drinking no wine.
And I know in my heart
That wherever I be
There will always be someone
Just waiting for me.

Jean Buthfer

Thoughts

Lifetime of memories, printed in gold,
Leaves scented delicate, never growing old,
Times of pleasure, times of strife,
But I would never change you,
Or the pattern of our life.

Eileen Brown

Pleasure

The smell most pleasing to the nose
Is not the lily, nor the rose,
Nor ocean spray, nor new-mown hay,
But mortgages, on burning day.

The sound most pleasing to the ear
Is not the voice of someone dear,
Nor songs of birds, nor words of praise,
But mortgages, when they're ablaze.

The sight most pleasing to the eye
Is not a sunset in the sky,
Nor mountain peaks, nor eagles' flight,
But mortgages, when they ignite.

Clarence Elliott

Jaded Desperation

Facile and weak
In my dark, misty sleep -
In these preludes of rain
In this after math of shame

When all strength disappears
And voices pacify
Virtuous... discerning...
Penetrating my mind

Eminent and languid
Obsessions devise
In this dim labyrinth of my spirit
In these gasps for the light

Until the last of calm I feel slipping
Into liquid places needless of time
Where only serene pangs of violence can
begin to wilt,
my nude, despairing lullaby.

Mercedes Sheri-Maye Friesen

In The Middle Of The Street

So solitaire,
in the middle of the street.
As still as a rock,
yet has a heartbeat.
As busy as its shadow,
lies the silhouette;
not a care in the world,
not a single regret.

A tiny black speck,
on this huge massive earth;
so insignificant,
since its very birth.

This inactive little figure,
in the sun,
filled with heat,
a simple housefly,
in the middle of the street.

Eliana Ricketts

Untitled

As I sit and watch
my boys at play,
I catch a glimpse
of their childhood days.
Seeing that sparkle
in their blue eyes,
puts a smile on my heart
that will last forever.

Cheryl Kountourogiannis

Untitled

As the day grows pale
In this wintry land
And the faces start to stare
Into the dark deserts of their hopes
As the night grows black
In this land of shiv'ring skeletons
And the eyes blush from too much wine
Time runs smoothly, unseen and silent

When spring with its juvenile force
Gives winter its final blow
In a storm of sun and rain
In wind and cold and new born flowers
One man stands with broken eyes
Alone out there in the fields still hard
And as he stares at no real sun
The birds pick on his worn out hat

Eugene Knecht

I'll Take You Home

Somewhere back in time it seems
Is a place I go to in my dreams
To a land I've never known
Yet, I feel, I'm going home.

There's a doorway I go thru'
Then it all comes into view
I hear a voice softly say,
"Come, walk the hills of yesterday".
"And as you wonder here with me
Think back, to how it used to be
This moment in time that you have seen
Is where your heart, has always been."

It's then I gaze into the face
Of one who takes me to this place
Somewhere, sometime, long ago
It's me I'm looking at, I know.

And, I'm no stranger to this land
I reach to take the outstretched hand
And hear a voice, so like my own,
"Come with me, I'll take you home."

Norma J. Suddard

Passion

   Each shared moment with you
Is embedded in my mind
And when thinking of you
Together we're one of a kind

   Our bodies and our souls
As one entwined gently
When making love with you
Feels so right and heavenly

   For being in love with you
Is so incredibly real
My feelings very ardent
To cry is what I feel

   And during our private moments
Your gentle touch, your kiss
For just being with you
Is everything I miss

   For every precious moment
I dream would last forever
I can't get enough of you
But this is my endeavor

Lynda Sprunt

Survivors

One who remembers
Is a survivor
Though we should not punish those who forget
I have never forgotten
But I am not a survivor
I am the one they remember
The one who makes them remember

I pushed them to a barren country
Where the smell of death stained their clothes

I regret what I did
But do I take it back
You don't know
And neither do I

Abby I. Miller

Friend

What I believe
Is in the true person
For they have a way
Of the passing of the day
Not unforgotten
Just missed
Because they are leaning
On a good composition
The question is where
But can it take a dare
With thoughtful care
Which is rare
what to do
Is to conglamorate
All the beginnings, middle and ends
Without the usual ledge
But cry in happiness
For all the friends you made
And saved the world for yet another day.

Laurier Preville

Life's Journey

Does your journey lead to an unknown land?
Is it guided by a strangers hand?
Think you've chosen a better way?
There will be a surprise on that final day.

Walking down the path of life,
Through a mist of trails and strife,
Heavy burdens you cannot bare,
Sorrows which you're afraid to share.

No matter which road you've journeyed along,
No matter the choices you've made which were wrong,
There's one who will always be waiting ahead,
To travel that road by your side as he said.

Open your heart and receive him today,
Place your life in his hands all the way,
The joys you'll receive for just trusting the Lord,
The smoother your journey the stronger the sword.

Your journey leads to the promised land,
Guided by the Lord's strong hand,
You have chosen the only way,
There will be no surprise on judgement day.

Monica Joan Frank

Way Of The Spirit

The way of the spirit
Is mystery.

Opened in glimpses
Serendipity.

Blessing
Not anticipated.

Intuitive knowing
Emergent.
Syphoned.

Expelled
From the depths of surprise.
Act of creation.

Born through the silence
Of listening.

Receiving the gift
Of the moment
Of open.
Link to origin.

Mary Angela Nangini

The Structure Of A Rose

The structure of the rose
Is that which to compose
The music of a love
Sent far from up above
Each petal soft and sweet
As two hearts come to meet
To join as one formation of beauty
To grow and thrive as its own duty
To build together, to exude such life
As uniquely felt between husband and wife
Only side by side may these petals create
A perfect whole, a union, a blessing of
love's fate

Lori Rose Forster

A Battle In Prison

The body is a prison, and what I scorn
Is the conviction for the crime of being born.
The walls of my body are all that I know,
And I fear to leave not knowing where I'll go.

Everyday, as the Judge hears my plea,
I find two beings sharing a cell within me.
There is a king fighting for his crown
A wizard whose magic holds the king down.

He'll attack as long as the clock in the cell ticks.
Excuse is the name of all the wizard's tricks.
When the king pierces him, believing he's won,
The wizard laughs: "I will never be gone!"

The struggle will continue until one of them gives in.
Hoping for victory is better than having illusion win.
But no matter how many illusions there may be.
They are lessons on the road to becoming free.

Albert Ter-Tovmasyan

To Be Born Free

To be born free,
Is to be born wild,
To be born free,
Is to be born ignorant,
To be born human,
Is to be born a slave,
Nothing in life is free,
And nothing is free in life,
We all play the game,
Where the stakes are high,
It's greater than the fates,
To live or die,
No-one is unlinked,
No-one has no ties,
We do what we must,
To live,
And survive

Nilesh Thanki

The Barren Fig Tree

They talked, and talk laughed;
It echoed on the wind and danced
Bruising the divine scales.
They laughed, and laughter laughed
Fruit of a barren fig tree.
They snickered, and snickers snickered
Darts darted from faceless forces.
A pointed finger pointed
A pilgrimage to a mirage.
Withered in withered darkness,
A withered finger withered.

Patrick Springer

Senses Of The Sky

The dark sky looms heavily above.
It tells a story of loss and love.
It tells a tale only you see.
It may be different for someone like me.
Tell me, tell me, what does it say?
Does it show you the path?
Does it show you the way?
Does it tell of love bordered with hurt?
Does it weep with the rain as it falls to the dirt?
And now do you see it soaking the earth?
Absorbing your soul and all you are worth?
Can it cleanse your soul?
Can it cleanse your mind?
Can it put all your troubles safely behind?
The dark sky looms heavily above.
It tells a story of loss and love.

Dara Mackay

Untitled

If the world could speak
It would tell of its darkness
It would tell of all its pain.
Take a look at the world and see its many sorrows.
There is trouble everywhere you turn
They talk about peace for the world tomorrow
They talk about a better world to come
   for everyone.
Continuously looking for a solution to
   solve every problem.
But the solution is only in the word.

Judith Taylor

The Pub

In an outback pub we stopped.
It was a shed made out of tin,
We were sitting at the bar,
When these yankies come on in...

They said, do you mind if we take some photos,
Your two Dinkum Aussie mates,
So we can show our friends,
When we get back to the states'...

(Not an Aussie drop between us,
Me and dad we both knew that,
The only Aussie thing we had,
Was dads Akubra Hat)...

Well, he tipped his hat,
And raised his glass,
He said, "Mate, give us another pot",
And he whispered,
"We won't only fool these two son,
We fool the whole darn lot"...

G. Tiefengraber

The Wanted One

I was passing by this little cafe.
It was very chic, the neon sign said, "My Life."
And in the window stood a sign that said,
"The wanted one".
And so I stopped to look in...

In the first window I saw my family.
But I was not with them. They looked so happy.

In the second window I saw my young friends.
But I was not with them. They looked so happy.

In the third window my friends had grown.
There were new people with them, and
    they were now in pairs.
As though playing some new game
    I'd never seen.
But I was not with them.

In the forth window the pairs were less.
And the space was filled with cheerful
    little angels.
They looked so happy.
The wind blew cold and the sun hid as I
    looked into the last window.
There lay nothing but a mirror in the
    middle of the room.
And in the mirror I sat, staring back at me
    holding a sign.
As the tears rolled down my face, I read the sign.
And all it said was...."The Wanted One"

Ian Rampersad

A Black Picture

This world is dark,
It's full of violence and hatred,
Everyone is in fear of death,
And I paint a black picture.

There is no colour here,
They all died yesterday,
There is no feeling here,
And I paint a black picture.

The people have one character,
The character is the same,
As the one that I am painting,
In my black picture.

Glenda Wells

My Granny

One descriptive word?
It would have to be grand
because she's sweet and she's kind
with a great helping hand

Two descriptive words
well they'd be patient and wise
because she's guided my life
with calm watchful eyes.

Three descriptive words
How about gentle and successful
with pride, because she's made it
through life, with one strong and
brave stride.
Four descriptive words.
Now they'd be sweet, valued wrinkled
and great I love her so dearly
and she's now sixty eight

Julie Solmosan

Quilters Plea

One stitch at a time Lord
It's so hard to do
One stitch at a time Lord
That's all we can do
So help us my sisters
To see us thru
Help us my sisters
We are depending on you
One stitch at a time Lord
Please help us to do
This beautiful quilt
We are making for you

Margaret Francis Weiland

To The Blessed Children

The poor little children
Just starting their day
The poor little children
Too young to pray

A kiss, a hug
And maybe a tear
By a parent when leaving
and feeling no fear

Oh Lord, why did you take them
So young and so sweet?
Did you take them to gather
Around your feet?

Talking to them
With voice calm and clear
Thank you, my Lord
For keeping them near

Now they are gone
And we are apart
They will always remain
Very dear in our hearts

Gladys O'Brien

Happiness

Happiness is a Loving God
It's something we've always had.
Happiness is a rich dessert.
A thought that makes you glad.

Happiness is a tiny spark
That starts a fire's glare.
It also is a friendly smile
And knowing that you care.

Happiness is a swimming hole
On a hot summer's day.
Happiness is a nursery rhyme,
Or a child hard at play.

Happiness is just coming home
After a day of stress.
And living life to its fullest;
Is true and complete happiness.

Bernice M. Keep

Earth

Please don't take my home away,
It's the only one I've got.
It's full of birds and trees and things
That I cherish quite a lot.

The roof is like blue topaz,
The floor is emerald green,
And all the features on it,
Are really quite a scene.

So why do they want to take it?
I've lived here all my life!
They just don't comprehend the fact
That it's like stabbing me with a knife!

Adriana Villela

Down And Out

I'm just a hard rock pussy cat
I've been around the town,
But my bones are getting brittle,
and those cool cats get me down

My attitude has changed a lot
so if to me you will adhere,
I'll not give you any troubles
and I'll sleep away the years.

My appetite is quite petite
I've learned to do without
I'll only eat a small amount
And you'll never see a mouse.

If that doesn't meet your standard
and with you there is no hope,
please pass the word around the town
and help this old puss out.

Marion Mortimer

Math

Math is fun,
Math is cool,
Math is an important part of school.
Some kids think it's boring,
But really, it's exploring
The numbers of your mind.
So find your joy in math.
You'll find it's really cool.
Math is fun,
Math is cool,
Math is an important part of school.

Laura Pearlman

My Opal

Within my opal
Lies the dream
Of a reflected ocean

Filled with mystery
Awakened by love
Colours rippling through
Like an icicle that drips
Emotions running
To the edges of the senses

While the soul of the stone
Receives the sun
Embracing it to the end

Christina G. Roberts

Why Count Sheep?

The doors are locked and bolted;
I've checked the windows too.
The T.V.'s off (made sure of that)
Nothing else to do.
Another day is over:
One not too bad, it's true.

Pull up the sheets and snuggle down
(It's freezing cold outside);
The pillow's soft; I've lost that frown,
Unconscious that I tried.
A cozy night ahead of me,
Tucked warm and safe as safe can be.

Peace and calm are precious;
Contentment; easy mind;
Clear conscience - nothing worries me;
Today is all behind.
Tomorrow is another day
Two seconds, and I'm far away.

Ian Christie

Memories Of You

Sorrow not what might have been, rather
Joy in our memories when time was with you.
Ours for a season, to hold with delight,
Love's loan now reclaimed to his home.

Lamb of God given in love for mankind;
Ours not by choice, yet yielded in raised reflection.
Our lives richer for the memory of you, my child;
Though, in vain, time's comfort fills this
   emptiness within.

Throughout our years together,
You carved a well into my soul,
Now filled with memories of you,
I reach down and draw them out, to pour
Over a heart thirsty for your embrace.

Still my soul sings through the strength of God's spirit,
With memories of you setting harmony to my song.
Though emptiness and thirst for a while are love's pains,
Each now is comforted in triumph o'er the grave.

Our lives now abiding in faith, hope and love,
Where God's grace allows us these
memories of you.

Brian Fryer

Romeo Is Bleeding

Romeo is bleeding all over Juliet's dress
Juliet slashes her arm to destroy the
sodden mess
lying in each others arm
Lovers of sweet, sweet doom
No one understood them
No one knew their gloom.

Hamlet sees a ghost that bleeds a sad sad song
But Romeo's still bleeding while the
reaper plays along
Juliet had died, and Romeo has too
And all of their sweet sorrow's have
turned to darkened blue

Natasha Keleher

A Special Friend

Everywhere's a crying soul standing in the rain,
Just like somewhere there's a special friend,
Trying to stop the pain,
It's that special friend that found you,
When others shut you out,
That always sticks right by you,
As you kick, and scream, and shout,
No other can replace that friend,
In good times and the bad,
'Cause that friend is with you all the time,
Even when you're sad,
You go together like a pair,
Until one of you dies,
Then even in your memories,
That special friend still lies.

Angela Bittner

The Ebbing Tide

The waves of the sea
   keeps rolling along.
As one disappear
   another comes on.
It teaches a lesson
   it seems to say.
You may not be here tomorrow
   though you are today.

In this sea of life,
   we are the restless waves
We rise in this world,
   just to ebb in our graves
So while we are here
   and keep rolling along,
Let us follow the waves
   and keep singing a song.

Cynthia Berkenbos

Little Girl Lost?

The day is finally here at last,
Kindergarten days have gladly past.
I am the little girl with big hopes and dreams,
Of special fun and large icecreams.
Leaving mummy for the first full day,
Seeing her cry, I'm on my way.
Watching her weep, I wonder why?
Perhaps a stray lash in her eye.
Grandma's so proud and daddy is too,
A special gift for the day, a ribbon of blue.
Remembering back to that emotional event,
I wonder is the little girl in me lost?
Or just spent.

Nadine Ribchester

The Tears Of The Rose

Do not wipe away the tears in shame
Let them fall like the rain
For each tear that falls from your saddened eyes
Are symbolic, just as the rose that you
hold for me

The tears that slowly trickle down
Are for the memories of laughter that followed us
The tears that race down
Are for the bitter-sweet moments passed

Watch the rose as it blooms
Think of the times we had while I watched you grow
When the rose dies
Do not let the memories of me die with it

Please do not be ashamed to cry
For each tear holds a moment of time
Think of me, and my rose will forever bloom.

Heather Dolby

The Assassin

A fanatic mad with rage and hate,
   lies with cradled gun in wait.
Crouched behind a pile of books,
   then peering down the sights he looks.

Waiting with the sights aimed high,
   to deal out death from out the sky.
Down below the crowd all cheer's,
   in one brief moment turns to tears.

Three shots have left the assassin's gun,
   the foul deed murder; has been done.
Now a man lies cold and still,
   throughout the world we feel the chill.

And wonder why this man so great,
   In the Rotunda; lies in state.
Then they start to take his stock,
   And know his loss the States will rock.

But we've learned from J.F.K.
   In every cloud there is a ray.
And we'll take a lead from him,
   his leadership will never dim.

Gerry Driver

"Life"

You puzzle yourself about life,
Life goes on.
You wonder why you are here,
But life goes on.

Life in itself is infinite,
From the smallest egg
to the largest animal,
nature embraces us all.

Life is an unbroken chain,
A life ends - another begins.
So why try to find the answer to life?
It is hard to look for something we already have.

Rob Cotterill

Forbidden Love

A star sprang into the darkness,
Lighting the shadows of our lives;
The world was great for the day
Our love conversed to say:

Teach us, O God to be tender,
Immerse us into full surrender
The glorified feeling of being one
Before your ire and wrath is done.

Let us nurse this flame of kindness
And not join the flock of mindless
Souls, whose hunger for lust
Lack our all encompassing trust.

Our day of love shall endure
And grow in its beauties allure
The feeling of wonder has no end
In our heart, till our lives are spent.

Hans H. Vogt

The Last Harvest

Dashed to the shattered earthen floor,
Like some bruised and battered god.
A ringing steel-toothed beast screams
into the dying desert of broken trees.
Split wooden limbs ricochet, flung as
harpoons into the oil stained air.

"Damn you Mother Earth! There hasn't
been rain since we first arrived!
The land is barren, the soil is dry!
If the forest cannot restore itself,
I'll be out of work and my sons will die!"

Small, meager clumps of rainforest
suddenly reach to the heavens; a calm,
sighed relief as Her tear drops fall:

"You don't know what it's like, dear
friend, to lose a million sons a day.
Every child I lose, I become a little
more numb to the pain...
Soon, my heart will be so hard
that you'll never, ever see the rain."

Jared Bielby

Lost In The Moment

Lost in the moment fears rises to the surface
Like the head in your glass of beer
You blow it away choosing not to drink it
Becoming part of the haze

Victory for a moment but fleeting it would seem
Fear that has not been dealt with
Will crawl back on its knees

And when you think you've beaten it
Fears rises to the occasion

You've only second guessed it
Now it's part of the equation

Fear casts a shadow over the soul
All you are and ever would be
Are reflected in the fears
You refuse to see

These are fears that you must face
Dreams that are fought hardest for
Will take shape and form
By challenging fear as it surfaces
And riding out the storm

Laura L. Lang

Untitled

People ask me questions
Like Who? What? Why? Where?
When?
But I've seen so many changes
In some three score years and ten;
  I just can't remember.

There were friends I used to know so well,
In different walks of life.
But names of those who meant so much,
In times of peace, or strife.
  I just can't remember.

There were times when I knew happiness,
And some when I shed tears.
But all that caused that joy or grief
In me throughout the years.
  I just can't remember.

Why they happened exactly where.
What day, or month, or year?
My mind is filled with memories.
But yet it's very clear;
  I just can't remember.

Mary R. Mayer

The Lady Of Sorrows

The lady of sorrows
Lives in a white house
With green shutters,
And a grapevine wreath on the door.

Her heart has been bothering her lately.
At five in the morning
She is awake, looking for the tablets
That will calm the troubled beats.

But what will ease the sorrows of her life,
When husband, friends and child
Have all gone, leaving her alone
In the white house.

At five in the morning,
She reaches for her rosary
To pray her way
Through another long day.

Paulette Lalonde

Reminiscence

On this day of November,
lives of men we remember,
who gave their lives in war.
In historic days of you.

Remember the shadowed past,
where our ancestor had cast,
where, our mistakes were made,
and where our memories fade.

Remember the men who fought,
the mistaken that were tough,
the tales of torturous battles,
and the end that now tattles.

Remember the people of peace,
until all wars do cease
which, then remember the present,
where we threaten the moment

After remember the future,
and what we may endure,
for history can repeat
and old problem begin to heat.

Lesley Manovich

He's An Indian And A Loner

He's an Indian and a loner,
Living in a whiteman's world,
And I wish that he'd share some of his
  time with me.

He's an Indian and a traveler,
Living in a world with love paved road,
And I wish that he'd take me when he leaves.

He's an Indian and a poet,
Oh he writes about the birds,
And I wish that he'd fly away with me.

He's an Indian and a nighthawk,
Spending those long night's alone,
And I wish that he'd spend those nights
  with me.

He's an Indian and he's gorgeous,
And he knows how I feel,
And I wish that he felt the same for me.

Well, he's an Indian and a loner,
Living in a white man's world,
And oh, how I wish that he'd share some
of his time with me.

Mary T. Smith

For Your Tomorrow

Fighting for heaven,
Living in Hell;
How long have we been here?
I can no longer tell.

Yelled at each morning,
Screamed at each night;
Told not to argue,
Taught how to fight;

Clasping our rifles,
Our hearts full of dread;
I wish death in battle
and not in my bed.

Adrienne de Souza

Children Of The Abyss

They sit squirming in their seats,
Look around, and kick their feet.
Bite their nails and twist their hair,
Give the impression they just don't care.

Report card time - their hands are shaking
Dejected and sad their hearts are breaking
The terrible words, "you just aren't trying.
Consumes them. Inside they're dying.
Oh how they long for a loving hug,
For their parents to say were proud of you son"
For their teacher to say, "a job well done."
These are the children with blank sad looks.
Who can't understand what's written in books
Computers and math, beyond comprehension,
Deep inside confusion and tension.
Their purpose in life is not learning, but teaching.
Trusting, simplicity, caring and giving.
Is the example mankind should be living
They justly can stand proud and tall.
The children who try the hardest of all.

Evelyn Wallace

The Other Day

I turned around the other day
looking for your face
I caught myself the other day
looking for a trace
a laugh
a whisper
a smile
from you
and I remember that you're gone
to a better place they say
you tore apart my world
it was built around you
it all came crashing down on me
just the other day.

Dana Bertram

Showain Neme'shin

Showain Neme'shin - pity me
Love blinded me 'til I couldn't see.
Nenemoo'sha - sweetheart, I did name him,
For all time, pledged my life and limb.

Shah shah - long ago, in the distant past
We cherished each other, and remained steadfast.
Kena'beek - a serpent in the garden of Eden now?
I believed your promises - your vow.

Showain Neme'shin - pity me
Love blinded me 'til I couldn't see.
Mishe Mokwa - the great bear, hug me to rest.
Shangoda'ya - a coward, now I'm put to the test.

Segwun on a way - spring awake
It is the time to give, and the time to take,
Nenemoo'sha - sweetheart, I did name him.
For all time, pledged my life and limb.

Patricia Deban

Secrets

Hidden deep in the caverns of my soul
Lurks darkness lying in wait for a chance
To escape through the softness of my mouth
And ricochet through someone's hollow mind

Seeking a golden opportunity
To escape the iron bars of my mind
Painful darkness throbs and wrestles my will
To leave in the tears streaming down my cheeks

Senseless garble in my brain begs me speak
But these are secrets never to be told
No matter what toll they take within me
So, my mind stands vigilant, guarding the dark

Secrets I have never told anyone
They shall cause my sad heart to stop beating
I will lie in a shroud of cold grey mist
Buried with the secrets I never told

Heather Evans

Rockport

The thirsty smell of the sea
Makes me want to breathe faster
To take in all the coolness
It comes as far as the main street
Narrow and cobblestoned
Full of people and flower boxes
White picket fences and stone walks
Lead straight to the harbor
The sailboat spotted cove
Weathered shacks decorated
In hanging nets, shells, starfish
The heat gets worse
Now I want to live out on that sea
Away from the clam shell, hook covered
docks
To be with the men in hip-high rubber
boots
Who look like bowling pins
In front of the sun
I feel dizzy and faint
And climb back into
The air-conditioned car

Jenny Sharp

The Tragic Story Of Mary Jane

One fine, sunny day,
Mary Jane was playing
In the garden and her
Mother was saying,

"The way you're sitting,
Your dress will get wrinkled."
Mary Jane didn't reply
While the wind chimes tinkled.

High above,
Foreign men in a plane
Were going to drop a bomb
On Mary Jane!

She didn't hear the whistle,
Until it was as loud as a roar,
Then little Mary Jane
Existed no more.

Jasmin Islam

Untitled

When cosmapekadekulators,
mate with Diskumbobulators,
results are quite dramatic,
as you know.

But when Treskadelipolymars,
begin to copulate in pickle jars,
electrocompalated jelly,
starts to grow.

It's green with little wiggly bits,
and will grow very large,
so buy a great big shovel,
and load it on a barge.

Then tow it down the river,
until you reach the sea,
where Astrodokalopticus,
will eat it - greedily!

The moral here, I'm sure you'll see,
is clearly very plain,
are Treskadelipolymars,
now breeding in your drain?

Geoff Warner

Unspoken Words

Useful words
meant to discuss and solve
shaky moments in life and love.

Bitter words
spoken in angry tones
in disagreement and rage.

They speak,
they yell,
and nothing's gained until.

A hand is raised
and with each wordless blow
come painful throbs.

Which soon become
unresisting agreement.
CAN A HAND REALLY SPEAK LOUDER
THAN WORDS?

Lori Maser

"Neighbours"

Why were neighbours, long ago,
more friendlier, than today,
was it because, they were mostly your relatives,
who kept in touch each day.

But now, if you're ill, and needing help,
your neighbours don't seem to rare,
Yet years ago, when they made a meal,
they'd bring you, in a share.

And if your children misbehaved,
as youngsters always do,
Your neighbours, would chastise them,
and then report to you.
But now, People don't seem to take the time,
to stop and chat any more,
So you're very lucky nowadays,
if you know the folk next door.

Jean Hendrie

Special Words

Those words mean so
much,
She has longed to hear
them,
So full of fear but still
excited,
She slips into her dress,
pretty but plain,
She's in love and today
she'll make it known,
She wants her new life
to begin today,
Today she's saying I do
to the man she loves,
and this day will stay
forever in her mind,
He opened his heart and
let her into love
him.

Melini Fralick

The Sound Of Love

My first time ever I saw your face
My heart stood still in wonder
And in the silence I could hear a sound
It filled a void within my soul
And bade me live.

How strange a sound, a rhythmic rasping
As of sand and sea, crashing against
A far off lonely shore, insistent, primitive
And urgent, it made the tremble with a
Passion unknown to me before.

And from your hand I took the cup
Which held the sweet and bitter wine of love
And in return I gave to you
The one and only thing I owned
My love, tender and true.

O, come to me beloved heart
While my tomorrows are still a golden
Light across the sky
And let me stay within your arms and
Love me, now and forever till the end of time.

Karin Kuskis

Mare Hydrangea

My whitecapped sea,
my MARE HYDRANGEA...

In July's warm night-time obscurity
I let myself become washed over
by the fragrance from your spumous surface
of clustering flowers,
while in your cool, emerald depths
my thoughts, like kelp
swaying slowly, try to ascend
to meet the currents of nocturnal
winds and waves.

Thoughts, which as the seaweed itself
are firmly rooted in the ooze -
the dreggy sediment at the bottom of my soul,
where life and death are fighting
their neverending struggle for power
over the bodily imperfection...

In this state of serene passiveness
I will be waiting for, and once more
salute, the daybreak...

Per-Magnus Jeppson

Mosaic

Don't care me what I am.
Not be worthy
to dazzle with itself
in the attempt in vain to admire
what made, what was, what has.
I pride me, yes,
that what I wasn't
only thus I can be most light
and see besides the sun,
because from the deceptions that I didn't suffer
and from the frustrations that I didn't have
to me and the others I spared
among so partings,
amities unmade or loves unfinished,
rested me the road
and the strange, ineludible sensation
to be always incomplete.

Ronaldo Cagiano

Parenthood

"Oh babes" how you've grown,
My memory keeps holding on,
To the day first you entered my life,
Though the years have come and gone.

I always cared and loved you,
Though sometimes you didn't make this easy,
And perhaps protected but embarrassed you,
Making you feel a slightly bit queasy.

I gave you life and never did I regret,
Having known and cared for you,
As you came to know more about yourself,
Your uniqueness came shining through.

When it was time for you to venture out,
I comforted but laid awake.
My heart wanted to stay without a doubt,
But I am your parent for Pete's sake!

As my parent before me always said,
"It's harder for me to say no"
It's history repeating itself once again
Instead of saying yes and letting you go.

Dianne Camire-Griffiths

Hold Me

It's been a long time since my pen saw a page.
My struggle with life is an undying rage.
I'm heading to nowhere, somewhere far beyond
Where most of my friends lived but now
   have moved on.
My pain is unnamed and my fury so deep
What is my problem? What can I keep?
Why am I crying? What is the key?
Where am I going and who is me?
What is the point of this being alone?
I'm tired of this fight. I just want to go home.
I need you to hold me. To make it okay
To take my hand each day by day.
Why have you left me? I need you now.
I'm losing the battle, the war, somehow.
Please return to my tattered old heart
It can no longer stand to be falling apart.
Hold me and rock me until the sun
Convince me I am still someone

Eileen Bona

What's Happening

Our love is dying day by day
My thoughts tell me run away
I have a feeling down deep inside
I can't explain the reason why.

I know love has its ups and downs
You see its presence all around
I guess that's just the way love goes
It wilts then dies just like a rose.

He doesn't even care at all
He walks around so proud and tall
He will not look me in the eye
For fear he'll see the hurt inside.

Each passing morning as I wake
I lay there wondering what it'll take
To stop this broken heart of mine
From seeing how our love had died.

Elaine Walter

Gethsemane

I am alone
   no one speaks to me
      I hear nothing.

I sit
in
   vast, empty
      spaces
   and weep.

My voice
   echoes
in hollow
   wastelands

Desolation
   is my
      home.

There is nothing
   There is no-one
      and
   I weep.

Barb Bjorge

Humble Thoughts

I have never sought a spotlight,
Nor made any claim to fame,
People will never know my talents,
And won't even know my name.

I've not aspired to win my laurels,
Or reach for any brass rings,
Because in life's true story,
These are not very important things.

Seek peace, freedom, and brotherhood,
Are a few near the top of the list,
We must all stop and smell the roses,
A pleasure busy people have missed.

If I had to live life over again,
I would never change a thing,
The simple truths I still would seek,
And still be happy as any king.

When your tomorrows seem like yesterdays,
Or your humour is running low,
Give thanks for all your blessings,
And get all those ducks in a row.

John Downey

For You, Just Because

There can be no goodbyes,
Not for us.
Just because.

We are similar in our hopes
But different in our ways.
I allowed you access to my self,
You invited a response.
Thus we engaged in a dialogue
Sometimes eloquent in its silence.

Absence will not deter our communication.
The mutual bond by which we are linked
With withstand, because of its intensity.
A sound, a word, an image, will suffice
And transmit from one to the other.

So, you see,
There can be no goodbyes,
Not for us,
Just because.

Michele Bourbonnais

"While Hedgerows Freeze"

Clouds, splenetic, wrap roll-thunder.
North herald pinks fork-lightning streaks.
Hail-showers pelt rime-crystals, under
Winter's notch-cut, wind-sawn peaks.

Brindle cat yawns, independent,
Warm-snuggled, stretches, curls to purr,
Prinks with lambent licks, resplendent
Her silken-satin sheen of fur.

Breakfast sizzles as coffee roasts.
Teacups chatter, round kettles wheeze.
Tavern logs blaze, mine landlord hosts
Our New Year fun, while hedgerows freeze.

Effulgent, lustrous stars, bestrewed,
Ponder chill breath-blown tingling days,
Where amethystine lakelets, dewed,
Sun-dance through silver-shivered haze.

Old folk shawl their slippered shuffle.
Dark, dormant countryside 'neath snow.
Breadcrust scavenger-birds ruffle.
Trees sleep, stark, veined, 'gainst twilight glow.

Michael Roy

Tomorrow

You are leaving tomorrow and I be here.
Not able to see you and hold you near.
With the thought of it I shed a tear.
Since we've been one you've been so sincere.

In five weeks we will be one.
I don't know how fast it will come.
Fast and slow days, there will be some.
But our happiness is the outcome.

Tonight the last night we will be,
Intimate, just you and me.
In five week we will see,
How bad I'll want to make love to thee.

I will miss you while you are there,
And I hope that you'll take care.
When you do have time to spare,
Think of me and the life we'll share.

Grace Moyer

Untitled

In a vast majestic field,
Not far from your home,
Randomly scattered patches of green
grass grows -
Millimetres to miles high.
Hills roll to the West,
Where the sun repeatedly dies.
East is a mighty willows home,
Awaiting the arrival of dawn.
Whose tranquil light dances with Tree,
And melts away the storm.

A secret place this has remained
without society,
nor human vane.
No rulers telling us where to breathe,
only our lives are left to lead.

Amber Mann

Peace Talks

Well now friends you all talk of peace.
But then we see nuclear testing increase.
You're considered the most highly educated.
You are the world leaders, and the worlds greatest bleeders
Of those not nearly well-fated.

But do you really talk peace? For killings don't cease,
You are not the corpse at the top of the heap.
And oh what a bitch you're all very rich
So at night you can peacefully sleep.

Yes, you've talked peace for fifty long years,
Born with forked tongue, but minus you're ears,
But to feel any pain, one must have a brain,
And that you don't have, it appears.

You've talked for too long but simply done nothing
Spending tax payers money just huffing and puffing.
Of course you don't fool the one who is most high
But perhaps you've forgotten that you are going to die
And there's always a front seat in hell.

Peace? Peace love and humanity. Why that talks insanity
But war? That's different. Well! Well!

Edith Jensen

Damp Memories

Eyes flutter as the white light escapes through my pours
Frozen in pain as it rips out, the angel inside bursts free.

In the years my white light has grown dark, all the hatred
and suffering that man has inflicted, has turned me against them.

Shuttering as night falls, once more I close my eyes,
and bow my head.

The anguish is too much, I run and run as the sorrow washes
through me.

I collapse and bitter sorrow grasps me as I lie down and wait,
for my final breath to be taken.

My blood grows thick and slow as my heart beats with all its
might. As my head grows light my eyes blur.
Nothing can be changed now, how I wish for another chance.

My entire life runs, scene by beautiful scene,
I cry as all the people I love vanish and the darkness slowly
encroaches upon me.

I wish the best for all of them, and hope, that someone,
somewhere will remember me and feel love.

And as I closed my eyes, my light arose bright, once again.

Cassandra Crosbie

The Rudder I Want To Hold

Paper boats I have put into the brook; Look!
They are being carried downstream by the current.
Where are they bound for?
What is going to become of them?
No one knows.
Their fate is in the hands of the Goddess of the River.

I refuse to consign myself to a wooden boat,
And let the current of time take me wandering.
The rudder of life I want to hold!
To have complete control over where I go!
Either heading downstream or upstream,
All is for me to decide.

Hsiao-Wen Wu

Mon Ami Quebec

I love you, Quebec, mon ami, my heart extends to thee
I mourn for your fragile spirit shattered at Meech
Feeling rejected by Canadians you desire to fly free
To be recognized for your distinct and unique society
Separation of our country is a fearful thought to me
I love poutine, tortier and Grandmere's secret recipe
I love Monsier Bon Homme and your majestic scenery
I love your eloquent tongue and cultural diversities.

Your roots are firmly planted in Canada's family tree.
If you choose to sever these limbs we both shall bleed
We cannot erase history when our eyes refused to see
Our ancestors embraced ignorance and evil racial bigotry
Our generation must not inherit their insidious disease
We can heal our wounds together, plant forgiveness seed.
Understanding and faith must guide our future and destiny
When the referendum booths open please do not vote "Qui"
Do not bequeath your farewell kiss upon my salted cheeks.

    Elaine Irwin

His Match

Striding around being the king he is,
nobody can deny that the forest is his.
Then one day a brownie strolled in,
there was an eerie silence as they stared
deep within. As the king stepped up,
challenging him, they all knew the fight was
to begin. Bodies smashing, dancing and prancing,
each trying to stop the other's teeth from slashing.
At this time the king knew that the brownie was
stealing his forest domain. If the brownie were to
win he would no longer remain.

They battled for hours, spilling blood on the ground,
still no winner had been found. After awhile there
was a lethal slash, and the brownie's jugular
vein was bloody gash. The king was the winner
and the forest was once again his domain, for years
on end he would remain.

    Clint Pendleton

Rainbow O'er The Sables

Against the cold, the bitter bitter cold; I know,
In pain the youngster responded; then parted;
On the icy ledged shore of the Sables below.

Leaning forward and on one bended knee;
Distressed, reaching forward, one arm had he/she offered thee.
Perilous were the moments; then from above;
Colorful and goaded, a rainbow offered love.

"Go back! Don't go! Come back! Stay away!"

The two in the water were related, 'tis sure I know,
To the youngster above. They reached, kissed, let go.
Then they swam strongly across the pool.

"Oh Pandora you're simply no fool."

He slumping backward, summoned her soul.
Then dove she o'er into the boiling frigid depths.
Strange was the feeling watching their deaths.

"Oh mighty river Sabled and sleek;
This messenger of mercy knows Pandoras your keep.
Where mighty river is that child today?
As mysterious as your rainbow wouldn't you say?"

    Carol Ann Hart

My Little Man

I look down upon you and watch closely as you sleep,
I smile and look ahead as you begin to creep.
I'll make life as simple and as good as I can,
I want you to be happy, my little man.

No hate, no sorrow, no fear do you know,
This will all come later when you begin to grow.
Don't bother to worry, no need to plan,
We'll talk about this later, my little man.

Your whole life and future is laid out for you today,
And mom and dad will see nothing stands in your way.
Smile my little one, smile as long as you can,
I want you to be happy, my little man.

Your cries of frustration and hunger I hear,
Somehow you seem to know pet when I draw near.
I'll care for you and love you just as long as I can,
Sleep peacefully now, my little man.

    Dorothy MacKay

Great Aunt

I have been Great Aunt Louise to three
For certainly a lengthy time you see
So you can really imagine my surprise
End of the year I was great aunt to five

In February, my greatness increased to six
For none of my nieces or nephews are fixed.
I really believed I had gone to (great) heaven
When in April the quantity increased to seven.

You should really understand I am truly great
When last month the count had grown to eight
So let's all celebrate with a bottle of wine.
You guessed it, in the fall there'll be nine!

    Claire Chapeski

I Love You Mom and Dad

I've been through a lot you know
And your love and caring surely shows
I know it pains you to see me cry
Asking God oh why
Parents are special for every child
They can change your tears into smiles
I'm pleased God chose you for me
Through my eyes I know you see
My love for you sets deep in my heart
Even when we are apart
I know that I don't often say I love you
But I want you to know my love for you is very true
We've had our share of ups and downs
Smiles, laughter, tears and frowns
Our love is draped in silk and lace
No one can ever take your place
I love you dearly Mom and Dad
I'm glad I'm the daughter that you had

    Celia Unger

Friendship

Such a rare and precious jewel,
it shines with good care, but usually breaks with wear
So fine.. I thought it was mine,
I thought I had found this special jewel.. .. oh so cruel..
the truth hidden away... and then with a burst of wind,
the crackle of lightening.. and then.. the rain
all of my memories of my special jewel gone in a day
such a price to pay.. what can I say?
I turned my back and saw the crack growing wider and darker..
so confused.. were you amused?..
my trust abused! I closed my eyes as I cried..
something inside died.. why all those lies?..
Did I really deserve?.. So absurd!..
I heard it all.. why didn't you call, out to me..
did you lose your key?..
I will never see that rare and special jewel again... it's gone
shattered like fine glass
I don't know if it will ever mend,.. my special friend
I cry as I say good-ye.. I turn my back and vow to never look back..
Friendship.. I don't believe I will ever see, like that.. again

Gwen Rathbone

Love

God gave his most precious special gift called, love.
In bond of Marriage, man and woman become truly one.
A pure and holy unity, blessed by "Jesus," his holy son.
To benedict the marriage with children, love, and fun.

He created, this gift, holy matrimony, with all his love.
This sacrament, he blessed, through the trinity, above.
A man, in love, must leave this parents, his good home.
Woman, her family; to be united with husband her own.

The unity, in marriage will become one flesh from two.
Vine, enwrapped, clinging, in rapturous love, known by few.
Therefore, a husband, must love his wife dearly like himself.
A married woman, her man comes humbly first before herself.

God, please consecrate all marriages from heaven, above.
Bless them in purity, and holiness, committed in love.
We thank you for this eternal gift from your precious son.

M. Evangelista

Late Summer, Cool Dawn

Dew clings to grass in silvery drops
Light breeze carries beginnings of fall
    Scents of wood smoke and leaves.
The orange goddess peeks over the horizon
    her rays reveal a sea of amber
A vast carpet d'or, stretches as far as the eye can see
    A lark, warbles to its mate over the prairie
Gentle wind rifles the gold, like waves on the sea
    New sounds now, the low rumble of
    some great mechanical beast
    A loud rustle is heard, as the golden soldiers
nod their crowns, once more to their queen
before being sucked into the maw of the beast
The goddess rises high now, her face all but
    obscured, by a veil of choking dust
thrown high into the azure prairie sky.

Marvin M. Shell

Exploring

Exploring, searching for something,
Not knowing exactly what,
Perhaps one day you will know,
By chance or by skill,

In caves and in caverns,
In holes and in tunnels,
The crevasses of rocks,
The shadows of the waters,

Not knowing where,
Or how,
Or even why,
But someday...,someday,

To work hard,
But not to be obsessed,
To venture,
But taking time for yourself and others,

The pride,
The glory,
The wisdom that comes with these,
Starting the adventure again.

John Roy

"A Mother"

She brings us into this world,
Not knowing what life may hold for us,
But she is committed on doing her best,
And raising us as the best she can,
She is a mother.

She does not dwell on the past,
But tries always to look to the future,
Knowing that she is responsible for that little life,
Which she alone has brought both into this world,
She is a mother.

She know's deep inside,
That she may face hard times
And she will undoubtedly make mistakes
But we as children,
"never really growing up,"
In her loving eyes,
Must stand by her side, always.
And try to endeavor to return some of the cherished devotion,
that she has always shown us.
She is a Mother.

Keith E. Kyle

Dolphins

Dolphins playing in the water,
On the shore I rest and watch.
Leaping, frolicking in shining waters,
Playing, resting amongst the rocks.
High waves come in which dolphins swim,
I love to watch them coming in.
Night has fallen, all is dark,
Silence has come to dolphin park.

Erin Fong

Brandy

I have a friend she is so true,
She's always there when I am blue,
Her Golden hair is like the sun,
She's always ready to have some fun,
I tell her all my thoughts and dreams,
She listens well and never screams,
I love my friend with all my heart,
And hope to God we'll never part.

Tracy Foden

Untitled

I am but a fantasy,
  not reality.

So I'm not real
I do not exist.

I'm but a liar,
  not truth.

I should know better
  I don't know

The liers make excuses.

I'm but a dream
  With lies and wishes

I ran with fantasies
I run into loneliness
  stumbled into the past

An unhappy heart
like one of a joyless child

Soon this dream will fade
  the truth of myself

will not exist..... until I face reality

Karmyn Luciani

Band Of Gold

Once young and strong
Now old and grayed
Love has come and gone
Wish it had stayed

Time stands still
A broken heart cries
Only memories remain
As love's light dies

Years slowly pass by
This heart went cold
All that is left now
Is a little band of gold

Rachel VanDer Weide-Church

My Dream And Desire

We have waited so long
now the battle is over
though the country's more strong
I'm not exactly in clover

For

My business has gone
washed right down the drain
though the damage is done
I can sing this refrain

When

With nothing to lose
I can live without pressure
And carefree would choose
To retire and seek treasure

Where

To search for a place
With political freedom
And leave the rat race
For a trouble free kingdom

Just to have the right to a harmonious
twilight

Evelyn Parker

Untitled

As we reminisce together
Of all the days gone by
Many have made us laugh
And many made us cry
The places that we've been to
All the friends that we have met
Paint a beautiful picture
We could never forget

Every bend in life's road
A new chapter in life's book
Gives us strength, gives us pride
In all the chances we took
All the caring, all the sharing
Precious memories never fade
We can look back and be contented
Knowing what a difference we made

Maureen Morrison Baxter

Things That Might Have Been

I paused awhile to think again
Of all the things that might have been,
Within my heart there beats a need
For something more than just routine.
Were I a singer I would compose,
Something to dream on before you doze,
But that's not me so I'll pick up my pen,
Before the idea is gone again.
Each one has a gift, be it ever so small,
A measure for one, and something for all.
To want what we have is more enduring
Than to have what we want and need
reassuring.
It takes only a moment to write this down,
Before the idea's forever gone.
Before it's too late I want to say,
I'm glad for whatever has come my way.

Eileen Sharp

The Moon

A golden girl
of grandeur
waltzes
across the ballroom sky.
Slowly
she takes a step,
then hesitates.
Then she slips away
hidden by her playmates;
on and on she dances
across the way.
The little candles dim,
and
flicker,
in the distance.
The floor is crowded
with admirers.
She takes a long look back
then,
glides into the darkness.

Marleen Ackerson White

"Above And Below The Mist"

To pass through the mist,
Of mountains and slough,
To see a bright sky
Of an indigo, blue,
Up the dirt trail,
Of the high hills we go,
A silvery sheen through
The wolf willows blew,
Along the road banks
A lovely red hue,
Where sweet and delicious,
Wild strawberries grew,
To grades in one room,
Of Peace Prairie school.
Back through the mist,
from an indigo blue,
Down the sleep trail.
horse and buggy flew,
Back to the ranch,
Of the home I knew
from an indigo blew.

Iola Haftner

Blessings Of The Sun

On the velvet tipped wings
of proud bird on high,
lye the answers to all questions
that one wonders why.

Yet, in each we seek wisdom
to be happy and be content,
But the colors of some souls
are tainted rainbows of repent.

The blessings of the sun,
are warm and full of hope,
as a child's heart is pure and free,
and needs love and faith to cope.

The green grass, the blue skies,
the butterflies in flight.
Are all from heavens canvas of stars,
that dreams have brought to life.

To see, to feel,
to be all as one,
is why God created you,
And sent blessings from his son!

Brian Cullen

Remembering

It is the eleventh hour
of the eleventh day
of the eleventh month

I gaze at the solemn faces of the veterans
And their loved ones
Fifty years later,
They still fight back
Tears

What are they remembering

Because they believed in
The cause of peace
They gave selflessly
They gave with courage
They gave their youth
They gave their love
They gave their lives
To give us freedom

We give them, once a year,
On minute of silence

Cairine Caughill

For All Our Todays

I pledge allegiance to the flag
Of the Free County
And to the Republic for which
It used to stand,
One nation under God, indivisible,
With liberty and justice for all.

I pledge allegiance to the flag
Of the United Races of the World
And to the peoples
For which it stands,
One humanity under God, indivisible,
With liberty and justice for all.

Bridget Pearson

The Mystic Sea

I sat on the old craggy cliff in awe
Of the wondrous scene Mother Nature did draw,
The thunderous waves rose like a vulture in flight
Converging and ravishing all in sight.

If foamed and frothed, it was an angry sea
Well hidden secrets from you and me,
Within its depths many an anguished soul
Was laid to rest while the sea took its toll.

The Winds that thwarted the sea below
Became a gentle breeze that let me know,
After a stormy sea there comes a calm
Its peaceful beauty like the words of a psalm.

My fellow man learn a lesson here
If you harbour anger you will drown in despair,
There is peace at the shores of a tranquil sea
To nurture the soul of you and me.

Barbara Barbour

Foresight

I had a vision
of times long gone
and dreams undone
a time when I could smile
and feel the sun on my face
there was a time
when I thought of the future
and you
my people yet to come
of faces fresh
and a hunger for knowledge
a passion for the past
inspiration
and a lust for life
drive me on my journey
to leave a marker worth tracking
find me
so I can find you
someday

Kim Kemsley

The Rapids

Water rushing down in torrents;
So beautiful; so turbulent.
Frothing, rushing, bubbling, swift
Tumbling over the rocks.

Two canoeists battling the current,
Paddles dipping rhythmically;
Slowly progressing forward.
Around the river's bend they go,
The turbulent peace restored.

Wyn Kochie

Summer

Flower, flower, everywhere,
Oh, what a lovely sight!
No matter where I turn to look
The garden's a delight.

Sparrows sing out merrily,
Fragrance fills the air,
Ladybugs and butterflies
Go flitting here and there.

Robins hunt the ground for worms,
Squirrels chatter from the tree,
Honeybees and tiny ants
Are active endlessly.

Relaxed by sun and cooling breeze,
Whiling away the hours,
I serenely sit and contemplate
Among the garden flowers.

Helen Miller

Memories

When the wind blew cool
On our burning mouths
Shivers slid on me as you were
Quivering for love at my breast.
Your eyes sang joyfully all your
Feelings to me
As I totally fell into your soul
Giving you every secret emotion
I had.

Why, why, why arc you not here
Anymore with me
To keep my hand tenderly
To steal hugs and kisses?
Where have they gone our lost days?
Never, never, never had memories
Danced more intensely
On the edge of an unforgettable
Moment.

Daniela Kustrin

My Dad

A man got married and with his wife
on their honeymoon did go
To meet a man he never met
But knew about so long ago.

The meeting place was at his house
A handshake welcomed us inside
Soft, spoken words, a friendly drink,
And then it was a wave goodbye..

And to his family all grown up
I wish to cause no strife
But when we first looked eye to eye
I knew him all my life.

A feeling deep inside my heart
That makes me want to say,
I always will be proud of him
until my dying day.

But when he died, I wasn't told
This really makes me sad
For every few really knew
This great man was my Dad.

Garnett Johnson

The Silt

I come down to the river bed
Once down there I would like to rest
But pushed are the things that are dead
As river flows though I resist my best
Settled are most by the mouth of the sea
Settled am I and others like me

I mingle with leaves twigs and bricks
With gravel stones mud and sticks
The river flows in criss cross
Breaking everything she comes across
Settled are the broken as she slow
Our number increases with the flow

What fall must rise seems like a plan
Together we will rise to form land
Breaking is the river's game
Though we shall rise again and again
I will keep falling in the river bed
I may be down but I am not dead

Robert Lee

Winter's First Snow

Winter is here with first fall of snow,
Once drab, dusty lanes flaunt a mellowy glow,
Castles of crystal, patterned in lace
Iridescently shimmer with beauty, with grace.
Icicles hanging from thick frosted eves
Sparkle like diamonds on snow laden trees.
Snow on the mountains, o'er valleys and leas,
Evergreens cradling their burden with ease,
Meadows aglimmer 'neath full moonlight
Accepting winter in glowing delight.
'Mid crunch and crackle of runners on snow
Gay bursts of laughter and shouts of Hello!
Mufflered and mittoned against evening chill
A sleigh filled with children glides over a hill.
Blithe spirits of winter with cheeks all aglow
Enjoy the delights of winter's first snow.

Colleen M. Noble-Nason

The Stump

Years ago in the ancient Pacific Rain forest
once, stood this gregarious old cedar tree.
Surviving centuries of drought, wind and fire
shading flora with its dense high canopy.

Monument; this hewed ragged remain
strangely, portraying its beauty, once grand.
Stumps appear in the rain forest each year.
Nothing can stop the disruption of man.

Scarce pools of water out on the desert
surrounded by surviving Palm trees.
Desert dweller's call that, "a lovely Oasis."
Being true, what would a rain forest be?

Wilma Mary Mitchell

My Mom

She is Heaven in my eyes
She is a halo in the sky
She is a twinkle in the stars
She is a glow in the dark
She is a lamp in my heart
She is my mom, God bless her
I love her, my mom

Bev McCollom

The Kiss (Boy Meets Girl)

Were I to use a word,
One that describes you the best;
A word tho' often heard,
It stands out from the rest.
This aptly describes you
You do not pretend
Always true blue,
You're my *friend*.

Faithful as the sunrise,
That starts a brand new day.
Your soul spoke thru a sigh
Mine listened to it say,
"My heart is yours my *friend*"
Metamorphosis
Heard it again
In a kiss.

Cecil A. Dorsett

Watchful Care

The night was dark and cold
Only images were seen
Muffled sounds floating in
From where images had been.

As I stepped out of my door
A small wisp of cool air
Blew past in an eerie way
Just enough to move my hair.

Fastening my coat up snugly
Against the cool of the night
Hurried on toward the car
Suddenly noticing a light.

Brightly shone from high above
Millions of tiny lights
Sparkling, twinkling, dancing
Causing quite a wonderful sight.

Gradually, understanding
God's watching care over me
From the marvellous sight
God meant for me to see.

Evelyn F. Robinson

Her Eye Through The Telescope

Miles below the razor cliff two white
opposing yacht bisect the circle
in her view.

A bowl of turquoise calm
streaks paler tints where wind
and current play. All matter floating

In spectral grace, heaven gleaming

minutely off riffling waves
so she never sees
two yacht crossing.
They glide in silent luminosity,
always approaching
never meeting.

Ramsay Wood

Void

The eternal unfeeling
the greatest suffering
that one cannot remember
is sleeping without dreaming.
Our frozen heart has stopped
it's clockwork.
Time has stopped and so the seasons,
timeless time is the birth of stillness
like birth itself, unconscience.

Raymond Ezra

Metamorphic Assault

My circle of seasons surrounds me
Oppressing my options of growth
Deficient of that joyous equal
Misplacing a share of my worth.

Festered with heights of enmity
Which perpetually unites with it's source
Overwhelmed by it's impressive summit
But incompetent to recover my force.

Deceived by this orb of reflection
Apprehending it's ideals as untruths
Absent of the degree of intensity
Essential to acquit my disputes.

A weak trace of promise sparks faintly
As I catalogue this earnest entreat
Discouraged by it's boundless insistence
With the possible risk of defeat.

Brenda Lee Leclair

Poem For A Chopper Pilot

Is that the sound of my heart beating
 Or is it the chopper that will bring you to me.
Hope is jumping around inside
 as I get up to look out the window.
I see the red and white bird in the sky
 and I am very anxious.
I want to be near you and touch you.
 Do you feel this way too?
Only time can prove your intentions
 But, I know in the darkness
 you will call for me
 wanting me too
So, until darkness comes......

Debbie Webb

Highway Of My Life

Sometimes I speed along
other times I cruise
upon the highway of my life
yesterdays are my exits
tomorrows my entrances
but crossroads are my today
at which I must make my choice
have passed others
have been passed myself
and in passing have felt
the influencing wind
of many a different personality
still I travel on as I must
searching for a rest stop
seeking a hideaway
where my life can stand still
and I can trace
with wisdom then
the route along
my life's highway

Calvin K. Preddie

Nothing

Nothing is iron clad,
Or roughly cast in stone.
Nothing can be felt,
Until the truth is known.

Nothing lasts forever,
Or so I'm often told.
Nothing could be better,
Seems further down the road.

Nothing ever happens
When you sit and wait.
Nothing really matters
When you see that it's too late.

Nothing ever seems right
When dreams take too long.
Nothing could be harder
Than doing it alone.

Nothing can hurt you,
Although it usually does.
Nothing makes more sense
Than nothing ever was.

Rosalie Ferris

Angel's Letter

Watch your step for you cannot get
out of here without your heart clear

Go up and find the light
there waiting for you
now the time is right
to develop into a angel
others have succeeded, so will you

Before you realize, your time is through
so wisely develop, prosper, and grow
for we need as many angels to go
back into darkness to spread white light
then those who've forgotten
will come too into Sight

Bring peace and love, surround yourself
as a blanket of warmth protecting the soul
we love you dearly and watch your every move
It is great joy when new wings unfold smooth.

Robin Eizner

Touch

He, bent before me,
over the pink lily-padded pond.
I poured amber water over his soft dark curls,
cool amber water over his soft warm curls.

He, bent before me,
over the shallow pool.
My fingers furroughed his hair, made channels,
moved between the water and his soft
warm hair.

He, bent before me,
over the gravel bottomed pond.
I took the water and touched him
closer then fingertips.

I, touched him, as he bent,
over the pond,
beside the trickling beaver damn,
by the large lake.

Here in this quiet place
I touched him.

Mae Vermeulen

Sonnet

Through countryside that I have seen before
Pacific Stageline country leaves me tired.
But trying something new it keeps me fired
And doesn't leave me broke down to the core.
I doze off while Pacific hits the trails,
Up the highway, past the Wedding Dog;
Familiarity breeds a heavy smog,
But trying something new, it never fails,
City bus is slower, half the cost.
I feel accomplished after I am home,
I feel a seasoned traveller, free to roam
And have survived the fun of being lost.
Something new is always fun to try,
If you haven't, then you'll wonder why.

Gillian Shirreff

See Not Its Secrets

The rose is so delicate:
Pale pink fades to white,
The petals forming layers of protection
'Round the vulnerable centre of secrets.
Petals will wither and fall,
But some will always protect the centre.
They wrap around it to keep it safe from
prying eyes.
Only by plucking away
Each petal,
Will the centre be revealed.
But that would kill the gentle rose
And the secrets
Would no longer be real.
Yet it would rather die
Than leave open its heart and soul
To the world's harsh touch;
For every time after
That you looked at the rose,
You would see not its beauty,
But its secrets.

Dawn Hunter

Waiting

He waits for her return
Patiently
As she travels the world
Searching
   For what? He had asked.
She had no answer.
But stared into a mirror instead

Postcard after postcard
Filled his letter box
   Egypt is beige
   Amsterdam is blurry
   I made a wish in Rome
   She wrote

He waits for her return
Patiently
How long has it been now?
   Forever. He sighs.
   Forever.

Palma Dell'Anno

The Birth Of An Idea

   With pen in hand passion pours
pearls of wisdom inside.
   Captured and held by dignity,
tangled by false pride.

   Thoughts too complexed, unite
to create the image held in vain.
   Once buried deep in quiet chambers,
can no longer reign.

   Exploding out in ink or lead
a writer's dream takes form.
   The birth of an idea becomes real,
and a poem is born.

Rose Ann Haeussler

Reflection

Your music is truly a gift to me
Pour out your message then stand by and see
That some will express it to those who will listen
Mirroring hopes, baring hearts' ambitions.

Disguise truth in your song, blend in a dream
Season with mood and trim at the seam
Allow it to flow from the few who create it
To the hearts and the souls of the ones
who await it.

Music entwines us throughout our lives
As we live, as we leave from the time we arrive
Echoing our laughter, love, soothing our pain
Listen now, I want to hear it again.

Stay away from "show biz" marketing schemes
Weave in your art but say what you mean
Choose the right path for dollars today
Will fade tomorrow in history's wake.

Serenade on, let me float in your dream
Make me rise, make me fall until it seems
You have touched my heart and I will feel
Enriched and at peace in a reflection revealed.

Carol Camara

A Different Life

I was planted by gentle hands,
Pushed into the hot dry soil.
Light was taken away from me.
I was left alone to find my own way.

As rain fell, sponged by the earth,
The droplets found their way to me.
In the darkness, there I began to grow.

"Painfully I pushed my knotted roots."
I opened to a world of bright light.
My beauty now revealed.
I swayed in the hot breeze for attention.
My colours and scent perfume the air.

Clouds blanketed the sun.
The rain had not come.
I began to wilt and weep.
Hanging my head in sorrow.

My bloomed beauty gone,
You will take me away,
Replace me with another.

I was planted by gentle hands.

Kim Mines

No One

The stars are in the sky
Quick foot steps on the ground
Wind blowing violently
But no one hears a sound

Peace is found inside
But nowhere in the air
No one can tell
No one cares

Listening to the quiet
Wondering if it will stop
The moon slowly rises
As the sun sadly drops

Sometimes he talks to me
stories of every thing he tells
But about no one does he speak
No one quietly dwells

No one is a man no one is afraid
who knows him the answer is nil
"Regretfully," he says
"No one never will."

J. Leah Rowan

The Quest

I search
Quiet mountains,
Sitting in prayer,
Waiting
For peace
With one and all.

I search
A darkened room,
Holding her close,
Hoping
For something greater
Than the dead just done.

I search
Deep in my mind,
Wading through thoughts
Looking
For myself,
The truth of me.

I search for love.

Martin Woods

Winter Fatigue

The season of unseasonal temperatures
return, and blue
anxieties are frozen to the untrue North
not strong not free

Scarlet memories
hip-hop waves of pedestrian slush
shadowed by neon reflections
unwarmed by green-blue swells

Silently, a child
floats in drips of sun beads
plucking seagrapes

equatorial dreams
capped by icebergs

J. Chang Alloy

The Last Encounter

Put me to rest ye Welshman, where the
fresh sod lying,
Reveals earth of a rich and nobler hue,
When brave fiery Celts, with Owen
Glyndwr were dying,
Making bloody the valleys, primed by the
morning dew.

Shroud me not in martial cloak, nor mark
where I repose,
Awaiting Judgement's call with warriors
now free
From mortality, but friend a prayer
compose
On Saint David's Day, that he will
intercede for me.

Put me to rest my comrades where yellow
daffodils
Grace grassy slopes, and the corn
shimmering vales
Become steeped in the stillness of the
sentinel hills
Be the cause lost, let us have died for
peace in Wales.

Roy Loveluck

Search

My flashlight shining through piles of debris.
Searching for life in this desolate place.
The smell of dust thick on my lungs,
Light shining in through cracks in the walls.

It's another world in here with only one way out.
People missing their loved ones as I try to help.
My search is unending with many to find,
The biggest fear is I won't get there in time.

I can't comprehend how these two people thought,
To steal innocent lives and then run and hide.
The pain I hold deep in my heart I withhold,
For others my strength is an example and hope.

The children so innocent had so much ahead,
But that was all gone in a blink of an eye.
Their lives filled with cheer, love, laughter,
Came abruptly to an end with this awful disaster.

Not many survivors came out of this plot.
There are hundreds of wounded, missing or dead.
These two that are guilty when both are caught,
Should be appropriately punished for the
deaths they have caused.

Brianne Woolley

Friendship

A true friend is one of a kind
Something like a precious gem
Very rare and hard to find

An eternal close playmate
Who shares intimate secrets
Ready to do battle or whatever it takes

We have our creator, kin, and country
That fills a certain need
But a loyal pal has a unique chemistry

A bosom buddy would save you in a fire
So show me a person who has two good friends
And I'll show you a liar

Ken Thomas

Loving You

Touch my lips
 soft as skin.
Loving you,
 is a sin.

Watching you,
 is a crime.
Loving you,
 takes only time.

Holding you,
 keep me warm,
Loving you,
 is like being horn.

Being together
 is what it means.
Loving you,
 is not what it seems.

Krystyna Kemp Jr.

Fabrics Of Memory

Whisper thin
shadows dance,
veiled in
papery
outlines,
barely visible,
waning
with each
glassy peek
behind.
I trace their
murmurs
from
swollen reminiscence,
engraved
for as long
as my
always is.

Cyndi Girouard

The Drive

We look to the sky
See not a star in sight
And we wonder why
This is a very dark night

We go for a drive
See people by street light
Like bees in a hive
Oblivious of dark night

As we drive along
Some were putting up lights
Now we hear a song
Carollers come in sight

Down in the next block
We see bright lights galore
We get out and walk
Nativity scene explore

We walk across the street
Reflecting, Jesus birthday
Visit people we meet
Then we were homeward way

Ella A. Olson

Death Of A Flower

The radiant April sun
Shines brilliantly upon
Moist fertile soil
And a flower is born
From the earth's womb.
Sprouting, emerging erect.
Growing, dominating
Absorbing Earth's offerings.
Selfishly stealing
Whatever it can reach.
Waiting, waiting
For the light.
Fighting, fighting
The wind's torment.
Growing, growing
And taking.
And on the brightest day,
The best day,
A man sees the flower
And plucks it from the earth.

Jacob Johnson

Dandelion

Dandelion
Slept all winter
Under white snow
And gray sky

Like a surprise
The little yellow buds
Silently woke up
Under spring rain

It's time again
Colorful Tulips
Flashy show their coats
Under sunlight

Poor Dandelions become white
And send their seeds
For continuing life

Wandering in the field
I remember the wild smell
Like an early smile
That Dandelion gave me
In a gloomy day!

Ann Lee

'Delicately Dawn'

Delicately, dancing, deciduous branches,
Sliding silently, sidelong
Into the morning shadows.

The unchaste lending to
A foretold future of
Well-trod paths.
Deliberated.
Then eroded and smudged
 by the elements.

Foamed-filled furies flourish
And dissipate the dawn frozen dew.
A clean palette.

Pauline Morgan Kuciak

Snow Ghosts

Cold, brisk winter
snow ghosts in the sky
I see them overhead
from the bank on which I lie

Whispering in response
to the shifting winds that blow
I hear them overhead
this I feel they know

With watchful eyes,
and attentive ears, I ready for reply
the snow ghosts shake themselves
snow falls from the sky

Upon my lips I feel the cool
of winters' chilly frost
I taste, but for a moment
what my snow ghosts have lost

Cold, brisk winter
snow ghosts in the sky
become a part of me,
and the bank on which I lie.

Julie A. Cybanski

The Countryside

The sun was shinning
so bright in the sky,
oh my, it is so high.

Oh... but there is
nothing at all to do,
just sit here and listen
to that annoying cow moo.

The countryside stands
so very still, there has
not been one car or truck
drive up the hill.

But wait - is that a deer
I see, how beautiful he does look!
He caught my eye so very well,
a picture I should of took.

Now the day is almost done,
I guess in a way I had some fun.
I'll go to bed and say
my prayer's now, gosh it sure
sounds nice to listen to that country cow.

Ashley Brazeau

Canada In A Frame

Baffin Island to the Niagara
Span the depths of a dozen nations,
Holding in the arm of security
The tongues of a thousand.
Daily we drink from the cup
A treasury that avails to all.
Mythical lands are not her rival,
Nor is the rich man mine.
I am part;
My roots lie buried,
Deeper than the seed of the farmer,
Who from fertility feeds the world,
Many in worlds of barren waste.
The painter's canvas, the poet's pen,
Cannot capture the profusion of color
Among the woodland evergreen
Bursting into the gallery,
Framed in ocean green and blue sky
Hanging to the north pole by a ribbon of ice.

Parker D. Langley

Love Come Alive

Brittany, our little ray of sunshine
So warm, loving and sweet
Arrived into our lives in 1993
Into this world of sorrows and pain
On her daddy's birthday, she came.

A flashing glance from big brown eyes so clear
Brings a smile to grandpa's face
To my eyes, a tear
She brings back memories of one so dear.

Though she is dark and he was fair
This uncle she will never know
For he has been gone these many year
Her smiles and sunny little ways
Bring thoughts of him ever near.

She is our granddaughter, youngest of five
Spoiled by brothers, sisters, grandparents alike
Hard to say no! To this little sprite
A near little package of love come alive.

Carolyn Cruickshank

Flip The Coin

I find that life is happy and bright,
Some find it very grim,
I feel happy for myself,
And very sorry for them.

There is so much in this world,
For everyone to enjoy,
I'm told I've smiled my way through life,
Since I was a little boy.

My outlook is a cheerful one,
By this tenet I abide,
When trouble strikes, I flip the coin,
And see the brighter side.

Life is short, as we all know,
There is little time for sorrow,
Today it may be rainy and dull,
But the sun will shine tomorrow.

Bill Ott

True Friendship

It's hard to choose friends these days
Some will use you in so many ways,
You'll be lucky if you find a true friend
One that will be with you till the end,
I think I have found a friend like that in you
I hope you will feel the same about me too,
I have felt this way once before
But I don't feel the same anymore,
All my friends think I would do anything
for them but that's
    not true
The only one I would do anything for is
the one and
    only you,
A lot of my friends take my friendship for granted
Please don't do that to me too!

Michelle Walls

"A Special Someone"

One I was afraid I would never find
someone to really care about.
I wanted someone perfect, at least for me.
A special kind of talking
An honest way of listening
Not being afraid to laugh or cry, show
kindness understanding.
Someone who would lift my heart, with joy.
I may expect a lot, but I am believer
Someday, someone particular magic will
transfer me.
Inspite of all the waiting, all the almost
giving up it was worth it
Worth while, for, wishes and dreams
do come true.
Because what I wanted is not a dream
or wish no longer...
    It is you!

Billy Copenace

Autumn Showdown

Showcasing Autumn is God's gift to man
Splashing reds and golds wherever He can
Flooding folks brain waves with mixed memories
Flashbacks of Fall Fairs and clowns expertise
Supplanted by scarecrows still in the field
Raggedly guarding grain crops second yield
Magic-Lanterned scenes of teen's back
    seat fumbles
Complicated by parents be careful mumbles
Choking whiffs of burning leaves and circus debris
Waken dreamers to Autumn's stern reality!

Mildred Dowd Collins

"Tree Fungus"

A velvet shroud, for soul of a tree,
swaying no longer, with breezes free,
fallen by an axe on a spree.

Feathered ruffles by a Holy Hand,
covering the ruthlessness of man,
who hears not, the silent plan.

Silky, delicate, these brown fantasies!
house tiny insects, with velvet canopies!
as Nature watches with conformities.

Trees are gone, stumps dry and dead,
it still protects their tiny heads
so oft times lost, neath mans blind tread.

As we muse through dingles, or dell,
let us listen, for their whispering elves,
natures togetherness hears them well.

Pearl Elizabeth Moorhouse

Life

The sky above us is blue.
The clouds as white as can be.
The sun a vibrant yellow.

But if should come a storm.
The blue sky would become gray.
The white clouds would become black.
The sun hidden beneath.

And so I think our lives are much like this
There are happy times and sad times

Laurencelle

Transformation

Such a weird guy he was!
Telling lies was his habit;
Gambling was his favorite.
He told splendid stories, but all were false.
He betted a lot of money, but all was lost.
Preventing all friends and relatives to approach.

But now, everything is changed from head to toe!

Such a nice guy he is!
Learning to love and care for others.
Shedding all bad practices in the past.
Inviting all friends and relatives to appreciate.

With my effort, I transform him in full!
With our effort, we become associated in full!

Jannie Yau

Man And A Tree

I'm a tree, a giver.
Spreading my branches wide with green
thick leaves,
I bring you rain
And generate the ever indispensable water;
And cleansing the air
To sustain your life.

Giving greenery, flowers, fruits,
shades and shelter,
I bring you warmth, beauty and joy;
Endeavoring to control the natural hazards
To save your life.

But in return, you indiscriminately destroy me
With axes, knives, hand-saws and fire;
I profusely bleed and burn
And I silently cry in agony
When I think of your world tomorrow,
Without me.

Embrace me now,
Save me today
To save your world of tomorrow.

Lyangsong Tamsang

"One Lost Soul"

He who has no destination,
Stands alone with little hope;
With scattered thoughts,
and clouded judgment,
he finds it hard to cope.

The road ahead seems endless,
tired feet that now give in;
He falls at where he's standing,
And whispers, okay, you win.

A shadow appears before him,
That carries him to his feet;
"Come with me my tired one"
The voice cries as he speaks.

No longer must you walk alone,
For I shall walk with you;
And keep you safe, always,
As I teach you what to do.

No more shall your feet get tired
No longer do you have to roam;
For I will take you in my boy,
And "one lost soul" goes home.

Wendy L. Hatfield

The Kissing Bridge

In a quaint little town named Montrose
Stands an old covered bridge worn and old
And there are those who claim on clear
    moonlit nights
As you stroll cross the bridge at the
    midnight hour,
You'll suddenly hear on the bridge
    straight ahead
The sound of buggy wheels drawing near
Then come to a stop, so close you can hear
The murmured endearments of the lovers within.
As locked in a passionate embrace,
    stilled by time
Their hearts beat as one, unaware of the light
That falls through the window to heighten the view,
Of this couple in love, forgotten by time.
Look quickly, for in a heartbeat or less,
This vision of tenderness swiftly fades out.
But listen, for off in the distance not far
One can hear the sound of wheels
    travelling on,
Perhaps to other spots held dear to their hearts.

Cathy Nash

Thoughts On Reincarnation
Before Conception

They stir gently in my mind, my little ones
Still waiting for new life,
Unborn children reminding me, persistently,
Of promises I made:
A chance to try anew lessons
Unlearned in lives lived long ago.
Rustling in the caverns of my mind,
Prodding me to action, to give them birth.
Hush now, my little ones, only whisper softly
Like a soft summer breeze.
I will be faithful. Safe in my mind,
Soon, soon to be safe in my womb.

Patricia E. Sherry

Youth Eternal

Fingers strong, that once were nimble,
Struggle now to hold a thimble.
And hair which once was raven-black,
Has turned to gray; its lustre lack.
Complexion that was smooth and fair,
Is ravaged with the lines of care.
Body that was once so agile,
Now is stooped, so bent, and fragile.
I shed the tears of sad lament.
To look upon her body spent,
And anger rises in my soul
At time which took its mighty toll;
That we who are still young, and bold
Will one day be gray-haired and old.
But then I look into her eyes,
And I am filled with great surprise;
For in those aged eyes I see
"Eternal Youth" peer back at me!

Darlene Dolan

Woe

Voices of dark clouds arose,
summoned with joy as they marched,
stalking for an onslaught.
The lonesome soul,
the white heart of the night,
the victim.
Shrouded by the dark curtains,
beleaguered and obscured,
his warm brightness began to fade.
A thunder,
a loud slaughter symphony,
the moon was destined to bleed
Clear blood cascaded,
auditioning its dance before my window,
I commemorated his carnage with a glass
of red wine.

Jason Chua

Daisy

Soft as the wind blow,
Sweet as the rainbow,
Lovely as the moon glow;

    Fresh like a daisy in the morning dew,
    So gay in a lovely face,
    Bees are singing with lovely gaze,
    To see daisy sweet as honey dew;

Daisy, how quaint you were made,
Lovely as it sees,
with golden crown and gems,
Stand solemnly against the wind.

Sujono

Shining Crystals

Beautiful crystals, on the hanging limbs
Swing slightly, side to side
Seems a little more breeze
Would break the ones beside

Before my eyes, a bright red bird
Tries its wings, and then slips
No matter when I see her
I get happy inside

Trees bent so low
That I look twice
Is the limb broken?
No its just the ice.

Next day, the sun breaks through
Yellow, blue, green, on every tree
Every where I look, diamonds all around
And all this for free?

Mary Matvenko

Untitled

Klick, the phones dead
The waves come into the shore,
toaching more rapidly than ever before
talk to them, they speak back.
Can you see the black mountains of coal
they've always been there.
Feel my heart beat more
Oh God! This war.
Send me the wave and I'll swim back to shore.

Andrea Padjen

This Cloud

What is this cloud
that I doth see
which is looking
back at me
it is gently floating
in the sky
with an attitude that of
I do not really care
if it rains everywhere
now if it suddenly
begins to rain on me
it is this cloud that you see
I shall blame
for raining on me

Albert Hapichuk

Ageing

I'd rather die while in my prime
Than falter at a later time

Your eyes don't see, your ears don't hear
The thought of that instills great fear

Your legs no longer briskly walk
Your speeches tremble when you talk

Your teeth no longer are your own
They sit in a glass when you're at home

Arthritis hits your body joints
And pain increases at these points

Your hair turns grey and some falls out
Your slender figure be - comes stout

Your friends, they dwindle one by one
Your loneliness is not much fun

You wither like a drying prune
And know that death is coming soon

I'd rather die while in my prime
Than suffer through that ageing time.

Georgina Breed

Ode To Ode, Faded Touch

'Tis a beautiful day and a beautiful pen
That flows on the paper below,
And where were you my love on this
    beautiful day
To help me flourish,
To help me grow.

I waited for you
With wind blowing in my face and
    through my hair,
And as I thought for one moment
    when you were nowhere to be seen
I swore you did not care.

A tear so clear rolled down my cheek
And as your ghostly finger tip tried to
    catch what it could not,
I smiled.
It is now that I know our souls will
    be entwined forever
Or at least for quite awhile.

Rebecca A. Bridgeo

"Keep Me In Your Heart"

Keep me in Remembrance,
That is all I ask of you,
Think of me as one who is,
Devoted, fond and true.

Do not let the passing months,
Blot out that memory,
Or dim the Recollections,
I have prized so tenderly.

Hold me in Remembrance,
So that when you come again,
I shall find you as you were,
My own may you remain.

Let the old love still continue,
Though we are so far apart,
Do not fail, forget me not,
And keep me in your Heart.

Michael Arthur Gillingwater

How

How do you fix a broken heart
That just won't mend
How do you wipe the tears from crying eyes
That just won't stop

How do you tell your heart
That the one you love just said goodbye
How do you tell yourself
That you must go on with your life

How can you make the hurt
That you feel disappear
How can you ease the pain
That throbs in your throat every time he passes by

How do you teach eyes to look away
That always stare at him
How do you teach a heart not to fall in love
That falls so easily and blindly for him
again and again

Amanda Mitchell

Fragments Of The Heart

Countless are the cracks
That line the walls of my heart
Each one representing
A pain that tore it apart

It has never completely shattered
Always picked up every shard
A courage deep within me
To hold their frailty hard

But every now and then
Hope lets the bonds grow thin
And courage opens the door
Allowing love within

As always it comes to pass
The signs are far from new
A single crack is forming
And this one is for you.

Patricia Blanchette

Vagabond Self

Drawing in the tattered shawl,
that never created much warmth at all,
just merely another wall,
standing tall —fortified.

Pursed lips and tightly knit eyes,
that stunted voice and blunted sight,
just merely another way to spite —denied.

Weak ankles and badly bruised feet,
that hadn't much choice than these streets,
just merely another of the
universal fleet —abandoned.

Fisted left hand, no wedding band,
that could contest to cliche dreams,
just merely the way
it should of been —unseen.

Setting sun and winters cold sting,
that could only lead to sunrise and spring,
Just merely another sure thing —eternal.

Christine Yvonne Delaney

Anger

Not a care in the world,
that's I
No emotion at all, just carefree,
The calm before a storm.

It comes
Thought and emotion that lay dormant
Come alive.
Meeting, conflicting, and seemingly
tearing my mind apart.
I turn wild and free
A man possessed.
The anger reigns-
It does not stop, but grows worse.
Someone greets me, and I snarl
They turn away, frowning.

My family,
friends turn away
from my anger from me.

Oh, why can't they understand?
If only they knew the conflict within.
The storm
With no wind to blow away the clouds —
The clouds, the demons that haunt me.
Oh, why can't they understand.

Matthew Fehr

Future

And through the maple
The cleric is clear
And all are familiar above
The gestures of sadness trouble me not
My bonds to reassure me
The faces here now from centuries past
Welcome me into their throng
And allow me a glance
At all I once was
And all that I could have been.

A. A. I. Anderson

Padstow

The harbour full of mud will soon fill up.
The boats will once again be bobbing high,
And gulls will swoop from roofs above the walls;
The grey clouds roll from sea across the sky.

The Custom House stands strong against the wind,
Firm and inviting, solid against the hill.
Past shell shops up the cobbled streets and stores,
To tea shop up the steps above the forge.

The nets and lobster pots spill out the fishing shed.
Above, the gulls will screech all afternoon.
The sun pours gold across the slated tiles,
And cars will queue at car parks without room.

This Cornish town holds magic in its streets.
Its secret hobby horse will hide behind its wall.
The magic is our memories which repeat,
And years gone by, which only they recall.

Michael J. Bolan

Strings

What there lies beyond
 the boundaries
of great love so fond?
Such tenderness I'm held
within warm hands so strong
and far in scope.

What ancestral bond
all flees
away from me
and then returns to bring me home
to tie me long
with such short rope?

As if it were some chord
in me that sings
and binds me to the instrument
of my own song -
and so I must play it out.

Ian E. Macfarlane

Yesterday

It seems like yesterday, yet long ago,
The breeze was soft and wafted to and fro;
We strolled together 'neath the shady trees,
Our arms entwined, our thoughts enfolded,
In the pristine breeze.

It seemed that time had stilled all thoughts
 but these,
Muted with the rustling of the leaves.
We murmured not a word, our hearts were one;
Our eyes conveyed our deepest thoughts,
Expression like a spider's web, just spun.

We lounged upon the fragrant grass
By mutual consent,
Our love was pure and meant to be,
As tho 'twas heaven sent.

I fell into his fond embrace,
He kissed my eager mouth, my neck, my face.
He whispered to me softly,
As he held me oh so near
And murmured that he loved me
And I knew he was sincere.

Rachel L. Hartland

All Good Things...

All times dwell together,
affecting everything.
The continuum of time surrounds
And holds its captives.
The barred windows of memories and
dreams provide a link
Ahead and behind;
But where in the fabric of time is dawn?
Where is dusk?
Who can define past, present and future,
If all are a single entity?
Time is not a thread, but many threads
Woven on a loom of being.
It is the governor of all existence,
But upon what span of time
shall a life depend,
And must all good things
come to an end?

Robert Geddes

Just An Act

Hi Clown...
The curtain's drawn - you're on stage
now with me
Your role - there is no need to tell
I'm sure you will perform it well.

Gosh! what you just did - was that part
meant to be!
Or was it just part of your act, merely to
impress me?
You know, you're doing very well
Be careful not to fool yourself.

Hey, wait - you can't do that
Right in the middle of our act!
I'm reading through your lines you see,
Instead of two, I now see three.

It's time for me to take my cue
There's only room on stage for two...
What?...why didn't I tell you that I knew?
Forget I was in the scene with you?

I couldn't bring the curtain down
Until your act was through.
 ...Bye Clown
Mae Samuel

To A Violin

Beneath the drawn bow vibrates the string;
The dead wood shivers into life;
Its cry cuts the air with shimmering knife:
A soul has found a voice with which to sing.
Life's core lies hid in each created thing
And therein lies the enigma of life:
What will not yield to the dissector's knife
Now stands revealed by a violin.
These shining notes that quiver on the air,
Define the indefinable in man;
They scale heights unscaled by his mind
And search the deeps wherein all being began,
Leaving unspoken mysteries behind.
The music soars; the soul of man lies bare.

April Britton

Dawn, The Break Of Day

The sun starts going down and
the edge will soon be here!
The darkness dims the light,
Like the tear drops of a clown!
As the sound turns to the silence of the night,
The sun has come and gone!
I find myself a sleep dreaming
As the world goes around and round!
Dawn is on the wake
And the sounds are crystal clear!
The wind blows through the trees,
Closing in are the soft foot steps of a deer.
The sun rise's up past the edge of the earth.
With ease, birds whistle of
The morning light the thoughts they kept all night
Dew in on the grass as temperature rise in degrees!
My dreams come back to me, in memories
 of the past
My face indoors the breeze.
This I hope will last!
Another day of light day break, dawn has come
And another day has gone!
Time the grain of sand!
In the blue ski, this is where I fly

James D. Cronk

Her Final Farewell

Her eyes...reflecting the midnight sky,
the fear...the wanting...the love.
Her mission; a quest that was not one of woe,
but only because she loved him so.

She then ducked behind a tree,
and scanned the grounds frantically.
And when she felt the time was right,
She then slipped down out of sight,
to the spot where her husband lay,
quiet...and waiting.

She then told him in whispered tones,
how much she wished that he'd come home.
As the moon shone through the clouds,
the young lady lay crumpled on the ground.

Her trembling fingers reach in her coat,
and a hopefully cry escaped her throat.
But her husband, he didn't make a sound,
And so; sobbing, she lay her head down.

As she turned and walked away,
on the grave a red rose now lays.
And with the hope, leaving all the fear,
on it shined a single tear.

Jon J. Turton

Memories

There is a face I would love to see
The laughing eyes just meant for
The tender touch of a gentle hand,
A ring of gold a wedding band,
The day that I met him,
I knew from the start,
That we would never be apart,
How did I know, how could I tell?
It was love at first sight,
That magical spell,
My lover, my husband, my best friend,
After many years, came to an end;
The gentle heart, that beats no more
Today, God called and opened heaven's door.

Ivy Brittain

Separation

The vote she come.
The French they say
No longer care
About our Canada.
We Anglos care.
For many years
We were brothers.
Together we tamed this land,
Charted the rivers
And planted the grain.
Shoulder to shoulder
In the wars for peace
Our blood intermingled.
Let us embrace
We will kiss your wounds
And together
We will tame the rivers
Of the future.

J. D. Harvey

The Great Lakes

Superior: Regal, granite, forever;
the giant, brooding, cold water killer.

Michigan: American, cities, skylines;
scenic northern coast a sporting paradise.

Huron: Georgian, Saginaw, Sarnia;
the rugged, rocky Bruce Peninsula.

Erie: Haunted, shallow, tropical;
pollution problems are international.

Ontario: Toronto, canals, harbors;
Niagara, Islands and Stateside borders.

Great Lakes: Freshwater, inland, unique;
silent keepers of dark secrets indeed.

Fifth Coast to remain shiny, valued jewel
or degrade into black putrid cesspool?

David Dicaire

Diversity

Starting into an endless tunnel of darkness.
  The glow of reality strikes hard.
The pain flows swiftly along forgotten river.
  Pureness lost in a realm ahead of time.
    Forgiveness a custom of the past,
    as religion fails the faithful.
Society lost in the madness of technology,
  as internet swarms its victims.
    Life as we know it, forgotten.
Simplicity evolving to a complex prophecy.
Living for your spiritual being a necessity,
as society becomes aware of individual diversity.

Amber-Dawn Stark

My Favorite Star

The sky at night is the blackest of blacks,
The sky at noon is the bluest of blues.
Even on the stormiest nights or the
cloudiest days,
Even with all those stars and clouds
blanketing the sky,
There will always be one special star for me - YOU!

Camillo Delli Pizzi Jr.

"Life Light"

Empty, hollow inside
The light flickers, and slowly dies
No one hears me, my desperate cries
The light flickers, and slowly dies
I stand up proud
make my final stand
they just turn away
and don't lend me a hand
I gave it my all, and I have lost
my heart and soul were the cost
bow my head
close my eyes
the light flickers, and slowly dies

Lenard Coull

Seasons Change

As the season's change,
the heaven's try to arrange,
a love that soon will bond,
that's why I wrote this song.
From me to you, with love,
with help from those above.
I know I was but a boy,
For treating you like a toy.
I'm trying to say I'm sorry.
You mean everything to me.
And if you don't forgive.
I'll love you all the same.
Because faith finds away,
As the seasons change

Joe Vieville

Farewell Friend

I'd remember nights when we'd stay up
The moon being our witness
We'd talk for hours about odd things
Ideas, our past
Comings and goings we had never shared
Moments of wonder
Of humour and of pain
Sometimes, we'd laugh for no reason
I'd comfort you as you cried
Advise you in your moments of despair
And now,
As I dwell on our last sharing
I wonder how you are now
I remember saying goodbye
Knowing that this may be our last time...
Together
Things may be different if we ever met again
But I'd know to tell you
I've missed you
And I wish you well.

Corey de Laplante

Dog Fights

The dogs look sternly at each other as
their masters open the kennels. They
run out and clash with each other.
Blood starts running down one dog's leg
It moans and groans as the other dog
digs its jagged teeth into the front
leg of it's opponent. Suddenly
it grabs the other's neck, ripping
its throat open. Choking on blood they
both fall to the ground, Not moving
because the pain is so intense.

Jarrod Dowdall

Teenagers

One minute you love them,
  the next you're not sure.
Their ever changing behavior
  is yet to endure.

They spread their wings
  to gain independence.
A parent learns to let go
  but still give them guidance.

Wild clothes and purple hair
  and ever constant phone calls.
Is part of growing and acceptance
  among their peers, that's all.

They think they know everything
  that adults couldn't know.
Love, support and encouragement
  is what they need to grow.

Dating, parties, choice of music
  and getting good grades in school.
Are many challenges of being a teen...
  soon they'll learn the golden rule.

Cheryl L. Law

Choices

There's a fork in the road that you must choose,
The one to win or the one to loose,
Your given a chance to make up your mind,
It's your true desire that you must find,

Nothing in life is easy you know,
But the road you choose is the way you go,
Make the decision that will be the best,
For you to experience life's given test,

You can open your heart and give out love,
And whatever happens will come from above,
There is no temptation that you can't pass,
For life to anyone is no simple task,

Life is only of what you make,
Happiness in life is for you to take,
Make that decision, turn over your will,
It may not be easier but in may be still,

Your true beliefs will help you feel,
There is no dream that can't be real,
All it takes is for you to be whole,
For the day will come that you'll reach
  your goal.

Cindy Embury

Flight Of The Giants

Oh clapping giants skyward bound
Ushering breezes my way and crowned
With noble beauty alive before me
Destined for true glory.
In a moment captured breath doth flee,
Surrendered by your majesty.
You reach for Heaven; I'm so rendered
Awestruck by such towering splendor.
Whisper tales of time dearly spent
Of years, and youth and sentiment.
Reflecting ages of reason and rhyme,
Forever soar higher; oh, peaceful sublime.

Kristy A. Roberson

The Memory

Thank you for the memory
The one where you shared your lullaby —
I sensed it came from the love in your heart.
Hearing it almost made me cry.

When I saw the look in your eyes
As you strummed your special song,
I wanted nothing more at that time
Than to simply sing along.

But I did not know what notes to sing
Or the melody.
So, I sat back to watch you perform
And I listened oh so carefully.

As your words and music flowed
I was carried off to far away places
Filled with happiness, and love,
And smiling faces.

The moment the song was over
And your voice was no longer heard
I hoped you would help me to learn to sing
Every note...then every word.

    E. C. Anderson

Rainbows Splendor

The red of our anger,
The orange of hesitation
The yellow of cowardice
The green of ignorance
The blue of depression
The violet of unbelief
The indigo of mourning
So that our human weakness may be
  changed,
Into the rainbow's splendor
Bringing the beauty
Through thy love.

    Gilles Phillip Losier

Hurting

The torments linger inside your heart
The pain wills it to stop
Eyes clouded over,
Hands trembling
But it will not stop.
A storm is brewing inside your brain
The madness, the pain
When will they learn
that voices can be heard.
voices ripping at your heart
Wanting to bring you down
The rain pours down,
The lightning crashes,
The thunder rolls,
And it all comes to an end.

    Lisa Alcorn

Aurora

I once saw Aurora dancing
through the frost-chilled Arctic night,
in soft robes that glowed and shimmered,
softly dimmed, and then flared bright,
as they hissed through deep magenta,
icy green, then sapphire blue,
she rejoiced in gay abandon
as she had, when Earth was new.

    Earl R. Knight

Live Your Life

Try and remember, try to forgive
the past, yourself
time may not heal, time won't erase
the pain, the deeds
remember the good in the past
there was
remember the person you were
you are
forgive the wrong that was done
to you
forgive yourself, you're not to blame
heal in the time that it takes
for you
heal in the care and the love
it takes
erase the doubts that you have
of you
erase the hold that it has
on you
live your life

    Diane Brazeau

A Wondrous Thing

A wondrous thing
the rainbow
arched high
proud
in the sky
amid thunderous clouds
of black and gray
'tis frail, I wonder why

Wind and rain
and sun
make clouds shimmer
and colours glow
'tis autumn
skies are heavy
now, o're fields
the cattle low

    Polly Tracey

Cocoon

Out of the egg into the green
the shining cool and strange
light like needles - tingling

And into the blind cocoon
it holds us warm and smothered
instinct and inertia
like so many filaments of fly paper
wrapping around us

And we -
seeking
always seeking -

Are greedy in our identical cocoons
feeling only what we have always felt
lazily restless
we grope blindly in the wrong directions
remembering only duly the tingle of life
running from the light that scares us
sinking happy into the pacific sameness

Never understanding or seeing
the trap

    Denise Moline

February

The days are getting longer,
The sky is deeper blue,
Lake ice is freezing stronger,
The snow is not so new.

The moon gives nighttime beauty,
Snow gems reflect it back,
While Jack Frost does his duty,
Makes tall trees snap and crack.

Planes rush through crystal clearness,
Write contrails on the sky
While icicles from nearness
Reflect the sun on high.

Tho' still 'tis Winter's inning,
This short month's omens show
Green Spring will soon be winning
The Battle of the Snow!

    Carle A. Rigby

Spring

The sky is blue the clouds are white
The sun is shining bright.
To look upon a day like this
Brings all the world to light.

Where have you been you smiling flowers?
I did not plant you there!
Yet here you are with patterns fine
And colours bright and clear.

Hello, sweet, singing bird
Perched high upon the tree,
Your nest is made, your mate sits there
With spotted eggs she laid.

The trees sway gently in the breeze
Their gowns in shades of green
Delight the eye o'er all the land
And shelter all with outstretched hand.

    Dorothy Currie

Love In A Dream

Walking down the path, along the field of wheat,
The sun was so bright and shining, and
warm air around you.

Sit on a huge rock, staring the crooked creek,
Playing with the wheat stalk, relax in the shade.

Heard a sound behind somewhere, your
heart begin to beat fast,
Stood up and spoke to her, she giggles
and being so shy.

Wondering yourself, sat on a bank of a a creek,
With hand holding together, Will our love
ever last longer?

Love at first moment, Love at first sight,
Love was so real, Love was so true.

You are just a dreamer, hopefully it comes true.

    Calvin Poortinga

A Walk In The Woods

As I walk through the fields on cold winter's day,
The woods beckoned to me with their unmoving
    limbs.
I was captured in wonder by their fragile fingers,
Reaching out to touch me with their icy grasp.
I walked in the woods and saw the snowbirds fly,
Was awed by nature's living statues of quail.
I was struck of a sudden by the beauteous quiet,
And I wanted to hold this moment forever.

Wyn Kochie

The Truth

The truth behind the lie is poetry
the truth runs wild beside our secrecy
the loathsome undying realness
is our living nature - phases of sickness

Running clear thru silence -
the beauty of sound
Creating us and what can be found

I feel it warm sunshine
browning my skin
Not cruel but sudden in it's path
giving soft wisdom wherever you are
A movement from deep silence
Vast endless promise

Night time liquidness
embraces our structures
until we're tied safely down
Witnessing truth's inanimate wonders.

Jeff Roth

"Night Of The Moon"

Lies, deception, death and deceit,
The world is born at my feet,

Demons and gargoyles, religions and Gods,
Yet the world suffers and people starve,
Wizards, sorcery lightening strikes twice,

Fantasy, reality, alive in ones mind,
Witches, black magic full moon in the night,
Potions, and poisons in every bite,

Traveling souls, in bodies so blind,
Just hanging around waiting for their time,

Stars, and astrology, planets in space,
Gravity, the moon, the tide on the race,

Rituals, curses, blasphemy lies,
Getting ahead no matter what dies,

The world is alive, with violence and rage,
It shows in our history books, on every page,

So save our world, its a wonderful place,
Would have been, if not for our race!

Ross Draper

In Memory Of Marco Eloio

Death is something we'll never
understand, especially when it is
the death of a friend.
We know in our hearts we will never see
the beauty he was and always will be,
but yet we hold dear to our hearts the
memories we have and never let them part.

Karen Clifford

To That Youthful "Pupil Pen": Tell The Tale

When Putting Pen to Paper
There is My Hearts Desire
My Inspiration's Motivator.

'My Heart,' I'll name the Paper.
This Pen, give the label 'Thought'
With my True Heart devoid of Feeding.

In Substitute, I'll Touch this Paper
Gently rub its Surface with my Thought
And Give to Most My Heart.

bbb

Goodbye Mom

You gave me life as it was meant to be
Then loved me deeply for all the world to see

Now I must close my eyes to see your face
Your smiling eyes and feel your warm embrace

The memories I keep within are mine
Never to be forgotten - till the end of time

My life has stood still since you've been gone
Your love will stay with me, where it belongs

To see you again, just one more time
And hold you close and say you are mine

I love you more as each day goes by
Why did you leave me alone to cry

The loneliness that comes from within every day
Is more than I can bear or begin to say

I love you Mom with all my heart
Next time we meet, we will never part

Fanny McNair

My Sisters

When I was just a little girl
Then the world seemed big and new
But in my life I have three friends,
My sisters, I bet you knew!

Some scary nights and fun filled days
When we lived all together,
They would try to hide or get me lost
And tell me then that they're the boss.

From oldest sister Sharon, to Brenda, then
Cheri-Lynn,
I love my sisters dearly,
Because they're my best friends.

People always tell us
How much alike we are.
I know that that's a blessing
And thank my lucky star.

If you have any sisters
Then call them on the phone.
You may not live together,
But you'll never be alone.

Michele Stableford

A Moment In Time

There is such happiness:
There are hours to which perfection clings,
The sweetness of life, so often rare.
Though brief they be, only then the strings
Controlled by each puppet hand forbear
To hold the tautness, and loosely lie.
It is then we count our lives more dear,
And the quickening breath becomes a sigh
Of wonder, hope, and forgotten fear.

We knew such happiness:
Beneath a pine tree, dark silhouette
Against the moon, we watched the valley
Fade from sight, the calm repose beset
By the last light of day. Then slowly
Did your head descend upon my breast.
Surely did the love communicate
Into our minds everlasting rest,
That only our dreams may imitate.

Godfrey Davies

You Can Bring Peace To Another

You can bring peace to another;
There is a kind word you can say.
You can show love to your brother,
And love to your sister today.

Then with the touch of an angel,
Caress and erase someone's pain,
Or like an infant chid's mother,
Sing someone a gentle refrain.

You have a door you can open,
To welcome the wanderer home.
Lift up the latch just a little,
Perhaps with a verse or a poem.

Then with the love of a father,
Rekindle that family flame,
And with the joy of salvation,
Just do it again and again.

Are you still hoping and yearning,
To bring peace but just don't know how?
Then ask the good Lord to guide you;
He'll bless you as He shows you how.

W. Diane Van Zwol

Daddy's Hands

Daddy's Hands are big and strong.
They always help me when I've
gone wrong.

When I cry
He's always there
With open arms
Full of concern and care.

When I go to bed
At night, I always pray
For Daddy's life.

But I know
That God does care
Because He's always there.

Christina Charles

Gunslingers

The gunslingers of yesterday
They know the code of the west
It's the Colt Peace Maker
Dead or alive, their the best

Man and machine as one
their fast with the thumb and finger
With the Colt Peace Maker
The legend will linger

Six shots of .45 lead
How fast can you draw?
Six shots of .45 lead your the first to fall

Shiver and shake, your life's at stake
With Jessie James and the Kid,
your life's at stake
With the Colt Peace Maker
  and a quick draw
Your dead! that's their law

For the love of money,
For the love of money, they kill!
For the love of money,
their dead on Boot Hill

The gunslingers live hard and fast,
  they die young and alone
With the Colt Peace Maker
  the legend will out last

Dean Gore

Mogadishu

I died in a place that sounds like a sneeze,
they told me "don't fret!
It's walk! It's a breeze!
They'll never withstand us;
they're youngsters on dope,
we're fighting marines;
their nation's last hope."

I believed them; I smiled; I expanded my chest.
I picked up my guns and my bullet proof vest,
and followed my sergeant, gung ho all the way,
and raced up the beach at the dawn of the day.

And behold, they were right. Resistance was nil,
we spread in formation and charged with a will.
The warlords were gone with their truck loads of loot,
leaving anxious invaders with no one to shoot.

But one stayed behind with his armalite gun.
He fired a burst and my battle was done.
I'd come here to help, heard humanity's pleas,
and I died in a place that sounds like a sneeze.

Carleton Davis Bell

Temptation

Sniff sniff sniff sniff sniff sniff sniff
ti ti ti ti ti ti ti ti
Sniff sniff sniff sniff sniff
ti ti ti ti ti ti ti ti
SSnniiff, sssnnniiifff, ssssnnnniiiiffff
ti ti ti
snif
ti ti
ssnniiff
ti
SSNNAAPP!!!!!!
  (A high price to pay for a piece of
cheese).

Bob Walsh

Fall Romancers

The northern lights are out tonight
They're playing their silly games
They chase each other and dance around
And fill the earthly plains.

I see the bright green glow o' bursting
I see the dark green shadows rising
They break apart and start their dancing
Hoping for some more romancing.

Their colors are different, shapes are rare
They seem so near yet so far
Would like to touch them and feel their life
As they fill the skies each day and every night.

Let's watch awhile, let's share their fun
They won't stay long, they'll soon be done
This time of year they seem to say
It's a fall, it's fall and we'll be on our way.

We're not sure where you come from, not
sure where you go
But to see your lights
During the long fall nights
Keeps our imagination aglow.

Margaret Kastrukoff

Perfect Love

Wondering through my life's memories,
Thinking it's deja vu,
on and on to this day I've come,
learning to love my way through.

Hopes and dreams they seem to be,
the mysteries of life,
in the distance not to far ahead,
it's no more the weary strife.

The paths I chose have lead me here,
with spirit guides I see,
my fears, my rage, my hateful abode,
I'm learning to set them free.

My greatest thoughts they seem to be,
a struggle inside to know,
a way to give a perfect love,
for you I'd really show.

Patrick Littlewood

Sounds Of The Soul

A wellspring transporting the soul and the mind
This dynamic power - pervasive, refined
Touches our lives with joy and elation
Uplifting the spirit through scores of vibration

From classical beauty to discordant sounds
In various forms of expression surrounds
And enhances the tone of our days
With accents of rhythm in myriad ways.

Creating a mood, a thought, intense feeling
In vibrant formation - arousing, appealing
Resonating through depths and peaks of sensation
Great MUSIC inspires the soul to ovation!

Betty R. Rimm

What Is It All About?

What on earth is it all about?
Those who think they know all shout
"Salvation! The blood of Christ alone
Can bring you to that awful throne,
Where judgement then shall be dispensed.
If black (or white) then life eternal.
If red, beware, then fires infernal.
Robbie Burns warned Tam O' Shanter,
Robbie always loved to banter,
"In Hell they'll roast you" he warned Tam,
Tho' Rab himself ne'er cared a damn
For "pentance stool" nor hell's damnation,
These he deemed imagination.
"Love thy neighbour, help each other,
Treat each man he were your brother.
Hold your head high, enjoy life,
Live at peace, avoiding strife!

Peter Lyon Nicol

My Soul's Spirit

My spirits' currents rushes like a tidal wave
through my living soul,
The flesh is weak,
oh but my living spirit is so strong,
My heart racing to keep up with the pace
  of my spirit,
My spirits are blended by love, life, sorrow,
pain, disappointment, happiness and yes
  hope,
roll all these emotions up and my spirits
  speaks within.
Life is spirit on a permanent electrical charge,
coming back to its source of energy time and
time again only to be recharged with new
  strength to face tomorrow,
oh my spirit carry me to my journeys end.

Barbara Thomas

Nature

Nature's sun is ready to rise
Through the clear bright blue sky

The autumn breeze singing soft and mellow
Caresses forest trees of red and yellow

The morning dew in the air
Leaves a soft and foggy glare

The first morning fisher's are on the bay
And won't return home till the end of day

The bears are up looking for their honey
But seem only to find a full grown bunny

The fox has found a porcupine to chase
But decides not to creep up just in case

Nature's day has to end
But still will return again

The sun has decided it's time to rest
Knowing that she has done her best

The animals have laid down it seems
And shall sleep through with sweet dreams

If you stop and look on the peer
You will hear the winds whispering night
is drawing near.

Brandy Yeo

The Graveyard

I was going home
Through the graveyard I went
It was light
Suddenly it went dark
I got scared.

The fog grew
It got damp
I heard some rustling noise
I started to run.

I ran faster and faster
Until the path came to an end
I had taken a wrong turn.

Somebody hit me on the back
I turned quickly
It was my mum
Now I wasn't scared.

Adam Leslie

Untitled

My heart in this place cannot remain;
'Tis dying from a long and lingering pain.

It knew long ago, a sweet refrain
With never a thought to complain.

But now, that the Die is cast,
Regarding another's misdeed, long since past;

With no hope of any reprieve;
And in time, with time, only to grieve.

The heart struggles against inner death
With only it's own fast, dissipating breath.

Can it find its way through the gloom?
So in time, with time, gradually resume

That lovely Refrain, that it had sung,
In a time, with time, when its beat was young.

Jan Anderson

The Approach Of Winter

On the Green, it seems to me
'Tis not the blasting wind,
    that bows those trees
Perhaps t'is their own desire to escape
    the breeze
That chills the sap and strips the leaves
T'is a conspiracy among the timbre
To up root feet and march from winter
The winds not the culprit, who's causing
this southerly swaying
Pulling, stretching, urgently aching
'Tis man with his axe
That's committing the slaying

Glenn Brown

The Mare

Slowly
Trotting
Gallop begin
The wind and rain
Take me in
Over the meadow
Across the field
The mare is my weapon
Her gallop my shield.

Eve Bleile

Our Family

I wonder what one has to do
To be as rich as some
To whom you're born, the lucky breaks
The lotteries those have won.

For we're a suburban family
The amount of us is four
I have a lovely husband
And two boys that I adore.

Sometimes it's a struggle
To make the money last
For we both get paid monthly
And the sum isn't all that vast.

But we're a happy family
And that means everything
For people that seem to have the cash
Don't have a wedding ring.

Lesley Rix

A New Day

Take each new day as another birth
To begin once again on this God given earth

As the dawn approaches we leave our nest
And venture outside in search of our quest

Frightened and unsure we move with caution
Wondering what this new day will bring
As far as learning and precaution

As the day unfolds hour upon hour
Our eyes see beauty our ears hear song
Our touch caresses the tenderness of a
    budding flower

Yesterday forgotten, tomorrow miles away
We live each precious moment waiting, hoping
For love and joy to come our way

As the sun settles silently in the evening sky
Our minds and bodies weary
But our hearts and souls soaring high

For another day, another birth
Makes waiting and hoping
For life, for love, for joy, filled with worth

Shirley Sarafinchan

The Magic

Bring me the magic,
To change my perception of day,
Bring me the magic,
To laugh, to sing, to play.

Bring me the magic,
Then, I will have my own way,
Bring me the magic,
To pass the time of day.

Bring me my magic,
To wipe my teary eyes dry,
Bring me my magic,
So I may see the stars in the sky.

Bring me my magic,
I, then can be filled with wonder,
Bring me my magic,
Then, I on life can ponder.

Paulette Joseph

Untitled

I am looking for something
To define...
Something like darkness,
something like time.
An abstract notion
Intangible, too
Foreign to the senses
Invisible to view
Yet it is an essence
Time on my hands, oh my!
Moments are precious,
As time goes by.
Is it back to the future?
Or forth to the past?
No, my friend, it's the eternal present
The future won't last.
Weightless and measureless,
Not the when nor the how;
Whenever you grasp it,
The time is now: eternally now.

Mary J. Callahan

Untitled

...All of a sudden the black clouds move apart
To flee far away shoved off by the wind
A golden beam illuminates the scene
With outstretched arms standing on the shore
Delighted that the dreadful storm is retreating
Gazing toward the sea toward the open sea
Lost in this island in the vast ocean
Amid this crowd surrounding me
On planet Earth
I shout my joy to all who wants to hear
There now I wander no more
Purified I become again as
I will be and I was long ago
Life is not always as
What we thought is not like it was
This hope inhabiting our hearts grows
    swells and overcomes
Taking us out of guard suddenly
    comes to life
This fleck on the beach immobile
    and dwarfing
Is me it was I say to myself
    while soaring away

Nicole Herold

I Wish I Had A Flower

I wish I had a flower
To give to you someday
I'll marry you whenever
No matter what anybody says

I wish I had a flower
To hold up in the wind
And as soon as I can press it
It's a sign that our friendship will never end

And if I had a flower
I'd give it right to you
To show my love so greatly
To someone so strong and true

I hope our love is like this poem
So sweet and secure and true
Your a person just like this
And if you would ask
I would be honored to marry you

Laurina Kennedy

Anticipation

I'd like to be the can opener
To pierce the first hole
And cleanly cut
Around the edges
Of your outer self.
To open and expose
That part of you
So deftly hidden
From all around you.
To release the emotions
Vacuum packed and sterile.
That you've built up and developed
Through childhood to adulthood
What a pleasure for me
To share the contents
And enjoy
The birth of a new soul

Patty Herrick

Quiet Day

Thank You God, for this quiet day
To rest, to dream, to plan, to pray.
No one called me on the 'phone
I might have been in the world alone
Except for the sparrows in my tree
Who always share their songs with me
In Gratitude for a tossed out crust.
In Thee, Dear God, they put their trust.

To-morrow I must join the race
And be in my accustomed place.
To-morrow I must punch a clock
But now my feet are on a rock
That will not move; and thus I can
Be gentle with my fellow man.
This quiet day has been my crust
In Thee, Dear God, I put my trust.

June L. Moore

My People

Disfigured, devalued, misshapen and odd,
To the lives of these people I have been called.
Their beauty, their warmth,
    their love goes unseen,
For so few take the time, their value to glean.

Hurting, ruined, beyond their control,
Their circumstances of life have dealt
    them a blow.
They do feel, they do hurt, they do agonize,
Only to find out, they have been categorized.

Helplessness, hopelessness,
    and even despair,
Have haunted their footsteps
    and keep them impaired.
Is there any mercy, is there any grace,
Has God forgotten the special place?

There will be mercy, there will be grace,
When we show them acceptance,
    it shows on their face.
They ask so little, yet give so much,
Our attitudes of love will speak of our touch.

Ardelle Quigley

Beating Drums

My heart beats
to the sound of a drum
soft and slow
as delicate as a child
should be embraced
yet a child is harmed
lets stand tall
together and put away
the pain....anger... sorrow
teach our children well
stop the cycle
violence...alcohol...silence
my heart beats
to the rhythm of drums
keep the circle strong
with peace...love.. harmony
and let there be more
who are brave enough
to joined our circle of
beating drums

Flores Fay Knife

Love Lost And Found

True love can be lost for so many
To them an emptiness worse than any
No words to explain this erie feeling
Only in time will there be some healing

The good Lord has smiled upon me I know
Our love for each other each day it grows
Good times and bad we both share
And the rough days are handled with tender care

We go through life in what it has to offer
Content with the love we give each other
There is no obstacle that we deplore
We embrace each other
    and know we can endure

The first day of our encounter is clear in my mind
When our eyes met no words I could find
My heart seemed to pulse an irregular beat
And my days of loneliness would go
    down in defeat

After all these years we are still together
No doubt in my mind we'll last forever
Understanding and forgiveness is a mutual thing
That's part of the secret to our well being.

Bradley Campbell

Seasons Of Love

Our love had its root in the spring
to unfold and grow.
And carry us on the journey
through the seasons of love.

But our covenant
tarnished as the leaves of autumn fell.
Now the soul is as the barren tundra
as spring bowed to the winter solstice.

So the blossom withered
perished in the winds of discontent.
Never to rejuvenate, alas,
that brumal animosity
shattered the dreams of spring tide.
And all is at a standstill
as the wintry enmity
Knells the seasons of love.

Patricia Long

Just A Poem

When I write a poem I have a chance
to write of love and romance
I could put all my feelings from the heart
down or paper for a start.

Some from love, some from hate
line by line they all state
Some are happy some are sad
Some are good and some are bad

They make a statement of a sort
Some to women that they court
Poems on trees, bees and grass
on the love of a lovely lass

Creating a poem is like magic
making words happy or tragic
From the future or the past
Poetry is here to last

Line after line we do our best
To create a poem to pass the test
Give me an idea I need a start
To write a poem from the heart

Brian Murray

Nature's Pathway

Special place, beautiful dreams
Tranquil space, pleasant vibrations
Buoyant thoughts aloft
Motionless trees, meandering stream
Whispers over the rocks
Quiet lullaby
Mellow dew like raindrops caress
flowery shrubs
Bees busy sucking nectar
Green-grass cushions, contours
the rolling landscape
Sweet fragrance permeates the air
Birds chirp, harmonize
Ah! enraptured, such symphony

Imagine the joy, romantic feeling
Sentiments of love

Glen G. Davidson

Unclear Divisions

Multinational of the human psyche
Tribulations of the human plight
Vipers nestling in the womb of racism
Showing a facade of welcoming acceptance
Shouting an avalanche of verbal intolerance
Conditional equality amongst all
Ensuring boundaries between our backyards
Sparkling toothpaste smiles we share
Exchanging superficial dialogues
Continuing to protest the moral
    outrage of difference
Declaring solutions and delaying answers
Who is at fault?
Are we all victims?
Waves of hope and mountains of failure
We are all contributors to this colorful canvas
Placed upon this universal campus
Instead of enlightenment its lip service given
As long as we remain in our backyards
A tolerable distance is maintained
Now we can become superficial friends

Dale Reece

When I Close My Eyes...

I close my eyes at night,
Trying to hold you near,
But when I open them up again,
All I feel is air.

I whisper the words 'I love you',
Wishing you were here,
To take me in your arms,
And make love to me so dear.

During the day,
I look around.
Hoping to see your smiling face,
But all I see around me,
Is a dark and empty space.

I cry aloud 'I need you',
Wanting you to come,
And take me far away.

Miranda Elston

Unemployed Down And Out In London

Eating food out of the dustbin
trying to stay alive
no money there in the coffers
my fears I am trying to hide

I've had enough, for I'm sleeping rough
and there's nothing but cold and the rain
I feel like turning to drink,
while here on the brink
but I haven't a bean to my name.

I've tramped the streets,
looking for work days and weeks
and my feet they are tender and raw
no roof over my head, not even a bed
I'm weary and tired of it all

No one cares how I feel,
when I'm down at heel
and my clothes they're all tattered
and torn when wanting a meal, I've
begged, borrowed and stealed
I've wished that I'd never been born

Oh! When will there be a turn of the tide
when will my ship come sailing in
out of work - made redundant
eating food out of the bin.

Gladys E. Weaver

Sunrise

The sun peaks over the shimmering
mountain tops,
Turning the snow to gold,
Then he bursts forth,
Exploding with radiant color,
For a moment he plays with the clouds,
He reaches his arms out to cover the earth,
Flooding the surface with welcoming warmth,
Bringing joy to a new day!

Crystal A. Williams

My Love And I

Twenty five years together for my love and I
Two souls that join as one in the blink of an eye
Time has now made us old and grey
Soul mates of the past and of today,
But when our lives are done
You'll find us going into the next as one.

Two soul mates we will always be
For my love, I am you and you are me.
A smile a touch of the hand
Time will not hold us to this land.
For we shall meet again in another time
And once again I will be yours and you
    will be mine.

A love like ours so-so strong and and true,
Past, present and into the future too,
We have loved many many life times
For our souls are the ones that binds
You to me and I to you.
So when we die don't be sad you blue
For in the next space and time
We will be as one, your soul and mine.

Joan Lewis

Life Depends On Us

In one day, one hour,
Two will see the world separately
Each will view it differently
Perhaps one happy, one sad
The world is the same
Except that feelings blur our sight
Whether it be rose coloured glasses
Or the fog of tears
Life depends upon us...

Marni Kyle

Make Yourself A Home

A house is not a home
Unless it is held by love
Not full of hatred and anger
But of happiness above

The four walls that surround it
Are made of wood and nails
But to make a home a happy one
Love will never fail

A house is not a happy home
Without the sound of laughter
Sharing our love with others
Makes memories for everafter

So make yourself a home today,
Fill it full of love not tears
Its sure to bring you happiness
For many many years

Donna Simard

Dead Falcon

A falcon soaring in the air
Was shot down; he fell to the ground-dead.
Now the hills are tumbling
And the walls are crumbling -
Falling down to the river bed.
The grass is growing high
And the wind rushes by
Carrying no sound of voices or laughter.
And feeling the eeriness of the place,
You think -
Why did the falcon have to die?

Marie Brown

Time

What is the time is your life
Up in the morning off to work
Or school you have to be in time
When I see you walking down
The street mademoiselle you
Know you look so sweet
I feel I want to hold your hand
But its only time
"O" what beautiful day the
Sun is shining brightly sorry
I can't stay I have no time
Love is in the air love is every
Where take my hand take my hand
For now is the time

Every where is war and more war
We want peace now is the time
God is love God is peace of mind
Many people don't believe in God
But it's only time, help the old
Help the children now is the time

Michael Robinson

Painting Of Life

They painted a picture for us
Using a dark grey colour
To depict the mysterious dark tunnels
Of the future that lies ahead.

We journey along the detours,
  hoping they will
Slowly lead onto the highway of life
As we do, we begin to notice
The innovation in colours:
Every shade a symbol in its own.

Blue for the hardships that bring tears
Red for the love shared in times of anguish
Black for the course of despair
Brown for the muddled states of mind.

But midst the novelty of these tones
You'll soon find the painting to hold a
  special amulet

Look in the center of the portrait
You will discover the light to that tunnel
The road sign to that highway
And the vision of happy, successful days
That colour is yellow.

Giosi Tortorici

Beaches In Summer

By our very impermanence
  we are forced
  to leave impressions.
In order to feel our own substance
we fight for memory
like a footstep in the sand.
There, for a moment;
then gone,
like a whisper of laughter.
Scarcely imagined
lifted from the pages of reality
leaving the beach a blank page.

Donna Kavin

Billboards

The wisdom of the open mouth with no
  violence emanating.
Language by billboards.
The variety show a roadside.
Silent films faxed on red brick walls.
Advertising.
Information numbers for you to call.
Street wise eyes ignoring the screen sex sells!
Focusing your attention through
  the man hole steam.
The picture yells.
Three D clowns without red noses.
A man chasing a women with a dozen red roses.
The impulse to rise above it all.
The philosophical message for the day.
Lead my demize
Florescent symbols projecting evaluation
Blue boxing the answers to mankinds.
Pollution.
Mass hysteria counting down
The answers to life written down town.
Right in front of your face.

Christine Gravel

Teachers

Teachers touch the lives of many
Wandering through their youth,
Giving time, knowledge and motive
To seek a path and learn the truth.

Teachers are criticized unjustly
For society's errors and woes
Replacing a missing parent and guide
Comforting, caring - as everyone knows.

Teachers are more than educators
Putting youth at ease
They continue to grow with youth
Frowning upon values that displease.

Teachers have always made the world
A place that we understand.
Through strife, success and pleasure
They lend a helping hand.

Marie Huss

Tears

Wet,
Warm,
Spilling,
Slowly
From red-rimmed eyes.
Wet,
Warm,
Coursing down
The furrows
Of my cheeks.
Nothing to dam them,
No resting place,
No shoulder.
Just stains
On the blouse
Enclosing
Unfondled breasts.

Lynette Graham

Quiet Moments

The wild beauty of the Northern land
Was created by the Master's gentle hand,
Where scarlet red and golden leaves appear,
As nature sheds a silent, golden tear.

Birds sing like tiny echoes in the sky,
A sweet song, or an evening lullaby
Dark eyes peek amidst the shaded pines,
Where deer trials and creatures do entwine.

Lakes like blue velvet touch the shore,
Then like ruffled lace they ebb away once more
Deep echoes fill the wilderness at night,
Where wolves howl in the pale moonlight.

The call of the loon from the lake near by,
Sounds through the mist of the morning sky,
The scent of pine drifts from the towering trees,
Carried on the wings of a gentle breeze.

Take a quiet moment let nature be your guide,
To listen to a bird's song, or watch the eventide,
Pick up a fallen leaf, hold a blossom in your hand,
Just take a quiet moment to really understand.

Joan Beth Clark

Genuine Love

Ever since the beginning of time there was love,
like a lily among the thorns it always
seemed to stand out.

But like a diamond,
genuine love is precious
but very rare,
it's like an emerald
that's far beyond
compare.

Many have tried but never succeed,
to conquer this love from all other
emotions your heart must be freed.

Although you sleep
your heart must always be awake,
Because this love comes in mysterious ways.
Many waters themselves are not able
to extinguish this love, nor can rivers
themselves was it away,
genuine love remains unconquerable,
inextinguishable, unpurchasable.

Pheleeto Carpenter

The Voyageur

Is it a particle of snow to be
When I return from eternity;
In this rekindling of the Lords design
A white knight riding upon the brine.
My steeds arched hooves my pointed lance
Etching out this other chance
To touch the rock of history
With my fellow calvary.
Whose might is not in that of one
But many to the sky have come;
For this long moment briefly past
A winter fragment coldness cast.
  Or is it on some other spare
  That God has willed to set me free?

David Hobberlin

Remember Us

Remember us,
we're those who died
who fought in the war
we tried and tried
sometimes we were blown up
other times we were gunned

Now we are up where
the birds fly high
looking down at you cry and cry.
We still hear the gun shots,
we still feel the pain.
when we cry up here.
To you it's rain.

We were bombed and shot at
we were tricked and tricked.
Where the poppies grow now,
not one is picked.

Telling this poem has made me healed
but remember the poppies,
in flander's field.

Abra Leigh Johnson

Bright Blue Eyes

Bright blue eyes,
Watching, wondering, waiting
Taking in everything,
Yet nothing at all.

Fear, like a life for you,
All that you've known.
The same in your eyes
Bright blue eyes.

From hatred
To horror, to sorrow, to love
Asking for help,
No one hearing.

Acting like you
Don't understand, yet all is
Taken in by your eyes.
Bright blue eyes.

Finally, someone who
Cares enough, rescues you.
To be held, and understood
to be loved.
With your bright blue eyes.

Meagan Hughes

An Enigma

Shall I ever know this gentle man
Who drifts along like a winding street
Wandering, waiting, for what was lost
To return again, to make his life complete.

Shall I ever know this gentle man
Who wears a mantle of bon vivant
So none can see what lies behind
The drape across the alcoves of his mind.

Perhaps some day that drape will open
When he finds what he is seeking
I only know I just keep pondering
Shall I ever know this gentle man.

Delores E. Dillon

"In The Void"

In the void that is the future
We know not what lies ahead.
Many will look upon the unknown with happiness
Others will look with dread.

All in their own ways try to find
Some guidance o'er the roads of life,
Something that will give them direction
In this world of care and strife.

A share of good fortune helps a lot,
Good kind friends aid too,
Enjoying good health and peace of mind
With happiness pulls you through.

The Lord in his many ways will give
Guidance to you where you go.
If you pause in your daily struggle
To faithfully ask Him so.

So worry not of your future
That is still unknown to you,
For by asking the guidance of the Lord
He will pull you through.

E. G. Clark

Crossroads

Sometimes at the crossroads
We stop to pause
Wondering what happened to years;
Years that have gone
With cause.

Faces blur and dreams fade
Irretrievable, beyond repair
Some fragments remain;
Some jade
And wear.

Then we start weaving
And building new hopes
Hopes that no longer darken;
No more sighs and groans
Plain fresh hopes.

No eternity, no beautiful dusk
Maybe autumn leaves
And some pain remains;
Buried in your heart
Immortal and grave.

Arpita Bhawal

A Poem For My Dad!

In tears we saw you sinking
We watched you fade away,
Our hearts were almost broken
You fought so hard to stay.

If tears could build a stairway
And memories could build a lane,
We'd walk that road to heaven
And bring you home again.

May you always walk in sunshine
And God's love around you flow;
For the happiness you gave us
No one will ever know.

It broke our heart to lose you
But you did not go alone;
A part of us went with you
The day God called you home.

A million times we've needed you
A million times we've cried,
If love could have saved you
You never would have died.

Natalie Herold

Desire

With craving passion, WE Desire.
WE seek, WE fancy, WE adore.

There is this great perpetual desire.
A need to want, to satisfy this fire.

WE are engulfed, in ceaseless torment.
Because of need, of this sheer discontent.

Can WE ascent to greater heights?
By satisfying our longing, that feed desire?

A vision most intense, it feeds the spirit.
It floats us high above the sky.

Will Poetry achieve our dream so reckless?
So outlandish, with no remorse?

WE need so many, many new ideas.
With lots and lots of splendid ventures.

We need Symphonic gestures.
Delights of vision, smells of glory.

WE need some rhyme, WE need some swing,
To get ahead and be succinct.

There is a need for grandeur vision.
With delicacy yet not told.

Nikolay Brovcenko

The River

Rolled like little pebbles
We turn from day to day;
Till our heart's reflect like mirrors
Of dreams all washed away;

Starting from a trickle
Where all is young and free,
Where life seems just so simple
And ends where sun meets sea;

Burning with desire
To be the first to know,
We race with gay abandon
Through fire, sand and snow;

We waste our precious moments
As if it will never end,
Passing withered branches
Around each growing bend;
Swelled by ageing wisdom
but slowed by weary feet,
We try to change the current
before our time's complete;

Rolled like little pebbles
we turn from day to day,
Till our heart's reflect like mirrors of
dreams all washed away....

Ken Moss

Welcome!

Welcome into my beast!
Welcome new comes!
Welcome in a new start
Of love in this summer!

Welcome into my spirit with a fresh air
Welcome new comer!
I like together to share
The flowers of summer

Welcome on the beach!
Welcome new comer!
If you is loving change each
Winter on summer...

Welcome on the beach!
Welcome new comer!
If you are loving change each
Winter to summer...

Not bring me the moon
The moon, on the sky!
Bring me just trust!
And soon, TELL ME:
That really happiness and you, is mine!

Eugenia Radu

Forgetting

You cross my mind in the red brick garden
where sun paints shadows among the ferns.
Your habit of coming and going
while tinkling piano notes
drift haltingly on the wind.
Now, you keep still and silent
like the stone unicorn kneeling over
some blue flower,
the name I keep forgetting.

Marie Serdynska

A Silent Cry

You don't hear their screams and cries.
You don't see the tears that flow from
those frightened eyes.
Too scared to sleep in their beds at night.
Too scared to speak in broad day light.
The pain is too much to bare
The thought is just a scare.
Their cries are silent and no one hears.
The question is; is there anyone who cares?

Natasha Indarjit

The Blue

Where would you be it
you were nowhere
Somewhere that you didn't
Know
When you were always,
In a place where
You know
What
To do and what you could
do with,
You
Re-self and to be free to be
who you
Are

Derek Tomicki

Shattered Silence

I went for a walk through the woods one day
When a deer happened to come my way.
With eyes so blue, and hide so brown
His giant antlers were like a crown.
He looked sharp and then he turned,
The cruel wind his face it burned.
Then came a shot from far away.
It hit the deer and he started to sway.
And as he dropped and looked up at me.
A bird's sad song came from atop a tree.
The hunter came to claim his prize
I looked at him with burning eyes.
He wouldn't like someone to take his life,
Take him away from child and wife.
But yet he kills one of God's own beings,
As if he thought a deer had no feelings.
A man such as this should be denied.
The privilege of keeping his own self pride.
For one of these days he'll walk by
And see nothing .... but what has died.

Debra Lynn Bethune

Back In Those Penny Post Card Days

Back in those penny post card days,
When a soda pop cost but a nickel,
The live'n was rough,
'cause the times were tough,
Heck, the general store sold a two penny pickle.

You worked all day for a quarter or so,
And a man's wallet was perpetually thin.
The clothes that were worn, were tattered and torn,
That's why the ragamuffin look was in.

A trip to the river with your sweetheart in tow,
Was best Sunday morning, right up to late fall,
The cost of our date, in pennies, just eight,
But a great time was had by us all.

With Christmas coming, you worked twice as hard,
And your presents for giving, your own hands made,
Our parties were long, our voices raised up in song,
And our drinks were pink lemonade.

But now all I have are good memories,
And some are covered with a dusty old haze,
But oh what I'd give, if once more I could live,
Back in those penny post card days.

T. Clifford J. Boswell

Quest

The night is dark, she stands alone
While the river runs quiet
And the winds softly moan.
The moon rises slowly,
Clouds block it's path.
Thoughts ramble aimless
In the dead of night.
Whither she goest, there is no light
For what does she search
This wraith in the night?
Family, friends, love bereft
For people like her there is no rest.
Why does she wander
This maid in the night?
Searching for answers
For all the world's peace.
This lady seeks peace.
It is a long, long road
For peace is elusive
And a very heavy load.

Joan Ryan

Bad Cat

I am so cute, I prefer handsome
When I am called I never come

I live with two dogs, they are my friends
When I'm around their fun never ends

I like to tease them when I know they are tired
Then I jump up on a ledge once I've got them wired

I keep this game up till I get bored
When will they learn that I am Lord

Dogs are so stupid, their brains are so small
It's a wonder to me how they get along at all

In my house I'm known by many a name
It depends on my mood and the name of my game

Trouble is my mission you can count on that
So most often you'll find that I'm called bad cat.

Lisa Soderberg

Answering Machine

Why are so many not at home
When I decide to use the phone,
The money's in and then oh 'no
I'm told to speak after the tone.
Surely asses have more sense
Trapped my body is all tense,
Mind a blank completely dense
There goes the last of my ten pence.
Should I stay, or should I go
Or attempt to face my foe,
Once more into the booth I go
Courageously I say "hello."
Feeling like I'm someone else
I'm definitely not myself,
Message over as by stealth
Now concerned about my health.
Of all the things that I have sen
In some places that I've been,
Afraid of no one or one thing
But this horrid mean machine.

Katie Munro

Like A Bird

Sometimes I wish a bird to be,
where I could fly above the sea,
I'd fly to places where no man's gone.
I shall wish for my friends to come along,
All woe's on earth would seem but small
For up there in the sky I'd have a ball
I've wondered what life would be like,
If I were so free,
Without a care in the world, a place I'd
truly be me,
I'd search for the beauty.
The simple pleasantries life brings,
Oh how I'd soar high above.
Feeling so much peace and
Tranquility,
Out loud I would sing,
Forever then
I would know deep in my heart
How God wished this
for us right from
the start

Luana McDowell

Bluebird Bay

It was early in the morning.
When the Captain came my way
He took me on his lovely boat.
And we headed for Bluebird Bay.

The sky was getting black.
The sea was getting rough.
All I could see ahed of me
Was a group of very high bluffs

I got so very sea sick
I really thought I'd die
And had to grasp a railing
Or I'd gone up to the sky.

Then the Captain came to me
And said
"little lady you'd better have some tea"
But I was too sick of any to partake
And I shall never forget that night.
That horrible night on the lake.

Blanche Stewart

When I Pray

I like to walk in mossy trails
Where deer or moose have trod,
There I can walk and ponder
Where I commune with God.
And I say thanks as best I can
I feel He's close beside
He knows my ways my very thoughts
There's nothing I can hide.
So I will keep on walking
The trail's still there to see
No fear of roughly falling.
That's when He'll carry me.
With silence all around me
I feel His presence near
I'll walk back home, contented
What more have I to fear.

Edith Mae Simpson

If Time Could Stand Still

My children are growing out of my life
Who can tell
How they'll be
Where will they go?

Lord,
I can't stop them from slipping away
If time could stand still
Just a little while longer
If time could stand still
Just for a minute longer

After all they are part of me
Part of my life
My most beautiful sight
If time could stand still, I wonder...
I could have them, a little while longer

My child,
All of my children are borrowed
Love them, cherish them,
Each and every moment
For one day, you will have them no
longer...

Lise Bedard

O, How I Would Like To Be

O, how I would like to be on the other side,
Where there is brotherly and sisterly love,
Where there is everlasting happiness,
Where there will be no anger, hatred, liars,
   thieves, sorrow,
deceivers, dishonesty and death.
There will be beloved, truthful, innocent
  and joyful people.
Those who are old, will be young again,
   those who are sick will be healed.
A place that is magical, because the trees
  will be singing
In a loud clear voice to our Prince and King.
There will be sweet tasting water,
delicious fruits and everlasting life, and
peace and goodwill to all men.
That place is called Paradise my friend.
Will there be such a special and lovely place?
Will there really be?........
Yes my friend there will be.

Camille Grey

Tears In Heaven

His tears drop,
Which he cannot hide,
The sadness he holds,
The anger inside.

He cannot forget,
That horrid day,
When half of his life,
Was taken away.

If he could see his son
For just a moment,
There would be
No more Tears to Heaven.

But life must go on
And he must accept the past
And think of the future.

His son may of died,
But his soul stays alive.

Katherine Jolin

Grief

He's gone! He won't be coming back.
Who can understand eternity?

For thirty years we loved and laughed;
We fought and cried and raised a family.

I see him on a busy street
I hear his voice, his laugh and turn to look.

I know he won't be back and yet
There's news to tell him, grandchildren to meet.

Only those who survive this loss
Understand the awful loneliness.

The quiet house; the empty chair;
No one to know my fears, my joys, my tears.

But I must move ahead and learn
To live and laugh without my friend.

To start again to find a life
That won't included the one who meant so much.

I must accept reality
He's gone! He won't be coming back.

Linda Riding

The Lovers

Where lie the promises of happiness
Whispers of a Summer night?

Winter hammers our deserted courtyards
With his steel gait

Impassioned, the lines where laundry hung
Cross-rule unvanquished space

A lost cat disappears with haste

Somewhere,
between the harbor's warehouses
Whistles a dismasted wind

Shadowless ships caught in rings of ice,
lie motionless
Appeased, at last the River
Embraces his winter City night after night
A City stripped of her glitter, undressed,
abandoned to
   elementary forces
Did we dream her strange beauty?
Had she ever been so loved?
Far away, bridges thrown into the night, fall asleep
Where two rows of candelabrum glow and die
Refractions of a thousand fires burning bright
Mystical dogs guard the gates of a kingdom

Francine Prevost

Untitled

I think I know
Why a bud needs to reach high
   when an Easter sun
    warms it ever so softly;
Why it wants to burst forth in glory
   when a robin chirps by.

And I think I understand
Why the wind gentles it sharpness
  to zephyr in and out;
Why the greens brighten
  and background the wild flash
   of springtime scarlet and gold.

Don't you?

S. Neil Kardian

When Angels Fly

Little brother don't cry
wipe your weeping eyes
because Daddy isn't there
to touch your lonely heart
and Mama is all you have
to cherish and to love
so be content little brother
and dry your weeping eyes
for someday your dreams
might come true
in the middle of the night
when the stars are bright and angels fly
you might probably hear Daddy say
I LOVE YOU.

Marcel Winter

Pollution Pollution

This earth is a wonderful world
With all it's trees and plants.
With it's lady birds, it's beetles,
and it's little ants.

The pollution in this world of ours.
Will wash these things away.
Put your rubbish in the bin,
Just don't throw it away.

The noisy factory has made it worse.
It's just been like a curse
All these things we've tried to do.
Pollution got their first.

The animals in the forest,
Are just as scared as us.
The streams are oily, thick and black,
The animals leave and fear they won't be
coming back

You and I live on this earth,
And we're not going to pollute it.
We'll put our litter in the bin,
And do our best to save it.

Kimberley Nelson

Untitled

Love can make the
world go around.

Give a child a hug
Or a kiss and there
Will be no dismiss.

Money can only last
For a time but one's
Love can last forever.

Love can provide you,
The security and stability
That can turn your
Life around.

So why not spread your
wings and let love begins.

Linnette James

Today's Dreams

Today's dream are tomorrow's memories,
Yesterday's gone, today has come.
Why do we worry just sing this song,
And you'll be happy, as you carry on.
When we were young, we made our plans,
Dreams of tomorrow, of things so grand,
But now there gone, our days near the end.
Although we wonder, we don't understand.
We wonder what happened to all our plans.
Things that we wanted, wanted so bad.
Now that we're older we understand,
Dreams are only thoughts in our heads.
The time has come, our day's drawing neigh,
All of our dreams are passing by.
All we have left, are memories of them.
Oh how we wish we could be young, again.

Leo S. Peters

Ghost Girl

I sit in class surrounded by people
Yet no one sees me
Longing to escape my insanity
I am the voice that no one hears
The silent streaming tears
Condemned to my own fears
I am the ghost girl.

I beg and cry and plead
Hear me, see me, speak to me
Release me from my destiny
Accept me in reality
For I am the ghost girl.

Nina Raike

A Nurse's Thoughts

You sit in silence, you do not see,
Yet once you had interests just like me,
Once you were newly wed,
Working hard to earn your b read,
You had a family, were a wife,
Had a full and happy life,
Now you sit staring straight ahead,
Do you dream of the life you once led?
You sit there in a geriatric chair,
So quiet we often forget you're there,
We speak to you, your name we call,
From you we get no response at all.
We keep you clean and dry,
And we often wonder why,
This thing has happened to you,
And yes, a fear it could be fall us too,
When the time comes for you to go above,
Perhaps you'll know we showed you love.

Anne Mathers

Pain

With you, there was happiness.
You are gone and life has turned back to
    darkness.
Around me, there is only pain,
Now that sorrow is back again.

There's a strange fear
which is flowing through my veins.
I try to wipe away my tears
but all of it, is still in vain.

Why should life be so unfair,
I can't become the one I really want to be.
Living in a world where no one cares about me
and life has no meaning to me.

To an unjust life I'm tied.
And I will find no way out.
I want to make my last ride
To a land where I will have no doubt.

I'm still so unsure
And it makes me feel insane.
For my sadness, there is no cure
and there's no way to stop my pain.

Nisha Devi Juggessur

For My Husband

As the day turns to night
You are in my minds sight
To have and to hold
Our story begins to unfold

To the dear sweet man
The other half to my silver ban
I want you to know
How much I love you so

Since the day we said "I do"
I have fallen deeper in love with you
My heart, my mind, and my soul
Are here for you as time grows old

To the dear sweet man
Who shares my silver ban
I want you to feel
That our love is real.

Karen Leblanc

Forever And Always

Five years ago
You got down on one knee
At the top of the world
And proposed to me.

Ever since then
It's been candy and flowers,
But what means more
Is all of the hours
We spend together.

We've taken great trips
Since I've been your wife,
But the greatest of all
Is the path of life.

Now we've had children,
The hours are less,
But of these times
We make the best
For quality time together.

I want you to know for the rest of my days
I'll love you my best forever and always.

Jennifer C. Hibbert

Pass You By

Yesterday, a moment passed you by.
You just didn't seem to know.
But if you knew then, what you know now.
Would you have let it go?

Who knows where that moment led.
Or where you would be today.
Would you be somewhere wondering
If a moment had passed you, along the way.

One day you will realize,
Because you know it's true.
Those moments that passed you by,
Will never again, come back to you.

Make the most of all your tomorrows,
Cherish today, and the moments to come.
For you should know by now,
Those moments fade like the sun.

So don't let the moments pass you by.
They are so precious, and few.
Fragments of time lost forever,
If you let them get by you.

June Liscombe

All Year Long

You were like a spring breeze
You made my heart swing slowly in the
    green scene
Leaving me with the sign of new love
Telling me that I will fall in love with you soon

You were like a summer ocean
You sparkled brightly under the endlessly
    shining sun
Making my blue eyes almost blind
Surfing through my mind with an invisible
    shadow

You were like an autumn leaf
You flew silently to a place I can never reach
Hurting my heart like a wounded child
Throwing "good-bye" from a sky high above

You were like a winter snow
You covered my heart sadly with a pure white start
Knowing that I can't start over without you
Hoping that I'd forget you someday

You were in my heart for all year long
You were my life for all the four seasons
Crying like a new born baby, I swear by the stars
Remembering you is the last thing I'll never do.

Mari Sakai

The Void

I often dream of how things would've been;
You, my father, I shall never know;
Yes, you are gone forever but...
I've so many questions to ask,
But only you can give me the answers I need.

You've passed on with dignity, please
    know I forgive;
For it was a long, tough journey; for us both;
Coming to grips with your demons and
    inevitable death;
Do you feel cheated and lonely as I;
Cheated out of our father/
Daughter relationship?

I love you Dad, and think of you often;
Your Son holds you in a precious part of
    his heart; as I;
Know that your greatest legacy is our mother,
She has been the strength, motivation and
    has always given us more than I can say,
You now have been gone for 26 years,
I guess that is the reason I still cry.

Michele MacLean

Sweeter Than Warm Honey

When I think of you
Your presence envelops me
Slips over me
Silky as the smoothest satin
Sweeter than warm honey
More tender than the violin's song
    as the bow gently caresses her strings
Burning like liquid fire
Brightly as a field of twinkling stars
That is how I think of you

Elizabeth Galbraith

Remembering Dr. Patricia Anne Devolder

You suffered long in silence,
You never asked Him why,
But I beg it of Him daily,
Why'd my sister have to die?

You needed a heart and set of lungs,
And a lot of help from above,
But now could you need someone else's heart,
When your own overflowed with love.

You knew that you were leaving,
How I wish you could have stayed,
You left us all with a message though,
"Be not afraid"

A life-force that's gone empty,
A strong will that has run dry,
I held your hand so gently,
Then softly kissed you good-bye.

I know that time and love can heal,
And hearts can make amends
Chance may have made us sisters,
But it's LOVE that made us friends!

Karen Schram

For You

You spoke of learning,
You spoke of joy
A joy so sweet but delicate.
You spoke of being scared,
Scared of losing what you had found.

You spoke of searching
Searching for a better way
You spoke of escaping
Escaping from the tyranny of conformity
Conformity in work and dress and thought.

You spoke of being shaped by four
blissful years;
A whole new world opening up
And I listened to every word,
Enthralled by what you said,
You were expressing me.

And now I miss you intensely.
My time with you was so short
But very special,
Very real and very connected,
And worth so much to me.

Helen Gregorczuk

This Morning I Watched You Laugh

How do I tell you I watched you laugh
You were a creature of majesty
your head poised with the grace of an animal.

What does the painter do when he is
unhappy with his work
as I with my poem.
Does he throw his canvas to the floor,
begin again,
or blend another color.
Poets like painters create beauty through
pen or brush
with a masters movement.

how do I tell you I watched you laugh
and just because of it I wanted to paint
you a poem
and have you understand,
this morning I watched you laugh.

Diane Phillips

The Butterfly Effect Or World Rendez-vous

In the Valley of the Yangtze a butterfly
Wakes from her dreams, bursts her cocoon, lights on a bloom
A lazy lady drying her wings in the sun

One thousand miles away a typhoon desolates
The shores in the Sea of Japan, flash fires flare
Across the main in the forest of the North West

Ill-seasoned snows shroud the prairie in the heartland
Of the States extinguish the lights in the East coast
Whilst unrelenting hurricanes rage in the South.

Earthquakes upheave the foundation of the Andes
Untimely monsoon turns lowlands into quagmires
In India, Sri Lanka, Bangladesh and Malaysia;

What world rendez-vous predesigned is in progress?
What stirs up the sands in the deserts of Iraq
And Arabia? What chanced, closer home, in Berlin

Swayed Central Europe and in Moscow what transpired?
What fell in ten days on the unsuspecting world
That in Tiananmen Square failed to get under way?

In the Valley of the Yangtze a butterfly
take flight from a flower to start a brief life on
bright-coloured wings dried by the sun.

M. T. MacLean

Enchanted Kingdom

I was taking a walk along the woods one night
To breath fresh air and perhaps take a few sight,
When suddenly out of nowhere I heard a sound
Coming from behind the trees along the way down-
Where I was standing on the edge of a steep cliff
On which I've estimated to be a thousand meters deep

Below the cliff I have noticed a vast green plain-
On which a kingdom stood and villages abound it,
Happy people filled every streets and every lane
Singing, enjoying, with music and sounds of every beat
The huge and beautiful castle was elegantly decorated
With balloons and banners, the best of those over made

There was a great carnival and colorful lights shined
Everybody, young and old seems to be celebrating-
Everywhere there is fun and joyful are everything....
Then with a wink of an eye it disappeared out of my mind
Like the mist of a cloud passing by the moon above
It was an enchanted kingdom, a paradise of love!

Elaine Mae C. Yu

Beautiful Morn

'Twas a beautiful morn and the first day of
spring was again reborn,
I was awaken to the world by the sweet melodious
song of a lone bird
who seemed to be calling me so I rose from my bed
and started off the day feeling that the world
was today friendly
Yes, it was a beautiful morn
I stumbled over to the windowsill that was before
bare and now seemed to have collected the whole
of mother nature's family there
and as I looked around I felt overcome with loving
cordiality for watching them had made me forget
all the horrors of reality,
the lone bird whose sweet melody had awaken me
had caught my eye, so I gently reached out and
touched his wings as they soared up into the spring sky.

C. J. Trebb

When We Miss The Harbour So Completely

But I am not unhappy
   To have been twisted before my time,
to have witnessed the sun target your pale skin
   like a curious suburban binocular boy,
only to forget it.

But I am not unhappy
   to have been frightened by the mirror,
To have stepped off our roof into a rising sky
   all to become my own raven. Flying for wingless dreamers
everywhere, only to awaken.

I shall not orphan the city with my absence
   for I will suppress my discomfort and become one with
Coffee, sex and all pleasure addictions
   in God's great kitchen.

And I am not unhappy
   to have waited a thousand years
Nor to have dreamt in our dusty attic
   with the bat-ticks, whose intentions are warm.
I will stay until they call me,
   forever ordering womb service for life, love and popcorn.

   Don McGugan

Promises

Promises, promises! Oh how many I've heard,
With so many broken, I should now have been cured.
Some promises were broken through no fault of their own.
With the best of intentions, their plans were just blown.
No explanation, not even mention was made,
Most often empty words, even lies, I'm afraid.
Then is when, "I'll call you soon." becomes weeks of gray,
And when 'ten minutes later' is turned into days,
Or a promise to dinner is simply ignored,
Only fools continue to believe in their word.
And when hope slowly fades while I wait, I have found,
In oppression and depression one becomes bound.
Should one dare not allow to hope in another?
Experience shows promises broken, why bother?
To eliminate trust, and faith in the other,
To protect ones self - is it worth it? I wonder.
The obvious way to avoid disappointment,
Is it count on no one - to be independent,
Self supporting, self sufficient, self reliant.
Ah then, what a self-centered lonely existence!

   Janet L. Wearmouth

A Gaelic Lord

In Matthew is a Gaelic lord I heard my father say
When often speaking of you, that's the picture he portrays
I'm counting on a child's world to help me reminisce
About the days when we flew out of Scotland o'er the mist
I want to start the day we left again now that I'm grown
Into a man much like yourself, a man I've barely known
Whose eyes are softly speaking in the shades of grey and blue
Whose quiet sense of humor keeps the world around him new
A soldier on the battled seas when bondage to defeat
For peace to be the sovereignty and war to not repeat
A cunning operator when the cards are in your hand
You savour every moment when the tournament is grand
If I could see this gentleman, particular and proud
I'd tell you that I miss you, Uncle Matthew, right out loud

   Diane E. Babcock

Stars

As their five points glimmer and the beauty of them glow,
the freeness of the starlight watching them go.
No shadows left behind, no sorrow in their soul,
the only thing they say is a whispering glow.
The beauty in the moonlight, they light up the sky,
no one can see them, only the naked eye.
They wonder here and there, without a care,
the freeness of their lives, they can go anywhere.
A million miles away,
most beautiful stars will come out and play.
The stars are like little angels, watching us at night,
we only look at them in the moonlight,
and we only see them as stars, but years from now we will say,
that they were our guardians watching us everyday.

   Natasha Ferrari

A Fervent Hope For Peace

The state of the earth is too much pollution
The poor of the world face dire grim starvation
Some nations embark on their nuclear testing
With greed others kill with obvious unfeeling
Perhaps they believe their race is superior
Or that their religion makes others inferior
So what is the good of man's cornucopia
If man's precious life is lost to his paranoia?

It is too much to wish to attain Utopia
If man is content without my phobia
To live in this world with enough sustenance
Not wishing to grab all things in abundance
To live simply in life with one's family
And hope to depart with love from progeny
For having done his best and proven his worth
Humanity gained because of his birth.

   Leonor R. Dy-Liacco

The Breath I Consume

Every little breath and wastefully inhale
the desire in me for you would never fail,
around you my co-ordination double - take and
   my language double - talk,
sometimes it's a puzzle why you still stand there,
   most people would walk,
I hope its just a "phase" if this continues - soon
   you'll see my doom,
for whenever you're around me I ignore every little
   breath I consume.
every little breath I dervastly intake.
I only see you in my dreams until I'm awake,
just the "thought" of losing you would drive
   me in a state of catatonic,
the slightest headache you feel makes me panic,
if this is what love feels like, if this continues - soon
   you'll see my doom,
for whenever your ground me, I ignore
and neglect, the very breath I consume

   B. Theresa Evans

Affinity

She walks the halls of life with easy step,
'Twould seem unhurried, yet with purpose clear,
As though, with careful thought, the way is seen,
And now the path to follow will appear.

But if you closely look, and listen well,
The almost unseen marks of stress are there,
For she has had her doubts and sorrows too,
But somehow found the means to thwart despair.

There is another facet to her style
Which, consciously or not, presents allure:
The little tease, the comment bright, the look
Of interest, disdain, or smile demure.

All these and more, bestowed on you, will break
Your firm resolve and high objective schemes,
And you will lose your heart, yet cannot tell
Just when, or how, she penetrates your dreams.

John Comrie

The Elephant In The Tree

An elephant sat in a big, old tree
With an unopened book laying there on his knee.
An owl flew by, sat on the elephant's nose
And said to himself, "Why do you suppose
An elephant sits in a big, old tree
With an unopened book laying there on his knee?"
The elephant heard; made this teary reply,
"I can't read the words no matter how hard I try."
"Why, I can teach you, but not in one day."
Said the owl, to the elephant, in a wise owly way.
So day after day the owl flew to the tree
Where the elephant sat with the book on his knee.
And day after day in the big, old tree
The elephant learned from the book on his knee.
Some words were hard; some were not.
Some he remembered; some he forgot.
But the elephant practiced and soon he knew
How to read the book, all the way through.
Now the elephant sits in the big, old tree
Reading the book, that lies open, there on his knee.

Audrey McKenzie

A Time To Remember

The battles first and second, and many wars before,
Tell the tales of sorrow, tell the tales of gore.

Many soldiers fought, even more grieve their deaths,
With certain hope and pride, they strained their last breaths.

A time to remember, let us not forget,
These troops fought to protect, from future threat.

Prelude and peace, the fantasy of war,
A quest with no meaning in battlefields galore.

A war of surrender, a bitter aftermath,
Our country had prevailed, theirs left in wrath.

A culture with desire, a nation with no shame.
A joyous community, with victory to proclaim.

Not only should we remember the injured and the dead,
We overcame the horrors of war, to victory we were led.

Let us as a people, bow our heads and pray,
For both death and victory, on Remembrance Day.

Kathleen Riddell

The Day That Kurt Cobain Died

The sound of a single shot tore thru' the night air,
Yet no one heard the end of one man's despair.
The lonely cries had gone unheard.
Did not one of us ever listen to his words?
He wrote of dying, pain - undescribable
The smile had left his eyes.
As tears burned unshed, as he gazed at us.
His face revealed his emotions.
The inner turmoil his soul struggled with each day.
Yet we did not hear - we tuned out with a deaf ear.
We loved his music as he touched our soul
But we ignored the man himself.
The torment he held inside.
Was just too much to bear
So when Aprils wind blew his way
He took a gun and left us that day
To search for the peace that eluded him here
The day that Kurt Cobain died.

Kelley Hazel

Overrated

Andrew,
The lonely child
slowly
emerges from his room below the attic and
creeps
down the squeaky, noisy stairs of the house,
hoping
to see what lies hidden in the heart of the basement.
His mother told him there's nothing
to discover
in the dusty rooms below.
But he still finds *life*
an adventure, and so he will descend
the stairs that lead to the
cob-webbed walls, though
disappointment
will appear on his mother's face.
The *results*
will not be new.

Efthalia Lidakis

Christmas Time

Christmas time is time to cheer for loved ones for,
so far and near. For little ones with eyes so bright
who wait for Santa on Christmas night with
snow so deep crispy and white his reindeers fly with
all their might.

As Santa sings of love joy, he means it all for
girl and boys. His little elves they work all night and
never sleep on Christmas night, they sing their songs
of love and good cheer, and wish us all a happy new year.

He leaves your toys at the foot of your bed, and
leaves by the window or chimney instead.
He flies back to Lafland all snowy and white
and will see you again Christmas night.

Robert Neill

Dear Grandpa

Dear Grandpa

Nobility shall bear your name
   Your dignified fire lit by a courageous flame

You fought in the war so that we could be free
   You loved your family ever so devotedly

Your radiant personality always burned bright
   As does the luminating white moon in the contrasting
   night

You never sacrificed honor for deception
   You were a soul of purity that demanded no correction

Your comfort in simplicity gave you your charm
   Your calm, even temperedness set off no alarm

You have taught me a valuable lesson in pride
   To walk each painful step in a powerful stride

To face each day with your chin up to the sky
   To not give up but to give it one last try

And so dear Grandpa, I'll treasure what I've learned
   For my respect and my love, you deserve and have
   earned

    Jason Jackson

"Velvet"

From the two black abyss, the diamonds trail in your velvet.
The recondite secret was ajar.
And then in the aurea of your soul, there was a storm
the premonitions of an uncertain destiny.
And the black lady, cuddle both of us, and the stars
in her cloak, where inviting with hope.
The ambient was formed with scents, a warm and
untouched wing, caress us, taking away the unseen flowers.
The dream to see both our silvers end.
It is the illusions of my yesterday, that still are,
with memories without echo.
And I continue my short trip, as if a leaf in the
wind that was, laying dry and deserted, alone.
And yet, your hands where in mine, trying to pass a
consolation, that couldn't be. To help me in your faraway
your memory is here.
But your velvet, is gone.

    Alejandro Castelli

A Song For Enzo: A Diptych

Going to see a dying man, a friend;
out of pity, curiosity, or to view my own mortality?
Like the face in the mirror after a shower's end
or crushed glass on black asphalt.

What do you say to him he has not heard before?
What tears can he cry for me? What word?
O yes I can play the clown, a frown, a smile,
in calico or black, in satin or in serge;

But with his mother's wail, my pathetic sighs
ever salve the mystery of these shredding skies
rent in two across the void, leaving this shell
apart from that drifting soul or justify this hell
holding hands in a black bed while white figures trace
the halls and alleys of my face?

Enzo is fragile like fading lily petals
but he sits up valse-like, crystal-eyed
gripping your hand like there's no tomorrow
and sings to you a song that settles
even my cynicism; a shaky tremolo, but a tide
that rushes in to erase all sorrow.

    Jim Head

The Day Begins

A pale moon torn by black clouds,
Sphere of purest light, distant and free.
Timeless, enchanting, released from life.
But slowly fading...as the day begins.
Lace clouds cover the moon commanding it to flee,
Back to the realm of darkness,
For dawn is breaking, and black turns to grey,
Light reclaims his throne, as the day begins.
Soon the sky is on fire with light,
A great lion tossing his head,
Colours that have no name, entangled with crimson and gold
In a sudden surge, the sun rises and night is no more
For the day has begun.

    Eilidh Talman

Untitled

Your eyes are the kind that weaken my knees,
Your smile is even better it always makes me freeze.
Your soul is as gentle, as the angels above,
The first time I saw you, I knew I was in love.
I would love to run my fingers, through your hair,
If only you knew, how much I really still do care.
Sometimes I feel lonely, even blue,
But to cheer myself up, I remember back when I was still with you.
Your heart is a lot more precious, than a handful of gold,
My love for you, will never go cold.
Seeing you kiss another, is tearing me apart.
We went together perfectly, like a horse and it's cart.
Why can't we be together, just you and me?
Oh Jonathan, if only you'd come back to me.

    Lorraine Scorsonelli

The Prairie

"Miles" don't express the distance I see
the earth laid before me, not even a tree,
a glimpse of the universe without having
to be on top of a mountain or out on the sea.

The colours are vivid and constantly changing.
Non-prairie folk have said it's amazing — the
abundance of green, rich browns, golds, and blues,
The crops and the grasses submitting their hues.

Out on the prairie, on a warm balmy evening,
with soft breezes blowing, sweet scents in the air,
there's a feeling of peace — who can describe it?
Thank you, dear Lord, for this moment we've shared.

The full moon, the sunsets, the big sky above
all add to the beauty and splendour you see.
If you're from the forests, mountains or coastlines,
come to the prairie—and share it with me.

    Emily I. Stillwell

The Opening Ceremony

At four o'clock we waled with much excitement to the stage
I could not believe the watching faces as we came to our seats

I held my breath until they called my name, my heart beasting fast
Iwalked to the middle of the stage ane prepared my words

No one was prepared for the color of the night
The shadows overcame and we spoke with much laughter

Cold night walking on to the moon after the ceremony
The way home in black and white like it's a wonderful life

We swam that night in ouir imagination and held our breath
Like fish without gills I asked myself to breath, but I couldn't

    Tomison Demmel

The Residence Of Sex

I am the Mayan snake,
the one that inyects its eyes
in the deep blue of its long nights.

But you, Eva, you are fire that extinguishes every day.
I dye your shame with this yellowish green
while Adan has fun among the other Divas.

In what residence will you hide your sex
wet of weeping, Eva?

Wrap your vulva
with this peeled fragment of snake.

Rub your breasts with naphthalin
and don't proclaim yourself beautiful,Goddess or attractive.

Nymphs are neither snakes nor Evas.

You and I are the exiled,
the ugly dolls
the females for a while
the most beautiful vagina for a myope.

Adan is going to fecundate a star
meanwhile, we,
we are drawing small paper boats in the exile.

Cristina Gutierrez Richaud

I've Lost My Sense

Walking through the jungle of this time,
The hatred, the destruction, distorting my mind,
Attacking me from in front, at my side and behind.
Only if I knew where I am going, for I'm blind.

I've drank of the blood, of those who had gone in haste,
I've drank of the water, polluted with waste,
I've ate of the food, poison, but could not trace;
For my tongue, it has lost the taste.

The sting of the air, just to inhale,
My nose, it cannot tell.
Clean, unclean, fresh or stale,
I do not know, for I can't even smell.

If someone were saying in my ear,
What about the living and dying cries of the air?
How could I know, what words can I share?
For I cannot read lips, nor can I hear.

I've even touched the eyes of the living,
Their fears and tears, they cannot conceal,
But what could I do, how could I comfort?
Oh, I only wish I was able to feel.

Elroy Yearwood

The Last Chapter

You were the ones, who held me tight.
You tucked me in bed, every night.
You sang me songs.
You rocked me to sleep.
You calmed me down, when I began to weep.
You always told me, "Everything will be O.K."
and that Mommy and Daddy would be here to stay.
I am more than lucky to have parents like you.
Reliable and supportive.
Helping me through.
These moments of laughter, love and fun,
it now has all ended a new chapter has begun.
Of misery, hurt and emotional pain.
I wish I can stay, but I will not remain.
Please remember me when I disappear,
and remember my presence will always be near.
I promise to stay strong until my life fades.
The doctor just told me I am dying from A.I.D.S.

Beverly Bilusack

Words Of A Common Woman

I've always felt that written words were music to my ears
And whether fact or fiction, they stirred me thru the years.

To have the gift of written words was something I desired
But due to my fear of rejection, I have sat, solidly mired.

To set my thoughts to paper and to write what's in my heart
Has always been a problem of knowing where to start.

Some thoughts are very funny, others filled with tears
And some recall the memories of my childhood years.

Words can be used to harm, they can be used to heal
And sometimes what I write will hurt, because that's how I feel

I've never fought with my fists, I've always fought with words
And though I haven't always won, I have at least been heard.

What I right may entertain, may make you stop and pause
May bring a tear to your eye, may stir in you a cause

I do not mean to offend, nor cast dispersions on the lot
But the things that are the dearest, are the things we've hardest
  fought.

Suzanne L. Hurley

"Illigitimi Non Carborundum"

"Don't Let The Bastards Wear You Down"

A thought can and will control your mind
Start daydreaming, wondering how far you have to climb
The hill in front of you grips your spirit with fear
Choking your desires that once were clear

Quandary controls your every move
Life begins to spiral into a deluge
Constantly bombarding rationale you once possessed
Delving deep into ones soul you become enmeshed

Searching takes on a major role in your life
Often combating ridicule and strife
Battling yourself is one of life's toughest chores
Fighting in the trenches - Waging daily wars

Always allow turmoil to be followed by peace
Caress your mind with the soft gentle touch of fleece
Happiness is derived from inner strength
You must be willing to go to any length

Mental toughness should never be underestimated
Focusing on the positive will not leave you decimated

It's the ninth inning and you are on the mound
Remember - "Don't let the Bastards wear you down"

Thomas J. McCann

The Day We Turned TOO Fast

I'll never forget that day
           the day we turned too fast
                      and nearly lost our cargo

I just watched the door swing wide
                      what a ride
                 I nearly lost my intuition
                      with the cargo nearly falling
                      out the back swinging wide
                                too fast doors.

Keryn Mulluch

247

'The Future'

Is it being formulated
somewhere in the firmament?
Perhaps, the main thing is...
it's here... Coming at us
relentless in fashion,
skimming oceans, mountains
and valleys.
Whether at the gate in San Francisco
or knee deep in Buffalo grass
in Nebraska, it's best to face it,
face the Northwest,
that's where the wind comes from,
surely the future rides on the wind.
Revel in it.
For the future can change atoms, molecules
and minds.

John R. Porter

Beautiful, Beautiful Sky

If I could watch you every moment,
Oh, the changes I would see.
It's almost like you can't decide,
Just how you want to be.

Whatever the time, whatever your mood,
I'm always sure to know,
That if I pause to watch you,
You'll put on quite a show.

So stunning you are wearing diamonds at night,
So many times you change colors each day.
At every glance you are such a magnificent sight,
But each pose so elusive, I fear looking away.

Though I hate to let one stance get by me,
So fleetingly they fly.
Oh, how you mystify me,
Beautiful, beautiful sky.

Nell Moore

Unspoken Thanks (of a tired tree surgeon)

Some days, when pain makes life no fun
You wearily walk, see no sun.
Shut down are engines of the mind.
The eyes squint, too, but are not blind.

They welcome, always, those who care,
Those who speak, where some don't dare,
To tired, dirty, stooped old men,
Making them "like new" again.

William E. Twombly

God Bless This Child

God bless this child night and day.
Let him be able to run and play.
God bless this child with Holy Grace,
Shine you're light upon his face.

Let him be able to see the stars that shine at night,
Let him be able to see the morning sunlight.
God bless this child with all you're might,
Please cherish him and keep him in you're sight.

There's a lot of love, joy and care,
That we all have to offer and want to share.
We want to share it with him for a lot of years,
So let him be safe and ease our fears.

God bless this child's holy name.
While we all continue to hope and pray.

Tessey Davis

'How Excellent Is Thy Name In All The Earth!'

When I think on all the things you've brought me through,
O, GOD "How excellent is thy Name!"
Be it sunshine, or be it rain,
"How excellent is thy Name!"
Stormy weather, cloudy days, your LOVE remains the same.
"How excellent is thy Name!"
I have loved and lost, I have lost and gained,
O, "How excellent is thy Name!"

There are many moons between life and death,
So many twists and turns our lives take after that first breath!
I've stumbled through valleys, and climbed over hills,
And He is always there to say, "Peace, Be Still!"
Through this ever changing, winding race called life,
I've come to know HIM in the power of HIS might.
Whether things go right or whether they go wrong,
HE is my inspiration and my song.

I will hold fast to the hand that will NEVER change,
O, "How excellent is thy Name!"

Anne Crump

That We Whose Willed Lands

That we whose willed lands were shed by polyps,
The chalk-white ooze fermenting tawny soil,
With forebears sorely wracked in slavers' ships,
Ultimate chattels of inhuman toil —
That we, mixed blooms of Ethiop'a's rape
Should violate anew our implied trust
In this, our island-brother's firm handshake,
Again, for spittle on old Europe's crust,
Fans ireful flames in this West Indian heart.
O mad conflagration! Must Treason's
Bleak auction-block ever keep us apart?
"Never!", the cry that echoes proud and free;
A clarion-call to each emerging nation
That will enjoin a renewed Federation.

Harold A. Beckles

Untitled

Your body tingles with excitement.
 Your heart pounds with joy.
You are in love.

The sky is a never ending blue
    reaching out until the eye can no longer see,
    past the horizon and into eternity.

The sun is a glowing ball of light
    thrusting forth its rays of mitigating ardor,
    deep within the soul and touching a tranquil candor.

The breeze is a melodious ballad
    caressing supple and yielding tendrils of hair,
    placid in a sense and not having any care.

The sand is a piece of elderly shell
    building pathways for life to bend and see all,
    forever stretching and unceasing to be tall.

The wave is a lolling majestic sight
    ascending into whitecaps to break onto the shore,
    life mingles within and is left with wanting more.

Your spirit is in peace. Your mind is able to be in repose.
You are in love...with the ocean.

Jamie Evert

My Mother's Gift

As spring warms the earth and life bounds anew
I remember the walks I once took with you
The hours we spent on old country lanes
Watching new lambs and calves romping in play

Sometimes we were lucky and saw a new foal
Struggling to stand; life's very first goal
The bird's would be singing high up in the trees
As they tended so carefully their little ones needs

At the pond we would watch the tadpoles and frogs
And salamanders sunning themselves on the logs
On the soft springtime breezes the butterflies danced
And we marveled at how the young deer would prance

From the hilltop we watched the Severn flow by
And spoke often of Wales over on the other side
In the valley the church we just had to see
For the old pipe organ filled our hearts with glee

These walks we shared taught me how precious life is
And how all we experience is truly a gift
That treating all living things with love and respect
Would make my life rich and free of regret

Heather D. Larsen-Price

The Alarm

Rrrrring! The woman stirs from her bed.
She enters the bathroom and looks at the mirror.
The face is not old, yet it appears weathered.
She desperately tries to look beyond the crows feet.
Suddenly, she sees the face of a child.
She bows her head, terrified that the child will not
recognize her.

She raises her eyes, ashamed that she could not face a child.
The girl's face becomes tear stained.
Memories flood the woman's brain.
  Dreams she once had
  Convictions she had the strength to hold true
The power to believe without seeing
The anticipation and excitement of entering adulthood.
She is an adult now and reality leaves little time for dreams.
She looks at the clock; it's time to get ready for work.
She passes the mirror as she enters the shower.

Michelle Colford

For Kathy

You are the juggler of my timid heart:
Tossed high, then passed, I nearly thought it'd stop;
A simple core that'd never been apart
From me—in your hands never once did drop.
You are the smuggler of my meeker soul:
Now spirited from behind this weak wall
Of flesh to seek release in union whole
With yours—in whose wings climbs but does not fall.
You are the keeper of my better self:
Who does exist outside the bound'ries fixed
By chance, but who this fool did find with help
Of Fate—delivered into you and mixed.
This truth like heart and soul I must confide:
You live in me as I in you, reside.

F. E. Balzac Jr.

Time In Writing

A clock of time moves within rhyme,
as hands express the words just right.
It runs away and while in flight,
a term inscribed, one second's mine.

The minutes come, there is a line,
as hours change, each passage fights.
A clock of time moves within rhyme,
as hands express the words just right.

As the hours wind, thoughts come to mind.
One day is gone, but it's not quite
a story that you'd want to write.
Then change a line, and you will find,
a clock of time moves within rhyme.

Catherine Dunbar

The Weeping Willow Tree

Falling in elegant, dropping waves,
Its branches reach to dust the earth.
An aura of peace stands still around it,
Secure in its knowledge of long-lasting life.
Under its branches time stands still.
No beeping horns, no rushing 'round.
A young mind takes flight in its shadowy embrace.
Mystical creatures dance, with the willow's vibrant life.

Megan Kiraly

Snow

Snow, falling all around me
A whirlwind of white flies by
As I dance among these tiny ice crystals.
I fall backward, onto the snowy ground
In a puff of whiteness
Spreading my arms like the wings of an angel.
As I lie on the ground I am blanketed
by the falling snow.
And as I rise the cold envelops me
I turn to see what I have created
An angel of snow, a pure, white and
beautiful angel.

Gabrielle Weiss

Sit Quietly, My Little One

Sit quietly, my little one
and wait patiently for Daddy to come home.
He'll be home soon, for he only went
to the corner store for a loaf of bread.

Sit quietly, my little one
and wait patiently for news about Daddy.
After the robber shot him by mistake
your Daddy's in critical condition at St. Joe's.

Sit quietly, my little one
and weep openly, for this innocent
man who died was your Father...
for this beautiful man whom we love
is no longer.

Shelly Fox

Good Morning Long Island

GOOD MORNING LONG ISLAND
You're a great place to start a new day
The good Lord created Long Island
to make us rejoice and thank God we're alive.

Long Island has the best boating-golfing-fishin'-swimmin'
Many handsome guys with pretty women
And great lovers too.
We have cheery folks with DON'T-GIVE-UP-SPIRIT
Birdees singing can't you hear it
As they greet the new day along with you

GOOD MORNING LONG ISLAND
You're a jazzy place to work or to play
We have joyous music and dancin'
And good clean fun for everyone
GOOD MORNING LONG ISLAND
We're gonna make it a wonderful day
GOOD MORNING LONG ISLAND

Richard Anthony Stryker

Music

The old man pauses by the ole jazz house at ten.
He listen to the melody before hurrying on again.
Inside faded blue curtains hang from limp rods,
while the bass and saxophone sing.
The slow sweetness gently pervades the ears of many a listener,
recalling bittersweet thoughts to their tired minds.

The old man pauses by the orchestra at five,
and listens to the magic going on inside.
Great arched ceilings bloom from marble walls,
as the drums sound and violins hum.
The high cheerfulness falls on aristocratic ears,
bringing back the joy of passed years.

The old man passes by the rock concert at nine,
and hears a song of a different kind.
The sound of youth, loud and strong,
in the notes of that upbeat song.
He smiles and says to himself,
"To truly understand the joy of the human spirit,
all one must do is hear a few notes of music!"

Kristin Curi

The Toy Soldier

Wraiths of sable smoke arose from crimson's dying ember
    Like throngs of demon horde that revel in wan pyres.
    Acier cannons silent—amidst the blazing fires.
The victor was a lad with tousled lock of amber

Who gathered up rifles, gallant calvary, and tanks
    And tucked us all away in ornamented crate.
The child traipsed to bed for he knew the hour late
And I sought surcease 'mongst the weary ranks.

As oaken little soldier, always full of zeal,
    I marched in joyous triumph as loyal troop fought on
Until the day when hope was lost—alas, my boy was gone.
O time, ye vile fiend, auric joy you've sought to steal!

My boy remembered not his trifling time-worn soldier
    And I remained alone, silently forsaken
    By dearest, truest friend whom time at last had taken.
In world apart, alone I steadily grew colder.

Days and years flew past as my spirit slowly dwindled,
    Hoping all the while I'd see my boy's return.
Ends anew, wheels unbroken, and my hope's reborn,
For here within my old friend's son....Imaginings rekindled!

Stephen Perret

A Day Of Nothing

The darkness cools the night
and in the street light the snow reflects
and the tires peel the slush to the side.

The snow leaves a great place to hide
until I'm ready to join the crowd
and chase the night down
and watch the shadows cower
waiting for the light

So I'll stay here and think of my father while I sit
and watch the spit freeze on Jack Frost's mouth.
And think of today which I could of lived
with out

Adam Grabowski

This Old House

I didn't expect a palace, just a nice place to dwell,
But right after moving in, it became 'the house from hell.'

'Dollhouse' was built for Barbie, too tiny for a human.
Rooms were all much too small. It's no wonder I was fumin'.

The 'any wife's dream kitchen' was a horrendous nightmare.
Leaky faucets and plugged up drains spewed water everywhere.

When in need of a nice hot bath I'd wait an hour it seemed.
The water pressure was so low that only I was steamed.

All carpeting was so soiled that it could not be used.
Rip it up, sand and varnish the floors I foolishly mused.

The first few boards were fine. I rejoiced, "that wasn't too bad."
The next few had clearly been used to make the termite's pad.

"Close to entertainment area" unlike my happy thoughts
Meant county jail on one side, the other weed-grown lots.

With all expenses for repairs and reconstruction too,
I suffered much but learned a lot. Here's my advice to you.

If in the future you should wish to buy a home that's right.
Check it out in the light of day. Don't make that choice at night.

And when the handsome realtor invites you out to dine.
Resist his invitation for that second glass of wine.

Opal Hickman

As Time Goes By

As time goes by I wait for you
I think of the things we used to do
As time goes by I'll shed my tears
I pray at night for you to reappear
As time goes by and we grow old
I sit by myself, alone in the cold
As time goes by my love goes on
I dream of our love going through and beyond
As time goes by I see tomorrow
I lay in bed reminiscing in my sorrow
As time goes by I'll still love you
I'll be waiting, waiting and loving you
As time goes by

Lisa M. Carnevale

Remembering You

Thinking back on yesterday, I reminisce of when first we met
It was one of life's most happiest times I will never forget
You came into my life at a time I was feeling so down and low
Everything around me was crumbling, I had no place to go
Even though we was strangers, you could have walked away
But instead, you opened up your heart and welcomed me to stay
At first we were so afraid that things would not work out
But the first time I held you in my arms, I knew without a doubt
I knew that you had been hurt before, and I was hurting too
The feelings I felt when you were near, I knew my love for you was true
You are the one I longed to hold in my arms, and not in my dreams
Because destiny had brought us together, in times crazy as they seemed
Together we laughed, we cried, and together we had our cheers
The special bond shared between us helped conquer all of our fears
I recall the times I held you close, promising we'll never part
We became friends before lovers, and captured each other's heart
Then came that dreadful day I realized you had really gone
Now I have to face each day, broken hearted and so all alone
Because I love you more than life itself, I will have it no other way
But tell me where did we go wrong, or was I a fool to let you get
   away

   Charles F. Davis Sr.

I Am Lost

They are the lonely ones,
destined to walk the stormy nights,
tormented by their tortured souls,
committed to unholy plights,
Love is gone now all is lost.
I'll take my fate, forget the cost.
No chance at all, for they are blind.
Stares are harsh and words unkind.
Time has stopped at the midnight hour.
Silence so strong with darkness's power.
Night so black it caresses my fears,
with winds soft screams all that I hear.
My tears of blood have sealed my fate,
engulfed by the ever consuming hate.
I am so weak, my will is gone.
I can't resist, they are too strong.
Oh, there is nothing to calm my soul.
They've clawed apart all that was whole.
I start to cry, but that is all.
For now it's time to take my fall.

   Elizabeth Reuter

Christmastime

Christmas is a time for sharing—
Memories from the past and hopes and dreams
   for the future.
It is a time when our hearts and minds are
   filled with happiness and good-will.
It is a time of anticipation - of greeting old
   friends, family, and making new acquaintances.
It is a time of heavenly joy and a time
   of earthly sorrow - -
Joy to the world, for unto us a child is born.
sorrow for those dearly departed who will
   not share this Christmas on earth.
It is a time unlike any other time of the year.
Waiting eagerly for snow and attending church
   and singing on Christmas eve.
Dressing warmly against the bitter cold,
Hot chocolate, cookies, eggnog and home-baked goodies.
It is a time of remembering, love, joy,
   peace, and above all, it is the
   celebration of the Birth of a KING.

   Henrietta M. Peters

The Love In His Eyes

Through the eyes of the Morning Dove
   God is seen
In the Grey Tabby's eyes
   He lingers
From a Dog's eager shake
   He holds our hand
In a Butterfly's vibrant color
   He soars among us

Through the eyes of the Morning Dove
   He consoles us before Easter's song
   Green cat eyes know His sparkle
   Through troubled waters
      Run aghast
         as if the forest could see...

   Leslie Kaufman

Daddy's Little Girl

Daddy's little girl has finally grown up.
He's watched her ride a tricycle
And now he watches her drive away...
He's been there with bandaids when
She skinned her knee.
Now he's there with a handkerchief as he watches her leave.
No more braided pigtails, no more swingsets.
Now he sees a grown woman standing before him.
She's ready to move out and live on her own.
He hopes his daughter is successful,
But he'll still be there open arms
When she needs advice.
Daddy's little girl has finally grown up.
And as he watches her leave,
A tear trickles down his face...
A tear of happiness for the one
He brought into the world,
And a tear of sadness
As he watches her drive off
Into the sunset of a new world.

   Kimberly Hulett

Golden Conspiracy

Golden bars and a golden light shining through my windows and my life.
Golden eyes with blackened skin the statutory demon is pacing within.
And I don't want to be held responsible for the damage of the
producethat people sell to get ahead.
And in my sorrowful stained glass eyes,
there will be no more room for lies,
and there will be no more room for the ridicule.
Searing down golden clouds and the golden frowns
will we live to see the legacy of tomorrow?
I want to soar in gracious flight, but I'll have to dig up some will
to help me through those lonely nights.
And it's sad to say that blackness is my motto.
So raise me up just like a King;
raise me up so I may sing a wonderful
song that seals the gallows.
And as I peel those flowers from my face,
I know I'm being stalked with grace.
So get me out.
Let me out of this morbid place.
Before my golden bars just melt away
And before my thoughts of leaving fall astray.
Can't you let me in on the conspiracy?

   Allyn R. Tebeau Jr.

"A Love For Eternity"

I hear people say, "Nothing lasts forever,"
but I just can't believe it's true,
because no matter what those people say,
I see forever when I look at you.
I believe that you and I were always meant to be,
To go through life hand in hand,
and see all the things in the world to see.
We'll grow old together, still hand in hand,
and reminisce about our past.
Through all the years we'll do so much,
but time will still go way too fast.
So when our time on Earth is through,
we'll meet again at heaven's door,
and love each other like we did,
only then it will be forever more.

Angie Meyers

Memorial Day

The Sunday paper lay on the table there
I picked it up and found the nearest chair.
Young bright faces caught my eye
Soldiers from a day gone by.
One stood out from all the rest
He held a gun across his chest.
A determined look upon his young face
That he would free that taken place.
Did he die on that bloody shore?
Or did he hold his wife once more?
Did he make it past the enemy line?
Did he read his daughter a nursery rhyme?
In a darkened bunker did he meet his match?
Or go on to teach his son to catch?
Did it ever run through his mind, all that he had left behind?
The cost for freedom was very high,
That's why so many had to die.
As I sit this cozy place, I have no fear, not a trace.
I wish I could go back and thank those guys,
For the sacrifice they made, their very lives!

Karis Murphy

You

After awhile you learn your body's limit
   you know when to push yourself
     and when to slow down

After awhile you learn to interpret your feelings
   you know what makes you feel good and what causes pain

After awhile you learn how to benefit from your life
   you know when to cram the most into every second
     and you know when to sit back and enjoy the present

After awhile you learn to trust yourself
   you know you'll make mistakes
     but you learn to forgive yourself
       because you are you and nobody else
         people will come in and out of your life
           but you are what will stay constant

So get to know yourself
   life is a trial of education to understand you
     for you were created under someone else's will
       but you have the power to sculpt
         and to make the most out of what was given to you
JUST DO IT

Christina Kathryn Smith

What's It All For?

On such a bright and sunny day; what's it all for...
A child walks home without a care in the world; what's it all for...
A semi-truck is making a run to a stop; what's it all for...
A child starts to cross the street to meet his friend; what's it all for...
The driver swerves to miss the child; what's it all for...
But, this day it happens too late; what's it all for...
Without a cry, without a second chance to make a difference; what's it all for...
A small life is ended too soon; what's it all for..
The ambulance is called for help; what's it all for...
The Paramedic arrives only to find out it is too late; what's it all for...
There's nothing he can do; what's it all for...
Years of training and there's nothing he can do; what's it all for...
Only God knows why it had to happen this way; what's it all for...
The Paramedic stops and wonders...
What's it all for?

Randy D. Blocker Jr.

Alone At Night

I sit by the window at night,
Staring into the moonlight.
By myself with nothing to do.
No friends to see or even to talk to.

I wish I could go to another school.
One, where they have some better rules.
Where I can start all fresh and new
And make new friends, ones who care about you.

That's what I need, a new house and town,
So I can ride my bike up street and down.
Say "hi" to my neighbors, the ones I know.
And feel good about myself, no matter where I go.

Sheri Bedard

Chris

Thinking "love" I reach for you
You're slipping from my grasp
I cannot hang on any longer
I'll take you with me
If you start trying
To separate us in this thing
Our cosmic love
Please stop fighting
You cannot leave, you cannot win
If I go down, I'll take you with me
Trust me dear,
It's for the best
Please choose fast
I have no time for the frivolous things
That rule your mind
My obsessions run deep when I am near you
And so you see,
Either way,
We'll be together
Forever...

Carrie Ann Alford

Slumber

Slowly drifting into the night's
Unmerciful grasp slowly, slowly
falling into its trap as we
Drift away to far away
places that our minds have yet to explore...

April Bechtold

"Hallways Of Life"

As I walk through the hallways of
life, I find you standing beside each
doorway encouraging me to step through them.

Even though you know not what's on
the other side, you still encourage me
whether it be the right or wrong door to
go through. You just know if I don't try
and go through each and every one, I will
be possibly missing out on maybe something
very special in life.

I know you're there to encourage me.
But I feel you are there to help and love
me through everything I find, whether it be
good or bad.

So I know I will find you behind each
and every door you stand beside.

In the hallways of life.

Ricky Paul Zurfluh

Winter

The ducks are gone from the water, few birds are in the air.
The grass has turned brown, and the trees are bare.
The wind is blowing from the South and the North.
The clouds are filled with snow to bring forth.

Isn't it beautiful! Oh, what a sight!
Mountains of snow came down through the night.
It makes the world a cleaner place.
It puts a glow on everyone's face.

The air is crisp and clean, invigorating.
It's nice to have a big fire waiting.
With the aroma of wood burning in the grate,
One can sit and dream and contemplate.

This is the season of gladness and a time for reflections.
Time to think of others, and of our own imperfections.
When the time of rest is over, there is much for us to do
To bring love and peace and harmony to the world, to me and you.

Naomi Knirk

A Nurse

The clock is moving slow for you
    You're hoping soon for seven
Yet it is moving fast for him for he is nearing heaven.

You face will be the last he sees
    Your hand - his final touch
The comfort that you offer him will mean so very much.

At last he draws his final breath
    And closes both his eyes
He has not time for 'thank you's' or even last good-byes.

But to his God in heaven
    As he meet his Maker there
He tells Him so profoundly of your compassion and your care.

At last, the clock has reached its seven
    Your time to go is here
But the serenity upon his face is thanks to you, my dear.

Now your stressful day is over
    Put your troubled heart to rest
You can rally in the notion that you gave your very best.

Patricia L. Turner

Bridal Thoughts

She balances, all dressed in white
On the cusp of a fragile new something.
Unnerved.
Her shoulders feel so heavy!
Her life hangs - suspended in time -
Waiting, aching to change.
In an instant
They are one.
She slips from her balance and gently lands
Beside another pair of shoulders.

Stacy Souza

The Spring

Out of the rocks it comes tumbling down
    Wearing white foam for its delicate crown,
Leaping and jumping and hurrying along
    Bumping the rocks to sing its song

Sliding and gliding around the curve
    Through the willows and out again,
Slowing now to rock little frogs
    In their lilly pad nests

Gathering speed, it gallops along
    To play with the water fall's song.
Rolling down the face of the falls
    It kisses the willows with its spray

Now hurries on to join waters rushing
    To join waters going to the sea.
Oh what a lovely, wonderful,
    Beautiful day.

Mildred S. Sager

The Grandchildren

Their visit over, their mother
straps them into car seats, and turns to look at me.
She smiles.
You'll have peace and quiet again, she says.
Like pale, shy birds, small hands flutter their goodbyes.

The echoes of their chatter, giggles, wails, fade.
The walls absorb the whir of tiny motors,
the baby-doll's thin cry, the clatter of falling blocks.
I fold the highchair, put away the play things,
return the fragile figurines to their appointed places.

Peace and quiet.
The house and I sit waiting in the silence,
waiting for the grandchildren,
until their noisy return will once more fill
our empty shells with the clutter of life.

Frances Sonnabend

Untitled

Hopes and dreams
are in the air
running, hiding everywhere
wishing, there will be no more
will take them through a greater door
the ones who escape and become free
will see the light that everyone wants to see
but those who stay and stick around
will be forever in darkness without a sound

Angie Nelson

Wolves

The night winds blow and the ground
grows cold as the moon sails in the sky
A grey wolf howls and his mate she
grows as the ringing echo dies.
Tall pine trees sway, the wolf still
bays until he hears an answer nigh
The night comes alive with echoing
cries as the moon sailed in the sky.
Nearer and nearer the howling comes,
Then the pack takes off on a run
to plunder a herd near by.
To rip and tear with long fangs
bared, and eat until they no
longer dared while the moon sailed
in the sky
Then back to the hills from whence
they came as the moon began to wane,
leaving the herd all mangled and lame.
The winds still blowed, the ground stayed
cold as the moon sailed in the sky.

Mary Morris

Sharing

Loving is fun, it can be grand,
When you do it hand-in-hand.
Share each day, one by one,
Joys and sorrows as they come.
Think about what today can bring,
Do not contemplate tomorrow's thing.
Don't demand, expect, or anticipate
Anything that can not wait.
Tomorrow may not hold the same,
For life is just a gambling game.
Be thankful for what is now
Don't ask the questions why or how.

Share with each other what God is giving,
Be happy, enjoy, and share in living.

Paula F. Panart

To My Grandchild

A joy to hold, a child to hug,
This new born babe is cuddled by the mother
As the father hovers near.
A tiny little life that they must now protect,
As the infant grows and grows,
Always reaching for their help.
The safely given to that tiny child of their
Is full of love and comfort
In the life that they all share.
But when that Baby gets so big,
Its clinging days are over
And "Independence" is the game.
For now the time has come they must let go
But then that child so big and tall
Comes back for just a time to have a tear wiped dry
or to express some Joy or Sorrow,
Wanting to be gently held by mother,
Then hugged by father who is hovering near!

Lon E. Gable

A Troubled Society

Red, yellow, black, white, ignorance, fear, wars to fight.
Boy, girl, education is dead, no condoms for sex, diseases to spread.
Robbery, murder, guns for crime, too much death, running out of time.
So much prejudice and discrimination,
families are poor, government inflation.
People will die, false accusation,
the gun is raised, brutal assassination.
Sexual harassment, she's crushed from rape,
police brutality, corrupt minds to shape.
Lies and back stab, trust is broken, fists are raised, words are
    spoken.
Disputes, arguments, he, or she, used to be a friend now an enemy.
Drugs, alcohol, gangs, and violence, unnecessary hatred, society is
    tense.
Black and white, separation of races,
pollution of minds, insane mental cases.
Politics and bribery for all that it's worth,
improper pregnancy, deformity at birth.
Mute, crippled, deaf, or blind,
fate of the future yours or mine.
Deadly volcano ready for eruption,
hurricane, earthquake, massive destruction.

Richard J. Shepherd

"In Love"

What does it mean to be "In Love"
It's like you caught all the stars above.

Gathered them together one by one
And broke them open, just for fun

All the glitter and all the gold,
Is now yours to have and to hold.

For being "In Love" I'm told it's true,
Days go by and your never blue.

Do you know that I'm "In Love"?
I went and caught all the stars above.

I'll give them to you,
Cause right from the start.

I looked at you,
And you captured my heart.

Elaine Rudibaugh

Choice

Stand we now before our own judgment
Lest we not forsake the joy within
Our Higher Self that leadeth us
To Divine Poetic Bliss

Bear not the rancid fruit of unbridled passion
Nor rank primeval pleasure
For thou shalt carry thyself to bittersweet deception;
Thine own demise

'Tis the fool that declares:
"I have no choice"
For in this very decree
He hath chosen his destiny

And if procrastination be thy crutch
There too is choice rendered
For thou hath chosen not to choose
And to that very end, O friend! lies choice

To choose, or not to choose-
That is the choice........................!

Robert Hernandez II

Lady On The Bus In West Baltimore

The older woman walks onto the bus,
pays her change, and sits down
She reminds me of where I've been, what I am, and who I'll be
The burnt toffee complexion of her face is deeply creased,
especially around the eyes
Her hands look coarse and rough, She is tired.
I can see within her that She has probably raised many children
Those eyes have seen the Baltimore
before the Baltimore that I know
She has endured those hardships I've only read about.
It hurts me that I can relate to this woman with nappy gray hair
and dusty clothes, but She is my ancestry
My real-life, practical ancestry
it is SHE
not Queen Nefertiti
I would like to conjure up thoughts in my mind
about kingdoms and richness and beautiful heritage and culture
Countee Cullen's refined black women and regal black men
But it is the old woman on the 51 that is my history
the root I can relate to

Alicia Jones

The Gate

The entry gate now stands ajar,
Its weathered posts a bit askew.
Slight movements from the breezes are
Reminders of those who once passed through.

Hinges, now rusty, were gleaming bright
The day it was opened wide
And the builder with great delight
Carried in his bonny bride.

It seemed the children soon were grown,
Old age crept upon the pair.
Their death then left the house alone;
Upon decay, no one entered there.

'Tis sad the gate can never tell
Of what's happened in the past.
No need for silent sentinel—
All else is gone; it is the last.

I stop to muse beside the gate
That death, too, is such a portal.
Time goes on—it will never wait,
But we pass through to life immortal.

Allegra Zick

Horsemen

I've internalized waking at this time,
as if the alarm was simply a precaution.

A reminder of the past
when 4:30 found me still half-sated
from last night.

The dark of early day,
"Top of the morning", they say.

Maybe I'm genetically tied
to the time of 4:30
when only we are awake.

Kathleen M. Driscoll

The American Way

We decided to go potluck today,
    It is the good old American way.
It's done by the Swensons, the Burkowski's, the O'Learys and all the rest.
    But I still think ve-vell do it best.
Mother puts just the right seasoning in baking the beans,
    Sister Kate selects only the crispest of the greens.
They worry about this, they fret about that,
    The first cake they baked usually gets fed to the cat.
We have the biggest table of food I ever did see.
    I don't know why we always have to wait for Aunt Bea
When we eat, it always seems that the plates are too small,
    and how I hate it when the pickle juice runs through it all.
Everyone knew I had some of Aunt Ruby's famous Blueberry dessert,
    Cause I had it all down the front of my new red and white shirt.
But I knew I had nothing to fear.
    We'll do it all over again next year.

Roy Schroeder

The Faultless Ones

Whispers that dare come out
Often I wonder what it's all about.
A voice that brings me pain
A strong but destine one I can't explain.
The children: so sanitary and sweet, come to play
But the corrupt came to beat.
How to help the ones in need
What to do about the budding seed?
Please listen to them as the scream
Don't be blind, let them dream!
So many innocent dying away
By their hearts being shot by day.
When will there lives be stood still
And when can they rest without a chill?
Who really cared and listened
Now that they're gone, no more little ones that glisten.
The little ones came to play
In return abandoned and on to another day.

Sabrina Arneberg

Glimpse

The glimpse of an eye foretells of want,
the desire to see, a desire to be.
Where once rote fascinations,
emerge anticipations.
Comes a time, unknown knowable,
to be a plan, forces impending,
choices determined, desire imbued,
honor usurped, construction renewed.
Where for art thou sweet bliss,
on road, forge ahead, and miss.
That which endows, again embowels,
where coincidence, now magnificence.
The purpose, confinement of option,
designation of few,
tower occupant, another document.
Again, the eye whose unaware,
unabashed now, a chance to stare.

J. David Smith

What Is Heaven?

No one knows what Heaven looks like
but this is what it looks like to me,
Heaven is a place where people are free from
crime and hate. One day I will go there but
when I'm still a live I will try to be kind and
nice I won't care when I go there because
I know I will loved.

Heidi Mason

My Grandmother

My grandmother means a lot to me,
But I hate having to see her suffer
And not be free.
She's part of me down in my heart,
For since we've been together for so long,
We will never part.
She was so strong and out-going too
Now she is weak and can't do what
She used to do.
I will always love and remember her love for me,
When she's away and finally free.

Joy L. Faulk-Lyons

Kailua Beach, Oahu

Daily I run, barefoot, upon the sand on the beach of Kailua,
Where the waves, wind-driven, break at the crescent shore,
With a throb that echoes the heartbeat of ocean deeps;
Tumbling the heavy green coconuts, end over end;
Sliding salt water sheets far up the beach,
Across the holes of the little ghost crabs,
Sprinting fast as thought ahead of the waves.

Though my flying feet imprint
For miles the cool-damp sand,
Behind me the slate wiped clean.

I race, waves erase;
I run, waves overrun.

Have I really run this beach?
Only the sand knows,
And the restless sea.

Glenn Hackney

This Leaf

This leaf is still green,
it hasn't turned colors yet.
Does it feel lonely and afraid?
Or unique and happy.

This leaf must have a lot of friends,
at least fifty I would think.
Was this leaf sad when it had to leave?
Maybe it had a few friends to join it,
on the long way down to the ground.

Sometimes I wish I could be a leaf,
to be free, and to be able to fly in the wind.
But, would the journey down be as fun as I think,
or be sad to leave the home I've known all my life?

Michele Cyr

"Breaking The Barrier"

I feel as if I'm trapped in a box
Cornering me on all sides
All around me chains and locks
Keeping me like a prisoner strapped and tied.

But just when it seems there is no hope
To leave this burden behind
You find a great force that can help you cope
And soon the joys of life will come to mind.

This power will not make you beautiful
Nor will it fix cuts and bruises
But soon, together your heart will pull
And against your faith the pain looses.

It seems the power can set you free
And break this wall so immense
But to this puzzle there is only one key
And that key is self-confidence.

Kristie Soares

At Night

Here I am in the night
Alone in solitude. . . no friends
The world has died
A barren wasteland of darkness
All that exists is one soul. . . one life
One knowledge. . . one perspective
Lone sentinels arc over streets
Shedding fraudulent beams of sunlight
Ghost cars lie abandoned on the curb
Resting in swamp-gray light
And I, just one life. . . just one voice
Just thoughts of mine in the night
You might feel the same at night
Alone, forgotten
No one is alive to care
Only shadows that whisper quietly
Amongst themselves
Silent witnesses of the living darkness

Mark Otuteye

Dulce

A ray of sunshine on a cold winter's morn
Sunrise and sunset at her command
Her hair - an abundance of flames
Like a moth, I cannot resist
Her vibrance pulls me; I am captivated by her every motion
Do not smile at me! For it will be my undoing
I will lose what little composure I have
Her scent haunts me, I can think of naught else when she is near
Ivory, freshly cut roses
Just the thought of her makes my pulse race
Would that I may touch you, feel the satin of your skin,
Your heartbeat next to mine
I am tormented every minute of everyday with visions of you
For I love you, and I cannot rest until you know the depth
   of this love

Tianja N. Davenport

Lost Youth

What time has given, and we thought begot
Is not ours, for we have not
It slips away on silent wings
And leaves us without most of things
We wonder, oh where did these wrinkles come from
Why can't I see, what on earth's wrong with my knee
Don't depend on the fantasy of youth
For in it there's not one word of truth
What we thought was given,
Is taken away
And then you wake up old one day

Carol Hammontree

Mommy Is Gone

It's been three months since I've been born
Me and Mommy, apart we're torn
Mommy's gone and I'm alone
I lay here in an orphan home
In my heart is a terrible burn
Will sweet Mommy ever return
I've thought about her three months straight
Could this have been Mommy's fate
I wonder what could have been
I'm sure she had her reason
I feel so empty
Can't she see
How could Mommy abandon me

Christina Guillen

To Each Of Us

Troubles come to each of us,
  uninvited and unwelcome, alarming and draining.

Troubles come to each of us,
  sometimes in twos and threes, ranging from small to large.

Troubles come to each of us,
  seemingly unbearable, seemingly unending.

Because troubles come to each of us,
  families share them, families love us.

Because troubles come to each of us,
  friends help us, strangers support us.

Each of us bears our troubles, our troubles end,
  end means vanished pain,
    vanished pain means strength to go on,
      vanished pain means understanding,
      understanding,

Troubles are a part of living
  but so are love, joy, and happiness that come
  to each of us.

  Virginia M. Kerr

"Little Brother"

You are my little brother this
You will always be some things
never change, and this I am glad to see.

You are so very interesting
with all your qualities art
and fashion are your passion
and this is neat to me.

Not everyone knows where
you are coming from, but
this I really do so do
not get discouraged as
I am here for you.

Life is very tuff so get
ready for this game it
maybe a while before
you get your fame
I am a true believer of
Your work you see so
hang in there little brother!
You will complete this fantasy!

  Noreen Marchese

Untitled

The sounds that the earth makes as she wraps herself in her infinite
  Blanket.
The movements which the dreamer produces as she rushes from
  her solace
To creep across the surface of her domain.
She walks the nights and she lifts the waves high into the air.
She troubles those with no spirit and empties the broken hearted.
She reaches into the depths of the earth and pulls all of the life out
  of her.
She ceases to think and whispers in the ears of those who will listen
She creates herself and destroys all that can not, will not exist
  with her.
She is the essences of all that lives; for with out her
  the earth sits as a still picture.
She becomes the breeze that plays across the hearts strings
Yet, she is the torment or those who ache inside.
She is there always in the waiting, she is the wind.

  Julie Gregg

Time

The old woman rocks steadily
in her rickety chair on the front porch.
Life has treated her well,
but has left her lonely and desolate
these past few years.
She watches the children play ball happily in the street.
Her expression is unchanged, though.
There is only one person in the world who could
bring brightness to her bitter and empty expressions.
She has left this person's heart for reasons unknown.
A ball rolls in her direction.
As she stands and fumbles for the railing,
There is a crash.
The woman's body lies lifeless
at the bottom of the front steps.
A car pulls up.
A long - awaited visitor steps out
and learns his visit is moments too late.

  Lisa Cappano

Life Is Like A Rose

Life is like a rose.
The bud standing as a new beginning
The act of getting up again and again.
After the many times we fail in life.

The unfolding, crimson petals.
Standing as those happy times
Those times that we will always cherish and remember.
And the future that we are about to unfold.

The thorns standing as pain,
The words that pierce our hearts.
These thorns stand as our enemies,
Those that try to tear us apart.

A rose won't last forever.
Life won't last forever.

Just as a rose begins to fade,
So do our days grow dim; as a
Rose begins to die, so do we become weaker.

A rose is a rose
A rose is beautiful.

life itself, is beautiful.

  Sarah Danforth

Brotherly Love

Just thinking of you, this very day;
Wondering perhaps, if you would say:
'Neath all the stars that shine above,
There's nothing greater than Brotherly Love.

We all have differences, needless to say,
And make mistakes 'most every day.
No one is perfect, to stand so tall,
On the highest pedestal, only to fall.

So friend, let bygones be in the past,
And give thy Brotherly Love to last.
Do this today, and please don't wait;
One day at a time, may be a day late!

  Nelson D. Bartlett

Am I My Mother's Child?

I see the reflection of myself in your eyes
but I cannot comprehend.
For the reflection I see
is of turmoil from deep within.

The noise, the noise is so loud;
Yet, it's so quiet it shouldn't matter.
My melancholy moods are with me more each day,
running on a constant pattern.

They say there's nothing wrong with me;
Just plain ol' mean.
But, my mind constantly converses with itself;
Playing over and over, like a picture scene.

You say I worry too much,
but I got s**t to worry about.
I spend my day chasing myself,
Never catching me; my mind is always enroute.

I see the reflection of myself in your eyes,
but I cannot comprehend.
Am I my mothers' child?
All sanity close to the end.

Sharon Ross

The Lily

Where is the lily I long to see?
In my backyard waiting for me.
Under the snow it is praying for spring.
There it is doing a wonderful thing!

The snow now has left us, the growth has begun
It's lifting its head up, right under the sun!
The lily is growing, its height two feet tall.
The petals now forming are white but still small!

I'm getting excited but it's still got a while.
That flower is bringing to my face a big smile!
I am writing a book called, The Growth for Today.
My book takes place from April to May.

That flower's all grown now;
I picked it in June.
It's white with pink spots...
And it sits in my room!

R. Quinn Copeland

Untitled

It's a balmy night .... with thoughts abound
Like echoes in a valley... yet
there is no sound.
Hopes and dreams.. somehow
have taken flight.
An ache inside.. I feel this night.
The darkness outside, from the window I see...
Has somehow blended with that
... which is a port of me.
The sky... no longer seems so blue
I yearn for some of the joy... that
I once knew.

Ellie Stidham

Vagabond

What time have I for wandering thoughts
Thinking of the have and have nots
Sleeping in the park in dry spots
Aimless through the streets but not lost
It might not be enough
but it seems like a lot.

Aaron M. Sargent

Why....

God works in mysterious ways...
I know that now, looking at your grave.
I stand here all alone, and nowhere to go.
I regret your time on earth is done...
and all the fun times we won't have under the sun.
They say the good always die young...
that we here on earth must stay strong.
But I can't help but to cry...
and ask why?!
I honestly believe, God works in strange ways...
I guess that's why I'm here-on this sad and lonely day.
I know some day we will be together...
the next time forever.
But until then I live my life on earth...
And do my best, for all its worth.
And here on earth I will wait...
Until the time comes for me to meet you at
the golden gate... Called Heaven.

Leslie Hart

My Rock

My rock stands strong and proud against wind and wave,
yet is torn to bits by breeze and ripple.
The empty rock becomes a cave,
Turned in upon itself; ever a cripple.

In the world's eyes my rock is strong,
Within my heart I know they're wrong.
My rock, whom I know all about,
Your worry, strife, pain, and doubt.

Though many come for shelter and protection,
She receives no reward, only rejection.
No one, but me appreciates the rock, until she's gone,
And they are left to fight their storm's alone.

Then, oh then they will dare to grieve,
But I alone will know you did not leave.
For I am the sand at your feet.
Bit by bit we shall meet,
We shall be as one,
For sand is no less than worn out rock,
In spirit we have always been one,
For sand is no less than weathered rock.

Michael Wayne Nichols

To A New Neighbor

We do not ask you where you lived before,
Your pedigree, nor how you earn your bread.
We're not concerned if you have less or more
You're here to live, that's all that really need be said.

You're human kind, that's all that matters here,
You've all the freedoms that our land affords.
To live, to learn, without concern or fear,
To strive and work, and earn your just rewards.

We're not concerned with where you go to church;
What lodge you've joined, to what clubs you belong
That's your affair, we have no wish to search.
Nor lecture you about what's right or wrong.

You have the right to think and vote and choose,
The way you think is no concern of ours.
We've no desire to try to change your views.
Nor question how you spend your leisure hours.

Good luck, new neighbor, here's to your success!
We wish you well, that friendships you may win,
This is you home, may God your family bless
It matters not the color of your skin.

Ken Taylor

Untitled

In all the lands, this never before told
Of a woman, much more precious than gold

With beautiful eyes, her skin was quite fair
Midnight black was the color of her hair

Smooth as silk, soft as cotton, was her face
Like swans, she moved with elegance and grace

She had a certain sparkle in her eyes
She needed no make-up or other disguise

With a soft tone in her voice, she would speak
It made even the strongest men grow weak

A woman like this is sure hard to find
For she is unique and one of a kind

You may say there is no woman like that
So I thought also, until I met pat.

Winward Hines

"Come Unto Me"

Are you tired of living your life in sin?
"COME UNTO ME" and I all be your friend.
I am a friend that is faithful and true.
Accept me into your heart and I will change you.
I know you had some friends that let you down in the past.
"COME UNTO ME" and experience a friendship that will forever last.
I'll be closer to you than any relative, friend, or your mother.
Believe in me and I'll show you a love that surpasses all others.
Remember when society labeled you and you got into trouble too?
You were at the end of your road and you gave up on hope.
I stepped in to save you my friend from the midst of Satan's grips.
You thought you were lucky but actually you were blessed.
I gave you hope and a new life, you gave me love and trust.
I cried when I you replied, "Thank you Jesus!"
It pleased me so, the day you told all of your old friends to go.
Later that night, you prayed for the first time to me, Jesus Christ.
Then you said, "Lord, I'm tired of living my life in sin."
Without any doubts, I can enter your heart and work all things out.
Now, all who lives in sin can "COME UNTO ME," I'll set you free!

Dennis Waters

My Baby Girl

At age two she set out to discover what "hot" could do.
So she picked up my curling irons by the wrong end.
After that she refused to touch anything hot again.

At age three, she said to me, "Do the stars in the sky get
wet when it rains?" I simply smiled and she finally understood
after much was explained.

At age four, she set out to explore. She formed an interesting
theory that really got near me. Biologically speaking
she's correct which proves to me her mind is in effect. According
to her, all infants are born female and upon reaching
a certain age "some" turn into male. Now when you stop to
think about it, the timing is wrong, but hasn't it been all
along for the male to give off an X or Y chromosome?

At age five, she's learning to abide by all rules and regulations
set. She's getting closer and closer to being a young
lady with each condition met.

When she reaches six years of age, I'll be sure to turn the
page and record all the progress that she's made.

Janier Smith

Let The Flower Bloom

Love is like a flower to bloom
That needs to have special care.
As the sun shines bright it soon
Causes the flower to be and love to share.

Fix your heart to be aware
The hug you give is one to share.
Believe and trust the Lord to give
Love everyday you live.

As the flower blooms it gives its seed.
Plants like people need to be
Watered as from above indeed.
Our water comes from Jesus we can't see.

Jesus is the difference.
His special love is not just a significance;
But is the belief and fact is Jesus Christ
Is true love and God as his life he did sacrifice.

Jesus lived as man.
He is that solid rock.
Allow Jesus into your heart today
And let the flower bloom, I pray.

Ruby Arrington

Werewolf Night

Record.
My old tape recorder turns on and I put the menu down.
My eyes roll back into my head as the curious breezes of the
Werewolf Night play with my hair.
Pause....Record.
I push my tongue out into the damp air which tastes like the back
of the airmail stamp on my brother's postcard.
Belgium is benevolent this time of year.
Pause...Record.
Justin's room had floor boards like the ones in this cafe.
The dull wood under my chair mumbles to me,
"Embrace, embrace the night."
"WHAT ELSE DO YOU WANT?" the waitress interrupts. I respond.
"TABLE THREE WANTS A DOGGIE BAG!" she screams absurdly.
And I think she laughs at me. Pause . . . Record.
I claw my way through the city the moonlight my flashlight
Searching, seeking, solitude . . . at last.
And after paying the toll I throw the doggie bag
and the old tape recorder over the Bay Bridge as I embrace the night.

Patrice Quintero

Paradise

Cloudy souffle and purple mist,
Its desert shores are heaven - kissed.
The sun shines down upon the land.
The water rolls upon the sand.
The wildlife haunts the lush green trees.
Exotic scents flutter in the breeze.
The native songs float through the air.
It would take you some place,
But you're already there.
The barbecue is full of fun.
When darkness falls, the day's not done.
The natives guard the secret they keep.
They draw the curtain and let the world sleep.

Lauren Elizabeth Ready

Seeds Of Sorrow

These lines that trail our necks,
Beneath burrowed brows atop contoured faces,
Lines as bold as vanquishing rebels,
Are not the trails of peaceful passing years,
Nor the marks of wisdom's gentle pursuit.

These are the mad foot prints of sorrow,
  and... ..... of pain,

Marks of grief, of worries, and...
  ....of fear;
Of woeful abandon, and....
  .....of sadness deep,
Of wholesome despair and...
  ....of freedom starved.

We are as fertile lands ill-tilled,
Fields sown with solitary seeds of joy,
One hopeless grain flung far from the other few;
But broadcasted free with grains of grief,
Bushels of seeds of sorrow..... and...
  ....of death!

Ali Mansaray

An Ocean By Dark

The waves crash in, I cannot see
White explodes with splendorous glee
The rocks corrode with every blast
Water retreats back to the sea

I don't understand why they last
Because it's happened in the past
But still they stand with all their height
Formed together much like a cast

In my hand rests a beam of light
Dull compared to the moon's bright might
It shines upon the waves that arc
To expose the froth in the night

In my mind's eye, it made its mark
The rolling waves, the moon so stark
And should you ask, I will remark
That's why the ocean's best by dark

Kenneth Loechner

Deep Thoughts

My soul bleeds for inspiration
My life needs something new
My heart needs some admiration
My mind needs another view.

I'm in a world with much confusion
I never know where to turn
Happiness seems like such an allusion
While I'm sitting here waiting to learn.

As I sit in a dream world and wait
For knowledge to enter inside
It makes me wonder how long it will take
For a needful person to be recognized.

My soul is hurting so desperately
My life seems so dearly lost
My heart is filled with great conspiracy
My mind has paid the cost.

Angie Weekly

My Sculpted Dreams

Who was I yesterday?

After my first breath of life,
I became a daughter, twin sister, granddaughter, niece and cousin.
I was a delicate baby fighting for her life!

In my youth, I was a tomboy, student and baby-sitter.
I married and became a wife, lover and mom.
In my careers I taught elementary children, fought community fires and
provided care to sick children and adults as a certified
Emergency Medical Technician.

Who am I today?

My life challenges have strengthed my marriage, family, and faith,
My inner self keeps changing from day to day
like a kaleidoscope being turned in many directions
and never coming to a complete stop!

My heart, mind and soul reminds me of Joseph's coat of many colors.
I'm bright, beautiful and get a little crazy when I am cornered!

Who will I be tomorrow?

My life long dreams are in my own hands ready to be sculpted.
This sculptor dreams of becoming an author, a writer, and poet,
professional clown and Candlelighter.

Roselyn Sherman

Unknown Soldier

They say be bold,
They say be brave,
laying in an unmarked grave.

Fighting for what you through was real,
Your pain is what I feel,
Your country is your pride,
No one knows you died.

I hope there was no pain.
What did war gain?
Heartache? Men insane?

Slipping through the sands of time,
You are the glory,
You are the Angel's chime.

They say life isn't always fair.
Why don't people seem to care?

I didn't know you.
I do care,
Why is hate so unfair?

Sharon Parle

My Best Friend

Through all my decisions, through all my fears,
Through all my happiness, through all my tears.

We've been through it all and still we're together.
You are my best friend and will be forever.

Words that weren't meant have often been said.
But never ever have I wished you were dead.

I have never told you I feel this way.
But I love you more and more each day.

We've done so much together, our friendship grows in my heart.
But as we grow older we seem to drift apart.

Whenever I've needed you, you've always been there
No matter what's done, you will always care.

I've never told you that you are my best friend.
But you'll always be, right till the end.

I love you mom.

Tonya M. Schuld

I Have The Power

A long black train is hurtling down the tracks at
uncontrolled speed. I watch in terror as it speeds
down the line.

Somehow I feel I am the train. I have no control.
If I ever had control I certainly don't have it now.
I know there's only one conclusion: there is going
to be a terrible crash.

This train has lost its brakes and is speeding headlong
into disaster. It has to stop and it has to stop now.
Suddenly the train starts slowing down. It keeps getting
Slower and slower until it rolls to a complete stop.
It has run out of gas.

I look at the train and somehow I know I now have the power.
I am in charge; I have taken control. As I stand looking at the
train it transforms into a long black snake. The same snake that
has terrified me in my dreams. I will no longer live in fear of this
snake. I will chop it into small pieces. I will completely destroy
it. I will vent my anger and free my soul and delight in doing it.

I have the power.

Barbara L. Cooper

Hear The Clowns Laughter

The world of man mocks me as
I drown in the bitterness of my own hate!

I hear the clowns laughter ringing,
telling me not to fight so, but just
to exist!

Yet I struggle to save myself
for I've no wish to die by
swallowing man's discharge!

To no avail! Though I resist,
I am sinking to the river of the
hate I bread.

Then my soul leaps up vainly
to steal one final look before sinking
into death.

Gordon Morse

"Interstate With A View"

I've stood
uncasy for many,
many years awaiting
my slow demise. My arms so
extended across the void, with a burial
aching to cry. How tranquil I am, though, in
the various seasons, for the passersby keep me in
touch. And with the erosion of dirt and sweat, my uneven
foot hold is luck. So I have good days and bad days as humans
might see, my frame of mind shifts with debris. Ruins that are
tussled by others in route
who cannot see a
forest or trees.

Kelley Elise Thomas-Spoon

The Lighthouse

Alone, out on the grey-green deep, beneath the heavens starry sweep
with only gulls to hear my cries, I tremble when I realize
how small my boat how far I've roamed
Behold another star!
The Highland light. It's beam marks home

Pauline Cunert

Out Of Time

She is beautiful, wise, and fair,
Unto her, this love I share
I drink her love, I drink the wine,
With Rhythmic motion our bodies intertwine
Motionless without a single just,
I spring to her with a single thrust

I live my life upon a stage, Bring new life, come of age
The secret of love is to combine,
My love, my life, give me a sign
For with out you I would be lost,
and struggle the vine at any cost
Rapped around a soul endured,
To lead you thru a world that so obscured

Bring forth a beginning in a single strife,
For her beauty is to bring new life
To end a war of ungodly trust,
To make a decision between love or lust
Dismay, betray, look they rhyme,
I'm just a man out of time

I capture her innocence in a single tear drop!

Shane Graham

Mom

There are some moms who are near...and thought of once in a while,
by kids who take for granted...their undecided smile.
One day to their dismay the kids may look back and regret.
The things they did not say to their dear mom, and still yet,
their eyes may always hide and refuse to see the pain,
that's caused by their unspoken words that leave the longest sprain.

Then there are some moms afar and thought of ever hour, by kids
who feel their fragrant love like the warm sun felt by a flower.
One day to their dismay God might reunite their closeness,
in proximity if I may, but I dare not be outspoken.

Just what's in the minds of those who have never been apart,
after suddenly being jerked away and left with a hurting heart?
Happy in their life, oh sure, these people likely are,
but saddened by the distance lying in between them far.
Unsure of when they'll see again each other's smiling face,
they endure that thing called time until the next embrace.

My favorite thing has always been to be around you, mom...
you are the reason many times I'm able to go on.
Repayment never could be made for all the things you've done.
I'm in debt forever, but so glad that I'm your son.

Curtis E. Bradley

Welcome to the Center of the Earth

The child peeled herself from the sticky seat
Gorgelshnumphs and Herzoids clinging to her fusia hair.
Licking gongadoon she giggled and writhed
In the pumescent night air.

She was only about four or five mocktons old
Oblivious to the world around her.
Reeking of innocenz and tonzenoff.
A literal kangadoon in a ziprack.

Oh how I longed for her tonzenoff.
The world would seem so pinrod
If I could return to the timzant when I was like her.
It was a vast eon ago
When I first passed the sign reading
"Welcome to the center of the Earth."

Andrew Conant

The Question in the Answer

The light that blinds you into a bright darkness
the loud silence that is heard as you stand at the middle of a crowd
the phantom of pain left behind when you set down a load
the cry you can hear from miles away
the suffocation of an open field
the patterns on a clear window pane
the curves within a straight line
the harmony of an out of tune piano
the choir you hear in a single voice
the softness of water
the meter kept in the bark of a cat
the purity of snow made from acid rain
the artificiality of a field of grass
the slant of a postured back
the emptiness of a forever loved soul
...the question in the answer...

Leigh Tillman

Rejection Syndrome

If I act like a real loser
It's because I'm broke down in my chooser
But relax, God's not finished with me yet

If I've been a real stinker
I might have problems with my thinker
Just remember, in my ways I am not set

If I sometimes make you cry
When my feelers running dry
Just remember I still care and I still try

Won't you try to understand
These are symptoms I don't plan
Or the buried rejections of my past

Please continue to pray for me
That some day I will see
That the prison door is open and I'm free

But while I'm still acting bound
And I'm a pain to have around
Won't you please keep praying for me.

Katherine Sanders

The Unclean Serpent Spirit

Black wings rising, dark omen of pain,
The Unclean Serpent Spirit claims his name.

Living deep in my flesh's fiery cold,
Stealing his son's bastard soul.

Continuing, continuing, he begins and ends,
A truthful lie that can never blend

With the vision I saw in the birth of my youth:
A winged serpent, bejeweled and diamond toothed.

A God spector soaring above rapturous plains,
Sun gold visions spiraling to enchanted domains.

Now defrocked and debased, a mirror of night,
An illusion of God mocking the light.

A blur of vision, thought sight restrained,
A sonata of colors, lost and deranged.

Hovering, descending with serpentine claws,
He tears from my soul all honorable cause.

A scream in my consciousness, crescendos of woe,
The shadow winged form pulls me below.

Flying from my death to seek calmer tones,
The Unclean Serpent Spirit occupies my home.

Perry Pennington Douros

Tears Uncried

The candle flame pierced the dark
A mother's tear fell from the sky
A young child's laughter stops in the park
And asks the question, "Did my brother die?"

He never had a breathe of life
And his virgin eyes had never spied
This world so full of strife
Because my baby brother had died

They say that God will take us in our time
All through his passing, I tried not to cry
But emotions are hard
When God makes your baby brother die

So many times I've said that he's cruel and unfair
And I would scream why
If the shepherd is supposed to share
Then why did my brother die?

Michael A. Loffreda

Separate Ways - Common Days

We were friends and comrades in the weary times
forced to go our separate ways.

Never to see the same light of day.

We stood shoulder to shoulder in the turbulent waves
of hate, war and blacken rage.

Never to see the same light of day.

We felt the frost and tasted the sand, distances far
from love-n-care of hearts affair.

Never to see the same light of day.

Twilight has come and stars start to play,
and we have gone our separate ways.
Only memories hold the thread to heaven.

Never to see the same light of day.

Jeffrey Huff

The Death Ship

The swift ship speed along the
waters as quietly and unseen as a ghost
The only sound it made was the howling
of mast in the wind - death
This ship was known as the death ship
for when it was seen no one saw a crew,
it floated along as though it wasn't
there until one day it was seen along a shoreline
When it was seen everyone fled for only
when it was seen that people would die and
the village would become diseased
But even though they left they would still die for they
had been struck with the death ship disease
This disease only hurt the people who had
lived in that village never hurting anyone else
The ship was known the kill all evil
even now from time to time it is seen
along a shoreline, and that village
vanishes from the earth

Samantha Strevy

Yon Mountain Peaks

Yon lofty mountain peaks arise
In Haughty grandeur to the skies,
Serene above all earthly care
Their snow-capped tops do heavenward stare.

So straight they stand, unchanged by time,
Majestic beauty, peace sublime.
I gaze at them with human awe,
For in their splendor is no flaw.

They seem to claim pow'r over all,
O'er man, o'er beast, they seem so tall
Yet my heart knows that small they stand
Within the hollow of God's hand.

Elsa M. Stockton

Rain

I gaze outside my window, the pouring rain is all I see,
I prepare for my day knowing stormy weather is in store for me.

I scamper to my car, rain gear fully snug,
I see the people staring, they point and shoulders shrug.

I tune the dial on my radio to listen to the report,
the day looks bright he says, a halter, maybe shorts.

I wonder?

I reach my destination full of confusion and dismay,
I remove my rain soaked clothing and prepare for a long wet day.

As I walk throughout the hallways I hear of picnics and bar-b-ques,
of weekend plans of laughter and couples two by two.

When the day is over and the rain has never let,
while dawning clothing barely dry once again it is so wet.

I leave the building thinking how silly they must be,
the rain continues pouring and to see it, only me.

As I stare into my mirror just before I go to bed,
I see the rain still falling like a faucet above my head.

Then I pause to ponder, and I can't believe its true,
Is it really raining or am I merely crying over you?

I wonder?

Oliver Harrell

Bricklayer

Criticize, demoralize, make my body shake.
I see the skies through teary eyes,
How much can I take?
The knife goes in, no blood comes out,
I live in your life's wake.

I build up walls,
You tear them down,
Can you hear my calls,
Do they make you frown?

You are the Bricklayer.
Walls are rising you cannot see.
I'm the city's mayor.
Walls become buildings, buildings become houses,
Homes for the voices that talk to me.

You build the walls,
I hide them well.
We are building a city,
I call it hell.

David J. Lange

The Essence Of Beauty

Beauty is not a face
nor form,

Beauty is not monetary success
but a success out of the norm.

Beauty is not a voice to be heard
but a choice made without a word.

Beauty is the light from within,
a light shining so bright just
saying I can.

I can do great things
with the beauty that's in me,

That's why I call myself beautiful
you see.

The essence of beauty comes from
the depths of your soul,

The essence of beauty is the
silent strength all women of color know.

Carla Shelton

Untitled

I am quiet and open
I wonder why things happen the way they do.
I hear God's voice.
I see his face.
I want to be with him someday.
I am quiet and open.

I pretend that I'm a dancer.
I feel my grandpa's hand guiding me.
I touch him and am comforted.
I worry that I'm not good enough.
I cry when I remember how things used to be.
I am quiet and open.

I understand that life is hard.
I say "Why does it have to be like this?"
I dream of my children and love.
I try to treat everyone the way I want to be treated.
I hope the world will be a better place for my kids.
I am quiet and open.

Becky Phillips

"A Turkey Story"

Said one turkey to the other, "Well, it's Thanskgiving Day again, want to make a bet this year brother?"

No! We never win.

The humans are running to and fro, getting ready for the big day and they are fattening us up and watching us grow. That is the human's way. "Listen up you ole birds", said the lady turkey as she drew near. We should feel honored that we are chosen each year. You know Thanksgiving Day is special, and that makes us special too. "There's nothing that makes me gobble so as seeing one of us at the head of the table", she said. So, stop gobbling and be thankful that you bring families together on this special day, and that Thanksgiving comes only once a year.

Happy Thanksgiving Day!

Rita Marie Calloway Stigger

Dusk

Looking into the sunset I can't help but notice
that despite her beauty,
a sense of struggle and hopelessness surround the sky.
Deep inside you realize that this day is gone
and everything that it had brought is lost forever.
Every thought, every action, every dream, every hope,
every sight, every sound is gone.
There is no chance of ever being returned the same,
exactly the same.
For even memory has a limit to what it can capture.
Even memory has a limit to what it can retrieve.

And the colours in the sky try to entertain us.
One last act with painted smiles
for they too know that nothing can be done to save the day.
So futile their attempt to comfort our fear of the night,
our horror as we try to find our way,
like children who wander into a forest and never return.

I am ingratiated by the sunset because of her sensitivity
as she tries to push the darkness back for just a moment more.
But like so many times before.. To no avail!

David J. Ebner

Red Tide Off Sanibel Island

Sanibel off season baring her sandy flanks
Only to find them strewn with debris
Evidence of a lover's quarrel.
Bloated dead fish stinking:
Scattered by fingers of jealous tides
Impotent Neptune broods in the depths.

Bikini clad and ripe with youth
She dashes thigh high into the surf
Pursued by her middle aged lover
Who lifts his camera above the sure foam
Like a trophy and smiles as he snaps
Her picture.
He has stolen her youth as a cloud
Of seagulls drops in unison to print
The sand with webbed impressions
Of Neptune's trident.
Oblivious, she brushes a wet strand
Of hair from her cheek and emerges
From the sea as triumphant as
Botticelli's Venus.

Cynthia Baker

Infatuation

I think about thee day and night
The love I have for thee I cannot fight
When I see thee my soul takes an angelic flight
I picture thee as the savior of my wretched life
Thou act comfort me and relieve my strife.
I love thee as a summer's morn
Fresh, new, and warm
Does thou lovest me as I love thee true?
Until thine answer my heart and soul will be of the bluest hue
The illness of thou love grasps my heart and mind
Diluting my reason to kind
Enabling fantasy to reign in real time
Please lovest me with all thy heart and be innocent
For thou will nurture my life as a God sent.

Jason Carwell

"Bridging The Chasm"

So quickly, it seems, the years have gone by,
In just a few seconds or the blink of an eye.
So many things I had intended to do
And one of them was to make peace with you.

The letters I've written, again and again,
Never got onto the paper from pen.
The words which just flowed out from my brain
Never got printed to ease any pain.

Of people I've known, and there've been a few,
None were ever as special as you.
I'm really so sorry life pulled us apart,
But no one could fill up your place in my heart.

If it isn't too late could I please make amends?
Will you once again number me one of your friends?
I give you my word I'll try to do better,
And to show I'm sincere I'll start with this letter.

So here I am hoping, and wishing, and dreaming,
That all of my wanting and all of my scheming
Will fix us and mend us and make us like new,
'Cause I've never stopped caring what happens to you.

Sue Thom

Side by Side

I fear
That you are lying in the chill next to my night
Prepared to wound me with your absence
By my side
Where you are lying sighing softly, warmly
Lulling
Me to sleep against your gently heaving breasts
Then when
You scream I will awake into the madness
Of the lonely who, unguarded thought forever would just last
As if tomorrow
Could be counted on to be the measure of today
You'll go away
While I still sleep inside the warmth already cooling in our
sheets.

Walter Schimmerling

"Why"

I don't understand
All this hatred and pain in my head
All around me people say
There's no one to pray for us
All we do is try to survive, trying to keep alive
He put us here, I don't know why
While all this hatred and pain is nearby
Please tell me Lord
Why didn't you tell me about this
I don't know why we even exist
You put us here in this place, where every face
Says, there isn't a chance.
For the human race
We hurt the earth so many times
But now we are taking each others lives
Before it's over, there will be no one left over
Fast as we came, the quicker we go
Everyday, one by one, soon there will be none
And I still wonder why, why even if God is nearby
Please God tell me why

Danielle Hake

Words Of A Wise Man

A wise man once said - "Man is made like a
grain of sand sifting through an hour glass
Bottled, he will reach an end and be settled.
Though set free, he is lifted by wind and able to
search and grow."

A wise man once said - "A soul will search forever
for the peace he was so wrongly deprived of because
he was not his own man rather, let others be him."

A wise man once said - "Man's burdens are likes
the fruit which grows a tree. They may be plucked
and devoured when they become too heavy for one
branch do support."

A wise man once said - "It is only after death
reveals himself from the shadows do collect the
weary souls, can man's spirit gain the right to
exist in a world that is trouble free and peaceful."

A wise man once died.

Judy Hess

The Little Birds

I went outside walking around
I saw a little sparrow scratching in the ground
He scratched for worms so round and fat
He knew he couldn't find anything better than that

I saw a covey of quail running down a narrow path
Looking for grain that was hid in the grass
Then come the baby quail tip toeing thru the sand
Following their mother at her command
Mother said each one has to feed himself
Or else he may starve to death
I don't like the birds with legs as thin as a stalk
For one day they might want to do the Tennessee Bird walk.

Now I see the beautiful dove flying from the ark
Looking for a place that he might park
The water was still high so he flew back in
To tell Noah where he had been

The dove and the quail must be God's chosen birds
Because they are mentioned in His Holy Word.

Now if God takes care of the birds in the air and the fishes of the
Sea, He has a much better plan for you and me.

Thelma Letchas

Our Moments Shared

A single moment comes to pass,
like tides the are swept away.
As a space unlimited within our hearts,
sheds light on a stormy day.
No time that ever passes,
should be measured by loss or pain.
It is all just a new experience,
that gives knowledge from clouds of rain.
Looks not for answers unrevealed to you,
or for truths that are not there.
Take only what is given you,
only what you feel is fair.
Open your eyes to the beauty,
that surrounds us from head to toe.
Don't ask where the road has lead you,
for you may never know.
Catch the moments like snowflakes,
embrace them in your hand.
Watch them as they melt away,
then wait for the next to land.

Christopher Shawn Tappan

Shadows Of Fear

Creepy dark shadows of fear,
Often I see you in my mirror.

Deep red blood shot eyes,
You stand naked without disguise.

I listen to your evil talk,
Unremorseful to God you mock.

Withering face as wrinkles set in,
Bones and sinews deaden within.

You carry on about your cross,
You bear nothing and now your lost.

The devils coming to take your hand,
To bury you deep within the sand.

There is no hope for eternal rest,
You were wickedly evil and did your best.

John A. King

"Past The Apparent"

I often sit and wonder
of life and its ordeals,
From the visible corruption
To the emotions we conceal.

The fast and speechless crowd
on a city's bustling streets,
Whose day revolves around a clock
to accomplish several feats.

The children on a school bus
with eyes still half asleep,
Some complaining of their homework
while others in their thoughts are deep.

Yet beyond the common lifestyle
lies a family divided,
An abandoned wife and mother
and young children badly chided.

We're surrounded by wrong doings
And yet help is not insight.
So I ask, what have we come to
When a wrong can be a right?

Claudia Diaz De Leon

Untitled

Lost at sea
Break in the waves
Release
Soul flies
Crashing through
Lunging free
Shining above
Beyond gravity
I'm here for a reason
Just give me a sign
I need a mission
A direction
No more wading in, the pools of darkness
I want the gift of sight
What sentence?
What grievance?
Pay my dues?
Suffer in blindness?
In order to break free??
The time is now give me the eyes...

Tamara Wilson

Sanity Is All

Has your mind ever
walked through dementia?
Describe the landscape
as you see it when insomnia
is eating your eyeballs.
Go ahead, scream, but the sound
and its reverberations might rip your
vocal chords, to shreds; ear-drums might
shatter in the cacophony.
Don't slash your wrists-the spilt blood
will burn your flesh, and you will
need your hands to grab hold of
that elusive...Sanity.

Kevin Haywood

Beautiful Most Indeed

BEAUTIFUL MOST INDEED is what I say to thee.
Your beauty from head to toe impassions me with glee.

BEAUTIFUL MOST INDEED are your eyes my queen.
Bold, beautiful and bright beaming a splendid sheen.

BEAUTIFUL MOST INDEED are your lips I long to kiss.
Your soft caress and tender press submerge me in irrepressible bliss.

BEAUTIFUL MOST INDEED is your body I desire to feel.
So shapely, sexy and smooth, you are positively ideal.

BEAUTIFUL MOST INDEED is your soul oh lovely lady.
Goodhearted, charitable and kind - you make everyone so happy.

BEAUTIFUL MOST INDEED are you my destined bride.
In you I take pride.

Steven R. Adams

"Illigitimi Non Carborundum"

"Don't Let The Bastards Wear You Down"

A thought can and will control your mind
Start daydreaming, wondering how far you have to climb
The hill in front of you grips your spirit with fear
Choking your desires that once were clear

Quandary controls your every move
Life begins to spiral into a deluge
Constantly bombarding rationale you once possessed
Delving deep into ones soul you become enmeshed

Searching takes on a major role in your life
Often combating ridicule and strife
Battling yourself is one of life's toughest chores
Fighting in the trenches - Waging daily wars

Always allow turmoil to be followed by peace
Caress your mind with the soft gentle touch of fleece
Happiness is derived from inner strength
You must be willing to go to any length

Mental toughness should never be underestimated
Focusing on the positive will not leave you decimated

It's the ninth inning and you are on the mound
Remember - "Don't let the Bastards wear you down"

Thomas J. McCann

Untitled

Daddy's back.
Staring into the sunset hoping he'll return.
Hoping he's leaving forever.
Each time he calls or comes he rips me up.
Shreds my ego, crushes my fantasy.
Have to love him, never respect him.
Emotionally stunted.
Stole my ideal.
Can't say he's proud.
Must he push?
Disgust and desire have never entwined
So easily. All of this, staring at
Daddy's back through a watery haze.

Kimberly Knight

As The Hourglass Drips

As my thirsting lips suck the fount of time,
Like the white blood
Drips from mother's breast;
And bathe in a pool of liquid sand,
The sun slowly sips from my wine glass
The hot wax of my candle flame.

As Winter takes off his bitter coat
And hangs it over the sun,
Like the chattering winds
Bite the summer's breezes;
And drapes the windows of the lakes with lace,
The flower's petals fade away,
And loves me not my withering fig skin.

As my blood thickens quick to slow the loathing pump,
Like the broken trees
Choke the mountain's springs;
And fills the shallow creek of my veins with rocks,
The faucet runs dry to the last salty drop,
Dangling from my cracked lips.

Denielle Aukerman

Friendship Lost Forever

I saw in the paper today that someone I knew
Long ago in the forgotten rivers of my mind
Had died on Christmas Day.

She was a cheery woman
Whose quick temper drove a wedge between us,
So that we no longer spoke.

She became as a speck of sand in my life,
Drifting in with the ocean's waves,
And washing out with the tide to the vast sea.

Death now parts us forever;
There are no more goodbyes to say,
Yet memories of her spirit filter into my thoughts.

I have added one more New Year's resolution
To my usual list of diet and exercise,
And that is, to reach out beyond my innate shell.

K. T. Cohen

Love

There is a love that can be found
That makes your heart of pure gold,
For some people they are bound
To achieve this heart of gold before they are old.

This love lasts forever,
If you remain in this state of mind
You will never say never,
Because this love will make you kind.

For others to see this kind of love in you,
It makes them remember the love they've lacked.
This love is fresher than the morning dew,
This love will make you push forward and not turn back.

For some people this kind of love is cherished,
And in this earth it should never perish.

Aaron R. Riojas

My Father

My father's a man I've never
seen or met, the stories I've heard
I don't want to forget.

I don't have any pictures or
memories to hold, he was a strong
and good man so I've been told.

Will I ever get over not having
him here, at least a picture would
be something I could always hold dear.

He died for our country trying
to make things right, I wonder if
he hears my silent tears at night.

There will always be a hollow
that can't be filled, for the father
I would have known if he hadn't
been killed.

Everything he left for me has
been taken away, but the best he
put inside me and that's where it will stay.

Cindy Bundy

Plummeting Dreams

More than just someone to hold me,
More than just a friend,
Just someone I can love.

Pure white flakes plummet to the ground,
They elude the ears but not the nose,
The silent beauty of the snow.

Watching, dreaming, longing;
He sits by the window staring blankly,
The snowflakes pass the window, like the dreams in his mind;
Slowly a warm arm slides across his chest,
Without looking he clasps her hand in his,
Silently, she opens her heart and pulls him in.

Watching, dreaming;
He gives thanks for dreams come true,
and bids farewell to the longing.

Mathew T. Jett

Christmas Time

T'was the night before Christmas and I can't wait to see,
    what Santa has brought for you and for me.

The angel on the tree top is watching below,
    and the lights from our window has a warm friendly glow.

The weather outside is crisp and bold,
    poor Santa is out delivering toys in the cold.

So remember Santa tonight before you go to bed,
    leave him something to warm him from his toes to his head.

Now grandpa's not Santa, of that we'll all agree,
    But with that belly he could have fooled me.

With a wink of his eye and a tilt of his head,
    were you all good children, he said.

Of course they were, as perfect as can be,
    Just ask grandma and you'll see.

Now our tummies are full and time is drawing near,
    for us to open our presents like we did last year.

My family is together, what a wonderful sight,
    Merry Christmas to all and to all a good night!!!

Rita Nifong

What Friendship Means To Me

Friendship is having a friend who accepts you for how you really are,
Sometimes making you close like two peas in a jar.

Having a supporter who will stand by you for being wrong or right,
That's what makes the relationship tight.

A chum you can tell your secrets to,
Not that they'll chatter and make you blue.

A pal who lets you have a great sense of humor with jokes and
laughter, that's what makes it a happy ever after.

If anyone can do this for me,
Then I'll be totally devoted to them you see.

For balance and harmony fills me with glee,
Then there will be no doubt in my mind that my soul shall feel free.
This is what friendship meant to me.

Sharon Schock

Mom

Who is there to see your first tooth, get bigger clothes and
loose your first shoe?
Who is there to blow your first nose and clean between your toes?
Who takes care of you when times are tough and you looks are rough?
And who is there to break up your first fight and never loose sight?
Well it's mom, that's right MOM!

Brandon Kay

Number Three Cell

"Just looking for a hole," the rapist said,
To the little girl, as she screamed and bled.
He's back again in No. 3 cell,
Some days she's better, her nights are hell.

"Just looking for a hole," the rapist said,
To the neighbor lady, as she lay in her bed.
He's back again, in No. 3 cell,
The neighbor lady will never be well.

"Just looking for a hole," the rapist said,
To the virgin teen as he beat her till dead.
He's back again in No. 3 cell,
Perhaps this time for a longer spell.

Hazel Carmichael

Sleep Digression

Summer solstice.
  Season's slack-tide.
   Sleepless, I drift and dream
    Past midnight doldrums.
     Ceiling drama casts primordial images
      In its ample yawn,
       While a storm approaches,
        The west wind moans,
         And curtains arch like gossamer sails
          Upon the breaking dawn.

Defenseless, I linger here,
  In murky abeyance,
   Wrestling nameless fear and faceless foe,
    While the soul in this realm,
     Sputters fragments of
      Prayer, hope, and defeat
       Into the maelstrom of
        Churning merging reality.

    Kay L. Harrington

Scared

Searching through the mountains of angels
My heart looking for its missing link
I saw the future through a lonely soul
Love seen at her face
Love became an act of murder and blood
And I'm bleeding through my heart
Beauty projected, only to be a reflection
Now that you're gone,
I'm trying to swallow the tears
It was pure rejection,
Hidden in those words.
This is not how I want it to end
I'll never be truthful again
Don't step any closer
Do you really think I need you
I'll learn to pretend and smile a lie.
Having a more dreams to defend.

    Jason Bojan

Angels

God sends angels into our life
To help and love and care;
To offer support during times of strife,
To heal with the power of prayer.

These angels are special as they touch our hearts;
They walk in comforting light,
We know they've a mission and we are a part;
As their goodness and selflessness shine bright.

Thank you Lord for sisters and brothers;
Many angels who aren't even aware,
How their presence and guidance and ministry to others;
Have been their profound and powerful gift to share.

    Marilyn J. Becht

Lest We Forget

Crucified on a cross of wood.
His teachings profound, his words understood.
Two thousand years have passed since then.
The next coming of, we know not when.
Set free from bondage, slaves no more.
Still a myriad of needful poor.
The wonders of the universe obeyed his commands.
He welcomed his enemies with open hands.
His dieing words, "father, forgive."
Allowed all of mankind... this chance to live.

    David G. Rodriguez

"Self-Employment"

Always career oriented, eager and bright
Became self-employed without first seeing the light.

It seemed the perfect thing to become my own boss
Never realizing how close I'd feel to permanent mind loss.

The employees so troublesome wanting to be in command
Arguing and insulting in pursuit of the upper-hand.

Employee and employee always entwined in a fight
No schedule change or employee change will bring happiness in sight.

Endless dedication mentally and physically regardless the cost
Is not appreciated by anyone even though it matters the most.

New in business, unappreciated, exhausted and barely making a dime
I keep telling my determined self... it will all work out,
   it's just a matter of time.

    Sherry Palmer

"Nature's Beauty"

Nature truly holds thing for us, but only by
viewing it right. It's just as beautiful in the
morning as it is at night. It first brings us
winter snow so white when freshly fallen,
then right around winters corner spring
nature comes a call'n. With its humming
birds, wind blowing so fine, and flowers that
sprang into action, and its cost to absolutely
nothing, just time only a fraction. Cause
when we take that second look summer is
shining through, with everything that's
self entitled and romances old and new.
Then before we even notice, in steps the
fall of the year, with all its fancy colors
and bringing along its cheer. Nature is so
very sweet and brings us lots of joys,
and keeps on going through generations
for all our girls and boys. So lets stop, take
a few moments, out of our busy days, to
appreciate natures beauty, and the wonders of its ways.

    Linda M. Hall

Homeless Peoples

No where to go, no one to love,
No place to lay their heads.

No food to eat, no money to spend
No cover or no bed.

No shoes to ware, no clothes to wash
No friends to hang around.

Just homeless people's throughout this land
From City's and from Town's.

Maybe we should reach out to them, and give a helping hand...
To help one homeless lady, or one homeless man.

Tomorrow may bring a better day, if we all just stop and say.
I will help one homeless person, to find a place to stay.

    George Dawson

A Perfect World Would Be

A perfect world would be, I think,
No more drugs on the brink,
No more illness, sickness, or war,
No more solicitors knocking at the door,
Pollution no more in the air,
Peace in the world everywhere,
No more poisons dumped down the sink,
This is what a perfect world would be, I think.

    Michael Fontz

Wind

The wind tells many stories.
It tells stories of anger, delight, and terror.
You may hear the weeping of many strangers
or the screams of persons in fear
and waiting but no one there.

The wind tells many stories.
It tells stories of being true, kind, and real.
You may hear the joys of happiness when
a baby take his first breath
or the crying of a young girl who's lost her favorite shoe.
Help is what she's saying "please do, help me find my shoe."

The wind tells many stories.
It tells stories of wonders, sites, and fantasy.
You may hear the voice of wishes
or the singing of birds in the morning.
That's why the wind tells many stories.

Kelly Klobuchar

Wilhelm Tell - The Short Version

On the flagpole, in the square hung a hat, it wasn't fair:
Those refusing to bow low in the dungeon they would throw.
Then one day, the sun was high, Tell and son were passing by.
Head held high and nerves like ice, Tell ignored the vile device.
But just then, with horse and arms,
Gessler came with his gendarmes.

Snarling "let our hero show how good he is with yonder bow!",
he took the boy (this man was vicious)
and crowned him with a Red Delicious.
Tell aimed the crossbow at the lad and shot the apple off his head.
But Gessler thundered "there I see another arrow, meant for me.
Arrest this man and grant no bail,
and ship him off to Küssnacht jail!"

Alas, storms churned the lake that day,
our Tell jumped ship and got away.
After six weeks: Through woods and fog
Gessler went on his morning jog
when tell in wait, at ten past five
blew out the tyrant's flame of life.

Rainer Rungaldier

Glass Comes From Sand

Glass comes from the sand
and I know the roses are red, but
why is the spring grass always so dry and shaded?

Why does the tanned old grass remind me of that
cemetery long ago on the soft hill?
Of that strange funeral where we buried a man that
I never knew nor ever met.

What do I know?
What do I know?

I know that a catty cat, who I never liked,
has been dead these seven months past,
only now I know I miss him.
And I know that the snow now blankets both
the man and the cat in this muffled December.

What are the solid facts?
The snow still drifts down the same every year,
covering the memories till they lay forgotten and stilled.

The old thoughts are no longer fluid,
they are the frozen and quiet,
like the sand that became glass.

David M. Behsman

Christmas Dad

The bells are ringing in the Christmas Cheers,
But our hearts are heavy, faces curtained with tears.
For a very special friend, loved by one and all,
Received in April, his beckoned call,
To join his Lord, and sit on high,
And left us saying, "please tell us why."
It's not our place to question the Lord's reason,
No matter the year, no matter the season.
So we're left with memories of Christmas days past,
Then feel at ease, break a smile, for the shadow of love he cast
On those precious memories, filled with joy and glee,
For his suffering is over and he's finally free.
We're truly lucky to have an angel like Dad,
We all should now, he'd except no one be sad,
He'd want us to go on, celebrate just right,
To gain from his wisdom, to gain from his fright,
Be happy with each other, learn to love as he did,
Grab that can of magic and kick off the lid,
To remember the good times, and put away the bad,
We love him and miss him, OUR WORLD'S GREATEST DAD!

Brian Russell Shinault

Friends

Friends are a very special gift,
When you are down and out, they give you a lift.

A friend is a person who really cares,
One with whom you can freely share.

Whether it's the sadness or the joy's of life,
A friend supports, especially in strife.

A friend is one who plays a special part,
One who always warms the heart.

The love of a friend, a warm embrace,
Someone in your life who can't be replaced.

A smile on the face, just the sound of the voice
Can make the heart pound and your soul rejoice.

But if you aren't forgiven when you slip and fall,
It probably wasn't a friend at all.

Barbara Greenwalt

"America The Not So Beautiful"

Once again our nation lies in need.
She's suffered from hate, petty lies and greed.

Enormous debts act as heavy chains.
The weight that binds, the strain that pains.

Economy's weathered a potent storm
Now life in poverty is again the norm.

And nature too has taken its tolls.
Disasters take lives and try our souls.

Landfills are filling way too fast.
How much longer can this ol' earth last?

We polluted our air, water and soil.
I wonder . . . Can a planet not spoil?

Homeless are now more abundant than ever.
Help, it seems, is a non-profit endeavor.

We've lost compassion for our fellow man.
We must act quickly and form a plan.

Shelter, food and a shot at good health.
Is it so damn wrong to share the wealth?

Again Uncle Sam is due a face lift.
He's lookin' poorly, if you catch my drift. THE END...NEVER!!!

Beau Burkett

Life Is

A life without challenges oo what a terrible thing.
A life without chances is really no life at all,
for only thru chances can you know the thrill of
victory or the bitter taste of defeat.
A life without imagination is truly a lonely place to be.
For only in men's minds can they be truly free.
A life without love is truly the worst demon of all,
for a life without love by one person surely affects us all.
A life without love is a life without challenges,
chances, or imagination that's all.

Jeffrey L. Merritt

Look Into My Soul

The shell that you see
This isn't me this isn't me

You have to look into my heart
Then you'll see
This isn't me this isn't me.

You need to listen to my voice and
Then you'll know

Look into my eyes to find my soul
My body may have changed but the
Soul insides the same
This isn't me this isn't me.

So I take my life day by day
And every night I close my eyes and pray.
And when I go to sleep at night in my dreams I'm alright
Oh I can walk I can run, I can even touch the sky.
You know sometimes I can even fly.
And nobody passes me by with the look of pity in his eyes.

And I ask God each and every day give me the strength and show
me the way. To be the best that I can be. And rise above the shell
to find the soul in me.

Robin Wengert

The Race

Life,
Black, yellow and white,
Living harmoniously in al that is right,
Like the energy which gives us the light,
Seeing through the color of night.
A beckoning call to those who will be,
For it is the color of light which separates
You and me,
So let go of your worries, your troubles, your hate,
And send up a message of show all good faith.
It is without reason to care who was right
For there still will be those colors,
Black, yellow and white.
Life.

Matthew William Rayle

Willow

My soul lies hidden far and deep,
  (Who is the mom here, who is the child?)

Oh, rock my weary heart to weep.
  (You teach me to be strong and leave.)

We plant this tree, the earth may keep.
  (In you, in our hearts, love is.)

Now rest my child, now grow, now sleep.

Deborah Lemack

The Real World

A candle burning,
A feather falling,
The leaves as they turn from green to gold.

Things that should be noticed,
Things that make life
In essence,
Beautiful.

Downy clouds as they drift in a lazy sapphire sea,
Laced butterflies perched daintily on a flower's crown,
A winter's muted beauty.

Lunch with Phil at eleven.
English War Essay due Thursday.
Laura is in a fight with Amy,
And I can't find my car keys.

And then,
You're in college already?
Where did the time go?
It seems like yesterday.

War in Bosnia escalates.
A feather falls unnoticed.

John D. Phan

Friendship

The measure of life is often found
Where success and praise, accomplishment abound.
The pleasure of life is always found
Where love and laugher of true friendship resound.
The treasure of life that's greatest,
Where the heart is blessed, the soul refreshed,
  joy found —

Is not in the accolades of man
  or the trophies won by our own hand.
The lasting measure of life's main part
  is the imprint left on another's heart.

Sandy Sweesy

Springtime

When springtime comes I am sure to know
For the birds of the air seem to tell me so.
The robin with its majestic breast
Is ever so busy building her nest.
The sparrow though here year long
At daybreak starts chirping ever so strong.
The killdeer with its color of olive brown
Keeps swooping low to the ground
Wishing to fool all creatures
Where its abode is found.
The meadowlark with its melody of song
Is joyfully serenading the day long.
The magpie believing he is boss over all
Lets out with a harsh rapid call.
Now answer me my friend I pray
Is there any better way
To say spring is here to stay?

Ida Van Klinken

Untitled

Here I am
In that favorite of seasons
The harvesting years of my life
Full of gold and crimson light

When did I stop rejoicing
In that inner life of mine
Why did life unsettle my happy
    sunset of quiet glories
Made me to fight again
When I was to rest and gather years
    of struggle safely over

And yet there are those other moments
When looking round my heart is full
And other hopeful younger days take over
Bringing into my fall the smell of spring
    and heat of summer!

Dulce M. Castilla

Prime Time

Don't let the fear of growing older
    Haunt you day by day.
Carry the torch with pride and grace
    Tell age to get out of the way!

Don't worry about the strands of gray.
    They are your crowning glory.
A line, a wrinkle—wear them well,
    Each one tells a beautiful story.

Be thankful for God's gift of life.
    Don't start each day with tears.
Awake with a song instead of a sigh,
    Count your blessings not the years.

Your life is a part of the Master Plan,
    Not given by chance or whim.
Accept it with thanks, live it well.
    This is your gift to Him.

Dolores Flanagan Mason

Restless Reflections

The cold iciness I breathe in and out gasping loudly
as I run wildly across the slippery smooth surface
of the perfectly peaceful pond frozen in the clear night.

Star-studded sky shimmers on the icy dance floor
with a silver spotlight on me as I slide swiftly across
with arms waving at my lone lingering spectator moon.

The biting wind snaps at my face as I rush restlessly
towards the silent freedom found in twirling on the icy pond
and ignore the imposed loneliness on invaders intruding.

Legs aggressively gaining speed and skates slicing
into the once flawless frozen aqueous body and producing
outrageous scars faintly sparkling in silver light.

The conforming clouds capture my bright, happy friend
cheering me and the chastises his curiosities peeking past the
pristine pools of frozen perfection to stranger streakings.

Moons insists to shine slivers of his self on my silhouette
standing still amidst the fading frozen unity we shared
while reflecting our intriguing images on the icy pond.

Elisa Guyader

Ye Soldiers Of Uncle Sam

Up before the crack of dawn,
more motivation, the struggle is on.
Setting up our home of camo
then giving orders on the humping of ammo.
Plotting the course of our mission
then administering the decisions.
Tired and worn, but we can't quit
the battle's just begun, no time to sit
because onward and forward is our command
Ye soldiers of Uncle Sam.
Living in a field of green
civilian life can't be seen.
Weekend Warriors training hard
keeping the enemy out of our backyard.
Wherever God and nation shall lead
we are prepared to meet he challenge and need.
Tired and worn, but we can't quit
we must stay alert and physically fit.
Because onward and forward is our command
Ye soldiers of Uncle Sam.

Lisa Campbell

Ice Storm

Look, the tree branches captured by a sheen
Of ice glimmer like opaline sculptures,

Rustle against each other like windchimes
Discussing and exploring truth. The storm's

Intensity seizes everything it touches,
Wraps its glaze around mortal flesh

Holding it close, even time stands still.
The branches encased in ice turn into red

Arteries, coursing blood frozen in time,
Children caught in freeze tag; the red casts

A furtive rose glow against the gray horizon.
The limbs of trees bend under the weight

Of ice, tilling the soil, tying a shoe,
Frozen in the day's labor. Experience

Seals the dusk before letting go begins.
The rose turned mauve twilight freezes in memory

Before the storm relents, before the
Ice melts, before the laborers rest,
Before remembering begins.

Christie Chandler

The Mountain

A trail came from the rocks
And cut into the mountain
I followed its path traversing high walls
And narrow passes, deep and mysterious
Over moraines and across ravines
Sunbeams danced on the walls, shadows fell at midday
And followed my wandering ways
As I tread this virgin trail
Over the face of the rock
Stones moved under my feet
And centuries of stillness changed
Yet the path and stone remained the same
The mountain remains the same
It is I that changes, never to be the same
Swallowed up in a journey of time becoming
A kindred spirit of the mountain
Pondering this moment, it is I who is the trail
I am the rock, the mountain, this place
My soul never to leave

Randy Carter

Oh Red Deer, "Oh Canada"

I think about the wind a-blowing
  Across the Canadian plain.
Maybe it is snowing
  Or just a winter rain.

Are the mountain peaks clear and sunny
  Circled by trees of green?
Or are they cloudy and funny
  Enveloped in misty sheen?

It's Christmas in Red Deer
  With bundled shoppers singing
All the children from far and near
  Their holiday voices ringing.

So when I hear, "oh Canada" sung
  A part of me is drawn forth
To my other home though distance flung
  Calling my heart - Go North! Go North!

  Frank Holden

Mother's Poem

Mama, yes, that's surely you.
We know your name, your time, your hue.

Atwist, arrest in God's great view,
We grant no sloth in love of you.

We know as well, we'll span this reach,
You'll always offer time to teach.

To you, for now, we move along.
But, to return our gifted song.

  Adisa Ben Achaki 1992

Enroute

I cannot imagine my father ever walking into a room and wondering
  why he was there,
  retracing his steps to remember

Instead, he would see who was there and start talking with them
  or
  examine the architecture and detailing
  or
  pass through to another.

It was only close to the end, when he was immobilized and could not
  pass through
  that sadness reached his eyes, in the gloom, and he looked
                    aside.

Perhaps that is why grown men cried when they heard that he
  would never
          pass their way again.

  Gretchen Haller

Looking For Me?

Who am I and where am I going?
On restless nights at dawn, go to the sea.
The tides of tranquility await a happening.
Where the sky melts into the unrelenting ocean.
Cloud formations tell the evolution of thoughts.
They give direction, the verdict of truthfulness.
Life's commitments will fulfill an inner happiness.
All hopes and dreams become reality.
At last peace from a momentary disorientation.
Once again I know who I am and where I am going.

  Don Ponsky

Confession

Emptiness is all I see as I look up into the sky.
I try to solve each mystery, and answer every why.

Little star, that shines so bright, what troubles carry you?
If you carry merely one tonight have you strength to carry two?

Grant me confession of sin and indulgence,
Since bullets will beg to run free,
But so did his stick and often his hand,
And both of them chose to blame me.

To blame me for straining, back-breaking jobs,
And wistful stomachs too.
Since rifles could fire and end bedtime sobs,
Finally, I begged too.
So you see little star,
Why someone like me had to share all my troubles with you.

  Diana Rodriguez

If You Lent Your Heart

If you lent your heart to the one you love
Then they brought it back feeling like a wounded dove
Would you take it back with a willful smile
Then fly away with a wounded wing
Hoping and praying for the spring
Or would you take it back with a crooked smile
Having had fun all the while
Betting on the next one up
Would be the one to fill your cup
Or would you take it back and your frown be known
All that had happened the sadness had shown
Then staying away from the paths that cross
The ways in which we receive
Can teach us how to believe

  Maureen Vitale

Road To Wilmar

The land
tumbling on a track
rows of corn and soy
dead
falling to attention
monotony at the wheel.

Tundra sulking
slow repetition
of house, silo, fence
framed between the click whirr
of the unraveling
power lines.
Monotone lecture from the land
tells nothing
drawing me to sleep.

Road to Wilmar miles of drifts and sky.
Now sight confined
I burn to see forever
that barren
home.

  Philip Logan Waugh

272

My Dog

White and black, with shades of gray,
Eyes full of expression with much to say.
A coat smooth as silk with hair so fine.
Smaller ears that are coated with white inner line.

The color of your nose is as black as night.
Its wetness is felt by my touch, not sight.

Traveling with speed on legs so small,
Your paws often show the burden of it all.

A smile forms on your face when food is near,
Thanking me with a bark, a howl full of cheer.

People flock to you, to pet and to hug.
You embrace them all with your own precious love.

Four legged creatures, like you, are part of God's plan.
To give to a world of two legs, a helping hand.
A hand in love, which opens and heals
The hurts which two legs find hard to unseal.

Thank you God, for this gift you have given.
This four legged creature, a blessing from heaven.

Boni Locke

Oasis

Long ago he set his sails
Horizon-bound,
Wind his only guide.

Land became a memory
As sea and sky fused to form
A swathe of boundless blue.

The cycling sun wore down his will,
But just when hope would falter,
Horizon broke its endless plane.

A verdant isle it was,
Awash with foliage -
Watercolor painted on a canvas of stone.

He laughed, and as the gulls called greetings
He rowed his way to shore.

Gary Glass

Untitled

The spur of the moment the height of the fall.
The little movement that makes us love all.
The pulling of hate into darkness alive.
The love that allows us to joyfully thrive.
What makes us look over somebody's faults?
The love that makes rude remarks come to a halt?
Is it the knowing that indeed it is bad?
The knowing that this can make somebody sad?
Then what makes us so happy we laugh with glee?
What is the feeling that makes bad feelings flee?
What is the feeling that makes us kind?
Joyfulness, happiness, or love the blind?
I do hope you agree with me,
That it is indeed all three.

Dorothy Van Duyne

Lament

The wish of one born in cold December.
Oh, for balmy eternal June;
Oh, for sunny days at the beach,
With the waves gently lapping the sand;
The low flying glide of the silent gull;
The tide coming swiftly in seashells,
If you could only tell
The secret of the ocean blue.

Opal M. Martin

Spools

From the mind, a deep descent,
To caverns in the tangled night.
Where figures blurred and strangely bent,
Are hung from cobwebs, silk wound tight.

Within the caves the winds do sound,
The breezes keep the silk thread dry.
The twisting of the ones last wound,
Subsiding as the years go by.

The spiders tend the thread with care,
The new cocoons are all secure.
Within, the blurry faces stare,
And will for eons while they cure.

The spiders need more silk to spin,
They hear the babbling of the fools.
The webs are shaken by the din,
The silk forthcoming from the spools.

Ron Rossini

Mindfulness

Snowflakes, suspended in mid-air
Luminescent in the crisp December night
Like elusive fireflies in midsummer
    at desert midnight
    blinking over Mill Creek's perennial song.

Moments of our lives
As the snowflakes, seemingly suspended
Timeless fragments
That fall to earth
Creating a snowbank
    without dimension
While we, distracted, look away.

Snowflakes, one by one
Moments, one by one
Luminescent
Creating the landscape of our lives.

Elaine Velasquez

Darkness

I am dead inside, my feelings and joys are diminished.
There's no telling how soon my outside will take to catch up.
Pain forever resides where my heart use to be, happiness
will never return.
Redemption can never be made for the wrong I have done, for
the pain that I have caused.
Darkness sets over me easily now, sunlight will never shine
in on my blackened soul.
Ruining others lives is what I do best, so why not accept
the gift God has given me with open arms and a warm smile.
Though I am not proud of it, this gift from God has been
used well for its true purpose.
For those I have hurt, I am sorry about the wrong I've
caused in their lives.
The pain I've dealt our will never match the pain that I
continue to feel every day.
My heart of darkness is fading away, it's now my time to
pass on and live eternally in the hell I've created for myself...

Louis Allen Rifesi

Do You Know Me?

I dazzle like the most radiant of gems, yet, without me the most
vibrant color is grey.
My handiwork is fundamental but always intricate.
I have been abused of men and corrupted by humanity.
Although I am blind and I have no form, I will have touched you
at least once.
I can make the truth a lie and a lie the truth, for I am the
master of illusions.
I am reality and pain is my substance, still, I am the beginning
of a new dawning.
You can feel my presence but I cannot be touched.
I am the essence of life itself.
I am Love....!!!

Denise A. Butcher James

Eternity

A misty fog surrounds the future,
with the sun flickering uncertainly in the distance.
It appears too murky, so I dare only enter where the light peaks
    through.
Stepping through cautiously, uncertain of what may be lurking ahead,
I find a path with stepping stones, that seem to appear as I go.

Trodding along sure footed, careful not to fall off the given path,
I make my way through the mist, searching for what lies ahead.
I am teased constantly by smaller less stable stones,
that lure me off in some other uncertain direction.
Always I find my way back.

It seems my path has been crossed by another,
at several different points, braiding its way tighter.
The distance between the intersections are getting smaller,
and I feel as if at anytime I will encounter someone new.
Believing to be on my way to find what lies at the end of the other
    path, I continue on.

Suddenly we spy each other, meeting on the same stone.
As we touch hands, the fog begins to lift.
The sun takes over, illuminating two clear paths side by side,
to the end of eternity.

Katherine Molinari

The Spiraling Mind

Stumble down the broken stairs
From the corner darkness glares
Feel the warm breath on your face
As cold death sets the pace
Sunder your mind and take your power
Blackness grows with every hour
Taste the fear on which to feed
Galloping hard across the plain
In the dust blood falls like rain
Into the void; the center is near
Crumbling under the surmounting fear
Blackness; alone. Lie there and moan.

And when at last the darkness engulfed you, you died.
But as the light dimmed so did the world.
    And when you died you never lived
    All you said and all you did - lost
At the birth of your death
Your first of your death
Your first gasp and your last breath,
As you died you felt so odd
Finally realized that you were God.

Brad Umscheid

The Future

Here lies the time, for which has been undiscovered.
The thought, through which the passage of life has taken.
The future is what yet is to come;
and for many, indecisive is their path.
Sitting, awaiting and predicting, are not the keys;
but our strength pulled forward, with get you far.
The love deep inside each and everyone's heart,
will pull our destiny closer and closer each day.
If you look closely, to what this life has given you;
you will find not only yourself, but who you really are.
The seas surround us, forging us to combine;
and yet separated, we have no where to go.
So we shall go forward in time, to find not only ourselves;
but others, who will give us the strength to carry on.

Dawn Jones

I Want

I want to know what love is
And I want you to show me
I've only experienced pain
I hope that's not how it should be

I want you to open up my insides
But you'll have to find the key
Because pain has locked my heart, and the hurt has taken over me

I want you to show me true love, and I want all the games to end
I want an honest lover
Even more, I want an honest friend

I want you to be my man
I want you to stay true
I want you to control me, and I want to control you too

I want you to be honest
I want you to be strong
I want you to be weak, and admit when you are wrong

I want you to be hard
I want you to be smart
I want you to be soft, so I can trust you with my heart

Melanie Gallop

Mrs. Daisy Isabel King

When I'm in the room of memory I think of Mrs. Daisy King
a woman who was respected and loved by all the people in her
district of Hanover.

Mrs. Daisy King was mixed with Syrian, Indian and Black.
A widow who was mother and father to her seven sons.
Mrs. King gave a helping hand to family and friends by
taking care of their children.

Sis Daisy affectionately called by many was never seen entering
a bar, or wearing pants - she considered it a man's garment.
She never used profane language - it was just not "lady like"
she wasn't a saint, but indeed a lady.

This lady that so many people had grown to love and respect
is my grandmother.

I always remember her favorite saying "do all the good you can,
to all the people you can, in all the ways you can, just as
long as you can."

I never got the chance to know her as well as others. What I
know about her makes me wish I knew more.
Grandma, if you can hear me just remember that I love you.

Sophia M. King

Friends

Friends are special people you
keep inside your heart.
Some you stay in touch with
forever and some just grow apart.
Friends will listen to your problems
and will do anything for you.
Friend will get you out of trouble
and make you happy when you're blue.
Friends will teach you new
things and help you with your math.
Friends will teach you how to
sing and try and make you laugh.
Friends will give you courage to
do the things you've never done.
Friends will turn scary things
into a lot of fun.
Friends will do the weirdest
things that you could ever see.
Friends are very special, especially to me.

Jennifer Williams

United Love

I loved you from the time we met
You made my whole body tingle
For if fate hadn't intervened
I probably would still be single
I love you more every day
And can't keep you out of my sight
Follow you around the house
Or at the store's blue blinking light
Our honeymoon is every day
Not on a special occasion
For a great magnet draw us closer together
Without any added persuasion.

Anthony J. Custer

"Hear Me!"

"Hear me!" I want to scream.
I want them to hear me
   And realize what they have done.
I want them to see my pain
   And recognize the anguish they have caused.
I want them to hear me
   And realize I shall be quiet no longer.
I want them to see me tear out my hair, fallen to my knees
   And recognize the despair they brought into my life.
I want them to hear me sob, eyes burning
   As the tears pour down my cheeks
   And realize my silence is ended here
   And now I want them to hear me
   And realize what they have done.
   "Hear me!" I want to scream.

Michael Cedillos

Sunset Of Love

A colorful sunset with beautiful hues
feelings of warmth begin to ensue.
Radiating into the depth of my heart
expressions of love I give you this art.
Think of these words and feeling you get
when looking upon a certain sunset.

Brian A. Kisner

Job Life

Teacher Tricia. Beautiful grand! With a
new life kicking within. Just like my mama
had been ten times before me - once after
Said, today write us a poem:
   "Your first job for pay"

My first job for pay was when my life began
kicking my mama from within'
Momma hurry! Let me out so we can
see what I'm like and going to do

When she let me out, I started screaming,
   "When do I get paid?"

Ah son, already you're paid for being
so close to me. Hang on and
We will pay you more wherever
far away you may swing

Cecil H. Connell

"Starvation"

Within the wealthy confines of our
Great and mighty nation,
There exists a destructive enemy
Simply known as starvation.

It destroys human life and limbs
With a catastrophic and deadly force,
It causes physical and mental anguish
And all without the slightest remorse.

But with our stocked-piled commodities
And our wealth that is so vast,
We could so very, very, very easily
Make starvation at thing of the past.

For, to help others in house cleaning
And leave theirs with a lustrous sheen,
We must always make sure that our house
Is in order, food-stocked, and clean.

Let's pray to "God" that all great nations
Can get together, plan, and converse,
On any ways to end rampaging starvation
Through out our mighty universe.

Louis L. Williams

The Sea And The Sand

I always will be with no one but me
All alone with the Sea . . . And the Sand
There no one can see . . . All my tears but the Sea
And I know that the Sea understands . . .

By Her smooth pebbled shore
I would walk Evermore
But SHE waves goodbye with a smile
For She knows I'll return
For my strength to the Sea
I'll come back to the warmth
. . . and that smile

Now I've returned to Her side
As Her welcoming tide
Whispers Her wisdom to me
For She too is alone
And Her strength as a Poem
Flows through . . . And once more . . . Exalts me

I leave Her refreshed, As I ever will be
When I walk on the Sand by the Sea

Patricia Rodgers

"Dedicated To Heather"

In the back of my mind rattles the thought,
"Think of tomorrow, but live for today".
Was my life indeed created for naught,
At the whim of the God to whom I pray?

Upon this Earth, what is the goal?
Enlightenment of the brain? Enrichment of the heart?
Where is the Great White, the destination of my soul?
Which appears at the time when my spirit departs?

What can man do, as an insignificant oar?
Tell me God, thou who art at the helm.
Does he have any part in reaching the shore
Of the splendid sea that is Your realm?

Onward, my Lord! Pull closed my curtain.
A smile on my face as I lie cold in the hearse.
For I know one thing, of one thing I am certain.
In the race to Your side, I WILL be first.

Michael Paleos

Chemistry

Four to eleven feet;
(that's my temporal, spiritual height...)
Physically; I'm 5'7"
(With all my might...)
But it's all a matter of Chemistry.
Not a matter of Philosophy, Sociology,
Geometry, Trigonometry, nor totally
Biology... but Chem-istry

Take love, hate - passion, fate.
Intrigue romance - Hap-pen stance..
(It's all a matter of...)

War, peace - the Mid-dle
East ...

Chem-istry

Green A. Blocker Jr.

Angels

An angels love is always there,
When we cry out in despair.
Messengers who are decent
In a heavenly desert
They watch over us and protect,
When we have feelings of neglect.
Through the light they shine, oh so bright.
An energy that surrounds
And gives us love that holds no bounds.
For in this love we reflect
In caring ways a heart that's warm.
Given task to complete without suffering defeat.
We all have the power to love
Given to us from God above,
Let us not suffocate the power from within.
Use this power to connect to an angel
That's been sent, to guide us through
A life that's meant and to receive the things
That are heavenly sent.

Lillian Murphy

Peach

Nothing eats me like a breath of peach;
the incense seeps to regions out of reach
of reason or restraint, in fact they each
give way to sheer desire as I breach
all resolutions to resist
a taste of sweetened sun once kissed
by dryad lips, now mine insist
on peach.

Christine McMillin

Dimension Zero

Welcome to dimension zero;
Where tension zeros;
Level; ground zero;
Around zero there's zero;
Circumference zero;
Three, six, zero;
Three hundred sixty zero;
To many zeros become void;
Which leads to zero;
No heros just zero;
No heros just zero;
Planet zero; rain zero;
Sun zero; moon zero;
One zero makes a zero;
No seconds suspect zero;
Without a zero there is zero;
Without expression we are zero;
We enter dimension one leaving dimension zero;

Jeremy Elliott

The Ultimate Sacrifice

I'm so afraid
What should I do
If in fact you have been made
Please God, don't let this be true.

I don't want you to be
Yet I don't want you to die
But I have to do what's best for me
I only hope you can understand why.

Either way I'll be sad
But I have to pick one
Just please don't think I'm bad
Whoever you are, my daughter or son.

If only wishing helped
I'd wish so very hard
But you have to play the hand you're dealt
Therefore, I must choose to discard.

But no matter what else happens
I promise I'll never forget you
Because you'll stick in my heart like pins
And I'll forever love you!

Stephanie Migacz

Cat Symphony

The ragged can follows the sound
and peeks into the rusted dumpster
ignoring the stench of humanity.

The cat gives a feline grin,
arches its back
and walks off with the man's head in his mouth.

Hair and fur drag on the ground
in a futile effort to wash the dirt
from a place that wears it with pride.

Jason Mical

276

M e

What some only see when they look at me is a human
What some only see when they look at me is a person
What some only see when they look at me is a woman
What some only see when they look at me is a color
What some only see when they look at me is a struggle

Some limit themselves to what they can see
Others have no limit.

When you look at me I hope you see my ambition
When you look at me I hope you see my inspiration
When you look at me I hope you see my personality
When you look at me I hope you see my integrity
When you look at me I hope you see my sensitivity
When you look at me I hope you see my intellect
When you look at me I hope you see my culture
When you look at me I hope you see my uniqueness
When you look at me I hope you see a future

Looking at me from the outside I might seem bland
But from the inside I'm a completely different person

Tiffany Williams

Loss Of A Friend

The days seem long, they all feel the same
Yet many times each day I hear your name.
The friendship we had didn't run very deep
But the smile on your face I will always keep.
In my life and in my mind the funny things you'd say
In my heart and in my soul, your kind words will always stay.
You are in God's haven now, why? I can not understand
But with the faith of His love, you have taken Him by the hand.
To bask in the warmth and glory of His love
You have left our mortal world to join the angels up above.
How very much I miss you, you haunt my thoughts each day
The beauty of your being, why did it end this way?
Tomorrow is a new day, another without you
The days you were in our lives, sadly were too few.
The memories of you in my heart, I always will hold dear
Forever in my life you'll be, I feel your spirit near.
Someday I know I will you see you again
Constant in my memory, in life and soul my friend.

Elaina Lockery

Dream Of Perfection

Thumbing through her magazine, her dream of perfection begins,
compulsive exercise and dieting, soon her obsession sets in.
An airbrushed photo appearance is her ultimate goal,
the sleekness and beauty to make her life whole.
Never liking the image that the mirror reflects,
lose a pound or two more and she'll have no regrets.
Her uneasiness at holidays is outwardly shown,
the thought of fat grams and calories always keep her at home.
Always happy on the outside but dying within,
her continuing battle to be unreasonably thin.
Pushing loved ones away to keep her secret concealed,
fearing her dream would be lost if it were revealed.
The future so bleak and filled with despair,
as obsession grows stronger with each passing year.
While there are children crying from hunger all through the night,
she stares longingly at her plate, never taking a bite.
Her body grows weaker as each day passes by,
wondering how much longer she can keep living this lie.
Thumbing through her magazine, her dream of perfection comes to an end,
baggy clothes and starvation, she can no longer pretend.

Kathleen E. McEachern

This Child

As I look through the window; a child I see
So lost and alone, who can this child be?
Her pain and despair so familiar to me
If only I could help to set this child free
If only I could embrace her and give her a home
To let this child know that she is not alone
It's as if this child simply came from nowhere
Some terrible mistake - no one seems to care
Now here is this child, eyes dark as coal
The pain I see there consumes my soul
I want so desperately to help her, but I can't seem to get through
This child looked up inside, I don't know what she might do
I scream "Someone please help me - help me get through"
"Don't you understand, I don't know what she might do?"
But just like this child - no one hears no one sees - now I feel her
    pain too and it paralyzes me
Then this child turn toward me - our eyes finally meet - reality
    consumes me - knocks me off of my feet
Now I understand as I look deep in those eyes; we've known each other
    all of our lives
That's why I can't get through this window you see
It's a mirror not a window and this child is me
Still no one hears - no one sees - this child crying out - this child
    is me.

Judith A. Mason

Thoughts From Within

Walking around this yard of mine,
thinking of moments long past in time.
Oh how I wish I could do again;
different I would be to my fellow men.
To right the wrongs and correct the mistakes.
Towards all the people I once forsake.

Because of my past, I dwell in the future.
What will it hold, who will I be?
Where is she now, will she wait for me?
These things plague my mind, always twisted and intertwined.
Day to day, night to night thinking of then feeling contrite

I'm on a collision course to hell,
Where for eternity my soul will dwell.
There is a light I've heard about,
but in my mind I have much doubt.
Is it around me? I just can not see.
Is it within me; How can that be?

I only know but one thing.
One day far from now, my time will end, I don't know how.
Then I'll see what was to be, and finally my soul will be free.

Steven Young

Abtruse

Little drops,
fall up again as before
they form little pools of water
with a steadiness I can't ignore.
My attention drifts away
to games we used to play,
I look upon your face
and remember the place
where we first embraced.
Sounds of your joy I can recall
walls of steel in my six walled ball,
drips of tears fall from the floor,
they fall for you straight from my core.
For you this life I'll leave
Love laced with deaths taste
a life gone a worlds laughter
but I'll wait for you
in my rainy chamber.

Marlo Twitchell

277

Baby's Soul

Like trees swaying gently, a howl through the night,
A baby's cry so soft, softer than moonlight,
The skin so smooth, the eyes so blue,
The baby's so happy-happy and new.

Like a newborn child, all warm and loved,
Being held so securely in his mommy's arms above,
The sound of silence roams the room,
The baby is sleeping for an hour or two.

The mommy is wakened, the baby is playing,
The daddy has left and she is praying,
"Oh God please help me make it through the night,
The baby won't sleep and I'm in a fright."

The morning has come and baby's in bed,
The mommy is crying 'cause baby is dead,
Mommy's arrested and thrown in jail,
The face on the baby is so small and so pale.

They lay the baby down to rest,
The baby is happy - God says it was for the best.

Sandra Denser

Christmas At Dawn

Darkness disappears
   At dawn;
Stars fade into oblivion;
Things of earth take shape;
Lights go out in the village
   At dawn;
Birds begin their flight;
Clouds, puffy wisps, float by;
Colors develop into blue and pink
   At dawn;
Your name is legible in the stone, my son;
Dawn to dusk as life to death,
Temporal to eternal;
It all becomes clear
   At dawn;
Another day breaks open;
The day of Christ's birth,
   This dawn;
The dawn of another life, another dimension,
For you. Forever? Yes, my child, forever.

Dorrie Santorelli

Lovesong In Spring

I stepped aside as we passed in the park,
I deep thoughts thinking, you on a lark.
Tangled hair flying, teeth all in-braced,
Make-up dabbed on, eyelashes misplaced.
Budding breasts outlined against faded brown shirt,
Deep dimple showing, 'neath streaky black dirt.
"Hey, wait for me," you yelled to a friend.
My bewildered heart answered, " a miracle send."
God granted His grace, spread out on a star.
With you, I am... With me, you are.
Both free to explore the universe unknown,
The bud of a flower, earth's prism hued throne.
Search inside a cocoon, sense a hummingbird's breath,
Find freedom forever, and love unto death.

Merril Berg

Non Verbal

To speak the words I can not say
A verbal promise for another day
But words I can give you with all my heart
A promise a beginning a brand new start

For safe I have found a place in your arms
A haven of peace from all of life's harms
Someone who'll love me for all that I'll be
Someone who loves me for just being me

Different in ways many and few
Together content when hearts beating two
Words that you've said soft and sincere
Help to belay some of the fear

I'm cautious in how I let my heart live
But now I can say my Love I do give

Sheri Stewart

Celestial Utterance

She sings to them.
Expressionless God fearing souls,
uncomprehending to what alludes their eyes.
Her voice, soft yet fierce, escapes them.
Frustration spills a drop down her flawless cheek,
flooding her throat with silence.
The quiet perceived as a calm
in the raging storm behind her words.
Synchronized applause erupts,
filling the moment void of sound.
Exploiting her futile efforts to reach them.
They wouldn't listen,
indifference conquering her gentle plea.
They couldn't witness,
irresolute of her blinding purity.
Afflicted memories dismissed
the melody she wove with golden light.
Their thoughts fading into that silence,
Erased the impression of her angelic song

Mary Beth Sanders

Waking Autumn

Dawn drifts into the dark arbor
Gliding golden rays through dark foliage
Igniting crimson, tangerine and sulphur
Burning through the cold dewy blue

Boreas blows the night's grey fronds
Billowing Dawn's consuming fire
Pushing her dancing rays through knotted branches
Sucking her to the charcoal floor

Gaea grasps at Dawn's sweet beacon
Thawing the silver frosted grass
Waking the bluebird and diligent squirrel
Warming sleeping chrysanthemums

Tethys twinkles in early light
Magnifying aurora's strength
Reflecting Dawn's life in shimmering mosaics
Bending her rays to sunken depths

Dawn dances among silver clouds
Brightening pavonian skies
Blossoming into meridian's brilliance
Relinquishing to Helios

Kerri Brannan

A God Of Grace

And surely, O God, Your grace amazes all,
But none so much as me my sinful self;
For I have known the height of Adam's Fall,
Traversed the wicked clouds of Hades' depth;
Yet even in my dark and willing sin
You kept me from the Devil's Dark Edge
Where spirits of demons lay in wait of men
To pummel them, and then to take their heads.
But why will demons curse my steps and flee,
If not because You came to die for me?
To think of it I quiver in my soul;
To understand I'll praise You for Your grace—
A grace that's oceans deep and bodies full
And lacking nothing, not height, nor depth, nor space,
But pure in presence, and perfect in its form—
Eternally present, and presently warm!

Chad E. Brown

Bleed Red

A country built on freedom
A land we'll fight for in war
the people here make the melting-pot
mixed people together rich and poor.

The U.S. abolished slavery
yet we discriminate against one another
we still have fights over land
with our many Indian Brothers.

With all our Ethnic backgrounds
together on our land
it would be nice to come together
and join each others hand.

We've battled so long to gain
a mutual respect for our kin
it's a Battle that for some
is one we'll never win.

We all bleed red and live
with the ones we love.
To make our country strong
and free needs and a sense of, American love.

Dan Gnadt

My Mother

   Another day has come and gone. I
go to bed tired and weary, and think of things just past.
The happy time with laughter, and tears
of joy running down my cheeks,-while
facing my Mother, maybe for the last time.
I thank God for this day for I saw
that my Mother loved me as I do her-
As I once again said good bye with a
hug and kiss. She patted me as if I were still
a little girl, and told me to be careful and take
care of myself.
   I hope and pray that there will be
another day, for Mother and me.
   But if not, I will treasure her the
same way, as she will always be in
my heart

Yvonne Waterman

Fall

A leaf falls from a tree,
a symbol that is very important to me.
Geese fly over head,
while a bear lies down for bed.
For many animals it is time for a long rest,
for others a time to leave the nest.
A cold wind whips the air,
thousands of leaves soar here and there.
The sky is a strange orange color,
red and yellow are some others.
This is the greatest season of all,
Fall

Eric Cosselman

Apple Trees

Apple trees and wounded knees
Clear blue skies, the summers breeze.
Fairy tales in the afternoon,
Lazy days gone, oh to soon.

By the shore at the beach,
Coral and shells at my reach.
Rippling waters, I do know,
Roll on forever, to and fro.

When I was young I used to think,
Of hot summer days and lemonade made pink.
For it is said these memories are few,
I still remember them all, as if they were new.

The stars shine bright against the soft moon glow,
Time for bed, I must go.
For then in my dreams I do find,
The apple trees I have left behind.

Paul V. Przybyl

Christmas Eve

The warmth of family coming together,
the pleasure of seeing those who are part of us,
the comfort of a childhood shared
envelop me on Christmas Eve.

We gather one night a year
in kinship and caring,
reminiscing on the years and happenings gone by
and seeing each other in the faces of our children.

This ritual of joining and enfolding
is not for ourselves alone,
but for parents, grandparents and children.
Those who came before and those who are coming after.

Honoring the ones who taught us the meaning of family
through their devotion and love.
Passing the legacy to our children,
keeping strong the ties of blood.

Lynn Hauser

A Christmas Wish For All To Hear

On this hectic holiday with Yuletide joy
   Some children lose the meaning, and it's not about a toy
It's about a baby, a small baby boy
   Who came to this earth to give us much joy
So I plead with you, on this Christmas day
   To give us a reason, to give us a way
To bring some old clothes to your local retreat
   And many hopeful children will crowd around your feet
Needing and wanting nothing more
   To be your friend, or to be your benefactor.

Timothy Rodney

His Best Friend (The Beginning And The End)

"I'm a man," he says; and his point to make
His first cigarette he'll proudly take
And then it becomes his best friend.

"I'm a man," he says; and throughout his life
Through all the worry and the strife
His smokes mean more to him than his wife
How could she replace his best friend?

"I'm a man," he says; though a wracking cough
Tells him his body has had enough
Tells him that breathing is getting tough
But he can't give up his best friend.

"I'm a man," he says; but his lungs can't get air
He spends all his time in an easy chair
The oxygen tank is within reach there
And he's had to give up his best friend.

"I'm a man," he says; but his heart says, "No,
I've had too much work, and just can't go
So I'll slow and slow, and then go no more
And you can thank your best friend."

Joanne V. Eoff

We The People

Skin dries, wrinkles, cracks
Eyes fail to reflect-grow dull.
Muscles, nerves, blood, bone
Food-be theirs or to a sifting dust.

Looks upon wonders, aches life's throbs
Known bitter disappointments-gives loyalty instead.
Let laughter sorrow, plant and water
Food-trust trustworthy or beat useless disgust.

A mining-machine medical study in wonder
It blunders-then learns balance with others.
A gift given not for ego wallowing-of service
Food-must seek progress or canker in rust.

It cries for homage in a healthy body, one that knows
Only when faith sleeps-may the thief enter.
Ever in hopeful risks, never to lose itself
Food-O' honesty! Where Art Thou?

Jay Taylor

Ceremony Of Innocence

Stars glisten and become transients,
Not in a nocturnal sky but atop ocean crests
As vast as Creation's ability to conceive infinity.

One "star" rides a frothy wave, free-spirited to shore—
Its destiny? A ray a light for a sojourner new to this land.
Another beam couples with a sister to become eyes
   for an aged figure...lost in Time.
Like a butterfly, one perches on the thumbs of a babe,
   who issues forth gurgles of glee at its presence there.
Dancing like lovers at a disco,
   Several meld to become harbingers of Spring
   to a winter person whose weary soul embodies no hope.
Others, obviously child-stars,
   dart from spume-tip to spume-tip, playing leap-star;
None ever reaches shore; each is thrown, Sisyphus-like,
   into a larger, more-consuming wave.
A special threesome, going they know not where,
   Form a holy triad and hover protectively above a stable.

Day's delights are enfolded by Moon's maternity.
The ceremony of innocence has come of age.

Carol F. Heskett

Sunshine

Something about the rain,
It is holy.
It is a dream about to happen,
A nightmare just awoken from.
It has an inconstant depth, a hollow knowledge
That silences the leaves. It speaks in heavenly rhythm
For only a brief moment in time.
From a droplet to a deluge, it plunges,
Whispering to someone, somewhere,
Who needs to hear its voice.
It leaves behind only a memory
Which will evaporate into thin air,
A reminder of where it once was,
Where it shall once be again,
Whispering to someone, somewhere,
Who needs to hear its voice.

Kevin Herchen

Day By Day

If you live your life day by day
It could be great in every way;

To live as if today is your last,
Will help you forget the past;

'Cause you're living for today,
And nothing can get in your way;

Of making every second count,
With kindness in the up most amount;

So you're smiling, giving, and sharing,
For all those who were so caring;

And for all those with an attitude,
You'll give hope for a better mood;

So if one day was all we had,
We'd thank God, and not be bad;

For life is precious to all,
And day by day should be a ball.

Jennie J. Chapman

Broken Roses In Swollen Hands

Frozen
blood red
You were thrived on the dirt of this world
but I plucked you put in a rusted vase
and you have been wilting of late

Soiled my hands with blood and messy life
I should have let you be: Buried
But the delicate petals against the broken glass and mud
shattered my resolve

You die
and I too
And there is no consolation in the pleasure of dying
or breathing
anymore

Justin Blarr

280

Truth

What is truth?
The meaning given to children that we've taught
Correctness, sincerity and the need for authentic proof -
I, personally, think not.

What has been learned by this growing of age
Is the need for deceit, deception and sham
A crooked idea that what they set to page
Should by their truth mislead their fellow man.

And we, as elders, hide behind false accuracy
Unsuspecting, we believe in our credulity
Teaching on without ever knowing that in our infallibility
We have taught a corrupted truth of honesty.

Eldon A. Callaway

I'll Remember (1980-1995)

Megan I'll always remember the times we shared,
The good times, the bad times, and the times in between.
I'll remember all the things we did together,
Especially when we'd get in trouble for them.
All the walks we took and just ended up somewhere,
All the rides we went on,
All the pools we swam in.
I'll never forget the many times at the beach.
You and me,
Me and you.
I'll remember how we wanted to become famous together.
How we were going to buy a big house and throw parties every night.
Megan, when you came into this world became a big part of my life.
And when you left this world you took away that big piece and
left my heart destroyed.
You'll be remembered and loved by everyone,
But out of everyone,
I'll love and remember you the most.

Nicole Cote

Lay Her Down To Sleep

Insanity is said, to repeat your actions, and expect a different result.
So when your love, for him is shunned, why don't you rise and bolt?
Bolt for the door, get out of the house! He doesn't love you,
 never the spouse.
The colors of red, black and blue, are only the colors he sees for you.
Hit with accusations, his reactions to tell.
Was a promise broken to keep.
So when he hit and the hammer fell,
Then he'd lay her down to sleep.
His temper flares, and hands begin to fly,
Between her tears she apologizes
With her actions claims the fault, still just living inside the lie.
That's all it is, it's just a lie.
Mentally dead and emotionally dry.
Never man of the house, he breaks all the rules
King of the castle, in a house of fools.
Then one day, nighttime fell, this time he won't touch her.
All that was right, all but just left.
And before her hand was the trigger.
Hit with accusations, his reactions to tell
Was a promise, broken to keep.
So when she cocked and the hammer fell....

Duncan M. Bryan

From The Eagles Eyes

The state of our nation, as seen from the eagles eye
The spirit of our fore fathers he carries, wings dampened
 from the tears they cry

Gone are the buffalo, that once covered the plains
Memories of their masses, is all that remains

Windows barred, doors bolted, everything stolen from its place
The "Stars and Stripes" burned, whats happened to Amazing grace

The fear of trust, gunshots fill the air
Fighting in our streets, homeless people everywhere

A broken home, for the "Brave and the Free"
The big white house hides corruption, in its democracy

A thief is prowling, a dollar could cost you your life
No room in our prisons, for the madman who just raped your wife

So many years of defacing this great land
For "America the beautiful," do we no longer stand?

Alone and forgotten, hungry are the old
Helpless to their burden, as the years of their labor unfolds

Structures may not be worthy, but the foundation remains
Wake up America! It's time to rebuild and
give "Oh Glory" back her good name

William Harney III

Desert Storms

I'm walking through a desert storm not knowing where I am.
I take a glance through burned and puffed out eyes.
To take a look at what's ahead for I fear I shall die.

A desert storm has been chasing me,
all the way from no man's land.
For when I dare to open my eyes,
a gust of wind and sand blows sand till I am blind.

I crawl behind the rocks, where the snakes come out to bite,
and tried to hide under my blanket that the wind taught to fly.
My camel is weak so I will leave it here, upon this silky hot bed,
for I have far to go before I escape this aweful wind...
And I haven't long before I die.

Reva Morgan Brandt

Simplistic Pen

My mind thinks through a simplistic pen
Another may not; mine may still
Senseless mumbo-jumbo can not be described
I pity the one who reads my works
For they are dry and bland
Vigor and life has long escapes my mind
The pleasures of the past
Somewhat out weighed by the pain of now
Ecstacy is escaped
Mention me not; for the purpose has long escaped me
Some say worthless; others senseless
But I question them not
For they claim to be wise and well versed
And I claim not
Little am I to communicate with
Easy am I to speak with
For I speak with a simplistic pen.

Chris R. Andrews

Christmas Died, Oh Tina Dear

Winter has started, Christmas is near,
And he kept Christmas all the year.

Some saw him as different, they saw him as queer,
But his heart was of the hollys' cheer.

It came that day, at winter's start,
He lost a love, became cold of heart.

She told him that day, her love was not,
That is why, he is cold of heart.

He keeps Christmas not, from that time,
He says; "I am lost, she is never to be mine."

Oh Tina Dear, it was not known,
It was for you, he kept Christmas alone.

Oh Tina Dear, you did not know
For you have killed christmas -

He, Christmas, Died Alone...

Terrance Reilly

Wilting

I stand, I stand, rage rushing through my blood.
I turn, I turn, and go as fast as I can run.
There is pain I can't describe,
so I have to run and hide,
and there's one thing I can't decide,
is the real?

I run, I run, thoughts flashing in my mind.
I stop, I stop, is there something I cannot find?
Is this just a fantasy?
Where you and me are make believe?
Or is it that I just can't see,
am I blind?

I stare, I stare, tears forming in my eyes.
I fall, I fall, wondering how I can survive.
I don't know how I can arise,
and stare into those big brown eyes.
How can there be so many lies?
I don't know.
I don't know.

Sara Belding

Untitled

The shallow shades of those pools of blue
run deep in my heart. I am confused.
The fallow vein of barren ground
bears me naught. I am alone.
The sunburn red of the clockwork boy
is clouding my vision. I am ablaze.
Yet the soft brown warmth that is set in your touch
has found the truth. My depth has no equal.
And the cool green sighs that waft down like a feather
are touching my soul. My love is unsung.
For the sweet, sweet sound of my soul crying out,
And the long lost shepherd that longs to be near me,
These things above all. I have found in my life, none worthy.
I have found in my life, none blameless.
I have found in my life, none true.
I have found in my life, none just.
And yet perfection is all that you show me.
Everything is Everything.
Your world, can exist, no other way.

Alan Wesson

"For Angels Never Die"

On that day of the bombing, when many Loved Ones died,
    There were Angels quietly watching, as many people cried.

Those Angels looked toward Heaven and said: "Lord what shall we do?"
    He told all his Angels, "Bring them to me, with you!"

The Souls Left with the Angels, long before the last breaths,
    For Souls leave the body, I believe, before the deaths.

These times make us sad, we can't understand, we ask Why?....
    But if we could see in Heaven, we might see them passing by.

We could maybe see our Loved One's, with a glowing, happy face,
    To tell us of the New Home they have, such a Beautiful Place.

They would ask us to be happy for them, to try to know somehow,
    That they are Angels now.

They would tell us not to cry for them, to try to be happy instead,
    Because as an Angel...they will never be dead.

Remember, they are with you always, in your heart and at your side,
this isn't good-bye...
"For Angels Never Die."

Becky Chambers

Drifting on a Memory

Drifting on a memory, into a misty blue
my thoughts and memories, are all of you
for I remember back, to the times we did share
together at the beach, shopping and walking everywhere
with no destination exactly in mind
it was just so that we could spend the time
to talk and laugh, even sometimes cry
Oh! mi abuelita, te quiero mucho, why must I say goodbye
I know in my heart, where you're at there's no more pain
but, yet still my tear's seem to flow like rain
from the inner chamber of my heart, so deep within
my love for you will flourish, until my time's end
so hold on grandma, please wait for me
for one day we'll be reunited, just wait and see
there in heaven, together side by side
just like before, just like old times
so thus I lift my head high to the sky
and drift in your memory, with tears in my eyes
for you've found eternal peace, por vida, y siempre
may you forever rest in peace, in loving memory

Daniel Stark

Bryan

You say you the feel the sun's warmth tenfold.
Every rain is a thunderstorm.
The drums beat a little stronger.
Blood courses much faster.
Hues collide coupling with blinding light.
Muffled voices, sharpened noises. Cloaked
In your shroud of scented leaves and magic dust, you feel alive!
A phantom — nothing no one can touch.

Do I dare share with you my reality
Where greater pains exist than a needle's kiss?
I live like the man scorned by the Gods,
Pushing an unsympathetic boulder up a fog-obscured hill,
Rising higher and higher towards the summit
Only to achieve a flicker of triumph — nothing more.

What can I offer you?
Only a flock of birds cleaving the heavens in unison,
Gilded dandelions at home in a crevice,
Blades of grass dancing to the inaudible melody of the wind,
Peace...freedom...during moments unforeseen.

The choice is up to you.

Flordeliza Alagao

Mother Dearest

I love to hear her laughter
even if it's a short while
I love it when she gives me
that great, big, beautiful smile

I hate to see her frowning, and I hate to see her cry
I wish that I could help her
if only I knew why?

I love to see her feeling high
instead of feeling low
I love to see her beautiful eyes
shine with an amazing glow

I'm talking from the heart
and letting my feelings flow
I want this special woman, to know I love her so

Through all the good times
and all the bad, even if I'm angry
or hurt and sad

I'll always love this woman
for she's like no other
this woman is unique, this woman is my MOTHER
Olga Caballero

Tribute To A Step-Dad

You never held me on your knee,
Nor sailed a kite or chased with glee;
We didn't have tea parties, play with dolls
Nor hold through nightmares, nor kiss the falls.

These are some things a dad should be,
But you are much more than this to me;
You weren't there in my early years;
Yet, you've always tried to dry my tears.

Throughout this time I've spent with you,
You always knew the right thing to do;
A quiet smile, a tender embrace,
Helped me my problems to daily face.

You're kind, gentle, loving and wise,
Your dumb jokes make my spirits rise;
Whenever I've been very sad,
I've been blessed with this special dad.

Since I've been blessed seven times seven,
I send much love directly from Heaven
For God in His mercy knew what to do,
When He sent me someone as great as you.
Alice J. Smith

Winters Teachings

A rose grew outside my window one day.
Its red petals unfolded as it bloomed
Softly calling to me from where I lay
While its scent flowed freely into my room.

Passing neighbors stopped to admire it
Forgetting they had other things to do.
From my open window I could watch and sit.
Its tall stance outside was a perfect view.

Mother nature stepped in then with her cold
Causing painful echoes of helpless cries.
Where once there was great beauty to behold
Cut short of life, an empty stem now lies.

All because that's what winter demanded.
Choiceless, it died as it was commanded.
Traci Portugal

Marvin Tate

Marvin Tate,
   The King of Real Estate,
      Served as Bryan's City Magistrate.

Your service years were ten,
   taking time from your kin.

Reading with a school boy,
   brings you fulfilling joy.

Raising funds for charity,
   makes you a rarity.

No stranger do you know,
   you made this community grow.

When playing golf, you score an eagle;
   the dog you love is not a beagle.

I have seen you two-stepping with Cindy,
   on a day not too windy.

Marvin Tate,
   The King of Real Estate,
      You made a fantastic City Magistrate.

You have had a memorable past;
   I hope your future is a blast!
Patsy Lee Montana

Memories

   Pictures cover my table.
Photographs that hold memories of my past.
Memories, that I carry with me,
wherever I should go.
Memories mean so much to me,
moments of long ago.
Memories that I carry with me,
wherever I should go.
Memories, Memories mean so much to me.
Memories, of long ago.
Emma Diebold

"Words"

Words spoken... in the heat of anger,
Puts your heart... in needles danger.
Seldom do you say... what's truly in your heart,
Instead, you use words... that rips you apart.
Words of companionship, romance and love,
Are replaced, with the things... that hate comes from.
Then without a whisper... your temper is gone,
And for those that you have hurt... your heart so longs.
The hurt is so great... that's impossible to just forget,
But, you must try... or you'll always have regrets.
Love can lift you... from the flames of hell,
But, not until that special person... you do tell.
All of those plans... and treasured memories,
Are gone... washed away... and there are no remedies.
Numbers can not count... the number of hearts lost,
Because of words... thrown in anger,... at such a terrible cost.
But, if love has saved... just one heart... like yours,
Think of the possibilities... for this world of ours.
No more war... hate... or mass destruction,
Just a lot of love... a vital human function.
Earl Edwin Gobel III

"Child Of Mine"

Oh child of mine forever
How long will it take for you to discover
That things of this world can never
satisfy your longing, ever.

Your only peace of mind
Or any other kind
Can only come from God above
When you can accept his love.

All the things of this earth
Will be of little worth
Only in Jesus the Son
Can this search of yours be won.

When you are searching near and far
And never finding who you are
You are looking not above
To find your one true love.

So keep on searching out my dear
The one who will draw you near
And prove to you He's the best
Then you can at last, be at rest.

Edna Lindahl

Remains

No one knows the reasons why I let the dream go,
but the promises all remain.

I guess it doesn't matter what I say,
you'll still act the way you did that other day.

And now I just can't stay here anymore,
every smile just reminds me of the make believe;
that we never needed anything else but this.

But now it doesn't matter what I do
Because I'll never really get inside of you.
I just can't hold my tears the way you do.
And every time I try to hold on to my happiness,
as fast as I can reach, it's running out the door.
And I have to say goodbye.

It doesn't matter what I say...I just can't stay here anyway,
every forced smile just reminds me of the make believe;
that we never needed anything but this.

Every moment of pure bliss took me straight to heaven
now it's all broken promises.
But the memories all remain, the dream still stays the same.

Shelby Newhouse

A Tribute To My Husband

Long ago a friend did say,
  Whenever things are not O.K.
   Look at trouble, prepare to fight,
    Straighten up and then fly right.

For over fifty years we tried,
  My love and I. We laughed and cried,
   Then suddenly I cried alone,
    For he had left for another zone.

The days and nights still come and go,
  The rains still fall, the winds still blow.
   The earth still goes around and 'round,
    But my world now is upside down,

For part of me has slipped away,
  Never to return another day,
   I touch his face in the moonlight beam,
    And then I wake up from my dream.

Sarah Martemucci

Do Things That Have Never Been Done Before

I want to do things that have never been done before
For I want to live forever,
be famous, touch the sky,
fall through a cloud,
and do things that have never been done before.

I want to fly with the eagles,
swim with the whales,
I want to eat with the dinosaurs,
play with the lizards,
and do things that have never been done before.

I want to have a career, a family,
I want to know God and
know my true father
and do things that have never been done before.

I want to have a day with the Indians,
touch the stars,
hug the moon,
and do things that have never been done before.

Jessica Fassas

The Oils Of Life

The old wagon creaks noisily by, the wheels
moaning for grease, begging for lubricant.

Unoiled lives are much the same.
They run hard, with great complaining.
They are known by their lamentations, murmurings,
and the friction with which they function.

Like oil for machines, there is a lubricant
for our lives. If applied we would run smoother.

The oil is a mixture of kindness, patience,
thoughtfulness, and consideration.
These all should go into the heart, working out
from there, making daily life run smoothly.
If used rarely or merely applied to the tongue,
it will last for a short while only, and when soon
worn off be just as squeaky as before.

But if the kindness gets into your heart
it will come out in words and actions
until it is a continual blessing in the
household or workplace.

Arwyn Emhof

The Crooked Rose

As I looked up and away from my thoughts,
I saw through the veils of untruths.
Seated were you beside the crooked rose,
upon your visage a rapturous hue.

So gentle a caress touched your hair, your cheek,
with persuasion thus, an errant breeze did forth come.
In vain it sought to sway your thoughts,
your reverence to be undone.

Yet unwavering did your gaze remain,
and not a tendril blew astray.
In humility it bowed before you,
and by your feet for eternity did lay.

And by your hand I saw the rose,
its constant search long last at end.
Away from the thorned and crooked path of past,
straining upward, it would achieve heavenly ascent.

When perfumed whispers it softly spoke,
ambrosia filled my soul.
And as before me the rose bloomed anew,
through parted veils I saw that I was you.

Jasjit Kaur Gabri

Window Sweat

Window gazing
window thinking 'bout love
(it happens time to time)
window sweating
like a lover losing to the cold outside.
Window turning back the pages
window re-evaluating wrongs
   and rights

there's a heart that's sweating
from the warmth lying deep as the soul it ties,
there's a love that's searching for something much more
than nightsuponights
it isn't cold—
it's just not into leaving 'cause the love was a lie.

Could I believe in you?
Could you be into me,
would it satisfy all of your dreaming?

I'm getting into you,
you're seeping into me
there's a shadow in the window, dripping you . . .

   Edward Curlee

Bob Knight

Perceived as a wonder coach and a dictator.
A misty-eyed tequila mocking bird.
A sassy and exhilarating,
Unique blend of spontaneity.
A chair throwing lunatic.
A dazzling, innovative,
Son-kicking, head butting general.
Admirably unrestrained.
He sure knows how to make or break a crowd.

   Mike Luginbill

Beneath The Shadow Of His Wing

The dark clouds may gather-
And the thunder may roar;
But my soul stands firm-
And on the wind of faith it soars;
High above the storm-
Where all my hopes do cling-
As I rest beneath the shadow of His wing,

There are times I've been alone-
And there are times I had to cry;
Sometimes I have been tested by fire-
And I didn't know the reason why-
But I remain faithful;
Because I know God knows everything-
I have found peace and contentment-
Beneath the shadow of His Wing.

   Zeola J. Barlow

Family

Family
is a group of people that live happily.
They stick through times that are rough,
struggle through the tough,
but still enjoy the good times.
They work together
and love each other.
Their love
is as pure as a white dove.
That is my family.

   Stephanie Hanes

The Hole

I am a Hole
distant, and alone
I am filled with remorse and confusion
I don't know which way to turn
I am trapped
hopeless, helpless, hostel
The deeper I am dug the deeper the pain
pierces into my heart
My soul is drained of love and replenished
with neglect and disgust
As time passes, the light of hope begins to
seep through my hole hope of change
I no longer feel deserted and trapped
pretty soon my hole is dark no more
I am surrounded by the yellow warmth of the sun
I feel peaceful secure
The color of yellow is a blanket that covers me with warmth and peace
as long as I have this blanket around my soul I feel safe
I am complete, confident, content
I am whole again

   Jamie Zappan

World Of Despair

Have you ever been trapped inside a world of your own?
Where your mind and heart in two parts are torn.
Where only darkness and gloomy skies prevail and only the
Lonely hearts that's ship wrecked may sail.
Haven't you heard, or don't you care,
That this world of doom anyone can share?
It only takes a broken heart, a path that's lost or a mind
That's torn apart.
Who, can rescue these struggling souls, to bring them back
And make them whole.
Only love, trueness and peace can bring them around the
Happiness they seek.
Never to be trapped in the world of despair, but to
Have freedom of joy for they know God cares.

   Juanita Byrd

"My Anger is a Fountain"

My anger is a fountain
it bubbles from within

It's darkness is a state of mind
with which I cannot win

The rumble of a mighty thunder
rolls inside my soul

This kinesthetic plague intact
creates an empty hole

And in that hole I'll fall to death
where evil satan lay

For anger is a wanton friend
my being it betrays

   Stacia Jo Mullen

Autumn . . . What A Change!

Autumn's the time when summer's
air goes away and frost begins to bloom

Autumn's the time when leaves
loose their pigment and turn scenic colors

Autumn's the time of changing
from sunny to chilly
without notice

Oh . . . Autumn . . .
   What a change!

   Laura Oberne

Sweet Goodbyes

Mild the sky, how pale the blue
The sea it jumps, it shines for you
Silence my dear, listen to the sea
It plays a gentle song solely for thee

A song of hope and disaster few
Blessed are those who see what you do
The shine of tide and whisper of dew
Never will these things amount to more than you

I love you dearly my sweet love
The wishes of a star have granted above
That you fulfill my dying wish
A true love so that I will miss

Mourn not me in my passing
Remember my words of true love everlasting
Live on my sweet and know
　　That you must let me go...

　　Melissa Smith

You

A wondrous rose
Its petals so glossy and pretty
So thick and firm it has no pity.
Bright with a smile
That flower grows and grows,
Beautifying every moment
I look at it, touch its silky clothes.
I rub my finger down the stem
That I can't help but love,
But with sheer surprise
It causes me pain
That love thorn
And who's to blame?
My finger bleeds
Drops on the ground
The rose also falls
But it will be found
Naked on the concrete
Will you please pick it up, remove the pain
Patch me up and kiss me again.

　　Jennifer Ellinger

Awakening

I used to worry of times ahead;
would all go right? I fretted long.
But then I learned to worry not;
Live day by day, as in the song.

My stomach churned so often then,
I drove myself for glory's sake.
Achievement was my motto when
No other balm my lust could slake.

But inner peace I never felt
While troubled over future days,
Till one day hard my world did crash
And melted from my eyes their glaze.

For now I see the truth that lies
In fearing not the days to come:
Though strive you should for future good,
A waste it is to fear an unseen sun.

　　Stephen R. Marks

Finally

I couldn't believe what I heard
the news was so absurd
world peace, peace between the Nations
no more bombing of Haitians
could this be the twilight zone
only once before we've had a peace full tone
what's this going on here
I have no fear
Ireland as one
Now they can concentrate on fun
what is this now
"wake up, wake up you're late for school"
Man I was such a fool
I should have known that peace was but a dream
AKA a Mad Man's Scheme...

　　Garrett J. Seiple

Angel's Cake

I got a cake for my birthday.
It arrived just after midnight.
He wanted to be first with his wishes,
To send me his love and some happiness
And tell me everything would be all right.

The cake was big, twice as big as normal
And yellow, my favorite kind.
It was frosted in white butter cream
And the smell, the smell was delicious
Fresh baked, from scratch, the best kind.

To make up for all of the birthdays,
When he'd call but it wasn't just right.
"Awfully busy just now, your gift will be late."
But the thought was all that I needed,
Perhaps all I felt I deserved.

I got a cake for my birthday.
The smell was so strong, it woke me.
It lit up the room, than was gone.
You see my son is an angel,
But his caring and love lingers on.

　　Natalie A. Alberto

"Inverted Circle"

An isolate stare through transparent promises
suspended inside tainted bubbles
faintly splash into jaded teardrops
broken mirrors reflect vague shadows
as black lace cascades over silent memories
penetrating flashes emanate the precious truth
that's been captured in a chasm of echoes
simple whispers pierce the invisible secrets
this moment so filled with significance
inverts the circle
though symbolic silence dissolves
emptiness still lingers
and time listens intensely for progression

　　Sharon Rose

Wonders

Wonders. Who is that, that wonders?
Wonders are dreams, wonders are thoughts,
Wonders are views of very, very many hearts.
Day and night, night and day
Wonders are with you in very many ways.
A wonder is your conscience telling you right from wrong
Wonders help you make up a poem or a song.
Wonders tell you of the adventure ahead,
And more new things when you dream in bed.

　　Cheryl Chambers

Tell Me Sea?

Tell me sea, if you could talk.
What makes you free to move and rock?
Do you ask permission to make all that noise?
Are you sometimes naughty, like some girls and boys?
Do you spill your water, when there's company around?
Do you have a department for lost and found?
Do you ever get tired of the taste of salt?
Have you ever desired a chocolate malt?
Do you mind all those animal taking a bath?
What's your opinion of pollution and trash?
Are there really monsters in the dark and the deep
And when night time comes, do you go to sleep?

Virginia Chapman Pielke

Since You Are Now Gone

I can still remember that afternoon
the overcast fall sky and the thick humidity lingering.
The sun seemed to set very early,
How early, I still ponder.

The rain gently sprinkled the brown dead grass,
like the tears which fell silently down my face.
The day wasn't gloomy at dawn; the darkness
fell when we went to retrieve you.

My faith fell like the orange fireball in the sky;
My anger competing with its heat.
God and demons cannot touch me now, for they
are responsible for my loss.

Hatred permeates from my flesh, burning anything
which tries to get close to me.
My anger ends and replaced by loneliness.

Why did you choose to leave me that afternoon?
What made you choose to cross that bridge?
Was the reason me?

The answers I will never know,
since you are now gone.

Ruth Wallek

Dead Of Winter

Under the outstretched arms of the weeping willow,
finger-like branches sweep the ground casting spindly shadows.
I'm reminded by the delicate leaves draping the firm earth
around me that it will soon be winter.

My trips to the old willow soon to be halted
by the bluster of Jack Frost and his companions,
chilling the breeze and blanketing the forest with snow.
I will miss the gentle listener who never ignores
or disagrees only comforts.

Watching my breath as it freezes in mid-air,
I remember sitting on the old wobbly bench with my father
fogging up the porch windows and writing our names
on them until my mother would protest.

I would bury my head in the folds of his sleeve
trying not to let mother hear my giggles.
His musty coat dampened my cheek in a soft and familiar way.

My mind, like a recorder, rewinds and replays these memories;
the only parts of my father that the cancer did not destroy.

A sharp gust of wind jolts me back into reality.
My joints, now stiff and aching, dread the walk back to the house.
It's time to leave my old friend and face the lonely Christmas
that lies ahead.

Melanie Turner

Grand Delusion

A parched winter air greets the morning dawn
An arresting calm throughout the decimated camp
Sitting beside the bivouac's flame a solitary soul
Frozen in an eternal stare

Steamed lead darting through the tents
Awakening a slumber of utopic dreams
Embraced by loved ones far away and never to be again seen
Into the thick of battle, unknowing and without a hope
Men of vigor undaunted by death
Boys sent too early to their graves

Once they spoke of exploits and fame
Before the bullets pierced their heads
Celebrated and honored in name
Corpses lying strewn and bloody
Amidst a world of chaos set aflame by the winds of war

Once there had been a cause for which to die
Now there was a blindness in his eyes
At one time he had chased immortality
Now he sought an end to earthly pains
For the cold wind of death had extinguished his flame.

Alex Aixala

Silent Childhood

Stretching the limits of the pew I graze her beach stained hair.
Uncontrollable desires, excite and elevate my skin.
Incense of resurrection, smoke in our eyes, as we stare
at her lily white body before us. Waiting for her childhood to begin.

Once we ambled through the meadows, breaking into an all out run
or meandering by the sea-shore in a musing walk.
Our footsteps would trace the sand under the falling sun
and the mystical moon dance that ceased to halt.

Looking over the pew I gazed at how it use to be.
Now, a playground swings empty of your famous frolic
and the summer sun is swept away to the sea.
I will always remember those words when you were sick,

"For everyone must die
to mark their place in time."

ron j. ziembowicz

To Whom It May Concern

To Whom It May Concern.
They always say we can't do things right,
even the ones who're bright.

To Whom It May Concern.
They say it's justice, when they bust us.
They break down our doors
and storm through our homes and say
we're the ones who're wrong.

To Whom It May Concern
We're better than the rest,
even though we may sometimes take a rest.
No matter how hard they try,
our love for learning and earning
will never die.

Antonette LaQuita Harris

The Little Dancer

The day was crisp, the leaves were brown,
    the apple trees were bending down.
I woke upon a willful sun, a mother calling "Breakfast done!"

Wearily I rose from bed, pulling on my heavy head.
    A breakfast fit for royal ones, with Daddy's funny lack of puns.
They were hiding something new and then out popped a pair of shoes.
    Not just tennis, these were pink, oh... I didn't have to think!
    "Ballet shoes!" I cried with joy, but oh, I'd need a good decoy.
Lessons would be my next move, what else could I do with those shoes?

Before I could whimper and cry for more, Mother hit the chosen door.
    "Lessons start on Monday noon,
    you'll need a reason to own them shoes!"

The day is crisp, the leaves are brown,
    the apple trees are bending down.
And gracefully, yet out of whack,
I leaped from bed and loosing slack,
I turned a glide and smiled, with pride.

Laura Fleming

Untitled

The rain fails to cease.
The overflowing pools of tears, are not getting any smaller.
The intense feeling of grief, seems to be a lifelong visitor.
Your heart never really seems to be whole.

For he has left,
And packed up your heart with the rest of his things.
He still had yet to realize that in the midst of his dirty clothes,
Are the pieces of your broken heart.
Alone and frightened, you have to face the sympathetic,
Yet not understanding world.
In your mind, no one can share this feeling.

Heavy brick loads are weighing you down.
Time has not stopped,
But life cannot possibly go on.
An open wound cannot always be healed.

The pools have tipped over now.
You are drowning in your sorrows.
If only someone could take you out of this cruel world.
Only when you are with him, will you be at peace.

Amie Florman

An Observation

Feelings - within, without, surrounding
To deny is time, to pursue tainted
Cautions, fears, connotations...
Just to be! To clearly see
Life's filters confuse the honesty
The need for love is universal.
Words and interpretations, needless complications
All simply and met down with gentle touch
Cleansing the complications,
Removing the filters - purified souls, embrace
Therein can comfort, friendship, kindness and truth
be nurtured and bloom
Accepted and appreciated for ourselves...at peace.....
The walls crash.

Gwen E. B. Whitham

The Far East

I went to Okinawa, from there I went to Japan.
and here is what I saw:
Slant-eyed girls with long black hair
a lot of gold teeth with a few white to spare.
I went to Okinawa, from there I went to Japan
and here is what I heard:
Oh-Hah-Yoh Goh-Zah-EE-Mahs and Goh-Mehn-Nah-Sah-EE
Kohn-nee-chee-wah nah-sahn and go home G.I.
I went to Okinawa, from there I went to Japan
and here is what I think:
Now the only difference between these two foreign lands.
Is a skoh-shee bit of water between Okinawa and Japan.

Gary R. Mercier Sr., 1958

Work Escape

I looked out my window
to see what part of life was
passing me by as I work at
my boring 9-5.

I drew in a breath and let out
a sigh as I watched a hawk up
in the sky. He was riding the wind
like a beautiful kite without any
strings to inhibit his flight.

As free as the wind he seemed to
fly up to the bluest part of the sky.

I watched him so free and wished it was
me who could sail in the ocean blue sky.
As he glided away out of my view a tear
fell from my eye because I wished that
I could fly, too.

Kim Moran

scream

can not hear lifeless hopeless saintless
bent twig growing into a twisted tree

lifeless sitting in that chair
sipping on bottled despair
numbness creep'n into the mind

hopeless as the night seeps away
the mind's sight slipping into the past
that will last till mornings' cast

saintless knowing he can not turn to ask
as he sits in the wired chair
scrapping at his soiled soul

silence creeps across a wall of faces
hiding behind their power & lies
concealing their guilt ridden eyes

knowing they planted the seed
that grew into the twisted tree
screaming to be released

Wayne D. Klein

Distant Love

The wind blew softly thru the three, he ran his fingers thru her hair.
The sunlight warmed their bodies, I should know I was there.
The path that went up towards the sky; seemed to travel on and on.
I turned to look and suddenly he was gone.
I looked at a flower that was lying in my hand.
I looked down and saw footprints in the sand.
The path that he left I followed and my journey soon came to an end.
He was off in the distance, swimming to the sky, he was gone; my lover,
and my friend...

Sue Green-Cheesman

The Other Side

As I slumber in the night
Comes a white embracing light
Calling me to the other side.
I feel no pain, I feel no fear
Just a warm atmosphere
Calling me to the other side.
Should I answer, or should I stay
Who would care if I went away
Let God choose-take it all in stride
Calling me to the other side.
It's too soon, my life's not done
to enjoy my life I've only begun
So I'll awaken from the night
Continue on and shut off the light
It's nice to know death don't fight
Things will be great when the time is right,
And it will be pleasant to take that ride
and cross over to the other side.

Janet E. Chancellor

Posters

Walls
Four, hollow, walls
Yellow, pale and barren.
Punctured paint
Portraying a multitudes of tiny apertures
Deeply embedded in the scarred, stale paint.
Patterns emerge
Unique to the desires of their architect
Yet barely visible to the naked eye.
What once was...exists no more.
Childhood dreams of my yesteryear
Posted on my now vacant walls.
Torn and shredded
To bits and pieces.
Set free to roam
With spirits past.
Carried by winds
To direction unknown.
My walls.
Gone, but not forgotten.

Ellen S. Wilkkowe

Untitled

My best Friend died today.
now I can never really go home again.
Her home would only seem like
another house on the block, and
I would stand and wonder who lived
there now.
The high hedges we hide in
the play-house we smoked our first
cigarettes,
the porch where we played our card games.
Theses things would all seen so still.
New kids playing only seem to be intruders.
Now, no-ones on the swings, that I know,
and it's truly time to go
for my best Friend and I
said are last good-byes
very long-ago.

Monica Watson

Hugs In My Pocket

A special time during each day
I think of the hugs I have stashed away
Where did they come from you might say?
From two little boys who live far away.

My pockets are full on the left and the right
So I take each hug and hold on tight
Just hoping they'll last all through the night

The hugs in my pocket will not wash away
They have special names and are here to stay.

The hugs in my pocket are magic you see
They're all very special from them to me.

Bernadine Bell

Krissy

I cross the room to my chair
And see you already lying there
Gently with hands so soft I place you on my lap
You neither wake nor do you stir as I rock to and fro
Then I see you kick your feet and I wonder what you dream
Are you chasing balls our watching doves fly high above
I remember quite well as we romped
Trying to catch you as you ran till I fell in the sand
Regardless of your size you were always there
Barking, Growling, Protecting me as strangers passed by
You have been my faithful friend
Though thick and thin
Your breathing slows as you open your eyes
You tongue licks my hand as I hold your head
Then silence fills the room
As I hold you to my chest
Tears fill my eyes as I hum a lullaby
I know you are gone to join your sister far beyond
I'll miss you Krissy and I'll never forget
Your devotion and your love

Sharon Kay Van Y.

To Love Another Is A Gift Of Life

Love can be expressed in poem or song,
By a smile, or a wink, with a nod short or Long.
By a simple touch, on shoulder or cheek,
Or a passionate kiss, that leaves ones knees weak.
Love can be symbolized in a rose or a present,
Or in any such item which is suitably pleasant.

But most of all Love is in each one caring,
In knowing one another, and in each your dreams sharing.
Love is in seeing one another's true beauty,
Making sure your Love knows of their essence your duty.
Love is in Romance, feeling special together,
Expressing to your Love one another's true Measure.
Love is in simple moments spent with your one,
Seeing your Love's beauty reflected in the setting sun.

Love is a gift of Life, your Love's and your own,
Made greater and new, as together they are sewn.

Jonathan Trachtenberg

In Lightning

A blackboard bearing blunt, but beautiful bombardments
Subliminal scribbles skip across the sensational skies
Flash! A fantastic feeling of fear and fascination flairs
Intense illumination inspires important insight and impact
Thwack! Thunder tells its terrific and tingling tale
Electrical eloquence echoes elaborate emotions to educate
Zap! A zealous zigzag zips through the zodiac to its zenith
A delightfully dynamic and dangerous dance the darkness demonstrates
Lightnings's lingering lecture of lost love's lessons
Necessary knowledge needed from the nocturnal narrator

Gretchen N. Oswald

289

Life

Life is a challenge; life is a game,
Life has many different names.
Life isn't easy; life is hard,
You've got to know how to play your cards.
Life is happy; life is sad,
Sometimes life can make you mad.
Life can be boring; life can be fun,
Life can be anything under the sun.
Life is precious; life is a gift,
Life shouldn't be wasted; time shouldn't be missed.

Kim Theulen

Glitter

As I gaze down from the mountain to a glassy lake of golden sheen,
 The gleams of dawn cut through me, like shimmering swords of opaline.
  ...I catch the glitter.

As the schooner cuts a vibrant path thru the crystal Catalina night,
 a moonfish skins the silken surface, reacting with a phosphor light.
  ...I catch the glitter.

As I stride through forest cover among the ponds and blades of grass,
 I gaze before a fish of gold within a pool of liquid glass.
  ...I catch the glitter.

When I stroll thru Sunday City, stepping on kaleidoscopes of rain,
 I see a droplet strike and flow, as the dribble cuts the window pane.
  ...I catch the Glitter.

When I circle flying inbound above the foggy Friscan sky,
 the City lights glow thru the mist, a safety beacons to guide me by.
  ...I catch the glitter.

Then when I rise to venture wayward, above the effervescent feelings,
 the distance grows, the tingles tug me, I turn, I wince, my mind
  is reeling and then above my shoulder seeking...

I catch the glitter, the scintillating glimmer, the mesmerizing
 shimmer... in your neon sparkle eyes.

Oscar Lynn

Untitled

In our world,
 a day goes by,
 No one misses it,
  No one cries.
We're all too busy wishing for tomorrow.
We think about yesterday in pity and sorrow,
for all the things we might have done.
We were all caught up in games and fun.
A wasted life is how it ends,
We look for sympathy from our friends.
Soon there won't be anything left,
but memories from
 the wasted life we kept.

Deborah L. McNeil

Lifeline

With weary soul and disillusion,
He wades through streams to find ablution.
Standing hip deep in life's confusion,
He casts his line for resolution.

His casual hand blocks the sun's rays
That gently kiss his upturned gaze.
He spies the mountains in the haze.
His peaceful soul gives quiet praise.

Some see him as a quiet man
Who yearns to fish where rivers ran
Where bass and rainbow trout command
And tug the lifeline in his hand.

Margaret A. McHugh

Somewhere Beyond The Sky

Somewhere beyond the sky
A hand reaches out answering your every reply
And there's the deepest love that
anyone could want
For you may be lonely and in despair
But isn't it good to know that there is
someone who care
You may not be aware
That there's someone awaiting for you,
All you have to do is to have faith
And your hearts will do the rest
If you think there's no one, you are wrong
There is someone out there for you
To make your life a brand new song.

Denise M. Willoughby

Dreams

As the wind blows, it whispers his name
It follows me, click, click, sweep, sweep
Whispering, calling, pulling my heart towards him
I see a light shining in the distance
The wind whispers, pulling me up
I'm pulled towards the light and I see a face
He smiles and holds his hands and arms out to me
The light clears and I open my eyes
A dream in the midst of a heart ache
But, as I walk outside there he is
I blink and smile, he smiles back
A dream is a wish your heart makes
Now I know, dreams can came true
(if only I still wasn't dreaming)

Angel Martinez

Time Travel

The afternoon is young,
just before one.
I rest in a grove and listen to the wind murmuring through the pines.
My soul is quieted by the stark loneliness and solitude created
 by their croon.
I close my eyes and travel through time to 1965.
I never left...
I never grew to 42.
I am still the boy who tarries beneath whispering pines nestled on an
 old abandoned farm.
How peaceful it is here.
Life has no pressure,
it is not shackled by charge,
I am free for a moment in the city park.
Then I open my eyes,
and walk back to work.

Jesse R. Panzarello

Neglect

Remembering the sweet, sad, certain death of Spring,
Lilacs crushed and daisies blown,
Faded Summer's petals strewn,
A sacred glade in retrospect,
Now lost or overgrown.

The place was called The Garden of Delights,
We spent our days in it and all our nights.

Return to me my memory and play
The songs we loved and thought would never die,
Forgotten now, they say it goes that way,
But oh, the time was sweet, the mood was high.

Gone Spring, Summer fled, Winter tells us Fall is ending,
Yet Love our garden still awaits our tending.

Tom Gelinske

Christmas

There goes the pitter, patter of tiny little feet,
that means one of the Baril children is not fast asleep.
For all must be quiet and very still,
to listen to hear who's coming over the hill.
As it is only once in every long year,
that we celebrate this day with good cheer.
Santa may come by on his merry way
to visit all the good girls and boys today
Yet, the true meaning that we should share
is showing each other just how much we care.
For on this day we celebrate the birth
of God's Son, Jesus coming to our earth.
In a manger in Bethlehem many years ago,
this babe was born beneath a star all aglow.
As wise men and shepherds came from afar
following the leading of that bright star.
To see who it was that was born that night
they found the babe to be such a great sight.
And all across the earth great choruses sang chords
That Jesus shall be King of Kings and Lord of Lords.

Jacqueline A. Kendall

Legend

Gazing, looking, deep in thought, on the wall, a hat.
Sleek in design, gentle, old, portraying the legend
that never dies — Baseball.
Made of leather and wool,
it returns me to the soft protection, like the womb.
How comforting it is to know that it is waiting there for me.
It is a symbol of dreams long forgotten,
and aged long ago into dust.
"Shoeless" Joe Jackson and
Visions of my imagination, or not?
Waiting for a bright sunny day,
it can be my protection from the parching sun.
Playing outside with the young neighborhood boys,
I am reminded of those days.
Whipping around my hat, a ball flies by, and I look into
the well of my cap, and there, a ball.
It's string's ripped and shape demented,
And I begin to cry.

Erika Fehr

Hema

Beautiful buttered green beans
lay atop
this great glow of passion
and pain.
And through her bulging eyes
she laughs at
absurd life.
Only she is dazzled in the
back seats of buses
eating oreo pie.

Our love is secrets, flower shops,
and green-laced sneakers
a lush fold of forest and sky-lakes
as blue and bright as...

And always, always
the mirror falls
when I try to adjust my rectangular view.

Rebecca L. Pearson

What A Wonderful Mom

These words are seldom said to you
But it's all so wonderful and all so true:
Every day of my life you're the one that I choose
You're there beside me even when I lose
You cheer me on when I win
Because Mom you're my best friend

If a thousand Mom's were standing in line
The greatest one there would be mine
How I cherish your look when I've had a success
And I feel your understanding when I've made a mess

I'm grateful when I can show you my A's
And feel so sad when I've had bad days
Oh you're a wonderful Mom to love
So kind and gentle as a dove
Mom you always want the best for me
How I yearn to be what you want me to be
You are such a wonderful Mom!!

Marie Money

Old Sea Man

Old sea man listen to what I say,
You may have steered a ship in your younger days.
You may have done it very well,
But now it's too late for you to sail.
Your back is bent and your hands are unsure,
The tide's too steep for you,
To steer your boat so small,
Once on top you're bound to fall.
Give up the sea and take to the land.
Live your life the best you can.
Be sure of each step knowing you'll not fall.
Old man don't be a fool.
Give up that life you once knew,
It's now too hard for you to do.

Bonnie Luna

The Gestapo Eyes

As harsh words scorch me from soft lips,
The stench of my own burning hair
Fills my nostrils as gangrene fills dead limbs.
But worse is the betrayal in your Gestapo eyes.
I've dreamed your depth was love for me,
But under it all, the acrid stench
Of toxic love, noxious whispers, and poisoned admiration.
The fires of your passion burn holes in the world,
And here I am.

I hate and loathe your blackened eyes of Auschwitz.
How many years have I sacrificed to the purity of Us?
Through the mortars and the shells and the air steeped with cyanide,
I thank you.
So here we are, you and I, your cesspool love between us.
I turn away from your jackal eyes
To face a world stripped of glory.
Thank you, my Hitler.

Catherine Porter

For So Many Years

For many years we have changed the face of the earth
And for so many years dug the heart of mankind
As we dug the earth
To find the gold that would change the heart of mankind.

But do the birds know this who after so many years
Still know when and how to migrate together?
And do the waters care, who rush down the rivers
Like there's no tomorrow, yet take so many years
To change the heart of Earth?

Claire Becker

Reassurance

When I look up-out-around...I am in wonder...at the Openness —
the Vastness that surrounds me...AN INFINITY.

It is in this space...THIS UNIVERSE...that we are
A Part of a Whole.
Brothers Children ALL.

From what has past...I Release. The Expectations of...
The Wishes for...what might have been said - could have been done...
Dissolved. Gone. Gone into darkness. NO REGRETS.

From what has past...A CLOSING. I come out...To see the Light.
To see only Good.
To have Hope...I reach out...An Opening. A Reawakening.
RENEWAL.

For it is in this time...NOW...I hold No Fault—No Blame—
No Anger — No shame.

For it is in this time...THIS LIFE...I have EXPERIENCED...
I have hurt...I have learned...I GROW.

For it is in this time...NOW...I have only FORGIVENESS. I feel only
LOVE...Acceptance...Compassion...Understanding...CONCERN.

When YOU look Up—Out—Around...
When YOU reach out...Into the Light...
YOU will Find...YOU will See...
I am THERE...I am HERE...For YOU.
NOW...And ALWAYS.

Jeffrey Milich

Original Family Name

Written in the spirit to those who have
The problem with black, because they
Are not and those because they are

No! No! My lost brothers and sisters, I
Repeat my lost brothers and sisters there
Is no one in my family named that.

However there must have been someone
In yours. For I have heard many many many
Of your family members call many many many
Of my family members by what I truly
Believe to be your original family name

Nigger! Nigger!

Jamel Myers

A Christmas Reminder

Once again Christmas is here.
Time for gifts, family, and special moments
To share with our neighbors and friends
Who tend to drop by.

But, though these times are special...
What of those who may never have a Christmas?
Never sharing in the joy,
Never experiencing the love.
There only wish is for a place to sleep;
And some food for their kids to eat.

Who helps these people at Christmas?

That job is for you and I,
To give them some hope
And bring on a smile or two.
Not just on Christmas...
But everyday of the year.

Verlinda J. Allen

Palette Of Loss

My anger is red and my hope is black.
We once were a whole and now half is gone.
My mind screams your, name there is no answer.
My skin shivers in cold, missing your touch.

My mind is dullness.
My voice is silenced.

I reach my hand in the darkness - nothing.
My expectant eyes open, you are not there.
My life once had meaning, where is it now?
My anger is red and my hope is black.

Give me a sign, my love,
give me a sign.

Martha T. DiGioia

Peace And War

PEACE, a prayer
showing we care.
A kind of life
without guns, bombs, or knives.
A world with happy carefree creatures.
People of equal race and color features.
Where no nightmares exist because of no fears.
Where no tissue is needed because of no tears.
Where death is natural and heaven is open to all.
Where people are free and animals not hunted or mauled.
A place of no crimes such as stealing, rape, or even killing,
because who wants a place of pain, blood, and grave sites filling?
A place such as that is not worth hoping for.
Living with enemies is what you get and more.
When weapons are there for protection and reason,
for innocent lives were taken the season.
Lives that were fought for victory,
death done so very unmercifully.
A kind of death that is worthless.
A sin, WAR.

Carrie Hoyle

Genesis

You've seen the eastern sky before the sun has risen?
Reddish with a trace of gold
brushed on a blanket of black.
You see
a faint outline of the horizon
a hill, a steeple, a tree
maybe lovers walking by.
Who are they?
Do they know who they are?
The self resides in darkness
with minimal light.
You see a vague profile
of who you might be

James G. Owens

Life's Quest

As I venture through this life
I wish to always reach out to another in need
And that I'll give love
In a way to ease hurt in some small way.

As each day's journey progress
I hope to be mindful of opportunities
And that I'll give special service
In a way to make a difference in another's day.

As long as my life's quest continues
I pray to God for chances to help
And that I'll give of my being
In time to do whatever the season may say.

Bobbie Comer

Funny Valentines

Don't you think it's funny, Valentine
how we still get silly this way?
Impatiently giggling you tear open your gift
while I teasingly get out of your way.
Then reluctantly forced I cover my eyes,
as you impatiently giggle some more
while laying a card upon my lap
then ask "Well, what are you waiting for?"
So opening my eyes I pretend to be shocked
as I slowly examine the card.
Chuckling I comment "My sweet Sweetheart,
you shouldn't have worked so hard!"
Decorated with hearts, a lipstick kiss,
and that fancy way you write,
I slyly grin at the message inside,
"Darling, I'm your gift tonight!"
Then laughing together I hand you my glass.
You pour us both some more wine
and I think to myself, 'Did she kiss that card?'
as you kiss your funny valentine.

Shirley L. Creel

The White Dove

The peace and harmony that the Dove brings,
As I listen for it to gently sing.
It flies high in the mountains, the sky and above,
to bring me reassurance, hope and unconditional love.

When all else has failed and tears start to fall,
The Dove lets me hear a coo unknown to all.
Passed from Granny to Mom to me,
It is what lets us know the future will come to be.

It soars with out hearts in a time of need,
As God softly whispers, "Follow My Lead".
It's white as snow, like being born again,
It is purity without sin.
The hurt, the sorrow, all fades away,
As the Dove speaks and God brings another day.

Depression, divorce, abuse, that all comes,
But it all fades away with love from that Dove, our God,
    even a little or just some.

Started by our family a while ago,
Will be passed on until the end.
So our daughters will have the hope and love we know.

Elizabeth Ashley Osbourne

When A Friend Dies....

My world is left a sadder place
    that I can't look upon your face

And knowing that within a while
    there'll be no laughter or your smile

My heart feels it was so unkind
    for you to leave your friend behind

And yet, I'd rather risk that pain
    than never having known your name

Or looking in your sparkling eyes
    and seeing where your true self lies

So, you live on! Because...my friend,
    within my heart you'll never end!

Monika Starr Langguth

"Until We Meet Again"

I was with you up in heaven before I let you go to earth.
And I sent you down to visit, the only way was by your birth.
You will learn that you're eternal. You will learn both day and night.
You will travel on life's journey, and will fight the victor's fight.
You will build a strong foundation, and my love will shine through you.
As you plan to start your future I will guide in what you do.

When you search to find life's answer and you think there's no one there.
If you search me with your heart you will find I'm everywhere.
And if you need to know the reason why I made you into man.
If you ask in faith, in prayer, I will reveal my earthly plan.
For my love for you is stronger than the shores that bind the sea.
And when your journey's over I will bring you back to me.

Just remember is won't be easy, there are times that you will fall.
But I am a God of mercy, I forgive wrongs great or small.
If you pray and read the scriptures, go to church, follow my command;
Then at the time appointed I will take hold of your hand.
For in my home are many mansions and you too, will have a place.
When you finish what was started we will meet there face to face.

Debbie Carden Merinar

"Mother"

The sun sparkles in her eyes
And a radiance is reflected,
Brilliance dances around her
As she smiles.
Yet no words need be spoken,
All has been said,
As she steps back
Into the shade
To let others step forth towards the sun
All the while,
Never knowing
It was her.

Tara Laruffa

Reflective Recollections

Sonnets
surrender
surreal satiation.
Singing songs softly
some stretch soaring spirits
stimulating sensitive souls.
Serene satisfaction
silently sends
scintillant
sighs.

Poetry and prose, pristine and polished:
properly placed, perpetually powerful.
Preferring ponderings primarily primitive
perennial principles provide pageantry.
Profusion promotes pastimes present,
primordial passions pursue perfection.

Gregory A. Reeves

Filter Smoke

The taste of blood and smoke fills my mouth
Laughing like a lunatic
A grey encircling vale
Last words of a doomed man
"I love you"
That says it all

The glowing tip of a cigarette
Urgent, insistent rhythm
The ringing of the telephone
Looking forward to the warm
    darkness
I close my eyes

Troy Young

Queen's Prize

Symbol of his love a rose,
King gave to his Queen.
She placed it in a crystal vase,
Her King she did esteem.

Glorious and perfect rose,
Brought life into the room.
Holding true their wedding vow,
Forever sacred flawless bloom.

Ornament of affection,
Gained attention from those adrift.
Wanting to hold and touch the rose,
They battered and bruised this selfless gift.

Gripping crimson petals,
Tears poured from her face.
Queen cried to the King,
"My dear, our love's disgraced!"

"No, my precious", King so soft,
"The beauty of the rose must pass.
Embracing tight our treasured faith,
Our love will truly last."

Shannon Luke

Earth To Earth, Ashes To Electrons

I envy Marilyn and JFK, their mummified youth usurped decay
Eternal life in a funny way, a detached voyeur perspective
I saw a movie, film noir, was it Barbara Stanwyck of Hedy Lamarr
Could I fall in love with this moving star, this fluorescent
beam exploding
Ageless beauty, timeless poise, a seductive image for all the boys
Electron love or just white noise, the real cliche - perception
My ageing body tells me "no," I feel both pain and afterglow
from human touch, no after show analysis can nurture
Inter the net, it's kiddie porn, safe sex or delinquent scorn
Society is left to mourn organic evolution
I see the future intimate, devoid of flesh, inanimate
With on screen pimp degenerate, all credit cards accepted
Of Marilyn and JFK my envy drains - a time delay
Both coded, loaded, pimped away, my access mouse now vermin
The loneliness, electric love, in life they fitted like a glove
In death they sit with God above, hitchhikers on the hard drive
Can we complain, those still alive? We'll take the time to
proselytize when the throes of death declare demise, that it's time to
click on "roses"
Complacency, "just let it be", deny responsibility
Some day, maybe, we'll hit the key - to life, to love ...accidentally?

David M. Templeton

Realities Of Life

There's pain in knowing some new year
You will lose one near and dear.
Husband, child, mother or father
Makes you wish time could go no farther.

We cannot save each other from fate,
Only love dearly instead of hate.
Life is too short to be sad of heart,
So let's all try for a brand new start.

And pray to God
each moment is cherished,
That the love is strong
before we've perished.

For after death it is too late,
To try and wash a dirty slate.
So keep it clean and keep it nice,
It really is a wonderful price.

Michele LaMaster

Hope Slumbers Not

My hand rests now upon this life still in my womb he sleeps
And when his life has been complete of me what will he speak?

I pray, dear Lord, he knew my love in any circumstance
That with all odds against him stacked I always gave him a chance

His heart, they say, is hopelessly weak
He'll live - at the most - an hour
Calling me selfish and sick not to end it all now
For such a choice - I hold not - the power

Son, indescribable months of anguish and sorrow
Hold not a candle to your worth
God be God - what'er His will for tomorrow
I promise you the gift of birth

I only pray that you will sense my love
Should our eyes meet but in one tear-filled glance
A knowledge so sweet - to take with you above
That I forgot my life to give yours a chance

If death is your road - you will NOT wait alone
I will walk you to the gate
Kissing your brow till a hand reaches out
And in loves arms you are brought to your fate

Hayley Johnson

Gold Hands

That time of year when thrushes clear their flutes
To pipe a roundelay for swelling earth,
We wandered near the greening willow shoots
Where newly minted buttercups shone forth.
The day had signed with gold its fragrant page
And you had vowed to love till time was dead.
My heart was trembling, but my head, more sage,
Reminded me that kisses buy no bread,
And I must bend young dreaming to my will,
If I would have the treasures I had planned,
For you were poor, and I was poorer still,
But I had met a man with golden hand.
You found a constant heart; my hands are gold,
But why do winds, at sunset, blow so cold?

Barbara S. Gabbitas

"Excuse Me While I Wipe My Brow"

Winding roads, and heavy loads, have thus far been my reward
The trials, denials, and troubles in piles a jalopy, all I can afford!
Mountains to climb, crossed oceans in time motivation borderline
still won't be kept down, denied higher ground it will soon be
my time to dine.
Excuse me while I wipe my brow, excuse me while I wipe my brow!
Elbow curves, accusations undeserved, deeper how deep must I go?
Will I know when I'm there, moving forward I dare
should I pass it will I even know?
Obstacles I've overcome, remembering where I'm from
meeting each challenge with an open mind
not much do I rest until in my own nest and the knots begin to unwind.

Excuse me while I wipe my brow, excuse me while I wipe my brow!
Wisdom replacing, confusion erasing, the emptiness that I bore
bright lights now showing, I know where I'm going
I'll open my own door.
Winding roads, and heavy loads, full circle came today
weathering trials, and denials, and troublesome piles
they now listen to what I say.
Excuse me while I wipe my brow, excuse me while I wipe my brow!

Bruce R. J. Morris

Self Esteem

Self esteem, is the innermost sense of self worth and value.
When we show love, people have a favorable opinion of you.
When we let our light shine, we spread happiness to others.
We will be held in high esteem by our sisters and brothers.
Knowing that Jesus has unconditional love for us should be an
Inspiration to our daily living.
It should build up our esteem to know that God is compassionate,
Merciful and forgiving.
When you are suffering from low self esteem and you feel worthless
And disarranged, God sees your potentials and only he can motivate
Us to change.
My friends, if you want to get on board, we have to love ourselves
And love one another, so we can see Jesus Christ, our Lord.

Estella Chambers

My Fading Dawn

Moments that meant nothing
I missed what I could be
Slowly they have sunken
In memory I do not see

My drop of water missed the ocean
Todays have become yesterday
I walked that forgotten notion
That tomorrow would be my today

Could not keep the sands of time
From falling through the glass
Shattered now what was mine
The ground holds my emptiness

Yet I see the sunrise again as
Dawns have blessed my remembered past
Sit and wait for the coming sunset
Did not know it would be my last

Tomorrow never became my today
And what I could recall is gone
No vision of what was yesterday
I forgive the darkening of this fading dawn

Wayne Santoro Jr.

Today's Storm

Yesterday's gone — laughter, singing and sunlight,
Cottony clouds hung on a drapery of blue.
Now clouds darken, weigh heavy, birds are in flight.
God's warning, "Prepare! A storm's coming for you."

Make the gray of the day like a warm, wooly wrap.
Let the wind wrinkle the air, leaves feather the sky.
See icicles of lightening that sparkle the map.
Hear thunder that tumbles and rumbles on high.

Let first raindrops mark the pavement like polka dots.
Have them multiply till they curtain the land.
Let rivulets of water dance pebbles in stony spots,
And pioneer roadways in unblemished sands.

Let the song of the rain make a peaceful balm
That lullabies babies and old folks at rest.
Let the storm layer the world with a coating of calm,
Secure in the knowledge God's plan is the best.

Let a wisp of sun's rays part the curtain of rain.
Watch patches of blue dart about in the gray.
Pray that tomorrow will find rough places plain.
Thank God for making your storm gentle this day.

Carol Hartland

God Gifts Are Wonderful

How wonderful are Your gifts God
They come in so many ways,
A blink of an eye, a big smile
Or a cloud up in the sky.

How wonderful are Your gifts God
And yet, we seem not to know,
That they are the little things
That only You can bestow.

A grain of sand, a blade of grass
The softness of a baby's hand;
Reflections of water on a glass
And kindness to your fellow man.

We never stop to think
That these things didn't happen by chance,
A butterfly; a ray of sun.
And rain that seems to dance.

These are the greatness of Your love
These are the gifts from God up above,
We thank You God for things great and small
Thank You God, You made them all.

Audrey S. Owens

Bang! Bang!

I am troubled with the visions of violence choking this world,
The boy gripping the handgun, pointing it at the bully at his school,
The man beating up an another man who didn't want to give up his
    possessions,
The man holding a grenade in the sweaty palm of his hand with the pin
    clamped around his trembling finger, holding a hostage, all because
    his girlfriend left him,
The man that beats his family with no thought of pain for doing it,
    his pain hidden by the Devil's brew, but it only shows more to the family,
The blood being splattered on the tube that all men are strapped down to,
I can't see the good in most things because I am blinded by the violence,
I walk down the street and see a man get shot because another wants
    his shoes,
Show me the good, show me the hope, show me the will to survive.
I found it. I found it in the Bible, the answer to all the problems
    that face this sick world,
"I am the way the truth and the life," said the Lord. Look to him and
    he will give you the answers.
Love will be the cure for violence and many more problems.

Jeremy Carver

True Love

I am True Love.
Follow Me.

I stalk the ash-illumined streets
Where pale faces with glass eyes drift—
Ghosts swallowed in then mist.
I stretch My arms
Around My lover.
I stun him with My kiss.
I lead him through the dark alleys,
Breathing the sulfurous refuse...
Into My room—dim vacant corner
Infested with rats and insects
That scrape each wall
And crawl upon the wood.
I hurl My lover into My web.
I spin and spin him in My thread.
He looks at Me as I undress...
And consume him in My emptiness.

I am True Love.
Carry My cross, Deny yourself, and Follow Me.

Jeesue Kim

Love . . . With Friendship

A rosebush is most beautiful, with flowers fragrant bloom
from innocent buds to full array, such beauty knows no gloom.

The rose itself must stand upon, a stem strong in stance
covered with protective thorns, not seen at passing glance.

Within the sharp protective thorns, nourishing each rose
is the life supporting all, the beauty each rose shows.

And even though its fragile petals, may fall unto the ground
leaving not a single rose, where once they could be found...

In time the stem, if nourished full, will bloom a fresh new rose
with fragrance maybe sweeter, more beautiful it grows.

But always keep in mind, it may just really be
the rose that lost its petals, the one you've always seen.

As so is love, the rose, it blooms with beauty grand
the stem is called a friendship, on which the rose can stand.

And so I see these two the same, a rosebush and two friends
who both can see the beauty, in a rose that always mends.

Petals can fall like romance, but if you look within
you'll see the miracle growing, inside the nourished stem.

And perhaps just maybe, its beauty's all the more
because your faith in friendship, looks beyond what was before.

Colette S. Werner

Merry Christmas, Happy New Year

Hark! Do you hear what I hear?
"Silver Bells!" And "Jingle Bells!"
It's time again for "The Jingle Bell Rock",
And hanging up all those Christmas Socks.
"We Wish You A Merry Christmas,"
With a hug and kiss under the mistletoe.
Gathering with our friends and family at,
This most festive time of the year,
To give each other presents and,
Yes, to be of good cheer!
To usher in the most "Prosperous New Year",
And so we lift up our glasses to make a few toasts!
Then gathering around the piano to sing,
We croon the old song "Auld Lang Syne",
Wishfully hoping we sound just like Bing!
So, I just want to say to everyone here,
"Merry Christmas, Happy New Year!"
"See you all again next year!!"

Vera L. Dryden

Deep Mindstate

Deep, Deep, go deeper into my mind and you shall find
Thoughts, thoughts of pain, madness, awful temptation and rage.
Rage, a thunderous rage such as when clouds darken in a land.
Every second of my life seems a strategic battle plan.
Always paranoid that there may be another like me when I sleep.
I sleep, dreaming to awake
Listening to certain stories of misfortune, anger and hate.
When the pain and grief cloaks my mind
I take it day by day one step at a time.
My life is astrained with only one to blame,
A biological who didn't bother
To give away his title for being a Father.
My mother always told me that you learn to teach from your life
And from hurt, pain and agony you shall indeed
Struggle to become a better person inside.
Bend down on your knees, look to the heavens and ask God to provide.

Derrick B. Banks Jr.

This Condition Of Mine: A Poem In Prose

I am an enfeebled old man at age 25. There is a great dark, evil maelstrom raging inside of me. A black-hole that sucks the light out of my eyes, the holy out of my spirit, the flesh off my bones, the will to live from my heart. I suffer from headaches of such magnitude! And pain courses through my thin blood like poison. The marrow has dried up in my bones-brittle they threaten to break at each movement, however slight. My lungs rattle with death and struggle for breath, suffocating. Nightmares torment my sleep by night and linger on by day like some sadistic torturer, not yet satisfied that he has inflicted enough misery. I am exhaustion personified. All is lost, but Time, that ethereal butcher, who mockingly lingers on...shaving seconds off my life for his gluttonous feast with his razor-sharp pendulum; slowly, watching, waiting, asking, "How much more can he endure?"

David Michael DiVita

Untitled

i heard the Angels sing -
    in joy of one coming home.

i heard the Angels cry -
    the sadness for those who were left.

She touched us all - and again once more.

i saw Her with Angels in the mourning sky.

another heard and knew the awesome wonder
    Christmas Angels bring - the beautiful songs
      She would hear and sing.

another saw the rainbow, promise of colours
    in the sky - and knew of the beauty and love
      that She would now see.

a small angel brought the news on a
    quiet Christmas Eve -
      our Angel earned Her wings.

Maralyn D. Olson

Ode To A Family

  Hello there.
I see you're with your Mommy
Who is guiding your stroller while she takes a walk.
That is how I used to greet you
When you were really very new.

  Hello there.
Now I see you're with your Daddy.
Are you showing him that you can find the way home?
You are bigger now and with him you can walk.
He's happy that you know the way and both of you can talk.

  Hello there.
You are really getting tall and love to skip and run
And with your sister and parents it's just so very much fun.
You are happy to be with your family
Because, you know, all of you make just one -
  Family, that is.

Drew J. Thomas

Untitled

ALL through life you hear of love;
I found some stories true.
WANT to know a secret?
IS it just for you?
YOUR never to tell a soul,
LOVE is this secret of mine.
PLEASE read the first word of every line.

Brandy Darrah

296

The Bird

He flies through the air high and free
Winging, winging towards the sea
Wishing, wishing he'll last one more day
Hoping he'll make it all the way
Dreaming, dreaming he'll get there soon
Each day he'll be looking for someplace
Someplace special just for him
Somewhere where the sky is blue
And the sun shines brightest at noon
Where wings stay high and legs stay low
He'll be flying high and flying low
He'll be trying to find just the right way to go
And when he finally reaches his destiny
He'll jump up and down full of glee
He'll hold his head high
As rays of light shine down from the sky
He'll be flying through the air
But won't ever be in despair
One more day flying high through the sky
Now he's there and there he'll stay

Jennifer Lyn Stevens

Occupation: Mother

Most of the time you feel unappreciated.
We didn't turn out the way you anticipated.
You may get angry, but you never give up.
Though sometimes we fill you to the brim of your cup.
A lot of your purpose is all about us two.
And we've done just about everything but make it easy for you.
It seems you like challenges, and that's just what we've given.
Making us good young ladies is what keeps you driven.
You attempt to replace our "stinkin' thinkin'" with thoughts of positivity.
You push us toward achievement and away from negativity.
We may not be all good, yet we can't be all wrong.
Because on us you've worked too hard for too long.
We know you didn't think parenting would be a piece of cake.
But eventually it'll pay off, I hope for our sake.
Believe me, we listen to every word that you say.
 Although most of the time it doesn't seem that way.
But keep doing what you're doing and your blessings you'll receive.
We're almost young women, because you always believe.
Keep doing your job, and we'll do ours, too.
We'll all do what's right, because it's the right thing to do.

Ayesha Patterson

Halloween

There is a time of the year called Halloween,
It is a time to scare people and make them scream!

When the old witch on the broomstick flies across the sky,
she'll be out of sight in the blink of an eye.
It is the time when the ghosts all romp and play —
always at night and never in the day.

And there is the pumpkin all nice and yellow
made into a jack-o-lantern — a funny looking little fellow
with a nose and mouth and two big eyes,
there are big ones, little ones, and 'most every size.

Little goblins and ghosts knock on your door and say
"Trick or Treat!",
they have come to your house for a gift of something sweet.
They go to the houses of the young and the old,
wearing their scary costumes and always so bold.

It is a joy for the little ones with laughter and gleam,
and this is what happens on the day called Halloween.

Thomas H. Gilliland

Vision

We are blessed with pristine spheres of brown or blue or green.
With these comes an innocent mind, fresh and new and clean.
Sadly, with this beautiful mind comes human complication;
The crystal lenses are soon clouded with hate and aggravation.
Fast to teach and slow to learn, society is infected,
And greed and power persuade us to leave the errors uncorrected.
Still, through new generations, the decay can be curtailed,
And, on a blooming, new horizon, a glimmer of hope prevails.
Though society has regressed and the path is long and harsh,
We can and shall overcome the trials and cause the hate to parch.
Art and science and literature shall reign in the revived world.
Rich culture and religion shall feed society a cure.
War and hate and prejudice shall be compelled to cease,
And one united people shall rest in tranquil peace.
As children of a setting sun and fathers of a rising,
We can see the prospects of our vision and our striving.
The gentle rains of time shall come to cleanse our clouded eyes,
And we shall shed the hate and fears of our fathers as we rise.
The future is a solid rock and an endless sea,
And we are destined to explore it now that we are free.

Julie Field

Labor No More My Son

Time was quick in passing years of
suffering and woe, God looked down
from His blessed sky and said
"My child 'tis time to go."
Be not ye sad and mournful.
'Tis a life.
"Repent thy sins, reach out thine hand
and blessed will ye be."
Ye have suffered a lifetime to reach
my throne, and soon will live in thy heavenly home.
Hunger, cold and unhappiness, these ye shall never know,
for I held thee upon my loving breast,
thy blanket of warmth is tenderness
reach out thy hand my tired son,
Ye days of labor on earth are done.

Ethel McClure

Yesterday

Yesterday I did something that
could not be explained
Yesterday I did something that
made me feel insane

I said some words that made others feel bad
I also said some words that made me feel sad

Yesterday was a time when
nothing would go right
Yesterday was a time when
I was full of fright

So full of fright that I would lose a precious gift
A gift so precious it would always uplift

My soul, my mind, and my whole being
This gift was full of love that I thought
I could only feel when dreaming

Yesterday I realized
You never know when you would be surprised
By something so special and so terrific
Something like a best friend who is all
so perfect

Jazmine Cook

The Last Leaf

You died last fall - didn't you know?
Before November you were brown
Your fellows dropping to the ground.
Scarce notice of you there -
Of your triumph unaware.
But after cruel winter's snow
And raging winds to deal the lethal blow,
Did you not feel strange -
Anachronism - out of range
Of Nature's inexorable turn?
What fate decided you'd be
Hanging there 'til spring -
Strength gained by summer's nurture
Or fickle gods' inertia?

Ethel Atkinson

Everyday

Once a year there comes a day
When we honor Mother and are supposed to say;
Happy Mother's Day, Mother, a wish for you,
Which comes once a year, but how untrue.

Because, Mother, it's not only this day
But all the others, that we wish to say,
To banish your troubles and dry your tears.

At times we're angry and all upset
And maybe hurt you and even let
You think you don't matter at all anymore,
But you are the Mother we all adore.

So, Mother, now you know we love you dearly,
And we hope from these lines you will see clearly,
That we're trying to say in spite of all
You'll always have children upon which to fall.

Daniel L. Walsh

Always In Love

When we were young we were quite a pair
Some say young love won't last, but we didn't care
That day under the tree when we carved our names
Made people clearly see we weren't playing games
Always in love

Not a day passes by that we weren't hand in hand
Never saw a tear in her eye until the wedding band
Underneath the moon so bright I see her smile
Now everything's all right I'll be here for awhile
Always in love

We've been together for such a long time
We've had stormy weather and lots of sunshine
Wouldn't trade her for the world she means that much to me
So we renewed our wedding vows underneath that same ole tree
Always in love

Richard E. Shelor

Ice, Fire And Wind

Ice: Letting it melt again your lover's red hot lip,
Watching it melt to a puddle of tears from your lover's eyes,
Holding the cube of ice in her/his hands to let it drip.
When the two of you are frozen, let love go and try.

Fire: Like the warmth of your heart can make her/him dream,
When her body is in motion against the sound of your heart,
When she slows down, the body began to let out steam.
When you got the heat inside of you the bodies will never part.

Wind: Air from the strongest part of your lungs to your mouth,
When you let it explode in the open it can draw back in your face,
Letting the doors open in your heart, under the roof of your house.
Never blowing in the wrong direction when I'm in your place.

Rendell N. Kitzmiller

Beauty

God created all beauty for man to enjoy.
The world is ours for keeping, not to destroy.
The softness of kittens, the fragrance of roses,
The delicate spider web, the pearly dew discloses.
The joy of living, and the thrill of love,
The reward of giving and blessings from above,
The majestic mountains reaching for the sky,
The graceful motion of birds as they fly,
The babbling brook, the waterfall,
The rolling sea to the rivers call.
A baby's tiny hand and a mother's caress,
That brings such joy and peacefulness.
These are all things of beauty, created by God above,
For man to enjoy and live in peace with brotherly love.

Inez Sorensen

Value

Blessed are those of pure heart and true.
"We Care! We Care!" Look what we do.

Much treasure spent on house and place?
Exhausted hours changing our face?
Think we're too thin, perhaps too fat?
Say, "Gimme this or gimme that!"?

Souls starving, dying, gaze at stars.
Must we buy yet more toys and cars?
Disease plagues many rich or poor.
Want more furs, diamonds, gold to store?

Life or just things? Compare?... Absurd!
Love is Action; not just a word.

Michael Swenson

What A Bore

School is never any fun,
it feels as if it's never done.

Math is boggling in the mind,
and my homework I can't ever find.

History is too far in the past,
and my knowledge of this never lasts.

English has always been a bore,
I just can't learn anymore!

And what about Bible with its history too?
I just don't know what to do!

Band with me blowing my horn,
my eardrum is almost totally torn.

Science with things for me not to see,
is always too hard for me!

I just guess I'll never learn,
the things for which I do not yearn!

Mary Elizabeth Reed

"When First I Set Eyes"

She was the girl of my dreams, the love of my life.
The one I had prayed for, I'd make her my wife.
We started out great, with hopes and big plans.
Experiencing joys and heartaches through life's great demands.

The journey we started would test our purpose and might.
I never excepted it would be our most challenging fight.
It would surpass all of our reasoning, to the point of madness.
When she gave in to the world, it caused me unbearable sadness.

It's over now ... I often wonder how.
But like a wounded solider after all said and done...
"By his mighty grace, I shall overcome!"

Luis H. Ortiz

For Charlie

If you were mine for just a day
I would not waste a second of it!
I would build memories to last a lifetime.
Your smile will be my sunshine in the lonely days ahead,
Your eyes my skies of blue.
Your laugh will ring in my memory;
like church bells in the still of the early morning.
As the soft summer breeze stirs the leaves,
I'll remember the caress of your hand on my cheek.
Your voice I'll hear in the laughter of children,
and the singing of birds.
When the rain falls softly to earth,
I'll see again the tears—that fell from your eyes
When we had to say "Good-Bye"
At the end of "Our Day".
Of all the memories I will treasure
From that one day with you.
Your kiss will be foremost;
For your kiss has kindled a fire in my soul
That even the passing of time can not extinguish!

Linda Lee Klatt

Win Ten Million

Always smiling, Ed McMahon,
This is my heartfelt plea-not a pun.
I faithfully returned all your sweep- stake mail, just as you asked-
That alone, proved to be no small task.

I subscribed to your magazines, until they are all over my house!
They cover all my needs, even those of my spouse.
When will you ever say: "That's enough."
Or will I keep hearing from others,
   "It's all just a bluff?"

I could pay rentals and mortgages
   for my kids, you see -
Since, I don't have such things as I am debt free.
But, my days maybe numbered
   as to I what can do -
To make others happy - so why
   can't you come through?

Your part is so easy, as millions you've made!
You could send me one million and still rest in the shade!
Too bad, Ed can't read this (I don't know his address)
But he knows mine - still no million, alas!

Ila Phillips

A Strand Of Life

I am a strand of life hanging
Not wanting to let go
Dangling, blowing in the wind
Swinging back and forth
Letting the rain drum down on me
Letting the thunder yell
Letting the wind tell me its secrets
Allowing the sun to spread its warmth
Blowing from day to day, month to month, year to year
Facing fear face to mysterious face

Becky Twohey

I Cry Myself To Sleep

I remember looking deep into your eyes,
holding your hand, saying good-bye.
I never wanted to let you go, I never wanted to hurt you so.
Watching you walk away, my heart torn in two.
I needed you there beside me, no one else would do.
Now I lay alone at night in bed, crying to myself.
I can't get you out of my head.
You're trapped in my thoughts, my dreams my prayers.
I'm going insane, and no one else cares.
I finally drift away to sleep, with one last sigh, and one last weep.
My mind begins to wander, my heart begins to dance.
I can see you in the distance, I can feel the warm romance.
You wrap your arms around me, and whisper in my ear.
Falling softly from my cheek, was one small, gentle tear.
I blinked my eyes, and wiped my face,
but when I looked, I was in a view place.
Pillows surround me, blankets were scattered.
I had been dreaming again, and nothing else mattered.
This pain in my heart, this ache in my soul.
My head begins spinning, I'm out of control.
I don't know what to do, I don't know what to say.
I need you here beside me. Please come back and say you'll stay.

Michele Barthel

A Certain Beauty

Today I saw a little bird.
A tiny thing was he
With feathers brown, hollow bones,
And a prickly sort of beak.
He lacked a certain beauty though,
For his spirit was all alone.
His feet should rest on the meadowy plains
Where forever winds will drone,
Or atop a tree in the grove
Where oranges grow in mass,
Or in the sky above a stream
Where children's feet do splash,
For just as in Emerson's "Each and All"
Beauty is lost with space.
Everything has its own secret garden-
God has granted us a place.
For in this crowded world of ours,
It is the crowd that makes one's face.

Sheri Thomas

"Neighbor"

Noise! Confusion! Chaos!
   My eyes are open there is no peace;

Fears they thread upon my sleep
   They speak language beyond my understanding,
Is it a love affair bickering?

It calms, then suddenly
   It crashes in a dreadful scream!
The moaning of an innocent child
   Caught between a fearsome stampede;

Mommy! Daddy! As you hear
   That child weep,
The smell of blood flows
   With the wind

Stop - stop; sorry it's too late,
Sounds of siren pierced my ear,
   As the red lights flashed, it reflect on my pain

Father had died - Mother under arrest
   In a white, but soaked red dress
Leaving an innocent child
   In the centre of a family ship wreck.

Ryan Chandler

Pillar Of Love

Not so many years ago, a tiny boy child was born.
As a mother new, I promised him, I'd guard him from all harm.

Now faith in myself and heaven above might not have been so strong
that I'd forget that other things could guide him toward that wrong.

The enemies of innocent kids and those who aren't too wise,
will creep right in and steal their youth, ignoring parental cries.

Society harbors many things among the shadows dark.
A child can lose his innocence, engaging in a lark.

You can't protect a child from life, no matter what you do.
The values taught, depend upon just how the child will view.

You look and see a danger deep, and cry a warning out.
The child excited, runs toward fun, or what it seems about.

Oh innocents, have not much wisdom to go with what they seek.
They gladly run to Disaster Ridge, and then to trouble knee deep.

Your heart cries out for all the pain that you can't keep them from.
For when they hurt and comfort need, it's to you that they will come.

Parental love is a bandage, true. The medicine they have is you.
No matter what the trouble is, the Pillar Of Love is you.

Julia L. Dickson

Mirage

A tree,
Standing proudly
In the ocean of endless horizons.
Where no life was before,
And where no life will be again.
Its seed brought by some miracle,
Kindly welcomed into the loneliness of golden sands,
Trying to survive,
Desperately.
Its soul as that of a human
Craving another,
Always hoping,
Always dreaming.
Aware of its plight,
Its destiny,
Yet never giving up
Till there is no more.

Olivia M. Zmarlicki

Beyond April 15th

The tax forms to be filed each year,
They claim are as simple as can be,
But, because of the complex tax laws,
They are as clear as mud to me.

The taxes we pay to keep America strong,
Would willingly be paid by us,
But the way the government spends money,
Is enough to make you cuss.

Obsolete studies, programs and laws,
Should be firmly dealt with today,
The wasteful spending has to stop,
Not just in the future - but right away.

They need to live within a budget,
Like you and I have to do,
With them spending our money wisely,
It would be better for me and you.

So, let your Representative know,
How you feel today,
Then the country will be stronger,
Because the people will have their way.

Donald R. Taylor, Diamond Springs, CA

"Change"

I often find the trees at a time when they shed their leaves.
"Oranges."
    "Greens."
        "Reds."
            and "fluorescent yellow" are dominating,
this eminent period.

In a matter of weeks these colors have turned brown;
Evergreens have lasted this transition.
Why wouldn't they?
Evergreens are not subjected to change.

Evergreens we find in the forest,
Usually growing to the top of the canopy.
Not allowing the short-lived "rainbow" period to be noticed,
From an aerial perspective.
That is why one has to go within a forest.
Why?
To find the "rainbow" and experience it.

John Koubaroulis

"Spring"

The robins are hopping again
From a long adventurous winter flight
A sing that spring is in the air
Hopping on green turfs of grass
In search for a grab with an inward eye
Nothing to fear to hop on grass so green
So happy with merry twitter
Free from the long hungry quest
That winter came and left at last
For them to put on an emphatic call
And let their matins raise and ring (with delight)
To pierce the air with songs of praise
And give thanks to the one who cares
To fluff their feathers and fly above
To a place to heaven and still for the night
And be enveloped in silent sleep.

Gladys Cooper

What Do You See?

A flash?
Sunlight reflecting off the unicorns golden horn.
Bells tinkling?
Fairies going about their play.
A light in a cave?
A Dragon heating the day.
An old tree?
A wizard who is resting for a moment.
A rainbow?
An invitation to an elf's home.

How do you know what you see is truly real?

I know because:
    I visit with the elves at their home.
    I rest a moment with the wizard.
    The Dragon warms me when I am cold.
    I play with the fairies.
    The sun reflects off my horn.
If I am not real, what about you?

Donna L. Seemuth

Untitled

I'm going home to never return, I've gotten over this pained return.
It took quite a lot to get free from this feeling
To get off of that wheel that always kept turning.
I was hoping you'd follow and pick up your pace,
I kept holding your hand and kissing your face.
I'm going home now, where the feelings so fine,
Where I'll stay forever with those other friends of mine.
There's too much at stake for you to ignore my pleas
You never took yourself seriously,
And now on your knees, again and again I find you there begging,
I lift you back up and you act so assured,
But deep inside you just keep ignoring me.
Please, please take hold of yourself,
If you don't figure it out soon it will wear us both out
Because I'm gonna go home and you should come too,
I'm gonna go home where that feelings so fine,
I'm going home where the love is divine,
I'm going home and never returning,
I'm going home and that wheel will stop turning.

Terry Cadle

The Cliff

I stand on the edge of a cliff,
barely able to keep from falling off,
from falling down,
into depression,
into wanting to die.

The edge is always there,
always beckoning to me,
welcoming me with long warm and cold tenuous fingers.

I back away,
but darkness overcomes me,
and I fall once again...

Once down there,
how do I get out?
The walls are sheer;
I'm not very good at mountain climbing
and I've forgotten everything I know
about climbing the walls of cliffs.

Kate Johnston

I Thought You Should Know

Written For Kris

I thought you should know, you're my
summons to rise from sweet-night's slumber.
You're each and every step I take,
whether forwardly charging the fray,
side-stepping waylays or backwardly
stumbling from unforeseen blows.
You balance my amble of existence,
on this slender thread of chance.
You've tardied time to an unhurried ebb,
allowing me to live on this avenue of life.
You've selflessly given me warning and
direction upon magic forks in my path.
You're my highest flights, deepest pains,
broadest hopes, and most singular aim.
Your pleasant thoughts ushering me to evening's rest,
allowing dreams to order the day's chaotic clamor.
For this and more- you are my life,
I pray... soon to be wife,
And, I thought you should know.

Jerry Simmons

Reflection

This woman in the mirror that is staring back at me,
I closely self-examine, and this is what "I" see.
It's as if the surface was removed to let me see inside,
To gaze upon the memories and the things she's tried to hide.
Like a flash of brilliant lightning that lights a darkened sky
I see the visions of her grief that made her start to cry.
As I peered into her eyes, her glossy pools of green,
They overflowed and made the paths where pain and sorrow stream.
And far beyond her eyes, deep inside her brain,
I saw the many different thoughts that tried to hide the pain.
Her wishes, ideas, and dreams calmly came to form,
Then the thunders of reality clouded them in storm.
Her troubles are like the waves that come crashing to the beach,
Like a mighty hand they wash her hopes far beyond her reach.
Then I saw her heart and wrapped around it was a hand,
Gripping it so tight that the pain was hard to stand.
She wondered who would cause her heart to feel this way;
To deprive her of the happiness she could have felt each day?
But much to her surprise, this agony she's known,
Came from the retching hand she realized was her own.

Lene Nicke

Ode To A Bedpan

Never seen in a headline, nor a line of print!
Wish I'd never been exposed to one. Never had a hint
Until I heard those horrid words (and I could only pray),
"Roll over! Lift up! Let down! Stay!"
Sitting, waiting, grunting, groaning, wishing I could go!
Push, strain, relax, success! How was I to know—
Elimination, agitation, aggravation, stress;
The waiting game had just begun and I was in a mess.
Inhibition, modesty, were going out of style.
The nurse was a "no-show" as I waited for awhile.
If I could ever have my wish, there soon would be a ban
On the uncomfortable, odoriferous, hated, B-E-D-P-A-N!!

Hilda McGinnis Priestley

Reflections By A Shattered Heart

Lying here in the arms of love
Thinking about your ways.
The way you charmed me
Made me cry
and how you kissed my heart goodbye.
I'll never forget
The last words you said before you walked out my door,
Leaving my heart in pieces
On the floor.
"I wish I could change the way things have been
But what's done is done and what's been has been.
I can change tomorrow but I can't change today
So honey I'm sorry to leave you this way."
As these wounds unfolded
I denied they were true.
But now I've found
My life has no meaning
Alone, without you.

Wendy Broker

Truth And Beauty

Truth gives us power, while beauty gives us pause.
Beauty, the bright eye of the tiger; truth, its fangs and claws.
Truth gives us the pathway, beauty the flowers.
One, pain pounding walk; the other, pleasure for hours.
Truth grips our bodies. Beauty releases our soul.
One makes us valid; the other makes us whole.
Push truth with all your might; then beauty squeezes into sight.
Try the other way around. Push beauty far and truth is found.
I thank God who surrounds us, we've received such a sign.
The hard straight lines of truth - softened by beauty, divine.

C. Edward Dawkins

The Eternal Spring

Water bubbling from between the rocks
into its own special dipping place.

Out the notch in the springhouse,
where crawdads played
among the mussel shells
from long ago—empty in silent splendor—
out to its run through the greening pasture.

I wet my unstockinged shoeless feet,
feel its singular coldness—
for it is yet March.

The run goes to the larger branch
and to the creek, with its flooded scree,
to a larger river, to the ocean.

My wetted feet have wedded spring and sea.
Carolina Russel

Nothingness

I see things, and don't feel.
  I touch and can't feel...

Is it me who is touching?
  Or someone else, I am watching?
Why does it seem like another being
  And not me who is really living?!

Going through the motions, going through the acts,
  doing everything that society expects!
An empty touch, a soundless kiss...
  I can assure you, this isn't bliss.

Where is that person who used to feel!
  Hug and squeeze and kick her heels!?
In vain I've searched, just... couldn't find...
  Is she still hiding or, has she died?

I see things and don't feel...
  I touch and... can't feel...
    S. Van Lehn

Appalachian Spring

The snow melt brooks in chorus
down rushing stream valleys and out
through the nature brush working
on happiness colored rainbow meads.

Winter winds retreat in trumpet array
while warm whisper winds float softly
and soothe each in love notes
at the beginning of each new life.

Winter stillness expands into action
and feels its way to movement
buzzing in all around circles in sharing
the innocently gentle gift of beautiful life.

The silently smooth march of time
shows little difference in the way
it repeats itself and keeps on restoring
in never jealous abundance
explosively bursting
my heart.
  John A. Bishop

Purple

We quickly turn our faces aside,
For we cannot bear to meet your eyes.
Ashamed of our color and our sex,
And of our drab, ragged, worn-out dress.

"Rags are all you women deserve,"
Say our abusers, yet we yearn.
Fingers outstretched towards purple cloth...
Perhaps we deserve more than thought.

Instead of acceptance we should fight!
Personal happiness is our right.
It is time to don our purple robes.
Our discarded rags lie on the floor.
  Misty C. Okuda

Rain On The Roof

On a lonely Saturday night I fell for you
Full of containment and commitment
We trickled into each other's open spaces
Finding our way before we ran off

You found someone older and easier
Someone who needed less and could afford more
I returned to my safer single bed
And swam circles in the rain barrel of self-knowledge

Tonight I listen to the rain
As I once did to you
Simply, profoundly, without effort
I kiss you goodbye
As I did not at that last lunch
You talking yourself into relief
My black heart ripping open
To reveal the red underneath

I think of you still
Wounded and significant in your gestures
All the while refusing to cry along
On lonely nights with the rain on the roof
  Bart Wayne

Solitude

Snow falls in sheets now,
leaves are long since gone.
Trees are as dormant as my soul.
This is a winter of solitude.
It always arrives, freezing the heart.
Sometimes it never leave.

Tears are the rain of the soul's winter, falling.
The heart is the tree, losing all it once clung to.
This winter is cold, relentless. But it will pass.

The sun peers through the puffy clouds,
Warming the soft soil.
Flowers reach to the sun in thanks.
The ice melts quickly now, dripping from the blooming trees.
The buds expose themselves, again.
open to the harsh reality, vulnerable.
Buds must face uncertainty to flower,
and the flowers warm the world.
The heart faces many extremes.
but the tree cannot flower without the long, cold winter
and neither can the heart and soul.
  Mike Riggs

Self Worth

In the time that I've been given,
Have I accomplished any goals?
Have I done anything significant, that in the future might be told?
Have I helped carry someone's burden?
So they can reach the top, of the hill that they are climbing;
Or did I simply stand and watch?
Have I prayed for my country's problems?
And still not taken a part, in the needed work to solve them;
When change in every home is where is starts?
I can begin first with myself, then reach my family too;
And after I've succeeded there, then our Young People I'll pursue.
If I help even one to change his way, then I have met a goal and

left a mark that day!
If that one should help another turn from drugs, violence, and
crime, our country will be better, and many more youth will live and
   not die before their time!
If I haven't inspired another to accomplish a goal, and reach out
   and help someone;
Then all I've done is live, work, and die . . .
   and my " Self Worth" is None!

   Barbara T. Sherode

What Is Christmas To Me?

What is Christmas to me?
Is it stocking stuffing, music playing, song singing, or is it
   decorating the Christmas Tree?
Christmas to me is all the above and a lot more that I can see.
Some of the most important, is my family, my health, my friends, and
the best gift of all is the Birth of Thee.
I thank god for my best Christmas gift.
He came to me so quickly, and left so swift.
I finally realize who the true Santa Claus is.
Because all my life he came to me with gifts on his birthday and
   left me with a quiz.
I realize now why I couldn't see the very person I tried to stay
   awake for "Santa Claus".
The presents under the tree that I can see comes from love ones that
cares, but the gift that I can't see comes from God, with that I'll pause.

   Isaac Hilton Sr.

Family...

Having loved with a heart
The delicate illusion that flesh tried to make real,
Bruises, burns, and batterings built strong the wall of dreams
Until the vicious cycle twisted in and on itself
And long ago replaced my soul's ability to feel.

Excuses marked the days, fear punctuated nights;
Clumsy lies, fragile excuses, a buried will to fight.

I thought I was much smarter; my advice rang all too true
As I opined so many others of what they ought to do.

"100-ways-to-kill-a-man," I know them all by rote —
1 simple way to kill myself—this page a final note.

Dying with a mind that imagined a true love-
An impregnable fortress to withstand life's roughest storm;
Blankets, blocks, and bottles destroying fight-or flight
The 2 heartbeats of motherhood have opened blackened eyes
To see the need for Death's Salvation before a hopeless child is born.

   W. Gail Custode

It Doesn't Seem Right

You wanted away from Mom and Dad,
So you pretended to love this lad.

Your marriage vows meant nothing to you,
You just wanted something new

He needed your love, He needed your heart,
But you didn't want these right from the start.

You have destroyed someone precious to me,
Just so you could be free.

It doesn't seem right it doesn't seem fair,
That you could destroy someone who cares.

It breaks my heart and makes me cry
To see what divorce did to this guy.

   Linda McBride

My Little Boy

"O dearest boy, yet oblivious to the power of your charm
(for which your innocence should count virtue twice),
would that you could remain so,
longer to give such unspeakable joy."

In the morning, while he still sleeps,
I gaze upon him in awesome wonder.

"Where have you come from, my little boy?
Perchance, some angel traversing Heaven
has dropped a treasured bundle -
surely, nothing so precious could be of Earth!"

How blessed are my eyes just to behold
his tousled head pressed upon most envied pillow.
He stirs, he blinks little starflecks from
widening eyes that shine clear and bright,
And his awakening smile to my presence
lights up my life for another day!

Who is this so-adored one that he should
differ from another to receive such adulation?
Simply, that he has given me his guileless love
in exchange for mine - for a little season.

   Vernon Owen Anderson

Untitled

As you walked into the door the other night,
I sensed that something was wrong.
Smelling the strong liquor on your breath and cigarette
smoke on your clothes, I knew where you had been.
With tears in your eyes and the look on your face I
knew, right then, what you went through.
Yelling out for the answers to unanswered questions,
tears ran down your cheeks.
The gun that had been placed in the wrong persons hand.
The bullet that shot the friend of your life.
Where was the help you so longingly called for?
Had your friend realized that you tried?
As you look up into the sky asking for the answers,
   you search the sky.
The sky that was once blue no longer is blue,
the white fluffy snow no longer looks white,
the people no longer look kind, and everything you once had is gone.
The emptiness inside your body, your aching heart, and
fulfilled anger are crying out for comfort.
Some one to give you a hug and tell you
"Everything is going to be all right."

   Deidre J. Axt

You

I sit and wait
For you to call,
Yet hear nothing.
The silence echoes painfully in my ears,
While straining to hear you beckon.
I turn and look to find you
Standing in the door,
Dirty tears staining your cheeks.
You try to call out,
Yet no sound can be heard,
While you cry your pitiful tears.

Phoenix Krill

Thine Eyes Did See My Substance

My God has made the mid-day sky
The iris of His drawing eye
It allows the seeking soul to know
A glimmer of truth to both high and low

Night's are the pupils of God's eyes
And from within shines the stars
Yet, the celestial hues ever so bright
Are not as beautiful as His guiding light

Unlike the heavens that I see
There exists no cloud to keep Him
    from watching over me....

Alicha Marie Gaskin

Pink Balls Of Yarn

Activities room they call it.
I guess it's true,
but it hurts when we move.
So glad to be rid of that silly aide
who wheeled me down here.
She takes care of an old lady,
but talks to a child!
If I could speak clearly again,
I'd let them know, my mind grew up a long time ago.
I keep looking around the table,
but I see no empty spaces.
We all survived another night,
so these old bodies can be pushed to move one more day.
Why am I here, looking at pink yarn balls?
My hands jerk at them
with fingers bent and fixed.
I try to do as I am instructed.
I'm in pain and I grieve.
For the result of my activity today
is nothing constructed.

Beverly Finnerty

"Raindrop Memories"

I walk around the streets in the rain
And slowly it washes away all my pain
As I walk and brave the weather cold
I see before me my life unfold
I am reminded of people both here and gone
And of how hard it is to always carry on
I see each and every rain drop fall on my face
And I am reminded of relationships never to be replaced
As I walk a stranger passes by
And I stop and just wonder why
There are people I never took time to meet
And wonder if I had would my life be complete
Or would I still have to deal with all this pain
And then I continue to walk until there is no rain.

Michael E. Cullen II

Mirror

Before my mirror what do I see
There stands a child where a man should be
Little boy, eyes so blue
Are you me, am I you
Are we one or are we two
Do you hide in that secret place
In the room behind my face
With my poems and my rhymes
The memories of better times
Little boy with eyes so blue
You are me and I am you!

John Gray

Colours Of Life

Red is the color of my love, my heart beating, my life's blood
Blue is the color of your eyes, oceans so deep and wide
Green is the color of envyings, jealousies, longings too long
    locked deep inside
Yellow is the color of the sun, to its warmth and brightness I run
Orange is the color of Love's flames that cannot be quenched by
    the rains
White is the color of purity and light in which I want to be clothed
    and hide
Black is the color of the night in whose arms I sleep
Purple is the color of my passions which are stored up like good wine
Pink is the color of innocence that is to short a stay

Sharon L. English

I Dance To One Drummer

I dance only to one drummer
Who plays
Pulsating,
Throb-bing-bing Rhythms
Give me BODY POWER to
Leap, fly, and soar!
While Red, Bronze, Black and Golden Tones Splash
Inside of me.
Ooo-oo-oo-oo!

But sometimes...
I sway, trip and Crash!
When foolishly following another's B-B-Beat.
So, I must listen to those multi-rhythmic rolls and tumbles
inside of me.

And I wouldn't have it any other way.
For I dance to one drummer.
Like Thoreau, that's a drummer with a different beat.

Bea Copeland

Loving One's Self

Look in the mirror and guess what I see?
A beautiful young lady as happy as can be.
A lovely smile, teeth of pearls, hair
of long and beautiful curls. That was me
a long time ago. I may have changed
on the outside, but deep inside
my heart and soul, lies a beautiful talent
more precious than gold. The talent I
have you should have too. Learning to love
yourself is the greatest gift, and believe
me that's true.

Shontea Bell

Wheels

I remember you standing there
The breeze touching your hair
My heart skipped a beat or two
When you looked and saw me too

And instead of turning away
You smiled, that made my day
You came and sat next to me
Under that big old shade tree

We talked for hours, and then some
But before we knew it, night had come
You rose and you touched the night
Only to remind me of my plight

You stood and stared into the sky
Then our eyes lock, smile and goodbye
I watched as you walked out of sight
Then I turn and pushed with all my might

It's been years since that wonderful day
My own hair now has a touch of gray
But I'll always remember that breeze in your hair
And how you didn't even notice my wheelchair

Karl R. Schneider

A Feeling, For Christmas

I went for a card, late eve Christmas Day,
But the stores were all closed, they were all packed away.
So I thought I would write, to tell you the sway,
That was stored in my mind, waiting for me to say.
Words don't come easy, but the thoughts are all there,
Thoughts that go deep, but never are shared.
Thoughts like, "I love you", and "Please, hold me tight",
When the moment is perfect, may come out some night.
But till then, I'll save those thoughts in a space,
Where all of my feelings and thoughts lie in place.
Till then I'll keep showing you, in my own way,
That you're special and wanted, though nothing I say.
To me, it's important for lovers to be friends,
And cherish that friendship, to the very end.
To the time, when here we can't speak, to say what we feel,
But you'll know with a touch, the feelings are real.
So I've said what I wanted, with tears in my eyes,
As I sit here alone, late eve Christmas Night.
May God bless and keep you, till the moment you're here,
To hold me with love, and we share Christmas Cheer.

Billy E. Bagby

Tomorrow, at dawn...

Tomorrow, at dawn, at the hour when the fields whiten,
I will set out. You see, I know that you are waiting for me.
I will go by the forest, I will go by the mountain.
I can no longer stay far from you.

I will walk lost in my thoughts,
Seeing nothing outside, not hearing one sound,
Alone, unknown, back bent, hands crossed,
Sad, and day for me will seem like night.

I will not notice the gold of the falling evening,
Nor the ships in the distance sailing for Harfleur,
And when I arrive, I will place on your grave
A bouquet of green holly and flowering heather.

Wenda Stang

Father

I can't thank you enough
for all you do
Your kind heart and helpfulness
is the best part of you.

You've lent your strength
in times of need
Always coming through
with another good deed.

You start from scratch building a castle
with your intelligence and knowledge
You accomplish anything
without a hassle.

You share your life with no restrictions
appearing when needed, day or night
Always seeming to solve my problems
by shedding new light.

This is just my little way
of saying thanks
For being my Father and friend
today and everyday since my life began.

Candi Stansberry

On Bended Knee

Here I am on bended knee,
Scarlets and blues shine down on me.
You're as near as my breath, yet I cannot speak.
Am I strong or am I weak?

The others here are bent and gray.
Do they have a place to stay?
Could it be here they found a friend
And peace at last, nearing their end?

Hush me now, and silence my soul.
With a deep sigh I bow my head low.
I awake with a start, and come to my senses.
Have I been jumping with sheep over fences?

How long have I been gone? How long under
The sweet sedative you call slumber?
It's getting quite late. I must be on my way.
I didn't even tell you the things I had to say.

A gentle calming of my heart leaves me reassured
All my words not spoken haven't gone unheard.
When life's burden take hold of me
I'll be back on bended knee.

Anima K. Muehlberg

About You

My heart grows impatient
With this masquerade.
And in hiding these feelings
I don't want to hide.
I know not how; nor why,
But the emotion is high
And you feel something too.
Frightened of the feeling,
It's been so long -
It's all about you.
To live those wonderful feelings...
Joy and happiness - Excitement anticipation
Expression is high.
You're suddenly alive - all inside - again.
And I thank you my friend
For the life in just being you.

Azalea M. Sandoval

Cloud Faces

There are faces in the clouds, that float across the sky.
From Norse, or Greek mythology; surveying you and I.
And oft' I've mused; "Are these just clouds, which on the
winds do ride?" "Or souls of lonely spirits, that in
purgatory hide?" Who with thunderous shouts and lightning
bolts, plead "GOD, open up the door, and cleanse one soul of
earthly sin, so that it float no more".
For suddenly, they'll disappear, these mounds of misty white,
And sunshine's gold will shine on through, to lead one soul
to light.

Frances A. Kulik

Blossom

Awaiting the hidden sun; its warmth and its light
Though I know it's there, but it's beyond my sight

I stand there in darkness, so cold and alone
Looking forward to the dawn, till this light is shown

At times it lingers and its rays fill me with life
'Till darkness falls upon me and I stand without might

I have no choice; to remain in this soil
It must have been meant; to be in this turmoil

But one day soon I will surely blossom
When this light mine'll rise; up from the bottom

For its my strength, my hope and my source
that keeps my heart beating; with love at full force.

Nancy Vasquez

"White Lie"

I had a friendship that was based upon a lie,
And to my grave, upon my chest
A small white whisper on my lips.
As I lived, I breathed, I died.
What I could have told,
Had I been so bold,
To risk a shedding tear,
Of I myself, a mortal soul,
Kept silent by my fear.
I question what I could have done.
What subtly I could have used,
To tread lightly upon a broken heart,
Is not to trample, the same thing?
So I carried the weight,
Which bore me down,
Though through the years it graced me.
For I who told that one small lie,
ignored the greater sin,
of being lover...mistress,
To the husband of my best friend.

Becky L. Miller

Untitled

Today I am yours,
Today you are mine,
Today we are one.
Our paths of life have crossed.
Today they become one.
The walk of life is long and hard.
Times will come and go when we may stray.
Our love will bring us back to follow our path together.

Christine Esson

Feral Humanity

Alone after everything
her heart lets go a silent scream.
It fills the space left by the lies,
instruments of man's demise.

A rabbit's howl, a cry of pain.
A deadly struggle ends the same.
The slain are cast off to the side
Their souls exposed to silent crimes.

Crimes in secret, no one knows.
Cheating hearts, incestuous moans.
A child is made to feel the pain.
Her life destroyed, her child's the same.

A silent scream, a quiet heart.
And always man has taken part.
The beast inside, his will be done.
The wild kingdom claims her son.

Lorie Fiedler

Spring

The geese flew overhead today,
    Pushing their mates on the way
Honking ever impatiently,
    Flying fast, flying free.

Silhouettes, black against blue
    A chorus as they flew.
The day was February forth
    As the honkers journeyed north.

Fluttering wings, such a chatter,
    With their feathers all astir;
Announcing the coming of spring
    and all the beauty it will bring.

Spreading the word, trumpeters white,
    Shimmering against the afternoon light.
Frogs, crickets and critters abound,
    Awakened from the sleeping ground.

There can be no message better,
    Not by phone nor by letter,
Than that which can be heard
    From the call of the wild bird.

Irene Haas

Dear Lisa

Today's the day I want to speak my love to my one and only little dove.
In the future I see us together with hopefully having nice weather.
I think of you often, with one thing in mind
of you in my arms that I will find.
Together, forever we shall be in love always, O Gee!
Thoughts the same and bodies as one
Let's have a hot dog and forget the bun.
I hope you love me as I love you, because if you don't, Boo, Hoo, Hoo.
Thinking of you, I get excited;
My love so strong, I can't fight it.
Now I need you more than ever, oh baby, just grab my lever.
I know we will live in harmony forever and ever studying
    astronomy.
All I want is for us to be happy
Chop Chop Bolly Bolly, let's make this snappy!
Maybe one day, we will have kids
don't forget to put the garbage out and close the lids.
I want our life together to be the best,
    and I'll make sure it's nothing less.
Oh Lisa, I love you more than my fish!
believe me, you'll always be my favorite dish!

Michael Cangiano

Falling Snow

The snow looks like pure white angels,
As I watch it falling cuddled up in my chair.
Brrr! The cold weather brings chills to me.
Layer upon layer, the warm clothes I wear.

I sit by the warm fire to keep my fingers and toes,
White sipping my hot chocolate (yum, yum, yum).
The Christmas spirit dances around the house with joy,
Followed by the new year — young and hum.

Friends and I enjoy wild snowball fights,
Having fun while dashing down the hills on our sleds.
In our front yards we make snow angles and forts,
Then skate away on the frozen ponds up ahead.

At the end of the day, as we gather by the fire,
We share the fun times, that we've had with each other.

Neelu Tummala

My Best Friend, My Dad

I am very glad that you are my dad
We have shared good times and bad times
When I see the Broncos anywhere I always think of you
You can always tell when I am mad or upset
There is no other best friend I would ever have than you

When I am with you I enjoy being with you
I am glad that I am your daddy's girl
You can talk me through something that I can get upset about and
say that you understand what I am going through
There is no other best friend I would ever have than you

Whenever you need help around the house you know that I will be there
You taught me to be what I want to be
There is no other best friend I would ever have than you

When I hear Daddy's Hands on the radio is like the bond that we
share all the time when we spend time together
When I go riding in the truck I am grateful that I can do that with
you I am very happy that you are there for me
Don't worry I know some of you tricks and you will not beat me
There is no other best friend I would ever have than you

Casee Conner

Morning

Sparkle! Crystalline glitter broadcast randomly
On emerald blades of grass and lawn.
The sparkling spell magically echoed
In the mirror of water beyond.

A teardrop prism dangles perilously from a leaf.
Reticently releasing it's tenuous hold,
The liquid diamond falls unimpeded,
Shattering the glassy surface below.

Halos radiate from the fragmented facade,
Heaving a galaxy of stars at the shore.
Moving silently ever outward
Until they are seen no more.

A gold-trimmed peridot envelope
Cloaks the mysterious change
Of a forthcoming monarch who,
Over the flowers will reign.

The bejeweled silver filigree of an arachnid architect,
Links distant pieces of greenery
With strands usually hard to detect.
Magic evaporates as the sun rises up.

Nancy Y. Fuchs

Practice What You Preach

When you sing,
  "He's a mighty God!"
do you believe that God can do anything?
When you cry,
  "I couldn't keep it to myself!"
would you really tell someone about what the Lord has done for you;
or would you even try?
When you say,
  "It's time to make the change!"
would you make the change in your life today?
There are many many songs we can sing.
But, if that is all we are doing, it doesn't mean a thing.
The songs has a message as good as gold.
That undenying truth that cannot be sold.
The message is not hidden it's where everyone can see.
What is done with the message is up to you and me.
Time is winding down, as we all know;
now it is time for you to decide which way you will go.

You could keep singing and not do a thing;
or, practice what you preach and gain everything.

Keisha L. Cohen

Untitled

In my darkest dreams, there is a friend,
Who links me closest to my end.
His name is death and beside his throne,
My chair is waiting on its own.

His eyes are vacant stares of hate,
His hands are bloody, wet by fate.
His robe is blackened by the night,
His whole appearance does not affright.

My arms reach out to touch his hand,
But I can't reach his hellish land.
My heart is pounding filled with blood,
He tears my soul, I feel the flood.

Into his vacant eyes I stare,
His hand out-stretched, I see it there.
My heart has stopped, there is no life,
With one short stroke, he breaks the knife.

Within my empty chest he lays,
He drinks my blood and takes my days.
My insides are on the outside now,
The show is over, take a bow.

Bobbi Jo Stevens

Why

Why is there greed and envy
why do we run and hide
tell me show me
how you feel inside
    there must be some good
    under all of this sin
    teach me guide me
    where to begin
why is there fear and hunger
why do we lie and hate
tell me show me is this all just fate
    there must be some reason
    I don't understand help me
    take me hold our your hand
why is there pain and suffering
why do we steal and fight
tell me show me
how to show them the light
    there must be someone who is living out there
    teach me help me take the time to care

Deborah Heider

Song Of The Wind

The wind is like a song
That echoes through the night
It sings a song of beauty
'Till the dawns welcoming light

From morning to dusk
It sneaks over a dune
As if it were looking for something lost
With its lyrical and dreamless tune

And as I pass a field
And watch the grass dance and bend
I can still hear the harmonious cry
The song of the wind

Nicole Billings

Spiritual Growth

By GOD's spirit of holiness JESUS was conceived,
Became flesh for a while,
GOD's will to fulfill those who believe.

Then JESUS to GOD returned as HE said HE would.
And to us did send THE HOLY SPIRIT for our growth and good.
Spiritual growth scripture says
by GOD's word we are to be fed.

This I affirm!
Through THE HOLY SPIRIT,
I LEARN.

HE directs as JESUS expects, not of our own accord.
Not to images and idols galore;
Nor to stadiums the games of ball to chase;
Not to the maze of bureaucratic direction;
Nor to society's pretentious perfection.

But tis true indeed;
GOD's spirit-directed, life-giving, omni-presence we need.
Then grow we must as questions, problems, concerns, activities,
to HIM we TRUST.

Charles E. Emswiler Jr.

Special Time of Year

Winter is here, it's come at last
And the snow, is beginning to fall

For Christmas has come, to this land
And the bells, ring deck the halls

The children are singing, in the streets
Of peace, and harmony

And as they gather, around the trees
They sing, for you and me

Maybe it's this special time of year
Which makes one think, of those so dear

So I'll say, to all of you
  Merry Christmas, my friends
    And a lovely
    New Year

Steve A. McCarty

Attraction

This is our second interlude
under the devious demise.
It begins with tension in our souls
until we become enveloped with each other.

I am grasping the earth at this moment.
clutching with my nails at the rapturous bang
creating a surge of enamored feelings within me.
Time stands still and we become one within each other.

The sweetness in your lips
sends a quiver through my bones.
Your enticing touch jostles my flesh.
As my eyes close, I envision it an eternity.

Catherine Serao

Alone

A dark black circle of everlasting sorrow,
A long, rough, bumpy road.
The smell of emptiness, the taste of bitterness,
listening to the cry of your loneliness.
Alone, all alone, like an abandon child,
covered in a black cape,
your happiness trapped inside.
Not being able to capture the feelings
of the one you let go,
Not knowing what will happen
I feel your sorrow.

Amy Camblin

Crossroads-Invisible In The Black

Love is like a finely spun web,
That cocoons you from the inside,
Stray thoughts linger through your head,
And confusion becomes your guide.

For love never leaves you with an easy answer,
Because it pounds so loudly in your ears,
Telling you riddled lines for your mind to uncover,
Unaware of its delivery of smiles or tears.

Love leads you along an uncharted path,
Because your heart is leading the way,
Then it springs upon you, as if to ask,
"Do you know what your tomorrow will bring you today?

Love for the now, knows no tomorrow,
Unknowing of how, it reaps a futureless sorrow.
For the winds of emotions has thrown you in a whirl,
And love has its price in a complicated world.

The crossroads are waiting at my door,
Relentlessly knocking more than ever before,
I can no longer hold them back,
For I must choose a path, invisible in the black!

E. Carole Ogden

Why?

So many people ask why?
If you look inside then you can look in your
eye, to find the answer.
Don't be the problem not the solution.
Society can see everybody responsibility,
What about you? Are you do what you
should be done? The best of your ability?
The question come full circle, why?
Look deep in the mirror, very close in your eye,
Then maybe you will see the answer, why.

Marian E. Butler

Writer's Mantle

Snow, gentle gracious snow,
Covering the earth with your beauty,
Like a soft white cloud descended from heaven
To bring a moment of peace to the world.
How I love your stillness!
You lie upon the hills like a velvet mantle,
Flowing over every crag and peak,
Clothing every branch and bush.
Not the smallest twig is left untouched.
Just for a moment the world is calm and lovely
While we drink in the beauty
That lies so quiet upon the earth.
Drink deeply, everyone -
Fill the wellsprings of your souls
So you may draw upon them
When the snow has gone away.

Ruth R. Beeson

Untitled

In all my effort to find true immunity
    my soul, does it fail?
There is the great desire to feel whole
    and I do not.
The need for expression comes out ill
    yet you are able to see, and I am not!

I can only breathe what you ex-hale

I am but a blackened night
    highlighted in cream clouds...
holding an elegant memory
    that is no memory of mine
wrapped in my own frustrated realm of sanity
where my goals are set behind with the past.

Brandy Trujillo

Untitled

I love to walk in the evening,
in a soft gentle rain.
All seems quiet and the solitude
eases any worry or pain.
The hustle and hurry of the world,
gradually seems far away.

It always seems I am alone with my Lord,
wherever the place, and my small
problems are gone, leaving no trace.

I wish that all people could feel the
calm, and be aware that the Lord, holds
them in His palm.

He wishes to fill all our lives with His
gentle love and He shows us with His
peaceful rain from above.

Jerry L. Jackson

The Voice

Once everything was purified and refined,
Before all of Earth was dug up and mined.
The animals lived freely in the rough chain of life,
This was before the gun and the knife.
All forests were virgin and green,
Then man came in with ax and machine.
The air and water, now polluted and gray,
Were once clean and fresh like a morning in May.
"Help!" a voice cries from the air, land and water,
No one hears, but the deer and the otter.

Julie Haar

Evening Walk In December

"A storm is coming up but we'll have time to take a walk
Before it hits," I told my wife. So we set out. We don't talk much.
At seventy-five we've said it all before. We walk our dog
Past church, courthouse, and the funeral home where tombstones
Are on display. "The one I liked, the one with overlapping hearts
Joined in the middle, is gone; where it was is only bare ground now."
I thought about the new earth now exposed, here, and on a grave.
As we walked on, the sun came down below the storm clouds.
Nearly to the horizon now, its mellow evening rays
Promised no storm soon . . . But what is that? — A brilliance
From the east, up in the Green Hill Cemetery where graves
Date back to our nation's birth, it seemed that every marker was a star.
One in particular caught the rays with perfect angle almost blinding us.
It must have been a dual marker, one for "man and wife." We paused
In wonder, for it looked like stars of heaven clustering 'round the sun.
But stars don't shine in daylight. Now we come to Green Hill Road;
Tonight we are not going up to be among the gravestones,
But to the house we live in: to supper, evening news —
"and so to bed."

William E. Epler

Tenacious States

Why is cohesiveness called great?
Is it because "coh" and "3" are one?
Why is the word tough have degrees of rate?
Is it because tenacity is 7 worlds not one?

Why is adhesive another state?
Is it because we can either love or hate?
Why is this state such a sticky mate?
Is it also because this is defined as great?

Why is it a word so Strong?

Is it because our opinions can be rights?
Why is devastation thought of as wrong?
Is it because everything is thought of as black or white?

Why is any disease so patiently stubborn?
Is it because my free will can be so obstinate?
Why must I be so spiritually warm?
Is it because it can be stated with wit?

Why can any disease hide or retain?
Is it because my God is so strong in memory?
Why is any disease called inhumane?
Is it because some don't call it a part of humanity?

Mark Sabin

Lost In A Sea Of Misfortune,
A World Turned Against Me

Love, strong as the ocean tide, tears at my heart as if this tender
    vessel were a small, tattered sail boat
I used to follow the winds of love, until wind turned to storm-and
    overthrew me
I'm drowning in a world turned against me
No land in sight
I swim for days only to find, that I am still defeated
I no longer have a course to follow
My destination, I can only imagine
To the on-looker, I am an experienced captain guiding my ship
In reality though, I can only pretend
I am tossed and turned by the waves of misfortune,
    the waves of opportunity
The sky, oblique in its grayness, hides hope
There are no stars to guide me
I only endeavor to survive the day at hand and each day I pray
    that I will soon find my way

John Michael Wells

Mom Said...

I can't tell him...the words won't form.
Eye contact impossible - - Mom said I have to have it.

Sixteen years old; planned future destroyed...
A mistake I can't eliminate -
   Because, Mom said I have to have it.

Explanation attempted...no acceptance to be granted.
   If I died —would it die, too?
It doesn't matter - Mom said I have to have it.

Only eight weeks now — would it hurt?
I wonder what Daddy would say.
   I'm his baby — having one.
Mom said I have to have it.

Blindfolded by familiar tears; shaking in desperation and fright.
No one knows my confusion, they're merely observing a statistic.
I want to run and hide - 'till this nightmare goes away,
   But, Mom said I have to have it.

Made my thoughtless decision, in a passionate frenzy,
Now the outcome... no longer my decision.
I curl, and feel my cold legs against my chest...
   I am completely alone.
   Corie Vickers

Progenitor

Crossing the channel under a blue sky,
behind us the chalky cliffs, ahead France.
We sit atop the P and O ferry,
you and the girls, wisps of blond curls, windblown
smiles in butterfly colored coats. Somewhere
above the same water fifty years ago,
my father fell from the sky, lost forever,
and now as we cross paths, I ponder his
last view, puzzled by providence and time
realize I'm older now than he ever was.

The water like blowing leaves churns away
in the wake of lost memory. Later in
Paris, on the rue de la Harpe as I
hear the rain and the bells of Notre Dame,
I recall his last letter to my mother,
telling her of the lights of this city,
I listen for the drone of his engines, ghosts
in twilight, when I see your beautiful
faces reflected in the river as we are
carried on by the tides of remembrance.
   John David Brooks

Love

Love drives you to do your best,
Not to leave things undone.
It lasts forever,
And its feeling is second to none.
It is a teacher of patience and sacrifice,
Of compassion and of strife.
It stays with you to the very end of life.

It is like a seed you plant and water.
It starts out very small,
And every day it gets bigger
Until it encompasses all.

The more work and time you give,
The more your love will grow.
It will bloom into a beautiful flower
Before you even know.

Love is something you don't just get,
Something you just receive.
If you just serve the one you love,
You'll get more than you can believe!
   Darrell Whitmer

Views Of A Sunken Dream The Disaster Of The Titanic

A Reporter
It was all in perfect astonishment. The mighty indestructible beast.
Burdened with the unbearable truth
   That humans will never reach total perfection.
Many a life were drowned in man's pride
   his over confidence, his disdainfulness, his insolence.
Lost in a horrible reflection of man's flaws
   By a lesson taught by the most powerful teacher.
One that we paid for with our own blood
   One that will not soon be forgotten.

The Iceberg
It was all in perfect darkness that I began my long mournful journey.
Down toward the heated islands
   Where this life would quickly banish me.
But my trek stopped short by a blade
   A sharpness, a sting, a serration.
Disrupting the path I was travelling
   A titanic form loomed over me, thrashing in a struggle
With a frigid heartless ocean that would not let her free
   The surging sea claimed her prize then let me on my way.
   Kevin O'Neill

"Making A Difference"

The tide was out, the sand lay bare,
in the distance a man stood there.

He stooped and picked up something and gently
tossed the object into the open sea.

As he continued to do this, I became a bit confused.
My curiosity raised, I ran to him bemused.

"What are you doing?" I asked with some reservation.
He looked and said without hesitation,

"I'm saving the starfish from the baking sun, by
giving it to the ocean to live and have fun!"

I looked at the miles of beach and said to him,
"There are hundreds of starfish, you're on a whim!"

Nonetheless, he continued relentlessly,
Responding, "at least I'll make a difference for
the next two or three."
   Jeffrey J. Swan

A Journey Through The Mist

Do you understand the rain?
See it bless or does it stain?
On this brisk November night,
enter into its domain.
Release your hold; contemplate,
recall the past, envision fate.
Shining through the darkened light,
feel emotions it creates.
It trickles down the windowside,
like tears you know you just can't hide.
The pain is blind, so close your eyes,
do not fear and fear's denied.
Rain's severe, embrace the sun,
your mind and body have joined as one.
Rise above, and hurt no more,
for now your freedom has begun.
   Nicholas Gaudiuso

Single Mother

Single mother, that's me
I know no other way to be
for some that may be a crying shame
because they feel someone else should take the blame
but for me, it's all that I know
it's my two children that keep me aglow
single mother, that's me
I know no other way to be!

Tina Johnson

Untitled

Riverwalks...losing count the number of times,
we've walked along the riverbanks.
Magically-our walks always feel like, our first romantic stroll,
walking side by side-holding hands, stealing kisses.
Laughing, talking...about old memories, reminiscing of
things in our past.

The river has overheard us plan our future,
listening to the love and longing in our voice
as we shared our dreams.
Looking down into-deep, dark waters,
wondering silently what the future holds.
Smiling when we realize, we're thinking a like.
Our riverwalks will always remain part of our lives.
For our love grew, blossomed like a flower,
along the river banks.

Time has a way-of slipping by,
when looking out, across the waters.
It seems we just got here...now already,
it's time for goodbye.
Never wanting to leave, slowly walking back....
slowly away from the river.

Jessica F. Roberts

Color

The greenest color of the grass
The golden color of a horn of brass
The whitest color when a babies born
And the brightest yellow of fresh cooked corn
The pitch black color of the night
Sputtering red blood when people fight
The clear color of a tear rolling down
someone's cheek
The dull orange of a birds beak
The bluest color of the bright morning skies
And the disappearing colors when someone dies

But if you feel the world is getting duller,
Immerse yourself with lots of color.

Rachel Quatroni

Anamnesis

Harmed hearts have hidden places, locked with care
  Where demons drone dark mantras of despair.
For souls enduring this, one antidote:
"Forget!" an optimist naively wrote,
"Amnesia is the sole viaticum
Bestowing peace and ghost of freedom".
Deluded fools drink Lethe's dumbing draught,
Seduced by Oblivion's cunning craft.
Amnesia's fruit's annihilation,
But mem'ry's life's — prime denotation.

Ann Trinita Sohm

Untitled

In the beginning,
The sun rose,
Then there was a starry romantic sky.
After the sound of the ocean's waves,
He needed someone to enjoy it,
  So life began.
He didn't encourage the worry or hurt.
He never expected the greed or the ignorance.
Did we make Him sorry for his gift to us?

Deborah Zoppetti

Boss Lady

I call you Boss Lady, with utmost respect, you bet,
'Cause you're one of the nicest ladies I've ever met.
You have style, you have charm, you have grace,
Topped only by the loving smile always upon your face.

To your students, you are kind hand giving to their need,
Yet shaping them sharply to produce to and beyond their ability, indeed.
They love you, and appreciate the way that you care;
It's a talent that's very good, but also very rare.

Your co-workers all respect you and admire you, too,
'Cause when they have problems, they can come to you.
You comfort them and always seem to know what to do;
They know they can count on you to always see them through

Meeting you has touched me in a every special way;
You made me feel welcome that very first day.
Your listening ear to my problems of these troubled times,
Made me feel, at least, someone cares, and that was really sublime.

So, Boss Lady, let me finish by saying this too;
And I mean it sincerely, and it's really true;
Keep being the wonderful, loving, caring person that I came to know,
And believe me when I say, because of you, I really hate to go.

Rudolph L. Greaux

Can You Hear The Children Cry

Those of us on the outside looking in
  Close our eyes and pretend
Not to see; our ears do not hear
  The crying children with unmeet needs
The warning signs we do not heed
As troubled parents look around,
  They commit their crimes
They do not think, hoping to not be found
  As the children's blood cries from the ground.
For you see, this is the heritage
  The parents brought from home
It's all they've seen and what they do
  Is all they've ever known.
Those of us who are looking in,
  Heroes in our eyes
Reexamine ourselves, our lives,
  Our parenthood as we realize,
The potential for this crime of crimes is in us all
  God help us hear the children cry.

Verna Moss

On The Edge Of A Dream

They think that they have won.
Now, that this time has come.
But, still hold on fast.
One moment will forever last.
Look on, as you will move.
There is nothing to prove.
For, excellence is a process, my friend.
A dream we search for until the end.

Carmela Cantone

Who?

You ask me who sent me, and all I can say is that
one day I awoke and remembered who I was and why I am:
  A lover, a lover of beauty, in form and idea, of jubie-faeries
    and Celtic tragedies. I yearn for the glamour, for the
  kalos vitae which flows.
  Romantic beauty, sweet violinist of the night,
    your music thrums within my beating heart,
   and the power, the glory, and the majesty
    of *life* is "all I know and all I need to know."
Truth? Beauty? Of course, what else do I
  require? Only my passionate wings, my
    masculine strength, and...
    and perhaps you, to share with, to share
  life with...
            or just this moment.

  Marc-Tizoc Gonzalez

Awakened Dream

For Erin

From the day you were born in my eyes
one thought became clearer than bright
a flow of uneasiness to follow
yet a feeling that has never been touched
pride of self finally rising
words won't say what wants to be said
runaway, but someone will follow
runaway, but nothing will stay
deep colour red prevails throughout
seeing through blindness clears
holding you in my arms
is what emblazes my deepest feelings for you
you now own everything I am
the love for you is yet to be uncovered
being with you is a come true fantasy
scattering my mindless thoughts
from the day you were born in my eyes
one thought became clearer than bright
my love for you will last
for as long as we make one!

  Mike Krishman

The Pursuit Of Happiness

I look up to see you watching,
Your eyes promise what your heart can never give,
Inner feelings threaten to surface
I look away.

My heart breaks at every glance,
Emotions clamor in rebellion,
Where were you when I was down?
"Right by your side" comes the reply.

I hear you say that you care,
(are your feelings real-or only pretend?)
You talk so much—what are you saying?
You're a bundle of conflicting statements.

When I want to tell you the truth
Why do I run and hide from view?
I'm so scared of the pain...
I look up and find you gone.

  Christina B. Tutterow

Black Woman

In ancient Cush they were treated like goddess.
Worshipped for the royalty they are. Their skin baked
in the riches of oil, bright as a brass vase, at least
that is what the BLACK WOMAN is to me.

She is a sister to her brother, mother to her
child, for any man to look upon her beauty, would shiver
and fall, at least, that is the BLACK WOMAN who
gives her all.

In her day's of slavery, she was the eye of delight,
her master had to posses her, for the beauty
held insight.

Mother of a nation held in pride, for the BLACK
WOMAN to go on, how long must she hide?

  John D. Wilson

Eulogy For Hope

I plead, dear hopes, to still your stir.
Don't fumble like a nervous child.
Though years you've waited burning myrrh,
I fear your pyre is flaming wild.
Through nightly discourse you have knelt
And prayed for graves to close their folds
Far into which the past has dealt
Its miseries in future's mold.
What must you ask for in the dark?
Its love is foul when swallowed whole.
Yet pray I must here or embark
Against a world and not her soul.
Oh, yes, it's love that I do crave!
A passion felt by many here,
But me, a lonely beggar's knave -
I've naught the strength but gallant fear.
So, Hope, I turn to you of mine,
Oh, damaged friend preserved in rot.
Although you've died a thousand times,
Immortal your sweet saving thoughts.

  Robert Pickerelli

Aids Touches All

He told me of the night they shared
The love, the lust yet unaware

Our world has encountered a deadly disease
It takes away your hope- takes away your need

He said it wasn't a one night stand
He wanted to see him again and again

To share the love that two men feel
In a society that demands "This love is not real"

Neither one asked who nor did they ask why
Only knowing the fear that they soon would die

So he hides behind an image, to ride out the wait
Yet others still only see his ill fate

Our world together must find a way
To say that loving one another is really ok

This long dark journey - no end in sight
A battle cry against aids, won't end without a fight
Stand-up do your part whether you are gay or straight
Our world is about love not about hate...

  Mary T. Upshaw

Driving

They keep passing me by, one by one, color after color.
Many window's telling stories about the lives within.
Traveling anonymously across the concrete plains, hearts
and souls bond together inside their metal casings.
What are they saying?
Are they as one?
I'm surrounded but they don't see me, they don't hear me.
Just another passing obstacle in their path.
I have windows but there are no stories to share.
The airwaves are my only companion
    as I move solely out of their way.
How I yearn for such a window, a window with a story.
A window with dreams, hopes, a future.
When I do, then someday, someone will wonder what stories there
    are behind my glass walls.

Lisa Ann Joan Iacolino

Proposal

I've searched and searched for many years
And in that search I've shed many tears
I never thought the day would come
That I would find that special one
The love we share is so very true
I'm so glad I finally met you
How happy you make is easy to explain
Your always there to take away the pain
It's more than just love it's a friendship too
That's just one of the reasons why I love you
I've searched and searched all my life
To find the perfect woman to be my wife
I know in my heart how happy we would be
I love you, will you marry me!

Michael Raymond Sweeney

Are You Listening?

This is to real women out there
I speak to you and you shun me
You do not think I will respect you
I know who's a lady and who's a tramp I know exactly who you are
You are our mothers, our sisters, and wives
You are our cousins, our lovers and friends
For the true women out there not all men are players
If you believe that you don't know what you're missing
I got love to give please are you listening?
I just wanted you to know because it's lonely out here
I have respect for real women so why don't you believe me?
Give me one chance and I'll show you
There are real men out there you just have to listen
They usually won't have much but plenty to offer
They can show you things that money can't buy
They can fill your day with love that won't cost
The only price is your love in return
So when you get through playing games with all the players
I'll still be out there waiting but not forever
My heart is speaking... are you listening?

Jake Colston

Deer

Yesterday I saw a deer
Standing there with a stretched out ear
Maybe listening for a mate
Maybe waiting for a date
I saw another walk up on he
Then they hopped away, as if jumping with glee

Kyle Waggoner

Freedom of the Heart

Do you ever wish your heart was free
    Free to fly on the wings of the wind?
        Never to be touched by human hands;
            Never to be torn in vicious strands.
Left to soar above the clouds
    Rising to heights unknown.
        Never again to burst from your chest in agony and pain,
            Only to live in harmony with the dreams flowing from your brain.
The hardest thing to remember
    Is the lining on every cloud;
        To know that during every storm
            The sun is shining now.
For every tear your heart must bear
    Throughout life's little play,
        Your soul will know a joy so great
            Only you can find the way!

Noelle E. Adams

Until Darkness Is Gone

Your gentle hand brushes against my cheek,
Your words are those that lovers speak.
Your lips are sweet pressed against mine,
As your finger trail slowly down my spine.
My breasts are crushed against your chest,
My ears are filled with the sound of your breath.
My hands tangle in your soft hair,
Time has stopped, yet I don't care.
For with the sun, dawn with break,
And scorn this gentle love we make.
Hold me close, pretend nothing is wrong,
And love me until the darkness is gone.

Kelly A. Morin

To Mother

My mother is a nice one
Her love is bigger than the sun
Wider than the ocean
But being around her is not that fun

Or so it seems in teen years
As her life and mine are filled with tears
Our lives are filled with pain
As I try to take my own life's reign

To her I am just strange
Why I try, I don't know
Life's cool wind will blow
Then I will fall back on what she thought

A mother's love can't be bought
So, to my mother with lots of love
Watch your little Dove fly away
But three words I must say
I love you, and that's okay
And I will say I love you for the rest of my days

William Curtis Riggs

"Tears"

Tears so warm and salty, they flow across my cheeks.
    They are my silent comfort when I'm lonely, sad or weak.
They steal upon my pillow in the hours before the dawn.
    When as I'm fondly thinking of that loved one who is gone.
And when a word so hot and cruel has pierced my broken
heart. I then will seek a quiet place and let my teardrops start.
    Perhaps I then have tried and failed, in a task that has been mine.
    Or perhaps I'm sad and lonely for that loved one left behind.
Whatever been the reason, in the night or in the day,
    the teardrops will come softly...
    and wash my grief away.

Jay Stevens

Untitled

"Heavens mourn the reflection of life,
the sky cried gray tears.

From within the hush and hiss of the
smoldering steam of the street.

An outstretch hand pierces through
the screen of despair to capture a fragment of serenity.

A fresh puddle of heaven's tears bring relief,
cleansing the soul with the baptism of nature.

To scorn the death of friends last past?

Or to possibly celebrate the rebirth of others.

Healing seem these solemn, wishful moments."

Constance Rain

Tell Me, Sylvia Plath

Please tell me, Sylvia Plath
When you put your head inside the oven
Did you think of your kids? Of Ted, your Husband?
　　I really do not mean to pry
　　but knowing I will never try
　　to kill myself by suicide
　　I'd like to share your last impression
　　of masochism and depression.
　　So sensitive, you touched my senses
　　But your poems had their consequences
　　And your nakedness left you defenseless

Do you believe artistic sadness
Inevitably leads to madness?

Ming Nagel

Why Me?

Enclosed within a thick wall of crystalline
Impermeable to all who try to enter in
Cloaked by distrust and fear
Surrounded by a lifetime of tears
　　is my heart and soul

Wounded gravely by lies, broken dreams, and heartache
They are numb to all they see and hear
For they fear to trust
　　they fear to believe
　　　they fear to love
　　　　they fear to even live

Because one again they know they will be betrayed

They wonder what could have been
　　what might have been
　　what SHOULD have been
And what they know will NEVER be

In a little box in the corner is the dream
they both envisioned and longed for shattered
into so many tiny fragments, like tiny crystal beads
Locked in with the key of guilt with resentment stand guard

Denyce Dauwalder

Silence

He keeps me in my mundane cage
Flightless, frightened, struggling
Almost on my way to becoming
Almost...
Through the panes of glass
Distorted views of life
Like a story that I am
Somehow detached from
Only a viewer
Never belonging
My voice is forgotten in the silence
Only he is allowed to speak
This stranger beside me whose touch I once longed for
Now imprisons me with his arms
It has been so long since I have been allowed a say
A moment to be myself
That I cannot remember what my own voices sounds like
Silence...

Michelle Monty

Untitled

The waves, a lover's hands caressing the sand.
Sensations, so pure tingle over my flesh as the same wave submerges
my body in a warm bliss.

I close my eyes and listen attentively to every message being conveyed
to me by this land yet secretive liquid.

It tells me of people long past and their love of the sea
And how much it wants them back; but they're lost in this world.

It deplores me to search for its many lovers; yet it knows that no one
can ever find them. So it welcomes me with a grand ceremony of
senses, and pulls me into its warm embrace.

I don't ever want to go back; I don't ever want to leave
This peaceful haven; this hypnotic kingdom

The lives all around me so honest and pure are worth more than the
　　greatest of our great world.

I don't ever want to return; and leave my turquoise place
To go back to ruins of soil and dirt.

The sea is my lover; and it becomes to me; to be surrounded by it
　　till eternity.

And when the sun goes down; and night-time comes; the darkness of
my place is still so bright; for my serenity and happiness is able
to light a million torches and illuminate my life.

Sandra I. Shehadeh

Ode To A Cat

Somehow a cat landed in my house.
I wasn't aware if he would catch a mouse;
but you may be sure, he would about face
if he weren't able to catch a mouse in this place!

Somehow a cat landed in my lap.
I wasn't aware of even having had a nap!
But, you may be sure, even now he doesn't nap...
Without first jumping into my lap.

Somehow a cat has brought me joy,
And he's a mere feline neutered boy.
But, you may be sure, I can truthfully say
That cat has made my day!

Isobel S. Gridley

As Days Go By

She sat alone, and lonely
In the corner of a dim lit room
Recalling delightful memories
Of the years gone by too soon.

With the light from dirt
Stained windows washing over
Her wizened old face
Gave her the look of beauty and grace.

She remembers the days of spring
The sunshine, the flowers, and the pain
Her eye sight grows dimmer
Her hands begins to tremble
As she sat in deep reflection
of past hopes and expectation.

She remembers the long hot days of summer
Filled with laughter and slumber
Hot dogs sizzling on the grill
Children playing in the field
Looking back with a pleasant sigh
Remembering days gone by.

Mazie Williams

"The Wind"

I heard a voice on the wind
She said "I'll talk to you like a friend"
"We will walk where the road bends"
But forever I will be the wind

I walked to the edge
I thought I'd fall down
And all the world around had gone blind
The wind said I wasn't the only one she found

We stand back and worry about all we see
We stand back and worry about what we can't change
The wind says only think about what you can be
And leave alone the things you can't rearrange

The wind had taught me to fly
The wind heard me sigh
She dried the tears in my eyes
And told me "Your life is yours to try"

I heard a voice on the wind.
She said "This day is not the end"
When time comes for the road to bend
I will be there to be your friend

Jef Fern

The Acquaintance

I think of us as two strangers.
At opposite ends of a street,
  Walking...toward each other.

The more we traveled,
The closer we became.
Soon we were able
To recognize one another.
Then we met, and
We enjoyed each other's company.
  But still walking.

We continued to walk,
In opposite directions,
  Until...we were completely out of view.

Sarah Prindl

How Many Broken Promises?

How many broken promises have you made to me?
I can't begin to count them, too many don't you see!

Your reasons are so many and good ones they are too,
You think it makes it okay to cause the hurt you do!

It really doesn't matter, cause when I'm dead and gone,
I really won't take notice, if they go on and on!

I'm sorry I'm a bother, I guess it's sad but true,
I guess I thought you loved me the way that I loved you!

And as you read this poem please do not cry for me,
It really doesn't matter, for now I'm dead you see!

It really doesn't matter, cause now I'm dead and gone,
I really won't take notice if they go on and on!

Betty L. Ramsey

"They Don't Make Erasers Big Enough"

There are some things that I have done
And some things that I have said,
That I wish I could erase - and
Enter something else instead.

Oh! There have been times when nothing
Would have been a better choice
Than the unkind thing I did - or
The way I used my voice.

Have you wished to change a gruff word
Or a thoughtless, impulse act?
We wish we could rub them out but
I found this to be a fact.

No matter how I worked to change
An act or a word so gruff;
It didn't change a thing. They don't
make erasers big enough.

Jessie Geater

Ride Of Your Life

All aboard on a new adventure
the ship is about to sail
onto a new horizon
just not so close to the rail.

The water is somewhat choppy
as tides come in then out
occasionally the sea gets calm
and the sea gulls fly about.

Not certain of this strange new world
or what it has in store for me
but one thing I am sure of
is nothing in life is free.

Stop now and then to test the wind
and see which way it is sending you
if for some reason it's the wrong direction
turn a few degrees and continue.

Kelli-Ann Bliss

On My Own

When times are hard and things get tough
and surviving is difficult enough,
I think of days when I was young
and life alone had just begun.

To scrimp and save to pay a bill
was something hard to do at will.

Then marriage came and tough times past,
but the love we had, it didn't last.

So off I went set out to do
the best I could to start anew.

Working hard just to make a buck
blood, sweat and tears and a little luck.

And now I guess that you could say
things have finally gone my way.

And though you see I'm still alone,
I'm happy and I'm on my own.

Barbara Cullen

Untitled

There are some who've lived forever
In crawling, black-filled cells.
They've watched as the sun sunk
First into a liquid vase
Next slid behind a ground of cycad and ice.
And in swift scuttling movements
We strain to stretch long our cut of twine
Bound inevitably into the matrix
Of their den of stench and dark diaphanous shell.
Their curved back with crunched up limbs
Huddled in anticipation of the next catastrophe
Lasting on yet not living
Like a star withholding its light

Amy Anderson

Breakfast

A flash of green
bolts through the elfin forest.
A tangle of deformed, twisted trees
looming ominously overhead.
Weak shafts of unwarming, worthless sunlight
painted stained glass
on the carpeted, green forest floor.
A choking, musty, putrid darkness
hangs in the air
like a thick cloud of smoke.
The night has brushed the forest floor with dew.

Steel claws rip at every muscle.
A burst of pain shudders through every tendon
and then nothing
as the lifeless body of a lizard
is carried into the air

A victory cry arises
deep within the soaring eagle
and shatters the stillness
of the quiet mountain morning

Matt Adams

Your Tapestry

Everyone has troubles they've gathered along life's way
    Some have no solutions, some you handle day by day.

What you are and how you feel is written on your face,
    Don't carry all your burdens there as you travel place to place.

Count up all your blessings be they large or be they small,
    While you're at it, ask our Lord for help, He hears us one and all.

In our tapestry of life we see but the underside,
    Full of ugly threads so narrow, while others are so wide.

I know beyond a shred of doubt when our earthly life is through,
    God will then show the front side of your tapestry to you.

You'll understand the need for all the ugly thread,
    A scene of peace and beauty is what you'll see instead.

So as you go through life keep your tapestry in mind,
    Let the Weaver spin His magic as He's done for all mankind.

Madeline S. Roman

There Exist A Lonely Soul

There exist a lonely soul
A soul full of despair
Who will rest their eyes on ye
And save ye from thy hold.

It hurts thy heart to think so
hard, and know that no one cares
for this soul, this lonely soul is
full of dark despair.

Is there no one, no one at all, who cares
about my sorrow's
and laugh with me for a while on
the prospects of tomorrow

No reply, none I fear, for ye the
heart does sound.
For there exist a lonely soul and
that lonely soul is me.

Nancy Lee Taylor

A Tale of Crystal Bird

Come fly with me said the old bird to her little bird
one day. Let's fly over the city's and the fields, down to the
shores of Coden Bay, for there I know of a pier where we
can sat and rest and talk and laugh and be the best of
friends and enjoy the left over bait and shrimp the fishermen
caught and after we have rested a bit and the sun is setting
over the Mississippi sound, we'll fly a little more for you my
little bird are what Grandmother birds live for to love
and teach to fly high above this land, when I have flew
high into the sun and want be there to hold your
little hand? Now fly my little bird back over the fields and
city and don't forget to take the knowledge and memories
of Grandmother bird with you, and as you grow you will
fly with another. Fly him to you and your old birds favorite
place to the pier on Coden Bay where the fishermen catch
bait and as you rest there and talk and laugh of the
future, as you head back toward home, over the fields and
city's, as you turn toward Mississippi sound to see the
sun going down there you will see the sprite of the
old Grandmother bird all around, only one pier on Coden Bay.

Greta Knox

The Haunting

There's a phantom haunting my apartment
   it crowds my thinking
so I go lie down on my bed, but
   it lingers there, like a perfume, taunting me.
in the closet, too
   on the floor, or behind the door, waiting to jump out at me
I walk to the mirror to prove it's just my imagination
   but my "imagination" tugs at the belt loops on my jeans
and it smiles...

like it's about to get away with something and, it does...

"Stop teasing me!" I say
"It's not teasing if I follow through"
"Why now?"
"Because I want to now....
   and because I can."
there's that smile again... damn it...

   Isabel Fernandez

A Farewell?

Hello young boy. Hello lad.
I saw you leave that night which was as faithful to you as
   the stars in that very sky.
Did you see me?
Did you see me as fire came to burn and as hoof came to ground?
Did you sense me? Did you sense me at your doorstep
shedding an invisible tear and crying an inaudible wail?
Was it fate or destiny that led you to the sky?
Did you love me?
Did you love me with my hooded dreams and my sheltered fears?
All of your life you looked at the world through a child's
   eye and the world looked back with a grin,
Yet the world looked upon me with a clouded eye and a sneer
   from edge to edge.
Did you miss me?
Did you miss me a world away from the hearth that warmed you and a
   hand that guided?
Did you understand me?
Did you understand that my love for you was my body's only sustenance,
That you were the only soul to whom my heart would shine
   upon even though I did not long for your lips?
Now you are gone and to what my mind holds you'll never know..
   will you.

   Lauren N. Ward

Look Over Your Shoulder

Dearest daughter,
When you think it's the darkest of dark
And the sun will never shine
Look over you shoulder and smile.

When you have fallen and cannot get up
and you think no one is around
Look over your shoulder and smile.

When you think the bad times outweigh the good
And tomorrow will never come
Look over your shoulder and smile.

And when you look back, you will see
Four halos shining bright to show the way
Four outstretched hands to lift you up
On your darkest day
And when you look back, you will see
The four loving faces of
Daddy, brother, granny, and me.

Just look over you shoulder and smile.

   Terry Wayne Heck

Castles In The Sand

So this is what we come to
This life of yours and mine

The splitting of the property
Half is yours and half is mine

Lawyer's fees and family feuds
Crank phone calls, we pay our dues

Is this the happy ending
That we once imagined

Among wedding gowns and limousines
With friends and family all around us

The dreams we had, the love we shared
The home we built, it isn't fair

It's not supposed to end this way
We promised on our wedding day

To love forever 'till the end
But now we must begin again

The newness dressed in pearly white
With dreams preparing to take flight

Have come to pass and now we stand
To face the wind that dissipates our castles in the sand

   Lori A. Rocchio

Salt Poured In

The year was 1943
and I was as smart as I could be
at least that was what I thought.
I even knew more than I was taught.

As the go by.
I look back with a sigh,
and wonder where all that smart might be
all the things I knew in 1943?

Well, here it is 1995
and I am fortunate to be alive
with all the knowledge I thought I had
I can't even remember how to subtract and add.

The year was 1943
I certainly wasn't as smart as I should be.
My Mother used to tell me with a grin,
"It's just where the skin was split and a little
salt poured in."

   Louise Tomi Thomas

Higher Learning

The institute of higher learning
education and knowledge behold
a struggle to obtain information
a desire for a place to grasp onto,
a place to hold.
The institute of higher learning
the higher place in life, survival of the fittest
conquerors of the obstacles of life
striving to survive the differences
trying hard to fit in,
integrating with different races
struggling with the beasts trained within.
The institute of higher learning
the new experience of homosexuality and the isms represented
homophobia is not the solution
fear and violence's outcome have a history of pollution.
The Institute of Higher Learning
readiness for the free world;
Although, in the free world there are no handouts.

   Damond Atiim Butler

Thinking Back

Just thinking about the good old times,
Trying to come up with something that rhymes;
Remembering the guys and all the pretty gals;
The ones that did me wrong, and the ones who were my pals

All that energy that's gone down the old tube,
All that dancing, and all of that booze;
Remember the music, some good tunes, and some bad;
I'm telling you this brother, those were times that we had.

Now it's all over and slipping into the past,
Then it starts to sink in that nothing really lasts;
Except for the ghosts that continue to haunt,
The things you didn't get, the things you still want;

So just put it down now, you need to put it back,
Just get on with what your doing, hang the past on a rack;
But we can't do that, can we? If we did it would be a sin,
Cause how do know where your going,
if you don't know where you been?

Ronald E. Ewerth

The Poet

What gift will he share with his readers today?
Perhaps an old thought, that won't stay away?
Dreams, which he had long ago suppressed?
Memories, he can't now keep at rest?

A riddle, a question, to cause you to think?
An emotion, or feeling, to turn your face pink?
A picture, painted with colors like fire,
Tenderness and truth, passion, desire?

A song, for those unable to sing?
Music, for the one who can't hear a thing?
A voice for the oppressed, unable to speak?
A choice for those, whose future seems bleak?

A story, lost before it reaches his lips,
But found its way to his fingertips?
touching the hearts of those that he knew,
Listening to this, he may also touch you.

Rick Albrecht

Songs

America's songs persist on an ever rising wind.
Songs sung in wigwams and tee pees on the plains.
Songs that soothed Columbus on roaring rolling seas.
Songs Pilgrims sang as winter turned to spring.

Songs sung by trappers, and by rebels, and by slaves.
Songs heroes sang as they gave the final gift.
Songs sung in churches, where all the faiths were free.
Songs taught to children so they could sing them too.

Songs from Ellis Island and along the Rio Grande.
A harmony of rhythms merged into a single sound.
Songs that can't stop ringing in the ever blowing wind.
Songs sung of freedom in the fullness of our time.

Sing, "America I love you." Sing, "America love me."
Sing, "America, America set all thy children free."
Sing, "America I love you." Sing, "America love me."
Sing, "America, America God bless thy destiny."

Charles W. Bowser

Bloody River

Nearly a year to the day: Justice died;
Families, friends, even strangers cried,
The spectre of racism successfully hid
The truth about the crime someone did.
Now two spirits walk earth bound by a lie
And the world is left to question: Why;
What purpose did this betrayal serve,
How do we assure the justice all deserve?
As a calculating killer walks the streets free
We each ask ourselves: Could that have been me?
How could our system ever have gone so awry
That for the victim there are no tears left to cry
For as the river burned by the droughts sun
Sympathy and compassion dry have run.

B. J. McKee

Untitled

At night he walks past her window, oh so quietly,
It's the beat of his heart that she can hear.
She lays there in slumber without a fear,
The time he will come is growing near,
He walks the hill, his path a shape of a heart,
The start of a grin on his face.
His message in is mind growing stronger every step.
He thinks he's right when in truth he's never been so wrong.
He wants change but is afraid.
He's afraid of new, too used to the old.
Every night he walks by her window,
The window that can be shattered like the dream within.
The window is her dream,
The dream that goes on.
But as she awakes she faces her reality,
That in truth he'll always be far.

Danielle D. Kneller

Nature's Caress

In the heady greenness of the meadow in the morn,
In the dewy wetness of a new day that is born,
Underneath a sunny sky
Where hearts should soar so high, so high,
I try to mend the tatters of a heart that is torn.

Under shady branches of tall trees against the sky,
Under lacy wildwood vines meandering so high,
Caught up in the sensuousness
Of nature's passionate caress,
I lie languishing in limbo, contemplating why.

Over grassy hillsides basking in the noonday heat,
Over wild profusion of flowers beneath my feet,
Sinking down in grass so deep
I'm tempted to lie down and sleep,
Forgetting life's anguishes, replacing sad with sweet.

Within quiet woodlands, lying in eternal calm,
I respond to quietness as poor man does to alms,
Lying down beside a stream
I replace my life with a dream,
Revelling in the healing powers of this soothing balm.

Emily Daniels Butler

My Life In A Hole

I started my life the same as anybody
Having a good time and feeling like somebody
Then life suddenly took a drastic role
That's when I started my life in a hole
I only fell down about twenty feet
I started to climb, not about to be beat
I climbed up ten, then fell another twenty
I was still young, and life I had plenty
Climbing again, it happened the same
Going further down, with myself to blame
Been in this hole for a very long time
Need to get out, while I'm still in my prime
Looking up high at the world an above
Climb and climb to find someone to love
I don't like to bitch, I don't like to whine
But I need that one person to throw me a line
Pull me out of this hole to the world up high
So I can give my life, just one more try.

Shawn T. Oxford

Voyage

Touch of fire against my lips, eyes pressed closed
Dark shades of blue - you excite me!
Pulsing, pounding sound that pushes,
Moving my body as though sound was an entity
All its own...
And I have no control of the dance.
I am in your hands, so care for me well
Lead me through dark, shadowy passages
Where the voice of the cello holds sway
Enliven my spirit with the steel guitar's cries
You awaken me
Shivering in delicate abandon
I feel like a person in the spirit,
Taking to the sky, climbing to the clouds
Circling high above, where the music is...
Triumphantly weeping, I soar and cry out
One with the forces of making
The act and the climax of becoming all at once
And I know, through your song, that I am real.

Ariane Teply

My Son

A Young man of 19; easy going and good-looking, smiles when smiled at.
He is somewhat mysterious at that as you can feel the depths of his mind at work.

A deep thinker from his writings on life, but so illusive, you might think his brain scattered and light.

When he was a boy, wherever you would take him, he would always race ahead in a whim, in a hurry to get to his next destination; it never mattered who he left in the dust, it was get ahead or bust! Just try to reel him in and he'll take flight again.

A gentle person; he never yells — to some he cast his spells, but when called upon with his skills, in some manner of help, you'll find at best an evasive sell.

In pursuit of more stimulation, opportunity, and success lies ahead of him life's best.

A little honey bun, that's my son!

Debora A. Crandall

"Standing In His Shadow"

From the time of our birth,
  He has called us by name,
    While standing in His shadow.

He picked a special angel,
  To guide and protect us,
    While standing in His shadow.

He had someone to watch over us,
  When the cold world denied us,
    While standing in his shadow.

Gave His endless love,
  A loyal companion was He,
    While standing in His shadow.

He sees something in us,
  All other folks have missed,
    While standing in His shadow.

Many years have come and gone,
  With our shoulders bowed, steps slower,
    We still stand in His shadow.

We fear not the ... shadow.
  So dark and grim, we are still standing in His shadow.

Annie Katherine Pierce

Peace Wish

I wish that I should live to see
A world grown tired of misery,
Of hunger, wars, and deeds contrived
To plunder faultless, hapless lives.

I wish that I should live to find
A sense of freedom for mankind,
Where all may trod their neighbor's plot
And love, and share, and laugh a lot.

I wish that I should live to hear
Of fields of plenty, ever near,
Where skies are blue, and children play,
And wise men keep the hawks at bay.

And please, if I may sometime know
That on this earth God doth bestow
His kindest blessing, that of peace,
And warring everywhere will cease.

These are my thoughts; I trust that you
Believe in peace, and want this too.
For if we all believe, it seems
We should achieve these happy dreams!

H. W. Baxley

Fading Shades Of Gray

As my life fades to shades of gray,
I find that I can't find my way.
As what was sharp is now quite dull...
I wonder what's within my skull.
The life that's past is out of grasp.
But not the thought of my last gasp.
I once could climb any hill, any wall...
now I struggle not to fall.
As the flame turned to flicker, fades to a glow,
those around me seem to know.
And the words go unspoken...
the thoughts go unsaid...
for it's now all too clear, that the day I once dread...
shall come to rescue me.

James C. Rosebraugh

To My First Born Child And Grown Daughter

As I write these loving words this day,
    I want to you to forever hold close and dear.

I often wonder if you "really" know that I truly
    understand why you now cannot often be here.

These are those special times within your immediate
    family circle that will always vitally enrich your lives.

If only more parents today with grown children were blessed to
    more easily understand and prepare other ways to survive.

I understand way to well it would be selfish for me to ask
    for "times" you no longer have to give.

It's during these lonely hours, I need but ask, and God shows
    me a happier way in which to live.

HE... has always been my answer to all questions since a very
    young girl in her early teens,

As in the Holy scriptures, we but ask our great Parent,
    and He supplies more important "means"!

    Gayle Beckcom McCorkle

Debbie

Stay with me, my faithful friend,
For I am lorn at heart.
The north-wind 'round our souls does bend.
Helios speeds; daytime parts.

Nighttime wakes; evening draws,
We speak by the cloistered sea.
As soft waves crest then gently fall
You laud me for my sanctity.

But still does mount my bleating plight
To your hearkening ears.
Pikes of the heart I bare in twilight;
Safe am I in your presence near.

More honeyed words from your lips descend
To mend my sundry lesions.
Oh, in my breast that sorrow tends
May there take root their season!

But lucky I am, yes, lucky I say
That your fair flower blooms
Before my eyes; I thus proclaim:
Happy I am for the friend in you.

    Jeffrey Michael DiGeronimo

Renewal Comes Again

The parched ground invites the fully clothed wood
to untie its frayed yellow leaves;
A lonely skeleton remains,
fronting a quiet curtain of drought,
conceiving dormant life which the Hands of Truth brought.
Watch and listen closely . . . renewal comes again,
From dryness of heart, mind, and soul,
His sword moves about, swaying to and fro,
pruning dead branches giving life no more.
Within the time of season . . . renewal comes again,
As sleepy silk blossoms awaken on bent emerald stems,
there is a second chance for the heart to unfold;
And suddenly . . . Birds soar across the open sky, trees extend arms
with foliage so green, flower petals aerate with sweet perfume,
and fruitful valleys sing.
His living sword arouses the old to become new,
like the resurrected spring.
Yes, Renewal comes again.

    Robert Huffman

Neutral Colors

I wish the world was neutral with
blacks, whites, reds, yellows just being
mellow. I wish this world was made
neutral with love, peace and decent
morals. A neutral worlds with faith, hope
and wisdom. Where being a race isn't a
sin. I wish this world was a symphony
where only the heart and soul are composed.
A harmony with several instruments.
I wish this world was composed of love,
peace, hope, joy, wisdom and honesty.
I wish this world was made up of
love. A love of neutral colors.

    Janese Gault

Heavy

I have big dreams, hopes, wishes anew
Big overdraft in my Bank Account, too
Big plans, desires, a big voice to shout
Big dreams for which I have no clout...

Excess baggage, yeah, an excess load
Excessive obstacles on the road
Excessive anger, excessive doubt
Many excesses I could live without...

Massive thoughts cluttering my brain
Massive clouds above with torrential rain
Massive headaches and worries and woes
Massive reasons to grieve no one knows...

I have a heavy heart, heavy mind
Heavy burdens too easy to find
I'm heavy footed, could use a lift
I've been heavy duty and it's no gift...

All mixed with so much love and too much hate
It's keeping me down....I must lose some weight
Love-On

    Lisa L. Sweatt

Life

Delicately interwoven with one in the same,
    altering another and instituting its fame.

Existence brightly virtuous and unknowing at first,
    expanding uncontrollably, absorbing all and about to burst.

Participation with unimaginable creations yet to see,
    learning, discovering and becoming all it can be.

Dimensions of both tremendously large and excessively small,
    fashion a silhouette of geometry encompassing its all.

Conception within a passionate twinkling of bliss,
    to suddenly depart and be greatly missed.

Temporary definitions elude genuine appreciation here,
    once it's lost, the absolute essence is perfectly clear.

Anticipating the duration of a visit be it short, be it long,
    time is inconsequential as long as it exist with a song.

A reflection of the significance is very monumental indeed,
    within a smile begins the making of another healthy seed.

    Dale E. Wallace

The Daydream

I'm lying in a sun-lit valley,
my bed is made of willow boughs,
Moss is at my head I'm happy.
No moment is lovelier then this one now.

The sky is blue as foreign seas,
The sun a dazzling white
the dewdrops twinkle in the grass
like their cousin stars at night.

Daffodils sway and curtsey,
perfection's in the air, it seems.
Isn't it funny this royal moment
is just a common daydream?

Krista Jansen

The Spirit Of Christmas

To share his love for others free,
The Christ Child's gift to you and me.
To share His joy within our heart
A treasure that will never part.

To care amidst the toil and stress
For others under great duress
So that our heart won't turn to stone
The Christ child's blessings will atone.

The Magi with their gifts so rare
Inspire us all our gifts to bear
To those less fortunate than we
In turn these gifts to Him will be.

At Christmas we our voices raise
to the Holy Child our hymns of praise.
Please, may these songs ring loud and clear
Within our heart throughout the year.

We raise our prayers this holy day.
To heaven's portal we come to say.
Though many times we've gone astray
Forgive us Lord on Christ's birthday.

Ralph G. Wells

Our Mission

Our mission is to do good you know
as along our way each day we go
and seek out others that we can help
Far in this way Christ's will is kept.

To show Other our love and kindness
and in many ways from Him be blessed
this is His promise to us my friend.
As we travel through life to live again.

And as we meet others each glorious day
some have problems along their way.
Be ready to give a willing and helping hand
and recruit others to join this worthy band.

Some do not have medicine or good food,
To them let us show Christ's brotherhood
and give generously our means and love
Then we can claim His reward from above.

Russell G. Lawler

Morning Star

There were many nights when I waited
Alone, except for sleeping children;
Worrying, wondering, where was my love?
Our story was no different from others.
The big war was ended,
But there were little wars all over the globe.
Berlin airlift, Korea, African hunger,
Cuban crisis, Vietnam, Atlantic Rescue,
And the Transport Service was always called.
No roaring warrior was he, no headline maker
But a man of service who longed for peace.

As the years went by, I often went out into the dawn,
Meeting the plane that brought him safely home.
Many a time my way was brightly lighted
By the morning star in the east.
As years pass, I often seek
The star of early dawn. I think
Of gifts my love and I partook:
Faith, trust, loyalty, charity and wordless talk;
Lost now by death, but never gone.

Lee Meinersmann

Depression

Life moves more slowly now.
Fog enshrouds emerging colors; blends them into gray.
Hope is buried in apparent circumstance.
Music soothes by distraction rather than by melody.
Hopeful thoughts reach outward to blind dark alleys of emptiness.
Paths go nowhere, wavering along a deep and endless precipice.
Dark imaginations approach the edge and disappear.
Despair I could not comprehend in others inhabits my own soul.
Choking out love before it grows to word and action.
Take what seems to be alive and build on it.
Soon it shrivels in your mind and disappears.
Even breathing now seems purposeless,
Not something you do but something done to you.
Others' visions and excitement bring remembrances of life
Soon choked and laid to rest in the tomb of reality.
At least I wish them well.
May they never comprehend the randomness.
Help them, by their running to and fro,
To miss the truth that life is going nowhere.

Roger H. Kennett

Portrait Of Winter

Snowflakes come tumbling down winters art
decorating the earth with jewels from
heavens treasure,
Some flakes fell on the trees and adorned
them in a gown of white lace with silver
sequins projecting scenes beautiful beyond measure.
Icicles clinging on tree branches gave the
appearance of crystal chandeliers suspended in space,
Winter was putting on a performance sending
all of her natural beauty over hill and dale
with much dignity and grace.
A carpet of Ermine lay on the meadow and
valley so elegant one is awed by this spectacular view,
The essence of tranquility inspired by this
scenic portrayal of winters delicate hue.
The sky was filled with sprinkles of diamond
dust cascading down the mountain side,
Winters beautiful scenery was admired and
respected as we reclined by the fireside.

Annie Marie Knox

Dirty Hands

The Lords called him to loosen Pharaoh's hold
And lead his people to the promised lands.
In him we see a leader great and bold,
And not the murderer with dirty hands.

It happened close outside Damascus gate,
Gone there to persecute the faithful few.
A light did strike, and purged his souls of hate,
Those dirty hands now clean as morning dew.

The slaves he shipped were no concern at all.
Their fate was theirs, on that he would not dwell.
But then, on him Amazing Grace did fall
And saved this wretch from everlasting hell.

Those chosen for these works hands unclean.
So I, with dirty hands, myself esteem.

Jack C. Page

A Tenth Birthday Message

Knights and kites, pink-cheeked dollies and games
Endless toy people with make-believe names
Little dresses and shoes, a toy farm and small town
Lie still, with no magic, when you're not around

Yet someday ahead, you'll leave these behind
But buried deep in the dust of my mind
Entwined with bittersweet, gentle and mild
Stir the memories of you as a child

Enclosed in the picture of a tiny round face
Cherished thoughts of another time and place
Knitted and held by a little girl's smile
Enriched by time through years and miles
Relived again, and held close, for awhile

Daddy

Sonnet To A Spring Rain

She washes leaden skies of winter's lees,
And melts the icy crust of frozen earth;
Awakes the dormant life in buried seed,
And clothes drab fields with Spring's ambitious growth;
Bestirs the sluggish larva in the mire,
And warms the meadows for the mourning dove;
Turns out the sleeping bruin from musty lair
To satisfy his hunger and his love.
If bear, and bud, and beetle break
The fearful hold of Winter's icy grasp,
Then courage can the weary spirit take,
Endure a crabbed age with vigor past;
For baser life from its dead husk set free
Presage for man an immortality.

Edward J. Helwig

Chicks In Trucks

Little men with Popeye arms
Cops with mirrored shades
Truckers with their peeter flaps
Sluts on roller blades

Bullys on the school playground
Christians on the front line
Gangs of angry Mexicans
Beemers in the carwash line

Hooded men with torches
Skin heads with artillery
Shopping mall security
The power does impress me

Michelle Van Rhyn

I Am Creator

Call Me Whither
and I will fade
Call me sentience
and I will see

Be with my folly
and you will fall
Observe my perseverance
and you will soar

With the wings of constancy
and the wind of arrival
The still creation of common stance
will rise to the rainbow rebellion of reality

You Will Know My Name!

Philip F. Hardwick Jr.

A Mini-Biography In Trochaic Tetrameter

Many moons ago, and then some
In the shadow of the Kootenae
To the tepee came a squaw-babe
Came the little squaw Omah-ha.

Grew she like the willow sapling
Listened to the braves and wise ones
Talk with wisdom of the owl
Of the ways to bend the young twig
Teach to weave and tan the buckskin.

Then down to the restless water
Came Omah-ha full of wisdom
There to teach young braves and squaw-has
Work in lodge and tell the tribe lore.

More moons pass and now Omah-ha
Weary of the tribal chatter
Leaves the young to tribal wise ones
So, "Good-bye", to braves and squaw-has
"Keep the fires to learn ablaze",
While Omah-ha stalks new ways.

Omah Illeyene Parker

Colors

We are from two different worlds
You are Caucasian with hairs of curls.
I am yellow with eyes that slant.
Some will say this while I now can't
That a love like ours can never be
But their hearts are blinded so they can't see
That love sees no color of skin or race
But love sees the color of the heart and not the color of the face.

Chuong Nguyen

Frigid Moment

Cold as the keys on my pad of type
Cold as the lid above my sink on the jar
Cold as the iron scrapings I found on the way home
last night after chasing street lamps down
one way avenues on the high class side of town.
Cold as the frown on my lifeless eyes,
Watertown cold breezes in the parkinglots
of oceanside resorts
and a cold haunting dream.

Michael Nathan

A Single Rose

A single rose can mean many things, especially when it stands alone:
A beautiful memory or heart felt dream, from which a petal may haveblown.

The petals may be symbols of, rough times or mistakes we've made,
and when each petal falls from the stem, the memory begins to fade.

Nature, just as life, without the rose goes on, replacing an old memory with a new.
The Lord set up life in this way, I believe, because he wants the best for you.

Now life is not perfect, nor is the rose, with each having their painful thorns.
But with these painful parts in life, we can appreciate even more,
    thorny stem which we call life, the fragile rose adorns.

You and I may have had rough times, and the Lord may think we
    deservebetter,
So he pollinated our lives, with full intention that our lives would
    come together.

Now we are one stem, which this rose symbolizes, I give you this
    rose to take,
and should you decide to keep this rose, the future will hold
    beautiful memories, that will together make.

Mark Edwin Remme

I Love You, Bruce

I didn't see your face when I looked up into your eyes - I saw
your soul in a cosmic second, where all time stood still and speeded up
at the same instant. Then, like a baby ready to be born, the intuition
reappeared when I caught your glance and sensed your warmth, and
then I felt two levels of awareness stirring within me. I felt your
goodness as a man, as a person, in this world, in this space, in
this time; and I felt the wonder of your spirit in harmony with the whole -
a much larger endeavor - capable of being perceived only in small
doses at special moments. My secret excitement grew until we parted
and I settled into the knowing only - that I truly liked you.
   And so we met again, and so it followed that the awareness grew,
and at long last I dared throw caution to the wind and let it happen
and let it be, because the knowing told me our souls entwined in
perpetual embrace, and there was absolutely nothing you or I could -
or should - do about it but go with the flow, bask in the warmth,
accept the gift, treasure the love, for however long or brief it may
be, let it be, let us be.
   For surely such profound love can only increase the total harmony
that directly and indirectly rebounds and permeates over every soul
within the light. And so with strong heart and open arms I accept
you as you are, as you have been, as you will be, as you, as my gift
to myself and the world.

Vykki Ruvalcava

I Hate My Body

I live, one of many, in a strange land, I'm seen as a sore thumb on a
big white hand. I want to separate from the body and live, because it
seems that all I do is give. The mouth sits upon its high post and
does little but chew, why does the fruit of my labour create its teeth
anew? Then there is the lazy stomach, taxing me to support its
useless growth. I am the middle laborer, and I hate them both. We
are connected by our nationality, many different parts of the sick
body. Most bodies in this crowd are uniform in color but mine is
marbled, motley like no other. I once thought of choking the pale,
high class neck but I knew my fellow phalanges would not let me wreck
their free ride, manicures, and cocoa butter. Now I hate my fellow fingers,
sellouts to the others. How can I hurt the body, I thought, without hurting
myself? Into books of amputation I begged the brown eyes to delve.
Which part can we do without, who their duties do shirk?
In agony I learned we need every part of this quilted body to work.

Michael D. Romans Jr.

Ode To Dylan Thomas

Died the year I was born, you did
You poor precious bastard.
I have long suspected
The world was spared
Or simply refused to endure
Our simultaneous gasping.
Or was it our raving?
I have read yours.
I cannot help but wonder
What poor precious bastard
May read mine.

John McBeth

Gentle Rain

The sound of raindrops,
Nature's lullaby sweet,
They hit the rooftop
Like pattering feet

Give life to each plant,
The raindrops do,
Create the world,
Bright, shiny, and new

When it is over,
The world's full of shine
Water covers everything,
From grass to pine

And then the plants wait
For more nice showers
Which will wet the soft petals
Of all the flowers

Emily Herrin

Seasons

A flower,
Fragile, free yet fettered,
Fights a fate from nature's force
of wild whims and careless course.
To live to die,
Its life is like the breath of sky
that flickers fragrant fields,
Coming, going, absent reason,
Fading, robe of glory yields,
Ending, then, a flower's season.

A human,
Hopeful, held yet heartened,
Hews a fate for timeless birth
from choice of paths on edge of earth,.
To live to live,
This little life can greatly give
beyond what seems to be an end.
Aging, dying, all for reason,
After robes of dust descend,
Begins the endless season.

D. G. O'Shanahan

Untitled

Somebody,
I've thought about this a long time
And I've wondered why would anyone
Let alone somebody,

Want me to publish my stomach.

Keith Khon

What Time Is It?

When the voice of reason can not be heard. And decisions are made without morality in mind when the idea of self being the center of all living things. You cannot share what is yours, I will not share what is mine. I asked a man standing near "pardon me do you know the time." He raised his wrist, pulling back his sleeve, "it is a quarter to nine".

When Motherly affections, becoming a thing of times once gone by. And a woman can sell her young daughter, simply for a short flown high. Or Fathers with no desire to be the jewel in their children's eyes. When our leaders run for office for the profit they will gain. And preachers preach their own doctrine, and do it in Jesus name.

A woman walks towards me and I ask her for the time please. Cautiously keeping her distance she answers "it is a quarter after three."

I have stilled myself quiet and in thought observing the passing time. And find there is one who draws close to me, and opens my heart and my mind. Saying, "the evening is drawing nearer, and these things I said would be. Let not your heart be troubled, but draw closer now to me."

Du-Kane Cooper Sr.

Siren's Song

She excites men's souls, flaunting her charms before their whetted consciences. Her siren's song precedes her in battle, disciples faithfully following in her wake.

This fearless, enchanting lady of equality and justice haughtily, tauntingly parades before mighty giants, causing them to crumble and topple in defeat.

What is it about her that drives peoples to unite, defying torture, persecution, and death?

What mysteries does she whisper in their souls, that they stand naked before their armed oppressors, willing victory?

It is her promise of unity that encourage young and old to hunger for weeks, sustained only by their love for her.

It is her promise that all men are created equal under the eyes of God, that make humble men stand under the tracks of military machines.

It is her promise of freedom from tyranny, that send thousands to the streets, knowing death awaits.

It is her promise of individual freedom, of controlling one's destiny, that blesses the blood that has been shed in her name.

She is an elusive, inconcrete, unobtainable desire, that can be felt by men of conscience.

She is the shining, guiding light of the oppressed. She is so many people cry for, what so many people die for.
She is... democracy.

Maria Holguin

As You Sleep

Might it be possible, could you look more beautiful or more peaceful
as you rest.
As you sleep I wonder what you think of, perhaps it's me, the one who
loves you best.
Real love carries from dawn to dusk and even throughout every dark night.
Run to me if you're scared of the darkness, for, in my love, I will
protect you and hold you tight.
You dream of joy, you dream of life, and you dream of love, for
tonight they are unexplored.
May you always have good dreams of love and, as in my heart, be
forever adored.
Even in times of trouble you can always resort to your world of
dreams to take you away.
Given in your heart that the best decision is to flee rather than
to stay.
Eyes closed, heart slowed, breathing steady, hands shaking, and mind free.
Nothing to fear, no one can hurt you, because as you sleep you are here with me.

Christopher Lowe

Words

Words drifting down from a spiritual
ever-land
Thoughts whirling round like a
literary Big Band
Words welling up . . . full of love;
full of sorrow
Wrench you awake. Or drift in dreams
'til tomorrow.
Words piling up like dry leaves in fall
A creative heart stirs them . . .
they touch us all.

Dale E. White

Our Flag

Have you ever thought of living
Where the flag is not allowed
To rise and wave beneath the skies
The stars and stripes most proud

One might feel more patriotic
If he thought he'd never see
That beautiful flag a waving
So freely in the breeze

Lets stand a bit more taller
When we see our flag a-flying
And do the best we can to be
A bit more law-abiding

Gwen B. Burgner

Where I Tread

I buried my Mother today,
while my Father watched....
alone.

With steel and cement,
I pitched my tent;
and I sat upon my throne.

I've covered her eyes
with my vain and my pride;
and slipped a blanket upon her.

I've opened the sky,
yet still, know not why
my Father tans my hide.

D. Eko Fuhri

Thank You

I want to say thank you
for helping me out
I want to say thanks
for not having a doubt
I want to say thanks
for the things that you do

I want to say thanks
for just being you
I want to say thanks
for being there when
I needed you,
and not hesitating like
it was something new
you were always here
and I know you still will be
So here's a thank you
to you from me

Charesse Danielle Roberts

You

As you gaze your sensuous eyes upon me from head to toe.
Your smile hypnotizes me in a nice and affection way, that only you
can do. The way you take control of me is forceful, but yet tender,
and so very sweet. You demand an answer to your question in a strong
but charming and caring way that shows you care. As my mind wanders
off into space your eyes, smile, and questions pop into my mind like
I never left your side. It's funny that all the times we share
together have been warm and tender moments that I'll always treasure.
The gleam in the corner of your eye tells me you care for me without
saying a word. I want to spend the rest of my life with you and no
one else. No one can take your place, if it was yesterday, today or
tomorrow. All my energy and time are focused on you only. I think
of you when the sunrise in early morning, and when the sunset at the
close of every day. As I look up at the stars twinkling. As the
night slowly passes by. One thing that has captured my mind is a nice
romantic evening, just you and me to count the stars one by one, as
the night creeps by. Whispering in your ear the three little words
I LOVE YOU, as the moon lights up the night just for you and me.
Holding you so tightly never letting you go. You have done what
other woman dream of do in a matter of seconds. As I sit back
dwelling on you, a smile comes across my face about the things
you do to control me. Others would be gone in a blink of an eye.
You're the woman that I've always wanted to be by my side for the
rest of my life. I want you, no one else, just you.

John I. Mitchell II

A Crystal Winter Morning

I woke early in the graying dawn of a frosted winter morn.
Sat up in bed, rubbed my eyes, and watched the day being born.
But I quickly made a starting discovery as the sun let it be seen.
And with astonishment I couldn't help but wonder, where was all thegreen?

For overnight the downy pillows, hanging heavy in the sky,
Had burst into high spirits and let their fleecy feathers fly.
These softened diamonds, in mute fun, danced with grace up in the air,
While looking down at the world below, promenading without a care.

They twirled and swirled with practiced ease that was a heart-warming
  sight to view,
As they let their crystal bodies reflect the sun, changing their pale hue.
Their nameless dance went on forever, or until they fell
Upon the ground, all out of breath, pale, delicate, and well.

There they lay, pilled on the ground, for rich and poor to behold,
Now a heavy velvet blanket that the clouds had let unfold.
Upon every tree and bit of earth, the blanket, it was there.
Making that joyous, calm, crisp day both elegant and fair.

My eyes, too, watched the shown, and let winter lighten my heart.
And there I spent the morning, not letting the performance and myself part.
Oh, what a glorious pleasure it was to gaze into that magic sky,
And watch all those fairy, crystal snowflakes frolic merrily on by.

Caitlin Reid

"Sisters"

With a tick and a tock on the eternal clock, Sisters were created.
'Twas God above saw the much needed love, would be so appreciated.
They'd be Mothers and Aunts and Sister in Laws, with hearts of solid gold
Daughters and nieces and Grandma's too, who's love would never wax cold.
Throughout time, they'd touch hearts like mine, from boys on up to misters,
So that soon or late, all men will pray thinking the Good Lord for Sisters.
They forgive and forget without any regret, then welcome you into their home
They think that you're great, though you make mistakes, still you're
  one of their own.
They'll tell you strong whether right or wrong how they feel about
  something you've done
However, it's by your side, they stand with pride when everyone else
  turns to run.
When the battle is done, Ere you've lost or you've won they'll tend
  to your wounds and blisters.
For it's God's great plan; and blessed is the man that thanks the
  Good Lord for Sisters.

Mark King Taylor

Christmas Time

Christmas time,
and it is snowing
flowing, flowing, flowing.
Children are playing.
Having fun sleighing.
It is cold out there,
but nobody cares.
Because, it is Christmas time,
and it's snowing.

Travis B. Landers

My Hero

She taught me gentle kindness.
To be both tough and stern.
I owe her my everything,
What a lesson I have learned.
She worked hard both day and night,
To keep her baby fed.
She loved me and she kept me safe,
No matter what was said.
She loved me through the good times,
She sheltered through the bad.
I've loved her and I'll miss her,
And all the times we had.
Mother you are my Hero,
Though you probably never knew.
I wish that I had hold you so,
Before your time was due...

Sherrie Anderson

"I'll Fight It With Love"

I shall not walk alone,
I'm as happy as can be.
May the birds fly high,
But so high and not see me!

Hurrah for tomorrow,
As it will start a new time.
From in this lazy life of sorrow
Should this never really be mine!

The world is at my feet
And this cannot be wrong.
Oh how I have waited,
For years, and that is too long!

I'm really not crazy
So just leave me be.
If life's little tricks do become mazy
I'll fight it with love, you'll see!

Sandra Furstal

Caught

Caught,
trying to get away
from the terror that lies ahead.
Caught,
trying to get away
from the sadness
of myself and others.
Caught,
trying to get away
from the hatred upon the earth.
Caught,
trying to find the way
so I would not be
caught AGAIN.

Erica Midden

"Arabian Daze"

Dreams no longer hidden from my face, for reality has taken away the
most pleasant of taste. In a foreign land where sand has the right
to be free. It covers everything, including me. The sun is hot and
the wind is strong, even we don't get along. Did someone call my name,
or is my conscience playing a game? Dreams no longer hidden from my
face, for I'm floating on memories away from this place. Hiding
from reality and it's ugly taste. No, I'm not lost or in despair. I've
got to have something to keep me going here. So as the future dawns
and a new day clears, I'll be looking to enjoy the rest of my years.
Dreams no longer hidden from my face.

    Maurice McIntyre Sr.

Endless Journey

I've been down that road before
I may look like I've been rode hard.
But youth is in the mind
      of the beholder.
We go through life with our eyes closed
And then one day. . . .
Our eyes open. . . .
      To face reality,
The many roads we have traveled. . . .
    And the many roads,
      We've yet to explore!!!

    Julie Lundell

Our Treasured Friendship

Unicorns that fly, horses that roam free,
pot of gold at the end of the rainbow,
are treasures we'll never see.

Friendship is one of those treasures.
That's so rare and hard to find, just like a fallen star,
It only happens once in a lifetime.

We were like two lost souls, searching for a place,
neither of us completely whole,
until we met face to face.

You're so honest and caring,
sweet and understanding,
you'd give the shirt off your back if you could.

You're always by my side, and you never criticize,
you take me for who I am,
and you always understood.

Fate brought us together,
just like the lighthouse,
brought lost ships to the shore.

We will always be lost souls,
Who will search for a place no more.

    Claire Carpentier

Regrets

Time can not be turned back, as the clock keeps ticking away,
Hour by hour, minute by minute death comes closer, with the passing
  of each day.
As I peek through the door that was locked for so long,
Pain came out to choke the life that remains to right the wrong.
Forgotten memories overwhelmed me, as a storm attacking a peaceful night,
Where oh where are you divine power, to ease the stabbing dagger,
  causing great fright?
Many regrets came the remembrance, as tears streamed down the face,
All were forgiven, many were corrected, others pitfall lessons to
  steady the pace.
Along with regrets, old friends are lost and some we hold dear,
Replaced by new friend, places, events, and hope for others regret
  is near.

    Janet E. Roundtree

The Serengeti:
Moments In The Well Of Creation

It was another
Which had come,
As nature stirred
To greet the risen sun.

Life moving below
Upon the plain,
A tiny kingdom
In a vast domain.

There is pleasure here
But also pain,
For each mortal thing,
Some loss, some gain.

The wonder of life,
Living with grace,
In eternal time
And endless space.

Then sleep follows sun
As death does life,
When our strivings end,
And a day is done.

    Dann Stockin

Untitled

It can not be seen
though we may look.
It can not be touched
though we may reach.
It is the softest kiss
of a Lovers lips,
it is the painted sky
on mornings sun,
it is as ageless
as the first caress.
A tender memory held so deer,
when softly touched
may bring a welcome tear.
It is not of the mind,
for the mind can not move.
Poetry is of the heart,
for with the heart
true Love will prove.

    Ron Bell

The Gift

Ageless as time,
  mysterious yet divine.
Piercing our hearts,
  yet cleansing our souls.
Fulfilling our desires,
  while igniting our fires.
Quenching our thirsts,
  feeding our hunger.
Ignoring all others,
  while with one another
Liberating the mind,
  entrusting the heart.
Becoming as one,
  like flower and sun.
Remaining together,
  while separated, apart.
Let this be my gift,
  the love from my heart.

    Marc Trotter

Winter Dream

Climbing snowflakes
through
naked frozen
birch tree branches.

A climb jumps
up
into the flakes,
mouth open wide
to taste
the huge different
white sweet stars.

They singe his
red chapped
face, forehead, cheek,
and drunken nose.

He bounces
up and falls
slips
drowning in white
dream laughter.

Dominick Scarchello

Take Back My Toys

Christmas now is over,
Santa went away.
I watch my Mama and my Papa
Beneath quilts where they lay.
I wonder what has happened
To make them feel so sad.
I got a lot of presents
So it wasn't that I was bad.
My ears are filled with sirens,
They're screaming in my brain!
I see them handcuffing my Daddy,
I must have gone insane.
"Merry Christmas you thief!"
I heard echoing through the door,
While Mama stood there weeping,
We saw my Dad no more.

Jack Hotchkiss

Regret

Angels floating on a whisper,
Carried to a forgotten land;
Promises of love and laughter
Wash away in the sand.

Tell me you will stay forever,
Tell me you will be my bride;
But the earth took you from me,
Just like it took back the tide.

Now bitter winds brush back my tears,
And raindrops masquerade my pain;
And the life that flowed between us
Now flows deep within my veins.

Rhiannon Romero

"Life"

It isn't what we know, but
how we act, what we do, with what
we have, and that's the facts!

Mary L. Randolph

Untitled

Does my exuberance
frighten you?
My intensity intimidate-
My passion elude you?

I am not justified in my
anger with your complacency-

How can I expect to soar
the heavens, while I allow
my wings to be bound?

Lane Malone

Untitled

Poetry is a way of life, an art
form, nature's way of expressing
its desires and feelings. Poetry
which can be inscribed in one's
mind for the rest of their life. We
live and love poetry everyday of
our lives. We pass poetry on from
generation to generation not
only because we like it, or
believe it to be educational for
our children, but because it is the
building blocks of life; our way
of escaping the stress and
disappointment of daily life, and
gathering hope for a
brighter tomorrow.

Tiffany Marie Wilson

"You Didn't Mean To Make Me Bleed"

I know you don't realize
how strong I am being-

When you're not in the path,
of the demons I'm seeing-

Perhaps who is weak,
in your sight of view-

Could be shattered, yet bravely,
just breaks in two-

Judging what,
you don't understand-

Devastates those, who
reach for your hand-

I hope, someday, you'll
come to bestow-

Acceptance of what,
I pray you'll not know.

Susan L. Guthrie

Seasons

In summer...
  I sit facing the beautiful
  sun gazing down at me.
I fall...
  I watch the leaves
  changing colors before eyes.
In winter...
  I watch the snow falling
  Slowly sparkling in rainbow colors.
In spring...
  In run thru the high flowers
growing higher and higher.
  seasons.

Jessica Scheetz

Electronic Cupid

They quarrelled.
Whose fault it was, I cannot say.
He left.
And soon had passed the seventh day.
She wept.
Gone her resolve to cause him pain.
He waited.
He longed to hear her voice again.
She acted.
His beeper number was her choice.
Her message,
"Call me, 'cause I love you, Royce."
The problem.
A stranger's beeper heard the call.
Their future.
They failed to get together at all.

Morris Hallford

Clouds

Look up high
  Quickly now —
See those big things in the sky?
Jagged curved and bold.
  Lying ever so still.
Shimmering, sparkling like
  Diamonds so.
Watch it now!
  Here it comes!
Sweeping gusts of wind
They blow every way, it seems
  On just a puff of breeze.
They are most outrageous shapes of
Bears and snakes and trees and ships.
  They seem to represent
Any form you know — then
  Puff!
They are off again and gone
Shaping something new.

Nancy C. Hensler

As Time Goes By

Crawling through the trees,
Fighting for survival.
We have become animals,
Forgetting human needs.
Can death be a real solution,
Or just a needless end!

Sleeping,
  Now I am.
  Dying,
  Soon I will.
Life is just too precious.
  So Living,
  Is what I'll be!

Chris Burgess

Untitled

Don't Hesitate to validate
The person that you're with
With just a word, perhaps a smile
A hug or little kiss

Kindness is an act of God
So if these things you do
The person that you validate
May very well be you

Patricia A. Kulbeth

An Uninvited Ego

"Oh!
Please come in.
I didn't know—
It seems you're blest,
You've brought a guest.

"Have a seat.
So, this is your twin?
(Resembles a clone)
Yes, he's handsome—it's true,
And ever so brilliant too.

"Such a charmer (snakes I bet)
And rich—
How could he be anything less,
When millions of heads turn,
And so many hearts burn?"

"Excuse me, won't you?
I need to find myself a place...
With more room.
In here, I might smother
With you and your other."

Kristin Gissendanner

Space...

If you were the world,
I would be the Sun
I would revolve around you,
Shed light on you
Sometime, Somewhere
Anytime, Anywhere
I would be able to reach you whenever
you would need me.
I could just reach out
  to touch you,
  to warm you,
  to brighten you,
  to love you.
If I were the Sun,
you the Earth,
We would be separated only
by Space.
Inevitable Space!
Space full of my love for you!!

Tina M. Fitzmorris

Testing, Testing

Testing, testing,
  One - two - three.
Please, Dear Lord,
  Are you receiving me?
Just do something
  To let me know.
Am I speaking too loud
  Or much too low?

I've got a lot of problems
  That I've prayed about
But when I don't get answers,
  I begin to doubt,
If my prayers are really
  Making it through
To the one intended,
  Yes, You, Lord, You.

So please, Dear Lord,
  Put an end to my doubt
Send me some answers -
  Over and out.

Billie L. Kelly

The Great Pretense Begins

I am unknowable
You are unknowable
Heaven is unknowable
Hell is unknowable
Eat from the tree of knowledge
And the great pretense begins

Gary Glassmeyer

Emotion

Love
A mother hears her son's first cries.
Love
The acceptance in your eyes.
Fear
The emptiness of a lonely heart.
Fear
That love will someday depart.
Hate
The fear that I find near.
Hate
Everything when you're not here.
Anger
With the pessimist in me.
Anger
With love's hopeless destiny.
Death
Alone will take you away from me.
Death will bring you back in eternity.
Love.

Marian Monica Gray, Ed. D.

The Season Of Love

Listen to the sounds of Christmas
The sounds we know so well
And listen to the sleigh bells ring
And listen to the old church bell

The Babe is born and we rejoice
For it's known far and wide
That He is come to one and all
As we kneel down by His side

So sing your carols loud and clear
And praise Him from above
The world is saved for one and all
As we give to Him our love

Let us love one another
Let no man keep us apart
And let us love this little Babe
Who has given us a star

So on this day of Christmas
Let no man harm his brother
Let's all give thank's to Him above
And forgive one another

Bernard J. Colella

I Think

I am who I am I think.
Others think I am another but
I am, who I want to be.
Sometimes fearful, sometimes courageous
and quiet, loud.
Full of inner strength yet weak
paradoxical in my existence in order
to know the balance,
that makes me I....

Kevin P. Deckert

Feelings From The Heart

All of my life
You weren't there to see
All of the times
I wanted you to be proud of me.

You should have been there
To comfort me from fears,
To hold me in your arms
And help me dry my tears.

I would love to get to know you
But to you I'm just a bother.
I can't call you Daddy,
For you are just my father.

Lashley Morrison

"Winter"

In the icy air we see
Angelic visions dancing nearer.
Melodic singers songs
Sweep across blanketed dreams.
A shy sunbeam
Plays games with its light.
Fairies harden water and
Point the world with frosty brushes.
Children take haste
In building snow fantasies.
What is this place
That is dressed in icy splendor?
Winter is the place and
It is found in frozen memories.

Lisa Winter

Untitled

When fire and smoke of
  younger days
Had left my dreams lost
  in a haze
I looked around and tried
  to find
Within myself some peace
  of mind
But peace of spirit eluded
  me
And lack of self
  surrounded me
And what I felt was
  agony
With incomplete expectancy

So I studied deep within

And pondered the road
  back where I'd been
And decided then it was time to begin
The long trek back to where I'd been.

Arno L. Weatherford

Youth Of Yesterday

How I remember my youth.
Not so long ago. Time go so
fast I remember when my parents
seem ancient.
  Now comes my time I remember
my youth of yesterday.

Joe Toro

My Legacy

I hope when I have left this world,
That I have left behind
A legacy of love and peace
That eased some troubled mind.
I hope I'll be remembered
As one that really cared,
And left someone much better off
For having me around.
I hope the time I spent on earth
Made it a better place,
And that I made a difference,
And just didn't up space.
I'd like to think that all who knew me
Were blessed in some small way,
And that my having been here
Gave some a brighter day.

Margaret S. Hinz

Time

When we were young, and time
stood still.
A time when we would love,
and see that life was good.
But would we know that life
is short, and would not
stand still.
To see that time pass so fast
makes my heart stand so
still.
To see that time once again
would make my heart race
so fast.
To see your face from that
past, still makes my heart
beat so hard.
To hear your voice makes
me long for that time
when life stood still.

John F. Griffiths

Untitled

Today my cat died.
I know, some say I'm foolish
'Cause I cried.
"It's just a cat", they said.
No; 'twas not just a cat -
He was a friend -
A pal, a comforter -
I'll miss those scampering feet,
The loud "meow" -
The gentle purr of "thank you, friend",
The warm-soft fuzzy in my lap -
The gentle lick upon my chin.
I know — he wasn't human —
Though almost —
And there are cats galore —
But not like Isabelle.
And I'll get over it —
But thank you, Lord,
You understand, and care, because
Today, my cat died.

Chrystal E. Morgan

Life, In General

What is life?
...life in general.
God, time, and fate-
control the course of events.
Nothing is forever,
but everything can be always.
We walk around in a mediocre world-
looking for meaning.
So many of us lost without a hope...
without a dream...
without a cause.
What is a man without a dream?
A failure without hope.
Look into the dawn.
Watch the first gray light.
There's new life, and rebirth.
Every sunrise, every sunset-
marking each day of life.
But what is life?
A question unknown to man.

Andrea R. Schlender

Do You Believe In Love

Do you believe in love,
and the promise that it gives,
do you believe in love,
and all the feelings within,
do you believe in love,
do you know what love is,
it's a feeling of passion.
and you share that passion with the
person who means a lot to you,
you have to care for this person,
you have to love this person,
and you have to show it,
that's basically about what love is,
so,
do you believe in love?

Elisa Perssico

Untitled

Doors closed to me
Because of the parts I lack
Doors closed
Because of parts I have
Doors closed
Because of certain brain patterns
Doors closed
And if I play it right
Use what I have
They'll give me a key
To a door
to a place where
I don't wanna be
I've been locked out
Don't you dare ignore me!

Vanesa Beauchamp

Moon Rise

Lunar fullness — golden sphere
Float above my One so dear
Altho apart in time and space
Softly — softly touch his face

When last we saw you
Thru pines of peace
A sacred vow with
Yearnings deep

K. Alter

We're Proud

As you go for Marine Corps training
And you're far away from home;
Keep us in your heart and on your mind
And you'll never be alone.

We will wait for your letters
To hear your progress and such;
And we will write to you often
Because we miss you so much.

Just know that we're proud of you
We know you can do it;
Stay strong and be cool
It will help get you through it.

When your training is done
And they've molded you strong;
The road you just traveled
Won't seem so long.

May God bless you and guide you
In all that you do;
And bring you home safely
When your duty is through.

Ethel Osgood Fanning

Memories Of My Grandmother

A million times I've missed you,
A million times I've cried,
Because I couldn't say good-byes,
Be held, or look into your eyes.

The things I feel most deeply
Are the hardest things to say.
My dear unknown one, I love you
In a very special way.

I wonder about your December death,
And then came my February birth.
My love was enough to save you,
If only the months were reversed.

No one knows my loneliness;
No one sees my weeping.
And all the tears from my aching heart,
While others all are sleeping

If I had a lifetime wish,
One dream that would come true.
I'd pray to God with all my heart
For yesterday and you.

Brandi Mayers

The End

Sat by the fire
Danced with the moon
Held the clouds
Healed the wound
Found the secret
Destroyed by mankind
Felt the heartache
Caused by the mind
Watched the leaves
Fall to the ground
Watched the desert
Cry and die with no sound

Melissa Gibson

Drink And Drug

A child in small town lights...
is now a maniac in big city bright

From joking and playing...
came drinking, drugging and scamming

Once living, loving and laughter...
now a miserable, hatred bastard

Once caring for others...
now not even bothers

Once power and piece of mind...
now a man weak and unkind

Fit, wealthy and happy...
Now sick, poor and skinny

Things we could have had...
now make us sad

A man who could have lived large...
is now behind bars

Once he had it all...
now he's making a call

You may try to find happiness...
Drink and Drug and you will find this!

William John Beckmann

This Creation Of Gods

As I gaze upon her face
majestic and full of grace
so close but far away
feeling I can reach out
and touch her
on a clear winters day
she is something to behold
so majestic she stands
as her form unfolds
high above the valley
she graces so peacefully
the air so fresh and clean
as the wind blows
from her every ravine
her peaks sharp and fine
the white of her crown
and shoulders aglow
with fresh new blow snow
she is most beautiful
this creation of God's

Harriet L. Hillier

The Spots Of A Dalmation

The spots, the spots
the glorious spots
all mingling in black and white.

The world is filled with
black and white spots
that figure that they are right.

Yet all in all in this bright world
the spots are alike.

Michael Rashfal

"Snowflakes"

No...you are not as passive
Thought you slovenly float
Because each one of you
Stirs wordless, happiness and hopes
The ones that have been granted
And, those that have been lost.

Your heavenly fight against
The winds of time, and bitter cold,
The silent way you talk, and talk
Takes away my breath along with you
While watching when you fall.

You reign when dressing the plains,
Or mountains (not disturbed)
A canvas you become (doing your best)
Reflecting the masterpiece-reminder
Of, "The greatest Pact on Earth!"

Rafaela Guiu Peluso

Dziadza(Grandfather)

A man I respected and loved.
A man I grew up with
and learned everything from,
since I was a child.

Not a father, or a friend
something more a part of me.
Then all of a sudden
this part of me left,
like a feather in the wind.

The feeling wasn't hurt
It was more like an explosion
inside of me.
Torn into pieces like a puzzle,
never to be put back together again.

Though I am still not one
Dziadza still remains
In my heart and mind,
until we meet again
  For Eternity.

Renee Rinaldi

You

If I were a genie
And could have my wishes come true
My first wish of all
Would be to be with you

I would hold you close
And make you smile
Your thoughts come first
All the while
Someone to hold
And to care
Someone to trust
Who would always be there

These words of mine
All are true
These words I say
Just for you

Kenneth Glasscock

Living Death

When a loved one dies
As they sometimes do,
I think of you...

When I hear our songs
That make me cry,
I think of you...

When the rain falls
It's tears of hurt,
I think of you...

When I know your, "really" gone
And the hole gets deep,
I think of you...

When an ending comes
And it doesn't stop,
I think of you...

Judy Santos

Memories

You gave me white roses
To fill my vase of life,
Turning it to a sweet
Glittering chalice...
Healing the poison fires of hate,
And obnoxious conduct
Which had seared the vessel
Flame deep and cool pride which
Had charred the smoldering embers...

Then you left to receive
Holy orders, taking
The most majestic rose
With you for convent life;
But your chaste loveliness
Lingers still in slender
Silhouette against an azure sky
as memories.

Joseph Mamana

Beautiful People

Mismatched clothes and shaggy hair,
Shuffling gait, skin not so fair,
Scars on the body, growth on the nose
Lord, you love each one of those!

Please help me, Lord, to look within
Each person that I see,
To look beyond the quirks of fate
That others note with glee.

If I should chance to meet someone
Who's just not very bright
Help me, Lord, to love them more
And show them it's all right.

Faye Johnson

Thoth Pooh Worthy

Illustrate Kung-Fu Tao desire
Deliberate counter relax
Double-blind target-oologists
Re-cooperate mutually rebellious

Exagge(rant) prominent
Caricature signature fixture
Alum-chromic concussion
Tempered metallurgy

Dave Abdul

Near The End

Didn't know you could
til' you said you would
walk down the pier.

In all we had
in a world gone bad
now we live in fear.

How time was spent
working for the rent
freedom shed's its tear.

Who will say
that were gonna pay
now the end is near.

Walk now, live now, cry now
now the end is near.

Samuel L. Pivarnik

Unexpecting Unassumed

A rash void
Bolting
Stumble
A slashed abyss
Idolize the simpering
Court dissension
Connoisseurs hoard
Plenty wanes
Accelerate
Loathe
Plead
"Hail, oh versed of deception"
Foster the savage mass
Feign concern
Achieve full flaw
Desert stable foundation
Worship prestige and fame
Combat righteousness
Loll and woo the blood thirsty curs

Maureen Evans

The Good Life

What portrays the good life
  In Nebraska land today?
Time to savour blessings
  God has sent upon our way

Appreciation of life itself
  In animals and plants.
Love and care for others
  To receive the best God grants.

Our clean air's a treasure
  We protect with mind and might.
Abundant pure cool water
  God gave as our birth right.

Fertile soil that we may grow
  The food to keep us well.
People living, laughing, caring,
  Praising God this land to dwell.

Nevabelle Howe

Untitled

Oh yes now I am old
so I need to be bold
and re-read the large box
of WW II letters I unfold

As I proceed, it's easy to see
the things I missed when I received
these long, lonely, homesick messages
and now they just overwhelm me!

Why didn't I write more often
I did write a lot
but how they needed that mail
after all the battles they fought

Wars are not fair
we all know they deprive
let us pray - wars no more
so we can go on with our lives.

Dorothy J. Mizer

Independence

Together apart,
Separate but equal.
Under one roof
Shared space, unshared lives.
Trite, cliche, commonplace.
Lonely presences together,
Each ego cased in armor.
No penetration,
No communication.
As though the inarticulate
Were proper mode of being.
Scaffolding all, a longing:
Single self is incomplete.
Other is the glue of the whole.
Sometimes.
Otherwise,
Hesitant groping in regions of pain.

Jonas R. Mather

Autumn Leaves

Leaves
like a colorful patchwork quilt,
blanket the earth
brilliant souvenirs of brighter days
warm, golden days
when the sun warmed the heart
before the cold, sharp winds
and grey fog of autumn
sapped away their color.
Time and people
tred on the leaves
turning them brown
and they shriveled into
unrecognizable memories
of beautiful days
needing only to be
gathered into a heap
and buried
deep in the soul

Elizabeth A. Betsy Meehan

Thought

In the meadow of my youth
Was a river - rather wide
On its shore - this shore of my age
Was the sound of her tide.

"Come here!" said the river.
I heard;
Was astonished, astounded, afraid.
Until then
Never had I thought
A river could revere
My thought.

"River, river, my dear",
Said I.
"Does the sun shine forever
In the ripples of a river?
Gather me up a cover
So that I too may hear."

A. Muhammad Ma'ruf

The Mantle Of Love

The patterns of humanity
  as fashioned from above
Make garments of stability
  seamed with threads of love.

The love of God
  with its purest gold
Bonds love of neighbor
  in strands two fold.

For only when our fibers
  within ourselves are known
May strands of neighbor be endowed
  with the substance to be sewn.

And, the fabric of love's mantle
  must, above all else,
Be woven with the love of God
  your neighbor as yourself!

Grace Forsythe

A Lamp Shining In A Dark Place

Did you ever notice a house at night?
From outside in, the house is light.
From inside out the night is gray
But outside in, it's bright as day.

And when the gray of night has passed
The morning light has come at last;
Then outside in, the house is light
And inside out the sun is bright.

Oh for that morning, bright with sun
When inside outside, all is one;
And each house when you look within
Can look without, be free from sin.

Then inside will be filled with light
And day star rising true and bright
Will flood the house, oh glorious sight
When night is passed and all is right.

Blanche Moerschel

Refreshing Renovation

The rain slowly drips
off of the ancient barn roof.
The water renews.

Virginia Hovdestad

First Snow

Soft feather flakes
have been falling
gently all night;
early dawn reflects
an extra glow of light
that filters through
my bedroom window.
Muffled quietness
like a blanket of hush
descends on laughing
bundled children
while they tumble through
untrammeled snow.

Adelee Bonadurer

The Human Spirit

I am black white yellow and jew
I am brown and red I am you
I hold death and peace on my tongue
I am old and I am young
I am restless I am life
I hold peace and I hold strife
I am poverty or I hold wealth
Most bad I do is in the dark in stealth
I am kindness or I can be the means
Of good and bad in life it seems
I can bring joy or bring madness
Fill your life with hope and gladness
So who am I and whats my name
The human spirit wild and untamed

Georgia Rose McLane

Still We Shall Dream

  On what is life built
On this seething tumbling world
What is found in dreams?

Deep understanding
Of joined mutuality
More than difference

Blending and binding
Colors, forms and melodies
Growth of life visions

Sun within oneness
What can we build together
For best goals of life?

More than marching bound
Lock step directed to cliffs
Of despairing endlessness?

Churning - no path seen
But sudden termination

Still we shall dream dreams
Seeking peace and harmony
Past - now - and future

Drayton S. Bryant

God So Loved Me...

  The birds fly happy
beauty spattered in the clouds
  frolicing without sin
so I with my soiled soul
  will breach the gates
with angels welcoming
  and live forever there
while they fly higher and higher
  only to always be looking in.

Nellie Fern Tobey

Marriage

Marriage is a gamble.
Two hearts are put at stake.
A tug of war
Forevermore
In this game of give and take.

Dete Jacquelyn Shaw

"Remember"

Your face, a smile so lovely
  we met that way.
Strangers you and I, yet
  you were familiar.

Did we dance the night away?
  It seems so long ago,
only yesterday.

Will I hold you again?
  Your body forming mine,
hands intertwining
  lips so ever close

Your face, a smile so lovely
  we met that way.

Remember...

R. B. Inzerillo

Who Gave A Damn?

A world fell in shambles at my feet.
In smoldering ashes was my defeat.
A dead heart beating inside of me,
Dying a death that none could see.
Silently my life had passed away.
But who gave a damn anyway?

Cherry D. Finley

Symbol Of Love

Santa is a symbol
of giving, love and cheer.
A jolly man who gives to others
one day of the year.

But Jesus is the reason
We celebrate Christmas Day.
He was humbly born in a stable
Among the animals and hay.

From Jesus we learn to give to others
all year through.
We can share love, joy or time,
and heartfelt prayers, too!

So enjoy your Santa Symbol
but don't forget to give
Reverence to the savior
who died so we could live!

Tammy Eldred

Life's Question

Gazing across a wild frontier
a man of old asked why
whose hand has made such wondrous land
and whom shall it deny

Not all of us will make it
but those who do survive
will one day when they also grow old
ask the question why

David Williams

Hershey Hugs

I buy my 'Hugs' at Wal-Mart,
  Two packages for five;
Oh, thank you Mr. Hershey,
  For keeping me alive.

My lonely body cries out,
  "Please hug me, I am here;"
But why my friend denies me;
  Is never very clear.

No warmth from arms of humans,
  No loving Christian hug;
But as my loved one passes by,
  A lonely pit is dug.

They say my God is jealous,
  He wants me for himself;
So here I am in lay-away,
  Upon a Christian shelf.

When Jesus comes, he'll find me,
  Still longing for a touch;
'Twas long ago, He purchased me,
  No one else loved so much.

Julia Dixon Collett

Grandma West

My grandma smoked a corn cob pipe
And lit it with a coal
From the open fireplace.
God bless her frugal soul.

My grandma smoked a corn cob pipe,
And lit it with a coal;
The top was always charred
Above the serrate bowl.

She always had a pleasant way
To greet the folks who came
To her modest cabin,
And greeted friends by name.

She welcomed friends and strangers
And always greeted me
With a bear hug and a smile.
She died at ninety three.

If I ever go to heaven,
I'm sure I'll see her there
Grandma with her corn cob pipe
In her rocking chair

William G. West

Joy

Sunlight glistening on brightly
coloured leaves.

Running and jumping and
climbing to a low branch
of a tree.

Racing wind cutting us off from
the rest of the world.

Memories of the past, thoughts of
the present and wonderings of the
future.

In a place where no one but we know
the secrets.

Katie Belk

Winter Snow

White lace
  lying on the ground
sparkling and
  shimmering all around.
The snow has fallen
  and it's here to stay
for a couple of months
  and then go away.
The tracks of birds,
  animals, and man
are recorded in snow
  by natures plan.
The delicate designs
  found in each flake
Are lost in the magnitude
  the drifts do make.
I'm glad to reflect
  this beauty we know
And enjoy the white
  of the winter snow.

LeRoy B. Schwan

4 - Mom

You hold my hand as I
  walk through life
You'll be here when I
  become a wife

You know all about my hopes
  my dreams
You know all about me
  it seems

You'll be with me through
  the good and bad
You'll be with me when
  I'm happy or sad

I know these things will
  come true
Because I can't go
  through life without you

Lavaughn D. Riley

Grateful

You brought me company
when I was lonely,
just when I became accustomed
to fasting when I was hungry.

You brought me excitement
when I was wrought with pity,
only to dance the night away
in Mecklenberg's most famous city.

You brought me a young man
ten years of age when I had no desire
for commitment or someone others
off-spring at this stage.

You brought me renewal in faith
that can only prosper and serve
when I was in a situation
that instructed me to learn.

You brought me a miracle as
precious as a Dove - one like you
who is my ultimate Love.

Bill Cameron

Ungodly

I do see him from the inside;
In his masking ungodly form;
He wants to rule over people;
And brainwash them till they are his;

He - once again a hypocrite;
In belief, they confide in him;
Already told of his power;
But he hasn't any power;

He had an average childhood;
But still he exaggerates it;
He speaks of himself as a saint;
And gossips in his sinly ways;

It has been set in people's minds;
He is one who commits no sin;
Naively, they will follow him;
Though he will never be leader;

A christian sworn in hell's fires;
Led by his unknown dry deeds;
His actions make you feel good now;
But he will hurt you later on.

Sherida Duckworth

Creation Design

Flowers from my garden
  how can one compare, for
Gods own hands put them
  there.
For me to marvel in, for
  me to share.
Butterflies flitter over them
  with care, bees gathering
their honey was seen there.
To turn the soil, to plant
  to prune.
Only by the grace of God
I was here to smell
  their perfume.

Sherry Leigh Lewis

One Love

I once had a love
my one love was a
boy when I was in
sixth grade. He had blue eyes,
blond hair and wore cool
cloths. In seventh grade
he still liked me but things
changed, he changed my one
love was asking someone
else out. In eighth grade
he kept on changing, went
out with new girls, new
cloths every thing. I knew
he didn't like me any more.
My one love loved
some one else, my one
love hated me,
my one love, my one love
married his new love
me his one love.

Misty Lien

Delirium

Empty stares fill all the rooms.
Hardy glares and silver spoons
in the mix not made to match.
There's no fix for this crude batch.

Rusty thoughts of friendship sails
through the animated gales
where the billows do appease,
and the fellows only tease.

My core full of fearful rage.
My temperament in third stage.
Should I quit to ease the pain
or submit and let it stain?

My final count soon to pass.
Such relief without the mass.
When it comes, time will tell.
Then will break this hardened shell.

Charlotte E. Shell

A Friend

A friend is one who stands close by -
and helps you laugh, and lets you cry.
And gently, in a loving way -
assures you that the hurt wont stay.

A friend remains in times of stress -
and guides you back to happiness.
Now I thank God every day,
for sending you along my way.

Remember, when we're not
together - a friend to you
I'll be forever.

Blanche Thomasson

The Wonderful You

Every morning when I wake up
I sit and think how my life would be
If I didn't have you here with me.

It's hard to believe,
And yet so hard to see,
How a person like you,
Could choose one like me.

I have sat around and dreamed
Of having someone like you.
Now, finally my dream has come true.

We're alike in so many ways
Different in so very few
It's as if you are me,
And I am you.

I love you with all my heart.
I hope you can see it in my eyes.
In hopes that we may never part!

Robin Renee Dykes

Rain

We are not made from metal,
Not even from wood.
Humans are fragile as a petal,
Even when we thought we could.
Push life to the limit,
But be able to pivot.
Although everyone can try,
We all can also die.

Slava Thaler

"Just The Two Of Us"

Just the two of us
    under the stars.
Thinking of the future
    is what we did.
We said that when the
    time was right
We'd be together till
    the end of time.
We didn't care what
    our parent's said.
We'd be together forever.
    Just the two of us
    under the stars so bright
Under the stars we sat with a
    long kiss good night.

Jana Zirnig

Splendor

The bounds that set us far apart,
sets forth emotions from the
heart. Bittersweet sometimes it
seems, but along time of loving and
joy is my life's dream.

I go to sleep at night with the
vision of your face, wake in the
morning knowing it never could
be erased.

Hold tight to the love that lingers
in the air, circling our world
without a care.

Be brave my darling for
bittersweet it seems, love like ours
was never a dream. Complete-complete,
the heart has surrendered to
nothing other than pure splendor!

Deborah Boykin

Untitled

The sky.
The reflections of a smile.
His.
My own.
Oceans of liquid purity
Shining from within.
Pale cornflower
With midnight peering from behind.
Yet thunderstorm will often
Come to cloud the skies.
Darkness from within.
Grey as death.
Storming.
Raging.
Searching.
Longing.
The raindrops fall,
But I will stand by until the
Peaceful blue skies come again.

Sarah Elizabeth Wells

Untitled

Abraham Lincoln
was born in Kentucky
On February 12, 1809
everybody in the world
should keep it in mind.

William Lee Grisdale

Listen To The Moon

On the nights when the moon
is full and bright and glistens . . .

You will hear it tell of my love
if only you will listen . . .

The moon knows of all
that we share . . .

And is sure that nothing
can compare . . .

So, never doubt the power
of the moon . . .

As it will lead you
to me soon . . .

Kimberly R. Kukla

Maliki

Entrusted to us for safekeeping
Is the grave of more than a pet
We'll be on guard while he's sleeping
Against any danger or threat.

For many's the time in our memory
When the guardian's roles were reversed
He was the gallant defender
Between the danger and us.

His whole life to us was devoted
His intent was to lighten our way
He knew when to be quiet and consoling
Or when to be happy and play.

Time will roll on down the ages
We'll all go away bye and bye
He'll live in our memories forever
Our good friend and pup, MALIKI.

Vernol A. Jasper

Untitled

Twelve long years
one dream I've kept
a mother's love
the tears I've wept

But on this day
I move from past
heartache remains
love does last

But in the silence
I hear a voice
to stay in pain
is that your choice

My mother my mom
I love you both
one is gone
and one I know

E. Genie Curry

Untitled

Through many eventful years
Filled with joys as well as tears
Just your presence always cheered
and made others more endeared.
Past bouts with adversity
Were met with audacity.
Although you are now in pain
You will overcome again.

Robert Gorman

Every Grey

Season of wither
with nonchalant grace
draped in gold autumn
which masks a cold face.

Never the more bitter
than winter's embrace,
deceitfully cloaked,
designed for any taste.

Venture the beauty
it boldly displays,
search for the dying
it harbors from trace.

On its chilled breath
where the leaves fall prey,
see the earth shedding
evergreen-to-ever grey.

Ron B. Davis

When We Danced

I heard a singer singing
Some songs I wish I wrote
like "Beautiful, beautiful brown eyes"
and "Somewhere over a Rainbow."

For your eyes are as warm
as a mother's arms;
they subdue me like a hug.
And rainbows are so beautiful,
like the spectrum of our love.

James G. Vittek

A Dream

If I could take a dream
make it come true
I would dream that the heavens
fall down on you

Turning your lies to truth
your bitter to sweet
Take all your madness
send it a fleet

Then you would be
so kind, gentle, and sweet
I would mix you in the heavens above
Then you would be
such a beautiful love

Oh heavens fall!
Dreams come true!
I want to share
my life with you
I have always
Dreamed of you

Toni

For Ronnie

When she walks
Within her hedged gardens
Below the iris band petals
Who, in chorus, nod consent,
The grasses bow doubly low
In waves of pliant strength
that bear unbruised a tread
so familiar and light
their only discomfort,
the diffidence of her steps.

Jack McAndrew

Eternal Love

It must have been a dream
When you walked into the room
Because now,
I'm the bride and you're the groom
Making vows and sharing tears
Thinking of future years

Everything seems so right
Our future seems so bright
The way you hold me
And say that you care
And the way that you stare
Or think nothing is fair
You've become my life
Everything else,
Is a want not a need
So I guess it's all just a dream.

Rhonda Munz

No Words

Spoken in silence
Our pact of fear
Cried in silence
This painful tear
I watched in silence
As you died
Said goodbye in silence
You no longer need to hide
Now I sit in silence
Wishing you were here
Once again I cry in silence
My missing you tear.

Amber VanMeter

At A Glance By Change

At a glance by change
I saw her lovely face,
As a Angel out of space,
Dressed in blue just for you.
Her shoulder length hair
Brushed with care.
Flashing blue eyes
Minus white lies
With blushing red lips,
And slender hips.

T'was but a glance
Then a change
My body trembled,
My heart rumbled—
But comes the dawn,
She'll be gone.
Her memory lingers on.

Laurence L. Kirk

Name=Spoon

People measure people
With a measuring spoon.
You own a plastic spoon,
You are a nobody.
You own a steel spoon,
You are a somebody.
You own a silver spoon,
You are a "VIP".
No spoon, no name.
What a shame! What a shame!
Owner of a fancy spoon
Gets to have a fancy name!

Anu Subhas

The Bag Lady

The lady walking down
the city streets,
    A familiar sight I see,
the woman with a sad face.
    The shopping bags held
tight in her hands.
    I wonder who she is,
if she's even had a home?
    Why she was left in the
streets like this, sad
and all alone?
    But the streets are her home
with millions of others.
    The streets they roam
from day to night with
nowhere to go.

Lisa Ann Stearns

Erotic Sonnet

You walked by
And smiled the grey
Concrete became warm
Tar underneath my
Feet and burned inside

You fed my brain lines
With a ladle and I
Swallowed every drop
And licked the rest off my chin

Our tongues search
For intentions
At the altar I will receive
Flesh mountains
Covered in snow sheets

Kathleen Dunne

Conversation

An exchange of words
More often talk without purpose
Venting to another
Without listening
No opening
No ending
Voices without thoughts
Strangers passing
Without touching

Janice Collins

Faith

I love you God,
for the sun, moon
and stars.

For the sky, sea
and the people.

And for the priest,
the church and its
steeple.

But, most of all,
it's your gift of life
and who you are.

Pamela Davis

Green

Like two ships passing
in the night.
I go by and see your green eyes
that set of that baby face.

How can I ever talk to you
and tell you how I feel, when
I can't even tell myself.

Tried to talk to you
but every time my senses are
lost and I can't say a word.

I am slowly beginning to
feel that I would like to
get to know you but still
I sink away into a corner.

I wish there was away
but I can't tell. Maybe
one day it'll happen before
it's too late.

Jai Loushin

A Rose

Cool, refreshing moonlight from above
filters down through the clouds.
It touches a dead world of giants
stretching upwards from the ground.

A dark pool of liquid silver lies
in a clearing, but not alone.
A rose bush stands proudly
its arms outstretched toward the world.

With a closer look at this creature
one can see contrasting acts.
On one side petals dropping slowly
being picked up by the breeze.

On the other side of the creature
a young bud expectedly waits.
When its time too will arrive
for it to open into the world.

Jami Wireman

Untitled

In times of adversity,
    Times of despair,
It's good to know,
    You have friends that care.

Someone to lean on,
    A strong hand to hold,
The knowledge that friendship,
    Will never grow old.

Always you've been there,
    Through times happy and sad,
And that you are my friend,
    I'm eternally glad.

Eloise M. Wenzel

The Mind

The mind of man is arable
But you must plant the seeds,
If in the harvest you except
A crop of noble deeds.

The mind of man is fertile too,
If tilling it you'll heed
But if you let it sow itself,
You'll get a crop of weeds.

Lloyd E. Jones

Lonely

Could you wait?
I would like to talk.
You don't have time.
Sorry, sorry.
It's just that I'm
Lonely...

Wait, don't I know you?
Nope just my imagination.
Last time I saw her was...?
Well, back up North, I guess.
It's hard, too far away
Yet still so close as friends
At heart.

Tracy Marsyla

Eclipse

We watched, in happy harmony,
the harvest moon emerge from
chiseled hills, in bold affront
to skirting, fluffy clouds.

Then, remembering, we said:
"Let's find a dark, lost road
where we can park to watch
again this Lunar game of tag."

We smiled, recalling times we
spent in youthful, daring touching:
moonlight sport, fulfilling dreamy
hour for lovers, new and shy.

So youth has fled; gone shyness, too.
Love's touch remains to join the game
old Moon and Clouds still play
with lovers on dark, lost roads.

M. Lee Sherburne

The Farmer Feeds Them All

The farmer works from morn till night,
How nobly he doth toil
Making furrows long and straight
Through the rich and mellow soil.
Many a care the farmer knows
Many a hardship does he face
As patiently he onward goes
Rasing food for the human race.

Millions there are that look to him.
To furnish their daily bread
Through heat and cold the farmer works
That these millions maybe feed
By the sweat of his honest brow
He feeds both great and small
Rich man, poor man, women, and children
The farmer feeds hem all.

Ruby Parker Davis

Untitled

"O' mother, how pretty the
moon looks tonight, it was
never so charming before,
the two little arms so
shining and bright, I hope
they won't grow any more,
if I were up there with
you and friends, we
would rock in it nicely
we would see the sunset
and see the sunrise and
on the next rainbow come home."

Margaret Colson Booth

Untitled

I was standing
In the open door
My heart told my body
I could take no more
No more
Pain
Sorrow
Of a broken heart
But
Will it end tomorrow?

The game we play
Of love and hate
We all stand
At the starting gate
The gun sounds
We all start fast
A few will be last
Pulled down
By their hidden past

Steve Cooper

"The King's Highway"

The Holy Spirit leads me...
    as I walk throughout this life;
I listen to His still small voice,
    protecting me from strife.

We never need to fear tomorrow,
    when our trust is in The Lord;
He will guide our weary footsteps,
    as is promised in His Word.

The road leads ever upward...
    straight and narrow is The Way;
No turning to the left or right,
    as we walk The King's Highway.

Black darkness is on either side,
    pits and snares to fall into;
But our feet will never stumble,
    with His hand to hold on to.

Let us keep our eyes on Jesus,
    The Truth...The Life...The Way;
As He leads us ever onward,
    to a Home in Glory some day.

Judy Ann Downey

Our Land

Oh, foaming waves and darkened caves,
Of the Pacific Coast,
And purple grapes on,
Gnarled vines are,
Pressed into September wines.
And sandstone spires,
Pierce brooding skies,
On a limitless night,
As oprey take flight.
Skylines and coast lines,
Merge into one, of multi-hued blues,
That follow the sun.
And National treasures,
Of forests and glades,
Protects Eagles and bears,
On nests and in lairs.
And parched amber hills,
Now rolling in wheat,
Await the winds thresher,
On this land meadowsweet.

Susan Kelso

The White And Pink Poem

White is a
Canopy bed,
Power Rangers,
And pillows.

White is
Ice cream, clothes,
Snowflakes,
And bunnies.

Pink is a
Canopy bed,
Power Rangers,
And pigs.

Pink are
Flowers,
Bunnies,
And cheeks.

Pink and white make lots of things.

Alyssa Ann Groux

Untitled

I sit and gaze at the mirror
trying to find the culprit
why can't I be beautiful?
My anger at the world
is turned inward
I hate my body, my mind
myself
why can't I be like her?
She isn't all that smart, sure
but she is beautiful
and in our world
no matter what we tell ourselves
that's all that really matters
the outside
not the in
let me be thin
let me be pretty
let me be her
anyone but me
Elisabeth

Elisabeth Cler

One Small Step

Standing on a wind swept ledge—
    specks of humanity below me.
Demons bark at my feet
    as I let myself fall forward.
The world rushes past me now—
    the pavement hurries up to greet me.
Striking the cemented path—
    my descent suddenly halted.
While my body lies in a pool of blood—
    limbs and neck contorted.
My last earthly thoughts are of you
    and the gentle push you provided.

Marc Holma

'Me'

I have ten fingers and ten toes,
I have one back and one nose.
I have two ears and two eyes.
I have one stomach and one back
and the color of my hair is black.

Jennifer Howard

336

Echoes

Strolling along
misty eyed
the scenery ahead transforms
into a blur of colors.

Echoes
from a single set
of footprints
weigh heavy on my heart.

An affectionate breeze
embraces me...
leaving only too soon.

The silence of the evening
becomes a deafening sound
as a destination to
no one awaits.

Cindy M. Morelli

My Little World

The graveled rocks
  made sand,
I drained my barefoot feet
  then buried near
  to whistle with the wind.

The sun shed light,
I felt it on my arm;
I held it
  in the hollow of my hand.

It sank to rest
  in the ruins of my pebbles,
  more lasting than stone.

A thin moon
  laid atop the hill,
  and blackness.

He had hidden my light,
But I found it in the stars.

Luan Elizabeth Gordon

'Childhood Lost'

'I'm too big for that'
We've heard it time and again
Just one little statement spat
And the wheels of aging begin.

'I can't wait until I'm older'
Everyone has felt this way
The fire of youth begins to smoulder
Fading faster every day.

'Let mommy give you a hug
I love my angel so much'
Away the shoulders will shrug
The age of 'DO NOT TOUCH.'

'Leave me alone, I'll do it myself'
A tear comes from my eye
Toys sit untouched on the shelf
To childhood we wave goodbye.

The little things we do and say
We never contemplate the cost
Oh, but what a price we pay
When we find our childhood lost.

Mary K. Taylor-Pearcy

A Lesson In Life

To learn about life
Replete with struggle and strife,
Just look and observe
The manner of the athlete
Whenever they must compete.

John G. Laflamme

The Sparkle Edge

On the sparkle edge of night
We the day turns to dark,
Sunlight fades to magic hues
And nature's mystery makes a mark.

Yellow oranges and purple pinks
Move to lavender grays and deep blue.
Daylight slips away
And air slides into cool.

Earth balances day
As it tips into night
And liquid shadows grow
Into evening by starlight.

The vision through nature's window
Is never more clear
Than when embraced by twilight
And its enchanted atmosphere.

This is the sparkle edge,
An elegance of place.
When brightest day becomes the night
With brilliance and grace.

P. J. Humes

My Window

When I look out my window
I see the sky
And it reminds me
The there are other things in life
Than what's in front of me.
That the blue sky
Is innocent of what is to come.

When I look out my window
I see the grass
And it reminds me
That there are other things in life
Than what's behind me.
That the trampled grass
Cannot be the same again.

When I look out my window
I see some children
And it reminds me
That there is life.

Cassie Lint

COWBOY

Cowgirls are the same, I reckon.
Oregon's cattle grazing.
Wampum Indians running wild.
Bop'n Bronko's jump'n.
Oh, I want to be a cowboy! I want
  to be a cowboy!
Yeeh-Hah!!!

Jamie Piechowski

Fossils

T rex once strode upon this shore
..... No more.

And now at this late date
Our feet pause briefly in the prints
He left behind.

What mark will future passers-by
Look down to see that we were here?
Will claw and fang bring our demise?
Will blowing winds bare our bones, too?

Will Eden die for lack of hope
— For lack of will
— For beastly greed?

Harold Russell Lohr

By My Leave

The tools of my trade I lay down,
I leave my profession here in town.
The vexation and dubious
of each day's milieu
my co-workers and friends
I leave with you.
My per diem is now
the sunrise and sunset
the smile of a child
the wave of a flower.
The call of a bird
The toast of a friend.
The silence of evening
the feeling of Home.

Sue Woodworth Duncan

Alone

Alone at last
No one but me
Empty room surrounding my thoughts
No sound except for breathing
One, two, three
Collect your thoughts
Gather your mind
What to do?
What to say?
Speak of yourself?
Tell to others
What's or your mind
You speak
They listen
I said you speak
Someone please listen
Three, two, one
Alone

Scott Cichocki

A Teacher's Garden

Do the groundwork; turn it over.
Prepare the soil; prepare the sower.
Plant the seeds row by row.
Nurture tenderly, weed and hoe.
Give them water, sun, and space.
Though wind and storms they must face.
Some plants need shade,
Some plants need sun.
The gardener has to know which one.
Give it time, give it care
Soon the garden blooms so fair.
The plants mature in stance and grace,
And make the world a lovely place.

Alvera Litsky

Secrets And Memories

There is a place within
each of us
Where violence and hate
can live
The fear and pain of
our lives
Provide a shelter to
house it with
A foundation that's been
laid with secrets
An exterior formed
of shame
The walls are constructed
from the memories
And despair has formed
the frame

Luanne Colyer

Why Me To Love

You came to me from out the blue
with joy and love eternal true.

As I am one who knew not these
I fell in wonder upon my knees.

Who am I to be so blessed
when all my life I've failed the test.

The test I live from day to day
takes all I have just to pay.

I feel I can't expect to be
loved by you so readily.

Where are the fees that I should pay
to have you love me day by day?

Your love for me be not for hire
it burneth as eternal fire.

I am loved at last.

James F. Yeoman

Answered Prayer

Lord I come to you in prayer
Knowing just how much you care.
I ask for others, not for me
That your glory it will be.

Many years to you I prayed
For this son of mine who strayed.
Now his life is back on line
A better job he needs this time.

That he has a job at all
Once seemed impossible, as I recall.
Thank you Lord, I know you care
As you hear my heartfelt prayer.

I'm sure You're not impressed
With my puny righteousness.
Though I would stand upon my head
Quoting scripture I have read.

God, in Sovereign control
Does not change his shaping role.
My little prayer I now can see
Does not change Him, it changes me.

Marylin Matthews Reed

Sun, Moon

Everything stood still
as the rain began to fall
in sweet innocent drops
onto the hot pavement

Everything was beautiful
as the wetness clung to every leaf
and blade of grass
and when the sun came out
the smile of a rainbow began to form

The raindrops dripped
the sun shined
the clouds passed
and everything stood still

Jacki Marks

A Special Moment

Each day has a special moment
No matter how bad, how sad
Each day has a special moment

Each day has a special joy
No matter how short
Each day has a special joy

Each day has a special surprise
No matter what kind
Each day has a special surprise

Each day holds its own special moment
Each day holds its own special joy
Each day holds its own special surprise
Each day is your own special day.

Sandra J. Warner

Angel

Angel soaring ever so high,
Do you frequently hear,
My mother's sweet sigh?

Angel way up above,
Is your strength for me,
Gently being carried,
By a tender white dove?

Angel always surrounding me,
These visions of love,
Will I forever see?

Angel with your glorious promise,
To never part,
Your heavenly presence,
Will remain forever in my heart.

Michele Malone-Scarzella

La Vie est Comme Une Fleur

Life is like a flower
First the budding
Then the rose
Water helps "La Fleur" to bloom
To see the flower grow

Lucky are some who have so many petals
That's it's long before they fall
Some buds never live to bloom
And others bloom, we see, but
happiest are those who live
To see life's eternity

LaRue Gwendolyn Killorin

Abandoned Coal Mine

Abandoned,
pillars pulled,
drift mouth empty,
work ceased.
The humming of motors
silenced,
men come no more to enter
its deep, dark cavern
once abundantly filled
with black gold
where now, only ebony
dust remains.
The search for its
treasure completed,
this hole in the
earth's surface is
vacated, having
indeed produced
its quota.

Ida Lee Hansel

The Lady

There she sat
A Lady in waiting,
For Him to appear
So elated was she,
Together hand in hand
They spoke softly.

The two together
Never to part,
Silence was virtue
For thoughts at hand,
Love was a mist
The late delay
So happy were they.

Beverly Matthews

The Mouse

In my house,
I'm baking a cake.
I see a mouse.
I grab a rake.
I get a blouse,
Oh how I shake.
I captured that mouse
with a rake.
I'm out of the house
down by the lake.
I don't see a mouse,
I see a snake!

Jennifer Platte

My Love

Her hair golden
    as the streets of heaven
reveals her purity

Her body delicate
as the earth
reveals her virginity

Her heart immense
    as the midnight sky
reveals her virtuosity

She is my Sanctuary
she is my Lover
she is my Woo

Richard William Adams

Peacefulness

A leaf fell upon my car
Had it travelled very far?
Or did it fall from my big tree
That always tried to shelter me.

I sat beneath this tree one day
To watch some animals pass my way.
A squirrel, a possum, then a deer
I sat real quiet 'cause they were near.

My tree gave me so much shade
As I watched the animals parade.
I felt real close to my leaf just then
So I reached for this paper and my pen.

I'll hold my little leaf and say
"As you leave my hand and blow away
Think of me and this little rhyme
Until I see you come next spring time.

Anne Sornstein

Down Home

Circa 1840
The mother by the table sits,
With nimble fingers deftly knits;
The foot in ceaseless motion keeps
The cradle where wee Ella sleeps.

On Molly's lap Cook rests content
Hearing how piggy's to market went.
And clapping his chubby hands in glee
He marks his patty cake with T.

Jane, George, William, Ida and John,
Are gazing at the wall where on
The father with his fingers bent,
Throws shadows which well represents,

The rabbit and the cunning fox,
A baying dog or patient ox.
John too at shadows makes a try,
Twists fingers and with mouth awry.

By precepts taught in early days,
Lured them to walk in wisdom's ways
Temptation found them ever true,
Life's grief's this home ne'er knew.

Amos Densmore

A Father's Sin

My father's sin has darkened me,
Kept me far from reality,
Left me knowing not me,
Tarnished, tormented, damaged me.
I'm living in my father's sin.
Why must I suffer the wrath of his sin?
The Lord hast punished not him, but I,
And has left me here to pay the price,
Of his sickness that rules his mind,
That stripped me of my woman pride.
As life goes on,
I must be strong,
As I live the life of my father's sin.

Anna Parker

Majestic Melody

The majestic melody here in my
heart was placed by you
from the start.

Such joy I've never felt before,
with a sense of tenderness
and love evermore.

The moments we share
are forever a treasure.
May our hearts embrace this
"Heaven Sent" pleasure.

I thank the Lord for you, my friend.
Here's to a love that will
never end.

The majestic melody here in my
heart remains with me,
even when we are apart.

Robin L. Handley

"A Second Chance"

I trace my footsteps back to the
  time when I couldn't see
I can feel the guilt and the
  worthlessness closing in on me.
But times have changed
  I know now I can feel
I'm not numb anymore
  my feelings are real.
I can't forget what has
  happened in the past
The happiness I thought I had
  was not one that could last.
But now I've got myself and if
  I can find that peace within,
I'll give people a chance to see
  that I'm the best I've ever been.

Debra Gauthier

Essence Of Life

Life be not proud and boisterous
but humble and quiet full of
knowledge and wisdom.
For life is but a collage of
experiences for all who pass
through its doors to embrace.
Capture all it has to offer and
revel in its wonders and glories
Refuse its negative aspects that
will always be there to entice
your thirsty soul.
Share your spirit with all who
care to drink from your cup.
Always seek truth and light as
you travel the sea of life

Wynona Cantrell

Untitled

Through the years
and with all the stuff
we tried to hold back the tears,
but it was too rough
it was all very hard
so I'd just like to say,
Because we let down our guard
Is why our love is here today

Shari Goldstein

Silent Screams

CALLOUS and COLD
you LOVE is BOLD
it BEGUILES me,
meanwhile we
sit in SILENCE.

Curious to say
it goes this way
There's no DENYing it,
we've been TRYing it's
going NOWHERE.

HEAR me scream
CAN'T YOU HEAR ME?!

I'm in a RAGE
I'm in a CAGE
I'm in a SUICIDAL stage;
I've got no hope
I cannot cope
and I feel like...

You CAN'T hear ME!!

It's SILENT—

Cora V. Moore

Untitled

To the one I love more than
love. I cherish all the time,
every second I see your
face. Although the feeling
is not mutual. My
passion burns on like
the fire burning in my
heart. Flaming to see,
touch, feel your body.
The feeling I have is
stronger than tears.
Never fear of
losing my love.

Danielle Renee Etchells

"The Search"

Inspirations of Happiness,
  Visions of perfect beauty,
  memories of loves express,
  knowledge of human duty.
Frantic grasps for days gone by,
  clutching onto what has passed,
  reaching out for something new,
  wanting happiness that will last.
Persuing something very unknown,
  searching for a dream,
  containing something deep inside,
  holding back a scream.
Looking into faceless shadows,
  seeking elusive expressions,
  turning life completely around,
  journeys through transgressions.
Striving harder toward a goal,
  working toward an end,
  rejoicing freely for your reward,
  finding the perfect friend.

Kevin Lee Lowney

My Friend

Someone to love
Someone that cares,
Someone that listens
Someone that shares.

Someone to hold
When times get though.
Someone to shape you up
and give you a cuff.

Someone to trust.
Someone that's kind,
Better people
you will not find.

Tim Farrell

Paradise Is Missing

Paradise is missing.
It was once here,
  A long time ago.
  It was something quite dear.

Once there was green.
Once there was living.
  Now there is grey.
  Now there is nothing.

Paradise is missing.
It was once here,
  A long time ago.
  Now there is fear.

I watched them tear it down.
I watched them do it to pave.
  It broke my heart to see
  The living things go to their grave.

Paradise is missing.
It was once here,
  A long time ago.
  I wish it were here...

Elizabeth Poire

The Rose

A pretty, bright red rose is there
Its beauty overflows
It stands so straight, so elegant
As I watch it grow
It fills you full of pleasure
Just to sit and see
How full of life and significance
A bright red rose can be
Its petals are so perfect
So delicate and fair
It's scent so sweet and wonderful
Like perfume has filled the air
And while I watch this amazing plant
as it blooms and grows
It reminds me life is just as precious
As this single, solitary rose

Jenna Sickmiller

The Storm

Thunder rolls off black skies
Leaves floating on white water
Drowned by the boiling storm
Happiness hangs by a string
It hits you like a strong fist
We have lost peace and laughter
You cannot stop the violence
Friendship is left alone

Sarah N. Foeldi

Hate Isn't Always It's Just Constant

Who hate sorry to hate
inevitably late always hate
constantly hate and no letting up
leaving this world and going it alone
no one to talk to
no one to relate to; but always
hate
To hate is to love but love
does not always make sense
because the fence around
us does not allow us to flee
into another dimension of the
life of love
So above the fence amongst
the sky
lies the realm of life
in the midst of all hate.

Diz Rigatoni

In Remembrance

In my younger days, I was one with
  the Mother
In all of her glory
I ate of her fruit
I drank from her veins
I basked in the glow of her paramours,
  the sun and the moon
I made love in open fields
  with the clouds and stars
  as my witnesses
She was mine
And I, hers.
But now that I'm older
I no longer recognize her
Her beautiful form has given way
To expansion and greed
Her fruit is now bitter
Her veins are dying
There are no open fields
I am alone.

Felicia M. Yarborough

Waiting

Dark
And alone
Feeling so sad...
Why?
I know it will leave...
But when?
Waiting patiently for that day
It will come
Like a dark cloud
Lifting
From my soul.

Nona T. Covington

True Love

True love is like a deep-rooted tree
Swaying in the wind
Weathering the storms
Braving the bitter cold
and in the end,
it is still standing.

Lorraine Crennan

Untitled

I as the lone bee
flying up to taste the rose
do not notice the thorns
caught in the overwhelming
desire to drink you in
sick from your nectar
I scramble to escape
the sticky sweet trap
the beautiful bloom
so deceptive
I find I can still fly away
as I pass another lone bee
I fly on
the flower withers slightly
but does not cry.

Melvin Williams

Motherhood

One is all alone.
Two becomes one.
Three makes one complete.

Alma R. Laster

Checkmate

Looking for love
staring out death
wanting to feel
the treasure of life

Searching their souls
seeing the hate
wanting to hear
the story of one

Walking in time
viewing the end
wanting to see
the image of all

Finding your answer
moving towards him
dodging the hands
of the fallen one.

John Heida

A Funny Poem

The bees in the flowers
are taking their showers,
The birds in the trees are
humming in the breeze,
The ants on the ground are
carrying a pound,
The feathers in the air
Are glad they can fly,
The people in the house
are looking at a mouse,
The people in the house
pushed the mouse out!
Oh! How the mouse was glad
to be out of the house!

Jinni Esslinger

Talents

If talents you would gain
  Then talents you must use.
This lecture you disdain
  Then talents you will lose.

Daryl B. Fox

Do You Have A Favorite Place?

Do you have a favorite place
Where flowers and trees grow a
basketball hoop, a clubhouse where
many children go. So do you have a
favorite place where you and me can
go and climb up in the high high trees
and look down way below.

Julia Dillard

Cry Of The Laborer

As I walk through the streets
Pushcart in hand
My head hung low
It's ashamed I am
A donkey, a mule
that's what I be
No Future ahead
No Security
But I'll bend and I'll push
And I'll lift and I'll groan
But God! how I wish
that I could stay Home
But there's mouths to feed
And Bills to pay
So I'll just push...
the long long day

Alfred Anguera

From Me To You

A day in the springtime
I met a girl
She was a so pretty
And pure

She was so lively
With energy and
With lots of
Integrity

During the Springtime
We had lots of fun
We grew together
In the summer sun

There are things that happen
Whether they're supposed to or not
But times will be better
And maybe even greater

There was something in the air
From Heaven up above
That this was meant to happen
Because I think it's love!

Darrell W. Carroll

Girbaud

Sweet and innocent,
Till the day he died,
He'll be in my heart,
No matter what.

His little face,
As he lay there,
So cold,
So blue.

He's gone,
I miss him,
Poor Girbaud,
My little rabbit.

Jessica Snarr

"Be Of Good Cheer,
For I Have Overcome The World"

In Memory and Thanks to All American Soldiers

Our hearts go out to you in deep
   love and gratitude
For your great sacrifice in giving
   your all for us;
And may we all rejoice this blessed
   Eastertime
In the wondrous message of the Cross.
Christ is ever ahead to show the way
He's taken away the sting from Death,
The victory from the grave!

Christ has showed us how to live, to
   die, to live again,
And upon the Cross our sins He's
   borne.
Giving eternal life for all who
   believe on Him,
And for them, there awaits a
   Glorious Resurrection Morn!

Ruth Ekholm

My Psychic Cat

In the middle of the night
I was wide awake,
I slipped into the bathroom
To take a puzzle break.
Back to bed I came,
After working two or three,
Now, Shorty (cat) sleeps
On the corner of my bed,
And never bothers me.
This time he awoke
And came up to see
If I needed him. I didn't.
Instead — he kneaded me.

Wanda M. Bland

A Glance At Mother Nature

Have you ever taken a stroll?
To some distant uprising knoll.
Where one may cast
his eyes and gaze,
over the crops that
farmers raise.
Or casually stroll
along some river,
how the wind will
make you shiver.
And in the woods
the countless trees,
that swing and sway
where'er blows a breeze.
See rabbits running
"To and fro",
the dashing of
a Buck or Doe.
All the things that we make love,
were provided by, our God above.

Edward J. Hotujec

Life

New world,
New sights,
First steps,
The beginning:
Birth.

Long waits,
Big times,
Education,
Lost innocence:
Adolescence.

New awakening,
Old beginning,
Hopeful promises
Of a lucky day:
Adulthood.

Old world,
Outdated wisdom,
Last steps,
The end:
Death.

Dustin K. Bennett

An Experience

I pulled open the richly
Carved doors of the old
Church and stood within.
Soft mellow ray of fading
Sunlight sifted through the
Oval stained windows and
Lingeringly touched the lustrous
golden pillars and
massive walls. Silently I
waited in this vast space of
receding light, for what I
knew not. Slowly the peace
of a thousand years
gently enfolded me and
communed with my soul -
and I knew fear no more!

Elva Stringer

Two Sunsets

Death is not a stranger.
Fear not, after all,
Time, like the ocean,
Before we were here,

Stretched to forever,
Through spring and through fall.
As it did, as it does, it will do.
Why fear?

The world turned before us.
Our lives are new.
Past, future...certainties.
Now is unclear.

Time and tide, far and wide,
Flow on, yet other lives
Will not behold them
Until they are here.

Vaughan Burton Jr.

Angel In The Sky

Looking up in the
sky I saw an angel,
waving her wings
and saying goodbye
She took an adventure
up in heaven, with a
white little pony
flapping it's wings
swaying up in the
big, long, sky
far, far up until
I couldn't see that
    beautiful angel
        anymore.

Lori Granados

Mystery

Something out there.
In the darkness
waiting, watching,
knowing.
It cannot think,
has thoughts formed for it by another.
It cannot move,
has someone move for it.
It is just a puppet in a
vast play,
just as we are all puppets in the game
of the world.
What is it, you ask?
I do not know.
To find out, you must let in the light.

Jessica Rack

Goodbye To My Love

The sun shined bright,
There was no rain.
When you were here,
I felt no pain.
Now the sky is dark.
There is a storm.
And you're not here,
To keep me warm.
I wish this pain would go away.
Everyday, I pray and pray;
To see your face,
With such loving grace
Would bring me joy
In this dark place.

Autumn M. McNamara

Youth Speaks

The greatness of man is not measured
By the wealth he may hold in this world
But by the rule of his kindness
He extends to some boy or girl.

It's felt in the clasp of a handshake
It's heard in a "How Do You Do".
It's observed in a day of labor
In a day of relaxation too.

As I look to the years before me
And run the race of this life through
What part of life's greatness
I may attain
Could have been inspired by you.

Clarece D. Hunt

Untitled

He loves me, he loves me not
Let me count your petals.

(Pluck!) He loves me.
(pluck!) He loves me not.
Emptiness fills your vacant spaces.
(pluck!) He loves me.
Blackness engulfs your open mind.
(pluck!) He loves me not.
Sing to me sweet melodies
About the life you used to lead.
Come close and hear my secret
Let me hide in your basket.
Come listen, come hear
I'll tell you all about it.
Come close, come near
And let me tell my side.

Melanie Deman

Windmill

If God commands the wind to blow
This old mill would surely go
Doesn't need the power of man
Just the will of God's good hand
It pumps water from earth below
It pumps man's greatest treasure
To go without would be displeasure.
God knew this ages ago
So He made wind to always blow
So if you ever have a thirst
Pray for wind to be its worst
Look around find a mill
God will always work His will.

Victor T. Kearney

Just Like The Sun

The love I had finally found
Disappeared today,
Just like the sun
On a cloudy day.

No words were spoken
He was just up and gone,
Just like the sun
After the dawn.

He had loved and held me,
Kept me safe and warm,
Just like the sun
After a summer storm.

He stroked my hair
And kissed so lightly my lips,
Just like the sun
Shining through the mist.

The love I had finally found
Disappeared today,
Just like the sun
On a cloudy day.

Angela Bohringer

Dark Flash

In years gone by I'd often fly,
With the eagles in the sky.
Now I sit and wonder why,
I have lost the will to cry.
Eclipsing days travel by,
Threading through the needles eye.
My soles run dry in my feet,
for ten years now with little sleep.
Sorrowful moments I would find,
gazing at the passers-by.
My strength is gone as I retreat,
quiet now I feel the heat.
The sea, the sand a woman's hand,
Still figure softly in may plan.
All alone I wonder why,
I still have the will to fly.

Richard P. Astukewicz Jr.

The Muse

The muse escapes me
    As I sit here
    As I worry
    As I mourn.

Peace and joy
    Gives away to fear
    As hearts are hardened
    I am torn.

Eyes of darkness
    Start to leer
    As fear subsides
    Thoughts are born.

The muse returns
    As sleep is near
    As I find peace
    And others mourn.

James L. Wilkerson

Eulogy To A Small Boy

    It's hard for me to come to you
    At this time of deep sorrow
    And say I care, and hug you
    When I know you'll hurt tomorrow.
The sadness that has seized your heart
And haunts you night and day
Now fills the place that was the part
Where one small boy's love - lay.
    Remember all the smiles so brief
    Do not forget the laughter
    Now is a hard time full of grief
    Sweet memories live ever after.
But one day when you think of Brad
You'll picture God with him
No greater love you've ever had
Than knowing both of them.
    A great crowd here has gathered
    Jesus loves me fills the air
    Thru tears we've said goodbye Brad
    Angels bright will greet him there.

Kay Holsman

My Grandmom And My Grandpop

My grandmom cooks
And reads me books.
My grandpop plays nintendo just fine
but I still beat him all the time.

Brandon R. Butler

Poetry Of Life

Sentenced to life when born
Like a prison to a body
assigned,
Then from her body torn;
A name given, matters not.

A minute, day, decade or
four score,
Never mind, after that we know
no more

Death is our sentence served;
Don't bother to keep a
score;

Released to forever go,
Where?
We never know;
To eternity,
to life
no more.

Richard Davis

I'm Inspired

I'm Inspired.....

By the first ray of sunshine
after a cool morning rain.

By the sound of ocean waves
beating upon the sandy shore.

By the tenderness of your touch
and your encouraging words.

Inspired.....
to the limits of my abilities.

Leslie A. Carrasquillo

Killer's Dream

Ghastly scars,
Left on the flesh.
Ghostly stares,
Came from the rest.
Bloody stains,
Stayed on my hands.
They would leave,
Given the chance.
I would not let them,
If I could.
I would keep them;
Not that I should.
And when it was done,
I stood awake.
All of them vanished.
No more they could take.

Rebecca Raskie

Freedom Of Emotion

If soft moonlight sees me unfit
  Then, so be it
If bright sunlight wants me
  Then, I shall have me

I will not retain anything!

All my love is to you
All my hate is to them
  All my anger-
  is to me.

Al Lonchiadis

Again

The black sky waits in silence.
The moon glares back mournfully.
The maple leaves fall gently
and ride on an easy breeze.
The grasses collide with the wind.
the rocks huddle on the slopping bank.
the water ripples impatiently
and laps against the reeds.
then slowly the sky brightens
and welcome the morn
with a shower of color.
the sun passes the moon smiling.
The day begins once more.

Brianna Miller

Just As

Just as light touches dark
to bring about the day,
so too your gaze upon me
draws my breath away.

Just as rain touches parched earth
to bring about a stream,
so too your lips upon mine
mold a heavenly dream.

Just as flame touches barren wood
to bring consumption entire,
so too I yearn for you
with the heat of hottest fire.

Just as grapes pounded underfoot
bring the finest wine,
so too your touch upon my skin
fills this heart of mine.

The time I spend apart from you
brings bleakness most sublime,
just as that spent with you
is the finest of my time.

Roberto Luis Gorena

Family Values?

A screen door
sways
outside a boy
plays
other holds her head
high
Daughter waves
bye-bye
Daddy...
on his knees
begins to
cry

Kenneth J. Brown

Beach Views

Hair flying in the breeze,
Feeling totally at ease.
Wind wafting off the water,
A man hugging his daughter
Children screaming with delight,
As each wave comes into sight.
A woman lounging in a chair,
Not a worry or a care.
Everything seems bright,
Just like the sunlight.

Louise Perkins

The Miracle

I saw a rainbow in the sky,
Its colors were so bright.
Before I caught another glimpse,
It faded out of sight.
I ran across a troubled boy,
Whose life was filled with sighs,
And was awed by the beauty that
I saw within his eyes.
I heard a haunting melody,
Too nice to comprehend.
And found myself still singing it
Long after it did end.
I saw a sun rise kiss the sky.
I saw a star shine bright.
I smelled the sweetness of a flower.
I saw the darkest night.
And all these things I've come across,
I've thought of long and hard,
And can't deny the miracle
That all of them were God.

Sherrie Sushko

A Christmas Poem

Who is this babe
Who came to earth
That night so long ago?

Who is this child
A Carpenter's son
More than the scholars he did know?

Who is this man
Who calms the stormy seas
And tells sickness and sin to go?

Who is this king
Who hangs on a cross
And shows satan He has lost?

Who is this Savior
Who ascended to heaven
To remove from earth all the dross?

His name is Jesus
And His life is from God.
He paid penalties for sin
And taught us to love
So that eternal life we can win.

Mary Becerril

Untitled

Forgiveness lasts and dreams
  Come true when you believe
Trust lies dead when you give up.
  At the end of a long road.
Love enlightens all that try
  when life itself comes to an end.

Amber Delgado

Nightmare Of Hell

With my skin burning,
I was running and turning,
Though scared of what was up ahead
For death I was yearning,
But fear I was learning,
Realizing I'm already dead.

J.A.Y.

The Best Of Me

The best of me, is gone you see.
What's left, will just have to be,
Enough to help me make it thru.
I lost the best, when I lost you.

The years we had seems such a few.
But thirty nine will have to do.
When God called you, an he left me,
He took the best, for it was thee.

Our parting came, thru pain and so,
We both knew, that you must go.
And when my soul is joined with thee.
Forever it'll be, the best of me.

Eva Mae Chavis

The Crash

Night time, Good time
Cruisin', music playing
Friends laughing
Feeling, knowing freedom
Time is outside in.

Cresting the hill
Small lights flash, floating
Body and mind react
Downshift, swerve
Time is but the moment.

Sliding, skidding
Sounds but no sound
Random, flashing picture thoughts
Turning, turning and turning
Time is inside out.

Awareness, Panic
Not knowing
Friends are hurt
Outcome unknown
Time remains twisted and bent.

Joe Stokes

The Potting Bench

Daria, Daria
You cleaned the area
Over there
By the potting bench.

Because we all care
No one will dare
Make a mess
By the potting bench.

Your presence is felt
But we need your help
Over there
By the potting bench.

Please stop in and see
And have lunch with me
But please not
By the potting bench.

Shirley A. Mitsko

Last Words

Please,
Don't kill me,
Mommy.

But,
I love you...

Really.

Jane Frady

A Tear

Much more than a raindrop
Born unto that young china blue eye;
A looking glass
Searching deep
Into another realm:
A restless ocean
Where pain rocks
The dark torrential waters,
And eminent storm clouds
Threaten the light,
Threaten the fragile happiness.

Brittany Dawson

Heaven

I need not know what heaven is
Nor even where it be;
It is enough for me to know
God has a place for me.

And in that heaven there may not be
The bounds of time or space;
The only bounds that we will know
Will be the bounds of God's embrace.

Florence P. Kendall

The Sounds Of Life

The sounds of life about the house
  Begin, crescendo, shrill.
The children come, grow up and leave,
  So soon the house is still.

The sounds of life about the house
  Are like a muted song,
The months and years flow swiftly by,
  And only the days are long.

R. Norman Crowley

Love

Love is like a rainbow,
that shines on and on;

Love is like a rose,
so beautiful and strong;

Love is like a snowflake,
so pure and so bright;

Love is like a star,
shining oh so bright;

How do you express this LOVE so
strong and so true?

Simply by saying

I LOVE YOU

Katie Helmer

The Holy Man

The Holy Man
stood on Holy Ground
and he Spoke
his Holy message
in silence

Linda Fuller

Christmas Around Here

The christmas tree is hung
with love and care
The christmas ornaments
are hung and bulbs
burn clear
It shows us that it is
Christmas around here

The packages are wrapped
with paper new and old
Colors are arranged
Red, Green, and Gold

So from our heart
that we know Christmas
is here
That's how you know
it's Christmas around here

P. J. J. Randall

My Little Angel In High Heeled Shoes

Some say an angel must be big.
Some say he must be small.
But my idea's different
From one, and from them all.

My angel dresses in purple
From her head down to her toes.
And if you just do one thing wrong,
By golly, Joe, she knows!

Her eyes are the color of hazel,
Her hair the color of the sea.
Her skin is the color of coffee,
Just like me.

Yes, that is my angel
The one that I choose.
She is my little angel dressed
In high-heeled shoes.

Chantal James

Pelagic Heaven

Blue warming, though it's cold autumn.
Amber trees stand upon a mountain top
breathing, virgin, northern breeze.
Anxious sky holds furnace light
to warm my heart along loves plight.
God carries me above the sea
like a billowed cloud forever free.
A colored world left astray
from the busy people caught in the day.
What buried feeling deep inside,
peeks from fertile seed of pride?
With only silence consoling me
the candid wind whispers reassuringly.

Robert Patrick Murtha

Untitled

Its my time to say goodbye.
I wish for you not to cry.
I can not stay any longer,
But our love will still grow
much stronger.
I want you to know I'll forever care,
and that I'll always be right there.
Please don't try and wonder why,
For its just my time to say goodbye.

Mandy Ferrara

A Welcomed Friend

Oh death....oh death...
come greet me

I welcome you
with open arms

Visit me not as
a thief in the night

But as a welcomed
friend to behold

Days are long
the nights cold

In my pain I grow
weak and old

Oh death...oh death
come greet me

My mother cries
at my bedside

She holds my hands, wipes my brow
And speaks softly of things that passed
She whispers gently in my ear
The end is finally near...

Patricia Schmidt

The Rush

Twinkling eyes at play,
eyes that still hold hope
for their future, to them,
   is still unknown.

Their laughter is the sweetest sound
that stirs a soul.
they are unaware of what
   lies ahead.

At play they pass no judgment.
Race and color matters not
to them at this point
   in life.

Too soon the smiles fade,
the laughter stops,
play becomes competition
   all grown-up...

John B. Francis

Walking Toward The Light

Christ said love your neighbor
treat him good and kind
He may not be the neighbor.
that you had hope to find
If his life is filled with darkness
and nothing seems quite right
give him a glimpse of Jesus
by walking toward the light

There's no respect of persons
everyone could be good and kind
If they will come to Jesus and
find this peace of mind
By faith accept His promise
Turn from wrong to right,
Oh there's such a difference
walking toward the light.

Margaret D. Lee

Helping

You don't
Need to go
To the store

There should
Be enough
In your drawer

To help the
Homeless
And poor!

Sarah Catherine Gover

Why Must I Cry?

Why must I cry
I cry and cry and cry
But don't know what about
I try to hold it in,
And not let anyone know
I pass myself back and forth in my room
Covering my eyes,
And telling myself not to cry
But no matter what I do
The tears come streaming out
I try to wipe them away
But they keep coming back
I wonder if its good to cry
Does it help you
Does it express how you feel
That's a question I must find out
But till then
Why must I cry?

Natalia Samudousky

The Face Of Love - Disfigurement

The face of love - disfigurement!
   Distorted, stressed and strained!
'Tis not the face you might expect
   The face of hope but drained!

The face of love with beauty burst
   Yes, that's what we would see!
A face - calm, clear, with placidness,
   Yes, that's the face for me!

But that is not the face we see,
   But one that's stained with tears,
A face that's heavy, weary, worn,
   And old beyond its years!

His face is aged for love of thee,
   His brow is wrinkled, worn,
His features scarcely recognized,
   As they with love are torn!

David P. Wilson

"No Return"

Solemnly I sit and rot away
Youthful death brings slow decay
Fight as I do, it does no good
No hope of regaining my childhood

What to do now-get a job, settle down
As naive ambitions fall to the ground
Fight as I do, it's all in vain
Nothing overcomes such sorrow and pain

Digging myself into such a hole
Trying to comfort this broken soul
Fight as I do, there is no control
Can't turn back, I'll just grow old.

Joshua Meier

The Words That Hurt

The words that hurt are words
of a good be.
The words that hurt are words
of a lonely man.
The words that hurt are words
of pain and jealousy.
The words that hurt are words
of a man crying.
The words that hurt are words
that say its over.
The words that hurt are words
of love being pushed away.
The words that hurt are words
of a babies cry for help.
The words that hurt are words
that let you go...

Lisa Klock

Kaleidoscope Of Grief

With your death
The eyes of my soul
Became firmly affixed
To grief's kaleidoscope,

And the crystalline shards
Of glass that gash and gouge me
Combine and recombine
At the end of
Grief's long tunnel
Into the shapes of pain.

Clattering together
With my every turn,
Intermingling in
Countless combinations,
Displaying every
Jagged edge and angle
Of the emotional
Diversity of grief's
Colors, shapes, and contours.

Jessica Dahl

"Snow"

Snow, a spirit of cleansing.
   A powder of white power,
   Sweeping away sin from the earth.
   Making the dark light,
   As it falls as one.

Snow, a spirit of cleansing.
   Soft as cotton,
   On a child's skin.
   A dust from the heavens,
   As a sign of peace.

Snow, a spirit of cleansing.
   It comes and goes,
   As visitors do.
   Sometimes leaving its remains,
   To stay in our hearts forever.

Snow, a spirit of cleansing.
   Even though gone,
   It's soul is always here.
   Until the white spirit,
   Returns again.

Jeffrey Manheimer

Wind

Wind is about the earth,
above the ground,
across the sky,

after the moon,
against the trees,
along the water,

among the people,
around the bend,
as the earth turns wind is there.

Thomas Mullin

Night Is Woman

Night is woman
And man is but a creature to her will
Yearning
For the pleasures of her soul.

Woman is mystery
Who veils her magic
Like mist at dawn
Passing light in time.

Black is her gourd
Of sweet heaven-bent petals
Fragrantly teasing
The tortured scent of man.

Enriched
In all the sweet care
Of a spring
Running trickles on the
Lips of sweet ecstasy,
She gives of her holy treasure trove -
Gratefully abandoned.

Richard N. Friedman

Jackie Robinson Apartments, Brooklyn, N.Y.

"Don't run inside"
says the lady
who lives in the apartment
built over the path
Robinson blazed,
head down, heart up
hook slid into home,
now only a home
where obedient children
(whose feet feel the echoes)
can't run.

Eleanor M. Scott

Reality

The sadness of reality,
Knowing that I cannot have
The happiness that I long
and to sing the glorious song of love.

It's so hard,
To be able to grasp,
and yet not to hold
These feelings of old
that I cannot escape.

This yearning has made me mad
I'm crazy so they say,
It's the wall I cannot break
The fight for my own sake,
And for it I pay in loneliness.

Kelly Dobbins

Untitled

I heard a call from desert
   begging water,
And rushed toward
   to save, to help, to heal.
I ran like hell, at first,
   then stopped in order
To judge: Who? When? And why?
   And is there a big deal?
Then ran again, then stopped
   for herbs and berries —
I'll bring with water
   treasures of the Earth!
That who is longing for my come
   in desert debris
Will be in safety,
   back to life and mirth.
The voice weakened,
   pleading in a wait.
I urged again...
   and all the same was late.

Natalie A. Kalinina

Refined

A young girl's love how innocent
   A teenage love, how dear
A young woman's love, how cherished
A mature woman's love, how refined,
   For loving so much.

Eleanor A. Allen

Reality

Summing, running, sledding,
Ball games, fishing
And Church on sunday
Sunday school, school
Friends, sodas, boy friend
Girlfriend, and country drive
Mom, dad, sisters, brothers
Jobs, career, money
Money, root of all evil
Pressure and growing up
Rent, car, and bills
What else, the reality of death
The final payment on life

Lonnie Pack

Untitled

I thought I saw you yesterday
When the butterfly passed my way
Not a word did he utter, he kissed
each shrub and every other.
I thought I saw you yesterday
only I found a child at play
I watched him chase the butterfly
in the distance a plane passed by
was it you in disguise?
I thought I saw you yesterday
gathered at (Moms) on "Mothers Day"
I felt your presence all around
you were no where to be found
I thought I saw you yesterday
God is in charge (he's taken you away)
I thought I saw you yesterday
I felt the wind, the sky was grey
I felt the tear roll down my eye
Angel Michael - why oh why

Filomena Kask

Closer Than A Sister

We are very different-
Yet we're nearly the same,
Though not related
By blood, looks, or name.

She is quiet and feminine
With a subtle air of grace;
While I'm reckless and wild—
On me a dress is out of place.

We know the other's thoughts
As if our minds were shared;
No words need to be spoken,
We simply are aware.

She is willing to comfort
Sometimes, just by being there
Or by giving a hug
To let me know she cares.

And when we're not together
She knows that I miss her
For this friendship we share
Is closer than a sister's.

Sandi Pitts

The Wall—Written After A Conversation With My Friend Violet

Although mother died some years ago—
At dusk
I often drive past
The pink pebbled wall
Where the ladies sit.

Warmed by the sun
They hug the wall!

There is my mother!
Still dressed in her
Plaid hat and coat!

Nodding as always
To her neighbors
The same conversation!
"It is hot"
"It is cold!"
"Summer is almost over"

I turn to wave
No one is there-The wind scatters
The dry leaves in front of the wall -
All is still

Violet Weiss

Ending

An ol' worn body sitting there
A whisp of gold still in her hair
Autumn crisp breeze takes but a spray
And blows that gold to yesterday.

A porcelain face of beauty rare
No hand to hold, no love to share
No sadness in her eyes of brown
Forgotten years can find no frown.

No movement in her pale pink lips
Or want of taste of joy or bliss
A solemn silence shared by one
Belittled by the warming sun.

A leaf round her gentle falls
As passing time that reaches all
A touch of winter's knowing breath
Will put that yesteryear at rest.

Ruth Campbell Eddy

Me

Sunsets by the lakefront
Starlights by the sea
These are just a few of the things
That always fascinate me.

Kittens playing with their tails
Puppies racing down the trail
Eagles soaring through the sky
Makes me wonder how they fly.

Children playing in the street
Running barefoot on their feet
Raindrops falling from the trees
Why do birds fly south to leave?

Church bells ringing at 12 noon
School time coming way too soon
Sometimes I wonder what I'll be,
And that itself still fascinates me.

Cynthia Kennedy Moorhouse

Plastic Paradise

Faceless futures
Of death defying feats,
And helpless ages,
Wrinkle free.
Come drink the milk
Of youthfulness
And pry upon the hefty mistress.

No such luck
To gratify,
A pretty glance,
Synthetic eyes.
I see before me
Figures fade,
Brushing back
The fate that's made.

Oh, be weary
To what you see,
The fragile features
Aren't shatter free.

Brenda L. Link

"I Remember You"

I remember you
You're the one I love
And each night I thank the Lord above
Thank him for your love.

As I close my eyes
I can see your smile
Hear your voice within my dreams
So, please, let me dream a while.

When the morning comes, Dear,
I recall my dreams
Welcome each new day, Dear,
And the joy love brings.

Jeanine C. Benson

Untitled

To get his wealth, he
spent his health, and
then with might and main
he turned around and
spent his wealth,
to get his health
again

Ciria M. Medina

Evergreen

Northwest, land of dreams,
Protected by mountains
Covered by tall greens,

God gave you the ocean,
Prairies, hills and rivers,
Wilderness and beauties

Friendly, hard work people
Have marked nice features
Like strong, brave ancestors!

Land of future's dreams,
Exploring unknown
Stars and galaxies...

More and more I'd write
Presenting my land
But - the best you'd see
When you'll come here!

Irica Hertog

For My Valentine

These few lines of poetry,
and lines of prose.
Will explain, if you're wondering;
where's the twelfth rose?
I begged and I pleaded,
"I need only eleven."
The most beautiful one,
was sent here from heaven.
Now hopefully it's becoming,
a little more clearer.
If not, please sweetheart,
go look in the mirror.
There you will see,
what these words had to say.
And for me, I wish you
Happy Valentines Day!

Brian Brecht

To Be

A poet!
To be a poet!
To be, to say,
To use and see,
The words, so powerful,
Joyous, delicious, thrilling!
To paint clearer pictures
Than human eyes can see.
To feel, to feel,
And bring forth from my soul,
That very ray, precise,
To touch your soul.
And from that radiant connection,
To spin a brilliant tapestry,
Ever changing, ever true.
To console or challenge or haunt,
But never, ever to leave!
To be a poet!
To be!

Kathleen Chilenski

Untitled

At times I look at life
like a string of pearls
each pearl beautiful yet
different.
When times are tough
the string has broken.
When it is restrung there is
a new and slightly different order.
Same pearls, new strings,
different order.
If I want my life to change
I must throw away the pearls.
Yet I probably will wind up
with a new string, different
pearls, different order, same life.

Jo-Ann Rifkind

Viva Las Vegas

I feed the metal mouth
Start to find a rhythm
Feel a bit of a technique coming on.
A spewage of coinage
Accompanied by noise like
Trains on tracks; a noise that warms
My ears.
Allowing, even encouraging this
Oh! So sweet seduction
I sit closer, lean a little nearer,
With cocky confidence of muscle
Movement I try and quell the
Metal monster's hunger.
Rewarded just enough;
I try again and again . . .
And again . . .

Sarah Jane Wisehart

Obsession

Obsession without release.
Erotic dreams and fantasies
I'll hold through waking hours
Tho' it does little... but to tease
My body relentlessly aches
With wanting and desire
And in the night it awakens
To burn...
... as one on fire
Day dreams of a rendezvous
Decadent sensual interludes
To want you without having,
Obsession...
...no release

Gloria A. McNabb

Once A Baby Boy

You are my baby boy,
I fed you, cleaned you, kept you warm.
Gave you comfort in a storm,
You were my baby boy.

You ate like a man,
Yet you played in the sand
Now my baby boy,
has taken another's hand.

As I am old and gray.
You have no time to play.
My baby boy you will stay.

Teresa Nash

Who Are You

Sitting on the bench
Sifting through the trash
do you have a house
or do you live in that box

Were you in the war
found out killing was not the answer
or you lost your love
maybe you never found her

Were you a king
maybe an inventor
did you invent the bomb
and feel sorry after

Does it get cold at night
when you are all alone
do you think of the good times
or was there none

I wish I could help
but I am just one
I guess the help of one
is better than none

Raymond B. Kuhn

Prayer Whispers

Softly murmured in the morn
Gently held upward and out
Reverently applied within
Prayer whispers are left to adorn

Humbly sent to a majestic high
Emotions of deep content
Brush against his face so clear
Received with passion unending

Laughter of sweetness
Smiles of joy
Rest beneath my weary body
For the horizon holds my infinite soul
Against prayer whispers untold

Octavia Yvonne Webb

When Love Is Gone

When love is gone,
  so is my mind.
I keep thinking of you time after time;
I keep searching, hoping to find,
  that piece of love so precious
  and kind.
My heart is filled with emptiness;
  I just long for one of
  your hugs and a kiss.
I long for all the dreams that
  won't come true;
I long for my one and only you.

Jimmy Marshall

For My Daughter Dianna

Day after day,
Is each different
And it also
Never come back
Never the same
Again.

Kimlan Phan

Madeline

Madeline your birth brought
  laughter and joy
At last a girl, we have two
  boys,
Your smile is sweet as is your
  cry.
For food to fill, that brings a
  sigh,
Pray your life bring good and
  kind,
And you will strive to fill
  your mind,
With all things beautiful,
  Kindness brings.
A song we'll teach you so your
  heart sings,
So as this ode to you unfurls,
You're first and foremost,
  the only girl!

Jean Kachin

Untitled

Infinity.
Eternity.
Creation and dissipation.
Rotation, coagulation,
and solar radiation.
Planetary formation.
Geology, biology, chemistry.
All this from infinity?
Biological evolution,
neural constitution,
mental cognition.
The ability to remember,
what a selective advantage,
a connection to the past,
but an isolated continuity,
the sense of separate identity.
But it's really one with infinity.
This illusion, so great,
of isolated ego,
what a lonely fate.

Kenneth N. Sharpe

Untitled

In my selfish prayers
I ask for a vision,
As if all I've seen
Isn't enough
To make me believe.

I ask for more possessions,
Never satisfied
With the abundance
Of things I already have.

As my cup runneth over,
I beg for youth of body and face,
Lest my last bit
Of vanity escape me.

Ever ungrateful,
I long for yesterday,
Hope for tomorrow,
And never appreciate
The gift of today.

Darla Dawn Martin

Longings

Some men long to see the view
From the loftiest mountain peak.

Some men long to see the mysteries
Of the ocean deep.

Some men long to see the worlds
That fill the endless skies

I long to see forever
My reflection in your eyes.

Joyce Nicholson Booth

Like A Flower In The Sun

It was a chance encounter
such a long time ago.
Who would have thought it-
that our emotions would flow?

Building our trust,
our honesty, our compassion,
these were the first steps
toward laying our foundation.

We did not try to force it,
we proceeded so slow.
Our efforts were focused
so our feelings could grow.

Through patience and time,
and a lot of hard work,
I learned how to love you,
especially that smirk.

I will embrace your warmth
like a flower in the sun.
I'm at peace with my world
for I know you're THE ONE.

Gregory D. Lovse

A Vision Of Art

A machine gun blows
An Easter dress
Trigger-happy and full of bliss.
Explosive patterns of red and white
An artist's dream screams with delight.
Innocence bursts
A confusing scene
Patterns of wickedness
A wildman's dream.
A flower falls
A child dies
Another creation will yet arise.
The loss and grievance will sustain-
An orgasmic bliss of creative pain.

Nikki Jade

Anticipation

The sun slowly sets disappearing in the
solitary horizon. An albatross takes
flight chasing the remains of the day.
I sit and watch while nightfall gently
caresses me, holding me in its immense blackness.

With eyes closed I see the sun
shimmering in your gaze. I follow it
and it warms me.

The darkness of the night lies only in
the intensity of your eyes, where
innocently my dreams are lost,
justifying my uncontrollable desire for
you, as I await your return.

Katherine Suhay

Wherever Life Takes You

Wherever life takes you
Make the most of everyday
Not content to just be there
Live by what you say.

There is joy and contentment
In helping others see
Happiness is within us
Not dependent upon what is to be.

There is love all around us
We only must open our eyes
Ask God for guidance and wisdom
He is always by our side.

So live to your fullest potential
In everything you do
And happiness you shall find
Wherever life my take you.

Judy H. Gambill

"A Rose"

Ones than was arose. That
Was no watered by a hose,
And that was selled by a rose.
And they chose to pick it.
And it closed.

Natalie Erin Hill

Brimstone And Fire

Barbed wire.
Bright lights.

Brutal guards.
Bemused superiors.

Brave parents.
Befuddled children.

Bludgeoned heads!
Busted limbs!

Brief respite.
Broken showers?

Barren faces!
Bloodied faces!

Burning flesh.
Bygone dreams.

Backward beliefs?
Belated remorse?

BASTARDS!!!

Errol Putman

Goodbye

Goodbye seems so final
A word I seldom use,
But in this case it's proper
Because I'm so confused.
I told you how I'm feeling,
I really spilled my heart
It must have been to no avail
For now it's tearing me apart.
I'm in real pain my darling
That can't be hard to see,
For you have told me nothing
You could have said goodbye to me!

Anthony D. Mattson

A Road I Share With A Friend

We shared a narrow road,
because our lives, were the same
in many ways, when we were
growing up, our mothers were the
same in many ways. That's
why we share our moments just
about everyday. They are emotional
to our feelings, that we just want
to cry. I'm glad we're friends
because we help each other
threw our emotional treads.
Our roads will someday change
because we are working with
our lives, if we weren't helping
each other, we wouldn't be friends
with each other that's why we
have our own little road.

Jillian Oleary

"Letting Go"

O! The pain I feel
when your memories run
through my mind.
It's so hard for me to
let go this time.
Your memories is all
I have left of you.
There's no flesh and bones
to hold on too.
If only I was there
to say "Goodbye!"
Then letting go would
be easy to do.
But this is my goodbye
to you, my love.
And to let you know,
Letting go wasn't
easy to do.

Bobbi Nantz

Today People

Today people fight.
Today people die.
Today bad people, scare people.
Today people are afraid.
Today people just get f***ed.
Today people don't know how to love,
except for maybe in their dreams.
Today what is real?
Today, not people.

Tomorrow People

Tomorrow people care.
Tomorrow people give.
Tomorrow people love.
Tomorrow people love to live.
Tomorrow people feel.
Tomorrow people are real.
Tomorrow people, I hope I live.

Jeff Small

Garden Of The Gods

Ah, Garden of the Gods,
how awesome you are to me.
When in you, I see, my
ancestors looking back at me.

Shirley N. Bryson

My Grandma's Kitchen Window

She washed the breakfast dishes,
Looked out at a brand new day;
Altho she never mentioned it,
I think it was here my grandma prayed.

Out that window was sunshine,
Grandkids and meadows of hay;
Sometimes she just watched for papa,
With a real sweet smile her face.

That window was her favorite place,
To view her world and dream her dreams;
And tho she never traveled much,
She knew a lot or so it seemed.

Today I stood at my kitchen window,
Looked out at a brand new day;
A different world stared back at me,
And like my grandma I started to pray.

Carol Robertson

The Compass

I see a glimpse of you
In my mind.
For some time, you're in color.
Then you leave
    Again.
I feel your lips on mine
White hot breath.
For a moment, the little death.
Must you leave
    Again?
You're melting into me
I'm on fire
For a while, sweltering flesh
Begging pleeease
My friend
    Aagaaain.

You're killing all that's left
I'm bleeding
You're still needing, I scream No
But you want to. And you can.

Andrea Rene Moschella

Miracles Do Happen

Miracles do happen
You know this to be true
Just too many coincidences
To just come out of the blue

Miracles do happen
Take a look around
I can see miracles
As easily as hearing a sound

Miracles do happen
And happen everyday
For many angels are watching
The earthly miracles display

Miracles do happen
And they happen to you
You must pay attention
And you will see them to

Miracles do happen
I thank the good Lord and pray
That the miracles that happen
Will never fade away!

John E. Tynio

Shadow Dreams

Deep in my heart I wish we
are never apart, I remember
the subtle hints of love whispered
threw the night, that seemed
to make all dark things light.
Fading away this dream we
call reality. And threw the night
with my vision in sight our
two hearts beat as one. You
hold my hand as I begin to
understand the power of your
love. The shadows call our name
will we ever be the same

Nate Butala

The Surgeon

Silent - seriously intent
Masked, gowned and gloved,
On healing bent,
He guides the knife.

Steady hand -Steady gaze,
With nerves of steel
Life and death,-
He parts the ways.

Calmly he works with his team
His hand guided from above,
At last to relax he seems,-
The work is done.

Edith Taffet

The Lost Little Puppy Dog

There he stands
with his head to the sky.
The lost little puppy dog
with a tear in his eye.

He looks into a sky of clouds
for a single ray of sun.
Now that he doesn't have it
he knows what he has done.

He took that ray for granted.
He didn't appreciate what he had.
And now that he doesn't have it
the puppy dog is sad.

He thinks that if only
To see that ray of light.
He hopes and prays that someday
and someday he just might.

Darrell Bennett

Once I Fell In Love

Dedicated to Ken Nadeau
Once, I fell in love;
And we were like
Romeo and Juliette.
The rose and it's color.
The sun and it's rays.
The sparrow and its song.

After all this time,
My heart still aches.
There will never be another
To take the place of you.
I'll never forget you,
Because once I fell in love;
Once and only once.

Hope Whittemore

Black Man

Out of my nightly slumber,
I am taken from my home;
Taken to the strangest of lands,
I am left to stand alone.

Will I survive?

Fighting with all I had,
I was soon set free;
Having no one to turn to,
And no one who would believe in me.

Will I survive?

In a crowd I marched,
Wanting my civil rights,
All the while I am so afraid,
Cause death usually comes at night.

Will I survive?

I now know I can make it,
I will just give it time;
No one can take away the fact,
This world is also mine;

I will survive!!!

Alvin R. Fritts

Do We Belong To The Earth?

The earth brings us life
Like a mother
Giving birth to children
Daughters and sons

The earth feeds us
Like a mother
Nourishing her children
With her milk and affection

We live on the earth
Our whole lives
Like lichens clinging to rock
Until they expire

But on behalf of dust
We always wonder:
Does the earth belong to us?
Do we belong to her?

Minh-Vien

Too Late

I wanted to walk with you tonight
Under the fat, orange-faced moon.
I wanted to listen with you tonight
To all the sounds of summer.
To watch the mists roll in
On silvery, silent feet.
And catch the quicksilver
Of a thousand flashing fireflies.
But then there comes a hugh
The very earth holds its breath
Standing tippytoe in moonlight.
Then softly and plaintively comes
The haunting call of a whippoorwill
And I thought my heart would break
Too late—too late for love.

Ethel Ellis

Life....

I guess its just a state of mind,
the more you try to avoid things,
    the harder it becomes
the more you more ahead in
life, the more you feel behind
    the deeper you fall in love,
the less you feel carefree
the more the money, the more the
greed
    the less the money, the more
the need
    the more the pain, the more you'll
grow,
    But is it all true, we'll
never know!!

Katherine Campoli

Heartbeat

Mama's only pride and joy,
Is nothing but a little boy,
Who spends his waking hours,
Climbing trees and water towers,
Catching frogs and water snakes,
While Mama stays behind and bakes,
Little men with smiling faces,
And baseballs with golden laces,
But sooner or later he becomes a man,
And releases hold of Mama's hand,
He finds himself in a foreign land,
Filled with blood and arabic sand,
A boy of youth and innocence,
Is Mama's special little prince,
The wooden box is of plain lumber,
Where he resides in eternal slumber.

Christine Lellis

The Crow

The crow, black and sinister,
evil eyes of ebony.
A clever thief, slyly sneaking,
creeping into the farms.

Ron Narozny

The Mind Deceiving Satan

Deep beneath the surface
In the caverns of my mind
Incessantly dwells a demon
A being of another kind

He flits around inside my brain
From here to there to yonder
Try as I might to subdue him
He rends my thoughts asunder

The devil is an awesome force
That science cannot halt
He's ever-present within me
As through this life I walk

But thanks be to almighty God
The father of us all
He sent his son to die for sin
And help me lest I fall

Yet to be a saint of God
And finally go to heaven
I must fight with all my might
The mind deceiving satan

James Berry

Trying

Sipping timidly the warmth
I close my eyes, hold my breath
there stains no red upon my lips
there comes no pink to my cheeks
no blush of innocence from the
white sin of a child
adolescence upon me,
there appears a purple haze
my green desire has made me drunk
we taste again the sweetness
of first love

Amy L. Helsel

The Path

At the end of the rainbow
   which is so hard to find
Is the secret of happiness
   for most of mankind
The form doesn't come from that
big pot of gold
   But from people themselves
   not things that are sold.
So take what you have
   and not what you want
Build a good life
   put your family in front
Follow Your Dreams, aspirations
   and hopes
Just leave all the nonsense
to the losers and dopes.

Michael N. Petroski

Gift Of Love

I have all the feelings
bottled in my heart,
   Hoping to tell you right
from the start.
   But where to begin I
have so much to say
   To you a Mom who
can brighten my day.
   Our friendship we
have is one I cherish.
   You've opened your door
and let me in,
   never to judge just
be my friend,
   Like the love I have
for you never to perish.

Paula Blackburn

Untitled

The light within
glows like a flame
Give it breath
to maintain
feed the will and
you want be still
use control and
you want be sold

James R. Jones Jr.

Pondering The Imponderable

When this universe I ponder,
I just never cease to wonder.
Can I contemplate such wonder
As I ponder things out yonder?

Just how far does it extend?
Does it even have an end?
Did this wonder once begin?
Will it ever have to end?

As bodies orbit everywhere,
What is the glue that holds them there?
Of what did God create this mass,
Or will He do with it at last?

Can mortals, with a certitude,
Appreciate such magnitude?
Can scion of mortality
Comprehend an eternity?

When these thoughts I put asunder,
They come back as loud as thunder.
And I wonder as I ponder
Can I ponder such great wonder.

A. V. Wallace

My Dad

There will never be another
   Greater than he
No one could ever know
   What my father meant to me

His will was strong
   This was proven every day
His will to survive
   Amazed everyone, in everyway

He was always there
   When and if need be
My fishing buddy, my coach, pals
   My dad and me

He taught me so much
   In so many ways
A man of great knowledge
   I'll always treasure those days

Although his life was taken
   A blessing in disguise
You can always see my father
   Just look into my eyes

Alice M. Paslick

Teenager's Lament

The alarm rings,
I open one eye.
6 a.m.
I'm gonna die.

Up 'till late,
Big exam.
So much material,
Cram, cram, cram.

School's creator?
Who was this fool?
Probably insane.
Definitely uncool!

My school has
One saving grace.
Good looking babes,
All in one place!

Sandra Sepe

Within

In vain does the Mind seek
What the Heart already knows.
No edge to age a matter gray
God's mysteries to disclose.
The joyous heart is a laughing child
Born free of braining blows.
In pain does the Mind seek
What the Heart already knows.

Francis J. Cavano

Untitled

I'm in love with you!
You have brighten my world
Your eyes lighten my live
You have given me reason
to live more lives.
Your smile makes me smile
Seeing you smile give me feeling
I can't hide you have open
A new door to my live a door.
which nobody has ever done.
You shown me more to live
then just one.
You have given me feeling I can't
explain your walk is so gentle
your tough I'm longing to feel
knowing that wouldn't be a enough
You have shown me happiness
will in my heart. But you have
also shown me silence which
keeps us a part.

Debra L. Camillone

To My Late Husband

Mid the shadows of this lonely room.
   I see your precious face
I feel the warmth of your tender kiss
   And the love in your strong embrace

Its only a dream I know my love
   Where I feel you close to me
But my aching heart keeps yearning
   For the days that used to be

C. P. Sutphen

A Mother's Peace

No peace could 'ere come over me,
No words yet to be said,
Like the peace that washes over me,
Standing by her little bed,
When sunlight draws its last shadow,
Like a single golden thread,
And I am standing silently,
One hand on her silken head.

Valerie W. Watkins

Gift For Mommy

Dear Mommy, I am small you know
And town is so crowded too
But with my love, here is my gift
That Daddy picked out for you.

And if, by chance, it's incorrect
And not as pretty as could be,
Then, Dear Mommy, fuss at Daddy
For he picked it out for me.

Virgil T. Albright

A Little Boy With Aids

It wasn't Ryan's fault
  But still he got caught
    With the aids virus

Everyone would avoid Ryan
  He got very annoyed
    With the aids virus

He went to school
  They called him a fool
    With the aids virus
He went to court
  To get some support
    For the aids virus
The hospital tried
  But still he died
    With the aids virus

     Allyson Reynolds

Earth Is A Classroom

These eyes can see beyond a doubt
These eyes can see what life's about,
The need to live, the need to die
The need to laugh, the need to cry
These eyes can see and tell you why,
There is a reason why we're here
Most don't know and most have fear,
Earth is a classroom, a place to learn
Some live their lives with no concern,
The clock just ticks their life away
The only path they take is play,
Spread your wings, take your flight
God still shines throughout the night,
Let life's song to you come through
That others matter, not just you,
In this world of make believe
There is truth, please hear me,
Yes. I falter, just like you
But these eyes can see just why I do
I am here to learn and so are you!

     Judith Veneziano

Life's Setting Sun

Shadows hasten with the hour
Of the twilight's setting sun,
Children gather to the bower
Of a dream when day is done.

Clouds of beauty drift in Heaven
Colored by the hand of God,
While the flowers, still adorning,
Fold their blooms and slowly nod.

Day is dying, crossing over
Where the stretching shadows lie,
Dew drops gather on the clover,
And the silver in the sky.

Gentle zephyrs gather sweetly
Essence from the goldenrod,
While the fireflies of the twilight
Start their evening promenade.

Oh! The lamp of light is dying,
And the evening tide is deep,
And a day of life goes flying
Like a flower gone to sleep.

     Russell E. Phillips

It's The Truth

Some people get you down,
And make you feel like you're nothing.
Let me tell you this,
Everybody's something.

You may not feel the same,
But, you know, I understand.
Because, everybody's something,
Even the poorest of man.

It may be hard to be around,
Someone from the streets.
But, nobody gets attached,
To everyone they meet.

So when you're feeling down,
And you think that you're nothing.
Just remember this,
Everybody's something.

     Melissa R. Henson

Are You There?

"Oh, help me God", he whispers
I'm not God, not even close.
But he believes
Are you there? I'm not sure.

How could he make him suffer.
For what. Did he do something to
deserve this?

Death with dignity-Hospice says.
I want to help him now
get better. This can't be the end.
He taught me about living-not dying.

He told me everything has a reason
Love, Hate, War, Peace.
How did he know?

Is this the circle of life
Do I believe? I want to.
God, you have to be there
My dad needs you now.

     Ann Hacic Hoffman

Spirit Dancer

Spirit Dancer in the sky
  dancing to and fro
    searching for his soul mate.
She is earth bound until
  he takes her hand.
His touch energizes her soul,
  lifting her to the sky.

Together they embrace
  dancing on moonbeams
    all through the night.

Morning comes showing
  all earth's splendor.
He puts his arms around
  her knowing love's decision
    has made him earth bound.
Together they ride the last
  moonbeams to earth.

     Winona Stevens Sweet

Staring

Every one is staring
they are staring;
down at me.
I am under pressure to answer #3.
#3, #3,
why did they pick me?
I'd better answer it
right
or they will laugh
at me!!
I'd rather be in bed,
my face is turning
red.
Every one is
staring
they are staring;
down at me.

     Megan Peterson

Baby-Busting

You understand
You care
You know what it's like
You've been there

You stood for love
But have none
You want peace
But pack a gun.

Self-righteous
You're no better than me
Not like them,
You'll not see your own hypocrisy

I will not be like you
Oh great idol of mine
I will not be like you
I will not be like you

     Dana Lobelle

Woman's Price

He wants me, he cannot feel me.
He wants me, he cannot hear me.
He wants me, passion in body
never in spirit.

He wants;
less feeling,
less thought,
less strength,
less clarity.

"Don't shine
and I will love you forever."

My bones and veins ring with
thought, feeling and expression.

I keep;
Full voice,
Full feeling,
Full expression,
Full clarity.

And my aloneness.

     Donna Blanc

Oh, Be Careful

Oh, be careful little tongue,
be careful what you say
Speak only words uplifting
to folks you greet today.

Do not say those words
that will cut and hurt
Always be on your guard
be careful and alert.

You know hurt feelings
take oh, so long to heal
And you know just how bad
that one can really feel.

So may the words you say
be cheerful and kind
Use Christ as your example,
always keep this in mind.

Oh, be careful little tongue,
be careful what you say
Speak only words uplifting
to folks you greet today.

Ruth F. Clifton

Bees

Head full of liquor dreams
Clocks laugh in my face

Room spins upside down
Turquoise walls look into bloody eyes

Fragrant spring breeze
Tiptoes across my non-virgin neck

Pina Colada wine coolers
Tiny bees buzzing in my head

Empty faces stuck in purgatory
Appear through vacant mirrors

Devil has a tea-party
With drunken philosophies

Acid rain
Drip...drop...drip.... drops

On your bloated face
Melted pieces float down sewer drains

Furry rats pick at the remains
Of your perfumed flesh

My bees stopped buzzing.

Amy L. Smith

The Phone

Ring, darn you, ring!
Don't just sit there
And taunt me, you cruel
nasty instrument of torture,
You know I feel helpless
and far away, yet filled
with wonderment and joy,
Will it be a girl of a boy?
You ring, you ring again,
"Hello, hello", I say,
A tired voice answers, your
son's voice,
"It's a girl mom, everything's
okay"
I lovingly hold the phone as
I place it in its cradle

Betty Lake Hutchinson

Darkness

So black the night.
So long the night,
Takes me many places.
Many lives, many faces.
in Darkness.
Takes me many places,
Live many lives, see many faces.
Dreams?
Nightmares?
Reality?
Will I ever know?
What is real?
Whom I am?
Surely some night
Light will be there
To guide me through
The maze, that is my night, my life.
Help, oh please help.
So many years, so many tears.
My Lord my Lord.
Save me from the darkness.

May Kuhn

Football Dilemma

My thoughts are on a subject
    that's popular today;
A lot of wives despise it
    and wish it'd go away.

I'm indulging as I pen this
    and must admit I'm hooked;
Football is an attraction
    I cannot overlook.

Whether college team or pro,
    the TV must be flipped;
All else is put aside
    So I can see who's whipped.

These weekends in the fall
    that used to be but few;
Have now become so numerous
    there's little else to do.

Harry F. Wilson

Changing Moods

Why is it in the morning
when the suns first rays peep through,
we feel so wonderful,
the day begins anew;
Our future is filled with promise,
who knows what lies in store;
Bird songs are in the air,
waves lapping at the shore;
As evening comes upon us
and the searing sun sinks low,
the heat of the day is still with us,
our voices are gruff and low;
Tension of the day makes us weary,
tempers flare at the slightest things;
Where is the elation of early morning,
that makes us feel like kings.

LaVerne Rubus

Untitled

Mind blown,
Heart crushed.
World gone —
Life is dead.
Lift me.

Nettie R. Stoer

Another Day

Have you ever been up
late at night when everyone's asleep
To gaze up at the starlit sky
and then begin to weep?

For you then begin to realize
that up from beyond the sky
the Lord looks down upon us,
His protecting eyes.

Thus through the long, long
night he does stay, to protect
us; we, who wake to sin
another day.

Joan Buchko

I Saw A Woman

I saw a woman
standing tall and strong

Perfect, there was no wrong
Until I reached into her mind
tears and pain left for me to find
from a childhood torn
bleeding clothes everyday worn

Dried stains no longer seen
hidden resurrection of a human being
A shining star, once was dim
erased, memories of him

I heard a woman now, clear and strong
listen, she speaks no wrong.

Dane George

Reflections

Children playing in the salty sea air
Ribbons tied in little girl's hair
Watching reruns on TV
All bring back the memory
Of my childhood.
When everything in life was good
And Mom and Dad were always there
And I never had a care.
But now that I have grown
I face the world alone;
For all I have are these memories.

Krista Giovacco

My Poem

My poem is
a train gliding on the tracks

My poem is
a child playing cars in the street

My poem is
the day dawning into night

My poem is
a majestic cat prowling in the fields

It is time for all children
to say good night

Megan Kesselring

Untitled

There once was a thing called money
People loved it as though it were honey
They crammed it in jars.
And spent it at bars.
And laughed as though it were funny.

Thomas Dyer

Questions

As we travel each day
A stretch of life's course,
We try to live freely
And with no remorse.

Along the twisting road
We'll think as we pause,
Why are we here?
Is there truly a cause.

The thought of fear
Travels our mind,
When there's no tomorrow
Will we be left behind?

Lifes long journey
Is another long quest,
With unanswered question
And no time to rest.

So travel wisely
And keep your life straight
For your deeds in life
Will choose your fate.

Randy Holt

Chasing Sunsets

If I had a wish, just one little
wish that I could make come true,
I'd wish everyone could chase sunsets
Like mother and I used to do.
I'd wish they could sprint down
the beach, feeling the grains of sand.
I'd wish they could collect seashells,
Or just walk hand in hand.
If you're on a beach and you have
just run out of things to do,
Why not try chasing a sunset
Like mother and I used to do.

Angie Brooks

"It's A Good Day To Live"

My heart feels light and gay.
My troubles seem so far away.
I looked and then I listened,
Now; I know what I have
been missing - living

Morris J. Griffin

My New Year's Poem

New me.
New you.
New year's Day
   is just as special.
   As special me
      and special you.

Emily Bradley

My Mommy

The special one
who loves me dear,
She hugs me close
And calms my fears.

So full of love
She'll hug and kiss,
Catch every chance
without a miss.

My mommy,
She's the very best,
without a doubt,
She tops the rest!

Lori A. Bennett

Miracles

Once you were a dream
Now you are growing inside of me
With every push and move
You are truly amazing.

You have your good days
You have your bad days.
But mostly they are good ones.

Life seemed so hopeless
Not worth living for
Till you, my little miracle,
Came along and made
My life worth hoping again.

Miracles do happen to those
Who wait for them
My little miracle is wonderful
And I can't wait till you
are in my arms so I can
Show off, my little miracle.

Sandra Slonaker

Free As A Bird

To soar high...
   To swoop low...
      No one to clip my wings...

To fly where these wings will soar...
To heights abound...where
   no soul can touch

Is but to be free as a bird

So....if one loves thee....set
it free....if it was meant
to be....it will soar back to
thee....

Go take flight...soar away
into the night.....just
remember....I loved thee.

Charlotte Rogers

Love Affair

Enthralled by your
   persona,
Captured by your
   romance,
Addicted to your
   passion
A hold but by chance

Charles J. Metscher

Untitled

Time

We live and learn
Happiness and sorrow
Yesterday is gone
Tomorrow is borrowed

Time

It is all we have
Someday not today
We will learn to live
And not pass time away

Time

It is all we have
Some say time is money
And money is time
A sad crime

Time

Is life and life is time
Use it well develop the mind
Body spirit this is the route
To happiness and everlasting time.

Jeremy Welch

A Single Flower

A single flower in my garden
on one summer's day.
I think about her always
but yet she stays away.

A single flower and a card,
but roses are so few.
Not everyone likes a perfect rose
like my love so true.

A single flower is like someone,
someone you really know.
They can go within your heart
where love and flowers grow.

A single flower sways in the wind
when it is left alone.
Sort of like my poems,
the one I call my own.

Belafonte Dewilde Gulledge

Prairie Winds

Daylight awakens across
The vastness of waving grass
Prairie winds gently rolling,
Grasslands perfume fills the air
With reflections of golden amber waves
Of penetrating light
Conjuring with imagination, autumn
Nearing with all her splendor.
A distant feathered friend twists
And turns, tempting minds eye
From a high sky of blue
With white tufts of upsurging
Scintillating cotton, floating
To the great beyond.
This majestic throne of undivided space
Will forever test man's abilities
Against the overwhelming elements.

Mitchell O. Skaggs

A Beautiful Day

Now that you are one my son
I sit and watch how well you run
Your little body has grown so strong
What a beautiful, beautiful day

Little legs now firm and fast
Little feet that move so quick
Arms that reach and reach and reach
What a beautiful, beautiful day

You smile and speak in your own way
Oh, how it makes my day
Little teeth are peeking through
Oh, so much joy I have through you
What a beautiful, beautiful day

Love has brought you my way
Now I hope and I pray
That I will see you with yours play
What a beautiful, beautiful day

Millie Welch

Timbuktu!

Out in the Sahara
    wit the wind blown sand
Under a sky, large
    and, oh, so grand
The camels - two by two
    of Tim and I went
To TIMBUKTU

Tim and I a camping we went
    when we came across a tent
Three wenches inside dressed in blue
I "Buk" one
    TIMBUKTU!!

Gregory A. Harrison, PhD, P.E.

Perpetuity - Life's Fund

How far I've come,
So much to do,
I don't know if,
I'll make it through.

I try and try,
Then get kicked again,
I'll try once more,
I'll wear a grin.

I play the game,
To get on top,
Once I am there,
That's when I'll stop.

Now I am here,
Still much to do,
I don't know if,
I'll make it through.

Lorin Blair Millard

The One I Love...

The one I love has left me blue
how much I loved him I never knew.
Till the day he said,"good-bye"
I had no cares to make me cry.
When I think of his loving face
it sets my heart at a faster pace.
Now it's over and I'll never know
how much our love would last and grow.

Noelle Taylor

This Feeling Unknown

People keep telling me
What good I've done
They're so damn proud of me
I'm everyone's son

I should be so happy
No clouds in my sky
But in all reality
There's not many smiles

I keep bringing me down
I just don't know why
Something is missing
Lost deep inside

What could it be
God only knows
I'll keep on searching
Till the end of the show

Peter C. Grimm

Untitled

I have a good friend.
The river runs wild.
Ever since I was a child.
Let us not defend.
For it is called the end.
My good friend, the end.
It comes like the rain.
It takes away all pain.
The troubles here do exist.
We must make the mist.
Let's live every breath.
For we do not know death.

Jim Harmon

Who Is King

A preacher man at the church
Pulpit was commenting on
A certain person at hand

That person rose from the
Pews and said I am the
King of my castle -
Let no man purpose to change it.
For I am - pause - the King
The priest said in reply
Sir! We are all brothers and sisters
We all have to answer to one King
Thus God Almighty
Repetition of mankind
Over and over and over and
Over and over and over......

E. Friis

My Grace Is Sufficient For Thee

"My grace is sufficient for thee,"
The answer to sinner's plea.
Take heart again, ye fallen man
Repent and in Jesus stand.

Make haste then, for time is speeding
Don't be your starved souls feeding,
Unhealthy doubts, for don't you see,
His grace is just right for thee.

Are you man enough to face it?
Lay down your pride - embrace it.
Put heav'n before dignity
His grace is enough for thee!

Emma Jo Miller

Where I Live

Where I live,
It is not my house,
Where I live is not a state,
Nor is it a country or a hemisphere.
Where I live is not a planet,
When you guess a universe,
I must tell you no.
For where I live is what I make it.
Where I live can be in my head,
Or in my heart,
Where I live, it is in my soul,
Where I live connects,
To where other people live,
Where we live is in each other,
When you ask "Where do you live?"
I reply, "I live in you."
I live in you.

Sarah Reeder

"Car-Radio Tunes"

As I drove to work this morning,
On the road the snow did glisten,
I reached and turned the radio on,
And to country I did listen.

Well I listened to Randy Travis,
And also to Charlie Pride,
And of course ole Dolly Parton,
She is known far and wide,

Those ole tunes they got me tapping,
My ole foot down on the floor,
As they sang about the well to do,
And also of the poor,

Tunes about "Ka-li-jah,"
And even "Diggin' up bones,"
Straight-out crying and misery,
With cheating under-tones.

Well I arrived to work this morning,
In the early of the dawn,
I reached to turn the radio off,
And found it was never on.

Daniel Moorhead

"Our Senior Scare"

It's unfair to us
It's almost impossible to bear
Knowing our school's curse
Our own senior scare
There's no way to avoid it
There's nothing we can do
All that we can say
Is I hope that it's not you
That's a scary thought though
There's nothing to prevent it
Even though we know it's coming
We're still surprised to see it
Now we realize what's lost
A valuable person to many
Our own dear senior
Our friend, our Katie.

Jacob Jones

My Prayer

Show me the way,
  and I will follow.
Show me the path,
  that I must travel.
Take my hand,
  and I will follow.
To the ends, of the world,
  loving you.
Though, there be pain,
  I must endure.
And things,
  I cannot change.
Give me the strength,
  to see it through.
And I'll leave this world,
  loving you.

Muriel Sauber

Christmas Time

'Tis absolutely great,
Christmas time is here,
No longer must we wait
For our favorite time of year.

Yes, there are special treats,
And beautiful fruits to share.
The aromatic foods we'll eat,
Put sweet smells in the cool air.

Our child, in and around us, lifts
Our spirits to the season's high,
As the moment we give our gifts,
Slowly, but expectantly, draws nigh.

Now as our presents we lovingly give,
We're inspired by our hearts so near,
To remember, we abundantly live
Because of God's Son so dear.

His Son He affectionately gives,
To each whose heart will invite,
Christ's life in each to live,
His life, liberating and bright.

Mike Samford

We Never Said Good-Bye

Although two years have passed us by,
I still remember vividly in mind,
My dear young friend,
Who died in her prime.
I can still see two little girls
Wild with play,
Never thinking of such a terrible day.

I never said I was sorry
For anything I did,
Or ever forgave you for
Our arguments and fights.
But, I won't lie
What hurts the most
Is that we never said good-bye.

Cicely Althea Rowe

Friendship

I meet you as a stranger,
I leave you as a friend,
I hope we meet in heaven,
Where our friendship will never end.

Lue A. Estes

Your Feelings

You laugh, you cry,
but never know why.
But then you sigh
and never try.
But through your laughs,
your cries, and your sighs,
You must know why
and always try!

Brandi Norton

Silenced

Windows full of raindrops
Dust on shelves of glass
Empty, old antique shops
Parched and dead brown grass.

Toppled down old windmills
Weeds grow through the cracks
Moss-encovered window sills
Rust-encrusted tacks.

A school where no one teaches
Street lights shine no more
A church where no one preaches
One hinge for every door.

The grandness is forgotten
The wreck that once was fair
Mahogany warped and rotten
A town that now is bare.

No one hears its sad lament
Of the life it led before
Dreams buried under hard cement
Destruction of a war.

Emily Livadary

Friends?

When I first met you I knew,
We would be friends.
  We have so much in common.
  We agree on everything,
Even though we like different things.
  But something changed.
  Now we are more than friends.
  We are family, you are
Like my twin.
  I now don't think of you as
Just a friend, but as
A sister too!

Vicki Plunkett

And Then You Came

My life was like a heavy cloud
Dark, dreary, sullen, full of rain;
With sleet and snow, with wind and hail
  And then you came.

My heart was bitter, stony cold
Untouched by love's pure, sacred flame;
With naught to make it sweet and light
  And then you came.

Now life good and full of light
My heart, now, never aches with pain;
It's flooded with sunshine and love
  Because you came

Out of the dark you came to me
Out of the hail, and sleet and rain
Now, my chaos is turned to light
  Because you came.

Vivian Lovelady

Night

The crook of your arm
Is an easy fit
In our warm, soft bed.
The feel of your body
Sends me yearning
For the passion and
The unspoken "I love you"
Seen even in the
Lazy left eye.
The unconscious naturalness
Of our molded bodies
Provides instant comfort
Or instant rapture.
The abandoned side
Smiles at the knowledge
That its abandonment
Is love.
I feel your heart
You are my heart...

Chantelle C. Normand

When Winter Comes

I can't hold back the tide
Or stop the tide from flowing
Or keep a rose from withering
Or still a wind that's blowing

And time cannot be halted
In its swift and endless flight
For age is sure to follow youth
Like day comes after night...

For He who sets our span of years
And watches from above
Replaces youth and beauty
With peace and true love
And then our souls are privileged
To see a hidden treasure
That in our youth escaped our eyes
In our pursuit of pleasure

No matter how the winds buffet
No matter how deep the snow
Life's beauty outweighs its bitter
Because I know it's true.

Erskine Venable

Sisters

Creamy skin and eyelash miles
a quiet voice that I hear sometimes
she is the moon and I the sun
or maybe each the other one

Green eyes brew
crocodile tears
that seem more real
than all I fear
She is the fox and I the hound
I do not wish to hunt her down

Soft within and soft without
a softness of a peaceful kind
a softness I may never find
She is liquid silver and I am pyrite
together we are colors bright

She wants children and a house
She seems to have it figured out
She is a bridge and I a river
I flow on and she delivers.

Karoline M. Ross

The Diary

I am something very old,
You can see all the stories
I hold.
Some people lock me up,
some people just put me up.
People use me everyday
to write down what they
did that day.
If you find me at certain
times, I can tell you of tales
behind.
I get treasured in museums,
sometimes, I have no end.
I continue with no stop.
I can sometimes reach the top.
So if you take care of me,
You will be surprised
what will become of me.

Melissa Ann Bledsae

P.S.

Life
is my Postcard.
Glossy and lovely
for all to see.
Behind
the Brilliant Cover
Written Banalities
Mask the anguish
So often
in this senders soul.
Unseen
Unsensed
Unheeded.
Wish you were here?
Oh no.
I wish only for
long ago yesterdays.
P.S. I Love You?
Oh no.
I love no one.

Patricia Zoch Ferguson

A Whim of the Wind

Isolated, yet dominant
Towering amongst its peers,
Lifted toward a more powerful
Force,
The gingko fans the arid air.

Still rooted in its rock,
Encrusted in a corn field.
Unmoved
By reaches of loftier heights,
The gingko sways near earthly stalks.

Power weighs against roots,
entrapped.
Untold strives seek achievement
Within and without its element.
The gingko exists alone.

Next generations will also be
A whim of the wind.

Annette M. Magid

Tears Of The Heart

The tears come down my eyes
from the sadness of my heart.
Because it feels like my whole
life has been torn apart.
Children crying, people dying is
what goes on in my head from
the looks of what goes on the
earth this day.
Murderers, evil leaders, gangs,
you must all pay.

Maria Stratman

Age

When does it really matter?
It's only making me sadder.

I ask you how a law,
can keep me from what I first saw.

When I found out,
I wanted to scream and shout.

My friend tried to help me,
and all I could say is leave me be.

It's like I never had a chance,
there went any of my romance.

I couldn't call you a jerk,
because no one knew if it would work.

If only I knew you liked me,
then maybe we could wait and see.

Why won't you just call,
that's really all.

Oh well I guess,
this won't make my life a mess.

Maybe it's a stage,
or could it only be my age.

Gloria Ragsdale

Far Away Soldier

How much longer will it be.
I hate when we're apart
even now I crave to be by her side
tho distance keep our hearts
can't wait to hold her in my arms again
and kiss her tenderly
my wife, my woman, my love, my friend
how much longer will it be?

Eliot Freeman

Amelia's Plea

I'm sorry, oh, so sorry!
  I didn't mean to do it,
The deed you thought so very bad,
  So please don't misconstrue it.

My little hands are clumsy
  And my memory can't recall
All the things you bid me do
  Or should not do at all.

With patience when I disappoint,
  Recall your learning years
And temper imperfections
  With more love than cause for tears.

Agnes M. Cowan

Aftermath

There is a great upheaval
to all of life.
It comes at the end, but
causes little strife
to those who partake in this
journey out of time.
Only in those who are
left behind
can the changes be noticed:
A faraway glance,
a lingering tear, or a more
thoughtful stance.
We are told time is the healer
of all wounds.
It helps us to forget and let
new memories bloom.
But to those left behind after
the upheaval of death,
time - cruel time - is all that
is left.

Greta P. Banks

Closet

There is this closet
to which I hold the key,
it's not in a hallway,
but inside of me.
It's where I hold my failures,
my doubts and my fears,
and all other bad things
built up through the years.
I hold all those times
when I wanted to cry
wanted to run
or wanted to die.

My closet is getting full now,
there's not much room for more,
and soon my wooden door will break
and out my troubles pour.
Now, I give you the key to this closet,
but you best beware,
for if you fear the darkness,
you're in for quite a scare.

Gabriel D. Gomez

If We Looked Through God's Eyes

If we looked through God's eyes
What would we see?
Arguments between everyone,
Even you and me.

If we looked through God's eyes,
Could we understand,
What everyone meant,
And forgive every man?

Stephanie Diane Mexia

Eulogy For A Marriage

To what we have
We have no more
We've gone and shut
The open door
No long goodbyes
Or farewell tears
To bid adieu
To all the years

Angela L. Short

357

Fate

How could we not have seen?
It was right before our eyes.
We met accidentally,
and love seemed to pass us by.
The more we shared we knew,
the time had come to find,
the feelings that we held,
no longer kept in mind.

Our hearts completely filled
the confession of love unwinds
emotions flow so greatly,
they must be cleared from the eyes

Finally, I do
and now the time has come.
To spiritually combine.
For life, as one.

Misty Gray

While I Was Looking Up

While I was looking up
I saw a bird,
It flew like lightning
on a thunderous night,
It flew in and out
Like a bee in a bee hive,
I wanted that bird I really did,
So I ran home and told my mom
She said don't be absurd,
But one fine morning, I awoke
To find a porcelain bird.

Laurel Hoffman

"Love"

Love is a gift from heaven.
Love is something that
Exists in each of us.
Love is a strong feeling
That we share for each other.
Love is something that we
Let into our hearts and souls.
Love is a type of happiness
That we all desire.
Love is something that we
All want to appear in our dreams.
Love is a powerful force
That overcomes all evil.
Love is a special, wonderful feeling.

Rachel Bishop

Jerome's Art

Stars accent your light's
hazily scenes on twinkles
a mesh they come together
lookout, contemplate your size
gold currency, false riches
for dreams come alive, inspires
variety spiced, little for abundant
Day's in past, slipped by
people walk in wonder
span light and silhouettes
Reflecting windows of site
hear nothing but what you see
busy streets close away
depicted, picture the words
look-in-site, feel your peace
one Jerome's art, in elevation

Arthur

Green Angel

The snow is white on my lawn.
It falls all night
and blankets dawn.
It covers leaves
I forgot to rake,
and hides the ants
on the piece of cake
I left on the bench
yesterday.

I'll miss the grass
until spring comes back.
Let winter wait
for just one day.

I'll make an angel
in the snow,
move arms and legs so fast
until I touch the grass.
Maybe a green angel
will make winter pass
fast!

Samantha Marie Tait

An Imitation Of Dawn

I like 7 o'clock on winter mornings.
Dawn is balmy and bold.
It forces its way.
Night must yield to day.

As the sky lightens, I awake;
So I can see the world:
The world of pain and poverty,
Struggling for security and joy.

Night must yield to day:
Warmer days, brighter days.
I like 7 o'clock on winter mornings.
I like to imitate the dawn.

Dayne Walling

May God

May God shine
And strengthen you the more
And lift you to the top
Of the mountains

As if you were
And eagle in flight
Guiding you through the country
Side by day and by night

And when you come down
And the obstacles appear he
Will anoint you strong as a Rhino
and swift as a deer

So there's no need to fear
He will sustain you
Through out every year

Dwight L. Davis

Moonlight Stars

Moonlight stars moonlight stars
Dancing, sparkling through the dark
Yellow shining in the night
Watching us through the light
What do we see, what do we see
But yellow stars like Christmas trees

Lindsay Martinson

Shadows

Are you there?
Peering from the darkness
Are you there?
With watchful eyes
Are you there?
Waiting for the light
Are you there?
Wanting to be seen
Are you there?
Dancing in the night....

Terri E. Priester

Desire!

Grant me one wish went through her mind
As she watched the snowflakes fall,
The pain she silenced in her heart
Deepened when she recalled.

How light of heart she felt within
When she danced across the floor,
Longing for days, she dared to dream
when life held so much more.

Raising her head, she sadly looked
into his tear filled eyes
Staring back were reflections of
those moments swiftly gone by.

Tilting her head to the side
The tears fell one by one,
Deep down inside an awareness rose
Her time had finally come.

Jaquie R. Riccio

Your Smile

I will walk a mile for
your smile.
To me your smile is
compassion, concern and trust.
Do you know that this could
Be a sure beginning for us?
I often think to myself, if
someone should ask, "what
helps me perform my most
gruesome task?"

I will look at him and
Without hesitation, I will
Reply, "My lover's smile."

And for that smile, I will
walk a mile.

Easter M. Rhodes

Nature's Way

Gentle breeze blowing free
Come on down and speak to me
See me standing here so small
Near to oak tree, great and tall

Merry laughter like a brook
Escape my lips with every look
To see, to hear to feel each sigh
Oh dancing breeze from way up high

From gentle breeze to raging wind
That makes majestic trees to bend
I would ne blind could I not see
It's nature's way to talk to me

Suzanne C. Kaercher

Tree

Goldenrod leaves
  tinted with shades of rust,

Falling from one
  lonely tree, crowded

By office buildings
  slowly turning to dust.

Beauty of nature is not overlooked,
  but shrouded.

Stacey Graham

Angel

There was a time I felt,
You,
You were an angel to me,
And I saw myself in a new way.
We cried together,
We laughed together.
I felt like your wings
Rose me up to the sky.
But things changed,
And I don't see an angel anymore,
Although I still see,
You,
You as a friend
Always filling that
Empty space in my heart.

Eva Tuminski

Life

Life a dream,
I do believe.
Think and dream,
Work and play,
do and say,
We think we know,
what going on,
But do we?
No one knows;
Except there own life.
What is life,
what is dreams?
And dreams reality or
is life a dream?
Is life a dream or
just a fake?
What do you think or believe?

Laura Stokes

Death Is Upon Us

The skies turn dark.
The flowers begin to wilt.
The tears begin to fall.
The streams stop flowing.
The rivers stand still.
The oceans go dry.
Death is upon us.
It will take us one by one.
The older ones first.
The young ones last.
The lovers stop loving
The dreams stop dreaming
The peace maker stop making piece.
Death is upon us beware
Pray that you are not the first to go.

Carrie Schyan

A Tribute To Dad

Gentle, loving and caring
  he alway's was with me.
Taught me that sharing
  was the way it ought to be.
The apple of his eye was I,
  his one and only pride and joy.
He'd wipe away tears when I would cry
  and men for me my broken toy.
He spared the rod and spoiled his child
  but raised me to honor and respect.
His manner was so meek and mild
  yet he always was ready to protect.
He taught me the importance of family
  and always found so me time for me.
The days we shared so merrily
  forever in my heart will be.
God really gave me one great father,
  of this I will not argue.
I could not be a prouder daughter.
  Dad, I send my love and "thank you."

Lucille H. Tanguay

I Look at Him

I look at him and
start to cry.
  For I know that he
is soon going to die.

I was never really nice,
and always quite bitter,
  and the thought of that
made me just shiver.

I hung my head down,
in disbelief, and wished I was nicer,
and not always in grief.

There was always such pain,
and now even more,
  For he's going to die,
and then there'll be nothing more.

In part of my heart,
there'll be a big empty space
  left by him and his lovely face.

Amanda Whalen

Reflections

Do you believe in the Soul?
Do you practice Self-Control?
Do you constantly Doubt?
Do you share principles without?

Do you have the Will?
Do you know the Way?
Does your past stand still?
Do you know what to say?

If you knew then
what you know now.
Mistake not again
the difference somehow.

Be willing to chance
like your first romance.
Your answers hold true
how people remember you.

Dirk Schroeder

Untitled

Hair of natures harvest,
looking upon my face,
radiant beauty
casting shadows
creeping around my feet,
your body surrounds me,
Why do you treat me so wrong?
To you the Gods will sing,
To I they laugh and curse,
Please speak to me
in your God-like words
Let me hold your hand
in this terrible world
so that I may have a peace of heaven.

Mindy Basler

Untitled

Thy father dies
Thy father tires
Thy father gone
Tears of joy
Light as a feather
Fresh innocent face
The past is gone
The weight has been lifted
Feel anew
Close to nature
My distant friend
Has come back again.

R. M. Fedak

A Tear Of Blood

As the blood trickles down my hand
I weep in sorrow
for there is no hope in pain
afraid to know what is tomorrow
my eyes are like an eagles
I look down on my life
from the cliffs above
I see nothing but confusion
I lay here silently
waiting for the dawn
It is all just a game
I am just another pawn
Alone in a hole
that I'm falling forever
I never hit ground
that would be better
I cannot breathe
for death is my fear
all I can do
is express one tear.

Christin Vyas

Fox And Baby At Midnight

I looked out one starry night
And saw some foxes looking
In the light, There was a mama
And a baby, I think they saw me
Maybe, The baby fox was chasing
A fly and motioned to its mom bye
Bye, I love the sight of foxes playing
And I know that you do too!

Julie Plyler

My Best Friend Once.....

My best friend once told me
"You need to be controlling"-
I just laughed in his face.

My best friend once asked me
would I do the hanky-
panky with him.
I told him in May.

My best friend once protected me -
Really, quite effortlessly -
from myself in this cold,
Dark, frightening world
Where I could get lost in the mist.

And my best friend once left me
To go home to his family
I think of him everyday.

Denise P. Donahoe

Days

The days will on and on
with words spoken and
unspoken
Someday to meet again
confident of lifes joys
and sorrows
Coming and going without the
too muchness
As it has already
happened
with you.

Barbara Johnston

Meaning It

Every touch
means I long to be with you,
in your arms
want our bodies pressed together,
touch you lips and taste you.
Every glance
means I want to know your thoughts.
I want to know your hopes and fears,
to share your souls deepest desires
Every laugh
mean I'm happy when I'm with you,
I didn't know true happiness
until I met you.
My heart will not feel joy.
Until reunited with yours
I mean I love you
with every part of my body
with all my senses I feel it.
Whatever it means; I love you.
In you I see you mean it too.
And in you, I see, you mean it, too.

Jennifer V. Doll

A Better Day

Come with me, I'll show you the way,
I'll take you back to a better day.
A day of peace, a day of love,
a day you'll recall from up above.

So rest your head and close your eyes,
you'll see a place with no more cries.
Just look real close and try to see,
but don't look far and there I'll be.

Erin Rogers

I Will

I will help you out.
I will follows Jesus in his word.
I will praise his name.
I will be happy and nice to people;
That how much you mean to me.

I will cries when you cried.
I will reading the bible.
I will respect my parent and other;
Take a walk with Jesus.

I will love everyday.
I will love everyone.
I will love to follow Jesus.

Tereasa Cummings

Ode To A Steak

Oh you big red steak
Done well done rare
Once most desired

The sight of you so admired
The first taste
Ecstasy and pleasure

Self indulging
To a full measure
Without care or worry.

That's a faint memory now.
It has been so long ago
Like a dream somehow.

Oh you once so beautiful,
Have you turned old
Or unattractive

Or have I?
Have your cholesterols
Changed me

And a simple green salad
Replaced thee?

Leo Gutreiman

Feelings!

Beyond love,
Open your eyes,
New and improved,
Deep in thought,
Yonder the light.

Can't you see,
Awaken me,
Now with a soft tender kiss,
Next I feel filled with love,
Open your thoughts,
Next to me.

As I walk through the door,
Night shines through,
Depending on you.

Make such sense out of this,
Even though it's true.

Devon Craddock

Sitting In The Dark

Sitting in the dark,
searching through the shadows,
looking for a light,
at the end of the tunnel.

Sitting in the dark,
hiding in a corner,
looking for peace,
that never seems to come.

Sitting in the dark,
listening for a voice,
haunting my dreams,
through a sleepless night.

Sitting in the dark,
waiting to be rescued,
longing for security,
a day approaches.

Michele Lindsey

The Edge

As I walk toward the Edge
I wonder if I'll fall
And is the ground hard and
Is the cliff tall

I hang my toes into nothing
Or rather into air
And wonder if when I'm gone
Anyone will care

As I go over the Edge
The wind goes rushing by
The thoughts run fast in my mind
As I travel thru the sky

As I face imminent impact
And subsequently death
I call to someone to miss me
With my dying breath

I went and really did it
I fell down to my doom
I went right off the Edge
Inside my padded room

Glenn Linder

The Empty Chair

It seems on every holiday,
When the family gathers round
The empty chair at the table
Is the ghost that's to be found.

When loved ones get together
To celebrate and cheer,
The empty chair at the table
Seems to bring a little tear.

Each time we get together
We often wonder then
If the empty chair at the table
Can ever be filled again.

At first the lose is great
But the others must live on.
The empty chair at the table,
The loved one who is gone.

We try and try to picture him
At the table up above,
Where God is taking care of him
With tenderness and love.

Maureen Lique' Oppe

Messed Up In Holliston He Committed Suicide

He was my friend
For that I know
I could talk to him
And he wouldn't say "so."

With him I was happy
With him I was glad
We were happy when friends
But now I am sad.

Why did he do it?
Didn't he care
His mind was messed up
His feelings he wouldn't share.

I knew he was crazy
I knew he was bad
But being his friend
Was a good thing he had.

He is not in this world
I won't see him again
I will remember him only
The one way I can. In my mind.

Caitlin Ippoliti

Let's Open Up Our Windows

The world is full of sorrow
The world is full of sin
Let's open up our windows
And let the sun shine in

Open up our hearts
And chase away the fear
Let the love start flowing
Know that God is near

Tell him what we're needing
Share the good and bad
Tell him what we're wanting
Thank him for what we've had

Let's open up the windows
To our heart and soul
Plant a flower garden
Feel our spirit grow

Nurture it with kindness
And as it reaches for the sun
Its beauty will surround us
Till life on earth is done

Jeanine Gould

"Walking Alone"

Do you know how awful
jacob must have felt when
he left Haren, I sure can his
father was disappointed in him,
his brother hated him, his only
friend wan his conscience.

I know now that feel, I remember
the time I stole a dollar from
my father, I didn't sleep for
a week, finally I had to confess,
I don't stop living for God,
I had to get up and keep going.

Tasha James

Feelings

I loved you
You broke my heart
I knew right then
that problems would start
I called you up
When they got bad
But all you could say was
"Oh how sad"
At first it was love
And I thought it was true
But I found out later
You didn't love me too.
I sat in the corner
I thought I would cry
You tore down my dreams
When they were so high
I thought you were the best
from the very start
I loved you
And you broke my heart.

Gayle Goetz

What You Are To Me

Of all the world's precious gems
you're the diamond shining bright
of a hundred billion stars you're most
radiant of the light

Of all enchanting songs
you are the flawless melody
of doors to brand new worlds
you are the magic key

Of all the quiet oceans
you're the tranquil setting sun
in all this imperfection
you are the perfect one
Of all the fragrant flowers
you are the sweetest smell
of all the things we hope for
you are the wishing well

Of all the peaceful seashores
you're the castles in the sand
of all the warmth I'll ever need
I have your little hand...

April Crabtree

The Walk

I have found my place
   in the world.

Time is my friend, no,
   need to be concerned.

Every day a to b is the
   answer.

Personal status has its
   rewards, making me a
   kinder and gentler person.

After all is said and done
   the flow of time is
   like fine wine.

Edward T. Lyons

Untitled

You are the light
in the midst of my darkness
the beacon to my soul
your smile lights my mornings
your laughter makes me whole

You are the flame
that ignites my passion
burns it through the night
I hunger for your kisses
your touch feels so right

You are the brush
that paints my life with color
the rainbow in my rain
you wash away the bleakness
cleanse away my pain

You are the man
I've been waiting for
the dream I've dreamed so long
you put music in my heart
you are the words to my love song

Susan Dickert

Portrait Of A Memory

On a kaleidoscope of browns and green,
My frosted toes rest gingerly,
As my heart soars light and freed
By the remembered moments told to me.
Knitted blankets, paneled walls
And frozen figurines,
Take me back, warm me up
And make the stage complete.
Outside the ice fairies dance and twirl
And watch with moonlit eyes,
The silent laughter, thoughtful smiles,
And a moment pulled from time.

Shannon O'Neill

My Prison

To wander through the meadow fair,
How the memory calls,
Down the darkened stairs
And through the prison walls.

I hear the children laughing,
Playing in the street,
Pitching balls, girls crafting
All in the summer's heat.

My life before the sentence;
Oh, happy and joyful reverie,
But now I hold acceptance
For this bateful world of potpourri.

Remember however, youth is grand,
Yet, no one is at fault;
For age comes quickly to a stand
And life to a spiraling halt.

Brian Turner

What If...??

What if the sun were blue?
What would you say? What would you do?
And what if ocean waves were pink?
How would you feel? What would you think?

Now picture clouds of fluffy green
And bouncing rabbits of tangerine.
Silver bees, a yellow sky
And a polka-dotted you and I.

Valerie Ann King

Broken Hearted

As I see him walk by
My heart beats on by
And say "Damn he's fine"
But I can't say something.
Cause I'm too shy
I wait for a little while, but
I find out he's not mine.
I feel pain inside,
He says we're not the same race
But does he really mind?
He's nice and funny and have someone
But I wish I was the one.

Demeley Arcilla Sarmiento

Nita

With her fur coat, suede shoes
and hat to match
    Just a struttin'
With her gold watch, gold chains
and diamond rings
    Just a struttin'
With her big pretty legs, as she steps
and Tailor-made suit, as if poured into
    Just a struttin'.
As she walks into the club, everyone
stands to get a better view
    Just a struttin'
Everyone running to find out her
name
    Just a struttin'
Then there's a whisper, Nita, Nita
who? Nita, none as sweeta

Theodore Allen Richardson

Poisoned Thoughts

You infect me like a virus on
a dark and rainy day.
With my weakend mind and
shattered heart I know you
like to play.
I try to wash your impurity
from my sullen soul.
Yet you cling to me like fire
on a burning, ember coal.
You try to break my spirit,
I try to set it free.
With bars of fear, you now
imprison me.
You laugh is spite,
my face goes white.
You plunge the knife.
You decide to end my life.
Crazy people, crazy days
violence always finds its way.
in the end, somebody pays.

Jeanette Deyoc

Summer's Knell

The crickets chime in, Summer's knell
    A winding down, a warning bell.
The leaves of green turn one by one,
    And wave farewell to Summer sun.
Flocks of birdsong in the sky,
    Cries of come on, and good-bye.
As they fly to Southern climes,
    Amid the knell of cricket chimes.

Paul B. Dobbins Jr.

"The Bird"

While sitting by my window dear
I saw a bird sitting near
singing all the wondrous songs with
which God had graced him.
He sang of joy and sadness
Love and hate
fear and security
all of which were struggling
within him. Not only him,
but in me also.
And somehow he knew he was
not alone in his struggles.
He knew someone shared
his pain and his joys and
so he shared with me his song
as I shared with him the
feelings that had been buried
so long within.

Amber N. Martin

Untitled

The day you rode your bike
without the training wheels.
I watched you, and inside my heart
I said; my son is growing up, what a thrill!
The time we played baseball with
my friends and their sons.
I watched you hit that ball out
in the field, and made a home run.
I said, that's my son! I'm so proud,
and that time I said it out loud.
You are having a birthday today,
and I just want to say that all
the accomplishments that you have made.
Makes me a proud dad in every way.

Ardella Foster

Untitled

From the forest
like a feather falling in the wind
calling her name,
a deepening sigh of beauty
    she walks alone.
With a rose in her hand
    that I once gave her
she looks up to the sky
    with hungry eyes
    and her thoughts roam.
The change of colors in her eyes
    green for the fields she grew up on
    she walks on,
    and she goes on a feeling.
Believes in the land
holds beauty in her hands
    in her mind
    in her laughter.

Adam Gandolfo

Conformist

He lights the fire
    I watch
He fills his cup
    I fill my cup
He hates
I hate
I love
He lights the fire.

Andrew Dougherty

Understanding...Me...III

I am the lover of
your world and mine.
I am the lover who,
married good and fine.
I am the lover, who is
true to himself.

I am the lover who
loves life.
If life is wife,
I am the lover.
If life is love,
I am the lover.

I am the lover whose
love is all.
I am the lover whose
life is all.
I am all...Life and Love!

Understanding all is life and love.
Understanding life is me and love.
Understanding love is me!

Laurent Dorion

How Do You See Me

How do you see me
Am I as transparent as glass
Do you look into my eyes
And see my tainted past

How do you see me
Am I as opaque as steel
Do you look into my face
And think I do not feel

How do you see me
Can you scale the wall I've built
Do you look into my eyes
And see my shameful guilt

How do you see me
Are you blind to my soul
Do you look for my heart
And find only an empty hole.

Kimberly C. Blankenship

The End

What happened to love;
Did it turn to hate?
What happened to forever;
Or what it not fate?
You told me you loved me,
And you really cared.
You promised me happiness,
The kind we could share.
We had something special;
You said you would not let go.
Distance didn't matter;
Something only time could show.
But things soon changed;
You made it quite clear.
Forever was over,
And love disappeared.

Dawn Lavender

Trace

I feel your hand clasped in mine
Through my fingers the sands of time
Upon your faith I rest my head
No kinder words have yet been said
I feel your touch throughout my fear
An impossible dream drawing near
Forever looms - presents despair
Nothing to do with you my dear
Fear consumes and cuts to size
Preach and primp and paralyze
Never can do without
An ingrained seed of constant doubt
If you weren't all I ever wanted
I will still remain undaunted
For you, my dear, I promise this
I'll gather strength from every kiss
I'll feel your love and gain reserve
And give you all that you deserve.

Dennis Linehan

The Legend Of The Dove

This small white dove
You can hold in your hand
It carries a message
Across the land.

As its wings unfurl
Its beauty we see
A sign of peace
For you and me.

Alone he flies, fast and high
A silhouette, beneath the clouds
In the sky.

The small white dove
Is God's gift to us
A symbol of love
From Heaven above.

The flight of the dove
Has done, what God has asked,
To spread his love to everyone.

It's a legend, we all share
as we bow our heads in prayer.

Wynnett M. Pontzious

Friends

Dedicated to Mandy Penrose
When tear drops are familiar
And some days never end,

Some friends just desert you
But I'll always be your friend,

Even on those awful days
When smiles seem far away,

I'll try to think of many ways
to make it all ok,

And if your heart has sunk too low
I'll find a way to lift it,

I'll lift it till it back in place
And never let it go.

Jamie Biesboer

The Last Piece

A one-thousand piece puzzle,
Sitting in front of me,
I've finished nine-hundred
Already you see.
I have only,
A few more to go,
'Till I get done,
And you'll have to know,
I'm down to there now,
And I can't finish it!
I've lost my last piece,
And I'm throwing a fit.
I'm getting real mad
I've come all this way,
I guess it just isn't,
My lucky day!
Well, I've finished my puzzle,
Or tried to at least,
But it is just too bad,
That I've lost my last piece.

Jocelyn Rogers

Where To Go

Who are you to ridicule me?
When through my eyes
you can not see.
Branching pathways for me to follow.
Roads to darkness,
in blood I'll wallow.
Grasping for God,
his hand is near.
Concepts of knowledge,
for knowing his fear.
But still I wonder from the light.
The hand that feeds me,
I shall bite.

Michael Warren

He's In My Sight

The light's were low
but the gleam of his
eye's excited my soul.
They say there's love
At first sight.
I never believed it till
he caught my sight,
on a cold dark winters night.
I vowed to keep him in my sight.
His eyes upon me felt so right.
That I wanted to hold
ower moment's all night,
And remembering he's
In my sight.

Sue Hall

Me

Do you know who I am, I am ME
with emotions, hopes and dreams,
Look at ME as I am, not as you
want me to be. I have my faults
and have made mistakes, but that
will never change who I am,
ME

Mary J. Garhartt

Untitled

Master shows his evil face
to no one but myself,
As I lie awake at night I wonder
are there others like himself?
The beast he lies real deep
way down deep inside
And when the beast comes forth
it's like Master had done died.
Then master comes alive again
when the beast is through.
He may be gone, but scars remain
a lifetime - maybe two.

Shakira Torres

Rain

Come and go as you wish
Your feelings change all the time
How am I to know
You won't show me
what you think
why you're here
why you're not
Be there when you're needed please
otherwise
everything dries up
emotions are hindered
they hover endlessly
incessantly asking for you
will you come or
is it not important right now
but it will be later
when it's convenient
maybe it's just not real

Natalie Peretsman

The Growth Of Faith

The only plants that grow here
are tangled thorns and weed.
Sprouted because of evil,
bitterness, and greed.

Each day the sun shines brightly
and fills the vast blue sky.
And without a word of thanks or
praise, we let it pass us by.

Each day a raindrop falls, though
the water has grown sour.
And still we're blind and do not
see God's ultimate love and power.

But beyond the fence of prejudice,
in the dry and tired ground.
Among the old, brown, trampled grass
a tiny flower can be found.

The tiny flower grows in us
if we let it stay.
This flower is faith that changes our
lives and shows us all God's way.

Rachel E. Rodkey

Life

Life is but a dream
Just awaiting to awake
But just like all dreams
It must come to an end
And to a new day you awake

David S. Eckberg

Lifesongs

I sit on the hillside
'mongst the dry, summer grasses.
Breezes mingle with the hot sun,
Sweat dampens my brow.
Birds soar in the canyons below,
And the day is an offering of peace.

I sit on the hillside
'mongst the dry, summer grasses;
and cry.

I am a plaything of the afternoon.
It delights in me
    as I roll in the fragrant grasses,
    and romp in its radiant warmth.
Then it tires of me,
and leaves me to the evening stars.

Marilyn Jossens

Love

Is it the gentle petals of a rose
    or the sharpness of a knife?
Is it like a summer afternoon
    or the harshness of a winter
    night?
Is it beautiful like the sunset
    or threatening like a thunder storm?
Is it a merry little brook
    or brutal like the sea?
Is it painful like the stabbing of a
    pin
    or painless as a cushioned fall?
If it is hate, can it be love?

Christina Seti

Imagination

I'll make a wish for you
and hope it will come true
cause I know a flower blooms...

It's in your imagination
like a backwards thirteen
You see it isn't true, you know
It is all a dream.

The sun is always shining
in the morning, in the night
You need to learn to protect yourself
but it isn't nice to fight.

A tree grows in the morning
the wind blows in the night
Will someone please teach me
how to fly a kite?

I know it's just imagination
cause I thought of it, it's true
You all should have a special mind
Just the way I do...

Jana Katz

The Key

I see from high above
but I'm not a dove
I do give love
When soaring down into a sea
I find a key
When placed in my heart
It could never be torn apart.

Nirvani V. Mootoo

Friends

Through the changing seasons
    and the passing years.
Never questioning the reasons,
    never forgetting the fears.
You will always be a part,
    always listen and hear.
The ache of the heart,
    the drop of a tear.
You will always be there
    to console, hold and love.
You are always fair,
    never putting You above.
Being a friend is not easy,
    you took the challenge.
You believe in who I am;
    you accept me as a friend.

Karie Scoughton

Tourist

Westminster Abbey
feeling crabby
then there she was
inside a box
ashes to ashes
what a loss.

Long since rotted
to bone alone
shock waves of centuries
struck my own
the hourglass dark from years of sand
and I stranger in her land.

Queen Elizabeth
red hair, lust
passions to ashes
is there peace in your dust?

Your shining moments
calling my name
between dust and dust
empires are gained.

Faith Nielander

A Promise

Their faces show their pain.
Their tiny bodies so ill.
What went awry?
I ask myself,
How could this be?
So tiny.
So precious.
So innocent.
But, amazingly strong.
They comfort me.
Assure me.
They dry my tears.
And all they ask,
Is a promise of my return.
To play.
But, in my heart,
I know.
They can't promise they will wait.

Katherine J. Diaz

Jacob A.

In the dark of the morning
Hi Grandma
The voice on the phone
My son
He's here
All ten fingers
All ten toes
No known weight yet
He's beautiful
He's life.

Denise M. Urban

"The Decision"

We two are lost it seems,
The darkness closing in.
We came by different roads,
By different roads may leave.
Whichever way we go—
Together, or alone—
A lasting love we've seen.
Since once we found the other,
Each other we'll always have.
When we, out of darkness come,
The light of love to find,
We'll know—we are forever one.

Erik Pratt

Farmer's Rain

In your arms
    is a place long sought,
    unlike any other I have been...

And in your eyes
    is the woman I thought I knew,
    who'd given up any hope of you.

Like a good, farmer's rain,
    You've touched my life a new,
    I am complete, whole;

And in the warmth of your arms
    lies the peace of my dreams,
    and home had found
    this wandering soul.

Victoria L. Link

Perfection

A perfect rose,
With a perfect pose,
Pedals spreading their wings.
A perfect rose
In perfect place,
With too much space.
A perfect rose,
Is starting to shrivel,
About to cry,
A perfect rose,
Just bowed its head,
And died.

Mary Beth Rawlins

The Arrival

I anticipated your arrival
For better or for worse
So anxious to meet you
I thought that I may burst

And when the day finally came
I held you close to my heart
And I knew in an instant
That we would never part

I'm so thankful for the angel
That God has entrusted with me
You'll never know black or white
Hatred or bigotry

You'll never be asked to make a choice
To know that I'm there for you
You'll never have to wonder
If my love for you is true

For you truly are a miracle
Sent from the heaven's above
Sent to make my life complete
Sent for me to love

Ren Humphreys

Untitled

I'm not the type of person
Society calls a poet
I can't even write a sonnet.
I'll never be a song artist
The words are good
But I have no voice.
And I'll never serenade you
Because I know nothing about music.
There'll never be a ballad or symphony
For you to tell your friends of.
I do however, believe in love
and how I feel about you.
And though I may not say much more
Than a simple "I Love You".
I'll hope you always know deep down
It flows beneath the surface.

Brea McLeod

Self

As it closes in
surrounding all exists
all entries, all hope.
A black hole of nothing
Reaching, grabbing to take you in
Much like the night
with no dawn.
No light at the end of the tunnel,
Nothing but yourself,
the sound of the rain,
and the swell of your heart.
As it reaches for someone,
Anyone who will have it.
But like the lone rose
No one takes it
Leaving nothing but one.
The ache that is left,
that always remains.

Amber Ward

For Janet And Emil

Great Spirit we look to thee
To bless this place we stand
To see this couple here before you
Gazing upward, hand-in-hand.

Give to them, Great Spirit,
All the joys of joining.

Care for them as stalwart trees
Always swaying to each other
Always standing each alone
Always singly, yet together,
Never one before the other.

Give to them, Great Spirit,
All the joys of joining.

Bless their onion o'er the years,
Give to them a sweet content.
Make their life a joyous journey,
Years unmarked by sad lament.

Give to them, Great Spirit,
All the joys of joining.

Janet Hartman

What If

What if we all walked backwards
   no need for memory
For everything that we would see
   Is what we used to be
In the light of everything
   we soon begin to see
That everyone and everything
   is what we wish to be
The past is soon forgotten
   buried down at last
For if we all walked backwards
   I think we'd miss the past

Tina Bethea

I Never Knew

I didn't think we would happen.
I never knew we were to begin.
Until a special light shown upon me
and I let you in.

I let you into my life,
A world of peace, love, and despair.
Then I got to know you and realized
We should've been born a pair.

You opened up your soul,
Then you proved me wrong.
Now you have the key to my heart,
You had it all along.

I never thought we could happen.
Now in my heart you'll stay.
Because now I'll always be for certain
My love for you will never fade away.

I dedicate this to you,
The one who makes me never want to end.
I write this only for you,
The very best kind of friend.

Roni Ann Parshall

Music

I hear your sweet notes,
They seem to flow deep into my soul,
The warm, enchanting melody takes
me away,
I flow through my dream world of
the sweet tune,
Thoughtless and free,
It seems as if I'm lifted off the
ground floating with the beautiful
notes all around me.
I feel your elegance in my soul,
I am the song,
I am the music,
Slowly as your sweet music ends I
will slip back to reality,
Once again I am me,
You are the music,
We are separate.

Amy Jo Richter

La Leçon

Suprême sauce simmers
on the Wood Stanley,

As a man presses dough
into tart molds.

Beside him, his daughter,
in a Douglas chair, peels potatoes.

The sauce surrenders white wisps
of steam that rise and evanesce.

He wishes they were making
breakfast.

Arthur Handley III

Looking

   You may have a problem,
and not have an answer...
Maybe there is no answer,
Maybe there's not even a problem,
to have an answer for...

If you do find the answer,
that your looking for...
Don't let go of it..
It just maybe the answer,
To your whole life!

Melissa Drinkwater

I saw you cry

I saw you cry
   and it touched it me
deep inside
   where my emotions are free
to soar and dip
   or ride the winds
of erratic storms
   too intense to unleash
upon unsuspecting hearts
   I've grown to love.

Joy Jones

The Light

I often think
of times and dreams
of moon rays and sun beams
of my state and of my town
and of this great world around

I sometimes wonder
who made the sky
and when things were formed
why people die
and why are we born

I always have a question
people say there's no answer
but why is there affection
and who gave us cancer

They say they're insoluble
my inquiries can't be solved
but they're too vulnerable
I know why things evolved

Once I learned, I couldn't go amiss
for I saw the Light, in Jesus Christ

Brandy Pfister

Out The Window

Look out the window
What do you see
There green trees
blue sky.
A yellow sun.
But look beyond that
and tell me what you see
Crime, drug, and murder.
And unhappy people.
But look beyond that
and tell me what you see
Someday hope, love
happiness a much brightest
happy day.

Zelda M. Cox

Shadows In The Sun

Shadows in the sun
Come down upon me now
Blue tears in rainbows
Are meeting me somehow.

Ask what I have done...
Put nightmares in my dreams?
How could I have known
That broken silence screams?

I left what meant most
A unity so strong
What was real fades fast
Could I have chosen wrong?

Weeds in a rose bed
Are shadowing my mind
Thorns among petals
Escape would be so kind.

I need you to know
My love has always won
But while we're apart
There are shadows in the sun.

Susanna J. Flores

Lost Love

The hours are longer
But now I'm stronger,
No one to drag me down

I'm just standing around
Waiting for someone,
Only to find no one

I'm alone;
All by myself
Nobody to talk to,

I'm surrounded by the memories
of me and you.

Tabby Hefner

Dreams And Wonders

I see you sitting there
And I wonder
Are you dreaming
Dreaming of a place down under
Or are you just sitting there to wonder
Wonder about the fantastic places
Places we think about
And no one will ever see
Do you wonder or do you dream
I wonder, I wonder about
Dreams
Dreams far away no one
Could hardly ever dream
A place called dreamer
Cause you always dream
Dream about the places
People could be
Or could never be

Rhonda DeLello

Goddess

The gulf's blue skies brighten to
a yellow sunshine on an ocean hued
o'er in shades of green endlessly
waver among'st the mighty seas.

Whence in the ocean, the Sea Goddess
hast taken salt to cleanse my wounded
soul of all inequities that take
froth among the foamy sea shores.

Sunshine sparkles in shimmering
warmth; shan't she ne'er stray while
walking upon the ocean waves and
I along the shore.

In membrance I shall forget you not;
for I have a shell you see that when
put to my ears tides of tranquility
fill my eyes to a sun set ablaze
upon seas of emerald green that
twilightingly wear an autumn horizon
for all to see.

Kevin J. Rodden

Erbiums Prayer

Ireland breathes a heavy sigh
as night unfolds before her eyes,
and lays a veil of slumber o'er
her rocks and glens.

Sleep Ireland, sleep,
for in the mist of morning
you will show your brilliant green,
as if reaching up to heaven in prayer.

Maria T. Hogan

Still Here? I Hope!

Do you exist beyond my thought
owning a place in time
beyond the point
a group of lines
XYZ
you make your space
dreams made real,
beyond my thoughts
from a pulse of light
to the beat of a heart
where's your path
flesh and blood.

Philip Warren

A Walk With Jesus

Jesus walked upon this earth
    And everywhere He went
Those who trusted in Him
    Knew He was heaven-sent.

Blinded eyes were opened,
    Those with deafness heard,
Miracles and healings came
    By touch or spoken word.

He pulled Himself away from crowds
    To spend much time in prayer.
He walked upon the water
    And bid Peter follow there.

Keeping eyes on Jesus,
    He walked on water, too.
He sank when sight took over;
    Jesus then walked him through.

Although my tests and trials
    May rise like mighty wave,
Jesus bids me come to Him:
    With outstretched hand He'll save.

Roberta M. Spinney

If I...

if i were to wrap my arms around you,
    would you push me away?
if i were to love you,
    would you reject it?
if i should even care,
    would you?
if we should make love,
    would you regret it?
if I should love you,
    would you love me back?

M. G. Zehner

A Tiny Creation

GOD made me, a tiny creation.
I was but one in this great nation.
I became blind, I could not see.
My last days on earth,
Were made very happy,
By a sighted brother,
Because he loved me!

P. R. Friedrich

Memorial Day At
Arlington National Cemetary... 1995

I'm here once again son
 At your home on that hill
The sun is now shining
 And the gloom is now gone

This makes me feel better
 As the sun warms my face
Drying my tears.

The gut wrenching pain
 Of your untimely death
 Now diminished.

Gives way to the gnawing pain
 In my heart.
There's a hole there you know
 That can never be fixed
 And I hate it!

But this is my future!!!

I lean and kiss your stone
 As I say goodbye....
 again.
Susan Winters

Wind Song

When all around are sleeping,
Work of the day is done,
To lie in the darkened shadows,
Night's symphony has begun.

Air conditioner turned off,
Window opened just right,
"Tis then the symphony opens
Wind's lullaby in the night.

Each season the music is different,
One must listen with senses alive.
In summer it's softly gentle,
In winter, noisy and wild.

Spring wafts a fragrance with breezes,
In autumn we hear the leaves die,
But always the wind is rhapsody
From God's star-studded skies.

Praise to the Great Creator,
Maker and giver of life.
Praise to the Great Conductor,
For the wind's symphony in the night!
Eunice Sharpe Simmons

Vicissitudes

If love's ardor wanes when
heavy winds abound

And tempests try to turn
direction round

Stay steady-coursed as Eros
points the prow

That surges on the crest
and then puts down

For faith in love it's true
direction finds

And so reclaims the gentle
winds in kind.
Katherine Gansell

Love

At a table for two in the
midnight air you say to each
other I love you with a look in
your eyes with only a sigh
The guy sitting before me has the
same look in his eye as we turn
to each other to stare at one
another we realize we were meant
to be together as we grow up and
become husband and wife we look
back on that very same day with
the look in our eyes with only a
sigh when we turn to each other
to stare at one another we
were meant to be together.
Jolita Tackett

The Promise

Seek not the splendor of tomorrow
When you gaze into my eyes,
For you'll find only this moment,
Or else a facade of lies.

There is a lure with siren's strength
For moments yet unlived,
Yet here and now is truly all
That is ever ours to give.

So kiss away the crystal tear
That glistens on my cheek.
I'll watch the sun rise in your smile
And dance within its heat.

I can't promise you tomorrow.
It's not mine to give.
But I'll carry your name upon my soul
As long as I shall live.
Barbara Myers

Untitled

Loving you always with an
open heart giving all my best.
Forever in a lifetime, I'll
be there by your side, lending
a helping hand or a shoulder
to put a tear drop on.

Whispering softly "I love you"
or a thoughtful kiss or giving
you a hug to make your
day brighter.
Neville Porter

"Autumn Leaves"

Autumn leaves are falling
 falling to the ground
The feel of your soul falling
 never to be found
Empty and isolated
 deep beneath the ground
The feel of loneliness
 echoes all around
If tears at your heart
 and your mind seems bound
No one to talk to
 Thou people are all around
To sit all alone
 silence is an empty sound
Edith D. Thurman

"While You Were Out"

The candle is lite
And the room is still.
There's a small cool breeze,
I feel it, still.

Quiet and calm...
A restful place.
No more noise
That rattles and quakes.

I look for love
And wonder, well...
Is there meaning
In life's deep well?

I can't wait for tomorrow
Or life's cool rain.
I just want to say...
I'm back home again.
Bruce Jones

Adam And Eve

When God made a mountain
and then made a tree,
He saw someone standing all alone
and that someone was Eve.

He said "I think I'll make someone
for that girl to love."
So he gathered up some sugar
and many stars from above.

He mixed them together
and molded up a man.
He gave him the breath of life
and then touched his hand.

He said "I'll name you Adam
because I know she'll like that name."
He said she sure is beautiful and
you looked and felt the same.

So you see God put them together
for he knew they'd love each other.
And everyone would see the meaning
of loving and caring for one another.
Jeffrey S. Ruddell

"Secret Thoughts"

When the night is so still
 With the quietness all around,
I will travel to my place
 And never hear a sound.
Sometimes I travel to foreign lands
 I'll cruise the oceans wide,
Then climb the highest mountains
 Without leaving my husband's side.
A place to dream my dreams
 At times I steal away,
To think my secret thoughts
 At the closing of the day.
I know a place where I can go
 A place no one can find,
A place that I can be myself
 The place is called my mind.
JoAnna Barker

"Soaring Eagle"

Fly high as an eagle
    soar to be free
Looking over the valleys
    gliding over the trees
Hear the wind whisper
    and echo your name
Rumbling down through the canyons
    dancing over the plains
It's a feeling that takes you
    to a place all your own
Where your spirit and mind
    can quietly roam

Janet M. Haynes

"A Day In Life"

Wake to the sun
    Stumble to greet the day
Deadlines to meet
    Hurry all the way
    New people to see
No time for me
Appointment to keep
    Letters to answer
Rushing to meetings
    Giving apologetic greetings
Wishing for quiet
    Telephone sudden ringing
Answered in haste
    Your soft "Hello"
Instant exhilaration
    Peace of mind
End of day
    Beginning of you....

Sharon L. Riggs

Jesus

Jesus generates His Almighty Power,
Through everything that Is.
His magnificence is indescribable,
In my weakness He is strong.
His divinity is my strength.
He will never leave me.

In my hour of need,
I approach his throne.
His brilliance is abounding,
His energy is ever present.
I am in awe of Him.

I humble myself before Him,
In the presence of His Eminence,
I kneel down and pray.

Through His Majesty,
He answers me.
His Divine Love surrounds me,
And I know that I am blessed.

Trudy Di Mattia Monroe

Little Trees

Little tree's of purple and blue
We all know this cannot be true
For if you take this little pill
The world before you, becomes quite ill
In this ill-found place of choice
Every mind wonders with each voice
But little trees of purple and blue
May exist for me and you

Erik Thomas Shelton

I'm Dreaming

I'm dreaming of a place
Where we don't judge a man
By the color of his skin
Or his face
I'm dreaming of a time
When we learn to love
The person within
And become blind
To the color of skin
I'm dreaming of a different world
A world that's kind
A world without hate
This world blows my mind
I know it's my fate
To make this dream come time
For me and you
I'm still dreaming

Gretchin DuBose

Plain

You enter this world
Naked and plain
With no mark of distinction
Not even a name
The first sound you make
Is a resounding loud cry.
With luck you are loved
And sometimes know not why
You live and you learn
To somehow get by
To make of your life
Whatever you must
To leave it again
And become just dust
Leaving just memories
That soon fade in the rain
It's sad that life is so justly plain.

Charlien Queen

Love's Kettle

Let us put loves kettle on
then watch the passion boil
rising steam, a heavy cloud
of coagulating trouble.
Tear sized drops tumbling down
one after another,
splattering upon the ground
Then clinging to each other.

Once a rising, steaming cloud,
now just soggy puddles
lying woefully around
reflecting on loves kettle.

Karen Western

The Ultimate

To attract others you don't know, to
laugh and love with a continuous flow,
always learning from all they do,
growing stronger and closer to that
inevitable dream, two halves no more
now they are a hole

G. Pello

A Visit

Love has come calling again;
This dear, near forgotten friend.
At heart's door, the beckoning knock,
The timeless serenade.
Yet! I sit silent as a rock,
Trapped tenderly
In the seductive safety
Of freedom's arms...

Then, reflect on the option,
The real reason for tears:
To be a slave to caution,
A martyr to my fears.
Still do I waver...

Love leaves in mock chagrin;
A telling farewell glance,
A whisper on the wind
Sing
Soon again we will dance.

Lorne Smith

A Fall Day

Here I sit outside
on a cold wooden
bench with a breeze
that gives me a chill.
I hear leaves falling
from the trees with a
crackle. I am looking in
the cold fall blue
sky and I am watching
long white stringy clouds roll by.
The black birds glide past
in the sky with the wind pushing them.

Edward R. Pawlick

Winter

Snow is swirling
round and round
white flakes on
the ground
thicker socks
on our feet
getting ready
for some sleet
hail pounding
on our heads
staying warmer
in our beds

Jessica Lee Janecek

Unity

The world becomes small
when you open
your eyes,
mind
and
heart
to
the
oneness
in
us
all.

Maria A. Gallo

Miles Away

Boredom is my shadow
Time is my enemy
Thoughts are my only companion
When I'm away from your love

Night comes over the Earth,
And takes away my love
My love is lost in space,
And no one can hear its screams

I wait, slowly, till day comes
To be rejoined with your love
I am filled with vastly riches,
Which no one else can contain

I am reborn once again,
I am Christ
I will not live without your love,
But I will die with it!

Michael Salmieri

My Caretaker

Nourishment from her breast
    tenderly given
Understanding from her gaze
    tenderly given
Compassion from her heart
    tenderly given
Love from her soul
    tenderly given
Memories from her existence
    tenderly given
Care given, care taken
    tenderly given

Jules R. Jacque

Hidden Sources

Our hidden sources come from above
and here on earth it's a mother love

From the moment we are born
There is no other touch
Like the mother we have
Who loves us so much

She strives each day to make our way
As easy for us as she can
Through good times and bad times
She is always there
Trying to help us through our demands

The hidden sources we can't do without
The heavens above, a mother's love,
These are worth writing about.

Omie Ree Dillon

"Birds On High"

Our feathered friends flock
to and fro—

Skimming the sky up so very
high—

Yonder they go with such a
soar, and we wonder where
they finally go—

Tweet, tweet we hear from
afar, as they complete their
journey ever so far—

Bye Bye Birdies.

Mary D. White

Dad

I forgot I had a dad for a while,
It was silent for so long
He never called to talk to me
Did I do something wrong?

He hurt me inside and out
As I cried and tried
In my mind I had no doubt.

His silence walked on my broken heart
My life is not the same,
The crack in my heart needs a new start
because he always puts me to blame.

I want our love to end now,
    forever till this day,
I can not end it,
    I don't know how
But I'll find out how to do it someway.

Alexia Coggin

The Soul Unmasked

The soul when it is alone and
    unbared is like
    the blackest night:
Out of it pours the fear of a dawn
    which will not come.
Alone it faces the fear of its deepness
    unrealized.
It sees a things potentiality, brought to
    the edges,
it finds no consolation in that
    (other) souls are unchanging.
Unchanging is it with the light,
It's eternity to face never-ending
    nights.

Anne Marie Sarutto

"Awaiting Birth"

Who are you
to say I'm late,
no one talked to me
When you set the date.

I've heard your world
is like a rat race,
I might be cramped
but this is a pretty nice place.

To leave this warmth
and share your cold,
I'm not sure I'm ready
for a step so bold.

It's no secret,
I'll come out to play,
but it's my choice,
and I'll pick the day.

I know your ready
but please don't rush,
Just a little more time,
then give me a push!

Clifford Yawn

Stray Dog

Yellow dog
    go away
The pack is full
    you can't stay

I hate dogs
    can't you see
The love in your eyes
    you melt me

I hate dogs
    go away
One more look
    ok, ok stay.

Jean T. Wood

Cookies

Cookies cookies are very sweet
They are good to eat
Yummy to my tummy
Give it to a bunny
It'll hop like a pop, eat it at the top
Give it to a mouse
It'll eat in a house
Give it to a goat
It'll eat it on a boat
It will float
Cookies are good to eat!

Stephanie Romine

This Darkness

This darkness is unyielding,
but to fear it is to be foolish.
For though it masks its secrets,
blinding one to the dangers,
It also hides oneself.

Everyone of us is lost,
traveling amongst this darkness.
Some have the insight to lead,
others the patients to follow.
Still others choose to walk alone.

All will be hurt by the unseen.
Those with the courage to continue,
and the strength to persevere,
someday find the truth.
All who stand unmoving, fearful, die.

Daniel J. Proctor

Nobody's Alike

I have brown eyes and you have green.
He is nice, and she is mean.
I like blue, and you like pink.
He likes pencil, and she likes ink.
I am nine and you are eight.
He has a friend, and she has a date.
I like to walk, and you like to run.
Now I am done, and this was fun!

Mandie Nicole Catalano

New

Curious young
Wondering feeling beginning
Life isn't the same forever.
Knowing changing ending
Done elder
OLD

Becky Dill

The Visit

They met in time
Though not too late
But time cautioned
Still another wait

He bared his soul
She seemed to know
What fertile ground
For love to grow

Time seems longer
As love grows stronger
Being apart brings such pain
Please God,
Let love reign
Together, forever, again!

How much longer
Time will tell
Till rescued from an early hell

A day in time and they will mate
They'll love in full
let heaven wait.

John S. Murphy

Untitled

Who can define friendship?
Who would be so bold
As to place restrictions
And requirements untold
On those, once only acquaintances,
Who knew you as only a face?
Now through time and companionship
They trust you as a base
For love and confidentiality
Without defining it as such,
And for support and encouragement
Through that untouchable touch.

Who can define friendship?
Who would be so bold
As to say it's too exhausting?
We dare not be so cold!

Christa Bartsch

Pictures Of The Soul

Mothballs, wool coat, raven's wings
Sunshine, fireflies, guitar strings.
Fragments, images seem swift to fly
Across the inner mind's internal eye.

Seemingly dissimilar at first glance
As much in common as flat tire or ants.
But to the person whose mind recalls
It's part or pictures of life overall.

Wool coat of mothball's pungent smell
Recalls a dearly beloved Uncle so well.
Raven wings, a crow and a favorite pet
In sunshine's golden memories seen yet.

Fireflies aglow on hot summer night,
Twinkling like fairies in glow-light.
Guitar strings rise up to again fill
Soothing away hurt of a childhood ill.

Memories etched on the mind of a man
Snippets of life in hourglass's sand.
Memories are the pictures of the soul
Carried by each of us as we grow old.

Joyce J. Ruskuski

Waiting

Smoky room,
  Nervous man,
Sweating brow
  Shaking hand

Worn out carpet,
  Steady beat,
Tired legs,
  Tired feet.

Open door
  Woman in white
Soft quiet voice
  Cheers of delight
  a boy!

Nancy Walters

Four Breaths

Spring's pink picture moon
is a petal of light
My blue friend.

Sweet summer mist whispers
through hot drunken gardens:
Let's watch the sky.

Autumn's death delirious
its purple languid shadow
frantic for the sun.

Goddess of winter dreaming
shakes black sleep
from her milk dress
above the storm.

Karen Pugliese

The Glory In You

A lily is a lily
Before it ever blooms
And GOD's love spins its garments
On nature's secret looms

It is no less a lily
Before it knows its worth
And with no hint of glory
Lies earthly in the earth

GOD's child, you are GOD's child
Rejoice in it and know
You have a glory in you
Though you have far to grow.

Dorothy Green

Feel

Feel my heart,
feel it race,
feel my love
keep its pace.
do not leave me,
do not go,
if you do I will not know,
what to do or
what to say or
how to stop thinking of you each day.
So do not go,
just stay right there,
stay with me don't let me scare.

Marc Fardink

To The Family

I never missed you so much
like I'm missing you today
I feel so sad and lonely
ever since you went away

I wake up from dreams about you
and I'm crying like a child
I cannot fill this void you left
my emotions running wild

I remember all the love you gave
and the good times that we shared
and everything you taught me
in that special way you cared

I can feel your love in my heart
your face in dreams and mind
your voice is in my memory
it's always there to find

I never will forget you
and your pictures I will save
I'll love you all forever
and put flowers on your grave

Richard T. Gregory

Life

A joyful power that has no
reason but it's own. Live a life
with love and sharing, and live
a life of endless gifts. Always
reaching your dream giving back to
what has been given to all.
A peace of time to hear all who
call a breath is all you need
to find joy a passive day to hold
a raindrop a snowflake the sun a
moon a friend to run to with
the waves of life. A child's face to
make you smile in your own fall to
see reality, a cry of pain and the
strength to make you see. But
there is no other life but you and me.

Mark Viola

The Ride Of A Lifetime

Love a state of being in love
a feeling love for your children
unconditional love for your mate
love for your soul mate, true love
love is a miracle
sometimes frightening
sometimes confusing
always beautiful
you can feel low in love
or like a bird in flight
love hits you like a hammer
and cuts deep in your soul like a knife
it rips you open and invades you
and only true love heals the wound
love it's a roller coaster ride
the ups and downs can kill you
but if you survive the hellish ride
love is the most beautiful mystical
blissful experience of one's life
don't miss the miracle

Kathleen Olson

To My Children

When I leave this happy world
And my world is happy dears,
I have no gold to leave behind
No wealth for all my years.

I have not made a flight in space
Nor plumbed the ocean's blue,
My contribution to immortal time
My dears, the two of you.

I'm not good at inventing
Don't excel in anything I do,
But I boast of one accomplishment
My pride's in both of you.

Each thoughtful thing I see you do
Each kindness for another,
Brings me mentally to my knees
How wonderful to be
      Your Mother
Violet Marie Unger

Throughout The Land

A prayer was said
   throughout the land

A tear was shed
   throughout the land

Hearts are full of pain
   throughout the land

A ribbon was tied
   throughout the land

To remind us who died
   throughout the land

Holding one another
   throughout the land

As sisters and brothers
   throughout the land

Joined together
   throughout the land

To try to make things
   a little better
   throughout the land...
Carrie Banwart

The Day We Met

You were just a face
in a crowd. Until
now you stick out.
You we're the only
one who cared and
listened. I knew
we'd be together
forever after that.
The other guys we're
telling you to "not
stay" or "go away"
but you didn't
you went ahead
and said "Hi"!
Aimee Mott

Nightmare

I awake in a cold sweat,
Frightened,
  Thinking,
Remembering,
  Horrified,
Nightmare becoming a reality,
Falling,
  Dropping from a cliff,
Watching,
  Splat - Hit the ground,
  Did not hurt,
Sick to stomach,
Get back up
  Wash away the fear,
Realize it's not real,
  Just having a nightmare,
Unfrightened, Unhorrified,
Not remembering, not thinking,
Not in a cold sweat,
  Asleep, forever.
Saurina Watson

The Window

Looking out looking down
I see the empty faces
Raindrops fall
Silently
Stopping
When they've reached their places
To know their freedom
That they've known
While dancing up in blue
Or black
Whichever it may be
But in their thoughts
That they knew
They'll reunite as one
To be drawn back
As a whole
To dance
Together
Again.

Josh Edward Battey

To My Grandchildren

  Speed and greed of yesteryear
have given way to plodding.
  No dollar gain or titles call
to quench the ego's prodding.

  Slower pace of golden age
with no schedule to be met,
  Allow my charges to keep up -
my pledge of time is kept.

  Bent and gray with aches and pains
forgetting today's events,
  Remember well those days of youth
spent with my grandparents.

  So, little ones, bear with me
as sight and memory fail,
  Because one day you too may share
the old grandparent's tale.

Greg Gresenz

Angel Of Mercy

Angel of Mercy, up and down the halls,
with a gentle face,
soothing hands,
soft words for all.

With a smiling face
She does all she can
to bring comfort to those
of the Land.

She brings you food.
She gives you a bath.
Helps you overcome
the worry and the aftermath.

Helping others brings her joy.
She never thinks of herself.
It is others she thinks of,
and others she strives to help.

God looks down on her
With a smiling face.
Your reward will be great,
Angel of Mercy, Lady of Grace.
Nannie L. Parker

Dew Drops And Moonbeams

The early morning dew
reflects off the grass.
This world spins very fast.
Hear the many mist drops
through the trees.
Free - falling hitting leaves.
Finally reaching the ground
quenching the earth's thirst.
The sun rises inch by inch
singing brightly with glorious rays.
Climbing up through the day
always bringing further changes
of growth your way.
Sunset comes showing soft colors
of warm lullabies.
The time is near for diamonds
to appear.
With hopes and dreams on moonbeams.
John F. Tierney

My Hill

  The cold gray rain is slanting down,
The barren fields are sere and brown.
But here and there a sudden blaze
Of color pierces through the haze
Of autumn which has not yet fled
Before winter's advancing tread.
High on the hill above the town
I brave the storm and nature's frown.

I see the flaming red of bittersweet,
The fields below, the corn shocks neat,
The village houses, row on row.
I leave my hill and go below—
But I can look from window sill
And see my lovely, lonely hill.
Above the petty cares that be
I know it's waiting there for me.
Bonnalie Childress

The Spiteful Watch

In your ticklings and your tickings
I discern quite hateful mockings.

You tick and tock and on and on,
Droning like your mind's quite gone.

One more tick or one more tock,
And I'll crush you with my rock!

Bang and smash! It's all over!
At last my mind begins to sober!

If this act be called a crime,
I plead my guilt for killing time.

David S. Auer

Dream Of Mine

A star's light, burning bright,
in plain sight,
so near, it holds dear,
a dream of mine.

In my sight, under moonlight,
such delight,
a tear of dew, thinking of you,
a dream of mine.

A dream to share, do I dare,
it's only fair,
words to say, oh please stay,
dream of mine.

I give to you, to be true,
never blue,
all my heart, never to part,
dream of mine.

William J. Ciccone

A Gathering Of Strangers

The road is coppered in the sun
of August's polished sky.
It shimmers to the water's edge
and disappears
where dinghies and old fish nets
tatter half the cove.

This is the place of one's imaginings
of summers past, but now
a scene of ghosts,
a streaked awareness
hanging in the mind
between two words.

No tide here, no splash of fish,
no reek of oyster shells,
but only recollections,
hermetically sealed for display
and, somehow, cleansed
of life's betrayals.

Patricia Bell Ellis

Not Much Time

As the birds fly by, by the minute
  The butterfly's flutter until dawn
  The flower's bloom in the morning,
   and the petals wilt at dawn
   from the blazing sun
  Not much time for you and me
  The winter, spring, summer and
   fall
  No time at all

Kathleen Schoefer

Dreaming In The Sun

As I sit by the window sill
very relaxed and very still
I dream of places I may go
far, far beyond the snow
I dream of castles on mountain tops
I dream of land covered with lollipops.
I dream it's sunny and it's warm
I dream we're not in a blizzard storm.
though the snow will be here awhile
I think I'll make a snow crocodile
That's a good idea I say
I think I'll go out to play

Vanessa Marchese

Down Life's Highway

Hand in hand together
Traveling life's highway
We find the journey pleasant
Sharing day by day.

Sharing the sweet and the bitter
Sharing the pleasure and the pain
We take the shadow with the sun
Laugh the silvery rain.

We laugh at the storms and brave them
Seeking to understand
We find the fruit of life sweeter
Traveling life highway hand in hand.

Pamela Fishwick

Bonding Of Souls

One is intertwined
of two faces.

Hearts are joined
by understanding
our self.

Hands are put together
from inner strength.

Bodies touch from
being one.

Pamela Fincham

Tis Naught

The world has said to me.
Tis gone...forget.
Bury it deep.
But no!
My dream's not dead.
Nor shall I ever weep.
For Love in its awakening
Bears such a precious gift.
That it matters not.
To where the sands...may sift.
It is the seed,
That wears the crown.
So what...if the stem has thorns
And the flowers are trodden...
To the ground!

Alda Ligia Palmer

La Doncella

An ageless glow surrounds her
And all suffuses who wait.
Great energy and power
From her do emanate.
Dreams become reality
Although not without much change.
Of risks there is no paucity
And a star is in her range.
The star is firmly fixed
To glow in her Tiara
Ah, Viva La Doncella.

Margaret V. Harold

Grackles!!!!

Large black grackles,

Squawking
Shrieking
Clacking ...

Large black grackles

Thieving
Messing
Yakking ...

Large black grackles

Disgusting
Loathsome
Hopping

Eternal chatter, never stopping ...
Of all the things God did create,
This is one I've come to hate!!

Large black grackles,
Really do raise my hackles!!

Charlotte A. Schaefer

Lost And Alone

A river flowing
as it searches a sea.
The wind is blowing,
is it looking for me?

I stand alone
in a crowded place
I look around,
is there a friendly face?

I feel a touch,
or was it a bump?
Although it was gentle,
I do still jump.

The moon is rising
gone is the sun.
Where am I?
What have I done?

My family is gone,
it's alone I stand.
Why am I here?
In a foreign land?

Jan Markulin

Industrial Revolution

Society is an industry
Manufacturing our heads
The sun manufactures the trees
The trees manufacture the leaves
Love manufactures me
Confusing my mind
Till it bleeds manufactured blood
Given by my manufactured parents
With blinded awareness
Hiding even from themselves
Throwing their real dreams upon
   dusty shelves
I pray my manufactured brain will die
So, all my manufactured thoughts
   will be crucified

Tara Lynne Havard

"World"

      A man is shot;
   a cocaine-addicted baby cries;
    a teenage girl is raped;
   the world spins, life goes on

   a classroom is taken hostage;
   a young man contracts Aids;
     a bank is held up;
   the world turns, life goes on

    a car collides with a van;
   a driveby occurs next door;
     a child is molested;
   the world rotates, life goes on

   a couple is mugged and stabbed;
  a drunk driver kills a family of four;
    a man beats his wife;
   the world revolves, life goes on

     species kills species;
      race kills race;
    mankind kills mankind;
   the world orbits the sun...

Kelly Quick

The Resting Step

A little boy sat on a step
With one hand on his chin
He thought about this world of ours
And everything within

He thought about atomic bombs
And things that are to come
He thought of people running things
And why they act so dumb

He thought of all the soldiers
Being oh so young
And how they have to go to war
Just to carry a gun

He thought of all the times
When things did not go well
Then he thought of all the times
When all the tent posts fell

And as he got up and walked away
He knew that he'd been blessed
Because he'd been given
His little step to rest

Elaine Moore

"My Life Goes On"

As tears fall from my face
I remember the days
of picking up cans for food

Watching our money go to alcohol
watching alcohol go into anger
watching anger go into rage
watching rage go into fights

The fights gets worse
first throwing things
then watching my brother get hit
next hearing my dad strangling my mom
finally hearing my dad
say I'm not his

Now I found the truth
found happiness
and found you

The holidays are better
family is still torn
memories are still strong
but my life goes on

Christina Lawson

Who Minds A Little Dirt

A little boy so brave and strong,
   the joy of every day,
with twinkling eyes and dimpled chin
   will steal your heart away.

No one will mind his dirty cheeks,
   his grass-stained jeans and shirt,
   a little smile is all you need.
    Who minds a little dirt?

He wanders off to creeks and ponds
   to capture toads and frogs.
   He runs from field to field
with his faithful, watchful dogs.

With faith and hope he meets each day,
   with courage, each tomorrow.
He always keeps his cheerful smile
   through happiness or sorrow.

Marilyn Thomas

Best Friend

The hours we've spent together.
The tears I've surrendered to you
The thoughts we've shared, how
   can I ever thank you my friend.

Your order, your warmth is like a
   cradle of love that only a
   good friend can generate.

I wake up in the early morning
   mist and you're there to greet
   me like a good friend.

If only the world knew that
   my best friend is my kitchen.

Magali Strada

The Music Plays On

Slowly dancing saxophone;
Picking with drummer
Blurred person walking down the street,
Madly playing a beat
Trash on the street all around.
The winds wildly
Tapping feet
Harsh notes hitting the air
Running fingers on the saxophone...
Carelessly running pass
The vandalized tire in the street
Fussy flute humming
Words briefly flying
Crashing waves
The foaming shore
Warm sunny weather
Harsh winds rapping at the door
Frightening expressions of musicians,
Madly striking the abused keys...
They are the ones in pain.

Fallon Wesley

Night

Why cry
Shed no more tears

Gloomy, dismal shadows
Lurking among the patches

Where do you go
When the day turn to dusk

As a silent animal
Waiting for the kill

Pray for your existence
Call to his majesty

Look upon yourself
Through the eyes of the dawn

Sarah Connolly

Singed

It was more than a twinkle in his eye
It was a flash
A dance of lightning
I was singed

I drew closer to the warmth
Of this dangerous flame
A fiery manifestation of
His passionate soul
His love of life
His joy in being
In each moment

Words were superfluous
My eyes revealed
My perception
My confliction
My dimming spark

He gently blinked
I looked away, smiling
Invigorated by his spirit
Rejuvenated by his shine

Karen M. Thompson

Birds Of A Feather

Birds of a feather flock together
   the old saying says
of all breeds, animals and humans
   have so little confidence
of self to self from all,
   Together at once a child is born
in the figure of love from two kin
   without a frown of sweet
the thought of young for forbidden
   forever is time to never be
detached, to stay close to feel
   them breathe.
Too much will make them stray
   from the flock of the same
feather together.

Renee A. Johnson

The Unfamiliar Stranger

Lost in the chaotic world
I find myself running at top speed
Passing its changing faces
In search of the unknown
At every turn there is a riddle
The answers lie within
Filled with bewilderment, I run on
Following the path of destiny
I can make no sense of this place
Overwhelmed by fear and despair
I shut my eyes to it
But its presence is still felt
Through other channels it creeps inside
Corrupting my heart and mind
I fight the good fight
But it has captured my soul
Leaving me with emptiness
As my last breath lay upon my lips
I open my eyes one last time
To the unfamiliar stranger before me

Rosanna Mauro

The Carrousel

I sit,
Huddled in his warmth,
And kissed by spring's first softness.

Before as grinds the noisy honky-tonk
Organ of the carrousel,
Mingling with the laughter of children.

It speaks of many years.
like us.
But youth does not hear age,
Nor does it see.

As we remember,
As we remember, when.

Alice J. Mylett

Mermaid

I saw on the horizon
That she was in the sea;
She raised her arm in greeting,
Beckoning to me.

I walked into the water,
Searching for my love;
Now I am there forever,
While she is free, above.

Pauline M. LaRue

To Go There

I rise to this occasion
dressed in fear
not cool
just cautious
cause to just go there
can not
be so easily repeated
I want to be free
I will be free
I am free
to remain so
is the illusion I need
to create balance
continual growth
for serenity
peace to us
let's do this equally
with fun
let's go there
together

Toni Wallace

Empty

I'll be your soulmate
I'll be your slave
I'll be your Goddess
Your one and only
But you won't love me
'Cuz love is empty, just like me

Share our secrets, heal our fear
Tell our lies and take off the disguise
Love each other 'til one of us dies
But you won't love me,
'Cuz love is empty, just like me

Dance 'til the stroke of midnight
Hold each other tight
Only you could make it seem right
But that was just a dream
'Cuz you won't love me
'Cuz love is empty, just like me

Michelle Progar

Buried Treasure

There is a treasure
buried in her

a special treasure worth;
more than diamonds, silver
or any gold.

There is a treasure buried
in her worth more than
a king's ransom.

There is a treasure buried
deep within that needs
to be found; but it's too deep

And that treasure is
a remarkable gift called love.

Michelle Evonne Warts

Until We Meet Again!!

Goodbye my love, goodbye.
Our paths have crossed,
   and may never cross again.
Goodbye my love, goodbye.

We take with each other
   something no one else has ever had,
Our souls, my love, goodbye.

We part not in sorrow, but in joy.
Knowing we will be stronger
   for knowing one another,
Goodbye my love, goodbye.

And if, by faith, our paths may
   some day cross again,
We will know, my love.

For our souls will say,
Hello my love, hello!

George J. Walker

Little Liar

Well, you said you loved me,
and you said you cared.
I was so blind I couldn't even see
there was nothing really there.

I only thought I loved you
until I saw your lie.
I guess it's nothing new,
and I'm glad we said good-bye.

You're a user,
a player, and an abuser.
My heart is still mine,
stay away from me, and I'll be fine.

I was just another victim
of your thoughtless crime.
I'll warn them of your system,
hope you won't hurt anyone this time.

Kaylee Lund

Parents

My parents now are older
and we children cause them pain,
though often we don't mean to
sometimes do — just the same.

To say the things that mean so much
like "Thanks" — we forget to say.
A better life they both have shared
with each of us each day.

Though self involved we seem to be
our lives have really changed,
for we are parents now you see
our time is rearranged.

Let us not forever forget
to say what we feel to be,
sometimes it's difficult and yet
I hope it is said to me.

"I love you Mom and Dad" you know
are never said enough.
These words we seldom seem to show
along with other stuff.

Mary M. Dostie-Ladd

"Love"

I really wish I knew
　How to say I care,
If only I could show you
　Everything we could share....

Time can only show if I will
　Ever feel your kiss,
Or know if you can love,
　And show me tenderness....

If to hold you once in my arms,
　I would surely fall in love,
Just to feel you near me,
　And to know,
That you the only one I dream of.....

Kermit Shane Thompson

My Time

My time is real precious
I'd like to have all I can
For I find time is mine
And time is what I am.

If I chose to waste my time
I can sit and brood all day
Well, I can't get that time back
It has permanently gone away

If I chose for greedy time
And want results too fast
The things that come are soon forgot
My greedy time has past.

If I chose to value my time
The results might come sometime later
But if I'm careful and take my time
the rewards are that much greater

Patty S. May

Time

Time stands still for no one
on a splinter of light
darkness stumbles in
at a flash
the light returns

Sometimes we take life for granted
we have so much but then
did you ever take time
　to look around you
　smell the flowers
　look into yourself

We are so busy with life
we don't care because
time is forever

Sometimes simple things in life
　our health, happiness love-
no one can buy these things

Time stands still for no one

Shirley Casey

Searching Sleep

A slow flowing river,
　a laced lawn chair,
　　a silent copse
　　　and contemplation.

A rushing back
　but the way is lost—
　　a narrow bridge
　　　recognized but forbidden.

Retreating and returning,
　to a house on a river bank,
　　to old friends' advice,
　　　to a wise, silent teacher.

Old music played
　on the porch—
　　a forgotten tune
　　　on a black cassette.

Beautiful dreamer
　awaken to me,
　　a haunting melody
　　　of searching sleep.

Wilda Kennedy Hoffman

Old Treasures

In going thru old treasures,
Wrapped and put away from dust
With dimly faded pictures
In a tin box old with rust,
Many precious memories
One can always find —
Within a locked up mind —
All begin to surface once again,
As trembling hands do hold.
With tear dimmed eyes,
One sees to reminisce with love
Old stories they unfold.
Accumulation of years gone by
Will never come again.
All may be found one day soon,
One never knows just when.
Place back high upon the shelf —
Left for others to explore —
Back to present time and place,
And quietly close the closet door.

D. Nelle Andrews

Everyday Memories

I wake in the morning
its hard to ignore so
many memories from the
days before.

The glass is filled with moisture
we've all seen in the past as
we take our hands to clear the
glass.

Dew settled in from the night
that past leaving sparkling little
droplets on the blades of grass

The sounds of bells start to blast
to let us all know its now half
mass these fond memories of day's
that past

As the night draws near and
your thoughts are clear
Memories of the past become so dear.

Robert Kelly

Impossible To Forget

From the first time I saw you,
I never forgot you.
The smile on your face,
The sparkle in your eyes,
The touch of your hand,
And the laughter in your eyes
　when you are happy.
You are very special to me,
And no matter how much
I try to forget you it is impossible.
The night that we kissed,
Was very special to me,
It was my first and I will never forget it.
It was the most wonderful thing
I have ever felt and experienced.
I hope someday it will happen again,
But no matter what happens,
If we never kiss again,
I hope we will always be friends.
You are such a wonderful person,
You are Impossible To Forget....

Lynnel Bethel

In This Day And Age...

What is humanity, when the public figure
is the one who represents all that we
have been brought up to hate?
Are we really good?

With the sanity of society
tied into material goods
rather than family and friends.
Are we really sane?

When too much is not enough,
and too little
can drive even the happiest
of people to the grave.
Are we really caring?

What good is our way of life,
when the way in which we achieve it
threatens existence itself.
Are we really living?

We are not good.
We are not sane.
We are not caring.
We are not living.
Therefore... We are not human.

Ryan McConnell

Candid Interview

Do you smoke?
No.
Walk straightlines on the pavement?
Yes.
Talk in crowded bars?
No.
Have some tea?
No, thank you.
Know what time it is?
Yes.
Can you tell me?
Yes.
Are you going to?
Oh, sure, ahh 4:27.

David Brunswick

Watch Her Play

Watch her play and throw her ball
A picture of purity, but you know nothing at all.
Eyes filled with wonder, a smile so bright
Too young to know if his touching is wrong or right.
She learned the hard way, which no child should,
About the realities of life she had not understood.
It's getting dark, it's time for bed,
Tell her a story and kiss her on the head.
Tell her you love her, then turn out the light,
Watch her roll over and sleep through the night.
Years will go by with no sign of a trace
But the wounds are too deep and the pain she will face.
She won't be a child forever and then it will begin
Everything will seem so difficult in a battle so hard to win.
It'll seem she's out of control, constantly she'll be acting out
Her feelings are of insecurity, shame, unworthiness and doubt.
She'll always be pretending, her depression will go on for long
It was never her fault, though she feels she did wrong.
She may not entirely remember, with moments she can't forget
So keep her young for now; her future's already been set.

Julie Ann Wright

Physical Image

Beyond the physical image there is a clear screen,
a place of fantasy no one has ever seen.

No matter how quick or how hard you try,
you can't see it, for it's behind the eye.

A place of wonder, a place of peace, a place where evil can't crease.

No matter where you go or angle your at,
it's always there, under the place you just sat.

Beyond the physical nature, under the deepest hole,
lies a place beyond the north pole.

This is a place where gypsies and unicorns fly,
a place where fairy tails are inside.

A place of wonder, a place to understand,
a home for imagination land.

This is where stories come about, no place for a child's doubt.

Grown-ups should come to realize,
that there is a place behind a child's eye.

To take them back to the innocence of a dream,
a place when young they have seen.

So when reality becomes to hard to handle,
remember the place brightened by a candle.

Melissa Quinlan

Spirit In The Sky

They tell me it won't hurt, but then what do they care.
An old shack down the Mill, that's where I go each day.
My Arm out stretched once again, then my body will shiver with pain.
Darkness I will see for awhile, then the sun will shine.
Now I'm just a spirit in the sky.

No more dark corners for me, no more do I fear each day.
Free, Free, as a Bird, up up in the sky I will fly.
I feel love, I feel joy, please let me stay a little longer.
I feel darkness coming once again, perhaps one day I will be stronger.
Until then, I'll just be a spirit in the sky.

The pain then the darkness, my dreams just fall apart.
This can't be for me, Dear God, my arm outstretched with despair.
This time a little more stick, my eyes are burning inside.
My body aches, then becomes light, this time I fear I'm hear to stay.
No more living by the mill, for now I'm flying night and day.
I'm flying so very high, I'm just another spirit in the sky.

Micheal Byrne

All Is Forgiven

She plunges and twists the kitchen knife; finally striking bone.
Above them thunder flashes; lightning claps.
The streams of sweet summer rain dilute
His thick flowing blood.
He lies in a pool of himself
Feeling his wasted life slip away;
She can smell impending death.

There are no tears in his burning eyes,
No remorse on her chiseled face.
She leaves him to watch the fading rainbow.
Deaf to his urgent reaching for her,
Blind to the sound of his struggle to rise a final time,
She only feels his once welcome touch on her arm.
He falls against her, staining her with his liquid.

Just as his soul withdraws from the world,
He whispers in her delicate ear that he understands.
The stringless puppet collapses around her feet.
She kneels beside her passionate transgression,
Kisses his wintry cheek and smooths his dull hair.
Smiling, she retires to cleanse her soiled blouse.

Janna M. Green

Faith, Hope And Love

Faith is important we strongly believe
Alleviating our sorrows, tears, pain we grieve
Internally distraught within
Tomorrow never to begin
Hopes and dreams shattered once again.

Honoring your courage, wisdom, the love you shared
Opposing negative feelings to remember how we cared
Pleasurable reminisces we reflect upon to reunite ourselves with our
    son.
Everlasting love given each and everyday the sweetest of
    memories have only begun.

Love and faithfulness meet together
Only to be cherished now and forever
Vast disappointments we face once more with pain
Endless confusion, our hearts cannot explain.

Kimberly Hartman

Remembering...

Alone. I sit and watch the endless night drift by,
and from my windows, see the barren trees lift empty
branches to the sky.

I hear them plead for morn' to come, and wake them from
their sleep, from this long winter vigil that they keep.

And in the street below, remembered faces of my youthful
    yearnings smile,
And beckon to me, faces of the past, and ghosts of love gone by,
reach up, and call to me, and years of days and nights pass by
my eyes, and I am in my child years for awhile.

And I am not alone, for in my mind I see the friends I knew,
when I was young, and laughed and played, and thought of no
    tomorrow, past to-day...
I hear the music of their laughter, and I feel the pain of sweet
"HELLO, that brought me to the growing years, of love,
    and feelings new...
And suddenly, the street is dark, and no one hears me as I cry,

where are the ones I loved? Some never said good-bye....

Like me the trees reach up with empty arms up to the moon,
and wait, as I, for morn to come, oh, Please, make it be soon.

Betty Weeks

Reflections

It's dark. I'm rising gently, floating outward as a cloud,
and naught, can I see around me, as surrounded by a shroud.
With my eyes I'm peering, straining into never ending depth.
My arms are every groping; yet I feel myself inept.

Now there, so far before me, a faint glimmering of light,
so far, and yet so welcome after hours of clammy flight.
At last, it's drawing nearer, not ahead - but "there below",
All around I feel a thickening, see a growing eerie glow.

"But wait!" I've stopped, I'm standing in a vastness that surrounds.
I see figures moving ghostlike; hear heart-rending wails and moans.
Like a piercing knife, its in me; knowledge of the place I dwell,
and my bowels tear deep within me, "My God - I've gone to hell."

Then I stopped, I sat, I pondered, my life's parade and sighed,
   This is not the end I wanted,
      But the end is justified.
   John W. Leithwood

Playing Golf

Golf is a game for gentlemen and ladies bright and bold,
And people who are golfers just don't seem to grow old.
Maybe they're like old sailors who simply sail away,
Or maybe like bright sunbeams that fill a summer day.

Of course I've seen some golfers who swear and throw their clubs,
Especially when that little ball performs the dub-a-dubs.
But mostly they're a cheerful bunch from duffers up to pros,
Except when someone hits a ball that lands close to their toes!

The game has lots of hazards - there's water and the rough.
It's hard to smile and keep your style if things get bad enough.
But oh those days of glory when everything goes well.
Your swing's a sweet old story; at Hole Nineteen, you'll tell!

I've known lots of golfers and played the game myself.
It really is amazing how golf can grab oneself.
They say the game was started by clannish, frugal Scots;
But it's got so expensive, and money - you need lots!
   William M. Wismer

Many Leaders

Many leaders, to make their place on top with good name
And to drop other leaders reputation to blame.
They force poor to make violence in society,
As they have nothing in them like humanity.

A bomb is blast here and a bomb is blast there,
Many die and left ones, have all sorts of hardships to bare.
Some money is given to show sympathy,
To become nice in front of world they show artificial mercy.
Money for some time can buy milk and bread,
But money can neither buy life nor even a single breath.
These kind of things happen mostly every day,
But no one takes actions even all this they pay.

They take false promises day by day.
They are so cruel that no one dares to ask what they say.
These well dressed leaders have no feeling in their stone heart.
They encourage terrorism for their victory forgetting AL-
MIGHTY LORD.
They enjoy their cruel victory so their faces are bright,
But till when they will enjoy with the hearts that have died.
   Asia Saleem

The Celluloid Window

Lush green trees in an ever expanding river of waste,
Animals pushed forward as they are unceasingly chased.
Look, was that a giant Panda running in flight?
Or was it just maybe, a trick of light.
For as you watch you see the machines reek havoc
Cutting, slashing, tearing the heart from the planet.

Visit the poor quarters of the cities, and stare
At the hovels, called homes, of the people who live there.
It's not for greed these people tear the guts from the land,
They don't know the earth will eventually turn to sand.

Now, see elsewhere, gaze in jealous wonder at the blazing sun,
White sands, tropical Palms, set in a paradise made for fun.
Hear the animals roar as they roam, searching, killing for food,
As great herds of Zebra, elephant and giraffes, change the mood.

Travel to the mountains and stare in wonder
At the magnificent splendor made for man to conquer.
Then on to the poles, a full world apart,
Then STOP, re-wind, and press re-start,
Don't leave your armchair, just sit and watch
As the power of the camera is yours at a touch.
   Francis Allan Hoggarth

The Clock

For most the clock is the reality in their clockwork lives.
As the gears of the clock move, the hands move.
As the hands move, the masses move, for the clock is their guide.
It instructs them when to do what throughout their lives.
The clock accounts for their every action.
Obsession makes their pitiful minds believe in the clock
And what its movements hold for them to do.
They would be lost without it.
I think they could function much better on their own.
To watch the clock is to believe it,
To believe it is to live by it and let it dominate
The thoughts and actions of those who perhaps disagree.
But the masses will try to push their constant "Reality" on others.
But the only reality is that the very machine
That they made to organize life has now taken over their lives.
It tells them everything, they do what it says
I will refused to be operated.
When I die there will be no more masses, no more rules,
No more dictatorship, no more of their insanity, no more clock.
For me the clock on the wall has nothing to say.
   Leslie (Les) Gully

What Now

In the inner reaches of the mind mysteries unfold
As we grow old, textured tapestries appear
And eerily the past becomes the present.
The future brushes lightly on the now then disappears from sight,
Should we give up the ghost or stay and fight?
Oh time slow down thy days
To ease the dark vexation of this inner soul
The mirrors cracked wherein we gaze
For stressful life has taken of its toll
We cannot see what once there was
Ah if the hands of time would only pause
So we could reminisce and live again our youth,
But who is there to listen to the tales we firmly speak as truth,
Fiction now for us becomes our facts.
Interwoven pieces of our lives, we call these memories
They survive, but in what context, time and place.
The name has gone but we recall the face.
The blurring of the edges of our days, our every thoughts a puzzle
As we search for ways just once, to make it all seem right
Before we are forced to enter that long night.
   W. Pantony

Green Flash

I espied a green flash in the sky before dawn,
Before reds and pink-purples of day could be born
The new shade the sky made as of Jade...and was gone;
-I felt sure that good luck would be struck from that morn!

We were 'teens' with love's fires, and desires, to be quelled
A dark grey, (as like clay), was our dawns early sky,
-Suddenly, the green flash...and this ash was dispelled!
We did grope, with green hope, to our GOLD: You and I!!

Ah but envy looks green, and we've seen what is wrath,
With dour 'friends' to such ends as would keep us apart;
And the years are gone by as if thorns in our path!....
-What's lost-love but blue veins...yet for swelling the heart?!

As we planned I now stand on the sands of twilight
Contemplating, while waiting, the light-mating Sea;
-Of a sudden green flashes!....an em'rald delight!!
They quick clear,...you stand there:-you do care!-Love will be!!

Casimir Mekdeci

An Inward Journey

I return, once again, to the same ole place
bound by the terrible laws of time and space
far too many painful memories I simply cannot erase
  such a total disgrace
No one, nothing left to embrace - gone without a trace

Enveloped in a melancholy blackness, a void so deep
  a constant aching, a longing for eternal sleep
  so I sit on this lovely bar stool and weep -
  never knowing what to keep...
  following you around like a lost sheep
  looking up at the cliff, so steep - inch by inch, I grope, I creep

So slow and pathetically painstaking
  whatever am I making as my heart is breaking?
  From this awful nightmare am I waking?
  Who am I kidding, I'm only faking
  was I giving or always taking?
  Why this torture, this raking...

After all I've been here before
  I read all the related lore
  Seen it all turn to gore so now I close that door!!

David Warren

Your Unseen Friend

When family and friends surround you, you feel safe and secure,
But in those many hours alone, you're not so very sure
That life has got much meaning, it's then you kneel and pray
To your Heavenly Father who loves you, and is not so far away.

His arms are always open to draw you by His side,
The scriptures telling of His works bring comfort and great pride.
Your's one of His chosen children, with tasks that have to be done,
And every hour that passes can mean another victory won.

Do you know you have a friend that's with you every day,
That stays close by you always, asleep, at work, at play.
He will guide you gently onward, and whisper in your ear,
And when the road gets bumpy, the pathway he will clear.

This friend he is not mortal, but when you need him the most,
If you are in tune and do but ask,
Your companion will be the HOLY GHOST.

Grace A. Wilkinson

When I Sleep Alone

You never wanted to hear the screams or the crying.
By day you engross yourself in work to the point you bring
it home with you.
  But at night; alone, cold, you hear it.
Sometimes its so loud it wakes you up and you lay there
hugging yourself or the pillow until you doze off and the crying
is only a faint whisper.
  Then finally one night its so unbearable; the screams and
crying, you wake to search it out.
  There is your one room cell; your mind is as if it an
apparition, shows you your loneliness and despair - cowering in a
corner in tattered clothing, shivering in the cold you sleep.
  Letting go of it, now you cower in the corner, shivering at
the wind of despair and loneliness, with only a blanket to hold
you and a pillow for you to hold.

John P. Byrns III

Mission

At a quarter to ten the Mission bell rings,
calling all the followers to count their blessings.
Yes that's where life happens and where it ends.
Mission keeps on calling like a long, lost friend.

Smilin' Gordie was a fisherman. He loved to sing.
Laughter to each moment did Gordie bring,
to everyone except himself...
His suicide lays on a shelf... in the big, red barn down the bay.

At a quater to ten the Mission bell rings
Callin' all its followers to count their blessings.

Townfolk celebrated their first "RAILROAD DAY."
Twelve bucks to Vancouver all the way.
Kids munched cotton-candy, local merchants showed their wares.
Oh, what a lovely day to go enjoy the country fair!

That's where life happens and where it ends,
Mission keeps on callin', life a long, lost friend.

Jumping off ole railway bridge is common-place these days,
Had three deaths this year, three more likely on the way.

That's where life happens and where it ends.
Mission keeps on calling like a long lost friend.
At a quater to ten, the Mission bell rings, callin' all its followers
to count their blessings

L. Richards

The Cavern

I was in a cavern; it was wet with stalactites and stalagmites
  everywhere.
It was quite a large cavern, with lots of room to move around,
But it was cool and very damp: the walls, the ceiling, the floor,
  the dripping and rivulets of water running down.
I was alone, and in semi darkness; the water the only sound.

Far above me I could see an opening; a light.
And a sheet of the light floated down and around to engulf me.
And I could feel, "Are you sure you are ready to go?"
My mind screamed and begged, "Yes! Yes! Please!"

But something interfered, I do not know what or why.
There was a pull from the opposite direction, as if on my coat tail,
And a feeling of discomfort from within.
The light began to retreat; the echoes of "You are not ready" left
  its trail.

But I can still see the opening at the top of the cavern.
Though small and high, it lets the light in, and the clean air, and
  lets me 'be'.
But it is there! I am not in complete darkness!
As a deep breath of air flows into my body to rejuvenate me.

Maria H. Groenen

Memories

Hundreds of blazing street lights, hundreds!
Exhausted, dragging its hem, snow stretches out on pines,
Changing faces, purple, blue dusk, immaculate pearl white.
Long wings clasp together in a green mirror, deeply, shattering glass,
Sinking down among yew tree branches, grown out of jasmine scent
Reigning there, before dry hydrangeas came, before maple trees went,
...Vanishing among trembling fingers, stuck to the arabesque of glass,
Each piece cleaving flesh down to the heart...
Wingless, the body of the swan fell to the ground.
(Yellow, rusty rags of velvet scattered all around).
Its quiet traces on the water weigh heavily within my soul.
Two-faced mirror, one of yesterday, one of today,
Who is the fairest in the world?
Yew trees bowed in the wind, beaks sipped weedy water.
We divided one heart into two: one for me, one for you,
Loving children of the world, learning the first lesson of paradise.
Then, the shadow called on us.
At the second lesson, we set Eden ablaze.
The third one, then...shattered glass, sinking wings, fall of the swan
Now...hundreds of blazing street lights, hundreds - the snow settles
   upon.

Eva Acqui

You Say My Love For You Is Not Real

Live the vile evil veil; reality as illusion.
Existential subsistence; depression, suffering, confusion.

Lotus Blossom sits in a pleased cool pool of blue.
I sit - waterside - admiring my reflection.
Lotus Blossom is beautiful they say.
I see me and I agree.

Pictures, two meanings display; words double entendre convey.
A desert mirage and a camouflage; to know, I play and replay.

Goddess of Humanity; couched in Lotus Blossom's thousand petals.
She strikes me blind, for I cannot look at her.
Goddess of Humanity is beautiful they say.
I cannot see and I agree

Peace, purity and I are lost; lies to self and therefore others.
My sculpture of life turns to sand; I no longer call men brothers.

You look at me and you see me. Odd, queer, and queerer;
I look at you and see myself - between us a one-way mirror.
dedicated to Dr. I. Elizabeth Solyom

Laurie Moran

It Was Black As Pitch

The tears followed the raindrops freely down her face,
Falling and melting into the ground.
Slowly she crossed the green, uncertain why she had come.
That magical night, half a century past, still remembered - in her
   mind alone.
They had agreed on that night that they would return;
To remember, to reflect, to relive.
Alone, she shivered in the darkness, trying to forget her solitude.
Touching the band which she refused to surrender, she remembered;
The beauty of the day, the excitement, the love,
And she could see herself, the white of her gown, the gleam in her eyes.
He stood before her, face glowing and ever so dapper,
"I do", he had told her, "and I always will!"
The roll of thunder relayed her to the present,
She stood alone, tears acknowledging her solitude.
Looking toward the clouds, she allowed the rain to wash the age from her face.
Feeling a damp chill, she realized that her reunion with time was ended.
"I do", she whispered with a slow smile, "and I always will."
Turning to retreat from the wrath of the clouds,
A sudden flash of lightning froze the moment in time,
And there, in the light before her, he stood.

Alexandra Dillon

Reciprocated Weather, Nurturing Bodies

When I ponder into your eyes I see endless summer suns rippling and
   glowing off gently deep waters
I rest and let be shone upon while your eyes
   evaporate up ideas to breeze
I will move my plates with slow persistent passion for you
   till you crest my shores with silky storm sounds.
Rest your head upon my chest so I can feel your waves of
   weather crash
upon my heart's mind and rinse my filthy pronged fjords.
Let your thoughts coagulate like chords of mystic wisdom,
   mix to pure crystallized perfection, and snow down in white
   wordliness to freeze in perpetual snow capped resonance
   my burning mind and body.
Let the snow melt from my mountains, thawing my sense of touch
   with yours, streaming tearing off my shoulder, fresh and exhilarating.
Whisper up clouds of sentiments and emotions to glide
   smoothly over your mouth.
Touch your lips to my neck and breathe deep
Gust words down my chin to fall in the craters of my eyes and ears.
Rain down on my dry barren fields to fill my lakes so I can slake
   my reproachful thirst.
Water trees and lively concepts with your worldly torrent of weather.
Whisper over my burning prairie chest so I will hear
   for no cloud brings bad weather when you are forecasted for me.
You are beautiful wisdom so when you talk, I will listen

David J. Wittman

Wordsmith

Wordsmith, whose couplets link with ease
graciously answering without reply

each motion of your instrument is cool precision -
with every jot and tittle

nothing is amiss no movement want for waste
how I wish to emulate you from my very marrow

you carve and sculpt your wood the word whittling away a tune
poetic verse you versify, poetic poetizer

your limericks glisten off envying poetasters' eyes
whose sonnetized disasters render them mere rhymers

I watch your essence rise and linger off the page
guiltily despising, me wishing you were I

for the coveted joy of your effortless abandon this soul will surely
wait to pierce the unknown unbroken barriers -

where unimpeached hides thy weighted word
and cloaked mysteries spring alive unveiled in your revelations

I struggle to compare amidst such utter shame
scribing my superfluous vanities I try to define sublime

while thereabouts in nowhere where somewhere the light shines
the Worthsmith works with his wood the word whittling away a tune

Robert Clark

Love

On a moon kissed evening when the earth was bathed in it's rays
I search for my image in your eye
Since you carried me wedged inside your eyes
The night was spent floating in a dream
At that moment speaking of magic of love in the world
It struck me, a love poem has never been written to worth while

Today as my middle aged life stretches sorrowfully
My eyes has been flung so far from yours
Seeking our images you soak your-self in liquor
Neglected I keep vigil on this dream-less night
Poetry, songs and dramas of the world ringing of the magic of love
Dawns on me now they are so much greater than love

Monica Ruwanpathirana

Except Time

Time... Endless, dreamlike and ever-living.
Hard and rugged with the knowledge of a thousand wise men.
Meaningless, yet purposeful.
Thrown into a reluctant journey, an adventure of relentless pace.
Time sees all crimes, ghastly, disastrously horrific and twisted.
It has experienced all atrocities.
Time has conquered the strongest fortresses,
it has loved beyond love and slept with the devil.
It has beaten all the records,
been on the forefront of discovery,
and ended the lives of countless souls.
Joy, fantasy, a flood of ecstatic excitement and happiness.
Time has cried and laughed, screamed in pain,
wallowed in endless self pity,
and bathed in an ocean of dreams.
It has deserted no one. Time tells all.
It is a universal voice,
the speaker for generation upon generation
of tiny insignificant creatures.
Damned to roam the earth, forgotten for an eternity.

Warren Mayes

Eye Of The Storm

They eyes of the oncoming storm, howling by the taint little
house. "I am the wind, for I am the storm, let me in, let me in
or I shall do more!"

I shuddered at the fact, but my ears did hear so, "could this
voice be for real?" "or is it a voice I do not know?"

Let me close the curtains and lock all the doors, turn off the
lights or my destiny soars.

The wind crept upon my taint little house. "Have mercy on me,"
I begged for I own no more.

Then suddenly with no indication, it all stopped. The wind
had listened. I peeked through my curtains, the sky appeared bright.

My heart stopped trumping for I realized everything would be
all right.

Reatha M. Freeman

Loneliness

Do you know how lonely I get in the Winter days?
How cold I get sitting at home in my dark old house.
I open my mouth to speak, but then I remember that no one's there.
I hear a noise.
Then realize it is only the swaying of the trees and the heavy
    downpour of the rain.
Now it is getting dark out, so I reach over to turn on the lights,
but the electricity is not working.
I reach over for the phone, but there is no dial tone.
I walk over and light a few candles.
I stare for hours at the burning light.
My vision gets blurred, and I think of you and the times we shared.
At this moment you would sit and comfort me.
Now I sit all alone, huddled in a ball staring with bewildered eyes
    and frustration,
wondering where you might be.
I lay down and stare at the blank walls.
I remember that I will always be alone.
The loneliness, is the thing that frightens me the most.

Bonnie Stringer

A Night Goddess

I am shimmering lavender, silvery in the moonlight.
I am gentle, pastel soft; edged in metallic, sharp and
    strong.
I am very feminine - like lilac flowers,
I feel spiritual and mysterious; I touch like pastel pink, blue and
    purple.
I am a tone not a shade - I am not a forceful primary color.
In tone, I'm sweetly pale mixed with silvery white.
I'm seen in ocean waves touched by the sinking sun.
I am not common and I am exquisitely beautiful.
I am the highlight on a dress, the edge on a shawl, and in my dream
    an entire ao dai in lilac silk.
My color is seen on snow kissed mountain's twilight hour,
    inaccessible and rare.
In gardens with a fragile scent the lavender blue, silvery purple can
    be felt, delicate and cool.

Jacqueline A. Colquhoun

Journey

I hear the voices in the wind, that seem to call me
I hear the echoes of a long forgotten time
I hear the music, I must follow, yet no one else seems to hear
I feel a beauty so beyond us
I feel a life that's not from here
I grasp a reality of being, that my brothers did not share
I hear the chants of distant meaning, of a time so long forgotten
Of a world peaceful beauty and of everlasting love
Take my hand so you may follow
Touch my mind so you may hear
Close your eyes so you may see
For my world is not of here
Walk through the door I open
Take the path I guide
Hear the song I sing, just for you in a special way
Rest with me within my Garden
Feel the peace, within your mind
If only for a moment
Take the journey through my mind

Jim Conrad

My Lovely Habit

When I wake up each morning before I get out of bed,
I think of all the funny things inside my sleepy head,
I go to work each morning, I hold my head up high,
I am so bright and cheerful to everyone who passes by.

I've got this lovely habit of whistling through the day,
It makes me really happy and helps me on my way,
I probably get on people's nerves but, it doesn't bother me,
The only time I'm quiet is when I stop for tea.

It's very windy where I work, everywhere I go,
My friends would think there is something wrong, if they didn't
hear me blow,
I can whistle any tune, when I buff the floor,
I'll blow them all to kingdom come then I shall blow no more.

Frances Llewellyn

Life

Life is like a black hole.
It is dark and scary.
You can fall deeper and deeper and there
Is no one to catch you.

You fall deeper and deeper until you don't wake up.
You can fall and fall until someone catches you,
Or fall and fall without ever stopping, never ending just falling.
In the black hole of life there is no love and no friends to guide you!

Bettina Baker

A Piece Peace Of My Heart

As I travelled in to meet you, and the road curved back and forth;
I thought of how life's twist and turns had happened to us both.
Years ago, I closed a door for a child, that could not be.
I never dreamed the curve in life would bring you back to me.

Then, I though, as I sped along; there was so little time.
You could not know, that in giving you up, was really a gift of mine.
A piece of my heart, and empty arms, and moments lost for good,
Prayed that someone would love and treasure you, as I wished that I
  could.

Arriving in the parking lot, and walking to the door,
I breathed a sigh of anticipation for what was in store,
But, the moment that I saw you, I felt all my love explode.
It was as if I never "lost" you, as I watched the years erode.

Oh what joy! You're giving me, in knowing you each day.
The pain of loss has disappeared; replaced by you to stay.
A peace, and overwhelming love, wells up in me; in fact,
Because I know now, what it's like, to have a daughter back.

Lee Anne Lansi

The Spider

I am but a tiny spider weaving this web of mine.
I wait in silence, not moving, slowly does pass the time.
As I sit and watch my work of art, spread from branch to branch.
My eyes droop heavy as my mind falls into a trance.
I must concentrate though, for my prey is soon to be here.
Entangled in my delicate creation overcome with fear.
Their wings and legs tearing as they struggle to break free.
Perhaps it will be a fly, a beetle, a mosquito or even a bee.
Then I will come forth from my perch
and wrap them in my fine silk thread.
To dine at my leisure, then I will repair my web.
The fight will have left me weary, my energy almost spent.
And life will continue, as was nature's intent.

Naomi Ivanic

Our World

Spinning on its axis slowly round and round
In the beginning it was perfection
It was rare and quite unique
There for all of us to use what a treasure to be found

It gave to us the air we breath the water that we drink
the soil to grow so many crops for the food we eat each day
It cared for us though all season in a very special way.

So why have we in our carelessness taken more than we should need
We have destroyed such beauty with our lustfulness and greed
We cared not for those to come in later years as we planted human seed.

Oh mighty Creature I stand before you and say
Forgive us of our ignorance give us one more chance to mend our ways
Let us save our one and only world
for yet another day.

Ruby Jenkins

The Anniversary

He sent her flowers for their anniversary,
Red carnations and golden somethings
Prettily tied up in cellophane
Silently thanking her for all the pain of years,
And all the tears she inflicted upon herself and him.
The sham facade enlightened by the way they sat at dinner
Glowering at each other across the flower filled, candle lit table.
Between sickly sweet smiles the hate rippled and gurgled.
Don't send me flowers unless, to you I have been all things.
No hate, no tears or bitterness.
For even a bluebell from the garden would be a travesty.
Better to have no flowers, but the flower of love.

Jean Moyra Layden

Censors Ode

Jungle storm lions breath, bird of prey cries in nest
Inky blackness erie gloom, death does rise from black lagoon
Fear and nausea, desperation and pain, a lowly pawn in an evil game
Baying wolf banshee's wail, bedtime story spinsters tale
Evil lurks in minds of men when artists pallet threatens them
Mortal fear immortal prey, imagination lives this way
Righteous souls and bleeding hearts, nuns habit preachers march
Barred soul heaving breast, moral sins God's test
Faccist weapon commy torch, protectant mother deadly force
Evil lurks in minds of men when artists pallet threatens them
Canvas and paint or pad and ink, celluloid derision lyrical wink
Pictures that move words that speak, music that talks minds that think
Wonderous images stories that scare, naked bodies length of hair
The poet, the thinker, the candlestick maker lutist perverse, actor faker
Evil lurks in minds of men when artists pallet threatens them
Light the torches build the fire, monsters death funeral pyre
Flames ignite the prisoners doom, books will burn flames consume
Sentence passed courts adjourn, verdict stands with God you learn
In Christ's name you will fear not, a heretic with an evil thought
Evil lurks in minds of men when artists pallet threatens them

David Kinsman

Friendship

It is the love that is shared between friends.
It is something that will continue through the years.
And be an everlasting friendship.

It is something that can very easily be tossed to the winds.
Friendship is visiting people that may be sick or disabled.
Showing you care about them.

Some friendships are very special.. .
Friendship between parents and children are important.
Friendship can open many doors that otherwise may stay closed.
Friendship is needed in every day of our lives, in work or play.
Friendship helps people live in harmony with one another.
Friendship is being a good listener when a friend needs to share
  something.
Friendship is making a new neighbor feel welcome.
Friendship is extending your hand as you welcome people into your home
  or church,
Friendship is showing love and understanding in times of trouble and
  adversities.

Friendship is getting together with friends.
Friendship is offering to babysit for a friend.

Friendship is something that cannot be bought.
Friendship carries no price tag.
Friendship is free; the most wonderful thing in the world.

Beverly F. Bradley

Christmas Treasures

The snow is piled upon our roofs, and deep along our paths
It's beauty sparkles everywhere, like pieces of broken glass.
Amidst the cold, the wind and snow, a little star does shine
To remind us one and all once more, "It's truly Christmas time."

A time when loved ones gather, in peace and love and joy
To celebrate that special birth, God's only son, a Boy!
Sent to this earth in human form, to die upon a cross
For our salvation, yours and mine, he truly paid the cost.

This gift so freely given, ours to receive
If we just humbly ask, and truly do believe.
May you share this Christmas story to all you may hold dear
That they might bask in peace and joy, not doubt nor loss nor fear.

My wish for you this Christmas time and yes the whole year through
That the peace and love the Christ-child brings t'would be alive in you.
Perhaps one day around the world, we'll hold each other's hand
And God's amazing loving grace, will spread across the land.

Marian Sarafinchan

The Limerick

The limerick's a terrible verse
Its humor is droll, but what's worse
Is trying to create
These poems that I hate
'Cuz the last line always has to be something cute that rhymes
with the first two lines and still keeps the stupid meter steady

The last line creates the dilemma
Without it there'd be no problema
And so I propose
For this type of prose
To eliminate the last line because it's a pain in the neck, and
besides, it sounds silly to have a type of poem with five lines in
each stanza anyway

Glenn McFarlane

Autumn For An Artist

When we see it's autumn and the leaves are burnished gold
It's time to get the oil paints out, all artistry enfold.
The foliage, curled and aged forms a carpet for our tread;
No more to sway in greenery, they're golden, tanned and red.

In spring they had their debut when shooting forth so new,
In summer they were fresh and green and with the breezes blew.
But, seeing nature's shedding is bliss to the artist's eye
A vision full of color and with skill he can apply.

From tubes of paint to canvas he works there full of hope
As dying leaves enshroud him, his love's in every stroke.
A picture then emerges of stately trees laid bare
Beneath the golden yellow sky, it's beauty all can share.

A feeling of tranquility invades and fills the mind
When plying paint to capture the scene he'll leave behind.
But, now he sees the sun go down and precious light ne'er stay
So time to pack and leave this place
At the close of an artist's day....

Patricia McGowan

Valdez (12:04 A.M.)

March 24th, the best equipped tanker in Exxon's fleet
Leaving Valdez for Long Beach, 5 days and a catastrophe away
Prince William Sounds and the Bligh Reef to meet
Unexpectedly, yet predictably, lurking amidst the fray.

Glacial iceflow into the Sound, 987 foot tanker
1 million 200 thousand barrels of North Slope crude.
Captain Hazlewood's orders have been strictly anchored.
Remember the plan of reaction, forget the front of being shrewd.

The ocean set up blindly on a date rape
Bergs in the dark, a drunken walk in the park
Oversight influenced ill fate
The hull, the reef, the blasphemous bark.

Ten million gallons, nothing corresponding with oceans
26oz. of vodka mean little to marine birds.
alaska wilderness bleeds a cringed security notion
To think it would never occur seems the most absurd.

Below the surface there's little room for mistake
Little wonder why veins never bleed clear
After the fact is too late to remonstrate
"Well I guess it's one way to end your career."

Mike A. McLean

At Home On Clover Point

The sea, furious and grey
licks the shoreline and my feet
staring into nothing, and everything, the sky
meets the liquid life, no distinction between the two is found

Heavy haze lifts slowly from the surface, hanging,
suspended like clouds atop its own unique sky
a lonely beacon post stands, not yet consumed by the waves
or the ever approaching shroud

The cliff sides are bruised, scarred, by years of this
ritualistic abuse
carved and created, they take shape, one not yet complete
but forever being developed, molded

The bush and trees that sit along the edge
are in a permanent bow, bent by the power, the incoming rush
the occasional one will fall, torn from its home
for no other reason than it became to fragile to fight

It did not ask to receive the torture
it merely did the best it could, to hold on
to withstand the blows, the fear, the pain
but sometimes that just isn't enough.

Eddy Piasentin

The Victims

Body and soul defiled, hours-on-end, through hours unended;
living through it all reviled, as if they condescended.

Women strike with emotion, verbally hurtful at best,
as cowardly men in motion behind closed doors and a fist,
attack the young molested in their tiny virgin state;
their innocence divested, as are others badly raped.

Each shameful act disdainful; resentment no salvation,
from loathesome ploys and painful blows, all ending in damnation.

.........TERROR..........TRAUMA....
................UNDEFENDED.......
.........BEATEN...BROKEN...TORN...
................UNMENDED........

And submitted to the wrath
of terrible attractions,
silent, in the aftermath
of bludgeoning reactions;

Abandoned victims prone
to invisible abuses;
sadly feeling left alone,
enveloped in the bruises.

Martin Crew-Gee

"Ode To Earth Mother"

Once, belonging only as an Avatar, still
strands of starlight found me longing yet for cradled
Hands of Shepherd tenderness to soothe my Pilgrim
Brow, that Eyes could meet, behold each moonstretched fireflung
Prayer, embrace the mist strung Legacy which Spring
Bestows, lips could whisper petalled themes of Prismed
Heights, their Harvest Rays impassioning arms to crush my
hunger, filling need for need, like wine in crimson
Wonder. Then, Saintly Shrouded in the Altared Husk, we
would Reflect in mirrored Reverence, Seas of the Sage from
Elysium, Cathedral pebbles pearled by the Hymns from the Tides of
Grace. Our Homage holds the Polar Gold of Light
Meridianed, to guide the rhythms of the Lanterned Night
such Chords of Glory weave transcending Tapestries
of Guardian Souls within, unfolding Seasonal Galaxies.

Ann Creer

To You

Love is forever love is a dream
Love is something I can now see
Beneath the moon beneath the stars
Love is something that can now be ours
The caring, the sharing the saying I do
Have made it all possible my dreams come true.
Your hair, your eyes, your touch, your feel
Have somehow made it seem all real
You're the one the one to say "Come on girl!
Don't let them bring you down
Don't let them stand in your way
Together we shall make your stand side by side, and hand in hand"

You sit me down. You comfort me
You listen to all my hopes and dreams

We share a bond so deep inside now we both know love never dies

So when I walk down the isle to you
I only hope your dreams will come true

And when I look into your eyes
Please believe I'll never lie because with these words
I say to thee I truly love you to you love me

> *Deann Marie Simard*

The Best Part Of Christmas

The smell of roasting turkey, mixed with spices, fills the air,
Love ones home from far away, and friends that come to share.
All these things are part of Christmas. That is very true.
But, the best part of Christmas is you.

Many things make Christmas bright, like sleigh bells in the snow,
Choirs out singing Christmas carols, and shoppers on the go.
All these things make Christmas merry, like a gift or two.
But the best part of Christmas is you.

You make the Christmas shopping list, and decorate the tree,
Then cook a meal fit for a king, that every eye should see.
And so I take this time my dear, to state my point of view.
That the best part of Christmas is you.

Christmas is a rosy fire, 'neath stockings hung with care,
Santa Claus, and Mistletoe, and Holly everywhere.
If you weren't here to share these things, I don't know what I'd do.
'Cause the best part of Christmas is you.
To My Wife Natalia

> *Ronald D. Cotton*

Her Hands Were Hills

I was born in an ocean.
My mothers belly was thick and warm.
I immediately reached for her long piano fingers.
Her hands were hills. Damp.
Smell of hay is so sweet.
Her belly was my ocean, it was warm and thick
and I was well fed.

I immediately reached for her hands. Her hands were hills.
Long drawn out landscape with tired eyes.
I stretched out her skin. I pushed my way out. It was too cold.
I immediately reached.
Her hands were hills.
Thin blue valleys of river flowed
over her paler than cream skin.

It was more than damp.
My ocean is my memory. Drink to the bottom.
The salt is sweeter than a spring.
My ocean is vast and fresh with dew.
I will not drown. I will swim.
I will breathe.

> *Kim Dawn*

The Cattle-Shed At Bethlehem On Christmas Day

("The Cattle Are lowing, the babe awakes...")

Old Cow: You did hear Mary say to Joe again...
Old Bull: Yes, that the child was born without a pain.
Black Cow: My calf as well is strange. My third right here
           Unlike before, was popped and not a paining.
Young Cow: Come off, you Bull, less haste. I want to hear
           What 'tis the shepherd's saying. Angels singing?
The Bull: Hold on, the moment now is ripe my dear.
           Don't move away. You shan't be virgin longer.
The Calf: I'm hungry Ma, I want my milk o'mother!
           Remember me and Him were born tonight.
Castrated Bull: I now don't mind if they may slaughter me
           For now, what more than this is there to see?
           Behold, my sight is bless'd with angels bright!
           Let them enjoy and eat my flesh outright.

> *Gerald M. M. Matovu*

Home To Stay

I could write a song about love and what it means to me
or I could tell you about the strength I draw from family
but ask me how I feel right now and I wouldn't know what to say
its the day my baby child came home to stay

He looks at me with bright blue eyes, he seems to know my face
He's got my father's features, he's got his mother's grace

He reaches out his little arms as though he's trying to say
that he knows today is a very special day

I will try to be all that I can be now that I'm living for this
treasure in my arms
and now I know how to live and laugh and grow and I learned it all
from the smile my newborn son

His grandfather carved an angel to watch over him from above
while his mother rocks him in her arms with tenderness and love
I'm watching every moment trying hard to make them stay
for I know in an instant that he'll grow up and move away

Now the lights are dim in the nursery and I'll rock my son to sleep
when he finally closes his little eyes I'll pray the Lord his soul to keep
I know my life has changed today in oh so many ways
on this day my baby child came home to stay

I know my life has been blessed today in so many wonderful ways
on this day my newborn son came home to stay

> *Kevin Toone*

The Reward

What a disappointment, to find when day is done,
    That the whole day went without a deed of kindness being done.
With all those opportunities to lend a helping hand,
    Or even give a cheery note to one who's feeling bland.

I could have even called someone upon the telephone,
    And asked them how they fared today, while spending it alone.
I could have had my neighbor in to watch the TV show,
    Because they haven't got the funds to get their own, you know.

And at the "Home for Aged" there are people rich and poor,
    Who'd love to spend the day "outside" with a kindly visitor
Who'd take them to the Park to watch the children playing games,
    And feed the birds and squirrels and give them all a proper name.

Alas for me! I was so wrapped up in my own affairs
    Of washing clothes and making cakes and dusting down the stairs,
I hadn't thought of those who are less fortunate than I,
    Whose wish is for some pleasant days before "night" passes by.

I swear, tomorrow I will do a deed of kindliness.
    I'll wear a smile and chat a while with new made friends, I guess.
Oh thank you Lord, for helping me and showing me the way
    Of making life rewarding with a Good Deed every day.

> *Chris Ross*

Moratorium

On this small culture island, they call "the rock"... many fisherman,
pains to walk, from a shaker style house, he calls his home, to the
shoreline of a friend, he thought his own. Now not long ago, not long
in the past,...cod stocks were plenty and plenty nets cast... from
small floating boats, which blemished her skin, cradled her body, and
churned her within. Up in the morning, way before dawn, the kettle
was boiling, the curtains were drawn... out through the window, his
small eyes could see, a friend in the ocean - calling "come, play with me."
His small boat lay resting, his net graced her side, handmade precisely,
with precision and pride... When out through the narrows, she declared
her devotion, her small engine churned with a putter of motion.
 Harbour lights - with bright eyes and voice that moaned, a portal
for man of grave face, and hands of brimstone... for 500 years his
fathers before him and he lay their claim, to a life of hardship,
sorrow and pain. Now with the err of man, and man-made machine,her
harvest fatigued, and the loss of her dream... to cradle wooden
playmates, she tossed and carried, lay abandoned on her shoreline,
tattered and dreary. Oh, Fisherman, Fisherman, take your nets from
the sea, what once was your bounty is now misery... what could you
have been, with a change of the wind, oh fisherman, poor fisherman.

   Cora C. Gallant

Quiet Lake

When seated by a quiet lake, a thought occurred to me.
Praised be the Creator, of this beautiful lake and trees.
And then it seemed in answer, to this thought profound,
That all surrounding nature gave off with a sound.
First, it was the whispering leaves and branches of the trees,
Gently swaying in harmony with the softly blowing breeze.
The trees, they stood with branches raised like arms towards the sky,
As if waving to the sun, or clouds, that happened by.
And then my attention was focused on another sort of noise,
A blue-Jay sat upon a branch, he looked so proud, so poised,
He was dressed up in such finery, all blue, black, and white,
His beauty was breath-taking, he truly was a sight.
he chattered and chirped for all he was worth,
He sang with all his might.
And joining in were other birds, blending in their songs so bright,
Till it seemed to be a symphony, of sound, song, and sight,
Which filled my soul, and lifted me, to raise my voice in chorus,
Thanking my Creator, for the lake, the birds, and forest.

   David Scott

Moments Past

I remember the tears that came to my eyes
Seeing you lying there,
Crying and screaming at the same time
As I cuddled you

It felt like nothing that I had ever experienced
As I held you in my arms,
It felt so right to have you there
I stared into those eyes looking for some sort of recognition

You slowly stopped squirming, then settled in against my chest,
I was sure you could hear my heart pounding
As I slowly brought you closer to my face,
Your mouth seemed to open for that first kiss

As I look back at these moments,
The tears still come to my eyes
You are the life's breath, of my own self
You are my child

   Leonard G. Familton

The Dilemma

Think you I should act GOD and give a quick release?
Should I let GOD take over but give her mind no peace?
Thou shalt not kill is GOD's law but is it just the same
As letting life depart with ease and freedom from all pain?
When the body is in agony and pain has no relief
Should not cure be death itself and the span of suffering brief?
Whether death comes from man's wicked works or illness
   sounds the knell,
Is pain to be a penance? It's still a taste of hell!
So where oh where is the line drawn when pain and death combine?
Should not death be swift and sure and dignified and kind?
GOD give you strength to make the choice if ever you are pressed,
For rights and wrongs of good intent can never be assessed,
If life is kept unasked for, through pain and tortured breath,
You're not prolonging life my friend, you are prolonging death!

   Lewis Mackie

Today's Life Like Is Going

Oh! Our life has many pains,
So many problems bring us to a bitter end.
We are crying at our place, and nobody can come to our help.
Where are you friendly society?
Our life takes after a ship, which want to capsize.
We are crying at our place, and nobody can come to our help.
Why do we abandon our brothers whom suffering from AIDS?
Why do we let our yougoslavia brothers killing among themselves?
We are crying at our place, and nobody can come to our help.
Let us make haste! To assist our brothers who are in bad situations.
And let us shout for universal peace, so that the war get
   a stop in the world.
We are crying at our place, and nobody can come to our help.
That domestic worries finish all along the Earth.
That enemy shake hands.
That segregation disappear in this world, in order that
   calm and love prevails.
We are crying at our place, and nobody can come to our help.

   Mafolo-Nkulu

Epitaph For A Lover

slip and slide, a cigarette bitten
tattered hand, it's hard to walk
with braces and laces, bondage
two same feet stepping
towards the edge, a one-time eternity.

tumble and roar, hear the water
between my teeth, white equine eyes eclipsing
the moon, side stepping, sliding like a small rock from very high up.

a midnight pegasus
soft shadow lunar forgettings
feathered fingers tearing torn air, falling
the engine idles, splutters, then dies.

"It's time" he said, me laying crushed, flailing
octopus arms scrambling for contact
cut by rough edges and still falling
expecting the salty swallow like a ribbon.

but not instead iron to the mouth
cold spoons and cleats
bent carefully, lovingly fitted, and landed
one foot amputated, small shoe sinks beneath the waves.

   Anita Slater

The Desert Storm

The swirling sands will cover the path
That has been trod this day
The sculpted dunes hum saddened tunes
As the viper devours its prey
The grains of sand roll with the winds as they are swept out to sea
And as they are sinking seem to be thinking
Why me, why me, why me?
The boundless dunes quietly shift their forms creating desert ghosts
That seem to be calling eerily
While capturing their wandering hosts
If you discover the Shangri La where the sunlight horizons abound
And the desolate murmur is heard on the wind
And formidable nomads are found
If you hear voices hauntingly call on the winds that tap your face
And visions float by in a wink of an eye
Of indigo and fine lace
And when the skies darken all around
And the shadows of camels pass by
Grab on to their tails while they wind their way
Lest the grains of sand blind your eye

Ellen Hopkins

Waking Up To Vietnam

Waking up. In the first light. Good. Morning. Morning dawns.
The clock yawns. The street trembles. In sun rising traffic's din.
Steel beams of glowworms in motion. Flood the cracked concrete.
Veins fill up with a streetbeat. Aorta chokes in the overflow.
Smog bites! Memory stroke! Surveillance camera watches.
Intersections of quicksilver. Fire tide runs through the rifts.
Infrared detector interrogates. The rolling coaster of feelings.
For eventual hospitalization. Resuscitation of hope fails.
Wobbling pedestrian stumbles on the fast walkway. Defeated.
Dazed and confused! Morning!! Good morning!!! Vietnam!!!!!

Juliusz Zajaczkowski

Where Love Grows, Courage Flows

What is courage but a humble heart.
That never questions where to start.
An unselfish act without the merriest thought.
With threatening dangers that have been forgot.
The heroes I know come from selfless acts
Yet to others have life changing impact
We meet them in every walk of life, usually having been through
   their own share of strife
Our mission in life seems to start out slow, but the angels among
   us always know where to go
A special spirit was sent to earth, with a special mission of love.
When He enters a room you feel a presence from above.
He is a man, a friend, a son, a brother and a father.
He only thinks of others feelings and with His own
He does not bother.
My brother Chuck is that symbol of love where courage overflows.
He seems to never question what comes, but excepts that God knows.
Never questioning His illness faithfully moving along, though each
   stage takes its toll.
And the love that people feel when their near Him is real unknowingly
   healing there soul.
Unless a miracle comes along His life left with us, will not be long.
But His mission of love will carry on until the light of life has gone.
Then once again He will be in Gods arms cause you see, that is always
   where He belonged.
But His love is here to stay, we will share it along the ways as His
   courage lives on and on!

Marcella Leasok

My Son

Baby Boy of blue and red, of pink and white and grey
That's how you looked to me my son, on that very first day.

You slipped into this world, my son, of giant imperfections,
But always turn to me sweet boy, when you need affection.

You slipped into my arms so warm where I'll hold you tight and never,
Let you go 'cause in my heart you'll remain my son forever.

Tears of joy not sorrow, were shed for you my love.
Always remember I'll be here for you, like a guardian angel above.

When God planted this seed in me, in my body so young.
He must have known how it would feel to love you and call you my son.

Always remember, my darling son,
my love is here to stay
It all began late that night and it'll never go away.
So when you're all grown up, my dear
and have a son of your own.
You'll realize what I mean by this and my feelings will be known.

But even when you're grown sweet boy,
my son you'll always be,
For there is no greater love my son,
as the love I feel for thee.

Karen Sheard

The Firmament

Nights black as black can be, blaze forth for those with souls to see.
The city, far remote, is but a glow-worn seen afar but dim.
Its absence brings to life the dark of uncontaminated sky.
Whence came these pricks of light that tell of galaxies unknown
That smash imagination's bonds and free unfettered thought to soar
Star-trecking through the void.
Where fancy leads can dreams be far behind?
But gaze in wonder at these beckoning lights
And lead the race 'cross stepping stones of stars.
Let mind go boldly now where none has gone before.
Each voyage unique to who would dare to go.
Where fancy leads reality will follow soon and riding chariots of fire
Man picks his way across the firmament
And spreads God knows not what 'cross hitherto unsullied space.
Praise God our thoughts may pass the speed of light
But bodies here by mass are held.
Until, please God, morality outpaces greed
And we no longer foul what gives us life.

Malcolm Kelly

The Return

He walked along the back roads, on tired, aching feet,
The late summer sun low in the sky, and pale;
Close to the hedgerows in fear of those he'd meet,
Who may wish him harm, or throw him in jail.

Sinking behind the crest, its warmth gone with the light
The sun's exodus paints the clouds purple and blood red.
A chill runs through him, facing another long night
With the same dreaded question, will he find a bed.

The wandering lane makes way for a town. What a welcome sight!
But the people stare and point and shout "Get out, get out o'here!"
Compassion is forgotten, for they are full of fear and fright
At this shuffling old man, his eyes filled with briny tears.

Head bowed low, he leaves in disgrace. What has he done?
He couldn't fathom this place! "Worse than a stray dog I'm treated"
He sighed, "in the town of my youth, once home, sweet, sweet home!"
But no-one remembers, and nobody cares. He leaves, again defeated!

"Don't go!" called the voice, as he stumbled down the lane.
"Here's a room, with warm blankets, a shower and hot food!"
He turned.....They found him next day, laying out in the rain,
A look of serenity that none could explain, but dead, just the same!

Kathleen M. Hall

A Falling Autumn Leaf

It was past one on a grey cloudy night.
The howling wind rustled the crisp autumn leaves.
Its icy cold gust penetrated my soul eventually dying to whispers.
Nearby, I could hear the low murmurs of a pair of warm embraced
    lovers.
Under the soft light of a street lamp I was studying DNA, the genetic
    blueprint,
Wondering why I hadn't inherited the Einstein genes.
Again, my mind was on medical school as the drowned Score broke my
    heart.
I wanted to ask the trees, the clouds, and the mountains,
Why has my LORD forsaken me?
What have I done wrong to incur this suffering?
As a young passionate geneticist, I dreamed of discovery and healing
    the sick.
Now, my life faded like the falling brown leaf,
Torn asunder by the wind of competition,
Landing on the cold pavement to be crushed by the pace of society.
Would my brown leaf ever green again?
All the hard work... all the sacrifice...
It was for nothing... nothing at all...

   M. Waleed Khan

Susan: My Daughter

Sunrise brought your departing smile and through my tears
The sunlit haze revealed you were no longer mine.
Your tiny sweetness lingered; on this day not so fine,
Unaware of my sadness and emotional fears,
Waiting for time to heal the emptiness over the years.
Only once, the cloud lifted and our meeting enabled my sun to shine.
Togetherness gave strength that I would become thine.
Distance played havoc as you grew with your peers.
Would you ever be mine to cherish and hold?
Your sweetness and charm blossomed; but my love would you forsake?
Triumphs and hurts enveloped you, yet my influence was not to mold!
Independence and defiance merged as you realized there were decisions to make:
Your enchanting beauty and realization of life invited me in from the cold.
Serenely our hearts joined and lovely daughter no more will they break.

   Allan J. Wearmouth

"My Little Room"

   All my life I have lived in this little room
There is no door; just a window.
I'm all alone in this little room
I would press my face against the window and
Wonder why I couldn't to go out and play.
There was no door to go out; the room was dark.
   Then one day my room was shattered
The walls all fell down. I sat around huddled in the rubble,
Trying to hide, trying desperately to put my room back together. I couldn't
   My room is now back together.
My room now has a door, an open door.
It took me a very long time to get into the doorway of my little room.
I have stood in the doorway of my little room looking at the world.
I have ran back into the safety of my little room and hid in a corner.
But the door remains open; ready for me, patiently for me.
   I have ventured a few steps away from my little room.
I have sampled the world.
I venture further away from my little room ...
And I have run back for security.
   I don't need my little room so often now.

   Mona Bruce

Waiting At The "Doc's"

   I went in with high hopes to see "Old Doc", and get the pill.
There were all strangers there looking like me, over the hill.
Across the way, sat a gal with unkempt straggly brown hair,
She kept scratching her crotch, hoping no one would look or stare.
Beside the gal with the scraggly hair, was a man with a battered
face, dressed in the best of attire.
His hand was broken and talking to himself, referred to everyone as a liar.
Next to him a little gal with black hair tide in a bun, kept
groaning, I hoped she would not have her child there.
Between those groans she would look around and glare.
The next in line was a Miss dressed in pants so tight,
she could not bend or barely walk, what a sight.
In that seated line was a man who had not bathed, dirty socks,
   and smelly feet.
That odor almost knocked me off my feet.
My "God, Doc", I only wanted the pill.
Sitting here has made me ill, we all will die but never know when
Home I shall go and forget my friend, "The Doc", and sit and
   read my book all about the wily wren.

   L. Evans

Letting God

Hanging on to yesterday is an easy thing to do,
there will always be 'those memories'
so much a part of you.

And though many 'things' remind you of the pain you felt so real,
it's those very 'things' around you
that will help your wounds to heal.

So when you come across, an old familiar sorrow,
face the sadness and the pain
and you'll grow stronger for tomorrow.

Soon you'll come to realize, the pain you held so near,
no longer has a hold on you
for you've let of the fear.

It's when you realize this, that you'll also come to know,
that as your wounds are healing
it's a time for letting go.

So as you let go of the past, and build your life a new,
take each day as it comes....
....and do the best that you can do.

   Lisa Norris

Maryland In The Fall

The glorious trees spread all around as far as the eye can see
Thickly clothed in orange, yellow, red and mulberry
Through this Autumn wonderland the quiet road winds down
Picturesquely strewn with leaves by gentle breezes blown
Sunlight filters through the branches, warming with it's rays
Casting out the shadows from the darkened woodland ways
Overhead a flock of geese on leisured wing go by
Their noisy clamoring breaking the stillness of the sky
Countless squirrels dart about this quiet countryside
Always busy in their search for food and nuts to hide
Rushing rivers run their course in the journey to the sea
Whilst in the distance mountains reign in quiet majesty
A sense of peace pervades here mid verdant land and sky
A spiritual refreshment and I'm so glad that I
Was privileged to be a part and see these sights first hand
And never will forget that special time in Maryland

   Betty Janet Curnow

Your Beginning

It starts as baby... wonder, vulnerable, sweetness - hold
this young life so precious.

The growing for little angels - we are your caregivers to hold
you to ease the pain.
Life is for you, each breath is yours given with love.
your eyes at me with needing, wanting - oh, I want to
enclose your pain, keep it deep within my body of health.
A young child fighting this war of pain with no weapons.
You are such a tiny warrior fighting, fighting with such painful hope.
We are in this battle with you - fighting with you, fiercely, tenaciously.
This gift of life was given to you and it will not be given back easily.

Irene Willadsen

Innocence Past

To see through the eyes of yourself, as a child once more.
To cast your eyes upon the beauty you saw for the first time,
All those years ago.
Laying in the green grass, seeing so many different shapes in the
cottony, white clouds above.
Envisaging a dandelion, as the most beautiful of all flowers.
Picking a bouquet for a special loved one,
They were so pleased when you handed them your special gift.
When did the simplest pleasures leave the child, too become so lost
    in adulthood?
To the child - the one we left behind,
So carefree and looking at each new day as an adventure.
Awakening one day and realizing how cold and uncaring life really is.
Finding our little niche in the world, known as life.
We try to be caring and giving, and get nothing in return.
After a while, you learn to protect yourself and the child inside,
Who is looking out, with tears streaming down it's face.

Debbie Turnbull

Soul Reflection

I smell the sea wind in the air, the damp unfiltered mist;
Touch the earth and taste the dew on roses gently kissed;
I feel the morning cold with rain, wet sand beneath my feet;
And understand the peace within where heart and soul should meet.

Beyond the grey of rocky crags, and blue of highland skies,
A hunger drives me higher than the golden eagles flies;
Beyond the purple heather or the thistle or the clan,
A passion holds me stronger than the love of any man.

Here soars my spirit in a sphere of wilderness untamed,
And sees beyond its mortal death, a life and time unnamed,
Unlocks the key to distant realms, possesses all my past,
And calls me home, across the sea, to find its rest at last.

Salem Cross

My Friend

I wonder what it is, that keeps me by your side
When the thoughts that enter in my mind, are ones I have to hide
I wish that I could say the things that wallow in my mind
But if I did I'm sure I'd leave a friendship far behind
I just don't understand how I can feel the way I do
I wish I wanted someone else, I wish it wasn't you
But somehow you have taken down the shield I had on me
and now I float above the glass and watch in misery
What I mean is that I knew the outcome, from the very start
That there would never be a place for me within your heart
I don't mean for a friendship, no I hoped for more you see
Though deep inside I knew, that it was never meant to be
I hope you realize if you'd look, into my heart you'd know
The friend that I can only be, is trying hard to grow
I only hope you realize, what it is I am inside
For when you need a friend just look, and I'll be your side

Janice Sear.

Breaking The Silence

We on earth have but only one life, and hating will never win,
We have to break the silence, but where would one begin.
One could start by not passing judgment, based on the color of my skin
One could look a little deeper, to see what lies within.
One should not frown down on me, while looking at my face,
One should come to realize, there's good and bad in every race.
One should question of themselves, how race came to a thought,
One should try to ponder, from whom that it was taught.
One should ask, was it in my home, where my parents rule,
Was it at my local school, where kids can be so cruel.
Was it on the city streets, where I got my views,
Or was it from the T.V., reported on the news.
Wherever it did come from, you have to send it back,
You really don't have any right, to slander and attack.
Give me a chance to prove to you, that I can be a friend,
The only person I want judging me, is God, when I am at my end.
I am a part of your world, I am filled with pride,
I ask of you, but one thing, to set your prejudice aside.
When we all look up at a rainbow, we all marvel at the sight,
Colors blend together nicely, why can't red, yellow, black and white?

Kathy Wilson

Kinder, Gentler Times

Oh for the days of long ago - those Kinder Gentler times
When life was easy, life was slow, in Lazy Hazy climes
Unknown then the traffic tie ups, Hectic Days and crazy nights
Corporate climbing, wheeling dealing - journeys trains and airplane flights
Sometimes, sitting, meditating, my imaginations soars
Leaving briefly urban jungles - ending up on unknown shores
Where all is pleasant, so serene -
peaceful brook and rippling stream
Sailing, sailing far away - on a cloud of misty grey
Oh, for the days of long ago - I ponder, but indeed I know
That I must live in modern ways and dream in vain those bygone days.

Joyce Minard

Untitled

Embrace me you say, but I cannot.
Who are you to ask such a thing of me, at this time?
When the film of my arrogance has melted away,
And the delusion of being special has vanished,
Scrambling out the back door.

Embrace me you plead, but well you know I cannot.
We are rivals in a tiresome contest, or is it a battle?
Repeated through the years, often when others are fast asleep.
Those who managed to reclaim their souls,
Or are fortunate enough, to not know the difference.

Embrace me you command, but I cannot.
You have found me again, too easily.
Naked, exposed to your ritual haunting.
I am alone in your presence.
Can you smell the change in me?
I do not tremble (too much), I do not sob (out loud).
Still, it is not yet time to be all one, with you.

Leave me now, for I am weary
Of this nightly stalking.
And would shun your embrace, once again, for now.

Anna C. Bernardo

Untitled

The dawn approaches while the wind blows
    water drops from desert flowers.
We sit staring, you and I, fixed with steady intent.
Starry-eyed and glassy,
Waiting.

Bob Happenstance

The Mariner

He walked slower now this mariner,
Who had sailed through life weathering storms
Whilst sleeping neath noon day sun's, but now he was weary
For the years had dwindled as sand through an hour glass,
And as the bow of his mistress cleaved the crystal waters
He reflected only upon the good times, when he had been filled
Wit the bread, and drunk on the sweet passion called love
Whilst gathering gifts from life's tree, per chance,
To glimpse shadow of himself as he separated grain from millet
As life's river ran dry,
For he had skipped ocean's as a child skipping pebbles across a
   stream,
But now, he knew his belongings were bound by solitary dreams
And the mark to be, the boundaries of his own truths
For the reaper stood upon the sea wall, his anchorage was made
   steadfast
The full measure had fallen about him, and in his great sorrow
He saw himself one more time a lad, skipping stones across a stream,
And as he placed his hand within that holding, he knew
He would sally forth alone upon that endless running sea
For all his nets had be cast.

Helena Starr Keddle

Mother Nature

A solitary raindrop falls like a teardrop to land upon the earth.
With the innocence of a child, she bears the eyes of an old woman
   who's seen it all.
She sits and watches as the world rushes by, unable to turn her back
   on the needless suffering.
She views the racism and hatred burn and eat people up inside until it
   lashes out in war.
Confusion shows in her eyes as pollution slowly kills off everything
   that is life.
A shuddering sigh escapes her lips as the anguish battles around and
   inside her.
To her, it is the physical and emotional pain of a mother who's child
   is dying before her eyes.
Trying to cleanse the world, a single teardrop falls like a raindrop
   to land upon the Earth.

Amber Gill

Tribute

Here's to the people who created me,
Without them I would not exist.
   They were there through every tear and smile,
And molded me with honesty, faith and truth.
   They taught me the significance of humility and pride,
And the wisdom to know the difference.
   Through them I learned the virtues of purity,
And the arts of earning friendships.
   They gave me the gift of dreaming,
And the determination to make dreams come true.
   They passed on to me the knowledge of being humble,
And the good graces to stand on my own two feet.
   Somewhere along the line they slipped in the golden rule,
And revealed to me the secrets of its understanding.
   Then they mixed in a little patience and a whole lot of love,
And delivered to me the importance of them all.
   So now I take the time to say "Thank You".
   For making me who I am!

Angela Wilson

Superstar

You are born with the moon and the midnight star
You adore fast car and other such things.
You sing, play, you do it just for a big hit.
And when you miss it you loose it all, instead of being six feet tall
you are simply small.

Sometimes the world just hate you because of the things you do, or
some people just wish they could be just like you.
You say it's hard and you have no privacy and people are
simply using you for your money.

You have all kind of honey coming to see you.
So instead of having the blues and taking those drugs to sweep
everything under the rug, you should take a trip to your real
neighborhood and see the true world.

Yan Hakim

My Precious Diamond

When you have something very beautiful in your arms,
You tend to shield it and protect it from the open environment.

It takes so much of your attention
That your own pressure is causing strain.

The pain goes unnoticed for sometime, until a fracture develops.
One tear develops into another, until a small river runs down her face.
It is only then, he realizes her situation and eases the pressure.

By that time, severe damage has already taken place.
He uses all of his abilities to repair the damage
Unfortunately, it's irreversible.

He has made a costly mistake,
One which he'll regret for the rest of his natural life.
To him, she was a diamond of great value and beauty,
No other woman could possibly possess.
Value - for her hard surface and sharp edges.
Beauty - for that soft sparkle in her eyes.

But now flawed...
He values his precious diamond even more than before.
Probably, because he knows the true value of his love.

R.A.M. — (94)

Another Spring

You've stood before the window, and gazed upon this scene.
You've tried to see the beauty ever day.

But winter month grow weary, with the sameness of each day.
And at some point you cease to see what's really there.

You become aware quit slowly, of the warmth the sun is bringing
And you know it should mean something, to your brain.

Then like a curtain lifting, your mind begins to clear.
You know that you will see another the spring.

And suddenly new promises, like soft new blades of grass.
Become a gentle whisper, in your ear.

The snow it is reseeding, from beneath that old rose bush.
And soon the buds will swell for all to see.

It warms a place inside you, and you feel the stirring deep.
And you open up your mind and welcome spring.

Marlene McMann

Who would want to sieve the sea

Who would want to sieve the sea of grimless sand from time to dusk
of everglowing nursery chimes in spite of kite to be ignited to fire
and heaves of candelabras in hovering fearful tasks engendering thongs
of multiplied and magnified beauty for Zeus' sake the firestorms
honderborns mugworms in holy bordergnomes at homes of renegades that
seem to be oscillating policemen in regards to my honest regards of
a jokingly finest reader of warphead incorporated the storm is over
boy and put yer finger back in place the times of everchanging finance
howlers to cut down the prowlers inoxidized oysters try to climb the
backyard of my feathered intestines please! please relax! your mind
not your throat or kidney my friendly fiend, you'd be exhausted right
before dark the dark hits me like a stone a thorn an oxen a priest a
wedge, come back into pools of rusty roses and glands. only the brave
will overvive but surlive the thunderbolt in their own belts operating
ushers in musty muddy munchy cellars containing monkeys of a glamour
never ever seen of course it is too keen to joust through the course
of life in an intimidating distance haunted banks by herself himself
oneself gargoyled down the drain.

Fernando Tiberini

Dedicated To The Hunt

Once Upon A Time:
A family resided at the base of a rugged mountain,
a wilderness yet to understand! Staggering shots break the silence, a
succession in dispersion of peace. Max, a black terrier patrolled "his
territory," from dawn to dusk deterring intruders that roamed this
area... a decree, "Shoot any dogs on sight!" was expressed among
hunters. It is said, "dogs run their game off," on the un-named
mountains-hunters claim Their own!

Once Upon A Time
High in elevations wild game experienced famine,
harsh elements, were preyed upon daily,
or singly wounded by poaches-often impending long suffering,
until their death! The hunters shot echo's dissolution... in
distortion of surprise the elk bellows his foreboding cry on to the
earth... hunters busily carve their trophy while exerting their
visions of taxidermal mountings, rugs or "some" meat in the process.

Once upon a time:
Grizzlies patrolled "Their territory "to protect their family and game
from intrudes.. for survival! The hunters are fiercely
attacked in horror, and buried with their kill, disguised in game scent
and camouflage, game wardens duteously, now avenge the death
of "the hunters!" Results were, three bears exterminated on "their site,"
branded as intruders by mankind!

Once Upon A Time:
In reality of the Fatal Hunt!

Patricia Palmer

Our Doctors

M.D.'s and specialists many years they train. To mend the body and
heal the brain. They are not given the credit due to them. By the
likes of me and you. Our Doctors

For those in pain, sometimes in vain. They work and surely feel the
strain. At night they answer a sirens call. While we into a deep
sleep fall. Our Doctors.

From coughs and sneezes to rare diseases. We expect them to know
just how to treat us. Give needles and pills for various ills and
advise when we need it. This wonderful band. Our Doctors.

It is so easy to forget that they are human too and yet what would we
do without them all. To answer an urgent duty call. Our Doctors.

In hospital twenty-four times I have been. Many are the doctors I
have seen. Without them I would not be here to-day. So, for them all
Dear Lord I pray. Our Doctors.

They've a dedicated life to lead. Like their patients they too have a
need. For understanding from the likes of me and you. I salute them
all. How about you? To Our Doctors.

Joy Stonelake

My Sleeping Father

A tall gray haired man
lying on a blue couch,
head nestled on a small pillow.
A crossword puzzle held loosely in his hands,
a crossword puzzle book lying on his stomach.
His eyes closed
and a faint noise
coming from his mouth.
Step closer,
you can smell the mints
he always eats.
This man has seen many things,
through those closed eyes,
traveled to many US states
and foreign countries.
Hikes everywhere
for the perfect photograph.
I don't want to wake my father up,
he needs the rest.

Kelly Pickering

Dragons

A dragon is imaginary.
A beast, ferocious and cruel.
It runs rampant through your peace of mind
And tries, your life to rule.

The hurts you feel help make it grow.
The fear to be just you
Causes the dragon to grow so fast
It colors every view.

There's one sure sword to kill the beast.
Reality is its name.
Face the facts as they really are.
Refuse to play the game.

Kill the dragon by knowing just
What caused the fear and torment.
You'll find the effort of fighting the thing
Has been worth the time you've spent.

Look to reality for peace of mind.
Kill the dragon that tortures you.
Look head, down life's great road
Without a dragon to spoil the view.

Nancy Linderman Buchanan

Powerless

It is so easy to allow yourself to
Be pulled into the cavern.
To be swallowed up,
To no longer need to fight for control.
To just let your body go.
Let it float away silently.
No struggle, no screams.
Floating carelessly toward the cavern.
A slow drifting motion quietly pulling,
Careful not to disturb you.
No struggle is necessary, the drift lulls you.
It is so easy to allow
Yourself to be sucked downward.
Feeling secure until your
Head is below water,
Until you can no longer breathe,
Until you have no chance of survival.
It is so easy to stop fighting,
To let your life go,
To let destiny control.

L. J. W. Woodworth

Mama And The Sugar Sack

One winter evening as I was sitting, with no one around
I wondered what can you do when you are lonely,
And I thought of the pictures I had found.
Mama in a bonnet and bloomers, trimmed with lace galore
Looking wishfully at the camera, wanting to run for the door.
It was her first photo, times were very hard back then.
Mama Gip put the lace on the bloomers, there was no money for a store.
The lace came from her wedding dress made a few years before.
It looked fresh as a daisy, wrapped in paper so it would not fade
And saved for her first child to have her picture made.
One picture was all they could afford as Daddy gip drove for a rolling store
And Mama got one piece of gum a week, and rolled it in the sugar sack
Til the next Saturday came around and the store came rolling back.
I believe in the picture, she had the gum in her mouth
For one cheek seemed much fuller, not a smile I saw, but a pout!
When the picture taking was over, she most likely got a new piece of
gum, as Daddy Gip rolled in at dark, always with a whistle and a hum.
For as poor as they were, they were rich in some ways
Love was the key as it should be today and I looked at the picture
once more, Mama in lace bonnet and bloomers, in the sugar the gum
was rolled before

Lynda Graham McCormack

Feelings

You are born one sex but want to be another
It's so complex you are afraid to tell your mother
You carry this burden around with fear
Lie awake at night many times shedding a tear

As you grow older, get more courage and grow more mature
You don't care what people think of you, you learn to endure
You go out into the world as you see fit
Express your feelings, not caring if anyone doesn't share your drift

It's your life and you have to do what you want to do
No one can tell you how to live your life or what is best for you
There is no reason for being ashamed, you aren't hurting anyone
The world is a big place, there is room for us all when all said and done

There is a partner for everyone in this life
Whether it be of the same sex or as husband and wife
Go make a life which is best for you
And live any way you want to

Just hope and pray for continuous good health
Along with happiness and maybe a little wealth
Live as you wish and always be content
Having a good life is heaven sent.

Anita Korn

A Birthday Wish

"Rise," cried the morning sun.
The gentle rays kissed your soft face upon.

"Sing," said the lovely bird perched.
Your name is whispered in Eden's holy church.

Blessed are you another year.
To seek your fortune and shed never tears.

For the wise grow old,
and the trivial grow cold.

Distess not at how the years, beauty is taken.
For yours is timeless, a glow within.

And I, bask in the brightness
fortunate among men.
To be here and call your friend.

Hugo Jaramillo

My Grandaughter-Dena Marie

Dena Marie is my grandaughter's name
The fourth day of April is the day that she came
She came straight from heaven, all dressed in pink
To add to our family, a precious new link
Ten little fingers and ten little toes
With daddy's blond hair and mommy's cute nose
We're happy you came to this family of boys
Where trucks and trains were their favorite toys
Now there'll be dolls wrapped in blankets of pink
And little tin dishes piled high in the sink
Dean and Rachelle are your proud parents names
They'll teach you to play all the little girl games
Mommy will sing lullabys in a song
And daddy will teach you to know right from wrong
We love you so much, we wish you were near
We'd hold you so close, brush away every tear
So until I can see you, and hold you on my knee
Take care of your parents and hug them for me
Yes, the year '81 is so special to me
That's when Dena Marie came to our family tree.

Joyce Bunnell

Never Say Goodbye...

The time has past, and now you've came to rest.
We stay behind to keep you forever in our minds.
Our hearts are filled with love, hurt and pain, as our
tears fall like the rain.
Your sweet smile, your tender loving care, will be a
memory, a memory for as to share.
The pain is so strong, that some times makes me wish I
was also gone.
But as we live in this world today, we live to never say
goodbye in many special ways.

Ana Vargas

Challenger Flight Crew

Seven wandering ones sought space;
Space which would enrich their lives.
To questions asked by a wondering world
They would find the answers in the skies.
They moved upward with the thunder;
Thunder from the tower of flame
That would carry them to new heights,
And enshrine their names in fame.
They never knew of the explosion
That forestalled their flight to space.
They just appeared before God's throne,
And met Him face to face.

Arnold A. Puckett

Forbidden Love

When you love something so much
One shouldn't be punished.
This love not forbidden, nor taken away.
For this is your strength of tomorrow,
And the belief that brightens your day.

But by chance ones refusal of this pleasure;
One goes on and the love is set free.
For your heart is blinded forever;
In the hopes that he will never forget me.

Jeanine D. Conway

No Title Yet

Roaming discovered it by the Jersey Sea,
a body washed up by the gore like a fish.
The picture is lit now for all to see.

The returns are in, the winner must be he
who has thrown godless scars like nickels in the dish.
My government is trying to embarrass me.

The bubbles of a girl who was Mary Joe Kopechne,
lay broken like a virgin in the best of rich parties,
the picture is lit now for all to see.

The harem of the large lord over the wee
like worms in a gondola,
my government is trying to embarrass me.

The narration, like a garter, is slipping by degrees,
underneath whole bodies are waiting for the itch,
because the picture is lit now for all to see,
how my government is trying to embarrass me.

Robert D. Teitelbaum

Music

Music is beautiful to my ears.
It is not filled with lies.
It takes away my fears,
and I am sad when the music dies.

Music tells stories of old.
It speaks the truth.
Its lyrics are filled with gold,
and remembers the years of youth.

Music fills my heart with joy.
It expresses the feelings of love.
Some think love is merely a toy.
I believe it is a peaceful dove.

Music calms the harshness of the sea.
It makes still waters.
It shows what world harmony could be.
It is what should pass to our daughters.

Music, it brings us clearing skies.
The world seems happy with tunes.
Yet, the sound always dies,
and again we wait for other moons.

Kirsten J. Snyder

A Friend

A person with a heart one who never turns away
And when things fall apart they help you find your way
Someone who is real an not a bit fake
One who helps you deal with all your mistakes
A person with a love so very warm an tender
It's like a message from above you'll always remember
Someone with feelings but smart and wise
And when your lifes not appealing
They help you open your eyes
You'll find that tomorrow is much better than today
Because they help the sorrow
Just up and go away
Life is so worth living when a friend is in need
Because people are giving something you can believe
Weather it be advise or a shoulder to cry on
Its always nice to have someone you can rely on

Christine E. Ketchel

My Life's Journey

As I travel down the journey of life
Please God don't walk too fast
I must make my way slowly, but sure,
And hold to your hand at last.

Be patient with me and forgive when I fail
Pick me up when I fall, and steady my feet
Lest I take the wrong turn down the
wrong way street.

Each step I take will take me closer home
If you will guide my directions in every turn
If my path gets rough and bumpy and
I forget to go straight
Take hold of my hand Lord and guide me
through the gate.

Harriet S. Bolick

'Something Black'

There's an endless supply of light
    in everything that's black
When you stare into the nothing
    there's something staring back
This something's here to help, how much is up to you
Take a look inside your head
    from this something's point of view
Understanding comes easily
    when your on the outside looking in
The blackness supplies the light
    the something takes it all in
Putting everything in perspective
    holding your emotions in check.
Keeping us from losing our grip is simply something black
Everything is clearer when you look through something black
Inner-peace in nearer, this something's looking black
So if grief has you a member and things are starting to look dark
Always remember there's an endless
    supply of light in everything that's black

Joseph Scott

Give Life A Song

My life was a classroom for many years.
I experienced the children through laughter and tears.
Each child had a story; some fiction, some true.
With a hope for the future, some old and some new.

Each morning our voices would rise in song,
Every child made a music book, so they could sing along.
Each child had a favorite song to sing and praise,
Their voice was so precious it brightened my days.

Our life can be music, if we let it sing.
Just watch your step and see what it brings.
Keep up the spirit and let life flow,
You've got a million miles, so let life ago.

Reach for the ultimate, let it soar.
Be kind in your spirit and expect much more.
God is our keeper and watches our fate.
Keep up your standards before it's too late.

Give praise to the person who brightened your life.
They were there to guide and lead you through strife.
Hold fast to the notes as life goes on,
Keep music in your heart and sing that song.

Charlotte Wiger-Achttien

Thoughts Of You

The joys of spring, the smell of flowers.
The joy of robbins, and sweet spring showers.
The beauty of nature, when the skies so blue.
All come to mind when I think of you.

The wonders of winter, so quite and serene.
The beauty of snow and the proud evergreen.
A soft winter night, and a fire so low.
Bring visions of you, how bright they glow.

The miracle of fall, color rules all.
The football games, the dance in the hall.
All memories so sweet, and memories divine.
Bring thoughts of you, that are very, very fine.

The freshness of summer, ol' sun shining bright.
The splashing of water until late at night.
The bikinis and tans, and girls galore.
Can't make me forget you, the girl I adore.

William L. Harris

See You Later

With fire in his eyes he stalks the night
Slipping through the water looking for a fight
He lies low to the ground
And makes a deep hissing sound
Hiding in the dark mirk
He studies you slyly with an eerie smirk
He doesn't dare to make a move
Just lies there motionless, wedged into a groove
His thick tail begins to swish
Then suddenly and violently his jaws are filled with fish

Karen P. Johnson

Although

Although I,
It is nice to know
To set my dreams——with the feeling of joy
It can be done
To set my goals——with a heart comradeship
It can be done
To set my price——I gasped to recognize
It can be done
To be vain and dishonest———is it necessary to triumph over others
Although I have not done——it can be done.

Yrma Camilla

Untitled

If you're young and black or even just a minority,
like me you're probably familiar with adversity.
Obstacles come in many forms,
be it peer pressure, finances or uncertainty
but we must learn to weather our storms.

For those that are fortunate
it's always first and ten.
On the other hand, there are the unfortunate
Who are constantly faced with third and long.

In the meantime just continue to prepare
for the opportunity of first and goal.
Then, when you have scored your
touchdown in life, the fruits of success
shall be your song.

Herbert J. Reid III

Life Is...

Life is such a beautiful thing,
As many singers so often sing,

We may encounter problems now and then,
But what would we do without them?
Life would be a constant bore!
With nothing but your everyday chores,

With nothing to learn or achieve,
How would we ever come to succeed?
Without the lessons we learn from day to day,
People would become weak and run away.

The love we have for so many,
Should be shared with those who haven't any,
The departure of our loved ones causes despair,
But the memories and love will always be there.

For all of the above are God's desires,
For his world to be entire....

Life is short,

   So live each day,

      In your own very special way!!!

Shelby Perine

Welcome

Weaving this blanket of feelings to wrap around you,
we share the colors of birds flying in the morning.
Strong and gentle, bright and learning your mother whispers,
I already love you so much.

Holding the knowledge of our fickle universe
your parents offer integrity, joy and kindness.
Reaching inside themselves for awareness and wisdom,
laughing and crying easily, they will dance your dances with you.

Little one, tucked into your mother's belly,
knowing the beat of her heart,
basking in the love your parents have for one another,
feeling, growing,....living out of sight,
we welcome you with stories to tell.

Leaving our own childhoods behind,
knowing in our hearts we are all parents to all children,
we give you ourselves.

Hummingbird Berreyesa

Jim

Jim looked at the roses at the hospital door
Like one who was leaving his native shore
He reached out and picked one that was his own
He knew he soon would be under a stone
He turned and looked, in his eye was a tear
He knew we were thinking about an earlier year

He knew he was leaving his fathers hall
Soon to be under a purple pall
He was going to heaven a journey new
Was talking our love, which always was true
Jo wept inside laid her hand awhile
On face a mothers comforting smile

A thousand thoughts of all things dear
Of his family he was leaving here
It was leukemia, he fought his best
He closed his eyes and went to rest
He is still here in sunbeams and roses
It is in God's hand my son reposes

William L. Roberts

The Light In Death

In death there is light
One that is said to shine bright
In death there is a certain darkness
As those who mourn feel such emptiness
As time passes, the light returns
As the floods of memories brightly burns
At 61 he is now gone. Wasn't really much past dawn
A man who gave his heart and soul to all
Departed from us one warm day early fall
Left behind such memories to burn bright
So we the living could feel the warmth of the light
Missing him and all he was
But knowing he'll never really be gone
For through us his memory will always linger on,
In death there is light
Where love has always shown bright for love never dies
No matter how it tries. The good in life is always preserved
Within the memories so richly deserved
So let there always be light in death
For without it how could we the living go on.

Valerie Sweeney

Beloved

The leaves are green
The air is crisp
And the grass is covered with dew
The sky hovers above, covered with blue
I saw it once, I saw it again
It was hard for my eyes to conceive
I saw something so quaint
It left my face with nothing but a blank
I stumbled, then I fell
I sought comfort, I was not alone, I was not well
I got my strength and made a stand
Then I felt the warmth of a gentle hand, Mom

Gerrie Barentine

Odyssey Of A Feather

I am a wispy vagabond on dicey winds,
A vagabond. Perhaps I stem from healing wings,
Crippled wings, landlocked wings, or soaring wings.
I touch and tickle only scattered, fellow plumes.

This frail pilgrim scribbles marks with chalk and lead
And writes its brittle legacy of dust and dusk,
Constructs its residence of only wind and quill
While whisking, brushing others at tangents of their lives.

What flight! These transient wings to distant, fertile lands,
Has drifted through fjords and climbed far mountain slopes.
Through atoms, castles, canyons, poems I have danced.
On pulsing guitar strains this fleeting down can soar.

From Shakespeare to the Serengeti breadth,
Safaris shall be roused, new symphonies are played.
From Internet to realms of inner space,
Undiscovered mystic trails still summon me; Explore.

A yet more lofty voyage beckons me to risk
A subtle stroke of love which lifts a friend in flight
Where scarce are sparks igniting fires within,
Where no trumpet sounds, no trophies are proclaimed.

Paul Langley

His Own

Green leaves and barren deserts,
Blue skies and gray mountains,
These are the things in this eyes.

Leath tigers and graceful lions,
Sleek dolphins and majestic eagles,
These are the things in his movements,

Molten lava and searing fire,
Rushing rivers and calming seas,
These are the things his touch sings of.

Sweet melody of the wolf,
Powerful song of the stars,
These are the sounds of his voice

These have created him and given him life.
These are his own.

Shanna Wendt

Dare To Discover

Dare to discover what you can discover,
over the mountains and beyond
   the trees.
Dare to see what you can see,
   beyond the rainbow and the skies of blue
Dare to say what you want to say,
   your opinion should be heard.
Dare to be what you want to be, beyond your wildest dreams.
Dare to save what you can save, the earth and all the leaves.
What you do is up to you. Dare, wait, and see.
Dare to discover what you can discover,
over the mountains and beyond
   the trees.

Stefanie Frank

Love Company

The dark sea and narrow rockey land;
The owl eye full moon large and high;
Splashing waves at the shore.
In fiery rings at their doze,
As I gain the cove with pushing prowess,
And quench its speed, I, the slushy dirt.

Then a mist of cozy sea-scented bay;
Four fields across, a cabin appears,
A pound on the old broken pane,
A bright spurt of lighted match,
And a voice less loud through its happiness
And fears, than two hearts beating
one to one.

Lacey Mason

After The Season

They lay there in ditches, on streetsides, and front lawns
Turning from green to shades baring colors of fawns
Lonely and useless, they wonder their purpose
What brought great beauty and homes for forest guests in acres,
Becomes trash by the wayside left with remnants of their brief
   material dress
They are no more part of human display nor social
   consciousness
Only christmas tree memories abandoned that way
For what reason?
Pretentious people would say,
It's the end of the Season

Sue Van Wazer

The Hand Above The City

There was a giant hand hovering above me last night
In the city's blackened sky
A hand
Fashioned by some broken ridges
In the pressing cloud line
With four jagged fingers
Bleeding out the miles from a hazy palm
And a thumb jutting forth
Violently
Into the nearing dawn
It belied the city's calm
This presence
So ominous
That I couldn't escape from
Though I tried
This giant hand
That could've easily clenched
Into a fist so wide
To crush an unwary city
While the dreamers slept inside.....

Matt Claymore

No, Not Today

Many times I've heard the wind call to me
A gentle breeze whispering "Come. Follow me."
A howling storm screaming "Come. Come. Come. Follow me."
I always answered, "No, not today."

Many times I've looked out at the mountains
I hear them say, "Come.
 See the adventures that wait on the other side."
They beckon to me with lush green meadows
Or white capped peaks.
I always answered, "No, not today."

Many times I've seen the ocean
Small swells tugging at me, "Come. See what lies below."
Crashing waves bellowing,
"Come. Let me show you my secrets."
I always answered, "No, not today."

Many times I've listened to the birds
An eagle calling, "Come. See all the beauty that I see."
A seagull crying, "Come. See all the wonders that I see."
I always answered, "No, not today."

But today no one calls, beckons or tugs
For I have gone to see
All that's been promised to me.

Bev Reis

If

If there ever was a day that kept the homefires burning,
If there ever was a night
That shed warmth on the recipients of its darkness,
Then I believe there is hope.

If there ever was a dying child who found comfort in a mother's touch,
If there ever was reconciliation
To the desperation of the poor by the drop of a coin,
Then I believe in love.

If there ever was a time a smile broke through your tears for
   another's sake,
If there ever was a moment
You shared hope and love through the pain of your own breaking
heart,
Then I believe in you.

Reggie Bannister

My Beautiful Field

As I stand and gaze upon my beautiful field,
I see the lovely birds on their flight, stop and
Sit upon those twigs that cover my beautiful field.

Such beautiful songs they sing as they fly in
My beautiful field.
Black and white, blue and red fill the skies in
My beautiful field.

At night they stop their flight and perch upon
The twigs and sort of sing a lullaby and we know
It's time to say goodnight in my beautiful field.

One morning as I was gazing, I heard an eerie cry.
I looked and saw machines plowing my beautiful field.
Their home has been destroyed! Where will they go now?
To another beautiful field?

But for me you see, I can no longer gaze upon them or
Hear their lovely songs. I can only remember that
Special place—my beautiful field.

Agnes Funaro

Wally's Poem

Come, sit here awhile with me.
Listen to the birds as they sing their melodies.
Hear my voice in the breeze.
I'll tell you why I had to leave.

No time to grieve, no time for tears.
My life was brief but filled with good years.
Friendships unforgotten, a peaceful home; I had so much.
Joy, laughter, my loved one's touch.

The path I have taken is new you see.
No more pain, no more agony.
I heard the call. I could not stay.
I took His hand. He led the way.

It's time to go and live a new.
Another life, another view.
So, goodbye and peace to thee.
We'll meet again when he comes to set you free.

Geneva Woehler

Untitled

You are an enigma to me.
I don't know much about you. You
   don't volunteer.
We go out a few times. You tell me
   you enjoy my company.
Then absolutely nothing. Nada.
If it's games you're playing — don't.
I'm done with them.
Played them too often.
If you're sincere, then I'd like to see where this
   will lead.

Diane Lennox

"Young Love"

I think of him night and day.
And pray he's thinking of me too.
That cute little smile makes everyone else disappear.
That sweet voice makes my heart melt.
I dream of his warm touch and adorable brown eyes.
So many things I feel.
Could it be love?
Could it be real?

Lara Gallaway

After The Storm

After the last snow flake has fallen
and the sky has turned a Carolina Blue,
there is a peace in the air
a peace that reminds me of you.

The snow is now covered with seed and nuts
that were placed there with your loving touch.
As the water bowl is being refilled,
the squirrels come and start there drill.
In their uniforms of blue and gray,
they run across the snow covered grass
and back up high into the tree.
They look like policemen walking a beat.

The birds start to fly from branch to branch.
They sing as the wind blows beneath there feet;
because now they, too, may begin to eat.

As the day turns to darkness
and I prepare for my night's sleep,
I think of Christ's son that was born
and the peace after the storm.

Lee Edward Kye Jr.

Sunshine On A Midnight Flower

Within your light all darknesses are drowned.
As I set forth, this journey is my test.
The glowing bud erupts from frozen ground.

The sacred search goes on without a sound
and from your bliss all promises are blessed.
Within your light all darknesses are drowned.

There shines nothing but blight within my mound,
but brilliant beauty soon must be confessed.
The glowing bud erupts from frozen ground.

Through murky tunnels, toward the light I'm bound.
While on this journey, there's no time to rest.
Within your light all darknesses are drowned.

The brazen path to glory I have found.
My frightened heart, your gentle hand caressed.
The glowing bud erupts from frozen ground.

With golden warmth, my wary heart you crowned.
The scorching sunlight pounds inside my chest.
Within your light all darknesses are drowned.
The glowing bud erupts from frozen ground.

Rebecca L. Davis

My Time

My time will come, When? No one knows-
My heart will stop. My eyes will close.

Once before I've had my time,
My moment of birth was only mine.

The years between the when? And then-
Are filled with memories of a curious blend.

I've had my ups, I've had my downs-
I've strived, I've faltered, I've stood my ground.

Beyond the dreams, My life fulfilled-
I wait for Father Time.

Not knowing when, but it will come-
And it will be My Time.

Emma Spoolhoff

Jealousy

Jealousy is a dark black sky.
You hear the sound of thunder and lightening.
You can taste a rotten apple.
It smells like a burned out fire.
You see bent and broken trees.
You feel left out.

Adam Olp

Darkness

At night after the sun has set the light fades
away, I sit alone to think.
I start to walk down a street, I hear something
behind me. I turn! It is darkness creeping up behind
me. As I watch it come slowly but surely as the last
rays of light fade away. I run and try to escape it,
but it follows me. Now I am starting to become tired
and let the darkness close in on me.
After a while the darkness fades and gives way
to the light.

Matthew Pollard

Lee

When I look in the mirror, this is what I see.
I see me, but how can this be, mommy says thank
goodness there's only one of me.
So who, who, who could this be? I guess he's my friend
I'll call him Lee.

Each time I go to the mirror Lee is always there, same
eyes, same hair, Lee and I always have on the same
  thing to wear.
How, how, how can this be? How does he know so much
  about me?

I wish Lee wouldn't always hide.
My wish came true one day while I was taking a ride.
There was Lee in the mirror staring at me.
And I guess I'll never ever know where he's been and
  where he'll go.

Lindsay Loup

A Simpler Place

The world was once a simpler place,
with simpler people too.

The air was fresh, the rivers clean,
the skies Carolina blue.

People knew their neighbors well,
milk came to the door

Grocery shopping was a special trip
to Mr. Carroll's general store

Children played hide and seek,
Dinner was eaten at the table

Entertainment was a family affair
like the sharing of an Aesop fable.

Each family had just one large car,
each town just one small bank

Church bells rang every Sunday morning
as we gathered to give thanks

Yes, the world was once a simpler place
with simpler people too

I truly miss that simpler time
I really, really do.

John Kermit Lomax

Under The Ironwood Tree

I have travelled the world over
and been most everywhere.
But the place closest to my heart
is forty acres on the shore of the
Little Glen at the foot of Sleeping Bear.
To see the sun come up on the Bear
as the whole thing turns to gold,
is one of God's miracles
and beauty to behold.
As a child I wandered the Bear and
Glen as happy as I could be,
and watched the sun come up
from under an ironwood tree.
And when my days here are over
and I go to the other side,
I will pray God will let my heaven be;
a chance to watch the sun come up
on the "Bear", under an ironwood tree.

S. Plowman

The Backward Girl

Once I knew this backward girl
They called her Senga Nylòrac -
When young, her life was a whirl -
Then, older, life became a wreck -
   In school she was bright but bored,
She chose to be close to her friends,
Who were on the wrong road.
20 years later, the road took a bend.
   After many husbands and children
Someone told her: "Life can be better,
Drug free life is not bewildering,
God in your life is what matters."
   Senga learned by working hard to recover,
To change her friends to ones in control of their lives.
To step away from her past much to discover
God would guide and console her, free from strife.
   Yes, Senga learned and she did it!
She's not backward anymore.
You can tell by her name, get it?
Agnes Carolyn turned her life around for sure!

Sylvia Pate

You're Not The Boy You Used To Be

Why do I find myself thinking of you?
We've broken up, so long ago too.
You're different now, that I can see,
You're not the boy you used to be.

I still love you but I don't know why,
I just want to sit and cry.
But crying does no good you see,
You're not the boy you used to be.

I still care for you,
Oh, how I wish you knew,
But there I am feeling blue.
I know you're different, so then why am I here, ready to cry?

I'm all alone in pouring rain,
As I wish for you in my bitter sweet pain.
I'm in love with a boy I used to know,
Somebody help, I fell so low.

I listen to song we used to know,
And I remember how it used to be,
when I loved you and you loved me.
But you're different now that I can see,
You're not the boy you used to be.

Gina Marie Grieco

Rastatter Or Rastatt

There's a big confusion when we chat
about which came first Rastatter or Rastatt

Were we named after the city
or was the city named after we

The thought is a foe
tricking us so that we will never know

Changing the answer when we are close to finding out
moving it away and all about

I guess there is no reason why
we shouldn't take a plane and fly

To Rastatt and tell them all but this verse
and then we will know which came first

Trevor Rastatter

Chant Of The Iroquois

The Iroquois chief wore the skin of a bear,
as he moved his tribe here and to there.

Basket nets were used to fish,
and they ate their meals out of a wooden dish.

Out in the fields grew large yellow corn,
and the women used needles made out of horn.

They were usually at war with another tribe,
Algonquians by name with their tribal pride.

Brethren of the long house, their nations were five,
They sided with England with arrows and knives.

Cayuga, Mohawk, Oneida are gone,
Onondaga, Seneca have seen their last dawn.

Where are the Pine Trees, the village, the clan,
they're gone from the mountain, the councils so grand.

One last trip on that river so old,
and we say goodbye to the warriors so bold.

Jeff Choens

Valley Of Ashes

My dreams are gone, they've seeped out through my gashes,
they drown, sinking out of my grasp.
I am stuck in the valley of ashes.

Stomped and walked upon,
pushed aside and ignored.
My dreams are gone, they've seeped out through my gashes.

Screamed at and hit,
surrounded by reality.
I am stuck in the valley of ashes.

Oozing out my wounds,
never to return,
My dreams are gone, they've seeped out through my gashes.

Broken and damaged,
can't speak a word.
I am stuck in the valley of ashes.

Suppressing and stifled,
Hurting inside and out,
My dreams are gone, they've seeped out through my gashes,
I am stuck in the valley of ashes.

Sarah Phillips

October Day

Amber twisted fingers of a powerful hand
pertrude from the regretful dying grass.

Wind blown leaves stick to the fence
as if painted on.

The evergreen remaining ever green
opposite be headed flower bodies.

Sounds of children, rustling through the
leaf piles, echo in the lazy haze of
autumn air.

Wistful gray clouds pass before a
full golden glows of moon and soothes
me off to sleep.

Penny Nava

Renata

Renata, reborn and always new,
Unbound and elusive as a butterfly;
You would be tethered
By neither insincere embraces
Nor the stifling ideas of small minds;
A fiery proud demeanor and confident air
Belie the well of pain and vulnerability
Deep within your soul,
From which flow streams of creativity,
Courage, and passionate idealism.

Judith Turano

Untitled

I sent you six red roses today
But times are different and situations change
Six red roses was my way of saying
I love you
Not all things will last forever
Not even the six red roses I sent you today
Their delicate petals and silken touch
Their breath of sweetness on the air
Eventually all life begins to fade
Flowers wither and die in slow death
The memory of six red roses
And something beautiful are all that remain
Images I remember today
Are of times that were once new
The closeness when our bodies entwined
The promises we whispered when we cared
Your smile and the scent of your hair
Are distant thoughts that go no-where
In time these will fade away
Like the six red roses I sent today

Douglas G. Walton

"1996 Blizzard Victims"

Blizzards, Blizzards by the score;
Stopped the traffic and some more;
People watched without a clue;
What Nature intends to do;
Blows smooth white blanket to the sides;
Piled so high we feel victimized;
Relief at last with a prayer or two;
Snow shovels push right on through;
Back to work in crowds confused;
Some quiet, some amused;
Next day more so what the heck!
Nineteen Ninety Six is now a wreck!

Julia B. Markland

Wishing Well

Love brought us to a wishing well.
    To be or not I could not tell.
Are pennies not enough for luck.
    Now I am asking, 'what the F—?'
Could it be we used it all the day we met.
I think maybe sometimes wishing wells forget.
    Damn you wishing well!
Into each other's love we fell.
    In dire need you nurtured well.
Soon all your hope had turned to love.
    You felt it like you never huv.
Could it be that wishes die like we have to.
I think maybe sometimes wishing wells laugh to.
    Damn you wishing well!
Once tears of joy now tears of pain.
    Sunshine had left me to the rain.
With no one there to kiss goodbye.
    I wish to let the feelings die.
Could it be that life is all it's meant to be.
I think wishes never meant so much to me.
Damn you wishing well!

Michael V. Anello

Endless Beaches

Tropical breeze's and endless beaches
with hot white sand oozing out from
between our toes,
aqua blue crystal clear water silently
splashes upon the shore.

As we walk arm and arm in the warm moonlit
summer night: a bright star setting
far off in the sky, uninterrupted by the
sparkle in your eye.

"In a stolen moment" I steal a kiss!
and my mind sail's off into peaceful
bliss, the touch of your hand shoots
sparks thru my being that brings on a
warmth of security in the warm summer night.

Putting a glow on my face and your tender
embrace holds my entire attention, as we
stroll thru this part of our live together
we make plans for the future to combat the
trials and tribulation as one.

Charles O. Reese

Same Story

A poisoned dart broke a precious string.
A heart was pierced and a cry did ring.
Twice before has this fate befallen
and twice before the heart has fallen.
Every time a new dawn came
and life carried on with
that feeling of same.

Sean F. Toomey

Ravenswood El, Winter

The squealing, grinding clamor
Measures the morning way to patient death
Leans close to tired walls
Strums acrid air
Flakes rust on storefronts where
Empty eyes stare.

Herbert Channick

No Love

Bodies fill my eyes once again;
Women, children, and a lot of men.

Blood and body parts, fills the trail;
Dropping and rolling as they fell.

Am I machine or man?
In this lonely and desolate land.

Is this the beginning or the end?
Or is it, merely all pretend?

I feel so lost, and all alone;
Sometimes; I think I'm better off gone.

Bodies fill my eyes and mind;
While the sun(high in the sky)still shines.

The terror that fills my eyes;
I'm the last to see, before I die.

Dear God; be with me and help me forget;
All the memories and thoughts of this debt.

Please don't let me turn to stone;
Because there is no love — I'm all alone.

R. Wayne Pritchard

Untitled

My love is yours in crystal cove castle.
Our love dims the light reflection on the crystals dazzle.
Can you speak our love for me for as we crystallize our love.
I express my feelings for you in seven words.
You are as sweet as a dove.
Crystals powers forms plans for our love between our hearts.
If my love was measured my feelings would fill eighteen carts.
Oh oh my darling oh my love you are my flame my only one.
If I was mercury oh how I'd like to rotate around you my sun.
Crystal light isn't as pretty as your face is to me.
How may we present our love so the world can see.
You are the only one my love who could fill my love with joy.
What would I do my love if you were a sailor that said "ahoy."
My darling love will grow from our hearts to our lips.
My love you aren't like my old flame,
 he had a problem with his finger tips.
Hate is a foe, my love mustn't be hostile.
You are so sweet.
Your voice in a high pitch my love
is like a baby bird singing tweet tweet.

Ferrer

"May We Have This Dance"

Demons never hiding under the bed
Forever dancing in my head
Why to me? What did I do?
I am age two still new and you
Take my dreams so full of light
Your evil rage darker yet, so alone my fright
I twist, turn, yes toss trying to fight - like nights past again this night
Gives way to falling - forever falling to your delight
A cold hard floor opens my blue eyes so bright
Can you now hold me if I climb back to bed
Will you stop dancing in my head
I'll give you my tears, my dreams full of light
All that I am - all I can be take all, yes all
But please, oh please - please leave me this night
Forgive me - forgive me - my tears, my plea full of fright
I do forget - all that I am blue eyes so bright belong to you night
 after night
And yes my days are now darker than my sorrow, my fright
I fear to dream dreams so full of light
I now know the demons not hiding under my bed
Love dancing, dancing forever in my head

Robert Downs

An Angel Sent

I close my eyes and always find myself in this same room
Dark, scary and quiet, it's filled with such sadness and gloom
I'm running, looking, searching, there seems to be no way out
After a while I must escape, but I can't, I begin to shout
Decades feel as they've gone by
With no windows, no light, I feel as though someone's left me to die
Then suddenly a noise is heard, I'm calmed, a door suddenly appeared
Footsteps are heard, am I dreaming? Someone has neared?
The door opened and I stood in disbelief
That someone was leading me out of my sadness and grief
As I walked through the doorway, I wondered if the door was there
 all along
With all my self pity blinding me, maybe it was there and I had
 been wrong
But now with this chance given me, I know in the future, shall I
 try - I will succeed
For sometimes we are overwhelmed, with our feelings of need
But while I was holding that hand I felt my own strength to move on
 and survive
So I let go, looked up, and thanked God for the precious gift,
 of just being alive.

Linda M. Dessipris

I Wonder

I wonder where the time has gone
when things were bright and new.
 When my horse had rockers, and my guns had caps
and my friends were honest and true.

I wonder where the time has gone
when my heart was filled with glee.
 When my dad would play his little tricks
as I sat upon his knee.

 When teachers taught and children learned of
both new and old.
 When English, math and science were taught by
the rule of gold.

The prom night dance was a night of joys, where
hands were held a kiss exchanged by wide girls and boys.

All gone now to the work day week, new joys to
conquer, new jobs to seek.

As I look back now at these childhood days
and wonder what went wrong
 I can't help but wonder, where all the has gone.

Thomas D. Roberts

Girl On A Mountaintop

I once met a girl on a mountaintop
Standing on the edge of a cliff
Her sheer dress flowing white as she stood so stiff
Had she bought it at a wedding shop?

She was the picture of elegance and grace
And there was nothing there for her to brace
I asked her was she intending to jump here
(Was her boyfriend angry and going to dump her?)

Then as she turned to me with a sigh
She smiled and asked, "Would I?"

"You mean jump her?"
"No." I said with fear.

She may have been a real beauty
But I told her jumping was not my duty

So I left her there in her white gown
I hope she made it down.

Timothy L. Spriggs

Make The Best Of It

We're only here for just awhile,
So let's take heed of our lifestyle.
If we put God first in all we do
The secondary things will follow through.

The Lord has plans for us, you know -
So let's not disappoint Him with thoughts of woe.
Be happy and thoughtful in all that we do,
And the love of God will come shining through.

With a smile on our face and a song in our heart,
We can do our best to take our part,
And give to our neighbor a helping hand
And then on the right hand of God we'll stand.

The angels and all the heavenly host,
But foremost the Father, Son and Holy Ghost
Will welcome us into the holiest place -
God's kingdom where we'll meet them face to face.

So keep smiling throughout the rest of your days,
And stay on the right path in all your ways.
Sing praises to God in all that you do,
And God's blessings will all come back to you.

Dianne Nichols

Ocean

Oceans with their waves so high,
Waves that seem to touch the sky.
Oceans with their waters of blue,
And sand that's damp from morning dew.

On a hot summer day, when it comes about noon,
The beach will fill soon.
Children running playing,
"You need more," lotion parents are saying.

Suddenly the sun starts to sink,
The waves slowly calm, as if there might be a link.
The children leave, and the waves sink low,
Without them the waves loose their glow.

The night creatures come out to play,
Until dawn they shall stay.
Dawn sneaks up without a sign,
The water unicorns now have their time.

Finally, day begins once more,
And, look, up on the shore,
The people ready to come again,
To once more fill the ocean's day with its friends!

Sami Smith

David (Age 7)

Alone on my narrow low cot
Looking up to the bed of my loving Grandpop
I enquired if he had money a lot
To buy a three pillowed bed?

Why? Was his answer
Two's enough for Grandma and me.
Well, with three I could sleep
There between Grandma and thee.

With smiles and laughter
The covers were raised
And I snuggled in warmly
Between Grandma and he.

Dorothy Lancaster Braswell

Untitled

It's the silence that kills me.
Speak louder, speak true.
Understand me. Respect me. Love me.
Teach me everything you know.
Let me in. Let me in.
Sat what you mean, mean what you say.
Hold me dear. Don't lose me. I'm falling.
Don't make me laugh, I want to forgive you.
I need to be mad. I need to hurt.
It will help me understand. It will help me understand.
Tell me you need me- I will believe.
Relieve me. Seize me. I'm just out of reach.
What you see is not what you get.
There is so much more. There is so much more.
You want to be different, but in that you're the same.
So insane like the falling rain.
Time only tells- I hear screams not your dreams.
The future rings clear- I need to be there.
The world is an oyster. Who is your pearl?
Let me know now. Let me know now.

Laura Zinch

Paths

There are paths of love and hate which some people choose to ignore
There are paths old and new which some have yet to explore
Paths of achievement and failure contain an equal amount of each
Paths of success and perfection are the toughest ones to reach
A path of knowledge can be gained at any type of pace
A path can be long or short the outcome similar to a race
Each path will form a shape making its own design
Each path will become history in a certain moment in time
There are paths of anger which sometimes are very intense
There are paths of loyalty for those with good sense
A path of loyalty can lead to happiness
A path of crime will lead only to loneliness
A path of patience is one dedicated with lots of devotion
A path of joy is decorated with fulfillment in emotion
Paths of individualism are ones of which you can roam
Paths of marriage are different and have a beauty of their own
A path of love makes you feel especially nice
A path of friendship is worth taking at any price
Each path chosen in life has a lesson it will give
Each path you choose will determine how you live

Anthony Demarco

"The Beast Within"

My dream is to be a poet. My words for all to read.
To educate and illuminate. God plants the poet's seed.

I'll write about our universe. Equality and Peace.
I'll try to soften, the hearts of stone. Destroying "The Evil Beast"

If I succeed in doing that, through the words I write.
The Beast will have nowhere to go, for I have won the fight.

So, Evil Beast, don't show your face, your emotion being hate.
With God's help, I'll soften the hearts. Soon you'll meet your fate.

I'll free the hearts, that you possess, through the words I write.
They'll be free, from you evil emotion. May they see the light.

Listen, evil beast within. You don't have a chance.
I've beaten you many times before. Again, I take a stance!

Do what you will do in life, as I write my mighty words.
Souls will turn away from you. For my message, will be heard.

Susan L. Kline

A Pair Of Soles

Her feet grew longer than her shoes,
her face a mix of purple hues.

These cool shoes will take me places,
if I can learn to tie my laces.

Instead I stumble along my way,
if I had velcro I'd be okay.

They laugh and mock and say how queer,
but can't they see I'm standing here?

I love my shoes so why don't they?
Because they can't accept the way.

I walk around, proud of my feet.
Look at my shoes; aren't they neat?

People all make fun of me
because my shoes look differently.

Why is it so hard to see,
that beauty lies in variety.

Hello my friend! Shall you borrow a pair
and together we'll walk everywhere.

And all the people stop to say,
there goes a pair with some very strange ways!

Tracy Atkinson & Bobbie Woods

Disappointment

Tired of tedious course of study,
Sad, when most my friends had gone
To answer country's call to duty,
I was alone, too much alone.

I must go and bravely join them
In some country fraught with war.
I must too contribute service
In some exotic land, afar.

When the weary war was over,
With few laurels yet to earn,
I would return to my dear homeland.
Triumphantly, I would return.

All of those I left behind
Would be waiting there to welcome me,
With open arms, as I had left them.
But this would not be. This could not be.

"Absence makes the heart grow fonder."
I angrily dismissed with great chagrin,
And sadly learned, as one before me:
"You cannot go back home again."

Harold Hoskins

The Man Who Carried The Cross

I followed the man, who carried the cross down the road
Saw the pain and suffering on his face, knew that he had a heavy load
Felt sorry when I saw him stumble and fall
Wondered why nobody came to his aid I recall
Finally I asked the man next to me
He said the one you followed is Jesus of Nazareth, the almighty
Saw the roman soldiers, who took the saviours garment away
They did not want him to live another day
It was a sad sight to behold, three crosses side by side
Jesus being in the middle, light around him had nothing to hide
He said father, forgive them for what they have done
I know in my heart, that the battle has been won
When you ever decide to go back to the Holy Land
Wonder if you will ever find the hill, where the crosses used to stand

John Geffen

Just Open Your Eyes And See

An incredible day is beginning
Shades of pink, orange, and dark blue with gold streaks
Skies are warm with brilliant colors
As the sun comes up, colors fade away
Just open your eyes and see

Dazzling shades of green covering the earth
Magnificent blue grey mountains getting further and further away
Butterflies in all different colors fly everywhere
Blue skies look like oceans without waves
Just open your eyes and see

Dark blue mountains outlined with bright pink, purple, and yellow
Brighter and brighter is the world as the sun goes down
Colors swirling around the earth
Magically the sky turns black
Just open your eyes and see

Sparkling lights look like bits of a colored chandelier strung
    across the countryside
Stars perfectly silhouetted against the pitch black sky
Half moon giving off a bright orange glow
An incredible day is ending
Just open your eyes and see

Jaima Katherine Atterholt

An Inspiration

A lonely man sat on a bar stool.
Smoke and spirits filled the air.

He gazed out the foggy window,
at a heartless world out there.

While reflecting on false friendship,
folks who wouldn't lend a hand.

He ordered up another drink,
pulled out a book he didn't understand,

And began to read the scriptures
of a man from Galilee.

He learned this man was Jesus,
that he'd died to set men free.

Suddenly, he felt quite sober.
The liquor glass had lost it's glow.

So, he paid his tab and
left for home, through the icey snow.

He arrived back at this door step,
went inside, sat in a chair,

And, remembering those wise words he read,
hung his head in prayer.

Donna Lynne Van Harreveld

Mixed Child

Love against the odds is what I symbolize.
Love against society and yet not a surprise.
It takes true love for someone like me to come to be.
Love is color blind but unfortunately people aren't, you see.
True courage and true love are two great qualities,
I, a mixed child, am a product of these.
A child is God's way of sending a smile at birth.
A mixed child is God's hope against the hate present on earth.
I am growing up and understand more of what I see.
How some people do not like me because of my diversity.
The world is like a giant rainbow, or so I've come to see.
The point at which the colors blend is where I, a mixed child,
    will be.

Courtney Kano

Always A Dream

I will always have my dreams to keep me safe and warm
They would guide me to paradise in the middle of the storm
As I cease to see the real world my eyes still envision the light
For I will always have a dream to guide me through the night
Whenever I wish to escape I'll lay down to sleep
Dream over and over the memories I wish to keep
If I never get to fly or touch the farthest star
If I never get to love or reach something so far
If I never get something I have always wished for
If I never see a smile like the ones I've seen before
I'll close my eyes and try as hard as I can
To leave everything behind, to leave this precious land
For I can dream of anything I can dream of anyone
I can dream about the future and things I never done
I can dream about a place where there is no right or wrong
I can dream about a world I can hold in my palm
I can dream about floating up through an orange sky
I can dream about dancing on the wings of a fly
There will always be a dream to keep me going on
There will always be a dream to keep me going strong,
    always a dream.

Jennifer Cabral

Of A Woman

Gracious in both success and failure
Courageous amidst suffering
Adventurous in search of knowledge
Compassionate to the ignorant
Supportive of those in need
Quietly wise and secure in the womb of chaos.

Alma A. Mariano

Piety

I choose
to extinguish the sensitive
sableness of the unnecessary;

For critique
of ample sensuous silk,
of the power your sweetness confounds...

My
saber, sable teeth may remain sober when
sinking into the sensational
seventh
sense of your sexiness.

I surrender
only the fact that my heart shall never be sour
at the sounds of your
savage soliloquies...
of
Love.

Warren J. Atkins Jr.

Life Of A Dream

As a river flows in idle motion,
its droplets dance on the water
catching that radiant caption from above,
giving life to the dance.
Moments portray the innocence
of the dream.
A dream of life, not death.
Created in the depths of
the shallow mind.
Alone in this world with his dreams.
Able to live, breath, and survive.

Melissa Ann Kuecker

Over The Hill, And Away We Go!

Whenever you're told that you're over the hill,
But to slow the descent, you should take a pink pill,
And you really should think about writing your will,
You can be well assured, you will get a big bill.

Now the doctors and lawyers are waiting in line,
Then next, politicians, technicians, morticians align;
They all have one purpose, as if by design;
They're after your pension, your Medicare, and mine.

The fixed income vultures abound in the land,
They circle, and circle, and hold out their hand;
When they get all you've got, then they've got all you get,
But try not to worry, your credit's good yet.

Your Security that's Social, amounts to a pittance,
But the tax men, indifferent, say, "Send your remittance."
Whether balding or gray, it's sure safe to say,
That they're all out to get you, if you're able to pay.

So heed this advice, all you obsolete kids,
Don't crawl in those boxes and pull down the lids;
Just stay in good health 'till age ninety-three,
Then jump in the sea, for you see, that is free.

Forest G. Seeley

"On Our Way?"

We were up in the dark at three A.M.
Our hopes were the snow storm we would stem,
The car was packed the night before,
But we still looked for space to pack away more,
On looking out the window snow covered the ground,
Everything in sight was white all around,
We turned on the weather channel on the old T.V.
To watch the storm line to see if this trip was to be,
While having breakfast a decision had to be made,
So it was back to the T.V. and our plan was laid,
The storm well covered the route we would take,
Bad weather was predicted to last two days before a break,
The time was now five A.M. so I went back to bed,
Snow or no snow I was not to be led,
Up again at quarter to nine to wash and shave,
Smiling to myself our friends would not have to wave,
The weather and my wife have come down with a cold,
You can always give one away but a cold can't be sold,
So we will wait for a more favorable day,
Then say adios and be on our way.

Gene Mason

Promises Never Kept

I never sky-dived
Or climbed a mountain
Or skied down a cold white slope
I never rode the crest of a billowing wave
Or dared the rapids
Or felt the salty spray of the sea from a fast moving boat
I never felt the tranquility of the fisherman
Or the solitude of the forest
Or explored the dappled sounds of a hidden waterfall
Or the scampering of a startled deer in the brush
I never soared the skies or played the wind on a hang glider
or brushed the clouds alone in a small, spirited plane
I never galloped a high-spirited steed in wood and glen
Or dived off the high-board into a pool of shimmering blue water
I never water-skied on the edges of a blue-green ocean
Or plumbed the sea
Or mingled with it's silent spawn
I never raced the pounding surf of a desolate beach
Tomorrow....Tomorrow....Tomorrow....

John Kent

Home Before Dark

When we were very young, long ago,
We'd ask our mother if we could go,
On soft summer evenings to play in the park,
And she'd say "yes, just be home before dark."

In later days, when in your prime,
We'd dine at nine, then dance and have a good time.
Sometimes we'd even party all night,
And not get home till morning light.

Now, in our declining years,
Due to night blindness and various fears,
Like auto breakdown or being mugged when we park,
We go to "early bird" dinners and we're always home before dark.

Rose MacLean

My Song

Living a world ruled by fate. Living with love, living with hate.
I feel the music of my life, I sing the songs of joy and strife.
The notes I hear, the tones I sing, seem to be my everything.

The feeling seems to endlessly change. Long phrases and trills,
the life remains. Times of climax, times of peace. Times of glory,
yet still defeats. Some songs are happy and some are sad.
Just like our lives, not one is bad.

You can be good, you can be bad, the choice is one the soul has had.
I have not lived so long to show, the feelings that I feel I know.
I live them in my music, and see them in my dreams.
I sometimes take them to extremes.

To express your feelings freely, to take good as well as woes,
    is when the music has crescendos and decrescendos.
The times of fear, some of regret, these are the times we don't forget.
The loudest point, the
sudden silence, this is the way we deal with violence.

The random songs of which I sing, are the wonders this world brings.
I don't regret, nor have one complaint.
My songs are joyous, they give me strength.
I love my life, though some things are wrong.
I sing for you my humble song.

Kristen Long

Thanksgiving Aftermath — Twice I Cried

The rose on the desk,
Still standing pert and tall.
Now in full bloom - to slightly fading—
Yet sending out a message of love and beauty.
A quiet reminder—
Of life's eternal purpose.

Then the little thimble
Perched on the book shelf,
Midst the jumble of books and cards—
Reminiscent of the last hiding place
Where it was to be spied by the playful ones
Who never tire of childhood games
Played other years with romping cousins.

Margaret E. Callahan

Silence

Yes, still waters do run deep
and you've miles to go before you sleep.

Tell your tales and alone you'll be -
they don't really want the truth, you see.

You have viewed the emotional range of humanity's indifferent face.
Disclose your heart and live in disgrace.

Julie Harper

November Deer

November Deer gliding in the air
    fast as a rushing river
Calm as a light cool breeze
    lighter than a snowflake that falls
    in late December
Gnawing the grass that is almost yellow
    sliding on the hard solid ice
    dancing in the crystal clear stream,
Wondering if it should run or be still
    November Deer looking at you
    through the window.

Crystal Leigh Johnson

Untitled

A song proclaims "the innocence is gone"
It's sad, but it is true.
You've crossed that line, made the turn,
It's time to start anew.

Move forward now with the knowledge
He has forgiven you.
His plans for you are great indeed,
to give hope and a future too.

Whatever your hand finds to do,
do it with all your might.
Be the very best you possibly can.
In the darkness, shine His light.

Listen to your heart.
It'll tell you what is right.
But you must always trust the Lord
and keep Him in your sight.

He'll lead beside still waters;
weapons against you wane.
Jesus' promises are sure and true.
For you, the lamb was slain.

Daryn A. Honda

A Walk With Nature's Sounds

The shady pathway was narrow and dim;
I pause to listen to the sounds that where glistening;
A gentle breeze blows all around;
Brittle leaves fall gracefully to the ground;
An owl sitting on a limb, spreads out its giant wings;
A group of birds begin to sing;
Up in the tree tops squirrels begin to chatter;
Why? Does it really matter?
Two chipmunks, run out on an old tree trunk;
The air is filled with love;
As a flock doves land in the trees above;
Yet through all the comotion came a magic potion;
Suddenly I felt a peace; that I hope would never cease;
Yet, I dare not sigh nor shoot a gun;
For nature's sound is loud enough.

Danny E. Johnson

The Weight Of The World

Today is the day I turn old.
I've been around so long, I'm growing mold.
My teeth are starting to fall out,
And in order to be heard, I need to shout.
I can't see well out of my peepers,
So now I have new spectacles - jeepers!
Whenever I try to do things fast,
I somehow always end up being last.
Now it seems whenever I go out,
There is always someone hovering about.
And whenever I'm feeling blue, I'm told,
"That's what happens when you turn five years old."

Christine Azzario

On The Outside Looking In

Day after day I felt kind of lonely,
Day after day it was him and him only,
He's a part of a world I'd never be,
This is how it's always been,
I'm on the outside looking in.

My eyes filled with tears,
Afraid of something that haunted me all these years,
I would pray for a miracle,
Pray that someday you would take me away,
From the pain.

I've been strong,
It didn't take long,
For me to realize,
Time won't heal this hurting human soul,

It seems as though I've always been,
On the outside looking in,
I've come so far,
I'm still reaching for the stars,
I'm not going to fall to my knees,
'Cause they'll never know the real me

Shauna Heide

My Amber

My pretend little sister, she was a beautiful girl.
I would play with her and read to her, we'd have so much fun.
She would always stay for supper, and often spent the night.
I would take her to the store, and in the summer to the park.
She would often ride on my lap, for she was very small.
The two of us put-put home away before nightfall.
We shared good times at Disneyland and also Ports of Call.
Fun in the backyard and playing with the pets
Is one of the things I remember best.
When her growing older had just begun,
Her normal life now was done.
Instead of parties, and dances,
Her life was chemo and blood transplants.
No more school; doctors and nurses now stood by her side.
She tried to fight, but the battle was hard and she wanted to hide.
Though she had grown, she looked little and frail.
Before long she got much worse. Then one day she was gone.
I will always remember my little sister, who now is not alone.

Frances Lee Johnson

Would The Sun Shine?

Would the sun shine
If the world was blind?
And no one could see its
fingers of light
Caress a cheek?

Would the sun shine
If it gave no warm showers of yellow and white
Onto our mournful
Faces of blind?

Would the sun shine,
If clouds muffled its voice?
Forcing echoes into ocean blue,
And letting no words enter our ears
To come through?

Would the sun shine if the rain drowned
Blackness into our minds?
And form our hearts and souls,
The joy and happy sound?

And would we live to see how blind we are
To never notice how the sun shined?

Angela E. Chang

An Ode To My Pinehurst Friends

Before one retires you will travel far and wide
Checking on various locations - your spouse by your side.
Situated in North Carolina - in the County of Moore
Is the Town of Pinehurst - offering everything you were looking for.

Your first impression of Pinehurst - "too good to be true"
Naturally you spend time to make certain - it's "red, white and blue".
The friendly residents and the area - leave little doubt in ones mind
All previous places visited - lacked the feeling you were able to find

Pinehurst and the Village - is something to behold.
Midas had the touch - and turned everything to gold.
The flowers, dogwoods and azaleas compliment grass - so neat and green
The drive to the Clubhouse - is one beautiful scene!

Now for the employees of the club - their friendly greetings a delight
Be it early in the morning - or later at night.
They take great pride in their work - and with people like this
Put it all together - Pinehurst and our Club doesn't miss!

How does one describe people - so thoughtful and kind?
There aren't enough words that can be put to rhyme.
That's sufficient poetry - so I propose this toast
Here's to Pinehurst and the residents - THEY ARE THE MOST!

Henry Hill

Time

Years ago when I was child,
It seemed time stood still for a while.
I'd dream of the day when I'd be grown
And have all the freedoms I'd call my own.

Very slowly through teenage years,
Time crept amidst my trials and tears.
College came with new friends galore,
One of whom I could not love more!

Our marriage has been like a dream,
Producing bright children whose love it seems
Increases with their trials and pain,
Which mirrors me before God's reign.

Today with grandchildren so sweet,
Retirement now makes life complete.
Time suddenly is speeding by
But won't stop no matter how I cry.

But happiness still reigns in my life
With God in control I have no strife.
Now I dream of my home in the sky
Where time won't matter in that by and by!

Jessie Butler

"Softly We Say"

From the radiant warmth of the noon-day sun
Two wayward seagulls took to flight
I briskly turned my head to see
What seemed to be a catastrophe

Intensely I watched with utter silence
Two butterflies in the bushes mating
Is it not strange but you should know
How careful in their actions go

Creative doubtful working trying
The common honeybees always flying
Their queen in slumber at her leisure
Her workers spare no time for pleasure

The sun now sets the day is over
Our workers count their daily treasures
All on this coast can safely say
We'll sleep and wait for another day

Lloyd Gajadhar

The Parting

Old body so weary, but in faith ever strong,
The power of love is guiding me on
I'm promised that it won't be long,
Until love delivers me safely Home.

Old body, you say you can no longer go on,
And I will have to go on, alone.
Unspotted by sin, in faith planted strong,
Trusting his grace to take me safely home.

Don't weep old body, for surely you know,
Your precious cargo will never grow old.
Soon I will wear a crown of pure gold,
That is the hope of this trusting soul!

Old body, this soul, in faith ever strong,
Soon you can stop, but I want to go on!
No tears are falling, it won't be long,
Until He comes in glory to take me safely Home!

Bonnie J. Gullick

The Silent Mountain

Towering into the sky, for thousands
of years it stood untouched by
man's hand. Now as the mist
envelops its grace, there upon run
trails of trodden ground, scaring its face.

Men on black wings circle high
and believe as though they may
place claim, but it endures, and
after all else it will still remain.

Who are we to judge against
wrongful deeds for one without
a voice? What right does man's
race have, destroying one without a choice?

Terri L. Clyde

Falling Water

The knowledge of the soul is resonant, autonomous, and true
unchallenged by mortal questions of heart and mind.
Where passion and adoration for another lie enmeshed
within the depths of one's existence without circumscription-but
boundless, infinite, and eternal.
Where the likeness of your beings smile, reflecting
back at one another in astonishing simplicity.

Canopied by dreams drowning in desire, ungoverned by precept,
but spurred by the magnificence of memory's vivid imagery.
All knowing and acceptance, the core
the miracle of humanness is in the captivation and mergence of two
souls, albeit unbeknownst,
until a bond emerges which transcends all earthly obstacles.
Intangible movements of space and time render
powerless against such union.

And when apart in empty solitude,
both souls restlessly thrash in search of the other,
yearning for the solace and serenity
that is only found in rejoining.
Convergence the goal. Ecstasy the reward.

Maria Scialla

Sonnet One

A point of silver light, a jet, shot by
framed half by hope, half by a maple tree;
and made me wonder who might ever be
paid honor to, whatever arcs we fly,
we kindle needs we never satisfy;
along whatever blue periphery
(my love for you and yours for me;
the line that marks off land from sky).

Whatever we've called up we've called by name
to take life fully, to participate
in cosmos, fuse in flesh and bone;
object and observer both grown tame,
committed to dynamics inchoate
in darkness, ineluctable as stone.

CherylAnn Whelchel

Christmas

Christmas is a special time of the year,
There is no fright, hatred, or fear.

During Christmas there is not trouble or fuss,
Christmas brings out the best in all of us.

Getting the gift that you wanted can bring you much ease,
But remember it is better to give than to receive.

During Christmas there are many things to buy and sell,
people on the streets singing songs and praising Noel.

Getting the best gifts seems to be our top priority,
when we should be concentrating on the less advantageous minority.

Christmas is filled with people who are praising
and throughout this great holiday the prayers are raising,

During Christmas other events in life are put on pause,
as we enjoy Christ, new life, love, and Santa Claus.

During Christmas there is a sort of loving feeling, a sort of a tingle
because of the love, caring, laughter, and the gifts from Kris Kringle

Some people think Christmas is just a myth,
but for those of us who believe it is on the twenty-fifth.

During Christmas there are many things people think they need,
but the one thing they need is to believe in a Christian creed.

Tyson K. Wollert

God Has A Plan For Us All

Life has a special to us all
The happiness and joy of living, from day to day
We never know what the next day will bring,
Because God has a plan for us all.
He wakes us up in the morning with thoughts on our mind;
Of living our lives to the fullest until it's out time,
To start our lives all over again.
We never know what day and time
That God will call us home.
But be ashore at any given time
You're bound to go home.

Leonard Sanders

The Asking

The asking of the river is only that we join it in stillness,
we lie on warm sun rocks staring a sky which turns the water blue,
even the children sit mute and watch the fisherman,
the fisherman's silence to the river's abyss.

The asking is not one voice but a myriad of overlapping sounds,
the first sound was a drop of glacier water echoing a canyon,
before the whisper could travel beyond ears another replaced it,
the river's eternal refrain sings like silver summer peace rain.

We lie on warm sun rocks and hold the hymn in paper cups,
even the children sit mute in tis arms and sing along.

Nathan Lund Eastman

The Cycles Of My Life

There's an aching down in my soul, that's tearing me apart
It haunts all of my dreams and breaks my giving heart
It's the passing of my mother and just the passing of time.
Fills my days with emptiness where's the reason or rhyme.
The visions of my childhood so totally wrap around
The essence of my mother that's now nowhere to be found.
Try as I might to find them, her memories will not come.
But a hunger for a time forgotten, continues to go on.
So I look for things in the present tense to remind me of my past.
They joys of youth that once were mine, I always thought would last.
I see them in my daughters eyes, the way they look at me.
Reminds me how I felt towards Mom and the times she shared with me
So I search for meaning 'tween the cycles of my life.
And I look for clues for life beyond my sorrows and my strife.
Sometimes I wish I could walk through the door of time long past.
And be with Mom in heaven above in blessed peace at last.
Though life now is filled with pain, it need not always be,
I have my wife and my sweet kids they are my family.
I only hope before I pass beyond that distant shore.
I rest assured that life goes on and will forever more.

Thomas W. Crider

Bring Back To Me An Old Christmas

Bring back to me an Old Christmas
    that I once knew as a boy
When everyone shared that deep feeling
    of warmth, closeness, and joy.

There was a certain calmness in the air
    Because the spirit was real
        and I could feel
        The presence of God there

Bring back to me and Old Christmas.

Tommy G. Killingsworth

Blue Christmas

This Christmas won't be like the ones in the past -
I hope this one goes quickly, I don't want it to last.

My son is in the hospital, he won't be here-
I can tell you it will be a blue Christmas this year.

He has an illness the doctors can not seem to pin down-
It has taken us from year to year running us all around.

My son is not at home, for he is still gone from here -
I can tell you it will be a blue Christmas this year.

The cold wind has come from far and near-
To make it seem more like Christmas is here.

The time should be jolly, but I can't bring myself to cheer-
For my Matthew is not with us, it will be a blue Christmas this year.

Melody Johnson-Sartor

"Strength Through Reflection"

Sitting and starring, I'll tell you a short tale
A man and his boat, in the Islands they sail

Left behind the mainland, away from the grief
Mother Nature will challenge, from storms to a reef

Society has left him, to struggle all alone
Damage was done, from his back to his leg bone

However anger and spew, will not be his way
No matter how bad, goes the week or the day

He remembers strengths, from beliefs he had formed
For whenever he struggles, his religion has warmed

Now seeing short comings, a long future with fights
He ponders all day, and all through his nights

So sailing for life, no work to be found
Only strong for a day, only his past is sound

Well a man like this, could be angry with ration
But instead he believes in, love and compassion

Okay one may argue, that he has the great life
Truth is great pain, no money, I'm prone to just strife

Capt. Rex Gallant

Mind's Sweet Slumber

It is my heart which bears the burden
when my mind sleeps.

While in sweet slumber my heart takes control
voicing itself upon my sleeve.

I have not the logic to resist
the oncoming encumbrance of foolish love.

Sweet, sweet somber mind,
wake from your lapse of unconsciousness
so that this unwinged bird may take to flight.

Phyllis Baio Pappa

If Only

If only the world would be a better place,
If only the world would smile.
If only there were no more wars
for a long, long while.
If only people would share,
If only people would care.
If only all of the dreams came true,
and peace spread everywhere.
The world would be a better place
if only we would try.
If only people were nicer,
and if only people won't lie.
If only the world would be a better place,
If only the world would smile.
If only there were no more wars
for a long, long while.

Jamie Weissman

Storm

The rainbow comes after the rain is gone
but what if once the storm raged on and the
black clouds in the sky were always there
this is a thought we do not dare
but what if all this were near and all of our
beauty were to disappear
what would you think then

Heidi Hiatt

Just A Picture In A Frame

Two sisters went out to an auction.
They stood together side by side
They listened as the sales continued
The auctioneers mouth opened wide.

The farmers tools sold very quickly,
to the young men standing near.
Next to go was all the china
Pretty patterns — sparkling, clear.

The auctioneer held up the pictures
In his right hand the bride was lifted high.
As to her left her handsome lover
smiled a last farewell and a fond goodbye.

The items sold portrayed their lifestyle.
Their valiant struggles—their uphill climbs.
The old cook stove fed hungry children.
The storybooks read and night time rhymes.

One sister to the other whispered
"Some day we will end our reign
When all our things will be auctioned
And we're just pictures in a frame."

Colista Ledford

Elephant Dream

I was giggling inside, but I guess it got out.
Teri woke up and asked, What are you laughing about?

I scared that big elephant, didn't you see?
He swam under the bridge, then looked right over at me.

I scared him so bad, he let out a scream!
I'm too small to scare him, wouldn't it seem?

She laughed and then asked, well is it still near?
Shall we get up, and get out of here?

No, don't be silly, can't you just see?
He's run out from the river, he's behind that big tree!

Well if he comes back, don't wake me you pup.
I have three more hours, before I get up

Dale Hooper

Magic Pen

  A magic pen writes down the words of my life,
of how I became a daughter, mother and wife.
It puts into sentences all my anger, fear and pain,
always reminding me that this life is no game.
It never tells my physical side just what's in my mind.
It passes the moments but, its words are frozen in time.
All my emotions put into words that no one ever hears,
Writing out all the nightmares of my fears,
Putting on paper with out knowing all the danger.
Scratching out so much never stopping my anger.
Only the ink and paper will ever understand,
Just what makes this woman take this stand,
Its helping me to find myself with out credit.
I write down these words hoping I never regret it.
So many words I write down when I cry,
This magic pen will make me remember why.
It writes down sentences reminding me,
What my life was and what it could be.

Shannon Mills

The Dawning Of A New Day

The prisoner wait for the pardon that never comes,
The hunger child waits for the food that never comes,
The homosexual waits for the understanding that never comes,
The abused woman waits for the help that never comes,
The actor waits for the break that never comes,
The woman waits for the promotion that never comes,
The transplant patient waits for the organ that never comes,
The mother waits for the child that never comes,
The college applicant waits for the letter that never comes,
The victim's family waits for the justice that never comes,
The homeless man waits for the home that never comes,
The girl waits for the boy who never comes,
The war stricken nation waits for the peace that never comes,
Turn to the horizon, the sun comes,
And a new day begins.

Julie Grill

Whispers

The crack in the shade allowed me to see
I peered silently out at the world
I heard the soft whisper of the wind
It seemed to call out secrets... the eternal meaning of life
But when the breeze stopped
Reality crept its way back in
And though I may never feel this way again
Somewhere inside I'll always retain
The secrets the wind has told me

Jill R. Bagley

Conjugation

When drops of Eternity fall on Mortality
  We, who waltz, find the dance floor darkened and barren;
For the tune that keeps the time Slows, Changes,
  Uncontrolled like ashes stirred by wind in the chimney.

Youth, in us for a time, passes, leaving photographs of
  Memory; and the photographs, like the tune, keep the time.

So, Having the still life of memory, youth remains.
  Mortality and Immortality come together on the instant,
Whispering and promising a certainty that mortals may
  Speculate upon, but will know only once.

Those who have not met this conjugation must await the
  Stirring of the ashes. And, who can deny that they must be.
  stirred?

There remains work for mortals! Photographs must be kept
  free of dust.
The tune must be set right!

And the waltz?
  The waltz must begin
Again!

Stephen E. Reynolds

Darkside

On a cold and colorless windswept shore
Amongst the stench of civilized waste and corpses
Lay a rock.
Ordinary
Worn by water
White.
I turned it over with silty suction resistance
Revealing the dark underside of natures gore
Why?
When no one cared to see it before.

Bryan L. Delvin

In A Class By Himself

I sat in my seat and wondered
How such a man would manage
If one day - just through sheer misfortune
His wife with great aplomb and daring
Should pass out at his feet
Stone cold
I imagine the Almighty struggle he has
Bringing this thing across and prayed
That he be spared so great a weight
But then I wondered about his daring
In taking such a mammoth task
Upon himself
The pealing of the bell interrupted my thoughts
And I dismissed him

Haye Lewis

The Little Empty Den

Whatever was, whatever is
whatever the season brings
nothing ever changes this
nothing can it seems

Sometimes I think of what once had been
and I walk up the stairs to this little empty den
in the corner where he lift them
his toy army stands in a line
across the roam his electric train you'll find

And here I stand in awe again
Watching as his train takes off
And his soldiers all pile in

I know I see these things I see
So are my eyes fooling me
Or is this whatever once had been.

Nancy Marek

"About Me"

A view from the outside can only reveal;
A guess and a wonder of how I really feel.
The actual pain can only be experienced when
someone is handed the real deal.
Though I may receive sympathy and compassion
from a select few;
I wish no one to feel my pain until the
time that it is due.
However, this pain did not start at birth and
we are not punished on the basis of what we
are worth.
Nevertheless, this million years of pain inside
is the equivalent to hell on earth.

Alan C. Coy

Napoleon Bonaparte

Napoleon Bonaparte a brave and daring man
went off to war with sword in hand
his mind was set on conquering the land
Through europe he marched
winning battle after battle
oh how the guns would rattle
although a short man, he sat
tall in the saddle
He was a brave man, this is true
fought many a battle and won them too.
But about his future, little he knew.
The day was cold, snow and wind blew
but important it is, yes it is true
This was the day, Napoleon met his waterloo

Robert A. Sexton

Evening News "Listen"

Do you hear the words God gave,
  Or the final moans of the brave?
To those who cry in the night,
  Hoping to stop the blight?
To the whines of those mistreated.
  Because they feel defeated?
To the roars from an angry crowd.
  Fury for being let down?
To the thrashing and screams of infants.
  Born with addictions?
To the howls from Black and Whites
  Demanding their birth rights?
To sobs of those who feel hunger
  Can they be deprived any longer?
To the hoots at those who are different?
  Their life is ever-lacerant
To the sudden loud clap of thunder.
  Perhaps its time to ponder.

Millicent R. McCoy

On Growing Old

What do we have in common?
This I can say for sure;
As a day passes we grow a day older,
Life's battles to endure.

From birth through school days
Is a step along the way;
Time moves so very slowly
Adulthood seemed so far away!

My hair shows gray, my face has lines
But each day is excitement filled
And in spite of growing clumsy
I feel (deep within) no different still!

There's always a tomorrow,
With numbers now on mine
I feel no fear, no dread at all
For the passing of time.

Lord, when you need me call
But I have so much to do
Please let me finish things down here
Before I go to you.

Frances Alloway

Tim's New Home

Tim built a new building to house his new cars.
Now he invites you to come out, it's not far.
Go north on the trail, about two miles I'd say
And see all the new fords he has on display.

We aims to please, I'm sure you'll like his deal
Some even say, "is he for real."
The "Country Boy" says, "Just give me a chance"
You call the tune and I'll try to dance.
The melody may have to be changed a bit
But sometimes changes are what make a hit.

You'll be proud of your ford, he'll be proud of it to
cause fords are his business, he's there to serve you.
He's got t-birds, XL's and LTD's
He's sure to have the model and color to please.

Do you want to buy a ford, is what he says when you phone
Please do him a favor and go see Tim's new home.

M. Helen White

Trees

Trees are those beautiful things
that seem to be dead during
the winter, but rebud
themselves in the spring.
Trees are those beautiful
things that as children we
use to climb, but now we
read under them in the summer, autumn, or spring.
Trees are those beautiful
things that small or large
animals either live in or feed off of.
Trees are those beautiful
things that we cut down
to make things out of, but we need to save
them for the fucture people.

Trees are those beautiful
things that we have to recycle.

Katrina Powers

I'll Always Go

My room is where I'll always go
to spend my night asleep
A wonderful place that I know
my belongings, just for me, here I keep

My room is where I'll always go
when things are not just right
And when I'm feeling kind of low
but then everything feels quite bright

My room is where I'll always go
a room that's just for me
Where I can simply sit just to sew
where I can begin to really see

My room is where I'll always go
where I can escape the outside place
Where I can simply just say "so?"
and where I'm always on home base

My room is where I'll always go
to talk on the phone
Where I can just pretend to sit and row
and simply call my own

Jessica Den Houter

Commencement Inspiration

Every new day shall bring a new dawn,
And many new ventures we can look upon.
And each dawning day has much to behold
New challenges and friends, gleaming with gold.
There will be so much to see, so many places to go,
So much to do, more than anyone can know.
And though we must bid our farewells for now,
We know that someday, somewhere, somehow,
We'll be together again to fondle the past,
To remember those things which in our memories still last,
And to look toward the future with spirits aglow,
As our love, respect, success, and memories grow.

Paul J. Fronapfel

Strength Without Love

A ship sailed away on a breeze.
With it my heart was carried on the seas.
My love had gone,
But what remained was strong.
My strength comes from yours.
Our bodies being shared as one,
Together, a child is formed.
She fills the void of love long gone.
You left me, for the freedom to love.
Flown away, on the wings of a dove.
The child was too binding, you could not stay.
The ships have now sailed, the birds have long since flown.
My love is gone, taken by you,
Yet what remains is still strong.

Joy D. Miller

"The Stars"

What destines do the stars hold for me?
I don't know, I'll just wait and see.

Am I destined for greatness and to be in it all?
or just be another someday who happens to be tall

What will I become, no one knows
Will I become another one of lifes lows?

The stars hold so much that we just can't see
I wonder if someone might hold my key.

A pattern, a web, that we're all part of
So release it in kindness; in peace; in love.

We weave our own pattern in the great circle LIFE,
But someone can tear it apart, just like a knife.

What secrets do the stars hold for all,
I'm not going to be a lowlife, I'll make sure I don't fall.

Heather Thomason

What Christmas Is Not

Christmas is not the gift you buy, but it is the time you spend
wrapping it with just the right paper and the special bow
you put on top.

Christmas is not the tree with all the presents under it, but it is
reading the name tags five thousand times with out any one knowing.

Christmas is not the lights that line the house or hang from
the shrubs, but it is the way they twinkle against the nights
curtain of blue.

Christmas is not the big meal with all the trimming, but it is
the hands that prepared it and the smells that remind you of long times past.

Christmas is not a little man dressed in red with a long white beard,
but it is the magic of dreams that live in the faces of children.

Christmas is not the carols that you hear at the malls, but it is
the sound of small voices just a slight bit off key at their first Christmas pageant.

Christmas is not just one day, one time of the year, but it is
sharing, caring, remembering and loving family and friends all year long.

Dorothy I. Walker

My Wife Is An Angel

There once was an angel sent from above
whose beauty and kindness was as great as her love.

When you looked into her eyes, you knew
there was a chance that there would be no
turning back from this romance.

After she captured my heart and became
part of my life, I decided to marry and
make her my wife.

James P. Jernigan III

Find You Love

Someday I'll Find You Love wherever you may be,
I'll search the world to Find You Love and pray you'll come to me,
And when I do come Find You Love I'll never let you go,
To Find You Love to become one to live and learn and grow.

To Find You Love and grow with you to build a world together,
Then live each day to Find You Love and treasure you, forever,
I want to much to Find You Love and never say goodbye,
To Find You Love and know it's you I'll burst into the sky.

Together when I Find You Love to share each others dreams,
To Find You Love and share the joy I'm sure is what God means,
Life's meaning when I Find You Love will turn in new direction,
The feelings when I Find You Love will bloom with great affections.

Knowing when I Find You Love that dreams sometime come true,
And knowing when I Find You Love my dreams will start with you,
The Feelings when I Find You Love to cherish you and live,
My feelings when I Find You Love to share and want to give.

Until the day I Find You Love I'll dream of you at night,
And until the day I Find You Love I'll think of what is right,
With God willing I Find You Love I'll know just what to do,
First Find You Love then thank you Lord and give all my love to you!

Harold Jack Blakemore Jr.

"Say No!"

"Listen closely for I can not speak,
what voice you hear is slow and weak.
I know your friends and one I am,
to you a favor that you command."

"By many names I have been called,
some good, some bad, some big, some small.
Cocaine, white horse, crack this, crack that,
no matter the name, forgive, forget."

"I'll strike a deal with you alone,
to make you rich, respected and strong.
After all is done, and you're well pleased,
it's my way then, bankrupt, diseased."

"All promises fulfilled and up-to-date,
your soul's now lost, no time to wait.
Swiftly we lived, hidden hunger to die,
"Happy" I hope, I'd wished you'd try."

"I am that of which you were warned,
with words so wise, words you did scorn.
Now taste of that you did not believe,
your life - your soul, this I now receive!

Jackie M. Love

Sunset And Illusion

If you look close you too can see
the hourglass, lifted, turned, and set again.
Pinks and reds and yellows, reflected off the sand,
dropping behind the curtain of sight.

Blues and purples-edged with darkness
soar above our caged souls like the nighthawks
although nighthawks, truly, know no boundaries.
They know of ours-and lend the dark.

For, till that orb rises in the morning,
and once more outlines — so clearly — our regrets,
once more brands memory "a coward's home" -
till then we can forget to mourn.

Yet staring into nothingness
cannot, alas, outlast pain, for it will wait for us...
neither can it purge the bile from the mind.
The nighthawk's scream tells us nothing...
nothing we can understand.

Brian P. Croft

Happiness

During my marriage happiness wore away
Like beaches in the curve of a swift stream pounded
By the constant torrent of abuse.
I felt without love and separated from family.
My will bowed in shame and silence.
I suffered
To become a human hollow shell with fixed eyes.
I went through the motions of life.
I was trapped
In the spinning storm that my world swept
Through leaving me raped and naked.
I got up although confused, to gather the pieces and
I found within myself the happiness I wanted.

Wanda Clois Wilkinson Rodgers

Lost

Creative genius stifled,
Trammelled in the world of ordinary
Quaint complacency,
The mother of safety,
Nestles her youth in morbid despair
Blinded by her shields,
Man is led to tasks of self
Employing all means necessary
Greed and fear, shakers of monetary reward,
Lurk in the dark alleys of our mind's crossings
Abandoned dreams fade out to sea,
Lost with the answer of what life was suppose to be

G. Scott Tedesco

Missing Time

So is the day, that turns as dark as night
when the jagged edge of memories, slice through its peaceful flight.
Gone is the present dream, of a life she can control
the victim walks alone, and plays an old forgotten role.
Meaningless is the journey, of footsteps that leave no tracks.
Time escapes its purpose, and the dreamer flashes back.
Can the light pierce through her blackened veil?
Will keys unlock her invisible jail?
Is it possible to see the sky, with eyes cast down?
Does anyone recognize the face, behind the painting of a clown?
She knows she's lost her way, though she can't recall just when,
the past come forth, and stole her right to live and love again.
"Go Away!" She screams out loud. "I have passed this stage."
"Go away," she whispers. "I'm so frightened of this rage."
Then through the blur of tear filled eyes,
comes a voice as clear as day...
"Just be here now, and you will see, that everything's okay."
Empowered by the moment she wakes up, - two months have past.
And she prays this time...will be the last.

Linda Surette

Mornings

Times ever changing hands
has taken it's toll on me.
I've been beaten, and pushed around,
and my heart has seen plenty
I have done all my wicked deeds
and I've wanted it all to end.
I have pushed myself to my outer limits,
and was alone, when I needed a friend.
I walked my own rocky ground
with my conscience as my guide.
And when I reached the end of the road,
I see my conscience lied.
So yet again I trust my faith
and I wake to another day.
And when the morning light touches the sky,
I know I'm here to stay!

Dana Totleben

The Butterfly

A lowly worm with universal scorn,
  Impending every mention of her name;
  Obedient to the impulse of her lame
  Instinct, suspended from a sword of corn,
  Her weight of ugliness.

And from the torn flat of the blade
  A coffin wove, wherein she curled
  And hid herself in sleep.
  But through the thin walls of her
  Slumber cell, encroached the morn of Summer.

The sun and motive of the world,
  Like master artisans within that house
  Patterned and built and painted, 'til the dry
  Promise of Autumn, like a bud uncurled,
  Let all the glory of the seasons loose
  And gave it wings

  A Beautiful Butterfly
  Walter C. Bruno

Grandfather

A man who speaks with wisdom,
Hands that are full of strength,
His mind remembers the stories of freedom,

Skin wrinkled with age,
A heart that holds yesterdays pain,
His good deeds could fill more than a page,

His presence with us is a glory,
Eyes that sparkle like a mourning dove,
His Life is an untold story,

For, He's a man I've grown too love.
  Charlotte Atkinson

Making Memories

What is a memory?
Is it a reflection of reality or is it merely a wish that you dreamed.
Can you touch a memory or is it a sensation that you once felt and
  lost forever in time
If your memories make you happy,
  why did you turn away when the pain was too much to bear.
And if they make you sad
Why do you forever seek to bring your memories to life
If our past is a teacher, showing us the pitfalls of the heart, why do
  we continue to make new memories, memories that grow from the
  emotions of our yearnings.

When we learn to love ourselves, and give of ourselves entirely
  without hesitation or fear
then and only then will our memories be a reflection of ourselves
  that we can leave on the doorstep of our past.
  Linda M. Sadler

The Loss

Through your eyes I've seen things
that I alone could never have seen.

Forever gone, memories treasured by no other.
Forever here, heartache from the loss of a lover.

The sickening smell of things that once were,
floods my senses like a cool mist-filled air.

Detriment for self - man's sure doom,
self-hate quickening - caught, in life's unescapable cage;

And now, now that your grave is in bloom,
the light reflects the gloom from my page.
  Michael E. Frost

Little Room

Oh little room you prevent me from fright;
I never knew you were here because you always keep out of sight.

So much I've learned about how not to fight;
Because you seem to teach things about taking a flight.

A little mean much with your colors of faces
decked in your walls and when allowed come out
like little clouds for all.

You embrace nonviolence with your warmth and laughter;
And go your way with children tucked in like baskets.

Oh little room you produce learning that is so
delightful just like yearning and yearning;
Giving out to all so tall and yet to others so small.

  I am so glad that I've been here;
  For I found something in dent;
  A particular spot where I can be
  Me and you can be you; such fun,
  games, clues everything seems to
fit like an old shoe.

  Walterine Woodard

"To A Lost Love"

Eyes of blue and gentle voice,
Thank you for your kind advice.
No, don't go! I'm so alone.
Don't you know, Special One,
I love you?

Love won't end. Can't you tell?
Love is heaven; love is hell;
Pain and sorrow, joy and bliss,
No tomorrow... come and kiss
My waiting mouth. I tremble with
Each gentle touch.

You hesitate. What do you fear?
Rejection? Betrayal? Please, draw near.
The words I speak are just for you.
The love I feel is just for you...
Love won't end. Can't you tell?
Love is heaven; love is hell.

  Mary Cowles

My Thinking Tree

My favorite place in the world to be
Is way up high in my thinking tree.
I sit in the branches, feeling the breeze,
And the songs of the birds put me at ease.
I look at the lake sparkling and clear.
The water seems to rock me gently as I sit here.
I see the golfers playing their game,
All silently hoping they have correct aim.
And as I sit high in my thinking tree,
I realize just how beautiful nature can be.
  Anna Hamilton

What Is Clear

Clear is the color we see everyday.
It is the color of water crashing into a bay.
It is the color of a diamond ring and just about
In everything.
Clear is the color in someone's eyes, when the
Fight is over and he cries.
  Douglas S. Knoll

Munao

The last time I saw her was a call from the blue.
Dinner and drinks at a place we both knew.
We talked of people we loved.

The invitation to laugh and dance seemed right,
And though tempting, fatigue ruled the night.
I went home... she seemed to know.

That night I dreamt of what was to come.
I guess that's why I awoke before dawn.
...A dawn that we did not share.

The thing that stands out is that she never said goodbye.
Everything was in place, but still I ask why? Why Munao.!

The years go by and I see my life anew...
The people, the places, and things we both knew...
Things are somehow different.

I guess in life, we all have a few...
People that come and go, whom we knew.
...But those people change our lives.

Years have since passed and I still feel the pain
But the lesson and knowledge is my constant gain.
Until we meet again... Munao.

R. W. Ligon

Mental Illness

A boss - yelling, screaming, and cursing
    at your employees

A boss - slamming doors, and drawers
    at your employees

A boss - insulting, belittling, and dehumanizing
    all your employees

A boss - sexually and mentally harassing
    the women employees

A boss - intimidating, undermining and threatening
    all employees

A boss - controlling, manipulating, and spying
    on all your employees

A boss - at work, at home and at play

A boss - employees, family, and friends life's
    are all... mentally ill... because...

A boss - is out of control and mentally ill

A boss - is this you?

Judy Cody

The Big Grey Ship

The big grey ship
Brought us all from the shores of Okinawa
To make a landing in Vietnam
To do battle with the Viet-Cong
And as I stood in the dawn's half light
I remembered how far we had come to fight
and soon upon these serene looking shores
The Marines will be going about their war chores
No more security aboard the big grey ship
Soon we will be at the mercy of God and man
As I stare upon this piece of foreign real estate
I remember the ride of our great forefather
who shouted the message to all patriots
"The British are coming, The British are coming"
And I wonder who is doing the same here
And I wonder if we'll ever know his name
How ironic this all seems to appear
For the name of my ship is the "Paul Revere"

William J. Feltner

A Mother's Pride

On the day you were born
    my heart was so torn
I wanted to keep to you myself
    hide you away on a shelf
I knew I had to share you
    because there were others who cared too.
You were a beautiful child
    full of laughter and guile
Before I knew it those years were over
    In the corner forgotten like your old friend Grover.
I tried through the years
    to hide all my fears
Now I can honestly say
    As I look back to yesterday
I had no cause to worry
    because my fears time did bury.
From your first breath
    until my last
I want you to know I'm as proud of you now -
    as I was in the past.

Sandra Deyarmin

Ode To A Daughter

Daughter of ours
Don't you pine
Because you're no longer 39
Dad and I predict and bet
These coming years will be the best yet
High school, college and then a marriage
A few years later a baby carriage
Some years ago you were a bride
When you left home your mother cried
Dad and I at times just sighed
But on the whole we've felt much pride
We think you have turned out just great
Did we help or was it fate?
May you know so very clearly
That you are loved so very dearly
And may you always keep on growing
With good things forever flowing
We hope that blessings will come your way
With you happier each passing day!!!

Helen Kiss

An Earnest Prayer

Lord, here I am again, asking forgiveness,
for my sins. I do not mean to worry you,
but I don't know what else to do.
    I try to be nice and do what
is right, but Lord I am weak, and
have no might.
    I want to be strong, to do your will,
but I need you, to help me up the hill.
    Give me the mind that was in
Jesus Christ, there is no other way
to live a righteous life
    Please make me strong, so that I
will do not wrong, and in my life, let
your will be done.
    This is my earnest prayer and heart's
desire, that you will come to my rescue,
so that I may serve you.

Hardy J. Perry

Dream States 1

Mind entwined,
Bodies rolling together;
She squeezed me tight,
I held her close;
The dreams of our souls united.

Caressing her hair,
Right down to her breast,
As she eased her way there,
And then came to rest.

As we peer into each others
Mirrored eyes;
Understanding eternity...
Though comprehension is lost,
So she spoke her Truth
Christ is in your eyes.

A moment too soon,
Too late to ask;
What do you mean?
For a bell was ringing,
It was my phone, you see... and the rest was a dream.

   A. Carlock

Adventure On Fifth Avenue

To stroll the shop-lined avenue
And gaze so ardently on fashions
While other strollers
With linked arms
And love's fires in their eyes
Pass you by
And seemingly become entwined
With smartly dressed mannequins
These faceless hordes
Look not in your direction
Their esoteric glances
Have meaning only to each other
And so you plod along
Seeking the companion for your stroll
Is she the one whose kiss is for another
Or rather,
The display of Bergdoff Goodman

   James Kotel

After The Storm

Rain pounding on the roof, wind howling in the trees
Lightning flashes, thunder speaks
Rivers roaring their way to the sea

After the storm has passed
I sit in the darkness safe inside this room

Candlelight flickering
My favorite music surrounding me with sound

Tiny flickers of light sway to the beat
Moving to the rhythms of song

Tall and wavering high, then settling low and fat
Dancing madly to the drums
Bowing to the applause it seems

I can see the music in the candlelight
Dark shadows wavering on the walls

Am I mad to see what I see
Beguiled by the magic of my imaginations
Of this candlelit stormy night?

Restored to safety
Lulled by the luminescence of dancing candles
Imagination has no limits on a night such as this

   Charlene L. Alves

The Sand Castle

I built a castle made of sand,
On the beach, beside the bay,
But the sea with its destructive hand,
Came and washed my work away.

The castle wasn't big and strong,
Nor was it fine and great,
But because I built it, it was mine,
And not the sea's to take.

I turned and walked toward higher ground,
Where no more waves could burst,
And there I built a castle far more sound,
With a memory of the first.

   Richard E. Eccles

"When You're Old And Grey"

My memory only takes me back to three
When you would let me roam outside so free
You always greeted me with warm spicy hugs
Fed me oatmeal and showed me lots of love
When I was sick and snotty, you nursed me to health
You bathed me and always put me before yourself
When I had problems using the toilet you trained me
You had patience when I ran amok tirelessly
Though I put you through hell mama
You were always for me

Now I'm grown up and you're still growing in age
"A nice old folks home will take care of her" they say
Some will turn away because your youthfulness is gone
I'll greet you with spicy warm hugs in our home
I'll feed you oatmeal kiss you and read you books
with love like you did when I was little
I'll teach you how to use the toilet all over again
When you get sick and snotty remember that nasty medicine
I'll take care of you no matter what they say
You'll still be my mother when you're old and grey.

   Donald Oakes

The Angel Of Seven

The oldest of seven
I was never alone then.

Tears joy, loyalty, love,
togetherness, caring tenderness and why?
All amongst the seven then.

The patriarch of the seven guided us.
The matriarch of the seven understood us.

Riches, smiles, religion, conviction,
sickness, attack, waste, rapid, and why?

The angel mother who consoled and gave unconditional love
wasted away beyond her seven's reach now.

The deadliest diseases is amongst her seven.
Far worse than the disease that raped the angel's body.
Prejudice, ignorance, fear, hate, so alive with the seven.

The oldest of seven
I'm now alone.

Who will bring the seven together again?
Who will unconditionally love us now?

Who will understand us now?
Who will be the angel of the seven?

   Roxanne Greco-Ashley

Priscilla The Spider

In the corner of the basement on web spun of silk
Sat Priscilla the spider drinking her milk.

Her legs were quite long, her lips rosy red
And her hair was pulled up on the top of her head.

She stretched first her one leg, then two and then three
The fourth, fifth and sixth leg she had to set free.

The seventh and eight which were covered in lace
Sent Priscilla dancing all over the place.

She danced first the Tango the Fox Trot then Rhumba,
She waltzed through the Polka the Cha Cha and Conga.

Her legs did the Twist and she danced the Mazurka
Priscilla the spider had gone quite bazurka.

As she crawled to the mirror and stood on all eight
she announced to herself, "I was really quite great".

Exhausted and tired and ready for bed
She returned to her pillow and laid down her head.

In the corner of the basement on a web spun of silk
Lay Priscilla the spider and new glass of milk.

Alicia Lazarz

The Crying In The Night

I close my eyes and listen to the silence
Anxious to dream a thousand dreams
And I wait, and wait, and wait

In the darkness the night comes to me
Befriending an old familiar friend
Embracing each other like lovers

Spiraling down out of my body my eyes open
I seek the deeper part of my dreams
The hidden mother father of my many lives

All of this is real in my dreams
Now I am free to feel and live and be
There is no fear here in the night

Silence is shattered by the sound of
Tears being shed down the face of innocence
The child within is crying out tonight

This is the crying in the night
My inner child longing for unity
Being called to remember the Light

Carla M. Norwood

Life...

I live for a reason that I know not of.
My life is in turmoil even though it's just begun.
Every time I get ahead, I just fall further behind.
People think my life is great, but I'm really living a lie.

My hands begin to sweat, the blood begins to flow.
It flows with such intensity that I wonder, why should I carry on?
My heart begins to race, anger bellows from within,
My mind starts to wonder, are there reasons for my being in this land?

Each day I have more anger, each Day I have more strength
Please, Oh please, can you tell me why this must be?

All the anger is gone, all my problems resolved
I've found a reason for living, the answer I've known for so long.
The answer lay before my eyes, yet I was too blind to see
What my life was missing, now my heart no longer bleeds.

Jason Lynn Wolfe

Hand In Hand

They were young and in love.
People said, "I don't know how they'll do it."
But that was over forty years ago.
And the hard times, they got through it.

They were holding hands years ago.
They still hold hands today.
They seem to grow closer all the time.
I know God planned it that way.

Now, Daddy's about a retire,
And Mama still cooks and sews.
But the most important thing they do
Is to love the Lord as they grow old.

Daddy writes poems of prophecy
And fellowship, of men.
So, as a reward, God, touch his heart,
And let him see his Daddy again.

Lord, when Your kingdom is here on earth,
And my parents are walking in,
For 'ole time's sake, can I have a glimpse
Of them, hand in hand again?

Mavis J. Cope

To Zelda

"Snowflakes are pieces of the moving dead."
Each flake is a part of a spirit that
once could walk and be heard. Silent, poignant
and beautiful now - nature's spiritual gift to the living.

If we watch and listen with our souls,
we hear the words of the snowflakes. The
slow, steady flakes say, "Take time to care —
life will be over soon."

The large fast ones say, "Feel the joy
of being alive - life will be over soon."

The blizzards, covering nature's canvas
with white starkness say, "Take time to make
your own rainbow - life will be over soon."

When my mortal life is over - listen
with your heart and soul and hear my messages.

Zelda, sweet, sad and lonely, I wish
I had known you and been able to tell you
that you were loved.

Pamela S. Johnston

My Blue Hawaii

I went to Pearl Harbor, went in '94.
I flew there in an airplane, had not been there before.
We flew there over water to a land of fun and sun,
But the visit to the harbor was the saddest one to come.
Those hundreds of service men, an unsuspecting crew.
They never knew what hit them, when the Arizona blew.
The Japanese kept coming, in their Kamikaze planes,
Bringing carnage and destruction to that watery terrain.
The men who lost their lives were every mother's sons.
So full of life one minute, and the next minute they're gone.
We rode to the memorial, with the sun upon our backs,
And stepped upon the dock, to view the memory kept intact.
Down through the ocean's depths, I could see the watery graves.
O Arizona, be the resting place, of those unlucky and the brave.
They have a list of all the men, who fought for us that day,
Etched in marble on the wall. We still come here to pray.
I saw that face of the man next to me, so full of sorrow and woe.
I knew he had lost a friend, and this was his way of letting go.
So many young men's lives, were lost to us forever.
From that one day of infamous action, they will be forgotten NEVER!

Marc R. Ridilla

True Love

If you love me, please let me live
God gave me this life and I must give
For in giving myself to others each day
I find joy and completeness along the way.

If a caterpillar were kept within its shell
No butterfly would come forth, its beauty unexcelled
To wing its way from flower to tree
For all of we mortals on earth to see.

If I were shut within four walls
Not be able to go when my God calls
To spread comfort and cheer to one downcast
How long would my life be able to last?

Let me give out if only a smile
To help someone walk just another mile
Perhaps a word, a song, a prayer
Oh, let me not fail that one in despair.

Vivian J. Harris

Two Marble Crosses

I walk among the crosses, to be among old friends.
I try to visit often to read the names again.
The promise that I made I made each one, is on my mind today.
To always stand beside them, there is no better way.

The rules of war are very hard, the end result severe.
The thoughts were never on our mind, our own end might be near.
The friend that stood here yesterday, just isn't here today.
He never had a chance to speak, he seemed to fade away.

As I walk among the crosses, I am tired now and old.
My hair is gray, my breathing poor, my body bent and cold.
There must be room for one more cross. Maybe on the end?

Next to the one that has no name, I want to be his friend.
The flag is neatly folded, two shiny bugles blow.
My cross will be right on the end, beside a friend I know.

Leon Sawyer

"Locked Up"

I never did like her she was mean to me.
She never had fun.
Always stiff as a tree.
She never laughed, I never saw her cry.
The sad thing is I didn't tell her goodbye.
She has a disease that's affected us all.
I don't remember her big, she was just small.
I do remember a woman, tell her one day
About when she was little and used to play.
Told her she was fat.
I thought "Oh dear, you didn't need to say that".
I've read so many stories on this type of girl.
They're obsessed with their bodies
Putting us in a whirl.
They think they are big and count every fat gram.
That gets on my nerves, just go eat some ham.
She's in her own world now.
She's better off there.
She has her mother,
To give her care.

Maggie Parker

Sometimes

Sometimes people lose things.
Sometimes they are little, insignificant things.
Sometimes they are priceless.
Many times people find what they have lost.
Others can only hope that someday they will.

I remember when I lost a treasure -
But the memories are fading,
The colors are turning black and white.
Sometimes people lose things.
A handful of daydreams are all I have left...

Thanksgiving at his house.
The smell of turkey flavors my memory.
Sometimes, it is priceless.
Christmas with Grandpa and Grandma.
Dinner scents fill my mind.

My memory becomes a photograph.
Blurred and fading, the edges, torn and tattered.
Sight has gone, leaving only the smell of dreams.
Many times people find what they have lost.
Others can only hope that someday, they will.

Kristin Garling

The Garden

Please be quiet when you enter here,
because the corn, it has an ear.
Don't hurt those lovely butterflies,
or the potato will see you with its eyes.
Don't disturb the flowers red,
while they are sleeping in their bed.
It wouldn't be very smart
to rip out that artichoke's heart.
Or punch the lettuce in the head,
because something will happen that you dread.
The tulips will give you a kiss,
and you will not be dismissed,
until the onion makes you cry.

Anthony Zannino

The Only Rose

We talked for a moment, few words were spoken
About trivial things, the topics were token.
acquaintances, weather, fashions and such,
We knew when we said them they didn't mean much.

I spotted a rose, one single yellow gem
Alone on a bush where others had been.
I mentioned that beauty like that can't be bought.
You reached out and picked it with nary a thought.

A thorn pierced your finger, a drop of blood fell.
If you felt the pain, you never did tell.
You handed it to me, a gift of the heart
To take home with me, since we soon would part.

I kept to myself what that rose meant to me,
But time passes quickly, and I want you to see
That few friends in life are as special as those
Who would pick for you their only rose.

Beverly Deirfield

Manatee

Manatee, manatee did you come from the sea?
You're a very gentle, sentimental creature of the waters.
Mother and daughter swimming together forever in harmony.
Slowly creeping, often sleeping in the sunlit ocean.
Watch out, a boat! Oh good it's only a float.
You're safe once again.
Be careful manatee

Katie Cameron

A Mythical Creature

A mythical creature,
or so they say
For came and took my breath away
With merciless teeth,
and eyes so untrue
I felt the seize of the sharp two
And as my life was being past
My new life began, I say alas
With curtain in hand and down on knee
I heaved the curtain with a sigh of relieve
The sun did bathe my body bright
As I smiled and cried and wailed in delight
Then I heard the bell ring
And felt what the mourning had to bring
I jumped from my bed
and heaved yet another sigh
for what an end
To a beautiful night

Jamie Lynn

What Is Calling Way Out There?

Beyond the desk we sit and stare.
What is calling way out there?

A freedom search, quite possibly.
In wilderness, we long to be.

Where all around the boundaries gone.
In solitude from dusk 'till dawn.

A quiet search for self-reliance.
To continue on - no small defiance.

Our choice to make, should we turn back?
Not from fear nor courage lack.

But search we must, inside the lines.
For freedom lies within our minds.

What is calling way out there?
An echo from a calling near.

Mike Kayes

Logging

Missed are the icy cold mornings
With loggers gathered over hot coffee
Pulling on corks for the days cutting,
Quiet murmurs of chain oil and bars.
Old blue fired up and running, ready to
go to the mountain and the woods.

Missed is the logger, raw-boned and muscle tight,
Smelling of p**s fir and diesel
At the end of the day
Cold winter sky already leaden with dusk.

Fir decked, clean limbed
Long butts huddled in piles
Waiting for the loader.
Elk step cautiously past
Low new stumps, pawing the snow for
Oregon grape and roots in the moonlit night.
The logging grouse warms herself in the bush
Feathers fluffed, bustling with importance
When the crummy crests the rise at the lake,
For then keen saws will sing and trees will fall.

Lucinda Russ

Where Is Temple Star Of David?

Where is the temple, where I can worship God?
This wandering jew is tired, as onward I trod?
I find no peace in worship, for I've no sacrifice.
No alter for the lamb, no blood to pay the price.

But God sent me a vision "I send you to a man.
Draw this triangle: The best that you can.
Then ask him what it means to him or any other man?
If he don't know, there show to him God's plan.

The draw another triangle, draw it upside down.
Draw it over the first one, the reasoning is sound.
This makes the star of David. All jew hold it dear.
Relate to him it's meaning, make it very clear.

The father, the son, and the Holy Ghost.
Are the meaning of the top triangle.
The spirit, the water, and the blood
Are embodied in the lower triangle.

The father gives to us his son, our sacrifice.
The son became God's word. And paid the price.
The Holy Ghost gives us His spirit, once we believe.
Salvation is complete, when Jesus we receive.
    PRAISE THE LORD!

Thomas L. Tex Glazebrook

Winter Sun

Sunlight eased her fingers gently
Through show laden boughs
Carelessly sweeping a small spray of glitter
And raining it down on the featherbed earth.

And as her warm hand caressed my face;
As I watched silently aware...
The subzero breath of Winter
Was replaced by feelings
Of Security...
Warmth...
And
Love
Radiating from her touch.

Lorrie J. M. Reynolds

Spirits Of The Deep

The waters rush past me as I steer my boat,
The waves crash in front of me and leaves a trail behind.
I look out to the horizon seeing the gold sun appear,
A feeling of warmth spread through my body and mind.
I focus my eyes upon the dark blue water,
Hoping to see the spirits of the deep.
Suddenly, they take me by surprise,
With a deafening blow and a tremendous leap.
The beautiful killer whales swim beside me,
Perhaps to an ocean far, far away.
The powerful bulls, followed by cows and calves,
Travel non-stop till the end of the day.
With the splash of a tail, my cheeks are wet,
Salty water on my face as if I weep.
The red sun lowers as I return to the shore,
Leaving the fish-smell ocean and the spirits of the deep.

Jia-Mei Qian

What Can I Say? What Can I Do?...

...To let you know my heart is true?
...To remind you of the day we said I do?
...Say three simple words I love you?
...When things fall from the way side and I forget about you?
...To bring together the distance between me and you?
...When to hold you in my arms is not enough for you?
For all that was said, for all that was done, the answer
to my question can only be one.
What Can I Say? What Can I Do?
Only to accept the real you.

Ephraim Badea

Firm And Tall

I am a black woman
I stand firm and tall,
Many have tried, and tried,
To bring me and my ancestors down
To make us fall
Still I stand firm and tall
In my life I face many obstacles
That block my every path and my every door;
    to success
Still I will try and do my best, because
I am a black woman
I stand firm and tall

Latisher Varnado

The Elements Of Life

The sea turns, and swiftly I melt into it
I no longer care that my choice was stolen away
There is only the wet warmth and stifling pressure
I am an ocean, forever shifting and writhing...

The air blows, and like the wind, I am free...
I howl and whisper, caress and rip at all
There is nothing like my kiss, and when I die, silence rules
As I breathe, life loves me, and makes me over...

In the earth I am born, as solid as reality and truth
I shudder and scream as my flesh is torn
In all reality, only I stand alone, I am forever
My love nourishes and embraces, and all return to my womb

In my pain I am the flame, and I burn because I must
My edges are many and few, and I am as lonely as death
Destruction is what I do, yet I am more loving than any
As I sear and murmur, all is torn down and made anew...

I whisper to life and draw what I must from it
Composed and structured from all, I am man...I am all.
Born of the earth, sustained by the sea, given wisdom through the air...
It is to the flame that I am called, to be returned to what
I was, and will yet be...

Erik S. Goudsmid

Untitled

My hearts been swept away, like the wild wind
    blows the leaves.
My love grows more each day, like the giant
    maple trees.
My feelings are so bold, just like the mountains
    stand.
My eyes they see the light, behind loves dark
    and secret band.

My heart it knows no wrong, like an innocent
    baby's cry.
And one day just like a bird, my heart will
    spread it's wings and fly.

April Krampotich

Vision Of Love

VISION may just be a word,
But to some, it is reality.
You see it, then it goes away,
Only to hope, it comes back some day.

You see, it is what makes life a dream,
Which is what we all truly need
It adds peace and calmness to us all,
Or would it be better just to dream—silently.

Imagine a vision meant for you alone,
Someone who loves you, deeply and forever
A person with a heart so warm and tender,
That tells you, they'll love you always.

Then the vision ends, the dream is over,
Is it better to be loved part-time,
Or not at all—no vision, no dream,
Maybe the time has come to end the scene.

But how? Is it ending life forever?
Or must we just keep going on,
Hoping that very special vision,
Will live in our hearts, without reason.

Janice J. Tumbleson

2756

Sea of love
Love is like a grain of sand
Waiting for a high tide on shore.
When least expected, a great wave crashes
And joins with the grain of sand.
For a while, they foolishly frolic
And let time go on without them.
Before long, they are in too deep,
And the salty water begins to sting.
In frustration,
The tide dumps the grain back on the shore,
And coldly crawls away.
All the grain has left to do
Is dry up in the sun,
And wait for another high tide.

Michelle R. Croteau

"A Changed Man"

His eyes were as black as the stones on the land
He stared in awe as I extended my hand
I could see the fear within each eye
as he looked to the ground he began to cry
then he fell to the earth and I said, "Do not fear
for the presence of the Lord is right here"
the sky turned blue after a dark, dismal gray
he looked up at me and we began to pray
when we were finished he stood up and grinned
for the peace of salvation was within

Becky Carter

Christmas Eve

On window panes, the icy frost,
Leaves feathered patterns, crissed and crossed.
But in our house, the Christmas tree
Is decorated festively.
J.B. is now fast asleep,
On his back and dreaming deep.
When the fire makes him hot,
He turns to warm his neutered spot.
Propped against him on the rug,
I give my friend a gently hug.
Tomorrow is what I'm waiting for,
But I can wait a little more.

Martin Thomas Hougham

"A Long, Lonely Night"

Sometimes when I am all alone
I wish you were here, to be my own
And then I remember how it used to be
Eye to eye, we could never see.

And again I remember how you sometimes would care
And the fun and laughter that we would share
All of a sudden, sadness would return again
And I wondered if this monopoly would ever end.

So, I sit here awake, night after night
Praying for a way to make things all right
Tossing and turning sometimes pacing the floor
Wishing and hoping you'd knock on the door.

Finally it's morning and I can see the sun rise
I'm thankful to close my red, tearful eyes
while falling asleep, your sweet face I can see
and I know that someday, you'll return home to me.

Edna Mae Shine

My Quest

Now I am elderly
What does that mean?
No longer needed, no longer dream?
No urge for laughter, no song to sing?

Oh, no, my heart says
Now this time is best
Children, grandchildren surround my nest
Friends gather round with love and respect.

A long life of caring
Turns back on itself
and now I no longer
Feel sad and bereft

'God's in his heaven'
all's well with my life
No longer sad yearnings, no questions left.
Happiness suddenly ends my quest!

Virginia Cross Ford

Life

It is true life is so short,
I can remember when we did court.
It was so special when it was new,
Until the day you made me blue.

Life they say can be so great,
Swinging through the pearly gate.
But live your life so fine,
God will take you in your time.

Living our life to help others,
Especially dear God your sisters and brothers,
Try to live your life so pure,
And maybe God will make you secure.

Try to make life worth living,
and always my children be giving.
Keep prayers in your life,
Always be good to your wife.

My children life is worth living good,
I pray to God that you always would.
So my children live your life with prayer,
or my darlings I would not bare.

Patricia Chauvin

So Let It Be

Without my consent or will
here I am on planet earth.
Had no input, if I wanted to
be here or not, but here I am
on planet earth, a life to live
like it or not, so let it be.

From day to day I survive with
food to eat and water to drink
all from planet earth.
As I grow from day to day,
I realize that this life I must live
was planned by one much greater than I
so be it bitter or sweet from day to day
I say so let it be.

Not lived before this life I must live
tis mine to live each moment of each day.
So as I live from day to day I pray that
my creator will give me strength to accept
night and day, riches and poverty
and in all things not my will but his will, so let it be.

John A. Curtis

The Man On Stage

A tall, strong man steps onto the stage, the years have been kind.
He grows better with age.

A wisp of a smile crosses his face, he just raises his hand and
the band ups the pace.

No words have been spoken, for there is no need.
This man is a showman, a showman indeed.

Every now and then the "real man" peeps thru.
That's the one I'd like to know, just between me and you

He sings "Hard To Handle and, oh yes "T-R-O-U-B-L-E too.
And then comes "Can't Help Falling In Love With You."

We have all wished we were part of the song,
God knows we love him, and will from now on.

His dark eyes just dance, like the stars in the night.
And a kiss from his lips sends your heart into flight.

The man on stage is special indeed, he is so full of love,
and he has special needs.

He needs to be trusted, wanted and loved, he loves all the people
and God up above.

May God guide each step, all the days of his life, and may Wayne
always listen so he'll have less strife. So if I might say, just one
thing to Wayne, its "Hey little darlin'" don't you ever change!!

Tricia Wilson

Christ, The Gift

That night in Bethlehem He did
so freely give,
A child - His son - a Savior, so man
could truly live.

A hope was born beneath that star,
a promise to all men, that we might
know our father and count Jesus as our friend.

So as we celebrate tonight one more
Christmas eve, let us know within our
hearts, it is Christ whom we believe.

And let us thank Him for His love,
for His devotion free, and walk with
Him while on this earth until in glory be.

Kathryn J. Finley

Carlitos

Amid frightful clouds chased by breeze
An insult rages towards me.
I do not complain. Silently I recoil from it
Swallowing the bitter taste of a battle kept still.

Words stumble, and as if in a tight fist
I hold fast on to my urbanity.

Yet questions agitate in my mind:
Do I humble myself? Do I heed my pride?
Do I retaliate? Do I retreat?
Will I regret what was or was not replied?

Confused becomes my conscience.
Furiously rushes my impatience.
But propriety prevails in sobriety and sense.
...Awareness obscures a disquieting thought:

That all that's left in the depth of my soul
Is no more than a faint-hearted, proud self.

Urania Lieb

"Happy Hearts"

Hearts are always very red.
With a heart, there is nothing to dread.
Hearts are nice and beautiful, too.
Follow your heart and your love will be true.

Valentine's Day was started by Cupid.
People say he is not stupid.
With arrows, he shot people in the heart.
He hoped that they would never part.

We all love to celebrate.
We think that this day is great.
Our homes look festive with decoration.
We fill our hearts with adoration.

Some wish it could last and last.
We love this holiday that came from the past.
This day brings many people together.
Sharing and caring is meant to last forever.

Bev Baciak

Away From The Maddening Crowd

Away away, I want to be; away away,
There, where there is hatred and sorrow, away away.
Away away I want to be; away away,
There, where insecurity and hostility lies, away away.
There, where love is unheard of, where envy and greed is, away away.
In this place, where there is no conscience nor content, away I want
to be.

There, where there is love and compassion, there I want to be;
Where there is brotherliness and happiness, there I want to be;
There, where there is joy and contentment, there I want to be;
Where I will find peace, understanding and care; there I want to be,
Far away from the maddening crowd;
Where sharing and caring reigns, there I want to be.

Chinedum Austin Otigbuo

Prayer

The act of prayer, is a gift alone
To pray and receive, is an act will done.
With patience and fortitude, the
right path you shall trod,
in humble submission, you act;
to the will of God.
It is love and adoration, coming
straight from the heart,
an act of true faith, also
playing a part.

Mary L. Redman

Why He Loves Me

It's the twinkle in my eyes
It's the braids in my hair
It's his kisses on my cheeks
My fingers, my toes, the
    Souls of my feet
It's the fullness of my lips
It's when we took our first sips
It's the whiteness of my teeth
It's the softness of my skin
It's the lightness of my touch
It's the way I dance for him
In my high heel shoes and
    Red fringed jacket
It's the firmness of my thighs
It's the things I do to please
It's the words I say to him
It's my look, my smile, my body,
My color, my taste, my scent, my difference
It's the fact that I am simply a woman
It's the perfect love we share

Carrol Roberts

I Know, Do You?

I know that I know that I know that I know
That Jesus lives in my heart!
I know that I know that I know that I know
That He will never depart!

I know that I know that I know that I know
That Jesus is coming again!
I know that I know that I know that I know
He will take me to heaven with Him!

Do you know that I know that Jesus wants you in Heaven too?
That God gave His son for you and me is what I want you to see!
Just open your heart and ask Him in is all that you have to do.
Then you will know deep down within, He has forgiven you!

Do you know that you know that you know that you know
That once you trust and believe!
Do you know that you know that you know that you know
God's promises you will Receive!

Do you know that you know that you know that you know
When God's peace fills you from within!
Do you know that you know that you know that you know
Then Jesus's love has no end!

Jean Wadsworth Barnett

Revelry

The Whirlpool spins its deadly web
Atomic age and on again
Where power, pride and greed prevail
Deafening ears to justice wails
And then . . .
S
I
L
 E
 N
  C
   E
A drop of sunlight filters through
Encased in haze yet somehow true
Illuminating caves and canyons of the blind
It sweeps aside cobwebs that hang within the mind
Then comes . . . Life's Essence

Tina Sacco

Pain

I don't see how you could
hurt me so, how could some
one sink so low.
The things that are dancing
around in my head get
so bad that I wish I were dead.
Not once did you think
of my feelings, nor did you try.
Sometimes I think you love was a lie.
I can't help but wonder if you still think of me
the things that are going on, I just can't let them be.
Each night when I lay myself down to sleep it's
our memory that hurts way down deep.
If we could just go back into the past
maybe just maybe our love would have last.

Corey Mitchell

Heart's Delight

Garage sales, garage sales,
Oh, how I love garage sales!
Pots and pans and sheets for the bed,
Buttons and bows and hats for my head.
Boots for the hubby, toys for the kids;
I might even find some Tupperware lids.
One never knows what one may find,
That's the "draw" of the garage sale sign.
Maybe I'll find an antique chair
Or a kewpic doll from a past state fair.
Just turn me loose, don't slow me down.
The weekend's here, I'm going to town!
I've driven on tar and wash-board gravel.
When its garage sale season - oh boy, do I travel.
The bargains are out there, there's treasures galore.
A garage sale sign...I cannot ignore.
So clean out your closets, take all you discard,
Add some price tags and set it out in your yard.
Put up a sign telling me when and where
And, honey, count on it, I'll be there!

Marjorie Borgerding

Daddy

Daddy I wake up this morning,
With you so deeply
On my mind.
This is not the first,
I have done this many, many times.

Spiritually, mentally
and physically you were there,
No matter what situation occurred,
No matter what time or place.
Daddy you always showed you really, really cared.

You left me daddy, but I know in my heart,
You have gone to a better place to rest.
Now, I have to stay until I take my test.
Because I know only I can express,
Whether there's a dad coming from
the south, north, east, or west
Daddy, my dearest you were one of God's best.

Lula M. Hinton

Mom

I look at Angels with love
I look at Angels with hope
I see myself on the wings of a dove
Often touched with a familiar gentleness...

Why does love feel so good?
Why does hope excite me?
The answers, no one knows for sure...BUT

My angel of love
My angel of hope
My angel of gentleness
IS MOM

Pat James

Northern Flight

Who in the night has not awakened
  to the thrill of a northern flight
Who has not heard from formations above
  the call of the Canada, the Snow
and the Blue
  And who, as he listens, has not wondered
of these regal, mysterious travelers
  From where do they come, What do they say
White Angels on high, revere our presence
  protect our role
and on Earth, peace and good will toward men

Joe Gray

Life (Lost In The Wind)

Lost in the wind
Knowing not destination if is one
Sudden, undaunted and divine
Having eyes but can not see what's ahead
Showing direction without a path
Hopelessly patient and consistently unsure
Full of wisdom yet still hazed
Strong as a beastly lion and fragile as a
squeaky mouse
Unpredictable it is very unpredictable
Filled with emotion of despair from
start to finish struggling for freedom
Lost in the wind
But not lost eternally

Titus B. Walker

We Used To Be

We used to be a unity that packed our minds and souls
But this is long since gone we've lost our value so bold
What happened to the speeches of equality that were left
  indented in our thoughts.
The words that once meant freedom have all since
  perished; are lost
Our once strong feelings of peace are buried deep in our hearts
The fights and struggles within will now just tear us apart
We used to be in tranquility, no worries that were ours
Our voices now stand silent and imprisoned behind thick bars
We know not what liberty contains and know not that it is for all
We once could rise upon our feet but now are sentenced to crawl
When will the time exists that this will be no more
When was the time that all our joy could upon this land outpour
The chance to change tis in the past right now we have not this
The explosions of our aggressions are slowly beginning to hiss
Where are the protests for peace that so much fought for that cause
For now all this is gone, change in this time has created these flaws.

Lucia Lopez

Retirement

To be retired is such a joy.
I am going on a cruise, ships ahoy.

I have looked forward to this day for fifty years.
Believe me, people, I shed no tears.

I liked my work I gave it my best.
Now it is my time to rest.

Do not feel sorry for me, now that I am sixty three.
It's a new beginning, a whole new life,
Without that everyday struggle and strife.

There are places to go, places to be.
A visit to my grandchildren in Texas you see.

Oh! I feel happy! I feel so good!
I have time to talk to my friends in the neighborhood

I am not in a rush, not in a hurry, I even took
A ride in a surry.

So much to make happen so much to do.
There is no time to feel blue.

I am not regretful I am not blue, I am looking
forward to a happy retirement life. And a
happy new year too!

Antoinette McGregor

Pathway To Hell

Today, I learned of an old friend's death,
I shall miss her to my final breath.
Her desperation, the darkness I know so well,
Still guides me along my pathway to Hell.

Today, I learned of my first love's death,
I shall miss her to my final breath.
My desperation, the darkness she knew so well,
Still drags me along my pathway to Hell.

Today, I learned of sweet Mary's death,
I shall miss her to my final breath.
Our desperation, the darkness we came to know so well,
Still bids to me, "Come travel my pathway to Hell!"

Dawson B. Grant

Our Little Kings

One is 'Six', the other just 'Two' —
   With eyes so big and round,
One has eyes of deepest blue —
   The other has eyes of brown.

The 'six year old', a little man —
   Takes care of all their things,
Helps Mommie look after little 'Dan!'
   They are 'Our Little Kings!'

They awaken so early in the morn—
   And hurry around in the early light,
Hurries out to their pile of sand—
   They have so much to do, before tonight.

Their days are free from any care—
   As they go about their play,
Won't take time to comb their hair—
   There is not enough time—to-day.

Night is coming, and time for rest—
   They have picked up all their things,
For little boys, they are the best—
   Because they are,—'Our Little Kings!'

Norris H. Smith

Untitled

The branches are waving in the summer's light wind.
The ferns rustle lightly, oblivious of him.
Through the forest of lightness and darkness;
He walks.

Soft moss for his seat, a tree at his back,
Lightness before, darkness behind.
At the edge of a meadow with soft grasses waving;
He sits.

The serrated ferns, the veins of the leaf,
The soft fur of the friend who lead him here.
The heaviness of the soil, the lightness of the air;
He feels.

A chattering squirrel, a singing bird,
The wind in the trees, the mice on the ground,
The shriek of a hawk, the chaos of noise;
He hears.

He cannot tell that the field is a lake.
He cannot tell a fir from an oak.
He cannot tell the brown from the red;
He is blind.

Ry Strohm-Herman

The Key To Your Dreams

When you finally realize your dreams...
Will it be too late?

The tasks you must complete, if left undone
kinder your journey through the golden gate

The value of knowledge, like a glittering diamond
Never decreases or tarnishes with age

Don't close this precious book of opportunity
Boldly turn to the next page

Fill your mind with all that you can absorb
For you will eventually see

Happiness and success in this world are yours to have
Education is the magic key

Cathy Brewer

Who Is This?

Who is this that stares back at me?
This impudent child with the laughing brown gaze.
This small creature demanding only love,
And yet, receiving my disdain.

Who is this that meets my gaze?
Looking into my eyes in that piercing way.
Seeing the hurt youth beneath my brave facade,
And understanding completely when I cry for my lonely life.

Who is this smiling at me so?
Grinning in that magnetic way.
Teasing me with her witty and intelligent gaze.
Flashing me a sensuous pout before she showers me
   with the huskiness of her laughter.
I reach out to touch the alluring woman I see,
But under my fingertips is only cold, unyielding glass
reflecting back the image of me.

Suzanne Hughes

God's Greatest Blessing

God gave me the blessing
of a love that is strong.

A love that has existed in the good
times and been with me through the bad.

A love that has eased the pain with
thoughtful words or a helping hand.

A love that has gracefully shown me
right from wrong.

A love that has taught me to be
heard but also to listen.

A love that gives me pride in myself
but helps me to know I am not perfect.

A love that believes in me and gives me
faith in all that is beautiful.

God gave me,
My Mother's Love.

Kimberly A. Martin

Grandma's Apron

Grandma's apron played a big part in Grandma's life.
As common to wear, for being a housewife.
Grandma's aprons were made by her family by the score.
Neighbors and her friends always gave her more.
Grandma used her apron to gather eggs at the end of the day.
Also used her apron to pick her vegetables to can and give away.
In her apron she gathered wood chips to make a fire.
And she never took her apron off till she, at night, retired.
She folded her hands on her apron as the blessing was said.
She put her apron, when it was raining, over her graying head.
She wrapped and wrapped her apron around the children when they
   were cold.
And used her apron to wipe their runny nose.
Grandma's apron was a faithful servant through sad and happy years.
Grandma used her apron to dry the children and her tears.
Through all the seasons, summer, winter, fall, and spring,
Everyday Grandma wore that Thing - her Apron.

Hazel Gruver

At Dawn

All alone
On a deserted road
Without this heavy load
On her frail shoulders
Without the tiresome company of her elders.

The sun is rising
She is not crying
Since her father died she is not living
Not anymore. She is merely surviving

When she was eighteen years old
She fell in love for twenty seven year old
American guy. He stole her heart
And now her heart is broken.
Maybe it was in her chant.

She has got no token
Of his love for her
She tried everything to find him
She knows it is useless; but she still loves him
She will love him forever and ever.

Florence Renaudin

"Birth Of A Butterfly"

Just trying to do what I know I should
Wished I realized sooner that change is good...

Abused in my own way, I pick who I would abuse
the next day..

"Almost around the loop"
I change therefore I grow

I opened my mind to different people, and
now I know...

I traded abuse for love
a vulture to dove
like a hand in a glove.

And that dove flew high
birth of a butterfly...
"I got out of the loop"
   What bliss
METAMORPHOSIS

Stevan A. Holmes

Why Wings

One day I met a caterpillar-
The next day he had changed.
He went through metamorphosis;
I guess he's not to blame.
He was now more brilliant,
A winged flower was he!
He could fly, he could walk-
Or he could just be.
I remember how he was so
Estranged the very next day.
He didn't know how to spread his wings,
He didn't know what to say!
Yet, I can still recall his complex simplicity-
Before he went through metamorphosis,
Before he flew away from me.

Erika Dawn Brown

The Ladder

There are the steps you take in life to help you as you grow,
Learning things like discipline, respect and just plain—NO!
Taught to us by inspiration-A quality to succeed
Reaching goals and accomplishments-A kind of interneed.

There are the steps you follow that no one has to discuss,
It just seems to come naturally because it's part of us!
It starts out with love and security and grows with trust and praise
Education, Marriage, Parenting...Children to raise.

These steps just seem to happen no one can replace
Comes from Generations - Memories of the Human Race.
These steps of Life pass day by day, A never ending Process,
To enjoy every moment and do your very best!

As you look down as you reach the top
A pause for a moment, making you stop...
Wondering what these steps were used for
Unreachable, simple task made easier to endure.
For each spill and paint glob, holds a memory of time
To remember hardworking, ambitious, Grandparents such as mine!
These steps that have been given will help us to see,
The capable hard workmanship passed down from History!

Tina Sutter

Tomorrow's Mommy

I love to have that little girl
  come calling from down the block,
With dress up clothes and beads galore
  and that very colorful frock —

"Just stopped in for coffee," I hear her say
  as she parks her buggy outside,
Brings in her dolly, "Had a little cold,
  but well enough for a ride."

"My husband's at work, he's a foreman y'know
  and Junior's the pride of our school,
Have you heard about Megan - dyed her hair, they say
  but y'know, I don't talk as a rule" —

Twenty years from now this little girl down the block
  will relive this little scene,
And smile to herself, as I'm smiling now.
  I think you know what I mean.

Leonard E. Bjella

"Jesus My Heart"

Lord I love you with all my heart!! Though at times
I'm not to smart, you've picked me up and taken me in.
When I was down and out and in sin.

Oh! How wonderful the Lord you are, magnificent in
all you do, let me lay my head upon thy breast
as I rest, just for a little while. You are so sweet
and so divine, your word is my favorite dish all
the time. Need me oh Lord I'm hungry for you and only you.

Lord I love you with all my heart! Chaos, pain, loneliness,
and heartache occurs when we are apart. I've had
wounds of many years gone by, but when I found you
Lord you healed me and put me on high.
A high that I never could have experienced with drugs or alcohol,
downers, speed, cocaine, acid or marijuana.
Lord you've picked me up and turned my life around, around
and around and now I can be found...with you.

Lord keep me I pray always in thy sight, may I gain strength,
courage and wisdom for the fight against the forces of principalities
and wiles of the wicked in dark and unimaginable places!
Lord allow me to fight a good fight against faces.
Lord I'll never be the same and now I have a new name...
Christian

Gregory T. Wah

The End

Sometimes I wonder if anyone thinks about the end
I know it's coming soon
The world's a great big balloon waiting the burst
But still it thirsts for love
All we need is a little help from the Lord above
The end is coming soon
People are killing
Sick children's stomach need filling
Isn't there anyone who cares
There's so much crime, and too little time
Children cry at night
While others fight with one another
Why can't we all just get along with each other
So many diseases
The devil this world pleases
The world is ending soon
Watch out for the bursting balloon

Michele Elaine Moore

The Fallen Eagle

Like a great and fallen eagle stricken down in flight
I came upon you in the darkness and shared your pain and fright.

The confusion and the loneliness often glistened in your eye
As you searched for understanding, as you kept asking "Why?"

But part of you was fledgling that had not yet taken wing
And I knew the wounds you suffered would teach you how to sing.

For I saw in you what you could not and as you struggled to break free
Your unsung song moved upon my soul and played its silent melody.

It sang of freedom and of love, it sang of tenderness and peace
It sang of truth and understanding, it sang of strength and of release.

When the song subsided, I looked upon the man
And knew the great and fallen eagle would soon begin to stand.

And standing he would find his strength not hidden anymore
Then waking, running, flying, my God, and then to soar!

Somewhere between the mountain tops, the valleys and the streams,
Perchance we'll meet again my friend, and stop to share our dreams.

Rose Moore

"Lost Delight"

Loving you wasn't a job
Getting love back, now that, was hard
Knowing love was just a word,
Wondering why it was only heard
When you said you loved me, you didn't mean it
When I shared affection, you didn't feel it
I wanted to please you, fondle and caress you
I was deeply devoted to nothing, but when it came
to leave or stay,
You left, sidappered, strayed away
I was left alone, with nothing more to be known.
You'll never know love like mine, never love as fine
Mine was true to the end, why the end came before
we could begin!

Sheryl R. Wayne

Reborn

The sprouting of a limb can live from day to day
The beauty and its color can make you
"Thank the Lord" and Pray
The Blossoming of the Colorful leaves are beautiful to see
For it is God's handwriting That He created for you and me.
But some of them may suffer, dry out and leave our sights
Its roots live on————
Spreading and developing all through the night.
And even in the winter
When the beautiful leaves shrivel and die
If you look up above, Up, way—up high
You are filled with great strength and relief of a sigh
For just in three short months
The leaves have come, my friend
And the Blossoming process starts all over again.
So to die is not dead
And it is not meant for us to mourn
Cause everything that is dead
Is actually REBORN.

Patricia Richardson

The Wonder Of The Great Lakes

The Great Lakes, dividing two great lands;
With a supply of fresh water, on demand.
Water more precious as the years go by;
As our cities and states need an ample supply.

Water is needed for our daily lives;
Needed, forever, if we would survive.
Lake Superior, largest link in the chain;
Lake Huron, next link, one of the main.

Lake Michigan, giving Chicago, Milwaukee,
   their daily supply;
Billions of gallons water, as weeks go by.
Lake Erie, pouring its surplus over Niagara Falls
With all its roaring beauty, one recalls.

Lake Michigan, giving Chicago, Milwaukee, their daily supply;

Lake Ontario, last of the five;
Keeping Buffalo, Rochester, and Oswego alive.
Water for so many of us, living on the lake;
often we do not realize what a lucky break.

When one thinks of women walking miles
   with a gallon of water on her head;
Then think of the gallons of water we use each day, instead.
To live on one of our Great Lakes is a privilege, indeed;
And have all the water one can use, for every household need.

It's good to have the water of the Great Lakes, keep it clean;
For the use of future generations, this is what I mean.

Albert Noyes

Wish

If I had a wish
My wish would be this
For you to be here with me
And for you to make love to me.
But that's every lover's fantasy.
And my dream is to be with you forever.
And I dream when we made love that first time.
So when I'm writing this poem
I'm thinking of you
And our love, how its meant to be.
I hope my wishes come true.
Because I love you.

Virginia Sanchez

A Cowboy Dream

In the fall of the year, with just the right girl-
with God looking down, and some luck.
We'd back up a few things, but not very much-
and get out of this town, in my truck.

We'd head toward the west, just taking our time-
and we'll stop where we want, long the way.
We'd get to Montana, God's country it's called-
and in the bed of my truck, we will stay.

She'll lay in my arms, neath the bright stars and moon-
and stare into these blue eyes, so deep.
The coyotes will howl, and the crickets will chirp-
and a fire will crack us to sleep.

Then the morning would start, with a sunrise of gold-
and the dew cross the prairie will glisten.
The deer will be moving, and there's the hoot of an owl-
down by the stream, if you'll listen.

To top off my trip, though it may sound insane-
in the bed of my truck, we would kiss in the rain.
Now it may never come true, though they don't so it seems-
but till the day that it does, that's This Cowboys Dreams.

Matt Barton

To: My Man Of The Hour

It's one in the morning, the movies have ended, each love that was broken is once again mended. The TV's turned off and the room is quite dark, I guess into night we once more embark.

It's two in the morning and what will I do, I can't get my bearings for thinking of you. You're sweet and you're tender and many more things, and each time I'm near you my happy heart sings.

It's three in the morning, and I'm wide awake, if I don't do something, I'll jump in the lake. Lying here thinking will do me no good, I want to get up and I think that I should.

It's four in the morning, oh, why can't I sleep, each minute I lie here, my heart skips a beat. I watch my dear hubby lie still on the bed. Look! Don't get me wrong, I didn't say he was dead.

It's five in the morning, my God, am I tired. If I sleep at my desk in the morning, I'm Fired!! But it's useless to sleep when I can't shut my eyes. If it's something I hate, it's this I despise.

It's six in the morning, the alarm just went off. I think he is waking, he just made a cough. Well, so much for sleeping, it's time to arise, wash out those sleepers from my bloodshot eyes.

The air is quite cool and I'm freezing to death. Each time that I breathe, I can see my breath. As I prepare eggs and plenty of bacon, logs are the only thing, my man is makin'.

But it doesn't matter cause I know he's mine, and if I should need him, I know he's the kind, Of person who'd jump when he's needed in strife, by his half-wit, and weary, and very tired wife.

Suzanne Sink

Celebrate Life's Milestones

When I was young I'd often scoff at pomp and circumstance. To wise was I to don a cap and gown or be seen at the senior dance.

Big weddings and funerals were all for show to my disdaining eye. I thought I didn't need a group to watch my life go by.

But then I lost one dear to me and in that searing grief I came to know a love that changed and deepened my beliefs.

Friends, relations - old and new - came near to share their hearts. Their words, embraces - solid presence - gave comfort and soothed a soul wrenched apart.

So now I know the value of the gathering of friends to mark the milestones of our lives - to laugh, to cry, reaffirm, begin again.

Celebrate the rituals. Light the candles, sing the songs. Weep in mourning, dance delirious - fight the fights and get along.

For in those times together we learn to see ourselves anew. Through the loving eyes of others we find strength to see us through.

Sherri Michael

Colorblind

A black and white world
Country's flags unfurled
A grave division no one wants
Brave few
Who stand up to those with taunts
They stand tall
Work hard
To break the color wall
The colorblind leading the blind
To a more harmonious earth
Helping everyone see
Another persons worth
No one black, nor white, nor even purple
Shall be discriminated against
When the blind, the deaf
Learn to be led by
The colorblind.

Torea J. Schauer

Memory Cloud

"What do you see in the cloud up on high?"
I ask my boys as we look at the sky.
A favorite game the four of us play
on a memory-making kind of a day.
"It looks like a big running dog," offers Jay.
But Alan is going to have his own way.
"It looks like a galloping horse," says he.
"That's what it really looks like to me."
Tommy looks up with his three-year old eyes,
and his brothers laugh and laugh as he tries
to picture a dog or a horse or a pup.
He's too little to know he can just make one up.
The older boys argue of angles and size,
and things that Tommy could never surmise.
I watch as his poor little brain tries to think.
When he looks up at me, I give him a wink.
The older ones tease and tease him until
the tear in his eye threatens to spill.
But he opens his mouth, 'cause he's had enough,
and he smiles as he says, "That cloud looks like puff."

Anita Prieto

Baseball-Just A Game

Do you remember this pastime, when it was a game?
It got into your blood, never leaving you the same.

The smell of the diamond on a hot day in July;
The thrill of your hit as it disappeared in the sky.

Do you remember the feel of a glove on your hand;
Or just barely stealing second, sliding through the sand?

The crack of the bat as it hit the ball
Sending it back, way back, just over the wall.

Do you remember the feeling the first game you won?
How sweet was the victory, but it was only for fun.

Through the years much has changed, but one thing's the same -

Baseball.
It was,
It is,
and always,
will be just a game.

Becky McClellan

The Beat Goes On

Some things we just become too accustom to
  Like rainy days in the summer,
    A cricket's song at night,
      Chilling winds in the winter, the sounds of a beating heart.

We forget each one's special meaning until
  Drought kills the crop in the field,
    Quiet looms in the dark outdoors,
      The winds bring no winter snow, and the heart beats no more...

Our lives move too quickly, our minds engaged in the
  Every day mundane chores of life, we forget to be aware
    That "He" is there...

"He" can stop the rain,
  "He can quiet the song,
    "He" can calm the wind,
      And "He" can still the beating heart...

  Sometimes forever
  Sometimes for only a moment
Before "He" gently urges it back into life
For "He" isn't ready for your coming yet...
He just needed to Remind us

  That "He" is there
Dusti Rhoades

Comfort In You

My thoughts go back to the time
When my happiness was overflowing
My dreams were within reach
The love in my heart, still growing.

I was at peace within myself
And you were there to protect me
I never felt so safe as in your arms
Your loving touch put my soul at ease.

There will never be anything in my life
As beautiful as what we shared
I think of you often, your soft gentle face
The faith you instilled showed me how much you cared.

Our lives are different, I know...you know
And I'll never forget the passion you inspired
I understand that things can't be the same
But the discovery of genuine love was what I desired.

I wish I could have back the comfort I felt
Every moment that I spent with you
My feelings for you are still the same
And the love deep within is still true.

Lisa Dian Salts

The Drinking Man

The drinking man is a great pretender.
Until he wakes and finds a dented fonder,
He thinks he's the greatest of lovers.
Until by chance his wife discovers.
He thinks he can beat any big louse.
Until he lands on the floor of the drinking house.

His children he often neglects.
While he sits and drinks without regrets.
He spends all his hard banned money,
Then finds out it's not so funny.

He thinks he can drive with skill,
Until he finds out a child he did kill,
He tells of his problems big and small.
Then awaits a divorce in the courthouse hall.

He drinks from every saloon,
Some end up at the bottom of a lagoon.
God help all of those like he,
Who leave the bars higher than a kite in a tree.
Please Mister please
Don't let yourself become a drinking man.

Mabel Downs

My Soul Spoke To Me

My soul spoke to me, today and said
"You don't love him so."
  My soul said "Let him go, leave,
unleash, yourself from his grasp.
  My soul said "His love means not
a thing to you." "It said, you were his
queen and he was the king, but now
it is over, it is done, the candle burnt
out, the flame is gone."
  And with these words I left,
head held high, even though there was
tears in my eyes.
  My soul spoke to me today
and said something I never found
before but now have...
  Myself.
Danielle O'Neil

"In Her Eyes"

She lifted up the knife,
and stabbed it in without a tear.
She knew it was the end of her life,
and she faced it without a fear.

I remember the size of her heart,
for the people in it were rare.
They scraped her off like dirt on a cart,
but to live on she would not dare.

Their words burned like fire in a dream,
praying by her bedside she would kneel.
The knife dug deeper, but there was no scream.
Even though every ounce of pain she could feel.

Her body was bruised from battering,
the way she loved it, it was as if she were blind.
She held herself to keep from shattering,
for happiness she never could find.

Now she lay with a knife in her heart,
in the middle of an open field.
For love could never play a part,
and protect her like a shield.

Bekki Johnston

Desperado

It was a warm and still summer night, when I got a call that left me
   in a fright.
All I could think was suicide, and how could he have died.
I didn't know what to say or do, but follow in his foot steps too.
My hurt and anger came out as one, and all I could do was run.
My hurt turned to annoyance and my anger to agony, as I was filled
with simplicity and ignorance.
I fell to my knees, pleading please help me God, please.
Then I saw the clamminess in his skin and his cold shut eyes as
I walked through the door. I felt
   like falling to the floor.
Then I asked God why Rusty, now?
Why?, and I couldn't help but to cry.
The ceremony was calm, even I myself was calm.
But then I heard it, Rusty's all time favorite...
Desperado
I was o-kay at first, until I listened to each verse.
It never seemed to have so much life,
   but then it did and still does.
It is Rusty's life.

Brandy Ward

He Should Have Known

He had a little too much to drink,
As he was driving down the street.

He should have known not to drink and drive,
Then my friend would still be alive.

Everything would be all right,
If he would have been sober,
And on the right side of the road that night.

Why should one less person be alive,
So one can learn not to drink and drive?

Tamara Lynn Kment

Untitled

The snow beats down on a winding path
And there is no sun
With twists and turns and not much warmth
One learns after he's begun.

He may find a rock to sit on
Or stop at if he will
But he must continue on
He knows to avoid the chill.

Some pass him in their man made warmth
Of cars and luxury
They may move fast and seem so smart
But do they know as much as he?

He has gained through many years
A perception that is deep
And though others may travel faster
Their knowledge of the world seems cheap.

Jennifer L. Fogg

Truth , Tears And Pain

Truth, tell the truth, not
the lies, stop for a minute
and analyze.

Tears, stop and think of
who you ruin, the tears that run
down our face, when you get us moving.

Pain the pain we deceive, doesn't
add up to all we receive, please
stop the tears and please make it go away
before it rains.

Crystal Collins

Forgiving Is Healing

Oh, the healing that comes from forgiving
   What bountiful joy that resides in your heart

All evil thoughts are dead their graves
   Kindness and caring will reign in their place

Gentleness and tenderness bud forth in your spirit
   The luxury of a soul filled with peace and love

All bitterness, hate, and malice will flee
   Replaced with gratitude, joy and serenity

Oh, the healing that comes from forgiving
   Brings purity and peace of mind

Elgeva Kiser Hutto

The Night I Met You

I'm remembering the night I met you,
Even then I didn't have a clue,
You gave me a friendly smile,
Then sat to talk to me for a while.

I could tell you were one of the nice guys,
When I looked into your big blue eyes.
And now I am beginning to see,
That you are far more than I thought you'd be.
You've given me friendship, respect, and love,
Sometimes I'm convinced you were sent from above.
I wasn't looking for love it's true,
But love is what I found the night I met you.

Briana Warren

Fantasy Walker

Come walk with me through my fantasy where dragons and unicorns both roam free
Where fairies twinkle their dust to stars and elves spin tales of what heroes are
Where dwarves whirl in dizzying dance and centaurs perform their graceful prance
Where wood nymphs wither without their trees and sirens sing their souls to the seas
Where wizards cast their patterned spells changing the destiny of all men's delves
These are the beings of the Light - All things good - all things bright.

Come walk with me through my fantasy where evil too weaves its tapestry.
Where fiends and demons stalk the night in endless attempts to douse the Light,
Where harpies screech their vile oaths and ogres enjoy all that is loathe,
Where ghouls and goblins darken your dreams and trolls and vampires utter shrill screams
Where monsters plague us in all shapes and forms and sorcerers conjure up earthshaking storms
These are the denizens of the dark who desire a land gloomy and stark.
Come walk with me through my fantasy and let us see what is to be
Hopes and dreams peace and light? Despair and darkness terror and fright?
Come walk with me through my fantasy and let us see what is to be
Hopes and dreams, peace and light? Despair and darkness, terror and fright?
Come walk with me through my fantasy, I welcome your warmth and company...

Barbara Mantell Schneider

Ex Animo

You are the bright spot of my existence.
The beam that comes round as if to warm the passersby, "Crags Are
Here! Look Out! Beware!" And we discuss the metaphor: I in my boat,
hole in the floor, bump on my head, broken ore, tossed by waves and
spray, while you, Beacon, circle round to warm me once, twice, and
more, yet I do not heed. The beacon that beckons me through the dark,
and through the rocks that still I do not see. "Look Out!
You'll be OK!"
Yet
My hopes dip the water. My back labors against them.
Waves throw me
pursuing my dreams that dipped, and my back strains against them to
pull and splash.
Stroke. Reach the light then...and then...and then one's broke!
The irony of Odysseus comes to me as I'm tossed. "Courage,...and
pointed to the land". Yeah right.
"You'll be OK!"
"This mounting wave will bring us..."
I don't know when I've been more unsettled.
The gleam from the shore applauds: "You broke an ore!"
There's a hole in my boat, and I am out of "infonlys" to plug it up.
Bleep comes the beam. Bleep!
And still I dream.
Perhaps I can swim?
"You'll be OK!"
Yeah, but you can walk on water.
"And you will be..."

Thomas W. Fiske

"Our Fallen Officers"

We will not forget you, though your name may not be known to all.
With dignity and pride we remember, and mourn, through and
  beyond the days of your final fall..

With all the courage and strength, the symbol that is known, we
  carry with pride.
The duty and cherished commitment you so boldly held on to,
  for which you died..

For some to understand why you sacrificed so much, is far from
  being understood.
Your presence will be missed, your spirit passed on, as it should..

As you look down on those of us who walk in the shoes you once did,
  we hold your memory with cause.
Remembering our "Fallen Officers", we pray for the family, bow our heads,
  and for a sacred moment...We Pause...

Jennifer K. Schmidt

Untitled

Flames shoot high into the sky,
Children die; people ask why.
All was quiet, nothing in sight,
They kept wondering why the fight.
Lives have been lost — a country torn,
And the only question was why the scorn.
People are blind to the matters that be,
This is the reason that they cross the sea.
If only we could make things right,
Maybe everyone could sleep at night.

Kristi Fredritz

Love Can Be

Love can be like a bird
spreading its wings learning to fly
Love can be like a rainbow
its beautiful colors shining so bright
Love can be like a knife
it can make your heart bleed
Love can be like a shattered window pane
it can break your heart into thousands of pieces
Love can mend your heart
but it can break it just as easy

Rikki Riggs

"If Time Could Talk"

If time could talk what would it speak of?
Would it speak of pain and hurt?
 or would it speak of joy and happiness.
Would it tell us about wars and revolutions,
or would it tell us
about mystery's hidden deep in time.
Would it speak of nothing more than how
we destroyed what we once had and now
how we want it back?
I don't know what time would tell,
but I know that time is starting to
run out.

Linda Estrella Padilla

The Cleansing

I arose this morning to a beautiful sight,
God had sent a cover of snowy white.
It covered the ground, no soil was seen,
So soft, so lovely it looked so clean.
I thought of Jesus how sweet and pure.
Then I remembered what He had endured
When He went to the cross and shed his blood
He washed me in the cleansing flood.
He gave me life and set me free.
To live forever with him, in eternity
With snow He washed the earth so clean.
For me He gave life, eternally.

Betty Karas

Impossibilities

Dreams coming true.
Goals achieved
A tearless eye clouding one's view
An unkept promise destroys the hue.
Last out on the realms of space
Searching, reaching for an inner grace.
Life! An untrue fate.
Invisible the way out gate.
Ends all hope of never more
Wandering on an unknown dark endless shore

Joyce S. Savage

Silent Noise Makes Me Deaf

I see the brightness of a moonlit night while walking through a warm, moist forest,
smelling the sweet fragrance of the flowers and the fresh, piney scent of the evergreens.

I see the darkness of an empty, deserted road that I wander aimlessly
    down, with no destination in mind,
On a bitter, wintery night, feeling the gentle breeze of the frigid air.

I hear the soft, melodious song of the ocean as I walk along the cool, wet sand
At the edge of the warm water on a hot summer night.

I hear the silent noise of the wind as it softly calls my name, while
I sit on a majestic mountain top,
Staring down at the brilliant colors in the sky at dawn,

And I sense the peacefulness of the town that lingers in the air
before the hecticness of the busy day begins.

The emptiness of my cluttered mind makes we want to scream and shout;
But still I am silent.

The brightness of a dark, vacant field makes me want to run away as quick as possible;
But still I am motionless.

I am deaf, but I hear. I am blind, but I see.
I cannot speak, but I scream.

I am unable to feel, but still I know the beauty that surrounds me
every where I turn, and every move I make,
Because beauty is not in sight, sound, or touch.

It is a feeling that is unique to each of us, which we hold deep within our hearts.
And it is a feeling that lets each of us know that even when our
dreams seem so far out of reach,
If only you believe...anything is possible.

Cynthia A. Grace

"The Visitation"

Now what would I do if God came to visit, would I ask Him "Dear Lord
how is it that You have picked me to come to visit?" Would I silently
bow my head in prayer, would I be aware of the purpose of His visit?
Would I know that God had taken my hand, on that journey we call the
promise land. Would I be ready willing and able to partake of the
meal He had served up at my table. Am I ready to be wrapped in His
blanket of love, would I know I had already become a dove. Resting in
the crook of His arms filled with love. Ever moving to the light that
was shining for me, could I leave behind my earthly matters. "Oh
Lord, could you please give me a minute, I'm only human and fearful
not knowing what's in it. But out of the nest my babies have flown
into adults fully grown. I have done for them my very best now it is
my turn to take a rest. Take my hand Lord I'm ready to go to that
special place that only you know. As a mother you helped mc take a
stand, as a fellow human, you helped me to keep reaching out my hand.
You helped me take those unsteady steps on my own, now our hands are
joined I will never again be alone. If my only crime on earth be
showing kindness to others, then Thank You, dear Lord, for helping me
to discover... I'm not afraid anymore if Your inevitable visit, you
helped me set my soul free. Now I am a peaceful spirit! No I'm not
afraid of the light anymore. For alas... I see your silhouette with
Your hand reaching out to me in it...

Marcella Leasak

Malady

The silence is never too much for my hollow mind.
The gripping loneliness holds apathy close to my heart.
I never dream anymore, what is the point? Dreams, are my mind's
hopeless to attempt to fog out the glare reality.
The endless fire of hope that burns in everyone's soul is smothered
by a drowning awareness; a thick, dark, clock of silk fibers
strangle the mouth of the fire with in my soul.
I, you see, am not blindly lead by the hand of mother fortune, rather,
I am dragged unwillingly by the arms of father fate.
I will always remain in this abyss; in this limbo of sorts.
The only struggle that greets me like death each time I am forced to
open my swollen eyes, is to continue to appear unscathed as you see me.

Marie Morrissey

A Christmas Rose

There's a rose blooms at Christmas time
And nearly the whole year through.

It's colored a deep and velvet red
And sparkles in the morning dew.

It brings joy to the hearts of many
Even when winter time is here.

It lifts the spirits of those who are down
And fills their hearts with cheer.

Six lucky hearts are richly blessed
With this rose their whole life through.

Those six hearts, your children, Mom,
For our Christmas rose is you.

Irene Chastain Kitchens

The Japanese Magnolia

Every time I see its bloom
I think of him

How ironic, it comes to life
on the eve of his death

Bringing to life beauty;
a rebirth of his soul

In the rain, its blooms
hold the tears I've cried

Every time I see its bloom
I'm reminded of the joy of him

The petals fall,
only to be reborn in the coming Spring

Then, I will think of him...
When I see the blooms of the Japanese Magnolia.

Heather Bradley

The New Hermano

What crazy vida, mi hermano
so many of you choosing to forget
and you go on
dressing, talking and thinking
pretending not to understand me.
I've seen you at the barrio
being someone you are not
avoiding the amigos from back when
que pena, my brother
Justifying who you are!!
Why the shame? Mi hermano.
Listen with care
Listen with arrogance
Listen with pride
the drums beating inside us are not lies
the anguish of our history, the struggle of our past
Our might.
Teach our children, mi gente
Don't let them forget the stories
Remind them of our reasons for pride.

Larissa Nunez-Cuevas

At The Beach

At the beach it is silent and peaceful,
Like the wonderful surrender and peace heard after a repulsive war,

At the beach a sweet smell of the salty seagull sea,
Reminds me of when children get to eat their favorite candy out of the
    cupboard after their dinner of a wedge of cheese, a slice of
    homemade country sourdough bread, and a tall glass of sweet tea,

At the beach the soft sand squished between my toes,
Like milk from a dairy cow being poured out of a glass container into
    a cereal that pops when moisture touched its fragile foundation,

At the beach you may find dolphins at play jumping in and out of the
    breaking waves,
Like fish going down waterfalls seeking survival and food for the next
    generation.

At the beach the seagulls hover in the sky for food,
Like condors of the west trying to find a dead carcass along the
    desert terrain,

At the beach turtles come forth their birthing grounds to seek the
    new world's treasures,
Like scientist discovering a new cure for a deadly virus or disease
    that would change the worlds thinking forever,

The natural beauty of the world today is mostly found at the
    peaceful, silent beach
Amber Jenkins

Canadian Confusion

We are a people from far away lands seeking a right to be who we are,
Not wishing to impose upon those who have settled here before us. Oh
Canada, my heart breaks for you, your people do not know who they are.
Strangers struggling for identification in a place far away from home.

Our belief in culture is so strong, blinding us to what went astray,
For our hope is greater than the needs of all others who've made a claim.
Oh Canada, where is the understanding that peace comes from within the heart.
A stranger's compassion must come forth from pain that desires to no longer exist.

Your language is insignificant— your hopes irrelevant, for we must be
above all others or we shall never survive. Oh Canada, the meaning of
diversification is the ability to respect the other's thinking. A
stranger's rights must never exceed those of a stranger seeking the same rights.

Why did we come to this county—to escape the bonds that held us
captive. For peace could never be ours and we fled in fear of persecution.
Oh Canada, does the peace we love so much mean we rise up against a neighbour?
Can peace be accomplished when one's dreams become greater than another's!

Now that we are here it's our duty to ensure that future generations,
Mature is suspicion and hatred toward others seeking what we now have.
Oh Canada, the answer is a simple one—for peace survives within the mind.
As strangers if we implement our views we lose our own respect.
Monica S. Kehler

Growing

When he was a small boy, he had dreams and fantasies of growing
up and becoming a man like his dad.

When he was a teenager, his thoughts, his feelings, his emotions,
were confusing. At times he was happy, and other times he was sad.

When he became a man, his hopes, his goals, his ideals sometimes
seemed out of reach, like the sand castle he once built as a boy,
just to watch a wave destroy it and wash it down the beach.

Then one day he became an old man, with much wisdom, with much
knowledge, and with many memories, some full of sadness and other
full of joy.

His dreams and fantasies had changed thru the years, for now they
were of growing young and once again becoming a small boy.
Larry Zufelt

"My Fondest Memories"

Her smile, her laugh
the way she wiped my tears,
her long, beautiful hair
the way she soothed my fears.
Her warmth, her kindness
her total understanding,
her unconditional love
the way she was never demanding.
Her patience, her caring
the old clothes that she'd wear,
her bright, shining eyes
the gentle way she'd comb my hair.
Her voice, her hands
the problems she helped me bear,
the way she made me
realize for me she'd always be there.
Kate Meyer

Where Are You Going

Where are you going?
I've already been there.
With the lynching and church burning.
And the K.K.K. every where.

Where are you giving?
I've already been there.
Sitting in back of buses.
And no one to care.

Where are you going?
I've already been there?
To Auntie boy and uncle.
That's what we had to share.

Where are you going?
I've already been there.
Disintegration a threat to our children.
A cost that's hard to bare.

Where are you going?
I've already been there.
With racism so prevalent.
Something's are changing; but bad times are still here.
Burnardine Flanagan

A Christmas Tree

Out in the woods we went,
to find a tree that was not bent.
We crossed the meadow and the brook,
And in all directions we looked and looked.

Some were too skinny
Others, the limbs were too many.
But at last our search was ended
It held us breathless and winded.

We saw it standing there,
Its arms reaching into the air.
Not a twig was out of place
And it had a smile on its face.

"I've been waiting for you," it said,
With a twist of its saucy head.
I'm glad you found me
Cause I've always wanted to be,

A Christmas Tree."
Joe Reese

Seasons

God gave us the seasons to show us the way to live, be happy and grow.
He started with Winter, when He sent us His Son to guard and guide
  each and everyone.

Winter brings the first blanket of snow
So pure and clean making the earth all aglow.
We can learn from the Winter Season how to be clean and pure
By living and keeping God's Law forevermore.

Spring is time to start anew, as God's painting of nature in bright
Pastels and hues, gives us hope in God's promises true.
Spring is the time to plant seeds of love, kindness and all that is
good; help alleviate pain and sorrow from our neighborhood.
Giving us a feeling of awe, knowing we are following God's call.

Summer with it's lazy days, tells us to relax and sing God's praise.
Praise for all the wonderful things He has done, giving His graces
And blessings to everyone.

Fall is the season I like best: Because it shows us
What takes place as we come to our final rest.
God gives the leaves their beautiful colors, to tell us that death is
Nothing to shudder; but just a phase from one life to another
A higher life is ours to attain with our heavenly Father; and in His reign.
We are all invited to join Him above; in His everlasting light and
  banquet of Love.
        Eleanor A. Bower

My Christmas Gift To My Wife

Children's dreams are complete when
wishes of cars and toys and things that are neat are found
All wrapped up under the tree waiting to be opened Christmas morning.

Children's feelings of love and security are symbolized
by what they ask for and then how they play with the toys that they
find and the games that they play to express the love they know.

As the years go by, the toys and knick knacks fall by the way
because in the place children are, the security and love remains the
same allowing the children to remain loved and secure without the
  symbols they used.
If not loved or secure, the dreams never were complete.

A child's lifetime needs were realized when
all his wishes, dreams and desires were met, his symbols realized,
completed within the Christmas package that is you.

I no longer need toys, gee gaws and trinkets, my dreams are complete.
My Bethsherta gives me the security and love that I need
to put away those childish things and concentrate on those that matter:
Her and I and the rest of our lives.

Love Always and Forever.
        Robert J. Doherty

Sorrow Of The Heart

I clasped my hand to your hand and gave you comfort for a while
I saw the sadness in the beauty of your face and gave you hope for a
while like sunlight warming the morning's dew
So deeply calm the hidden grief which softly veils your face
You brightened every moment and softened every heartache till it
soothed me like fairest skies of cloud-filled summers
I cannot lift the pall that God has draped upon your grave
Memories and silence prays me mourn you
Your spirit shall not leave me, your image I retain
While Heaven divides us
        Kathryn N. Bender

Future

I sat down,
and looked at the screen,
and I said to it,
"Who are you?"
and it said back to me,
"I am the future."
I sat back,
and put my bare heels, up on the keyboard,
a voice came out of nowhere,
was it, it, or was it me,
"Please don't do that."
I took my feet off the keyboard,
I was puzzled,
"I don't like you."
It said, "Too bad."
"Why's that?" I asked.
It told me,
"Because I'm coming
whether or not you want me too.
        Jennifer Weaver

Dream's

    Past, present an future, who has not had them.
Some good or bad of hope,
those day's gone by. Dreams for our
children. Some happy or shattered
even long, forgotten an faded.
A face, place or time, those
that warm our heart, an other's
that chill our souls. One's when
lying in the shade, on a hot summer's
day, or on a cold wintery night.
But really all dreams are made
of are the past, present an future.
        Dartha Gibson

A Sailor's Sights

Tranquil, pacific bouncy waves
blond hair closely shorn
posturing in the soft whirling wind
on breathtaking early morns

Smart, quick color spurts
Flashes of purple, orange and pink
Catapult across the awesome sky
greeting busy white hats or blue work caps

God's ceiling, my floating boat-home and me
That's all there is
That's all I see
For days
        Mary J. Williams

Cupids Arrow

With eyes of darkness and a beauty to behold
I've often wondered what lies in her heart,
If I may be so bold.
A voice as soft as an angel's whisper brings
my heart to attention. Might she utter the
words my soul has waited for her to mention.
Could those lips of a most Ruby hue speak
the words my heart so desires, rekindling
long dormant fires.
'Tis love that I speak of, I know it well. It
has power beyond any magic, charm, or spell.
'Tis love that has hit me on the mark.
Please help me understand, don't leave me
in the dark.
        John Garcia

The Loving Tree

Because our ten-day courtship was coming to an end,
We needed a living symbol to allow our romance to grow.
After walking the rows of evergreens and shrubs,
We spotted our "Loving Tree"......
For only Ann to see.

It was early morning when I walked out to see,
That "Loving Tree" before I planned to leave.
I wrote a note upon a card and placed it in the pot,
For only Ann to see.

The note was short and to the point.....
It said, Dear Ann.....
   "My true soulmate...keep it alive while I'm gone...
   Always loving you"......Our "Loving Tree,"
For only Ann to see.

But now my friends, with school bells in the air,
I have returned to see the "Loving Tree".
And what a tree to see...Her loving care to share,
That "Loving Tree", for only Ann to see.
And for me to be,
The proud owners of the "Loving Tree".....

Dennis L. Johnson

I Don't Do Anything

I don't do anything but stare at the ocean
and watch the birds skim the water
like stones skipping across moments of time.
I see their wings reflect in wet sand
like mirrored images of lives turned upside down.

A remembered peace encourages my pain,
taunts and teases it,
reminding me of happiness long sought
but rarely gifted.

The wind whispers it, birds scream of it,
the ocean contains it.
It's soft, it touches and caresses me, and it eludes me.

And it's elusiveness welcomes my obsession.

So the wind whispers to me now and I can't hear it.
The sun caresses me and I can't feel it.
The wind blows stronger, the waves pound harder,
the birds scream louder, and I can't hear it.

I hear one name.
I see one face.
I have one thought the wind can't chase.

Carolyn L. Weidell

Popularity

I'm not that popular but I don't care.
I mean what is popular?
All I think it is, is when some really
hot guy asks you out then
everyone likes you, and you think you are popular!
But then the really hot guy leaves
you for another girl who becomes popular and you,
you're left very lonely, lonely and depressed, thinking,
I'm such an idiot, why did I say yes?
Did I raise my ego too high?
I don't think it would be your ego.
I think it would be him!
He was probably conceited, just liking you for your looks!
Me, I'm not poopular, and I don't care, I feel
fine! I mean what's wrong with not being popular?
I have friends, I like them, I may not have billions of friends,
but a few is enough for me.
I may only have a few friends, but at least they're true friends!
But you can still have a few friends, which is fine,
and not be popular! What is popular again?

Dana Finger

The End

The world is quickly coming to an end,
there's so many problem's people can not
mend.

Strangers roam the streets and homeless in
the alleys, people walk around holding protest
and rally's.

The world is just so far in debt, there's
so many deadlines that can not be met.

People sit alone and sigh, as another lonely
Person let's out their last cry.

Gangs roam the streets looking for trouble,
as the death rate in the world begins to
double.

So sit back, relax, and enjoy it while it
last, because one day soon it will all be
in the past.

A page in the history book is all that
will be left behind, if people in this world
don't stop wasting their mind.

Molly Haschemeyer

Your Coming

How pleased and blessed I felt with you coming just for me!
I love you so much and delight in your presence, those beautiful
blue eyes so full of God...

What a joy you are to me. My heart is complete in you love!
It's home when you are here, or when I'm with you.

Your visit is like a gentle breeze on a hot summers day, and
the delight of flowers which lingers even after you go to warm
my heart.

Ruth Seeley

Stop

Before you sell your car and stereo
Before you take yourself away from me
I'd like to tell you something
Don't you know that God cries with you
Don't you know you'll take a piece of me away with you
I don't think you're that selfish—I hope I'm not wrong
Yes I know it hurts- I've been there before
Nothing to live for,yet so much to cry for
Tell me one more time before...
Don't you know that God cries with you
Don't you know you'll take a piece of me away with you
I don't think you're that selfish—I hope I'm not wrong
Why didn't you trust me with whatever it was
You didn't have many friends
But the ones you had would always be there for you
Wasn't that enough
Didn't you know that God cried with you
Didn't you know you took a piece of me away with you
I didn't think you were that selfish
I guess I was wrong

Nicholas Almer

To Pray

When it's time to think, and contemplate on my day,
This is when I pray.
I've found living requires thought each minute of the day,
This is the time to pray.

Phillip Courvelle

Discovery

She ran along the roadside in her search
to find her fallen stone of shining gold
but though she peered between each blade of grass
and underneath each crackled leaf's shelter,
She could not find her precious heart's token
so sat down on the curb with head in hands.
But in a moment her worries slipped away-
She found joy far exceeding mere token-
For from the barren ground she focused on
had sprung a flower, colored by the earth
and perfect even in its imperfection
with radiance of unexpected blooms.
She pulled the flower loose from its green bed
and tucked it softly behind her jeweled ear...
Forgotten golden stone was left to sink
into the soil to yield another dream.

Adrienne Riggs Thompson

Symbol Of Deceit

Strolling down the street,
up in the sky, a symbol my eyes did greet.
Something that was dazzling and tantalizing,
urging me to deceive.

Four eyes that were ablaze with fire,
a body shaped like metallic barbed wire.
It had no mouth but still it spoke,
"You have nothing and your life is a joke."
My head started to ache and my body felt like
rings of floating smoke.

I stood in a trance, unable to move,
gazing at this procreation.
It danced back and forth.
In its eyes I visioned death and misery.
It raised my body into the air,
lifting me off of my feet.
I rose into the black clouds, dissolving
into the symbol of deceit.

Michael Andrew Baglione

One Love

My heart takes wing and flies each time
your angel voice sings my name;
and freeing my soul from life's troubled ends
gives sight to the passionate flame
that yearns to escape and engulf in whole
the embodiment of wonder and grace
that came to me in vision bold
and radiates from angel's heavenly face.
Time and distance can't mask our love,
the connection, our hearts strongest chain,
will forever stretch to the ends of the earth
as a shield to all drowning pain;
and I'll carry with me long after my end
the memory of love warm and pure
that was showered on me by my angel of light,
one love, in our eternity, so sure.

Richard Vise

Friends

Friends are people who stay beside you.
Who never leave you, but always guide you.
Friends are people who tell the truth,
Keep their promises for them and for you.

Anna Gilliam

Untitled

Down the fools road
or upon the path of wisdom;
In confusion I hesitate.
Though the way to take seems simple enough,
my instincts I seem not to partake.
Tempting and enticing the fools herald
Hail! Come join us kindered of heart.
In our company you shall see
how it is and
the world as it ought to be.
In dreams I see as it is.
So simple really.
One we are and no right or wrong;
together, apart,
it matters not.
Our choices are what binds or unbinds us.
Is there freedom in either or are both the same?
Will each path lead to the destiny?
Through the mere facts and reality I try to look beyond
to follow my heart on a wave of ecstasy.

Kath McGee

Loneliness

Though its mark is not left on the face in the form of bruises
...so someone would show concern

Though an x-ray in a hospital can't be placed over a neon background
...so a doctor can see the scarred tissue of a broken heart

Though there is no plaster or cruches to declare the injury
...so someone would bother to ask

The hollow, screaming blackness cries out from the depths of one's
soul, only to reach the coldness of the world in the form of a tear,
quickly wiped away
...so no one will see

Kevin B. Noonan

Respect, Power, Greed

Causing respect, power, greed
One reason for murder, one of the roots of all evil

Causing respect, power, greed
Survival can hardly be without it.

Causing respect, power, greed
The more it is had, the more it is craved.
One taste is not enough.

Causing respect, power, greed
Shadows groveling, asking for a piece of the pie.

Causing respect, power,greed
Pages written, pictures taken, stories told.
People dreaming, wishing for it.
Stares and glares coming from hopeful but hungry eyes.
People praying for it, wanting it.
Doing anything and everything for it.

The cause of respect, power, greed.
Is it worth the price?
The loss of morality.

Heather Kayer

Sending Pictures To Heaven

No matter where I am, no matter what I do,
I will always think of you.
Not only my mother, but my best friend,
We share a lifetime of memories that will never end.
The memories are like pictures in my mind,
They will travel on with me through time.
The memories of your children at home and at school.
All become pictures you can take with you.
When your time has come and you leave this place,
You will have many pictures to take heavens gate.

Kirsten S. Brown

More Than Words Can Say

For all the feelings never to be spoken
and all the acts never to be played
Too numerous the words I never let go of
not knowing how or was too afraid.
Give me the courage to move forward
for tomorrow has become today.
Loving you is not an emotion
I love you more than words can say

I want you, but I don't want to lose you
I need you, but I don't need the pain I must pay
I like you, but I don't like not being without you
I love you, I love you more than words can say

All that words cannot say
I know I'm feeling inside
The energy held deep within me
is too much for one heart to hide
A slave for whenever you need me
it is your command that I obey
Sanity I have lost completely
I love you more than words can say

Jon L. Nikaido

Family

As far as families come and go
the best is of course the one you know.

For all the troubles that have come and gone
the family is always there and beyond.

With all the love that is shown and taken
don't ever forget it, or let it be forsaken.

On this Earth there are such little things
but its our family that gave us our wings.

So remember even when you're young and old
you can always come back into the fold.

The love that was there is still yearning to be shared
for everyone on Earth let them know you cared.

My family has all these wonderful things
with each and every year, it grows like tree rings.

The love that's been shown has carried me through
and forever and ever, it will always be you...family.

Elaine H. Tyson

Castles In The Sand

When you were a little girl you loved to hold my hand;
When we crossed the street; played a game, or just on command.
Now that you have grown, I want to hold your hand.
I want to keep you here with me, and not let you go as planned.
But I know, I have to let you go to make you own castles in the sand.
Perhaps one day, you will have a daughter of your own,
And she will hold our hands,
And we will watch her together,
As she makes her own castles in the sand.

Debra S. Gee

Our Tree

A tree as straight as can be will never bend accept for the wind.

The branches of a tree comes in many shapes putting each
tree in style as it grows.

The world full of beauty awaked our sight to see the many
wanders a tree can bring.

Yes! The mighty Oak, Maple, Spruce and many more hope to
save them generations to come.
Sit under them with pride and love they will always be our friend.

Helen Jagiello

Torn Love

Whenever rain falls is when I think of you.
Rolling over in bed and I smell your perfume;
Oh, I miss you day after day,
Alone and on my own once more.

Raindrops on my window are like the many tears
I want to cry.
When thunder cracks, it's like the sound of
my heart breaking.
Lightning flashing is like the anger and pain
I feel every time I look at a happy picture or hear a sad
song playing on the radio,
and when I do something you would have loved to do.
A burning fire only reminds me of when we would make love.

Oh, how I miss you and the times we would have had;
Oh, I wish it would rain because I think of you,
And feel the pain.

Amanda Swiger

Angel Eyes

Warm, sweet summer night,
I can feel her presence as I prepare to sleep tonight.

Far beyond the moonlit light,
She spreads her wings with joy and delight.

As I lay me down to sleep,
I pray my guardian angel will watch over me tonight,
for I fear such a terrible fright.

Please keep me safe from harm tonight,
As you keep my presence in your sight.

Warm, sweet summer night,
You can hear her voice whisper ever so softly tonight,
Sleep soundly my child don't be afraid,
I will watch over you just as you prayed.

Vincent J. Prisco

Sounds Of Day

Opening my eyes to the sun,
I stretch to touch the clouds.
The children play joyously,
Their laughter and pitter pater feel the warm air.
The k9's howl makes you jump with excitement for play.
Following faithfully by their master,
They remain loyal as the promise of the
Ever coming waves to the ocean.
The sounds of life feel the surroundings,
Birds chirps are songs of love that
Fill the day with a jovial experience.
The sounds of light slowly diminish
Into a dark sleepy hollow.
Having the hero of enchanting darkness
Sweep his caper above us,
We fall into slumber with
The sounds of day slowly dying
To evolve into a whole new life.

Amy Riley

Every Once In A While

Every once in a while you meet someone
  And you wonder...
    Why is this person special?

Every once in a while you let someone affect you
  And you wonder...
    Why is this person special?

Every once in a while you let someone become important to you
  And you wonder...
    Why is this person special?

Every once in a while you try to figure it out
  And you wonder...
    What makes this person special?

Every once in a while you realize...
  That when someone is special to you
    it's because being together makes you
    feel very special too!

  Jan Garvey

Hail To The Butlers

On an evening when there is no snow
And when perhaps the wind won't blow,
An opportunity is provided to go,
To a dinner place I think you know.

But "Why?" you ask do I feel the need
To send you off to relax and feed.
It is these words I hope you'll heed,
Your kindness and courtesy is admired indeed.

The ongoing efforts displayed by Zell,
Who clears the endless snow so well,
The worries of homeboundness you quell,
After several inches of snow which fell.

And so I say without further ado,
Whole-hearted thanks go out to you.
Kind neighbors like you lead me to cheer,
Merry Christmas to all and a Happy New Year!

  Sue W. Kittredge

The Truth

I will not lie,
I think about you and sometimes want to die!
Maybe everyone's right
It's not my fault and about time I see the light.
But what still lingers in my mind,
Is what is left to find.
Love was there, and you didn't take the dare,
I'm not an expert, but yet I'm no blind.
You were so sweet, so gentle, so kind.
Life may go on, and we still have a bond,
I will wish all I can,
That once again I'll be in your hand,
It may take a few try's,
But it won't be built on lies,
I know how I feel,
I guess I should kneel, and pray to God,
That you will nod,
Yes,
Yes to my question of love,
It's about time I see the dove.

  Mindy Klinger

First Love

A boy's first love cannot be forgotten,
No matter how much time goes by, he will think of her often.
From the first time that their eyes did meet,
And he experienced a feeling that nothing could beat.

To the first time that their hands intertwined,
From the point on, she was always on his mind.
Finally to the time when their lips came together,
That is when he knew, he would love her forever.

But his true love for her he could never explain,
Until the day she left him in the cold bitter rain.
Now he wonders looking for something new,
While his heart is aching, broken in two.

Looking for something that will give him healing,
Once again looking for that special feeling.
But so afraid of being hurt once more,
He takes the key to his heart and locks the door.

  J. D. Keene

Two Calls

Back in its cradle
The second child considers the third's report
"He's leaving," the interpretation
Rises swiftly to pack a dark blue suit
Ninety miles without a word

Dented doors crash inward
Not a single white or green notices
Erratic beeps disturb the sterile silence

Waiting...

The first child needs a bottle

Waiting...

A large green and white team rushes past
The first child can not be found
Generations attempt awkward assurances

At home, the second child
Raises the first from the slumber of spirits
"He's gone," the realization
I have no recollection of packing a tie
Back in its cradle

  T. Michael Kenney

Puzzle Of Life

Sitting in the wooden chair beside the old oak table
He stares at all the puzzle pieces looking quite unstable
Finally sets one piece in the center of the table
Tries desperately while screaming to reach outside the cradle

Blackened coffee, stain-rimmed mug sits by him softly steaming
He pushes glassy focals on his nose and starts to dreaming
Yet another piece is placed to finish all the seaming
Now flying in the first world war, his plane the engine screaming

Gleaming-stare turned glossy-eyed, he gazes out the window
The ticking of the ancient clock removing him from Limbo
Pulls another piece to place-'does not belong!'-will not go
He sees his loving wife and children floating towards a rainbow

The sunset slowly shining, splashing colors in the skies
The aging day still darkening with the moonlight on the rise
He looks into the distance, sees the light without surprise
And places the piece to bind them and slowly shuts his eyes.

  David B. Butvill

My Dad

'Twas hard to beat, the man of steel
I wish I could tell, just how I feel
A smile and help for everyone
It seemed his work was never done
One relative dying, another lying
Someone he knew, he just found crying
With each new task, his solvers stance
He would handle well, with a smiling glance
No reward would he ever ask or need
For everyone he knew, his heart would bleed
So much of himself, did this man give
I suppose he was destined, not long to live
One heart so warm, and always giving
Gave out one day, and he ceased living

Terry Fox

The Victorian Age

The dances, the balls, the grace of a time
When "socials" and "fetes" were the rage;
The powdered white wig, the "bow from the waist;"
How grand the Victorian Age.

The landau, the livery, the drawing room "teas;"
The hoop skirt and pinching of stays;
The manners and charm, the "bold cavalier;"
Ah, yes, the Victorian Days.

The carriage of black, the plume on a horse,
The clop of a hoof near the front;
The riding crop, coattails, and blare of a horn,
The scent, of the fox at the hunt.

The meeting of eyes over fans at the dance;
The fingertips pressed to the lip;
The tie and cravat, the Wellington hat,
White billows of sail from a ship.

We need a look back to a gentle, sweet world,
To the safety and freedom from crimes;
To the taffeta swish, God grant me one wish,
To live in Victorian Times.

Marlene Meehl

Racism

God, creator of all that exist,
Creator of earth and of seas;
Created man to live in harmony and grace,
Not develop racism which has spread like a disease.

In the beginning was the word, and the word was God,
In the beginning among the living dwelled peace;
In the beginning was no racism or prejudice of the sort,
But in time all of this goodness came to cease.

Racism developed among this human race,
Dividing us by our intellect and our creed;
Racism transformed all peace into hatred,
Transforming truthful sharing into greed.

Racism defined is discrimination and prejudice,
Ignorance of any color of any man;
We were created by God to not hate but love,
We were created to live in amity on HIS land.

God, creator of all that exist,
Did not create any superior humans,
We as a people must stop this racism,
And come together before all is in ruins.

John E. Norris III

Faces

Who can tell at a glance, or by the look in your eye
Emotions you are hiding, what makes your temper fly?
No one can see through the faces you wear
Cannot tell by guessing hate? Love? Or fear?
It is up to each person, up to you and to me
What we want to tell others, what we'll let them see
The games people play, trying to be what they're not
When they're pretending today, who is filling their slot?
I am sure that someday, it will work itself out
Do you know who you are? Or is there still a doubt???

Dwayne Kosch

"The Mind Of A Child"

When I was a child, about nine or ten,
I heard people tell of places they had been
They spoke of places, in lands far away,
All these places, I swear, I'll visit someday.

I'll be a king, with a house on a hill,
Just thinking of it gave me a thrill
I'll own all of this when I am a man
I made myself castles, molded in sand

I built great cities and roads in my mind
I'll conquer the world, just give me time
But all of our wonders last but a while
Like yesterday dreams, in the mind of a child.

I still vision a lad as he was back then,
With a heart full of dreams, around nine or ten
Those yesterday's thoughts now bring a smile
Of the life and dreams in the mind of a child.

Henry Strahan

Age

Some say you don't look your age,
You sure have taken care of yourself.
My! What nice words, but maybe I
Need a badge for courage and for
stability, for burdens I've taken on and tried.
But still things went wrong.
You don't look your age, when sometimes I'd
like to scream with rage.
And wonder how I took care of myself
When so often I longed to cry for help
anybody's help.
"You don't look your age" well nothing that
lives can go without visible change, just like a page
keep turning it and soon it will lose its
sleekness, any surface changes in time.
Even though I don't look my age, time and
everything that goes with time, has changed
me like a page.
Age? I'm not ashamed of mine!!

Guidie B. Hubbard

Epiphany

Darkness of the soul is sometimes irreversible.
It can not be written down, nor can it be explained away.
It takes over like an inner fire, and consumes the very life
    out of a tremblingly remorseful creature.
Therefore, it can not be separated from the being it infects.
It becomes a part of them, just like their leafy brown hair.
Is it darkness that evades the out-stretched hands, or rather fear?
Perhaps loneliness?
The walls build up so high.
Bricks, or stone?
Either one is impermeable.
Safe in the darkness for yet one more day.

Heather J. Barnes

Too Far Too Fast

To all the young lovers here's a little hint
And it's really not too big of a task
So if you're in love and want it to last.
Here's a little bit I've learned from the past
Love is like driving - if you speed you wreck
Love is like cooking in haste you burn, the food
you throw it away, and it's a waste.
When you burn the food no compliments are won
When walking too fast you stumble and fall
So take it slow and easy and you're hear well done
Young lovers don't look for love
in all the wrong places
And the fake smile on phoney faces
give love a chance to grow and blossom
if it's true love it will stand the test
you'll be strong, and it will last
slow and easy, slow and easy
don't go too far too fast remember if it's true love
it will truly last please don't go too far too fast

Doris Goldsberry

Destroying Cycle

Another forest is leveled off,
Another animal's habitat is demolished.
Another glorious flower is dead,
Another tree is now a mere stump.

A cloud of smog with a charcoal hue,
floats above a crimson, brown smokestack.
The gloomy heaviness unnoticeably glides,
into the earth's deteriorating atmosphere.

The blazing sun beats through the ozone,
much fiercer than years before.
People wonder why a common sunburn,
is emerging into an agonizing fatality.

We are killing ourselves,
and we don't even realize it.
The death of forests is the birth of construction,
that birth is our death.
Peace out!

Sara Wilson

Christmas To Me

Christmas is family and friends that you love
Celebrating the birth of our father above
Coming to earth as a wee baby boy
Together we listen as our hearts fill with joy.
Pretty poinsettias all in a row
And candles that set the church all aglow
The look of an angel on a little child's face
As he hears about God's magnificent grace
When he sent his son to save us all
Born as a baby in a lowly stall.
People in costumes as in days of old
Acting out the greatest story that ever was told.
The choir singing the carols we love to hear
Especially "It Came Upon a Midnight Clear"
Kneeling to pray as the shepherds did that night
Beside baby Jesus in the starry light.
This is what Christmas is to me
Not lots of presents under a tree
Having my family and friends worship with me
Makes my Christmas the best it could ever be.

Joy A. Bryant

Ode To Buddy

One day while walking down the street,
    A black lab kept running 'round our feet.
No collar did adorn his neck,
    Yet he listened when we spoke as onward we trekked.

Thinking that he was lost, we took him to the pound.
 Someone would certainly look for him and our "Buddy" would be found
The allotted time passed and a call came to say,
    No one claimed the lab so he'd have to be put away.

We remembered the bright eyes of our "Buddy" that danced
    with a longing to play.
    How full of life he had been the day when we first met.
Death wasn't an option for this playful pup,
    So we claimed Bud as our pet.

He found his place within our home,
    He'd already wormed his way into our hearts.
Off to Obedience classes the three of us went,
    And his 2nd place ribbon proved the time was well spent.

A true friend to us our "Buddy" is
    And we couldn't imagine life without him.
These last three years have been filled with great joy
    From "Buddy", our wonderful boy.

Barbara Ann Trivelli

"Mom"

Mom, when I was little, I needed you so much
I needed your loving guidance, sometimes just a touch.
You left when I was young, mom, to pursue your dream
I wanted you and looked for you, all in vain it seemed.
I tried to grow up right mom, to make you proud of me,
It seems you didn't really care, and you couldn't see.
The many things I tried to do to get your attention,
I ran away, skipped school and cried and even got detention.
When I grew up and became a mom, I thought about you a lot,
But mom, I still didn't understand you, and we always fought.
And now my kids are growing up and there is so much to do,
And Jesus love has helped me to forgive, but mom, I still need you.

Jeanette McMillan

Untitled

Friendship runs very deep
like a mountain oh so steep
A true friendship lasts forever
And always seems to just get better.
Our friendship is like that,
One that lasts and lasts.
There's no one to come between us
And nothing could cause any kind of fuss.
Yes, we'll have our ups and downs
But we'll always smile and chase away the frowns.
Our friendship is most important to me
Through everything, this you'll see.
We may have once been more
And maybe again we'll be
But you and your friendship is all I'll ever need.

Cara Meskow

"An Oblivious Soul"

Two souls have parted, yet only one is so very sad;
One had a lot of love that the other never had,
One was deeply loved and the other was used,
One had such sincere feelings that the other abused,
One left before the hurt grew, the other had no remorse;
One had broken free before things had gotten worse.

Reni L. Medina

Emergence

Insecurities
like blood drip from my open wounds.

At last! My search for help is over -
I see
a face in the distance;
one that seems
nearly as pained as my own.
help, I cry out...
the face does not reply,
but does not turn away as I limp towards.
slowly I make my way to my rescuer -
the only one who can save me.
finally, I reach my destination.
the face returns my shocked stare,
then shatters as I
scream in agony -
breaking the looking glass,
and the image of
the only one who can save me.

Megan Weber

Tamara-Lynn

Five foot five, green eyed friend, Tamara-Lynn;
how she makes me laugh and
grin, where no one could till then.

How would I know 15-long years ago,
a broken tooth and piece of gum,
would lead me back to my Tamara-Lynn

For her and I have been through so much
good and bad; my pretty five foot five
green eyed, Tamara-Lynn

Oh, Lord - in this hour of my life, please
tell her, how much I care and love her!

For she and she alone, lifted the darkness
from my heart and made it sing - 5'5"
green eyed pretty Tamara-Lynn

Dennis Ditlefsen

Prejudice

It sneaks in like a slithering snake.
You try to fight it; there is no escape.
You try to run; you try to hide,
But somehow it still sneaks inside.
It gives no warning; it gives no dues,
But there it is inside of you.
No one claims it or seems to know,
How, when, or why it started to grow.
It spreads as fast as a raging fire
While it never seems to tire.
With nothing else left to gain
It only causes hurt and pain.
You say that this can not be
Something so wrong growing in me.
Yes, I say it is already there
Even if you are not aware.
So now while you are young and can
Get rid of prejudice before you're a man.

Noah C. Landy

The Puppet

Oppress the views of the puppet
  who hangs upon the strings of time.
Ridicule the hope of the fool
  whose spirit is confined by the court of fools.
Fight the suppression of the spirit
  before it smothers the fire of the fool puppet.

Darrin Hochhalter

Life's Stanza

As I look beyond the shadow of time,
Now in search of that thing which conquers all.
Not in jest or even a simple rhyme,
I patiently await that beckoned call.

In your eyes I see my souls reflection.
And momentarily my mind wonders
In search of yet another reaction,
To your smile, new emotions it conjures.

For your company I will always yearn.
Your soothing brilliance calms my troubled heart.
Your love and trust I hope to someday earn,
From your sweet embrace I can't be apart.
Tell me, can I entrust my heart to you?
Am I destined to be forever blue?

Richard D. Campbell

"Thank You"

They are small words. Let's take them all apart.

  T is for all your THOUGHTFULNESS
and H is for the big HEART that you own.
  A is for the ADMIRATION we have for you.
and N is for the NICETY you've shown.
  K is for the KINDNESS you have given
and Y is for the YES you always do.
  O is for the OTHERS that you think of.
and U is for the UNIVERSAL letter meaning you.

AFTER AL OF THE ABOVE WE ARE RIGHT BACK TO THE START
  saying "THANK YOU"

Lucille Parisi

"Mystery Owl"

You wise old owl with your savory looking eyes
Tell me the reason in the daylight you hide
Then when its night you come on your flight
You're preachy in that tree and you're asking questions through the
Night just what is it that keeps you up in the tree
Just what is it that such a mystery
Or could just be a question of your own
Just who will it be to leave me and
my haunting tree alone?

Leslie Breaux

Hurry Away

Bird, bird fly fly away in a very hurry.
Frog, frog jump jump away in a very hurry.
Spider, spider crawl crawl away in a very hurry.
Fish, fish swim swim away in a very hurry.
  Because if you don't a great big CROCODILE
  will come and go

Snap!!
  Snap!!
  Snap!!

Brooke M. Halstead

Governments Don't Raise Children... People Do

Governments don't raise children... people do;
So, what are we doing to make children dreams come true?

Are we engaged in their conversations, school work, and friends?
Do we spend time with them before the day ends?

Or, are we so busy working, trying to make a living;
That we are over looking the most important thing, the time that we
   are not giving?

Children need a foundation that is laid with attention, love and
concern; It is something innate, that each child yearns.

The luxuries in life are not as important as the time we give;
So let us give children a meaningful life to live.

Tell them they are loved and very special too,
And that we want to be a vivid part in making their dreams come true.

Because, governments don't raise children... people do!

   Ruth N. Segres

"Destiny's Demand"

I stood upon a foreign land
and wondered "Why am I here?"
I came by destiny's demand
to witness life in another sphere.

I stared about and saw pain,
poverty and woe.
I asked myself "Will I ever be the same again?"
To myself, I answered "No!"

Most of us when given much
are inclined to ask for more
until the day we touch
a distinctly different distant shore.

Then we look around us
and see lives far worse than our own,
and we thank the fate that found us
for we never would have known.

Fools like I need yardsticks to measure our fortunes by.
Fools like I need to be shown
or we foolishly shake our puny fists at the sky!

   Edward G. Donnelly

Innocence Stolen

Innocence stolen, now nothing's left
I'm but a shell, blind, dumb and deaf
All to a world, a world never known
All hope was taken when I was shown
All of the bad that mankind will do
To one another, to me and to you;

Innocence stolen, my will is now gone
A will to survive, sustain, carry on
What is the point to the life that I live?
I can't ever change things, though myself I give
So I'll leave all behind now, go off on my own
Never to add to the evil I'm shown.

   Joshua I. Hilbert

Family Of Two

Family of two was once that of three,
Not a moment left of joy, happiness, or glee.
When a smile comes across my face,
Is it wrong for me to feel such disgrace?
All of the people, they all mourn the same,
Later will they even remember his name?
They mourn for him, as though they should,
Now, almost a year, would they cry if they could?
Memories of my family will always make me sad,
For I loved him very much, the one I called Dad.
The money that came, is it worth the cost,
For the precious life of his that was lost?
Two days after my sixteenth birthday,
I knew what my tearful-eyed mother was going to say.
Two horrible days in the hospital filled with pain,
Now all we have left is his picture in a small, wooden frame.
I think we'll be okay, maybe we'll even be all right,
I know this though, I'll have trouble getting to sleep tonight.

   Ann Elise Pyles

My Pleasure

On most days in the wee hours of the morning,
I awake refreshed, immediately praising the Lord,
For another day that will soon be dawning.

Oh how I love this special time of day,
The calming quietness throughout the house,
Gives me a will to want to work,
And plan for the activities in the best possible way.

With so many things to do,
It is sometimes difficult to prioritize,
But I rest assured that everything planned,
Will be organized.

I know the Lord will be near,
To strengthen and help in time of need,
Even though it may seem that He is not here.

These pleasurable wee hours of the morning,
Give me great comfort and joy,
I keep the Lord stayed on my mind,
He'll keep me in perfect peace,
Knowing today I'll be so busy,
I'll need Him to keep me at ease.

   Marilyn Hodge

A Moment Ago

Do you see
The darkness of that winter day?
   Of moments lost, with a nothing left to say
The reflections on my sense of loss?
   Of memories past, so like an aging moss
Do you see the times I talk of it so low?
   Of quiet periods, a moment ago

Why now did the darkness of death come here?
   And leave with me this deep, aboding sense of fear
Why now am I no longer able to give, to see?
   And leave me with a loss, so quickly given to me
Why now does nights passing take too long to go?
   And leave me lonely, a moment ago

Can you feel the sorrow in the loneliness of my heart?
   To let me know, though we are now apart
Can you hear my silent cry on many quiet nights?
   To let me see precious, wonderful, familiar sights
Can you give to me my wish and make it so?
   To let me live my past again, just like a moment ago

   Leon Ray Fennessy

"Fate Awaits"

Her eyes appear dark and hollow;
Crying out for us to let her go.
As the evil growth eats at her insides;
Forcing her to lose the battle long fought.
Her hands are cold and clammy;
sweating out her beautiful life.
Her breathing grows calmer;
as a smile crosses her face,
she thinks about her past:
Her loving husband returning from war,
Her glorious first child born a year later,
Holidays, family gatherings, her pampered garden
Her mind, a treasure chest of the past.
Her smile slowly fades as she realizes it is time to go.
The power above welcomes her impatiently.
Her family is puzzled as she weakly begins to laugh,
Then they begin to cry.
They realize her fate is clearly in view,
and it awaits her, finalizing her battle.
She is now free of pain, residing in her safe new haven.

Kristi Smook

David

I am not the white in the clouds
Nor the pink in your eye
Nor the yellow of the sun

I am the blue of a flame
Lighting everything

I am not a grizzly bear
Nor a peaceful bird in the wind
Nor a cuddly cat

I am a roaring lion
Laying in the grass

But for one day
I would like to be a peaceful bird in the wind

For just one day
I would like to be a cuddly cat

David Tobin

Owen's Bench

Just an ordinary bench as they waited for the bus
the three of them together, Norman Rockwell with a brush.

Now usually where three souls meet, triangles come together
but truly what transpired there, resembled alpine heather.

Affection, flare-ups, rich regard-will you imagine with me
sunshine embracing thunderclouds; unusual yet no really.

Based upon our calender, May always precedes June
but when it comes to Owen's bench — the two are equal soon.

Owen loves June dearly, comrade in arms are they
synchronized in timing, mesh together in life's fray.

Now consider May and Owen, very different melodies
when at odds the two of them create disharmony.

But when they come together with an olive branch that's frail
the song they sing together goes beyond the written scale.

Concern for one another, a tender, warm embrace
harmony now restored — discordant notes erased.

Waiting at the bus stop, represented by these three
are many of life's hopes and dreams, heartfelt humanity.

They symbolize the very best this cold world has to offer
for out of different points of view—come acceptance, warmth and
    laughter.

Tracy McGee Jaeger

Haunting Cries

20 years 200 years 2000 years of moans
Haunting cries muffled wails of defiled women
Generation by generation
Greeted with silence
1 Heart breaking, 2 hearts broken
Generations of hearts heavy with the dark memories

The heavens fill with their cries
The skies deluge with sorrowful weeping
The earth shivers with sorrow
The people turn away silently

The silence is deafening

Lights going out one by one
Generation by generation
Innocence lost in bruised bodies
Broken children
Souls stolen in the night
In the daylight.

One more child moans in the darkness
Haunting cries
One more light went out tonight.

Pat Stewart

Some Day

Why'd you have to leave us early that one sweet day,
when things were going great in every little way.
The lightened skies were clear, not a cloud to be seen,
birds were even flying, and the grass was still green.
When the sun broke the plains and shined bright on your face,
wish I could have told you what was about to take place.
We started the morning the way we always do,
but it all changed quickly when we no longer had you.
It began to get cloudy, then the birds disappeared,
you laid their motionless without shedding a tear.
I wanted to know why you had to leave us right then,
but how can I argue, you're where we've never been.
It's funny how the world has to treat us that way,
but I'll go on knowing we'll see you again some day.

Aaron Rose

My Thanksgiving Prayer

HEAVENLY FATHER, I'm thankful for each sunrise
That I can still behold
And for the love I've found here
More precious now than gold.

You've guided me to mountain tops
And rivers that run clear
Although I didn't know your name
I've felt your presence near.

You offer far more beauty
Than this world can ere embrace
I thank you for your sacrifice
And marvel at your grace.

Please protect and guide my loved ones
Each day they spend on earth
Please bless their hearts with peacefulness
And fill them with self-worth.

Help us all to spread your love
And accept the trials you send
For your love shows us no boundaries
In JESUS' name. Amen.

Donna Robins

The Mighty White-Tail Deer

Translucent ears erect, tips only scarcely dense,
Ethereal velvet nose twitching,
Commanding elegance and eminence
In one swift glance.

Legs as robust as an onion's smell,
Corded muscles and veins tracing their way,
Enabling her to romp to and fro in a secluded dell
Or from a hunter's rifle.

A more innocent form there never was,
An appealing fawn with white spots
On its baby fuzz.
It waits in a concealed glen for Mother.

Soft eyes glazed over, all life gone,
Legs secured in rigor mortis.
Leaving behind the baby fawn,
The mighty white-tail deer is no more.

Searching for any minute fault,
The hunter attentively scrutinizes the doe.
Taxidermy the ultimate insult to life, staunchly refuses to
Contemplate its lifeblood, its soul, only its carcass.

Melissa Lunn

Feelings Of Love

Dreaming...falling fast sleep
Waiting...praying for your eternal soul
Hoping...for one more breath of life
Laughing...for the sun to set upon your golden boy hair
Crying....for one more chance to see you smile
Wondering...why you cry like the sea at dusk
Caring..for your lifeless body one more time
Grasping...for the key to reality
Trying...to understand why the flame went out before it even
    began to glow
Burning...for your hot body
Tasting...every breath you breathe
Pondering...every liquid moment
Growing...inside with unspeakable thoughts of passion
Telling...you I love you with all of my heart
Seeing...if you even comprehend my spoken words
Sharing...all the deep, dark, secrets that I have within me
Giving....you my eternal flame of love

Amanda Mary Thorp

A Monologue On Monologue

Words
We trade in words
Yet deal in lives
And seldom guess
How few can play our games

While verbiage our skillful tool
Restores the identities
Of a small articulate number
Who hope they understand

Our verbosity as we counsel voluminously
To keep from facing
The myriad nonverbal minds
Who have no counselor

For they deal in action
Unnamed feelings
Unlabeled fears and unspoken agony

They are the nonverbal
To whom we have much to say, little to communicate
Who unspellable problems we must ignore
Lest we know failure not unlike their own

Karin Bergwall Stratmeyer

Thou Loveth Me In Eternal Slumber

Why do they relish my eternal slumber?
Why do thou giveth love to my everlasting hunger.

I ask for nothing of what I receive from thee not for your desire
to seek that of which lye inside me.

But still thou wonders in wondrous fate, how time with time can
sculpture and create. Such bliss in eternal slumber, I cannot
give thee what lye inside me, I cannot give that what I cannot see.

But with time and fate thou sculpture and create,
thy blissful hunger in my eternal slumber.

Daniel Harper

Return To Love

Our world is like a raging sea
Hate takes over where love should be
Lord we pray, don't let us down
Put our hopes back on solid ground.

It seems everybody is a victim
Nobody takes responsibility
Let all of us take a little blame
And try to solve our problems through love.

Once I asked, how hard could it be
Growing up, reaching for the stars
Looking for the truth
And embrace the world with an open heart.

If we could see the world with children's eyes
Still innocent, with a tender heart
The way God wants us to see
What a better world it would be.

August H. Kraft

Old Man Fate

The storm tonight has the waves, riding high upon this cliff.
I stand alone with the rain on my checks, and toss across your gifts.
By your own choice you chose to leave me, here on this cold rock.
I'm left alone to think in the dark, by a door which has no lock.
The way to you cannot be barred, by such a thing as a lock.
I'm kept at bay by Old Man Fate, and the sands of his hour clock.
I wait for the day when the sands run out, and I'll have to
    stay no-more.
Once again we'll be together, when Old Man Fate unlocks the door.
I won't kill myself the way you did, suicide is a burden to bear.
I don't want my loved ones to carry chains of guilt, like the
    ones your family still wears.
They ask themselves, "What could I have done, to make you want to stay?"
Instead they hear your silence, as they begin, yet another day.

Joyce Waltman

Let Me Be A Friend

Let me be a friend who will lend a helping hand.
Let me be patient when I do not understand.
Let me take time to listen to, someone else's woe.
Let me not hurry and tell them I have to go.
Let me have compassion to share, someone's pain.
Let me always remember when my pain was much the same.
Let me be tolerant of someone's defects I may not like.
Let me always keep in mind, they may be fighting a hard fight.
Let me be a friend, trustworthy kind and true.
Then I will always be that friend, that I have found in you.

Theresa Whynot

"Return"

I think it's time for all to return,
To the Babe of Bethlehem,
To go back to the very first Christmas
And all to sing a hymn.

A hymn to Christ who gave His life,
For the salvation of all mankind,
Instead of just stumbling down life's road,
As if we were truly blind.

It's really oooh-so simple,
To just do what God did ask,
To live by His rules - such an easy school,
It's truly not a hard task.

And now 1996 is here,
And some folks will never learn,
With their foolish pride and selfish ways,
They refuse to make that return.

That return to the Babe of Bethlehem,
Who was born that first Christmas night
To follow His rules and do what He asked,
Then life won't be such a fright.

Connie Cunnington

The Lessons Which You Have Taught Me Mom

You have taught me love
To never take things for granted
By always giving me love
I am able to love.

You have shown me compassion
Whenever I needed a friend
And you have made me see right
In my wrongs.

You have taught me confidence
To believe in myself and my true potential
By your love and support
I have become the person that I am.

You have had faith in me
When I lost faith in myself
And you have made me see promise
In any situation.

Most importantly, you have taught me
To give all of my heart
And because of your lessons
I am a good mother.

Shelby A. Myers

My Angel Sister

Happy Birthday, my sister so dear.
This is going to be an angel year.
You are so sweet and good you shall never fear
There's always a Guardian Angel near.

In your heart you are especially kind.
In this troubled world its hard to find.
For other's feelings you always care.
You are always concerned how the world fares.

The Lord records this with a smile.
And for you, will go the extra mile.
He takes these things into view,
Because you are among the special few.
With you, the Guardian Angel can always be found.
And you, sister dear, with our Lord...
Will wear a shining crown.

Rachel Orrell

Another Buffalo Gone

It seems we met such a short time ago.
You looked up at me, needing me so.

Through long days we fought the fight.
Though there were trials, you never lost sight.

Like the buffalo you stood your ground
Silent tears, quiet anguish, yet never uttered a sound.

We all watched, prayed, hoped, and cared.
Only for a moment did we see you were scared.

When fear finally found its way to those blue eyes,
Away they drifted, searching for Heaven's skies.

Once they were filled with laughs and love,
Then confusion clouded and away flew our dove.

God answered; today he made you free.
An honored guest in Heaven I've no doubt you'll be.

Though there are tears, I have to find a smile
At the thought of your laughter echoing beyond the miles.

It comes to me and holds certain peace.
It makes me calm and my inner soul finds release.

Goodbye seems so final and farewell like the end.
But my heart holds the memory of your life, my friend.

Jill Nuckolls

Changing Seasons

Snow, snow, beautiful snow
Ole' man winter is really
Giving us a blow
Just two more months and spring will be here
With lovely flowers and lots of clean air
For the past seventy years
I have been in awe of the changing seasons
And what they stand for
I may not be around to see many more
So I do appreciate what they have in store
As I see it, this old world doesn't
Have much to offer except the
Changing seasons from winter to fall
Each season has its own beauty
And I try to enjoy it to the fullest.

Betty Evans

Human

Wild, curious eyes
    dance behind our closed masks
housing cruel lies.
Words of pain
    run through our evil mouths
waiting to stain.
Bright white teeth
    smile to our unsuspecting friends
hiding what's beneath.
Terrible tearing thoughts
    bounce around in our minds
seldom getting caught.
Carefully combed hair
    groomed and made to cover all
that's under there.
From blood to skin
    we are all imperfectly human, wondering
    where to begin.

Elton R. Piper

When I Saw You

The pounding of my heart grew louder
As vibrations of emotions grew stronger
When I saw you

I dreamt your kiss
Overshadowed by the midst of your caress
I awaken feeling refresh
When I saw you

I've created a song
Within my shadow and devotion
And a story I rhapsodized
Over passion and affection
When I saw you

A tingle ran through me
A moment of paradise you laid upon me
When I saw you
I was free
To wander the sky
To even swim or fly
I knew when I saw you
I fell in love

Marc Joethom SanLuis

Am I Worthy

Am I worthy of thy friendship, thy care, and thy love,
have we not gone silent and broken the spell?
The hurt intense to some with behavior ill,
thus we learn wisdom.
Rigid as a wall, enclosing to suffocate, at rescue you stand,
with weapons of love, bearing down the wall,
To conquer a soul in despair, hail to him for not
just fate has brought you here.
A bond he instilled for us to share, to grow older,
to die in peace.
For then we lived, for compassion and empathy
shall be the way to Heaven.

Sylvia Reygers Curtis

The One

I have nothing to hide
Please believe what I say
Wanting to hold you
For just one moment in time
It seems so everlasting
I know in my heart
That you can't erase a feeling this strong
It's only a matter of time
Your soft heavenly eyes gazed into me
There were no words for me to find
I stood there beside myself
I could see you and no one else
When I saw you
I could not breath
I fell so deep
I would never be the same
The love just rushed in
And all at once I knew
You were the one for me.

Margie Kriescher

To My Beautiful Bride On Our Special Day

Today is the day we become one
you are so beautiful that I am awe-stricken.
I love you so much
words just can't say,
how special and beautiful you are to me
each and every day.
I surely was blessed when you came along,
you showed me how to love with your wit and charm.
As we go through life,
sharing the good and the bad,
maybe we will be blessed and
I'll be a Dad.
And when we are old and
our love ever so strong,
with me you will always be number one.

Randy Yaun

You Made Me...

Believe in dreams that were unbelievable
To see visions that were unseeable
To hear music that was oh so faint
To feel emotions that were never to be felt

Whispers of thoughts
Imagines of colors
Dance inside my head
What a lucky man I am

Empires have fallen and men have died
for the love that fills me

You made me believe in the stars, the heavens,
and in Gods own angels
YOU MADE ME....

Greg Ruppert

Life Near Death

I wonder what would happen if I were ill and in bed.
Would my family and friends come around out of love,
or duty instead.
Would they share with me my remaining days.
Or would they show their feelings in other ways,
like flowers and cards and calls on the phone.
Would they say their sorry or
wait until I'm gone.
Wouldn't they know I'd need them now.
No matter how small or large or how.
Give me yourselves now, do not wait.
Show me you care, before it's too late.
Break down these barriers of love and hate,
give me your time, yourself, don't wait.

Barbara Dale Boynton

Love

Love is the quickening of my heart
When your lips touch mine
The feeling of your strong arms
pulling me close
The sweet smell of your body
close to mine
The touch of your hands against
my skin making me shiver with excitement
The soft whisper of your breath in
my ear saying I love you
love is the joining of one boy and
one girl for all eternity.

Michelle Folkenson

Angels

Floating through the air
Are we dead?
Or is our body just resting?
Is that a light that draws us near
Or is it life, all pain, misery, and feat?
Will the earth grow bitter and cold?
Can all human live to be ripe and old?
Who is watching us night and day,
Gliding us along life's dismal way?
Given to all, zero to one hundred eleven.
A small guardian angel
Straight from heaven.

John Richard Blaylock

Good-Bye To A Friend

When we first met we used to talk till dawn, you were ignorant of
your aristocratic ways. Now it isn't my fault that we never talk
because you learned to be special. You were born to be
princess; to be, in your mind, revered by all. To good to be
touched, to proper to be loved, and to good for an old poor
friend. Now when grow old and find out that you never lived,
only went through your daily routine of nice cars, nice friends
and nice boys, please remember the one who ever judged you.
remember the one who never condemned you and took you for
what you where, not what you have become but what you could
never be again; innocent.

Jeff Mitchell

Hunting - Cache - Bottoms

He died at 13, after giving me his best years
we went to many trials and won and lost
he and I drank beer and boy did it cost
he was the best anyone has ever seen
he didn't have a stitch of mean
after 13 years of giving me his best,
I now have his grandson that has so much zest.
Maybe after he gives me many good
years, we too can sit and talk, and drink beer.
I love him so, and he's so young
his little life has just begun.
I miss his grandpa, and it makes me so sad
he makes me so happy he's my new little LAB!

John Thomas

Untitled

Oh dear, how can it be
Yesterday I was a size 12, today I'm a 20
First, a few pound added, which I can easily drop
Year after year, it has become a lot.
How can that ice cream, Hagen Daez too
Add so much pleasure but be mean to you.
That little glass of wine - to make you relax
Brings the calorie count up to the max
A few cookies for energy - they can't count
Add a handful of candies - who knows the amount.
The skirt is no longer a little "Too tight"
It is the "Impossible Dream" - what a sight
The pants choke you at the inseam
A size 18 would be a dream
The big ladies department will never see me
Unless I rip out the size as fast as can be.
"Until the fat Lady Sings" scares me a lot
People look in my direction - although fat I'm not.
Everyone loves a fat girl is not quite true
But 1996 is time for a diet - I promise you.

Mary Westman

Nature's Gallery

Nature, a gallery
of wild, wondrous fair —
the salt of Gaea's care.

Time, elements, invisible forces:
Tools of creativity

In a domain where
life and death are nature's complimentary ways.

Spruces - statuesque in their green, grandeur
within their roots left to time.

Stocks - carved and tempered
by een's seasoning graces into permanence.

Sharp senses, acute instincts - ancient in the wild
a pup forages

Among these age-old roots
for saps and chews couched in grass and greenery.

She selects her treats:
Kelp, shells of crab, sea urchins —
harvest cast ashore.

In season's spirit,
life is young and timeless in nature's gallery.

Paula M. S. Ingalls

Golf

I shouldn't play golf, no sir, not me
There are so many things to do and see.
Who wants to swing at a ball all day
Following its path wherever it may stray?

Hook it, slice it, dribble off the tee;
Keep your head still, but bend that knee.
Hit into the water, hit into the sand;
Don't pick up your head to see where you will land.

Left arm straight and cock your wrists too;
Swing it nice and easy and follow through.
Putt it soft and straight and put it in the cup;
Keep your head down and don't look up!

I love to play golf - I do, you see.
Try it just once and I think you will agree
Nothing is as pretty as seeing that ball soar,
And the game is even better when you are keeping score!

Special woods and irons, wedges, balls and tees,
Head covers, golf bag, and lessons if you please.
The game of golf today is really not that hard
All that is required is a valid credit card!

Therese A. Gaudreau

This Is Not A Message

Staring at a picture on the wall...
Tears stained cheek
Glistens
Sunset through
The beveled glass window
Prism corners refracting
Staining walls,
Pictures
With ephemeral rainbows

He is blind to it
Like the eyes of her face
In the family picture
Look without seeing
Forever

It is an Image

Charlie Starr

Seasoned With Love

Where e'er we go,
What e'er we do,
We want to honor the Lord above,
And do everything seasoned with love.

As we go about our daily deeds,
We should always care about other's needs,
So as we carry on, push and shove,
We want to season everything with love.

Each day as we care for our family,
And sometimes, we think we want to flee,
We just throw our head back and look above,
And pray to God we will season everything with love.

When life seems to get us down,
And no one else seems to be around,
We take flight on the wings of a dove,
Then we can season everything with love.

When our life on earth is o'er,
And we are called to that hallelujah shore,
We will know then, why we reasoned
That it was with love, that everything should be seasoned.

Linda Johnson

Letting Go...

My heart feels the pain, my mind plays the game
but I just don't seem to know,
Being in love and wanting to be loved how do I ever let go?
The one I love and hold dear to my heart,
can I ever start anew?
While I'm existing outside yet dying inside
what am I to do.
Torn between confusion
not knowing what's really true,
Keeps me from moving on or to stay in love with you.
Wanting you completely
to love with all my being,
but to face the truth and know
that seeing is believing.
Where does it end, when does it stop to just go on with my life,
To wake up one morning and not feel the pain
like you're cutting me up with a knife.
It's anger and love, it's twisted emotions
that I just can't seem to control,
And wanting it all with you in my life please tell me how to let go.

Terri Phillips

Paradise

Morning dew
rolling down a rose petal,
dripping into a sparkling mountain stream.
It finds its way
over moss covered rocks,
and down crystal water falls.
At the bottom,
in a paradise lagoon,
A snow white swan swims by a baby deer
Steeling a drink from mother natures tears.
The day has past,
and a golden sun sets
in the high snow covered mountains behind.

Gregory D. Buckland

"More"

I don't understand how this love came about
But with these feelings of mine. I have no doubt
that the love that I feel is not shared
And my feelings were not spared.

I'm not quite sure what kind of spell you cast,
But I'm sure that it will make the hurt always last.
With these feelings of mine that will last so long
I'm not sure that I will ever again be strong.
The stress you've caused makes me so tired
But the pain in my heart won't let me sleep.

My nerves of which used to be made of steel
Have now turned to mush with the pain that I feel
I've tried so hard to hide my pain behind a smile,
But now I realize that my efforts were vile.

If I had to do it all over again, I would have offered more
I would have realized my love sooner and then opened the door.
I don't understand how the pain you've caused
Just makes me want you more!

Poet Le Evans

Rapture Of Love

While thinking of the woman in gold;
The rapture of love, touched my very soul.

The rapture of love reaches deep into my bones;
I find it hard, to leave this woman alone.

You see, rapture of love is pure;
cause the woman with love knows, that this is the cure.

Rapture of love, what else could it be;
For I've found it in this woman you see.

And it feels, so good to me!

Robert M. Barnes Sr.

Be Aware

Keeping yourself informed is a big must,
which sometimes requires a little bit of thrust.
A thrust of ambition to check things out,
or important information you'll do without.
Don't let your head to awareness be dead;
if you do you'll miss important stuff that's been said.
Spend sometime each day of the week
and pick up a paper and take a peek.
Maybe a TV would be better for you,
whichever is best just be sure to do.
Pass this on to youngsters down the road,
for it may help them to bear the future load.

Rory Sewell

Untitled

Envy, touch our joy of relationship
Know why thy dwellest where love ne'er abides;
Watch, O jealous tongue that you dare not slip
Discontented and lonely voice that chides.
Come near to our torch of passionate flame
Warm thy cold tongue in the bath of our heat,
Partake in fellowship sharing the same
Freely loving, knowing nothing of cheat.
Wish thou to own what has always been free?
Possess all alone ubiquitous love?
Can love be owned like estate property
Granted sole to wealth and those from above?
Come, share, eat, for the table's now spread
For two? No - now three; for envy's now dead.

Jeff Shade

A Sister's Love

We grew up together
The future seemed so bright
I walked in the light
He walked in the dark
Now we are apart
But only in body
Our love is the same
We are still as one
For I believe there is a God
Who kept him safe thru the years
I speak to my brother thru a glass
To show my love and my support
Years have passed; still bending my knees
One day soon I pray
This will all be over
He will come back
Walking in the light
For I live by what I believe, not what I can see
Your freedom is near; I'll see you soon!

Angela M. Moore

This Old House Has Struck A Leak

When I was younger,
I used to go out to wine and dine.
Now I am old and in a bind.
This old house has struck a leak.

My eyes are dim
I can't see as well as I use to
My heart is growing weaker day by day
My legs are not strong as they use to be
Because Old Uncle Arthur has taken a hold on me.

When I was younger I liked a devils life
Then one day I heard a voice within me
Saying come unto me all ye who
Labor and are heady loden and I will
give you rest.

I listened to the voice within me
and obeyed the gospel of Christ
I am happy and glad I did because when
This old house has fallen down and
stand no more I won't have to worry
because I will become a new house in heaven.

Addie A. Stedenson

The Spring And You

Winter is gone, with its ice and snow;
The spring is here, to stay I know.
I love you, dear, you know I do;
It's all I have, the spring and you.

Spring is here, the skies are blue;
I love both, dear, the spring and you.
The birds are here, I hear them sing.
Every Sunday, the church bells ring.

Winter is gone; with it's cold, cold days.
The sun is shining, I can feel it's rays.
The flowers bloom, the lakes are blue,
Still I love only, the spring and you.

After the spring, comes the summer sun;
Without you dear, life would be no fun.
Spring is so much like you it's true
nothing can compare, to spring and you.

Jack Morgan

Desperate No More!

From the big city streets
To the eastern sea shore
I will cry aloud
I'm desperate no more!
I've found myself, I like myself, I love myself
This is for sure
So I can say it proud
I'm desperate no more!
The type of woman I am any man would adore
And I can shout it loud
I'm desperate no more!
Jesus is the answer
And He gave me exactly what I was looking for
And now I can say
I'm desperate no more!
Ask the Lord to help you look inside yourself
To find the love that is pure
So you can also say
I'm desperate, no more!

Chanta Barrett

Spring

Beckoned by the warm sun she
awakes from her slumber and steps
slowly from her thresh hold.
In her swopping gown of green grows
flowers, and in her flowing hair the buds
of blooming trees.
When he sees her the old man trembles.
The ice taken from his breath and the
frost from his heart, he loves her but
knows he cannot stay.
So with a melted heart and grieving
tears he gathers his robe of white around
him and quickly melts away.
She certainly is beautiful!

Matthew Withem

Forty Three

You begin to see things differently,
When on your birthday, you're forty-three.
To yourself you think, it really doesn't
bother me, bother me, bother me.

There is a different outlook about your life,
Your actions show more sincerity.
You begin living much less carelessly,
And start enjoying history.

You want more than prosperity,
And you hope for serenity.
You think of others, not only thee
Concerns of others, you begin to see.

You think about your destiny
And wish the world more unity.
Your thoughts are more for family
And ways to avoid calamity.

You don't think so narrowly,
And try to live more merrily.
Anyway you're forty three and barely,
Live and hold your life dearly.

Ed Gandy

Today I Thought Of You

Today as I was sitting with nothing else to do
I shut my eyes, kicked off my shoes
And started thinking of you.

Of course it was amazing that in my mind you did appear
I thought that you were in my past what are you doing here?
When was the last time that I saw you?
Just what did you wear? Why are you on my mind?
I never thought I cared.

But the vision of you is so vivid
My heart begins to skip a beat.
Could it be that I am not quite over you?
Could my life not be complete?

If that is the case I am worried
Because I know you won't believe it is true
But today as I was sitting
Today I thought of you.

Gene Ann Scarpa

In Memory Of Puffy

A puffy fat face, oh how she made me smile.
Never going too far from home, maybe a mile.
A joyful sound of meows coming across the street,
A puffy fat face and four white feet.
The warmth and compassion she gave me at all loneliest of times,
Her incidental death should be a crime .

It took one time for her to let her guard down,
When one fast car flowed her to the ground.
Now my emptiness is full of sorrow,
My puffy face cat with no more tomorrows.
People may think it's odd to grieve so, over a cat.
But believe me, puffy was much more than that.

Puffy was her name, and she meant the world to me.
I protected her inside, but outside is where she preferred to be.
I miss her so, and it hurts so bad,
My puffy face cat was all I had.
May her soul rest with God now, I pray day and night.
Take my advice be a good pet owner, keep your cat in sight.

Diane Mack

Friend

Oh God! They say you are up in the sky
Is hell a better place than the world of my?

You have left me with a difficult task
Can't distinguish between a man and his mask
Is the man real or his mask
A question I am afraid to ask

You meet a man and confide in him
You tell him your worrying things
You confess your rights and wrongs
But then you find he picks up the wrongs
From every side you are bitten with pairs of prongs

Everybody now thinks that you are bad
And you can't help it except being sad
There are tears in your eyes
And everybody laughs at your sight
The man now sits with his lips tight
Leaving you with a tearful night

Later the news comes which breaks your heart
It was your 'friend' who did that all.

Medha Bodas

Dark Night

Each day she fades
soon God will have a new angel
disease is killing her
a memory haunts her
one night of passion -
for a lifetime.
Her dreams are filled with beautiful children
sadly smiling.
The boy she loves slips a ring
on a ghost.
Her future lies in the heavens
her heart aches
regret overpowers pain now
she trusted him
a single moment of ecstasy
instead of hopes....
Dreams...
Living...
The angels are calling...

Michelle Sollars

Who Am I?

I am flesh and bones.
I have a soul and a mind.
I am not one hundred percent right all of the time.

I have feelings.
I have desires.
I want to see myself through others' eyes.

I am compassionate and full of love.
I am striving to be like the Almighty above.

I am honest and practice being meek,
but I don't always turn the other cheek.
I treat others with respect,
so when I look in the mirror I have no regrets.

So, who am I?
I am a person full of love,
striving to be like the Almighty above.

JoAnn G. Davis

"Kicking Her Boots"

I was a yellow "Rose" of
Texas bright and full of joy but,
life in Texas is fading fast
and this yellow rose of Texas
wanted nothing to do with Texas
I will always remain a yellow
rose of Texas but, are
love has faded and so will this
yellow rose of Texas and I
wanted to kick my Texas boots
somewhere else cause like
the San Antonio Rose I, don't
want your faded love but,
I'll always be the yellow
rose of Texas kicking my
boots somewhere else so
for that San Antonio rose and
the yellow rose of Texas
she's kicking up her boots somewhere else.

Barbara Jean Priestley

445

Let Me Be

Let me be your wings
To carry your worries, your suffering, your pain.
Let me be your shade from the sun,
Your lighthouse at night, your shelter from the rain.

Let me be your flowers in spring,
Your ocean to sail, your elixir to drink.
Let me be your fire in winter,
Your clouds in the sky, your awakened dream.

Let me be your castle in the sand,
Your rock to lean, your summer, your dove of peace.
Let me be your prose, your verse, your rhyme.
Let me be the wind in your hair, your moonlight,
Your mourning prayer, the thoughts in your mind.

Let me be the smile that brightens your day,
Your guardian, your shield to keep troubles away.
Let me be the music that chants your name,
Your ladder to ascend, the water you bathe.
Let me be your confidant, your lover, your friend.
Let me be your heart beat until the end.

Manuel R. Borrell

Just A Thought

As I sit here alone in my room I begin
to wonder what do I want to do with my life.
It seems as though times are getting harder
and each moment makes me want to holler.
Education is the key! Education is the key!
How can education be the key when people
are still being judged by their skin, race and creed?
They say everyone looks out for their
own kind. Well how come my kind hasn't
spared me a dime or a moment of their time?
Although this poem may leave you in a
daze, you must understand that I am going
through a depressing phase. And this
poem was just a thought.

Marie G. Durand

Eminence

With the deserted house
laughter breezed through halls
and music billowed across vast land.
The front porch droops,
exhausted by dancing shoes of the wind.
The sagging door howls, long forgotten,
in need of repair.
The chimney crumbles as Mother Nature disciplines.
Weary eyes close, dreaming of youth.
Whispers that circulated through walls,
hush as Father Time accelerates years.
Untamed ivy and itchy vines
crawl toward the decaying roof,
leisurely strangling the breath of the house.
Clutching its last shred of hope,
it waits to be revived.
As overwhelming murderous forces take command,
the house releases a gasp and surrenders.

Kate East

Reflections

It's that time of year when branches are bare
Twigs responding to the echoes of the wind
Boughing in all directions
And I am thinking of the tumult in the world

We need to learn again how to reach out
Caress each other with our eyes, hands, minds.
To develop a sense of being
Become each others 'best' friend and neighbor
Help ourselves to earn happiness,
Happiness beyond our wildest dreams for all our children.

I dream of serenity and love between us.
Of the glorious colorful plants that add spice to our eyes
Ecstasies to our tongues, odors to our noses

Creating words so sweet, mellow
Developing dignity, worth, integrity, trust, love.
Building blocks of eternal peace on earth....

Philip Sosis

Untitled

Jesus Christ was born that day
For all our sins he came to pay.
King of Kings, ruler of all
Many believed his story tall.

He lived and died for you and me
So that from sins we could be free
To live with him and God above
As was granted through his undying love.

Now Christmas is celebrated once a year;
Congregations gather collectively to cheer
This day, as remembered, the birth of Christ,
And His promise to grant us eternal life.

His life is forgotten sometimes on this earth,
As well as the reason for God giving birth
To the King of Kings, Ruler of All
Whose story is far from being tall!

William D. Cox Sr.

Love Lost

How many days has it been since your phone call?
Seems like years since that day.
Seems like years since being with you and always wondering...
Are thoughts of me in any part of your day?

The pain in my heart is so very deep.
Each second of the day is spent wondering about you.
It's so hard to imagine days without you...
Not to spend another night by your side.

The tears have not yet come. I will not let them.
I cannot let go...so afraid if tears fall, the end will be true.
Never again to see you, or hear your voice.
Never again to be with you.

Barbara J. Pate

The Sound Of The Angels

Whistling winds, harsh rain.
The chimes are singing,
"they've come again!"
The angels are here.
Oh, sigh of relief,
for their arrival, releases my grief.
I feel in my heart, the presence of good,
telling me, "it's alright child, you are understood."
As they drift away, "thank you," I say,
for bringing peace, in a single day.

Tasha Martinez

Untitled

The monarchs are back
Signaling that fall is upon us
Bursting with color and gentle movements
of welcome and joy,
Heading south for the mountains of Mexico;
Millions of them going home as if being drawn
By an unexplainable faith.

My soul is ravished by doubt,
Seeking answers that prove there is more...
Always coming up short.
Until I saw
The beauty and patience of the monarch
Lingering gently, holding back the cold,
Telling us and showing us that
Faith is indeed a tangible reality,
As it moves ever so surely on its pre-destined journey,
Guided by the eternal radar of life.

Donald Sbarra

America

America, the BEAUTIFUL LAND OF THE FREE!
God created; regardless of race, religion or creed.
Obey the law and do as you very well please.
God gave His only son to die for you and me.

Let's daily thank God for love to share.
For family, health, shelter and food to care.
And may the people everywhere,
Go beyond the family they just hold dear.

Freedom is responsibility shown in love.
Sinners we are until God sent the dove.
And created a new heart for you and me.
That we all might live in eternity.

Anita Thomure

No Color

There is no color in this race
Only form and the changing of the pace
Work, work, work, when will it end?
When my bones can no longer stand straight or bend
Maybe when I am old crippled and thin
Then society will see me as a waste
Hey will say I can not keep up with todays Pace

Why should they reach out to destroy my soul?
Just because I have grown old
I think I deserve to be heard and respected
Definitely not overlooked and rejected

After I have worked for years until my body yearns to rest
I will want my dues I have done my best
There is no color in this race
Only form and the changing of the pace
Only another burden I must face.

Christal M. George

Dedicated To Mom

Words can never express the tender feelings inside,
of love and sheer joy, for a mother like you.
Though time has changed our lives, it's still so easy to see,
the mom who listened tirelessly, still cares so much for me.

It seems like only yesterdays, when you took good care of me,
and now the tiny hands you wipe are all my little ones.
But even though my needs have changed, you're still right there to care,
to listen, guide or lend a hand in an ever gentle way.

So Mom, please know I love you and that I always will,
and I'll always be here for you,
just like you've been there for me.

Melody Wagner

A Peaceful Solution

Look up from where your kneeling friend
Your ready to expire.
And gaze out into yonder fields where
The lilies never tire.
Their heart's are never laden down with
Burdens huge and endless.
Their stems reach up into the sun their
Beauty is quite breathless.
They never toil, they never spin,
They never hurry around.
But you never catch them without a scent
Their heads are never down.
How do they do it my weary friend ask
Them if you must.
Then listen closely and hear them say
"The father said to trust"
For what you do in your own strength
Will never be the best.
Just come to him weary and heavy
Burdened and he will give you rest

Keith Bolt

Outcast

Do you know there are those who despise this dawning "rose"
That God made?
They won't have it in their yard, they don't want it in the glade,
They spurn it, they scorn it,
Some even say this early Morning Glory should just go away.

They, so much of beauty missing; first gleams of sunlight gently kissing
The dews deposited from the heavens thru the night.

A drop of wine he gave to one,
A drop of sky to others,
To some a drop of pearly-white,
A drop of ebon' to their brothers.

Splendor shrinks of anger senseless; folding, hiding in the leaf,
From the heat of hate defenseless;
Unearned, unmerited bequeath.

When all are called to go where we've not been before,
When all the petals gone, only left the bleach-ed bone,
Minus then exclusive claim;
Left, homogeneous fragile frame.
For a drop of this or that the one earth-life of a race, outcast...

Joyce G. Sutherlin

In My Dreams

He comes to me often in my dreams
Always smiling and laughing it seems.
I wrap his memory around me tight
And sob on quietly through the night.

I miss him Lord, I truly do
Tho I know he's happy there with you.
I think of his face, his bright blue eyes
And of his fate, how young he dies.

I miss the times we would have had
He as my husband, the kids calling him dad.
I don't quite know how to go on ahead
With an empty heart, in my lonely bed.

Lord, I know you've a reason for calling him home
And leaving me here to walk all alone.
Right now I can't grasp the reason why
Although I'm sure I will as time goes by.

Please help to make me stable and strong
To sleep again peacefully all night long.
Keep me in line, my faith being true
So I can spend eternity with my love, and you.

Kathleen Braden-Liles

Night Reflections

When everyone else dreams
With quiet minds and closed eyes,
I see things best forgotten,
With clarity of vision and pain.

Tired of body and needing rest
Oh God, not now - I need to sleep.
My heart thrusts fingers into the eye
Mercilessly ripping hours of peace away.

Watching him sleep deeper away
I need to talk - I need to hold.
You need to share this nightmare world with me
Maybe our hands would close my eyes.

Instead, the sounds of night sing along
Interfere with reasoning and drown my calls.
Tense arms and legs won't move, can't try
Afraid he'll wake and ask me why.

Marian Hutto Blaylock

Marigolds

With chilled hands I pull up the marigolds,
long gone to seed and sprawling from the bed,
their summer brilliance faded into rust
like once warm sunshine when the day is gone.

It is a labor I do not enjoy
old friends uprooted and then cast away
as though the need for them was but a time
that somehow lost its reason to be so.

I planted hundreds of bright bulbs for spring
anemones and tulips - daffodils
to color cool days after winter's hand
has held the world so long in black and gray.

The bulbs are only evanescent things
that burst upon the land and quickly go,
with petals lying shriveled on the ground
and naked stalks that once held blossoms, dead.

But then, as summer comes back once again
I'll plant a host of small green marigolds
and variegated yellow blooms will rise
in every weather - like old friends come home.

Roger T. Burson

The Hero

Ollie was a soldier, tall and straight and true,
He sat before the congress and told them all he knew.

He promised to be truthful, to lay aside the lies.
He spoke of love of country, for which he'd do or die.

He told of how he broke the law that wasn't meant for him,
Of how he planned to give the aid and wash his soul of sin.

The country was in crisis and congress couldn't know,
For surely they would leak the news and spoil Ollies show.

He always sought approval from those who sat on high.
A simple J.R. on his memo and the law he could defy.

He spoke of Commie threat and how we must react.
No matter what the means he'd use, the end would stay intact.

Oh yes he was convincing, for many did believe
That Col. Ollie was a hero, it was his duty to deceive.

Shirley Newsham

The Tale Of The Rose

A single rose shall tell the tale and not another told
A rose shall sing, a rose shall laugh, a rose shall cry
I have never heard it . . . how sad
A single rose shall tell the tale and not another told
The rose must live . . . the rose must die
But who shall know it was so?
The one who sees, the one who hears, the one who loves
I know him not . . . are you sure?
A single rose shall tell the tale and not another told
Why shall this be done? . . . because he is the only one!
So begin . . .
The single rose shall tell the tale and not another told
What shall we do when the rose dies? . . . shall we mourn?
Why? . . . it is dead . . . is he? . . . look again!
Hear him sing, hear him cry, hear him laugh
Can you? . . . I can! . . . Do you understand the words?
Yes! . . . How? . . . I listen . . . I hear nothing!
Listen with your heart . . . what does he say? . . . LOVE!
A single rose shall tell the tale and not another told
It is done! . . .Rest in his love.

Rebecca Mortimer

Five

Five points in the same plane, five me's in the same name
find out which way you want me, confused or medium intensity
can't stand to see my tears flood, out onto my face to get stuck
pass the tissue called my sanity, not much left so use it sparingly
fly high on your broken wings, trip, fall down, under everything
try not to chip your teeth, you'll need them to attract a thief
brush, comb, until there's nothing there,
strands of me sticking everywhere.
Five tries in the same, chance, five looks in the same glance
figure out which time you made it, never stop to see if it fits
skip stones on my damned up stream, love lies within my childish dreams
if I could dig it out again,
I'd have to cry about what might've been
my breath forms little question marks, in the cold, defensive dark
feel my flushed revealing cheeks, every time my conscience speaks

Five leaves on the same stem, five breaks in the same bend
pluck each one out, he loves me or he loves me not
it always ends so negative, and I never know for whom to give
kiss me and you'll turn to stone, I guess I'll entertain alone
smile at the anxious expression,
upside down and inside out oppression
a perfect bunch of ripened efforts, can't begin to count them separate
Five lives out of nine asunder, five is just an ordinary number

Annalisa Harrington

Touched By The Sunshine

All a sudden the rainfalls softly
to the ground, drip drop like the sound
of a down, that is being hit it starts
rapidly them all a sudden the climate
changes, and the snow flurries are
seen falling swiftly form the beautiful
lights blue sky. The birds fly south
for the winter in a swift retreat
wasting no time but resting occasionally
before they fill the warm sunlight
touch them from far away.

Lisa L. Berry

Armageddon (Revelations 19)

In the valley of Megiddo there I saw Him;
His face toward a battle straight ahead;
His eyes were like a flame of fire
His vest was dipped in blood, a scarlet red

He sat upon a steed of white;
His name is yet unknown;
Many crowns he wore upon his head;
In the distance far beyond the mounts,
and descending from the sky:

Were the armies of Jehovah
Waiting for a signal to be led.
From His mouth there went a two edge sword;
In His hand a rod of iron,
With which He come to rule the world
And all those faithful to His word.

Run children run to your master
Run children run to your king
Behold the Lion of Judah who has come to fight for you.
He has come to win.

Helen Securo

The Warrior Breed

They came from every walk of life
Know heartbreak, bitter strife, this fraternity of mine.
They climbed the hills, crossed the plain,
Left love behind and knew the pain,
The boys that laid it on the line.
They are the warrior breed.

Their hearts were true and above it all
Not a single one refused the call
Of their country, right for wrong.
They kept the faith with honor bright,
Tho wronged at home, still fought our fight.
Lured to their death by the harpies song.
They are the warrior breed.

Now in some future year ahead,
When all these valiant men lay dead,
Who will answer to the bugles trill?
Hold up the nation when spirits sag?
Stand tall beneath our blooded flag?
And through it all feel the patriots thrill?
Those of the warrior breed.

Harold D. Kellams

Untitled

Oh, the sad and soulful eyes of winter
are staring their icy stare,
and the cold breath from her mouth
has encompassed us everywhere.

I look out at the stark and barren trees
now so grayed with cold,
remembering the fresh green of their summer-
it makes them look so old.

Listen to the sounds so sharp on the winter earth,
footsteps like a hammer on stone....
winter's frosty fingers reach inside our hearts,
it's not the season to be alone.

It's time to start the fire glowing in the hearth
and listen to the crackle of pungent wood.
And touch hands and hearts in this warmth,
oh, if you an I only could!

Gretchen Kane

Grandma

You were like a river.
A river that flowed forever and ever.
You were strong, but not rough.
You'd never hit any of your family.
But you'd always be there helping and caring, whenever you
    were needed.
To me, you were the river that flowed in my heart.
Whenever I saw you I would become stronger and see that
    since you never gave up I wouldn't either.
Like a river, fresh and clean, glistening in the sun, warm
    all through the year, you will always be remembered.
You will be remembered for a beautiful caring person, who
    ran through our hearts, showing us the right way to go.
Grandma, I love you with all my heart.
You will always be he river that runs through our hearts
    and our memories.
For the rest of Eternity you will always flow.

Cindy Hughes

Wasted Days

i put a hand to my head,
and hold back the tears.
Once again i have promised
to never unleash my fears.

i see myself standing scared in the Garden of Hell,
looking upon those i thought i knew well.
only to find remorse
in the nakedness of my naiveté.
just to please one last person,
for one lonely last day.
and then I'll find myself filling
the shadow of that scared naked soul—
one last day, just gone to waste.

McCain Tyler

Untitled

When I think of you, after our relationship
has long since ended, I think of what
I may have done wrong to make you leave me.
No matter how long I think about it
I can never find a good answer.
I sit up day and night, always alone,
trying to find the problem with me.
I always will remember the days where
All we'd do is curl up on the couch together
And watch movies or whatever wc do.
I miss all of those wonderful days and
that one very special night that we
shared ourselves with each other so lovingly.
Now, when I see you out around town,
I like to think that we an still be friends.
To my surprise, when I see you, after
two years of not knowing anything, you
act as if we were old friends. Your behavior
baffles me but you have taught me to
expect the unexpected from anyone.

Melinda Woodall

The Sea

The sea is wonderful
Its dark, blue waters flow gently
the fish swim quietly under the surface
the oysters sit on the rocky bottom
bubbles float to the top of the calm waters
as the sand and seashells descend to the ocean floor
the tides rise and fall, silently and gently
I sit there and watch
amazed by the beauty and grace of —— The Sea

Chiara Grenaway

The Irony Of Who I Am

Oh how I wish I was completely free,
to be whatever I wanted to be.
But, I'm so tied down by society;
living in the land of opportunity.
My life is so full of all of these rules,
unlike the eagles, or fish in their schools.
I'm created greater than all of the beast;
Yet, even I can be made of the feast.
I have the ability and potential to learn,
But lack grace and beauty, like flower and fern.
Said to be greatest of all living things
and yet, I envy Robin in flight as he sings.
I'm amazed by hummingbird and bumble bee you know,
yet I can conquer blistering heat and bitter cold, so
no matter what I say or no how I may act,
It will never change the ever present fact,
That I am of the family they call "Mankind."
Though mass-destructive, a more wondrous family I'll never find

Jim Junkin

The Christmas Story

Christmas is a joyful time
people spending every dime
relatives to visit and see
presents for everyone and me
watching kids received their toys
parents putting up with all the noise
but is this what its all about
let's not forget old Herod's pout
for in a manger in nazareth lay
a baby boy which was there to stay
Jesus was his name and that's no doubt
but many people didn't know what he was about
He came here to save everyone
to free us from sin when it was all done
He was nailed to a cross and made fun of
but He did it because of love
He would come back one day for all of us
to live with Him so have no fuss
for where we would stay is a beautiful place
to live with God face to face

Joshua J. Correia

Halloween Party

Oh, what a frightful night it's gonna be —
Another Halloween party for you and me.
There'll be plenty of darkness for your spirits to roam—
So, jump into your costumes and leave and little gremlins at home.
There'll be fun and refreshments at this blood-thirst feast-
So come on out, and dine with the deceased.
There'll be monster, witches, and goblins galore —
And lots of graves for you to explore.
It's gonna be a horror fun night; Oh, what a thrill!—
Come as you are, or come dressed to kill.
So hurry out to the old homestead——
Party among the living and the dead.
We'll be expecting to see you on this eerie-night of blood and gore——
So arise from your coffins and be seen once more!

JoAnn Mullis

A True Friend

You pick me up whenever I fall;
Morning or night I know I can call.
A shoulder to cry on a hand to hold;
I know you won't tell what you've been told.
I would always do the same things for you;
That's how I know our friendship is true.

Bri

God's Serenade

I heard the music of the spheres
But once during all my years.
It was enchanting and sublime,
Transporting me through space and time.

Far too mystical to explain,
I still hear its faint refrain;
And since that inner rendezvous
My days have dawned more bright and new.

O how I've learned, above all else,
From this cosmic, throbbing pulse,
There is One Heart, below, above,
Singing God's serenade of Love!

Norman V. Olsson

Jack And Bobby

Two brothers are together now,
while on earth two widows their heads do bow,
A mother holds her grief inside,
And a father wishes he had died,
Instead of two so close to him.
Whose loss makes our worlds future dim,
An unborn babe is also sad,
It's tough to be born without a Dad.
For another father far away.
There is also grief on this dark day.
He did his best with what he had,
How could he know his son was bad
How could a man with future nil.
Fire a shot to forever still
A heart so big, a head so bright.
Who had a future of peace in sight
Are there wise men who can reason why
Small men want big men to die?
And now my plea to you is please,
Don't judge all men by such as these.

Virginia L. Bothroyd

No One Can See

With the hurts and pains inside of me.
And all the wounds that no one can see.
It gets worse everyday.
And hurts more in every possible way.
No one has the pain or hurts the way I do,
And no one understands or really cares to.
So I sit in my dark world, I sit alone,
I sit in the dark and no light is shone.
I dream of a life that's rich with love
and no one gets hurt, and no one falls down.
I dream, in my own little world, my
own little town.

Laura Bailey

Untitled

'Tis the human touch in this world that counts,
The touch of your hand and mine.
It means more to the fainting heart
Than shelter and bread, and wine!
Shelter is gone when the night is over
And bread lasts only a day,
But the touch of your hand,
And the sound of your voice
Sing on in the soul always!

Polly A. Dickey

This Boy Dreams

He dreams of how this world should be.
He has a hope that more people would agree.

He had dreams of people on streets being
fed and not so many people dead.

Dreams of things people say and knows it
shouldn't be this way.

He dreams of all the people that are killed
and all the self-esteem teens need to build.

He dreams that love wouldn't sometimes, be
a heartbreak and wishes people would have
the heart to give and not take.

He dreams of people trying to succeed and
therefore not so many people would be of need.

He woke up and realized there was no change
but the sad part was, that wasn't to anyone, strange.

Michelle Teakell

Inspiration

Inspired by the mood
  my mind opens free to elude.

I seek out the smallest of images
  unseen by most with the naked eye.

Placing confusion and illusion with reality
  In a way that all who read may sigh.

Perception magnified, I conquer the describe.

Breaking down the complexity
  I write to suppress the insanity

I bring into normal view
  the lives of me and you.

A golden kiss sent
  is my gift I wish to present.

The inspired wish to know
  for this very reason this message is to flow.

Kevin L. Kexel

Heartbroken

We used to be close
but times got tough
I thought it would be best to leave him
and think I've had enough
I knew that day, at that time
that it wasn't what I wanted.
I only wanted him

Now he doesn't talk to me or even tempt to stare
It's only that mean awful glare
I really like him, even though he doesn't know
but in time I will tell him I need him
He might say something
or hold me once again
but it will take time
to break the thought of being apart because
In my heart the love will never leave

I only wish that he would come back
Talk to me; set my mind free
of the guilt and worries I hold
and the bad memories I see

Lisa Street

Count Your Blessings

We gather together as folks did of yore
to reminisce what last year had in store.
But wait now a minute, the slate is wiped clean,
A new year has dawned, see what I mean
our errors, and mistake of last year we can forget, a clean page is
before us, we need not regret.
Hold on to your hats, everything comes so soon,
This year is anew baby, holding on to a spoon
Your attitude in life keeps the spoon empty, or full,
If your chin drags on the ground your life will be dull.
Smile, and cheer up life can be happy, even though you
may be a granny or pappy.
Rejoice with the things that you have been blessed.
Your home, food, and even in the clothes you are dressed.
Look around you so many haven't got it so good,
and most of them are happy, and in a fine mood.
God has given us blessings galore,
so thank Him, and praise Him — HE has much more in store.

Helia Aho

A Penny's Worth

A penny's worth was not enough
For expressing him my feelings.
There is not many words to be described.
I only know it is revealing.

In the world, there is not a nickel
For him quite as silver.
The skies turn grayer by the day
As winter makes us shiver.

Of the dimes inside the universe,
Compared to him, there was none as nice.
So, that season, when snow falls,
Remember I am not cold as ice.

With all the quarters in the galaxy,
More there would have to be to have fun.
If that were the case, with every penny,
Nickel, dime, and quarter, he is the one.

Susan Killewald

Our God-Given World

Somewhere beneath the extended murky air lies the
beauty of the world and all the serenity of nature.

The fowls soar like the breeze, hard and cold. The
rugged mountainous lands crumble underneath my feet as
I marvel at the vicinity that beset me.

I wondered: "Why Heavenly Father, have we deserved this
lovely home we call Earth?". That question will
possibly never be answered.

Angela Marie Haney

Now

I climb down derelict ladders
Into beds of withered flowers and twigs
And hope the road will be smoother
A few steps down I will find the pleasant
I grope at dreams that lie beyond my stretch
And bend over backward to kiss the past
Wailing voices of a thousand destinies I could have reached
Echo within my passage
A little stronger, a little swifter, a little higher
And I could have built an empire of fulfilled desires
Holding a tiny depleting drop of time
Ripe and delicious with all its charm and promises
I live everywhere, but in it.

Sumitava Chatterjee

Our Savior

I was just a little guy,
When I heard the triumphant cry.
Jesus Christ was born today.
Born to take our sins away.
God sent his son down to the earth,
To give our souls a new rebirth.
Stay with Jesus and you'll know,
Gods love will follow you where ever you go.
Walk with Jesus and you'll see,
The final victory at Calvary.
Yes Jesus Christ was born today,
Just to take our sins away.
Talk to Jesus and you'll know,
God's love will follow you where ever you go.
Remember Jesus and keep your path straight.
For your final reward will be heavens gate.

Joseph P. St. Clair Jr

"The Name Jesus"

If I was to write the name Jesus;
it would not be on a cloud;
For man would be to low to look up and behold the name Jesus;
I would not write the name Jesus on the sands of a beach;
For man would only came along and trample it;
I would not write the name Jesus on the trunk of a tree;
For some strong arm lumber jack would come along and cut it down;
If I were to write the name Jesus;
I would dip my pin in His blood and write it up on each and
   every heart.

Freddie Walker

Untitled

Story is about to begin.
With cold chills running through
my bones. Let us start.

Growing more mature each day.
I wonder how many times life has somehow
played these tapes.
Over and over again.

In what chases.
The odds against making and remaking
the same choices.

To look at the stars with such awesome power.
To think the stars will always be a novel.
The beauty of the heavens, portrayed by endless time,
and unharness freedom of spirit.

Light does dance softly on the moon.
How swab and graceful, slipping in and
around a full moon.

Let your eyes focus on the fine lines.
Open Hearts and unleashed mines.

Lydia Newberg

To Mom

Your eyes so loving and kind are sought,
Very wise through ages taught
Only few will know you are a treasure,
Now and always giving pleasure
Never will your happy heart mar,
Ever bright your shining star.

Maxine R. Rogers

Your Imagination

Your imagination is there, in whatever you do,
Without it, you would not have a clue.
You use it when you walk,
You use it when you talk.
It is there when you sleep,
It is there when you weep.
It can take you to a place that does not exist,
Or somewhere that has a cool Spring mist.
It can let you be who you want to be,
Or just close your eyes to see what you want to see.
It is in your dreams,
No worries, no schemes.
You use it to express yourself,
It may even bring you great wealth.
It is not something you find in your gene pool,
It is rather powerful.
It forms your personality,
It is beyond reality.
It is a form of creation,
It is your imagination.

Nicholas L. Fryer

Little Ones

Up in the morning, awake with the sun,
Rise little sleepyheads, a new day's begun.
Nighttime is over, it's now after dawn,
Gently they stir and softly they yawn.
Out of their beds on two little feet,
Out of their rooms, the morning they greet.
Their days are filled with fun and play,
Games and adventures through out the day.
Upside down and inside and out,
Here, there, everywhere, they run all about.
Giggles and laughter, shouts of glee,
Oh to be young, what fun it must be.
Happiness and good times, had by the tons,
Oh the lives of those little ones.

Rhonda Johnston

Lover

Restless hours tormented thoughts,
my heart beats faster my breathing stops.
Close your eyes feel my touch,
a candle lit light quivers with us.

Love has no rules....
It can rear its ugly head
it can make you kiss the sky,
one never knows what it can do.

Love casts its doubts,
it leaves its scars.
But in one breath...
it's who we are.

Albert Roppolo

Lost

I float in space, that left its mark
A dot, a ray, pulled from the dark
A breath of life, grazing the globe.
to acquire knowledge, to learn to probe
The mystery on earth, the challenge, the intrigue
The truth of creation, I try to seek.
Where does one start, my mind is racing
Its tearing me apart.
My blood is throbbing, my heart it pounds,
I feel myself sinking, I shudder, I scream,
My eyes, I open, it was only a dream!

Anny Walters

Brown And Blue

Falling water kisses glass, like a whore it does not matter.
Side to side works the wiper.
In a bar, poison fills the Viper.
Flesh and bone move in metal.
Hand in hand, Brown and Blue travel.
Warm as sunshine, Blue gives a kiss Brown shall miss.
Intoxicated, comes the Viper.
His headlights pierce through the wiper.
Somewhere a grave grins at you.
Stung by a tear, an angel cries my dear.
A twisted embrace, leaves Blue without a face.
Two become one, death leaves one.
Torn, skin creates warm rivers of red, which stream south
and lay on the Devil's bed.
Curtains of flesh cover Blue, forever eternal are you.
Silence tells all, wet kisses remain in the red rain.
What was still is, hand in hand.
Meat and metal rot, with one last thought Brown forgot.
What was still is, four wings and a flame.

Mitchum N. Ray

Time

Time, oh thou cursed mistress of men;
Must thou devour every morsel of life,
Engulfing it with ephemeral brevity,
Ticking away the days of youth towards senile decay.
Thou create dismay, hungrily grasping for each momentum,
Gaily capering along when thou should hold thyself motionless,
Then lagging at ease, in spiteful wickedness, when thou
   are most wished to hasten.
Obscene as thou art, smirking through eternity
At your mournful victim: mankind.
Cease this dreadful rambling!
Surrender forever this paused moment to me -
   And my love.

Victoria A. Molinari

New Love

With sensual tempo and leering sight
It rises strong in hideous delight
Each new time refreshed and young
The story of love: unborn, unsung.
Thus new love.

Though flesh of past still cling
Love takes flight on bony wing.
And circling builds a hollow shell;
Imprisoned lover in heavens hell.
How best to win what can't be kept?

Then with love comes question lured
The heart goes on: the love's assured.
What now gives the heart more faith?
Love's an old and sickened wraith.
Should the being of love be worn or shed?

With quickening hope and dropping fear
It dries again another's tear.
This time there is no doubt, no end.
The love its lovers will defend
Thus new lover.

Gerald W. Allen

A New Angel In Heaven Tonight

There's a new angel in Heaven tonight,
   There's a little boy in a man's body who gave up the fight.
There's a beautiful dark haired boy knocking at Heaven's door,
   Who has come to see the light that had frightened him before.
There's a mischievous comedian who's ready to go beyond,
   who leaves behind so many who share in him a bond.
He stayed on earth to touch the lives of all he'd come to know,
   He stayed on earth because his loved ones needed him so.
Heaven will be proud to have Travis in the fold,
   For when the child was born, they threw away the mold.
So God, we ask this prayer of you as we let go of Trav,
   We only want the best for him, and that we're sure you have.
So open the door and let him in-he'll tell a joke or two,
   He's saved them up for years, you know, to tell them all to you.
We'll see him in the sunrise and in the flowers that bloom in spring,
   We'll remember him with fondness when we hear a robin sing.

Delana D. LaHue

A Friend For A Life Time

The trees in the distant view
reflect the golden rays of the sun
   In the late afternoon
we recall the morning of fun
   You have to leave
I understand that
   but what I don't know
Is when you'll be back
   I only wish I had more time
To ask you the questions that have been on my mind
   We gaze into the dusky blue sky
   hoping that it will not turn into night.
   we knew we were born the day we met
   to be each other's soul mate even in death
   but this is worse than any thing like that
   as we now lay in the place we had sat.
"It's time to go," you say just then.
"I will miss you my dear best friend.
"Who will be there when we part?"
"I will my dear, I'll be in your heart."

Cherish Masters

Image

The image of space, it seems so dark
Through the corner of my eye I catch a spark
Temporary blindness, a rain of sweat
Adrenalin flowing and great contempt

A light I see, a glow so faint
A star maybe, a motionless state
I'm at the point of no return
Moving closer, the light, it burns

A rage revolves in fluent streams
Sentimental, but not reprieved
Compulsive screams. like howling wolves
Echo back in galloping hooves

In my head a thunder roars
A deterrent fate around me soars
Fear, depression, undenied
'It's an illusion', my mind replied

My mind and body disarrayed
With a feeling of decay
With a jerk, I arise
To an empty scene before my eyes

Hinor Doko

Untitled

I'm often left to wonder why
my driest days are filled with rain
I cry the tears that "Men don't cry"
I bear the marks that "Tears won't stain"
I'm often left alone to cry
my truest love you do disdain
Your truest love-the blackest lie
the greatest pleasure-the greatest pain
I'm often left in sad goodbyes
too many dreams for one man's brain
You came to me and asked me, "Why?"
Your tears conveyed my death again

Stephen Daugherty

Entanglement

I think that into every verse of rhyme.
There goes a bit of you each time.
You labor on, yet unaware,
Of what you've really written there.

Upon the page and woven thru and thru,
For all to see, is much of you.
You cannot hide behind the pen.
Transparent, there you are again.

Tho' verse displays your handsome, high ideals,
Numerous faults it, too, reveals.
Yet, sympathetic readers find,
Their own shortcomings brought to mind.

Alba E. Schulz

War

My love is gone and I am here
Left, all by myself
The only thing left of him is the picture on my shelf
When he left, he took part of me
A part I'll never have back
They sent my love to an early grave
For that I am so blue
For he is gone and I forgot to say
"Darling I love you"
For he had gone and been so brave
But, that won't bring him back
For War is guilty and it's wrong
It's Justice that they lack

Cheryl D. Costello

Shadowed

A peaceful existence is very untrue
to the one to whom the peace belongs

The awareness of ones self is troublesome to the
outlook of reality

To face the understanding of ones true identity
can be so transparent
yet only be revealed within your shadow

Looking in the mirror will not explain your affliction
being that you only fancy what is lying
on the superficial

The key to inward content
is to cast away shame and doubt and to remain
...forever shadowed

Jennifer Jennings

Words

They can set the soul free
They can create our destiny

Words
They can calm a stormy night
They can make wrong seem right

Words
They are our only way to connect
They help us express what we think

Words
They are building blocks of the mind
They give us space, order, and time

Words
They control all that we are and can become
They shelter our hope, bring love to some

Words
Never say it was only words...

Zoe

The Wind

When I was just a little girl, I loved the wind to blow;
I loved the trees and flowers, swaying to and fro.

The clothing on the clothesline would wave and leap and dance,
the tapping all about the house would cast a lazy trance.

Mama always loved the wind; she said it cleaned the air,
and spread the seed upon the earth for nature's gentle care.

I loved to run against the wind, and hold my coattails high;
my feet would almost leave the ground; I felt that I could fly.

The Summer wind was very soft, and gentle like a breeze;
the fall wind was much stronger as it danced among the trees.

The Autumn leaves with colors bright would swirl and fill the air,
then come to rest upon the earth, and Winter would prepare.

The Winter wind would howl and moan and make the air so cold,
the snow would drift about our home in shape and form untold.

But in the Spring it settled down, and tapped upon the earth,
and woke up all of nature to give Spring its new birth.

Carol E. Baumfalk

Burning Solitude

Calm and solitude filled the air.
The school was quiet with not a rustle,
The teachers stopped and talked without a care.
Coaches walked and did not hustle,
As the day was peace filled, yet, they were unaware.

Slowly the wind blew and picked up speed,
Quickly the air shifted from a breeze
And evil thoughts and evil things did what e'er they pleased.
Their movement was guarded by the wind
Gusting the crippled leaves, oranges, reds and dying browns
Would soon leave bodies all around.

Hideous creatures and ghastly beings
Shed blood and tears on shadows and living things!
Spreading fear and hate so far
That men can't run but must stand in stupor's tar!
Hell's gates are opening its fire is steaming
Satan is jumping his demons are screaming,
Chants and rituals go up in fire
As the new soul bows to our leader, our sire!

Andrew S. Park

Message For A Footprint

Virginal white covers the frigid wintery ground
There is only an angel like whispering sound
Till a footprint appears and defiles the crystallized surface
Awakening the lightness of its flakes with heavy footing
Branches of God's trees are flocked with the snow
A family of birds fly down to seek nourishment below
The wind nips at any flesh that is standing in its passage
And mounds together like a jigsaw puzzle pieces of snow

    Calling it a drift
Icicles formed on an old roof top suspend four feet to the ground
Until the chillness fades some and it turns into a waterfall
    Condensing into an ice rink

    The footprint appears once again
This time to collapse on top of the clear covering that
   is no longer virginal white
It speaks to the gray sky with a pain in its eye
    Fall, fall, why I
Footprint, you have taken away the snow's purity
Now all the footprints shall follow and this makes me cry

    Eileen L. Zigmont

Summer Time In May

The grass is green high enough
to now. I eat a bite then
outside I go. I grab the gas from the
shed an gas up the riding mower.
   As I got on the mower and
put it in gear it would not go.
   Off I got and look under
neat it was a brown fat ground
hog sleeping. So I got a stick and punch
the ground hog in the rear end, an away he
ran. I got on the mower again.
   Mowing around the house and down threw
the hollow. Looking up toward a bank down
came a black racer, running faster ahead of my mower.
   With chills running up an down myself. I mowed
two acre as an headed for the house.

    Ruth M. Kinney

"A Golf Widow's Omen"

I wish I were a golf club, I'd know just where I stand,
Cause if I was a golf club, I'd never lose my man.

I'd even like to be the ball, thou he'd knock me off my tee,
But I'd be sure every time that he would follow me.

In the weeds and woods and through the mud
He'd keep on searching for his true love,

Hot or cold in rain or snow,
He'd always want me-that I know.

If I were the course so nice and green
'Twould be of me he would always dream.

For hours he would trample all over me
And stay all night if he could see;

I thank my stars for just one thing,
That they don't have lights on those greens

Just a Golf Widow is all I am,
And what I have to say is, Damn!

    Margaret Land Sauls

Memories Of The Past And Dreams Of The Future

Today is a beautiful time in which no one sees,
To most it's filled with future dreams and past memories.

The sun rises and the moon and stars begin to fall,
There is no present time, only the past to recall.

Life is much like a storm with a rainbow at the end,
Only the worst is seen, then the beauty now and then.

It takes one wrong decision; one breath to end this day,
Why do we look for tomorrow when we're not done with today.

So live each day of this life as if it were the last,
Not dreams of the future nor memories of the past.

    Tracy Wisdom

The Sound Of Silence

Have you ever listened to the silence?
Its cry deafening
As subconscious thoughts imprisoned speak out
Sounding like a mighty lion's roar —
Disturbing
Reaching the remote regions of my soul.
Then, the madness drifts in
Creeping in ever so slowly like an incoming tide
Swishing back and forth
Flooding my mind —
Drowning.
Upon its retreat
The only thing left is the desperate cry of solitude.

    David Brian Fambrough

Homecoming Is Such Sweet Sorrow

To hear a quick and distant call,
On pane of glass, in light of waterfall,
Upon the lips of a flower-red carnation,
And flush your stone-white, blushing cheeks in my direction...
To promise me this at a later date...
Or a content dance on the banks by the moonlight,
To waste away with me by the call of night,
And attempt this bleak and weary, hopeless romance,
Would you, with me by shadow of a solemn chance...
Perhaps, maybe me at a later date...
Or streaked in silt, sweat and sorrow,
A day to wreck and more to me to borrow,
A final dance to wilt and wane,
as its ringing tones stand placid among you in the rain...
Perhaps, maybe me at a later date...
Or shimmer to mingle, the whispers a-single,
The gales of the flowing moon in you to mingle,
To forget, yet not to be late,
or lift away the fear and hesitate...
To run out of time... perhaps at a later date...

    Tyler Ritter

Dear One

Oh the excitement of when we first met.
To behold that instant and yet
here we are 40 years later,
after the beginning - and end of dreams.
Still hand in hand, it seems
that electricity still connects
attitudes, beliefs and love - a oneness.
We've huddled many fences, oh yes,
and gained strength one from the other.
We grew in many ways closer to each other
so that two becomes one - a wholeness.
The caring and sharing grows even more
'cause God granted us the nurturing of time
for a special love - my love dear one.

    Elaine K. Sheehan

The Storm Internal

Her forehead pressed against the glass;
her tears matched the rain
streaming down
unyielding.

Furious flashes
of light came from within.
She questioned.
How could be he do this—
Again?

The sting of his fabrications
in her mind drowned out
the rhythmic pattern
of the deluge
upon the glass.

Nothing settled
with the slam of the door
the squeal of tires..
during the storm.

Her forehead pressed against the glass.
Dodie Lynn Jarvis

The Avon Baseball Team

We're coming home losers, the seventh game in a row.
If we're gonna keep losing, then I would rather not go.

But I can't voice my opinion, there's nothing I can say,
It was just another baseball game, where I didn't get to play.

Our record is 2 and 7, our winning streak is gone.
We're making a lot of errors, and doing a lot of wrong.

COACH SIDES can't understand it, he says there's no excuse
Yea! We should be winning, but every game we lose.

We loaded the bus for the game, and then away we went,
Coach Sides says— "Fellows I don't ask much, just a 110 percent."

We've played for four long years and our seasons close is near,
When you find there is no place on the team
For you — your Senior Year

So Underclassmen take warning, if you find yourself in a pinch,
Give the coach a 110 percent, and you too will sit the bench.

Jeffrey Scott King

My Mother

   My mother is very kind,
my mother is always on my mind.
My mother is encouraging and sentimental,
My mother is ever so gentle. I don't
need another sister, or a brother, all
I need is my beautiful, wonderful mother
My mother has the fragrance of a rose
in the spring, I wouldn't trade my
mother for anything. Her eyes are dark
brown and pretty they are, they open
like sunshine and twinkle like stars.
Her skin is as velvety as a kittens
fur, I want everyone to know I love her.
I'm proud to have such
a mother, I wouldn't trade her for any other.

Sean Hildreth

Andrea

You're the bestest sister I ever had
Actually you're the only one, and I'm glad
Because if there was another one like you
I wouldn't know which one to tell my secrets to
And what if I had a nightmare in the middle of the night
Whose room would I go into to cuddle with and take away my fright
I wouldn't know whose white shirts to stain
Or who to annoy and be a pain to
Whose long hair will I brush
And whose room will I clean when they're in a rush
What if I want to take a walk
Or I just want to talk
Tell me which one would I give this poem to when I'm done
Because you can't put as much LOVE into two as you can into one
So you can see why I'm glad there's only one of you
Otherwise I wouldn't know what to do
For nobody in the world covered ever take your place
In my heart for I've covered it with ribbon and lined it with lace

Erin Moslener

Love Is Heaven, Love Is Hell

Love runs the gamut of human emotions
From gentle caring to total devotions.

Giving and taking, doing and sharing,
A special commitment with tender caring.

There are times you begin pleased and smiling
Only to end in tears - gently crying.

Sometimes it's anger with sparks a flying;
Frustrated, confused, hopelessly dying.

It's then you remember the effort it takes
To accept or correct the human mistakes.

But love is worth all the effort it takes
Bending and shaping for each others' sakes.

For suddenly the soft, warm feeling begins
And spreads like wildfire carried on the winds.

For though beginning deep within your core
It soon encompasses you from head to floor;

Searching and scorching and all consuming;
Cleansing your heart where pain was rooming.

It's only then you'll understand so well that
love is heaven, love is hell.

Marie Tatina

The Pleasure Of Your Company

The pleasure of your company is multifaceted,
It is the pleasure of seeing you...
The pleasure of hearing you laugh and talk softly...
The drama of watching your actions,
your likes and dislikes and adventures...
The pleasure of catching you when I call,
And the delicate warmth I feel when you call...
The pleasure of your company is multifaceted.

The pleasure of your company fills me with joy...
It is measured in nature by the lakes, streams and cloudless skies...
The restful quiet of the mountains through renewal of our souls...
The beauty of my world shines through,
The pleasure of your company.

The pleasure of your company creates a sincere strength..
It is the security of knowing you care...
The practically of creating something unique...
The true happiness from sharing favorite thoughts...
The peace that provides needed strength through,
The pleasure of your company.

Eleanor McNamara

In Memory Of

A loved one from us has gone, a voice we loved is stilled
A place is vacant in this home, which never can be filled.

He lived a life of service, and was true to God and man,
so let us follow his example and do the very best we can.

He loved the little children, and they to, loved him so well,
And how glad he always was, the story of Jesus to tell.

No night was to dark and dreary, no day to hot or cold,
to render his good service to those of whom he was told.

How we miss his footsteps and his prayers, as they reached the throne.
For those who were sick and suffering while he had sorrows of his own.

He never shirked his duty, always lent a helping hand,
now he's gone to his reward to that bright and happy land.

He's gone to be with Jesus and the blest angel band,
some day we shall meet him when we to, leave his pilgrim land.

Doris Walker Hargrove

Parting

I did not know
  what you were feeling
  as you stood and watched me go.

I was twenty-five or thirty;
  you were sixty-five or seventy.

The sadness in your heart then
  (I imagine it was so)
  is the sadness I now know.

I am thirty-plus years wiser,
  and I'm sad to see you go.

O, the you who parts is different, surely,
  but the you who stays is all the same.

And I watch and watch and watch you,
  as you watched me down to the road...

When the drying leaves of autumn
  swirled a veil across the screen.

Charles S. J. White

The Tiger Swallowtail

From where, to where? Prince of the skies.
Effortless and without ties,
Sipping nectar as you go,
You rise and fall - blow wind blow.
You flutter high among the trees,
Then settle down wher'er you please,
You wait no welcome, take no leave,
You give no one the time to grieve,
Don't worry what the morrow brings,
Today hear how the Robin sings.

Your tailored suit of bright yellow,
Laced with black, no somber hue;
You are quite the gaudy fellow
With brilliant jewels of orange and blue.
Now rest awhile on our dogwood,
And taste the honey waiting there,
Precisely where my Ginny stood
This morning in the cool spring air.
She smiled at me and all was well,
What more, my friend, is there to tell?

Don L. Jacobs

Self Discovery

I have lived many lives, all chosen for me.
I have traveled many roads, all chosen for me.
I have seen may sights, all chosen for me.
I have heard many sounds, all chosen for me.
I have felt many emotions, all chosen for me.

I have followed, I have obeyed, I have existed.
The pattern has been identified, forgiveness has occurred.

I now live the life meant to be lived.
I now travel the road meant to be traveled.
I now see what is meant to be seen.
I now hear the sound of my own voice.
I now feel the passions meant to be felt.

I now choose, I now lead the way.
I now soar to heights beyond comprehension.

The energy of yesterday has been released and a new soul is born.

Deanne Moore

Untitled

There once was a girl named Marjorie Grace
Who had long blond hair that looked of lace

As she grew older she grew wiser
For now there is KEN who stands beside her

God has created this woman and man
And now there's a baby who holds out its hand

May the baby you carry so close to your heart
Help us remember just how life starts

Now you are a mom and KEN is a dad
And for this reason I am so glad

For I have three children all of my own
Who have filled my life with a happy home

There may be times when you're all flustered out
For sister I LOVE YOU and I have no doubt

For remember the saying I mentioned above
I have three children and they're all full of love

Now it is time to be on my way
But always remember my thoughts for the day

You three will always be deep in my heart
For remember Margie it was you and I from the start.

Tammy Hilbig

The Night Visitor

Suddenly, we were enveloped in an opalescent garment
Spun of gossamer thread
The fog embraced us edges were lost and found
Ugliness was blurred in the delicate weave
Lights were haloed, glowed and became veiled stars.
Footfalls were muffled, danger lurked
Crime had an accomplice eeriness, beauty, grace
Paradoxical—at once warm and protective
Then cold, deceitful, dreaded it curled, it floated
It penetrated, enriched, demoralized, mystified
It flowed, then stagnated
There was a fragile, luminous gauze about us
We created, envisioned dream-like characters
In an opaque world
Somewhere, in the distance, strains of a familiar melody
Instilled a loneliness, a poignancy,
The magic ended when morning came,
The mist hugged the earth, then crept away
With the first rays of a shy sun,
Leaving a world of diamonds in its wake.

Ann Kostura

The River

The river runs deep, and has peace within,
Harmonious and focused toward only one end.
It's energy is channeled as one moving stream;
A cascade of voices pursuing a dream.

To focus one's energy is the first seed of greatness,
Edged like a river and flowing with straightness.
Clarity of purpose, vision and being,
Simplicity of effort unswerving within.

Go with the flow and roll like a stream,
Reap generous rewards in pursuit of your dream.
Ebbing and flowing with rhythm and tide,
'Til the fruits of your labors are plenty and wide.

Stewart Bronaugh Jr.

God's World Awakens

Leaves are falling in the breeze.
Amber shadows cover the trees.
Puffy white clouds float in the sky,
changing shape as they scurry by.
Flocks of birds are flying south
as every squirrel packs his mouth.

Cold winter's creeping very near.
God's little creatures never fear.
Instinctively they seem to know,
even when earth is covered with snow,
that spring will come bringing rain
to wake the sleeping world again.

When all our time on earth has passed,
we'll reach our heavenly home at last.
Until that time God's world will sleep
and awaken each spring when flowers peep
to see what beauty they can bring
to add to God's eternal spring.

Alyse O. Spencer Hunt

Goodbye

Loving you have hurt me so bad,
Pain fills my heart and makes me sad,
Grief now flows in my veins,
All my happiness you have drained.

I have been trying so hard, I've grown old,
Yet your heart has remained ice cold.
You wanted more than I gave,
You almost sent me to my grave.

I have to give up, I am tired and torn.
I have gotten so weary, I am sore and worn.
I have to protect what's left of my heart.
Goodbye my love, we have to part.

Lorraine Clacken-Knowles

"The Heavens Declare The Glory Of God"

O . . . Beyond a beautiful, sunset, is
    the master artist of all time
    his brush is never still
    each and every evening, he creates
    yet one anew!
O . . . ranges of blues and purples, beyond
    compare
    renderings of yellow and rose
    and the bright orange sun, sinking
    into the horizon
O . . . the heavens declare the
    glory of God . . .

Jack Wallace

Rotation

Each year the seasons come and go, and each one tells a story,
They each start out so mildly, and end in bursts of glory.

The snow white blanket of Winter, slowly melted all away,
To reveal the brand new sprouts of green, that say, spring is on the way.

The plants all reach out to the sky, the animals bear their young,
And put their notes onto the page, writing songs that will be sung.

The gentle times of Summer breezes, and rains that quench the thirst,
Of all the living things that thrive, upon the mother earth.

They live their cycle, each in it's way, and move on to make room,
And the greens all turn to golden hues, and flowers loose their bloom.

The process quickens un-announced, the leaves began to fall,
And all at once it's Autumn, and mother nature takes roll call.

Each thing has had a slice of life, and each thing did it's best,
Mother Nature smiles on everything, and says thanks, it's time to rest.

With that remark she waves her wand, and skies fill up with flakes,
That slowly drift down to the ground, and a furry blanket makes.

As each and every spark of life, turns into a soft glow,
And rests and gathers up new strength, beneath the cover of snow.

Not moving, but just waiting there, until the rays of the spring sun,
Start the cycle, once again, for each and every one.

Joseph M. Bower

Untitled

When you start to dream of trivial things
unconscious on the floor
you notice that what has brought you there
isn't nothing anymore

You stoop so low to remember things
that used to mean so much
you've got yourself and so do I
that used to mean so much

And it seems to you the thing to do
is wish it all away
so nothing here can make you stay
it's okay
there's nothing left here anyway

And I won't wait without good reason
my heart and mind change with the season

John Ashley Shreffler

The School Custodian

For most of days, "Mr. Fix-It" he be
And pride in his work, you'll see.
He pushes that broom; and he swings that mop
Of floods, fires & daily trash, he is on top.

He rids graffiti; he dusts window sills
Inside and Out, all over the place, he mills.
Or wearing plastic gloves and a nose mask
Only God knows the hazards or a task.

"Yes," each day's chores reach their gain
Be he happy, sad, or twitchin' with pain
He's somebody's brother; he somebody's son
Who's stiffled dignity and work's battle won.

Be it required to scrub toilet
Or clean up that stinking ole vomit
Never forget how necessary that he be
And kindly remember a person like he

Donna M. Baker

The Love Slayer

Why does it drive me crazy so?
Sitting in my bedroom all alone?
Shredding the thoughts of you in my mind.
Love less lost, no chance to resign.
No Fault by me? Tis what eats at my brain.
The voided question left to the sane.

My voices are churning, echoed and burning.
Whispers of you left lost in my sheets.
I shudder in silence, lost in my sleep.

Awaken to find my void still there,
I cry to the Night King to send a love slayer.
A slayer as big and as bountiful as my love.
To strike it down, and drown it in the tub.
Why yes! Undoubtedly that's what I need.
A slayer of love to help me sleep.

Paula Chastain

My Summer Place

Come to my summer place, where paths run quiet
And gently embellish the Maestro's
    Sands
Where love lives, and I within
Come hear my song begin.
Come to my summer place
    And play
Relive my dreams but once and stay
They're there to share
    With you.
Escape to my summer place. You will find me there
Kissing the path where I want you to walk
To share your song
    With me.
I will be there forever—for you
Will hear my song but once.
Come to my summer place
    And play.
Come to my summer place, and stay.
    But come!

Robert L. Stempin

Taxes Ode

Here's to the Voter, the common man:
    Taxed to his death according to plan!
They taxed his house and taxed his bed,
    Then taxed the bald spot on his head!
They taxed the shoes right off his feet
    And found ten ways to tax his meat!
They taxed his oxen and his ass.....
    And double-taxed his car and gas!
They taxed his duck, his cock and goose,
    Gouging each red penny loose!
Each year they tax his house and lands,
    Then tax the blisters on his hands!
They taxed his cow, her milk and her calf,
    And taxed again just for the laugh!
They double-tax his water and well,
    Doing their best to make life Hell!
They tax his weather, foul or fair....
    Spending his money on free welfare!
Just who "They" are, nobody knows....
    But "They" cause all our gov't woes!

Jack Ledford

The Path

She heard His soft voice, calling her name
Come quickly my child, out of your pain.
Following the pathway to the brilliant light
Feeling His love was the greatest delight.
The pathway was long but at her side
Was her wonderful Mother, to act as her guide.
The light grew stronger as they went along.
The air was filled with a beautiful song.
She could see the flowers, all radiant blooms
Their colors so brilliant and to her surprise
She suddenly knew, she had two perfect eyes.
Her pain was all gone and her body was light
Everything in this world was perfect and right.
To the end of the pathway and into the light
The love of Jesus was gloriously bright.
Her sojourn on earth has come to an end
A beautiful new life is about to begin.

Ava A. Comeau

My Son

I look and see a partially grown man,
With a turned down lip and a dark even tan.

I study his face and see a boy,
Too young to love, yet too old for a toy.

His face is covered with trouble and woe,
Yet he'll never quite begin to know...
    how lonely he will stay.

He stays the same and yet unknown,
and goes thru life, living on his own.

He'll be famous, I myself say,
And yet I know his price to pay

His price is neatly woven in a plan,
That will someday reveal a full grown man.

Beverly Graham

Sylvio's Cry From Alzheimers

Please look within me, feel what I feel
For it's a burden I carry, one that's very real.
I'm still a person, very much like you
I just can't remember the things I once knew.
Look into my eyes, deep into the fear
For I've somewhat forgotten those so dear.
I don't ask for much, just a warm, friendly smile
A brief shake of my hand, just once in awhile.
When I try to speak, there's no sense of what I say
And I live with this frustration day after day.
I'm a warm, gentle person with eyes of baby blue
Someone who has needs, complaints I have few.
I can whistle a tune, hum a song, clap my hands
I may dance a step or two, draw an image with my crayons.
I did not choose this lifestyle for me
You see, it's my illness that won't set me free.
But no one can strip me of my dignity and pride
All I ask is a hand to lead me and to guide
Into a world I'm not quite sure of, but a life I feel a part of.
So please look within me, feel what I feel and I hope like me, you
find it's very real.

Dolores Denette

Sandy

Crying as she climbs the hill,
Not tears, but choking sobs,
Gasping at air for her lungs to fill;
Leg muscles feeling like knobs.

Beside her plods a faithful friend,
As close as he can be,
Keeping watch around the bend,
And stopping at every tree.

Some walks are happy, some are sad,
Depending on the mood,
But even when the day is bad
Her friend is usually good.

Brown and white, ears held high,
Listening for unknown sounds
Of deer, rabbits or maybe a fly,
In this his territorial ground.

She looks at him, as they walk along;
Her crying stops, she laughs and smiles,
How could anything be wrong?
With him, she will go on for miles.

Mariana B. Heilman

Waiting For You

I call you every single day
But do you hear the phone
I waste my life to talk to you
But are you ever home

You said you'd call you said you'd write
But I don't hear a thing
I sit and wait for you to call
But the phone will never ring

You never called you never wrote
But it is so unfair
That I cry and then I blot my tears
But you don't even care

You said I never loved you
But I loved you for so long
I really thought you loved me too
But I guess I was so wrong

I gave you all my heart
But you broke it into two
I guess there will never be a time
When you love me as much as I love you

Michelle A. Morse

There Was No Thunder

Staring out the window I was
    shut out of the storm
        One without warning
            Lightning strikes without thunder
Observation of ungraspable truth
    inevitably   undeniable
I can't believe   Why can't I understand
            Lightning struck without thunder
    there was no reason
        no warning
        no thunder

Sara Alayne Hudson

"Rainbow Man"

Are you laughing in heaven? Is there so much fun?
So many people singing praises to Gods Son.
Yes I imagine you are, so close and yet so far,
I can't even imagine just where you are.
Is your mansion on a hill?, Is it near a creek?
I really don't know where God keeps the meek.
The angels are flying high all around you now Dad,
It still amazes me why I'm happy, yet sad
I guess its really true - life is but a vapor
'Cus all I can do is put thoughts on this paper
So many more chapters to put in life's book
The thoughts of you are in my heart - the way you look
You have a perfect body you're handsome as can be
I hope when my lifes over, you'll recognize me
I'm the image of you Dad, the impression you made on me
I know in times of depression to still stay happy
My time here on earth will also soon pass by
I'll be looking for you in heaven high in the sky.
Until then Dad enjoy heaven and all its grand pleasures
Thank you so much Jesus for giving Dad his treasures

Helen Woodruff

Heaven Sent

Upon this earth they ascend.
To our problems they attend.
When all has been made right,
Into heaven they take flight.

These bearers of peace.
Their good deeds will never cease.
Sent by the Almighty One,
They look like a radiant pieces of sun.

These magical creatures come like the first shower of snow.
Before you know it they come and go.
These guardian angels are heaven's gift,
To give both good and evil a spiritual lift.

Karen Halladay

What Is A Daughter To A Father

A daughter to a father is a treasure and joy
and down down deep inside, he hopes she never meets a boy
He watches her from birth as she grows to be his gem
There's no one quite like her, she's his perfect rose and stem.
She can twist him round her finger from the day she learns to speak
Just by looking at her daddy, makes him melt and very meek
And then when she gets married, he tries to act so tough
because whatever boy she marries is never good enough
And still her daddy worries, is her husband good to her
Does he feed her well, protect her. What bills does he incur
And so it never really stops, because that's what dads are for,
to live and love forever, The Daughter they adore.

Cy Symons

For John

Like a box of chocolate, I can't resist
Your eyes, your touch, your wonderful kiss
I mark each day with you I miss
Your love, your smile, so much - all this.

The chances of finding a love this rare
As precious as each tiny chocolate square
To melt in my heart as I hold you there
I love you, I need you - I promise, I swear

The cards, the flowers, the chocolates, a day
Lovers in love swept happily away
I'm remembering the moments, I remember today
Happy Valentines, my love - forever, always.

Marcia Kay Roberts

Man And Woman

She wore only a pink apron
and talked about fulfillment
as she stood around and
blew perfect rings of smoke.

He paced the floor in worn
out Levis, all the while looking
at his tired, unshaven reflection
in the windows that passed him by.

He asked her if he could leave;
as if he had asked her a
thousand times before.
Anxious sweat beaded across
the small of his back.
She did not hear him.

Her legs were long and slender like the hind legs of a cat,
her fingernails pointed and poised. And her tongue, sharp
and wet, sprayed saliva as she scolded him.

He did not hear her.

They silently sat and shared a bottle of Jack Daniels,
listening to the beating of each others hearts quicken with
the jolts of wild thunder.

Erin Fee

Fear Of Love

When love is what you fear,
you cannot see or hear the dangers that surrounds you.
You'll never find a heart to hold —
your fiery fear will show too bold
to attract the one you want and need.
You seek and search, but
as you lurch on, you feel
that real love is too far gone;
you trip and stumble through your sad, sad life;
it soon will be dawn,
but you wallow on in grief, and
fail to see the singing dove.
You feel hopeless — when
it is fear you love.

Heidi Elizabeth Hewitt

Rob

Just don't think about him;
it's the only way to win
The battle of a broken heart.

Tears don't fall!
Keep your eyes dry!
Demands made upon myself
In order to get by.

I should overcome the sadness
that wallows inside of me;
but visions of *him* I constantly see.

"You'll be OK in time."
The redundancy of sympathetic advice
from family and friends of mine.

"I don't have a new girlfriend."
"I still love YOU."
Statements proven false...
and **nothing** I can do.

I want to believe your lies.
Why am I clinging to a ghost?
You are gone from me forever - but you can never die.

Elaine M. O'Gara

My 2nd Heaven

When I see you, my eyes shine so bright
Like the stars on a clear summer night

My heart beats to the rhythm of a sad love song
Because you're the one I've desired for so long

Someone says your name and my soul soars through the air
Only wishing to show you how much I care

I praise about you to my family and friends
For the love I built for you seems it will never end

When I'm alone, your always on my mind
Searching for that chemistry of love, I can never find

My image of life has a small empty space
Which long's to be filled by the beauty of your face

Waiting for love can take so much time
But in my heart I know someday you'll be mine

To stand together like the one's in 11
To come together as 1, would be my second Heaven

E. Donovon Collins

"The Meaning Of Your Words"

I see you as the person that can change my life,
Without a word or a broken smile - I know you're there.
You often said things that would stick in my mind -
    and will forever
But to you they probably had no effect.
I guess once that happens, you kind of know
this is the person you can tell anything to.
I can't explain it but the meaning of your words,
and the way you say them, is like seeing a shooting star
for the first time in your life. You don't realize
it has meaning until after it's already been said or done.
It's kind of like a memory you will never forget,
one that was never meant to be remembered,
but one that can never be forgotten.

Melissa Maccarelli

Love

Love is an emotion with which we are blessed,
God placed it within us, then we must do the rest.
What we do with it is our own choice,
But life would be much easier, if we listened for His voice.

There is the love of a mother as she holds her child to her breast.
She caresses it gently until in sleep the little one rests.
And the love of a father who labors and toils
To provide a home for his little girls and boys.

There is the love of a friend, who is always kind and true,
Understanding us, no matter what we do.
Through trouble and strife, good times and bad,
They're always there to cheer you, when you are sad.

There is the love between husband and wife,
Created by God to last through our lives,
To lighten our load as we travel this road,
With this great emotion we are bestowed.

But the greatest love this world has ever known,
Was the sacrifice Jesus paid that day all alone.
He was beaten, nailed to the tree and left to die,
He gave his own life, because He loved you and I.

Wynona Kuntz

Care Shows

As the saying goes, "Caring is Sharing" is quite true
But there is more to this meaning than just a word or two
To give, understand, help, and obey
For doing all these things, a better friend you will stay
To cherish and trust what you believe
Is the key to God's love and care to receive
Caring is a great way to express your feelings,
To love, protect, and show all your willings
Caring is the time you spend together
It's all the love you show
And then and now, it's good to know
You have a friend forever

Lynette Pinson

Karate

Two ways to go,
Win or Lose.
Fight or flight,
Just do what's right.
But I have questions in my mind,
The answers are real hard to find.
If I stay and fight a kid,
Will I be sorry for what I did?
If I choose to run away,
Will I always wish that I had stayed?
I don't really know what to do,
But I'll continue to train, wouldn't you?

Andrew Capone

Natures Promise

Today will be tomorrow when the new sun
breaks the clouds.
Nature will awaken from its silence
on the ground.

Tall trees will feel the affection that the
brightness will send down,
the smaller of them will patiently wait
until it filters down.

The warmth will awaken Natures
rested souls.
Sounds will break the silence
as anticipation grows.

Today has now began again,
Natures promise now has came.
All creatures great and small rejoice..
the promise will never change.

Angelina Halseth

Negroid

I am an intimidating factor
Naturally strong and high-minded
I was born of African descent
from kings and queens
Instilled with strong goals, a free mind,
and my own deserved dream.
I have thick lips and broad features,
Born to be a doctor, lawyer, president, and a teacher.
With my tightly curled hair
and brown or black eyes
Youngest to oldest, I was taught to be wise.
Born to be free, then taken as a slave,
I am the chosen nation, and will be
the last to go to my grave.
Who art thy?

Alex Taylor-Smith

In Writing

Is this my fate? A trap, a hate
This Knot tied tight with time.
I'll not be subdued
I'll not let go
I'm torn between the two
An overwhelming love for you
A sense of sliding behind.
It would have been easily done
to depart in the romantic past
Now time's brought me pause and an unsound shade
With bonds intense and duty deep
To discard the gold would be a laborious task.

Susan McMillon

The Way Life Used To Be

Old woman in the rocker please talk to me.
Tell me about the way life used to be.
When there was no violence or gangs on the streets,
When kids hung around ice cream churns waiting for
Frozen treats.
When bread was a nickel and milk a dime.
When you could hear the sound of old church bells chime.
Tell me old woman so I can know,
So I can tell my child as I watch her grow.
Old woman you may leave,
But I'll still see,
The way that life used to be.

David Heyman

Oh Troubled Hearts

Oh troubled hearts, weep no more
For a long lost love, you can't restore
Or dream about what might have been
If your past, you could live again
But look a head and you will find
More love and happiness, than you left behind

So dry your tears and smile again
Can thou change the sun, or stars, or wind.
Nor can you relive your yesterday
But you may help someone else, along this way
And in helping others, you will find
More joy and peace, than you left behind

Annie Mae Thompson

The Shark

On the ocean floor,
There is a shark,
That is so mean, it will eat tree bark!

He slunk through Russia's door,
With his head hotter than the sun's core.

He destroyed Moscow,
But no one really knows how.

The czar said,
Without any pain,
That it was,
The end of his reign.

The shark soon swam away.
(Much faster than a blue jay!)

No one knows what happened to him,
But many think he turned into a wren.

Joel Chasan

Don't Be Afraid

I am the innocence lost in love, I am the hatred that burns your
soul. Feel the power, taste the waves, did your hands into
the silent hole.

Reach up and take my hand. Lead me with your loving light. Guide
me with your outstretched arms. Teach me, please, what's wrong and right.

Open my eyes so I may see, please don't be afraid of me.

Your eyes they change from blue to gray, as a dark light slowly
passes by. One by one I hear them coming; one by one I hear them cry

(Don't be afraid, it's only me.")

I am the shadow in the night, I am the darkness that they made. I
am the dream that life has told.
I am the reason they're afraid.
    Reach out..
    Reach out and touch me. See my emptiness, hear me sing.
    Reach out, reach out and be me. Hear my laughter through
    hallways ring.

Once you feel and once you see,
(Don't be afraid, it's only me..")

Anna Nicole Moyer

One Of The Few

When our world falls down in shambles and the tunnel darker gets,
We want to reach for others to share the load a bit.

We need some help in sickness, just to know there's comfort near,
Yet it calls our brothers to witness that there are things we all
    do fear.

It's enough to send friends running, and oh, the gaping hole that's left.
They could have filled that hole with kindness, lifted me up - just a bit.

Do they think this is something I prayed for or could control of my
    own freewill?
Many think it can't happen to them - others fear that it will.

But these are the many I'm speaking of, I thank God it isn't all.
For a few stood by without flinching, they listened, helped cushion the fall.

They lifted the load when my arms were too weary, encouraged me not to give in.
They told me they loved me, showed that they cared and
prayed that my battle I'd win.

Yet, what if this happened to one of my friends?
What if this happened to you?
We could all be part of the many, you know -
    or perhaps we'd be one of the few.

Nancy K. Fields

The Strength From With-In

I SAT ON THE EDGE OF THE LONG WOODED PIER
glaring down on the moon's shadow, down the river, so crystal clear.
I felt the calmness through-out that warm summer's night,
as the early morn's sun peaked from behind the mountain,
with an eagle in flight.

MY FRIEND, YOU'VE RETURNED,
with the tide that drifted in, you've heard my silent cry,
through the rhythm of the wind.
I've lost the strength that come's from with-in,
have you come to remind me of where it begin's?

HE FLEW DOWN FROM HIS SKIES OF FREEDOM,
and stood beside me with his head held high,
showing pride, and giving wisdom through his glassy sculptured eye's.
Then he rose, showing strength come's from with-in, find the love
and peace in your heart, this is where it will begin.

MY FRIEND, I'LL RETURN,
with the strength from with-in, I will hear your silent cry,
through the rhythm of the wind.

Deanna Sue Higgins

Winter Gazing

The white cold snow falls down on me,
So gentle, so sweet, so happily.
I look at all the children running,
Snowball fights, happy snowmen being made.
I look around me, children shoveling snow,
Just to get paid.
I hear sniffles, coughs, and even sneezes,
I hear spills of puzzle pieces.
Then I look at my home, it is the happiest of all domes.
So I trail inside,
Having a lot of pride,
Sit down at the fire and admire
The wonderful joy I have.

Ashley Kay

The Shore Of Life

The shore of life is funny, bringing people to your heart
Like grains of sand the sea washes in,
People rush into your life.

All kinds of people for every grain of sand
Some you love and some you hate
But all are a part of His plan.

Then you catch sight of him as the sea rushes in
You know that you'll love him
Until the time the earth will end.

You love him, you love him as time passes by
while cupid stands watching,
laughing as he's breaking your heart.

Then as suddenly as the sea brought him in,
it's outgoing tide compels him
to leave you again - alone.

Though the sea may take him
from your sight, never can it take him
from your heart, your heart.

The shore of life is funny,
bringing people to your heart, to your heart.

Kathleen E. Wall

Rough Exterior

A smile that sings sensitivity,
Eyes that shows true understanding.
A heart you know wants to be loved.
Another soul longing for companionship.

With a gentle whisper you can hear sweet
    romance flutter to your heart.
A laugh that barely is ever heard breaks
    all the fear built in armor.
With one true glance,
You can't help but we mesmerized.

The show of outer strength and non-caring
    truly overcomes the want of happiness.
The beast called peer pressure rears it head
    every corner he encounter.
Until the battle is won by someone's true heart,
The longing for companionship will grow.

The advice of the great one says that if
    you search for what you want; you shall receive.
The one's with the rough exteriors,
    and the loyalty shinning through.

Krista M. Cagle

463

A Nurse And A Purse

"All he'll want is a nurse and a purse!" A friend told me that, in a
voice that was terse. I laughed, of course. I know my guy.
He's strong; he's generous; he's sweet as pie. The "purse" part' ok.
I pay half of the bills. We agree on everything, food, trips, frills.
The "nurse" part, though - I'm not so sure.
Have I bitten off more than I can endure?

First, he fell down, two vertabrae crushed. To hospital for x-rays we
frantically rushed. Six months followed, full of pain. I had never
heard anyone else complain in a non-stop manner, from morning 'til
night. You'd think he'd shut up, grit his teeth, fight! But no -
fuss and fume, just about cry, cranky as sin, my, oh my.

Again he fell, a smashed-in nose, cracked rib, contusions, blood
head to toes. I cleaned up the blood, bandaged the sores; tried to be
strong to keep up with my chores. He's healing at last; the scrabs
are dying; he's finally decided that he's not dying. As soon as
he's well, I should get out fast. If anything else happened, I wouldn't
last. I really and truly am glad he's alive; but, if anything else
happened, I wouldn't survive.

If the tables were turned, would he help me? Absolutely! I'm sure!
I'm positive! Yes! (If I'm wrong, God help me; I'm in a real mess.)
My friend warned me, "a nurse and a purse."
How right she was; but, what's even worse - I love him so much,
I can't even curse. I'll stick to the end, even if it's a hearse!
that's my story - chapter and verse. I'll stick with him for better and worse!

Ruth Wendorff-Fair

Sun, Flowers

Sometimes,
When life knocks you down and you can't stand up straight and you
can't move your feet and you can't turn around and you don't know
what to do and you don't know where to go and you try to breathe
but the air won't go in and you try to sleep but your eyes won't
shut and you try to swallow but your throat won't open and you try
to move yours arms but they're glued to your side and your heart
races around a neverending track in the darkness and it feels like
it hit a brick wall that it didn't know was there...
Then, Take time to relish the scent of cigar smoke in the arcade.
Let the wind twist your hair into curious shapes, and the grass tickle
   your bare toes.
Absorb the warmth of a sunflower through your fingertips,
   and cherish the delicate swaying of a tiny green clover sprouting
   between a crack in the pavement.
Hug your fingers with your palm and feel the vitality within them,
   and then pick your head up and move on.

Debralee Dembling

Epiphany Unbound

The foudroyant sky shimmers above my brow; a silver hand moves
through me. I look down. I see through the mist all is laid before my sight.
The moment is cathartic, the breath surreal inside this borrowed glimpse,
Lingering, watching the kaleidoscope twist, understanding the meaning of all.

The chasm we fear becomes a brook, lapping at new shores undiscovered.
The twists that seem to meander, how undimensional the mortal faculty.
Clearly now, the fruit is not knowledge. We are with eyes, yet unable to see.
How trivial, how conceited and vain, lingering in a linear space.

Awake! Shake off the empty perceptions, cast off the bridle you've been fed!
Locked in deafness, hearing only pettiness, how pathetic the infantile ego.
Forgiveness, how unworthy your sight. Eternity's glistening cord is surely weakened.
The weight of our imperfection, how it must hinder the expanding vapors.

The sphere unfolds. I see beyond all horizons. As the curtain is raised, I laugh at the simplicity.
Standing, staring at the answers I see. They have always been present, merely forgotten.
Everything known now was known before. How confining the practiced perceptions.
We see only that which we are told to see.
We practice at becoming the past, learning nothing.

Thomas Day

Why?

You were here,
But now you're gone.
You left me here,
Singing my sad songs.
It isn't fair,
The way you left,
I hate you for it,
But I love you to death.
I wish you could come back to stay.
Don't you understand,
I need you here, rightnow - today!
Why did you have to do what you did?
I don't understand,
Do you want to be dead?
Weren't the people who loved you enough?
Why did you turn around and do that stuff?
Well now you are dead,
And I must go on,
But I will always love you,
And sing my sad songs.

Elaina Stretch

Beyond My Book's Binder

On a damp, rainy early morn
I find a child's book, yellowed and torn.
I seek out a cozy window nook
In which to ponder my old book.
Settled and reading into the past
I have sweet memories awakened at last.
Not just of the story within my book's binder,
But of a time when life seemed so much kinder.
My father reading to me after work one day,
While waiting for supper before putting my book away.
And after mother tucked me into bed at night,
She read me my book, to my delight.
So with my book now in hand
I start to really understand;
It wasn't just the story I wanted to hear,
It was having my parents ever so near.
So remember when a child wants you to read them a book,
Take time to do so, maybe in a cozy window nook!
It will not be just the story the child will boast,
But the caring person reading, making it the most.

Barbara J. Potts

Gone

Gone are the days of happiness,
Gone are the days of sorrow.
Gone are the good times we have had,
Gone are the bad times.

Gone are the friendly visits,
Gone are the friendly chats.
Gone are the fights we have had,
Gone is the joy of making up.

Gone forever is the love and happiness we have shared,
I will always miss you.

Kristin Maze

"Forever"

Forever is a very long time!
But for you and me that's what I've got in mind!
Everyone says we will not last,
But the thing that proves we will is our past!
We've been through laughs, quarrels, and fights.
But through it all, we've held on tight.
We're here right now and that's how it should be,
Together forever, just you and me!

S. Caleb Mortimer

Realism

When her soul was just a newborn to the world
I had the privilege of holding her in my arms
Her fragile body stirred, yet her eyes remained tightly shut
Forcing the harsh world of reality away from herself
She was mine, but in a way didn't belong to me
I was not hers, I had no owner, home or loved ones
Now she grows into a willowy young women with her eyes still closed
She fights against a storm of remembrances to search for belonging
I still own a part of her, deep inside my heart
It's there somewhere locked away amongst the shadows and cobwebs of my past
It pains her whenever her eyes are cracked open and the world seeps in
The screams all go unheard except by my ears
How do I comfort this child, still a babe in the womb?
She keeps herself tightly closed off, afraid to allow people inside her heart
She fears the pain of isolation and rejection
I fear the self-afflicted hatred she has grown within herself
I must show her the world through unadulterated eyes
I must look upon her abstract world of mindless thought as a flame
This is my duty as a friend, mother, keeper and lover
Realism is nothing but what we make of it

Beth Maul

Your Love - Crazy Love No. 1

Your love is like Satan. Mean and menacing, forceful against my
 virgin - like skin. Wrong and sinful.
Your love is like Hell. Deep and cruel. Interrogating, penetrating
 my body, burning my interior.
Your love is arrogant. Knowing it can break me open, crumble
 me into frantic seizures. Painful pleasure.
Your love knows no bounds. Scorching me every time we become one.
 Moving together with flames of passion.
Your love is one-sided. Dirty and dangerous. Too distant, devious to be real.
Your love is no love. Hollow when we get out of bed. Deceiving me.
Your love fades away whity preoccupied boredom. Scarring me forever.
Your love is gone.

Kira Jelincic

A Poem For My Parents

Parents aren't chosen, they're a gift from above; A Father and
Mother who shower us with unconditional love; They care for, nurture,
and raise us with pride; And occasionally, of course, they smack our
backside; They love us forever and in so many ways; Yet we take them
for granted most of days.

This poem is a tribute to you, Mom and Dad; You reared me from
scratch, And I was quite bad; You guided my actions, but gave me
freedom to grow; And taught me the answers to questions I didn't
know; Now that I'm older I realize that I'm guilty too; I never sat
down and told you, Thank You;

This poem is that THANK YOU with big letters in bold; If they gave
medals for parents, yours would be gold; Thank you for loving me all
through the years; For kissing my bruises and wiping my tears; You
nudged me so gently and showed me the way; Without your love, I
wouldn't be who I am today;
You are both special people and so dear to me; I hope you hang this
proudly for others to see; This poem is a tribute that I give to you;
For all that done and that you do; I'll love you forever and never forget;
While parents aren't chosen, I got the best you could get; Thank you

Harry B. Parks

A Cold Night, The Family In Winter

The cold wind on my face.
The warmth that is felt sitting in front of the fireplace.
The wind whistling on a cold winter's night
The stars shining oh so bright.
Outside my window the trees are bare
I can see snow everywhere
The children are sleeping peacefully in their beds.
After their bed time story has been read.
There is nothing in the world that seems so right.
As your family safe and warm on a cold winter's night.

Mae Hendeson

A Friend Is....

A friend is a friend
nothing more nothing less.
They'll help you through life
and let you de-stress.

A friend will be there
when you need a good laugh.
Just remember you too
must do your fair half.

A friend is someone
who you trust and rely on,
whose shoulder is there
to rest and to cry on.

Friends are the ones
who teach us to give.
they'll listen, advice,
and always forgiven.

A friend is the one you turn to in trouble.
They'll fix up your lie and pick up the rubble.

A friend will be there whether you need them or not,
And deep in their heart you'll have a special spot.

Tamara Tsark

Warmth Of Winter

One year ago today was a very special day
New life sprang forth like the flowers of May
The deep cold of winter could not subdue
The warmth of summer that shown through
And though winter is here once again
Please be reminded my dearest friend
That all through life as you have need
Soar's the eagle waiting to support and please

Kenneth E. Stipes

Silence

And the walls came crashing down.
No longer could his strength withstand the
ever growing force that built up all around.

He now lay in silence on the earth,
which was loved ever so, with a look of
bliss across his cold, darken face.

This was neither a hero nor a martyr.
Only someone striving to go just a little further,
to ascend the wall and go farther.

Many were in despair at the sight they saw.
A man, just a boy, whose silence allowed the
walls to come crashing down.

Jonathan Fields

Fantasy Girl

I don't know your name, but I do know your face.
This picture I have, from a time and a place.
Your beauty is stunning, your beauty is pure.
And maybe some-day, I'll come knock on your door.
I really want to meet you, how much you don't know.
But I'd travel forever, through rain, sleet, or snow.
These things that I say here, are straight from the heart.
If I were a cupid, I'd fill you, with love from my dart.
My name is LA, and I will not attack.
So pick up your pencil, and please write me back.
For now I must finish, this poem I wrote.
But please always remember, this one little quote.
I'm a straight forward person, and honest you see.
Ask me anything you want, I'll explain straight to the tee.
Your love machine T-shirt, is what caught my eye.
But for now I must go, so I'll just say goodbye.

Lowell Abrams

Don't Let Me Regret

Lancer, my son, do I forget sometimes,
with the hustle and bustle of life,
to tell you how much I love you, my son,
with the noise, the worry, the strife?

Bradley, child, do I fail to hear
when what you say is important to you?
Is sleep more important because I'm so tired?
Have I not heard a word when you're through?

Kim, sweetheart, do I fail to realize,
even though you are grown up and wed,
that you're still a babe in so many ways,
that you still can be counseled and led?

Oh, you three little children of mine,
I guess what I'm trying to say
is we all need love, we all need attention,
and time to study, to work, and to play.

To live, be thankful, to laugh, and to cry,
to love each other ere time passes us by.
Lord, the blessing I want seems so hard to get,
Lord, the time with my children, don't let me regret.

Dickie Sue Kitchens

Wolf River

My Father's hands, always beautiful...tug catfish lines
    against a muddy river bank.
Manicured nails on chiseled fingers glisten like oyster shells.
    Moonbeams lay splendor against young faces.
White bellied fish glow in the dark.
    Silver tipped tails turn perfect pirouettes.
Hooked, bleeding mouths blow iridescent bubbles.
    Echoes of screams fall silent...
    Bank against the edge.
The bridge that crossed Wolf River is gone now...
    Making liars of us all.

Beverly Hays Simpson

Lovers

The pain has to stop.
Do you remember when you used to love me?
I do. How long has it been?
Why did you stop loving and start hurting?
I love you and always will.
But the pain has to stop.
Goodbye.
Wait.
I have to tell you something. (It's too late)
I love you, too.

Sean Hendershot

The Fortunate Child

A child born in early Spring, by Fall I was alone.
My Mommy never said, "Goodbye", her life was now her own.

My Daddy tried, a month or so, to make a life for me.
But there was also little Ken; it just was not to be.

A man alone, try as he might, could not be Mommy, too.
So each in turn, we left his life, and he began anew.

The time passed by and once again, it was the early Spring.
The strangers came and took me in, and said, "What joy I'd bring."

And though they did not give me life, I was one of their own.
They sheltered me and gave me love, where once I was alone.

They guided me with gentle hands, and did not let me stray.
The morals and high standards taught, stay with me yet today.

And now they guide me from on high, death not did sorrow bring.
For I will join them once again, one day in early Spring.

Patti Shannon Byrd

My Prince

Like a snow princess I have been waiting
And wondering, how will we meet and when?

When I was little I used to pretend I would
meet a handsome prince who would kiss me
and take me away to never-never land.

Yes my darling I know its you, you have
awakened me to make my dreams come true

You don't know how many treasures I have stored up
inside, while waiting to become your bride.

I've been waiting for you to unlock the doors
So we can share our dreams and so much more
Our laughs, our tears, even our fears.

My heart tells me this is real, when you
touch me you can't believe how I feel.

I have waited such a long time for you
This hand some prince of mine.

Carol Ogden McGinnis

Lost Love

My heart is a fountain, whose water no longer flows,
A leaf in the wind, away from my lover I blow.
No signs are left, nothing within me remains,
For love was stolen from me, and it was taken in vane.
But why does it bother me so, and make me sick this day?
For another will come along, and it may not be too far away.
But soon to be healed, I must not forget this state,
It is only a part of the play, and it decides not my fate.
I will give not forgive her, nor will I ever dismiss,
But will I never forget the sweet warmth of her kiss?
While the dejection and rejection bothers me no more,
I must not be ashamed, for there is too much in store.
A lost love can scar like an unforgiving and brutal bout,
But better off am I than he who lived without.

Andy Hippensteele

A Passing Thought

In your most private moment you will close your eyes
and ask yourself why, because
failure is life's way of bringing a perspective to reality
it makes you aware of the smallness of your ambition over
the consequences of your success,
yet you will strive to accomplish what little reward you
may muster because,
what little there is to failure it is the praise of
success that motivates the being.

Randolph Schimmenti

Of Corpulence and Calories (With Apologies to Lord Byron)

Roll off, O full-blown flabby fatness, Roll!
Ten thousand lymph glands in a queasy hell;
Ten million blood cells shrieking out their soul
Midst ganglia and protoplasmic gel
Fain wouldst be free, no human haunts to dwell!

Farewell to crapulent intumescence.
With calorie counts obesity dispel!
And, as the ugly blubber's penitence,
Let muscles bulge 'neath epidermal shell!

Philo Wilson

And It Was Good

The lamps in the sky have been dimmed;
the cold breath of September wind just blew;
the cheeping sounds from the trees welcome both-
and the lights in this room are getting brighter

Love and anger are hugging each other here
flowers crumble into rust on a battlefield
and the fist is eased by the touch of silence-
which is a gift everybody has been granted

The lights just exploded into sparks and disturbed dust
and like leaving your house into the bitter, winter air
the moonlight angled itself through the window panes
leaving the room painted a soft blue and dark

leaving the room quiet and forbidden.

Charlie West

Following Shadows

The darkest shadows in the alley came to life one day.
The lonely apparition right before my eyes just would not go away.
I watched intensely as it clung next to me.
It frightened me immensely;
It would not let me be.
Everywhere I walked, the figure walked as well.
Was it just my shadow?
This, I could not tell.
As my pace quickened, my heartbeat raced with fear.
I saw the shadow hurry and now was very near.
I walked out of the alley and right into the light.
The shadow quickly vanished and evaporated from my sight.
I looked around and sighed with great relief.
All this time it was my shadow that had given me such grief.

Elizabeth Steele

Never Again

We looked him in his eyes for the very last time.
We saw his last appearance before he said goodbye.
He didn't want our help though we wanted him to live.
It's really sad that he thought he had nothing more to give.
His music was our voice for the words we couldn't find,
So they picked him for a spokesman and said he didn't mind.
What they didn't know can never be explained,
Except by the man himself, the one who was in pain.
But with a single shot he's gone forever.
I shed a tear so I can remember.
Never again will he smile at me.
It's only an important memory.
Never again will he see his wife.
For the beautiful man took his life.
...Never Again... Never Again...
Never again will he sing for me or you
So say goodbye to the man you once knew.
Goodbye dear Kurt... goodbye for good.
I'll take care of the ground where you once stood.

Jamie Cassin

Untitled

In the deep of the night
In creeps my deepest and darkest fears
They come to me by the pale moonlight
I've fought them hard, over the years
But now, the time has come
To battle them, for forever victory
Through God's strength, I know what's to be done!
For tonight, God, for me, will makes history
The demons of mind are just that
Imaginations are these gouls
But God, my Lord, will not let them get fat
He knows just what to do
As I kneel to pray
He puts to end my fears
As breaks the light of the new day
No more shall I fear over the rest of my years

Derek K. Sharp

Fired

The vacuous stare in the eyes of each subordinate
  betrays privy knowledge about your fate,
    be it from professional or mortal hate.

The letter left in your chair
  greets you at eight and assigns things in your care
    to those who only stand and wait.

The intruder sent to make camp
  at your office phone
    is ordered to rubber stamp
      what you left undone.

You clash with the source
  of your decline and disgrace—
    his effusion of courtesies
      taking brutal force's place.

The paid leave, the ouster sabbatically,
  programs you to leave less dramatically.

The self-abuse that follows,
  currents of anger, denial, and sorrows—
    you plunge into them absent of scheme
      only to surface happily downstream.

J. V. McCrory

Cool Shudders

I look around, my anxiety builds,
I start to tremble my body chills.
I joke and have fun, time will pass,
And I turn to see my face in the glass.
No longer can I hold it inside,
I turn to run there's nowhere to hide.
Their accusing eyes burn my skin,
My pulse is racing, again and again.
In turn to the vase and pull out arose,
I brush the silken petals against my nose.
I turn this time to face the crowd,
I am the soulful one that they surround.
I call to them with my alluring eyes,
And I leave the room with pitiful sighs.

Vanessa R. Curtis

My Eternity

I can only see the darkness of which
  the glowing light seeps inside of me.
I fail to find the heavens that guide
  me to the beauty of the flawless sea.
Consumed by the nectar, I bleed to the
  grasp of a thousand angels
Melting soundless names to my eternity.

Skye Penny

A Thought For Today

As we arise each morning with a new day ahead,
There shouldn't be a thing in life that we should dread.

For we have a special planner that is totally in control,
As long as we follow his lead we'll always be on a roll.

With love and understanding he will always lead us thru the day,
For a pure and happy life we must always follow his way.

For our mistakes and wrong doings just by asking he'll forgive,
Those of us who know him know it is the only way to live.

Happiness with smiles and laughter is a gift he gives us all
If we will just respond with an open heart when he gives us a call

Those of us who think we can make it totally on our own
Are in for a rude awakening at the end when we are left totally alone.

Always remember for us in life he has already set our goal
Following his guiding hand our hearts will still be young when
    our body's growing old.

So an example for others Lord please help me to be
That I may be an inspiration for all the world to see.

So this day thank you Lord for being our guiding hand and master
For without you in my life it would be a total disaster.

Leon Mullen

Country Living

Country living, it's in style
Patches of green, mile after mile
A quiet summer rain, the rolling hills
You can almost make, the time stand still.

In the morning, a songbird calls
The sunflowers, stand so straight and tall
Another day, that's so new
A rose bud, with a touch of dew.

On your face, feel the warming sun
You know the day, is almost done
Late afternoon, a gentle breeze
The rustle of leaves, in the trees.

The sun sits, with a artists brush
Take your time, no need to rush
Country living, that's for me
There's no other place, that I'd rather be.

Patricia Burns

Our Grandpa

We loved our grandpa, we knew him well
When we needed it he would give us hell
He was always happy, never sad
He always knew how to make us glad
He left us today and we did cry
It was like we had only seen him yesterday
He knew we loved him from far and near
We will always have his presence here
We cried for all the times he was there
We cried for all the times he shared...
Telling us stories and making us laugh
He was the grandpa that we loved best
He always had this little sparkle in his
eyes that would always shine no matter if
in good-times or bad.
We all loved our grandpa and this he knew
Our memories of him will live on through and through.

Brenda Frederick

Divorce

That sound could be a skull shell caving,
alone a madman raving
harried house
no longer sojourn

That click could be a baby rattle,
against your nipple bottle
harried store
no longer sojourn

That whirr could be you hailing smiling,
broken cyst, calmly crying
harried woman
in the grey goodbye.

Pete Brush

Storm Swallows

A wounded snowflake I am in a forgotten storm,
Falling endlessly downward without fear of the warm
Air curtsying its breath on my pointed ends,
Though I know if this happens I will finally make amends.
Storm swallows swiftly, surfing I this air
And those all around me don't know to beware
Of the fire within me, even under the snow,
They will ask "Did this happen?" or "Could it be so?"
I am not a judge, not an accuser, nor crook,
But I will be convicted as all three when it occurs to them to look
In my pat, in my drawers, in my words to them all
That the answer I've looked for I found in my fall.

Jennifer Hayden

"Far Beyond The Sun"

How can I hold you when there's blood on my hands?
How can I tell you what no one understands?
How can I die, and leave you here alone?
How can I live, knowing what I've known?
How can you cut yourself
When you know I'll feel the pain?
How can you sit and watch
When all my dreams fall down like rain?
How can you catch me
When you don't know I'm fallin'?
How can you come
When you don't hear me callin'?
How can you save me
When you don't know I'm dyin'?
Why do you believe me
When we both know I'm lyin'?
Cause I've walked the lake of fire
And I've got my race to run,
Rising higher, I won't tire
'Till I'm far beyond the sun

Joseph Moghabghab

Creation

Using imagination and the uniqueness of our ideas
Beautiful feathery phrases are fabricated.
Stanzas of rhyme, rhythm, and meter,
Provoking our innermost human emotions.
Heart-wrenching lines bleed from our pens
Forming poetry of all kinds.
Our minds join in synchronicity
For a brief moment of creation
Developing a single togetherness of images and metaphors.
The whole of our existence
Is composed of the individuality of each,
With unparalled thoughts, feelings, and dreams.

Nealie Rae Mondi

Seasons Of Perfection

Golden and red, leaves of brown,
 Twirling and swirling to the ground.
Clouds of blue are filling the sky,
 With white puffy ones hanging near by.

I wonder about the order of things.
 How do crickets know when to sing?
Why do humming birds fly far away,
 And then return on a special day?
How do birds know how high to fly,
 When they are soaring in the sky?
Do bees know they hurt when they sting,
 While gathering pollen and doing their thing?
Does it hurt the rabbit when they
 full out their hair,
To line their nest for their babies so fair?

But the Lord above, in His perfect plan,
 In His creation of creature and man.
Made everything for a purpose and reason.
 For us to love and enjoy.
 in His perfectly timed seasons.

Frances A. Osborn

The Afterlife

Slowly I have been fighting this battle throughout my young adult life.
When finally I decided to end it all with a restricten knife.
Things aren't what they used to be,
My soul has excited from me.
My heart is left in this warped world,
Where bodies, and minds cringe and curled.
Leaving a life I could not understand,
Leading my life was an invisible hand.
I can now see a light red from above,
Taken away are things that I loved.
A voice heard and not seen from the shadows,
Tells me his games and how to overcome his battles.
He had taken my had into his restricted morgue,
Where things were left to praise his Lord.
His Lord never to be seen had taken my hand,
Into the darkness of this unknown land.
My life lie before me then burned to coals,
Excited my mind were unwanted souls.
One who are to good to be taken to burn,
I can't escape this HELL that I have so earned.

Anastasia J. Weingart

Tony

 When I'm lonely and broken apart,
thoughts of Tony come straight to my heart.

 His dark eyes are so beautiful reflecting
God's love so true. Sooner or later I'm no
longer feeling blue.

 I've tried to explain to Tony just how
much I care, but it's often just too much for
his spiritual mind to bear.

 Tony is special. That there is no doubt.
I'm waiting for the day he'll let me kiss him on
the mouth.

 I want to be with Tony twenty-four
hours a day, but Dawn always approaches to
steel my Tony away.

I'm at the end of my rope. I just can't
cope. Without Tony there's just no hope.

Fredrick P. Hoefert

"Calendar Pages"

I've tried to distance myself
from the rumors and reasons
and the demons, life's shown to me

In the act of defenses
I've defiled my senses
in the eyes of life's sham drudgery

Oh, it's not the time wasted or the time going by
or my body and mind in decline

I've devised my own reasons for believing my deceivings
and been content watching it all from the side

These calendar pages
keep changing the faces
of the people all passing me by

And I can't help wonder
had I listened to thunder
I might be six feet under now

Yeah, the calendar pages turn like the tide
they never surrender or ever subside

Yeah, it's not the time wasted or the time going by...
just that I've been content watching it all from the side

Robert J. Dixon

Life Goes On

A trace of light slowly disrupts the darkness
like the passing of the guard as time marches on
with eyes now open to the strangeness of reality
and twisted knowledge of how so many things go wrong
life goes on
I look forward to the insights of the morning
no time to question events of yesterday
with another new day just over the horizon
life's chance for new meaning with the new day
life goes on
An oak stands sentry over the empty frozen field
its gnarled branches exposed without their leaves
the morning sunrise silhouettes the unique features
as younger branches wave in the gentle breeze
life goes on
I see nothing new yet something is different
is it perspective, or timing, or just state of mind
as it quickly passes I wonder if it really matters
another distant thought with the passing time
as life goes on

Shane Johnson

Land Of Anarchy

Its world is a dark, desolate place,
Everyone wears a mask to hide their face.
The ruler is a beast of rage and terror,
Filled with cruelty and horror.

Few have seen it and lived,
Death is the only thing it has to give.
It kills those who won't obey,
soon others will become its prey.

The nightmare spreads its poison as it grows,
How it kills, no one wants to know.
No one can escape its wrath,
For death marks its path.

Peace cannot be found,
In a land where the Nightmare walks the ground.
It rules by a hellish monarchy,
In a world poisoned by its anarchy.

Jeff Rhoades

"Christmas Eve In The Country"

It's Christmas eve in the country,
Those little towns are rolling by
We're homeward bound this Christmas eve,
The wife, the kids, and I.

Those little towns are all adorned,
With lights of red and green,
And the moonlit snow, gives off a glow
Like a Christmas card I've seen.

The kids are sleeping side by side
Between the seats they lie,
Their sleep I'm sure is filled with dreams
Of Santa on the fly.

I hold my wife our hands entwine,
She's never felt so dear,
Then on her face I feel the trace
Of a small but happy tear.

We thank you God for all your gifts,
The wife, the Kids, and I
It's Christmas eve in the country
I'm so happy I could cry.

Dave Darmody

Boy...Wonders

If I ever grew up, can I still be a boy?
When I learn how it works, can it still be my toy?
Will I still talk to puppies, who don't understand
or hold a frog in the palm of my hand?

Can I still dream of big ships that sail on the seas,
castles with Kings, houses in trees,
or cities alive in the depths of the ocean?
Will I still believe love, is more than just an emotion?

Will I think about flying to the moon and the stars,
swimming in mud holes, and shiny fast cars?
Will I still throw rocks at cans in the dirt?
Can I cry big tears, when ever I'm hurt?

Can I still kiss my mom without people talking?
Will I still skip and run when all the others are walking?
Can I think I'm the hero, who'll save the world,
the one who fights off bad guys for the heart of a girl?

I ponder these things, as I play in the sand,
with trust and love I clutch at his hand.
Dad..., I wonder, if the world will ever see
through the eyes of the little boy who lives in me?

Richard King

"Runaway"

Mother the echo of it sears my heart like a burning ember.
Dreams, hopes and plans that will now never be, I remember.

I cry warning, guard the comfort you now feel.
The world is at work your loving memories to steal.

Can my love which is still so alive be buried?
Stones of accusation have been cast, yet my love still tarries.
Can the mantle of mother be wrenched from the one who bore it
  from the start?
and be carefully manipulated and arranged to fit another
  woman's heart.

Your life I have carried and felt your heart beat within my womb.
My mothering you have cursed sealing me alive in my tomb.
Yet for eternity my love will remain true.
You can reject me and leave me, but I will never leave you.

Sally J. Knight

Untitled

The feeling I feel deep inside
oh is much to real to real to hide
you tell me every thing is fine
you need not worry I just need some time
with love there is no hurry
Well baby baby I love you so, oh
and if you leave me these tears will still flow
all the pain and all the sorrow
will stay the same until tomorrow
you tell me to wipe these tears from my eyes
continue on that's life
cause no one cares about the pain I feel
when nothing goes right and I see no light
There nothing wrong, just let me be
I don't need no help, no sympathy
I feel so alone so I close my eyes
continue on that's life

Shon Sparks

Expectations

Sometimes people think, sometimes they wonder
   Things change and set their lives asunder

Time will pass and they keep pondering
   Only to wake up realizing that they've been wandering

Who's to say what they've done was right or wrong
   Living regretfully, the heart sings a sad song

As wisdom grows, so does the urge to be great
   If there is a strong desire, it's not too late

Wisdom and intelligence are gifts not to waste
   Look into your soul and be strong; make haste

Gaze through the past; remember how it was pale
   Find your dreams, contemplate the future and set sail

Don't fall back; grab your hopes and hold them tight
   Strength, courage, love, persistence and you'll be alright

The only thing stronger than dreams is love
   If you have them both, you shall rise above

Reach the zenith of your dreams; remember how it used to be
   Then look down, reach out, and share true wisdom with
   someone like me.

Paul F. Harbin Jr.

Alpha And Omega

A new ("self") arrives; (sunshine)..."star;"
To start the Journey of "Who We Are."

All is Yesterday, Now, Tomorrow;
Sometimes Happiness, Joy, or Sorrow.

As we (dream) of "Never Endings;"
And justify our "Pretendings."

"Journey" ends before it Starts!
While we cling to chosen "Parts."

Then we leave with What we came.
Our Soul, Our Love... Our Name!

Anthony Piacentino

Loving Misery

How can the love of your life be the reason
there is no love in your life?

As I tear down those wonderful years, I wonder
Were those wonderful years?

If so, what does the future hold?
Wonderful years of pain?

If so, may I remain miserable.
Please.

Tina L. Robinson

The Nightmare's Realm: There's No Peace In A

"A Stranger Out of the Night"

A stranger came out of the night,
where the shadows melted my sight.

I smelt' the spark of steel against flint,
and saw in his hand a metallic glint.
His face was smudged with reflection
as he delivered a blow unto my midsection.

A stranger went into the night,
where the shadows melted his flight.

I felt a caliginous claw at my gut,
and longed only to escape this necrophilic gamut.
I was loath to let this my journey disrupt,
for the earth here was corrupt.
But, I was constrained to stop at 6th and centrail.
I glanced back and found the trailings of my bloody entrails

A stranger laughed in the night,
where the shadows melted my mortal plight.

Kevin Oliver

Loss

Dwelling lonely on the sand,
Now strangers in our strange new land
Remembering back to long ago
The fields we used to reap and sow,
When mountains ridged the azure sky
For miles eagles soared on high
Praying to the God of rain.
But all our hardship was in vain.
We toiled and labored with fertile ground
Until intruders came around
Forcing us to leave.
Tearing us to leave.
They didn't understand
Our land beat as our heart.
Left open in an empty shell,
Forgotten and neglected, made prisoners in our own home,
From society rejected. Almost forgotten
With earth and sea
The ancient spirits
of wounded knee.

Shanna Merola

At The Cemetery

At the cemetery it was a different world.

Even though the rain poured, flooding the grounds,
a peaceful stillness and dignity remained.

The graves were covered with flowers
as if they wanted to be hidden
from the unassuring outside world.

Survivors mourning their loved ones walked dismally,
quietly, and carefully - seeming to dread every step.

Lorie S. Kouba

Something To Consider

The crows, like black dry-rotted fur, have gone
Away to places full of shadows. Deep
Below their wings a worm does sing a song
Of life and joy that he is there for keeps.
Still, now until the wind will stir, a bird
Comes from the tree of mood and purity.
The worm knows not of games gone on behind
Its helpless skin, but only sees the crows
Who leave life's long suspense throughout their flight
To those left on the ground. I see the pain
Within the worm-its mixed and twisted thought.
For trickiness, the tree, I guess, is old

And wonders not what thoughts live in the cave
of crows and worms as, in this haze, do I.

Denise Russell

"Escape"

I listen to the creaking of the oars,
    As patiently I row against the tide.
My destination is a distant shore
    Where dreams come true and cares are cast aside.
Why is it that my fantasies in life
    Rebel against the logic of my mind?
Seeking to escape the turmoil and the strife
    And leave the "Real World" problems behind.
On eagles wings my spirit yearns to soar
    Into the upper reaches of the sky
To find the "Peace of Mind" I'm searching for
    And watch the mad, mad world go rushing by.
My conscience then gives forth a strident call
    "Come back, you'll find your Shangra La at home,
Surrounded by your love ones and your wife
    No need to joust with "Wind Mills" all alone",
YET — deep within the cockles of my heart
    A tiny spark refuses to expire,
Patiently awaiting the inevitable hour
    To burst into an all consuming fire.

Hampton Allen

AIDS

AIDS is killing the people of this world.
Not just our men and women.
But, now it affects our young boys and girls.

Our future being born without a chance of survival.
Shut up in a thunderous room of hate.
Searching, looking, no where to escape.

Right under your noses someone could be suffering.
But, with death ears.
Who could ever listen only if it hits home.
Is when it will grab one's attention.

I have seen the wondering eyes for no more discomfort pain.
So silently trying not to complain.
The joy you and I can continue to give.
Is to be a friend.
Because it will be the only thing to offer at the end.

Angela Robinson

My Window

If you look deep into my eyes
you can see my soul, but don't look too hard,
I don't think you could handle what might unfold.

You might see the laughter of memories of old
or may be the pain I have left untold.

Don't look too hard if you don't want to see,
for everything inside is my reality.

Darla R. Harris

Your Birthday

The giver of gifts has given to you
Another birthday with His love so true.
He will also guide you from day to day
Through many more birthdays along
    life's way.

He speaks to you daily amidst the world's mass
But listen and hear him in the rustling grass.
His spirit will guide you through each
    trying hour
And make your life as beautiful as his handiwork
in flowers.

Since you have the key to these spiritual
    blessings
You must conform to His transcending messages.
Then your key will be used to open the door
Where earthly birthdays will be no more.

Beverly G. Pace

Song For Shayne

I pray, she kiss me with kisses of her scarlet gold lips
    so fine!
Her intoxicating embrace, sweeter than the finest wine.
    I wish to drink in her beauty till the end
    of time!
Her beauty is more colorful, than the peacock's plumage
    in full bloom.
Her name is an enchanting tune played upon the reeds of
    the wind swept Nile, drawing me as I follow,
    beckoning me for her kisses to swallow.
With her, I would rejoice and exult,
    I would extol her love; it is beyond time:
    how rightly she would be loved, if she
    were mine.
This song was played upon a psaltery and harp. . .the tune
was strummed as the words emanated from my heart!

Richard Anthony Dore

Peace Of Mind

I used to feel discouraged by the hand that life had dealt;
I seemed to think no one on earth could know how bad I felt.

I often felt that I was bad and God was mad at me-
That I had sinned some unknown sin that only God could see.

One day I stopped to realize God was holding to my hand;
And if I was to make it through. I had to take a stand.

I stopped to count the things I had against my pain and strife
And the blessings that I found I had gave new meaning to my life.

I no longer feel afraid to live, or die, when my time may come.
An earthly tomorrow is not a blessing that is promised to anyone.

I was the one that went away, God never left at all.
And now I've put my trust in Him, and He'll catch me when I fall.

If I only look with an open heart, God's blessings I can find.
No matter what the future holds, I can still have peace of mind!

Linda Wheat

Untitled

Old man in starched shirt he brings me
tales of heroes, ships and things
while mama sings the silence down,
weaves bedding quilts and wedding gowns
Together, they recall no less
than yesterdays of happiness
What joy! That time has finally blessed
the bad years with forgetfulness.

Teresa Fowler

The Look

The summer breeze is slowly blowing,
Through the spring air.
You and I are talking.
The look of true love is being given.
No one notices the look.
You are looking into my eyes.
Your eyes are still for the moment.

You and I give each other,
The look.
When I stare into your eyes,
I can feel my whole world.
Coming alive, my soul is reaching out,
For you, my heart is open.
The look will be there for all eternity.

Time will make the look stronger.
You and I will be there to give it.
Only true love can make the look.
We must have true love.
The look is between us.

Candace Finklestein

Did You Ever Meet A Tiger

Graceful creatures, stripes of black on gold.
Ferocious! That's what I'd been told.
Flashing teeth that would rip you apart.
I believed that with all my heart.
With awe I'd look while at the zoo.
What he was thinking, only he knew.
The rest of this poem, you may not believe.
It is the truth, I do not deceive.
I met a tiger face to face.
It happened at an unusual place.
Small and cuddly, coy and smart.
The meeting took place at Wal * Mart.
It was love at first sight, for me at least.
Who wouldn't fall for this wonderful beast.
Now he has grown to one full year.
Two hundred pounds, but not to fear.
A great big baby, Bahl-Shoy's his name.
Although he's grown, he's still the same.
Believe if you will, I know that It's true
You'd love this tiger as much as I do.

Bonnie Stone

God's Angel

One day God made an Angel
He borrowed sunbeams for his hair and blue skies for his eyes
He made velvet for his skin and a blanket of love to wrap him in
Then He lent him to earth for a little while.

He arrived one warn spring day
He was my son, I was His mom
And I knew a little bit of heaven had come my way.
And with each passing day
He begin to grow and learn and play
And so often I would hear him say, "Look Mom! Look at me!

Then one cold dark winter morn
Just twenty short years after he was born
God said, "Son, it's time to come home now."

With a sigh he was on his way
But he made one short delay
To slide down a moonbeam, swing on a star
And dance along the milky way

And I can almost hear him shout
As his wings begin to sprout
"Look Mom! Look at me now!"

Gail Kusturin

472

Whiskers Bark

A kid 2 years old had a cat twice her age;
set up a scene looked like center stage.
This cats name was Whiskers Kitty,
and OH OH what a pity.
For the kid yelled out like a shark,
Whiskers Kitty; please, please, bark!
The cat sat in amazement for the kid stood next to the door
shouting and shouting over again
Whiskers aren't you my friend!
She sat from noon till dark,
shouting out Whiskers won't you bark!
pacing back and forth,
She even tried it sitting on the porch.
she tried in the kitchen and saw a few cans
but because it was dark,
and Whiskers wouldn't bark,
the kid tripped over a pan.
The kid yelled out a big OW!
and you know what finally; Whiskers, said "Meow".

Veronica Valasek

Lifemap

Roads of choice vein a blasted land
that rolls forever with tomorrow's sand
laid upon an earth of love and life
covered with obstacles crowded tight
to confuse the way or offer shade
on our way past days that forever fade

As we navigate we encounter roads
that others made on the way they chose
and if we're lucky our way stumbles on
another person struggling on then gone
But before they go they will impress
a thought or idea we must address
that will change the course our road will go
for better or worse our way will grow

And so through new lives and old
our roads of life will constantly unfold
constructing a view of the world at hand
that show's us when or where we stand
in good times and bad in fortune or mishap
we continue to lay out our own life map

Alan Anderson

The Visions Of Her Lonely King

Sitting on his flush red velvet throne,
the lonely King closes his weary eyes.
The reflection of a marvelous white stallion
graces the now cracked and weathered window.
A new-born baby girl spins naked
in a pool of black air,
and one fierce yellow eye watches
from the shadow which has swallowed
the only corner in the round stone room.
In the other corner stands a sterling white book
crested with golden letters which read "HOLY BIBLE".
Leaning on the front of the great Book is a sword.
The handle glitters with gold, diamonds, and gems,
the blade saturated with the fresh blood
of a lesser man.
A brilliant red cardinal sings his song
from the other side of the empty room.
And beyond the bolted wooden doors,
the beautiful Queen weeps,
for she has lost her lonely King.

Steven Abate

Autumn Nights

Have you noticed,
Dawn keeps getting late
And sunset all too soon

That your nighttime dreams
Make little sense, as they wake
You to the harvest moon.

Do your daytime naps
Last all too long then
You wonder where days have gone.

Are birthdays coming all too fast
As you count them racing by
Yet the pain lasts all too long.

Is spring the only time of year
That gives you very much joy,
Or has your memory left you in the past.

I wonder just how long it goes on;
These short days and long nights,
As the golden years turn to brass.

Richard E. Miner

Broken Am I

Tonight I lie awake. My thoughts entwined with restless fears.
Hoping you will still be here as I search through my tears.
I strain to see your shadow on the wall, deep in the night.
I hope that all I live for won't just vanish out of sight.

If I should ever lose you, would my life be worth a dime?
Could I face each day forever? Would my grief subside with time?
I can't think of life without you; to my heart you hold the key.
I wish that life were perfect like I thought that it would be.

It only hurts a moment when your anger lashes free.
I take each blow with patience - hold my pain inside of me.
Bruises come, they go again. Time fades away the sting.
I can't let go; I need you so. You give me everything.

When I'm alone, I think of you - the center of my world.
Remember when you held me tight? Called me your little girl?
You used to be so kind and sweet. Now that time seems strange.
What happened to that time gone by? What brought about the change?

Each day I ask myself if I deserve all that you give.
My spirit has been broken to the point I just forgive.
Just when I'm sure the strength is there to help me break away,
I end up breaking down instead. My destiny's to stay.

Maria Yonika

Snow Is Like The Sea

Snow is like the sea,
It is awfully wet,
And way too cold for me.
Children enjoy the snow as long as they can,
Just like the sea, when they play in the sand.
There are many creatures in the sea,
Quite as you know,
But in the wintertime
You might just see a doe.
And since your childhood goes by fast,
And you want those seasons to always last,
Remember the snow is like the sea.
And the sea is like the snow,
So fun for you and me
Will never end.

Erin McCarthy

In The Mood For A Thunderstorm

Were you ever in the mood for a thunderstorm?
When the lightening flashes, the thunder crashes
                    and the house shudders?
The rain slams against the windows and the lights
                    flicker a warning.
The sky turns black; shadows fall where shadows
                    never fell before.
In the darkness of the day your room becomes smaller
                    and wraps around you.
You sit, enfolded within yourself;
                    And the melancholy leaves;
                    And the loneliness leaves;
                    And the emptiness leaves;
I'm in the mood for a thunderstorm.

Anita Di Sisto

Untitled

God filled my cup with the Holy Wine from Heaven.
I drank by the tilt of His Heavenly Hand.
It purified me from within.
It filled me with the thirst of my desire.
It filled me with the peace and calmness that can only come from Him.
It pushed out my sorrow and my woe.
It chastened my thoughts.
It purified and calmed my tribulations.
Praise be to God.
Praise the Holy Name of Jesus.
Praise be to the Anointed King.
For He uplifts my spirits like an eagle in the eye of a hurricane.
Praise be to God for the joy He has brought me.

Mary Saville

I'll Always Be There

I gave birth to you, my child
From the moment I felt you
To the moment I held you
I knew I would always love you

I was there when you took your first breath
There when you took your first step

I was there when you rode your first bike
There when you had a fright

I was there when you drove your first car
There when you went to far

I was there don't you see
As I always will be

Mozelle Cook

"An Ode To A Brother"

Once I had a brother,
Who was nice as he could be,
I don't know what happened,
But he turned his back on me.

I loved to hear his music,
And he always stayed in key,
I'm afraid his tune has changed a lot,
Because he turned his back on me.

We grew up as friends, and now we're old,
Things are not the same, you see
Because of a foolish misunderstanding,
He turned his back on me.

Flora Fielstad

"The Draft"

We place our faith and trust in the protectors of our land
We see them marching off to the beating of the band
The foot soldiers to follow the generals to lead
to kill and be killed and let their country succeed
Young men and young women in the prime of their life
see companions die through America's strife
But when the world is struggling and in need of a war
You must give up your life
and be willing to do more
Your heart and your soul
are a small price to pay
when your country finally sees
the victorious day
The love of the country
through the battles and fight
keeps the military strong and our spirits stay bright
So if your country should summon
you must rise to the call
for united we stand
and divided we fall

Regina Raleigh

Family

As we all sit at the table,
Each of us telling our days fable,
There's that sense of sharing,
To listen with a special warmth of caring.

It's that unity of togetherness,
That carries on through the times of sorrow and happiness.
It allows us to compromise,
And allows us to sympathize.

There's compassion and tears,
There's security and fear,
There's felicity and joy,
Along with modesty and coy.

We're individuals brought together by a mother and a father,
And fulfilled be sisters and brothers.
Our love for the other keeps our strong,
To be a family, generations and generations long.

Kathy Schultz

Untitled

Crisy, Crisy, with eyes of blue,
How long I long to be with you,
Crisy, Crisy, with hair of brown,
Wear a smile, not a frown,
If we were close, if we were near,
We can sit in the woods and watch the deer,
Writing poem's is not hard to do,
All I have to do is think of you,
Crisy, crisy, shy little thing,
With a smile only sunshine would bring,
If you hide, if you seek,
Every day is a brand new peek,
So don't be blue, don't be sorrow,
Think of all the good in tomorrow,
I will leave you with this thought,
The grass is greener on the other side of the hill,
Forget about the past and start a new,
Hang in there baby, you'll pull through.

James Masen

Chrissy

On the day she was born,
The first of September
What a day of surprises,
I can't even remember
We all expected a regular child,
She almost was, her difference was mild
They said "Spina bifida",
What a picture to paint
Problems with the spine, walking would be her restraint
We didn't care, we'd love her despite,
All we wanted to know was that she was all right
That was some years ago and she's almost thirteen,
My sister, Chrissy,
The greatest of God's miracles I've ever seen

Rebecca L. Walker

One

One day we'll hear the same whisper.
Feel the same wind through our hair,
Cringe from the same sting of our tears.

No longer will there be the uncertainty and fear.
Our feelings will remain profound and near.

We will no longer feel coarse sand
Sifting through our feet.
But feel the same rushing tide
Foam around our toes.

We will both know and understand.
No more waiting for the other's silent demand.

We will be equal,
Feel what the other may feel,
Nothing to hide or to reveal.

No more troubles, no more lies.
Just love, and the same sweet sigh.

Kate Marcus

Poor Black Man

Ready...Aim...buck goes the sound from the
gun of the white cop, "Stop where you are!
Don't move! Freeze!"

The black man who's running never made it to the bus-stop,
the poor black man fell straight to his knees.

"Is the black man dead? Is the black man dead?" was the
question from the crowd in the street.

While they all stood around, as the black man bled,
The black man's body lay stranded on the concrete.

"Someone call the doctor!" yelled the girl with the blonde hair,
"I think he might still be alive."

As tears ran down her cheeks with the feeling of despair,
thirty minutes later, the medic does arrive.

"Please save the black man," says the girl with her white dress,
shaking cause the little girl's in fear,

While the medic look at her and says, we'll surely do
our best, drip, drip, drip goes her tears.

As the cop sees the little girl, he grabs her by surprise, he can
feel the pounding of her heart beat. He looks at the girl with his
dark and somber eyes, and says...
"It's just one less negro in the street."

Donell Buggs

The Scary Page

Some suffer silently...some are crying out loud
Waiting for someone...that will make them feel proud
They've eaten their roots...cast the seeds onto a stone
Today they are trembling...their food is all gone.

Now they stand there..saddened faces in the dark
The place they feared...feared the seeds would start
Losing the comfort....with the emptiness in their head
Will they now miss them...and the gifts they once shed?

On their own decision...they tore out the page
It frightened their spirit...to live on this stage
And when it was over...they bred me their shame
Dividing their anger...demanding me the same

I will not let their anger...burn within me
It's something for tyrants...they will never be free
I conquered their hatred... and felt all their pain
So, will it make any difference
if I rewrite that page?

Anthony T. Quernemoen

Adoption Day

When you lose a part of you,
you will always stay blue,
knowing that special someone,
is in someone else care on keeping.
You can't sleep at night for your
insides are shaking and
you just need that company
to bring back love to me.
    Someday you know you'll
see him and maybe before its
time, you can come back
home again and everything
will be fine, till you
have to say goodbye, because
your time on earth is over.
But just because you do you know
your love will never die, and
so you cover her up never
to see her again, but
maybe in the new world you can be best of friends.

Laura Moore

The Promise Of Summer

After weeks of cold, wet, blowy showers,
We sure look forward to summer's flowers.
After so many grey, wet, rainy days,
We're ready for summer's sunny rays.
After a winter of stark, bare trees,
We're ready to watch those birds and bees,
As they flit from bloom to bloom,
Dispelling the last season's gloom.
Gathering nectar as they go along,
Accompanied by the cardinals song.
To this song we plan our flower beds,
Using all colors, oranges, yellows, blues and reds.
Orange marigolds, yellow daffodils,
Putting lots of color in those hills.
Blue delphinium, red roses, pink coral bell,
I'm sure it's going to turn out well.
Humming bird, drawing cleome, morning glory on the vine,
See, every things turning out just fine!
Thinking of the past season, I think! What a bummer!"
I'm sure looking forward to the promise of summer.

Dorothy L. Bauman

As The Sun Sets

Never again will I ever see as wondrous a sight,
None as beautiful, magnificent as the one I've seen tonight.
Up on a hill between two trees, I sat amongst the leaves,
As pink clouds passed above me, floating in the breeze.

Leaning forward to look down to the lake, I watched water slowly sway
And then decided for the night, it was here that I would stay,
To watch the sun as it slowly fell and behind the mountains before me
Hid itself not again to be seen until tomorrow morning.

As I closed my eyes and layed down my head looking forward
   to tomorrow,
I laid my hand upon the grass and felt a bit of sorrow,
For never again would I ever see as wondrous a sight,
None as beautiful, magnificent as the one I've seen tonight.

Amanda Lisbeth Vaiden

A Piece From My Mind And World

I see a light shined I follow it?
Will it lead me to life?
To some unknown world
Where dreams really do come true my dreams
Where I am living them, touching them.
Breathing them deeply in,
And exhaling life and encouragement to others,
To follow me
And believe in me, who I am
What I can become
What I have become
Where I am not afraid to live as me
Where my heart will never be broken
And my mind is at peace
And so be this world

Tanya Smith

Silent Communication

You left in anger, like a fire in a windstorm, sparks followed you,
hot and stinging, Now you plea, "Let's talk!" But can we?
You have so many preconceived thoughts, you truly believe we talk.
And yet the words I spoke are not the words you heard.
They are not an expression of my thought,
For you painstakingly filter each word
Through your new found prejudice.
You never heard my silence. The heavy, long, painful, screaming silence.
How could you ever understand my words
If you don't feel the silence?
Please, just listen with your heart!
For it hears my words, but also joins
with my grieving heart in stunned silence.
And deeply mourns the precious moments now lost forever
Sometimes to communicate must not involve words.
They only become obstacles to overcome,
to move beyond, to avoid. The pure, honest truth of
silence allows each heart to touch the other and communicate deep,
unquestioning love!

Jeanne Rafferty

God's Son

It isn't Jesus that I speak of when I call the child God's Son,
My womb brought forth this gentle boy; I was the chosen one.
But he left this life too soon...too fast...to see what it could give;
And without my son, the pain I breathe makes it difficult to live.
So in God's Arms, He'll hold my boy and stroke away all pain,
Please make him happy once again, the Host will entertain.
My son. My son is yours my Lord, at least for now it seems,
But he comes to see me every night, I soothe him in my dreams.
With the dawn he's gone once more, cold emptiness fills my heart,
There's distance from the clouds to me that's keeping us apart.
Lord, when my time here is no longer, and my suffering's at an end,
Please, remember who you gave him to, and give him back again.

Mary Bowen

Love's Insanity

Oh, for your love I gave my all to thee
till naught was left till at some distant time,
when all of love and all its passion be
less overpowering of soul and mind.

The first consuming throes of love doth change
the unsuspecting flower within its grasp
into a mindless wonder so deranged
that all in life is love and its repast.

Somewhere within this orb of senselessness
the mind rebounds and seeks for sanity.
How can one new at love's games ever guess
that time and time alone will be the key?

Though love lives on forever in the heart,
of life it's only one consuming part!

Geneva Roberts

Wise Old Man

Grandfather, Grandfather what can I do?
My girlfriend stole my heart and she tore it in two.
"Listen up young fella for I'm wise in my ways
I know what you're feeling you'll be hurting for days,
But I know a remedy, I know the cure
Follow the path for true love is so pure,
Find you a girl who will stick by your side,
One that is faithful, has nothing to hide."
Thank you old man for your words are so true
Now that I know exactly what to do,
I'm gonna go out to the fish in the sea
And find that girl so special to me.
"It's not that easy to find the right one
Especially if you hurry like a bullet from a gun,
Let time take its course she'll come around
Take a hold of your heart, bring it back to the ground."
I will Grandfather, you are so smart
Just know that you too have a place in my heart.
"Thanks sunny-boy now be on your way,
Remember what I told you and you'll be the king of the day."

Javier Yzaguirre

Peace In The Mornings

In the spring: I love to rise before dawn, a cup of coffee in hand,
go outside and wait for the first bird to sing.

   One by one they all burst into song, and it seems like
   the trees sway as they all sing along.

I think: This is how God intended it to be, but all to soon the
city awakes and the birds flee, and I feel as empty as the trees.

   Reality sits in, as the noise of the city prevails and I wonder
   what this day will bring as in the distance, a siren wails.

Troubles and woe are the norm for the day.
This world is a jungle, and near by, little children play, and I
wonder will one of them be the prey:

   I try hard to block out the pain and despair as the news comes
   out over the air, and look forward to a new day when once again
   I can go just outside my door and find solace and peace in the
   morning there.

Shirley Davis

Our Minds' World

Our minds are strange, yet wonderful creatures -
They can stretch and they can feature
Yet, will reason and reflect - Comprehend the intellect!
Understanding at time, enough to judge
But opinionated, and often throwing mud —
Recollecting through the years, contemplating many fears,
Concentrating on the good, giving attention to things we should -

Elaine Van Horn

The First Day Of School

The first day of school
is anxiously fun.
You miss your t-shirt and umbros,
I hate to see the summer undone.

You miss sleeping in,
My sister can't get her hair right.
I can't find my shoes so I look in the den.
So you say to yourself I wish it were night!

The teacher said we will have a math test tomorrow,
So I start to freak out.
I want to know how to borrow,
But I don't know my route.

The teachers overload you with stuff,
The things is you don't even know it.
When you get home from school you think it's enough,
You try to do your best so you don't blow it!

Liz Paullin

"A Fallen Stone"

Where goest thou' there so will I be
soaring away far into the sky
Let not thou love wanderer alone,
For so be it a fallen stone.
Cry no more, trust one in the other, bless your
Cause, reach out to touch, it was now is,
to give thy love there no more never so
be my friend ever there. Let not for get in despair
seems no end. Cry, cry so alone, tho thou fright.
Night is darkest nite,
Farthest a way there is that light.
Shining o'so, glow, oven land across a sea
o'er to thou strongest guiding hand
reaching out, hear my plea, only hope
time is never to be ever alone,
never to be a fallen stone.

Wylene K. Terrell

Uncle (And Angelic Overtures)

He's not bad for a man
who can hear only what he sees.
His eyes stare through me with the strength of
a mirror that never seems to age.

Our uncle shakes from his ailment,
his nerves must thrash about inside
like loose coins in a pants pocket
that slip between the fingers of a spring hand.

His face is filled a warm smile, precious wrinkles
delicately inscribed around the cheeks and mouth,
fighting zealously to free the subdued teeth
from the loneliness that incarcerates them.

My uncle lives for Thanksgiving and the family he loves.

His heart rises furtively as he peers about the room, leaning into his cane,
his words broken and unattended, but direct in their goodness —
and within the soft angelic overtures he offers do I find
that the weight of his diction is proof of his divinity.

Matthew Nierenberg

You

Wanting you.
Feeling the pain,
Letting it hurt.
Dreaming of you.
Feeling the loneliness,
Letting it take over me.

This all happens.
I wonder why?
I love you.
This all brings pain to me
Not knowing you but loving you.
Why did I let this happen?
I didn't have a choice.
The love for you fell over me.
Now I'm crying and dying every night.
Hoping for you is all that is left for me.

Eleni Andreou

Shadowy Trail

Shadowy trail of my past,
with dreams that didn't last.
Shadows I sometimes see,
shadows of you and shadows of me.
In the dark and dismal night,
I knew that things did not feel right.
To you my heart I had lost,
And now my soul will pay all cost,
This war within myself I fight,
And pray, Dear Lord, to do what's right.
Now the shadows linger in the dusk,
They darken deeper with mistrust.
The love we shared is dead and gone,
It's buried within the day's new dawn.
Shadowy trail of my past,
Those dreams of hearts that didn't last.
Shadows I sometimes see,
shadows of you and shadows of me.

Edith S. Holbrook

Cheryl Lee (My Wife)

You came to me with a trouble soul,
Your life full of hurt that I tried to console.
You lifted me up from the troubles I'd seen.
Tried to show me the things that real love could mean,
To share in life's moments, the good and the bad.
I never really knew what I already had.
My eyes were not open to the things you were showing.
My ears did not hear when you said you were going.
I wake up each day now with a feeling of fear,
Not knowing if ever again you will be near.
My heart will be with you as each day goes by.
I want you and need you to be by my side.
I love you, I miss you, please come back to me.
I'll try to show you everything we truly can be.
My heart is so full of sadness and regret,
Not knowing if another chance I will get.
To show you I hope you and want you to believe,
To give you the happiness you deserve to receive.
I'll carry these thoughts because of so much you gave,
Through the rest of my life and then on to my grave.

Peter D. Baril

"I Don't Wanna Die"

I was on my way to the store
and I heard shots ring out, bang! bang!
I ducked, cause I was afraid of being shot
and most of the other kids on the street ran too
but some of them didn't make it
and when the shots died down
I looked around the street
there was a little girl on a stoop
covered in blood, probably dead
nothing I could do
I knew the police wouldn't come
(they don't come around here no more)
and I saw this kid lying in the street
covered in blood like the little girl
but he was alive and I could see him moving
and he was crying
and he looked up at me and said,
"I don't wanna die."
And I knelt down in the street and held his hand
while he died

Lauren Atkins

The Key

I found the key to unlock our minds,
And all the secrets that we have inside,
About the future of mankind,
Can we find the wisdom inside?

The key you have to unlock your door,
It's so simple, so hard to ignore,
Find the secrets you have in store,
To peace, security, and much more,
If you'll only open that door.

Some people may never unlock their door,
That's what this poem is for,
Come on people, we can do more
To save our world from a nuclear war,
So let's go people, open the door.

People, people, why can't you see,
The wisdom is in your and me,
If we all act as one, then we will see
A peaceful future for you and me.

Rand I. Nichols

The Squire

There came a time a knight received a blow.
It was not fatal, but his son did know
That to the knight's brave bedside he must tend,
And to the doctor's needs attend.
The lad was filled with double grief,
For he preferred to wander as a leaf.
Tis 'not to say he did not love the noble man
But working day and night was not his plan.
Yet 'soon the old brave knight let out a yawn
And fell asleep not long ere dawn.
He left the knight secure in sleep
And walked off towards a hut through forests deep.
He struck a note upon his lute,
Then played a song, 'twas almost mute.
And soon the peasant's girl appeared, so shy,
That did a pang in his poor heart lie.
A ray of sun streaked over now,
And she approached and kissed his brow.
As she into her hut retreated,
Then he turned back, his father to be heeded.

Max-Joseph Montel

Yesterday's Love

For a life to live through
You never new how much I loved you
Tears pouring down my face in disguise

My heart broken into pieces
My happy smile turning into a frown
Love pouring out of me as fast as can be.

My eyes redding as I cry
The floor wet
Yesterday's love comes from yesterday
Today's love comes for another day

Waiting for a sign
for you to rescue
me to hold me in your arm
and say

I love you

Krystal K. Reinke

"Saying Goodbye"

Throughout all the laughter and all the tears,
   it was apparent to all, mom had no fears.
With her love, her humor, her wit, she
   displayed grace and dignity that wouldn't quit.
What an honor to be one called to her side,
   to be drawn into her as her arms opened wide.
She had so much to give, so much to recall;
   joy overwhelming, love abounding for all.
How are you this morning? Well, I'm still here!
   We laughed, we hugged, we wiped our tears.
It was difficult to watch her slip away;
   if only we could stop it and make her stay!
But God was calling her to His side,
   where forever she would be His bride.
What joy, what peace, what love she'd find there;
   no pain, no tears, her life eternally in His care.
Saying goodbye, what a painful task. But what a gift,
   What a blessing; what more could one ask?
Thank-you God for giving us this one last chance to cherish
   and be cherished; our hearts, our lives forever enhanced!

Cynthia M. Reed

The Princess Of Nothing Special

The princess of nothing special sits and dreams
Her eyes fixed in a far away world
No one knows of what she dreams of
Her slight smile and sparkling moon-lit eyes only give you a taste

The princess of nothing special sits and dreams
Her life can not be as empty as her surroundings
Walk through her forest and understand
Sit and feel her presence
Her kingdom unlike others

The princess of nothing special cries softly
For no one is with her
Tears speak the truth of her realm
Dreams are her only escape

Christine Weisheit

"Always"

There will always be
   Oceans and mountains,
   Children's love of puppies and Christmas.

There will always be
   Friendships that never fade,
   A past, present and a future.

There will always be
   You and me in my heart.

Stan Waszak

Meditation Cove

Take my hand and come with me
To a sheltered cove down by the sea
We'll walk over the rocks - then find the path
That leads to the sound
Of the sea's great wrath.

Nature vents her anger by slapping the shores
With whips of water — lashes o'er and o'er
Again and again and again and forever
It's sure as can be
That she'll cease it never.

This is my place but today you may share it
Get away from the world
When you simply can't bear it
Sit in the sand — let the wind blow your hair
Isn't this wonderful — this spot that I share?

My place to remember whatever I feel
The spot where I dream dreams quite unreal
Quiet and peace and rest for my mind
Restore my desire for thoughts of mankind
This is a marvelous spot, you will find.

Phyllis Edsall

Peaceful Sleep

My Lord, last night I woke up late,
And wondered where you are,

I know you told me that you would always,
Be close and never far,

Sometimes I doubt your closeness Lord,
And for a moment I feel fear,

But somewhere in the dark of night,
I know that you are near,

"I'll never leave you child," you say,
"I'll always be close by,"

And so I close my eyes and rest,
And never wonder why,

I know my doubts won't last for long,
I know you're watching me,

I'll sleep the sleep of peace tonight,
For you said that's how it will be.

Carmen Lee Scott Comer

Snake

He was a snake.
A slimy, sleazy, slithery snake.
A snake with a mind.
A snake with a heart.
But, a sneaky snake.

A snake who did wrong,
but wanted to do wright.
A snake that wanted to be good
and be loved, but wouldn't.
A snake that was addicted to bad,
but wanted a cure to be good.

A snake that couldn't get a chance.
A snake that needed a chance.
The snake was good - deep down.
He couldn't get out of the bad snake body,
but wanted out.

Gary Ingham

Home A Healing Place

Our conception into life begins by the love of two people
Who choose to love and protect us giving us our first home
Through, their nurturing and guidance
We move on to our future place of home a beautiful gift
Given to us by no choice of our own

But to achieve this comforting secure place no one told us
The road blocks and detours to avoid to get to this sanctuary
But life give us experiences of sickness, pain, hurt,
Heartaches and sometimes desperation
So we may appreciate where we are going
    while we are searching for it

When we think we finally reached that place
As we conquer those bridges in our life
And think we have achieved love, comfort, warmth and peace
Our life comes to a startling realization that our time is up for
searching for our home leaving all the crossroads we took to get there

We begin another journey yearning for that wonderful home of bliss
We known as a spirit child and as we get closer to our healing place
We find it frightening and unable to freely reach for it
Which has always been waiting for us that most powerful being
Who has offered it to us, guides us back home to our healing place.

Roseanne Betancourt

Faces

I see poems in faces.
Thoughts expressing
concern, wonderment, surprise,
joy, thoughtfulness. Smiling,
frowning, eyes open wide.

These faces are mixed, as our country is. Some
check bones are high, the lines curving up or down;
Small noses or large; The goatee, the beards;
the clean shaven; the hair styles; the handsome
and beautiful. They all are worth watching,

As they walk down the streets in our fair cities;
as they are seen in our rural towns, in our
grocery stores, or in groups all over our land.
The shapes and sizes of their faces, the long
or short hair; Whatever one finds.

Faces are poems, that's what I see. The sweetness
that shines in someone's eyes; the sadness
of life being lived; the tears that flood the eyes and roll
down the cheeks. The heart that has been touched
by a word, or a song.

E. P. Frasure

When Will The Killing Stop?

A century coming to an end, with its wonders and
Its miracles, and its progress, too great to portend
In the shadow of this lightness, and in the background of
The brightness, in all corners of this planet, children
Crying, people dying, "Who will hear us, who will save us,
When will the killing stop"?

A world with all its beauty, its vastness and resources,
Countries and their peoples, already changing courses.
New hearts given, in place of the old, a trip to the moon,
Ever so bold. Too many weapons to take away life, too
Little money causing much strife, and in all corners of
This planet, children crying, people dying,
"When will the Killing stop"?

Can we be silent, just for a moment, and look into our sad Souls?
Can we bring back to this planet, our well defined Goals?
Each and everyone of us, the responsibility to
Share, to make this world a better place, and really
Start to care.

Rita Valerie Goldstein

"Ship of Envy"

I have sailed to thy harbor many a time
On the will of dreams and aspirations.
I have crossed thy sea many a time,
but to never see thy victory torches glowing.
I run from thy wretched shadows.

I have pierced thy destiny for thee,
but the stars has rewritten our fate.
"Destino" thy destined a victory once more.
Envious jade, color of thee eyes
Who sees, thy sin shadowing your sail
Destined by your fate.

Thou shall not swim past seas of despair?
For thyself? For thee?
Love has veiled thy eyes and
fogged thy mind, love is evil
lust is sin. Costly and earthy.
True love is spiritual.

Sail. Thou's life is a journey.
I a metaphor. Speak kindly, listen beautifully
love eternally.

Audie V. Case

"Fear-Obea"

Why do I fear the end of day
As dusk begins to fall
Why do I wake from a troubled sleep
As though I've heard a call
I shake I tremble like a frightened bird
From a fear that is yet unknown
But then somehow I seem to feel
A strange indifferent tone
If only light seek-out the dark
And the drift of voices near
I would fall into a peaceful sleep
Not caring it was here
But alas my hopes aren't granted
This darkness has just begun
My thoughts sink deeper my heart beats louder
From a fear I have not won
As dawn approaches I open my eyes
And give a sigh of relief
For I have no longer fear nor cause
Only the memory of grief

Virginia F. Sill

Those Forgotten

Some shovels shine ready to dine on the earth
while others sit and rust from the damp of the dirt.
Past, present, and future all matter in time.
Happy, sad, good, and evil, uncaring and kind,
all sorts of thoughts run through minds mind....

Rain keeps on falling when its cold turns to snow,
ice storm's eyes seeing in hail.
Sun shows shadows and mirrors reflection through clear glass.
Eyes crying inside of some deaths while you laughed.

Some things smell dead, spoiled, pi**y and rotten,
when one dies will you miss them if not leave forgotten.

Don't feel sorry for yourself... or for me... at that, no one.
If you really do care then just simply show them...

Justin Hatten

I Use To Be

It's cold outside, I have no coat, the
wind blows harshly against my face, I
stand in the rain, wet homeless, I have
no place to go, my Belly hungers, I
have nothing to give, I'm invisible
to those who see me, they call me crazy
that must be my name. In door ways
and boxes I lay, lost are my dreams.
It's cold out side, in a crowd I'm alone
when I wake I cry, the streets are my
home, my clothes are old, dirty, torn, I'm
pitied and despised, I see it in their eyes.
I know nobody, nobody knows me, it's cold outside all my wines gone,
I've taken all the drudges, I'm escaping from my
prison called me, but when I screen no
ones, comes near, it's cold out side I'm no longer
real, I'm not in your files I carry no ID
My family pretends their not home when I knock
at the door, I fall to my knees and plead
with God to think no more of me.

Aaron Williams

Oh Most Beautiful Creation

Floating down softly
as an infant's eyes. Small, simple and yet not.
Huge and so much not expressed.
Unable to show complex
features hidden in a mirage of simplicity.
Each a perfect work of art.
Receiving each the steady hand of the creator.
Flawless.
Never ending works.
Diamonds in his hands.
Complexity beyond comprehension.
In our hands a simple glass portrait.
Simple but yet not expressed
All floating,
Softly.. as an infant's eyes.

Phillip A. Rau

"Unknown Outcome"

She goes by the name of Tracey.
Uplifted, god-gifted is her beauty and my heart.
Looking lovely, like a goddess of moonlight
Shining like a diamonds, she does ever night
We are just friends and nothing more.
I wish everyday, every night we were together.
Should I tell her that? A risk, a gamble.
With my heart as delicate as a feather.
I keep my feelings, my emotions quiet.
And watch her, an angel she is with wings.
I would give her the world if I could.
She means to me more than everything.
Sounds of music being played for her.
Chocolate, a dozen roses, a poem to remember.
Is the only way I can express my feelings.
Maybe, I could tell her by the month of December.
That what I feel for her, will never leave.
I will never hurt her and I want her to see.
That my feelings and emotions are pure and well.
Never change, for the one I love eternally.

Brian Chieppo

Come With Me

Come leave with me let me show you the way.
We'll make the world our own private roadway.
You'll discover places you'd never dream of:
From the falls of En-Gedi to the city of Kirov.

Come laugh with me let me show you the way.
Act like a kid, if you wish, or read Hemingway.
We'll go to the Opera to see Don Giovanni,
Or listen to Kurt Masur conduct a symphony.

Come love with me let me show you the way.
Not for an hour, a week, a month, but everyday.
Peer into my mind and observe my devotion.
Kiss my lips and feel the depth of my passion.

Come live with me let me show you the way.
Come and stay for good and not day by day.
Soon all your apprehensions will be gone
And we'll call the preacher on the telephone.

Vaughan J. Horasan

Calm Seas

I am sitting, dangling my feet in the cool water.
I can feel the icy drops of water splash in my face.
I get up.
I put on my sweat shirt.
I gently push the hair out of my face.
The sun starts to sink in the magenta sky.
I turn my sails to go home.
I get inside the harbor.
I hook on to my mooring.
I fall asleep as the breeze ruffles my sails.

Kara Buban

In Your Eyes

In your eyes, as a young child I could see
Only love, hope and joy
Faith and security.

As I changed and grew taller
That bright light in your eyes
Seemed to grow smaller

A lot of that hope and joy grew very slim
And that light, yet still there,
Was very dim

And now looking back on those days
That seemed to last so much longer
The light I was hoping for, came back
And this time, even stronger

As a child I always looked to you
As a teen I looked away
And now as a woman and a mother
I look to you again, and say,

"Thank you Daddy, for showing me the way
of the light, that shines so brightly,
in your eyes."

Stacey Marie Venditti

Regrets

In youth the hard knocks scarred me.
In middle age the barbs cut deep and to the core.
In older years the bad memories haunt me,
Leave me hurting, tormented, and pleading, "no more!"

Only time can erase all the heartaches, mistakes, and all the cares.
So until merciful death releases me,
To a fairer land than this
I will seek forgiveness, and long for eternal rest.

Helen Luigs

Untitled

Sometimes I feel as if the world is passing me by
There's nobody there.
Nobody cares.
I'm just lying here waiting to die.

So young and yet, so old.
I came in this world alone.
No one understands.
Can't meet my demands.

On the outside looking in.
My world is falling apart.
The walls are wearing thin
On the barrier of my heart.

There are footprints on my face
Where the world walked over me.
My confidence misplaced
I'm drowning in their sea.

Amanda C. Black

The Comfort Of Rain

Tears from heaven dance upon my flesh
tepid droplets spilling down my cheeks reduce my loneliness
unwanted sadness,
red stained face,
icy pain and bitter taste
so insane....I cannot believe
Wet and dreary, cloudy skies...
take it away from me

Nicole C. Lynskey

The Gate

I'm standing on a threshold
Attempting to be bold.
I don't know where to look,
Who to talk to, or if it's in a book.
Some days I giggle and pretend
That childhood will never end.
Other days I worry and fret
A plan for life I soon must get.
I'll have to step right through that Gate
And enter Adulthood, my beckoning fate.
What will happen to my childhood?
A time of life so filled with good.
Must I leave it all behind
To answer the questions on my mind?
A wise old woman told me once
Laughter's the best weapon on life's battle fronts.
I'll take it with me from the past. I'll bottle it and hold it fast.
Humor will guide me through no matter what I decide to do.
Now I'm ready for that Gate,
I'll cross with confidence, not hesitate.

Margaret Durfee Allen

Memories

You brought me happiness as no one else could.
With your love of life, and sense of good.
Our quiet talks, and hours spent on dreams,
Were not wasted words to be forgotten
When morning comes, and life rushes on like
A cold mountain stream.
You are gone now, far from these eyes
That looked deep into your own, and saw love,
Far from these hands that touched the
sunshine in your hair
I see you when now raindrops cover my window.
When autumn leaves fall softly to the
forest floor, and when footsteps come to
My lonely door.

Robert Ragan

Pam

To my baby sister
Whom I love so dear
News about your health has come
A day that I did fear.

I have no words to let you know
The feelings that I feel.
Remember that I love you so!
These words will be our seal.

Today we found out some very sad news,
My world suddenly stopped today.
I try to place myself in your shoes
And I thought of some things to say.

Yes, you will be just fine
Your strength is in the One it should be.
He will see you through this time
Due to prayers from us, you see.

I love you a lot!
And I can't wait till you're better!
I'll never leave your side,
We'll go through this together.

Cindy Watson

Seems Like Yesterday

Seems like yesterday I found your love
Midst lollipops and flowers
And as the stars danced in your eyes
We spent those magic hours

You said that you would walk with me
And told me of your wishes
To give your love and hold my hand
And share a thousand kisses

We traveled fast, took each new path
In sunshine and through showers
We laughed and cried and shared our dreams
Like petal-painted flowers

I wish you happiness and joy
And all the things you wished for
When I was young and didn't know
What life and love were meant for

Seems like yesterday I gave you gold
With cold intrinsic powers
For now I give you all my love
With lollipops and flowers

Martin Michael Leahy

Sleeping Dogs

Animals of the night roam freely through your home.
The streets are fogged in past blind parking meter row.
City cats look far and wide, searching for their prey.
Dogs dissolve into shadows, hiding from the dark of day.

Freedom's lost — freedom's won, depending on a chain link fence.
Running so fast, can't be seen. No one gets a need rest.
Lights of flash fill the mist — glimmer at your town's graffiti walls
No one hears a cry for help — dragged down by mankind's call.

Sleeping dogs — they howl
At the whiteness of the midnight sun.
Their cries are heard everywhere.
Only silenced by the gun.

S. R. Klein

"Decisions"

We are humans and the earth is our only place.
It is up to us to overcome hatred, prejudice and problems of race.
The world is getting smaller and yet together we have to live.
We must believe in ourselves and know that we can learn, help and give.

People are different but respect is the same.
Education will help along with trust in our Father above.

Never allow bias or judgment to control your thoughts,
ideas and capacity to love.

Jacques Russell

Sorrow

The air, thick and damp,
A horse lies still in the distance.
There is no movement, only the, flutter of a bird,
Closer, closer I walk,
Still no movement, but now there is sound
Heavy beating strained by saliva,
Cold and damp to the touch,
Pale are the gums,
Response is only in the eyes,
Pain and sadness darken the morning light.
The brush is matted; all expressions dim,
A blanket is laid on an old friend.
Time creeps as help is beckoned,
Help comes with death laughing.
Efforts are made, hope shows its face,
An old friend goes to sleep.

Todd W. Bosworth

"People's Country Home"

Country home it's ours you see, miles and miles of empty space.
Just look out the window, it's the way it should be,
     to plant and sow God's grace.
We all need some room on this earth, I'll share it
     with you sister and brother.
And this site before you behold its mirth, if
     you'll promise to give some to another.
There's plenty of room to spare, don't waste what
     you've been given.
As long as nature gets carried on there, we'll continue
     to grow and go on livin'.
So lets all replant, all that we've learned into
     the earthly plains
With the peace of mind we've richly earned,
     just a small seed to sprout through our remains

So that next generation to step foot on the ground,
Will have a fresh start, anew,
And they'll know in their hearts, where they are bound
Cause from our kindness and love

     they grew.

Diana Stephens

Winter

Winter is cold, freezing as it turns
into frost for this icy city that
has caught the publics eye of Old
Man Winter's return from hibernating,
the snow pouring outside has piled the
once busy streets by turning it into
a mountain of snow, a snowy hill is a
site where children play, with their sleds
they plummeted down the icy slope
only to cope with the impact of fun
and laughter as a true season of
beauty.

Brian Flinchum

My Christmas Prayer

I pray that Jesus will give you and me:

Enough COURAGE to challenge injustice when we encounter it.
Enough FAITH to keep hope alive in our hearts.
Enough HAPPINESS to enjoy every minute of every day.
Enough TRIALS to keep us strong and alert.
Enough DETERMINATION to make each day better than the last.
Enough FRIENDS to give companionship and comfort when needed.
Enough GENEROSITY to become God's special gift to others.
Enough FAILURE to teach us humility.
Enough INNER PEACE to bring hope to a friend in his or her darkest hour.
Enough SUCCESS to keep us enthusiastic to face life's challenges.
Enough WEALTH to meet our needs and to share it with others.
Enough QUIET TIME to reflect on God's countless gifts and to say
  Thank You.
And WISDOM to keep circumstances in their proper perspective.
Enough SORROW to keep us sensitive to the dreams, hopes, needs, and
  feelings of others.
Enough COMPASSION to listen to others, thus giving them the
  opportunity to Be.
Enough LOVE to bless everyone we encounter in a healthy and positive way.

S. J. Womack

"The Dentist"

My dentist is an okay guy
But enjoys inflicting pain, don't ask me why,
He took the syringe out of its pouch
And before he even jabbed me, I said "Ouch!"

He said, "Now, Kathy, open wide"
I see the needle coming, no place to hide,
As he draws nearer I see a gleam in his eye
Drawing deeply on the gas I give a resigned sigh.

Relief from the pain is on its way
"Will this take long?" I try to say,
To my surprise my mouth is numb
And whenever I speak it sounds really dumb.

"I can't feel anything", I try to say
and saliva drools out to my dismay,
He laughs and says," This won't hurt at all"
He laughs again, he's having a ball.

It's finally over I'm glad to say
He'll do a checkup another day,
The pain was minimal when he used the drill
But it hurt a lot worse when I got the bill!

Kathryn Harger

Winter Is A Joy

Winter is a joy
to have, to hold, to understand
fallen are the leaves
that walk together, hand in hand
and naked are the trees that embrace
the feelings no one wants to notice

But death provokes a spark of life
and in the healthy bosom grows
passion, desire, strife
these three things she shows:

The trampling of a blade of grass beneath a careless shoe;
the wisdom of a lesser day; the life I almost knew

Timothy Achan Gates

Freedom

Freedom is desired, yet limited,
  seldom given without earning trust and responsibility,
Those who have it must work to keep it,
  yet those denied must suffer.

It's rated by age, measured by love,
  and poured with all strictness.
Boundaries surround it like a locked gate,
  and it's given slowly with each test of adulthood.
Many in the end receive it, but some seldom achieve it.

Those who experience it, become fuller and more confident.
Those held back, miss a born luxury.
If taken for granted, life is simply an empty pasture.
If treated as a rare flower, in blooms into a beautiful bouquet.

Kristen Suzanne Graham

Love's Course

You are my star, my guiding light,
  beauty against the darkness, illumination to my soul.
I long for you.
Your eye's beam pierces the roughness of my hardened shell,
  my protection from the world, armor against nature.
Your warmth, your heat, draws me from my shelter, my cocoon.
I emerge, seeking, and am drawn to your flicker.
A female of the murkiness, I seek my sparkling diamond in the rough.
My winged path, though newly birthed, acknowledges no other flight
  except to you, my glimmer in the gloom.
My velvet wings, bright with bold colors, seek to gather your
  translucent rays.
I long to hold your evanescence close to my heart, my soul.
But, oh, how my love does burn, for all stars, alas, are flame.

Norma J. H. Patterson

Nike Of Samothrace 190 B.C. Louvre, Paris

Remaining through the centuries monumenting a piece of
ancient art. Stone, cold statue still standing through the rubble
and ruins of the aching heart. Isolated and deserted, standing
proud of being untouched and not being knocked down; but the
tear that has been frozen on its face by waiting for that warm
embrace shows a different feel to that stone, cold texture.

A vital Eagle circle above and sweeps down to grab hold of the statue.
Fly, free, high up in the clouds they pass through time...

...As years go by of my mortal life, I had the opportunity to love;
but I had let it go - for what reason why? I do not know! As I
stand in this time while looking in the mirror, I see a scar shaped
of a teardrop on my face and I realize it is time for me to depart.
The eagle returned to my windowsill waiting to take me home,
where no mortals walk through the rubble and ruins of my aching heart.

Laurie-Ann Lanberg

Little Ones

Sing a song and try to be strong
For the little ones they're all gone
Whisked away in the blink of an eye
No one knew it was their day to die
We all sorrow and some of us cry
We look for help from heaven above
We also get it from our fellow man's love
Many have labored, long and hard
Sweaty, hungry, dirty and tired
We hope and pray that maybe someday
Mankind will put his anger away
But we all know that while the children play
They'll also be the ones who pay...
God Bless Oklahoma

Charles E. Hill Jr.

Before And After February 26, 1995

I have always loved the beach.
Sand beneath my feet.
Essence of salt air.

Never imagining,
It could be more momentous.

You are near me.
Waves crashing before us.
Motioning us to stay near.
In awe of the power before us, we are hypnotized.

Now as I stand,
In the places we stood.
I feel a sense of loss coupled by a sense of gain.
I have my hand in yours.
I steal a glance at your face.
Our blue eyes meet, lingering on each other.
You pull me closer.
A warmth shoots through my body.
Your lips gently press to mine.

My awareness reclaimed, a chill passes through me.
You are gone.

Jennifer L. Hornsby

The Music Plays On

Go swift through the dank of the midnight haze!
Hold fast 'neath the sting of the white moonrays!
Lend a kind hand to others; Be true to your ways
While the music plays on and we live in our days.

See more than the limits of your time present!
Love all who surround; I believe that's what's meant!
Face the facts, my brother, it's all a bit bent
While the music plays on as if heaven sent.

Climb over the wall of the This and the That!
Run through the Why valley and never combat!
Swim faster, sweet sister! Grab hold of the mat
While the music plays on, all dance 'round the hat.

Be one with the land on which you reside!
Traverse the waters of the merciless tide!
Truth is seeker from which one can't hide
While the music plays on and the time seems to slide.

Dive deep in the bottomless scorching blaze!
Jump over the who is right who is wrong maze!
The truth's plain to see though it be like a craze
For the music plays on till well after our days.

Dante Golio

Life's Treasures

How can I ever hope to heal
    the wounds of others I do not feel?
If my eyes are dry and I never weep.
How do I know when the hurt is deep?
    If my heart is cold and it never bleeds
how can I know what others need?

For without crosses to carry
    and burdens to bear.
We dance thru life
    that is frothy and fair.
And only thru tears
    can we recognize
The suffering that lies
    in another's eyes.

So spare me no heartaches,
    or sorrow, dear Lord
For the heart that is hurt
    reaps the richest reward.

Bonnie Goin

"The Immortal Vampire"

In the deepest hours of the night, I rise once again to walk,
the land I've learned to love, where the soft, gentle wind talks.

The moon hangs overhead, like a shiny Christmas bulb,
and the breezes across the lakeside seems very cold.

I stray over to the woods whose voices echo my name,
when there upon a hilltop to a castle I came.

I glided up to the front doors, and they opened before me,
I looked ahead for some one, but no one did I see.

I followed the infinite hallway to another set of doors,
this time they did not open, I knocked and was ignored.

As I turned around to walk away, I noticed a dark figure ahead,
the man whispered my name, and to him, he led.

The storm outside began to show its rage,
the rain poured down heavily, encasing us in a cage.

The man spoke simple words, saying, "Come unto me..."
"hasn't your heart desired to be mortally free?"

As I drew nearer still to my surprise I saw,
the most mysterious man, in my dreams, I'd often call.

I realized in that moment I'd seen the eyes of "Eternal Fire,"
He is the one, my love, the IMMORTAL VAMPIRE.

Jennifer L. Zimmerman

Annihilation

Faces screaming, crying, agonizing
I feel nothing
I wanted to know if my son was all right
Mom's shaking me, "He is dead! Cry it all out baby."

This strange feeling of being someone
I don't know what I am supposed to say
Everyone is watching to see if I'm crying
To see if my life's falling apart

Friends stop over, consoling, watching
Wanting me to break down, yell, anything
My calm face makes them nervous
Why am I so strong?

It all comes out in spurts
You know he was not loyal to you
What? Yes it is true, we are sorry
They watch for the tears that will never come

I feel a strange relief
I am glad it's over completely, a clean break
No haunting divorce to torment our lives
I feel free, and know no remorse.

Madhu Prabhu

In Remembrance Of Marlene Scruggs

I remember
Short chubby legs and eyes so blue.
Sweet little mouth that said I love you.
Tiny sweet kisses, just for me.
I remember
Little skinned knees, trying to climb the trees.
Christmas morning delights and just
holding you tight.
I remember
fights with your sisters. Your trying to run away
laughter and tears nearly every day.
I remember
your growing up years
all the laughter, all the tears.
And I'll never forget all my fears.
I remember.
I love you always Moma

Nina B. Fowler

Progress (Some Things Never Change)

Piercing blue, solar rays resplendent;
Layers thick with hunter's hue.
Scintillate here, softly there;
Gaia consistently inviolate.

Innovation buzzes to and fro,
Noxious gas, materials she did not intend.
Careless operators see not the gravest sin,
Despoiling air and earth with crafted apathy.

Information reigns supreme,
Invisible connectors whir and beep.
Omniscient CPU's know more;
Never shall we wake from this technocratic dream?

Cicero's tongue no longer holds
The key to eloquence.
Forgotten past, tomes lay dead;
Gates a hero, oblivion for Rimbaud.

To what end, this limitless frontier,
Human contact lost?
Loss of self not lagging far,
My love, my saviour whispers in my ear.

Todd Powers

The Life Of Colors

In the distance a young girl dancing freely in the wind,
Reminded me of a child once dancing frantically alone.

I stood in wonder at the colors in her dress
Just as if a blind man saw his first sight.

The spinning colors were like flashbacks of Spanish
Paintings to my witnessing eyes.

It seems to be a maze that the circular lines on her dress
Spun around my eyes until they drifted into a daze.

Even though the shadow of redness appeared to my soul,
The sight for me was overwhelming.

As my excitement grew the greens seemed to focus my eyes
As though they had seen spring on a mountainside.

Before my eyes shooting streaks of yellow seemed
To perform a dance.

Among the colors, the blue stripes filled the dark spots
Of my imagination.

Together these colors reminded me of a child once
Dancing frantically alone.

Maribel Perez

"Glory Of Love"

Set beside me and tell your story
Find all the points of conquest and glory
We shall hear the inner tones of your tale
Panning off in life's narrow trails
I can tell the false from the true
Can you see how much, I love you?
Life hold its mysteries with full embrace
Then there is me to set my place
Set beside me to say the true story
Telling all of youth and glory
I can tell the false from the true
I can tell that, I love you!

Elaine Hines

First Watch

I see the faintest hint of morning.
The night slipped by with little warning.
My thoughts have kept me locked away
While waiting for this brand new day.

The sun appears in all its glory.
This day begins another story.
My thoughts now turn to other things
As somewhere an alarm clock rings.

I pledge my efforts to this day.
In gratitude, I go my way.
Yet, in silence, passions burn
As I long once more for night's return.

I view again the night-time sky.
I am alone, my thoughts and I.
In hope, I wait for early morn
To bear witness to the day re-born.

Cheryl Lynn Allee

Follow The Sun

I've earned my wings, I can not fail
Trust yourself, that's my contention
As we lifted off the ground
I had no need for His direction
My Navigator never looked
The path I took it did not matter
His goal was simple, find a way through stormy weather
Then all at once, through hail and sleet
My confidence had left me cold
Our aircraft fell the speed of heat
Unfolded was the faith I needed
Follow the Sun was all He said
Through the reign of fear and doubt
I trusted Him in times like these for He can surely get me out
It's then I looked upon his brow
and saw the Son I follow now
The knowledge gained, the friendship found
Is all that matters off the ground
Follow the Son is my contention
All you need is His direction

James Kendall Galloway

Ignorance Can Be Lovely

I see the flowers bloom
The animal's play
A just wedded wife and groom
An Honest man's pay

Great seas of blue
Families of joy
Morning's fresh dew
The new child, a boy.

I can go on to state more pretty, plain things
But at a second look, much more this brings.

I see the flowers die
The animal's kill
Matrimony's great lie
Self murder of will

Poisoned waters throughout
Families that hate
Scandals running about
The boy jailed by state:

For everything lovely, there is another side
Keep away from ignorance; don't let the truth hide.

Lora E. Kirn

The Garden

Somehow I need to find a way to tell you of the change..
The unfolding of myself since you are in me.
There always was this wellspring of love in me,
I know it was there, but, of course, it had to be hidden..
    protected..Life hurt.
Like a walled-in rose garden no one could see; then you!

How you climbed inside I surely don't know, can't understand.
But in some wonderful, magical way
You take away the yesterdays and let me see tomorrow.

What key were you given that no one else had ever used?
Was it in the door all the time and no one ever turned it?
You tear down walls with simple words and touches..
And make me feel free-flying, but God, so vulnerable.

Do you mean to clear away the walls and nurture the garden..
Or is the wall the challenge and the space for leasing?
The last stones to clear away are the boulders, buried deep, buried yesterday.
If you clear them, you are honor bound to work the garden.

You can close the door, turn the key and leave.
Please take the key with you.
No one should ever walk in here but you.

Nancy Purcell

If We Must Live

If We Must Live, let us live promoting the spirit of race
    relations, love and freedom for all.

If We Must Live, let us live administering to and assisting
    the needy.

If We Must Live, let us live helping young men and women
    further their education.

If We Must Live, let us live conducting a worldwide commercial
    and technological enterprise.

If We Must Live, let us live as registered voters at the polls,
    voting in every election.

If We Must Live, let us live voting for those individuals who
    are sensitive to our needs.

If We Must Live, let us live preparing a new generation for
    the struggle as we move toward the 21st century.

If We Must Live, let us live helping those adolescents out of
    control, desperate for attention to their problems and
increasingly willing to resort to violence to get the attention they crave.

If We Must Live, let us live as productive citizens in
    our communities.

Willie Cosdena Gunn

Ocean's Broken Waves

Waves are coming in
they hit the beach... Broken Waves
Undertows entice sand
pulling away from our beach... Broken Waves
Wet sand shows every footprint
until undertows erase it away... Broken Waves
A cool breeze sails through
sun catches ripples
and with a touch of highlight
brings ripples to life... Broken Waves
As water sparkles this wave comes along high
colliding with a rock in the cliff... Broken Waves
Whales jump up to catch a sun ray
they moan and let out an ear piercing screech
as their bodies hit icy..cold...sharp water... Broken Waves
That sound...that scare is a relief to all sea life
Now that whales have broken waves
waves burst apart and meet at the beach where they all die

Erin Leigh Springer

St. Patrick Church

A quaint old church peering at the skyway,
Structured so firmly with walls of brick,
Numerous steps are rising to the doorway,
Calmly you enter the house of St. Patrick.

High altars so light are picture perfect,
With artful handiwork and detailed crafting,
Life like statues create a graceful effect,
With stations of the cross quietly mourning.

Stained-glass windows reflect the colors,
As the sunshine glistens beyond compare,
Musical notes float down from the choir,
While parishioners assemble for a prayer.

Our celebrant prays and leads the service,
His homily impresses the attentive crowd,
Receiving communion lifts one's office,
A new day begins on a lily-white cloud.

This is the home of our heavenly father,
Where everyone visits for solemn adoration,
Rewards are generous for those who gather,
Reminding us all to express appreciation.

Francis Lesica

Myself

    Inside myself, I'm locked
away. The days, the nights, the still.
    I listen oh so carefully, but the
words alone; can not set me free.
    To look outside myself, and beyond
is much to lonely as life goes on.
Inside myself is trust and faith,
dependability and good grace. Myself
is safe, but also destructive. I want
to unlock myself you see but most
looks gray instead of blue seas.
    The beauty is disappearing, all
that's left is locked away, inside myself
where it can be safe. Inside myself,
I'm locked away.
    I can't find a key, that fits
myself, it appears as though someone
locked that away. May I never find the
key, because I will always be safe, inside
of me.

Theresa Caccano

Remembrance

A sparkling illusion of agua on a tar-paved highway
In a valley, sloping, rising, into los verdes cierros de las montanas,
La vista es tan hermosa, I think I once fell in love here
    con el cielo y el desierto
I do remember holding tight, so tight it squeezed fresh lagrimas
    de mis ojos
My heart broke once, it has never felt the same,
Where? El Paso, PHoenix, Dallas, Las Vegas - all here en mi corazon
Wide stretching desert, speckled with cactus, sage, backdrop of
    longing
A soul searching within wild freedom
A whitened cactus, guardian del desierto
    los blancos nubes en el cielo azul
Soy triste,
so very, very sad
Mi vida no es Ilena, necesito algo para mi,
solamente pare mi.

Stacy Kehner

Moonflower

There once was a seed planted with care
on a lot in Neosho where the yard was all bare

With some days of sunshine some rainstorms and drought
through months of mistreatment there appeared a small sprout

The days had been dry but the nights made her strong
the gardener had loved her though his care was all wrong

Through hard work and love and after a soft shower
she perked up one evening and sported a flower

One late summer's evening just around midnight
while the stars looked out came a butterfly from flight

The first time he saw her it was love at first sight
together they shared love and danced into the night.

Mark Mente

My Brother

I have a brother who is sometimes mean,
most every day we fight,
The color of his eyes is green, I love him with
all my might!

In the summer we play in the sand,
I like to give him hugs!
Every day I hold his hand,
Except when he picks up bugs!

He always has a belly ache
And I really am his friend.
He tries to eat all the chocolate cake!
I know our love will never end!

Rachel Lyn Bellinger

God's Hands

I ache for the things that might
have been - for the things that
have passed into eternity
God is in control - all is in God's hands.

I experience what is today,
The many happenings of a new born day.
God is in control - All is in God's hands.

I am anxious of what is yet to come,
what lies ahead for each and every one.
God is in control - All is in God's hands.

There is no comfort in aching for what might have
been - no need in resisting what today brings.
Most of all there is futility in fretting about
Tomorrow's unknowns.
God is in control - All is in God's hands.

Anita Middleton

Ill Desires

Lust, the root of all evil;
The ache of a broken heart in strain
Seems to be possessed by the devil.
For a heart can withstand but so much pain.

The longing and endless desire
Of a heart raging desperately with need,
Will slowly and helplessly tire
Of endless pain causing the heart to bleed.

If peace is the heart's ultimate goal,
Love should bloom only from the soul.
Love a person for mind, not physique,
Making love the passion mystique.

Desire not, for too long;
For a broken heart cannot mend alone.

Teresa Edenfield

Futuristic Reflections

Faces pass in front of blind eyes
never to be seen again.
The faces move on, then separate
and go their separate ways.
The only thing that we must cling to,
The only thing of which we may be certain,
Is the uncertainty of the future.

I depend on my ignorance of things undone
to lead me through existence.
As I close one chapter in life's novel,
I open another and continue on,
bouncing and depending upon,
our communal cloud of ignorance.

Raindrops catch in my palm
A pretend pool cooling the warmth within.
I create futuristic reflections of any sort
which quickly disintegrate
as I let water fall onto a place
where one day
I may or may not walk again.

Irene H. Kim

Medicine Horse

The trees whip in the wind
The storm stalks us up the mountain trail
The horse lifts his nose to the wind
The red spots on his flank shimmer

Always, we ride this trail
Always, we quicken our pace, straight up
He arches his neck and blows at the wind
Nothing catches the medicine horse

Dust clouds chase us
The storm growls behind us across the desert
The marks of the sacred shimmer on his flanks
Like bloody prints on snow

We dream together of forever
We ride the winds across the land
His hoofbeats are the heartbeat of the world
Ancient magic, medicine horse

N. Far Well

Bethlehem

Thou who art the smallest among the nations
Sunken low in God's creation
Home of harlot and unbalanced fee.
What good can come out of thee?

Can a gain be made to erase thy waste?
A culture be born to whet thy taste
For nobler life? What can compensate
To lift from thee the stifling weight?

Can a single course-changed star that rests,
And points to the end of a Kingly quest,
Bring new light to a shepherd's eye,
When that star points to an animal's sty?

Oh Logos, let us see the new birth there
Let Jacob's ladder with its angelic stair
Fade before its pure radiant light.
Interpret for us, blot out the night.

Bethlehem, Bethlehem, for such as thee He came
To forgive thy sins; to make straight thy lame
And while thy multitudes with indifference hummed
The God-Man line must needs be plumbed.

W. E. Fitzgerald

Without

I want to fly high in the sky without
Any wings to help me get there.

I want to be buried in the sand without
Getting dirty.

I want to sink in the sea without
Getting wet.

I want to love someone without
Falling in love.

I want to have a sweet dream without
Going to sleep.

I want to lay under the sun without
Getting burned.

I want to live tomorrow without
Having to live today.

Courtney Watts

Sporadic Reminders

Some mornings at our house, the hum of lying minds ceases
when father's plane takes off
from the upstairs runway.

Rattled floor boards signal to
pealed back luggage stickers.
While dawn resists the shaft beneath our door,
it all makes mother weary.

   "A brittle canopy is not meant to be cradled"
I hear her say.

Like the tissue paper lamp shade my father
returned to China.

Jess Marshall

Puppeteer

Visions of emerald, ruby, and sapphire
Engages the scene into motion
For all creatures to admire.

Blissful movements of a silhouette
Engulfs the imagination into pure splendor
To delusions of gold that we reflect.

A glimpse to the dazzling lights
Emotions flutter into entanglement
Confusion dismays the heavenly delight.

Moisture of dew induces a fall
The trend yields to a slumber
Anticipating the drapery call.

Sheila L. Hall

Basketball

When running down the shiny court it takes a lot of speed.
I like to look at the score board to see us in the lead.
I'm five foot three as you can see that isn't very tall.
But I can shoot three monster points, in all girls basketball.
We practice hard, we play our best in every single game.
It doesn't matter win or loose, but that my family came.
My sister is our biggest fan, she cheers us on all night.
She tells me what I'm doing wrong and what I'm doing right.
The time goes fast, the scores are high and a moment's never dull.
When you're running down the court in all girls basketball.

Jacqie Schoenfeld

The Tree Of Death

I'm sitting on the branch of the tree of death.
I'm a lost soul, going nowhere, doing nothing.
I don't know who I am, or I was before.
I'm just sitting here on the branch of the tree of death.
Here there are no seasons, just nights filled with treason.
Howls and screams are the sounds I hear.
Burning flesh of sinful souls permeate my nose.
I'm lonely and filled with dread, sitting on the branch of
the tree of death.

Maria Garcia

"Of Reflections And Dreams"

When it is that I reflect, about the things I see
   About the type of person, I'd really like to be
      The kind of life that I enjoy, of things I like to do

My mind transcends with scores of dreams
   My heart then feeds the need to see
      Intensive feelings start to grow
         The spark called life begins to glow
            That causes depth immensely felt

Then comes to birth of things surreal
   Which from the start were so concealed
      From human logic not conceived
Need now fuels sure attainment, all detractions disappear

      Now the dream seems very near

As I start to reassess, this is a dream that I possess
   I realize with glowing feeling,
      This is the future I am seeing
When reflections turn to dreams, then reality it seems,
   Takes these dreams not preconceived

      To make a future well received...

L. Aubrey Bentley

One Tale Of Mental Illness

Donald doesn't like to change
his clothes. It requires too much
time. Instead, he wears
a forgotten mouth and weeping willow hair.
His gait slide-shuffles,
   feet in phantom chains,
shoulders forward hunched
   as if to hug himself.

Off his meds, he's restless
as a nightmare; a dreamer maddened
by the light. Uneasy and unquiet,
his independence sounds a stream
of gleeful public pee.

Kathleen Grove Scott

In My Heart

In my heart, the love I had for you will always be there.
Because in my heart, you know I'll always care.
In my heart, I often sometimes cry
Because in my heart, I miss you more as the days go by.

In my heart, sometimes it aches so very much!
Because in my heart, I miss your gentle and loving touch
In my heart, I know you are feeling Glorious and Grand!
Because in my heart I know you are in God's hands!

In my heart, I know from above with your eyes you can see
Because in my heart, I can feel the warmth of your love surround me!
In my heart, sometimes it's hard to go on without you but I do.
Because in my heart, I know you would want me to be strong just like you!

In my heart, when I sleep my heart, mind and soul are at ease.
Because in my heart, I know your heart, mind and soul are at peace.

Byron Miller

Matthew's Vacation

I asked God about a year ago or so ago
　If my time was due to take a vacation.
He smiled, and said, "When it's time, I'll let you know—
　And I'll let you pick your own relation.

It seemed like months and months that I looked around.
　God made so many nice people everywhere!
I looked at Moorhead — my Mom and Dad were found!
　Six months ago God said, "Go now - and - take care."

My Mom is Linda - and my Dad's name is Doug.
　Grandmas and grandpas and aunts and uncles too!
And do you know what?　Grandma K. sure can hug!
　To make them laugh - all I do is Coo!

I hated to tell them my visit was to end.
　"Come, little Angel Matthew," I heard God say.
Maybe some day I can arrange to help send
　A brother or sister for a longer stay.

Will you tell my sitter I just fell asleep?
　I love you all — I'll miss the whole relation.
The hurt will pass — and you can smile — not weep!
　'Cuz, that was the bestest of all vacations!!!!"

　　Jeanie Brennan

My Silent Alarms

I have often been told that a watchdog would be,
　The very best way to protect little me.
But how could they know of the secret weapon I have,
　One is named Buddy and the other is Sir Galahad.
They're my silent alarms with whiskers and fur,
　Too small to catch criminals, but deadly with birds.
The interesting thing is that when I'm alone,
　Not a sound goes undetected with "the boys" guarding my home.
Cause suddenly they "snap to" with wide-eye distress,
　Letting me know there is something amiss.
Forewarned and forearmed we all sit around,
　Trying to hear noises, not making a sound.
And when their eyes droop and their tails stop to flutter,
　I breathe a sigh of relief, and still, no word had been uttered.
And when someone speaks up and says a dog is man's best friend,
　I just smile and think of my two silent alarms,
Always ready, prepared to defend.

　　Mary Elizabeth Sheffield

The Rose

She stands there so silently not moving a bit.
She is so beautiful
She just arose from her long sleep
She yawns and stretches when she sees the sun
She waits for her friends to come.
She just stands there,
silently waiting.
When time passes, she suddenly feels weak.
She droops her head low,
　as if she's bowing.
It seemed like an eternity.
Her hands get hard and dry.
I guess she's tired again.
She goes back to sleep, waiting for the warmness
　of the spring sun, once again.

　　Sharifa Diaz

"New Year's Eve"

Snowflakes on branches and icicles on rooftops.
Stars shine through darkness and show prints are everywhere.
Inside the tree lights flash on and off quickly.
Gold hearts and red tinsel shine in the night.
Family being together brings forth such a feeling
of joy, love and warmth.

Eating and drinking
and giggling and smiling,
hugging and kissing
and talking and whining.

While piles of glistening snow
pours out from the sky.
Outside there's a chill that stings
ones face and ones eyes.

There's much excitement and anticipation
of waiting for midnight and the grand celebration.
The time is ticking away
and a New Year begins... 1996.

　　Patricia Refugio Holguin

Serenity Prayer For Parents

Oh Lord let me glide and flow with the tide
As my teaching days are swiftly passing me by
The markings on their minds are indelible, I hope,
That which I tried to impress is now behind.

You have made us each different and unique as we are
It is not easy to watch each slowly drift apart.
We must hold tight to the memories we share
and never forget our love's in Your care.

The world is so vast, there's so much to explore
With the ships that sail or the planes that soar.
It's endless, it's breathtaking for them to behold
Each child's dream will soon lead him onto the path
　where he's called.

Whether they stay or whether they go,
You have shown us "The Way, The Truth, and The LIGHT"
Now together we stand, your strength is our need
Whilst one by one You'll guide each off in their near
　or distant flight.

　　Priscilla M. Krivitz

Balsam Flowers

In many, many bygone years
My aunt's eyes were full of tears
My cousin's fingernails were crimson
Many balsam flowers were in full bloom

When the balsam withered
My cousin got married
And my aunt got a son finally
The moon in the court was beaming brightly

When frogs were croaking
I wandered off from home again
To an unknown land to browse
Ever longing for the balsam flowers

Now when frogs are croaking again
What am I searching for alone...
Am I going to roam the world over...
But may the balsams bloom for ever

　　John Y. Sohn

Angel's Blue Sweater

Angel has a sweater which is dark blue.
It was her great grandmother's, this is true.
She wears it — oh — every once in a while,
And it goes so very nice with her smile.

It's the prettiest sweater, although it's not new.
Why she doesn't wear it more, I don't have a clue.
It's so full of magic, just like herself,
I wonder, did it once belong to a good elf?

It's darker than the ocean, and also the sky,
But more beautiful than both, and I know why.
It belongs to someone more precious than gold,
And if she keeps it always it will never grow old.

It's a sweater that only Angel should wear,
For with anyone else, would never form a pair!
Whenever she wears it I think oh-my.
It looks so nice on her that I simply must sigh.

Jerry R. Tindal

Influence

Modern conveniences she never had
She washed our clothes by hand
Mother struggled for many years
Taking care of eight kids and her man

Mother felt her religion strongly
She was sure that Heaven waited
Her attempts to teach us right from wrong
Was persistent - and continued unabated

The night she lay on her final bed
No hope to ever recover
Her body was so weak - she could hardly speak
But we still got a smile from Mother

In the aftermath of her departure
Lay sorrow - tears - and pain
The years have come and gone
But the heartaches still remain

Should her children find success in life
And happiness in fulfilled dreams
We'll owe more than a little part
To Mother - and her genes

Billy W. Lang

Laurie

When first we met I asked you to give
me your pinky.

You asked why.

I said "it's a pinky wish"

You just smiled in your own cute way,
and put your Pinky out to me.

As I took it I said "Someday I might get
lucky enough to have the rest of your hand."

Now, my dreams are becoming a reality.
When I lift your vale today I will
awaken my princess and give angel
wing's to my heart and your's

True love is a treasure seldom found

I have found that treasure in you
my Princess

Brian Keith Holman

The Beach

The beach, what a tranquil visualizing
sight. The cool breeze sweeps you in a
crying swoosh. Resisting in irresistible. Your
hair blows in the superb light of dawn. Skimming
on this smooth surface bring's consensus
moments of sensational respite all over again.
The feminine side releases into the shallow.
Sea crabs scatters to the cackle of sea shells.
Reliving the moment of expectation happens
momentarily. The beach, so frequently in motion
captures the soul within.

Jahmarle A. Greene

"Melting Pot"

In the waking hours of night
When heavens cease their eternal light
And God almighty lies in spite
A curse sets in that's bound below.

For the hatred, war, and bleeding
Curse to scourge the needless needing
And to life its sin impeding
A curse for all mankind to know.

Its birth became what had to be
What mankind's sight failed to see
For the inflictor life's a small fee
Ignorance is the seed which bears its fruit.

Shackled and drudged by oblivious chains
In this land where carnage reins
Suffering through life's solemn pains
Peace and love are its pillaged loot.

This taker of life who hides within
Whose eyes see the different blend in sin
Bears no color, tint, or skin
And plagues the world with its Hate.

Ryan J. Lewis

The Plea

Sinners of this wicked world, why do you turn away?
    Do you not believe the things you hear and see each day?
You sinners live from day to day, no memory of Christ's name,
    When he should be the answer to the things you can't explain.
He heals the stricken baby, and makes the blind man see,
    And hearing to the deaf man, and churches to the free,
Why do not believe the words the Bible tell so dear,
    Of things already passed, and of others, oh, so near.
For judgement day is coming, but, yea, I know not when,
    As I am but his angel, yes, from heaven I descend.
I'm pleading and I'm begging, please, sinner, change your ways,
    With fire ad fury close at hand, be saved before that day.
If you still do not believe the things that I have told,
    May God in heaven me, have mercy on your soul.

J. W. Kemp

Untitled

I was sitting thinking, hot and stinking,
About the blizzard way up North.
The weather man stood, his teeth a clenching,
In two feet of white stuff, snow of course.

Than the picture changed to a different stage,
A tornado was knocking on my front door.
As it beat the house with a terrible rage,
I yearned for the snow, just once more.

J. Carlton Moorcroft

The Crossing

Poised like a ballerina,
In that infinite moment of the soul's longing
When fortune flashes on the tips of my fingers
And power arcs the night like lightening,
I move out onto the ropes uncertain,
Feeling the gravity of the decisions,
My heart spinning over and over
As destiny turns on the toss of a dime.

What awaits me at the close of this crossing?
Can I cross, if I look up and see only solitary sky?
Will I freeze, if I listen to the melange of voices below?
I close my eyes and just begin the dance
In the way of all beginnings — with one tenuous step
Awaiting the gift of trust in outcomes unknown.

Then life moves me.
One foot swift in front of the other.
And as the terrain shifts beneath me, I know
I will not fear again in this incarnation and nothing,
Nothing will ever be the same as the footfalls
Of my crossing echo into tomorrow.

Diane-Marie Blinn

Sonnet One

Always too hard to reach
like the ripest apple clinging
tightly to its branch. For when I search
my love has gone. Leaving me waiting
and longing to have someone close
everywhere I can see other's true love
never have I asked for the most
just someone to call of
I'm told that out there somewhere
there's another just like me
who has been waiting to hear
of a love that will always be
I've felt too much pain
true love, I have yet to attain.

Dawn Wertman

Lost Time

You said you loved me before,
then you just walked out the door.
God, I loved you so,
and was forced to let go.
I always thought wed be together,
then you left and I thought it was forever.
Now your back in my life,
I want you but gotta think twice.
I don't want to get hurt again,
can you promise we'll never end?
So, give me sometime,
cause my hearts on the line.
A lot of time has gone by.
I missed you so, so hard I cried.
So, here you are at last,
and now I think of our past.
We have a lot of catching up to do,
give us awhile will catch up me and you.

Sherry Freas

A Conversation With An Angel

I miss you girl, you being gone
    Has changed my whole world
It's hard to explain the way that I feel
    Sometimes my head spins out of control
Just like a spinning wheel
I think about your mother
I think about your dad
I think about the precious wonderful
    Times that we had
I'm very angry at him Liz
But the Lord says that
    Vengeance is his
Your birthday is coming up
    You would have been thirty four
Celebrated with the angles Elizabeth
    And when I get there
We'll celebrated some more
    I miss you girl...

Jeanne Brock Martin

Untitled

Tuesday, January 28th, 1986,
"Full throttle up" the command.

In a moment, in a twinkling of an eye,
An explosion, fire and smoke ripped the sky.

The U.S. challenge was gone.
It carried five men, two women along.

It all vanished, we know not where.
There before our eyes, up in the air.

1st Corinthians 15:52 states:
In a moment, in the twinkling of an eye, dead and alive
Shall be caught up to meet Jesus in the air.
With a loud shout and last trump all will be there.

In a twinkling all will be changed,
As in a twinkling the challenger was changed.

I wonder if Almighty God gave us a picture
Of the rapture sometime soon or in the future.

The shouts, the command,
The challenge would never land.

All vanished as if it has never been
Likewise the raptured saints will never be seen again.

Irma J. Straub

"Autumn Beauty"

  When Autumn sheds her leaves of gold
Oh! What beauty to behold! With every little
gentle breeze; they fall so graciously from the trees..

  From the highest mountain, or lowest vale.
So many colors, no one can tell; just stand in
awe and try to describe the serene and beauty
falling everywhere...

  Even when the last leaves are sheds, there
is still beauty just ahead..... with children
laughing and squealing with glee, watching the
snowflakes drifting through the trees...

  We know by the stillness in the air..
that winter is here with her frosty glare..
Then comes spring again once more, pushing
little flowers through summer's green moores!

  The season's come and go so fast, makes one
wish they could forever last! But if there
were no changes for us to enjoy.... then
autumn would be just another tomorrow!

Ruth E. Light

I Dreamed About Daddy Last Night

We first noticed Daddy's illness in 1962.
It was hardening of the arteries.
There wasn't much they could do.

He didn't remember things we talked about, as early as yesterday.
But something that happened 50 years ago,
To him, was clear as day.

Well, daddy died in 1964.
The last time I saw him was when they closed the casket door.

The other right I was dreaming Daddy just appeared.
We had so much to talk about.
It had been over thirty years.

I told him how he would love this place;
How I missed him all the time.
And when I work the garden, he is always on my mind.

I walked right up and hugged him.
There was a smile on his face.
Now in my dreams at sixty-two, finally, we embrace.

They say a picture's worth a thousand words.
Well, I think dreams are, too.
Cause when you dream of loved ones, they seem so real and true.

Kenneth W. Harp

Unreachable Goal

My heart races with excitement.
The thrill of victory, the agony of defeat.
Voices pierce the air,
Yelling, screaming, unforgettable words.
Running far, far away,
Away from the pain.

Silence is restored once again,
The salty taste of tears,
Silent sobs,
Years of yearning,
Yearning for that one thing,
That one thing that seems so close, yet so far away,
Peace

Erika Hofe

"Yesterday"

Growing up I have always felt awkward when I told
someone about my father and they came back with
an I'm so sorry, how is a person supposed to
respond to that?
  I found out yesterday...
I've often wondered how a widow with small
children manages to tell them that their father died.
  I found out yesterday...
I've heard of our soldiers being killed in action,
dying on our highways and I've thought of how I
would react to such an awful crises.
  I found out yesterday...
Because yesterday, I heard many I'm so sorry's,
yesterday, I was the widow who told her children
that their father died, yesterday, I handled the
biggest crises of my life, because yesterday, my
soldier, the dearest man in my life, died, yesterday.

Marybeth Barker

"Why Oh Why?"

We spent our whole life together,
before God took you away.
The question I ask now is,
why did he want me to stay?
I can't seem to do anything with you gone,
because we were both as one.
If I wanted to call, you called me first,
if you wanted water, I quenched your thirst.

Our friends are sweet and they do try,
I pray and pray, but I still cry.
You are not there to hold me tight,
so I lay awake all through the night.

Dear God in heaven above,
you took away my true love,
so give me the answer,
if you can today,
to the question I ask,
why do you want me to stay?

Jeanne Tremer

A Christmas Wish

Christmas doesn't have to be
Presents piled high, under a big fir tree
With glitz and glitter so brightly adorned
We forget that it's to celebrate the day that Christ was born

And I don't need a magnificent feast
With all the trimmings and tasty treats
I'd rather see some other reasons
To celebrate the holiday seasons

I'd like to see people all offering a hand
Hearts shining brightly throughout every land
Lending a shoulder and drying a tear
Holding on tight to dispel loneliness and fear

I'd like to see people, all colors and creeds
Working on solutions to each others needs
Giving up prejudice, selfishness, greeds
Living and sharing with peace, hope and dreams.

Nora Graner-White

Untitled

When you are in need of a friend
someone in whom you can rely
A good neighbor can be your best bet
and that's something that money can't buy

A warm friendly greeting is essential
to send a message his way
That you too are a good neighbor
with only the best things to say

We must forgive our shortcomings
in lifes rapid changing course
And remember only the good that is done
in this way only, can we allay remorse

So let's go out and make a new friend
"A friend-in-need, is "A friend indeed" they say
You may be lucky and find a good neighbor
in your neighborhood-just a few doors away

Don't say, I should have - just do it!
you may be very surprised in the end
He too sought to find a good neighbor
and also to make a good friend

Alfred T. Masch

"Twenty Years In The Past"

They say Vietnam's over, it's twenty years past
They say you done your duty, and war is twenty years past
It's time to let go of twenty years of the past
They say be proud, your a vet, twenty years have past
You done your best for now it's time to rest
Vietnam may be twenty years in the past
But our twenty years of hell is not in the past
For our peace just don't last, can't believe twenty years have passed
The memories and horror seem it's just yesterday
The smell of a spring rain can bring back so much pain
The loss of three cousins and good childhood friends
Among the 60,000 names of twenty years of past
The pop of a firecracker or the flight of a chopper
Our eyes go searching for things twenty years in the past
On a calm winter night oh such a good deep sleep
A blast from the past we're in cold sweats
From a firefight of twenty years past
All this unrest and heavy hearts
Even today we're still not accepted
Are you sure Vietnam is twenty years in the past

Steven J. Simpson

A Loving Father

He was a handsome fellow; strong and brave and true.
All the neighbors needed him to do a thing or two.
The county's only blacksmith with muscles to abound
While receiving honors for growing cotton from the ground.

He could build a house to stand through any kind of wind.
And worked hour after hour running the county cotton gin.
With all his accomplishments he still had time to be
A little girl's loving father; so proud of him was she.

He rode her on his tractor; bounced her on his knee.
Carried her on his shoulders so farther she could see.
Always there in time of need as ages moved along.
This loving father, so brave and true and oh so very strong.

His steps a little slower; his eyes a little dim.
Twas a happy moment with the grand children 'round him.
He could still make them chuckle or clap their hands with glee.
As he told them his stories and bounced them on his knee.

With a smile on his lips; a twinkle in his eye
His thoughts of a reunion with loved ones in the sky.
He's gone to be with Jesus and the one he loved so dear,
But all the fond memories will ever linger near.

Christene C. Blaylock

"My Dad Is Thinking About Leaving"

My dad is thinking about leaving,
It's scaring me to death.
My dad is thinking about leaving,
and I'm saving my last breath.
My heart is breaking, Can't he see?
Doesn't he even care about me?
I've cried all day, then arose a thought,
Why, all needs in his heart is God.
Why doesn't he care about how I feel?
This isn't a nightmare, it's very real!
Why isn't anything going swell?
Doesn't he know I'm going through HELL?
I hope and pray everyday,
That somehow I will find a way,
To keep my daddy hanging on,
and make sure that he'll not be gone.
I love my daddy, Can't he see,
What all of this is doing to me?

Lisa Marie Buckner

The Clipper Ship

Around the horn in the early morn
Sailed the three masted ship,
All sails were out as she came about
Through the water, how easy she slipped.
Long and sleek and made of teak
A clipper, who rode so proud,
All sails unfurled, she sailed the world
Carrying freight to a waiting crowd.
Up the coast, faster than most
She carried 'Frisco's mail,
With salt and beans and mining machines
And '49ers lining the rail.
She docked at night in the harbor's light
Her deck were emptied fast,
With a load of gold now in her hold,
Back around the horn she passed.
Over miles untold, laden with gold
At last she was headed home,
At Boston town, her home renoun
She docked, at last, at home.

Larry Crowell

Hidden Passages

To Mom and Dad

The old chest passed down through generations
Filled with pictures and lace
Expressions of loved ones left upon each face

Treasured through the years
With loving care and grace,
Memories of treasures shared
Of hidden passages in time
That have not been erased.

The old chest sachets of fragrance filled the air
of presence of loved one's surrounded
Still there
Homemade rugs, quilts, music boxes, wooden toys,
Building blocks, poetry and songs,
In times of slower pace

As picked up through the genes
Her eyes, her smile, his nose, his voice
Like Mommy's like Daddy's, like grandma's and great grandpa's

And the works of art
God has gifted each one down in line
Shows and shares the hidden passages of time

Faye Ann Hirvi

Operation Desert Storm

At first it was Operation Desert Shield,
Then it became Operation Desert Storm,
Led by General Schwarzkopf —
Known to some as Stormin' Norm.
Five-hundred-thousand American troops,
Plus allied support from around th world,
Fought in the sands of the Persian Gulf
To free Kuwait from Iraq's peril.
Around-the-clock air attacks caused great devastation
To the Iraqi troops and their whole Arab Nation.
America's Patriot Missiles destroyed the Iraqi Scuds,
And the "Mother-of-all wars," predicted by Saddam Hussein,
Brought great destruction to his oil-rich domain.
But praise be to God! For he answered the prayers
Of those who sought peace everywhere.
The war was soon over... the victory won!
And the troops have returned safely home.
With casualities so few and morale so strong
Praise be to God all the day long!

Joni C. Massey

Isaac

All alone - my thoughts and hopes become dimmer
As the life inside me grows more each day
so does the sorrow
still young, with a lifetime to go
so much left to experience - now only one
destination lies ahead...
Love promised for eternity - has changed to resentment
goals for a future - now only a memory
parents that were proud - overcome by embarrassment
applications to colleges - cast into my trash bin
friends having fun - while morning sickness engulfes me
dreams of a white wedding - turn to nightmares of a shotgun wedding
the honeymoon to Hawaii - will be a trip to the delivery room
oh God, will I ever get through this?
The life inside me, growing each day, unaware the pain he causes
unaware of a father who doesn't want him
and unaware of the struggle it will take to keep him
your name is "Isaac" because I know
you'll give me the laughter and happiness
I've always wanted... I love you.

Amber Ward

The Signs Of Summer

The breeze is warm, yet moist to the skin,
The air is still and the clouds are moving in.
The daylight is longer and darkness is short,
I love the summer days of this sort.

The sound of the creatures all lively and aware
Are enough to make you realize the wide world out there.
The smell of fresh cut grass, the sounds of the childs laugh,
And flowers in bloom with no signs of doom.

The gray and gloom of winter is gone,
Although we thought it'd last all year long.
And suddenly when you couldn't take anymore snow
The signs of summer begin to show.

How long will it last? Not long enough for me!
Summer all year long is what I'd like to see.

We absorb the greenery and flowers that surround us here,
And hope that we'll remember it until the same time next year.

Carrie Eileen Campbell

Alone I Walk The World

I walk the world alone
Through today, tomorrow, and yesterday.
I know its ways, but not well enough.
I know its sorrows all too well.

Its sorrows are all too many; its joys, are all too few
Killings, massacres, wars galore; morals gone - the world no more.
A candle is burning,
When it goes out, the wick smokes and furls.

The candle is helpless, defenseless.
One person gives it life,
Another takes life away.
The candle is helpless, defenseless.

The candle is like the children of the world.
Helpless, defenseless.
One person gives a child life,
Another takes it away.

I walk the world alone
Through today, tomorrow, and yesterday.
I know its ways, but not well enough.
I know its sorrows all too well.

Gina Danielle Toto

Grandma

All grandmas are sweet.
All grandmas are kind.
Some grandmas are spunky, (like a peacock)
And like to drink wine.

There is one grandma,
Who stands out from the rest.
True, her name is Boring,
But she's clearly the best!

When deadlines are close,
And we are in need, she comes to the rescue,
And does her good deed.

She'd 76, but it doesn't show,
Cause when a grandchild needs help,
She's run through the snow.

When the government shuts down,
She drives into town.

And when you think she might lose,
She shows up on the news!

What would I do? I'd go insane,
If it wasn't for her, I'd miss the plane!

Amy Boring

The Ocean

Waves rolling upon the beach,
splashing ever softly,
wonders underneath to reach,
clear as glass,
pure as the earth,
my words shall flow with the water,
and deep beneath the surface,
with tides rolling in and out,
the real wonders of the sea shall roll before us,
beautiful marine fish,
streaming tails like silk scarfs flowing behind them,
otters with their satin fur,
everyone working together,
like another earth,
forgotten and peaceful,
waters glistening in the sunset,
reflecting the dying sun,
if only earth could be so wonderful.

Christina Gargiullo

Strangers Are The Best Critics

Someday soon, I shall fall.
I shall fall from atop my perch.
I can hear in the distance someone is singing,
beckoning me, but the name she sings is not my name.
She is calling me home but I don't know where home is
and they don't even know my real name.

Some day soon, I shall digest
the parts of me that are not real.
My poet's heart and my lyricist's soul
Will be extracted to make room
For be realist's liver and kidneys
and the analyst's mind and heart.
I will breathe with the lungs
of a man without dreams and I'll take on my life as it comes.

For some day long ago, I learned
that only poetic hearts get broken,
and the only pain that is truly real
is not in the verse at all.
The realist makes it in today's society,
while the poet gets eaten and the idealist gets digested.

Jared Kitchens

Blackhooded Gulls At Barnegat Light

I knew, I was in a gulls paradise this day
The moment the lighthouse loomed in the bay
Gulls fly to the land, gulls fly out to sea
Wherever I look, it is they I can see.
Gulls fold their wings into place when they land
Poise on the beach and walk on the sand
One provoking gull laughs at me
As his web feet shuffle a two or three.
Gulls line the fence posts like sentinel guards
Watchful scavengers sojourn from ship lane boulevards
Chattering noisily, they have much to say
Of their next scheduled flight out over the bay.

Nina Carol Vicar

The Tiger Lays At Night!!!

It lays at night
　　Beneath the slow mid sky.
　　　As a spite of fright creeps nearby,
　　　　But only a bright few pinches of light remained calmly,
　　　　　As the beast-like creature spies nearby!

Rachele Manning

Untitled

A front runner in life
　no regrets of the past
Looking forward beyond the stars
Reaching for a dream
Standing in a circle
　with no hatred, nor lies
Looking around feeling safe
A loved person loved by many-loved a many
So wondrous so full
No wonder you did not see
Thy stood alone beyond the circle in which you stood
Out in the world, looking in
With a blink of an eye thy was missed
Beauty lies within so one could not resist
To bad the world won't take a risk
　what the world wants most
Lie hidden outside thy circle
Look around, not for beauty but beauty in thy eyes
So lost in a world, thy could not become
　the meaning of love to be love in the world we must become

Erin Lance

My Mark

As you go through life you should hope to leave a mark.
Something that will shine as brightly as a spark.
Letting the world know you were truly here.
In your time spent on this special sphere.
Your mark should be set in more than stone.
Rather it be set in minds alone.
You may have already done it, but haven't read the score.
Your accomplishments may be many but how many will endure.
A mark on this world should be for one of spacial deeds.
One who fought for the rights of others and their needs.
One disagreeing without malice while keeping mind alert.
Knowing malice only leads to more, while getting someone hurt.
If I were to leave a mark it would have to be this advice.
Never make your mark in foolish things such as ice.
For most probably the memories will too finally melt.
And the world will only wonder how you really felt.

Richard G. Connors

Untitled

Leaves
Frail, colorful, crisp
Falling, spiraling
Swirling downward to the frozen ground
Frosty leaves crackle soft in children's gloved hands
Leafage

Lauren Sanders

A Christmas Forever

It was Christmas so long ago you see,
a special day for my two brothers and me.
We peeked under the door almost a fight.
To see who got the shining new bike.
A little train going around the tree,
for my dad and brothers, what a sight to see.
A new walking doll for a special little girl,
had my color hair, including the curl.
Our Grandma's and Grandpa, their love to share,
the aunts, uncles, and cousins were all there.
It's the birth of our savior, Jesus Christ,
a special day, and it's really nice.
It was the 50's, now 90's, and we still give a holler,
cause we were all born with me the proud name of "Mahler"

Judy Mahler Franklin

The Gray

The past haunts like a relentless ghost-
Uncertainties clear in the gray.
No black or white.
Tomorrow forever unknown-
The dawn brings the clean canvas.
The bright white of the undone present
Bounds in upon us-
Frightening all souls who dare to dream.
Untouchable wishes and hopes that crash -
The dark grows so easily.
Time heals all wounds-
Or so they say.
A soft velvet feeling of peace it should be.
Healing turns out to be forgetting-
Long enough to go on.
The canvas-gray in reality.
The dark forever hovering in the back.

Cheryl Fluke

A Moment In Time

Summer was half over when the beginning came.
No one knew or considered the consequences,
As sweltering love has a way of consuming
all rational thought, and time stops....
Autumn came and disappeared,
The secret now was known to some....
But winter revealed the news to the world
That even snow and frost were unable to keep hidden
In spring she came...
The golden child received a
Name of her own.

So unique is each life
As it plays out its own role... as in
a game of chess, a brand new king or queen
with friends and foes; challenges and goals
and an ever present family.
No one knows how it will end
But alas, someday it will... Poof

Virginia J. Hamshar

Magic Window

Take a look through the magic window
feel the illusion of what once was
as the wind blows through your hair
Taking with it all bad thoughts and memories,
only a blank stare, preparing to refill
with a new dare.
A peaceful and loving image appears
out beyond the stretched horizon
taking shape of shooting stars
realizing the magic window is just a
simple state of mind.

Roland Carrizales

Like An Eagle In Flight

Lord let me soar to the mountain top,
like an eagle in flight, up to
the mountain high.
Carry me Lord up high on eagle's wings,
up where the spirit soars.
Let me soar in the spirit; upon
the mountain top; up to the heavens high.
Let me run and not be weary.
Let me walk and not faint.
Like an eagle in flight soaring
up to the heavens high.

Marcia McAllister

"Answered Prayer"

Last night I tossed and turned
  and sleep refused to come.
With aching heart and spirit low
  I prayed to God to ease my pain.

With fevered brow and tearful eyes
  I dozed and dreamed of you.
From out the past you came to me
  and held me in your loving arms.

We spoke no words, I couldn't see your face
  But you were here, no doubt of that!
Your love surrounded me and eased my loneliness
  For God does answer prayer!

Though we are worlds apart your love still comforts me.
  I know we'll meet again some day,
And in this veil of tears you'll come to me again
  For God does answer prayer!

Penny Bowers

Untitled

Rumors aren't nothing but a bunch of lies
Like the rimers that make tears fall from my eyes
About a boy and a girl so deeply in love
A match made in heaven by angels above
Until the rival of the girl told a lie that meant diddle
A fight between both girls leaves the boy in the middle
In love with his mate and for the other no love at all
But she tries to force out our love so hatred will fall
She thinks she'll be mine when our love is through
But the jokes on her my love is invested in you
Locked in tight of the heart that only you own
Always and forever my love will be known
So when you're not sure if I still care
Look deep in your heart my love will always be there
Let me tell you a rumor that I promise is true
About the undying love I'll always have for you

D. J. Gentry

The Battle Within

Like the wind that rocks a ship upon a stormy sea,
there is a battle going on; deep inside of me.

I'd love to believe about the
place some people say we'll go,
a place with streets paved with gold, no worries or woe.

Yet these same people who
tell us of this place; this promise land;
they do things to people I just don't understand.

I know there's something out there;
something from which we came.
I know we have a creator of sorts, regardless of the name.

I feel there is a time set aside for all of us to go,
it happened the day we were born, only our creator knows.

Just as the wind keeps the clipper ship assail across the sea,
tis the breath of my creator that keeps the life in me.

I think the end will be as the calming of the sea;
the wind will cease to blow, the sun will be setting low,
my creator will reach out his hand and say;
come my child, it's time to go.

Juanita Bragg

Reflections

Wants and needs doesn't all boil to greed, wants and needs
Who'd believe, that you'd be deceived.
For filling what we believe all of us need
Wants and needs reflect on faces that we see on fast steeds,
Moving purposely thru arid and sometimes melancholy breezes.
Some apparent, some not, some wishing, what it is not.
Want and needs.

Derrick A. Capers

When Dickens Comes A Knocking

When Dickens comes a knocking
The whole world will hear,
A loud, hard knock
That influences us every year.
The ghost of christmas past
Will watch you through your life,
And when you least expect it
It will appear to you one night.
The Ghost of Christmas present
Will make you chuckle with delight
And the ghost of Christmas to come
Will scare you with fright.
So, if I were you I would be good all year,
Or the Ghosts of Christmas will come
And teach you Christmas cheer.

Stefanie Peters

"On Farm Bird And Vines"

Your red flight caught my eye
As you went swiftly by,
In my lonely solitude you came,
Bringing me joy,
When you were tame.
And purple morning glories in early dawn,
Waving your beauty from sun to sun,
Dressing my fiance many times,
While dew drop diamonds deck your climb.

Offie Parsons

Love Is....

Love is a flower when it blossom, a fragrance of beauty
beholds our sight.
Love is a morning sunrise, it brightens your day.
Love is a ocean wave, when the tides is low,
Love is pleasant and calm.
When the tide is high, love is exciting and passionate.
Love is a rainy day, the rain washes away the hurt and pain.
Love is a rainbow that appears full of radiant colors, that
makes the love of your life bright and high-rising above
anything else.
Love is a pink rose, the sight of softness reminds me of
your touch, that penetrates my heart, mind, body, and soul.
Love is a person, place, or thing, love is how you feel
deep inside your heart, and true love is ever-lasting and
unconditional.
Love is like a song, you may forget the words, but the
melody always stay in your heart and mind.

Violet Hall

The Garden

I planted my love a garden, filled with beautiful things.
But she refused to walk there, and enjoy the pleasures it could bring.

For somewhere she had walked in a garden, and been bitten by a snake.
Now she is wary of beauty, and fears repeating her mistake.

So I walk alone in this garden, and water it all with my tears.
I cannot convince her it is safe, I cannot weed out her fears.

Now I am alone in the garden, the one I created for her.
The fragrance and colors are wasted, her feelings of love they
can't stir.

I have become a prisoner of this garden, I can go no other place.
For wherever I go, I carry it with me, and her absence I cannot erase.

So I can but tend this dear garden, in hope she may someday come near.
As I wait and pray in her garden, I pray she may conquer her fear.

Bob Davidson

Born With A Halo

I was born with a halo, shiny and new
As I grew bigger, my halo did too
Full of innocence, was this heart of mine
But that all changed, in a matter of time
As I grew up, and became more aware
Of all the things, I could get into out there
Mom and Dad said for me to beware
Something inside of me, just didn't care
People, places, things I could do
Where I would start, nobody knew
It grew more exciting, as time went along
And much to much fun, to ever call wrong
Not paying attention, to this halo of mine
It no longer held, it's luster and shine
Tarnished, battered, broken too
Wouldn't you know it I ran out of glue
They say you slow down the older you get
I couldn't tell you I haven't gotten there yet

Tricia Martin

A Country Boy's Lament

Today will be yesterday, tomorrow.
Next week will be ten years without you.
We thought we'd put away the sorrow;
but, now, I know it isn't true.
You said you thought you loved another,
you had to leave to find the truth.
An 18 - wheeler stopped you're searching.
Now I'm just lonely and blue;
because, — (start again at top)

William E. Stoudt

Child Of Life...

While he waits upon his bed,
child's prayer not alive nor dead.
Seeing what can only be,
father of humanity.
Lights around the child that lie,
will he live or will he die?
Questioned truth on resting spot,
will it come true, the prayer he sought?
Brown eyes wait upon the day,
rise in air praise them who pray.
Machines won't help it may appear,
God will be your only cure.
When it's time wrap him in lace,
let heaven be his resting place.
But it's not your time you may not come,
your life on earth has just begun.

Jennifer Moretti

Ripples

As I sit here beneath the twinkling
of the stars and watch the waves upon
the water, I can hear you say
"I love you, my darling".

Yes, I can still hear you though the years
have gone by saying,
"Get the net, this is the
big one of the night."

I can see the glitter of your boat
as you try for that one last strike,
knowing, my darling, you have had
a good night, just riding the ripples
of the water on a starlit night.

The dawn is breaking
and I realize I was only dreaming,
as I wipe the ripples of water
from my eyes.

Velma Lake

Lord Give Me A Tender Heart

When my brother is blind and cannot see,
And he stumbles and falls and cries out to me.
May I show him the way in this world of sin.
May I hold out my hand to take him in.
Lord, give me a tender heart.
Lord, give ma a tender heart.

When my sister is crying and filled with fear,
And there's no one to care or to dry her tears.
May I hold out my hand in the stormy night.
May I lift, her up to the Master's light.
Lord, give me a tender heart.
Lord, give me a tender heart.

When a child is hungry and has no bread,
And his home is lost and his mother dead,
And there's no one to love him or to take him in,
May I hold him close in this world of sin.
Lord, give me a tender heart.
Lord, give me a tender heart.

Catherine Ashbaugh

"Grace"

What a beautiful thing to have grace.
For grace you are truly alive, you are really living.
With grace your whole life is so much richer,
    your outlook on life is so much brighter.
All things seem easier.
There is a peace that flows within you which no man can see but
    is aware of its presence there in.
Oh that all men may have this grace that gives you peace that
    we all long for and that which the world can not give.
For you to can receive this grace by lifting up your
    mind in prayer to God who gives grace freely to those who call
    on Him with a sincere heart and who are sorry for the wrong's
    in there life and want to start a new.
You to will share in this gift of grace if you just look up to God in
    prayer for he is waiting for you, for he loves you more than
    you could ever know.
Have faith and believe and you will feel that grace no man can
    see but is aware for its presence there in

Roland J. Crouch

Another World

    As I look at his face, I see a face that was seen by
most as stubborn old man, a man that thought his way or the
highway. But as the hour glass ran out of sand, I took a
closer look and I saw something else. A Grandfather that
needed not to give me money to make me happy, but a man who
always had time for me. He always had time for me to stay
with him in the summer. Time to play with me, and most
important time to be my friend.

    I sit here and wonder is he really gone, or is he just in
another world? I wonder why my hour glass ran out? I never
had time to play anymore, and now it's to late. I never had
time to be his friend. But I hope that people will see some of
him through me. He still is a friend that's gone, but not forgotten.

    I realize he is not in another world, but he is in my
world walking with me still. When the road gets rocky, he will
be there ready to catch if I fall as only a Grandfather can do
for a Grandson.

Jason Miller

Tears

What is a tear? Does anyone know?
Why they come, and where they go.

The color is always so crystal clear,
they say they come from within caused
by loneliness, pain, and fear.

Sometimes they come slowly, and sometime fast,
from happenings in the present, and thoughts from the past.

There are some that are happy, some are sad,
but never are there any that are shameful or bad...

From young and old, they come from many of such,
and even sometimes they come from a warm, loving,
and caring touch....

Tears? Yes they are very strange;
that is one gift, that time nor man will ever change.....

P. Diane Martin

Twenty Twenty

Ten-thirty's the time for a good look at you
for both the coming from and the heading to.

You look great, you feel young, your at your best
of course twenty-twenty can still pass the test.

Experience, that's what you have to offer
thirteen puts lots of that in the coffer.

Kids don't know good from bad from a catcher's mitt
forty knows the story, at least most of it.

Oh sure there are some times when things just go wrong
and fifty minus ten may just go along.

There are days when just getting up out of bed,
sixty minus twenty has aches in the head.

There's a struggle to get up and work to survive
seventy minus thirty's glad it's alive.

Ages can never do much about the past
and don't know how long the game will last.

Perspective and attitude both must be right
to age all enjoyment from morning till night.

James F. Rogers

Time

    A summers nigh eve has come to an end.
And the chilling winter's breath has just begin. I
struggle to keep myself warm at night, and the nightmares....
I've only started to fight.
When you left a whole new
world started for me. A world of fear, heartache,
and Broken dreams.
    Struggling to stay alive with only letters and
a hollow voice. A voice that can not show love, sympathy
or care by choice. How I wish you were near me in my
time of need. A life we started together, but ended
up in separate homes. How I hate this loneliness that
fills my heat, mind and soul. I keep the tears
and hurt inside. Knowing in my heart will be together
for the rest of our lives. But time is killing me
slowly day by day. So I'll just wait and pray.

Jamie Frizzell

Save Us From The Violence

Save us from the violence that sweeps across our land.
Stop the rage that seems to guide too many a hand.
Lead us back to You and peace to quiet the minds
That blindly rage on and on and so often cross the lines —
The lines of love and kindness and caring —
The lines of trust and decency and sharing.
Stop the random shootings and the senseless lootings,
The uncaring choices and the abusive voices.
Help us know that within us all lies the power
To end this reign of terror and the selfish cower.
Return us to prayer and love of Thee and our fellow man.
Save us from the violence that sweeps across our land.

Nanette LeMaster

"chelsea"

wrought iron, sidewalks and brick
dust and stadiums places I've never been
vines saturations
a life never lived
women violated
there, not men
hotel rooms
    cobblestones

brian samuel knutson

Old Friends Like Roses In The Snow

Life seems all wrong, my smiling is gone, as depression takes hold.
I wonder sometime, where is peace of mind, as I lose control.
Old friends come around, when life gets you down, to help you when you are feeling low.
When you need a friend, they will come back again, for old friendsare like roses in the snow.

Roses will bloom, when life is out of tune, in the coldest, deepest snow.
One came by today to spend time and pray, just when I needed him so.
Often my life with all of its strife, like a snow storm that never goes away.
And when I am feeling bad from the problem I've had, old friends
   drop by to spend the day.

Roses have thorns, they say. You can work right through them as you pray.
Through melted snow, roses will grow. Friends are like robins that sing.
Old friends are there, to lift you in prayer, adding color like roses in the spring.
Problems are growing while it is snowing, but friends are like roses in the snow.

   Don H. Tallison

Do You See A Rainbow?

Rainbows are a special thing. They appear as a background during the
daylight, glistening as they shine their beauty for all beholders to
see after a nice rain. Much like a special girl who out shines
all around her without revealing her beginning or end.

For a rainbow never starts and never ends, but represents the tears of
innocence with an array of colors: Red, blue, and yellow. All of
which are primary. The red signifies the warmth of love, while blue
represents the flow of emotions, and yellow defines the inner peace
which comes from within when we are together. While all colors may be
seen when I gaze at you, just a mix is all that is necessary for meto see the rainbow.
Although many only see it for a brief moment, that is all that needed for a lifetime.

All seems the same if one's eyes are not filled with the pigments
necessary to separate the colors. And especially sad is when onccan
only see shades of gray because it tends to disillusion their heart.
They only can see the peripheral of a person and not their true colors
The tears that come in that special moment are the pigments necessary
to separate the colors. Only the colors are the real feelings which
are always their but may be hidden depending on who is beholding.

The next time we behold each other please ask yourself:
Do I see the rainbow or do I see shades of gray?

   Robert Newberry

A Simple Question

Far in so many ways:
Distance — over lands; love — from the hands; thoughts — about a man
Yea — a man we say
Is there still love today? I wonder that often... often... does he?
Nay... at times — times of madness. Yeah... at times — times of sorrow
Sorrow to harsh to bear.
To look out there, a far — over the trees of green, lakes of blue
Will we ever see You
Another question to arise? Do we..do we want to see you?
We wonder,it is true,as I can see in the blue seas of my blood
I am sure he also sees wonder in my seas of hazel too
Our lives will go on either way
Whether we see you today or from the years of yesterday
Our souls will soar far above as eagles do — over the ocean blue.
There in so sibling rivalry... never here..nothing, not even despair
All that is here in our oceans blue, hazel and gray is the wonder of
the day...is it nay or yea?
We are both moving on with more...both joining others in '94.
One of us in the Spring and the other in the Fall.
Our lives will continue as new souls we'll bear.
Yours is dormant — with questions in there.

   Halle J. Nero

Getting By

Didn't ascend a towering tree
Couldn't cross the wildest sea
Never mounted the highest tower
Failed at growing the most luring flower

Ambition to me wasn't sent
But my time was most richly spent

   Albert Neil Steck

Untitled

For a girl named Tair,
Who lives very far from here.

Put your hand in the sea, as you stand on the sand.
Then than little drop of water that touched your hand,
Will cross the ocean and travel far
To the shore in Florida, where we are.

Then one morning, we'll walk on our beach,
And hold out our hands, and reach and reach
'Til we find that drop of water you touched,
Like a bridge of love from you to us.

   Louise Schwartz

Mother

I admire my mother,
Because she is like no other,
My mom reads me books,
She's a really good cook,

She's so special she loves me so,
She's like a present with a beautiful bow,

I love my mother she is so nice,
She's just like sugar and spice,
She's so pretty I don't know what to say,
She gets prettier every day,

My mom likes to bake,
Every birthday I help make cake,
My mother likes to read,
She always tries to succeed,

My mom likes to help me,
She's as pretty as she can be,
My mom likes April showers,
And beautiful flowers,
That's all I can say,
About my mother on this very beautiful day.

   Jason Christopher Peters

Legacy

Selfishly, living
beyond anyone's reach,
Feeding ducks from the dock,
Watching brim lengthen in the lake.
Carelessly, basking
In summer sun-filled gardens.
Sinking into cool waters at dark,
Watching for venus, waiting for Orion—
Learning the owl's secret night language—
Listening to muffled wail of the bobcat
Through symphony of tree frog.

Inherit experience—
Rewarding yourselves freely as bats at dusk,
flitting over waters, selfishly, swooping—
scooping up life in voracious gulps.

   Jan Evans

Isabel Dominicane

Honeysuckle lips sang softly with vigor. Rainbow eyes watched grace
place long thin stemmed flowers of swan - white with dim red love
transparent veins - into the soft avalanche hair of African friends.
Emperor, empress, counts, vampires, spirits, and swords feasted
around a dense mahogany dining table of gourds, fruits, brie,
wonderful breads, lamb; mushrooms, majesty, sorcery, MC 900 foot
Jesus, orchestra, classics: a mimicry of Greek God's. The rustic
room of cold cement was filled with scarlet velvets, silks, tapestries, pastries
Widows silently and calmly mourning; widows fornicating, drunk men
belching, screaming, sucking, frolicking, hibiscus narcissism opium
floral, tiled acid cackling weasels
These humans, as Victor Segalen brilliantly says of an artwork in
Paintings, "unfold the pathetic vulgar tale - in the guise of popular
heroics...." Such was Henry VIII and many others of sixteenth century
immorality. Volunteers of risk, pride, pridelessness, challenges of
the suggestion, rather than the challenger were possessed with the
liquid grape vine of rich drink
Plump woman, chandeliers, sweet breasts, and rocks penes - were
reinforced by a blackbird perched on an olive branch, pumping its flat
metal tail
"Price Alpert, come hither and make love to me darling." And he
replied full of breath and charming repression, "To bathe in lovely
beds of dew, honey, and milk with you would give me nothing more
than pure pleasure. And to watch your lips quiver..."
he then neared her flesh and said, "good bye."

Tara Cuccia

"Man Will Dominate Man"

On scarlet hills asunder lie, their thoughts and hopes and dreams did die,
O'er all the land lay a silent sigh, no longer hear their battle cry.

The white man came and saw and took, whatever he thought was good and look!
A beaded shoe, a fishing hook but especially - land.

The Indians heard the wild call, they fought the land belonged to all,
The old pine tree so proud, so tall, hear the gurgling splash of the waterfall.

How could mere man these things own? Not man who is made of flesh and bone,
Only are these things we use, a loan, to the chieftain's tribe this fact is known.
But those men whom we call civilized, deceived the Indians with their lies,
With notions of treaties as their guise, they stole what the Native American's prize.

Finally these people could stand no more, they remembered old stories and lore,
Of battles fought with pride, not gore, with that in mind they went to war.

But 'gainst bullets their arrows quickly fell, no longer could they go home and tell,
Their kin of conquests that turned out well, instead their wives heard a last death knell.

There are still members of this noble breed, of this battle their children now read,
But many more wars will they see, for "man will dominate man to his injury".

Korina Lois Flint

Love's Doors

Love has two doors: One small and wooden, the other hellacious and
made of iron. Many, will choose the easier path, and unlock the
wooden door.
But, in time, those many will only believe in a hollow love.
A love, that threatens the mind, the body, and the soul, with a pain
unlivable for any human. But, those who take the less taken path,
and unlock the iron door;
Those few will find a key to all their deepest desires. They,
will find a love pure and true; a love that restores the soul with
such perfection, that one might believe they were in heaven.
   But, sadly, in the end, there are those who will live their whole
lives without ever coming upon the two doors. Those, who know no
love, shall forever feel the love they lack. But, the love they
lack may be their only true salvation.

Connie N. Chavez

The Trail

It's just a path from the house to the pond,
through the woods and back in time,
To when children played and ran around,
And the dog was close behind.

It's peaceful here, and I like to watch
as the bunnies scurry home,
And a woodpecker knocks on a rotted tree,
while the birds sing me a song.

I'll stay here awhile on top of the hill,
while visions play on my mind.
Then I'll walk back down that path in the woods
And leave yesterday behind.

Priscilla Galeski

Marriage

A wedding band does not mean a thing,
Unless love and devotion in a marriage you bring.
Many a time things do not go right
Never, but never go to bed angry at night.
Be sure to accept your husband's family
In return he will respect yours - you will see!
Marriage is a two may street
Not a casual "Hello" when you meet.
Understand and compassion are part of the game
You show it to him - and he will show you the same.

Eva J. Bookman

Untitled

The night winds would tell me of you.
The chill would scare me.
But they'd whisper your name and I'd feel free.
I'd walk aimlessly towards them.
My body uncontrollable.
All I knew was you.
And with that on my mind I walked.
Walked.
The winds urging me on.
Taunting me with your smile.
HELL I had to go through to get to you.
But no matter.
I got through it.
And in the end you were in my arms.
Forever.
Never losing you.
Always loving you.

Birk Farnum

Struggling To Survive

Living with grief is more than I can bare
Waking up each morning knowing
    that my son won't be there
Yes my memories are my treasures mine forever to keep
But those memories aren't enough
    and I still begin to weep

The hours go by while I'm busy at work
Then I stop for a moment and I begin to hurt

No matter what support
    and family members are by my side
No one can feel my loss I've bottled up inside
My loss to me is something that only I can feel
Nothing in this lifetime could ever come close to heal

Beneath this stone my son doth lie
He now rest in peace and never-ever will I
    Struggling to survive

L. Wayne Ochoa

Priceless Legacy

Wealth and gifts of money and gold, I did not receive as heir
Nor stocks and bonds or mutual fund, nor estates to divide or share.

My dad was poor if measured by wealth,
    and never a learned Rhodes scholar
But the gift of honor and truth that he left,
    would match dividends dollar for dollar.

Though my mother possessed no minks or furs,
    but purchased her clothes on sale
I continue to have her quite grace, long after the savings and loans field.

The world owes you nothing so use what you have,
    is what my parents always said
Learn to develop a relationship that endures,
    long after your treasures are gone.
Don't blame the world for things you control,
    is the word that passed through our home
If you reach for the stars and fallow your heart, you will never be left alone.

All is not fair but you don't make the rules, so pursue the things you can change
And be willing to risk being unorthodox, and considered by some to be strange.

You are who you are you make your own choices,
    you turns at the fork of the road
When you are at peace with the person within, you'll have
    found the treasured mother-lode.

And finally instead of a name of renown,
    on a hospital or university hall I've received
a lifetime of memories of love, the most treasured legacy of all.

Ruby L. Burney

An Ashtray's Life....

The puff floats through the air-like smoke, it really stings my eyes.
Yet people repeat it as though it's a joke. I wish I could ask them why.
Then they tap ashes, upon my head, oh why can't they let me be?
I'll burn, I'll flame, and soon be dead, just open your eyes and see.

Day after day I watch people smoke, doing it as though it's death or life.
Bringing themselves closer to when they will croak, it would be
    quicker to just use a knife.
They're also to selfish-to even have thought, that their smoking could
    be hurting me.
Not to mention the money they've spent on packs that they've bought,
    just open your eyes and see.

To end this wretched thing would be a hit, although I doubt it would
    ever come true.
People say it's very hard to quit, look in the mirror — it's all up to you.
I'm longing for smoke free world, it's something I wish we all could see.
I hope that one day it will happen, but for now just open your eyes
    and see.

Kavita Seth

I Have Lived It True

Oh, Lord; I have lived it true; to get close to you. Without any
kind of feeling that makes up a normal mind.
    They look at me and see inside the hell I paid with my pride and
the soul inside.
    It shows on me like the raw on my hide. The way I lived and the
way I crawled to get to where the good LORD, calls. To me; and here
is what was said.
    The only way to get back here is the way I say and the way I
clear for you to go. And to waste away is to go back to where you pay for
the crimes of life. Which only the Lord can take away. With the
hell in the mind with FIRE and the good Lords love of desire. Down deep
inside without any kind for a normal mind.
    I strode to take a righteous stand against all reason. Which
went, against the evil of my soul. When it feels like the ripping of the
fabric of my thoughts. Two worlds colliding in one world of thought.
There is no easy way; one or the other the evil or the good. One destroys one creates.

Eli Devich

Construction

If I could build the perfect man
I would build his heart with red rose petals
Delicate, passionate, sensitive
I would build his mind with marble
Pure, strong, traditional
I would build his soul with water
Soothing, changing, cleansing
I would build his testimony with gold
Durable, everlasting, perfectible
If I created the perfect man.

Barbara Gayle Babylon

The Lighthouse

We discovered the beach
Guarding the lighthouse
It flashed a warning to us
Beware . . . pause . . . beware
Love lies ahead
The stars became instigators
The surf, a pounding aria
Of undeclared love
Aware of my vulnerability
You made me aware of you
Your salty kiss descended to my lips
Gentle as the circling fog
The sea joined our celebration
Sending its mist to embrace us
The lighthouse beam carried the message
For twenty-six nautical miles
Love is here . . . pause . . . love is here

A. Frances

Weeping Willow

When the weeping willow weeps
    and its silent tears fall to the ground,
Like a crying child in the night,
    with no one to hear, does it make a sound?
With every picture painted
    a thousand words will speak,
But they're never actually heard,
    like when the weeping willow weeps.

Melissa A. Beatty

Believe

If God can take the crimson stain,
    And wash it white as driven snow;
Why then should I in sin remain,
    Since worldly folly brought me low?

If God can by His Word command,
    The night to yield to golden day;
Can I not on his promise stand,
    When labor's fruits in ashes lay?

If God observes the sparrow's fall,
    And clothes the lily of the field;
Can I not trust to him my all,
    E'en tho' the future seems concealed?

Since all these things of Him are true,
    And naught of faith shall be denied;
Can I not trust that He will do,
    The thing for which my heart has cried?

Believe, my soul, trust in His word,
    Take up faith's shield, and Spirit's sword;
The trusting soul knows no defeat,
    There's vict'ry 'round the Mercy Seat.

Willard J. Van Dree

Thoughts At The Wall

We were the finest, America's youth
We came from far and wide
We asked not what our country could do for us
We answered when duty called
We chose to serve our country
We went when the president ordered
We fought with bravery and honor
We bled our life's blood for the cause
We suffered in cruel prisons
We died when required
We endured the wrath and scorn of the ungrateful
We saw our sacrifices given away
We are consumed with frustration and rage
WE ponder how those who did this to us sleep
We weep bitter tears for our fallen
We pray it will not happen again
We will forget.....NEVER

William Jerry Upshaw Jr.

Change

As the mid-summer moon casts its glow upon the orchards,
A wind begins to stir. The lush, green leaves
Transform into autumns majestic
   Scenery.
Harvest-time crops disappear
Only to make their appearance sooner than man
   Expects.
The changing wind arrives on cue
To howl a loud note of winter. Then, while the end of the
White, blustery confetti tumbles to join its forerunners, the
   Changing
Wind brings drops of transparent moisture.
Tiny blossoms spring
From the
Unfamiliar patches of visible, green springs. The mid-summer
Moon will once again evolve and the
   Feelings
Of change will once more be relived
By those who understand, accept, and make memories of them.
   Change.

Erin Elizabeth Schneider

Life Without Life

You said you'd stand by me through thick and thin,
But left as soon as I had a life within.
Too scared to raise a babe alone,
I rid myself of the seed you'd sown.
Guilt over myself made battlefield,
I cry for the life that I have killed.
I hope that God will understand,
Why I took that life with my own hand.
With God's blessing and our love, we did create
The same subject that the courts debate.
At the time I killed, I did not know,
That a mere operation could give such a blow.
I feel empty, shallow, and so cold
My body young, my spirit old.
I wish now I had not chosen this way,
But life goes on, or so they say.
I just wish I didn't have to face it everyday.

Audra Hough

Time

Time goes forward and never back
It's like a train on its track
It leaves you wondering if you're late
All because of realities fate
I've always wondered what time really means
If it's truly reality or just in your dreams

Kim Arsenault

Trails

A honey-haired darling at Daddy's knee
Is out in the snow, pacing games from our tree.
Her breath, measured puffs, charts her energy spent
And small drifts of snow is a treasure-trail meant.

Some forty fractions of an hour will pass.
The snow design fades as the trails amass.
The doll-child turns from her latest trail crossed
And gazes at crystals ablaze in the frost.

A surge of emotion, her life is so sweet.
This day in the future, my memory will meet.
How precious the thought when my sweetheart has grown,
Loving fox-and-geese trails from a child of her own.

Jim Keech

Thank You Father For The Children

Thank you Father for the children
   so innocent and sweet.
Thank you Father for their lives,
   because they made our lives complete.
Thank you Father that your Angels
   had and still have charge over them.
Thank you Father that we will soon
   see them again.
Thank you Father that these
   little ones so fair, will always
   know how much we loved them
   and will forever care.
Thank you Father for keeping them
   and holding them under your wings.
   While around them, your Angels sing.
Thank you Father for these children
   that touched our lives and for all
   the children of this Nation.
They are all your precious creation.

Elizabeth E. Pittman

History Re-Al (Reeal)

To America the Mayflower brought one hundred and two
But Galleons deposited thousands, more than a few
With pride we claim lineage of the one hundred and two
But deny blood ties with the thousands, more than a few
My truth, your truth and the truth is our history re-al.

Vagabonds, vagrants, felons and neer do wells
Are our ancestors, a truth upon which we neer will dwell
Bondsman, slave, indentured, serf, to the master were all equal
Half breed, mulatto, quadroon, mestizo, all an american original
My truth, your truth and the truth is our history re-al.

One people, one nation under God, the slogan says
How true, but so few, admit the errors of our ways
We celebrate and laud, the glory of our two hundred years
But forget the misery, the poverty and the ocean of tears
My truth, your truth and the truth is our history re-al.

To appease, to cleanse our souls, to redeem our lives
Millions more must march, together with our wives
And trace our children, despite the color of skin or eyes
And proclaim to the world, we are one, it is our lives
My truth, your truth and the truth is our history re-al.

Rupert Marques

Untitled

There are lots of girls, but none like you
to me your the most glamourous, intelligent
and beautiful to, I can't help it that your
so fine, I love you, I love you, and wish
you were mine.

Newton Toney Jr.

Thoughts

Life, death, love and hate are all the same.
Forget the world and love
the cross to me is just a game.
Time to love and time to feel.

Why do we have the pressure of tomorrow?
As each day passes tomorrow is today.
What will become of me tomorrow,
will it be just like today?

In the quiet, unholy years of my life.
What will I be faced with?
Am I really here or am I
just a figment of His imagination?
Time is the best form of torture,
the cruel stopwatch of life.
It weighs me down like the world upon Atlas shoulders.

The credibility gap is bigger then expected.
They have brainwashed us into being
all activists in its fascist way of thinking.

Don't be sentimental, be efficient.
Beauty is only skin deep...

Alison Merritt

Oneself

One in self-companionship of confinement
Latitude in thoughts of attainable acknowledgements
Transcends the grandeur of reverberating expressions
Perpetuates beyond most superficial impressions.

Strength and courage flow in quiet solitude
Wisdom and perception invigorate with aptitude
Love and joy linger the course of heart
A consummation manifest in comfort and art.

Scope and magnitude blossom in oneself
Inspiration and devotion in loneliness are dealt
A preponderance within of the matter cherish
Exuberatese a dream, a hope, no perish.

Stride graciously with desire arbor
Amalgamate the ratified seclusion and exposure
Glow profusely into omnificent bountifulness.
A radiant life, a whole, a consciousness.

Drift confidently beyond self-contemplation sublime
Expound on the gratitude society stime
Wedge stilted within the fabric of its threshold
Participate and contribute fervently and bold.

Mahendra Persaud

Faith

Though you do not understand me,
Believe in me.
Though you can not see me,
Hear me.
Though I act in strange ways,
Don't lose faith in me.
Though my words seem foreign,
Listen.
Though you feel abandoned,
I am here.

Though you don't know what role you are to play,
Remember we are called upon in different ways.

Courtney Dunlevy

What Do You Know And What Does It Matter?

Do you know the happiness that one little smile can bring?
A smile given to a poor child, one who is cold and wonders why
He wonders why he has no food
He wonders why he doesn't have a home
He wonders where his parents went and when they're coming back
He wonders who has the answers, so he asks, but nobody knows
And yet there you are at home wondering why your hair
 looks like it does
Wondering what to wear while looking at a closet full of clothes
Do you ever think of others before thinking of yourself
If every time you thought of yourself, you thought of others
 3 times more...
I guarantee that you wouldn't think that you had any problems

Ana Almeida

Bullet

Eternity exploded in his face
 and he died in silent compliance.
Without objection, he quit this place
 at the request of sudden violence.

The adamant invitation was sent
 to a common "whom it must concern,"
Without an appending supplement
 that required reply or return.

Just before he died, he spread a sheet
 of claret red on the chilly ground,
Then he rearranged his hands and feet
 to ease the strain of the earthen-bound.

His conformation was superb
 when reconciled to the burial trench,
And the only hint that he died disturbed
 was the fist he forgot to unclench.

Stephen H. Keuchel

As It Is

To live as life has run
Since the tale of time begun
Existing never to die.
Laughing, loving, only to cry.
Live as it is

Flying, soaring, never ignoring the little things.
Picking, prying, at instances denying your very wants and needs.
Bringing. taking, awakening the feelings you conceal inside.
Faster, farther, around, higher souls fly.
Live as it is.

Dewan Keesee

My Love...

You have touched me with the truest
 emotions my heart has ever felt

You have made me tremble as your
 gentle caress has crossed my naked soul

You have reached in and taken hold
 of my love with such a burning
 passion it blazes into the actual
 depths of my entire being

You have lifted me with arms of
 tenderness and truth to unknown
 heights of ecstasy

You have shown me feelings in
 their purest form creating a
 sense of worth unmeasured
 by human understanding

Kimberly A. Haney

A Word From A Former Fool

A wise man knows what he is and what he is not, excepts
the reality of what he can be, knows his limits of go's and stops.

SEEKS council and instructions, correcting wrongs to right,
repenting in yonder years of night,

PONDERING over ancient wisdom, of where inspired
visions lie, never to ask why, why, why, of a fool's saying not I, not I.

IT is in best interest to invest wisely these words to decision
make, for the wise heart and strong will, that prison keepers
cannot break.

BY his own deception, proverty will be his bread, and hell
will he go to make his foolish bed. Stung by his deceptive lip
so often finding his own foot to trip.

A fool says there is no God, not considering the Deity's
wrathful rod, heed these words from a former fool, beware,
beware, just yesterday, I came from there!

ONLY FOOLS DECEIVE THEMSELVES!
FROM A FORMER FOOL
John William Baker

A Child's View Of Christmas

Chirstmas thru the eyes of a child
is a wondrous sight to behold
The pilgrimage of Mary and Joseph
as the events of Christmas unfold
They witness the star of Bethlehem
and the stable behind the Inn
where the birth of the baby Jesus
on the first Christmas morning was given
The baby was wrapped in swaddling cloths
a manger of hay was his bed
The children were amazed at the radiant light
that shined brightly above his head
The shepherds are the first to appear
the Wise Men and then the Kings
from distant lands they followed the star
to pay homage to the King of Kings
Christmas thru the eyes of our children
is the story that never grows old
The gift of God's son is the reason
the Christmas Story is told
Larry H. Erickson

Oh Beautiful Sun That We May Be One

O'er thy warm embrace, beckoning from afar,
   all have stooped
 in amazement
   and steepening awe.
Skin-claddened, eye hooded
   worshippers dare whisper
     of birthing legends and magical myths,
       habitual rites, spiritual nights,
       to mollify light.
Dancing through space, linear waves speed past
   the heroic remnants of greece.
Bound by RA
       to brighten darkness
         and maintain earth's fecundity,
   an impeccable assembly arrives at once,
standing slowly, dappling waves, caressing wheat, nimbly down,
silhouetting everything it touches, making a mold out of the model.
   Although some would revere and others might revel,
this light - distant traveller
       does all that we need.
Scott Michael Potter

Lessons

As a child, I asked my mother
"Please tell me, what is life?"
Throughout my lifetime came her answer:
"It's happiness with a mixture of strife.
It's holding on to hope and prayer
When it seems that's all you've got.
It's running the race ahead
Whether you're ready or not.
It's learning to love and letting go
As the seasons of life go by.
It's making the most of every God given day
Because I warn you time will fly.
It's living, laughing, learning, growing;
It's believing, loving, and sharing.
In life there is frustration, pain, and heartache.
But don't forget joy, peace and caring.
This and much more comprises life.
Daughter, do you understand?"
"I think so Mom," was my reply.
"I'll just hold God's hand."
Donna Willoughby

The Longest Day

I invite you to spend a day with me. Leave the comfort
of your world. Come and see my life astray. Where the world
changes on this side of the tracks. Where the day seem's to
keep coming back the same. Over and over and over again.
My day takes me through hunger, sickness, and pain. Where
children cry, it seems in vain.

Where mother's try and try each day, trying not to let life
just stray away. We pray, we pray, oh! Yes, we pray, although
God heard our prayers. Soon, afterwards he sees my crying.
My tears run like the ocean deep. This day you see
is not strange to me. This day you see in my life.
Patricia A. Ogbuew

Transformation

The forest, changed over night
   from barrenness to beauty.
Ice clinging to branches - shimmering
   like silver-frocked fairies
   in the tree tops.

All nature glistens
   as the sun's rays
   proclaim the handiwork of God.

Ice glazed streams seem like giant mirrors
   reflecting images of passers-by.
Wilted, drooping branches are caught
   in unsuspecting poses,
   frozen like statues.

Suspended they wait
   til mother nature waves her wand
   and melts their frigid bonds.

The forest, transformed overnight
   another masterpiece,
   a miracle - no less
   of the supreme artist and change maker.
Carol J. Folwell

Is Seeing Believing?

In the dim lit caves
I walked in anticipation,
Stretching my mind,
Searching for a translation.
Could the cave men really have tried
To decorate with pictures of things alive?
Having read, and having seen in books
Wasn't enough proof to skip the looks.
Once seeing the bulls
And ink finger prints on the wall,
Didn't help to answer
My questions at all.
But here they were, right in front of my eyes,
Wouldn't primitive paintings be hard to disguise?
If they'd been here for centuries
Wouldn't they be fainter than these?
Was this for real...no jokes?
Was this for real...and not a hoax?

Doris Spaude

Mother

Like a stone in a wall
The keystone to the wall of a castle
A castle held together by a stone
As the castle grows older, the stone begins to wear
The sharp edges replaced by softer curves
When the dust from the stones's edges fall, it becomes soil
And in soil is life, which with a seed produces a vine
The vine grows until it is what holds the castle together
The vine then produces the most beautiful of all gifts -a rose
So, Mother, just as the castle grew older and more beautiful with time,
    so do you.

R. J. Brackin Jr.

I Can't Explain

As I lay here on my bed
I think about things in my head
I can't seem to fall asleep and
All of a sudden I start to weep
Why do I feel this way
These feelings don't seem to go away
I can't explain why I act the way I do
Things happen so fast out of the blue
Maybe it's friends, family, or love
Or it could be some kind of message from above
People probably wonder why I look so sad
I wish I could tell them why I feel so bad.

Lisa Kahle

The Beginning Of The Day

The early morning is what I like most
As the sun comes up and is warm as toast
The birds are chirping their stories to tell
The flowers are spreading their petals with a
    wonderful smell
It is the best time of the day to start with
Whether it is work or play
You will always remember the beginning of the day.
The grass is always pretty and green
And we wonder what is in store for us that day
There is always a nice smell and a pretty sheen
We can plant more flowers and hope that they grow
We know when it trains there will be a story to tell
After spring, summer and winter comes on the scene
With all the blossoms falling
And the grass turning to brown
We will always remember the beginning of the day.

Marjorie O. Mitchell

Reflections Of Narcissism

What is this madness?
Does not care.
Narcissist concern takes ME there.

Depart without a hint of time.
Your pain, not MINE.
Child's eyes see the dark of night.
What will they be, what they see.

Mom's eyes look. Don't speak.
Intimate with my own flesh and blood can be.
They hurt, okay, as long as you are with ME.

Children re-enact what they have seen.
Worry sent, returns.
Done in the dark, rises to the light.
Be true to self. Where will I take flight?

Right. Wrong. Love is gone. Does not matter.
All said and done, fun for ME or fund of ill spent.
Continue on or repent.

Consciously asleep, swimming in an open sea.
Have I become what has happened to ME?

Denise Labrie

"On Grief"

I am a pretender; I pretend to get
    through the day because others
    depend on me to be me,
But I'm hiding in a dark place now
    where only the faintest glimmer of
    light filters in and out unexpectantly.

For those moments—when the light comes—
    I remember the world colored a brighter,
    safer place;
And in the remembering, I feel the light of
    day fall on my face; it is only at
    this moment, I breathe deeply once again.
I feel it's my last deep breathe and the first
    of many small steps I must take to be
    happy once again.

Kay Gunter

The Glass Wall

Remove yourself from the pedestal
You put yourself upon.
Now you've no army or artillery.
You'll face yourself alone.

Trying to break the mirror
That reflects the side concealed.
Your hands left sore and bloodied.
Your efforts to keep from being revealed.

Lashing out in frustration.
Only causing yourself more pain.
You've constructed this wall,
This shell to try to hide your shame.

If you now destroy the wall
The shards will cut your flesh.
You'll see the last ray of sun and
Breathe the last sacred breath.

Reduced to a quaking child
A tear in your eye and sweat on your brow.
Such a pity, you've destroyed yourself.
What a shame, no one can save you now.

Courtney Le Bel

Greetings To My Former Mate

Greetings to my former mate
The best you did for me was reject me
No, I bear no hate
Had you not gone, I would not be able to reflect me.

We were two different people—you, pessimistic; I, optimistic
You mistrusted, I trusted
It was inevitable that our love was a sieve.

Had you not gone, I'd know not joy today
Today I love
I am loved, I love!

The comfort I feel is indescribable
He applauds my growth
You were afraid of its prescription.

Had you not gone; I would have
Our union was mismatched
Now, you've not been replaced
You have been surpassed!

Patricia Bennett Castellini

Untitled

Daydreamer
focused on the movement of my thoughts
rapidly swelling and crashing
and swelling and crashing
like an ocean whose waters are on fire
and then
I slow to the pace of a blade of grass growing in the sunshine
and I place my cheek to the earth
feel the coolness of the soil and the heat of the moon
burning like an icicle on my lips
and I fall...tumbling through a million galaxies
darkness cushions my swirling descent and my final contact
as I startle to awareness and this reality attacks me with its
silence
its stillness is my anxiety
there is no thought in the moment
the instant before catastrophe...devastation
but it cannot even expel a breath on me
because my thoughts continue to race wildly
because I am a
daydreamer

Emily Ortega

Jimmy

The sun was out shining,
The trees were swaying in the wind.
The clock struck three,
And the little boy walked home in the wind.

His heart was beating fast,
He could not stop running.
The man chased him in his car,
But the boy kept running.

Someone grabbed him from behind,
The man, no doubt about it.
The boy screamed and kicked him hard,
But no one must have heard it.

The boy was laid to rest,
His lovely name was Jimmy.
What will happen to the man, I don't know,
For I mostly think about the young angel, Jimmy.

Jamie Diptee

In The Mist Of Time

In the mist of time we hear
no sound at all, in minutes
later we could hear rain drops
falling on the roof top.
In the mist of time, we walk out
side in the dark and look up to the
sky and we see a bright shinning star.
In the mist of time in our life we
fall in love, we have moments and moments
and years and years of happiness and
sadness and laughter of all the times we have had together.
In the mist of time, we may hear
a little voice crying out for
mom and dad.
In the mist of time, it all has
to come to an end.
In the mist of time we all have
to say goodbye to someone that we love so dear.
In the mist of time, don't worry
God is always near.

Darlene Hanvey

My Friend

God put a love in my heart for my friend
Whatever you want me to do Lord I intend

With no idea what this friendship would mean
Time brought the Word through our lives to be seen

Bondage's of the past threatened our spiritual future
Deliverance, trust in God, we needed it for sure

We courageously opened our hearts to one another
Usually thinking we were being a bother

There for each other sunshine or rain
Lifting the heart, seeing it through pain

Taking joy, one in the others success
Trying to bring out the others best

Sometimes hurting and pushing help away
Often no idea what words to say

Thankful we have God's Words to speak
Ours are not always humble, most are rarely meek

We cherish the time we spend together
Making memories we'll keep forever

I thank God now, and at its start
For putting that love for my friend in my heart.

Lorraine Hawkins

Lovers

Lovers laying in each others arms,
They know they're protected from all harm.
In the dark they whisper each others name,
She says, I love you, he tells her the same.
Lovers covered in sheets of lace,
They find, they touch, that special place.
Places secret that they would never share,
They're given now, because they care.
Lovers laying side by side,
The joy, the passion, they ride the tide.
The fear is gone of all things new,
Because their love is deep and true.
Lovers, together by choice,
Their love gives them just one voice.
They do things they've never done before,
They've awakened their minds, opened passions door.
Lovers sing their song together,
Of now, tomorrow, and forever.

Tina Marie Fox

Hay Hauler's Dream

We were sittin aside an alfalfa field, —near Bakersfield
My truck and I,—just put a full day in
We truck 15 hours, - give or take
Haulin Hay up and down the Interstate
I shut that truck and trailer - d o w n,
Right there - bout -16 miles from town

As I lay on the truck bed between the hay ropes
Starin up at the moon and the deep night sky
I could smell the sweet scent of fresh baled hay
But morning comes early with my hay hooks and chaps
Got 426 bales to hand load and perfectly stack
Then we'll go down the road with a straight load of green

We truck the backroads all over the west
Haulin feed or freight, or whatever she'll take
Deliver to the Dairy farm, or the track at Holly wood Park
Unload the next mornin and hope we get back before dark
If you come for a ride, you'll see just how it feels
Riding a long green shiny hay wagon with 18 shiny wheels

When you're on the road and meet a perty load a green
You'll know that's my "Hay Hauler's Dream"

Randy Oliver

Ode To Heidi, My Pet

My pride and joy.
You were a girl, not a boy.

Thirteen years you lived with love
    that I showered on you, and you on me.

Sad eyes you had when out the door I would go.
Glad eyes greeted me when I returned, with a
    question I could see.
As if saying "What did you bring me? Some good
    food that I hunger for?
I have loads, but I always want more!"

She's up in pet Heaven, that I know,
And is now with all her loved ones that she
    grew up with,
And perhaps is looking down at those
    who are below here on earth
Who miss her and loved her so.
My pride and joy

Dot E. Trupiano

Untitled

The days have passed now years gone by
What once was my youth has been lost
Depression overwhelms me for what I've not tried
Living strictly for the future simply has its high costs

I've listened to authority and played by their rules
While friends have all strayed and had their fun
My losses remain the jewel of all jewels
Experiences not experienced are my smoking gun

Keep waiting for tomorrow and you'll lose today
Soon tomorrow comes, the wait is over
And your regrets become known as yesterday
I've got to pick up the pieces of my life's disorder

I've passively allowed the sand drain through the glass
With nothing to show for my many years of age
I've no stories to tell, because I've sat on my ass,
Soon the world will be minus one bird in a cage

Stephen Doherty

Mind And Heart

My mind, reassuring me that the love we shared was that in vain,
Still coincides with my heart
As it continues to feel the pain of yesterday.
Anger and sadness, intertwined as one,
Making life somewhat more difficult to bear.
I take responsibility for my pain,
As I allowed myself to become vulnerable to you
Once again.
Being lead into the darkness,
As I should have known from the start.
Your regret shall come at a time when it is,
Least expected.
You shall begin to wonder what was truly in your heart.
In the dark of night, my name shall be the one you repeat.
Whether it be your frustrated silence,
Or your voice echoing to me,
I shall someday know the truth.
Only then, it will be too late.
You cannot mend a heart
That you have broken one too many a time.

Nicole Nostramo

Memories

Memories; they come so fast, yet go so slow, memories

Memories; they hurt so bad, yet feel so good, memories

Memories; some people say they go away,
others say they always stay,
but memories, my memories

I once was young, but now am old;
I once felt good, but now feel cold . . . from memories;
my memories;
sweet memories

The world we had has long since gone,
only our dreams still linger on,
in memories, my memories

I used to laugh, but now I cry;
I used to wonder when and why, but memories,
my memories, sweet memories of days gone by.

Jesse Keen

School's A Drag

School's a drag,
It makes me gag,
I'm tired of carrying that same old bag.

Get up early,
Go to bed late,
Oh no, I'm going to be late for my date!

Go to class,
If we have a party,
We have a blast.

Study for tests,
Try my best,
Even if I don't get any rest.

In May,
We get out for many, many, days,
"Hip, Hip, Horray!" Is what I say.

I can't wait till summer vacation is here,
And I'll tell you this dear,
School's a drag, but if you stay in school then your
really, really, cool.

Stephany Robinson

I Deserve You

How lonesome I felt before I met you
Thanks, for taking me out of the blue
I know, I am having a hard time to trust
but, to have you I know that I must
Never thought someone as nice as you
Could ever happen to someone so blue
Me deserve you?
Yes I do!
You are so exciting
I find you quite inviting
Yet, our relationship so new
I cannot get enough of you
Two broken hearts, hopefully have found,
A home together so sound
Two lonely souls,
Have but, only one goal
Which is to be with each other
And, to care about one another

Doreen Fri

Natures Golden Moments

As I gaze into the deep lustrous
color beneath the mist that rests
upon the mountain peaks.
A cool sparkling stream makes its
way down over the rocks to the valley below.
I notice an Eagle soaring
high up near the top of the
mountain peaks, gliding along
on a gentle breeze. She sweeps
down to rest upon the trees,
which stand like mighty towers
along the mountain side. Their
leaves are like a warm fire aglow,
in a magnificent array of beauty.
Tiny animals scurry along the
ground beneath the trees, searching
for food. They know it won't be
long before cold Weather Arrives.

Natures finest moments can't be bought,
but they can be cherished within our hearts forever.

Lamar Pettit

The House On The Hill

The house on the hill is so quiet now,
Since Jesus called Daddy home.
Mama is lost without him,
And grieves since he's been gone.
We try to comfort Mama the best we can,
Sometimes the empty feeling is more than we can stand.
We all share the loss of the one we loved.
Jesus understands and gives comfort from up above.
I just can't stay away from the house on the hill.
For when I'm with Mama, I can feel Daddy there still.
With God's loving comfort, we lifts our eyes to the sky
And Jesus dries our tear stained eyes.

Geraldine Hill

Pretty Words

I was going to sit down and write pretty words for you,
but none would come into my mind.
I thought of all the things that man-kind had said since time began
but all that seemed too familiar to write about again,
so I decided to run away for a few days to see if you miss me.
And if you do, then I'll write for you the prettiest words of all..
I love you,
but if you don't, then I guess I'll just write
Good-bye.

Sharon Holloran

A Child

A child's laugh fills the heart with smiles
A child's chatter fills the mind with great expectations
A child's songs fill the air with joy
A child's hug fills the soul with love
A child's parents fill their world with security.

A Child's Abuse
Deadens their heart
Bruises their mind
Destroys their love
Crushes their soul.

Karla Van Horn

Reflections

The house sits empty.
The walls are bare; the rooms are vacant.
Memories begin to race though my mind.

Mother's chair sits by the window,
Her knitting bag beside it.
The penetrating heat from the fire warms my back.
The old player piano sings a sweet melody.
The stuffed cat perched on top smiles warmly.
Laughter echoes through the hallways.

The tall grandmother clock
Ticks softly from the corner.
Polished oak floors gleam
With the brightness they once had.
A lamp's soft glow
Spreads across the pale peach walls.

A beckoning voice interrupts my daydreams.
My reflective thoughts vanish.
I take one last look.

The walls are bare; the rooms are vacant.
The house sits empty.

Melanie Karelse

'Share The Broken Dream'

I grew up with Superman, The Lone Ranger...then came Gilligan
homerun wiffleball, these lost days I recall

I'm in my forties sit'n in my lazyboy, daydreaming still somehow
I'm Micky Mantle with a three an two count
The bases are loaded, two outs, and low-an-behold I knock one out!

I'm round'n the bases wave'n to the fans
They're give'n me a stand'n ovation
round'n third...but I never reach home
I'm interrupted by the telephone

Dad....can you come pick me up?
Try-outs are over...I didn't make the cut
...There's silence...on both ends
...until I realize my son needs me to be....his best friend

Dreams....ah dreams....they're not at all what they seem
Whether it's baseball or homecoming queen
When they break they break the heart
But by sharing the pain...you grow together...not apart

Dreams...ah dreams....they're not at all what they seem
Barbie and Ken are this world's elusive ideal
It's the love shared...that's what's real

Steven Mark Hamlet

Winter In My Soul

Why does winter hold only shades of gray?
Why do I feel tired, empty, redundant today?
Does winter have a purpose, a reason, a goal?
Is it meant to give rest to the weary soil, the weary soul?
To let the land rejuvenate, so that in spring color will return to
   this gray scape;
To let my soul lay barren, so that with spring the emptiness can escape?

Some winter days the sun shines, and the world becomes brighter.
And then, my heart, my mind, my soul seem lighter.
Why can't the sun shine everyday?
Is it because to appreciate color, one must first experience gray?
To feel the true heights of joy, one must first know the depths of sorrow?
To know that after the grayness of today, lies a brighter tomorrow?

I thank God for the shades of gray,
For the long, seemingly endless, winter day.
For when spring returns to the earth and my soul,
I'll see the grass and the flowers, and I'll know
After winter, comes spring; after rain, the rainbow,
And after winter's emptiness, my soul's joy will overflow.

   Karen Elaine Stubert Gangl

Mom's Tear's

I don't know your name, but I do know your pain.
Day's and night's you watch your
child, you pray for your baby, (no matter what age.)
You cry for them and with them.
The doctors and nurses do their job.
Endless needles and tests and expect us MOMS to sit by
and comply: To all the pain ...voiceless.
But that's not their child. They
don't feel the pain of their tears.
Of course. They care for our children.
or they wouldn't do what they do.
But they are just not MOM!
We, as moms, don't want to be, selfish, mean or uncaring.
But the endless hours of sleeplessness
the waking of a sleeping child, who's only peace is sleep.
and the numbness you start to feel.
becomes a part of your heart. And you wish someone, anyone
could understand, your pain and your tears.
Each night I say a silent prayer for you, MOM.
because, I know your pain.

   Love and improving health
     to your child.
   and a caring heart to you!

   Cammy Harper

The Falling Crystal

A color of tranquility and a relaxing sound
as our very life begins to tap on the ground
while they try with relentlessness to purify
and there are many of them to lend each other a hand
when their commander the rain maker cast them upon the land
The tranquility is a lost stare and a moments peace
not conceiving in ones own mind that it will cease
while the pattern of its sounds go hand and hand
with its invisible color
It ask your ears to rest fore a moment as you hear another
Many will run and scatter to find shelter
as it can be kind and gentle yet a powerful force
and while it rains from the heavens to meet earth
These beads of crystal return to the place of their birth

   Anthony Fornari

My World

Where did the Universe come from? Where is it going?
If all should continue? It could start all over again.

Was it random, thrown out or developed to be in perfect order?
Drop a cup and saucer, it breaks and flies all over.

Could that be the beginning. All pieces scattered and thrown about
Could they all go together like a jigsaw puzzle? No doubt.

From it all! Man's thoughts and ideas of every lasting Earth.
Days months years are all time - and man sets the scale for time.

All things above and around are signs of measurement.
For man to see and use. He says birds can fly and so can be.

Sun expands - could use its light
Stars burn out and disappear from sight.

But the universe - its just there - the part of yesteryear.
Today is now, the future tomorrow - it may still be there

Men must stop running, stop walking, stop talking
And listen to the world. See things today that are not there tomorrow

   Marcia Whalen

Thy Will O'God

When I stand and look unto the hills
I realize everything is under God's will
The moon, sun, and stars obey you
Birds, animals and fish too.

The plants and flowers bloom in summer
So many blossoms you can't number
The grass so beautiful and green
The prettiest sight I've ever seen.

The sun in the day, the moon by night
Obeying God and giving us light
As I look around me
I behold God's goodness in everything I see.
Jesus made the wind and waves obey
He knew to them just what to say
People every where, let Jesus have your life
He will cut sin out just like a knife.
Clouds floating so white in the air
Sky so blue and oh so fair
Birds all flying high and low
Singing sweetly as they go to and fro.

   Alice Lee

Tides

Weathered and gray my grandmother stands.
Eyes holding a sea of love.
Laden and weary, she carries her loss...
Images of days gone by sweep through her mind,
Like grains of sand against the salty ocean wind.

Waves lap afoot...a memory surges:
Like a beacon of light she calls to him.
A young soldier rushes to shore
Breaking the horizon with his ageless face.
Her love for him will always be
A love of hope, to see another way...
To make it through the clouds,
Like the war of his time and hers of today.

Standing seaward, she senses time and love,
Like the tides.

   Tyler D. Hammond

Special Date, My Birthday Or Special Date, Special Child

On a cold October night, I was born at eight o'clock.
On the twentieth day of thirty eight.
I didn't come one minute too soon nor one minute too late.
Mother wrapped me in a blanket on that special date.
To keep me warm and cozy and away from worldly harm and hate.
She knew too well how to take care of her child,
For I was the ninth of her pile.
Mother didn't know what my out come would be.
But she was so proud and showed me to all the family.
At night she would bath and feed me and put me to bed
And pray that I would grow up not to be bad
But to grow in love and be loved by all who know me.
That special child my mother had?

Elsie Irene Ford

Second Thoughts

Lying on my bed, listening to music.
Identifying with every song.
Waiting for the phone to ring.
I know better, I know this is pathetic.
One step down the road of letting someone else run your life.
Forgive Eva Braun, forgive Rachele Guidi- they were in love.
Not that I'm in love; no, definitely not that word.
What then?
The possibility of love?
The aftermath of a love-type thing?
Memories of events that only really happened in your mind.
When movies and books merge with your subconscious.

Amy E. Hurtz

Secret Identity

My life I'm not that certain with, but my name and age I am.
I don't know much about myself,
I've been living a secret life
I'm living a secret identity trying to hide my dark and scary past,
A secret to me that no one shall know, a nightmare that shall one day
  be put to rest,
I'm afraid to tell for I am a shame,
If I tell anyone they'll shut me out like a cold winter storm,
I've been living a lie for so many years,
I the person me doesn't really exist,
One day this lie will destroy me make me bitter and cold,
The day I tell anyone, will be the day I come to peace with me,
Myself and the people who put me through this living hell.
I wish I would of told my secret when I was young now it's to late.
It caught up with me and won the race,
It's destroyed at last, I thought I was strong enough to win
The day it came to rest was when I came to say goodbye.

Paulamarie Bryant Hill

Just A Dream

I lay in bed wondering what life would be like
If I wasn't hated and hit all the time
Where hugs and love replaced the pain
Where I had a family who wouldn't refrain
From showing caring and tenderness
A family full of laughter and happiness
Each day waking up with a smile on my face
A kiss on the cheek to end the day
For no reason being told "I love you"
Every second being a wonderful memory forever
Then I wake and see reality, it was just a dream
Life isn't always the way you think it's suppose to be.

Rachele Holden

"You Should Have Been There"

You should have seen the fireworks
from the beach with me last night,
The water was so cool and still
and the moon was full and bright.

It brought back lots of memories
as I walked the beach alone,
I thought I heard you call my name
but wait....you were at home.

I couldn't help but dream of you
when I went fast to sleep,
Of all the time that we have shared
and the secrets that we keep.

I dreamed that you were with me
on that beach so long and wide,
You held me close and kissed me
as we walked along the tide.

Still...you should have seen the fireworks
from the beach with me last night,
The water was so cool and still
and the moon was full and bright.

Sandra G. Cook

My Love

My love looks at me
with big blue eyes-
wide open,
innocent and as bright as any child's.
My love cuddles
and purrs sweet nothings in my ear.
His body curls close to mine
to share the warmth left in our bodies
as the early morning chill tries to steal it away.
He kisses me softly-
not to wake me so early in the morning.
But his tongue is like sandpaper and
his whiskers tickle.
I wake smiling to the sky
paling with the colors of dawn.
My faithful kitten, Sealy, by my side.

Cara Minardi-Pettersen

Weeping Willow

Crying
with my mother getting her clean
white shirt wet as if she bathed
in a lake of tears. I lay on her
soft quilt, the smell of her faint perfume
I can't shut off my tears.
Wiping my tears away but one
returns after the other is gone.
She tells me that she
will never leave and we will always
be together, even though daddy
is with his new family, I will
never start one without you.
  You can always
return to my quilt. You can
always bury your head in my arm.
You can always be
a weeping willow with me.

Carly Short

The Arrival

We wait for the holiday train
And a long lost relative, missing for millenia.
With bided time we laugh, we cry, we hope, we fear;
Anticipation kills.
His luggage will be heavy: redemption, forgiveness.
In a corner the mood turns ugly;
Where lines of concern were,
Scars of anxiety increase.
They cry out — what if, what if...
Let's form a party, unify, unify!
Crack that whip.
Those in the family with blemish: be gone.
Those with conscience and mind: sit up straight.
they weep: Alas! The master is come!
Make haste! Clean house!
We choose the dust, and name the dirt
Make way for our Lord, our Master.

Pray for the mind's own child, pray for the innocents;
Cry for light
Thirst for wisdom.

Charles Wright

Untitled

To Luc
Today my son you are 5 years old
where's the little boy I used to hold
time flies so they say
as I watch you getting bigger day by day
I see so much of myself in you
Your passion for sports and your brown eyes too
I wish I could give you more than this
but my love for you son you will never miss
now as we turn this page in your life
emotion's so thick you can cut it with a knife
and no matter what happens from this point on
your stars are the brightest have ever shone

Rick Couvell

Dreaming...

I rest and wait..on the doorsteps of time..
with eternity ahead of me...

This dreamless state I cannot wake..
I smell the breeze through the trees....

O wonderful star..for heavens abode..
for galaxies far and near...

Weightless sleep and endless awe..
for dawn will soon be here..

I dream of fields and prairies green..
and flowers pure as milk...

Of skies aglow and puppet shows...
caressing soft as silk..

With diamonds in hand..and streams of gold..
and water that runs like time..

Flame without heat..endless treasures I seek..
but my clock begins to chime...

I crack one eye so that I may spy..
a glimpse of the dawn at hand..

INSTANTLY...FLASH!
with a boom and a crash... I returned to the world of man.....

Michael V. Cowan

Brother

The night was cool and calm
The moonlight illuminated the sky
When I started to think about you
I began to cry
I knew you were far away
But that you would be back again one day
And on that special day
We will sit and talk like yesterday
But yesterday is far away
Never to come again
But i should feel no sorrow
For we will always have tomorrow
Tomorrow, tomorrow
There will always be tomorrow

Mike Terrell

Search?

I opened my mind and all my thoughts
feel out,
I searched for answer, where there
were no questions,
I hid myself from all the world, only to be
found by everyone,
I feel the hurt, but there is no pain,
I face the sun to find only darkness,
Where is my world going? -
The flowers grow among the weeds -
Their perseverance is strong -
And so find, what's inside of me?
There lies the flowers of my secrets.
My world - My life - My infamy -
My search.

George Broughton

"The Mysterious Sea"

The sun is now setting on the never quiescent sea,
The birds are heading for shelter as the light of day ceases to be;
In the distance, as the waves continue to beat the distant shore,
There is a feeling of loneliness I never felt so strongly before.

As I look out over the waves of darkened blue
There is nothing but water and birds a few,
With an occasional gull moaning it sad story
To a lonely shrimp boat or passing dory.

Then as night continues its journey across the sky,
The waves bounce freely; their hands reaching high
Only to be thrown back into the sea
By the strong arm of an ocean breeze.

Then on the far off horizon as the sun shows its face
And the world begins its normal pace;
In its continuous pace and mysterious ways
The never quiescent sea, in all its splendor, faces a new day.

John W. Tilghman Jr.

Woman

She has a warm blooded heart, which opens up to anyone.
Her skin is as soft as a baby's bottom.
Look at her but please don't touch.
Admire her grace, style and presence.
Look in her eyes and tell me what you see.
Listen to her laughter and look at her smile.
She is pretty inside as well outside.
She is independent and can stand on her own two feet.
She deserves respect and won't settle for less.
So treat her with kindness and love her for just being the woman that she is.

Tessie Y. Graham

My Hero

Sixteen! What happiness when I met you!
Blond hair, eyes of blue, a smile hello, how do you do?
Ah yes! I knew, I knew! You were meant for me.
And I was meant for you.

Thirty-two years of love, wonder, embrace.
Years of trying to stay in the race.
Three wonderful children, a pet or two
And then, the world "fell in" on me and you!

The big "C" was staring us square in the face.
Something we could endure only by "His embrace."
You never lacked courage though looking Death in the face
And you conducted yourself with the utmost grace.

You didn't sit idle and poor health chide;
You were too busy securing the future for your long-time bride.
You were always determined that I have the best
And you made sure of that before your internal rest.

I sit here with beautiful memories of years gone by
And I hold you in my heart, where you'll never die.
Handsome, loving, honest, and true,
I delicate this poem to my hero, my husband, you!

Billie H. Guth

Colors

Red and orange, southward bound, not resting long
The cold north wind whipping into action
Vigorously pushing everything in and out of its way

Robins headed south flying on that crest of wind
Leaves trying to follow in broken formation
Not capable of keeping up, unescorted, lastly engulfed by winter

Savage days of winter's brilliance, scourging the land
laying waste to all falls within its range
Covering up its destruction with a layer of white

Red and green, rushing up through the bleakness
To burst forth in helter fashions
Chasing out the winter with gentle southern breezes

Robins and tulips, relish in the virgin spring
Hurrying to be the first in their own greatness
Delighting in the sun and displaying to us their beauty

Rich Wells

Reflections Of My Life

If I were to die tomorrow
what a waste the people would say
what a tender young age to go away
But none of life is ever wasted
Life's experiences have made me richer
I've known love in the roles of a
Mother, a daughter, a sister, a wife
Though the pain of the loss of a loved one
Has caused me much strife,
I savored in the strength and support of good friends
How greedy to reach out and cram it all in,
But isn't that what life's always been,
Love, meaningful relationships, some work,
Some play, a sense of humor and
A small piece of immortality through
Our most treasured loved ones, our children
Life, our most precious gift is never wasted.

Suzanne Grayson

Thank You, Suzie

Unexpectedly, thick, gray clouds slowly began covering the sky.
I opened all the doors and windows, and turned all the lamps on;
However, still, despite all my efforts, dimness finally took over
My life, and I felt afraid, insecure, lost in the mazes of fate,
Entangled in the mysterious webs of existence,
Trapped in a hostile world, where I fought
With phantoms and shadows, and always failed...
Suddenly, in the middle of the night,
Suzie appeared like a ray of sun in the midst of the darkness,
Took my hand, and guided me to the land of light and hope,
Of joy and opportunities, where we now together walk over forests
And valleys, crossing mountains and rivers...
Thank you for everything, Suzie;
Thank you, my precious seeing eye dog...

Irena Franchi

Tonight's Mirage, Tomorrow's Reality

In the midst of a morning dawn
the very bright sun reminds you soon
that what went on past eves,
was just a game; last nights debts,
are due at noon.

If a mirage is a nocturnal day,
what then is sure to last.
And what you think is yours today
tomorrow is gone and lost away.

Empty dreams built in vain
of what was here today,
There may not be a remain
After the bottle is finally drained.

Should you not enjoy today?
After all, illusions are the soul's prey.
Tomorrow, may be better than today,
but while it comes, adore living today.

J. Antonio Aldrete

I Felt The Baby Grow

I've felt the baby grow,
It's a feeling every woman should know.
To have someone inside.
To cuddle be it's guide.
Some mornings it makes me sick
to feel the baby twist, turn and kick.
Oh to start a life,
hoping to be a good wife.
Always wondering and not to know;
I'm happy to say, "I felt the baby grow"

Jennifer Lewis

Solitude

In Solitude, I cry with gushing tears
While lamenting my demise and its miseries,
For the affliction is like all fears
That haunts anon, at your rich memories.
When am alone in my own wilderness
With the chaste gifts of mother nature,
yet my mind flees into forgetfulness.
And, like sailor Selkirk, endures the adventure.
At the visible dust of twinkling stars
I gaze avast into the inconceivable void,
For wanting to be there as Mars
Like a luminous satellite or an asteroid.
It's God's will to lay a stone
A resting place you care to trace,
Engrave these words, here rest a soul.
Who made a garden in rocky waste.

Andrew Sonne Hill

Cool Summer Night -1969

Cool summer night -1969.
Cutoff bluejeans and dirty bare feet.
Running down the sidewalk with my best friend.
Playing Batman.
Open garages and chainlink fences,
Windows glowing gray with TV light.
Neighbor's dogs, as familiar to us Andy and Opie and Aunt Bea,
dance at backyard gates as we go past.
A street lamp's pale yellow glow lights our way.
A new car dealer opening across from the mall;
their search lights circle the evening sky.
The Batman Signal!
We run faster.
Enjoying the night.
The neighborhood is our Gotham.
And we are safe.
And content.
On a cool summer night - 1969.

Ron A. Ridley

Reflecting On The Cross

What do I see on the cross made of Wood?
As I looked up at the cross from where I stood.
I see a face so drawn, agonized with pain.
Who is the man? Jesus The Christ, is His name.
Eyes looking out on a world so filled with sin.
He opened The Way, for all to enter in,
When God, "His Father", sacrificed Him.

I see thorns for a crown they had made
pushed into His head; til from the wounds He has bled.
Nails in His hands and feet—Oh, so cruel.
Blood streaming from a stab in His side.
Why, Oh why must this Jesus have died?

Where are His friends? There's just His Mother and one;
Is this His reward, to earth He had come?
With Love of His Father, He said,
Forgive them all, and then He was dead.

But I look again and I see the cross is bare
and in place of a body, a light shines there.
For Jesus had died; risen and lives
Joy, Hope, Forgiveness and Everlasting life to us He gives.

Harry R. Howells

Faith

Remembering as a child
lying in the beige talcum desert sands of Arizona.
My horse, my father's horse
nuzzling each other quietly nearby
my father
in old dusty denims and short sleeves
turning in circles spinning
dancing, feathers of eagles
wrapped in long black braids
the bones of eagles
in strong brown hands, arms
outstretched
talking to spirits with strange names
our horses quietly kissing,
my legs, two booted triangles
my arms behind my head
looking up at the pinks the oranges marvelling
at the aquamarines violets of the setting sun

watching, waiting,
for the rain to come.

Colette Tisdale

The Dove

The dove came to the door.
It hit the hard surface and
a feather did drop.
It flew to a pine tree and
sat for a while.

An ordinary meeting you say when
I tell of the dove. A tale of
friendship and love I relate.
For in the sight of the dove, the Lord
in His goodness appeared.

For you see in that moment of time when all
hurt and sorrow stood so still,
my friend and my love died and her soul
took the form of the beautiful
dove to fly with the angels for all
of eternity.

Loretta A. Shemeley

Sounds Of The Seasons

Listen to summer, what does it say?
I hear splashing in water all day.

Beach balls bouncing, diving boards squeak,
Riding my bike until I'm weak.

Listen to fall, what does it say?
I hear leaves falling every day.

Orange, yellow, red, and brown,
Falling crisply to the ground.

Listen to winter, what does it say?
I hear snowflakes night and day.

Crunching in the ice and snow
Or skiing a slope is great you know.

Listen to spring, what does it say?
I hear green things growing each day.

Stormy storms or gentle rain,
The cold is over and it's warm again!

Shirley Willoughby

Christmas

The brightest beam, the star of bethlehem shone down.
It brightened the night while the world slept sound.
Guiding the pathway for shepherds that night long ago.
To the babe in the manger, and voices singing low.
The star weaves a rapture of a christmas that will never end.
It's a symbol from our creator for eternity he will send.
Along with angel eyes, the surrounding stars gave a glow.
To the blessed scene of two heads bending low.
Shining on the Christ child, who has that power over that star.
That divine light that unites the world near and far.
It's ours this christmas ever, before that star fades away!
As it's brilliance of holiness vanishes to christmas day.
Let us unite with that star, and gather our good deeds.
To weave a halo of love from ancient hebrew reeds.
It's your star and my star this christmas eve!!!
Let's together carry it to the world to come.
The bright, the beautiful, joy-giving world!

Marcella J. Wolha

Friends

Friends are people that stand by you
Even times when your feeling blue.
Friends are people that are always there
When others say I don't care.
Friends are people who don't turn away
When you say can we talk today.
Friends are people who don't turn on you
And go find someone new.
Even though these things a friend can't always obey
A friend is always there to stay.
And you know that in the end
You'll always have a very good friend.

Teresa Danielle Hall

Forget

Forget the boy that meant so much.
Forget his kiss, his gentle touch.
Forget his lips, his loving eyes.
Forget the time he told you lies.
Forget his laugh, his funny smile.
Forget everything that made life worthwhile.
Forget the long walks in the rain.
Forget the love that cause you pain.
Forget he said I'll always care.
Forget the fun you both shared.
Forget the way he made you smile.
Forget the awful kiss goodbye.
Forget the pain that's in your heart.
Forget these things and someday you'll
Forget the pain you feel today...

Angela Rose Huizar

"My Feelings To Mattern"

Have you ever taken a walk on a beach
Took pleasure in a single shell on a shore
Or stood on a mountain cliff at dusk
And stared at the sun
If you haven't you must

Have you ever been inspired enough to cry
Have you ever been fearless enough to try
Have you ever dared to journey
Without a map
Have you ever stood out in the rain
And longed

Are you afraid to hear
What you don't want to know
Is there anywhere at all
You're afraid to go

You're only inhibited
By your physical form
Till the moment of "death"
From the day you were born.

Ashleigh Marie Metcaff

Untitled

How sweet are those memories of days gone by,
When I was a boy in Burkesville High.
I went for a year and tried to excell,
I made straight A's, I'm proud I can tell.
But next year I met a beautiful girl,
The prettiest, I thought, in all the world.
She had a pair of sparkling brown eyes;
She attracted others, but that's no surprise.
So along came a boy very handsome and tall,
When he took my girl, he took them all.
And before I knew it, the year was past,
With me at the bottom of the sophomore class.

Russell Bow

Best Friends

You are my best friend.
Our friendship will never end.
You have been so nice to me.
Just watch and you will see,
How our friendship keeps growing,
From hot weather to when it's snowing.
I enjoy lifting your spirits high.
Way, way up there in the blue sky.
Secrets we will keep,
Especially ones that are very deep.
We meet all over the place,
But a bully you will never face.
'Cause you help me and I help you,
In all of our subjects, sports too.
We love to joke, we love to laugh.
Our friendship will never be torn in half.
Friends stick together that's how
Best friends forever, best friends now!

Erika Goodwin

United

The destructive technology that's taken over has no name,
And yet it causes so much pain.
When it comes to our home we act nonchalant,
For it to disappear is what we want.
But all we need is for nature to survive,
To pass any obstacle until every one has realized,
Nature must always live on,
Till the last day brings forth the dawn.
One night when the technology sleeps deep,
We all move towards it at slow creep.
Our heart beats accelerate so we feel it pulse in our mind.
We have trapped technology, it is technology's time.
Nature explodes with a unbelievable wrath
We have chosen our own destructive path.
Technology is dead for nature has claimed the land,
And we all lie dead in God's great hand.

Kelli Frondle

The Storm

The hawk flies low, and hovers above the grasses;
Its wings stop, and slowly move, until it dives, and passes,
Through the air, straight down for its prey.
This time it appears, the mouse or rabbit has gotten away.

The sheep seek shelter, as the rain begins to fall;
They get under anything, even feed bunks, not so tall.
The dog has run for shelter;
The birds are flying helter skelter.

The lightening, through the sky is fierce;
It appears the ground, it does pierce.
The ground shakes, as the thunder rumbles;
You can almost feel, the leaves from the trees tumble.

The sky becomes slowly lighter;
As the sun peeks through, making the world seem brighter.
Look to the east, and you can see the rainbow;
So, now the spirits lift, and we go back to the daily flow.

Jane J. Wiseman

"Extermination At Auschwitz"

There is a land that time fell still.
No living among its scores.
No breeze, no light, nothing, darkness,
but the face of death smiles from its floors
Here is a river of scarlet, red as blood.
No living dwells in its stream.
The flow of mortality it drained in flood.
Drained as the chosen screamed.

Jeffery Lance Westbrook

514

My Crime

I have nightmares all the time,
All about my crime.
My crime is that I know you because of what you did,
With the first shovel of dirt on my grave you digged.
I wish you could feel all my sadness,
Because it was all you that made this badness.
You're always on my mind,
Why is it I'm still doing time?
I was dead long before I lived,
The one thing I have learned is that I will never be able to forgive.

Amy Urban

"The Unattended"

As I sit here in my sterile surroundings,
    wall to wall carpets and cold chrome,
both to the eye and the touch

Your pencils stand tall and erect
    ready to meet the needs of the
ensuing day, and another urgent call
    of "Jean bring your book"
they too are cared for

Your plant is well watered,
    its leaves shining brightly
under your watchful eye and care
    if a brown spot appears,
you're the first to know it's there

But what about you,
wherein lie your needs,
your many calls gone unanswered

How do you express the deep regret
    of a heart gone unattended.

Jean Nichols

Play

In 1960 it is said
That Webster's was your dolly's bed.
In '95 we buy the things
Imagination used to bring.

A folded kleenex for her head
A bottle cap for bites of bread,
Her brides dress cut from mother's glove
Her veil a hankie pinned with love.

My brothers made to stand for hours
And hold the sheets for playhouse towers,
And sometimes they could play a part
In games that came from in my heart.

Sometimes I'd dress long-suffering cat
In frilly dress and pretty hat.
He knew pretending was my way
Of hoping dreams come true some day.

Is it better to provide
A ready-made tower in which to hide?
A child is at work in play
To learn to face the world some day.

Sharon Kossayda

Songs

A little child came up to me one day and said, "Sing me a song".
Instead I told him to listen to the wind.
The wind always sings a beautiful song.
On the wind ride the songs of birds.
It carries the cries of the newborn child.
Listen now and hear it rustle through the trees.
The leaves are singing about the life of their tree.
Happy notes in spring and lively notes of green in summer.
And then the coming of autumn, and the leaves sing no more.
In the cold, clear air of winter hear the wind whistle.
And in snows hear it howl out in mourning.
Shall I sing you a song now?
Rather hush, be still and listen to the songs riding always on the wind.

Michelle McCann

Just Words

All those things you said to me
Keep running through my head you see
And I have to remind myself
That it's just words, and it shouldn't hurt
Cause it's just words.

That's what you always say - Why do people care anyway?
It doesn't make sense why they get so tense
Get so overworked, become such jerks...over words.
Cause it's just words, just words.
Oh, but I know what I heard, and it wasn't just words
Cause I think of what you said
And get this feeling something's dead.

And it seems so obscure, you see I'm not really sure
Do I pick and choose which words are true?

And then you said you loved me.
And suddenly... I could see
As all those words came back to me
What you said was true, and I knew
What I just heard, it was just words.
Just words.

Yvonne M. Brunet

In Loving Memory Of My Grandma

The way that I felt, the day that you died,
Could not be explained, by the way that I cried.

To see you so peaceful, was such a relief,
To know you're not suffering, from anymore grief.

The hurt that I felt,
The sorrow was real,

Nothing can explain.
This pain that I feel.

To see you in pain, was so hard to do,
I can't imagine, how it felt for you.

It's to hard to take, one day at a time,
Without you here, to keep me in line.

You will always mean the world to me.
And so very much more.

Now that you, are no longer here,
My heart will always be sore,

I will think about you everyday,
And love you more than I can say.

One of these days, we will be together,
Until that day comes, I will love you forever.

Jennifer Poff

Untitled

I see before me this gentle one.
He is a teacher of true power,
with grace and humility.
He teaches as an exceptionally good parent,
who patiently allows the child to learn.
He needs not draw power nor fear from others,
for through supreme dominion he retains his own.
In turn, the student gracefully bows her head
in appreciation and respect,
for the lessons gratefully learned
from this gentle one.
Alas, the student wishes to say,
"I feel richer for knowing you"

Beth Elworthy

The Bartender's Lament

Too many hours behind the counter,
So he winds down on the other side.
Another night, and it's been hell on him,
So he takes a ride.

A woman, a drink, and a game or two,
Then he'll head on down the line.
Somebody else is waiting on him,
And he's got to go make it all fine.

He thinks about the future,
Plans he has for himself.
But like the liquor bottles,
He keeps putting them back on the shelf.

It's always gonna be tomorrow.
Then the day after is already here.
Trying to get it going on,
While he wastes another year.

It all sounds like insanity,
but it's the life he'll live.
and all the world expects of him
Is all he's got to give.

Karri R. Roper

Technology

Technology really has me up a tree,
It is very difficult for me to see.
What others rave is a great change,
To me - it seems that I'm in a cage,
There's no more retaining one's privacy,
Everything is out there for all to see,
It's hard for me, advanced in years,
To understand all the hoopla and cheers,
Of those who participate in the new age,
And think the new technology is all the rage,
What is happening on internet or super highway,
Is something to which I have nothing to say,
Except where's the privacy we once enjoyed,
When all nosey people we could always avoid?
Today everyone's life is a wide open book,
Those wanting information have an easy look,
At everything and anything all about you,
And the privacy I once knew has gone askew.

Chatherine F. Seidel

Grandparenting

It's difficult for me to say
All that grandparenting means to me
But after you've read the following
Hopefully you will see!

When you become a parent
With compassion, you really care
But with the birth of a beautiful grandchild
It's a feeling beyond compare!

You have the warmth and enjoyment
But none of the work to do
How much you get involved in their lives
Is usually up to you!

Maturity has made you wiser
Be supportive in all that you say
In the blink of an eye, they'll be adults
So enjoy them in every way!

Dee Dee Bowers

We Cannot Tire Of War Too Quickly

We cannot tire of war too quickly
   hate kills the source from whence is sprung
   our life and love and peace, undone
Yet some must lift the burden weighty
   and all too oft we them forget
   while still the drumbeat rolls

We can't lose sight of those before us
   their sacrifice would then be vain
But stocks are up, exchange is good
   the fertile land and hay to truss
So all too oft we them forget
   and still the mortars fall

We can't forget the sufferings gone
   the anguish there by torture fed
   hope torn apart and death a friend
Their lives were snuffed from earth in their dawn
   and all too oft we them forget
   while still the deathbells toll

Deborah L. Gatrell

Don't Give Up

DON'T GIVE UP on yourself, my friend, don't throw yourself away,
lift your chin, throw back your shoulders, hold your ground and stay.
There's no one who'll forsake you, all others count on you,
no one else will ever doubt the many things you do.
Alone, you hold the power; the key to how you fare,
and you can travel far and free if only you will dare.
A set back here, a mistake there, a failure now and then,
is no excuse, so pick right up and get back in again.
You can do it if you want to, you can do it if you trust,
and if you wish to prosper, to grow some, then you must.
The world is yours, it's out there, waiting for your touch;
your abilities and talents, goodness sakes you have so much!
To throw yourself away, my friend's, to slap the face of God,
and then continue on as the wretch, the fake, the fraud.
You have so much, you are so much, God's raised you up so true,
that every step achieved in life is toward the real you...
So catch that ball, then toss it, and then catch it once again—
don't put it down and turn your back and declare that it's the end,
For it is never over, since you have all the say—
so DON'T GIVE UP, no matter what, don't throw yourself away.

Cathe O'Donnell

Storm

The wind is in a rage, turning
the green leaves inside out.
They show silver underbellies stark
against an indigo sky.

Sunlight recedes further, heightening
vibrant greenery. That, too, recedes.
The leaves turn black as the shaking
branches become spider arms against
an eerie backdrop.

The thunder shouts, the lightning
shrieks, the wind moans as rain
bullets assault the windowpanes and
gutters. My heart thuds in
accompanying rhythm.

Suddenly calm descends, the storm
spent. Remaining is darkness, wind
whispering the leaves. And a little
lightning cloud on the television screen.

Mary Louise Gabrysh

The Season Of The Rising Sun

The long . . . cold . . . winter bids us fond farewell,
As the hope of springtime within us, swells.
Little children . . . soon . . . hard . . . at play,
Will herald the changes of April and May.

The trees will bud and the flowers bloom,
As the air is filled with Spring's perfume.
The insects will buzz, the baby strollers appear,
To echo a warning that summer is near.

The beaches will welcome the folk with delight,
As the crowds greet the tide both morning and night.
Steel gray skies will give way to blue,
Sunshine abound, as it dries morning's dew.

For this is the season of the rising sun,
When spirits are lifted, the doldrums are done.
A time when all cares seem to melt away,
The season of Hope . . . the Creator's new day.

Suzanne M. Perkins

Untitled

Once upon a time a long ago,
Her story had begun, her voice was low.
A story of a baby, love's purest light,
His birth would have been a miraculous sight.
His mother Mary made for him a manger bed,
A little pillow of hay on which to lay his head.
This little baby, so seemingly insignificant,
Would do things that were, oh, so magnificent.
He would raise the dead and heal the lame,
Help blind to see and mute to talk again.
Jesus, God's beloved son,
Would die for the sins of everyone.
This little baby born on Christmas Eve,
Is the son of God, won't you believe?

Laura Caldwell

Waves Of Love

Love is much like the ocean,
   for in it's depth there is beauty.
Beyond the depth there is fear.
   Million's of emotion's expressed by waves
dancing in the moonlight.
   The anger being splashed upon the rock's.
There is so much understanding,
   yet so much left misunderstood.

Leisa Mielke

The Rose

I put a rose on my grandfather's grave one Father's Day.
As I set it down I felt the power, the fear, and the love of my grandfather.
I felt like I was holding his hand.
The rose's dew felt like my grandfather's tears.
And the thorns were like his anger.
And the petals were like his face smiling at me.
And the smell was like his glory and his achievement.
My grandfather was kind and considerate and had a sense of humor.
I will miss him.

Frank Harris

"Oh Mother Of Mine"

As I look to my days of youth...
They are only filled with memories of you.

Your warmth and tender love always
embraced me, filling my heart with
pleasure and happiness.

When troubles seemed to bother me,
you always had words of kindness
and comforted me.

When others abandoned me or I lost
favor from them, you drew near to me.

You were always there with a smile and encouragement.

A rose is beautiful, it buds, the blossoms,
but only for a short time, then it fades away.

But you love in enduring present and
eternal, nurturing, touching everyone with love.

These are the feelings out of my heart
for you "Oh Mother Of Mine"

Frank Trojanek

My Angel

Mother is like an angel; she protects me from harm.
She nurtures and cares for me in her loving arms.
She is there to guide me because she knows what is best;
And make me do what is right, even though I protest.

She is always with me, through the good times and the bad;
And looking back I'll see how I miss those times we had.
She goes out of her way because to her, I am so dear;
A sense of security is felt just knowing she is near.

Her love is unconditional and it will not sway,
Knowing she'll still take me in when I've gone astray.
I can always look to her in my time of need,
Or tell her a little secret and know to it she'll heed.

She is there to console me when I'm feeling down.
It's comforting to know that she'll always be around.
For even when she leaves this life her spirit will remain;
As Mother becomes my angel and helps take away my pain.

She'll still be my watchman until my time is through;
And I become an angel for someone just like you.
So in prayer I say "Thank you" to the Father up above,
For granting me this "Angel" that I so dearly love!

Stephanie Louise Coker

Bugs In The Basement Broom

There are two bugs within the broom.
They thru the whisks do zoom, zoom, zoom.
They love the dark and dankness there.
They'll raise a family - where?
In that dark dank old broom, of course.
There'll be more bugs
Which will be worse!

Fay M. McCarthy

A Feast For The Senses

Rich was the pattern that you could not see,
You thought, "far too intricate, for a novice like me."
The threads were eclectic, some were old, some were new,
Some brightly colored, some just pale blue.
The textures were varied, some were plush, some were fine,
All woven, painstakingly - unparalleled design.
To the touch, it was enticing, it would ebb and then flow,
A feast for the senses, kindling imagination aglow.
It was my own pattern, that you could not see,
Alive, with a life, that took shape within me.
This pattern, the fabric of my heart and my soul,
My dreams woven through it, sacred intimacy, its goal.
A true soul mate could sense this, what you could not see,
Feel its warmth, love its tenderness, grasp its significance to a tee.
With its fantasy and providence and aura all it own,
Utilizing mind and the spirit as its needle and thread, sewn.
One day you might see it, or feel it, who knows?
When awakened by your touch, it might unfold as a rose.
So, give heed to your senses, feign neglect and you'll miss,
The patterns you might cherish, live peacefully, know bliss.

> *Carol Ernstein*

Spinning

Just down the road, in my neighbor's shed
Filled with bikes, balls, leftovers of childhood,
A spider's web hangs over a red child's sled,
Battered, broken, seemingly discarded.
But it wasn't the sled I watched as I stood
(Though to any who asked, that's what I'd have said).
I thought of all the times I had brushed down
Other webs. And I knew, too, that this one
Was probably not the first this same brown
Spider had woven, nor likely his last.
Intricate patterns, organic steel strands
Proof that, although beauty is so often cast
To cold earth and shattered, through faith and love
We can create again, our tender hands
Fashioning all the joy we can dream of.
And I, whose fragile heart has so often bled,
Smiled to think of what my love again could
be. By a small brown spider I was led
to spin again — to join my soul in dance
with the moon, the stars, the rain and the sun,
trusting in love and the "could be" of chance.

> *Peter Goss*

Little White Moth

You took a trip with me, little white moth
I plucked you from a place, far away
You Rode so snugly in a venetian blind
And kept your balance in the wind.

I took you to a foreign land
They didn't ask if you were there
And when my house was opened then
You came and flew you were my friend

Tonight before I go to bed, I'll send you out into the world
In hopes you'll find a life out there.
And spread your wings, across the land
And find a friend that you can love
And know I cared enough to let you go.

I grabbed you, oh so gently, and let you out the door
I watched you take flight my friend
I'll see you never more.

Please tell whomever you shall meet
that you once had a friend
Who cared enough to set you free
to roam the earth again.

> *Joyce H. Carpenter*

Sweet Each Day

Jesus wonderful shepherd and Guide,
you've been with me all of the way
You've lived in my heart since I was a child

And you are more precious today
you sought me out
a little lost lamb
and gathered me into the fold
and are still leading on at a genther pace,
Now that I'm growing old
And I thank you, Dear Lord for the
rivers we've crossed
That you never left me alone
That your beautiful presence grow
sweeter each day
on the way to my heavenly home

> *Mary Frances Osborne Harber*

D-R-C

Modern words make it sound better!
It's called, "Down Sizing", when
Your job is taken away from you.
You're not laid off, you're down sized!

When they give you two jobs to do,
In the same amount of time,
It takes to do your own job;
It's not slavery, it's "Restructuring"!

When you loose all the added
Benefits you worked for over
The last 16 years, and you're reduced
To tears; it's called a "Changed Of Policy"!

I guess by now, you can tell
That non of this rhymes!
It's cause I'm DOWN SIZING,
RESTRUCTURING and CHANGING MY POLICY!

> *Minnie Candle*

Broken Dreams

Looking back through the years things have never changed,
I'm still looking for lost love and searching for my dreams.
After years of wanting and hoping, I'm still lost within myself,
Needing to touch and hold, and be loved for what I am.

My heart burns deep inside, raging like my anger,
Deeply wanting what they hide because their pride is too strong.
Expressing what I feel is impossible to do,
They deprived me of my needs; my heart is made of stone.

The tears in my eyes sting like the growing pain,
Burning out like my hopes, making me turn cold.
Now it's far too late to tie the broken ropes
I'll never love again, or want what isn't there.

If only they knew about the love that they denied,
They have dragged a woman to a cruel and selfish child.
More tears will be shed for what I've longed for,
But never will I forget the pain inside my heart.

Now they will be memories, pictures in my past,
Soon they'll turn to dreams that never will come true.

> *Lindsey Inaba*

Trust

What should I call this thing,
Delicate like angel wings.

Hard to get and hard to keep,
Its rewards are hard to beat

Once you have it, there's no doubt,
A treasure you hold, so don't give it out.

Trust, the thing I'm speaking off,
Is a gain to keep at all cost

Cherish it and treat it well,
Once it's gone, this is your hell,

Because you can't seem to get it back,
It's lost for good, imagine that.

So nourish it, each single day
So it may never go away,

This delicate thing called trust,
A treasure to savor from dawn to dust.

Margitta Evans

Tracks

Standing on shallow ground, afraid to take another step
I know where I've been though it's not clear where I'm going
The (clock) hands keep ticking away, pounding like cannons of war
Unable to move, will I stand or fall? Maybe if I just stand still
The world passes by while dust batters my face
Visibility is low, tolerance is high, debris collects at my feet
Some things I am proud, some...I regret. The best seems far behind
Questions and fears no text can answer
I am blind to the future, deaf to the present, do I survive?
I am not living, I merely exist
The paved roads lead where others have already been
Follow me, my way is best - they do not know me
The wind is fierce - I struggle for breath - I close my eyes

Kris Crawford

A Tragedy

Why, when I walk the streets,
Must I don the mask of hostility?
I just want to be your friend,
But you're the one who could bring me to my end.

To live in peace I must kill
If only with my eyes.
And nothing hurts more than knowing
You're scared of my disguise.

But where I eat and where I sleep,
Survival is a crime.
I'm not allowed to defend myself;
I'd end up doing time.

And you don't choose to understand
These words I choose to speak
Because your eyes can't pierce the darkness
Of the world in which I creep.

So I'm doomed to yet another act
As the hero of this play
When all I want is to remove the costume
And live in your world for the day.

Jared Rhea

Hopeful Heart

I want to take the love in my heart, open up your life and
pour it in until it fills you.

I'd love to take the worried look on your face and with a touch turn
the frown into a look of complete contentment.

I'd be your rock, your comfort.

If my love had wings they'd lift your spirits to the
clouds erasing every trace of hurt you've ever felt.

I'd give you peace so you would sleep like a child who has
not a care in the world.

I'd bathe you in the warmth of the morning sun and refresh you
each night like a cool autumn breeze.

I'd be your lighthouse, chasing away all the darkness.

I'd fill your soul with joy and laughter or
be a shoulder for your tears,
I'd share the burdens great or small.

If my love had arms they'd reach to you
wherever you might be and hold
you, never too tightly but always secure.

Safe within my hopeful heart.

Cathy Coplin Benson

Dreaming

It was off the rocky, windy shore of Donegal
That I met my first true love
She was perched on a stone far out from shore
With a light rain coming from above

My heart went out to greet her
And she smiled back at me
In a moment a wave came in
And washed her out to sea

I returned today to that very same spot
To get one more glimpse of my ocean queen
I searched the strand from end to end
But nowhere could she be seen

I learned today what I should of known back then
It was only an Irishman's dream.

Thomas B. Moriarty

Rocking Chair

When, I go down town, I walk, pass, a store,
A, little, rocking chair was, sitting
all by, itself, in the window
As, my eyes, got a look, it
It brings back, a lot of memories of when
Grandma, would sit, rocking her grandson
goodnight, sleep, children were laying
next two, her heart, she sing
hymns, like, Jesus, love's little
children, and tell-a story of her
days, as a youth, going to school
riding her father's mule, that just
plowed, the field's and garden day before
She lived, without, used a coal oil lamp
Electric she had no, running water in her, home.
She cooked, baked, canned her own food home, made corn bread
just like mothers, on a old, coal stove iron skillet
they, cut, fire, wood, put in side of stove
in winters she sat for better days
cold air will flow in the house as she read the bible and prayed.

Roger L. Spencer

Begin Another Day

I wake up early morning to the fall of a summer rain,
And thru my open window, I hear the call of a distant train.
And I lay here a while, wishing in bed I could stay.
With the car breaking down, and the bills piling up,
Each day I'm getting older and there's nothing in my cup.
But I put my feet to the floor and rise, so I can begin another day.

The rain is falling harder as I pass thru the rooms.
The house is still, there's no one here to tease
away the gloom.
And I mutter to myself, "I don't care what happens anyway".
So I make the morning coffee and I sit alone to eat.
I'm off to work for 8 o'clock and I'm still half asleep,
But I shower, dress and find my keys, so I can begin another day.

But then I see the rain is easing,
And I hear singing in the trees.
By the time I hit the road, I smell roses on the breeze.
And I know there's sunshine around the bend!
And this good feeling will stay with me, until tomorrow,
When I wake early morning, To begin another day again.

Joyce R. Breen

Friendship Forever

There are things in life that bring people together,
Especially when life is going through stormy weather.
The night we met I thought my world was felling apart,
We both had become victims of a broken heart.
We do what we can and try to rearrange,
But some things in life we just can not change.
Our friendship grew and helped each other when down.
we seemed to be walking on some common ground.
This emotional tie can get carried away,
as I look back on that one particular day,
Our friendship was extended and I growing inside,
I had to tell you as I called to confide.
There are just too many reasons I could tell you why.
This life inside me can not die.
Time is now something we lack,
as you hold the torch that she may come back.
Your chances may have changed but please be my friend
I hope this friendship will never end.
and when that day comes this a child I'll deliver
I know then that friendship can be forever.

Caren M. Kenny

The Flower

Love is a seed planted between two people
Their trust, support, and care start the seed's growth
When the seed has sprouted,
And its blossom has come into bloom,
It is the most beautiful thing the eye can behold
But only continued love,
Can keep this plant alive
If this flower does die
What is left.
This bitter feeling
A bitter taste
The feeling of the lie
Spoken once to you
But never again
I love you.

Scott Davis

Unique As A Snow Flake

Snowflakes fall at the school house door and make me slip and slide.
Children build a fort of them and they crawl inside to hide.
Snowflakes grace my collar on a long coat made of wool.
Children follow in my steps as I make my way through school

Snowflakes soon form snowballs and in play at some are hurled.
And, some are now a snowman in this spontaneous winter world.
Snow flakes number billions as the snow reaches to my knee
yet, individuality all unique if I take the time to see.

The students that I teach each day gather near me, at my feet.
I pray to God, give me the strength, their expectations I must meet.
Lord, let me not ignore the gentle soul and mind
don't let me duck those hardened ones thrown at me from time to time.

Allow the fort they chose to build to occupy my room.
It soon will melt. It will be gone, no need for doom and gloom.
Allow them to build their snowman in a likeness that they choose.
Let me provide the opportunity and the tools that they use.

Unique as a single snowflake in the raging blizzard of life
make me content within the knowledge, education must match the life.

Steven L. Kittleson

Above All - January 4, 1996

I have my health, my work, my hobbies
I have my life
Above all, I have my children and my love

I have my faculties, my mother, a roof over my head,
Food on the table
I have my life
Above all, I have my children and my love

I have friends, true friends
I have a past, a present, and a future
I have my mother, again
I have my health, again
I have my life

Above all, I have my children and my love

Patricia J. Crosby

Snowmen

On Christmas Eve,
I tossed and turned,
I looked out the window and then I learned,
That snowmen do come to life.
So I went outside into the night,
The cold wind hit my face,
And snow was blowing all over the place,
Then the snowman took my hand,
I began to understand,
That he was taking me for a ride,
We were flying high in the sky,
When we landed I started prancing,
Because the snowmen were all dancing,
At the strike of midnight we went home,
Then I slept the whole night long.

Laura Elizabeth Crevier

Help

What happens to our futures, depends upon our pasts.
Lessons unlearned the first time, we will repeat at last.

So let's not rush forward mindless, but plant each foot solidly,
to keep ourselves from falter, and create what is to be.
For our futures lie in our own hands, our fates and destiny's.

So let's make peace amongst ourselves, and walk on hand in hand.
Feel the LOVE of GOD shine in to help us understand;
that we all have our own hills to climb, but help your fellow man.

Richard L. Thornburg

Untitled

I wish I could heal you
My American friends
I wish I could set you free

We all should get out of this place
Create a new kingdom, see a new dawn
I don't know though
I'm just dreaming on
But what's wrong with dreaming?
Reality is gone
So if you want to come, come right along
Your mind is free from all that is unpure
At Panacea, the Universal cure
The mystery maiden and your totems reign
To protect you and release deep pain
Pray to the sun and the moon of night
Bathe within their sacred light
Nearby at the top of a tropical hill
Is the temple of your soul
Go and gather your ancient gifts and talents
And share them with your friends in the village below

Rob Barclay

"This Was The Week"

This was the week that the trees became bare,
In the frost and the chill of the November air.

The sun is going down now in the late afternoon,
the warm summer sunshine is gone all too soon.

A few leaves are still hanging only by a thread,
As the sweet smell of burning wood enters my head.

The sunset is orange peeking through the field,
Barely showing through out stalks of the bountiful yield.

The trees all surrender those last stubborn leaves,
The cold days of NOvember upon them like thieves.

The night is so quiet the birds you can't hear,
It signals the end of another passing year.

Soon the cool days of November will go,
They'll pass into memory making room for December snow.

Joseph J. Toppi Jr.

Marriage

Marriage is like a phantom book
In the Library of life,
Co-authored and co-edited,
By a loving husband and wife.

The book is bound by heartstrings
And humor, of course, is the glue.
The pages are printed on purest soul,
Invisible ink will do.

The final chapter is written:
You have come to the "Death do us part"
But you will recall every twist of the plot
For the contents are carved in your heart.

Joan T. Muller

Your Life is Like a Rose

Your life is like a Rose,
it starts as just a tiny seed,
then it grows and leaves from important parts of our lives.
Every once in a while we come across a thorn,
some sharper than others, but soon enough it smooths back out and
only helps us to become better people.
As we grow and discover our true colors, a blossom blooms
and out comes the most beautiful thing you can ever imagine...

Jessica Rizza

Childhood

Thirty years of bittersweet youth
Has come and passed.
Time seemingly races with unwarranted haste
Towards tomorrow's uncertainty.
Innocent childhood...forlorn...
Forgone...but unforgotten.
Vivid sights in the mind
Embrace unsurpassing glimpses
of yesteryear's blissful moments.
Reverberations of youthful joy
Echo loudly
In my ears of hopeful regression.
Still, childhood runs away from the present
As if it were but a speck
In the realm of a lackluster dimension.
Yet that speck incessantly fulfills the happiness
That would forever remain
Within the memories of my life.

Arthur Nieves

"The Cane Cutters Ballad"

Am I your cane cutter
swinging a machete like a pendulum
like my father, my grandfather and his father
please, forgive me
if I am not like the others

I will sing hymns and psalms to praise your beauty
to the beat of oxen hoofs
pulling cane filled carts
so that everyone
across this land will see
what I already know
and as I sing
I will be thinking of when our lips touch
in a sweet embrace
because your lips are like a medicinal tea made with honey
healing my wounds
giving me strength
as I cut sugarcane beneath the Caribbean sun
tanning my neck
marking my cane cutter status

Michael S. Borrero

M.L.K.

Happy Birthday M.L.K.
Sorry, still no change today.
With candy coated attitudes
we believe a different life exudes,
for still when we come face to face
we fixate on our brother's race.
Changing some, eluding race.
the pain still tears the hearts of mothers.
Happy Birthday M.L.K.
we'll try again some other day.

Mark Patterson

Untitled

Today I came to the woods with Beth,
before the cool of the evening disbursed,
and walked with her along the well-worn paths,
but pretended that she and I were the first.

Our hours, they passed, as flittering seconds,
as we talked of the creation of such grace.
Never supposing any other could be true,
for God's image was reflected on natures face.

Jason M. Curtis

Love Conquers All

A soft summer wind blows in the night
while the birds and crows are startled with fright.
A faint song of help is heard in the air, the crows take off as the
birds just stare. Into the night they fly like a hawk
straight to the call, just one huge flock.
They land by a weak tiny baby dear, as the mother is there shedding
a tear. The mom looks at the crows as if to say,
"please help my poor only baby today."
The crows bow their heads, there is nothing to do.
A long horrible pause sets between the two.
As they hoped and prayed for a miracle that day,
the baby stood up and walked away.
The crows looked up with love in their eyes
as the mother watched the baby with tear filled eyes.
The baby walked to his mother and nuzzled her cheek.
The mother could tell that he was no longer weak.
As they all sat there with question in their mind,
they all knew that love saved the little boy.
Love was the cure, love did it all
We all count on love when someone falls.

Karissa Miller

Lassitude

Little more than silk
Lost in my abeyance
Flicking my song westward
My mouth is easy turning
What wraps a note
Around my tongue
Floating a word past my teeth
Portraying all that whistle
While this stillness lets me humble
As I've humiliated self-pity
Comes to me once and then to score a job
A well-had resentment
And set its fingers upon me
As dismayed as that puppet
My confinement is convenient
Lacking in the comfort
Cloaking all the demons
The possessions that I know of
My walls have faded them now

Jessica Earl

Free

The world turned its back on me
and took my wings so I will never be free
The world fed on me like a parasite
and now I do not have the courage to go out and fight
My life has no certain direction
or any serious intention
All my liveliness has been shunned out
and my life is now just a crooked route
My deepest thoughts worry me
because I don't know if they will come true for
everyone to see
Every night I cry myself to sleep
because what I have to overcome is so deep
I will probably fail
and the whole world will just look at me and stare
My soul is becoming small
every time a tear decides to fall
All my hope has been strangled out of me
please world, turn back around and let me be free

Andrea Kajder

"Let's Get Ready To Rumble"

Twas the night before the fiesta bowl under a Tempe sky
All big red huskers celebrating, getting tipsy and feeling high
Morning came upon them, eager for the game to begin
On and on the hours went, it seemed forever to them
Some had their faces painted red and white
Others completely decked in red, what an awesome sight!
Finally it was kick off time, and Florida was the first to receive
Our big red defense prevailed in the end, with unexpected ease
The NU blackshirts shut them down rolling over like tanks,
You can't have any fun in your gun when all you shoot is blanks!
The huskers played tough and hard till the gators couldn't take
anymore Florida didn't even phase then, the final "62-24"

Juanita J. Byers

Christmas '95

The Holiday Season is once again upon us,
    Tis time for us to make a fuss.
The leafless trees stand as the wintery winds blow,
    While some places are white with fresh fallen snow.
The houses are trimmed with garland and lights,
    To make way for the Festive Holiday nights.
If you're from the North, the South, the East or the West,
    A joyous Christmas celebration is always the best.
As the families gather and prepare to celebrate,
    The children are all stationed for a Santa wait.
Whistle a tune or sing a song,
    As the countdown to Christmas goes along.
Peace, health, happiness and love,
    Are the wishes we wish from God above.
Extend your hands and a glass of cheer,
    For Jesus's birthday and the ones we hold dear.
Whether our loved ones and friends are far away or near,
    Have a Merry Christmas and the very best in the New Year.

Rose Serrano

Flower

Beautiful, fragrant, flower
Across the garden I saw you
Your stem, your petals, your smell
All more magnificent than the rest
How your beauty extinguished me
Your touch was that of heaven
Your fragrance was that of pure euphoria
But your thorn was sharp
Cautioning me of your independent existence
So I left you be
Leaving you in your garden home, to bloom and grow
But oh, how I wanted you
You beautiful, fragrant, flower

Brennan Cipollone

Untitled

Funny.
I can hear your silence.
I can hear the cries of your inner most thoughts,
And even the heart felt rhythm of your soul.
I can see the pain in your face and deep into your eyes.
Those eyes...I look into them and I am lost.
I lose track of time and place and find....only now.
This moment. As if I am suspended in time.
Hanging by a thread. I gasp for air.
I find none. I reach out to you and you move away.
I'm falling....Help me!
At the last moment, you reach out to me.
I feel safe at last, but am I?
Can I trust you? Do I really want to - again?
I'm at a loss. The world spins and continues
Not knowing, and not caring,
that I dream...that I am afraid.

Teresa P. Bowman

Song Of The Soul

As evening falls with sun-swept fire,
I lay in wake, driven by man's desire.
Among the cliffs of rock so sheer,
There lies in hiding my inmost fear.
It has burdened me day and burdened me night,
But with God's power, I'll keep it from sight.
To my God alone I lift up all praise,
For He is pure in all of His ways.

Oh earthly beauty and all spacious sky,
I seek out your face, to look in your eye.
So full of wonder and so full of grace,
All I can think of is God made this place.
The sweet smell of the grass and cool evening dew,
They remind of your touch, so soft and true.

I picture mountain tops and valleys below,
I sit there and ponder over all that I know.
There in a field your light shines so bright,
Like a lily among thorns-is your beauty this night.
You're a flowering rose in the desert of life,
Unexpected splendor, so soothing to strife.

Matt Jackson

Our Love

Our love is the truest,
we feel it in our hearts.
Every time I look in his eyes,
I want to fall apart.
    He makes my life worth living
always loving,
always giving.
    He is the best that's happened to me,
I know we'll be forever.
Just as long as he loves me,
my love won't stop - not ever.
    He makes me as happy,
as I could possibly be.
Never thinking of himself,
before he thinks of me.
    I am his world,
and he is mine.
As long as we stay together,
We'll both be just fine.

Melanie June Fooks

There Once Was A Guy....

There once was a guy
Who dreamed of coaching football when he looked up at the sky

He wondered and worried and prayed everyday
Until the right people came around his way

For then it was Martin, a Clipper he became
And with that, Coach "O" was his name

He studied the defense, watched tape after tape
He ran the boys ragged, and himself got in shape

He believed in hard work, no guts, no glory
And the first game was won, 32-0 was the story

The hard times hit, team spirit was down
But Coach "O" fired up, "Son, wipe off that frown."

This coach they respected and loved to poke fun
Through discipline and toughness, the last three games were won

This coach grew and learned more than just football and reason
For now, on the field is where you'll find him each and every
    fall season

There once was a guy who said, "I can."
Where there once was a guy, there now stands a MAN.

Shana Daily

"Gently, Please, God"

Turn back the clock, oh hands of Father Time!
Allow my heart a quicker beat
    my feet a lighter step...and yet,
Do not settle me into a
    bygone world where life
    was tedious and difficult.
Do not leave me in the days of worry...
Sorry I had spanked a little boy.

Do not take away the creases from my cheeks
Or the look of wisdom within my faded eyes.
What then, you ask...where will you take me?
Only on a brief journey that will not last
Into that youthful past...

For I have seen my yesterdays
    and choose to stay in the present.
Without a fear for tomorrow
    when you, Time
Will take my hands in yours
And the ticking ends

Elaine S. Stevenson

Teaching

I went to college to learn to teach,
Children's minds I was going to reach.
And when at last, with diploma in hand,
I got a job, I thought life was grand.

Into the classroom I marched with pride,
To unlock the potential in each child's mind.
I taught from books each word with care,
All my knowledge I wanted to share.

But as the years went flying past,
I felt something missing, just out of my grasp.
Yes, I knew all the "book words" to say,
But there was more than that needed each day.

So now I awake each day with a prayer,
"Please God, let me know YOUR peace to share.
To teach and instill this peace to all
And that on you, Lord, we can surely call.

At the end of the day with the setting sun,
Let me rest in the knowledge that it was done.
That I spoke and acted in a kindly way,
And passed it on to all others today.

Fran DePatie

Time in the Garden

Measured in lengthening shadows
Not for the sake of numbers of hours:
But for how many birds come to nest;
Vivid bunches of fresh jonquil, sweet roses
and pungent asters as they wax and wane.
Leaves let go, first a few and then many
Like the first snow fall,
Marked and measured.
In our memories with marriages, the birth of children,
the aging of friends, death of a parent.
Year upon year,
Familiar.

Margo Anne Sosa

It Happened After 40 Years Of Marriage

It happened after 40 years of marriage
It's what we now so often hear and see!
I found out that my wife's lover
Is a much younger man than me!!!

He now has the nerve to come to the house
And last night at the door
My wife met him with a kiss
God - I can hardly take no more!!!

I went to see my lawyer
And said, "put the divorce papers in the mail."
I'm still in shock - don't know where I'll go
Lord, how did my marriage fail?

My lawyers laughed and said to give it more thought
And I'm glad I listened because I realize it's true
The "Big guy" who has stolen her love
Is my two year old "Grandson" too!!!

William T. McIntyre

The Swing

I see you in the twilight;
your rusty frame hovering,
creaking with each breath the wind takes.
I smile to myself,
remembering their taunts and jeers—
"you're too old, you're too old..."

I run to you
and jump into your steel grasp—
your hug of youth.
You are so old, I am so childlike.

"Look at me, Daddy!"
I giggle, close my eyes...
Ride you higher and higher
until my tiny hands grasps a star.
"I can do it, Daddy!"

A falling tear, a slight grin,
and childhood returns.

Elizabeth A. Carle

The Wonderer

Weary mind, eyelids a-dropping,
wondering
pondering
about the dark infinity that is the night

Never sleeping, quietly fading,
wondering
contemplating
about the dark infinity - the night

Slowly departing, the heart rejoicing
slumbering
reposing
finally being one with his dark love - the night

Desiree Ong

When I Meet And Met Him

The scintillating warmth of his smile
And eyes that give me all
The encouragement for awhile
To answer my own inner call
To create from what's in me
To write and to dance and to play
Riding the crest of fired energy
I found in myself, through him, that lay
In me all unbound, can it be,
When I meet and met him, on that day.

Trisha Fike

Something's Lost

There's something lost in my mind
That's confusing and hard to find.
Is it faces of people I see each day?
Is it my thoughts or the words I say
That tumble out in spasmodic order?
It's looking down an empty corridor
With rooms on each side of the hall
That frustrate, confuse and yet call
Me from the safety of my little world.

I hide behind a gaping smile
While feelings are allowed to pile
In mountainous heaps upon the floor
Of my mind — shut to the door
That won't open and let people in.
As my body slowly turns to tin,
I giggle, laugh and play the role
Of an infamous actress whose lines I stole
To keep me in the safety of my little world.

There's something lost in my mind
That's confusing and hard to find.

Carol L. Hottman

Walking With The Lord

I took a walk with the Lord today,
it was my special way to pray

I knew he was walking beside me, as we looked over
the land, he gave me a hug and held my hand

You can't imagine how I felt that day, as the Lord
and I began to pray

We knelt together and we looked toward the sky,
things aren't so bad he said, and there was a twinkle in his eye

He said dear father help these people here on earth
especially the ones you have just given birth, Satan
is ever present with his cunning ways, letting sin
look enjoyable so your people don't pray

Help all your children who believe in your spirit
and light, be with them always both day and night

We rose together and as He walked away,
He said remember I will return for you all again someday

Audree Trombley LaFontaine

Desire

Impatient with vagueness,
Angry with lack of definition,
Unable to see the beauty
Of fluid and formless emotion;
You forced our misty longing
To congeal and coarsely condense
Into passionate desires
Of fully known starkly palpable sense.

From the edges of shadows
You found a definition of fire,
When the dance of turbulent softness
Calmed into the naked clarity of desire.
An innocent stream caught
And enclosed by an unyielding dam,
To forever watch and possess
Its own steady reflection of sham.

Cold eyes of a vulgar day
In search of my sorrow and shame,
Stab into my empty depth
Which is now your desire's rigid frame.

A. K. Sen

Coffee Break

I am, for whatever reason, sitting down
and drinking coffee and talking to the INNER MAN.

"And what's wrong with that?"

I am after all, a SUPERVISOR in this vast and
crappy CONGLOMERATION. ORGANIZATION??

Run by Baby Boomers...?

Who say "I'm 50 plus by God".. who walk and talk
in limited vocabulary... "Like you know.. and COOL...
and like, you know???

I look askance. It's tough to verbalize.. you know."

I reflect. I can remember.. back to last November...
when the sun was shining overhead and my Lap-Top
SCREEN WAS CLEAR AND CLEAN.. and I sit and sip and
watch the BOOMER APPROACH...

"FRIG them windows" he says. WE'RE CLEAN SWEEPERS"
he says. "ESP guys" he says.

"I'm a firm and steady guy" I say... "On a coffee
break..." He stares and I smile..

I drink my coffee and leave.

Robert Baker Davis

The Search For Atlantis

I smile at my situation
A bittersweet happiness occupies me
A cheerful sadness
Love, success, money elude me but loom on the horizon
And what broad horizons they are
I sigh
Maybe Jack Kerouac had the right idea
Holden Caufield is someone whom I look up to
But I know I must be true to myself.
The only thing important in this life is to share it with someone else
I fall in love fifty times a day but never get anywhere
The only thing important in this life is to leave
your mark on this world
I dream of the great contributions I will make to society
What am I doing?
Writing in a notebook.
I would chuckle, but I worry about being a
hypocrite to myself.

Fred Kontur

To Wish To Dream

There's ne'er enough time to do as I'd wish,
A cool mornings walk in the woods thru the mists.
A sail on a lake that is stirred by the wind,
To lay by a fire in the dusk of days end.
To live someone's life thru the words of a writer,
To wake with the thought that this day will be brighter.
No rushing about, no schedules to meet,
To paint if I'd like, hear music so sweet.
A cat purring softly, the flowers in bloom,
Rain on my face, to look at the moon.
To dream in the day of the night coming warm,
The passion of lovers to build as a storm.
Then break with a flood of exhausted release,
To drift into sleep, side by side, so at peace.
I know I can't to all the things, I would like,
But, through wishes and dreams, I may find some respite.

Dona Hawley

Let Brotherly Love Continue

The flame of the candle burns straight and erect as he stood
    until the silver cord loosened.
The Lord's Prayer silently recited as the flame glowed
    in memory of my brother...
Who's spirit returned to God on this seventh day of December '94
the day made infamous for the Japanese attack on Pearl Harbor '41.
The day will forevermore have truer meaning for those bereaved.
Knit souls...
    We were companions in many lives and will be again.
    Love was never voiced, only in thought and deed.
    Lives joys and sorrows took on an aspect privileged for brothers.
    Gemini, both, our personalities blended...
        few words were needed, few actions taken.
The voice of my brother's soul
    trumpets in my head...
    whispers in the night...
For he was written in the Book of life.

Thomas E. Yaudes

Untitled

You and I were meant to be, in love with you I fell
I love you darling more each day, I hope that you can tell
I want so much to be with you on this journey we call life
To share it with you always, one day you'll be my wife
I'll stand by you, in all you do, show you that I care
Together we can live and love through experiences we share
With love that comes so naturally, love that remains true
No other will I ever love as long as I have you
I do know we will have hard times, disagreements now and then
But I know we can work through these, I know you as a friend
Friends and lovers, companions are we, we're really quite a team
You're everything I want and more, beyond my wildest dream

Robert R. Blake

Our Walk On The Beach

Sadness
  It is black
  Surrounding the heart
  The beat goes on
  Yearning to lift the darkness
Today
  God's creation broke through
  The sun shone warming the sand and feet
  Tinting the body and sky with hues of red
  The water cooled the feet and spirit
  The endless waves took the black out to sea
Tomorrow
  The black may come back
  God's creation will be there the blue sky
  The green grass the yellow flowers
  The rainbow to again lift the darkness
  And bring back the calm

Joanne Kamps

Atlas

One day mighty legs will grow weary
and the dreariness of the earth
becomes too much for one to bare.
So he rips that weight off his back
tearing and ripping the world in half
from its hottest seam he pulls and yanks.
Colliding cold winds from above and below
meet in the center and embrace.
Now I stand freezing and cold.
Unable to tell young from old
and I do not know snow from snow.
So what else could I possibly know?

Harlan Kroff

Moonview

I passed with laughter through the gate
knew I was arriving late
hoped to hide some bitter tears
hoped to lose a bag of fears...
    and discovered to my woe
    beyond the gate, a field of snow
and in the ice these words were writ
"It's not the time for this bulls**t!"

And so, I emptied out the bag
scrutinized my every pain
visualized my every hand...
    lived the anguish once again.
    Discovered shades that wine had dimmed,
The little nightmares, fit and trim.

And then my tears became a flood and washed away the snow
    the bitterness was strong as p**s
    and WOW that field did grow.

Nurtured now, and manicured
    I've civilized that space
    but as we speak I swear to God, Another gate is in my face.

    Eve Van Syckle

The Rest'rant

The table seemed too big for her.
She sat alone a woman with white hair, glasses.
A purple flowered blouse.
Her face, wrinkled, with her cheeks full
and her expression lonely.
The look in her eyes was haunting.
I've said in the past that the elderly were "old and withered"
For this I apologize.
Her face wasn't withered - only wrinkled,
and yet I could feel the softness of her cheek.
The Anonymous Patron.
I looked at her. I wished I could sit with her.
Talk to her. Keep her company. Yet I couldn't.
All I could do was look.
And she finally looked at me. And I smiled.
And she smiled back, nervously, and went back to her meal.
And I felt for her so much.
But there was nothing I could do.
Except remember ana never forget
the look on her face and the story her eyes told.

    M. David Lopez

Untitled

Why must children learn to weep?
Why must pain be taught at an early age?
I know that maturity only comes through tears, but why?
A child's smile is the rainbow's pot of gold;
a child's tear can tear out the heart of God.
Life can be beautiful
(or so I seem to remember),
children can be happy
(or is that only a dream?)
and love does exist
(if only in bloody brows and dying words
Why have you forsaken me?)

Children, be strong.
Forget the pain.
Laugh while you can,
because when you forget
beauty will forever die.

    Jeremy Hedges

Virtues Of A Skunk

I'd like to write a poem, on the
virtues of a skunk, and if it doesn't
sound so good, we could just say it stunk.
    They eat a lot of insects that damage
our tomatoes, and we can be real thankful
that it doesn't eat potatoes.
    I ran into a mother and six
little ones one day. She gathered
them around her and then said "let us pray"
    Don't get too friendly with the cat or
even try to pet it, for if it
mistakes your intent, oh boy you
sure will get it!
    With their unique protection, they
do not have to bite, they're easy to
identify, they're always black and white.

    Oliver P. Walston

Untitled

I always like to look at the ocean
and to hear the sounds of the waves. It makes
me feel so relaxed and forget about everything.
Sometimes, I think my feelings for Billy are like
the ocean. It seems to have no end. The
motions of the waves and changing time of the
tide sounds like my passion that I feel for
him. The water is so clear and clean that is
the way my love is for him. My feeling for
Billy will last as long as I live; because
they are like the salt; It's solid and Crystalline.

    Rosa Rosales Szulewski

Paint And Thinner

Paint and thinner and thinner and paint,
All around me, within me, below me,
Touch me, I said to her, and then she touched me
With her paint and with her thinner,
Oh.... I know all there is to know about paint.
Feeling paint, feeling and paint and demons,
In a green and blue and round room so full of demons...
And propaganda and Hitler and Arjon - what a great leader
    to cry during battle.
Half Indian, Half Man, Half White, Three Halves equals one.
Many mathematicians are now proven wrong.
I laugh at three halves equals one,
Why do I want to tell, to make me seem different or exotic or
    strange or normal or Arjon.
Khan pops into my head so often. I'm not sure why.
I hate using the word why and the word hate.
Here comes morning, and with it the light.
Here comes the light too fast to comprehend, too slow to see.
It makes me cry, I'm so emotional I cry.

    R. C. Ohlson

Renewal

The sun, red as fire, slowly melted away resistance
against the cold world.
Crisp cool air, whipped about by lashing winds, scarred
the hill that was once brazen with wild flowers.
The soul of the earth was touched by sorrow.
Broken and battered, yet not quite smothered completely.
A droplet, strewn by the tears of an Angel, fell upon the ruin.
Tiny, yet ever so powerful, it grew, spawning rivers and oceans.
Mountains, once again were green with life
Birds returned to singing and natures balance was almost again.
Peace overcame the harsh world that was.
I sighed inside for I knew I had been touched
in heart to dream such a dream!
Renewal

    Dianne M. Lee

Pages

As the warm soft sun peeks over the meadow and
gently awakes God's creatures great and small, I
think how wonderful...
In the pages of my mind I dream of days gone by.

I remember the gentle touch of your hand and the
warm brush of your lips and I weep.

The ravages of time has made its claim, and I
wonder why I feel the same warm glow.

Now it's late and we will go, but I'll remember my
love of long ago in the pages of my mind....
Always

Antoniette V. Rando

The Brightest Star

Heaven needed one more angel;
I know God this is true;
Because you chose my Grandpa;
To come and live with you.
I'll miss his voice, I'll miss his laugh;
I'll miss his smiling face;
I know there'll never be a man;
Who could ever the his place.
God take care of my Grandpa;
And show him lots of love;
As he did for us on earth;
And now does from above.
As much as I will miss him;
I know he now can rest;
He's safe from all the evil;
Taken care of by the best.
So when I look up late at night;
And see the brightest star;
I'll know it is my Grandpa;
Shining down from afar.

Tina A. Michael

"Love"

Did you ever love someone
but knew they didn't care?

Did you ever feel like crying,
but knew it wouldn't get you anywhere?

Did you ever look into their heart
and wish that you were there?

Did you ever try to move on
knowing life's not fair?

You live your life in misery

You almost go insane

There is nothing in the world that causes so much pain.

Kymberly J. Clifton

My Great Grandson

I count my blessings, name them one by one
Then say a prayer for my great grandson.
Little smiling man with his sun kissed hair,
Tho he's far away in my heart he's here.
May he grow up tall, stand above the crowd,
In all that is good be stalwart and proud
No general, president, big tycoon or
Astronaut who'll walk an the moon.
I want him to become a good man
And meet life bravely, the best he can.
In years to come amidst both good and bad
The Nation's fate hangs on such a lad.

Catherine L. Grizzle

Gods Most Precious Gift

O how I love this frosty morn
The day our precious Lord was born
The shepherds following the light
Came to see the wondrous sight.

There the new born baby lay
Wrapped in swaddling clothes on the hay

The angels watching over him
Because he was such precious gem.

The angels watching from above
Their hearts were so full of love

So on this cold and frosty morn
Let's all remember who was born.
For it is christ Jesus who gives us love
From his wondrous home above.

Evelyn Raby

Beside The Still Water

I walked through the meadow one day
    where all nature in beauty doth lay
and where all nature seems to meet
    in a realm of blessed retreat.
I walked beside the water so clear
    and felt that the Lord was surely near,
and our Lord's words I did utter,
    "He leads me beside the still water".
I thought of our Lord as he walked by the sea
    beside the waters of blue Galilee
where he, too, found a blessed retreat
    to prepare for the throng he soon would meet.
By the shores of his tempest-stilled sea
    they knew he was sure to be,
eagerly coming from far and near
    His kind and gentle words to hear.
Here he taught them his every truth
    to rich and poor, to age and youth,
and here their troubled hearts calmed he,
    beside the waters of blue Galilee.

Martha F. Wells

Steelmill

i remember margret
her freckle punched face
absorbing concealing revealing

tears pain anger secret

her straight uniform needle tipped hair jagged
molded square at the shoulders forehead protecting
helmet guarding approach touch
her cutting blue eyes chiseled sculpted slits
warning penetrating slicing the intruder
her uninviting closed narrow lips bound shut
honed razors mutated muted never telling
never witness to her creator manufacturer
never testimony to her assembly process abuse
her welded tight silence shame guilt knowledge
of who forged her steel pounded her shield's shape
hammered the rivets into her armor shrouded innocence
erected her impenetrable fortress secreting from the world
a beautiful ten year old girl adorned with a party dress

R. E. Shenberger

527

The Faith Of Sisyphus

Once when I was still small in school,
they showed us a strange picture;
among a seemingly senseless mass of dots,
they said you could see a certain face.
Well, I looked until my eyes overflowed,
but all I ever saw was random squirming paint.
Everyone else seemed to see this mystery,
so I smiled to conceal my shame.

The memory recurs from time to time;
like an avalanche of sickening suspicion,
thoughts of stupid splattered paint
smash all the living hopes I have
and sweep away all the faith I've built.
But like Sisyphus I simply shrug
as once more I try to roll my stone
up toward ultimately unattainable heights.

Roslyn Coates

"Total Recall"

I ventured out to work at the mall,
And found that my car had been recalled.
My boss says, "Because of your lack to work at all,
Your present employment has been stalled."
Broken heart and appalled,
I trek into the chilly fall.
Arrival at my apartment tall,
I find my things out in the hall.
This note I find tacked to the wall,
"Your marriage has been annulled."
To me it seems to take a lot of gull,
To be thrown out at your first downfall.
Then a southern, dreamy voice seems to call,
"Be not alarmed, I had a ball;
Now start over, wake up ya'all,
This dream has just been — recalled!"

Vernon W. Goodrich

Love Grown

When we met, we were so young
Just sixteen years of age,
When big romance was a high school dance
And the whole world was our stage.
I caught his eye and he caught mine
And I guess that's how it starts,
When a spark so new and so unsure
Finds its way to two young hearts.
The spark soon grew and so did we
Grow closer along the way,
And that's when passion became our fashion
And we planned our wedding day.
We've been through many things since then
Through our wedded years,
And have kept that spark of love alive
'Tween diapers, joys and tears.
We tend our marriage like a garden
That we never take for granted,
With patience, faith and energy
For that seed of love once planted.

Cyndi Futch

"The Love Of A Lifetime"

Like a tiny little pebble in the master's hand,
To the smallest mound of clay in the potter's plan,
The love of a lifetime begins with a dream,
An answer to prayer on bended knee.

It enters its magic with God's gentle nudge,
And grows from a whisper to a mountain of love.
No mortal can explain how it all begins,
The creator of the universe only knows when.

Across the ages it spans like a mighty ocean breeze,
And soars through the heavens where the angels sing.
But gently one day it touches the heart
With a passion so tender no words can impart.

Its majesty lingers in every human soul,
For the joy of its splendor will never grow old.
Awesome wondrous grandeur could not begin to touch
Just how it feels to be in love.

Then when life's journey on earth is done,
On the wings of a dove Angels carry it home.
Back to its beginning in God's divine scheme,
Where the love of a lifetime began with a dream.

Nancy Carolyn Wilson

Untitled

A light breaks through the trees.
All the while,
The rain throws its pelting drops
down onto the earth.
A hunger wells from within,
But the food on my plate
Does not soothe.
All the while,
The rain throws its pelting drops
down onto the earth.
The wars of the world,
and the inner-city
burn with rage.
All the while,
The rain throws its pelting drops
down onto the earth.
The humans' reign upon the earth,
has ceased to be.
All the while,
The rain throws its pelting drops down onto the earth.

Robin Dzvonik

I Would

If I could I would hang the moon,
for you this I would do.

If I could I would take the sun,
and make it shine just for you.

If I could let you touch the stars,
I would give you the whole array.

When you wanted I would make it rain,
cooling you night or day.

If you wanted the skies, the land, the life, and the sea,
I would give them all to you,
if that could only be.

If you wanted color,
a rainbow I would unfurl.

For you know that if I could my love,
I would give you the whole world.

Angela Lynn White

Simpler Times

In this fast paced, harried life
filled with work, worry, and strife,
I often think that it is sad
that we have lost sight,
of the simpler things in life.

To work we rush, we've bills to pay,
no, we don't have time to play.
Our babies left with strangers
still, we need more money to get our fill.

The precious things in life must wait until some far
off future date, when we may have some time to spare.

So off they go to daycare malls,
a group of little lost soul dolls,
until the end of day is near,
then we appear to dry their tears.

The sitter says Sue said "bye-bye" and
Johnny's shoes he's learned to tie.
Oh simpler times when we could be
the ones to hold those memories,
I long for simpler times.

Kathleen O'Brien

Missing You

I've never met a friend as special as you,
you made me happy when I was blue.

Someone like you can't be forgotten or left behind,
because you are in my heart and always on my mind.

I can remember the good times and even the bad,
but we will always be friends happy or sad.

Please don't forget me because I won't forget you,
you are a great friend and that I say is true.

Tears you may weep but that is always okay,
as long as those are happy tears of our long gone days.

Laraine Vogel

You Can't Hide From The Moon

Sometimes a party can be so silent
In a way you're always alone
You can't hide from the moon
In the end we all must come home
In the way you know the August heat
Will give way to Autumn frost
In the way you escape reminiscent old nights
Good memories can bear a high cost
Sometimes a party can be so silent
Sometimes the night comes too soon
Every good thing has a darker side
No one can hide from the moon

Jason Parker

Husband And Wife One

God loans us children for such a short spell,
   to guide them through life, to teach them well.
But, then all to soon they're gone from our care,
   leaving our hearts with an empty place there.
I see now as man grows older in life,
   So also should grow the bond with his wife.
When God made the husband and wife one,
   He planned that, when their parenting was done,
Together, hand in hand, they'd end life's quest,
   In each other's arms when called to their rest.
And thus God decreed they should end their years,
   Not clothed in loneliness, stained by their tears.

Jose A. Cardoso

Sometimes Wonder

So lonesome, but please don't cry
what do you need from me?
Do you sometimes wish you could fly?
Fly so high above everything
have no worries
spread your wings
fly higher then a bird
do you sometimes wonder if you really know?
Do you ever wish you could be a turtle?
When things aren't going right,
you hide away in your shell
don't have to come out
if you don't want to
take your time.
Go slow don't care what they think
they don't have to know
what are you thinking: What are in your thoughts?
Do you sometimes wonder what its like to run forever?
Never stopping not for anything at all
do you ever wonder what it's like?

Valerie Hawks

Reach For The Light

In darkness I was formed
Then I searched for the light.
Affliction beset me like a cloud,
Then God delivered a silver lining.

Disabled though I remained,
I learned to reach for the light.
Self-confident and determined,
I would not be deterred from my goal.

The loss of a loved one brought despair,
But remember, I reach for the light.
Though the stumbling blocks be many,
I am strengthened by my faith.

The door of opportunity has opened,
Now I truly can reach for the light.
Though my goal has taken me far away,
I know it is a part of His great plan.

Others can be encouraged by my fight.
Learn to reach for the light.
Ice skating has given me hope.
I now reach for the light of Olympic Gold.

Carolyn J. Bearden

Untitled

I sleep at night without dreams,
Awake in the morning with nothing to look
   forward to,
I wait by the phone but no ring.

I sit and wonder shall I be lonely forever?
Shall I never find the love of my lie?
Will I always be alone?

I shall soon sleep with dreams,
Awake to something to look forward to,
And I will hear voice on the phone.

I shall no longer wonder if I'll be lonely,
No longer worry about the love of my life,
And no longer worry about being alone.
One day all my dreams will come true and
   all my worries will disappear.

Keri McManis

Love

Your love I miss,
I remember our first kiss.
When I think of our love,
I see a dove.
When I feel your presence near me,
I wish I could melt so far away into the sea.
I think of everything we did together,
I wish it could always be that way forever.
I feel your touch,
And than I realize that I needed that so much.
You have to know how much I need you,
Because I know you feel that way too.
I see your face,
I see it every place.
I need you so bad,
Without you I'm sad.
You are a part of me,
Without you I will melt into the sea.
Just be with me,
For eternity.

Kara Keding

Mother's Day Eve

My goodness the day before,
My emotions are confused
What if I don't?
Will my true feelings be misconstrued!

Will I get flowers,
Will I get card,
What will I do?
Maybe a flower from the yard!

Maybe it is duty,
Maybe it is tradition,
What is the reason?
For something that is in God's petition!

For you are a good mother.
For you are a good wife,
What has God shown?
Because it is obvious by the fruits of your life!

Because it is time now to rest,
Because through Him I know,
What is it then?
That our love will continue to Grow!

Richard Wewerka

One

As a homo sapien, be a paragon.
For beyond the ramification of ethnicity and
geographic diversity; in the realm of ethics,
there is something that is called right. And
there is something that is called wrong.
Let your life be a shining light.
Deal with what is right; - which is the way
towards psychological enrichment positive truth
and the state of quintessential love.
Open your heart with adoration towards all people.
And let your crowning point be the
concentration on the good that comes from within.
Be you black, white, yellow, red, or brown; we are
all brothers and sisters under our sun.
And even in a deeper dimension, — in the
the eyes of the Creator we are one.

Benjamin Clark Mantherudder

The Ponytail

Something in me wants to pat her ponytail.
A playful tug, perhaps. A simple touch
On this symbol of her girlish being—
I rest my case before the world,
Am I asking much too much?

I marvel at her shiny, bouncing braid
That seems to sweep the air
With every movement of her head.
If only I could tell her how
She's made my day. But I'll stand still,
And just enjoy the sight, instead.

Louis F. LeBlanc

The Rose Bush

In the beginning it's small, fragile and innocent.
It is planted with care, watered often, and treated with love.
The roots are delicate, its future uncertain, but he desire to live strong.
Through the first year, its life is hard.
The sun is hot, the winter is cold, and the rains are hard.
but through it all, this bush refuses to give up.
Its root grow stronger, the stems get bigger, and leaves begin to appear.
As the years pass by, its life gets harder.
The winters become colder, the frost grows thicker, and the summers get hotter.
This bush will endure good times and as well as bad times.
Some stems may need trimmed and extra care is required.
But, as every spring arrives, you can always be certain it will
produce one of the most beautiful and precious things on this earth...
A rose.

Steven Craig Albers

Waiting

Killing time with my thoughts.
Patience is a good friend.
And though silence occasionally interrupts,
She listens to what I have to say.

I'm well acquainted with loneliness.
It seems I know more about her than anyone else.
The exception, of course, is reality.
I can't seem to rid myself of her.

Jealously stopped by but couldn't stay.
Ambivalence betrayed me, but I came to the
Realization that Hatred was my bitter enemy.

So I wait with Patience.
Of course, with an occasional interruption from Silence.
Love... now that's someone I'd like to meet.

James P. Snow

Getting Well

The joys of life,
they're coming back to me,
as I once felt so trapped,
now I feel free.

Free of the land,
with so many promises unkept,
and I know that land must have been,
the valley of the shadow of death.

Like a fish out of water,
I was gasping for air,
so many people trying to help,
but I just didn't care.

And I guess my life is still kind of strange,
but a lot of things have been said and done that only
time will change,
so now that this bolder's been moved,
to me the only way I can come out is improved.

Carrie Rankin

Winter

When the sky transforms from satin blues to smoky greys.
When trees no longer stand still but swing and sway,
When through a darkness you see an Glistening light,
When what seems like half started days turn into night,
And gusts of whistling sky and he flapping clouds of
  feathered wings whiz by,
When the air smell of fresh pine and a pinch of spice,
And where ever eyes look there is a carpet of white,
When pointed trees and sparkling lights help brighten up
  cold chilly nights.
When all these graceful sighs appear,
Fall is long over and WINTER is here!

Althea Crichlow

Mood

It's a waste of time trying to be who you are not,
You live inside a crystal ball,
And the minute someone touched it, it breaks,
You're on your own now,
Nothing protects you.
As vulnerable as a child,
As delicate and soft as a rose,
Afraid of what will happen next,
Of what you want,
Of where to go,
Of who you are.

Teresa Ledesma

David - My Friend

A voice, resonant and strong,
  Whether speaking or singing
Clearly reciting God's love for all to hear

A smile, brighter than most light
  Inviting others to participate in
Life and its many options

A laugh, full-bodied, mischievous,
  Sincere, infectious
Able to change attitudes in a positive way

A hand, strong, supportive, helpful, caring
  Completing countless projects
For the good of others

An ear, listening, tuned, ready, attentive
  Able to discern truth

A heart, large and full, overflowing
  With God's love for everyone
Brimming with boundless energy for
  Life's daily tasks

Roger C. Beason

Untitled

Slowly receding from the depths
  of her soul,
He withdraws from her with a
  tender pull.
Then in the eve he'll come again
To wash upon her lovely sands.
Gently at first, then with
  stronger intent,
He feeds her until they've both
  been spent.
Lapping softly, thrusting eagerly,
Giving to her what she needs.
Their spirits have entwined
Since the beginning of time.
He is the sea, and she is the sand,
Forever walking through life, hand in hand.

Vickie Kaye Schmelzer

Looking Back

As a chilling wind
brisk, yet unpredictable
the days, the time
whisper and howl
as a spirit
may present itself
if to offer a feeling
of comfort or warmth
yet only the opposite will reside.
The chilling reality
may be that
only to some
while others
will breeze through paradise
savoring as a Chardonnay, the melancholy
with frugal attempt
searching past the wretched vines
in hope to unveil
the coveted truth.

Leslie Perih

Purple Snow

As daylight slipped into twilight
  And the clouds were painted by the fading sunlight,
From out of the Southwest
  The light reflected on the Purple Snow.

The snow was colored by reflections from the clouds,
  Brought to Earth by sunlit shrouds.
Orange, yellow, gold, and rose,
  And the most beautiful purple, reflecting on the snow.

God, set the theme, provided the colors,
  Placed the sun behind the clouds,
And opened just the right amount of space
  To let the brilliant purple, shine on the snow.

The snow had fallen on a Southwest slope,
  Providing a reflector for the "Color of Hope"
This, supposedly, was the color of JESUS' robe
  As brought to Earth by the Creators Hand showing us the Purple Snow

The color was there for only a few seconds, for us to see
  Then, it disappeared, into eternity.
But, for those seconds, we watched in awe,
  The beauty of GOD'S painting, of the Purple Snow!

George C. Steidel

"Yahweh Just Before The Rain Falls"

The stains of November rain drops smeared
Their souls on my windowpanes
And their crawling intricacy mimicked capillaries
On clear, crystal - cold plains.
My breath slowed and shallowed inside,
Was out-roared by the raping wind.
I knew somewhere above,
God's looming face and looming lips
Gave birth to this roar,
This magnificence that stripped and made bare the lands,
That stirred black oceans to sway and spit in rebellion,
Whose power flattered copper
Colored leaves as if run through
By a stiff and glorious comb,
And who will with a last and furious
Strength bend the mightiest of trees
To dip back and forth
From the twin milk saucers of heaven
Before fading and moving
Slowly upwards unto the eager lips of God.

Elizabeth A. Eslami

Untitled

You do not see what thine eyes behold
You do not hear what your ears are told
You do not feel the pain
Of a world gone insane
   Isolated, no feeling
Everyday a child dies
Everyday a mother says goodbye
   But tomorrow.
Will it be your child that dies
Will it be you saying goodbye
   Isolated, no longer
Will you finally see what thine eyes behold
Will you finally hear what your ears are told
And will you finally, feel the pain
Of a world gone insane

   Cindy Jo Byington

I Am In Love

I can see you before me,
   flesh and blood.
Your eyes, pools of warm sincerity.
Your lips, zones of sensuous pleasure.
Your body, strong and firm, presses against mine.
   I am in ecstasy.

I can feel you beside me,
   Heart and soul.
Your presence surrounds me.
Your spirit penetrates me.
Your passion, powerful and true, overwhelms my being.
   I am in love.

   L. A. Quinn

I am a Mall Maniac

I am a mall maniac
I wonder if I'll ever get tired of shopping
I hear cha-ching of a cash register
I see awesome clothes and dazzling jewels
I want more money
I am a mall maniac

I pretend I'm the Queen of the mall
I feel hurt when I have used all my money
I touch the silk coats and say how pretty
I worry when my bank account is empty
I cry when I miss a day of shopping
I am a mall maniac

I understand when there's a sale and I'm not there
I say I own the mall in one room
I dream of my own mall
I try to spend all the money I can
I hope the store doesn't run out of clothes
I am a mall maniac

   Jessica Gillen

Private Thoughts

O, the sweet bliss of one moment alone with non-spoken thoughts,
Radio blasting, starting a train of unconscious musing.
Brief respite from the humdrum of routine
No automatic responses here,
Only a trip over the rainbow through pastel shades of space.
How lovely, the mellow yellow, next to the cool blue
With a pale of lavender beckoning your soul to come and see
The other side.
No free ride, just a change of pace.
Floating away over the clouds, where time has
No meaning and no one is leaning on the shoulder of your life.

   Shirley Heckard

Bad Dog

The humor in it escapes me,
and yet you insist that we play,
a game of cat and mouse.
Your brown eyes dance in taunting shades,
just daring me to play.
My resistance to engage causes you to tease,
creating in me a reactionary rage.
Your eyes wear a coy smile,
laughing as you come so close,
but then you dart a mile,
and I am left to scratch my nose.
The humor in it escapes me,
as my blood pressure rises high,
as my voice looses all controllable tones,
while you race by once more with those eyes
that laugh.
At the end I throw my hands to the sky,
asking myself, why! Why! Why!

   Parrish Kathy

"My Mother"

My mother means so many things to me.
The M-means the many things she says and does
The O-means outstanding how well I know it's true, and mother I
Knows there's only one like you.
The T-means tender loving care
She has always shown.
The H-means how great I think
She is with hands so soft that do everything.
The E-is for everlasting
The R-for radiant which she always is.
My mother will always do and do, and I know she's wonderful kind, and true.
I could never repay her know matter what I do, and I'm proud to
Say she's number one and the greatest to.
God bless her and keep her she's one of a kind.
I love you mother and glad you're mine.

   Priscilla M. Boas

Lifetime Friend

Have you ever looked into your soul
Have you ever wondered
That if you look deep, if you could actually
   reach with the greatest story ever told.

The story of a man
That traveled the Holy Land
He talked with people near and far
This man was fighting a sin war.

Did you ever think about what it would be
Did you ever dream
Of a life without HIM to intervene?

This man is great
HE is the one and only NO ONE can ever duplicate
HE is the soul Supreme
This man HE, your soul, can redeem.

Would you like to know
Would you like HIM
To plant the seed inside that will forever grow?

HE loves you my friend
And HE is one whose love never ends.

   DeJuan N. Knighton

February

So soon. Again, Aquarius doth mourn,
Old February's passing in the rain;
His heavy, earthly scent is water-borne;
His tears of parting streak my window pane.

O shadow; brief and fleeting; stark and cold—
I watched time hang suspended in thy dawn,
Until the blaze of noon; impulsive, bold—
Subdued your morn, then it, too, traveled on.

A gentle sorrow lingers deep inside
As I reflect on this analogy;
O February, sudden ebb and tide;
O still, small portion of eternity;
To live so short a span, and then to die;
Reluctantly,
   Releasing,
      Soft.
         Goodbye.

  Shanti Adams

An Inkling

There was a narrow white line
around the third finger of my left hand.
Gradually the line
faded, from my finger, and my thoughts.

Cold wet spring
became summer, fall, winter.
The seasons cascaded
one, upon another, upon another.

Sometimes
I am surprised
to discover myself
rubbing the side of my finger with my thumb.

The same way
I used to rub the gold hand
that left the white line
around the third finger of my left hand.

  Dennis Moore

The Dove Bled Red

I thought we'd ride the waves of love
With courage to soar like God's great dove,
And on the crest, with raised steel blades
We'd fight through all the barricades.
Until at last, the glass showed all,
A way through the maze to stand up tall
And proud, and full of heart - 'till death do us part.

But you never warned the glass would break,
Nor that your heart of jewels were fake.
You swam away to a different shore
While I fought on, 'till I could stand no more.
And on my knees, your sword at my side
I'm drowned by dreams, by words that lied.
You promised a heaven with you as King,
The Queen has fallen, you forgot one thing,
You never said the dove bled red.

  Christina Pagano

Fist Time

Looking at you for the first time,
Was part of that sunshine that I always dream of
Being with someone I love.
Not knowing we would be together,
Not saying it would last forever.
It was good just looking at you for the first time.
Baby, I never knew we would love, touch, or hold each other.
But time went away, wasn't meant to stay.
I just can't say things I used too,
Because your love has gone away,
From me,
From me,
But the first time I saw you it was good,
And I will never forget the look on your face.
That sunshine that I just can't erase from my mind.

  Calvin Carson

My Lord

Lord, each day I long to see your face,
To know the one who took my place
I look to the skies so fluffy and white,
Hoping for a glimpse, a sign or a sight.

I remember all the roads and the dark places I've been.
My past was so cloudy, filled full of sin.
I ask myself how I made it thus far?
And tremble at the thought of not knowing who you are.

I long to do your will, to be pleasing in your eyes.
But I know I still have a long journey which in the future lies,
Lord, I just want you to know from my heart,
That I love you so much, it shall never part.

What you have done for me from the beginning of time,
There are no words, no songs of poems that rhyme.
For Father, you are the reasons I must carry on.
Dear God, grant me the wisdom and show me the way.

I yearn to know and grow closer to thee each day.

  Detra Jones

Angela

There is one who is far away.
As far as Michigan is to California.
My love transcends to her far away.
I in Michigan, she in California.

Each day I think of her.
I sit with pen and paper and write.
My feelings I put down and send them to her.
Many times there are tears as I write.

She is so far away.
I want to tell her to her face how I feel.
I wish we were not so far away.
It's hard to express on paper how one feels.

Someday we will be together.
She and I sharing our love.
Married and forever together.
Forever sharing each others love.

  Harold J. Laymon Jr.

A Late Christmas Wish

To my Partner:
　As year pass by, New Year says "Hi"!
　But Christmas 95 not yet behind,
　With gifts and cards under big pine,
　Wishing you have wonderful times.

　I love you much and appreciate your love,
　Sometimes forgot to "Thank you", though!
　But in my heart, my dear Partner,
　It always beats, always remembers.

To my Partner's daughter:
　May everyday you discover,
　The wonder-touch of love's power,
　That makes you laugh, that keeps you comfort,
　From all of us who love you forever.

To my Partner's son:
　Christmas comes and goes with cheers and tears,
　It passes through your heart years after years.
　Take them all and keep smiling,
　They help you grow as human-beings.
　　　Peter Nguyen Bao Thu

Where I Am Being Kept

I flow in its green sphere,
Hell that dreams of deep heaven.
Behind thin, filmed windows,
I quietly think,
Drink softly,
So I can look at her beautiful airline,
She is....

And when I'm thinking steel gray,
Like clouds, afraid.
Windows, unwilling, opaque.
I see swing sets, tear dropped.

Alone, she spins recklessly, calm,
And in black, in the folds of her dress,
There are hungry nothings.

Only twice she spoke,
Of covered eyes and activity,
Of revolution at three-hundred and sixty degrees,
Burning planets,
Burning places,
Lovers in threes.
　　　Michael Murphy

Joey

Look at all the children play
They're happy as can be
But one of them, is not so lucky
It's Joey, he cannot see

The other children, dance around
They make fun of him
But God is standing, by Joey's side
He's watching all of them

God's making a place, in Heaven's doors
For Joey, one day soon
The cancer is eating, away at his body
As he looks on towards the moon

I hope that Joey knows how lucky
As one day soon he'll see
Cause all those children, playing on the playground
They're as blind, AS BLIND CAN BE
　　　Birdie Spears

Lemon Meringue Pie

Are you ready for a luscious treat, naturally sweet?
We've got a "C-o-o-l" dessert that just can't be beat!
Quality and care are definitely our bill O' fare.

Indulge our Lemon Meringue Pie for a taste bud burst!
A filling so "yummy" to excite your appetite at first!
Sweetened condensed milk, eggs, and squeezed lemons, yes please.
An awesome pie surrounded with fresh baked cookies, a real tease!

These pies are "so good, they named a street after it."
Lemon Lane captures the pride of Edwards Pies, a hit!
"We top the pie with a f-l-u-f-f-y egg white meringue."
Guaranteed to bring taste appeal to your hungry gang!

A tempting Lemon Meringue Pie top, toasted to a "golden brown"
So, get ready to share the Oohs and Ahs, reversing any frown!
"These pies are fully prepared and ready to serve."
"Homemade look and taste," a thrill guests truly deserve!

Now you're anxious for the luscious taste of our "C-o-o-l pie,
So please, give our famous Edwards Lemon Meringue Pie, a try!
What is the secret of Christopher Edwards Baking Company, you bet?
Our business hub has "The Lord of The Harvest," whom we've met!
　　　C. Ray Tucker

I Am Surrounded By These Ghosts

I am surrounded by these ghosts,
　Here in the silent night.
Their names and faces form the hosts,
　I long to bring to light.

And I wonder what hearths they tend,
　Now that their years are past,
And if laughter they ever blend,
　Or have they laughed their last?

Do they warm to any fires,
　Where we could sit beside,
Do their hearts conceal desires,
　Like we are apt to hide?

When twilight embraces the day,
　And slowly dims the light,
Do the dreams in their souls still play,
　Or has hope lost the fight?

By these ghosts I am surrounded,
　In vain for them I grope,
Tho' the longer they lie grounded,
　The stronger grows my hope.
　　　Richard K. Bridgford

Mr. X.

Someday, I hope not far away,
I'll meet a someone new.
A someone sweet in every way,
Who'll make my dreams come true.
He may be tall, he may be short,
He may be thin or stout.
He may have money or none at all
But all his love I will not doubt.
I've waited long for Mr. X.
To come along my way.
That certain one of the opposite sex
　　　- To say he's come to stay.
Until my dreams of love come true
　　　- My life will be complex
　　　- And never will the sunshine through
'till I meet my Mr. X.
　　　Helen Stopera

"Why"

Why enter my life repeatedly shutting the door when you feel
Why the tears on my face, my heart sulking and my mind beginning to
reel. Why just leave me memories, hopes, whispers of words not true
to you why talk in secret keys, passionate looks, then steal away
    making me blue

Should I leave my sane and enter the world of make believe and dreams
Getting through the spell like laughter of waves on the earth sun
beams I feel that I live in an empty shell, I tried reaching out
you would take for me romantic mist and sky rockets, you could leave
    it all - all is my mistake

I believed in my heart, mind and soul you were mine in all simplicity
I wait and let time take it's place, can I wait for all infinity
I let you play your little games like you always have before - for I can't resist you
The feeling inside is one I will always have, the feeling I have is nothing new

Although the time is short, the way I feel seems like it has been life-long.
How can I express myself, no words can tell, not the music to a song.
My life resembles the seasons; spring, summer, fall and winter.
Spring were fragrant, summer were alive, fall were wilted, winter were gone

Jacky McCarty

"In Between Hours Of Dusk And Dawn"

Beneath sheets of white silk I lay, untouched by the night asleep at rest.
Left unknowing of a world around me I drift to dwell in the midst of my mind.
A sweet breeze off a summer's night Creeps in.
Hovering over...endlessly watching.
Alone, I am not in these hours of slumber.
Halfway between dusk and dawn does he come.
Never to know that he may be there I am left to doze in his presence.
He winds a kiss to greet my cheek by this blissful act I wake
In a silent night with bloated tears I big him, "stay".
His thinned weightless body sits at my side.
My wild eyes refuse to relinquish of their hold,
afraid to lose this prisoner of the past.
Through my window dances the last shadow of moon.
The first signs of morn follow quickly led by streaming colors
full of spectrum finger painted across the changing sky.
My heart throbs, knowing he must go
yet I cling to a lifeless hand.
but when I wake the windows closed
and he has never been.

Melissah J. Falavorito

The Garden Above La Mer

In memory of Lt. Cdr. Ronald W. Dudge, USN
In silent lines white crosses stand, serene in their eternal hours;
Sorrow stalks, and in her hand there blooms a bright bouquet of flowers.
Across the high and windy hill, row after row of graven signs,
Naming boys they sent to kill, in row after row, in endless lines.

Sorrow walks, she knows not where, nor what she seeks, what comfort find;
She knows his stone will not be there, nor bones, nor skin, nor soul, nor mind.
Sorrow talks to silent stones. She kneels down and reads the names,
Sorrow weeps for rotted bones of boys betrayed by old men's games.

She kneels and gently puts a bloom on the stone of a boy she didn't know,
She weeps at the sight of his lonely tomb and Sorrow's garden begins to grow.
Up and down the rows she walks, leaving her flowers, one by one;
No one is listening as she talks to the boys whose lives were too early done.

She stands at last atop the hill. She saved for him her final flower;
Loving him then, and loving him still, through the anguish of his final hour.
All prayers are said, all tears are wept, one final thing that must be done;
She takes the flower that she kept and flings it toward the setting sun.

Valerie Sansone Kahn

Divorce

Dreadful, frightful, cruel,
Insane.
Voices that cry out in pain!
Oratory
Rape that scars to the bone.
Cry out; hold it in.
Evidence has it you'll never be the same.

Charlotte Schonert Watson

Just How Much Do I Mean To You

When I drove by your house, I saw "his" truck in your drive,
Please baby don't say it's true,
Because now you're making me turn blue,
I didn't mean what I said last night,
Give me another chance to turn the wrong into right.

I cried until my last tear fell,
While you and him were in there,
But when you called me, and said you made a mistake,
My cries turned to joy,
After you assured me that I wasn't just your toy
But your entire life,
I realized how much I mean to you.

You showed me how much you cared,
I finally see; how much I mean,
I'm so sorry for misinterpreting you,
Now all of that doesn't matter anymore,
Because you do; truly love me,
And I will always love you,
Forever; because I know
Just how much I mean to you.

Jasmin Treanor

Not Grief

My life is a flame, a spritely, dancing blaze
Spiking upward with red, licking tongue.
Blue-tipped and white hot at the vertex
The highest culminating point its strength.
Long ago it quivered, sputtered, became
Shrouded in smoke, pencil thin, so cold
In its dimness that extinction beckoned smugly.
The while from one dead coal's still living
Center a wiry spurt of raging red flew up
Incredibly persistent, denying its demise.
Fresh thrusts of red, rust, yellow etched
The darkening coals, restoring warmth to
Chilled, charred embers, sudden reprieve
From black oblivion. Time will be spent,
The flame will die. No need for sadness.
Cool and content the still ashes will
Remain a feathery, heaped up mound
Tokens, not of grief but gladness.

Joan T. Myers

Beauty And Love

Beauty is a pure heart, not a pretty face.
Love is trust, caring, tender, patience, understanding.
Hides all faults, forgiving, sincere.
I can erase a miss spell word.
I can blot out unpleasant memories,
But you will always have a special place in my heart.
I cannot blot out nor erase.

Annie H. Graves

Hemingway Look-A-Like Key West Papa

The judges in their places, all in a row, quiet and calm,
watching a show of men standing tall with twinkling eyes,
in khaki and turtlenecks and hope in their strides
as they approach the microphone to reveal,
in words of their own why they feel,
they should be chosen the one the judges like best,
year after year it's a repeated quest.
And I'm jealous as I can be, of hemingway look-a-likes, for you see
I've loved the real man since I first read "farewell to arms"
and a "natural history of the dead".
I've been watching this contest now for years
and do admit I've been brought to tears
by camaraderie, sincerity and the bonding of men
so it should be no surprise that I harbor the trend
to wear khaki and turtlenecks too and get on the stage
and do what they do
But forgive me my sisters I must draw the line here
let girl scouts be boy scouts I really don't care
but here in the land between Atlantic and bay
let men be real men like Papa Hemingway

Maxine A. Meitz

Seems Like Forever

Seems like forever I have loved you, though my memory's not quite as clear,
As it was the first night I held you — my darling, my Lenia dear.
Seems like Forever and a life time, though time has so swiftly gone by.
Many were the times that we laughed together and many times did we cry.

Seems like forever you have loved me, though not seldom I have wondered why.
I should fall at your feet, your highness I bow now in wonder and sigh.
Seems like forever since we were young and fresh and free and careless too.
Though still I see that same young bride in things you say and do.

Seems like forever since you told me our firstborn was on the way.
Seems like forever and a life time but it's as fresh as yesterday.
Seems like forever and that's a very long time. We supposed it would always be,
The blush of youth, the warmth, the glow, the immeasurable eternity.

Seems like forever since the hot summer days. But winter can't smother the fire,
That we once started in the days of our youth, of love's passion and yearning desire.
Seems like forever but time does not linger. It falls through the hourglass like sand.
Yesterday, today, tomorrow and forever we love and walk hand in hand.

Seems like forever I have loved you, though my memory's not quite as clear.
But my heart is full and my life is too. I'll love you forever my dear.

Jerold Posey

a thrombic retroperspective

this weight i carry in my chest gave cause one day to sit, to rest
with back braced against the oak, recouping breath, and understood:
         "to soon might be my Death."
to be sure, a gloomy, bleak, and selfish notion; began reflecting
         upon plans in motion
left wanting for a finishing part or, perhaps worse, a start.

a child not hugged, a pond unswum, beaches not walked, a song unsung,
a hand not held, a task untried, roses unsniffed, a tear not dried,
sad to leave thus unshriven, so unexpected; scant time for apologies
         neither given, nor accepted.

plumes of breathe on winter's air; the excitement of the fireworks faire;
the smell of the spruce on a rainy day; returning home after time away;
watching clouds' ballet of shapes; or seeing the moon dance on a lake;
if these joys be absent tomorrow, a greater regret: not sharing your sorrow.

now recovered and doing well, the ministrations successful,
a memory shifts, and i am then, recalling branches in a gentle wind,
         parting now and again.
piercing my fog, the heavens i viewed and marveled at a light so
         bright and a sky so blue.

Stephen Eric Fey

If Only

I wish to express a piece of poetry of mine
To speak it with glory, to watch myself shine.
I accept the good and wrong of me.
If I were you I would envy me.

My mind tries so hard
To keep my values strong.
To provide a warm heart for others
To spread laughter, not harm.

Not all the weak become strong
Nor do all the rich become poor.
For all that does not change
May be cursed to stay the same.

Three wishes per every star
Cannot take the pain away.
We wake in the morning
Not to hear the birds chirping
But to see that another child has been slayed.

I cannot change what I must see
All goodness and harm will be.
As man I wish to declare myself free.

Amber Henry

What Is My Purpose?

I have no present, no future, no past.
It's all suppose to have a center point.
But it can't be. If it did we wouldn't
Have war. Don't get me started.
I have no culture, I arrived, from a
glutton of confusion, curiosity, pain,
pride, passion, anger, and hate.
It's all suppose to add up to one
center point, but I don't see how.
If it did we wouldn't have war.

What has war done for me?

Confused my present.
Destroyed my future.
Distorted my past.

Sonya M. Sherow

Ghost In The Mountains

These mountains are lonely without you
I can feel your presence everywhere I roam
I keep seeing your face in my wonderings
The ghost, my love will never be home.

Why did you have to leave me so suddenly
We meant so much together didn't we,
If I could have you back I'd do so
The ghost, you meant the world to me.

So I will stay right here in my loneliness
And see your face everywhere I go
No one will ever take your place with me I promise you
The ghost, the love, forever will show.

Vionne L. Freeman

Love

Love is not some thing that grows on trees.
It is very sensitive,
it can break a heart,
that has just been fixed.
Love hurts.
If you know where the key to my heart is,
you will earn my love.

Kimberly Joslin

I Am One

I talk but no one listens, I'm afraid but no one cares.
They say I'm BLIND, but yet I can see what others cannot.
I listen clearly to the words that are spoken, but when questioned
I am MUTE in fear of the worst.
I feel speech at work on the cells of emotion, the PAIN is unbearable.
But when the triumphant horns of courage sound
With the rage of an angry lion and the speed of a runaway locomotive
I am unstoppable, the meer thought of being scared is no more.
I can climb story after story to a cliff at the top of the clear blue sky.
I am victorious for I have over come my first fear, but suddenly
an unthinkable thought comes to mind. Like horses on a track messages
flee through my brain. I begin to strip articles of clothing one by
one from my body until I am completely bare. In a diving position,
I plunge into the endless waters. As I glide freely through the air
feeling the wind caress my every curve, my time to pierce the water
awaits my entrance. My heart is massaged with the fear and worry
that once left me. There is no turning back my conscience tells me.
Surrounding me are the soft whispers of reality speaking and letting
me know this: YOU ARE ONE, YOUR OWN INDIVIDUALITY.
A NEWBORN HIGHER AND LEADER THAT LETS NO ONE
STAND BEFORE YOU.
YOU'RE
ONE

Latina Smith

My Serenity

A peaceful place, complete silence, a walk on a quiet beach.
Sand filling my toes as I scuffle along, smelling the freshness of the air.

I hear only the sounds of chirping birds and waves splashing against
the rocks. Sea gulls claim this haven for home.

I look up at clouds laced with ribbons, each a uniqueness of its own,
dancing along at a pace I dare not keep, as I want to keep this
peacefulness, a slow and still like walk.

Wind tussles my hair as the sun peaks through the clouds, warming my
flesh and hugging each part of me, with a love I yearn to feel.

My mind and soul combine a search for precious memories that long
have past. My first love. The birth of my children, the sounds
of their cries at night as I hold their tiny bodies close to mine.
Tiny footsteps at my side, their love reaching and tugging deep
within my heart. Their first day of school, and then so soon, those
lonely feelings as they wave and say goodbye to journey on their own.

How wonderful you've stored my thoughts dear Lord, engraving them
within my soul and giving me this special day, a pain free walk, a
walk of life, a walk of love, allowing me this freedom as I touch
the peace I yearn for every day, MY SERENITY.

Joanne Perry Cox

Legend Of The Lame Wolf

Winter snows and years of cold have dimmed his heart and eye,
yet on a lonely night with the moon full-bright,
you can hear his mournful cry.
He left the pack many winters back, more from selflessness than scorn
and as he prowled the night, surviving each new fight,
he felt the beast within reborn.
He lost his speed and his right to lead to a man-made trap of steel.
He knew right away that he could not stay for the leg would never heal.
Gone from the pack, upon an unknown track he wandered off alone
and while he roamed the woods and hills, new skills he began to hone.
His cunning and his silent stealth helped him to survive and
though the tale is very old, they say he's still alive.
And so my child, heed this lesson well and listen for his call.
Beware the lame wolf in the night, for he's the deadliest of all.

Jerry B. Smith

Bad Love

You get with the wrong crowd it seems
like the right one, you hook up with a
fine guy and think nothing could go wrong.
But then problems start to happen and the
way he treats you hurts, he calls you a
slut and treats you like the same, you thought
that's what you wanted but you thought
wrong again, you better get out before the
hatred gets to strong, your scared to go he
acts to rough, maybe next time you should
think things through enough.

Juliana Woehl

Another Life

As cold as the dead flowers in the breeze,
as harsh as the words of hatred floundering around us,
as calm as the nearby winds. He is there listening,
watching our every step, waiting to make his move.
For we are just a game to his amusement.
Death is a spy of life, a messenger of God,
and also a dream. For you really do die, but remember
faith is the key to your second life.
When death comes I'll be waiting with my arms open,
and my feet crossed!

Jacob Cockrell

Nothing Lasts Forever

Few times in your life
Will you have the chance to find,
Something so very special
It will overcome your heart and mind.

Most often it is a person;
Sometimes it is a thing.
You will know you have found it
By the happiness it will bring.

But nothing lasts forever
And the happiness will fade.
You must always keep close to your heart
The memories you made.

Always treasure the special times
Of that something so special and true.
And never, ever forget to say
How much it means to you.

Jackie Campbell

The Blizzard Of 1996

Our day began in the usual way
After breakfast, we start a new day.
We're moving along at such a pace,
We then realize, we forgot to say grace.

We forgot who to thank for our daily bread,
Our health, and all that we own,
For without God, try as we might,
We cannot make it alone.

The blizzard, was God's way of reminding us,
That He is still in command.
God put a "Stop" to everything, He is in control,
He holds the whole world in His hand.

Joan Rhinehart

"The Sign Of The Time"

It's the Devil's latest device that he's pulled deep from beneath
his rug; his new deadly spirit in a powerful addicting drug
   It's his device which he calls the latch;
   known to us as the drug called crack.
Now it is so powerful that when it is took;
deep inside your soul his latch is hooked.
   At that time it becomes your biggest concern;
   as it begins to take everything that you've ever earn.
A very strong addicting desire that needs to be fulfilled everyday;
and whatever the Devil tell's you to do get it you will definitely obey.
   Because it is you that Devil is abusing;
   and your mind he is totally confusing.
Now there's never really a time when you can say that you're finished;
because the addicting desire is a constant replenish.
On a woman this device has a greater effect;
because as a lady she loose's all of her respect.
   It will make all individuals stoop low and steal;
   and if necessary just to get it they will lie and kill.
Now in this century it is the main reason there's so much crime;
So please don't get hooked on crack because it's the sign of the time.

   Efren Z. Burton

Paroled

I am going to kill for God's sake, return me to my cell
that which has suckled me as a mother rearing me in the ways of death
discrimination that has no face or sex but finds its way through my sweet mercy.

Return me to society, bleeding hearts, sing my rehabilitation and repentance
for all those nightmares I have created, allow me freedom to roam your streets,
stalking, waiting, exorcising life's spirit from your sons and daughters.

Moving to fulfill prophecy from the mouths of conservatives screaming for justice
while liberals beg for leniency, pleading for my return
to a world that turned its back on me long enough to allow the plunge
of my dagger and sweet taste of blood for my sins.

I am wise to the ways of death more than you, bleeding hearts,
and the inability of this or any generation to save me.
I have been saved. Spared the hangman's knot
around my neck to become a millstone around yours.

Allow my freedom to disable you and I promise
to raise sons and daughters that will carry on where I leave off.
Bow your head, say your final prayer
do not mind the coldness of the steel as it separates your body.

   S. Petersen

Untitled

Welcome my friend, to a let down day.
The sun was so bright, but now it's grey.
Now that your company has gone far away, you sit there and
realize that you have to stay.

Look out your window; the street is so bare.
Is there not one person down there who cares?
If loneliness only were riches to store,
I would have riches and riches galore.

Love, I will share, that in me resides. Oh friend,
will you come and sit by my side? You are so busy
and have so much to do. Please do forgive me, for I bother you.

I am not good, but neither am I bad. Just a low friend who is
feeling so sad. Reach out your arms and stretch them to me.
Please let me know I need not be lonely.

The tears that run down a lonely, sad face must surely be hid to hide the disgrace.
Look out your window; is someone down there?
Will they shout up and tell you that they really care?

Look at the clouds, so high in the sky. Remind me to pray and then
I won't cry. Even though the clouds are so high up above,
I'm gently reminded of His perfect love.

   Teddie Peterson

Desires

Present to me a thought,
A treed, mountainous wilderness,
I'll make it into a flat suburb,
With only the slightest hint,
Of what used to be before.

I'll rip out its entrails,
Line its insides with concrete,
Decimate its forest,
Wholesale slaughter its beasts.

I'll plant leafless trees,
That burn white fires all night,
And race roaring demons,
Around mazes you people call streets.

Now no more wolf,
Now no more bear,
It's human's growing on top of one another,
In a dirty play pen of defeat.

   Christopher J. B. Lineman

The Apple Tree

It started out just you and me
And the apple tree in the back yard.
Then we added a few children
And times never did seem too hard.

Our children grew up and moved away
To start new lives of their own.
Now our kids have their own kids
And those kids are almost grown.

Through the years there have been many changes
So many lives have come in and out that door.
Children who only knew this place
Who won't know this place anymore.

Though we love this place, it's time to go
But we'll take with us the memory,
Of the way it all began
With just you, me and the apple tree.

   Carrie S. Hester

Craftsman

The balsa wood employed in adolescence
to create worlds now's collecting dust.
Imagination, which once conceived of wood
as wanting flight, has itself flown and, long since
caught in wind sheer, crashed to concrete,
splintered like so many of his dreams.
His hands, once graceful, disciplined,
are veined now, splotched with liver marks,
and tremble, not in anticipation of some
sweet surprise like naked flesh compliant
as his wood, but of the vast unknown.
No chisels, knives, sander, awl or lathe can
reshape what lies ahead—not simply being shelved,
he's already experienced that, but finding himself
inanimate, like one of his blocks of wood, dependent
on some unseen other craftsman to give him life,
or let him fall, no longer usable.

   Ed Devany

My Paula

You make your mother proud to tell
Now you're manager of Super Eight Motel.
The years were long and the struggle a brute.
If you couldn't climb a mountain
You dug a tunnel through it.
Scratch and dig and climb the walls,
Now you're queen of the hallowed halls.

   Ruth C. Reiten

Ode To A Great Man

Was he born, or was he sculpt from fiery
Stones of Life on some Olympian height?
Heaven's gift he came, Prometheus-like . . . a
Lonely force in Freedom's smallish troop, and
Built his temples grand of noble tones with
Soaring strains of true, profound emotion,
Loos'ning ancient chains of lifeless form and
Leading man to dream aspiring dreams.

Was he born, or was he sculpt from fiery
Stones of Life on some Olympian height?
Heaven's gift he came, Prometheus-like . . . a
Lonely force in Freedom's smallish troop, and
Towered taller far than all his peers . . . the
Greatest Titan of his time — BEETHOVEN!

Hugh W. Shankle

Color Us Together

I see in you, young girl, like me
White, black, brown, pink
Your hue so bright
How well you laugh when friends are kind
When siblings dance, when peace is high
And hope is ripe.

I see in you, young boy, like me
Black, pink, brown, white
Your tint so proud
How hard you cry when nations war
When parents fail, when drugs and guns
Bring down your hopes.

But we the young
Move forward here and there
No blush, no shade should color what we feel
Nor change our flight
No hue or tint should blot our rainbow dreams
Which paint tomorrow's future
For all of us,
Together.

Kherra Tanyike Bennett

Dear Mom, I Miss You

In Memory of Theresa Matthews
I think of you often when times appear hard
Sympathize with all that you've been through
I know not an easy life have you had
Your heart weeped inside cold and blue
When others rejected your undying humanity
It made me ponder endlessly why
Were they so selfish to really perceive
For true love you'd give up your life
They treated you wrong and never said sorry
Maybe that would change your heart
So proud to say it did not persuade you
Your love was as good from the start
Please don't go away, I wanted to whisper
Your love is just one of a kind
O like a diamond in the rough
Shining brightly all of the time
Could you just stay here in my world
Filling it with pure joy and love
Although I know it's just much too late
Being your child is a gift from above

Gail Matthews

Winged Flight

The planes are like tiny toys within the skies.

Upon the hills,
Upon the rise,
It hurts the eyes
To watch the tiny planes within the skies.

The winter winds are on the rise.
The wings rise and fall upon the chest
in Peace or War.
The wings rise and fall upon the chest.
The wings are silver
And they emboss the gold upon the chest.
They rise and fall with every breath.
The flight is like magic on the chest.
The winter flights leave Logan now,
hour by hour,
The country's planes; they now fill the air.
When boarding now, we trust the flight.

Muriel Zitowitz

I Love You Too

Her eyes are black, her face is bruised,
She stands up and says: "I love you too".

All her life she heard them say
You're a mistake, you're not worth a damn,
She stands up and says: "I love you too".

From her father to her husband
It's all been the same
With tears in her eyes and ice for her hand,
In front of the mirror she would stand.

Her eyes are black, her face is bruised,
She cries and says: "I love you too".

As she stood there looking, she sees something new:
It wasn't a stranger within all the black and blue
It was me, a person, a mother, a friend...

As reality hits me, I see through the smoke: I stare at the truth.

Promises are of words and are easy to break.
But now I finally something to say:

Good-bye
Because "I love me too".

Sherri D. Wright

Laid Off

Wouldn't it be nice if work could be trusted,
To feel safe and never get busted?
Do what you can, and be proud of what you do,
And hopefully, this won't happen to you.

I worked for them for many years,
Through good and bad times, and even some tears.
The job was secure or so I thought,
Time and experience is what I brought.

Then one day they called me at home,
And what they said was "You're all alone."
To keep your job doesn't make sense,
So please consider it - past tense.

Looking for work was real yucky,
But now I'm making a lot more bucky.
What they did I thought was wrong,
But now I happily say "So long."

Dudley Genter

A Castle In The Mist

This journey has taken us far.
We've found many friends; we've left loose ends.
We've faltered at many pitfalls.
We've even felt great pride in these symbolic halls.
We've heard millions of times,
"Enjoy this journey for it will be your greatest one."

We've taken that advice and most of us have had a heck of a lot of fun.
We've kept our heads up when others would have buried them.
And when others would ridicule us, we would find a way to beat them.
Many obstacles we have overcome; and yet, there will still be some.

However inconceivable, we will have to face the inevitable —
we will have to leave the ones we love.
Whether we accept it or not.
We are ready even though we don't know a lot.
We have battled through the journey's hardships
and galloped through the easier times.
And we have not quit, but have learned from it.

Now, as time runs short, we pull our Mighty Mustangs to a halt
Striving for each moment and each sweet thought.
And now we are standing, looking over a cliff
Finally seeing our goal — a castle in the mist.

Scott Coones

Longing

Down, down in the depths of my heart
Feeling I should surely come apart
Alone, alone as I can truly be
Why, oh why is not someone there for me?

Is it too much for one to ask
In the warmth of love to bask?
Yearns my aching soul a turn of fate
To birth my feeling for a mate.

And yet she must be simply unique
This fragrance of heaven that I seek.
Not ANY woman can quench my thirst
She must be a gentle lady first!

Yes, and kind and loving and a friend
For such an angel I'd go no end
In vain I look where sun has shone
And that is why I pine alone.

Alan Sanderson

What Is Fear?

What is fear?
Why does it exist?
Is it the actuality of knowing not
What you may or may not miss
Is fear the expression on someone's face
When hearing of a strange and unknown place
Does fear thrive on the human soul
Would that be the reason why
This world is so evil and cold
Could fear by any chance be
The origin of all hate
Lying quietly beneath the surface
In the face of you and me
Can we blame fear
For the mistreatment of others
Causing us to abuse, slander and ridicule
Our unique but identical sisters and brothers
Or maybe fear is just in the mind
Waiting to overcome you
At any place or given time

Zelia Michelle Woods

It's Winter

It's Winter! It's Winter! That's all you know,
The earth is covered in a sheet of snow,
If you look over the hills of everlasting white,
You can find much more if you go at night,
Crickets a leaping,
Rabbits are sleeping,
The earth is covered in silence
Nothing dreaming of violence,
It's Winter! It's Winter! The earth is covered in snow,
Animals nestled in the earth below,
The sun will be shining,
There's no time for whining,
The snow will be melting,
The church bells loud "Ding",
It's Summer! It's Summer!

Christopher Chapogas

Untitled

If granted thus the time to see.
A world of peace and harmony..
Of which there is no fear.

No longer seeing young lives stand still.
When childrens' dreams are all fulfilled.
With high hopes everywhere.

A time when all men are aright.
A time when all the earth is bright.
No cause to be despair.

When all men stand together as one.
In unity they walk or run.
With strength beyond compare.

Working together side by side.
Standing tall as each one stride.
His brothers' load to share.

Taking hold his brother's hands.
Showing that he understands,
The need for ALL to care.

Lillie M. Gathers

Ten Little Indians

Ten little indians, going down a line
One crossed over, that left nine

Nine little indians fishing in a lake
One fell in, and there were eight.

Eight little indians, trying to race eleven
One looked back, and there were seven

Seven little indians, trying to get a fix
One got too much, that left six.

Six little indians, talking the jive
One talked too much, and there were five

Five little indians, one was a bore
They got rid of him there were four

Four little indians climbed a tree
The tree limb broke, there were three.

Three little indians, didn't know what to do.
One shot a cop, there were two.

Two little indians, one smart, one dumb
He tried to hitch hike, there were one

One little indian left out of ten
Found some playmates to start over again.

Alice Brent

Wanting

It sometimes seems I have the weight of the World on my two shoulder.
With each passing day the pressure increase as I grow older.
And I began to notice the many things around me.
Some I've seen before, yet some I've just begun to see.
I wonder if maybe time isn't really on my side.
That I'm on an emotional roller coaster ride.
I want to have the speed and finesse of a cat.
And do all the things I haven't done yet.
I want to be as fearless as a great black bear.
To have the courage to do all things no one would dare.
I want to be as free as a bird and sprout my wings and fly.
The only limit I'll have is what's beyond the sky.
I want to feel the wind at my feet.
I want to smile down on the people I meet.
I want to close my eyes and float to the great beyond.
And when I reach Heaven then, I'll know my journey is done.

Vickie Rushing Terrell

John Henry Gallo

Though I must say Good-bye now to
my brother and friend
I know in my heart we'll be together again.

Though your spirit is with God, it also lives
in my heart
So we are separated, but never apart.

Though I know you are in a safe and
peaceful place
I still long to hear your voice and look upon
your face.

Though I have photographs capturing your
every grace
I still miss very much your big Huggable embrace.

Though memories of you are etched in my mind
I still wish we could have had more time.

Though there's an emptiness inside me
Along with the endless tears I fend.
I know my life was blessed having you as
my brother and friend.

Joanne Gallo

Life's Many Clouds

In our life are many clouds.
The dark cloud when we lose a loved one.
The joyful cloud at the birth of a baby.
The cloud of anticipation when we meet that special person.
The cloud of envy when we see others who have more.
The cloud of happiness when we see our children grow.
The cloud of fulfillment when we look at a loving spouse.
The cloud of satisfaction when we reach the goal we set.
Look and see life's many clouds.

Ron Henry

Bunker Hill

Inside the darker tunnel dwell
He who hath lived a thousand years
And shed with it a thousand tears.
"No man can live as I do here.
His heart would into a thousand pieces tear."
No mortal will partake of he,
He who has never crossed the sea
Nor traveled fields and roads abroad,
Nor seen the shepherd with his rod.
Immortal who has lived here since
Has none but regret and consequence.
And forever more shall be here still,
He who lives in Bunker Hill.

Amber Daniel

Memories

We walked alone on the beach
hand in hand
Pausing just long enough to write our love
in the sand
As time passed on we knew we
couldn't stay
How sad, the tide had washed
our love away
Now we have but fond memories that make
us laugh and cry
But how I remember those beautiful times whenever
I watch the seagulls fly
Today I walk those same beaches alone thinking
beautiful memories, time and time again
Always wondering what life together
might have been

Clint Moses

falling hard

the Feeling surged with smile-swept sensation,
into my quaking hands It was hurled.
i was drenched with a storm-punch of emotion,
shaking my china-cup world.

i fell hard for your Spirit, your Beauty, your Grace.
in every bone and thought i held You.
now i soar on an air stream of dizzying space,
in a sky of more honest blue.

with finger-thrill touch i flung to a wanting,
a buoyant miracle dive.
a new beauty brilliant, i'm warm with a haunting,
all flutter-wonderful alive.

the Voice of your Eyes holds a fragile power,
a pillar of swaying moonlight.
i wake up in Van Gogh's yellow sunflower,
and spin under his Starry Night.

so i wait, and want, and wish for a dream
of the two of Us dancing a lifesong.
a Duet of stream and sunlight beam,
and rainbow-rides till dawn...

Stephen Cornell

in the middle of life Crisis in the middle of life

I may just dry-up and blow away someday
like a puddle left by summer rain:
The sun comes out, heats the pavement hot,
and poof, the puddle's gone.
She gazed at the green-stoned ring on her left hand,
the red-stoned ring on her right —
I'll give this green ring of my young girl,
the red ring to the older;
They've spoken for them already - why wait till I die?
All that red tape-they'll pay too dearly for their rings —
high taxes and legal fees
Yes, I'll give them the rings now; I can enjoy their delight.

But you have many more years of life, I said —
unless you know something I don't.

She lifted the tea cup to her lips
Conversation died away to silence
Gravely lowering the cup to its place,
She stretched her hands before me.

Look, she said, a lizard's claws adorned with jewels —
what a bizarre, even repulsive thing.
Her green eyes stared stonily at mid-life thoughts.

Joan Vestal Ellis

The Message Of The Cradle

The message of the cradle is a tale that never ends.
It holds the true meaning of Christmas and what it really means.
For there in Bethlehem was born - our Savior and our Lord.
He came as a gift from God - a gift of eternal love
To show us how to live our lives and how to treat each other.
He came to show the world and all, that we are sisters and brothers.
Oh, Holy night; oh, blessed day; oh, what joy our hearts discover,
To know that Jesus came to be our savior
To help our souls recover.
The message of the cradle in all its love and joy
Discovered in a manger - in sweet little Jesus boy.
Blessed angels hover as they did in days gone, and past.
About that little manger scene - a cradle that will forever last.
For God gave us His only son - to love and to forever cherish
That we might live a life of love and never truly perish
He lives today as surely as He did in that day of yore.
He lives in you - He lives in me - He lives forever more.

Peggy Guthrie

My Blue Crayon

You were my favorite of the whole bunch,
always waiting for me after lunch.
I used you on the walls and mom took you away,
but sure enough you were back the next day.
An imagination of your own,
sometimes color my entire picture blue,
but I promise you one thing -
I always respected you.
I didn't mean to hurt you when I accidentally broke your head,
I was in a rush to finish and thought you would never
return from the dead.
You were soon back - as good as new.
I never knew a crayon who was a
great friend like you.

Jeanine Reed

Old Goliath

Much has been written about David —
David, the shepherd boy, David, the king.

And of David and Goliath,
the giant Philistine.

Each of us is David
And Goliath — our sin.

Each day brings new battles
Without and within.

And daily we strive
And we try to do right.

Asking Lord Jesus to
Calm us in fright.

Old Goliath, get behind us.
Trouble us no more.

Christ Jesus has risen —
And settled the score!

Linda Szymik

Eyes Of Blue

I had two babies with eyes of blue
I brought home two babies in blankets of blue
I had two babies eyes of blue, I diapered them in diapers of blue
I sent them to school all dressed in blue
I watched them graduate in gowns of blue
I watched them marry eyes of blue
I saw them bring home babies with eyes of blue

Linda Kela

"A Lover Without Tear Drops"

No matter how you could love me,
or have a running tear down your face.
Just remember how I loved you —
more than ever before,
or with anyone else.

My love will always be with you,
even though I can't keep those tears
from dripping now and then,
I rather have those tears,
than lose you forever.

Even if you never loved me,
without any loving tears,
making my heart beat astray.

Who is the stronger one?
The one with lots of tears?
Or the lover who never had one?

I rather be a teary-eyed mate,
than face a wild grizzly bear.

And you sweetie, an African killer bee -
for not having a lonely or two just for me.

Russell Dye

Ones Life

Ones life cries out for something new,
Like a desolate ship without a crew,
In search of a word, a song of some rhymes,
To fulfill ones wants that have been empty at times.

Ones life cries out as if in pain,
For things in our heart that should be plain,
But our soul struggles for things in the past,
To tear out your heart for the present to last.

Ones life cries out for the world to hear,
But the world is deaf and it doesn't care,
My problems are mine and I should know,
What's right and wrong and which field to sow.

Ones life cries out and it has no voice,
Searching through memories trying to make a choice,
But the path ahead seems straight and clear,
Thinking all problems could be solved in a year.

Ones life cries out and time passes by,
Looking for courage to act and reply,
To our wants in life and pamper our tears,
And make the life we've waited for years!

Emmanuel Pelekanos

My Son

Just imagine the joy,
When the doctor, told me that I have a baby boy.
I loved you then, and I love you now,
To you my son, I solemnly pledge you this vow.
We've had our problems you and I,
I'll always love you, until the day I die.
I pray for you night and day,
That you would never go astray.
I will always be at your side,
Hoping to look into your eyes, with
    such loving pride.
What happened to my little boy,
The son I treasure with such pride and joy.
My son, my son, what more can I say,
I love you in every imaginal way.
To me you still are that baby boy,
The son that always gave me such joy.

Rose M. Harris

Sounds of the Heart

In the dawn of light
  shimmering rays of sunshine
  glisten in midair
  falling softly into nowhere.

Then it happens, unaware at first,
  unsure of your own being
  until the sound becomes barely audible,
  but clear and distinct,

    Heartbeats. . .
    one, then two,
    heartbeats.

Words are not needed,
  because our thoughts are as one,
  and without knowing, or wondering why,
  we begin to hear and feel our own

    Heartbeats. . .
    one, then two,
    heartbeats.

    strong, rapid, forceful,
Until our souls become one heartbeat. . .
      Christina Devor

Without You

The unfeeling evil, does its work so well
Without pity or concern, it makes our life living hell

We hope and build our defenses, holding firm and strong
Praying that this time apart, won't last too long

It tries to steal the memories, we cherish and hold dear
The moments we kissed and loved, and held each other near

Time, our enemy, the only friend of despair
Will try to make us suffer, but I don't care

I could laugh at death, I love you that much
If only I could see you again, and have your hand to touch

Our love is forever, my heart beats only for you
My life is empty and meaningless, I must have you

I'm determined to have you, no matter what the cost
Without you I have no life, without you I am lost
      Justin Sidney Henderson

"Yours And Mine"

It's been a long, long time
  since we said "What's mine is yours, yours and mine"
It's been quite awhile since
  we woke up and saw one another smile.
Changes have come along
  but our friendship will never be gone.
I've shared with you
  things no one ever knew.
You've shown me things
  no one else could see.
We've shared love, harmony and
  the greatest friendship of all
    "Yours and Mine".
Now once again, it's time to say Good-bye
  and if I seem to cry it's only because at least there
    is still love when we look eye to eye.
So in my heart,
  no matter how far apart
    at least we will always have "Yours and Mine"
      Sean Kavanagh

Alone

What happened to warm hugs and soft kisses?
Were they just my dreams and wishes?

What happened to long nights lying united as one?
Was it something special to you or merely for fun?

What happened to the soft words spoken?
I guess they were just empty promises now broken?

What happened to the love we shared?
Or am I wrong, was it only me who cared?

I know there is no reason for to cry
But it's hard not to when I don't understand the
  answer to the question - why?

Even though I still wish you were here with me
I now realize that it is not meant to be.

I am me and you are you
and no matter how hard I try, we will always equal two.

Two. Two separates. Two pieces apart.
Never to be joined or united at the heart.
      Mary Louise Reilley

Botanical Garden

Behold as you walk into this tiny jewel
A sense of leaving outside your cares,
Your worries, your concerns;
Serenity and beauty enfold your very being,
Your soul sings with contentment.

Here a towering tree plays music with the wind
There a low bush outdoes itself with flowering beauty,
Seeming to mock the taller stems, smiling to itself.

Hibiscus, trumpet flowers, lilies, orchids,
The bonsai and soothing waters of the Japanese garden,
The waterfall murmuring to itself with memories of
  engagements, marriages
And the small feet of wondrous children on the tiny bridge.

The quiet comfort of the bench beneath the tree:
One contemplates those who have so freely given
To make this haven a reality.
The joyous songs of the birds and quiet rummaging
Of squirrels gladden our hearts.

God's beauty, giving to us fleeting moments of joy,
A precious jewel, giving us peace.
      Cynthia Goring Shaw

"Old Memories"

They say that love at first sight comes only to the young.
But they were wrong and it was fun.
When my eyes met yours for that very first time.
A light lit in my heart and you were mine.
And thru me went a warmth and glow,
That this could happen to me was not so.
This warmth that I thought had long gone by,
But alas — all I could do — was sigh.
Because what I felt was for me alone,
I knew that once you left it could never be,
You would turn into a memory again for me.
But 'twas nice that for a little while —
I saw the radiance of your smile,
'Twas ever meant that we were to part,
But in my memory forever shall be hidden,
And in a corner of my heart.
      Ethel L. McNeill

Freedom Lost

Thousands fled, but I remained.
Tears I shed on land blood stained.

I ask you why so many men
were sent to die, you tell me then,

"For freedom. Haven't you heard?
We've lost some of our precious earth."

"What earth?" I say, "just soil beneath
was worth the slay of these lives for thee?

How can this bring the freedom you tell?
Hearts no more sing after they've fell.

Where is this freedom you say they have won?
Not a mother, numb, after losing her son.

When will I feel this freedom you sought?
Wasn't it real, the war that they fought?

"I don't really know", is your only reply.
"I reckon it's so. No one had to die."

"If we would have cared, we wouldn't be said.
We could have shared in all that we had.

Now we have learned, but it is too late.
After greed churns, the loss is so great."

Julie Weide

A Sunset Closer

As I board the plane for home, my heart leaves me.
I think of you as we fly over the clouds and the sun displays
   its awesome talent to paint the sky with its rays.
Your love has painted my life with colors I never knew existed.
My soul longs for the day that we'll be one,
Just as the sky and ocean are on a moonless summer night.
I long to walk along the beach with you as the tide embraces the shore
And the breeze spirits away the warmth of the day.

I see your smile, which could warm the coldest heart,
And your deep blue eyes that could read the most guarded soul.
Your love warms my heart like the sunshine on a autumn morning,
And has left its fingerprint on my soul.
I can feel your spirit next to me, transcending the miles between us,
Knowing Time will join our hands again in the near future.
For now, I watch the sunset on the desert, with all its awesome hues,
And find solace in knowing I'm one more sunset closer to being with you

Elizabeth M. Sanchez

The Birds

Fly, fly ever so high
Up over the trees-in the sky
I wonder what you think
Pushing yourself to the brink.

Wings so fragile, yet so strong
Always whistling a beautiful song
If you should ever change your ways
It would be awful for the rest of our days.

Mitchell Sizemore

Winter's Song

The faded leaves and crumpled flowers
Call an end to autumns hours
For winter slams a door on autumn's glory
But sings to all a different story
Of life that's pared so spare and lean
With open spaces in between
Then all is muffled by the snow
And drifted by the winds that blow
Do not follow after autumns fire
   Stay with me and sing to winter's lyre.

Frances Anne Prince

Where Are You?

   As I look around each day, I search for you
in some small way, hoping I'll find you close at
hand, instead of miles across the land.
   Thinking how when we first met, the discovery
isn't over yet. I have so much to say to you. I'm still looking
where are you?
   Your smile, your touch, the look in your eye, remembering
as I look across the sky. Wishing a twinkle of star dust
to fall, upon my heart, not to keep us forever apart.
   When you first touched my hand, I didn't really
understand. What would be between you and me, only
time will let me see.
   As time goes by it becomes clear, I wish for you to be
near. To hold you close so you can feel what words may
not reveal.
   While we hold each other near, the miles between
will disappear. For you have found the star dust sprinkled
on the ground and where you are I have found.

June Curry

Sandman

An invisible little madman
sprinkles golden dust on sleepy eyes.
He travels through the night air
listening close for drowsy sighs.
His line of work is odd to some
but to him it has its meaning.
His life is spent creating worlds,
while everyone else is dreaming.
He, himself does never slumber,
so from house to house he flees.
Leaving a luminescent trail
sparkling between the trees.
He is so small he cannot be observed
through the naked eye alone.
He says no words, he makes no sound, just an eerie, quiet monotone.
There are no words to describe his speed,
he is far quicker than any fire fly.
Most people believe it to be the wind, when he comes spiraling by.
Yet, even though so small is he, this tiny little magician,
cannot be resisted by man, or woman, infants, or even children.

Jennifer Goodson

A World Of Hatred

Our children are being raised in a world of hatred and violence.
As parents we need to spend more time teaching love and guidance.

What difference does it make the color of one's skin?
It is only a layer, it is not what is within.

All must stop, the drugs, violence and abuse.
We need help, because there is no excuse.

Our children need to be nurtured and loved.
Not shot at, shot-up, pushed or shoved.

An end must be put to the Racial Wars.
We must help, make it one of life's biggest chores.

God made us all equal, he created us all.
He did not stop, because some were short and some were tall.

Teach your children of race, color and creed.
It need not matter, when someone is in need.

The hatred needs to come to an end.
Take your neighbor and make them a friend.

This world is the place our children must grow.
We need to teach them, hatred must go.

Michele Richner

"Think"

"Use your common sense!"

There are some words and phrases that will always stick with a person, some good... some bad.

"Don't stand there and do nothing!
Always think of a way to help your partner."

The good and the bad change through time
bad thoughts become good and vice versa.

"Was what you did wrong?.... Was what you did right?... Why?"

Age plays a hand in this switch
some call it wisdom.

"Think before you do!... Use your head."

Sometimes, the more I "use my head"
the more confusing things become.

Some people fight this chaos, others embrace it.
I am learning to live with it.

When this confusion engulfs me I need only remember one thing;
I can almost hear your voice telling, sometimes yelling, the
difference in tone is naught, the message is still the same....

"Billy, use your head... THINK!"

I believe it is that phrase that has made all the difference in my life.
So basic, yet so profound.

"THINK."

Bill Kennelly

The World

I look around and all I see is pollution, hate and prejudice.
A person's skin should not matter, yet it does. Why?
We fear those who are different than we are.
Is white better than black? How do we judge? God made both!
We ponder long, the answers does not come easy.
The earth and sky are littered. Noise deafens. Smoke chokes.
Newspapers are read and thrown away;
some containing remedies.
Today we read, we think, but do we act?
Will we wait while the world wasters away?
I must do something? But what?
Stop smoking, don't litter? Will it help?
It begins with me and goes on from there.
Some hate those with long hair and different ideas.
But hate is sin, so why do we feel this way?
We have to be taught by our elders.
But we should think for ourselves.
I hate war, I also hate communism.
So the sin is in hating the good but not the bad.
Sometimes we can change the bad to good by hating
It is a lot to think about.
And the thinking is the beginning!

Kerry Rogozinski

The Gift

Have faith for the best is yet to come
There is a kingdom in my home for you when thou deed is done.
These were the words I heard and with you these things I share
For God so loved the world the greatest gift he bear.
Those who felt it was his son, true a great gift was he
but I still say the greatest gift of all is for everyone to see.
You can't find it in the water or in the lands afar,
The kindness of a lover's heart or in a drinking bar
This wonderful thing you see can't be found in a mall
The greatest gift is the chance for Heaven given to us all.

Terrance Hunter

"The Saddest, Sweetest Story"

Easter morning used to be a day to go to church and see;
the easter bonnet's gay and bright; and hope that
we were dressed alright.
    But, Good Friday morning, some year's ago, I felt
there was more that I should know. I have been
forgiven for my sins, now I wanted knowledge
and wisdom within. I picked up my Bible;
not knowing where to find that story I knew
was there and where it opened I was so surprised;
there was that story before my eye's!

    I read of His sadness and His strife; Oh! the sorrow
I felt when they took His life! The tears come down;
I thought my heart would break; to think, how they -
MY JESUS LIFE DID TAKE! I felt I died up there with Him!
He did all this, just for my sin's!

    Then after three days, "HE AROSE"! He
walked on earth with men to teach them how
to live for God, till He comes back again!

    It's the saddest, sweetest story that ever has been told -
the saddest sweetest story - It never will grow old!

Janice K. Harlow

Little Boy Gone

    My little boys gone, he left to live at his daddy's place
the sadness, the hurt, so unbearable for me
His voice, his touch and love, the sight of him no more each day
to hear, to feel, to see
I call his name, but get no reply please come back
I love you I cry
And though my life goes on it's empty now, lonelier too
My little boys gone
goodbye my love, my dearest son, goodbye to you.
Mommy

Gilda A. Tisa

Leave All Doubt Behind

Darkness fell upon us giving us night,
Changing everything around us into shadows and fright.
A mind is like the darkness,
Full of doubt and fear.
It's when we give it knowledge and love,
All frightening things disappear.
When a mind is used it's as if,
A new day has begun.
Full of sunshine and brightness,
Just as the morning sun.
Look for the morning,
Soak up the sun's rays..
For the darkness of night is near.

Ann M. Barnes

You Slipped Away

We stood there watching as day turned to night,
but with you beside me the darkness seemed bright.
I turned to you slowly and saw something there
the warmth of your smile showed that you cared.
You told me you loved me and then held me tight,
and slowly as you slipped away the darkness turned to light.
I still feel your presence and the love that you bore,
but I know we'll meet again on the steps of heaven's door.

Kelly Seig

God's Refreshments

Warm the summer morn came dawning,
Raindrops falling unrestrained
Joy of Joys God's love surrounds me.
In the midst of this worlds pain.

Sometimes we're forced to lie in pastures
By waters still, as David did.
To see God's rapturous, glorious beauty,
That from our eyes is oft time hid.

What precious time to spend with Jesus,
In Him alone, His presence share
To learn the secrets through life's Valleys,
How He will all our burdens bare.

I will not fret, or even question
Why my life is dealt with so,
I only know that I will trust Him
To guide my path, where ere I go

Peggy Corbitt

Wildfire In The Sky

Midnight blue with sparkling specks of yellow and white.
The gentle winds blow, the tall grass sways back and
    forth like the ripples in the water.
Bright shells decorate the cool, moist sand.
Tiny pebbles trace the tide line along the beach.
The indigo ocean foams.
White waves crash on rocks peaking out of the water offshore,
    leaving a never-ending mist floating in the air.

In the distance, the deep blue skyline changes to shades of purple,
    getting lighter as time goes on.
As darkness fades from the sky, a glowing tangerine peaks over the horizon.
The color bleeds, bright orange runs like wildfire across the sky.

Now, the sun is fixed high above the sea.
It is just a yellow ball, sending its heat down to Earth.
The winds have died down.
The waves have left for distant shores.
The ocean remains a deep blue-green.
Flocks of seagulls fly into the crystal blue sky.
Even the clouds have drifted away.

Brenda S. Machado

Separated Again

Our worlds are different and so far apart.
To see your face would warm my heart.

I can recall your image but soon it fades.
I sit here waiting and wondering as I count the days.

I wish I was with you; just to hear your voice.
If only I had made that simple choice.

Our separations are endless and seem so many.
I miss your humor, your jokes, and your being funny.

Our love is now and forever lasting.
To love me is all I am asking.

Tenia M. Torrey

Nightfall

The hills are still dappled in moonlight;
The grass not yet moist with dew.
The lakes still ripple with shadows;
Red roses still blooming new.
A shadow of darkness covers
All land within human view.
A sphere of light discovers
A place; to me, new.

Monica Vickers

My Sister Karena

To my little sister, we've been through so much.
My hair in your hand, your neck in my clutch.
But as we got older we began to realize,
We became friends, what a surprise.
We've grown through the years sharing laughter and tears.
You've been my best friend when I needed you near.
I'll love you always, even though we're apart.
And this is coming straight from my heart.
I'll always cherish our memories so dear,
And please don't forget if you need me I'm here.
I'm glad you chose Rocco, he is a good man,
I know he'll protect you the best that he can.
And when you have children I hope you agree,
That they'll be as close as we've come to be.
My dear baby sister, it's so hard to let you go,
Twenty-two years is a long time you know.
But I wish you and Rocco a long happy life,
You've been a great sister and you'll be a great wife.

Andrea L. Piserchio

Everlasting Life

I made the mountains, I made the rain,
And the love I have for you
Is stronger than the strongest chain.
For as the sun rises in the east and it sets in the west,
The strength I give to thee, it will never rest.
So I sent you My Son, you needed a sign.
The love He has for you, it is endless in time.
For He is a Teacher, both knowledge and Truth.
He'll search your hearts, give you back your youth.
His words are straight, His sword is you.
Your testimony in Him will be clear and true.
So tell of His works...In God You Trust,
How righteous, how clean, He will never Rust.
So pick up your cross for your least of sin.
Your walk with Jesus, It's His heart you must win.
For if you deny me in Him, You deny him of me.
Water and Spirit, it's your life, it's your key.
You have a short time so practice what you preach.
The Ten Commandments and Miracles...
It's heaven you will reach!

Christopher Alan Wood

Cybelle's Spirit

I remember still the way she shone,
the day we shared sunset.
Her fiery afterglow of burnished gold,
that graced her cheek, still wet.

Her touch was like a gentle breath,
an invisible angel left behind.
In musky grass, amidst wildfire blooms,
it burned to know she was my kind.

We strolled golden grasses, a multi hue,
as two new apart will sometimes do.
We dreamed of a time that was not ours,
when our loves hope could spring anew.

We walked saddened fields, in poppies red,
with burnished gold above her head.
I cherished her hand and watched her walk,
we neither one had any talk,
    in sunsets glow, so red.

Dante B. Kun

Surrender To Serenity

Telephone, television, trauma,
Static invades the human heart.
Over-load, over-worked, over-extended,
Communication breaks down.
Tragedy strikes.
Tension mounts.
Life crumbles.
Pause, reflect, connect,
Believe that there is a power that transcends space.
Release the Power dwelling within you.
Communicate in silence with the creative marvels of God.
Relax before a quiet stream.
Receive the peace of God.
Nurture your starving spirit.
Be still.
Listen. Look.
Respond to the delicate, beautiful symmetry of flowers.
Reflect on the majestic stature of trees.
Communicate with the natural rhythm in nature's music.
Quietly breathe in Power, the peace of our Creator, God.

M. Jovita Hatem

Why Do You Hurt Me?

Why do you hurt me? Why do I care?
Why is loving you so hard to bear?
Why do you hurt me? Make me understand!
Why is staying like a time bomb in sand?
Why does leaving hurt so deep inside?
Why can't I just go some place and hide?
Why do you hurt me? Why do I care?
Please! Please tell me, tell me if you dare!

You say you want me, then you go away.
Just as quickly you are back, sometimes for just a day.
Falling in love was never in my plans,
My restless soul yearns for distance lands.

Help me, help me to go my own way
I must keep my journey from going astray.
My life is lonely, I know not what to do!
My heart has been searching for someone just like you.
God in heaven looking down to earth,
Sees and knows all our worth.
Hurting each other was never in His plan
For this He did not create man.

Helen Faye

Untitled

She awakes to the sounds of engine thunder and
the crunch of gravel beneath rolling wheels.
With a pounding heart she runs to the window.
She sees who she thought was her man, steal away
without a backward glance.
Surely she must have known there is a greater power
than the love of mortal woman, which owns his
gypsy soul. The wind; he'll always return.
He cannot deny her charms nor does he want to.
She takes his breath from him, as she whispers in
his ears words only he can understand.
She lovingly caresses his skin with her cooling fingers,
and scents his hair with her sweet perfume.
She holds him firm in her grasp as he flies along
black ribbons of road and highway.
For him to ride with her is to love, and to live.
She watches him from the window, until he is
swallowed up by space and distance.
His legacy to her is his memory and the hot tears
on her cheeks. She fell second to the wind.

Jim Lyman

The Ride

The metallic machine under me
    moves and moans
carrying me breathlessly across its path
    growling and groaning
vibrating beneath me, against my skin
    pulsating inside me
pulling us rhythmically toward the wind
    blowing fiercely, in the gentlest way
whirling by me, familiar scents
    and sights not seen from there,
where the metallic machine under me
    moves and moans.

Judith Sherrow Conde

Just A Lifetime

A picture perfect setting for such a special night,
the feelings that abounded were pure delight;
It began with a spark and ended with a fire,
the song that was sung by a heavenly choir,
especially for the four of us there;
the comfort received with the touch of your hair.
Holding you closely, delicately in my arms,
wanting to love you and keep you from harm.
How beautiful you looked and how beautiful you'll be,
now and forever until eternity.
That night, tomorrow was the least of my cares,
all that I needed were your sweet loving stares.
Later that night while lying in bed,
memories of you still fresh in my head,
I prayed and asked God, "Is she the one,"
"I need her, oh God, like the earth needs the sun."
    There exists no deed that I would not do,
    if He would just grant me a lifetime with you.

Kyle Scott Barrett

Love

    Love is as close as a mother and her calf
Love is as close as a cry and a laugh
    Love is as delicate as a feather
Love is as special as the weather
    Love is always telling the truth
Helping out when a friend lost their tooth
    Love is supposed to come from your heart
So give someone love and don't depart

Chrissy Long

Just Yesterday

Time passes so swiftly, it seems like just yesterday
When she looked at me and with nota word
Answered a cry in the night barely heard
A diaper change, a bottle of milk
Those cool mornings, those fishing trips
Just yesterday

A small boy, a little girl outside at play
Bring thoughts of those many sun filled days
Then there was grammar school preceding a teenage world
With the roughness of a boy, the gentleness of a girl
Just yesterday

Just yesterday has given memories that are stored in the
    hearts of mom and dad
That brings not a time of sadness, but a time to be glad
For when tomorrow comes, we can proudly and with love proclaim
Like yesterday, a new daughter, a new son, we've gained...
    Just yesterday

C. W. Vantreese

Ocean Liner

Here aboard an ocean liner I truly love to be,
As we move across the ever changing surface of the sea.
I like to hear the sea gulls scream and feel the whistle blow.
I like to wonder where I am and where we're going to go,
The chug chug of the motor at the bottom of the boat;
The wind that blows across the bow and makes me want my coat.
I like to watch the water as it rushes past the side.
I like to see the buoys that mark the channel and the tide.
I like to stand above the big propellers at the back
As they turn and churn a foaming wake into a V-shaped track.
And when the birds have left us and the land is far away
I can watch the wind tossed water and can taste the salt sea spray
Then my heart expands within me and my joy is so complete
It can never quite escape me though I walk a city street.

Frances C. Andersen

God Knew

God knew what he was doing
when he created a child.
A tiny little soul
so complete and mild.
With skin so soft and tender
to the touch.
No one could imagine
you could love them so much.
Their little eyes so trusting and true.
While their tiny hands find so much to do.
No where in the world
is anything so sweet.
As a baby sent from heaven
made so complete.

Karen L. Reed

From The Heart

I have some things to tell you, and I'm not sure where to start,
    but be assured of one thing, they're genuine, from the heart.
There are memories that I'm fond of, in the passing of the years,
    when you offered me your loving hand, to wipe away my tears.

"This too shall pass" you always said, when I was feeling sad,
    a moment later, I could go on, life wasn't quite so bad.
There had been so many times as I was growing older,
    when I needed to feel loved, to cry on someone's shoulder.

So let me try just one more verse to complete what's on my mind,
    just how I feel down deep inside, and say them so they'll rhyme.
I have a "special" friend in life, perhaps you now will see,
    she never asks for anything, she's just always there for me.

Renee A. Thomaier

Water Song

Vertical rush from chrome tap, or slow drip.
Ice-shock to the swimmer.
Spreading circle from a stone
Beneath the bridge a glimmer viridian.
Foaming white mares pound a beach,
withdrawing at whim of moon-pull.
A leaning willow drops a swirling leaf
in limpid cool, our lifeblood.
But listen, sheer therapy when it falls
hypnosis, glint and shimmer.
Tumble, shamble, riffle, tremble.
Music.

Yvonne Koolhof

Barrister

With eyes that run straight to the flaw...
Finding fault, where perhaps only error lies,
why turn my stance into sound?
Sheathing swords that never cower the
    wicked eyes,
Yes, tell them! Of flags left
    on the ground...

Like "Taps" steadily haunting, from the
    bugler's cursed horn,
Only I know what I've left on the shelf;
And their trappings and rewards only delay
    and warn:
"There's beauty, and everything else."

Pray for the nobles in a different war,
For He shuns the merchant without goods;
I think it was hades that bathed me on
    a welcome shore,
the day,
they trained me, and my eyes
to run to the flaw...

J. Scott Colesanti

Held

I remember the night.
When I held you in my arms,
Your head upon my shoulder
As I took you in my arms for I was no longer lost
As your sweet breath thawed that heart of ice
As we danced, real close
In the dimly lit room
Clinging to each other
As we only had eyes for each other.
Our expectations were that
Of priceless moments in time
Envisioned in our hearts forever more
Quietly, oh so quietly
Time slipped on by
And the precious wonderment's
That we had faded, faded on away
As I remember the night
You came into my life
And I held you tight
All through the night.

Philip W. Haywood

Closed Bud

This dreary cold summer day will soon be passing
The leaves are busted out in full.
As the flowers begin to bloom.
Only I feel the cold and loneliness
And know within there's never an end
No one to reach out to - no one to touch
Enclosed in this small bud
But never, will I, be able to blossom.

Shirley Harrah

Untitled

My days were once filled with depression
and my heart with solitude
My mouth spoke nothing of hope
and my mind thought nothing of happiness

Until the day I found the Lord
he filled my days with meaning
and my heart with love

Now my mouth speaks nothing of despair
and my mind thinks nothing of sadness

Benjamin D. Sweatland

Taking The Lead

I can see the frustration as he turns each page,
I brace myself for one of his fits of rage.
He is like an animal in a cage,
Trying to fit in with those his own age.

What is it that holds this child back?
Is it his upbringing, or rather the lack?
Whatever it is, the odds seem to be stacked,
But I won't give up on this kid who takes me aback.

I'm not sure why I've become so attached to this child,
Maybe it's the eyes that look up at me, so big, so wild,
Or it might be the way he attempts everything with his own style.
Whatever it is, to say I've grown to love him is putting it mild.

So what do I do with a child that can't read?
A child who has so many a need...
Do I listen to those who have done little indeed?
Dare I listen to my heart and take the lead?
Yes, I think he shall succeed.

Michelle E. Lierz

Siblings

I held you in my arms- clumsily inexperienced,
  yet I was careful, because I could feel how fragile you were.

We held hands walking through the park,
  and picked the flowers with their earthly sweet fragrance.

We were friends from birth you and I-
  we shared our love, laughter, and our eagerness to learn.

Now reliving the good times, after the nightmares of the bad,
  I cry for you in my sleep- each tear a shattered dream.

The two of us were sworn as one,
  now we're torn apart by another's discontent.

The endless nights of fighting still linger in my thoughts,
  and the silent screams still fill my head.

How could they have been so blind?

We were two of a kind you and I,
  until you followed our father down a separate path.

The man we loved and respected but whom we now both despise.
  He changed you and left you forever scarred.

His way was wrong-abusive and abused,
  and now you live disillusioned-abusive and abused.

But dear brother, I forgive you because I was there too.

Christy Kreymborg

Why Did I Die!

So young was I, "when I died"
So full of hopes and dreams "before I died."
So many friends and loved ones I had "before I died."
But I can't understand "for the life of me" why I died."

Such a pretty day it was "when I died".
Walking with my friends, singing songs, playing laughing
And joking as we walked along. "before I died."

Everything to me was just perfect, "before I died."
Until I heard shouting and cursing, "before I died."

Run! "they said before I died".
"Why" I said "before I died"
"Why" the last word I said "when I died".

  And I can't understand "for the life of me"

  "Why I died"!

Aretha Franklin

"Alys"

I said it quite as plain could be,
the Lord takes care of you and me.
You must believe and you must see,
that nothing's impossible, not for he.
Yet while we prayed, I knew he heard,
Our plea for life, It's in his word.
God always knows what we don't know,
And chooses the very best way to go.
As we laid the rose buds in the snow,
We blessed his name and thanked him so.
A new little angel flies the skies,
And we are grateful he is so wise.
They'll come one day that spirit back home,
For us to hold and call our own.
A well land healthy child in form,
Another babe in "spirit born.

Joan True

The Battle

As I watch the battle proceed,
I feel the anger, hatred and greed.
As my brothers and fellow countrymen bleed.

The shouts of the battle now rage louder than ever,
"Don't retreat! Just fight better!
Oh, how long will this bloody curse endeavor?

As the smoke from the cannons and guns slowly rise,
I still hear the moaning of battle cries,
As the men lie losing their lives.

Now the victory flag rises slow,
Over the new fallen bloodied snow,
But the victory cries are low.

A new day will turn this one will end;
But the victory cries will stay low,
For they killed men they didn't even know.

Pamela McLoughlin

See How America Loves Her Children

That body, toted off to doctors, dentists. opticians, physicians,
Impregnated with wheat germ, cod oil, sunshine and vitamins.
Thanks to Spock, a mother's BA, Dad's hard-earned pay,
The finest body of the century, Shaw's Superman with 70
  year life expectancy
is now wracked with cigarette cough and hack.
(Hearing it by dark, I know, at least, my son is back).
That Tabula Rasa, never sullied by color book, nor TV dead or alive,
A mind, on which each citizen taxpayer yearly spends three
hundred five, and which we've humored, encouraged, expanded,
improved and enriched to our debt——
(Did we think a perpetual infant, when we played at Papal roulette?)
is now zapped on speed, uniformly LSD's, and high on grass
without regard to race, creed, color or class.

Virginia Soetebier

Searching

Searching and looking for that priceless thing,
Demanding what I have struggled to win.
Requiring things which make my heart rejoice!
A child's heart, yet a woman's life.
Leading onward, not knowing where,
Just searching and looking for that priceless thing.
I've had a glimpse;
I want it now, but it seems my trees' too high to climb.
I should like to rise and go back to where my apples grew,
But I've been grafted to newer branches-
I'm neither the old nor the new.
My search goes on. Searching, Searching.....

Willie Bell

The Lake

Always you were there for me, reflecting my mood.
Wind whipped waves rushing ashore, cold sand
up to my ankles. Gray somber clouds, feeling
alone, yet a part of you.
A cool bright morning, you and me swirling
twirling whirling with the wind; running in
the sand til my heart beats in my ears. Breathless;
Sun twinkling on crystal whitecaps.
You knew when I was in love, you looked even
more beautiful then. Purple clouds and orange
sunsets; the swell of waves in the evening- memories in the making.
You felt my loss and you grieved with me.
but you didn't stop changing with the seasons;
you showed me life goes on - time is unstoppable.
I will grow older but you will remind me of how
young and hopeful I once was.
You are the place my memories and secrets live,
while my life marches on.
The birds may fly away - the sun will grow distant
But you will always be there.

Suzi Carmody

Dear Little Turtlehead

There's another woman in your life,
But there's a chance you won't know me.
I long to hold you in my arms
And to press my lips to your sweet cheeks.

I wish I could see you walk
And to hear you're voice ring with laughter.
To see you run into your Daddy's arms
With a puppy barking at your heels.

To see you climb a mighty oak
And to hide out in your tree house,
And to climb down the ladder
To plop into your sand box.

I wish you all the best that life can give.
May you grow big and strong
And nothing in your life go wrong,
And the dreams you dare to dream come true.

Oh, my little one who I love so much
There's so much that I could give you,
But I probably won't get the chance.
Maybe one day you and Daddy will come home.
                    Love,
                        Stepmother

Charlotte McMillan

Opaque But Clear

Everything moves along too slowly, living life through other's eyes.
Why do we go along with life? With all its troubles, all its lies.
I sometimes sit and ponder, what life really is.
Times like now, my family went to see Les Mis.
I stayed home, of course, like I always do.
Pretended I was sick, caught some type of flu.
I think sometimes I really am sick, deep down inside.
My thoughts, my feelings, the ones I always hide.
It used to be sunny out the window, the sun had reflected in the pane.
But now the window's opaque, covered by a thick sheet of rain.
Always lived my life in solitude, always liked being alone.
A true brave man, could spend his whole life at home.
I am that brave man, I am scared of no thing.
I'm going to stand up on my hill, where only I am king.
Me, myself, and I, need not any of you.
I'm going to just stand up on my hill, till life tells me I'm through.
I'm here at my climax now, it's all downhill from here.
No time for second thoughts, no time for fear.
I slit my wrists swiftly, with an old kitchen knife.
I think it's safe to say, this was the best day of my life.

Jeff Algayer

A Noble Promise

In my mind's eye, I beheld a castle.
A palace of splendor, a palace of light.
Built brick by brick, for your every delight.
Of bird songs at morning
And star shines at night.
You are my Princess, I, your humble Knight.

The realm of your heart,
My kingdom it shall be.
The inner peace of your soul,
The quest calling I shall heed.
Some never have the chance,
Some never chance the dream.
So quickly now, give your hand to me.
And forever banded we will be.

I will complete you,
As you will complete me.
And with every drop of valor,
With a never ending faith,
Your protector, your Prince,
I'll pray to be.

Thomas E. Murray

The Lawman Of First Grade

Pictures were to be taken
At school that day
Mom stated, your not going dressed that way

With six shooters on my hip
And sheriff star pinned on my chest
I could not leave home
Until mom was at rest

So to the bedroom, I did go
Hiding the sheriff star
So it would not show

Needless to say
I wore the star on my vest
For a six-year-old
Live by the Code of the West

I was in first grade
When it all came about got my rear busted
The day school pictures came out

Years have long since passed, when the pictures were made
My parents still call me
The Lawman of First Grade.

Calvin Wayne Skipper

Time

Here I sit looking out my window.
The wind blows thru the trees, bending them making them shed their
Leaves and life.
The seasons are changing and so am I. Lonely, lost, no direction.
From today I can see yesterday but no tomorrow.
Life is good, but with no direction, I seem lost.
Like the leaves on the trees blown across the lawn going no place special.
But there seems to be promise in the wind.
Something special is near, there is love and love of life.
Bringing with it hope, happiness, and innocence of life.
Only the wind knows which way to go, blowing thru time with
     direction and power.
I would follow the wind but I don't know which way it would take me.
I'm afraid it would be the wrong way, but what is the right way?
Only time can tell, the hope of something special seems to be near.
The wind seems to be holding a message.
Only time will give the answer.

Bear Carney

Where Is Paradise

But FATHER, Where is Paradise, Please let me tell you my Child.
Paradise is in the peaceful blue and azure of the skies
Paradise is in the beauty of an innocent child's eyes.
Paradise is in the trees so gold, red and green.
Paradise is in the color of friendship so true and serene.
Paradise is in the flutter of the wings of gulls.
Paradise is in the sounds of the waves against the ships hulls.
Paradise is in the birth of the new born child.
Paradise is in the strength of the marriage long and mild.
Paradise is in the snow glistening and white.
Paradise is in the sounds of children skating in the moonlight.
My Child, Paradise is everywhere.

Ruth I. Magdzinski

God, Our Eternal Flame

The Lord Almighty is a forever light;
He has come to impart unto the wicked the way of the right.

His precepts are a burning candle for His chosen;
From His unfathomable sacrifice salvation is offered to all men.

Though the sun of earth may melt away someday;
The Son of God will forever more stay.

God's children each an amber of His love;
We will ignite the world from the glory of Him above.

No passionate fire could equate His brilliant glow;
His plan of splendor is proclaimed from the earth tops above
to the valleys below.

Our Father carried the hurting, burdensome torch to the end;
So that our hearts, yours and mine, He might mend.

Do not forsake this Jesus the unquenchable light given to all;
For without this light we like sheep will stumble and fall.

Matthew Phinney

"Time"

We started with all we thought we'd need, our youth and love to share.
But life held other fortunes, we'd got caught up in its snare.
We slaved to what we're taught; the right things for us to know.
Like winter's desolation, our dreams were buried in the snow.
It drew us through the coming years, their passing taught us nil.
Our love became a fleeting word; passion's flames died in the chill.
Yet somewhere in the middle a second chance we knew.
It gave us one more season, the child inside you grew.
But fools can never see the start of something good again
And all to soon its passage led us back the way we'd been.
The trappings of the life we shared glittered in the glowing sun
And all of those 'round us believed in just how well we'd done.
But in the darkness of the night, we could see the clearest then,
Loneliness vainly pointed the way to lead us from our sin.
The distance grew between us; it moved us in divergent ways.
We'd left once more lessons of just livin' simpler days.
Now granite marks the ending, your passage through is through.
I wish only now, with reddened eyes, I'd spent more of It with you.

Time.

Tony R. Hall

When I Looked At You

When I looked at you.
You looked like you had the flu.
That's when I fell in love with you,
I asked, you your name.
You said, "David Fame"
When I asked you out.
You said, "There's no need to pout,"
You said, "Yes, don't wear a bow."
That's when I fell in deeper love for you.

M. Kuhn

A Night At Liberties Cafe

Cozy tables,
Shaped in circular discs of Wedgewood blue.
Poetic Patrons,
Brimming with oceans of notions,
Murmuring with conceptions and impressions,
Uttering expressions of sparkling inventions.
Rarely personal,
Sometimes impersonal,
Nevertheless, all eternal.
Eyes twinkling,
torsos twisting,
feet itching, to mount the podium, under the lectern.
Eager to declaim a poem,
Perhaps to share an angst.
Perchance to stir a dream, or two, into each steaming potion of
    coffee brew.
Yearning to imbue,
in this wholesome venue, a more gentle soul,
to forever dwell within the heart of you.

Tony Mazzara

Christmas

'Tis the season to be jolly,
or at least that's what they say.
    Deck the halls with boughs of holly,
on this wonderful Christmas Day.

    Santa Clause will be here soon,
with his sleigh all filled with toys.
    But you better watch out and don't you shout,
he only comes to good girls and boys.

    The reason that we celebrate,
our joy on Christmas Day.
    Is because of the tiny new born king
who was born upon the hay.

    He gave us life, and took our sins,
on his shoulders he did bear.
    To give us everlasting life,
to live in his kingdom there.

    When you open all your presents,
and turn on your blinking lights.
    Please remember the real reason we celebrate...
the birth of Jesus Christ.

Debra Wilson

Lisa

Forever yours is the best in me,
Love for love, just let it be
The shine of a star
The dream of a child,
Oh, can you see?

Lisa,
Like a tranquil breeze you came along
Opening my heart, whispering a song.
Lisa,
You soothed my soul and lighted the way
Tearing down my sorrows, cheering up my days.

How can I forget
Your smile wiping my pain,
Healing this hurting heart of mine,
Bringing joy and the best of times?
To love you, Lisa, was to live again.
Your love, Lisa, was the best to get.

Benedict Loredo

A Day's Work

Muscles straining, nostrils flared,
Hooves stamping, tail whipping in the air.
Circling, turning, rearing, pawing,
The roan hears the day's work calling.

The steps get nearer to the pen, a noose is readied, twirled and thrown.
Caught! Over the head goes the bridle, the blanket is placed high on
    the strawberry roan.
Leather, soap, saddle, man, he twists his head to catch a smell.
In the domain of man and horse, all is well.

Eager for the run, flesh quivers, ears point ahead.
The cinch is tightened, prancing, out the gate he is led.
Mounted, headed, trotting, galloping, full run
To the herd in the pasture, his day has begun.

Bawling, running, dodging, calves try to escape.
Roping, throwing, cutting, marking a brand, no time for a break.
Without any commands, both roan and man move as one.
The horse and man complete the job. Well done.

When the sun began its short journey to the plain,
The team turns and lopes toward home.
Satisfied, tired, hungry, glad to be back again
Is the man and his strawberry roan.

Mary McCrury

My Mother's Death

The days my mother left me, I was just a wee, wee girl.
 It happened oh so suddenly and she spoke not a word.

I stood and wrung my hands as I cried and cried.
Then came the next morning and I wished I too had died.

There was my little brother. He came up to me and said, while
We hugged each other, what will we do? She's dead.

We had our grandparents, many aunts and uncles too.
There was also our stepfather but none of them could do.

To take the placed of one so kind and full of love and care.
Such a one to fill that void no other can compare.

Clonda Thomas

The Marsh

I miss the marsh, the marsh is gone
    and windswept fragile reeds of gray
    bend downward to the sand and grieve
    the loss of nest for gull and tern
    which we can never more retrieve.

The marsh is gone, and in its place
    new hills of garbage mounds disgrace
    the shore with rows of look-like homes
    replacing all we loved before.

I miss the marsh, the tidal flat
    patrolled by Horseshoe Crab and rat.

The marsh is gone. It's gone to hell.
 I miss the stench, the blessed smell
 of ebbtide mud and rotting shell.

Joseph M. Goliger

Silent Gifts

 Once a dime fell from the sky
and hit the street with a silent noise.
Nobody heard it or saw it. The dime
just lay there. Plenty of cars and
bikes ran over it, but the dime still
didn't move. The following day a
boy found the dime, and spent it on
candy, and the dime still lays silently.

Alison Bland

The City The Sun Sets Upon

Seeking out across the ocean
to find the city the sun sets upon
Hearing waves cause a comotion
I gaze in your eyes and then move on

Looking deeper into the night
to find the city the sun sets upon
Searching for my way, by light
I gaze in your eyes and then move on

Moving on, forth I venture
to find the city the sun sets upon
Engulfing the sea adventure
I gaze in your eyes and then move on

Moving on, I will no further
I found the city the sun sets upon
Gazing in my eyes, the sun shines forever
As I gaze in your eyes, our love goes on

Donnamarie Theberge

Separate Worlds

We may be walking side by side
Even be looking in each others eyes
But the truth of the matter is my pearl
We are living in separate worlds

Occasionally our world may intersect
For a moment our bodies may connect
We'll experience pleasure and ecstasy
But soon we'll be apart and you'll be a fantasy

I'm waiting hungrily for our worlds to turn
So together again our bodies may burn
Then our love can melt and keep us warm
On those lonely days when apart our worlds are torn

Rose Stephens

My Dad

My dad will always be my hero
No one will ever take his place
He has always believed in me
Without questions or doubts
My dad will always be with me
Throughout my life
Always giving me advice
Never doubting my choice
My dad will always be special
Being close or far away
His presence will always be near
In my heart and soul
My dad will always be my confidant
Giving me answers
Believing in me
Strengthening my beliefs
My dad will always be my source of strength
Helping me through time
Preserving new experiences
Leading me through my life to eternity.

Joyce Pimentel

Immoralities

You're blind, but you can see.
You're deaf, but you can hear.
Your heart is black, yet still beats.
You speak, but the words mean nothing.
My heart cries out to you, but you don't answer.
You cry, but no tears fall
You have emotions, but no feelings.
And you truly hurt mine.

Bonnie Barnhart

"Who Am I?"

When I walk across the room, what do you see?
You see a strong Black Woman, and that woman is me.

Whether I'm dressed in blue jeans or in a suit;
My goals and achievements are always in pursuit.

I have been the anchor and backbone for so many years;
During that time, I have been tired and shed several tears.

My strength is determined and my mind is strong;
With my head on my shoulders, what could possibly go wrong?

The tools that I've used can be acquired by anyone;
Education, Confidence and Determination are just to name some.

I consider myself a role model for those to see;
One look at me and this is what they can one day be.

Women like me have paved the road for others to follow;
Despite the prejudices that they had to swallow.

Let my legacy continue on for years to come;
'Cause being a Black Woman, my work is never done.

I will always proceed to follow my dreams;
Afterall, success isn't has hard as it seems.

So, the next time you ask yourself "Who Am I?";
You're that beautiful, strong Black Woman reaching for the sky!

Lynette Lobo

Just 2 Of Us

Everything seems to be quiet,
    Just 2 of us.
Wondering how life will be without your desire.
Cause I'm a victim of your touch, your fire.
You burn me deep inside.
I can feel your touch from far away,
Cause without you, I'll be nothing. Do you remember?
All the good times we've had,
    Just the 2 of us.
We've become man and a woman,
Tonight it is Just 2 of us.
Holding each other forever.
Smiling, laughing and weeping a tear,
Knowing that we live without fear.
As our affection grows, between the 2 of us.
Our happiness will be for us.
Now are feelings are so strong,
That nothing can go wrong.
No one can break our bond ever,
That's why we'll say to each other, I Like You.

Sue D'Amalfi

Reading

Reading, an EYE, seeing through my eyes, blazed across the page.
Was a Spirit of an Ancient Age.

Frightened, Curios, I continued my glaze.
Through the eye of that Ancient Age.

AWAKEN! No Death. No Sorrow. No Sage.
Was the promise from that Spirit, of an Ancient Age.

Frozen In Fear. Least not I move, and loose that Spirit, of an Ancient Age.

"Divine Intelligence." Peaceful spiraling lights of
totality, flooding every molecule of my being. 'TWAS GOD!
That Spirit of an Ancient Age.

Jan Boyd

Look For Good Things To Do

I sit and watch the days go by,
Often I've asked myself, and wonder why.
How could I made a mistake so bad,
To make my family, so damn sad.

I know that what I did, was wrong,
So I am asking, please, help me to stay strong.
And as I sit here, to look at the moon,
I hope and pray all of this, will be over soon.

I think of being home with all of you.
Then I start to get so blue.
Mom, I wish I was still a kid,
So I could try to do better, than I did.

I sit here and look at the past,
And wonder how things will last.
Now and time again,
I wish my life would end.

I know that is wrong to say,
Still I look forward to another day.
When I get out, and this is true,
I will look for good things to do.

Joel Maisel

A Child's Prayer

One night I listened to my child
As he spoke to God in prayer
And the touching things he had to say
Made me glad that I was there

"I ask that God bless Mom and Dad
And my little brother, too
There's something else I'd like to add-
Dear Jesus I love you..

You helped me through my loneliness
When my daddy died last year
You made me strong so I could cope
And face the things I fear

Thank you Lord, for all you do
I'm glad that you're my friend
Watch over me and keep me safe
In Jesus name I ask— Amen."

Brenda Dobson

Moving Closer To The 21st Century

Less than four years from now
    will be the year 2000
        wow!!
Every day we're moving closer,
    closer to the 21st century.

Will rocket Science reach the stars?
Will an astronaut land on Mars?
What will be the occupants on planet earth's
    most popular cars?
As we move closer to the 21st century.

As family members in house earth
    are all members pursuing their self worth?
Is mother nature and father time,
    using earth's hungry, homeless and hurting
    to show a drastic decline,
    in members caring for another thru
        tough times?
As we are being watched, moving closer
    to the 21st Century.

Eugene Williams

"Love You"

I really Love you with all my heart, and
can't stand to be this far apart.
Wait, wait, wait, seems all I ever do
to be able to share my Love with you.
Be ready, soon the day will come when
in each others arms we will again become one.
Your kiss I miss each morning, and every night, and
arms so strong that hold me tight
again and again I have to say, I pray you will come back to stay.
I Love you more every day.
Love is what I need now to be fine...
You need to read the first word of every line..

Jennifer Janell Reaves

Beauty

Thousands of days blend as one. With each setting of the sun,
Her one mission in this life is closer of being done.

A trembling and withered hand slowly pushes
The once silky brown hair out of her eyes.
Now it is gray strands
Limply hanging.

Her lonely and weary eyes stare blankly in thought
World Wars, the Depression, the Baby....
Tears form, but her over-used tissue absorbs them.
Is she hurting, or just aging?

How much she has to teach
This world!
If only it would slow down and
LISTEN.

Her wrinkles cheek bones and forehead, her colorless mouth,
Her calm breathing with the exception of a spontaneous whimper,
This is the price she pays for her experience.

Yet she is beautiful.

Thousands of days blend into one. With each setting of the sun,
Her one mission in this life is closer to being done.

Lori K. Lieb

The Road To Vernon

We are mortal - a dot in the universe,
longevity of a firefly, no more
than a flash in the firmament...
welcome to Mephistopheles waltz.
Winding ribbons of road divide
the jutting monoliths on either side
as slivers of sunlight slash across
the slate rock to embellish the raw
artistry of the natural sculpture...
The somnulant stone, cast in variegated
violets and royal blues, blends artlessly
into cool purples and night-shades
of ebon-black sheen, to intertwine
in a rapture of splendour, ascending
majestically into a periwinkle sky
Witness to eternity, tabula rasa
to ages past, the record keepers of
a thousand and one eternities,
humanity, rendered a blip in time.

M. Mickey Turnbull

"Imagine"

As the beauty of a flower is in it's blooms that slowly
opens up to an array of colors and fragrance to the
delight of onlookers, so too, let your life continue to be
a positive uplifting influence of love and happiness in
service toward others.

May your countenance always shine like the warm
bright light of the sun, your dreams and goals be realized,
your life in the following months soar like an eagle.

Giving your best in the creative endeavors you
take up is soothing and peaceful to the soul, just
like the sight and sound of a sparkling gentle flowing
water stream, which produces life in all it touches in
abundance, brings gladness and kindness to smiling hearts.

Remember, that in faith and hope there is strength
of purpose and all things are possible if you only believe.

Patrick A. Moats

Blooming Brings

To dwell upon the lavish of love brings forth the desiring need to be loved.
To sacrifice a heart and soul shall not bring forth weakness.

Solitude that must surely come to pass
to enrich the soul with such bliss and comfort not to
compromise alone in a whether of silence, but to bring about
the inspiration of hope that once surged so freely.
Sacrifice not the ability to survive on ones entity
bring fourth passion and compassion
surpass the shadows of despair.

Blooming upon the waters deceive
the reflections of within, bring forth tranquility
and face courage to the fear
for a new beginning is no longer wilted.

Mary M. Louk

To Izzy On Your 80th Birthday

Sing a song of joy today
Brimmed with adoration;
For gentleness wipes tears dry,
Sparkling eyes make a soul fly,
Warm conversation over tea
Tames nervous waves into a cozy sea,
Like an aged wine in the cellar
Seasoned and savory,
Priceless, mellowed over time.

A flag flutters in the winds on the road we travel
The road, creation of divine hands
Whose artist molded heaven and earth.
Subliminal scheme indiscernable
To mundane minds - we become weary.

When the pilgrimage is over
And if only a few be chosen to heaven
I'll pray that you'll be one.

Grace Varner

Once More

If I could live my life once more,
I would do the same thing again,
The sadness and sorrow and happiness too,
My heart has been broken and I'm crying inside,
But I'd do it again with tears in my eyes,
If I could live my life once more,
I would not change anything,
Please give me more time,
I can't leave you now and feel like I do,
I would do it all over again
Just to be here with you.

Doris Viator

Untitled

To: My Family
On this day we celebrate the birth of our Savior.
For he purified us from our sins and behavior.
He sacrificed himself for us and all of God's creations.
So we could have these families for many generations.
But most of all, I have this one, which I would not trade for.
They bring me happiness, love and care, and also much, much more.
So that is why I wrap and give to you with all of my perfection.
These gifts from me to you showing all of my affection.
MERRY CHRISTMAS!!!
I LOVE YOU!!!

Enrique Frias

Panning For Gold In California

Panning for gold in California,
Like looking for a needle in the hay.
The water is cold and swiftly moving,
The rocks are slippery, wet, and hard.
Fool's gold flickers in the water,
Mica sparkles like diamonds bright.
The water makes everything look brilliant,
The rose quartz catches your nervous eye,
Your pan floats off down the creek!
Real gold is dull and yellow.
The black sand isn't gold at all.
But that's what all the gold dust hides in.
You think you'll find a big gold nugget,
But all that glitters isn't gold.
So you find out broken hearted,
Pyrite's golden, mica's shiny,
Quartz is lovely, rocks are slippery,
But the gold is dull and yellow.
Panning for gold in California,
Is not what it would seem!

Gary Tiemeier

Best Of The Day

Best of the day when the ice clinks her glass
and the rest that is clear can be poured from a jug
in a straight line.
No kids, no man,
red light's on the machine but no phone calls.
Earrings off, shoes off,
lights off almost everywhere except in the bathroom;
where one window open,
cut in slats that shift up when you push to widen them;
ashes in a corner of the sill, and smoke now and a cigarette
since her cigarette's there while she stares.
And that face that hasn't changed looks so similar,
and that pin box in the corner
where she lifts it unopened
still closed,
still there.
Someone added this room to the house
before we came,
and now I'm here.
I'm here.
I've been added.

Jo Scott

Candy Cane Sky

On Christmas morn when I awoke
  and saw the sky
I thought that it was evening tide
The sky was dressed in candy-cane stripes
With just a glimmer of daylight
And God in His Heaven must have smiled

Ruth Carr

Kids

Do you wonder where your toys go, the
one both big and small?

You buy them by the bag full, box and
the lot.

Then when you go to find them,
they're in the toy box—NOT!

I think they go to Whosville, the
place by Dr. Seuss stolen by the
gremlin, mean old Mr. Grinch.

So when you try to hide them and time
is in a pinch, remember who will get
them—that mean old Mr. Grinch.

Picking up your toys is not so hard
to do, especially when you remember your
toys belong to you.

So always put your toys up each and
every day and always in your toy box,
your toys will be to stay.

David Collins

Mother's Day

Mother's day is an appreciation day,
You receive thanks in all kinds of ways.

But you mother's name, will always be my mother to
My heart,
We live different lives now, but we will never be apart.

You've taught me the road to success,
How to stride, hold my head up high, and be the best.

You've given me everything a child need love, caring,
Understanding, but most of all when I needed you, you
Were there to whip my tears.
You were there at night to help me get over my fears.

Now, I've bloomed into motherhood with all the teachings
That you've taught me,
And I know next to you I will be the best mother there
Could possible be.

Vikki D. Lincoln-Broussard

Insane

An apple falls far from a tree
It's the same as you and me
I am different from the rest
I'm an outcast at my best

In a world of trees I am the apple that is lonely
I am beautiful in god's eyes only
There is no one to understand my pain
Thus, I will never be one of you the sane
I live my life day after day
I try to act the normal way

No! I'm sick of living a lie
I lie awake at night and cry
Can't you try to see
I just want to be me

I don't want to be some one I'm not
at once you knew me or so I thought
You are one of the sane
I am the one lying here in pain

Emily Zentgraf

Reality

I see it, yes, I do.
It's up there just past the clouds.
It may take me years to reach it.
But at least I know it's there.
It's always been there for me.
Just covered up by reality.
Finding it has been a long journey up hill.
Battling reality all the way.
Though I've been cut, bruised, and broken,
It has not stopped the fight still left in me.
Now I'm armed and ready to face the battle, the hill, the journey.
But, reality, are you ready to face me?
For I shall make it past the clouds to my star.
The star of hope, love, and friendship.
The star of reality.
I always knew it was there for me.
It's for everyone like you and me.
All you have to do is want to succeed.

Brenda Masset

Night Song Of The Motherland

Dancing to the beat of the old man's hands,
Cloth as smooth as the nile water draped
Around the coal black silhouettes

Eyes like the tiger who roams the wild plain
Plays 'round the circle looking for the souls
To take within the dimension of happiness
Where no forsakes are ever heard

No mere mortal can resist the pounding of the
Old man's hands
So they'll twist and turn until the dawn
When freedom is no more

Pamela Muldrew

The Sanderling And The Sea

We hear the waves pound,
Sledge hammers on the sand, thunder in the night
The ocean heaves, the sea surges, again and again

Steady, unrelenting rolls move tiny grains of sand
to the east, to the west
To form a new land, drown an old beach.

The tiny Sanderling scampers at the water's edge
Chases the retreating waves like a clockwork toy
Searches for a morsel served by the sea

Your rows of boulders eight feet tall, two hundred feet wide
Set by three ton bull dozers
Your revetments revenge

But the sound of the ocean reverberates
The sand buries the bottom step of the steep stairs
that climb to the top of the cliff

Your silence is ice. Your rebuttal is screeching.
Your television is out of tune. Your sermons are stale.

But the rhythm of ocean, the beat of Her heart
Echoes and re-echoes
Bringing savored rations to the Sanderling

Priscilla C. Brown

Slightly Grey

Grown-up angst, childish disillusion
left them behind in the dust, used to be together
longed for unity, yearned for freedom
fell apart along the way
one by one
left to right, back and forth
one will make it others won't
two by two, three by three
file up in line, get shot down
only they shall roam the earth
others sucked into the cracking ground - hot and full of lava
exposing, expanding, extrapolating,
don't miss the point - there is none that is evident
greyscale images of things, full color movies of people,
real life of events oh, how I love it!
Hidden messages in purple skies, amethyst clouds and pollution
the air is cleared of my soul
it is the beginning of the end
the end of the beginning
does it matter?

Sarah Raillard

Demons

These are not spirits.
Not loving, caring or welcomed,
As implied.
These are demons
That change knights into dragons,
Always dreaded.

I watch the fire spreading through your veins,
Taste the tears falling from my eyes.
Grabbing you tight,
Trying to stop what has already begun.
As if my touch alone
Could clean your blood.

I await the sunrise,
The calming of the flames,
And know it brings another day.

Kara D. Smith

Even

Every night I pray to God and get down on my knees.
I thank Him for the life I have, guarded from disease.

I thank Him for protecting all the people that I love.
He guides us with His angels that He sends from up above.

My mom, my dad, my family, and all my special friends.
He holds us in His holy hand until the very end.

My soul belongs to Jesus Christ, God's one and only son.
The lessons I have learned from Him will never be undone.

To know that God is caring from the heavens in the sky,
Is something I will always feel until the day I die.

When I am done praying, I say "Thank You" for this stuff.
But I often feel that these two words are never quite enough.

So I tell the Lord that my whole life is something that I owe.
And I know someday He will collect and then I'll have to go.

Hopefully, that night won't come until I'm old and gray.
When all my dreams have been fulfilled and my heart has lost its way.

I'll sadly look upon my life and all that I'll be leavin'.
I'll stand before my Lord and thank Him,
And then we will be even.

Marc Colagiovanni

Sir James

Just a hint of your essence,
as you, dared not to share!
My Lord! You grew to the.
Essence, everywhere! Like a wildflower
Sunlight in Thy Hair, My Love,

"I could, so easily share! Yet.....
I.... vowed a friendship!!!
Sir Cleveland,
a Man, tall in stature, well armored!
With a love...... well dared.
My love! "I, could love you?

Yet you're silencing.... a friendship
that a love, wouldn't grow from there!
A love... I felt.
Yet you promised not to share.
My love....... why didn't you question it?
My Lord! Yet, you dared not too!
Our secret is well kept, I promise and I swear!

Janette Fletcher

Untitled

The corner of a vast maze that contains me swiftly grows
to reveal a hole lighted by a dream of some other mind.

Mountains, abound with trees swaying in a warm morning breeze,
hear the call of an eagle in search of prey,
feel the scratch of a small creature's search for food.

A small cabin, isolated from the clutter of another world,
sits patiently waiting,
as a young couple walks along a path they are making their own.

The sky, painted in a brilliant array of colors
not to be matched by any artists brush,
knows the day is coming to an end, as is the dream.

The hole darkens once again, as the maze takes a tighter hold
on the soul it has captured for its own.

RoxAnna Rhoten

The Sage's Song

I walked the dark ways of the world, fear always in my heart,
Never sure of my destination, my mind ever in confusion.
The world, impatient and unkind, finding I was lagging,
Turned its back on me, and left me wandering far behind.

I was lost and tired, I was without hope,
In desperation, I prayed for Divine Grace.
Years went by; it seemed I had sung Heaven's Praise
In vain; and then it came, the glorious day,
Joyous laughter rose from the depths of my soul,
For the Voice of Heaven had whispered therein,
"Bound by chains of ignorance, you sleep and roam
The dream-ways of a dream-world and know it not.
Awake! Arise! Let the sun of knowledge shine,
It will show you the way of Truth and of Light,
It is the way of the Spirit, its single
Destination, the Sea of Eternal Bliss."

Then did I exult and loudly proclaim, "Farewell, dream-world,
I'm awake, I rise, I am lost no more, my way shines bright; the chains of
Ignorance I break, they fall off, I am free, and turning
My back on you, I leave you and your dream-ways behind me."

Sipra Mukherjee

Tears From Heaven

I look around at the world today
and I see myself in a world of flame.
Held aloft by my faith in God,
My heart is filled with endless shame.

The world awash with hate and pain,
the people scorched in Satan's flame,
Praying for God's forgiving rain
to fall on them, to ease their pain.

Tears of heaven fall to earth,
and still we fail to see our worth.
The tears come down like a waterfall,
but yet we fail to see them all.

Often we ask, "Does God care?"
But his only son died aware,
of the pain we've caused and were yet to do.
His only motive was his Love for you.

Jonathan Prock

Knowing Keara

On that April morning, when the clouds didn't move
and the sky was blue and the grass was green,
I was somehow cold.
We drove through the cemetery to the new-drug grave
that pulled my mother toward it.
That grave in that silent cemetery where no one dare whisper.
That grave, that stone grave that made
my father cry, my mother weep.
I should have hated that grave, that piece of stone.
And yet I felt attached to it,
somehow attached to it,
and to her,
that angel who left as she came,
quick like a perfect dream.
And somehow I knew that she was
thinking of me
and watching me
and smiling.

Tami Thompson

Untitled

My heart is not numb
of course I feel.
So when someone hurts me,
the pain never heals.
you took away my happiness.
I have to live in sorrow.
you took away my life,
I'm scarred of tomorrow.
Because I know it'll hurt more.
The pain is not gone, it's forever sore.
I can't stop myself from crying.
I can't help but think of dying.
There's no one in my life,
They're all withdrawn.
There's no one in my life,
Their all gone.
You left me alone.
With so much neglect.
You left me alone.
This I'll never forget.

Carrie Coolidge

Father

I dreamed I walked with Father,
He took me by the hand.
He took me up above the world,
And showed me all the land.

He showed me lakes and rivers,
and laughing bubbling streams.
I saw soft breezes blowing,
And heard their fondest dreams.

Of a world full of sunshine;
And birds on happy wings.
The flowers bright and merry,
That true happiness only brings.

My heart was full of sorrow,
For this my troubled land,
But I knew that things would be alright,
'Cause Father held my hand.

Herbert Lynn Green

Who Am I?

Life has torn me into many different shapes
It has taken me through many phases
It has drenched me through the thorns of hell
From the top of my head to the end of my toes
My blood thickens, my blood not be pure but that of lie and sin
Who Am I?

Day to day I awake to this world and still sadness is within me
Happiness they say will take its toll
But through my eyes I cannot see it to be
For only when my eyes shed sleep, I hope the next day not be
For only in my dreams, happiness I do see
Who Am I?

My desires can be that of money, that of power,
That of another like me
They can be, that is my desires, envy and hate towards others
Greed can be my desire, even that of death
Who Am I?

I have lied and or sinned, I pursue to find happiness,
And to fulfill my desires
Who Am I? Man.

Jesus Miranda

Lily, Under The Storm

Lily, under the snow,
pale, white hands at rest
among the pearls on her breast,
is now at ease from all her woes.

Twice lately I have thought of her.
Snow fell lightly once upon her brow
and melted in her hair,
as I stood there one Christmas Eve
and asked her in
to listen to her dreams.

There was another time the year before.
It was the summer when she asked if I believed
sleep was a cure for every ill on earth.
I had no answer for her ears...
no handkerchief to wipe her tears.
I pale to think I could not think
and give her words of hope.
I did not know the scope of hope.
I did not know the usefulness of verbal skills
that still the soul.

Pat O. Cooper

Too Close

So close to me that I could touch you
Yet so far away I can barely see you
I so long to touch you
But there is only the air between us
I touch but can not feel
I'd do anything to see you again
There is so many miles in our way
As I look you are not far from my home
But the miles in my heart
Is farther than the touch of the breeze
If only I could reach your loving hands
I'd take them and never let them go
But the reach is farther than the moon
It will take some time to get to you
But I will wait until I see your eyes
So close to me that I could see right through them
Every time I see you my heart beats faster
Yet each and every time my heart beats
Is it one more step farther from your eyes?

Linda Ellis

Big John

I walked out on the porch one moon-light night
There sat Big John a little to my right
I sat down and Big John got up
I knew then he was feeling his stuff
I got my horn and got in the truck
I told Big John, I believe they had done struck
I went to the barn and there was the old gang
All but Homer, because I forgot to give him a ring
I sat down on the ground and I couldn't hear a
sound, not even a hound
The fellows don't want Big John around
Big John known for his strength and his speed, these
guys know when Big John runs he is gonna be in the lead.

Goodson Peveler

The Encounter

As I watch you dance across the floor
your grace and beauty I cannot ignore
Although there are others in this room
all my attention is drawn to you

Too once catch your eye would still my heart!
My god. When I look at you I fall apart
I cannot move, or speak, or catch my breath,
My heart goes still... Is this death?

No, it can't be I've never felt more alive!
I would take on the world with you at my side

Like a flower in the Spring, you dance on the breeze
to blossom in the Sun beneath the oak trees
Your smile is like a star that shines through the night
glistening off the waters... what a beautiful site

From here to there and back again,
time stands still will there be no end

I see the future... I see you holding my heart,
will you embrace it gently or will you tear it apart

I will take this risk of this I'm sure
because what I have, I have and there in no cure

Gary L. White

The House On A Woodbine Hill

Just out of town on a Woodbine hill,
Stands a beautiful home serene and still.
But it was not as it looks just now, you know
Blood, sweat and tears, helped to make it so.

Many hands were used in the work,
As no one had any time to shirk;
For behind each man was a girl with light hair,
Saying, no! Put it here! No! Put it there!

But that's all in the past and a home it did make,
With love and compassion, and all that it takes.

Then one day from an overcast sky,
Came the fiercest of storms and did not pass by,
But shattered the windows and wet all the floors,
Destroyed all the crops and rattled the doors.

The rain came down with hail like a ball,
Destroying houses, churches, cars, and all.
After the clean-up, fix-up and such,
A lesson was learned, that GOD is in touch.

W. Ray Brown

Thank You Lord

Thank you Lord for salvation so rich and so free
Thank you Lord for your son Jesus who first loved me

Thank you for the moon in the sky
Thank you for the clouds that go floating by
Thank you for a love that will never end
Thank you for the dove that use to be my friend

Before the fall the world was in sink and perfect
and now it just stinks and it's soon time for you to dump it

You've fill me with things I've looked elsewhere for
when all along they were right here at my door
Your word will stand when all else fails
for you have said everything else is sinking sand

I thank you Lord that you never change
for the same Lord that said: "let there be"
Will be the same Lord that says; come my child
I'm taking you home with me.

Ylonda-Renee Holts

Precious One

The first time I felt your heartbeat,
it took my breath away.
Instantly, I fell in love,
as I felt you growing day by day.
And with each little movement,
I thought it a miracle, a God given grace.
You had a personality all your own,
and I couldn't wait to see your precious face.
When I saw you for the first time,
I was overwhelmed with love and joy.
To me, you truly were an Angel,
my precious and loved - baby boy.
From this moment on I'll be there,
so very proud of all you'll become.
Because there is a love so special,
between a mother and her son.

Brenda Waters

Darkness Before The Light

The Angels came in the quiet of night,
To gently guide me into the light.
My soul endures no more pain or grief,
The time has come for my relief.

The time I had was not well spent,
Before I knew it, it came and went.
Somehow I thought all the time,
Someday I'll catch up and won't be behind.

The plans I made I'll do someday,
And before I knew it, time had slipped away.
This life passes in the blink of an eye,
And when it's over, we wonder why.

The regrets we have it's now too late,
There's no more time for us to wait.
This life we lived whether wrong or right,
Was clouded with darkness before the light.

Rita Walker

The Wee One

Tottering in heels high
Up on tiptoe, a mere 48 inches tall
This person small
A gnarled branch the cane
Moving quickly, discreetly, quietly
Blonde and slight, an unusual sight

Ha! 'Tis not an old woman small
But a child, a boy, just four foot tall
His skirts he picks up, the shawl clutched tightly
To deceive with a scarf on his head
Why oh why little boy

Hurrying, just rushing, this tiny one
A glance over the shoulder, with timid expectation
Shrinking with panic, must fade out of sight
If seen by another, paralyzed with fear and despair
Hastening, directions reversed
Obscurity sought, alone to be

Again on the morrow, out and about
With skirts and shawl, high heels and cane
Tottering and teetering once again

Betty Jean K. Goold

Shaman

Appropriational overseer
for the prodigy in us all
Enigmatic figure forever seasoned
an enlightening skyscraper
standing tall

Diverse in achievements
A natural born genius
Patience uncompromised with care

Givingly teaches as well as to be taught
Refuse a lost student, he thinks not
Many knew, he unveils whatever we thought not there

So in my journey of recollection
My thanks, I give, in encouraging pursuit of education
and guidance you've given so well

Alas comes to call to rest in peace
from a life once lived so bittersweet
I bid thee, fair colleague, farewell

Patrys Destin

O God Act

I am . . . an actor
True, I don't get many acting roles
But, over the years, I find that
I am . . . right where I must be . . .
What is mine will always be mine.
That moment will arrive for me
It might be one word . . .
Or just my face, my presents is needed-
For that play, that movie for it to be perfect.
I am . . . alive . . .
My destiny is there, waiting for me . . .
Don't give up, don't lose my heart
Someday, who knows, my rent might be paid on time-
Now, this moment, I am a survivor
I love acting God gave me a great gift . . .
I promise, never . . . never curse the road
I had chosen in life to follow . . .!
Even if I must die an unknown actor . . .
But I will die praying for the "others" . . .
To act . . . oh God . . . to act . . .

Vincent Palmieri

A Tribute

I lost a very special friend today,
Death came quietly and took him away
To a beautiful land up in the sky,
Where he'll know no pain and bluebirds fly.
Our sixty year friendship, stood the test of time.
Many cherished memories are cemented in my mind.
Now that he's gone, I'll miss him so,
But his memory will live in my heart, that I know.
Yes, I lost a very special friend today -
Death came quietly and took him away.

Romie Clouse

Untitled

A man is only human,
   neither endowed with supernatural powers nor even truly unique...
He can fool himself into thinking he's special, and even boast of his
deeds, he can look down upon others - upon himself...a majestic gaze...
He will aspire to the top - taking all from those below,
   look past the physical - the mental capacity is where the true
   danger lies...
In his synaptic macabre, be warned, all who enter hither,
   you know not for whom the bell tolls...
With secrets gathered, never to be let known,
   he will not pass the gauntlet... now... or ever...
He will ride the great black beast to the crest of the summit,
   laughing as he looks in his wake...
Take heed to the level of death in those dark eyes, that dark face,
   ice running through veins that pump a frozen heart...
And a smile parts the lips of the dark beast,
   at those who try to cheat him...
For a man will flirt and walk with death,
   laughing along the way...
But as all living things will come to realize,
   the Reaper knows no favorites.....

Christopher J. King

Wrinkles Of Time

Somewhere in the Autumn of one's life
the reconnoitering of time pursues itself

What seemed to be so impossible for
someone so young has now slid in on
the wrinkles of time

While the resonating sounds of youthful
love can still be heard in the beating of
one's heart

Gerry Rae Schultz

Romance 'Til Nothing Is Left

Romance me with flowers
Romance me with candy
Romance me with candlelight dinners
Diamonds are just fine and dandy

Spend all your money
Max out your credit card
Go borrow all you can
it really isn't all that hard

Romance me for a month
or even a shorter while
Romance me for a long time
or just take me on a cruise of the river Nile

Now you're flat broke
Not a nickel to spare
think you're going to hold on to me
I would not take the dare.

Madeline Medley

The Morning Dew

The morning dew "Oh it felt so new",
as it pressed upon my face of old.
Where did the time go? I want to know.

So many reasons to conquer treasons
of the ones you loved for all seasons.
I did not know - he wanted to go.
He did not tell me - he wanted no more.

He always made me feel so unsure
and for this I could find no cure.
Had I known, I would have left him alone and
then by now - he would be gone!

No more years to spend in vain,
with someone who caused so much pain.
I did my best - but he couldn't care less.
Be very glad to have gotten rid of this mess.
Now feel free to tell the rest!

"Oh morning dew - I do thank you."

Geraldine Currington-Whitaker

"I Remember"

To Marcia Ellen Fulmore 12/22/45 - 2/2/94
Each Day I think back 2 the Day when it Happened -
There after this Day, My Life has been Saddened.
I remember Her PAIN and also Her Grief -
48 years, in My eyes is Brief.
I Remember Her STRENGTH & WILL in Our Battle -
If it were U, Do U think U could Handle?
2 know U will DIE in a Matter Of Months -
Wasn't caused by Cigarettes, Drugs, or Blunts.
As I count ALL the Days and Months of a Year -
I wonder sometime, Is GOD really there?
Grew Old B 4 Our Eyes, each Day a Surprise -
The whole situation, I wished they were Lies.
The Disease was Slow & at the same very Quick -
4 Months was how long My MOTHER was Sick.
My MOM would ask Y, but GOD would not answer -
A tumor she had, A Disease called CANCER.
She suffered a Seizure and went into a Coma -
Missed My Graduation & High School Diploma.
As I proceed, No need 4 Weed -
No Cuts or Bruises, It's Inside that I Bleed.

Charles W. Fulmore

Images

It's only a poem, it doesn't make scents;
the timing is awkward, obscure, even rigid-
The lines are all focused on what has been hidden ...
Leaving something so tense.

So don't be amazed
should it glow with a sparkle or light with a blaze
for the words are mere image, the meaning untrue,
conceived in an instance, perceived in a few,
and you stare, and you gaze, and what stays is so tense-
it's lacking a purpose that wouldn't make senseanyway.

Out of something so awkward, unheard of and calm
might arise a new mourning - shall we sing a new song?
For the new day is dawning, we haven't seen yet,
and the thoughts that we cherish so soon we'll regret.

Paul Baker

Forgotten Memories

Do you know of the memories that haunt
Those unforgiven tracks of time
When life held you against your will
And fault with deception when handed a raw deal
I know of this place inside the mind
It fades oh so ever slightly in good time
It is here we hold onto our past
Whether good or bad we decide what lasts
But it is with old age that our mind decides
What stays and what's no longer left inside
And everyday I am sadden to see
That my own mother has many many forgotten memories.

Tina Victoria Leon

Working The Night Shift

The work is hard and never ends.
The doors swing open and never close.
One shift over and another begins,
I'm ever so tired but on it goes.

Now here's Sister with her theme song,
"You'll have to stay, your relief is sick."
OB is calling, they can't wait long...
Leave this one with me and go...be quick!

"Breath into the mask... breath in and out.
Hold your breath and push! Push and hold it!
Relax, little Mama, and please don't shout!"
Catch the slippery baby! The blanket! Unfold it!

Hold the wet bundle close and wait.
He frowns and pees and begins to cry!
Check color, reflex, and heart rate!
"And now, little Mama, breath out a sigh!"

Suddenly I know why I'm here!
I feel alive, my fatigue is gone!
I'm so euphoric I shed a tear.
A job well done... and soon... the dawn!

Frances Burks Reeder

My Love For You

My love for you, is bringing a smile to your face, from a warm memory.
My love for you, is leaving you a poem, telling you I love you.
My love for you, is bringing you roses, for no special reason.
My love for you, is giving you a kiss, in the kitchen, in the back yard, in an elevator.
My love for you, is calling you in the middle of the afternoon. telling you I miss you.
And because my love, is so strong, and so pure for you, before I die,
   I will give to you,
   my last breath.

Bill Morris

"I'm Glad You Are Here"

I'm glad I am here to be a part of your days.
You are part of mine in so many ways.
I think of you sometimes, from my face emerges a smile.
And makes my day all the more worthwhile.

When I am down and start to feel blue,
From my mind comes the image of you.
Before I lie down and fall to sleep,
I pray to the Lord for your soul he'll keep.

And as long as there is light, the birds and the wind,
There will be two people you can always depend.
For Jesus and I will always be your friends.

   I am glad I am here to be a part of your days
   For you are a part of mine in so many ways.
   James Allen

Envy

We are the essence of man.
Look for my brother in the eyes of the hungry,
and the abodes of the indigent,
He is the embrace for parents
who sit in vigilance over their children.
He is also the flickering of a lost cause,
He is never lost, His epithet is hope.

The dammed have lost her,
My sister is the bond between the virtuous, the wicked
and the unpleasant which makes this plethora of wills humanity.
She has no social, ethic, or political boundaries.
You can not touch, feel nor can you see her, but she is as real,
and as beautiful as the sunlight which beckons a new day...
She is Faith.

"I am the elder of the three, and I stand alone.
I long for acceptance, as are my kindred, but forsooth,
Pandora's pride thwarts my bequest,"
We are three, and I am the Third... the extra.
Sometimes... I am hard to find. It seems,
Scarcity is my middle name, but I am the best part of humanity.
I am tangible, and the forgiving.
I feed the children, and bear the cross.
I am alms for the poor and the benevolence of God toward man,
I am affection, good will, and the love of man for his fellow man...
I am brotherly love,
We are Hope for the world, the Faith in mankind, and I, the third, I
am that which binds my brother and sister together.
I am Charity.

W. A. Lamb

Necessary People

As you enter into this brand new year
To continue your endeavor in patient care
To stretch the muscles, and pop the bones
To study the pains, the moans, the groans

You're necessary people that just must be
To turn our injuries into victory
Though we lay shaken, broken and full of pain
We'll go it with Jesus all over again

Necessary people we also must be
When we're all mended, and returned to society
No more therapy, and no more pills
We're back to normal, and life's many thrills

We give our thanks to you superstars
You cured the pains, but you left the scars
When you return home for your much needed rest
Be at peace with your conscience,
   you gave your best

Harold R. Dickerson

The Indians Dance In The Heat Of The Sun

The ancient feast is about to become
only one can make this all happen
So hurry and forget your weapon
a peace ceremony is what this is about
You might not take part but never doubt
The spirit of the ancient land
as the Indians dance in a circle of sand
rain pouring down from the sky above
But the Indians still dance in a ceremony of love
Be happy this festival is going on out here
don't feel nervous there's nothing to fear
The clouds clear up as the sun shines down
But only in this Indian town
Peace and love is what they now know
now it's my turn to enter their show

Jerry Thurman

For My Friends

In Loving Memory of Kevin P. McDermott, Sep. 17, 1961 - March 15, 1994
I walk in the shadows now, not to be seen in the light.
Once I was a handsome young man, now I am unrecognizable.
I've felt life course through my veins, now death follows that same path.

I see today a new challenge, and fight like hell to see tomorrow.
I am very frightened at times, but I hide behind my jokes and
laughter so no one will know.

What I would do to change the past, in hope to alter the future.
there is no time left to hate, just to forgive the ignorance of the
world. My body and mind are now shutting down, the walls of
life are now closing in.

My family and friends weep for me, but i will be fine. Free from
the anger, hate and pain. It is for them that I weep, for my path
has been chosen. It is they who will have to fight the struggles
of the world. Who would have thought that for a single hour of
pleasure would leave behind me a lifetime of pain!

John J. Serra

The Gift

God gave His gift, born not of our flesh but of our hearts,
The gift of a son, a gift of a lifetime, a gift of love.

Memories of laughter and hugs and wonders,
Memories of dancing eyes and wide-eyed questions,
Gifts that time can never erase,
Gifts that God gave, not ever forgotten.

God gave His gift, a Child of God, A Blessing, a gift from above,
The gift of a son, a son He shared, a moment in time.

A son who touched those around,
A son who lived to love those he found,
A son who though he is gone in body remains in spirit,
Gone from our sight but not our hearts.

God have His gift our son, a part of our lives, our family, of us,
Always to be a part of our thoughts, our memories, our joys.

A better place he has gone,
No more sorrow, no more pain.
Now he shares in Heaven the gifts he shared with us,
The gifts of smiles, laughter, and love.

God gave His gift, His son, our son, our son together,
A son we now return with love for the moments we shared as one.

Dean Nelson

My Garden

There is a place, very dear to my heart,
Once I am there, it seems so soon I must part,
    Filled with bushes, flowers, and trees,
Also birds, lady bugs, and very busy bees,
    I can be there with family, or alone,
For when I am there it feels like home,
    It may be morning, noon, or night,
Being in my garden, always seems right,
    Hands in the earth, new plants in view,
Some I have seen forever, others are quite new,
    God gave me a place, a special place to be,
When he gave me my garden it was to be free,
    I love going there, it's always a pleasure,
Never knowing what I'll find, but knowing it is a treasure,
    Gorgeous in color, words can not explain,
Beautiful in sunshine, or after a rain,
    Winter finds me in a planning state,
But now spring is here, and I can not wait,
    So, now, for me you must please pardon,
It is time to work, and just be in my garden.

Shelly Champion

Fading Feelings

There is a love in poverty that isn't in affluence, there is a
yearning to please and a yearning to give that is lost in wealth.

The feeling of helping and being useful in any way possible is paramount.

The sincerity of prayer and the legitimacy of a handshake, the pride
in refusing something you wish for with all your heart.

A special love and a closeness grows in the family, a feeling of
tremendous accomplishment for anyone who makes a strive forward.

The simple things that bring so much joy at Christmas
with very little but song and good cheer.

The friendship of helpful neighbors, the closeness and love of
mother and dad, the deep concern by all when one of the family is ill.

The heartaches of hardship bring enormous love and feeling for one
another that only the very poor can understand.

There's much more to be said but no more needs to be said for those
who have lived in these terrible but loving and caring times.

Daniel F. Toomey

Golden Dreams

You know there are all kinds of dreams that we all have
some are very happy, and some are very sad
And some even make us feel very very glad.
But a golden dreams is what's deep down inside you
yes this dream will either make you or break you.
It is within you from the rising of the sun
until the time that it goes back down.
Take this golden dream and make it to the top
because you've made it when you're happy or sad
with what you've got.
Many people will come to you and say
you won't make it till you do it my way.
I've heard them all I guess I could say
but no one will ever take mine away.
As for golden dreams they are for a real
so from your heart break away that bitter seal
and watch what your golden dreams will always reveal.

Isaac B. Garcia

Come, Sweet Spring

I am weary of the snow,
Weary of this vast outspreading
Glow of white and nothing more.

Dormant lies my soul within me
And my heart gives hardly a flutter
In this frozen land around me.

Come, sweet spring, bring the flowers,
Perfumed breezes, azure skies
And caressing April showers.....

Hark! It is already Spring;
The buds are swelling on the trees,
The Robin- I have heard him sing!

Come thrush, come lark, come mocking-bird-
Come all joy-loving beings on earth
And form the chorus to be heard

Around the world. Come and sing-
Sing to the sun, to life, to love
And welcome back life-giving Spring!

Helen Cassimus

The Fool

"Where is my fool?" shouted the king.
"Bring him to me to dance and sing!

Let him speak of despair and woe
Let's hear him tell of friend and foe.

I want to know of ladies fair
Of great knights and the deeds they dare.

I want a song of grassy knolls
Of meadows green and hills that roll.

Let us make sport of the silly fool
With his clothes of rays and his scepter of jewels

Let him do tricks like a dirty old dog
Let him chirp like a bird and leap like a frog

Make him roll in the dirt and beg at our feet
Watch him smell of the cistern and tells us "how sweet"

"Bring me my fool!" the king then said
But alas for them, their fool was dead.

Sylvia Kosalko

Wind Whispers

Wind whispers in my ears, it tells me
everything I want to smell and hear.
Ah! Sweet flowers in the field, I hear
the laughter of my little girl near,
The sun, oh how warm you feel, surround
me with your beam of light and hold me near.
The wind will whisper till end of time,
and I will tell you oh! how your sun
will ever so shine.

Diane C. Bragadin

You Think

You think that you are strong but you are weak.
It takes more strength to cry... admit defeat.
I have truth on my side, you have deceit.
You think you can leave but be by my side.
My heart aches; not this time.
Now I'm free; I can fly.
You think I'll never find myself again.
My soul is strong, I know who I am.
I have a goal and I will win.

Brandy Blanton

Untitled

You were gone one day
gone and changed like an autumn leaf.
Covered by the snow and
disappeared with the winter.
Why love is so hard to sustain?
Why your absence is so unbearable?
I cry every night
and look for you everywhere.
I dream and think only of you
I live only for you.
Your voice and face is unique
and your presence is joy.
How can I function?
How can I survive?
How can I reduce the pain?
I miss your smile and all the happy moments.
Did I drive you away?
Or overvalue what I don't have.
All the elements are there...
and springs only bring new leaves.

Gerty J. Jacques

She Feels

She sits in her corner playing with her doll.
She hated to be alone, but she was afraid of them all.

She's stronger and wiser, all grown up now.
She wonders how could he do that; how, how, how?

When he wouldn't wake up, she used to be scared.
Even though he doesn't sleep anymore, he still isn't there.

He's sobered up now, but she's still scared.
He hasn't changed that much and her life is bare.

Now he's leaving, maybe it won't be so bad.
She loves daddy, but she hates seeing mommy sad.

Brother thinks that mommy didn't give him a chance.
She stuck in there for 19 years, there is just no romance.

Daddy has a job and will be fine on his own.
We'll still get to see him, but she's there and mommy's not alone.

Elyssa Bragg

No Past At My Back

There can be no past at my back,
So I must journey without goodbyes.
Nothing but forward must I see;
The quest will take aeons to apprise.

My seeking soul must not be bound
By things that hold me to the past.
Thoughts of yesterdays, quenching a thirst,
Are all I can afford to allow to last.

My searching needs to my back the wind,
And wings, when my feet have slowed,
Afforded by the eagle, whose visionary eyes
Have watched and loved and known,

That this wanderlust is a child of God,
Who hears the Spirit's whispering call,
And seeks the knowledge, to fully understand,
That the universe is one and one is all.

Fern Rupert Piner

The Whole

As we walk the earth, we're not quite complete.
Not knowing what lies ahead or who we might meet.
Afraid of death, as well as life,
burdening our souls with mountains of strife.
We comfort our minds with imaginative stories,
and comfort others with tales of false glories.
Too proud to admit ignorance,
too ruthless to admit arrogance,
yet all are aware of one sacred question.
The answer is vague and scarcely known.
What are we?
All I can tell you is that all that
exists are part of the whole,
for the rest of the answer is buried in
the depths of your soul.

Contessa Vaupel

My Thoughts Today

Where rivers flow and fish swim by,
where wheat turns yellow, God is nigh.

Where flowers bloom, where birds do sing,
where a butterfly finds that it has wings.

When a child is born, where beauty is found,
we feel God's presence all around.

Where sorrow was, now laughter is,
we've learned that God did freely give.

Kathleen A. Canute

Hummingbirds

At the first sign of spring come the minute jeweled fellows
    with their gossamer wings.
Their tiny shrill squeaks fill the air as they fight for their lady fair.
Off they go in all directions to build their thimble-like nests
    of cobwebs and lichen.
Honored only with their presence after the wee eggs are hatched.
We soon lean their fearless courage cannot be matched.
Later come the babes so innocent and new.
To fly and play among the flowers of blue.
All too soon they take to wing and we know we will not see them
    again till spring.

Bev Beaumont

Invisible Joker

Etched on my soul permanently
These scars on my body, deep within my soul
The mind captures hidden messages as the ear listens
In my thoughts, I wonder through the clutter which burdens my soul
Discarding the worst, holding on to hope
Maximized pain combined with mental suffering fades
    but remains in one's mind
You play hide-n-seek; as does a child at play or
    boogie-man, which leaves me fearful and helpless
Sometimes I'm more afraid of living than of dying
Desperately, I reach for strength through my goals
    and dreams; through my faith most of all
You don't care about emotions or my state of health, do you, Joker
The Joker takes life for granted, and advantage of it
Spewing riddles and patterns to decipher
Never stopping to see the damage unfold
Don't trust the Joker, it's not as it appears
Cause the Joker, tears you apart and feeds upon your fear
Skin cancer is my Joker; what is yours?

Kathleen Collins

Sadness

Into the dark the girl steps,
Nobody sees her, nobody cares.
She looks back to the light,
where everybody is happy and bright.
She cries out, wishing to be one of them.
She calls out for somebody, anybody...
but nobody pays attention, except for one.

A boy hears her cry.
He steps carefully toward the darkness,
not certain about what could happen.
He steps to the border between light and dark,
and holds out his hand - she grasps it.
He pulls her out of the darkness and they walk toward the
    light together, hand in hand.

Emma Goldenberg

A Plea For Dionysus (From The Greek Of Anacreon)

O Zeus, thou who art ever prone to incite
Ever-winning Eros, the young and smiling god of love,
The painting dark-eyed nymphs gifted with graces of the dove,
And the golden-haired and beauteous Aphrodite,
Together with countless other deities:
Pan with his harmonious pipe, Lyceus with his melodious flute,
Apollo with his celestial lyre, and Orpheus with his comforting lute.
O king of gods, reclining on your Olympian couch so lofty,
The slightest nod of your eagle-like sceptre.
Could shake the universe, I beg of thee be tolerant
And aid the divinities who guide the fleecy clouds.
O heed my prayer and grant this favor to a god by nature proud:
I entreat thee, o powerful Zeus, around Dionysus' brow entwine
A wreath of grapes, a living garland from the vine.

Victorine P. Chappen

Life's Legacy

You pray to the morning light in the sky so high above,
For all your unselfish needs and God's undying love.
Humans tend to stray and desire the tempting greeds,
Forgetting to touch the roses and ending up with just the weeds.
Heartfelt kindness and true friendships are the easiest to see;
Envy and hatred beckon to make you stray and flee.
But, in your heart the emotions keep you from the errors of today.
In a world of discontent, its hardships cause to stray.
We must find within ourselves the answers to our pleas.
Forget the calls from evil's doors and tend only to your needs.
A smile to show your kindness in an understanding way -
This could help to ease the moment of pain in someone else's day.
Dig deep within your soul to find the meaning of life itself.
When life's quest is over, your spirit is your wealth.
So to live each day with sunshine and tears enough to spare,
When our life is over, may the love we shared be there.

Phyllis G. Bennett

Who Said That?

The fire in my stomach starting to spread.
It has gone past my shoulders and is now in my head.
It is burning my face and is now in my mouth.
It is still a hot fire that developed deep down south.

I didn't mean to swear. I was pushed to the limit.
It may have been different if I had thought for a minute.
Now I stand in you're stare, my head dropped in shame.
My mouth is washed with soap. That hot fire is to blame.

Lanelta Armetta Thomas

The Call

We heard the call for black men to come.
The message itself was loud and clear,
   although the messenger, to some, was not so dear.
With our women in full and total support,
   we knew the mission would not abort.
Female voices in harmony saying,
"We got your back, go black man, you are free to act."

Wow! One Million Black Men.

The drive was oh so very long,
   and the media made the call seem so very wrong.
Gas peddle all the way down, nothing but nothing can stop us now.
Men from everywhere, assembled at the DC mall,
   all for one and one for all.

Wow! One Million Black Men.

In the sixties we were Black and Proud,
   and shouted it out oh so loud.
Something changed us in those thirty since years,
   but today we got it back with clinched fist and tears,

Wow! One Million Black Men.

   Glenn Miles

The Day After Today

Is it worth the wait?
As if we had a choice
Can't be put off
It's inevitable,
destined,
written in the book of fate.
We know it's coming;
It's unstoppable;
Sun goes into hiding;
artificial illumination begins;
Sensation of noise modified;
Night creatures come into view
For some it's the time of riches and crowns;
for others, dread, horror, trepidation.
Projectiles commence shattering dreams;
heavenly bodies reveal themselves.
Yet; all coming closer to that final moment;
of the anticipated, but ever changing......
TOMORROW.

   Constance Braxton

Fly Long Tee

Suddenly coming out of a hole non ventilated
Here is reviving my will,
After these seven years of hibernation.
Thus revive all these sensations

Which were underground
Locked in this black greenhouse

There it has been seven years long
In hollow of darkness of blood
Surrounded of false songs,
Now retrieving its strength, it's row.

There cloistered in this deep seven long years
Without being able to extirpate from these animated unhappiness,
Which little by little are removing from my skin, like to a jelly fish
Like to an octopus hanged by cunning.

There it is free,
Able to the free air to extirpate stoned,
And think and fly skillfully,
Happy, full of love, my dear will, my blood.

   Chanoz Fabien

My Favorite Day

I discovered a sun that I never knew;
It was so beautiful in a sky of bluest blue.
This sun was shining on a lake so clear;
It made the fish seem ever so near.

The loon was drifting, seemingly asleep;
It was a day of days that I wanted to keep.
The eagle was soaring, high in the sky;
While back on the shore, a squirrel scurried by.

Here I sit on this long wooden pier;
Watching the wooded shoreline for a passing deer.
My spirits are high, my heart is filled with elation;
How did you guess, I'm on VACATION!

   Shirley M. Grimm

Anything At All

When the sun starts to rise and the morning dove cries
And the windows light up with the sun
I'll be thinking of you, do you think of me, too?
Or am I the only one?

When the trees come alive and the flowers survive
And the new grass is covered in dew
That's when I wonder when I will see you again
And you'll make my life feel new

But I sit and I look out my window
As I dream my eyes start to fall
Will I ever tell you what I'm longing to do?
Will I say anything at all?

When the wind starts to blow and the sky looks like snow
And the last leaves of Autumn hang on
That's when I think of how I can't be with you now
And my arms ache to hold you again.

When the clouds start to clear and the darkness is near
That's the time you appear in my mind
Do you know I am here, that I long to be near
To a place only we can find?

   Celeste McKenzie

Demons Of The Mind

In the dark we see demons,
they loom over our beds waiting
for us to sleep so they can
feast upon our flesh and bones.
In the basement there are demons,
ready to attack you and bite you
they want to taste your salty but yet
sweet tasting blood.
In the attic they walk around
up there and you hear creepy
noises they want you to go check
and see what's up there they hide
and then while you're looking around
they shut the attic door and corner you.
Then they tear your body to shreds.
But it's only the demons of the mind,
but why does the mind play those
mean tricks on you? To scare you? To
make you cry? To make you scream? Just
remember it's only the demons of the mind.

   Rachel Tidwell

Hi Mom

On a quiet afternoon while everything is still,
I lie looking out the window staring towards the sky,
  that is cast by an old oak tree which is reaching way up high.
While peering through its branches and looking high above,
I can see a face formed in the clouds,
  a face I will always love
He's grinning and looking at me and in the wind
  I can hear a faint whisper, "Hi Mom."
For a moment my fears and emptiness had disappeared,
Then a tear rolled down my cheek,
Oh! If I could only reach out and touch him as I heard him speak.
Suddenly more figures appearing one by one,
They are all your children a daughter or a son.
And as the clouds begin to fade,
I see your children of every shade
And with my son are many souls,
Some very young, some not so old
I can sense they have all bonded in this very special place,
Children from every walk of life and of every race.
Now they are all free from this earthly bother,
And have found peace with God and with one another.

Maureen Condon

Angel

An angel's love is like the full moon at night.
An angel's shine is like the bright warm sunlight.

His glorious white wings are trimmed in gold,
With a heart full of love for you to hold.

A golden halo circles his mane of hair,
And he helps you through the deep pits of despair.

His long white gown flows by his feet as he walks,
And through the acts of kindness is how he talks.

A dazzling smile placed on his angelic face.
Coming to your aid in a time of disgrace.

Giving you a helping hand he starts to smile,
That helping you and knowing God is worth while.

DeeDee Davis

Wax Wings

Let me fly, Mother, let me fly.
Let me spread my wings and fly.
Let the sun heat my wings and melt the wax of Icarus.
Let the wind lift my soul and let me soar
Through the depths and widths of my mind.

The sun is so hot, Mother.
Flames lick with infinite care,
But they burn so, Mother, they burn so.
Touch me with your hands of ice and melt the sun.
Cool the heat, Mother, so that I may sleep.

I had a dream yesterday, Mother.
I had a dream that I could not sleep
For fear that I would not wake.
Should I close the curtains to the windows of my mind?
Illuminate the world, Mother, and shine.

For you are the sun, Mother, as am I.
We are the warmth that thaws life
From the ice and water that is the Earth.
Shine with me, Mother, for you are the flame,
The giver of life, the giver of love.

Tehnaz Parakh

Grandfather

As I look at my grandfather sick in bed
I see a young man
A young man without fear in his eyes
A young man of the war
A young man feeling that just being there
would help change the outcome for his country
A young man dreaming about being a hero,
saving lives, and getting medals pinned on him
A young man without a thought in his mind
of my father, much less of me
A young man without a thought in his mind
of going home and meeting the girl
that would soon be his bride

As I look at my grandfather a smile crosses his face,
and a tear touches my eye
As I smile back, I realize my grandfather
was a young man like I am today
Not always knowing where you're moving on to,
but always moving one foot in front of the other
A big grin on your face and a feeling that no one can stop you

Lance E. Duhon

Adrift

The tides of time run swiftly till they break
  on eternity's shore.
Such was your Fate.

Love washed into our hearts so long ago
Mingling our life streams; lifting us on its current;
Carrying us, together, to a quiet pool of oneness
Along the riverbed of life.

The fruits of our union, like shining stones,
  dropped into the smooth surface of our lives,
  making growing circles that reached to the very edge of time.
Living produced swift undercurrents:
Life's jutting rocks of trial and error, joy and sorrow,
  slowly white capped our aging heads.
Hardly aware of the growing momentum, we clung together,
  rapidly approaching our separation.
As you were swept into the rushing unknown.
  I was hurtled into the empty eddys along the shore
  where I wait for the current that will bring me
  to where you are.

Mary E. Smith

Teaching

You bless me, Lord, with the young minds in my care.
I thank you, Lord, for my opportunity to share.
My charges grow like wild flowers in the sun.
Who knew that teaching could be this much fun.

Struggles and frustrations do at times abound.
But these are overshadowed by the young "beings" found.
I work to light the flame of curiosity.
They strive to lift my teaching out of mediocrity.

Challenged and nurtured their minds do grow.
The fruits of my work are beginning to show.
I can see their individuality taking shape.
Growing and maturing at differing rates.

We grow and learn about the world and life.
We work to find answers to end strife.
I learn to appreciate an inquiring young mind.
They patiently endure my weaknesses,
and are at times, extremely kind.

Teaching is a partnership, the student and I.
I try to interest them, they surprise and fascinate me.
We grow together, each in our own way.
Hoping each will remember the other, far longer than just May.

Jeffrey L. Bell

Mind Time With Mean Meanings

Why do memories fight to exist?
Anger aura born around my fist.
I suppose they color our emotions,
Trying to erase them,
Always results ion a genocide of distortions,
If only I knew about the next coming rain,
Neglecting all my desires before drowning peacefully in my shame.
Gazing at the waves of logic, with the tides of wisdom filing a claim.
Soaking wet is the disturbing vision of blame,
Ugly scars over my bleeding heart filter away the fame.
Climbing out of the moist shore will kill who I became,
Kindness burning down to ashes by my hateful flame,
Something tells me I'll never come out the same...
Suddenly the aroma of love disturbed my rage,
Offering me life's greatest mysteries was the spiritual sage
Shaping my stalking past into a circular object,
    as he finally opens the lid
"Trust your future to bounce the ball, be patient as you skid;"
Omitting the explanation to this dream, as I awake his presence
    disappeared
"Place the beauty of existence above you, and remember
    the trails you feared
Invite the uncertain to destroy the horrible boredom..."
Tasting this dramatic poetry may bring your hungry mind the
    key to nature's soul.
        Ethan R. Shalom

Up Wedding

So enter into this union with the blessing of the Lord.

O mighty king of kings unto thee do we pray to bless our life on
    this our wedding day.
For in this life if any marriage is to stand it has need of the
    touch of Thy loving hand.
So enter into this union with the blessing of the Lord.

With the giving of this ring we ask Thy blessing O mighty king.
Wherever you will go no matter what the land I will go with you
    walking hand in hand.
So enter into this union with the blessing of the Lord.

Hear that robin sing his love song as our wedding bells play along.
We lift our face toward heaven and smell the flowers in the air it
    is our wedding day there is beauty everywhere.
So enter into this union with the blessing of the Lord.

When trouble comes a knocking just a beating at your door remember
    the beauty of this day and be in love forevermore.
Walking down the road we call life never forget
    he's your husband she's your wife.
So enter into this union with the blessing of the Lord.
        Michael G. Allen

Beyond

Look beyond what the eye can see,
    and see with a new sense of awe.
Feel beyond the human touch, and
    feel your senses soar.
Think beyond all human reasoning,
    and know an intellect far
    greater than the scholar of scholars.
Hear beyond the whispers of the soul,
    and hear the voice of the unknown
    presence, and know He is He.
The one who takes our eyes beyond,
    sight, our touch, beyond feelings,
    and our minds to a greater plain.
For if we hear His voice, we will
    surely see His presence, in all
    the unseen places.
Just look Beyond.
        Cheryl McCarthy

To Win

Was there ever a time when the world looked blue?
    And all of your troubles to Mountains grew
When you felt that the effort could never gain
    The slightest chance in the world of Fame?

Was there ever a time in your wildest dreams
    When you visions a future and started schemes;
And made up your mind that the price you would pay
    Striving to finish your job some day?

Was there ever a time when you stopped to think
    And ponder what brings the success we drink;
What tireless efforts and ceaseless strife
    Follows us on through a much filled life?

Indeed it is hard! But you'll gain much worth while
    Glad when you finish you won with a smile;
A confident knowledge you've kept in the right,
    And surely through courage you deserve your delight.
        Marion Scarborough

What Then....?

I've never been to Bethlehem, where Christ our Lord was born,
I've never seen the manger bed, where He slept that Christmas morn.

I did not see the wise men, as they followed the shining star
Nor heard the host of angels, that formed the heavenly choir.

I've never walked beside him, when He walked in Galilee,
Nor talked with His disciples, as they stood beside the sea,

But I was there that awful day, they nailed Him to the cross,
And heard His cry of agony, as He knew His Father's loss!

My mother-heart was broken, with the tears His mother shed,
As she gazed upon her loving Son, and saw the blood He shed.

I heard the frightful mockery, of those who gazed on Him,
And shouted, "He saved others, now let Himself save Him!"

When on that glorious morning, they found the empty tomb,
I knew that He had risen, to drive away sin's gloom!

Now I own Him as my Savior, this One who died for me,
And I'll dwell with Him forever, blessed Lamb of Calvary.

And when in realms of glory, they sing that new, new song,
I'll tell the old, old story, of the One I have loved so long!
        Gladys M. Gaines

"I"

I am your fantasy extra ordinary...
I am your darkest dreams come true...
I am the most foreign of strangers...
Nevertheless—I am a part of you...

My temptations are ritual—endoctrinating all that wish to play...
Share my sorrow with your soul—forever and a day...
I am often denied credit for the chaos that I bring...
I am the meekest of paupers—nevertheless I am the king...

Contemplate my identity—I am the predecessor of nations...
Curiosity trickles down the corner of your imagination...
I dictate the struggle of man—and all pitfalls...
I am the extravagant flowers—the beautiful waterfalls...

I paint the world beautiful in lovely shades of lavender...
I break the hearts of all—I am the wickedest of scavengers...
I am the epitome of euphoria—deserving much acclaim...
Nevertheless—I am the tears of pain's deepest rain...

Hearts of blackness and skins of mesh...
Discover my demons...explore my flesh...
I lurk within the shadows—nevertheless plain to see...
My name is Reality...
        Ronald Gittens

The Wind

Colorful leaves drop from the tree one by one,
Swaying back and forth,
They land on the soft, fertile ground
Winds whistle by, pick up the leaves in caring hands,
Taking them off to a world
Familiar, yet, so far away.
Walking to the trunk of the willow,
Resting its long limbs on the edges of the pond.
Caressing the water, the tree moves back and
    forth over the surface.
Close The eyes and cross the legs.
Now, sitting next to the loving tree,
Envisioning wind... into spiraling breezes.
Experiencing, touching, beauty surrounds.
Feeling the leaf within.
The reddish, greenish, yellow leaf glides through
Layers of the sky,
Passing through clouds and flying over mountains.
The wind dies down and the leaf softly floats
    to the ground.

Christina Martin

Ocean Of Tears

You see a person sitting on the beach,
staring into the ocean while crying.
You wonder what she's feeling,
what she's thinking,
what is it that is rushing through her
    mind that is making her cry this way?
As you come closer to her,
you want to say something,
but don't know what.
You want to comfort her,
but don't know how.
You don't even know her,
yet you feel compassion towards her.

Suddenly, you realize that she is a
symbol of everyone who knows
pain or has been hurt in some way.

Gianina Giovanazzi

Picture Of Love

As I lay here trying to sleep, thoughts of
you keep running through my mind. I only wish
you were here with me, to feel the warmth of
your body next to mine.

When you call the sound of your voice excites
me. And when I see your smile, and feel the
warmth of your embrace as you hold me close,
my love for you overwhelms me. For when I'm
with you, I feel the love and warmth I've
always dreamed of sharing with someone.
When you hold me close and make love to me,
you enter my heart and soul and I feel as
though we are one.

Once again too often, when you are gone, I
toss and turn trying to sleep. My ears reach
out for the comfort sound of your breath in
the still of the night as you sleep.

When we are together, I feel as though
my prayers have been answered.
When we are apart... my heart aches for you.

Joyce L. Palmberg

Light

Love is what she gives and
    What she receives from me.
    Granny is like no other
    As far as I can see.

In my room every day
    She taught me my first word.
    Turn it on, turn it off,
    Throughout the house it could be heard.

Granny had the patience
    That every grandmother needs.
    Over, and over, and over again.
    On her patience I did feed.

How I learned it, I don't know?
    It's more than a mystery.
    But every morning it would be turned on
    And soon I began to see.

The word is light but really it's love
    I learned this as a baby.
    My very first lesson in my small life
    Was taught by my dear Granny.

Kristin Michele DeBusk

Untitled

I'm poor, but not just because of a hole in my sock
But because of worry that I just can't stop
Will they take my car, can I pay the rent?
I'm scared as I count every dollar that's spent

I'm poor, but not just because they might turn off my lights
But the hunger I feel late in the night
The places I'll never visit
And the people gone unseen
Lost of my hope and forgotten are my dreams
Smothered with despair before it could grow
And yet I still live, why I don't know

Yes I'm poor, but not just because of a hole in my sock

Twana K. White

Have We Overcome

Form Emancipation to Incarceration
From Freedom Rides to Genocide

  HAVE WE OVERCOME

From Marcus, Medgar, Malcolm, and Martin
To Murder, Mischief, Mayhem, and Manslaughter
From Leadership to Leaderless

  HAVE WE OVERCOME

From Physical Chains - To Crack Cocaine
From the Coming of Age - To the Coming of A.I.D.S.

  HAVE WE OVERCOME

From the schoolyard - To the graveyard
From growing from boys to men - To becoming
Boys-n-the-Hood

  HAVE WE OVERCOME
  HAVE WE OVERCaME
    -OR-
HAVE WE BEEN OVERTAKEN

Martin Price

Valentine's Day

I have a sweetheart so precious
And life for me is so sweet,
Especially when she holds me
So wonderfully I discrete.

While looking into her tender eyes,
I see such loveliness.
I fee a joy deep within my soul
That words can never express.

So while I take her close to me
I caress her tender charms,
I feel a touch of paradise
Entwined within my arms.

So please heart don't stop beating
And end this priceless joy,
Cause I don't know any other place to go
To invigorate this little boy.

  S. P. Ewing

Rush Toward Your Dreams

Rush toward your dreams child — Awake or asleep
To far away places or just down the street
Sunshine or shadow — chaos or calm
Rush toward your dreams child
They're on your way home.

Rush toward your dreams — they're many and sweet
In faces of loved ones and friends that you meet
Laughter or sorrow — you're never alone
Rush toward your dreams child
They're on your way home.

Rush toward your dreams child — to treasure and keep
They slip through your fingers and play hide and seek
They ebb and they flow, child
They ease and they grow
Just rush toward your dreams child —
You're on your way home.

  Dana Boyington

Emptiness

His stride told the whole story
Her belongings in a hospital bag
A nurse stops him and says "we're sorry"
His shoulders heave and sag

Can we ever be prepared
For us that time will come
We feel the love they shared
She was his special someone

Her time had come
The decision had been made
It's still so hard on some
Their memory will never fade

He looked back at us all
His little wave said "thank-you"
No words were spoken
His pain was felt by all.

  Ana P. Correia

Thoughts Of Lollipops

Take a walk in the park with me.
See the starlight through the waving trees.
Feel the softness of the evening breeze.
Smile your caramel eyes at me.

Slip slowly down in the steaming bath,
And feel my hands upon your back.
When the water cools and the bubbles fade
We'll fall asleep on the bed I've made.

Let's takes a swim in the velvet night
And throw shadows with the water light.
Let's dance alone to the radio
And leave ourselves to the musics flow.

When the rain in falling
And the thunder calling,
Lay with me on a bed of down
While the storm is raging all around.

We've done these things, let's try for more.
Let's take the chance. Don't be unsure.
Just think of all the things we'd see
If we'd quit fighting it and just be.

  Theresa Drum

Higher Math

How high the wall?
How long the road?
How fast the pace?
What size the load?

Quantify to qualify
measure greatness by its size.
Value science, so precise
for each difference maximized.

Listing, naming each in sequence
categories short and tall.
Place in order, organize
separate names for each and all.

But what of tulips in the sun
and faith in unseen mysteries?
Shall we always measure distance, space apart
or sometimes favor filling in, the pilgrim's empty heart?

  David A. Lombard

Never, Now

You once told me never to say "Never".
You once told me never to run away.
You once told me never to hurt parents,
You once told me never to do drugs
You once told me never to be like our mother.
You once told me never to put my self down
Now you said "Never".

Now you run away
Now you have hurt our parents.
Now you are like our mother
Now you fell off the pedestal which I put you on
Now you must STOP!!!

You never did drugs.
You never will, I hope
You were on a main road, but I guess you fell off
You must not heard the thump
Sis, I loved you. But now I hate you.

  Jessica Bolin

Friendship

Friends can be both family and peers,
A relationship which can last for years.

Friends are there through thick and thin,
Always revealing a loving grin.

Friends kind words uplift the spirit,
Listen hard you can almost hear it.

Compassionate, thoughtful, caring and kind,
Friends like these, come hard to find.

Keep your eyes open, don't let them get away,
You need to cherish them every single day.

Jennifer L. Morrill-Mayer

Surrender In The Sand

Slowly, I remove my outer layers,
drop my warm environment,
as I ready for the cool of the water.

I feel the granules between my toes
as my feet begin to sense the security
of the terra firma beneath me.

Forward I move, into the waiting body of life.
It teases me as the waves break at my feet.
Cool, oh so cool.

I push forward against the breaking waves.

Suddenly, there's a stinging sensation -
the water slaps my legs as if to let me know
nothing in life is without its pain.

Harder, harder it comes at me.
The sand beneath my feet gives way.
My security is drifting out to sea.

I no longer fight the flow.
I lie still as the cool water covers
my feet, my legs, my body, my mind.

I surrender to the power that surrounds me.

Lisa Romer Math

Thru the Window

In the early hours of the morning
You hear the birds sweetly singing
Welcoming you to the day's beginning
And then you hear the clock begin ringing
Time for me to be a showering

As you rise from your sleepy bed
And begin thinking of what's ahead
There's the family to be fed
And today a dentist appointment you dread
Alas a chapter you haven't read.

Looking thru the window and I see
A bird on a branch singing a melody
A squirrel playing in the grass alert to flee
Wind thru the willow branches blowing free
A big brown rabbit nibbling grass watching me

For now the house is empty and silent
And thru the window sun light glint
I can smell the beautiful roses with ruby tint
And begin to wonder where the day went

Ann Marshall Heath

My Heart Only Beats For You

Forever my life has been intensely complicated
and forever and a day scientifically I waited
for logic to drop a casual hint upon my heart
but my condition was so irregular
that it increasing fell apart.
I wanted to eliminate constant thoughts of you
as a motivational incentive to do what I wanted to.
The negotiation took place between my heart and my mind
meanwhile the bargaining failed to allow me to unwind.
I was confident that my creative thinking was a form of art
but all the thought created a pounding of my heart.
I estimated that a strong love for you would take a year
but my plans and thoughts have been relinquished
and the time is presently here.
My heart has overcome and claimed victory over my mind
and I honestly have to admit
    that I was in love with you the whole time.

Terry Moore

Don't Let Yourself Drown

When life has its ups and downs,
You learn to either swim or drown,
Smiling when you really don't want to,
Looking for happiness although you're blue,
To know there is a positive in all things,
No matter what life has to bring,
These things help your hold your head up high,
Although deep inside you may want to cry,
You must give your all when times get tough,
Even as that uphill battle seems so rough,
For at the top of the mountain you will find,
A sense of relief and peace like no other kind,
As you complete things with a special pride,
A feeling of joy arises inside,
And when spreading this joy wherever you go,
There's a magical gleam that comes out with a flow,
Hopefully this will inspire others to try,
Instead of breaking down and starting to cry,
So remember when things seem to bog you down,
Either you'll swim or you just might drown.

Brenda K. McClellan

People Born of Yester-Year

History is etched in the hearts of babes,
This what I'm told
By the people born of yester-year;
Born of the days of old.

    They tell stories of the slavery days,
Of the boat ride over here.
The tears and blood that was shed,
Of people chained and filled with fear.

    Sun up to Sun down they worked in fields,
Men and women all the same.
Babies strapped upon their backs;
With death the only victory claimed

    They lifted their hearts unto God,
Cried for mercy upon their poor souls.
These are the stories I've heard tell,
By people born of the days of old.

This history is etched in my heart,
It paints a vision of blood and tears
I cry out in pain for my people;
The people born of yester-year!

Charlse McGary

Gran'pa

Gran'pa... why are you so tall?
Gran'pa... why am I so small?

Gran'pa... can you hide under there?
Gran'pa... under the dining room table chair?

Gran'pa... why is it dark, at night in the sky?
Gran'pa... if I flap my arms like a bird, can I fly?

Gran'pa... I skinned my knee yesterday, when I fell down.
Gran'pa... can we take te "Vickie" out into town?

Gran'pa... what did you whisper into my ear?
Gran'pa... I sang so loud I couldn't hear.

Gran'pa... you are the best Gran'pa that I know.
Gran'pa... I'm glad you're here, to watch me grow.

Gran'pa...

Margo Lorraine

Interesting Conclusions

If we give a serious thought
It reflects in ordinary straight lines
Curvatures impress us almost always
Human characters become very attractive
From display of facial emotions
This gives feelings to serious acting
Politicians are recognized by certain quirks
Which are portrayed by cartoonists
For the public to think seriously
Of what they actually want
Artist's pictures bring out character
Both in humans and animals
That are usually not evident
When identification is casually made
We love our mountains and wild country
But what do we actually see
For their overwhelming scenic grandeur
And fail to observe deeper
Careful searching reveals intriguing features

John Wallace

The Edge Of Everything, Your Eye's

Lives of old (those untold)
Again ignite kindred souls
An Autumn day set free.

Our passion plays,
Remembered days,
The color of the sea...

Came sweeping like a gentle wave
Wordless, sharing all we crave,
So unexpectedly.

From one with hands and eyes of fire,
The world had disappeared.
No one but you and I were standing here.
Upon the edge of everything, so far and then so near.

All things we dream and dare believe staring back at me.
Like grains of sand pass through our hands,
Inevitable memory (will it never let me be?).

The afternoon was setting sun.
It was and wasn't meant to be,
This frozen moment (pleasure/pain),
Like two eternally.

Andrea Walker

Love's Gold

Thirty One years to look back on—
Mem'ries of love and good times,
Hardships, worry, sick children
All shared with You, Husband of mine.
Our lives have weaved us a pattern,
Some dark threads, some light, some grey
Some silver highlighting the dark ones
and Love's Gold binds securely today.

You've worked hard, unceasing your labor—
Building, providing the care—
The roof, food, small and great pleasures
    for the family you hold most dear.
You've earned all the joy and satisfaction
Life can give to you,
Such
    a One!
It's God, You and Me
    in the future and more happiness in the next
    Thirty One.

For Life can only be better
When we love god supremely and then
We love each other more dearly
Than when our love first began.
For each new day brings another
Opportunity for each to show
In some little way "I LOVE YOU"
    and only Eternity to grow.

Marjorie D. Dunn

The Wedding: Vicci And Curtiss

I remember a phone call a while back,
    you said Curtiss had something to say,

And when Curtiss came to the phone he asked:
"Will you give your daughter away?"

You will never know the great feeling, whether it be early or late in life,

When a man tells a father, I want your daughter to become my wife.
So on October 16, 1993, among the happy, joyous tears,
A commitment of love, trust and understanding,
    that will be with you throughout the years,
But just remember one thing Shug,
    no matter who you are married to,
There will always be one man in your life,
    your pop, who will always love and care for you.

Bob Tarvin

Wisteria

Soaring higher and higher,
Always reaching for the stars.
With love to guide it, it shall rise
To unbounded heavenly heights.

Never ceasing in its search
For a peace everlasting.
With a blight spirit, does it climb.
Fiercely seeking with unconquerable hope and faith.

Oh, radiant wisteria,
You cling so unwaveringly and proudly to life.
With God's loving hand, I too shall soar
    to sovereign spheres.

Donna Chapman

A Life Without Reason

People say that things happen for a reason, well what's the reason.
All the pain and death in the world are caused by something.
The pain in lives of unborn children to lives on the death beds, why all this pain?
  The pain in the world is here to stay.
  People think it's just normal, but oh Lord make them see that it's not.
Every hour people die by the thousands, but many more are born.
Yet many are born to future deaths and horrible fears to overcome.
Something has to cause all this death, oh why all this death?
  Death has been for many centuries and will be for many more.
  How to cope is the question, oh God how!
People should stand up and just start living.
But it's so hard to live when the future looks as pale as the moon.
And the earth loses its life a day at a time waiting to break.
Oh Lord help! God help us!
  Life is born every day and we give it all away.
  All is done and has yet to begin, for many years come much more sorrow.
The lightning strikes and the thunder rumbles the life away.
The glory is gone and what's once is no longer.
What will be will have to be and is carved in stone.
For death and pain is on the way, the way to stay.

   Justin Yacinich

Sorrow Of Sacrifice Cliff

In the distant blue horizon, galloping at breathless speed.
Clouded by powdered, dust, shielded by the sun's scorching glare.
Two painted ponies, panting hot, wet to the touch, push to succeed.
Forcing fleet hooves to pound Mother Earth's green breast bare.

Upon these vibrant steeds, two warriors return after years of war.
Fought courageously in the Dakotas against the dreaded sioux
Leaving behind their fallen comrades, who are lost for evermore.
In their heated pursuit, they seek their fate, of which they'll soon rue.
Hunger grips their inside, thirst has parched and cracked their lips.
Tired, worn, deeply scarred by the ravages of battle and hellish dreams.
Our weary warriors soon feel the chilled touch of death's finger tips.
Swiftly, boldly they ride into the village, oblivious of the survivors screams.

Throughout the shadowed village, the stifling stench of rotted flesh fills the air
Frantically our warriors search for the living among the silent dead.
"Wait! Wait!" is the cry of the surviving mourners,
  but the shield of the deaf lay everywhere.
All is lost, all are gone, there is nothing left to fear,
  there is nothing more to dread.

In blind senseless fury, veiled in madness, cloaked in suffocating sorrow.
The grief stricken warriors mount a blind folded frightened steed.
Straight to the cliff's edge they charge, forgetting all memory of tomorrow.
Soaring down over the edge, connecting earth and flesh as one,
until their tortured souls are freed!

   Alice Marie Lien Shows

Untitled

I'm a world that seams so bleak, we should listen
to what we speak.

No more drugs and peace on earth, but things
change with every birth.

Education is dropping fast, why can't things be like the past?!

When our parents were young like us, there really
didn't seam to be a fuss!

In the schools you had to learn, now most kids
want to burn!!! Out!

   Jeff Herbert

Sharing God's Gift

Our little precious gift from God,
I watched you from the start.
You were growing in mommy's tummy,
But living in her heart.

Mommy loved and tried to keep you,
But that was impossible to do.
So she gave you to another,
Who she knew would love you to.

She cried and was very sad,
It was so hard to do.
She wanted such a better life
Than she could offer you.

We all hope you'll be happy,
And never shed a tear.
Of course you will, and she will to,
With each and every year.

I love your Mom, as I love you.
So please remember hon',
She was my baby as you were hers,
You both are number one.
LOVE FOREVER GRANDMA

   Sue Maude

The Unknown

Sunset, sunrise,
All but an expression of the unknown.
The moon goes round the earth,
The earth goes round the sun.
And so it goes 24 hours a day.

The tide ebbs and flows.
While a single, lonely, shinning star
Solemnly reflects an innocent child's
Wishes for the future.
And so it goes, a single blooming flower,
an isolate starfish.

All have significance.
All begin as one.
All become one.
And all end as one.
In a world of natural
Inspiration and phenomena.

   Alessandra Cerroni

"Hearts Entwined"

When hearts are destined to entwine
Then love must find a way
To make the world go around in tune
With the games that lovers play

If fate should deal a cruel hand
And cause one heart to break
Look up dear heart, and you will find
That new friends you will make.

Among those friends, perhaps there'll be
A heart that's tried and true
Just waiting there, to be entwined
With someone just like you.

   Mary S. Patterson

Love Signs

Walks in the dark, listening ears;
finding no fault, wiping away tears;
Understanding and caring without any doubt;
That's what pure love is all about.

   Todd Ballard

The Streets Are For The Children

How can we stop the crime?...They kill many in their prime.
The city's become a fortress, with guns and drugs and corpses.
The streets are not safe to walk, and people so scared to talk.
A neighbor is now suspicious, for could they be mean and malicious?

As nights come alive with terror, the police now become the bearer...
Of news that we've lost another: A father, sister, mother or brother.
Why can't our system be tougher, and all of the judges be rougher?
Stop revolving the doors of our jails, put an end to parole, higher bails.

Then if guns are used in a crime, you'll spend many years serving time.
With no parole for good behavior, just years of lost memories to savor.
Let's restrict selling of guns today; aren't there laws to take dangerous toys away?
We'd stop senseless fighting and killing, returning the streets to our children.

If only one day there'd be no news of murder, terror and abuse.
Perhaps if publicity on TV rewarded more good deeds of humanity.
What's happened to life's pleasures: The love, the kind hearts we treasure?
A smile and a pleasant "good morning," our children desirous of learning.

Let's clean up the streets today, and plant some trees where the children play.
For as their limbs reach toward the sky, with purpose and strength we all shall try...
To replace fear and dread hereafter, with the joyous sounds of our children's laughter.
For then our neighborhoods truly shall be, filled with love and concern for humanity.

Leah W. Miller

Metamorphosis

When thoughts awake you and you wonder what it is that lies ahead
Remember God's own quiet lesson to humanity instead
About life's changing forms and faces which we all can see
When we watch the metamorphosis of a butterfly from captivity.

A butterfly will stretch and struggle from a caterpillars tight embrace
And when he's won the hard, hard battle he finds he's in a better place
Once he only lay upon the ground...and had a narrow vision
But because he let go of what he knew...a tiny prison
He soars above the earth with wings in ecstasy
His vision ever widening...beholding wondrously.

So smile and know my spirit's with you when you glimpse a butterfly..
He went through such a struggling metamorphosis to find he didn't die
He only found another way to live...as God has shown so perfectly
My soul has only left its shell upon the ground...I too am soaring free.

Nancy Rose Glotz

Intrinsic Epitome Of Another Man's Tears

Sad man of youth, who's reflection is aged.
self observant, in peering out through an iron cage.
Reminiscing the story of his long past glory.

Oh, wayward sorrowful man, of reversed image.
Bowed low in a corner. A wastrel, wretchedly hungry and timid.
I feel your pain, pregnant with fear of hopes, dreams commandeered.

For I, also witnessed the irony of lawlessness and decay;
through alcoholism, drug abuse, immorality, and dismay;
even to the very edge of sanity, I dare to venture and stray.

Cries! Cries! Of errie warning, with a spine chilling barrage
of jeers, calls my ears to attention. All around lurks temptation.
Beguiled by bait, that beckons, calling my name;
I reach, seemingly into a date with my own destination creation.
The dangling encitement of bait. -
A seemingly date with my own destination.

But, then comes another voice, I'm given a choice.
A way of escape, or warnings of guilt and exile through hell's gate.

I'd been warned before, but chose to ignore. now paying the cost of folly.
Actions which made me truly sorry.

So I imagine I made my bed by looking for paradise in the bottle of strife.
This bottle which we call - the good life!

Eugene W. Burns

Teen Wishes

I have to live with myself and so
I want to be fit for myself to know
I want my looks to do me proud
I want to feel adequate in any crowd
I want to strike verbal abuse off my list
I want to keep my cool when the heat resists
I want to take time to respect truth in all
I want to be myself but listen to my Master's call
I want my soul all clean so that God is proud
I want to represent God well in every crowd
I want to be able to sort out the good from the bad
I want to accept the happiness, but handle the sad
I want to hear whispers, "There goes a good teen"
I want the experience: not all teens are mean
I want to shun funky deeds that are never real
I want to grow graceful in right way GOD! Please reveal
I have to live with myself and so
I want to be fit for myself to know.

Bess Shannon

The Rhythm

Chubby pink hand
Resting in the callused palm
Of a hero.

Sorrow-blue eyes
Mirror the faded ones
That see him as his eternal baby girl.

Quick two steps
To his steady one
That walk them though the growing years.

Strong thump thud
Of two hearts
Beating out a father-daughter rhythm.

A soothing universal rhythm
That provides an escape
From the job of growing up.

Sarah Hollimon

That's Love

If love is the answer to the world's problems,
then where is the love?

If love is the ingredient needed in the world's relations,
Then where is the love?

If love is the answer for peace in the world,
Then where is the love?

Love is where you are,
Deep within yourself,

So reach inside yourself and supply
the love that is needed for the
World's problems
And the world's relations and world peace.

It begins with you giving what you have —
That's love.

Sharon Young

Echoes In The Wind (Abused Children's Cries)

You've seen too few loving smiles, felt too few warm and gentle caresses
How many soft, soothing lullabyes were sung in your ear?
None, my guess is.

You've shed too many stinging tears, been robbed of youth's carefree years
You'll never grow old enough to hear; "You're still wet behind the ears."

You'll never get to play tag or baseball, never skate, or ride a bike, or go on a date

because people didn't want to interfere, help came far too late,
you were imprisoned behind those doors, to face a terrible fate

entrusted to people who had no comprehension of the word: "Nurture"
people who abused you, used you as an object for torture

We ask, "Who's to blame?" Then say, "What a damn shame...

that you've fallen between the cracks,
become a shadow in the almanacs,

never knew anyone kind, that your cries became echoes in the wind...
that you died."

Marianne Dimmick

Angels Never Fall

If I could be an Angel, how glorious it would be, to soar above all
earthly things and know that I am free, to tend to matters of the
heart instead of worldly things; I'd touch the souls of all created,
each and every being.

I'd whisper words of gentle song to take away all fear, I'd capture
pain and suffering and wipe away all tears. I'd cradle the child who
cries to deaf ears, no more will he cry - - his special tears.

With my wings I would blanket this child who is cold and forever
and ever as the child grows old, all memory of pain would endlessly
cease while the innocent child lives - always at peace.

For those who wander aimlessly through darkness and despair,
I'd shine a brilliant light of Hope for them to see it there,
To follow it and then I'd tell them oh, so tenderly, "This time shall
pass but God's pure love will forever BE."

And then I'd breath warm words of comfort, God's simple message to all;
"Please, do not fear, for I AM here, and My `Angels Never Fall'"' . . .

Dianne Windsor

Will It?

The strain on the mind of the multitude of thoughts,
From the outermost light, meaningless musing, to the deepest turmoil
of self-examination.
The wonders of the world, yet not the same wonders so commonly known
to the people of our society today.
An infinite number of questions about anything, everything, and the
existence of nothing at all.
I ponder about all of the people on Earth and their unique personas
and how my actions today will eventually affect them or their
great-grandchildren; about who may be standing in the spot I
am in, in a hundred thousand years from now, if
this spot is still available to stand in.
And as I say this to you, do you understand my meaning, and do you
interpret it the same as I, and does it sink into your soul,
and will you remember it tomorrow?

Will my words be passed along or will they perish as the candle
extinguished by the mightiest of winds?
Does anything I think or feel or say matter at all?
Will it ever?

Aimee Fisher

Terry Fox

A blank white wall is all I see
A partition for my quest and me
Is this my coffin, this hospital bed?
So many thoughts rush through my head

Now that I can not run no more
My run's dear cause will they ignore?
Now that I've stumbled on this rope
Who'll end the Marathon of Hope?

Cancer, why did you return?
Will you never ever learn
That I'll soon be back on my feet
And you will have to face defeat

Faithful people, worry not
I so fast will not be caught
Give me time, just one more day
And I'll come back to lead the way

Everybody run with me
We'll cross the nation, sea to sea
And continue on if I take a dive
For though my body's dying, my dream's alive

Sangeeta Bhadra

Dawn

I stand alone at the edge of the beach
looking out over the ocean of my past life and loves.

In the distance the dark sky begins to fade into a purple-grey
and a faint glimmer of light nibbles at its edge.

As orange bands infiltrate and highlights the sky,
a stillness, a serenity settles over the scene.

The coolness of the night begins to warm.

I feel a gentle presence beside me,
a soft hand slips into mine.

Have you come to watch my dawn?

Or, am I here to share yours?

Roberta L. Young

Turn around look at me
For I am only you
I may be hard to see
So I'll tell you what to do
Don't let our life be wasted
Being stubborn all the time
I don't want to live this way
I would like to kind
People say we are heartless
Now they are talking about me
I want to give my heart out
But me they cannot see
They say we think of no one
So double thinking I have to do
I do my thinking of others for me
And try to think of others for you
One time please think of me
By going to the mirror and looking at you
Because you and me are all in one
I'm just your conscience trying to get through
YOU AND ME

Patricia A Palmer

574

Belief

Who is this God in which we believe?
Who is it to whom we cleave?
I believe He's always with us, and hears what we say.
He brings us the night and another glorious day.
he created all things in Heaven and Earth.

Can't you see him in the miracle of birth?
I see Him in the trees and flowers.
He brings us those needed spring showers.
He gave His beauteous son for our souls to save.
Who rose on the third day with keys to Death, Hell, and the Grave.
Jesus gave His life so that we may live.

What else should this God have to give?
In Him we say we give our trust.
But with the things we say and do,
Can he believe in us?

Kevin Tauber

Unheard Cry

Their cries go unheard to the world around them,
    It is silenced by pain and then death.
There were millions of them and more yet to come,
    Why won't you allow their first breaths?

Their fingers are tiny, their toes are yet smaller,
    And they long for your love and your care.
They feel your swift movements, your laughter and fear,
    They love you, dear mothers, but why don't you care?

I know you could have chosen an abortion,
    As many a heartless women have in the past.
But instead you eagerly counted down the days,
    Lovingly awaiting my arrival at last.

The pain my birth brought you became a thing of the past,
    As you held me, your newborn, to love me at last.
Although I can't say it clearly quite yet;
    My happy gurgles mean "I love you" and "Thanks, you're
the best!"

Betsy M. Hammond

A Well Kept Bargain

The sights of eighty years must have gone past his eyes.
His gait was steady; his diction was a bit slow.
He spoke; there seemed to be a few frequent sighs.
He was well-dressed, and his hair was white as snow.
Sadness had recently penetrated his heart.
He seemed to have forgotten his I.D. card;
You could tell he wasn't himself from the very start.
Someone called his name and the message was hard.
His wife was very ill; her condition was grave.
He had to put her on the machine to save her;
Tears ran down his cheeks, although he tried to be brave.
What a beautiful marriage he must have had with her...
The girl at the desk said, "May I call a preacher?"
After a while he asked her to call the neighbor.
Oh, such a distraught and miserable creature;
But how sweet it must be to fulfill the labor.
"Til death do us part's" true meaning in the man's eyes
Reverberates in my heart each and every day
To help me to realize the tears in God's eyes
Each time a couple parts and there's good-bye to say.

Louis H. Adams

In Search Of Forever

Have you ever mused the haunting waves of deaths impending tide;
Will it be an ethereal journey in eclipsing the final divide;
Or shall it be a turbulent quest on the reins of an angry steed;
Will we embrace our ultimate horizon or beckon to recede.

I have heard there shines a radiant essence that abrogates time and age;
An ambiance of serenity that will quell life's scornful rage;
I ponder the chance to grasp the core of this supernalic force;
And be ensconced in the clairvoyant peace of its eternalistic course.

But indeed I harbor a thwarting fear of deaths forever path;
As I've seen its aura embark with blyss and inflict with scourging wrath;
And when our mortal hour glass has tapped its final sand;
Will we only have our faith and soul to help us understand.

When I call to mind my proclivity of reaping fruitless seeds;
I succumb to the question of consequence of my many thoughtless deeds;
But in my heart there lives a God who is absolute and true;
And so in His hands I will rest my search of forevers life anew.

Frank J. Ryan Jr.

Or So It Seems

So long to the bright blue sky on a Summer's day.
So long to children's laughter and the games they play.
This is all part of growing up they say.
The end of innocence and living day by day.

So long to ice cream on the end of a child's nose.
So long to running in and out of a water hose.
It is those living day by day that should know.
These things are necessary for us to grow.

So long to mud pies and the gleam in a child's eye.
How many tears must he cry?
Just because he is to scared to try.

Growing up is not what kills our dreams.
It is forgetting about ice cream or
so it would seem.

Annette Lynne Pentes

Title Why?

Dear Lord please help me life's so unfair,
Why did You give me such a heavy cross to bare?

My child He answered turn and look around,
So I did and couldn't believe what I found.

My cross was not heavy in fact rather small,
There were times I found I had no cross at all.

Why are others so happy their life so easy,
Why Lord why couldn't that of been me?

I've heard You only give us what we can take.
Please Lord I pray give me a break.

Times I feel so alone like no one cares,
Please give me a sign that You are there.

Take away these awful feeling sand salty tears,
Strengthen my weakened spirit consul all my fears.

Show me a reason to go on,
Give me courage make my heart again strong.

Lighten this burden please help me cope,
Give me a sign renew my hope.

Thank You for listening to what I've had to say,
Please help me through another day.

Andrea Pawlikowski

My Little Man

I look down upon you and watch closely as you sleep,
I smile and look ahead as you begin to creep,
I'll make life as simple and as good as I can,
I want you to be happy, my little man.

No hate, no sorrow, no fear do you know,
This will all come later when you begin to grow.
Don't bother to worry, no need to plan,
We'll talk about this later, my little man.

Your whole life and future is laid out for you today,
And Mom and Dad will see nothing stands in your way.
Smile my little one, smile as long as you can,
I want you to be happy, my little man.

Your cries of frustration and hunger I hear,
Somehow you seem to know pet when I draw near.
I'll care for you and love you just as long as I can,
Sleep peacefully now, my little man.

Dorothy MacKay

"Without Her"

I feel the tired daybreak in morning,
Beat upon my skin.
The cold rain soothes the tired eyes,
As I look for a key to her soul.
She's trapped, her form of body in a trance,
They tell me there is no way I can reach her.
Her mind had been set to an ease as
The night time fell dark.
Her heart needing love reminds me of myself
When the black vultures fly overhead.
Its strange how sometimes the white seagulls do appear.
They come with no entrance, they come with
No warning they just appear.
I can see them in her eyes.
I can see you in her eyes, dancing to the
Songs of a moonlit star.
You may dance without her but images will be glued to your memory.
Until that same darkness interrupt your pure dreams of an innocent child.
She appears only when her state of mind
Is clear and the night time is no longer dark.

S. Candy

Change Of Heart

After awhile you learn the subtle difference...
Between holding a hand and imprisoning a soul.

And you learn that love doesn't mean security,
While you begin to understand that kisses aren't binding contracts.

Words or gifts aren't promises of forever
You accept defeats in reality.

With your head held high and your eyes open wide,
Take it as the grace of a woman, not the grief of a child.

Then you learn to build all your roads on today,
Because tomorrow's ground is too uncertain

futures have a way of failing in full flight,
After awhile you learn that sunshine burns when you get too much.

So you plant your own garden and decorate your soul,
Instead of waiting for someone else to bring you flowers that will whither in the wind.

It's then that you learn to endure... and endure...
Endure even more

You discover that you really are strong, a survivor.
And you learn that you really are worthwhile...
You learn and learn... that's life!

Jay Warren Downs

How Selfish Have I Been

The Lord took my only son away, this happened just the other day
People came to pay their respects, they're hurt too, from what I detect.

Some brought cards, flowers, and money
Others brought meat, bread and honey
Some gave kisses, while others gave hugs
Lord knows, some wiped their feet
While others tracked dirt on my rugs

Some folks called from local, some from long distance
I had several out-of-town people arrive in an instant

So tell me Lord,
How selfish have I been, when others were in need?
How selfish was I, when others needed me?
How selfish was I, when my neighbor lost her kin?
How selfish was I, and where did it all begin?

Lord, only you have the answers to my questions above
I know what you'll tell me, "it's all about love"
So Lord now that you have my son "J.R." in heaven
Everyone can dial 431-6647
Cause if ever they need ne, I'm a phone call away
For no more will I be selfish, starting today!!

Cheryl Ann Young

"Lady In Red"

Send me some forget-me-nots; anybody, that would make my day
Forget-me-nots from the lady in red with the blinding blue eyes
For her and the governor to deliver my pardon, now that would
    truly make my day!
But who could this lady be?
I have touched love with many;
Chris, the dashing red bone with the black and grey eyes,
Rose, the shy, gentle dove who carries a piece of my heart
    around her neck
Diane, the adventurous chick who can turn around on a dime
    and give you eleven cents change
Cindy, the snow girl, who looks at me everyday within a set
    of twins
Holly, the only pecan tan to ever propose to me
Evil, a gentle teddy bear with a lust for life and second to none
Rhonda, a tenderoni, on a quest for a no-static-love
Laverne, the lith tigress who can devour a heart at the
    blinking of an eye
But Red, the most understandable woman in the world
Pound for pound, she's untouchable
Oh how I wish for a future or even a past with the Lady in Red
Let the victor come forth and claim their prize.

Grant Rogers Jr.

My Harvest

I planted seeds so long ago, and watched for them to sprout.
I watered them with tenderness, and weeded all cares out.
I nursed them, not always wisely, but always with love to spare
They grew so fine in stature, so handsome and so fair

And then came harvest time, for me to reap what I had sown
I gave them understanding, and they gave me joy unknown.
I gave them love and love came back to me a thousand fold
They brought to me such happiness, worth more than any gold

Yes, I have reaped my harvest, more than my heart can hold
For now my plants have little sprouts beginning to unfold.
I hope they bring their parents, the joys that I have known
So when their harvest time comes 'round
They'll reap what they have sown

Dorothy Farnel

Paradox

My heart is lost in the night of loneliness, wandering aimlessly about.
No stars are there to guide its way;
The moon is hid by clouds of doubt.

My soul I have sown to the four winds,
the storm of indecision raging high;
Saint or sinner, which shall I be?
So undecided — Sinner, then, am I.

There is no halfway place for us; the way is all or none.
A lonely sinner's dark of night
Cannot blend with Saint's bright dawn.

Saintly One, citizen of the dawn, painter of the day's golden hue;
You could not sink to the halfway mark,
Or you would then be sinner, too.

O! Saint, will you wait for my lost heart to escape the loneliness
    of night;
Wait for my soul its sin-chains to break
And enter the Saint's dawn light?

Where my heart and soul can reach out and touch your heart and soul,
O! Saint;
Where I may live beyond the dawn —
Completely yours, without restraint.

   Billie A. Cooper

Untitled

I close my door
and walk beneath a soft blanket of majestic elms,
maples and oaks
Now hued in golds, crimson and scarlets.
Their last show for the season.

I close my door
and slowly drive past mile after mile
of corralled fields and pastures
flecked with stallions and mares and cows bursting for milking.
Nature at her best.

I close my window
after paying the toll that permits me to drive mile after mile after
mile of blacktop with the white line whizzing by me.
Mesmerizing me.
Enticing my thoughts from the industrial warehouses
and train yards I pass.

I close my door
and start my 8 hours for which I get paid.
A mere pittance that is supposed to enable the other 16 hours
not to be a struggle.

I open my window as I drive the blacktop home
to my country paradise and you
to let in the smell of fall
and rebuild myself back to a whole person again.

   Anne Raimondi

Mirror Mirror

Oh Rose, you are what I see each morning when I gaze into the mirror.
My roots are my parents, my foundation for life.
The soil is my husband, how he gives me nourishment to grow and live.
Like you, my stem is my strength, it helps me mature, to rise above my
down falls, to tower above my thorns.
My bud is my child, a new birth as I encourage her to blossom into a
   young women.
My petals are my arms, how they keep on opening the doors to my heart,
   my soul, allowing people dearest to me to come into my world.
When your leaves dry up, I get wrinkles, when you become weaker,
I grow older, but we can look back and see the seeds that we are
   leaving behind, "The seeds of a new generation."

   Sheri Baity

A Fallen Star Returns To Heaven

A star from heaven once visited the earth. It was small but fairly
bright...it slowly grew and became brighter as the days went by.
This star was loved by many and the world was in her hands.
But a tragedy dimmed her light forever...very close to her heart a
bullet hit...and soon she was no more.
The world in purple black was dressed and many tears were shed...
Angry and puzzled and uncertain of this crime...how can anyone be so
cruel and so unkind?

The world less bright will be...because her presence will
no longer light the dark corners of our hearts.
But her music and her songs will forever entertain our souls.

Sometimes when the night is quiet and still I seem to hear a gentle
voice uttering from above... "Please don't grieve for her my dear
children, she is happy in her new home. She came to me when I needed
her the most, to light the universe and make your long dark night a
little brighter. If you should miss her still...in the darkest
night look up to the heavens and among the twinkling stars, you'll
see a bright light winking as if to smile and greet you all!

   Maria G. Perkins

The Ancient Ruins

Boldly sitting, staring at history, and daydreaming.
Dismissing knowledge of things more important than... me.
Could it possibly be?....yes
One has withstood time. One has experienced so little.
A tangible breathing being - a distant memory.
So obvious which's more worthy of attention...the here, the now, no!
What once was carries more weight.
The ruins possessing more substance than petty, everyday,
"all-important" life. Time, so obvious in everything.
Aging both but only distorting one.
Changing both slightly but only killing one.
Which will survive longer?...
Not a question but sarcastic mockery.
Others, daring to ignore the greater of the two,
The victor continuously laughing at the weak, the lowly, the
fleeting moment in history.
Choose to learn or be complacent....no matter.
Choose to be enlightened or remain in darkness....who cares.
A personal choice with no one to hurt but yourself.
Accept the sad truth....
One will remain. One will not even be remembered.

   Jennifer Pukach

Ashlee

Oh Ashlee, of the ash tree meadow,
From an ancient kingdom long forgotten.
Now remembered in your birth.
With beauty, and color, wonderful smells of spring.
So were you my dear, so were you
Just when all the flowers of spring would bloom.
They are born in May, just like you.
Ivory skin, soft to the touch, and your smell,
I was sure you were Ashlee.

A great princess lost in the past, born again today,
to redeem her promise, the promise of spring, of the ash tree.
The beauty you held at one glance took my breath away.
It could only be compared to a flower, at first bloom.
Tiny little hands that went pinch, pinch.
Your eyes turned from a baby blue, to a brilliant green.
The green of the sea.
Like two big emeralds they followed me, watched every move.
Oh Ashlee, just as all dreams are possible you were born.
You are my spring, my princess, my dream.
As all the spring flowers were born in spring, so were you, my flower.
   My Love,

   Gladys Fox

"Aids" "Wanted Dead Or Alive"

Aids is a disease most commonly known
given little understanding it comes
into your home. Its doesn't care if you
like it or not, it's there to ruin your life.

Aids is not bashful, nor is it shy it comes
in all colors, shapes and size. It doesn't worry
of whom the next victim will be, not caring
that it is a deadly disease.

Aids is something that does not discriminate,
if given the opportunity it diminishes your health
this can be very gruesome you see. Let's pull
together in peace and harmony.

The muggers, the robbers, prostitutes and pimps, the crackheads,
and gangs or no exempt. Aids has no respect for you
or me so now we must look up towards heaven
for God is our only key.

Delisa Phillips

Cold Wood

I walk on top of the cold wood floor and consider:
I do not have heels of forever,
The winter will be gone very shortly
And I can no longer feel myself to be simply preparing
For the next winter.

I want spring and yet fear it because it rushes on and reminds
Me that I do not have winter's excuses,
I think of how spring once was:
The fishermen no longer wore their heavy gear
And smiled as different birds flew above their bows,
And boys played ball in streets
With little cares,
And young girls played hopscotch and skipped rope,
And hot pies cooled on ledges.

There was always strong rain
And puddles which when mixed with gasoline looked even better than
The rainbows which the sun formed above on large billowy clouds.
Yes, spring with all its newness and exposing ways.
I never worried then but now have had many winters
And no longer the hope of forevers.

Baron Drexel

Cold Wood

I walk on top of the cold wood floor and consider:
I do not have heels of forever,
The winter will be gone very shortly
And I can no longer feel myself to be simply preparing
For the next winter.

I want spring and yet fear it because it rushes on and reminds
Me that I do not have winter's excuses,
I think of how spring once was:
The fishermen no longer wore their heavy gear
And smiled as different birds flew above their bows,
And boys played ball in streets
With little cares,
And young girls played hopscotch and skipped rope,
And hot pies cooled on ledges.

There was always strong rain
And puddles which when mixed with gasoline looked even better than
The rainbows which the sun formed above on large billowy clouds.
Yes, spring with all its newness and exposing ways.
I never worried then but now have had many winters
And no longer the hope of forevers.

Baron Drexel

Stigma On Humen Faces

My heart filled with desires, limit is sky;
My head tilted with dire consequences to fly.

My pen filled with ink, obsolete to repeal;
My decree charged with authority, stigma to peal.

My people willed with oriflamme, to do or die;
My people, Ah! Himalayans, commandments to defy.

My world, Ah! yet patronizes the mafia and apartheid;
My U.N., Ah! yet "justice delayed, justice denied".

My world, yet patronizes the ignobles and heinous:
My world, yet patronizes the irresponsible and insidious.

My brothers and sisters in siege before Serbians and Somalians:
And mass massacred before the Bolsheviks, Nazis and
Rwandans!!!

My world is Beirut, Gaza and South of Africa;
My world is Afghanistan, Kurdistan and Horn of Africa.

My orgy is loot, arson and riots in Kashmir-desh:
My Biharis' camps' ordeal and episodes in Bangladesh.

I'm, a bitter fact, not supposed to be, sinking in shame!!!
I'm, in fact, supposed to be, Deputy to God, ranking in fame!!!

Shah Salim Ahmed

My Picasso Painting

I stood in the doorway watching the sun rays flitting and slithering
    over my hands, outlining the heavy veins under the
    creepy skin.

The rays expanded, dancing and skipping, piercing the window to
    embrace the dimpled glass vase, forming tiny opalescent
    bubbles and flashing lights.

My reflection started at me through the concave surface, the features
    retreating into a sunken bowl-shaped face, the nose
    peeking from behind the daisy stems.

Turning the vase to the convex side, my face suddenly arched like a
    cupid's bow, a sickle-like nose touching an ear, the
    eyes dancing on my brow, the wrinkled neck
        pulsating to the rhythm of each heartbeat.

I was relieved when the rays retreated and drifted away. Then the
    water was calm and all I saw were fresh yellow
    and white daisies.
BUT - the faces are still remembered.
I think I shall finish this poem when I meet Picasso in my next life.

Efimedia Raptis Kent

Has anybody ever? No never! Tell it!

Never ever sever my life until I tell He lives
There's no other treasured gift like Our Saviour gives
No sinner finds that Christ will not take him
All human kind finds He won't forsake them
No other friend so meek or so lowly
No night so dark that His love can't cheer us
No time-period so pointless that He will not hear us
No one else can heal our Soul's diseases
Now is the appointed time — He gathers when he pleases
He knows everything about our life's battle won
He'll ever guide till our final day is done
He'll never sever our life — not ever
If we believe on Him the victory is begun
Contentment will be my crown — I crave no earthly glory
Within my lowly spot — I want to tell God's wondrous story
I want to tell it again and again — implore
Salvation's story repeat o'er and o'er
Till none can say of the children of MAN
Nobody has ever told me that before

Bess Shannon

Wake Up!

We have differences with each other all the time,
Somebody is always drawing territorial lines.
Brothers often distinguish their own neighborhoods,
It somehow seems to do them good.
But, now, it's a call for peace,
So, let's chill on the violence on our streets.
Because, we're only taking our own men down,
And it's not that many around now. The fight is not with each
other,
We're suppose to get strength from our brothers.
The enemy is the Destroyer, who comes in different packages
and shades,
And he doesn't care how he takes you to the grave.
You see, cigarettes, liquor, drugs and guns all kill
but, they don't come in human shades,
So, while we're busy fighting each other they slip away.
They're taking us out one by one,
While we're smiling and calling ourselves having fun.
Regardless, how good it feels,
What does it matter if it's a feel that kills.
Hey, My Brother, don't be tricked!
Loose yourselves from the devils grip. And wake up!!!

Natalie Stovall

Mommy And Daddy's Love

Today your just a little boy in Mom's and Daddy's eye.
Tomorrow you'll start growing more and then you'll wonder why
Mommy's really silly and daddy's really sly.
Soon you'll be getting bigger and you'll be sure you know
Better than your mom and dad cause they're just growing old.

But while your thinking all these things remember one big fact.
That mommy brought you up and Dad knows where it's where it's at
Of course you know, it's really true, mistakes you'll have to make.
Just like your Mom and Dad, you'll have your own heartaches.
But while your doing this, remember they did too.

But remember this dear Grandson;
Of all the things above
You never will have done them,
Without Mom's and Daddy's love.

Katherine Ruprecht

So Near

Now as the time comes near we will always love.
With our friendship we will remember the times of fun and sorrow,
For, there will always be a tomorrow.

Patricia A. Curran

World of High Officials is a Maze of Amazings

More than a hundred fifty Nations,
Without Geneva accord signings ___:
At; twisted talons and inter-twigs of fateful... step-care,
and longings for...
   Earlier, care-free times that ne'er may ere be again!!
   Whom are these people... partly sailor.
Wot; A biped. O'cr, Mosaic—E-D:
Because... are these people, the rates of exchange
of anything of value! Since Porto Bello...
of the Carribbean? Prayer, or appeasers!!
Christmas week; A.D. 1995, a fire in upper duplex;
And Easter week... Spring fever fishing abounds:
Caught 3, snow now, so a wait for scads more — or less!
Late winter found a rare animal from somewhere in dawn's light —
Circus; or something unusually migrating along river!
Times of wax-bean lunches... the animal twice heavier,
Claw tracks in mud, than I! Dangerous Bush-Type Animal
Of the wild — living in sewers ... perhaps!!

Richard C. Miller

Women

Women are special, unique in a way.
Women are happy and sad everyday.
Women are fun.
Women are different in all different ways.

Different races, different hair,
Different hands, different feet,
Different family and friends.

Women stand barricaded at the wall of freedom.
No work, no feeling.
Destruction, discrimination, stand at the door.
Women can't get away.
Going into the 21st century, still barricaded, still sad, women stand.

Women can't see, but women can hear.
The questions, the answers, they're not right, they're not true.
Women are heroes like you and me.

Women are the ones that can always tell.
When you're sad, when you're mad, all women can tell.
Mothers can, sisters can, aunts, grandmothers, all women of the world.

Women are special, unique in a way.
Women are happy and sad everyday.

Whitney Leader-Picone

Natural High

It's a place we like to hike up in the mountains high,
The two of us together, but a feeling of alone.
At first it is dark and cool; the trees are our Protector.
We follow the stream as it rushes by, its sound is our music.

We step out of the woods and into a giant bowl,
Our yard a field of flowers, our fence the mountains.
Above a hawk makes a passing sweep searching for its prey,
While just below a critter hurries for its home.

The trail begins to narrow almost lost amongst the rock,
Our map becomes the mountains, lakes and valleys afar.
As we climb those final steps we gaze around in awe,
This is the top of our world; we give Him thanks for all.

Marilyn Steen

Softball

S oftball is not for the novice.
O ccasionally you'll be diminished by
F orfeit or loss.
T he attitude you have must be unaffected by defeat,
B ecause you're out there to hurl the ball, get that runner out
A nd win the championship! This is how my sister,
L aura, thinks as a catcher. She
L oves the game.

Leeanne Jagusch

To War

I cannot help but think of war
And all the ills it brings
For I can sense that some day too
I shall feel its stings.

But if to leave and fight I most
I'll always fret and wonder
That fate will play a wicked trick
And cast me far asunder.

But then I think with brighter views
Which makes my heart so free
For there will a day when I'll return
And you again I'll see.

Bernard Taub

I Won't Ever Pay for Stress Again!

First it's just a bad day where everything seems to go wrong,
Maybe you just got out of the wrong side of the bed.
The next day, bills come in and some are singing high prices song,
So try to pay as much as you can but it gets to your head.

Third day, an illness has struck you like a ton of bricks,
Children defy you and argue everything you ask,
Next day, unexpected death of a loved one has really made you sick.
Following week, best friend plays headgames and tolerating is even a task!

Wake, Funeral, and confusing emotions drain you to no end.
After, nerves are worn to the hilt and you cannot sleep,
A fight with your husband and neither will bend...
Three days later a terrible flu makes you weep.

News comes that your beloved Nana must be operated on in order to survive,
and it's a good chance she can't even take the operation.
1:30 A.M., you are rushed to the hospital for a severe migraine that thrives.
HAD ENOUGH OF TOO MUCH STRESS AND TOO MUCH COMMOTION!

NO MORE BLACK CLOUD WILL BE FOLLOWING ME!
I took my vitamins, ate well, and slept for an entire day.
Promised myself when the first signs of stress come, IN ANY WAY,
I'll take the time to find peace with myself and it, SO I WON'T PAY!!!

Laurel Barron

Grandma

You are a great person and no one can take your place. We will really
miss your face. When someone special is no longer here today, the
pain inside will never go away. I would give you the moon and the
stars, so remember me this way. Your family has the best Grandma,
your husband has the best wife. There's no one who can replace you.
When it comes to death, there is nothing you can do. You are the
greatest card game ever dealt. Without you the sun coming up at the
beach won't be the same. No one will forget you, not a soul, not a
name. Who will feed the birds in your yard? Who will send you a
Mother's Day card? There will be many hearts shattered. I'll miss
you so much, that's what's the matter. I will climb the highest
mountain just for you. Even sail the sea's you've never visited.
The most important point is:

I LOVE YOU!

Melinda Shaw

Sarah

A feeling of hopelessness and hurt the pain of the wait the time
passes by never knowing is she gonna be okay the betrayal act of
others who just don't know how to cope. You can't understand her
you don't know how you can help. All you can do is be there feel
your feelings live the joy, laugh the laughter. If you lose your
humor they'll be nothing left. It's okay to hurt, it's okay to cry,
it's okay to know when your gonna die, it's okay to be angry but
let your grudge go. Forgiveness is everything when you only live
once. Hate is to murder as murder is to hate death will come for
those of us who wait to let go of pain, misery and despair if you
do go please warm me first. We won't forget the memories we share
they connect us as one. You will be with me always as I will be
with you. Let go of me but I won't let go of you. I'll keep you in
my prayers and remember to think of you as the rest of us continue
through. I won't give up hope. No, not till we know more and when
she lays weary and tired. I'll give her the rest of my strength on
me and when all is over and everyone is well we'll do the things we
used to and everything will be swell.

Lorelli Taylor

Le Reveil Comme Cyranno

Drowning in tides of ugliness
Tears become my only refuge;
I cry myself a beautiful girl
Succumbing unto them.
Her perfect, glossy lips uttering only deception
Pretending she's comforting me
As if she's my salvation,
As if she knows how I'm feeling
Disgusted with myself.
The skin around my lips slowly begins flaking,
Someone's tearing me apart repulsive
    layer by layer,
Revealing new flesh
As if there's something deeper:
Deeper than my face,
Deeper than my skin,
Deeper...

Katie Kristensen

Mother's Day

It's midnight now
no sleep for me,
I hear the cries
the silent cries
of children
neglected left-alone
They cry for mother
Mother Nature
she answers gentle teardrops
washing away
the guilt
guilt of the people
people who don't
need to worry
their mother will help
always there to cleanse
to hold
to wipe away the tears

Mike Wszalek

Two Pine Trees

Two stately pine trees
    swinging in the breeze
one holding the other
    because its got weak knees,
hold on tight the tall
    one seems to say
and maybe just maybe
    you'll last another day
but there comes the wind
    blowing oh so high
down goes the pine tree
    with a great big sigh.

Alice C. Van Cour

SUDDENLY

Suddenly I am a senior citizen!
Suddenly I am without wages!
Suddenly my life changes!
Suddenly I feel I have no identity!
Suddenly I am out of everything!
(Pay checks, union benefits, food, etc.)
Suddenly I am alone and sad, not to
Mention being in pain and disabled —
Suddenly I find out how really cruel
    Humanity is!
Suddenly I learn that long suffering
Makes you a Spiritual person
And suddenly I AM GLAD!!

Mrs. Beryl Singho

Metamorphose At Eckley — for Dave

Just before dawn the old company house is desolate, no paint,
side porch collapsing from the weight of a hard Pennsylvania winter,
supported only by two 4 x 4's leaning toward it.

The sun begins to rise, the reflection of light off the windows
revealing the tulips just breaking through the ground. As the light
intensifies, the new grass shows itself, a grasshopper hopping about.

The form of an apple tree appears, just sprouting its buds, soon to be
white with flowers. If I close my eyes I can picture the red round
fruit and then imagine the smell of cinnamon and apple in a newly baked pie.

As I glance toward the broken porch, I see a little nose poke out,
then another and another. A litter of kittens makes its way out into
the day. They roll about with each other until Mom comes and swats
one's nose. They then follow their mother to a morning feast.

Now the sun is fully risen, I look up into the cloudless sky with its
shades of azure and sapphire unmarred by man, made glorious by nature.

I look again toward the house to see that the door is painted a bright
green, the color of hope. The house looks no longer desolate, it is
such a beautiful, wonderful house.

Lynda L. Woolf

"Sons And Fathers"

My sons, my sons, a father's love, how bright their fires burn.
How proud I am, how proud I was, to watch them grow and learn.
When they were young, I held them close, they meant so much to me.
I'd never known such love before, they were my destiny!

Until the times when they arrived, my soul was quite adrift.
To see them smile, to laugh and play, was just the greatest lift.
We hugged and kissed and wrestled 'round, and said our prayers at
night. And there were also many times I'd have to stop a fight.

If I could bend the hands of time, and visit them at play,
I'd pick them up and dance around, for but another day.
The joy they brought, and yet still do, keeps filling me with pride.
Alas, they've grown and gone their ways, I'd like them by my side.

The kisses, hugs, the acts of love, somehow can't be accepted.
We're all men now, It's now the same, it's quite the unexpected.
Sons and fathers should not fear love, it's part of our existence.
The times we had can't disappear, there shouldn't be this distance.

It's up to me to start anew, to tell them how I feel.
After all, they are my sons, my love for them is real.
I beamed with pride, and joy, and love, as I watched you grow.
To each of you, I love you Son, I always have you know.

Robert Montgomery Thomas

Matt Lee Vierling(In Loving Memory)

Matt was so full of life when he was around he made things more fun.
How could anyone take you're life, and then take off and run
He was more then just a regular, everyday type guy
Why someone so unique as him has to go God just answer me why?

There was so many good, things he could say to make other feel good.
Because he felt that way.
Thinking about you could bring a smile to someone everyday
You're someone that had friends, you had so many.
Losing you is just like not having any.

You had the sweetest personality that can't be beat.
You always looked nice and dressed neat.
Always when you were around you're friends would feel near.
We will never be able to heard you sing loud music in our ears.

Its hard on everyone that you were close to.
Its going to be different without you.
Losing Matt we lost so much more.
Matt had everything to live for.

Leslie Kay Frederick

Ambition

Heartless, swirling smoke of the big city
Choking with unseen hands, life's ambition.
Concrete pavement, tell me where's your pity?
Throbbing, crushing, rushing population,
Traffic going nowhere, quickly, sickly
Crowding, shouting over frustrated screams.
Dripping sweat on nights hell-hot and prickly,
Reaching, chasing after aborted dreams.
See him there among the many, trying
To be seen here where none can stand
For very long. Laughing, crying, dying,
Fighting against the daily ruling bland,
  Never ending humdrum, dumb existence.
  Excitement gone without some assistance.

Lorraine Kay

My Monster

My monster Fred lives under my bed
His head is full of sand

He makes a mess which we all dread
But I think he's just grand

He moans and groans and whines all night
It really is a chore

But even though he's such a fright
I couldn't love him more

He makes me laugh until I cry
He's never seen me sad

I'll love him till I die
In spite of mom and dad

So if you've got a dust ball pal
Who lives beneath your bed

Maybe he's a she named Sal
And maybe she'd like Fred.

Stephanie Kirsten

Dark Boomerang

Tri colored memories of sadness more
  devastating than the bombing of
Pearl Harbor so merciless and utterly unkind
Spasmodically fluttering the hemispheres
  of my once becalmed mind
Drown deeper into lonely grief imprisoned
  by it's bind
Disturbed by a ploy to destroy
The discovery of recovery
So I serve you notice of eviction
Drawn from my inner souls' strong conviction
I cast you away for as long as I live
My life to you no more will I give
Inside of it you'll never ever reign
Your efforts are all counted as vain
Like a boomerang return to your domain

Mary Antoinette Morgan

My Friend

I have a friend who's very dear.
He helps me get through every day.
And when I have a problem he is near
To solve it in his own special way.

When sorrows weigh heavily on your mind
And you think people are too busy to care
Open your heart and you will find
My friend "God" very willing to share.

Denise A. BedardMy Friend

"Praising the Field"

The excitement is kept alive
Driving in a winning run
Sweat sinks into the leather
A hero shines tonight

Happiness fills their smiles
A love for the game
Fans applaud this living legend
An inspiration for us all

The giant lit up that night
And left many memories
An old record has been broken
Their tears revived the glory

Doing the best you can
This is a very special gift
Dreams have praised the field
A desire to compete

Francisco DaCunha

Like Flowers In December

I was alone/all I needed was ...
your love and a home/you
said a home I cannot give you

But you wrapped me/in your
arms/quilted me in the feathers of
your love...and took me home...

I hear no whispers/like
flowers in December/rare and beautiful

I was homesick
you made homesick a
memory and took me home/
I hear no whispers...
like flowers in December/rare and beautiful

Saundra L. Williams

"Sparks"

I'm not sure that what I feel
   could be construed as right
But I know how you make me feel
   and I hope you see the light,
From my life you brighten
   my days so gloomy and dark
My love for you now deepens
   and it started from just one spark,
That spark is now an eternal flame
   that keeps my heart so warm
I get my strength from you my dear
   for my heart is now reborn,
Do you know just what you mean
   to me why can't you see
You're the only one I want
   you're everything to me,
For I'll be there when you're lonely
   and I'll always be your friend
I'll fight all odds to serve you
   and I'll love you to the end.

Patrick Sliwinski

My Friend

I have a friend who's very dear.
He helps me get through every day.
And when I have a problem he is near
To solve it in his own special way.

When sorrows weigh heavily on your mind
And you think people are too busy to care
Open your heart and you will find
My friend "God" very willing to share.

Denise A. Bedard

hand me downs

silver names on silver chains,
lost but found again
and almost forgotten,
smiles and hand squeezes,
dreamily she asked if she will be remembered.

memories stuffed in old borrowed socks,
never to be worn again by the same person,
the stale candy in a jar
but the flowers are gone, the dirt is bad,
we will remember.

candles are lit
and the wind blows,
fire stays in the hearts
of the children looking on,
we will remember.

the procession moves on,
eyes come out of a daze,
minds return to the present,
gripping the blood pumping muscle,
i will remember, always.

Naomi Tarle

Untitled

When I throw a penny
in a wishing well
I wonder if my wish will come true.
I stand there for a second
and listen...
SPLASH!!!
The penny falls down.
I look.
I say to myself
this wish will stay in my heart
forever.
Will it come true?
I wait,
and I wait - until it does.

Michael Sohn

Everyday Memories

I wake in the morning
its hard to ignore so
many memories from the
days before.

The glass is filled with moisture
we've all seen in the past as
we take our hands to clear the glass.

Dew settled in from the night
that past leaving sparkling little
droplets on the blades of grass

The sounds of bells start to blast
to let us all know its now half
mass these fond memories of day's
that past

As the night draws near and
your thoughts are clear
Memories of the past become so dear.

Robert Kelly

Nature's Way

I like it when I am alone with nature
for I feel nearer to you God
whom I so often neglect

I see the magic in the garden
the beauty in your flowers
the soft swaying and rustling
of the coconut and palm trees
Your small creatures moving so carefree
the gentle push of your breeze
blue skies above
Your sun's golden rays beaming down
the ocean swollen and magnificent
blue and turquoise ripples
your people around me
so different yet so same

My being is overwhelmed
I am filled with awe and excitement
and the wonder of YOU
I feel your presence God you are with me
You who have never failed me we are one.

Bonniel L. Nauyen

Untitled

I want to tell you about
a very special place that everyone has.
A place that makes your dream come true.
Where you can make yourself a pirate or
even a kings knight.
You and your friends can be stranded on an island.
Even you in an animals point of view.
If you would like to eat dog food
   you are welcomed to.
Would you like to know why?
Well, because silly you can eat anything you please.
You could dress in fish scales or even
amphibian skin.
It's all up to you, because it's your
imagination.
Won't you come and imagine?

Nicole Ball

I Saw God Wash The World

I saw God wash the world today,
All dirt and slime were washed away.
Every blade of grass was clean,
Making the lawns cleaner than I had ever seen

The birds and beasts all got a bath,
But to count them all would be a lot of math.
God has the power to do all things,
including cleansing ponds, rivers,
streams and birds' wings.

When I see how clean all outside things are,
I feel as if I am seeing them from afar.
Oh! how I wish God had also washed me,
As clean as He did that old magnolia tree.

Modine G. Schramm

Untitled

When I met you I knew not of love,
It was something in song and stories alone.
Since I met you I have learned of love,
It is real indeed. It's not something you see or do,
It's something from the heart that emanates within.
You are so full of love it rubbed off on me,
Now I know for sure what love is so
I'm writing this to say to you, I love you.

Richard E. Deily

Have You Ever

Have you ever held a dream in your hand
and awed at you hold,
Never had you thought,
one moment you'd hold gold.

Have you ever cherished paradise
and painted one of your own,
And added so much to it
every year you've grown.

Have you ever released freedom
and latched onto something grand
That something being so special
it inspired the dream in your hand?

Ever year you live
there's so much more to give
And someone to give it to,
that gift and dream is you.

Elizabeth Herron Rowley

Eight Point Five

The dog was acting strange,
and far from the epicenter
there walked a mountain range.

It's your fault, San Andreas, it's your fault.

When the nation shakes its tail,
8.5 on the richter scale
goodbye, California, goodbye.

In dreams you'll still enchant us
golden sister to atlantis
we'll cry, California, we'll cry.

It's your fault, San Andreas, it's your fault.

Fate has written your epitaph
on the scroll of a seismograph.
Goodbye, California, goodbye.

When the nation shakes its tail,
8.5 on the richter scale.
we'll cry, California, we'll cry.

Richard Applegate

Daddy

It's been a year ago since daddy died
and left one more time.
But it was different for me,
he was really trying to be a little more kind!

I had seen him before in a lot of odd ways,
but he had been my daddy those last two days!

I could see the love and wear in his old blue eyes,
as if he was saying to me I love you but
I've got to say goodbye!

There both gone now and now in my life,
I have to be strong they say
and pray pass this strife!

I cry to myself and talk to them each day,
please Jesus let them here me.
For I miss and I love them more
than my words can say!

Brenda Sexton

I Thank You

There are all the happy times
And the many hours of joy you give
And for all the ways you care
I thank you, my friend, I thank you
Every lovely letter you send
For your gentle, giving, tenderness
For each and every warm embrace
For all these things I thank you

For all the dreams you helped me dream
For all the ones that came to life,
And the ones that passed us by
Just making memories that pushed me on
For all these things I thank you

You've given me strength,
Revived my heart,
Helped me to continue on,
You've kept me strong,
For all these things and many more
I thank you, my friend, thank you

Jean Isham

Words Within

These words in my mind
   Are flowing all the time

These words within are like a rush,
   They are a part of me

Where have they come from?
   Where have they been?

These words within are like a certain spint
   Appearing and disappearing,

Coming from the depths of my soul
   They cannot wait,

For they are strong-willed, you see,
   Trying to escape, the master of my fate.

These words within, my words
   I'm glad they are here.

Catherine Frazier-Allison

Angels of Space

God be with you, Space Angels,
as you ascend into flight;

Your hearts beating wildly,
apprehensive with fright.

Piercing the Heavens
and territories unknown

Pilgrims of bravery,
your discoveries abound.

Know our hearts here on earth
go with you beyond

as He reached out to welcome you,
your earth missions done

Missions greater now waiting,
for it Be Thy Will,

for you Mike, Dick, Judy,
Ron, Christa, Greg, Ell.

Oh, heroes of mankind,
may you all know God's Grace

Pilgrims of bravery,
Angels of Space.

Judy Schmidt Herbst

The Perfect Rose

I think it's only God who knows the living
beauty of This Rose.
Whose lovely petals were so pressed for
all my guilt and sinfulness.
Whose blood was shed on Calvary's hill;
He is the Rose of Sharon stll.
His sweetest fragrance fills the air,
   breathes grace and mercy everywhere.
What Wondrous Rose so fair, so pure
   blooms in my heart-salvation sure.
Such splendor, beauty glory rare
   excites my soul His love to share.

Such worship, praise and joy of heart
   His faithful promise n'er depart.
Touched by His grace — God only knows
   my deepest love for this His Rose.
This song of love and honor goes
   to this Majestic, Perfect Rose.

Amazing Graze, Redeeming Love
   yearns for your heart in Heaven above.
The Way, the Truth, the Life is He;
   Repent, believe, His child you'll be.
Lord, Saviour, Priest and King 'tis true-
   This Perfect Rose died just for you.
      Jesus — The Perfect Rose.

Bessie Evers Gooch

My Indian Heritage

Fe Fi Fo Fum, I hear the beat of an Indian drum
Calling me from far away, another place,
another day.
Genes I carry of ancestors from the past
Are manifesting themselves at last.
As I think of them, I heave a sigh
When I remember those days gone by.

The Indian was treated with shame
And I often think I can feel his pain
As he was chased from place to place
Because of the greed of the pale-face.

I have always had a soft spot in my heart
For those wonderful people who had such a part
In forming the history of this beautiful land.
My heart aches for the sorrow and pain
Brought to them again and again
By the thoughtless treatment of the white man.

I am proud of the Indian heritage my
Great-Grandmother gave to me,
Yet, I don't think I would like living in a teepee.

Ruth Mills Grant

"Party-Party"

Party, party, out 'til three
Celebrate your victory
Dance and babble all night long
Soft-shoe steppin' high on song.
Don't do drugs don't do crime
Feast on winning dine on "fine"
Dance on ceiling prance on stair
Shake-twist body whirligig hair
Party, party, out 'til three
Celebrate your victory.

Katherine Meris

Untitled

As the souls touch one another, they
can not feel the warm embrace.
There is a wall they can not grasp for
is not the time nor the place.
As winter rushes in to fill the empty
space, there is a place in eithers heart,
that shall remain untouched, not even
filled by grave.
There is a time when both shall part,
for their love was not meant to be.
The thought though hard to come by.
Both shall clearly see, united they shall
never be.
Only memories of the heart shall warm
his pious face, and the fight will end,
as the cold story eats at him. He shall
on imagine her sympathetic embrace.

Tracy Joyce

Numen

There is a quality in music that
cannot be named by man, eluding to
Immortal planes where melody and thought
are one, where every biding strain construes a
concept more exact than simple sound.
What is it that in music causes kings
to weep and babes to let scorned sleep surround
their hearts and minds?
 And why, when robins sing does
Spring return with eager haste to brush
a shaded winter scene with songs of brighter hue?
 And why did Heaven cease its hush
when Christ was born, all darkness to deter?
There is a power lies in music that
no dark, no light, no mortal can combat.

Rebecca McGovern

911

I don't want the sad times, the bad times
Daddy please stay away
Mommy's out of the hospital and we're okay
I begged her, please mommy
don't let him come home

Too Late...too late...Someone call 911
Mommy where are you, please come home
In the dark my voice whimpered...impossible
Daddy cut her to the bone

Now mommy's in heaven, daddy's in jail
And I'm in foster care
Who can I call, who can I tell
How can I make you aware

That children should be loved and nurtured
Not abused and abandoned to a strangers care
Do you the parents not realize
That we the children are the future

How desolate I feel
Can you not nurture me, care for me
Are you deaf, dumb and blind
Can no one read the tragedy in my mind

Sharon von Micks

Untitled

When I see you
falling or in pain
I help you with
all I've got.
When I see you
crying and in shame
I help pick you up.
When I see you
reach your goals
I'm happy;
and for you
I stand up.

Casey D. Wilkinson

Feathered Song

Stay you silent as you are,
Far and lofty as a star,
I should ever lift my eyes
Bearing love that never dies
To your frozen, gleaming throne
Which you wish to hold alone.

Will your winter hold out long
'Gainst my thrilling, lilting song?

Rise you farther up above,
After you, on wings of love,
Rings my voice to melt your heart,
Pierce it with Love's flaming dart
That in fluttering pain you fall,
Waiting for my rousing call.

Would you die whilst you could hear
Love's sweet voices in your ear?

Gloria Socrates-San Agustin

White

White is a puffy cloud
Floating in an endless sky
White is a crystal ball
White is a thin piece of paper
waiting to be written on.
White is a ghost on Halloween
Frightening young children away
White is a picture in your mind
a calm feeling in your hollow head.
White is a heavy mist rising
out of a graveyard.
White is the color of heaven
and the color of an old man's beard
who is waiting to die.

Erich Kahner

Untitled

His face is gone,
Forever and back.
His few belongings,
Preserved in a sack.
The pictures hurt,
More than I can explain.
Why can't anyone,
Understand my pain?
His body was alive,
Yet dying inside.
Nobody knows,
How much I've cried.
They think it's funny,
Like some big joke.
But they don't understand,
How my heart broke.

Melody Hartke

Nurture

By whose volition are my seeds sown.
For my hands remain untarnished -
immaculate and gentle
Within nature's bed.

Still, to entrust growth in seasoned fields,
As my virgin earth pleads?

I know what care is required!
What direction to cast!
But voracious beasts -
or tainted light,
In time they will vanish.

For your hands hold too tightly
To tend eternal gardens.

Relentlessly clutched,
We may never bloom.

Randall O. Hamilton

Portraits

Borrowed relatives
From the antique store
Decorate walls.

Formal attire
High-necked apparel
Are carefully arranged.

Personal gazes and
Intimate glimpses
Tell of wistful remembrances.

The frozen images
Capture the
Untold stories.

A portrait
Belongs in an album
Not sold in a store.

Colleen Hansen

Messy

Juice from a lemon, juice from a lime
Ground carrots, onions, sage, and thyme,
Moldy cheese spread, covered with dirt,
I guess it's time to change my shirt.

Stepped on berries and their leaves,
Sap that dropped down from the trees,
Old honey that is crawling with ants,
It may be time to change my pants.

Tomato juice that was spilled on the floor,
Purple gum that was stuck to the door,
All kinds of mold, gray-green and blue,
It's probably time to change my shoes.

I'm in this state, it's really true!
Gray-green and purple, red and blue.
I think you'll agree its probably best
To tell me that I am a mess!

Ingrid Sakrison

War

Anger, destroy
 Weapons, deploy
 Enemy, dies
 Family, cries
 Hurt, pain
 Victory, shame
 Question, why
 Living, lie...

Mark Spencer

A Song Of Melody

With joy I sing a song to you.
It rings within my heart so true.

With a melody of ultimate peace,
my life responds to sweet relief.

The pain I struggled with was so hard to bear,
but love released the burden of despair.

This song rings continually: it will never depart,
it is deep within the corridors of my heart.

Frankie L. Smith

"I Am"

I am a kind and fun loving person.
I wonder what life would be like in the year 2000.
I hear the cries for help from young
women and children.
I see a Leprechaun hiding his pot of gold.
I want to stop all the violence and drug abuse.
I am a kind and fun loving person.

I pretend to be older than I really am.
I feel the desperation of starving and
homeless children.
I touch the sky wishing for world peace.
I worry about the future of the world.
I cry for the homeless, starving, and
battered children.
I am a kind and fun loving person.

I understand that no one is perfect.
I say all races are equal.
I dream all of the wars would end.
I try to get along better with my siblings.
I hope all of the fighting would stop.
I am a kind and fun loving person.

Nicki Jo Agro

The Pain Inside

The pain inside, the pain I hide,
I feel it in the inner me.
The me that people cannot see.
I cover it with happy smiles and silly frowns
that I carry mile after mile.
When I am alone, I shed a tear, a tear
full of sorrow, a tear full of fear.
The fear of not knowing what's next?
Not knowing what to expect, not knowing
if I am too early, not knowing if I
am too late. But until I know, I'll
just have to wait, wait until that
special date, wait until I have
no more tears, scary thoughts,
dreadful fears, that I carry year
after endless year. I am not the
same person, that's the sad part.
All I have left is two pieces
of a broken heart.

Jennifer Power

Uhh, That Feel

Hellen I would love to whisper;
    sweet nothings into your lovely ears.
And oh, how I would like to kiss you;
    like a fire that's hot.
Each tantalizing lick shaking me
    even more.
Until one moment I am playing,
    you like an organ.

Marc Roberre

Moving

Some have it down to an art and
others just don't know where to start.

The closets? What a clutter.
It takes an excavation expedition
for the finishing rendition.

And at the end your carefully
stored possessions become the
tax deductible property of
the Salvation Army's Non-Profit
Organization.

Ivet Perez

Rain

Heat without movement, still and bright
Grass burnt brown and curled up tight

The air smells of dust and things dry
Everything lingers under the clear sky

The hush is patient and long has been the wait
Without moisture soon, for much it will be too late

Something is different, it has a smell
Moisture is a tease and only time will tell

The air makes a move, ever so slight
The sun still bakes everything in sight

The scent is real and ever so sweet
The move is now a breeze shifting the heat

So small and so precious, it is the first drop
Hope consumes all, will it continue or stop

The brightness dims and then a streak of light
A splitting crack then rumbles from great heights

Rain is here in torrents and with a great rush
Replenishing those who had waited with
    patience and trust

Howard M. McCain

Appreciation

Hospitable.
How
You made me feel -
So comfortable
Like a meadow walk
on a just-right summer's day.

The worries pause
And realize
They're not so important
And they stop clambering for my atten-
tion.

The mad pace
Pauses
And while there remembers
What the goal was
in the first place.

All because
You are so
Hospitable.
You make me feel so welcome here.

And I thank you for this space to simply be.

Wrennie N. Warren

I Dare To Discover To See Beyond...

To see beyond myself
how I can explore the world
how far I can go
where I can travel on the path unwinding

To be the best I can be
how I can be it.

To see what is in my heart
how it feels to be proud of myself.

Each time I think of something new
the Earth shakes for my love and affection.

Each time I see snow fall
I feel a twinkle in my eyes.

I DARE TO DISCOVER WHAT IS BEYOND.

Erin Weimer

Vision Of Beauty

The day is done, the night is near
I close my eyes to sleep
I wish I could hold her
But my thoughts are what I keep

Her beauty is always there
To her it is so unknown
She gives love from her touch
For no one to be alone

She's more than just a woman
She's one who is always giving
My life without her goes to empty
A life simply worth not living

She begins to walk away
I feel as though I've died
My God I feel I'm losing her
I wake up and she's by my side

Frank V. Grieco

Life Eternal

Oh child of my love
I give to thee without end
Whatever your heart should want
Whatever aid my aged body can lend
What time I have in this mortal attire
My eternal soul when my life expires

Child of my dreams
Your potential is without bounds
Whatever the road you might choose
Whatever cause you may of found
You cannot help but to succeed
In making mankind a better breed

Child of my hopes
My immortality rests in your hands
Those ideals I hold most sacred
I hope you come to understand
For long after I'm gone and forgot
In you I shall live in what I've taught.

Henry Skvzypkowski

My Garden

God gave me a beautiful garden,
I was too busy to enjoy the garden.

I did this and that from dawn to dusk,
I saw nothing else but my own task.

Then one day I felt really sick,
I could not do much at my desk.

I opened the curtain of my window,
I could see flowers in the meadow.

As one flower would be a Heaven,
My garden should be an Eden.

In the worldly hot pursuit I lost my Garden;
In a quiet wonderment I found my Eden.

I do thank God for my garden,
The once lost but now found Eden.

Micah W. M. Leo

Underneath The Skin

Love comes from underneath the skin
In a place we call the heart.
Always we must look from within
So as to never drift apart.
Disparaging comments and nasty looks
We can never let them take their toll
Two halves once not together
Now in marriage we are whole.
From a calm, colorless sea
Emerges a storm quite great
Protests of black
Ignorance of white
Both reap and sew their festered hate.
I ask myself will the day ever come when
I feel the hate no more
Only now to gaze in our own child's eyes,
wondering what life has yet in store.

Melissa Amatulli-Crain

"A Child's Vision"

I lay upon my bed to sleep,
in a tent grown old and worn.
I could not help but sigh and weep;
my heart was so forlorn.

Tomorrow I must go away,
from the parents I held so dear;
for they upon their sick bed lay,
and could not calm my fear.

With brothers, I must go and stay,
with people strange and new.
I knew not then, how long 'twould be;
but the days would not be few.

As I lay upon my bed,
fearing the unknown,
to my breaking heart and fear filled head;

A moonbeam streamed down through a hole,
and my aching heart restored.
It eased the pain of my lonely soul;
for there, was Christ our Lord!

Barbara J. Benson

Loneliness

Loneliness holds me
in its empty arms.

It speaks to me
with its silent voice.

It draws me deep within
a hollow place of darkness.

Clutching me tighter and tighter,
I cannot escape its grasp.

It suffocates me
with its dark cloak.

I feel myself falling
deeper and deeper into its silent emptiness.

Cynthia Soliz

Life

Footprints
  in the sand of Life.

Memories
  of times that once were,
  but can never be again.

Wilted flowers
  telling of dreams that
  came true.

A broken mirror
  reflecting life's horrors.

A rainbow
  giving hope
  and promises for tomorrow.

A pillow for a casket;
  Rest for the Weary.

Debora H. Leonard

A Friend

A friend is one you can count on
In times when you are down.

A friend is one who deeply cares
And will be there to share your fears.

A friend is always true to you
No matter what you are going through.

A friend sticks by your side
And will not shy away your sigh.

A friend does not put you down
Even though at times you may do wrong.

A friend will guide you along the way
So you will not go astray.

A friend brings laughter to your heart
And is sure to make you feel glad.

A friend is always eager to believe the best
And is never ready to expose the worst.

A friend will help share the bad times
And will love you at all times.

A friend in deed
Is a friend we all need.

Veronica Phillips

S.P.C.A.

My love of freedom
is still in my heart.
I feel the rhythm
and I hear a hum.
But now I am restricted.
Swishing my tail,
hoping to be found,
Sitting on a paper bed.
I've been here for a whole year,
and not more than a glance
has ever been sent my way.
No-one wants an old hound.
The man in the white coat,
fiddling with his ring of keys,
and opening my cage,
drags me by my fur coat.
"Let's go for a walk," he says.
So we go down than hall,
his footsteps, echoing around me.
My bed will be empty tonight...

Chrissy Sittig

Abraded Hope

What keeps him from that misty death,
is time; days of which he claws his way,
reaching for his life.
There is no place to hide at all,
for death shan't be denied.

And as he waits this fortnight's hell,
all else remains the same, unchanged.
When each night the stars flash by,
he can feel it come - the angst,
as sure as the birds, they fly,

And if he sings, it is real low,
for these walls echo greatly the sound,
of a grown man weeping; tired and
morose,
awaiting time to wind down.
They know not what they chose.

Mark A. Robertson

Rae

A beautiful smile;
Large pretty eyes.
Soft skin to the touch,
A wonderful mother of mine.
Now you are older;
With problems of your own,
I find my own arm around you,
Guiding the loved one that I knew.
Helping the lady that I know.
I love you Rae;
Until your dying day.
May I bless you,
With God's love.
Upon my lips I pray.

Janice A. Steinberg

Where?

The Gnomes and the Pixies,
live in Mushroom land.
Where mother nature watches,
and lends a hand.

The Unicorns and Dragons,
aren't that far away.
Just over the mystical mountains,
in the Enchanted Bay.

There is a wizard, who lives
not to far.
Just down by the river, then
towards the North star.

The Dwarves and the Elves all
live together, and the
Sorceress on the mountain
commands the weather.

This is the place that I belong,
since my Father was the last
Leprechaun.

Garrett Nelson

"Gazing Toward Heaven"

As I gaze toward the heavens
looking for God's face,
I'm searching for an answer
that has put me in this place.

With struggles before me
and triumphs behind,
I know that with God's help
the answer I will find.

God is always faithful
and is looking after me,
even when His plan
is something I don't see.

I know that it is written
that all things work for good,
so I'm trusting in the Lord
the way I know I should.

When this battle's over
and another war begins,
I'm know that God is with me,
and I will surely win!

Annette Pitts

Use "Me"

Lord, I give this day to You...
    May I be pleasing in all I do.
Guide my thoughts, words and deeds,
    Let me help... someone in need!

There are those that are without hope
    Who've never MET Thy holy Son.
Oh help me listen well, and obey...
    Lord, let me PLANT a seed today!

Use "me"... Lord, to work for You...
    Let Your light shine through me.
My desire only, is that through grace
    OTHERS will today... seek Thy face!

Then thru faith, their victory won -
    And salvation's a gift of Thy son
Oh may they never, never stray...
    Oh, Lord... from... Thy holy way!

Ruth Emily Newman

Tears and Pain

The tears I cry, are caused by pain,
    My life has been violated,
With fear and shame.

Nights I cry, not knowing why,
    My heart aches,
With tears and pain.

Others see my loving smile,
    Not seeing the hurt,
That I've had for a while

My life is in a turmoil,
    From flashbacks and memories
My life is not the same,
    I'm going insane.

LORD, give me strength, and make me whole,
    And LORD, deliver me from,
The tears I hold.

Linda George

"Turn On The Lights"

Turn on the lights of my heart,
My lover and I are torn apart,
I have given all and received small.
Turn on the lights of my heart,
I feel alone, hurt and in the dark.
I have tried to forget, but the memories
    won't let me quit.
My love is so deep, it is for real,
    forever and for keeps.

Turn on the lights of my heart,
So that I may see another road, and shed
    these painful memories, and this heavy load.
Turn on the lights of my heart,
so that I can make a brand new start.
My heart is imprisoned, in chains and pain,
    bound by this one love.
Release, release, let me go, so that I might
    see what the future holds for me.
Please, turn on the lights of my heart.

Thepencia McNeil

Untitled

Smile even when your heart is broken...
No one can hear words not spoken.
Cry when you are alone...
It is a long journey not letting
feelings known.
Patch your heart daily, it is a throne...
It knows the torment of life all alone.
Shackle the heartache and hide the key...
How soon again we are brought to our knees.
Turn your head from the ignorance and all
the hurting things people say....
Does it really matter? Just walk away.

Connie Gilmore

Not Much Time

As the birds fly by, by the minute
    The butterfly's flutter until dawn
    The flowers bloom in the morning,
    and the petals wilt at dawn
    from the blazing sun
    Not much time for you and me
    The winter, spring, summer, and
    fall
No time at all

Kathleen Schoefer

My Special Love

I'm sure I've had a special love
Not many's had the same
If never more I see your face
Alone I had became

I'd know I've had the fullness
The gift from God above
Of life's most special treasure
I've had a special love.

A lot of people seek for it
Through all of life they look
It's something rather rare they say
Like some old care, worn book.

For many years I never knew
The gift from God was mine
Yet like a book, it takes the years
To finally be fine.

I'm sure I've had that special love
The love that ne'er grows old
That year by year with tender care
Grows stronger, dear and bold.

Mildred Kelley

To

Her whose gentle voice did ring
Of painted flowers in the spring
And to my heart did swiftly bring
Mem'ries of the dawn

Away she flew on wings of rain
Echoing my silent pain
Alas! to be alive again
I wish my soul to be

The sunshine of her tumultuous hair
A flowing chaos in the air
A radiant, soulful, brilliant glare
But now these days are gone

So here I sit at last reclining
For her soft hand and warm heart pining
Like a star her soul left shining
Into the distant sun

And thus upon the blackened shore
Remembering bygone days of yore
Her laughter to echo no more
And I am left alone

Jeremy T. Glover

Us?

We've been together for 10 years
or so for a good reason you won't
let me go. I'll admit it's not easy
we do have a son. The imprisonment
I feel in my heart is not fun.
I love you dearly to this very day
but my wanting to leave just won't
go away. I can forgive you for the
physical abuse, the way hurt me most
is saying I have no use. I know
how deep and boundless I am
heart and soul. My limitless
potential to the world I'll show
and nothing will stop me from
reaching my goal. When I'm on
top of the world where I was
meant to be. I don't really
know if I'll want you with me.

Rachel Smith

My Family

My husband and my sons have brought
The kind of love that I have sought.
Today I am so glad to see
The joys of you, my family.

Whene'er I feel the least bit blue,
I only have to think of you,
To know that life is still worth all
The ups and downs with its pitfalls.

You've given me the kind of home
So that I'll never have to roam.
My hopes and dreams securely set;
I'm settled in with no regrets.

For you, my loves, I live and breathe;
I find my utmost is achieved.
When working or playing for you I strive
To give you back the joys I've derived.

My husband, my sons, I see as One,
One complete and total sum,
For whom I want to always show
My life is lived your love to know.

Brenda R. Fullerton

Today

If I were an angel,
tell me where I'd have to fly

If I were a page in time
in which sentence would I die?

For do you think that all you see
is here but for today
In small men's minds
the waves of time
Chase all they fear away

For those who live each day as if it were their last,
Redeem a peace of mind
For the shadows they have cast
On their hearts and their souls
the scars no longer heal
The raven calls, the white dove falls,
the truth is no longer real
But here today I do stand
to face all that will arise
Turn the page, tell me my love,
in which sentence will I die?

Jill M. Spillett

The Web

Have you ever watched a spider
Spin its web?
How the finest threads are used—
The symmetry of line complete
As he passes round and round,
Pausing here to secure a thread
Before he takes
A leap — with gossamer line
Right over the flower bed —
Alights on the leaf of a chrysanthemum
Whose flowers are golden and high,
Transmit their glorious rays of sun
On the silken thread,
That the spider spins
So fine ————

Juhli T. Bonn

Untitled

As darkness comes to rule the night
Shadows dance in the dim moonlight
Of angels of demons I do not know
For this love has taken a piece of my soul
What spell she had on me I can't explain
For on my heart I carry scars of sorrow and pain
And as I lay my head to sleep
Memories of the past slowly creep
And as the night passes by
My screams echo throughout the sky
To be written in the realm of time
Of loves greatest crime
Sometimes I wonder if
I should stand and fight, or just
Walk away
And let her demons have their way
For nothings really what it seems
When you live your life in such a dream
Now night has broken, becomes the day
And in my mind she fades away

Anthony Weygandt

"My Son, Close To Me"

Oh my son, my first born,
So little and small was thee.
When they first laid you in my arms,
I cradled thy head to me.

And when you were just a little boy,
And fell and skinned your knees,
I kissed those tiny little hands,
And drew you close to me.

When you grew to manhood,
And moved so far from me.
My thoughts were with you daily,
And I know you thought of me.

And now my son, God has called you,
To "Come up hither" to be with thee.
And though I don't understand it,
I'll see you one day indeed.
And then you'll always,
continuously be forever, close to me.

Wanda Kay Wright

"I Am As You"

Lakes water holding deeply within,
    quenching life's thirst.
Streams flowing and glowing in the wild,
  I am as you!
Trees shading places and faces
    silently saying;
Spend a few moments with me,
    I need your company, I am as you!
I am strong and seem aloof but I am
    fragile within; I am as you!
We are all in kinds, in beauty and
    purpose.
I am as you, in human reality.

Linda Hager

"For The Moment"

  If I had a moment
to make a wish come true.
I would wish for someone as loving as you.
  With trust and honesty and all that's fair.
  I would hope that you
will always be there.

Geri Cennimo

Little Girl

You can't have him.
Tall with blonde hair and blue eyes.
He's a savior little girl.
Don't even think about him that way.
You shouldn't hurt yourself and talk to him.
If you wanna try to get him,
Get in line little girl.
What makes you think you could?
Did his eyes make you cry?
Stop yearning little girl.
He could have any woman he wants.
What makes you so special?
Do you believe he thinks about you
    and your imperfections little girl?
You think he's perfect,
    he doesn't even think about you.
He may talk to you
    but don't let it go to your head.
Your just a little speck in a big man's
    world little girl.

Michelle Verdon

A Note To Me

You look for honesty but do not trust;
Seek out love but settle for lust.
Expect compassion while bearing a grudge,
Ask for opinions but will not budge.
Pursue freedoms with lock and key;
Search for God without bended knee.

Stupid human, can't you see?
You look for freedoms, but will not free.
You ask your questions, then close your ears...
You're the only one you want to hear!

Stupid human, don't be mad;
It's no wonder that you're sad.
It's always the things, that you don't see...
That are resolved so easily.

Cindy Tkach

The Shadowlands

Another night I lurk in the shadowlands;
  The shadows of regret for what might have been.
It seems like no man understands
  The vast depression I am in.

Shadows haunt me from the past;
  The things I wish I would have done.
Now my numbered days are in overcast
  That yesterday can't be undone.

Shadows haunt me of the future;
  The things I'll never do or know.
It scares me that I won't endure
  To live to see tomorrow.

Now no more lurking in the shadowlands;
  My time has come to accept the blow.
Yet I fear less now as I disband
  To know we are but dust and shadow.

Eric S. Smith

Life's Death

Empty quagmire world of disillusion,
where all tangible possibilities
are dependent on possibilities.
To never exist, except to wait and see
if what you live
you had in fact chosen
or washed up beside you somehow.

Silvia Kindl

A Mother's Cry

It's a boy! It's a boy, the doctor said.
Precious little baby boy I said.
So big and strong and healthy too.
I'll protect you and love you through and through.
She watched him grow from boy to man.
You'll always be my baby, one day you'll
    understand.

My baby, my boy
My world, my joy.
I remember the years and hold back the tears.
You were taken away without any warning.
Early one wednesday morning.
I still expect to see you come through the door.
But I must realize this will be no more.

My baby, my boy.
My world, my joy.
Now I can't see beyond the tears
And I remember all the years I cared for
    you and loved you so.
Oh why oh why did you have to go?
This way, this time, this day, this year.

It's a boy! It's a boy the doctor said.
Precious little baby boy, I said.

Rita Shields

Untitled

I sat on the cold, hard three legged stool
the tall table in front of me,
the mound of clay
sat on the white paper plate
lifeless and dull, like a loaf of bread
waiting to be woken up and taken
to another time and place
when it was alive and well.
But clay you think
does not live like me,
but it does.
I need to create a beautiful
master piece with my clay
and I do.
I create a redwood tree
a giver of life,
because I am something
so I create.

Lisa Marie La Plant

Just For Me

Why are they hanging on my wall-
    their life-size yellow roundness
    opening to dark centers,
    depths I still can't penetrate
With glossy petals of sun filled color
    brighter than their background world
    and textured edge deceiving.

I can almost imagine if I try...
 I'm in a field and want to pick one out of paint.

But no,
I'll save them
Let them grow
    his art, my sunflowers
    inside myself.

I wonder- did he paint more just like these?
But I know he gave this one to me.

Mary Franc

Horizon

This old earth is spinning pretty fast
we want to make each day last and last
but the future comes quick and soon is the past
occasionally remembering
this old earth is spinning pretty fast
when the stars are out late at night
we pause and loose a little sight
and while sleep time slips away
then by the bright light of day
the morning sun through the window cast.
Occasionally remembering
this old earth is spinning pretty fast.
We jump from one age and stage to the next
we love to eat and sometime we fast
while hoping our fortunes to be vast
occasionally remembering
this old earth is spinning pretty fast.

Edward D. Valdez

If

If I were yours I'd learn to find
    the rainbow thru the clouds.

If I were yours I'd see the sun, the grass,
    the trees and flowers.

If I were yours, birds would sing more sweetly
    with each dawn; and every wave
    upon the shore would echo on and on.

If I were yours I'd learn to love
    now and evermore and with each breath I'd
    learn to live better than before.

If I were yours true peace I'd find, and with it
    I would bring, all the hope and all the joy
    and love you give to me.

To you I'd give all these things
    and hopefully much more.

If I were yours I'd love you true
    now and evermore.

Mary A. Blair

In Eo

Peace until the midnight hour
when St. Paul grows angelic flowers
while earthly beasts round the land scour
seeking whom they may devour.

Slowly move the hands of thyme
and still the second hand is myne,
and still the hands spin rainbow band
placing Venus on the stand,
the golden crown of morning planned,
like games of Puck
and pipes of Pan,
elusive vapors tame the pride of man.

And prayers of Paul bring peace to power
while adding bricks to Babel's tower
causing beasts below to cower;
    final bows
    to final bower...

Patzi Kozlakowski

The Setting Sun

A fiery ball of blinding light
We all named it the SUN,
It streaks along before the night
When it's day's work is done,

In haste it sinks beneath the deep
From those who watch it set,
It leaves treasures for us to keep
One not so many get.

The scenes produced by light and cloud,
What beauty to behold,
Almost they'll make you shout aloud
Watching such wonders all unfold.

It hastens to another land
To rise to start another day,
It demonstrates the MASTER'S HAND
Burning the earth with scorching ray.
As if to leave a gift behind,
The waiting clouds stood in it's path,
What light and scattered clouds combined
Can even silence our wrath.

Seymour Palmer

Now And Then

Reflections lace through misty eyes
where those I knew appear
a treasured haven safe from time
for dreams and joyful tear

Long I beckon to behold their voice
and feel their caring touch
to share once more an I love you
with those who meant so much

No more beauty he created
than the warmth within their heart
the bonding ember etched by faith
so that never more we part

As autumn sheds her joys of life
petals such are we
called home with him to blossom
who once he shared with me

Forever now they grow for thee
flowers without end
a bouquet of memories yet remains
I love you now...and then

Michael Soroka

Stars

To gaze upon hopeful dreams
To make a wish in a cool, crisp breeze
To search for an answer you cannot find
To catch up where you fell behind
To laugh at all the mistakes
To cry about your last heartbreak
To create a new beginning
To build a life with sacred meaning
To escape the harshness of reality
To feel your pride and dignity
To believe in yourself and your goals
To free your isolated soul

Julie Swaim

Nature's Magical Moments

What do we see in the bright shining Sea?
    Reflections of beauty for you and for me.
What do we see when we rise at the dawn
    On a cold Winter morn looking out on the lawn?
'Tis a beautiful blanket of crystal white Snow
    With fresh little tracks, where did those Bunnies go?
As we gaze up the Valley at the dazzling Sun
    We're reminded of Jack Frost with his paintings all done.
While he rests and prepares for his next busy shift
    His fine etchings we treasure, oh my what a gift!
And what do we see after Winter is o'er?
    Mother Nature's achievements right at our back door.
Blooming buds on the Tulips, sprouting Leaves on the Trees
    Coaxing Spring to return with its' sweet balmy breeze.
Then what do we see on a hot Summer day?
    Farmers gathering Hay and the children at play.
What do we see on a gorgeous Fall morn?
    Magnificent hues......Thank God we were born
To enjoy God's creation, an original art
    We count all our blessings of which we're a part!

Betty Ann MacPhetridge

In the Winter

In the winter,
the tall oaks are bare.
Exposed, to the cold and the snow,
they are an open book to the world.
Oaks are not like pine, those who hide
their defects.
An Oak by nature - shows all.

I was looking out my frosted window and
I saw old man winter.
The oak trees are bare, but the pines
don't care!
It seems peaceful outside, hiding the cold
from my eye.
Curious, I step outside.
Is old man winter...
Just...
Cold in my mind?

David Makowski

Mommy, Mommy Please Don't Go

Mommy, Mommy, please don't go,
stay a little longer and watch my show.
Kisses on the cheek and a wave good-bye,
off to work with a tear in my eye.

Most of my friends children are grown,
but mine I'm afraid are home alone
Responsibility beacons here and there
and choices to be made for my ones so dear.

Beaming little eyes on innocence fed
and everytime I leave is the time I dread.
Daddy's not around to tuck them in at night,
never there to hold them during a stormy fright.

Now Mommy has to leave to work another job,
I see understanding eyes, but tearful sobs.
Mommy, Mommy, why do you work so hard,
you're minutes away, but it seems so far.

Children, I don't have an answer for you this time,
be patient, Mommy loves you, and we'll be fine.
I promise you: Someday I won't work as hard as I do,
and I'll be home, loving, spending time with you.

Shirley Johnson

Anniversary Poem

We're gathered here together on this very special day
to celebrate the love you share in your very special way.
It must seem like so long ago when you first said "I do",
your hearts were young, smiles were bright, and love was so brand new.
That day began your lives as one to share, to hope, to dream.
To endure all that love would impart and all things in between.
The children you were blessed with, they filled your happy home.
Life just couldn't get much better, now you'd never be alone.
Through trials and tribulations together you would stand.
Never letting things divide you, or questioning God's plan.
Now here you are - you've made it - fifty years gone by.
You've shown us by example ..... true love will never die.

Kathy Rea

Grandpa

Holding Grandpa's hand, one last time,
The warmth and strength, still there,
His eyes were closed, his breathing light
Yet, he squeezed our hands, to show his care.

Tears filled the eyes of the family in the room,
We watched as his life peacefully faded away;
Goodbyes and I love you's filled the silent air,
To see him at peace, no one begged him to stay.

Years of memories passed through each mind,
Bits of laughter, mixed with tears.
The love and pride for his family was known,
An honorable man, to so many, through his years.

Quietly he left us, his hands still gripping ours,
But somehow when his heartbeat was gone,
A warmth filled the room, drying my tears.
Death to grandpa came quickly, as he wanted all along.

Sure I'll miss my Grandpa's Head, very much;
He's been a big part of my life -
He left the struggles and pains that came with age
Yet, he left us his wonderful wife.

Brenda Head Lasch

Life As Lived

I saw a field of tiger lilies
They stood straight and laughed in the bright sun.
I was six it made me a cockeyed optimist
At eight I was allowed to punch down the weekly bread dough.
At fourteen I realized that there were darker sides of life.
At eighteen I started life, love in Marriage with great hopes.
Then there was the war; five hearts to watch and wait for.
When I was twenty one I lost the hope and part of my heart.
I lost a baby boy. He died.
Another beginning, another love, two beautiful daughters as rewards.
At forty three a miracle son; my cup runneth over.
At forty six I lost my love. He died.
Now I'm seventy two, I grow tiger lilies;
They stand straight and laugh in the bright sun.

Letha Elizabeth Hadady

Spring Morning

Blossoms rest on emerald beds wrapped in silvery dew.
Fragrance fills the air of Spring quickening all anew.
Winter packs away the chill to return another day.
Music now invades the morn in feathery array.

Sunlight lifts the morning mist on silent, amber wings.
A quiet pond reveals a loon adrift on gentle rings.
Creature sounds embellish every corner of the glade.
Rendering a symphony in sunlight and in shade.

Sue A. Murray

Bonnie Rae

Bonnie Rae was a young girl,
Hair of auburn and eyes of brown.
She was just a tomboy, who made life full of joy.
Bonnie Rae was a young girl, when God took her that day,
Awards she hadn't seen, and the years of being a teen.
She showed me one day, how to jitterbug the time away.
Her love of Elvis and Johnny Ray, I laugh to this day.
My sister, I remember our times of yesteryear,
But now, your an angle in the clouds.
The year 1958, and the summer had just begun,
Why did God take you before our fun was done?
Bonnie Rae, my sister, I miss you everyday!

Jane Grodi

The Dance Of The Banshees

It was the midnight dance of the Banshees.
They were having a loud riotous ball.
The pale moon was sailing above the trees.
There was much strutting by both big and small.

Someone would rear back her head and holler.
It was a bay to the sliding wolf-moon.
It soared on high full of fitful choler.
The wild crescendo made an eerie tune.

They did a wide sashay into a prance.
The deep throated howls and yowls were blended.
They jigged and yawed about in frenzied dance.
With elan that grew and never ended.

Higher and higher came the feral cries
As they swirled and dipped and spun about.
They were panting and sounding grunting sighs
Which dissolved into the next screaming shout.

They dance and wail as they shrieked of old
With never a thought of making amends.
Their keening cries will never lose their hold.
Hee-hee-hee. I don't care. These are my friends.

Frank Ducat

"Faith"

And the angel sat upon the rock, holding
tight his position; while his peers in frolic,
he wished he could play - but knew the then
would stray; losing his grip from the rock
of clay. Silently he mumbled words of faith,
knowledgeable of the only one truth. His heart
unfailing, his mind prevailing, his spirit
unveiling the havoc between angels of dark
and angels of light... and in his mind voices
of deceptive channel talk. Oh come play with me
come play with me - we'll have so much fun
in the untamed sea! No-stay on the rock,
the rock of clay, the angel of light continues
to say! The wisdom of truth and knowledge
is here on the rock, always with you willing
to stay. So hold tight to the rock - your
rock of clay, where the angel of light
continues to pray.

Denise M. Kelley

Little Puppy Dog

One day when I went out for a walk
To be by myself and to gather a thought
I saw a little puppy dog waiting at a gate
In hopes that his master would not be late

There he is coming down the street
He knew for sure that he would get a treat
His tail was wagging he could hardly wait
For his master to get up to the gate

Being so excited he could not be still
So he tried and tried using all his will
When his master got by his side
The little dog leaped with love and pride

The little dog jumped on his master's chest
This little dog knew his master was sure the best
He licked his face neck and ears
His master was so happy you could see his tears

This master loved his dog so much
Together they played and did things and such
So the little puppy stands at the gate
And hopes that his master will never be late

Tondalaya Lapthorn

Untitled

Come, come with me back in time
To that sunfilled happy close
Walk hand in hand down that leafy dappled lane
Hear the simple music once again
The wind sighing gently through the trees
The bird song wafted on the breeze
Hear the childrens laughter while at play
Oh! lovely, lovely day
Just wandering not wondering what lies ahead
Dreaming, thinking, words left unsaid
To speak would break this peaceful spell
Which of your thoughts would you care to tell
Never again will there be moments quite like these
Carefree, pleasant so much to please
The world's sounds muted seeming distant
Come with me, be not resistant
Oh! I know it is all in memory
But for a little while we can pretend, can't we?

Sylvia Elfman Classic

Sweet Mother

This is a poem to my mother, who is a sweet mother,
Whose love for me, remains a source of inspiration.
Oh!, my sweet mother,
When I was hungry, you gave me something to eat.
When I was sick, you prayed that I got well quick,
You spent sleepless nights, taking care of me,
You will not sleep, until you've lured me to sleep.
All that you did for me, will run pages.
Ebony black, mother you are beautiful,
You are sweet, sweet mother.
I cannot forget that early January morning,
When the cold hand of death, snatched you away from me,
You died,
When I needed you most,
Unwilling, you went to the world beyond.
So, I write this poem for love, for life, in memory,
As a tribute to you my dear sweet mother,
Who died nine years ago,
Struggling to educate me.
Sweet mother, the struggle continues.

Michael Nnaemeka Okonkwo

591

The Untangible

The unimaginable has happened
and oh what a blow is struck to the future stricken.

However no one knows
What the future holds
How quick or slow

The plot will thicken.
Oblivious are we to when it will arrive.

No woman, no man, or breach in plan
Can break its stride.
Reality is everyone's first love
And everyone's first heartbreak

Its mystery leaves you
Blind in mind, blind in sight:
To see how much more you can take.

The unimaginable has happened
and oh what a blow is struck to the future stricken.

However no one knows
How the future holds
Whichever way the winds blow,

The plot will surely thicken.

Myrah Torres

One of Those Days

Ever had one of those days when things don't
    go just right?
Well I had one and it gave me a fright!

Last week after my first patient
I thought I was going to get blown up!
The gas fumes in the truck cab were so
strong - I thought I was going to throw up!
So— I held my nose - put the window down,
drove to my second patient's house with a
frown - I thought to myself - this just isn't
right!!! I called my son and traded rigs
He said, "Gee Mom, your sure lucky that this
didn't blow!", the gas was certainly not
leaking slow!, but a steady stream, just under
the hood — we both know, that that wasn't good!
Well, I guess you'd call it my lucky day, the
problems all fixed and I'm on my way!!!!

Janet Frey

My Anger

From the halls of mind, to chambers of my heart
My anger consumes me; it's tearing me apart.

Eating away my emotions, feeding on my pain
Like a group of hungry buzzards tasting corpses in the rain.

The rain is tears falling from my eyes,
Everyone is dirty,cheap, and pack full of lies.

"Help!" My body screams at me.
"Help me, save me, set me free."

The hole is getting bigger, black and rotten to the core,
I'll take it no longer I'll take it no more.

Lying in white sheets, but blackened inside,
My pain, now evident, from doctors I cannot hide.

"Help me doctor, it hurts to cry,"
Now I need to ask myself, I need to wonder Why?

Eileen M. Casarez

To Maureen, With Keats' Poems

I cannot give you what some men can give
Gowns made of silk, glittering rings of gold,
And though I could, I wouldn't. Primitive
Is that which greedy men love to behold.
I cannot make to you the vows which warm
The coldest hearts. I cannot say "My Love,
You are so sweet that bees around you swarm
And angels fear they've lost you from above."
But what I give shines infinitely bright
When Sleep or thought have cast their silent spell;
When snow is falling on a Winter's night
But Summer's joy within you starts to swell;
Or when in Spring, you see a flower bloom
And think of Autumn dreaming up its doom.

Jamison Ashley Oughton

My Linda

Always caring always giving
Never wanting anything in return
Maybe all she needs is a little love
From someone that cares

Someone to hold her close to give her warmth
To care for her more than anyone should or could
Someone that could wait forever but should they
Wait till the end of time
Yes they could

She was beautiful when I met her at twenty
She was warm and tender at thirty
She was caring and understanding at forty
I hoped she would be my wife by forty five

Comme Ci, Comme Ca
As the french say whatever will be, will be

I should sweep her off her feet
and take her away
From all her hurts and problems
To live very happily ever after with me

My song for you my love
Some day our day will come

Kelsie R. Gates

Longings

Outside the winds of winter blow, how I long for mild
    breezes and the whispering willow.
To see lowland flowers blooming in wide, grassy hollows,
    bees sucking at honeysuckle, the black-winged swallows.
How I long for the summer to clothe the fields in rye,
    yellow cornfields waving to the sky.
And birds by rivers that glide along, and in words that
    echo their rapturous song.
Puffy clouds, like snowy, billowing sails, plying the
    skies o're hills and dales.
Happy reapers out early binding sheaves, the sun brightly
    shimmering through the trees.
How I long for the soft, unclouded night, of starry clusters
    shining bright.
Of summer shade and sunlight glowing, of green hill-tops
    and sea winds blowing.
Joyous skies where sunny pinions soar, a rainbow water-
    fall's surf-like roar.
Where no sorrowing clouds cry, the air ripples and sings,
    with warmth, dancing light, and swift-rushing wings.

Dee E. White

The Girl in the Mirror

Until we met, I never knew the girl in the mirror...
  Never thought she was pretty enough,
  strong enough,
  smart enough...

Then for a very brief time you came into my life...
  And you gave me the hope and courage
  to live,
  to love,
  to trust...

No one has ever touched my soul the way you did...
  Even through your sickness and pain you
  were strong,
  and gentle,
  and knowing...

You accepted me for who I was, no questions asked...
  And you forced me to do the same,
  wity love,
  with grace,
  with regard...

Dad....I wish you Godspeed, till we meet again, so long.

    Melody Smith

"Death Of A Friend"

The church hall was crowded with people you knew,
everyone was sad, some were crying too.
As the Minister said his last words of grief,
I looked at you lying there and began to weep.
I couldn't believe it was true,
I couldn't believe we were parting from you.

Tears filled my eyes
as I heard all my friends say their good-byes.
As I stood there in line,
memories of you went through my mind.
All the things we'd been through together,
and all the good times.

I knelt down on the step below,
and said good-bye, silent and slow.
As I reached over to touch your hand,
I said "I love you" once again.
Then next to your heart, I placed a red rose
and the tears came again
as the lid was closed.

    Karen McGlade Millett

Sliding Slam-Dunk Into Sixty

O - As my mother's newborn, I didn't know a sister, a
    brother, and sixty were coming.
10 - With friends, I was laughing, jumping rope, and chumming.
20 - I had finished high school, and was enrolled in college.
30 - Married, a B.A. Degree, and a parent of three, I
    was certainly adding to my knowledge.
40 - I began vengefully searching for the one who said,
    "They are fabulous years!'
50 - An M.S., two precious granddaughters, and a
    divorce, brought cheers and tears.
60 - Two delightful grandsons have arrived and I am
    busy counseling and teaching.
    Having slid, here I sit, slam-dunked, midst sixty helium
    balloons tied to cards. For the stars, I am still reaching.

    Peggy Lindley Ewing

She's Back And Safe — Again

She came home today, after an absent spree
From a disease her family tries faithful to see
Our daughter, our sister, our lovely Lea.

One day at a time, never two the same
Her troubled spirit she tries hard to tame

When very young, headstrong and so gullible
Her life before her leading only to trouble

Conduct that persisted through out the teen years
Drugs and alcohol continued our fears
Watching and waiting with worry and tears

No future, no peace, only constant running
An altered mind, unstable and cunning

While the devils persisted to rape her mind
And steal the peace she only knows a short time

Ever searching, but finding no place to go
Until a higher power intervenes with the foe

With constant vigilance and a family's love
Reaching and praying to the power above

That peace and serenity and love unfurl
Around our loved one, until we leave this world.

    Freda Hurley

When A Loved One Passes Away

The loss of a loved one is the most painful thing
anyone should have to face.
The sense of helplessness,
and the question, "Why?"
Which never seems to be answered completely.

The pain is physical, as well as emotional;
The arms that ache to hold someone,
The empty feeling inside,
The memories that are held so close,
To keep them from getting lost.

The memories of the times together;
Really, they're treasures that will always be there.
And the feelings when we notice something
Which would interest someone we still love,
"I've got to remember to tell you about this..."

I think they already know.

    Allcla Suenaga

Sleepless Nights!

Thinking at night, your eyes
wide open all night long can
really put a troubling feeling,
turning, tossing, sitting up
or even walking around with
your night clothes on, thinking
your problems be over. The
only way to handle them is do
what you have to do to clear
your mine. And sometimes
marcials do happen when you
believe in them, and most of
all be happy, your life we be
a lot stronger then you think,
sleep will things be okay you'll see.

    Shirley J. Courtorielle

Gates and Fences

Developing a relationship is a process not dissimilar to the task of building gates in a stone fence. The purpose of the gate is to allow access while preserving the security of the treasures within.

Gates, as the fences they bisect, come in a variety of styles and shapes. But in every case, the gates are constructed to swing freely swinging inward and outward. All gates can be closed and locked. Some gates are solid, while others allow for visibility even when they are not open for entry.

One gate is labeled trust, another is called honesty, while a third bears the name of constancy. Other gates are known as courage, sharing, and empathy. There are gates embossed with the titles of understanding, caring and acceptance. Some gates allow entrance to the past, some to the present, and still others lead to the future.

All gates are opened by the latch of communication and swing on the hinges of spiritual, emotional, social and physical values. The maintenance of the gates require gentle words and warm smiles with an occasional hug for good measure.

We've started to build a relationship. So far we have traveled through the gates of trust, honesty, empathy, and caring. There are still many portions of our mutual fences that remain closed, but the hope of future gates is strong. Thank you for being a friend, a companion, and a diligent gate builder.

Gerald D. Adams

The Booger Ballad

He was sitting in church with a problem, that nobody else could know.
He was extremely uncomfortable, there was a huge booger stuck in his nose. He wanted so badly to pick it, but somebody else might see.
For placing your finger up your nose in church would be far too disgusting. He placed a finger over his left nostril, and blew with all his might. Then that humongous booger came exploding out the right.

There was a woman in front of him, that wasn't even aware,
that the humongous booger had landed in her hair. He thought he oughta pick it out, before that booger dried. But when he missed and pulled her hair, the woman screamed and cried. Everybody turned around and saw that booger there. Then he felt responsible for that booger in her hair.

When he got home he felt so bad, he gave the woman a call.
But she was in the hospital, she had taken a nasty fall. For when she washed the booger out she stepped on it and slipped. She had fallen on her side, and broken her left hip. The next day he called to check up on her and much to his surprise, because of his big booger, an innocent lady died.

Scott Fleischer Nelson

High Flying Experience

Although I watched it flying, I could see it had no wings,
From a gust of wind it started rising, and a hand held ball of string.
As my father began to run, it kept rising ever higher.
I stood silently in awe, while thinking this was something to admire.
My father handed it to me, and told me to hold tight and run.
As I ran across the field, I remember smiling and having fun.
All at once the wind died down and the sun crept through the trees.
My flying friend came swooping down, like it had been stricken with disease.
I heard my father yell out to me to pull tightly on the cord.
Curiosity overwhelmed me and my father's orders went ignored.
On that day I watched it crash from where it flew so high.
Although I felt discouraged, dad just smiled and said "good try".
Even if it was not me up there, I still feel I touched the sky.
It gave me confidence to think that I, too, one day could fly.

Jason Klenetsky

Untitled

You have touched my heart.
You have touched my soul.
Tell me who you are.
Tell me what you are.
You have enriched my life.
You have indulged my lust.
Tell me where you are from
Tell me why you have come.
You have enlightened my spirit.
You have surrendered my essence.
Tell me how you have come to be.
Tell me when you are going to leave.

Linda Macleod

Myself

Myself is myself
Yourself is yours,
But don't you understand
Ourself is ours.

For in ourself
Is a self
Who knows ourself
Better than ourself.

For if ourself
Knew ourself,
There would be no need
For the self within ourself.

For the self within ourself
Is helping ourself
Follow that self
And you will find
Yourself.

Mark D. Howard

The Death Penalty And Willie Francis

The memories haunt you day and night
Your head was shaved, your body
    strapped down
The collage of faces all around.
The switch was pulled, your body lurched
But something went wrong - you did not die.

Your poor father contacted an attorney to help you.
Over the coming year he will go to many
    courts on your behalf.
But you will again be condemned to die
For a crime you may not have committed.
Is this not cruel and unusual punishment?
Double jeopardy?
Punished twice for the same offense?

It's Louisiana in 1947.
Does it matter that you are poor and black?
Newspapers say you are illiterate.
But you can read and write.
Does demeaning you justify the act?

Again you are facing the spectre of death
Knowing full well the grim fate you will suffer.
And you are only seventeen.

Carolyn Toenjes

One Day At A Time

One day at a time my love, that we would soon meet...
 At a place where a beautiful green valley lies with peace and eternity.
 At a time when all glory is given to you and your light shines brightly.
At a situation where you and I would reach out to each other hand in hand.

One day at a time my love, will I follow you...
 Till the day you come when I see your lovely face.
 Till the hour you come that my pain and sorrow will be gone.
 Till the minute you come that everything will be left behind.

One day at time my love, that we'll live for eternity...
 Where there is everlasting love in the air.
 Where there will be no more hurt, pain and despair.
 Where you and I will be one.
 Where you and I will be together at last.

 Even if this world crumbles into pieces.
 Even if this world turns away from me.
 Even if this world tears me apart.
 Still my love, I'll wait for you One Day at a time...

 Billie Oller

Listen It Is Morning

Listen, it is morning
A new day has begun
There is no sound
Only the whisper of God speaking

Listen, it is morning
One by one God's creation awakens
Birds sing songs of praise
To herald the risen son

Listen, it is morning
Peace reigns supreme
Take time to pray as you start this day
Wrap yourself with His spirit of peace

Listen, it is morning
God is speaking to your soul
Will you take the time to listen
Feel His warming presence flow

Listen, it is morning
This is our time
Come and share this special moment
For it will never be again.

 Marguerita H. Johnson

Drinking Into Your Death Bed

You get a call late at night,
a party is on at a brand new drinking sight.

You hop in your car going a slow mode,
but what you didn't know was tonight is
the last time you will ever see that road.

Your going at least so when you hit the spot,
people sitting down drinking and even smoking pot.

So you joined the rest and had a lot to drink,
you headed for your car, not stopping to think.

You thought you were sober enough to drive your car,
but as you hit a telephone pole you
know you didn't make it that far.

Now you're found in a cemetery lying to rest,
all because you got into your car and,
failed life's greatest test.

You thought you were so cool and oh so hip,
but now your dead all because of that one last sip.

 Trish McKellar

My Days

I was leaning on the parapet of summer
a day when enchantment falls
fast as garment
round the feet of happiness.

I was watching the water
float the image of my face
against the swaying forms
of schooner hulls,
my mind a bay of briny dreams.

I was reflecting on the pallet
of Renoir; the richness of his umber
the burntness of sienna, the parasols
and poppies of his fields.

Sweet never-pausing summer days
when flapping leaves wave
at the sun's ascent and fall,
not nothing weeks and months
that age their edge with raw sienna
till they drop and float like schooners
on water where my image was.

 Alan Pearson

Is There A Place?

Is there a place where a mother, mother's?
A father, fathers? A child with all their innocence
is free to be a child?

Is there a place where any man, women or
child of each and every race, culture or religion
be respected for the person they are?

Is there a place where gangs do not exits,
only groups of friends. Weapons become tools
of the trade for all the jobs, careers and
opportunities available for everyone.

Is there a place where honesty and rewards
replace crime and punishment love and
attention, delete drugs and alcohol.

 Lisa Madrigal

The Black Jaguar

The forest grew silent at the passing of the a head back as shadow.
A long red tongue lolled out of a wide-open panting mouth,
 displaying cruel teeth.
Small rounded ears pricked to the slightest sound as it scented
 the air for prey.
It's sleek, dark hide rippled elegantly in passing, though its padded
 paws made no sound on the leafy floor.
Not a spit of colours graced its coal-black coat, except small dark
 lines which suggested rosettes on its flanks.
A long rounded tail flicked impatience as it slid slowly out of the
 toward its prey.
A crackling, a sudden terrified squeal from some doomed animal
 and it's all over.
The creature slinks back into view, carrying a young peccary.
Shining claws are calmly withdrawn into silken pads as it passes
 silently back into shadows.
This is the domain of the black jaguar.

 Tracey McGowan

Spring Contentment

She bows her head where roses grow
And plants her seeds in many a row,
She feels the warm earth in her hand,
And knows the wonders of Gods Land,
God brushed her cheek, she heard God say,
It is another fine spring for you: Dear Kay:

 Irene Hansen

Here Today, Gone Tomorrow

We once were together
A place far far away
Somehow I knew
You would not stay

You left me there
Left there for dead
Killing it all
The love I had said

The tears flowed
So full of sorrow
My own happiness
May not see tomorrow

Why am I
The one to cry
No one cares
Or wonders why

Trapped in here
For life it seems
You only appear
In my dreams

Mark Desormeaus

Sepulchral

Tomb, obolus and tablet thrice here bound —-

First? Dark-eyed Homer's Acropolis lies
A plundered museum 'neath sable skies.
Upon? Shakespeare's gallery once was hung
With season waning and twilights begun.
At center? Raised up, on Parthenon stacked,
Spy you Keat's zoo where the codes have been cracked
By wraiths whom from out the wastelands attacked,
To fall upon wise-flavoured game they had tracked.
Through pallid gall'ry with treasures they've won,
Past dim, Promethean gifts, spectre run
From the museum, each shade with its prize
Cleaved to breast, breathes one poignant breath and dies —

Buried deep in words, rapt therein to drown.

Richard McLay

"The True Casualties Within"

A child born, clean, blank and unaware
A spirit seemingly unaware of his surroundings
Indoctrinated and a name given.
Begins with the orientation of the world physical reality.
The senses becomes stimulated towards logic and reason.

The growth of conscious reality subjugates his being.
He grows, getting immersed in a mirage of worldly teachings
He becomes plagued by fears, feelings and anxieties
he goes searching to consolidated on his own kind
Awakened by the truth within, asks the use if existence.

He identifies with the Universal spirit, to seek spiritual essence
all these lies, in the salient truth within.
The true casualties is the new child born within
These's children reached out the parts, which was the beginning
of existence

The society, as the interpreted ideals of those who have experienced.
That is the child without colours at birth.
He is the true casualty within.

Ekhator Osemwengie Victor

The Voice

Ahhh! The voice answers.
A voice full of caressing warmth and
steadfast truth.
A voice that causes time to stand still
with just a whisper.
A voice who's laugh carries my spirit high into
the heavens.
A voice of comfort in times of darkness and
rejoice in times of glory.
A voice overflowing in wisdom and never ending
friendship.
A voice I long to hear at any given moment.
A voice belonging to you.

Jarmila Palicka

"When Love Leaves Your Life"

When love leaves your life you feel so empty.
A void so large that nothing can fill.
You miss all those moments that you've shared together.
You have to move on and you hope that you will.
Then conscience takes over and makes you feel weary
of fighting your feelings because you want them to stay.
But knowing the joy in having had such pleasures
Keeps you alive in a glorious way.
Now in this moment at this point of time
You have to let go, you know that you must.
To allow your life to refill with laughter,
to allow your heart to refill with trust.
It could be your fault that things are what they are
but that doesn't matter, the past is all gone.
You have to start thinking of how you'll continue
You need to press through it,
You've got to go on...

Tangerine Hasani

Longing

Married You are, not to anyone
able to talk to You, like no one
You are the One
who fills my wakening hours
You are the One
who is missing from my dreams

I can not enter into your dream,
when you are awake -, miles away
Yet - You fulfill the emptiness
which surrounds me.

I listen to a heartbeat -
that is not mine, comes -
from out of sight
I sigh -, may it be YOURS
like I AM.

Erika Fazekas

Last Goodbye

You taught me the way,
and I thought you would always stay,
But never would I before,
think of you as rotten to the core.
As my eyes fill with tears,
A river rushes through me,
no one can hear.
As you close the door behind you,
I know I will never find you
The emptiness of my heart.
Takes what once was filled with what
you had start
And even though it is true,
I still love you.

Vivians M. Nunes

More

Inspired by the best of them
Acquired by all the friends
On fire, we watch while you condemn
Require more pieces ends

Shifting through he pile of ash
Drifting, far away
Uplifting currents make you crash
If tingling more today

Propagate the see for life
Stop hate before it starts
Drop fait clean, with tempered knives
Too late, more bleeding hearts

Again we see those wielding moves
Explain why just you see
The rain defies and quickly proves
Retains more rights to be

After time slows down somewhat
Laughter fills the air
Craft teary eyes from deeper cuts
Cold draft more way out there

Tom Granger

The Girl And The Woman

You are alone in the field,
Alone at harvest, alone in song.
Your only company is a chorus of crickets.
They grieve with you.

This summer, too, will pass, and many another,
And you will be alone.

Under your silk shirt you wish, you say,
To preserve your breast untouched.
Ample like ripening quinces,
Rising like the waters of spring.
In your voice the security of fire.
Probably from the colour of your face.

You lift a golden sheaf of wheat
And fall to the ground on well-rounded knees.
Knees anxious for yearning.
You do not care for anyone or anything.

Summers will follow summers and harvests will pass,
Harvests of wheat and youth.
Do you wish to be visited by flocks of fireflies?
Will you greet them and send them away with a song?

Mustafa Jahic

Your Son

As a new circle of life is starting,
and your first child has been born,
remember the feelings that have made you smile,
and the ones for which you were torn.

Use all of those feelings that you have had,
to help guide you in your ways,
your ways of teaching those rights and wrongs
of how he will live and play.

Remember this is a joyous event
and tough times are still to come,
and when you want to give up on it all,
remember he us "Your Son!"

But the one thing you must never forget,
is that, your son - is not you;
remember he will be his own self,
so love him, for all he will do.

Glenn Moriarty

Searching Within

Searching within, brightness so thin,
Always looking for the way out.
Acknowledging feelings with a doubt,
The best things being left behind,
For fear makes most blind,
Reminiscing of the toll love took,
Wondering how a soul can be shook,
Listening to what the heart longs for,
Doing ignorant things when the mind thinks more.
A soul shut behind a door,
Afraid to see what life has in store,
Like a child wanting to be free,
Shy because of the implications one sees,
Why do actors play their roles so perfectly
When all they're feeling is misery,
Feelings so strong and so hard to describe,
When one's feeling so alone and scared inside,
The future holds a hope, but vague and thread like thin,
Continuing a deep search,
Searching for something within.

Dilani Joharatnam

Phases Of Infinity

Juxtapose the night and day
An equinox some might say
A quarter moon a shooting star
Time and space infinite they are

Heaven and hell, black and white
Opposing forces within the conscious fight
The good, the bad, some joyous some sad
Round and round a revolutions had

Within your soul, upon your heart
Desires and dreams need a place to start
The beginning and end, the bottom and top
A finish line that never stops

Young and old, far and near
A clouded sky begins to clear
Harmonious intentions for the good of man
Only from the resurrection of the faith in hand

Divine intervention laced with eternal temptation
Pass through the phases of infinity, the last revelation

Curtis Julien

To Be With You

To be with you, is my dream come true
And I will love no one but you
To have opened my heart to a new kind of love
One I had not known I was capable of

You have promised with me, you'll always be
With those four words "will you marry me"
So I will give my heart, which is full of love
To the man I have always been dreaming of

I'll spend the rest of my life in your embrace
And awake each day to your smiling face
To kiss your lips and hold you tight
Is what I'll want from you each night

We'll share our dreams and build a life
With you as my husband and me as your wife
Together, forever, just you and me
That will be our destiny

Lisa Bernstein

Dark

Where light never shines
And noise is but
A far off echo
Reminding man of a time
That once was and now
Has past from his forever.

The cold and damp
Slips through the cracks
Of the boards which were
So securely nailed
But time has conquered
And softened to its will.

The dust which remains
Marks the memory of a life
Which so long ago did
Walk and breath and enjoy
The wonders of the earth
That he has now himself become.

Sharon Bailey

The Sea And Me

I gaze with awe and wonder at her beauty on display
And see her gentle kisses lapping up on yonder Bay
Children test her waters and frolic in the sun
Dolphins dancing in the foam. A world just made for fun
A sail boat in the distance tips her mast in a salute
And a jaunty perky ferry gives a friendly happy toot
Sharing in her bounty serene and calm and still
In the mood for giving and you can take your fill
Remember while your feasting she has another side
And her mood can quickly shift with the changing of the tide
Currents hidden with her treasures in the darkness of the deep
Can surface with a fury that makes mighty Captains weep
So if one day I smile at you when I am feeling grand
And while in the mood for sharing, offer you my hand
Don't take my gift for granted - don't feel you have the right
To feast upon my boundaries from morning until night
The subtle shifting current buried deep with in my soul
Can surface without warning and often take there toll.
So don't abuse the blessing for any given space
And you will see more often the bright side of my face.

Marjorie L. Reynolds

Worry

Have you ever gone to bed with a troubled mind
and stayed awake trying to find
an answer or solution to your plight
until that early morning light
peaks through the bedroom window blind
when the problems still weighs on your mind?

Nothing is resolved so late at night
when you're alone unable to fight
that feeling of vulnerability
from fatigue to think quite logically.

Worry can be dealt with readily
when a rested mind can clearly see
a problem in the light of day
not magnified in that strange way
that a tired mind often tends to do
when sleep is lost the whole night through.

So every time you go to bed
think only positive thoughts instead
of dwelling on worries or other strife
and be assured of a longer life...

Terence F. E. Giles

With Love

Today with love from the stars
and the moon I cross my heart to
you, and when the storms begin
to brew just remember my love for you.

Patricia LaCroix

We Own This Earth

We trample this earth unaware,
And trample this earth without a care,
As if we owned it, say what? You dare!

A thousand steps this way, a thousand that,
Do we care?
We own this earth!

New shoots split parched earth,
Drops of dew, quenching thirst.
A beetle crawls,
Surviving another day,
Night time falls.

Sleeping pebbles,
In sands bed,
Only to be disturbed,
As across open beaches,
We tread.

We own this earth!...

Jack A. Bradbury

Teardrops

A teardrops shed for loneliness
And yet I wonder why
You still can make me think of you.
You still can make me cry.

A teardrop shed for tiredness
For all our endless fights
For all the times you didn't call
For al the sleepless nights

A teardrop shed for time that's lost
And now I think I see
That I'm clinging to a dream
And a memory

A teardrop shed for friendship
A friendship from the heart
A friendship based on trust and faith
A friendship torn apart.

And finally a teardrop,
Because all of this is true
A teardrop just to let you know
These teardrops are for you.

Vanessa Scarrow

Untitled

I'm looking at you now
But I don't know what to see
I can only see the clouds
Then it was only you and me.
I don't know what to do for another brother.

I don't know what to see
I can't see your body
Because your body just disappears
And it's sort of sad and it's sort of happy
I don't know what to do.

Christopher G. J. Eades

From The Depths Of The Night

An innocence lost with a flicker of light,
As dawn spreads it's wings from the depths of the night,
Awakening from a slumber where perfection gleams,
Soaring high from realities cold turbulent streams.

A haven of safety is life within dreams,
Untouched for a moment from hearing the screams,
Barriers broken with a sliver of thought,
A heightened awareness of what is sought.

Searching for strength and yearning for hope,
Leaving the past while attempting to cope,
Fearing the future gathering guidance within,
The body awaits a new day to begin.

The calmness of peace envelops the soul,
Replenishing the spirit as it reaches it's goal,
As the sun stars to rise and the moon to sink,
The body awakens and the mind to think.

Fantasies fulfilled with intense inner fire,
Created in a mind by a thought or desire,
Secrets unveiled without benefit of sight,
Survive and live from the depths of the night.

Sherlynn Birtles

Friendship

I know what I'm looking for
As I have wandered, and wandered over the years
I seem to be more with my feelings,
I seem to be more obedient. Caring, graciously
Giving to all whom come my way
I feel your warm embrace
I feel you leading me on
Through the hard times.
To were that never ending river flows
When so still. So still.
You seem to have a special hold on me
You are always there for me
You know my every thought
You just seem to be there at the right moment
I have found what I am looking for
True friendship cannot be bought
This is giving so freely of itself
I have found what I am looking for
True friendship.

Gloria Froystadvag

Untitled

Their mouths opened wide
  As if gasping for air

Faces etched in stone

They look down on us
  Those silent rulers of this world

Knowing they'll be here
  Long after we are gone

Silently waiting, watching
  As the end seems to close in

Some seem to laugh others frown
  Most care not

They do not feel emotions
  Never have, never will

They see all they know all
  Their secrets never to be told.

Shelli L. Rawn

Breaking In Battle

Burned like a whip.
As if great spears were breaking in battle.
Spray that flew around there looked like blood.
As the victor drags the vanquish.

Leah F. Friedman

The Clock

For most the clock is the reality in their clockwork lives.
As the gears of the clock move, the hands move.
As the hands move, the masses move, for the clock is their guide.
It instructs them when to do what throughout their lives.
The clock accounts for their every action.
Obsession makes their pitiful minds believe in the clock
And what its movements hold for them to do.
They would be lost without it.
I think they could function much better on their own.
To watch the clock is to believe it,
To believe it is to live by it and let it dominate
The thoughts and actions of those who perhaps disagree.
But the masses will try to push their constant "Reality" on others.
But the only reality is that the very machine
That they made to organize life has now taken over their lives.
It tells them everything, they do what it says
I will refused to be operated.
When I die there will be no more masses, no more rules,
No more dictatorship, no more of their insanity, no more clock.
For me the clock on the wall has nothing to say.

Leslie (Les) Gully

Untitled

The heart beat no longer
As the soul slipped away
A journey to heaven
Or hell far away.

Through clouds and wonder
For us to behold
A lifetime of pleasures
If we are so bold.

Onward to somewhere
Of mystery and dreams
A place for forever
No heartache or greed.

We see all the answers
To our heart's desires
But is this a heaven
Or a joke of our mind.

The questions are answered
As the world turns to hell
The moments surrender
To the reality of fear.

Tamar Bainbridge

Expression

A heart,
Broken, shattered, off beat
A soul,
Lost, alone, crying out for love
A mind,
Confused, depressed, unfunctional
A boy,
Exhausted, drained, limp
A love,
Abandoned, deserted, worthless
A dream,
Buried, forgotten, completely out of reach.

Rena Murray

599

A Chair Without Malice

Frame bent upon Frame,
Bald skin to fuse with metal,
A gallery of faces afore; benign, listless.
Eyes without malice. Dutiful.
Set not, to see me die.

The lonely chair embraces me
Chaplain preparing a wanton soul for slave,
By thrust of current,
Of a hooded man without malice. Dutiful.
Set not, to see me die.

A crown of metal descends upon me,
Leather bindings for nails,
Impotent rite yearning kinesis,
Of a warden's retinue, without malice. Dutiful.
Set not, to see me die.

Gathered round, so many final faces
Transfixed upon my unholy throne,
With purpose, without stake, without glee. Dutiful.
Now delivering me from this life. Why?
With malice not, they invoke my death.

Scott Bark

Thanks God ... Life Goes On Again!

'Tis the time to hit the sand,
beat the heat and make some fun,
get a lazy sleep after a dip
only to wake at barbecue's incense sweet.

Summer is a date everyone can't forget.

Air is cool and maples turn colorful,
apples' scent so sweet and leaves start to fall.
Rain puts a strike as unfriendly hurricane displays its might,
but when 'tis gone friendly breezes weary heart and mind.

No doubt, Autumn is nature's best kaleidoscope!

Now nights are long and days are short,
clocks seem to tick so low and so soft,
a sleeper's favorite but not to avid of sports,
a hockey, or soccer to basketball in a covered court.

Yes, winter can be fun or even be a feast with salmon or roast beef
from a sizzling pan.

But cold snow must go and spring must begin
so fields and praises continue their food givin'.
Kids get their playin' and adults their laughin',
for indeed, the world and all creatures are back to life again.

Thanks God for summer, fall, winter and spring ... life goes on again!

Gabrielito D. Garcia

Dreams

Dreams are the best they say;
Because in them we do what we may;
And in full control we end each one;
But from our mind they're never gone;

Some say we dream of to-morrow;
But in my dreams, I want no sorrow;
For to-morrow maybe good or bad;
So I'll dream of today and be glad;

Cause in my day-dreams I get by;
And work with out asking why;
For I've got this lousy job to be?
Cause in my dreams I'm the boss too!

Margaret A. Nesbitt

Roses And Pain

If Roses are the flower of love, then thorns must be the pain,
because why would lovers come back again for just more of the same.

The beautiful Roses that smell so sweet, can cause our love
    to stand defeat.
We think that our love can take no more, then the one we
love comes through the door, a big bouquet of Roses in hand,
    can our love still take a stand.
Or, will we fall like the Roses so grand, and the thorny
    thorns just cut our hand.
Will our love end, and be no more, or can we stay and
    close the door.
What makes us stay for just more pain, what do we think
    we can regain.
Like the Roses so sweet, we try to fight our defeat, and
    all our love problems, we try to delete.

L. Martin

My Soul Of The Living

My soul of the living
    breath thy mighty air deep and long
Grasp as much life as you can
Feed us its limited duration

My day at death's door
I fear, I wish of all things I have not done
    would forgive me in time
The day in a life we must seize with fulfillment

A pleasure, a coldness of panic
    I stand before you Lord
Knowing you see guilt
    Only you knowing my silent world

Forgive me Lord on my imprisoned habits

We're born, we're tortured
    we're mislead, we're dead
We live, we think,
    we try, we hope

Terry Pippy

A Farmer's True Worth

"He's just a plain farmer", I heard them say,
But that doesn't make him less for a day.
He works a hard life and wished they knew,
The many things he must be able to do.

By studying the soil and watching the sky,
He's sure to tell you the right time and why.
Then he plows and he sows, inspecting the crop.
Knows bugs and diseases - bottom to top.

Some buy machinery, brand spanking new.
And if it breaks down, he's a repairman too.
Imagine the books farmers must keep.
Income, expenses, taxes recorded 'fore sleep.

If cattle he owns, 'to buy or to sell?'!
Is the question only a farmer can tell.
He's busy with calving, and if a cow's sick,
He's in his ol' pick-up' to get medicine quick.

He has no degree or initials oft his name,
But is human and needs respect just the same,
Could it be God chose farmers to care for his earth,
For he truly understood a farmer's true worth?

Vivian Nemish

But Was It Wise?

I detect the brilliance in your eyes,
beneath the ominous winter skies,
as they search for a more discrete disguise.
But were you wise to seek sanction
with such a heavenly institution?

I still see your anguished cries,
transcending truths of starlit nights,
transformed through chaotic fireflies.
But were you wise to seek silence
through such passionate, self-directed violence?

I heard your screams change to sighs,
as you thought and began to realize,
how hasty you were to self-inflict demise.
But was it wise to let part of my spirit die
on the night yours passed us by?

Tanya Dahms

Give Me Strength

You told me that you loved me,
but then you keep on taunting me
You told me that you cared,
but then you keep depriving me

You said our love would grow endlessly
until the end of time
You said our problems wouldn't matter
as long as you were mine

You used to try to console me
every time I cried
You always seemed to worry
and said without me you would die

You said all that really mattered
was the love we've shared for years
But then something came out wrong
and suddenly, you weren't free

Sheryl Mirra Koo

I Tried

I tried to touch the sky and to reach far beyond the stars,
by treating my body unkind
I tried to expand my mind
But as it is I failed at times I thought I was there,
I don't know really where
Maybe I wasn't any place at all and maybe I was, who really knows,
right now I don't but later I will
find out if I was somewhere or if I was ill.

How can I explain what went on in my brain
So time goes on and on and on...
Will time ever stop
Will time reach a certain top.

What happens to a person who is dead
What happens to all the thoughts they once had in their head
I tried to die without dying I guess, but learned that you can't be
alive and be dead at the same time I confess.

Peter Bachlow

Flying

To soar is to fly like the wind
Embrace the air and ye shall find
The meaning of freedom of flight
As it sees the distant lights
Above, in the crisp autumn night
Take care, because what is sees is
A glimmer of hope

Tony Mohan

Broken Child

Broken Child, Bleeding heart, forsaken love, lost mind,
Can't you see what is happening to our children everywhere?
Sad eyes, lonely faces, where are the parents?
Where are those who care?

Mommy had to go to work today.
Tonight her friend comes. I must stay away.
Daddy left long ago, I'm not sure I have a daddy.
The neighbors say I'm in the way, don't come here.
The businesses say get out child, you cannot loiter here,
Grandma lives so far away.
Alone, I seek the blackened streets to hide my anguish,
But the dark cannot blot out the fear inside.

Somewhere out there a child is crying,
Can't you hear his weeping?
Somewhere out there a child is pleading,
Can't you see his eyes?
Somewhere out there a child is searching,
Please someone, help me! Please someone, love me!

Ruby Paull

Inverted Conscience

Vultures in the sky above
    Communicate with death;
They scorn the denizens below
    Oblivious of the threat.

Rosary's turning, eagerly in
    The over-reachers hand,
Whose vile heart, knowing no virtue
    Replicates decay.

Self-seekers wishing full support,
    On pleas of competency,
Remain unable to decipher
    The enigma:
Selflessness withstands.

We slay our conscience knowingly,
    Providing ambrosia,
To scavengers.

Humaira Aslam

Path Of Life

Our path
    could be plain,
        rugged,
            at times - rocky.

Along the way
    we might grope . . .
        crawl . . .
            even fall.

These matter not,
    provided -
        we try to walk
            steadily upright . . .
        before reaching
            our
                destiny.

Flor Del Rosario

Thoughts

I relax and dreams by a small moving river.
Many thoughts of hurt and sorrow travel on this lonely water with a quiver.
Silently the water glides on, then suddenly
sighs and gurgles, falling into the turbulent sea.
Taking all the taunting memories and leaving me free.
Vanished are all those wild disturbing thoughts,
into the wild, and whimpering sea of nought.

L. Evans

Save The Children

As children around the world dream peacefully in their sleep.
Dreaming of what will be, on this night I lay to weep.
The thunder has come and gone. Taking those we thought were strong.
I hold a candle in my hand, but it play's my and only friend.
Standing all alone in the night. Hoping this candle will be the light.
I look up to the sky hoping that there is a heaven.
I start to pray that there is someone that will listen.
I have lived my life long enough and soon my time will come.
But please save the children.
They are not to blame for what we have done.

Marcos Abrantes

Learning To Let Go

The memories will always exist,
even though your gone.
I will always remember the laughs,
even through the tears.
I will remember the love,
even though it is over.
For I now know,
sometimes love is learning to let go.

Tiffany Spurling

Betrayed

My broken heart
crashes
like waves shattered
against
ageless rocks
as bleeding drops
they bubble
their way back
to the sea
vanishing
in the numbness of
the cold
in freedom of
their pain
while sails in
the distance
dance their way
in silence
with a reason
to forget.

Avaleen McIntosh

Illustrious Dawn

Dawn of day
Darkness of twilight
Babies first cry, illustrious and bright

A child's persecution
So often denied
A parent's pain concealed, destiny leaves no where to hide

Rings on fingers
Promises to keep
Fragile dreams - dared, we seek

As elder we discern
Benevolence in this world must overtake irreverence
So as to conserve our cherished existence

As sure as light leaves us at the end of our day
I my flesh worn, am too tired to stay
Tomorrow without me, the sun will rise
and prayers will be said for new little lives...

Sandra K. Pruden

Capricious April

Capricious April
Doing things at will
Swinging both ways
On alternate days
Back into Winter
Forward to Spring
One day it snows
Next a breeze blows
Many heads shake -
Say for goodness sake
Where are the showers
And the pretty flowers
Mother Nature please
Don't be such a tease
Tell capricious April
Not to give us a chill

Susanne Noordyk

Believe In Your Dream

I'll always believe in you
Don't be afraid to try something new

J... ust another way of staying alive
E... veryday she works so hard to survive
N... o use complaining, it's a facts of life
N... ow y' know, what's it like working in a city
I... heard that "Cafe Verde" is a place to be
F... resh baked muffins serve with hot coffee
E... veryone knows by now, she's a special girl
R... eady and determined to take on the world

I'll always believe in you
Even when you're sad and blue

D... o you want to share your dream with me
E... ver wonder how it will turn out to be
B... et your dream is a very special kind
O... h, how I wished I could read your mind
C... an you tell me if everything is fine
K... indly take me away from this "waiting line"

I'll always believe in you
Wish there's something else I can do

Yandhi T. Cranddent

Mugs Are Like People

Mugs are like people I think you could say
  Each one is special in it's very own way.
There are mugs that are thin, and some that are fat
  Some that say this and some that say that.
Some mugs are more special, I would dare say
  They're designed to express a wish for the day!
Some advertize business, some mugs portray fun
  Some are for the older, some for the young.
Some mugs from the church, and some from the hall
  Some from the city, and some represent baseball.
Some mugs are from near, and some from a far
  All are quite interesting from wherever they are.
There are mugs that are short, some that are tall
  In various colors, a mug to please all.
Yes, mugs are like people I think you could say
  Each one may be different yet useful in it's own way!

Elsie G. Sheffer

"June"

June what a beautiful month you are
Enfolding in your clasp
The promise of return of Spring,
The warmth of summer (Sun) at last.
You are the month of (Roses),
This beauty you possess.
You have a special honour,
We put you to the test.
We know you'll do your best,
With culture and repose.

I feel (The Rose) portrays the depth
No other flower knows.
A special gift we can enjoy,
Each of us to our liking.
The "scent", the "touch",
Can mean so much,
To help us hold our trust in God and man.

Aulda Roberts

To Alethea At 13

I sometimes wish for days gone by
E're boldness gave away to shy.
When outstretched arms a hug did plead,
A hug to answer a human need.

A diaper change helped form a bond,
With touch and smile, a magic wand.
Memories of these precious days
Lie gentle on the heart... always.

Your teens now stare us in the face.
This wrinkled skin, which lacks in grace,
Although accepted well by some,
Is strange...abhorrent to the young.

I demand a hug when e're we meet.
That contact, still, is pure and sweet.
The furrowed skin plays no real part
And hugs will warm this ancient heart.

Love is ageless and has no bounds
As birthdays make their endless rounds.
So enjoy the years as they hurry past,
The years will fade... but love will last.

Thomas Fugler

Secret Emporium

Shadowed lights stare through an open window
Every line in your face is picked up by the dimness of the moon
Dimness yet brightness, there is no difference
Still where were we when the beginning began?

Misty mornings full of dew and faint breezes
Every strand of your hair is blown by the calmness of the wind
Calm and ferocious it blows across your soul
Still where were we when the beginning began?

East of the west and north of the south
Mountains rage over your world of dimensions
Rage yet caress the simple silence of life
Still where were we when the beginning began?

Darkness falls one the plain face of light
We escape the realm of the dreaming
Reality reaps through the skin of our hearts
Still where will we be when the beginning ends?

Virginia Dimoglou

Tears Of A Clown

He laughs, he smiles, he jokes around,
everyone tells him, he never frowns.
You make me laugh, you brighten my day,
is what I've head, many a person say.
You're a very happy person, does nothing sadden you.
If only they looked close enough, if only they knew.
For behind that smile the tears are there.
A broken heart, a clown just cannot share
lonely tears of a clown are the saddest of all,
for that painted smile becomes their wall.
Lonely tears of a clown, that no one sees,
if only they knew, that crying clown is me.

Ann Mackenzie

Over The Sky

Faint on the dark sky gleaming,
Faint on the roaring seas.
And it held down the glory.
And it hasten the day if peace.

The glory, the peace, hers bringing,
The king who comes from far;
And to him who overcometh,
He will give the morning star.

Some day I'll tell the story
And I'll lay burden down.
Some day I'll meet you in glory.
And wear my golden crown.

Effee Stewart

"My Strumpet"

He said, "Fortune is a strumpet,"
Favours all, constant to none.

I seek favour,
Not constancy;
As constancy is just a word,
Insubstantial, blurred.

Every belief shatters,
Every entity perishes,
Every morning's sun matters,
But with varied intensity cherishes
Its blaze.

I gaze
At my strumpet
That never favours me,
Just glances,
At my chances
Of being comforted.

Peerzadah Salman

Lesson

Ludwig Van Beethoven
love of one's music like bourn
like play a note "Sol" from bandsman
liking for play with feelings to boon

Learn about him a musician born
"Let It Be", he's blind in Bonn
life is alive to his spirit for brain
look to paint from me for Beethoven

Van Ngoc Nguyen

Glitched

Here I sit in my wheelchair,
Feeling everyone's cold bitter stare.

Looking at me as if I'm a freak,
But keeping their distance so we don't have to meet.

Scorned and shunted in today's society,
Asking myself, "How can this be?"

They call me disabled, something bewitched,
I consider myself, and everyone, to be glitched.

For no one is perfect, just look around,
And in others you see, problems can be found.

Vision that is blurred, words that are slurred,
Imperfection in everyone, I am assured.

We are individuals, recognized by our trait,
Seeking livable comfort, until that final fate.

Ask now how to get rid them,
But how can I be your friend.

Because friendship is a hard thing to achieve,
Whether you're young or old, or people like me.

Tony Kirkpatrick

Silky Silver Moon

Silky silver moon
Fill me with silly silky dreams,
I dream of movies they went make of me
Silver castles I won't build.

I dream the softness of silk,
Silk I went own,
I spill out my leaden heart.
Turning it into soft silk.

Silky silver moon,
Define my silky dreams.
Let the stars bear witness,
As I climb the stairs of my dreams,
Let the cool breeze whisk me to my dreams,

Silk silver moon
Let the silky dreams warm my heart.
Carry me to silky happiness.
Let me dream of happiness,
Happiness for the whole world

All these are silky silly dreams
Dreams that bring soft happiness soft as silk.

Mpumelele Michael Siphambill

Year Passing

Walking in the autumn breeze
  hand in hand by the riverside.
The smell of perfume, with brown hair tumbled,
  and soft lips smiling, your arm in mine.

Embracing on a winter's eve
  beneath the blankets - snuggled tight.
The warmth your flesh, with brown hair tumbled,
  you naked closeness, we spend the night.

Silent on a fine spring morn
  side by side - no words we find.
Your eyes look away, with brown hair tumbled,
  we rarely touch now, love's left behind.

Lonely on a summer day
  my arms hold nothing but thin air.
I'm dreaming of you, with brown hair tumbled,
  my hand reaches out, but you're not there.

Roger J. Smith

The Dove

Flying, flying in the sky
Flying, flying passing by
You see that time is passing by
Flying, flying in the sky

You can't hold on, you loose your grip
You realize your going to die
You start to sigh good-bye to life
Flying, flying in the sky

The bird of peace called the dove
He comes to save your dying love
He takes you to where you belong
Flying, flying in the sky

He flies up to heaven his home
To rest in peace up above
Then you try to say good-bye
Flying, flying in the sky

As you watch this peaceful bird fly
You realize God was by your side
Knowing how lucky you were, you start to say
Thanks so much for flying by

Erin Ruxton

The Night I Committed Suicide

The night I committed suicide, the joy it did bring.
For I sat in silence, except for the laughing at nothing.
I brought the knife close to my chest and said to myself,
"It's finally time to rest."

I cut myself lightly watching myself bleed.
Thinking of only the poems I used to write and read.
To myself not sharing with anyone.
They might think I'm crazy for what I've done.

I jabbed myself right into my heart.
Not for the end of life, but for death, the start.
My mother walked in looking right in my direction.
And she grabbed the knife, only for my protection.

I looked in her eyes as she started to cry.
And I thought to myself why couldn't I just die.
I looked around the room as it started to fade.
Then I looked down to were my body was laid.

Pictures of my life started flashing by.
Reminding me why I really wanted to die.
I wanted to feel something deep inside.
But there was nothing there, no feeling to hide

Aleisha Birch

Summer Night

Sitting, sipping, dark rum sweetened with exotic, tropical juices
from a straw, in a long frosted glass.
She looked very elegant; her profile
rather art deco ——
like the glass, the long, straight, stunning lines.

There, on the veranda under the stripped umbrella, shadowing
her bare arms from the fading rays of the setting sun,
she could distinguish the base notes of the sax filtering
out of the ballroom, over the drone of the
patrons at cocktail hour.

The leafy, green vines covering the old, brink hotel
provided the perfect backdrop for ——
her hat, her hair, her nose, and her dress which
motioned in sync with her slender body as she
rose and descended the granite stairs.

Leaving the glow of her eyes
embedded in my heart.

Shauna Bisgaard

Steel Nails

I watched His back rip open
From the whip, then I heard his yell,
I watched His blood run down His cross,
As He carried it and as He fell.

I watched the guard raise the hammer,
I watched His body curl in pain,
I watched the tears run down His cheek,
I watched the guard repeat this twice again.

I watched the thorns piercing His brow,
I watched His chapped skin crack,
I watched the water and the blood run out,
I watched the sky turn black.

I watched the crowds not their approval,
I watched as His weeping disciples spoke,
I watched His blood stained body hang limp,
I watched and then I awoke.

It was just a dream, or so I thought,
'Till I noticed blood smeared on my bed rails,
Then to my horror, I looked in my hands,
And beheld a hammer and three steel nails.

Troy Reeves

Jonah

After springing the blood
From your man's head
With a needle stiletto,
He was given time
To iron himself out.

Needless to say, seven
Seven years was too long
To make any difference,
And now he's back scaling fish
In occupied territory,

Jonah with the whale inside him.

Conor Carville

Light's End

Breaking through an opening
Glittering down across the sea
Darkness falling around
Clouds closing in.

Seagulls flying by
Waves settle down
Darkness falling all around
Clouds closing in.

No breaks nor an opening
No glitters across the sea
Darkness fell all around
Clouds closed in.

Shirley Hofley

Hope

Has given incentive and courage to start,
Healing and comforting my tense anxious heart.

Originates in the Lord's blessed love,
overcoming despair by faith from above.

Provides me with power to live calmly today,
Perspective to see some potential way.

Effective in seeking my purpose and goal,
Essential to enduring peace for my soul.

Mary Gay

Love Is...

Driving down a deserted country road.

We pull off and park.
Hand in hand we run,
through a wheat field slanted with a soft breeze.
Up a grassy hill to our favorite place.
We lay down under the big old tree,
Head to head, hands always as one.
Through the widespread arms of the ancient one,
We look up at the sky and absorb each others dreams.
Nothing is to silly, nobody is ashamed,
we just talk, laugh and dream.
For Love is itself can be a dream come true.

Back in reality, people never have true dreams.
There is to much clutter in the brain.
Love sometimes has trouble getting through.
Reality destroys love, a little piece at a time.
You don't even know it is happening.
People need to lay down under that tree.
No matter how far they have to go to get there.
For in the right frame of mind, it is closer than you would imagine.

Paul Heyden

Just To Have A Home

Midnight cried and I was left alone.
He had compassion and took me in,
I became his son and had a home.
Midnight cried with fervor once again.
She too took me in with softest love,
And stayed by my side with sweet refrain.

The nights were safe and totally secure,
Now I had a loving father and a mother,
Who with fragrant love removed all fear.
Midnight cried long and loud once more.
For I was to leave my home forevermore,
Openly weeping and heaving as I shut the door.

Midnight vainly protested when they died.
Now only album pictures show their love and smiles.
A sweet memory and wrenching sorrow make me cry.
Gently her petalled hand will never let me roam,
As she shows me our grandchildren faces so divine.
Oh the wonder of it all, just to have a home.

Michael G. Peacock

"Us"

I am the loveliest dream of your mind,
I am the rose blossoming in the morning dew,
I am the symbol of your sensitive thoughts,
I am the partner of your happiness and sorrows,
You are made for me and I for you.

You are the tower of my strength,
You are my protector from evils,
You are the fountain of love,
You are the world's best lover,
We are made for each other.

They are combinations of you and me,
They are part of our souls,
They will flourish our family,
Through them we will be remembered forever,
They will honour us for eternity.

Sneh Thakore

Aftermath

I am more powerful then the rays of the sun.
I have broken more hearts then all the doctors have tried to mend.
I have caused hundreds of tears to spill.
I have been compared to the high tide of the ocean, for I have
   swept away so many dreams.
I have the force of an earthquake for no ground is solid
   when I am present.
I am as strong as a hurricane for I have destroyed so many homes.
I find my victims among all men and women alike throughout
   this universe.
I carry the torch of your yesterdays and of your tomorrows.
I have played the trump card and throughout the palace.
No soul is guaranteed freedom from me, for I am coming of age.
I am what some may call the emotions of love.

Gabriella Reischl

Suicide Is Not Painless

I know suicide is not painless
I have spent agonies in my soul denying it, but
it creeps behind me and
I feel the cold breath of death upon my neck,
I hear it whisper foul and obscene taunts in my ear

A doom descends and seeps into my mind
into my organs, especially my heart
but I pay the price when I wake and feel the blankness in my bones

I yearn to yield to sleep forever, so
I may stop running to and fro on the track of misery

At times in my life I have glimpsed
far, far above me chinks of bright, white light
and always while they beckoned I followed
yet now I look up and see nothing, a black void

As the years have passed with no end in sight
a chill has encircled my heart
and slowly but surely
squeezed all belief out with bony fingers of ice

Nothing, no-one can save me now

Suzette Yael Woolley

Children Are The Future

As each day walks by,
I look at all of you and I see who you've become.
Bright, beautiful, outgoing little girls, filled with hopes and
dreams that I hope someday will come true.

Your smiles bring me peace, your hugs and kisses
fill me with your love which money could never buy.
I knew when you were born that you change my life for the better.
I understand the future is yours, I hope and I pray you can
change the future, for it is your to keep.

Darlene Bailey

My Father

   I always want to see your smile, I love your big bear hugs.
I want to tell you how I feel, to have a dad like you.
We didn't always see eye to eye, or always get along.
But I know you always loved me, know that I will always love you.
We were a pair, you and I.
We sometimes hurt ourselves, and each other, by simply not
   communicating our true feelings to one another.
I'm truly sorry, please forgive me.
You could brighten even the gloomiest days with the magic of
   your smile.
As we go through the years life brings us pain, it brings us tears.
Now your gone so far away, but I think of you everyday.
I feel the pain everyday, pain that just won't fade away.
I look deep inside and I can see, although we can not be together
   always, DADDY we will never really ever be apart.

Brenda Lee Metzler

Untitled

I love you and there's nothing more to say,
I love you and I wish that you could stay
With me marking every passing day
Until the end of time

I can't take this, I love you with all my heart,
And far inside I know we'll never part,
And without you I know I'd only start
To hate life without you

And there's nothing you can say
That will lead my soul astray,
Please don't ever go away,
Because I love you.

And there's nothing you can say,
Nothing I can say,
Please don't ever go away,
Because I need you.

Tim Coleman

Silent Tears

I looked outside my window today;
I saw a tiny bird, so helpless with its broken wing.

I looked outside my front door today;
I saw a small, brown leaf beaten by the wind.

I looked out at the end of my lane way today;
I saw a short twig dried out by the sun.

I looked up the road today;
I saw a tiny, gray kitten crushed by technology.

I looked at the town today;
I saw a small child abused by society.

I looked in the mall today;
Is aw the unwanted crust of a sandwhich upon a table.

I looked inside a store today;
I saw a newspaper full of broken promises.

I looked at the world today;
I saw only grief where joy should be.

I shut my eyes to the earth today;
Nobody saw the silent tears that flowed down my cheeks.

Victoria L. Donald

Untitled

As the candle burns down
I'm overcome with emotions
a wave of confusing reaction, about going home

I feel guilty, that I want to escape
but responsible in the neediest place
when I fall a sleep, I am numb
beyond the Horizon with my Heart unfold

When I talk to the Children
my Eyes are filled with Tears
I tell them about the happy Life, that I live
for those who get supported
I see a glimmer of Hope
for those who stay Orphans
the new beginning is for.

So we should all provide a foundation
for the future of these Children
desperately trying to escape the Horror's of War,
as we prepare these little ones
getting away from the cruelty
that we have begun

Monika Buchmann

"The Ghost"

On a dark and stormy night,
I see a vision on my wall,
I blink just momentarily,
Then it's not there at all.

It appears again just faintly,
All white and with a glow,
It's floating gently in the air,
Just how I'll never know.

I reach out to touch it,
But it's like its not even there,
What appears to be something ghostly,
Had me pulling out my hair.

I tried to scream so loudly,
But all I did was fail,
My fear inside was growing more,
I was turning very pale.

Was I going crazy?
What does this ghostly figure mean?
Is it all reality?
Or is it just a dream...

Brenda St. Coeur

To My Children's Children

When I listen to music I see, what no one else can see.
I see the dying world, it's destruction all around me.
I see the earth exploding, hate and war unfolding.
Why is there so much hate?
Maybe our sin is our fate.
To bad people can't see, in music of what I see.
That we are all related in some special way.
The simple care that can warm us like the sun's ray.
To bad the world resorts to violence, greed and the gun.
What about love, peace and the future of our children?
I see greed and no thought, because this is now and
Not our children's children.
I wish people would leave things alone,
We are moving to fast listen, hear the earth moan.
The trees are calling out, the creatures dying out.
The oceans are gasping for air, the land is beginning to tear.
I admit I am afraid to die this way, but,
I am more afraid of the thought that my
Children's children will live by;

The very thought that we didn't care.

Tammy Mulder

Broken Heart

As the leaves fall, and the snow comes down.
I think about the past and true love.
The winter is cold and dreary, and so is
my heart. The cold air on my face reminded
me of that day, when everything changed
and I realized my love was gone and
so was his, he took it away as quick
as he gave it. People say the past is the
past and move on. But I can't, it's just
to hard. It's been almost a year but yet
it seems like an eternity. I miss him.
No one who knows me knows what's going on
in my mind or my heart, I feel
sad and lonely that it's all mine.
I want to share my thoughts and
emotions with someone I love, I want to be
one again with that special someone. If he
only new how I felt, if he only cared he'd
be here right now.

Rachel Yurasek

On Parting

I think of the day that I met you,
I think of the love we have shared,
And now that the times come for parting
Its a comfort to knows that you cared
I dream of our life together
Of the happiness that we have known
And I marvel that down through the years
Our love has simply grown and grown
I think of the times down the years
When we have known sadness and tears
And I thank God that we were together
So that we could overcome all our fears
And I know that whatever may happen
Our love will stay strong drown the years
So try to remember the good times
And try to forget those that were sad
For we had more of one than the other
Yes, remember the good times we had.

R. Martin

Gone To Memories

You left me before I could say goodbye
I was too young to know
That you couldn't stay forever
My beloved I miss you so!

What pleasures we shared together
Hours beneath the sun
On a lake sometimes stormy and rough
But you never faltered, kept true to your course
My beloved I miss you so!

A grand old lady they called you
While inner ailments increased
Beyond repair they let you die
And you disappeared from my life!

Forever will I remember
The adventure and pleasure you gave
Engraved on my heart is your beauty
As you sailed from port to port.

S.S. Cayuga remembered by passengers and crew
Beloved we miss you always
In memories won't let you go!

Carole M. Lidgold

The Person I Am Inside Of Me

The person I am inside of me
Isn't the person outside that you see;
Inside I am young, in love, full of life,
Not the Grandmother, Mother, and forty - year wife!

The person I am is ambitious and gay,
The person outside, you see is grey;
Inside I have talents, and numerous skills,
Outside I battle, discriminate corporate wills;

The person I am inside of me,
Is not the person outside, that you see,
Inside there is wisdom, gained through the years,
Outside you see, an old woman with fears;

The person I am, inside of me,
Isn't the person, outside that you see;
Inside please look, and you will see,
The other person, inside of me.

Catherine M. Laurie

What Is Silence?

Is silence absence of noise or absence of pure sound?
Is silence absence of music or absence of vibrations?

"Silence is golden", they say! Why is silence so golden?
Why is silence so dear, so precious to those who listened?

If silence is deemed to be absence of something, why
Does it have a value? Why pay a price for something
Which may not even exist? Why pay the unknown owner?

Or might we be wrong? Might silence mean "fullness"
Instead of"emptiness"? Might silence be vibration?

Why do we often think of silence as some form of
"Stillness"? Yet, whenever we are still and silent,
Our internal ear feels incredible energy flowing
Within the depths of our inner being, our soul!

What is it that we truly hear? What is it that
We truly sound? What is it that we truly feel?
Might it be the voice of our silent self? Might
It be the gentle spirit of our Silent Creator?

Simply remain still and silent! The divine and
Sacred sound of silence is soon to be heard or
To forever remain silently silent in your heart!

   Raymond D. Tremblay

"Unknown Destiny"

Like the tiny seed that's planted, its destiny unknown,
its fragile fate determined by the elements alone

She knew she was merely existing, in a world where others lived free,
but her roots were never secure enough to safely support the tree

So her life had been a paradox of decisions beyond her control,
but her heart was well protected by the walls around her soul.

Still her world appeared to be settled in a package that seemed very
neat, and those who knew her loved her, yet her life was incomplete.

Then by some visit of fate she left the fear of the unknown,
and she knew that she had entered an unfamiliar zone

Her carefully constructed walls come helplessly undone,
and she knew that she could never stop what had already begun

She could not love him any less, nor love him any more,
for she had truly fallen, like she never fell before

But his heart would never belong to her for it was not his to give,
someone had taken it long before and left him alone to live

But falling in love gave her courage to set free her heart and her
soul, and strength to see that self respect survives with self control.

Though the tree has lost some of its branches, it still stands as the
loose leaves are blown, like the tiny seed that's planted,
   it's destiny unknown...

   Cathy Mucklestone

Harmony

Let us change a desert into a rose garden
Let's see a stranger become a friend
Let's convert our exile to a homeland
So let us get united
Then the strangers of exile
Suddenly become acquaintances
Loving each other is the cure for human miseries
And the clouds carrying pure emotions will rain again
Ending the thirst of lovers to love
The good-hearted people are the shells holding the most
Beautiful pearl of ocean of life

   Parvaneh Sadrian

Winter Scene

A bubbling, laughing brook tumbles and somersaults along its
merry way, not yet restrained by the winter's cold.
Joyfully, it chuckles and gurgles like a child at play.
Splashing playfully, it laughs and giggles amidst silent trees
bowed low with their burdens of snow.

The trees smile gently at this rambunctious child.
Their branches, hanging low, extend delicate ice-coated fingers
to tickle and caress as it squiggles and wriggles by.
Branches laden with glistening snow; like frosting on a cake;
stretch heavenward in praise and thanksgiving to God,
our wondrous Creator.

A touch of joy amidst the somber solemnity of winter's stillness.
So too is faith, amidst the somber solemnity of living.
A strand of glistening, leaping hope within bodies burdened with trials.
While hearts, lifted up in praise and thanksgiving,
yearn and ache and seek union with their wondrous Creator.

   Tara Miron

At Okuno's Church It's New Year's Day

At Okuno's church
it's new year's day,
rock and roll chants
but nary a sway.
Hundreds of believers,
on bended knee,
Buddha their way
to eternity.
Hypnotic nothingness,
sanskritized hum,
waves of hard faith
to kingdom come.
Never a quiver,
never a budge,
song sound sensation
cleanses all drudge.

This is the church
that faith gilt,
the church of the father
and son to the hilt.

   Howard S. Levy

Desire To Play God

Once I asked the Pharaoh. "Why proclaimed God?
Just a particle of dust and that's all you are.
Someday you will fall and get lost in the past.
You are a man after all, like any one on Earth.
You eat like a man, you drink like a man.
All your needs are like those of a man."
"Why! But you never stopped me." The Pharaoh smiled.
"You bow down before me. And I get the thrill.
I push you down more, you go down on you knees.
I push you further down and you kiss the ground.
And, by God! That's what makes me feel like God."
"But that is not fair." I protested with fear.
"Ah! What nonsense is fair!" The Pharaoh frowned.
"There is a God in every man, however you deny.
You are a God for those whomever you command.
All you need is power, power over human being.
The more power you get the more drunk you are.
It's too intoxicating for you and me to digest.
Once you get the power, with no limits and bonds.
You won't be what you are, you too will play God."

   Nazir Uddin Khan

My Friend

When I consider how my life is spent
  Lodged with me useless, though my soul more bent
I always wanted to die
  This, my friend... I won't deny.

From the very start, I feel a pain
  A pain that makes my heart cry like pouring rain
How long can I hold my tears not to fall?
  The pain I have is the common pain of all.

My friend... how long can I stand?
  These aren't part of my life's plan
Bear the pain, the ache, and the sorrow
  How can I face the challenges of tomorrow?

I'm tired enough or everyday strife
  But you are these to brighten my life
In your mysterious way
  You've given me peace and joy during my troubled day.

That's what I've been waiting from the beginning to end
  And I found it in the heart of a true friend
My friend... the things you've for me
  Will bring me peace and joy till eternity.

    Lynn J. Ponsaran

"Given The Eagle"

...I am given the eagle
might've been the dove
(but you decided the legal
was to monitor our love!)

Note the distance between us
(to quiver and shattering arrow)
Grow cows cannot comfort you
(oh soft and sullen sparrow!)

I'm as hard as flint inside
I scream when I want to cry
(ackward aching abandonment
encapsulates each eye!)

I've seen my latest reflection
"And o how much I've changed!"
(The bold one's a species now
whom we thought so de-arranged!)

We sit our nets to in share him
but he perceives them from a far
(and continues to soar so freely
the sky of the northern star!)

    Mark Curtis Farell

Northern Beauty

Northern beauty,
My eyes bounce across your shorelines,
I hear the breeze move in your silence,
The calmness of your water flirts with my soul,
Day begins here in no hurry,
Clouds show the energy of the night.
Here my heart is absorbed by the essence.
Northern beauty,
Your sounds confess no secrets,
Your ecstasy labors with the trees,
You are whole with man's temptation,
Your soul has no inner quarrels.
Northern beauty,
Pass through my emptiness,
Teach my yearning to accept,
Fly my heart upon your breeze,
Cleanse my heart with the calmness of your water,
Be with me when I need you.
Northern beauty,
You can live within my memory forever.

    Victor Finnie

Listen A. A.

When I first came to A.A. and tried to stop that drink,
My God, I can't go through with it that's what I use to think,
I was always thinking too far ahead and was getting no where fast,
Until I started listening and took things in at last,
It really made a lot of sense what those people they all said
They spoke of things what not to do like thinking too far ahead,
They spoke of living just for that day,
Then I knew just what they meant,
If I could really live this way,
I think I could really be content,
They say to remember some of the past,
And don't worry what you did,
Just put it in the garbage can and seal it tightly with the lid,
Just live your life for only today don't think what's coming tomorrow,
But please don't plan too far ahead it could bring you lots of sorrow,
So to all new members I have this to say,
Just live your life from day to day,
And if you live your life the way A. A. says,
You will have a lot more, brighter, brighter days.

    Duncan Wilson

The Proposal

You are the apple of my eye, my love
My heart is yours forever
And the only thing that I do wish
Is to spend our lives together

Every day would be a special day
And I would honour all your dreams
I'd lay my love like an open book
So never a doubt would be

I would be your lover
I would be your friend
And I would always let you know how much I love you
Then I would let you know again

Without any hesitation
For you, I'd offer all my life
And give all my tender warmth
To comfort you at night

These words are not filled with broken promises
And my thoughts are not laced with lies
I'd give you everything and more, my love

Will you be my wife?

    William A. Johnston

Suicide

I rush to the waves as they pour and out pour...
my mind has suddenly turned to the ways of discuss.
A mirror of how it seems some what better than before,
it is now a corps...

As I look up at the sky I think I see I smell how wonderful life is
and how I should not take my own.
I pear up to the cliff thinking and dreaming dream not yet dared.
It's towers have such length, it's sympathetic jump is so far yet it
seems to be the answers to me.

As I sit along the beaches with that cliff near by, I don't know
yet, if I should stay behind or say goodbye. If I stay here I am a
statistic, and if I leave, I will become rancid.

    Lourdez White

The Lonely House

Those house no longer laughs with joy,
No child in sight or broken toy,
No happy sounds or cries of pain,
I strain my ears and try in vain,
To catch an echo of it's past
When love and life were here to last,
No future had it now I fear
It's expectations drawing near,
To end it's days without the grace
The family always gave the place,
So here it stand and weeps some more,
It's search for life worth waiting for.

Sally Ann Irvine

Leaves: In Memory Of My Father

Today, the leaves spring lush as youth with green,
not yet sun-tough or dark, but innocent, supple,
rippling back and forth in a sibilant echo of the breeze.
They burst like dreams from within their winter-hardened branches,
unashamedly crowning their tree with fresh promise.

But you lay quietly, eyes closed to wasted worlds,
your hand pulling at the pallid sheet,
skin blackened by blood bruises,
bones bent by time into gaunt, gesticulate body-shadows.

I watched that hand go back, go forth,
clutch at the white sheet and then the catheter tube,
and I gently stretched your crooked fingers,
seeking to pry the plastic free.

Your eyes flickered open
but recognition dulled into oblivion like a sun sinking,
and the restless hand moved again, in its inexorable voyage,
back and forth, back and forth,
brushing the sheet so that it, too,
bent forth, bent back,
like a blanched leaf mutely searching for its vanished sun.

Anthony Whittall

A Cry In The Dark

The cry for help will reach the ears
Of all who stop to listen,
We will hear the cry, see the tears
Not for gold or things that glisten.

The Mothers' frail, take firm hold
Their tiny babes unnourished,
The air is hot or be it cold
All around, their world impoverished.

Take heed you folk with much to spare,
Give freely of your bounty
To those who need some special care
In Cities, Towns, or County.

While we see the signs, despair and hunger,
Do we pause awhile to think
Of the older folk or of the younger,
Who starve for food and drink.

Those of us who feel we're bored
With eternal care or sorrow,
Just spare a thought, a gift or prayer
For those with no tomorrow.

Janet Margaret Battisson

Love Flows Like A River

I inhabit on the upper-stream
    of the Pearl River,

While you dwell on the lower-stream
    of the same river.

Everyday I don't see your visage,

But I dream of your image;

And but we drink the same water
    from the same river.

When could this water be exhausted?

When could it come to a pause?

Only would I wish your heart
    being identical as my heart.

So it would never stop
    the ever-flowing love into us.

Hor-ming Lee

Where The Seed For Life

Where is the seed of life?
Oh, tell me, tell me, where oh where.
Where lies the seed for life?
Stop looking out start looking within.
You will find it hidden in your life.
There lies the seed for life.

We asked the elephant slowly moving
Oh, tell me, where is the seed for life
Dawn, looking he asked. "Where are you roots?"
There lies the seed for life.

Stop looking out and start looking within,
You will find it hidden in your life.
There lies the seed for life. We asked the sages,
sages oh, sages, where is the seed for life!

Showing the books they whispered in ears
You are a world inside
Love this world and do good to others.
These lies the seed for life.

Juma Marwa

Forgotten

As I observed the children play,
On that beautiful sunny day.
I noticed one child all alone.
How can anyone of this condone?

That while all of the other children have love,
This child is by himself; alone little dove.
He looks on with such longing,
Only if he was belonging.

This is the child who will go home in fears!
In one so young there should not be such fears.
Of having to be alone.
Oh, how can anyone of this condone?

Tammy Gowan

Feeding Birds In High Park: A Tanka

Half-Peanut in hand.
Rock dove comes and picks it up.
    Bird comes back again.
No peanut remains in hand.
May your hand prove different.

Owen Malone

Love Never Dies

Thought a life may end
On this earth here below
Love never dies
In my heart you know

Sadness and sorrow
Sickness and pain
Can never alter
The love I've gained

Through thick and thin
It lasts on and on
Even after those dear ones
Have finally moved on

To a world so wondrous
High up above
A place so special
Filled with God's own love

Though years may pass
And days creep on
Love ever changes
It keeps holding on
Diane Kennedy

Untitled

Two strangers inside of me
  one a child
    the other an adult
fighting to take hold of me.
Eventually the adult will win
but, in the meantime,
there're two strangers
and a lost me yet to be found.
Sometimes I'll put myself down
and then bring myself up
because that's what I want.
I want to be an adult, not a child.
I want only one stranger who will turn into me,
    and not be lost in a fight
    between two strangers inside of me.
Melissa Kolej Allen

Broken Pearl

One broken pearl
One shattered world
Among the many shouts of joy
One cry of pain to destroy

From a sunset and a sunrise
A love, a life but still those cries
Between a dawn and a night so far
A sun, a moon and a star

One broken pearl
One forgotten world
Cruel hopes of a paradise
A prince, a queen, a sunrise

You were my sunrise
But veiled under two lies
Of the Sun, the moon and the star
But a broken pearl, and a scar.
Steven Keays

Metamorphic Assault

My circle of seasons surrounds me
Oppressing my options of growth
Deficient of that joyous equal
Misplacing a share of my worth.

Festered with heights of enmity
Which perpetually unites with it's source
Overwhelmed by it's impressive summit
But incompetent to recover my force.

Deceived by this orb of reflection
Apprehending it's ideals as untruths
Absent of the degree of intensity
Essential to acquit my disputes.

A weak trace of promise sparks faintly
As I catalogue this earnest entreat
Discouraged by it's boundless insistence
With the possible risk of defeat.
Brenda Lee Leclair

Untitled

Life in a blue funk
Or life in a purple haze
Life in the clouds
Or only on sunny days

Drug induced stupor
Parachute trooper
Millions with game boys
Chant isn't this super

Why yes it's super, one two and three
Oh doctor, is the princess really that sick?
"Of course she is lad, don't you question me
Your wallet's too thin and your head is too thick"

But grandmother's comatose, and grandpa just overdosed
"It isn't my fault" the doctor replies
Yes sir I know it, you're just easy to blame
The problem has long hair, big ears and my eyes
S. Micklewright

I Love You Jason

All the tears in the world will not make you better
Our prayers are not being answered

I see you slowly slipping away
I no longer see my brother, but a stranger

Please know that if you must go
That I will understand

Don't be afraid, there are loved ones waiting for you
This is not goodbye forever

We will all once again be together
In a place that is full of love and free of pain

You will always be in my heart and soul
In my memories, and in my dreams

Although you will not be here, you'll never be far
Just a thought away

We will be sad at first, then happy...
Happy that you are free

Happy memories will replace the tears
Don't be afraid Dear Brother, be free
I love you
Tracey Johnson

Alive And Breathing

I spend the day sailing
over Vancouver streets, an ocean of cappuccinos
baiting the breeze; Greek bakeries trolling with spanakopitas
and espressos and baklava: fishing for customers.

Cars swim through hidden currents
all lefts and rights, brake lights blinking in waves.

I flash on — a swordfish arching in the dying sun;
scales bright, weaving through traffic on two wheels.
Handlebars gripped.

The city is alive and breathing, this city of wine and winos where
salvation armies march, weaving, lurching and sometimes stumbling
   across

Fields of concrete; bumping into stockbrokers who
check their watches and walk when it says YIELD.

Mountains bunch up to form a backdrop, sharp notes of
a million cash registers rising
in crescendo high above the city,

Echoing across distant peaks
until they are lost in remote valleys
where bright green salmon spawn under a blaze of northern lights.

Absolutely no refunds without proof of purchase.

   G W. Rasberry

Thorns Of Rose

Aches for Ale,
Pains for Pastries,
To drink and to chew
Is the luv in-between.
Still gristles to grind,
More shackles to shear,
To swallow and be free
Is the luv in-between.
Oh! Luv's Ave;
Honey's empire.
Sweet to tread,
The Roseanne's pathway.
Sweats of suffering,
Luv's labour proved.

   Francis Anat Okolo

Son Of The New World

To you sir, he may be just another number to be sold up river,
Part of this cargo of misery sailing from freedom-
Shackled to and grasping at a new world.

To me, he's a miracle, my son born of no master!
The only sunlight that shines through the filth of this suffocating
   dank hull.
The greatest child ever born,
Inseparable from his mother's love.

Nothing can taint the meaning of this timely birth,
The dignity of his life.
Although you shallow, swamp merchants try to colour God's people-
The spirit of love carries us down through the ages.
Our will to resist the future with hope.

For if life was left to these superstitious sailors of treachery,
Their ships would never reach those hallowed shores.
They would fall off the edge of a darkened cube.
Saved by onc soul's prayers in spite of themselves-
One word to God from a little heart, so true it manifests destiny.

   Michael K. McLeod

Despair

People crying
people dying
everyone has long lost all their hope,
and it seems
that all their dreams
went with their ability to cope.
People don't care
we forgot how to share
our visions are clouded in black
for now we can only strive
to try and stay alive
for we may never gain our humanity back.

   Louis A. Theroux

The Need To Find The Truth

The need to find the truth has every man's mind
Preoccupied,
Demands for a just world trouble every one's mind.
Charters are put to save man's breath.
Still a just act is never fulfilled
Is it a crime to come close to a place where God strength
Abides? Where evil dreads to come close to or sinister care to reside
Where only a victorious soul lies peacefully deep inside.
Never ceasing to say "no" to an earthly lie.
Where justice is bound to free every man's mind.
However, truth is man's far fetched sigh!
He may never reach it without a courageous try!

   Safa Abu Assab

Ab Ovo Usque Ad Mala

Out of the darkness a consciousness that does not think,
Regarded with indifferent love
Opens it's heart and mind
Unleashing the waves of genius over a dry path.

This is the acephalous man in his blunt armour
The weight of the Gods is a heavy burden,
As Nodens himself knows in his windy mansio
Where anvil clouds throb daily under the sun.

The companionable zephyr and the chill waters
Are nourishing yet blameless agents
Inattentive spectators in the rows
Sometimes taking an Herodian part.

Mummers sowing in the byeways
Near an altar foreboding the harvest nemesis,
Recall the image of a goitrous season
Black saplings are it's fruit.

   Paul Catherall

The Colour Of My Dreams

The colour of my dreams,
The colour of rainbow,
But there is there is no pot of gold
   at the end of the rainbow.
No reflection of beautiful colours.

In the colours of my dreams,
I am like an old Romeo.
An old Romeo standing in the rain
With nothing to gain.

The colours of my dreams
The colours of rainbows.
But no fog has lifted in my dreams.

   Mpumelelo Michael Siphambili

I Think And Sigh

Save thy innocence save thy emotions
Saving thy energy, actions, relations,
do or die, don't be shy.

Look little birds, pretty and nice
Sailing with ease in the skies
How thy fly? Don't be shy.

Rain is over, clouds are gone
neat and clean as white house lawn
see blue sky, don't be shy.

Dreams will kill you
Totem or taboo.
That is a lie, don't be shy.

Kiss 9'm mailing in the envelope
Though unseen, unknown, let to developed
O Love! Just reply, don't be shy.

Cheap n priceless peace no-where
Murderer, Hunter every where
I, think and sigh- don't be shy.

Shams Soomro

The Poster On The Wall

He sights a poster on the wall,
Sketched in shades of black and grey.
A young man leans against a door,
And at his feet smashed dishes lay.

Crouched in a chair, near a phone,
Are two small boys in a woman's arms.
She holds them close - looks far away,
He knows she wants them safe from harm.

The telephone receiver is in her hand.
She is picking it up or placing it back.
Their happy smiles are upside down,
And her pretty eyes are circled black.

Above their heads, "BREAK THE SILENCE,"
Below their feet, "IT'S NOT TOO LATE,"
Telling him, "YOU CAN MAKE THE DIFFERENCE,"
Help free them from this helpless state.

Well he knows this CYCLE OF VIOLENCE,
For that's his life on the office wall.
He drops his head in tearful sorrow,
And he finally tells his therapist all.

Karen Kinslow

Tribute

I was just getting to know you again
so many years we were out of touch
you living your life, I living mine

I thought of you often
wondering if you knew I still cared
then we found each other
and 'twas though we'd never parted
silver hair that once was gold
but that same sweet smile I'd always remembered

Now the final parting has begun
but no more will I wonder
for we had a second chance

We tried to make up time that was lost
I just needed more

Anita Osborne

Bright Shining Star

Sometimes I wish that I was a star,
So that I can shine wherever you are.
To fall from the sky, and know that you cared,
And remember the wonderful nights that we shared

When you wish upon this lonely star,
Please know in your heart that I won't be far.
Because love is a feeling, a natural high.
That's what they say, don't ask me why.

It might be the way you look in my eyes,
The tears that I feel, the heart pounding cries.
So just take a look, when your afar,
I'll be that big bright shining star...

Bill Siemens

Monotony

Faceless dolls in an eternity of
soleless shoes.

Salt-water tears shed from
sweet angel eyes.

Somber giants with thorns in
their toes; cry softly to the
tasteless world beneath.

Wind-up clocks wasting away
With time. Long, dusty roads
that too many travel.

Angry cacophony sang by
screeching gulls. Gone are the
good times, only heart-lacking
metal for the future.

Amanda Williams

Bubbles

They take me to the place where
souls are left to die.

Reflecting windows of color, pop, pop
popping!

Floating slowly toward the sun they
wetly kiss, the sky.

They waltz to their silent minute and
cast an evil spell.

Memories wash over me. I'm sine again

How painful is the macabre ballet
that I am destined so follow over and
over again.

Leslie Richards

Untitled

Happy Birthday Sister
Many more may they be
Along with this little gift
And a wish from me
I know you like bread pudding
So I up and made you some
Hope every bite taste real good
And you'll end with yum, yum
If by chance its not just so
And don't want second or thirds
Well open up the door
And feed it to the birds.

Thelma Lynch

Red Sky Women (Misskwann - Quad - Do Kwe)

I am captured by your enchanting radiance!

The western sky manifests your entity creating tranquil ambience.

A soft velvet red robe extends glorifying your presence!

I long to live and express my passion, your immortality touches the
    spirit of my innocence.

I was a child of purity, born from my mother's womb.

My defenseless child became confused by cruelty and violation!

In the solitude of the night I wept, my aching heart resigned to
the loneliness I felt.

A cold harsh wind slapped around my body, I trembled recalling my
    tormenters!
Momentarily, I caught a gentle smile, it tugged at my heart
    flowing me to melt.

My healing journey started many days ago, I began to hear and
    listen that other women have cried and suffered, too!

The child within has forgiven and is full of love, her spirit is
    free to soar just as the eagles do!

I walk proudly with integrity, grandfather's hear the song in my
    heart, it yields a joyous beat!

Red Sky Women, your serene elegance is majestically powerful!
I've shared my pain to women of whom I am grateful to meet.

Glenda Snache

Dear Life

Standing at the foot of your incredible expanse
Stirs something deep inside of me, I want to learn your dance

Uncertain, I begin to take a small but steady stride
My heart beat new, I'm overwhelmed with feelings if such pride

I'm ready now to meet head on the challenged your present
I'll stumble, but I'll get back up, my time will be well spent

Believing true with all my heart, endeavors I shall win
I'll overcome my obstacles so new hope may begin

For with each path I choose to take, my journey starts anew
On my own judgement I'll depend, I know I'll make it though

No matter how I feel inside, you magnitude elates
You wrap me in your gift of joy, contentment this creates

Your deep dark caves, your open skies, your rivers and your trees
Your gusting wind which overpowers, becomes a calming breeze

Soaking in the splendor of your crests and valley deep
Humbles me, inspires me, inside I gently weep

Entranced by all your beauty when I listen to your song
Encourages this feeling that I truly do belong

So challenge me with all your might and know I'll not give up
I'll drink as long as you allow from Nature's loving cup

Carrie Steeves

Once

We were young, once.
We had sunny skies, once.
We laughed together, once.
We cried together, once.
Now I sit alone
And cry alone,
Just once.

Roderick L. C. Thomas

Hope

I rested on an icy alpine peak
taking in the magnificent view,
as the world entered into a new day.
Behind me, under a thick crest of snow,
a young pine tree reached up to heaven
with its delicate fingers.
And in the east, the morning sun shone
in all its radiance, giving life to the
shadows of the night.
As I sat there is rapture, hope entered me,
giving my spent soul strength.
I could sense her gracefully lifting me up.
Gently, she touched me and gave
my spirit flight.

Steve Bourgeois

The Love Of God

There is no greater love
    than the love of God.
He loves us so much He
    gave His son to die for us.
His love is so continuous,
    "For He has loved us with an
everlasting love".

His love is so sacrificial,
    "There is no greater love than a man
would lay down his life for his friends".

His love is so steadfast, He
    admonishes us to, "Continue ye
in my love".

That agape love, so genuine,
    we are reminded", now abideth faith,
hope and love, but the greatest is love".

Sharlene E. Gibson

Pressure

Pressure is the terrible feeling
That you're being crushed,
Squashed flat by a
Heavy metal bulldozer from above,
And a rising slab of concrete from below.

I t can overwhelm you completely,
Blocking out even the minutes ray of sunshine,
Make you feel that every single problems is insurmountable.

It will make you resign
Lose faith in yourself,
Until all that is left is a vegetable miniature
Of what used to be sparkling, vivacious person.

Resist the pressure
And you will see as most beautiful sun emerge
From behind the drab gray clouds.

But it is you who has to be the aggressor,
It is you who has to
Take yourself in hand;
You'll be surprised at the pleasure
The little things in life can offer.

Shulamit Davis

The Late Melodies

"The morning stains by tender colors
The ancient moscow Kremlin's walls.
The soviet powerful colossus
Wakes up gaily for new battles"...

'Twas summer in Siberia, I was a snotty lad
Of everbusy mum and ever absent Dad.
In shady tiny room with old huge gramophone
I played this only song, sat on the floor alone.

My limping grandpa and I'm at his hand
Liked listening to the March of air-force band
In park: "Wait, girl, with all your might and main
And soldier comes back to you after rain".

I do try to recall at my full tilt
"We're the pioneers of the soviets" lilt
From Granny's all-waves radio
On summer sunlit patio.

Cadences bother my tired brain.
I hear Chaikovski and Rubinstain.
I feel a sweet scent of that far June.
There is not the S.U. I remember its tunes.

Alex Medvedev

Fourteen

A very magic age attained
The beginning of being adult
Time to understand world problems
And consider the actions of others
The change is not easy
To progress from normal fun
To where we must consider
The difference in our behavior
Sports are still quite important
This appreciation will hopefully remain
The other sex now emerges
To dominate our changing ways
We resist the change happening
It has appeared very rapidly
Going dancing now takes over
And all activities involve others
We feel proud of our achievements
And strive to prove ourselves
As being suitable for adulthood
We now mature very rapidly

John Wallace

Reflection

The sun sets on this chapter.
The blue sky turns to fiery red,
Then black.
A vast nothingness sparkling with often unseen potential;
A result of the transition from colour to black and white
Which leaves us mourning the rainbow.

The stars are scarce;
The space they reside in infinite.
Yet our focus has to lye on their wondrous beauty
And we must remain oblivious to the surrounding
Emptiness
From which they seem to have stolen all life.

Although few and far between,
The mere knowledge that the stars exist and the sparkle is real
Fuels our survival.

The sun sets on this chapter
Yet in that same instant,
It rises on the next.

Laura Varndell

Night Music

Listen to the music of the night
The call of birds late in flight
A roll of thunder crackling lightning bright
The click and slap of rushing feet
Splashing in the rain as it travels to the drain
Traffic flowing to and fro
People all on the go
The drone of an aeroplane
The rumble of a car going
Down the bumpy lane
Gradually the music plays its self out
And all that is left is drop and plops
Of silent rain until tomorrow night again.

Mary Climie

Grading Day

The door is opened wide at last,
The children are set free,
Their voices rise upon the air,
Their eyes are filled with glee.
All but one - how sad he looks
His head is bent so low.
He hasn't made the mark , and
So his heart is full of woe.
His steps are slow, his throat is full.
His eyes, they over flow.
He tries but fails to swallow,
The hurt, but all in vain.
And so he trudges home ward, in disgrace, and in his pain.

His friends, they cannot meet his eyes.
And so they look away.
They hate to see him crying
On this their grading day.
They cannot share his failure, they wouldn't want to try.
To understand would end their youth.
And so they just deny.

Virginia Laffin

"My Favorite Place"

Soft whorls of dust beneath my feet on a path through cedar trees
The crows so raucous overhead they drown the humming of the bees
Leading to my favorite place
A quiet gentle dreaming space

The pond glistens and shimmers in the cooling breeze
Swift dart and weave the surface with ease
With orange hues breast and tiptilted wing
They dance a ballet of grace to welcome the spring

The apple trees blossom in flowered perfection
In the pond is mirrored their glistening reflection
On dandelion puffs the butterflies light
Birds chorus their songs for exclusive delight
As I absorb with ears, eyes and heart
This my favorite place for spring to start

Audrey Otter

Angels

My Guardian Angel has
wings of pearl.
A smile of sunbeams and
a halo of gold.
She surrounds me with white
light, gives me her hand to hold.
My Guardian Angel is a
connection to comfort me in the
dark of night.

LuJuan Bartlett

The Missing Piece

A piece of my heart was taken by God
The day that you were born;
He took it and placed it next to yours
To help him lead you home.

He used my tears to help you sail
Through the storms that came your way;
And he used my love to give you hope
As you journeyed toward that day.

He used my smile to light your path
For he knew that you could see...
The piece of broken heart you had
Was the piece that belonged to me.

Ann Hale

The Breath I Consume

Every little breath and wastefully inhale
the desire in me for you would never fail,
around you my co-ordination double - take and
    my language double - talk,
sometimes it's a puzzle why you still stand there,
    most people would walk,
I hope its just a "phase" if this continues - soon
    you'll see my doom,
for whenever you're around me I ignore every little
    breath I consume.
every little breath I dervastly intake.
I only see you in my dreams until I'm awake,
just the "thought" of losing you would drive
    me in a state of catatonic,
the slightest headache you feel makes me panic,
if this is what love feels like, if this continues - soon
    you'll see my doom,
for whenever your ground me, I ignore
and neglect, the very breath I consume

B. Theresa Evans

Like A Bed Of Flowers

Today the sun came beaming down, it made my face feel warm
The flowers in their bed took shape, beauty creating form
They overflowed with life it showed, they fluttered in the wind
As one bud finished blooming wide, another one would begin
So what if my life took such form, and grew so wild and free
My true colors then would show, from deep down inside of me.

And what if things were easy, then we'd have no need to fight
And what if times weren't rough but smooth, like day changed into night
And what if dreams always came true, everything would be so good
But what if we just worked real hard, we'd reach those dreams we would
What if we were all rich inside, we'd all wish we weren't the same
And what if we knew we could win, would we still want to play the game.

Cause just as life seems so right, when good things shouldn't change
The sun that brought the flowers out, has suddenly changed to rain
Uncertainties creep right black in, desperate to alter facts
But tomorrow's sun will brighten minds, and bring the joy right back
And flowers form their beds again, as the sun warms up the earth
Making us glad for what we're got, no matter what it's worth.

Eugene Cantwell

Three Roses

I am giving you roses on this special day
Three roses that can do more than words can say
Roses that will steal your heart away like a thief
Roses with a touch of love as tender as a kiss
Roses that will give life to the colour that you miss
Three roses that smell as clean as you
Three roses representing the three words, I love you...

Sabrina Bool

Who Is Right!

The trenches are stagnant and damp,
The gun fire rings in my ears as a constant reminder of the hats
    all around,
The smell of blood is a laced remembrance of the long battles,
No more that a star risen past,
Yet so long ago,
All of them lost none of them won all lost
The barb wire tears at the flesh,
But there is no pain here,
For the sorrow binds my wounds in black furrows,
I am seventeen years old this day,
But no joyous song do I hear,
But thoughts of drunken soldiers,
And no luscious food do I taste,
Stale bread and bitter porter are all I relish,
No love do I feel,
Loneliness is my only comrade,
But still I fight for my country I fight for Germany,
For freedom for liberty,
Because we are right,
Right?

Shauna Dawn Smith

Dreamers

Stillness around
the night has
closed in to
find its dreamers.

We are dreamers
of broken illusions
we dream the dream
and hope the thought
of what might, but isn't.
We care to dare
what could - but wouldn't.

We are dreamers
but the night
    won't last ...

Ursula Tillmann

The Village

Here was a village. Once, its people spent
the quiet hours. In the soft descent
of even', by its ancient tower, the groups dispersed.
The old bell tolled the hour,
as here, in peace and quietness as old
as quiet hills, the river, swift and cold
ran from those snow-capped sentinels to slake
the thirsty olive slopes. Slow, in its wake
the peasants, blue-smocked, faces goldly brown
paced slow behind their laden beasts. Far down
the valley - where, in even rows of green
grew fruitful vines. This village. Peace hath seen
and peaceful now, lies shattered in the gloom.
The tower, shell-riddled, saw its sorry doom.

George Alexander Macdonald

Untitled

A sight of hopeful becomings
In a sky of changing surroundings
Silence of a distant voice
Searching for its place of rejoice
A walk in a season of breathless skies
An ocean of beauty seen through her eyes
A flame of desire in a burning field
Radiance of the light makes his shield
Clouds of somber rain passing by
A white dove begins to die.

Jason K. Roy

The Long Of A Bird

In through my window early each morn
The song of a blackbird floats.
He sings such a cheerful chorus of dawn
Such a trill of tuneful notes!

He's the first to awake each day
And with his melodious chirp
He sets the tone, that come what may
No bad feelings or through can usurp.

How can he stay so free of care
No matter what foul wind blows?
Maybe he has a secret to share
Or a story that he alone knows.

Whatever the reason may be,
As free on the wing he glides
I'm glad he comes back to his beautiful tree
To help me feel good inside.

To whenever you're feeling blue or sad
Think of my small feathered friend
And if you can keep a smile through the bad
Your day will be bright beginning to end.

Madeline Christy

Untitled

Have you ever heard
    The sound of the death. No?
It comes silently, snatch away your beloved
    It leaves you crying, helplessly?
But the death has its own voice,
    It has its own voice, haven't you ever heard?
Than, what was that when you were standing
Just opposite the wall
    On the other side, kids were crying,
Crying for the help, crying for the life,
    Wasn't that a sound of death?
But you were helpless.
    Alas, you could hug a child,
You could save the life you could become the shield
When running feet were
    Trampling to the innocent flowers,
But you were helpless.
    Alas, you could save that smile
But the tearing eyes are saying
    We were hapless, we were hapless.

Indu Mehra

Living Poor

As the sun sets, on the blue horizon
I wonder what life holds way beyond....
I hate to be poor, I say to myself
Born in poverty
Raised in poverty
Raising kids in poverty
In a poor neighborhood
You get no respect when you're poor
You're looked upon, worse than an unpainted door
My body trembles with chills, cause I have no skills
But, no matter the cost, I will have it all
So my kids won't drag no ragged cross
Against no ragged wall

Yvonne B. Forbes

Why Can't You Believe?

Why can't you believe
The things that you can't see
Why do you to doubt everything

Why can't you believe
The things that I say
Your life would be more complete with a little faith

I'm getting tired of telling you
Getting tired of preaching, too
There are too many things that you can't explain

So, open up your heart
And clear out your mind
There are beautiful things out there for you to find

If you give it chance
I'm sure you'll like what you see
This world can be beautiful if your heart is free

With your eyes open wide
And a heart that can care
There are a lot of wonderful things out there

I just want you to believe in the things that you can't see
Because life can be beautiful, take it from me

Steven Vegh

Negatively Positive

I a so fat!
    there are two seats for me
I am so ugly!
    girl don't trouble me
I am so dumb!
    there is all vacation for me
I am so short!
    people can't face me
I am feelingless!
    there is no pain for me
I am non existent!
    life doesn't bother me

Amir Riaz

Lover's Lament

Running through the darkest days
There were times I changed my ways
Sweat in the noon day sun
And hoe to hear from my only one

She cut off her hair which I used to love
And thinks of herself a wet above
Poems of her I've written and lived
But her love for me she'll no longer give

We used to be so close every day
Then I cried and our love went away
Ignoring me was her way to say goodbye
And I often questioned myself as to why

Normon Chiosson

Warm Nights

Candles, lamps and lanterns that light
Having you here to warm the night.
Little windows of gold
glitter by the firelight.
Nowhere to go
-nothing to do.
Thank God for warm nights
and comforting thoughts of you.

Debbe Behnke

The Derelict

He's not respectably dressed
There's liquor on his breath
He has abandoned what is cherished by some
To become a vagrant and a bum

Old friends have become a soft mark
Home is oft a bench in the park
If all his connections fall through
There's always the street to turn to

He'll save the day with a practiced line
"Could you please tell me the time?"
"I need a cigarette, or two"
And, "Say Mister, could you spar a dime?"

When all his resources, he has used
He'll hock his socks, or his shoes
He'll eat in the soup kitchens of "Sally Ann"
And drink stolen cologne in place of booze

The established order he defies
Will give him money, and criticize
But, deep in the soul, guilt lies
"Thank God, it's not I", humanity cries

Sandra Cipriani

Poetry Is No New Truth

Poetry is no new truth
Though truth it may be
Poetry is no new story
Yet a story it may be
Poetry is saying anew
What may be familiar
Unveiling fresh vistas
On a well-worn canvas
It may well be new songs
Wrought of dated tunes,
Startling with language
Arresting with usage on
What may be commonplace

Iboro Otongaran

Nativity Of Christ

Virgin birth of Jesus Christ is amazing and wonderful
Thoughts of it is source of joy for blessed human souls
Humbled himself to dwell in the womb of Mary, Virgin lass
Born of Holy Ghost to save men from Adamic sin.

Days of yore, prophet Isaiah fore-told of this noble birth
Sign of the son, taking birth from a holy virgin
He will be called 'Immanuel', meaning that "God is with us"
Truly happened at the time of Herod, the great King.

Men of wisdom, came from far East, guided by the then born star,
Uttered in joy that they had seen star of the born Jew King
Fell on the face, worshipped and put gold, incense Myrah
Admitting him as their king, priest and also prophet.

It was on a pretty night of moonlight that the shepherds heard
Angel preaching news of great joy for all universe
Glory to God, peace to men Christ's born in David's town
Child in swaddling clothes, can be seen in the cattle shed.

Jhoma

How People Find Time To Hate When Time Is Too Short For Love

Two stars trying to shine their way
through the chaos of darkness
were crushed in hatred
and drowned in the pool of blood;
Two flowers waiting for a chance to bloom
but withered away in the enmity surrounding them;
Two humans trying to crawl out
from their tangled chain of love;
were confined in the web of evil
Two hearts singing the same song
were tuned down by the shelling of jealousy;
Two lovers whose body lay in their ghost town
in the obscene reflection of insanity;
Two souls now free from their imprisonment
stand by the doors of heaven
and look back in discreet
as their dews fall in a sparkle
and their lips wet with urge .....
..... How people find time to hate
when time is too short for love!

Zoon Saeed

The Tree

There once was a seed that made its way up, deep from the underground.
Through the winter it waited long to find the warmth of the sun.
When it passed into a sprout, the tiny tree had hopes and dreams,
for someday he would touch the sky and show the rest in the forest green.
Others thought he'd be a pine, but he ignored them and their joke,
because of knowing from the start, he was meant to be an Oak.

Days went by to months and years, the people watched it grow.
That tree did wait so patiently, and survived the many snows.
As seasons come they also go. When spring comes it also knows,
to draw within much Sun and rain, so it can replenish it's leaves again.

It's now a Century old from birth, time is passed its due.
Now that it's blessed from mother earth, it's made his dream come true.
That tree which was little seed, some made him as a joke,
but tried until he did succeed... to be a mighty oak.

Lise Tunold

Peace And Brotherhood

Peace O Lord, let there be peace,
Throughout the lands,
North, South and East and West.
Let the children of the world know
A life without tears,
Without strife, without fear,
Let them not hear the fall of bombs,
The sound of gunfire,
Let them not go hungry,
Or without shelter or warmth
Let them know the love of family,
Teach us how to keep the peace,
To live together......
In brotherhood.

Joan Sinclair

'The Going'

A dawn of realization and a
Time never spent in me.
An aftermath of your mystique mind,
And yet - you remember!
Remember the times of tomorrow
Last yesterday
When the earliest of the Intellect began to question
It's own worth and being.

And yet you can still recall it
And label it - "Time".

Thoran S. Kuciak

618

Irish Magic

It seems that on St. Patrick's day
'Tis everyone' desire
for the wearin' of the green,
And Irish songs inspire...
Could it be the Little Folk
Cast a Magic Spell,
And we're all Irish for a day,
'Faith now, who can tell?
'Tis then, in the early dawn
You're sure to see a leprechaun,
And on that day, for awhile,
'Tis the Magic of the Emerald Isle.

Joyce A. Heasley

50 Years Ago

Oh, to the men that crossed the sea in the steel ships;
To gain a freedom for you and me.

Giving up the best years of their youth
And not even sure of their return;

Planning, training; the course is set; we'll cross
The English Channel in the biggest invasion yet.

Hitting the beaches of Normandy and some came up the boot;
But gaining even a mile or two cost some their lives that day.

For thanks to our dads who landed on Juno and into Italy,
We have today in Canada the greatest country you know.

Happy to remember this day; to honor those who fought;
Their lives changed forever; but that's how freedom's bought.

And that was back then, 50 years ago.

Our lands are still full of evil men; led by unseen enemy
And while Christ has died to lead the way, smart men still go astray.

Our call to arms is still maintained as in 50 years ago;
As we battle on in victory, we overcome the foe.

But thanks to our dads, who gained some ground for us
And gave us time to enjoy what God so richly planned.

Thanks dads, for 50 years ago.

Sigurjon Eiriksson

Daddy's Little Girl

When I was young he left the light on,
To guide my way up the stairs at night.
A gift to let me know of that special day,
When I was brought into this world of life.

A little smile on the side of his cheek,
To let me know that he approved of me.
Of those times he had come into my room,
To check on me as I slept the night away.

Now he stands and looks into an empty room,
Looking at an empty bed beside empty walls.
As now I am the adult, living on my own,
I never stopped to realize the effects on him.

But I will always know there is a light on,
Just in case I so happen to need my Daddy.
A gift to let me know of that special day,
When I was brought into this world of life.

A little smile on the side of his cheek,
To let me know that he approves of me.
And that no matter how old I get,
I will always love being his LITTLE GIRL.

Nancy Engleder

Prejudice Or Precaution

Must it require black and white racial prejudice
    to justify our intelligence?
Or must it require rich or poor status precaution
    to justify our existence?

Must be our prejudicial provision
    to avoid our vulnerability be exposed to the others!
Or must be our advanced precaution
    to avoid our talents be superseded by the others!

Should we forget our faith and education
    to hold prejudice against our new comers?
Or should we insist our misconception and precaution
    to hold grudge against our new comers?

Should time be wasted with our blindfolded prejudice
    in our beautiful world?
Or should time be saved with our dedicated precaution
    in our endangered world?

Should we determine to have our prejudice
    vanished into our limited fresh air?
Or should we persevere to have our precaution
    energized in our diminishing clean air?

Pauline Chu

Oh Chirac, Please Wake Up

I wish I could invoke the muses
To wake you up from your slumber
You seem to have lost your senses
Why else would you let us ponder?

You have breathed fresh life into sirens
Who seduce men into terrible war
Decades can't erase the mental scar
Of the Japanese, victims of these sirens

Fail not, to open thine eyes
Lest you are raped by your own sirens
Attempt not, to close others' eyes
For they have been excited by sirens.

Dare not, to rape an innocent child
And burn its dream to become a virgin
'Peace' is still a very small child
Who longs to live and die as a virgin

Fifty years is too short
For a child to become a real lady
Dare not, to be over smart
And kill it's hope to become a lady

Arun H.

Perfection

Total perfection is an impossible day dream!
Total perfection is not in Nature's scheme!
He who brought light brought along shadow;
He who doesn't think can't open this window!
Total goodness fine though, is not possible,
Total evil will make all life impossible!

Those who desire light remove darkness;
Those who need darkness welcome darkness!
World, we can't think of without devils;
World survives only by countering evils!
For the humans' survival oxygen is the best!
For the growth of plant life c.o. two is a must!

Both of these need to be in a proper mix;
But for this, the whole world will be in a fix!
Where hangs the clue to this amazing balance?
Where lies the limit of this strange tolerance?
All the problems have answers they deserve;
Answers dawn only to those who observe!

R. Janakiraman

Lady Autumn

Autumn glides in on golden wings,
Trailing her scarlet gown,
An aging beauty with painted lips,
She lures the boys to town,
With air as sweet as summer wine
she permeates your soul,
"Come with me" she whispers "let joy
become your goal!"
Crispy days and smoky nights drenched
in Autumn's pleasures,
With no regrets she beckons you to
view her greatest treasures,
Through Rainbow-coloured foliage you
praise her vibrant noon,
Then dance with wild abandon beneath
her harvest moon,
Too soon it seems we hear the sound
of winters silver bell,
A gust of wind,
A puff of smoke and Autumn bids farewell.

Elizabeth Waltham

What Goes Around Comes Around

I live to survive on the streets of New York.
Trying to stay alive, cause no one would hire me to work.
My pocket ran out of luck.
And I'm down to my last buck.
Now I'm living the streets as a homeless.
Cause I've got no place to go.
So one day, I'm walking minding my own business.
And what do you know. I get busted.
Busted for walking the streets.
Busted for being a citizen. Ain't that a down fall.
It seems like no matter what I do.
I'm always crashing through the wall.
Give me a job I said. They looked at me like I was dead.
To them I was just a piece of meat.
All they had to do now. Was step on me with their feet.
As far as they were concerned.
I was a nobody. But that's okay.
Someday they will be just like me.
And that's when I'll say.
What goes around comes around.

T. J. Way

Sights

Bright city lights
twinkling - inviting
all modes of thought.

Sparkling - glittering
various hues and designs
reminding of never - never land.

Radiating good wishes and dreams
animating animals and humans alike
inspiring vacant stares.

Brilliant - bobbing points of luminescence
dancing and swaying seductively
sparking seldom used imaginations.

Altered focuses - blurring
reflecting off vehicles and windows
showing distorted images.

Eyes twinkle mischievously
as ideas silently creep
and night beams - onward.

Saadia Kendall

The Abyss

Many thoughts dance across the barren landscape,
Twirling, taunting, tantalizing.

I sit in my chair in the midst of this forgotten abyss,
Staring out into the blackness that has engulfed me,
Trapped me.

I try to capture those dancing messengers
    that carry the answer to my sanity,
Or the cure to my insanity.

I strike out into the abyss to strike down and recapture,
The long lost components of my sanity.

Still I only find its cause,
But not its creation.

As insane man fighting for his sanity,
A sane man locked in the abyss of the human mind.

Trevor Mulligan

A New Beginning

Here I lay nothing at all
Two individuals get together for the call
    To become one, they must engage
For the thrust of love must occur
    Like a dove, pure and soft
To endure one's feeling of emotion
    the out trust a loud, with the winter
white cloud up above.
For I am united with the goodness of love,
    a great bonding.
As I grow throughout the months,
    the warmth shines through; but to
everyone's sense I am find.
No matter of any was and downs; the days
are final for one to come.
    So beware of any pain, I am on
the way out.

Nick Chiaromonte

Our Mission

My brothers and sisters, don't you know?
    We have no other place to go
Mother Earth will soon come to an end,
Don't you have a helping hand to lend?

    Recycle paper, cans and more
        Clear up garbage
That clutter the floors

Prevent extinction,
Let the animals live
You know much you and me can give.

Save our ozone,
Stop pollution.
If we work hard, we'll find a solution.

Somehow, sometimes, someday
We'll all look up and be able to say
"We've saved our home today!"

Unite in the reconstruction of Mother Earth
And you'll be helping in her re-birth.

Bana K. Qabbani

Mall Love Event

Fish me from this tank.

"Date me by machine bank.
Wed me in cool bed furnishings.
Kill me not with love. Stationary or Optical
I must swim the whole mall free."

Pledge me your troth.
To love, honour and to shop
till debit death do us part.

A promisory note.
Your wafer thin plastic silver embossed,
that now lies spent, after the vast possession
sliced and skimmed through calculator scanner pads
honing the sharp edge of pleasure.
Heat in my trembling hand.

In defiant disgust I toss you up
over the brink, you flip, you float. Then sink
in a pet store fish tank. I cower away
drooping through a drowning mall.

Malevolent still you call to me

"Fish me from this tank."

Jocelyn Boileau

Untitled

Hand in hand
We'll abandon our respective communes
Since it's stopped raining
And the grass is wet
Wouldn't it be just splendid
If we lied down and
Made love in the dew,
Say, under a tree
While the raindrops fall
Upon our nakedness
From the green leaves above
Let nature cleanse the sweat
From our renounced corpses
Let's become one with the temporal moisture
Soaking up the earth and metamorpho-size into
The puddle the stream the brook
The river the lake the bay the ocean and
The ultimate current.
We'll become the torrent and concur in
The making of the abyss.

Mark Douglas Talbot

First Love

When you told me that you loved me
When you made my world shine
When you promised me the moon and stars
I thought we'd outlive time
I thought you meant forever
But forevers been and gone
The scenery changed, the characters died
And the mirror shows a pawn
The road that we once travelled
Has long since turned to dust
Yet still I am searching
For a love that turned to rust
It's been so long since I swam
In your eyes of blue
You've cast a spell upon my heart
Have I done the same to you?
After all the fights, after all this time
I still can't turn away
And to hear you whisper stay

Jenna S. Stevenson

Nature Rambles

Where the gentle breezes blow,
Where the golden geese sings,
Where the farmers come to sow,
Where the ploughman's furrows make rings,
There the greenfields look afresh,
Glistening with nature's diadem,
Listening to the sweet music when I ramble.

Where the busy birds are nestling,
Where the flora and fauna are much alive,
Where each flower dance so sprightly,
Where the swans swim so gracefully,
And the ducklings after them,
There is where my heart should have been.

Where the mountain goats walk wearily to their home,
Where the shimmering snow knows no bounds,
Where the lifeless valley becomes alive,
Where the seasons change,
Beyond any range,
And then again everything alters,
When I take my nature rambles.

Moses Albert Michael Jacob

"Beautiful Roses"

Beautiful roses carries petals
which is precious to the heart,
protect your petals
allow them not to be fatal,
for it is a value highly prize.

Beautiful roses carries thorns
which are the spikes to what you attained,
the privilege is yours, make it a choice,
favourable opinions, respect and regards
thus amending all the others.

Beautiful roses carries spikes and petals,
guard your roses with your spikes
avoiding heartaches, pain and grief
for in every color of the flower
is a message yet to follow.

Beautiful roses carries hate, death, love
virginity and purity,
guard your roses with your spikes
and wait upon the Lord to strike.

Dorothy Reid Richard

If Time Could Stand Still

My children are growing out of my life
Who can tell
How they'll be
Where will they go?

Lord,
I can't stop them from slipping away
If time could stand still
Just a little while longer
If time could stand still
Just for a minute longer

After all they are part of me
Part of my life
My most beautiful sight
If time could stand still, I wonder...
I could have them, a little while longer

My child,
All of my children are borrowed
Love them, cherish them,
Each and every moment
For one day, you will have them no longer...

Lise Bedard

Tribute To Terry Fox

There once was a young man, named Terry,
Who had a heavy load to carry,

But he didn't have any time to despair,
He showed us all what it means to care,

He labored each and every day,
Trying to lead us, along the way

Upon his face he wore a smile,
And it grew bigger, with each passing mile

But giving up was not his way,
He started to fight, and learned to pray,

In his strength, and in his youth,
He sought to show us all, the truth,

He did more than fulfill a dream,
He left us all with an inner gleam,

But the battle grew, both hard and tough,
And in the end was just to rough,

So growing tired and needing to rest,
Terry soared to heaven, to rest with the best.

Marion Pinsent

True Love Never Dies...

For all this time,
   You're such a wonderful guy to me,
The love that you gave me
   was the dream of my heart,
Never cry for anything
   'coz true love never dies...

My one and only love,
   The cute smiling face
      was the cutest thing I've ever seen,
Since the time we've been together
   thing started to change,
Never care what people say
   'coz our true love never dies...

My one,
   So please don't make me sad,
      'coz the sad will burn my heart,
      then into my eyes,
I'm gonna start to cry for you...

Never feel like this before since you,
   cause I love you and I really do...

Faezah Yahya

Resemblances

The flaming red sunset,
Your passionate love.

The frost on the windows,
Your striking and icy gaze.

Λ warm summers breeze,
Your embrace.

Fall leaves,
Your changing temperament.

Nature,
You.

Crystal Shields

Anum Dear

Anum is a nice girl,
who has achieved the status of a family pearl.

She befriends alike small and big,
And always gives the impression of being a big wig

She looks like a queen in her best,
But always avoids greed and lust

Everybody likes her indeed,
For her noble and admirable deeds

She is normally always in her best,
But when angry listens to nobody when bust

She would accept any task,
She keeps her head up as a mast

There s fragrance around her which gives good musk,
Frolicking around looks like a family musket

At times she feels she should must,
But parents and nobody can stifle her when bust

She would work up any family and school task,
And keeps her head always high like a mast

Muhammad Aslam

The Barber

There are many men
who were once lifted upon your High Throne
and were crowned with a haircut
that wa the mark of many a stubbled comment.

The big mirror is now gone
that holds forever the images
of our tiny heads gripped in a battle
as you clipped your way to victory.

Memories now itch away
at the back of our necks
reminding us of that cool breeze
you kept employed outside the shop door.

Now your High Throne sits empty
protected from the cool breeze and the rain
yet from time to time in some man's mind
a childhood thoughts sits upon it again.

Thomas Campbell

A Guilty Heart

Why is this pressure so hard to bear?
Why can't I except the people who care?

I need someone, yet I need to be free.

Why is it that no one can hear my plea?

I don't want to be hurt, or hurt the one who's best.
But I'm afraid that I'm worse than all of the rest.
I'm evil yet sweet, innocent yet wild.
I'm smart and wise, yet still a child.

If only you understood the way that I felt.
You wouldn't find me so bad, or the heart which did melt.

I'm sorry if my misleading ways caused you pain,
but my loss may be another's sweet gain.

Don't hate me for the grief I have brought.
From your love, I've learnt a lot.
And when I'm ready to commit my soul,
Remember you helped me along to be whole.

Simone Marie Bouchere

Why

Why Daddy why did you cheat and you lie?
Why did you have to make Mommy cry
Mommy say's we can't keep you where you don't want to stay.
Why Daddy why, did you hurt us this way?

Why Daddy why, did you love us then go?
Please tell me Daddy is it me? I don't know.
I miss the times when we'd sit and talk
Throw a ball or go for a walk

Why Daddy why, I was such a good boy,
You said I was your special little pride and joy.
Why Daddy why, is Mommy always so blue?
She says that you hit her because you couldn't be true

Why Daddy why, did you leave us alone?
Its my birthday today and I need you at home
When I blow out my candles and make wish
One will be for your hugs and a kiss.

Why Daddy why,I long for your touch,
Mommy and I, we love you so much
Why Dadd why, did you make Mommy cry
Why Daddy why, do you have to get high?

Denise Smagata

Pro-Life Or Pro-Choice?

It's my baby living and still
Will I love it or will I kill?
It's my baby, it's my choice;
But there is still that little voice.
I hear it when I think at night
No matter how I try to ignore with my might.
Crying and striving for life and peace,
Will the wailing ever cease?
Can I do this, destroy a life?
Or will my soul bleed as if cut with a knife?
I am a big girl.
I can handle this world.
An abortion is nothing,
And my baby is something.
I hear you my darling. I now listen to you.
I will let you live and let your dreams come true.

Myra M. McPhee

A Question

Someone asked me, "Why the obsession
  with bones and skeletons?"
I replied, "I feel like a little boy
  that can not sleep on Christmas eve...
It is a present - it is
  God's creation wrapped up in skin."

Patrick John Mills

Pure Magic

I love to watch the clouds roll by,
What a perfect splendor in the sky.
How thankfull we are that we can see,
God's perfect beauty, that was meant to be.
Life on earth can be a blessing on a strife,
It's all up to us and the strength of our night.
We are the product of our thoughts,
They do determine us our lot.
Let the light shine through and strengthen our faith,
For then the days to come will not be a weight.
Life is not meant to be so very tragic,
But to unfold a purpose that is pure magic.

Shirley M. Fisher

Lost Together

How long I have slept?
Twenty, thirty, hundred years, or a century!
With dwelling of passion, love and desire.
In a crimson coated lonely room, I woke up and found,
world is tight, small and restless.
I cannot weep, I cannot breathe, I cannot sink.

Then I thought, for whom the lotus opens the eyes!
For whom the window utters the sound!
Then it happened, lost in wilderness I met a vagrant thirsty deer.
And I read in his sleepy eyes, the thundering, rolling, creeping
storms; written on winds, carved on stones.

I ran after him, fast and fast.
And at last we stopped together.
Our eyes met and crossed the woven lines of time,
splashing and flowing the juicy lime!!

Then I thought.
Who can sleep and cross the dreams!
Who can touch the shining beams!!

For centuries, I and deer have ran and thought.
And together we are lost, lost and lost.

Ishrat Roomani

"Aching Heart"

It pours from deep down,
within her aching heart,
the agony of bitter sweet pain.
Of love that she has lost.
Memories of her beloved.
Pass often through the mind,
the loneliness unbearable,
as time keeps passing by.
In quiet moments she recalls.
His gentle loving ways.
A touch upon her shoulder,
reminder of his love,
not a day has she regretted,
sharing the years together.
He her husband, she his wife,
now he has gone forever.
She believes in her aching heart
that one day they will meet.
to continue the happiness,
they saluted in their youth.

Meryl Keswaui

Togetherness

How, we've grown so close
Year's have flown so far.
We're a pair the both of us.
We think the same all the time.

I really enjoyed my time with you.
And, I know you truly have too.
All the things and gifts you've bought.
Brings me tears sometimes a lot.

You're my knight in shining armors.
I'm your Queen of hearts.
The places and stuff we did together.
Makes me love you forever and ever.

Some days you get upset and disturbed
I try to talk and make it all better.
But, it doesn't help and you still depressed
Giving a hug and kiss then you rest
Togetherness always.

Valerie Bradley

Hello

Hello is such an easy word
yet often hard to say;
and now I find my lips can't move each time you pass my way.
A mere hello could start off fine and work it's real smooth
If only I could find the strength,
to force my lips to move.

I say hello one thousands times,
I hold my lips real tight;
But when I see you in the halls
I feel my lips turn white.

If only I could know for sure
that you wouldn't turn and walk away,
Then maybe this mere simple word,
wouldn't be so hard to say!

Nancy Horowitz

My Child

I look into your eyes and I am filled with awe and wonder
You are the creation of millions of wishes
You were born of prayers, hopes and dreams
You are my child, innocent and dear.

I look at you and see the future
You are the glory of generations gone long ago
You are the final branch of a fading family tree
You are my child, alive and well.

I long to protect you and keep you safe
You are my heart, my soul, my very being
You began a seed that has been nurtured and loved
You are my child, my flesh and blood.

I look at you and see an individual, distinct and unique
Free of all past injustices and guilt
Free of spirit, thought, and idea
You are my child, strong and free.

I see in your eyes a light that shall endure
You are a glow in the darkness
You are my star on earth
You are my child, full of promise and hope.

Salmana Mellick

The Good Shepherd

Come home, come home the Good Shepherd said
You have wandered too far you are being mislead

Come here, come here where the sweet waters flow
and rest for a while till the cobwebs all go

Be still, be still by the soft rippling stream
and the wisdom you'll find will answer your dream

Then listen, just listen for the voice you will now
and He will give you direction on just where to go

Then follow, just follow the footprints I leave
and your sure to find home when you truly believe

Remember, remember when you just follow me
there's peace and contentment so let yourself be

Anon, anon as you travel along
secure in My love you will burst into song

Your home, your home you will find you say
and wander no more from the Good Shepherd's way

Sarah Innes Bell

Those Visions Your Heart Can See

Dreams are fragile thing
You hold in the palm of your hand,
Like looking through an hourglass
Washing away the sand.

Dreams sometimes seem an illusion
Simply too hard to make come true.
Too far out of reach
You feel there's nothing you can do.

Dreams are often just dreams
To comfort on a dreary day,
When things become too much
They find that elusive sunday .

But dreams can't live without
For without them what is left?
Your destiny left unfulfilled
As the soul has silently wept.

Don't throw your dreams,
Those vision your heart can see.
Follow those visions
For your heart holds the key.

Sandra Parker

The Deer Hunter

I seek you in the shadow of your days,
You of the cloven hoof play fast and loose
With my weak senses. Lost in veils of spruce
I follow through your dim and mossy ways,
Until I think that I should strike a truce
And leave the encumbered reaches to the Jays.
November's sun is cold but still your track
Draws at my huntsman's spirit, on and on,
Deep in the labyrinth of tamarack.
T'was so with a red leaf'd October dawn,
When a quick chipmunk mocked me in your wake
And Autumn painted pictures on a lake.
I saw you and before the bow was drawn
Your swifts glance signalled "Fool" and you were gone.

Frank MacGregor Caswell

Tragedy

Stay and have another one
Your car will always wait
Stay and have another one
Now it's time to chance your fate

You've got to leave the bar now
You say, "I've only had a few"
Come on! Hop in I'll drive you home
Let's see what this bucket of bolts will do

We headed home then
Never thought someone would die
Hit a bump in the road
Was that a baby cry?

We killed a little kid
My life will never be the same
It was a little baby
I've got to live with that pain

I've had to dictate this
I'm paralyzed from the neck down
It would have been better if I had died
But I'm left alive to drown.

Sheila Churly

624

O Dolce Vita

O sweetness of life
Let me breath in
The life-giving oxygen
To see the world anew.
I sigh with relief.
I am not dead.
I am reborn.
Everything is new:
A blade of grass,
A petal on a flower,
The petal of a rose.
The iron mist entered my soul
Is gone from my breath.
In peace I can rest
When time runs out
Put until then
I will rage, rage,
Against me dying of the light.

W. B. McDade

Be Valiant

Be strong, Be brave
Let this spirit shine through
We must try and save
Those left are but few

One by one they are falling
Amid the fray in their jungles
Victim, they are all ailing
From a virus of rainbow bubbles

For this is the ME world
Idolizing and venerating stardom
Filled with vice and demeaning mores
All disguised in the name of freedom

So we must help reassemble
All their parts and edifices
Make them all more capable
In their reasoning and wishes

Be strong, Be brave
We must remain constant
We've no more need for slaves
Stand firm, Be valiant

Marcelle Dakin

My Thoughts

Empty, my life empty
Nothingness, like a bottomless pit.
Disappointments and betrayals
In a world full of trials.
Self destruction I thought of
But then: What about my God above?
Would he forgive me?
I hope that he would,
For to end my life I wonder if I could.
Would it be worth it?
Sometimes I think yes,
But what would God say?
Maybe I am bless
To have him to talk to,
Otherwise what would I do?
Without him I'll be doomed.
Thank you god for listening;
I'll start a new beginning.
Accept myself for who I am
Or else I'll be damned.

Gloria Franklyn

A Dream

My child you dear
I wish you exsisted
In my hearth you are near
Often I had a dream
A son a daughter who knows?
You would be given all the understanding
You wishes of tenderness and love
Be guided to be yourself
Honest and faithful
Good to your fellow man
Strong to stand against temptations
Clear the life's difficulty
So good it is possibly
This was my dream.

Solveig Olsson

I Would Dream

When I was young,
I would make believe.
I would dream,
About how I would look,
How I would talk,
When I was older.
I don't make believe.
I don't dream.
Who has time?
Now I sit and think
About where I went wrong.
How I was supposed to change.

I'm not a child, why should I dream?
I can't change how life is.
I don't make believe.
At least not anymore.
There's no purpose.
Now I can only plan and fix my mistakes
I made of on the way here
What to do, how to act, how to dream.

Allisha McFarlane

Unrequited Love

My hands start to tremble,
If you glance my way;
A simple smile from you
Will brighten my day.

When I close my eyes,
I see your face;
I feel the heat
Of your embrace.

But reality hits me
When I wake;
The absence of your love
Makes my heart ache.

This hole in my heart
Refuses to heal;
Without you near
The pain is real.

So although I know,
The love isn't true;
In my heart I feel
I will always love you.

Stacy Lavery

Feeling Rough

Come home today feeling rough
I had juts about enough
Sat down in my easy chair
Because I wasn't going anywhere
Then all of a sudden I heard "hi"
Couldn't figure out from where and why
Then I seen this gorgeous bird
Then I head another word

And there I was sitting and amazed
Just wondered what and dazed
It was a parrot and told me so
Lonesome to I did not know
Said it did not have a home
And was too tired of having to roam
It took my feelings all away
What I had when I come home today
And now this parrot is with me
And we're as happy as can be

Tom Flottorp

Remain(s)

Wandering across untamed gardens
I hear the sound of my breath
The once lost city wardens
Now resurrect from death

Trees cross near-gone paths
And silence is pressing on my breast
Rocks reflect the sun that casts
Rays through an old eagle's nest.

I see the birds fly away
Fast and accurate aimed
In the beauty I cannot stay
It's bound to be untamed

Stefan Dreverman

The Empty Nest

As I look out in my window today,
I see a sparrow in a tree
Her head is down, I wonder why
I then see her children fly
They soar up to the bright blue sky.
My head is down, I wonder why
My children waved and said good-bye.
The sparrow has left her lovely tree
And I think to myself that she is free
We both have shared that lovely tree
The Empty Nest, the Empty Nest.

Sharon Watson

Life In Brief

I wake up in the mornings light,
I go asleep in the dawns light,
And If I die before I wake
I beg God my soul to take.
My life and soul are all alone
My family and my friends are gone
and when I prey to get. Them home
It doesn't work at all, bet when I
get my life a grown I fall
asleep to hear It all. In brief my life.

Jacqueline Murray

Confusion

Everything the same yet different
I don't understand
Today I feel I've grown
Yet I still know not enough
Doing the same thing as always
But for the first time
Acting different to a known situation
Meeting new people
You've known all your life
Don't know what I'm thinking
But still thinking to much
Mind is racing
With different thoughts and emotions
I feel love
But for who
I'm alone.

Lisa Hendry

Living In Isolation

The mass of darkness held no light.
I existed in permanent isolation
Enduing crucifixion.
My faith dwindled in the wind
Replaced by fear and hopelessness.
My soul shattered with shame and grief.
My mind disappeared.
I carried my cross everyday.
It weighed my spirit down.
My life was a journey of blackness
Blindly, leading top my final crucifixion.
Then she gave her hand.
She carried my cross.
Her voice became my salvation.
She soothed my mind
And calmed my spirit.
She became my saviour.
She bore my burden
And endured my pain.
She gave me life again.

Vanessa Tarsia

Resolve

You weigh heavy on my soul.
I feel your loss, I feel your anger,
And I cannot bear it. I want to try,
But my fear holds me back.
It is your burden, and I have no influence.
I feel your touch, I feel your love,
And I cannot bear it. It stings and
smacks...
And I wait for collapse.
I cannot live in your past.
I will not be haunted by your ghosts.
I cannot bear them.
My soul is struggling to remain free,
strong...
And you weaken me. I have doubt,
And I cannot bear it. It is not from
weakness,
But my choice.
My ghosts are buried, my loss recouped,
My anger gone, my soul...weightless.
So what am I to do?
How can I to live: With or without you?
I cannot bear it. And yet I know, I will.

Victoria Harrison

For You

As long as you love me
I'll stay by your side
I'll be your companion
Your friend and your guide
I'll bring you the sunshine
I'll comfort your fears
I'll gather up rainbows
To chase all your fears
As long as forever
My love will be true
For as long as you love me
I will always love you

Teresa Reeve

Mother

The gate was open
In fact it was just a jar
Of coagulated fetuses.
Aborted by
The unmakers
Of life.

You quit!
You stopped
Having children.

Thanks be to St. Peter
He left the gate, not
A moment too soon.

The crack was so small
I nearly lost you all.

Maria Rottluff

Lost

The pain, the anger, the hurt
It's all here
Buried deep within my heart
Sometimes at night
When I'm asleep
It creeps from it's hidden depth
To torture me
I thought that I could bury it
The pain, the anger, the hurt
Deep, deep within this soul
I am sad; I am lots
Oh Lord, my soul cries
For freedom long ago lost.

Leona A. Naylor

With This Hand

With this hand
I've held onto hatred, and
with this hand I've painted more
than a stranger, with this hand
I've stolen for profit, and with
this hand I've pointed in
anger, with this hand I've
rejected warm tidings, and with
this hand I've forsaken my neighbor,
with this hand I've dealt in
deception, and with this hand I've
played with seduction, with this
hand I now find hand to live
with, and by this hand I
must pray for forgiveness.

Jim Walters

The Fae

Moonpale, her skin trembles at his touch.
Her pulse, a caged butterfly
Beats in her throat.
Her kiss is nectar sweet
As morning dew.
In night's velvet embrace
Holding the mortal she lays,
With breezes caresses,
With rose petal touches
She loves the mortal.
They are Ophite symbols,
Translucent bodies twining on the grass.
She will be gone
In the morning,
Born away on Seetie wings.
And he will wander,
Will find his cottage,
A hundred years later
That day.

Lila Bender

Untitled

Hello, my little angel,
How are you, today?

Are you happy,
Full of fun,
And are you ready to play?

We have toys,
We have laughter,
Running, jumping
And lots of noise!

So won't you come
and join in
With all the girls
and boys!

Hello, my little angel
How are you, today?

Sherrie Collins

Untitled

This house
I can sit and stare at its walls forever
forever is mighty long time for a family
Striped
Of all warmth
I left it
Checkered
They left it
Raped
He will never leave
It was a beautiful home
Where is home
I am so sad for the
Bareness
This house
Graves
For the loss of a family
For the loss of feeling
This house
Was my friend.

Carla Wilkie

Nature's Natural Wonders

A sprinklings of shimmering gold-dusted stars suspended low in the
Heavens fill me with awe and delight,
On his warm still evening of a mid summers night.
As I gaze up in wonder at what God's imagination has wrought,
I am humbly reminded of earthly treasures "created:, not bought.
A shooting star spiralling downward, the moon "Dipper" and Milky Way".
All for the viewing each and every day!
The beauties of nature surround us majestic mountains, seashells,
    tropical rainforests, valleys, crystal-blue seas,
Translucent rainbows, magnificent sunsets and sky-blue Robin eggs
    nested on a branch in a tree.
The quiet hush of winter's frozen landscape beneath a mantle of new-fallen snow.
And in Spring-time, renewal, rebirth
    and refreshing rainshowers making everything grow.
Golden fields of grain ripening and swaying in the sun,
And the blessing of a bountiful harvest over and done.
The cool days of Autumn when leaves of orange, gold, and red are falling,
While over-head migrating geese can be heard honking and calling.
In viewing these natural wonders it is difficult to deny,
The existence of a supernatural "being' far greater than you or I.
This world, this Universe of splendor did not just happen to "be".
I was carefully planned and orchestrated by our "Creator" for the
    inspiration and enjoyment of you and me.
So thank you God for these "snapshot" moments" we revel in and savour.
May be continue to find, hope, peace and happiness as we remain in
    your love and favour!

Bonnie Baker-Leuser

Poetic Heart

Oh poetic heart,
Now that your blue candle eyes set-off flames that scorch my heart,
And your almond scented sighs extinguish whispers that we do not part,
You give me sweet content, and woo me much more.

And now that the sweet berry dew dawns on colored rainbow shades,
And the lovely moon, taps its silver slipper shoe to vow your love
    within its fairest cascades,
Your pearly white hands tickle my nights in the calmest slumber,
And your pearly white fangs suck at my heart to feed your hunger.

Oh poetic heart,
I can now hush the tempered tone and possess the poet's tongue,
So I may scrawl this like dream poem to place our love within this song.
Colour in the toneless rainbow with velvet red and peacock
blue and paint with gentle strokes this morning maiden dew.

Dip in the pleasures beside the river in pearly trickles and silver
shades pillow the journey of the falling stars on dusky sketches and
tranquil cascades. Outline the smiles in the picturesque spring for
the red-red robin to play in the autumn wind, and the echoes of the
rustling green-leafed dishes shall whisper my heart of wishes.

Elaine Mary Dutton

Tired After a Night of Writing

I'm so very tired after writing all night
            last night
                my eyes are dripping way below their sockets
                into the half-empty cup of coffee on my desk

    I can see the grinds in the bottom of the cup
      The marbleized paper I'm now writing on is wet
          with warm ideas
            and still born thoughts of evening
              and sleep
                and sleep
                  dear sleep counting white sheep
                    as the lunge through my open wide eyes
                    into my coffee
                    plop

Andrew Derringer

Stephen F, Austin, The Great Explorer

Moses had a plan of colonizing,
But at his old age, his health was failing.

Stephen F. Austin was the man,
Who carried out his father's plan.

With the Old Three Hundred, Austin came,
While doing this, he earned some fame.

They continued down, farther south,
They reached two rivers, near the mouth.

There in between the two rivers,
They ate deer, even the livers.
6the rivers were Brazos and Colorado,
This was definitely the best place to go.

He then left for Mexico City,
When he returned, the land wasn't pretty.

Many problems faced Austin when he returned,
A serious drought had occurred.

Finally Austin and Bastrop settled the land claims,
He wrote them down there were so many names.

After competing the contract, at age 31,
Stephen Austin said, "At last, it's done!"

Michelle Tiemeier

BIOGRAPHIES
OF POETS

ABALLI, MAXINE WITTE
[b.] August 8, 1931, San Diego, CA; [p.] Irish and stepfather Ralph Sawyer; [m.] George J. Aballi (Deceased), January 30, 1976; [ch.] Former marriage: Gary, Ronald and Russell - all married and on their own; [ed.] Brawley Junior High School, Woodbury College in LA, now Woodbury University in Burbank; [occ.] Retired; [memb.] In the past: Eastern Stars (Demitted), Republican Women's Club - All in LA Area. In College: Alpha Iota Sorority. Here in Arizona: I belong to a group trying to get recognized as a church of religious science.; [hon.] When working several sales awards had the honor to be introduced to the Calif. Senate and Assembly for work AA quiet American re: The Pledge of Allegiance. I was the 1st Miss Imperial Valley in 1950 to participate in Miss California Pageant the year before Miss Universe. I also trained a young lady - entered her in the 1994 Miss Calif Pageant she was one of the top 5.; [oth. writ.] I entered your contest last year, was told I won the Editor's Choice for "My Daddy is in Heaven" printed in "Mist of Enchantments", invited to join the International Society of Poets. Have sent them several poems.; [pers.] I believe strongly in faith and the God given ability that we are what we think our biggest challenge is keeping a positive attitude. God's Law is as we think we put into action we create our own situation.; [a.] Lake Havasu City, AZ

ABATE, STEVEN
[b.] September 28, 1976; [ed.] Patapsco High, West Virginia University; [pers.] Enjoy your own company and live by God's will and any problems that arise will resolve themselves peacefully.; [a.] Baltimore, MD

ACEVEDO, JUDITH
[b.] July 17, 1948, Brooklyn, NY; [p.] John Acevedo and Epifania Vazquez; [ed.] High School Graduate (Eli Whitney High School); [occ.] Legal Secretary; [memb.] International Society of Poets Poetry Society of America; [a.] Brooklyn, NY

ACHTTIEN, CHARLOTTE WIGER
[pen.] Char W. (I sign on oil paintings); [b.] November 28, 1931, Donnelly, MN; [p.] Grace and Julius Gilbertson; [m.] 1954-1981 to Don Wiger (Now deceased) 1988 to present John Achttien; [ch.] Debra Geraghty, Charles Wiger, 5 stepchildren; [ed.] BS in Elementary Educ. plus 1 year graduate work, plus Kdgn. Educ.; [occ.] Retired Teacher taught 38 years - first grade and kdgn.; [memb.] Active Member - Luth. Church of Christ The King, Retired Teachers of Moorhead, and Ream-Retired Educators Assis. of Minn.; [hon.] Treas.-Mate Moorhead Ass'n. of Teacher Educators, - 2 years. Bldg. Rep. to Mea.-Moorhead Educ. Ass'n. - 2 yrs. served, 2 years on Effective School Comm. of Moorhead.; [oth. writ.] None published; [pers.] I always try to reflect a positive attitude toward anyone I encounter. I wished for each child to have positive successful days by the attitude I set forth. People and life experiences have influenced my way of thinking.; [a.] Moorhead, MN

ADAMS, LOUIS
[pen.] Henry Louis Adams Jr.; [b.] August 4, 1971, Atlanta, GA; [p.] Henry Adams, Alma Adams; [ed.] Shamrock High School (Decatur, GA) Career Development Institute (Atlanta, GA); [occ.] Minister, Minister called to the office of a Prophet; [memb.] Dekalb United Pentecostal Church (Stone Mountain, GA); [hon.] Inspiration Awards; [oth. writ.] Several poems recorded and put to music for the sole purpose to glorify our Lord and savior Jesus Christ!!!; [pers.] The poetic ministry of Louis Adams is a division of the ministry of Louis Adams Inc. The sole purpose of the poetry is to be a channel in which God can communicate to ones spirit and encourage them with a word from on high!!!; [a.] Atlanta, GA

ADAMS, STEVEN R.
[b.] August 22, 1965, Quincy, IL; [p.] Donald and Sally Adams; [ed.] Quincy Senior High School, B.A. University of Kentucky, J.D. Salmon P. Chase College of Law; [occ.] Attorney; [a.] Cincinnati, OH

AGRO, NICASIA
[pen.] Nicki Jo; [b.] Spetember 5, 1984, Voorhees, NJ; [p.] Angelo and Rosalie Agro; [ed.] In 6th Grade at Voorhees Middle School; [occ.] Student, 6th Grade; [memb.] Junior Episcopal Youth Club - St. Bartholomew's Episcopal Church, Cherry Hill, NJ; [pers.] "I am a kind and fun loving person..."; [a.] Voorhees, NJ

AHMED, SHAH SALM
[b.] February 12, 1941, Calcutta; [p.] Dr. Wali Ahmed and Mrs. Marium Wali Ahmed; [ch.] Shah Fahim Ahmed (name has been changed) Abducted and missing with my ex-wife.; [ed.] Islamia High School, Calcutta, India., Quaid-E-Azam College, Dhaka, Bangladesh, Long Island University, Brooklyn, N.Y.C.; [occ.] Self Employed; [memb.] General Secretary: Pakistanis' Well Wishers' Association, N.Y.C.; [hon.] Award of Merits on services rendered to Pakistani community, received from the hon. Chief Justice of the Supreme Court of Pakistan in Columbia Univeristy, N.Y.C. in 1992, Couple of Certificates and Awards were receive from the National Library of Poetry and International Society of Poets, Maryland, USA.; [oth. writ.] One great book in Urdu Language named "Ehsaas-E-Zian" got published from Jung publications, Lahore, Pakistan. in 1992.; [pers.] It's my study, the best religion in the world is human-conscience, or say any religion which practices human-conscience and conscience only, is the best religion. Beware of fear and favour, prejudice and passion, and stay Holy and Clean. Like a prophet.; [a.] New York City, NY

AHMED, SHAH SALIM
[b.] February 12, 1941, Calcutta; [p.] Dr. Wali Ahmed and Mrs. Marium Wali Ahmed; [ch.] Shah Fahim Ahmed (Name has been change) Abducted and missing with my ex-wife.; [ed.] Islamia High School, Calcutta, India, Quaid-E-Azam College, Dhaka, Bangladesh, Long Island University, Brooklyn., N.Y.C.; [occ.] Self Employed; [memb.] General Secretary: Pakistans' Well Wishers' Association, N.Y.C.; [hon.] Award of Merits on Services rendered to Pakistani Community, received from the Hon. Chief Justice of The Supreme Court of Pakistan in Columbia University, N.Y.C. in 1992, Couple of Certificates and Awards were received from The National Library of Poetry and International Society of Poets, Maryland, USA; [oth. writ.] One great book in Urdu language named "Ehsaas-E-Zian" got published from Jung publica-tions, Lahore, Pakistan, in 1992.; [pers.] It's my study, the best religion in the world is human conscience, or say any religion which practices human-conscience and conscience only, is the best religion. Beware of fear and favor, prejudice and passion, and stay holy and clean. Like a Prophet.; [a.] New York City, NY

AIELLO, CAROLYN M.
[b.] April 1953, Los Angeles, CA; [p.] Frank Aiello and Jean O'Reilly; [occ.] Real Estate Broker, Owner of C.M.A. North Bay, Santa Rosa, CA; [memb.] President, Northwest (NWCA) Community Association, Chairperson, (SMHS) San Marcos High School, Class of 71, Reunion Committee, California Assoc. (CAR) of Realtors, National Assoc. of Realtors (NAR); [hon.] Daughters of American (DAR) Revolution Good Citizen Medal, National Junior Honor Society, Rotary Club Out-standing Achievement and Leadership Award, P.T.A. Outstanding Academic Achievement, U.C. LA Scholarship; [pers.] I was inspired by my personal experiences proceeding the death of my mother to write this poem in an effort to comfort a friend.; [a.] Santa Rosa, CA

ALDERDICE, LAURA BRATENAHL
[pen.] Laura Alderdice; [b.] August 29, 1949, Berkeley, CA; [p.] Alexander and Roberta Bratenahl; [m.] Dr. Mark Alderdice; [ch.] Alison and Monique Alderdice; [ed.] Polytechnic HS, Pasadena Pomona College, Claremont, UC Berke-ley, BA Music; [occ.] Musician and Boat Captain; [oth. writ.] Several poems published in Pt. Reyes Light, Pt. Reyes, CA; [pers.] I have spent my life uncovering harmony and harmonic connections, helped by many, many teachers. Harmony is what I would express, and gratitude.; [a.] Watsonville, CA

ALEXANDER, DENISE
[pen.] Alex; [b.] October 25, 1980, Concordia, KS; [p.] Dennis Alexander, Patricia Bosserman; [ed.] Clifton - Clyde High School; [occ.] Dairy Farm Assistant, Alexander Dairy, Clifton, KS; [memb.] FBLA.; [hon.] Most Outstanding Language Arts Student; [oth. writ.] A couple published in poetry newspapers.; [pers.] I write it how I feel it.; [a.] Clifton, KS

ALEXANDER, WALTER
[b.] December 2, 1929, Obion Country, TN; [p.] Knox and Zelma Alexander; [m.] Anne L. Alexander, May 26, 1950; [ch.] Sheila Stella (43), Mike Alexander (40), Sandra Greganti (37); [ed.] Graduate Martin High School-Martin, TN, Gradu-ate University of Tenn. - Martin, TN; [occ.] A. and W. Design (Semi-Retired); [memb.] Church of Christ, Hermitage, Tennessee; [hon.] Past Member of Sales and Marketing Executives (Numerous Sales and Leadership Awards); [oth. writ.] Several poems in my possession, none of which have been published.; [pers.] I strive to be a helping and caring person. I try not to expect more of others than I do of myself.; [a.] Mt. Juliet, TN

ALI, SAYED HUSAIN
[pen.] Sakib; [b.] January 6, 1953, Amalner, Jalgaon Maharashtra; [p.] Late Samad Ali, Shahdutt-bi; [m.] Shaheen Bano Sayed Husain Ali, November 16, 1988; [ch.] One son, another is daughter.; [ed.] Passed M.A. with English from Bombay Univer-

sity, India; [occ.] Postal Clerk in a mail center; [memb.] No where. except your library.; [hon.] Nothing at all until now.; [oth. writ.] In URDU, My mother tongue - Poems and stories. Hindi Poems and stories. English Poems and stories.; [pers.] I have been encourage by you only for publishing my poems. As Philosophy on life. Happiness, the way. Words of wisdom, Don't Quit.; [a.] Tanajib Dhahran, Kingdom of Saudi Arabia

ALKIRE, ARJAY A.
[pen.] "Wahoo" (Wahoo Ranch); [b.] December 21, 1963, FL; [p.] Richard James and Peal Anna Alkire; [ed.] John I. Leonard High, West Palm Beach FL; [occ.] Truck driver, writer and poet; [memb.] Shady Grove Baptist Church; [hon.] Recognized and first discovered by: The National Library of Poetry; [oth. writ.] Currently writing novel, "Whoever, Wherever You Are" to my daughter adopted at birth. Story and poems published in the "Suwannee Democrat." Seeking discovery and career in writing.; [pers.] My novel will be my life: From nowhere to live and nothing to eat, to being in a movie and commercial, and no longer on the street. Writing poems and entering contests. Putting my talent to work. And hoping for the best.; [a.] Live Oak, FL

ALLEE, CHERYL LYNN
[b.] June 3, 1959, Charlotte, NC; [p.] Uriel Sylvan and Mary Ingram Allee; [ed.] Myers Park High (Charlotte, NC), Queens College (Charlotte, NC), University of North Carolina at Greensboro, The American University (Washington, DC); [memb.] American Political Science Assoc., Mortar Board National College Honor Society, Presidential Management Alumni Group.; [hon.] Various academic honors and awards during formal education years and professional recognitions during recently-completed tenure as a federal government employee.; [oth. writ.] "The Impact of Disabilities on Federal Career Success", with Greg Lewis, Public Administration Review, July/August 1992.; [pers.] I write in celebration of life in all its aspects but with a particular appreciation for life's many ironies and subtleties.; [a.] Alexandra, VA

ALLEN, ALYSON
[b.] May 31, 1981, The Bronx, NY; [p.] Neville Allen and Doreen Allen; [ed.] Public School 121, Middle School 144, Brooklyn Technical High School; [memb.] The American Museum of Natural History; [pers.] Life is nothing more than good and bad memories.; [a.] Baychester, NY

ALLEN, JAMES
[pen.] James Allen; [b.] November 21, 1952, Helena, AR; [p.] James Oren and Earline Allen; [ch.] Leah Jo Allen; [ed.] Associates in Electronics, General Class FCC License; [occ.] Technician-Coca-Cola Columbia, South Carolina; [hon.] 2nd Place South/East Arkansas Song Writing Contest; [oth. writ.] Once a week daddy a song for mama, close to my heart and I close my eyes.; [pers.] Want my songs and poems to touch people's hearts.; [a.] Columbia, SC

ALLEN, MRS. DIANNE R.
[b.] September 21, 1948, Chicago, IL; [p.] Mr. Thedore R. and Mrs. Wanda M. Vincent; [m.] Mr. Thomas G. Allen, September 23, 1972; [ch.] Mrs.

Victoria E. Halberg; [ed.] St. Sylvester Elementary, Madonna High, St. Vincent De Paul Infant Asylum; [occ.] Unemployed; [hon.] Degree - Child Care Technician; [oth. writ.] Short Stories: "200 Hundred Dead", "Victoria", "Dad", "Angel", "Working For Your Present" - short articles, "Thanksgiving Preparation", "California Bomb Scare", and "Street Incident" - Poetry, "Two Weeks Before Christmas", "New Year's Eve Planned", "While I Sleep", and "Stranger In My Room".; [pers.] "To writers - if you're going to dribble, play basketball".; [a.] Chicago, IL

ALLISON, CATHERINE
[b.] February 16, 1947, Havana, FL; [p.] Mrs. Rossie Huntley; [m.] David Allison, January 19, 1970; [ch.] Steven, Timothy, Kelvin, Jefferey, David Jr., Angela; [ed.] Graduate Havana Northside High, Associate of Arts Degree Nova Southeastern University, Presently Attending Nove SE and Fla. A and M University to attain Bachelors of Science Degree; [occ.] Presently Employed, Godsen County School Board - Havana Elem. Sch. Teacher Assistant; [memb.] New Bethel P.B. Church, North Florida Reading Council; [hon.] Dean's List Nova Southeastern University. Certificate of Appreciation 5thGrade Department; [oth. writ.] Spiritual Warfare, Joy Cometh In The Morning, Conquer The Dream, Mama's Baby Boy, Giving Something Back.; [pers.] It is not the smart or the swift who survives the continual ups and down of the experiences from life. It is only the strength of endurance, given from God's grace to behold the winner of the race.; [a.] Havana, FL

ANDERSON, CLEVE
[b.] June 27; [oth. writ.] A Book entitled: The Nuclear Threat that Dwarfs the Bomb plus many articles on plutonium including my most recent one - Defusing Weapons Plutonium; [pers.] I share the belief of the Hopis, a peace loving Indian tribe, "There are many paths to the Summit but there is only one God. Tolerance of people with different beliefs is an important step toward word harmony".; [a.] Green Valley, AZ

ANDERSON, ELIZABETH C.
[b.] October 30, 1957, Toronto, Canada; [p.] Robert K. Anderson, Rose E. Anderson; [m.] Divorced; [ch.] Michael Joseph; [ed.] Michael Power, St. Joseph's Secondary School, Humber College of Applied Arts and Technology, Etobicoke, Ontario; [occ.] Administrative Assistant, Royal Bank of Canada; [hon.] Several Special Achievement Awards (Royal Bank); [oth. writ.] Many poems written for personal pleasure.; [pers.] For these I strive: To lead the good clean life, To keep a song in my heart, And to try to do things right.; [a.] Etobicoke Ontario, Canada

ANDERSON, RANDY
[b.] May 18, 1962, Toronto, Ontario, Canada; [p.] Barb Keown, David Anderson; [m.] Rhonda James, Engaged; [ch.] Ashlynn 3, Lindsay 9, Gabe 13; [ed.] Sutton District High 1 year Senaca College; [occ.] Courier Driver and Network Marketing.; [oth. writ.] This poem was the first poem or story I have ever written; [pers.] The May 1, 1995 Edition of News week Magazine were a picture appeared on its cover with a fireman cradling a small child named Baylee in His Arms, was the basis for my poem the

strength and courage of Baylee's mother truly inspired me, that is why I dedicate this poem to Baylee's mother. Hobbies: Hockey, Darts, Waterskiing, Reading.

ANDERSON, VERNON OWEN
[b.] May 23, 1920, Kenosha, WI; [ed.] University of Wis., BS, '50, MS, '51; [occ.] Taught Art and Enlish, mader career in Advtg. Dir. - Public Rel. Dir. for food distrib. corp. in Southwest, wrote PR copy and and monthly col. for nat. food journals. "Evolution of Food Industry in USA." Currently retired, organist in local Bible church, write and publish biblical commentaries on current world affairs. Continuing writing personalized poetry for weddings, birthdays, retirements, etc. recreate on organs playing music of Big Bands; [hon.] Phi Eta Sigma Hon. Soc.; [pers.] I am eternally grateful for life of good health and spiritual well-being.; [a.] Riverside, CA

ANDISMAN, MARCIA
[b.] June 22, 1945, NY; [p.] Mollie and William Andisman; [ed.] Theo Roosevelt H.S. 1963, Hunter College 1967; [occ.] Executive in Fashion Industry; [memb.] Fashion Group NYC; [oth. writ.] Numerous poems about friends, special occasions, my life etc.; [pers.] Yesterday is history tomorrow is a mystery, today is a gift that's why it's called "The Present" Enjoy those you love; [a.] New York City, NY

ANDREANO
[b.] August 30, 1972, Madder Than, MA; [p.] Sun, Moon; [ch.] Secret, Spider, Devil, Dance; [ed.] This life and my previous 7.; [occ.] Martyr; [memb.] Friends of the Anti-Gravity Program, Violet Voodoo, Gina's Tiny Head; [hon.] "Mad Rocket of the Disenchanted Comet Parade of Enlightened Perception"; [oth. writ.] In 1991, wrote pilot episode of "My Little Hedgehog Friend" which, unfortunately, never aired.; [pers.] Blast from the live. It hurts too. Outlined by your best side. The fat black of the trip drips before you. Miniaturize. Rise like a tide.; [a.] Milford, MA

ANELLO, MICHAEL V.
[b.] March 26, 1973, NF Memorial; [p.] Mr. Matteo Anello and Ms. Jeri Anello; [ed.] Undergraduate at U.B.; [occ.] Billing Department Assistant; [pers.] The poem Wishing Well is solely dedicated to Julia Maurren Hope - who, for a time, was the source and focus of all my love and inspiration.; [a.] Niagara Falls, NY

APPLETON, MIRIAM
[b.] November 1, 1974, Camp Lejeune, NC; [p.] Miriam and David Appleton; [ed.] High School - Toms River North, Toms River, NJ College - U of MS. and Trenton State College; [occ.] Jewelry Sales; [oth. writ.] 1st time published

ARTHURS, KEVIN LINDSEY
[pen.] Kevin Lindsey Arthurs; [b.] April 23, 1961, Mendota, IL; [p.] Mr. and Mrs. A. L. Arthurs; [m.] Ex-wife: Amy Lynn Saunders, February 14, 1985 (Valentines Day); [ch.] None to my knowledge; [ed.] Grade School: Blackstone School, Middle School: Northbrook Jr. High School, High School: Mendota High School, Graduation date: June 6, 1979, Illinois Valley Community College from

1982 through 1992, all located in North Central, Illinois, LaSalle County; [occ.] Helping to run a Subway Sandwitch Shop, located in Roswell, NM; [memb.] Unfortunately none currently, my work and personal life don't allow me much time. Currently have a hastings books and records card and two library cards.; [hon.] Various art awards, during High School. I also was involved in Drama and music, during my Soph., through Senior Years in High School. Showed Art work, during both High School and college years.; [oth. writ.] I had about eight poems published, in a Junior College Newspaper (Kaleidoscope) during the two years, which I attended in 1986 through 1987 - Kishwaukee Jr. College, located in Malta, Illinois. Lots of unfinished, unsubmitted material.; [pers.] I am a firm believer in destiny. I believe that all we do and say, has lasting results and we touch lives, long after we are among the living. In the infinite universe, our thoughts and our souls continue for an eternity and are kept alive by the ones we love.; [a.] Roswell, NM

AS-SALAAM, JAMAAL
[pen.] A.K.A. William L. Williams Jr.; [b.] April 20, 1955, Albany, NY; [p.] William and Helen Williams; [m.] Divorced; [ch.] Mieko, Kwende, Shani, Jamaal; [ed.] S.U.N.Y. at Albany, S.U.N.Y. at Purchase, University of Northern Colorado; [occ.] Poet, Actor, Photographer playwrite; [memb.] AFTRA, SAG; [oth. writ.] Chapbook: Philopena, Close to the Heart, Facing East, Screenplays: Liemert Park, Lightland Caravan, Plays: The Muse, Persona Suite; [pers.] To strive for excellence and live everyday as though it is your last day on earth.

ASLAM, ALHAJ DR. MAJOR MUHAMMAD
[pen.] Sheattles; [occ.] Medical Doctor, Practicing Gender Choice Theory of American Doctor Sheattles, for a male issue, a great necessity of East; [memb.] Exporting Precious Stones. Pakistan can boast of super quality Precious - Semi Precious Stones. Available at very competitive prices; [oth. writ.] Free lance writer. Several poems, articles published in local and Foreign Press. Write on Kashmir, Sikhs Greatness, Education, Defence Medical and other Sciences.; [pers.] Aim of life should be love for humanity two pieces of Photographs of ANAM are enclosed, which may please be inserted with the poem Anam is a nice girl.; [a.] Lahore Cantt, Pakistan

ASLAM, HUMAIRA
[pen.] Humaira Aslam; [b.] February 6, 1969, Peshawar; [p.] Muhammad Aslam and Rasheeda Aslam; [ed.] Master in English Literature, University of Peshawar; [occ.] M. Phil Student, English Literature; [memb.] Member of Public Library, Directorate of Archives and Libraries, Government of N.W.F.P; [oth. writ.] I write poetry occasionally but have not published it.; [pers.] I strive to lay bare hypocrisy and advocate equality for all.; [a.] Peshawar NWFP, Pakistan

ATKINS, LAUREN
[b.] December 17, 1982, U of M, Ypsi; [p.] Ron and Kathy Atkins; [ed.] Henry Ford Elementary and St. Francis Middle School; [occ.] Student; [hon.] Hudson's Black History month essay contest (10-13 category); [oth. writ.] Black Angel (Essay Winner) Susie's Ghost, I made (Anthology of

poetry by young Americans), Slave Voice, etc.; [pers.] I don't write because I have to. I don't is it for fun. I do because some things just need to be said; [a.] Ypsilanti, MI

ATTERHOLT, JAIMA KATHERINE
[b.] March 21, 1986, Prescott, AZ; [p.] John and Wendy Atterholt; [ed.] Abia Judd Elementary School; [occ.] Student, Horse Trainer; [memb.] Girl Scout Troop 405-Az. Cactus Pine, AYSO, American Morgan Horse Assoc.; [hon.] '94 Abia Judd Cultural Arts, Fair Finalist (poem), '94 Az State Award of Excellence, '96 Abia Judd Cultural Arts, Fair Finalist (poem), National PTA Reflections Finalist; [oth. writ.] "If I Could Give The World A Gift", A variety of poems and short stories for school.; [pers.] I write because I enjoy it and I like to express what is important to me.; [a.] Prescott, AZ

ATTO, HELIA E.
[b.] August 12, 1921, Angora, MN; [p.] John and Emilia Nelmark; [m.] Benjamin L. Atto (deceased March 9, 1992), October 15, 1940; [ch.] Six children - three boys and three girls; [ed.] High School Graduate Correspondence Course in Literature; [occ.] Homemaker; [memb.] Senior Citizens, Bowling League, Tops Club, Church; [oth. writ.] Several poems published in local papers - poems published in following anthologies - Arcadia poetry spring 1993, summer 1994 Treas. poems of America summer 1994 paths less traveled 1990.; [pers.] Most of my poems have a spiritual bent - or may be humorous - my writing is done in the wee hours of the morning - must be my inspiration hour.; [a.] Babbett, MN

AUER, DAVID S.
[b.] September 23, 1969, Saskatoon, Saskatchewan, Canada; [p.] Paul and Carol Auer; [ed.] Swarthmore College; [occ.] Hope Technical Sales at Aladdin Software Security, Inc.; [memb.] Habcore, Inc.; [hon.] Bausch and Lombe Medal, National Merit Scholar; [oth. writ.] Several poems in school papers.; [pers.] Dear Ed, I wish we had had more time.; [a.] Middletown, NJ

AYMER, GINGER ADKINS
[pen.] Ginger Aymer; [b.] April 25, 1975, Michigan; [p.] Mary Lynne Rose; [m.] Dale E. Aymer, January 19, 1996; [memb.] International Society of Poets; [oth. writ.] The huge oak tree in Mists of enchantment and have you seen me in best poems of the 90's coming out soon.; [pers.] Never stop trying. Dreams are never out of reach I've learned this from my very supportive husband Dale, thanks. And to my Mom, and thanks for sending me courage.; [a.] Owens Cross Roads, AL

AZZARIO, CHRISTINE M.
[pen.] Abby Kline; [b.] January 8, 1971, Rochester, NY; [p.] David Azzario and Joanne Azzario; [ed.] Hilton Central High School; [occ.] Cake Decorator for Wegmos Food Market; [hon.] Business Student of the Month - 1/88; [oth. writ.] Though, this is my first poem that's being published, I write on a regular basis and plan to submit more writings in the future.; [pers.] I'd have to say that the person who influenced me the most was my eight grade English teacher. He would assign a story at the beginning of the week and we were to have

it finished by Friday. It was then that I knew I was destined to write.; [a.] Hilton, NY

BABCOCK, DIANE
[pen.] Dedan; [b.] September 14, 1955, Comox, BC; [ch.] Tyler Austin, Babcock; [ed.] Gr 11; [occ.] Office Manager; [hon.] Best Waitress Award, Three Editors Choice Awards from National Library of Poetry; [oth. writ.] Book - 'Charges' Carlton Press 1994. Poems also in National Library of Poetry's 5 other. Anthologies - After the Storm, Best Poems of 1995, Garden of Life, The Path not Taken, Mists of Enchantment.; [pers.] 90% of my work is written on request by people who have a deep need to express something but, don't know how. These are my greatest challenges, as in order to speak for them, I find myself on extreme emotional levels that I would have never experienced otherwise.; [a.] Nonaimo British Columbia, Canada

BACHLOW, PETER
[pen.] Extra Ordinary Poet; [b.] June 17, 1957, Newmarket; [p.] Maria (Siberia) and Alex Bachlow (Russian); [ed.] Grade 12, Dr. GW Williams, Aurora, Ontario; [occ.] Carpenter, Tinsmith; [hon.] Army Cadets, Queen York Rangers, Music Band, Cubs; [oth. writ.] The Priest From The East, It Occurred To Me, Crazy Show, Hang On Honey; [pers.] We are all born young to grow old. Sometimes we laugh, sometimes we cry, but in the end, we all die.; [a.] Richmond Hill Ontario, Canada

BAFFORD, NICOLE DANIELLE
[b.] December 18, 1977, Baltimore, MD; [p.] Richard and Evelyn Bafford; [m.] Jason Davis; [ed.] Sandalwood High, Florida Community College of Jacksonville; [pers.] Love the world, and the world will love you.; [a.] Jacksonville, FL

BAILEY, DARLENE B.
[b.] July, 19, 1919, Edmonton, Alberta, Canada; [p.] Daisy Bailey; [ch.] Kayla Daisy, Kirsten Paige, Kelsey Claudette; [ed.] Grade 12, Hotel and Restaurant Management Certificate The Career College, Nait Contuting Education Business Services.; [occ.] Receptionist/Secretary; [oth. writ.] A Woman of Life (In memory of Barb Pooley), Kitty Cat Prayer; [pers.] I'd like to thank Barb Pooley the one person who inspired me to write freely and spirtually.; [a.] Edmonton Alberta, Canada

BAILEY, SHARON
[pen.] Samantha King; [b.] November 22, 1948, Ottawa, Ontario, Canada; [oth. writ.] Poems published in local newspaper.; [pers.] In my writing, whether poetry or short stories, I endeavor to make the reader think about the pure and simple things in life.

BAIRD, RICHARD
[pen.] Richard Baird; [b.] June 8, 1920, Pittsburgh, PA; [p.] Arthur W. and M. Ethel Baird; [m.] Robbie A. Baird (Nee Smith), October 29, 1983; [ch.] 5 Grown, (1) six yrs. old; [ed.] High School, On Job Training, in Steel Industry, and Electronics, Operated Construction Equipment for several years.; [occ.] Retired from Honeywell Inc.; [memb.] Orange Springs Community Church and Civic Center, Internat'l Society of Poets, Support Groups for Seniors; [hon.] Grand prize: Honeywell Nat'l Contest: (Winning Edge), many poems published

in Regional Pamphlets issued my honeywell. Poems published in anthologies, published by "The National Library of Poetry.; [oth. writ.] A collection of 88 poems entitled (Poetic Potpourri), have begun another collection.; [pers.] My talent is a gift from "God", originally used for romantic poems for my lovely wife, now used to express appreciation and philosophy.; [a.] Orange Springs, FL

BAKER, CYNTHIA
[b.] July 29, 1946, Hanover, NH; [p.] John F. Goodman, Gwendolyn V. Goodman; [m.] Perry N. Baker, December 29; [ch.] Seth, Jessamyn, Jed; [ed.] American College in Paris, University of Maryland, University of Maine, Seminole Community College School of Nursing; [occ.] Free lance artist, Licensed Practical Nurse; [memb.] Episcopal Church of the Resurrection, Rain Forest Alliance; [oth. writ.] Articles for "Bittersweet" magazine of Maine, Illustrated and self-published "Moose Family Christmas," a children's book, have written lyrics and music to pieces performed at my church.; [pers.] As an artist, I approach the process of writing poetry as visual metaphor, as a songwriter, I appreciate the rhythm of language, and as a nurse, I hope to convey compassion for the human condition.; [a.] Longwood, FL

BAKER, DONNA M.
[pen.] Donna M. Baker; [b.] February 12, 1936, Norman, OK; [p.] Loyd and Aline Vanderburg; [m.] James C. Baker, February 6, 1971; [ch.] Two (sons - by first-husband - M. L. Brown); [ed.] High School Grad. (and School of Hard Knocks); [occ.] High School Custodian was Waitress for 41 years (13 years was in Las Vegas, NV); [memb.] Union Local #226 Las Vegas, NV; [pers.] Always place: "Principals before personalities" and try to be open-minded.; [a.] Oklahoma City, OK

BAKER, JOHN
[pen.] John W. Baker; [b.] August 31, 1951, Redstone Township, PA; [pers.] A word from a former fool was inspired by unnecessary lessons earn and learned. Success and failure begins and ends with attitude.

BAKER, MABLE JO
[pen.] Mable Jo Baker; [b.] January 26, 1910, Sterling, NE; [p.] Arch and Anna Mary Borland; [m.] Henry R. Baker, April 22, 1929; [ch.] Bruce - Gene - Shirley; [ed.] H.S. - Liberty NE. Post - Grad 1 yr. French and Bus. Math; [occ.] Retired - doing art work at home; [memb.] Church of God 7th day. Located Denver Co. Light Bearers Club. Woman's Association International Society of Poets; [oth. writ.] Ed. children's Missionary 6 yrs - Stanberry MO. 2 small poem books. Just finished a poem - story book and illustrated for my 26 great grand children wrote poems for (After glow).; [pers.] Words have power. Thus, God grant me a mind to use only up lifting words.; [a.] Chatsworth, CA

BAMHART, BONNIE LYNN
[b.] December 6, 1980; [a.] Elmwood Park, NJ

BANKS, GRETA P.
[b.] June 30, 1958, Shelby County; [p.] William Burrow, Geraldine Burrow; [m.] Arthur G. Banks, September 14, 1985; [ch.] Adrian, Jaydin, Camaryn; [ed.] Bolton High School, Christian Brothers College now called Christian Brothers University); [occ.] Customer Service with U.S. Postal Service; [memb.] Good Samaritan United Methodist Church, Alpha Kappa, Alpha Sorority (Mu Epsilon Chapter); [a.] Memphis, TN

BANWART, CARRIE
[pen.] Carrie; [b.] October 24, 1951, Watonga, OK; [p.] Earl and Colleene Burton; [m.] Robert C. Banwart, August 12, 1972; [ch.] Christopher Kelly Banwart; [ed.] Southwestern Oklahoma, State University, Weatherford, OK; [occ.] Computer Operator, Clerical Clerk for City of O'Keene; [hon.] Numerous Art Awards, Art Scholarship, Employee of the Month; [oth. writ.] Poems published in College Newspaper, "Poems and Prayers" Book, local newspapers.; [pers.] For all the victims and their families I wrote the poem "Throughout the Land" for the Oklahoma Federal Building Disaster of April 19, 1995. Oklahoma people joined together with every human being in the universe to show the sorrow we shared this day.; [a.] Hitchcock, OK

BARDELLA, MARIA
[pen.] Leondra James; [b.] July 28, 1958, Rome, Italy; [p.] Giulio and Assunta Bardella; [ed.] Diploma of Primary Education Bachelor of Education; [occ.] Primary School Teacher; [memb.] Member of the Arabian Horse Society of Australia, Riding Pony Society of Australia; [hon.] Editor's choice award for "Ode to the Arabian horse" poem featured in "Walk Through Parodise"; [oth. writ.] First poem written was 'Ode to the Arabian horse' and was published in walk through paradise. Have also written a science fiction novel for which I am seeking a publisher titled "Warrior Queen" and am in process of writing second novel "Drinkers of the Wind"; [pers.] My writing philosophy is that I write about the things that I love and I try to express that love in the words that I write both in poetry and in prose.; [a.] North Dandenong, Vic

BARKER, MARYBETH
[b.] June 11, 1963, Milwaukee, WI; [p.] Patricia, Morgan; [m.] Ssgt. Stuart L. Barker, July 17, 1982; [ch.] James - 13, Jonathan - 11, Nakita - 9; [pers.] I wrote this poem the morning after May 31 yrs. old husband died unexpectedly. He had been in the military for 12 yrs. and was to be honorably discharged in three weeks.; [a.] Whitewater, WI

BARNETT, N. JEAN WADSWORTH
[b.] October 3, 1933, Wichita Falls, TX; [p.] Otto and Pauline Wadsworth; [m.] Divorced; [ch.] Linda Gail, Phillip Brooks, Carol Jean (also four Grandchildren); [ed.] Wichita Falls Senior High School; [occ.] Benefits Representative, MBNA Information Services, Dallas, Texas; [memb.] The North Church, Beta Sigma Phi Sorority, International Society of Poets; [hon.] Editors Choice Award presented by the National Library of Poetry; [oth. writ.] Poem "The Ending of Pain" published in "A Delicate Balance" by the National Library of Poetry.; [pers.] May my writings show to others that God's love never fails and his mercy endureth forever.; [a.] Farmers Branch, TX

BARON, RICHARD
[b.] September 20, 1949, Brooklyn; [p.] Solomon and Alvira Baron; [ed.] Bishop Ford High School, St. Francis College - B.A., City College of N.Y. - M.A; [occ.] Mathematics teacher, William Alexander Middle School 51, Bklyn, N.Y.; [memb.] Contributor American Museum of Natural History, Member of Association of Computer Educators, Member of World Wildlife Fund, Member of the American Bowling Congress, Member of the United Federation of Teachers; [hon.] Who's Who in American Education, Small Grant Recipient from Citi Corp, Phi Alpha Theta Theta Nu Chapter (History Honor Fraternity); [oth. writ.] Short story published in Trace, the Journal of the Association of Computer Educators, Curriculum writer, editor, for the New York City Board of Educations Mathematics Unit.; [pers.] The structure, meaning, and visual presentation of my poetry is rendered through the little, the central theme of my poetry is the commonalty of humanity. We are born, we live, We perceive, We work, We suffer, We love, We die; [a.] Brooklyn, NY

BARRETT, CHARITO
[pen.] Chanta; [b.] January 19, 1970, Philadelphia, PA; [p.] Toni Barrett and Henry Gossette; [ed.] High School Martin Luther King, Trade School Gordon Phillips Beauty School; [occ.] Salesperson and Cosmetologist; [oth. writ.] A collection of approximately 21 poems, which continues to grow as often as my spirit is moved to write; [pers.] The poems that I write are a pure gift from God. He blesses us to be a blessing to others. These words which flow from my heart, through the spirit have truly blessed me. And I just want to share God's gift in hopes that others will be blessed like I have.; [a.] Charlotte, NC

BARTON, GARY TREVOR
[b.] October 1, 1968, Bedford, England; [p.] Graham and Janet Barton; [ed.] High school, '0' levels, currently writing tuition being taken, I also have a certificate in Horticulture.; [occ.] Unemployed writer and poet; [memb.] World Wide Fund for Nature, International Society of Poets; [oth. writ.] I have a few poems published in Anthologies in England me and some friends are publishing a book of short stories poems and haiku called Brainstorm, 2 stories Stevie (Romance) and Hitchhikers Tale (Horror) I've included in this book.; [pers.] I like to help people with whatever problems they have. I believe in love and peace as being our natural state and work to bring joy into peoples lives.; [a.] Norwich Norfolk, England

BASARABA, GLADYS S.
[b.] March 25, 1950, Fisher Branch, Manitoba, Canada; [p.] Mary Basaraba; [ed.] Fisher Branch Elementary and Collegiate, Fisher Branch, Manitoba, Canada, University of Manitoba, Winnipeg, Manitoba; [occ.] Substitute Teacher, Winnipeg School Division, Winnipeg, Manitoba; [oth. writ.] 11 experiments in the Pesticide Research Report, 1973.; [pers.] As life continues undaunted so creativity exudes from it, for not only does life breed creativity, but creativity breeds life. Life's many wonders never cease, so take time to appreciate and to create.; [a.] Winnipeg Manitoba, Canada

BATTEY, JOSH EDWARD
[b.] August 6, 1959, Portsmouth, VA; [p.] Hunter and Nancy Sterling; [m.] Bernice Lutz Battey,

August 16, 1982; [ed.] Norview High/No Formal Education; [occ.] Journey Man, Carpenter; [memb.] Carpenters Local 613 Norfolk VA.; [oth. writ.] In The End/Brutus/My Love; [pers.] It was a dark period in my life and I found comfort in writing... in memory of my fear friends.; [a.] Norfolk, VA

BATTISTE, MRS. MURIEL J.
[b.] February 7, 1933, New York City, NY; [ch.] Deborah Louisa; [ed.] In Junior Year working towards degree in Business Management - University of the District of Columbia, Washington D.C.; [occ.] Office Management Assistant, Laboratory for Astrophysics, Smithsonian Inst.; [memb.] a) The Writer's Center, MD, b) The International Women's Writing Guild, c) American Guild of Organists - National, d) St. Matthew's Evangelical Lutheran Church, e) American Association of Retired Persons (National and Local); [hon.] Recipient: University of the District of Columbia's Creating Writing Award only recipient - 1993, Dean's List; [oth. writ.] Works nearing completion: a) book of poetry, b) a seven - year recount of my childhood experiences during World War II - book will soon be ready for printing.; [pers.] Take time to observe the wonders of nature, the revelation reopens the heart to love humankind.; [a.] Washington, DC

BAYS, TRACY ALAN
[pen.] Alan Tracy; [b.] July 1, 1972, Portsmouth, OH; [p.] David Lee Bays; [m.] Helen Louise Bays; [ed.] Portsmouth High, Vocational School (Electronics); [occ.] Former U.S. Marine Writer; [hon.] National Defense Medal, Sea Service Deployment Ribbon, and Good Conduct Medal; [oth. writ.] No previously published material.; [pers.] People should use more common sense, and stop trying to dictate how other people should live. We are not Gods.!; [a.] Pierz, MN

BEAUCHAMP, VANESA RENEE
[pen.] V. Bea; [b.] May 28, 1979, Henderson, NV; [p.] Divorced; [m.] Dave De Perrot (fiancee); [ed.] I am now in my 11th Grade Year and attending Horizon South High School; [memb.] I am a member of the human race, so I'm told; [oth. writ.] I wrote a poem about my Cabage Patch kid in 3rd grade and it was put in the paper and performed as a skit.; [pers.] I'm a girl, a lover, a daughter, and now a published writer.; [a.] Henderson, NV

BECERRIL, MARY L.
[pen.] Mary L. Becerril; [b.] December 9, 1943, Dallas, TX; [p.] Isaac and Josie Fowler; [m.] Luis E. Becerril (Deceased), December 19, 1973; [ed.] Royse City High School Texas Woman's University B.S. 1965, Ph.D. 1985, Ph.D. 1994 Boston University - M.S. 1969; [occ.] Professor of Counseling Dallas Baptist University; [memb.] Chi Sigma Iota, National Counseling Honor Society, Who's Who in the Southwest, Tau Alumnae Association, National Association of Pediatric Nurses and Associates. American Association of Christian Counselors, Christian Counselors of Texas; [hon.] "The Exchange" in the treasured poems of America, (Sparrowgrass poetry forum, 8/96), "Friendship" in mirrors of the soul (Modern Poetry Society, Spring, 96).; [hon.] I write poetry in order to express my personal experience with people and events. I hope others relate to my poems through their similar experiences; [oth. writ.] De Soto, TX

BECKER, CLAIRE
[b.] January 13, 1964, Paris, France; [occ.] Painter-Sculptress; [pers.] I write when words are more than words and need to be breathed into my soul, to this world where fear his taken over most of the words we speak and hear, I offer those words of love and compassion, hoping that they will be heard.; [a.] New York, NY

BECKLES, HAROLD A.
[b.] November 23, 1963, Barbados; [p.] Wilfred Beckles, Pauline Beckles; [ed.] Barbados Community College, College of the Bahamas, North Carolina Central University; [occ.] Student at N.C.C.U. (Junior in English Literature); [memb.] Past member of the Association of Literary Artists (ALA in Barbados), The Smithsonian Associates, Cystic Fibrosis Foundation; [oth. writ.] "The Barbados Advocate" newspaper - various stories, 1982-1983, "Banja", No. 5, 1989/1990 (In Barbados), "At Random", Vol. 1, 1990 (C.O.B.), "Ex Umbra", Spring Sem., 1995 (N.C.C.U.), "Ex Umbra," Spring Sem. 1996 (N.C.C.U.); [pers.] An artist's work should paint to both a politically and spiritually progressive path for any community with which he or she maintains a dialog.; [a.] Durham, NC

BEDARD, DENISE A. LAPALME
[b.] January 27, 1961, Sudbury; [p.] Albert-Desneiges Lapalme; [m.] Richard L. Bedard, October 29, 1983; [ch.] Alec Bedard February, Anik Bedard; [ed.] Health Care Aid, Cambrian College, Sudbury Ontario; [occ.] Mother and House wife.; [a.] Sudbury Ontario, Canada

BEDARD, LISE
[b.] November 1, 1955, Sudbury; [p.] Paul and Estelle Daoust; [m.] Gilles Bedard, September 20, 1974; [ch.] Paul, Gilles, Chantale; [ed.] Grade 12, diploma; [occ.] Housewife; [memb.] Parents Association at St. Dominique School in Sudbury, Member of the International Society of Poets; [hon.] The Editor's Choice Award for Outstanding Achievement in Poetry presented by the National Library of Poetry 1995; [oth. writ.] "Two Sons and Mama" published in 1995 anthology "Sparkles in the Sand."; [pers.] I believe that you are never alone!; [a.] Sudbury Ontario, Canada

BEHEN, ANNE MARIE
[b.] May 1, 1912, Pittsburgh, PA; [p.] Francis X. Behen (Deceased) and Mary H. Smith Behen; [ed.] Corpus Christi HS (1926), U of Pittsburgh (BA, 1979), Duquesne U (MA, 1982), Duquesne U (MA, 1986); [occ.] 1929-1975 Secretary: Gimbel Brothers, Mellon Institute, Gulf R&D Co.; [hon.] Phi Alpha Theta (Epsilon-Phi chapter), 1981, Duquesne U; [oth. writ.] Author wrote several poems during her retirement years.; [pers.] This poem was written by author about her own funeral and was read at the author's funeral in 1988.; [a.] Pittsburgh, PA

BELL, CHRISTINE MARIE
[b.] December 4, 1947, Philadelphia, PA; [p.] Antoinette Tarquinio Palmer, George Joe Palmer; [m.] John W. Douglas; [ch.] Margaret Douglas Garcia grandchild Kasandra Lynn Garcia (Lynn); [ed.] Graduate: Strasburg High School Strasburg Ohio; [occ.] Inspector, AJ Heinz Fremont Ohio Company; [oth. writ.] Book, Ellis Came Home,

Barbara Baur Agency; [pers.] Margie, Kas, Chris we will always remember the joy Gabrielle brought us.; [a.] Greensprings, OH

BELL, JEFFREY L.
[b.] October 19, 1953, Wheeling, WV; [p.] Faris and Helen Bell; [m.] Michell D. Bell, August 5, 1972; [ch.] Misty L. Bell; [ed.] B.A., Bethany College, Lindsburg, KS, 1981 M.S., Kansas State University, Manhattan, KS, 1988; [occ.] Social Studies, English, Publication Teacher 7th-8th grades Salina Middle School, South Salina, KS; [memb.] KAMLE, Kansas Association of Middle Level Education, P.T.A., Parent, Teacher Association, NASSP, National Association of Secondary School Principals (Middle Level); [hon.] Who's Who Among American Teachers 1996, Academic Dean's List, Bethany College, NAIA All-American Defensive Lineman 1981; [oth. writ.] "Just Try, Middle Level Physical Education", KAMLE Karavan 1990; [pers.] Teachers walk in the shadow of the future. If you truly want to enjoy life, find what you love to do as a profession. It is hard to consider something work, when you have fun doing it.; [a.] Salina, KS

BELL, REBEKAH
[b.] October 11, 1974, Fort Ord, CA; [p.] Bradley and Barbara Bell; [m.] Brian Carr; [ed.] Kearns High School, International Correspondence School/ Journalism and short Story Writing; [occ.] Nanny; [oth. writ.] This is my first publication; [pers.] I have always enjoyed reading poetry and now I hope I can bring such joy to other people.; [a.] Foresthill, CA

BELL, RON
[pen.] Vincent Logan; [b.] Long Beach, CA; [p.] Buck and Bey Jahnke; [ch.] Adam and Roxanne; [ed.] Fullerton College, Fullerton CA; [occ.] Security; [oth. writ.] Strength is a Tender Rose...

BELL, SARAH INNES
[b.] January 17, 1934, Glasgow, Scotland; [p.] Thomas and Margaret Eccles.; [m.] May 28, 1960; [ch.] Liana Jean and Robert Campbell; [ed.] Whitehill Academy Glasgow - Scotland.; [occ.] Semi - Retired.; [hon.] Editor's choice award 1995 - the National Library of Poetry for "God's Vast Memory" poem.; [pers.] This Psalm is one of several I wrote during a very trying time in my life. In a way they were my journey of faith. When your need of God is great, he gives you what you need, not what you want.; [a.] Mississauga Ontario, Canada

BELL, SHONTEA NICOLE
[pen.] Shonny; [b.] September 27, 1979, Willow Grove, PA; [p.] Shirley Bell and Paul Talaferro; [ed.] Ninth Grade, Lincoln High School; [occ.] Student; [memb.] Arthritis Teen Club of Philadelphia; [hon.] Handwriting Award; [oth. writ.] "There sits a child", "Brotha's and Sistas", "Shattered Pictures"; [pers.] "The poems pop into my mind as a certain word and build up from that word. My poems are about love and life."; [a.] Philadelphia, PA

BELLINGER, RACHEL LYN
[b.] February 17, 1984, Mishawaka, IN; [p.] Diana, Greg Bellinger; [ed.] Currently in grade school at St. Mary of the Assumption, South Bend, IN.; [pers.] I am just a kid, but I love to write poems and stories!; [a.] South Bend, IN

BENNETT, DARRELL D.
[b.] May 28, 1953, Kansas City, MO; [p.] Gerald Bennett, Wanda Bennett; [m.] Jodie L. Bennett, March 10, 1995; [ed.] Lincoln - Way H.S. Central Piedmont Community College Stanly Community College; [occ.] Student; [hon.] Phi Theta Kappa; [oth. writ.] None published; [pers.] I attempt to fill the sun shine through on a cloudy day.; [a.] Gastonia, NC

BENNETT, DAVID A.
[pen.] David Arthur Bennett; [b.] February 18, 1953, Leeds, England; [p.] Frank Bennett, Monica M. Bennett; [ed.] St. Peter's, Agnes Stewart School/s, Park Lane College, Leeds, England; [occ.] Media Specialist (TV and Radio Broadcaster); [memb.] British Equity, Friends of the Earth, R.S.P.B., National Campaign for Arts (NCA), A.A.C.A., Friends, A'deen Art Gall Museums, A.I.Y.F.; [oth. writ.] Poems published in numerous anthologies. Short stories. T.V. and Radio Scripts, Newspaper copy.; [pers.] 'The written word often gives opinion and observation, credibility,; [a.] Aberdeen Scotland, United Kingdom

BENNETT, KHERRA TANYIKE GRACE ANN
[b.] July 18, 1983, New York; [p.] Judith Bennett Crowe and Bobby Crowe; [ed.] Am in Elementary School, 6th Grade, will enter Jr. High School in September, 1996; [occ.] 6th Grader; [memb.] Fairington Student Council, Sisters of the Circle, Fairington Strings Orchestra (Viola), Jr. National Geographic Society, Soapstone Performing Arts (Ballet and Tap), Dickerson Performing Arts Theater, N.Y. (1987-89), Fairington School Chorus; [hon.] Creative Writing Excellence Award for excellence in writing, creativity, and vision, for 1994 books: "Mystery Camp" awarded jointly in 1995, by: Turner Broadcasting Station, KSL TV 5, Teach for America, Greenlight Communication, Hollywood for Children, Marine Midland Bank, Bonneville Production Co., Kids for Kids, won a DeKalb County, Georgia, top ribbon for Social Studies writing/display presentation in Sociology, The Rastafarians, 1996, Placed on the Principal's List (surpassing Honor Roll) from entering Elementary School to present time for excellence in academic and behavior achievements, Sole representative chosen from Fairington School for American Red Cross Georgia Safety Conference, 1995, numerous school awards and certificates for various achievements; [oth. writ.] Book: "Mystery Camp" kept in Fairington School Library, DeKalb County, Ga, poem "Color Us Together": Selected for a publication page in 1996 edition of the Anthology of Poetry by Young Americans, poem, "Martin Luther King, Jr." published during Black History Month in The Panther Press, 1995.; [pers.] "Your parents can only guide you. What you are now, and what you become are your responsibilities."; [a.] Lithonia DeKalb County, GA

BENNETT, PHYLLIS GAR
[pen.] Gar for Art Work; [b.] August 14, 1947, Great Barrington, MA; [p.] Willis and Shirley Cottrell; [m.] Rick Bennett, May 12, 1988; [ed.] Saratoga Springs High School graduate, Albany School of LPN Charcoal Artist; [occ.] LPN Charcoal Artist; [oth. writ.] Numerous poems, personal handmade cards, charcoal drawings; [pers.] I have found that gifts from the heart are so deeply appreciated. Our talents should be shared to make this world a better place to be.; [a.] Saratoga Springs, NY

BENSON, JEANINE C.
[b.] September 28, 1948, Omaha, NE; [p.] Cecil Anderson, Jean Anderson; [m.] Warren W. Benson, January 7, 1973; [pers.] Teaching piano and organ for fifteen years, I gained appreciation for the fact that poetry, like music, deeply touches people's hearts and minds.; [a.] Omaha, NE

BERNEY, SANDRA
[pen.] Sandra Deschene; [b.] March 10, 1956, Atchison, KS; [p.] Barbara J. Ehret and Marcel E. Deschene; [ch.] William E. Kloepper; [ed.] Graduatedn from High School in May 1974, Graduated from University of Missouri at Kansas City in May 1996 with Bachelor's degree in Sociology.; [occ.] Mail processor for the U.S. Postal Service.; [memb.] Member of "Promoting Postal Pride" Committee.; [oth.writ.] Various poems and Prose would like to publish a children's bppk entitled "Joey's Teddy Bear".; [pers.] I believe that I am a writer -not because I earned some degree in journalism or English, but by virtue of the simple fact that as I am compelled to express myself, I write, naturally.; [a.] Independence, MO

BERNING, MARILYN

[pen.] Marilyn (Bublitz) Berning; [b.] July 27, 1938, Winona, MN; [p.] Donald and Helen Bublitz; [m.] William E. Berning, September 13, 1958; [ch.] Jeffrey Wm. Berning, Jason D. Berning Peggy Lynn Berning (now deceased); [ed.] Spring Valley High School (1956) Spring Valley, MN., 55975 also, some additional classes; [occ.] Small Business Co-Owner and Homemaker; [memb.] International Society of Poets; [hon.] National Library of Poetry (Editor's Choice Award - 1996); [oth. writ.] Several Publications - Other Anthologies also, may work at song writing as a hobby; [pers.] To express one's feelings thru a poem - Is like sharing part of one's soul; [a.] Stewartville, MN

BERNTSEN, THOMAS
[b.] August 6, 1965, New York; [p.] Joanne and Ragnuald Berntsen; [ed.] B.A. Syracuse University 1988, M.S. Indiana University 1991, Ed. D. University of Massachusetts 1998; [occ.] Math/Science High School Teacher; [oth. writ.] Article entitled, "What If" in The Science Teacher (Feb. 96). Article entitled, "Let It Snow, Let it Snow" in The Physics Teacher (Nov. 95) Fifteen other poems have ben published. Working on 2 books: A Journey To Victory and You Can Go Home; [pers.] Home is one of the sweetest words in the english language. Sometimes young children loose their homes and families and grow up to be like Nomad Man. But the search he has taken gives hope to all of the orphans searching for their righteous path in life, their home.; [a.] Brattleboro, VT

BERRY, MISS LISA L.
[pen.] Peatie or Sweetness; [b.] July 30, 1964, Beckley Hospital; [p.] Lillie Mae and Charles William Berry; [ch.] Roy Edward, Charlott Mae Green, Barbara Annpenn, Samuel Alexander; [ed.] I graduated from the 12th grade from Woodrow Wilson High School, I graduated in the year 1983; [occ.] Disabled; [hon.] I received an award of merit, an Honorable Mention from National Library of Poetry for a poem called The American Eagle.; [oth. writ.] When president Ronald Reagan was in office, I sent him a letter of my poem I wrote called The Flag of Justice, he told me my work speaks clearly of my time and effort such acts of friendship are truly encouraging.; [pers.] I believe that if you do not succeed first in your goal and you are given a second chance, then maybe you will make it the second time.; [a.] Mabscott, WV

BERRY, VICKI ANN
[b.] February 18, 1963, Fairfield, CA; [m.] Stephen Berry; [ch.] KarenDanika, AlexanderStarner and KristenAdele; [ed.] Lowell High School, San Francisco State University City College of San Francisco; [occ.] Home manager and Mom; [hon.] Best Penmanship -2nd X 6 grade, Best Mathematics - 9th grade, Annual Poetry Review "The Grand Age of Manuscripts" Honorable Mention "Fantasy Dreams...Dare to Risk"; [oth. writ.] "Epigenetic Love" "Perfection's Creed" "Praise Worthy"; [pers.] Fatherless since age 8 - due to freak accident, I grew up quick. To become an independent perfectionist...who hates the word "Should" because it makes me feel impose upon.

BEST, DR. ELIEZER MOSES
[b.] March 5, 1915, Bombay, India; [p.] Moses (Father) and Rebecca (Mother); [m.] Ivy (Abigael), November 14, 1948; [ch.] Dr. Lael-Anson, Ashbel; [ed] M.B.B.S., M.D., F.C.P.S.; [occ.] Retired; [memb.] Inspector on behalf of Medical Council of India - Inspected Lucknow, Kanpur, Manipal, Hyderabad, Kornool Calcutta, Udaipur, Jaipur, Meerut, Nagpur Aurangabad, Goa, Miraj, Sholapur, Jamnager Baroda, Bombay (3 Colleges), Poona; [oth. writ.] "The problem of "P" published in "Times of India" a daily Newspaper in Bombay, dated February 27, 1872.; [pers.] Started life as demonstrator in psychology - later professor, then Dean, B.J. Medical College and super intendant of Civil Hospital, Ahmedabad and last deputy director of medical education, Gujarat State - India.; [a.] Ahmedabad, Gujarat

BHADRA, SANGEETA
[b.] February 23, 1979, Brampton, Ontario, Canada; [p.] Asish Bhadra and Tamal Bhadra; [ed.] Enhanced Honour Student at R.H. Lagerquist Junior High, Grade 10 Enhanced student at Turner Fenton S.S., Brampton, Ont.; [occ.] Grade 10 Enhanced student at Turner Fenton S.S.; [hon.] Accepted as piano major at Mayfield Secondary School of the Arts, passed Gr. 8 piano and Gr. 2 Theory with first-class honours (RMC); [oth. writ.] A collection of poems, first play in the making, original paintings and sketches, Disney drawings, nothing published yet.; [pers.] They'll push me down but I'll bounce right back and keepm on running on my tough track; [a.] Brampton Ontario, Canada

BHAWAL, ARPITA
[b.] June 11, 1969, Calcutta, India; [p.] Dwijendra Bhawal and Manju Bhawal; [ed.] B.A. (Hons.) in English Literature; [occ.] Copywriter/Advertising, Self employed.; [hon.] The 'Big Bang Award' '96 for excellence in advertising for a product film on real estate called "Oxford Serenity" - entry made in the general category, by the filmakers, 'Forsee Multimedia'.; [oth. writ.] Several poems,

shorrt stories and essays 9 not yet given for publication0 - also working on a novel.; [pers.] The most important thing to me, is human relationships. Without it, I would have never been able to write. It is after all, important to feel and then tell the world what it is all about.; [a.] Bangalore, Karnataka

BIBBY, LILLIAN F.
[pen.] Libby; [b.] November 20, 1957, Orlando, FL; [p.] Deceased; [ch.] Benjamin Fnazworth, Kevin B. Nazworth; [ed.] High School; [occ.] Waitress; [hon.] Champion Billiard Trophy; [oth. writ.] Several poems unpublished and short story's.; [pers.] I have been through some very rough years, but I always strive to better myself.; [a.] Danielsville, GA

BIELUCZYK, MONIKA
[b.] March 6, 1965, Hartford, CT; [ed.] East Windsor School System East Windsor, CT, grades K-12. University of Hartford (attended only, never earned degree); [occ.] Guitar instructor and housecleaner; [pers.] As a poet, my poetry reflects nature and simplicity with a spiritual theme.; [a.] Ellsworth, ME

BILUSACK, BEVERLY
[b.] September 2, 1977, Windsor; [p.] Violet and Bryan Bilusack; [ed.] Walkerville Collegiate Institute; [occ.] Student; [pers.] I find writing poetry is a relaxing pastime. I have written other poems, but this is the first time I have ever submitted any of my compositions. Your acceptance of my poem has greatly inspired me!; [a.] Windsor Ontario, Canada

BISGAARD, SHAUNA
[b.] November 19, 1953, Vancouver, British Columbia, Canada; [p.] John and Nancy Carr; [m.] John Bisgaard; [ch.] Leighla and Dustin

BISHOP, JOHN A.
[b.] November 24, 1949, New York City; [ed.] Dartmouth 1971; [occ.] Accounting; [oth. writ.] Various Articles and Poems, Book on Tax Law; [pers.] Keep the faith; [a.] FL

BIVENS, HUNTER
[pen.] Schmitty, Will the Doorman; [b.] December 27, 1996; [occ.] Janitor, Student; [memb.] International Socialist Organization; [hon.] The President Seal of Academic Fitness in 1989, rejected twice for PA Governer's School of the Arts.; [oth. writ.] "The Binary Tree", "Locomotor Aphasia", "Untitled No. 5", and "Submarines" — oh, and "Ritual #8"; [pers.] A poem is the grounded interaction between the first and second person singular pronouns, having nothing to do with truth of social responsibility. Have been greatly influenced by Austrian rock singer Falco, and Thomas Pynchon.; [a.] Philadelphia, PA

BLACK, AMANDA CLAIR
[b.] March 31, 1980, Charlotte, NC; [p.] Joseph E. and Kayren B. Black; [ed.] A sophomore at North Mecklenburg High School in Huntersville, NC. Hoping to receive my Master's degree in Business Administration at Appalachain State University in Boone, NC.; [memb.] Latin Club, Spanish Club, Red Cross; [pers.] Current interests include reading, writing, war history, and foreign language. I have

been a resident of NC all my life. My family has lived here for nearly 200 years.; [a.] Huntersville, NC

BLACK, CRYSTAL
[b.] February 1, 1950, Kittanning, PA; [p.] Finley-Phyllis Klingensmith; [m.] David W. Black, April 15, 1970; [ch.] Tamerin Renee, Brian Christopher; [ed.] Ambridge Area High School; [occ.] Full time mom - Housewife, former Dance Teacher/Dancer-Choreographer, Dental Assistant; [memb.] Distinguished member of the International Society of Poets; [hon.] Editor's Choice Award-from The National Library of Poetry 1995; [oth. writ.] This very day in The National Library of Poetry's Anthology Windows of the soul - In Light of the Poets in The National Library of Poetry's forth coming the Best Poems of the '90s; [pers.] I have personally found dance and poetry to be of close band. Each a form of unique expression. One through motion of body the other written word and voice. As one who needs an out let for self expression, I am happy to find the two harbor no jealousies. They are indeed the sisters to my soul.; [a.] Freedom, PA

BLACKBURN, PAULA
[b.] May 19, 1969, Gladwin, MI; [p.] David Vickery and Marge Dings; [m.] Curtis Blackburn, April 7, 1990; [ch.] Trisha, Dennis, Christen, Katrina; [ed.] Although I never graduated, my life has educated me greatly.; [occ.] Domestic House Engineer; [memb.] I am a Board Member of C.H.A.D.D. support group; [hon.] My honors and awards are the family I have which awards me everyday of my life.; [oth. writ.] I have numerous personal writings of thoughts and life experiences.; [pers.] My writings are based on true life experience's and feelings.; [a.] Pontiac, MI

BLAIR, LINDSAY
[b.] September 10, 1979, Edmonton, Alberta, Canada; [p.] Ken and Spencer Blair; [occ.] High school student; [hon.] First Class Honor Roll, Alberta Honor Band, Canadian Honor Band (flute); [oth. writ.] Several personal poems; [pers.] Philosophical statement...? Just go out and have fun!!!; [a.] Medicine Hat Alberta, Canada

BLAKE, DORNA
[b.] June 30, Westmoreland, Jamaica; [p.] Roy Sleugh, Adlyn Sleugh; [m.] Donovan Blake, August 2, 1980; [ch.] Jodi Blake, Rashaud Blake; [ed.] St. Elizabeth Technical High, Jamaica Shortwood Teachers' College, Jamaica Moneague College, Jamaica; [occ.] Remedial Teacher, Clement Howell High, Turks and Caicos Is.; [memb.] Jamaica Cancer Society, Kendal Shiloh Apostolic Church Youth Group/Women's Auxiliary Group; [hon.] Prize for Magazine Cover Design - Moneague College 1988, Hons Diploma in Teaching; [oth. writ.] I have written poems and songs for my Church's Youth Group, some have been submitted to other poetry organizations.; [pers.] Life is whatever you make it.

BLAKEMORE, JR., HAROLD JACK
[b.] January 8, 1957, Philadelphia; [p.] Harold and Maria; [ch.] Desiree', Jesse, Peter; [ed.] BSEE Wider Univ., Chester, PA.,; [occ.] Engineer; [memb.] ISA, IEEE, DAV, FOP; [hon.] Deans list, Army Commendations, Professional Commenda-

tions; [oth. writ.] Personal Collection; [pers.] While walking along lifes way don't forget to stop and smell the flowers!; [a.] Philadelphia, PA

BLALOCK, JOEL R.
[b.] June 9, 1967, Atlanta, GA; [p.] Robert and Kathryn Blalock; [m.] Marsha Len Blalock, March 31, 1990; [ed.] Palmetto High School, LA Grange College, West George, A. College; [occ.] English Teacher, Frank McClarin High School, College, Park, GA; [memb.] Modern Language Assn., Professional Assn. of GA Educators, Omicron Delta Kappa; [hon.] Member All State College Chorus; [pers.] I am a graduate student concentrating on Victorian Literature. My writing in influenced by both the Victorians and the Romantics.; [a.] Fayetteville, GE

BLANC, DONNA
[b.] June 1955, California; [ed.] Graduate of Holy Names College; [occ.] Classical Musician (Cellist), Teacher; [pers.] As a dyslexic, I found great success with the nonverbal communication of music. After bridging nonverbal and verbal communication, I experience written expression equal to musical expression. Using a pen or my cello changes only the texture of my statement. I continue to help college instructors understand the literary needs of there dyslexic students.; [a.] Oakland, CA

BLANCHARD, DAVID ALLEN
[pen.] David A. Blanchard; [b.] August 23, 1960, Lewiston, ME; [p.] Connie and James; [m.] Jill Blanchard, September 7, 1996; [ed.] Telstar High School, Associates Degree - 2 years Trades Degree - 2 years, Braodcasting 1 year; [occ.] Boiters, Boiler Operations in a Power Plant; [oth. writ.] 100 poems while I was in college, 1st publishing, 1st entry of any written.; [pers.] I wish to have peace and harmony in the world! Family values are most important to me.; [a.] Holks, ME

BLAYLOCK, JOHN
[pen.] John Blaylock; [b.] June 16, 1996, Sumter, SC; [p.] Richard and Morele Blaylock; [ed.] Freshman in Flour Bluff High School; [occ.] Student; [hon.] Presidential Outstanding Academic Achievement 1995, Flour Bluff Junior High School A-Honor Roll 1994 and 1995, Outstanding 8th Grade Bandsman 1995, President Sports Award 1995, A and A-B Honor Roll at Flour Bluff High School; [pers.] In my writings I refer and reflect on people and events who have shaped my beliefs concerning life and death. I just like to write and see where it goes.; [a.] Corpus Christi, TX

BLINN, DIANE MARIE
[pen.] Diane-Marie; [b.] May 4, 1945, New York, NY; [p.] Grace Hargrove, the late Richard Hargrove Sr.; [m.] Gar S. Blinn, May 2, 1980; [ch.] Rob Blinn; [ed.] AB, Vassar College, Ph.D., University of Chicago; [occ.] Educator (Walden University, Norfolk Public Schools); [pers.] Poetry has always been in my heart. Crafting it and sharing it are new midlife experiences.; [a.] Norfolk, NE

BLOCKER JR., RANDY D.
[b.] May 9, 1969, Columbia, TN; [ed.] Ben C. Rain H.S., Troy State University, Trenholm for Paramedic Degree; [occ.] MEDLIFE EMS in Mobile, AL as a Paramedic, ALS Supervisor, Education, and

Head of Q&A; [memb.] Phi Mu Alpha Alumni, E.M.S. volunteer, computer games and computers, and work.

BLOCKER JR., GREEN A.
[pen.] Greensleeves; [b.] March 22, 1956, Elgin, TX; [p.] Mr. and Mrs. Hayward McNeil, Rev. and Mrs. Green A. Blocker Sr.; [m.] Ms. Rachel M. Blocker, August 1, 1993; [ch.] Jacinda, Regina, Arlin Jr., Beverly, Rochelle, Dan and Christopher; [ed.] Elgin High School, Southwest Texas State University, Regional Training Center, Lackland (Air Force Base), Lowery (AFB) Technical School; [occ.] Telemarketing Associate with AT and T; [memb.] U.S. Air Force Vet., Who's Who (Among High School Seniors), Seniors Class Pres., (High School), member of NAAGP... (Baptist Minister's Assoc.); [hon.] Basic Training graduate (Air Force), Marksman expert, (M-16 Rifle) Air Force, $300.00 Scholarship, Eastern Star, (Green's Delight Group...) Lodge; [oth. writ.] (Those Gals Of Spring And Summer): April, May and June... and numerous other poems... i.e., D.D.A. (Ode to J.F.K.).; [pers.] I believe in live and let live... and I'm pretty much of an African - American version of will Rogers... (maybe I am him reincarnated...).; [a.] Austin, TX

BOAS, PRISCILLA MARIE
[pen.] Pris; [b.] November 19, 1942, Lancaster, PA; [p.] Lloyd LeRoy and Rose Marie Laukhoff; [m.] Milton R. Boltz-fiancee.; [ch.] Michelle wife of Brian Emerick, Joanne wife of Jeff Williams, Karen wife of Greg Rice, Teresa fiancee of Kevin Draughon, Frank S. Doman III - deceased; [gr. ch.] Jackie, Jeffrey, Lindsay, Tara, Mclvin, Amanda, Troy, Austin, Krystal and Jeffrey.; [ed.] J.P. Mc Caskey High School Received G.E.D.; [occ.] Retired from Armstrong World Industries as dock leader and relief supervisor.; [memb.] Lewes Rehoboth Chapter 1814 W.O.T.M., American Legion Auxiliary Post 0017, and Girl Scout Leader for 18 years.; [pers.] I wrote this poem for my mother in 1969. Since then she has died.; [a.] Lewes, DE

BOJAN, JASON
[b.] November 4, 1976; [p.] Natile Bojan, Martin Bojan; [ed.] Syosset High School, Farmingdale Community College, Florida Atlantic University; [occ.] Student at FAU, Drummer, Songwriter; [pers.] I am greatly influenced by my own emotions. Everything I write is based on true personal experiences. I give my greatest respect and happiness to this moment to Lorrine Bossang, my English teacher who influenced me in the art of poetry.; [a.] Delray Beach, FL

BOLIN, JESSICA LEIGH
[b.] January 24, 1982, Cleveland, OK; [p.] Tim and Cansee Bolin; [ed.] Heaton Elementary, Ft. Miller Jr. High; [memb.] Church of Jesus Christ of Latter Day Saints, Civil War Re-enactment Society, and 1996 Math-o-Rama Team; [hon.] Honor Roll 1991, 1992 and 1993, Principal's Awards 1994, Soroptimist International Service Award 1994, Hyperstudio Drug Education Outstanding Project 1994; [a.] Fresno, CA

BONA, EILEEN
[pen.] Bella; [b.] June 30, 1967, Sydney, NS; [p.] Florence and Clarence Bona; [ed.] BSC in Psychol-ogy - Partially finished an M. Ed in Educational Psychology from the University of Alberta.; [occ.] Behavior Management Specialist in Private Practice.; [memb.] Psychologists Association.; [hon.] 1st place on Medical Courses 1 and 2 C the National Defence Reserves where I served 2 yrs as head Medic to an Infantry Unit and 3 years as a Medic in the Med Coy.; [oth. writ.] Real Riches, on our way, our world, a friend, take care, the bride, the boy in the bush, farewell, where is me, raging black, Elfie 1 and 2, why you?, the beast, I always will, my feelings and more.; [pers.] I believe in focusing on solutions, not on problems. If I'm not happy, I change something, or everything. My changes have made my life a colorful adventure. My writing is a reflection of the pain I experience while striving for happiness.; [a.] Edmonton Alberta, Canada

BONNOR, CECILIA
[b.] July 3, 1974, Rosario, Argentina; [p.] Hector and Maria J. Bonnor; [ed.] Stratford High School, University of Texas, B.A. in English in May 1996; [occ.] Student; [memb.] Sigma Tau Delta, Gamma Beta Phi, Phi Kappa Phi Golden Key National Honor Society, Phi Beta Kappa, Alpha Delta Tau, Amnesty International; [hon.] Anne Frank Human Rights Award, 1986, Musabelle Book Award 1992, Dean's List 1992, 1993, Scholar's Day 1995, Scholar's Day 1996; [oth. writ.] Several essays and reviews published in Dreaming Out Loud and a poem published in Chrysalis.; [pers.] I am captivated by the existential life of individuals. The struggle is as important as the achievement and I am moved by this. In fact, I care deeply about the juxtaposition between literature and politics because herein is the essence of human strivings. I have been deeply touched by Shakespeare, James Joyce, John Lennon and Sinead O'Connor; [a.] Houston, TX

BOOI, SABRINA
[pen.] Sabrina Booi; [b.] July 23, 1978, Curacao, NA; [p.] Anna Abdalah and Gerry Booi; [ed.] I.L.C. Pacific High School, 12th grade, afterwards U.F.; [oth. writ.] Several poems written for just my friends and family.; [pers.] I like to express what I feel inside through my poems. I have been encouraged by my dear mom and the greatest friends.; [a.] Nymegen, Holland

BOONE, JOANNA
[b.] January 15, 1984, Woodstock, New Brunswick, Canada; [p.] Kevin and Barb Boone; [ed.] Grade 1-5 Central Carleton Elementary School, Grade 6 Hartland High School; [occ.] Student; [hon.] 1st Place for Remembrance Day Story from Hartland Legion - 1994 Hartland, NB, Merit Award for story from Mactaquac Provincial Park - 1995 Mactaquac, NB; [oth. writ.] What Christmas means to me walk through paradise.; [a.] Hartland New Brunswick, Canada

BORDEN, GEORGE
[b.] December 17, 1935, Nova Scotia, Canada; [occ.] Retired Military (CD, CM, CM); [memb.] Black Artists Assoc (Nova Scotia, Can.), N.S. Song Writers Assoc. (Can.), Christian Writers Assoc. (Halifax, Nova Scotia, Canada); [oth. writ.] Canaan Odyssey, 1988 ISBN 0-921201-06-0 and footprints images and reflections, 1993 ISBN 0-921201-11-7 Re the black experience in North America-Canada; [pers.] Find most joy in writing Southern Gospel songs for professional artists.; [a.] Dartmouth Nova Scotia, Canada

BORGER, DONNA J.
[b.] January 4, 1970, Kentucky; [p.] Donald and Judy Gerding; [m.] Arthur W. Borger III, February 28, 1992; [ch.] Eric, Artie, Garrett, Keith; [occ.] House wife; [pers.] I would like to dedicate this poem in loving memory of my father-in -law, who was a true inspiration to me, and an example of what if means to have been a true Christian.; [a.] Cincinnati, OH

BORRELL, MANUEL R.
[b.] January 22, 1961, Madrid, Spain; [p.] Osvaldo Borrell and Miriam Garrido; [m.] Nancy Borrell, September 3, 1982; [ch.] Shannon and Michelle M.; [ed.] University of Puerto Rico (BA), Central Michigan University (MS); [occ.] U.S. Army officer (Major); [memb.] American Hospital Association; [hon.] Graduated Magna Cum Laude from College; [oth. writ.] Many works yet unpublished.; [pers.] My poetry express the emotions of the human spirit. It reflects the endless psychological conflicts of reason and logic versus passion and desire.; [a.] Peachtree City, GA

BORRERO, MICHAEL S.
[b.] July 7, 1974; [ed.] Carnegie Mellon University; [memb.] Society of Hispanic Professional Engineers; [hon.] Carnegie Mellon Ramon Bentances Award for Leadership; [oth. writ.] Several poems published in Dossier and Tertulia Literary and Design Journals.; [pers.] My poetry attempts to bring the Puerto Rican identity and struggle to the American Literary and Mainstream Communities. I have been most influenced by poets such as Langston Hughs, Claude McKay, and Nicolas Guillen.

BOUCHER, ROBERT J.
[pen.] RJB; [b.] August 3, 1966, Brockton; [p.] Richard and Victoria Boucher; [ch.] Jaime Celine Boucher; [ed.] Bridgewater State College; [occ.] Arborist/Land Clearing; [memb.] VFW/American Legion National Arbor Day Foundation; [oth. writ.] A poem entitled "As Far as I can see" published in across the universe; [pers.] This poem was written in the sands of Saudi Arabia during the gulf war which I was in for seven months. I wrote it while thinking of friends and family I missed dearly.; [a.] Brigewater, MA

BOUCHERE, SIMONE
[pen.] Sika, Smocha, Mone; [b.] February 24, 1976, Downsview, ON; [p.] Albert Bouchere, Adele Bouchere; [ed.] St. Charles Garnier Elementary, Regina Pacis Catholic High School, Centennial College; [occ.] Customer Service Representative, Highland Farms, ON; [hon.] Most Improved Student Award, Business English Award; [oth. writ.] Several poems for personal collection. To be published one day.; [pers.] My inspiration comes from the one true love of my life M.R. true love never dies, it only grows strong (June 25, 1994); [a.] Richmond Hill ON, Canada

BOURGEOIS, STEVE
[b.] July 25, 1979, Iroquois Falls, Ontario, Canada; [p.] Don and Jocelyne Bourgeois; [ed.] I am currently in grade 11, and will graduate in the next 2 years. I am attending Iroquois falls secondary school.; [memb.] I belong to the Mountain Equipment Co-operative.; [hon.] I have received numerous top-academic awards, communication awards, and math and science awards.; [oth. writ.] Short stories, poems on various topics, essays.; [pers.] "Apply your heart to instruction, and your ears to words of knowledge" - proverbs 23:12; [a.] Iroquois Falls Ontario, Canada

BOWER, ELEANOR A.
[pen.] E. A. Bower; [b.] May 11, 1936, Philadelphia, PA; [p.] James J. and Mary C. Kelly McKeffery; [m.] Charles A. Bower (Boots), November 10, 1989; [ch.] Paul A. (James J. and John R.) Identical twins and Laurianne; [ed.] Saint Monica's Elementary and So. Phila. H.S. - some college credits from Williamsport Area Community College (Nowkons Pa. College of Technology); [occ.] Semi retired - Domestic Engr.; [memb.] Hospice Vol., Prison Vol., Red Cross Blood Donor, St. Boniface Roman Catholic Church and Lector; [oth. writ.] Unpublished poems. This is my first attempt at having any of my writings published I have a book started on my dog, Minerva of 19 yrs. I intend it to be a children's book and dedicated to my grandchildren.; [pers.] I have always been impressed and fascinated by Nature and the Universe. Also, my teaching nuns. IHM, have influenced me. My philosophy is to try to see the beauty in everything and everyone.; [a.] Williamsport, PA

BOWMAN, RASHIDA T.
[b.] March 2, 1973, Columbus, OH; [oth. writ.] I have more scraps of poems, songs, and stories than I care to think about. Will they ever be published? I hope so.; [pers.] I may not be the best writer, but I think I'm doing something half-way right.; [a.] Columbus, OH

BOWMAN, TERESA
[b.] April 19, 1956, Winston-Salem, NC; [p.] Bib T. Priddy, Jr. and Nina B. Martin; [m.] Charles R. Bowman III, October 26, 1974; [ch.] Jonathon Lee and Justin Ray; [ed.] Forsyth High School, Forsyth Tech, Rowan Community College; [occ.] Data Entry Clerk; [pers.] I look for the best in people and in life and writing is a wonderful way to express my feelings. Many ideas come from my family, as they are truly the source of my inspiration.; [a.] Concord, NC

BOYER, JUDY
[b.] August 20, 1936, Vidalia, GA; [p.] Lois and Monroe Davis; [m.] Kenneth H. Boyer, September 2, 1956; [ch.] Deborah Kaye and Kenneth Jed; [ed.] Vidalia High School, Valdosta State College; [occ.] Art Teacher; [memb.] Ft. Bend Co. Art League Richmond, Texas, The Church of Jesus Christ of Latter Day Saints; [hon.] Coffee Co. (Alabama) Art Merit Award; [oth. writ.] Published in local newspaper.; [pers.] I strive to reflect the love and interaction in family relationships.; [a.] Richmond, TX

BOYER, KENNETH J.
[b.] February 23, 1961, Bethlehem, PA; [p.] Kenneth H. & Judy Boyer; [ed.] A.A.S./ Criminal Justice; [occ.] Student; [memb.] DAV / Disabled American Veterans, CLEAT/ Law Enforcement; [oth. writ.] They Came in Peace, A Christmas Ditty, The Cowboy Spirit; [a.] Austin, TX;

BRADBURY, JACK A.
[b.] December 2, 1942, Peterborough, Ontario, Canada; [p.] Mr. and Mrs. P. A. Bradbury; [m.] Mary-Jane; [ch.] Roxanne, Marilyn, Chandelle, Daralynn, grandchildren Rhalynn Corbin; [occ.] Letter carrier Canada Post; [hon.] Editors Choice Award for "The Shabby Little House" 1995 I.S.P.; [oth. writ.] Eighty-five to ninety poems. Summer passing, legends to be published in Beneath the Harvest Moon - Summer 1996; [pers.] "Plastic Words" A computer I don't have to push a button and find a thought that I had it simply raced my mind.; [a.] Prince George British Columbia, Canada

BRADLEY, BEVERLEY
[b.] September 11, 1934, Arcola; [p.] Mrs. Blanche Stewart; [m.] Edward Bradley, March 6, 1959; [ch.] Allan, Robert, Wesley Ruggles, Carrs Frederick, Joycelin Elaine, and Edward, Murry Lynne; [ed.] Grade 9; [occ.] Housewife; [memb.] Carly Community Chapel Sask. Seniors Association.; [hon.] 2 Red Ribbon, 5 for unpublished poem not the one sent another one.; [oth. writ.] Poem sent senior paper; [pers.] I am a small town housewife and mother of grown up and married children I love tow rite prose, poetry and monologues, when spirit moves me.; [a.] Arcola Saskatchewan, Canada

BRADLEY, TIM
[b.] May 23, 1955, Mebane, NC; [p.] Roy Bradley, Lucille Bradley; [m.] Victoria Anderson Bradley, August 3, 1980; [ch.] Jennifer Lynn, Allison Rosa, Caroline Anderson, Jessica Dawn; [ed.] Assoc Applied Science Electronics, B.S. Fire and Safety Engineering; [occ.] N.C. State Fire Commissioner; [memb.] Mebane First Baptist Church, Bingham Masonic Lodge, International Fire Service Accreditation Congress; [hon.] Executive Fire Officer, Who's Who in State Government; [oth. writ.] Assorted poems, published in local journals.; [pers.] Most of my poems reflect personal experiences in my life.; [a.] Mebane, NC

BRADLEY, VALERIE
[pen.] Val; [b.] June 1, 1961, Grande Prarie, Alberta, Canada; [p.] Victor and Muriel Amiro; [m.] Calvin Bradley, February 2, 1985; [ch.] Aaron Bradley; [ed.] Hillside High School-Valleyview, AB. Correspondence through I.C.S. to finish my education and get my diploma too; [occ.] Was a waitress, now staying home as a moment and wife.; [hon.] Received one award for a poem, I submitted to The National Library of Poetry, for 1995.; [oth. writ.] I love to write. My ambition is to be a professional writer and a poet. I want more out of my life, than being a waitress.; [a.] Fox Creek Alberta, Canada

BRADY, DARREN
[b.] May 4, 1963, Osawatomie, KS; [p.] Elaine Mounger; [ed.] Osawatomie High School, Washburn University of Topeka, KS; [occ.] Musician, Sound Mixer, Composer; [memb.] ASCAP; [hon.] Outstanding Civic Duty - City of Los Angeles, Charitable Contribution Award Los Angeles Food Bank, Los Angeles Marathon '95 and '96 various music scores for film, video, and stage.; [pers.] Listen to hear the unspoken!; [a.] Sherman Oaks, CA

BRAGADIN, DIANA
[pen.] Dee Dee; [b.] December 20, 1959, Detroit, MI; [p.] Billy Perry, Carol J. Perry; [m.] Nick Bragadin, July 30, 1988; [ch.] Missy Bragadin; [ed.] Wood Haven High School (graduation "1978") Dearborn Continental Studios, Middle Eastern Dance "1978"; [occ.] Domestic Engineer (Housewife); [hon.] Middle Easter Dance Top of the Class "78"; [oth. writ.] I have written for the Monroe Evening News; [pers.] I strive to express my feelings about the people I love most, my daughter, husband and family. I have been greatly influenced by my father, and mother, both, romantics.; [a.] Monroe, MI

BRAGG, ELYSSA
[b.] September 30, 1982, Greenville, SC; [p.] Phil and Cherie Bragg; [ed.] Addison Elementary and Rawlinson Road Middle School; [occ.] Student

BRAGG, JUANITA M.
[b.] August 12, 1948, Beckley, WV; [p.] Charles and Ilene Bragg; [m.] Edward Loren Bragg, September 5, 1970; [ch.] Paul Brian and Jessie James; [ed.] Lincoln West High School; [occ.] Homemaker; [oth. writ.] I have written many poems, mostly for family and friends, a few were published in our local 71 journal.; [pers.] I've never fancied myself as a poet, but I love to write about things that touch me in some way. I am just an ordinary person writing about ordinary, everyday feelings.; [a.] Sheffield Lake, OH

BRAITHWAITE, CATRIONA LAIDLAW
[b.] December 31, 1944, Calcutta, India; [p.] Hannah-May and Thomas Smith; [m.] Dr. Desmond Braithwaite, August 16, 1980; [ch.] Damon, Thomas, Isamu, Yasuda; [ed.] John Knox School, Preston Lodge College, Royal Academy of Dane; [hon.] Several writing awards at college; [pers.] I have been tremendously influenced in my daily life by the writings of Kahil Gilbran and other Winter of Philosophy many of my poems are created from some personal emotional trial.; [a.] Mississauga Ontario, Canada

BRAITHWAITE, LOURIE
[b.] February 28, 1964, Kamloops, BC, Canada; [p.] Karen and Bill Braithwaite; [occ.] Clerk Typist, Edmonton Public Schools, Edmonton, Alberta; [oth. writ.] Published in Sparkles in the Sand; [pers.] Missing my brother, friends and kin, my beloved mother these are my inspirations; [a.] Edmonton Alberta, Canada

BRANDT, REVA MORGAN
[b.] July 12, 1983, Saint Paul, MN; [p.] Rita and Warren Brandt; [occ.] Student; [memb.] Girl Scouts, 4-14, O.M., 100% Club, Jason Project; [hon.] Presidential Academic Fitness Award, Young Authors Wisconsin Award, My biggest award was being selected to go to Florida by Earth shuttle; [oth. writ.] "A Special Place for Me", Gypsy Cab Press, Anthology of woman Writers, "God's Creations," "Free," "Have You Ever Wondered," "Murder," "Making Mistakes," "Darkness," and

"What Is".; [pers.] I have eager Alan Poe and Robert Frost. My goal in life in to write 1 children's book, chapter books, and a novel.; [a.] Prescott, WI

BRANTLEY, LILLIAM
[b.] February 1, 1951, Augusta, GA; [p.] Juanita and John Shanks; [ch.] Brandon, Brantley, Angela Everett, Juannita Walton; [ed.] T.W Josey High School, Augusta Technical School 26 yrs of Medical experience; [occ.] Lab Technician Medical College of GA; [memb.] MT Calvary Baptist Church, Clyde Hill Senior Choir.; [hon.] Recognize by the Hospitals single out Committee, as an out standing employee.; [pers.] In memory of a Good Friend.; [a.] Augusta, GA

BRAUN, ELLEN
[b.] February 1, 1948, Niagara Falls, NY; [p.] Fred O'Callaghan, Joyce O'Callaghan; [m.] Mel Braun, September 17, 1966; [ch.] Vicky, Chris, Steven; [ed.] Niagara Falls High School, Niagara Falls, New York; [occ.] Booking Clerk, Lincoln County Board of Education, St. Catharines, Ontario; [memb.] Church of Christ; [pers.] People are the essence of life. It is their experiences which have determined history, will determine the future and influence the present.; [a.] Saint Catharines Ontario, Canada

BRAXTON, CONSTANCE VERONICA
[b.] September 24, 1933, Brooklyn, NY; [p.] Frances Martin, William Jenkins Sr.; [m.] George Braxton, March 24, 1950; [ch.] Debra, Patricia, Constance, Robin, Melody, George and Dionne; [ed.] My Tech College A.A. Degree in Liberal Arts, Empire State College, B.S. Degree in Human Services; [occ.] Freelance Writer of Stories and Poetry and Coordinator for 1180's Retiree's Newspaper; [memb.] American Association of Retired Persons AARP, National Council of Senior Citizens NCSC, Local 1180 Retiree Members Club; [oth. writ.] 1st Prize Literary Short Story Contest published by Brooklyn Woman, a Brooklyn Journal Publication. Numerous articles published in Daily News Voice Column.; [pers.] I love to write stories and poetry because it gives me the opportunity to reflect on my experiences and in hindsight, to figure out why they mean so much to me. The remembered feelings let us reflect our own successes, failures, needs and frustrations. All in all, its a great feeling to share.; [a.] Brooklyn, NY

BRAZEAU, ASHLEY R.
[pen.] Doniqua Lilian; [b.] March 27, 1983, Pembroke, Ontario, Canada; [p.] Steve Brazeau, Christine Brazeau; [ed.] Our Lady of Lourdes, Elementary and Bishop Smith High School; [hon.] 3rd Place Public Speaking, 1st Place in Math Olympics and went on to higher competition, in Ottawa, Ont.; [oth. writ.] I am processing a children's story book.; [pers.] I am the type who always has plans and I look forward to the future and hope one day I will be well-known for my writing.; [a.] Pembroke Ontario, Canada

BRENT, ALICE K.
[b.] December 29, 1948, Wayne Co.; [p.] James and Bessie Kendrick; [m.] Gregory Brent, November 5, 1990; [ch.] Derrick, Danina, Deanna; [ed.] Wayne County High School; [occ.] Factory

General Electric; [oth. writ.] I have written other poetry, but I haven't had any of it published before.; [pers.] I have reflected some of my religious background of myself and others in some of my poetry, and in some I try to reflect the lighter side of life, laughter smiles and joy.; [a.] Lexington, KY

BRIDGFORD, RICHARD
[b.] March 24, 1960, Anaheim, CA; [p.] Anan and Janet; [m.] Sison, July 18, 1988; [ch.] Four; [ed.] Stanford B.A. 1982, Stanford Low JD 1985; [occ.] Trial Attorney; [oth. writ.] Many poems

BRINTZENHOFF, CAMILLE
[b.] May 16, 1978, Reading, PA; [p.] Virginia Brintzenhoff; [ed.] At this time, I am attending Exeter Senior High School as a Senior.; [occ.] I am a High School Student at the present time.; [oth. writ.] My only other writings are and were for school related projects.; [pers.] My mother has played an important part of my life, she is my inspiration. Everything I write, I write out of love for whoever inspired me.; [a.] Birdsboro, PA

BRITTAIN, MRS. IVY
[b.] October 20, 1919, Bolton, Lancs, England; [p.] Beatrice and John Wilding; [m.] George F. Brittain (Deceased 1992), December 9, 1939; [ch.] Three (2 Boys and 1 Girl); [ed.] Grade 9, High School; [occ.] Housewife; [memb.] Life member of Royal Canadian Legion and Executive member. Member of Moose Lodge (Formerly); [hon.] Honorary Life Membership Award from R. Can Legion; [oth. writ.] Short Stories, never published though; [pers.] Care about children and their rights and the environment and rain forest and third world children; [a.] Hamilton Ontario, Canada

BRITTON, APRIL
[b.] April 1, 1933, Norwich, England; [p.] Sidney Britton, Daisy Britton; [ed.] Northern Vocational School (in Toronto), A-R-C-T in Violin, from Royal Conservatory of Toronto; [memb.] I'm a member (for 28 years) of an Intentional Spiritual Community at the Canadian HQ of "The Emissaries", an International Spiritual Organization.; [hon.] High school scholarships and prizes, Kiwanis Festival of Music Awards. By invitation, I took part in three concerts with a fellow poet and classical chamber choir, reading a selection of my poems.; [oth. writ.] Various poems published in local newspapers, and in poetry journals. An article on playing chamber music: "Friendship A Magic Formula", published in "The Emissary". Poems and articles in "Northern Light", an annual Emissary Journal.; [pers.] When I touch the inherent beauty in the creation, I touch the very presence of God. It's the divinity in me, seeing the divinity all around me. And that is unalterably present, even in the darkest days of the chronic illness in my life.; [a.] 100 Mile House British Columbia, Canada

BRITTON II, DANIS B.
[b.] September 20, 1967, Biddeford, ME; [p.] Linda Borruso and Danis Britton; [ed.] Andover College, University of New England Pre Law Major; [occ.] Service Specialist Blue Cross, Blue Shield of Maine Portland, ME; [hon.] Deans List; [pers.] "Believe in yourself and all will be possible."; [a.] Saco, ME

BRODD, NADINE ANZURES
[b.] June 29, 1955, Williams, AZ; [p.] Ida Wallace and Alphonso P. Anzures; [m.] Michael Paul Brodd, March 25, 1996; [ch.] Four (Three Girls, One Boy) (Two Grand); [ed.] Associates Degree in Electronics. Need Completion of Business Degree; [occ.] Car Sales Representative, Rich Ford, Albuquerque, New Mex.; [pers.] I have been greatly influenced by my first and only love of my life, my husband, Mr. Brood. He gave me love, hope, and life... purpose. I strive to reflect my life in hopes of more openness in man's way of thinking....; [a.] Albuquerque, NM

BROHMAN, JEAN
[b.] Toronto, Ontario, Canada; [p.] Jane Merritt, A.W.J. Russell (Deceased); [m.] Edward James Brohman, December 11, 1943; [ch.] Darlene Flynn - Edward (Jim); [ed.] Public School, Night School, Classes in Crafts, Papertole Bunka Oil Painting etc.; [occ.] Homemaker; [memb.] Parks Recreation Crafts; [hon.] I received a certificate for flying in a 1941 Wacoupe - 7 - Bi Plane. Also for going up in a hot air balloon. I also went up in a glider; [oth. writ.] I have written several humorous poems and some that are both humorous and serious but have never submitted any; [pers.] I have 5 grandchildren and a dog named Bear.; [a.] Scarboro Ontario, Canada

BROOKS, ANGIE
[b.] May 2, 1978, Bowie County, TX; [p.] Michael Brooks, Judy Brooks; [ed.] Arlington High, Abilene Christian University; [memb.] North Davis Church of Christ, Arlington High School Student Council, Arlington Citizens Police Academy; [oth. writ.] Several personal Journals of Poetry (not published); [pers.] I have written poetry for many years. It is the one true way I can express how I feel.; [a.] Arlington, TX

BROOKS, VIRGINIA CHAMBERS
[pen.] Ginny Brooks; [b.] February 27, 1933, Harrisburg, PA; [p.] Mr. and Mrs. Frank Vucenic; [m.] Peter J. Brooks, March 11, 1978; [ch.] Kathleen Marsh, Joseph Chambers and Mary O'Donnell; [ed.] High School - Harrisburg Catholic High School, many life experiences; [occ.] Homemaker; [memb.] St. John of Arc Church Hershey, PA, Assist with special Olympics Local Area; [hon.] Editors Choice Award, National Poetry Society; [oth. writ.] Editorials in Patriot News Paper Hbg., PA., Book of Fiction called Anthony. Now writing a book about the Harrisburg, PA. Police dept. unpublished at this time. Wrote articles for "City news" years ago.; [pers.] Most of my writings are of the human spirit and the confusion of politics. I never run out of subjects. My husband encourages my writing, for this I am thankful.; [a.] Hershey, PA

BROUSSARD, VIKKI LINCOLN
[b.] April 5, 1973, Houston, TX; [p.] Willie Zepher, Lorrissa Lincoln; [m.] Herschel P. Broussard Jr., September 17, 1994; [ch.] Je Quila Willis; [ed.] Booker T. Washington High Sch., Huntsville High Sch., will be attending Transworld Academy April 29, 1996.; [occ.] Signing Supervisor Spec. for Target Dept. Store; [pers.] Through my poems, I express my inner-most feelings. Most of my poems are from life experience.; [a.] Houston, TX

BROWN, ANNE GREENWOOD
[b.] September 29, 1967, St. Paul, MN; [m.] Greg Brown; [ch.] Samantha Ruth; [ed.] St. Olaf College (Northfield, MN), William Mitchell College of Law (St. Paul, MN); [occ.] Lawyer; [memb.] Phi Beta Kappa; [pers.] As a Medieval Studies (undergraduate) major and recent convert to Catholicism, I am intrigued by religious traditions, customs, and motifs.; [a.] Stillwater, MN

BROWN, CHAD E.
[b.] March 22, 1969, Oklahoma, OK; [p.] Glen Brown, Sue Brown; [pers.] "One far off divine even toward which the whole of creation moves." Anonymous.; [a.] Kennesaw, GA

BROWN, ERIKA DAWN
[pen.] Erika Dawn Brown; [b.] June 10, 1973, NY; [p.] Kathy Taylor, Joel Brown; [ed.] University of South Florida, International Exchange Sr. Year — University of Brighton (England), B.S. English Education; [memb.] National Council of Teachers of English (NCIE), Poetry Society of America (PSA); [oth. writ.] Several poems published "Another Drag of a Cigarette" (modern poetry society), song lyrics — Edlee music and East coast records.; [pers.] Poetry is like a photograph. One being a verbal impression the other a visual. Each captures a moment in time. neither need justification, defense nor explanation.; [a.] West Palm Beach, FL

BROWN, FLORENCE M.
[pen.] Brownie; [b.] January 29, 1909, Union, OR; [p.] George and Claro Jerwilleger; [m.] Russell J. Brown, April 2, 1939; [ch.] Bruce and Russell; [ed.] Sacramento High School San Francisco National Training School, University of Redlands Major Sociology - 15 years as Social Worker 21 years as Teacher; [occ.] Retired Educator; [memb.] Calif. Teachers Assoc. Calif. Retired Teachers, National Retired Teachers; [hon.] Certificate Exemplary Service - North Sacramento School District 2-A one woman show of oil landscapes - Sylvan Oaks Library - Selling paintings; [oth. writ.] Poems written for enjoyment and to use in school when teaching to help children see beauty in Words, Language Arts.; [pers.] I try to remember "there but for the grace of God go I"; [a.] Sacramento, CA

BROWN, KENYA B.
[b.] December 15, 1977, Poway, CA; [p.] Blanche Cates, Jesse Barrett, Ken and Doll Brown; [ed.] Graduated Ramona, Ca H.S. 1995. Currently College Freshman; [occ.] Grocery/Vitamin Dept; [memb.] Concert Choir, Glee Club, Volley Ball Team, Community Service Program, Grace Community Church; [hon.] Lettered in Music H.S., Honor Roll; [oth. writ.] Arizona Moon, I realized - Love and various poems.; [pers.] I hope that my poems reflect the beauty in the world around me.; [a.] Grants Pass, OR

BROWN, LAURA B.
[b.] October 24, 1934, Saxe, VA; [p.] James E. and Mattie I. Moore; [m.] The late George E. Brown, May 2, 1953; [ch.] George, Clinton, Gary, Timothy, Carol; [ed.] 12th Grade; [occ.] Children's Aide; [memb.] New Shiloh Baptist Church; [hon.] Saturday Church School, Teacher of the Year 1987-88, New Shiloh

Baptist Church, Woman of the Year Award April 16, 1989; [oth. writ.] The Empty Place; [pers.] Through the poems I am inspired to write, I try to show others the strength and power of having God in your life.; [a.] Baltimore, MD

BROWN, MALVIN L.
[pen.] Malvin L. Brown; [b.] August 30, 1912, Sparta, TN; [p.] Malvin E. Brown and Elizabeth Lylis; [m.] Ola Moseley Brown, November 24, 1938; [ch.] 2 girl and 1 boy (Deceased); [ed.] High School Graduate and several sessions of nite school, controler of construction 42 years; [occ.] Mgr. small Grocery; [memb.] V.F.M. Dav. former Mayor of Sparta, former Comissioner of White Country Court for 14 years; [hon.] Served on TN Board Director of Dav. also served on Board of Glows of TN Boxing Association.; [oth. writ.] Numerous poems and personal skits of philosophy several songs all unpublished; [pers.] I enjoy writing skits and poems also songs of local interest; [a.] Sparta, TN

BROWN, PATRICIA H.
[b.] July 7, 1943, Milwaukee, WI; [p.] Harley and Delores Rust; [ch.] Five; [ed.] 12th Grade; [occ.] Lab Laborer; [oth. writ.] The System, Devils Riders, Mama's Angel Wings, Superstition Mountains, and others.; [pers.] I specialize in song writing - I've written over 300 songs. I hope to someday sell my songs to a publisher, who in turn will have a big star sing them.; [a.] Afton, WY

BROWN, RONALD G.
[pen.] Ron Charlot; [b.] November 3, 1946, Pittsburgh, PA; [p.] Karl P. Brown Jr., Ruth M. Brown; [m.] Barbara H. Brown, August 26, 1967; [ch.] Christopher Joseph; [ed.] The Florida State University, 1968, The Culinary Institute of America, Hyde Park, NY, 1980; [occ.] Self-employed Caterer, Owner: First Fruits Catering; [memb.] 1.) Calvary Bible Church and Maplewood, PA; [hon.] The Gospel Puppeteers, Hamlin, PA (Child Evangelist Gospel Ministry); [oth. writ.] Local newspaper articles about my Culinary Specialties and Charity Banquets; [pers.] As my business name indicates, and according to (Prov 3:9-10), I desire to use my God given abilities for his honor and glory alone. As he has so abundantly blessed me, I now attempt to share these "fruits" with others. My prayer is that those who "taste" my work will desire to "see" for themselves the goodness of God (Ps 34:8); [a.] Moscow, PA

BRUMAN, DAVID L.
[pen.] Harry Owens; [b.] May 17, 1951, Brown City, MI; [p.] Mary and George Bruman; [ch.] Shawn Amanda Brandy; [ed.] 1 yr. Vietnam; [occ.] Disable Vietnam Vct; [memb.] MOPH, DVA, VVA, GSVV, VFW; [hon.] Purple Heart; [oth. writ.] Don't Get Close, OK To Cry, and many more unpublished.; [pers.] The forgotten ones would not be forgotten if we did forget, POW/MIA; [a.] North Branch, MI

BRUNO, WALTER C.
[b.] April 2, 1920, Pittsburgh, PA; [p.] John F. and Anna C. Bruno; [m.] Clare F. Bruno, December 26, 1953; [ch.] John G. Bruno; [ed.] St. Catherine's Elem. Sch. La Salle Milatery Academy LI NY Mt. Union College (B.S. Deg); [occ.] Retired; [memb.]

Bowling Writers Assoc. of America (BWAA) National Rifle Assoc. (NRA) Inst. for Legal Action Phi Kappa Tau Fraternity Smithsonian - Nat'l Geographic; [hon.] BWAA - Honorable Mention, World Champion Endurance Bowler; [oth. writ.] Remembering (Poetry) Vomo Della Morte (Autobiog) National Bowling Illustrated Beach Comber (Magazine) Mia, Fla.; [pers.] Poetry, is the Panorama of the Soul.; [a.] Pittsburgh, PA

BRUSH JR PETER N
[pen.] Pete Brush; [b.] June 22, 1970; [p.] Peter and JoAnna Brush; [ed.] MA Univ. of Maryland, 1995, BA Univ. of Vermont, 1992; [occ.] Internet Wire Editor, Associated Press; [oth. writ.] (None published): "Philly and the Bandits," children's story, "The Corridor", a novel, "The Plank", a play and other poems.

BRYSON, SHIRLEY NELL
[b.] February 11, 1929, Ft. Payne, AL; [p.] Eula and Ollie C. Hairston; [m.] Ronnie M. Bryson, July 16; [ch.] Cecilia and Shelia; [ed.] HS and College and Leadership Training, Cosmetology; [oth. writ.] Two books (Children's) published 1995 "Secrets In The Beginning" "The Little White Rabbit"; [pers.] Always dream and be truthful.; [a.] Rossville, GA

BUCHMANN, MONIKA
[b.] February 16, 1953, Germany; [p.] Johann and Therese Ruffing; [m.] Josef Buchmann, December 9, 1975; [ch.] Andre, Maika, Tanya; [ed.] Completed Grade 12 in Germany, Meerbusch; [occ.] Bench Craft/Kitchener, Leather Sewer - Belts; [memb.] National Geographic Society; [hon.] The Friends of Algonquin Park, The Valuable Contribution of the Centennial Ridges Trail; [oth. writ.] I have poems and stories written, never published.; [pers.] I God inspired through my Dad, my first story I put down on paper in 1982 it was a sad one, most of it is a German. Pictures give me the go.; [a.] Kitchener Ontario, Canada

BUCKNER, LISA MARIE
[b.] August 10, 1981, Muncie, IN; [p.] Randy and Vicky Buckner; [ed.] Freshman at Blackford High School; [occ.] Student; [memb.] Drama Club, Science Club, BADD Club, Swimming, Diving, and Tennis Teams"; [pers.] I'm dedicating this poem to my father Randy, when he was talking about leaving my mom and I, which he did about 1 month after I wrote the poem. I would like to thank my Drama teacher "Mike Clossin" for inspiring me to write poetry.; [a.] Hartford City, IN

BUIL, JOSE A.
[b.] April 7, 1934, Ponce, PR; [p.] Alfredo C. Buil, Waldina Velez; [m.] Iris Frye, May, 28, 1959; [ch.] Joseph (Deceased), Michael, Katherine; [ed.] Attended Central H.S., Santurce, P.R. Earned BSCE from A&M College, Mayaguez, PR, Attended U. of Kansas, U. of Missouri, and U. of Cincinnati where he earned a MSCE in 1972.; [occ.] Retired Professional Engineer, after 33 years of Federal service as a Civil Hydraulic Engineer with the U.S. Corps of Engineers and a Hydrologist with the Ohio River Forecast Center, national Weather Service. Consulting Engr.; [memb.] Past mem. Missouri, Ohio, and National Societies of Professional Engineers. Member Toastmasters International. Owns many copyrights and a Trademark.; [hon.]

Two high performance awards from the Corps of Engineers. Outstanding Performance Award from the NWS/NOAA. ATM Award from Toastmasters International Registered Professional Engr. (Mo.) Founded own Public Speaking and Consulting firm.; [oth. writ.] Author of numerous technical papers published in International Journals. Numerous poems and articles incl. "A Father's Legacy Remembered."; [pers.] "Wisdom is attained by mastering our knowledge.... knowledge is obtained by living loving experiences..." all that ever remains is beauty as a result of such living...; [a.] Cincinnati, OH

BUNDY, CINDY
[pen.] Cindy Bundy; [b.] December 14, 1964, Concord, CA; [p.] Ron Baker and Gail Baker; [m.] Ken Bundy, July 30, 1994; [ch.] Gina Lynn, Janelle Lee and Billie Ann; [ed.] Concord High School, Loma Vista Business School; [occ.] Front Office Sales Diablo Glass Co, Inc.; [pers.] The poems I've written are from the heart I will always be a part of me.; [a.] Concord, CA

BURNEY, RUBY L.
[b.] May 29, 1953, Tallahassee, FL; [p.] Elie and Maggie Walker; [m.] Donald C. Burney, August 17, 1974; [ed.] High School Graduate, Business School; [occ.] Administrative Assistant Thermo King Corporation; [memb.] Interamerican Society; [hon.] 1992 Market Share Award - Westinghouse - 1995 Thermo King Corporate Quality Achievement Award; [pers.] Used what you have to improve your life and those around you, and take responsibility for your own course in life. My parents have taught me that I have many choices.; [a.] Montgomery, AL

BURNS, EUGENE WALTER
[pen.] Mr. 007 "Gadget" Chowhound Gene (Walt) Burns; [b.] August 25, 1959, Terrytown, NY; [p.] Crawford E. Burns, Audley B. Burns; [ed.] Deluherta High, College of Acronautics, S.C.S. Tech, Maritine-Trade, Fairchild Industries, Coast Guard Aux.; [occ.] Maine Dept. Tops Buffalo NY, "Free Lance", Fine Artist, Song Writer, Musician, Inventor, Engineer, Mechanic,- Plumber, Carpenter, Poet, Martial Arts Instructor, Electrician, Painter And Actor; [memb.] President, and Sole Proprietor of Combined Minds Co., UFCW Local 2; [hon.] College of Aeronautics Honor list summer of "79", Fairchild Industries 5 year Gold Pin Service Award "85"; [oth. writ.] Pending; [pers.] I draw on my short yet vast experience, and that of my family, friends, and colleagues a long with my educational background to provide the fuel or foundation for the works on which I write, but the true influence that ignites this fuel comes from God, his word (The Bible) and the love of my family in my christian upbringing. E. B.; [a.] Buffalo, NY

BURR, JEFFREY M.
[pen.] Matthew Burr, Jeff Burr; [b.] May 2, 1976, Vancouver, Canada; [p.] Daniel and Karen Burr; [ed.] Glendora High School, class of '94, Azusa Pacific University current.; [occ.] Bellman/Driver, Embassy Suites Covina CA.; [oth. writ.] Several poem's published in "The Muse" high school magazine and a few songs written and recorded by Eagle Recording Studios; [pers.] I desire to show that people are limited only by themselves, for

what we try we do and what we do not try we can never do. I give all honor to God who has given me this talent; [a.] San Dimas, CA

BURTON I, EFREM ZIMBULIST
[pen.] Efrem Z. Burton I; [b.] January 3, 1961, Atlanta, GA; [p.] Mr. and Mrs. Henderson Burton Jr.; [m.] Separated, December 20, 1980; [ch.] Efrem Jr. and Christopher; [ed.] Southwest High School, 1979 Brewton Parker College, Mercer University, Macon Tech. 1989-93; [occ.] Carpenter, Drywall Contractor, Chef, Poet, Song Writer, Business Man; [memb.] "Disabled American Veteran" (D.A.V) 730 Peach Tree St. Atlanta GA. Student of Arabic and Theology and Philosophical Studies; [hon.] Theology, U.S.R.A.B. Ft. Riley KS, I.E.C, Military Cook Schools, drafting; [oth. writ.] "Today Has Come To Pass" "The Truth and the Key", "Lukewarm" "The Vision of Deliverance", "He's Coming Bac", "There's soem difficulties Up Ahead" "Sacrifice for God", "Children of the World". "The Devils Prostitute" Etc.; [pers.] The Price of Success is perseverance, but the price of failure comes cheaper, however, success doesn't come to you, but you must go to it, therefore, I strive to rise...to the divine majestic heights of prosperity, Spiritually, Intellectually and in every aspect of my life, through God Almighty.; [a.] Altanta, GA

BURTON JR., VAUGHAN
[b.] February 11, 1966, Cartersville, GA; [p.] Vaughan and Frances Burton; [ed.] Western Guilford High, University of North Carolina at Greensboro (B.A.); [occ.] Commercial Artist, Guitar Instructor; [memb.] Greensboro (N.C.) Artists League; [hon.] National Art Honor Society, Art Club Scholarship, Dean's List; [oth. writ.] Lyrics, poetry, music; [pers.] Guitar player, recorded on several independent compact discs. I feel that emotion is ultimately the driving force in all art. Special thanks to Lori Simon.; [a.] Greensboro, NC

BURTON, LEAH MICHELLE
[pen.] Leah Burton; [b.] June 5, 1976, Los Angeles; [p.] Wanima Joyce Marsh; [ed.] Associates of Arts, Degree in Psychology, Los Angeles City College; [occ.] Full-time Activist; [memb.] San Francisco Women Against Rape, Peace Action For A Sane World; [hon.] National Lincoln Douglas Debate Gold Champion; [oth. writ.] None other published; [pers.] I live my life one day at a time, but my entire being is devoted to the world struggle for justice and freedom for all oppressed peoples.; [a.] San Francisco, CA

BUSBY, ANGELA
[pen.] Angela; [b.] December 19, 1980, Wauchula; [p.] Herman and Vickie Jones; [ed.] Starke Elementary, Starke and Trenton Middle, Trenton High; [occ.] Writing song's for singing ministry "Gospel Four"; [memb.] Bell Church of God; [hon.] An award from Modern Poetry Society for poem "Baby Jesus" (Nationwide). A copyright on song, "The Lord Is My Helper."; [oth. writ.] "Baby Jesus", song "The Lord Is My Helper."; [pers.] Thanks to my mother Vickie Jones and father Herman Jones for the love and support they have showed and gave to me, also special thanks to my sisters, Kimberly, Lucretia, and Monica.; [a.] Trenton, FL

BUSTER, ANN LEE TICE
[pen.] Ann Lee; [b.] February 6, 1932, Fort Worth, TX; [p.] Floyd and Glady-Tice (Both Deceased); [m.] Divorced - 1979; [ed.] Crowley, TX, Elem. Burleson - Senior - High TCU, TCJC - North West Campus; [occ.] Retired - Nurse - Health-Care of Elderly (also 2o years of retail Clerk Cashier); [memb.] Baptist Church; [hon.] Certificate of Award Merit By-Ted-Rosen for recognition of outstanding lyric-writing ability, also certificate of appreciation youth - department from inspiration church of God Eastland, Texas Church Pastor Larry Smith Youth Director - J. L. - Blackstook; [oth. writ.] Unpublished - my grandfather life story "Man Behind The Plow."; [pers.] "Never forget from whence we came, who we are, and the loving hand that guides us through life" this statement from my grandfather many years ago the old red haired Irish nod, carries me thru life.; [a.] Fort Worth, TX

BUTLER, BRANDON R.
[b.] May 16, 1987, Philadelphia, PA; [p.] Cheryl and Boise Butler; [ed.] 3rd Grade Student at the General Francis Nash Elementary School; [occ.] American Kenpo Karate Assoc. "Blue Belt"; [oth. writ.] "Bears" (unpublished); [pers.] I like all of the following sports: Football, Soccer, Basketball, Base Ball, "T" Ball and Kickball. My favorite school subjects are Science, Spelling and Math. When I grow up I will either be a Scientist, a Policeman or a Firefighter.; [a.] Harleysville, PA

BUTLER, JESSIE
[b.] May 30, 1934, Clovis, NM; [p.] Robert E. and Lola Swinford; [m.] Wright Butler, June 7, 1954; [ch.] Randi Chase, Karla Glass, Greg Butler; [ed.] B.A. and M.A. in Elementary Education from Eastern New Mexico University; [occ.] Retired teacher - 30 years in Elementary Education. 10 of those 30 yrs in Special Ed.; [memb.] Member of Christ Community Church in Alamogordo N.M., Former Member of Ojai Valley OVTA - Calif. Teacher's Assoc. NEA; [hon.] National 4-H Club Winner in 1953, Scholarship from Kerr Glass Corp. Teacher of the Year Meiners Oaks Elementary School; [oth. writ.] Wrote many poems on cards and gifts - wrote plays, stories, and songs while I was teaching.; [pers.] I am a Born Again Christian. I base my life and my works on my faith in God.; [a.] Alamogordo, NM

BUTLER, MARION E.
[b.] July 2, 1935, Chicago; [p.] Author Clay; [m.] Arnold Butler, July 2, 1958; [ch.] Arothee Butler, Kathy Meeks; [ed.] Graduate High School, AAD; [occ.] Homemaker; [memb.] Access of living Hearn Horner Senior Citizen and Handicap Club; [hon.] City Ward Poetry Pernece Attendance HCX; [oth. writ.] Poetry excess; [pers.] Be true to yourself. Cut the crop and get to the bottom line. And get to the bottom line. And don't waste no time.; [a.] Chicago, IL

BYRD, PATTI
[pen.] Shannon; [b.] March 13, 1951, Tacoma, WA; [p.] Lonnie and Evelyn Doll; [m.] William, August 21, 1982; [ch.] Kathy, Kevin, Kris, Renee, Traci; [ed.] Napa High School, Napa Ca. Diploma: "General Law Enforcement" North American Correspondence School; [occ.] Correctional Of-

ficer State of Oregon, Salem; [pers.] To my husband bill, for all his love and support. To Mom and Dad, for teaching their children to be they very best they can be. To Gary and Kent, thanks for not laughing.; [a.] Salem, OR

BYRNE, MICHEAL
[b.] September 2, 1951, Ireland; [p.] Mary and Micheal; [m.] Noreen, December 24, 1972; [ch.] Peter 22, Paul 13, Shane 6; [ed.] Leaving Cert Standard De Burgh County Sec School; [occ.] Irish Army/DJ; [memb.] Catholic Boy Scouts of Ireland, Musical Cecilians; [hon.] Bronze Medal of Meret for the G.B.S.I. Also Unpeace Medal for Service to Peace Twice Served disease; [oth. writ.] In the process of finishing two childrens short stories book (Awaiting on a publishers) also 40 other poems etc., the rose/my child/poems published an local newspapers.; [pers.] I write all my poems about life and I strive to let people see the inside of my feelings I hope one day to publish a book of my poems.; [a.] Limerick, Ireland

CABRAL, JENNIFER
[pen.] Jennifer Cabral; [b.] June 5, 1979, Bermuda; [p.] Barbara, Terry Cabral; [ed.] Prep School and now still in High School; [occ.] Student; [memb.] The LITE Society (Liteature for Individual Thought and Expression), Need to join Greenpeace.; [hon.] A class scholarship in 9th grade: an athletics award.; [oth. writ.] One other poem published, the start of a book and over 150 songs, poems.; [pers.] "Without freedom of choice, there is no creativity. Without creativity, there is no life." -Star Trek; [a.] Virginia Beach, VA

CAGIANO, RONALDO
[b.] April 15, 1961, Cataguases, MG; [p.] Dario Albuquerque Barbosa-Terezinha, Cagiano Barbosa; [m.] Claudia Viviane de Souza Barbosa, April 7, 1992; [ch.] Murillo de Souza Cagiano Barbosa, Rebecca de Souza Cagiano Barbosa; [ed.] 10 Grau: Colegio Estadual de Cataguases-MG, 20 grau (idem). Grau Universitario: Universidade do Distrito Federal (UDF), Curso: Direito.; [occ.] Advogado e Assessor da Presidencia da Republica; [memb.] Associacao Nacional de Escritores (ANE), Sindicato dos Escritores do Distrito Federal (SEDF), Sindicato dos Escritores de Minas Gerais (SEMG), Casa do Escritor de Sao Roque (SP), Associacao de Escritores do Amazonas (AM); [oth. writ.] Livros publicados: "Palavra Engajada" (1989), "Colheita Amarga and Outras Angustias (1990), "Exilio" (1990) e "Palavracesa" (1994), Editor do jornal "Escriba" (informativo do SEDF). Correspondence dos jornais: "Folha de Cataguases" e "Correio da Cidade"; [pers.] O autor e adepto da corrente modernista da literatura. No entanto, e um estudioso das diversas escolas literarias. Filosoficamente, tem predilecao pelos escritores existencialistas e do "nouveau romain". Politicamente, se define como socialista democratico.; [a.] Brasilia DF, Brazil

CALDERONE, MARY M.
[pen.] Mary M. Calderone; [b.] March 16, 1921, St. Johns, Nfld, Canada; [p.] Phillip and Mary Healey; [m.] Ross Calderone, November 26, 1939; [ch.] Carolyn and Dennis; [ed.] 8 years grammer School, 4 years high school; [occ.] Retired; [memb.] The international Society and Poets; [oth. writ.] Assisting my grand-daughter Michelle in compil-

ing family background - to publish a book she's writing on her heritage to pass on to her family.; [pers.] My poetry reflects my feelings about our world and life around us. To give hope and a smile to all. "Never give up" - look for the positive side. Have memories - But grow too!; [a.] Las Vegas, NV

CALLAHAN, MARY J.
[pen.] Mary June; [b.] June 30, 1920, Woodstock, New Brunswick, Canada; [p.] Daniel L. and Elva A. Callahan; [ed.] Deerville Elementary, Woodstock High School, (1939) Graduated: Mount Carmel Academy, (1948) B.A. University of New Brunswick Fredericton, (1955) M.S. in Education, Fordham University, New York; [occ.] Retired Teacher; [memb.] N.B.T.A., New Brunswick Teachers Assoc., for 57 years I have been a member of S.C.I.C., Sister of Charity of Immaculate Conception in Saint John, N.B. Canada. I live in a Nursing Home (Ruth Ross Residence) at 105 Burpee Ave., I have taught all grades (kindergarten to University between the years 1945 and 1969.; [hon.] Certification of Degrees and Licenses; [pers.] A powerful pen is a two-edged sword, it sites - it heals.; [a.] Saint John New Brunswick, Canada

CALLAWAY, ELDON A.
[b.] February 29, 1964, Inglewood, CA; [p.] Eldon H. Callaway, Carolyn Callaway; [ed.] Pacifica High, Goldenwest Junior College, University of Southern California; [occ.] Data Processing, Real Estate Trainers, Santa Ana; [memb.] The Planetary Society The Challenger Center; [pers.] My deepest gratitude to family and friends, present and past, who have helped me realize that there is more to life than material things.; [a.] Garden Grove, CA

CAMACHO, JOEL
[b.] March 29, 1938, El Paso, TX; [p.] Francisco and Otilia Camacho; [m.] Dorothy; [ch.] Elizabeth, Joel Jr., Tammy; [ed.] High School Graduate at James Lick High San Jose; [occ.] Welder, Technician; [hon.] Won Several contents for poetry, some have been recited on spanish radio such as "La Carta De El Soldado"; [oth. writ.] Have written several songs for local bands translated some poems from spanish to english.; [pers.] I have always been interested in writing about early History of Mexico during the Revolution and write poetry on actual incidents and accounts that happened during that period.; [a.] San Jose, CA

CAMACHO, LEILANI M.
[pen.] Leilani; [b.] June 26, 1972, Concord, CA; [p.] Kim Camacho, Tere Daane; [ed.] Basic High School, Community College of Southern Nevada; [occ.] U.S. Navy; [memb.] Rainforest Alliance; [oth. writ.] An essay call "Lethal Ocean" published in the school creative writing book called "Shattered Reflections".; [pers.] I have always loved poetry and writing, one of my greatest dreams is to have my words immortalized on paper. Dreams do come true...; [a.] Las Vegas, NV

CAMILLONE, DEBRA L.
[b.] March 25, 1963, Bronxville, NY; [p.] Jean and John Camillone; [ed.] Horace Greeley High School Chappqua New York; [pers.] Poem, was written for some one special to me "L.G.K"

CAMPBELL, BRUCE A.
[pen.] "B.C," Bruce C.; [b.] October 22, 1947, Trenton, NJ; [p.] Bernard and Hawra Campbell; [m.] Patricia Plank Campbell, December 18, 1976; [ed.] B.A. English - U of Wisc., Madison, Wisc, June 1969, M.A. - English - New York university - N.Y., N.Y. June 1971, M.P.A. - (Master's in Public Administration) USC - LA, CA., June 1991; [occ.] Federal Civil Service, AIDS and Substance abuse specialist, U.S. - D.H.H.S. - H.C.F.A. - Medicaid Division - Region IX - SFCA; [memb.] A.P.W.A. (American Public Welfare Association); [pers.] "Never, never, never, never, and I do mean, never, give up on your creative vision! If you need companionship, get a pet, if you need love pray!.; [a.] Rohnert Park, CA

CAMPBELL, KATHERINE LEAH
[pen.] Leah Campbell; [b.] March 4, 1978, Florence, SC; [p.] J. E. Campbell III and Catherine M. Campbell; [ed.] This is my senior year in High School. I will be attending Clemson University in the Fall.; [memb.] National Beta Club; [hon.] Governor's School at College of Charleston '95, Lt. Governor's Award for Prose, Duke Talent Identification Program; [oth. writ.] I have a large collection of unpublished poems and a handful of short stories never released to public eyes.; [pers.] Poetry, like love, is a raindrop on a silver ocean, expanding its beauty with every shimmering ripple.; [a.] Blackstock, SC

CAMPBELL, LISA
[b.] November 13, 1964, Omaha, NE; [p.] Chuck Campbell and Cheri Campbell; [ed.] Colstrip High School, May School, Montana State University; [occ.] U.S. Army reserves, Seasonal Grounds keeper, Colstrip parks; [memb.] The Believer; [hon.] National Honor Society, Employee and District Employee of the Month, Soldier of Annual Training, Army Achievement Medal; [oth. writ.] Book review published in local newspaper several poems and fictional stories in the works.; [pers.] Follow your dreams, for the backbone of this great nation was founded on dreams. My goal is to be the best writer that I can be, by writing from the heart. Garth Brooks said it best, "Dreams are the roots of reality. Go for it."; [a.] Colstrip, MT

CAMPBELL, RICHARD
[b.] October 15, 1966; [ed.] BA in Chemistry 1988 Brooklyn College, Brooklyn NY, MD from State University of NY at Brooklyn, NY 1992; [occ.] Anesthesiology Resident at State University of NY Brooklyn; [memb.] NYSSA, ASA; [pers.] The Shakespeare sonnet form has been a passion of mine since I font read his collection in high school.

CAMPBELL, THOMAS
[b.] May 23, 1958, Enniskillen, Northern Ireland; [p.] James and Rita Campbell; [ch.] Kelly Sarah Campbell; [ed.] St. Michael's Primary School, St. Michael's Grammar School but finished school at age 16 and left Ireland to work in England; [occ.] Transport and General Workers Union - District Officer; [memb.] Amnesty International, Anti-Racist Alliance; [oth. writ.] Various poems published in local and national anthologies and readings on local radio.; [pers.] I believe in human rights for all. I am very committed to civil liberties. I am very opposed to any form of

racism or sexism. I believe in the dignity of the individual and work for a better life for everyone.; [a.] Aberdeen, Scotland

CAMPOLI, KATHERINE
[pen.] Katherine Campoli; [b.] July 20, 1975, Mount Vernon, NY; [p.] Josephine De Martino and Vincent Campoli; [ed.] Blessed Sacrament Saint Gabriels High School, College of Mount Saint Vincent; [occ.] Full-time college student, Part-time Sales Reps.; [hon.] Academic excellence in Foreign Language (Spanish), 1st and 2nd Honors in High School, Academic Excellence (for 3 yrs. to present) Award at College, Persistence Award (College); [oth. writ.] Various poems written for pleasure, (no publication) in leisure time. (As hobby); [pers.] In my poems I express life experiences such as: Death, love, pain, and wonder. My beloved brother Sal, and my loving, never-to-be forgotten mother have greatly influenced all the words expressed in my works. I hope others can too, identify in all of life's wonders good and bad.; [a.] Mount Vernon, NY

CANGIANO, MICHAEL
[b.] November 1, 1968, Plainview, NY; [p.] Jerry and Diane Cangiano; [m.] Lisa Cangiano, July 9, 1994; [ed.] Associates Degree, Farmingdale College NY, Bachelor of Science, Hofstra University - NY, Masters of Business Administration - Dowling College NY; [occ.] Transportation Management; [pers.] The older you get, the quicker life goes by. We must all learn to stop and cherish what life is all about. Life is not about how successful you are but rather how happy and beauty you are.; [a.] Deer Park, NY

CANONGE, RITA L. AUBREY
[b.] March 5, 1943, Lafayette, LA; [p.] Biological Mother (Deceased), Father (resides in LA), Guardians: Mrs. Laura Aubrey and the late Mr. Wilson Aubrey; [m.] Mr. Benjamin Lucien Canonge Jr. (Deceased, March 10, 1988), October 30, 1965; [ch.] Yolanda M. Canonge Peterman, Benjamin L. Canonge III, Janaia A. Canonge; [ed.] Holy Rosary Institute, 3 1/2 yrs. at the University of Southwestern Louisiana (USL), and received Child Development Associate Certificate for Head Start Program (CDA); [occ.] Teacher Coordinator Head Start, Green T. Lindon Elem. Sch., Youngs Ville, LA in Lafayette Parish; [hon.] Certificates of Appreciation for Services in the Head Start Program, Participation in workshops, Certificates of Appreciation for services rendered in Teaching Sunday School, Vocation Bible School, and NBC at Progressive Baptist Church in Lafayette, LA, Most honored to be a Christian.; [oth. writ.] Other poems to be published in the near future.; [pers.] "I have been inspired by the Holy Spirit to write this poem to all children who may have lost a mother in death. And in memory of my mother, Mrs. Lumanna A. Normand, who died March 2, 1990. The Lord has blessed me with this talent and I'm so very grateful."; [a.] Breaux Bridge, LA

CANUTE, KATHLEEN A.
[b.] January 14, 1953, Bay City, MI; [ch.] Carmen K., Misty Lynn; [oth. writ.] Several of my poems were printed in local churches and news papers. A collection of my poetry

was aired on family life radio Midland, MI.; [pers.] I wish to dedicate this poem in memory of my grandmother Elsie who gave me lasting memories, humorous moments which will always live in my heart. I am also most grateful and proud to be a small part of this book.; [a.] Pittsburgh, PA

CAPPUCCINO, JEANINE
[b.] November 4, 1964, Exeter, NH; [p.] Robert and Joan Bibeau; [m.] James Cappuccino, April 11, 1992; [ed.] Pratt Institute, Brooklyn, NY, New England School of Art and Design, Boston, MA; [occ.] Estate Manager, Graphic Designer; [oth. writ.] "Black Clouds" published by the Mile High Poetry Society in a book titled Ariel.; [pers.] Growing up in New England I have been truly inspired by nature, which lends itself willingly to the art of writing Haiku.

CARDER, KATHY
[b.] July 23, 1945, Marion, IN; [p.] Alice and Charles Carder; [ed.] Elementary and High School in Fairmount IN, the home of late actor, James Dean, Bachelors Degree in Sociology from Manchester College, North Manchester, IN; [occ.] Adult Services case worker with Indiana Division of Family and Children; [memb.] International Society of Poets, United Methodist Church Worship Comm, Marion Easter Pageant Chorus; [hon.] Poem, "The Birds Song", published in the National Library of Poetry's anthology, "Walk Through Paradise".; [oth. writ.] "The Innkeeper's Wife", a story of Christ's birth as seen through the eyes of the Innkeeper's wife. Some other poems: "The Flight", "Tribute to Mid-Life", "Buford, The Blue Goose"; [pers.] Always think the best of a person until they give you reason to believe otherwise. Then, give them the benefit of a doubt.; [a.] Marion, IN

CARLOCK, ARTHUR G.
[b.] October 1, 1953, Hackensack, NJ; [p.] Deceased; [m.] Elyn, October 1, 1994; [ed.] Poli-Sci/Psych-B.A. 1976 Boston College, Boston, Mass., Juris Doctor - 1979 The George Washington University Legal Center, Washington DC; [occ.] (Retired) Attorney-at-Law in the State of New Jersey; [memb.] Int'l Al Jolson Society, Am. Phil. Society; [oth. writ.] Several poems published in magazines, a poem published by Sparrow grass Poetry Forum; [pers.] The purpose of all of us is to Love One Another

CARLSON, TOM
[b.] January 10, 1979, West Berlin, East Germany; [p.] Terri and Christopher Madison; [ed.] Am presently a Junior at New Kent High School, New Kent, Virginia; [occ.] Am currently a page at the West Point Library; [memb.] Beta Club; [a.] West Point, VA

CARPENTER, JOYCE HUBBARD
[pen.] Joyce Hubbard Carpenter; [b.] February 15, 1928, Swampscott, MA; [p.] Rita and Walter Hubbard; [m.] Donald Townley Carpenter - (Deceased), June 16, 1960; [ch.] Hadley Whittemore, Ronald Whittemore, Donald Carpenter Jr. Claire Dickey and Fred Carpenter - Deceased; [ed.] Amherts, MA. High - School, Assoc. Degree from Leland Powers School, of Radio, Theater and T.V.

Att. Boston Univ School of Music - 3 yrs. at Berklee Union) College of Music - Boston (formerly Schillinger School); [occ.] Retired, writing a book and completing a full length musical.; [memb.] Daughters of the King - D.A.R. Blue Ridge Camp Club - Episcopalian Prison fellowship, and C.O.P.E. (Coalition of Prison Evangelists.); [hon.] (1) Governor's award as volunteer of the year for N.C Prison work. (2) Award for 20 yrs service with mentally challenged children - Jr. Welfare Club. (3) Honorary Lion - for 30 yrs work with blind projects - by producing and writing seven full length musicals. All proceeds went to Lions Club - for Blind.; [oth. writ.] Wrote for newspaper (Springfield Union) Did commercial copy for radio. Compiling my own book of poems and writing a book. Have had recipes published - writing a cook book. Just finishing musical called "Look Towards"; [pers.] Life experiences have given me volumes of material. I still have goals which I hope will touch other lives and make a difference - I am a Christian, and that has made a difference in my writing.; [a.] Hendersonville, NC

CARPENTIER, CLAIRE T.
[b.] March 24, 1963, Woonsocket, RI; [m.] Marc E. Carpentier, November 10, 1984; [ch.] Joshua Carpentier; [ed.] Graduated High School; [memb.] Globe Park PTA Officer for 3 years.; [hon.] Honorable mention in the 1994 National Library of poetry contest.; [oth. writ.] Several poems published in local newspapers. Also a poem published in 1994 and 1995, 1996 Anthology.; [pers.] I have been greatly in flounced by songwriter Paul Williams, whose writings have touched and inspired me for twenty two years.; [a.] Woonsocket, RI

CARR, RUTH BROWN
[pen.] Ruth Brown Carr; [b.] October 19, 1917, Union City, NJ; [p.] Charles and Mary Brown; [m.] James Carr, February 5, 1950; [ch.] Three girls, two boys; [ed.] St. Agnes N.Y.C., Cathedral High N.Y.C., N.Y. Business College N.Y.C.; [occ.] Retired; [memb.] Bayshore Senior Center, St. Catherine's Prayer and Praise Group, Bayshore Community Church Organist, Retired Senior Volunteer Program, Sharing and Caring Salvation Army; [hon.] 200 Volunteer "Dollie" shows in J.C., Mayor McCann's Photography Contest J.C., Lector at St. Catherines, Middletown, V.J., R.S.V.P. Sewing Hospital Pads; [oth. writ.] 1. Candy Cane Sky, 2. Our World Without End; [pers.] Like Etienne DeGrollet, knowing we pass this way but once, I try to be kind always.; [a.] Middletown, NJ

CARTER, RANDY
[b.] December 18, 1947, Stillwater, OK; [p.] William C. and Mildred T.; [ed.] B.S. Southwestern Okla. State Univ. Cook College, Rutgers Univ - Public Heath and Environmental School; [occ.] Public Health Inspector Trenton N.J. and Princeton NJ.; [memb.] N.J. Environmental Health Assoc. Sunshine Foundation.; [oth. writ.] My first every published my thank, to Lynn and Lourdes; [pers.] Mankind exists in a wasteland of talent waiting to appear like stars in the western sky but only a few ill glow in the morning sun.; [a.] Trenton, NJ

CARTY, MERCEDES PAZ
[b.] April 30, 1939, Cochabamba, Bolivia, South America; [ch.] Margarita, Maria Eugenia, Monica,

Ximena, Maria Ines, Edward, grandchildren: Kimberly, Robert, Nicholas, Philip, William, Carolina; [occ.] Medical Laboratory Technologist, Georgetown University Hospital, Washington, DC, Former Language Instructor, English and Spanish, Centro Boliviano-Americano, United States Information Service, Cochabamba, Bolivia, South America; [memb.] The Washington Society for the Psychoanalytic Study of Film, The Washington and Virginia Societies for Jungian Psychology, Library of Congress Associates, Italian Cultural Institute, Washington, DC; [hon.] First place, poetry — Germanna Community College, Spring 1994, Second place, poetry — Germanna Community College, Spring 1993; [oth. writ.] Several editorial comments concerning Hispanic issues published in local newspapers. Poem published in local newspaper article dealing with area poets.; [pers.] In my writing, I try to express the hidden beauty of ordinary people and ordinary things. My favorite poets include Pablo Neruda, e.e. cummings, Rainer Maria Rilke, and John Keats.; [a.] Lake of Woods Locust Grove, VA

CASE, AUDIE V.
[pen.] Barakiel Eros; [b.] February 24, 1976, Gravette, AR; [ed.] Bentonville High School, University of Arkansas; [occ.] Student; [hon.] Who's Who Among American High School Students 94-96; [pers.] To write poetry is to philosophize life.; [a.] Bentonville, AR

CASEY, SHIRLEY
[b.] December 9, 1935, Manhattan, NY; [p.] Donald Baker and Susan Baker; [m.] Joseph Casey, September 12, 1953; [ch.] Joseph, Susan, Emma, Donald and Bonnie; [ed.] Pawling, NY; [occ.] Volunteer Astor Head Start, Sharon Hospital; [memb.] Cancer Support Group.; [hon.] Wassaic Development Center, Project Head Start.; [pers.] I have written this poem to express that life is so precious. I feel that time does not stop for anyone. In a splinter of life it can be gone.; [a.] Dover Plains, NY

CASTELLINI, PATRICIA A.
[pen.] Dr. Pat; [b.] March 25, 1935; [p.] Alice and Ben B. Bennett, Jr. (Deceased); [m.] William (Bill) M. Castellini, December 17, 1994; [ch.] Barbara Lee Ragland, Bruce Bennett Welis (Nabil Subhani); [occ.] Dr. Pat (Wells) Castellini, A.A., B.S., M.S., Ph.D., is Commissioner of the Lafayette Economic Development Authority and currently serves as treasurer. She is the former Executive Director of the Enterprise Center of Louisiana, Inc., a not-for-profit small business incubator. Dr. Pat is Emeritus Professor of Management at Oregon State University. She taught courses in Management, Organizational behavior, Managerial survival, and Human Resources. Prior to coming to Louisiana, Dr. Castellini served as executive Director of the Business Enterprise Center, Inc., a not-for-profit business incubator in Corvallis, Oregon and has engaged in business consulting since 1976.; [memb.] She is member of many professional Organization and has served as President of five such Organizations, one on the National and one on the International Level. She served as the 1983-85 President of the Oregon Conference of the American Association of University Professor and as the 1984-85 President of the Association of

Business Communication, an International Professional Association. Pat served in the Corvallis Area Chamber of Commerce as Vice-president during 1985-86, as president-elect in 1986-87, as President in 1987-88, and as Chairman of the Board in 1988-89. Dr. Pat was President of the Board of Directors of the Boys and Girls Club of Corvallis for 1991 and 1992, was the 1991 Benton County Campaign Chairman. She was a member of the Board of Directors of Corvallis Mediation Services, served on the Corvallis City Leadership Forum, the Economic Development Committee, and the Benton County Budget Committee. She was a member of the Benton County Board of Equalization.; [hon.] Dr. Castellini was presented with the Connections "Career Achievement Award for 1995" and was named from a membership of 105,000 and from 1900 chapter nominations in 1980 as National American Business Woman of the Year by the American Business Woman's Association. She was chosen as the OSU "Boss of the Year" by the Personnel Association in 1981. She is a Fellow of the Association for Business Communication. Pat is listed in Who's Who in the West, Who's Who Among American Women, Who's Who in the World, Who's Who in Business and Finance, and Two Thousand Notable American. She has received many awards including the prestigious D. Curtis, Mumford Faculty Service Award and the Chamber of Commerce's George Award.; [oth. writ.] She has written many management articles. Dr. Pat has written a monthly advice column on solving problems at work for over six years.; [pers.] Finding love so late in life is a wonderful gift. God has given me so much, in turn, I owe much.; [a.] Lafayette, LA

CATALANO, MANIDIE N.
[b.] July 28, 1986, Brooklyn, NY; [p.] Faye and Tom Calatano; [ed.] South Bay Elementary, 4th Grade; [memb.] Girls Scouts Soccer; [hon.] National Physical Fitness Award 6/95, 5th Place Horse Back Riding Show; [oth. writ.] Grandma's House School, My Dad, My Mom, My Aunt Robyn, My Teacher; [pers.] I enjoy putting my feelings into my poetry.; [a.] West Babylon, NY

CATHERALL, PAUL
[b.] August 30, 1977, Chester, UK; [p.] Darell Catherall, Doris Catherall; [ed.] Elfed High, University of Wales at Wrexham - currently studying Primary Education with majors in English and Art. (B. Ed); [occ.] Student in Primary Education (Fulltime); [memb.] Amstrad User Society, Methodist Church, Various Poetry Magazines, Wrexham College Literature Society, 'Circle of Poets' - informal local group. Adam's Poetry Page - Internet.; [hon.] 'Advanced Level', 'Merit' in Literature (General Certificate of Education (High School)). 1st Place in Internet Page List - 'Adam's Poetry Page.'; [oth. writ.] Internet Pages, especially 'Adam's Poetry Page' on internet (Contributions).; [pers.] My poetry reflects the often negative aspects of man's behavioral nature - as discussed in the works of blake, plath and fisher.; [a.] Buckley Clwyd Wales, United Kingdom

CAUDLE, THOMAS A.
[b.] January 16, 1934, Wadesboro, NC; [p.] Deceased; [ch.] Julie 31, and Kristin 26; [ed.] BBA Wake Forest College MBA Wharton School of

Finance and Commerce, U. of PA; [occ.] Real Estate Broker Commercial Properties; [memb.] DeKalb Board of Realtors; [oth. writ.] Several real estate related articles in local real estate periodicals.; [pers.] This is my first poem submitted for consideration. I love to write about the inner beauty and goodness of the human spirit I study the Koran and early mystics Rumi and Kabir. In recent years Meher Baba has been the greatest influence. I love love stories.; [a.] Stone Mountain, CA

CAVANO, FRANCIS JOSEPH
[b.] May 24, 1941, Kingston, NY; [m.] Carol Holland Cavano; [ed.] BA - Marist College 1963, MD - Creighton University 1967; [occ.] Psychiatrist; [memb.] Alpha Omega Alpha - National Medical Honor Society; [hon.] Alpha Omega Alpha - National Medical Honor Society; [oth. writ.] "Real Visions" - Psychiatric Opinion - February 1980; [pers.] I see myself as a spiritual writer who believes that life is eternal. I write to inspire and encourage myself and hopefully, others. Am a student of "A Course In Miracles."; [a.] Saratoga Springs, NY

CEDILLOS, MICHAEL
[b.] July 20, 1981, Berkeley, CA; [p.] Gail and Raphael Cedillos; [ed.] Las Lomas High School; [occ.] Student; [memb.] California Scholarship Federation, California Association of Peer Programs; [pers.] It's always there right from the start, each poem comes right from my heart. Can you hear my heartbeat?; [a.] Walnut Creek, CA

CEJKA, CHARLES RAYMOND
[pen.] Franklin Scott Hayes; [b.] January 9, 1979, Brooklyn, NY; [p.] Dennis Michael Cejka, Frances R. Hale; [ed.] Bartlett-Yancey Senior High School (Completing 11th grade - graduation, '97); [oth. writ.] Several unpublished poems (Death being the first written and published), working on a novel.; [pers.] I wish to only reflect to people of the things of nature and God. "Poets speak with a voice. Poetry is a voice poets speak." I have honored and been greatly influenced by J.R.R. Jolkien.; [a.] Yanceyville, NC

CHAMBERS, CHERYL RENE
[pen.] Summer Brieze; [b.] December 6, 1983, Columbus, MS; [p.] Howard and Janice Chambers; [ed.] 1st - 6th grade at Starkville Academy, Starkville, MS; [occ.] 6th grader through May, 1996, after that 7th grader at Starkville Academy; [memb.] First United Methodist Church, Starkville, MS; [hon.] Starkville Academy Elementary School Honor Roll; [oth. writ.] Other poems named "The Limit", "Time" and "Wind" and a short story "Blue Rose" and a funny story "A Life as a Shoe".; [pers.] Writing is a river because words flow into verses like rivers flow into oceans. I want to donate as much water to their river literature as possible to keep it flowing.; [a.] Starkville, MS

CHAMPION, SHELLY
[b.] November 11, 1965, Hayward, CA; [p.] Ronald Farr, Juanita Quintana; [m.] David Champion, February 5, 1983; [ch.] Amber Renee, Jo-Anne Michelle, and Haylie Nicole; [ed.] Washington High School; [occ.] Homemaker; [oth. writ.] Poem published in newspaper, poem read on radio station.; [a.] Fremont, CA

CHANDARLAPATY, RAJ
[b.] May 12, 1970, Toronto, Canada; [p.] Dr. Sri and Mrs. Chandarlapaty; [m.] May 1, 1968; [ch.] Myself and Sarat 24; [ed.] Graduated, Bachelor of Arts, Vanderbilt University, 1992 - European History. University of Arkansas, Master of Arts - English literature - in progress.; [occ.] Student; [hon.] Semifinalist, National Library of Poetry, 1996 inclusion in New Anthology "The Ebbing Tide"; [oth. writ.] No other published writings to date.; [pers.] My only altruistic goals as a writer are to empower those choosing alternative lifestyles and to create for them (and me) Positive framework for Literary Comprehension and love of literature.; [a.] Eugene, OR

CHANDLER, CHRISTIE
[b.] October 26, 1958, Cleveland, OH; [m.] John Stahl; [ch.] Hattie and Samuel Stahl; [ed.] BA Sociology, MA Anthropology Northwestern University; [occ.] Poet; [hon.] I have been awarded language, research and teaching fellowships

CHAPMAN, RICHARD
[b.] February 5, 1942, Miami, FL; [occ.] Partner in investment management form of Bohlen-Chapman Area.

CHASTAIN, PAULA
[pen.] Elemenohpe; [b.] October 22, 1977, Kennesaw, GA; [p.] Sam Chastain, Cheryl Chastain; [ed.] High school - North Cobb High School; [occ.] Student; [memb.] PETA, People for the Ethical Treatment of Animals; [hon.] Reflections Poetry Contest, Honor Roll North Cobb H.S.; [oth. writ.] I have many other poems, short stories, and essays published in an undergrand literary magazine, Zeit Guist. Which a friend and I publish together.; [pers.] Poetry is the personal reflection of feelings and emotions. Those of us who cannot elaborate these become the poets, artists, and madmen.; [a.] Kennesaw, GA

CHAUVIN, PATRICIA
[pen.] Pat Chauvin; [b.] March 17, 1942; [p.] Glenn Pettry and Rita Pettry; [m.] Donald Chauvin, November 24, 1965; [ch.] Joseph Wayne, Pamela Jean, Darleen Marie, Ronald George, Robert Francis; [ed.] Beckly High; [occ.] Resort Hostess; [oth. writ.] Many poems not published as yet.; [pers.] I have been writing poetry all my life off and on. What inspires me is the love for life. And I want people to understand that life is suppose to be beautiful. Poetry lets me express my feelings.; [a.] Norwich, CT

CHAVIS, EVA MAE
[pen.] Eva; [b.] October 11, 1934, Robeson County, NC; [p.] Rhoda J. Harris, Hunt and Arron P. Hunt; [m.] Paul W. Chavis, November 8, 1951; [ch.] Four sons and two daughters; [ed.] High School; [occ.] Semi Retired; [memb.] Huckabbe Grove Emmanuel H. Church, Laurel Hill NC; [oth. writ.] For our church monthly paper and just for own scrap book.; [pers.] I like reading, writing, and learning new things, and going to new places. I am a Native American of the Lumbee Tribe of NC.; [a.] Gibson, NC

CHEESMAN, SUE
[pen.] Sue Green - Cheesman; [b.] May 8, 1959, Pittsburgh, PA; [m.] Walter G. Cheesman, May 12,

1979; [ch.] Justin Thomas, Cody Austin, and Tyler Gordon; [ed.] Seabreeze Sr. High School, all aspects of banking - teller, Sr. Bank Rep, Loan Officer, Exec. Secretary; [occ.] Helping Hand Advisory Service Inc., Owner/President Retired 17 years banking; [pers.] Nothing compares to a child's love: A small hand held tenderly in yours, a big hug and wet kiss on your cheek, four little words spoken honestly, I love you Mom!; [a.] Ormond Beach, FL

CHERKIN, ADINA
[b.] November 22, 1921, Geneva, Switzerland; [p.] Dr. Herz Mantchik; [ch.] Della and Dan; [ed.] UCLA BS and Master in Russian Linguistics; [occ.] Retired-interpreter in 5 languages, Russian, French, Germany, Spanish, English; [memb.] Head of Amity Circle in L.A. (A cultured forum for Yaweth issues), Citizen Diplomat of the International Visitors Council.; [hon.] Los Angeles City Council Award for "Contribution to the Community"; [oth. writ.] Poetry published at Cal. Tech and Univeristy of Michigan Press; [pers.] My greatest satisfaction comes from helping others.; [a.] Los Angeles, CA

CHESROW, WILLIAM
[pen.] Curly Bill; [b.] March 13, 1917, LaGrange, IL; [p.] Frank and Mary Chesrow; [m.] Pearl Chesrow, October 25, 1938; [ch.] Three; [ed.] Two years Crane H.S., Chicago Illinois; [occ.] Semi retired, Beer Coil Service Work; [memb.] Teamsters Union Local 710 Chicago Il.; [hon.] Dale Carnegie, Freight Traffic Management, Spector Freight System; [oth. writ.] Other poems: "Will Power", "Still Here", "Beautiful People", "Bashfull Birds", "Beautiful Snow", and more.; [pers.] Always enjoyed writing poetry for other people with their names in each poem. Wrote poem for a graduation class with all persons names and teachers names in it.; [a.] Chicago, IL

CHIEPPO, BRIAN ANTHONY
[b.] February 18, 1976, Fremont, CA; [p.] Pat Chieppo and Sharon Chieppo; [ed.] East Union High School; [occ.] Crew Person, Carls Jr. Restaurant; [oth. writ.] 2 poems published in expressions magazine in 1995.; [pers.] The way I express myself in writing comes from 2 sides of a coin. The good and the bad.; [a.] Manteca, CA

CHRISTIE, KESHA
[pen.] Kesha Christie; [b.] August 3, 1979, Toronto, Ontario, Canada; [ed.] Grade 9-10 and Midland Avenue Collegiate Institute, Grade 11 at Exeter High School, studying at advanced level; [occ.] Student; [oth. writ.] An avid poet with other published poetry in newspapers, magazines and pamphlets.; [pers.] I feel poetry is the perfect vehicle for commenting on society. I have been influenced by Maya Angelou and thanks go to all who support me.; [a.] Ajax Ontario, Canada

CHRISTY, MADELINE IRIS
[pen.] Maddy; [b.] August 30, 1947, Kettering, England; [p.] Joan and Len Green; [m.] Hira Christy, June 22, 1968; [ch.] Seven, (five sons, two daughter); [ed.] Graduated from Church College of New Zealand 1964; [occ.] Computer Operator for Northern Publishing Co; [memb.] Active in Church of Jesus Christ of Latter-day Saints as a teacher - member. Also involved in porcelain doll making; [oth. writ.] I have written about 25 other poems

over the last couple of years. I have never entered any in any other competition, so this is very new to me!; [pers.] I started writing poetry as a way of sharing my feelings with others. If it has the ability to help someone else deal with the problems of life I will be satisfied.

CHU, PAULINE
[b.] May 6, 1955, Hong Kong; [p.] Chue Ming Fah, Chue Wong Yuk Fong; [m.] Separated; [ch.] Derek Tat Kai Chow; [ed.] Concordia University, Montreal, Canada Bachelor of Commerce (Magna Cum Laude) Data Processing Major; [occ.] Looking for job; [hon.] 2 years champion at Hong Kong Management Game (team Leader) 1987-1988; [oth. writ.] This is my first attempt.; [pers.] They reflect my life experiences. They are also my teachings to my dearest son.; [a.] Richmond Hill Ontario, Canada

CHUANG, D. ALEX
[b.] 1959, China; [p.] King C. Chuang, C. H. "Sue" Chuang; [m.] Sophie Lin, February 6, 1993; [ed.] Bronx Science, Virginia Tech Penn.; [occ.] Management Consultant; [memb.] IEEE, Colorado Springs Sister Cities International; [pers.] I would like to leave the world a better place for our children.; [a.] Castle Rock, CO

CHURCH, TAYLOR
[pen.] Raven; [b.] September 22, 1947, Peach Bottom, PA; [p.] Webb Church, Mary Church; [ch.] Paul Taylor, Philip Eugene; [ed.] Solanco High School, Rockford Barber College, Empire Beauty School, Empire Beauty School-teacher; [occ.] Currently recovering from major surgery.; [memb.] American Legion, Disabled American Veteran, Wakefield Bible Church; [hon.] Bronze Star, Purple Heart, 4th place Barber trophy, Student of year-Empire Beauty School; [oth. writ.] Numerous works unpublished.; [pers.] I have been influenced by Edgar Allan Poe's writings. Never except things at face value. Be gracious in face of rejection.; [a.] Peach Bottom, PA

CLARK, BETH ANN
[pen.] Beth Ann Clark; [b.] October 20, 1972, Temple, TX; [p.] Judge and Mrs. Patrick A. Clark; [ed.] Graduated from West Orange Stark High School and Miss Wades Fashion Merchandising College.; [occ.] Orthodontic Manager; [memb.] Dean's List in College.; [a.] Orange, TX

CLARK, JOAN E.
[pen.] Evelyn Sefton; [b.] August 21, 1924, Liverpool; [p.] Frank and Olive Leeson; [m.] Widow; [ch.] David, Paul Lucinda, Joanne; [ed.] Convent, State Registered Nurse and Health Visitor; [occ.] Retired; [memb.] Conservative Association; [oth. writ.] "The Broach", an historical romance published 1995, poems published by local magazine further two books awaiting publication; [pers.] The beautiful countryside of Wales inspired me to start writing, when I retired there. Your anthologies also inspire he and I wish all those who contribute success in their writings.; [a.] Wales, United Kingdom

CLARK, LINDSEY
[b.] October 4, 1984, Indianapolis, IN; [p.] Robbin Clark and Rhonda Leap; [ed.] Central

Elem; [occ.] Student; [hon.] Honor Roll; [a.] Indianapolis, IN

CLARK, MARYLIN J.
[pen.] Marylin J. Scull Clark; [b.] April 12, 1932, Ocean City, NJ; [p.] Thomas J. Scull and Minnie Mumford Scull; [m.] Leonard E. Clark Sr., June 2, 1950; [ch.] Thomas, Sandra, Van and Michelle; [ed.] High School; [occ.] Wife, Mother and Grandmother; [hon.] "My Children" were my Greatest Award; [pers.] "My Miracle" was inspired by my first born on the eve of his wedding.; [a.] North Cape May, NJ

CLIFTON, KYMBERLY
[pen.] Kymberly Clifton; [b.] February 14, 1980, Chicago, IL; [p.] Lynda and James Clifton; [ed.] Currently Enrolled in Atlantic High as a Sophomore; [occ.] Teacher Assistant for Dance at "Academy of Fine Arts"; [memb.] "Academy of Fine Arts" "Dance Mautica" Dance Troup; [hon.] Finalist for Volusia County - Short Story Entry 94, Finalist for Volusia County - Poetry Entry 95; [oth. writ.] "Ladle of Death" - short story.; [a.] Port Orange, FL

CLIMIE, MS. MARY
[b.] February 19, 1964, Ballymena; [ch.] 9 year old daughter; [ed.] Primary and Secondary school and college until age of 18; [occ.] childminding, housekeeping, gardening; [oth. writ.] Songs and poems writing is one of my hobbies.; [pers.] Quiet confident mature mother with a keen interest in environmental issues especially those concerning nature and wildlife.; [a.] Northern Ireland

CLOUD, RONALD L.
[b.] September 6, 1935, Bradenton, FL; [p.] Mr. and Mrs. R. L. Cloud (Deceased); [m.] Gloria D. Cloud "Cookie", August 7, 1975; [ch.] Seven daughters - one son; [ed.] Hillcrest Hi S.C. Plant Hi Tampa Fla.; [occ.] Cert. Weldor and Mechanic - Florida Power Corp.; [memb.] P.B.A. member Senior Tour Veterans of Foreign Wars; [oth. writ.] Several poems - Righteous - sent through churches in St Pete, Fla. unpublished; [pers.] I strive to write story poems, that touch the heart. Love poems and righteous poems that also touch the heart. I love poetry, and the effect it has on people; [a.] Tampa, FL

CLOUSE, ROMIE
[pen.] Romie Clouse; [b.] November 30, 1914, Baker, MT; [p.] Deceased; [m.] Eugene L. Clouse, June 23, 1946; [ed.] High School graduate Mead High School-Spokane, WA; [occ.] Retired; [memb.] Several Animal Organizations and Penpal clubs.; [hon.] Won many prizes and awards in flower shows pairs and photography.; [oth. writ.] Have had works in several anthologies, newspapers and magazines; [pers.] I love animals and have helped many homeless and uncared for creatures over the years. It is so rewarding to see the fear and loneliness in their eyes, change to love and trust.

COATES, ROSLYN
[b.] August 7, 1967, Dallas, TX; [ed.] University of North Texas; [occ.] Paralegal; [memb.] ACLU; [a.] Dallas, TX

COBB, OFFIA
[b.] January 30, 1910, Ashdown, AR; [p.] Charley Cobb,

Syble Cobb; [m.] J. C. Taylor, February 11, 1927; [ch.] Wayne, Charley; [ed.] Harvey High - Texarkans Texas-Jur. College; [occ.] Retired Licensed Nurse; [memb.] Missionary Baptist Church, Ladies Club, PAV; [hon.] Desineda Quilt an made for USA, went to Republine Convention et President Regan Autograph et.; [oth. writ.] Household Hants for Grit Magazine; [pers.] I try to bring learning for honor to the youth.; [a.] Mena, AR

CODY, JUDY W.
[pen.] Judy W. Cody; [b.] August 15, 1951, Asheville, NC; [ed.] Athens High, Graduate of Georgia Real Estate Institute; [occ.] Realtor, G.R.I. in the state of GA., First Class Realty-Athens, GA.; [memb.] National Association of Realtors, Georgia Association of Realtors, Athens Board of Realtors; [a.] Watkinsville, GA

COGGIN, ALEXIA
[pen.] Lexi; [b.] January 10, 1981, Dallas, TX; [p.] Kim and Kevin Coggin; [ed.] Forney High school, Forney, TX; [occ.] Baby sitting and a student; [hon.] A/B Honor roll, Perfect Attendance; [oth. writ.] Jailer, homeless which has been published too.; [pers.] I am glad people had time to appreciate my work. Thanks to my family and best friend Robin.; [a.] Forney, TX

COGGINS JR., JOHN D.
[b.] August 20, 1931, Oklahoma City, OK; [p.] J. D. Coggins Sr., Pauline D. Coggins; [m.] Zoe Ann Coggins, October 13, 1955; [ch.] Mark, John III, Lynnette; [ed.] High School - New Mexico Military Institute Bachelor Degree, Business - U. of N.M. - MBA - North Western; [occ.] Financial Consultant, Freelance Writer; [oth. writ.] I write essays and poetry, usually with a moral theme; [pers.] My business career did not permit much time for writing until recently. Now I am giving emphasis to a hobby of 20 years duration.; [a.] El Paso, TX

COHEN, ELEANOR L.
[pen.] "Nova"; [b.] October 15, 1945, Newark, NJ; [p.] Rovena and James Levell; [m.] Divorced; [ch.] Erik C. Levell; [ed.] 1979-1983 Bachelor of Science in Nursing, Rutgers University, NWK, N.J. 1970-1973 Associate Applied Science in Nursing, Essex County College, NWK, N.J.; [occ.] Retired Registered Nurse. Student Home Course, Medical Billing.; [memb.] Board of Nursing, NWK, N.J., Consumer Affairs Div., Trenton, N.J., Rutgers Alumni, NWK, N.J., Long Ridge Writers Alumni, CT. N.J., Honorable Member of The International Society of Poets, MD, N.J.; [hon.] Medical Transcription Cert., CA., Professional Award, Overlook Hospital, Summit, N.J., Scholarship RN Award, Greystone State Hosp., N.J., Editor's Choice Award, 1994-1996, Poetry of Merit Award, 1995., Cert of Recognition ISP, 1995, 1996, Sparrowgrass Poetry Forum, 1996, NW, Who's Who in New Poets, NY., Iliad-Meditations, 1996.; [pers.] I was divinely inspired by Jehovah God to pen each creative expression from within. I mind search the universe as I write with pen, to unfold rare virgin flowers to share as gems!; [a.] Morris County, NJ

COKER, STEPHANIE LOUISE
[b.] January 19, 1978, Greenwood, MS; [p.] Joseph and Maribeth Coker; [ed.] Pillow Academy; [memb.] Faith Fellowship Church, Light

Brigade Youth Group, National Honor Society, Varsity Cheerleaders, G.G. Dance Troupe; [hon.] Valedictorian, Louise B. Mayhall Award (for poetry), Talent Search - 1st place Creative Expression Division; [pers.] I praise God for the gift of poetry that He has given me. "My Angel" was written as a gift for my mother who, like myself, enjoys collecting ceramic angels.; [a.] Morgan City, MS

COLAGIOVANNI, MARC R.
[b.] August 7, 1973, Providence; [p.] Robert V. Colagiovanni, Sharon Colagiovanni; [ed.] University of Vermont; [occ.] Senior at the University of Vermont; [oth. writ.] Several poems written/non-published; [pers.] Regardless of lifes obstacles, anything can be accomplished with hard work and determination.; [a.] Cranston, RI

COLLETT, JULIA DIXON
[b.] September 3, 1923, Saint Louis, MO; [p.] Irene Rives and Forney Dixon; [m.] Leslie Collett (Deceased), July 17, 1944; [ch.] Juleta Burrell, Melissa Freeman, Stephen, Douglas and Rosanne Collett; [ed.] Normandy High School Grad. 1941, Wash. univ. Psychology Courses; [occ.] Retired Exec. Sec. and Administrative Asst., Seniors Dir. YMCA; [memb.] St. Louis Generalogical Society, Distinguished Member, International Society of Poets; [hon.] National Library of Poetry Editor's Choice Award for Outstanding Achievement in Poetry 1995.; [oth. writ.] Published in: At Water's Edge, Best Poems of The 90's, The Ebbing Tide and Through the Hour Glass; [pers.] Writing since 1931. My writings read like a saga of sadness journaled as therapy for self and the reader.; [a.] Saint Ann, MO

COLLINS, DAVID E.
[b.] December 8, 1954, Ottumwa, IA; [p.] James E. and Charlotte L. Collins; [m.] Yulanda Kay Collins, April 1, 1993; [ch.] Gage A. and Tyson L. West; [ed.] Life long process; [occ.] Laborer; [pers.] Look to the future with an eye on the past. The life that you're living goes by in a flash.; [a.] Centerville, IA

COLLINS, ERIC DENOVON
[pen.] Eric Donoron Collins; [b.] December 24, 1970, Louisville, KY; [p.] Earl Collins and Charlotte Collins; [ch.] Zachary Allen, Henning - Collins; [ed.] Bullitt Central High, Communications Inst; [pers.] The mystery of God and Life itself is the key to my writing. Though I have a passion to meet our God someday, I have an equal passion to live forever. Knowing I can't do the latter, I have the talent for the next best thing, I will leave my thoughts and images on paper for everyone to read forever.

COLLINS III, WILLIAM M.
[pen.] Dore; [b.] August 24, 1972, Norfolk, VA; [m.] Shantal Collins, July 7, 1997; [ed.] Univ. of Maryland at College Park; [occ.] Program Coordinator Martin Luther King, Jr. Family Life Ctr; [oth. writ.] "Love Speaks about the End."; [pers.] Keep steady and look within for the end is near. Love with "all" your energy. I love you; [a.] Chesapeake, VA

COLLINS, KATHLEEN E.
[pen.] Gypsy; [b.] December 22, 1951, Augusta, ME; [p.] David and Maxine Glazier; [m.] Kenneth Farrington Sr., Frank X. Collins; [ch.] Kenn Jr., Ginni and Patrick Farrington; [ed.] Winthrop High School, Winthrop Maine, Class of 1970 graduate; [occ.] Unemployed due to a rare form of cancer (Lieumyosarcoma) found in the intestines and liver.; [oth. writ.] None published until now.; [pers.] Always find the best in any situation and learn everything you can because life is very fragile. Become passionate about life and you will learn positive thinking skills.; [a.] Chelsea, ME

COLLINS, MILDRED DOWD
[pen.] M. Dowd Collins, Polly Dowd; [b.] Fibre, MI; [p.] Albyn and Anna Dowd; [ed.] College-graduate Ypsilanti, Mich. Summer School-Marquet, Mich. to study play production correspondence courses eg. story writing, NIA. Newspaper, Lewis Motel Hotel Training, Shepherd and American Contest courses; [occ.] Taught English at Rochester, Mich. High School 4 yrs. operated (owned) Motel Traverse City, Mich. Owned and Operated Ladies Style Shoppe in Sault Ste Marie, Ontario for 9 years each. Now retired; [hon.] Have won over 50 contest (Last lines, naming, 25 or less words Why I Use Products. 100 words How I Would Remodel Home Room etc. sponsors eg. Swift, Kraft, Betty Crocker Maico etc. Editors Choice Awards - Tears of Fire 1994, Best Poems 1995; [pers.] Tell it like it is!!; [a.] Guelph Ontario, Canada

COLSTON, JAKE
[pen.] J.R.X.-1; [b.] March 9, 1976, Memphis, TN; [p.] Hal Colston, Rita Colston; [ed.] Millington Central High, Tresevant Vo-Tech; [occ.] Security Guard; [oth. writ.] Several poems, one book untitled and several songs.; [pers.] I feel that the truth must be exposed in everything I write. The reason being is because truth and knowledge is power.; [a.] Millington, TN

COLYER, D. LUANNE
[m.] Calvin Colyer; [ch.] Aaron, Brittani and Tristian; [ed.] Currently attending Methodist College in Fayetteville, N.C. major - micro and cellular biology; [occ.] Student; [oth. writ.] Poetry, short stories, children's stories; [pers.] It's not what you accomplish, as much as what you overcome.; [a.] Fayetteville, NC

COMARCHO, COWAYNE
[pen.] Dubble C!, Co!, Co-Co!; [b.] September 11, 1977, Nassau, Bahamas; [p.] Almarie Comarcho; [ed.] Harbour Island All-age-School (Harbour Island - Bahamas), Centreville Primary, Sandiland Primary), L.W. Young High, the Training Center (Computer School); [memb.] The Bahamas Writers Society, Ova Da Hillimprovement Association, Olympia Track Club (200m - 22.7 sec.) The International Society of Poets (I.S.P.); [hon.] Poet of Merit (I.S.P. 1995), National Poet Winner in Voice Speaking '96. J.A. SK Run. U20 Male 1st Place 93. Poem Published in Local Newspaper. Read at Governor-General's House, U.S. Ambassador (Sidney Williams). Minister of Youth (Algernon Allan). School Perfect - 1993-1995.; [oth. writ.] Short stories, and song writing, I strive to reach the 'youth' of the Nation.; [pers.] "I can do" all things through Christ, who strengthens me. I hope to take part in the future olympics, and I'm presently seeking scholarships. (Cowayne Comarcho - PO Box N

3913, L.W. Young High School Nassau Bahamas).; [a.] Nassau, Bahamas

COMBS, GRANT J.
[b.] August 5, 1976, West Chester, PA; [p.] Grant Combs and Barbara Combs; [ed.] St. Joseph Education Center, Bishop Shanahan High School, Twin Valley High School, Penn State University of Berks Campus; [occ.] Full time student, Penn State Berks; [memb.] Penn Players; [oth. writ.] Several articles and poems published in Raiders' Signals Newspaper; [pers.] I would like to thank: My family, George, Brenda, Mrs. Murphy, and Mrs. Spleen, all of whom are present in my writing. I believe unreturned love is the biggest waste of natural resources known to man; [a.] Honey Brook, PA

CONANT, ANDREW D.
[pen.] Xavier Mikhail Summers; [b.] March 31, 1975, Owosso, MI; [p.] David Conant and Sandra Conant; [ed.] Owosso High, University of Michigan; [occ.] Student, English; [memb.] Phi Mu Aloha Sinfonia, Tau Beta Sigma, Michigan Marching Band, Michigan Men's Basketball Band; [pers.] There is always time to change. The question is do we really need to?; [a.] Ann Arbor, MI

CONDE, JUDITH SHERROW
[b.] October 27, 1948, Danville, KY; [p.] Mary Hamm Hollon; [ch.] Lola, Renee; [ed.] Franklin Co. High School and Berea Foundation High School, B.A. Berea College, Diploma-Universidad de Guadalajara, Mexico, M.A. University of Kentucky, Ph.D. University of Kentucky; [occ.] Spanish teacher, Western Hills High School, Frankfort, KY; [memb.] American Assoc. of Teachers of Spanish and Portuguese, Ky Assoc. of Teachers of Spanish and Portuguese, Ky Council on the Teaching of Foreign Language; [hon.] Sigma Delta Pi, National Spanish Honor Society, National Endowment for the Humanities Fellowship Grant, PEW Charitable Trusts Project Grant, Goals 2000 Teachers' Grant, Outstanding Alumnus 1993, Franklin County High School, numerous travel and study grants received; [oth. writ.] Published: Book - Poridat de las Poridades - vocabulario etimologico, numerous articles in scholarly journals, book - Top-notch Tips for Teachers (this book not yet published); [pers.] Writing poetry is a reflective, therapeutic exercise for me. Through poetic expression I believe we can recreate our reality so that it can be more easily experienced and understood.; [a.] Lexington, KY

CONDON, MAUREEN MCCALLUM
[pen.] Maureen Catherine; [b.] March 7, 1937, Boston; [p.] John and Marie Arbuckle; [ch.] Richard, Patrick, Colleen, Thomas, Erin; [ed.] Charleston High School, Massachusette, Aquinas Newton College, (catholic special need education) Sancta Maria Hospital Cambridge, Mass.; [occ.] Hospice worker, EMT, (I care for elderly, homemaker); [memb.] Grandparents United for Children's Rights Inc.; [hon.] Patient Care award Central Hospital Somerville, Mass., certificate - Teacher of Special Needs students Holy Cross Cathedral Boston, Mass.; [oth. writ.] Many poems published in our local newspaper. One poem composed into music, Michael, Poor Soul, Christmas in Heaven, Welcome Home, etc.; [pers.] Many of my writings are spiritual, my Holy

Spirit guides my hand. My love for God and children inspire my poems.; [a.] Quincy, MA

CONNELL, CECIL HARDEE
[pen.] Cecil Connell; [b.] February 4, 1903, White Rock, Med River Co, TX; [p.] Alexander Connell, Alice Maddon Connell; [m.] Esther O'Shields Connell (Deceased, 1982), July 3, 1927; [ch.] Elizabeth Connell Clement; [ed.] Clarkes Ville, TX. High School, Univ. North Texas BS, Texas Tech. Univ. MA, Univ. Iowa, Ph.D. Graduate Study, Teaching and Rearch in Fields of Environment Health and Pollution Control; [occ.] Retired Professor, writing memories: (Hope ere too late); [memb.] Life (50 yrs.) American Chemical Society, American Water Works Association, Water Pollution Control Federation, Honorary Member - Texas Water Utilities Association; [hon.] Honorary Water Drop Drop: Award-American Water Works Association Honorary Science Fraternity, Sigma Zi Honorary Chemical Fraternity - Phi Lambda Upsilon; [oth. writ.] Some fifty publications in fields of Water Treatment and Water Pollution Control. Hundred (plus a few): Memories Stories and Poems (some so in character and tradition read like fiction).; [pers.] Life is search for identity, Who am I? What, where, when, how come? Most important, Why?; [a.] Georgetown, TX

CONRAD, JAMES
[b.] November 14, 1949, Halifax, Nova Scotia, Canada; [p.] Muriel and Roy Conrad; [m.] Norma R. Conrad, January 1, 1983; [ch.] Four; [ed.] Secondary and Post Secondary; [occ.] Sales; [hon.] Your publication; [oth. writ.] Educational essays for children with learning disabilities. Also some science fiction, not published.; [pers.] Influenced by the Human Spirit. Its continues journey to find the way home.

COOK, MOZELLE
[b.] September 23, 1954, Austin, TX; [p.] James L. and Dorothy Jean Pogue; [m.] Herman Alvin Cook (Al), August 30, 1986; [ch.] Jesse L. Hotz Jr.; [ed.] Roosevelt High San Antonio, TX; [occ.] Acct. Sect.; [a.] San Antonio, TX

COOK, SANDRA
[b.] October 12, 1953, Bristol, VA; [p.] Juanita Ross/ Johnny Glass; [m.] Chad Cook, March 31, 1973; [ch.] Joseph G. Cook; [ed.] Satellite High, Satellite Bch., FL., Polk Vo-Tech, Lakeland, FL.; [occ.] Unit Coordinator at Ramadan Hand Institute, Lake Butler, Fl.; [pers.] My inspiration comes from life's daily experiences with friends and family. Writing lets me reflect on the good as well as the bad times years after the events have unfolded.; [a.] Lake City, FL

COONES, SCOTT D.
[b.] October 26, 1977, Freeport, TX; [p.] Winston and Connie Coones; [ed.] High School Graduate Nixon-Smiley High School Plan to attend University of Texas to major in physical education; [occ.] Student; [memb.] First Baptist Church, Nixon Fellowship of Christian Athletes Future Farmers of America Student Council; [hon.] Varsity letterman in football, basketball, academic all-district, FCA officer and homecoming beau, FFA V-pres., FFA Outstanding Achievement Award FCA Outstanding Huddle Member Honorable Mention Christian Athlete of the year, Honor Roll; [oth. writ.] Numerous poems and essays for school assignments and activities; [a.] Nixon, TX

COOPER, BILLIE
[b.] October 25, 1927, MO; [p.] W. S. and Sarah Cooper; [ed.] Univ. of Colorado; [occ.] Retired Telecommunications Specialist; [memb.] Valley View Bible Church, and DAR.; [hon.] Beta Gamma Sigma; [oth. writ.] Poems and other writings in church publications; [a.] Phoenix, AZ

COOPER, BRENDA MONA
[b.] October 24, 1946, Ottawa, Ontario, Canada; [p.] Clifford and Mona Smith; [m.] Martyn Cooper, April 13, 1968; [ch.] Ian, Martyn, Mona, Shannon; [ed.] Moira Secondary School Belleville, Ontario; [occ.] Assist. Husband in Family Business.; [memb.] Salvation Army Church, West Haldimand General Hospital Auxiliary.; [oth. writ.] Several poems nothing published.; [pers.] I'm thankful for the words God has given me. Many times they have helped me cope with life situations, just by writing them.; [a.] Jarviz Ontario, Canada

COOPER SR., DU-KANE
[pen.] The Watchman; [b.] January 7, 1955, Detroit, MI; [p.] Lonzie and Ruby Cooper; [m.] Charlotte E. Cooper; [ch.] Delfeen, Dukane Jr., Diallo and Danielle; [oth. writ.] None published; [pers.] Seeing things from another point of view.; [a.] Detroit, MI

COOPER, GLADYS
[b.] June 10, 1914, Thornton, KY; [p.] Wyatt and Clarinda Cooper; [ed.] College; [occ.] Teacher; [hon.] KY Society of Poetry Pub., KY "The Perpetual Laurel Hills" Pub. "Doodle Bug" - Pub - KY, The Fox Chase - Golden Award; [pers.] Depths deep but poor landing. Never thought about publication.

COOPER, MR. W. D.
[pen.] James Edgehill; [b.] January 8, 1925, Kingstree, SC; [p.] Thomas and Flora Cooper; [m.] Divorced; [ch.] 2 girls, 1 boy; [ed.] High School Grad; [occ.] Master Craftsman, Fine - Upholstery - Self-employed; [memb.] American Legion, St. Albans Congregational Church, NAACP; [hon.] Nothing outstanding; [oth. writ.] Un-published writings for a future book and extensive un-published poetry and poems over many years.; [pers.] "We strive to excel at most endeavors"!; [a.] Westbury, NY

COPENACE, BILLY
[b.] February 27, 1978, Rainy River; [p.] Ernest and Karen Copenace; [ed.] Grade 12 of the Rainy River High School.; [occ.] Student; [hon.] School Awards, ex. Attendance, behaviour, etc.; [pers.] I strive to reflect my true feelings in poems and whatever I write comes from the heart.; [a.] Morson Ontario, Canada

CORNELL, STEPHEN
[b.] April 7, 1963, Pittsburgh, PA; [p.] Darrell and Sue Cornell; [ed.] Serra High, Point Loma Nazare College, B.A. in Liberal Studies, Teaching Credential.; [occ.] Elementary school Teacher, Shadow Hills School, San Diego, CA; [memb.] California Teacher Association, San Diego Museum of Art.; [pers.] I have been influenced by E.E Cummings and Annie Dillard, and I am inspired to write by the voices and spirit of nature.; [a.] San Diego, CA

COSTER II, CHARLES W.
[b.] April 2, 1945, Cleveland, OH; [p.] Charles Coster - Ruth Coster; [ed.] Aurora High School Litschert School of Photo Retouching; [occ.] Manager - Aurora Auto Wash. - Aurora, Ohio; [hon.] Akron Beacon Journal's Student of the Week, April 1963.; [oth. writ.] High school newspaper "Coster's Comments" (A personal newsletter).; [pers.] To my lovely Kathleen. My poetry would still be deep within my heart had it not been for your love and inspiration. Thank you my darling.; [a.] Aurora, OH

COTTON, RON
[pen.] Ronald D. Cotton; [b.] November 30, 1937, Calgary, Alberta, Canada; [p.] Charles and Alice Cotton; [m.] Natalia Jo-Ann, August 22, 1964; [ch.] Tim and Jeff; [ed.] Grade 12 Graduated 1963, X-Ray Tech (Medical), Grade 9 Violin Royal Conservatory of Toronto.; [occ.] Technician Physics Dept University of Alta.; [memb.] Natl. Library of Poets; [hon.] Thesis award - X-Ray Edmonton Society X-ray Techs 1963. Three medals Violin (Royal Cons) Highest mark in the province B.C. Twice once in Alta.; [oth. writ.] "The of Loving You" Published in Sparkles the Sand" Have other poems not yet submitted. I'm also trying to write a book have about 15 chapters (SCI FI); [pers.] "With God's love in each heart war would suddenly end" - quite from my poem "Let them live" (25 or 26 lines); [a.] Edmonton Alberta, Canada

COULL, LENARD
[pen.] Mush Room; [b.] December 5, 1973, Lachine, Quebec, Canada; [p.] Peter Coull, Penelope Coull; [ed.] Bishop Whelan High, Champlain College; [occ.] Pharmacy Lab Tech., Pharmaprix, Lachine, Que.; [memb.] Royal Canadian Legion

COURTORIELLE, SHIRLEY
[b.] May 18, 1968, Peace River; [ch.] 3 kids; [ed.] Grade 10; [occ.] Mother at home!; [oth. writ.] I made a few poems and I'm thinking of writing a book!

COX, JOANNE PERRY
[pen.] Joanne Perry; [b.] September 23, 1936, Egg Harbor, WI; [p.] Lloyd and Nora Perry; [ch.] Dennis Olson, Daniel Olson, Lance Olson, Loren Olson; [ed.] Gibraltar High School, Fish Creek, Wisconsin, Oakton Community College, Skokie, IL; [occ.] Admission Coordinator, Mariner Health of Tallahassee; [hon.] Essay, I speak for Democracy; [oth. writ.] Poems published in local newspapers and published in local newsletters, essays and short stories; [pers.] My writing reflects my deep love of self and genuine love for those around me. I have been greatly influenced by my father, Lloyd E. Perry (deceased) retired principal of Elementary Schools, Fish Creek, Wisconsin.; [a.] Tallahassee, FL

COY, ALAN C.
[b.] February 13, 1974, Maryville, MO; [p.] Thomas G. Coy and Janice K. McGinnis; [ed.] Maryville High, Northwest Missouri State University, and Law Enforcement Training Institute at the University of Missouri.; [oth. writ.] Other Unpublished poems include "Confusion finally put in perspective and "trust".; [pers.] In most of my poetry I attempt to depict the true reality of a certain topic which in turn is left to the imagination of the reader.; [a.] Maryville, MO

CRAFTON, VALERIE LEA
[b.] February 12, 1967, Lubbock, TX; [p.] Monty and Mary Ellen Cooper; [m.] Shane Crafton, July 15, 1987; [ch.] Tyler Lane Crafton, Ryan Drake Crafton; [ed.] Jacksboro High School, Jackboro, TX - Tarleton State Univ., Stephenville, TX; [occ.] Assist. to Business Mgr. J.H. Office Aide, Henrietta I.S.D., Henrietta, TX; [memb.] First United Methodist Church, Henrietta, TX; [hon.] Received a (BBA) Bachelor of Business Administration; [oth. writ.] I have written several other poems about the changes in my life as well as family and friends.; [pers.] I write poems to work out my feelings, whether they be happy or sad. I find it easier to express my feelings in words, instead of talking about them.; [a.] Henrietta, TX

CRAIG, MONICA C.
[b.] February 25, 1976, Philadelphia, PA; [p.] Brian and Pauline Craig; [ed.] Temple University; [occ.] Full time student; [memb.] Public Relations Student Society of America (PRSSA); [hon.] Dean's List, Vice President of PRSSA; [oth. writ.] Several articles published in newsletter "The Wire," a publication of the Public Relations Student Society of America; [pers.] My finest expression of life is shown through my writing. Pictures may capture the sight but only words express true feelings.; [a.] Philadelphia, PA

CRANDALL, DEBORA ANN
[pen.] Debbie Deneb; [b.] February 5, 1956, Burlington, VT; [p.] Loretta Piche and Franklin Hubacher; [m.] Richard Crandall; [ch.] Sean; [ed.] Degree in Business with emphasis in Humanities and Journalism; [occ.] Communications Specialist; [memb.] MSJ Business Honary; [hon.] Business Honary, College of Mount St. Joseph, Third prize winner in the Carnation Slogan/Poem contest, several Editorial Achievement Awards for Technical Proposal work; [oth. writ.] SH Stry: "The Trip", others in outline.; [pers.] We are all connected in the vast realm of cosmic consciousness. Life is what you make it and that will improve by transcending positive thoughts and words to our fellow beings which in turn can only enhance the best in us all.; [a.] Cincinnati, OH

CRAWFORD, HELEN L.
[b.] March 3, 1917, Champaign, CO; [p.] Thee Watt, Mary Loyd (Both Deceased); [m.] Clark M. Crawford, July 3, 1935; [ch.] Three girls plus a girl deceased; [ed.] Tolono High School 1935, Ielini Beauty School 1945; [occ.] Retired; [oth. writ.] Many I've written over the years about family, friends and things I love.; [pers.] I've been married to the same man for 60 1/2 years. He is ill now and I thank my God I am able to keep an care for him in our home.

CRENNAN, LORRAINE
[b.] January 12, 1956; [m.] Jack Crennan, October 15, 1983; [ch.] Stacy and Tara; [ed.] Comsewogue High School Blake Business School for Court Reporting.; [oth. writ.] Children's book accepted for publication.; [pers.] I love to write about nature. Those who can live with nature, and not go against it, are the wisest of all.; [a.] Ridge, NY

CREVIER, MRS. LORAINE
[b.] July 24, 1942, Chatham, Ontario, Canada; [p.] Mr. and Mrs. Steven Hofmann; [m.] Mr. Ralph Crevier, March 11, 1962; [ch.] Five; [ed.] Grade 9; [occ.] House wife, EG Domestic Engineer

CRIDER, THOMAS WYATT
[b.] October 13, 1958, Oklahoma City, OK; [p.] Vera F. and Thomas E.; [m.] Glenda D. Crider, November 12, 1983; [ch.] Lindsay Kate, Chelsea Lynn; [ed.] MCHS, Rose State, OU, BA. Psy.; [occ.] G.M.; [memb.] UAW Local 1999, FBC Norman; [hon.] Husband, Father, Son, Grandson and Friend; [oth. writ.] Available upon request; [pers.] There's time for grieving, time for laughter, time for wonder, and time to love if we will only take the time.; [a.] Norman, OK

CRITCHFIELD, LORI JEAN
[b.] May 24, 1968, Berwyn, IL; [p.] Allen and Connie Klicka; [m.] Robert Harlan Critchfield III, June 1, 1996; [ed.] A.A. Degree, Orange Coast College, and currently an undergraduate Biology Major, Cal State Fullerton.; [occ.] Environmental Lab Technician, and pre-veterinary student for (Horses) equine medicine.; [memb.] CSUF Student Health Professions Association, World Society for the Protection of Animals, and the V.S. Recreational Ski Association.; [hon.] (1981 Honorable Mention in the Color it Orange Art Competition, Laguna Beach.) (1994 Certificate of Excellence, Biology Teaching Assistant- Orange Coast College.); [oth. writ.] Poems: "A letter of Impatience", "The Shower Poem," "Thoughts for the New Year", "Crooked," and essay "Evolution of the American Dream."; [pers.] When people tell you that you'll never reach your goals, they're right...the very moment you stop trying. Don't give up! Lori Critchfield.; [a.] Garden Grove, CA

CROFT, BRIAN PATRICK
[b.] May 30, 1973, Omaha, NE; [p.] Clancy and Barbara Croft; [ed.] Northwest High School currently attending the University of Nebraska - Lincoln; [occ.] Student; [hon.] Eagle Scout, Dean's List; [pers.] As this is my first published work, I dedicate the poem to my parents and to K.M..; [a.] Lincoln, NE

CRONK, JAMES D.
[pen.] Freelee; [b.] September 13, 1963, Winnipeg, Manitoba, Canada; [p.] Mary Hellen Cronk, FLorence Hunt (Adopted mother); [ed.] Grade 12 Tec - Voc High School Winnipeg, Manitoba, Canada, (I Study Aromatherapy), Play High School Football, Member in Choir; [occ.] Shielded Butterfly Ent. (Self Employed) Advertizing; [memb.] A distinguished Member of the International Society of Poets! Former Member of Forum Art Institute, Still A Member of Forum Art; [hon.] In my heart it has been a honor to have my works acknowledge by the T-N-L-P and I-S-P (International Society of Poets)!; [oth. writ.] The first PCS in painted is called the Shielded Butterfly, a PCS of sirealism showing the art of change. The first PCS I wrote is called People are People; [pers.] As the World Peace goes around, World Peace can be Obtained by the turn of the Century time the Grain of Sand People (Peace); [a.] Winnipeg Manitoba, Canada

CROSBIE, CASSANDRA
[b.] September 2, 1977, Oshawa General Hospital; [p.] Norman and Kathy Crosbie; [ed.] Grade 13, completing at Eastdale C.VI in Oshawa Ontario; [occ.] Student; [hon.] Horsemanship and competition ranging from Grand Champion to 6th place. Honour role for grade 10.; [oth. writ.] This will be my first publication besides a poem in my grade 5 news letter.; [pers.] I hope my poetry will let other adolescents know that they are not alone in their struggles and that my sanity was kept by the ink of my pen.; [a.] Oshawa Ontario, Canada

CROTEAU, MICHELLE R.
[b.] November 26, 1976, Montreal, Canada; [p.] Lucille Croteau and Marc Croteau; [ed.] Wellington High School, FSU College; [occ.] Student; [hon.] Southern Scholarship; [oth. writ.] Other poems; [pers.] Life is a stage - I must give my best performance.

CROUCH, ROLAND J.
[b.] July 8, 1935, New York; [ed.] Elementary School Killingly Public Danielson Conn - 1951; [occ.] Maintenance Magnani and McCormick Inc. Color Lithographers Enfield Conn.; [memb.] Parishioner of St. Michael's Cathedral Springfield MNSS member of Nocturnal Adoration Society St Thomas West Springfield Mass; [hon.] A certificate of completion of religious correspondence course in my Catholic faith. New haven October 7, 1975 student number 23114 Honorable Discharge 1953-1956 us army 82 air borne also 187 air borne; [oth. writ.] The mysteries of life the spirit of life faith is believing the human side of life a new beginning today I found a friend my walk in the Christian faith; [pers.] My faith in God and his inspiration to me that enabled me to write my poems. My life has been enriched with new meaning and purpose, with an awareness of God's love for me. It is my hope who ever reads my poems will also share with me a sense of awareness and love God has for us all.; [a.] Springfield, MA

CROWLEY, BRENDAN
[b.] October 10, 1970, Brattleboro, UT; [p.] Joseph Crowley, Sheila Crowley; [m.] Lily Patterson; [ch.] Albry, Anthony, Kiah; [ed.] B.U.H.S. (Brattleboro high school); [occ.] Janitor Country, Kitchen Bakery (Bratt UT.); [memb.] Insight Recitation Society, Buddhist Studies; [pers.] I write from within. It's an emotion only the pen understands. Poetic energy is nothing more than mere love for words.; [a.] Brattleboro, VT

CRUMP, ANNE M.
[b.] Arkansas; [p.] Guy Metcalf and Maggie Metcalf; [m.] C. W. Crump, June 27, 1968; [ch.] Inga Crump and Shawn Crump; [ed.] River Rouge High School, Henry Ford Comm. Coll.; [occ.] Emply. Dctroit Municipal Credit Union, Det., Mich.; [memb.] Assist-Pastor of Zion Pentecostal Church Ecorse, ML of (Mt. Zion Holy Churches of America; [oth. writ.] Do personalized writings on request.; [pers.] My writings are inspired by experiences in my life.; [a.] Detroit, MI

CRYER, MELISSA
[pen.] Missy; [b.] October 22, 1979, Houston, TX; [p.] Lillie Cryer; [ed.] Sam Houston H.S., and American Home School, Graduate 1996; [occ.] Day care Teacher, Melrose Baptist School, Houston, TX; [memb.] North Central Baptist Church, Youth Dept., Honor Society In H.S., Student Council; [hon.] Many awards in school, too many to mention!; [pers.] I would like to say thank you to all the people who helped me make it through all the hard times in my life.; [a.] Houston, TX

CRYSTIAN, CAROL M.
[ch.] Sean, Caira, Jasmyn Crystian; [ed.] Associates in Arts, Bachelors in Science, and Masters in Education; [occ.] Teacher - ITL Milliones Middle School - Pittsburgh, PA; [memb.] President of Just Us Investors Corp.; [oth. writ.] I have written other poetry. Possible book in print. (Pending); [pers.] I strive to write my poetry in a simplified manner, so my students and others can relate and understand. I also attempt to give a message or tell a story.; [a.] Pittsburgh, PA

CULLEN II, MICHAEL E.
[pen.] Michael E. Cullen II; [b.] August 28, 1977, Toledo, OH; [p.] Michael E. Cullen I and Malinda Cullen; [ed.] Central Catholic High School, Toledo; [memb.] Today Productions - Christian Theatre Group. I was Vice President of Drama Club and President of Art Club my Senior Jr. and Member all High School.; [hon.] I have been Awarded many Local Awards in the field of Art, I have also received many Honors in the field of Drama.; [oth. writ.] I have many other writings, but none have yet been published in any other publication. I do plan to have them published soon though.; [pers.] The belief I have in life is to be original. "Be different be your self." I write my poetry to try to capture the emotions of depressed anxiety of young adults.; [a.] Toledo, OH

CUMMINGS, TEREASA YVONNE
[pen.] T. Williams; [b.] December 22, 1977, Memphis, TN; [p.] Mr. and Mrs. Earl and Sandra Cummings; [ed.] Westwood Elementary - Westwood High School; [occ.] Taco Bells Fryer Cooked and helping on the register and on the lines; [memb.] Memphis Partners, Glee Clubs, Westwood Chorus, Welcome Committee, Big Brother, Big Sister Program and Jobs Tenn of Graduates; [hon.] Students Councils, Citizenship, Honor Roll and Who's Who among American Students; [oth. writ.] I write several poems in the Literary Magazines; [pers.] I like thinks about something good in my heart. And I love Jesus because he first love me and died for our, sin forgiveness.; [a.] Memphis, TN

CUMMINGS, TEREASA YVONNE
[b.] December 22, 1977, Memphis; [ed.] 12th grade Westwood High School; [memb.] Who's Who Among American Students, Big Brothers Big Sisters, Programs, Glee Clubs, The Chorus, Jobs Tenn Graduates and 12th year Club. I take of offering at church and a Welcome Committee.; [pers.] What happens to me longtime ago and what heart about God. And sometime love and romance. My Church: I like go to church every Sunday and reading my Bible. My church at Union M.B. Church.

CURLEE, EDWARD
[pen.] Edward Curlee; [b.] February 26, 1953, Pueblo, CO; [p.] Justina L., Mom; [ch.] Ditto; [ed.] Cathedral High, Denver, CO, Metropolitan State College, Denver, Colorado Institute of Art, Den-

ver; [occ.] Administrative Assistant and Researcher for Department of Energy. I've also produced a local TV show and am shopping product for sponsorships.; [memb.] Colorado Association of Black Journalists (Membership Coordinator, Society of Professional Journalists); [hon.] Awards in Speech, Drama, and poetry.; [oth. writ.] Previous poems published in community newspapers, with 2 published in Anthologies that were distributed nationwide.; [pers.] I push to write in different styles to reflect the different influences of life (the dark side vs. the light, the notion that out of evil comes good). Personal influences include e.e. cummings, Maya Angelou, and Jimi Hendrix.; [a.] Denver, CO

CURRIE, DOROTHY
[b.] April 30, 1932, Aberdeen; [p.] George McL. Cobban and Georgina Cobban; [m.] James Currie, August 3, 1956; [ch.] Graham William, Stuart Robert; [ed.] Local Schools, Aberdeen College of Education; [occ.] Retired primary teacher specialized in Children with learning difficulties; [oth. writ.] This is my first article to be published; [pers.] My inspiration frequently comes from the countryside of hills, glens, rivers and lochs, colour plays a large part, but I often find I am writing for children about animals and make believe.; [a.] Aberdeen, Scotland

CURRY, DEBORAH
[pen.] Debbie Turnbull, D. A. Hobart; [b.] May 21, 1951, Ohawa, ON; [p.] Donald and Ferne Curry; [ch.] Alesia, Ferne and Grant Roland; [ed.] Ottawa Ont. Highland Part High, Holland College Charlottetown, PEI; [memb.] Executive Secretary for Separated, Widowed and Divorce Grp. Member of Self-Help Depression Grp. (Mental Health) Instructor for Continuing Education.; [hon.] Justice of the Peace, Charlottetown Provincial Court. Award for 1st yr. Instructing Continuing Education; [oth. writ.] Poem - "No More" published in Treasured poems of America, Sparrowgrass Poetry Forum Inc. copy right 1995; [pers.] My written words come from that which I have lived and experienced. They are my gift to myself to those who can see into them, whose souls can relate to mine!; [a.] Summerside PI, Canada

CURTIS, H. SYLVIA
[pen.] Sylvia Reygers Curtis; [b.] August 4, 1947, Indonesia; [p.] Henry S. Reygers, Maria H. Reygers; [m.] John L. Curtis Sr., March 5, 1974; [ch.] John Lewis II, Maria Louise; [ed.] High school and part college; [occ.] P.H.D. Professional Home Director, caring for 95 years old mother, Family and Home.; [memb.] With luck and God's, Grace....Heaven....I hope.; [hon.] Just from my family, which have been rewarding and from our Father above.; [oth. writ.] A few short letter forms of anecdotes. I've always been intrigued by an author's talent to lead a reader into the world of creative tales.; [pers.] The fascination with words, connected to the mind, brings forth an explorative challenge, which then can be described in poetry or a story, to be absorbed by an other person's mind. Words, a commodity taken for granted, yet they are the beginning or end to many things.; [a.] Las Vegas, NV

CURTIS, JASON M.
[b.] October 22, 1973, Alexandria, LA; [p.] Willis Ray Curtis and Kathy Stanley; [ed.] Silliman High School, Currently attending Stephen f. Austin

State University; [occ.] Student; [oth. writ.] Poetry published by "The Advocate" And "Explorer".; [pers.] If you have built castles in the air, your work need not be lost, that is where they should be. Not put foundations under them.; [a.] Lufkin, TX

CUTHBERTSON, DARYLA YOUNG
[pen.] Daryla Young; [b.] May 15, 1948, Montreal, Province of Quebec, Canada; [p.] Audrey (Blampied) and Donald Young; [m.] James Cuthbertson, September 19, 1987; [ch.] Four; [ed.] High School - Gladstone, Vancouver, B.C.; [occ.] Federal Government Employee; [memb.] The Channel Island History Society, Thyroid Foundation of Canada; [hon.] Top Ten Volunteers in British Columbia 1984; [oth. writ.] None published.; [pers.] Follow my conscience in all things. Write what I feel.; [a.] Hope British Columbia, Canada

CYR, MICHELE
[b.] February 24, 1983, Waterbury, CT; [p.] Ivan Cyr and Mary Woodward; [ed.] Junior High School; [occ.] Student; [pers.] Books like "Where The Sidewalk Ends" and "A Light In The Attic" by Shel Silverstein influence the way I write poems, instead of thinking heavily about the poem, I let the feelings come to me naturally.; [a.] Watertown, CT

DACUNHA, FRANCISCO
[pen.] Frank; [b.] February 13, 1971, New Bedford, MA; [p.] Antonio and Olivia Dacunha; [ed.] Master's of Social Work, University of Pittsburgh, 1995, BA., Umass at Dartmouth, 1993; [occ.] Youth and Family Therapist; [memb.] United States Army Reserve, International Society of Poets, Reserve Officer's Association; [hon.] Commissioned as a second Lieutenant for the Medical Service Corps in the United States Army Reserve, July 19, 1995.; [oth. writ.] Book entitled words published by American Literary Press, Maryland, 1993.; [pers.] "Always plan when you're going and focus on how you got there but never forget where you came from"; [a.] New Bedford, MA

DAFFT, ROBERT E.
[b.] January 25, 1954, DeLeon, TX; [p.] Joseph E. L. Dafft II, Nova H. Bryan Dafft; [m.] Maria A. Gandaria Dafft, December 30, 1983; [ch.] Christopher J., Tabitha M., Jennifer E.; [ed.] Comanche High S. Grad., Tex. St. Tech. Inst. Grad., U.S. Navy Res. Hon. Disc., Barber College Grad.; [occ.] Barber Stylist, Evangelist Prison Minister, Writer; [memb.] Full Gospel Business Men's Fellowship Int., Door of Hope Christian Church, Five-Alive Inc.; [hon.] TX. St. Class D. Bowling Champ "77-78" 100 Gold. Blood Donor, 100 Pheresis Donations.; [oth. writ.] Burns with fear, true providers, just can't see, the coolness came, the room is full, and she was praying and about 50 more ready for publishing. I've been accepted to write children stories.; [pers.] I memorized EA Poe's Sepulchers by the sea, when I was in H.S. and from then on, I kind a hated poetry, and thought that I would never write. But we just never know what kind of plans God has for our life. "So please never say never." S.D.G./K.I.T.; [a.] Alamo, TX

DAHMS, TANYA E.S.
[b.] April 14, 1967, Guelph, Ontario; [p.] Dr. Fred and Mrs. Ruth Dahms; [s.] Michael Riem; [m.] May 27, 1994; [ch.] none yet...; [ed.] B.Sc. University

of Waterloo (Honours co-op Biology and Chemistry), Ph.D. University of Ottawa (Faculty of Medicine, Dept. Biochemistry); [occ.] Post Doctoral (NSERC) Fellow Purdue University; [memb.] The Biophysical Society, American Crystallographic Association, Canadian Society of Chemistry, The Dance Network (Ottawa), Canadian Society of Biochemistry and Molecular Biology; [hon.] Ontario Scholar, Post Graduate Scholarship - NSERC, University of Ottawa Scholarship, Post Doctoral Fellowship - NSERC; [oth. writ.] "Today i see the Moon" In Ph.D. Dissertation: "Conformational Heterogeneity and Secondary Structure of Proteins" University of Ottawa, 1996. Various scientific research papers...; [pers.] This poem was written in 1984 for J.P. An abundance of knowledge clouds the imagination, biases any observation, and dampens the sense of pure wonder: Learn it, let it go and when you need it again, discover it yourself.; [a.] West Lafayette, IN

DAILY, SHANA
[b.] February 14, 1975; [occ.] Graduate Student in Psychology; [pers.] How you think determines who you are, who you are determined what you do.; [a.] Kalamazoo, MI

DALLAS, KATHERINE ELIZABETH
[p.] Katie, Kati and Kat; [b.] October 16, 1982, Greenvill, SC; [p.] Michael Dallas and Deborah Dallas; [ed.] Gulf Beaches Elementary School K-5, 16th Street Middle School Magnet for the Arts - 6th grade, W.G. Sugg Middle School - 7th grade; [occ.] Babysitter, prep-cook; [memb.] Suncoast Girl Scouts, Kurt D. Cobain Memory Fan Club; [hon.] Pinellas County Mathematics Pride Awards 93-94 school year; [oth. writ.] Back to me, Demons in my view, My life, and many many more.; [pers.] Good friends don't come along very often, so my friends tend to inspire my poems. Kara Pasick is my biggest influence.; [a.] Bradenton, FL

DALLMANN, NANCY
[pen.] Miss Pitty Ross; [b.] November 22, 1938, Elroy, WI; [p.] Clarence and Hilda Ormson; [m.] Kenneth Dallmann, May 2, 1964; [ch.] Dawn, Vick, Carrie; [ed.] Elroy, WI High School; [occ.] Wife, Mother, Grandmother, Real Estate Entrepreneur; [oth. writ.] Local Newspaper; [pers.] I see my poems as a diary of my life... sadness, laughter and everyday life... influenced and cheered on by my husband, daughters and two sisters Sara and Marge.; [a.] Oconomowoc, WI

DANSO, ROBERT VAN-EARL
[pen.] R. D. Van-Earl; [b.] June 19, 1950, Begoro-Akim, Ghana, West Africa; [p.] Robert Aboagye, Margaret Asiedva; [m.] Selina Beadiwaa Danso, April 1, 1981; [ch.] Kofipaul, Awo Sarah, Rebecca, Joe, Sharon Doreen; [ed.] Salvation Army Elementary Sch- Begoro, Akim Ghana, Kwahu Ridge Secondary School, Abuakwastate College, Kibi, Ghana; [occ.] Evangelist/Missionary resides in Connecticut, U.S.A.; [memb.] Spoken Word Ministry, International Society of Poets, Born into the Universal bride of our Lord and Saviour Jesus Christ.; [hon.] Certificate by Arts Council of Ghana (First National Youth Festival- 1976).; [oth. writ.] Beyond The Curtains of Freedom, published by the Watermark Press Owing-Mills MD.; [pers.] God gives inspiration through the

holy spirit to encourage the follow up of the footprints to righteousness. These nuggets lies in the volumes of his word, yet blindness and modern science have weakened his power to protect.; [a.] New Haven, CT

DAUGHTRY, WILSON G.
[b.] October 31, 1921, Hertford, NC; [p.] Lorenzo and Isabelle Daughtry; [m.] Salina Leigh Daughtry, October 31, 1948; [ch.] Four; [ed.] High School Plus Two Years at Kerpel School of Dental Technology; [occ.] Retired; [memb.] Member of Bethany Baptist Church for more than thirty years, and a Member of the Men Chorus.; [pers.] I like to write about things around me, things I can see, and people. A long and fruitful life maybe our goal. Many times we came up short before we are old. I am please I know my poem is being publish on its merits.; [a.] Brooklyn, NY

DAVENPORT, TIANJA N.
[b.] March 2, 1976, Philadelphia, PA; [p.] Robert and Shari Wilkes; [ed.] Oscar Smith High School, Tennessee State University; [occ.] Student majoring in History Africana Studies; [memb.] Tennessee State University Aristocrat of Bands, University Honors Program; [hon.] Dean's List, Tennessee State University Aristocrat of Bands Scholar and Section Leader; [oth. writ.] 5 other published poems in various publications.; [pers.] In my writings, I seek to capture the essence of what love and beauty is, in their every form.; [a.] Chesapeake, VA

DAVIDSON, GLEN G.
[b.] September 14, 1951, Jamaica, West Indies; [p.] Walter and Dapne Davidson; [m.] Sharon Davidson, March 25, 1972; [ch.] Nicole Charmaine; [ed.] Secondary - Ardenne High School, Kingston, TA, George Brown College, Toronto, Ont., York University - several undergraduate courses; [occ.] Sales Representative; [memb.] Ardenne Past Students Assoc.; [oth. writ.] One poem published in local ethnic newspaper - "Share" 1985; [pers.] Poetry is a creative form of expressing life experiences.; [a.] Bowmanville Ontario, Canada

DAVIS, LOIS LINDSEY
[b.] August 7, 1913, Devine, TX; [p.] P. E. Lindsey and Etta O'Neal Lindsey; [m.] Louis M. "Red" Davis (Deceased), November 1, 1931; [ch.] Justin Davis, Louis E. Davis, Darlene Davis Crain, James L. Davis; [ed.] Devine High School graduate 1 year SWTX Teachers College; [occ.] Homemaker; [memb.] Order of the Eastern Star Chapter #43; [hon.] High School District Declamation and Spelling Bees, College recognition by a teacher who kept one of my poems because I was late to physical ed class in college.; [oth. writ.] Several unpublished poems; [pers.] Strive to help the underdog.; [a.] Devine, TX

DAVIS, PAM
[pen.] Pamela Davis; [b.] November 13, 1965, Dallas, TX; [p.] Susan Hufsey and Jim Hufsey; [m.] Marvin Davis, October 8, 1993; [ch.] Justin Aaron Cowan; [ed.] South Garland High; [occ.] Wife, Mother, Prophet; [memb.] National Geographic Society National Arbor Day Foundation; [hon.] Only one - Life; [oth. writ.] Non published Fantasy Writings and Poetry; [pers.] Grasp Love and everything else falls into place.; [a.] Richardson, TX

DAVIS, RICHARD
[pen.] Ricardo; [b.] July 18, 1931, Cleveland, OH; [p.] Josephine Legat, Clifford Davis; [m.] Jennie Davis, June 25, 1956; [ch.] Craig Davis; [oth. writ.] Several poems but never published. Also working on a book of short stories.; [pers.] After my wife passed away in the summer of 1994, I found myself with a deep desire to write poetry in remembrance of my Dear wife.; [a.] Mayfield Heights, OH

DAVIS, SHIRLEY ANN
[pen.] Shirley Ann Buck; [b.] December 8, 1936, Gladewater, TX; [p.] Maurice Buck and Greta Buck; [m.] Briane Lee Davis, August 5, 1968; [ed.] Huntington Park High School CA. Cypress College—CA; [occ.] Retired-Rockwell International Corp.—Anaheim, CA Senior Analyst Configuration Specialist; [memb.] Calvary Chapel-Yorba Linda Church Yorba Linda, CA; [hon.] New Age Thinking Honor, Investment in Excellence Honor, Operations Improvement Program Achievement Certificate, Organizational Excellence Honor, Chairman Team's Award, Ronald Reagan Presidential - Tennis Sports Award; [oth. writ.] Poems published in local newspaper; [pers.] The Love, guidance and encouragement from my husband, Briane, and my inspires me to paint in oils, participate in sports and God gives me the ability to achieve. My prayers are that some day, man will realize that we are only a small entity in this world and we must preserve it.; [a.] Yorba Linda, CA

DAVIS, TESSEY
[b.] February 20, 1971, Macclenny, FL; [p.] Charles Ward, Joan Hurst; [m.] Bonnie Davis Sr., March 25, 1991; [ch.] Amber, Ronnie Jr., Charles; [ed.] High School Graduate Baker County, FL.; [occ.] Housekeeper, Mariner Health of Macclenny; [hon.] I was chosen by my co-workers for employee of the month and year in 1994.; [oth. writ.] I write poems all the time and keep them in a folder at home. This is the first poem I have ever sent off.; [pers.] This poem is special because I wrote it for a friend of mines grandbaby that was in the hospital. God bless you all.; [a.] Macclenny, FL

DAVIS, WILLIAM R.
[b.] April 13, 1926, San Bernardino, CA; [m.] Maria Davis, July 24, 1965; [ch.] Robert, Peter, John, Christina, Elizabeth; [ed.] Univ. of Oregon; [occ.] Sales Consultant; [memb.] Knights of Columbus; [oth. writ.] Mann Poems; [pers.] My poems reflect my own thoughts.; [a.] Petaluma, CA

DAWSON, GEORGE ARTHUR
[b.] August 5, 1957, Kinston, NC; [p.] Louise Dawson, Mary Murrell; [m.] Susie M. Dawson, September 15, 1990; [ch.] George Dawson Jr., Carlos Murrell; [ed.] Kinston High School (US), Army (SGT); [pers.] To the memory of my loving father Leroy Dawson Sr. Who always told me, you can do anything in the world. If you have trust in the (Lord).; [a.] Kinston, NC

DAY, JOAN
[pen.] April Day; [b.] April 28, 1941, Ottawa, Ontario, Canada; [p.] Helen and Roy Day; [ch.] Bruce Tutchings; [ed.] High School - Glebe Collegiate, Reg. Nurse - St. Mary Abbot's Hosp., London, England, B. Th. - St. Paul University, Ottawa;

[occ.] Theologian; [pers.] I write to bring out the joy of living in this beautiful world that God has given us. To me, writing is sometimes a form of prayer.; [a.] Nepean Ontario, Canada

DAY, THOMAS
[b.] March 26, 1968, Atlanta, GA; [p.] Thomas and Liane Day; [m.] Jennifer Day, April 7, 1990; [ch.] Isabella Brianna Day; [ed.] Auburn University, Georgia State, CFA; [occ.] Financial Analyst; [memb.] Perimeter Presbyterian; [oth. writ.] A lot of unpublished items due to my irrational face of allowing others to wade through my mind. Included among these: Tem Jihad, a lonely view, tis true you are an angel, the limpet, yada, yada, yada.; [pers.] Accept nothing. Question everything. All is not as it appears to be.; [a.] Atlanta, GA

DE BELLIS, DOLORES
[b.] March 27, 1932 (Easter Sunday), Sharon, PA; [p.] Margo Markick-Gaich; [m.] Michael Joseph De Bellis; [ch.] Marle, Michele, Desiree, Thomas-(dec.), Christopher, and Gerard; [occ.] Educator - Parochial School Teacher; [memb.] Association with the Sisters of St. Joseph, Orange, CA.; [hon.] Lady of the Rosary Cathedral - San Bernadino, CA

DEAS III, HENRY
[b.] December 25, Charleston, SC; [ch.] Michael, Brian, Demian, Gary; [ed.] Baylor Prep, The Citadel Strasberg, Warner Robertson Acting Sherwood Oaks Experimental Film College; [occ.] US Director moving pictures; [oth. writ.] "The Hall", Italy "Romano Sembre", "Romance Made in Heaven" published for "Airlift to Africa"; [a.] Los Angeles, CA

DECELLO, RHONDA
[pen.] Rhonda; [b.] July 28, 1983, Lubbock, TX; [p.] Richard and Nollia DeCello; [ed.] 7th grade Atkins Junior High; [occ.] Student; [hon.] A, B Honor roll; [oth. writ.] Have others haven't sent in. I need a publisher.; [pers.] I love to write. "I strive to write what is in my thoughts which comes from within my heart so everyone can know what my dreams are all about."; [a.] Lubboch, TX

DEHAVEN, DESIREE L.
[b.] October 22, 1971, Chester Country, PA; [p.] Dorothy M. Burkey; [m.] Charles DeHaven, February 28, 1995; [ch.] Heather DeHaven and C. J. DeHaven; [ed.] Graduated in 1995 through the I.C.S. Newport Pacific High School Scranton PA currently attending Lancaster School of Cosmetology.; [occ.] Student of Cosmetology; [hon.] Made Instructors Honor list at Lancaster School of Cosmetology; [pers.] The poem's I write are written form my heart. I lost my mother in a car accident when I was 14. All the poems I write are written about the loving and beautiful person she was. My Rose is dedicated to my mother.; [a.] Lancaster, PA

DEL ROSARIO, FLOR
[pen.] Flor, Florecita, Jasmine; [b.] Caridad, Cavite City; [p.] Atty. Quirino del Rosario and Encarnacion Custodio; [ch.] Alvin (R.A.); [ed.] B.S.E. (English Major), Litt. B. (Spanish Mayor), Few Units in the Post Graduate Course; [occ.] (Former) College Instructress Spanish - English Translator; [oth. writ.] The gift of life (exposition) poems unrestrained emotions parting memories - parting memories solitude the mystery of life, etc.; [pers.]

I find serenity and contentment whenever I write about the marvelous (creations) of our greatest creator.; [a.] Cavite City, Philippines

DELAPLANTE, COREY
[pen.] Coco; [b.] September 27, 1971, Hearst, Ontario, Canada; [p.] Real DeLaplante and Fleurete Rigoden; [ed.] College diploma in Fine Arts, Heritage College (Hull, Que, Canada), currently studying for BA Ph. at Dominican College (Ottawa, Ont., Canada); [pers.] All forms of art tap into a fundamental existential element of which we as human beings could tap into. Art is the most universal medium of communication.; [a.] Hull Province of Quebec, Canada

DELGADO, AMBER MICHELLE
[pen.] Jasmine; [b.] October 20, 1984, Palos Heights; [p.] Susan Delgado, John Delgado; [ed.] Oakridge Elementary School; [a.] Palos Hills, IL

DELL'ANNO, PALMA
[pen.] P. S. Dell'anno; [b.] March 3, 1970, Etobicoke, Ontario, Canada; [ed.] Attended Sheridan College (Ontario), courses included Fiction Writing and Write to Publish; [pers.] Poetry takes one moment in life, emphasizes it, and tells a story.; [a.] Etobicoke Ontario, Canada

DELROSARIO, PAMELA L.
[pen.] Pamela D.; [b.] November 7, 1955, Jeffersonville, Indiana; [p.] Maxine A. Lawrence; [m.] Divorced; [ch.] Lori DelRosario; [ed.] Graduated from Milton High School in 1974, (Milton FL) Attended Pensacola Junior College.; [occ.] School bus driver; [oth. writ.] I have written two books of Christian poetry and I am currently working on an autobiography. I am not yet a published author. I am just beginning to introduces my work to the public.; [pers.] A writing career is not something I spontaneously decided to pursue. It seems to be something I was destined to do. My mother had been an English major in college. She was always encouraging me to write. I've always has a weakness in the area of math. Whenever I've felt the desire to better myself, I've studied what I know best and avoided my weaknesses. My favorite areas of study have always been the English language and writing. I have a great love for communication. I feel that if all of mankind would sharpen this skill, we could solve many of our problems. When we express ourselves with words we often create artwork that is as beautiful as a painters creation. The credit for what I create belongs to God. A close walk with him inspires my work.; [a.] Milton, FL

DEMAIO, KIMBERLY
[b.] March 24, 1975, Livingston, NJ; [ed.] Junior at Monmouth University in West Long Branch, NJ, majoring in English/Education; [hon.] Kappa Delta Pi, Lambda Sigma Tau, Dean's List; [oth. writ.] One poem published in High School Literary Magazine; [pers.] My poetry usually reflects personal experiences I have had and I try to use poetry to express the deepest and most honest part of myself.; [a.] Westbury, NY

DEMBLING, DEBRALEE
[b.] May 31, 1974, Long Branch, NJ; [p.] Marc and Las Ann Dembling; [ed.] Morristown H.S., Morristown

NJ, B.A. in English from the University of Michigan, December 1995; [occ.] Title Searcher, Liberty Title Co., Ann Arbor, MI; [memb.] Sigma Kappa National Sorority, Consider Magazine, Associate Editor; [oth. writ.] Several articles published in the Michigan daily.; [pers.] Through my writing I am able to express my heart, and my greatest hope is to reach the hearts of others.; [a.] Ann Arbor, MI

DENEEN, JOSEPHINE F.
[pen.] Jo Deneen; [b.] May 3, 1943, St. Cloud, MN; [p.] Frances, Vincent R. Schyma; [ch.] Charles V. Deneen, Gena M. Deneen; [ed.] Foley High Foley, MN NY School Photography NY/NY, NJ Inst. of Photography NJ. Marine Corp. USA Llept; [occ.] Life Education of Owner JD's Photography and Hwy 34 Kennel, also employed at frigidare Inc. St. Cloud, MN; [hon.] Merits Honorable Mention World of Poetry; [oth. writ.] Highest Mountain; [pers.] To laugh often and Spread Laughter, To appreciate nature and life, To know one life is easier because I have existed. My favorites poets are John Donne and Loid Byron; [a.] Pierz, MN

DENETTE, DOLORES E.
[b.] October 9, 1955, North Adams, MA; [p.] Ruth E. Stokes, Fay E. Stokes; [ch.] Timothy A. Denette, Eric J. Denette; [ed.] Drury High School Berkshire Community College; [occ.] RN Nursing supervisor for Alzheimer Unit - Sweet brook Care Centers Williamstown, MA.; [hon.] Dean's List - Graduated with honors Art of Caring award and the margaret S. Kennedy Memorial Nursing Award upon College Graduation; [pers.] I find that writing is very therapeutic. It allows me to express and elaborate on my innermost thoughts and emotions; [a.] Clarksburg, MA

DEROO, ROBBYN
[b.] October 26, 1977, London, Ontario, Canada; [p.] Robert and Elaine Deroo; [ed.] Valley Heights Secondary School; [occ.] Student; [memb.] Student's Council President, Community Theatre, many sports teams; [hon.] Ontario OAC Scholar; [oth. writ.] Poems published in high school newspapers.; [pers.] I'm inspired by love. Lost, present, and future loves.; [a.] Langton Ontario, Canada

DESOUZA, ADRIENNE
[b.] July 13, 1977, Edmonton, Alberta; [p.] Sandra and Phillip DeSouza; [ed.] Albert College in Belleville, Ontario and Royal Military College of Canada in Kingston, Ontario; [occ.] Student and Officer Cadet; [oth. writ.] A lot to friends, but that may not actually be what you mean.; [pers.] This was a deviation from my usual style. I just hope my other works get such a warm welcome!; [a.] Kingston Ontario, Canada

DEVOR, CHRISTINA
[pen.] June 13, 1952, Fort Belvoir, VA; [p.] William Devor, Charlotte Devor; [ed.] Graham High, Martin High, Via Tech and Research Institute, Houston Community College; [occ.] Project Manager, Financial Systems - GC Services LP - Houston, TX; [memb.] Houston Area Women's Center, Texas Gulf Coast Chapter of the Lupus Foundation, National Association for Female Executives (NAFE); [hon.] Dean's List, NHS, 1st and 3rd place correspondence awards; [oth. writ.]; [pers.] I feel I am doing something worthwhile

when I write poetry. If only to express something that someone else has experienced, this is the real joy of writing.; [a.] Houston, TX

DICKERSON, HAROLD R.
[b.] December 31, 1939, Cox's Creek, KY; [p.] Deceased; [ch.] Patrice L. Dickerson; [ed.] U.S. Air Force University Extension, the college of Education in Ellensburg, Washington; [occ.] Poet/Writer, Crane Operator through Pacific Maritime Association; [memb.] Artist Embassy International, and Who's who in Poetry; [hon.] Five Golden Poet Awards, one Silver Award, three Honorable Mentions, and one Master of Poetry Certificate. Outstanding Poet for 1994; [oth. writ.] "Reflections From The Heart", love poems. "Gather your Roses," Religious poems, up and coming.; [pers.] In one manner or another we are dependent upon each other and as we entertain our connection, help someone with his perfection.; [a.] Oakland, CA

DICKSON, JULIA
[b.] August 1, 1944, Sacramento, CA; [p.] Arsanuel and Ida Dickson; [m.] John C. Jackson; [ch.] Blended family of 5 girls and 4 boys; [ed.] Sacramento Senior High School and Consumes River College; [occ.] Office Assistant for The California Youth Authority; [memb.] International Toastmistress, National Children's Cancer Society The Garden of Paradise Church of God and Christ; [hon.] Department of Youth Authority employee recognition Award, World of Poetry Golden Poet Award, Silver Cup for Speech Contest, Toastmistress Club Level, 2 Regional Speech Contest; [oth. writ.] Two short stories for children and several poems written for Black History celebrations and special occasional events.; [pers.] Born in Sacrament and have lived there most of my life. The oldest of eight children. I started writing poetry, short stories at age 13. I have been designing cards for 10 years. I have 15 grandchildren, several of who are artistically inclined. Presently collaborating on book with husband.; [a.] Sacramento, CA

DIFETERICI, JOSEPH
[b.] October 29, 1949, El Paso, TX; [p.] Joseph DiFeterici, Alicia DiFeterici; [m.] Eileen DiFeterici, February 14, 1990; [ch.] Erik, Paul, Aaron and Rachel; [occ.] Construction Engineer; [oth. writ.] Numerous other poems but nothing ever submitted for publication; [pers.] All of my poetry is connected to my children and my family. In this poem I tried to convey to my children (now all children) the connection between them and all living things surrounding them.; [a.] Washington Township, NJ

DIGANGI, YVETTE A.
[pen.] Anne De Machery; [b.] July 27, 1923, France; [p.] Mayo Maurice Yvon, Gabrielle Yvon; [m.] Edgar Parsons (Deceased), Salvatore DiGangi, May 31, 1986; [ch.] Jack Parsons, Eric Parsons and Mary-Frances Schempp, Step-daughter: Angela DiGangi; [ed.] Educated in France, taught myself how to read and write English; [occ.] Housewife; [memb.] For a while, I was part of the Women's Bell Choir at the Middleburg Heights Community Church; [oth. writ.] Many poems written in English and in French and working on my autobiography.; [pers.] Most of my literary work is the result of my life long experiences.; [a.] Middleburg Heights, OH

DINARDO, LAUREN MARIE
[b.] August 8, 1983, Bridgeport, CT; [p.] Mark DiNardo, Diane DiNardo; [ed.] Seventh Grade, Ripon Christian Schools; [occ.] Student; [oth. writ.] School newspaper, literature class, journal, and pleasure writing.; [pers.] I like to think that, "Life is a Picnic and I'm starving."; [a.] Ripon, CA

DIPBOYE, V. LORRAINE
[pen.] Lorry; [b.] September 2, 1911, Van Buren, AR; [p.] John and Emma Coleman (Deceased); [m.] Jesse J. Dipboye (Deceased), January 1933; [ch.] Raymond Vance and Jesse Jardin; [ed.] 9th grade Oak Grove, Arkansas, employed for many years as a book keeper and typist. Up there; [occ.] Retired; [memb.] Up There up there, up there stood lonely me beneath the tall mist-laden tree. I felt a presence close to me. I heard a chorus of crickets drone standing beneath this misty dome. I felt a breeze thoughts roamed. Behind that veil is He and I am not alone; [oth. writ.] I have a book filled with simple poetry that I have written over the years.; [pers.] All poems that I have submitted were written by me.; [a.] Richmond, VA

DITLEFSEW, DENNIS LEE
[pen.] Zachary Maxwell; [b.] October 28, 1946, Fond du Lac, WI; [p.] Bob and La Vera Burchell; [oth. writ.] Assessment 49 Job-less, One Dream Two Hearts, Words and Swords, Salvation Light, Time Trans Parent, Lockington Wood, Dark Haired Brown Eyed Ann, Tobi-Awn; [pers.] Knowing is understanding and understanding is doing!; [a.] Tomah, UT

DIXSON, ROBERT J.
[b.] October 6, 1959, Carol Gales, FL; [p.] Ann and Joe Dixson; [ch.] Barbara; [ed.] High School; [occ.] Fire Fighter, Paramadic Dade County Fla.; [memb.] AFL CIO Local 1403 Five Dept Dade County Fla.; [oth. Writ.] Always Known, Kind Eyes, If I Could Cry Santa Teresa; [pers.] Lone philosophical mentor and influence singer, songwriter Jackson Browne.; [a.] Key Largo, FL

DOBSON, BRENDA M.
[b.] March 19, 1951, Battle Creek, MI; [p.] William R. and Dwanna J. Dow; [m.] Mark D. Dobson, September 23, 1994; [ch.] James E., Timothy A., Tracia M. Jones; [ed.] Harper Creek High; [occ.] Switch Operator for the Pillsbury Plant in Buckley, Michigan; [oth. writ.] Have had several poems published in a Local Church Bulletin.; [a.] Mesick, MI

DOHERTY, STEPHEN
[b.] June 10, 1976, Brockton, MA; [p.] John P. Doherty, Geneva Doherty; [ed.] Westboro High, New Hampton School, Saint Michaels College; [a.] Westboro, MA

DONALD, VICTORIA LYNNE
[b.] June 6, 1968, Strathroy, Ontario, Canada; [p.] James and Percelle Donald; [ed.] East Elgin Secondary School, (1st yr) New Liskeard College of Agricultural Technology; [occ.] Horse Trainer, Riding coach, Morgan Horse Breeder; [memb.] Ontario Morgan Horse Club, Rainbow Morgan Horse Club; [hon.] Canadian Morgan Horse Assoc. Outstanding Youth Award, Outstanding 4-4 Member (horse) numerous Championships and Year-End Awards in Ontario

Morgan Club, Canadian Equestrian Federation and computation.; [oth. writ.] Until recently, my poetry, stones, etc. Have been a reflection of my own personal life and shared with family, close friends.; [pers.] Our most valuable treasure is today's youth, Yesterday's Followers, Tomorrows Leaders we must inspire them, Support them and allow to follow their dreams if tomorrows generation is to be better than ours.; [a.] Glencoe Ontario, Canada

DONISI, HOLLIS LEE
[b.] March 29, 1949, Youngstown, OH; [p.] Fred and Donna Miller; [m.] Greg Donisi, January 31, 1980; [ch.] Timber and Brentner, Jennifer and Kathy; [ed.] Northmont High School 1967; [occ.] Sales Clerk Bay shore, Clothing and Small World Marathon FL; [pers.] Without the love, support and encouragement of my husband and sons, I would still be "hiding" my poetry.; [a.] Marathon, FL

DONNELLAN, JAMES
[b.] December 6, 1960, Massachusetts; [ed.] St. Francis Xavier University, Antigonish, Nova Scotia; [a.] Ballston Spa, NY

DONNELLY, EDWARD G.
[b.] July 13, 1929, Brooklyn, NY; [p.] Michael and Mary Donnelly; [m.] Margaret Perry Donnelly, May 22, 1971; [ch.] Mary Beth, Stephen, Barbara, Eileen; [ed.] Nativity Grammar School, St. Leonard's Academy (2 year High School) Erasmus Hall Evening High School, St. John's University (Graduated January, 1959); [occ.] Retired Court Clerk Specialist, New York County Surrogate's Court; [memb.] Knights Of Columbus New Hyde Park Council, Catholic Court Attache's Guild; [hon.] Commendation Ribbon with Metal Pendant from the U.S. Army (Korea); [oth. writ.] None that have as yet been published, but I have other poems and songs that I have written over the years.; [pers.] I believe in the beauty of nature as a manifestation of God, and that this world is a testing ground for an even more beautiful world to come.; [a.] New Hyde Park, NY

DORAN, BRAD
[b.] April 29, 1973, Boulder, CO; [pers.] I would like to thank the absurdity of modern day society for the inspiration to write my poems.

DORSEY, JANETTE F.
[pen.] Janette Fletcher; [b.] September 14, 1958, Austin, TX; [p.] Mr. and Mrs. James Fletcher Sr.; [m.] Donald Dorsey, April 1, 1990; [ch.] Glen, Leticia, Ja'Reem; [ed.] Reagan Senior High at Austin TX; [occ.] Dallas Area Rapid Transit; [memb.] TX Film Comm. Zacdry Scott Theater; [oth. writ.] First submitted; [pers.] I strive to reflect the goodness of mankind in my writing, I have been greatly influenced by early romantic poet, this is my beloved Walter Benton.; [a.] New York, NY

DORTON, JAMES MCARTHUR
[pen.] Franc Y. Volpe; [b.] March 28, 1942, Mooresville, NC; [m.] Mary Ann Jefferies Dorton, November 21, 1965; [ch.] Matt, John, Laura; [ed.] BS - The Citadel, Charleston, SC, MA - Kansas State Univ., Manhattan, KS, MA - US Naval War College, Newport, RI, MS - Salve Regina Univ., Newport, RI; [occ.] Staff - The Citadel; [hon.] Retired Colonel, US Army - 30

years service; [oth. writ.] Other poems and items published, various media, several limited publication Research papers and booklets published for Dept. of Defense organizations. War Poetry Anthology A Soldier Can Be Gentle Too, approx 200 personal experience poems - In Progress.; [pers.] Life is an adventure too short not to attempt to experience as much as possible.; [a.] Mount Pleasant, SC

DOUGHERTY, ANDREW
[pen.] Relt Script; [b.] January 4, 1972, Omaha, NE; [p.] Larry Sharon Dougherty; [ch.] Hannah Alexis Dougherty; [ed.] Uncompleted BA in Accounting; [occ.] Proof operator; [oth. writ.] Retribution (Novel), Mislead trio (Novel), Isolation (poem), Lies (poem), Eternity (poem), Little Boy Blue (poem), Crucify (poem); [pers.] Loneliness and unhappiness has inspired me the most, but writing fulfills me I've always felt I had talent, but it pleases me to hear it from someone else.; [a.] Omaha, NE

DOWNEY, JOHN ANDREW
[pen.] John or Jack Downey; [b.] November 1, 1925, Ireland; [p.] James Downey, Margaret Jones; [m.] Patricia Dunne, October 23, 1954; [ch.] John Alexander, Patricia Marie, James Norman; [ed.] St. Coleman's R.C. Ireland, St. Mary's High, Ireland, Bathurst Collegiate, Canada; [occ.] Retired (1986); [memb.] Irish Red Cross, Seniors Association, Canada; [hon.] Irish Festival Awards, First and Second Place (1949) - (1950), Male Choir Division. Long Service Award. De Havilland Aircraft (Canada Ltd); [oth. writ.] "The Four Seasons", "Requiem for a Pilgrim" published in sparkles in the sand anth. National Library of Poetry 1995. Also "Destiny", "Heavens Above" other poems to newspapers and radio stations.; [pers.] I have been greatly influenced by Irish writers and poets. Poetry always seeks a way to find the truth.; [a.] Guelph, ON

DOWNS, JAY WARREN
[pen.] Matthew Lovell Downarian, Sterling S. Silverpeace; [b.] September 6, 1936, Reading, PA; [p.] Paul S. and Ethel A Downs; [m.] January 25, 1958; [ch.] Patrick Jay, Brian Scott, Michael Allen, Kevin Glenn, Denise Ann, Kathleen Lynn; [ed.] Readinf Sr. High, University of Wisconsin; [occ.] Commercial Transportation Director, ARCO Industries Inc., Milwaukee, WI; [memb.] International Brotherhood of Teamsters, American Trucking Assoc., WI Trucking Assoc., National Safety Council, National Assoc. on Transportation Safety, American Fellowship Ministries, Alliance Church, Milwaukee, WI; [hon.] National Safety Council, American Trucking Assoc., Teamsters Union/ Local 200, State of Pennsylvania, Carnegie Hero Award, Univ. of Wisconsin-Literature, Milwaukee Writers Club.; [oth. writ.] Publishers/ Associate Editor of Christian Light, Reaching Out, Words From Within, Numerous Articles, Essays, Poems and Short Stories Pub.; [pers.] I am committed to making a worldwide contribution in literature one poem and one person at a time. As a youth I was influenced by the great classics, they are responsible for the accomplishments I enjoy today - Thanks, Dad!; [a.] Milwaukee, WI

DOWNS, MABEL
[b.] July 8, 1934, Freedom, PA; [p.] Louis and Mabel Kossler; [m.] John Downs, June 22, 1975; [ch.] Four; [ed.] 10 1/2 yrs. plus a G.E.D.; [occ.] Retired; [oth. writ.] Poem - title Thirteen and Halloween.; [pers.] I have copy rites for the drinking man and Thirteen and Halloween the fare also converted into country gospel songs.; [a.] Harrisburg, PA

DOWNS, MARTHA B.
[pen.] Martha B. Downs; [b.] November 18, 1910, Georgia; [p.] Wm. Eli and Victoria Bradswell; [m.] John V. Downs (Deceased) 1988, February 19, 1939; [ch.] One daughter; [ed.] Kaigler's Business College Macon, Ga - Bachelor in Univ. Studies 1976 Univ. of N.M. Albuquerque, NM; [occ.] Homemaker Former Nuclear Physics Microscopist at Natl. Lab in Los Alamos, NM; [memb.] AAUW, Church Women United, AARP, United Methodist, Southern Poverty Center Montgomery, Ald, Nat'l Wildlife to others; [hon.] Valiant Woman's Award Church Women United, Outstanding Citizen Award by St. of N.M. recommended by town of Los Alamos, N.M.; [oth. writ.] 130 poems (some published) Autobiography "Lest I forget", Biography of my brother, History (35 years) of Church Women United in Los Alamos NM, papers on (1) World Hunger, (2) Enthanasia; [pers.] Life is not easy. It is not meant to be in-used muscles atrophy. We grow and expand by using hard - knocks to widen our horizon. The maker of Heaven and Earth wants only good things for us.; [a.] Lindenhurst, NY

DOWNS, ROBERT A.
[b.] August 2, 1943, Trenton, NJ; [m.] Patricia, January 17, 1963; [ch.] Three; [occ.] Comic/Dramatic Actor; [memb.] AFTRA; [oth. writ.] "This Love For You It's Always True", "Civil War Tribute", Children's story "The Little Girl Who Never Had Christmas"; [pers.] Thank You God for always being with me especially those times I have not been with You; [a.] Trenton, NJ

DOWRICK, BRIDGET
[pen.] Bridget O'Dubrick; [b.] January 25, 1974, Media, PA; [p.] John and Julie Dowrick; [ed.] Graduating December '96 from Neumann College in Aston P.A. and going to graduate School soon after.; [occ.] Home Quest, tracking down troubled youths who live at home, in Norristown P.A.; [pers.] There will be another me so I'll make the best of myself.; [a.] Springfield, PA

DRAHOZAL, OLGA M.
[pen.] Sindelar; [b.] June 26, 1927, Cedar Rapids, IA; [m.] Wesley J. Drahozal; [ch.] Ruth, Wesley M, Walt, Art, Denise, Becky, Pete; [ed.] St. Wenceslaus High School, Mount Mercy College; [occ.] Teacher; [memb.] Czech heritage Foundation, Czech School for Children, Sokol, Czech Heritage Singers, Czech Plus Band, Federation of Gech Groups, National Czech and Slovak Museum and Library.; [pers.] A deep and abiding faith and trust in God is an inheritance from our parents and grandparents which we value highly. This gift, we pray, will someday be accepted and held lovingly by our children and grandchildren.

DRIGGS, ANA R.
[b.] April 4, 1964, Miami, FL; [p.] Guillermo Driggs, Ana Driggs; [ed.] Our Lady Of Lourdes Academy High School, BS and M from Florida International University; [occ.] Teacher at Sweetwater Elem, Miami, FL; [memb.] Zoological Society of Florida, The Nature Conservancy, Habitat for Humanity; [hon.] Award for Outstanding Academic Achievement from FIU, 1997 Finalist Dade Country Teacher of the year; [a.] Miami, FL

DRYDEN, VERA L.
[b.] November 24, 1934, Dayton, OH; [p.] Twyla and Charles Kerns; [m.] Aldren D. Dryden, October 24, 1960; [ch.] John and Amy grandchild (Mike); [ed.] Farmesville High School, Ohio State University (1 qtr), Miami-Jacobs Business College, Miami University Extension (Night Classes); [occ.] Co-owner of Tennessee Control Systems; [pers.] My belief is the same as my grandmother's "Everything works out for the best". Also "our past is the springboard to our future".; [a.] Smyrna, TN

DUBOSE, GRETCHIN
[pen.] Michaelle Brannon; [b.] January 25, 1980, Orlando, FL; [p.] Jhan Brannon, Stephen DuBose; [ed.] DuBose Day School; [occ.] Waitress; [memb.] Michael Jackson International Fan Club and The Free Willy/Keiko Foundation.; [oth. writ.] Two poems printed in books and several other poems and songs.; [pers.] Never give up your dreams. If you want something, go after it. Peace.; [a.] Lake Lure, NC

DUFF, COLLEEN
[b.] February 11, 1956, Bell Island, Newfoundland, Canada; [p.] Louis and Bernice Costello; [m.] James Duff, June 24, 1978; [ch.] Angela 16, James Jr. 14; [ed.] Bathurst High School, Bathurst NB, Memorial University of Newfoundland; [occ.] Home Maker, Quilter, Craftsperson, Seamstress; [memb.] Oromocto Quilter's Guild; [oth. writ.] Currently working or two books that I hope to publish; [pers.] I write from the heart. It is how a subject affects me that cause the end result. Justice for all concerned is truly what I strive for in my writing - even for myself and my family.; [a.] Oromocto New Brunswick, Canada

DUGAL, JILL
[pen.] Jill Dugal; [b.] January 15, 1952, Ottawa, Ontario, Canada; [p.] James Rivers, Marion Kenney; [ed.] Champlain High; [occ.] Secretary and Corresponding Secretary; [memb.] National Italian American Sports Hall of Fame Chicago Land South - Women's Division; [hon.] Member of the year for N.I.A.S.H.F.- Women's Division; [pers.] I strive to bring encouragement and a closer relationship with God to all who read these writings. I have been greatly influenced by reading the Bible. Also writings from Helen Steiner Rice.

DUHON, LANCE E.
[b.] March 6, 1979, Lake Charles, LA; [p.] Vaughn and Elizabeth Duhon; [ed.] Sophomore in High School; [occ.] Student; [memb.] Three yrs. in Speech and Drama Class. Two years in Spring Production. On Varsity Football Team; [oth. writ.] First poem written. Wrote it for English to honor my grandfather; [a.] Sulphur, LA

DUNN, GLENDA FAWN BANGS
[b.] November 8, 1951, Norfolk, VA; [p.] Lester Meredith Bangs, Jr. and Shirley Rose Corbett Bangs; [m.] Calvin Humphries Dunn, September 30, 1978; [ed.] Indian River High, Longwood College, Old Dominion University; [occ.] Librarian, Mount Zion Elementary School, Suffolk, Virginia; [memb.] Eastminster Presbyterian Church (P.C.A.); [hon.] National Honor Society, Keyettes, graduated cum laude from Old Dominion University; [pers.] I am forever grateful to the Lord, my Shepherd, who lovingly cares for each sparrow that falls, unceasingly blesses through His caring concern for the intricacies of our lives, and reveals His artistic handiwork through Nature's touching tapestry of creative colors and detailed designs.; [a.] Chesapeake, VA

DUNNE, KATHLEEN M.
[pen.] Caitlin Duffy; [b.] December 1, 1972, Boston, MA; [p.] Charles Dunne, Nancy Dunne; [ed.] Waltham Senior high school, Purchase College (State University of New York); [occ.] Hardware Administrator, Parametric Technology Corporation; [hon.] Dean's List, Kingsbury Temperance Poster contest 2nd place, Kingsbury Temperance Scholarship recipient, Certificate of Achievement for Distinguished Recognition in Feminist, Studies in Arts and Letters from Purchase College; [oth. writ.] Climbing The Ladder of Experience, A Comparative Study of Women in Contemporary Literature (Sr. Thesis), 2 poems published in a local literary magazine, 1 poem published in high school magazine, various poems and articles published in college literary magazine; [a.] Waltham, MA

DWIGHT, DAVIS
[b.] March 18, 1973, Jacksonville, FL; [p.] Earl and Shirley Davis; [m.] Tawana Davis, February 5, 1993; [ch.] Kayla Charisse, Dwight Jr.; [ed.] William M. Raines High; [occ.] Truck driver, Winn Dixie; [memb.] Faust Temple Church of God in Christ; [pers.] With Christ in my life as the chief corner stone, my goal is to bring more people into the knowledge of Jesus Christ. And to remember "Can God - God can, and he will!!!; [a.] Jacksonville, FL

DYE, RUSSELL R.
[b.] March 21, 1933, Indianapolis, IN; [p.] (Deceased), Rector and Dorothy Dye; [m.] Betty J. Dye, May 5, 1990; [ed.] One and half years, Indiana University, took up Acting 1 and Acting II; [occ.] Screenwriting—Pending "No Greater Love", Working on Second screenplay; [memb.] Rock Club-Springfield, Oregon—Moose—American Legion, Writer's Digest Book Club; [oth. writ.] More unpublished poems.; [pers.] There are some people out there that shouldn't get involved by getting accustomed in using other people so much in a wrong sense to benefit themselves financially, and etc., by taking advantage of people's weakspot to the point that the other person may become so blind to see what is actually happening, like for example, "coming in between a married couple from a prior friendship, relationship, and etc." One way for a villain or a hero to get a woman on your side is to tell her your troubles what another woman did to you!"; [a.] Eugene, OR

DYER, JOY
[b.] June 14, 1982, Brooklyn, NY; [p.] Leonard Dyer, Audrey Dyer; [ed.] Manhasset High School; [occ.] 8th grade student at Manhasset Middle School; [memb.] National Junior Honor Society, Student Government, Elim International Fellowship; [hon.] 1st place Nassau Writing Poetry Contest, High Honor Roll; [oth. writ.] Poems submitted to Merlyn's Pen Magazines Manhasset Press, and school newspaper, A Children's Book of Writings; [pers.] I attribute all my writing talent to the Lord Jesus Christ who has enabled my mind to be creative.; [a.] Great Neck, NY

DYER, THOMAS ROUILLARD
[b.] December 19, 1996, Swinefurt, Germany; [p.] Art and Lucy Dyer; [m.] Timothea Dyer, August 5, 1996; [ch.] Levi Streeter Dyer, RoiAnna Naomi Dyer, Arthur Cole Dyer; [ed.] 12 grade High School; [occ.] Batchmaker wax factory; [memb.] Member of the Dyer family that enough for me.; [hon.] Honored by being a member of the Dyer family; [oth. writ.] None but have several small Notations in the 1200 Book Library I have in Each Book I've read all books of actually happenings no fiction; [pers.] Life is like the wind you, can't see it coming and it can change directions on you in the spur of the moment.; [a.] Columbus, GA

DYMOND, LEONARD
[pen.] Uncle Binchie; [b.] March 29, 1936, London, England; [p.] Richard, Minne Dymond; [m.] Mary, June 30, 1973; [ch.] Son Patrick - daughter Michelle; [ed.] Brecknock Sec. Mod. School London, England; [occ.] Retired (ex trucker); [hon.] 1 Million Mile Award - 4 awards from Nat. Small Bore Rifle Ass.; [oth. writ.] Poem "Where" published in "Sparkle in the Sand"; [pers.] Poem "Missing You" in memory of the woman teacher who started me in poetry with the poem "I Must Go Down To The Sea Again".; [a.] Windsor Ontario, Canada

EAST, KATE
[b.] January 23, 1976, Kalamazoo, MI; [p.] Walt and Marilyn East; [ed.] Gull Lake High School, Kalamazoo Valley Community College, Michigan State University; [occ.] Student majoring in Broadcast Journalism; [hon.] Poetry Finalist of America's Best, 1994 competition, Attended Summa Institute for the Arts; [oth. writ.] Several articles in College Paper and Kalamazoo Gazette; [a.] Richard, MI

ECCLES, RICHARD E.
[b.] November 5, 1948, San Diego, CA; [p.] Ruth and Edward Eccles Jr.; [m.] Katherine M. Eccles, August 10, 1970; [ch.] Wendy and Chris; [ed.] Emporia HS AA University of Maryland 2 yrs at Austin Peay St. Univ.; [occ.] Retired Military Jrotc Teacher: Muhlenberg North HS Greenville, KY; [hon.] Deans List MD. Univ, Dcans List Apsu, Summa Cum Laude; [pers.] Retired from the U.S. Army February 1, 1992 as a Command Sergeant Major; [a.] Clarksville, TN

ECKBERG, DAVID S.
[pen.] David S. Eckberg; [b.] November 4, 1975, Soringfield, IL; [p.] Penny Eckberg; [ed.] Currently an undergrad At DePaul University Major: Communications; [occ.] Life Guard; [memb.] U.S.L.A. (United States Lifesaving Association); [hon.] Deans List; [oth. writ.] Many other poems I wrote while in highschool, most of which got lost during a move, yet, a few remain in my memory.; [pers.] I enjoy helping and engage in community service often. I live through the faith of God to achieve my best in all areas of life.; [a.] Chicago, IL

EDDY, MS. RUTH CAMPBELL
[pen.] Ruth Campbell Eddy; [b.] January 16, 1936, West Virginia; [p.] Chester and Mary Campbell; [ch.] Ash, Aaron, Jessica, Amy; [occ.] Office Manager Washington Landmark, Inc., Marietta, Oh; [pers.] I write only for pleasure.; [a.] Marietta, OH

EHSAN, ZAREIAN
[pen.] E. Z.; [b.] August 6, 1959, Persia; [p.] Seyoaga and Khanom Zareian; [ed.] B.S. in Agricultural; [oth. writ.] Published a short story in International Persian Newspaper.; [pers.] Watching journey of the present. Watching it amused by what futures hold. Nothing but love.; [a.] New York, NY

EIRIKSSON, SIGURJON
[b.] November 1, 1948, Sherridon, Manitoba, Canada; [p.] Kris and Helen Eiriksson; [m.] Janet Eiriksson, July 9, 1988; [ch.] Victor Eiriksson; [ed.] B.S. Brandon University, Teaching Certification, University of Manitoba, Power Engineering Class IV Calgary, Alberta; [occ.] Teaching Assistant and Log Home Builder; [oth. writ.] Writing poetry in various meter forms and verse since 1964. First poem "Rhyme Of The Ancient Mariner." Poem about the mariner IV spacecraft to Mars. Over 100 poems written to date.; [pers.] Real life situations, moral and ethical values, life struggles and conflicts. Recent writings centre on Christian values and my faith in Jesus as Lord and Saviour.; [a.] Brandon Manitoba, Canada

EKHOLM, RUTH
[pen.] Ruth Ekholm; [b.] August 25, 1918, Lake City, MN; [p.] Ellen and Paul Bryngelson; [m.] Wilford Ekholm, September 12, 1942; [ch.] Carolyn, John, Paul and Lori; [ed.] High School, Business Course, Art Classes, Bible Courses; [occ.] Housewife, (Retired); [memb.] 1st Covenant Church, Elim Covenant Church and Bethany Covenant Church - all in Minneapolis; [hon.] I was one of the 4 girls chosen as artists to draw a N. York model at the Minneapolis Auditorium on the 100th Anniversary of Minneapolis; [oth. writ.] I was secretary for Y.P. at 1st Cov. Church and in charge of the WWII service men's paper. I also wrote for Elim's Paper WWII and Bethany's newspaper; [pers.] I had deep spiritual roots from my grandparents and parents. My Grandpa Bryngelson was a pioneer preacher from the Mission Church in Sweden. He established churches in Miss. and Mn.; [a.] Minneapolis, MN

ELLIOT, CLARENCE
[b.] September 8, 1921, Saint Joseph Island, Ontario, Canada; [p.] Nelson and Laura Elliot; [m.] Isla Lawrence, May 13, 1955; [ch.] Accepted by four children, who were joined by a later arrival; [ed.] Secondary; [occ.] Enjoying retirement; [oth. writ.] Several other poems dealing with issue that affect us - numerous poems of anniversaries and retirements.; [pers.] Enjoy life and feel an interest in my fellow man.; [a.] Sault Ste Marie, Ontario

ELLIS, JOAN V.
[m.] William S. Akard; [ed.] B.A., W.A., UT Knoxville, TN, M.A., Chicago Theological Seminary; [occ.] Instructor in Speech Communication Dept., UT Knoxville, TN; [pers.] I write about a human's relationship with God - a struggle of ecstasy and pain.; [a.] Knoxville, TN

ELLIS, ROBERT
[b.] May 11, 1965, Cardiff, Wales, United Kingdom; [p.] Mr. Robert Alan Ellis, Mrs. Mary Ellis; [ed.] University of Nottingham, England, (also University of Wyoming, Laramie); [occ.] Student of American Studies (Nottingham Uni.) B.A.; [hon.] Dean's List University of Wyoming.; [oth. writ.] Poetry - short unpublished book of poetry - "Retrospective" and a book of short stories entitled "the Kinoath" Illustrations by Ms. Susannah Bulpin. (Unpublished); [pers.] I hope at some point I will be able to reflect just a little of the passion I have for my beloved wales (CYMRU) and my blood link with the peoples of the passamaquoddy.; [a.] Cardiff South Wales, United Kingdom

ELSTON, JOSEPH GORDON
[b.] January 16, 1925, Lincoln Co, Stanford, KY; [p.] Charles Benton Elston, Josephine Carpenter Elston; [m.] Christine Robson Elston, March 2, 1956; [ch.] Joseph Gordon Elston Jr.; [ed.] University of Kentucky 1947, Memphis Academy of Arts 1948-52, Art Institute of Chicago Summer 1948; [occ.] Pink Palace Museum Preparator 1957-1991; [hon.] 1987 Good Conduct Metal 30 years Service, City of Memphis; [oth. writ.] Poem: "Love Birds", University of Kentucky, 1947; [a.] Memphis, TN

ENEMUOH, DONALD CHUDI
[b.] March 8, 1971, Nigeria; [p.] Peter and Tina Enemuoh; [ed.] College Senior University of Wisconsin - Madison; [oth. writ.] Lyrics written and performed with the help of music.; [pers.] Too many times we often ignore the struggles of the less fortunate. We are all filled with greed and selfishness, but it differs among individuals. It is time for a universal agreement to end all sufferings of man, for we are the cause of our own pain.; [a.] Madison, WI

ENGLISH, REBECCA
[p.] Becky; [b.] March 15, 1950, Newfoundland; [p.] John and Rebecca English; [s.] Reginald Smeltzer (Deceased); [m.] October 12, 1968; [ch.] Reginald, Jr., Christopher; [ed.] Grade 10, Accounting; [occ.] Stay at home Mom; [oth. writ.] Working on other poems and hope to have them published. [pers.] I wish to express in my writing, love and pain which is what all people feel, throughout our lives, understanding for others. [a.] St. Hubert, Quebec

EOFF, JOANNE VIEVA
[b.] Denver, CO; [p.] Carl and Vieva Kjeldgaard, Big Springs, Nebraska; [m.] Gene Eoff; [ch.] Michelle, Carl, Larry and Brian; [ed.] St. Olaf College—two years U. of Wisc. —one summer U. of Nebr.—grad. B. of A in English Literature; [occ.] Vice President of small Corporation; [memb.] Kappa Delta Sorority, Good Shepherd Lutheran Church; [hon.] Regents Scholarship U. of N. qualified as under-grad for Phi Beta Kappa, ROTC Queen, Calendar Girl; [a.] Goleta, CA

EPLER, WILLIAM E.
[b.] April 15, 1920, Parkersburg, WV; [m.] Juanita Rockhold Epler, February 12, 1940; [ch.] Rosalie, Paul, David, Richard; [ed.] B.S. (Sociology) Weber State U. Ogden Utah 1970, Graduate Studies Harding University, Graduate School of Religion, W.V.U. Graduate School of Social Word; [occ.] Minister, the Church of Christ; [memb.] XAP, 0K0 Rotary, American Legion; [hon.] Neville Award for Scholarship, Cum Laude; [oth. writ.] Religious Journals, Essays; [pers.] If I win a prize, call and I will type for publication and forward the fee.

ERB, MARY EUNICE
[b.] November 11, 1956, Buffalo, NY; [p.] Francis J. Engler, Evelyn E. Engler; [m.] David L. Erb, July 6, 1991; [ed.] Kenmore East Sen. High School; [occ.] Champion Products; [oth. writ.] I have six poems already published. Five of which in books edited by Eddie-Lou Cole. Such as Today's best poems, Great poems of The Western World to name a couple. One poem in reflections on a rainbow by P&L productions. (Poetry of Hawaii); [pers.] My inspiration to write began in the lovely state of Hawaii. The poems "Destiny, Illumination, The Answer Lies, There's Always Tomorrow, God, Hawaii Sounds" were all written there. God's beauty can only bring out the heart's joy.; [a.] Castile, NY

ERDLEY, TAMARA
[pen.] Jessica Reynolds; [b.] October 20, 1970, Buffalo, NY; [p.] Howard Erdley, Bonnie Erdley; [ed.] East Aurora High School Plattsburgh State University; [memb.] Sigma Tau Epsilon honor society; [hon.] Listed in 1990 edition of "The National Dean's List"; [oth. writ.] Feature Editor of "The Tor Echo"; [a.] East Aurora, NY

ERHABOR, OLAYEMI ABDU
[pen.] Olayemipan; [b.] March 17, 1938, Nigeria; [p.] Deceased; [m.] Deceased, March 17, 1962; [ch.] Five boys, one girl; [ed.] General Certificate of Education, Diploma London School of Journalism and television; [memb.] Nigerian Labour Congress, Nigerian Union of Journalists, WFTU (World Federation of Trade Unions); [pers.] In the palace of your heart plant naught, but the rose of love, and from the nightingale of affection and desire loosen not your hold. Treasure the companionship of the righteous and eschew all fellowship with the ungodly.; [a.] Brooklyn, NY

ESSON, CHRISTINE
[b.] September 21, 1966; [m.] Michael, September 21, 1985; [ch.] Maddie, Adam; [pers.] My pen is the window into my heart.

ESTRELA, STEPHANIE
[pen.] Steph Estrela; [b.] December 19, 1981, Oakville; [p.] Delta and Joe Estrela; [ed.] Grade 9; [occ.] Student at Don Bosco School; [oth. writ.] I enjoy writing short stories and jokes and songs.; [pers.] Writing let's me express myself. It also helps me find solutions to my problems.; [a.] Etobicoke Ontario, Canada

EVANS, BETTY
[pen.] Betty Evans; [b.] March 14, 1925, Cols, OH; [p.] Glenn and Garnet Mosier; [m.] Edward Evans, December 23, 1944; [ch.] Susan J. Havice and Edward Evans II; [ed.] Central High School 12th Grade; [occ.] Retired; [oth. writ.] Outside of writing poems for my family, this is my first attempt at publication.; [pers.] I like to be creative and maybe at the same time, leave a legacy for my children and grandchildren.; [a.] Cols, OH

EVANS, GERALDINE BURGESS
[pen.] Jan Evans; [b.] April 8, 1945, Atlanta, GA; [p.] Deceased; [m.] Dr. Art Evans, December 17, 1993; [ch.] Cluis, Steve, Amy; [ed.] BA, English Literature, State University of New York; [occ.] High School English Teacher; [memb.] NEA, AARP, Georgia Assn. of Educators; [hon.] President's List, Dean's List, Cum Laude; [oth. writ.] Numerous unpublished.; [pers.] The art of the Italian Renaissance and the pre-Rupees, along with the literature of the Romantics have greatly influenced my thinking and writing style. I share to express my new of life through poetry.; [a.] Jasper, GA

EVANS, KIMBERLY R.
[b.] March 6, 1968, Houston, TX; [p.] Tommy L. Evans and Barbara A. Turner; [ed.] John Foster Dulles High School, University of the Incarnate Word (formerly Incarnate Word College); [occ.] Program Specialist, Metropolitan Orlando Urban League, Orlando, Florida; [memb.] St. Mark A.M.E. Church Music Ministry, Deaf Ministry, Alpha Kappa Alpha Sorority Inc.; [hon.] Dean's List; [pers.] I challenge all to let the vision of your dreams lead to your success and dare you to confront what you have only imagined.; [a.] Orlando, FL

EVANS, L.
[pen.] L. Evans; [p.] Welsh; [ed.] College; [memb.] St. John Ambulance private; [hon.] Serving Officer in St. John Ambulance; [oth. writ.] Short Stories, Crystal Wedding Glosses, Poems Circle Of Life, The Urn, Man On The Stairs, Stronger The Rocking Choice, Little Brown Church; [a.] Edmonton Alberta, Canada

EVANS, POET LE
[pen.] Poet Le; [b.] September 8, 1981, Waco, TX; [p.] E. J. and Bobbye Evans; [ed.] Midway High School; [pers.] I write from the heart.; [a.] Waco, TX

EVANSEW, THOMAS J.
[b.] May 10, 1946, Scranton, PA; [ed.] University of Scranton B.S. Secondary Education Marywood Education College M.S. Special Education.; [occ.] Special Education Teacher of Educable Mentally Retarded; [oth. writ.] "Silent Veterans" a book of poetry dealing with my experiences in Vietnam; [pers.] "We must learn that war is not the answer."; [a.] West Pittston, PA

EWERTH, RONALD E.
[pen.] Ren; [b.] December 9, 1937, Lincoln, NE; [p.] Agnes and Earl Ewerth; [m.] Jewell A. Ewerth, March 1, 1958; [ch.] Scott and Ron Ewerth; [ed.] High School; [occ.] Sign Maker; [oth. writ.] Various poems and short stories, children's stories. Biographical work about experiences in my life. Many published in Trade Magazines and Local Newsletters etc.; [pers.] I believe the things we do (the important as well as not so important) should be written down so that those that follow can get a grasp of who they are and where they came from.

EZRA, RAYMOND
[b.] January 3, 1963, London; [ed.] Diploma (Urban Community Studies) Birbeck College, University of London.; [occ.] Creative painter; [oth. writ.] Poems published in local newspaper.; [pers.] A painting may also reflect poetry. I included this concept when I developed a new style by the name of animationism since 1996.; [a.] Medinaceli Soria, Spain

FABIEN, CHANOZ
[b.] July 19, 1988, Cannes, France; [p.] Jacques and Suzy; [ed.] To the Third French Grade; [occ.] Helping the "Amigos Pe cos ninos" Society in Honduras; [oth. writ.] Clameur Fertile new poems.; [pers.] God is love, let's all look for Him, and we will find Him.; [a.] Nuevo Paraiso Paraiso, Honduras

FANNING, DAVID MYRON
[b.] September 6, 1980, Naval Hospital, Portsmouth, VA; [p.] Charles Edward Fanning Sr. and Delores Joyce Fanning; [ed.] Western Branch Elementary, Middle Schools and is currently attending Western Branch Senior High School, Chesapeake, Virginia; [occ.] Student in the Ninth Grade Western Branch Sr High School; [memb.] Member of the Western Branch High School Varsity Basketball Team, Member of the National AAU Boys Basketball from Chesapeake, Virginia playing under the BOO Williams AAU Summer League. Member of the Children Bowling league in the Western Branch Section of Chesapeake Virginia; [hon.] Has won man awards for playing Basketball, Basketball where I have been playing since age of six. On the Honor Roll at Western Branch High School.

FARDINK, MARC JARRETT
[b.] December 5, 1981, South Weymouth, MA; [p.] Roger and Sherry Fardink; [ed.] In last year of Jr. High; [occ.] Student in Jr. High; [hon.] Several in compositions and art work; [oth. writ.] Daggar of Dealth, Composition Award: Fair Housing Essay Contest: Composition Award; [pers.] If you don't try, you cannot get anywhere.; [a.] West Palm Beach, FL

FARRELL, JOHN J.
[b.] July 8, 1923, Astoria, NY; [p.] John Farrell, Edith Farrell; [m.] Beatrice Christie Farrell, January 27, 1952; [ch.] John, Mariann, Steven, Robert; [ed.] Immaculate Conception (Elem) Long Island City High, New York University; [occ.] Ret. Elem. Tchr. P.S. 166 and 136 Queens N.Y.C, Health Educ. Tchr. Thomas; [memb.] Various Teacher Organizations; [hon.] Recommended Rho Chapter of Phi Delta Kappa N.Y.U.; [oth. writ.] Several published sports features for "The Las Vegas Sun." Local newspaper, numerous poems.; [pers.] In these pomes I try to focus on the memories (things we all remember either sadly or fondly) of events and experiences of people we love with emphasis of those shared by the extended family.; [a.] Las Vegas, NY

FARRELL, MEGHAN
[pen.] Meg; [b.] October 15, 1985, Manhasset; [p.] Josephine and John Farrell; [ed.] Is currently in the fifth grade 95/96; [memb.] Distinguished Member of International Society of Poets; [hon.] Editors choice award, ISP; [oth. writ.] Sadness, Untitled, Across The Moon, Open Your Eyes And See, The Clouds, Patricia's Poem, Horses.; [pers.] I would

like to thank my fourth grade teacher, Miss. Goldman and my third grade teacher, Mrs. Wolitz for introducing me to writing and I would like to thank my parents for their undying support.; [a.] Baldwin, NY

FARRELL, TIMOTHY P.
[b.] November 22, 1956, Milwaukee; [p.] Norm and Marilyn Farrell; [ch.] Amanda Farrell, 5 years old; [ed.] Achieved G.E.D. on February 29, 1996, Currently Working on HSED, Certified Welder and Machinist; [occ.] Machine Operator at Ripon Foods Inc. in Ripon, Wis; [hon.] Trophies in Pool Tournaments 2nd and 3rd place; [oth. writ.] "The will to win", "Friendship", "My Friend", Remember Your Dreams", some poems for some friends wedding. A poem for my dad on Fathers Day called, "I really appreciate you dad."; [pers.] 1.) Never give up no matter how tough life gets. 2.) You get the best out of others, when you give the best of yourself. 3.) Try to get the most out of life. 4.) Face your fears and you like your dreams. 5.) Be patient your dream may take time; [a.] Green Lake, WI

FATH, TAMMY
[b.] September 20, 1966, Saginaw, MI; [p.] Richard and Delores Kohagen; [m.] (Divorced) Donald Fath Jr.; [ch.] Amanda 7, Donald 2; [ed.] New Lothrop High School Delta College Nanny Program; [occ.] Nanny; [oth. writ.] Poems Written for family and friends in process of writing my first children's book; [pers.] My poems are mt feelings and my heart on paper. They usually reflect something going on in my life. This poem is in loving memory of my younger brother Chris.; [a.] Chesaning, MI

FAUBLE, TINA L.
[b.] August 17, 1962, Cheyenne, WY; [p.] Albert Solomon and Darline Eikum; [m.] Richard D. Fauble Jr., August 20, 1988; [ch.] Brandon age 11 and Britanny age 5; [ed.] Hot Spring County High, Bay Area Legal Academy; [occ.] Bed and Breakfast Owner/Innkeeper "The McFarlin House Bed and Breakfast in Quincy FL, and full-time Legal Secretary; [oth. writ.] Published in local newspaper.; [pers.] I hold a great admiration for simple life and simple poetry.; [a.] Quincy, FL

FAZEKAS, ERIKA
[b.] January 16, 1954, Hungary; [p.] Olga Smid, Sandor Alex Gergely; [m.] 1977; [ch.] Elizabeth, Andrew, Victor; [a.] Toronto Ontario, Canada

FEHR, ERIKA
[b.] May 6, 1975, Saint Paul, Minnesota; [p.] RoxAnne Fehr, Jon Fehr; [ch.] Phantom my dog, Moby the chameleon, Abbey the cockatiel and Cristobal and Cabot the Solomons Island Skinks; [ed.] Coronado High School; [occ.] Artist; [memb.] Arizona Society for the Prevention of Cruelty to Animals (ASPCA); [hon.] Rotary Scholarship; [pers.] To be loved in all the wrong ways is not to be loved. It is to be jailed - never knowing when you'll be pardoned. To those of you who have loved me in all the right ways - look what love can do! To those of you yet to learn - trust in love, don't deny love.; [a.] Fountain Hills, AZ

FEHR, MATTHEW
[b.] May 20, 1982, Steinbach, Manitoba, Canada;

[p.] Peter and Viola (Wiens) Fehr; [ed.] Art Instruction Schools, Mitchell Jr. High School; [memb.] Art Instruction Schools; [hon.] In grade 7, I was on the honor roll 3 out of 4 times; [oth. writ.] Working on novel, hope to publish.; [pers.] I believe that any art, whether through writing or drawing or whatever, is the best way to express your feelings to others and to yourself.; [a.] Steinbach Manitoba, Canada

FENNESSY, LEON RAY
[b.] July 21, 1943, Charleston, SC; [p.] Leon E. and Olive R. Fennessy; [ch.] Heather Elizabeth, Gerald Stuart; [ed.] Milby H.S., University of Texas and University of Houston; [occ.] Tax Accountant; [memb.] National Order of Garlic Ireland; [hon.] Creative writing Achievement - University of Texas; [oth. writ.] Published Essayist, short stories - "The Frog Who Had No Legs", "Billy Butterfly", "Golden Flakes", Novels - "The Messiah Code," "Shadows Before Dawn".; [pers.] Write from your heart, with emotion, otherwise you contribute nothing worth reflecting on related to life experiences.; [a.] Houston, TX

FERCHLAND, MRS. CATHERINE
[b.] November 1, 1964, Sydney, Australia; [p.] Mrs. Anne Hunt; [m.] Mr. Marcus Ferchland, June 17, 1994; [ed.] Busby High School - Sydney, Sychey Technical College; [occ.] House wife and author; [memb.] Red cross. The Volunteer Connection; [hon.] 1995 Editor's Choice Award (The National Library of Poetry), Volunteering Today Community Services, Welfare Awards.; [oth. writ.] A poem in (Walk Through Paradise). Two books one "End of the Path" on all of my poetry. A short story book named "Wing's of love" both books are unpublished.; [pers.] The love and support I have from my husband Marcus, is all the inspiration and influenced I need to have for my writing and the confidence come's all from my husband Marcus.; [a.] Soest, Germany

FERGUSON, L. JACKIE
[b.] February 5, 1946, Michigan; [p.] Roy and Rosa Renegar; [s.] R.T. Ferguson; [ch.] Wendy, Rick and Steve; [ed.] San Jacint High School, Houston, TX.; [occ.] Choreographer/writer; [memb.] M.S. Society, Seek and Rescue (self start support group for victims of various types of abuse), Baptist Church; [hon.] Dance congenial, sales, TV, radio and Media Coverage. [oth. writ.] Articles and poems in various papers.; [pers.] Through trials we witness,m build and character and strength. [a.] Houston, TX

FERNANDEZ, JOHN
[b.] March 22, 1960, Woodland, CA; [p.] Sam and Gloria Fernandez; [ch.] Corrine Nicole Fernandez; [ed.] High School Graduate 1978, 2 yrs College; [occ.] Warehouse Supervisor (Abertsons Distribution); [pers.] I believe you can do anything you want to do. If you really want to. Believe in yourself, work hard, and go for it. (The world does not meet you halfway.); [a.] Woodland, CA

FESSLER, MARTHA E.
[b.] September 24, 1917, Indiana, USA; [p.] John and Ina Cubert; [m.] Quincy C. Fessler, June 1, 1941; [ch.] 4, 11 grands and 1 greatgrand; [ed.] Nurse graduate - Registered California 1942 - Refresher Course San Antonio, TX - 1978 - Lutheran Hospital; [occ.]

Retired Missionary Nurse (30 yrs. Mexico and Asia and Europe); [memb.] Oakland Evangelistic Association and Alumni - Wishard Memorial Hosp. Nursing Alumni Assoc.; [hon.] President of my Nursing Class 1938-1941; [oth. writ.] None other published but I have a large file of devotions, poems one line thoughts and have started writing of God's working in our lives while in Mexico as missionaries.; [pers.] All the people in this world should know salvation thru Jesus Christ. My desire is to help those in need regardless of age, color or creed, and to let them see the beauty of Jesus in me.; [a.] San Antonio, TX

FESTOFF, LUZ E.
[b.] May 24, 1966, Arecibo, PR; [p.] Enrique Lopez, Monserrata Jimenez; [m.] Robert J. Festoff, April 7, 1990; [ch.] Mathew Festoff; [ed.] Lorenzo Coballes Grandia High, Interamerican University; [hon.] Magna Cum Laude; [pers.] Life is a poem itself. I have been inspired and supported by my loved ones.; [a.] Williamstown, NJ

FIEDLER, LORIE WAYNE
[b.] March 30, 1976, Liberty, TX; [p.] Carolyn Taylor and Larry Fiedler; [ed.] La Porte High School, Texas A and M University, Kingsville; [occ.] Residence Hall Desk Clerk; [memb.] National Honor Society, who's who of America High School students 2 yrs in a row.; [hon.] High School, most outstanding Junior in Science, Presidential Academic Fitness award, U.I.L. award, Cum Laude High School School graduate.; [oth. writ.] A poem published in my high school literary magazine. Won an essay contest about how Texas A and M University Kingsville can better celebrate Martin Luther King Day, 2nd place.; [pers.] Remember your dreams!; [a.] Baytown, TX

FIKE, TRISHA
[b.] February 6, 1962, Anchorage, Alaska; [p.] William Jewell Fike and Frances Thomas Fike; [ed.] BA Philosophy - University of Washington, Seattle, MA Philosophy - Stanford University, MA Humanities - Stanford University, MA Film and Television - University of Southern California; [occ.] Writer (articles, screenplays, nonfiction books; [memb.] American cinematheque, Phi Beta Kappa, Mensa, Sierra Club; [hon.] High School Valedictorian, Howard Prize Book Award, National Merit Scholarship, Andrew W. Mellon Fellowship, Daily Trojan Newspaper Best Staff Member Award; [oth. writ.] 85 entertainment articles published in the Daily Trojan Newspaper, San Diego Review and Venice Magazine. Various (so-far) unproduced screenplays. In progress: Nonfiction book Killers of the Cure: The Medical Monopoly's War Against Your Health; [pers.] I want to be a loving and healing force for all humanity and to help others to be the same. May we all feel our common identity and connection with all that is.; [a.] San Diego, CA

FINDLAY, LEAH B.
[pen.] Leah; [b.] June 14, 1943, Plumwood, OH; [p.] Gladys (Justus) and Albert C. Glass; [m.] Robert G. Findlay, July 19, 1986; [ch.] Andrea Lee, Haelan, Shannon, Sherry; [ed.] Jonathan Alder High School (1961), (Plain City Ohio), Ohio School of Career Technology (Columbus, Ohio); [hon.] High School - Senior Scholarship, Quill and Scroll, Noma Spelling Award; [pers.] If everyone would practice

the old-fashioned morals our country grew up with, we would all be blessed with a safer, healthier, and happier environment.; [a.] London, OH

FINK, SANDY
[b.] August 9, 1935, Chicago, IL; [p.] Jeanette Walker Deike and Harry Walker; [m.] John Fink, October 15, 1987; [ch.] Perry Hornkohl; [ed.] Major in Philosophy and English, Minor Psychology; [occ.] Retired; [memb.] Distiguished Member (Life Member) Internaional Society of Poets Life Time Membership in Florida Freelance Writer's Association, Annual Membership in the South Florida Poetry Institute and the Rockford Writer's Guild; [hon.] Numerous Competitive Poetry Awards including first, second, third and honorable mention in Oregon, Florida and other States; [oth. writ.] I've written and been published in newspapers, magazines, newsletters, brochures and television (T.V. commercials). Key Images, a book of poetry (with illustrations and in my calligraphy) was released by Distinctive Publications January, 1992; [pers.] I'm at my best in distillations of any kind, especially when I can apply humorous twists to material. I enjoy paradox caught within a person's life, and the individual way it plays out. I'm hooked on the written word and go through life trying to make as much of it mine as possible.; [a.] Chiefland, FL

FINLEY, KATHRYN J.
[b.] July 27, 1950, Rockford, IL; [p.] Robert Finley and Shirley Finley; [ed.] Northern Illinois University - 2 yrs also attended Rockford Memorial Hospital School of Nursing; [occ.] Medical Transcriptionist; [memb.] National Right to life Organization; [pers.] To be reconciled to God through the saving grace of Jesus Christ transcends all other experience after which we have a heart to love God and live with our fellow man in true peace and harmony. We were designed for such a relationship of love - as such, without it thee is no happiness.; [a.] Rockton, IL

FINNERTY, BEVERLY
[b.] May 5, 1939, Waterloo, NY; [p.] Ellsworth and Jennie Jones; [m.] Richard, September 27, 1958; [ch.] Two - Jacqueline and Edward; [ed.] M.A. Western Michigan University; [occ.] Student M.A. English - Xavier University, Cincinnati; [hon.] High School Citizenship Academic Scholarship to W.M.U. (Partial); [oth. writ.] None published with exception of freelance human interest and local news stories.; [pers.] Everyone has a voice. It is in hearing it that we can appreciate the value of our fellow humans, prose, poetry (spoken nor written) music, painting or sculpture each one unique therefore valuable.; [a.] Cincinnati, OH

FISHER, SHIRLEY M.
[b.] October 16, 1931, Hamilton, Ontario, Canada; [p.] Marquis Fisher, Cindy Fisher; [ch.] Linda, Bill, Debbie, Cindy, Laura; [ed.] Westdale High; [oth. writ.] One of my poem are "A Baby is Born" has been published by the National Library of Poetry in the book, "Beneath the Harvest Moon" also it is on a cassette called "The Sound of Poetry" also by the Society; [pers.] I always loved to read poetry, however I never wrote anything until I started to go to unity and study metaphysics, which was about fifteen years ago. When I sit in the quiet

go within me, the poems come through.; [a.] Hamilton Ontario, Canada

FISKE, THOMAS W.
[pen.] Elliot Rosewater; [b.] May 23, 1954, Santa Fe, NM; [m.] Mary Catherine Wenstrom Fiske; [ch.] Tobias and Simon-Dean; [ed.] B.A. Elem Educ. (Minors in History and English) Some post grad work. Edu. Adm.; [occ.] Farmer/Farrier; [memb.] AFA, PSIA, Nea St. James Episcopal Church.; [oth. writ.] A day at plains, the unofficial Autobiography of Elliot Rosewater.; [pers.] "You can be in my dream if I can be in your's" Bob Dylan said that.

FITZGERALD, WILLIAM EDWARD
[b.] September 14, 1914, High Point, NC; [p.] Reid and Nell Speneer Fitzgerald; [m.] Evelyn Craven Fitzgerald (Deceased), July 1, 1919; [ch.] Linda F. Raims and Carol F. Lowery; [ed.] Children's Home Of Methodist Church, R.J. Reynolds High School, High Point College, Duke University; [occ.] Retired United Methodist Minister; [memb.] Shady Grove United Methodist Church Lions Club, Retired Member United Methodist Conference Methodist, Active member of Alumni Assoc. of the Children's Home Winston-Salem, NC; [oth. writ.] Poems; [pers.] "I will always be grateful to the United Methodist Church and for the Methodist Children's Home"; [a.] Winston-Salem, NC

FLETCHER, TAMMY M.
[b.] January 5, 1964, Wiliberty, KY; [p.] James and Ella Stacy; [m.] Steven A. Fletcher, December 17, 1983; [ch.] Michael, Justin, Derrick; [ed.] Middletown High School, Middletown, Ohio; [occ.] Asst. Manager for Local Restaurant; [memb.] Boy Scouts of America; [hon.] Several Awards for service as Den Leader in Scouts.; [oth. writ.] Other non published poems one I like "Lord Tell Me"; [pers.] I was greatly influenced by my high school Science teacher who make me believe in myself. I hope I can do the same thru my scouting endeavors.; [a.] Middletown, OH

FLORES, SUSANNA JOY
[pen.] Susanna J., Susanna Unger; [b.] December 2, 1977, Delano, CA; [p.] Greg Flores, JoAnn Unger; [ed.] Home schooled - American School; [memb.] The local "Writers' Club" in California City; [oth. writ.] Poems published in local newspapers, and in "Write to Fame" magazine.; [pers.] For me, writing is a spontaneous and powerful expression of self. "Shadows in the Sun" is dedicated to my brothers: Joseph, Joshua, and Jacob. May we always be together in spirit.; [a.] Tehachapi, CA

FLOTTORP, TOM
[pen.] Flip Rue; [b.] May 7, 1920, Bulyea, Saskatchewan, Canada; [p.] Lily and Robert Flottorp; [m.] Beryl Flottorp, December 20, 1945; [ch.] Three; [ed.] Grade VII (too much farm work after I was twelve years old, an diversified ten times) never fired. Farm WWU-Telephones - Furniture Railway - Inventor, lyrics, seamster, leather mitts draw.; [occ.] Retired (I love to innovate) to not be active someways, is the wrong way to go.; [hon.] Editor's Choice Award of this same company last year for "When I Was Just A Little Boy". I have a framed certificate to drove it. First time ever.; [oth. writ.] Poems - lyrics poems for

greeting cards not yet accepted. Lyrics for songs - have been asked to send three a month to Nashville now for two years. To keep sending.; [pers.] I enjoy doing this it helps me to keep my mind off my body because of disability problems - arthritis - muscle spasms - diseased lungs - blood pressure.; [a.] Regina Saskatchewan, Canada

FLOWERS, CHARLES R.
[p.] The "Angel"; [b.] July 2, 1933, New Orlens, LA; [p.] Frank E. Flowers and Montie Flowers; [ed.] 8th Grade; [occ.] Paint Contractor; [oth. writ.] Tracy, The Journey Home, "Images", Have I Touched Thee Oh! Sweet Mama, The Angels Song, Sometime Today All Of Tomorrow, Tell Me That You Love Me and countless others.; [pers.] Write not for fame or fortune! But! to touch lives that your life might not be a waste of "God's Time"! Make a difference in this world! And try and find humor in pain and suffering.; [a.] Slidell, LA

FLUKE, CHERYL
[pen.] Cei; [b.] November 3, 1969, Cherokee, IA; [p.] Lonnie and Pat Hanson; [m.] David, July 23, 1988; [ch.] Jessica, Dylan; [ed.] Buena Vista University; [occ.] Assistant Controller Sioux city Hilton Hotel, Sioux City, Iowa; [memb.] AICPA, ISCPA; [pers.] I write what I feel. My poetry is the expression of myself.; [a.] Washta, IA

FODEN, TRACY ANNE
[b.] July 11, 1963, Toronto, Canada; [p.] James Foden, Thelma Foden; [ch.] Tiffany Erin, Jennifer Lynn; [occ.] Desk top publishing; [oth. writ.] One of many poems in my collection. Second to be printed by National Library of Poetry.; [a.] Mississauga Ontario, Canada

FORBES, JEREMY LEE
[pen.] Smoke King; [b.] May 30, 1978, Warner Robins; [p.] Randal and Connie Forbes; [ed.] High School; [oth. writ.] 30 poems including a collection of poems that I have dedicated to my "Shining Star", Tarah Jane Moore.; [pers.] My poems are about experiences that me, and too many other people have been through, about the injustices of the world, and about how much love overcomes.; [a.] Centerville, GA

FORBES, LINDA L.
[b.] January 11, 1957; [p.] William and Marjorie Forbes; [ed.] Louis C. Obourn High, Monroe Community College; [occ.] Auto Technician; [memb.] V.F.W. Derinton Memorial Ladies Auxillary; [oth. writ.] Wrote many other poems which I use for greeting cards; [a.] East Rochester, NY

FORBES, YVONNE
[pen.] Barbara; [b.] July 12, 1962, Jamaica, West Indies; [p.] Leslie Burke and Elain Martin; [ch.] Andreen Therese, Phillip Dean and Zadeckie Lemoire; [ed.] Burnhamthorpe Coll, Medger Even College; [occ.] Program Instructor; [hon.] Certificate of Merit, Medger Even's College, New York; [oth. writ.] Several children's book, with two about to be published.; [pers.] I use writing as a healing therapy to connect me with my inner self.; [a.] Weston Ontario, Canada

FORD, ELSIE IRENE
[pen.] Elsie I. Ford; [b.] October 20, 1938,

Spartanburg Co Landrunt SC; [p.] Henry Thomas, Angeline S. Ward; [m.] William E. "Bill" Ford (Deceased), October 13, 1962; [ch.] Barbara "Kim" Ford, Kerry Ray Ford; [ed.] 12th High School diploma, Music lesson piano - 4 yrs. singing or voice 2 yrs; [occ.] Disabled retire; [memb.] Assembly of God Columbus NC; [hon.] Sing Church Solo's An Honor; [oth. writ.] 6 songs - 12 poems 4 Canvas country paintings "Non Published"; [pers.] I wrote a poem on Columbus friends want me to publish in local news paper for 4th of July. I strive to put my feeling in my songs and writings some poems written for children; [a.] Columbus, NC

FORD, VIRGINIA
[b.] January 6, 1914, Little Rock, AR; [p.] Dora and William Cross; [m.] Gerald K. Ford (Deceased), October 15, 1937; [ch.] Two sons, Kenneth and Frederick; [ed.] Davenport College, Lenoir, NC, Southern Baptist Theological Seminary, Woman's College; [occ.] Retired and enjoying the pleasant life in Florida; [memb.] First Baptist Church, Tequiera, Florida, Member and Teacher of Adult Women; [hon.] Former State President of Woman's Missionary Union, State Convention of Baptists in Ohio, have been honored for Service in many Christian activities through the years; [oth. writ.] None published expect - have written many articles and other material pertaining to Christian activities as a ministers wife and mother to my sons - they have been published in denominational publications.; [pers.] I hope my life has been a blessing to all it has touched in any way especially to my sons and wives, their children and great-grandchildren.; [a.] Tequista, FL

FORDHAM, RICHARD C.
[b.] October 26, 1964, Butte, MT; [p.] Lauvic P. and Effie L. Fordham; [m.] Louise M. Fordham, November 22, 1986; [ch.] Michelle N. and Brittany E.; [ed.] Pike County High University of Maryland (A.A.) Temple University; [occ.] Pharmacy Tech; [memb.] American Legion; [a.] Philadelphia, PA

FOREMAN, JAMES
[pen.] James Foreman; [b.] November 22, 1962, Philadelphia, PA; [p.] Mr. and Mrs. Alan Bergey; [m.] Jennifer Foreman, October 21, 1995; [ch.] Son on the way; [ed.] Ged. 1 1/2 yr. College; [occ.] Kitchen Mang. Minnos Fasta Express Newhall Ca, 91321; [hon.] 4th Place in one of Your Contest (Book) Tear's Of Fire; [oth. writ.] Just one published by the National Library of Poetry.; [pers.] I think everyone has the creative ability to do good, it's just a matter if figuring out what's good and what's bad.; [a.] Newhall, CA

FOSTER, ARDELLA
[pen.] Dell Foster; [b.] July 16, 1952, North Carolina; [p.] Liddell Davis

FOSTER, GARY J.
[b.] July 27, 1961, Philadelphia, PA; [p.] John Foster, Betty Foster; [m.] Tracy A. Foster, October 19, 1985; [ch.] Kristen Marie, Sean Michael; [ed.] Frankford High School; [occ.] Service Manager; [memb.] Masonic Lodge #292; [hon.] Senate Good Citizenship award; [pers.] To my wife and children who I love, thank you. To my father who I miss everyday, I'll see you in my dreams.; [a.] Pipersville, PA

FOSTER, RITA
[pen.] Rita Foster; [b.] August 29, 1944, Burt County, NE; [p.] F. Lloyd and Violet Richards; [m.] John W. Foster, September 3, 1993 (Second Marriage); [ch.] Four daughters; [ed.] 2 yrs. toward BA in Sociology; [occ.] College Student; [hon.] Recognized internationally for work as rural activist during Agricultural Depression of the 80's. Honored by Gov. R. Kerry and Farm Aid Rep. Willei Nelson. Featured: In US News and World Report, on BBC radio in London, National Newspapers through Assoc. Press and Syndicated Columnists, Nat'l Church Periodicals and Videos, President's Honor List - College; [oth. writ.] Rural Folk Composer/Performer, Produced Two audio cassette tapes of music. Tapes in 16 countries. Articles published in College newspaper on Social issues. Published in Nat'l and world church Periodicals.; [pers.] Having lived most of my life in a rural setting and bonding with the natural earth as a spiritual resource, my perspective of self, as more than a physical creation with limitations, has shaped my belief that we as individuals have a purpose and our unique influence makes a difference in the outcome of human events.; [a.] Norfolk, VA

FOWLER, LAWRENCE S.
[b.] January 26, 1955, New York, NY; [p.] C. L. Fowler, Kathleen Mavis Lawrence; [occ.] Human Resource Director, Upper Manhattan Mental Health Center, New York City, NY; [memb.] Board of Directors: Bronx AIDS Services Inc., Community League of West 159th St; [pers.] I pray the best I will be is not the best I have been.; [a.] New York, NY

FOX, TINA MARIE
[b.] March 27, 1965, Manassas, VA; [p.] Thomas Wortman, Barbara Wortman; [m.] Charles E. Fox Jr., "Rusty", September 23, 1995; [ch.] Charlie, Justin, Angela, Jennifer, Heidi, Heather; [occ.] Certified Nursing Assistant; [oth. writ.] Numerous poems never submitted for publication.; [pers.] I have been writing poetry my whole life. My recent works have been inspired by finally finding peace and happiness with someone I love dearly, and the beautiful little town we live in. "Lovers" was written for, Rusty, my true love.; [a.] Catlett, VA

FRAME, BARBARA
[pen.] Bobbie Korte Frame; [b.] June 12, 1937, Breslau, Germany; [p.] Deceased; [m.] Gary, November 29, 1985; [ch.] Two boys - Two girls; [ed.] College 3 years, various courses and seminars - trade school; [occ.] Investigation; [memb.] H.B. Athletic Club; [hon.] Employee of the month three times for: designed a tracking system with codes and forms, outstanding customer service. In recognition of outstanding achievement.; [oth. writ.] Poems: The Fugitive - Meine Mutter - Dawn Of New Hope - A Bitter Lesson - Frozen In Time - The Mythical Wolf - The Civilized Stranger - Novels: Repercussions Of A War - From East to West to U.S.A. - The Children She Lost; [pers.] I like to build a bridge from me to the reader. Giving them enjoyment and escape. Also, to have a philosophy behind each creation and to stir reader's imaginations.; [a.] Huntington Beach, CA

FRANCIS, JOHN B.
[b.] June 12, 1974, Saint Louis, MO; [p.] Garrell and Lita Francis; [ed.] Hazelwood West Jr/Sr High Central Texas College; [occ.] U.S. Marine; [memb.] A.I.M., Greenpeace; [oth. writ.] Published poems in High School Lit. Mag.; [pers.] Follow your dreams, for some of us thats all there is.; [a.] Camp Lejeune, NC

FRANK, MONICA J.
[b.] June 13, 1958, Edmonton, Alberta, Canada; [ch.] Nadia Nicole Frank; [ed.] M.E Lazert CHS, Edmonton Secretarial College; [occ.] Landlord and Tenant Consultant Community and Family Services, Landlord and Tenant Advisory Board, City of Edmonton; [memb.] Beulah Alliance Church; [oth. writ.] Though this is my first published writings, I have written an extensive amount of poetry.; [pers.] My poetry is a result of trials I've faced in life. Expressing my emotions in my writings helps in dealing with difficulties. So my poetry reflects my life and issues of concern. I strive to write uplifting and encouraging words giving the glory to God my heavenly Father.; [a.] Edmonton Alberta, Canada

FRANKLYN, GLORIA
[b.] October 1, 1951, Bridgetown, Barbados; [p.] Mr. and Mrs. Alphonsa Franklyn; [ch.] One son; [ed.] St. George's Secondary-Bar Housecraft Career Institute - CAN, Durham College - CAN; [occ.] Private Nurse's Aid; [hon.] Diploma in Nurse's Aid, Diploma in Home Economics; [pers.] I am an avid reader, I express my feelings better in writing. I also enjoy good poetry.; [a.] North York, Canada

FREAS, SHERRY
[b.] April 23, 1979, Kannapolis, NC; [p.] Bill and Cindy Freas; [ed.] 10th grade; [occ.] Cashier; [hon.] To have my first poem published by the National Library of poetry.; [oth. writ.] Poems as a hobby hope to be published again soon.; [pers.] Deepest and most treasured emotions to come to paper. My friends, family and loved ones are my inspiration.; [a.] Kannapolis, NC

FREEMAN JR., ROBERT
[pen.] Eliot Freeman; [b.] September 22, 1954, Chester, PA; [p.] Robert and Nettie Freeman Sr.; [m.] Denise Marie Bennett; [ch.] Robert Eliot, Yasmin Denise, Errol John, Dorlisa Michelle; [ed.] Chester High; [occ.] Texas Dept. Criminal Justice, Mark W. Stiles Unit Beaumont, TX; [oth. writ.] No other published or written. I write songs. "Far Away Soldier" began as a song but instead ended up as my only poem written in 1974.; [pers.] My greatest influence is my father, Bob Freeman "The Lonesome Stranger" An Entertainer at heart, who, like Gershwin, had the music and I the words.; [a.] Beaumont, TX

FREEMAN, REATHA M.
[b.] June 24, 1966, Windsor, Ontario, Canada; [p.] Orville and Alice Freeman; [m.] Single; [ed.] Midland CI graduate in 86. Graduate of Investigation School 87.; [occ.] Literacy Tutor; [oth. writ.] For "Depressed Anonymous." Several articles throughout 1995.; [pers.] To write how I really feel, makes the best message to my readers.; [a.] Toronto Ontario, Canada

FRI, DOREEN ANN
[b.] October 3, 1957, Fremont, MI; [p.] Donald White, Delores White; [ch.] Samantha Marie, Krystyn Lea, Brittany Lynn, Kyleigh Jo; [ed.] Fremont High, Ferri State College, Commercial Art Program; [occ.] Computer Tech at Amway Corp., World Headquarters, to put to get the Labels for Major Brands; [oth. writ.] Several poems but never tried to have published and would like to.; [pers.] I strongly believe in fairness, kindness love, a special thanks to John Anes who inspired me to write this poem as Garth Brooks wrote "You are not free unless you can love whom you choose."

FRIEDMAN, RICHARD N.
[pen.] Richard Friedman N.; [b.] July 13, 1941, Philadelphia, PA; [p.] Martin Harry Friedman and Caroline (Both Deceased); [m.] Catherine Helen, November 7, 1970; [ch.] Melissa D. - 21; [ed.] University of Miami - B.A., 1962, J.D., 1965, Georgetown Law Center, LL.M. in taxation, 1967; [occ.] Lawyer, entrepreneur; [memb.] The Florida Bar, District of Columbia Bar, Screen Actors Guild, Society of Founders, University of Miami, Associate Member, The Academy of American Poets; [hon.] Awards Received: Certifs. of Merit from Dade County Bar Assoc., plaques of appreciation from Sunrisers and Sunrise Community for the Retarded, numerous Certifs. of Appreciation from service organizations such as Rotary International, Kiwanis, Lions, Optimists, Jaycees, etc., Richard N. Friedman Week, City of Homestead, April 3-9, 1978, Citizen of the Day, April 8, 1980 by WINZ Radio and Citizens Fed. Svgs. and Tennessee, June, 1970.; [oth. writ.] Columnist, "Securities Today", Miami Review (1971-73), Business Leader (1974-76), Associate Editor and Columnist, The Market Chronicle, 1984-87, Feature articles writer, 14 Community Newspapers, 1988-92. Poetry Published: College and other newspapers, first book of poetry to be published, 1996.; [pers.] Each of us is a poet and each of us has poetry in our hearts. People can be poets if they reach down inside themselves and memorialize their thoughts or emotions in writing.; [a.] Miami, FL

FRIESEN, MERIEDEGG SHERI-MAYE
[oth. writ.] 'Dream an Inspiration' published in High School year book and 'Escape the Madness' in Canadian Anthology - "Scaling the Face of Reason."; [pers.] I'm a progressive rock singer/keyboard player working in the creation of my band "Catras Matrix," I realize time and again through my writing, these words that pour from my soul are most often, my only light of breath and sanity.; [a.] Milton Ontario, Canada

FRIIS, EUGENE A.
[pen.] Geno; [b.] July 26, 1931, Omaha, NE; [p.] Holger Friis - Edna McFarland Friis; [m.] Divorced 40 yrs ago; [ed.] 10th grade; [occ.] Retired Building Maintenance Engineer; [memb.] AARP; [oth. writ.] A recipe for kitchen dinner published 1965; [pers.] To believe in the Lord and Mean it this will produce compassion Love and respect for your fellow Human Beings. This will produce clean thoughts clean mind - equals good writer; [a.] Omaha, NE

FRITTS, ALVIN
[b.] April 8, 1968, Oak Ridge, TN; [p.] William and Hazel Robinson; [ed.] B.S. Electronics Engineering Technology; [occ.] Operation - T.V.A.; [memb.] Alpha Phi Alpha Fraternity Inc.; [a.] Oliver Springs, TN

FROSURE, E. P.
[pers.] When I am comfortably resting, I let my thoughts turn naturally to God and then hearing His words, my poems come quietly to my thought.; [a.] Colorado Springs, CO

FRYER, BRIAN H. S.
[b.] August 21, 1952, Vancouver; [p.] Stan, Shirley; [m.] Theresa; [ch.] Aaron, Toby, Josh, Jesse; [ed.] B. of Music - U.B.C.; [occ.] Teacher; [memb.] Surrey Teachers Assoc.; [oth. writ.] Several other poems and short stories.; [pers.] I trust that my writing reflects the hope and faith that we all can share.; [a.] Surrey British Columbia, Canada

FRYER, NICHOLAS L.
[pen.] Nick; [b.] February 20, 1978, Cumberland; [p.] Stephen and Catherine Fryer; [ed.] Four Years of Art, College English, History, and Art.; [occ.] Wal-mart; [memb.] National Art Honors Society, K of C, Who's who among High School Students, American Legion Boy's State; [hon.] Glenville College Art Exhibition, Potomac State Mention, Art Published in High School Senior Magazine and Star Wars Galaxy Magazine; [pers.] "I believe do everyone should be happy. Do what one can to happy. Do what one can to make them and the people around them happy. Life is a small portion of existence".; [a.] Ridgeley, VA

FUHRI, D. EKO
[b.] May 28, 1970; [p.] E. Patrick Haberman, Sara Haberman; [m.] Colleen Fuhri, October 31 1993; [occ.] Graphic Artist, Composer; [pers.] Universal survival depends upon everything taking only what is needed and giving back everything that they are.; [a.] Coral Springs, FL

FULHAM, CHRISTINA M.
[pen.] Christina M. Fulham; [b.] December 28, 1982, Arlington Heights; [p.] Deborah and Thomas Fulham; [ed.] Grade school, Middle school; [occ.] Student; [memb.] U.C.C. Church, Soccer, Softball, Basketball; [hon.] Two years of an honor roll student, a writing essay award, young authors essays, many sports awards.; [oth. writ.] Winning a D.A.R.E. essay award, young authors awards, poetry published in North West Daily Heralds, other poetry, poetry published in memory book.; [pers.] I wrote this pride poem because my sister died on October 25, 1995, from the Fox River Grove bus/train crash to I dedicate this to her.; [a.] Fox River Grove, IL

FULLER, KATHERINE HELEN
[b.] August 8, 1984, Morristown, NJ; [p.] James W. and Kelly H. Fuller; [ed.] Alumnus of Moravian Academy, Bethlehem, PA; [occ.] Student; [hon.] 24 Challenge Champion 1995 (National Math Contest), Merit Award for Academic Achievement, 1st Place Athletic Awards 1992, 5-time Country Fair Award Winner; [oth. writ.] Other works of poetry published in Moravian Academy's Annual Publication of Literature.; [a.] Hellertown, PA

FULLER, LINDA
[b.] August 3, 1946, Earth; [p.] Art & Evelyn Sizemore; [s.] Ted Fuller; [ch.] Krystal Kauney; [ed.] Living & Loving with a degree in "Touch" & "Gentleness"; [occ.]Touching and Loving - Promoter of "One Ness"; [memb.] Member of the Brotherhood of Mankind.; [hon.] Wife, Motherhood, Friend, Daughter, Sister, Comforter, Holy Child of God.; [oth. writ.] Article appeared in "Mothering" Magazine; [pers.] "What is the same can not be different, and what is one can not have seperate parts"; [a.] Lakeland, FL

FULLER, MAXCINE
[b.] July 31, 1940, Diboll, TX; [p.] Malissia Randolph, Paul Fred; [ch.] Beverly, Anita, Tyrone, Crystal; [ed.] Temple High Valrie Hand Beauty and Business, College; [occ.] DISD Custodian; [memb.] Perry Chaple CM and Church, The International Society of Poets; [hon.] Editor's Choice Award, the International Poet of Merit Award; [oth. writ.] Angels Whisper, Old Dusty Road, Poverty, Save the Children, To Someone Special; [pers.] I direct my mind to seek wisdom in the day of prosperity be happy.; [a.] Diboll, TX

FULMORE, CHARLES W.
[pen.] Intrigue (The Verbal Architect); [b.] November 8, 1978, New York, NY; [p.] Kenneth B. Fulmore I, Marcia E. Fulmore; [ed.] Queens Lutheran School, Long Island City, Queens Borough Community College; [occ.] Travel Agent, Travel by Tiffany, NY., NY.; [memb.] Black Pride Committee Varsity Basketball, Pal (Police Athletic League) and Track; [hon.] Honor Roll, Student of the Month, Sports Awards; [oth. writ.] First publication, many other works still seeking notoriety; [pers.] I'm inspired by life itself and the opportunity to experience and accomplish everything possible and learn "absolute attention is absolute being!"; [a.] Queens, NY

FURBEYRE, STACEY
[b.] June 16, 1982, Elkhart, KS; [p.] Rodolfo and Nellie Furbeyre; [ed.] From elementary to middle school in Sacred Heart Catholic School. Moving into first year of high school.; [occ.] Student, eighth grade; [oth. writ.] Have written many other poems but none are published. Currently working on a 300 page book about the T.V. series the X-Files.; [pers.] People say they dream of the impossible. Look at the world and people arounf you. Now how many dreans of impossibility are there?; [a.] Jacksonville, FL

FURSTAL, SANDRA
[b.] Hammond, IN; [p.] Sophie Stiles, Frank J. Stiles; [m.] Gyula Furstal, October 29, 1992; [ed.] Barton Co. Comm. Col., Marymount Col., Bethel College of Ks. Valparaiso U of IN.; [occ.] Nursing, English Tutor; [memb.] Literacy Program of Lake Co. In. Tutor Training for ESL/Basic Reading; [pers.] My aim is to help others and to show the positive side of life.; [a.] Lowell, IN

GAINES, GLADYS
[b.] June 20, 1911, Mountain Home, AK; [p.] Ewen and Lillie Merrell; [m.] Troy Leonard Gaines (Deceased), November 23, 1929; [ch.] One daughter; [ed.] High School Graduate, Business College; [occ.] Bible Class Teacher; [memb.] Only Church;

[oth. writ.] Several poems published in Denver Post (Colo.), Colorado Springs (Colo.) Gazette, Tucson (Ariz.) Daily Citizen, Local News Paper, Escondido Times Advocate; [pers.] In my poems, I seek to call attention to the beauties of Nature, and above all else, to glorify God.

GAJADHAR, LLOYD
[pen.] Lloyd Michael Byron; [b.] July 5, 1951, Trinidad, West Indies; [p.] Byron and Doris Gajadhar; [m.] Louise Gajadhar, June 21, 1980; [ch.] Anne-Lynn and Alexis; [ed.] B.A. Hons. University of Toronto, Registered Nurse, Pitt Community College, Greenville N.C.; [occ.] Reg. Nurse in the field of Substance Dependency; [memb.] Gamma Beta Phi (Alumni) Greeneville Racquet Club Aquatics and Fitness Center, National Geographic Society; [hon.] President Gamma Beta Phi at Pitt Community College; [oth. writ.] "The Test of Time", "My Woman, My Friend and My Wife", "My Little One", "Tell Me Why"; [pers.] "If patience and knowledge can nurture our minds. We'll hurdle all obstacles in the test of time."; [a.] Greenville, NC

GALAZKA, KATARZYNA
[pen.] Kasia Galazka; [b.] April 19, 1965, Warsaw, Poland; [p.] Helena Luszcz and Tadeusz Galazka; [ch.] Miriam Elena; [ed.] XVI Ginnazjum N. M. Senpolowskiej in Warsaw, Poland; [occ.] Business Manager; [oth. writ.] "Talks with Uriel" poetry - unpublished "Free to Survive" unpublished "Without Mother" unpublished "Cosmic Prince" unpublished; [pers.] "Celestial expression of human form/ abandon to levitate/simply I name the eternal quest/ for freedom of spirit" "Within all burning desires of soul/the quest for freedom/has the undeniable power of victory".; [a.] Jacksonville Beach, FL

GALESKI, PRISCILLA
[b.] May 6, 1934, Tyngsboro, MA; [p.] T. Wendell Watson, Ethel Watson; [m.] George, May 6, 1952; [ch.] Joy, Cynthia Jean, Lisa Ann; [ed.] Clinton High - Fisher Jr. College; [occ.] Retired; [memb.] Mustang Club of New England; [pers.] Any talent that I may posses, I owe to my late father and noted poet, T.W.W. Watson.; [a.] Berlin, MA

GALLO, JOANNE
[b.] September 4, 1956, Artesia, CA; [p.] Joseph Gallo Jr., Elma A. Gallo; [ed.] Downey High, Cerritos College; [occ.] Self-employed - Partnership Lil' House of Cakes, Downey CA.; [memb.] Downey Chamber of Commerce National Wildlife Federation; [hon.] 1st Place City of Downey Chamber of Commerce Anniversary Cake Contest; [oth. writ.] Handmade Birthday Cards for family and friends, poems about Beloved Pets; [pers.] I strongly believe that all animals are God's gift to mankind-to beautify our World. It greatly saddens me to see the distraction of the animal kingdom without regard to its importance.; [a.] Downey, CA

GALLO, MARIA A.
[b.] August 9, 1955, Artesia, CA; [p.] Elma and Joseph Gallo Jr.; [ed.] Downey Senior High School Cerritos College, California State University, Long Beach BA, National University MA; [occ.] Elementary School Teacher Oceanside, California; [memb.] National Educational Assoc., California

Teacher's Association, National Parks and Conservation Assoc., RE 1 Member; [hon.] Alpha Gamma Sigma, Dean's List, Kappa Delta Pi; [pers.] Let every moment count. Life is too short to just work. Travel and learn about people and the world to enrich your life.; [a.] Laguna Niguel, CA

GALYON JR., JOHN D.
[b.] September 6, 1965, Augusta, GA; [p.] John and Mary Galyon, Sr.; [m.] Sonja A. Galyon, September 6, 1992; [ch.] Anastasia, Andrew, Adriana; [ed.] Guilford Technical Community College: Advertising Design; [occ.] Artist: Graphic Design, Cartoon, Poetry, song writing; [memb.] Promise keepers; [hon.] Nominated to Who's Who of America, Phi Beta Lambda; [pers.] God is our father, friend, teacher, wisdom and love. These virtues are expressed in his written word, the bible, and exercised daily in the Birth of a child, the blossom of a flower and the sunrise of tomorrow.; [a.] Manchester, NH

GAPP, EVELYN CARIE
[pen.] Eleven; [b.] November 20, Portsmouth, VA; [p.] Jack and Kay Olson; [m.] 1976; [ch.] Valerie Kay Gapp; [ed.] Graduated from De Tour High, Mich. Graduated from Chef's Training, Sault College, ON; [occ.] Cook, Amway Distributor, Custom Baker, Nature Photographer and Home Office Cleaning Egos is the name of my business. Evelyn Gapp's Own Style; [pers.] God is the reason I am here. Jesus saved he woman in the tree by taking her heavy burden upon his own tree. He gives me the word and the word lives in me.; [a.] Guelph Ontario, Canada

GARCIA, MARIA
[b.] March 11, 1978, Guerrero, Mexico; [p.] Alicia and Manuel Garcia; [ed.] Currently High School Junior at Roosevelt High School; [memb.] National Honor Society Member, Oregon State Volunteer, Volunteer at a Computer Learning Center for children member of Oregon Leadership Institute; [pers.] Writing poetry has perfected my mind and soul. I now perceive things differently. I notice detail and deep emotions. I write what I feel inside.; [a.] Portland, OR

GARTON, WILLIAM H.
[pen.] W. H. Garton; [b.] January 31, 1929, Ohio; [p.] Jack and Vesta Garton; [m.] Kaye, December 1955; [ch.] David, Christopher, Deborah, James; [ed.] B.A. - Muskiwguw College - Ohio University Southern Calif.; [occ.] Physical Therapist; [memb.] American Physical Therapy Assoc.; [oth. writ.] Biofeed back research - Medical Journal; [pers.] My inspiration couples from my God, family and love of the romanticism of the Old West.; [a.] Riverside, CA

GASKIN, ALICHA MARIE
[b.] June 24, 1975, New Port Richie, FL; [p.] Jack Watson, Christina Watson; [ed.] Hermitage High, Hermitage Tec., Bob Jones University; [occ.] Full time student; [memb.] Mount Calvary Baptist Church, Beta Epsilon Chi Literary Society, Honorary Thespian Society; [hon.] Honorary Thespian Medalion, Principles Medalion for Dramatic Excellence, Hermitage Technical Center Scholarship; [pers.] "My God" refers to the one true Lord and Savior Jesus Christ, with whom I have a personal relationship.; [a.] Greenville, SC

GATHERS, LILLIE M.
[b.] December 26, 1935, Sumter, SC; [ed.] Saint Michael H.S., Wedgefield, SC., Cass Tech H.S., Det Mich., Detroit Practical School of Nursing. WCCC Detroit Mich.; [occ.] LPN - License Practical Nurse for 27 yrs.; [memb.] A.A.R.P.; [hon.] Recognized by "Whose Who" in Field of License Practical Nursing for my Achievement in Scoring 530 Ft., of 600 ft on the exam.; [pers.] My writing reflects my feeling toward all mankind. My favorite book and inspiration is the Bible.; [a.] Detroit, MI

GATTS, JASON THOMAS
[pen.] Thomas Beck; [b.] June 18, 1977, Latrobe, PA; [p.] Judith B. and Arthur Lee; [ed.] North Carroll H.S.; [occ.] U.S.M.C. cook; [memb.] Millers U.M. Church M.D. Christian Tae Kwon Do Assoc.; [hon.] Whose Who in American H.S. Black belt in Tae Kwon Do National Youth Leadership Forum Boys State; [oth. writ.] Poetry in school publications.; [pers.] The greatest influences on my life have been Jesus, Krishna, Mohammed, Siddhortha Gatauma, as well as Gandhi and Paramohansa Yogananda.; [a.] Millers, MD

GAUDIUSO, NICHOLAS
[pen.] Nico; [b.] January 8, 1980, Brooklyn, NY; [p.] Pietro Gaudiuso, Maria Gaudiuso; [ed.] Xaverian High School, Brooklyn, NY, St. Athanasius Elementary School, Brooklyn, NY; [hon.] First Honors in School; [oth. writ.] Poems written in a personal log; [pers.] I write about personal experiences and about my impressions of my environment. "You have nothing to fear, but fear itself", "Hakuna Matada"; [a.] Brooklyn, NY

GAULT, JANESE
[pen.] Jenave Glossar; [b.] June 6, 1980; [p.] Janice Gault and Dwight Gault; [ed.] Amherst High School Student; [occ.] Literary Volunteer, Poet Book Writer, Singer; [memb.] Universal Life; [hon.] Writing Award, Blue Ribbon for Running Track and Lead soloist in a school play; [oth. writ.] Book's Princess Aluwna, Honey Friends 4 Life, Cleo and Craig ectalon Poems," "Love me" "Unexpected Love" "Our Love", "Hearts Cry" etc.; [pers.] I believe the poetry is a good given gift so then for we should always write from our souls.; [a.] Snyder, NY

GAUTHIER, DEBRA
[b.] June 24, 1952, Springfield, VT; [p.] Charles W. and Mary Parker; [m.] John Gauthier, September 6, 1975; [ch.] Jaime Lee; [occ.] Factory Inspector; [oth. writ.] A few poems and articles published in local papers.; [pers.] I find that writing is a release and a means of putting my feelings in perspective. Anyone can write if they look deep enough inside themselves.; [a.] West Rutland, VT

GEDDES, ROBERT
[b.] February 6, 1978, Sydney, Nova Scotia, Canada; [p.] Andrew Geddes, Mary Geddes; [ed.] Breton Education Centre; [occ.] Student of St. Francis Xavier University; [hon.] Lieutenant Governor's Award; [oth. writ.] Poem published in magazine, local newspaper.; [a.] New Waterford Nova Scotia, Canada

GEE, MARTIN CREW
[b.] April 15, 1942, Shifnal, England, United Kingdom; [ch.] Jason and Lara; [ed.] St. Michael's College, Hitchin, UK, De Montford University,

Leics, UK; [occ.] V.P. Design Warner's of Warnaco Canada Ltd.; [memb.] International Society of Poets Dist. Member; [hon.] Design Diploma (Hons), Top Students and Student of the Year Award (finals), Courtaulds Design and Clutsom-Penn Awards (1st Place); [oth. writ.] "Epitaph" sparkles in the sand.; [pers.] Thank you to Evie, for everything, especially for her appreciation and understanding. Her encouragement for this apprentice poet to keep on trying to improve his craft has made the challenges immensely gratifying.; [a.] Gatineau, PA.

GENTNER, CHARLOTTE M.
[b.] November 5, 1926, Ravenna, OH; [p.] Warren Beverlin, Mildred Beverlin; [m.] Donald H. Gentner, October 7, 1964; [ch.] Hal Christopher, Mark H. Matthew Leonard; [ed.] North High School, Jennings Junior High, Bettes Elementary; [occ.] House Wife (retired); [pers.] I have always written poetry but never sent any in to publishers, out I write from my feelings inside. I've always loved poetry. Poetry comes to me when I'm alone.; [a.] Doylestown, OH

GENTRY, D. J.
[pen.] Don Juan Gentry; [b.] June 13, 1980, Floyd Memorial Hospital; [p.] Michael and Lisa Gentry; [ed.] Three Years of Honors English; [occ.] Student; [memb.] Charlestown Road Southern Baptist Church; [hon.] Won a Young Author Award for a Poem, I have a large collection of Football Trophies and Wrestling Metals; [oth. writ.] Several better poems only read by family and friends.; [pers.] I strive to have the reader feel my emotions and the emotions of the people I write about.; [a.] New Albany, IN

GEORGE, JOHN CHARLES
[pen.] John C. George; [b.] September 20, 1924, Port Huron, MI; [p.] John C. George and Georgeina George; [m.] Catherine George, or Kitty, August 27, 1961; [ch.] Gina L. Wilquet; [ed.] High School, Mich. State University, school of labor and industrial relations; [occ.] Retired, tool and die maker; [memb.] Life, member, D.V.A.V.F.W. and American Legion, 101 St. Airborne Division Society Skilled Trades Union President, 66, 67, and 68; [hon.] World War Two, Bronze Star, two Purple Hearts, 101 St. Airborne Division, 506 regiment, D company; [oth. writ.] Poetry, Passion For Commitment, Our Flag, The Beggar And The Rose, and a novel, I hope to get published, called, Cross Roads At The Complex; [pers.] I firmly believe that if mankind could devote, only one half of the effort, we take to condemn each other, and turn that effort into love and compassion, through poetry and writing, we would all have a better world to live in.; [a.] Fairview, MI

GEORGE, LINDA J.
[b.] October 30, 1953, Cleveland, OH; [p.] Joseph and Willa Williams; [m.] Rurrell A. George, August 24, 1974; [ch.] Ebany S. Jamal A., Brionna N. (Granddaughter); [ed.] John Hay High School; [occ.] Data Entry Ft. Myers Police Dept.

GERAGHTY, PATRICIA
[b.] December 17, 1945, Astoria, NY; [p.] Bernard Geraghty, Dorothy Geraghty; [ed.] Lexington School for the Deaf, Palm Beach Junior College, University of South Florida, Western Oregon State College, Lewis and Clark College, Junior High School Teacher, Phoenix Day School for the Deaf, Phoenix, AZ; [memb.] Alexander Graham Bell Assoc. of the Deaf, SW Phoenix Deaf Woman's Organization; [pers.] Despite of my deafness at birth, I fear not to challenge my creativity in writing as I will always allow it to freely inspire me to become a better possible writer.; [a.] Phoenix, AZ

GERALD, STEPHEN B.
[b.] November 13, 1972, Columbus, OH; [p.] Nella Gerald, Fred Gerald; [ed.] BA - University of Baltimore Pikesville High; [hon.] Member of PI Sigma Alpha - Political Science Honors Society; [pers.] I attempt to conglomerate the conscience with the subconscience; [a.] Baltimore, MD

GERBER, JARED
[b.] November 23, 1971, Oberlin, OH; [p.] David and Claudia Gerber; [ed.] B.A. Psychology SDSU, M.S.W. U.S.C.; [occ.] Counselor; [memb.] Sierra Club, Cal Pirg, N.A.S.W., N.P.C.A.; [hon.] Honor Roll L.A. Marathon; [oth. writ.] Over 200 poems, never shown, unpublished; [pers.] I write to express the deepest passions of my soul, and to describe the universal archetypes and syncronicities which are shared in the emotional center of our being.; [a.] Venice, CA

GHANSAH, RACHEL KAADZI
[pen.] Icy Blue, The Roach; [b.] December 29, 1981, Indiana; [p.] Rickie L. Sanders and James Ghansah; [ed.] Greene Street Friends Middle School; [occ.] Student at High School; [memb.] The World Wildlife Fund "The Mt. Airy Triplets"; [oth. writ.] I write for the school newspaper, and once for Germantown courier; [pers.] I am influence by every unique person. We all carry something. I think women influence me the most and shock me with their many traits and gifts. I love my mom, Diane, Bjork, Carrie, Lindsey, Tim, Lucy and G'mom for chunks of support up and for catching me when I am falling. Love, The Roach.; [a.] Philadelphia, PA

GIBSON, BRENDA
[b.] Biloxi, MS; [p.] Charles and Agnes Banks; [m.] Charles Gibson, October 15, 1991; [ch.] Alisa, Kendall, Doniver, Latanya; [ed.] 33rd Avenue High Phillip's Business College, Jefferson Davis Jr. College, Houston Community College; [occ.] Nursing - Veterans Administration, Houston, TX; [memb.] Winsor Village United Methodist Church - The 700 Club; [hon.] Dean's List; [oth. writ.] Sense Beyond the Beauty published in Shadows of Light; [pers.] "Our Eyes can not see the truth that lies within the heart"; [a.] Houston, TX

GIBSON, SHARLENE EVANGELINE ELLIS
[pen.] Sharlene; [b.] December 25, 1955, Bimini, Bahamas; [p.] Dr. and Mrs. Robert Ellis Jr. (Deceased); [m.] Richard Edwin Gibson, December 17, 1988; [ch.] Rishea; [ed.] R.M. Bailey Secondary School, College of the Bahamas; [occ.] Manager, Clothing Store Muck-A-Mucks Limited; [memb.] Mt. Tabor Union Baptist Church; [hon.] Received Jesus Christ as Lord in 1987, Diploma, La Salle University Chicago, Illinois (Correspondence) in Fiction Writing 1978, Asst. Manager, Chicken Unlimited Ltd. Fast Food Restaurant 1987; [oth. writ.] When The Devil Comes To Church, Picked Out To Be Picked On, A Look Around From The Shoulder Down, A Check Up From The Neck Up, The Love Of God part II, many, many other poems and dramas.; [pers.] God has blessed me with the gift of writing. The poem, "The Love Of God" is not merely words to me. I am a born again christian who has experienced the love of God in my life. I pray that through the publication of this poem, people all over the world would be convinced that there really is no greater love than the love of God.; [a.] Nassau NP, Bahamas

GILES, TERENCE F. E.
[b.] May 2, 1929, England; [p.] Edwin Giles, Lillian Boswell (Deceased); [m.] Jean Mason, June 3, 1950; [ch.] Lynn Ann, Karen Kay; [ed.] Wellingborough School, England. Extension Courses, McMaster U. Hamilton, Ontario.; [occ.] Merchant Seaman, 1945-1946. Royal Navy 1948-1950 Emigrated to Canada 1954. Technical Representative, Precast Concrete Company, 4 years. City Building Inspector, 16 years. Commissioned in the Royal Canadian; [mem.] Engineers, transferred to the Ontario Regiment (Armored) 28 years in City Planning Dept. Retired in 1994.; [memb.] Rotary International Paul Harris Fellow; [hon.] Started to write traditional Poetry depicting historical events etc.; [pers.] Inspired by Rudyard Kipling, Lt. Col. John McCrae, Oliver Wendell Holmes, Sgt. Joyce Kilmer AEF, Robert Service.

GILLIAM, ANNA MARIE
[b.] October 23, 1984, Cedar Rapids, LA; [p.] Jerry and Kristin Gilliam; [ed.] Still in Grade School, 5th Grade; [occ.] Baby sitting; [pers.] My true feelings are what I like to write about. My best work comes from my heart.; [a.] Blairstown, LA

GILLILAND, THOMAS
[b.] April 27, 1919, Yellow Jacket, CO; [p.] William Thomas and Eva Stevenson Gilliland; [m.] Dorothy Gilliland, November 15, 1938; [ch.] Bill, Judi; [ed.] Eight Grade; [occ.] Farmer; [memb.] Masonic Lodge - 32nd Degree Lewis Grange, Colorado State Grange, Farm Bureau, served as President of Board of Directors of Lewis-Arriola Fire Protection District for 18 years; [hon.] Numerous Agricultural Awards; [oth. writ.] Various poems and local history articles.; [pers.] My writings are based on my memories of growing up in a pioneer family and life experiences. My mother and my uncle were both writers who had works published.; [a.] Lewis, CO

GILMORE, CONNIE
[b.] December 27, 1946, Attica, IN; [p.] William Poet and Florence Poet; [s.] Robert H. Gilmore; [ch.] John and Shana; [ed.] Attica, IN; [occ.] Human Resources Assistant for Columbia House in Terre Haute, IN; [pers.] As a tribute to my son John. The purpose of my writing is to help others find an inner peace. [a.] Terre Haute, IN

GILSTRAP, PAUL P.
[pen.] Paul P. Gilstrap; [b.] September 29, 1958, Wichita, KS; [p.] Jess and Joyce Gilstrap; [m.] Kimberly Ann Gilstrap, May 22, 1992; [occ.] Out Placement Consultant/Writer, First Impressions;

[memb.] Immanuel Lutheran Church; [hon.] National Directory of Who's Who in Executives/Professionals, Dr. Daniel J. Caliendo "Life Worth Living" Award Nominee; [pers.] To my precious wife, partner and soulmate, I love you!; [a.] Wichita, KS

GIRON, ELOINA
[b.] July 19, 1955, Dunkirk, NY; [p.] Luz M. and Ventura Martinez; [ch.] Zaida, Jose, Jenette, Tammey; [ed.] Austin High School, El Paso TX, Kean College, NJ; [occ.] Certified Court Interpreter (Spanish); [oth. writ.] More poems I've written in Spanish. In small community newspapers.; [pers.] I have been greatly influenced by mostly Spanish writers, such as Gabriel Garcin - Many years where I can release in verse my restless spirit.; [a.] Buffalo, NY

GIROUARD, CYNDI
[b.] October 24, 1959, Barrie, Ontario, Canada; [p.] Joan and Sam; [ch.] Joshua David; [ed.] Gaspe, Quebec, Canada; [occ.] Artist/Exec. Secr; [pers.] To Josh: Witnessing the miraculous metamorphosis of seed to babe to child and onward into your unwinding destiny is the privilege of this grateful participant. Deep gratitude overwhelms as I observe the priceless unfolding of your young, life. Awe rouses unrestrained pleasure experienced through this interchange.; [a.] Kitchener Ontario, Canada

GITTENS II, RONALD G.
[b.] December 21, 1968, Fort Lauderdale, FL; [p.] Ronald G. Gittens Sr., Louise Gittens; [ch.] Francesca N. G. Gittens; [ed.] Boyd Anderson High, Broward Community College, Private studies in hypnosis and meditation.; [occ.] Entrepreneur/Salesman; [memb.] Fort Lauderdale Film Festival; [hon.] MBNA America, Market U.S.A.; [oth. writ.] Three screenplays which include, No More Secrets, Tripper, Hidden Agenda, and a myriad of poems published in the Mind-Works Literary Magazine.; [pers.] I journey within my writing to bizarre and brilliant places, I aim to take my readers along... with my words leaving traces... The fibers of ones character are defined from moment to moment.; [a.] Fort Lauderdale, FL

GLAISTER, MURIEL DYAR
[b.] January 24, 1928, Hamilton, AL; [p.] S.C. and Bula Dyar; [m.] Joseph W. Glaister, January 26, 1952; [ch.] Ira Glaister, Jerome Glaister, Debra Glaister, Sherri, G. Hendrix, Melissa Glaister; [ed.] Hamilton H. S. BS Liberal Arts BSN Nursing MA Ed, M.A. Clinical Counseling; [occ.] R.N. Clinical Counselor. Retired.; [memb.] Biology Honor Society, Education Honor Society, Al. Nurse Assoc. ANA Med. Aux. State of Al, National Med. Aux.; [hon.] Dean's List UNA, UAH; [oth. writ.] Collection of poems. A collection of short stories.; [pers.] As I am in the Late Autumn of my season I becomes more appreciative of having lived in the USA. My entire life and I become more appreciation of my strong healthy children and grandchildren.; [a.] Florence, AL

GLASS, GARY
[pen.] Kimber Gray; [b.] February 15, 1973, Downey, CA; [p.] Everett and Geraldine Glass; [ed.] Thousand Oaks HS, UC Santa Barbara; [hon.] Regents Scholarship, AFL-CIO Scholarship, Conejo

Valley Little League Scholarship; [pers.] Poetry is an art of subtlety and emotion, and I strive to embrace both facets in every poem I create.; [a.] Thousand Oaks, CA

GLASSMEYER, GARY L.
[b.] February 26, 1952, Cincinnati, OH; [occ.] Newspaper Production Manager; [a.] Cincinnati, OH

GLAZEBROOK, THOMAS L.
[pen.] Tex Glazebrook; [b.] May 29, 1994, Minneapolis, MN; [p.] Grace Howard and T. Lafayette; [m.] Margaret, February 17, 1979, Colleen (deceased), December 10, 1945; [ch.] Dedra Kay Tiger and Tama Glazebrook; [ed.] GED plus 2y Okla School Buss. Ambassador Bible College; [memb.] California 250th Coast Artillery members Organization, San Luis.; [hon.] WW II 70th Infantry, Bronze Star Medal, Purple Heart Medal, 275th Infantry, Wire Team; [oth. writ.] 2 Volumes 316 poems 9 volumes of poetry (never published) Soul Winners hand book! Temple Star of David Evan. Numbers of Bible Lessons.; [pers.] There three that bear record in heaven! There are three that bear witness in the earth! Salvation is by Grace!; [a.] Bartlesville, OK

GLOTZ, NANCY ROSE
[pen.] Nancy Rose; [b.] October 12, 1940, Marquette, MI; [p.] Rev Robert, Gladys Shahbaz; [m.] Carl P. Glotz, May 10, 1984; [ch.] 2 children, 6 stepchildren; [ed.] Alderson Broaddus College Philippi, WVA BSN; [occ.] Registered Nurse; [pers.] Metamorphosis was written in memory of my twin sister, the Rev Dr Marilyn Winsor, who died suddenly September 9, 1995. It was inspired by her love of butterfly's and my faith in God.; [a.] Richmond, VA

GOAD, LENSI
[pen.] Lensi Goad; [b.] August 31, 1979, Bakersfield; [p.] Kathi and Steve Goad; [ed.] West High School; [occ.] Dance Instructor; [memb.] North Bakersfield Dance Co., Kern Youth Council, National Honors Society, CA Scholarship Federation; [hon.] Junior Miss of Bakersfield Scholarship, Dean's List, Honors Education Program; [pers.] My work reflects my emotions and passions in life. I hope to connect with others with others who share similar sentiments.; [a.] Bakersfield, CA

GOETZ, GAYLE
[b.] December 7, 1980, Atlanta, GA; [p.] Charles Goetz, Betty Goetz; [ed.] Parkview High School; [pers.] I'm a 15 yrs. old student who strongly believes in Christ. Let your heart guide you in your decisions as well as your mind.; [a.] Lilburn, GA

GOLDMAN, JEFFREY M.
[b.] September 3, 1939, Brooklyn, NY; [p.] Martimer and Juliette Goldman; [m.] Lucille Jacinto, February 14, 1974; [ch.] Justin Michael and Sarah Lucille; [ed.] Andrew Warde High School, Quinnipiac College; [occ.] Sales Representative; [oth. writ.] First Writing; [pers.] Married on Valentines Day. Always considered myself a true romantic; [a.] San Diego, CA

GOLDSTEIN, RITA VALERIE
[b.] August 4, 1932, South Africa; [m.] Sam Goldstein, August 18, 1957; [ch.] Steven and Gary;

[ed.] Two grand-children; [pers.] I am inspired to write what I feel in my heart. I have been studying self-actualizations for many years and working on self growth and empowerment. In the spiritual dimension.; [a.] Atlanta, GA

GONZALEZ, FEBE
[b.] September 28, 1929, Arecibo, PR; [p.] Juana Perez and Vicente Gonzalez; [ch.] Julie Ann and Michael S. MacFarlane; [ed.] Arecibo High School - Piano Studies. Advanced-Three Scholarships.; [pers.] My Father Vicente Gonzalez, a poet, was the greatest influence and inspiration in my life. This inspiration in my life. This encouraged me in my dedication to write poetry.; [a.] Hialeah, FL

GONZALEZ, MARC-TIZOC
[pen.] Kalos Vitae; [b.] May 12, 1975, Sacramento, CA; [p.] Alfonso Z. Gonzalez, Petra Valadez de Gonzalez; [m.] (Fiancee) Ame Naomi Berkely; [ed.] Will Graduate From UC Davis with B.A. in Psychology in June of 1996; [occ.] Student Portrait Photographer, Writer, a man.; [memb.] Psi-Chi-National psychology honor society; [hon.] The National Dean's List; [oth. writ.] Previously Unpublished; [pers.] Humanity lives in a shared world. Here darkness exists within light, and wisdom is gained through sorrow. My art, my life is an attempt to share the kalosvitae, the beauty of life with the whole.; [a.] Sacramento, CA

GONZALEZ, MICHEL
[b.] May 13, Havana, Cuba; [p.] Eduardo Gonzalez, Celia Rodriguez; [ed.] Vedado High School, Havana Cuba; [pers.] My favorite poets are Mario Benedetti and Pablo Neruda. My poetry has been heavily influenced by the lyrics of the Beatles and the Doors.; [a.] Newark, NJ

GOOD, MARGARET
[b.] February 4, 1933, Torrance County, NM; [p.] Claude and Bertha and Emeline Brown; [m.] Paul W. Good, March 16, 1962; [ch.] Three; [ed.] Finished Two Years College; [occ.] Retired Secretary; [memb.] Church of Christ, International Society of Poets, Cross Timbers Gem and Mineral Club, Word Runners - The Writers Club; [hon.] New Mexico Girls State - 1950 Salutatorian of High School Graduating Class of 1951, Scholarship to Harding College Searcy, AR; [oth. writ.] "Wings of Flight" - my first book of poetry published in two high school and one college anthologies of poetry, two times in sermon's in poetry, world treasury of great poems, todays great poems, famous poems of today, best poems of 1995, best poems of 1996, 17 other anthologies by NLP, vessels, local newspapers.; [pers.] I credit my 7, 8 grade teacher Eulah Watson, for getting me started writing poetry. My writings consist of things with which I am familiar, specific events, people and religion.; [a.] Stephenville, TX

GOODWIN, HAZEL J.
[p.] Polly Anna Pleasant; [b.] April 15, 1946; [p.] Ollie Thomas-Powell and Albert W. Thomas (dec.); [s.] Divorced; [ch.] Arthur L. Goodwin, Jr. 9dec.0 and Kevin Michael Goodwin; [ed.] B.S. Bus., Eastern Illinois University, Charleston, IL. Lincoln Sr. High, E. St. Louis, IL; [occ.] Consultant in info. systems and HRD-Human Achievement Recognition; [memb.] Con-

cerned Black Parents & Citizens of South Brunswick (NJ), Church-Unity Center, NYC.; [hon.] Who's Who In Finance & Industry (1981-82), Who's Who In The East (1972-1980) Carol Chapman Memorial Award - 1982, Outstanding Sales Awards (1981-84 & 1987 and 1988); [oth. writ.] Chapbrook - "Thoughts to Help You Ride The WAVE of Change", Chapbrook - " You Have My Blessings As You Leave", In Progress - " Skeletons From My Closet"; [pers.] I believe the nature rehythms of poetry "speak to" and "stick to" people. I write poems that "ooz" from my soul to heal me and then share the common experience with others.; [a.] Kendall Park, NJ

GOULD, JEANINE
[pen.] Grandma Jeanine; [b.] June 28, 1942, Duluth, MN; [p.] Foster child too many parents; [m.] Divorced; [ch.] Curtis, Jerry, John and 1 grandson Nicholas; [ed.] High School Diploma Life was my real Education; [occ.] Manager of a Burger King; [pers.] I have written many personal - spiritual and inspirational poems in the last 20 years. I've had some published in a small newspaper - mostly I give them away. I also write songs based on life and feelings. Writing makes my heart sing, sharing them gives me greater joy yet.; [a.] Farmington, MN

GOWAN, TAMMY
[b.] November 9, 1968, Hagersville, Ontario, Canada; [p.] Carl and Margaret Gowan; [ch.] Meghan; [ed.] Grade 12, Diploma of Journalism, Short Story Writing; [occ.] Assembly line worker; [oth. writ.] Poem, Grammy; [pers.] Live life to the fullest.; [a.] Brantford Ontario, Canada

GRABBER, BEN
[b.] October 1, 1980, Canyon, TX; [p.] Patricia Grabber; [ed.] Currently Freshman in High School; [memb.] Canyon High School Band, Canyon High School Football Team, Canyon High School Power Lifting Team, St. Ann's Parish, St. Ann's Choir; [hon.] Member of UIL all region band, numerous awards for band, rifle, athletics; [pers.] Always do right and trust in God and things will be right in the end.; [a.] Canyon, TX

GRABOWSKI, ADAM
[b.] February 3, 1981, Springfield, MA; [p.] Michael and Amy Grabowski; [occ.] Full-time Student; [oth. writ.] Published once in a book of young American poets when I was twelve.; [pers.] A fairly strange individual, Adam sees himself as a cross between Jack Kerovac and "Weird" Al Yankovic. When he's not pondering the meaning of life, Adam spends his time listening to the likes of R.E.M. dead Kennedy's and Tori Amos and trying to sell his poems to earn enough money to send his parents to Florida when they get really annoying.; [a.] Springfield, MA

GRAHAM, ANASTASIA
[pen.] Anastasia, Graham; [b.] November 14, 1979, Trinidad, WI; [p.] Randolph and Eldila Graham; [ed.] Palm Beach County School of The Arts, 10th Grade Communications Major; [occ.] Student; [memb.] Very Special Arts Gospel Chorale for Palm Beach County School of The Arts, Spanish Honors Society, Artist of the month of August 1992; [hon.] Top Mass Media Student #1 Student in Computer Technology, H.P.A. of 39 Honors

Award, Top Honors Award, Top Soprano Vocalist for the Voices of Praise Choir; [oth. writ.] Journalist for state of the arts news paper at school of the arts poems published in school's literary magazine; [pers.] My purpose in life to achieve full spiritual development and during my experiences to achieve this goal, help others along their path of life.; [a.] West Palm Beach, FL

GRAHAM, LYNETTE
[b.] September 4, 1943, Manly, NSW, Australia; [p.] Norman and Doris Evans; [m.] Geoffrey Graham, June 10, 1967; [ch.] John, Peter, Keren, Andrew; [ed.] Moorefield Girl's High; [occ.] Advertising Production Clerk, Sydney Morning Herald; [memb.] Friends of the Royal Gotanic Gardens Sydney Inc - Friends of Sydney Philharmonia Choirs - Friends of Art Gallery of New South Wales; [oth. writ.] Numerous poems - unpublished; [pers.] Dedicated to Frank McGivern my friends, encourage and mentor.; [a.] Carlingford NSW, Australia

GRAHAM, ROXANNA
[b.] February 23, 1971, Springdale, AR; [p.] Tommy and Ellen Graham; [ed.] University of Arkansas, University of North Carolina at Charlotte, BA English; [occ.] Model, Professional Cheerleader; [memb.] National Registry of Authors, Golden Key Honor Society, Sigma Tau Delta H.S., Alpha Episilon Tau Delta H.S., Alpha Episilon Delta Honor Society, Gamma Beta Phi Honor Society; [hon.] Chancellor's List, National Dean's List, Honors Program, Academic Scholarship, Academic Festival, Honor Roll; [oth. writ.] I have had other poems published in anthologies.; [pers.] Childhood makes lasting memories.; [a.] Charlotte, NC

GRAHAM, STACEY R.
[pen.] Stacey Davis; [b.] November 13, 1967, Ripley, TN; [p.] Frank and Mary Alice Davis; [m.] Robert E. Graham, March 21, 1993; [ch.] Sloane (2); [ed.] Graduated with honors 1985, Lithia Springs, H.S., currently enrolled in Children's Writing Course through Correspondence at Institute of Children's Literature; [occ.] Cust Suc. - Square D Company; [memb.] Georgia State Poetry Society, since 1995; [hon.] HM Award for my poem "Love Is" by New Hampshire P.S., 1st poem published, "Little Red Ball," in "Inspirations," Cader Publishings, 1995. My poem, "The Meeting" was selected for "Reach of Song - 1995" by the GA State P.S.; [oth. writ.] I am currently working on a murder mystery, and have recently submitted a few of my children's short stories to magazine publishers.; [pers.] I have been writing since I was eleven. I submitted my 1st poem in Jan. 1995 and have enjoyed continued success in my writing since then. I enjoy entertaining people with my creative imagination.; [a.] Douglasville, GA

GRANT, DAWSON B.
[b.] October 5, 1966, Prattville, AL; [p.] Charles and Mary Grant; [m.] Virginia D. Grant, December 22, 1995; [ed.] Prattville High School, Central Texas Community College; [occ.] U.S. Army Engineer/Instructor; [pers.] I would like to be remembered as a man who wished to simply express the joys and sorrows of everyday life to understanding hearts. Peace and love to all.; [a.] Leavenworth, KS

GREEN, JANNA M.
[b.] August 12, 1975, Charlottetown, Prince Edward Island, Canada; [p.] Allison and Judi Green; [ed.] Senior, University of Prince Edward Island - English Major Fine Arts History Minor; [hon.] Awards from Royal Canadian Legion Remembrance Day Contests - 1988, '90, '92, Creative Writing Award Kinkora Regional High School 1993, UPEI's Dean's List 1994-95, 1995-96; [oth. writ.] Published in anthologies from West Prince Arts Council, PE, Sparrowgrass Poetry Inc, the Poetry Institute of Canada.; [pers.] I try to write the kind of poems are non-specific and open to many interpretations. One of the reasons for my writing is that poetry is so unlimited. For one moment, I can write about roses and springtime while turning to dark images and moods the next moment.; [a.] Albany Prince Edward Island, Canada

GREENAWALT, BARBARA
[pen.] Barbara Greenawalt; [b.] June 3, 1935, Manheim, PA; [p.] Martha and Henry Greenawalt; [ed.] Manheim Central High, Moody Bible Institute, Chicago, IL; [occ.] Retired; [oth. writ.] Several poems have been published in Church and local publications. My book, "A Penny for you thoughts" will soon be published.; [pers.] Although I write for pleasure and to share my thoughts and feelings with others, I strive to bring enjoyment in my poetry, insight in my subjects and help and comfort to those in need.; [a.] Lancaster, PA

GREGER, TERRY LEE
[pen.] Terry Lee or Langenkamp; [b.] August 4, 1947, Bassett, NE; [p.] Frank and Kay Greger; [ch.] Tracey Lynn, Lisa Jo, Kathleen Marie, Ginger Leigh; [ed.] High School grad from St. Joseph in Atkinson, Nebr C.L., Certified Lawman; [occ.] Non Drug Ag Consultant DBA Tleeco over 30% of Nebr; [memb.] F.O.P., N.R.A., L.A., D.A.R.E., Master of Chi TA; [hon.] Who's Who in Poetry 90, Golden Poet Award '88-92 in angers for company in top 500 in the 90's; [oth. writ.] Thanksgiving, Easter, Christmas, Good and Evil, The legends of kid vicious, I'm a lover relationships. The scout eight son cassette Looking Back and Reminiscing; [pers.] What we first observe is not always reality look for truth it free us; [a.] Central City, NE

GREGORY, RICHARD T.
[b.] April 24, 1951, Wilkes Barre, PA; [p.] Deceased; [ed.] Completed numerous courses in Pest Management - Food Processing and Sanitation from Cornell and Purdue Universities; [occ.] Senior Pest Control Technician; [memb.] NY State Dept. of Environmental Conservation - Certified Pesticide Applicator; [hon.] Certificate of Achievement Billboard Song Writing Contest 1990; [oth. writ.] Wrote numerous songs and poems as the lead singer of the "liquid nite blues band."; [pers.] I have been greatly influenced by Jim Morrison - brother Dave - Michele, Mark and Ray.; [a.] Buffalo, NY

GREY, CAMILLE ATASHA
[pen.] JoJo or Josephine; [b.] November 16, 1979, Montego Bay, Jamaica; [p.] Mrs. W. Watson and Mr. E. Grey; [ed.] Completed Elementary School Presently at High School; [occ.] Student; [oth. writ.] I do short stories in my spare time belief is

if you are determined in.; [pers.] My personal belief are 1.) If you are determined in life you will achieve your goals. 2.) You should never be doubtful when you are doing something, because without faith you can't expect a miracle.; [a.] Saint James Montego Bay, Jamaica

GRIDLEY, ISOBEL S.
[pen.] Toni Gridley; [b.] November 30, 1923, Buffalo, NY; [p.] Wilson W. Scrimshaw, Janet Scrimshaw; [m.] Clifford H. Gridley, April 17, 1948; [ed.] Southside High, Elmira Business Institute, "School of Hard Knocks"!; [occ.] Retired; [memb.] AARP, Gettysburg Presbyterian Church, O.E.S. #323, Big Flats, NY, Retired Public Employees of PA; [hon.] Editor's Choice Award, National Library of Poetry (1993), Past Worthy Matron of Excelsior chapter #323, O.E.S.; [oth. writ.] Letters to the Editor, Patriot-News Co., Harrisburg, short story submitted in contest, to PBS, Harrisburg; [pers.] I would like to create poetry to fill the spirit like that which listening to music gives me, and to fill the body the way satisfying food does. (I have entered numerous cooking contests without striking it big!); [a.] Gettysburg, PA

GRIECO, FAITH L.
[b.] September 20, 1956, New York, NY; [p.] Elias Jennett, Hattie Jennett; [m.] Ronald A. Grieco, May 29, 1993; [ed.] Fordham University - Bronx, NY; [pers.] This gift I possess is from God, built into me, made a part of me, to be used for the benefit of others and for His glory.; [a.] Sunrise, FL

GRIECO, FRANK VINCENT
[b.] January 3, 1962, Brooklyn, NY; [p.] Nicholas Grieco, Beatrice Grieco; [ed.] St. Agnes High School, St. JOhn's University College; [occ.] Letter Carrier United States Postal Service; [pers.] Feelings from the heart are better expressed through words than not expressed at all.; [a.] Seaford, NY

GRIECO, GINA MARIE
[b.] September 20, 1973, Elizabeth, NJ; [p.] Leonard and Dawn Grieco; [ed.] Arthur L. Johnson Regional High School, Clark, NJ, and St. John's University, Staten Island, NY; [occ.] Customer Service Rep. at Prudential Mutual Finds, Edison, NJ; [memb.] Accounting Society; [pers.] "Tomorrow is not promised to us, so let us enjoy today and make the bet of it!"; [a.] Clark, NJ

GRIFFIN, MORRIS J.
[b.] July 11, 1952, Vancouver, WA; [p.] Edward and Evelyn Griffin; [m.] Daymien Flevry, February 25, 1995; [ch.] Four dogs, one cat; [ed.] 2 yrs. College; [occ.] Retired; [memb.] Founding Father of Human Rights Group - "T.D.A. - USA, Total Devotion and Allegiance - To Human Unity"; [hon.] GEO - Griffin - Kerske, Human Unity Lifetime Achievement Award, Honorary Member - The Leather Men/Atlanta; [pers.] If we would give each person the basic human rights - there would be no need for all the different special rights, such as woman, black, gay, straight or children rights!; [a.] Atlanta, GA

GRIFFITHS, DIANNE CAMIRE
[b.] April 17, 1957, Kenora, Ontario, Canada; [p.] Madeline and Adrien Camire; [m.] Bruce Griffiths,

January 13, 1979; [ch.] Nancy, Anthony and Amber; [ed.] Beaver Brae and Lakewood Secondary's, Niagara College, Sault College, University of Waterloo and Lakehead, Entrepreneurial Development and Computer training.; [memb.] Canadian Hearing Society; [oth. writ.] "Satisfaction", "Day's Duty", "My Mark", (published); [pers.] "I want to make a difference in the way people think of themselves by giving them hope and teaching people to like themselves."; [a.] Kenora Ontario, Canada

GRIFFITHS, JOHN F.
[b.] February, 25, 1948, Somerset, IA; [p.] John and Rachel Griffiths; [ch.] One son, John, three daughters, Rachel, Robin, Rebecca; [ed.] Was a student at Crowder College, Neosho, Mo; [memb.] Vo-Tech Club, Phi Betta Kappa Honor Society; [hon.] Dean's List; [pers.] John died shortly after he wrote this poem, from injuries sustained in an auto accident. This poem was read at his funeral. Time now stands still for John.; [a.] Fairview, MO

GRILLO, GERALDINE
[pen.] Geraldine Pascale; [b.] 1899, Italy; [p.] Vito Pascale and Rosa Pascale; [m.] Salvatore Grillo, 1924; [ch.] Benita Hargrove; [ed.] Hunter College, B.A. 1921; [occ.] Teacher of History, Literature, New York City Schools, retired at age 96, enjoying works of geniuses from the beginning of time.; [hon.] Awards scholarship work on Dante's "Divine Comedy." Award: "Life of Savonarola" Scholarship - Woman's Law Course, New York University.; [oth. writ.] Short stories to "New Story Magazine", England. Occasional Verses, Local Periodicals.; [pers.] Man's nobility consists not in never failing, but after each fall, rising higher and higher to reach the beneficence of the "Great Provider."; [a.] Island Park, NY

GRIMSTEAD, DR. JAY
[p.] Bilbo Baggins; [b.] February 2, 1935, Bismarck, ND; [p.] Ruth Deemer and Joe Grinsteiner; [s.] Donna Hoffman (Grimstead); [m.] December 14, 1963; [ch.] Julie and Guy; [ed.] B.S. Sterling College, Th M Fuller Theo Seminar, D. Min Fuller Theo Seminar; [occ.] Theologian & Publisher of Crosswinds Magazine; [memb.] Evangetical Theological Society, Fellowship of Christian Ministries; [hon.] E. Stanley Jones Ministry- at- large award;[oth. writ.] Book "Let's Have a Reformation", articles in magazines, short stories in His Magazine "A Theological Science Fiction"; [pers.] The Bible has all the answers in principle to solve all momland's problems in the fields of Law, Government, Economics, Education, Science, Arts, Family, and Psychology.; [a.] Sunnyvale, CA

GRIZZLE, CATHERINE
[pen.] Catherine L. Smith; [b.] February 21, 1905, Oakland, IN; [p.] Tom and Annette Smith; [m.] O. John Grizzle, April 15, 1922; [ch.] Gail and Peggy; [ed.] "Public High School" Grad. 50 yrs, an avid reader, read all of bible and prose and poetry of all sort and times.; [occ.] Retired - (Photo Dark Room Technician); [oth. writ.] A short story of my very young life precious memories", was published in news paper. It was selected over other entries, in 1995; [pers.] From the time I learned to talk and rhyme two words, poetry has been with me. In good

times it adds to happiness and in sorrow it brings solace to my soul.; [a.] Hillsboro, TX

GROSSMAN, RANDI M.
[b.] December 13, 1975, Brooklyn, NY; [p.] Stuart Grossman, Judith Grossman; [ed.] South Shore H.S., Kingsborough Community College, Brooklyn College; [occ.] Genovese Drug Stores; [memb.] Institute of Children's Literature, Computer Applications, Research and Technology Program.; [hon.] Associate of the Month by Genovese, public school graduation chorus; [oth. writ.] Not as of yet published: Sally Gets Lost, Black Sky, Frolicking, Mystery.; [pers.] I dedicate this poem to my father. Who not only told me to try my best, he also lives within my spirit.; [a.] Brooklyn, NY

GRUE, SHEILA
[pen.] Sheila Grue; [b.] February 26, 1948, MN; [p.] Theodore and Lorraine Gamboni; [m.] Derald (Dewy), July 17, 1974; [ch.] Jeramie, Jeffrey, Denise; [ed.] White Bear Lake Jr. and Sr. High; [occ.] Ceramics, Poetry, House wife and grandmother; [memb.] Ladies VFW Auxiliary National Library of Poetry; [hon.] Poets Society 20 year pin, Ladies Auxiliary; [oth. writ.] Survival, You Took My Breath Away, Then I Looked At You, Don't Give Up Hope, This Old Jelopy.; [pers.] The Poem "Don't Give Up Hope" was written because it is what happened. Her finding me filled with an emptiness that was in my heart, that nothing else could have replaced. I loved my new family. Especially my grand children Stefanie and Danielle and Son-in-Law Dan.; [a.] Circle Pines, MN

GULLICK, BONNIE
[b.] November 25, 1932, Falkner, MS; [p.] J. C. and Bessie W. James, (Deceased); [m.] James B. Gullick (Deceased), January 20, 1962; [ch.] Deborah (Mrs. Harry) Bowman; [ed.] Falkner High School; [occ.] Retired from "Federal Reserve Bank, Memphis Branch"; [pers.] Any writing talent I have is a gift, I thank the Giver!

GUM, BRIAN
[b.] April 12, 1979, Seoul, South Korea; [p.] Ho Kyong Gum, Hae Yon Gum; [ed.] Harvard-Westlake High School; [occ.] Student; [memb.] Admissions Committee, School Newspaper (Chronicle), School Foreign Language Literature Magazine (Foreign Outlook Magazine), Junior Statesman of America; [hon.] Honor Roll, Humanitas, Certificate of Merit Music Achievement Award, Award for Editorial Writing in Journalism; [oth. writ.] Currently writing a novel on the Asian-American Immigrant Experience.; [pers.] I try to express a different point of view in my writing. I believe that it is a writer's duty to make known the minority opinion or any other side to an issue. I strive to make readers think of various aspects before having them form an opinion.; [a.] Granada Hills, CA

GUNN, WILLIE COSDENA
[pen.] Cassie Gunn; [b.] December 24, 1926, Seneca, SC; [p.] Fletcher and Mattie R. Gideon (Deceased); [m.] Willie James Gunn, December 24, 1975; [ch.] Dr. John Henderson Thomas III; [ed.] B.S. in Biology from Benedict College, Columbia, S.C., M.A. in Education from the University of Michigan at Ann Arbor, M.S. in Counseling and Guidance from the University of Michigan at Ann

Arbor.; [occ.] Retired Educator, and a Licenced Professional Counselor; [memb.] Ebenezer Baptist Church, Community Education Network Project, American Counseling Association, Director of Dr. Bryant Sebastian Sharp Scholarship, Tri-County Technical College Comprehensive Studies Advisory Board, Access and Equity Advisory Board, Life member of Zeta Phi Beta Sorority, National Sorority of Phi DeltaKappa National Association of Media Women, Top Ladies distinction.; [hon.] 1998 National Media woman of the Year, 1989 Counselor of the Year, Phi Delta Kappa Mid-Western Regional Educational Award, Zeta Phi Beta Woman of the Year and inducted into Zeta Phi Beta Hall of Fame. Panhellenic Council Woman of the Year, Flint Michigan Editorial 1988 Outstanding Achievement Award, Flint Michigan Literary club Literary Award of the year.; [oth. writ.], Booklets: "Career Planning" "Count down to College", for high school students, "Achievement Register", Co-authored a book of poems "Feelings", published many professional papers, served on the Charles Stewart Mott Adult High school Committee to write the first 900 reading series for adult education in Flint, MI.; [pers.] Poetry is therapy. Reading and writing poetry helps me to tap into the imagery and depths of feeling found in poetry that I might not be able to articulate in my everyday speech.; [a.] Seneca, SC

GUSTAFSON, SCOTT K.
[b.] August 10, 1971, Napa; [ed.] Justin-Siena High School, Sonoma State University B.S. Energy, Minors - Chemistry and Philosophy; [occ.] Self-employed, student; [memb.] Electric Vehicle Assoc., Ideas to Market; [pers.] Dare to dream, if you don't no one will do it for you. Live your dream, life is too short to do otherwise. Create your dream, the key to its realization.; [a.] Santa Rosa, CA

GUTHRIE, PEGGY C.
[pen.] Peggy C. Guthrie; [b.] November 23, 1923, College Station, TX; [p.] Leonard D. and Aurora N. Trevino; [m.] James (Jimmy) Guthrie, April 7, 1946; [ch.] Sandra Lynn and Pamela Ann; [ed.] A&M Consolidated Elementary, A&M Consolidated HS, TWU, Paris Jr. College, Texas A&M, East Texas State University; [occ.] Retired Bi-Lingual Spanish Teacher; [memb.] RSVP, AARP, Retired Teachers, Co-Ministry, United Methodist Church, United Methodist Women, Little Black Book Poetry Society, Littleton-Hite Bible Club, Aerofit-Swinging Srs. Eastern Star; [hon.] Paris COFC Finest Teacher Award, United Methodist Women North Texas Paris, Sulphur Springs District Poem, Devotion Booklet and Newsletter, NE Texas Emmaus Newsletter; [oth. writ.] "Without Him", "A Glimpse of God", "An Agape Prayer", "Five Little Widows", "The Third Dimension", "On Eagle's Wings", etc.; [pers.] God's love, His grace and His many blessings besides my family, church and friends are my inspirations.; [a.] Paris, TX

GUTREIMAN, LEO
[b.] March 17, 1923, Poland; [ch.] Three; [ed.] Elementary; [occ.] Former Carpenter Builder; [oth. writ.] Poems prose Chronicles of my Life's Experiences in 3 continents; [pers.] At this time in my life the pen is more creative than the saw and hammer; [a.] New Haven, CT

H, ARUN
[b.] January 29, 1968, Kerala, India; [p.] T.K. Hari and Mrs. Mohana Hari; [ed.] B. Sc (Maths), A.C.I.B. (London); [occ.] Credit Officer (United Arab Bank); [memb.] Distinguished Member of The International Society of Poets; [hon.] Recepient of Editor's Choice Award from The National Library of Poetry, USA.; [oth. writ.] I run my weekly columns Gulf-Weekly of Dubai, UAE. Junior-News of Dubai, UAE. Times of Oman of Oman.; [pers.] 1) I believe only in humanism. 2) Time is the most precious thing for me. 3) I believe in the concept of " One World", I am against all wars. [a.] Sharjah, UAE

HACKNEY, GLENN
[pen.] Glenn Hackney; [b.] December 22, 1924, Erieville, NY; [p.] Arthur Hackney, Beatrice Hackney; [m.] Esther Hackney, December 8, 1946; [ch.] Glenn Alan, Arthur James Hackney; [ed.] Cazenovia Central High School, Cornell Univ. (1 year); [occ.] Retired; [memb.] National Republican Party, AARP, Presbyterian Church, Running Club North, Madd, Gallups Island Radio Assn.; [hon.] Former Alaska State Senior, Senior Citizen of year (1994), Olympic Torch Bearer (1996); [oth. writ.] Poetry in local newspaper, verse for many local organizations.; [pers.] I deeply enjoy building poems. The mating of words is an endless and sensual joy.; [a.] Fairbanks, AK

HAEUSSLER, MRS. ROSE ANN
[pen.] Rose Ann Haeussler; [b.] May 20, 1961, Windsor; [p.] Florence and James Ferguson; [m.] Richard Haeussler, June 26, 1982; [ch.] Jenifer, Adam, Emily, Charles and Eric; [ed.] Saint Claire College; [occ.] Housewife; [memb.] Recent Member of Women Writers of Windsor; [hon.] Editor's Choice Award, The National Library of Poetry for 1995 Poems, 1. Embracing the Light, 2. Communication, 3. Fences; [oth. writ.] 1995 Publishings in Sparkles in the Sand - Communication Path not taken - Embracing the Light Shadows and Light - Fences; [pers.] I hope my poems bring the readers as much pleasure as I have making them for their enjoyment.; [a.] Windsor

HAFDELIN, LAURA ANN
[pen.] Tzigane; [b.] March 20, 1970, Bloomfield, NJ; [p.] Arthur Hafdelin, Linda Hamilton; [ed.] Meadowbrook High School; [oth. writ.] This is my first published work. I have written for myself all my life.; [a.] Richmond, VA

HAFEEZ, ZEBRA HASAN
[pen.] Zeba Hasan Hafeez; [b.] September 30, 1960, Karachi; [p.] Professor Mushtaq Hasan and Zubaiba Hasan; [m.] Mohsin Hafeez, September 16, 1987; [ch.] Two daughter, Sahar and Sarah; [ed.] Medical Doctor, MBBS, MCPS (Dermatology); [occ.] Skin Specialist (Dermatologist); [memb.] Pakistan Association of Dermatologists; [hon.] 2nd Prize in English poetry competition, American Centre, Karachi, 1985. First Prize in English short story writing, American Centre, Karachi, 1984. Second Prize in English poetry competition, Arts Council, Karachi 1981. First Prize in Jane Townsend poetry competition, American Centre, Karachi, 1980. Editorship of Dow Medical College Magazine "Dowlite", Karachi, from 1980 to 1983.; [oth. writ.] Articles, short

stories, poems published in Dowlite, local newspapers and magazines. "World Poetry", India, 1983. NE Europa (Luxemburg), a literary magazine covering arts, letters and sciences, published in English and many European languages, 1987.; [pers.] Poetry writing enables one to explore vistas of one's imagination and, at times, accept the cold reality. A poem, thus, is heightened to the stage of being an externalization of one's deep thoughts and intense emotions. I have been encouraged and guided particularly by my late Aunt Mrs. Bilquis Siddiqui (Educationist).; [a.] Karachi, Pakistan

HAFTNER, IOLA
[pen.] Iola Haftner; [b.] November 14, 1926, Sylvania, Saskatchewan, Canada; [p.] Cliff and Francos Townsend; [m.] Divorced; [ch.] Three girls and one boy; [ed.] Grade 10; [occ.] Retired; [memb.] Have written to published articles for the Natural History Society on Nature and Wild Edibbe plants and flowers.; [oth. writ.] The poem came from a book "Beyond The Misty Mountain". I'm writing about The Peace River Valley in Northern Alberta, I grew up on Deep Creek Ranch as a real Cowgirl, I've also composed about 300 songs but can't afford to record them.; [pers.] Taken Botany and Harticulture am an avid gardner Naturalist and Botanist, study health and vitamins, have a wild flower stamp collection, play scrabble and read all non fiction.; [a.] Victoria British Columbia, Canada

HAKE, DANIELLE
[pen.] Diva; [b.] January 11, 1981; [pers.] I have been greatly influenced by Melissa Etheridge, because she is not afraid to be herself and stands up for what she believes in. Therefore she is my "Hero."; [a.] Coral Springs, FL

HALL, DARIUS
[b.] February 10, 1977, Gary, IN; [p.] Rosalind Hall, Darius Halls Sr.; [ed.] Cosmetology, Arts, Music Humboldt High; [memb.] Nevordisc Music; [hon.] Cinco de Mayo Art Award; [oth. writ.] Two poems published in school newspaper; [pers.] I try to write poems to fit everyone's emotions. I mainly faces on the relationships of today; [a.] Saint Paul, MN

HALL, LINDA
[b.] October 26, 1961, Columbus, OH; [p.] Theodore and Dottie Good; [m.] Lee Hall, February 27, 1993; [ch.] Donivin Dawayne, Roshawn Scott, April Renee; [ed.] South High School, Pacific College of Medical and Dental; [occ.] Sewing Machine Associate, Vanity Fair Mills, Milton, Fla.; [memb.] Jordan St. S.D.A. Church, Sabbath School Teacher, and Superintendent; [hon.] Sabbath school teacher, medical school, first place music award; [oth. writ.] One of my poems titled "He Lives" was sung by the Maranatha choir in San Diego, CA. Another one won first place in a poetry contest.; [pers.] I thank God from whom all of my blessings flow. And my mom for all of her encouraging words, and for lending an ear to hear everyone of my poems.; [a.] Milton, FL

HALL, MICHELE
[b.] August 3, 1953; [ed.] Cypress Jr. College; [occ.] Evidence Technician; [memb.] California Association for Property and Evidence; [pers.] To find a sense of grace and dignity to

life through the love and passion of language.; [a.] Buena Park, CA

HALL, SHEILA L.
[b.] May 31, 1961, Fort Belvair; [p.] Ralph and Sylvia Kiner; [m.] Win C. Hall; [ch.] Ory Joel, Donaphon Win, Tessa Machell; [ed.] Polk Community College; [occ.] Homemaker; [hon.] Dean's List; [oth. writ.] "The Power of Time" in a Sea of Treasures of the National Library of Poetry.; [pers.] I dedicate this poem to Sylvia, my mother.; [a.] Canton, TX

HALL, TERESA
[b.] January 29, 1983, Fargo, ND; [p.] Pam and Gerry Hall; [ed.] I'm currently in 4th grade and I'm an a student.; [occ.] I'm in school.; [memb.] I'm a member of the YMCA; [hon.] I've had 2 physical fitness awards and spent a day with the Gov. of N.D.; [oth.] I have written more poems and also a book on boy family.; [pers.] The children of the world are sometimes not noted for the great talent they possess and I thank you for noticing my poetry.; [a.] Oxbow, ND

HALL, TONY R.
[b.] October 24, 1953, Akron, OH; [p.] Tommy and Marie Hall; [m.] Mary Lou Hall, May 1993; [ch.] Joshua and Laura; [ed.] Mechanical Engineering B.A., Electrical Master Carpenter; [occ.] Writer/Wood Worker; [oth. writ.] Numerous Technical article's for various fortune 500 companies.; [pers.] "Don't Quit"; [a.] Mercer, PA

HALL, VIOLET Y.
[b.] January 28, 1969, Jacksonville, FL; [p.] Mr. and Mrs. Earnest Hall; [ch.] Latiancian T.K. Clinton; [ed.] William M. Raines Senior High School, Jones College, Florida Community College of Jacksonville; [occ.] Clerk - Supervisor of Elections Office, Jax, FL; [hon.] Employee of the Month Cargill Inc., Head Coach for the Hoya's Cheerleaders YMCA 1994; [pers.] My poems reflect on how I see God's creations as a sight of love and beautification that is revealed morning, noon, and night.; [a.] Jacksonville, FL

HALLER, GRETCHEN
[b.] December 2, 1941, Pittsburgh, PA; [p.] Fred E. Haller and Genevieve Sanford Haller; [m.] 1966-1987; [ch.] Tabitha S. Pearson, Linnea H. Pearson; [ed.] Rosemont College, Carnegie Institute of Technology, Univ. of Pittsburgh; [occ.] Free Lance Writer; [memb.] Preservation Pittsburgh, Phg. Assoc. for Arts in Education and Therapy, Education Writers Assoc.; [hon.] Intl. Assoc. of Bus. Comm. (IABC), PA Sch. Bds. Assoc. (PSBA), Nat. Sch. PR Assoc. (NSPRA); [oth. writ.] Articles published in The Pittsburgh Press, Pittsburgh Post-Gazette, Vermont Life Magazine, coeditor, Sarah: Her Life, Her Restaurant, Her Recipes, for Pittsburgh History and Landmarks Foundation; [a.] Pittsburgh, PA

HAMILTON, DEBBIE
[pen.] BBB; [b.] October 3, 1968; [p.] Sheila Rourke and Jean-Marie Hamilton; [m.] Nil; [ed.] I have been subject to many different levels of schooling which has unconsciously prepared me for the inevitable Consciousness of the underlying Subliminal of a Social Collective Belief System,

i.e., the Male-Perception dominated Structure of the World of Images, I have no Love for the conflict-structured, literary Text-Book, but it has enabled me to "See": Comprehend, the Truth found in it's Opposite Possibility.; [occ.] Administrative Assistant; [memb.] Alliance Quebec The International Society of Poets; [hon.] To be accorded the 'Ability' to "See" the veil of the Imaginary.; [oth. writ.] Have had several poems published by The National Library of Poetry, Various articles published in a local magazine.; [pers.] 'Thoughts' - itself derived from the beginning of Natural Experienced - has three times: Opinion, Perception, Experience. The sole Purpose of 'Thought' is to equate the Mind to all things instinctively - whether Person or Idea - for the Reason of Comprehension. From this comes the Authentic Authority.; [a.] Montreal, Quebec

HAMLET, STEVEN MARK
[pen.] Steven Mark Hamlet; [pers.] A true legacy of Love experienced by the author from his father (Robert B. Hamlet). And handed down as a love letter to the author's son (Jeremiah J. Hamlet); [a.] Jenison, MT

HAMMOND, TYLER DAVID
[pen.] Tyler David Hammond; [b.] April 30, 1975, Spearfish, SD; [p.] Dan and Robyn Hammond; [ed.] Graduated from Pullman High School with honors 1994. Currently a sophomore at WSU majoring in theatre.; [occ.] Full time student at Washington State University; [memb.] I am currently a member in the Washington State University Concert Choir. I'm also involved with a Summer Palace Theatre Co. and Theatre Education Workshops.; [hon.] I have received many acting and speech related awards. I was chosen as lead vocalist in my jazz solo division at the '94 Lionel Hampton Jazz Fest. I received solo entry to his evening concert.; [oth. writ.] Have written numerous poems as well as a full length play. I have had writing as well as art work published in "The Prairie Winds" magazine (local to the black hills of SD.); [pers.] Experience brings poetry. I strive to capture moments of my experience, that would otherwise be forgotten. I speak especially of love where mutual self giving can be intensified and clarified through verse. Thus, poetry is an art of interpretation.; [a.] Pullman, WA

HANEY, ANGELA M.
[pen.] Angie; [b.] November 18, 1977, Key West, FL; [p.] Noah F. and Joyce L. Sanders; [m.] December 14, 1981; [ch.] Alex, Crystal, Angela, and Keith; [ed.] Cottondale High, 11th grade; [oth. writ.] Other non-published poems, including one published in the school yearbook.; [pers.] I love to write because it is a very rewarding way to express my feelings and emotions. I hope to inspire others with my writings, and my accomplishments as a result of my writings.; [a.] Cottondale, FL

HANSEL, IDA LEE
[b.] December 28, 1933, Hazard, KY; [p.] Howard and Ruby Stacy; [m.] John T. Hansel Jr., July 5, 1952; [ch.] Sharon, Michael, Deborah and Jonathan; [ed.] Commercial School Graduate, Plus Courses and much, much experience; [occ.] Just retired Legal Assistant; [hon.] I feel too minor to list

although I have been writing poetry and short stories since I was a teen, I got serious about it when I got much older and have received acclaims, but none I think would be major; [oth. writ.] Short stories, Prose and Poetry, published in newspapers, periodicals, anthologies in U.S. and England, (This is not to be included but just a short statement, "I have been told that I have poems possibly in Kennedy, Eisenhower and Nixon Museums), working on my first book of poetry and prose, "Come Walk A Country Road"; [pers.] I love putting words into poetry and most of them reflect on the good days of yore, personal experiences, some derived from years of working in the courtroom and legal field at large. I love people and write hoping someone will reflect on the "Good Ole Days" when reading my offerings. I worked for years in an outdoor drama based on John Fox, Jr's, the little Shepherd of Kingdom Come. I am so glad that I entered your contest.; [a.] Spartanburg, SC

HANSEN, LUCILLE M.
[b.] Rigby, ID; [p.] Elmer and Melbie Waters; [m.] Jewell Hansen; [ch.] Marjorie Vaughn, Lynn, Lyle; [ed.] Rigby High School and classes at Ricks College and Columbia Basin Community College; [occ.] Retired (Civil Service 2nd Washington State); [memb.] WAES (Washington State Assn of Educational Secretaries) 2nd MLAES (Moses Lake Assn of Educational Secretaries) and church groups; [hon.] Being asked to write for programs, and having my writings published is a great honor for me.; [oth. writ.] Poems and articles published in 3 different church magazines, several rural magazines, three different daily newspaper, and in the Burr Pioneer History Book; [pers.] I write to express and preserve my deep feelings and observations of people and nature in a brief poetic way. Finding the right words and expressing myself poetically fascinates me.; [a.] Rexburg, ID

HAOVE, MR. IKRAMUL
[b.] April 30, 1937, Raipur, India; [p.] Not alive; [m.] Mrs. Shakila Shabnam, May 5, 1971; [ch.] Five; [ed.] Bachelor of Arts Degree, Bachelor of Laws Degree from University.; [occ.] Station Manager, Pakistan International Airlines, Frankfort Airport.; [oth. writ.] Poem published in sparkles in the sand.

HARBIN JR., PAUL F.
[b.] January 30, 1977, Warren, MI; [p.] Roberta Jean Harbin, Paul F. Harbin; [ed.] GED, trying to make my way to college. Would like to either write and/or go to an Art College.; [occ.] Receiving crew member at a warehouse distribution center in Atlanta, GA; [oth. Writ.] The Wrong Side, Sleep Walking, multiple poems which are part of a book not yet completed.; [pers.] A man's experiences are his greatest teacher. His understanding of them can make him an honorable student of life.; [a.] Mableton, GA

HARDWICK JR., PHILIP F.
[b.] June 3, 1973, Durango, CO; [p.] Philip Hardwick Sr., Dianne Sue Hardwick; [ch.] Leorah Ganesa Hardwick, Aliya Hardwick; [ed.] '91-94 Plymouth State College, Psychology/Philosophy; [hon.] Sweet Rewards; [oth. writ.] Nothing officially, officially nothing.; [pers.] You say my poems are poetry? They are not. Yet if you understand they are not

- then you see the poetry of them - Ryokan.; [a.] Northfield, NH

HARGROVE, DORIS WALKER
[b.] August 6, 1935, Lonoke, AR; [p.] William and Maydelle Eagle; [m.] Jackie R. Walker (Deceased), August 19, 1952, Marvin R. Hargrove, March 5, 1994; [ch.] Randall, Sharon, Jackie Anita, Mark Barbara; [ed.] Midway High, Cabot, AR, Univ of Wisconsin Banking Degree; [occ.] Vice President - Bank of Cabot Cabot, AR; [memb.] Lions Club, Methodist Church, U.S. Postal Committee; [oth. writ.] This was my first attempt.; [pers.] I love nature and most of my thoughts will be on nature. I am also a very sentimental person like the thoughts in my poem, "In Memory of".; [a.] Cabot, AR

HARLOW, JANICE K.
[pen.] Jan Harlow; [b.] Alderson W. VA; [p.] Clyde Feamster; [ch.] Sherry, Gail and Brent; [oth. writ.] Write poem's and song's about my experience's had song published; [pers.] Go to wildwood Baptist Church Kennesaw, CA, - Hoping that my gift will be an inspiration to other's; [a.] Kennesaw, CA

HARMAN, EFTALON
[b.] July 28, 1946, Hornsey, London, England; [p.] Ramiz and Suzan-Harman; [m.] Sue Mehmet Harman; [ed.] Hornsey College of Art Hornsey, London; [occ.] Artist; [hon.] Bachelor's Degree in Fine Art, Editor's Choice Award '91, '91, '93, '94, '95, '96. 'The National Library of Poetry'; [oth. writ.] Qairn poem sketches - 1983 - qairn sonnet sketches - 1987 recorded album of sonnets 'Visions' by The National Library of poetry; [pers.] Goodwill to all my 'Brethren'.; [a.] Islington London, England

HAROLD, MARGARET V.
[b.] June 5, 1918, Lorain, OH; [p.] Steven Latran, Honor Latran; [m.] Frank C. Harold M.D., April 11, 1941; [ed.] Oberlin H.S., Oberlin College University of the Andes; [occ.] Retired Foreign Language Teacher Columbus, Ohio; [memb.] AAUW, Delta Kappa Gamma, MLTA, OMLTA, AATSP; [hon.] OAS Scholarship (Cuba), Full-bright Scholarship (Columbia); [oth. writ.] Writer of oral history for senior theatre and production. Oral history and poetry for family and friends.; [pers.] The personal background of four languages give me an in depth source of appreciation for the poetry of many cultures and help me to express honestly my thoughts and feelings.; [a.] Columbus, OH

HARP, KENNETH W.
[pen.] Kenny Harp; [b.] November 16, 1933, Lexington; [p.] William and Gertude Harp; [m.] Katherine M. Harp, October 25, 1952; [ch.] Two boys, Two girls; [occ.] Retired; [oth. writ.] A Journey with the Covenant Cloud Prophecy, Follow his Example, Mama's Feast Time Story, Trust and forgive, "The Great I Am" For the Rainbows Promise, God's Chosen Soldier, Comfort, Mr. Adams Wift, The Lesson Within.; [pers.] I like a simple life. I love our farm, and my life there. I am a God fearing Man. And the Lord is always first in my life. And I've always liked to write poetry.; [a.] Cameron, MO

HARRINGTON, KAY L.
[b.] January 27, 1947, Stockton, CA; [p.] Hal and Ellen (Carlson) Van DaGriff; [m.] Fredric T. Harrington, August 23, 1987; [ch.] 6/8 Grandchildren; [ed.] Baptist Bible College, Springfield, MO, Framingham State College, Framingham, MA 80's, Aurora High School, Aurora, MO; [occ.] Secretary/ Development Office at Regis College in Weston, MA (past 7 months); [memb.] Tremont Temple Baptist Church in Boston, MA; [hon.] 11 Years of Service to Babson College in Wellesley MA as Administrative Assistant in a Managerial Position/Award January 1995; [oth. writ.] Freelance writing for local newspaper enjoy poetry and all types of writing had thesis published at BBC and more recently, wrote for children a cook book, "Grandma's recipes and more."; [pers.] My desire is to write in such a way as to impact the lives of others positively while upholding christian precepts.; [a.] Wayland, MA

HARRIS, BELVHA LEVALLE
[b.] April 13, 1951, Springfield, MA; [p.] John W. LeValle and Belvha F. LeValle; [m.] John C. Harris, December 23, 1972; [ch.] John Cowan Harris Jr.; [ed.] Commerce High, University of Massachusetts; [occ.] English Teacher, John F. Kennedy Middle School, Springfield, MA; [memb.] Bethel African American Episcopal Church; [hon.] Mass Mutual Inspirational Teacher Honoree 1995; [oth. writ.] Published in the National Library of Poetry Anthology "Tomorrow's Dream."; [pers.] My writing reflects the love and strength of my mother, who taught me to cherish each member of my family.; [a.] Springfield, MA

HARRIS, ROSE
[b.] February 3, 1932, New York City; [p.] John P. Sim, Julia Sim; [m.] David J. Harris, December 19, 1977; [ch.] Patricia Joyce, Karen Sue, Debra Ann, Edward Jr.; [ed.] Washington Irving High School; [occ.] Housewife; [pers.] I have been influenced, by the poems by "Elizabeth Barret Browning", and "Emily Dickenson". I enjoy reading about poetry. I am greatly inspired by "How Do I Love Thee".; [a.] Flushing, NY

HARRIS, STARR RUSSELL
[b.] November 2, 1977, Louisville, KY; [p.] Candance Russell, Richard Harris; [ed.] Washington College Academy, Lewis and Clark College; [occ.] College undergraduate Eng. Major, Gender Studies Minor; [memb.] AIDS Awareness Group; [hon.] Senior English Award; [oth. writ.] I have had poems published in high school and college literary magazines.; [pers.] Poetry is my way of seeing, tasting, feeling, and being. It is the air I breathe and my purest love. I write about the moments in life that touch me, that touch others. I very much thank my parents, my three sisters and those I love for continued material and inspiration.; [a.] Portland, OR

HARRISON, GREGORY A.
[b.] July 16, 1946, Baltimore, MD; [p.] Harry M. and Marie C. Harrison; [ch.] Have 4 cats; [ed.] BS Fire Engineering US/Md, MS Civil Engr US/M, MS Admin, GW Univ, PhD Safety Engineering Kennedy - Western Univ; [occ.] Forensic Engineer; [memb.] ASSE, NFPA, SFPE, BOCA, Registr. prof. engr. Md/VA/ CA; [oth. Writ.] Numerous Technical Articles; [pers.] Whenever possible, I strive to make the person next to me laugh. I am motivated and influenced daily by Sarnetle Wagner.; [a.] Gaithersburg, MD

HARRISON, MR. KIM L.
[pen.] A. Tarr and Professor Feather; [b.] April 11, 1952, Hickory, NC; [p.] Clyde and Mary Harrison; [m.] Katrina Gregg Harrison, October 16, 1973; [ch.] Melissa, Trevor, Kale, Sage; [ed.] Lee's Summit MO. High and "The World at Large"!; [occ.] Professional Driver I also Teach Motorcycle Rider Education; [memb.] Freedom of Road Rides Inc, Motorcycle Safety Foundation, American Motorcycle Association; [oth. writ.] I wrote a monthly satire intitled "Hey! What's The Deal" for the F.O.R.R. `Freedom' Press for four years. Several short stories, and news letter columns.; [pers.] My imagination explodes when I'm with my word processor and I have the ability to see life from a unique perspective. I think life should be uncomplicated and fun. I can't wait to see what the future holds!; [a.] Independence, MO

HART, CAROL
[pen.] Rosa; [b.] October 26, 1951, Cornwall; [p.] Denzil and Chloe Hart; [ch.] Sean Butcher, Ian Burtcher, Andrew Hart; [ed.] Includes various post - secondary Certificates but neither a Diploma, nor a degree; [occ.] Registered Practical Nurse; [memb.] College of Nurse of Ontario, 1st Morrisburg Colony - (Rainbow) Beavers - Scouts Canada Leader, Presbyterian World Services and Development Representative - Presbyterian Church of Canada, Commissioned Sunday School Teacher, St. Matthews Presbyterian - Ingleside Ontario; [oth. writ.] A shadow dance, cold Frenzy, Ode to A winner, Flaner - No "S" plus: Half - way home (published in "Sparkles in the Sand - 1995 Anthology Semifinalist), also Rainbow o'er the Sables: What is a poem? - Philosophically; [pers.] What is a poem? - Philosophically. Between the rhyme of each line, is release for the feelings experienced o'er time. A release like magic of what is sometimes tragic, but no less it is renewal of in freedom, to behold and reminisced."; [a.] Morrisburg Ontario, Canada

HART, LESLIE
[b.] February 5, 1966, Greenville, KY; [p.] Linda and Marion J. McFarland (Deceased); [ch.] 2 Tiffany and Timothy; [ed.] Attending College for Accounting; [occ.] Manager Trainee Hucks/Martin and Bailey; [hon.] Young composers-1976 state and National Awards for Health Occupations students of America-1982, 3rd place young artist-1976; [oth. writ.] I have written several poems - none that I have had published, but I have never had the chance to enter them until now.; [pers.] I write poems that come to me they are from my heart, my pain, my future, and my past. This specific poem was wrote for Chris Beasley a 16 years killed from a gun accident. My love to you, Chris; [a.] Mount Vernon, Indiana

HARTLAND, RACHEL L.
[pen.] Jennifer Greeve; [ch.] Four daughters; [ed.] I completed my education, as well as a commercial course and Secretarial course in Richmond/ Vancouver, BC.; [occ.] Writer and volunteer works.; [memb.] Royal Canadian Legion, Society, for Retired and Semi-Retired, Calgary Co-op. AMA/ CAA plus church of England.; [hon.] "Editors Choice Award", C.V.S.M. "Award of Excellence" "Certificate from city of Nawanio B.C. for work with Seniors."; [oth. writ.] "Yesterday", "Lovers", "God's Masterpiece", "Looking upward",

several short poems as well as and article on SLE known as systematic Zeepus Eurethematosis.; [pers.] Also an article on "Drugs in the home and used where children are preserved" - distributed across and Canada. Also keep busy in mind and believe in oneself.; [a.] Alberta, Canada

HARTMAN, JANET
[b.] February 2, 1926, Downsville, NY; [p.] Velma Price Nee Whoehrle, Fred Price; [m.] Widow of Charles Hartman, November 24, 1966; [ch.] Gay Baker, Melody Currey; [ed.] Downsville Central High; [occ.] Retired from New York State Legislative Bill Drafting Commission, part-time telemarketing; [memb.] Democratil party, supervisor retired public employees association Inc.(Life Membership), AARP, Commander's club, National Veterans Association National Wildlife Association, Smithsonian; [hon.] Legislative resolution of merit from senate and assembly, NY State, Citation from Connecticut General Assembly; [oth. writ.] Poems published in news papers, instruction manuals for state job, political newspaper column; [pers.] To me, poetry is the essence of all things, sister to the hymn of living!; [a.] Albany, NY

HARTSELL, JAMES C.
[b.] December 6, 1933, Rocky Comfort, MO; [p.] R. A. Hartsell, Pauline Hartsell; [m.] Larri Shannon, August 20, 1993; [occ.] Director, Hartsell Home; [memb.] ISP Distinguished Member; [oth. writ.] Several published poems, 1 book of poetry "Visions From the Trail".; [pers.] Good poetry must reflect the unique voice of the poet.; [a.] Alington, WA

HASKELL, MARGARET H.
[pen.] Margaret Dewey; [b.] April 28, 1923, Boston, MA; [p.] Charles Howard, Katherine Howard; [m.] Widowed; [ch.] Damon H. Ball; [ed.] Radcliffe College A.B., Columbia University A.M., Boston College School of Social Work, M.S.W.; [occ.] Psychotherapist and writer; [memb.] National Association of Social Workers, Harvard (University) Institute for Learning in Retirement, Marblehead Yacht Club, Marblehead Club of Small Gardens; [hon.] A.B. Cum laude, Radcliffe College, awarded Best of Show for fiction, Marblehead Arts Festival, 3 Superior Performance Awards from the Lowell, Mass. Veterans Administration Mental Hygiene Clinic; [oth. writ.] Several poems published by the Literary Supplement, Harvard University Press, a short story published by Writers World, Marblehead Festival of Arts, another story by Marblehead Magazine; [pers.] I want my poetry to convey the immediacy of experience, and to present both sides of a conflict, keeping the opposing forces caged within the poem like boxers in a ring.; [a.] Marblehead, MA

HATEM, S. M. JOVITA
[b.] June 18, 1925, New Straitsville, OH; [p.] Joseph and Faduah; [ed.] B.A. Ursuline College, M.A. Creighton University Omaha, Nebraska; [occ.] Writer/Teacher and Principal Facilitator of Spirituality; [memb.] NCEA/CTA, O.S.U./ASCD/ #1 Active Member of Ursuline Community Facilitator - Rainbows for all God's children; [hon.] Nominated for Principal of year in Ohio and Kentucky Advisory Council Live Oaks (Ohio), Participant in First National Gifted and Talented

Organization Administrator Perceiver (SR1) taught 10 Courses at Creighton University; [oth. writ.] Several letters to editors in Ohio newspaper - dedication address for new church prayer services and poems in Ursuline Publications two books for children: Activities for advent, a walk with Jesus, Lenten Activities and Prayers.; [pers.] I am a fully alive christian deep faith. As an Ursuline teacher and administrator I practice a contemplative love of God resulting in an openness and eagerness to serve the needs of others. I believe love, care, concern, joy should exude from the school environment.; [a.] Louisville, KY

HAWLEY, DONA S.
[pen.] Dona; [b.] June 9, 1940, Dallas, TX; [p.] Martrue and Don Sterling; [m.] David Hawley, January 5, 1985; [ed.] Highland Park High, Southern Methodist University School of Arts; [occ.] Working owner of a Floral and Catering/Party Service; [memb.] Friends of Fair Park (an organization for the historical preservation of "The Texas Centennial grounds and buildings, etc" (currently known as "The State Fair of Texas at Fair Park"; [hon.] Full page story in the Dalls Morning News re: my art work, especially my sculpting.; [oth. writ.] Numerous poems and one children's book with illustrations - all unpublished as yet.; [pers.] I can't say I have any great philosophy, just live and let live. I tend to see life thru rose colored glasses, make strong emotional commitments and have deep feelings for the beauties of my surroundings and attempt to communicate this thru creative endeavors.; [a.] Dallas, TX

HAYWOOD, CATHRYN
[b.] December 8, 1935, Windsor, Nova Scotia, Canada; [p.] Hedley Brown, Delta Brown; [ch.] Christine, Andrea, Peter (Deceased); [ed.] Windsor Academy, School of Business, Nursing Asst., Psychology of Adulthood and Aging; [occ.] Personal Care Worker, Northwood Care, Inc., Halifax, N.S. Can.; [memb.] Leila Rebekah Lodge #59, Missionary Oblates of Mary Immaculate, Compassionate Friends; [hon.] 30 yr Jewel - Leila Rebekah Lodge #59; [oth. writ.] Several poems published in the compassionate Friends - A newsletter for Bereaved Parents.; [pers.] I began writing after the death of my son in 1989 and it has proven to be a very special therapy.; [a.] Darthmouth Nova Scotia, Canada

HECK, TERRY W.
[pen.] Terry W. Heck; [b.] September 5, 1949, Evansville, IN; [occ.] Truck Driver; [pers.] Look over your shoulder is my first and only poem to date, I wrote this poem in twenty minutes, on a Saturday afternoon. I was thinking of a friend who had just lost her mother, the rest of her family had already past on, I felt her pain, in doing this. I wrote this poem from my heart. Now its time to share it with you.; [a.] Evansville, IN

HECKARD, SHIRLEY L.
[b.] March 28, 1932, London, England; [p.] James and Olga Carewe; [m.] Widow, September 22, 1954; [ch.] Mark, Randy, Jennifer; [ed.] Laguna Beach High School USMC; [occ.] Massage Therapist, Notary, Minister, Secretary; [memb.] IMA, NNA, WMA; [oth. writ.] Poems, stories for VCLA Extension creative writing

course.; [pers.] Always in touch with the healing power of massage.; [a.] Fullerton, CA

HEDGES, JEREMY
[b.] May 15, 1973, Fort Lauderdale, FL; [p.] Stephen Hedges, Wendy Hedges; [ed.] Hallandale High, Palm Beach Community College; [occ.] Student, Education Major; [pers.] This poem reflects my experience as dorm parent and English teacher at an orphanage in El Salvador.; [a.] Lake Worth, FL

HEFELE, ANNA M.
[pen.] Anna M. Hefele; [b.] January 23, 1943, Montreal, Province of Quebec, Canada; [p.] Alex Hefele and Margaret Bernath; [ch.] Daryl, Jessica, Christine, Michael; [ed.] St. Patrick's High School, Alexander Bus. College, University of Alberta (2 yrs), Fine Arts; [occ.] Administrative Assistant; [memb.] C.O.L.D. Club for person with Chronic Obstructive Lung Disease Respiratory Rehabilitation Clinic; [hon.] 1983 Nomination for Citizen of the Year for starting the Alberta Chapter of Thyroid Foundation of Canada and helping many hundreds of people better understand this illness.; [oth. writ.] Many poems and short stories as yet unpublished, most of them on the subjects of antisemeticism, racial issues, and prejudice.; [pers.] I write about things I know, feel and see within the circle of life. I believe our personal circle should not be so confining as to not allow new people, experiences, adventures to enter.; [a.] Edmonton Alberta, Canada

HEIDA, JOHN KENNETH
[b.] January 21, 1970, Ithaca, NY; [p.] James and Janet; [ed.] Eastern Christian High B.A. Business Administration and Computer Science, 1993 Calvin College, Grand Rapids, M.I; [occ.] Supermarket Sales; [memb.] Sussex Christian reformed, Sussex, NJ; [hon.] High School Varsity - soccer, tennis Calvin College Varsity - Soccer, Teams USA - U 17 NJ-Soccer in europe Concertmaster - North Jersey Regional Orchestra 1984; [pers.] "The Lord is my shepherd, I shall not want" "There is an intelligent arranger of everything." (Diogenes); [a.] Wayne, NJ

HEIDENTHAL, HEATHER
[b.] May 14, 1985, Brooklyn, NY; [p.] Debra Heidenthal; [ed.] St. Edmunds Elementary School; [occ.] Students; [hon.] Citizenship Award; [oth. writ.] My first published writing.; [pers.] I hope that my writings show my feelings about the sadder parts of life but I believe that things will always get better and we should learn to love one another.; [a.] Brooklyn, NY

HEIDER, DEBORAH A.
[b.] June 5, 1067, Kenmore, NY; [p.] Ronald Mitchell and Joan Mitchell; [m.] David Heider, June 24, 1995; [ed.] Kenmore West Sr. High; [occ.] Secretary, Amherst - Tonawanda Orthopedic Center; [pers.] I dedicate this poem to those of us who strive help others in strive to need. I have been enlightened by the writings of Shel Silverstein.; [a.] Orchard Park, NY

HEILMANS, MARIANA B.
[pen.] Bunny Heilman; [b.] February 7, 1920; [p.] William and Eleanor W. Bray; [m.] Deceased; [ch.] Harrison B. Hoffman, Dlamela Onyx; [ed.] High School; [occ.] Retired

HEITZER, TIFFANY
[pen.] Alice Dee; [b.] March 21, 1982, Johnstown; [p.] Robert Heitzer, Donna Heitzer; [ed.] Somerset Junior High School; [occ.] Attending School; [hon.] Presidential Academic Fitness Award and Honor Roll in School ever 6 weeks; [oth. writ.] I've never had any of my stories or poetry published before.; [pers.] I wrote my poem for an English assignment in school originally. I wrote about my hero Jerry Garcia who passed away. I feel that Jerry's death is a shame and an end to an Era and legacy of The Grateful Dead.; [a.] Friedens, PA

HELWIG, EDWARD J.
[b.] May 27, 1926, Connellsville, PA; [p.] August and Germaine Helwig; [m.] Verna, October 9, 1954; [ch.] Marybeth, Robert, Donna; [ed.] B.S. Chemistry Diquesne U. Graduate Studies U. of Pittsburgh and Pennsylvania State U.; [occ.] Research Chemist - Retired Consultant; [hon.] Honorable Mention in Woman's Day Essay Contest 1976, AISI Medal for Best Technical Paper 1988, Humor Article Selected for "Selected Papers of J. of Irreproducible Results" Third Edition 1986 ISBN O-930376-42-0, Qualified Parachutist 82nd Airborne Division 1945; [oth. writ.] 23 Technical papers published in various journals, one poem in cycloflame vol XIX 1971.; [pers.] Our greatest right is to be free to do our duty. Honesty, compassion, and humor are the three prime virtues. Nostalgia is depressing so don't look back.; [a.] Tarentum, PA

HENDERSON, HEATHER NICOLE
[b.] August 2, 1986, Tucson, AZ; [p.] Vince and Rita Henderson; [ed.] 4th grade, Pikeville Independent Elementary School, gifted/talent Creative Writing program; [memb.] Pikeville Elementary Choral Group, Wing Chung Martial Arts; [pers.] I write my poetry for my daddy, he is my true inspiration.; [a.] Pikeville, KY

HENDERSON, JUSTIN S.
[pen.] "Jive"; [b.] July 20, 1953, Lexington, KY; [p.] Sidney R. Henderson, Carrie J. Grubbs; [m.] Caroline J. Henderson, August 19, 1993; [ch.] Justin S. Henderson Jr.; [occ.] United States Air Force Supply Superintendent; [oth. writ.] Several hundred unpublished poems about my life and love.; [pers.] Don't worry it won't change anything. Everyday is an opportunity to experience more than you did yesterday.; [a.] Montgomery, AL

HENDRIE, MRS. JEAN
[pen.] Jean Hendrie; [b.] July 2, 1929, Dundee; [p.] William and Jean Simpson; [m.] John Hendrie (Deceased), February 10, 1948; [ch.] Sheila (Deceased) and Ian (44 years); [ed.] Butterburn Primary School, Rockwell Secondary School, Stobswell 'Night' School; [occ.] Retired Secretary; [memb.] 'Saga' Club, 50 Douglas, Dundee Club, 'Solitaire' Pen-Friend Club, Anchors Aweigh Poetry Mab Club; [hon.] 4 Mensa Cert's. I.Q. 127, 131, 137, 146, Shorthand Certificate, Typing Certificate; [oth. writ.] Poems published (last nine months), poetry books (inc-3-int poets London, others in poetry now anchor books, rhyme arrival (2 Nat Lib USA), local newspapers, magazines; [pers.] I started wrting poetry nine months ago, after the death of my only daughter in June2, 1995. I had my only

been a widow for 5 years. Putting my thoughts and life in verse, helped me overcome some of my grief.; [a.] Dundee, Tayside

HENLY, RACHEL
[b.] September 6, 1975, Saint Paul, MN; [p.] Dorothy Henly, Thomas Henly; [ch.] Anthony Thomas, Thomas Scott, Nicholas James; [pers.] I have always put my heart and soul into my poems. I started writing poetry at a young age. Edgar Allen Poe has always had a great impact on my work and, has influenced me in many ways.; [a.] Vadnais Heights, MN

HENSLER, NANCY COLLINS
[pen.] Faye Collins; [b.] March 13, 1953, Clarksdale, MS; [p.] Clinton H. and Fannie B. Collins; [m.] Harry E. Hensler Jr., March 17, 1990; [ch.] Jane Kubecka, Tracie Shaw, Thomas Shaw, (grandchildren) Hannah and Jonathan Kybecka; [ed.] Brenau University; [occ.] Administrative Clerk/Auditor for State of GA - Dept. of MHMRSA; [memb.] National Association for Female Executives (NAFE); [oth. writ.] Variety of short stories - (not published yet).; [pers.] The consequences of today are our choices of yesterday.; [a.] Sugar Hill, GA

HENSLEY, ELIZABETH
[b.] September 27, 1980, Charleston, SC; [p.] Darrell Lee Hensley, Lorene C. Hensley; [ed.] I am currently in my sophomore yr. of high school at Fitch Senior High in Groton CT; [occ.] Student; [pers.] Life is a very precious thing that shouldn't be given up for any thing. Be yourself always, and never let anyone pressure you into changing. You are the only one that can help yourself. Remember.; [a.] Groton, CT

HERNANDEZ II, ROBERT
[b.] June 30, 1953, Bronx, NY; [p.] Robert and Carmen Hernandez; [ch.] Melissa Jennifer; [ed.] James Monroe High, Bronx, NY, Open Stage Theartre Company, N.Y.C.; [occ.] Aspiring Actor and Reiki Master; [oth. writ.] A potpourri of poetry, songs and short stories; [pers.] "From moment to moment, from year to year, embrace your self-judgements and make love to your fears." Thank you Mom and Dad for believing in me. "Your creation now creates." I'll love thee eternally.; [a.] San Francisco, CA

HEROLD, NATALIE
[b.] December 10, 1976, Canada; [oth. writ.] Several poems written in notebooks of mine! I write poems because I enjoy it! And in some ways they comfort me from my biggest fears!; [pers.] This poem was written in memory of my father George Raymond Herold, who died March 17, 1995. He was born in Hanna Alberta, 1935 and died 59 years young! "Although he's no longer here. I feel him, he is near"!; [a.] Mississauga Ontario, Canada

HEROLD, NICOLE
[b.] Brest, France; [p.] Theodore Leon Herold and Germaine Mellou; [ch.] Raymond - John Jean Gabin - Tina Azerad; [ed.] B.A. of Art French - Archeology Simon Fraser Univ. Burbany, Diploma in Translation (University of British Columbia) Vancover; [occ.] My translation company: "Les Mimosas" translation services; [memb.] National

Geographic Society of B.C., French Alliance, Earth Mag, Outdoor Club, etc.; [hon.] In France: 1st Prize in Drawing/Painting with honor also received books as awards for my writings (in high school), Awards for Good Scholarly Results at Simon Fraser University S.F.U.; [oth. writ.] Short humoristic articles in French in the local French Newspapers, over 60 poems in which in French 50+3 (in English) sent to: "Prix Roger Kowalski" in Lyon France, awaiting in find out the publications date, short stories; [pers.] I look at the comical situations of today's life in my short articles and stories, my poems reflects the high intelligence and suffering of our elders from the dawn of humanity, the disastrous effects of the actual civilization, and the rising of spirituality that will eventually correct the situation, my life.; [a.] Burnaby British Columbia, Canada

HERR, PANG
[b.] October 6, 1982, Denver, CO; [p.] Seng P. Herr; [m.] Chao V. Herr, July 23, 1977; [ch.] Tong Herr, Cher Herr, Mai Shoua Herr, Pang Herr; [ed.] Front Range Community College, Westminster, Colorado; [occ.] Electronic Assembler/Technician and Life Insurance Agent.; [memb.] Denver Hmong Alliance Church.; [hon.] 2nd Pl. Dare essay, Table of Honor Award, A and B Student Award, Most Sparkliest Award and Perfect Attendance Award; [a.] Arvada, CO

HERRERA, KAREN
[b.] August 22, 1952, Douglas, AZ; [p.] Jack Black, Doris Black; [ch.] Keri Wright, Erica Painter; [ed.] Saguaro High School, Austin Community College; [occ.] Student - pursuing English degree Southurst Texas fall 1996; [hon.] ACC Dean's List; [oth. writ.] Five poem and five short stories in five issues at the River's Side (A.C.C. Literary Journal 1993-1995), 2 poems Borderlands 1996; [a.] Austin, TX

HERRIN, EMILY LAUREN
[b.] March 24, 1981, Munster, IN; [p.] David and Joy Herrin; [ch.] Beth; [ed.] I am currently a student at Munster High School; [occ.] Student; [memb.] President of Student Council in grade school, Cheerleader 3 years; [hon.] Outstanding Academic Achievement Award, (President's Education Awards Program), National Honors, National Piano Playing Auditions, 1990-1995, 41-4 G.P.A., Munster High School; [oth. writ.] I have always loved to write stories and poems, but this is my first publication.; [pers.] I would like to dedicate my poem to everyone in my family. They are a constant source of love and support.; [a.] Munster, IN

HERRING, JUSTIN W.
[b.] June 25, 1924, Garden Grove, CA; [p.] Ralph Herring, Joan Herring; [ed.] Yosemite High; [occ.] Student of Performing Arts; [memb.] SADD, National Red Ribbon Week; [hon.] Several High Honors in Music (Marching, Symph); [oth. writ.] Several unpublished poems.; [pers.] I would like to thank my mom and dad, also to Shar Kimes for everything she did to help me through school. To my best friend Ryan Vincent thanks bro, we've both come a long way!; [a.] Sacramento, CA

HERTOG, IRICA
[b.] February 18, 1948, Romania; [p.] Joan and Elisabeta Vasilescu; [m.] Mihai Hertog, December

30, 1971; [ch.] Emanuel, Gabriela, Corneliu, Mikaela; [ed.] Chemistry College - 1970, Nursing - 1989; [occ.] Nurse; [pers.] My Romanian sole found peace and happiness in God's great salvation. A big thank you to all American friends who encouraged me to write poems.; [a.] Seattle, WA

HESTER, CARRIE S.
[b.] October 8, 1973, Tulsa, OK; [p.] Fred and Susie Simms; [m.] Doug Hester, May 22, 1993; [ch.] Lakyn Daria Hester; [ed.] Owasso High School Tulsa Vo - Tech; [occ.] Nursery teacher; [memb.] Garnett Church of Christ; [oth. writ.] Several poems and songs never submitted for public use.; [pers.] I write a lot of what I feel and even more of what I think others are feeling. I have been influenced by day to day happenings and God.; [a.] Tulsa, OK

HEWITT, SCHLERETH
[b.] July 23, 1936; [ed.] BA, Wesleyan University, 1958; [oth. writ.] Commonsense Celestial Navigation, How to Buy a Sailboat; [a.] Milford, CT

HEYDEN, PAUL
[b.] April 21, 1968, Guelph, Ontario, Canada; [p.] John and Marlene Heyden; [m.] Jodi Crewson, August 27, 1994; [ed.] Guelph Collegiate-Vocational Institute (High School), Conestoga College of Applied Arts and Technology (Mechanical Engineering Technician); [occ.] Certified Mechanical Engineering Technical; [memb.] (OACETT) Ontario Association of Certified Engineering Technicians and Technologists, (SME) Society of Manufacturing Engineers; [hon.] Society of Manufacturing Engineers Student Scholarship Award. Ontario Association of Certified Engineering Technicians and Technologists (Certified Engineering Technical); [pers.] It is impossible to be sad while smiling, smile always.; [a.] Elora Ontario, Canada

HICKEY, HELEN K.
[pen.] Helen Davis; [b.] February 26, 1923; [p.] Isabel M. Hicket, Kieran J. Hickey; [ed.] Waltham High School, Boston Univ., Sargent College B.S. 1950, B.U. School of Educ. M.S. 1954, Honorary D. Sci. Regis College; [occ.] Self employed Entrepreneur - Body Work, Counseling, Book Seller; [memb.] Am. Physical Therapy Ass., Assn. Schools Allied Health Profes., Assn. Humanistic Psychology, Boston Computer Society Senior Net, Habitat for Humanity Easter Seal Society, Daptive Environments; [hon.] Boston University Alumni Award, Sargent College Twinness, Presidents Award Am. Sor. Allied Heath Professions, Lucy Blair Service Award - Am. Physical Therapy Assn., Warren J. Perry Leadership Award - Univ. of Buffalo, Honorary Doctoral Degree - Regis College, Pi BDA Theta Honorary Soc. March of Dimes Leadership's Award, Mass. Paralyzed Veterans Award, Sargent College Dudley Allen. Sargent Award, Honor Auxiliary of Sargent College, Fellow Award Am. Soc. Allied Health Professions; [oth. writ.] Career monographs, grant applications, career recruitment flyers, guidance material. Some other poetry - unpublished.; [pers.] My life of service, networking and facilitating the activities of others has given me great riches, fun and fulfillment.; [a.] Waltham, MA

HICKS, EDWARD
[b.] April 2, 1932, Floyd Co, GA; [p.] Ernest L. and Nellie Mae Hicks; [m.] Betty Nell Hicks, March 12, 1975; [ch.] Seven; [ed.] 10th grade - Police Academy - GED; [occ.] Retired Police Officer currently City Marshall; [hon.] Letters of Commendation for Lifesaving, Letter of Commendation for Professionalism; [oth. writ.] Poem published Hawkinsville Georgia paper. Title - Public Servant #1; [pers.] I have been greatly influenced by nature and the great West.; [a.] Hawkinsville, GA

HIGGINS, KATHRYN M.
[b.] November 27, 1957, Tucson, AZ; [p.] Neil and Muriel Higgins; [ed.] Business Adm. College, LMP; [occ.] Researcher; [memb.] MS Society; [pers.] Poetry is song, from the depth of the soul.; [a.] Tacoma, WA

HIGGINS, N. LOY KUHN
[pen.] Loy; [b.] August 2, 1944, Lousville, KY; [p.] Arthur Louis Kuhn (Deceased) E. Nina Waller Kuhn; [m.] Dr. David Michael Higgins, November 27, 1990; [ed.] DuPont Manual High School, Louiville, KY, Class of '62, Eastern Kentucky State College, Richmond, KY, '62-'64, Miami Dade Junior College, Miami, FL, 73-74, AA Degree, Fine Arts/General, U of the State of New York, '86, as liberal Arts and General Sciences (Regents Program), conferred Jan '87, Scottsdale Community College, Scottsdale, AZ, '95, Studio Recording and Electronic Music; [occ.] Writer, Musician, Teacher, National, Desktop Publisher; [memb.] International Society of Poets, National Authors Registry, Adult Recital Series of AZ State Music Teachers Assn., Alliance Francais, Senior Friends; [hon.] Poems published in the "National Library of Poetry's" anthology "A Voyage to Remember," the Modern Poetry Society of Dunnellon, FL's volume of modern poetry "Mirrors of the Soul," and Iliad Press Literary Anthology "Crossings," Honorable Mention, Pine Hills, NY Poetry Competition 1995, Superior and Excellent Awards National Federation Junior Festivals '93, '94, '95, and membership in the National Fraternity of Student Musicians, Student Division of American College of Musicians and Piano Hobbyists, ASMTA, Central District, 43rd Piano Ensemble, '95; [oth. writ.] Poems, humorous short stories, songs, and lyrics. Writer and publisher of Poetry Lines series. Arranger and performer of several keyboard cassette recordings, recorded in my home studio in Scottsdale, AZ; [pers.] Creativity is driven by emotion — be it joy, sorrow, love, hate, or fear, therefore, indifference is rarely found in the arts.; [a.] Majuro Atoll, MH

HILL, ANDREW S.
[pen.] Sonne Hill; [b.] February 27, 1925, Trinidad; [p.] Mary and Martin Hill (Deceased); [m.] Bernice Roma Hill (Deceased), September 5, 1953; [ch.] Dawn, Ryan and Jacqueline Hill; [ed.] Elementary, Secondary, Tertiary Management Studies Course at British Management Asso (Employment Law) and American Management Asso (Industrial Relative, Negotiations), New York, Continuing studies, University of the West India - Campus St. Augustine; [occ.] Professional Accountant, retired 1986, Hobbies: Painting, Drama, Writing - Short stories, Plays and Poetry; [memb.] National Scouts Association of Trinidad and Tobago, Association for Retarded Children of Trinidad and Tobago, Notredame Sports Club (Football and Hockey) of Trinidad and Tobago, National Chess Association - Knights Chess Club of Trinidad and Tobago; [hon.] Medal of Merit - Scouting, Certificate of Service - Mental Retardation, 2nd Prize - National Competition - Trade Winds Professional, Group - University of the West Indies - for 'Play' Sweet Auburn', Life of Martin Luther King, Jr. - Civil Rights Leader - Book of Plays 'Jack Dilemma and other Local Plays'; [oth. writ.] 1) Building Together - Scouts Jamboree, 2) Notredame - History of 50 yrs. 3) Phantom on the Cemetery Wall and other short stories, 4) Jack's Dilemma and other Local Plays, (published in 1995); [pers.] Solitude is about peace, loneliness and isolation - to be alone, quiet and will to be with God in communication - to wise up one's mind and heart to God in prayer - in the end to seek peace and happiness in God's image and perfection.; [a.] San Antonio, TX

HILL, NATALIE
[b.] July 28, 1976, Birmingham, AL; [p.] Jo Ann and Jerry Hill; [ed.] Springville High, Moody High, Alabama School of Massage Therapy, Leeds Beauty School; [occ.] Beta Club, Mu Alpha Theta, Tai Yoe Quan, Zhong Wuyi; [memb.] Who's who among American High School Students; [oth. writ.] Grass at Sea, etc.; [pers.] Thanks Mama Mama and Grand - Daddy; [a.] Birmingham, AL

HILL, PAULA
[pen.] Paula Marie; [b.] June 12, 1974, Everett, WA; [p.] John and Carmen Warren; [m.] William Marshall; [ch.] Daniel Glynn, Aaron Robert, Jordan Taylor; [ed.] West Mesquite High, Richland College; [occ.] Housewife and proud mother, loving daughter; [memb.] University interscholastic league, NCA Recording Company; [hon.] Award from the UIL for Solo-Small Ensemble ROTC; [oth. writ.] Many unpublished poems; [pers.] I've been writing and studying poetry for twelve years and the legendary poets who brang them to life. It's an honor to have my amateur poem published by the NLP.; [a.] Balch Springs, TX

HILL, RENEE JEANNETTE
[b.] July 9, 1961, Sacramento, CA; [p.] Eaddie and Ellis Moore; [m.] Andre Li Hill (Deceased), September 10, 1985; [ch.] Janee Rose Hill; [a.] Sacramento, CA

HILLIER, HARRIET L.
[b.] June 9, 1931, San Jacinto, CA; [p.] Perry Waggoner, Lulu Waggoner; [m.] Stanley E. Hillier Sr., August 30, 1952; [ch.] Stanley Edward Jr., Harriet Loretta, Diane Mareen, Debbie Marlene; [ed.] San Jacinto Elementary, Montebello Junior High, San Jacinto High, attended Woodbury College of Los Angeles, CA- Whatcom Community in Bellingham, WA; [occ.] Retired; [memb.] Winnebago of Nebraska Tribal member, Bellingham Covenant Church.; [oth. writ.] Poem for class reunion year book.; [pers.] Our Lord has created so much beauty out there, from the rugged mountains, to dry desert and ocean shores. It is a pleasure to relay it to those who do not see it or look for it. Our Lord is the beauty of it all.; [a.] Ferndale, WA

HILTON SR., ISAAC
[pen.] Big Ike; [b.] December 29, 1958, Charleston, SC; [p.] Samuel Hilton Sr., Mable Hilton; [m.] Divorced, June 7, 1980-August 21, 1994; [ch.] Angel, Pamela, Ranell, Isaac Jr., Joseph, Ezekiel; [ed.] Baptist Hill High, US Navy - Boiler Tec 8 1/2 yrs, Trident Tec College - Welding, Burning school (Summer of 88); [occ.] Utility Operator Foster Wheeler RRI "Boiler opp"; [memb.] Baptist Hill School, Parent Patrol, attend different church but not a member of any; [hon.] High school diploma 1977, US Navy 79-87, Navy achievement medal - appo. 83, Honorable Discharge Navy 83 and 87, trophy - boxing (94); [oth. writ.] I'm currently writing a book of poems. "Life Advice in a Poem, from the Heart". The only one to be publish is "What is Christmas to Me?" (to date); [pers.] My poems comes straight from the heart. I hope and pray that one day my work will be published in a book form to be read as a deterrence from violence among mankind.; [a.] Charleston, SC

HIRVI, FAYE ANN
[b.] April 11, 1957; [p.] Walfrid and Vieno Honkavaara; [m.] Alden, September 25, 1982; [ch.] Daniel and Megash; [ed.] Jeffers Senior High School '76' Nurse's Aide; [occ.] Housewife; [oth. writ.] I also write short stories I have written since the age of five, and since the loss of both of my parents, within three years I've written over eight hundred poems. My Secret Willow Tree, published in the spring of 1996 edition of poetics voices of America; [pers.] I love poetry and songs because, it's a part of the inner me that can be expressed so deeply and freely; [a.] Toivola, MI

HOBSON, PAMELA ROSE
[b.] January 14, 1939, Hull City; [p.] Olive and James Arther Hynes; [m.] Divorced; [ch.] Julie Ann; [ed.] Secondary Moden School; [occ.] Living alone spend 20 years looking after animals; [oth. writ.] "I have just finished a book called revenge is sweet Rebbeka about a Victorian girl do you know anyone who would like to look at it.; [pers.] I have always wanted to put my feelings in writing I am writing a book now about Victorian girl called Rebbeka, my grand father came from the States Irish American.; [a.] England

HOCHHALTER, DARRIN
[b.] August 29, 1973, Denver, CO; [p.] Rose and Merlin Hochhalter; [ed.] Dear Trail High School; [occ.] United States Navy, Hull Technician

HODGE, MARILYN
[b.] April 15, 1945, Dallas, TX; [p.] Samuel and Alice Robinson; [m.] Clarence Hodge Sr., September 21, 1963; [ch.] Clarence Jr. and Sametra; [ed.] Dallas Baptist University; [occ.] Self-employed Bookkeeper/Clerical Work; [memb.] Executive Secretary of Greater Love Chapel Church of God in Christ, Everman Independent School District Trustee, Highland Hills Neighborhood Association, Fort Worth Citizens Police Academy; [hon.] Several Certificates of Appreciation from Church and Neighborhood Association, School Board Recognition; [oth. writ.] Article published in local newspaper (the newspaper paid me 75.00), I have written many "Letters to the Editor" of our local newspaper.; [pers.] I want to live my life in such a manner that I will be worthy to enter heaven.; [a.] Fort Worth, TX

HODGES, GLENDA
[b.] November 8, 1958, Macon, GA; [p.] Glenwood McMullen Sr., Almeta R. McMullen; [m.] Cornell Hodges, April 27, 1979; [ch.] Andy Hodges, Angel M. Hodges, Ashleigh Hodges; [ed.] Southwest High School, Mercer University; [occ.] Housewife, last occupation - Restaurant Manager; [memb.] Bloomfield Baptist Church Macon Volunteer Service; [hon.] Quality Service Awards; [oth. writ.] Several unpublished poems during teen life.; [pers.] I strive to encourage the maintenance of family unity. The struggle to keep and show our love is challenged all too often. I intend to encourage mankind to keep what's good and cling to family structures.; [a.] Macon, GA

HOEFERT, FREDRICK P.
[pen.] Ashley James Cromwell; [b.] September 1, 1969, Milwaukee, WI; [ed.] Pulaski High School: Graduated - June 1987, Milwaukee Area Technical College: Degree - Administrative Assistant Information Processing (June 1991), currently studying religious history at the University of Wisconsin - Milwaukee; [occ.] Administrative Assistant; [memb.] Self-Realization Fellowship; [hon.] Muscular Dystrophy Association's 1990 First Place — "Flash Typist" at MATC's South Campus; [pers.] Enjoy this dream and don't take its apparent tragedies seriously. On writing: The most successful writing comes from the heart — what you feel and care about.; [a.] Milwaukee, WI

HOFFMAN, HEIDI
[b.] November 29, 1968, San Francisco, CA; [p.] Ernest E. Hoffman, Hildegard Hoffman; [ch.] Cheyenne Hoffman; [ed.] El Camino High, Heald Business College; [occ.] Account Coordinator, Mediacopy, San Leandro, CA; [hon.] High School: Certificate of Honor for Outstanding Achievement 12-96 and 5-87, Outstanding Achievement Student of the Year 1986-1987, Certificate of Merit 7-94, Business Course (Padgett/Thompson); [oth. writ.] Several poems written while in high school, one published in high school, creative writing magazine, few poems written last couple years none published.; [pers.] Poetry has always been a big part of my inner self. Always hope give others inspiration with my words and thoughts.; [a.] American Canyon, CA

HOFFMAN, WILDA JEAN
[pen.] Wilda Kennedy Hoffman; [b.] May 4, 1932, Wharton, TX; [p.] Henry H. Kennedy and Emma L. Peebles; [m.] Max Richard Hoffman III, February 15, 1950; [ch.] Michaelee Hoffman Franz and Carl Hoffman; [ed.] B.S. Education minor History M.A. English Literature Concentration Poetry — M.A. Thesis Original work of poetry — "The Springing of the Well"; [occ.] Very occupied and happily occupied grandmother; [memb.] First Baptist Church Alvin D.A.R. Mary Rolph Marsh Chapter; [hon.] Bachelor of Science Cum Laude University of Houston at Clear Lake City, Master of Arts University of Houston at Clear Lake, Honorable Mention Carol Ann Riordan Memorial short story contest Pepperdine University 1983; [oth. writ.] Many poems not a part of the thesis—short story—devotional writing; [pers.] Through the use of literary language, the poet carefully constructs her experience into a form that has the power to communicate heightened perceptions of a moment in time in ways that involve the reader's senses emotions, intellect, and imagination.; [a.] Alvin, TX

HOFLEY, SHIRLEY HOEFLING
[b.] October 6, 1955, Castor, Alberta, Canada; [p.] Fred Hoefling, Vi Hoefling; [ch.] Jason; [ed.] Sedgewick High School, Eastglen Composite; [occ.] Purchaser, Fieldco Mfg. Inc. Edmonton, AB; [pers.] When I write, the words come from my heart and soul on how I feel love and life should be. And hoping someday, more will feel this way, then better the world will be.

HOGAN, MARIA T.
[b.] May 27, 1964, New Hartford, NY; [p.] Alexander and Rosemarie Chiffy; [ch.] Sean Hogan; [ed.] Saint Mary of Mount Carmel Elementary, Notre Dame High School, Mohawk Valley Community College; [occ.] Secretary for the Utica City School District, Special Education Dept.; [memb.] Member of the National Trust for Historic Preservation, The Library of Congress and The Smithsonian Institute; [hon.] Daughters of the American Revolution - Excellence in History Award; [pers.] I always listen to my inner voice. It sings to me and I write down what I hear.; [a.] Utica, NY

HOINO, KAREN
[b.] January 10, 1963, Lynwood, CA; [p.] Ray Hoino, Bonita Hoino; [ed.] Downey High School, Cerritos College - Fashion Merchandising; [occ.] Human Resources Manager; [memb.] Alumni Lambda Phi Sigma Sorority, American Compensation Association, Volunteer Work for the American Heart Association; [pers.] I have been touched by certain turns in my life and have recently found a voice within that allows me to express, through my writing, what I so vividly see and feel.; [a.] Irvine, CA

HOLBROOK, EDITH S.
[b.] August 2, 1979, Dallas; [p.] S. "Kae" Paetin and Jimmy Lynn Paetin; [ed.] Fredonia and Carpenter, Elementary School - Nacodgoches, Intermediate School - T.J. Rusk Jr. High - Nacodgoches High School ALC and Nacodgoches High School; [occ.] Genealogical Research Asst. Genealogist and Sales Rep - Hobby Lobby Inc. Florist; [memb.] First Families of Texas, East Texas Families, Woodmen of The World Fraternal Society Bell Baptist Church; [hon.] Piney Wood Fair '93 - 1st Floral, 1st Improders, 1st Hot Sauce, Piney Wood Fair '94, 1st Ceramics, 1st Floral Arrangement, 1st Hot Sauce, 6th Embroidery, 1st Pepper Relish, Piney Wood Fair '95, 1st Ceramics, 1st Crockett-Afagan, 2nd Hot Sauce, 1st Floral; [oth. writ.] Several Genealogical Research Books published, poems published in area quarterlies, I'm compiling for parting publications, poems form local teens into poetry booklet for publication.; [pers.] How life has it's ups and downs and how people can pick themselves up and move on our life. This one poem is about a first love in someone's life how they hope they do what is right.; [a.] Nacodgoches, TX

HOLGUIN, MARIA
[b.] April 14, 1965, Los Angeles, CA; [p.] Manuel and Liz Holguin; [ch.] Adam Neil Dominguez; [occ.] Author; [oth. writ.] Collection of poems.; [pers.] This poem was written in dedication to the

ladies of all the red light districts of the world. To the lady of Amsterdam.; [a.] Santa Rosa, CA

HOLLENBACH, ROBERT Z.
[pen.] Arzie Aitch; [b.] March 26, 1918, Hatfield, PA; [p.] Paul Hollenbach, Elsie Zepp; [m.] Louise P. Hollenbach (Deceased), September 4, 1950; [ch.] Thomas B., Mark R., Ann M.; [ed.] Cooper Union Night School of Engineering (46-50), M.I.T. (SBME 52), R.P.I. (M.S. 59); [occ.] Retired Professor of Mech Eng. (from U of Mass at Lowell); [memb.] A.S.M.E., A.S.E.E., Pi Tau Sigma, The Society of the Sigma XI; [hon.] First Prize for Best Work in Principles of Physics (6-8-48) Prize for the best work in Engineering Drawing (6-20-49), (both from the cooper Union); [oth. writ.] Spoonfed trigonometry Triangle Solutions Pythagorean Numbers and Instant Geometry The Eulerline and Nine Point Circle Various Poems (All of the above not published); [pers.] As shown by "other writings", I have a special interest in geometry and trigonometry also, I like to read history; [a.] Needham, MA

HOLLIS, MARY JANE
[b.] July 27, 1938, Lebanon, TN; [p.] Clifton Tribble and Beatrice Moore; [m.] Mack Hollis, October 23, 1957; [ch.] Louis Kyle and Loring Kase; [ed.] Lebanon High, Middle Tenn State University, AD in Nursing; [occ.] Retired Registered Nurse, presently Manager Equine Breeding Program; [memb.] Wilson County Child Abuse Board, Prospect Development Review Committee; [hon.] Honored for naming Lebanon's Cedar Fest; [oth. writ.] Several poems in process of writing children stories.; [pers.] Life is an experience that lends us the ability to express our thoughts, memories and ideas for future generations to enjoy.; [a.] Lebanon, TN

HOLMAN, BRIAN KEITH
[b.] August 30, 1971, Troy, NY; [p.] Robert E. and Patricia A. Holman; [m.] Laurie, December 16, 1995; [ed.] 8th Averill Park High School Averill Park NY; [occ.] Work on Sign's Operate B and L Signs; [memb.] Future Farmers of America; [hon.] Future Farmers of America; [oth. writ.] None really just thoughts, I write what I feel in my heart.; [pers.] I write what comes in my heart as I feel it.; [a.] Ormond Beach, FL

HOLMES, GREG
[pen.] G-Money; [b.] July 2, 1974, Little Rock, AR; [p.] Charles and Bernice Holmes; [m.] Dawn Holmes, March 31, 1995; [ed.] Noah Little Rock H.S. and Oak Grove H.S.; [occ.] Install Sand, and Finish Hardwood Floors (McDaniel Hardwood) floors; [memb.] I'm one of Jehovah's Witnesses. For my whole life.; [oth. writ.] I write poems for my wife. Because of the love I have for her.; [pers.] I look forward to a time when "the wicked one will be no more, but the meek ones will possess the earth and find their exquisite delight in the abundance of peace.".; [a.] North Little Rock, AR

HOLMES, LORRETTA
[b.] May 8, 1977, Etobicoke, Ontario, Canada; [p.] Wayne and Elizabeth Holmes; [ed.] Martingrove Collegiate Institute, attending University of Toronto in fall of '96.; [occ.] Student, striving toward teaching degree.; [hon.] Earned silver and

gold pins for academic achievement in high school, is an Ontario scholar.; [oth. writ.] First publication; [pers.] I share my feelings through the words that I write. I enjoy life and I want the world to love it to.; [a.] Toronto Ontario, Canada

HOLT, NANCY VANESSA BROWN
[pen.] Nancy Vanessa Brown-Holt; [b.] August 24, 1963, Baltimore, MD; [p.] Ruth Payne Brown, Harts Morrison Brown; [m.] Harry William Holt Jr., June 29, 1985; [ch.] Nancy Elizabeth Holt; [ed.] Brown University, SCB-Biology 1985, Johns Hopkins University School of Medicine, MD 1989; [occ.] Obstetrician - Gyne Cologist; [memb.] Alpha Kappa Alpha Sorority, Inc., Diplomate American Board of OB/Gyn, Fellow American Medical Association, New Shiloh Baptist Church; [hon.] Wellcome Company Leadership Award for Resident Physicians, Baltimore City Africian American Heritage Society Pacesetler's Award in Medicine, SNMA Chairperson's Award for Service, Aka National Leadership Fellows Program, Governors Citation for Civil Service and Scholarship, Mayor's Citation for Civil Service and Scholarship; [pers.] Poetry is a lifelong, personal expression of God's wonders in your life that is sometimes shared with others to give them joy and understanding.; [a.] Woodstock, MD

HOLT, RANDY LEE
[b.] March 9, 1972, Mentor, OH; [p.] Gary and Barbara Holt; [m.] Suzanne Holt, February 25, 1995; [ed.] Mentor High School; [occ.] United States Air Force; [oth. writ.] None other than my own poetry.; [pers.] Let no one ever tell you, you cannot do something because one day you may just believe them.; [a.] Valdosta, GA

HORTON, MARY E.
[pen.] Mary Horton; [b.] September 16, 1920, Pittsburg, MO; [p.] Thomas and Edna Milam; [m.] Jesse A. Horton, August 8, 1944; [ch.] Michael, Patrick, Timothy and Maureen; [ed.] High School; [occ.] Retired Pacific Telephone Co. Employee; [memb.] Telephone Company Pioneers, and Senior Citizens of Orange; [hon.] "Mother of the Year," "Most valued Employee"; [pers.] At age 75 I am filling a lifetime desire. (Writing poetry) the essence of the poems, strictly down to earth, family, and everyday living.; [a.] Orange, CA

HOSKINS, HAROLD
[pen.] R. H. Hoskins; [b.] January 15, 1927, Pineville, KY; [p.] Mr. and Mrs. Steve Hoskins Sr.; [m.] Phyllis A. Ramsey Hoskins, May 18, 1973; [ch.] Charles J. Hoskins; [ed.] M.A. Education History and English Union College, Barbourville, KY.; [occ.] Retired Teacher, Bell Co. School System, Pineville, KY. English and History; [memb.] NEA - K.R.T.S. - Board of Directors Bell County Historical Society - K.H.S. member; [oth. writ.] Legend and History of chained rock published Bell County History Edit/Writing - Trophy APR for Publication Kentucky Explorer (Mdg.); [pers.] From: "Trophy" I had rather express just one great truth I'm poem or prayer of hymn that would capture the hearts and minds of more trophies to present to him.; [a.] Beattyville, KY

HOTUJEC, EDWARD
[b.] June 1, 1928, Kansas City, KS; [p.] John and Mary Hotujec; [m.] Mae (Griffith), July 10, 1971; [ch.] John Hotujec; [ed.] Bishop Ward High, St. Benedict's College, Rock Hurst College; [occ.] Retired - 41 years, Armour - Swift Eckrich Materials Control Mgr.; [memb.] Order of Moose, American Legion, St. George Society; [hon.] Bronze Star (Korea) 1951-52; [oth. writ.] Wrote a book of unpublished poems, as a hobby.; [pers.] Fond of the beauty of Nature and the outstanding characteristics of mankind.; [a.] Saint Charles, IL

HOUSEY JR., JOSEPHUS
[b.] March 24, 1975, Springfield, MA; [p.] Jeanette and Josephus Housey Sr.; [m.] Natalie T. Smith-Jacobs; [ed.] Putnam High School, University of Massachusetts Amherst; [occ.] Asst. Director of Housing and Student (Full-time); [memb.] Non-Voting Member of One Hundred Black Men of Greater Springfield; [hon.] NAACP High Academic Award (1993), Jewish War Veterans of U.S. Brotherhood Award (1992), Daughter of American Revolution Good Citizens Award (1993), Who's Who Academic Achievement Nominee (1991-92); [oth. wit.] Flight Of The Dreamer, Going Down; [pers.] "Difference comes only from those who chose to make it." I try to keep in mind those who mean the most to me, who more God, my fiancee, and my family.; [a.] Amherst, MA

HOWARD, KYALO
[pen.] Kylus; [b.] February 8, 1976; [p.] Sharon K. Garrett/step father, Charles Garrett; [m.] Adina Sjoselius (Girlfriend); [ch.] Jordan Sjoselius; [ed.] Finishing school at this point and next taking a few course's for mech. drafting. Hoping one day to design new house's and I also wish to Invent a few future helping things.; [occ.] Seasonal construction worker and part time poet with out any schooling for poetry.; [memb.] To me my friends and the world are the people that I am a member of, it is them who I wish to be a part of and help. I select Adina, Steve, Andre and Billy for the loving support they give me. I give you all my love!; [hon.] Never won anything or received a honor or award but what I do earn is people's love and respect. This to me is the biggest award in the world and also the honor to be able to write poetry that I feel God has gifted upon me for all to read.; [oth. writ.] I'm in the process of writing a book of poetry titled Poetic Thought's. These poem's are based on true feelings I have about daily problem's. I hope to have this book published some day in the near future. This contest that my poem got selected for, The main important thing about it was for it to be seen through the world and I wish to have Poetic Thought's follow in the same path way.; [pers.] My goal is to help save this world. To me all can change for the better. God has granted my wish to put my poem in a place for all to see, not for just he but for the world. This is the only thing I wanted to have happen in this contest. For some reason most of poems have to do with the Lords judgement about the people and problem's of faith, so world think about how God work's.; [a.] Brooklyn Park, MN

HOWELL, LORI MICHELLE
[b.] October 5, 1967, Terre Haute, IN; [p.] Jane and Allan Burris; [m.] Donald Duane Howell, Novem-

ber 7, 1989; [ch.] Ricky Duane Howell and Tiffany Nichole Howell; [ed.] Kaiserslautern American High School - West Germany; [occ.] Housewife; [memb.] Palo Duro Baptist Church; [hon.] My first honor is The National Library of Poetry for publishing my first poem.; [oth. writ.] A handful of writings (poetry) that are not published yet.; [pers.] My reason for writing is to remind people of God's nature and love. And of the beautiful things in the land.; [a.] Wildorado, TX

HOWERTON, MIKE
[b.] October 8, 1979, Fridley, MN; [p.] Greg Howerton and Cathy Howerton; [ed.] Ottumwa High School, Buena High school; [oth. writ.] Many untitled poems and short stories.; [pers.] I have many bottled up feelings on how to make the world a better place. Writing is one of the few ways I can express those feelings. Maybe someday somebody will read my writings and act upon my expressed feelings.; [a.] Sierra Vista, AZ

HUDSON, MELISSA
[pen.] Melissa Hudson; [b.] June 1, 1983, Memphis, TN; [p.] Linda Chambers; [ed.] Alcy Elem. - Grades K-6 Currently attending John P. Freeman Optional School; [memb.] Norris Ave. Church Youth Choir; [hon.] State Certified as Gifted Clue Student (Creative Learning in an Unique Environment for Gifted Student) Editorial printed in local newspaper, and Publish-A-Book Merit Award, John P. Freeman Honor Student (Optical School) 1st Place Winner in Church Essay Contest; [oth. writ.] Editorial printed in local newspaper, publish - A - Book honorable mention contest winner Church Essay - What Christ Means To Me"; [pers.] Life is like a rubber band: Harder you go forward, harder you snapback. So do not make slip ups. I try to remember this especially in my writing and I think in every day life.; [a.] Memphis, TN

HUDSON, RICHARD ANTHONY
[pen.] R. A. Hudson; [b.] May 13, 1968, Suffern, NY; [p.] William Hudson III, Dianne Hudson; [ed.] Chaminade High School, Barry University, Broward Community College; [occ.] Paramedic Student; [oth. writ.] Poems and thoughts written about personal experience of life, love and friendship.; [pers.] "For you, Luli, my poem, my heart, my love." "Your thoughts are never seen unless you act them out, never heard unless you speak, never felt unless you write them down, express yourself."; [a.] Hollywood, FL

HUFF, WILLIAM JEFFREY
[pen.] Jeff Nuff; [b.] March 4, 1966, Winchester, VA; [p.] Howard Franklin Huff Jr., Justine Nana Huff; [m.] Patricia Vansisy Huff, June 21, 1993; [ch.] Nathan Riley; [ed.] University of La Verne; [pers.] One must look at life from many rear view mirrors.

HUFFMAN JR., RICHARD W.
[pen.] Rick Huffman; [b.] March 16, 1956, Augusta, GA; [p.] Richard and Rosalinde Huffman; [ch.] Richard W. Huffman III; [ed.] Richmond Academy; [occ.] Lab Technician; [pers.] Greatly inspired by the lives of Byron, Keats, Shelley. Special thanks to Evelyn Easler for encouragement to express myself through my writing.; [a.] Augusta, GA

HUMES, P. J.
[b.] January 23, 1953; [occ.] Artist, Homemaker; [oth. writ.] Although I have written several other poems/songs, this is the first one ever submitted for publishing of any kind.; [pers.] Most of my writings reflect simple observations of life on this planet.

HUMPHREY, OWEN EVERETT
[b.] October 25, 1920, Wautoma, WI; [p.] Marion and Flora (Helms) Humphrey; [m.] Billye Cox Humphrey (Deceased), April 6, 1946; [ch.] Reba (Humphrey) Rick, Ivye Humphrey; [ed.] B.S., Univ. of Wis./Whitewater, M.S., Univ. of Ark./ Fayetteville, Ed. Sp., Univ. of Ill./Champaign, Add. Grad., Southern Ill. Univ./Edwardsville.; [occ.] Retired School Administrator.; [memb.] Association for Supervision and Curriculum Development (Life Hon.), National Education Association (Life), Kappa Delta Pi Honorary Society, Phi Delta Kappa, Collinsville Theatrical Society, International Society of Poets.; [hon.] Biog. sketches: Dictionary of International Biography, Who's Who in the Midwest, Who's Who in American Education, Two Thousand Men of Achievement, Creative and Successful Personalities of the World (Creativity Recognition Award 1972), Granite City Area Council PTA Award, 1979, I-Search Certificate of Recognition for writing 5-County Curriculum for Prevention of child Abduction, 1987, Phi Delta Kappa Service Key Award, 1983, Kappa of the Year, 1984, George H. Reavis Associate Award, 1991.; [oth. writ.] Author, The Greening of Gateway East, A History of PDK Chapter 1097, contributor, IASCD Newslatter and Illinois School Research publications, 1969, 1970, 1971, 1973. Poetry: "On the Death of An Infant," in A Delicate Balance, "The Poem Sculptor," in A Tapestry of Thoughts, "The Best Dog in the World, in Carvings in Stone, "America's Renewal," in The Best Poems of the '90s (National Library of Poetry Anthologies).; [pers.] Most of my writings reflect a love for humanity and a longing to see this great country erase the violence and return to its original role as protectorate of all mankind.; [a.] Granite City, IL

HUNT, CLARECE
[b.] December 27, 1922, Pineview, GA; [p.] John B. and Alice R. Dennard; [m.] Hewlett J. Hunt, January 13, 1938; [ch.] James T., Robert L., Alice H. Ramsdell; [ed.] Jr. High School; [occ.] Retired - Professional Seamstress and Accountant; [memb.] Pineview Finleyson Methodist Church; [oth. writ.] Poems - Beloved Georgia and our America published in Georgia - Images and reflection - of poets and authors. The family Doctor published by the National Library of Poetry - at Waters Edge; [pers.] This poem youth speak is dedicated in memory of Eric P. Staples Past Principle of Perry Schools in Houston Co. Georgia. He was loved by students and faculty and was a true builder of character in the lives of parents and children alike. Including Sam Nun Jr. - Member U.S. Senate

HUNTER, DAWN
[b.] February 10, 1969, Toronto, Ontario, Canada; [p.] Mary Hunter, Thomas Hunter; [m.] Roger Pappaert; [ed.] University of Toronto, Honours B.Sc.; [memb.] Editor's Association of Canada, Canadian Campaign Association; [oth. writ.] Books reviews in Camps Canada, poem published

in Occasional News; [pers.] If my poetry strikes a chord, triggers a memory or, maybe, eases the pain in a reader, then I have succeeded.; [a.] Toronto Ontario, Canada

HUNTER, ELVIS JOHN
[b.] December 19, 1958; [p.] Jessie Mae Hall, Biological Mother; [ch.] Aaron and Amber; [oth. writ.] One nation under God, United we stand, place of birth.; [pers.] Threw my writings I wish to someday contact my three biological siblings; [a.] Wauconda, IL

HUNTER, TERRANCE J.
[pen.] Terry; [b.] April 14, 1974, Mobile, AL; [p.] James and Peggy Hunter; [ed.] Associates Degree in Art/Science from Bishop State Community College of Mobile, AL; [occ.] Employed by Tailored Foam of Alabama; [memb.] Member of the Greater Mount Hebron Baptist Church, Phi Theta Kappa Member; [hon.] Phi Tetha Kappa Deans List; [oth. writ.] Other unpublished poems dealing with Egyptian Culture (Ancient) Pride, and Struggle; [a.] Mobile, AL

HUTCHINSON, ROBERT
[b.] October 17, 1919, Congress, Saskatchewan, Canada

HUTCHISON, RANDI JO
[pen.] Randi Jo Hutchison; [b.] May 12, 1969, Trumann, AR; [p.] Johnny L. and Phyllis D. Hutchison; [ed.] Trumann High, Arkansas State University, Art Education B.S.E.; [occ.] Former Jr High and Sr. High Art Teacher, Currently Computer Operations; [pers.] Live, Love and Laugh make each moment a truly special memory.; [a.] Springdale, AR

HUTTO, ELGEVA K.
[pen.] Elgeva Kiser Hutto; [b.] May 5, 1943, Charlotte, NC; [p.] Heath Kiser, Sr. and Mary Kiser; [m.] William Carroll Hutto, June 2, 1962; [ch.] William Scott, William Timothy, Michael Todd, Matthew Philip and Christopher Kelly; [ed.] Garinger High School Graduate (Family-to-Family training (Dayton-Hudson)); [occ.] Child Care (Owner-in-home) (Am retiring end of 1996); [memb.] Family Child Care Assocation American Association; [hon.] 1991 selected to attend National "Save the Children" Conference in Atlanta, GA.; [oth. writ.] I just published a book: Titled: I Am Your Rest, Your Peace, Your Stillness, in 1995.; [pers.] Most of my poetry is twofold: To glorify God and to bring healing, peace, and rest upon those who read it.; [a.] Charlotte, NC

HYNES, HEATHER
[pen.] Marie Kelly; [b.] July 25, 1984, Bend, OR; [p.] Theresa and Kelly Hynes; [m.] Single; [occ.] Currently in 6th grade; [occ.] Middle school student/writer (in free time); [memb.] Boys and Girls Club; [hon.] 3.86 student on the Honor Role; [oth. writ.] Children Story; [pers.] "A feel for writing" is dedicated to my dad - William Kelly Hynes (goes by Kelly) for always believing in me! - 2 sisters, 1 brother Amanda, Justine, Sean; [a.] Bend, OR

HYSEN, GORD
[b.] December 16, 1974, Hamilton, Ontario, Canada; [p.] Bernice and Sonny Hysen; [ed.] Ath-

letic Therapy Student at Sheridan College; [occ.] Student; [memb.] Canadian Athletic Therapy Association; [hon.] Ministry Award for Outstanding Achievement. Editors Choice Award for Poetry; [oth. writ.] "The Love" published in sparkles in the sand and many poems for keep sake purposes.; [pers.] My poems are dedicated in the memories of Monika Kalmar, and Jennine Akanas two beautiful girls that I love and I will never forget. Keep shooting for your dreams Carolyn (Brook Basketball) Luv ya!; [a.] Hamilton Ontario, Canada

IMAMURA, SCOTT DARRYL
[pen.] Mr. Imam; [b.] January 17, 1958, San Jose, CA; [p.] Mitsuru Imamura, Shizue Imamura; [m.] Single; [ed.] West Valley College A.A. - Arts San Jose State University - B.S. International Business. San Jose State University - BS. - Finance; [occ.] Tax Accountant; [memb.] Spartan Foundation San Jose State University, San Jose State University Alumi. Assoc. Yuki. Tetkei Haiku Society Deans List at West Valley College; [hon.] Won 3rd Place in National Library Poetry Contest - Songs on the wind. (1995); [oth. writ.] Many Editorials Published in San Jose Mercury News (Local Newspaper) and various newsletters. Have own newsletter "Imamura's I'd quarterly" - self-help news letter; [pers.] Every capable human being should try to better him or herself everyday to reach his or her Potential and dream. To make this world a better place to live.; [a.] San Jose, CA

INDARJIT, NATASHA STACY
[pen.] Speck, Tasha, Shorty; [b.] September 7, 1980, San Fernando, Trinidad; [p.] Maureen and Premchan Indarjit; [ed.] Forest Glen, Glenhaven and Glenforest Secondary (High School); [occ.] Volunteer at the Hospital; [hon.] Principal's Honors, Attendance Awards; [pers.] Life's short! So live it to the fullest!; [a.] Mississauga Ontario, Canada

INGHAM, GARY
[b.] March 28, 1975, Georgia; [p.] Mr. and Mrs. William McLaughlin; [ed.] Rumsey Hall School Washington, Ct. Valley Forge Military Academy Penn.; [occ.] Student; [pers.] I wrote this poem which I was a student at Rumsey Hall School in Washington, Ct. age 15 - I am currently attending College and live at home with my parents. I am the youngest of six children.; [a.] Watertown, CT

INNES, JAMES
[b.] June 15, 1941, Aberdeen, Scotland; [p.] James Pittendriegh, Mary Ann (Nee Smith); [ed.] Middle Junior Secondary, College of Commerce, Aberdeen; [occ.] Nurse - Ward Manager; [hon.] "Retail Business Studies", "Registered General Nurse", "Registered Mental Nurse"; [oth. writ.] Other poems published by U.K. Publishers.; [pers.] Some good can be found in everyone, some make it easy to find, some make it a challenge.; [a.] Aberdeen Scotland, United Kingdom

INZERILLO, R.B.
[pen.] Inzy; [b.] May 14, 1937, Kansas City, MI; [p.]J.C. & T.I. Inzerillo, Sr.;[ch.] Loretta, Chimene, Marcus, Mario, and Angelo.; [ed.] Electronic Eng'g., Mechanical Designer; [occ.] Mech Designer (contract); [memb.] C.E.T. (Certified Engineering Technician), ASCET- Association for the Society of Certified Technicians, Eagle Scout, Former

Assist Scout Master. [hon.] Art Scholarship, Veteran; [oth. writ.] Poems - non published; [pers.] I believe in every person's life, there is a time of peak awareness and creativity. For me the awareness of my enviroment and the creation of a few chosen verses to share to share hopefully with pleasure to others, took place.; [a.] Greensboro, NC

IRVINE, SALLY ANN
[b.] January 3, 1940, Devon, England; [p.] Jack and Dorothy Briggs; [m.] John Lewis Irvine, February 15, 1958; [ch.] Heather Ann, Sandra Lee, Christopher John; [ed.] Scholarship to Barn Staple Girls Grammar, then Rhuapahu College, New Zealand; [occ.] Part-time Pharmacy Ass.; [oth. writ.] Several poems published in local newspapers and magazines.; [pers.] All my poems have been inspired by true life experiences and I didn't start writing until a year ago when we moved from New Zealand to Western Aust. is an inspiring place.; [a.] Perth, WA

IRWIN, ELAINE M.
[b.] June 17, 1962, New Brunswick, Canada; [p.] Earl and Evelyn Thompson; [m.] Brian Irwin, September 1, 1990; [occ.] Registered Practical Nurse; [pers.] This is my first entry into a writing contest and I am absolutely thrilled to be published in this attempt to make my dream a reality. Believe in yourself and try your best.

ISON, JACQUELINE
[b.] March 17, 1961, Lorain, OH; [m.] David McCarty, April 23, 1983; [ch.] Jeremy David; [ed.] Lorain High School, Lorain County Community College; [occ.] Asst. Mgr. Property Mgmt Co., LandLord Leasing Service; [memb.] Fellowship Baptist Church Association with Lorain Real Estate Board, Associated with Amherst Sandstone Workshop Players; [oth. writ.] Some other poems currently being published; [pers.] I enjoy the arts, classical Music, opera (Rigeletto) being a favorite, playing the piano, singing and writing; [a.] Amherst, OH

JABBAR, SADIQUA AMATUALLAH
[b.] September 7, 1979, New York; [p.] Desarz and Zabriel Zabbar; [ed.] High School 11th Grade; [occ.] Student; [hon.] Children's Volunteer Award, University Hospital, I want to be a teacher.; [oth. writ.] World I, World II, People, Think of Others, Unwanted Touch, Some People Someone Special, Blackman, Test.; [pers.] To all children out there as long as you have an education there is nothing you can't do, with a college education you have the key to the world.; [a.] New Orleans, LA

JACKSON, RUBY J.
[b.] September 10, 1939, Fairfield, AR; [p.] Earline G. Chatman; [ed.] Associates Degree in Social Services; [occ.] Child Advocate; [memb.] Church Membership at First Baptist Church at Dewdrop, Sons and Daughters of Haiti - Order of Eastern Star - Lambda Alpha Chapter; [hon.] 1st Prize in Essay Contest 1986 - Kraft Essays; [oth. writ.] "Letter From A Black Mother", "The Jewel That Lust It's Sparkle", "A Christmas Ago"; [pers.] "Hug Me", was written after the death of my second son died of complications due to aids. After working with other aids patients and their loved ones, I have devoted my life to letting others know that help is available.; [a.] Pine Bluff, AR

JACQUE, JULES RAYMOND
[pen.] JRJ; [b.] May 17, 1951, Port Washington, WI; [p.] Nicholas F. Jacque Jr., Dorothy Rita; [m.] Susan Jayne Jacque; [ch.] Rebecca Sue, Rachel Nicole; [ed.] Port Washington, H.S., U. W. Oshkosh 2 years; [occ.] Disabled with special interests in Poetry, Woodworking, and Horses; [oth. writ.] Numerous poems written for Ma and Pa's keepsakes Stoddards Wis. 54658; [pers.] "My Caretaker" written in memory of Dorothy Rita Brainard Jacque. Personally speaking, poetry should be written in a picturesque and concise manner, allowing for reader participation and interpretation.; [a.] Stoddard, WI

JACQUES, GERTY J.
[pen.] Gerty; [b.] January 9, 1962, Haiti; [p.] Gertrude A. Guillaume; [ed.] Kingsborough College; [occ.] Insurance Broker; [oth. writ.] Several poems unpublished, short stories unpublished.; [pers.] Education can rarely deceive you, so stay in school. I'd like to dedicate this poem to a special friend, he's the only one who knows why. Love to mom Myrtha, Alix, Margaret, Joe and Alice.; [a.] Jamaica, NY

JADALI, CAROL SINOBEN
[b.] Guam; [p.] Tomasa and Anatolio Sinoben; [m.] Nader Jadali, 1984; [ch.] Shaheen, Jasmine; [ed.] Notre Dame High Graduate, DeAnza College-Dean's List; [occ.] Child Development Field; [pers.] You dream with your eyes closed. The dream becomes your destiny only with your eyes open.

JAGUSCH, LEEANNE
[b.] January 26, 1983, Southfield, MI; [p.] Kathy and Tim Jagusch; [ed.] K-2 Kinlock Elementary, 3-5 Round Elementary, 6-7 Farms currently in 7th grade Middle School; [memb.] Sierra Eagles/Crossroads Club, Hartland Equestrian Club, 4-H; [hon.] Livingston Country Young Authors, Student of the month 7th grade, Youth Appreciation Award, all A's Honor Roll 4th-7th grade; [oth. writ.] Several poems for school magazine and equestrian club newsletter; [pers.] "The world belongs to the energetic".

JAMES, DENISE A. BUTCHER
[b.] January 24, 1958, Philadelphia, PA; [p.] William L. Butcher, Juanita Butcher; [m.] Willie M. James, January 6, 1977; [ch.] Akira and Elon James; [ed.] University City H.S., Temple University, Penn State University; [occ.] Educator, Trainer; [memb.] "Eta Sigma Gamma, Professional Health Honor Society, "American Society for Training and Development"; [hon.] 1984 "National Dean's List", 1995 "Young Alumni Achievement Award", 1994 "Special Contributor's Award", [oth. writ.] "If We Could Talk, Just One More Time"- dedicated to the memories of my Father, brother and sister.; [pers.] I write when I am inspired and because writing is healing. Life and living inspire me to foster healing.; [a.] Mount Holly, NJ

JAMES, ELEANOR
[b.] January 1, 1947, Chester, England; [p.] Johnson Forsythe, Maureen Forsythe; [m.] Keith James; [ch.] Karen, Robert, Jenny, Stevan; [oth. writ.] The Carpenter, Tapestry, The Light, Timeless,

What Happened and other Poems.; [pers.] I try to express all kinds of love in loves many forms, be it joy or pain.; [a.] Whitby Ontario, Canada

JAMES, KELLI-ANN BLISS
[b.] August 13, 1969, Cranston, RI; [p.] Allen and Rose Bliss; [m.] Aaron W. James, October 14, 1995; [ch.] Aaron W. Bliss-James Jr.; [ed.] East Prov. Senior High; [occ.] Reject Claims Analyst-Brooks Drug, Third Party Accounting; [oth. writ.] Several works of poetry, and stories for pleasure and relaxation.; [pers.] Every person is the same, until that one moment when it's time to shine above the rest.; [a.] Providence, RI

JAMES, LINNETTE
[pen.] Leonie; [b.] January 28, 1976, Jamaica; [p.] Mrs. Venise McIntosh and Mr. Clive James; [ed.] Previuosly done GCSEs, currently studying media studies and English Lit. and language A levels; [occ.] Student, Composer; [oth. writ.] A song entitled I'm Sick Of Your Lies which is due to be release in the summer of 1996 by Hollywood Artist.; [pers.] I feel blessed and honored in having a piece of my creative work been published in your anthology.; [a.] Leicester, England

JAMES, TASHA SHAY
[b.] January 15, Monroe, LA; [p.] Walter James; [m.] Mrs. Rosa James, July 18, 1959; [ch.] 7; [oth. writ.] "Faith Walkers", Live The Way You Tray" and "Walking By Faith".

JAMISON, NICOLE EILEEN
[pen.] Nej; [b.] December 11, 1969, Abington, PA; [p.] Doris Lucera and Nicholas Lucera; [m.] David G. Jamison, April 23, 1994; [ed.] BA English/Secondary Education January 1992 Gwynedd Mercy College; [memb.] Dean's List; [a.] Willow Grove, PA

JASPER, VERNOL A.
[pen.] Vernol (Bun) Jasper; [b.] July 14, 1919; [p.] Thomas and Susie Jasper; [m.] Elsie Brown Jasper, December 26, 1939; [ch.] Roy, Bobbie, Douglas and Debra

JEAN-FRANCOIS, MARIE-CATHERINE
[b.] July 30, 1974, Brooklyn, NY; [p.] Jeveille and Phinelie Jean-Francois; [ed.] The Mary Academy, Hofstra University; [occ.] Full-time College Student; [memb.] International Society of Poets, Hofstra's Literary Magazine Club, Americanized Self-Defense School of Martial Arts and Science; [hon.] Dean's List ('92 and '95), Editor's Choice Award ('94 and '95), Eugene Schneider Prose Award (1995); [oth. writ.] Short stories, poems published by NLP including Mists of Enchantment and Best Poems of 1995.; [pers.] What inspired this poem was a wish to feel completely content with myself as well as with my life despite my everyday troubles and inconveniences. I haven't experienced this wish yet but I know I one day will.; [a.] Hollis, NY

JEESUE, KIM
[b.] April 27, 1968, Seoul, Korea; [ed.] Northwestern University, University of London, Cornell University; [occ.] Singer in an alternative band.; [memb.] Sierra Club; [hon.] Cornell Tradition, New York Forensics Finalist, Class of 1906 Schol-

arship, 1992 San Jose Film Festival - Animation Entry, College Scholar; [oth. writ.] 'The Maid', short story published in The New Press.; [pers.] I try to bring my experiences from South Korea, in the aftermath of a major war, to evoke humanity's loss of faith, in love, conflicts with morality and consciousness that seems to shift, reflecting the times.; [a.] Saratoga, CA

JELINCIC, KIRA LEIGH
[pen.] Kira Leigh Jelincic; [b.] January 15, 1978, Pittsburgh, PA; [p.] Dagmar and Frano Jelincic; [ed.] Graduating Radford High School in June 1996; [occ.] Student; [hon.] This is my first; [pers.] I believe, completely, in the tremendous power of words.; [a.] Radford, VA

JEMISON, MILDRED CLAUFF
[pen.] Mildred Clauff Jemison; [b.] February 27, 1904, Osceola, NE; [p.] Charles Clauff and Elizabeth Morgan Clauff; [m.] Earl Jemison, February 27, 1979; [ch.] Eugene and Darrell Adamson; [ed.] Rural Nebraska first 8 years High School Fullerton, Neb. College Nebraska Central College, William Pen at Oskaloosa in Iowa and Kearney teachers College at Kearney NE.; [occ.] Retired and manage my farm.; [memb.] Methodist Church, Fish and Wild Life. I have been forced to drop many groups because I can't drive now. My eyes are to poor.; [hon.] Prices on heedle work, also on my oil paintings. I am happy to belong to belong to International Society of poets. I have had such a busy life, raised my family in the dirly 30's. Now I have time to write paint and all I have been wanting to do.; [oth. writ.] Story for cappers weekly; [pers.] I love to study and discuss any thing that has to do with life in our Universe now, or past, or future. Also study of the soul.; [a.] Aurora, NE

JENCA, KIMBERLEE
[b.] July 21, 1968, Pittsburgh, PA; [p.] Michael Swidorsky, Dorothy Swidorsky; [ed.] Oliver High School, Columbus Middle, John Morrow Elementary; [occ.] Telephone Operator for an Answering Service; [memb.] Holy Trinity Luthern Church; [oth. writ.] One other poem published so far.; [pers.] I believe you must always try to do your very best, and the key is to never give up. You can achieve all your goals and dreams as long as you believe in yourself and go with what is in your heart.; [a.] Pittsburgh, PA

JENKINS, RUBY
[pen.] Ruby Jaye; [b.] Whangorie, UL; [p.] Christinia & James Smith; [ed] Auckland Girls Grammer School; [memb.] Life Member Tihai Venture School for Boys Member of Round Dance Clubs; [oth. writ.] Poem War published. Articles published in Wartkato Times and Hamllton Press, U.L.; [pers.] I am influenced by nature and it's natureal forms of beauty. I strive to give a clear message to mankind in my writing.

JENNINGS, CHARLOTTE J.
[b.] August 29, 1969, Chicago, IL; [p.] Roy Chandler, Charlotte Chandler; [ch.] David Lee, Amber Marie, Amanda Lynn; [ed.] Raymond William Wilmont High, Gateway Tech University of Wisconsin Parkside; [occ.] Waitress; [memb.] Distinguished Member of International Society of Poets; [hon.] Editors Choice Award from the National

Library of Poetry; [oth. writ.] Visions - as published in Windows of the Soul, Snowflake - as published in Treasured poems of America, several unpublished poems; [pers.] I hope to touch the hearts of others through my writing.; [a.] Kenosha, WI

JEPPSON, PER-MAGNUS
[pen.] Jeppes Penna; [b.] December 9, 1933, Uddevalla, Sweden; [ed.] Gothenburg Design School of Art and Crafts, Cont's Prep. School of Life Hardship; [occ.] Unemployed Interior Designer; [memb.] Swedish Architects' Association, Swedish Tourist Association (Member of the Local Branch Board); [hon.] None worth mentioning; [oth. writ.] None worth mentioning; [pers.] As a young boy I was silent - even at school, when matured I just talked and talked, now I am constantly trying to find something really essential to say...; [a.] Landvetter, Sweden

JOHANNSER, JANE
[pen.] Jane Johannser; [b.] March 10, 1944, Cleveland, OH; [p.] John and Elizabeth Donaldson; [m.] Richard H. Johannser, August 2, 1968; [ch.] Richard Alan, Neil Paul Johannser; [ed.] Fairview General Hospital (Diploma), BSN University of State of New York at Albany MSN Medical College of Ohio, Postgraduate Nurse Practitioner Case Western Reserve University; [occ.] Family Nurse Practitioner Ashland Family Practice, Ashland, Ohio; [memb.] Nurses Christian Fellowship, Sigma Theta Tau, American Association of Critical Care Nurses, American Academy of Nurse Practitioners; [hon.] MCO Graduate Nursing Award for Excellence in Critical Care Practice (1988 Lorpin YWCA Merit Award, Women of Achievement (1990) Who's Who in American Nursing 1993-94, 1996-97; [oth. writ.] "Self-Care Assessment: Key To A Teaching and Discharge Plan", Dimensions of Critical Care Nursing 11(1) p. 48-56, "Update: Guidelines for Treating Hypertension American Journal of Nursing 93(3) 42-49, "Chronic Obstructive Pulmonary Disease: Current Comprehensive Care for Emphysema and Branches", The Nurse Practitioner 19(1). 59-67; [a.] Wakeman, OH

JOHNSON, ABRA LEIGH
[b.] November 26, 1985, Prince George, British Columbia, Canada; [p.] Kevin and Mellody Johnson; [ed.] Grade 5 currently at David Hoy Elementary School, Fort St. James BC; [hon.] Certificate of Merit for Outstanding Citizenship -(Grade 4), A-honors in Music Festivals, 1st place (age 8-9) in Friends of the PR George Public Library Writing Contest (1994). Several awards for Speech Arts and Science held at David Hoy Elementary School.

JOHNSON, DANNY E.
[b.] March 18, 1960, Sparta, TN; [p.] Chester M. and Helen Willene Johnson; [m.] Theresa M. (Palmer) Johnson, February 17, 1987; [ch.] Kenny Crabtree, (Stepson) Anthony Wand, Legantye Johnson; [ed.] 12th grade graduate, Major F.F.A.; [occ.] Disabled; [hon.] Have received awards in: Public Speaking on Conservation, Forestry, Horticulture, Photograph, Speech on our Freedom Rights (essay).; [oth. writ.] Public Speech on Conservation. Several poems during school days. None published. Speech and essay on our Freedom Rights (1st place in High School); [pers.] I was encouraged to pursue poetry by English Teacher in

1976. Being from a small town I never thought much about it till now, I decided to give it a try. Couldn't hurt anything.; [a.] Crossville, TN

JOHNSON, DEBRA L.
[b.] February 9, 1953, Cleveland, OH; [p.] William Beasley Sr., and Loretta Beasley; [m.] Divorced; [ch.] Ron Jr., Tiffany Sherelle, Stephanie Charisse; [occ.] Secretary, Freelance; [oth. writ.] A host of poems and short stories for my family and friends.; [pers.] I write because I cannot "not" write.; [a.] Cleveland, OH

JOHNSON, DENNIS L.
[pen.] Dennis or Denny Johnson; [b.] March 26, 1996, MI; [p.] Walter and Constance Johnson; [m.] (Deceased March 7, 1995), June 24, 1962; [ch.] Heidi and Gretchen Johnson; [ed.] B.S. Degree in Education - Ferris State University; [occ.] Business Broker - Denny Johnson Enterprises...; [memb.] National Realtors; [oth. writ.] 2nd poem - I Looked Up And She Was There; [pers.] After my wife passed away in March '95, I met a special friend on a ski trip which inspired to compose the two poems from the heart... Also, brought me to New York (Long Island) from Michigan.; [a.] Rockville Centre, NY

JOHNSON, FLOYD A.
[b.] November 30, 1934, Wilmington, NC; [p.] Willie Johnson, Lela Johnson; [m.] Pearlinem Johnson, April 9, 1977; [ch.] Jennifer, Jewl, Anthony, Dillard; [ed.] 10th grade Mike, Sharon, Fred; [memb.] First Baptist Church

JOHNSON, FRANCES LEE
[b.] April 9, 1971, Knoxville, TN; [p.] Richard and Mary Johnson; [ed.] Attending university of California, at Irvine to get BA in English. I also plan to get a masters degree after graduation; [occ.] Full time student; [memb.] American Legion Auxiliary California Republic Party, Young Republicans; [hon.] Easter Seals Poster Child for Tree Years; [oth. writ.] I have written poems. Short Stories, and essays. This the first thing of mine that is published.; [pers.] I have had Juvenile rheumatoid arthritis since I was a year old, through hard work persistence and a strong faith I have been able to have many achievements because of my hospital experiences I was able to give amber support and love.; [a.] Desert Hot Springs, CA

JOHNSON, HAYLEY E.
[b.] April 24, 1974, Wortzburg, Germany; [p.] Hurry E. Johnson and Elaine Johnson; [ed.] Hammond High School, Columbia, MD - Catonsville, Catonsville, MD and Eastern Shore Community College, Melfa, VA; [occ.] Educational Interpreter for Deaf High Schoolers (american Sign Language); [oth. writ.] The Son's Flower, Be There, and Children's Literature; [pers.] I always try to have "delayed vision". Where millions of eyes fall together upon the same conclusion, I make an effort to find a side route to a new perspective. God gave everyone some redeeming quality and a purpose only he/she can fulfill.; [a.] Onley, VA

JOHNSON III, WILLIAM F.
[b.] May 31, 1978, Baltimore, MD; [p.] William Johnson Jr. and Terri Johnson; [ed.]

Williamstown High School, Williamstown, New Jersey, Hamilton Southeastern High School Fisher, Indiana; [hon.] "I dare you" Award, "Right Stuff" Award, 1995 US Air Force Academy Summer Scientific Seminar, Academic Excellence Award, Alternate Boy's State nominee (Indiana), Congressional Nomination for US Service Academies, Who's Who in High School Students, Who's Who in High School Athletes; [oth. writ.] Several poems published in local newspapers and anthologies.; [pers.] I strive to illustrate mankind's pain, hate and sadness as a characteristic of nature. The words in my poetry, to me, are like foot steps, because no matter what problem or fear I face, I can always find a place that comforts me.; [a.] Williamstown, NJ

JOHNSON, JACOB
[b.] April 1, 1977, Salmon Arm, British Columbia, Canada; [p.] Debbie Stephenson, Chris Johnson; [ed.] Returning High School Drop-out but plan to pursue a university education.; [occ.] Canadian Wildlife Federation; [pers.] I am a misanthropist, a budgie encaged by humanity. Waiting patiently for the day it can escape. Then, upon doing so, it sees that Earth has been destroyed by the cold hands of mankind and all it can do is live and die.; [a.] British Columbia, Canada

JOHNSON, MS. TINA V.
[pen.] "T.J."; [b.] August 14, 1955, New York City, NY; [p.] Viola and Eugene Johnson; [ch.] Tika and Bruce Johnson; [ed.] PS 28 M, IS 52, Louis D. Brandeis, H.S., Bronx Community College, Boricua College; [occ.] School Aide, Student Teacher; [memb.] P.T.A. President of IS '90, President of Student Gov't. of Boricua College in Spring of 1995; [hon.] Dean's List, Roberto Clemente Award, IS '90 Community Achievement Award; [pers.] To strive, to achieve my education, so that I may share what I've learned. To enhance the minds of children to want, to learn, by using a multi-cultural background, I will be able to touch any young mind, because I feel that any child can learn!; [a.] New York, NY

JOHNSON SR., DAVID I.
[b.] October 31, 1936, Columbia, SC; [p.] Mr. and Mrs. David and Thomasina Nesbitt Johnson; [m.] Sandra C. Learmont (now divorced), Dec 1960; [ch.] David Jr. and Lisa Diann; [ed.] BFA - Commercial Art Education - Drake University, 1962. MA - Art Education - University of Illinois (Champaign) - 1968. Additional study: University of Illinois, University of South Carolina, University of Georgia, etc.; [occ.] College Art Educator, Vocalist, Trumpeter, Commercial Pilot, Actor, Art Faculty, Shaw University, Raleigh, N.C.; [memb.] Kappa Alpha Psi Fraternity, Raleigh N.C. Alumni Chapter, Delta Phi Delta Honorary Art Fraternity - Drake U., Chi Gamma Iota - U. of Ill. Vetrans Frat., Omicron Delta Kappa Honorary Leadership Fraternity - Drake University. Former membership in USAF Reserve Officer Association, S.C. Wing Civil Air Patrol: Aerospace Education Director and Mission Pilot, Aircraft Owners and Pilot's Assoc., National Art Education Association.; [hon.] National Boy Scout Explorer Award Trip to Philmont Scout Ranch as high school student, senior class president and three year high school varsity track mile-run S.C. state champion

1952-1954. Drake University cross-country track Missouri Valley Championship team member 1961, USAF ROTC "Distinguished Cadet" Honor 1962. S.C. Governor's Merit Award for Aeronautics Education presented by Gov. Richard Riley, 1981. Poet of Merit and Lifetime Membership awards in the "International Society of Poets", 1991, 1992, and 1993 respectively.; [oth. writ.] Poems: "Charles Towne S.C." "Warm Ice", "Misty", "Mushroom Cloud", "A Semester Ends Begins", "Daybreak", "Power By Sunbeam", "In Memorial To Our Beloved Deceased", etc.; [pers.] Typically, in my poetry, the organic and inorganic are active vehicles, through contemplative theme and basic rhythmical alliteration, I seek to weave sound and subject, invitingly, to conjure up passions for caring.; [a.] Columbia, SC

JOHNSON, TRACEY LYNN
[b.] December 9, 1970, Edmonton, AB; [p.] Don and Linda Johnson; [ed.] Chemical Technology Diploma from Northern Alberta Institute of Technology; [pers.] This poem was written during my brother Jason's battle with cancer. He died March 8, 1995 and never got to read this poem. I would like to have it dedicated to him.; [a.] Edmonton Alberta, Canada

JONES, ALICIA TAMARA
[b.] January 3, 1975, Baltimore, MD; [ed.] Walbrook Sr. High School, Coppin State College; [occ.] Student/Secretary; [memb.] Beth Kappa Chi, McNair Post-Baccalaureate Achievement Program, Coppin State College Honors Program; [hon.] All-American Scholar (94-95), Minority Leadership Award (94-95), National Dean's List (Sp-93, F-94 S-95); [oth. writ.] A Fini, The Betrothed, Horizon, Cotton Tree, Misery Without Company, Hydroplaning, Black Moon Rising, Perspective The Secret, Sunkissed, Fists of Fury, An Episode, 5 Ways to Love Me; [pers.] "I just thank God for letting me bloom. I've been a seed too long."; [a.] Baltimore, MD

JONES, CARRIE A.
[pen.] Katz; [b.] December 18, 1979.; [p.] Wayne and Shirley Jones; [ed.] 2nd High School at Cabool High School.

JONES, CHESTER L.
[b.] October 28, 1965, Barren Co.; [p.] Garron Jones, Berniece Jones; [m.] Robin Jones, October 24, 1986; [ch.] Courtney, Bliss, Jesse; [ed.] GED; [occ.] Supervisor Collis Inc.; [memb.] Shady Grove Baptist Church; [oth. writ.] My Mother, Mother And Daughter, Family, As Time Goes By, God's Great Promise Land, Changes in the Weather, Christmas Day, Beginning a New Year; [pers.] Grandaddy was written in memory of my wife's Grandaddy, Emmitt Dallas Lyle. A good hardworking honest man. He lived a special life. He loved people and they loved him back! That's why he's in a special place, with God!; [a.] Center, KY

JONES, DAWN A'LEE
[pen.] Dawn Froysland; [b.] March 4, 1977, The Dalles, OR; [p.] Richard and Penny Jones; [ed.] Beaverton High School; [occ.] Desk Management At Valley Lanes Bowling Center; [memb.] (YABA) Young American Bowling Alliance; [hon.] Corky Talley Bowling Scholarship; [oth. writ.] Many

Poems and Short Stories un-published.; [pers.] I hope to fulfill each heart with strength and love through my poetry. Also, to inspire those to live by the moment and follow your dreams.; [a.] Portland, OR

JONES, DETRA
[pen.] Dee; [b.] November 13, 1958, Nashville, AR; [p.] Clell Turbeville, Hally Mitchell; [m.] Donald Jones, July 26, 1984; [ch.] Misty, Samantha, Amanda; [ed.] Nashville Elementary, Murfreesboro High; [occ.] Jordan Health Care; [memb.] Buchanan United Methodist Church, Liberty Eylau, P.T.A.; [oth. writ.] Several poems, 2 children's stories.; [pers.] I write for the glory of God. So that others may come to know Jesus.; [a.] Texarkana, TX

JONES, FLORENCE M.
[pen.] Florencia Prudence; [b.] April 11, 1939, West Columbia; [p.] Isaiah and Lu Ethel McNeil; [m.] Waldo D. Jones, May 29, 1965; [ch.] Ricky, Wanda and Erna; [ed.] Prairie View A and M. Univ. BS/1961 (Cum Laude) MED 1968 (same as above) Rice, University of Houston/Post Graduate; [occ.] Piano Instructor, Writer, Speaker, Story Teller Seminar Presentor; [memb.] Life/Texas retired Teacher Association, Tejas Story telling Association - Life, distinguished Life Member - International Society of Poets, National Women of Achievement Oak Meadows Church of God; [hon.] Letters of Achievement for Outstanding Contributions in Education from: President Bill Clinton, Gov. Ana Richards, Gov. George Bush, Congresswoman Shelia Jackson Lee, Lib. of Poetry Editors choice award, gold medallion National Women of Achievement 3/96; [oth. writ.] 1 Science modules for Houston Ind. School Dist., poems in NLP anthologies and sparrowgrass poetry forum, Follow Your Dream - Personal Growth and Dev. program; [pers.] Peace, a gift from above, generates a positive attitude leading to a positive approach to life. A positive approach (to life) enables individuals to achieve extraordinary feats.; [a.] Houston, TX

JONES, JACOB ALAN
[pen.] Jacques Broussard; [b.] November 22, 1978, London, OH; [p.] Alan D. Jones, Jo-Anne Jones; [ed.] Madison Plains High School; [occ.] Sales Associate at Phillips-Van Heusen; [memb.] 1994-95 Member of Who's Who Among American High School Students; [oth. writ.] I have had two other poems published in our school newsletter.; [pers.] Poetry isn't a talent, it's a gift. The good poet can open their heart and let their feelings do the writing.; [a.] South Solon, OH

JONES, MICHAEL M.
[pen.] M. M. Jones; [b.] July 10, 1956, New York City; [m.] Patricia, October 9, 1981; [oth. writ.] A compilation of twenty five (25) years of unpublished poems, prose and essays; [pers.] Love is...; [a.] New York, NY

JONES, RALPH
[b.] November 5, 1950, Greenville, SC; [p.] Helen Jones; [m.] Sharon C. Jones, January 30, 1982; [ch.] Amber 12 and Ashley 9; [ed.] High School; [occ.] Grading Contractor self-employed; [memb.] Masonic Lodge Church Member; [oth. writ.] "Head

of the House" and "My Son"; [pers.] These poems are dedicated to the memory of loved ones who have passed on.; [a.] Piedmont, SC

JONES, ROBERT J.
[pen.] Robert J. Jones; [b.] January 8, 1921, Rocky Forks Park Country, IN; [p.] John N. Jones, Blanch Jones; [m.] Louis Riggle Jones, April 12, 1946; [ch.] Robert, Vickie, Mike, and Steve; [ed.] 8th grade, Navy Storekeeping Schools, Building Trades School, Religious School; [occ.] Retired Stonemason; [memb.] Church of the Nazarene; [hon.] Sunday School Teacher Awards, Churchmanship Awards appointed to Brazil City Council served 5 years; [oth. writ.] Over 200 other poems some comical have 1st one written when 15 years old.; [pers.] I have been influenced by the old poets. Longfellow, Poe, Hemans Whitties and Whitman.; [a.] Brazil, IN

JORDAN, MONA A.
[b.] January 28, 1963, Boston, MA; [occ.] Astrological Consultant/Councilor; [pers.] Words are the solid form of the stirring of a soul.; [a.] Quincy, MA

JUEL, RICK
[pen.] Rick Juel; [b.] December 21, 1958, Sioux Falls, SD; [p.] Dale and Shirley Juel; [ed.] 1-5, in a one rm. Country School 6-12, Canton Public, Canton, SD; [occ.] Personal Fitness Trainer, Massage Therapist; [oth.writ.] Mother Nature, The Silver Haired Man, Mama's Little Girls, Silent Prayer, The Rancher, A Love We Can Not Hide, Young Man's Dream, A Lonely Heart's Walk, and The Fear Within; [pers.] What started out as a release of troubled emotions, from a young man's heart, has turned into a fulfilling and rewarding hobby. I love life, my health, and my happiness and I try to keep things very simple, stress and high drama free. God has given us a beautiful place to live, please help me save her!; [a.] Playa Del Rey, CA

JUSTICE, PEGGY
[pen.] P. D. Justice; [m.] John N. Justice; [ch.] John N. III, Susan Goodwin and James H.; [ed.] Lake Worth HS, BA and MA University of Texas at Arlington; [pers.] The versatility of words should be cherished. It allows us to explore the unexpected beauty often hidden among the mundane and sometimes painful realities of life; [a.] Athens, TX

KAERCHER, SUZANNE C.
[b.] July 9, 1942, Cleveland, OH; [p.] Clarence and Ella Slivka; [m.] Robert W. Kaercher, April 12, 1969; [ch.] Janelle Marie; [ed.] 2 years Elementary Education at Bowling Green State University. Associate RM degree from Columbus Technical Institute, Columbus, Ohio; [occ.] Home Health Care, Nurse and Case Manager at Choctaw Valley Home Health, Crestview, FL; [memb.] American Nursing Association, Good Shepherd Lutheran Church, Parish Nurses, Nurses, VFW Ladies Auxiliary #5450, Florida State University Boosters Club; [oth. writ.] Non-published children's stories written while taking a course with the Institute of Children's Literature as well as "Just For Fun" poetry.; [pers.] My philosophical beliefs can best be expressed as follows: The unceasing pitfalls of daily life need not to be a source of bitter strife choose wisely, carefully, don't delay now begin, today's the day!; [a.] Crest View, FL

KALB, KAMERON
[b.] October 15, 1960; [ch.] Candice Renee and Christopher Julian; [oth. writ.] Not one of my poems is committed to memory, every time I read them, it's like reading them for the first time.; [pers.] I am inspired by everyday living and by people in several neither of which are ordinary, so possibilities and ideas are endless. "I write more than I know," "I know more than I write."; [a.] San Jose, CA

KALCHTHALER, MAX
[b.] December 16, 1979; [p.] Robert and Laurel Kalchthaler; [ed.] St. Xavier High Cinncinnati OH; [occ.] Student; [hon.] Made it to State Finals in "Power of the Pen" Writing Competition in 1994, Ohio; [pers.] Poetry challenges us to·know ourselves better. We as human's struggle to express ourselves. In this search of self expression poetry is an excellent median. So many feelings, so many types of poems. Poetry is more than written expression, it's a way of living your life.; [a.] Laguna Niguel, CA

KALICH, KATHERINE LYNN
[pen.] Kathy Kalich; [b.] February 27, 1982, Houston, TX; [p.] Brian P. and Desiree C. Kalich; [ed.] Pre - K. through 5th Raymond Elementary School 6th Eckert Intermediate School 7th and 8th Aldine Middle School; [occ.] Student; [memb.] Girl Scouts, U.S.A. Student Council - treasurer; [hon.] Girls Scouts: Leadership, and Silver Awards (which is the second highest award given) school: Honor Roll, honors in attendance, and class room awards; [pers.] I've never had any of my poems published and I am genuinely proud of myself. Everyone who has a goal should try their hardest to achieve it.; [a.] Houston, TX

KAMENSKY, OLGA
[b.] March 14, 1986, Moscow, Russia; [p.] Alla Kamensky, Victor Kamensky; [ed.] 4th Grade of Salanter Akiba Riverdale Academy.; [occ.] Student 4th grade SAR Academy.; [memb.] International Society of Poets; [hon.] Editor's Choice Awards of Outstanding Achievement in Poetry (The National Library of Poetry 1995, 1996). An honorable Mention the cricket league poetry contest, August 1995; [oth. writ.] About 70 poems, a few stories. Published: My Lost Heart - The Garden of Life, 1995 p. 358 and The Riverdale Press November 23, 1995, p. A10. Night of the Nymphs is being published in best poems of 1996. Three poems published in school's newspaper.; [pers.] The poems was inspired by one of my fights with my best friend which to my regret occur rather often.; [a.] New York, NY

KASTLER, PAT
[pen.] Patrick Joe or Pat Kastler; [b.] January 15, 1960, Raton, NM; [p.] Paul and Marriane Kastler; [ed.] B.S. Civil Engineering Technology and Minor in Computer Sciences from N.A.U. (Northern Arizona University); [occ.] CAD Design Specialist for my own Business; [oth. writ.] "Images" - to be published in upcoming anthology "The Voice Within".; [pers.] I wrote the "Happy Mother's Day" pome for my mother who is wonderful mother, wife and classy lady. When I was a young boy, I had a sickness and my mother nursed me back to health by weighing my food, giving me my medication, and enforcing the doctor's or-

ders. She was a great role model of what a woman should be and what I should look for in a wife.; [a.] Phoenix, AZ

KASTNER, TONI
[pen.] Toni Robinson; [b.] October 15, 1960, Ardmore, OK; [p.] Johnny Robinson, Robbie Harmon; [ch.] Lesley Robinson; [ed.] G.E.D. - Dept. of Educ., State of O.K. Associate in Science - Murray State College - Tishomingo, OK., Sociology - East Central Univ. Ada, OK.; [occ.] Cook - J.D.'s Cafeteria Ada, OK; [oth. writ.] College Essays and Research Papers.; [pers.] My favorite topics to write about are social problems, human behavior, child abuse, and relationship. I place emphasis on expressing an image or thought, that the people can see, feel, and understand.; [a.] Ada, OK

KATS, EDWARD
[b.] July 18, 1946, Kiev, Ukraine; [p.] Sophia Rozel, Moses Kats; [m.] Klaudia Kats, December 17, 1976; [ch.] August, Jay Kats; [ed.] Elementary School, Kiev Urr Musical College, Kiev Ukraine; [occ.] Hardresser, Composer; [oth. writ.] Lyrics for Urbom "My Prayer", at present time I'm working on my book, "Guinea Pig from Silicon Valley"; [pers.] To be deeply hearted by abusive power one of the Government Organization, I as much as I can expressing pain and tension of my soul trying to rich peoples mind at the same time looking among of them for their support and understanding.; [a.] Palo Alto, CA

KAVANAGH, SEAN
[b.] April 5, 1968, Rochester, NY; [p.] Ronald and Debbie Kavanagh; [ch.] Jenna and MacKenzie Kavanagh; [ed.] John Marshall High School; [memb.] Poets Guild; [hon.] Publication in "Best New Poems Anthology" by the Poets Guild; [pers.] I enjoy writing, about the people I love and meet. Everyone has a quality and I always try to find it, in everyone and write about it.; [a.] West Columbia, SC

KAWAR, ISSA
[pen.] Desdichado; [b.] December 19, 1950, Ammau, Jordan; [p.] Nayef Kawar, Widad Kawar; [m.] May Kawar, October 3, 1986; [ch.] Nayef, Bassel, Luma, Leen; [ed.] Bachelor of the Mechanical Engineering from American University of Beirut (AUB) - 1973; [occ.] Managing Director Gemini Trading Establishment; [memb.] Royal Society for Conservation of Nature - Jordan Kawar Cooperative Society. Orthodox Club. Creative Writing Group of Amman; [oth. writ.] Several poems published in AUB's weekly outlook newspaper.; [pers.] Life is a winding road full of surprises at every bend.; [a.] Ammau, Jordan

KAYER, HEATHER
[pen.] Heather Kayer; [b.] February 23, 1977, Brownsville, TX; [p.] Viola Kayer; [ed.] Graduated first colonel, High school in VA. Beach, VA and attending Tidewater Community College in VA; [occ.] Student; [oth. writ.] I have never had, any of my writings published.; [pers.] I hope to bring enjoyments and enlightenment to those who raed my writing.

KEECH, JAMES H.
[pen.] Jim Keech; [b.] January 9, 1933, Allegan,

MI; [p.] Gerrit and Louthelle Keech; [m.] Ruth M. (Keillor) Keech, November 30, 1957; [ch.] Tim, Matt, Chris, Rachel; [ed.] Hartford Mich High School - 1951, Western Mich Univ. BA - 1960, Education Western Mich Univ. - MA Communications; [occ.] High School Social Studies Teacher, Watervliet (Mi) H.S.; [memb.] Nat'l. Soc. Studies Org., VFW Amer Legion - D.A.V., F&AM - Eastern Star, Phi Delta Kappa, Co-Producer of Legend Summer Theatre; [oth. writ.] Wrote a book titled "Gaijin Journal" about my teaching experience (English) in Japan 1986-87, have also has a number of cartoons published.; [pers.] This poem was written for my daughter, Rachel.; [a.] Decatur, MI

KEEGAN, JAMES W.
[pen.] James Keegan; [b.] January 16, 1946, Brooklyn, NY; [p.] James and Corinne Keegan; [m.] Marsha, April 26, 1980; [ch.] Charlene; [ed.] Miami Norland High School, Air Craft Electrician, U.S.A.F., Musician, 38 years, Electronics, Sales, Motion Picture, Post Production, Recording Studio Artist/Engineer; [occ.] Real Estate Sales and Musician and Technician; [memb.] Hollywood Board of Realtors, Child Reach, AAA Crime Watch Hollywood; [oth. writ.] The "Eclipse" collection "River Saint" Valley people collection "Shat" Collection, "Brats" book "A Merciful Kingmanship" song "Essence" song/poem, "Sweet Contagious Dreams" song.; [pers.] With brute strength us smile life's breathe, moving in the comfort of love like silk flowing with wind we are creations family!; [a.] Hollywood, FL

KEELEY, JENNIFER LEE
[b.] August 7, 1975, Smithtown; [p.] Diana J. Keeley; [ed.] Smithtown High School, Northport Wilson Tech (for cosmetology), S.C.C.C. Selden, NY, The Risk Academy, L.A., California; [occ.] Cosmetologist and student; [oth. writ.] 1. Making a Decision, 2. Finding Myself, 3. The Black Rose, 4. How Much I Love You. There are several others but "Afraid to Love" is the first and only one that has been published.; [pers.] All of my writings have been influenced by my own life experiences. Art, in any form, is always the best way to express one's emotions.; [a.] Ridge, NY

KEENE, J. D.
[b.] January 8, 1979, Pickerington, OH; [p.] John and Linda Keene; [ed.] Currently in Pickerington High School; [occ.] Sales Clerk at JC Penny Outlet; [oth. writ.] None of my poems have been published yet. They include "The Search", "Hope", and "Time" just to name a few.; [pers.] You don't know how much you truly love something, until you lose it. I have been inspired to write by the women in my life. I guess I am a hopeless romantic.; [a.] Pickerington, OH

KEESEE, DEWAN
[pen.] Dewan Keesee; [b.] November 9, 1975, Mount Home AFB, ID; [p.] Alvin and Vanessa Jernigan, Kenneth and Shirely Keesee; [ed.] Edmond Memorial High School, OK, sophomore - University of Tulsa, OK; [occ.] Student; [memb.] Lantern Honor Society, Student Assoc., Cabinet Programmer, University of Tulsa Wind Ensemble and Pep Band; [hon.] Cabinet Member of the Week, 2x Senator of the Week, Alpha Phi Alpha Scholarship, St. John Missionary Baptist Church Scholar-

ship; [oth. writ.] Thoughts of a Young Black Man - collection of poems - unpublished.; [pers.] I write in order to allow the reader to experience a taste of my daily buffet. By extending a piece of myself to the reader, I hope that he or she goes away with something moving and thought provoking.; [a.] Edmond, OK

KEKINO, LOVELYN M.
[pen.] "Love"; [b.] September 11, 1961, Honolulu, HI; [p.] Mr. Elmer and Mrs. Roseline Kekino; [m.] Perry Dane (Fiance) Rauch; [ch.] Dane Kekino, Lovisa Kaulana E' Kanani Rauch, Vagn Kaikane Rauch; [ed.] McKinley High; [occ.] Travel Consultant; [pers.] Poetry has been a feeling of impression, that I feel for others. I write what comes from deep within my heart. This poem "Rainbow" was written for my niece Danielle Alfapada, her teachers had ask the students to write in a poem about themselves, and this is what she presented... this name was given by her grandfather, Elmer, Lani Kekino.; [a.] Haleiwa, HI

KELLAMS, HAROLD D.
[pen.] Hal Kelly; [b.] January 21, 1931, New Albany, IN; [p.] Durward S. and Viola K. Kellams; [m.] Jonell K. Kellams, May 30, 1954; [ch.] Harold Kellams, Alomakirby, C.R. Kinsey, Doris Kinsey (deceased); [ed.] N.C. State and Charlotte College (3 yrs), Flying School, Real Estate and Numerous Military Intelligence Courses and School; [occ.] Retired (Disabled VET); [memb.] Veterans of Foreign Wars, American Legion and Fleet Reserve Association; [hon.] Nat. Def (2), Marine G.C. (2), Korean Service (2), Korea P.U.C., U.N. Service Medal, Armed Forces Res. M., Nav. Res. Meritorious Serv. M., S.W. Asia (2), Kuwait Med and Several Letters of Commendation and Appreciation FM 2 - Admirals and 2 Commanders, 1 - General; [oth. writ.] Have one other poem published (In a Fantasy Publication) and have written many others which were never published. Several poems were printed in the church publication.; [pers.] Most of my poetry is patriotic, religious or humorous. I usually write of my experiences and perceived exp. of others. I have been influenced by the classics and balladeers such as W. Service.; [a.] Charlotte, NC

KELLMAN, ANDERSON W.
[pen.] Anwerfield; [b.] September 19, 1949, Barbados; [p.] Isolene Sinclair; [m.] Margaret, June, 1982; [ch.] Don, Dan, Justin; [ed.] High School, College, Techn School; [occ.] Electrician, Electronic Technician; [memb.] MTL Barbados Bowling League; [hon.] Technical Diplomas; [oth. writ.] Many other songs and poems (unpublished); [pers.] Love was, still is, and will always be the answer.; [a.] Montreal Quebec, Canada

KELLY, TRACY
[b.] June 13, 1964, Los Angeles, CA; [p.] James Kelly, Virginia Love; [ed.] West Los Angeles College; [occ.] Executive Secretary; [memb.] Paradise Baptist Church; [hon.] Dean's List; [pers.] I listen to my heart, create from my soul, and write with my pen... "I can do all things through Christ, which strengthens me", (Philippians 4:13); [a.] Los Angeles, CA

KEMP, KRYSTYNA
[pen.] Kris; [b.] April 6, 1979, Maitland; [p.] Neil Kemp and Mary Kemp; [ed.] Telarah Public, Rutherford Technology High; [occ.] Student; [a.] Telarah NSW, Australia

KENDALL, FLORENCE P.
[pen.] Florence P. Kendall; [b.] May 5, 1916, Warman, MN; [p.] Charles and Mathilda Peterson; [m.] Henry Otis Kendall (Deceased 1979), January 25, 1935; [ch.] M. Susan, Elizabeth Ann, Florence Jean; [ed.] B.S. degree University of Minnesota Certificate, Physical Therapy Walter Reed Army Hospital; [occ.] Physical Therapist, Author, Professional Registered Parliamentarian; [memb.] American Physical Therapy Asso., National Asso. of Parliamentarians, National League of American Pen Women, Grace United Methodist Church; [hon.] Mary McMillan Lecture Award, APTA, Catherine Worthingham Fellow, APTA, Lucy Blair Service Award, APTA, Honorary Dr. of Science, Univ. of Indianapolis, Honorary Dr. of Science, Philadelphia College of Pharmacy and Science; [oth. writ.] Books: Co-author of Muscles, Testing and Function, Posture and Pain, Golfers, Take Care of Your Back (and numerous articles and films); [pers.] I believe that the greatest satisfaction in life comes from helping others.; [a.] Severna Park, MD

KENDALL, JACQUELINE A.
[pen.] Jacque; [b.] May 13, 1956, Detroit, MI; [p.] Arnold and Gertrude Kendall; [ed.] MSW, Univ S. Carolina, BSW, BS Education, Weber State; [occ.] Clinical Social Worker; [memb.] National Hospice Organization, Association of Oncology Social World; [hon.] Who's who among Human Service Professionals, 1988, Elizabeth Poet Award for Volunteerism from central so Carolina Chapter of the American Red Cross.; [oth. writ.] First submission for publication.; [pers.] I reflect my thoughts after serving others. Always putting others first. Keeping my eyes on Jesus, the author and finisher of my faith.; [a.] Columbia, SC

KENDALL, SAADIA
[pen.] Saadia; [b.] January 24, 1959, Chilliwack, British Columbia, Canada; [p.] Arlene Jones and Steve Millen; [ch.] Adrienne, Rene, Leslie, Kendall; [ed.] High school diploma, business college, teller training, journalism, short story diploma, Psychology certificate and diploma; [occ.] Home Engineer, student, poetess, and writer; [hon.] Received honors in many academic courses, and Lifetime Learners Awards.; [oth. writ.] Had several poems printed in the school newspaper and write fiction stories, some children's but mostly in the SF genre. Also had a poem published in your 1991 book - A Different Light. I greatly admire Edgar Allen Poe's work and Clive Barkers.; [pers.] Imagination is a wonderful thing, it can evolve individuality, and uniqueness and provides the enjoyment of the varied and beauteous things that life gives use it to the utmost.; [a.] Calgary Alberta, Canada

KENNEDY, CYNTHIA
[b.] November 25, 1950, Palestine, TX; [p.] Thurman and Rachel Kennedy; [ch.] Ricky and Laura Kessner; [ed.] High Island High School, High Island, Texas; [pers.] I like to write about God's creations, whether it be the innocence of His children, the humor of his animals, or the beauty of this wonderful world He created for us.; [a.] Rosenberg, TX

KENNEDY, LAURINA
[pen.] Laurina K. Levesque; [b.] January 19, 1981, Calgary, Alberta, Canada; [p.] Donna Mattern, Gordon Kennedy; [ed.] Fred Parker Elementary School, (1 yr.) Olds Elementary School, Deer Meadow Middle School, Olds J.H. School, Ernest Marrow Junior High School; [occ.] Student; [memb.] Student Against Drinking and Driving, Womens Institute Girls Club, Junior High Drama Club, Choir; [hon.] Women's Institute Girls Club Poetry Contest 1st place, Public Reading in grade 7 graduation assembly.; [oth. writ.] My own personal anthology of poetry.; [pers.] I strive to bring faith thoughts, emotions and feelings brought on by my own personal experiences and what I perceive in life and nature itself.; [a.] Calgary Alberta, Canada

KENNEY, MICHAEL T.
[pen.] T. M. Kenney; [b.] October 30, 1960, Dalton, OH; [p.] Terrence L. and Mary L. Kenney; [m.] Ann C., November 12, 1983; [ed.] Bachelor of Arts, Wright State Univ.; [occ.] Financial Consultant; [memb.] F and AM, Sigma Alpha Epsilon; [oth. writ.] A large collection of unpublished lyrics and poems.; [a.] Columbus, OH

KERN, CHRISTENA BRYSON
[pen.] Christena Bryson; [b.] October 19, 1919, Silver Lake, NH; [p.] Dr. Kenneth D. Bryson, Beulah Spencer Bryson; [m.] Dale A. Kern, October 24, 1943; [ch.] Bruce, Kristina, Gregory; [ed.] Wooster College, BA Baldwin - Wallace BS of Ed Kent State - Graduate School in special education Cleveland School of Art, 2 years (Ceramics); [occ.] Retired formerly: Teacher (Language/Math); [hon.] In first class of women officers in Naval Reserve at Northampton, Mass in 1942, a LT (J.G.) in Waves at Cape my Naval Air Base in Communication During WW II; [oth. writ.] Poems published in anthologies by young Pub. Co of VA, and poems in several anthologies published by the National Library of Poetry; [pers.] I have been writing poetry for 66 years, and finally decided to stop being a bud, and try to become a blossom. I love cadence in poetry, just as I do in music, and unforced rhyme, when appropriate.; [a.] Olmsted Falls, OH

KERPER, STEVEN M.
[pen.] Steven Kerper; [b.] June 20, 1969, Newport Beach; [p.] Phyllis and Bernard Kerper; [ed.] Wintersberg High School, Going to take some writing classes...; [occ.] Inspector at Factory. But my true love is writing; [memb.] I play drum's with a band, I've been playing drums for 8-9 years now (Jazz man!!); [hon.] To be blessed with a great mother and family!; [oth. writ.] Lot's and Lot's of Pomes, and I wright all the Word's in our Songs....; [pers.] Would it be a dream for a wish to come true and have no one there to share it with you?; [a.] Huntington Beach, CA

KESWANI, MERYL
[b.] February 7, 1927, India; [p.] George and Mavis Hiett; [m.] Deceased, December 22, 1957; [ch.] (Two) Daughter and Son.; [ed.] Matriculation (India); [occ.] Retired Home Maker; [oth. writ.] Not yet. Intending to write a book.; [pers.] I'm a quiet reserved person. Hobbies writing poetry do-ing ceramics and needle point. I like travelling in my country provinces and some in United States, New York and Montana; [a.] New York, NY

KETCHEL, CHRISTINE E.
[b.] October 26, 1949, Trenton; [p.] Edward R. Bell, June Bell; [m.] Raymond F. Ketchel, February 16, 1990; [ch.] Jason C. Scott; [ed.] Florence High; [occ.] Artist, repairing and repainting antique pottery, stain glass; [oth. writ.] FHS creative writing club.; [pers.] My writing comes from the heart, a feeling of love and happiness comes over me and I have to write.; [a.] Florence, NJ

KETTERMAN, WAYNE D.
[pen.] Wayne D. Ketterman; [b.] January 31, 1948; [p.] Harry and Eileen Ketterman; [m.] Kathleen Jo Schrader, January 23, 1980; [ch.] Kim, Keith, Kris, Kris, Kelly and Ken.; [ed.] School of Very Hard Knocks.; [occ.] Machinist by Trade; [memb.] I'm a member of the Family of God and also a member of the Human Race; [hon.] Boy Scout, Military Man, Vietnam, Vet. Disabled Vet, Ex Con. Washed in the Blood of the Lamb. My Only Hope.; [oth. writ.] Tears, Tripwire, It Only Hurts, Thoughts, Black Wall, Can You Hear Them, and Think. Published by Vietnam Vets of America, Chapter 34.; [pers.] Looking forward to the day They Beat Their Swords Into Ploughshares.; [a.] Akron, OH

KHAN, NAZIR UDDIN
[b.] December 21, 1939, Hyderabad Daccan, India; [p.] M. Sardar Khan, S. Mubarka Begum; [s.] Tanvir Atia Nazir ; [m.] April 4, 1973; [ch.] Sha-Hnila, Iffat, Tariq and Khalid; [ed.] None throught my educational institution. Master Mariner Class-1 (self acquired); [occ.] Master on a merchant ship; [memb.] Master Mariners Society of Pakistan; [hon.] Editor's Choice Award -1995, by The National Library of Poetry for the very first poem "Illusion of Right" published in "Walk Throught Paradise".; [oth. writ.] Book "Rainbow of Death" fiction based on true marine adventure (unpublished yet); [pers.] When men bow down before "Man In Power" they create the worst God for themselves and but one kind of slavery or the other.; [a.] Karachi, Pakistan

KILLINGSWORTH, TOMMY G.
[b.] September 28, 1948, San Angelo, TX; [p.] Dayton and Bobbie Killingsworth; [m.] Rebecca Killingsworth, February 23, 1974; [ch.] Dennis, Lisa, Ryan; [ed.] Edinburgh High School, Edinburg, Mississippi; [occ.] Truck Driver, City Delivery and Pick-up, A.B.F. Freight Systems, Inc.; [pers.] I have found that in working with other people, one of the greatest assets an individual may ever possess is respect, but it is only obstainable through a genuine respect for your fellow man.; [a.] Knoxville, TN

KILLORIN, LA RUE G.
[pen.] La Rue G. Killorin; [b.] December 28, 1943, Duluth, MN; [p.] Grace (Grayce) Bowe, Hanson Ahestrom, Harold William Ahestrom; [m.] Timothy John Patrick Killorin, September 14, 1974; [ed.] Wisconsin State College/ University Superior, WI 54880; [occ.] Disabled housewife; [memb.] Golf, figure skating, bowling, swimming, only taught figure skating, never taught

golf, swimming, bowling; [hon.] Golf, Numerous Awards in 1960's out of Nemadji Superior, WI Ridgeview, Duluth, MN, (ABC) Bowling (2) 1957, 1963-1964, no figure Skating Honors or a awards, however I was A professional and Johnson Ice Follies and taught a bit there after until marriage and then, just a little bit in Squaw Valley and Usma (West Point) (Superior, WI-Duluth and Bloomington, MN were prior to marriage); [oth. writ.] "Dear Snow", "The Trellis", "La Vie Est Comme Une Fleur", "Life Us Like A Flower"; [pers.] I consider Myself as an extremely, very flighty, individual never completing, joining continuously, one activity, mentioned to husband that my three Poems are all I wish to wrote; [a.] Fort Montgomery, NY

KIM, HAENG JA
[pen.] Haeng Ja Kim; [b.] March 9, 1948, Youngdong, Korea; [p.] Hu Kun Kim, Kyung Ho Sohn; [m.] Chong In Lim; [ch.] Steven Sung-Hoon, Christina Hyun-Jung; [ed.] Taejon Girls High School, Sook Myung Women's University; [occ.] Pharmacist, Harbor Hospital Center, Baltimore, MD; [memb.] Korean Poets and Writers Assoc. in the Washington Area, Korean Poets Assoc. of America, Maryland Society of Health-System Pharmacists, Korean American Pharmacists Assoc.; [hon.] A poem was selected as one of the best poems in the most prestigious New Years Literary works by "Joung Ang Times", Selected as the best poem "The Wave" in a poetry contest by the Korea Times in L.A., President of Korean Poets and Writers Assoc. in the Washington Area, President of Korean American Pharmacists Assoc. of greater Washington; [oth. writ.] Author of a book of poems: Image Of You In My Vision, Poems published in numerous magazines and newspapers including "Korea Times", Dong-A Daily News", "The Korean Weekly", "The Korean-American Life Magazine" and "Hyondaemunbak" (Modern Literature Monthly) etc.; [a.] Randallstown, MD

KIM, IRENE H.
[b.] June 18, 1973, Cambridge, MA; [p.] Chi-Jzon Kim, Kyoung-JA Kim; [ed.] Pine Lane Elementary - Parker, CO, Highlands Ranch Jr.-Sr. High - Highlands Ranch, CO, University of Colorado at Boulder: BA in English and Linguistics; [occ.] Student; [oth. writ.] Alumni Association - June '96 publication, which keeps all Alumni update with what's happening on and around campus, have been writing a novel for the past seven years, write in my free time on anything and everything - my favorite subject is life.; [pers.] My goal in life is to live every day to its fullest, so that every 24 hours become permanent fixtures in my memory, and not just disappearing acts. I believe writing to be both a challenging and necessary part of life. Words are one of the rare things that all of us share - a unifying force for humanity.; [a.] Boulder, CO

KING, JOHN A.
[pen.] John Alexander; [b.] July 6, 1965, Albuquerque, NM; [p.] Alex King, Linda King; [ed.] Manzano High, Associates Degree Allied Health Sciences; [occ.] US Air Force, Aerospace Medicine; [pers.] My influence is from Dad, my inspiration is from life.; [a.] Las Vegas, NV

KING, RICHARD L.
[pen.] Rk; [b.] January 25, 1953, Chicago, IL; [p.] Richard and Betty; [ch.] Stacey King and Zachacy King; [ed.] Douglas MacArthur Hs., Lincoln Land Comm College, Sangamon State University; [occ.] Marketing Director, Virkler Chemical Clt, NC; [oth. writ.] Over 300 poems 15 short stories. Several corporate brochures plus TV and Radio Ad Copy; [pers.] Life is what we make it. Live it and try desparately to seek love in all things. Every thing is relative...after all, from an airplane, even your uncle looks like an ant.; [a.] Charlotte, NC

KINNE, MERLE W.
[b.] September 23, 1917, Minnesota; [p.] Chester Kinne, Alyce Vandenberg; [m.] Patricia A. Kinne (Gooding), October 12, 1954; [ch.] Kevin; [ed.] High School, Minneapolis Dunwoody Institute, Minneapolis; [occ.] Retired/Oil Industry; [memb.] Heritage Foundation, B.P.O.E. (Demit)., International Soc. Of Poets.; [oth. writ.] Two articles - Intl. Bow Hunter. Three novels, Western and foreign intrigue. Epic poems of the old west and romance. 40 short stories.; [pers.] Flying, mining, horseman provide themes for much of my work. Enjoy drawing. A wild imagination helps my writing. At 78 I regret my writing so late in life, but enjoy it. Poetry relaxes the emotions.; [a.] Long Beach, CA

KINNEY, RUTH
[b.] June 9, 1937, Junction City, OH; [p.] Ben Baldy Flora Baldy; [m.] John Kinney, June 10, 1957; [ch.] Sharon Kinney, Steve Kinney; [ed.] 11 years High School New Lexington, Ohio; [occ.] Housewife; [pers.] I love reading poetry books, and writing poems.

KIPP, JENNIFER LYN
[b.] June 16, 1983, Coatesville, PA; [p.] Jeff and Zedra Kipp; [ed.] At present in seventh grade; [occ.] Student; [a.] East Fallowfield, PA

KIRKPATRICK, TONY
[b.] February 6, 1967; [p.] Harry and Philomena Kirkpatrick; [ch.] Skylar, Duncan, Jordan; [ed.] St. Joseph's Composite High, CDI College of Business and Technology; [occ.] Program Analyst; [memb.] Scouts Canada; [oth. writ.] I am honored to say that this is my first publication.; [pers.] "Life would be happier of people looked at each as friends, friends, rather than enemies."; [a.] Edmonton Alberta, Canada

KIRKWOOD, JON M.
[pen.] J. Duss, Morey Jensen; [b.] January 9, 1974, New Brighton, PA; [p.] Jon H. Kirkwood, Judy Kirkwood; [ed.] Center Area High School, Washington and Jefferson College, Community College, Community College of Beaver County, Indiana University of Pennsylvania; [occ.] Student; [hon.] East-West Soccer Ambassador International Team; [oth. writ.] None published; [pers.] Poetry is defined only by the imagination of the writer.; [a.] Monaca, PA

KITCHENS, DICKIE
[b.] June 7, 1936, Lubbock, TX; [p.] Burton Pruitt, Merle Pruitt; [m.] Willie Luther Kitchens, January 7, 1988; [ch.] Kim, Bradley, Lancer, 2 stepchildren Kirk and Cheryl; [ed.] Lubbock High School;

[occ.] RTD Southwestern Bell Telephone Company; [oth. writ.] The Taylor-Pruitt memories in poetry (A Compilation) The unveiling of Jesus Christ (A Discourse on the Revelation in Poetry) other unpublished works.; [pers.] I have been greatly influenced by the holy scriptures, John Bunyan, and Laura Ingalls Wilder.; [a.] Lubbock, TX

KITCHENS, IRENE CHASTAIN
[b.] June 4, 1943, Tivoli, TX; [p.] Melvin Bee and Addie Bell Chastain; [m.] Roger Paul Kitchens, August 8, 1981; [ch.] Martin - 30, Hunter - 26 and Reese Little - 24, Erin, Kitchens - 11 yrs.; [ed.] Tyler Jr. College, Tyler, Texas, Angelina College, Lufkin, Texas; [occ.] Housewife; [oth. writ.] Several other poems none have been published.; [pers.] My poetry is inspired by people, place, and things that I love. I write what I feel. My family and friends are very encouraging.; [a.] Lufkin, TX

KITZMILLER, RENDELL N.
[pen.] Renny; [b.] August 14, 1939, Huntertown, IN; [p.] Neal and Evelyn Kitzmiller; [m.] V. Jo Pounds-Kitzmiller, May 7, 1989; [ch.] Denny, Lisa, Kathy, Shawn, Norman, David and Nicole; [ed.] Huntertown School, Huntertown, Indiana, Adams Jr. High, Fort Wayne, Indiana, New Haven High, New Haven, Indiana, Polk Voc-Tech Center, Eaton Park, FL; [occ.] Cook, Photography and Drafting; [memb.] Former member of Houston Photographic Society, 1960 Photographic Society and 1960 PC Users Groups of Houston, Texas; [hon.] Won many 1st and 2nd place awards in photography.; [oth. writ.] Have on hand several unpublished poems.; [pers.] I enjoy Photography, Cooking, and Collecting shot glasses and writing. In my shot glass collection I have over 225 different kinds of glasses some of them are very rare and illegal to use in bars.; [a.] Houston, TX

KLEIBER, WILLIAM G.
[pen.] Billy Sal; [b.] December 23, 1949, Bronxville, NY; [p.] Mary Bowler Kleiber; [m.] Barbara Cellura Kleiber, November 26, 1983; [ch.] Billy Sal, Kimberly, Kelly; [ed.] Eastchester HS, Westchester Business Institute; [occ.] Senior Property Manager for City of Yonkers; [oth. writ.] Several other poems written as hobby reborn was the first ever submitted; [pers.] I write not for myself but to bring out the best in other people.; [a.] Yonkers, NY

KLEIN, S. R.
[b.] June 2, 1959, Aberdeen, SD; [p.] Richard and Jalois Klein; [m.] Alecia Atwell, November 25, 1994; [ch.] Shaun Lee Atwell; [ed.] MFA in Directing/Acting from Mankato State University - Mankato, MN, BA in Theatre/Political Science from Gustavus Adolphos College - St. Peter, MN; [occ.] Chairman of the Department of Theatre Arts - Cameron Universities; [memb.] Phi Kappa Phi, Southwest Theatre Association, Southwest OK Opera Guild, OK Community Theatre Association, TNT, Arts for all; [hon.] Research and Performance Award - Cameron University School of Fine Arts, Commendation in Directing ACTF; [oth. writ.] Plays which include: "Beanstalk," "Tales Tole Out!" "The Spiriting of Christmas," "Snip, Snap, Snout"; [a.] Lawton, OK

KLOBUCHAR, KELLY SUE
[pen.] Kel; [b.] September 1, 1980. Maryville, IL;

[p.] Joseph A. & Tammy Kay Gasparovic; [ed.] 10th Grade, Winter Park High; [occ.] Student; [hon.] Student of the month; [oth. writ.] Personal poems (non-published) 1st contest; [pers.] Poetry is an enjoyment to me. [a.] Winter Park, FL

KNAPP, SHIRLEY M.
[b.] January 23, 1932, Norway, MI; [p.] George R. and Irene Olsen; [m.] Earl E. Knapp, June 24, 1950; [ch.] Mary Lynn, Daniel Ray (Deceased); [ed.] Grad. Clintonville WI High School; [occ.] Homemaker; [memb.] All Non-Profit, Volunteer, United Methodist Church, Choir, Education and Worship Commissions, Music Librarian, AARP, WAHCE, NAFCE, WAHCE Chorus, Clintonville Woman's Club and Historical Society, Homemakers Club; [hon.] 52 years UMC Choir, 45 years WAHCE; [oth. writ.] Church newsletter, WAHCE update, wrote song for NAFCE; [pers.] Have written since a child. Always enjoyed life. Having survive 2 cancer surgeries, heart attack and 2 heart procedures, each day is treasured, as is family. God, family and rural living have been inspiration.; [a.] Bear Creek, WI

KNECHT, EUGENE H.
[pen.] Owen, Jeremy; [b.] March 24, 1963, Neuchatel, Switzerland; [p.] Ingrid Knecht Gentil, Eugene G. Knecht; [m.] Barbara Degano-Knecht, February 7, 1994; [ed.] University, Neuchatel, Switzerland; [occ.] Singer-songwriter; [oth. writ.] Lyrics featured on 2CDs (in Switzerland); [pers.] I watch and listen, try to transcribe my feelings. Catch a mood, a furtive glance, an involuntary movement.; [a.] Neuchatel, Switzerland

KNELLER, DANIELLE D.
[b.] September 28, 1975, Towando, PA; [p.] Samuel and Robin Kneller; [ed.] Currently a student at St. Bonoventure University. Major: Journalism/Mass Communication, High School: Troy Area High School, Troy, PA; [oth. writ.] Articles in the Bond Venture newspaper (College) and the Daily Review (Towanda, PA); [a.] Troy, PA

KNIGHT, KIMBERLY
[b.] November 16, 1973, Orange, CA; [m.] Cristopher Knight, July 29, 1995; [occ.] Hotel Reservations Manager; [a.] Glendale, CA

KNIGHTON, DEJUAN
[b.] January 17, 1972, Randolph County, GA; [p.] Clarence Knighton, Betty K. Horton; [ed.] Frederick Douglass High, Johnson C. Smith University; [memb.] Lupus Foundation, Charlotte-Mecklenburg Urban League, Book of the Month Club; [oth. writ.] Several poems in college literary magazine, Treewell.; [pers.] The most alluring existing likeness in the universe is expression. My most prized possessions on earth are pen and paper, with them I am able to communicate exquisitely.; [a.] Charlotte, NC

KNOLL, DOUGLAS SCHMIDT
[b.] March 14, 1985, Bloomington, IL; [p.] Deborah, Keith Knoll; [ed.] 5th Grader Center Grove Elementary; [occ.] Student; [memb.] Center Grove Soccer Club, Indianapolis Tennis Center; [pers.] I wrote it for school.; [a.] Greenwood, IN

KOENIG, DONDI
[b.] February 19, 1965, Harvey, ND; [ed.] Music Major, North Dakota State University; [occ.] Postal Clerk; [memb.] Amnesty International, Unitarian University Association, Disabled American Veterans; [oth. writ.] Poems of Life, Love, and Comrades remembered.; [pers.] I am a cynical Optimist, I believe that somehow, the world will eventually be a better place of what we do to it and ourselves.; [a.] Fargo, ND

KOHREY, DEETTE J.
[pen.] DeEtte Kohrey; [b.] June 8, 1934, Omaha, NE; [p.] Charles L. and Eva T. Puerson; [m.] June 6, 1905; [ch.] Mark, Stephanie Matt, Andy, David and grandchildren Seanna, Craig, Pierson and Avery Rose; [ed.] High School, Assoc. Degree Acctng. Jr. and Level at Univ. of Nebr-Lincoln; [occ.] Acts Payable Analyst at Nebraska BK Co - Boy do we have books; [memb.] Eastridge Presbyterian Church Stephen (lay) Minister, Deacon, Sigma Kappa Sorority; [hon.] National Thespian, Presbyterian Women Honorary Member; [oth. writ.] She should have been a butterfly to be published in Carvings in Stone in June.; [pers.] I originally wrote poetry in grade school and high school again when my daughter Stephanie was a teenager, it helped to get pts. across. Most recently when in a lot of pain.; [a.] Lincoln, NE

KOHSELL, DEETTE J.
[pen.] DeEtte Kohsell/Twitters of Life; [b.] June 8, 1934, Omaha, NE; [p.] Charles and Eva Pierson; [m.] June 6, 1954; [ch.] Mark, Stephanie, Matt, Andy and David; [ed.] High School, Assoc. Degree in Acctng. Jr. Level at UNL; [occ.] Accts. Payable Analyst at Nebraska BK Co; [memb.] Eastridge Presbyterian Church, Stephen (lay) Minister, Sigma Kappa Society; [hon.] National Thespian Honary Presbyterian Women; [oth. writ.] Many other poems; [pers.] I wrote may things in grade school and high school and college, one prof. said "I don't know what you wrote but I sure like it" Wrote poetry to help my daughter as teenager it seem to help her and started again recently due to pain and my it sure helps.; [a.] Lincoln, NE

KOMAR, MARIE ELAINA
[pen.] Marie Elaina; [b.] January 29, 1954, Sumter, SC; [p.] Marie and George; [ed.] St. Aloysios Academy, St. Peter's College both schools located in Jersey City, New Jersey; [occ.] Clerical/Computer; [hon.] "Twentieth Century Clown" - published in High School Literary Magazine; [pers.] Great is He who stems from royalty and retains His throne but, far greater is He who stems from peasantry and makes Himself King; [a.] Bayonne, NJ

KOTEL, JAMES
[pen.] Jim; [b.] September 1, 1930, Bronx, NY; [p.] George and Faye Kotel; [m.] Divorced (Janet Barker Graham), March 30, 1968; [ch.] William Graham Kotel; [ed.] Local New York City Schools in Washington Heights, 3 years of College; [occ.] Retired, former Sales and Marketing Mgr. at MacMillan, Harcourt Brace and Penguin Books in the 1960 era. Marketing Director for A Medical Products Development Firm and Ad Space Sales for a Medical Magazine in the 1970's and 1980's.; [hon.] Numerous poems. Some written with tongue in cheek.; [oth. writ.] I have always felt poetry to

be an instant response to a situation or an individual. Almost a gut feeling.

KOUBA, LORIE S.
[b.] March 2, 1973, Cedar Rapids; [p.] Gary and Barbara Gill Kouba; [ed.] Kirkwood College CR Iowa - AA degree, Mt. Mercy College CR Iowa - Business Management and Public Relations, Graduate in Dec. 96 Avant Modeling Agency Graduate; [occ.] Full-time student, part-time model and employee at Elmcrest Country Club CR Iowa; [memb.] P.E.O. Women's Society, Alpha Beta Gamma Business Honor Society, St. Paul's United Methodist Church, Business Club; [hon.] Alpha Beta Gamma Honor Award, Who's Who Among American College Students, National Dean's List, Future Business Leader's of Tomorrow Award, Mt. Mercy Academic and Leadership Scholarship Award; [oth. writ.] Feature stories for local college publications; [pers.] Writing is my way to express emotions of the past so I will have them to re-live and to hold onto.; [a.] Cedar Rapids, IA

KOUBAROULIS, JOHN
[b.] February 3, 1979, New York; [p.] Vasilios Koubaroulis, Matilda Koubaroulis; [ed.] Junior at Frank W. Cox High school; [occ.] Student; [memb.] National Honor Society, French Honor Society, Math Honor Society, Key Club, Young Democrats City Committee; [hon.] Student Ambassador to Japan, Australia, New Zealand. Attended National Young Leaders Conference, selected for boys state.; [pers.] Change is not easy for one to experience however with the ability to accept and be open minded it is possible.; [a.] Virginia Beach, VA

KOUNTOUROGIANNIS, CHERYL
[b.] March 29, 1970, Saint Catharines, Ontario, Canada; [m.] George, October 29, 1994; [ch.] Brian and TJ; [oth. writ.] Published 1992 selected works of our world's best poets, the world of poetry and 1995 walk through paradise, the National Library of Poetry.; [pers.] I dedicate to the wonderful men in my life. Brian and TJ for inspiring me and George for his encouragement and belief in me.; [a.] Niagara Ontario, Canada

KOUSHA, HASTI
[b.] June 23, 1983, Tehran, Iran; [p.] Karim Kousha, Zari Kousha; [ed.] Alexander Galt Regional High School; [occ.] Student; [memb.] Lennoxville and District Women's Centre, Intercultural Club of A.G.R.H.S.; [hon.] Proficiency in Language Arts Award and French Award from Sherbrooke Elementary School Musee des Beaux Arts Prized Work (drawing won a contest and was displayed in the museum for 1 month); [oth. writ.] Poems and stories published in school writings; [pers.] There is an inner soul inside each human being. It is this inner self that is reflected on the outside. All humans have the right of equality, regardless of race, religion, culture or beliefs. Each living thing would be useless without others. Life is too short, stop the hate, die in peace and pride.; [a.] Sherbrooke Quebec, Canada

KOWALEWSKI, VICTORIA
[b.] May 7, 1986, New York, NY; [p.] Katherine Verna, Stan Kowalewski; [ed.] 4th grade student at P.S. 99 in Kew Gardens, N.Y.; [occ.] Student at PS 99; [hon.] Student of the month November

1995 at PS 99; [oth. writ.] I wrote a song in honor of Martin Luther King and was chosen to sing it to our Principal at P.S. 99; [pers.] I enjoy writing, acting and sports. I hope to be a famous writer or actress when I grow up.; [a.] Kew Gardens, NY

KOZEE, KIMBERLY
[b.] May 21, 1964, Bellefonte, KY; [p.] Glenn Newsome and Rachel Melvin Newsome; [m.] Ernest Jeff Kozee, July 8, 1983; [ch.] Samuel Thaddeus; [ed.] Morehead State Univerisity, Eastern Kentucky University; [occ.] EBD Teacher; [oth. writ.] This is my first publication.; [a.] Danville, KY

KREYMBORG, CHRISTY
[pen.] Christy Caldwell (Maiden name); [b.] June 17, 1972, Tulsa, OK; [p.] Debbie Abels, Mike Abels, Brandon Caldwell; [m.] Skip Kreymborg, July 27, 1991; [ed.] Bachelors in Speech Language Pathology at University of Central Oklahoma, Currently in last semester of Masters Program at same University, (Graduate Spring '96); [occ.] Echo Parent Advisor for Families with Hearing Impaired or Deaf and full-time Student; [oth. writ.] I write because I enjoy it, and because the writing process itself has helped me to survive the things I write about in my poetry and short stories.; [pers.] Oklahoma City, OK

KROLL, RITA G.
[b.] October 21, 1938, Detroit, MI; [p.] Louis Kay, Ethel Kay; [m.] Dr. Edward G. Kroll, May 12, 1985; [ch.] April Joy, Jill Erika; [ed.] Central High School, Mercy College - B.S. Central Mich Univ. M.A.; [occ.] Dietitian - Housewife - writer; [memb.] American Dietetic Association Michigan Dietetic Assoc; [hon.] Kappa Omicron Phi - National Honors Home Economics Society Past Editor - Mich. Dietetic Association News Letter; [oth. writ.] Poems and short essays published in College Publications, several articles published in local newspapers; [pers.] My poems are a reflection of my inner life, I hope my readers look into the mirror of common shared experiences; [a.] Bloomfield Hills, MI

KRONE, KEVIN
[pen.] Kevin; [b.] June 29, 1961, Pensacola, FL; [p.] Irene and Robert Krone; [ch.] David Anthony Krone; [ed.] High School; [occ.] E5/QM2 US Navy; [oth. writ.] My book in the works now in untitled. I'm still working on new thoughts to write down.; [pers.] You must always keep yourself and your mind on a straight and even plane, stay in focus, and always remember that body and mind in harmony are combined together to form one... you.; [a.] Key West, FL

KRUTAN, LESLIE
[pen.] Leslie K; [b.] August 1912, New York; [p.] Ruth, George; [ed.] Rider University BA 1975; [occ.] Sales; [oth. writ.] Waiting Voyage to Remember; [pers.] "Hold onto the dream, no matter how far it takes you".

KUCIAK, THORAN S.
[pen.] "Boomer"; [b.] February 5, 1983, Calgary, Alberta, Canada; [p.] Jozef and Pauline; [ed.] Attending Millarville Community School; [occ.] Grade 7 Student, Ranch Work - Week-ends and

Holidays; [pers.] Life is a book. It's 365 pages to the chapter. Every fourth chapter there's a bonus page. Never stop reading.; [a.] Hamlet Priddis Alberta, Canada

KUN, DANTE BAYLESS
[pen.] Northern Skald; [b.] June 21, 1958, Durham, NC; [p.] Sarboche Miklos Kun, Linda K. Kun; [m.] Rhonda Kathryn Kun, May 7, 1990; [ch.] Dante, Tara, Kyle, Corey, Ryan; [ed.] Santa Rosa Junior College, Sonoma State University School, US Army Military Mountaineering School, Armorer School, Recondo Training Instructor.; [occ.] Case Manager at Pelican Bay State Prison.; [memb.] L.O.O.M., Recondo Club. (L.O.O.M. is Loyal Order of Moose.); [hon.] Star of Life Award for Bravery by State of CA EMS. Imjim Scout Award, US Army, Korea.; [oth. writ.] Short stories, poems, Haiku, epic poems.; [pers.] We are spiritual beings in human bodies, there really are no differences. We are a global village and my writings try to show this.; [a.] Crescent City, CA

KUNKEL, SCOTT A.
[b.] April 2, 1968, Toledo, OH; [p.] Jerry and Tricia Kunkel, Rosalie Ballinger; [ed.] Six years college education leading to Nursing Diploma and National Paramedic Certification.; [occ.] Flight Nurse; [memb.] National Flight Nurses Association, National Flight Paramedics Association; [oth. writ.] None published.; [pers.] My influence has been fueled by the individuals around me, the emotions, desire, and passion for everything that makes up our lives.; [a.] Portage, MI

KYE JR., LEE EDWARD
[b.] July 16, 1950, Forsyth County; [p.] Lee and Juanita Kye; [m.] Penny C. Kye, February 15, 1969; [ed.] Parkland High, Forsyth Technical College, National Fire Academy; [occ.] Fire Engineer (Retired) Volunteer Forsyth Hospital; [memb.] International Association of Firefighters, Winston-Salem Professional Firefighters; [hon.] Have received awards for my work with Forsyth Hospital, M.D.A., American Cancer Society.; [oth. writ.] Poems for my wife and family.; [pers.] I have been inspired to write by my wife, who is also, my best friend. I strive to write about nature and how it relates to our spiritual being.; [a.] Winston-Salem, NC

KYLE, KEITH
[b.] February 14, 1962, Blairemore, Alberta; [p.] Robert and Hazel Kyle; [s.] Connie Nelson; [m.] To be married July 26, 1997; [ch.] Christine Marie, Shawn Douglas, Terri-Lynn Marie, Michelle Lee, Sheyden Kane, and Cindy Marie.; [ed.] continuing; [occ.] Full-time student - Alberta Vocational College, Edmonton, Alberta.; [othr. writ.] Numerous poems of varying length and style. (23 at the time of this printing); [pers.] My inspiration comes from the ones I love and the ones I've lost. This one's for you Mom!; [a.] Edmonton, Alberta, Canada

LA MASTER, MICHELE A.
[pen.] Michele Rohlman and Lamaster; [b.] July 20, 1942, Reno, NV; [p.] Carolyn Elizabeth Douglas and Thomas Walker Tillman; [m.] Divorced; [ch.] Todd Alan Rohlman and Belinda Ann Rohlman; [ed.] Associates degree in Accounting from Western Nevada Community College in Carson City, Nevada,

Tungston Grammar School - Tungston Nevada; [occ.] Management analyst II for Nevada State Dairy Commission Reno, NV; [memb.] Tops NV 60, Sparks NV; [hon.] Governor's Meritorious, Citation State of Nevada; [oth. writ.] Several poems - none were published.; [pers.] Think positive. Enjoy the beauty of each new day.; [a.] Sun Valley, NV

LA RUE, PAULINE M.
[pen.] Pauline La Rue; [b.] 1905, Burr, NE; [p.] Loisethel and G. J. Kahl; [m.] Everett H. La Rue, 1921; [ch.] One; [ed.] High school - K.C. MO, - Peru Normal - Her course in Mech. Dwq. - night school; [occ.] Retired (from teaching country sch. from Mech engineering).; [memb.] M.E. church - Woman's Club at Htg, W.Va, (Chaired L.T. - Drama Dept.); [hon.] Poem the wind - in "Heritage of dreams" - Austin Texas Poetry set - (1976), am planing to set one at my last poems to music.; [oth. writ.] Write prose, plays and poetry - on all subjects. In daily life - subjects come to me from everything - usually in rhyme - None published - except "The Wind" - just for fun; [pers.] My mother wrote poetry as does my sister - Lois Kahl Davis, one of your contributors. We are pushing another sister Velma Kennell to write. Twice monthly I submit a poem to the poetry club here at the retirement home, where we live.; [a.] Omaha, NE

LABRIE, DENISE
[b.] November 22, 1952, Houston, TX; [p.] Whitney Calegon, Inez Calegon; [m.] Glen Labrie, January 31, 1976; [ch.] Michelle Denise, Glen Anthony, Jr.; [ed.] Phillis Wheatley High, Univ. of Houston, Liberty University; [occ.] Manager, Southwestern Bell, Bellaire, Texas; [memb.] Professional Women of Southwester Bell; [oth. writ.] Several writings of poetry and greeting card verse.; [pers.] I strive to touch the hearts and minds of others in a positive manner through my writing. I thank God for His many blessings.; [a.] Houston, TX

LACY, WENDY L.
[b.] September 7, 1954, Geneva, NY; [p.] Dick and Teena Prater; [m.] John W. Lacy Jr., March 8, 1985; [ch.] Patricia Lynn and Jill Amber (stepdaughter); [occ.] Housewife - gardener; [memb.] Nature Conservancy, National Wildlife Federation; [oth. writ.] One poem published in the Anthology "Carvings in Stone", several poems published in local papers.; [pers.] In the face of adversity - we must have strength, hope and belief. I believe even from the painful things in life - much good can come.; [a.] Coal Grove, OH

LAFFIN, VIRGINIA
[b.] July 10, 1949, Brasd'or, NS; [p.] Simon Fraser, Viola Burton; [m.] Patrick Laffin, August 31, 1971; [ch.] Tara, Cory, Molly; [ed.] High School, Brasd'or, Riverview, NS; [occ.] House keeper, St. Joseph's Brasd'or, NS; [memb.] Point Aconi Community Dev., Christopher Leadership Course; [oth. writ.] Numerous poems and short stories (unpublished).; [pers.] I only write when I am moved or touched by a person, memory or event, it's very personal, sometimes hard to share.

LAI, EVELYN
[b.] October 17, 1985, San Jose, CA; [p.] Tony and Esther Lai; [ed.] Currently Laurel Mountain Elementary 4th Grade; [occ.] Student; [hon.] 1st

Place Piano Solo Contest (Grade 2) Austin District Music Teacher Association, 1994, Outstanding Student (grade 1-2) Austin District Music Teacher Association - Student Association, 1994, One of the winners in "My Favorite Teacher" contest in Austin American-Statesman, 1996, Finalist in "Round Rock Independent School District Council of PTA's Reflection Contest" Texas, 1994; [oth. writ.] "My Favorite Teacher" - writing contest in Austin American-Statesman. "Curiosity of Cupids" - published in "Mystery an Anthology of Student Work," written by Students in the round rock independent school district talented and gifted program.; [pers.] I like to paint and write poems about nature. My wish is to have my poems and paintings put together. Someday...; [a.] Austin, TX

LAKSHMAN, BULUSU
[pen.] Bulusu; [b.] July 23, 1976, Vizag, India; [p.] Prof. B.S.K.R. Somayajulu and SMT B. Sita; [m.] Bulusu Anuradha, November 11, 1995; [ed.] B.E. (Computer Sc. Engg.) (Honours), B.S. (Math), (Honours), Utkal University Orissa, India; [occ.] Software Consultant; [memb.] Member and Distinguished Member of International Society of poets, Maryland, U.S.A.; [hon.] Editors Choice Award of National Library of Poetry, U.S.A., Elected Member of International Society of Poets, Maryland, U.S.A. 1995-96 (Honorary); [oth. writ.] My mother, my wife, look sharp, my friend, reflections of a Leper, beauty, Darling, emotions on tranquility, bliss of solitude, a bleeding heart, Nostalgia etc.; [pers.] Has written 41 poems to date and has been interest in reading and writing poetry. Greatly influenced by William Wordsworth, P.B. Shelley, John Keats, W.B. Yeats and Walt Whitman.; [a.] Lawrenceville, NJ

LALONDE, PAULETTE
[b.] 1943, Windson, Ontario, Canada; [m.] Darryl Lalonde, 1966; [ch.] Three grown sons; [occ.] Former Elementary School Teacher and Adult Education Instructor; [oth. writ.] New to poetry writing - in 1995, developed a manual for a women's literary course; [pers.] I believe in the "possibilities" or potential of people, things and situations. Mid-life, for me, has been a time of change and creativity. Writing poetry is one form of expressing this creativity.; [a.] Sudbury Ontario, Canada

LAMB, PAULINE ANN
[pen.] Pauline Lamb; [p.] Elmer Thibault, Marjorie Thibault; [m.] Gordon James Lamb, April 17, 1976; [ch.] Adam James Reynolds, Vera Marjorie Pauline,; [ed.] Quinte Secondary School; [occ.] Mixer Operator, P.C.V. Plastics Extrusions Inc., Napanee.; [oth. writ.] Poems published in local newspapers.; [pers.] This poem was written about my sister, Elizabeth Pearl King, who died of cancer.; [a.] Napanee Ontario, Canada

LAMBERT, WILLIAM J.
[b.] December 24, 1919, Camden East, Ontario, Canada; [p.] The Late Winnifred Holland, John Lambert; [m.] Evelyn Lambert, September 21, 1977; [ch.] Three daughters; [ed.] Very little, grade 8; [occ.] Propane Operator; [memb.] War Amps of Canada (Life membership); [hon.] National Library of Poetry, Editors Choice Award several

times also a distinguished member. Entered in "Poetry Elite" a 1985 anthology of Canadian poetry; [oth. writ.] I wrote for 2 years for a local newspaper "The Poet's Corner" and I have 3 books, volumes 1, 2, and 3 "Treasured Thoughts" volume 4 is about to be printed; [pers.] My inspiration's are as swift as the waters, nature is my education, the best teacher of man, looks back on his boyhood days and all nature, around him, he started to put his thoughts into poem.; [a.] Ontario, Canada

LANBERG, LAURIE-ANN
[pen.] Milady; [b.] September 11, 1971, Yonkers, NY; [p.] Joanne and William Lanberg; [ed.] Connetequot High, Suffolk Community College, Fine Arts; [memb.] Knights of Columbus, Columbiette; [pers.] Poetry is the only way I know how to feel, it opens my soul, and in order for me to speak, my pen glides across the paper - I am heard. Writings are my voice.; [a.] Ronkonkoma, NY

LANDY, NOAH COOPER
[b.] October 26, 1983, Nashville, TN; [p.] Dr. and Mrs. Stephen Landy; [occ.] Sixth Grader at Presbyterian Day School, Memphis, TN; [memb.] Crusader Club Second Baptist Church Presbyterian Day School Choir; [hon.] Wordsmith; [a.] Memphis, TX

LANG, LAURA
[b.] March 15, 1963, Victoria, British Columbia, Canada; [p.] Sylvia Lang; [occ.] CSR - Canadian Imperial Bank of Commerce; [memb.] International Society of Poets; [hon.] Editor's Choice Award, National Library of Poetry. Nominated International Poet of the Year (95) by The International Society of Poets; [oth. writ.] Masquerade, the stage of life, silence in the forest, and time all published.; [pers.] I would like to dedicate this poem to my brother John Land currently residing in Africa. Thank you for your love and support.; [a.] Salt Spring Island British Columbia, Canada

LANGLEY, PARKER
[pen.] Eagle Perkins; [b.] May 31, 1938, Seal Harbour Nova Scotia, Canada; [p.] Harold and Alice; [m.] Faye Marion Langsley Nee (Pledge), November 4, 1961; [ch.] Laura Lee, Deanna, Lana; [ed.] Grade II Mine Mapping and Survey, Heavy Truck Merchandising (C.M.I); [occ.] Retired; [memb.] Independent Baptist Church, Capebreton Volunteer Search and Rescue, Royal Cape Breton Yacht Club, Lingan Golf and Country Club.; [hon.] Life member is search and rescue assoc., 6 yrs in top 6 truck salesmen in Canada (Ford), 1st and 2nd prize in provincial public speaking competition, past Lt. Cov. Kiwanis EC and C Dist. of Kiwanis International; [oth. writ.] The Mighty Eagle and From The Eye Of The Eagle. (Both Unpublished) published the American Poetry Anthology (3) poems. (Today has been) (Faith) (John F. Kennedy); [pers.] I choose to write for a simpleman things that he can understand of the things that I can see because that simple man is me. Joy of the serene wilderness. Painting with my pen.; [a.] Sydney Nova Scotia, Canada

LANSI, LEE ANNE
[b.] April 12, 1944, Halifax, NS; [p.] Harry and June Eaton; [m.] Karl, September 3, 1966; [ch.] 'Joanne', Tracy, Todd; [ed.] Ryerson University,

Toronto, Registered Nurse, Certified Nurse Practitioner; [occ.] Obstetrical Delivery Room Nurse, and Birth Instructor; [oth. writ.] Over the years, I have written several articles and poems, but I have never submitted them for of my articles. However, I have used many of my articled for presentations, to make an impact or influence a situation. "The Pen is Mightier than the Sword."; [pers.] This poem is based on my personal emotionally charged experience of relinquishing my baby, as a unwed mother, many years ago and meeting her for the very first time two years ago.; [a.] Callander Ontario, Canada

LARLHAM, OLIVER J.
[pen.] Oliver J. Larlham; [b.] June 25, 1918, Greenwood Lake, NY; [p.] William and Della Larlham; [m.] Dorothy Lee, 1940; [ch.] Six-Four Living; [ed.] High school, Warwich, NY; [occ.] Retired iron worker; [memb.] Correspondence school of creative writing, Jehova's Witnesses; [hon.] The smiling faces of our children, when I wrote, in verse, the story, "Sneezy, the Honey Bee". Trying to get this published; [oth. writ.] Story for children in verse, and others.; [pers.] Getting old is only the golden years if we consider it an opportunity.; [a.] Dover, DE

LARSEN, BARBARA LYNN
[pen.] Barb; [b.] April 29, 1932, Calgary; [p.] Vicky Larsen, Cliff Larsen; [m.] Gilbert Wood (Divorced), February 24, 1973; [ch.] Steven Laverne Wood; [ed.] Grade XII, Nursing Assistant Course, Day Care Course; [occ.] Writing poetry; [memb.] Girl Guctes, Single Parents Club; [hon.] This is my first time my poetry has been recognized.; [oth. writ.] I have written over 200 poems.; [pers.] I just open my heart and the words flow on to the paper. The greatest gift God has given me is my friend and my rock Bob.; [a.] Edmonton Alberta, Canada

LARUFFA, TARA
[pen.] Tara Laruffa; [b.] October 21, 1978, Yardley, PA; [p.] Joan An Pascal Laruffa; [ed.] Stuart Country Day School Middle School, The Lawrenceville School: High School (class of 1997); [occ.] A student, for the most part; [oth. writ.] Occasional poetry and short essays, creative writing - none publically printed - until now.; [pers.] I never know what I'm going to write until my pen hits the paper, from there it just goes - it's amazing how much I never knew I thought.; [a.] Yardley, PA

LASKARIS, RICARDO D.
[b.] January 5, 1978, Toronto, Ontario; [p.] Polichronis Laskaris and Josephine D. Laskaris; [ed.] Islington Junior Middle School, Collegiate Institute, Toronto, ON; [hon.] Year V course proficiency award, writer's cradt; [oth. writ.] Several essays, scripts, and short stories.; [pers.] Cui Dono Lepidum Novum Libellum/ Arida Modo Pumice Expolitum?; [a.] Toronto Ontario, Canada

LAURENT, CONNIE
[b.] March 24, 1922, Mexico City; [m.] Gerard Laurent, September 30, 1946; [ch.] Michel, Pierre, Chantal, Marie-France, Genevieve; [ed.] British and American Schools, Mexico City, Seton Hill College, PA; [occ.] Teaching: Poetry Appreciation Course; [memb.] (ADK) Alpha Delta Kappa,

Honorary Sorority (International), Senior Centre, Benevolent Society, American Society of Mexico, International Apostolic Movement.; [hon.] Sigma Kappa Phi (National Honorary Language Fraternity), Emeritus Professor Award from University of the Americas, Mexico.; [oth. writ.] Poems in ADK monthly publication and in the ADK "Kappan", magazine published twice a year. Articles published in American Society magazine, "Amistad.; [pers.] I am interested in human nature. My poems are often a comment on human relationships and the forces which might affect or control them. I delight in the simplicity of nature, in natural beauty...; [a.] Mexico City, Mexico

LAURIE, CATHERINE M.
[b.] August 8, 1937, Niagara Falls, Ontario, Canada; [p.] Charles Schwab and Vida Schwab; [m.] Ernest W. Laurie, June 2, 1956; [ch.] Cynthia, Daniel, Christine; [ed.] Brighton High School, East Kootnay Comm. College, International Correspondence School, Kootenay Airways Aviation School; [occ.] Matron (Security Guard) Can. Corps of Commissionair's Alberta Canada; [memb.] International Society of Poets; [hon.] Business Administration Honors Degree; [oth. writ.] Several poems published in local newspapers, songs, recorded and sold across Canada, poems of personal nature for Birthdays Graduations, Etc; [pers.] "My emotions through time are recorded in rhyme". Loving and being loved and encouraged by my husband, makes me the person I am.; [a.] Whitecourt Alberta, Canada

LAW, CHERLY
[b.] December 21, 1956, Oshawa, Ontario, Canada; [p.] Divorced; [m.] Separated 18 years marriage.; [ch.] Rachel 15 yrs, Courtney 10 yrs.; [ed.] I went back to school after raising my girls to better myself and earn my grade 12 diploma.; [occ.] Hearing aid dispenser receptionist; [oth. writ.] This is my first poem entered into a contest. I have wrote other poems for myself and family members.; [pers.] I have just discovered a hidden talent and I enjoy creating poems. I am a romantic and would like people to share with my personal feelings.; [a.] Oshawa Ontario, Canada

LAWRENCE, DAVE
[pen.] David Marcell; [b.] September 10, 1975, Yumnia, AZ; [p.] Steve Lawrence, Judy Lawrence; [m.] Single; [ed.] Orange Park Hill, FL; [occ.] Commercial Air Conditioning Mechanical Installer, Student in College; [hon.] None to be noted.; [oth. writ.] None published yet.; [pers.] Be careful with love for its power holds no bounds. It can take years to find you yet in 5 seconds its can destroy you and all you hold as truth is lies at this moment all you have grown to hate you become.; [a.] Orange Park, FL

LAWSON, KIM DENISE
[b.] May 11, 1957, Houston, TX; [p.] Malcolm and Helen Lawson; [ed.] B.A. Music Education Baylor University; [occ.] Sales Manager; [memb.] St. Mark's Episcopal Church, Symphony League of Southeast Texas, Beaumont Interfaith Choral Society, Southeast Texas Kantorei; [oth. writ.] Poems for community events; [pers.] I strive to reflect the passions of life in my writing.; [a.] Beaumont, TX

LAYDEN, JEAN MOYRA
[b.] August 7, 1922, Batley, West Yorks, England; [p.] Norris and Elsie Farrington; [m.] Ronald Layden, May 19, 1943; [ch.] Graham, Howard; [ed.] Batley Girls Grammar School West Yorks, England (5 years); [occ.] Retired Poet, Painter, Photographer; [oth. writ.] At least 30 poems, 4 short stories, 2 childrens stories. Family History - in progress also 2 murder stories.; [pers.] I have always done my work as a hobby, (owing to the early demise of my mother and my fathers'. Remarriage unable to take offer of a place at Leeds University.) I love people and all my work is from life.; [a.] Brighouse West Yorks, England

LEA, SUE ELLEN
[b.] December 5, 1954, Flint, MI; [p.] Duane and Catherine Sholler; [m.] David Lea, June 26, 1976; [ch.] Catherine and William Lea; [ed.] B.S. degree and Master's Degree from Central Michigan University; [occ.] Speech and Language Pathologist in Infant-Toddler Programs in the schools (Shiawasee Resd); [memb.] Carunna United Methodist Church, Michigan Speech and Hearing Association American Speech and Hearing Association; [oth. writ.] This is my first published writing; [pers.] This poem came to me while driving in my car. I wrote it in approximately 20 minutes. It was a gift from God.; [a.] Owosso, MI

LEASAK, MARCELLA
[b.] December 11, 1952, North Battleford, Sask, Canada; [p.] George and Eva Frehlich; [m.] James Leasak, November 10, 1988; [ch.] Robin Denis, Jessica, Eva-Marie, Kasie-Jean Leasak; [ed.] Gr 1 to 9, Meota School, Gr 10 COCJ North Battleford Sask, Canada; [occ.] Wife and Mother of 3 children, helping to run our farm; [memb.] The Humane Society of Canada, "PETA", Protection Education Towards Animals; [hon.] "Editors Choice Award" for outstanding achievement in Poetry for 1995 given by National Library of Poetry nominated Poet of the Year and International Poet of Merit for 1995; [oth. writ.] Poem published in Sparkles in the Sand, by National Library of Poetry other poems published in local newspaper, many others not published.; [pers.] I thank God for my poem writing ability. He guides my pen, his constant love and my faith in him is what guides the messages in some of my poems it is like some things need or are meant to be said.; [a.] Edam Saskatchewan, Canada

LECLAIRE, BRENDA
[pen.] Buncasa Lee Jules; [b.] July 7, 1950, Sault Ste Marie, ON; [p.] George Ross, Estelle, Maria Ross; [m.] Paul LecLair, August 16, 1985; [ch.] Stephan Ross, Jason Graham, Melanie Nicole; [ed.] Sault Ste. Marie Tech. and Comm. High School, Sault College; [occ.] Secretary, A.F. of M. Musicians Assoc. Local 276; [oth. writ.] Designer and Publisher of Local Musicians "Vocal Chord" paper.; [pers.] Gained knowledge of the revolving matters of the mind are mirrored in my writings and my art.; [a.] Sault Sainte Marie Ontario, Canada

LEDESMA, TERESA
[b.] March 23, 1978, Canary Islands, Spain; [ed.] American School of Las Palmas, Canary Islands, Spain; [occ.] Student

LEDFORD, COLISTA
[b.] February 17, 1930, Staffordsville, KY; [p.] Frank and Mattie Spradlin; [m.] Homer Ledford, 1952; [ch.] Mark Ledford, Cindy Lowy, Julie Baker and Mattie Lee Conkwright; [ed.] BS degree in Bus. Adm. Berea College, Berea, KY; [occ.] Homemaker and Community Greeter; [memb.] President Clark County Unit American Cancer Society, Winchester Lioness Club, Past Pres. Daniel Boone Music Club - Past Pres. First United Methodist Church - Member of the Board-Staff Parish Relations - Chr.; [hon.] Honored by the American Cancer Society in 1991 for outstanding service in the crusade to conquer cancer.; [oth. writ.] Several other poems published in local newspaper.; [pers.] My greatest desire is to serve God and to be a help to others.; [a.] Winchester, KY

LEE, DIANNE M.
[b.] April 21, 1963, Saint Paul, MN; [p.] LeRoy Johnson, Joanne Johnson-Jensen; [ch.] Christopher, Amber, Olivia; [pers.] To touch but one heart and give hope of a less cruel world in our near future. My greatest influence is Dorothy Parker, not only her poetry but her belief in a peaceful society yet to come.; [a.] Saint Paul, MN

LEE, HOR-MING
[pen.] Hor-Ming Lee; [b.] November 29, 1929, Jiangmen, Xinhue, Guangdong, China; [p.] Yi-qian Lee, Zhing Shi Lee; [m.] Min-ya Liu Lee, December 25, 1964; [ch.] David Y. Lee (MD); [ed.] Taiwan Chung Hsing University; [occ.] Prof. of Directed Reading on Traditional Chinese Medicine, Director and Vice President of International College of TCM; [memb.] IPS; [hon.] International poet of Merit Award, 1995; [oth. writ.] Translation Works: Chinese Masso-Therapy, Symptoms and Treatment of Menses and Leukorhed. Articles: Psoriasis, Alopecia etc. Song poems translated.; [pers.] I endeavour to attempt to bring the world into a big family by way of poetry, and at living through the cooperation of East-West Medicine. I have been greatly influenced by ancient Chinese odes.; [a.] Vancouver British Columbia, Canada

LEE, HOR-MING
[pen.] Hor-Ming Lee; [b.] November 29, 1929, Jiangmen, Xinhui, Guangdong, China; [p.] Yi-Qian Lee, Zhong Shi Lee; [m.] Min-Ya Liu Lee, December 25, 1964; [ch.] David Y. Lee (MD); [ed.] Taiwan Chung Hsing University, M.A. Program of Asian Studies in Seton Hall University; [occ.] Prof of Directed Reading on Traditional Chinese Medicine, Director and Vice President of International College of TCM; [memb.] ISP; [hon.] International Poet of Merit Award, 1995; [oth.writ.] Translation works: Chinese Masso-Therapy, Symptoms and Treatment of Menses and Leukorrhea Articles, Psoriasis, Alopecia etc. song poems translated; [pers.] I endeavour to attempt to bring the world into a big family by way of poetry, and at living through the cooperation of East - West Medicine. I have been greatly influence by Ancient Chinese Odes; [a.] Vancouver BC, Canada

LEE, MARGARET D.
[pers.] I'm retired from G.E. and my husband and I try to do all we can, toward Christian work. I

thought perhaps this poem might help someone.

LEMASTER, NANETTE B.
[b.] April 21, 1938, Gaffney, SC; [p.] Charles B. and Etha P. Baker; [m.] R. Tommy LeMaster, July 23, 1959; [ch.] Mary Nan, Chris, Christopher Thomas and Tim Timothy Baber; [ed.] Gaffney High School, Limestone College (B.A.), Converse College (M.A.) with graduate work at University of S.C. Clemson Univ., and Winthrop; [occ.] Wife, mother, grandmother I recently chose early retirement after teaching English and French for 30 years - Gaffney High and Ewing Junior High; [memb.] Delta Kappa Gamma, Chi Delta Phi, SCEA-R, NEA-R, Cherokee, County Retired Teacher's Assoc. - Grassy Pond Volunteer Fire Dept - Ladies Aux., Charlotte Grigsby, Circle; [hon.] Delta Kappa Gamma (Corresponding Sec., 2nd Vice-President), Co-Chairman of GPVFD Aux. - Chairman of Circle - Dean's List, Editors of the Lantern, (College Newspaper), Kalosophia (Honor Scholastic Society), President of Chi Delta Phi, Who's Who; [oth. writ.] Poems published in College Literary Magazine as well as my Student's Publication Bits and Pieces - local newspapers and Sorority Publications I have a children's poem "(Grandaddy's Truck)" waiting for publication in both form; [pers.] I write when I feel deeply moved by something - other poems I've written reflect joy, love, and nature Emily Dickinson, Alfred, Lord Tennyson, and William Wordsworth are some poets I particularly enjoy as well as the Romantic Period Poets - (Heats Lord Byron, Shelly, etc.); [a.] Gaffney, SC

LENNOX, DIANE
[b.] June 24, 1966, Scranton, PA; [p.] Phillip E. and Carol J. Lennox; [ed.] Abington Heights High School, 1 yr. Keystone College; [occ.] Temporary secretary; [pers.] I write what I feel.; [a.] Clarks Summit, PA

LEWIS, DARRELL GARRETT
[b.] October 10, 1972, Orangeville, ON, Canada; [p.] Maxwell and Jewel Lewis; [ed.] Norwell District Secondary School; [occ.] Pursuing a Career in Writing and Theatrical Arts; [oth. writ.] Several poems and short stories, unpublished.; [pers.] This poem is dedicated to all those who believed in me and to my love Joanne, who inspires me to write from the heart and soul.; [a.] Mount Forest Ontario, Canada

LEWIS, JOAN
[b.] July 18, 1951, Comox Van. Is.; [p.] Mr. and Mrs. P. McGee; [m.] Jerry Lewis, November 19, 1971; [ch.] Paul and Cory; [oth. writ.] Other poems and two short stories not published.; [pers.] Counting my blessings rather than my bruises along my pathway through life.; [a.] Powel River British Columbia, Canada

LEWIS, RYAN JAMES
[pen.] Ryan James Lewis; [b.] May 3, 1979, Los Angeles, CA; [p.] Ronald and Maureen Lewis; [ed.] Junior year at a prestigious Military Academy in Texas, Marine Military Academy, Harlingen, Texas; [occ.] Student; [memb.] National Honors Society, Fellowship of Christian Athletes, Junior Statesman of America, McIlhenny scholar; [hon.] National History and Government award,

McIlhenny scholar; [oth. writ.] Various other magazines and books; [pers.] "To succeed you must attempt."; [a.] Chatsworth, CA

LEX, JESSE
[b.] May 12, 1978, Emerson Hospital Concord, MA; [p.] Jeanne and Dennis Lex; [ed.] Groton Dunstable Regional High School; [occ.] Student; [oth. writ.] Short story, "George" in out printed paper-back prose and poetry in school literary magazine articles in the school newspaper.; [pers.] I write what I feel and feel what I write some of my greatest influences in the best generation, the Franksters, and a lot of science fiction writers.; [a.] Groton, MA

LIDGOLD, CAROLE M.
[b.] January, 1943, Toronto, Ontario, Canada; [p.] Robert and Rhoda Thomas; [m.] Gordon A. Lidgold, May 7, 1966; [ch.] Lorraine, Warren; [ed.] High School - Gr. 12, Winston Churchill Collegiate; [occ.] Church Secretary, Writer, Editor, Publisher; [memb.] Canadian Authors Assoc., Scarborough Arts Council Authors; [hon.] 4 Time Winner in Gold Book Section of Authors; [oth. writ.] Magazine/Newspaper Articles, "Journey Into Christmas" (Book) Poetry Memories of Cayuga - Ontario's Love Boat (Book), short stories in "Authors"; [pers.] I write because I can't stop the flow of thoughts and ideas that force themselves onto paper.; [a.] West Hill Ontario, Canada

LILES, KATHLEEN BRADEN
[b.] May 27, 1958, Lake Geneva, WI; [p.] Brad and Joyce Braden; [m.] Divorced; [ch.] Sarah Kathleen and Aaron Michael; [ed.] Boswell High School, Courses taken at Cornell University and Colorado State University; [occ.] Breeding Mgr. on Horse Farm - Aledo, Texas; [hon.] Certificate of Accomplishment at Cornell Univ. and Colo. State Univ.; [oth. writ.] I have many more poems that have not been published at this time.; [pers.] I write only from my real life experiences, good or bad. My parents have raised me into the wonderful life of of horses and ranch life!; [a.] Aledo, TX

LINDER, BRANDI MAYERS
[b.] February 19, 1979, North Dakota; [p.] Rene and Gary Mayers; [m.] Terry Charles Linder, March 21, 1994; [ch.] Travis Clayton Linder (20 mo.); [ed.] 9th grade and GED; [occ.] First Admiral Cleaning Services (Bastrop, Texas); [a.] Dale, TX

LINDSEY, MICHELE
[b.] November 17, 1952, Holyoke, MA; [p.] Annette and Joseph Macon; [m.] Divorced; [ch.] Nicole Ann, Joshua Robert, Tonya Marie, Charlene Elizabeth, Elizabeth Ashley, Maria Del'Rosario, Cassandra Sabrina, Travis Taylor, Christopher Michael; [ed.] High School grad. 1971, Commerce High School, Springfield Mass.; [occ.] Seamstress; [oth. writ.] Never published - just personal poems, short stories; [pers.] I write to reflect how I'm feeling at the moment.; [a.] Liberty, NY

LINDSTROM, LISA MICHELE
[b.] August 8, 1961, Minneapolis, MN; [p.] Ward and Carol Engebrit; [m.] Jeffrey Rollin Lindstrom; [ed.] Charles A. Lindbergh H.S., Hopkins, MN - 1 Year University of Minnesota; [occ.] Poet, Housewife, Office Manager; [memb.] Distinguished

Member - Intl. Society of Poetry, Member - All American Eagles Racing Team; [hon.] Editor's Choice Ward for "Unfantasy" in "At Waters Edge"; [oth. writ.] Several anthologies through The National Library of Poetry. I also became a publisher to publish my 1st book of poetry entitled "Adequate Justice - beginning healing through poetry."; [pers.] Thank you Dr's Judd, D.C and Marvin Gladstone, M.D. for your emotional support.; [a.] Yorba Linda, CA

LINEMAN, CHRISTOPHER J. B.
[b.] June 18, 1973, Weymouth, MA; [p.] Ronald and Constance Lineman; [ed.] G.E.D. certificate, Life - "The Really Big One!; [occ.] Student/Peer Counselor for Vinfen, Corp.; [oth. writ.] Too numerous to mention... at least, 1,000 poems and some short stories plus 2 plays; [pers.] My favorite saying is one Thoreau wrote in Walden - "One must stand up to live before can sit down to write." I consider my poem "Desires" to be a good poem, but not my best. If the Library wishes over to see more of my works, many of which I believe to be equal, and even greater, in their artistry and power, I would love such correspondence.; [a.] Quincy, MA

LINK, BRENDA
[b.] July 18, 1973, Westwood, NJ; [p.] Ludwig and Ursula Link; [ed.] Bachelor of Science - B.S. Degree - (Psychology) William Paterson College Wayne, NJ); [occ.] Information and Referral Specialist - Bergen County; [memb.] CRC Helpline, Lambda Tau Omega Sorority, Inc., Community Gospel Church - Northvale NJ (Assemblies of God); [hon.] "Most Outstanding Greek" - 1994; [oth. writ.] Collection of poetry; [pers.] "It is by God's grace and love that a thought evolves, a word is spoken, a sentence is manifested and meaning comes to pass."; [a.] Hackensack, NJ

LITSKY, ALVERA
[b.] February 27, 1935, Donora, PA; [p.] Andrew and Genevieve Pykosh Litsky; [ed.] Donora Senior High School and California University of Pennsylvania; [occ.] Retired Elementary Teacher after 38 years, of teaching.; [memb.] Catholic Women College Club, Mon Valley Chapter of the Pittsburgh Opera, Polish Falcons Mixed Bowling League, The Valley of Hope.; [oth. writ.] I have written poems for the Donora Elementary Center.; [pers.] I would like to dedicate the poem a teacher's garden, to my sister, Genie Listsky Bogdan, who loves children and teaching.; [a.] Donora, PA

LOBO, LYNETTE
[b.] October 18, 1964, New Haven, CT; [p.] Alfred Lobo, Rosalind Lobo; [ch.] Earle G. Munroe Jr.; [ed.] St. Mary's High, Stone Academy; [occ.] Customer Service Rep., Blue Cross/Blue Shield of CT.; [memb.] Member, Eureka Chapter #2 O.E.S. Member, Arabic Court #95 Daughter of ISIS; [oth. writ.] Several poems written for people and special occasions.; [pers.] Poetry for me is a way of self expression. Through my writing, I hope others can grasp my inner most feelings. I have been greatly influenced by experiences and diverse issues. Many thanks goes to Martin Luther King Jr., Bob Marley and Maya Angelou.; [a.] Hamden, CT

LOCKE, BONI
[b.] November 12, 1948, Atlanta, GA; [p.] Jim Locke, Myrtice Locke; [ed.] Virginia Commonwealth University; [occ.] Freelance Artist, Teacher, Fitness Trainer; [memb.] Toastmasters International, First Unity Church Volunteer.; [hon.] "ATM" Toastmaster Award, "Black Belt Excellence" for community involvement in Karate; [oth. writ.] Newsletter articles as president of first Unity Church Board, Articles for Toastmaster Newsletter.; [pers.] To vividly express the inner and outer beauty of our environment and the positive effect on our life. My influence comes from Edgar Allen Poe and Native American Writers.; [a.] Saint Petersburg, FL

LONCHIADIS, AL
[b.] April 28, 1977, Worcester, MA; [ed.] Shrewsbury High, Worcester State College; [hon.] I have been honored by who's who in America and received honor from my family and friends, the highest honor of all.; [oth. writ.] Previously unpublished, writing for personal enjoyment and for those closest to me.; [pers.] True poetry, that comes from one's soul, should mean something different to everyone, every time is read. Conscious ideas have no place in poetry, poems are truth. And nothing besides.; [a.] Shrewsbury, MA

LOPEZ, NORA CRYSTAL
[b.] October 21, 1982, Toppenish; [p.] Hilario and Teresa Lopez; [ed.] I am going to school in Morris Schoot Middel School, I am in seventh grade.; [memb.] I am a member in the Healthy Kicks Club, it is for kids won't do drugs nor alcohol.; [a.] Mattawa, WA

LOSIER, GILLES PHILIP
[b.] March 26, 1983, Stratford, Ont.; [p.] Melten and Geraldine Losier; [occ.] Currently attending Ecole La Passerelee, Grade 7; [a.] Saint Isidore NB, Canada

LOVE, JACKIE M.
[b.] June 23, 1950, New Orleans; [p.] Benjamin and Julia E. Love; [ch.] Lamur, Raoul, Julian Love; [ed.] South Scotlandville Elementary, Scotlandville Jr and Sr. High School, Southern University, Palomar College, Baton Rouge Vocational Tech and Airco Tech; [occ.] Driver (Limo and Crab), Welder, Math Tutor, Writer, Post; [oth. writ.] "I Have Love", "Cocaine Alley", "Love Is", "What Kind of World is This", and others.; [pers.] If mankind is to be saved from itself, it can only be done by God and Y.; [a.] Baton Rouge, LA

LOVELADY, VIVIAN
[b.] October 4, 1916, Crockett, TX; [p.] Rev. W. M. Gardner, Adella Gardner; [m.] Tony Lovelady (Deceased), May 15, 1937; [ch.] James, William, Charles, Henry, Christine, Vivian, Minnie, Darsey, Percy; [ed.] Salt Branch Elementary, Crockett C. High School, Mary Allen Jr. College; [occ.] Retired; [memb.] Pleasant Grove CME Church, Jasper Cemetery Association, Class in Red Cross Home Nursing; [hon.] Honor grad. from Elementary School, High School and Junior College Class Poet of Mary Allen J.C. graduating class of 1935.; [oth. writ.] A number of poems written over the years few published, one published in The Garden of Life (National Library of Poetry).; [pers.] I do

the best I can and leave the rest to my maker so I can give life to my years, not just add years to my life.; [a.] Crockett, TX

LOVELUCK, ROYSTON
[b.] September 1, 1929, Bridgend, South Wales, United Kingdom; [p.] Edward Loveluck, Olive Loveluck; [m.] Meirion Loveluck, March 24, 1958; [ch.] Helen Margaret, Rosalind Catherine; [ed.] Technical College, Bridgend, University of Science and Technology, Cardiff; [occ.] Retired - Was a professional Chartered Engineer; [memb.] Member Institution Electrical Engineers, National Trust Membership; [oth. writ.] Several poems and articles published in local church of England Magazines.; [pers.] Much of my writing reflects my Welsh background and culture. I admire the poets William Wordsworth and Dylan Thomas.; [a.] Chester Cheshire, United Kingdom

LOWE, CHRIS
[pen.] Desperado; [b.] December 18, 1971, Woburn, MA; [p.] Russell Lowe, Joyanne Lowe; [ed.] Andover High School University of Massachusetts at Lowell; [occ.] Chemical Technician Millipore Corp. Bedford, MA; [hon.] Omega Chi Epsilon, Dean's List; [oth. writ.] None published.; [pers.] My writings are all inspired by a woman whom I love. Read carefully for there is a special message to her hidden within. I dedicate this poem to my love, Genevieve.; [a.] Andover, MA

LOWMAN, BEVERLY
[b.] February 16, 1945, Bronx, NY; [p.] Mabel Smith, John Seignious; [m.] Divorced; [ch.] Lisa Marie, Glenda Yavette and Philip III; [ed.] Newburgh Free Academy, Bronx Community College, Manhattan Bible Institute; [occ.] Pastor, Church of our Lord and Savior Jesus Christ, Brooklyn, NY; [memb.] Faith in Action Ministries, Precinct Clergy Council; [hon.] Community Service, Faith in Action Ministries; [oth. writ.] Articles: Amsterdam News, The Beacon, Poems: Several in local newspapers personal poetry broadcast, Germantown, MA, Tributes: Martin Luther King Jr., John and Robert F. Kennedy Gavin Cato, Recordings: Welcome back (Hostages), our Vietnam heroes, that child was my child (Atlanta children).; [pers.] All aspects of life's realities, pains and joys encompass my work. I write from personal experience as well that related by others. A lover of poetry since childhood, (a beauty and wonder outside my world) I marvel at its development within.; [a.] Brooklyn, NY

LOYD, HEATHER
[b.] September 20, 1972, Grand Prairie, TX; [p.] Janet Loyd, Leon Loyd; [ed.] Burkburnett High School, Midwestern State University, Institute of Children's Literature; [occ.] Student; [hon.] 2nd place State UIL journalism Several state and national awards for journalism, newspaper production, and writing.; [oth. writ.] Poems published in other anthologies. Articles printed in college paper.; [pers.] I have heard many people put down my part of the country, Texas, and its people, so I hope I can show others its beauty. I also want children to know they're not the only ones.; [a.] Wichita Falls, TX

LUCAS, MARY CHRISTINE
[b.] January 18, 1958, Kirkwood, MO; [p.] Frank

and Pat Lucas; [ed.] Just School Freshman Year; [occ.] Disabled; [oth. writ.] Many other writings; [pers.] I feel I've been given a gift from God. I touch others heart and lives with my poetry all the credit is the Lord's that's who I'm giving it to.; [a.] DeSoto, MO

LUIGS, HELEN FRANCES
[b.] July 3, 1921, Christian County, KY; [p.] Geo. D. Harned - Mamie B. Harned; [m.] Kenneth J. Luigs, June 20, 1942; [ch.] Joseph K. Luigs; [ed.] Bosse High School, Evansville, Indiana; [occ.] Active member Lakeland Regional Medical Center Auxiliary; [memb.] A.B.W.A., National Honor Society, Quill and Scroll, Scarlet and Grey, S. Fla. Ave Church of Christ; [pers.] Our family enjoys traveling, having been to Europe and Alaska, and extensive travels in the U.S.A. I find writing poetry is a creative outlet for emotions that are not otherwise easily expressed.; [a.] Lakeland, FL

LUX, JERRY
[ed.] VW-Milwaukee; [occ.] Landscaper; [memb.] Former Member: Amnesty International; [pers.] I enjoy reading Vonnegut, Leguin and Castaneda.; [a.] Lone Rock, WI

LYMAN, JIM
[b.] August 29, 1969, Middletown, CT; [p.] Cheryl A. Lyman, Jim Lyman Sr.; [ed.] High School; [occ.] Sheeter Helper in a Paper Mill; [memb.] Spent 4 yrs. in the United States Marine Corps., Desert Storm Vet.; [pers.] I wrote this poem to show that love is not a sure thing, and that we must make the best out of the experience. For we may never know if we will experience such a love again.; [a.] Dalton, MA

LYNAR-COHEN, ELEANOR
[pen.] Nova; [b.] October 15, 1945, Newark, NJ; [p.] Rovena and James Levell; [s.] Arthur Cohen (divorced); [m.] July 5, 1986; [ch.] Erik C. Levell; [ed.] 1979-1983 Bachelor of Science, Degree in Nursing, RN, Rutgers University, Newark, NJ., 1970-1973 AAS Degree, Nursing, RN, Essex County College, Newark, NJ.; [occ.] Disability-retired RN.; [memb.] Rutgers Alumni, Newark, NJ. Consumer Affairs Div. Trenton, NJ. Distinguished Member of The International Society of Poets, 1994-1995. Long Ridge Writers Group Alumni, 1993-1995, CT, NJ.; [hon.] Medical Transcription Certificate, CA. Professional Service Award, Overlook Hospital, Sumit, NJ.; [oth. writ.] Editor's Choice Award, 1994, 1995 - The National Library of Poetry. International Poet of Merit Award, 1995. Sparrowgrass Poetry Forum, WV. for 1996.; [pers.] I was divinely inspired to write poems for friends and families. When I reach out to help other races, I enhance my own unique consciousness.; [a.] Morris County, NJ

LYNN, OSCAR M.
[pen.] Chico Lynn; [b.] April 12, 1951, Guadalajara, Mexico; [p.] Luz Elena Lynn; [m.] Naida Lynn, June 29, 1976; [ch.] Anthony James, twins Jessica Michelle and Jesse Michael; [ed.] BA Business Administration, UTEP, AA Univ. Maryland; [occ.] MIS Manager; [pers.] Live life as happy and as fruitful as you can, without hurting others, if possible.

LYONS, EDWARD T.
[b.] May 9, 1946, Jersey City, NJ; [ed.] Rutgers

University 2 yrs - Business Administration; [occ.] Writer, Inventor; [memb.] The American Legion; [oth. writ.] The program of the good published by co-operative publishing Peterborough, New Hamshire January, 1984, Second printing Vantage Press, New York City, NY May, 1988, The Return Of The King, copyright 1986, 1987, will be published in near future.; [a.] Jersey City, NJ

MA'RUF, A. MUHAMMAD
[b.] January 9, 1944, Sri Lanka; [p.] 'Abdal Qadir, Rahmath Allah; [m.] Nihar, 1973; [ch.] Khaldun Zamani, Aishah and Adam Qutb; [ed.] University of Pennsylvania, University of Ceylon, Peradeniya, Sri Lanka, St. Anthony's College, Kandy, Sri Lanka; [occ.] Anthropologist; [memb.] American Anthropological Association, Brideton Islamic Centre; [oth. writ.] Several anthropoligical and Islamological papers.; [a.] Swedesboro, NJ

MACKENZIE, ANN
[pen.] Annie; [b.] November 24, 1956, Australia; [p.] Gorden MacKenzie, Elizabeth MacKenzie; [ch.] Lee Andrew, Lucinda Ann and Krystal Jade; [ed.] Wynham State High Narrabeen Primary; [occ.] Full-time mother; [pers.] I strive to write poems with inner deep feelings, everything in this world has beauty its looked at with the heart and not the eyes.; [a.] Colchester, England

MACPHETRIDGE, BETTY ANN
[b.] April 3, 1931, La Crosse, WI; [p.] Dan and Cora Young; [m.] Don MacPhetridge, September 10, 1955; [ed.] 12th Grade plus many development seminars throughout my career.; [occ.] My Business Training led me to secretarial duties at Trane Co. in La Crosse, WI where I retired in '88 as a Manufacturing Engineering Assistant.; [memb.] 45 years in PSI (Professional Secretaries International) and am very active in our United Methodist Church.; [hon.] Secretary of the Year in PSI.; [oth. writ.] Being very involved in crafts I design greeting cards and compose very personal poems to utilize therein. I enjoy coordinating parties form. Have written many Happy Ads for friends that are published in our local paper.; [pers.] Writing poetry, to me, is a neat way of truly expressing oneself and my wish is to inspire hopefuls. My belief in life is to enjoy every moment and to accomplish this it is imperative we care and share. But...Most of All.. and a daily priority, we must count blessings and Give Thanks!; [a.] Onalaska, WI

MADDUX, KELLY
[b.] July 6, 1981, Poway, CA; [p.] Linda Maddux (Mother); [ed.] 8th Grade student at Canon City Middle School; [memb.] A member of the Youth center of the First Methodist Church in Canon City, a member of the Canon City Middle School band, I play Trumpet.; [hon.] I have won medals for playing the trumpet in band for Solo and Ensemble contests.; [pers.] I enjoy writing poems about life as a teenager, it's pros and cons.; [a.] Canon City, CO

MAGDZINSKI, RUTH I.
[b.] April 24, 1927, Union Pier, MI; [p.] Emily and Joseph Konvalinka; [s.] John R. Magdzinski; [m.] May 24, 1947; [ch.] Kathleen M. Beldorth and Stephen A. Magdzinski; [ed.] New Buffalo High School; [occ.] Real Estate Broker; [memb.] 1) Southwestern Michigan Assoc. of Realtors. 2) National Assoc. of Realtors. 3) Multiple Listing Service of S.W. Mich. 4) Red Arrow Ride Assoc. 5) Harbor-Cuntry Chamber of Commerce. 6) Village of Lakeside Assn. [hon.] 1) Million Dollar or more sales awards for real estate - 9 years. 2) 25 years service - Vil. of Lakeside Assn. 3) Many more. [oth. writ.] Wrote history of union Pier, MI. for edition of Red Arrow Ride newspaper - 1993. Used this poem for Christmas letters as it depicted our small town character.; [pers.] Live for todayt because tomorrow could be too late - this was my mothers philosophy. She lived to be 86. I am 69 and still working full time as a real estate broker. Married 49 years - May 24, 1996.; [a.] Lakeside, MI

MAGID, ANNETTE M.
[b.] Cleveland, OH; [m.] Hillel Magid; [ch.] Suzie Tuchman and Jonathan Magid; [ed.] B.A. - Joan Carroll University, Cleveland, O., Suny at Buffalo - M.A., Ph.D.; [occ.] Professor of English, Erie Community College/Sough, Buffalo, NY; [memb.] NEMLA - Two year Colleg Rep. (Executive Board Member), MLS - Publications Editor, MYCLSA, AAUW, AACCW, NATE, NEA; [hon.] President's Award, Student Gov. Award for Advisor, Employee of the Month, Sabbatical Award, Student Gov. Award, Student Gov. Award for Dedication and Service to students, Who's who - College Professors.; [oth. writ.] Poems published in Images and Cathartic. Educational articles published in Eric. Editor Sci-Fi stories vol. 1-3.; [pers.] I enjoy writing in several genre: Poetry, Drama, Short Fiction. Each of us has poetry within. Writing enhances the rhythm of the heart. The victorian period is most fascinating to me.; [a.] Williamsville, NY

MAHULA, SANDRA
[b.] February 22, 1946, San Antonio, TX; [p.] Ernie and LaVerne Mahula; [ch.] Shelley Whittenberg (28), Leslie Whittenberg (25), grandchildren: Monica (8) and Samantha (4) Whittenberg; [ed.] Bachelor's Degree: English, Schreiner College, Kerrville TX, Master's Degree: Guidance/Counselling, TX, A and M Univ., Kingsville, TX, Vocational Counselling Certification S.W. Texas State San Marcos, TX; [occ.] Vocational/Career Tech, Counselor in Sam Houston High School, San Antonio, TX; [hon.] Graduated Summa Cum Laude, B.A. in English; [oth. writ.] Several other poems published in school district publications; [pers.] All of my poems have been a blessing of God through life experiences. They reflect the true nature of life and love as God has given us.; [a.] San Antonio, TX

MAISEL, JOEL
[b.] January 4, 1977, Pueblo, CO; [p.] Debra Rocco and Alan Rocco; [ed.] GED; [pers.] "Use mistakes to open doors of change."; [a.] Pueblo, CO

MALLETT, JAIME
[b.] February 1, 1977, Newport Beach, CA; [p.] Roy Mallett and Carolee Mallett; [ed.] Trabuco Hills High School; [hon.] Graduated top 10% of 1995 graduating class - Trabuco Hills High School; [oth. writ.] "Memories" published in Mists of Enchantment; [pers.] No matter what obstacles stand in your way, if you believe in yourself anything is possible.; [a.] Mission Viejo, CA

MALONE, OWEN CROZIER WILLARD
[pen.] Oeghan Maeloeghan, Ian MacLean; [b.] June 23, 1938, Toronto, Ontario, Canada; [p.] Alfred V. Malone Gwnteen and Jean Malone; [ed.] Grade Nine Weston Collegiate and Vocational School Grade Twelve Equiv. Humber Community College; [occ.] Living on Disability Allowance; [pers.] I am an anglican christian. My two greatest influences are the diverse Carl Sandburg and T.S. Eliot.

MALTA, RICHARD A.
[b.] March 6, 1943, Oceanside, NY; [p.] Dorothy Maltar; [m.] Alice Malta, October 11, 1985; [ed.] MS in Education; [occ.] Welfare Examiner; [memb.] Roman Catholic Church; [oth. writ.] "All or Nothing for the Handicap" On Sacred Ground, He came to Masada, Discerning Heart.; [pers.] There is a personal God who loves each of individually he wants each of us to come to him like a little child.; [a.] Freeport, NY

MANCUSO, DANIELLE
[pen.] Annabelle; [b.] July 2, 1985, Baltimore, MD; [p.] Andrea Brown and Scott Mancuso; [ed.] 5th grade, Joppatowne Elementary, Harford CO, MD; [occ.] Student; [hon.] 3rd grade poetry contest honor roll; [pers.] I write about children's like and dislikes.; [a.] Joppa, MD

MANE, VAISHALI N.
[b.] April 17, 1973, New York, NY; [p.] Nishikant D. Mane, Dr. Jayashri N. Mane; [ed.] Stuyvesant H.S., Barnard College at Columbia University; [occ.] Student; [hon.] Barnard College Student Leadership Award, 1994 and 1995, Junior Marshall 1994, Senior Marshall 1995; [pers.] Self-confidence and spiritual strength will take you as far as you can dream.; [a.] New York, NY

MANOVICH, LESLEY
[b.] January 22, 1976, Yorkton; [p.] Annette Manovich, Joe Klemm; [ed.] Graduate from High School; [hon.] I won awards fro Remembrance Day, and in school I won for the Best Attendance at school for grade 12.; [a.] Foam Lake Saskatchewan, Canada

MANSARAY, ALIBADARA MED
[pen.] NFA Kemoh Keita; [b.] Kenema, Sierra Leone; [p.] Sajoh and Adama Mansaray; [ed.] Kenema Government School, Fourah Bay College, Univ. of Sierra Leone, University of South Carolina: B.A. (General) from F.B.E. U.S.L. in 1993, MPH, USC, May, 1996; [occ.] Student: Masters, school of Public Health, Univ. of S, Carolina; [memb.] Black Graduate Students Association (BGSA), USC, International Student Association (ISA), USC, School of Public Health Students Association USC, The "Chosen Few" of Sierra Leone (CF).; [oth. writ.] `A Prayer In The', `A Voice From Yesterday', `We Are In Tears', `A Vanished Friend' and other poems, `the Luxury of sacrifice' and other storied. Novels: `A Piece Of The Earth' and `The Road so far' in progress. (All unpublished.); [pers.] I have been abundantly influenced by: the Teaching of my mother, the examples of my father and all I have known, read, loved and despised. My inspiration stems from: The glory and sacrifice of friendship, the beauty and blessing of family, the being and resilience of the world and the grace and eternity of God.; [a.] Columbia, SC

MARAZITA, CORY P.
[b.] February 19, 1958, New York; [p.] Mike and Mary Marazita; [occ.] Safeway Food Chain and Ukiah Fitness Center; [oth. writ.] First and only poem.; [pers.] I would like to all the viewers to understand what this poem means to me and can to you. To this day I continue to read and experience the spiritual feeling from this poem. I hope this poem flows through you, like it flowed through me.; [a.] Willits, CA

MARCHESE, NOREEN
[b.] January 10, 1971, Troy, NY; [p.] Eugene J. Bechard, Marion Bechard; [m.] Christopher Marchese, August 20, 1994; [ed.] Troy High School, Maria College Albany, NY; [occ.] Occupational Therapist Assistant, Lansingburgh School District; [pers.] I enjoy writing poems to express my thoughts in words to those I know and love.; [a.] Troy, NY

MARCHIANO, ROSE C.
[b.] November 14, 1923, Brooklyn, NY; [p.] John and Susan Cucurullo; [m.] Ralph T. Marchiano, April 15, 1951; [ch.] Thomas, Marian, Robert; [ed.] Brooklyn College - B.A. Degree; [a.] Staten Island, NY

MARIANO, ALMA A.
[b.] August 27, 1953, Manila, Philippines; [p.] Catalina Richards, Ramon Abanilla; [m.] Elpidio G. Mariano, June 20, 1975; [ch.] Elpidio Jr., Emily and Ecoterina; [ed.] Master's Degree in Education; [occ.] Adjunct Faculty Clinton Community College; [pers.] We are who we are and the sooner we know what makes us tick, the sooner we can enjoy living.; [a.] Clinton, IA

MARIOTTI, ESTHER DOROTHY
[pen.] E. Dorothy Mariotti; [p.] John and Ida Pollick; [m.] Louis Mariotti (Deceased), May 4, 1946; [ch.] Two (Marlene) and (Angelo); [ed.] High School Grad. and Graduate of Penn State University (B.A.) in Counseling; [occ.] Counselor in Crises Management; [memb.] PDDC - Mechanicsburg, PA, Ministry Speaker Credentials, Associated with A/G Clergy Ministerium; [hon.] 1993 - Keynote Speaker at Women's Convention, Counseling Seminars there also. Speaker at Valley Forge College to Senior Graduates in 1989; [oth. writ.] A tract (copyrighted) "Retirement." Not published as yet. Looking for publisher. Writing a book currently, to be finished soon. Readers will find their problems eased.; [pers.] Take time to push someone a step father. I am hoping to finish book compilation in 1996. Contents of book are relative to lifespan and problems common to each age segment. Applying educ. academia.; [a.] Cheswick, PA

MARLETT, ROBERT M.
[b.] July 11, 1973, Martinsville, IN; [p.] Dave and Nancy Marlett; [m.] Karen Sue (Stilwell) Marlett, April 24, 1992; [ch.] Bethany Sue, Michael William; [ed.] Desoto Co. High, Arcadia, Fl; [memb.] International Society of Poets; [hon.] Two Editor's Choice Awards from The National Library of Poetry; [oth. writ.] Over 2,000 poems including Everglades: Daughter Of The Wild, The Meaning Of The Flag, and A Search For Love.; [pers.] If poetry doesn't create in the reader the emotions of the author, it is a waste of time for both. Poetry isn't simply another form of literature, it is emotions in print.; [a.] Jacksonville, FL

MARQUES, RUPERT
[b.] January 5, 1935, Georgetown, Guyana; [ed.] South America, England and the United States. Qualified, certified and licensed in several disciplines. Alternates from periods of wanderlust to recluse.; [occ.] Dabbled In The Maritime, Military Medical Legal and Political Professions; [memb.] Experimental Aircraft Assoc., Aircraft Owners and Pilots Assoc., National Notary Assoc.; [oth. writ.] Frequent contributor of letters and articles to hometown newspaper.; [pers.] Life was, life is and life will ever be. There is neither a beginning or an end, only continuity. Everything is in a state of flux. Nothing is static. There is neither life or death only transition.; [a.] Okeechobee, FL

MARSHALL, JESSICA
[b.] May 28, 1977, Midland, MI; [p.] Rick Marshall, Becki Marshall; [ed.] I am a senior in High School at Marple Newtown; [oth. writ.] I have had publishing in Poetry Motel; [a.] Newtown Square, PA

MARSHALL, JIMMY
[b.] June 14, 1970, Kingsport, TN; [p.] Pat Marshall and Wayne Marshall; [ed.] Grad. Daniel Boone High School Grad. Rets Electronic Institute; [occ.] Elevator Apprentice for a large chemical company; [hon.] On Dean's List 4 out of 6 times at the RETS Electronic Institute; [oth. writ.] This is the first writing that I have ever submitted.; [pers.] I enjoy sharing and expressing my feelings through writing poetry and country music that the majority of people can easily relate to and understand.; [a.] Fall Branch, TN

MARTEMUCCI, SARAH
[pen.] Sally Martin; [b.] December 18, 1919, Connecticut; [p.] Rose-John Puccia; [m.] Frank Martemucci, July 2, 1939; [ch.] Rosemarie, Vincent; [ed.] Hunter College - N.Y. BA, MS; [occ.] Retired; [memb.] Holy Eucharist Bereavement Group, Country-Western Dancing, Organ "Double Sharps, Retired Teachers of N.Y.C.; [hon.] Phi Beta Kappa (Hunter College), Dean's List; [oth. writ.] Marty and Smarty (Children's book) Poetry for Occasions, Poetry for Original greeting cards.; [pers.] I endorse an enthusiastic approach to any undertaking in life, a positive outlook in any circumstance and good will in anything and everything you do.; [a.] Southampton, NJ

MARTIN, CAROL J.
[pen.] Caroll J. Martin; [b.] March 28, 1947, England, AR; [p.] Willie Lee and Calvin Moore; [m.] Divorced; [ch.] Two marvelous young ladies; [ed.] RN - Nursing school, incomplete undergraduate - Governor's Statell, Park Forrest, Illinois, New adventure - University of Vermont for Holistic Health Degree; [occ.] R.N. Friage Nursing at Audie Murphy Hospital and South West Texas, San Antonio, TX; [memb.] Friends of Elisabeth Kiibler - Ross Center (to be dissolved); [hon.] Peace Corps Poster Person in 1970, 3rd place Illinois State Short Story contest, Honor: To have known so many teachers in my lifetime, to have seen an angel, to have known Elizabeth Kiibler - Ross who told me 20 years ago not to compromise my writing.; [oth. writ.] Unpublished manuscript - Insight from the Doorstep - numerous poems, love, the forever essence (short stories) repro-

duced on tape cassette and filmed for PBS x2 for television.; [pers.] I am my greatest teacher. I choose to absorb the teachings. I am the master of my life. I am grateful to all who have entered my kingdom, thus clarifying who be I.; [a.] Lakehills, TX

MARTIN, CHRISTINA
[b.] December 23, 1979, Atlanta, GA; [occ.] Student; [memb.] PETA - People for the Ethical Treatment of Animals, Periwig, Pacific Northwest Ballet - performed in Seattle Opera House, Lawrenceville Singers; [hon.] 1st Place in Tang So Do Tournaments, High Honors, Theater Club, 1st Place in Ski Race. School Meeting Committee, Solo in Lawrenceville Singers Tour; [pers.] "The truth is known to all the world, yet all the world does not know of the truth."; [a.] Jackson Hole, WY

MARTIN, CYNTHIA THEA
[pen.] Cemp or Cint; [b.] January 9, 1957, Charlotte, NC; [p.] Margaret Johnson, J. B. Martin; [ch.] Ayesha A. Martin, Grand-Amber Martin; [ed.] Laurens Drist 55 High School Laurens, S.C.; [occ.] Wilson's Sporting Company, Fountain INN S.C.; [memb.] The Richard L. Harp Truth Club; [oth. writ.] Personal keep-sakes; [pers.] I have been influenced by the word of God, then, now, and tomorrow. A special lady help me get there, my grandmother - Josephine Martin of Laurens S.C.; [a.] Laurens, SC

MARTIN, KIMBERLY A.
[pen.] Kimmi; [b.] September 14, 1970, Cleveland, OH; [p.] Carolyn Jary-Heiman, Dennis Szymczak; [m.] Dale James Martin, November 21, 1992; [ed.] Garfield Heights High School, Cuyahoga VAlley JVS; [occ.] Route Accounting Clerk for Pepsi-Cola Bottlers; [oth. writ.] I have written many poems and a couple short stories but this is my first publication.; [pers.] All of my writings come from my emotions, the stories my heart needs to tell.; [a.] Maple Heights, OH

MARTIN, OPAL MCCLURE
[b.] December 22, 1922, Gary, WV; [p.] Bertha McClure, McKinley McClure; [m.] James H. Martin; [ch.] Lois, Glenn, Janice, Karen; [ed.] B.S. Education, MS Education, MS Library Science and Media Specialist; [occ.] Retired; [memb.] Delta Kappa Gamma, Roanoke County, Woman's Club, Salem Baptist Church, Roanoke Athletic Club; [hon.] President-Womans Club, Volunteer Medical Library, Volunteer Church Library, Chairman - Education Dept. Womans Club; [oth. writ.] Poems published in "Grapachat" College, Quarterly - Radford University; [pers.] Retired in name only - I am busy with clubs grandchildren, and volunteer work - after a cold winter my children and I can hardly wait for the sun and the beach.; [a.] Roanoke, VA

MARTIN, PATRICIA DIANE
[pen.] "Lady Di"; [b.] August 31, 1952, Dallas, TX; [p.] Joe and Geraldine Freeman; [ch.] Jason, Jimmy, Makyla, Idau; [ed.] R. L. Turner High University of Maryland; [occ.] Cosmetologist; [oth. writ.] Several poems written and put into stars and stripes during desert storm.; [pers.] A lot of my poems are my personal experiences. My

deepest feelings and thoughts through out my life. I have been influenced by God, and my children.; [a.] San Antonio, TX

MARTIN, TRICIA
[b.] February 11, 1971, Kingston, NY; [p.] James and Patricia Martin; [ch.] Steven Blake Shattuck; [ed.] 10th Grade - every day life has taught me the most things there are to know.; [occ.] PBX Operator; [hon.] Columbia University "For Writing"; [oth. writ.] Childrens Books that I wish to have published soon and a poem published in Central Florida Community College Newspaper.; [pers.] In a world where everyone is looking out for #1 we are loosing sight of our #1 proiority, our most valuable asset "Our Children".; [a.] Rock Island, TN

MARTINEZ, BOB G.
[pen.] Bob G. Martinez; [b.] June 7, 1949, Las Vegas, NM; [p.] Mrs. Mary Jane Martinez; [m.] Annette E. Martinez, February 10, 1973; [ch.] Lita R. Martinez (19 yrs); [ed.] North High School (Denver) in 1968; [occ.] Security Guard at the Denver Merchandise Mart; [memb.] Distinguished Member I.S.P., Mile High Poetry Society, and Columbine Poets of Colorado; [hon.] Four "Editor's Choice" awards, Voted: "Most likely to be handsome and sweet" by my wife and daughter; [oth. writ.] "My Time To Rhyme", a personal journal from childhood to day I became a grand father (302 pgs. unbroken single poem), "Sidetracks", Compilation of Poems; [pers.] One step at a time...Wherever He leads. Though mountains to climb, He grants all my needs.; [a.] Denver, CO

MARTINEZ, DEANNA LYNN
[pen.] Deanna Allen; [b.] January 27, 1971, Woodland, CA; [p.] Frank R. Martinez Jr. and Phyllis E. Blair; [m.] Mitchell A. Allen (fiance); [ch.] Andreia D. Melton and Elizabeth Rabouin Allen; [ed.] Graduate of Winters High School Class of 1988, American River College and Solano Community College; [occ.] Housewife, Mother; [memb.] Lifetime Member of the International Poetry Society, Girls Scout of America National Arbor Day Assoc. The Up Girls of American, Vaca Valley Christian Life Center; [hon.] Honor Student Graduate, Poet of the year Merit for 1996; [oth. writ.] Hundreds of unpublished poems. Poems publicized have included, radio jingles, weddings, funeral eulogies and several other special events. Published poems in books entitled: 1.) The Path Not Taken 2.) The Best Of The 90's, a personal compilation entitled "A Poet And A Prisoner" I hope to publish one day.; [pers.] I pray that through my writing, God, may allow my fellow brothers, and sisters to be reached, touched, encouraged, inspired, relieved and united. More so, I hope to relay messages of hope and faith, and to share with everyone, the incredible gift of love and life God has to us all.; [a.] Elk Grove, CA

MARTINEZ, MELISSA
[b.] August 14, 1977, Ogden, UT; [p.] Ed and Susie Martinez; [ed.] Box Elder High School; [occ.] Production Worker at Morton Automotive Safety Products; [memb.] St. Henry's Catholic Church, youth Group Aide; [hon.] Two time listed in Who's Who Among American High School Students, Eagle of the Cross Award; [oth. writ.] Several poems published in The Hive book of poems for the Box Elder High School.; [pers.] My writing is greatly influenced by the writings of Edgar Allen Poe and I strive to reflect the beauty of nature and mankind. I look beyond what lies on the surface.

MARTINEZ, TASHA MARIE
[pen.] T-poo; [b.] December 10, 1981, Pittsburgh, PA; [p.] Donna Johnson, Ricardo Martinez; [occ.] Student High School; [hon.] High Honor Roll, Effort Awards Participation; [oth. writ.] Assortment; [pers.] Dedication to my father (1954-1989)

MASCH, ALFRED T.
[b.] January 3, 1914, Bronx, NY; [p.] Both deceased; [m.] Dorothy, October 30, 1938; [ch.] Gary; [ed.] Hasbrouck Heights, NJ Elementary Schools, Cooper Union, NY Phoenix Art Institute, Kavagaugh School of Lettering, University of Indiana; [occ.] Graphic Artist and Miniaturist; [memb.] B.P.O. Elks (Past exalter Ruler), IGMA - International Guild of Miniature Artisans; [hon.] Elk of the Year - 1959, Hasbrouck Heights Citizen of the Year - 1991 Voted to "Fellow" status in IGMA; [a.] Hasbrouck Heights, NJ

MASON, DOLORES FLANAGAN
[b.] October 21, 1931, Baltimore, MD; [p.] Henry and Gladys Flanagan; [m.] Cornelius B. Mason (Deceased), March 18, 1951; [ch.] Eleven; [ed.] Paul Lawrence Dunbar Sr. High Class: June, 1949; [occ.] Retired: Office of the Public Defender - Baltimore, MD; [hon.] "Mother of the Year" (for) Afro American Newspaper - May 1968; [oth. writ.] Many poems and essays (non published).; [pers.] My writings reflect my personal thoughts and (my) experiences over the years.; [a.] Baltimore, MD

MASON, JUDITH A.
[pen.] Judy Mason - Judy Hinz; [b.] January 31, 1946, Detroit, MI; [p.] Marvin Hinz - Margaret Hinz; [ch.] Gail Sosnitza, Tracy Gatt, Trudy Mason, Joseph Mason, Carrie Mason; [oth. writ.] Several poems written since 1984; [pers.] My inspiration for the majority of my works was my brother Paul Hinz who died tragically in 1984 and my comparisson for abused children I am greatly touched by the writings of Kahlil Gibran; [a.] Dearborn Heights, MI

MASON, LACEY
[b.] December 19, 1985, Lincoln, NE; [p.] Sheila Mason; [ed.] 4th Grade Friend Elementary Friend, NE; [occ.] 4th Grade Student; [memb.] The Young Writers Club; [hon.] 94' - 95 3rd grade Book - it! Friend Elementary; [oth. writ.] I write lots of poems some my favorite ones are, "Angels", "It", and " The Knight", "It", and "The Knight Who Rode at Night".; [pers.] Poems are a great love eof mine. Even at age 10 I enjoy poems and feel they are an ideal way of expressing your feeling with out hurting another person.; [a.] Friend, NE

MASSEY, LETTIE CARDER
[m.] Donald Lee Massey 1933-1984; [ch.] Elaine Spahn, Vernon Massey, Karin Lingerfelt, Galen Massey and Landon Massey; [ed.] I graduated from Central High, now Garringer High and Charlotte, NC. I Completed a Dale Carnegie course in effective speaking and human relations in which I was awarded three awards, Reporting Award, Book Award, and Highest Achievement Award.; [occ.] Worked with my husband for 15 years in snack food business - the Dainty Nut company. I went to work in 1980 as a biscuit cook for two years, then into management with Spartan Food Systems, now Flagstar subsidiary - Hardees restaurant. I am still employed there.; [oth. writ.] I have written two other poems worthy of mention, one of which has been published.; [pers.] I believe that it is only children who possess the potential to guide our destiny. It is the duty of a parent to foster that potential into positive energies. I believe that my own greatest accomplishment shines in the lives of the five very respectful, highly achieved children whom Donald and I raised together with the help of God. They share a belief that their mother can accomplished anything.

MASTERS, CHERISH HOPE
[b.] March 8, 1983, Fairbury, IL; [p.] Virgi Bennett and Kim Masters; [ed.] 8th Grader; [memb.] Science and Math Club, Drama Club, YMCA, School Track Team; [hon.] 4th Place at County Spelling Bee, 3rd Place County Beauty Pageant, Accepted into Mid-America Beauty Pageant, 2nd Place Accelerated Reading Comp.; [oth. writ.] Friend for a life time is first published poem.; [pers.] Dream with your mind act on your heart.; [a.] Burnsville, MS

MATIAS, EDWIN
[pen.] Eddie Matt; [b.] June 25, 1966, Newark, NJ; [pers.] In my heart as well as mind - poetry is the examination of truth at its zenith - from the bible to a nursery rhyme - truth portrays beauty on a stage where the audience of perfection intertwines infinite applause.; [a.] Newark, NJ

MATTHEWS, BEVERLY ADELL
[pen.] Bev; [b.] December 15, Wake County, Holly Springs, NC; [p.] Mr. and Mrs. Raldy Matthews; [ed.] 2 yrs. College, Graduated: FuQuay Springs High School, FuQuay Springs, NC, Attended: ElCentro College, Dallas, TX, Real State: SMU Dallas, TX; [occ.] Secretary; [hon.] 1 Award; [pers.] A talent of discovered late is better than never knowing a talent existed.; [a.] Dallas, TX

MAUDE, SUE
[b.] May 23, 1951, Hamilton, Ontario, Canada; [p.] George and Marcelena Maude; [m.] (Fiance) Dave; [ch.] Rob, Lori, Lilia, grandchildren - Michael, Calvin, Kirsten, Justyne and Meghan; [ed.] Housewife; [pers.] Have wrote poems all my life. I love to read anything, and poetry is a favorite. Greatest inspiration is life. I also love to draw and make my own cross-stitch patterns.; [a.] Okotoks Alberta, Canada

MAXWELL, JOZETTE
[b.] April 15, 1968, San Antonio, TX; [p.] Allen Maxwell and Vickie Maxwell; [ed.] D. W. Holmes High School, Texas Southern Univ. (B.A.), St. Mary's Univ. (M.P.A.) (in prayers); [occ.] Process Analyst; [memb.] Delta Sigma Theta Sorority Inc., Christian Service Volunteer Corps.; [hon.] Judge-Poster Contest Character Education, Editor The Tiger (TSU Yearbook Publication), Assistant Editor - The Afroceutric Scholar.; [pers.] I thank God for his divine wisdom and power. "The Rage Within" was inspired by talks with fellow Christians who are "Waiting on the Lord". I want to

encourage everyone to be of good courage and always know that God's will be done.; [a.] San Antonio, TX

MAY, LISA
[b.] May 29, 1960, Teaneck, NJ; [ed.] Currently enrolled fulltime at Christopher Newport University as a Junior Majoring in English; [oth. writ.] Poem was first attempt at formal writing; [pers.] Whether life is cruel or enchanting, we should strive always to make ourselves better human beings.; [a.] Newport News, VA

MAYER, JENNIFER L. MORRILL
[b.] September 28, 1968, Detroit, MI; [p.] Dr. John and Amanda Morrill; [m.] Chad Walter Mayer, June 26, 1993; [ed.] B.A. Albion College, M.A. Candidate MSU, "Literacy Instruction"; [occ.] Elementary School Teacher with Logan Elem. (Detroit); [memb.] (CIS) Communities In Schools, (NCTE) National Council Teachers English, (SAA/COM) Student Auxillary Assoc. Osteopthic Medicine MSU, (MDRC) Metropolitan Detroit Reading Council; [hon.] Chairman of Various, Committees through Detroit Publics Logan Elementary; [oth. writ.] Poems published in "Dusting off Dreams" "Echoes of Silence" Quill Books.; [pers.] "My poetry reflects primarily on those close to my heart and soul."; [a.] Dearborn, MI

MAYS, FREDA M.
[b.] March 24, 1936, Kansas City, MO; [p.] Ferdinand D. and Ruth H. Brockington; [m.] Divorced; [ch.] Donald Birdwell, Brenda Smotherman 5; [ed.] Kansas City, Missouri Lincoln High School, Park College Grossmont College, La Mesa, CA Milwaukee Technical College, Milwaukee Wisconsin; [occ.] Retired/ Accounting; [memb.] International Society of Poets 1994-95, Queen of Sheba #19, Order of the Eastern Star; [oth. writ.] I have written a collage of poems, mostly true life experiences of my life and others. The poem that I have just submitted is regarding my mothers present situation. I like to reach others hearts and enhance awareness.; [pers.] I plan to write a collage of poems for publishing and plan to get my poems published in self help books and magazines.; [a.] El Cajon, CA

MAZZARA, ANTHONY S.
[pen.] Tony Mazzara; [b.] October 7, 1939, Brooklyn, NY; [p.] Frank and Lydia Mazzara; [m.] Lila M. Mazzara, November 24, 1973; [ed.] BA Economics, MS Labor Relations; [occ.] Retired NYCPD Lieutenant; [memb.] Police 10-13 Clubs, Disabled Police Officers Group; [hon.] National Dean's List 1982; [oth. writ.] Numerous published articles observing the political and social scene, including NY (NY Newsday) NY Forum piece describing how good men become corrupted cops. Led to books TV Movie (not by me) and changes in official attitude toward the corruptive process; [pers.] I write in order to broaden a perspective, to stimulate a humane act, or, to give pause to a hurtful behavior.; [a.] Boca Raton, FL

MCALLISTER, MARCIA
[pen.] Marcia McAllister; [b.] April 17, 1959; [p.] Merlin and Sylvia McAllister; [ed.] College Spring Community High School, College Rhema Bible Training Center; [occ.] Minister Missionary and baby sister. Just go and

back from Guatemala on a mission of our reach.; [memb.] Women a slow, Reb. Women; [hon.] Have one award in High School For Speech Contest.; [oth. writ.] This is my poem to to be published I am work on a children book to be published. Sometime soon.; [pers.] I believe it is importance to use the talent God give you. To bless other that what I have tried to do.; [a.] Farragut, IA

MCATEE, ROY L.
[b.] September 5, 1949, Covington, KY; [p.] Grace and Victor McAtee; [m.] Elizabeth Geary, July 26, 1980; [ch.] Emily Taylor, Nicholas James; [ed.] Newport Public High School, Northern Kentucky University, University of Cincinnati, The Union Institute, American Holistic College of Nutrition; [occ.] Technical Support, Cincinnati Beu Telephone, Cincinnati, Ohio; [memb.] Boy Scouts of America, Telephone Pioneers of America; [pers.] Sanity is the playground for the unimaginative... don't be afraid of the edge.; [a.] Cincinnati, OH

MCCAIN, HOWARD MITCHELL
[b.] August 5, 1935, Cleveland, MS; [p.] Howard McCain, Marguerite McCain (Deceased); [m.] Divorced - February 3, 1989, April 8 1967; [ch.] Dennis, Bonney, James; [ed.] B.S. Degree Civil Engineering, Miss. State University - 1957, B.S. Degree in Business Administration University of Southern Miss. 1962; [occ.] Employed by the U.S. Public Health Service; [memb.] Louisianna Engineering Society, American Society of Civil Engineers; [oth. writ.] Seven contributions to the reminiscences portion of: "Old Main-Images Of A Legend", Harmony House Publishers 502-228-2010, Library Of Congress Catalog No. 95-79213, Hard Cover Intern Standard Book No. 1-56469-018-8, First Edition Fall 1995, Copyright 1995 Ms. State University Alumni Association; [pers.] Words that rhythm delight the mind, through and through. But a poem must also be clear, and it might ring true.; [a.] Lafayette, LA

MCCALL, BULAH
[pen.] Beulah Messer; [b.] Ware Shoalds, SC; [p.] Lunia Messer, Gilbert Messer; [ch.] Donald Vance, Tammy Renae, Brannon J.; [ed.] Green Ville High.; [memb.] George's Creek Heights Church of God; [oth. writ.] Articles for Local Magazine Articles of Community Elem. School; [pers.] "The Autumn Must Be His," was written and dedicated in loving memory of my young niece, Tina and, for her parents, Nadine and Marvin Messer.; [a.] Greenville, SC

MCCANN, MICHELLE
[b.] February 17, 1950, Cleveland, OH; [p.] Michael Schobel, Doris Farinacci; [m.] Daniel McCann, October 19, 1973; [ch.] Michael, Kevin, Brianne, Mark, Scott; [ed.] Shaw High, Cleveland State Univ.; [occ.] Registered Nurse; [memb.] Aspo/ Lamaze, Icea, Ilca, Olca, Awhonn, Nann, Nola, Dona; [hon.] Sigma Theta Tau; [oth. writ.] Large personal collection of as yet unpublished poetry; [pers.] The art of self-expression through poetry. I wish to thank Mr. George Todd, my 11th grade English Teacher of so long ago for encouraging me to write.; [a.] Medina, OH

MCCLELLAN, REBECCA LEE
[pen.] Becky; [b.] July 6, 1980, Erie, PA; [p.] Michael and Lee McClellan; [ed.] Sophmore at Hillcrest High School - Honors Program; [occ.]

Student; [memb.] Hillcrest High School Varsity Softball Team - Catcher; [hon.] Beta Club "A" and "AB" Honor Rolls "National Merit Scholar"; [oth. writ.] "Grandpa" short story, "Lou Gehrig" poem, "I Am" poem, "The Homerun Cut" poem; [a.] Simpsonville, SC

MCCLURE, ETHEL L.
[b.] March 23, 1929, Charlestown, MA; [p.] Robert J. Davidson, Charline, Margarett; [m.] Robert T. McClure, October 28, 1948; [ch.] Three - Donna, Robert Jr., Lorretta; [ed.] To eleventh grade, Medford High School, Medford Mass., Durham Elementary School, Durham Maine; [occ.] I am terminal ill. I'm a volunteer reader to the second grade at the Durham Elementary School.; [oth. writ.] Have written other poems and many songs and children's stories. None published never did anything with them. I just love writing.; [pers.] Writing poetry songs, or children's stories. I always write poems exactly how I feel at the time. Also stories and songs.; [a.] Durham, MA

MCCOLLOM, BEU
[pen.] Muh Muh; [b.] Kirkland Lake; [p.] Deceased; [ch.] One - Jacqueline; [occ.] Retired GM, Trainer Brock University Hockey Team; [oth. writ.] All poems; [a.] Saint Catharines Ontario, Canada

MCCONNELL, RYAN
[pen.] Ryan McConnell; [b.] December 29, 1978, Lloydminster, Alberta, Canada; [p.] Malcolm and Alana McConnell; [ed.] Marshall School, Marshall Saskatchewan K-9 Llyodminster Comprehensive High School 10 - present currently attending grade 11; [memb.] Lloydminster Umpires Assoc., Lloydminster Judo Club, LCHS Barons Football; [oth. writ.] Many poems that I write are required in my grade 10 English class. Alot of my poems have no titles.; [pers.] I thank Ms. Francine Blyan for her extra effort in getting me started. Writing poems is a great way to express yourself.; [a.] Marshall Saskatchewan, Canada

MCCORMACK, LYNDA GRAHAM
[b.] September 18, 1941, Lewisburg, TN; [p.] Ms. Iroline Gipson Graham - J.B. Graham Jr. (Deceased); [m.] Rober Franklin McCormack (Deceased); [ch.] Robert C. McCormack, Chris G. McCormack; [ed.] Marshall Country High School - Lewisburg Tennessee. Attended Columbia Business College, Columbia, Tennessee.; [occ.] Retired from Faber Eberhard Lewisburg, Tennessee; [memb.] Westrue Church Christ-Lewisburg Tennessee; [hon.] A letter from Nr. Milton Berie is a prize possession. Nomination for Poet of the Year - 1995 International Society of Poets Selected to appear in the Best Poems of 1996. Poem published in Echoes to appear in Best Poems of the 90's. Poem published in Echoes of Yesterday Editors Choice Award - 1994, Award of Merit. 1990 world of Poetry Award of Merit - 1991. Poem published in at day's end. Golden Poet Award 1991 world or poetry - published Poem Modern Poetry Society 1996 Poems published in Heart and Home 1995 (Southern Christian Book); [oth. writ.] Poems published for Churches, loca l newspaper, Poems written for school paper selected to write the Senior Class will. Poetry written for 50th Weeding Anniversaries, Trib-

utes and Memorial.; [pers.] I feel it is a gift from God. My poetry comes from the heart. Writing poetry is part of my Heritage, for there were writer on both sides of my Families The Gipsons and the Graham's. I dearly Love to write Poetry. And Miss Florence Fitzpatrick, Mrs. Alfred Overholser, Teachers at Marshal Country High inspired me to "Press On."; [a.] Lewisburg, TN

MCCRURY, MARY HELEN
[b.] December 17, 1940, Lamesa, TX; [p.] Belland Dan Little; [m.] Darnell McCrury, August 24, 1958; [ch.] Michael, Shauna; [ed.] Ector High School, Sul Ross State University, University of the Permian Basin; [occ.] American History teacher - Nimitz Jr. High; [memb.] Delta Kappa Gamma Odessa Classroom Assoc. Nimitz Jr. High PTA; [oth. writ.] My writings have been for the enjoyment of my family, friends, and myself up to this print in my life.; [pers.] Traditions and beliefs held the generations of my family form the core of my stories and poems.

MCFARLAND, CAROLYN
[pen.] Carolyn McFarland; [b.] December 7, 1946, San Antonio, TX; [p.] Dorothy Brown, Gilbert Brown; [m.] Glenn E. McFarland, March 2, 1974; [ch.] Kerry, Kurtis, Kevin, Duane Chris; [ed.] Jefferson High School - San Antonio, TX, Sam Houston Univ. - B.S. Art Education; [occ.] CFS Dept. Specialist - Baroid Completion Fluid Services, Baroid Drilling Fluid Services - 17 years; [memb.] National Children's Cancer Foundation (5 years); [hon.] Cecil B. Sampson Award for Outstanding Service in Little League (2 years) Little League Volunteer of the Year Award (1 year). Involved in Little League for 18 years, including Tournaments and Play offs.; [oth. writ.] One poem published in "A Tapestry of Thoughts", one poem published in "Carvings in Stone".; [pers.] My poems are a special way of communicating thoughts and feelings.; [a.] Humble, TX

MCFARLANE, CHRISTINE
[b.] November 19, 1973, Winnipeg, Canada; [p.] Dr. Charles McFarlane; [ed.] I graduated from Kingsville District High School. Did four years of journalism print at college. I am going to be majoring in Psychology at University; [occ.] Student; [hon.] Editor's Choice Award for 1995 from National Library of Poetry, certificate from International Society of Poetry for 1995-1996; [oth. writ.] I wrote for school newspaper and wrote a poem and got published in Toronto, Ontario and Ann Arbor Michigan; [pers.] I strive to write straight from my heart, and reflect my innermost thoughts.; [a.] Windsor Ontario, Canada

MCGRATH, BRIAN J.
[b.] March 7, 1937, Sydney, NSW, Australia; [m.] Mary Una McGrath, March 31, 1964; [ch.] Mary Madeleine, Phillippa Margaret, Caitlin Una, Mairaed Llewella; [occ.] Lawyer Businessman; [memb.] Law Institute of Victoria (Australia); [pers.] Poetry for me is a hobby. It is a means of clarifying thoughts and recording feelings. Every one of my poems is a special memory, often I endeavour simply to capture and freeze a particular moment of experience.; [a.] Porto Heli, Greece

MCGREGOR, ANTOINETTE
[b.] October 19, 1933, Talladega, AL; [occ.] Retired Nurse; [pers.] I enjoy writing about the positive things in every day life. I enjoy writing positive verses, about my friends and giving these verses to them. It makes me feel good. Also the recipients of these verses.; [a.] Monongahela, PA

MCGUGAN, DON
[b.] March 17, 1973; [pers.] I've never quite adjusted to life on this planet... however, when the boredom junkies spat on me after I had lost my passport, I found there are at least some nostalgic moments.; [a.] Brampton Ontario, Canada

MCINTYRE, BILL
[b.] May 23, 1929, Lafayette, IN; [p.] Deceased; [m.] Dorothy Suttmiller, August 4, 1951; [ch.] Mike, Patty, Danny, Kathy; [ed.] Fowler High School, Fowler, Ind.; [occ.] Navy retiree - Part-time N.O. Steamship Co, New Orleans, LA; [memb.] Fleet Reserve Assoc. - Shetland Sheepdog Club; [oth. writ.] Poems and articles for Shetland Sheepdog Magazine; [pers.] Enjoy articles and poems in the humorous category.; [a.] New Orleans, LA

MCINTYRE SR., MAURICE
[b.] April 15, 1959, Brooklyn, NY; [p.] Mamie and William Knox; [m.] Tamera McIntyre, July 25, 1994; [ch.] Charleen, Maurice Jr., Doeneah, Sade, Jaboidia; [ed.] Martin Luther King High, Troy State University; [occ.] Postal Clerk, Wiesbaden Air Base Army Post Office, Germany; [hon.] Army Achievement Awards, Army Accommodation Awards, SW Asia Liberation Medal, Bronze Star, Overseas Service Ribbons, Physical Fitness Awards; [oth. writ.] Numerous unpublished poems.; [pers.] To fish in the river of knowledge which feeds our minds, hearts and souls. What not I do, only what am told. Forever flowing. Greatly inspired by Ralph Waldo Emerson and my beautiful wife, Tamera.; [a.] Philadelphia, PA

MCKAY, BEN
[b.] March 13, 1963, Halifax, NS; [p.] Ronald and Lena McKay; [oth. writ.] Brother Missed The Common Cold

MCKENZIE, AUDREY P.
[b.] December 26, 1937, Galt, Ontario, Canada; [p.] Charles and Helen Watson; [m.] Robert N. McKenzie, June 9, 1962; [ch.] Matt, Rob, Steven, John; [ed.] Galt Collegiate and Vocational School (G.C.I. and V.S.) Short Story and Journalism course, International Correspondence School (I.C.S.); [occ.] Part-time employee of Sobeys Grocery Store; [oth. writ.] None published; [pers.] As a non-published writer, winning a place as a semi-finalist and seeing my poem in print has given me great pleasure and bolstered my confidence to keep trying. You just never know, maybe, someday...; [a.] Cambridge Ontario, Canada

MCKENZIE, BERYL
[pen.] Anniebel Booth; [ch.] 1 Daughter; [ed.] Aberdeen High and Dip C. Ed. (merit prof subjects) teaching from age 20 as class teacher, French teacher, Music, A.H.T. (age 29) and D.H.T. pupils aged 4-11 (Nursery and Primary); [occ.] Song Writer and Ed. Book Rep.; [memb.] Scottish -

Helenic Soc, Interest, Ecology, Gardening, Scottish Heritage, Keyboard and Piano, Literature.; [oth. writ.] 'Anniebel Booth's Cameos D'Ecosse.' 10 songs of Scot, History incl. Melody, Notes etc, cassette tape 'Sense of Time' incl. and two sets of E.S. Songs for children - 1 Scottish, 1 intern at.; [pers.] As a busy D.H.T. I never had to time to write Music of poetry but often wished that this type of material was available. I am inspired by the Scottish Scenery Encouraged by Family and Motivated by love of language and music. (This is the first competition to be in the Final and now have the confidence to publish some of my other material.); [a.] Scotland, United Kingdom

MCKENZIE-KERR, RICHARD ALEXANDER
[pen.] Ram, R. Kerr; [b.] January 27, 1969, Ontario, Canada; [p.] James and Marie; [ed.] Chinguacousy High School, Sheridan College, York University; [occ.] Revenue Canada Mississauga District Office - Miss, ON; [oth. writ.] Sally-Jo, The Madison Pub and Tonight.; [pers.] I thank my parents and my brother Rob, for all their encouragement and support. This poem is dedicated to Amy Russell who set me on the road of creativity. Look for other great works/poems. By the simple Ivy known as Ram.; [a.] Bramalea Ontario, Canada

MCKINNEY JR., WILLIE
[pen.] Will-Ken; [b.] October 8, 1945, Texas; [p.] Willie and Martha M. McKinney; [ch.] Rochea A., B. McKinney, Lawrence J. T. McKinney and Qiana A. McKinney; [ed.] B.S., B.A. Degree, Suffolk Univ. Roxbury Community College, A.A. Degree, New England Conservatory of Music, Northeastern University Courses; [occ.] Engineering payroll, MBTA, Boston; [memb.] Rapid Investment (RIP), Partners, We Can N.I. Revelation Baptist Church, Father's Day, Mother's Day Message, Publicity Assoc. of MA, CDC Assoc., NAACP, Heart Assoc., United Way; [hon.] Roxbury Community College, 2nd Place Trophy Body Building, Gerard Duchaney Road Race, Medal - 1995, Member, Site Council, English High School (oldest Public High School In America), National of Poetry, Editor's Choice Awards - 1994, International Society of Poets, Distinguish Member, International Poet of Merit Award - 1995, Tufts Health Plan, on my own time Special Recognition for help us to Save the Children - 1995. Office of Economic Opportunity, Outstanding Achievement for Community Service, Roxbury Community College - First Chairman of College Screening Committee in the History of Community College System and First President of Student Government Association, Senatorial, Commonwealth of MA, Senate, Engineering and Maintenance, Employee of the Year 1995, Massachusetts Bay Transportation Authority Guest Speakers, 2nd Annual Black History Month Celebration; [oth. Writ.] United Together We Stand As One, My God, A Taste Of Love, Rise To The Challenge, A Special Message To My Son, My Whole World Is Falling Apart.; [pers.] I love by the belief that God is my greatest inspiration. It is through him that I have gained my ability to write poetry, because of that strong bond, I feel that I have the strength to endure that which I can't cure. My goal is to inspire the nation and reach people of all ages and nationalities and create a lasting memory in their minds. I write about life, relationships and reality, which all too opted

reflect the pursuit of, Truth, Citizenship, Education and encouragement in all endeavor of life.

MCLAUGHUN, DOUGLAS
[b.] November 21, 1971, Portland, ME; [p.] Janice and James; [ed.] Falmouth High School; [occ.] Server; [pers.] Poetry is the main tool in my struggle against not only the hypocrisy and injustice of our world, but also the struggle against personal anguish and confusion - literary therapy.; [a.] Portland, ME

MCMILLAN, CHARLOTTE P.
[b.] January 24, 1953, Knoxville, TN; [p.] Frank B. and Charlotte B. Potts; [m.] Wesley H. McMillan, July 1, 1988; [ch.] Cody A. (step-son); [ed.] Medical Laboratory, Technician; [occ.] Radio Chemistry Analyst; [oth. writ.] Poems for personal pleasure and published in school newspapers.; [pers.] True love backed by the power of God will conquer all.; [a.] Clinton, TN

MCMILLON, SUSAN
[b.] March 14, 1952, Pasadena, TX; [p.] James W. Cobb, Betty Cobb; [m.] Richard McMillon, September 27, 1975; [ch.] Robin Adele and Colleen Denise; [ed.] Pasadena High, San Jacinto College; [occ.] Homemaker; [pers.] My writing is moved by the intensity and complexity of the relationships that guide and govern man and nature.; [a.] Dayton, TX

MCNAMARA, ELEANOR
[b.] Fredericksburg, IA; [p.] Edwin and Lucille Spinden; [ch.] Michelle Smith, Michelle Gloeb; [ed.] Paradise Valley College; [occ.] Executive Director, American Institute of Architects of Georgia (AIA/GA); [memb.] Honorary AIA Member, served on National Board of Directors of AIA 1992, Advisory Board 1991-92 to Arizona's Office of Americans with Disabilities, Advisory Council of College of Architecture, Georgia Tech., Board of Directors Arizona Girl Scouts Hosting Committee Fiesta Bowl; [hon.] Honorary AIA (National), Award of distinction, Western Mt Region of AIA, National AIA Service Award, Listed in "Who's Who of American Business Leaders," "Foremost Women in Communication," "Notable American Women."; [oth. writ.] Author, Editor, Publisher of Arizona Architecture magazine, managing editor of Charles City Daily Press, Iowa, Free Lance Writer; [pers.] My writings express where I am in my life. Feelings are what direct my creativity.; [a.] Atlanta, GA

MCNEIL, DEBORAH LEE
[b.] January 11, 1968, Stuttgart, Germany; [p.] John and Geraldine Crain; [m.] Collin W. McNeil, June 28, 1986; [ch.] Christopher, Jonathon, Matthew; [ed.] Eisenhower High, Lawton, Oklahoma, Graduated 1986; [occ.] Student - Skagit Valley College, Mount Vernon, WA; [pers.] My inspiration comes from the love and encouragement of my family, especially the man who reminds me everyday what laughing, loving, and living are all about.; [a.] Sedro Woolley, WA

MCNEILL, ETHEL L.
[b.] July 10, 1910, Halifax, Nova Scotia, Canada; [p.] Ethel MacKintosh, William A. Dee; [m.]

George S. McNeill, April 18, 1934; [ch.] 1 Boy-George William; [ed.] High School Ethel Traphagen NYC School of Design, Human Relations - Night School; [occ.] Retired; [memb.] Afraid none; [hon.] Afraid none this is my first time. Could not believe I heard from you.; [oth. writ.] Have other poems have never entered anything before. My brother who was a printer, put some together which, I've been doing since 1931.; [pers.] Been active in school all the time my son was in school. Pres. of PTA worked in Hospitals as volunteer have been trying to write a book "Grandma's Were Young Once" but haven't done much so far.; [a.] Naples, FL

MCPHERSON, CHRIS
[b.] October 9, 1976, Cochrane, Ontario, Canada; [ed.] Grade 11 at Ecole Secondaire Cochrane High School; [occ.] Student, Security Guard, Bouncer; [memb.] Glad Tidings Pentecostal Church Cochrane Ont., Morning Star Ministries Iroquois Falls Ont; [hon.] Class Proficiency Award; [pers.] I usually write based on my emotions. However, lately, much of my writing has been inspired by two people who are very important to me. Jesus Christ, my Lord and Saviour, and Mary Nijp, my best friend.; [a.] Cochrane Ontario, Canada

MEDINA, RENI
[b.] August 17, 1977, Rota, Spain; [p.] Lexie R. Medina, Jay R. Medina; [oth. writ.] No other published writings, so far.; [pers.] I try to reflect real human feelings and reactions in my writings. I have been inspired by my own personal experiences.; [a.] Prunedale, CA

MEDVEDEV, ALEX
[pen.] Alex, Medvedev; [b.] November 16, 1952, Perm Reg, Russia; [p.] Maria Medvedev, Aleksey Medvedev; [m.] Tamara Medvedev, November 14, 1980; [ch.] Sergey Medvedev; [ed.] Sankt - Petersburg's Marine Academy Russia; [occ.] Radio - Officer; [pers.] English to all people!; [a.] Riga Latvia, Russia

MEEHL, MARLENE HYATT
[b.] November 6, 1940, Faribault, MN; [p.] Louis Hyatt and Mildred Hyatt; [m.] Charles Meehl, September 3, 1979; [ed.] Faribault High School St. Cloud University - Minnesota Dean's List; [occ.] Taxi Dispatcher - 1960-1979, Triplex Owner and LandLord Since 1967; [memb.] Faribault Eagles Auxiliary; [oth. writ.] "I'd be a flag" published in the Faribault Daily News in Honor of Pearl Harbor Day.; [pers.] The ending stanza of my poem "Tale of the Troubadour" is my believe Kingdom's are for kings, riches are for fools, the man who sings owns happy things and those are what he rules.; [a.] Faribault, MN

MEEKS, DENISE F.
[b.] August 23, 1963, Manhatten, NY; [p.] James H. and Mary Allen; [m.] Divorced; [ed.] I have a B.A. in Anthropology from the University of Tulsa, and I will be obtaining my Master's degree in Anthropology from The University of Tulsa in May 1996; [occ.] I work part-time as a Sales-Clerk in Retail.; [memb.] I am a member of the University of Tulsa Anthropology Club and of the Oklahoma Anthropological Society.; [hon.] Two of my poems received Honorable Mention Awards in the National College Poetry Contest in the Fall of

1995. President's and Dean's List at Tulsa Junior College.; [oth. writ.] I had two poems published in the American Collegiate Poets Anthology. Three other poems of mine were published in the Tulsa Junior College Student Anthology.; [pers.] Since I was a child, I have had a love affair with writing. I especially enjoy poetry, because I believe it allows one to express one's feelings and touch others in a most freely, creative literary venue. My favorite poets are W. B. Yeats and Sylvia Plath.; [a.] Broken Arrow, OK

MEGLIC, WILLIAM
[pen.] Vilko; [b.] April 13, 1972, Saint Thomas, Ontario, Canada; [p.] Joe Meglic, Katica Meglic; [ed.] St. Joseph's H.S., St. Thomas Ont Centennial College, Toronto Ont, Northwood University, Midland Mi, Fanshawe College, London Ont; [memb.] American Advertising Federation Knights of Columbus; [hon.] Dean's List, Cum Laude, Barrie Foundation Award; [pers.] It is noble to be superior over other men, the true nobility comes in being superior to your previous self. To my family who has helped me through so much - thank you.; [a.] Saint Thomas Ontario, Canada

MEIER, JOSHUA
[b.] March 7, 1977, Iowa City, IA; [p.] Jeff and Vickie Meier; [ed.] Tipton High School, Kirkwood Community College; [occ.] Full time student, part time grocery store stocker; [memb.] United Church of Christ; [pers.] I am greatly inspired by the lyrical genius of songwriters such as John Lennon, Jim Morrison, and perhaps most of all, Kurt Cobain. Although these men have left us, their music will live forever.; [a.] Tipton, IA

MENTE, MARK
[b.] March 17, 1957, Milwaukee, WI; [p.] Gordon Mente, Shirley Mente; [ch.] Miranda Jo, Andrew Patrick; [ed.] High School Grad., James Madison High, Milw; [occ.] Carpenter; [pers.] This poem was written for my current fiancee Dr. Laurie Boeten.

MERRITT, JEFFREY L.
[pen.] Jeff Merritt; [b.] October 1, 1962, Winchester, TN; [p.] J. F. Merritt Jr, Louise G. Merritt; [m.] Single; [ed.] Franklin Co. High; [occ.] Bill Collector; [memb.] Franklin Co. Republicans member of Franklin Co. Friends of the Library; [a.] Decherd, TN

MERRYMAN, BETTY J.
[b.] March 24, 1935, Wash., DC; [p.] Harry G. Merryman and Dorothy L. Merryman; [ed.] RN, Univ. MD, CRNA The Johns Hopkins Hospital, BA Interamerican Univ. MA Education, NYU; [occ.] Acute Psychiatric RN, VAMC, Reno, NV; [memb.] Sierra NV Celtic Society, U.S. Taekwondo Union.; [hon.] BA, MA are Summa Cum Laude; [oth. writ.] Articles in martial arts magazines, newspaper articles, poetry and short stories.; [pers.] Meditation and martial art training equal inner peace and outer calm.; [a.] Reno, NV

METZLER, BRENDA
[pen.] Brenda Lee; [b.] October 31, 1964, Kingston, Ontario, Canada; [p.] Linda Hosford, Donald Boomhawer; [m.] George Metzler, August 31, 1991; [ed.] Grade 10 at BCIUS, Belleville, On

Business Management, ICS, Montreal, QC Geriatric Care, NA, Panorama, Calgary, AB; [oth. writ.] Several poems. Nothing published before this.; [pers.] "I learned something early in life," "There are two great times of happiness - when you are haunted by a dream, and when you realize it. Between the two there's a strong urge to let it all drop. But you have to follow your dreams to the end.; [a.] Calgary Alberta, Canada

MEYER, CORY D.
[b.] February 18, 1976, San Jose, CA; [p.] Charles E. and Karen A. Meyer; [ed.] Presently a sophomore of Xavier University in Cincinnati. I attended Cathedral High School in Indianapolis as well.; [occ.] Employed by Cork W. Bottle in Newport Ky, but I will be transferring employment to Kings Island in Ohio; [memb.] Big Brother - Xavier University, National Wildlife Foundation, International Thespian Society, Children International Sponsorship Group, Delta Sigma Pi - Business Fraternity Xavier University; [hon.] Delta Sigma Pi - elected U.P. of Chapter operations. Also I had an article written about me in the Xavier Publication of Excerpts about the Big Brother Little Brother experiences.; [oth. writ.] Mainly I write to pass time and reflect on my feelings. Writing gives me a chance to step outside of myself and let my thoughts soar. I take this extra time and I have to write as medicine for the soul.; [pers.] My life has been a cinderella story... Each day I thank God for the many blessings he has given me. My parents, my friends and the less fortunate, all give me the inspiration to write poetry.; [a.] Cincinnati, OH

MEYER JR., NEFERTITI LOUIZA FLAMA
[pen.] Tribal Princess N. L. Flama Meyer of Bassa Tribe - Rivercess Liberia; [b.] April 9, 1946, Monrovia, West Africa; [p.] Ambassador George and Victoria Flama Sherman Sr.; [m.] Pastor Bishop Felix Meyer Jr., March 15; [ch.] Mictivic-Misheal and Lanla Mona Lisa (daughter), 1 son drowned - 1988 Liberia-Raphael.; [ed.] British Pan-African Graduate Briston and London Royal Academy, Theatre Dramatic Arts and music, Fine Arts Degree, L.R.A.D.A., during parent Globe-trotting assignments. On 3 continents, while attending Drama College Bristol (England), won many awards for "Elocution" Mime public speech... while in college. Starred as 1st African actress "Elina" in BBC 11 '68 1st TV movie "Wind Versus Polygamy" with 3 sisters "Flama Sherman Out.; [occ.] Worked as 1st black artist at Beatles Apple Music. Busy wife of Minister, mother... desires to finally published "long held" poems, short stories - seeks publisher, agent to publish plays, novels... left on "Back burner"... for years).; [memb.] For religious reasons is only member of "Church" but is actively as "Humanitarian" donator to many (involved), worthy causes ie: Red cross, good will, TBN, relief UN projects. Founded "Awareness Platform: for war refugees of Liberia. Produced, created many community projects from Hollywood to Texas.; [hon.] Winning official endorsements from city mayors, 1978 - Mayor Bradley, LA, 1992 - Mayor Lanier, Houston, Mary Ron Kirk, Dallas 1995 and Governor Bush - 1995, for successfully creating producing "God Bless Liberia Awareness Platform" raising "awareness" of media-forgotten war refugee plights.. for a nation founded in 1822 by freed USA slaves with closest

historic links to USA. Founded "Young Friends of Africa" Cultural and Theatre in 1980 Hollywood based. Often invited to lecture in public schs. Black History, and erasing "Stereo-types" Libraries, sings as solo in many churches, while husband speaks - daughter plays clarinet (Misheal).; [oth. writ.] "Santa Goes to Africa!", Youth Musical (Produced) yet to publish WK, wrote joint-songs with Sisters in Europe, "Move Me", "Super Day", "Where is He" in Europe. Have my solo work awaiting. "Afrika... Make War!", "Bassa Love" record '68, recording, singer, produced release 1979. Currently working on screen play (which she hopes will enhance race relations), "Spiritual Afrikan Truthodessey" seeks agent and publisher.; [pers.] "I trust my "God given works will enlighten readers... to soar above racism. Tribalism, and all forms of prejudices. I have also experienced all forms of during my travels from girlhood to womanhood on three continents. All people... same emotions... and all people have contributed to humanity... with "Godly knowledge and balance research in educating ourselves we will look at life with a third "Spiritual eye of faith" and with greater respect and appreciation. I hope my work reflects that spirit to "bless" and help uplift readers globally.

MEYEROWITZ, HELENE JOYCE
[b.] September 11, 1943, Bronx, NY; [p.] Ida Meyerowitz and Oscar Meyerowitz; [m.] George S. Ward, June 15, 1986; [ch.] David Everett Sheridan; [ed.] Wm. H. Taft High School, Bronx, NY, B.A. Hunter College, N.Y., M.A. Univ. of Maine; [occ.] Elementary Teacher, Warren, Maine; [memb.] NEA (Nat'l. Education Assn.); [pers.] Fear and faith together cannot live in the same house.; [a.] Rockland, ME

MICHAEL, SHERRI MARTIN
[b.] March 11, 1958, Wadsworth, OH; [p.] Theodore O. Martin Jr. and Chloeta F. Martin; [m.] Douglas Michael, August 31, 1990; [ch.] Savanna Fay, Stepsons: Aaron, Jason, Ryan; [ed.] B.S. Sociology - Univ. of Akron, Akron, Ohio, Juris Doctor, Univ. of Akron, School of Law; [occ.] Homemaker, Atty at Law; [a.] Canton, OH

MIDDEN, ERICA
[b.] October 26, 1979, Columbus, OH; [p.] Mike and Laurie Cateriny; [ed.] A tenth grader at DeLand High; [occ.] Student; [memb.] Beta Club, Juniorettes, Basketball team, Softball team; [hon.] I've received many athletic and academic awards; [oth. writ.] I have had no other writings published before; [pers.] To achieve we must dream, and to dream we must stay focused.; [a.] Orange City, FL

MIGUEL, REMEDIOS V.
[pen.] Cecilia (In honor of St. Cecilia whose feast is Nov. 22); [b.] November 22, 1924, Honolulu, HI; [p.] Saturnino Villanueva (Father), Basilisa Miguel (Mother); [m.] Segundo A. Miguel, April 2, 1965; [ed.] Graduate in Nursing in UP-PGH 1950, (Philippine General Hospital - University of the Philippines School of Nursing); [occ.] Retired Registered Nurse from Youth Guidance Med. Clinic; [memb.] 1.) Retired Employees of the City and County of San Francisco, 2.) University of the Philippine Nurses Assn. of Northern California; [oth. writ.] 1.) My Mother's Hands appeared in "The Guide" official organ of St. William's College

under the Fathers of the Divine Word, 2.) Prayer for friends, 3.) June, 4.) Lines to the Athletic Meet; [pers.] I strive to reflect and promote the moral and spiritual values of the youth, mostly by prayers and distributing prayer cards and pamphlets to parents and the youth, also by meditation.; [a.] San Francisco, CA

MILES, GLENN ANTHONY
[pen.] Bolt Freeman; [b.] February 8, 1944, Louisville, KY; [p.] William Ross Miles Jr., Anita Mae Miles; [m.] Divorced; [ch.] Glenda, Annette, Lynnette, Denise, Eric; [ed.] Bachelor of Arts (Pscychology) Calif. State Univ., Domingues Hills; [occ.] Photographer "Miles Smiles" Social Worker - Seven Counties/Photography Consulting Svc.; [memb.] Veterans of foreign wars, Telephone Co. Pioneers, Louisville Urban League, Yearlings - Men Club, Muay Thai Assoc. of America; [hon.] Honorable Discharge - U.S. Navy Vietnam Vet. Retired Manager Pacific Bell Telephone Co.; [oth. writ.] "The Ball"; [pers.] "To know me is the love me", is the spirit of brotherly love that I want my writings to reflect.; [a.] Louisville, KY

MILLARD, LORIN BLAIR
[b.] November 9, 1969, Elgin, IL; [p.] Darrell and Marjorie Millard; [ed.] University of Wisconsin - Whitewater Disney University; [occ.] Student, Field Representative, and Sales Representative; [memb.] Delta Chi Fraternity (AX), Mathematics Association of America (MAA), APICS; [hon.] Ray Kroc Award, Badger Boys State, "Ducktorate" degree from Walt Disney World; [pers.] Education is more than just academics. There is no adequate substitute for travel experiences. Some things must be experienced first hand.; [a.] Whitewater, WI

MILLER, BYRON W.
[pen.] Lyrical Byron; [b.] September 14, 1952, Baltimore, MD; [p.] Shirley and Marvin Miller; [m.] Rose Mary Miller, November 11, 1992; [ch.] Byron II, Ahmad, Kesha, Davina; [ed.] Admiral King High International Correspondence Schools - VCR and TV Repair; [occ.] U.S. Army Retired McQueary Drugs Warehouse; [hon.] Army Commedation Medal, Army Achievement Meadal, Army Good Conduct Medal, NCO Professional Development Ribbon Army Service Ribbon Overseas Service Ribbon; [oth. writ.] Poetry for my wife and mother, wife is my biggest inspiration and Critic; [pers.] Poems are for the lovers of life and the spirit to be free! And to be enjoyed by lovers of life, like you and me!; [a.] Springfield, MO

MILLETT, KAREN MCGLADE
[b.] December 31, 1968, Havertown, PA; [p.] William and Elizabeth McGlade; [s.] Robert J. Millett; [m.] November 7, 1992; [ch.] Thomas James Millett and one on the way; [ed.] Haverford High; [occ.] Secretary, Shelvin Financial Broomall, PA; [oth. writ.] "Happy first birthday my precious son" in The Best Poems of the 90's, also published by The National Library of Poetry.; [pers.] "My poetry comes from the heart and reflects some of my life's experiences. This piece is dedicated in memory of Kef, Handy, and all my other friends and family who are gone, but not forgotten."; [a.] Drexel Hill, PA

MILLS, PATRICK JOHN
[b.] November 4, Saint Jerome; [p.] June and John Mills; [ed.] Vancouver College, Concordia University B.A.; [occ.] Painter; [hon.] Editor's Choice Award, Best Poems of 1996; [oth. writ.] Several poems published.; [pers.] To my mother, June Viola Mills and in memory of my father, John Henry Mills. I love you always and forever - Patrick.; [a.] Montreal, Canada

MILLS, SHANNON
[b.] January 15, 1974, Lansing, MI; [p.] Mr. and Mrs. Donald Milliman; [m.] Ted Mills, January 20, 1990; [ch.] Kevin Mills - James Mills; [ed.] I am working on my G.E.D. Eaton Rapids Public schools; [occ.] House wife and mother; [oth. writ.] Emotions, Confusion, Fear From Beer, End Surfing, Blank Pages, Grandma, Poverty and many others that have not be published.; [per.] We must find peace within our self's to be able to find true happiness, I am still looking.; [a.] Lyons, MI

MINARD, JOYCE
[b.] Yorkshire, England; [m.] Cy Minard, September 20, 1969; [ch.] Diane, Fiona and Brett, (Step children) Roger and Sheila; [occ.] Retired, Telecommunications, Investigator; [memb.] Diabetic Society, Square Dance Association N.L.P.; [hon.] Friends of City Hall, Volunteer Award; [oth. writ.] Poem "Felines" published in "Sparkles in the sand" I.S.P. 1995 Square Dance Magazine, Friends of City Hall Newsletter.; [pers.] I write what I feel deeply, drawing from life experiences. Love early poets - Shelley Byron, Longfellow, traditional poetry.; [a.] Edmonton Alberta, Canada

MINARDI-PETTERSEN, CARA
[b.] Hartford, CT; [occ.] Writer, Student; [memb.] International Women's Writing Guild (Member); [pers.] My writing attempts to reach those in search of peace, as I am.; [a.] Boston, MA

MINER, RICHARD E.
[pen.] Rem; [b.] August 19, 1928, Springfield, MA; [p.] Charles and Marion Miner; [m.] Divorced; [ch.] Craig, Susan, Jeffrey; [ed.] Stochbridge School, Univ. of Mass.; [occ.] Retired, former occup. 25 years sales (On the Road); [memb.] Disabled American Veterans Life Member. CT Veterans Affairs Medical Ctr. Wittareu, CT Golden Age Olympic games from Member; [hon.] U.S. Service Medal, U.N. Service Medal, Korean War Service Medal, 2nd Div. U.S. M.C. Presidential Unit and Citation Salutatorian Class of 1954 Univ. of M.A. (Stockbridge School); [oth. writ.] The following poems "The Cowpoke", "Tony", "The Old Ballgame" and "Growing Up Fears"; [pers.] I have been in the theatre, and writing. Nowhere can, I believe, one get the deepest satisfaction than that which writing brings. It's a trip through life I wouldn't want to miss.; [a.] Hamden, CT

MINES, MARY SUSAN KIM BELAIR
[pen.] Kim Mines; [b.] September 29, 1979, Montreal, Canada; [p.] Yves Belair, Lynn Gale, Step father - Neville Mines; [ed.] Martin Belanger, Montreal Lyne and Longcress of E primary school, St. Anns Heath, Virginia Water, Surrey, Charters, Berkshire; [occ.] Student; [hon.] Commended by WH Smith Young Writers Competition and gave a reading in an Arts park both from the same person.; [oth. writ.] I have only just started to enter my poems.; [pers.] I do my best in everything I do, and if people cannot see the determination in my work than it is they who are the failures.; [a.] Warfield Berkshire, United Kingdom

MINES, ROSETTE
[b.] April 1, 1929, Brooklyn, NY; [p.] Samuel and Esther; [occ.] Own Bus. Cust. Serv. Inc. Printers; [memb.] Artist League of Brooklyn; [hon.] Artist League of Brooklyn sold two paintings one in a private collectors, Falling Honorable Mention World of Poetry National Library of Poetry Editors Choice; [oth. writ.] Poetic Eloquence, Feelings Magazine, Armondillo Poetry Press Poetry Motel; [pers.] Creating through writing or painting in my love sensing life, feeling air nature people bowling music the summary's being part of life.; [a.] New York, NY

MINGER, MICHAEL F.
[pen.] Michael F. Minger; [b.] December 28, 1956, Three Rivers, MI; [m.] Julie; [ch.] Adam, Nick, Ryan, Joshua; [pers.] My words are most influenced by Edgar a. Guest. A simple mans poet.

MIRANDA, JESUS
[b.] October 17, 1969, San Benito, TX; [p.] Juan and Maria Victoria Miranda; [ed.] Harlingen High School; [occ.] Section Coordinator Specialist; [oth. writ.] Currently working on concluding my first novel.; [pers.] Live life not as victim but instead as a survivor.; [a.] Dallas, TX

MITCHELL, DEBBIE
[pen.] Maliea Jorolan; [b.] May 21, 1979, Twentynine Palms Base Marine; [p.] Ron and Bonnie Mitchell; [ed.] Yucaipa High School; [occ.] Student/Day Care Worker; [memb.] Madrigals, Swimming Team, Church Youth Groups; [hon.] Golden State Exam. (Algebra) Varsity Letter Swimming; [pers.] I try to challenge people to think and see other perspectives than their own E.V. has been an enormous influence. Thank you.; [a.] Yucaipa, CA

MITCHELL, SANDRA F.
[b.] April 12, 1951, Dade City, FL; [p.] Mr. Chester Martin, Mrs. Ridenour; [m.] John A. Mitchell, June 23, 1979; [ch.] Julie and George (step-children), Christina and Victoria (step grandchildren); [ed.] HS Diploma from Halton HS Fort Worth TX, Associated Degree from East Mississippi Junior College; [occ.] Retiree, USAF Technical Sgt. Domestic Home Manager; [memb.] Ladies Auxiliary (VFW); [hon.] I have received Numerous Awards and Decorations during my Air Force Career.; [oth. writ.] The poem, "Prickly Pear" in A Delicate Balance.; [pers.] I seek to honor the code of the USAF Sgt. which is Duty Honor, country and the most important being love of God and family.; [a.] Columbus, MS

MITSKO, SHIRLEY A.
[b.] October 18, 1948, New London, CT; [p.] John and Lillian Gavaletz; [m.] Wayne E. Mitsko, April 27, 1968; [ch.] Scott R. Mitsko; [ed.] Waterford High school, New London Academy of Hairdressing, New York Botanical Garden, University of Hawaii, University of Connecticut; [occ.] Garden Center staff; [memb.] CT. Assoc. of Extension Master Gardeners, CT. Horticultural Society, National Trust for Historic Preservation; [hon.] U.S. Army Spouse award, U. of HI Master Gardener; [oth. writ.] One poem published in Community Newsletter; [pers.] Poems inspired by people and events in my life.; [a.] Groton, CT

MOCCIA, MS. MARIA
[b.] June 5, 1964, Hamilton, Ontario, Canada; [ed.] Sheridan College, York University; [occ.] English as a Second Language Instructor for Immigrants and Refugees.; [oth. writ.] Local Newspaper Columns, Newsletters, Articles for Local Newspapers.; [pers.] My writing is a reflection of the souls who have in some way, touched my life. Especially one, who was my bear on of hope - who gave me the strength to continue my journey.; [a.] Burlington Ontario, Canada

MOERKE, MEGAN
[b.] July 11, 1981, Fond du Lac, WI; [p.] Steven and Kristi Moerke; [hon.] United States Achievement Academy Awards, English, All-American, and National Leadership and Service Awards, First in National Word Masters Competitions, Iowa Scholar in Iowa Talent Search; [oth. writ.] Local Anthologies and Newspapers have printed my poems and short stories.; [pers.] Some people complain about roses having thorns - I think the thorns are lucky to have the roses.; [a.] Bettendorf, IA

MOERSCHEL, BLANCHE
[b.] December 2, 1915, Oak Park, IL; [p.] Henry, Estelle Hollnagel; [m.] Eugene Moerschel, April 17, 1943; [ch.] Richard, Paul, Eugene, Daniel, and Joel; [ed.] Oak Park High, Oberlin Conservatory, Cosmopolitan Sch. of Music, Chi. Musical College, U. of W. St. Point, WI Bach. of music in composition and piano; [occ.] Piano Teacher - Private; [memb.] N.M.T.A. Wis. Alliance of Composers; [oth. writ.] Book of poetry - some published in the New Creation Magazine.; [pers.] "When all things shall be subdued unto him, then shall the son also himself be subject unto him that put all things under him, that God may be all in all." 1 Corinthians 15:28 Maranatha! The Lord Cometh! Excelsior!; [a.] Waupaca, WI

MOLINARI, VICTORIA A.
[b.] August 14, 1945, Brooklyn, NY; [p.] Charles and Florence Marcellino; [m.] Michael Molinari, August 3, 1968; [ch.] Michael and Mark; [ed.] Mt. Vernon Hospital School of Nursing, Mt. Vernon, New York; [occ.] School Nurse for Multiply-Handicapped Children; [memb.] New York State School Nurse Associations, American School Health Association; [oth. writ.] Several poems and short stories.; [pers.] I tend to write about personal experience, often reflecting on the mysteries of life.; [a.] Staten Island, NY

MONCADA, IDANIA
[b.] October 28, 1977, Managua, Nicaragua; [p.] Olgarivera, Carlos Moncada; [ed.] Andrew Jackson Elem., Douglas Elem., Henry M. Flager Elem., Kinloch Park Middle School, Coral Cables Sr. High/South Miami Sr. High; [occ.] Student/Host; [memb.] F.B.L.A. Member Future Business Leaders of America; [hon.] Citizenship Award Outstanding (1 plaque), Contribution and Achievement, 2 plaques of each.; [pers.] My poetry is a reflection of my

soul and mind. I write of my own experiences and feelings of life. Thank you Hiram of your inspiration and encouragement.; [a.] Miami, FL

MONDI, NEALIE R.
[pen.] Nealie R. Mondi; [b.] May 24, 1970, Greenville, PA; [p.] Raymond and Susan Peterson; [m.] Frank T. Mondi Jr., September 12, 1993; [ch.] Thomas A., Bradley J., Logan R.; [ed.] Pope John Paul II High School Palm Bch. County Community College Indianna University of PA ICS - Master Art; [occ.] Freelance Artist; [memb.] Christian Coalition, North Shore Animal League; [oth. writ.] Letter published in Valley News Dispatch; [pers.] There is beauty in everything if you just take a moment to look. Always let the Lord lead you and you will never be lost.; [a.] Ford City, PA

MONTEL, MAX-JOSEPH
[b.] May 13, 1979, New York City, NY; [p.] Michael J. Montel, Jane Montel; [ed.] Ethical Culture Fieldston School (currently in Junior Year of High School); [occ.] Student; [memb.] Sierra Club, USTA - US Tennis Assoc., Organic USA, Fieldston Dance Company, Fieldston Cross Country Team; [oth. writ.] Various unpublished short stories.; [pers.] Without fiction, how can we see the truth?; [a.] New York, NY

MONTY, MICHELLE
[pen.] Miranda Blake; [b.] Norwich, CT; [p.] Agnes and Francis Le Page; [m.] Karl A. Monty, January 3, 1991; [ch.] Adam Anthony; [ed.] Mohegan College; [occ.] Personnel Manager Norrell Services; [hon.] Graduated Phi Theta Kappa, appointed to Dean's list; [oth. writ.] Several articles based on past experience, also short humorous stories. Currently writing a children's book.; [pers.] It is my opinion that all writing regardless of its nature should be a passionate journey of discovery.; [a.] Preston, CT

MOORE, DEANNE
[b.] August 29, 1954, Topeka, KS; [pers.] I tell a story of we experiences in what I write. From discontent to relation, a life time journey of the self. I wish to reach others who are struggling to final their way.; [a.] Dallas, TX

MOORE, ELAINE MARIE
[pen.] Elaine Marie Moore; [b.] February 9, 1935, Polo, IL; [p.] George F. and Urith G. Bunnell Wagner; [m.] Barker Douglas Moore, March 3, 1967; [ch.] Three and six stepchildren; [ed.] Graduated Minister; [occ.] I am employed by Walmart - right now Test Scanner; [memb.] Member of Moose Club Kissemmee FL; [hon.] The only honor I have is getting to know you lovely people. To me that's an award - Thank you and God Bless you; [oth. writ.] I write poetry and songs. But never published any till now.; [pers.] I think that reading poetry and writing it opens a very special part of people that they really do not know they possess.; [a.] Kissimmee, FL

MOORE JR., ROBERT JAMES
[pen.] Romeo, Bug, and Coach; [b.] May 22, 1957, Gastonia NC; [p.] Robert and Shirley; [ed.] C.P.C.C. For High School Completion, From Jesus Christ above not in that order of course.; [occ.] Machine Operator In A Plastic Plant; [memb.] Bible Way Holiness Church, P.A.L. Football League, and in heaven. Our Father Jesus Christ makes me and all of his Saints winners just like him, and I pray for the unsaved people.; [hon.] When I was 13 years old, I was on two championships basketball teams, the Saturday Morning League and the Classroom Championship. P.A.L. Asst. Coach Awards, In 1981 I was saved and Sanctified; [oth. writ.] All of my Love letters to my lady friends, none published even though they wanted me too? When I was ten years old I wrote a letter that made my grandmother cry. Jesus Christ gave me this gift and talent of expressing love to all his creation.; [pers.] In today's generation most men fail to realize how special women are, and I just wanted to bring that out in my poem. All women are angels. If you don't think, so, try to live without one for a long period of time.; [a.] Charlotte, NC

MOORHOUSE, PEARL E.
[pen.] E. P. or Elizabeth Pearl; [b.] September 6, 1917, Alberta, Canada; [ed.] Regular Schooling. Norman Rockwell School of Fine Arts; [occ.] Retired; [memb.] F.C.A. is the Federation of Canadian Artists, also, a Craftsman and Amateur Poetess; [hon.] 2 (two) scholarships from the International School of Fine Arts; [oth. writ.] By the way, I have a number of filler poems, if you should require them.

MORENO, CHERYL C.
[pen.] Cheryl C. Moreno; [b.] October 18, 1955, Long Beach; [p.] William and Deloris Sullivan; [m.] Eddle Moreno, September 28, 1985; [ch.] Robert and David Morgan; [ed.] Grad. Rancho Alamitos - Garden Grove, Goldwest J.C., Huntington Beach Major: Police Science and Public Relations; [occ.] Financial Service Rep. San Bernardino County Credit; [memb.] Victorville Chamber of Union Commerce; [hon.] Presidential physical fitness award 3 times 69-71, Bowler of the year 1980. San Bernardino County fair, 2nd Place baby afghan category 1994, "Best Costume" S.B. County Credit Union film festival 1995; [oth. writ.] First one published; [pers.] Thanks to Tim and Sue Krotz for whom the poem was written, for their strength and courage. "The ultimate heartache God can give is, for a parent to out live their child"; [a.] Victoria, CA

MORETTI, JENNIFER
[b.] August 12, 1980, Ocon, Memorial Hospital; [p.] Lynn and Al Moretti; [ed.] Oconomowoc High School; [occ.] Lorleburgs Hardware Store; [memb.] BMG, Columbia House; [hon.] Semi finalist in Miss America Pageant. I had a coupe poems published in a church booklet.; [oth. writ.] Black, What Relationship, Mine, Wild Hearts, Forever Lasting Love, Call Me Master, The Last Warrior, I'll Be There, Love Hurts, Your Hurting Me, U.S., Stcel and Stone, The Ones I Love, My Fault, My Luck; [pers.] My sister, Jackie Moretti has been my biggest inspiration for writing poems. And now that my sisters new baby, Chelsea Moretti, has been born I've had one more thing to write about.; [a.] Oconomowoc, WI

MORGAN, JACK F.
[pen.] Jack Morgan; [b.] January 23, 1926, Morris, OK; [p.] Minnie and Frank Morgan; [m.] Patsy Morgan, November 25, 1948; [ch.] Daniel, John, David, Janet and Susan; [ed.] 9th Grade; [occ.] Retired Operating Engineer; [hon.] World War II Victory Medal; [oth. writ.] I tied a-string around my finger - can't you understand these songs were not published); [pers.] I like to grow my own vegetables, and write poetry; [a.] Coleman, TX

MORGAN, TIMOTHY SMOKEY
[b.] February 5, 1974, Baltimore; [p.] Barbara Morgan; [ed.] Harlem Park Middle School, William Pinder Hughe Elementary, Harbor City Hearing Center, Current at Baltimore City Community College - G.E.D. diploma; [occ.] None - will like to be a Scientist; [hon.] Poem published in awaken to a dream - 1991; [oth. writ.] To the ones who see the good - awaken to a dream; [pers.] "For those who know of my words, has it been done to you, for those are my words, it will be done to you."; [a.] Baltimore, MD

MORIARTY, GLENN S.
[b.] May 17, 1972, Toronto, Ontario, Canada; [p.] Gerry and Pat; [occ.] Marketing; [pers.] This piece was written for the birth of Garrett Moriarty, first child of my brother Gregg and his wife Ray.; [a.] Oshawa Ontario, Canada

MORIARTY, THOMAS B.
[b.] September 5, 1914, Durham, NH; [p.] Maurice and A. Bertha Moriarty; [m.] Grace B., June 27, 1933; [ch.] Patricia and Thomas; [ed.] UN.H; [occ.] Retired; [oth. writ.] Dreaming, Waves, Reminisce, C.T.S., many others; [pers.] The love of poetry I get from my mother and when I travel I always drink the beauty of the land and the people when I get home I set down a few. Lines so as not to forget, then hide them away to reminisce and dream. Is what it is all about.; [a.] Durham, NH

MORRIS, CLINT
[b.] September 9, 1981, Augusta, GA; [p.] Darwin Morris, Marcie Morris; [oth. writ.] I also write short stories and essays and hope to someday write a novel worth reading.; [pers.] I strive in my writing to bring passion into a world where it's lost, and am greatly influenced by the words of Robert James Waller and the voice of Barbra Streisand. I also write poems from specific people in my life. This one is for Dena.; [a.] Appling, GA

MORRIS III, ARTHUR W.
[b.] January 2, 1980, Jackson County; [p.] Arthur Morris Jr., Elizabeth M.; [ed.] 9th Grade; [occ.] Student; [oth. writ.] I have other poems but there not published.; [pers.] I always liked to write stuff since I was little, and I still write a lot of poems. This poem, "tears" came to me at 5:30 in the morning when I couldn't get to sleep.; [a.] Jackson, OH

MORRIS, MARY V.
[pen.] Mary Riele Morris; [b.] October 14, 1921, Sacramento, CA; [p.] John C. and Ina C. Smith; [m.] Donald R. Morris, March 1, 1941, John Riele, October 12, 1977; [ch.] Frank J. Riele - John J. Roseina and Duffy Riele; [ed.] 2nd yrs. High School; [occ.] Raising grandchildren; [memb.] Eagles; [oth. writ.] One poem published; [pers.] I love the beauty and sounds of nature, and appreciate God's gift of eyes and hearing to enjoy with all.

MORROW JR., OZZIE
[pen.] AH-Z; [b.] September 11, 1953, Des Moines,

IA; [p.] Orsel and Nellie Morrow; [ch.] Dierra Morrow and Ozzie Morrow III; [ed.] Los Angeles City College; [occ.] Bakers Assistant; [hon.] I was awarded 2nd place in 1989 for my graphic art, and was given an honorable mention I'm art work in 1990, 1991 and 1992 at the Los Angeles County, Federation of labor art exhibits.; [oth. writ.] I have several short stories for children such as the adventures of mongie Bolongo, Mom he said it again! Papa don't stand no mess, and uncle squiggly and.; [pers.] I make a point, to make children laugh, and entertain them with character I established in my mind. It's so important to encourage kids to read now a days. And to keep their minds active especially when they read through the worlds of OZ.; [a.] Hawthorne, CA

MOSCHELLA, ANDREA RENE
[b.] October 13, 1973, Glen Ridge, NJ; [p.] Joan and Sebastian Moschella; [ed.] Hanover Park H.S. Univ. of Rhode Island; [occ.] Marketing Coordinator for Freedom Published, New York City; [memb.] Sigma Kappa; [hon.] Golden Key, Order of Omega, Psi Chi, Dean's List, Graduated Cum Laude. B.A. in Eng. B.A. in PSY; [pers.] Writing is my Catharsis. My thoughts are clarified in the written word - is this not true for everyone?

MOSES, CLINTON H.
[pen.] Clint Moses; [b.] July 17, 1942, Los Angeles; [p.] Mrs. Lois Moses; [ch.] Stephen Moses-29, April Moses-26; [occ.] Real Estate; [oth. writ.] None other than: "Sometimes God Chooses to Prime" from my life what I dern to be fruit and I move not why... thus...; [pers.] Sometimes it's wise to them reflect on the good times and go on for where there once was light, there is now approaching darkness best we walk away with what is left of the light so that we can.

MOSLENER, ERIN
[b.] February 13, 1982, Columbus, OH; [p.] Marti and Tom Moslener; [ed.] 8th grade; [occ.] Student; [memb.] National Jr. Honor Society; [hon.] Principal's Award; [a.] Annandale, VA

MOSS, KEN
[pen.] Gray Sunrise; [b.] March 1, 1965, Queensland, Australia; [p.] Ken Moss, Betty Moss; [ed.] Nambour High School Queensland Australia; [occ.] Surf Lifeguard Noosa Heads, Queensland, Australia; [memb.] Sunshine Beach Surf Life Saving Club, Nambour Amateur Swimming Club; [hon.] Lifeguard of the Year 1991-92 Queensland Australia. Extensive Athletic Background Including Professional Ironman Races (Surf).; [oth. writ.] Currently writing a novel - fiction. I have a large collection of poetry written in the past ten years. This is my first attempt at competition.; [pers.] Passion is the key to a life fulfilled. If you believe in something so strongly you know is right then pursue it no matter what.

MUDAN, PUPINDER
[b.] November 8, 1980, England; [p.] Kal Mudan; [ed.] Grade nine student at Essex high school. also enrolled in voice lessons and hopes of becoming singer and songwriter.; [occ.] Going to school at Essex high school; [oth. writ.] Poem published in the local paper; [pers.] I am influenced by the darker poets like Alan Poe and many of the

distruction and texture that happens in the world that we don't see. Something that needs to be noticed.; [a.] Essex Ontario, Canada

MUEHLBERG, ANITA
[pen.] Anima Muehlberg; [b.] September 6, 1958, Saint Louis, MO; [p.] Tom and Lorene Florence; [m.] Michael D. Muehlberg, September 8, 1980; [ch.] Michael, Aaron, Annalisa and Monica; [ed.] High School - Tulsa Central Graduate - 1977; [occ.] Receptionist, Tulsa Abstract; [memb.] Legion of Mary, Society of Childrens Book Writer's and Illustrations, Oklahoma Chapter of S.C.B.W.I.; [hon.] Judge for Diocesan Speech Contest - 1996, Secretary of School Board; [oth. writ.] Articles in the Tulsa Sentinal News paper, Eastern Oklahoma Catholic. School spirit song, St. Chaterine, Finalist for Local Radio Station, Jingle Contest; [pers.] When I'm not doing my other hobby, laundry, I like to write poetry, songs and children's stories. My favorite author is Helen Steiner Rice, My greatest inspiration comes from my own family.; [a.] Tulsa, OK

MULDER, TAMMY
[pen.] T. K. Mulder; [b.] December 17, 1971, Toronto, Canada; [p.] Elly Mulder and John Mulder; [ed.] Georgetown District Christian School, E. C. Drury high School, I.C.S. School of Art; [occ.] Prep-Cook, Artist; [memb.] Natural Science Book Club Humane Society; [hon.] Numerous Athletic Awards in Synchronized Swimming and Track and Field; [oth. writ.] Personal lyrics for songs; [pers.] I love to do art in any form. I believe sunsets, nature and all within nature are the most perfect of all art forms there are. My influences are Robert Bateman and Albert Casson.; [a.] Milton Ontario, Canada

MULLINS, STEPHEN WAYNE
[b.] September 8, 1950, Martinsville, VA; [p.] Keever C. Mullins, Frances G. Kerns; [ch.] Ashley R. Mullins, Maegan B. Mullins; [ed.] Campbell Court Elementary, Jacksonville High School, Lenior County Community College; [occ.] President, all points v/s, Jacksonville, NC; [oth. writ.] Several unpublished poems, "Christmas Wish" was my first attempt at publication.; [pers.] A personal note of gratitude to Doreen Couser, my inspiration to put my thoughts in writing.; [a.] Jacksonville, NC

MUNTAEN, JOHN MICHAEL
[b.] October 25, 1966, Erie, PA; [p.] Mr. John Muntaen and Mrs. Jean L. Semple-Muntaen; [ed.] Strong Vincent High Erie, PA. Lee Strasberg Theater Institute New York, NY.; [occ.] Actor/Model/Songwriter and Poet.; [memb.] SAG (screen actors guild) ASCAP (American Society of Composers, Authors and Publishers); [hon.] 'The National Library of Poetry Semi-Finalist. It is an honor to be published by such a distinguished organization.; [oth. writ.] Countless songs, Poems and other Various writings.; [pers.] 'Pain is the greatest inspiration for some of the purest poetry'. "Celestial Dream" is dedicated to Victoria N. Vonderbank. Bethel, Ct. USA.; [a.] Flushing, NY

MURPHY JUDY A.
[b.] October 14, 1951, Baton Rouge, LA; [p.] David and Judith Spencer; [ed.] B.S. Our Lady of the Lake Univ. San Antonio, TX; [occ.] Director, Human Resources Falcon Seaboard Resources, Inc;

[memb.] President - Houston Human Resource Management Association - 1995 - 1996; [pers.] My writings reflect my personal feelings about people, places or life in General; [a.] Houston, TX

MURPHY, LILLIAN
[pen.] Lillian; [b.] August 8, 1948, Cincinnati, OH; [p.] Mary Lawrence, Vernon Lawrence; [m.] Gary Ward; [ch.] Janie and Chris Murphy; [occ.] Licensed Practical Nurse Drake Center Cincinnati, Ohio; [pers.] My writings are created through the unconditional love my parents and grandparents have shared with me, along with the spiritual growth I have achieved.; [a.] Cincinnati, OH

MURPHY, MICHAEL
[b.] June 16, 1970, Oak Ridge, TN; [p.] Dennis Murphy, Edith Haddock Murphy; [ed.] Providence Day School, University of North Carolina - Charlotte; [a.] Charlotte, NC

MURRAY, THOMAS
[b.] December 17, 1969, Riverhead, NY; [p.] William Murray, Shirley Gonce; [ed.] Westhampton Beach High School, Florida Atlantic Un.; [memb.] Amnesty International; [pers.] It is true, when they save, no one stands alone. We all live in a kingdom call humanity. A nation that flies a banner as red as the blood that holds our mortality. There is for each of us, the noble duty to champion the cries of the helpless. For nobility is not a birth right but divined by one's actions.; [a.] Hampton Bays, NY

MURTHA, ROBERT P.
[pen.] Pilot Rabz; [b.] May 30, 1971, Newton, NJ; [p.] Joseph Edward and Carol Ann Murtha; [ch.] Ryan Patrick Murtha; [ed.] Mount Olive High, Post Graduate of Morris County Vo-Tech.; [occ.] Warehouse worker for wire cloth Manufacturing; [memb.] Member of: Mendham Hills Chapel, NJ, Member of Popular Hot, Rodding Association; [hon.] S.T.S. Car Service Centers Jack Apgar Leader Ship Award 1991, Morris County Vo-Tech. overall winner skills expo. 1991.; [pers.] Live Christ's Example, Where there is light there is shadow In the end find warmth in the light.; [a.] Budd Lake, NJ

MYERS, BARBARA
[b.] June 9, 1953, Providence, RI; [p.] Irving W. Perry, Lillian M. Perry; [m.] Divorced, October 13, 1973 - April 24, 1994; [ch.] Jeremy James, Jamie Lee; [ed.] Lake Worth High School, Palm Beach Junior College, Florida Atlantic University; [occ.] Language Arts Teacher, Lake Worth Community Middle School; [hon.] Outstanding Student in English - 1971, Phi Theta Kappa, Dean's List, President's Honors List; [a.] West Palm Beach, FL

MYERS, SHELBY A.
[b.] October 9, 1968, Bryn Mawr, PA; [p.] Edwin M. McGrath III, Judith A. McGrath; [m.] Timothy R. Myers, May 16, 1992; [ch.] Ashley A. Myers; [ed.] Shawnee High School - Medford, NJ, Burlington County College - Pemberton, NJ; [occ.] Owner and Consultant Ashleigh's Wedding/Affair Consultants; [pers.] This poem is dedicated to, of course, my mother who is also my best friend, my father and brother, my husband. Timothy, who is my strength and my

life, and to my daughter Ashley who is my heart and soul. I write from my heart and I am inspired by those who do the same.; [a.] Mount Laurel, NJ

MYERS, WILLIAM
[pen.] Jamel Myers; [b.] July 11, 1947; [p.] William, Pauline Myers; [m.] Shirley Walls, April 17, 1977; [ch.] Trinka, Jamel Myers; [occ.] Legal Tech Paralegal Co-Owner; [oth. Writ.] Simply Red, Property Of Three, What Blood Cell?; [pers.] How is the light most like the dark? How is the dark most like the light?; [a.] Oakland, CA

NAKHLE, THERESE JARBOUH
[pen.] T.J. Way; [b.] April 14, 1966, Lebanon; [p.] Assad Jarbouh, Georgette Jarbouh; [m.] Mark Alexander Dickson; [ch.] Crystal Rose; [ed.] High School; [occ.] Writing, Singing, Recording; [memb.] Harley Owners Group; [hon.] The National Library of Poetry; [oth. writ.] Poems published in local magazine and in the Garden of Life anthology of poetry, songwriter, singing, and recording.; [pers.] This poem is dedicated to those who are unfortunate and to the government for not damn seeing it promises, promises that's all we hear when will we ever learn and when will these problems finally disappear. I believe that sometimes catastrafies brings people closer to God.; [a.] Orleans Ottawa Ontario, Canada

NEIL, ARNOLD W.
[b.] July 23, 1953, Minneapolis; [p.] Walfried and June Neil (Deceased); [oth. writ.] "Operation Pronto" - The Arnold W. Neil Story. C. Unpublished. "Arrival", "Santa Clause Was Here." Hill Top Records, Christmas 1995, Published, the sounds of Christmas.

NEILL, ROBERT
[b.] November 5, 1963, Northern Ireland; [p.] Lena and Bobby; [m.] Alison, August 25, 1990; [ch.] April; [occ.] Airport Fighter; [pers.] I am proud and honored, that my poem has been printed in your book, I dedicated this poem to my wife Alison and daughter April.; [a.] Belfast, Northern Ireland

NELMS, BETTY L.
[b.] Knoxville, TN; [p.] Andrew Hinman, Clara Hinman; [m.] Easton Nelms, December 7, 1951; [ch.] Sharon; [ed.] Goodman College of Theatre Arts, Chicago, ILL University of La Verne, La Verne, CA; [occ.] Legal Secretary, Latham and Watkins, Los Angeles, CA; [memb.] Northside Theatre Group, Drury Lane Theatre Club; [hon.] Goodman Theatre Actress of of the Year Award (2 yrs), Northside Theatre Best Actress Award; [pers.] The path we choose defines the life we live, even sorrow can produce rainbows.; [a.] Chino, CA

NELSON, DEAN
[pen.] Dean Nelson; [b.] October 6, 1951, Columbia, SC; [p.] Lonnie and Margaret Nelson; [m.] Martha L. Nelson, November 29, 1975; [ch.] Stephanie; [ed.] BA, Newberry College, Newberry, SC High School-Denisville, Columbia, NC; [occ.] CFR Director, American International Group; [memb.] Advent Lutheran Church, Director, Lutheran Lay Renewal; [hon.] Dean's List; [oth. writ.] Several poems published in local publication; [pers.] My writing reflects the love I have for our Heavenly Father and it Honors Him for all He has bestowed upon me, my family and my friends.; [a.] Charlotte, NC

NELSON, SHAUN CHRISTOPHER
[b.] January 5, 1977, Phoenix, AZ; [p.] Zinda and Gordon Nelson; [ed.] So far High school soon College then medical school (that's my goal); [occ.] Disable from the accident.; [memb.] Near Death Experience Group; [hon.] 1st entry; [oth. writ.] Artistry also and poems.; [pers.] I was in a serious car wreck, should be dead. I saw God, now I'm getting better and I've became a prolific poet writer since the accident. My near death experience has given me a new insight to my writing.; [a.] Tucson, AZ

NEUBACHER, FRED
[b.] March 19, 1937, Australia; [p.] Elizabeth, Roman Neubacher; [m.] Valerie Anne Taller, July 3, 1995; [ch.] Roman Manny; [ed.] High school student under Prof. Heinz Galle; [occ.] Self-employed Artist (Painter)

NEUMANN, CAROL E.
[pen.] Carol Baumfalk-Neumann; [b.] June 17, 1939, Stratton, NE; [p.] Francis Baumfalk, Ella Baumfalk; [m.] William R. Neumann, August 16, 1959; [ch.] Brian, Christy and Cathy; [ed.] Stratton High, McCook Junior College, Denver-North Community College; [occ.] Retired; [oth. writ.] Poems published in local newspapers, a book on my childhood memories; [pers.] I was raised on a farm in Nebraska with loving parents, two older sisters, and a younger brother. My writings are influenced by fond memories of my life on the farm, and inspired by my Mother's gentle love for her family, tremendous zest for life, appreciation of nature, and love for the Lord.; [a.] Fort Pierce, FL

NEWBERG, LYDIA
[ed.] High School Grad.; [occ.] Equine Manager; [hon.] Poems published in local paper.; [oth. writ.] Disturbing Dream, Our Love, Faces And Places Reality, Unveil, Work Words World, The Deformed Heart, Candles, Hurt, Endless Thoughts, Touching Jade, Listen, Toast, Sun; [pers.] Read explore learn to embrace your passions, be a willing student life has mach to teach.; [a.] Salem, OR

NEWBERRY, ROBERT
[b.] November 13, 1967, Huntsville, AL; [p.] Mr. and Mrs. Murl H. Newberry; [ed.] B.S.E.E. University of Alabama in Huntsville; [occ.] Electrical Engineer; [pers.] I try to glorify God with my life, only his word should be honored.; [a.] Huntsville, AL

NGUYEN, BONNIE LYNN
[b.] February 4, 1955, Nassau, Bahamas; [p.] Nam Hein and Cynthia Nguyen; [ch.] Kya Simone, Khristy Laural; [ed.] The Government High School, University of Waterloo-Canada, University of West Indies - Jamaica; [occ.] Training Manager - CIBC Bahamas Limited (Bank); [memb.] President - Bahamas Human Resources Development Association, Member - ASTD Member - Bahamas Library Association.; [hon.] CIBC Area Manager's Award for "People Management" - November 1995; [oth. writ.] Poems read at local writer's Association Public meetings, Book of Poetry and Short - Stories soon to be published.; [pers.] "To thine own self be true.." I strive for excellence in my work but I take the time to play and be with those I love.; [a.] Nassau, Bahamas

NGUYEN, PETER
[pen.] Nguyen Bao Thu; [b.] September 7, 1961, Vietnam; [p.] Thap Nguyen and Chi Thi Do; [ed.] Bachelor of Science in Electronic Engineering (B.S.E.E.), pursuing Chartered Financial Consultant (Ch. F.C.); [occ.] Life Underwriter and Registered Representative; [memb.] National Association of Life Underwriter (NALU); [hon.] Executive Council Member of New York Life, Million Dollar Round Table (MDRT)'s honor; [oth. writ.] "The Seven Magic Lamps of Life Insurance"; [pers.] "The Seven Magic Lamps of Life Insurance" is a book that I wrote in bi-language to contribute to my community and to the Vietnamese-American younger generation as well. Insurance history and it's huge development today is an interested thing to know. I am working on finding a sponsor to publish this book soon.; [a.] Placentia, CA

NGUYEN, VIEN MINH
[pen.] Minh - Vien; [b.] January 18, 1940, Vietnam; [m.] Huong Ngo Nguyen, 1969; [ch.] Khoi (Son) and Daisy (Daughter); [ed.] Saigon University, Vietnam; [memb.] Vietnam P.E.N. Center Association of Free Vietnamese Writers and Artists, The International Society of Poets; [hon.] Editor's Choice Award (1994), The International Poet of Merit Award (1994), Editors Choice Award (1995); [oth. writ.] (Published works of Poetry): The Moon, Vietnam: A Nightmare War, Blue Rain, Saigon: The Unhealed Wound; [pers.] Poetry lives inside the poet and the poet lives on poetry.; [a.] San Francisco, CA

NICHOLS, MICHAEL W.
[pen.] Nic; [b.] December 29, 1959, Mount Airy, NC; [p.] C. Albert and Mary Bowman Nichols; [m.] Carolyn Simpson Nichols, August 20, 1978; [ch.] Dusti Amber (Amber) 11 years old; [ed.] East Surry High, Pilot Mtn., N.C.; [occ.] Drafting Manager; [memb.] American Welding Society; [hon.] National Honor Society Fatherhood; [oth. writ.] Several none published, poems and short stories.; [pers.] There are no absolutes, the only constant is change.; [a.] Matthews, NC

NIELANDER, FAITH
[pen.] Faith Nielander; [b.] April 9, 1966, Indianapolis; [p.] Gary and Elizabeth Nielander; [ed.] Columbus North High School, Indiana University, Ambassador College, Pasadena, CA.; [occ.] Publicist; [hon.] NCTE Writing Award, Honors English at I.U.; [pers.] Silence to me, is like death. To be alive is to be heard, no matter how difficult it is to speak or how mundane the subject.; [a.] Pasadena, CA

NIERENBERG, MATTHEW
[b.] September 19, 1970, Los Angeles, CA; [p.] Alvin and Marilyn Nierenberg; [ed.] Los Angeles (enter for Enriched Studies High School), V.C.L.A. and V.C. Santa Barbara (B.A.), V.C. San Diego (Prof. Certification in Spanish); [occ.] Student; [memb.] Heal the Bay, Santa Monica, CA, Surfrider Foundation, CA, Windansea Historical Surfriding Association, La Jolla, CA; [pers.] "The world is not imperfect or slowly evolving along a path to

perfection. No, it is perfect at every moment... Everything is necessary, everything needs only my agreement, my assent, my loving understanding..." —from Siddhartha, H. Hesse. There is no beginning, no end... just our recognition of the huge space in between left empty for us to fill with things designed to make our journeys more pleasant and heartfelt.; [a.] La Jolla, CA

NIMCHUK, JANICE K.
[pen.] Jan; [b.] January 17, 1949, Minneapolis, MN; [p.] Einard Hasti, Nell Hasti; [m.] Robert Nimchuk, May 5, 1978; [ch.] Scott Christopher, Daniel Jeremy, Holly Elizabeth; [ed.] Osseo High School, University of Minnesota; [occ.] Homemaker - church volunteer; [memb.] North Heights Lutheran Church; [hon.] Church Deaconess; [oth. writ.] Other poems - journaling; [pers.] Poetry has helped me to express some of my deepest feelings. I have collected special poems for years.; [a.] White Bear Lake, MN

NIX, KEVIN B.
[b.] September 16, 1971, Rome, GA; [p.] Ronald and Jo Ann Nix; [m.] Leslie Cook Nix, June 3, 1995; [ed.] Shorter College, Rome, GA 1989-93 Psychology Major, BA; [occ.] Carpenter; [oth. writ.] Published verse in local literary magazines; [a.] Cartersville, GA

NOORDYK, SUSANNE
[b.] May 1, 1942, London, Ontario, Canada; [p.] John and Edith Taylor; [m.] William Campbell; [ch.] Jacob, Anne-Marie, Irene, William and Willy; [ed.] Oakville - Trafalgar High School, Mohawk College; [occ.] Housewife; [memb.] Hamilton Society of Model Engineers - O Scale, Skyway Blue Grass Club.; [hon.] Member of year 1990 - Skyway Blue Grass Club; [oth. writ.] Friday the Thirteenth; [a.] Hamilton Ontario, Canada

NORRIS III, JOHN EASLEY
[b.] July 23, 1977, Fort Leonard Wood, MO; [p.] Mr. John E. and Mrs. Sheila J. Norris Jr.; [ed.] Freshman in College; [occ.] Student; [hon.] Honor Graduate of Northeast High School, Clarksville, TN., Oberlin College Scholarship; [oth. writ.] Several oems where selected for publication on campus.; [pers.] I write to express the truths of what is actually taking place within our society today. I try to express the ongoing cry of unity among "our" race, not the black race, not the white race, but the right race, the human race.; [a.] Clarksville, TN

NORRIS, JOHN R.
[b.] January 2, 1926, Winnsboro, TX; [p.] Deceased; [ch.] Three; [ed.] 9th grade; [occ.] Writer; [oth. writ.] Short stories, poetry, songs; [pers.] Money's good is you have it and use it. It will buy some happiness. It can also buy your way to hell, but won't bail you out. Served in World War II, raised as a orphan by aunt and uncle.; [a.] River Oaks, TX

NORRIS, LISA DIANE
[pen.] Greta; [b.] Vancouver B.C.; [p.] Tom and Bev Norris; [ch.] 2 Rottweilers - Arnold and Lucita, 1 Persian cat - C-fer; [ed.] Criminology diploma studying herbal medicine.; [oth. writ.] Have been writing poetry since high school and am

currently writing a book - hopefully to be published one day.; [pers.] I am dedicating this poem to my Aunti Greta, whom I know would have been very pleased to learn of it's publication. She always said it should be published - I'm sure she knows!; [a.] Vancouver B.C., Canada

OABBANI, BANA
[pen.] Bianca Kaleil; [b.] August 17, 1980, Amman-Jordan;]p.] Khalil Oabbani, Leila Oabbani (2 sisters - Shima Oabbani & Shatha Oabbani); [ed.] Cambridge High School - Dubai - U.A.E.; [occ.] Student; [hon.] Arabian Regional Painting Award (world enviroment day), School: Endeavour award & Academic award, Recycle model award; [oth. writ.] Several poems not published, articles in school newspaper.; [pers.] It is never too late to restore happiness, peace and prosperity to the world. Yet, both willingness and unity must exist.; [a.] Dubai - U.A.E.

OBIE, SANDRA C.
[pen.] Ellen Lillian; [b.] Billings, MT; [p.] Agnes Hoag McDonald and Alfred F. Collins; [m.] Donald L. Obie, 1991; [ch.] Damon Obie, Krisobie; [ed.] Montana State University at Billings, and Rocky, MTN college at Billings, MT; [occ.] Apolescent alcohol and drug counselor; [oth. writ.] Other poems in "Cats, Canines and other criteria" "Seasons of the Heart," A children's poetry series and stories and poems in progress.; [pers.] I seek to capture an event and a feeling from the event to make them real, and once on paper, alive for all to share.; [a.] Winifred, MT

OCAMPO, ELVIRA DIAZ
[pen.] Vera; [b.] December 8, 1949, Laredo, TX; [p.] Isabel Diaz, Trinidad Guerrero; [m.] Santos Ocampo Rojas, August 20, 1977; [ch.] Daniel Cortez Jr., Jennifer D. Marton, Sarah I. Ocampo, Stephanie M. Ocampo; [ed.] Raymond and Tirza Martin High School (1968); [occ.] Legal Secretary, Schechter and Marshall, Houston, Texas; [memb.] Notary Public, State of Texas; [oth. writ.] Bi-lingual writer, several unpublished poems and stories; [pers.] "A Rose In My Garden" was written in memory of my niece, Julissa D'Anne Gomez (1970-1989), A gymnast who aspired to win an Olympic medal. She lives in the hearts of those who loved her.; [a.] Houston, TX

OGDEN, ESTHER CAROLE
[pen.] Carole Ogden (Esther Maupin); [b.] January 4, 1967, Oregon; [p.] Carolyn and Ted Maupin; [ed.] I have a B.S. Degree in Special Education and Regular Education Univ. from currently I am working on my Master's Degree.; [occ.] I am a 4th grade school teacher at Selma Bartlett Elem.; [memb.] Beading Association; [hon.] I have received 2 awards for merit and nominations for dedication work. I graduated college with honors.; [oth. writ.] I have written several poems, but this was the first time to enter my work in a contest.; [pers.] My poetry is a reflection of my soul. Therefore, when I'm writing, my inner thoughts seem to pour out onto paper and I'm guided by some powerful, emotional force.; [a.] Henderson, NV

OGUNDIMU, TARA L.
[pen.] Babyface; [b.] January 4, 1977, Oakland, CA; [p.] James and Teresa; [ed.] Chula Vista

Junior High Marston Middle School Muellar Elementary School Rend High School; [occ.] Assistant Manager; [memb.] Leader of Governor Bob Millers Youth Action Team (Dance Group) Lover's Grove Krew. (My own dance Grew); [hon.] CJSF (california Junior Scholarship Federation) Outstanding Scholarship Federation Outstanding Students of spring Quarter 91, Outstanding performance, Student Star Award, African American Reflection, Certificate of Honor; [oth. writ.] A collection of other poems in my book at home and a few songs.; [pers.] Nothing's impossible. Dreams do come true. Never give up and your best critic is yourself. Keep your head up.; [a.] Reno, NV

OKOLO, FRANCIS ANAT
[pen.] Boy Anat; [b.] March 4, 1970, Unth, Enugu; [p.] Ichie John Okolo, Lady Carol Okolo; [ed.] Higher National Diploma in Applied Chemistry of the Institute of Management and Technology Enugu, Nigeria; [memb.] Chemical Society of Nigeria. Nwagu Age Grade of Abor Town; [oth. writ.] Several poems published in local newspapers in Nigeria.; [pers.] Self-discovery is the deity of any duty which creates it's tentacles to source every talent.; [a.] Enugu, Enugu

OLDENBURG, MARSHALL C.
[b.] April 19, 1964, Madison, WI; [p.] Norman and Florence Oldenburg; [ed.] University of Wisconsin - Madison; [oth. writ.] No other publications. Multiple works currently under construction. "The Sane Observations Of An Insane Man."; [a.] Madison, WI

OLIVER, KEVIN
[b.] June 22, 1979, Alexander City; [p.] Tony and Martha Oliver; [occ.] Student - Pell City High School Junior; [memb.] Poetry Club, 4 H Member, Art Club; [hon.] National Honor Society; [oth. writ.] No other publications but I have several more poems and I'm writing a book; [a.] Pell City, AL

OLIVER, RANDALL W.
[pen.] Randy Oliver; [b.] August 9, 1954, Oakland, CA; [p.] George L. Oliver, Jordeen Krabach Oliver; [ed.] Valencia High, College of the Siskiyous; [occ.] Electronics Ed. Equipment Business Owner/ Operator-Oliver Hay and Supply; [memb.] MANA (Manu. Agents National Association) CITEA (CA. Industrial Tech. Ed. Association); [oth. writ.] Poems (18 Wheeler Cowboy) (Tex Respect); [pers.] Its not always how much education you have, or how many letters you have after your name, but how you apply the knowledge and talent you have to contribute to society. Many highly educated and non-educated people learn to reap the benefits from society without ever contributing.; [a.] Modesto, CA

OLLER, BELINDA THERESE
[pen.] Billie Oller; [b.] January 15, 1973, Philippines; [p.] Guillermo, Milwyda Oller; [ed.] Mountain View High School, Los Angeles Trade, Technical College; [occ.] Proof Machine Operator, Wells Fargo Bank; [memb.] Grace and Mercy Christian Fellowship; [hon.] Dean's honor roll: High School and College Fr. (Spring) Fall '92, Spring '94; [oth. writ.] Newspaper articles (O) from High School to College newspapers

and articles from Mid-Valley News.; [pers.] I live to be an artist for the glory of my Lord, Jesus Christ.; [a.] Baldwin Park, CA

ORME, MAILE
[pen.] Sufiya; [b.] October 2, 1950, Honolulu, HI; [p.] Olga and Frank Orme; [m.] Halfuji, 1996; [ch.] Pono and Precious; [ed.] Punahal High Sch. Hon. Hi, University of Mi., L'Ecole de Commerce, Switzerland, Beau Soleil, Switz and extensive World travel over 10 years period exposure to many cultures and art forms.; [occ.] Creative and performance artist, also involved in healing arts; [memb.] D.U.C.K. Club, Honomuni Yoga Society (Committee Member), Shifting TS. for a Better World, Pres.; [hon.] Honomuni School of Healing Arts (hon.); [oth. writ.] Lady Truth, Aphrodites Cups, Ode to a Duck, Fuji and the Mermaid; [pers.] How to express the profundity of being truly alive on this precious earth? My writings and all creative expression have come from a need to express a life that can't be contained, the source of inspiration is a creative stream as mysterious as an exotic flower emerging from the ground unannounced, seeded by unseen hands.; [a.] Kula Maui, HI

OSTROW, JOSEPH
[pen.] Joey A. Smith; [b.] December 11, 1977; [hon.] Poet of the Month, Betny published.; [oth. writ.] An unpublished poetry anthology called "The Dictionary of Love and several short story anthology called, The Hitch Hiker and other Scary stories.; [pers.] Life is a game the more serious you take it, the harder the rules becomes; [a.] West Babylon, NY

OSTRUNIC, CYNTHIA SUSAN
[b.] February 23, 1959, Euclid, OH; [p.] Robert and Catherine Ostrunic; [ed.] Euclid Sr. High School; [occ.] Support Coordinator/Switchboard of Operator Progressive Ins. Co.; [hon.] 1993 Editor's Choice Award from the National Library of Poetry for a Poem Titled: Heart and Soul; [oth. writ.] Heart and soul, and respect published in National Library of Poetry Anthologies. A true friend in the process of being published in another National Library of Poetry Anthology.; [pers.] In my writings, I strive to uplift and touch the hearts of everyone. May God bless you always, in always!; [a.] Euclid, OH

OSWALD, GRETCHEN N.
[b.] August 29, 1967, Holyoke, CO; [p.] Janice and Robert Oswald; [ed.] University of Colorado, B.S. in Journalism/Broadcast Production; [occ.] Computer Software Sales at Exchange; [oth. writ.] Two other poems published in hometown local newspaper.; [pers.] My basic philosophy is live to learn, learn to love, love to live.; [a.] San Francisco, CA

OTIGBUO, CHINEDUM A.
[b.] June 25, 1977, Dublin, Ireland; [p.] Engr. and Mrs. Ik Otigbuo; [ed.] Federal Government College OK., Nigeria. Fresno City College. Fresno CA; [occ.] Currently attending Fresno City College. Accounting Major; [memb.] Associated Student Member Fresno City College; [oth. writ.] Several collections of poems pending publishing. Also including short stories.; [pers.] I always look at

poetry as a very strong and important form of human expression. I am also influenced to a great deal by the great poets of our time. I think poetry is a passion.; [a.] Fresno, CA

OTTER, JEANETTE WELD
[b.] May 6, 1919, San Jose, CA; [p.] Elwin H. Weld, Idabell A. Weld; [m.] John Delaware Otter, April 16, 1942, Baltimore, MD; [ch.] Lee Worth Otter, Marjorie Sue (Bruneau) John D. Otter Jr., Nancy Clark Otter, Robert Weld Otter, Alice Rebecca (Fontes); [ed.] 1940 A.B. San Jose State University, Major-Education, degree minors-Art, Music, Psychology, Credentials - General Elementary and Kindergarten Primary; [occ.] Housewife; [memb.] Society of Mayflower Descendants, California Native Plant Society, The Nature Conservancy, Big Sur Land Trust, Planning and Conservation League, Sierra Club, Monterey County Geneological Society, others; [hon.] Delta Phi Upsilon, Kappa Delta Pi, Poet Laureate, Monterey Peninsula Herald, 1968; [oth. writ.] Several poems published in local newspaper. Family History (in progress); [pers.] Love, Family, Nature, Social Commentary: Often a short poem can make a point more succinctly than a long report. A good poem becomes not only the Message but also the Messenger when it brings the reader's own thoughts and feelings into focus. That's the Glory of it!; [a.] Carmel, CA

OVERTON, EDNA
[pen.] Edna "Bree" Overton; [b.] June 7, 1946, Buffalo, NY; [p.] John Overton, Roberta Overton; [ch.] Dayna Antoinette Overton-Burns; [ed.] D'Youville College, Erie Community College City, Bryant and Stratton Business Institute; [occ.] Registered Nurse; [memb.] Naomi Chapter 10 Order of the Eastern Star, Prince Hall Affiliation of the Masons, Inner City Lions Club, Friendship Baptist Church, NAACP, Editor of the St. Columbo Square News Letter; [hon.] Scholastic Achievement Award, Dean's List; [oth. writ.] Written over 100 poems and short stories; [pers.] My sincere gratitude to my sister Janet Harbin - Mack and Aunt Jazzetta Kempt for encouraging me to write. My heart smiles when someone is touched by my poetry.; [a.] Buffalo, NY

OXFORD, SHAWN T.
[b.] May 3, 1977, Ventura, CA; [p.] Mike and Kathleen Oxford; [ed.] Buena High, Ventura Community College; [occ.] Student, Store Clerk; [hon.] 1994 Golden State Examination Academic Excellence Award; [oth. writ.] Confused mass of unpublished work; [pers.] Poems are nothing but feelings on paper. Everyone has feelings, so everyone's a poet.; [a.] Ventura, CA

PABON, ANA N.
[pen.] Ana N. Pabon; [b.] July 26, 1949, Fajardo Puerto Rico; [p.] Lauro Medina Sr., Rufina Medina; [m.] Divorced; [ch.] Jose, Monique, Rubin, Shalimar, Edwin, Joana Pabon; [ed.] Morris High School Bx, N.Y. Degree in early childhood; [occ.] Co-owner of Pabon Clearing Service Inc.; [memb.] Foster Parent Association; [hon.] 10 years of service award from Foster Parent; [oth. writ.] I have written several poems that I have not published yet; [pers.] What influence me the most in my writing are my children my poetry is a reflection of our everyday life.; [a.] Harrisburg, PA

PACZKOWSKI, ROSALIE S.
[pen.] RSP, Patches; [b.] October 30, 1950, Bayonne, NJ; [p.] John C. and Helen Paczkowski; [m.] C. Robert Gerimroth, July 6, 1990; [ch.] L. Alexander Tamasi, Nicki L. Germany; [ed.] Mt. de Sales Academy, Catonsville Community College, U. of Md.; [occ.] Registered Nurse; [memb.] Phi Theta Kappa, 1st Md. Infantry Battalion C.S.A, Friends of the National Park at Gettysburg; [hon.] National Honor Society, Dean's List; [oth. writ.] Several poems and short story published in school publication.; [pers.] Life is the most accomplished ironic comedian for it has all eternity to learn the exact timing. My poems reflect this lesson and come from the heart of a human struggling to snatch the moments of happiness due us all.; [a.] Baltimore, MD

PADILLA, LINDA ESTRELLA
[pen.] Estrella Padilla; [b.] December 8, 1978, Magna, UT; [p.] Lind and Victor Delgado; [ed.] Junior in high school; [occ.] School; [memb.] Mesa - Math, Emerging, Scinee Achievement; [hon.] Mesa honor award most improved student; [oth. writ.] Without You, Love, I Want, Disar, When I Lost You, I Loved You, A Small Death, Rain, Laty, Everytime; [pers.] I play the cello, on my spare time. I like the outdoors and things that are adventure.; [a.] Magna, UT

PAGANO, CHRISTINA
[b.] October 27, 1971, Seattle, WA; [p.] Francia and Robert Pagano; [ed.] B.A. in English, minors in Physics and Corporate Economics, Middlebury College, 1994. Currently attending the University of Chicago's Graduate School of Business.; [occ.] Professional Basketball Player in Queensland, Australia. Graduate Student at the University of Chicago's Graduate School of Business.; [hon.] Graduated High Honors in English. Second Team all American, 1994 (Basketball). Australia's CBA all Star National Team, 1996.; [oth. writ.] Bedouin Faces, a photo graphical journey into the lives of the South Western Bedouin tribes. Amour Vincit Omnia, a historical romance novel, yet to be released. Currently working on a modern-day romance novel.; [pers.] The need to be loved, the dire to feel wanted, the fear of being alone: These are the issues at the heart of human motivations. My poetry and stories give voice to these subconscious emotions. My family is my inspiration.; [a.] Queensland, Australia

PALMER, PATRICIA
[b.] June 10, 1949, Didsbury, Alberta, Canada; [ch.] 3 children, 4 grandchildren; [ed.] Mount Royal College, Calgary, Alta; [occ.] Massage Therapist (14 yrs.); [memb.] Distinguished Member, International Society of Poets; [hon.] International Poet of Merit Award 1995 - (3) Editors Choice Awards since 1994, Greatest, joy being mother to Jeff, Anjia, James and in-law to Vaughn and Sandra - grandmother to Nicole Alex, Mikel, Stephen; [oth. writ.] Church mag. - Ensign Memories of an , Auto-biography - Unheard Cry (in progress), Anthologies - After the Storm, The Path not taken, Best Poems of 1996; [pers.] I feel in writing experiences - thoughts will reflect on enlightenment for knowledge while extenuating a positive attitude to rise above personal discouragements. Providing a foundation of hope in life's

testing ground for growth - encouraging tools of love for self and others to draw from.; [a.] Creston Bristish Columbia, Canada

PALMER, SHERRY
[b.] July 30, 1954, Neptune, NJ; [p.] Marjory Palmer and Charles Palmer; [ed.] Wall Township High School Wall, NJ; [occ.] Owner, Wall Pizza and Deli, Wall, NJ

PALMIERI, VINCENT
[occ.] Actor; [oth. writ.] I wrote my first novel that took me 40 years.; [pers.] I feel one moment can change your life. My daughter wrote a poem, "Arising In Me... I was born of seekers but they are too scared to seek..." That poem changed my life. I am finally seeking... thank you, Deborah. I love you. Dad; [a.] Hollywood, CA

PANZARELLO, JESSE R.
[b.] December 14, 1953, New Carlle, PA; [p.] Edward and Frances Panzarello; [m.] Alison L. Panzarello, October 28, 1978; [ed.] BS Horticulture, The Pensylvania State University; [occ.] President, Wall Coverings Inc. Pittsburgh PA; [hon.] First time approach into poetry. I hope to gain momentum; [oth. writ.] Personal memories.; [pers.] Poetry paints pictures with impressions invoked by words creating not only thought in the reader, but an emotional response that evokes relative memories or revelation of the present human condition. I write about the celebration or tragedy of life and am inspired by the quotes of anyone who will revealed their humanity thought them.; [a.] Pittsburgh, PA

PAPPA, PHYLLIS A.
[pen.] Phyllis Baio-Pappa; [b.] January 31, 1965, Hartford, CT; [p.] Angeline Prete Baio and Michael Baio; [m.] Michael J. Pappa, September 6, 1982; [ch.] Michael J. Pappa Jr.; [ed.] South Catholic, Bulkeley, Three Rivers Community College; [occ.] Early Education Teacher, Norwich, CT; [memb.] St. Mary Youth Group Committee, Bereavement Society, Children's Liturgy of the World Coordinator; [oth. writ.] Reported for old Saybrook pictorial, clinton recorder, poems published in project learn newsletter currently working on a compilation of poetry for future book.; [pers.] My heart pumps ink through my veins when my soul is compelled to speak. My fingers merely make the movements commanded by my spirit.; [a.] Voluntown, CT

PARDON, LAFAIR
[b.] January 8, 1952, Birmingham, AL; [p.] Emmett Pardon, Ruth G. Pardon; [ed.] Huffman High School; [occ.] Chief at Morrison Restaurant; [hon.] Gold Certificate of Volunteers Service in Public Schools. Certificate of Recognition of Attendance at Birmingham Public School Parent Education Program; [a.] Birmingham, AL

PARISI, LUCILLE
[pen.] "Lucille Parisi," "Grand Malu"; [b.] September 25, 1929, Little Ferry, NJ; [p.] Amelia and Henry Ahrens; [m.] Joseph C. Parisi, April 30, 1950; [ch.] Three children, six grandchildren; [ed.] High School graduate, Business Courses, Insurance Courses, Art Courses; [occ.] Bookkeeper Otterstedt Insurance Agency; [memb.] Independent Insurance Agent of American, Holy Name Hospital Foundation, Englewood Cliffs Democratic Club (My husband is Mayor); [hon.] National Honor Society in High School, "Women of the Year" - Eng. Cliffs Chamber of Commerce; [oth. writ.] "Notes from grandma Lu" which are poems, letters, notes etc. for each of my grandchildren.; [pers.] Writing poetry has a peaceful and calming affect after a busy day at work.; [a.] Englewood Cliffs, NJ

PARK, ANDREW SCOTT
[pen.] Harlem Scott; [b.] September 30, 1976, Lafayette, IN; [p.] Joseph E. Park and Nancy C. Park; [ed.] Jefferson High, Indiana State University; [occ.] Student at I.S.V., and Actor and Ventriloquist; [memb.] Theta Alpha Phi, American Red Cross, Jefferson Players, Evergreen Wesleyan Church; [hon.] Theta Alpha Phi, Performance and Creative Arts Scholarships; [oth. writ.] Several articles published in local Newpapers and Magazine, Produced Playwright.; [pers.] Conformity kills the child to make a man. My poetry rejects the societal molds revealing the burning impulses and secrets of my soul.; [a.] Lafayette, IN

PARKER, ANNA
[pen.] A. Lynn Reed, A. Lynn Burke; [b.] Sanford, ME; [p.] James Parker, Carol Parker; [oth. writ.] Besides standard poetry, I write rhymed narrative children's books.; [pers.] I write to touch others. To inspire thought and feeling in those who have never considered my subjects before. To those who have personally witnessed them first hand, know that you are not alone, and others do understand.; [a.] Dover, NH

PARKER, EVELYN
[b.] June 9, 1925, Manchester, England; [p.] Edwin Lee and Louisa; [m.] (Separated 1976); [ch.] Allison Carol and Simon Brett Parker; [ed.] Manchester High, Eng. Peter St Commercial, Eng. Can. Sheridan College, York Univ. and also Ryerson - FRI - Further also advanced courses; [occ.] Real Est. Investment and Prop. Management; [memb.] REIC - FRI MDSA (Exec Secty), (Landlord Assoc.) Since 1972; [hon.] None Letter from queen Elizabeth RE. WLA Service, expressing appreciation - 1943 to 1947; [oth. writ.] Am presently taking a writing course with the institute of children's literature; [pers.] I am happily expecting my first grandchild towards the end of this year. I have always wanted to write, but have not had the opportunity and time before.; [a.] Toronto Mississauga, Canada

PARKER, JASON
[pen.] Jay Parker; [b.] April 8, 1972, Riverside, NJ; [p.] John and Denise Gazaway; [ed.] Delran High School, Burlington County College; [occ.] Vid's Deli, Reverside; [memb.] Delran Emergency Squad; [pers.] I try to focus on the little thoughts that are over shadowed by the big ideas.; [a.] Delran, NJ

PARKER, MERCEDES
[pen.] Sadie; [b.] March 27, 1984, Atlanta, GA; [p.] Phyllis Parker (mother); [ed.] Mary McCloud Bethune Elementary, McNair Middle School; [memb.] Wings of Faith Usher Board, Youth Choir, National Beta Club; [hon.] National Junior Beta Club, Certificate of Perfect Attendance, Scholarship Award, Mathematics Award, Spelling Bee Winner, has been a Honor Roll Student throughout my Education Term; [pers.] I strive to reflect the goodness of God as we walk in his presence. I hope to influence other children's lives, so that they may seek the hand of God and prosper.; [a.] College Park, GA

PARKER, NANNIE LEE
[pen.] Nannie L. Parker; [b.] February 7, 1919, Wolhow, NC; [p.] Maggie and Joe Pressley; [m.] Johnny Parker, August 17, 1935; [ch.] Four; [ed.] 10th Grade; [occ.] Home maker and Jack of all traid, croft write sew cook; [memb.] United Methodist Church; [hon.] Never entered any thing be fare now; [oth. writ.] Lots here at home but this one poem is the only thing I have every entered in anything; [pers.] I write mostly, love, hearty and God and mankind

PARKER, SANDRA
[b.] April 22, 1974, Burlington, ON, Canada; [pers.] The simple act of being kind and tolerant of others is all we really need, but when we can each stand before our own God's then we shall be free.

PARLE, SHARON LOUISE
[b.] May 27, 1978, San Jose; [p.] Walter and Ann Parle; [ed.] Los Gatos High School; [oth. writ.] Several poems never published.; [pers.] The poem "Unknown Soldier" was written in loving memory of my Uncle Chuck, whom I never got to meet because he was missing in action in Korea.; [a.] Los Gatos, CA

PATE, SYLVIA
[b.] May 8, 1929, Beeville, TX; [p.] William and Lilie Ezell; [m.] Charles Pate, December 10, 1946; [ch.] Three boys and two girls; [ed.] High School grad. P.S.J.A. in Pharr, Texas. Lots of self study and reading; [occ.] Retired and sitter; [memb.] For the older people. Who need me.; [oth. writ.] I wish to write and publish a small book of short stories and poems. With American - Beehemian or Czechoslovakian back ground.; [pers.] I like to write true to life material. This experience could well be the beginning of something big and great.; [a.] Clanton, AL

PATTERSON, MARK
[b.] April 17, 1960; [oth. writ.] Numerous other poems and prose catalogued, but as of yet unpublished.; [pers.] It is our obligation to seek out our uniqueness and then use it to change the world.; [a.] Murrieta, CA

PAWLICK, EDWARD R.
[b.] October 29, 1982, Flemington, NJ; [occ.] Student

PEACOCK, MICHAEL G.
[pen.] Francis Gravenorst; [b.] December 14, 1942, Republic of South Africa; [p.] Arthur and Caroline Peacock; [m.] Geraldine C. Peacock, June 4, 1966; [ch.] Caron and Michael-Paul; [ed.] Livingstone High (RSA), Wesley Training College (RSA), Certified Gen. Accountants Ontario, York University (Toronto); [occ.] Teacher, Bus., Math and History at Scarborough Christian High School (TOR); [memb.] Certified General Accountants Association of Ontario, Canada; [hon.] Hicth School - Award for Highest Mark in Biology, College - Awarded Education Bursary; [oth. writ.] Have been working on two volumes for publishing: South

African Autobiography, A Biblical History of Israel; [pers.] Suffering should bring out the best in any human. One voice speaking truth can change 300 years of history. Poetry is one of those voices.; [a.] Scarborough Ontario, Canada

PEARSON, BRIDGET
[pen.] Poirson Brigitte; [b.] August 5, 1951, Dole, France; [occ.] English Lecturer; [hon.] 4 Awards for poetry published in Paris (France). One book of poems published in New York (USA).; [pers.] Poetry is an experience that unites, a search for human unity and dignity.; [a.] Navenne, France

PEARSON, REBECCA L.
[pen.] Becka Pearson; [b.] November 5, 1977, Princeton, NJ; [ed.] Honors student, U of Hartford; [memb.] Honors Association, U of Hartford, March of Times Volunteer, Jerry's Kids Volunteer, Walk America Volunteer Educational Main Street Tutors; [oth. writ.] Publication of poetry, prose, and artwork award-winning magazines in Parauax, aspirations; [pers.] In writing, I try always to create life-images in my poetry of all the sweetnesses and blacknesses of life that grip all of us at once time or another.; [a.] Hamilton Square, NJ

PEATROSS, MARCIA I.
[pen.] Mip; [b.] March 12, 1946, Philadelphia, PA; [p.] Alexander Jago, Lillian Jago; [m.] William L. Peatross, July 26, 1992; [ch.] Ronald Pelikan, Tracy Pelikan; [ed.] Germantown High; [occ.] Administrative Assistant to the Dir. Software Engineering at Cardone Industries, Inc. in Phila., PA; [oth. writ.] Several poems written for people for special occasions, weddings, birthdays, a poem I wrote for my husband that was put to music and sung for him at our wedding; [pers.] My poetry, I believe, is inspired by, and reflects the love I am surrounded by in my relationship with the Lord Jesus, my wonderful husband and children, grandchildren and friends.; [a.] Philadelphia, PA

PEEL, LYNN
[pen.] Lindsey Beale; [b.] September 5, 1950, Ashland, PA; [ed.] B.S. PA State University, MA, Columbia University; [occ.] Sales Support Coordinator; [memb.] CT Poetry Society, Sono Poets Society; [pers.] My poems reflect the joys and sorrows of life. I love to dance, run, write poems. Be young with my children Aimee and Joshua and travel a spiritual journey with my soul mate, best friend and love - Michael.; [a.] Norwalk, CT

PELUSO, RAFAELA GUIU
[pen.] Felita; [b.] January 3, 1923, Oriente, Cuba; [p.] Manuel Guiu Emperador; [m.] Dominick D. Peluso, January 4, 1950; [ch.] My only son died in 1964; [ed.] Finished H.S. "Public School #1 Won an scholarship in 1942, In 1942 I won, but I lost, because the attire and books were too expensive, it was Private School.; [occ.] Retired, I live with my mother, 93 yrs old and counting, her name is Mercedes, that is my occupation, besides reading and studying, Greek, and Ru; [hon.] Won $30.00 in silver at George Jensew for a drawing used in meaning, and assign reality, "New Gark, Thodes Council and Halet Association N.Y. Coly Inc.", "George Jensen Dic. 1964"; [oth. writ.] I have some in English and Spanish, I think some are good. The only writing I published in New York was an

opinion about the death of kid Paret Angilist; [pers.] When I was 5 yrs. old I could read and write, when I started school I was a third grader, study at home, that's why. The happiest days of my life was the birth of my son, and to salute the flag of the United States, in a ceremony of "The Waldon of Astria" in the Bicentennial. That was an experience!; [a.] Miami, FL

PENDLEY, ROBERT R.
[b.] May 5, 1965; [p.] William and Anne Pendley; [m.] Susan S. May 25, 1988; [ed.] A.S. Degree in Law Enforcement Certificate in Paralegal Studies; [occ.] Freelance Paralegal; [pers.] Learning, disabled students are not stupid, in fact most are brilliant. Life is not always fun or fair the key is to persevere.; [a.] Naugatuck, CT

PENNEY, HELEN SILKA
[b.] June 24, 1934, Canada; [p.] Doris MacWhirter Bazan Radomska, John Cybulka; [m.] Charles Penwill - Armstrong - Penney; [ed.] B.A. (Univ. of Windsor), Masters Courses (Univ. of Windsor), Post-grad. (Univ. of Toronto); [occ.] Teacher (experienced in all levels from K-Univ. level; [memb.] Women Writers of Windsor, Can. Author's Assoc., International Society of Poets, the Scottish Club, Can-Am. Friendship Centre, Windsor Home and School Council, Royal Country Scottish Dancers; [hon.] Teaching Award from parents and students, Toronto, Ont., Social Studies Award (100% Av.)- W.B. Lane S.S., for top class teaching marks in law (1986) from husband Charles, Poet of Merit Award (International Society of Poets), Editor's Choice Award 1995 from The National Library of Poetry, Past Recognition in 1962 by letter from Queen Eliz. for "Gems of Peace"; [oth. writ.] Gems of Peace (1962)- all poetry Devon, Eng., in progress "Wee Bobby of Greyfriar's-short story, - India Catholic Journal-short story (Univ. of Chicago Journal) many general writings yet to be published and written; [pers.] I try to instill in my readers an appreciation for the aesthetic qualities found in creation and in all creatures, also I hope tat readers will learn to appreciate the necessity of all cultures to practise the "Brotherhood of Man" idea.; [a.] Windsor Ontario, Canada

PERAGALLO, CATHY
[b.] June 6, 1956, New Jersey; [p.] Mary Anne and Joseph; [m.] Ricky, July 14, 1985; [ch.] (Two) Dawn and Jacqueline; [ed.] North Bergen High School, New York Institute of Credit Religious Education Institute Scranton, PA; [occ.] Assistant Accounts Payable Supervisor; [memb.] I am currently a Board Member of the Winona Lakes Property Owners Assoc. having served as past secretary and treasurer. I'm active in our church community, too.; [oth. writ.] None that have been published; [pers.] I hope this is a direction to the future of having my work published, and I thank God for all my blessings and my family.; [a.] East Stroudsburg, PA

PERKINS, SUZANNE M.
[pen.] Suzanne Silva; [b.] November 24, 1949, Manchester, NH; [p.] Manuel J. Silva, Rollande Belisle-Silva; [c.] Dedicated to Faydra Moul; [ed.] St. George High School 1963 to 1966 Manchester Central High School 1967; [occ.] Job Title "Unit Senior Resource" V.S. Bankruptly Court District of

New Hampshire; [memb.] Saint Anne's Guild, Campfire of America, National Bankruptly Clerks; [oth. writ.] "Love is a shining thing" published Central high orange spring 1967 various poems published in N.H. Court Colloquy.; [pers.] To live each day to the fullest, to support my family and friends to the extent I am capable. To make one person laugh or smile each and every day.; [a.] Manchester, NH

PERRET, STEPHEN
[b.] February 4, 1979, Bethpage, NY; [p.] Robert and Lydia Perret; [ed.] Currently attending Chaminade High School, Mineola New York; [occ.] High School Student 11th grade; [memb.] National Honor Society, Assistant Editor of Skylight Literary Magazine, Chaminade High School Science and Social Studies Club, Writer for Chaminade H.S. Newspaper; [hon.] Honor roll, 9,10,11, Science awards, 9,10, Finalist: Lincoln-Douglas Speech and Debate, 1995, 2nd Place: Lincoln-Douglas Speech and Debate, 1995, Bishop McGann "Best of the Fair" Science award 1993; [oth. writ.] Several poems published in skylight literary magazine, several articles published in school newspaper.; [pers.] I wish to express that through nature and relationships with fellow man, mankind finds true meaning of life. My greatest influence has been the undying devotion of my family, friends, and the invaluable assistance of my uncle James.; [a.] Sound Beach, NY

PERRY, HARDY JAMES
[pen.] Hardy James Perry; [b.] May 25, 1941, Hampton, VA; [p.] Lula Mae and Wilford Perry; [m.] Francina Delores Perry, November 27, 1980; [ch.] Lula, Kim, Mary, Denice, Beverly, Harvey, James, Richard; [ed.] 12th Grade; [occ.] Retired; [hon.] Pastor, Elder Hardy Perry - Pastor of God Fellowship Temple #1 and 2; [oth. writ.] My friend Dwright and a list of others.; [a.] Newport News, VA

PERRY, LILLIE
[b.] January 29, 1943, Tahlequah, OK; [p.] John and Nancy McCarter; [m.] Arthur E. Perry; [ch.] Leslie G. Kirkpatrick, Farrell Eugene, Steven Keith; [ed.] Tahlequah High School, Haskell Institute, Northeastern State College; [occ.] Environmental Officer for the Cherokee Nation; [oth. writ.] Poems published in the Cherokee Advocate and the Oklahoma Highway Patrol, Public Safety Magazine; [pers.] To me a written poem is a way of expressing my thoughts which can't be expressed verbally. My writing tablet is my sounding board.; [a.] Tahlequah, OK

PERSAUD, MAHENDRA
[pen.] Mahendra Persaud; [b.] October 11, 1947, Guyana, South America; [p.] Rampersaud, Janie; [m.] Kristy, March 23, 1969; [ch.] Vij, Shelly, Minty; [ed.] 1. High School Graduate, 2. Agriculture College Graduate, 3. Hotel Front Desk Procedures-Cert. -Lindsey Hopkins' Tech.; [occ.] Hotel Front Desk Clerk/Night Auditor.; [hon.] 1. 1965 most qualified C.P Exam student - Lion's Club Award. 2. 1990 - awarded $1500.00 by Guyana Sugar Estate's "Field Operations Manual"; [oth. writ.] 1. See #2 left below, 2. Written several unpublished poems.; [pers.] Application and dedication to any task/assignment make that differ-

ence in the result, I believe and practice.; [a.] North Bay Village, FL

PETERS, LEO SAMUEL
[pen.] L. S. Peters; [b.] January 7, 1947, Catalone, C.B.N.S; [p.] William Leo and Mary Peters; [m.] Allena, July 5, 1975; [ch.] Two girls, one boy; [ed.] Grade 12 GED and academic upgrading level IV, April 28, 1995; [occ.] Part time work, and writing poems, and songs; [memb.] Faith Baptist Church and a Member of Socan Society of Composers, Authors and Music Publishers at Canada; [oth. writ.] I have written many other poems and songs close to a hundred, some of my songs have been play on our local radio station C.B.C. and CHER radio. I have about 25 songs on demotapes sung by different singers.; [pers.] I believe someday the Lord will show someone my poems and songs and they'll be published. I know my songs are as good or better than a lot of music played on radio today. Some of my songs have real meaning and are mend for Forcerin Pleple.

PETERSON, CECILE
[b.] June 23, 1912, Saba, NA; [p.] Deceased; [m.] Deceased, August 28, 1928; [ch.] Five living, two deceased; [ed.] 6th grade, available at that time; [occ.] "Ordinary Mom" and "Grandma" "20", and great grandma "12"; [oth. writ.] Several, none ever published.

PETERSON, DARLENE DURHAM
[b.] December 10, 1955, Vineland, NJ; [p.] Ophenia Peterson; [m.] Carl M. Durham Jr., July 2, 1983; [ed.] Cumberland Co. College; [occ.] Nurse; [hon.] Editors Choice Award from the National Library of Poetry.; [oth. writ.] God looking down on America, my Aunt Fannie going Astray.; [pers.] I want my poems to touch the heart of men, so that it may reflect upon the goodness of God.; [a.] Vineland, NJ

PETERSON, TEDDIE
[pen.] Teddie; [b.] January 13, 1946, Harrisburg, AR; [p.] Irvin Peterson, Lois Peterson; [ch.] Troy, Dawn, Scott, Brock; [ed.] Blooming Prairie High, Brainerd Vo Tech Brainerd MN, American Inst of Business, Desmoines IA. Pine Tech College, Pine City, MN Various Correspondence Courses; [occ.] Shipping and receiving clerk, Orsckeln farm and home, Owatonna, MN; [memb.] Former Commander Award Club Aitkin' MN, EMTA Blo. Pra Ambulance. North American Guesmith, Guild, NRA. Life, pistol, shotgun instructor, MN firearms safety instructor, IOWA and MN police and peace officers association; [hon.] Metal and Trophy for placing 3rd in hand skills competition in VICA. Five state area.; [oth. writ.] Started pine tech gunsmith guild news letter in 1985 (Poem) take out the garbage, published in Fountain centers news letter life line winter 1995. 32 unpublished poems.; [pers.] I try to reflect the pain and joy I have had or am having. To let others know they are not alone someone else also feel their pains as well as joys. Life is just that some pain, some joy but in either case it should be shared with others.; [a.] Blooming Prairie, MN

PETRIC, ANDREEA
[b.] February 22, 1978, Bucharest, Romania; [p.] Marilena and Gabriel Petric, Maria Ungureanu;

[ed.] College of New Rochelle (graduated high school in two years, at 16); [occ.] Student; [hon.] Who's Who Among American High School Students, The National Dean's List, nominated for the All American Scholar award, the fourteenth place as an Individual scorer in the Catholic High School's Math League Competition; [pers.] Favorite quote: "By all that's wonderful it is the sea, I believe, the sea itself - or is it youth alone." Who can tell? But you here - you all and something out of life: Money, love - whatever one gets on shore - and tell me, wasn't that the best time, that time when we were young at sea, young and had nothing, on that sea that gives nothing, except hard knocks - and sometimes a chance to feel your strength, that only is what you all regret. (Joseph Conrad, Youth).; [a.] New York, NY

PETRUCCI, FREDRICK A.
[b.] January 4, Miami Beach, FL; [ed.] Fresno State University Fresno, CA; [occ.] Teacher - Industrial Technology, San Marcos High School - Santa Barbara, CA; [oth. writ.] Short poems Reflecting on Life, Love, Romance and Nature. Previously published "Dead Meeting Syndrome" in the voice within.; [pers.] Life's not an emergency - take the time to open your eyes to what's around you and touch people's lives. The journey's so much sweeter with company.; [a.] Lompoc, CA

PFISTER, BRANDY
[b.] October 14, 1980, New Orleans; [p.] Cathrine and Gerald Pfister; [hon.] Honors Students at Andrew Jackson High School; [oth. writ.] I story written for mobile contest.; [a.] Arabi, LA

PHILLIPS, DELISA I.
[b.] April 17, 1963, Lufkin, TX; [p.] Mr. and Mrs. Johnnie F. Roberts; [m.] Gregory R. Phillips, October 6, 1984; [ch.] Gregory II and De'von Phillips; [ed.] M.B. Smiley High School Houston Community College; [occ.] Domestic Engineer; [memb.] American Heart Association American Lung Association; [hon.] Great Mothers Award of the year; [oth. writ.] A Housewife, East of the Sunrise Love is, My Everything Recited by Gregory and De'von Phillips which took 1st place trophies. The Man in my Dream, The Wondering Child.; [pers.] I take one day at a time asking God for strength to do the task of the day to the best of my ability which inspires me to relax and write.; [a.] Houston, TX

PHILLIPS, PETER H.
[b.] September 9, 1957, Queens, NY; [ed.] University of Pittsburgh; [occ.] Elementary Teacher Penn-Middle School Jeannette PA; [a.] Pittsburgh, PA

PHILLIPS, VERONICA JONES
[pen.] Bero; [b.] June 4, 1950, Trinidad, WI; [p.] Clement Jones and Agatha Jones; [m.] Andrew Phillips, July 9, 1977; [ch.] Mark Andre Phillips; [ed.] Trinidad West Indies sacred heart providence amow's secretarial; [occ.] Home Maker; [oth. writ.] Several poems not published

PICONE, WHITNEY LEADER
[b.] August 20, 1983, Berkeley, CA; [p.] Malcolm and Linda Leader-Picone; [ed.] Thousand Oaks Elementary School, Franklin Entermediate School

and Martin Luther King, Jr. Middle School, Berkeley, California.; [occ,] Student; [memb.] Berkeley City Ballet; [hon.] Martin Luther King, Jr. Middle School Honor Roll, invited to read my poem "Women" at the dedication of the mural "Maestrapeace" at the San Francisco Women's Building on September 25, 1994.; [oth. writ.] None published; [pers.] My friend Edythe Boone , a muralist, asked me to write a poem to celebrate the dedication of the "Masterpeace" which decorates the outside of the San Francisco Women's Building, I Like to put feelings into my poems, to bring the meaning of the poem.; [a.] Berkeley, CA

PIERCE, GORDON C.
[b.] October 27, 1918, Atlanta, GA; [p.] Dr. Carl F. and May S. Pierce; [ed.] Graduate, Greensbury High School Graduate, Carnegie-Mellon University Degree: Bachelor of Architecture; [occ.] Practiced Architecture for 40 years in Greensburg, PA-now retired.; [memb.] The American Institute of Architects, Pennsylvania Society of Architects, National Trust for Historic Preservation, Greensburg Art Club, Preservation PA, First United Methodist Church, Greensburg; [hon.] Charles McKenna Lynch Essay Award, Eternit Emaille Award, Kapelle Op Den Bos, Belgium (Foreign Travel), Redstone Highlands Award (Poetry); [oth. writ.] Journal of the American society of church architecture (articles on religious architecture of the Orient).; [pers.] Write principally of nature and the world about is, the earth, seas and skies. Also memories of past events as experienced.; [a.] Scottdale, PA

PINER, FERN RUPERT
[b.] February 26, 1920, El Dorado, KS; [p.] Mason Rupert, Edna Rupert; [m.] Willard E. Piner Sr. (Ascended), January 24, 1970; [ch.] Linda Lamb, Allen Lamb; [ed.] Haynesvilled (LA) High Learning has continued through reading, lectures, speeches, courses, discussions, etc. Western Union School; [occ.] Retired Western Union Service Representative; [memb.] Poetry Society of Texas (former member), American Association of Retired Person, Western Union Keep in Touch Klub; [hon.] My poem "Memories" was laminated and used as favors for seventy guests at our AARP 25th anniversary party. Reading at WU Kit Klub; [oth. writ.] 82 page unpublished book of poetry entitled "Part Of It All", 41 page book entitled "Thoughts and Essays by Fern Rupert Piner" unpublished.; [pers.] To quote myself, "I can never be small, I'm part of it all." Is my philosophy. Much of my work flows through me so fast I can hardly keep up and comes in perfect form. These poems are never changed. The giver of the gift needs no help from me.; [a.] Dallas, TX

PIPPY, TERRY GORDON
[b.] April 11, 1966, Halifax, Nova Scotia; [p.] Gordon and Violet Pippy; [ed.] Sir John A. Macdonald High School from 1982 - 1985; [occ.] Musician/ Writer/Producer; [memb.] Membership with The International Society of Poets; [hon.] Five Science Awards presented to me in 1979, Junior High school, 1995 Editor's Choice Award for outstanding achievement in poetry presented by The National Library of Poetry.; [oth. writ.] In walls of wisdom - unpublished 1991. Poetry published in Dalhousie University paper Halifax, Nova Scotia

Canada April 2, 1992.; [pers.] I hope thru my poetry I can encourage and inspire others to direct their pain and anger in positive and in non-violent ways.; [a.] Halifax Nova Scotia, Canada

PIVARNIK, SAMUEL L.
[b.] October 10, 1969, Stamford; [p.] Charlotte Lillian Montlick; [ed.] Fairfield High School, Served 4 years with U.S. Navy; [occ.] Sheet Metal Mechanic; [oth. writ.] Black Top Course, The Waiting, No Coins; [pers.] My writings are a reflection of events that take place around myself. Written in my view.; [a.] Fairfield, CT

PIZZINO, NICHOLAS S.
[b.] March 5, 1985, Bethlehem, PA; [p.] Gail and Sal Pizzino; [ed.] Currently in 5th Grade at Asa Packer, Elementary School, Bethlehem, PA; [memb.] Student Council, Staff Writer for Puma Press (School Newspaper); [hon.] Certificate from the Johns Hopkins University for Young Students Talent Search, Finished in top 10 of the National Geography Olympiad for two years; [oth. writ.] Winning entry for Mother's Day Contest published in Local Newspaper; [pers.] I was inspired by a Professor of poetry who presented a lecture to our Fifth Grade class.; [a.] Bethlehem, PA

PLANTE, KATHERINE
[b.] October 16, 1976, Livingston, NJ; [p.] Gail C. and Brian Plante; [ed.] North Hills High, pursuing undergrad at Cornell U.; [occ.] Student; [memb.] Cornell Tae kwon Do Club, St. Paul's United Methodist Church, Johns Hopkins U. Alumni Assoc.; [hon.] Phi Sigma Pi, Dean's List, Rachel Carson Book Award, National Merit Finalist, AP Scholar with Distinction; [a.] Pittsburgh, PA

PLATTE, JENNIFER LEE
[b.] February 14, 1984, Rochester, MN; [p.] LeRoy and Nancy Platte; [ed.] K-6th at Readlyn, Iowa Elementary (Wapsie Valley School District); [occ.] Student; [memb.] Three Years of 4-H, 6 Years of Ballet, Tab and Jazz Lessons; [hon.] First place D.A.R.E. Essay Winner, 9-year old Honorable Mention on "Fire Safety in my Home" booklet at 4-H fair; [pers.] I enjoy writing stories and poems.; [a.] Readlyn, IA

POIRE, ELIZABETH ANN K.
[b.] March 20, 1981, Kailva-Kona, HI; [p.] Gordon and Edy Poire; [occ.] High School Student; [memb.] Member of the Arts Council Co-op (ACCOP) and Operatio 'Ohana (a registry for native Hawaiians); [hon.] An honorable mention from the Fair Housing Project House Contest and an Award from the 1991 Aloha Week Art Exhibit and an honor in Science by the United States Achievements Academy in 1995; [oth. writ.] A story awarded by the Hawaii Council of Teachers of English (HCTE) in the 1992 Language Art Showcase; [a.] Kailva-Kona, HI

POLLARD, ROSA CLARISSA
[pen.] Rose Pollard; [b.] February 15, 1903, Edmonton, Alberta, Canada; [p.] Francis Pollard, Annie Bedard; [m.] Francis C. Pollard (Retired Coast Guard Officer), July 23, 1972; [ch.] Sister Mariam Pollard Mt. St. Marys Abbey, Wrentham, M.D.; [ed.] Edmonton High School Alberta Business College; [occ.] Retired from Foreign Service

1965, Administrative Officer in Tangiers and Honolulu; [memb.] AARP, NARF, Scuba Diving Club (in Hawaii), Friends of the Library, Holy Family Catholic Church Bonsai Culture, 10 years ago Rosa became blind and dictated the poem to her nurse.; [oth. writ.] Golden Gate Bridge poem My Home - Blue Door; [pers.] If you loan toward poetry, music of art, cultivate it. It may sustain you in your old age.; [a.] Seal Beach, CA

PORTH, TINA L.
[pen.] Tyler Liegh-anna; [b.] March 15, 1979, Pennsylvania; [p.] Debra & Peter Porth; [ed.] Western Wayne High School adn future college at Johnson Technical Institute; [occ.] Cashier; [memb.] Several poems published in local circulars.; [oth. writ.] 152 other personal writings and continuing to write.; [pers.] For the love of poetry and the peace it brings upon all those who understand it, I hope to further my writings in my own book.; [a.] Hamlin, PA

POSEY, JERALD
[b.] November 16, 1946, Oneida, TN; [p.] Arvel Posey Sr., Vivian Posey; [m.] Lenia C. Posey, November 12, 1966; [ch.] Donna M., Mary A., Paul S.; [ed.] Oneida High School Crossroads Bible College, Christian Bible College; [occ.] Pastor, Evangelist; [oth. writ.] Poems, Newspaper Articles; [a.] Vilonia, AR

POWERS, TODD R.
[b.] October 30, 1971, Boston, MA; [p.] Kenneth and Suzanne Powers; [ed.] University of Delaware (grad. cum laude B.A. in Medieval History), currently attending Boston University for M.A.T. in History Education; [occ.] Student Teacher, Newton North H.S., Newtonville, MA; [memb.] Massachusetts Council for the Social Studies; [hon.] Phi Beta Kappa, Phi Alpha Theta History Honors Society, Academic Scholarship to Boston Univ.; [oth. writ.] Poetry and short stories (as yet unpublished); [pers.] I write for a catharsis - attempting to release my qualms with humanity and society. I would like to acknowledge those who provided love and inspiration: my parents, my Lazebniks, and my other self, Anna Lazebnik.; [a.] Boston, MA

PRATT, ERIK
[b.] August 24, 1973, Alamosa, CO; [ed.] Embry-Riddle Aeronautical University, University of Missouri at Kansas City; [occ.] Actor; [memb.] Smithsonian Institution, Boy Scouts of America; [hon.] Eagle Scout, Tomtom Beater in the Tribe of Mic-O-Say; [pers.] It's the meaning gathered from words, rather than the words themselves, that touches lives. I offer my words for your interpretation.; [a.] Kansas City, MI

PRECIE, MONICA
[pen.] Monica Precie; [b.] November 24, 1982, Koma Kinda; [p.] Mary and Robert Precie; [m.] February 10; [ch.] Genevieve, Robert Jr., Michael; [ed.] Colton Jr. High Middle School; [occ.] Student of Cotton Jr. High, and recreation softball.; [hon.] School District Art Award in drawing. (pencil art); [oth. writ.] Poems have been published in school news paper.; [pers.] The way I write my poems is how I feel all these poems come from the mind and heart. I've written many others for school.; [a.] Colton, CA

PRELL, ELIZABETH ANN
[b.] March 26, 1980, Fremont, NE; [p.] Richard R. and Ruth A. Prell; [ed.] Sophomore - attend Fremont Senior High, Fremont, NE; [occ.] Student; [memb.] Civil Air Patrol, Band (concert and marching), Choir, Track, Cross - Country; [hon.] Young authors, track, cross-country, Saxophone Solos, Honor roll student; [oth. writ.] Have written 20 poems and still writing.; [pers.] I've been writing poems for 3 years. A few months ago I found out my birthday is the same as Robert Frosts. Poetry, to me, is away to express my feelings. If I get the urge to write something, I write it down and it just comes out in the poetic form.; [a.] Fremont, NE

PRESLEY-ROY, MICHAEL
[pen.] Michael Presley-Roy; [b.] April 20, 1928, London, England; [ed.] Upton Grammar, Berks, UK (1939-44), Newland Park College, UK (1967-70), Hornsey College of Art, London, UK (1973-75); [occ.] Professional artist and poet.; [hon.] Oxford University School Certificate (1944), Art Teachers Certificate, Reading University (1970), Diploma in Art Education, London University (1976), Diploma, 1993/4, International 4th Poesia - Visual Bienal, Mexico City, poem "Aubade" published M.L.P. `Best poem of 1995', poem "Ostrakon" published N.L.P. `Best poems of 1996,' (Editors choice award certificates and bronze (rd prize) medallion.; [oth. writ.] Books, "The Role of the Art Teacher", published London, 1976, "The Art-Lark", published southampton, 1992.; [pers.] "We endeavour to sustain with fortitude through our spirits wintering's, knowing that in Spring's soon-to-come `Whispering May', (wordsworth) there will be the refreshment of our soul through renewal and rebirth."; [a.] Southampton, England

PREVOST, FRANCINE
[b.] June 26, 1953, Leigne Sur Usseau, France; [oth. writ.] La fiencee du Mississippi, Sequences, Nobi...; [pers.] A poem is "un lieu de memoire" Montreal in winter, a time of memories, fleeting and insubstantial, lived and dreamt.

PRICE, HEATHER D. LARSEN
[b.] May 12, 1954, Furth, Germany; [p.] Walter L. R. Larsen, Thelma N. Larsen; [m.] Christopher D. Price, December 9, 1989; [cd.] Kailua High School, Rockhampton School of Equatation, Kapiolani Community College; [occ.] Owner Windsor Equestrian Center, riding instructor/trainer; [memb.] American Horse Show Assoc.; [hon.] B.H.S.A.I. 1973; [oth. writ.] Published once in Quill Books, "All My Tomorrows" volume VIII 1994.; [pers.] I write of the things that touch my heart and soul, good and bad, happy and sad, and in this way create lasting memories of the events in my life.; [a.] Redmond, OR

PRIESTER, TERRI E.
[b.] January 27, 1974, Charleston, SC; [p.] Sheree Chumney; [ed.] 1992 Graduate of Carrabelle High, Carrabelle, FL; [occ.] United States Navy Sardinia, Italy; [oth. writ.] "Shadows": Meditation and Poetic Voices of America. Unpublished words include "Tomorrow", "The Abyss", "You", "Darkness".; [pers.] Personal experiences which affect me deeply inspire some of my best writing.

PRINCE, FRANCES ANN
[pen.] Frances Ann Poince; [b.] Toledo, IA; [p.]

John Ihos and Frances Keily; [m.] Richard Edward Prince, August 17, 1951; [ch.] Anne Louise and Richard Edwin III (Deceased); [ed.] AB, Berea Coll., 19951, Postgrad., Kent School Social Work, 1951, Creighton U., 1969, MPA, U. Nebr., Omaha, 1978.; [occ.] Instructor flower Arranging Western Wyo. Jr. Coll., 1965 - 66, Editor Nebr. Garden News, 1980. Editor Emeritus; [memb.] State Camping Com., 1959-61, bd Dirs Wyo. State Coun., 1966-69, Chmn. Community Improvement. Green River, Wyo., 1959, 63-65, Wyo Fedn. Women's Clubs State Library Svcs., 1966-69, U.S. Constitution Bicentennial Comm. Nebr. 1987-91, Omaha Comm. on the Bicentennial 1987-91, Wyo State Adv bd. on Libr. Inter-Co-op., 1965-69, Nat sub Con. Commn. on the Bicentennial of the U.S. Constitution, 1986-91, bd. Dirs. Sweetwater County Libr. System, 1962, pres. dd., 1967-68 Adv. Coun. Sch. Dist. 66, 1970-, bd. dirs. Opera Angels, 1971, fund raising chmn., 1971-72, V.P., 1974, bd dirs. Morning Musicale, 1971-90, (Organization Disbanded) Bazaar Com. Children's Hosp., 1970-75, Docent Joslyn Art Mus., 1970-85, Nebr. Forestry Adv. bd., 1976-, Citizens Adv. bd. Met. Area Planning Agy., 1979, Nebr. Tree Planting Commn., 1980-, bd. dirs., U.S. Bicentennial of U.S. Constitution bd, dirs. United Ch. Christ. Recipient Libr. Svc. award Sweetwater County Library, 1968, Girl Scout Svcs. award, 1967, Conservation award U.S. Forest Service, 1981, Plant Two Tress award, 1981, Nat. Arbor Day award, 1982, Pres award Nat. Coun. of State Garden Clubs, 1986, 87,89, Joyce Kilmer award Nat. Arbor Day Found., 1990, awards U.S. Constn. Bicentennial Comm. Nebr., 1987, 91, Omaha Comm. on the Bicentennial, 1987, Nat Bicentennial Leadership award Coun. for Advancement of Citizenship, 1989, Nat. Conservation medal DAR, 1991, George Washington silver award Nat. Commn. on Bicentennial of U.S. Constitution, 1992, Mighty Oak award Garden Clubs of Nebr., 1992, AAUW (Vol. of Yr. Omaha Br. 1989), New Neighbors League (Dir. 1969-71), Ikebana Internat, Symphony Guild, Omaha Playhouse Guild ALA Nebr. Libr. Assn. Assistance League of Omaha, Omaha Coun. Garden Clubs (1st v.p. 1972, pres. 1973-75, Nat. Council 1979-, pres. award 1988, 98, 90), Internat. Plattform Assn. Nat. Trust for Hist. Preservation, Nebr. Flower Show Judges Coun., Nat. Coun. State Garden Clubs (Chmn. Arboriculture 1985-90. Chmn Nature conservancy 1991-93), Nebr. Fedn. Clubs (Pres 19781), Board of Directors 1963-69, Exec. Com. 1966-69); [oth. writ.] Poems Chmn. Lone Troop Copun. Girl Schouts U.S.A., 1954-57, trainer leaders, 1954-68; [pers.] To work in my garden brings me intouch with the elemental forces of the earth the sun the wind, the rain, the change of seasons and how they affect us as we live and love and are earths caretakers it gives us a sense of and closeness to the eternal.; [a.] Omaha, NE

PRINCE SR., KEVIN T.
[pen.] "Q-Man"; [b.] December 16, 1961, Jacksonville, FL; [p.] John and Betty Prince; [m.] Renita V. Prince, August 8, 1987; [ch.] Kevin T. Prince Jr.; [ed.] Ribault Senior High School, Jacksonville Florida, Morehouse College, Atlanta, Georgia (B.S. Biology 1985), University of Florida (D.M.D. 1992) Gainesville, Florida.; [occ.] Dentist; [memb.] American Dental Association, Omega

PSI PHI Fraternity Inc., National Naval Officer's Association.; [hon.] Navy commendation Medal, National Defense Service Medal.; [oth. writ.] Several poems for special occasions, musical lyrics for publishing and recording, and short stories, articles for newspapers and magazines.; [pers.] My mission is to bring those who read my writings into the work, and have them feel the emotion, intensity, and determination which goes into that particular piece of work. I am forever striving to stimulate thinking and discussion thru my writing.; [a.] Chesapeake, VA

PRINDL, SARAH E. R.
[pen.] Sarah Eve; [b.] March 10, 1971, West Allis, WI; [p.] Douglas and Renee Roth; [m.] Travis Prindl, July 8, 1995; [ed.] Waterford Union High School, University of Wisconsin, White Water; [occ.] Safety Professional, Janesville, WI; [hon.] Northeastern Illinois ASSE Chapter Scholarship, Silver Scroll Senior Honor Society, Dean's List; [oth. writ.] A couple poems published in bank calendars.; [a.] Milton, WI

PROCTOR, DANIEL J.
[b.] August 8, 1976, Chewelah, WA; [p.] Jerry Proctor, Elizabeth Proctor; [m.] Johanna Proctor, July 8, 1995; [ed.] Colville High School, Spokane Community College; [occ.] Student, Spokane Community College, Spokane, WA; [pers.] "This Darkness" is my first submitted work and my first published work. It has given me the courage to continue writing.; [a.] Spokane, WA

PROCTOR, EVELYN
[b.] November 4, 1950, Modesto, CA; [p.] Jessie Ames, Edward (Deceased); [ch.] Kristopher R., Elizabeth L.; [ed.] Modesto High, Modesto Jr. College Calif. State Univ. Stanislaus; [occ.] Student; [hon.] Cum Laude, Dean's List; [pers.] My poetry is an expression of my growth through life.; [a.] Sonora, CA

PROVINCE, NICHOLAS BRYAN
[b.] July 25, 1979, Parkersburg, WV; [ed.] K-10, presently a Junior at Northwestern High School; [pers.] Every step we take each day writes another line of poetry and I think all of us have very interesting stories to tell.; [a.] Rock Hill, SC

PROVITT, CLINTON
[b.] May 19, 1946, Montgomery, AL; [p.] Clinton Provitt and Berdic M. Provitt (Deceased); [m.] Ozzic L. Provitt, Februry 11, 1995; [ch.] Concetta, Rico, Tony, AngeL, Diane; [ed.] Atlanta Metropolitan College, Atlanta Music Business Institute; [occ.] Musician/singer, pianist, organist for church; [hon.] Who's Who in American Jr College 1976-77, Music Appreciation Award, Dean's List; [oth. writ.] I've written some religious songs I've gone to the bible and put the melodies to some of the psalms and taped them. I also sing them; [pers.] I am a "citizen of life", owning my allegiance to God, country and humanity. I write mostly through inspiration springing from the waters of my soul.; [a.] East Point, GA

PRUITT, MISTY
[b.] December 17, 1978, Elk City, OK; [p.] Loyd

and Carla Pruitt; [ed.] I am a high School Student of Elk City High School. I'm in the tenth grade.; [memb.] Chorus (select choir); [oth. writ.] I have a poetry journal that I have kept. There aren't that many, but what I do have I'm quite confident that they could do as well as "I am" has.; [pers.] I believe poetry is a way of expressing unexpressed, maybe hidden feelings in your soul. I have been influenced by 2 special people former teachers. Mrs. Adkinson and Mr. S. Carpenter.; [a.] Elk City, OK

PUKACH, JENNIFER
[b.] November 24, 1968, Aliquippa, PA; [p.] Marion Pukach, John Pukach; [ed.]Quigley High Duquesne University Masters Degree in Criminal Justice Duquesne University; [occ.] Retail and Wholesale Business; [hon.] American Legion Award National Honor Society; [pers.] Three statements have helped me in dealing with people and life. You can't change the spots on a leopard. To thine own self be true. Do it now.; [a.] Pittsburg, PA

PUSKAR, MICHAEL BRANDON
[b.] October 23, 1977, Baltimore, MD; [p.] Daryl and Deborah Puskar; [ed.] Liberty High, Class of 1995 - Western Maryland College, Class of 1999; [hon.] Carroll County Arts Council, 1995 Creative Writing Award, Dean's List - Highest Honors; [oth. writ.] Columns, Poetry, Comic Strips (High School Newspaper, Paw Prints), Column, Comic Strips (College Paper, The Phoenix); [pers.] I want to ameliorate the problems of the world and hope that my poetry will be revelation in the eyes of mankind. I accredit my desire to write poetry to one of the greatest lyricists of today - string.; [a.] Sykesville, MD

PYLES, ANN ELISE
[b.] April 2, 1978, Arlington, TX; [p.] Paul and Judy Pyles; [ed.] Senior at Martin High School; [occ.] Work at an advertisement company.; [oth. writ.] Nothing published, I just write for myself to express how I feel.; [pers.] "Family of Two" was written in memory of my father who died April 4, 1994. I loved him greatly and miss him very much.; [a.] Arlington, TX

QIAN, JIA-MEI
[b.] March 12, 1980, Shanghai, China; [p.] Hong Yu; [occ.] Student in Millburn High School; [pers.] You are never too young.; [a.] Millburn, NJ

QUATRONI, RACHEL
[b.] November 14, 1985, Bronxville, NY; [p.] Yvonne and Thomas Quatroni; [ed.] Siwanoy Elementary; [a.] Pelham, NY

QUIGLEY, ARDELLE M.
[b.] December 13, 1945, Hanover, Ontario, Canada; [p.] Norman and Bessie Klages; [m.] J. David Quigley, August 23, 1969; [ch.] Daphne, David, Joel Evangeline and Esther; [ed.] Nursing, Diploma in Theology, Bth. in Theology, C.A.P.P.E. - Chaplaincy Training; [occ.] Chaplain in Continuing Care Center; [memb.] Canadian Association for Pastoral Practice and Education, (Chapliancy-Pentecostal Assemblies of Canada a (Minister); [pers.] I believe God can relate to each individual, no matter where they are physically, mentally, emotionally and spiritually.; [a.] Edmonton Alberta, Canada

QUINN, LAURA
[b.] August 16, 1969, Bronx, NY; [p.] Eamon and Patricia Quinn; [ed.] Acad. of Holy Angels, University of Delaware; [occ.] Graduate Work in French Literature; [pers.] Poetry is an expression of and an exploration for the depth of my own sensitivity, regarding the pain and joy brought to my soul by life's experiences.; [a.] Wilmington, DE

RAGLE, MATTHEW WILLIAM
[b.] April 8, 1967, Annapolis, MD; [p.] Dwight and Barbara Ragle; [ed.] B.A. Psychology, Eastern Connecticut State University, Willimantic, CT.; [occ.] Self-employed Entrepreneur.; [memb.] N.R.A.; [hon.] 1st Degree Black Belt in Tae Kwon-do; [oth. writ.] Several articles and poems published in college newspapers.; [pers.] "To get the most out of life, you must first get the most out of yourself".; [a.] Farmington, CT

RAHMING, CHARLENE H.
[b.] November 7, 1969, Nassau, Bahamas; [p.] Freddie Rahming (Father); [ed.] Uriah McPhee Primary School Donald Davis Junior High School R.M. Bailey Senior High School; [occ.] Computer Sales Clerk; [pers.] Anything that come to my mind. Anything in general.; [a.] Nassau, Bahamas

RAILLARD, SARAH
[b.] August 24, 1982, Aix or Province, France; [p.] Pierre and Marie Raillard; [ed.] Riverfield Elementary School, Tomlinson Middle School; [occ.] Student; [memb.] Audubon Nature Society; [hon.] High honors; [oth. writ.] Several poems published in local newspapers finalist in the reflections contest, writer of an electronic underground newsletter; [pers.] One of my favorite poets is Poe. Like him, I like to make things in my poems obscure, or at least, to have a different meaning for different people.; [a.] Fairfield, CT

RAIN, CONSTANCE
[pen.] Cheryl Anderson-Eulo; [b.] October 3, 1956, Jersey City, NJ; [p.] Brenda and David Anderson; [m.] Gerald A. Eulo, September 15, 1990; [ch.] Chelsea Ann, Robert; [ed.] American Academy of Dramatic Arts, Kingsborough C.C., Essex County College; [occ.] Physical Therapist Assistant; [memb.] Phi Theta Kappa, American Physical Therapy Association, Aquatic Exercise Association, Youth Division of U.S. Soccer Federation, Harley Davidson Owner's Group; [oth. writ.] Over time I have accumulated an entire collection of work, however, I never had the nerve to present it for publication, until now.; [pers.] "Breath each moment deeply, for it will never pass again."; [a.] Nutley, NJ

RALLI, SUSANNA
[b.] January 26, 1964, Washington, DC; [m.] James Ralli, October 17, 1993; [ed.] Wellesley High School, Boston College; [occ.] Freelance Editor, proofreader writer; [memb.] Women's Business Network, Women in Publishing (Boston), Freelance Editorial Association; [hon.] Member of the Alpha Sigma Nu Jesuit Honor Society; [oth. writ.] Several articles published in local newspapers.; [pers.] Natick, MA

RAMPANI, ROBERT MICHAEL
[pen.] "Bob"; [b.] July 1, 1928, St. Louis Co., MO;

[p.] Michael and Etta Rampani; [m.] Divorced, October 23, 1950; [ch.] Steve, Gene, Ralph, Aaron, Roberta; [ed.] Graduate of Pattonville High School 12th Grade; [occ.] Retired From McDonnell Douglas; [memb.] Greater St. Louis Archaeological Society the International Society of Poets International Association of Machinists and Aerospace Workers; [hon.] Poetry Award NLP-ISP many Archeology show awards Missouri State Champion Tree Award write up in "Home place, Bridgeton Missouri" Book write up in "St. Louis Post Dispatch" newspaper Baseball Awards.; [oth. writ.] Several poems published in news letters and newspaper. Articles in archaeology Journals. Have written 150 poems as yet released. Other poems submitted to ISP-NLP and poets Corner. A poem "God's land" sent to to the President and V. president of the United States.; [pers.] I write from the heart in an experienced way, about the past, Gods creatures, beauty of our land and preservation of it. Whatever I write will be heartfelt for I live it. Concerned greatly about destruction of our natural land, Indian sites and all wild life.; [a.] Bridgeton, MO

RASHFAL, MICHAEL
[pen.] Michael Rashfal; [b.] January 26, 1980, Tucker, GA; [p.] Irina and Rafail Rashfal; [ed.] The Paideia School; [occ.] Student - 10th grade; [memb.] U.S.A.B.D.A. (United States Amateur Ballroom Dance Association); [hon.] Various Awards for Dancing, 1st Place at the Georgia Music Educators Association Solo-Ensemble Festival.; [oth. writ.] Various poems submitted for school.; [pers.] Be yourself and always strive for the top.; [a.] Tucker, GA

REA, KATHY
[b.] January 16, 1959, Mount Clemens, MI; [m.] Anthony Rea, August 1, 1987; [ch.] Lauren, Alexander; [ed.] Lakeview High School; [occ.] Labortory Receptionist at Bon Secours Hospital in Grosse Pointe, MI.; [memb.] Head of Fundraising effort for abused children residing at the Macomb County Youth Home; [oth. writ.[Currently writing a book to promote the "Make a Wish Foundation" and dedicated to terminally ill children.; [pers.] "Everything I've ever written comes from my heart and is a direct result from some experience that I've had".; [a.] St. Clair Shores, MI

REAVES, JENNIFER JANELL
[pen.] Jennifer Reaves; [b.] August 11, 1970, Lawrence, KS; [p.] Judy, Earl Fisher, and Gary, Jeanie Reaves; [ed.] Mayde Creek High School, graduated 1987, Texas School of Business, 1989; [occ.] Secretary, at Fisher Industries, Inc.; [memb.] Charter Member of the Houston NW Optimist Club; [oth. writ.] Not, at this time. But I am presently working on a Children's Book.; [pers.] I dedicate this poem to Layton Taylor, my Fiance.; [a.] Houston, TX

REDMAN, MARY L.
[b.] December 14, 1931, Madison, IL; [m.] David E. Redman, December 26, 1950; [ch.] Michael, Joan, Helen, Debbie, Patty, James (Deceased), Sandy and Laurie; [ed.] High School; [occ.] Family Aid Specialist Child Abuse (Retired) Child Neglect State Agency; [memb.] Our Lady Queen of Peace Church

Prayer Group, (Memb.) American Diabetes Assn., Cancer Survivors; [pers.] I Hope to light one little candle, by expressing my faith in the power of prayer. When one recognizes a higher power all things are possible.; [a.] Bethalto, IL

REECE, DALE
[b.] May 22, 1953, Grenada, West Indies; [ed.] Verdun Protestant High, Vanier College, Concordia University Montreal, Canada; [occ.] Special Care Counsellor, Care Giver; [memb.] National Geographic Society Doubleday Book Club; [hon.] Bronze Fitness Award; [oth. writ.] An article published in High School Newspaper; [pers.] I try to promote good human relations by approaching everyone I encounter with politeness and respect.; [a.] LaSalle Province of Quebec, Canada

REED, MARY
[b.] May 7, 1982, Dallas, TX; [p.] Albert Reed, Dianne Reed; [ed.] Trinity Christian Academy (K-8) will enter High School 96-97 at Trinity Christian Academy; [occ.] Student; [memb.] Dallas County Pioneer Association Northwest Bible Church Orchestra; [hon.] Headmaster's Honor Roll (5-8), Spanish Award (5); [a.] Dallas, TX

REED, MARYLIN
[pen.] Marylin Matthews Reed; [b.] August 14, 1939, Pasadena, CA; [p.] Burt E. Matthews, Gussie Matthews; [m.] Gary W. Reed, June 28, 1958; [ch.] William G. Reed, Sharon G. Sherman; [ed.] Paramount High School, Paramount, California; [occ.] Wife, Mother, and grandmother; [memb.] Southwest Bible Church, Beaverton, Oregon; [oth. writ.] Short story - Scripture Press Publications, Inc.; [pers.] The only solution to humanities downward spiral is Jesus Christ.; [a.] Beaverton, OR

REEDER, FRANCES BURKS
[b.] September 24, 1920, Mississippi; [p.] Mr. and Mrs. Edgar S. Burks Sr.; [m.] Stephen T. Reeder, 44 yrs. ago; [ch.] John Michael Reeder; [ed.] High School, Lake Ms., RN Vicksburg Hopt. V'burg, MS, OR Post Grad Johns Hopkins, MD, CRNA Baylor Univ. Hopt Dalls, TX; [occ.] Retired Nurse Anesthetist; [memb.] Methodist Church; [oth. writ.] Short essays and compositions for family and friends - some poems and original greeting cards (unpublished); [pers.] I like to write personal and meaningful articles to people that I love and respect. This poem "Working the Night Shift" is dedicated to my teacher and mentor Ms. Emma Easterling she is 90 yrs. old.; [a.] Big Sandy, TX

REEDER, SARAH M.
[b.] September 29, 1982, Medford, OR; [p.] Cathy Nash, Joe Reeder; [ed.] Current Student at Talent Middle School; [memb.] Science Club, Math Team, National Junior Honor Society; [hon.] Honor Roll; [a.] Phoenix, OR

REESE, CHARLES
[pen.] C. O. Reese; [b.] February 5, 1941, New York; [p.] Willis Reese and Leonora Reese; [occ.] Retired; [oth. writ.] Cardinal Medeiros Center Boston senior citizen center monthly - St. Helena's Boston - monthly St. Francies house a poem framed and hanging in the dinning area Boston - reflections of light at waters edge.; [pers.] My interpretation of poetry is! Using

words in paraphrase and sentences that may mesh together or not - about nothing in particular, may be something specific that stimulates your trend of thought in a short space of time.; [a.] Boston, MA

REETHS III, ARTHUR J.
[pen.] Arthur James R.; [b.] April 4, 1954, Yorktown, VA; [p.] Art and Pat (Schultz) Reeths; [ch.] Shannon and Jamie Reeths; [ed.] G.C.C. (Glendale Community College) AZ and the Hair stylist Barber College... a Licensed Hair stylist, for 17 years; [occ.] A (U.S. West Cellular Phone Rep.) Incottonwood, AZ; [hon.] Honorably Discharged Vietnam Viet. served early 70's last draft of Vietnam 72-76; [oth. writ.] Two different articles in my hometown paper, "The Glendale Star" titled "Remembering Wifer" 2 other poems being published with the Nat. Lib. of Poetry titled "In Your Eyes" and "Jerome's Art" or "Stained Glass."; [pers.] I was blessed with a 2nd chance in life, and decided to pursue other avenues of personal achievements. One would be my writing, and drawing. I would like to see the real beauty and dispositions and attitude: Goodness that man could produce.; [a.] Jerome, AZ

REEVES, GREGORY A.
[b.] September 6, 1953, Havre de Grace, MD; [p.] Allen Reeves, Beverly Longenbach; [m.] Michelle Reeves, June 11, 1988; [ed.] Parkland High, LeHigh County Community College, U.S. Navy, U.S. K-9 Academy, Allentown College, numerous Seminars and Workshops; [occ.] Business Owner: Dog Training, Boarding, and Grooming Faculty; [memb.] Association of Pet Dog Trainers (APDT), People for the Ethical Treatment of Animals (PETA); [hon.] U.S. Navy: Good Conduct, and Humanitarian Awards, LeHigh Community College: Dr. and Mrs. Berrier Achievement Award for Most Outstanding Male Freshmen Student, Dean's List; [oth. writ.] None published - Working on various others.; [pers.] I am a vegetarian with strong beliefs in human and animals rights. An enigma of romanticism and realism pervades my philosophy.; [a.] Hellertown, PA

REEVES, GREGORY A.
[b.] September 6, 1958, Havre de Grace, MD; [p.] Allen Reeves and Beverly Longenbach; [m.] Michelle Reeves, June 11, 1988; [ed.] Parkland High, Lehigh County Community College, U.S. Navy, U.S. K-9 Academy, Allentown College, Numerous Seminars and Workshops; [occ.] Business Owner: Dog Training, Boarding, and Grooming Facility; [memb.] Association of Pet Dog Trainers (APDT) People for the Ethical Treatment of Animals (PETA); [hon.] U.S. Navy: Good Conduct, and Humanitarian Awards, Lehigh Community College: Dr. and Mrs. Berrier Achievement Award for Most Outstanding Male Freshman Student, Dean's List; [oth. writ.] None published - working on various others; [pers.] Pro human and vegetarianism and Animal Rights. An Enigma of Romanticism and Pragmatism pervades my philosophy.; [a.] Hellertown, PA

REEVES, TROY
[b.] January 13, 1978, Lahr, Germany; [p.] Suzanne Mayes and Chris Reeves; [ed.] Student at Prairie Bible College; [hon.] Graduated with honors from Halifax Christian Academy in Nova Scotia.; [oth. writ.] I have written many poems which I'd like to get published, one of which, "The clock of Life," has been published by the National Library of Poetry, and it was inspired from a gospel tract untitled, "The Clock"; [pers.] All credit belongs to my Lord and Savior Jesus Christ, who by His grace, has blessed me with this talent. I want to glorify Him with my poetry.; [a.] Three Hills Alberta, Canada

REID III, HERBERT J.
[b.] February 11, 1969, Kansas City, KS; [p.] Herbert and Tommie Reid; [m.] Olivia C. Reid, June 18, 1994; [ed.] AGS Kansas City Community College BS Health Services-Wichita State University; [occ.] Youth Care Worker, Aspiring Physical Therapist; [memb.] Who's Who 1994, 1995 Colleges and Universities; [hon.] Arthur Ashe Award-1995, Leadership Council 1995-1996, Alpha Eta Society December 1995; [oth. Writ.] Seasons Of Love, Retro, Mr. Bachelor, He's There, He's There; [pers.] Fear is the mental lactic acid that put one's esteem into deprivation.; [a.] Wichita, KS

REIS, EUSTACE HENRY
[pen.] Ric; [b.] December 8, 1913, Guyana, South Africa; [p.] Alfred Reis and Julia; [m.] Enid Gabriella Reis, February 16, 1952; [ch.] Guy and Christopher, Michelle Reis Cotteir; [ed.] Bachelor of Arts, Open University, United Kingdom, Diploma in Theology Dip. Theo. University of St. Michael's College, Toronto, Canada linked with University of Toronto, Canada.; [occ.] Retired British-Colonial, Civil Service and British Local Government Service London, England; [memb.] O.B.E., Order of the British Empire awarded by Queen Elizabeth II herself in 1966 New Year's Honours Member of the Royal Commonwealth Society (Toronto branch).; [hon.] O.B.E. as above. The National Library Poet's Choice Award for contest entry as published in shadows and light.; [oth. writ.] Several poems (not yet on offer for publication) including odes on "A Philosophy Of Suffering, Saving The Children, and an ode relating to the Oklahoma Tragedy, and several religious poems in prayer/hymn form.; [pers.] A practicing Christian, who greatly respects other religions, especially the Budhist, Jewish, Hindu, and Muslim religions, and hope to see all some day on a common platform urging love and peace worldwide.; [a.] Scarborough Ontario, Canada

REITEN, RUTH C.
[pen.] Val E. Paul; [b.] June 9, 1915, Minnesota; [p.] Pauline M. Reiten, August 19, 1939; [m.] Paula, Val and Virginia; [ch.] B.S. Degree El.Ed 15 yrs. Exp 2 writing courses wrote gardening column for local news. Wrote Col for R.E.A. mag.; [ed.] Retired; [hon.] Keep Am beautiful a word, honor dairyman a word.; [oth. writ.] Spires west - poetry book I need a friend (Psy of Friendship) Chips and Chuckles book. (Numerous, Historical of '50's in Minn.); [pers.] When we drag against the grain of nature we get slivers.; [a.] Billings, MT

REMICK, DAWN A.
[pen.] Dar; [b.] May 25, 1949; [p.] Henry and Shirley Rollinber; [m.] Ralph B. Remick III, August 15, 1991; [ch.] Christopher Alan Hoffman (Deceased) Constance Marlo Hoffman and Ralph B.

Remick IV; [ed.] Bachelor's Degree, Northwood University will graduate May 1996; [occ.] Contract Specialist; [memb.] National Assoc. for Executive Women, Federal Employed Women, Doberman Pinscher Club of Mich. and National Society for poets; [hon.] NTL Society for Poets; [oth. writ.] Dreams and I Remember, other poems one published one just submitted. Wrote in high school and for Doberman Pinscher Club of Michigan newsletter; [pers.] My writings come from my heart that has been filled with brief for the loss of my son in June 1995 to a senseless murder.; [a.] Sterling Heights, MI

RENAUDIN, FLORENCE
[pen.] Milicent Forbes; [b.] December 2, 1968, France; [p.] Francois Renaudin, Claude Renaudin; [ed.] Instituted L'Assumption ecoredes Hautes etudes Ensosociales LA Sorbonne Nouvelle Paris III UCLA Los Angeles; [occ.] Hand Model, Amateur Writer; [oth. writ.] Poems, novels; [pers.] I try to write about different topics using many different genres from poetry to novel; [a.] Palms Springs, CA

REYES, RIZALYN
[b.] April 24, 1980, Calgary, Alberta, Canada; [p.] Ramon and Flordeliza Reyes; [ed.] Currently enrolled in Gr. 10; [hon.] Honor Roll, Royal Conservatory of Music Piano Studies (Finished 3 grades with honors); [pers.] Everything that they comes, from the heart is beautiful.; [a.] Calgary Alberta, Canada

REYNOLDS, LORRIE J. M.
[b.] May 21, 1953, Kansas City, MO; [p.] Dr. Carl K. McMillin, Norma Buchler McMillin; [m.] Edwin J. Reynolds III, December 28, 1992; [ch.] Alisa Nora, Mary Kathryn; [ed.] BSN University of Delaware, Newark, DE; [occ.] Home School Teacher and Mom; [pers.] Giving God the glory - Praise his Holy name.; [a.] Dublin, OH

REYNOLDS, STEPHEN E.
[pen.] Seryn; [b.] July 17, 1936, Jersey Shove, PA; [p.] Willard Reynolds - Vivian Perry R.; [m.] Cathy, March 25, 1960; [ch.] Brent, Kevin, Glenn; [ed.] William Carrie College, MS; [occ.] Maintenance Planner, Blue Grass Army Depot, KY; [memb.] Pen and Sword Society, 1st Baptist Church, Music Clubs of America, Boy's Town, NRA; [hon.] Various military honors, Achievement Awards for Public Service.; [oth. writ.] College Anthologies, news articles about skin Diving (many years Ago), one song recorded.; [pers.] Do all you can for those around you - be the best you can - and don't worry about that which is beyond your control dream!; [a.] Winchester, KY

RHATIGAN, RACHEL
[b.] May 15, 1971, Council Bluffs, IA; [p.] Roy and Linda Rhatigan; [ed.] Abraham Lincoln High School, Indian Hills Community College, U.C. Berkley (Extension); [occ.] Laser Technician at Coherent Laser Group; [memb.] Sierra Club, World Wildlife Fund; [hon.] Dean's List, IHCC Student Senator, IHCC Foundation Award; [a.] Santa Clara, CA

RHEA, JARED
[b.] January 16, 1977, Colorado Springs, CO; [p.] Ronald and Beth Rhea; [ed.] Graduated of Vallejo

Senior High; [occ.] Shipping Clerk for Real Time Solutions in Napa, CA; [oth. writ.] Working on a chap book with Joel Grandholm.; [a.] Vallejo, CA

RIBSCHESTER, NADINE
[b.] September 26, 1971, Victoria, Australia; [p.] Robert and Janine Evans; [m.] Ian Ribschester, March 25, 1995; [ed.] Lilydale Secondary College; [occ.] Computer Operator, Binney and Smith Australia P/L; [oth. writ.] Various unpublished works.; [pers.] The majority of my writing is influenced by my own personal feelings and past experiences. The fight against animal cruelty is something we should all support.; [a.] Boronia Victoria, Australia

RICE, YVONNE MARIE
[pen.] Y. R.; [b.] September 30, 1943, San Luis Obispo, CA; [p.] Victor Beze and Bonnie Calvin; [m.] David George Rice, December 21, 1962; [ch.] Yvonne, Yvette, Jeanette, David; [ed.] A.A., Theater Arts Major, Certified Stephen Minister, Mary Mount University for Certified Spiritual Director, State of California Life Insurance Lic.; [occ.] Funeral Director/pre-arrangement counselor. Spiritual Director; [memb.] Roman Catholic Church Lectors Guild. Stephen Ministry. Association of Christian Therapists. Sophia Women's Groups. R.C.I.A., Catholic Ch.; [hon.] Support Recognition award from Calif. State Univ., Dept. of Social work. Best Actress award, "Tobacco Road" El Camino College; [oth. writ.] Children's stories: "Waterbaby Much Afraid", "Little Bird", Funeral poems for Bereaved families.; [pers.] Life is filled with a thousand endless journeys...I have travelled most of them and have completed quite a few.; [a.] Redondo Beach, CA

RICHARD, CRISTINA GUTIERREZ
[b.] June 15, 1956, Guadalajara, Jalisco, Mexico; [ed.] Hoth's Classical Ballet Academy; [hon.] She has been a coordinator in literacy workshops, she has also given courses, during several years, on "Literary appreciation". She participated to the board of authors of Televisa. She has a diploma in Philosophy for the Panamerican University. In June 1986, she got the first place in The National Contest of Poetry at the "Festivities of May" In Puerto Vallarta Jalisco Mexico., In August of the same year, she got an honorific mention in the National Contest of Scenic Expression of Jalisco with her drama work titled "Linaje De Baro" ("Lineage of Clay."); [oth. writ.] She writes poetry, theater, story and essay. Beside that, she recently finished her first novel titled "Mujer De Cabellos Cortos Y Buenas Piernas" (Women With Short Hair And Beautiful Legs"), soon to be published., In 1987, she publishes and book of poetry: "Las Sombras Que Refleje Manana" ("The Shadows I Reflected Tomorrow"), at the publishing unit of Jalisco State Government (UNED). In 1988, she is part of the anthology in the book "Flor De Poesia En Guadalajara" ("Flower Of Poetry In Guadalajara"), published by the city Council of Guadalajara 1986-1988. In 1989, her work appears again with the book "Poesia Reciente De Jalisco" ("Recent Poetry of...") collection of the Center of Literary Studies, published by the University of Guadalajara. She takes part in the volume III "Teartro Mexico Del Siglo XX" ("Mexican Theater Of The Twentieth Century") 1900-

1986. Catalogue of Theater plays, published by the Mexican Institute of the Social Security (I.M.S.S.). In 1992, part of her poetry can be found in the book poets from Jalisco-. State Council of Culture and Arts (C.E.C.A.). In 1993, she publisher a story book titled: "Sin Mi Me Muero" ("I'm Dying Without Myself), published by the State Council of Culture and Arts. This same year, she publishers a new poetry book: "De Angels Y Cegueras" ("From Angels And Blindness"), La Luciernaga Publishers, as a commemorative publications and Latin American Women Writing. Her poetry was set to music in the compact disc "Con Rostro Propio" ("With Own Face"), from the composer and singer Lucia Ramirez. Besides that, it is compiled in the book Io. "Poesia, Enciclopedia Jaliscience De Lecturas Escolares" (Poetry, Jalisco Encyclopedia of Scholar Readings), La Luciernaga Publishers. Anthology in the book "Presente Y Precedente De La Literatura De Mujeres Latinoamericanas" ("Present And Precedent Of Laten American Women Literature"), La Luciernaga Publishers, Guadalajara, Jal., 1994. Part of her poetry appear on the Book-Catalogue of Lucia Maya's painting work "Al Filo De La Vida" ("On The Edge Of Life"), published by the Puerto Rican Institute of Culture, San Juan de Puerto Rico, 1994. "Nombrario/Namery" (Bilingual Edition), published by the P.E.N. Club International, as an official sample of the foundation of Pen Club Guadalajara, which one was approved during the General Assembly in the sixty-first Prague Congress held in November 1994. Special numbered edition "La Sal De Los Silencious" ("The Salt Of The Silences"), 1994, Lucia Maya/ Cristina Gutierrez Richaud, Sistole Diastole Publishers. Works to be published: "Sophie's Silence" and "Lineage of Mud". (Theater). She has written several short stories for infants and some theater plays for children. Some of them have been staged.

RICHARD, DOROTHY AUGUSTINE REID
[pen.] Dor.; [b.] March 28, 1952, Jamaica, WI; [p.] Loretta and David Reid; [m.] Lloyd Richard, August 29, 1992; [ch.] Five; [ed.] College Graduate in the following Arears Health Care Aid, Recreation Therapist for Seniors and President for the Family Training hour in my Local Church.; [occ.] Recreation Therapist; [oth. writ.] Songs; [pers.] My heart felt feelings capture many forms of love: And thus I expresses it in qualities that pleases the mind.; [a.] Toronto, Canada

RICHARDSON, EVELYN
[b.] May 24, 1979, Natick, MA; [p.] Marci McPhee and Bert Richardson; [ed.] High School year of graduation 1997; [occ.] Student; [memb.] Massachusetts Youth Ballet, Natick High School Jazz Ensemble; [hon.] National honors Society, Honor Student, Flute Section Leader; [oth. writ.] Several poems published in The Writer's Bloc Literacy Magazine; [pers.] "To be great is to be misuderstood". - Thoreau.; [a.] Natick, MA

RICHARDSON, THEODORE ALLEN
[b.] November 21, 1948, Dayton, OH; [p.] Mr. and Mrs. Earl Richardson; [m.] March 10, 1975; [ch.] Two daughter, one son; [occ.] Writer; [hon.] Honorable Discharge USMC, Purple Heart, Gold Star, Wright State University Certificate for Completed Vietnam Era Veteran Program; [oth. Writ.] "Clear To Me You See", "Love In

Large Portion", "After Effect (Vietnam)", "Anniversary Period", "Miss D Miss Delicious To The Taste"; [a.] Dayton, OH

RIDDELL, KATHLEEN
[b.] March 11, 1981, Ottawa, Canada; [p.] Jamie and Ernest; [ed.] High School Student, Holy Trinity Catholic High School: Kanata, Ontario; [hon.] English Award, Grade 8 Graduation: Female Athlete of the Year, 1992-93 at Holy Redeemer Elementary School - World Awareness, Award (92-93) - Valedictorian; [oth. writ.] Poetry; [pers.] Poetry is one aspect of my life. In my poems I try to capture the romanticism and tradition of our past.; [a.] Nepean Ontario, Canada

RIDDLE, WESLEY ALLEN
[pen.] Keoni Aloha

RIDLEY, ELAINE
[b.] March 17, 1946, Lewiston, ME; [p.] Carroll and Emma Webster; [m.] Divorced; [ch.] Mary Ann, Carrie Ann, Clayton Delfred, Michael James, Paul William; [ed.] Wales Central, Monmouth Academy, Farmington State Teachers College, University of Maine (Lewiston Auburn, Augusta); [occ.] Home maker; [memb.] First United Pentecostal Church; [hon.] Phi Theta Kappa, Dean's List; [oth. writ.] Poems written to friends or family indifferent situations. Letters of encouragement, exhortation. Stories of life experiences dealing with range of topics. Life with children with ADD.; [pers.] I draw on my own life experiences and attempt to make reader feel as if he were there. I am a born again Christian and try through my writing to convey His wonderful power in our lives. I write about feelings.; [a.] Sabattus, ME

RIGGS, MIKE
[b.] January 1, 1971, AZ; [occ.] Writer, Student; [pers.] Thank you family and friends for making me who I am and thank God for 44th St.; [a.] Newport Beach, CA

RIGGS, SHARON
[pen.] "Sherry" Riggs; [b.] July 31, 1947, Knoxville, TN; [ed.] College; [occ.] Legal Assistant for Law Firm.; [oth. writ.] Short stories - poems published in "Anthology of Poctry" from the Center for Today's Women - Cerritos College.; [pers.] I am an artist who loves to paint in oils, write, and am an American Indian of the Cherokee Nation, Eastern Band. I write what I feel in my heart and see with my eyes.; [a.] San Diego, CA

RIKER, KRISTY
[pen.] Lonely Heart; [b.] November 15, 1978, Sullivan, IN; [p.] Randy and Diana Riker; [ed.] Currently a junior in high school; [hon.] Honor Roll in the 9th Grade; [oth. writ.] "Dreams", "Regrets", and "Colors of Life"; [pers.] "Love - those who have it, write about it. Those who don't - read about it."; [a.] Terre Haute, IN

RIPLEY, DENNIS
[b.] August 3, 1944, Amherst, NS; [m.] Madelyn; [oth. writ.] Silent Mission published in Sparkles In The Sand, The Buriel published in The Path Not Taken.; [pers.] Poetry is a wonderful way to record ones memories and perceptions.; [a.] Calgary Alberta, Canada

RIVERA, BRANDON
[b.] August 26, 1974, Bemidji, MN; [ed.] Thief River Falls, MN-Northland Community College, 2 years; [pers.] I have several poems although not published public. I've been greatly influenced by the writing of the poet Jim-Morrison.; [a.] Bagley, MN

RIX, LESLEY
[b.] March 16, 1953, Middlesex, United Kingdom; [p.] Christopher and Edna Aveson; [m.] Ronald, December 27, 1975; [ch.] David and Graham; [ed.] Woodlands Girls School Basildon; [occ.] Factory Worker at Henderson Mobile; [oth. writ.] Poem printed in Sparkles in the Sand. Western novels and poetry.

RIZZA, JESSICA J.
[b.] December 8, 1981, Helena, MT; [p.] Sandra and Jim Rizza; [ed.] 8th grade; [occ.] Student; [memb.] Junior National Honor Society; [hon.] Student honor role, student of the month; [oth. writ.] In the Works; [pers.] Beauty is within us all. We just have to uncover it.; [a.] Avondale, AZ

ROBERTS, CARROL
[b.] June 13, Jamaica, West Indies; [p.] Thelma and Uriah Roberts; [ch.] Andrew Scott and Kevin Scott; [ed.] St. Hugh's High School, College of Arts, Science and Technology; [pers.] To Mark: Thank you for the love and happiness you give to me. You are an inspiration.; [a.] Boonton, NJ

ROBERTS, CHARESSE DANIELLE
[pen.] Reese; [b.] July 27, 1982, Philadelphia; [p.] Yolanda and Eugene Roberts Sr.; [ed.] I started my education in Primasens Germany, Then I attended Smith Elementary School for grades 2 thru 4, now I attend Barratt Middle School 8th Grade; [memb.] I am a member of the Focus Club which is for Honor Roll Students I am a member of The New Bethany Baptist Church where I am on the young adult choir and on the educational committee; [hon.] I have received numerous award such as the principals award along with trophies for music and other citizenship awards; [oth. writ.] My other writings I have are not yet published except for one that has been published in the 1994 issue of Anthology of Poetry For Young Americans titled My Cousin; [pers.] This poem is dedicated to my mother for always being there and helping me out and most of all guiding me through the tough times and allowing me to write my feelings into poetry where it may be an inspiration to someone else who reads it.; [a.] Philadelphia, PA

ROBERTS, CHRISTINA G.
[b.] March 29, 1972, Toronto, Ontario, Canada; [p.] John Peter Lee Roberts, Christina Van Oordt; [ed.] University of Victoria (British Columbia), Universite du Quebec a Trois-Rivieres (Quebec), University of Montreal (Quebec), (U.Q.T.R.); [occ.] Full-time student and Seasonal tree planter since 1993; [hon.] Public Speaking Award, U.Q.T.R.; [pers.] Writing, for me, is a way of seeking truth and holding onto my dreams. I would like to acknowledge the works of Van Morrison, Michael Timmins and Anne Hebert.; [a.] Vancouver British Columbia, Canada

ROBERTS, KIRI A.
[b.] November 4, 1966, Portsmouth, VA; [p.] Mr. William R. Roberts Jr.; [ed.] Pensacola Catholic High ('85), FL Jacksonville University ('89), FL BFA in Visual Communications; [occ.] Research Analyst - Medical Billing, Jacksonville, FL; [memb.] Zeta Tau Alpha (Collegiate Alum); [hon.] Editors Choice Award for Outstanding Achievement in Poetry 1995.; [pers.] I dedicate my poetry in memory of my mother Norma J. Roberts...I'm fascinated with the aesthetic qualities of texture and the different moods it can convey. I try to implement these qualities in all of my life, my art and my poetry. My writings show a different way of seeing, personal reflections on an ambiguous journey through life and it's conflicts.; [a.] Jacksonville, FL

ROBERTS, THOMAS D.
[b.] May 13, 1936, Hartford, CT; [p.] Louis and Dorothea Roberts; [m.] Linda M. Roberts, September 4, 1982; [ch.] Raymond and Chris, and Stepchildren; [ed.] High School; [occ.] Disability Retirement; [memb.] Masonic Lodge, Scottish Rite York Rite and Shriner; [oth. writ.] I have written many other Christian poems. As yet I have done nothing about them; [pers.] I believe we should take time out to look back at our lives correct our short comings and put our trust in God.

ROBERTSON, MARK ALLEN
[b.] May 28, 1968, Los Angeles, CA; [p.] Geary Lee and Mary Lou Runnels; [ed.] Williams High School; [memb.] Lamp of Hope: Anti Death Penalty; [oth. writ.] Poems published in the following books, "Seasons to Come" (poem: Incommoded) "Out of the Night" (poem: So many Times) and other minor publishings in "rag-bags" and small papers.; [pers.] Living on Death Row has been a curios business. In society's garbage can I have discovered my own mortality, my spirituality and most important my humanity. We are then men judged incorrigible, yet we love, live and suffer when we see those die around us. For some death row is the end of the road, for others it is only only beginning. Being a death row inmatye, I have met many men, who were judged incorrigible. I find this appalling for the intrinsic value of human nature is to develop, learn and prosper. To abandon this philosophy and kill a man by law is to abandon humanity itself.; [a.] Huntsville, TX

ROBINSON, CHRISTINE YOUNG
[b.] March 19, 1955, Columbia, SC; [p.] Celess Young, Ruby Young; [m.] Joseph Robinson, September 7, 1974; [ch.] Rahim Robinson, Nishika Robinson; [ed.] University of Islam, New York Tech College, RCA Business School, Ace Business School; [occ.] Civil Service Disability Retiree; [memb.] Shades of Impact Women's Club, sponsor of Unique Girls Club; [hon.] Veterans Administration Outstanding Performance Award, Veterans Administration Superior Performance Award, Creative Writing Award; [oth. writ.] Process writing and publishing a Black Comedy Book, Unique Girls Club Newsletter.; [pers.] With God as my guide I can accomplish what I will. My writing is dedicated in loving memory of my cousin, Gloria Yvonne McCornell.; [a.] Columbia, SC

ROBINSON, HELEN E.
[b.] March 2, 1908, PA; [p.] Harry and Laura Gohh; [pers.] This poem is very serious to me as I have had seeing and hearing problems along with my many experiences in life. To appreciate look to the clouds when reading.

ROBINSON, MABLE AUGUSTA CARTER
[b.] May 9, 1945, Waco, TX; [p.] Jesse and Freddye Carter; [m.] Nehemiah Robinson, July 18, 1971; [ch.] Nikki Robinson; [ed.] A.J. Moore High, Paul Quinn College, BS in Elem. Ed. Prairie View A and M College, Med. Post grad. study, Kansas State U. and Emporia State College of Kansas.; [occ.] Kiddie Kollege Primary Teacher K.C.K.; [memb.] Church of God in Christ, Life Mem, N.E.A., Zeta Phi Beta, Business and Professional Women's Federation of KS. East C.O.G.I.C.; [hon.] Who's Who among students in Am. Univ. and Colleges, 64-65, Outstanding Young Women of Am. 77.; [pers.] Being engaged in the ministry I strive daily to live by Prov. 3:6. In all thy ways acknowledge Him, and He shall direct thy paths. I put God first.; [a.] Kansas City, KS

ROBINSON, MICHAEL S.
[pen.] Michael S. Robinson; [b.] July 29, 1945; [p.] Vernon and Jean Robinson; [m.] Divorced; [ch.] One son, Mark Robinson; [ed.] East Croydon High School, London, England; [occ.] Musician; [oth. writ.] I have just finished writing a book of 200 pages of my life, and 12 songs for an album, who ever will sing them I am writing now a book for children.

ROCCA, ANNA MARIE
[b.] January 20, 1967, Santa Ana; [p.] Peter Rocca, September 2, 1995; [ed.] Rim of the World High, Orange Coast College; [occ.] Singer, Song Writer, Artist; [hon.] Artistic Showcase Award 1982, OCC Drama Award 1988; [oth. writ.] Dreams - an anthology of poems.; [pers.] Through my writing, I endeavor to enlighten and inspire others. I find writing poetry to be a magical experience.; [a.] West Hollywood, CA

RODER, BERNICE
[pen.] Bernice Gilge Roder; [b.] March 5, 1934, Rib Lake, WI; [p.] Julius Gilge and Martha Gilge; [m.] Conrad D. Roder, September 13, 1952; [ch.] Diane, David, Dawn, Debbi, Kelly; [ed.] Rib Lake High School; [occ.] Homemaker, Farmer's Wife; [memb.] Trinity Lutheran Church of Chelsea, WI. and Women's Group; [oth. writ.] One poem published in local paper, several unpublished poems.; [pers.] I wrote this poems as a tribute to the nurses at Memorial Hospital of Taylor County, Medford, Wisconsin.; [a.] Rib Lake, WI

RODGERS, WANDA CLOIS
[pen.] Wanda C. Wilkinson; [b.] February 14, 1944, Memphis, TN; [p.] Cullie and Naomi Wilkinson; [m.] Divorced, June 23, 1970; [ch.] Heath Devlon, Brian Delane; [ed.] BS and MS University of Memphis; [occ.] Art Teacher at Horn Lake High School; [hon.] Who's Who in Ed. 1996 (according to pre-publication information), WOTR "First Submission", Contest Winner in Writers on the River, Fall 1992; [oth. writ.] Short Stories, "The Grave Robber", Writers on the River 1992, "The Frog Princes", Writers on the River

1993 or (1994); [pers.] My poetry and story writing are merely tools to relieve my pain. I have been beaten on the head, burned to a crisp, and emotionally stepped on while I was down by the systems that were supposed to protect me. However, God always provided someone to place a stepping stone for my heart as I passed along the way. A small act of kindness can build a mountain of hope and courage.; [a.] Southaven, MS

RODNEY, TIMOTHY J.
[pen.] Timothy J. Rodney; [b.] April 9, 1980, Hospital, Scranton; [p.] Barbara Rodney, Michael Evanick; [ed.] Sophomore North Pocono High School, Moscow, PA; [occ.] Student/Musician; [oth. writ.] "Don't Fall Asleep" a short story that is unpublished written under the pen name H. F. Simon.; [pers.] I was greatly influenced by writers such as Stephen King and Peter Straub, and by poets such as James Thurbery Ogden Nash.; [a.] Moscow, PA

RODRIGUEZ, DAVID
[b.] February 18, 1950, Las Animas, CO; [m.] Sharon Rodriguez, December 24, 1971; [ch.] David Jr., Jason B., Daniel; [ed.] Las Animas High School, Rangely Jr. College; [occ.] Retired D.V.A.; [oth. writ.] Several poems and other writings unsubmitted/ unpublished at this time.; [pers.] Priceless knowledge and experience I gained - simply by doing! Priceless youth and time I lost - simply by assuming!.; [a.] Las Animas, CO

ROGERS, JR., GRANT
[pen.] Lamar; [b.] June 3, 1958, West Virginia; [p.] Carrie and Grant Rogers, Sr.; [m.] Single; [ch.] 3- Robert, Teresa and Tommy; [ed.] 1 year college; [occ.] Librarian; [memb.] Live and let live club; [oth. writ.] Seasons Change, Tearing Down The Walls, Lost in The Sungle. [pers.] Give more than your willing to recieve, and always be better than, the best you can be. Also inspired by my baby girl.; [a.] Bluefield, W.VA

ROGERS, MAXINE R.
[b.] November 4, 1939, Winchendon, MA; [p.] Arthur B. Rogers, Yvonne A. Rogers; [m.] William D. Noel (Divorced/deceased); [ed.] Gardner High School; [occ.] Military Personnel Staffing Technician, AMEDD Reserve; [memb.] AARP, Eagle's Auxiliary, National Geographical Society, Wildlife Conservation; [hon.] Work related only; [oth. writ.] None at this time.; [pers.] I believe we are all the same because we come from the same place, even though the threads of our life may look different from others, if only means the threads of our lives are woven into interesting patterns and if we take the time to look we will find ourselves in others. When we can accomplish this then how could we hurt, kill anyone, after all who would harm themselves?; [a.] Gardner, MA

ROGOZINSKI, KERRY
[pen.] Potthoff, Marty; [b.] May 25, 1955, Mineola, NY; [p.] June McNeil - Philip Potthoff; [m.] Anthony Rogozinski, September 27, 1981; [ch.] Toni Philis Rogozinski; [ed.] East Meadow High School; [occ.] Data Entry Operator; [memb.] Sunday School Teacher, Secretary Executive Board - CSEA Union Local - 852, Hampton Bays Republican Women Volunteer; [pers.] I try to just make people happy, to see that God made

everything and everybody equal - "Keep smiling"; [a.] East Quogue, NY

ROMANS JR., MICHAEL D.
[b.] February 5, 1977, Tallahassee, FL; [p.] Carrie C. Romans; [ch.] 2; [ed.] Druid Hills High, Atlanta, GA; [occ.] Student in College, Stevens Institute of Technology; [memb.] Greenforest Church, Decatur Library, Usher Board; [hon.] Selected for Who's Who Among High School Students. Presidential Scholar, National Merit Scholar; [pers.] Aim at the sun. You may not reach it, but you will fly higher than if you never aimed at all.; [a.] Atlanta, GA

ROMEOS, OLGA V.
[b.] September 30, 1962, Montreal, Canada; [p.] George and Stavroula Romeos; [m.] Vasilios (Bill) Siozios, March 16, 1986; [ch.] Diana Siozios, Georgios Siozios; [ed.] B.S. Computer Science M.S. Computer Science (Course work); [occ.] Sr. Systems Engineer; [pers.] The peace enjoyed by many starts with the peace found by one.; [a.] Silver Spring, MD

ROMERO, RHIANNON
[b.] February 25, 1978, Paramount, CA; [p.] Armando Joseph and Gloria Romero; [ed.] St. Joseph High School; [occ.] Student; [memb.] National Honors Society, California Scholarship Federation; [hon.] National Hispanic Scholar, third place in the Los Angeles times annual scary story contest; [oth. writ.] "Scarlet Vengeance"; [pers.] Writing, like my other art, is a form of self-expression. When a writer creates, that person exposes a part of him or herself between every line, within every word, of his or her text.; [a.] South Gate, CA

ROOLEY, SARAH CROY AVAN
[pen.] St. Croix; [b.] October 9, 1967, Morristown, NJ; [p.] Ronald and Kate Croy; [m.] David Brian Rooley, June 19, 1993; [ch.] Johnathan Rooley; [ed.] McGavock High, Institute of Children's Literature; [occ.] Homemaker; [memb.] St. Philips Episcopal Church; [oth. writ.] Stained Shoulder, 1990; [pers.] As for my life, I will give no answers, no regrets. I am what I have lived - and what I have taught myself to be. How can I apologize?; [a.] Mount Juliet, TN

ROOPE, MICHAEL S.
[b.] August 31, 1970, North Wilkesboro, NC; [p.] Fred and Helen Roope; [ed.] North Wilkes High School, Wilkes Community College (A.A., A.S.), Davidson College (B.A. Psychology), Appalachian State University (Post Graduate); [occ.] Teaching - Parent, Wilkes Boys town; [pers.] I am captivated by the romantic and intellectually idiosyncratic depictions of everyday life — they breathe life into open minds and new experiences.; [a.] North Wilkesboro, NC

ROPER, KARRI R.
[pen.] Roxy Leavitt; [b.] July 16, 1968, Easley; [p.] Mr. and Mrs. William R. Roper; [ed.] BA in Psychology at University of South Cardina, Associate in Human Services at Midlands Technical College, Master in English at Clemson University; [occ.] Writer, Food and Beverage Consultant with the A. Ivey Corporation; [oth. writ.] Three novels in progress many poems,

lyrics, and special occasion pieces.; [pers.] I write mostly about bars, bands, and trying to get life right. "The Bartender's Lament" was written for Johnny Raines, and friend we call "The Best Across the Bar."

ROPPOLO, AL
[pen.] Stevie London; [b.] January 21, 1963, Boston, MA; [p.] Sal and Salima Roppolo; [occ.] Song writer/poet; [a.] Brockton, MA

ROSE III, ROBERT L.
[b.] September 19, 1974, Georgetown, TX; [p.] Robert Rose Jr., Cecile Rose; [m.] Carrie R. Rose, September 24, 1994; [ch.] Micah R. Rose; [ed.] Pflugerville High, Community College of the Air Force; [occ.] United States Air Force; [hon.] Pflugerville Performer of the Year 1993; [oth. writ.] Published songwriter, co-writer and director of plays for various organizations.; [pers.] My work is generally Christ-centered and explores the emotions associated with serving Jesus Christ. He is my inspiration and the reason I have a talent to share.; [a.] Austin, TX

ROSS, CHRIS
[b.] April 20, 1026, Hartney/Farm; [p.] Laurence and Gladys Thomas; [m.] (2nd) Ken Ross, (1st) September 20, 1950, (2nd) July 1, 1958; [ch.] Evalynn, Freda, Marlene, Helen, Beverly, Christopher, John and Curtis; [ed.] Grade 7 Melgund School.; [occ.] Housewife, grandmother, owner and manager of a goatherd of purebred Alpines and Nubians. Formerly a horsewoman; [memb.] Seniors for Seniors Writers Club, Brandon. Reston Art Club of Painters. Teaching basic art of animals.; [hon.] Trophy of Appreciation from the Manitoba Palomino Horse Association. Trophy of Appreciation from the Brandon Goat Show Committee.; [oth. writ.] Article - Two articles published in the magazine "Palomino Horses" official publication of the Palomino Horse Breeders of America. (Many years ago). A letter of appreciation of a friend in goat business, published in Dairy Goat Journal, the official publication of American Dairy Goat Association. (A couple of years ago).; [pers.] I let my love of God's creations of nature and animals show up in my poems and stories, and also in my paintings. I am attempting to get as much in print or picture as I can remember, or have time for. It is because my children will someday want to know these things, and I won't be here to tell them, unless I get it down on paper or canvas. I am not trying to become famous, or make a living at it. I am only doing it so my children will have it in a keep able form.; [a.] Hartney, MB

ROSS, SHARON
[b.] December 24, 1957, Dallas, TX; [p.] Merlene and Enoch Ross Jr.; [m.] Johnny Johnson (Deceased), September 28, 1973; [ch.] Timothy and Nadia Johnson; [ed.] Working on BFA at New Mexico State University, G.E.D., Associates of Arts, New Mexico State University.; [occ.] Certified Nursing Assistant; [pers.] At the age of thirteen I heard the poet Nikki Giovanni recite her poetry. After hearing her I started writing poems myself.; [a.] Las Cruces, NM

ROSSBY, JOSSTEIN
[b.] December 12, 1941, Harstad, Norway; [p.]

Hans Rossby, Gudrun Rossby; [occ.] Translator, Crossword Maker; [memb.] The Church of Jesus Christ of Latter-Day Saints; [oth. writ.] Limericks, poems and articles published in some local and national magazines and newspapers in Norway.; [pers.] The truth is in here.; [a.] Moss, Norway

ROSSI, PHILOMENA DOLORES
[pen.] Chookie; [b.] October 6, 1931, Latrobe, PA; [p.] Anthony Peter De Primio and Viola Katherine Brasili; [s.] Anthony F. Rossi; [m.] July 11, 1950; [ch.] 4 - Michael, Jessica, Patrick and Antoinette; [ed.] Grade School to 2nd year of Jr. High. Had to go to work to help family.; [occ.] Housewife, Pres. of Entertainment Services & Promotions Agency.; [hon.] Editor's Choice Award. Outstanding Achievement in Poetry by The National Library of Poetry. Nomination for one of poet of year 1996 award. Aug. 2 - Washington, DC (Whitehouse).; [oth. writ.] Story Book " Stories for children of all ages" with 2nd book now in progress. Poems: " I walk Alone", " Keys", "Winter's Grief", "Aseed", "With You Eternally", "Where Would You Go", "Do You Remember", "Winds", Pittsburg Steelers Here to Stay", "Do You Hear The Rain", and "Time". Article published Catholic Accent Christmas Focus.; [pers.] Always wanted to write. Did so throughout childhood but nothing ever accomplished by it, except lessons learned. Now that I am older, this need is still in me, so I following my heart.; [a.] Greensburg, PA

ROSSINI, CARMEL
[pen.] Carmel Rossini; [p.] Alfred Alcaro and Margaret Greco; [ed.] Fordham University Walton High School Bronx, New York City; [occ.] Pianist-Artist Teacher; [memb.] Thomas Wolfe Society; [hon.] Carnegie Hall, Diploma-New York, Received Classic Accademia "Nobel" of the Accademy of Science, Letters and Art of Milan Italy; [oth. writ.] Poems and Articles Now Preparing First Novel; [pers.] Books are jewels to be revered. People who read many good books can never lose their way in life.; [a.] North Miami, FL

ROWE, KIMBERLY
[b.] April 17, 1969, Canada; [p.] Lorenzo, Barbara Rowe; [ed.] Port Colborne High School, Brook University; [pers.] I personalize all my poems and deal with life experiences. I truly believe that I can reflect the unheard voice of many women through my poetry.; [a.] Brooklyn, NY

ROY, JASON K.
[pen.] J. R.; [b.] September 29, 1976, Edmundston, New Brunswick, Canada; [p.] Donald Roy, Audrey Roy; [ed.] C.D.J. A.M. Sormany; [occ.] University of Moncton (Student), (Maj. Computer Science, Min. Physics); [memb.] Poets' Guild; [oth. writ.] Poem in the poetry anthology "Best New Poems" (Poets' Guild).; [pers.] My poetry is a self-expression of what I wish for, of what I feel.; [a.] Edmundston New Brunswick, Canada

ROY, JOHN
[pen.] John Roy; [b.] June 25, 1980, Halifax, Nova Scotia, Canada; [p.] Alain and Diane Roy; [ed.] Charles P. Allen High School, grade 10 student, Bedford, Nova Scotia, Canada; [occ.] Charles P. Allen High School - grade 10 student, Bedford, Nova Scotia; [memb.] Volunteer Youth

Club Leader - Fall River, Nova Scotia, Fall River Community Bible Chapel, Fall River, Nova Scotia; [hon.] Graduate Honors George P. Vanier Junior High School 1995, Fall River, N.S. Canada, 1994 Kiwanis Music Festival Gold Award Vanier Jazz Band (Trumpet), 1995 Kiwanis Music Festival Gold Award, C.P. Allen Grade 10 Band (Euphonium); [oth. writ.] (The Eel-Kimberlines), 1994 publication of poetry selection "The Eel" in Kimberlines by The Association of Teachers of English of Nova Scotia.; [pers.] I write poems to express my feelings in writing.; [a.] Fall River Nova Scotia, Canada

RUBUS, LAVERNE
[b.] June 26, 1933, Cleveland, OH; [p.] Harry Boege, Lillian Boege; [m.] Robert Rubus, December 21, 1957; [ch.] Lilliam, Deborah, Theresa, Rachel; [ed.] John Hay High; [occ.] Administrative Assistant Retired; [pers.] The beauty of the written word has always touched me deeply; [a.] Eastlake, OH

RUDDELL, JEFFREY
[pen.] Rude Moose; [b.] April 12, 1977, Burgaw, NC; [p.] Charlie Ruddell, Debbie Ruddell; [ed.] Pender High; [occ.] United States Postal Employee; [hon.] Eagle Scout, Who's Who Among High School Student '92, '93, '94, '95; [oth. writ.] Several screenplays, short stories and poems.; [pers.] Always look and do your very best, you never know who's watching you!; [a.] Burgaw, NC

RUIZ-DIAZ, ELENA
[b.] April 17, 1942, New York City; [p.] Lorenz and Olga Bauer; [m.] Oscar M. Ruiz-Diaz, 1967; [ch.] Andreas and Daniel; [ed.] B. A., City College of New York, MSW, New York University; [occ.] Clinical Social worker; [memb.] N.A.S.W., various nature and wildlife consevency groups; [oth. writ.] Unpublished poems; [pers.] My poems reflect the every day situations, dilemmas and feelings of people. In my work, I try to help people with these same phenomena.; [a.] Stamford, CT

RUVALCAVA, VYKKI CAPLAN
[b.] January 24, 1956, Los Angeles, CA; [p.] David and Sarah Caplan; [ch.] Shandi and D. J.; [ed.] Los Alamitos High School, Whitley College of Cart Reporting, AA Chaffey College, BA National University; [occ.] College Instructor, Cerritos Community College, Dept. of Court Reporting, Norwalk, CA; [memb.] California Court Reporters Association, National Cart Reporters Association, Faculty Association of California Community Colleges, Team of Advocates for Special Kids, Church of Religious Science; [hon.] Court Reporting Certified Shorthand Reporter, Calif., Registered Diplomate Reporter, Certified Reporting Instructor, 1996 Who's Who of American Teachers; [oth. writ.] Misc. poems and letters published in local newspapers. Wrote a letter that On Laura Schlessinger read on her radio program (1994).; [pers.] I want to contribute to the good things in our world.; [a.] Los Alamitos, CA

RUWANPATHIRANA, MONICA
[b.] February 26, 1946, Matara, Sri Lanka; [p.] D.H. Ruwanpathirana, Sisiliyana Liyana Jayawardene; [s.] Gunaratne Ramanayake; [m.] December 27, 1973; [ch.] Amila Ramanayake; [ed.] Sangamitta Girls College, University of Sri Lanka, UN University;

[occ.] Poet, University Lechturer, Expert on development; [memb.] Advisory Council on Television, Commitee on Broadcasting, Council on Drama, Council on Literarure; [hon.] Indipendent Cultural Award for best Poet; [oth. writ.] Poetry books-seven, collection of short stories, literature revision book, children poetry book, several poems and articles published in newspapers and other publications.; [pers.] The main theme of my poetry is give courage to humankind. I have been highly influenced by great poetic traditions of the world. [a.] Colombo, Sri Lanka

RUXTON, ERIN
[pen.] Pooter; [b.] January 21, 1984, Edmonton, Alberta, Canada; [p.] Keith and Carrol; [ed.] Grade 7; [occ.] Student; [hon.] Passing honors fr. gr. 1-7, Dancing Awards (Tap, Jazz), Scholarships for dancing.; [oth. writ.] Have a few but they were done for school.; [pers.] I would like to thank Mom and Dad for always be proud of my writing and encouraging me to write.; [a.] Edmonton Alberta, Canada

RYAN JR., FRANK J.
[pen.] F.J.R; [b.] December 3, 1954, Bronxville, NY; [p.] Gloria and Frank J. Sr.; [m.] Jane Joan Ryan, June 26, 1988; [ch.] Lauren Marie born 8/1993; [ed.] Iona Preparatory School, New Rochelle, NY Condoria College, Bronxville, NY; [occ.] Regional Manager/Circulation Operations for Gannett Co,; [memb.] Westchester County Medical Center Heart Club; [hon.] 1994 and 1995 Winner of hte New York Post Valentines Day Prose Contest; [oth. writ.] Many Editorial Articles published in Major New York Newspaper and National magazines including Time Magazine. Prose and Poetry published in New York Post. Current event and sports articles published in The White Plains Reporter Dispatch, Yonkers Herald Statesman abd Standard Star.; [pers.] "Writing is the ultimate power to the immortal expression of ones passions and opinion. Time may erase cherished words once spoken, however writing is the indelible stamp of remembrance to those words".; [a.] Yonkers, NY

SABATINI, ROBERT A.
[b.] February 21, 1957, Louisiana; [p.] Mr. and Mrs. V. J. Sabatini; [occ.] Civil/Structural Design Engineering; [memb.] Ducks Unlimited Conservation Group, International Society of Poets; [oth. writ.] Poems in "The Garden of Life" and "Mists of enchantment".; [pers.] Greatly influenced by writer Jack Kerovac and singer/songwriter/poet, Jim Morrison of "The Doors" Fame.; [a.] Houston, TX

SABOL, JACLYN
[pen.] Jacqui; [b.] December 9, 1982, Rockland County, NY; [p.] Kenneth and Elizabeth Sabol; [ed.] St. Augustine Elementary School, Academy of the Holy Angels High School; [occ.] Student; [memb.] St. Augustine Student Council, and Yearbook Committee; [hon.] High School Scholarship, Dance Scholarship as well as winning many dance competitions.; [pers.] Anything can be achieved if you strive for it whole heartedly, greet it with open arms, and embrace it willingly.; [a.] Pomona, NY

SADRIAN, PARVANEH
[b.] May 1935, Tehran, Iran; [m.] Divorced; [ch.] Four; [ed.] B.A. Science, Literature; [memb.] Board Member of The Iranian Women's Org., The Iranian Senior Citizens Comity and also a board member of the Iranian's Arts Org.; [hon.] A large number of awards and prizes in a variety of Iran TV/ Radio Contests such as "Quiz" shows and so on.; [oth. writ.] Parvaneh is one of the few writers who's articles are seen printed on a number of community newspapers. She is also a painting artist and also an excellent mother of four.; [pers.] Parvaneh wishes that all the people of the in the world live happily and peacefully together. "We Are All One".; [a.] Toronto Ontario, Canada

SAEED, ZOON
[b.] March 27, 1973, Karachi, Pakistan; [p.] Dr. and Mrs. Muhammed Saeed; [ed.] B.A., Major in English Literature; [pers.] I pray for peace, a word that speaks for itself, a word that possesses great value for human life. It teaches those indifferent to love one another. It is the most noblest gift one can share with the other. I pray to God that peace shines in every ones heart and soul.; [a.] Karachi, Pakistan

SAGER, MILDRED G.
[pen.] Millie-Mino; [b.] February 17, 1902, Indiana; [p.] Hattie and Richard Saylor; [m.] Carl W. Stephens, June 1, 1924; [ch.] 2 girls, 2 boys; [ed.] Two terms normal, grade-high school; [occ.] Retired, making dolls; [memb.] Baptist Church; [hon.] U.S. Postal Service honorable discharge Feb. 29, 1964; [oth. writ.] Writing descriptive papers for Realtors to use in their advertising work; [pers.] War one called two of my brothers to serve in military I became my father's boy. I love the outdoors and nature, birds especially.; [a.] Westminster, CO

SALMAN, MOHAMMED
[pen.] Peerzadah Salman; [b.] April 14, 1970, Badin; [p.] M. Younus, Shamim Younus; [ed.] M.A. (English Literature) from University of Karachi; [occ.] Sub-Editor, local weekly; [oth. writ.] Articles for the news (daily), MAG Weekly; [pers.] So far, an Agnostic, influenced by Shakespeare, Eliot, Sartre and Ghalib.; [a.] Karachi, Pakistan

SAMFORD, MICHAEL JAMES
[pen.] Mike Samford; [b.] December 14, 1950, Las Cruces, NM; [p.] Archie Marvin and Dorothy Ann Samford; [m.] Judy Lou Huse Samford, December 30, 1979; [ch.] Michael James Jr. and Jessica Ann; [ed.] Three Years Las Cruses, Mayfield H.S. and Alamogordo H.S. (68-71), Ged-72, 2 years NMSU at Alamogordo, NM, 2 1/2 Years Wayland Baptist University, BA - 1977; [occ.] Eligibility Specialist with the Texas Dept. Human Services; [memb.] Indiana Ave. Bapt. Church, Lubbock Chess Club; [pers.] My writing gift, as my life, belong to the Lord Jesus. May he be lifted up and glorified, in my life and writing, everywhere he leads me. I hope and pray someone is touched and inspired when they read what I write.; [a.] Wolfforth, TX

SAMUDOVSKY, NATALIA L.
[b.] December 30, 1983, Wheatridge, CO; [p.] Barbara and David Samudovsky; [ed.] Canyon Middle School - class of 2002; [occ.] Student;

[hon.] Honor roll, student of the month, Stanton math general; [oth. writ.] "The Beach", anthology of poetry by young americans 1995 edition. "What is Respect" Canyon Communique, February 1996; [pers.] I try to put all of my felings and emotions into my writing!; [a.] Castro Valley, CA

SAMUEL, MAE AILEEN
[b.] May 22, 1951, St. Kitts, WI; [p.] Basil and Alexandrina Samuel; [ed.] Epworth Junior School, and St. Theresa's Convent High School in Basseterre, St. Kitts, West Indies; [occ.] Unemployed due to illness. (Former Office Clerk); [memb.] Grace Church of the Nazarene, The Canadian Sickle Cell Society; [oth. writ.] Other poems and song lyrics, never been published. Most of my work was done solely as a hobby or pastime during periods of recovering from illness.; [pers.] My inspiration comes from God, and things that happen around me from day to day. When writing song lyrics, I am mostly inspired by country music. I love making others happy.; [a.] Saint Laurent Quebec, Canada

SANCHEZ, ELIZABETH M.
[b.] May 27, 1966, El Paso, TX; [p.] Joe and Elena Sanchez; [ed.] University of Texas at El Paso BBA Accounting Currently working Toward A B.A. in Literature at same University; [occ.] Billing Clerk for Watkins Motor Lines; [pers.] Read every chance you get. Many of life's lessons can be great poets and authors.; [a.] El Paso, TX

SANCHEZ, VIRGINIA A.
[b.] March 4, 1982, El Paso, TX; [p.] Virginia Sanchez; [ed.] Riverside Middle School; [hon.] For writing story's; [pers.] I'm 14 years old. I live in El Paso, Texas; [a.] El Paso, TX

SANDISON, PAUL C.
[b.] March 28, 1947, South Africa, Durban; [p.] George Sandison and Joan Sandison; [ed.] BA Hons (Natal), M Cert Ed (UPPSALA), B Soc Sci, M Soc Sci, B Soc Sci, B Soc, Sci (Stocholm), MA (Bath); [occ.] Educational Author and Consultant; [memb.] University of Natal Alumni Association; [hon.] Gabriel Massey Speech prize 1962, Distinction: M Cert Ed 1983, Distinction: B Soc Sci 1986, Distinction: M Soc Sci 1986; [oth. writ.] Articles for newspapers, journals, book reviews, MS for School Radio Programmers and Magazines Translations and the book "The Key To A New Educational Strategy", publ. by Shadow, Rivonia, South Africa 1994, ISBN 0620186860; [pers.] A new threat of dictatorship in appearing in Europe in the form of the European Union - A huge European State run by a council of ministers supported by a Mondlithic Bereaucracy. The court of human rights in Strasbourg is infiltrated by dictatorial scandinavian lawyers who put appeals from the victims of human rights infringements in Sweden into the note this please!; [a.] Durban, South Africa

SANDY, GIL
[b.] October 6, 1946, Lanark-Scotland; [p.] Mary Smith & John Smith; [s.] Divorced; [ch.] Gary Sandy, James Sandy, Peter Sandy; [ed.] Comprehensive - no qualifications taken; [occ.] poet - writer; [memb.] None; [hon.] None; [oth. writ.] Poetry published in England 'East Midlands Poetry

Now', 'Riveacre', Poetry Institutze of British Isles and soon of course in the 'National Library of Poetry'; [pers.] I adore traditional poetry Keats, Browning, Shakespheare, etc. My outlook on life? Open mindedness, hold the moment, expect nothing that way you will never be let down. I believe in life and me.; [a.] Nottingham England U.K.

SARAFINCHAN, MARIAN
[b.] November 13, 1944, Bonnyville, AL; [p.] William Iverson, Agnes Iverson (Both Deceased); [m.] James Sarafinchan, January 29, 1966; [ch.] Quentin James, Tamara Lee, Derrick Charles, Darrell William; [ed.] Ardmore High, St. Joseph's School of Nursing, Vegreville; [occ.] Office Manager; [hon.] Loyalty Award in Nursing; [pers.] The depth and content of my writings are influenced to a large extent by my love of God, my appreciation of nature as well as my intrigue and amazement of the scope and range of human emotions.

SARAFINCHAN, SHIRLEY ANGELINA
[pen.] Virginia Frotten; [b.] April 18, 1947, Winnipeg, Manitoba; [p.] Rosario & Nettie Gauthier; [s.] Kenneth Sarafinchan; [m.] August 19, 1989; [ch.] Jeffrey , Lori Rose, Corey & Christy; [ed.] Grade XII St. Mary's Academy; [occ.] Payroll/Human Resources Administrator; [memb.] United Way of Canada, St. John Bosco Parish & CWL; [oth. writ.] Several poems not yet published; [pers.] My poems reflect life, family & love of nature and mankind. I have been influenced by God & his wonderfull creations; [a.] Edmonton Alberta, Canada

SARGENT, AARON
[b.] November 2, 1973, Cincinnati, OH; [p.] Ronald and Nora Sargent; [ed.] Anderson High School, and life itself; [occ.] Technical Support Specialist (Computer Operations); [oth. writ.] Unpublished short stories including Left, Empire and The Last Soldier, and a varied collection of poetry.; [pers.] Man's greatness has been achieved through divergence, not repetition.; [a.] Cincinnati, OH

SARUTTO, ANNE MARIE RITA
[b.] February 2, 1950, Brooklyn, NY; [p.] Michael and Margaret Sarutto; [ed.] Lafayette High School, Galveston College, Texas A&M University, Graduate with B.A. degree in Meteorology (1994), University of St. Thomas, City College; [occ.] Post Graduate Student in Meteorology at City College (1995-1996); [memb.] American Meteorological Society (1995, 1996) American Mathematical Society (1993-1996), New York Academy of Sciences (1996), American Petroleum Society (1996) Dean's List (1978-1980); [hon.] FXXM on Geological Scholarship ($250, 1975), Phi Theta Kappa (1978), English Honor Society (1991), University of St. Thomas, American Apological Minority Scholarship A Ward (1993-1994), Nasa Summer Intunship, Atlanta, (1991); [oth. writ.] I have had selections of my poetry, philosophical, theological and scientific writings copyrighted and submitted to the Library of Congress (1991). The title of my work is: Works in Progress, volume I and II.; [pers.] The writer must have authority in order to convey his or her ideals to those who want to hear. Poetry is the realm of universals. Whosoever strives to grasp the truth of poetry must accept this university.; [a.] Brooklyn, NY

SAVAGE, JOYCE S.
[pen.] Tillie; [b.] October 14, 1953, Tunica, MS; [p.] John and Annie Sherman; [m.] Emmett Louis Savage, June 7, 1973; [ch.] LaShonda, MarKeisha, Krystle; [ed.] Rosa Fort High, Shelby State Community College, Union University; [occ.] Registered Nurse, VA Hospital, Memphis, Tennessee; [memb.] Boulevard Church of Christ First Aid Committee Boulevard Church of Christ. One poem published by National Library of Poetry; [hon.] Hands and Hearts Award, Top 100 Nurses Award; [oth. writ.] It aint that way no more: Thats my Son Hanging on the Cross, I raised You The Best I Could, The Devils Funeral Jaye; [pers.] I strive to reflect the Godness of God in my life and I keep him first in my life as well as in everything that I do. I realize that I am who I am because of Gods Grace and Mercy and I thank for my ability to compose.; [a.] Memphis, TN

SCANLON, JOSEPH C.
[pen.] Arctic Casey; [b.] January 2, 1926, Boston; [m.] Ex (Jane Cronin, March 5, 1953); [ch.] Justin, Mary, Anne, Edmund; [ed.] Boston College, B.S., M.S. Polytechnic Institute of Brooklyn; [occ.] Retired Physicist Presently: Math Teacher; [memb.] Past Member: Amer Chem. Soc., New York Acad. Science, Amer. Optical Soc. Amer. Crystallo Graphic Assoc.; [oth. writ.] About 100 Scientific publications (See Chem. and or Phys. Abstracts, 1975 Et Seq.). Poems in the Chesterton in the Chesterton review, the wanderer, selections in m/s; [pers.] "In Samland" my poetry (hopefully) includes humor satire and religions "Ceitmotivs"; [a.] Highland Park, NJ

SCARCHELLO, DOMINICK
[b.] September 26, 1970, Hagerstown, MD; [p.] Barry and Margaret; [ed.] B.A. Philosophy, Univ. of Maryland; [occ.] English Tutor; [pers.] The totality of experience is encompassed differently in every individual.

SCARZELLA, MICHELE-MALONE
[b.] August 13, 1964, Elizabeth, NJ; [p.] John and Terry Malone (Deceased); [m.] John Scarzella, August 3, 1991; [ed.] St. Mary's Grammar School, Rahway High School, Union County College, Kean College (Majored in Elem. Ed. and English); [occ.] 3rd grade Teacher St Mary's School, Hackettstown, NJ; [memb.] Developmental Committee - Grants Team Member; [hon.] National Honor Society Rahway High School Dean's List - Kean College; [oth. writ.] A Short Story titled "The Heavenly Flight" was published in Karen Goldman's book - "Angel Encounters"; [pers.] One night I had a dream about Angels. The next day, I woke up, and wrote this poem. I always reward my students with "angel points", for work well done.; [a.] Belvidere, NJ

SCHAFFER, WENDY S.
[b.] March 26, 1952, Summit, NJ; [p.] Dorothy and Theodore Schaffer; [ch.] Laura and Nancy, (grandson) Jairek; [ed.] Morris Hills H.S. 1 year - Palm Beech Junior College, 14 years Licensed Insurance Agent, 3 years President of Advance Insurance, Inc.; [occ.] Disabled; [hon.] Phi Theta Kappa, Dean's List SBAC Consumer Advising Board of Palm Beach County, 1995 Women Entrepreneur of the year; [pers.] I wrote my poem in memory of my beloved step-daughter, Robyn.; [a.] Fort Lauderdale, FL

SCHALK, WAYNE CRAIG
[pen.] Wayne Craig Schalk; [b.] June 7, 1951, Seattle, WA; [p.] Stanley R. Schalk and Alica Schalk; [m.] Susan Schalk, October 6, 1995; [ch.] Mathew and Adam; [ed.] Rowland High, Golden West College; [occ.] Pipe Fitter and Welder; [memb.] United Association Local, 364 Colton Calif. - Lyons Club - Moose Lodge; [hon.] United Association District Council No. 16 Meritorious Activities Award for Courage, Dedication and Leadership; [oth. writ.] To be released upon my earthly departure.; [pers.] If in doughty of our heavenly father, then take a closer look at the many colors of the things that are natural.; [a.] Hemet, CA

SCHMELZER, VICKIE
[b.] April 1, 1970, Muscatine, IA; [p.] Richard and Sally Kerr; [m.] Todd Schmelzer, May 16, 1986; [ch.] Alexandra Leigh, MacKenzie Kerr Jean, Jesse James Howard; [ed.] Muscatine High School; [occ.] Homemaker; [pers.] In my writing I've tried to convey the beauty and tenderness that nature has to offer us, if we only take the time to see it.; [a.] Muscatine, IA

SCHMIDT, MARY ELLEN
[b.] September 6, 1951, Rhinelander, WI; [p.] Adam Schmidt, Lorene Schmidt; [m.] Michael Jackson, September 25, 1975; [ch.] Step Sons: Edward and Scott; [ed.] Textile Sales, Velcro-Texline; [occ.] National Multiple Sceerosis Society, Cystic Fibrosis Foundation, Special Olympics; [pers.] I thank my friends and family they are my gold.; [a.] Pasadena, CA

SCHMUTZ, KIM
[b.] April 22, 1984, Stettler, Alberta, Canada; [p.] Lynn and Klaus Schmutz; [ed.] Grade 5 at time of writing, Grade 6 now; [occ.] Student; [hon.] School writing awards.; [oth. writ.] Another poem "School is life" My friend and I in grade 3 wrote a poem that got published in a news paper.; [pers.] I write to express my feelings, or what I think of something.; [a.] Athabasca Alberta, Canada

SCHNEIDER, BARBARA MANTELL
[pen.] Barbara Schneider; [b.] November 17, 1947, Bergen County, NJ; [p.] Roger and Anna Mantell; [m.] Mark Frank Schneider, December 28, 1968; [ch.] Matthew Mark and Christopher John; [ed.] Ramsey High School, N.J., Palm Beach Community College, FL; [occ.] Legal Assistant; [memb.] Florida Bar, General Practice P.A.D.I.; [oth. writ.] Currently working on the Book, "Fantasy Walker", several poems and children's stories; [pers.] For the endless joy and vast vision I thank Master Tolkien, Neil Hancock, Brian Jacques and my husband, Mark.; [a.] Palm Beach Gardens, FL

SCHNEIDER, ERIN ELIZABETH
[b.] February 8, 1982, Ann Arbor, MI; [p.] Richard and Deborah Schneider; [ed.] Presently attending Salem Lutheran Grade School (8th grade/1996) next year will attend Michigan Lutheran Seminary (High School/1996-2000); [memb.] Trinity Lutheran Church, Girl Pioneers, Varsity Blues Drama Club, Saline Writing Forum, Salem Sports teams, (volleyball, basketball, and track) Dance Alliance Advanced Jazz; [hon.] (No writing awards), The A/B Honor Roll for the past five years, Several track and field awards, Free Throw Champion and Hot Shot Winner in Basketball. This is my first publication of a poem and it is a great honor.; [oth. writ.] Several unpublished poems such as "A Special Heritage", "The Babbling Brook", "A Colorful View", "Gold", and a short children's story (A Case of the Left Out Blues); [pers.] I have been extremely encouraged by my loving family and friends. I would specially like to thank Carly Ferch for keeping me going. I believe if something is wanted badly enough, it can be accomplished.; [a.] Ann Arbor, MI

SCHOEN, WALTER ALAN
[b.] November 8, 1961, Lethbridge, Alberta, Canada; [p.] Joe and Rose Marie Schoen; [ch.] Nathan (Joseph) and Stephen (Anthony); [ed.] Warmer High School, S.A.I.I. Chemical Process Operations, Lethbridge Community College -Law Enforcement - Business Law-Data Processing, University of Lethbridge - Conversational French; [occ.] Private Investigation Consultant; [pers.] Through my writings and songs I try to reflect the different perspectives of life through my eyes as well as my mind.; [a.] Lethbridge Alberta, Canada

SCHROEDER, DIRK
[b.] September 10, 1959, Bad Godesberg, Germany; [p.] Manfred and Ulva Schroeder; [m.] Kathy Horvath, April 4, '89; [ch.] Kyle and Erick; [ed.] Nauset Regional H.S. (Cape Cod), Florida Junior College; [occ.] Real Estate Brokerage Firm Owner/ Manager; [oth. writ.] I enjoy writing poems and meaningful children's stories.; [pers.] Good conscience is the love within us, bring it out in perpituity!; [a.] Saint Augustine, FL

SCHULMAN, JOSEPH ISAAC
[pen.] Yossi Schulman; [b.] July 12, 1987, Madison, WI; [p.] Michael and Nancy Schulman; [ed.] Now in 3rd grade (1995-1996) at the Chai Center School of Ithaca, NY; [occ.] Student; [memb.] Tzivos Hashem Organization for Jewish Children, World of Good Campaign; [hon.] Highest Rank (General) in Tzivos Hashem; [pers.] I encourage everyone to be part of the world of Good Campaign, which promotes acts of kindness among all people. It was inspired by the Lubavitcher Rebbe, who said that "Moshiach is ready to come now. Our part is to add in goodness and kindness."; [a.] Ithaca, NY

SCHULTZ, JUDITH F.
[pen.] Judith F. Schultz; [b.] January 16, 1931; [p.] Kathryn Christensen and Harold Frederiksen; [m.] Robert G. Schultz, September 15, 1951; [ch.] Kathryn (S.), Whitt, Julie (S.), Clippard, Melody (S.) Colt, Angela Schultz; [memb.] Four Seasons Garden Club, St. Pauls Episcopal Church, Past Sunday School Teacher, Altar Guild, Kitchen Guild, every member Canvas, Volunteer NC Baptist Hospital, Secca; [hon.] Won a Kiwanis Award my Sr. Year in High School for a Paper on what I wanted to do after High School; [oth. writ.] Poems - titles of a few, friends, my aunt, my husband, 1951, christmas, my legacy, grand girls, our doctor, tutor (and more).; [pers.] My poems are inspired by my deeds feelings about life, love of family and God - friends etc. I started writing this past September instead of only thoughts I decided to put them on paper.; [a.] Winston-Salem, NC

SCHULTZ, KATHLEEN M.
[pen.] Kathy; [b.] March 6, 1966, Minneapolis, MN; [p.] Douglas J. Schultz; [ed.] A.A. Waldorf Lutheran College Forest City, IA, B.A. (Health, Phy. Ed) SSU, Marshall, MN., B.S. (Physicians Assistant) UTHSCSA San Antonio, TX; [occ.] Physicians Assistant; [memb.] U.S. Army; [hon.] Magna Cum Laude graduate from SSU, Marshall, MN., Who's Who Among Collegiate Scholars. First team all regional volleyball at Waldorf Lutheran College soldier/NCO of the year.; [oth. writ.] Over 50 poems and saying, none published until now.; [pers.] I've been writing poetry since 1981. It enables me to express my thoughts and feeling which is otherwise difficult for me to express verbally. My heart allows my mind to express my emotions.; [a.] Westbrook, MN

SCHULZE, JENNY
[pen.] Lamseben; [b.] April 2, 1922, Danmark; [p.] Carl and Helga Pedersen; [m.] Bruno Schulze, April 1, 1944, Germany; [ch.] William, Helga, Bernd; [ed.] Danish Public School System; [occ.] Retired; [hon.] World of Poetry, Sacramento, California, 1. Gold Award "Praying Hands", 2. Silver Award "Knowing My Lord", 3. Gold Award, "Where My Cradle Stood"; [oth. writ.] Book of Poems and Prover my Biography, If you should be interested I would be happy to forward my book of poems to your attention.; [pers.] Our Lord, Our Lord is never far away, remember that always because you need Him everyday in your heart he stays.; [a.] Kitchener Ontario, Canada

SCORSONELLI, LORRAINE
[b.] May 11, 1981, Adelaide; [p.] Raffaele and Corazon; [ed.] Currently doing year 10 at Findon High School; [occ.] Student; [hon.] Certificate of Academic Achievement Australian Music Examinations Board-Pianoforte Australian Music Examinations Board - Theory of Music; [oth. writ.] Poems published in school yearbook "Finmag"; [a.] Adelaide, South Australia

SCOTT, DAVID WILLIAM
[b.] October 25, 1942, Saint Catharines, Ontario, Canada; [p.] William Scott, Lena Towers; [m.] Suzanne Richard, August 17, 1963; [ch.] Andrew Eric, Nancy Marie, Patrick Michael; [ed.] High School, John Abbot College Police Tech., 2 1/2 yrs. Theology Courses, Adult Christian Training, Loyola Campus, Concordia University; [occ.] Retired Police Officer 30 yrs. Service; [memb.] Various - Christian Fellowships Prayer and Counsel Ministry; [oth. writ.] Some Poems, Songs in Christian, News Letters - Montreal Region; [pers.] In my songs or poetry I try to express the love I have been shown or experienced through creation or creator, with another being, hoping they too, will come to know as well. And be blessed.; [a.] Chateauguay Quebec, Canada

SCOTT, JOSEPH
[b.] February 2, 1967, Philadelphia, PA; [p.] Bernadine Scott, Joseph Scott Sr.; [m.] Single; [ed.] Father Judge H.S.; [occ.] Owner and Operator of Joseph P. Scott Plumbing and Heating Co.; [oth. writ.] Numerous Poems and Song Lyrics.; [pers.] I believe in the power of positive thinking, I've looked death in the eye and never once thought of dying.; [a.] Philadelphia, PA

SCOTT, MEL
[pen.] Mel Scott; [b.] March 1, Toronto; [p.] Pauline and Frank Scott; [ed.] Student of Astrology and Mysticism; [occ.] Film and TV writer; [memb.] Writers' Guild of America, Screen Actors' Guild of America, International Society of Poets; [hon.] Ontario Arts' Council: Film Grant award. An 1995-'96 National Library of Poetry "Editor's Choice Award", awardee.; [oth. writ.] Journalism, Radio, Television, Stage. Roving freelance columnist 7 years with the Toronto Telegram. Wrote column: "Mel Scott in Hollywood", and theatre reviews.; [pers.] Quite often, from musing moments is learned that too much concern on all the things we should have has blinded us to much we can have.; [a.] West Hollywood, CA

SCOTT, MICHAEL
[b.] September 24, 1945, Orange, CA; [ed.] M.A. in Philosophy; [occ.] Professor of Philosophy at Orange Coast College; [oth. writ.] Pidgeon Feet Sand Etchings, Mind Cuisine, Yellow Brick Destinations, Ruckwartsburg, The Pistadoubs; [pers.] Like a musician, a poet should become conversant in all the forms and styles of the art.; [a.] Hurtington Beach, CA

SCOTT, TERESA
[b.] July 25, 1968, Mt. Clemons, MI; [p.] Meredith and Dan Terry; [m.] Darnell V. Scott, June 21, 1992; [ch.] Clara Jean Scoot, Daniel Darnell Scott; [occ.] Respiratory Therapist; [hon.] Communicator Bi-monthly Newsletter for Kansas Avenue SDA Church. (I hope to write much more poetry and stories in the future.); [oth. writ.] Much of my inspiration I adopt from a beautifully written masterpiece... the Bible. I enjoy writing anything that will impart joy into the heart of the reader. "Oh, that men would give thanks to the Lord for His goodness, and for His wonderful works to the children of men! Psalm 107:31, thank you, Lord for my gifts from you.; [pers.] Farmville, VA

SEELEY, FOREST G.
[b.] December 22, 1921, Hastings, NE; [p.] Claude Seeley, Alice Seeley; [m.] Emoline Seeley, April 18, 1967; [ch.] Philip Seeley, Kenneth Seeley; [ed.] BS Hastings College; [occ.] Rctired; [memb.] Elk's Club, Lion's Club; [hon.] Science Writer's Award; [oth. writ.] Approximately 30 scientific papers and journals articles.; [pers.] Poetry has been one of my hobbies. Keeping it humorous tends to keep perspective.; [a.] Oak Ridge, TN

SEELEY, RUTH ELIZABETH
[b.] December 2, 1937, Spokane, WA; [p.] Mr and Mrs Bernand Flanigan; [m.] Frederick Michael Seeley; [ch.] 5 children, 6 grand children; [ed.] High School; [occ.] House wife - want to write - I love it!; [memb.] Door of hope church fairbanks Alaska; [oth. writ.] Have other poems etc; [pers.] With God all things are possible! Keep looking up! Walking up! Thinking of Good things - Looking for the best in others.; [a.] Fairbanks, AK

SEGRES, RUTH N.
[b.] June 27, 1971, Kingstree, SC; [ed.] Rocky Mount Senior High, Edgecombe Comm. College, St. Augustine's College Trinity College of Quezon City, Manila Philippines; [occ.] Counselor Swift Creek Elementary; [memb.] Sisters With A Pur-

pose, founder, Alpha Eta Omega Christian Fellowship, NAACP, Homer Honor Poet Society, The Cactus Generation, The St. Augustine's Players, African-American Student Forum; [hon.] 1st Poet Laureate of St. Augustine's College, Dean's List, MLK, Jr. Oraltorical Award, Young Adult Leadership Award, Community In School Award, AIDS Service Agency Award; [oth. writ.] Published: The Falcons Quill Magz., The Carolian, The News and Observer, Chic Magz., Philippines, Harmony Magz., Philippines; [pers.] People influence my life, but I decide what choices to make.; [a.] Rocky Mount, NE

SEPE, SANDRA WOODRUFF
[b.] CT; [p.] Gloria and Edward Woodruff; [m.] Thomas, January 1974; [ch.] Two Boys Jason and Justin; [ed.] Three yrs Nursing School RN Waterbury Hospital creative writing in psychiatric nursing; [occ.] Registered Nurse Health Director Adult Day Care; [memb.] Team mother for prospect, CT, Little League Baseball, PTO, and church group; [hon.] Honor student thru school - Literary Committee member for high school year book wrote articles and speech high honor student in Nursing School; [oth. writ.] Short stories and poems; [pers.] Fascinated by the power and complexity by human emotions and the responses they illicit from people. Love to view life through the eyes of children.; [a.] Prospect, CT

SERDYNSKA, MARIE
[b.] December 13, 1946, London, England; [m.] 1969, Divorced in 1987; [ch.] Two grown-up daughters; [ed.] McGill University; [occ.] Coordinator Social Services, International Cooperation; [oth. writ.] Several poems, unpublished; [pers.] I seek to write about the human condition with observations of daily life. I have been inspired by W. H. Auden, John Betjeman among others. I am also influenced by images captured on film, is photographs and paintings.; [a.] Montreal Province of Quebec, Canada

SERRA, JOHN J.
[b.] December 31, 1970, Medford, MA; [p.] Mr. and Mrs. Dominic and Maria Serra; [ed.] Medford High; [occ.] Superintendent of Senior Citizen Apartment Building; [memb.] Greater Boston Association for Retarded Citizens, Names project, Mothers voices, and Aids Action; [hon.] Greater Boston Association for Retarded Citizens. In appreciation of outstanding service.; [oth. writ.] One other poems published in the names project news letter.; [pers.] I like to use feeling in my writing to reflect on emotions that people may not be able to express at times.; [a.] Medford, MA

SETH, KAVITA K.
[pen.] Kavi; [b.] June 9, 1982, Panorama City, CA; [p.] Gulshan K. and Veena Seth; [ed.] Ladera Vista Junior High, Troy High School (Fullerton); [occ.] Student; [memb.] National Junior Honor Society; [hon.] Presidential Academic Fitness Award; [oth. writ.] Several Humorous, Poems (Mostly Family Oriented), Published in School News Paper; [pers.] The wisdom given to us through poetry, is greater than any gift money can buy!; [a.] Fullerton, CA

SHAFFER, EARL VICTOR
[b.] November 8, 1918, York, PA; [p.] Daniel

and Frances Shaffer; [ed.] William Penn High School, York, PA (1935); [memb.] Appalachian Trail Conference; [oth. writ.] "Walking with spring" first end-to-end trek on the Appalachian trail (1948).; [pers.] During World War II as a signal corps installation crewman I always carried three books: A bible, a dictionary, and a volume of kipling poems. "High Frontiers" was written in 1945 in Hawaii, as one of many through out the war.

SHAROLLI, ALI
[pen.] Ali Sharolli; [b.] September 23, 1980, Dallas, TX; [p.] Ab and Linda Sharolli; [ed.] Currently a freshman in high school; [occ.] Student; [memb.] National Junior Honor Society; [hon.] Presidential Physical Fitness Award, Academic Achievement Award; [oth. writ.] An Eend To All, Inferno; [pers.] Make the best of what you have.; [a.] Fairfax Station, VA

SHARON, CHELSEA CREO
[b.] May 9, 1984, Pittsburgh, PA; [p.] Leonard and Claudia Sharon; [ed.] Sixth Grade (presently) Waynflete School, Portland, ME; [oth. writ.] A poem "Fuschia" and two letters to the editor in my local newspaper; [pers.] I enjoy to write because it gives me a voice for my opinions, ideas and feelings.; [a.] New Gloucester, ME

SHARP, JENNY
[b.] June 13, 1974; [m.] George Sharp, August 26, 1995; [ed.] Fenelon Falls Secondary School Trent University; [occ.] Student; [a.] Haliburton Ontario, Canada

SHAW, CYNTHIA GORING
[b.] August 14, 1931, Boston, MA; [p.] Gordon E. and F. Enid Shaw; [m.] Widowed; [ch.] Julie, Jeanne, Paul, Victoria, Mark; [ed.] Roslindale High School (Coll Prep) Boston, Mass. Teterboro School of Aeronautics, Dept of State Foreign Service Institute, U.S. Army and Air Force Schools, Imam M. ibn Saud Islamic Univ - Islamic and Arabic Sciences in America; [occ.] Retired; [memb.] Heathcote Botanical Gardens, Scottish Society of the Treasure Cost; [hon.] U.S. Army Meritorious Civilian Service (Bravery), U.S. Army Civilian Award for Humanitarian Service, Woman Flyers of America Scholarship (Essay), Beta Sigma Phi Sorority Awards; [pers.] I follow the Golden Rule.; [a.] Fort Pierce Hutchinson Island, FL

SHAW, DETE JACQUELYN
[b.] Midlothian, IL; [ch.] Linda Shaw Byerly and John Wallace Shaw; [ed.] Northern Illinois University, DeKalb, IL; [occ.] Songwriter, Teacher; [memb.] ASCAP (American Society of Composers, Authors and Publishers), SGA (The Songwriters Guild of America), University Women's Club; [pers.] I'm a fatalist: I believe everything happens for a reason. (Like you are reading this.); [a.] Sun City, CA

SHAW, SARAH
[b.] August 29, 1923, Lake Geneva, WI; [p.] L. J. Kirk and Ruth Kirk; [m.] Bob Shaw (Deceased, 1978), March 22, 1942; [ch.] Gary, Laurel, Elaine, 6 grandchildren, 7 great grandchildren; [ed.] High School, Business College; [occ.] I've been a housewife, helped run a farm, a mother and grand mother! Volunteer in Missions.; [memb.] Jerome

United Methodist Church - Lay Delegate and Lay Speaker. Albion District United Methodist Team Officer. A Volunteer in Missions. serving at red bird mission Ky McCurdy Mission School, N. Mexico.; [oth. writ.] I have writing poems, songs and dramas for our church activities for forty years. Every year for 20 years I have written a poem to honor the graduating High School Seniors at our school. Also poems to honor events in our families life I have received a certificate of achievement and a cash prize for the best poem in "Spiritual" category from modern poetry society. I have had my poems used in U. M. W. papers and in McCurdy School, and red bird mission publications.; [pers.] Life is an adventure for me, that I share with God. I feel very blessed, and to express the joys and the sorrows and challenges, I must write!; [a.] Jerome, MI

SHELL, CHARLOTTE
[b.] September 6, 1972, Hunstville, AL; [p.] Dr. Ron and Evelyn Shell; [ed.] B.S.ED., Athens State College, Athens, AL; [occ.] Elementary School Teacher; [hon.] Dean's List, President's List; [pers.] Life is full of experiences, good and bad. My responsibility is to appropriate wisdom and knowledge from both. Poetry is an effective and meaningful way of expressing my feelings and thoughts about those experiences.; [a.] Cheyenne, WY

SHEPHERD, MATTIE
[b.] October 5, 1945, Calvert, TX; [p.] Mrs. M. Jergo and Rev. C.B. Shepherd; [ch.] Karole Lynn and Roy La Vann; [ed.] Tucson High School, Mallincrodt Institute of Radiology, Washington University; [occ.] Human Resources Manager, Governor's Office of Emergency Services; [memb.] Am. Soc. of Prof. Plrns: Nat'l Coordination Council on Emerg. Mngmt. Phi Theta Kappa; [hon.] Honorary Colonel of Armenain Air Force, Women's Intn'l Inner Circle of Achievement, Who's Who Worldwide, Intrn'l Certified Emergency Manager; [oth. writ.] Various Technical Papers on Radiation, Emergency Management Article for American Society of Professional Planners, Radiological Emergency Mngmt Guide, New Employee Orientation Guide; [pers.] Teach our children for they are our future, save quality time for you, the quality of your life depends on it, spend each minute wisely, for learning is a treasure.; [a.] Galt, CA

SHEPHARD, VALERIA F.
pen.] Valeria F. Seay Shephard; [b.] June 28, 1932, Brunswick, GA; [p.] Ethel seay; [m.] Johnnie l. Shephard, Sr., Decembber 24, 1954; [ch.] Johnnie Jr., Melvin, Harold and Carol; [ed.] Risley High School (Validictorian) Brunswick, Georgia, two years at Clark College, Atlanta, Georgia, two years at Clark College, Atlanta, Georgia, 50-51, 51-52, made Dean's List three semesters; [occ.] Retired; [oth. writ.] I have a collection of poems called "Ponderings", they have been written over the past 20 some odd years; [pers.] If I should in any way achieve anything concerning my poems, I would like to recognize Mrs. Constance Treloak as mentor. She has motivated me tremendously. [a.] Daytona Beach, FL

SHERBURNE, MARGARET L.
[pen.] M. Lee Sherburne; [b.] April 8, 1990, Scobey, MT; [m.] K. S. Sherburne November 1942 (1st), October 1975 (2nd); [ch.] Charles L. Hollis and Marnee J. Hollis; [ed.] High School, Scobey, MT Colleges: U. of MT. Northern, Havre, MT., Pacific Lutheran Univ., Tacoma, Wash. Education degrees, Grad. work/endorsements, Language Arts: Secondary level.; [occ.] Retired..do performance of dramatic writings (mine) spend much time writing, rewriting, reading, remembering.; [memb.] Academy of American Poets, P.E.O., O.E.S., Delta Kappa Gamma, Pres. Church (elder).; [hon.] Meritorious Civilian Service, 1944, Certificate for Outstanding teaching service (2) Outstanding service state of Nebraska Council for Extension work, Ms Senior Nebraska, 1989, listed speaker/member Nebraska Humanities Council.; [oth. writ.] Poetry in anthologies, news papers, feature stories, editorials, scripts, researched writing: Performance, children's stories, thematic speeches.; [pers.] Poets should never preach, no use for second pers. pro., Poetry reflects observations, tells stories, describes realistically, metaphorically nature and everyday living. Lean toward philosophy. Grateful for privilege of pulling ribbon to untie gift of each new day—good or bad, happy or sad.; [a.] Humboldt, NE

SHERER, MARY ALICE
[b.] February 22, 1945, Scranton, PA; [p.] Felix J. and Elizabeth M. Krohn; [m.] Divorced; [ch.] Joseph F. Statkiewicz Christopher R. Statkiewicz and Terry R. Sherer, Jr.; [ed.] A.S. Degree from College of Allied Health, Professions of Hahnemann University, Phila. PA, School of Radiologic Technology, Hahnemann Univ. Phila. PA, Hazleton Senior High School, Hazelton PA.; [occ.] Medical Author, Radiologic Technologist at Columbia Summit Medical Center; [memb.] American Society of Radiologic Technologist (ASRT), Past-President of NJ Soc. of Rad. Tech's, Past-President of Mid-Eastern Conf. of Rad. Tech's; [hon.] Fellowship from the American Society of Radiologic Technologist (ASRT) awarded 06/90. Two first place awards for Technical Essays at Mid-Eastern Conference of Rad. Tech's.; [oth. writ.] Primary author of "Radiation Protection in Medical Radiography" 2nd Ed. Mosby-Year Book, Inc.-St. Louis, 1993 author "Q and A Preparation for credintialing in Radiography" W.B. Saunders Co. Phila, 1992. Articles published in National and State Scientific Journals and biweekly News Paper; [pers.] "The Wall" is dedicated to the Vietnam Veterans who gave their all.; [a.] Mount Juliet, TN

SHERODE, BARBARA T.
[pen.] "B" or Barbara Trumbo, Tucker; [b.] January 22, 1953, Louisville, KY; [p.] John W. Trumbo Sr., Zella Trumbo; [ch.] Jimmie Lee, Shanee Alise; [ed.] Parkland Jr., High, Male High School, J. Graham Brown Edu. Center; [occ.] Assembly Line Worker; [oth. writ.] Several unpublished poems and a few personal commentary papers, written for and most of the time, simply shared with friends or strangers. In nature the subjects range from spiritual, to sympathy, to friendship and romance.; [pers.] I write only when I am inspired by people, or circumstances. My goal is that my writings bring hope, faith, encouragement, strength, peace, and love. This is my gift to my world!; [a.] Louisville, KY

SHEROW, SONYA
[b.] February 20, 1967, Dallas, TX; [m.] Timothy Williamson, September 24, 1993; [a.] Houston, TX

SHERRY, PATRICIA
[b.] December 19, 1937, Portsmouth, England; [p.] Raised by my grandmother Enid Stafford; [m.] Divorced Eons ago; [ch.] Six; [ed.] Grammar School, England Avery Hill Teachers College, London, England Queens University Kingston, Canada; [occ.] Writer/Homemaker; [oth. writ.] Poems, short stories childrens stories and nature articles letters to the editor; [pers.] My great love is nature. I have always been interested in religious and scientific thought and have often wondered about the possibility of reincarnation.; [a.] Kingston Ontario, Canada

SHINAULT, BRIAN R.
[b.] January 3, 1959, Riverside, NY; [p.] Patricia and Eugene Shinault (Deceased); [m.] Theresa Martin Shinault, December 2, 1989; [ch.] Tiffany Elaine and Andrew Charles Shinault; [ed.] Oldham Co. High and The University of Louisville; [occ.] Administrative Coordinator for KHESLC; [pers.] Most of my writings reflect true human emotions and the realism of everyday life. My father, wife and children inspire most of my writings.; [a.] Pewee Valley, KY

SHINE, EDNA MAE
[b.] May 18, 1944, Polkton, NC; [p.] Ollie Mae Sturdivant and Will Shine; [ch.] Johnnie, Shirley, Pamela, Patricia, Lisa, Clarissa, Elizabeth; [ed.] Northwest Sr. Hi., G.E.D. at C.P.C.C., Clerk-typist Certificate, C.P.C.C.; [pers.] I am an incurable romantic. As my poem shows, I haven't found the real thing yet. So, Kenny, this one's for you!; [a.] Charlotte, NC

SHIRREFF, GILLIAN
[b.] September 30, 1941, Vancouver; [p.] Lucy and Douglas Harlee, Betty (Step Mother); [m.] December 28, 1981, (Widow); [ed.] Victoria Read Society Project Literacy Victoria, Victoria College of Art; [occ.] Poet and Artist; [memb.] New Hope Baptist Church Project Literacy Victoria Friends of Schizophenics Friends of Government House Gardens, Victoria; [hon.] Student Reader, Victoria Read Society's, Writes of Spring, 1995, got a standing ovation there; [oth. writ.] News letters "The Hillsider" Schitz support Soc. magazines, Read Society Publication, other Lib. of Poetry publications; [pers.] I will revert to my "mother" Betty's Cliche of when I first met her "It is better to be kind than rights" also everyone is beautiful in his own way!; [a.] Victoria BC, Canada

SHOWS, ALICE MARIE LION
[b.] December 10, 1946, Billings, MT; [p.] Thomas and Louise Yarlott Young; [m.] Thomas Louis Lion Shows, June 25, 1976; [ch.] Louie, Tomie and Ottie; [ed.] Bachelor of Science in Lion Shows Elementary Education, and a Bachelor of Science in History and Social Science; [occ.] I am a Elementary School Teacher for grades 2nd 3rd and 4th. In addition, I also teach a Sunday School class; [memb.] Montana Education Association, National Science Teachers Association, National Arbor Day Foundation, W.E.A., Participant in the National Sci-

ence Foundations, Finest Field Based Instruction for Native American Elementary Teachers, and NEA; [hon.] Two of my poems, "Mystery Of Medicine Wheel," and "An Invisible Warrior," will be published in the upcoming volume of Treasured Poems of America. To be published in both the Treasured poems of America and The Ebbing Tide Anthology is a very important honor to me; [oth. writ.] "Mystery of Medicine Wheel", Indian Reservations, A Tragic Invention", "A Tribute to Native American Women", "Lament Of A Warriors Mother", "A Matriarch Society, An Honored Tradition", "Mother Earth, The Sustainer Of Life", "Plenty Coups, A Legacy", "A Beautiful Treasure, The Elders Of Our Society", "Bishee, The Substance Of Life", "An Invisible Warrior", "The Big Horn River", "A Mystery Of Life", A Mighty Hero, Grey Blanket, "A Day Of Infamy, June 25, 1876. And many more; [pers.] Poetry is an exquisite way to express your creativity, by using spirited imagery, emotion invoking words and glorious imagination. The important elements of poetry give the writer a high level creative power over the written word. Whether writing a piece of work with a whimsical nature, satire, or intense sensitivity, poetry is rhythmical, Captivating and very beautiful!"; [a.] Lodge Drass, MN

SICKMILLER, JENNA MARIE
[p.] Jenna Sickmiller; [b.] December 7, 1984, Mansfield, OH; [p.] Edward and Carol Sickmiller; [ed.] 5th grader at Northmor - Iberia Elementary School; [occ.] 5th grade student; [memb.] Pleasant Grove Church of Christ, Country Clovers 4-H Club, Member Conflict Management Team; [hon.] Iberie Elementary 1996 Spelling Bee champion, All A's honor roll; [oth. writ.] Anthology of Poetry by young Americans "I Like Fall" pg 78; [a.] Mount Gilead, OH

SIEMENS, BILL
[b.] July 28, 1976, London Ontario; [p.] Frank & Margaret; [ed.] Valley Heights Secondary School; [occ.] Part-time worker at Little Ceasers, Tillsonburg, Ont.; [hon.] Arts Award (Visual), Basketball Award (Bronze Medal); [pers.] "Thoughts left unwritten, can disappear in the mind." I started writing poetry only a year ago, and it has helped me to find myself,and I thank a special person for helping me find this gift.; [a.] Langton Ontario, Canada

SIEVERT, MARY E.
[pen.] Mary Elizabeth Sievert; [b.] May 17, 1962, Allegheny, PA; [p.] John Elmo Holleran and Nancy E. Whaley; [m.] Chris Sievert, October 7, 1989; [ch.] Erica, Justin, Brandon, Brittany and Shawn; [occ.] Homemaker mother of five beautiful children; [oth. writ.] I am a poet who reflects feelings of the lives of others. I try to reflect there life experience by putting myself in there place. Everyday life is man I write.; [pers.] Poetry is a feeling that needs to reach the depths of the souls of those who read it. If it does not then I was the poet I have failed at my job.; [a.] Oak Park Heights, MN

SILL, VIRGINIA FRANCES
[pen.] Ginny Sill; [b.] July 31, 1923, Oneonta, NY; [p.] Fred and Dora Spafford (Both Deceased); [m.] Bernard; [ch.] One son; [ed.] High School (2 yrs.); [occ.] Homemaker; [oth. writ.] "My Dad", "23", "Memories"; [a.] Parish, NY

SIMARD, DONNA
[b.] November 19, 1959, Birtle, Manitoba, Canada; [p.] Ardena and Allan Pizzey; [m.] Jean-Marie Simard, April 16, 1977; [ch.] Calinda, Stephanie, Justin, Robert, Stacy, Amanda, Joel, Patrick Mark and Kristian; [ed.] Foxwarren Elementary and Junior High, Birtle High School; [occ.] Homemaker; [memb.] St. Lazare Pro-life Group, St. Lazare Catholic Church; [hon.] Diploma from the institute of childrens literature under the direction of Hilda Stahl; [pers.] I feel very blessed. My writing has been greatly influenced by my wonderful parent ten children and husband. My busy life is full of great ideas.; [a.] Saint Lazare Manitoba, Canada

SIMMONS, JUANITA
[b.] August 9, 1982, Charleston, SC; [p.] Mr. Reginald Brown and Ms. Jacqueline Simmons; [ed.] Currently an 8th grade student at Cross High School, home of the Mighty Trojans; [occ.] No memberships, but a JV Cheerleader for School's JV Football and Basketball Teams; [memb.] Many awards for school. Bank no 1 in class.; [oth. writ.] Many other writings but none published.; [a.] Cross, SC

SIMMONS, SIMONE
[b.] Melbourne, Australlia; [ed.] Kingswood College, Box Hill Tafe, Melbourne College of Decoration.; [occ.] Higher education worker, Swinburne University of Technology, Hawthorn, Australia.; [memb.] British Institute of interior design (Australian Chapter) - experience extension scholarship.; [oth. writ.] Short stories: From College to Crocs, From College to The Coast, Heaven Save us Granny Davis.; [pers.] I enjoy music, theatre, opera, photography and aqua aerobics. I am influenced by te rhythm of the sea, the beautyu of the moon and stars and the never ending cycle of nature.; [a.] Melbourne Victoria, Australia

SIMS, GELOIS C.
[pen.] Lois; [b.] October 21, 1946, Hindsville, AR; [p.] Robert and Annie Collins; [m.] Joe W. Sims, November 7, 1965; [ch.] Daughters, Sonia, Evelyn and Warda; [ed.] High School Graduate Lanier High; [occ.] Central Tech. Certified St. Dominic Hosp.; [memb.] National Institute for the Certification of Healthcare Sterile Processing and Distribution Personnel; [oth. writ.] Breaking Barriers, Satan Vs Holy Spirit; [pers.] God has given me a gift to write and my message is to reach people who are lost in a sin sick world.; [a.] Jackson, MS

SINGHO, BERYL
[pen.] "Precious Gem"; [b.] March 16, 1920, Lynchburg, VA; [p.] Edna and Richard Cardwell; [m.] Rodney Singho, December 28, 1983 and (2nd time) July 15, 1991; [ch.] One son (deceased), one stepdaughter Queens; [ed.] H.S. Graduate - 1 yr Queens College Courses Med. Terminology; [occ.] Retired City Worker Heart and Hospitals (Med. Secretary); [memb.] NAACP, YRBM League AARP, CSREA Mother Hale Aids, Cancer Research; [hon.] 32 yrs. Service Hearth and Hospitals Vol Schools Pediatric Wards (hosp.); [oth. writ.] Usually writing have other poems, this the first I submitted! My mother and grandparents were educators.; [pers.] I have had a network of sorrow in my life, the worse being the murder of a most worthy son and only son on his birth day. My motto is it can always be worse and to

"Forgive the unforgivable" God sent me my husband 2 to the Bate of my sons murder. Our love is unconditional, He is almost half my age we married twice! For love.; [a.] Queens, NY

SINHA, ANJULI
[b.] March 26, 1985, Louisville, KY; [p.] Suman and Sunil Sinha; [ed.] 5th grade; [occ.] Student; [hon.] 1st place in Math competition city wide, (KUMON), straight A honor student at school.; [oth. writ.] A Garden, I Got An F Today, Something Upstairs; [a.] Cincinnati, OH

SINK, SUZANNE M.
[b.] September 14, 1956, Baltimore, MD; [p.] Irene G. and Harold D. Kanipe; [m.] J. W. Sink, February 24, 1977; [ch.] Angela and Jerry, Jr.; [ed.] A.S. Degree from Bluefield Baptist College; [occ.] Office Manager for McGuadrey and Pullen, LLP; [pers.] I enjoy writing poems for my husband.; [a.] Charlotte, NC

SITTIG, CHRISSY
[b.] May 25, 1979; [p.] Pat Howlett and Martin Sittig; [ed.] McCaig Elementary School and Ecole Primaire Alpha; [occ.] Senior student at Rosemere High School; [hon.] Other prose and poetry published in Spring Journal (annually released composit of local student's literary talent.); [pers.] My English teachers tend to complain that my work is of a slightly morbid tone. They seem to expect me to create a fairy-tale land on paper. And cannot understand why I strive for the brutal veracity of life, in my poems and stories.; [a.] Rosemere, Quebec

SIZEMORE, MITCHELL
[b.] May 2, 1963, London, KY; [p.] Ernest Sizemore, Dorothy Couch; [ed.] Clay County High, Eastern Kentucky University, B.S. in Education with Emphasis in Social Science and English.; [occ.] Substitute Teacher, Self Employed in Construction; [pers.] I am an avid hunter and fisherman. I enjoy being outdoors. I try to write about things that are associated with the outdoors and my surroundings.; [a.] Garrard, KY

SKIPPER, CALVIN WAYNE
[pen.] C. W. Skipper; [b.] May 20, 1950, McLean, TX; [p.] Milton and Maurine Skipper; [m.] Jackie L. Skipper, May 7, 1987; [ed.] College - Amarillo Jr. College Palo Duro High School - Amarillo; [memb.] Amarillo Masonic Lodge #731 Amarillo Commandery #48 Knights Templar Bonita Chapter #184 O.E.S - Amarillo Friendship Baptist Church - Amarillo; [oth. writ.] "An old Cowboy Pondering" "Thumper - Rodeo Clown", "First Pair of Spurs" "The Blizzard of '62", "English Class" "Hometown Church", "The Lady"; [oth. writ.] For a country boy, the chance to say thank you to my parents, my wife, the National Library of Poetry, and my God.; [pers.] For a country boy, the chance to say thank you to my parents, my wife, the National Library of Poetry, and my God.; [a.] Lubbock, TX

SLUTSKY, JORDAN
[b.] August 13, 1980, Bronx, NY; [p.] David and Natalie Slutsky; [memb.] International Society of Poets, Ice Skating Institute of America, High School Clubs, Drama Club Newspaper Staff (cre-

ative writing editor), Student Council, Varsity Tennis; [hon.] High Honor Roll; [oth. writ.] Several poems and short stories.; [pers.] My poetry represents my honesty... maturity can only develop from truth.; [a.] Ellenville, NY

SMIT, ALLAN DOUGLAS
[b.] February 11, 1916, East London; [p.] Douglas and Charlotte Smit; [m.] Norah, November 11, 1940; [ch.] Five; [ed.] Bachelor of Medicine, Bachelor of Surgery (MB Ch. B.) University of Cape Town, Fellow of the Royal College of Surgeons of Edinburgh (FRCSE); [occ.] Semi-Retired Orthopaedic Surgeon; [memb.] Rotary Club of East London; [oth. writ.] Various mina contributions to the South African Medical Association.; [pers.] Born November 5, 1916, Cape Town MBCHB 1941, FRCSE 1948 Retired Orthopaedic Surgeon.; [a.] Stirling, Republic South Africa

SMITH, ERIC SHANE
[b.] May 19, 1974, Ft. Lauderdale, FL; [p.] Fred W. Smith and Denise C. Smith; [ed.] Graduated from Florida State University with Bachelor of Science degree. Graduated from Bay High School, Panama City, FL.; [occ.] Currently undergoing EMT training while applying to Medical School.; [memb.] Pre-Medical Honor Society [hon.] Dean's List - FSU; [oth. writ.] Poems and short stories published in Bay High School's Literary Magazine; [pers.] I'd like to thank my high school creative writing instructor, Mrs. Hodges, for inspiring me to search deep within myself to find this gift that I can share with others.; [a.] Panama City, FL

SMITH FRANKIE L.
[b.] February 23, 1943, Tifton, GA; [p.] Mr. Frank Smith and Ruby Smith Reese; [ch.] Linda Smith-daughter; [occ.] Retires-U.S. Postal Worker; [pers.] I strive to keep a loving relationship with Jesus Christ.; [a.] Miami, FL

SMITH, JERRY B.
[b.] March 8, 1954, Raleigh, NC; [p.] Lavern and Magalene Smith; [ed.] South Johnston High, Johnston Community College; [occ.] Police Detective, Clayton Police Department, NC; [memb.] Johnston County Colonial Militia Re-enactment group, Lafayette Longrifles, NC, Law Enforcement Officers Assoc., Police Benevolent Assoc., Johnston Co. Law Enforcement Officers Assoc., Johnston Co. Crimestoppers; [hon.] Competitive Shooter in Police Combat and Primitive Weapons, Awards at local, state and national levels. Five High School letters in football and track. The "I Dare You" Award for Leadership. Most Dedicated Award for High School Athletics.; [oth. writ.] Short Stories and poems in local newspapers. Period songs for Colonial re-enactment group.; [pers.] The poem in this book is a metaphor of my life. I was severely injured in a motorcycle accident at a young age and told that I would be crippled. Through will power and the love of others, I overcame obstacles and made my life what I wanted it to be. Like the Lame Wolf, I became a survivor.; [a.] Benson, NC

SMITH, LATINA
[b.] May 31, 1980, Newark, NJ; [p.] Michael Duhart, Fontina Duhart; [ed.] McGuire Air Force Base Elementary Schools, Northern Burlington Jr., Sr High

School, Barringer High School; [occ.] Sophomore student, Barringer High School; [memb.] 4-H Club member; [hon.] Attended Citizenship Washington Focus, attended Governor's Inaugural Ball; [pers.] I write my inner feelings and personal experiences to express my words in my writings.; [a.] Newark, NY

SMITH, LAURIE L.
[pen.] Lls; [b.] May 4, 1960, Hobbs, NM; [p.] Howard and Rozetta Smith; [ed.] Clear Lake High School, Texas Tech University; [occ.] Part of corporate America; [memb.] International Poets Society; [oth. writ.] Poems published in the following books: Sparkle In The Sand, Walk Through Paradise, A Delicate Balance, Soul Of The Window, Best poet of 1996, a tapestry of thoughts, and poetic voices of America.; [pers.] All my writings come from my emotional feelings and experiences I have encountered due to my family, my extended family of unique friends and especially from past and present relationships. My writings are my way of dealing with life in general, as far as what is worth blowing away using a breath of kindness.; [a.] Lewisville, TX

SMITH, MARY T.
[b.] October 27, 1970, Prince Edward Island, Canada; [p.] Ken and May Smith; [ch.] Atheania, Catherine and Adrian; [ed.] Grade 7, Sunny Brea I.A.U. at Community College G.E.D.; [occ.] Homemaker; [oth. writ.] I have written about 250 poems but this is the first one to be published.; [pers.] My poems are written from the heart. They are about how people and things make me feel and what I see when I look at something or someone. The poem in this book was written when I was 17 years old.; [a.] Moncton New Brunswick, Canada

SMITH, NATASHA L.
[b.] April 15, 1977, Virginia Beach, VA; [p.] Ronald D. and Dyra L. Smith Sr.; [ed.] Salem High School, Norfolk State University; [occ.] Secretarial; [memb.] New Horizon Outreach Ministry; [hon.] Certificate of Recognition for Academic Achievement, 1995, Certificate of Appreciation for participation in community programs.; [pers.] Fear is a form of ignorance restraining us from excelling — Fear only God.; [a.] Virginia Beach, VA

SMITH, ROBERT R.
[pen.] Roop; [b.] December 22, 1972, Fullerton, CA; [ed.] Millikan High School, Cypress College; [occ.] Server - Networker; [oth. writ.] None published; [pers.] Your mind determines what's real, not someone else's limitations.; [a.] Long Beach, CA

SMITH, SARAH GRANT
[b.] January 22, 1962, Walterboro, SC; [p.] Annie E. Brown and Willie Whitlock; [m.] February 28, 1985; [ch.] Diemisha, Jerry, Tocara and Jerard; [ed.] Charles A. Brown High School, Farah's Beauty School, Texas College, Low Country Nurses Aide Training School Inc. and Trident Technician College; [occ.] Nursing Assistant; [memb.] Sigma, Shadow Organization of Phi Beta Sigma Fraternity, Inc. Saint Peters Ame Church Young Adult Choir - Student Council; [hon.] University of S.C., Division of Continuing Education, Certificate of Recognition and Service; [oth. writ.] Several poems, but only "Alone" have been published in The Chronicle Local Newspaper; [pers.] This poem is

dedicate to Ms. N. C. Williams, Mrs. M. Provost, Family and special Friend Mr. Gripper Polite; [a.] Goose Creek, SC

SMITH, SASKA M.
[pen.] Saska M. Smith; [b.] February 26, 1976, Martinez, CA; [p.] C. Edward Smith and Alice Junis Smith; [ed.] Shore Acres Christian School, Pittsburgh High School; [occ.] Care worker; [memb.] X Files Faw Club; [pers.] I want to thank all the people in my life for being good influences. Making me write what I feel on paper. Thank you C.E.S., R.S.M, B.F, D.K and Ms. Ovick; [a.] Pittsburg, CA

SMITH, SHAUNA DAWN
[pen.] Shauna Dawn; [b.] December 21, 1979, Red Deer, Alberta, Canada; [p.] Norma Smith, Richard Scown; [ed.] Presently attending Lindsey Thurber Comprehensive High School; [memb.] Treehouse Youth Theater; [hon.] Kiwanis Festival of Performing Arts Awards, The Royal Conservatory of Music Grade 4; [pers.] I'd like to dedicate this poem to the most influential people in my life Norman Merry the greatest teacher and my Mom Norma Smith. "And remember always follow your dreams."; [a.] Red Deer Alberta, Canada

SMITH, SHERIDAN
[b.] April 14, 1977, Reno, NV; [p.] Steve and Linda Smith; [ed.] Reed High, University of the Pacific; [occ.] Student; [memb.] St. Paul's Episcopal Church, VOP Women's Soccer Team; [hon.] VOP Scholarship Award Recipient; [oth. writ.] Poems, short stories etc.; [pers.] Life is an adventure. Live each moment to the fullest and Smile Moment while you're doing it!; [a.] Sparks, NV

SMITH, VIRGINIA E.
[b.] Rome, GA; [p.] Deceased; [m.] Billy Joe Smith; [ch.] Billy Joe Smith Jr., Ernest, Smith, Daisy Wilson, Anna Ware; [ed.] High School; [occ.] Retired; [memb.] Church of Christ, (NSAI) Nashville Songwriter International; [hon.] Church plaques for dedication and appreciation; [oth. writ.] I write poems for church bulletins and special occasions. I wrote and recorded one record. I write all types of songs and want to get my own poems published in book form.; [pers.] The world is my subject but God is my inspiration.; [a.] Rome, GA

SMITT, ROBYN
[b.] November 29, 1977; [p.] Robert and Debra Smitt; [ch.] Jordyn Renae; [ed.] I am currently attending Wayne State University in hopes of receiving a degree in Special Education

SMOOT, ELEAN K.
[pen.] Venus; [b.] May 6, Winston Salem, NC; [ch.] Grandson: Pierre, Monique, Tangee; [ed.] Degrees: Exec. Sec., Science, Computer Technology; [occ.] Office - Home Consultant, Import and Export Enterprise, Mortgage Broker; [memb.] Major's Hon., Violence Task Force, Legal Sec. Assoc., Prof. Sec. Assoc. NC Notary Public, Dual NC Insurance Licenses: Property and Casualty, Life Accident, and Health, etc.; [pers.] "For life to come to blossom, you must feel both joy and pain, flowers cannot burst forth to color with just sunshine and no rain."; [a.] Winston-Salem, NC

SNACHE, GLENDA
[pen.] Northern Lites; [b.] March 18, 1945, Ontario, Canada; [p.] Dora Sylvester, Ramie Sylvester; [ch.] Derrick, Paula and Andrea; [pers.] Mother Earth, her compelling magnificent beauty and rage captivate me creating an interaction to connect with human kind and nature.; [a.] Toronto Ontario, Canada

SNOOK, DANIEL JOHN
[b.] May 2, 1937, Layton, NJ; [p.] Albert and Mary Snook; [m.] Patricia Ann Snook, October 26, 1963; [ch.] James Jude and David John; [ed.] Newton High, NJ, Arkansas Comm College, East Stroudsburg Univ; [occ.] Retired; [memb.] American Hypnosis Assn., Flying Hams Club, Masonic Lodge F&AM; [oth. writ.] My first poem. I wrote for the contest.; [pers.] The answers we all seek are already within ourselves. Already within our selves. We must find a way to focus our energy within and the answers will come forth.; [a.] Bushkill, PA

SNOW, JAMES P.
[b.] July 17, 1970, Salt Lake City, UT; [p.] James R. Snow, Patricia M. Snow; [m.] Kara Helena Snow, April 6, 1996; [ch.] Eric Leland Snow; [ed.] Vista High, Mira Costa College; [occ.] Currently Disabled; [memb.] Lutheran Church of New Hope; [hon.] My wonderful wife; [oth. writ.] "Just A Stone's Throw Away"; [pers.] "A little adversity is the spice of life, for too much comfort can confine one to complacency, the bitter enemy of growth and imagination."; [a.] Oceanside, CA

SOGG, EMILY ELIZABETH
[b.] March 19, 1985, Los Angeles, CA; [p.] Kenneth J. Sogg and Carol Kapuza Sogg; [ed.] Franklin Ave Elementary, Wonderland Ave Elementary, Immaculate Heart Middle School Los Angeles CA; [occ.] Student; [memb.] Girl Scout Troop 771; [hon.] ICAN Associates 10th (1995) Annual Child Abuse Prevention Month Poster Contest - Finalist, ICAn Associates 11th (1996) Annual Child Abuse Prevention Month Poster Contest - Finalist; [oth. writ.] Poem published in anthology of poetry by Young American's, 1996 edition.; [pers.] Anyone can make a difference.; [a.] Los Angeles, CA

SOHM, ANN TRINITA
[b.] July 26, 1950, Staten Island, NY; [p.] Patricia Balmaine and Harold Sohm; [ed.] M.A. Liberal Studies CSI, CUNY B.A. Music, Richmond Coll. CUNY; [occ.] Teacher, Music and Art, Professional Classical Singer; [hon.] N.Y. State Legislative Award "Woman in History" for lecture concerts of historical music, CSI-CUNY Alumni Hall of Fame Award, graduate Faculty CSI-CUNY Award for Outstanding Academic in relation to M.A., various juried art shows of paintings.; [pers.] As a poet, singer and artist, I try to share the beauty and compassion which nourish our lives and souls in ways nothing else can.; [a.] Staten Island, NY

SOLLARS, MICHELLE L.
[pen.] Peanut; [b.] January 19, 1984, Flemington, NJ; [p.] Ernest J. and Danielle L. Sollars III; [ed.] 6th Grade, Readington Middle School; [occ.] Student; [memb.] Girl Scouts, Super Cub (5-years in a row) at Whitehouse Elementary School; [hon.] Honor Roll at Readington School; [oth. writ.] Explorer, November Poem, Dark Night, Writer for School Newspaper; [a.] Whitehouse Station, NJ

SONNETT, RACHEL MARIE
[b.] January 22, 1981, Pittsburgh, PA; [p.] George Sonnett, Sharon Sonnett; [ed.] High school Freshman; [occ.] Student; [memb.] Girl Scouts, Marching and Pitt Band; [hon.] I am currently working on my Girl Scout Silver Award.; [oth. writ.] Numerous poetry and short stories.; [pers.] I find writing an excellent release from tensions and daily anxieties.; [a.] Slippery Rock, PA

SOOKRAM, NARINE DAT
[b.] December 2, 1975, Guyana, Berbice; [p.] Nandrachand and Mohanie Sookram; [ed.] Ontario Secondary School Graduate, Presently attending College for computer studies; [occ.] Machine Operator; [hon.] Gain Royal Nobility Status in 1975. Nominated as Citizen of the Year 1995 by Prince Kevin. Nominated for the K-W Arts Award. Awarded two Life Time Royal Jewellery, one in 1995 and one in 1996; [oth. writ.] Most of my writings are done in the form of poems; [pers.] Writings are something and really enjoy doing. My future goal is to publish a book with the combination of all my own writings. This will include my personal biography in more details.; [a.] Kitchener Ontario, Canada

SOOMRO, DR. SHAMS-UD-DIN
[pen.] Shams Soomro; [b.] January 6, 1954, Dadu Sindh Pk.; [p.] Ghulam haider Soomro 9late) & Aaisha-Haider. [m.] Mrs. Halema Noor Soomro, September 18, 1980; [ch.] Saima 'Afrien', Sehrish, Aisha.; [ed.] M.B.B.S.; [occ.] Medical Practice; [memb.] Chairmain Basant Arts Council Secretary General S.A.S.S. (Sindhi Adabi-Sangat Sindh) Member P.A.L. Islamabad. Hon. Sec. Ed. Board Monthly WAIJ Key. Member Exec. Com. Pak. Med. Asso. Key.; [hon.] Best Science Eassay writter Award 1973-74.; S.A.S.'S. Best Writer Award 1994-95.; Best Essay writer or Shah Lateef Award 1991.; Sarwan (Leader) Gold Medal Award as best Sindhi Critic & Short Story writer 1995.; [oth. writ.] Various short stories, Daily columns and essays published in Sindhi Periodicals, Newspspers and Magazines.; [pers.] Intellectuals and writers remain very close, despite continental distances, their intellect creative power and artistic work become their sole identity even though they never meet or see each other.; [a.] Karachi, Pakistan

SORENSEN, INEZ
[pen.] Inez Sorensen; [b.] December 1, 1924, Georgia; [p.] Ben and Mary Powell; [m.] Deceased; [ed.] Tom P. Haney School, Gulf Coast Comm. College, Fla. State University, West Fl. University; [occ.] Retired R.N.; [memb.] A.A.R.P., Sigma Theta Tau, Kevin Trudeau Marketing Group; [hon.] Graduated with honors from Gulf Coast College and Fl. St. Univ.; [oth. writ.] Poems some have been printed in Church papers.; [pers.] The material I write I feel very deeply. I find it difficult to write a jingle. It has to be something that moves me. I've been privileged to travel and I've seen so many lovely things to write about.; [a.] Panama City, FL

SOSIS, PHILIP
[pen.] Phil Sosis; [b.] September 13, 1914, New York City, NY; [p.] Dora Alper, Isadore Sosis; [m.] Suzanne Gluck-Sosis, April 7, 1995; [ch.] Richard, Philip - Louisa, Fred; [ed.] Graduate of Montalar State College Cum Laude - 1979; [occ.] Retired;

[memb.] Ethical Culture Society of Essex; [hon.] Accepted by the N.V. English Teachers for poetry - 1995; [oth. writ.] Books of Poetry - The Rookery 1995, Preludes, Probes, and Dreams 1992, Sonata for 3 Voices 1977, Pub. Canopus Press - Phil Lohman, Designer; [pers.] A lower cost side child orphan asylum Bully turned athlete helpers on much for 17 cent per hour during depression, power brake depection/mechanical/shop foreman/charter member of Univ/Husband - Father Grandfather/ HS Teacher - Vocational Guidance Counselor, retired at 77 to composer language - mean words.; [a.] Elizabeth, NJ

SOUTH, BETTY
[b.] January 28, 1946, Garland, TX; [p.] Dan Lillie and Mae Davis; [m.] Ralph W. South, September 8, 1952; [ch.] Four Children - Rodney, Candy, Ronnie, Vickie; [ed.] 11th; [occ.] Nanny

SOUTHARD, JEFF
[b.] October 21, 1962, Culpeper, VA; [p.] Claude W. Southard and Mary Lee Brown Southard; [m.] Candice R. Tennant, December 10, 1994; [a.] Culpeper, VA

SPAUGH, STEVE
[b.] September 4, 1923, Concord, NC; [p.] Mary Spaugh and Hubert Spaugh; [m.] Dorothy; [ch.] David; [ed.] BA Degree, Cent. High, Wash, D.C., LaSierra Univ., UCLA, Northwestern Univ., Univ. of Texas; [occ.] Pres. and CEO, Spaugh Ent. Corp. (RE Broker, Consultant and Investor); [memb.] Life Mbr. SA Chamb. of Comm., Life Mbr. SA Counc. of Pres., Life Mbr SA Safety Counc., Nat. Assoc. of Master Appraisers; [hon.] World War II-Bronze Star; [oth. writ.] his first published effort was in 1949 in America - 1949 Anthology of College Poetry, Pub. Nat'l. Poetry Ass'n., 3210 Selby Ave., Los Angeles 34, Calif. (Poems: Iin the House of My Friend.) This was followed by another publication Anthology Of The Verse Of American Youth, Robert Shaw-Wilson, Ed., Twentieth Century Press, Los Angeles, Calif. (Poem: First Snow). Next was a play in 1954 published Ivan Bloom Hardin Company and The Dream Shop, 109 14th St., NW, Mason City, Iowa (Play: A Kiss For Henry). Numerous poems, storys and articles followed through the '50s, '60s, '70s and '80s published in newspapers, church papers, and various other periodicals. Then in 1982 the publication Our Twentieth Century's Greatest Poems, John Campbell, Ed., world of poetry press Sacramento, Calif. carried (Poem: An Act Of Love (a sonnet). In 1984 two items in The American Poetry Anthology, Vol. Iii, Number 3-4, Fall/ Winter, John Frost, Ed., The American Poetry Association, Santa Cruz, Calif. (Poem: Ode to Jude-a tribute to Thomas Hardy's Jude The Obscure). In 1985 the Hearts On Fire: A Treasury of Poems on Love, Vol. II, John Frost, Ed., The American Poetry (Poem: Bon Chance, Milady). In 1986 Masterpieces Of Modern Verse, Selected Poems From The 1985 Summer Poetry Contest, John Frost, Ed., The American Poetry Association, Box 2279, Santa Cruz, Calif. 95063 published: (Poem Dadd - to my son David). Most recently Steve Spaugh has had two articles published in the House Organ of the National Association Of Master Appraisers

(1991): (The Personal Touch in Property Management, and Kernels of Knowledge From A Counseling Broker, Winter 1991, Vol. IV No. 4); [pers.] I consider my self a classical type poet after the order of Byron and Shakespeare. I have six Volumes of yet to be published poems.; [a.] San Antonio, TX

SPEARMAN, CHUCK
[b.] August 24, 1968, Seneca, SC; [p.] John and Frances; [m.] Emily, November 14, 1992; [ch.] Jonathan, Montez; [ed.] West-Oak High School, Tri-County Technical College; [occ.] Electrician-Greenfield Industries, Clemson, S.C.; [memb.] Reedy Fork Baptist Church; [pers.] My wife is my greatest inspiration. This poem was written after our first date. It didn't look like there would be a second, but after this poem... the rest is history.; [a.] Seneca, SC

SPECKEL, JULIE L. BEST
[b.] December 7, 1960, Bourne, MA; [p.] Ted and Gloria Best; [ch.] A quiver full; [pers.] To Mom, thank you for teaching me to believe in myself. And to Dad, for the rewards of learning to look beyond, to see within the heart. In all things, my thanks to God and my parents, for the gift of life.; [a.] Coon Rapids, MN

SPENCER, ROGER
[pen.] Roger Spencer; [b.] November 2, 1957, Campton, KY; [p.] Orba, Margie Spencer; [ed.] Powell Country High School; [occ.] Unemployed; [memb.] Methodist Church; [oth. writ.] Personal; [pers.] My writings embrace my heart and soul and delivers it to the paper via pen. Simply reflects my world. Which I hope to share with all that have a desire to enter.; [a.] Clay, KY

SPRAGG, LUKE
[b.] January 25, 1970, North Vancouver, British Columbia, Canada; [p.] Catherine and Graham; [ed.] Ontario Secondary School Diploma, Grade 12, Life.; [occ.] Supervisor, Rogers, Cable Systems; [oth. writ.] Personal Poems, Short Descriptive Prose.; [pers.] Write from your hearts and you'll be amazed biggest inspiration is life and living. Influenced by heartache, joy and flagrant disillusionment of people in power. Many thanks to Josh, Dion, Friends and Family.; [a.] Toronto Ontario, Canada

SPRIGGS, TIMOTHY
[b.] January 24, 1957, Ft. Worth, TX; [p.] Marion Spriggs and Raymond Spriggs; [ed.] Western High School (Anaheim, Calif), Express Community College (Cypress, Calif); [occ.] Truck driver; [hon.] Honor Society in high school - entire junior year. Dean's List at Cypress College; [oth. writ.] Represented Western High School in national writing contest (one of five student entries); [pers.] Poets and Musicians - two sides of the same creative coin.; [a.] Albuquerque, NM

SPRINGER, PATRICK
[b.] August 12, 1953, B'Town, Barbados; [p.] Darrell Springer and Anne Springer; [ed.] High school graduate some university courses, Correspondence Queens University and the University of Waterloo.; [occ.] Production Operator General Motors of Canada Oshawa; [pers.] I have been

writing poetry and songs for about twenty-three (23) years. I never tried to publish any of my writings. At my older brothers persistence, I relented, and entered this competition. Thank you for the opportunity.; [a.] Toronto Ontario, Canada

SPROUSE, PATRICIA
[b.] April 13, 1961, Fort Leonard Wood, MI; [p.] Shirley A. & Richard D. Snow; [m.] Stan Sprouse, August 30, 1986; [ed.] Cottonwood High, I failed every Writing and English class I ever took; [occ.] I have a blood disorder and am disabled; [pers.] My mother was my best friend and taught me that I could do anything I set my mind to, she passed away only ten months after I was married. But she is still the greatest influence in my life; [a.] Salt Lake City, UT

STANG, WENDA
[b.] January 5, 1943, New Orleans, LA; [p.] George St. Peter and Bobbye Nelson St. Peter; [ed.] Upper Columbia Academy, Walla Walla College, La Sierra College Year Abroad at Collonges-sous-Salove, France, Wash. St. University School of Veterinary Medicine, University of Denver; [hon.] Degree in French with very high honors, High School Graduating Class Salutatorian, Vice President, and Editor of School Newspaper; [pers.] My poem, "Tomorrow at Dawn..." is dedicated to Dr. Geoffrey B. Heron, who encouraged me in my decision to translate French Poetry after the death of my beloved dog, Buffy. Buffy was my inspiration for this poem, the first among many now completed.; [a.] Denver, CO

STARK, DANIEL
[b.] July 17, 1975, California; [p.] Dave and Cecilia; [ed.] High School, EMT Training and Certified Currently in College; [occ.] Emergency Medical Technician (Ambulance); [hon.] Honor Roll in High School; [pers.] This poems is dedicated to my grandmother Inez G. Saavedra, because I was inspired to write it the night of the passing away.; [a.] Hawthorne, CA

STARKEY, MELANIE JEAN
[b.] March 30, 1950, Oak Harbor, WA; [p.] Herbert Emison O'Neal, Rosa Lee O'Neal; [m.] David Ray Starkey, June 26, 1993; [ch.] Angela Starkey and Karl Starkey; [ed.] Lake Taylor High, Norfolk, VA, personal spiritual studies, course in miracles; [occ.] Student; [memb.] Unity Center for positive living 3101 Lombard Everett, WA - we receive tapes from our minister weekly.; [hon.] I have written several other poems that I have not yet tried to publish.; [pers.] I was used as an instrument and expression of our creative source, whose only message is love.; [a.] Florissant, MO

STEIDEL, GEORGE C.
[pen.] Gorge C. Steidel; [b.] January 28, 1924, Saint Joseph, MO; [p.] George E. and Ida V. Steidel; [m.] Marjorie Ann, (1st April 13, 1943), (2nd February 14, 1979); [ch.] Three daughters; [ed.] Elementary 1at-6th, Jr. High 7th-9th, High School 10th thru 11th 2 years Business College; [occ.] Retired after 34 1/2 yrs. at Wire Rope Corp of America; [memb.] Masonic Lodge #189 AF and AM Post Master of above (1992) 32o York Rite Mason, HI Twelve Club, American Legion Post #359

(World War II) Post Master's Club; [hon.] Achievement Award - Grand Lodge of Missouri (1992); [oth. writ.] Wrote short story for Capper's weekly when 10 years old. Article on events of war - young at heart magazine section of local newspaper. Currently working on short stories for children. Also had poem published in American poetry anthology; [pers.] I write of things of God and nature. By doing so, it is hard to go wrong and draw too much criticism. After all, God gave us these subjects. What better way to glorify his name?; [a.] Saint Joseph, MO

STEINBERG, JAY MICHAEL
[pen.] J.A.Y.; [p.] Alicia Sue Dwoskin, Jerry Steinberg; [ed.] High School Grad., attending Junior College for Perlussion Techniques; [pers.] My life's goal is to change the world through poetry and music. To make all the fake people real, like during the hippie generation. I'm gratefully dedicated to the ongoing search for peace love, and happiness, for life is too short and you have to enjoy it while you can.

STEMPIN, ROBERT L.
[pen.] Robert L. Stempin; [b.] December 8, 1936, Wilkes-Barre, PA; [p.] Leo and Minnie Stempin; [ed.] G.A.R. Memorial High School; [occ.] Staff Specialist Duke University; [memb.] The Dramatists Guild, Inc.; [oth. writ.] Several plays: "Annie: The Story Behind Hellen Keller, performed at the Wilkes-Barre Little Theater, "Dearest Teacher" a new musical of the life of Annie Sullivan, performed for the Wilkes-Barre Lions Club, "Angels Twice Descending" and "The Sky Is Low, The Clouds Are Mean" both currently in the works.; [pers.] This poem is dedicated in loving memory of Gilda, and in honor of Max, both of whom are responsible for my new children's book: Maxie Waxie and the Double Yellow Christmas.; [a.] Durham, NC

STENGEL, PAUL A.
[b.] November 11, 1966, New Jersey; [ed.] Fort Lee High School; [occ.] Boiler Engineer/Handyman; [oth. writ.] 50 or so unpublished writings. No titles; [a.] Fort Lee, NJ

STEPHENS, DIANA O'CONNELL
[pen.] Gerard; [b.] December 12, 1958, Paterson, NJ; [p.] Robert and Helen O'Connell; [m.] William Stephens, February 25, 1984; [ch.] Robert, Tammy and James; [ed.] Graduated from Ridgewood High School, Ridgewood, NJ - 1976; [occ.] Trying to get my poems published; [memb.] Outstanding at Carmel Middletown, NY; [oth. writ.] "My thanks to you," "The door," "The changes in a year," "The tiny elves," "Without you," "Strong wind blowing," "Minds in the country," "The hurt deep down," "A fathers love," "Day lillies," "Apologies," "Robbie," "Tammy," "James."; [pers.] My Lord, my husband and my children are my inspirations in all of my writings.; [a.] Middletown, NY

STEPHENS, ROSE
[b.] May 22, 1959; [p.] Mother Enid Latibeaudiere; [occ.] Business Woman; [pers.] I am in my 'write' mind; [a.] Miami, FL

STERLING, MAURICE D.
[pen.] David; [b.] November 13, 1930, Boston, MA; [p.] Both Deceased; [m.] Mrs. Mila Sterling, October 22, 1980; [ch.] Jennifer Lynn Sterling; [ed.] 4 yrs. College (Under G.I. Bill), Holy Angeles - University - Angeles City Philippines, 2009; [occ.] Retired (U.S. Army); [memb.] Retired U.S. Military Phil. Assoc., (RUMPA), Life, Member of VFW Angeles City Phil. American Legion Post 123 MacArthur Hwy. Angeles City; [hon.] To many to list from 20 years in army; [oth. writ.] I would like to try to write my life story (Which includes 6 marriages (2 Americans and 4 Pilipina).; [pers.] I'm just interested in giving the world some good stories so late in my life... I probably missed my calling sort of to speak!! I hope not?.; [a.] Angeles City, Philippines

STEVENS, BOBBI JO
[pen.] BJ Stevens; [b.] August 12, 1973, Needmore, PA; [p.] Elmer and Joan Hann; [m.] Robert K. Stevens Jr., February 13, 1993; [ed.] Mt. View Christian School; [pers.] Death fascinates me and I try to write about what it might be like. I am influenced most by the poet, Edgar Allen Poe.; [a.] Big Cove Tannery, PA

STEVENS, JACOB
[b.] February 19, 1982, Saint Louis, MO; [p.] Julie and Greg; [ed.] I am currently in the 8th grade, I was in 7th when I wrote the poem I was 13 years old; [hon.] Just sports trophies, and plaques, mostly sports things. I am a member of the Junior National Honor Society.; [pers.] Always be yourself, no one can change you.; [a.] Florissant, MO

STEVENS, JENNIFER LYN
[pen.] Jennifer Lyn; [b.] February 11, 1983, Raleigh, NC; [p.] Roger and Patricia Collins Stevens; [ed.] Cleveland School; [occ.] 7th Grade Student; [memb.] Beta Club, National Honor Society, Art, Chorus, Girls Athletic Association, Dare; [hon.] Honor roll, Academic Achievement Award, Star Student, Terrific Kid, Local Art Showings; [a.] Angier, NC

STEVENS, JOANNA
[pen.] Jodie; [b.] December 27, 1945, Toas, New Mexico; [p.] Paul & Marina Gaunder; [m.] Bill Stevens, August 6, 1981; [ch.] 7 - 5 children and 2 step-children; [ed.] High School GED; [occ.] Home Habitation Aide, Therapist Technitian II - Texas Dept. of Mental Health & Mental Retardation.; [memb.] Hospice Volunteer (former), Anerican Red Cross Volunteer - not curently; [oth. writ.] Some poems, non-published; [pers.] To be the best that you can be - no matter your lot in life.; [a.] Graham, TX

STEVENS, JUANITA
[pen.] Jay Stevens; [b.] February 14, 1934, Ralco, VA; [p.] Father (Deceased), Mother left; [m.] Paul J. Stevens, May 15, 1971; [ch.] Four girl's by 1st marriage; [ed.] 2 years college for Nursing; [occ.] Writing and playing guitar and singing.; [oth. writ.] Many poem's and song's over two hundred. Many of spiral nature. Blue's, Country, Contemporary many over twenty lines, and they are beautiful; [pers.] I love people and like writing about real thing's as well as the people I meet. Word's form in my mind and so does the me lady if it is a song

and not a poem.; [a.] Las Vegas, NV

STEVENS-SWEET, WINONA
[b.] September 20, Philadelphia, PA; [m.] Deceased; [ch.] Jesse Wm. Lawson III; [ed.] Jacob Lorne Institute, Port Deposit Md. (12 grades) courses at Univ of Dayton Okie and Harford Community College, Bel air, Md and Maxwell AFB, Ala (Civilian); [occ.] Chief, Whites Wolf Band, Southeastern Cherokee Confederacy for Md.; [memb.] Board of Directors Conversation Society of York, Inducted into Native America Hall of Fame (1990). Lifetime Previous, Indian steps museum, Airville, PA as of 1986; [oth. writ.] Several poems published in the Harford Post, Bel air, Md are poem published in "Mists of Enchantment by the National Library Poetry 1995.; [pers.] Poetry dedicated to my brother John Reuben "Red Fox" Stevens who had me submit my poetry and inspired me.; [a.] Havre de Grace, MD

STEWART, PAT
[b.] 1941, California; [ch.] Robert Merrill, Lisa Merrill; [ed.] BA UC Berkeley Ca. High School, Garden Grove Ca.; [occ.] Owner of Tax Preparation and Consulting Business, also State Worker.; [memb.] Nat'l Assoc. of Enrolled Agents, United Church of Christ Sebastopol (former moderator); [oth. writ.] Several sermons for church services, words for music performed in church, dramatic one-woman presentations. Writings appear in "Chelsea" by Paul Ogden and "Cry of Tamar" by Pamela Cooper-White.; [pers.] I strive to bring power/sexual abuse issues to awareness and I work to empower women and children. Power comes through the voice and the word.; [a.] Santa Rosa, CA

STINNETT, PATRICIA
[pen.] Pat; [b.] January 10, 1947, Washington; [p.] Herbert and Dorthy Thomas; [m.] Dan Stinnett, July 31, 1965; [ch.] Dan and David; [ed.] Crook County High Prineville, OR, Bend Community College Bend, OR - Major Math; [occ.] 21 Dealer have been for 24 years.; [memb.] B.M.I writer for music lyrics; [oth. writ.] Won a local contest to rewrite song of Reno. Several published poems locally - some songs I've written are recorded; [pers.] Writing poetry - song lyrics or cards for friends bring me extreme pleasure to feel others enjoy my thought - My dream in Life is to write for a living.; [a.] Sparks, NV

STIPES, KENNETH
[pen.] Kenneth Stipes; [b.] January 16, 1944, Knoxville, TN; [p.] Thomas (Deceased) and Ethel Stipes; [ch.] Kristy Delapp, Kandy and Tony Stipes; [ed.] Gibbs High School, University of Tenn., Knoxville Business College, American College of Life Underwriters, C.L.U. designation; [occ.] Solid Rock Christian Ministries, Minister; [pers.] To "Reach the Unreachable" for Jesus Christ my Lord!; [a.] Covington, TN

STOCKIN, DANN
[b.] Beatrice, Fred; [p.] Lula; [ch.] Thea, Erick, (Grandchildren: Rachel, Erika), (Great Grandchild: Lacy); [oth. writ.] I will begin writing one or more manuscripts in 1996.; [pers.] I was given a purpose in my teens from reading A. Carrel's Man, The Unknown. Since then I have continued to search for the truths to the nature and meaning of our human existence.; [a.] Seneca, SC

STOCKTON, ELSA M.
[b.] March 5, 1923, Colorado; [m.] Homer A. Stockton, August 20, 1945; [ch.] Sharon, Thomas (Deceased); [occ.] Retired Executive Secretary, Tutor for "English as a second language"; [memb.] National Wildlife Federation, Los Angeles Greater Los Angeles Zoo Association (GLAZA). Former deacon in Presbyterian Church. I am legally blind since 1994.; [oth. writ.] Many poems, religious articles of Pasadena Star News (Freelance); [pers.] My poems and writings are very personal and were written over a 46-yrs period. This is my first attempt at publishing, some have been in church paper.; [a.] LaCrescenta, CA

STOCKWELL JR., MARSHALL FREDERICK
[pen.] Fred Stockwell; [b.] August 26, 1956, Springfield, MA; [occ.] Ice Cream Production; [oth. writ.] Never published.; [pers.] Fred Stockwell is prematurely gray and rapidly approaching 40 with dread. His literary influences include Jack Kerauge, Captain Beefheart and Dr. Seuss, his interests include cooking, drawing, appreciating fine ales, playing the ukulele and receiving cash awards in poetry contests.; [a.] Springfield, MA

STOPERA, HELEN M.
[b.] August 15, 1929, Cohoes, NY; [p.] Helen Flavin, Neil Keefe; [m.] Robert J. Stopera, October 12, 1952; [ch.] Four daughters, one son; [ed.] Cohoes High School; [occ.] Retired-former Salesclerk - Teacher Aide; [oth. writ.] I have written many poems over the years.; [pers.] I have been able to put my feelings into words that rhyme. I love to write.; [a.] Cohoes, NY

STOUDT, WILLIAM E.
[b.] March 17, 1933, Bethlehem, PA; [p.] Emma J. and W. Edwin Stoudt; [m.] Gladys March 31, 1929, December 25, 1952; [ch.] James, William, Thomas, Kenneth, Sael, Steven; [ed.] AET, BSEE Purdue University; [occ.] Retired; [memb.] NRA, Fleet Reserve Assoc., American Legion, VFW, AARP; [hon.] Listed in "Who's Who in Computer's and Data Processing", US Navy Citation for Computer Programming 1972; [oth. writ.] L-Tran (Lesson Translator), Basic Computer Programming 1963, Utilities for Regis Cruisers, Basic Computer Arithmetic; [a.] Mount Laurel, NJ

STRETCH, ELAINE
[b.] August 18, 1979, Somers Point, NJ; [p.] Rosemarie and John Steven Newman; [ed.] Presently going to Mainland Regional High school (Linwood, New Jersey); [occ.] High School student (sophomore); [hon.] Receiving an A (95%) on my Term Paper dealing with Teenage Pregnancy; [oth. writ.] Some other little poems.; [pers.] No one knows what is going to happen tomorrow, so don't regret what you do today!; [a.] Somers Point, NJ

STRYKER, RICHARD ANTHONY
[pen.] Rick Anthony "Stryker"; [b.] March 24, 1936, New York City; [p.] David and Mary Stryker (Mother's Maiden name (Duggan); [m.] Sylvia Sue Stryker, June 18, 1955; [ch.] Patrick - John - Gloria (5 grandchildren); [ed.] High School, 1 year College Chofstra; [occ.] Proprietor of Employment Agency since 1949 still working more than; [memb.] Long Island Association, Bellmore Chamber of Commerce; [oth. writ.] 34 poems written since the

1940's I have composed music to accompany all of these poems. 23 of these songs have been included in an original musical comedy drama which I wrote titled "Baby What I Couldn't Do With Plenty Of Money And You." Many of writings have been discussed and heard on radio and TV and discussed and praised by prominent people, out as yet none has been published nor have they been financially successful.; [pers.] I have written 2 other songs poems praising Long Island. 1) Long Island Has Everything 2) Jones beach Is The Greatest. Most of writing are happy and convey fun and truth, some are serious. All of my profits from one of my poem songs will be contributed to creating happier and more lasting family relationship. This song is "Always be lovers." I have also written poem songs about family members (Mothers, Dad, Daughter, Wife, Grandchild) Also marriage - Brotherhood, also romantic humorous normal - Healthy - sexy songs. My poem "Time To Be Happy Is Now" is very positive thinker writer. My writings have been praised and also ridiculed by negative people who like to make distasteful humour. I am one of those "Cherry Folks With Don't Give Up Spirit" that I write about in my poem "Good Morning Long Island" who still has high hopes that writings will receive financial and artistic acclaim when I find the time to promote and circulate them.

STUCHELL, BRIAN M.
[pen.] B.; [b.] May 28, 1969, Eugene, OR; [p.] Phil and Beverly Stuchell; [ch.] Isaac Daniel; [ed.] Creswell High, Lane Community College; [memb.] Member of The National Library of Poetry; [oth. writ.] Several works published by World's Too Heavy Press. Works published in the following anthologies, Between the Raindrops, Carvings In Stone, and Through the Hourglass. All anthologies published by The N.L.P. Much thanks to them!; [pers.] Spending time with my son, Isaac, is like holding the hand of God. Together they give my soul true, unwavering peace. Because of them, and the utter joy they bring me, I am able to write words of love in spite of my everyday tortures that my paralysis shoves on me. Thank you, God, for the blessing of my son, Isaac.; [a.] Eugene, OR

STUDLEY, HELEN ORMSON
[b.] September 8, 1937, Elroy, WI; [p.] Hilda and Clarence Ormson; [m.] William Frank Studley, August 3, 1965; [ch.] William Harrison III; [ed.] Elroy High School, Pat Stevens College, Madison Vocational College, L.A. Valley College; [occ.] Artist Writer, Designer, Poet, Teacher; [memb.] Sons of Norway, Lutheran Brotherhood, Emmanuel Lutheran Church; [hon.] 1980 and 1984 Lithographs display "Olympics", Golden Poet Award 1987-1992, Named Finalist in competition for the John Simon Guggenhsion Fellowship, Special Art Award, "Flowers for Ruth", "Love is all Colors", "Show Award", Diamond Pin Award" (1991-1992) Carter, Hawley, Hale; [oth. writ.] "Changes", "If you Care", "Tiger-Pool goes to the Circus", Love is Care", "Super Body, Super Mind," "I Love my Texas Cowboys," "Asper Love..."; [pers.] "To know of your love of writing is one thing, but to write the poetry and songs you love, care, and feel about is the only thing special to do"...; [a.] Sherman Oaks, CA

STURDIVANT, WILLIAM R.
[pen.] Bill Sturdivant; [b.] February 22, 1952, East Chicago, IN; [p.] Marie and Randall Sturdivant; [m.] Mary H. Sturdivant, August 7, 1990; [ch.] De'Andre, Denton, Reseda, Regina, Eric; [ed.] Westside High, Midwest Insurance School, Building Mainti Electrical Vocational Tech.; [occ.] Lead Person - Adia Employment Services; [memb.] Faith Christian Center, (Musician) Guitarist (Oshkosh); [hon.] Award for Excellence American General Life and Accident Insurance Company, 6 awards for Christian study; [oth. writ.] Reason One Day - poems, From My Heart songs, Your Life, My Rendition Of Heaven, Memory, Beauty To Me, If You Feel The Need, Shout For Jesus; [pers.] I strive to project love, peace, and joy the way God gives it to us. I am influenced by deep personal feelings and worldly beauty to reflect on what is good and right.; [a.] Oshkosh, WI

SUDDARD, NORMA J.
[b.] April 13, 1940, Oshawa, Ontario, Canada; [p.] Alice and Joseph La Porte; [m.] Kenneth Suddard, August 2, 1958; [ch.] One daughter, Karen Lee; [oth. writ.] Tread Softly As We Trespass, Santa Carried An Umbrella, Don't Look For Sadness, Wildflowers, Battlefield Scars, Awaken In An Old Fashioned Kitchen; [pers.] I have written over 300 poems and short stories on a diversity of subjects. From a word, phrase or scene, a concept begins to take shape in my mind and the urge to formulate my feelings compels me to record them on paper.; [a.] Oshawa Ontario, Canada

SUHAY, KATHERINE
[b.] January 13, 1965, Naples, Italy; [p.] Ernest and Maria Suhay; [ed.] In Italy; [occ.] Sales and Marketing for European Import Company; [oth. writ.] Several other poems, currently working on a fictional children's book.; [pers.] In the depths of our souls, we all have a song to sing, a message to send out. Mine are of love and passion. When the core of my being is truly touched by a person or an event, that is when I'm most inspired poem, which he inspired and I thank my dear friend Steve, for encouraging me to send in this to who I dedicate with all my love.; [a.] San Francisco, CA

SUJONO
[pen.] Sujono; [b.] March 27, 1978, Jakarta; [p.] Loka Indra; [ed.] Bunda Hati Kudus Senior High School; [occ.] Student; [memb.] Pat-Djiu Wu-Shu Martial Arts Organization, and local Poet Society by the name "SS Enterprise Love Poet Society" as the executive committee.; [oth. writ.] Several poems published in school magazine and also some short stories published by the same media.; [pers.] God doesn't want us to be the best, but to do our best.; [a.] Jakarta, Indonesia

SUTTON, EMMIE
[pen.] Salem Cross; [b.] September 14, 1950, Leiden, Netherlands; [p.] Ann and Joe deKoning; [ch.] Catherine Anne; [ed.] Georgian College; [occ.] Journalist; [memb.] SOCAN (Society of Composers, Authors and Music Publishers of Canada); [oth. writ.] Folk Album of Original Compositions Recorded Feb., 1996 (Folk Songs, Guitar Playing by Salem Cross); [a.] Stroud Ontario, Canada

SWEENEY, MICHAEL RAYMOND
[b.] January 4, 1964, Nassau County, NY; [p.] Marilyn Bella and Raymond Sweeney; [m.] Virginia Elise Sweeney, May 2, 1993; [ch.] Jennifer Anne, Michael Jr.; [ed.] West Babylon Senior High; [occ.] U.S. Navy (10 years) Machinist Mate Second Class Petty Officer; [hon.] Operation desert Shield, Storm Veteran Navy Achievement Medal (2) Navy Good Conduct Medal (2) Navy Expeditionary Medal (2) National Defense Service Medal (1) Armed Forces Expeditionary Medal (2) southwest Asia Service Medal (1) Kuwait Liberation Medal (1); [oth. writ.] I have written several poems, most of which I wrote out at sea during operation desert shield/storm.; [pers.] Every poem I write comes from the heart; [a.] Plainview, NY

SWEET, CASSIE LYNN
[b.] July 19, 1980, Homestead; [p.] Vickie and Philip Sweet; [ed.] Currently in High School; [occ.] Student; [a.] Miami, FL

SWENSON, MICHAEL
[b.] April 5, 1966, Los Angeles, CA; [p.] John and Susan Swenson Jr.; [m.] Nane Swenson, August 10, 1995; [ed.] 6-9 years of Diversified Collegiate Studies; [occ.] Minister of Jesus Christ, Entrepenuer, Inventor; [memb.] United Christian Ministerial Association; [oth. writ.] "Gift Michael and His Angels" (large volume completed as yet unpublished); [pers.] All I possess and all that I am are God's, belongs to God, and is given to me by God. May this bless Him and others innumerable. Amen.; [a.] Boulder, CO

SWIGER, AMANDA
[pen.] Amanda Rae; [b.] December 10, 1978, MI; [p.] Donald and Helen Swiger; [ed.] Junior in High School; [occ.] Maid at Foothills Motel; [memb.] Tae kwondo, placer high chorus.; [hon.] Who's Who Among American Teens Achievement Award, Chorus Awards, Placer Letter Men; [oth. writ.] Trail of tears which is unpublished.; [pers.] My inspiration for writing this poem came from my older brother Jeffrey Pontius. I would like to dedicate it with love to him and my nephew Carson.; [a.] Evart, MI

SWITZER, BARBARA
[b.] September 24, 1941, Hot Springs, NM; [p.] Wesley and Goldie Hobbs; [ed.] Some College Courses, G.E.D. High School Equivalency; [occ.] On Disability; [memb.] Living Word Baptist Church; [hon.] My honors and awards must go to the Lord for giving me the gift to write my poems.; [oth. writ.] The Lamb - published in "Walk Through Paradise", A Friend - published in "Mists of Enchantment", Gift of Love - soon to come out in this book called "The Ebbing Tide", Trust in Him - coming out in "Carvings in Stone", also three other poems unpublished, The Shepherd, The Blessing, and Angels; [pers.] God has been my inspiration to write because of all the beauty He has given us in this world to cherish. All we need to do is open our eyes, hearts, and mind to enjoy and share all of God's love and grace.; [a.] Los Lunas, NM

SZULEWSKI, ROSA ROSALES
[b.] April 28, 1968, Managua, Nic; [p.] Maria and Salvador Rosales; [m.] William A. Szulewski, April 22, 1995; [ed.] Elizabeth High School,

Berkeley College, Union Country College; [occ.] Executive Manager, Bloomingdale's, Short Hills, NJ; [memb.] Hand-in-Hand Festival Committee, Church of Saint Anthony of Padua, Eastern Paralyzed, Carnegie Hall Membership; [hon.] Elizabeth High, Dean's List and trophy Bilingual Club Vice-Pres. 1987, Berkeley College, Dean's List 1988, Golden B Award and Plague - Best Shortage - Bloomingdale's 1992-1994; [pers.] "I am convinced that life is 10 percent what happens to me and 90% how I treat to it. And so it is with you...we are in charge of our Attitudes." By Charles Swindoll; [a.] Elizabeth, NJ

TA, KIM ANH
[pen.] Ann Lee, Kim Lan Anh; [b.] November 22, 1956, Saigon, Vietnam; [p.] Van Ta, Thuan Dang; [m.] Tuan Le, December 18, 1981; [ch.] Nam Le, Anh Ta, Minh Ta, John Le; [ed.] Elementary Teacher, Post Secondary School; [occ.] Housewife; [oth. writ.] Poems published in School Magazine, Vietnamese Newspaper; [pers.] I have the aspiration to describe my love and emotions towards the beauty of Nature and Humanity.; [a.] Ottawa Ontario, Canada

TALBOT, MARK DOUGLAS
[b.] June 5, 1974, Montreal, Canada; [pers.] She gave me all I could ever ask for, and then took it all away.; [a.] Montreal West Quebec, Canada

TALLISON, DON H.
[b.] July 31, 1935, Benton, AR; [p.] Stella-Hermon Tallison; [m.] Vivian V. (Harris) Tallison, August 26, 1955; [ed.] Duachita Baptist University in Arkadelphia, Arkansas, Southwestern Baptist Theological Seminary in Fort Worth, Texas; [occ.] Retired Southern Baptist Missionary to Alaska; [memb.] Retired Missionary Association SBC of America, (Executive Board, Central Baptist Association of Arkansas); [hon.] Received many honors and rewards for Pioneer Chaplain work I did in prison and hospital work in Soldotna, and Nome, Alaska, I was honored for being Memorial Day Chaplain in Nome, by the city.; [oth. writ.] Many of my poems have appeared in religious papers and newspapers both in Alaska and Arkansas many of my poems are used as songs in many Churches., [a.] Prattsville, AR

TALLMAN, EVELYN
[b.] November 13, 1922, South Westerlo, NY; [p.] Mrs. Hazel F. Mabie; [m.] Deceased, January 23, 1940; [ch.] One; [ed.] Greenville Central High School National baking School 835 Diversey Parkway Chicago, Illinois; [occ.] Retired and write; [memb.] Social Service with Albany Country, Social Security Benefits; [oth. writ.] World of Poetry 701 Dixieanne Ave. Sacramento, California 85815

TAN, POH KOK
[b.] August 24, 1956, Kuching, Sarawak, Malaysia; [p.] Mr. Hung Siow Tan, Mok Ju Kho; [ed.] Louisiana State University, Baton Rouge, USA; [occ.] Sole Proprietor; [memb.] Malaysian Red Cresent Blood Donors Association; [oth. writ.] Several poems published in The New American Poetry Anthology and American Poetry Anthology; [a.] Kuching Sarawak, Malaysia

TANGERINE
[pen.] Tanji; [b.] April 29, 1972, Vancouver, British Columbia, Canada; [p.] Randall Beaudin, Lisa Burnstein; [m.] Divorced; [ch.] Aziza Ashley; [ed.] Bradford High; [occ.] Poet/Phychic; [hon.] "Editors Choice Award" and " Member in Good Standing" Certificates from National Library of Poetry.; [oth. writ.] Poetry/Articles published in local newspaper. Interview on local newspaper. Interviewed on local cable show. This is second time, published in Anthology books.; [pers.] I write what's in my heart, hiding nothing - yet revealing only a portion of my soul.; [a.] Hawkesbury Ontario, Canada

TAPPAN, CHRISTOPHER SHAWN
[pen.] Chris Me!; [b.] October 15, 1965, Everett, WA; [p.] Diane Viola Tappan, Bob Tappan; [ed.] Inglemoore High School Graduate, Army Honorable Discharge Avionics; [occ.] Lead Cook at a nursing home retirement center; [oth. writ.] In the process of writing a book of poetry... have written over 400 poems have only sixty, that still hold the original impact!; [pers.] The emotional pool is created by blood, sweat, and tears... within this pool, are the boundaries, and limitations, set by God...For us all!; [a.] Everett, WA

TARLE, NAOMI
[b.] October 26, 1980, Santa Monica, CA; [p.] Marci and Norman Tarle; [ed.] Graduating from Santa Monica High School in June 1998.; [memb.] Member of the UCLA Junior Rowing Team; Member of Delians - the Santa Monica H.S. chapter of the California Scholarship Federation.; [hon.] Principal's Honor Roll.; [oth. writ.] short story "Oatmeal Cookies", published in Young Voices magazine; poem -"Memorabilia", published in The Voice Within", The National Library of Poetry.; [a.] Santa Monica, CA

TARSIA, VANESSA
[pen.] Vanna and Alto; [b.] June 9, 1976, Ottawa; [p.] Maria and Ted Tarsia; [ed.] St. Pius X High School; [occ.] Receptionist, Garvey Construction Ltd., Gloucester, Ontario; [hon.] St. Pius X High School Certificate of Achievement for achieving first class honours in grade 11, 12 and 13; [oth. writ.] A poem published in the high school year book entitled "Silent Visit".; [pers.] I attempt to express my opinions and emotions through my poetry. At times I find it very therapeutic and it becomes a coping mechanism when life becomes difficult.; [a.] Nepean Ontario, Canada

TATEM, JENNIFER
[b.] May 26, 1953, New York City, NY; [p.] Dearie Tonnchill, Clarence Bowden; [m.] Widowed; [ch.] Five sons; [ed.] Attended Monroe College currently attending the College of New Rochelle - major is Social Work; [occ.] Working towards opening my own business.; [memb.] I truly thank the National Library of Poetry for giving me the opportunity to display some of my work in their books.; [hon.] Received a certificate for Assisting the Federal Emergency Management during the aftermath of Hurricane Hugo. This storm taught me how precious life is.; [oth. writ.] My son Elroy and his best friend Mitch wrote a children's story called The Cheetah is

taught a lesson. I thank his teacher Ms. Picket for encouraging this project, Flags 98.; [pers.] I love writing and its also a release of everyday pressures. I thank God for giving me the ability to put words down on paper reflecting my personality. In the near future I will write a book of poetry in hopes of warming everyone's heart.; [a.] Bronx, NY

TATINA, MARIE
[pen.] Wisdom; [b.] December 17, 1939, Chicago, IL; [p.] William and Eleanor (Nee Karczewski) Tatina; [ed.] Jaeger Jr College, Chic. Teach College, No. Chic. Music Cons. BS and MS Calif. Western Univ. 1978; [occ.] Owner, Designer, Engineering for Artistic Designs Innovators in Stained Glass Art; [memb.] Benedictine Oblate, Stained Glass Assoc of America, Eucharistic Minister - St Marks; [hon.] People Choice Award 1986 for "Iris" 3rd Stained Glass Window and 1st place for Autonomous Panel "Flu, study of a nightmare, Heavenly Award survived Brain Surgery after in Aneurism burst September 1, 1991, God gave me life again; [oth. writ.] Work books for the learning disabled. Life accomp school teacher 22 yrs, Principal Boys School 7 of those yrs also own music studio 5 yrs and choir 6 yrs, last 17 yrs founder, owner of Stained Glass Studio Artistic Designs; [pers.] Throughout my life I have lived the Benedictine Motto "Ut In Omnibus Glorificetur Deus" that in all things God may be glorified. Do only your best, give more than you take, and never lose your integrity. Honesty is the only sleeping pill you'll even need.; [a.] San Marcus, CA

TAUBER, SHARON
[b.] August 6, 1969, Queens, NY; [p.] Leonard and Marcia Tauber; [ed.] Masters in Education with a specialization in Rehabilitation Counseling.; [occ.] Job Coach, Job Developer; [memb.] National Rehabilitation Counseling Association, TASH; [hon.] Graduated Cum Laude, Certificates for Outstanding Poetry from The National Library of Poetry.; [oth. writ.] Other poems published by The National Library of Poetry.; [pers.] To truly live, one must be allowed to grow. To truly grow one must be willing to risk!; [a.] Woodbury, NY

TAYLOR, LORELEI
[b.] April 13, 1980, Graham, TX; [p.] Tim and Dawn McDonald; [m.] None; [ed.] Currently a sophmore at Kenowa Hills High School; [occ.] Student; [pers.] This poem is dedicated to my dear friend Sarah Gitchell, who is fighting cancer with love, Lorelei.; [a.] Walker, MI

TAYLOR, MARK KING
[pen.] M. K. Taylor; [b.] April 18, 1961, Denver, CO; [p.] R. E. Taylor and Diane W. Hanson; [m.] Nancy J. Taylor, December 31, 1982; [ch.] Shawn, Jennifer, Benjamin, Bobbie; [ed.] Cucamonga Elementary, Los Amigos Junior High Cucamonga Calif., Chaffey High School Ontario Calif., Tulsa Junior College Tulsa, OK (Marketing); [occ.] Journeyman Code Welder Fabricator; [oth. writ.] Unpublished country and western songs in modern style and religious songs christian style. Some titles - "Fit to be Tried" "Starting New so Soon" "Brief Case Under the Bed" "Partners" "Thank You Jesus" and more.; [pers.] Being recognized as a talented writer by the National Library of Poetry

is one of the greatest things that could have happened to me. I wish my Dad could have lived long enough to enjoy it with me. He always told me to pursue a career as a song writer. That's my dream.; [a.] Salem, OR

TAYLOR, MARTHA J.
[pen.] Jay Taylor; [b.] May 15, 1914; [m.] Edward Taylor, (Deceased 1982), March 14, 1943; [ch.] Ron Taylor, Dee Rouk, Martha Mersiovsky; [ed.] High School, 2 yrs Business Ed.; [occ.] Retired; [memb.] United Methodist Church; [hon.] Poem in "Best Loved Contemporary Poems" in 1979, titled "An Orphan's Christmas."; [oth. writ.] I am working on a novel based on "Whats in a name. Nothing! Until you find yourself without one."; [pers.] Some books are to be tasted, others to be swallowed, and some few to be chewed and digested - Francis Bacon, Ah! To be a book! a book! Fair and questionable: Acheingly - try withstanding all four above - Jay Taylor.; [a.] Temple, TX

TAYLOR, NANCY LEE
[b.] February 6, 1955, Hartford Hospital, CT; [p.] Gloria S. Taylor, Robert L. Taylor (Deceased); [ch.] Nathan Terry Taylor, Lacey Nicole Taylor, Lacey Michael Edwards II and Brandon Lee Taylor; [occ.] Student at: Quinebaug Valley Community Technical College.; [pers.] In dedication to my late sister Janet Taylor who passed away October 20th 1995 and of the most important persons in my life besides my loving children, my children's father: Mr. Lacey Michael Edwards Sr., my dearest and best friend Cheryl Olden and son Zacheriah, Sharon Glass, Dat Milhamma and Charlene Scott.

TAYLOR, ROBERT L.
[b.] June 1, 1932, Bracken, KY; [p.] Raymond Taylor, Ruth Kidwell Taylor; [m.] Meralyn Taylor, December 13, 1953; [ch.] Lynette Davidson, Jeffery Taylor, Lori McKnight; [ed.] B.A. Transylvania University M.Ed. - Xavier University (Ohio), Juris Doctorate - Chase College of Law Northern KY University; [occ.] Attorney; [memb.] Kentuky Bar Assn., Phi Alpha Delta (Legal), National Education Assn., KY. Education Assn., Bar of U.S. District Court; [hon.] 8 years Elected School Board Member, President - Covington Education Assn., Scholarship Award Sr., year at Transylvania College, President High School Sr. Class, Captain High School Basketball Team; [oth. writ.] Kentuky School Reform (Published Kentucky Poet Newspaper and the Kentucky School Bd. Journal) Professional Negotiations in the Public Sector (Published in the Kentucky Education Journal); [pers.] I would like to say in poetry that which is not possible to say in prose; [a.] Park Hills, KY

TEITELBAUM, ROBERT D.
[b.] April 11, 1949, New York, NY; [p.] Nathan B. Teitelbaum, Shirley; [m.] Theresa, April 21, 1979; [ch.] Lauren, Jenna, Caitlin; [ed.] Lafayette H.S., Brooklyn N.Y., Cornell University, N.Y. College Podiatric Medicine; [occ.] Podiatrist; [memb.] American Pediatric Medical Assn., American College of Sport Medicine, American College of Foot Surgeons, NYCPM; [hon.] Goldman Award in Biochemistry, Phi Delta, Graduated Cum Laude NYCPM; [oth. writ.] Contributing editor "sport performance report," several journal articles on

topics in podiatry.; [pers.] Expanded perception leads to the development of the poetic voice.; [a.] Naples, FL

TEMPLETON, DAVID M.
[b.] December 26, 1952, Northern Ireland; [p.] Malcolm, Ann; [m.] Joan, June 23, 1978; [ch.] Jonathan, Jacqueline, Emma; [ed.] University of Ulster, University of Warwick; [occ.] Parent; [oth. writ.] Some songs, poems and other ramblings.; [pers.] Played, wrote sang and recorded with the Irah fold ensemble Resistance Cabaret in the Mid Seventies.; [a.] Middlebury, CT

TEMPLETON, VICKIE A.
[b.] August 19, 1965, Denver, CO; [p.] John and Peggy Lowery; [m.] October 13, 1984; [ch.] Wesley, Teara Templeton; [ed.] Livingston High School, Angelina College Texas; [occ.] Graph Artist; [memb.] Vice Chairperson Student Govt. Angelina College, and Editor of Chaparral 95-96 Angelina College; [hon.] TIPA Awards for Illustrations in the Pacer Newspaper and Computer Graphic Illustration in The Chaparral Yearbook; [oth. writ.] Short stories (The Pacer) "Dreams of Christmas" (Chaparral); [pers.] I wrote "the man" for my papa after he died, to show him all the ways he touch my life, and that he always will.; [a.] Livingston, TX

TEPLY, ARIANE
[b.] February 26, 1966, Chapel Hill, NC; [p.] Zia and David Charnack, Larry Heller; [m.] Mark Teply, January 29, 1995; [ch.] Caitlin Teply; [ed.] Redwood High School, College of Marin; [occ.] Client Services Representative, GE Capitol Life, San Rafael, CA; [memb.] Glide Memorial Church (San Francisco), Former Member of Glide Ensemble, Names Project Contributor; [oth. writ.] Two independently published books, poems published in the Nuvo Review and College of Marin Echo-Times; [pers.] Poetry comes through me, and from deep within. It is a spiritual and cleansing process for me. I could no sooner stop writing than I could stop breathing.; [a.] Sonoma, CA

TER-TOVMASYAN, ALBERT
[b.] April 22, 1970, U.S.S.R.; [ed.] A degree in Nuclear Medicine Technology.; [occ.] Nuclear Medicine Technologist; [pers.] In life there are no failures, only experiences. The only true failure is giving up. For then learning stops. Without learning there is stagnation. And where there is stagnation, there is no life.; [a.] Toronto Ontario, Canada

TERRELL, ELIZABETH YOKLEY
[pen.] Beff; [b.] January 24, 1908, Davidson County, NC; [p.] Charles and Cora Conrad Yokley; [m.] Frank Terrell, August 15, 1938; [ed.] AB Degree - High Point Uni 1930, Uni, N.C. Chapel Hill and UNC Greensboro changing certificates from Elementary Edu. to High school. Traveled - all continents except Antartica.; [occ.] Retired teacher - very busy volunteer - church, hospital, college scholarship.; [memb.] Delta Kappa Gamma Society, Lexington Woman's Club, Retired Teachers Org., N.C.F. Music Club, Civinette Club, United Methodist Church, Business - Professional Woman's Club; [hon.] Presented life membership in N.E.A. - Distinguished service award in Womans

Club - chosen for a judge on team for Southern Association of Edu. - Helped train student teachers, asked to edit State Magazine for Classroom Teachers, served as President for all above organizations School of Arts College scholarships for Fed. of Music Clubs; [oth. writ.] Skits, plays and programs for programs in school work Editorials for Classroom Teacher Organization Letters to editor for local papers Won District and State recognitions for poems, essays, etc. for Womans Club Art Festival - no publications.; [pers.] As a teacher I hoped to be the great teacher as described by Wm Arthur Ward. "A mediocre teacher tells, The good Teacher explains. The superior teacher demonstrates. The great teacher inspires." Children should be taught to dream - day dream travel is fatal to bigotry and hatred.; [a.] Lexington, NC

THAKORE, SNEH
[ed.] A Master of Arts degree and a Bachelor of Education degree. She has also attained a Scholarship in Painting. Applied Fine Arts.; [occ.] She is a Teacher. She has taught in India, England and in the elementary school system of Ontario. She also enjoys painting and cooking.; [memb.] She is a member of the Scarborough Arts Council and the International Society of Poets.; [oth. writ.] Locally, her writings are published in 'Hindu Dharma Review,' 'Kavya Kinjalk', International Hindi Smarika' and 'Sangam'. Her writings are also published in the 1995 National Library of Poetry book and 'Vishwa Vivek' in the Unites States.; [a.] Scarborough, Ontario

THOMAIER, RENEE A.
[b.] December 29, 1956, Elizabeth, NJ; [p.] Raymond Pfaff, Helga Pfaff; [m.] Robert C. Thomaier, September 13, 1985; [memb.] Officer-Born Free Wildlife Care; [oth. writ.] Letters to editor - local newspapers; [pers.] We all must be a part of the solution. There is no time to waste. The time is now.; [a.] Mountainside, NJ

THOMAS, BARBARA P.
[b.] September 27, 1959, Bermuda; [p.] Grace and Calston, Pat Simmons; [m.] Allison R. Thomas, April 20, 1980; [ch.] Takiyah and Chelsey Thomas; [ed.] Bermuda College, Warwick Secondary; [occ.] Secretary, Inpatient Services, St. Brendan's Hospital; [memb.] Volunteer for St. Brendan's Hospital, working with patients during my free time.; [pers.] I write to express my deepest thoughts from within. I also write to let people know that I care about their well being, and to share my joy and happiness.; [a.] Bermuda

THOMAS, CLONDA
[b.] March 22, 1939, Antigua, WI; [p.] Una Phillip, David J. Nelson; [m.] David A. Thomas (Deceased), December 31, 1983; [ed.] St. John's Girls' School T.O.R. Memorial High School, Holberton Hospital Nursing School - St. John's, Antigua; [occ.] Nurse; [oth. writ.] I have written a few more poems. I started writing in December 1995.; [pers.] I believe that the Almighty God is the Creator of all mankind and the Lord Jesus Christ came to redeem all men. I have received Him as my own personal Savior. He directs my life.

THOMAS, JESSIE SPARKS
[b.] May 17, 1928, Clarkston, UT; [p.] Gertrude and Lawrence Sparks; [m.] John J. Thomas, December 23, 1945; [ch.] Jana, Jamie and Joanna; [ed.] High School Boise, ID., Courses in Indiana State Univ., LPN School in Terre Haute, IN.; [occ.] Legal Receptionist, Former Nurse; [memb.] Daughters of the Utah Pioneers Teach Genealogy Classes; [hon.] Have Written Historical Biographical Sketches for DUP and SUP (9) Awards received, several poems published in National Library of Poetry; [pers.] I have written many poems concerning my family and their lives. Poems for friends are fun also. My grandmother has been a great influence on my poetry writing. She also composed songs. My self expression comes through in many of my poems.; [a.] Brazil, IN

THOMAS, LANELTA S.
[b.] November 28, 1959, Nakina, NC; [p.] Willie and Dessie Smith; [m.] Willie Jackson Thomas, May 7, 1995; [sib.] Pembroke State University Master Degree in Reading Ed.; [ed.] Communication Skills Teacher 6th Grade; [pers.] I strive to reflect the message that we are in control of our life in my writing. If we are on the wrong trade simply change tracks!; [a.] Nakina, NC

THOMAS-SPOON, KELLEY ELISE
[b.] March 3, 1966, Knoxville, TN; [p.] Drs. Bob and Connie Thomas, brother - Michael [m.] David Todd Thomas-Spoon, December 26, 1993; [ed.] University of Tennessee, B.S. Marketing, Honors Roane County High School, Highest Honors; [occ.] Training Specialist, Roane State Community College; [memb.] American Marketing Association, Audience, Response Movie Critic, Knoxville Area Theatre Coalition Member; [hon.] Phi Chi Theta, (Business Honor Society), mostly likely to succeed, Faculty Who's Who, Optimist Club Outstanding Youth Award, Salutatorian; [oth. writ.] Have been writing poetry since I was 16 years old. Have got a book of poems with over 70 poems in it.; [pers.] My writings establish "notes in time" which help myself, and hopefully others, experience the strong emotions of life and life's beings.; [a.] Knoxville, TN

THOMAS, ROBERT MONTGOMERY
[pen.] Montgomery Thomas; [b.] August 20 1943, Philadelphia, PA; [p.] Robert Alexander and Gilda Katherine; [m.] Divorced; [ch.] Alexander and Robert; [ed.] 1 year college Lib. Arts. (USAFI), Central High/Olney High - Phila PA H.S. Ged (USAFI); [occ.] Kitchen and Bath designer and Remodeling Contractor; [memb.] Elected town meeting member, appointed by law review committee member, former member habitat for humanity constr. Committee and Volunteer, former Treasurer Milton, MA Lions Club, Member Weymouth Town Republican Committee; [oth. writ.] Poetry published in Local Print Media from time to time; [pers.] My works are inspired by personal experiences, political occurances, and Kipling's "If', along with Grellet's "Ode to Passage". ("Works" include writings and personal life); [a.] Weymouth, MA

THOMAS, STEPHANIE
[b.] September 8, 1977, Effingham, IL; [p.] Russell and Jo Thomas; [ed.] Graduate from Effingham High School in 1995 and I am a current student attending Lake Land College; [occ.] Student;

[memb.] I am a 1st Degree Black Belt in Tae Kwan Do. I am a Assistant Instructor Trainee at Effingham Tae Kwan Do which is a school that I attend.; [pers.] "It is a dream of mine to be successful in life and meet the Beatles.; [a.] Effingham, IL

THOMPSON, ADRIENNE RIGGS
[b.] March 13, 1979, Charleston, SC; [ed.] Porter-Gaud School (presently in 11th grade); [occ.] Student; [a.] Mount Pleasant, SC

THOMPSON, KERMIT SHANE
[pen.] "Jim Little Crow"; [b.] May 31, 1975, Columbus, IN; [p.] Flora Mayfield and Kermit Coy Thompson; [ed.] Romeoville High School and Joliet Jr. College in Romeoville, IL; [occ.] Machine Operator at M.E.M.C. Electronic Materials Inc.; [pers.] My writings have been greatly influenced by famous Rock 'n' Roll Poets of the 1960's and 70's. And further influenced by my own personal experiences in life. I hope everyone enjoys reading my work as much as I enjoyed writing it.; [a.] Troy, MO

THOMPSON, MRS. LOWELL
[pen.] Phyllis Thompson; [b.] February 14, 1934, Clear Lake, SD; [p.] John and Ida Klemm; [m.] Lowell Thompson, December 13, 1953; [ch.] Joe and Jill Thompson; [ed.] Grade School, 4 yrs High School, 6 WRS College Course in Teaching; [occ.] House Wife; [memb.] Trinity Luthern Church, Madison, SD; [oth. writ.] One for every occasion in hopes of putting them in Greeting Cards - Sympathy - Valentines Day, Get Well - Anniversary etc.; [pers.] On my grand daughters confirmation, I wrote her a special note that turned into a poem that moved the mother and other grand mother to tears. Later they had compliments and praise for my work it is religious.; [a.] Winfred, SD

TIBERINI, FERNANDO BENJAMIN
[b.] December 26, 1974, La Jolla, CA; [ed.] Clark High Las Vegas, Kantonsschule Baden, University of Zurich; [occ.] Student of English and German Literature and Linguistics; [hon.] Clark Star Awards for writing; [oth. writ.] Several pages of unpublished poetry.; [pers.] I am indebted to James Joyce for diction and to Dylan for rhythm.; [a.] Baden, Switzerland

TIDWELL, RACHEL LYNN
[pen.] Sunnie; [b.] September 21, 1981, Saint Joseph, MO; [p.] Janice and Charlie Tidwell; [ed.] 8th Grader at Coronado M.S.; [pers.] To whom ever reads my poem thank you for taking the time to read it! Your friend Sunnie.; [a.] Kansas City, KS

TIERNEY, JOHN FRANCIS
[b.] January 29, 1970, Montclair, NJ; [p.] Edward and Gertrude Tierney; [ed.] Montclair High School, Monmouth College Biology Major; [occ.] Garden Center and Book Store; [memb.] Tau Kappa Epsilon; [pers.] I enjoy social events, I love going to a variety of places in nature. Take in the experiences and become inspired. Then write them down as soon as I can.; [a.] Upper Montclair, NJ

TILGHMAN JR., JOHN W.
[pen.] J. Warren; [b.] January 17, 1937, Fruitland, MD; [p.] John and Doris Tilghman; [m.] Evelyn

Henley Tilghman, April 16, 1960; [ch.] Mary Elizabeth Tilghman Etheridge; [ed.] High School, some college, many Technical Schools in Electronics, Instructor Training, Course Writing; [occ.] Semi-retired Burroughs/Unisys Corp, (30+years) AABC Baseball Umpire: Dum-Dum the Clown: Radio Shack, Comp-Cons Computer Consultant; [memb.] NRA, AARP, Mason; [hon.] Ordained Southern Baptist Minister; [oth. writ.] Poems published Navy Times, High School Annual, and used as memorials. Written some articles for small newspapers.; [pers.] I strive to glorify God and reflection his creation. I desire someday to write professionally.; [a.] Forest Park, GA

TILLERY, CHRISTOPHER
[pen.] Christopher Tillery; [b.] January 28, 1979, Houston; [p.] Jim Tillery, Sharleen McDonald; [ed.] Derby High School; [occ.] Osco Drug Store, Studying for Law School; [memb.] Derby High School Football Team, Student Council; [hon.] Derby High School Nominee in all USA, USA Today Academic Team; [oth. writ.] Several poems published in school newspaper along with articles, poems and short stories, not yet published.; [pers.] I have studied and admired the works of Byron and Tennyson and have striven to reflect my own views and ideas through my work. I would like to thank Sarah Heiskull for her help in developing my poem.; [a.] Wichita, KS

TILLMAN, LEIGH
[b.] October 8, 1981, Columbia, MD; [p.] Ned and Kathy Tillman; [ed.] 9th Grade at Centennial High School; [occ.] Student; [memb.] Cross Country Team and Track Team at Centennial High School, YRUU Youth group; [oth. writ.] "Do we have the right?" published in the Sandy Spring Friends School literary magazine.; [pers.] Hello World! Shaba. Splits at the neck.; [a.] Ellicott City, MD

TILLMANN, UTSULA
[b.] March 5, 1951, Germany; [p.] Germans; [ed.] College in Alberta Diploma of Fine Arts Journalism Administration; [occ.] Free - Lance Journalist; [hon.] "Golden Poet" 1991 in New York "Features Award" Nationwide in Germany in 1989; [oth. writ.] Short Stories and poetry in english and German; [pers.] Look at the nature and reflect to understand; [a.] Canmore, Canada

TISDALE, COLETTE
[b.] December 19, 1970, Buffalo, NY; [p.] Ann Wagstaff, Celes Tisdale; [m.] Shawn Davenport; [ch.] Alexa Blue Davenport; [ed.] City Honors School, Texas A and M University; [occ.] Owner of Star Tutoring; [pers.] I'm always careful to stay true to my own voice and not be influenced by poetic trends.; [a.] Buffalo, NY

TOPPI JR., JOSEPH J.
[b.] February 27, 1962, Cambridge, MA; [p.] Sheila Orr (Mother); [m.] Marilyn Morales, June 23, 1985; [ch.] Joey and Sean; [ed.] Bachelor of Science in Management - Golden Gate University 1089; [occ.] Operations Manager - United States Air Force; [memb.] Air Force Association, Air Force Sergeant's Association, Non-Commissioned Officers Association, American Legion; [hon.] Decorated with the Air Force Commendation Medal 5 times, and the Air Force Achievement Medal

once.; [pers.] Always treat your spouse and your children with respect. Tell them you love them every day, and never forget that they are all that really matters, everything else is secondary.; [a.] Bellevue, NE

TORO, JOSEPH L.
[pen.] Joe - Lucky; [b.] July 20, 1928, Brooklyn; [p.] George and Rose; [m.] Maryanne, January 7, 1956; [ch.] Two daughters; [ed.] Public school High School 1 year Technical Training; [occ.] Retired Cadillac-Mech. (General Motors); [memb.] Church Club Westinghouse - High Dance Groups O.T.B.; [hon.] Expert-Rifleman-in (Army) Tack-in-High School Spelling-Bee's Penmanship - Award; [oth. writ.] When I was dating to my wife - poems of love sincerity; [pers.] I just love the outdoors the nature of things is beautiful.; [a.] Brooklyn, NY

TORRES, ROBIN D. S.
[b.] July 18, 1965, Norfolk, VA; [p.] Robert and Barbara Scott; [ch.] Lisa Torres - 4 and Dominique - 2; [ed.] Lake Taylor High, Norfolk State University (Early childhood Education); [occ.] Computer Mail Correspondent IV Broadcasting Network; [hon.] Numerous Awards for Excellence, Integrity and Innovation, 10 year Service - Honor - Broadcasting Network, National Junior Honor Society, Achievement Awards, Leadership Award, Suggestion Awards; [oth. writ.] Was the Dream Worth The Wait Of The Reality, Wounded Heart, Special Friend, The Puppet, The Master and the Overseer Beyond The Mountain

TORTORICI, GIOSI
[pen.] Giosi Tortorici; [b.] January 14, 1973, Montreal, Canada; [ed.] Lester B. Pearson High School, Dawson College, Concordia University; [occ.] Student of English Literature, Concordia University; [oth. writ.] Other writings published in Arcady, college publication circulated in 6 countries, comments in local magazines, newspapers; [pers.] Letting thoughts pour out on paper is for a composition of emotions into a song of words: every work expressed is an emotion released, a memory surfaced and a reflection that will never be lost.; [a.] Montreal Quebec, Canada

TOULSON, DOROTHY L.
[pen.] Dottie; [b.] August 8, 1946, Baltimore, MD; [p.] Rodmon Richardson, Pauline Mack Richardson; [m.] Herman L. Toulson Jr. (Deceased October 1984), June 20, 1968, Honolulu, HI; [ch.] Cecelia St. Anne, Lynette Leilani, Noelle Felecia; [ed.] Church Home and Hosp Sch. of Nsg. 1965-1967, Comm. Coll. Balto. AA 1975, Coppin State Coll. BSN 1993, Goucher Coll, Loyola Coll., Columbia, Md.; [occ.] Registered Nu BNSC, Comm. Health Nurse - School Nurse, Episcopal Lay Minister; [memb.] Amer. Nurses' Assoc., MD Nurses Assoc., Nat. Assoc. of Sch. Nurses, Md. Assoc. Scho. Nurses, AFSCME #558 Union; [hon.] Outstanding Young Woman of Amer.; [oth. writ.] "O My Soul", "Perhaps - Who Knows"; [pers.] Center of my belief: I belong to God. Jesus is my Lord and Savior. He commands to not forbid his precious children to come to Him, to love my neighbors (the world humanity) as myself and to feed His sheep - His Word, my bread and His wisdom.; [a.] Baltimore, MD

TOWLER, PAMELA
[pen.] Pam Kostas; [b.] May 8, 1950, Winston Salem, NC; [p.] Dolores McGee, Dempsey Bullock; [m.] Michael Papakostas, June 27, 1995; [ch.] Marc Jason Towler; [ed.] BA Shaw University 1986 - Raleigh, NC, Presbyterian Church Newsletter; [occ.] Substitute Teacher/Card Designer; [pers.] I am a wonderer... so long the city I desired to reach lay hid... but I had seen the city, and one such glance no darkness could obscure. Browning's "Paracelsus"; [a.] Winston Salem, NC

TRACHTENBERG, JONATHAN
[pen.] Noj; [b.] June 21, 1973, Boston, Naval Hospital; [p.] David and Susan Trachtenberg; [ed.] North Gate High School, Diablo Valley College, University of California at Santa Cruz; [occ.] Programmer and Information Manager, Valu Comp, Goleta, CA; [oth. writ.] See http!/www.artisia com/ Jonathan or the world wive web.; [pers.] My poetry celebrates romance. I am most often inspired by interactions with people, be they friends, lovers, or strangers who pass by my life for only a moment, compassion is the driving force of my life.; [a.] Santa Barbara, CA

TRAILL, TED
[b.] June 4, 1942, Toronto, Ontario, Canada; [p.] George Traill, Gertrude Cannon; [m.] October 5, 1985; [ch.] Stacey; [ed.] B5C, 1966, University of Toronto, Canada; [occ.] Self-employed woodworker, log builder; [memb.] North American Guild of Timber framers, U.S.A, National Air and Space Museum - Smithsonian, U.S.A.; [oth. writ.] Samples enclosed. No effort to publish any.; [pers.] God bless America, land of opportunity, for suggesting I might be a poet. I'm honored.; [a.] South River Ontario, Canada

TRAMMELL, JOHN
[pen.] John Shreffler; [b.] December 8, 1969, West Palm Beach, FL; [p.] Joe Shreffler, Susan Trammell; [ed.] College Freshman, Kennesaw State; [occ.] Record Store Manager; [oth. writ.] Have written about 60 poems in 6 years. None have been previously published.; [a.] Marietta, GA

TREBILCOCK, DOROTHY WARNER
[b.] July 8, 1926, Lansing, MI; [p.] Grace and Harold H. Warner; [m.] James M. Trebilcock (Deceased), August 25, 1950; [ch.] Amy Trebilcock Frost, Robert Trebilcock; [ed.] Oberlin Conservatory of Music (44-'46), Michigan State University ('48) B.A. Michigan State University ('78) M.A., Arizona State University ('81-'83); [occ.] Writer/teacher. Columnist and U.S. Correspondent for the Korea Times newspaper Seoul, Korea; [oth. writ.] Fiction, non-fiction, poetry in a range of publications from children's magazines to denominational, sailings magazines, newspapers, etc. Most recently have focused on writing about Korea as a professor at Yonsei University in Seoul, Korea. Publication in Lions Magazine, Far East Traveler, National Parks Magazine, Korean Culture Magazine, etc. Shield Of Innocence, a paperback original, (1978); [pers.] Having been a writer/teacher for many years, I've had the opportunity to share ideas with hundreds of them. I think that is what my berth poem is about.; [a.] Ludington, MI

TREMBLAY, JENNIFER J.
[pen.] J. Jan; [b.] November 11, 1957, Ottawa, Canada; [oth. writ.] Sweet Affection, A Space Inside, (All never published) Trust, Giving Thanks, Special Feelings, etc; [pers.] Jenny's Prayer is the only poem of many that has or will be been published as these Windows To My Soul have rarely been read.; [a.] Kanata Ontario, Canada

TRIGG, CHRISTOPHER L.
[pen.] Christopher L. Trigg; [b.] May 12, 1963, Green Castle, IN; [p.] Lincoln, Jessie Trigg; [ch.] Providence, Ann, Nattlie L. Trigg; [ed.] Green Castle, High; [occ.] Factory Worker; [memb.] NAACP; [pers.] To make people think with my words; [a.] Green Castle, IN

TRIVELLI, BARBARA ANN
[b.] March 21, 1948, Lansdale, PA; [p.] Phillip and Ruth Calamaro; [m.] Anthony J. Trivelli Jr., September 19, 1970; [ch.] Anthony III; [ed.] Wildwood High School; [occ.] Buyer, Dow Chemical Co.; [oth. writ.] Won a poetry contest in 8th grade at St. Ann's in Wildwood, NJ. Wrote poems throughout high school.; [pers.] I enjoy expressing my feelings through written words; [a.] Newark, OH

TROJANEK, FRANK
[b.] April 19, 1953, Charlevoix, MI; [p.] Clarence and Rose Trojanek; [m.] Single; [ed.] Grand Valley State University, B.S. in Criminal Justice 1996; [occ.] Student, part time work for J.C. Pennye's Co; [hon.] Art award in 1971 from East Jordan High School, East Jordan Mich.; [pers.] I try to convey the different facets of the human emotion in my writings and see people through the heart and eyes as God would see them.; [a.] Grand Rapids, MI

TRUS, DOROTHY A.
[pen.] Dorothy Ann Crean; [b.] May 23, 1940; [p.] Sheila and Hugh Crean; [m.] Michael, June 23, 1963; [ch.] Mike and Tania; [ed.] Sion Hill Convent Country Dublin Ireland; [occ.] Housewife; [memb.] Dublin Writers Workshop, Dublin Ireland, international Society of Poetry's Owing Mills Maryland U.S.A.; [oth. writ.] "Winning" published in "Walk Through Paradise", published through Ireland.; [pers.] I believe there is a poet in everyone, but few of us are fortunate enough to have the time to unite. Most of my poems are from personal experiences; [a.] Toronto, Canada

TUCKER, JO
[b.] September 28, 1941, Dallas, TX; [p.] Joseph and Robbye Doucet; [ch.] Timothy, Jesse, Cody; [ed.] UTA, Arlington, TX; [occ.] Admin. Asst.-Genesis Center, Manchester, CT.; [memb.] AARP, CCF; [hon.] Ordained Minister; [a.] Manchester, CT

TUNOLD, LISE
[pen.] Tofauna; [b.] May 17, 1966, Surrey B.C.; [p.] Olaf Tunold and Eva Tunold; [m.] Bob Roberts; [ch.] Robert, Heather and David; [ed.] Johnson Heights, Selkirk College; [occ.] Artist; [oth. writ.] A collection of poems compiled from 15 years.; [pers.] The soul searches for its destiny, Life is riddled with mystery, energy is fueled by desire to learn adn thus endows my mind and pen in hand. So

from within the spirit speaks and onto paper ink will flow.; [a.] Osoyoos, B.C.

TURANO, JUDITH
[b.] December 29, 1939, Silverton, CO; [p.] Angelo Turano, Ruth Turano; [m.] Robert Gregori, May 2, 1964; [ch.] Renata Marina, Andrea Teresa; [ed.] University od New Mexico; [occ.] Opera Singer and Voice Teacher; [hon.] Leading artist in many world premieres and prestigious performances.; [oth. writ.] Collection of poems, some of which have been published in area publications.; [pers.] Poetry, like music, reaches deep into the soul and links mankind together.; [a.] Philadelphia, PA

TURCIOS, ERICA
[pen.] Erica Turcios; [b.] October 6, 1983, Berkeley, CA; [p.] Bob and Janet Turcios; [ed.] 7th grade, Christ The King Catholic School, Pleasant Hill, CA; [occ.] Student; [memb.] Ayso Soccer, Christ The King Student Council; [hon.] Certificate of Achievement - creative writing Christ The King School; [a.] Martinez, CA

TURNER, DAVID G.
[pen.] Gemini; [b.] June 6, 1939, Salt Lake City, UT; [p.] David S. Turner, Arlene V. Turner; [ch.] Seven; [ed.] Olympus H.S., Brigham Young University, University of Utah, University of Maryland, Gardvers School of Business; [occ.] Special Consultant to State of CA on Training (Apprenticeship); [memb.] AARP; [pers.] My favorite poet is Eugene Field.; [a.] Santa Rosa, CA

TURNER, JAMES A. ALVAREZ
[pen.] James Turner; [b.] January 27, 1975, Fajardo, Puerto Rico; [p.] Hilda E. Turner; [m.] Divorced, June 27, 1994; [ch.] Dominique R. Turner; [ed.] The Streets of the S.L.S.; [occ.] Data Processing, Hip Hop Lyrical Production; [memb.] Het Productions, Latin Club; [hon.] President's List; [oth. writ.] Several raps have been requested for publication by record companies and Songwriters Clubs. One has been aired on the radio.; [pers.] Every individual on the face of the planet has the power to control his or her own destiny. Although no one could ever plan events to come, working within the current of life will get you where you want to go.; [a.] Orlando, FL

TURTON, JON JOSEPH
[pen.] J. Joseph Turton; [b.] March 18, 1970, Beaumont, Alberta, Canada; [p.] Robert and Patricia Turton; [ed.] Northern Alberta Institute of Technology (N.A.I.T.); [occ.] Architectural Design Technologist (C.E.T.); [memb.] Alberta Society of Engineering Technologists (A.S.E.T.), Eastern Seals Ability Council; [hon.] "Irrelevat... life is rewarding enough"; [oth. Writ.] Personal Anthology Of Romanticizes, Personal Autobiography, The Ebbing Tide (The National Library Of Poetry), Jon's Book Of Knowledge I.; [pers.] "A writers limits are never to bold, because the power in the pen is ours to hold. "4 is 5".; [a.] Lloydminster Alberta, Canada

TWITCHELL, MARLO
[b.] October 28, 1977, Cedar City, UT; [p.] Robyn and Kim Twitchell; [ed.] Junior at Cedar High School; [occ.] Room Service/Prep Cook at Cedar Citys Holidays Inn; [oth. writ.] No other writings,

yet; [pers.] Poetry is a way to convert a feeling into words which otherwise wouldn't even be recognized. The spirit cannot speak to the human ever but from spirit to spirit.; [a.] Cedar City, UT

TYSON, ELAINE H.
[b.] December 14, 1954, Twentynine Palms, CA; [p.] Jack Darby, Jeanne Darby; [m.] Dee G. Tyson, March 4, 1974; [ch.] Nicole Marie Tyson; [ed.] Hemet High, San Bernardino Medical and Dental Assis. School. Editor school news paper senior year.; [occ.] Registered Dental Assistant; [oth. writ.] Berkeley Toy Boats, published in boating magazine.; [pers.] We are, ourselves, creations. And we, in truth, are meant to continue creativity by being creative ourselves.; [a.] Fallbrook, CA

UPSHUR, LONNIE
[b.] March 14, 1957, Marionsville, VA; [p.] Charles Edward and Mary Lena Upshur; [m.] Kimberly A. Upshur, May 1, 1981; [ch.] Lauren K., Whitney G., Eric R.; [ed.] Hamilton High West, Mercer County Community College; [occ.] Electrician, Student; [hon.] President's List; [pers.] Poetry may be found in any human experience. Thank you, Dr. Goldstein.; [a.] Trenton, NJ

URBAN, AMY
[b.] March 18, 1976, Danbury, CT; [p.] Michael and Joann Urban; [ed.] Graduated from Bethel High school, Bethel, CT; [a.] Bethel, CT

URQUHART, STEVEN J.
[pen.] K. J. Craigs; [b.] May 2, 1956, Exeter, NH; [p.] Gordon and Dorothy Urquhart; [m.] Janine Kennedy, December 12, 1982; [ch.] Jordan, Shannon, Craig, Kyle; [ed.] Marshwood High, University of Maine, McIntosh Business College; [occ.] Manager - Bell Window Service Concord, NH; [oth. writ.] First writing submitted for publishing.; [pers.] The intentions of my writing is to bring out the thoughts or feelings of the reader, which would otherwise be unexpressed or repressed in everyday living.; [a.] Franklin, NH

VALES, SHARA
[b.] May 29, 1979; [p.] Robert and Audrey Vales; [ed.] High School (Junior); [memb.] USTA member, Peer Helper, Jr. Class Committee, Outdoors Club, Ski Club, Bible Club, Student Forum, Newspaper Staff, Interact Club; [hon.] Varsity "C" Club at Carlynton H.S. Gate, Letter in Varsity Soccer, Tennis, and Track, National Honor Society, High and Distinguished Honor Roll, 1st place in Jets Competition at Bethany College.; [oth. writ.] "What America Means To Me" (essay); [pers.] "Do the best you can, with what you got, where you are."; [a.] Pittsburgh, PA

VAN COUR, ALICE CLEMONS BEYER
[pen.] Alice C. Van Cour; [ch.] Mitch, Ethel, Joanne, and Judy; [ed.] Lester, Carl Beyer and Denise Van Cour; [occ.] Retired ran a small Hotel; [memb.] Cottage Inn in Copenhagen for years which I enjoyed very much doing. Customer's called Ma Alice.; [hon.] When you down and feeling blue published in Famous poems of today, famous poetry Society 1995; [oth. writ.] Poem Our Home published in National Library of Poetry

at Water Edge Editions choice award poem Bed of L. Fe published American Poetry, Anthology Summer 1995 by Arcadia poetry press; [pers.] My advise to anyone writing poetry is to send it to contest etc - Hey you never know and it's worth a try.; [a,] Copenhagen, NY

VAN KLINKEN, IDA CLASENA WILLAMINA
[b.] February 10, 1928, Oak Harbor, WA; [p.] Arnold Diederick Arends, Jantina (Bierling) Arends; [m.] Albert Gerritt Van Klinken, December 22, 1950; [ch.] Susan Jane, David Gerritt, and Karen Marie; [ed.] Prosser High School; [occ.] Very Active Homemaker; [memb.] Christian Reformed Church; [oth. writ.] First time entered; [pers.] As I love to write, one of my greatest desires is to come up with a book for publication.; [a.] Prosser, WA

VANY, SHARON
[pen.] K. T. Marshall; [b.] February 12, 1943, Flint, MI; [p.] Duncan Vany, Virginia Vany; [ed.] Flint Northern High School; [occ.] Assembly worker Delco Electronics; [memb.] National Wildlife Federation- The Human Society of the United States and the P.E.T.A.; [oth. writ.] I am attempting to write a novel.; [pers.] I enjoy writing about animals. I also like to reflect on nature.

VEGH, STEVEN
[b.] May 24, 1972, Toronto, Ontario, Canada; [p.] Loretta Thomson, Robert Haire; [ed.] T.L. Kennedy Secondary School; [occ.] Packer, Confectionately yours Inc.; [oth. writ.] Many unpublished songs, poems, and stories; [pers.] Just because you can't see it, just because you can't hear it, just because you can't feel it, doesn't mean it isn't there.; [a.] Toronto Ontario, Canada

VENEZIANO, JUDITH A.
[pen.] Judith; [b.] June 23, 1942, Waterville, ME; [p.] Robert Thomas, Barbara Thomas; [m.] Robert Veneziano, June 23, 1963; [ed.] Graduated - Waterville Senior High School; [occ.] Housewife; [oth. writ.] I have written other poems but never had any published; [pers.] I wish that every human being ever born would be "Born Free". My greatest joy is giving to or doing something for others!; [a.] Madison, ME

VICKERS, CORIE
[b.] January 17, 1970, Wichita, KS; [p.] Thomas and Rhonda Vickers; [ed.] Hollins College (Roanoke, VA), Univ. of Denver; [occ.] Actress, Los Angeles CA; [pers.] There is creativity in every human being. I am in constant pursuit of a life full of self expression, so as to share it with the world.; [a.] Los Angeles, CA

VIGORITO, CARMIE T.
[b.] September 25, 1935, Paterson, NJ; [p.] Carmine F. Vigorito and Helen Vigorito; [m.] Patricia M. Vigorito, October 21, 1967; [ch.] Karen Marie, Kelly Ann and Brian Michael; [ed.] Central High, Paterson, NJ, Seton Hall University-BA and LLB; [occ.] Attorney at Law; [oth. writ.] Numerous poems and short stories.; [pers.] Life's most distant horizon is possessing the courage to be ones of self and and do ones best, heedless of gain.; [a.] North Haledon, NJ

VILES, FLORINE MARIE
[pen.] Marie - Marie Ann Friend; [b.] Kansas; [ch.] Three children - five grandchildren; [ed.] High School graduated, graduate of: Licensed Practical Nurse's Training - Neo Jr College Miami Okla; [occ.] Retired Licensed Nurse; [memb.] First Southern Baptist Church Del City Okla, Frank LauBauch - Literacy Link Volunteer Creative Writing Classes Rose State College, Midwest City, Oklahoma.; [oth. writ.] Several poems published in magazines. Several being held by publishers for possible future publication. Also meditations personal essays; [pers.] I strive to be reflect the greatness of God, the goodness of Mankind the wonders of nature in my writing and relate these truths to the reader. I have great respect for the poets - Robert Frost and Carl Sandburg: For the Novelists, Ernest Hemingway and William Faulkner.; [a.] Midwest City, OK

VILLANUEVA, CLAUDIA
[pen.] Claudia; [b.] June 20, 1973, Lima, Peru; [p.] Carlos Villanueva, Maria Romero; [ed.] S.S.C.C. Belen Catholic School, San Agustin Technological Institute; [a.] Lima, Peru

VITALE, MAUREEN
[pen.] June 4, 1960, Detroit; [oth. writ.] Several; [pers.] To share any insight on feelings from the heart, that my words can convey.; [a.] East Points, MI

VOGEL, LARAINE
[b.] September 6, 1982; [p.] Lydia L. Gorrell, Dave Vogel; [ed.] Attending Central Valley Intermediate School. In the 8th grade now.; [hon.] Principles Honor Roll 2 years straight, (Straight "As" all years), Honor Roll for 7 years, Greatest Achievement Award, Outstanding Citizen's Award, Royal Reader Award, Outstanding Penmanship Award; [oth. writ.] A 29 page hand written story published in the 6th grade.; [pers.] Only the best is acceptable. Nothing less is worth anything.; [a.] Redding, CA

VOGT, HANSH H.
[b.] October 27, 1925, Germany; [p.] Hans and Anna; [m.] Irma, September 15, 1951; [ch.] Ludwig; [ed.] High School in Germany Ryerson College, Radio College, Seneca College, all in Toronto; [occ.] Writer for German Publications in Canada and Germany; [memb.] Bonhoeffer Lutheran Church German Professional Association Stiftung Naturschutz, Hamburg Deutsche National stiftung, Home Owners Association, Kettleby; [hon.] Honors Seneca College on Computer Science and Spanish Language; [oth. writ.] Poetry in the German language Essays on History and Science Short stories, presently working on a novel.; [pers.] Influenced by Shakespeare, Goethe, Thomas Mann writers to give meaning to life by example, to show this world can be made better by own personal effort.

VOGT, TONYA
[b.] September 19, 1985, Dunedin, FL; [p.] Kurt and Judy Vogt; [ed.] Attend Suannee Elementry East School, I am in the fourth grade.; [occ.] Student; [hon.] 96 Suwannee County Fair, I placed 2nd on my poem named "Springtime" and 3rd on my drawing named "Rose Garden."; [oth. writ.] "Springtime"

VONDERHEID, MILA
[b.] December 27, 1942, Wilkes Barre, PA; [p.] Helen T. Lynch and William C. Vonderheid; [m.] June 18, 1966 and December 29, 1990; [ed.] "Penn State University" The Pennsylvania State University; [occ.] Receptionist; [memb.] None currently at PSU: Sorority: Alpha Delta PI; [oth. writ.] "Untitled/Unsigned" in where dawn lingers; [pers.] Those consumed with survival/greed cannot know love.

VON MICKS, SHARON
[b.] Toronto, Ontario, Canada; [p.] John Von Micks; [ch.] Leigla and Duke Von Micks; [occ.] Writer, Movie Scripts, Poetry Reiki Practitioner, I'm currently working on a book; [oth. writ.] Two (2) movie scripts, "The Block Rose I its sequel, The Black Rose II. I so - wrote the scripts with my daughter Leigha.; [pers.] Realization leads to awaren awareness leads to action, Action leads to help my poem "911" was written to bring you to awareness, rest is up to you.; [a.] Missisauga Ontario, Canada

VOWELS, IRENE
[b.] November 13, 1927, Chicago, IL; [p.] John and Catherine Gajda Guida; [m.] Robert Joseph Vowels, November 13, 1947; [ch.] Daughter Yvonne - Grandsons Joseph Nolan; [ed.] Primary - Old St. Stephen Secondary - Holy Family Academy College - Loyola U, - School of Liberal Arts - Rome, Italy; [occ.] Retired; [memb.] A.A.R.P. - Coalition of Retires - Route of Club - Golden Pioneers Happy Hearts - Hydro Exercise - Chicago Park District; [hon.] In Dr. Ross Faloaico's Class (He's a published poet, his father was in Italy) I received an I in Poetry; [oth. writ.] I love written several and nature articles for N.S.A. - If a child as young as 8 years old I completed lost line lemericks for magazines I had a tray full of perfumed prized; [pers.] In my rare Alpha moments poetry is the way I express and preserve my finer thoughts where I attempt to reach above my mud dane existence.; [a.] Chicago, IL

VUJASINOVIC, MILOS
[pen.] Misho; [b.] July 22, 1971, Belgrade, Serbia; [ed.] Faculty of Law, University of Belgrade; [occ.] Private Investigator, Painter (Fine arts); [memb.] Few, 'Alfa Market International'; [oth. writ.] Novel "Happy Hunting Grounds", Novel "Bottomless Well", Collection of Psychological Studies, "Psychic Powers", Novel "Bronx Canyon", Novel "Secret Agency 'Scandal'"; [pers.] Founder of symbolism in fine art of painting, - chromotherapeutic movement where artist acquires natural high designing certain color combinations while at the same time, in comparable mastery, his subconsciousness and visionary character, sends passionate and vibrant, entirely characteristic message, through the exotic, rebus-like symbols.; [a.] Philadelphia, PA

VYAS, CHRISTIN C.
[pen.] Christin Vyas; [b.] February 10, 1981, Pittsburgh; [p.] Debra Vyas and Chand Vyas; [ed.] Ladue Horton Watkins, High School, St. Louis, MO; [occ.] Student; [hon.] I have won two Art Contests for the Saint Louis Symphony. In 5th grade I was elected a captain of a flag football and led there to be champions for a lunch time league.; [oth. writ.] None published; [pers.] Writing helps we heal my inner-self.; [a.] Saint Louis, MO

WAGONER, ROSE
[pen.] Bonnie Kiki; [b.] August 12, 1962, California; [p.] Jimmy Wagoner, Alice Wagoner; [ch.] Nicholas Verando; [ed.] Morningside High, and Lost Angeles City College; [occ.] Insurance Broker, Wagoner Insurance Services; [memb.] Life Underwriter Training Council, Stop the Violence Increase the Peace Ass.; [oth. writ.] Actually this was my first poetry contest, I have been writing since the age of eleven, and thank you, I will continue.; [pers.] Universal love is my inspiration for writing, it come's from within, and may my poem touch you with a gift of life.; [a.] Los Angeles, CA

WALKER, FREDDIE
[b.] January 8, 1944, Montgomery; [p.] Mr. Wilmer Walker and Mrs. Emmett Williams; [m.] Emma Walker, June 2, 1992; [ch.] Anthony Walker; [ed.] GED attended Alabama State University and Trenholm Technical College; [occ.] Retired from the army (also disabled); [memb.] Vietnam Veterans of America, disabled American Veterans (D.A.V.); [hon.] National Defense Service Medal, Army Commendation Medal Vietnam Service medal (4) Purple Heart, Army occupation medal; [a.] Montgomery, AL

WALKER, MARCELLA J.
[b.] December 14, 1931, Janesville, WI; [p.] Edward and Evelyn Murphy; [m.] Robert E. Walker, June 30, 1956; [ch.] Johanna, Robert, Amanda, Paul; [ed.] Janesville High, Mercy Hospital Sch of Nursing (R.N.); [oth. writ.] Numerous poems and writings.; [pers.] I have been writing christmas and famous holiday poems for the last twenty years to bring tidings of peace and happiness to my friends.; [a.] La Grange, IL

WALKER, RITA
[b.] April 17, 1953, Huntington, WV; [p.] Oliver and Edna Barry; [m.] Archie Walker; [ch.] Brandon Flannery, Melissa Walker, Adrienne Walker, Andre' Walker; [ed.] Fairland High, West Virginia Career College, University of Maryland; [occ.] Administrative Assistant, Staff Sergeant, United States Army; [hon.] Nu Ta Sigma, Dean's List, Joint Defense Meritorious Award, Joint Defense Commendation Award, Joint Defense Achievement Award, US Army Commendation Award, US Army Achievement Award, Pershing Professional Award; [pers.] All thanks to God for giving me this talent and hoping that this is only the beginning of much more to come.; [a.] Gallipolis, OH

WALKER, TITUS B.
[b.] November 22, 1974, New Orleans, LA; [p.] Aline Walker and Walter Battles Jr.; [ed.] Fremont High - Oakland, CA., San Jose State University (3 years), San Jose, CA.; [hon.] Top Student in my High School Upward Bound Program; [oth. writ.] I'm generally a songwriter but I love to right poetry.; [pers.] I was inspired to write when a friend of mine in high school died and I wrote a poem about him. It was for a class assignment and I got an A. Ever since then I have been comfortable writing poetry. Life is to short live it and respect what it has to offer.; [a.] Memphis, TN

WALL SR., ALTON
[pen.] "Pop"; [b.] August 11, 1964, Durham, NC; [p.] Claudie Cameron and Evelyn L. Parker; [ch.] Almesha Wall, Alton Wall Jr., Antonio Daye; [ed.] Northern High, Watterson Diesel Inst; [occ.] Master Mechanic, City of Durham, Durham, NC; [memb.] Mt Olive Missionary Baptist Church; [hon.] Work published by NCCU Newspaper. Recognized as guest speaker at the Mt. Gilead Baptist Church; [oth. writ.] Many poems that I continue to resight with hopes to try and make a difference in the community that which I live. "Mother to Mother" was printed in the N.C. Centrals Campus Echoes newspaper; [pers.] I hope that my writings one day give me the opportunity to meet famous poets and to share my thoughts and visions of Life, Love and the preservation of humanity; [a.] Durham, NC

WALLACE, ANCE VIRGIL
[pen.] Ance Virgil Wallace; [b.] November 26, 1913, Moselle, MS; [p.] Anderson and Annie Wallace; [m.] O'Lean Hulsey Wallace, February 25, 1939; [ch.] Dortha, Richard and Donna; [ed.] College 2 yrs., and ext. work; [occ.] Retired; [oth. writ.] Essay and Poems I, Essay and Poems II, Moon, Sun and Tides, Orbiting Matter, As I Remember; [pers.] Time is limited don't waste it. Do what you can while you can.

WALLACE, DALE E.
[pen.] Dale Wallace; [b.] July 21, 1961; [m.] Diana, August 31, 1991; [ch.] Frantically working on it; [ed.] Cranial expansion limited; [hon.] Currently being considered for publication in "The National Library of Poetry"; [oth. writ.] Bogus notes for Acquaintances to Skip out on Current Obligations.; [pers.] Watching old cartoons while eating sugary breakfast cereals and washing it down with extremely thick coffee is the only way to faster true creativity.; [a.] Richland, WA

WALLACE, DILLON
[b.] October 13, 1977, Oklahoma City, OK; [p.] Frank Wallace, Margaret Rose; [ed.] Floyd E. Kellam High School; [memb.] American Museum of Natural History, National Geographic Society; [oth. writ.] Mostly personal, some poetry published in high school literary art magazine; [pers.] Nature is the eternal source of individual freedom and satisfaction, as well as being our maternal guardian.; [a.] Virginia Beach, VA

WALLACE, TONI
[b.] September 14, 1960, Los Angeles; [p.] Avril Wilkerson; [occ.] Courier; [a.] Los Angeles, CA

WALTON, RICHARD L.
[b.] July 12, 1953, Tucson, AZ; [p.] Glean and Opal Walton (Deceased); [ed.] Catalina High School; [oth. writ.] Publications of the National Library of Poetry as follows, Beyond The Stars (JDNI), Beneath The Harvest MDDN- (no one else), The Ebbing Tide - (Promises Given); [a.] Tucson, AZ

WARD, BRANDY
[b.] August 19, 1982, Rochester, MN; [p.] Debra Ward and Edward Ward; [ed.] Byron High School; [occ.] Student; [memb.] American Tae Kwon Do Association; [pers.] In my writing I try to show my feelings as well as I can. In this poem, my inspiration was the death of my foster brother.; [a.] Byron, MN

WARD, LAUREN N.
[pen.] Lauren N. Ward; [b.] May 26, 1981, Pittsburgh, PA; [p.] Sheryl and Wesley Ward; [ed.] McKeesport Area High School; [occ.] Student; [memb.] First United Methodist Church, Mckeesport Area High School Band, ATP/compressed program, Kisan Production (ballet, jazz, toe), high school newspaper, ASIST tutoring program (as a tutor); [hon.] United States Achievement, Academy National Mathematics Awards, United States Achievement, Academy National Merit Awards, Colleges and Scholarship Program, High Honor Roll; [oth. writ.] Articles and a poem printed in the school newspapers.; [pers.] Imagination is limited in the real world, but in poetry, imagination is boundless.; [a.] McKeesport, PA

WARNER, GEOFFREY K.
[pen.] Mav'rick; [b.] January 14, 1946, England; [p.] Stanley and Beatrice Warner; [m.] Patricia A. Warner, March 25, 1967; [ch.] Karen and Dean; [ed.] School of Commercial Studies, Bristol, England; [occ.] Distribution Sales Manager (for a weekly shopper publication.); [memb.] Netmar President's Club. Wilderness Preservation Society.; [hon.] University of Oxford General Certificate of Education (GCE) for English Language. (4 time) Netmar President's Club Award for superior sales and customer service.; [oth. writ.] The Vexed Vet. A Valentine's Lament. A Dickens Of A Carol and others.; [pers.] I see humour in everything and try to reflect that in most of my poetic works. There is a serious side to my personality, particularly where the degradation of the environment is concerned. That is very disturbing.; [a.] London Ontario, Canada

WARREN, BRIANA MICHELLE
[pen.] Bri, Julie, Baby Boo, Pooh Bear; [b.] October 17, 1981, Goshen, NY; [p.] Sharon and Harold Cushing; [ed.] East Coldenham Elementary Valley Central Middle School 8th grade; [occ.] Full time student; [hon.] Photogenic Winner of the International Galaxy Pageant in Middletown, NY for 1993 eligible to attend Grand Final. Several Trophies from Braeside Camp, Middletown, Ny. Chosen as a potential model by model Search America; [oth. writ.] This is my first poem ever to be published.; [pers.] Love is something you love by luck is just a number.; [a.] Walden, NY

WARREN, DAVID
[pen.] DJW; [b.] May 4, 1971, Hospital Ottawa, Canada; [p.] Rodney Warren, Ruth Warren; [ed.] BA Hon. English; [occ.] Unemployed, a poet wannabe; [oth. writ.] I have hundreds of personal poems, can and will write poems for special occasions. I have written for funerals, births, marriages, the pastor's departure from our church, friend's family etc.; [pers.] I have been wasting my talent. I am a poet who touches people. Stop wasting your talent. If you love poetry - write!!! But always offer hope in your stuff because the world needs it. If you want a sample please write me.; [a.] Ottawa Ontario, Canada

WARREN, PETER J.
[pen.] Mugwort Turtle; [b.] August 19, 1957, New York City, NY; [p.] Peter K. Warren, Maria Alba Warren; [m.] Peggy D. Warren, July 17, 1981; [ch.] Peter A. Warren, C. Aidan Warren; [ed.]

Bronxville Schools, Denver University, New York University. Certified in Public Speaking, Philosophy of Kashmir Shaivism, Massage Therapy, T'ai Chi Ch'uan.; [occ.] Wellness Consultant; [memb.] MC for Steamboat Springs' Poets Corner, Smithsonian, Veterans of foreign wars.; [hon.] 1st Kyu brown belt in Kyokushinkai-Kan Karate, student of Jung Yuen Temple Taoism 20 years; [oth. writ.] Published a poem entitled: "Pashupati's Dream" in the Dream Network Journal, pub. "What is the Sound of Distant Waves and Wind" in the Seaside Times; [pers.] "If you could trust your life enough to simply pour it back into the ocean of existence, you would find that somehow, mysteriously, it continues. Don't fear it, embrace it." Life, just as it is, has been my best friend and most honest teacher.; [a.] Steamboat Springs, CO

WARREN, W. N.
[pen.] Warren B. Nichols; [b.] April 3, 1953, Kansas; [p.] Ezra Warren, Florence Warren; [m.] Divorced; [ch.] Westley Warren, Jordon Warren, Jaimee Warren; [ed.] Tonganoxie High School; [occ.] Director Plant Services; [pers.] I write what I feel. I feel pain, I write pain, I feel love, I write love. I feel nothing, I write nothing.; [a.] East Stroudsburg, PA

WASHINGTON, JOYCE
[b.] August 25, 1962, Washington, DC; [p.] Elizabeth Barnes and John Barnes; [m.] Ricky Lee Washington, April 28, 1987; [ch.] Sinitta, Charnele, Devonte, LaVonda; [occ.] Housewife; [oth. writ.] Songwriter, (Love is a wonderful thing).; [pers.] Life situations can be overwhelming at time, but I learned that our load can be lighten if we look for answers to cope with our problems. Those answers I come to learn can be found in the bible.; [a.] Chesapeake, VA

WASSERMAN, MARTIN M.
[b.] October 12, 1980, Milwaukee, WI; [p.] Lew A. Wasserman, Laurie Moeckler; [ed.] Milwaukee Jewish Day School, Nicolet High School; [occ.] Student; [memb.] Chapter Solomon A.Z.A. B'nai' B'rith Youth Organization (B.B.Y.O.), Congregation Beth El; [hon.] Nicolet High School Dean's List, First Prize, Milwaukee Jewish Community Holocaust Essay Contest; [oth. writ.] Many poems published in local magazines and local newspapers, and the novel Nova (In progress, the play Dies Irae, Dies Illa, several songs.; [pers.] I endeavor to show people my views of our world. Most of my poetry reflects this, using what I call "Mind pictures."; [a.] Glendale, WI

WATERMAN, LEWIS
[pen.] "Waterlew"; [b.] June 4, 1941, Cranston, RI; [p.] Lew Sr. and Harriette; [m.] Carol, August 20, 1988; [ch.] Derek-13; [ed.] High School; [occ.] Carpenter; [oth. writ.] Yes?; [pers.] When you can't bang nails write poems!; [a.] Waterford, CT

WATERS, DENNIS
[b.] November 28, 1953, Flint, MI; [p.] Joseph Waters, Mary Jackson; [m.] Stephanie Waters, May 8, 1992; [ch.] Juwana Tate, Ruby Tate, Rou Maeo Tate and Tamasha Tapia.; [ed.] Flint Northwestern High School 1 yr. Baker Business College; [occ.] G.M. (General Motors) A.C. Delphi/West Employee; [memb.] U.A.W. 659

Local Family Worship Center Church; [oth. writ.] Several Poems and Auto - Biographical writings never published.; [pers.] I am so encouraged to write about the goodness of God, and how He has changed my life! I also love writing romantic poetry as well as how true life is lived in today's Society.; [a.] Flint, MT

WATKINS, VALERIE W.
[pen.] Ebb; [b.] May 22, 1958, Richmond, VA; [p.] Tony Ortega, Janet Ortega; [m.] James A. Watkins, November 21, 1992; [ch.] Page MacKenzie; [ed.] Amelia Academy; [occ.] Executive Assistant, Quantum Solutions, Inc., Bellevue, WA; [hon.] Salutatorian 1976; [oth. writ.] Never published in any form; [pers.] I write about what I feel and the way I see the way I see the world. I always wanted to give something to my daughter - an impression of my real self. That is the deepest purpose of my writing. It's just an expression of me.; [a.] Bellevue, WA

WATSON, LORRAINE E.
[b.] July 11, 1940, Malta, MT; [p.] Arthur and Etta Schlieve; [m.] Thomas L. Watson, November 14, 1961; [ch.] John, Lorna, Barbara; [ed.] Graduate Malta High School Adult classes in Art at present I am learning to play the guitar. My husband plays the Fiddle and he is my teacher.; [occ.] Bookkeeper 24 years at Equity Co-op; [memb.] Phillips Country Cattlewomen, Attend: Elim Lutheran Church "Tops" Malta past Secretary for District 35 Fiddlers Association; [hon.] 5 years Leader Award in 4-H, 20 years Plague for Employment at Equity Co-op. I have 7 grand children that is the best honor anyone could ever have.; [oth. writ.] Wrote an article for self magazine and sent photo. My picture was published along with 100 others to use in an article "Portrait of the American Women" I was the only one from Montana.; [pers.] Poem dedicated to: Daughters Lorna, Krause, and Barbara Christofferson, and grand daughters: Larae and Lindsey Krause, Brianna and Carlee Christofferson. I love them so much.

WEATHERFORD, ARNO LEE
[pen.] Samson Kendrix; [b.] December 3, 1954, Fort Worth, TX; [p.] Arno Weatherford, Mary Weatherford; [ch.] Lydia Amber; [occ.] Carpenter; [oth. writ.] None published.; [pers.] I hope people get as much out of reading my poetry as I get out of writing it.; [a.] Las Vegas, NJ

WEBB, DEBBIE ROSE
[b.] October 18, 1970, Nain; [p.] Henry Webb and Andrea Webb; [ed.] Level III, Labrador College; [occ.] Manager of Webb's Gift Shop and Boarding House; [memb.] Canadian Rangers, Labrador Inuit Association; [oth. writ.] Everlasting Love published in 'The Space Between"; [pers.] Poetry writing is something I love to do, although I don't get much time to do it anymore.; [a.] Nain, Canada

WEBB, JAMES ROBERT
[pen.] James Robert Webb; [b.] June 25, 1970, Nashville; [p.] Frank and Rita D. Webb; [m.] Tracey D. Webb, May 7, 1994; [ed.] Hunter Lane High School, Middle Tennessee State University (M.T.S.U.) and Tennessee State University (T.S.U.); [occ.] Administrative Assistance for a Mental Health Organization; [hon.] Dean's List, Who's Who in America, Junior National Honors Society;

[oth. writ.] "A tender-almighty God" and "Through the Dust" published with this organization; [pers.] "Seek the kingdom of God first and everything else the Lord will provide."; [a.] Nashville, TN

WEBB, OCTAVIA YVONNE
[pen.] Yvonne Webb; [b.] December 6, 1954, Knoxville, TN; [p.] Leon Ivnes, Katie Ivnes; [m.] James E. Webb Jr., July 10, 1982; [ch.] James E. Webb III, Lakesha Webb, Tiffani Webb; [ed.] Bearden High, Knoxville Business College; [occ.] Administrative - Assistant, Robert Half International and Accountemps; [memb.] Lovell Heights Church of God Ladies Ministry Board, Knoxville Christian, Cultural Ministries, Knoxville; [oth. writ.] "Heavenly Scents" a collection of poems inspired by my relationship with God through life experiences.; [pers.] If we meet and you forget me you've lost nothing, but if you meet Jesus Christ and forget him you've lost everything.

WEBER, MARY MICHAELA
[ed.] Queen's University, Fine Arts, Silent Ground Research and Retreat Center BC, Canada: intensive meditation, Taoist alchemy and chikung, perennial philosophies, classical song, poetic speech, eurythmy (Movement Art), Jana Yoga, Zen, Anthroposophy - 7 years training; [oth. writ.] Performance work, articles for healing journals; [pers.] My poetry is born out of the inner meditative journey. It is rooted in the traditions of the minstrel, the band, of Homer and his Lyre. I seek to reach into the realms beyond concept and image. Sounds, wearing through rhythm and word into language, elucidating the conceptual elements, can illuminate into the unutterable regions of the human spirit.

WEIDE, JULIE
[pen.] Julie Weide; [b.] February 3, 1959, Belmond, IA; [p.] Raymond Larsen and Betty Hansen; [ed.] CAL, NIACC; [occ.] Construction Fareman; [memb.] United Methodist Church; [oth. writ.] "Eternity Won," "Stepping Stones," and other poems, shared with friends, but unpublished.; [pers.] Whether nothing a letter, book or poem share your view of the world, your feelings and a bit of your soul.; [a.] Grafton, IA

WEIDELL, CAROLYN L.
[b.] April 24, 1955, Long Beach, CA; [p.] Charles Weidell, Jacqueline Nay; [ed.] Long Beach State University B.A Anthropology; [occ.] Senior manager; [pers.] I have been strongly influenced by nature, and by the writings of Edna St. Vincent Millay.; [a.] Mercer Island, WA

WEILAND, MARGARET F.
[pen.] Margaret Francis; [b.] December 17, 1914, Bridgeport; [p.] Fred and Florence Wickens; [m.] August 21, 1937; [ch.] 2; [ed.] Commercial 3 years; [occ.] House Keeper

WELCH, JOY SHIREE
[b.] October 27, 1980, Lansing, MI; [p.] Fred and Phyllis Welch; [ed.] Spring High School; [occ.] Student; [memb.] North Park Baptist Church; [a.] Spring, TX

WELCH, MILDRED E.
[pen.] Millie Welch; [b.] September 15, 1933,

Washington, DC; [p.] William Edwards, Rosa Golden Edwards; [m.] Widow; [ch.] Lynn W. Nicholson, Karin L. Welch; [ed.] Cardoza High, Temple Bus., USDA Grad School, DeKalb College, Federal Executive Development Program; [occ.] Retired Budget Analyst, USDA, Artist - Realistic Oil Paintings; [memb.] Senior Leadership Charlotte, USDA Travel Club, American Red Cross, Friends of JCS, NAACP, Arts and Science Council, The National Museum of Women in The Arts.; [pers.] I always tell my children and grandchildren to never set limitations for themselves because you can do anything you want to do and you can be anything you want to be in this life if you are willing to work hard and to persevere. Never feel that it is too late in life to begin.; [a.] Charlotte, NC

WELLS, GLENDA J.
[b.] September 6, 1972, Toronto, Ontario, Canada; [p.] Mr. and Mrs. James Wells; [m.] Mr. Mark Pycha (Fiance); [ed.] Grey Highlands Secondary School; [occ.] Receptionist, Office Clerk; [oth. writ.] Several poems and one children's story, writing from the of seven until some time into the future.; [pers.] A true poet is one who writes through inspiration, that is what I do best.; [a.] Toronto Ontario, Canada

WELLS, JAMES A.
[b.] April 28, 1938, Corner Brook, Newfoundland, Canada; [p.] James and Fannie Wells; [m.] Joy Wells, February 10, 1960; [ch.] Lucinda 33, Melinda 32, James 31, Roderick 30, Lawrence 28, Glenda 24, Debra 22, Wayne 18, Amanda 15, Rebecca 12; [ed.] Complete H.S., Trained in First Aide (Amalgamated Regional High) St. John Ambulance Instructor/Trainer; [occ.] Retired; [pers.] I have had an ease with poetry. White about things close to me or I knew about. I have a number of children who have followed my ability to verse.; [a.] Dundalk Ontario, Canada

WELLS, MARTHA
[p.] Peter and Agnes Blanksma; [m.] Frank Wells; [ed.] Educated in Brookings County So Dakota schools.; [occ.] Homemaker; [mcmb.] United Methodist Church, Methodist Organizations, Lay Speaker in Churches, Certified; [hon.] Several certificates of merit and awards; [oth. writ.] Several poems.; [pers.] The Bible says give honor where honor is due, I try to honor God in my writings.; [a.] Sheridan, MO

WELLS, SARAH E.
[pen.] Sarah Van Dreese, The Clan; [b.] March 26, 1974, Milwaukee, WI; [p.] Laurie Van Dreese and David Van Dreese; [m.] Mark S. Wells, December 31, 1995; [ed.] Auburn High, Augustana College, Rock Valley College, Chadwick University; [occ.] Student; [hon.] Alpha Phi Omega, Dean's List, Placed First in State Illinois Future Problem Solving Bowl Group Competition and Second in the Individual Competition; [oth. writ.] Various poems published in "The Cutting Edge," essays blind smiles, please hear what I'm not saying, with memories gone can life go on?, Finding the extra in the ordinary, various other untitled poems.; [pers.] I find my voice in my writing - a voice too often stifled in childhood. I hope that its message reaches across the page to be heard and be helpful to others.; [a.] Rockford, IL

WELSH, CHRISTINE
[b.] November 8, 1957, Orange, NJ; [p.] John and Mary Olson; [m.] Frederick Welsh, August 18, 1984; [ch.] Casey and Colby; [ed.] Skidmore College, BA Dance and BA English; [occ.] Advertising and Marketing/Thompson and Welsh; [hon.] Dean's List, Professional ballerina; [oth. writ.] Copy for ads and brochures; [pers.] Writing is a creation, spirit-filled thoughts balanced by the dance of words.; [a.] La Jolla, CA

WENDT, SHANNA
[pen.] Pheonix Avinor; [b.] June 10, 1979, Dos Maines, IA; [p.] Christine and Gregory Wendt; [ed.] Derby Senior High School; [occ.] Student; [memb.] National Honors Society; [pers.] My only dream is to write something that no man has written before and to bring back the greatness of all the writers who how been forgotten in the pages of time. I want to see mankind reach his future and remember only the truth about his past.; [a.] Derby, KS

WENGERT, ROBIN
[pen.] J.S.C.; [b.] April 10, 1962, Alton, IL; [p.] Warren Clendenn and Rachel Clendenny, (Deceased both); [ch.] Shane and Kevin; [pers.] This poem is a dedication to Christopher Reeve and all his struggles. Also for everyone else who has some type of handicap.

WENZEL, ELOISE M.
[b.] March 22, 1966, Vancouver, WA; [p.] Paul and Eva Wenzel; [m.] (Fiancee) Chris Stitely, June 15, 1996; [ch.] Areal and Sara; [ed.] Woodland High School; [occ.] Mother and Housewife; [pers.] Ever when things look bleak, remember love conquers all.; [a.] Miami, FL

WERNER, COLETTE S.
[pen.] Emily Rain; [b.] July 18, 1973, Riverside, CA; [p.] Gene and Marianne Werner; [ed.] Leigh High School, San Jose City College; [occ.] Adoption Counselor. Humane Society of Santa Clara Valley; [hon.] Graduated with honors, Dean's List at San Jose City College; [oth. writ.] Waiting for their time, (if it's meant to be,) to be shared with those who also appreciate the individual perceptions of life through poetry.; [pers.] My friend, let me share with you the happiness... Let us bring about some laughter in our lives...; [a.] San Jose, CA

WEST, CHARLIE
[b.] February 9, 1979, Glendale, CA; [ed.] Graduated High School in September of '95 with my G.E.D.; [occ.] Dishwasher and janitor at a local Cafe; [memb.] New Hampshire's Young Writer's and Publisher's Project; [oth. writ.] Hundreds of other poems and several short stories, but nothing published.; [pers.] Writing helps to release and sort out a lot of pain and confusion, as it taps into the inner turmoil I have. I've always dreamt of sharing it with the world, hoping it makes somebody feel normal.; [a.] Concord, NH

WETZEL, LUCINDA M.
[pen.] Cindy M. Ballantyne; [b.] July 24, 1962, Pittsburgh, PA; [p.] Joseph and Shirley Ballantyne; [m.] Walter C. Wetzel Jr., June 18, 1993; [ch.] Walter Charles III, Joseph John; [ed.] St. Peters Elem. School, St. Benedict Academy (High School),

Community College Allegheny County; [occ.] Wife and Mother and striving writer and artist; [oth. writ.] Other works of art sold and painted by me are "The Light House" - 1979, "The Farm" - October 1979, "The Retriever" September 1976; [pers.] As a member of the human race it is my daily goal and responsibility to make each and every day, a little brighter, happier and better for each and every person that I may encounter.; [a.] Pittsburgh, PA

WHEAT, LINDA
[pen.] Linda "Bird" Wheat; [b.] June 26, 1947, Gainsville, MO; [p.] James Bird, Ina Collins Bird; [m.] Kenneth Wheat, June 2, 1965; [ch.] Lisa Lynn; [ed.] Dora High School; [occ.] Home maker; [memb.] Sparta Church of Christ; [oth. writ.] This is my first published poem; [pers.] I love to write about my faith, family and friends; [a.] Sparta, MO

WHELCHEL, CHERY ANN
[pen.] "Iloveeverybody"; [b.] September 18, 1958, Gainesville, GA; [p.] James D. and Patricia J. Whelchel; [m.] Divorced; [ed.] Forest Park High Clayton State College; [occ.] Disabled by Multiple Sclerosis; [memb.] Dem. Nat'l. Committee Nat'l. Multiple Sclerosis Society; [hon.] Included in: World "Who's Who of Working Women" Eleventh Edition; [oth. writ.] Short stories in electronic book format for anyone using internet, several parodies and satires published on internet. Poems in local newspaper and library.; [pers.] Stumbling blocks are really stepping stones. Use them wisely.; [a.] Atlanta, GA

WHISKIN, ROBERTA
[b.] August 12, 1951, New Westminster, British Columbia, Canada; [p.] Bob and Peg Whiskin; [occ.] Receptionist for Weyerhaeuser Canada Ltd., Okanagan Falls for 22 years.; [hon.] Being selected in this contest is probably one of my greatest honors.; [oth. writ.] Several poems published in our small town newspaper.; [pers.] I try to find the lighter side of situations. I think everyone should have one good laugh a day. It tends to keep you young at heart and its something you can pass along.; [a.] Okanagan Falls British Columbia, Canada

WHISSELL, GWEN
[b.] November 23, 1931, Sudbury, Ontario, Canada; [p.] W.S. Bill Beaton, Isla May Robertson; [m.] Joseph Alfred 'Gerry' Whissell, September 18, 1950; [ch.] Robert, Gary, Bev, Rick, Miles and 3 grandchildren; [ed.] Alexander Public Sudbury High, S.M.T.S. Confederation; [occ.] Clerk Valley East Library Synchronized Swimming Coach; [memb.] ACBL, Wood Carving Confideration, Sudbury District Authors Guild; [hon.] Swimming, Paddling Reciting Poetry; [oth. writ.] Poetry Guild, poems published in Sudbury Star, Vision church; [pers.] Encouraged by family, friends at Valley East Library - Encourage to learn by my father.

WHITAKER, GERALDINE CURRINGTON
[pen.] "Gerry"; [b.] August 14, Sheilman, GA; [p.] Floyd and Minnie Currington, IN; [m.] Alford Whitaker IV, July 3, 1986; [ch.] Andrea and Alford V; [ed.] Randolph County High - Cuthbert, GA, Albany State College, Albany, GA; [occ.] Senior Customer Service Advisor, Public Utilities Dept., Jacksonville,

Fl.; [memb.] Alumni State Alumni Assoc., Jacksonville Branch; [hon.] Award for Outstanding Volunteerism (Certificate) for the City of Jacksonville; [oth. writ.] None published; [pers.] "Live the life you want repeated" what you present is what you consent.; [a.] Jacksonville, FL

WHITE, ANGELA LYNN
[pen.] Angela Lynn; [pers.] No matter your past condition, present situation, or what you've been told your life will be, we are all destined for greatness. This poem is for Bruce. Thank you for the love and belief that is my inspiration. For today and every tomorrow, "I would."; [a.] Corpus Christi, TX

WHITE, BARBARA
[pen.] Bea Copeland; [b.] January 9, 1954, Cleveland, OH; [p.] Elizabeth White and Robert White; [ch.] Ranahnah White; [ed.] York College of the City University of New York (BA) New York Univeristy (MA); [occ.] Speech Improvement Teacher for New York City Board of Education/ P.S. 191-Brooklyn; [oth. writ.] Presently working on book of original poetry.; [pers.] I strive for world peace. I believe that our children should be exposed to less violent art, especially in riders and film.; [a.] Bronx, NY

WHITE, CHARLES S. J.
[ed.] Ph.D., Divinity School, The University of Chicago. I have studied medieval Hindi poetry, Spanish poetry, and English and American literature.; [occ.] Retired professor of Philosophy and Religion, The American University, Washington, D.C.; [oth. writ.] Several books in the field of history of religions, including Ramakrishna's Americans, The Caurasi Pad, Transformations of Myth through Time (Anthology about Joseph Campbell), and numerous articles in scholarly journals and encyclopedias.; [a.] Washington, DC

WHITE, CHERYL BROWN D.
[pen.] Aquarius; [b.] February 5, 1954, Philadelphia, PA; [p.] William H. Brown and Catherine P. Brown; [ch.] William A. White, Desare M. White and Tylecia D. Brown-Bryant; [ed.] Dover High School - Dover, Delaware, University of Delaware Newark, Delaware Community College of Philadelphia - Philadelphia PA Graduated May 1989; [occ.] Writer and Mother and Grandmother; [hon.] Editors Choice Award - National Library of Poetry; [oth. writ.] A play - Woody's playhouse a book of poetry - the heart of an aquarius a fictional novel - dreams can come true.; [pers.] Granddaughter - Diamond U. Jones, you can be whatever want to be. Don't be afraid to dream and go after your dreams, because if you don't, you sell yourself short, for dreams can come true.; [a.] Philadelphia, PA

WHITE, DEE
[pen.] D.E. White; [b.] December 29, 1941, london, England; [p.] Elizabeth and Frederick Lambert; [m.] Jack White, May 12, 1967; [ch.] 1; [occ.] Writer, Poet and Artist; [oth. writ.] Written two manuscripts, and now writing book of poetry - was a columnist for newspaper, and A 'Contributor' writer for the Britannia magazine.; [pers.] Like the winter and spring, poetry is a lamp that cast's light upon the heavy shadows of despair, and the sun, to lift the damp

mists of sorrow.; [a.] Georgetown Ontario, Canada

WHITE, MARGARETTE HELEN
[pen.] McHelen White; [b.] July 5, 1923, West Chester, PA; [m.] August 5, 1946; [ch.] James, Stanley Jr.; [ed.] Oceanside High School, Oceanside L.D. NY, Navy Wave - US NR - 3rd Class Petty Officer; [occ.] Retired

WHITHAM, GWEN E. B.
[pen.] Gwen Evelyn Beebe; [b.] May 18, 1963, Hartford, CT; [p.] Gordon Beebe, Rita Beebe; [ch.] Jason Whitman; [ed.] University of Connecticut, Westfield State College; [occ.] Systems Consultant; [memb.] Alpha Chi National College Honor Society, United States Tae Kwan Do Federation; [hon.] Alpha Chi National College Honor Society, Dean's List; [pers.] Life is my mentor, love is my life. I'd like to dedicate this poem to Jason, Paul, and Einstein.; [a.] East Granby, CT

WHITMER, DARRELL
[b.] October 23, 1977, Beaumont, TX; [p.] Evan Whitmer, Ruth Whitmer; [ed.] Deer Valley High School year of 96; [occ.] Student, Red Cross Swim instructor; [memb.] Church of Jesus Christ of Latter-Day Saints; [hon.] Eagle Scout Award; [oth. writ.] One other poem published, many poems just given as gifts to friends; [pers.] I try to touch the heart of the reader. To uplift and give hope to those who need it.; [a.] Phoenix, AZ

WHITNEY, DANENE
[b.] April 14, 1950, Aberdeen, WA; [m.] Perry Whitney, September 1983; [ch.] One son - Sean, 2 step-daughter's Pat and Debbie, 2 Step Sons - Matt and Josh; [ed.] Weatherwax High School, Dewitt's Beauty School (Licensed beautician); [occ.] Housewife; [oth. writ.] Have written 2 fairy tales and over 100 poems to be copy - nighted had "The Secret" published last Oct. by Local Newspaper along with Cover article "The Bogeyman" and Several through national Library of Poetry.; [a.] Montesano, WA

WHITTEMORE, HOPE
[b.] November 24, 1972, Biddeford, ME; [ch.] Chantel Mariea; [occ.] Front and Shift Leader, Shop-n-Save, Saco; [oth. writ.] Currently working on a book of poems called "Come, See My World"; [pers.] I like to write poems based on my life experiences.; [a.] Saco, ME

WILGANOWSKI, JOAN M.
[b.] October 22, 1953, Houston, TX; [p.] Fred Muzyka, Margie Muzyka; [m.] Henry J. Wilganowski, July 15, 1972; [ch.] Nathaniel Lee, Tara Colette; [ed.] St. Pius X High '72, Houston Community College, A.A.S. '89, Le Tourneau University, B.S. ('96); [occ.] Sales/Purchasing Agent, Jake's Finer Foods, Houston, TX; [memb.] Nat'l Assoc. of Female Executives, Houston Women's Bowling Assoc; [hon.] Phi Theta Kappa, Alpha Beta Gamma, Dean's List, Certified Food Service Professional - Level 1; [pers.] I enjoy the ability to communicate with others through several mediums.; [a.] Houston, TX

WILLADSEN, IRENE
[b.] July 12, 1942, Aberdeen, Scotland; [m.] Paul Willadsen, October 17, 1970; [oth. writ.] Various

letters to Toronto Sun Newspaper Re: Letters printed that I wish to comment on.; [pers.] Employed as Admin. Assistant at Scarborough College, V. of T. from 1966 until 1990 when multiple sclerosis (M.S.) was diagnosed.

WILLIAMS, JENNIFER
[b.] September 19, 1981, Chile, South America; [p.] Maryann and Lawrence Williams; [ed.] Brewster High School; [occ.] Student, Dancer, Tap and Jazz Teacher; [memb.] Ursus Writing Club, J.V. Tennis Team, High School Band - Flute Second Chair, Community Service Volunteer; [hon.] Student of the Mouth November, Honor Roll; [oth. writ.] Essays and short stories published in school paper. My favorite poets, writers are Poe, Dickinson and Montgomery.; [pers.] If I can dream it I can make it a reality.; [a.] Brewster, NY

WILLIAMS JR., HENRY
[b.] August 6, 1949, Florence, SC; [p.] Mr. and Mrs. Henry Williams Sr.; [ch.] One daughter (Shawanda); [occ.] CRT Operator RJR Nabisco; [hon.] Cash Prize for Safety Slogan Focus and Stay Alert Practice Safety And Don't Get Hurt; [oth. writ.] Chap book of poems. Poetic expressions.; [pers.] Make lay while there is sun do what you can while you can, you may never get this chance again.; [a.] Winston Salem, NC

WILLIAMS, MARY JO
[pen.] Mary Guglielmo, Mary Tomaszewski, M.J. Williams; [b.] February 1, 1945, Philadelphia, PA; [ch.] William A. Michael P., Scot J.; [ed.] Villa Maria Academy, Malvern, PA; [occ.] Executive Secretary, SEPTA-Suburban Operations, Upper Darby, PA; [memb.] Writer's Club of Delaware County; [hon.] Life's Special rewards: My three grand daughters: Noel Marie, Tiffany Natasha, and Theresa Gabriele Tomaszewski; [oth. writ.] Editor of the Suburban Star Newsletter - Quarterly publication SEPTA-Suburban Operations; [pers.] To preserve the innocence of small children always and to never forget the child in all of us. To realize that no matter what mistake we make in life, there is hope for our future. "Failure is an opportunity for Learning."; [a.] Aldan, PA

WILLIAMS, MAZIE
[b.] January 30, 1930, Mississippi; [p.] Elvis and Daisy Johnson Lawhorn; [m.] Willie Williams (Deceased), May 24, 1948; [ch.] Seven; [ed.] High School and College Graduated as a nurse; [occ.] Retired Nurse; [memb.] D.E.S. Eastersill Society, Pres., American Legion Aux., AARP URGE, Disable Vcts. of American, Rep. Floyd Clack Advisory Comm.; [hon.] Outstanding Usher in Church, Work award for Perfect Attendance, Merit award Church work, Distinction Jury Adaro, Merit award Pres, American Legion Aux.; [oth. writ.] Valentines, and Christmas cards and birthday card for family and friends. Essays.; [pers.] I believe a person one it to themselves to be all they can be, and to served their country, and fellow man and God to the best of their abilities.; [a.] Flint, MI

WILLIAMS, MELVIN
[b.] July 27, 1953, New Bern, NC; [occ.] Designer, Custom Yachts, Hatteras; [pers.] Our life's blood

flows onto the page in a rhythmic description of joy and pain, love and anger, hope and despair, by writing we understand.

WILLIAMS, MICHAEL

[pen.] Michael Williams; [b.] December 16, 1960, Temple, TX; [p.] Dorothy Brooks and T. W. Williams; [ch.] Sharniqua Myical Williams; [ed.] Temple High School, Gray Job Corps., Temple Jr. College, Clover Park Voc-Tec Ins., Windham Voc. School; [occ.] Self-Employed; [hon.] Silver and Golden Poetry Awards; [oth. writ.] "Splendor of Life" and I am compiling my poetry to publish a book of my own.; [pers.] I write about the world around me and about life's experiences and how they've affected me.; [a.] Temple, TX

WILLIAMS, NINA

[b.] January 14, 1950, Harviell, MO; [p.] Arvel and Lucy Pennington; [m.] Floyd E. Williams, November 20, 1986; [ch.] Keyla Lloyd - Jonathan Lloyd; [ed.] Neelyville High School, Ozark Cosmetology College; [occ.] Rentals; [memb.] American Legion; [oth. writ.] Only for family members.; [pers.] I write from the heart, doing so as a form of relaxation.; [a.] Poplar Bluff, MO

WILLIAMS, RICHARD G.

[pen.] Rick; [b.] June 15, 1941, Fort Monroe, VA; [p.] Bill and Marie Williams; [ch.] Glenn and Amy Williams; [ed.] Rancocas Valley Regional H.S. - 1959; [occ.] Retired U.S. Army - 1980, Medically Retired and Security - 1988; [memb.] American Legion; [oth. writ.] "A time after," futuristic", a "Time in Life", "Transparent," "Exciting Eyes", "It comes as a dream", "Storybook Lady", and "What if."; [pers.] Everything I write is from personal experience and lessons learned in life. My sincere appreciation to 3 of the most beautiful women, people, teachers in the world. Thank you Linda, Toby and Nikki.; [a.] Phoenix, AZ

WILLIAMS, WILLIAM H.

[b.] November 6, 1922, Pembroke, GA; [p.] John and Mamie Williams; [m.] Doris Cudlipp Williams, June 1, 1950; [ch.] Bill, Bob and Bonnic; [ed.] Georgia State Univ., BA, 1955; [occ.] Dept. of Corrections, State of Georgia; [memb.] Georgia State Poetry Society; [pers.] I writes to praise God and edify the church.; [a.] Covington, GA

WILLIAMSON, FRANCES

[pen.] Fanny McNair; [b.] May 24, 1941, Niagara Falls, Canada; [p.] Ted Manders and Fanny McNair; [m.] Dennis Williamson, May 14, 1960; [ch.] Stacey, Dennis, Terry; [ed.] Niagara Falls Collegiate, Vocational Institute graduated grade 12; [occ.] Buyer, Manager Theme Park; [memb.] Toronto Humane Society, Being with my family; [oth. writ.] 'A Mother Tear', Pub - sparkles in the sand; [pers.] I put in words what I feel in my heart yet can not express.; [a.] Niagara Falls, Canada

WILLOUGHBY, DONNA

[b.] December 11, 1973, Birmingham, AL; [p.] Raymond and Judy Willoughby; [ed.] Hanceville High School, current University of Alabama of Birmingham (UAB); [occ.] Student in Occupational Therapy School at UAB; [memb.] Student Occupational Therapy Association, Alabama Occupational Therapy Association, American Occupational Therapy Association; [hon.] Dean's List, President's List, Golden Key National, Honor Society; [pers.] I am inspired greatly by my family. My favorite bible verse, which serves as a source of motivation and guidance, is Philippians 4:13: I can do all things through Christ who strengthens me.; [a.] Hanceville, AL

WILSON, ANGELA

[b.] June 19, 1971, Chatham, Ont.; [p.] Debra Hawes, Arthur Wilson; [ch.] 1 son - Curtis R. Girard; [ed.] I have successfully completed my Ontario Secondary School Diploma through correspondence; [occ.] I'm currently employed at Olan Mills Portrait Studio; [pers.] I enjoy writing about events that molded my life. It provides me with great comfort to later glance back and reflect on where I've been, and where I'm confident I'm going.; [a.] Chatham Ontario, Canada

WILSON, DAVID P.

[b.] June 13, 1930, New York City, NY; [p.] Norman and Emily Wilson; [m.] Alma, May 10, 1955; [ch.] Hall Mark and Victoria; [ed.] Hope College, Western Theological Seminary; [occ.] Pres. And CEO Trinity Travel and Tours, Inc. Also: Writer, Composer; [hon.] Official Commemorative Poem for 50th anniversary of Rip Van Winkle Bridge on the Hudson River in NY, Poetry put in time capsule in one of oldest towns in America - Stephentown, NY Wrote wedding hymn for Prince Charles and Princess Diana of England.; [oth. writ.] Books: His Hallmark Is Love 100 Tantalizing Tales Of Yore, Calvary - Where The Cost Was Counted And The Price Was Paid, The Issue Of Bethlehem, The Coroner's Verdict, and 15 other books.; [pers.] Poetry tends to be a lost art - with lost interest for the most part. Partly due to lack of skill and purpose in writing and preoccupation with other things on the part of the reader. Poetry that exalts Christ seems to still be the best poetry: The Psalms, as example.; [a.] Pine Bush, NY

WILSON, KATHY

[b.] July 29, 1957, Brantford, Ontario, Canada; [p.] Eugene Wilson, Katherine Wilson; [m.] Christopher Urbanowicz, Eight years; [ch.] Many wonderful nieces and nephews; [ed.] B.C.I., I.L.C., Mohawk College; [occ.] Purchasing Agent; [memb.] Volunteer for the Canadian Red Cross Society, Ontario Slo-Pitch; [oth. writ.] Several poems in local newspaper; [pers.] I strive in my writings to convey love and compassion. My greatest love is my family, those who are here, those who are not, as they influence me to write from my heart.; [a.] Brantford Ontario, Canada

WILSON, MARJORIE

[b.] August 1, 1945, Bigfork, MN; [ch.] Jennifer; [occ.] Director of Compliance Betsy Johnson Hospital, Dunn. NC; [pers.] Life is an adventure, to be Journeyed through with an open mind and a free spirit.; [a.] Dunn, NC

WILSON, NANCY CAROLYN

[b.] September 11, 1945, Winnfield, LA; [p.] Mallory and Lottie Jenkins; [m.] Glenn S. Wilson Sr., October 10, 1987; [ch.] Tina Reed, Sherry Cox, Robin Noel; [ed.] High School, Winnfield High School, Winnfield, LA; [occ.] Medical Transcriptionist American S.I.D.S. Institute, Atlanta, GA; [memb.] First Baptist Church Morrow, CA; [oth. writ.] The Skylight Series, a compilation of 20 poems touching the brilliance and beauty of "Heavenly Creations of Light." "The Makers Masterpiece", "When Jesus Died", and "When Daffodils Whisper."; [pers.] I try to write much of my poetry in a "full circle" style. It carries your mind from beginning to end. And expresses your innermost feelings of the heart at great depth at every level in between.; [a.] Morrow, GA

WILSON, PHILO

[pen.] Philo Wilson; [b.] January 29, 1924, Westfield, MA; [p.] Carroll Wilson, Doris Carl; [m.] Kathryn M. Elsden, September 25, 1947; [ch.] Pamela C., Karen M., John E.; [ed.] Westfield High, Williams College (AB), Cornell Univ. (MS), Wash. State Univ. (Ph.D.); [occ.] Retired Geology and Oceanography Prof., Oneonta State (NY); [memb.] Previous Professional memberships have been allowed to lapse; [hon.] Chancellors' Award for Teaching Excellence, Distinguished Teaching Professorship, Earth Science Dept Chairman; [oth. writ.] Geology Laboratory Manual, a couple of professional papers, poems for family occasions; [pers.] Staying young in spirit will keep one young in body.

WILSON, TAMARA

[b.] November 13, 1972; [p.] Karen Fontaine, Bruce Wilson; [ed.] Livermore High School, Las Positas Junior College, California State University, Hayward; [memb.] American Morgan Horse Association; [hon.] A.A. Degree with highest honors, American Morgan Horse Association's, Saddle Seat Medal - 1988, '89 and '90, United Professional Horsemen, Association's Challenge Cup - 1989 and '90; [oth. writ.] Too many to say; [a.] Livermore, CA

WILSON, TASHA M.

[b.] September 10, 1975, Columbia, SC; [p.] Coretta Harrell, David Brannon; [m.] Anthony C. Speach, April 9, 1995; [ch.] Tyrell Speach, Tuneel Speach; [ed.] Spring Valley High, Columbia Jr. College.; [occ.] Home maker, Student; [hon.] Deans List; [oth. writ.] Articles in the upward bound newsletter of USC.; [pers.] Mother Nature Creates pure beauty. I strive to reflect the beauty of her creations in my writings.; [a.] Columbia, SC

WILSON, WINSTON W.

[pen.] W. W. Wilson; [b.] January 27, 1968, Jamaica, West Indies; [p.] Urshel Wilson, Rita Jackson; [m.] Shirley Velinor, September 2, 1993; [ed.] H. S. Accounting and Economics - 1991 B.S. Accounting - 1990, (Brooklyn College); [occ.] Auditor - CS First Boston; [memb.] AICPA American Institute of certified Public Accountants NABA - National Accountants.; [hon.] Summa Cum Laude Graduate Brooklyn College, Dean's List 8 Semester, Danielson E. Myers Awards, Mitchel Titue Award, Ford Colloquium Scholarship (2 years) for College Teaching.; [pers.] "Eat the mountain bite by bite".; [a.] Monmouth Junction, NJ

WINDSOR, DIANNE

[b.] January 20, 1942, Chicago, IL; [p.] John and Mary Windsor; [ed.] Moraine Valley Community Coll. Palos Hills, ILL, U. of Chicago Cytology School, Chicago, IL; [occ.] Cyto-Technologist; [memb.] American Society of Clinical Pathologists, Defenders of Wildlife; [oth. writ.] None published; [pers.] Words written of kind repose, along their journey give eyes to the blind, song to the deaf, voice to the silent, alas, they are my friend.; [a.] Streamwood, IL

WINTER, LISA M.
[b.] January 26, 1982, Pottsville; [p.] Nicholas and Lisa Winter; [ed.] 9th Grader at Nativity B.V.M. High School; [memb.] Chorus, Cheerleading, Newspaper, School Play, Forensics, Math Club, French Club, Honor Roll; [hon.] 50 Savings Bond from Schuykill County Council of the Arts for "Published Poem" Citizens Award, Presidentional "Academic of Excellence" First Honors "Who's Who" National Math Society, National French Society; [oth. writ.] Three articles in the call Schuylkill Haven paper Editor of The Saint Ambrose School paper.; [a.] Auburn, PA

WINTER, MARCEL
[pen.] Yanz - Malkovich; [b.] April 6, 1962, Saint Lucia, WI; [p.] Joseph Thomas, Esther Winter; [m.] Francine Depont, January 15, 1991; [ch.] Miguel Winter, Stephanie Nadeau, Maika Winter; [ed.] Vieux-fort R.C. Boys School; [occ.] Journalism, Short Story Writing; [memb.] Distinguished Member of the ISP; [oth. writ.] My first poem was recently published (entitled My World) with The National Library of Poetry in the Anthology "Sparkles in the Sand".; [pers.] You are unique in your own way, there is no one like you in the entire world. You have just one enemy and one friend, look into the mirror and tell me who do you see... Well, that's your worse enemy and your best friend, for only you have the power to love yourself or hate yourself, and that's reality.; [a.] Granby Province of Quebec, Canada

WISEHART, SARAH-JANE
[pen.] Sarah-Jane Wisehart; [b.] April 14, 1970, Salford, England, United Kingdom; [p.] Francis Joseph Donelan, Patricia Ellen Donelan; [m.] Marc Merrill Wisehart, March 31, 1994; [ed.] Turton High School, Wigan College of Technology, Salford College of Technology; [occ.] Waitress, Lyons, Sacramento; [oth. writ.] Monologues which were performed, along with two plays by my College Theatre Company - Edinburgh Theatre Festival.; [pers.] When I wrote my first 'Good Poem' I was hit with a feeling - I could talk without having to explain myself! But what fascinates me is the 'possibility' behind words, therefore I intend to listen, to think - to learn.; [a.] Sacramento, CA

WISEMAN, JANE J.
[b.] February 25, 1938, Nora Springs, IA; [p.] Benjamin and Irene Hart; [m.] Clifton E. Wiseman, February 29, 1992; [ch.] Mark Lowry, Stepchildren, Suzanne Miller, Melvin, Wayne, John and Tom Wiseman; [ed.] Charles City High School, Iowa State Teachers College, Iowa Falls Junior College, Simpson College; [occ.] Retired from 5 years factory 6 years teacher of special ed. 5 years NH 6 years hosp. 211/2 yrs Medical Ins.; [memb.] Past years - church affiliated activities; [hon.] Superior Performance Award Veterans Administration Hospital, Iowa City, IA; [oth. writ.] Published a 60 page hard copy book of poems and prose, "A Shake of a Lambs Tale and other thoughts", Another poem book "A to laugh" is

being published; [pers.] I believe that good happens even in the most tragic of happenings, and most of my writings reflect the good.; [a.] Sheffield, IA

WISMER, WILLIAM
[b.] September 13, 1913, Jordan Station, Ontario, Canada; [p.] Philip and Minnie Wismer; [m.] Margaret Katherine Anna (Chalmers), June 16, 1938; [ch.] Margaret Katherine; [ed.] Bachelor of Arts (B.A), Bachelor of Laws (LL.B); [occ.] Retired Lawyer; [memb.] Ontario Club, Toronto Board of Trade; [hon.] Queen's Counsel, Honorary Member of the Law, Society of Upper Canada, Phi Delta Phi Legal Fraternity, Canadian Who's Who; [oth. writ.] 327 Old-Timer's Homespun poems in poetical rhyme.; [pers.] I never cease to marvel at the beauty and versatility of the English language.; [a.] Toronto Ontario, Canada

WOEHLER, GENEVA R.
[b.] September 18, 1944, Covington, TN; [p.] Lansing and Josie Smith; [m.] Wallace M. Woehler (Deceased), May 7, 1965; [ch.] Michael, Christophern and Robert; [ed.] High School; [occ.] Secretary to the School Nurse Supervisor for San Diego City Schools; [oth. writ.] Have since written approx. 20 poems/verses related to my experience in dealing with the sudden death of my husband. My goal now is to write the "In-between" information that lead to my poems and be published as a self-help book.; [pers.] I was to be the kidney donor for my husband. He died two weeks short of surgery. My poems written for him. However, I believe he had a hand in writing it to relate a message to me. The poem is engraved on a bench at his office.; [a.] San Diego, CA

WOLCOTT, ROBERT
[b.] February 28, 1981, Santa Monica, CA; [p.] Deane Wolcott, Elvira Wolcott; [ed.] Newbury Park Adventist Academy, Newbury Park, CA; [occ.] Student; [hon.] Academic Scholarship Newbury Park Adventist Academy; [pers.] Robert wrote this poem the day after his grandfather's death. He was in 8th grade age 14 - at the time.; [a.] Thousand Oaks, CA

WOLLERT, TYSON K.
[b.] July 4, 1981; [p.] Mr. and Mrs. Keith Wollert; [ed.] 8th grade Wiley Schools, Willey; [occ.] Student; [memb.] No memberships. I am in student Council and on the accountability I also play any sport you can think of; [oth. writ.] 'Panther' Published in Anthology of Poetry by, young Americans, '1994' edition; [pers.] To me poetry is a bunch of nouns and adjectives placed together perfectly to make them beautiful.; [a.] Lamar, CO

WOOD, MR. JEAN T.
[b.] December 28, 1928, Lynchburg, VA; [m.] Emily J. Wood; [ed.] E.C. Glass High School Lynchburg College VA. Tech.; [occ.] Retired Construction Engr.; [pers.] As a boy I would race home to hear Ted Malone read poetry on the radio. Started writing poems after I was 62 yrs. old.; [a.] Victoria, TX

WOODARD, WALTERINE
[occ.] Fourth Grade Teacher (Cleve. Public Schools); [oth. writ.] I Can See, A Trail Of Success, The Stillness Of The Night, and My Color, which

you have; [pers.] I encourage people along the way, I also give two-thirds of myself to others as I go along life's way.; [a.] Cleveland, OH

WOODS, HILDA G.
[b.] October 18, 1941, Belgrove, LA; [p.] Clarence C. Green and Susie B. Felder; [m.] Henry Woods, July 15, 1961; [ch.] Dennis Woods, Cherly Woods, Karen Turley; [ed.] Booker T. Washington High School, Meadows Draughon B. College; [occ.] Poet and Writer; [memb.] Household of Faith Full Gospel Baptist Church; [oth. writ.] New voice in American Poetry 1977, 20th Century's Greatest Poets 1982 A book of poems by Hilda G. Woods 1995; [pers.] Hilda G. Woods is an inspirational writer and poet. She has been blessed with an unique and awesome gift. Her speciality, "Poetry in your Name" is able to capture the most intriguing qualities and personality of an individual having to know little about that person. She praises God for her gift.; [a.] Metairie, LA

WOODS, ZELIA MICHELLE
[b.] August 20, 1978, Memphis, TN; [p.] Melvin and Stella Woods; [ed.] Trezevant High School; [memb.] Business Professional of America, Yearbook Staff, School Choir, Christian workers in action; [hon.] National Honor Society, W.H. Sweet Honors Award, Who's Who Among American high school students, United States National Journalism Award (USNJA); [oth. writ.] I have a personal collection of original poetry.; [pers.] My writing reflects the many ideas about life and emotional feelings that exist within me.; [a.] Memphis, IN

WORRELL, JESSICA
[pen.] Jessica; [b.] July 7, 1985, Kissimmee, FL; [p.] Katrina and Curt Worrell I.; [ed.] Spanishburgh Elementary School; [memb.] Camp Creek Baptist Church; [hon.] I've won several Young Writers Week Contests at school. I have also won a money award from contest at a library off of a poem.; [oth. writ.] Several other poems and stories written.; [pers.] I hope my writings will influence other people who haven't yet discovered their talent. I hope to be a professional writer in the future.; [a.] Spanishburgh, WV

WOTELKO, VICTORIA
[pen.] Victoria Elkoe; [b.] February 6, 1912, Elizabeth, NJ; [p.] Stanislaw and Anna Gibas Wotelko; [ed.] Theodore Roosevelt School-Elizabeth, NJ, Battin High School 2 yrs., Commercial Course and some evening classes- Elizabeth, NJ; [occ.] Retired; [pers.] I did not think my poem would make it this far.; [a.] Roselle, NJ

WRIGHT, CHARLES
[b.] July 8, 1953, Springfield, VT; [p.] Edward and Esther Wright; [ed.] Fall Mt. Regional High School; [occ.] Contract Data Entry, U.S. Dept. of Labor; [memb.] Anthroposophical Society; [oth. writ.] Short stories, Novellas illustrator if children's book and cartoon History of Consciousness; [pers.] The arts reflect our spiritual origins. Human beings are the balance of microcosm and macrocosm and the act of artistic creation verifies humanity's uniqueness.; [a.] Cambridge, MA

WRIGHT, DEREK
[b.] February 24, 1947, Wakefield, United Kingdom; [p.] Stanley and Edith Wright; [m.] Renate Mohrbach Wright, July 31, 1981; [ed.] Univ. of Reading 1968-71, Univ. of Leeds 1971-72, Univ. of Keele 1972-73, Univ. of Queensland, Australia 1982-85; [occ.] Associate Professor of English Northern Territory University, Darwin, Australia; [memb.] Assoc. for Commonwealth Lit. and Language Studies, Africanist Association of Australasia and South Pacific; [hon.] Choice Outstanding Academic Book Award, American Library Association, for Ayi Kwei Armah's Africa (1990); [oth. writ.] Five books on African writing including studies of Wole Soyinka, Ayi Kwei Armah, Nuruddin Farah and contemporary fiction. 85 journal articles on English, American and Commonwealth Literatures. Books reviews, poems in journals in Australia and South Africa.; [a.] Darwin Northern Territory, Australia

WU, HSIAO-WEN
[b.] September 25, 1977, Taiwan; [p.] Chin-Mu Wu and Liu Chun-Chiao; [ed.] Chin-Ou Girls High School, Country Day School planning to attend Indiana University; [occ.] Student dream on becoming a doctor; [hon.] Distinguished Team Scholastic Award, Outstanding Achievement in French Scholarships for Outstanding Academic Achievement; [oth. writ.] Memories; [pers.] Be bold and courageous. When you look back on your life, you'll regret the things you didn't do more than the ones you did. Be willing to lose a battle in order to win the war; [a.] San Jose, Costa Rica

WUTTKE, MARC
[b.] September 20, 1965, Braunschweig, Germany; [p.] Renate Domroese, Wolfgang Wuttke; [m.] Linda Wuttke, June 12, 1989; [ch.] Maurice Quince, Cameron Quince, Joe Quince; [ed.] B.A., Liberal arts, Germany, Bachelor of Engineering Electronics in Progress.; [occ.] Library Aide; [memb.] Elmhurst Seventh-Day-Adventist Church; [oth. writ.] Exercise book in progress.; [pers.] Draw to God because with Him, on your side nothing is impossible! "Behold, The Fear of the Lord, that is wisdom, and to depart from evil is understanding."; [a.] Oakland, CA

WYNNE, MARY BOYCE GWALTNEY
[b.] November 5, 1916, Isle of Wight County, Smithfield, VA; [p.] Wallace and Elsie Gwaltney; [m.] John Fleming Wynne, April 10, 1941; [ch.] John Boyce and Mary Fleming; [ed.] Smithfield High School (1935), AB Degree - College of William and Mary 1939; [occ.] Taught 2nd grade - 20 yrs. in Virginia - Retired; [memb.] Bethany United Methodist Church, Colonel William Allen Chapter - D.A.R.; [hon.] Senior Class Poet (1935); [oth. writ.] Just a personal poetry scrapbook. Nothing published.; [pers.] "No man is an island" - Communicate! People can't read thoughts. Help others and be willing to let others help you. Children and animals and birds I enjoy.; [a.] Smithfield, VA

WYNTER, DAVID JOHN ARTHUR
[pen.] Fredro Star; [b.] October 17, 1978, Jamaica Hospital; [p.] Ms. Carla Seals, Vata; [m.] O My Luve's; [ch.] Kidnamesake; [occ.] Crazy - rhyming; [memb.] I met life; [hon.] That for being articulate, The Comptrollers Award; [oth. writ.] Not yet published, P.S. to thine mighty one L.L. Cool J. who I gaze into capturing scene as so.; [pers.] Love comes once, if you are lucky then twice. I most desire works of America's Golden Age.; [a.] New York, NY

XAVIER, IRENE THERESE
[b.] October 23, 1928, Hongkong; [p.] Viriato M. Xavier, Maria L. Xavier; [ed.] St. Mary's School, Hongkong, Santa Rosa Lima College MACAU; [occ.] Administrative Secretary (retired). Distinguished member of the International Society of Poets.; [memb.] Distinguished Member of the International Society of Poets; [hon.] Poems published in seven anthologies by the American Poetry Association. Received Honorable Mention Certificate and Golden Poet Award (1987), along with a trophy from world of poetry. Received Editor's Choice Award from the National Library of Poetry 1993, for outstanding achievement in poetry.; [pers.] When depression gets one down, poetry expresses the emotion and soothes as a balm.; [a.] Daly City, CA

YANEZ, DONNA LEE
[pen.] Donna Lee; [b.] April 4, 1959, Edison, NJ; [p.] Grady and Loretta Waddell; [m.] David Yanez, February 14, 1988; [ch.] Robert, Nicole, Lindsey; [ed.] Edison High School; [occ.] Creative writing short story - Poetry; [memb.] National M.S. Society; [pers.] Cherish your visions and your dreams as they are.; [a.] Milltown, NJ

YATES JR., F. ROBERT
[b.] December 2, 1951, Wash., DC; [p.] Jaunice and Francis R. Yates Sr.; [ch.] Francis III, Jason, Karce; [ed.] MBA in Health Services, B.S. Biology/Chemistry Administration Board Certified - college of Health Care Executives; [occ.] Health Care Executive; [memb.] American College of Health Care Executives, American Association of Health Care Administrators, National Association of Health Care Executive, Medical Group Practice Management.; [oth.writ.] A Windy City, The Dove, A Velentine Gift, Contrast of Fate, Two Lovcis Journey, [pers.] Success is integrity and balance in one's life.; [a.] Columbia, MD

YEO, BRANDY LEE
[b.] February 8, 1981; [p.] Linda and Dave Yeo; [ed.] Grade 9 and a student at Arthur Voaden Secondary School.; [occ.] High school student; [hon.] I have received a Science Award and a honour roll award.; [a.] Saint Thomas Ontario, Canada

YEOMAN, JAMES F.
[b.] February 28, 1942, Bellaire, MI; [p.] Jane and Ernest L. Yeoman; [m.] Mary M., July 3, 1983; [ch.] Tim, Deb, Natalie, Rachel, Jeffery, Robert; [ed.] High School Dip./Electronics degrees. Alumni of school of Hard Knocks; [occ.] Blue Collar Worker; [memb.] Patron Member National Rifle, Assoc. Life Memenber Northland, Sportshands Club, Life Member Whittington Center Gun Club, Member of Several Conservation/Sporting Groups.; [oth. writ.] Several letters to news papers expressing my views on issues. Most are published.; [pers.] "A man becomes a fool when he believes he has learned all he needs to know."; [a.] Gaylord, MI

YORKS, JANET M.
[b.] October 21, 1960, Springfield, MA; [p.] William Haynes, Josephine Haynes; [ch.] Tara Marie, Kyle William; [ed.] Armijo High School Fairfield - California; [occ.] Noon duty supervisor, Amy Blanc School, Crossing Guard, Cleo Gordon School Fairfield - California 94533; [pers.] I have been greatly influenced by the love of my children and my family. I love you all very much.; [a.] Fairfield, CA

YOUNG, CHERYL ANN
[b.] November 18, 1963, Danville, IL; [p.] Kenneth H. Young II, Marcella M. Young; [ch.] One son (Deceased); [ed.] Danville High School, Danville Area Community College; [occ.] Records Technician, Danville Police Department; [memb.] Carter Metropolitan C.M.E. Church; [oth. writ.] "A Years Past"; [pers.] This is dedicated to my darling son in heaven - Travis L. "J.R." McCullough. The expressions of sympathy and love from my family, church, friends, co-workers and community inspired me to write.; [a.] Danville, IL

YOUNG, KERRY R.
[b.] September 2, 1972, Pittsburgh, PA; [p.] Laverne Young and Edward Brown; [ed.] Sto-Rox High and Edinboro University of PA; [occ.] Assistant Girls Basketball Coach; [memb.] Leukemia Society's Team in Training; [hon.] Softball and Basketball Scholarships (Edinboro University of PA); [pers.] Writing to me is a feeling, I try to write about what I'm feeling or how I want to feel. It's a passion!; [a.] Pittsburgh, PA

ZAJACZKOWSKI, JULIUSZ M.
[pen.] J. Maciul; [b.] May 29, 1955, Wroclaw, Poland; [p.] Stanislaw and Czeslawa Zajaczkowski; [ed.] Wroclaw Technical University (MSC), Poland, University of Queensland, Australia; [occ.] Mathematician; [memb.] Queensland Multicultural Writers' Association; [oth. writ.] Poems published in Australian Literary Magazines: Idiom 23, Northern perspective, social alternatives, Australian writers' journal. Poems and short stories in the anthology "windows", 1993.; [pers.] I am concerned about passing of time, why we are here and where we are going, and about a place of human individual in the universe. Walt Whitman's "I Sing the Body Electric" is a guiding light in my writing.; [a.] Brisbane Queensland, Australia

ZANNELLI, LISA
[b.] June 18, 1982, Poughkeepsie, NY; [p.] Robert and Alfraetta Zannelli; [ed.] North Junior High School 8th grade (13 years old); [occ.] Student and babysit; [hon.] Bowling, Cheerleading, all district, for Violin, and a Spelling Award; [a.] Newburgh, NY

ZICK, ALLEGRA
[b.] July 18, 1931, North Freedom, WI; [p.] William and Margaret Shale; [m.] Albert Zick, June 9, 1951; [ch.] Aaron Zick, Amy Zick Seiler; [ed.] BS - Education - UW Platteville, WI, MS - Administration - UW - Madison, WI; [occ.] Elementary Educator for 40 years - now retired; [memb.] American Association of University Woman, Woman's Christian Temperance Union National, State and Local Retired Educators Associations, Lay Speaker for UM Church; [hon.] Pi Lambda Theta (Honor Association in Education) Women Leaders in Ed. Award by AAUW; [oth. writ.]

Sermons - local newspaper articles.; [pers.] God puts something beautiful in all of us and all around us. Poetry enables us to communicate this to others.; [a.] North Freedom, WI

ZIEMBOWICZ, RON J.
[b.] May 21, 1968, Detroit, MI; [p.] Alison Faitel, Leo Ziembowicz; [ch.] Jessica Lyn; [ed.] Edsel Ford High Dearborn, School-Craft College; [oth. writ.] Essentially the writings of life, love, hate and death, as foreseen through a 'Twenty Somethings' eyes.; [pers.] The use of experimental poetry has an intriguing pull on me. Words in verse are as passionate as the Gods in the garden.; [a.] Lincoln Park, MI

ZIGMONT, EILEEN L.
[pen.] "Minikin"; [b.] September 30, 1950, Trenton, NJ; [p.] Clarence Snell, Dolores Snell; [ch.] Heather 18 yrs., Timoji 13 yrs.; [ed.] Hamilton High West Vogue Modeling School 1 yr Voice Lessons and Dance Acting and Writing Classes; [occ.] Writer, Entertainer for Children; [memb.] Minikin the Clown Party Entertainment; [hon.] Won writing contest for NY Times Newspaper, "My most memorable time with my father", Re: Fathers day contest. Personal letter from the president Bill Clinton Wash. during Oklahoma Bombing.; [oth. writ.] Poems pub. in sev. anthologies, few in newspapers. I write all my own rhymes to perform for children.; [pers.] My goal through my writing is to reach as many people worldwide that I can through words. I am along with God to be an advolate to touch other peoples lives.; [a.] Cranbury, NJ

ZIMMETT, TERESA E.
[pen.] Teresa Trapeano; [b.] November 15, 1912, Damacus Township, Penna; [p.] Eliz and John Trapeano; [m.] Geo Zimmett Sr. (Divorce), July 30, 1935; [ch.] 4 Children - 2 Boys, 2 Girls 8 Grand children, 6 Great - Grandchildren; [ed.] High School; [hon.] I volunteered in school for 12 years teaching Kinter Garden in 3 schools My teacher had the book of poems written for me and my children; [oth. writ.] Written about 25 poems in all about my family and other people.; [pers.] I wrote a few poems during the war 1944 - for my brother and friends who were in the war.; [a.] Buffalo, NY

ZMARLICKI, OLIVIA MARIA
[pen.] Olivia Zmarlicki; [b.] January 23, 1965, Poland; [p.] Hieronim and Krystyna Zmarlicki; [ch.] Steven Harbist; [ed.] Associate in Business Management; [occ.] Claims Adjustor, ITT Hartford, Southington, CT; [hon.] Dean's List, President's List; [oth. writ.] Several poems published in local newspapers; [pers.] To embrace every second of life as if it was your last.; [a.] Farmington, CT

ZOPPETTI, DEBORAH
[b.] October 27, 1960, Rochester, NY; [p.] Irene and Robert; [ed.] Bachelor of Architectural Engineering, Penn State University; [occ.] Assistant Project Manager, Barclay White Inc.; [a.] Wrightsville, PA

ZWERDLING, PEARL
[pen.] Pia; [b.] December 26, New York City, NY; [p.] Rose and Max Zwerdling; [m.] Divorced; [ed.] High School graduate of Abraham Lincoln in Brooklyn. One year Brooklyn College.; [occ.] Clerk - Typist, Green and Weiss - Accounting firm.; [memb.] Young Israel Synagogue.; [oth. writ.] Poetry reflecting child hood memories. Did not submit for publication yet. Trying to make poems into book, form with illustrations.; [pers.] Watching Charlie Rose show on Channel 13 on night, guest interviewed was Calvin Trillin, He read some of his great poetry. I was very impressed and decided to try writing some of my own.

INDEX
OF POETS

Index

J

J.A.Y. 343
Jackson, Angela R. 192
Jackson, Darrell 114
Jackson, Jason 246
Jackson, Jerry L. 309
Jackson, Mario Concepcion 91
Jackson, Matt 523
Jackson, Minnie 95
Jackson, Ruby J. 117
Jacob, Moses Albert Michael 621
Jacobs, Don L. 457
Jacque, Jules R. 369
Jacques, Gerty J. 563
Jade, Nikki 348
Jagiello, Helen 432
Jagusch, Leeanne 579
Jahic, Mustafa 194, 597
James, Barbara W. 29
James, Chantal 344
James, Denise A. Butcher 274
James, Linnette 241
James, Pat 419
James, Tasha 361
Janakiraman, R. 619
Janecek, Jessica Lee 368
Janell, Jennifer Reaves 554
Jankowska, Marie 205
Jansen, Krista 321
Jaramillo, Hugo 390
Jarrell, Robert B. 97
Jarvis, Dodie Lynn 456
Jasper, Vernol A. 334
Jean-Francois, Marie-Catheline 114
Jefferson, Dorothy 25
Jelincic, Kira 465
Jenca, Kimberlee 34
Jenkins, Amber 428
Jenkins, Cassandra 124
Jenkins, Ruby 381
Jennings, Charlotte J. 110
Jennings, Jennifer 454
Jensen, Edith 219
Jeppson, Per-Magnus 218
Jernigan III, James P. 408
Jett, Mathew T. 267
Jewell, Janice L. 185
Jhoma 618
Johannsen, Jane M. 44
Joharatnam, Dilani 597
Johns, Scott H. Jr. 158
Johnson, Abra Leigh 238
Johnson, Amy 47
Johnson, Bill 82
Johnson, Clark 129
Johnson, Connie J. 46
Johnson, Danny E. 402
Johnson, Debra L. 126
Johnson, Dennis L. 430
Johnson, Faye 330
Johnson, Frances Lee 403
Johnson, Garnett 223
Johnson, Hayley 294
Johnson, Jacob 226
Johnson, Karen P. 392
Johnson, Kristen Anne 148
Johnson, Lemuel Kwame 86
Johnson, Linda 443
Johnson, Marc 98

Johnson, Marguerita H. 595
Johnson, Michael Curtis 112
Johnson, Michelle Christine 43
Johnson, Renee A. 374
Johnson, Roberta 208
Johnson, Shane 469
Johnson, Shirley 590
Johnson Sr., David L. 106
Johnson, Tina 311
Johnson, Tracey 611
Johnson, Walter Randolph 68
Johnson-Sartor, Melody 405
Johnston, Barbara 360
Johnston, Bekki 425
Johnston, Kate 301
Johnston, Pamela S. 413
Johnston, Rhonda 452
Johnston, William A. 609
Jolin, Katherine 241
Jolly, Mary Lou 155
Jones, Alicia 255
Jones, Bruce 367
Jones, Carrie 53
Jones, Chester 61
Jones, Dawn 274
Jones, Detra 533
Jones, Donna Foy 11
Jones, Dottie 111
Jones, Florence 4
Jones, Jacob 355
Jones, Jenica 101
Jones, Joy 365
Jones Jr., James R. 351
Jones, Judith Lyle 109
Jones, Lloyd E. 335
Jones, Michael M. 41
Jones, Ralph 92
Jones, Robert J. 121
Jordan, Maliea 138
Jordan, Mona 112
Jorgensen, Susan 116
Joseph, Paulette 235
Joslin, Kimberly 536
Jossens, Marilyn 364
Jowers, Alice P. 123
Joyce, Tracy 584
Juel, Rick 154
Juggessur, Nisha Devi 242
Julien, Curtis 597
Jungic, Zoran 193
Junkin, H. L. 108
Junkin, Jim 450

K

Kachin, Jean 348
Kaercher, Suzanne C. 358
Kahle, Lisa 505
Kahn, Valerie Sansone 535
Kahner, Erich 584
Kain, Ruth 152
Kajder, Andrea 522
Kalb, Kameron F. 81
Kalbach, Hope 60
Kalchthaler, Max 172
Kalich, Kathy 107
Kalinina, Natalie A. 346
Kallio, Leila Lisebet Tuori 77
Kamal, Mohammad 83
Kamensky, Olga 38
Kamps, Joanne 525

Kane, Gretchen 449
Kano, Courtney 400
Kantor, Anatole 8
Kanze, Jonathan 41
Kapner, Miriam 107
Karas, Betty 426
Kardian, S. Neil 241
Karelse, Melanie 508
Karl, Christine J. 107
Karlen, Monique 140
Kasch, David 187
Kask, Filomena 346
Kastler, Pat 19
Kastrukoff, Margaret 234
Kathy, Parrish 532
Katz, Jana 364
Kaufman, Doris A. 155
Kaufman, Leslie 251
Kaupp, Shannon 110
Kavanagh, Sean 543
Kavin, Donna 237
Kawalewski, Victoria 171
Kawar, Issa 208
Kay, Ashley 463
Kay, Brandon 267
Kay, Lorraine 581
Kayer, Heather 431
Kayes, Mike 415
Kearney, Elaine 65
Kearney, Victor T. 342
Kearns, Julia F. 101
Keays, Steven 611
Keddle, Helena Starr 388
Keddy, Kelly Lynn 203
Keding, Kara 530
Keech, Jim 502
Keegan, James W. 172
Keeley, Jennifer Lee 135
Keen, Jesse 507
Keene, J. D. 433
Keep, Bernice M. 214
Keesee, Dewan 503
Keeterle, Michael 64
Kehler, Monica S. 428
Kehner, Stacy 486
Keill Sr, Fred Charles 144
Kekino, Lovelyn M. 103
Kela, Linda 542
Keleher, Natasha 215
Kell, Alice B. 20
Kellams, Harold D. 449
Kelley, Denise M. 591
Kelley, Mildred 587
Kellman, Anderson 197
Kelly, Billie L. 328
Kelly, Eleni 204
Kelly, Malcolm 385
Kelly, Robert 375, 582
Kelly, Tracy 81
Kelsey-Gilbert, Gloria 207
Kelso, Susan 336
Kemp, J. W. 490
Kemp Jr., Krystyna 226
Kemsley, Kim 223
Kendall, Florence P. 344
Kendall, Jacqueline A. 291
Kendall, Saadia 620
Kennedy, Diane 611
Kennedy, Laurina 235
Kennelly, Bill 545
Kennett, Roger H. 321

Kenney, T. Michael 433
Kenny, Caren M. 520
Kent, Efimedia Raptis 578
Kent, John 401
Kern, Christena Bryson 175
Kerns, Peter 178
Kerper, Steven M. 86
Kerr, Virginia 257
Kesselring, Megan 353
Keswaui, Meryl 623
Ketcham, Chrystine 144
Ketchel, Christine E. 391
Keuchel, Stephen H. 503
Kexel, Kevin L. 451
Khan, M. Waleed 386
Khan, Nazir Uddin 608
Kho, Jennifer 132
Khon, Keith 323
Kidder, Sandra Kay 109
Killewald, Susan 451
Killian, Kay L. 183
Killingsworth, Tommy G. 405
Killorin, LaRue Gwendolyn 338
Kilroy, Jeanne 122
Kim, Haeng Ja 59
Kim, Irene H. 487
Kim, Jeesue 295
Kindl, Silvia 588
King, Charles 130
King, Christopher J. 560
King, Elizabeth 196
King, Jeffrey Scott 456
King, John A. 265
King, Richard 470
King, Sophia M. 274
King, Valerie Ann 15
Kinne, Merle W. 31
Kinney, Ruth M. 455
Kinslow, Karen 613
Kinsman, David 381
Kipp, Jennifer 77
Kiraly, Megan 249
Kirk, Laurence L. 335
Kirkland, Jillian Lea 85
Kirkpatrick, Tony 604
Kirkwood, Jon M. 190
Kirn, Lora E. 485
Kirsten, Stephanie 581
Kiser, Elgeva Hutto 425
Kisner, Brian A. 275
Kiss, Helen 411
Kitchens, Dickie Sue 466
Kitchens, Irene Chastain 427
Kitchens, Jared 494
Kitchura, Kerri 205
Kittleson, Steven L. 520
Kittredge, Sue W. 433
Kitzmiller, Rendell N. 298
Klassen, Jennifer 193
Klatt, Linda Lee 299
Klein, S. R. 482
Klein, Wayne D. 288
Klenetsky, Jason 594
Klimszewski, Jeanette 97
Kline, Susan L. 25
Klinger, Mindy 433
Klobuchar, Kelly 269
Klock, Lisa 345
Kment, Tamara Lynn 425
Knapp, Shirley M. 146
Knecht, Eugene 212